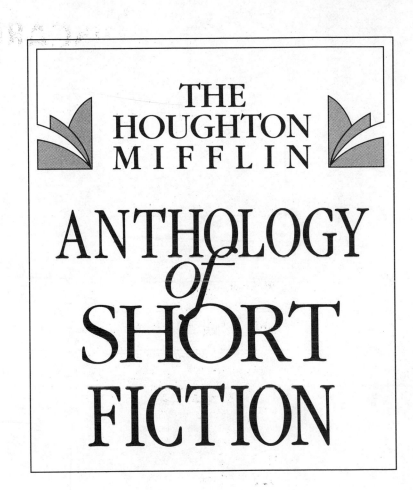

THE HOUGHTON MIFFLIN

ANTHOLOGY *of* SHORT FICTION

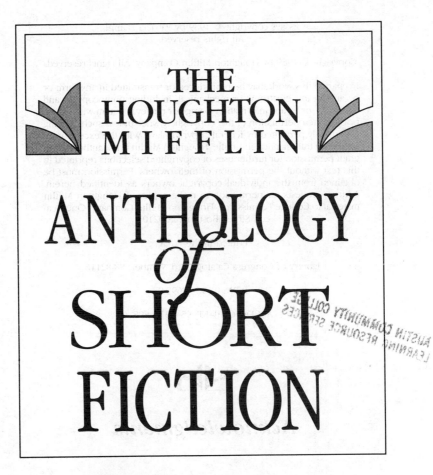

THE HOUGHTON MIFFLIN

ANTHOLOGY *of* SHORT FICTION

PATRICIA HAMPL

University of Minnesota

with the editors of Houghton Mifflin Company

HOUGHTON MIFFLIN COMPANY   BOSTON

allas   Geneva, Illinois   Palo Alto   Princeton, New Jersey

Library of Congress Catalog Card Number: 88-82116

ISBN: 0-395-49695-0

ABCDEFGHIJ–KP–9543210–898

Acknowledgments

Chinua Achebe:
"Chike's School Days" from GIRLS AT WAR AND OTHER STORIES by Chinua Achebe. Copyright © 1972, 1973 by Chinua Achebe. Reprinted by permission of Doubleday, a division of Bantam, Doubleday, Dell Publishing Group, Inc. Published in Canada by Heinemann Educational Books Ltd. Used by permission of David Bolt Associates.

Alice Adams:
From "TO SEE YOU AGAIN" by Alice Adams. Copyright © 1982 by Alice Adams. Reprinted by permission of Alfred A. Knopf, Inc.

Hans Christian Andersen:
"The Wild Swans" from HANS CHRISTIAN ANDERSEN: THE COMPLETE FAIRY TALES AND STORIES. Translation copyright © 1974 by Erik Christian Haugaard. Reprinted by permission of Doubleday, a division of Bantam, Doubleday, Dell Publishing Group, Inc.
Published in Canada by Victor Gollancz Ltd. Used by permission.

(*continued*)

Ethan Canin:
"Star Food" from EMPEROR OF THE AIR by Ethan Canin. Copyright © 1988 by Ethan Canin. Reprinted by permission of Houghton Mifflin Company.

Truman Capote:
Copyright 1948 by Truman Capote. Reprinted from SELECTED WRITINGS OF TRUMAN CAPOTE, by permission of Random House, Inc.

Angela Carter:
"The Bloody Chamber" THE BLOODY CHAMBER AND OTHER STORIES by Angela Carter. Published by Victor Gollancz Ltd. Copyright © Angela Carter, 1979. Used by permission of Rogers, Coleridge & White Ltd and Victor Gollancz Ltd.

Raymond Carver:
From CATHEDRAL by Raymond Carver. Copyright © 1981, 1982, 1983 by Raymond Carver. Reprinted by permission of Alfred A. Knopf, Inc.

Willa Cather:
"Paul's Case" from YOUTH AND THE BRIGHT MEDUSA. Published by Alfred A. Knopf, Inc.

Anton Chekhov:
"Gooseberries," by Anton Chekov, translated by Ivy Litvinov. Reprinted by permission of the Estate of Ivy Litvinov.
"The Lady with the Pet Dog": From THE PORTABLE CHEKHOV, trans. Adam Yarmolinsky. Copyright 1947, renewed © 1968 by the Viking Press, Inc. Copyright renewed © 1975 by Avrahm Yarmolinsky. All rights reserved. Reprinted by permission of Viking Penguin Inc.

Joseph Conrad:
"An Outpost of Progress" from TALES OF UNREST by Joseph Conrad. Published in 1898 by Doubleday, a division of Bantam, Doubleday, Dell Publishing Group, Inc.

Julio Cortázar:
From END OF THE GAME AND OTHER STORIES by Julio Cortázar, translated by Paul Blackburn. Copyright © 1967 by Random House, Inc. Reprinted by permission of Pantheon Books, a Division of Random House, Inc.

José Donoso:
From CHARLESTON & OTHER STORIES by José Donoso, translated by Andree Conrad. Copyright 1971 by José Donoso. Reprinted by permission of David R. Godine, Publisher, Boston.

Andre Dubus:
Reprinted by permission of Philip G. Spitzer Literary Agency. Copyright © 1983 by Andre Dubus.

Louise Erdrich:
From THE BEET QUEEN by Louise Erdrich. Copyright © 1986 by Louise Erdrich. Reprinted by permission of Henry Holt and Company, Inc.

William Faulkner:
"Barn Burning": Copyright 1939 and renewed 1967 by Estelle Faulkner and Jill Faulkner Summers. Reprinted from COLLECTED STORIES OF WILLIAM FAULKNER, by permission of Random House, Inc.
"An Odor of Verbena": Copyright 1938 and renewed 1966 by Estelle Faulkner and Jill Faulkner Summers. Reprinted from THE FAULKNER READER, by permission of Random House, Inc.

Gustave Flaubert:
From THREE TALES by Gustave Flaubert, translated by Arthur McDowell. Published 1924 by Alfred A. Knopf, Inc. Reprinted by permission of the publisher.

E. M. Forster:
"The Story of the Siren" from THE ETERNAL MOMENT AND OTHER STORIES, by E. M. Forster, copyright 1928 by Harcourt Brace Jovanovich, Inc., renewed 1956 by E. M. Forster, reprinted by permission of the publisher.

Carlos Fuentes:
"The Doll Queen" from BURNT WATER by Carlos Fuentes, translated by Margaret Sayers Peden. English translation copyright © 1969, 1974, 1978, 1979, 1980 by Farrar, Straus and Giroux, Inc.

Mavis Gallant:
"The Cost of Living": Reprinted by permission of Georges Borchardt, Inc. and the author. Copyright © 1957 by Mavis Gallant.
"The Ice Wagon Going Down the Street": From HOME TRUTHS: SIXTEEN STORIES by Mavis Gallant. Copyright © 1981 by Mavis Gallant. Reprinted by permission of Random House, Inc. Reprinted by permission of Macmillan of Canada, A Division of Canada Publishing Corporation.

Gabriel García Márquez:
"Death Constant Beyond Love" from INNOCENT ERINDIRA AND OTHER STORIES by Gabriel García Márquez. English translation copyright © 1978 by Harper & Row, Publishers, Inc. Reprinted by permission of Harper & Row, Publishers, Inc.
"Monologue of Isabel Watching It Rain in Macondo" from COLLECTED STORIES by Gabriel García Márquez. Copyright © 1968 in the English translation by Harper & Row, Publishers, Inc. Reprinted by permission of the publisher.

Natalia Ginzburg:
The Mother by Natalia Ginzburg translated by Isobel Quigly from ITALIAN SHORT STORIES edited by Raleigh Trevelyan (Penguin Parallel Texts, 1965), translation copyright © Penguin Books, 1965.

Nadine Gordimer:
"Africa Emergent," SELECTED STORIES by Nadine Gordimer. Copyright © 1971 by Nadine Gordimer. All rights reserved. Reprinted by permission of Viking Penguin, Inc.
"Sins of the Third Age," SOMETHING OUT THERE by Nadine Gordimer. Copyright © 1982 by Nadine Gordimer. All rights reserved. Reprinted by permission of Viking Penguin Inc. © Penguin Books Canada Ltd. 1982. Reprinted by permission of Penguin Books Canada Ltd.

Thomas Hardy:
Published by Macmillan London Ltd.

Mark Helprin:
"The Schreuderspitze" from ELLIS ISLAND & OTHER STORIES by Mark Helprin. Copyright © 1977 by Mark Helprin, originally published in *The New Yorker*. Reprinted by permission of DELACORTE PRESS/SEYMOUR LAWRENCE a division of BANTAM, DOUBLEDAY, DELL PUBLISHING GROUP, INC.

Ernest Hemingway:
Ernest Hemingway, "In Another Country" from MEN WITHOUT WOMEN. Copyright 1927 Charles Scribner's Sons; copyright 1955 Ernest Hemingway. Reprinted with the permission of Charles Scribner's Sons, an imprint of Macmillan Publishing Company.

Zora Neale Hurston:
Reprinted by permission of Turtle Island Foundation.

James Joyce:
"The Dead," DUBLINERS by James Joyce. Copyright 1916 by B. W. Huebsch, Inc. Definitive text copyright © 1967 by the Estate of James Joyce. All rights reserved. Reprinted by permission of Viking Penguin Inc.

Yukio Mishima:
Yukio Mishima, DEATH IN MIDSUMMER. Copyright © 1966 by New Directions Publishing Corporation. Translated by Geoffrey W. Sargent.

Alice Munro:
From THE BEGGAR MAID by Alice Munro. Copyright © 1977, 1978 by Alice Munro. Reprinted by permission of Alice Munro. Reprinted by permission of Alfred A. Knopf, Inc.
"The Beggar Maid" by Alice Munro, Copyright © 1977 by Alice Munro. This story is the title story of THE BEGGAR MAID which is available in a Penguin edition. The story originally appeared in *The New Yorker*.
"Oh, What Avails" by Alice Munro. Copyright © 1988 by Alice Munro. Originally published in *The New Yorker*.

V. S. Naipaul:
From THREE NOVELS: THE MYSTIC MASSEUR, THE SUFFRAGE OF ELVIRA, MIGUEL STREET by V. S. Naipaul. Copyright © 1957, 1958, 1959, 1982 by V. S. Naipaul. Reprinted by permission of Alfred A. Knopf, Inc.

R. K. Narayan:
"Naga," MALGUDI DAYS by R. K. Narayan. Copyright © 1972 by R. K. Narayan. Originally appeared in *The New Yorker*. All rights reserved. Reprinted by permission of Viking Penguin Inc.

Joyce Carol Oates:
"The Lady with the Pet Dog": Reprinted from MARRIAGES AND INFIDELITIES by Joyce Carol Oates by permission of the publisher, Vanguard Press, Inc. Copyright © 1968, 1969, 1970, 1971, 1972, by Joyce Carol Oates.
"Raven's Wing": From RAVEN'S WING by Joyce Carol Oates (A William Abrahams Book) Copyright © 1986 by the Ontario Review, Inc. Reprinted by permission of the publisher, E. P. Dutton, a division of NAL Penguin Inc.

Edna O'Brien:
"A Rose in the Heart of New York" from A FANATIC HEART by Edna O'Brien. Copyright © 1984 by Edna O'Brien. Originally appeared in *The New Yorker*. Reprinted by permission of Farrar, Straus and Giroux, Inc.
"Sister Imelda" from A FANATIC HEART by Edna O'Brien. Copyright © 1981, 1984 by Edna O'Brien. Originally appeared in *The New Yorker*. Reprinted by permission of Farrar, Straus and Giroux, Inc.

Tim O'Brien:
Reprinted by permission of International Creative Management. Copyright © 1986 by Tim O'Brien.

Flannery O'Connor:
"The Artificial Nigger" and "A Good Man Is Hard To Find" from A GOOD MAN IS HARD TO FIND AND OTHER STORIES, by Flannery O'Connor, copyright © 1955 by Flannery O'Connor, renewed 1983 by Regina O'Connor, reprinted by permission of Harcourt Brace Jovanovich, Inc.

Frank O'Connor:
From COLLECTED STORIES by Frank O'Connor. Copyright © 1981 by Harriet O'Donovan Sheehy, Executrix of the Estate of Frank O'Connor. Reprinted by permission of Alfred A. Knopf, Inc. Reprinted by permission of Joan Daves.

Sean O'Faolain:
From THE COLLECTED STORIES OF SEAN O'FAOLAIN by Sean O'Faolain. Copyright © 1957 by Sean O'Faolain. By permission of Little, Brown and Company.

PREFACE

*T*he Houghton Mifflin Anthology of Short Fiction has been created for readers in a range of literature courses that study the many forms, voices, and motifs of the short story. Collected here are 98 stories by 79 writers — traditional, contemporary, and international. They are presented alphabetically by author; a chronological table of contents (page xxi) provides the historical sequence. Each story (or, in the case of writers represented by two stories, each opening story) is preceded by a brief discussion of the writer's life and writings.

Two essays offer an extended examination of the heart and soul of the short story in general and this collection in particular. The first — "Celestial Process: The Private Life of the Short Story" — explores the not at all preordained paths by which a story finds its way onto the page. "An Introduction to This Collection" is an in-depth profile of this anthology.

It is a pleasure to thank those individuals whose advice helped shaped this collection: Ray Anschel, Carleton College; Carol Bly, University of Minnesota; Patrick Bratlinger, Indiana University; James Catano, Louisiana State University; Robert Creed, University of Massachusetts, Amherst; Barbara Christian, University of California at Berkeley; Larry Danielson, University of Illinois at Champaign–Urbana; John Dick, University of Texas at El Paso; Gary Handwerk, University of Washington; John Hanes, Duquesne University; Robert Harlow, University of British Columbia; Glenda Hudson, Vanderbilt University; Marjorie Lewis, Texas Christian University; Diane Lichtenstein, Beloit College; Herbert Lindenberger, Standford University; Margot Livesay, Carnegie–Mellon University; Keith Maillard, University of British Columbia; Michelle Massè, Louisiana State University; Michael Meyer, University of Connecticut; Eric Pankey, Washington University; Steven Weisenburger, University of Kentucky; and Karl Zender, University of California at Davis. Thanks also to Stephen Plumb, reference librarian at the James J. Hill Reference Library, St. Paul, and Robert Rulon-Miller, Rulon-Miller Books, Minneapolis.

CONTENTS

EUDORA WELTY

EDITH WHARTON

VIRGINIA WOOLF

MARGUERITE YOURCENAR

CHRONOLOGICAL TABLE
OF CONTENTS

CELESTIAL PROCESS

The Private Life of the Short Story
Patricia Hampl

A brief cautionary tale: One day some years ago, after I had published a book, I was asked for permission to excerpt a piece from it in an anthology. Delighted, I wrote back.

As it happened, I used this anthology in a course I taught. I admired its selections, and found the study questions helpful. Not that I used the study questions much, I suppose, but I directed my students to them from time to time. They seemed purposeful and not foolish. I was pleased about being included in the next edition of the book, imagining students not just reading my work, but *studying* it.

About a year later, the anthology arrived. Snappy new jacket (better than the first edition, I thought), well-designed pages, clean type. And there was my name in the table of contents, right along with several of my heroes and various high-flyers.

I skimmed through my piece. No typos — good. And there, at the end of the selection, in those shivery italic letters reserved for especially significant copy, were the study questions. There were several under the heading "Questions about Purpose." One will do: "Why does Hampl establish her father's significance to her family before she narrates the major incident . . . ?"

Beats me, I thought.

I had no idea what Hampl's purpose was. All the study questions looked quite mad to me.

Remember those grade school IQ tests, when the teacher would say soothingly, "Just relax, and answer with the first thing that strikes you as correct. You can't fail this test." My heart always sank; I knew instinctively something worse than failure awaited me. Fate was lurking in those intelligence tests and I might as well surrender to my middle-range score before I picked up the magnetic lead pencil.

This same sinking sensation swept over me reading the study questions. *My* study questions. If anyone could answer them, it ought to be me. They were not unreasonable. They were questions very much like the ones in the first edition (and how many other textbooks over the years?) that had struck me as useful.

Like a shady accountant, for years I had been keeping separate books on the imagination. In one ledger I logged questions about writing that proceeded from the completed work, treating it as the source and arbiter of itself. The story was the story. Period.

In the other ledger, apparently written in invisible trick ink, I wrote my own stories and poems. In that ledger, everything was up for grabs. "Hampl" had precious few intentions, except, like the charlatan I suddenly felt myself to be, to filch whatever was loose on the table that suited my immediate purposes. Worse, the "purposes" were vague, inconsistent, reversible under pressure. And who — or what — was applying the pressure? I couldn't say. The best I could say was that this pressure gave me the sharp nose of a scavenger, not the keen mind of a thinker.

It wasn't long before I switched the shameful behavior onto the study questions, of course. They were at fault, not me. They were simple-minded, they were pointless. The truth, as usual, was somewhere in the middle. It still amazes me that I could be so startled, that I could so instinctively go about learning to write one way, and yet look at writing that moved me in another, far more decorous way.

For decorum was part of the problem. I was unwilling to admit any mess into the workrooms of the stories I loved. I was unwilling to admit there was a workroom. For me and anything I wrote — yes, of course, a workroom that sometimes felt like a sweatshop. But for the writers of the stories I read — no. As a reader I preferred to consider the finished products of other writers.

I wasn't even aware I was doing this, maintaining the enchantment at the expense of learning something about the magic. I thought I was studying the parts that composed the story when I considered plot, narrative voice, when I charted a rise in action and was able to identify a point of conflict. Yet, here I was, unable to answer questions about something I had written myself when I had been quite diligently answering them for other people for years. I was face to face with a strange sort of double life of the mind.

Call it an unwillingness to face facts — as if these stories by others, stories I had loved and studied, were fresh flowers. And I had filled the house with beautiful bouquets but refused to accept the information that all these real flowers have their natural home in dirt.

It was the fact of roots which I had denied. I wanted the blossoms, all right, but not all that knobby stuff they sprang from in the dark. For the moment, holding that anthology, I had no idea how I had written my own story in it, but I had the spooky feeling that I would still be capable of standing in front of a class and earnestly show them how another story had been written by someone else.

Every story has a story. This secret story, which has little chance of getting told, is the history of its creation. Maybe the "story of the story" never *can* be told, for a finished work consumes its own history, renders it obsolete, a husk.

Isn't that the point? Fiction, that ingenious architecture, hangs above life, suspended by the invisible tensile wires of the imagination. It glitters and winks up there, impossibly aloof, and performs its chief duty, which is the confirmation of enchantment. Don't mess with the veils and curtains, ladies and gentlemen; give the magician a little room, please.

But another piece of conventional wisdom insists that the best stories come from "life," from "experience." This sends a person scurrying back to the notion that where it comes from and how it all happens must have an essential bearing on what fiction *is*. An unbudging belief asserts itself that the hinge between life and story exists — and matters.

Life and experience have the disadvantage of being big, cloudy words. Who is to say where experience occurs — exclusively in the flat-footed world of literal autobiography? What about observation — can it *become* experience? And memory — should it be trusted as experience? Doesn't it have the soul of a pick-pocket, slipping here, dipping there, to get what it wants? Will anyone argue that fantasy is not experience, although it never "happened?" And dreams, how about dreams?

Every reader, no matter how successfully enchanted, senses that the power of a story resides light years past the official words given to describe its parts — beyond plot, beyond character and dramatic conflict, beyond even the subtler conceptions of tone and voice. Why does an earnest consideration of these aspects of narrative fail to cast the bright light that would expose the lines holding the story aloft?

A stubborn hunch persists that those invisible wires are made of simple stuff, like the beautiful old guitars whose tone is complex and unforgettable, although the music comes from plucking strings made of catgut.

"The next best thing to writing your own short story," Raymond Carver says in his introduction to *The Best American Short Stories 1986,* "is to read someone else's short story." Yes. Carver's winning admission makes a happy jumble of writing and reading. He just doesn't see them as opposed, not even as generically different. The sense behind his statement is that writing a story and reading one are pretty much aspects of the same thing.

That thing is the imagination. It makes sense, I think, to erase for the moment the usual boundary between reading and writing in order to think about how a story actually comes into being. If you begin at the end — with the finished story open before you — it's possible to say a lot about what is there, how it affects you, what your response is. You can talk well about what "works," where the action turns; you can perhaps locate the climax, denouement, and admire the airy beams of certain turns of phrase which, on closer inspection, prove tough as tempered steel. The story is a solid object, observable and finite. A thing as tidy as the little brick of a book.

We must speak about stories in this way. For one thing, unless we are able to identify the parts of a story, we are unable to recognize its moral power. The theme of a story is not simply some literary jargon attached to the narrative after the fact; the theme rises up as the moral spirit within the work. The capacity to recognize the story's theme is akin to the ability to make a useful relationship between literature and daily life. No small business.

The same thing is true for many of the ways we learn to speak about fiction in classrooms. It is necessary to understand what "conflict" is in literary terms, and why some characters must remain "flat," though the bit players in our real lives may have the annoying habit of being all too rounded out.

But there is reason to look at stories another way, not as finished at all. To step back a bit to consider the messy faculty of mind which produced the story makes it possible to catch a glint off those hidden guy-wires suspending it. And in that glimpse of the imagination, the finished story itself is *placed,* given residence in a larger geography, one more lush than the territory reserved for discussions of plot development or the construction of round and flat characters.

In their notebooks and (a more contemporary and public form of writer's note-book) in interviews, writers often puzzle over how the imagination works. A distinction: *the* imagination, not their own personal, unique imaginations. There seems to be an implicit understanding that the imagination is not owned, not contained within oneself, even though the experience of it is intensely interior. As F. Scott Fitzgerald says in a rueful, self-castigating note in *The Crack-Up,* "I had been only a mediocre caretaker of most of the things left in my hands, even of my talent." This sense of being in the service of the imagination — not its master — is a trademark of an authentic experience of creativity.

After long and intimate contact, the imagination begins to be experienced as another. To Henry James it was, quite plainly, a pal. "Look also, a little, *mon bon,*" he recommends chummily in his notebook, "into what may come out, further, of the little something-or-other deposited long since in your memory — your fancy — by the queer confidence made you by the late Miss B." *Mon bon,* my good fellow. Sometimes he refers to the imagination as his angel.

The imagination, addressed as a friend, a guide and guardian, is also experienced as a process. Process does not inhabit space the way the image of an angel or good fellow does. It exists in time. In fact, the process exists *as* time, a special, unfettered experience of temporality. This accounts for the frequent amazement on the part of writers at the displacement of time: I looked at my watch when I sat down to work, and it was 9:30. The next thing I knew, it was 3 o'clock!

In the same notebook entry, James goes from addressing his genius as "mon bon," his good pal, to " — oh celestial soothing, sanctifying process. Let me fumble it gently and patiently out," he says of the story he is working on, "with fever and fidget laid to rest. . . ."

The process toward a story often presents itself hesitantly, not as a grand scheme, but as an uncertain question. James again:

"Isn't there a little drama in the idea of such a situation as A. L.'s — that of an extremely clever and accomplished man, a man much prized and followed up in society, a great favourite there as a talker and a 'brilliant' person, whose interior is 'impossible' through the dreaminess of his wife and children, their inferiority to himself, their gross, dense, helpless stupidity and common placeness. . . ."

Again and again in the notebooks, James teases out a story with an offhand inquiry: "Isn't perhaps something to be made of the idea that came to me some time ago . . . — the little idea of the situation of some young creature (it seems to be preferably a woman, but of this I'm not sure), who, at 20, on the threshold of a life that has seemed boundless, is suddenly condemned to death (by consumption, heart-disease, or whatever) by the voice of the physician? . . ."

"Isn't there perhaps the subject of a little — a very little — tale . . . in the idea of a man of letters, a poet, a novelist, finding out, after years, or a considerable period, of very happy, unsuspecting, and more or less affectionate, intercourse with a 'lady-writer,' a newspaper woman, as it were, that he has been systematically *debine,* 'slated' by her in certain critical journals to which she contributes? . . ."

These questions, tentative and unintrusive, bear the grace of a good host attempting to draw out a shy guest. No crude presumption or demand. This is not an interrogation. Inconsistency is perfectly okay, indecision ("preferably a woman, but of this I'm not sure") is no big deal. Just keep talking — mumbling is fine. In a sense, these inquiries are not questions at all. They are brooms sweeping a clear space for the story to sit and compose itself — only if it wishes, of course.

James is not unique, not even unusual, in his attentive courtesy to the imagination. But his notebooks provide one of the best paper trails ever charted to the creative process. His willingness to speak to the imaginative process as to a friend is almost childlike. The faith in the independent personhood of his ingenuity is striking. The vulnerability is breathtaking.

But vulnerability poses a threat. How does authority, that basic requisite of narrative voice, attach itself to someone so thoroughly humbled before the inchoate imagination and its imperious ways? In the story, it just won't wash to be iffy about the details. Sometime or other, James has to settle down and know whether that 20-year-old woman (or man?) on the threshold of life died of consumption or of heart disease. Dying of *whatever* won't do.

The lax habits of the free imagination exhibit an appealing open-door policy. But to counterbalance this extreme permissiveness, the celestial process had better employ some sort of disciplinarian, an enforcer, to maintain order. Where else does the famous restraint and brevity of the short story come from? In other words, there must be a plan, an outline. Mustn't there?

Raymond Carver, in his essay "On Writing," turned to Flannery O'Connor when he was mulling over just this question. In her essay "Writing Short Stories," she talks about writing as an act of discovery. Carver found that "O'Connor says she most often did not know where she was going when she sat down to work on a short story." Most writers, she believed, didn't know where they were headed when they began a story.

"When I read this some years ago," Carver says, "it came as a shock that she, or anyone for that matter, wrote stories in this fashion. I thought this was my uncomfortable secret, and I was a little uneasy with it. For sure I thought this way of working on a short story somehow revealed my own shortcomings. I remember being tremendously heartened by reading what she had to say on the subject."

We should all be heartened, readers as well as writers, for this "method" speaks to the act of *discovery* in writing. We are used to thinking of discoveries in science. We even require them; a real scientist, to bear the name, *must* be engaged in discovery. Otherwise, we are speaking of a technician. People may argue over the merits of technology (or even over where science ends and technology begins). And it is assumed that a scientist has technical expertise or at least the ability to judge it.

We seem to understand these distinctions when thinking of scientific endeavor and have little trouble comprehending that discovery *is* the point of the endeavor. We even speak of "pure science," knowing it to be the furthest reach of exploration where *what* will be found (not to mention its possible use) is unpredictable — and properly so. Modern science is said to rely on scientific method. But it may be truer to say that it is based, like all original work, on a hunch. Method comes later — and of course, stays longer.

Literature has a tougher time keeping this simple fact of its nature before readers — and even before writers. Raymond Carver's relief when he read Flannery

O'Connor's candid description of her working process is a writer's response. But it is also a reader's reaction to the mystery of the seamless garment which is a story. Writers, especially writers of a form as refined as the short story, come to the act of writing as readers too, people who already love many stories by other writers they admire.

It is not a problem to come to writing as a reader (which is how just about everybody comes to it) because you might be "influenced" by another writer. No problem with that, anymore than learning to speak English, rather than Latin, unduly limits you because you were born in twentieth-century America instead of third-century Rome. We learn to speak from those who speak to us. But before long, we say things they wouldn't be caught dead uttering. Count on it: Originality is unavoidable.

The inevitable trouble of coming to writing as a reader is, rather, that the finished stories we read and re-read, love and return to (or anthologize!), reinforce our sense of their immutability and unity. We see no clue to their process — and forget such a thing even exists. We are enchanted. And that is enough.

For a while. But when you are Raymond Carver, or any writer at all, another form of enchantment lures you. How to *do* it becomes the call. You have plenty of examples of how it has been *done*. There are days when it seems you spend most of your time on your knees to these canonized idols. Much literary energy is expended in reverence.

Nor is this question of process something that preoccupies only writers. It seems to propel the instincts of readers too, for different reasons than for writers but perhaps even more intensely (after all, writers have the satisfaction of sitting around talking and writing about "craft"; by now there is a long and accepted tradition of shop-talk of this sort).

Graywolf Press, a literary publisher, has reported that its all-time best-seller is a book titled *If You Want to Write* by Brenda Ueland. It is not a how-to book, but an essay about imaginative process. In just a couple of years and with very little advertising, Graywolf has sold 50,000 copies of this little book, which is neither a novel nor a collection of stories. The call for this book clearly does not come from a coterie of writers but from what Virginia Woolf calls "the common reader."

Readers want in on the magic, too. Who knows why? Maybe creation is always magnetic. In any case, readers have only the story before them, the tantalizing story which keeps its lip buttoned about its private life. A reader waiting at a bookstore to have a book autographed posed the question as well as anyone. "Where," she asked, "do you get your . . . um . . . ideas?" A little cloud of hopelessness attended the question, as if she knew in advance no bright answer would ever break through.

"Read it, read it, and you'll see how it's written!" Isak Dinesen crowed at an interviewer who asked much the same question about her story "The Monkey." But a particular kind of reading is called for, more investigative than the reading which is enchantment, less mechanistic and reductive than the mentality that speaks of "the techniques of fiction."

"The celestial process" suggests a different order of business. A writer must renew faith in that process as a regular exercise. Otherwise, the blank page is no invitation. It is the abyss. And the writer waits to be hurled into it. The offense? Not having it all figured out in advance.

Just because the goal is unity doesn't mean the method is going to look — or feel — smooth and effortless. I'm not talking about facing up to hard work or discipline, as if the problem were faulty willpower or a poor character. There is such a thing as sloth, and everybody knows what it feels like. It is a form of cowardice. But when it comes to the imagination, there is probably more sinning done in the name of discipline than by any amount of lazy daydreaming.

As Flannery O'Connor said in the passage that encouraged Raymond Carver, when she started her story "Good Country People" she had no idea "there was going to be a PhD with a wooden leg in it. I merely found myself one morning writing a description of two women I knew something about and before I realized it, I had equipped one of them with a daughter with a wooden leg."

Then she brought in a Bible salesman, also without any immediate occupation for him. "I didn't know he was going to steal that wooden leg," she says, "until ten or twelve lines before he did it, but when I found out that this was what was going to happen, I realized it was inevitable."

There's celestial process for you. Something a little hellish about it, after all.

Lest all this begin to take on the perverse aura of paradox: I am trying to describe (and lift descriptions from writers like James and O'Connor and Carver who have tried to express it) how the process is experienced. Not how it ought to happen, not how it might be better orchestrated, and especially not how it looks from the light end of the tunnel when the scary part — the writing — is over.

This question of where the story comes from and how it is made is not solely a "craft question," not a "technique of fiction" dilemma. The work of the imagination is too fundamental to belong to writers alone as if they were a bunch of inspired grease-monkeys tinkering with a hot rod, revving the engine and making a lot of noise as they turn corners, screeching the tires, annoying and amazing the neighbors with their flashy toy.

The obviously genuine reports of writers make it clear that the process that brings finished stories into being does not look like the stories themselves. The story is fluid; the process is given to fits and starts. The story speaks with poise and assurance; the process must fight fevers and fidgets, as James calls them.

So, if writers aren't thinking of plot and outline — if all that comes later or only in conjunction with something more fundamental — what is that more fundamental thing?

It's nothing much. Like a seed (I'm thinking of a poppy seed), it looks like a speck, but it packs a wallop. Life is in there, life and the breeding instinct.

"Caress the detail," Vladimir Nabokov said, "the divine detail." This is the atom that generates all the stars.

Probably every comp teacher living or dead has a heart inscribed with the phrase "Be Specific." Yet the generating power of the detail is too often obscured in discussions of writing. The detail is paid homage, of course; phrases like "a wonderful eye for detail" or "precise detail" are clichés of reviewing flattery.

But such talk sees detail as cunning ornament, an accessory to a grand ensemble whose design gives detail a proper place from which to shine. The detail as diamond earring, winking from the ear of a statuesque beauty.

Sometimes, detail is seen as the source of symbolism, even as rudimentary allegory. The earring "stands for" — fill in the blank. Once again, the mechanistic response is the wrong respone. Unfortunately, when detail is etherealized in this way, it loses power by the very inflation which attempts to sanctify it.

Literature engages in the work of transformation: a diamond earring can become a sexual wink, and in that glint, the earring breathes a soul and is an earring no longer. It becomes the shocking availability of the married woman wearing it. And so, yes, it becomes a symbol.

But the verb here is telling. Symbols *become;* they are figments of the celestial process, not techniques that *stand for* something or other. They don't stand; they carry. They are not static. As soon as they are imprisoned that way, symbols begin to die. It is simply sad, maybe pathetic, when this happens to a reader reading a story. It is lethal when it happens to a writer writing one.

That is why Nabokov's fervent command — *Caress the detail, the divine detail* — is a necessary caution. Creation is godly work. Well, but who is God? Nabokov once said in an interview that *his* characters were galley slaves. Yet when it is a matter of locating the godhead, even a writer as unabashedly imperious as Nabokov did not point to himself, but to the detail. Detail: the smallest, least organized unit of fiction. Next to grand conceptions like plot, which is the legitimate government of most stories, or character, which is the crowned sovereign, the detail looks like a ragged peasant with a half-baked idea of revolution and a crazy, sure glint in its eye.

◀▶

It comes down to faith. If, as Nabokov says, the detail is divine, there's nothing much to do but give yourself over to it as one properly does in worship. If there's any question about the divinity of the detail, by the way, think of that *one thing* which you can explain to no one but which is precious beyond expression. That is a divine detail. It is also a literary opportunity.

A woman once told me she could not listen to the Beatles' song "Here Comes the Sun." It reminded her of . . . (but it is her story to tell). If she was driving in the car and the song came on, she *had* to switch off the radio. At a party where someone played it on a tape machine, she had to leave. Even the Musak version made her exit elevators on the wrong floor. A clear case of a divine detail, that song.

This detail, only mildly interesting in itself, *led her* to a story. I would even say, led her against her will. She was a writing student and had "trouble with plot" (her phrase). I wonder if she did not actually have trouble with detail. Certainly, she was unwilling to caress *that* detail. Yet she knew, if confusedly, that it mattered. I think she was shy of making too much of it.

Certain questions of imaginative failure can be answered by looking at the larger structures (like plot) that fiction moves to for its sustained life. But many failures begin much earlier, in the smallest corners. And certainly the difficulty readers have in understanding creative process comes from a resistance to the humbled circumstances of the job. Or from a resistance on the part of writers to acknowledging the secret life of composition.

In his notebooks, Chekhov tries to describe to a friend how he writes a short story. "I write the beginning serenely, let myself go," he says, "but in the middle I have already begun cowering and fearing. . . . My start . . . is full of promise, as though I were beginning a novel; the middle section is difficult and broken up, while the end, as in a short short story, is like fireworks. In writing, therefore, one is bound to concentrate first of all upon the story's framework; from the mass of greater and lesser figures you pick one particular person — the husband or wife — place him in the foreground, draw him in and underscore him alone, then you throw the others about the background like loose change, and the result is not unlike the vault of heaven: one big moon and around it a mass of very small stars. The moon, however, cannot come through successfully, because it can only be interpreted properly when the other stars are understood; and the stars in the meantime have not been clearly explained. So what emerges is not literature, but something on the order of the sewing of Trishkin's coat. What shall I do. I simply don't know. I put my trust in all-healing time."

This is not so much an explanation as a wail followed by a philosophical shrug. "In writing . . . one is bound to concentrate first of all upon the story's framework." This would seem to suggest that detail is *not* the key element after all. However, it's strange to see that Chekhov immediately expresses his "framework" in metaphor, not in technical literary language. He is able to describe briskly the act of concentration, but his focus is not on "flat characters" and "round characters." He speaks of the moon and the stars. He is speaking from within the experience of writing, not from a theory about what a story is made of. What he comes up with, he says with obvious regret, "is not literature." It is (you can almost hear the sigh) a patchwork coat that a peasant might wear.

Those patches are details. And like Carver, like any writer, Chekhov is expressing here the frustration of emerging from the act of writing into the more orderly world of reading. Of course the story's framework is the writer's first and last wish. But if the story is engaged in discovery this framework is discerned over time. "I put my trust in time." Time spent cooped up with a pack of crazy details acting like juvenile delinquents, exhibiting no sense of responsibility but a lot of gorgeous random energy.

In the end, though, the story *is* seamless. We are enchanted again and again. If the story fails to enchant us, we are ruthless — or killingly kind (which can be crueller still). Just read the reviews in any paper.

So, somehow or other the divine detail gets caressed and coaxed into tumbling out its tale of woe and/or ecstasy. Is that it? More mysterious veils, more cranking of wires. Celestial process as stagecraft.

Chekhov put his trust in time which he, a physician, saw as "all-healing." Time spent with the sickness which was the virulent fragmentariness of the unwritten story, its chronic spinelessness. Time spent with details. Typically, it takes longer to write a story than anyone, including most writers, wants to admit. Fiction in the making is a patient prone to many relapses, requiring much hand-holding.

How then is that time spent? James provides a clue again in his essay "The Art of Fiction" when he speaks of "the rich principle of the Note."

He stakes a big claim. "If one was to undertake to tell tales and to report with truth on the human scene," he says, "it could but be because notes had been from the cradle the ineluctable consequence of one's greatest inward energy . . . to take them was as natural as to look, to think, to feel, to recognize, to remember."

Everyone knows about writers' notebooks. An essential piece of equipment for one in the trade. But as with the notion of "the detail," the notebook is not given a long enough look in this whole question of how a story gets itself written. Like detail, the note is seen as an accessory.

What is most striking about James's remark is the pedestal upon which he places the note. It is not a tool, not "useful." He does not treat the note as the result of a creative impulse. The note antedates the organizing impulse of art; its life is older, begotten of an ancient, primitive order. He goes so far as to say that in order to "undertake to report with truth on the human scene" one must *have been* taking notes. It is not merely a professionally expedient habit to be picked up and turned to good use.

The note is evidence of the drive for accuracy. It is also a safe-house where detail with its bit of intelligence can slip into a protected room, and be debriefed by friendlies. No questions asked. Just sit a while. Rest a moment. Tell the little you were able to pick up. And vanish as you must. Another operative will come along to take your place.

Adrienne Rich once wrote in a poem, "The notes for the poem are the only poem." That is the sort of faith I've been thinking about here.

The dedication to the fragment, which is not itself discipline, provides a writer with the driving passion to spend all that time, Chekhov's all-healing time, with what often feels not simply lifeless, but nonexistent.

For remember, the story is nonexistent during most of a writer's intimacy with it. That's the fact of the matter. That's what makes the detail so dear. It is the only flesh it is possible to touch in the whole alluring body of the story.

"I recall kneeling on my (flattish) pillow at the window of a sleeping car," Nabokov writes of a childhood train ride in his memoir *Speak Memory*, ". . . and seeing with an inexplicable pang a handful of fabulous lights that beckoned me from a distant hillside, and then slipped into a pocket of black velvet: diamonds that I later gave away to my characters to alleviate the burden of my wealth." This must be what James meant when he spoke of the habit of taking notes "from the cradle."

Everyone does it, in rudimentary form. Everyone has a memory with precious odds and ends tossed about. That is why we recognize this capacity for the note in others, especially in writers we trust. It may be why we are able to winnow the false from the authentic in our reading: we have an ear for the note. Like the musical note, the literary note has tone, rhythm, all the properties of expressive art which cannot be faked.

This view of life as a collection of shards introduces the inevitable thought that life is full of brokenness, after all. Life is not a fixed star, not a unity. That idea of certain unity is only a touching illusion. It makes sense that stories, for all their apparent seamlessness, should be formed of smashed, discarded bits. Scheherazade keeps going, on and on through the scary night, enchanting the ear of the king who would destroy her. Of course she must be steady, assured, of course the story must not hesitate. Her life depends upon it.

For all the misery of it, this work of writing stories seems to have to do with happiness, which even those who write stories best have trouble describing. "My own happiness in the past often approached such ecstasy that I could not share it even with the person dearest to me," F. Scott Fitzgerald writes in *The Crack-Up,* "but had to walk it away in quiet streets and lanes with only fragments of it to distil into little lines in books. . . ."

Maybe "the person dearest" cannot be, for a writer at such a moment, the wife or husband, the friend or lover of daily life. Maybe it is you, dear reader, stranger, who must be trusted with the ridiculous, broken bits that are held long in the hand as the writer struggles to tell the tale.

An Introduction to This Collection

*T*he anthology has become so thoroughly associated with classroom use that it brings to mind that other academic genre — the textbook. But the anthology has a more winsome lineage. The word *anthology,* coming originally from the Greek, means a collection of flowers.

Let's start there. Not for the charm of the thought, but to be reminded of the curious mix of objectivity and subjectivity that must go into the making of an anthology. The literary works themselves — in this case, the stories — are growing out there in the field, in astonishing variety, some of them tucked into remote, hidden spots. They're simply *there,* objective as flowers, whether they're gathered or not.

It's the gathering that makes for the subjectivity. A collection of flowers? All right, but *whose* collection? Gathered where, for what purpose? "Every reader is an anthologist," Alberto Manguel says in his essay "Sweet Are the Uses of Anthology." We all keep our lists. And one person's bouquet is somebody else's bunch of weeds.

But the formal anthology, intended both for reading and for study, has a strange relationship with subjectivity. Such a collection must have character, but avoid eccentricity. It should exhibit forceful choices, and be willing to go with a strong hunch about a little-known author or story — in order to represent a shared tradition while it inevitably nudges that tradition along an untried path. The anthology lives in history and therefore risks being dated, but its commitment is to its own period's sense of what is timeless and most valuable in literature. A tall order.

Ideally, the reader of a general anthology of short fiction should come away from the table of contents with a sensation of having been out there in the growing field too. Some of the names and titles will be as familiar as daisies, a part of our communal collection (what anthology of short fiction, for example, would not include Chekhov?). Some names that are less familiar may provide an introduction to a particularly vital literary culture (for instance, Cortázar, Valenzuela, Donoso from Latin America); another writer may address a contemporary issue that concerns everyone (Susan Sontag's "The Way We Live Now" about AIDS).

"On rare occasions," Alberto Manguel says, an anthologist must "be drawn not by a feeling of debt to the past, but by a feeling of debt to the future." The idea is not only to give the reader a working sense of what has been done in the past but "in the best of cases, [to give] the reader a sense of things to come."

Some of the stories here have been neighbors in other anthologies over the decades and are familiar not only to generations of readers but, it seems, to each other. Others meet here for the first time. Each story must stand on its own, of course. But living under the same roof, the stories gathered into an anthology seem to cluster, revealing common themes, narrative voices of striking similarity — or striking discord. They cease to be merely a collection, and begin to become a conversation.

That conversation has to do with something called "canon formation." In fact, canon formation is one of the hottest aspects of literary studies in our times. It is not simply fashionable, but hot as in burning hot. The phrase itself is new. "The canon" has always referred to what is agreed upon as our (or even, the) heritage, those works which are essential, lasting, and which represent the living tradition of our literature. As such, the canon has been thought of as a body of works received, not formed. That assumption has changed and continues to change.

Put simply: in the past two decades, as women, racial, ethnic, and geographic minorities (who, in fact, are sometimes global majorities) have asserted the values and experiences of their own populations, they have looked at standard literary anthologies and said, "We aren't here." And, more to the point, "We ought to be." This can be an explosive recognition.

It has also become increasingly clear that what is anthologized is what is studied; and what is studied becomes, finally, what *is*. As readers become more critical, the subjectivity of anthologies has properly come under closer scrutiny. Choices can seem outrageously limited. Women teachers and students, for instance, pick up an anthology and automatically do a gender count of the authors — so many men, so few women. In times of such cultural ferment, anthologies can begin to look more like battlefields than fields of gathered flowers.

Canon formation may sometimes look like one dustup after another, but at its best this process has more to do with discovering and reclaiming and paying strict attention to the widest possible field than to making the fur fly. The volatility of literary studies has also given a profound shock to anthologies. A good shock.

For one thing, the anthology has become a vital genre, not simply a classroom standby. Anthologies are powerful voices in the current debate. As the concept of a settled canon is superseded by a wider search for a literary heritage, the anthology ceases to be a museum. It is the meeting room for the debate itself.

In 1829, a man named Samuel Kettell edited and published a volume titled *Specimens of American Poetry*. His book is the first-known anthology of specifically American literature published in this country. "The following work," he says in his preface, "is the result of an attempt to do something for the cause of American literature, by calling into notice and preserving a portion of what is valuable and characteristic in the writings of our native poets."

The cause of American literature. A telling phrase. It is touchingly defensive, betraying an underdog's view of the literary scene. Until well into the twentieth century, in fact, merely to establish such a thing as "American literature" as a distinct entity seemed to be the biggest task any American anthology could undertake.

A protective tone invades most of the prefaces of these early collections. They refer to "specimens of native genius" and speak of trying "to foster native literature." As late as 1889 an anthology titled *A Library of American Literature* could give as its purpose a desire to provide "a general view of the course of American Literature . . . for popular use and enjoyment, and to occupy a vacant field."

The field is hardly vacant anymore. Following the principle of what-goes-around-comes-around, contemporary anthologies have to contend now with the opposite problem their predecessors faced. Not only must the contemporary anthology include "native geniuses"; it also must make sure that the rest of the world is represented too. Brave American anthologies used to try to give a place to home talent in the face of an established European, particularly English, tradition. Now the job is to discover Europe all over again — and Latin America, and Africa, and the ignored populations of our own country, and and and. . . .

Luckily, an anthology's purpose is not to fan out over all of world literature and pretend to represent it with bland neutrality, a miserly dram measured from all quarters. Every anthology is made from within a culture. The culture is the given. But its boundaries may be (should be, no doubt) permeable. The collection is made *from* the culture — but not only within it.

By what it includes, what it chooses to exclude or simply what it fails to notice, the anthology demonstrates the nature of literary curiosity in a given culture at a given time. This happens to be a particularly exciting time to be investigating that literary curiosity in America. It also happens to be a singularly vital time for the short story.

But whose literary curiosity is under investigation? Well, not exclusively the editor's. This collection was not made by a committee, but neither was it the work of a single reader. It is worth taking a moment to mention the process by which these stories — and not some others — came to be gathered into this anthology, in order to cast some light on the nature of contemporary literary curiosity.

The selection process was highly communal, but most of the players never met each other. That was the beauty of the method, perhaps. Everyone who gave a critique of the table of contents remained a reader, responding to stories without reference to what someone else might say. No one argued: everyone testified, often passionately, sometimes ironically, which could prove especially powerful. Most of this testifying was done in written correspondence to my editor at Houghton Mifflin, whose desk served as headquarters for the project.

She and I, through letters to each other and eventually via numerous telephone conversations, made and revised many lists of stories and authors. Other anthologies (both out of print and on the market) were searched and consulted, recent magazine and newly published books were sifted. We read individual collections by many authors. We re-read old chestnuts, we finally got to stories we had always meant to read but which had somehow escaped us before. We read stories by writers we had never heard of — on a hunch, on a tip from another writer or a colleague.

We began to notice preoccupations and traits rising from clusters of stories, as if from a hidden spirit within the emerging collection. We tried to follow the contemporary reader in search of a vivid, living tradition. This was especially true of our search for stories from other countries and other languages, which led us deep into Latin America, for instance. And figures who might have been deemed merely eminent elder statesmen astonished us with their immediacy and urgency — Henry James, perhaps most of all.

It was a period of special, quite intense reading. At one point, our telephone conversations sounded something like the talk between two collectors with a mitt full of baseball cards, working out a series of swaps to our mutual advantage.

Though we hammered out the final table of contents, we were not alone in this busy reading and story swapping. A couple dozen readers were recruited to write lengthy responses to preliminary versions of the table of contents. Some of these readers are fiction writers, but most of them are professors of literature who teach the short story in literature and writing courses at colleges and universities across the United States and Canada.

Their testimony, in their letters, deserves an anthology of its own. Certainly their correspondence is evidence of the passion that is being brought to bear just now on canon formation and on the short story as the stellar genre of the day.

One lively letter would tell us that some of the stories we were considering were "too often collected." The very next letter would applaud our intention to "widen the canon of the short story in significant ways" and would say of those same stories that they were less known than some of the standard sources, and so especially welcome.

It is in the nature of the genre that no anthology ever fully satisfies any reader, including its editors. The classic response to any new anthology is, "Why didn't you include . . . ?" In a way, it is an impossible question to answer. But, from our reading, a strong, compelling personality has emerged, no matter the wistfulness that lingers for a story cut or a culture not as fully represented as we might have wished (Asia has three stories here, including French writer Marguerite Yourcenar's treatment of a thirteenth-century Chinese tale).

A few statistics give a rough personality profile of the collection. There are 79 writers in the anthology, almost a quarter of them represented by two stories. That comes to 98 stories in all. About half the stories are Anglo-American, the other half international (other than Britain). Approximately 40 percent of the stories are by women.

Forty-one of the 79 writers are living. Thirty-five are from the United States, 4 black, 1 Native American. Ireland is represented by 9 stories (by 6 writers), Canada by 6 stories (by 4 writers). Africa has one story each by two black male writers and two stories by one white South African woman writer. From Continental Europe come 12 stories. England comes in with 13 stories, only three more than those by writers from Latin America and the Caribbean.

The oldest story may be the Taoist tale from which Marguerite Yourcenar retold "How Wang-Fo Was Saved" — or perhaps the folktale from which Hans Andersen wrote "The Wild Swans." The most recent is "The Best Place for It" by Richard Powers, which appeared in a magazine in 1988.

It is important to note that these statistics result from a few guiding intentions rather than from a master plan to include a certain number of stories from this or that category. We wished to be inclusive in a way that represents not only the best writers today, but the best readers — readers who cherish the stories of a common tradition and reach out to contemporary short stories at a time when the form is especially lively. But we did not want to represent the literature of other cultures only out of the abstract notion that this would be a good thing.

Rather, we were trying to recognize the fact of what readers — not simply ourselves but the informed readers we enlisted to give us long and spirited commentary — are already reading, and what they wish to see gathered together in one place. The demographics of the authors and the numbers of stories should be considered in this light. There was no quota system here. The pull came from the stories themselves.

The short story is acknowledged to be the most exquisite kind of prose fiction, requiring perfect craft, the form in which the smallest slip can bring the whole contraption — plot, character, narration — down in a crash. A delicate business.

When that is said and done, and everyone has been warned of the ferocious fragility of the short story, its elegant ways and its sly, spare habits, all the talk suddenly reverses itself. There is no salient definition, it turns out, for "the short story." More even than the novel, it won't declare itself formally, won't be corralled, ranging instead on open territory. The short story likes to pretend it isn't a genre at all.

To begin with, it isn't always short. It sometimes fattens up to novella size. Its voice, when the tale is told in the first person, is often scarcely discernible from a memoir. And then again, at times the narration is as aloof and impersonal as the sky it seems to come from. It is a hard form to characterize, which may account for its popularity: the flexibility of short fiction invites any number of voices, tales, and tellers.

Perhaps even more telling than the rough statistics concerning the demographics of the anthology are the binding ties of the themes and narrative techniques gathered together here. It would be dismissive merely to tick off figures about these matters, but it is worth noticing some general tendencies.

Narrative voice is one of the most striking distinctions from story to story. A general rule of thumb (not always observed, of course, but still interesting): first-person narration does not simply signal intimacy, but even more so the evidence of contemporary consciousness.

Third-person narration, however, can seem surprisingly memoiristic. Katherine Mansfield's "Prelude," told in the third person, still gives off the scent of a beloved commemoration, perhaps because of its episodic quality with its lingering attention to landscape and homescape.

Inevitably and yet still surprisingly, the major preoccupation of the greatest number of stories here is with family and its relationships. Nor should the word "family" necessarily bring to mind the middle-class American family. Just about all our identified population groups turn to this powerful source. The working out of family dynamics seems to magnetize writers as varied in culture and style as Baldwin and Bradbury, Joyce, Donoso, and Mann, Welty and Edna O'Brien.

On the other hand, we tend to turn to writers from other cultures, like Argentina's Valenzuela, Czechoslovakia's Kundera, and South Africa's Gordimer, for overtly political stories. North American writers seem, as a rule, to favor psychological insight, the epiphanic moment, and the meticulously retrieved childhood memory. There are exceptions, of course: Tim O'Brien's hypnotic piece on Vietnam, Sontag's grieving choral work on AIDS.

Of course, a powerful story should not be reduced to what it's "about." Edna O'Brien's "Sister Imelda," for instance, can be studied as a memoir story, the narrative taking its power from the quality of backward looking that is invested in the voice. But it is also a story about faith — the living experience of faith and its eventual desertion of the soul. It is, among other things, a love story. It is also a portrait of a teacher/student relationship. As such, it would make a striking companion to Charles Baxter's "Gryphon."

Other themes and voices present themselves. What is war for Hemingway? For a realistic writer like Cynthia Ozick? For a fantasist like LeGuin? How does García Márquez handle a story told in monologue? How does Welty try the same narrative voice? Some stories are stories wrestling with how to tell a story: Julio Cortázar's "Blow-Up," Ann Beattie's "Snow." Death is at the heart of many of these stories, too. Death and mourning. Carol Bly's "The Dignity of Life," Joyce's "The Dead," Mark Helprin's "The Schreuderspitze," and Alice Walker's "To Hell with Dying" form a powerful square.

There is quite a solid tradition of detective fiction running down the middle of the short story's history, as well. We have chosen to represent Poe as a detective writer rather than, as is often done, an early writer of horror fiction. Follow Poe through Conan Doyle, and eventually you get to Borges. The supernatural, too, has its pull. Writers as diverse as Thomas Hardy, Henry James, Elizabeth Bowen, José Donoso, and Mercè Rodoreda deploy it to powerful effect.

Another clustering that would be particularly instructive for Americans would be to consider the Canadian writers as a group. And what about gathering the Irish together to see what common preoccupations they have?

Well, the pairing and matching possibilities are endless — and worth pursuing. They extend the conversations that these stories, gathered intimately together here, are meant to have.

Short stories, it has been said, are like snapshots: a moment (or a day, or a year, or a realization) captured and fixed in time. Or, as Mavis Gallant put it, "A short story is what you see when you look out of the window." They're everywhere, stories.

Regarded one way, they're rather slender, sometimes hardly more than a sheaf of a few pages — certainly, they don't have the heft and orchestration of the novel. But, as Virginia Woolf said (of novels, as it happens), "Is life like this?" It *is* a matter of impressions, flashes, recognitions. In a way, the short story bears greater kinship to the lyric poem, which is another brief look out a window.

Literature has a way of adopting the forms that suit its times best. Our time has embraced the short story and found it wonderfully reliable. It is a small form, but not a minor genre these days. That's how it was for Chekhov, too. "On the whole," he said in a letter, "little things are much better to write than big ones: there is very little pretension and sure success ... what more does one need?"

P.H.

CHINUA ACHEBE

Chinua Achebe was born in Azidi, Nigeria, in 1930, the son of one of the first Ibo Mission teachers. Ibo is his native tongue, but he learned English — the language in which he writes — at a young age. After taking a degree in English literature from University College, Ibadon, in 1953, he worked for a time in broadcasting in Nigeria and England. His first novel, *Things Fall Apart*, was published in 1958. It has been called "the archetypical African novel" — one depicting the disintegration of African tribal culture at the hands of the white man — and is usually considered the most famous novel written in English by an African. Its story continues in two more novels, *No Longer At Ease* (1960) and *Arrow of God* (1964). Achebe's short stories are collected in *The Sacrificial Egg and Other Stories* (1962), *Girls At War* (1972), and *African Short Stories* (1985). In them, as in his longer fiction, Achebe is intent on communicating the ways of the Ibo to his Western readers; he does so by melding Ibo proverbs, thought patterns, and linguistic rhythms into his English prose style. In citing literary influences, he has mentioned Thomas Hardy and Joseph Conrad — both great spinners of tales — and the Bible, an echo of which can be heard even in the opening line of "Chike's School Days."

Chike's School Days

Sarah's last child was a boy, and his birth brought great joy to the house of his father, Amos. The child received three names at his baptism — John, Chike, Obiajulu. The last name means "the mind at last is at rest." Anyone hearing this name knew at once that its owner was either an only child or an only son. Chike was an only son. His parents had had five daughters before him.

Like his sisters Chike was brought up "in the ways of the white man," which meant the opposite of traditional. Amos had many years before bought a tiny bell with which he summoned his family to prayers and hymn-singing first thing in the morning and last thing at night. This was one of the ways of the white man. Sarah taught her children not to eat in their neighbours' houses because "they offered their food to idols." And thus she set herself against the age-old custom which regarded children as the common responsibility of all so that, no matter what the relationship between parents, their children played together and shared their food.

One day a neighbour offered a piece of yam to Chike, who was only four years old. The boy shook his head haughtily and said, "We don't eat heathen food." The neighbour was full of rage, but she controlled herself and only muttered under her breath that even an *Osu* was full of pride nowadays, thanks to the white man.

And she was right. In the past an *Osu* could not raise his shaggy head in the presence of the free-born. He was a slave to one of the many gods of the clan. He was a thing set apart, not to be venerated but to be despised and almost spat on. He could not marry a free-born, and he could not take any of the titles of his clan. When he died, he was buried by his kind in the Bad Bush.

Now all that had changed, or had begun to change. So that an *Osu* child could even look down his nose at a free-born, and talk about heathen food! The white man had indeed accomplished many things.

Chike's father was not originally an *Osu*, but had gone and married an *Osu* woman in the name of Christianity. It was unheard of for a man to make himself *Osu* in that way, with his eyes wide open. But then Amos was nothing if not mad. The new religion had gone to his head. It was like palm-wine. Some people drank it and remained sensible. Others lost every sense in their stomach.

The only person who supported Amos in his mad marriage venture was Mr. Brown, the white missionary, who lived in a thatch-roofed, red-earth-walled parsonage and was highly respected by the people, not because of his sermons, but because of a dispensary he ran in one of his rooms. Amos had emerged from Mr. Brown's parsonage greatly fortified. A few days later he told his widowed mother, who had recently been converted to Christianity and had taken the name of Elizabeth. The shock nearly killed her. When she recovered, she went down on her knees and begged Amos not to do this thing. But he would not hear; his ears had been nailed up. At last, in desperation, Elizabeth went to consult the diviner.

This diviner was a man of great power and wisdom. As he sat on the floor of his hut beating a tortoise shell, a coating of white chalk round his eyes, he saw not only the present, but also what had been and what was to be. He was called "the man of the four eyes." As soon as old Elizabeth appeared, he cast his stringed cowries and told her what she had come to see him about. "Your son has joined the white man's religion. And you too in your old age when you should know better. And do you wonder that he is stricken with insanity? Those who gather ant-infested faggots must be prepared for the visit of lizards." He cast his cowries a number of times and wrote with a finger on a bowl of sand, and all the while his *nwifulu,* a talking calabash, chatted to itself. "Shut up!" he roared, and it immediately held its peace. The diviner then muttered a few incantations and rattled off a breathless reel of proverbs that followed one another like the cowries in his magic string.

At last he pronounced the cure. The ancestors were angry and must be appeased with a goat. Old Elizabeth performed the rites, but her son remained insane and married an *Osu* girl whose name was Sarah. Old Elizabeth renounced her new religion and returned to the faith of her people.

We have wandered from our main story. But it is important to know how Chike's father became an *Osu*, because even today when everything is upside down, such a story is very rare. But now to return to Chike who refused heathen food at the tender age of four years, or maybe five.

Two years later he went to the village school. His right hand could now reach across his head to his left ear, which proved that he was old enough to tackle the mysteries of the white man's learning. He was very happy about his new slate and pencil, and especially about his school uniform of white shirt and brown khaki shorts. But as the first day of the new term approached, his young mind dwelt on the many stories about teachers and their canes. And he remembered the song his elder sisters sang, a song that had a somewhat disquieting refrain:

> Onye nkuzi ewelu itali piagbusie umuaka.

One of the ways an emphasis is laid in Ibo is by exaggeration, so that the teacher in the refrain might not actually have flogged the children to death. But there was no doubt he did flog them. And Chike thought very much about it.

Being so young, Chike was sent to what was called the "religious class" where they sang, and sometimes danced, the catechism. He loved the sound of words and he loved rhythm. During the catechism lesson the class formed a ring to dance the teacher's question. "Who was Caesar?" he might ask, and the song would burst forth with much stamping of feet.

> Siza bu eze Rome
> Onye nachi enu uwa dum.

It did not matter to their dancing that in the twentieth century Caesar was no longer ruler of the whole world.

And sometimes they even sang in English. Chike was very fond of "Ten Green Bottles." They had been taught the words but they only remembered the first and the last lines. The middle was hummed and hie-ed and mumbled.

> Ten grin botr angin on dar war,
> Ten grin botr angin on dar war,
> Hm, hm hm hm hm
> Hm, hm hm hm hm hm,
> An ten grin botr angin on dar war.

In this way the first year passed. Chike was promoted to the "Infant School," where work of a more serious nature was undertaken.

We need not follow him through the Infant School. It would make a full story in itself. But it was no different from the story of other children. In the Primary School, however, his individual character began to show. He developed a strong hatred for arithmetic. But he loved stories and songs. And he liked particularly the sound of English words, even when they conveyed no meaning at all. Some of them simply filled him with elation. "Periwinkle" was such a word. He had now forgotten how he learned it or exactly what it was. He had a vague private meaning for it and it was something to do with fairyland. "Constellation" was another.

Chike's teacher was fond of long words. He was said to be a very learned man. His favourite pastime was copying out jaw-breaking words from his *Chambers' Etymological Dictionary*. Only the other day he had raised applause from his class by demolishing a boy's excuse for lateness with unanswerable erudition. He had said: "Procrastination is a lazy man's apology." The teacher's erudition showed itself in every subject he taught. His nature study lessons were memorable. Chike would always remember the lesson on the methods of seed dispersal. According to teacher, there were five methods: by man, by animals, by water, by wind, and by explosive mechanism. Even those pupils who forgot all the other methods remembered "explosive mechanism."

Chike was naturally impressed by teacher's explosive vocabulary. But the fairyland quality which words had for him was of a different kind. The first sentences in his *New Method Reader* were simple enough and yet they filled him with a vague exultation: "Once there was a wizard. He lived in Africa. He went to China to get a lamp." Chike read it over and over again at home and then made a song of it. It was a meaningless song. "Periwinkles" got into it, and also "Damascus." But it was like a window through which he saw in the distance a strange, magical new world. And he was happy.

ALICE ADAMS

Alice Adams was born in Virginia in 1926, grew up in Chapel Hill, North Carolina ("a bookish town"), and was educated at Radcliffe College. For the last forty years she has lived in the San Francisco Bay area, the setting of a number of her novels and short stories. After working for a time at various clerical jobs, she turned her attention to writing; as she has ruefully said, "My mother read all the time, so I thought, 'If I'm a writer, maybe she'll like me.'" Adams' stories are invariably about the nuances of relationships — between lovers, between family members, between friends, between past and present. "Snow" touches in some way on all these relationships. Among Adams' novels are *Careless Love* (1966), *Families and Survivors* (1975), *Listening to Billie* (1978), *Superior Women* (1984), and *Second Chances* (1988). Her short stories are collected in *Beautiful Girl* (1979), *To See You Again* (1982), and *Return Trips* (1985); new ones frequently appear in *The New Yorker*, *Atlantic*, *Paris Review*, and other periodicals.

Snow

On a trail high up in the California Sierra, between heavy smooth white snowbanks, four people on cross-country skis form a straggling line. A man and three women: Graham, dark and good-looking, a San Francisco architect, who is originally from Georgia; Carol, his girlfriend, a gray-eyed blonde, a florist; Susannah, daughter of Graham, dark and fat and now living in Venice, California; and, quite a way behind Susannah, tall thin Rose, Susannah's friend and lover. Susannah and Rose both have film-related jobs — Graham has never been quite sure what they do.

Graham and Carol both wear smart cross-country outfits: knickers and Norwegian wool stockings. The younger women are in jeans and heavy sweaters. And actually, despite the bright cold look of so much snow, this April day is warm, and the sky is a lovely spring blue, reflected in distant small lakes, just visible, at intervals.

Graham is by far the best skier of the four, a natural; he does anything athletic easily. He strides and glides along, hardly aware of what he is doing, except for a sense of physical well-being. However, just now he is cursing himself for having dreamed up this weekend, renting an unknown house in Alpine Meadows, near Lake Tahoe, even for bringing these women together: a visit from Susannah, who was bringing

Rose, whom he had previously been told about but had not met. Well, skiing was a diversion, but what in God's name would they all do tonight? Or talk about? And why had he wanted to get them together anyway? He wasn't all that serious about Carol (was he?); why introduce her to his daughter? And why did he have to meet Rose?

Carol is a fair skier, although she doesn't like it much: it takes all her breath. At the moment, with the part of her mind that is not concentrated on skiing, she is thinking that although Graham is smarter than most of the men she knows, talented and successful, and really nice as well, she is tired of going out with men who don't *see* her, don't know who she is. That's partly her fault, she knows; she lies about her age and dyes her hair, and she *never* mentions the daughter in Vallejo, put out for adoption when Carol was fifteen (she would be almost twenty now, almost as old as Graham's girl, this unfriendly fat Susannah). But sometimes Carol would like to say to the men she knows, Look, I'm thirty-five, and in some ways my life has been terrible — being blond and pretty doesn't save you from anything.

But, being more fair-minded than given to self-pity, next Carol thinks, Well, as far as that goes Graham didn't tell me much about his girl, either, and for all I know mine is that way, too. So many of them are, these days.

How can he possibly be so dumb, Susannah is passionately thinking, of her father. And the fact that she has asked that question hundreds of times in her life does not diminish its intensity or the accompanying pain. He doesn't understand anything, she wildly, silently screams. Stupid, straight blondes: *a florist. Skiing.* How could he think that I . . . that Rose. . . ?

Then, thinking of Rose in a more immediate way, she remembers that Rose has hardly skied before — just a couple of times in Vermont, where she comes from. In the almost-noon sun Susannah stops to wait for Rose, half-heartedly aware of the lakes, just now in view, and the smell of pines, as sweat collects under her heavy breasts, slides down her ribs.

Far behind them all, and terrified of everything, Rose moves along with stiffened desperation. Her ankles, her calves, her thighs, her lower back are all tight with dread. Snow is stuck to the bottoms of her skis, she knows — she can hardly move them — but she doesn't dare stop. She will fall, break something, get lost. And everyone will hate her, even Susannah.

Suddenly, like a gift to a man in his time of need, just ahead of Graham there appears a lovely open glade, to one side of the trail. Two huge heavy trees have fallen there, at right angles to each other; at the far side of the open space runs a brook, darkly glistening over small smooth rocks. High overhead a wind sings through the pines, in the brilliant sunlight.

It is perfect, a perfect picnic place, and it is just now time for lunch. Graham is hungry; he decides that hunger is what has been unsettling him. He gets out of his skis in an instant, and he has just found a smooth, level stump for the knapsack, a natural table, when Carol skis up — out of breath, not looking happy.

But at the sight of that place she instantly smiles. She say, "Oh, how perfect! Graham, it's beautiful." Her gray eyes praise him, and the warmth of her voice. "Even benches to sit on. Graham, what a perfect Southern host you are." She laughs in a pleased, cheered-up way, and bends to unclip her skis. But something is wrong, and they stick. Graham comes over to help. He gets her out easily; he takes her hand and lightly he kisses her mouth, and then they both go over and start removing food from the knapsack, spreading it out.

"Two bottles of wine. Lord, we'll all get plastered." Carol laughs again, as she sets up the tall green bottles in a deep patch of snow.

Graham laughs, too, just then very happy with her, although he is also feeling the familiar apprehension that any approach of his daughter brings on: *will* Susannah like what he has done, will she approve of him, ever? He looks at his watch and he says to Carol, "I wonder if they're O.K. Rose is pretty new on skis. I wonder . . ."

But there they are, Susannah and Rose. They have both taken off their skis and are walking along the side of the trail, carrying the skis on their shoulders, Susannah's neatly together, Rose's at a clumsy, difficult angle. There are snowflakes in Susannah's dark brown hair — hair like Graham's. Rose's hair is light, dirty blond; she is not even pretty, Graham has unkindly thought. At the moment they both look exhausted and miserable.

In a slow, tired way, not speaking, the two girls lean their skis and poles against a tree; they turn toward Graham and Carol, and then, seemingly on a single impulse, they stop and look around. And with a wide smile Susannah says, "Christ, Dad, it's just beautiful. It's great."

Rose looks toward the spread of food. "Oh, roast chicken. That's my favorite thing." These are the first nice words she has said to Graham. (Good manners are not a strong suit of Rose's, he has observed, in an interior, Southern voice.)

He has indeed provided a superior lunch, as well as the lovely place — his discovery. Besides the chicken, there are cherry tomatoes (called love apples where Graham comes from, in Georgia), cheese (Jack and cheddar), Triscuits, and oranges and chocolate. And the nice cool dry white wine. They all eat and drink a lot, and they talk eagerly about how good it all is, how beautiful the place where they are. The sky, the trees, the running brook.

Susannah even asks Carol about her work, in a polite, interested way that Graham has not heard from her for years. "Do you have to get up early and go to the flower mart every morning?" Susannah asks.

"No, but I used to, and really that was more fun — getting out so early, all those nice fresh smells. Now there's a boy I hire to do all that, and I'm pretty busy making arrangements."

"Oh, arrangements," says Rose, disparagingly.

Carol laughs. "Me, too, I hate them. I just try to make them as nice as I can, and the money I get is really good."

Both Rose and Susannah regard Carol in an agreeing, respectful way. For a moment Graham is surprised: these kids respecting money? Then he remembers that this is the seventies: women are supposed to earn money, it's good for them.

The main thing, though, is what a good time they all have together. Graham even finds Rose looking at him with a small, shy smile. He offers her more wine, which she accepts — another smile as he pours it out for her. And he thinks, Well, of course it's tough on her, too, meeting me. Poor girl, I'm sure she's doing the best she can.

"You all really like it down there in Hollywood?" he asks the two girls, and he notes that his voice is much more Southern than usual; maybe the wine.

"Universal City," Susannah corrects him, but she gives a serious answer. "I love it. There's this neat woman in the cutting room, and she knows I'm interested, so she lets me come in and look at the rushes, and hear them talk about what has to go. I'm really learning. It's great."

And Rose: "There's so many really exciting people around."

At that moment they both look so young, so enviably involved in their work, so happy, that Graham thinks, Well, really, why not?

Occasionally the wind will move a branch from a nearby tree and some snow will sift down, through sunlight. The sky seems a deeper blue than when they first came to this glade, a pure azure. The brook gurgles more loudly, and the sun is very hot.

And then they are all through with lunch; they have finished off the wine, and it is time to go.

They put on their skis, and they set off again, in the same order in which they began the day.

For no good reason, as he glides along, striding through snow in the early California afternoon, the heat, Graham is suddenly, sharply visited by a painful memory of the childhood of Susannah. He remembers a ferociously hot summer night in Atlanta, when he and his former wife, mother of Susannah, had quarrelled all through suppertime, and had finally got Susannah off to bed; she must have been about two. But she kept getting up again, screaming for her bottle, her Teddy bear, a sandwich. Her mother and Graham took turns going in to her, and then finally, about three in the morning, Graham picked her up and smacked her bottom, very hard; he can remember the sting on his hand — and good Christ, what a thing to do to a little baby. No wonder she is as she is; he probably frightened her right then, for good. Not to mention all the other times he got mad and just yelled at her — or his love affairs, the move to San Francisco, the divorce, more love affairs.

If only she were two right now, he desperately thinks, he could change everything; he could give her a stable, loving father. Now he has a nice house on Russian Hill; he is a successful man; he could give her — anything.

Then his mind painfully reverses itself and he thinks, But I was a loving father, most of the time. Susannah's got no real cause to be the way she is. Lots of girls — most girls — come out all right. At that overheated moment he feels that his heart will truly break. It is more than I can stand, he thinks; why do I have to?

Carol's problem is simply a physical one: a headache. But she never has headaches, and this one is especially severe; for the first time she knows exactly what her mother meant by "splitting headache." Is she going to get more and more like her mother as she herself ages? Could she be having an early menopause, beginning with migraines? She could die, the pain is so sharp. She could die, and would anyone care much, really? She's *lonely*.

Susannah is absorbed in the problem of Rose, who keeps falling down. Almost every time Susannah looks back, there is Rose, fallen in the snow. Susannah smiles at her encouragingly, and sometimes she calls back, "You're O.K.?" She knows that Rose would not like it if she actually skied back to her and helped her up; Rose has that ferocious Vermont Yankee pride, difficult in a fragile frightened woman.

It is breezier now than earlier in the morning, and somewhat cooler. Whenever Susannah stops, stands still, and waits for Rose, she is aware of her own wind-chilled sweat, and she worries, thinking of Rose, of wet and cold. Last winter Rose had a terrible, prolonged bout of flu, a racking cough.

Talking over their "relationship," at times Susannah and Rose have (somewhat jokingly) concluded that there certainly are elements of mothering within it; in many ways Susannah takes care of Rose. She is stronger — that is simply true. Now for the first time it occurs to Susannah (wryly, her style is wry) that she is somewhat fatherly with Rose, too: the sometimes stern guardian, the protector. And she thinks, Actually Graham wasn't all that bad with me, I've been rough on him. Look at the example he set me: I work hard, and I care about my work, the way he does. And he taught me to ski, come to think of it. I should thank him, sometime, somehow, for some of it.

Rose is falling, falling, again and again, and oh Christ, how much she hates it — hates her helplessness, hates the horrible snow, the cold wet. Drinking all that wine at lunchtime, in the pretty glade, the sunlight, she had thought that wine would make her brave; she knows her main problem to be fear — no confidence and hence no balance. But the wine, and the sun, and sheer fatigue have destroyed whatever equilibrium she had, so that all she can do is fall, fall miserably, and each time the snow is colder and it is harder for her to get up.

Therefore, they are all extremely glad when, finally, they are out of their skis and off the trail and at last back in their house, in Alpine Meadows. It is small — two tiny, juxtaposed bedrooms — but the living room is pleasant: it looks out to steeply wooded, snowy slopes. Even more pleasant at the moment is the fact that the hot-water supply is vast; there is enough for deep baths for everyone, and then they will all have much-needed before-dinner naps.

Carol gets the first bath, and then, in turn, the two younger women. Graham last. All three women have left a tidy room, a clean tub, he happily notices, and the steamy air smells vaguely sweet, of something perfumed, feminine. Luxuriating in his own full, hot tub, he thinks tenderly, in a general way, of women, how warm and sexual they are, more often than not, how frequently intelligent and kind. And then he wonders what he has not quite, ever, put into words before: what is it that women do, women together? What ever could they do that they couldn't do with men, and *why*?

However, these questions are much less urgent and less painful than most of his musings along those lines; he simply wonders.

In their bedroom, disappointingly, Carol is already fast asleep. He has not seen her actually sleeping before; she is always first awake when he stays over at her place. Now she looks so drained, so entirely exhausted, with one hand protectively across her eyes, that he is touched. Carefully, so as not to wake her, he slips in beside her, and in minutes he, too, is sound asleep.

Graham has planned and shopped for their dinner, which he intends to cook. He likes to cook, and does it well, but in his bachelor life he has done it less and less, perhaps because he and most of the women he meets tend to shy off from such domestic encounters. Somehow the implication of cooking *for* anyone has become alarming, more so than making love to them. But tonight Graham happily prepares to make pork chops with milk gravy and mashed potatoes, green peas, an apple-and-nut salad, and cherry pie (from a bakery, to be heated). A down-home meal, for his girlfriend, and his daughter, and her friend.

From the kitchen, which is at one end of the living room, he can hear the pleasant sounds of the three women's voices, in amiable conversation, as he blends butter and flour in the pan in which he has browned the chops, and begins to add hot milk. And then he notices a change in the tone of those voices: what was gentle and soft has gone shrill, strident — the sounds of a quarrel. He hates the thought of women fighting; it is almost frightening, and, of course, he is anxious for this particular group to get along, if only for the weekend.

He had meant, at just that moment, to go in and see if anyone wanted another glass of wine; dinner is almost ready. And so, reluctantly, he does; he gets into the living room just in time to hear Rose say, in a shakily loud voice, "No one who hasn't actually experienced rape can have the least idea what it's like."

Such a desperately serious sentence could have sounded ludicrous, but it does not. Graham is horrified; he thinks, Ah, poor girl, poor Rose. Jesus, *raped*. It is a crime that he absolutely cannot imagine.

In a calm, conciliatory way, Susannah says to Carol, "You see, Rose actually was raped, when she was very young, and it was terrible for her — "

Surprisingly, Carol reacts almost with anger. "Of course it's terrible, but you kids think you're the only ones things happen to. I got pregnant when I was fifteen, and I had it, a girl, and I put her out for adoption." Seeming to have just now noticed Graham, she addresses him in a low, defiant, scolding voice. "And I'm not thirty. I'm thirty-five."

Graham has no idea, really, of what to do, but he is aware of strong feelings that lead him to Carol. He goes over and puts his arms around her. Behind him he hears the gentle voice of Susannah, who is saying, "Oh Carol, that's terrible. God, that's *awful*."

Carol's large eyes are teary, but in a friendly way she disengages herself from Graham; she even smiles as she says, "Well, I'm sorry, I didn't mean to say that. But you see? You really can't tell what's happened to anyone."

And Susannah: "Oh, you're right, of course you are . . ."

And Rose: "It's true, we do get arrogant . . ."

Graham says that he thinks they should eat. The food is hot; they must be hungry. He brings the dinner to them at the table, and he serves out hot food onto the heated plates.

Carol and Rose are talking about the towns they came from: Vallejo, California, and Manchester, Vermont.

"It's thirty miles from San Francisco," Carol says. "And that's all we talked about. The City. How to get there, and what was going on there. Vallejo was just a place we ignored, dirt under our feet."

"All the kids in Manchester wanted to make it to New York," Rose says. "All but me, and I was fixated on Cambridge. Not getting into Radcliffe was terrible for me — it's why I never went to college at all."

"I didn't either," Carol says, with a slight irony that Graham thinks may have been lost on Rose: Carol would not have expected to go to college, probably — it wasn't what high-school kids from Vallejo did. But how does he know this?

"I went to work instead," says Rose, a little priggishly (thinks Graham).

"Me too," Carol says, with a small laugh.

Susannah breaks in. "Dad, this is absolutely the greatest dinner. You're still the best cook I know. It's good I don't have your dinners more often."

"I'm glad you like it. I haven't cooked a lot lately."

And Rose, and Carol: "It's super. It's great."

Warmed by praise, and just then wanting to be nice to Rose (partly because he has to admit to himself that he doesn't much like her), Graham says to her, "Cambridge was where I wanted to go to school, too. The Harvard School of Design. Chicago seemed second-best. But I guess it's all worked out."

"I guess." Rose smiles.

She looks almost pretty at that moment, but not quite; looking at her, Graham thinks again, If it had to be another girl, why her? But he knows this to be unfair, and, as far as that goes, why anyone for anyone, when you come to think of it? Any pairing is basically mysterious.

Partly as a diversion from such unsettling thoughts, and also from real curiosity, he asks Carol, "But was it worth it, when you got to the city?"

She laughs, in her low, self-depreciating way. "Oh, *I* thought so. I really liked it. My first job was with a florist on Union Street. It was nice there then, before it got all junked up with body shops and stuff. I had a good time."

Some memory of that era has put a younger, musing look on Carol's face, and Graham wonders if she is thinking of a love affair; jealously he wonders, Who? Who did you know, back then?

"I was working for this really nice older man," says Carol, in a higher than usual voice (as Graham thinks, *Ah*). "He taught me all he could. I was pretty dumb, at first. About marketing, arranging, keeping stuff fresh, all that. He lived by himself. A lonely person, I guess. He was — uh — gay, and then he died, and it turned out he'd left the store to me." For the second time that night tears have come to her eyes. "I was so touched, and it was too late to thank him, or anything." Then, the tears gone, her voice returns to its usual depth as she sums it up, "Well, that's how I got my start in the business world."

These sudden shifts in mood, along with her absolute refusal to see herself as an object of pity, are strongly, newly attractive to Graham; he has the sense of being with an unknown, exciting woman.

And then, in a quick, clairvoyant way, he gets a picture of Carol as a twenty-year-old girl, new in town: tall and a little awkward, working in the florist shop and worrying about her hands, her fingers scratched up from stems and wires; worrying about her darkening blond hair and then deciding, what the hell, better dye it; worrying about money, and men, and her parents back in Vallejo — and *should* she have put the baby out for adoption? He feels an unfamiliar tenderness for this new Carol.

"You guys are making me feel very boring," says Susannah. "I always wanted to go to Berkeley, and I did, and I wanted to go to L.A. and work in films."

"I think you're just more direct," amends Rose, affectionate admiration in her voice, and in her eyes. "You just know what you're doing. I fall into things."

Susannah laughs. "Well, you do all right, you've got to admit." And, to Graham and Carol: "She's only moved up twice since January. At this rate she'll be casting something in August."

What Graham had earlier named discomfort he now recognizes as envy: Susannah is closer to Rose than she is to him; they are closer to each other than he is to anyone. He says, "Well, Rose, that's really swell. That's *swell.*"

Carol glances at Graham for an instant before she says, "Well, I'll bet your father didn't even tell you about his most recent prize." And she tells them about an award from the A.I.A., which Graham had indeed not mentioned to Susannah, but which had pleased him at the time of its announcement (immoderately, he told himself).

And now Susannah and Rose join Carol in congratulations, saying how terrific, really great.

Dinner is over, and in a rather disorganized way they all clear the table and load the dishwasher.

They go into the living room, where Graham lights the fire, and the three women sit down, or, rather, sprawl — Rose and Susannah at either end of the sofa, Carol in an easy chair. For dinner Carol put on velvet pants and a red silk shirt. In the bright hot firelight her gray eyes shine, and the fine line under her chin, that first age line, is just barely visible. She is very beautiful at that moment — probably more so now than she was fifteen years ago, Graham decides.

Susannah, in clean, faded, too tight Levi's, stretches her legs out stiffly before her. "Oh, I'm really going to feel that skiing in the morning!"

And Carol: "Me too. I haven't had that much exercise forever."

Rose says, "If I could just not fall."

"Oh, you won't; tomorrow you'll see. Tomorrow. . . ." says everyone.

They are all exhausted. Silly to stay up late. And so as the fire dies down, Graham covers it and they all four go off to bed, in the two separate rooms.

Outside a strong wind has come up, creaking the walls and rattling windowpanes.

In the middle of the night, in what has become a storm — lashing snow and violent wind — Rose wakes up, terrified. From the depths of bad dreams, she has no idea where she is, what time it is, what day. With whom she is. She struggles for clues, her wide eyes scouring the dark, her tentative hands reaching out, encountering Susannah's familiar, fleshy back. Everything comes into focus for her; she knows where she is. She breathes out softly, "Oh, thank God it's you," moving closer to her friend.

HANS CHRISTIAN ANDERSEN

Born in Odense, Denmark, the son of a washerwoman and a cobbler, Hans Christian Andersen (1805–1875) yearned as a youth to become famous in theater. His brief acting career was not exactly resplendent: the only time his name was ever listed in a program was for a walk-on role — as a troll — in an opera-ballet. He came instead to portray characters another way — in the fairy tales he wrote, which first began to be published in Danish in 1835 and in English translation in 1846. In his own time, as today, he was beloved for the charm and sensitivity of his stories, some of which were inspired by Danish folklore, many others of which were entirely of his own creating. Among his 156 tales are "The Ugly Duckling," "The Red Shoes," "The Princess and the Pea," "The Snow Queen," "The Emperor's New Clothes," and "The Nightingale." For Andersen, the fairy tale had to meld "tragedy, comedy, naive simplicity, irony, and humor . . . the lyrical note." And often, as in the case of "The Wild Swans," an Andersen fairy tale is the story of a pure heart enduring suffering and transforming it into something beautiful and fulfilled.

The Wild Swans

Translated from the Danish by Eric Haugaard

Far, far away where the swallows are when we have winter, there lived a king who had eleven sons and one daughter, Elisa. The eleven brothers were all princes; and when they went to school, each wore a star on his chest and a sword at his side. They wrote with diamond pencils on golden tablets, and read aloud so beautifully that everyone knew at once that they were of royal blood. Their sister Elisa sat on a little stool made of mirrors and had a picture book that had cost half the kingdom. How well those children lived; but it did not last.

Their father, who was king of the whole country, married an evil queen, and that boded no good for the poor children. They found this out the first day she came. The whole castle was decorated in honour of the great event, and the children decided to play house. Instead of the cakes and baked apples they usually were given for this game — and which were so easy to provide — the queen handed them a teacup full of sand and said that they should pretend it was something else.

A week later little Elisa was sent to live with some poor peasants; and the evil queen made the king believe such dreadful things about the princes that soon he did not care for them any more.

"Fly away, out into the world with you and fend for yourselves! Fly as voiceless birds!" cursed the queen; but their fate was not as terrible as she would have liked it to be, for her power had its limits. They became eleven beautiful, wild swans. With a strange cry, they flew out of the castle window and over the park and the forest.

It was very early in the morning when they flew over the farm where Elisa lived. She was still asleep in her little bed. They circled low above the roof of the farmhouse, turning and twisting their necks, to catch a glimpse of their sister, while their great wings beat the air. But no one was awake, and no one heard or saw them. At last they had to fly away, high up into the clouds, towards the great dark forest that stretched all the way to the ocean.

Poor little Elisa sat on the floor playing with a leaf. She had no toys, so she had made a hole in the leaf and was looking up at the sun through it. She felt as though she were looking into the bright eyes of her brothers; and when the warm sunbeams touched her cheeks, she thought of all the kisses they had given her.

The days passed, one after another, and they all were alike. The wind blew through the rosebush and whispered, "Who can be more lovely than you are?"

The roses shook their heads and replied: "Elisa!"

On Sundays the old woman at the farm would set her chair outside and sit reading her psalmbook. The wind would turn the leaves and whisper, "Who can be more saintly than you?"

The psalmbook would answer as truthfully as the roses had: "Elisa!"

When Elisa turned fifteen she was brought back to the castle. As soon as the evil queen saw how beautiful the girl was, envy and hate filled her evil heart. She would gladly have transformed Elisa into a swan at first sight; but the king had asked to see his daughter, and the queen did not dare to disobey him.

Early the next morning, before Elisa was awake, the queen went into the marble bathroom, where the floors were covered with costly carpets and the softest pillows lay on the benches that lined the walls. She had three toads with her. She kissed the first and said, "Sit on Elisa's head that she may become as lazy as you are." Kissing the second toad, she ordered, "Touch Elisa's forehead that she may become as ugly as you are, so her father will not recognize her." Then she kissed the third toad. "Rest next to Elisa's heart, that her soul may become as evil as yours and give her pain."

She dropped the toads into the clear water and, instantly, it had a greenish tinge. She sent for Elisa, undressed her, and told her to step into the bath. As she slipped into the water, the first toad leaped on to Elisa's head, the second touched her forehead, and the third snuggled as close to her heart as it could. But Elisa did not seem to notice them.

When Elisa rose from the bath, there floating on the water were three red poppies. If the toads had not been made poisonous by the kiss of the wicked queen, they would have turned into roses; but they had become flowers when they touched Elisa. She was so good and so innocent that evil magic could not harm her.

When the wicked queen realized this, she took the juice from walnut shells and rubbed Elisa's body till it was streaked black and brown; then she smeared an awful-smelling salve on the girl's face and filtered ashes and dust through her hair. Now it was impossible for anyone to recognize the lovely princess.

Her father got frightened when he saw her, and said, "She is not my daughter." Only the watchdog and the swallows recognized her; but they were only animals and nobody paid any attention to them.

Elisa wept bitterly and thought of her eleven brothers who had disappeared. In despair, she slipped out of the castle. She walked all day across fields and swamps until she came to the great forest. She did not know where she was going; she only knew that she was deeply unhappy and she longed more than ever to see her brothers again. She thought that they had been forced out into the world as she had; and now she would try to find them.

As soon as she entered the forest, night fell. She had come far away from any road or path. She lay down on the soft moss to sleep. She said her prayers and leaned her head against the stump of a tree. The night was silent, warm, and still. Around her shone so many glowworms that, when she touched the branch of a bush, the little insects fell to the ground like shooting stars.

That night she dreamed about her brothers. Again they were children writing on their golden tablets with diamond pens; and once more she looked at the lovely picture book that had cost half the kingdom. But on their tablets her brothers were not only doing their sums, they wrote of all the great deeds they had performed. The pictures in the book became alive: the birds sang, and the men and women walked right out of the book to talk to Elisa. Every time she was about to turn a leaf, they quickly jumped back on to the page, so as not to get in the wrong picture.

When she awoke, the sun was already high in the heavens; but she couldn't see it, for the forest was so dense that the branches of the tall trees locked out the sky. But the sun rays shone through the leaves and made a shimmering golden haze. The smell of greenness was all around her, and the birds were so tame that they almost seemed willing to perch on her shoulder. She heard the splashing of water; and she found a little brook, and followed it till it led her to a lovely little pool that was so clear, she could see the sand bottom in a glance. It was surrounded by bushes; but at one spot the deer, when they came down to drink, had made a hole. Here Elisa kneeled down.

Had the branches and their leaves not been swayed gently by the wind, she would have believed that they had been painted on the water, so perfectly were they mirrored. Those upon which the sun shone glistened, and those in the shade were a dark green.

Then Elisa saw her own face and was frightened: it was so dirty and ugly. She dipped her hand into the water and rubbed her eyes, her cheeks, and her forehead till she could see her own fresh skin again. She undressed and bathed in the clear pool, and a more beautiful princess than she, could not have been found in the whole world.

When she had dressed, braided her long hair, and drunk from the brook with her cupped hand, she wandered farther and farther into the forest without knowing where she was going. She thought about her brothers and trusted that God would not leave her. There ahead of her was a wild apple tree. Hadn't God let it grow there so that the hungry could eat? Its branches were bent almost to the ground under the weight of the fruit. Here Elisa rested and had her midday meal; before she walked on, she found sticks and propped up the heavily laden branches of the apple tree.

The forest grew darker and darker. It was so still that she could hear her own footsteps: the sound of every little stick, and leaf crumbling under her foot. No birds were to be seen or heard, no sunbeams penetrated the foliage. The trees grew so close together that when she looked ahead she felt as if she were imprisoned in a stockade. Oh, here she was more alone than she had ever thought one could be!

Night came and not a single glowworm shone in the darkness. When she lay down to sleep she was hopelessly sad; but then the branches above her seemed to be drawn aside like a curtain, and she saw God looking down at her, with angels peeping over His shoulders and out from under His arms. And in the morning when she awoke, she did not know whether she had really seen God or it had merely been a dream.

Elisa met an old woman who was carrying a basket full of berries on her arm, and she offered the girl some berries. Elisa thanked her and then asked if she had seen eleven princes riding through the forest.

"No," the old woman replied. "But I have seen eleven swans with golden crowns on their heads, swimming in a stream not far from here."

She said she would show Elisa the way and led her to a cliff. Below it a little river twisted and turned its way through the forest. It seemed to be flowing in a tunnel, for the trees that grew on either side stretched their leafy branches towards each other and then intertwined. Where the branches were not long enough to span the stream, the trunks had pulled up part of their roots, in order to lean farther out over the water so the branches could meet.

Elisa said good-bye to the old woman and followed the stream until its water ran out into the sea.

Before her lay the beautiful ocean. There was not a sail to be seen nor any boat along the shore. She could not go any farther. How would she ever be able to find her brothers? She looked down. The shore was covered with pebbles: all the little stones were round; they had been made so by the sea. Iron, glass, stones, everything that lay at her feet had been ground into its present shape by water that was softer than her own delicate hand. "The waves roll on untiringly, and grind and polish the hardest stone. I must learn to be as untiring as they. Thank you for the lesson you have taught me, waves; and I am sure that one day you will carry me to my dear brothers."

Among the dried-out seaweed on the beach she found eleven swans' feathers. She picked them up; to each of them clung a drop of water, whether it was dew or a tear she did not know.

Although she was alone, Elisa did not feel lonely for she could watch the ever changing scene before her. The sea transforms itself more in an hour than a lake does in a year. When the clouds above it are dark, then the sea becomes as black as they are; and yet it will put on a dress of white if the wind should suddenly come and whip the waves. In the evening when the winds sleep and the clouds have turned pink, the sea will appear like the petal of a giant rose. Blue, white, green, red: the sea contains all colours; and even when it is calm, standing at the shore's edge, you will notice that it is moving like the breast of a sleeping child.

When the sun began to slide down behind the sea, Elisa saw eleven wild swans, with golden crowns on their heads, flying towards the beach. Like a white ribbon being pulled across the sky, they flew one after the other. Elisa hid behind some bushes. The swans landed nearby, still flapping their great white wings.

At the moment when the sun finally sank below the horizon, the swans turned into eleven handsome princes, Elisa's brothers. She shrieked with joy when she saw them. Although they had grown up since she had seen them last, she recognized them immediately and ran out from her hiding place to throw herself in their arms. They were as happy to see her as she was to see them. They laughed and cried, as they told each other of the evil deeds of their wicked stepmother.

"We must fly as wild swans as long as the sun is in the sky," explained the oldest brother. "Only when night has come do we regain our human shape; that is why we must never be in flight at sunset, for should we be up among the clouds, like any other human beings, we would fall and be killed. We do not live here, but in a country on the other side of the ocean. The sea is vast. It is far, far away; and there is no island where we can rest during our long journey. But midway in the ocean, a solitary rock rises above the waves. It is so tiny that we can just stand on it; and when the waves break against it, the water splashes up over us. Yet we thank God for that ragged rock, for if it were not there we should never be able to visit again the country where we were born. As it is, we only dare attempt the flight during the longest days of the year. We stay here eleven summer days and then we must return. Only for such a short time can we fly over the great forest and see our father's castle, and circle above the church where our mother is buried. It is as if every tree, every bush, in our native land were part of us. The wild horses gallop across the plains today as they did yesterday when we were children, and the gypsies still sing the songs we know. That is why we must come back — if only once a year. And now we have found you, our little sister. But we can only stay here two more days; then we must fly across the ocean to that fair land where we live now. How shall we be able to take you along? We have neither ship nor boat!"

"What can I do to break the spell that the queen has cast?" asked Elisa.

They talked almost the whole night through; only for a while did they doze. Elisa was awakened by the sound of wings beating the air. Her brothers had turned into swans again. They flew in circles above her and then disappeared over the forest. But her youngest brother had stayed behind. He rested his white head in her lap, and she stroked his strong white wings. Just before sunset, the others returned; and when twilight came, they were princes once more.

"Tomorrow we must begin the flight back to our new homeland," said the oldest brother. "We dare not stay longer; but how can we leave you behind, Elisa? It will be a whole year before we can return. My arms when I am a man are strong enough to carry you through the forest; wouldn't the wings of all of us be strong enough to carry you over the sea when we are swans?"

"I'll go with you!" exclaimed Elisa.

They worked all night, weaving a net of reeds and willow branches. Just before sunrise, Elisa lay down upon it; and she was so tired that she fell asleep. When the sun rose, and the princes changed into swans again, they picked up the net with their bills and flew up into the clouds with their sleeping sister. The burning rays of the sun fell on her face, so one of the swans flew above her, to shade her with his great wings.

They were far out over the ocean when Elisa awoke. So strange did it feel to be carried through the air that at first she thought she was dreaming. Some berries and roots lay beside her. Her youngest brother had collected this provision for her journey, and it was he who now flew above her and shaded her from the sun.

The whole day they flew as swiftly as arrows through the air; yet their flight would have been even faster had they not been carrying Elisa. Soon the sun would begin to set. Dark clouds on the horizon warned of a coming storm. Elisa looked down; there was only the endless ocean; she saw no lonely rock. It seemed to her that the wings were beating harder now. She would be the cause of her brothers' deaths. When the sun set, they would turn into men again; then they would fall into the sea and be drowned. She prayed to God, but still there was no rocky islet to be seen. Black clouds filled the sky; soon the breath of the storm would be upon them. The waves seemed as heavy as lead, and in the clouds lightning flashed.

The rim of the sun touched the sea. Elisa trembled with fear. Suddenly the swans dived down so fast that she thought that they were falling; but then they spread out their wings again.

Half of the sun had disappeared when Elisa saw the little rock. Looking down from the air, she thought that it looked more like a seal who had raised his head above the water. Just as the sun vanished they landed on the rock; and when the last of its light, like a piece of paper set aflame, flared up and then was gone, her brothers stood around her arm in arm.

The island was so tiny that they had to stand holding on to each other all night. The lightning made the sky bright and the thunder roared. They held each other's hands and sang a psalm, which comforted them and gave them courage.

At dawn the storm was over and the air was fresh and clear. The swans flew away from the rock, carrying Elisa. The sea was still turbulent. The white surf looked like millions of swans swimming on a raging green ocean. When the sun was high in the sky, Elisa saw a strange landscape. There was a mountain range covered with ice and snow. Halfway down the mountainsides was a huge palace, miles long, made of arcades, one on top of the other. And below that was a forest of gently waving palm trees, in which there were flowers with faces as large as millstones. She asked if that were the country where they lived, and the swans shook their heads. What she was seeing was a fata morgana: a mirage, an ever changing castle in the air to which no human being could gain admittance. As Elisa stared at it, the mountains, the castle, and the forest disappeared. It melted together and now there were twenty proud churches, every one alike, with high towers and tall windows. She thought she heard their organs playing, but it was the sound of the sea beating far below. The churches, in turn, changed into ships with towering sails. She was just above them; but when she looked down, she saw only fog driven by wind over the waves. The world of the sea and the air is always changing, ever in motion.

At last she saw the shores of the real country that was their destination. The mountains, which were covered with forests of cedar, were blue in the afternoon light; and she could see castles and towns. Before the sun had set, the swans alighted in front of a cave; its walls were covered with vines and plants that had intertwined and looked like tapestries.

"Tomorrow you must tell us what you have dreamed," said her youngest brother, showing her the part of the cave that was to be her bedchamber.

"May I dream how I can break the spell that the wicked queen cast," she said fervently; and that thought absorbed her so completely that she prayed to God and begged Him to help her; and while she was falling asleep she kept on praying.

Elisa felt as though she were flying into the fata morgana, the castle in the air; and a fairy came to welcome her who was young and beautiful, and yet somehow resembled the old woman Elisa had met in the forest and who had told her about the eleven swans with golden crowns on their heads.

"Your brothers can escape their fate," began the fairy, "if you have enough courage and endurance. The waves of the ocean are softer than your hands, yet they can form and shape hard stones; but they cannot feel the pain that your fingers will feel. They have no hearts and therefore they do not know fear: the suffering that you must endure. Look at the nettle that I hold in my hand! Around the cave where you are sleeping grow many of them; only those nettles or the ones to be found in churchyards may you use. You must pick them, even though they blister and burn your hands; then you must stamp on them with your bare feet until they become like flax. And from that you must twine thread with which to knit eleven shirts with long sleeves. If you cast one of these shirts over each of the eleven swans, the spell will be broken. But remember, from the moment you start your work until it is finished, you must be silent and never speak to anyone — even if it takes you years, you must be mute! If you speak one word, that word will send a knife into the hearts of your brothers. Their lives depend on your tongue: remember!"

The fairy touched Elisa's hand with the nettle. It felt like fire and she woke. It was bright daylight. Near her lay a nettle like the one she had seen in her sleep. She fell on her knees and said a prayer of thanks; then she walked outside to begin her work.

Her delicate hands picked the horrible nettles, and it felt as if her hands were burning and big blisters rose on her arms and hands. But she did not mind the pain if she could save her brothers. She broke every nettle and stamped on it with her bare feet until it became as fine as flax and could be twined into green thread.

When the sun set, her brothers came. At first they feared that some spell had been cast upon their sister by their evil stepmother, for Elisa was silent and would not answer their questions. But when they saw her hands covered with blisters, they understood the work she was doing was for their sake. The youngest of her brothers cried and his tears fell on her hands; the pain ceased and the burning blisters disappeared.

That night she could not sleep; she worked the whole night through. She felt that she could not rest until her brothers were free. The following day she was alone, but time passed more swiftly. By sunset the first of the nettle shirts was finished.

The next day she heard the sound of hunters' horns coming from the mountains. They came nearer and nearer and soon she could hear dogs barking. Frightened, she bound the nettles she had collected into a bundle with the thread she had already twined and the finished shirt; then she fled into the cave and sat down on the nettle heap.

Out of the thicket sprang a large dog; then came another and another. Barking, they ran back and forth in front of the entrance to the cave. Within a few minutes the hunters followed. The handsomest among them was the king of the country. He entered the cave and found Elisa. Never before had he seen a girl lovelier than she.

"Why are you hiding here, beautiful child?" he asked. Elisa shook her head. She dared not speak because her brothers' lives depended upon her silence. She hid her hands behind her back so that the king might not see how she suffered.

"You cannot stay here," he said. "Follow me, and if you are as good as you are beautiful, then you shall be clad in velvet and silk, wear a golden crown on your head, and call the loveliest of my castles your home."

He lifted her up on his horse. Elisa cried and wrung her hands. The king would not set her down again. "I only want to make you happy," he said. "Someday you will thank me for what I have done." Then he spurred his horse and galloped away with Elisa. The other hunters followed him.

By evening they reached the royal city with its many churches and palaces. The king led her into his castle with its lofty halls, where the waters of the fountains splashed into marble basins, and where the ceiling and the walls were beautifully painted. But none of this did Elisa notice, for she was crying so sorrowfully, so bitterly.

Silently but good-naturedly, she let the maids dress her in regal gowns, braid her hair with pearls, and pull long gloves over her blistered hands. When she entered the great hall, dressed so magnificently, she was so beautiful that the whole court bowed and curtsied. The king declared that she was to be his queen. Only the archbishop shook his head and whispered that he believed the little forest girl to be a witch who had cast a spell over the king.

The king did not listen to him. He ordered the musicians to play and the feast to begin. Dancing girls danced for Elisa; and the king showed her the fragrant gardens and the grand halls of his castle. But neither her lips nor her eyes smiled. Sorrow had printed its eternal mark on her face. Finally the king showed her a little chamber. Its walls and floor were covered by costly green carpets. It looked like the cave where she had been with her brothers. In a corner lay the green thread which she had spun from the nettles, and from the ceiling hung the one shirt that she had already knitted. One of the hunters had taken it all along as a curiosity.

"Here you can dream yourself back to your former home," remarked the king. "Here is the work you used to do; it will amuse you amid present splendour to think of the past."

A sweet smile played for a moment on Elisa's lips when she saw what was nearest and dearest to her heart restored to her. The colour returned to her cheeks. She thought of her brothers, and she kissed the king's hand. He pressed her to his breast and ordered that all the church bells be rung and their wedding proclaimed. The silent girl from the woods was to become the queen.

The archbishop whispered evil words in the king's ear, but they did not penetrate his heart. The marriage ceremony was held, and the archbishop himself had to crown the queen. He pressed the golden band down on her head so hard that it hurt. But she did not feel the pain, for sorrow's band squeezed her heart and made her suffer far more.

She must not speak a word or her brothers would die. But her eyes spoke silently of the love she felt for the king, who did everything he could to please her. Every day she loved him more. If only she could tell him of her anguish. But mute she must be until her task was finished. At night while the king slept, she would leave their bed and go to the chamber with the green carpets, and make the nettle shirts for her brothers. But when she had finished the sixth shirt she had no more green thread with which to knit.

She knew that in the churchyard grew the nettles that she needed. She had to pick them herself. But how was she to go there without anyone seeing her?

"What is the pain in my hands compared to the pain I feel in my heart?" she thought. "I must attempt it and God will help me."

As if it were an evil deed she was about to perform, she sneaked fearfully out of the castle late at night. She crossed the royal park and made her way through the empty streets to the churchyard. The moon was out; and on one of the large tombstones she saw a group of lamias sitting. They are those dreadful monsters with the bodies of snakes and the breasts and heads of women. They dig up the graves of those who have just died, to eat the flesh of the corpses. Elisa had to walk past them. She said her prayers, and though they kept their terrible gaze upon her, they did her no harm. She picked her nettles and returned to the castle.

Only one person had seen her: the archbishop, for he was awake when everyone else was sleeping. Now he thought that what he had said was proven true: the queen was a witch who had cast her spell on the king and all his subjects.

When next the king came to confession, the archbishop told him what he had seen and what he feared. He spoke his condemning words so harshly that the carved sculptures of the saints shook their heads as though they were saying: "It is not true. Elisa is innocent!"

But that was not the way the archbishop interpreted it; he said that the saints were shaking their heads because of their horror at her sins.

Two tears rolled down the king's cheeks, and with a heavy heart he returned to the castle. That night he only pretended to sleep and, when Elisa rose, he followed her. Every night she went on with her work; and every night the king watched her disappear into the little chamber.

The face of the king grew dark and troubled. Elisa noticed it, though she did not know its cause; and this new sorrow was added to her fear for her brothers' fate. On her royal velvet dress fell salt tears, and they looked like diamonds on the purple material, making it even more splendid. And all the women of the court wished that they were queens and could wear such magnificent clothes.

Soon Elisa's work would be over. She had to knit only one more shirt; but she had no more nettles from which to twine thread. Once more, for the last time, she would have to go to the churchyard. She shook with fear when she thought of walking alone past the horrible lamias, but she gathered courage when she thought of her brothers and her own faith in God.

Elisa went; and secretly the king and the archbishop followed her. They saw her disappear through the gates of the churchyard. The same terrifying lamias were there, and they were sitting near the place where the nettles grew. The king saw her walk toward them, and he turned away as his heart filled with repulsion, for he thought that Elisa, his queen — who that very night had rested in his arms — had come to seek the company of these monsters.

"Let the people judge her," said he. And the people judged her guilty and condemned her to the stake.

She was taken from the great halls of the castle and thrown into a dungeon, when the wind whistled through the grating that barred the window. Instead of a bed with silken sheets and velvet pillows, they gave her the nettles she had picked as a pillow and the shirts she had knitted as a cover. They could have given her no greater gift. She prayed to God and started work on the last of the shirts. Outside in the streets, the urchins sang songs that mocked and scorned her, while no one said a word of comfort to her.

Just before sunset, she heard the sound of swan's wings beating before her window. It was her youngest brother who had found her. She wept for happiness, even though she knew that this might be the last night of her life. Her work was almost done and her brothers were near her.

The archbishop had promised the king that he would be with Elisa during the last hours of her life. But when he came, she shook her head and pointed towards the door, to tell him to go. Her work must be finished that night or all her suffering, all her tears, all her pain would be in vain. The archbishop spoke some unkind words to her and left.

Poor Elisa, who knew that she was innocent but could not say a word to prove it, set to work knitting the last shirt. Mice ran across the floor and fetched the nettles for her; they wanted to help. And the thrush sang outside the iron bars of the window, as gaily as it could, so that she would not lose her courage.

One hour before sunrise, her brothers came to the castle and demanded to see the king. But they were refused, for it was still night and the guards did not dare wake the king. Elisa's brothers begged and threatened; they made so much noise that the captain of the guard came and, finally, the king himself. But at that moment the sun rose; the brothers were gone but high above the royal castle flew eleven white swans.

A stream of people rushed through the gates of the city. Everyone wanted to see the witch being burned. An old worn-out mare drew the cart in which Elisa sat. She was clad in sackcloth; her hair hung loose and framed her beautiful face, which was deadly pale. Her lips moved; she was mumbling a prayer while she knitted the last shirt. The other ten lay at her feet. Even on the way to hear death she did not cease working. The mob that lined the road jeered and mocked her.

"Look at the witch, she is mumbling her spells!" they screamed. "See what she has in her hands! It is no hymnbook; it is witchcraft! Get it away from her and tear it into a thousand pieces!"

And the rabble tried to stop the cart and tear Elisa's knitting out of her hands. But at that moment eleven white swans flew down and perched on the railing of the cart; they beat the air with their strong wings. The people drew back in fear.

"It is a sign from heaven that she is innocent," some of them whispered; but not one of them dared say it aloud.

The executioner took her hand to lead her to the stake, but she freed herself from him, grabbed the eleven shirts, and cast them over the swans. There stood eleven princes, handsome and fair. But the youngest of them had a swan's wing instead of an arm, for Elisa had not been able to finish one of the sleeves of the last shirt.

"Now I dare speak!" she cried. "I am innocent!"

The people, knowing that a miracle had taken place, kneeled down before her as they would have for a saint. But Elisa, worn out by fear, worry, and pain, fainted lifelessly into the arms of one of her brothers.

"Yes, she is innocent!" cried the oldest brother; and he addressed himself to the king and told of all that had happened to himself, his brothers, and their sister Elisa. While he spoke a fragrance of millions of roses spread from the wood that had been piled high around the stake. Every stick, every log had taken root and set forth vines. They were a hedge of the loveliest red roses, and on the very top bloomed a single white rose. It shone like a star. The king plucked it and placed it on Elisa's breast. She woke; happiness and peace were within her.

The church bells in the city started to peal, though no bell ringers pulled their ropes, and great flocks of birds flew in the sky. No one has ever seen a gayer procession than the one that now made its way to the royal castle.

MARGARET ATWOOD

 Margaret Atwood was born in Ottawa, Ontario, in 1939. As she tells it, "six months [after her birth] I was backpacked into the Quebec bush. I grew up in and out of the bush, in and out of Sault Ste. Marie, and Toronto. I did not attend a full year of school until I was in grade eight." At the University of Toronto she came under the influence of critic Northrop Frye, whose theories of mythical modes in literature she may be said to have adapted to her own purposes in her prolific writing of poetry, novels, and short stories. Of her novels, *Surfacing* (1972), *Life Before Man* (1979), *Bodily Harm* (1981), and *The Handmaid's Tale* (1986) are perhaps best known. Her short stories are collected in *Dancing Girls* (1977), *Murder in the Dark* (1983), and *Bluebeard's Egg and Other Stories* (1986), and she edited *The Oxford Book of Canadian Short Stories in English* (1987). Much of Atwood's work explores the individual's imperative to sustain humane existence in the face of the tyrannies of nature, political institutions, and personal relationships. "The Grave of the Famous Poet" is a story of a failed relationship, to be sure — but also one of survival.

The Grave of the Famous Poet

There are a couple of false alarms before we actually get there, towns we pass through that might be it but aren't, uninformative stores and houses edging the road, no signs. Even when we've arrived we aren't sure; we peer out, looking for a name, an advertisement. The bus pauses.

"This has to be it," I say. I have the map.

"Better ask the driver," he says, not believing me.

"Have I ever been wrong?" I say, but I ask the driver anyway. I'm right again and we get off.

We're in a constricted street of grey flat-fronted houses, their white lace curtains pulled closed, walls rising cliff-straight and lawnless from the narrow sidewalk. There are no other people; at least it isn't a tourist trap. I have to eat, we've been travelling all morning, but he wants to find a hotel first, he always needs a home base. Right in front of us there's a building labelled HOTEL. We hesitate outside it, patting down our hair, trying to look acceptable. When he finally grits up the steps with our suitcase the doors are locked. Maybe it's a pub.

Hoping there may be a place further along, we walk down the hill, following the long stone wall, crossing the road when the sidewalk disappears at the corners. Cars pass us, driving fast as though on their way to somewhere else.

At the bottom of the hill near the beach there's a scattering of shops and a scarred, listing inn. Radio music and hilarious voices from inside.

"It seems local," I say, pleased.

"What does 'Inn' mean here?" he asks, but I don't know. He goes in to see; then he comes out, dispirited. I'm too tired to think up solutions, I'm scarcely noticing the castle on the hill behind us, the sea.

"No wonder he drank," he says.

"I'll ask," I say, aggrieved: it was his idea, he should do the finding. I try the general store. It's full of people, women mostly, with scarves on their heads and shopping baskets. They say there is no hotel; one woman says her mother has some rooms free though, and she gives me directions while the others gaze pityingly, I'm so obviously a tourist.

The house, when we find it, is eighteenth century and enormous, a summer residence when the town was fashionable. It offers Bed and Breakfast on a modest sign. We're glad to have something spelled out for us. The door is open, we go into the hall, and the woman emerges from the parlour as though startled; she has a forties bobby-soxer hairdo with curious frontal lobes, only it's grey. She's friendly to us, almost sprightly, and yes, she has a room for us. I ask, in a lowered voice, if she can tell us where the grave is.

"You can almost see it right from the window," she says, smiling — she knew we would ask that — and offers to lend us a book with a map in it of the points of interest, his house and all. She gets the book, scampers up the wide maroon-carpeted staircase to show us our room. It's vast, chill, high-ceilinged, with floral wallpaper and white-painted woodwork; instead of curtains the windows have inside shutters. There are three beds and numerous dressers and cupboards crowded into the room as though in storage, a chunky bureau blocking the once-palatial fireplace. We say it will be fine.

"The grave is just up the hill, that way," she says, pointing through the window. We can see the tip of a church. "I'm sure you'll enjoy it."

I change into jeans and boots while he opens and closes the drawers on all the pieces of furniture, searching for ambushes or reading matter. He discovers nothing and we set out.

We ignore the church — he once said it was unremarkable — and head for the graveyard. It must rain a lot: ivy invades everything, and the graveyard is lush with uncut grass, succulent and light green. Feet have beaten animal-trail paths among the tombstones. The graves themselves are neatly tended, most of them have the grass clipped and fresh flowers in the tea-strainer-shaped flower holders. There are three old ladies in the graveyard now, sheaves of flowers in their arms, gladioli, chrysanthemums; they are moving among the graves, picking out the old flowers and distributing the new ones impartially, like stewardesses. They take us for granted, neither approaching nor avoiding us: we are strangers and as such part of this landscape.

We find the right grave easily enough; as the book says, it's the only one with a wooden cross instead of a stone. The cross has been recently painted and the grave is planted with a miniature formal-garden arrangement of moss roses and red begonias; the sweet alyssum intended for a border hasn't quite worked. I wonder who planted it, surely it wouldn't have been her. The old ladies have been here and have left a vase, yellowish glassware of the kind once found in cereal boxes, with orange dahlias and spikes of an unknown pink flower. We've brought nothing and have no ceremonies to perform; we muse for an acceptable length of time, then retreat to the scroll-worked bench up the hill and sit in the sun, listening to the cows in the field across the road and the murmur of the ladies as they stoop and potter below us, their print dresses fluttering in the easy wind.

"It's not such a bad place," I say.

"But dull," he answers.

We have whatever it was we came for, the rest of the day is our own. After a while we leave the graveyard and stroll back down the main street, holding hands absent-mindedly, looking in the windows of the few shops: an overpriced antique store, a handicrafts place with pottery and Welsh weaving, a nondescript store that sells everything, including girlie joke magazines and copies of his books. In the window, half-hidden among souvenir cups, maps and faded pennants, is a framed photograph of his face, three-quarters profile. We buy a couple of ice-cream bars; they are ancient and soapy.

We reach the bottom of the winding hill and decide to walk along to his house, which we can see, an indistinct white square separated from us by half a mile of rough beach. It's his house all right, it was marked on the map. At first we have no trouble; there's a wide uneven pathway, broken asphalt, the remains or perhaps the beginning of a road. Above us at the edge of the steep, leaf-covered cliff, what is left of the castle totters down, slowly, one stone a year. For him, turrets are irresistible. He finds a scrabbly trail, a children's entrance up sheer mud.

He goes up sideways, crabwise, digging footholds with the sides of his boots. "Come on!" he shouts down. I'm hesitant but I follow. At the top he reaches his hand to me, but, perpendicular and with the earth beside me, afraid of losing my balance, I avoid it and scramble the last few feet, holding on to roots. In wet weather it would be impossible.

He's ahead, eager to explore. The tunnel through the undergrowth leads to a gap in the castle wall; I follow his sounds, rustlings, the soft thud of his feet. We're in the skeleton of a garden, the beds marked by brick borders now grass-infested, a few rosebushes still attempting to keep order in spite of the aphids, nothing else paying any attention. I bend over a rose, ivory-hearted, browning at the edges; I feel like a usurper. He's already out of sight again, hidden by an archway.

I catch up to him in the main courtyard. Everything is crumbling, stairways, ramparts, battlements; so much has fallen it's hard for us to get our bearings, translate this rubbish back into its earlier clear plan.

"That must have been the fireplace," I say, "and that's the main gate. We must have come round from the back." For some reason we speak in whispers; he tosses a fragment of stone and I tell him to be careful.

We go up the remnants of a stairway into the keep. It's almost totally dark; the floors are earth-covered. People must come here though, there's an old sack, an unidentifiable piece of clothing. We don't stay long inside: I'm afraid of getting lost, though it's not likely, and I would rather be able to see him. I don't like the thought of finding his hand suddenly on me unannounced. Besides, I don't trust the castle; I expect it to thunder down on us at the first loud laugh or false step. But we make it outside safely.

We pass beneath the gateway, its Norman curve still intact. Outside is another, larger courtyard, enclosed by the wall we have seen from outside and broken through; it has trees, recent trees not more than a hundred years old, dark-foliaged as etchings. Someone must come here to cut the grass: it's short, hair-textured. He lies down on it and draws me down beside him and we rest on our elbows, surveying. From the front the castle is more complete; you can see how it could once have been lived in by real people.

He lies down, closing his eyes, raising his hand to shade them from the sun. He's pale and I realize he must be tired too, I've been thinking of my own lack of energy as something he has caused and must therefore be immune from.

"I'd like to have a castle like that," he says. When he admires something he wants to own it. For an instant I pretend that he does have the castle, he's always been here, he has a coffin hidden in the crypt, if I'm not careful I'll be trapped and have to stay with him forever. If I'd had more sleep last night I'd be able to frighten myself this way but as it is I give up and lean back on the grass beside him, looking up at the trees as their branches move in the wind, every leaf sharpened to a glass-clear edge by my exhaustion.

I turn my head to watch him. In the last few days he's become not more familiar to me as he should have but more alien. Close up, he's a strange terrain, pores and hairs; but he isn't nearer, he's further away, like the moon when you've finally landed on it. I move back from him so I can see him better, he misinterprets, thinking I'm trying to get up, and stretches himself over me to prevent me. He kisses me, teeth digging into my lower lip; when it hurts too much I pull away. We lie side by side, both suffering from unrequited love.

This is an interval, a truce; it can't last, we both know it, there have been too many differences, of opinion we called it but it was more than that, the things that mean safety for him mean danger for me. We've talked too much or not enough: for what we have to say to each other there's no language, we've tried them all. I think of the old science-fiction movies, the creature from another galaxy finally encountered after so many years of signals and ordeals only to be destroyed because he can't make himself understood. Actually it's less a truce than a rest, those silent black-and-white comedians hitting each other until they fall down, then getting up after a pause to begin again. We love each other, that's true whatever it means, but we aren't good at it; for some it's a talent, for others only an addiction. I wonder if they ever came here while he was still alive.

Right now though there's neither love nor anger, nor resentment, it's a sus-pension, of fear even, like waiting for the dentist. But I don't want him to die. I feel nothing but I concentrate, somebody's version of God, I will him to exist, right now on the vacant lawn of this castle whose name we don't know in this foreign town we're in only because dead people are more real to him than liv-ing ones. Despite the mistakes I want everything to stay the way it is; I want to hold it.

He sits up: he's heard voices. Two little girls, baskets over their arms as though for a picnic or a game, have come into the grounds and are walking towards the castle. They stare at us curiously and decide we are harmless. "Let's play in the tower," one calls and they run and disappear among the walls. For them the castle is ordinary as a backyard.

He gets up, brushing off bits of grass. We haven't visited the house yet but we still have time. We find our break in the wall, our pathway, and slide back down to sea level. The sun has moved, the green closes behind us.

The house is further than it looked from the village. The semi-road gives out and we pick our way along the stoney beach. The tide is out; the huge bay stretches as far as we can see, a solid mud-flat except for the thin silty river that cuts along beside us. The dry part narrows and vanishes, we are stranded below the tide-line, clambering over slippery masses of purplish-brown rock or squelching through the mud, thick as clotted cream. All around us is an odd percolating sound: it's the mud, drying in the sun. There are gulls too, and wind bending the unhealthy-coloured rushes by the bank.

"How the hell did he get back and forth?" he says. "Think of doing this drunk on a dark night."

"There must be a road further up," I say.

We reach the house at last. Like everything else here it has a wall; this one is to keep out the waves at high tide. The house itself is on stilts, jammed up against the cliff, painted stone with a spindly-railed two-decker porch. It hasn't been lived in for many years: one window is broken and the railings are beginning to go. The yard is weed-grown, but maybe it always was. I sit on the wall, dangling my legs, while he pokes around, examining the windows, the outhouse (which is open), the shed once used perhaps for a boat. I don't want to see any of it. Graves are safely covered and the castle so derelict it has the status of a tree or a stone, but the house is too recent, it is still partly living. If I looked in the window there would be a table with dishes not yet cleared away, or a fresh cigarette or a coat just taken off. Or maybe a broken plate: they used to have fights, apparently. She never comes back and I can see why. He wouldn't let her alone.

He's testing the railing on the second-story porch; he's going to pull himself up by it.

"Don't do that," I say wearily.

"Why not?" he says. "I want to see the other side."

"Because you'll fall and I don't want to have to scrape you off the rocks."

"Don't be like that," he says.

How did she manage? I turn my head away, I don't want to watch. It will be such an effort, the police, I'll have to explain what I was doing here, why he was climbing and fell. He should be more considerate. But for once he thinks better of it.

There is another road, we discover it eventually, along the beach and up an asphalt walk beside a neat inhabited cottage. Did they see us coming, are they wondering who we are? The road above is paved, it has a railing and a sign with the poet's name on it, wired to the fence.

"I'd like to steal that," he says.

We pause to view the house from above. There's an old lady in a garden-party hat and gloves, explaining things to an elderly couple. "He always kept to himself, he did," she is saying. "No one here ever got to know him really." She goes on to detail the prices that have been offered for the house: America wanted to buy it and ship it across the ocean, she says, but the town wouldn't let them.

We start back towards our rooms. Halfway along we sit down on a bench to scrape the mud from our boots; it clings like melted marshmallow. I lean back; I'm not sure I can make it to the house, whatever reserves my body has been drawing on are almost gone. My hearing is blurred and it's hard to breathe.

He bends over to kiss me. I don't want him to, I'm not calm now, I'm irritated, my skin prickles, I think of case histories, devoted wives who turn kleptomaniac two days a month, the mother who threw her baby out into the snow, it was in *Reader's Digest,* she had a hormone disturbance, love is all chemical. I want it to be over, this long abrasive competition for the role of victim; it used to matter that it should finish right, with grace, but not now. One of us should just get up from the bench, shake hands and leave, I don't care who is last, it would sidestep the recriminations, the totalling up of scores, the reclaiming of possessions, your key, my book. But it won't be that way, we'll have to work through it, boring and foreordained though it is. What keeps me is a passive curiosity, it's like an Elizabethan tragedy or a horror movie, I know which ones will be killed but not how. I take his hand and stroke the back of it gently, the fine hairs rasping my fingertips like sandpaper.

We'd been planning to change and have dinner, it's almost six, but back in the room I have only strength enough to pull off my boots. Then with my clothes still on I crawl into the enormous, creaking bed, cold as porridge and hammock-saggy. I float for an instant in the open sky on the backs of my eyelids, free-fall, until sleep rushes up to meet me like the earth.

I wake up suddenly in total darkness. I remember where I am. He's beside me but he seems to be lying outside the blankets, furled in the bedspread. I get stealthily out of the bed, grope to the window and open one of the wooden shutters. It's almost as dark outside, there are no streetlights, but by straining I can read my watch: two o'clock. I've had my eight hours and my body thinks it's time for breakfast. I notice I still have my clothes on, take them off and get back in bed, but my stomach won't let me sleep. I hesitate, then decide it won't do him any harm and turn on the bedside lamp. On the dresser there's a crumpled paper bag; inside it is a Welsh cake, a soft white biscuit with currants in it. I bought it yesterday near the train station, asking in bakeries crammed with English buns and French pastries, running through the streets in a crazed search for local colour that almost made us late for the bus. Actually I bought two of them. I ate mine yesterday, this one is his, but I don't care; I take it out of the bag and devour it whole.

In the mirror I'm oddly swollen, as though I've been drowned, my eyes are purple-circled, my hair stands out from my head like a second-hand doll's, there's a diagonal scarlike mark across my cheek where I've been sleeping on my face. This is what it does to you. I estimate the weeks, months, it will take me to recuperate. Fresh air, good food and plenty of sun.

We have so little time and he just lies there, rolled up like a rug, not even twitching. I think of waking him, I want to make love, I want all there is because there's not much left. I start to think what he will do after I'm over and I can't stand that, maybe I should kill him, that's a novel idea, how melodramatic; nevertheless I look around the room for a blunt instrument; there's nothing but the beside lamp, a grotesque woodland nymph with metal tits and a light bulb coming out of her head. I could never kill anyone with that. Instead I brush my teeth, wondering if he'll ever know how close he came to being murdered, resolving anyway never to plant flowers for him, never to come back, and slide in among the chilly furrows and craters of the bed. I intend to watch the sun rise but I fall asleep by accident and miss it.

Breakfast, when the time for it finally comes, is shabby, decorous, with mended linens and plentiful but dinted silver. We have it in an ornate, dilapidated room whose grandiose mantelpiece now supports only china spaniels and tinted family photos. We're brushed and combed, thoroughly dressed; we speak in subdued voices.

The food is the usual: tea and toast, fried eggs and bacon and the inevitable grilled tomato. It's served by a different woman, grey-haired also but with a corrugated perm and red lipstick. We unfold our map and plan the route back; it's Sunday and there won't be a bus to the nearest railway town till after one, we may have trouble getting out.

He doesn't like fried eggs and he's been given two of them. I eat one for him and tell him to hack the other one up so it will look nibbled at least, it's only polite. He is grateful to me, he knows I'm taking care of him, he puts his hand for a moment over mine, the one not holding the fork. We tell each other our dreams: his of men with armbands, later of me in a cage made of frail slatlike bones, mine of escaping winter through a field.

I eat his grilled tomato as an afterthought and we leave.

Upstairs in our room we pack; or rather I pack, he lies on the bed.

"What're we going to do till the bus comes?" he says. Being up so early unsettles him.

"Go for a walk," I say.

"We went for a walk yesterday," he says.

I turn around and he's holding out his arms, he wants me to come and lie down beside him. I do and he gives me a perfunctory initial kiss and starts to undo my buttons. He's using only his left hand, the right one is underneath me. He's having trouble. I stand up and take off, reluctantly, the clothes I've so recently put on. It's time for sex; he missed out on it last night.

He reaches up and hauls me in among the tangled sheets. I tense; he throws himself on me with the utilitarian urgency of a man running to catch a train, but it's more than that, it's different, he's biting down on my mouth, this time he'll get blood if it kills him. I pull him into me, wanting him to be with me, but for the first time I feel it's just flesh, a body, a beautiful machine, an animated corpse, he isn't in it any more, I want him so much and he isn't here. The bedsprings mourn beneath us.

"Sorry about that," he says.

"It's all right."

"No, shit, I really am sorry. I don't like it when that happens."

"It's all right," I say. I smooth his back, distancing him; he's back by the deserted house, back lying on the grass, back in the graveyard, standing in the sun looking down, thinking of his own death.

"We better get up," I say, "she might want to make up the room."

We're waiting for the bus. They lied to me in the general store, there is a hotel, I can see it now, it's just around the corner. We've had our quarrel, argument, fight, the one we were counting on. It was a routine one, a small one comparatively, its only importance the fact that it is the last. It carries the weight of all the other, larger things we said we forgave each other for but didn't. If there were separate buses we'd take them. As it is we wait together, standing a little apart.

We have over half an hour. "Let's go down to the beach," I say. "We can see the bus from there; it has to go the other way first." I cross the road and he follows me at a distance.

There's a wall; I climb it and sit down. The top is scattered with sharp flakes of broken stone, flint possibly, and bleached thumbnail-sized cockleshells, I know what they are because I saw them in a museum two days ago, and the occasional piece of broken glass. He leans against the wall near me, chewing on a cigarette. We say what we have to say in even, conversational voices, discussing how we'll get back, the available trains. I wasn't expecting it so soon.

After a while he looks at his watch, then walks away from me towards the sea, his boots crunching on the shells and pebbles. At the edge of the reed bank by the river he stops, back to me, one leg slightly bent. He holds his elbows, wrapped in his clothes as though in a cape, the storm breaks, his cape billows, thick leather boots sprout up his legs, a sword springs to attention in his hand. He throws his head back, courage, he'll meet them alone. Flash of lightning. Onward.

I wish I could do it so quickly. I sit calmed, frozen, not yet sure whether I've survived, the words we have hurled at each other lying spread in fragments around me, solidified. It's the pause during the end of the world; how does one behave? The man who said he'd continue to tend his garden, does that make sense to me? It would if it were only a small ending, my own. But we aren't more doomed than anything else, it's dead already, at any moment the bay will vaporize, the hills across will lift into the air, the space between will scroll itself up and vanish; in the graveyard the graves will open to show the dry puffball skulls, his wooden cross will flare like a match, his house collapse into itself, cardboard and lumber, no more language. He will stand revealed, history scaling away from him, the versions of him I made up and applied, stripped down to what he really is for a last instant before he flames up and goes out. Surely we should be holding each other, absolving, repenting, saying goodbye to each other, to everything because we will never find it again.

Above us the gulls wheel and ride, crying like drowning puppies or disconsolate angels. They have black rims around their eyes; they're a new kind, I've never seen any like that before. The tide is going out; the fresh wet mud gleams in the sun, miles of it, a level field of pure glass, pure gold. He stands outlined against it: a dark shape, faceless, light catching the edges of his hair.

I turn aside and look down at my hands. They are covered with greyish dust: I've been digging among the shells, gathering them together. I arrange them in a border, a square, each white shell overlapping the next. Inside I plant the flints, upright in tidy rows, like teeth, like flowers.

JAMES BALDWIN

James Baldwin (1924–1987) was born in Harlem, the son of a preacher from New Orleans. In his teenage years he himself preached at a pentacostal church, an experience he later regretted but which marked his writing unmistakably. In 1948 Baldwin moved from the United States to Paris. There, in self-imposed exile, he found the power to write two extraordinary novels — *Go Tell It on the Mountain* (1953) and *Giovanni's Room* (1956) — which center on the anguish of being black and homosexual in a white and heterosexual society. Along with his novels, Baldwin's impassioned essays — published in *Notes of a Native Son* (1955), *Nobody Knows My Name* (1961), and *The Fire Next Time* (1963) — voiced outrage at racial and sexual injustice and, in the words of one critic, gave a public issue, "all its deeper moral, historical, and personal significance." "Sonny's Blues," published in his collection *Going to Meet the Man* (1965), reveals another of the central concerns of Baldwin's writing: the need for people, individually and collectively, to find healing through love.

Sonny's Blues

I read about it in the paper, in the subway, on my way to work. I read it, and I couldn't believe it, and I read it again. Then perhaps I just stared at it, at the newsprint spelling out his name, spelling out the story. I stared at it in the swinging lights of the subway car, and in the faces and bodies of the people, and in my own face, trapped in the darkness which roared outside.

It was not to be believed and I kept telling myself that, as I walked from the subway station to the high school. And at the same time I couldn't doubt it. I was scared, scared for Sonny. He became real to me again. A great block of ice got settled in my belly and kept melting there slowly all day long, while I taught my classes algebra. It was a special kind of ice. It kept melting, sending trickles of ice water all up and down my veins, but it never got less. Sometimes it hardened and seemed to expand until I felt my guts were going to come spilling out or that I was going to choke or scream. This would always be at a moment when I was remembering some specific thing Sonny had once said or done.

When he was about as old as the boys in my classes his face had been bright and open, there was a lot of copper in it; and he'd had wonderfully direct brown eyes, and great gentleness and privacy. I wondered what he looked like now. He had been picked up, the evening before, in a raid on an apartment downtown, for peddling and using heroin.

I couldn't believe it: but what I mean by that is that I couldn't find any room for it anywhere inside me. I had kept it outside me for a long time. I hadn't wanted to know. I had had suspicions, but I didn't name them, I kept putting them away. I told myself that Sonny was wild, but he wasn't crazy. And he'd always been a good boy, he hadn't ever turned hard or evil or disrespectful, the way kids can, so quick, so quick, especially in Harlem. I didn't want to believe that I'd ever see my brother going down, coming to nothing, all that light in his face gone out, in the condition I'd already seen so many others. Yet it had happened and here I was, talking about algebra to a lot of boys who might, every one of them for all I knew, be popping off needles every time they went to the head. Maybe it did more for them than algebra could.

I was sure that the first time Sonny had ever had horse, he couldn't have been much older than these boys were now. These boys, now, were living as we'd been living then, they were growing up with a rush and their heads bumped abruptly against the low ceiling of their actual possibilities. They were filled with rage. All they really knew were two darknesses, the darkness of their lives, which was now closing in on them, and the darkness of the movies, which had blinded them to that other darkness, and in which they now, vindictively, dreamed, at once more together than they were at any other time, and more alone.

When the last bell rang, the last class ended, I let out my breath. It seemed I'd been holding it for all that time. My clothes were wet — I may have looked as though I'd been sitting in a steam bath, all dressed up, all afternoon. I sat alone in the classroom a long time. I listened to the boys outside, downstairs, shouting and cursing and laughing. Their laughter struck me for perhaps the first time. It was not the joyous laughter which — God knows why — one associates with children. It was mocking and insular, its intent to denigrate. It was disenchanted, and in this, also, lay the authority of their curses. Perhaps I was listening to them because I was thinking about my brother and in them I heard my brother. And myself.

One boy was whistling a tune, at once very complicated and very simple, it seemed to be pouring out of him as though he were a bird, and it sounded very cool and moving through all that harsh, bright air, only just holding its own through all those other sounds.

I stood up and walked over to the window and looked down into the courtyard. It was the beginning of the spring and the sap was rising in the boys. A teacher passed through them every now and again, quickly, as though he or she couldn't wait to get out of that courtyard, to get those boys out of their sight and off their minds. I started collecting my stuff. I thought I'd better get home and talk to Isabel.

The courtyard was almost deserted by the time I got downstairs. I saw this boy standing in the shadow of a doorway, looking just like Sonny. I almost called his name. Then I saw that it wasn't Sonny, but somebody we used to know, a boy from around our block. He'd been Sonny's friend. He'd never been mine, having been too young for me, and, anyway, I'd never liked him. And now, even though he was a grown-up man, he still hung around that block, still spent hours on the street corners, was always high and raggy. I used to run into him from time to time and he'd often work around to asking me for a quarter or fifty cents. He always had some real good excuse, too, and I always gave it to him, I don't know why.

But now, abruptly, I hated him. I couldn't stand the way he looked at me, partly like a dog, partly like a cunning child. I wanted to ask him what the hell he was doing in the school courtyard.

He sort of shuffled over to me, and he said, "I see you got the papers. So you already know about it."

"You mean about Sonny? Yes, I already know about it. How come they didn't get you?"

He grinned. It made him repulsive and it also brought to mind what he'd looked like as a kid. "I wasn't there. I stay away from them people."

"Good for you." I offered him a cigarette and I watched him through the smoke. "You come all the way down here just to tell me about Sonny?"

"That's right." He was sort of shaking his head and his eyes looked strange, as though they were about to cross. The bright sun deadened his damp dark brown skin and it made his eyes look yellow and showed up the dirt in his kinked hair. He smelled funky. I moved a little away from him and I said, "Well, thanks. But I already know about it and I got to get home."

"I'll walk you a little ways," he said. We started walking. There were a couple of kids still loitering in the courtyard and one of them said goodnight to me and looked strangely at the boy beside me.

"What're you going to do?" he asked me. "I mean, about Sonny?"

"Look. I haven't seen Sonny for over a year, I'm not sure I'm going to do anything. Anyway, what the hell *can* I do?"

"That's right," he said quickly, "ain't nothing you can do. Can't much help old Sonny no more, I guess."

It was what I was thinking and so it seemed to me he had no right to say it.

"I'm surprised at Sonny, though," he went on — he had a funny way of talking, he looked straight ahead as though he were talking to himself   "I thought Sonny was a smart boy, I thought he was too smart to get hung."

"I guess he thought so too," I said sharply, "and that's how he got hung. And how about you? You're pretty goddamn smart, I bet."

Then he looked directly at me, just for a minute. "I ain't smart," he said. "If I was smart, I'd have reached for a pistol a long time ago."

"Look. Don't tell *me* your sad story, if it was up to me, I'd give you one." Then I felt guilty — guilty, probably, for never having supposed that the poor bastard *had* a story of his own, much less a sad one, and I asked, quickly, "What's going to happen to him now?"

He didn't answer this. He was off by himself some place. "Funny thing," he said, and from his tone we might have been discussing the quickest way to get to Brooklyn, "when I saw the papers this morning, the first thing I asked myself was if I had anything to do with it. I felt sort of responsible."

I began to listen more carefully. The subway station was on the corner, just before us, and I stopped. He stopped, too. We were in front of a bar and he ducked slightly, peering in, but whoever he was looking for didn't seem to be there. The juke box was blasting away with something black and bouncy and I half watched the barmaid as she danced her way from the juke box to her place behind the bar. And I watched her face as she laughingly responded to something someone said to her, still keeping time to the music. When she smiled one saw the little girl, one sensed the doomed, still-struggling woman beneath the battered face of the semi-whore.

"I never *give* Sonny nothing," the boy said finally, "but a long time ago I come to school high and Sonny asked me how it felt." He paused, I couldn't bear to watch him, I watched the barmaid, and I listened to the music which seemed to be causing the pavement to shake. "I told him it felt great." The music stopped, the barmaid paused and watched the juke box until the music began again. "It did."

All this was carrying me some place I didn't want to go. I certainly didn't want to know how it felt. It filled everything, the people, the houses, the music, the dark, quicksilver barmaid, with menace; and this menace was their reality.

"What's going to happen to him now?" I asked again.

"They'll send him away some place and they'll try to cure him." He shook his head. "Maybe he'll even think he's kicked the habit. Then they'll let him loose" — he gestured, throwing his cigarette into the gutter. "That's all."

"What do you mean, that's *all?*"

But I knew what he meant.

"I *mean,* that's *all.*" He turned his head and looked at me, pulling down the corners of his mouth. "Don't you know what I mean?" he asked, softly.

"How the hell *would* I know what you mean?" I almost whispered it, I don't know why.

"That's right," he said to the air, "how would *he* know what I mean?" He turned toward me again, patient and calm, and yet I somehow felt him shaking, shaking as though he were going to fall apart. I felt that ice in my guts again, the dread I'd felt all afternoon; and again I watched the barmaid, moving about the bar, washing glasses, and singing. "Listen. They'll let him out and then it'll just start all over again. That's what I mean."

"You mean — they'll let him out. And then he'll just start working his way back in again. You mean he'll never kick the habit. Is that what you mean?"

"That's right," he said, cheerfully. "*You* see what I mean."

"Tell me," I said at last, "why does he want to die? He must want to die, he's killing himself, why does he want to die?"

He looked at me in surprise. He licked his lips. "He don't want to die. He wants to live. Don't nobody want to die, ever."

Then I wanted to ask him — too many things. He could not have answered, or if he had, I could not have borne the answers. I started walking. "Well, I guess it's none of my business."

"It's going to be rough on old Sonny," he said. We reached the subway station. "This is your station?" he asked. I nodded. I took one step down. "Damn!" he said, suddenly. I looked up at him. He grinned again. "Damn it if I didn't leave all my money home. You ain't got a dollar on you, have you? Just for a couple of days, is all."

All at once something inside gave and threatened to come pouring out of me. I didn't hate him any more. I felt that in another moment I'd start crying like a child.

"Sure," I said. "Don't sweat." I looked in my wallet and didn't have a dollar, I only had a five. "Here," I said. "That hold you?"

He didn't look at it — he didn't want to look at it. A terrible closed look came over his face, as though he were keeping the number on the bill a secret from him and me. "Thanks," he said, and now he was dying to see me go. "Don't worry about Sonny. Maybe I'll write him or something."

"Sure," I said. "You do that. So long."

"Be seeing you," he said. I went on down the steps.

And I didn't write Sonny or send him anything for a long time. When I finally did, it was just after my little girl died, he wrote me back a letter which made me feel like a bastard.

Here's what he said:

> Dear brother,
>
> You don't know how much I needed to hear from you. I wanted to write you many a time but I dug how much I must have hurt you and so I didn't write. But now I feel like a man who's been trying to climb up out of some deep, real deep and funky hole and just saw the sun up there, outside. I got to get outside.
>
> I can't tell you much about how I got here. I mean I don't know how to tell you. I guess I was afraid of something or I was trying to escape from something and you know I have never been very strong in the head (smile). I'm glad Mama and Daddy are dead and can't see what's happened to their son and I swear if I'd known what I was doing I would never have hurt you so, you and a lot of other fine people who were nice to me and who believed in me.
>
> I don't want you to think it had anything to do with me being a musician. It's more than that. Or maybe less than that. I can't get anything straight in my head down here and I try not to think about what's going to happen to me when I get outside again. Sometime I think I'm going to flip and *never* get outside and sometime I think I'll come straight back. I tell you one thing, though, I'd rather blow my brains out than go through this again. But that's what they all say, so they tell me. If I tell you when I'm coming to New York and if you could meet me, I sure would appreciate it. Give my love to Isabel and the kids and I was sure sorry to hear about little Gracie. I wish I could be like Mama and say the Lord's will be done, but I don't know it seems to me that trouble is the one thing that never does get stopped and I don't know what good it does to blame it on the Lord. But maybe it does some good if you believe it.
>
> Your brother,
> Sonny

Then I kept in constant touch with him and I sent him whatever I could and I went to meet him when he came back to New York. When I saw him many things I thought I had forgotten came flooding back to me. This was because I had begun, finally, to wonder about Sonny, about the life that Sonny lived inside. This life, whatever it was, had made him older and thinner and it had deepened the distant stillness in which he had always moved. He looked very unlike my baby brother. Yet, when he smiled, when we shook hands, the baby brother I'd never known looked out from the depths of his private life, like an animal waiting to be coaxed into the light.

"How you been keeping?" he asked me.

"All right. And you?"

"Just fine." He was smiling all over his face. "It's good to see you again."

"It's good to see you."

The seven years' difference in our ages lay between us like a chasm: I wondered if these years would ever operate between us as a bridge. I was remembering, and it made it hard to catch my breath, that I had been there when he was born; and I had heard the first words he had ever spoken. When he started to walk, he walked from our mother straight to me. I caught him just before he fell when he took the first steps he ever took in this world.

"How's Isabel?"

"Just fine. She's dying to see you."

"And the boys?"

"They're fine, too. They're anxious to see their uncle."

"Oh, come on. You know they don't remember me."

"Are you kidding? Of course they remember you."

He grinned again. We got into a taxi. We had a lot to say to each other, far too much to know how to begin.

As the taxi began to move, I asked, "You still want to go to India?"

He laughed. "You still remember that. Hell, no. This place is Indian enough for me."

"It used to belong to them," I said.

And he laughed again. "They damn sure knew what they were doing when they got rid of it."

Years ago, when he was around fourteen, he'd been all hipped on the idea of going to India. He read books about people sitting on rocks, naked, in all kinds of weather, but mostly bad, naturally, and walking barefoot through hot coals and arriving at wisdom. I used to say that it sounded to me as though they were getting away from wisdom as fast as they could. I think he sort of looked down on me for that.

"Do you mind," he asked, "if we have the driver drive alongside the park? On the west side — I haven't seen the city in so long."

"Of course not," I said. I was afraid that I might sound as though I were humoring him, but I hoped he wouldn't take it that way.

So we drove along, between the green of the park and the stony, lifeless elegance of hotels and apartment buildings, toward the vivid, killing streets of our childhood. These streets hadn't changed, though housing projects jutted up out of them now like rocks in the middle of a boiling sea. Most of the houses in which we had grown up had vanished, as had the stores from which we had stolen, the basements in which we had first tried sex, the rooftops from which we had hurled tin cans and bricks. But houses exactly like the houses of our past yet dominated the landscape, boys exactly like the boys we once had been found themselves smothering in these houses, came down into the streets for light and air and found themselves encircled by disaster. Some escaped the trap, most didn't. Those who got out always left something of themselves behind, as some animals amputate a leg and leave it in the trap. It might be said, perhaps, that I had escaped, after all, I was a school teacher; or that Sonny had, he hadn't lived in Harlem for years. Yet, as the cab moved uptown through streets which seemed, with a rush, to darken with dark people, and as I covertly studied Sonny's face, it came to me that what we both were seeking through our separate cab windows was that part of ourselves which had been left behind. It's always at the hour of trouble and confrontation that the missing member aches.

We hit 110th Street and started rolling up Lenox Avenue. And I'd known this avenue all my life, but it seemed to me again, as it had seemed on the day I'd first heard about Sonny's trouble, filled with a hidden menace which was its very breath of life.

"We almost there," said Sonny.

"Almost." We were both too nervous to say anything more.

We live in a housing project. It hasn't been up long. A few days after it was up it seemed uninhabitably new, now, of course, it's already rundown. It looks like a parody of the good, clean, faceless life — God knows the people who live in it do their best to make it a parody. The beat-looking grass lying around isn't enough to make their lives green, the hedges will never hold out the streets, and they know it. The big windows fool no one, they aren't big enough to make space out of no space. They don't bother with the windows, they watch the TV screen instead. The playground is most popular with the children who don't play at jacks, or skip rope, or roller skate, or swing, and they can be found in it after dark. We moved in partly because it's not too far from where I teach, and partly for the kids; but it's really just like the houses in which Sonny and I grew up. The same things happen, they'll have the same things to remember. The moment Sonny and I started into the house I had the feeling that I was simply bringing him back into the danger he had almost died trying to escape.

Sonny has never been talkative. So I don't know why I was sure he'd be dying to talk to me when supper was over the first night. Everything went fine, the oldest boy remembered him, and the youngest boy liked him, and Sonny had remembered to bring something for each of them; and Isabel, who is really much nicer than I am, more open and giving, had gone to a lot of trouble about dinner and was genuinely glad to see him. And she's always been able to tease Sonny in a way that I haven't. It was nice to see her face so vivid again and to hear her laugh and watch her make Sonny laugh. She wasn't, or, anyway, she didn't seem to be, at all uneasy or embarrassed. She chatted as though there were no subject which had to be avoided and she got Sonny past his first, faint stiffness. And thank God she was there, for I was filled with that icy dread again. Everything I did seemed awkward to me, and everything I said sounded freighted with hidden meaning. I was trying to remember everything I'd heard about dope addiction and I couldn't help watching Sonny for signs. I wasn't doing it out of malice. I was trying to find out something about my brother. I was dying to hear him tell me he was safe.

"Safe!" my father grunted, whenever Mama suggested trying to move to a neighborhood which might be safer for children. "Safe, hell! Ain't no place safe for kids, nor nobody."

He always went on like this, but he wasn't, ever, really as bad as he sounded, not even on weekends, when he got drunk. As a matter of fact, he was always on the lookout for "something a little better," but he died before he found it. He died suddenly, during a drunken weekend in the middle of the war, when Sonny was fifteen. He and Sonny hadn't ever got on too well. And this was partly because Sonny was the apple of his father's eye. It was because he loved Sonny so much and was frightened for him, that he was always fighting with him. It doesn't do any good to fight with Sonny. Sonny just moves back, inside himself, where he can't be reached. But the principal reason that they never hit it off is that they were so much alike. Daddy was big and rough and loud-talking, just the opposite of Sonny, but they both had — that same privacy.

Mama tried to tell me something about this, just after Daddy died. I was home on leave from the army.

This was the last time I ever saw my mother alive. Just the same, this picture gets all mixed up in my mind with pictures I had of her when she was younger. The way I always see her is the way she used to be on a Sunday afternoon, say, when the old folks were talking after the big Sunday dinner. I always see her wearing pale blue. She'd be sitting on the sofa. And my father would be sitting in the easy chair, not far from her. And the living room would be full of church folks and relatives. There they sit, in chairs all around the living room, and the night is creeping up outside, but nobody knows it yet. You can see the darkness growing against the windowpanes and you hear the street noises every now and again, or maybe the jangling beat of a tambourine from one of the churches close by, but it's real quiet in the room. For a moment nobody's talking, but every face looks darkening, like the sky outside. And my mother rocks a little from the waist, and my father's eyes are closed. Everyone is looking at something a child can't see. For a minute they've forgotten the children. Maybe a kid is lying on the rug, half asleep. Maybe somebody's got a kid in his lap and is absent-mindedly stroking the kid's head. Maybe there's a kid, quiet and big-eyed, curled up in a big chair in the corner. The silence, the darkness coming, and the darkness in the faces frightens the child obscurely. He hopes that the hand which strokes his forehead will never stop — will never die. He hopes that there will never come a time when the old folks won't be sitting around the living room, talking about where they've come from, and what they've seen, and what's happened to them and their kinfolk.

But something deep and watchful in the child knows that this is bound to end, is already ending. In a moment someone will get up and turn on the light. Then the old folks will remember the children and they won't talk any more that day. And when light fills the room, the child is filled with darkness. He knows that everytime this happens he's moved just a little closer to that darkness outside. The darkness outside is what the old folks have been talking about. It's what they've come from. It's what they endure. The child knows that they won't talk any more because if he knows too much about what's happened to *them,* he'll know too much too soon, about what's going to happen to *him.*

The last time I talked to my mother, I remember I was restless. I wanted to get out and see Isabel. We weren't married then and we had a lot to straighten out between us.

There Mama sat, in black, by the window. She was humming an old church song, *Lord, you brought me from a long ways off.* Sonny was out somewhere. Mama kept watching the streets.

"I don't know," she said, "if I'll ever see you again, after you go off from here. But I hope you'll remember the things I tried to teach you."

"Don't talk like that," I said, and smiled. "You'll be here a long time yet."

She smiled, too, but she said nothing. She was quiet for a long time. And I said, "Mama, don't you worry about nothing. I'll be writing all the time, and you be getting the checks. . . ."

"I want to talk to you about your brother," she said suddenly. "If anything happens to me he ain't going to have nobody to look out for him."

"Mama," I said, "ain't nothing going to happen to you *or* Sonny. Sonny's all right. He's a good boy and he's got good sense."

"It ain't a question of his being a good boy," Mama said, "nor of his having good sense. It ain't only the bad ones, nor yet the dumb ones that get sucked under." She stopped, looking at me. "Your Daddy once had a brother," she said, and she smiled in a way that made me feel she was in pain. "You didn't never know that, did you?"

"No," I said, "I never knew that," and I watched her face.

"Oh, yes," she said, "your Daddy had a brother." She looked out of the window again. "I know you never saw your Daddy cry. But *I* did — many a time, through all these years."

I asked her, "What happened to his brother? How come nobody's ever talked about him?"

This was the first time I ever saw my mother look old.

"His brother got killed," she said, "when he was just a little younger than you are now. I knew him. He was a fine boy. He was maybe a little full of the devil, but he didn't mean nobody no harm."

Then she stopped and the room was silent, exactly as it had sometimes been on those Sunday afternoons. Mama kept looking out into the streets.

"He used to have a job in the mill," she said, "and, like all young folks, he just liked to perform on Saturday nights. Saturday nights, him and your father would drift around to different places, go to dances and things like that, or just sit around with people they knew, and your father's brother would sing, he had a fine voice, and play along with himself on his guitar. Well, this particular Saturday night, him and your father was coming home from some place, and they were both a little drunk and there was a moon that night, it was bright like day. Your father's brother was feeling kind of good, and he was whistling to himself, and he had his guitar slung over his shoulder. They was coming down a hill and beneath them was a road that turned off from the highway. Well, your father's brother, being always kind of frisky, decided to run down this hill, and he did, with that guitar banging and clanging behind him, and he ran across the road, and he was making water behind a tree. And your father was sort of amused at him and he was still coming down the hill, kind of slow. Then he heard a car motor and that same minute his brother stepped from behind the tree, into the road, in the moonlight. And he started to cross the road. And your father started to run down the hill, he says he don't know why. This car was full of white men. They was all drunk, and when they seen your father's brother they let out a great whoop and holler and they aimed the car straight at him. They was having fun, they just wanted to scare him, the way they do sometimes, you know. But they was drunk. And I guess the boy, being drunk, too, and scared, kind of lost his head. By the time he jumped it was too late. Your father says he heard his brother scream when the car rolled over him, and he heard the wood of that guitar when it give, and he heard them strings go flying, and he heard them white men shouting, and the car kept on a-going and it ain't stopped till this day. And, time your father got down the hill, his brother weren't nothing but blood and pulp."

Tears were gleaming on my mother's face. There wasn't anything I could say.

"He never mentioned it," she said, "because I never let him mention it before you children. Your Daddy was like a crazy man that night and for many a night thereafter. He says he never in his life seen anything as dark as that road after the lights of that car had gone away. Weren't nothing, weren't nobody on that road, just your Daddy and his brother and that busted guitar. Oh, yes. Your Daddy never did really get right again. Till the day he died he weren't sure but that every white man he saw was the man that killed his brother."

She stopped and took out her handkerchief and dried her eyes and looked at me.

"I ain't telling you all this," she said, "to make you scared or bitter or to make you hate nobody. I'm telling you this because you got a brother. And the world ain't changed."

I guess I didn't want to believe this. I guess she saw this in my face. She turned away from me, toward the window again, searching those streets.

"But I praise my Redeemer," she said at last, "that He called your Daddy home before me. I ain't saying it to throw no flowers at myself, but, I declare, it keeps me from feeling too cast down to know I helped your father get safely through this world. Your father always acted like he was the roughest, strongest man on earth. And everybody took him to be like that. But if he hadn't had *me* there — to see his tears!"

She was crying again. Still, I couldn't move. I said, "Lord, Lord, Mama, I didn't know it was like that."

"Oh, honey," she said, "there's a lot you don't know. But you are going to find it out." She stood up from the window and came over to me. "You got to hold on to your brother," she said, "and don't let him fall, no matter what it looks like is happening to him and no matter how evil you gets with him. You going to be evil with him many a time. But don't you forget what I told you, you hear?"

"I won't forget," I said. "Don't you worry, I won't forget. I won't let nothing happen to Sonny."

My mother smiled as though she were amused at something she saw in my face. Then, "You may not be able to stop nothing from happening. But you got to let him know you's *there*."

Two days later I was married, and then I was gone. And I had a lot of things on my mind and I pretty well forgot my promise to Mama until I got shipped home on a special furlough for her funeral.

And, after the funeral, with just Sonny and me alone in the empty kitchen, I tried to find out something about him.

"What do you want to do?" I asked him.

"I'm going to be a musician," he said.

For he had graduated, in the time I had been away, from dancing to the juke box to finding out who was playing what, and what they were doing with it, and he had bought himself a set of drums.

"You mean, you want to be a drummer?" I somehow had the feeling that being a drummer might be all right for other people but not for my brother Sonny.

"I don't think," he said, looking at me gravely, "that I'll ever be a good drummer. But I think I can play a piano."

I frowned. I'd never played the role of the older brother quite so seriously before, had scarcely ever, in fact, *asked* Sonny a damn thing. I sensed myself in the presence of something I didn't really know how to handle, didn't understand. So I made my frown a little deeper as I asked: "What kind of musician do you want to be?"

He grinned. "How many kinds do you think there are?"

"Be *serious*," I said.

He laughed, throwing his head back, and then looked at me. "I *am* serious."

"Well, then, for Christ's sake, stop kidding around and answer a serious question.

I mean, do you want to be a concert pianist, you want to play classical music and all that, or — or what?" Long before I finished he was laughing again. "For Christ's *sake,* Sonny!"

He sobered, but with difficulty. "I'm sorry. But you sound so — *scared!*" and he was off again.

"Well, you may think it's funny now, baby, but it's not going to be so funny when you have to make your living at it, let me tell you *that.*" I was furious because I knew he was laughing at me and I didn't know why.

"No," he said, very sober now, and afraid, perhaps, that he'd hurt me, "I don't want to be a classical pianist. That isn't what interests me. I mean" — he paused, looking hard at me, as though his eyes would help me to understand, and then gestured helplessly, as though perhaps his hand would help — "I mean, I'll have a lot of studying to do, and I'll have to study *everything,* but, I mean, I want to play *with* — jazz musicians." He stopped. "I want to play jazz," he said.

Well, the word had never before sounded as heavy, as real, as it sounded that afternoon in Sonny's mouth. I just looked at him and I was probably frowning a real frown by this time. I simply couldn't see why on earth he'd want to spend his time hanging around nightclubs, clowning around on bandstands, while people pushed each other around a dance floor. It seemed — beneath him, somehow. I had never thought about it before, had never been forced to, but I suppose I had always put jazz musicians in a class with what Daddy called "good-time people."

"Are you *serious?*"

"Hell, *yes,* I'm serious."

He looked more helpless than ever, and annoyed, and deeply hurt.

I suggested, helpfully: "You mean — like Louis Armstrong?"

His face closed as though I'd struck him. "No. I'm not talking about none of that old-time, down home crap."

"Well, look, Sonny, I'm sorry, don't get mad. I just don't altogether get it, that's all. Name somebody — you know, a jazz musician you admire."

"Bird."

"Who?"

"Bird! Charlie Parker! Don't they teach you nothing in the goddamn army?"

I lit a cigarette. I was surprised and then a little amused to discover that I was trembling. "I've been out of touch," I said. "You'll have to be patient with me. Now. Who's this Parker character?"

"He's just one of the greatest jazz musicians alive," said Sonny, sullenly, his hands in his pockets, his back to me. "Maybe *the* greatest," he added, bitterly, "that's probably why *you* have never heard of him."

"All right," I said, "I'm ignorant. I'm sorry. I'll go out and buy all the cat's records right away, all right?"

"It don't," said Sonny, with dignity, "make any difference to me. I don't care what you listen to. Don't do me no favors."

I was beginning to realize that I'd never seen him so upset before. With another part of my mind I was thinking that this would probably turn out to be one of those things kids go through and that I shouldn't make it seem important by pushing it too hard. Still, I didn't think it would do any harm to ask: "Doesn't all this take a lot of time? Can you make a living at it?"

He turned back to me and half leaned, half sat, on the kitchen table. "Everything takes time," he said, "and — well, yes, sure, I can make a living at it. But what I don't seem to be able to make you understand is that it's the only thing I want to do."

"Well, Sonny," I said, gently, "you know people can't always do exactly what they *want* to do — "

"No, I don't know that," said Sonny, surprising me. "I think people *ought* to do what they want to do, what else are they alive for?"

"You getting to be a big boy," I said desperately, "it's time you started thinking about your future."

"I'm thinking about my future," said Sonny, grimly. "I think about it all the time."

I gave up. I decided, if he didn't change his mind, that we could always talk about it later. "In the meantime," I said, "you got to finish school." We had already decided that he'd have to move in with Isabel and her folks. I knew this wasn't the ideal arrangement because Isabel's folks are inclined to be dicty and they hadn't especially wanted Isabel to marry me. But I didn't know what else to do. "And we have to get you fixed up at Isabel's."

There was a long silence. He moved from the kitchen table to the window. "That's a terrible idea. You know it yourself."

"Do you have a *better* idea?"

He just walked up and down the kitchen for a minute. He was as tall as I was. He had started to shave. I suddenly had the feeling that I didn't know him at all.

He stopped at the kitchen table and picked up my cigarettes. Looking at me with a kind of mocking, amused defiance, he put one between his lips. "You mind?"

"You smoking already?"

He lit the cigarette and nodded, watching me through the smoke. "I just wanted to see if I'd have the courage to smoke in front of you." He grinned and blew a great cloud of smoke to the ceiling. "It was easy." He looked at my face. "Come on, now. I bet you was smoking at my age, tell the truth."

I didn't say anything but the truth was on my face, and he laughed. But now there was something very strained in his laugh. "Sure. And I bet that ain't all you was doing."

He was frightening me a little. "Cut the crap," I said. "We already decided that you was going to go and live at Isabel's. Now what's got into you all of a sudden?"

"You decided it," he pointed out. *"I* didn't decide nothing." He stopped in front of me, leaning against the stove, arms loosely folded. "Look, brother. I don't want to stay in Harlem no more. I really don't." He was very earnest. He looked at me, then over toward the kitchen window. There was something in his eyes I'd never seen before, some thoughtfulness, some worry all his own. He rubbed the muscle of one arm. "It's time I was getting out of here."

"Where do you want to *go,* Sonny?"

"I want to join the army. Or the navy, I don't care. If I say I'm old enough, they'll believe me."

Then I got mad. It was because I was so scared. "You must be crazy. You goddamn fool, what the hell do you want to go and join the *army* for?"

"I just told you. To get out of Harlem."

"Sonny, you haven't even finished *school.* And if you really want to be a musician, how do you expect to study if you're in the *army?*"

He looked at me, trapped, and in anguish. "There's ways. I might be able to work out some kind of deal. Anyway, I'll have the G.I. Bill when I come out."

"*If* you come out." We stared at each other. "Sonny, please. Be reasonable. I know the setup is far from perfect. But we got to do the best we can."

"I ain't learning nothing in school," he said. "Even when I go." He turned away from me and opened the window and threw his cigarette out into the narrow alley. I watched his back. "At least, I ain't learning nothing you'd want me to learn." He slammed the window so hard I thought the glass would fly out, and turned back to me. "And I'm sick of the stink of these garbage cans!"

"Sonny," I said, "I know how you feel. But if you don't finish school now, you're going to be sorry later that you didn't." I grabbed him by the shoulders. "And you only got another year. It ain't so bad. And I'll come back and I swear I'll help you do *whatever* you want to do. Just try to put up with it till I come back. Will you please do that? For me?"

He didn't answer and he wouldn't look at me.

"Sonny. You hear me?"

He pulled away. "I hear you. But you never hear anything *I* say."

I didn't know what to say to that. He looked out of the window and then back at me. "OK," he said, and sighed. "I'll try."

Then I said, trying to cheer him up a little, "They got a piano at Isabel's. You can practice on it."

And as a matter of fact, it did cheer him up for a minute. "That's right," he said to himself. "I forgot that." His face relaxed a little. But the worry, the thoughtfulness, played on it still, the way shadows play on a face which is staring into the fire.

But I thought I'd never hear the end of that piano. At first, Isabel would write me, saying how nice it was that Sonny was so serious about his music and how, as soon as he came in from school, or wherever he had been when he was supposed to be at school, he went straight to that piano and stayed there until suppertime. And, after supper, he went back to that piano and stayed there until everybody went to bed. He was at the piano all day Saturday and all day Sunday. Then he bought a record player and started playing records. He'd play one record over and over again, all day long sometimes, and he'd improvise along with it on the piano. Or he'd play one section of the record, one chord, one change, one progression, then he'd do it on the piano. Then back to the record. Then back to the piano.

Well, I really don't know how they stood it. Isabel finally confessed that it wasn't like living with a person at all, it was like living with sound. And the sound didn't make any sense to her, didn't make any sense to any of them — naturally. They began, in a way, to be afflicted by this presence that was living in their home. It was as though Sonny were some sort of god, or monster. He moved in an atmosphere which wasn't like theirs at all. They fed him and he ate, he washed himself, he walked in and out of their door; he certainly wasn't nasty or unpleasant or rude, Sonny isn't any of those things; but it was as though he were all wrapped up in some cloud, some fire, some vision all his own; and there wasn't any way to reach him.

At the same time, he wasn't really a man yet, he was still a child, and they had to watch out for him in all kinds of ways. They certainly couldn't throw him out. Neither did they dare to make a great scene about that piano because even they dimly sensed, as I sensed, from so many thousands of miles away, that Sonny was at that piano playing for his life.

But he hadn't been going to school. One day a letter came from the school board and Isabel's mother got it — there had, apparently, been other letters but Sonny had torn them up. This day, when Sonny came in, Isabel's mother showed him the letter and asked where he'd been spending his time. And she finally got it out of him that he'd been down in Greenwich Village, with musicians and other characters, in a white girl's apartment. And this scared her and she started to scream at him and what came up, once she began — though she denies it to this day — was what sacrifices they were making to give Sonny a decent home and how little he appreciated it.

Sonny didn't play the piano that day. By evening, Isabel's mother had calmed down but then there was the old man to deal with, and Isabel herself. Isabel says she did her best to be calm but she broke down and started crying. She says she just watched Sonny's face. She could tell, by watching him, what was happening with him. And what was happening was that they penetrated his cloud, they had reached him. Even if their fingers had been a thousand times more gentle than human fingers ever are, he could hardly help feeling that they had stripped him naked and were spitting on that nakedness. For he also had to see that his presence, that music, which was life or death to him, had been torture for them and that they had endured it, not at all for his sake, but only for mine. And Sonny couldn't take that. He can take it a little better today than he could then but he's still not very good at it and, frankly, I don't know anybody who is.

The silence of the next few days must have been louder than the sound of all the music ever played since time began. One morning, before she went to work, Isabel was in his room for something and she suddenly realized that all of his records were gone. And she knew for certain that he was gone. And he was. He went as far as the navy would carry him. He finally sent me a postcard from some place in Greece and that was the first I knew that Sonny was still alive. I didn't see him any more until we were both back in New York and the war had long been over.

He was a man by then, of course, but I wasn't willing to see it. He came by the house from time to time, but we fought almost every time we met. I didn't like the way he carried himself, loose and dreamlike all the time, and I didn't like his friends, and his music seemed to be merely an excuse for the life he led. It sounded just that weird and disordered.

Then we had a fight, a pretty awful fight, and I didn't see him for months. By and by I looked him up, where he was living, in a furnished room in the Village, and I tried to make it up. But there were lots of people in the room and Sonny just lay on his bed, and he wouldn't come downstairs with me, and he treated these other people as though they were his family and I weren't. So I got mad and then he got mad, and then I told him that he might just as well be dead as live the way he was living. Then he stood up and told me not to worry about him any more in life, that he *was* dead as far as I was concerned. Then he pushed me to the door and the other people looked on as though nothing were happening, and he slammed the door behind me. I stood in the hallway, staring at the door. I heard somebody laugh in the room and then the tears came to my eyes. I started down the steps, whistling to keep from crying, I kept whistling to myself, *You going to need me, baby, one of these cold, rainy days.*

I read about Sonny's trouble in the spring. Little Grace died in the fall. She was a beautiful little girl. But she only lived a little over two years. She died of polio and she suffered. She had a slight fever for a couple of days, but it didn't seem like anything and we just kept her in bed. And we would certainly have called the doctor, but the fever dropped, she seemed to be all right. So we thought it had just been a cold. Then, one day, she was up, playing, Isabel was in the kitchen fixing lunch for the two boys when they'd come in from school, and she heard Grace fall down in the living room. When you have a lot of children you don't always start running when one of them falls, unless they start screaming or something. And, this time, Grace was quiet. Yet, Isabel says that when she heard that *thump* and then that silence, something happened in her to make her afraid. And she ran to the living room and there was little Grace on the floor, all twisted up, and the reason she hadn't screamed was that she couldn't get her breath. And when she did scream, it was the worst sound, Isabel says, that she'd ever heard in all her life, and she still hears it sometimes in her dreams. Isabel will sometimes wake me up with a low, moaning, strangled sound and I have to be quick to awaken her and hold her to me and where Isabel is weeping against me seems a mortal wound.

I think I may have written Sonny the very day that little Grace was buried. I was sitting in the living room in the dark, by myself, and I suddenly thought of Sonny. My trouble made his real.

One Saturday afternoon, when Sonny had been living with us, or, anyway, been in our house, for nearly two weeks, I found myself wandering aimlessly about the living room, drinking from a can of beer, and trying to work up the courage to search Sonny's room. He was out, he was usually out whenever I was home, and Isabel had taken the children to see their grandparents. Suddenly I was standing still in front of the living room window, watching Seventh Avenue. The idea of searching Sonny's room made me still. I scarcely dared to admit to myself what I'd be searching for. I didn't know what I'd do if I found it. Or if I didn't.

On the sidewalk across from me, near the entrance to a barbecue joint some people were holding an old-fashioned revival meeting. The barbecue cook, wearing a dirty white apron, his conked hair reddish and metallic in the pale sun, and a cigarette between his lips, stood in the doorway, watching them. Kids and older people paused in their errands and stood there, along with some older men and a couple of very tough-looking women who watched everything that happened on the avenue, as though they owned it, or were maybe owned by it. Well, they were watching this, too. The revival was being carried on by three sisters in black, and a brother. All they had were their voices and their Bibles and a tambourine. The brother was testifying and while he testified two of the sisters stood together, seeming to say, amen, and the third sister walked around with the tambourine outstretched and a couple of people dropped coins into it. Then the brother's testimony ended and the sister who had been taking up the collection dumped the coins into her palm and transferred them to the pocket of her long black robe. Then she raised both hands, striking the tambourine against the air, and then against one hand, and she started to sing. And the two other sisters and the brothers joined in.

It was strange, suddenly, to watch, though I had been seeing these street meetings all my life. So, of course, had everybody else down there. Yet, they paused and watched and listened and I stood still at the window. *"Tis the old ship of Zion,"* they sang, and the sister with the tambourine kept a steady, jangling beat, *"it has rescued many a thousand!"* Not a soul under the sound of their voices was hearing this song for the first time, not one of them had been rescued. Nor had they seen much in the way of rescue work being done around them. Neither did they especially believe in the holiness of the three sisters and the brother, they knew too much about them, knew where they lived, and how. The woman with the tambourine, whose voice dominated the air, whose face was bright with joy, was divided by very little from the woman who stood watching her, a cigarette between her heavy, chapped lips, her hair a cuckoo's nest, her face scarred and swollen from many beatings, and her black eyes glittering like coal. Perhaps they both knew this, which was why, when, as rarely, they addressed each other, they addressed each other as Sister. As the singing filled the air the watching, listening faces underwent a change, the eyes focusing on something within; the music seemed to soothe a poison out of them; and time seemed, nearly, to fall away from the sullen, belligerent, battered faces, as though they were fleeing back to their first condition, while dreaming of their last. The barbecue cook half shook his head and smiled, and dropped his cigarette and disappeared into his joint. A man fumbled in his pockets for change and stood holding it in his hand impatiently, as though he had just remembered a pressing appointment further up the avenue. He looked furious. Then I saw Sonny, standing on the edge of the crowd. He was carrying a wide, flat notebook with a green cover, and it made him look, from where I was standing, almost like a schoolboy. The coppery sun brought out the copper in his skin, he was very faintly smiling, standing very still. Then the singing stopped, the tambourine turned into a collection plate again. The furious man dropped in his coins and vanished, so did a couple of the women, and Sonny dropped some change in the plate, looking directly at the woman with a little smile. He started across the avenue, toward the house. He has a slow, loping walk, something like the way Harlem hipsters walk, only he's imposed on this his own half-beat. I had never really noticed it before.

I stayed at the window, both relieved and apprehensive. As Sonny disappeared from my sight, they began singing again. And they were still singing when his key turned in the lock.

"Hey," he said.

"Hey, yourself. You want some beer?"

"No. Well, maybe." But he came up to the window and stood beside me, looking out. "What a warm voice," he said.

They were singing *If I could only hear my mother pray again!*

"Yes," I said, "and she can sure beat that tambourine."

"But what a terrible song," he said, and laughed. He dropped his notebook on the sofa and disappeared into the kitchen. "Where's Isabel and the kids?"

"I think they went to see their grandparents. You hungry?"

"No." He came back into the living room with his can of beer. "You want to come some place with me tonight?"

I sensed, I don't know how, that I couldn't possibly say no. "Sure. Where?"

He sat down on the sofa and picked up his notebook and started leafing through it. "I'm going to sit in with some fellows in a joint in the Village."

"You mean, you're going to play, tonight?"

"That's right." He took a swallow of his beer and moved back to the window. He gave me a sidelong look. "If you can stand it."

"I'll try," I said.

He smiled to himself and we both watched as the meeting across the way broke up. The three sisters and the brother, heads bowed, were singing *God be with you till we meet again.* The faces around them were very quiet. Then the song ended. The small crowd dispersed. We watched the three women and the lone man walk slowly up the avenue.

"When she was singing before," said Sonny, abruptly, "her voice reminded me for a minute of what heroin feels like sometimes — when it's in your veins. It makes you feel sort of warm and cool at the same time. And distant. And — and sure." He sipped his beer, very deliberately not looking at me. I watched his face. "It makes you feel — in control. Sometimes you've got to have that feeling."

"Do you?" I sat down slowly in the easy chair.

"Sometimes." He went to the sofa and picked up his notebook again. "Some people do."

"In order," I asked, "to play?" And my voice was very ugly, full of contempt and anger.

"Well" — he looked at me with great, troubled eyes, as though, in fact, he hoped his eyes would tell me things he could never otherwise say — "they *think* so. And *if* they think so — !"

"And what do *you* think?" I asked.

He sat on the sofa and put his can of beer on the floor. "I don't know," he said, and I couldn't be sure if he were answering my question or pursuing his thoughts. His face didn't tell me. "It's not so much to *play*. It's to *stand* it, to be able to make it at all. On any level." He frowned and smiled: "In order to keep from shaking to pieces."

"But these friends of yours," I said, "they seem to shake themselves to pieces pretty goddamn fast."

"Maybe." He played with the notebook. And something told me that I should curb my tongue, that Sonny was doing his best to talk, that I should listen. "But of course you only know the ones that've gone to pieces. Some don't — or at least they haven't *yet* and that's just about all *any* of us can say." He paused. "And then there are some who just live, really, in hell, and they know it and they see what's happening and they go right on. I don't know." He sighed, dropped the notebook, folded his arms. "Some guys, you can tell from the way they play, they on something *all* the time. And you can see that, well, it makes something real for them. But of course," he picked up his beer from the floor and sipped it and put the can down again, "they *want* to, too, you've got to see that. Even some of them that say they don't — *some,* not all."

"And what about you?" I asked — I couldn't help it. "What about you? Do *you* want to?"

He stood up and walked to the window and remained silent for a long time. Then he sighed. "Me," he said. Then: "While I was downstairs before, on my way here, listening to that woman sing, it struck me all of a sudden how much suffering she must have had to go through — to sing like that. It's *repulsive* to think you have to suffer that much."

I said: "But there's no way not to suffer — is there, Sonny?"

"I believe not," he said and smiled, "but that's never stopped anyone from trying." He looked at me. "Has it?" I realized, with this mocking look, that there stood between us, forever, beyond the power of time or forgiveness, the fact that I had held silence — so long! — when he had needed human speech to help him. He turned back to the window. "No, there's no way not to suffer. But you try all kinds of ways to keep from drowning in it, to keep on top of it, and to make it seem — well, like *you*. Like you did something, all right, and now you're suffering for it. You know?" I said nothing. "Well you know," he said, impatiently, "why *do* people suffer? Maybe it's better to do something to give it a reason, *any* reason."

"But we just agreed," I said, "that there's no way not to suffer. Isn't it better, then, just to — take it?"

"But nobody just takes it," Sonny cried, "that's what I'm telling you! *Everybody* tries not to. You're just hung up on the *way* some people try — it's not *your* way!"

The hair on my face began to itch, my face felt wet. "That's not true," I said, "that's not true. I don't give a damn what other people do, I don't even care how they suffer. I just care how *you* suffer." And he looked at me. "Please believe me," I said, "I don't want to see you — die — trying not to suffer."

"I won't," he said, flatly, "die trying not to suffer. At least, not any faster than anybody else."

"But there's no need," I said, trying to laugh, "is there? in killing yourself."

I wanted to say more, but I couldn't. I wanted to talk about will power and how life could be — well, beautiful. I wanted to say that it was all within; but was it? or, rather, wasn't that exactly the trouble? And I wanted to promise that I would never fail him again. But it would all have sounded — empty words and lies.

So I made the promise to myself and prayed that I would keep it.

"It's terrible sometimes, inside," he said, "that's what's the trouble. You walk these streets, black and funky and cold, and there's not really a living ass to talk to, and there's nothing shaking, and there's no way of getting it out — that storm inside. You can't talk it and you can't make love with it, and when you finally try to get with it and play it, you realize *nobody's* listening. So *you've* got to listen. You got to find a way to listen."

And then he walked away from the window and sat on the sofa again, as though all the wind had suddenly been knocked out of him. "Sometimes you'll do *anything* to play, even cut your mother's throat." He laughed and looked at me. "Or your brother's." Then he sobered. "Or your own." Then: "Don't worry. I'm all right now and I think I'll *be* all right. But I can't forget — where I've been. I don't mean just the physical place I've been, I mean where I've *been*. And *what* I've been."

"What have you been, Sonny?" I asked.

He smiled — but sat sideways on the sofa, his elbow resting on the back, his fingers playing with his mouth and chin, not looking at me. "I've been something I didn't recognize, didn't know I could be. Didn't know anybody could be." He stopped, looking inward, looking helplessly young, looking old. "I'm not talking about it now because I feel *guilty* or anything like that — maybe it would be better if I did, I don't know. Anyway, I can't really talk about it. Not to you, not to anybody," and now he turned and faced me. "Sometimes, you know, and it was actually when I was most *out* of the world, I felt that I was in it, that I was *with it,* really, and I could play or I didn't really have to *play,* it just came out of me, it was there. And I don't know how I played, thinking about it now, but I know I did awful things, those times, sometimes, to people. Or it wasn't that I *did* anything to them — it was that they weren't real." He picked up the beer can; it was empty; he rolled it between his palms: "And other times — well, I needed a fix, I needed to find a place to lean, I needed to clear a space to *listen* — and I couldn't find it, and I — went crazy, I did terrible things to *me,* I was terrible *for* me." He began pressing the beer can between his hands, I watched the metal begin to give. It glittered, as he played with it, like a knife, and I was afraid he would cut himself, but I said nothing. "Oh well. I can never tell you. I was all by myself at the bottom of something, stinking and sweating and crying and shaking, and I smelled it, you know? *my* stink, and I thought I'd die if I couldn't get away from it and yet, all the same, I knew that everything I was doing was just locking me in with it. And I didn't know," he paused, still flattening the beer can, "I didn't know, I still *don't* know, something kept telling me that maybe it was good to smell your own stink, but I didn't think that *that* was what I'd been trying to do — and — who can stand it?" and he abruptly dropped the ruined beer can, looking at me with a small, still smile, and then rose, walking to the window as though it were the lodestone rock. I watched his face, he watched the avenue. "I couldn't tell you when Mama died — but the reason I wanted to leave Harlem so bad was to get away from drugs. And then, when I ran away, that's what I was running from — really. When I came back, nothing had changed, *I* hadn't changed, I was just — older." And he stopped, drumming with his fingers on the windowpane. The sun had vanished, soon darkness would fall. I watched his face. "It can come again," he said, almost as though speaking to himself. Then he turned to me. "It can come again," he repeated. "I just want you to know that."

"All right," I said, at last. "So it can come again. All right."

He smiled, but the smile was sorrowful. "I had to try to tell you," he said.

"Yes," I said. "I understand that."

"You're my brother," he said, looking straight at me, and not smiling at all.

"Yes," I repeated, "yes. I understand that."

He turned back to the window, looking out. "All that hatred down there," he said, "all that hatred and misery and love. It's a wonder it doesn't blow the avenue apart."

We went to the only nightclub on a short, dark street, downtown. We squeezed through the narrow, chattering, jam-packed bar to the entrance of the big room, where the bandstand was. And we stood there for a moment, for the lights were very dim in this room and we couldn't see. Then, "Hello, boy," said a voice and an enormous black man, much older than Sonny or myself, erupted out of all that atmospheric lighting and put an arm around Sonny's shoulder. "I been sitting right here," he said, "waiting for you."

He had a big voice, too, and heads in the darkness turned toward us.

Sonny grinned and pulled a little away, and said, "Creole, this is my brother. I told you about him."

Creole shook my hand. "I'm glad to meet you, son," he said, and it was clear that he was glad to meet me *there,* for Sonny's sake. And he smiled, "You got a real musician in *your* family," and he took his arm from Sonny's shoulder and slapped him, lightly, affectionately, with the back of his hand.

"Well. Now I've heard it all," said a voice behind us. This was another musician, and a friend of Sonny's, a coal-black, cheerful-looking man, built close to the ground. He immediately began confiding to me, at the top of his lungs, the most terrible things about Sonny, his teeth gleaming like a lighthouse and his laugh coming up out of him like the beginning of an earthquake. And it turned out that everyone at the bar knew Sonny, or almost everyone; some were musicians, working there, or nearby, or not working, some were simply hangers-on, and some were there to hear Sonny play. I was introduced to all of them and they were all very polite to me. Yet, it was clear that, for them, I was only Sonny's brother. Here, I was in Sonny's world.

Or, rather: his kingdom. Here, it was not even a question that his veins bore royal blood.

They were going to play soon and Creole installed me, by myself, at a table in a dark corner. Then I watched them, Creole, and the little black man, and Sonny, and the others, while they horsed around, standing just below the bandstand. The light from the bandstand spilled just a little short of them and, watching them laughing and gesturing and moving about, I had the feeling that they, nevertheless, were being most careful not to step into that circle of light too suddenly: that if they moved into the light too suddenly, without thinking, they would perish in flame. Then, while I watched, one of them, the small, black man, moved into the light and crossed the bandstand and started fooling around with his drums. Then — being funny and being, also, extremely ceremonious — Creole took Sonny by the arm and led him to the piano. A woman's voice called Sonny's name and a few hands started clapping. And Sonny, also being funny and being ceremonious, and so touched, I think, that he could have cried, but neither hiding it nor showing it, riding it like a man, grinned, and put both hands to his heart and bowed from the waist.

Creole then went to the bass fiddle and a lean, very bright-skinned brown man jumped up on the bandstand and picked up his horn. So there they were, and the atmosphere on the bandstand and in the room began to change and tighten. Someone stepped up to the microphone and announced them. Then there were all kinds of murmurs. Some people at the bar shushed others. The waitress ran around, frantically getting in the last orders, guys and chicks got closer to each other, and the lights on the bandstand, on the quartet, turned to a kind of indigo. Then they all looked different there. Creole looked about him for the last time, as though he were making certain that all his chickens were in the coop, and then he — jumped and struck the fiddle. And there they were.

All I know about music is that not many people ever really hear it. And even then, on the rare occasions when something opens within, and the music enters, what we mainly hear, or hear corroborated, are personal, private, vanishing evocations. But the man who creates the music is hearing something else, is dealing with the roar rising from the void and imposing order on it as it hits the air. What is evoked in him, then, is of another order, more terrible because it has no words, and triumphant, too, for that same reason. And his triumph, when he triumphs, is ours. I just watched Sonny's face. His face was troubled, he was working hard, but he wasn't with it. And I had the feeling that, in a way, everyone on the bandstand was waiting for him, both waiting for him and pushing him along. But as I began to watch Creole, I realized that it was Creole who held them all back. He had them on a short rein. Up there, keeping the beat with his whole body, wailing on the fiddle, with his eyes half closed, he was listening to everything, but he was listening to Sonny. He was having a dialogue with Sonny. He wanted Sonny to leave the shoreline and strike out for the deep water. He was Sonny's witness that deep water and drowning were not the same thing — he had been there, and he knew. And he wanted Sonny to know. He was waiting for Sonny to do the things on the keys which would let Creole know that Sonny was in the water.

And, while Creole listened, Sonny moved, deep within, exactly like someone in torment. I had never before thought of how awful the relationship must be between the musician and his instrument. He has to fill it, this instrument, with the breath of life, his own. He has to make it do what he wants it to do. And a piano is just a piano.

It's made out of so much wood and wires and little hammers and big ones, and ivory. While there's only so much you can do with it, the only way to find this out is to try; to try and make it do everything.

And Sonny hadn't been near a piano for over a year. And he wasn't on much better terms with his life, not the life that stretched before him now. He and the piano stammered, started one way, got scared, stopped; started another way, panicked, marked time, started again; then seemed to have found a direction, panicked again, got stuck. And the face I saw on Sonny I'd never seen before. Everything had been burned out of it, and, at the same time, things usually hidden were being burned in, by the fire and fury of the battle which was occurring in him up there.

Yet, watching Creole's face as they neared the end of the first set, I had the feeling that something had happened, something I hadn't heard. Then they finished, there was scattered applause, and then, without an instant's warning, Creole started into something else, it was almost sardonic, it was *Am I Blue.* And, as though he commanded, Sonny began to play. Something began to happen. And Creole let out the reins. The dry, low, black man said something awful on the drums, Creole answered, and the drums talked back. Then the horn insisted, sweet and high, slightly detached perhaps, and Creole listened, commenting now and then, dry, and driving, beautiful and calm and old. Then they all came together again, and Sonny was part of the family again. I could tell this from his face. He seemed to have found, right there beneath his fingers, a damn brand-new piano. It seemed that he couldn't get over it. Then, for awhile, just being happy with Sonny, they seemed to be agreeing with him that brand-new pianos certainly were a gas.

Then Creole stepped forward to remind them that what they were playing was the blues. He hit something in all of them, he hit something in me, myself, and the music tightened and deepened, apprehension began to beat the air. Creole began to tell us what the blues were all about. They were not about anything very new. He and his boys up there were keeping it new, at the risk of ruin, destruction, madness, and death, in order to find new ways to make us listen. For, while the tale of how we suffer, and how we are delighted, and how we may triumph is never new, it always must be heard. There isn't any other tale to tell, it's the only light we've got in all this darkness.

And this tale, according to that face, that body, those strong hands on those strings, has another aspect in every country, and a new depth in every generation. Listen, Creole seemed to be saying, listen. Now these are Sonny's blues. He made the little black man on the drums know it, and the bright, brown man on the horn. Creole wasn't trying any longer to get Sonny in the water. He was wishing him Godspeed. Then he stepped back, very slowly, filling the air with the immense suggestion that Sonny speak for himself.

Then they all gathered around Sonny and Sonny played. Every now and again one of them seemed to say, amen. Sonny's fingers filled the air with life, his life. But that life contained so many others. And Sonny went all the way back, he really began with the spare, flat statement of the opening phrase of the song. Then he began to make it his. It was very beautiful because it wasn't hurried and it was no longer a lament. I seemed to hear with what burning he had made it his, with what burning we had yet to make it ours, how we could cease lamenting. Freedom lurked around us and I understood, at last, that he could help us to be free if we would listen, that he would never be free until we did. Yet, there was no battle in his face now. I heard what he had gone through, and would continue to go through until he came to rest in earth. He had made it his: that long line, of which we knew only Mama and Daddy. And he was giving it back, as everything must be given back, so that, passing through death, it can live forever. I saw my mother's face again, and felt, for the first time, how the stones of the road she had walked on must have bruised her feet. I saw the moonlit road where my father's brother died. And it brought something else back to me, and carried me past it. I saw my little girl again and felt Isabel's tears again, and I felt my own tears begin to rise. And I was yet aware that this was only a moment, that the world waited outside, as hungry as a tiger, and that trouble stretched above us, longer than the sky.

Then it was over. Creole and Sonny let out their breath, both soaking wet, and grinning. There was a lot of applause and some of it was real. In the dark, the girl came by and I asked her to take drinks to the bandstand. There was a long pause, while they talked up there in the indigo light and after awhile I saw the girl put a Scotch and milk on top of the piano for Sonny. He didn't seem to notice it, but just before they started playing again, he sipped from it and looked toward me, and nodded. Then he put it back on top of the piano. For me, then, as they began to play again, it glowed and shook above my brother's head like the very cup of trembling.

TONI CADE BAMBARA

Born in New York City in 1939, Toni Cade Bambara entered Queens College at age sixteen, "in a great hurry to get my 'formal education' behind me so I could devote full attention to my anything-but-casual education that would clarify what my work in this world would be." By way of that learning, she took a degree in American Literature, traveled to Europe, returned to the United States to work in psychiatric and drug therapy, youth organizing, and settlement houses, and become a teacher, first at City College, New York, and later at a number of colleges and universities across the country. She edited two anthologies — *The Black Woman* (1970) and *Stories for Black Folks* (1971) — then her own short stories, which had appeared in various small journals, were published in *Gorilla, My Love* (1972) and *The Sea Birds Are Still Alive* (1977). Bambara's stories reflect the scope of her "anything-but-casual education" and are often told with humor (frequently sassy), in the tones and rhythms of street speech. Above all, they honor what Bambara learned from the women of Harlem: ". . . the laws of hospitality, kinship obligation, and caring neighborliness remain eternal, 'cause first and foremost there's us· community.'" "Gorilla, My Love," takes the reader to a place somewhere between laughter and heartache.

Gorilla, My Love

That was the year Hunca Bubba changed his name. Not a change up, but a change back, since Jefferson Winston Vale was the name in the first place. Which was news to me cause he'd been my Hunca Bubba my whole lifetime, since I couldn't manage Uncle to save my life. So far as I was concerned it was a change completely to somethin soundin very geographical weatherlike to me, like somethin you'd find in a almanac. Or somethin you'd run across when you sittin in the navigator seat with a wet thumb on the map crinkly in your lap, watchin the roads and signs so when Granddaddy Vale say "Which way, Scout," you got sense enough to say take the next exit or take a left or whatever it is. Not that Scout's my name. Just the name Granddaddy call whoever sittin in the navigator seat. Which is usually me cause I don't feature sittin in the back with the pecans. Now, you figure pecans all right to be sittin with. If you thinks so, that's your business. But they dusty sometime and make you cough. And they got a way of slidin around and dippin down sudden, like maybe a rat in the buckets. So if you scary like me, you sleep with the lights on and blame it on Baby Jason and, so as not to waste good electric, you study the maps. And that's how come I'm in the navigator seat most times and get to be called Scout.

So Hunca Bubba in the back with the pecans and Baby Jason, and he in love. And we got to hear all this stuff about this woman he in love with and all. Which really ain't enough to keep the mind alive, though Baby Jason got no better sense than to give his undivided attention and keep grabbin at the photograph which is just a picture of some skinny woman in a countrified dress with her hand shot up to her face like she shame fore cameras. But there's a movie house in the background which I ax about. Cause I am a movie freak from way back, even though it do get me in trouble sometime.

Like when me and Big Brood and Baby Jason was on our own last Easter and couldn't go to the Dorset cause we'd seen all the Three Stooges they was. And the RKO Hamilton was closed readying up for the Easter Pageant that night. And the West End, the Regun and the Sunset was too far, less we had grownups with us which we didn't. So we walk up Amsterdam Avenue to the Washington and *Gorilla, My Love* playin, they say, which suit me just fine, though the "my love" part kinda drag Big Brood some. As for Baby Jason, shoot, like Granddaddy say, he'd follow me into the fiery furnace if I say come on. So we go in and get three bags of Havmore potato chips which not only are the best potato chips but the best bags for blowin up and bustin real loud so the matron come trottin down the aisle with her chunky self, flashin that flashlight dead in your eye so you can give her some lip, and if she answer back and you already finish seein the show anyway, why then you just turn the place out. Which I love to do, no lie. With Baby Jason kickin at the seat in front, egging me on, and Big Brood mumblin bout what fiercesome things we goin do. Which means me. Like when the big boys come up on us talkin about Lemme a nickel. It's me that hide the money. Or when the bad boys in the park take Big Brood's Spaudeen way from him. It's me that jump on they back and fight awhile. And it's me that turns out the show if the matron get too salty.

So the movie come on and right away it's this churchy music and clearly not about no gorilla. Bout Jesus. And I am ready to kill, not cause I got anything gainst Jesus. Just that when you fixed to watch a gorilla picture you don't wanna get messed around with Sunday School stuff. So I am mad. Besides, we see this raggedy old brown film *King of Kings* every year and enough's enough. Grownups figure they can treat you just anyhow. Which burns me up. There I am, my feet up and my Havmore potato chips really salty and crispy and two jawbreakers in my lap and the money safe in my shoe from the big boys, and here comes this Jesus stuff. So we all go wild. Yellin, booin, stompin and carryin on. Really to wake the man in the booth up there who musta went to sleep and put on the wrong reels. But no, cause he holler down to shut up and then he turn the sound up so we really gotta holler like crazy to even hear ourselves good. And the matron ropes off the children section and flashes her light all over the place and we yell some more and some kids slip under the rope and run up and down the aisle just to show it take more than some dusty ole velvet rope to tie us down. And I'm flingin the kid in front of me's popcorn. And Baby Jason kickin seats. And it's really somethin. Then here come the big and bad matron, the one they let out in case of emergency. And she totin that flashlight like she gonna use it on somebody. This here the colored matron Brandy and her friends call Thunderbuns. She do not play. She do not smile. So we shut up and watch the simple ass picture.

Which is not so simple as it is stupid. Cause I realize that just about anybody in my family is better than this god they always talkin about. My daddy wouldn't stand for nobody treatin any of us that way. My mama specially. And I can just see it now, Big Brood up there on the cross talkin bout Forgive them Daddy cause they don't know what they doin. And my Mama say Get on down from there you big fool, whatcha think this is, playtime? And my Daddy yellin to Granddaddy to get him a ladder cause Big Brood actin the fool, his mother side of the family showin up. And my mama and her sister Daisy jumpin on them Romans beatin them with they pocketbooks. And Hunca Bubba tellin them folks on they knees they better get out the way and go get some help or they goin to get trampled on. And Granddaddy Vale sayin Leave the boy alone, if that's what he wants to do with his life we ain't got nothin to say about it. Then Aunt Daisy givin him a taste of that pocketbook, fussin bout what a damn fool old man Granddaddy is. Then everybody jumpin in his chest like the time Uncle Clayton went in the army and come back with only one leg and Granddaddy say somethin stupid about that's life. And by this time Big Brood off the cross and in the park playin handball or skully or somethin. And the family in the kitchen throwin dishes at each other, screamin bout if you hadn't done this I wouldn't had to do that. And me in the parlor tryin to do my arithmetic yellin Shut it off.

Which is what I was yellin all by myself which make me a sittin target for Thunderbuns. But when I yell We want our money back, that gets everybody in chorus. And the movie windin up with this heavenly cloud music and the smart-ass up there in his hole in the wall turns up the sound again to drown us out. Then there comes Bugs Bunny which we already seen so we know we been had. No gorilla my nuthin. And Big Brood say Awwww sheeet, we goin to see the manager and get our money back. And I know from this we business. So I brush the potato chips out of my hair which is where Baby Jason like to put em, and I march myself up the aisle to deal with the manager who is a crook in the first place for lyin out there sayin *Gorilla, My Love* playin. And I never did like the man cause he oily and pasty at the same time like the bad guy in the serial, the one that got a hideout behind a push-button bookcase and play "Moonlight Sonata" with gloves on. I knock on the door and I am furious. And I am alone, too. Cause Big Brood suddenly got to go so bad even though my mama told us bout goin in them nasty bathrooms. And I hear him sigh like he disgusted when he get to the door and see only a little kid there. And now I'm really furious cause I get so tired grownups messin over kids just cause they little and can't take em to court. What is it, he say to me like I lost my mittens or wet on myself or am somebody's retarded child. When in reality I am the smartest kid P.S. 186 ever had in its whole lifetime and you can ax anybody. Even them teachers that don't like me cause I won't sing them Southern songs or back off when they tell me my questions are out of order. And cause my Mama come up there in a minute when them teachers start playin the dozens behind colored folks. She stalk in with her hat pulled down bad and that Persian lamb coat draped back over one hip on account of she got her fist planted there so she can talk that talk which gets us all hypnotized, and teacher be comin undone cause she know this could be her job and her behind cause Mama got pull with the Board and bad by her own self anyhow.

So I kick the door open wider and just walk right by him and sit down and tell the man about himself and that I want my money back and that goes for Baby Jason and Big Brood too. And he still tryin to shuffle me out the door even though I'm sittin which shows him for the fool he is. Just like them teachers do fore they realize Mama like a stone on that spot and ain't backin up. So he ain't gettin up off the money. So I was forced to leave, takin the matches from under his ashtray, and set a fire under the candy stand, which closed the raggedy ole Washington down for a week. My Daddy had the suspect it was me cause Big Brood got a big mouth. But I explained right quick what the whole thing was about and I figured it was even-steven. Cause if you say Gorilla, My Love, you suppose to mean it. Just like when you say you goin to give me a party on my birthday, you gotta mean it. And if you say me and Baby Jason can go South pecan haulin with Granddaddy Vale, you better not be comin up with no stuff about the weather look uncertain or did you mop the bathroom or any other trickified business. I mean even gangsters in the movies say My word is my bond. So don't nobody get away with nothin far as I'm concerned. So Daddy put his belt back on. Cause that's the way I was raised. Like my Mama say in one of them situations when I won't back down, Okay Badbird, you right. Your point is well-taken. Not that Badbird my name, just what she say when she tired arguin and know I'm right. And Aunt Jo, who is the hardest head in the family and worse even than Aunt Daisy, she say, You absolutely right Miss Muffin, which also ain't my real name but the name she gave me one time when I got some medicine shot in my behind and wouldn't get up off her pillows for nothin. And even Grandaddy Vale — who got no memory to speak of, so sometime you can just plain lie to him, if you want to be like that — he say, Well if that's what I said, then that's it. But this name business was different they said. It wasn't like Hunca Bubba had gone back on his word or anythin. Just that he was thinkin bout gettin married and was usin his real name now. Which ain't the way I saw it at all.

So there I am in the navigator seat. And I turn to him and just plain ole ax him. I mean I come right on out with it. No sense goin all around that barn the old folks talk about. And like my mama say, Hazel — which is my real name and what she remembers to call me when she bein serious — when you got somethin on your mind, speak up and let the chips fall where they may. And if anybody don't like it, tell em to come see your mama. And Daddy look up from the paper and say, You hear your mama good, Hazel. And tell em to come see me first. Like that. That's how I was raised.

So I turn clear round in the navigator seat and say, "Look here, Hunca Bubba or Jefferson Windsong Vale or whatever your name is, you gonna marry this girl?"

"Sure am," he say, all grins.

And I say, "Member that time you was baby-sittin me when we lived at four-o-nine and there was this big snow and Mama and Daddy got held up in the country so you had to stay for two days?"

And he say, "Sure do."

"Well. You remember how you told me I was the cutest thing that ever walked the earth?"

"Oh, you were real cute when you were little," he say, which is suppose to be funny. I am not laughin.

"Well. You remember what you said?"

And Granddaddy Vale squintin over the wheel and axin Which way, Scout. But Scout is busy and don't care if we all get lost for days.

"Watcha mean, Peaches?"

"My name is Hazel. And what I mean is you said you were going to marry *me* when I grew up. You were going to wait. That's what I mean, my dear Uncle Jefferson." And he don't say nuthin. Just look at me real strange like he never saw me before in life. Like he lost in some weird town in the middle of night and lookin for directions and there's no one to ask. Like it was me that messed up the maps and turned the road posts round. "Well, you said it, didn't you?" And Baby Jason lookin back and forth like we playin ping-pong. Only I ain't playin. I'm hurtin and I can hear that I am screamin. And Granddaddy Vale mumblin how we never gonna get to where we goin if I don't turn around and take my navigator job serious.

"Well, for cryin out loud, Hazel, you just a little girl. And I was just teasin."

" 'And I was just teasin,' " I say back just how he said it so he can hear what a terrible thing it is. Then I don't say nuthin. And he don't say nuthin. And Baby Jason don't say nuthin nohow. Then Granddaddy Vale speak up. "Look here, Precious, it was Hunca Bubba what told you them things. This here, Jefferson Winston Vale." And Hunca Bubba say, "That's right. That was somebody else. I'm a new somebody."

"You a lyin dawg," I say, when I meant to say treacherous dog, but just couldn't get hold of the word. It slipped away from me. And I'm cryin and crumplin down in the seat and just don't care. And Granddaddy say to hush and steps on the gas. And I'm losin my bearins and don't even know where to look on the map cause I can't see for cryin. And Baby Jason cryin too. Cause he is my blood brother and understands that we must stick together or be forever lost, what with grownups playin change-up and turnin you round every which way so bad. And don't even say they sorry.

CHARLES BAXTER

Charles Baxter was born in 1947 in Minneapolis, Minnesota. He has been a teacher all his adult life, first in a high school and presently at Wayne State University in Detroit. His stories are collected in *Harmony of the World* (1984), *Through the Safety Net* (1985), and *First Light* (1987). Baxter once said of his fiction that it focuses on "threatened individuals"; in a way, "Gryphon" shifts the focus, to the threatening individual.

Gryphon

On Wednesday afternoon, between the geography lesson on ancient Egypt's hand-operated irrigation system and an art project that involved drawing a model city next to a mountain, our fourth-grade teacher, Mr. Hibler, developed a cough. This cough began with a series of muffled throat clearings and progressed to propulsive noises contained within Mr. Hibler's closed mouth. "Listen to him," Carol Peterson whispered to me. "He's gonna blow up." Mr. Hibler's laughter — dazed and infrequent — sounded a bit like his cough, but as we worked on our model cities we would look up, thinking he was enjoying a joke, and see Mr. Hibler's face turning red, his cheeks puffed out. This was not laughter. Twice he bent over, and his loose tie, like a plumb line, hung down straight from his neck as he exploded himself into a Kleenex. He would excuse himself, then go on coughing. "I'll bet you a dime," Carol Peterson whispered, "we get a substitute tomorrow."

Carol sat at the desk in front of mine and was a bad person — when she thought no one was looking she would blow her nose on notebook paper, then crumble it up and throw it into the wastebasket — but at times of crisis she spoke the truth. I knew I'd lose the dime.

"No deal," I said.

When Mr. Hibler stood us up in formation at the door just prior to the final bell, he was almost incapable of speech. "I'm sorry, boys and girls," he said. "I seem to be coming down with something."

"I hope you feel better tomorrow, Mr. Hibler," Bobby Kryzanowicz, the faultless brown-noser said, and I heard Carol Peterson's evil giggle. Then Mr. Hibler opened the door and we walked out to the buses, a clique of us starting noisily to hawk and cough as soon as we thought we were a few feet beyond Mr. Hibler's earshot.

Five Oaks being a rural community, and in Michigan, the supply of substitute teachers was limited to the town's unemployed community college graduates, a pool of about four mothers. These ladies fluttered, provided easeful class days, and nervously covered material we had mastered weeks earlier. Therefore it was a surprise when a woman we had never seen came into the class the next day, carrying a purple purse, a checkerboard lunchbox, and a few books. She put the books on one side of Mr. Hibler's desk and the lunchbox on the other, next to the Voice of Music phonograph. Three of us in the back of the room were playing with Heever, the chameleon that lived in the terrarium and on one of the plastic drapes, when she walked in.

She clapped her hands at us. "Little boys," she said, "why are you bent over together like that?" She didn't wait for us to answer. "Are you tormenting an animal? Put it back. Please sit down at your desks. I want no cabals this time of the day." We just stared at her. "Boys," she repeated, "I asked you to sit down."

I put the chameleon in his terrarium and felt my way to my desk, never taking my eyes off the woman. With white and green chalk, she had started to draw a tree on the left side of the blackboard. She didn't look usual. Furthermore, her tree was outsized, disproportionate, for some reason.

"This room needs a tree," she said, with one line drawing the suggestion of a leaf. "A large, leafy, shady, deciduous . . . oak."

Her fine, light hair had been done up in what I would learn years later was called a chignon, and she wore gold-rimmed glasses whose lenses seemed to have the faintest blue tint. Harold Knardahl, who sat across from me, whispered "Mars," and I nodded slowly, savoring the imminent weirdness of the day. The substitute drew another branch with an extravagant arm gesture, then turned around and said, "Good morning. I don't believe I said good morning to all of you yet."

Facing us, she was no special age — an adult is an adult — but her face had two prominent lines, descending vertically from the sides of her mouth to her chin. I knew where I had seen those lines before: *Pinocchio*. They were marionette lines. "You may stare at me," she said to us, as a few more kids from the last bus came into the room, their eyes fixed on her, "for a few more seconds, until the bell rings. Then I will permit no more staring. Looking I will permit. Staring, no. It is impolite to stare, and a sign of bad breeding. You cannot make a social effort while staring."

Harold Knardahl did not glance at me, or nudge, but I heard him whisper "Mars" again, trying to get more mileage out of his single joke with the kids who had just come in.

When everyone was seated, the substitute teacher finished her tree, put down her chalk fastidiously on the phonograph, brushed her hands, and faced us. "Good morning," she said. "I am Miss Ferenczi, your teacher for the day. I am fairly new to your community, and I don't believe any of you know me. I will therefore start by telling you a story about myself."

While we settled back, she launched into her tale. She said her grandfather had been a Hungarian prince; her mother had been born in some place called Flanders, had been a pianist, and had played concerts for people Miss Ferenczi referred to as "crowned heads." She gave us a knowing look. "Grieg," she said, "the Norwegian master, wrote a concerto for piano that was," she paused, "my mother's triumph at her debut concert in London." Her eyes searched the ceiling. Our eyes followed. Nothing up there but ceiling tile. "For reasons that I shall not go into, my family's fortunes took us to Detroit, then north to dreadful Saginaw, and now here I am in Five Oaks, as your substitute teacher, for today, Thursday, October the eleventh. I believe it will be a good day: All the forecasts coincide. We shall start with your reading lesson. Take out your reading book. I believe it is called *Broad Horizons,* or something along those lines."

Jeannie Vermeesch raised her hand. Miss Ferenczi nodded at her. "Mr. Hibler always starts the day with the Pledge of Allegiance," Jeannie whined.

"Oh, does he? In that case," Miss Ferenczi said, "you must know it *very* well by now, and we certainly need not spend our time on it. No, no allegiance pledging on the premises today, by my reckoning. Not with so much sunlight coming into the room. A pledge does not suit my mood." She glanced at her watch. "Time *is* flying. Take out *Broad Horizons.*"

She disappointed us by giving us an ordinary lesson, complete with vocabulary word drills, comprehension questions, and recitation. She didn't seem to care for the material, however. She sighed every few minutes and rubbed her glasses with a frilly perfumed handkerchief that she withdrew, magician style, from her left sleeve.

After reading we moved on to arithmetic. It was my favorite time of the morning, when the lazy autumn sunlight dazzled its way through ribbons of clouds past the windows on the east side of the classroom, and crept across the linoleum floor. On the playground the first group of children, the kindergartners, were running on the quack grass just beyond the monkey bars. We were doing multiplication tables. Miss Ferenczi had made John Wazny stand up at his desk in the front row. He was supposed to go through the tables of six. From where I was sitting, I could smell the Vitalis soaked into John's plastered hair. He was doing fine until he came to six times eleven and six times twelve. "Six times eleven," he said, "is sixty-eight. Six times twelve is . . ." He put his fingers to his head, quickly and secretly sniffed his fingertips, and said, "seventy-two." Then he sat down.

"Fine," Miss Ferenczi said. "Well now. That was very good."

"Miss Ferenczi!" One of the Eddy twins was waving her hand desperately in the air. "Miss Ferenczi! Miss Ferenczi!"

"Yes?"

"John said that six times eleven is sixty-eight and you said he was right!"

"*Did* I?" She gazed at the class with a jolly look breaking across her marionette's face. "Did I say that? Well, what *is* six times eleven?"

"It's sixty-six!"

She nodded. "Yes. So it is. But, and I know some people will not entirely agree with me, at some times it is sixty-eight."

"When? When is it sixty-eight?"

We were all waiting.

"In higher mathematics, which you children do not yet understand, six times eleven can be considered to be sixty-eight." She laughed through her nose. "In higher mathematics numbers are . . . more fluid. The only thing a number does is contain a certain amount of something. Think of water. A cup is not the only way to measure a certain amount of water, is it?" We were staring, shaking our heads. "You could use saucepans or thimbles. In either case, the water *would be the same*. Perhaps," she started again, "it would be better for you to think that six times eleven is sixty-eight only when I am in the room."

"Why is it sixty-eight," Mark Poole asked, "when you're in the room?"

"Because it's more interesting that way," she said, smiling very rapidly behind her blue-tinted glasses. "Besides, I'm your substitute teacher, am I not?" We all nodded. "Well, then, think of six times eleven equals sixty-eight as a substitute fact."

"A substitute fact?"

"Yes." Then she looked at us carefully. "Do you think," she asked, "that anyone is going to be hurt by a substitute fact?"

We looked back at her.

"Will the plants on the windowsill be hurt?" We glanced at them. They were sensitive plants thriving in a green plastic tray, and several wilted ferns in small clay pots. "Your dogs and cats, or your moms and dads?" She waited. "So," she concluded, "what's the problem?"

"But it's wrong," Janice Weber said, "isn't it?"

"What's your name, young lady?"

"Janice Weber."

"And you think it's wrong, Janice?"

"I was just asking."

"Well, all right. You were just asking. I think we've spent enough time on this matter by now, don't you, class? You are free to think what you like. When your teacher, Mr. Hibler, returns, six times eleven will be sixty-six again, you can rest assured. And it will be that for the rest of your lives in Five Oaks. Too bad, eh?" She raised her eyebrows and glinted herself at us. "But for now, it wasn't. So much for that. Let us go to your assigned problems for today, as painstakingly outlined, I see, in Mr. Hibler's lesson plan. Take out a sheet of paper and write your names in the upper left-hand corner."

For the next half hour we did the rest of our arithmetic problems. We handed them in and went on to spelling, my worst subject. Spelling always came before lunch. We were taking spelling dictation and looking at the clock. "Thorough," Miss Ferenczi said. "Boundary." She walked in the aisles between the desks, holding the spelling book open and looking down at our papers. "Balcony." I clutched my pencil. Somehow, the way she said those words, they seemed foreign, Hungarian, mis-voweled and mis-consonanted. I stared down at what I had spelled. *Balconie.* I turned my pencil upside down and erased my mistake. *Balconey.* That looked better, but still incorrect. I cursed the world of spelling and tried erasing it again and saw the paper beginning to wear away. *Balkony.* Suddenly I felt a hand on my shoulder.

"I don't like that word either," Miss Ferenczi whispered, bent over, her mouth near my ear. "It's ugly. My feeling is, if you don't like a word, you don't have to use it." She straightened up, leaving behind a slight odor of Clorets.

At lunchtime we went out to get our trays of sloppy joes, peaches in heavy syrup, coconut cookies, and milk, and brought them back to the classroom, where Miss Ferenczi was sitting at the desk, eating a brown sticky thing she had unwrapped from tightly rubber-banded wax paper. "Miss Ferenczi," I said, raising my hand. "You don't have to eat with us. You can eat with the other teachers. There's a teachers' lounge," I ended up, "next to the principal's office."

"No, thank you," she said. "I prefer it here."

"We've got a room monitor," I said. "Mrs. Eddy." I pointed to where Mrs. Eddy, Joyce and Judy's mother, sat silently at the back of the room, doing her knitting.

"That's fine," Miss Ferenczi said. "But I shall continue to eat here, with you children. I prefer it," she repeated.

"How come?" Wayne Razmer asked without raising his hand.

"I talked with the other teachers before class this morning," Miss Ferenczi said, biting into her brown food. "There was a great rattling of the words for the fewness of ideas. I didn't care for their brand of hilarity. I don't like ditto machine jokes."

"Oh," Wayne said.

"What's that you're eating?" Maxine Sylvester asked, twitching her nose. "Is it food?"

"It most certainly *is* food. It's a stuffed fig. I had to drive almost down to Detroit to get it. I also bought some smoked sturgeon. And this," she said, lifting some green leaves out of her lunchbox, "is raw spinach, cleaned this morning before I came out here to the Garfield-Murry school."

"Why're you eating raw spinach?" Maxine asked.

"It's good for you," Miss Ferenczi said. "More stimulating than soda pop or smelling salts." I bit into my sloppy joe and stared blankly out the window. An almost invisible moon was faintly silvered in the daytime autumn sky. "As far as food is concerned," Miss Ferenczi was saying, "you have to shuffle the pack. Mix it up. Too many people eat . . . well, never mind."

"Miss Ferenczi," Carol Peterson said, "what are we going to do this afternoon?"

"Well," she said, looking down at Mr. Hibler's lesson plan, "I see that your teacher, Mr. Hibler, has you scheduled for a unit on the Egyptians." Carol groaned. "Yessss," Miss Ferenczi continued, "that is what we will do: the Egyptians. A remarkable people. Almost as remarkable as the Americans. But not quite." She lowered her head, did her quick smile, and went back to eating her spinach.

After noon recess we came back into the classroom and saw that Miss Ferenczi had drawn a pyramid on the blackboard, close to her oak tree. Some of us who had been playing baseball were messing around in the back of the room, dropping the bats and the gloves into the playground box, and I think that Ray Schontzeler had just slugged me when I heard Miss Ferenczi's high-pitched voice quavering with emotion. "Boys," she said, "come to order right this minute and take your seats. I do not wish to waste a minute of class time. Take out your geography books." We trudged to our desks and, still sweating, pulled out *Distant Lands and Their People.* "Turn to page forty-two." She waited for thirty seconds, then looked over at Kelly Munger. "Young man," she said, "why are you still fossicking in your desk?"

Kelly looked as if his foot had been stepped on. "Why am I what?"

"Why are you . . . burrowing in your desk like that?"

"I'm lookin' for the book, Miss Ferenczi."

Bobby Kryzanowicz, the faultless brown-noser who sat in the first row by choice, softly said, "His name is Kelly Munger. He can't ever find his stuff. He always does that."

"I don't care what his name is, especially after lunch," Miss Ferenczi said. *"Where is your book?"*

"I just found it." Kelly was peering into his desk and with both hands pulled at the book, shoveling along in front of it several pencils and crayons, which fell into his lap and then to the floor.

"I hate a mess," Miss Ferenczi said. "I hate a mess in a desk or a mind. It's . . . unsanitary. You wouldn't want your house at home to look like your desk at school, now, would you?" She didn't wait for an answer. "I should think not. A house at home should be as neat as human hands can make it. What were we talking about? Egypt. Page forty-two. I note from Mr. Hibler's lesson plan that you have been discussing the modes of Egyptian irrigation. Interesting, in my view, but not so interesting as what we are about to cover. The pyramids and Egyptian slave labor. A plus on one side, a minus on the other." We had our books open to page forty-two, where there was a picture of a pyramid, but Miss Ferenczi wasn't looking at the book. Instead, she was staring at some object just outside the window.

"Pyramids," Miss Ferenczi said, still looking past the window. "I want you to think about the pyramids. And what was inside. The bodies of the pharaohs, of course, and their attendant treasures. Scrolls. Perhaps," Miss Ferenczi said, with something gleeful but unsmiling in her face, "these scrolls were novels for the pharaohs, helping them to pass the time in their long voyage through the centuries. But then, I am joking." I was looking at the lines on Miss Ferenczi's face. "Pyramids," Miss Ferenczi went on, "were the respositories of special cosmic powers. The nature of a pyramid is to guide cosmic energy forces into a concentrated point. The Egyptians knew that; we have generally forgotten it. Did you know," she asked, walking to the side of the room so that she was standing by the coat closet, "that George Washington had Egyptian blood, from his grandmother? Certain features of the Constitution of the United States are notable for their Egyptian ideas."

Without glancing down at the book, she began to talk about the movement of souls in Egyptian religion. She said that when people die, their souls return to Earth in the form of carpenter ants or walnut trees, depending on how they behaved — "well or ill" — in life. She said that the Egyptians believed that people act the way they do because of magnetism produced by tidal forces in the solar system, forces produced by the sun and by its "planetary ally," Jupiter. Jupiter, she said, was a planet, as we had been told, but had "certain properties of stars." She was speaking very fast. She said that the Egyptians were great explorers and conquerors. She said that the greatest of all the conquerors, Genghis Khan, had had forty horses and forty young women killed on the site of his grave. We listened. No one tried to stop her. "I myself have been in Egypt," she said, "and have witnessed much dust and many brutalities." She said that an old man in Egypt who worked for a circus had personally shown her an animal in a cage, a monster, half bird and half lion. She said that this monster was called a gryphon and that she had heard about them but never seen them until she traveled to the outskirts of Cairo. She said that Egyptian astronomers had discovered the planet Saturn, but had not seen its rings. She said that the Egyptians were the first to discover that dogs, when they are ill, will not drink from rivers, but wait for rain, and hold their jaws open to catch it.

"She lies."

We were on the school bus home. I was sitting next to Carl Whiteside, who had bad breath and a huge collection of marbles. We were arguing. Carl thought she was lying. I said she wasn't, probably.

"I didn't believe that stuff about the bird," Carl said, "and what she told us about the pyramids? I didn't believe that either. She didn't know what she was talking about."

"Oh yeah?" I had liked her. She was strange. I thought I could nail him. "If she was lying," I said, "what'd she say that was a lie?"

"Six times eleven isn't sixty-eight. It isn't ever. It's sixty-six, I know for a fact."

"She said so. She admitted it. What else did she lie about?"

"I don't know," he said. "Stuff."

"What stuff?"

"Well." He swung his legs back and forth. "You ever see an animal that was half lion and half bird?" He crossed his arms. "It sounded real fakey to me."

"It could happen," I said. I had to improvise, to outrage him. "I read in this newspaper my mom bought in the IGA about this scientist, this mad scientist in the Swiss Alps, and he's been putting genes and chromosomes and stuff together in test tubes, and he combined a human being and a hamster." I waited, for effect. "It's called a humster."

"You never." Carl was staring at me, his mouth open, his terrible bad breath making its way toward me. "What newspaper was it?"

"The *National Enquirer,*" I said, "that they sell next to the cash registers." When I saw his look of recognition, I knew I had bested him. "And this mad scientist," I said, "his name was, um, Dr. Frankenbush." I realized belatedly that this name was a mistake and waited for Carl to notice its resemblance to the name of the other famous mad master of permutations, but he only sat there.

"A man and a hamster?" He was staring at me, squinting, his mouth opening in distaste. "Jeez. What'd it look like?"

When the bus reached my stop, I took off down our dirt road and ran up through the back yard, kicking the tire swing for good luck. I dropped my books on the back steps so I could hug and kiss our dog, Mr. Selby. Then I hurried inside. I could smell Brussels sprouts cooking, my unfavorite vegetable. My mother was washing other vegetables in the kitchen sink, and my baby brother was hollering in his yellow playpen on the kitchen floor.

"Hi, Mom," I said, hopping around the playpen to kiss her, "Guess what?"

"I have no idea."

"We had this substitute today, Miss Ferenczi, and I'd never seen her before, and she had all these stories and ideas and stuff."

"Well. That's good." My mother looked out the window behind the sink, her eyes on the pine woods west of our house. Her face and hairstyle always reminded other people of Betty Crocker, whose picture was framed inside a gigantic spoon on the side of the Bisquick box; to me, though, my mother's face just looked white. "Listen, Tommy," she said, "go upstairs and pick your clothes off the bathroom floor, then go outside to the shed and put the shovel and ax away that your father left outside this morning."

"She said that six times eleven was sometimes sixty-eight!" I said. "And she said she once saw a monster that was half lion and half bird." I waited. "In Egypt, she said."

"Did you hear me?" my mother asked, raising her arm to wipe her forehead with the back of her hand. "You have chores to do."

"I know," I said. "I was just telling you about the substitute."

"It's very interesting," my mother said, quickly glancing down at me, "and we can talk about it later when your father gets home. But right now you have some work to do."

"Okay, Mom." I took a cookie out of the jar on the counter and was about to go outside when I had a thought. I ran into the living room, pulled out a dictionary next to the TV stand, and opened it to the G's. *Gryphon:* "variant of griffin." *Griffin:* "a fabulous beast with the head and wings of an eagle and the body of a lion." Fabulous was right. I shouted with triumph and ran outside to put my father's tools back in their place.

Miss Ferenczi was back the next day, slightly altered. She had pulled her hair down and twisted it into pigtails, with red rubber bands holding them tight one inch from the ends. She was wearing a green blouse and pink scarf, making her difficult to look at for a full class day. This time there was no pretense of doing a reading lesson or moving on to arithmetic. As soon as the bell rang, she simply began to talk.

She talked for forty minutes straight. There seemed to be less connection between her ideas, but the ideas themselves were, as the dictionary would say, fabulous. She said she had heard of a huge jewel, in what she called the Antipodes, that was so brilliant that when the light shone into it at a certain angle it would blind whoever was looking at its center. She said that the biggest diamond in the world was cursed and had killed everyone who owned it, and that by a trick of fate it was called the Hope diamond. Diamonds are magic, she said, and this is why women wear them on their fingers, as a sign of the magic of womanhood. Men have strength, Miss Ferenczi said, but no true magic. That is why men fall in love with women but women do not fall in love with men: they just love being loved. George Washington had died because of a mistake he made about a diamond. Washington was not the first *true* President, but she did not say who was. In some places in the world, she said, men and women still live in the trees and eat monkeys for breakfast. Their doctors are magicians. At the bottom of the sea are creatures thin as pancakes which have never been studied by scientists because when you take them up to the air, the fish explode.

There was not a sound in the classroom, except for Miss Ferenczi's voice, and Donna DeShano's coughing. No one even went to the bathroom.

Beethoven, she said, had not been deaf; it was a trick to make himself famous, and it worked. As she talked, Miss Ferenczi's pigtails swung back and forth. There are trees in the world, she said, that eat meat: their leaves are sticky and close up on bugs like hands. She lifted her hands and brought them together, palm to palm. Venus, which most people think is the next closest planet to the sun, is not always closer, and, besides, it is the planet of greatest mystery because of its thick cloud cover. "I know what lies underneath those clouds," Miss Ferenczi said, and waited. After the silence, she said, "Angels. Angels live under those clouds." She said that angels were not invisible to everyone and were in fact smarter than most people. They did not dress in robes as was often claimed but instead wore formal evening clothes, as if they were about to attend a concert. Often angels *do* attend concerts and sit in the aisles where, she said, most people pay no attention to them. She said the most terrible angel had the shape of the Sphinx. "There is no running away from that one," she said. She said that unquenchable fires burn just under the surface of the earth in Ohio, and that the baby Mozart fainted dead away in his cradle when he first heard the sound of a trumpet. She said that someone named Narzim al Harrardim was the greatest writer who ever lived. She said that planets control behavior, and anyone conceived during a solar eclipse would be born with webbed feet.

"I know you children like to hear these things," she said, "these secrets, and that is why I am telling you all this." We nodded. It was better than doing comprehension questions for the readings in *Broad Horizons*.

"I will tell you one more story," she said, "and then we will have to do arithmetic." She leaned over, and her voice grew soft. "There is no death," she said. "You must never be afraid. Never. That which is, cannot die. It will change into different earthly and unearthly elements, but I know this as sure as I stand here in front of you, and I swear it: you must not be afraid. I have seen this truth with these eyes. I know it because in a dream God kissed me. Here." And she pointed with her right index finger to the side of her head, below the mouth, where the vertical lines were carved into her skin.

Absent-mindedly we all did our arithmetic problems. At recess the class was out on the playground, but no one was playing. We were all standing in small groups, talking about Miss Ferenczi. We didn't know if she was crazy, or what. I looked out beyond the playground, at the rusted cars piled in a small heap behind a clump of sumac, and I wanted to see shapes there, approaching me.

On the way home, Carl sat next to me again. He didn't say much, and I didn't either. At last he turned to me. "You know what she said about the leaves that close up on bugs?"

"Huh?"

"The leaves," Carl insisted. "The meat-eating plants. I know it's true. I saw it on television. The leaves have this thick icky glue that the plants have got smeared all over them and the insects can't get off 'cause they're stuck. I saw it." He seemed demoralized. "She's tellin' the truth."

"Yeah."

"You think she's seen all those angels?"

I shrugged.

"I don't think she has," Carl informed me. "I think she made that part up."

"There's a tree," I suddenly said. I was looking out the window at the farms along County Road H. I knew every barn, every broken windmill, every fence, every anhydrous ammonia tank, by heart. "There's a tree that's . . . that I've seen . . ."

"Don't you try to do it," Carl said. "You'll just sound like a jerk."

I kissed my mother. She was standing in front of the stove. "How was your day?" she asked.

"Fine."

"Did you have Miss Ferenczi again?"

"Yeah."

"Well?"

"She was fine. Mom," I asked, "can I go to my room?"

"No," she said, "not until you've gone out to the vegetable garden and picked me a few tomatoes." She glanced at the sky. "I think it's going to rain. Skedaddle and do it now. Then you come back inside and watch your brother for a few minutes while

I go upstairs. I need to clean up before dinner." She looked down at me. "You're looking a little pale, Tommy." She touched the back of her hand to my forehead and I felt her diamond ring against my skin. "Do you feel all right?"

"I'm fine," I said, and went out to pick the tomatoes.

Coughing mutedly, Mr. Hibler was back the next day, slipping lozenges into his mouth when his back was turned at forty-five-minute intervals and asking us how much of the prepared lesson plan Miss Ferenczci had followed. Edith Atwater took the responsibility for the class of explaining to Mr. Hibler that the substitute hadn't always done exactly what he would have done, but we had worked hard even though she talked a lot. About what? he asked. All kinds of things, Edith said. I sort of forgot. To our relief, Mr. Hibler seemed not at all interested in what Miss Ferenczi had said to fill the day. He probably thought it was woman's talk; unserious and not suited for school. It was enough that he had a pile of arithmetic problems from us to correct.

For the next month, the sumac turned a distracting red in the field, and the sun traveled toward the southern sky, so that its rays reached Mr. Hibler's Halloween display on the bulletin board in the back of the room, fading the scarecrow with a pumpkin head from orange to tan. Every three days I measured how much farther the sun had moved toward the southern horizon by making small marks with my black Crayola on the north wall, ant-sized marks only I knew were there, inching west.

And then in early December, four days after the first permanent snowfall, she appeared again in our classroom. The minute she came in the door, I felt my heart begin to pound. Once again, she was different: this time, her hair hung straight down and seemed hardly to have been combed. She hadn't brought her lunchbox with her, but she was carrying what seemed to be a small box. She greeted all of us and talked about the weather. Donna DeShano had to remind her to take her overcoat off.

When the bell to start the day finally rang, Miss Ferenczi looked out at all of us and said, "Children, I have enjoyed your company in the past, and today I am going to reward you." She held up the small box. "Do you know what this is?" She waited. "Of course you don't. It's a tarot pack."

Edith Atwater raised her hand. "What's a tarot pack, Miss Ferenczi?"

"It is used to tell fortunes," she said. "And that is what I shall do this morning. I shall tell your fortunes, as I have been taught to do."

"What's fortune?" Bobby Kryzanowicz asked.

"The future, young man. I shall tell you what your future will be. I can't do your whole future, of course. I shall have to limit myself to the five-card system, the wands, cups, swords, pentacles, and the higher arcanes. Now who wants to be first?"

There was a long silence. Then Carol Peterson raised her hand.

"All right," Miss Ferenczi said. She divided the pack into five smaller packs and walked back to Carol's desk, in front of mine. "Pick one card from each of these packs," she said. I saw that Carol had a four of cups, a six of swords, but I couldn't see the other cards. Miss Ferenczi studied the cards on Carol's desk for a minute. "Not bad," she said. "I do not see much higher education. Probably an early marriage. Many children. There's something bleak and dreary here, but I can't tell what. Perhaps just the tasks of a housewife life. I think you'll do very well, for the most part." She smiled at Carol, a smile with a certain lack of interest. "Who wants to be next?"

Carl Whiteside raised his hand slowly.

"Yes," Miss Ferenczi said, "let's do a boy." She walked over to where Carl sat. After he picked his five cards, she gazed at them for a long time. "Travel," she said. "Much distant travel. You might go into the Army. Not too much romantic interest here. A late marriage, if at all. Squabbles. But the Sun is in your major arcana, here, yes, that's a very good card." She giggled. "Maybe a good life."

Next I raised my hand, and she told me my future. She did the same with Bobby Kryzanowicz. Kelly Munger, Edith Atwater, and Kim Foor. Then she came to Wayne Razmer. He picked his five cards, and I could see that the Death card was one of them.

"What's your name?" Miss Ferenczi asked.

"Wayne."

"Well, Wayne," she said, you will undergo a *great* metamorphosis, the greatest, before you become an adult. Your earthly element will leap away, into thin air, you sweet boy. This card, this nine of swords here, tells of suffering and desolation. And this ten of wands, well, that's certainly a heavy load."

"What about this one?" Wayne pointed to the Death card.

"That one? That one means you will die soon, my dear." She gathered up the cards. We were all looking at Wayne. "But do not fear," she said. "It's not really death, so much as change." She put the cards on Mr. Hibler's desk. "And now, let's do some arithmetic."

At lunchtime Wayne went to Mr. Faegre, the principal, and told him what Miss Ferenczi had done. During the noon recess, we saw Miss Ferenczi drive out of the parking lot in her green Rambler. I stood under the slide, listening to the other kids coasting down and landing in the little depressive bowl at the bottom. I was kicking stones and tugging at my hair right up to the moment when I saw Wayne come out to the playground. He smiled, the dead fool, and with the fingers of his right hand he was showing everyone how he had told on Miss Ferenczi.

I made my way toward Wayne, pushing myself past two girls from another class. He was watching me with his little pinhead eyes.

"You told," I shouted at him. "She was just kidding."

"She shouldn't have," he shouted back. "We were supposed to be doing arithmetic."

"She just scared you," I said. "You're a chicken. You're a chicken, Wayne. You are. Scared of a little card," I singsonged.

Wayne fell at me, his two fists hammering down on my nose. I gave him a good one in the stomach and then I tried for his head. Aiming my fist, I saw that he was crying. I slugged him.

"She was right," I yelled. "She was always right! She told the truth!" Other kids were whooping. "You were just scared, that's all!"

And then large hands pulled at us, and it was my turn to speak to Mr. Faegre.

In the afternoon Miss Ferenczi was gone, and my nose was stuffed with cotton clotted with blood, and my lip had swelled, and our class had been combined with Mrs. Mantei's sixth-grade class for a crowded afternoon science unit on insect life in ditches and swamps. I knew where Mrs. Mantei lived: she had a new house trailer just down the road from us, at the Clearwater Park. She was no mystery. Somehow she and Mr. Bodine, the other fourth-grade teacher, had managed to fit forty-five desks into the room. Kelly Munger asked if Miss Ferenczi had been arrested, and Mrs. Mantei said no, of course not. All that afternoon, until the buses came to pick us up, we learned about field crickets and two-striped grasshoppers, water bugs, cicadas, mosquitoes, flies, and moths. We learned about insects' hard outer shell, the exo-skeleton, and the usual parts of the mouth, including the labrum, mandible, maxilla, and glossa. We learned about compound eyes and the four-stage metamorphosis from egg to larva to pupa to adult. We learned something, but not much, about mating. Mrs. Mantei drew, very skillfully, the internal anatomy of the grasshopper on the blackboard. We learned about the dance of the honeybee, directing other bees in the hive to pollen. We found out about which insects were pests to man, and which were not. On lined white pieces of paper we made lists of insects we might actually see, then a list of insects too small to be clearly visible, such as fleas; Mrs. Mantei said that our assignment would be to memorize these lists for the next day, when Mr. Hibler would certainly return and test us on our knowledge.

ANN BEATTIE

Ann Beattie, who was born in 1947 in Washington, D.C., is often characterized as the chronicler of a generation that came to consciousness and its early maturity in the 1960s and to disillusion and subsequent ennui in ensuing decades. Her characters are sometimes accused of being unable to compel the reader's empathy, but in her uninflected depiction of truths as she sees them Beattie echoes something of an earlier seeker of truth in short fiction, Anton Chekhov. John Updike has said it well: Beattie's dialogue reveals "an uncanny fidelity to the . . . heartbreaks behind the banal." Among her works are two novels, *Chilly Scenes of Winter* (1983), and *Love Always* (1985), and several collections of short stories, including *Jacklighting* (1981), *The Burning House* (1982), and *Where You'll Find Me* (1986). "Snow" is, in a rare departure for Beattie, told in a second-person narrative, one which quietly and achingly sustains a central metaphor.

Snow

I remember the cold night you brought in a pile of logs and a chipmunk jumped off as you lowered your arms. "What do you think *you're* doing in here?" you said, as it ran through the living room. It went through the library and stopped at the front door as though it knew the house well. This would be difficult for anyone to believe, except perhaps as the subject of a poem. Our first week in the house was spent scraping, finding some of the house's secrets, like wallpaper underneath wallpaper. In the kitchen, a pattern of white-gold trellises supported purple grapes as big and round as Ping-Pong balls. When we painted the walls yellow, I thought of the bits of grape that remained underneath and imagined the vine popping through, the way some plants can tenaciously push through anything. The day of the big snow, when you had to shovel the walk and couldn't find your cap and asked me how to wind a towel so that it would stay on your head — you, in the white towel turban, like a crazy king of the snow. People liked the idea of our being together, leaving the city for the country. So many people visited, and the fireplace made all of them want to tell amazing stories: the child who happened to be standing on the right corner when the door of the ice-cream truck came open and hundreds of Popsicles cascaded out; the man standing on the beach, sand sparkling in the sun, one bit glinting more than the rest, stooping to find a diamond ring. Did they talk about amazing things because they thought we'd turn into one of them? Now I think they probably guessed it wouldn't work. It was as hopeless as giving a child a matched cup and saucer. Remember the night, out on the lawn, knee-deep in snow, chins pointed at the sky as the wind whirled down all that whiteness? It seemed that the world had been turned upside down, and we were looking into an enormous field of Queen Anne's lace. Later, headlights off, our car was the first to ride through the newly fallen snow. The world outside the car looked solarized.

You remember it differently. You remember that the cold settled in stages, that a small curve of light was shaved from the moon night after night, until you were no longer surprised the sky was black, that the chipmunk ran to hide in the dark, not simply to a door that led to its escape. Our visitors told the same stories people always tell. One night, giving me a lesson in storytelling, you said, "Any life will seem dramatic if you omit mention of most of it."

This, then, for drama: I drove back to that house not long ago. It was April, and Allen had died. In spite of all the visitors, Allen, next door, had been the good friend in bad times. I sat with his wife in their living room, looking out the glass doors to the backyard, and there was Allen's pool, still covered with black plastic that had been stretched across it for winter. It had rained, and as the rain fell, the cover collected more and more water until it finally spilled onto the concrete. When I left that day, I drove past what had been our house. Three or four crocus were blooming in the front — just a few dots of white, no field of snow. I felt embarrassed for them. They couldn't compete.

This is a story, told the way you say stories should be told: Somebody grew up, fell in love, and spent a winter with her lover in the country. This, of course, is the barest outline, and futile to discuss. It's as pointless as throwing birdseed on the ground while snow still falls fast. Who expects small things to survive when even the largest get lost? People forget years and remember moments. Seconds and symbols are left to sum things up: the black shroud over the pool. Love, in its shortest form, becomes a word. What I remember about all that time is one winter. The snow. Even now, saying "snow," my lips move so that they kiss the air.

No mention has been made of the snowplow that seemed always to be there, scraping snow off our narrow road — an artery cleared, though neither of us could have said where the heart was.

CAROL BLY

Carol Bly was born in 1930 in Minnesota, a homeland for which her devotion has never flagged. At times that devotion has taken on the tones of exhortation: frustrated with the narrowness of small-town mentalities, Bly wrote essays for Minnesota Public Radio's magazine, admonishing the inhabitants of rural communities to attend to their inner lives and to forget their fear of social criticism or ostracism. "Positive thinking," she wrote, "is a kind of naivete. People who practice or commend it are interested in feeling no pain." Those essays were published as *Letters from the Country* (1981), which essayist Noel Perrin (himself a keen observer of rural America) termed "a clarion call . . . meant to resound along a thousand Main Streets." Bly's short stories, collected in *Backbone* (1985), are at one with her essays in their themes and concerns. Told quietly, with affection and humor, they reveal the poignance and also the pleasure in sustaining self-reliance in a rural community. "The Dignity of Life" establishes as well Bly's deft sense of the comic.

The Dignity of Life

Two people stood quarreling in the Casket Showing Room. They were a sixty-three-year-old man named Marlyn Huutula and his unmarried sister Estona. She was so angry that she bent towards him from her end of the coffin.

"You really ought to keep your grimy hands out of that clean quilting!" Estona told him in a ferocious whisper. "As if you owned the place! As if Svea weren't lying dead this very minute, right here in this very building, and you showing no respect!"

Jack Canon, the funeral director, had been hovering near them. Now he gave a swift glance over to see how grimy Marlyn's hands were. He would let this grown brother and sister quarrel a moment; he meant to leave this end of the long Showing Room so that they would not feel self-conscious as they whispered furiously about prices.

Marlyn and Estona were buying a casket, and the service that went with it, for their aunt, Svea Istava, an old woman who had come down in the world. Svea had died alone in her wreck of a place just north of St. Aidan, Minnestoa. From the time she moved there in 1943, until she died in February, 1982, she had always had a few faithful visitors. They would pick their way through her sordid front farmyard, avoiding the wet place and the coils of barbed wire. Her place was what was called "inconvenient": that is, it had no water up to the house. But whenever someone visited — Mrs. Friesman to leave her idiot son Momo, or Jack Canon, the funeral director, or on Sundays during the football seasons, her nephew, Marlyn Huutula — Svea filled their cups with smoky coffee.

Her most frequent visitor, Momo Friesman, found her dead. Next morning, people sitting around the Feral Café traded information about Svea, making her a kind of random liturgy. They told one another how Svea had taken better care of that dog, Biscuit, than she took of herself. They told each other it was certainly hard to believe that Svea Istava had ever been the wife of a Lieutenant Colonel in the 45th Field Artillery, whose body had not been sent home because that was during World War II, not Vietnam. Mrs. Friesman had seen his Bronze Star and his European Theatre of Operations ribbon bar hanging on cuphooks in Svea's smudgy cupboard. Finally, people in the café settled to the most interesting thing about Svea: they said she was worth $500,000. In one booth, the sheriff was talking about her to the state patrolman who lived in Marrow Lake. The Marrow Lake man went past Svea's place nearly every day and had never seen such a dump. But the sheriff said that you could tell the true class of a person, though, by how they treated a dog. He himself had a handsome white shepherd bitch; that Biscuit, now, originally was a runt from one of his litters. He had taken it over to Svea because he knew she would make it a good home, and so she had.

Everyone thought that Svea had left the whole $500,000 (if she had any $500,000) to her nephew Marlyn instead of half and half to Marlyn and his sister Estona. Marlyn visited her once a week for years, whereas Estona talked mean about Svea. Estona, who ran the Nu-St. Aidan Motel, was always roping in total strangers, finding out what they did, and then asking their advice. With both elbows on the sign-in counter, her eyes trying to read their bank balances when they opened their checkbooks, her wrists supporting her cheeks, she would say, "So you're a sales representative? As a sales representative, would you please tell me if this sounds right to you? I mean, you're in a position to know . . ." Then she would explain about Svea's money going to her kid brother because he was a man and made up to her on Sunday afternoons. Recently, she had said to the new Adult Education teacher who stayed at the motel on Wednesday nights, "You're a humanities consultant? Now that sounds like something that has got to be about how people treat each other! Fairly or unfairly? Well, would you tell me as a humanities consultant — would you call it fair that this old woman, who keeps her place so bad it is amazing they don't get the countryside nursing people in to spray around, do you think it is right she would leave all that money to my brother and not my half to me?" Estona regarded the humanities consultant as another middle-aged woman like herself, who had to have picked up some sense somewhere along the line. "I don't know if this is in your field or not, but just looking at it humanly, can you tell me that he is making any big sacrifices for his aunt when he can check on his Vikings and Steelers bets as good on Svea's eleven-inch black and white as he could on his own remote control at home? Or maybe it's just me."

As Marlyn and Estona stood around the Casket Showing Room, Jack Canon thought of everything that had happened since Svea's death. Her body had been discovered by Momo: Jack had quickly gone out to fetch it. He knew Momo as well as Svea, because Momo liked dead bodies. There was scarcely a wake or visitation in the past ten or fifteen years at which Jack hadn't had a word with Momo — that is, he had had to take him firmly by the elbow. Then, after he took Svea's body to the chapel, twenty

or more youngsters went out to her place, apparently, and dug great holes all over
the yard. By the time the sheriff reached the place, the boys had tipped over Svea's
outhouse and were prodding the hole, looking for money. Another boy and girl had
got hold of powers augers and they were drilling into the frozen ground, like mining
prospectors, among the stacked snowtreads and fence-wire wheels. The sheriff
pulled them all in on Possession and Vandalism and then let them out again. He
called Jack and said he was going to ask the state patrolman to help keep an eye open
these next days. "If we are going to have any trouble," Jack told him, "it will be
during visitation days, not at the funeral itself." The two men talked to each other
quietly on the telephone, in the special, measured way of people holding the fort for
decency and dignity — while all the others give in to some horrible craze. The
sheriff said with a sigh, "Well, we'll manage! I've got to locate that nephew of hers
now, wherever he is!" Jack felt the respect the sheriff had for him, a funeral director,
and the disrespect he felt for Marlyn Huutula, who never had steady work in the
wintertime if he could help it. Like half the men of St. Aidan, Marlyn kept a line of
traps somewhere out east along St. Aidan Creek. Once he had tried to bribe the
sheriff out of a speeding ticket while the sheriff stood at his car window, writing.
Marlyn had picked up the rabbit lying on the passenger side and passed it up to the
sheriff. The sheriff had been busy writing, so he didn't look carefully: all he saw was
white fur and a little blood. At home, his shepherd had just had a new litter of white
puppies, so he mistook this animal. It was a full minute before he saw it was a rabbit,
not a puppy. He had been writing a Warning; now he tore up the yellow card and
gave the man a Citation instead. All day, as he later told Jack, his stomach churned.
Then he blushed. "I don't guess that would bother someone . . . in your line of
work," he added.

"Yes, it would bother him," Jack told him.

"I never had much tolerance," the sheriff said.

Jack Canon felt less tolerant every day now. He had started an Adult Education
course two weeks ago; he thought it would give him perspective, but it was just the
opposite. Now he minded remarks he heard that previously he would have passed
off as "the kinds of things people say."

He frequently thought of his crimson vinyl notebook that lay on his office desk. It
was labeled: HUMANITIES: ST. AIDAN ADULT EDUCATION PROGRAM — MOLLY GALAN, INSTRUCTOR.
Jack had never been a man who took notes on his life as it went by. Yet now, several
times a day, he said to himself, sometimes even aloud, since he was a good deal
alone, "I ought to put *that* into the red notebook!" or *"That* ought to go into the red
notebook if nothing else ever does!" And he looked forward to Wednesday night, the
night of his class.

Tonight it was to meet in his office, as a matter of fact. That had come about
because two weeks ago, on Registration Night, only one student had shown up to
sign for the humanities course — Jack himself. His teacher was a spare, graying
woman with a white forehead, who was unlike anyone he had ever known. He
glanced over her head, her figure — her long hands with thin, unremarkable fingers,
trying to say "It is in the eyes," or "It is the hands," or "It is how she *carries*
herself" — but he knew all his guesses were wrong. She leaned against the
second-grade teacher's desk, and Jack sat cramped before her in a desk-and-chair
combination comfortable only for small children. They waited for others to appear.
Through the schoolroom doorway, they heard shy voices, calls, remarks — people
signing up for Beginning Knitting Two, a continuation from the fall semester.

No one else came at all. Presently, Mrs. Galan explained that the guidelines of the course would allow the class to meet in private homes, if the class so chose. The following Wednesday, there was a blizzard, but Mrs. Galan made it on I-35 from St. Paul to the Nu-St. Aidan Motel, and to the schoolbuilding. This time she read off to Jack some of the course subjects approved in the guidelines. They might choose among Ethnicity, Sources of Community Wisdom, Ethical Consciousness in Rural America, Longitudinal Studies of Human Success and Failure, Attitudinal Changes Towards Death, or simply Other. They agreed that the following Wednesday, since no one had shown up again this time, they might as well meet in Jack's office. He explained to her that she should walk round to the back of the chapel, where the back door opened onto a concrete apron. It was kept clear of snow, he told her.

In his years and years of single life Jack had noticed that lonely people were either carefully groomed or remarkably grimy. He himself had to be immaculate at all times. It was a habit by the time he was fourteen — along with learning how to cover the phone. He would push his arithmetic problems against the chapel schedule board, keeping the phone where his left hand could raise the earpiece on the first ring. Then he spoke immediately and courteously into the flared mouth. By the time he was a senior in high school he was used to nearly all the work of the chapel: he knew how to lift heavy weight without grunting, while wearing a white shirt, tie, and suit jacket. He learnt to keep longing or anxiety from showing on his face. One October day, in 1936, he was sitting on the football bench at St. Aidan High School. The big St. Aidan halfback sat down next to him, for just a minute. Jack had been sitting there, knees together, chilled, for an hour. The halfback, a great tall boy named Marlyn Huutula, dropped down beside him when he was taken out to rest a minute, and his body gave off heat and the glow of recently spent energy. It was nearly visible like a halo — that great hot energy field around the boy. Jack knew enough not to look at Marlyn for more than a second; he must not let himself be mesmerized into staring like a rabbit at a successful boy, the way he had seen others do. So Jack had given Marlyn a casual grin and both of them turned to watch the field. Then the coach snapped his fingers at Marlyn, who jumped up right in front of Jack. The coach's arm went around the leather-misshaped shoulders; Jack overheard the friendly growl of instructions. The coach pointed into the field with one hand, slapped Marlyn's buttocks with the other, and the halfback swung away towards the players, his socks sunk below his calves, jiggling in folds around the strong ankles. For the thousandth time that autumn, Jack expressed manhood by not letting his face look sad.

But the next Thursday afternoon, just as he was helping his father transfer a casket from the nervous pallbearers into the hearse, Jack recalled the bad moment on the football field. His face jerked upward in embarrassment at the memory. When his father had closed the hearse doors, he pulled Jack aside. St. Aidan Lutheran's two bells kept tolling so the sound rang down nearly on top of them: the sidewalk was white and cold with afternoon sunlight. "I'm going to tell you this just once, but it is very important," Jack's dad said. "Do not put on a fake sad look — the way you did just now when we were taking the casket. Get this straight: they don't expect you to look sad — just professional. Just keep your face serious and considerate."

Jack became more and more carefully gauged in his appearance: he controlled his face, he maintained his grooming. But Svea Istava, whose body now lay in his operating room, had turned dirty as she aged. When Jack first knew her in 1943, she was a handsome woman of thirty-nine or so. She told him she had to give up the St.

Paul house that her husband's officer's pay had been financing. She asked Jack if the World War II dead were going to be returned to the United States. Next month, she bought an old, very small farmhouse on an acre of scrubland, about a mile past St. Aidan.

The first time Jack went out there to visit, his eyes passed over the turquoise-painted, fake-tile siding. He saw the string of barbed wire that someone had hitched to one corner of the outhouse and then stretched over to the cornerpost of the house itself. He supposed that Mrs. Istava would gradually have trash removed from the farmyard. He hoped she would find enough money to put in plumbing. He imagined the huge shade of the oaks darkening not these piles of rejected auto batteries and other trash, but new lawn. There was a distant view of both church spires, and to the north lay the pleasant, spooky pine forest.

To his surprise, Svea didn't remove the barbed wire; she took to leaning things against it — first a screen door that warped and she couldn't repair, next a refrigerator that stopped working. Its rounded ivory corners and its rusted base grate seemed natural after a while; Svea tied a clothesline length about it so that Momo Friesman would not climb inside and be killed. Sometimes she stood the way poor rural people stand, elbow bent, one hand planted on one irregular hip, and the face gazing vaguely past the immediate farmyard, as if to say, "There is life beyond this paltry place — I have my eyes on it."

In those days, Jack sometimes thought he would save Svea from all that. He imagined himself, in a square-shouldered way driving out one miserable winter night, when the sky would be black and the ground-storming of down snow nearly blinding. "Oh, how did you ever make it on such a night?" she would cry, and he would say briefly, a little sharply, "Come on — we're going to town! We're going to be married!" He imagined the reliable Willys pushing through all that darkness and whiteness.

It never happened. Svea never called a junk man to pick up anything in her yard. Instead, more junk arrived. Jack had to pick his way to the doorstep over corrugated-tread wheels of broken lawnmowers. Often, Momo stared at him from a pile of rubbish near the tipped refrigerator. He knew the child trapped mice and then buried them in a distracted, faithful way, among Svea's onion sets and carrots.

As the years passed, a rumor grew up that all this while Svea Istava had been and was still worth $500,000. The more unlikely her person and possessions, the more entrenched the myth.

Meanwhile, gradually, Jack began to lose confidence. He began buying more and more expensive clothing. By the 1960s, even his garden gloves were from L. L. Bean. He was the first man in St. Aidan to have a wool suit after a decade of Dacrons and polyester. By accident, he found out what was wrong with him. One evening, he sat with the sheriff down at the station. It had been a bitter February day, as it was now, and the sheriff was saying that the bad news in St. Aidan County was the rising crime rate but the good news was that more and more uranium leases were being let out around the area. Jack listened idly, leaning comfortably against the iron radiator, watching the heat move the window shades a little. The sheriff held several puppies on a pillow in his lap; his hands kept passing over the little dogs and the dogs kept rearranging themselves in a whining, growling, moving pile of one another. As Jack looked on, he felt that he was losing confidence because he wasn't touching other live bodies enough; he watched in an agony of envy as the puppies wandered with their fat paws into one another's eyes and ears and stomachs — he got the idea they were gaining confidence from one another every time they touched.

The next day he walked into the Feral Café to have lunch with the new Haven Funeral Supply salesman, Bud Menge. Haunted by the revelation of the puppies, he sensed that women looked up at Bud Menge as he went by, and rearranged their buttocks in the booths.

Bud was friendly, right from the first. After a year of their acquaintance, Jack said, "Couldn't you ever stop and let me buy you lunch without you trying to sell me something?"

Most dealing in St. Aidan took place at either the Men's Fellowship of St. Aidan Lutheran or at lunch in the Feral Café. Bud's face grew grave and considerate. "Listen, Jack, how would you like to discuss something that is absolutely new and different and will revolutionize your whole approach?"

In ten minutes, Bud sold Jack an industrial-psychology program that he had used ever since. The Casket Showing Room Lighting Plan, like all of Bud's ideas, was disgusting from the outset. "That's really revolting, Bud. Let's face it, Bud," he had said, "that is just about the worst taste I have ever heard of!" Jack had often made such remarks during Bud's first year as representative for Haven Funeral Supply. Later he was slower to speak. Bud never presented him an idea that was not absolutely profitable.

The first aspect of the Casket Showing Room Lighting Plan was simple. You lighted only those caskets you wanted a client to inspect. You placed small wall-bracketed lamps at six-foot intervals along the two long walls, and across one short end-wall of the Showing Room. These lamps had either rose or cream shades: you lit only those you wanted on each given occasion. Jack generally lighted the caskets that went with the $1500 service, the $2300 service, and the $4000 service. No one in St. Aidan ever bought the $4000 service, and in fact, it was not for sale.

This $4000 casket was an elaborate part of Bud's Lighting Plan. Jack saw that it was lighted, and left its cover up, but did not lead clients over to it. Bud explained the procedure: people shopping for caskets feel that they are likely to be cheated by the mortician. Even if the mortician is a fellow small-town citizen whom they have known for years, they still feel they must watch him like a hawk now that they are buying from him. They know perfectly well that their own harrowed feelings at the time of a death are the funeral director's pivot. They are on tiptoe against his solemnity. Therefore, Bud explained, clients want to wander around the Showing Room on their own: they feel they are getting around the funeral director if they look at caskets besides the ones he seems to want to show them. They want to be shrewd. Eventually, Bud explained, because it is lighted and open, the $4000 casket catches the client's eye. He goes over, and, wonder of wonders, finds this casket to be noticeably more elegant than anything the funeral director has shown him so far. Immediately, he thinks that it is probably priced the same as the caskets he has been shown, but simply is a better buy. He suspects it is being kept for some preferred customer of the funeral director, and that a comparative lemon is being pawned off on him at the same price. Bud told Jack, "You follow them over to the $4000 casket, but stay behind a little — as if you didn't really want to go over there. 'How come you never showed us *this* one?' they will ask. 'How come you never showed us this one when it's just beautiful?' they will say. So then you tell them. 'You're right — it is the most beautiful one, by far. It is the best casket we have ever had at Canon Chapel.'

Just tell them that much at this point. Let them hang a little. Sooner or later the client will stop staring at you and will say, 'So how come you didn't show it to us?' Now here is where you pull your act together," Bud told Jack. "You tell them, fairly fast, 'Because I don't want you to buy that casket, is why.'" Bud begged Jack to pause again, right at that point. "Stick with the pauses, Jack, I'm telling you. Pause right there. Every single client — I don't care if it is the middle-aged mother of an only son who just died — every single client will say, 'But why don't you want me to buy it? What does it cost?' Now you go right up to the client and say, 'Because it costs $4000. I know you can afford $4000, Mrs. So-and-so, I know you can easily raise that amount. Money isn't the problem. The reason I don't want you to buy it is that I'd a hundred times rather that you bought the $2300 casket and gave the other $1700 to church or charity in memory of' — and you insert the deceased's name here — 'I'd a hundred times rather you'd spent the $1700 extra that way than on a casket.' O.K., now, Jack, here is the third pause — don't make it very long — just a short one. Now you say, 'Or does that sound crazy, from where I'm supposed to be coming from?'"

Bud was right. No client ever said, "Yes, it sounds crazy." Men gave Jack a warm look and sometimes slapped his arm. Women sometimes came around the $4000 casket and hugged him. Everyone said, "Thanks, Jack, for being so square with us." And just as Bud had prophesied, not one of those clients ever bought the $1500 casket: they all bought the $2300 one. The whole point of the Lighting Plan was to switch people from the $1500 to the $2300 casket. During the whole sales procedure, Jack never had to lie. After explaining the Plan, Bud had paused briefly, then looked very straight at Jack across the strewn café booth table, with the chili bowls and paper sachets of coffee-whitening chemicals that both men had pushed away so they could lean forward on their forearms. "Some of them," Bud said, "I wouldn't bother to explain they don't have to lie — they wouldn't care. But with you, Jack, now that's a major thing."

The last point of the Casket Lighting Plan was to have one end of the Showing Room nearly dark. Jack made use of this point right now: he broke into the quarreling between Estona and Marlyn Huutula.

"Folks," Jack said loudly, "I am going to look over some odds and ends of paperwork. I'll be down at the other end of the room, so when you want me, give a call."

Clients needed the sense of quarreling privately. They needed to confer over how little they could spend without causing talk in town — talk about how cheap they were, after all that *he* or *she* had done for *them,* too. Jack always left people to have this quarrel, but he stayed within earshot so he could return at the right moment.

At a tiny writing table at the dark end of the room, just behind the county casket, Jack looked over an eight-page booklet showing full-color photographs of funeral customs all over the world. The photographs were on the right-hand pages, the "Discussion Questions" on the left-hand pages.

"What's the good of it?" Jack had said in the Feral Café, when Bud passed him the booklet across their coffee cups.

"It's the most practical thing we have come up with yet," Bud told him with his frank smile. "It solves the problem of the local necrophiliac. And every town has one."

Jack said, "I wish you wouldn't use that word in the Feral Café, Bud. In fact I wish you wouldn't use it at all. And besides," he added in the no-nonsense tone he used when he had to, his mind picturing Momo Friesman, "we haven't got anyone like that in St. Aidan."

"Every town has one," Bud said. "If you haven't got him today you will have him tomorrow. When some funeral director tells me his town don't have one, I look at the funeral director himself. Ha, ha! Just joking, Jack."

Bud opened the booklet to a page called *Funeral Practices of the Frehiti People*. "O.K.," he said. "Here's how it works. Your man shows up at a visitation or a wake."

"And who are the Frehiti People? What do we care!" said Jack.

Bud grinned. "How should I know who they are? They don't live around here anyway. Anyway, they're somebody. Some sociologists or humanities people or somebody did all the research — we know it's O.K. That's a point I'm glad you asked about, Jack. You know, the research in this booklet didn't come from our publicity department like most of the stuff. This is the real thing — you can be confident when you use this. Anyway, your guy comes up at the wake so you go up to him and you put your arm around his shoulder, the nice, teaching way a football coach throws his arm around you and you feel good because you know the coach is taking you into his confidence. O.K.? Didn't you say you played football for St. Aidan High? O.K. — then you know the way I mean. Now, with your free hand, Jack, you flip open this booklet. It is easy because they put this Frehiti People discussion at the center where the stapling is, so it naturally opens right there. So you keep your other hand on his shoulder, see, and you show him this picture, the one you see there, with the jungle huts in the background, and them carrying the corpse in a kind of thatch-covered chair with the feet hanging off like that, towards us. And the Discussion Questions at the left. So you don't have to tell this person, 'Look at the terrific picture of a dead body with the feet hanging off that kind of coolie chair or whatever it is.' What you get to say aloud is, 'I wonder, so-and-so — you want to use their name as much as you can, Jack, as you know — 'Hey, so-and-so, I wonder if you'd look through this new book and read these Discussion Questions. Maybe this is something that would help families get through grief — would you look this over and then tell me what you think?' And Jack, all the time you are saying all this, his eyes are glued onto that picture and his mind is thinking, if people like that think, There are other full-color pictures in the book, too, and I want to see them all! Then he hears you offering to let him take the booklet home with him. Now all this time, you are pushing him along right out of your funeral chapel and he is halfway home before he realizes he is no longer at the visitation. And that is fine with you. The last thing you need is someone trying any sensitivity games at a visitation."

Bud gestured toward the booklet in Jack's hand. "That little item may not have a lot of class like our bronze desk accessories and all, but it is one hundred thousand percent effective."

Now Jack sat at the dark end of the Showing Room, looking at the dead Frehiti in the photograph. The man's feet, whitened in the foreground, in sharp focus, were separated from the gloomy jungle village in the background; the feet had come to meet the viewer; the straw hut roofs, the gnarled equatorial trees, the smudgy broken grass of the village street — all that receded and lowered behind, like a cloud departing.

Jack heard Estona Huutula's voice rise in fury. He was used to family differences in his Showing Room, but this one was especially nasty. He listened, trying to decide when he should break in.

"I don't see how you can be so uncaring," Estona was shouting. "You know that when they open up that will, there will be a half million for you — probably for you, alone, too; you won't even have to share it with me, since you did such a good job making up to Svea all those years! You know what people will say, Marlyn! They'll say that there that nice aunt left him a cool half million and all he would buy her was the county casket."

"I never said I wanted to bury Svea in the county casket!" Marlyn shouted back.

The casket they referred to was a narrow, light blue coffin that St. Aidan provided for welfare clients when the family could afford nothing else. It was nicely made, but most funeral directors, including Jack, made sure it was locally referred to only as "the county casket" so that no one would contemplate buying it for a loved one.

"All I meant was," Marlyn said, "why go to $2300 when we can get the same service and a perfectly nice-looking casket for $1500?"

Jack rose from his small desk.

Estona said, "That's going to look just fine, isn't it, when you get all that money? I call it downright cheap!"

Marlyn grumbled. "We don't even know if Svea had any money anyway."

"All the worse for you then!" cried Estona with a slashing laugh. "All those Sunday afternoons you put in for nothing! Sitting there in her filthy kitchen letting her tell you how Chuck Noll should do this, Chuck Noll should do that, and how old age comes even to football players, and how Cliff Stoudt was a fool to hurt his arm. That one time I was there, you must have said it twenty times if you said it once: 'You may have something there, Svea!' I nearly puked. And 'Everything that goes up has to come down, I guess, Svea — even Lynn Swann!' If you weren't the sponging wise nephew of the sports-expert aunt! And the two of you drunk as lords before three in the afternoon, too! I nearly threw up listening to you — I'd say 'puke' except we're in a funeral chapel!"

Jack generally let relations quarrel until both of them had turned their irritation, by mere exhaustion, from each other to him. As soon as he felt all the anger coming towards him — none left for each other — he would spend a minute deliberately hardselling a coffin he knew they didn't want. Then they would concentrate on outwitting this awful funeral director for a minute or so. He let them outwit him. Then he decided which coffin they would really like, and usually wrapped up the sale, including choice of Remembrance folders, in fifteen minutes. The clients left in harmony with each other, which was good: the moment they left Canon Chapel the elation of having stumped the mortician would die and they would notice and carry their grief again.

"And another thing!" Estona cried. "You know, if you had *really* respected Svea's dignity in life or death, you wouldn't have been out tomcatting the very night after they found her, would you? There we were, the sheriff and I, trying to figure out where you were, with all those kids having dug up poor Svea's yard and all! Do you know that the sheriff sent the deputy down the river because they thought you were checking your traps? Finally Mrs. Friesman said she seen you driving somewhere with that Mrs. Galan from the Adult Education. 'Oh,' I said, 'he wouldn't be with her. She always stays with us at the Nu-St. Aidan Motel.' Well, yes, she saw you though, she said, so what could the sheriff do; he drove back out to your house and there you were in the middle of the night, the both of you! Of course I'd made a fool of myself, telling the deputy I knew you wouldn't be running around with her because she seemed like such a nice widow lady and very intellectual."

Jack now made his way slowly from the dark end of the room, like someone a little off balance. He approached the brother and sister standing under the yellow wall lights and took Estona by the elbow. He explained that they would now go into his office and have a sip of something that he kept, which sometimes helped people in times of grief. He led them around behind the chapel, past the door leading to the operating area, and into his office. Sunlight poured in, dazzling after the draped and shadowy Showing Room. Jack seated Estona on the couch; he put Marlyn in the conference chair, and opened a bottle of Pinot Blanc. Although everyone in St. Aidan knew that Estona Huutula turned on the NO part of the NO VACANCY sign at the motel each night around ten, and settled down with a whiskey, Estona said, "I don't use much alcohol, Jack, but a little wine *would* help me, I think."

Estona then allowed they ought to get the $2300 white-lined casket instead of the $1500 tan-lined one because it would be more cheerful for Svea to look out of. Both men looked out through the faint window curtains when she said that. She added, "Or maybe that's just me."

In the normal course of things, Jack would have let Estona sell Marlyn on the more expensive of the two caskets, but now he wanted this old high school classmate and his sister out of the office so badly he would have sold him a co-op burial-club service with a pine box for $34.50 if they would just get out. So he took it into his own hands. Ignoring Estona, who was tapping her glass for a refill, he spoke to Marlyn in a man-to-man tone, making fast explanations. He filled the man in on some of the side services provided in a funeral, such as getting police cooperation in case there was further trouble, or unwanted crowds to see the body of a simple old woman worth $500,000. He explained that his own man, LeVern Holpe, would park cars, assisted by the chapel man from Marrow Lake.

Marlyn responded exactly as Jack wanted: he tried to be snappy and intelligent too. Marlyn never mentioned the $1500 casket again. Then, just when Estona was beginning to look as if she felt neglected, Jack passed her the new Remembrance format that Bud Menge had brought over only the week before. Gone was the Twenty-third Psalm in Old English eleven point on the left-hand side: instead, there was a passage from *The Velveteen Rabbit* in a modern face without serif. Jack said to Estona, cutting Marlyn out of it: "Estona, I want your honest opinion of these. If you don't care for these new-style Remembrances, say so, and we will have the others printed up for Svea."

At last brother and sister were gone. Jack telephoned LeVern to say that he could come over and work any time now. He himself would have a catnap. He lay down on the small office sofa.

The winter sun, very bright and low at this time of year, sent its long webby light through the glass curtain. Jack fell gratefully asleep, still wearing his suit jacket. Sunlight fell onto his desk with all the accessories Bud had provided him — the bronze-tone plastic paperweight imprinted CANON CHAPEL: CARE WHEN CARE MATTERS MOST. The sun fell onto his red-covered humanities notebook, too. It fell onto his own face, and made his white hair nearly transparent and his skin luminous. Once during the following hour and a half, his young assistant, LeVern, looked in soundlessly and thought how sad the human face looks asleep; he decided that Jack Canon, in his opinion anyway, led a very crappy life. LeVern decided he could manage the job without waking the fellow, and called Greta at the beauty parlor when he was done to tell her she could come over and do Mrs. Istava's head now or whenever she was ready.

In his dream, Jack went to spend the weekend in a motel north of St. Paul. He was to meet a woman there who had exclaimed, "My God! I think I am falling in love again! I love you, John!" So long as Jack still believed she would show up, he patrolled the motel room, swerving round the ocean-sized bed and rounding the television set like an animal. Once he had decided she was not going to show up, he took to rereading all the materials in the desk except the Bible placed there by the Gideons. Everything he read swam and enlarged and darkened in his eyes. Everything had color swimming at the edges; even the papers he held were yellowed like church windows on Christmas cards. He read through the Room Service Menu with its appalling prices and his eyes swam with tears. He read the Daily Cleaning Services options with his eyes silvered with tears. He was reminded of something that someone at a Minnesota Funeral Directors' convention had once told him: the man had said that when he became Born Again, for the first few weeks, whenever he opened up the Bible, no matter at what place he opened it, his eyes would fill with tears. Jack was thinking that over, in his dream, when he waked to LeVern's tapping on the office door.

LeVern put his head around the door. "All set now, Jack," he said. "I'm going home now."

"Oh, then, you're ready for me," Jack said, trying not to sound slowed with sleep.

"No, it's all done," LeVern told him. "Greta's here working now."

Jack lay vulnerable in the huge sadness of his dream. The day was nearly over. All morning he had longed for the day to be over, because it was Wednesday, the night of his class. Now the joy was gone out of it.

Eventually, he rose and bathed and shaved and put on the best sports jacket he had. He looked at his gray eyes very carefully in the mirror, but it was O.K.: none of the dream or his own feelings showed.

He locked the front door of the chapel, making sure the twin lights for visitations were both turned off; people understood by that that Svea could not be viewed until the next day. Then he went round and lighted the rear yard light, which fell upon the private entrance to his office and the garage. At nearly eight o'clock, the bell rang. Jack cried to himself, "She came after all, then!"

He swung the door open to the cold night. Outside, Momo Friesman stood on the garage cement, his bulging eyes bright from the overhead light.

"I came to pay my respects to Mrs. Istava," Momo said quickly, "and don't you turn me away, Jack. I got a right. She was neighbor to me, and my mother and I was friends. She had me come keep her company once a week and I got a right to mourn her as good as anyone else."

"Visitation isn't until tomorrow, Momo," Jack said.

Then he recalled Bud Menge's little book of photographs and discussions. "There *is* something you could help me with, though, Momo. Do you have time to come in a minute?"

Momo's eyes shone. "I can help you in the lab, Jack!"

"No," Jack said firmly, "not in the operating room — but wait." He started to go to the Casket Showing Room for the booklet, but then remembered he couldn't leave Momo alone or the man might leap through the office door towards the operating room. So he put his arm around Momo's shoulder and led him to the sofa. When he saw Momo was all the way seated, he left.

Momo had the face of a twelve-year-old; he was forty-three, in fact. Every morning in the summer, his mother drove him into town and Momo went to all the trash disposal cans in St. Aidan, recovered *Minneapolis Tribunes* from them, and sold them up and down the one street of the town, shouting, "Paper! Paper!" All the business people sent someone out, a receptionist or whoever was nearest the door, to give Momo a nickel and take a paper. When he had gone the whole length of the street, from the Canon Funeral Chapel at one end to the Rocky Mountains Prospectors' office at the other, he would find more papers lying on top of the trash cans, so he sold them again — this time to the other side of the street. At noon he waited among the boxes that came into the Red Owl on the truck; the owner would shout, "He's here, O.K., Mrs. Friesman!" when his mother came to pick him up. Once a week she took him over to Svea Istava's place across the road, and Svea would let him dig in her piles of orange crates and used winter tires.

When Jack dropped the booklet into Momo's lap, it opened as Bud had promised, to the photograph of the dead Frehiti man in his grassy chair. Jack thought to himself, "It is eight-oh-five now. She hasn't shown up. She is not going to come. Well," he went on to himself, "everyone has to have some kind of memorial made in their honor. We shouldn't any of us die without someone's doing at least *something* in our honor." Jack looked down at Momo, who was bent over the photograph. "Well, Momo," Jack thought, "you're it. Svea let you into her place all those years. Tonight, then, I will let you into mine. You can sit there and gloat over that book for two hours if you want." Jack went and sat down at his desk. He said in his thoughts, "I don't suppose you'd understand, Momo, if I tried to explain to you that Molly Galan was supposed to be sitting here where you are sitting, not you. Well, anyway — it isn't her: it's you." Jack remembered how Svea remained kind to Momo even when, two weeks after her dog Biscuit died, Momo found the grave, despite the rusty refrigerator grille Svea had laid on top of it in hopes he wouldn't notice. Momo dug up Biscuit and brought the body into the house and laid it on Svea's oilcloth-covered table. Biscuit looked bad after two weeks in the earth. Even then, Svea did not lift a hand to Momo. She only telephoned Jack to ask if he ever had had any difficulty with Momo around the chapel. Jack confessed that he had to deal with Momo on various occasions.

Now he went through the little speech Bud had taught him, suggesting Momo take the booklet home. He need not have bothered. Just as Bud predicted, Momo was entranced by the pictures.

The doorbell rang again.

Jack went over to it, nearly faint with hope but still unbelieving.

"I didn't know if I ought to come," Molly Galan said. "I know you have had a death."

"Oh, but visiting isn't until tomorrow!" Jack cried. He held the door wide, but didn't offer his arm. Molly Galan explained that she was a little breathless from having walked over from the motel. Then Jack remembered Momo. "This is Momo Friesman," Jack said. He went over and stood near Momo's knees. "Momo is going to zip up his jacket now and take his book home, before it gets even later and colder."

"I want to stay here," Momo said.

"Let's see your book," Molly said.

"You give that back," he told her.

"I promise," she said. She sat down beside him, turning the pages.

"And now you must take it home with you, Momo," Jack said. "But first you must zip up your jacket because it is much colder again now."

Jack realized that in one minute Momo would be out of there, and the thought made him so joyous he nearly danced the man into his zipper.

"I don't want to go," Momo said.

Jack thought, "I could just strangle him until those eyes jump clear out of his head like twin pale spheres careening out into space and then I could pick him up and throw the whole mess of a man out the door." As soon as Jack noticed what he was thinking he backed further from the sofa. Anyway, he thought, retreating to the desk, what did he care if Momo chose to stay the evening? What good would it do *now* to have an evening with Molly Galan?

"Oh yes!" he cried to himself. "Look at that flushed face of hers! And that lively look in her eyes: that isn't from hiking over here in the cold! And her wonderful smile!" That smile was turned towards Momo, but how could such a smile be for Momo? Women of fifty did not look like that except when love was so recent the body itself still remembered it. Jack's anger narrowed and cooled and felt permanent. "And anyway," he added to himself, "all this is just a job of work for a woman like her." She was hired to tutor adult extension students in the humanities, so she tutored adult extension students in the humanities. She had agreed to meet in his office probably because that arrangement was simpler than anything else.

He said aloud, "Well, if Momo wants to stay, that would be all right, wouldn't it?"

She looked at Momo and said, "Of course. Momo, you can read your book and we will work on ours."

"And afterwards I will pay my respects to Svea," Momo told her.

"Not tonight," she said. "When I say it's time you will zipper up your jacket and you can walk home with me."

In the meantime, Jack walked rapidly back and forth between his lighted desk and the sofa. Perhaps Molly Galan was going to open her copy of the red humanities workbook over there, on the sofa beside Momo. She might do that, he supposed.

But she didn't. She came to his desk and sat down in the conference chair. She picked up a bronze marker stamped CANON CHAPEL and laid it back quickly. She said, "The Extension people would like to know which subject we're going to work on. And they want us to write an evaluation as we go along. This is a kind of pilot program, you see." She smiled at him. "They want to know what your expectations are."

How could Jack tell her his expectations? All week he had planned how she was coming and he meant to tell her part of his life story. Shamelessly, he had meant to. Jack had meant to tell her how all his life he had wished to be serious, not just solemn as he must be at his work, but serious. He wanted to tell her how here in St. Aidan, where he practiced a trade he had never wanted to practice, somehow he could not rise over the chaff and small cries of daily life into some upper ring of seriousness. He imagined this ring of seriousness, like Saturn's rings, almost physically circling the planet — but he couldn't reach it because he was caught down here, blinded in the ground-storming of old jokes, old ideas, old conventions, which no sooner were dropped than they were picked up again like snow lifted and lifted and dropped and lifted again by blizzard wind, blowing into everyone's face over and over.

Molly Galan smiled at him. She had placed the four fingers of her right hand between five pages of the humanities notebook, and she held these pages apart as if for ready reference; he saw the lamplight through the spread pages like a nearly translucent Eastern fan, collapsible, of course, but taking up its space as elegantly as sculpture does.

Jack thought, How can it be that anyone with such hands spent last night with Marlyn Huutula? How can that be, when Marlyn Huutula all his life had never done anything admirable except play halfback for St. Aidan in 1936? — and Jack saw, as sharply in his mind's eye as he had ever seen it, Marlyn's sweaty hair as he removed his leather helmet.

Now Jack bent towards Molly under the beautiful lamplight and shouted at her, "What I want to know is, why did you ever do it? How could someone like you go and, go and, oh how could someone like you for the love of God go and spend the night with Marlyn Huutula? How could you *do* it?"

"I know I did not just say that aloud," Jack told himself; "I know I did not. Nonetheless, that is what I just did. However, I must not have really said that aloud because men in their sixties do not ask humanities consultants why they spend the night with whomever they spend the night with. Yet it was my voice that said that."

Then he thought: "In one minute she will simply rise and leave without another word. She will go over to the couch and pick up her coat where she left it near Momo and she will leave. I shall offer her a ride home because it is so cold again and, oh, Christ, she will refuse even that!"

However, the ladylike fingers did not fold up the fan. Molly Galan shouted at him. "I don't know! I don't know why I did it! And what do *you* care, anyway?"

"I don't care! I don't care what you do," Jack said.

"Well," Molly shouted, "you just don't know how dumb it all is!"

She burst into tears.

Very far inside himself, in a place really too dank to nourish a spark of happiness, Jack felt a tiny warmth: "What do you mean, 'dumb'?" he asked. But then the snarl came back into his voice. "So what's that supposed to mean, *dumb!* What is that supposed to mean, 'How dumb it all is!' Anyone can go around shouting things like that!"

"You don't know what it is to be lost in the dumbness of it!" she shouted, still crying.

"You chose it! You chose it!" he said. "You chose Marlyn Huutula!"

Suddenly then her hands fell simply, faintingly, like snow onto the booklet in her lap. Her face and voice suddenly were completely serene. "Yes," she said, pausing. "That's right," she said in an agreeable, logical tone. "Marlyn Huutula. Now he really *is* dumb." She added in an even more peaceful tone, "That is a fact, you know. He is really *very* dumb."

"The dumbest person I ever knew!" Jack said. But then he leaned forward and said, "What do you mean exactly?"

He felt a hope taking fire in him too quickly. He did not want to lose his proper anger in this hope. Already, he noticed that Molly was sitting with her head tipped to one side, nearly daydreaming at him, and he, too, on his side of the lamplight, was tipping his head at the same angle. They regarded each other like two birds, with that great concentration and that great natural stupidity of birds.

Hope kept rising rather weakly in Jack, like a hand rising from a lap, with the fingers still fallen from the rising wrist, the fingers flowing downward like an umbrella.

Momo meanwhile had approached them, and now wavered, his face turning from one to the other of them.

Jack whispered, "Well, will we go on with the course, do you think?"

Molly said, "Of course we will."

Jack said briskly. "It is too cold for you and Momo to walk home. I will drive you both. Momo, it is time for you to zip up your jacket now."

The telephone rang. It was the sheriff. "Jack, I thought you would like to know. The Huutula family read Svea Istava's will early, and you know what? She didn't have two cents to her name! After all that fuss! So what we'll do, Jack — the Marrow Lake patrolman and I will kind of keep an eye out the next couple of days, and we'll make sure the news gets around, so you shouldn't have any crowd-draw to the visitation hours. I expect you'll just get the usual for an old woman like that." In the background, Jack could hear the sheriff's puppies barking.

Jack and Momo and Molly all sat in the front seat of his car. The night had dropped below zero, so their breathing frosted the windshield and the side windows as well. The defroster opened up only a small space in the windshield directly in front of Jack; he had to hunch down to see through it. He guided the car gingerly through the cold town out on the north road towards the Friesmans'. The black woods were not wrecked, but they were nearly wrecked. The greater trees had been cut over. The earth under the forest was not wrecked, either — but it was staked out. Here and there, invisible to ordinary people, were concrete-stoppered holes where the uranium prospectors had pulled out their pipes and left only magnets so they could find the places again. As the car crawled along the iced highway, Jack thought of the whole countryside, nearly with tears in his eyes. He kept peering through the dark, clear part of the glass, with his whole body shivering and his skin cold in his gloves and the whole of him beginning to flood with happiness. His own life, Jack thought — it wasn't wrecked completely, after all! It felt to him, since he was sixty-three and much was over for him — or rather, had gone untravelled — that his life was nearly wrecked. But not completely. He began to smile behind his cold skin. He started driving faster, feeling more jaunty and more terrific every second.

The patrolman from Marrow Lake, who had just left the St. Aidan station, happened to see the car tearing along Old 61 where it crossed the north road. He thought, "Oh, boy! Travellers' advisory or no travellers' advisory! Nothing stops some people! Car all frosted blind like that, tearing right along anyway!" Behind the car's pure white windows he did not make out the local undertaker and a comely woman and a middle-aged retarded man.

JORGE LUIS BORGES

Jorge Luis Borges (1899–1986) was born in Buenos Aires, Argentina, into a family in which both English and Spanish were spoken. English was, in fact, the first language in which he learned to read (beginning with Twain, Poe, Robert Louis Stevenson, and translations of *Don Quixote* and *One Thousand and One Nights*). In an autobiographical sketch, Borges wrote, "If I were asked to name the chief event of my life, I should say my father's library." Indeed, bookishness and erudition are hallmarks of Borges' style; he has been said to write "literature about literature," and much of his fiction concerns itself with philosophical inquiry, history, and the nature of time. In a Borges story, the characteristic tone, form, and manipulation of the illusion of reality — the appearance of "the work-within-a-work," the presence of footnotes, allusion to real people and events — often lead readers to wonder whether they are reading an essay rather than a story. Borges' short fiction is collected in, among others, *Ficciones* (1944; English, 1962), *The Aleph* (1949; English, 1970), *Dr. Brodie's Report* (1970; English 1971), and *Borges: A Reader* (ed. Monegal, 1981). He was interested all his life in the intricacies of detective fiction. His first collection of stories (*A Universal History of Infamy*, 1935; English 1972) told the lives of real and fictitious criminals, and his fascination shows in many subsequent stories, "The Garden of Forking Paths" among them. The second story here, "The South," was one of Borges' own favorites.

The Garden of Forking Paths

Translated from the Spanish by Helen Temple and Ruthven Todd

To Victoria Ocampo

In his *A History of the World War* (page 212), Captain Liddell Hart reports that a planned offensive by thirteen British divisions, supported by fourteen hundred artillery pieces, against the German line at Serre-Montauban, scheduled for July 24, 1916, had to be postponed until the morning of the 29th. He comments that torrential rain caused this delay — which lacked any special significance. The following deposition, dictated by, read over, and then signed by Dr. Yu Tsun, former teacher of English at the Tsingtao *Hochschule,* casts unsuspected light upon this event. The first two pages are missing.

. . . and I hung up the phone. Immediately I recollected the voice that had spoken in German. It was that of Captain Richard Madden. Madden, in Viktor Runeberg's office, meant the end of all our work and — though this seemed a secondary matter, *or should have seemed so to me* — of our lives also. His being there meant that Runeberg had been arrested or murdered.* Before the sun set on this same day, I ran

---

* A malicious and outlandish statement. In point of fact, Captain Richard Madden had been attacked by the Prussian spy Hans Rabener, alias Viktor Runeberg, who drew an automatic pistol when Madden appeared with orders for the spy's arrest. Madden, in self defense, had inflicted wounds of which the spy later died. *Note by the manuscript editor.*

the same risk. Madden was implacable. Rather, to be more accurate, he was obliged to be implacable. An Irishman in the service of England, a man suspected of equivocal feelings if not of actual treachery, how could he fail to welcome and seize upon this extraordinary piece of luck: the discovery, capture and perhaps the death of two agents of Imperial Germany?

I went up to my bedroom. Absurd though the gesture was, I closed and locked the door. I threw myself down on my narrow iron bed, and waited on my back. The never changing rooftops filled the window, and the hazy six o'clock sun hung in the sky. It seemed incredible that this day, a day without warnings or omens, might be that of my implacable death. In despite of my dead father, in despite of having been a child in one of the symmetrical gardens of Hai Feng, was I to die now?

Then I reflected that all things happen, happen to one, precisely *now*. Century follows century, and things happen only in the present. There are countless men in the air, on land and at sea, and all that really happens happens to me. . . . The almost unbearable memory of Madden's long horseface put an end to these wandering thoughts.

In the midst of my hatred and terror (now that it no longer matters to me to speak of terror, now that I have outwitted Richard Madden, now that my neck hankers for the hangman's noose), I knew that the fast-moving and doubtless happy soldier did not suspect that I possessed the Secret — the name of the exact site of the new British artillery park on the Ancre. A bird streaked across the misty sky and, absently, I turned it into an airplane and then that airplane into many in the skies of France, shattering the artillery park under a rain of bombs. If only my mouth, before it should be silenced by a bullet, could shout this name in such a way that it could be heard in Germany. . . . My voice, my human voice, was weak. How could it reach the ear of the Chief? The ear of that sick and hateful man who knew nothing of Runeberg or of me except that we were in Staffordshire. A man who, sitting in his arid Berlin office, leafed infinitely through newspapers, looking in vain for news from us. I said aloud, "I must flee."

I sat up on the bed, in senseless and perfect silence, as if Madden was already peering at me. Something — perhaps merely a desire to prove my total penury to myself — made me empty out my pockets. I found just what I knew I was going to find. The American watch, the nickel-plated chain and the square coin, the key ring with the useless but compromising keys to Runeberg's office, the notebook, a letter which I decided to destroy at once (and which I did not destroy), a five shilling piece, two single shillings and some pennies, a red and blue pencil, a handkerchief — and a revolver with a single bullet. Absurdly I held it and weighed it in my hand, to give myself courage. Vaguely I thought that a pistol shot can be heard for a great distance.

In ten minutes I had developed my plan. The telephone directory gave me the name of the one person capable of passing on the information. He lived in a suburb of Fenton, less than half an hour away by train.

I am a timorous man. I can say it now, now that I have brought my incredibly risky plan to an end. It was not easy to bring about, and I know that its execution was terrible. I did not do it for Germany — no! Such a barbarous country is of no importance to me, particularly since it had degraded me by making me become a spy. Furthermore, I knew an Englishman — a modest man — who, for me, is as great as Goethe. I did not speak with him for more than an hour, but during that time, he *was* Goethe.

I carried out my plan because I felt the Chief had some fear of those of my race, of those uncountable forebears whose culmination lies in me. I wished to prove to him that a yellow man could save his armies. Besides, I had to escape the Captain. His hands and voice could, at any moment, knock and beckon at my door.

Silently, I dressed, took leave of myself in the mirror, went down the stairs, sneaked a look at the quiet street, and went out. The station was not far from my house, but I thought it more prudent to take a cab. I told myself that I thus ran less chance of being recognized. The truth is that, in the deserted street, I felt infinitely visible and vulnerable. I recall that I told the driver to stop short of the main entrance. I got out with a painful and deliberate slowness.

I was going to the village of Ashgrove, but took a ticket for a station further on. The train would leave in a few minutes, at eight-fifty. I hurried, for the next would not go until half past nine. There was almost no one on the platform. I walked through the carriages. I remember some farmers, a woman dressed in mourning, a youth deep in Tacitus' *Annals* and a wounded, happy soldier.

At last the train pulled out. A man I recognized ran furiously, but vainly, the length of the platform. It was Captain Richard Madden. Shattered, trembling, I huddled in the distant corner of the seat, as far as possible from the fearful window.

From utter terror I passed into a state of almost abject happiness. I told myself that the duel had already started and that I had won the first encounter by besting my adversary in his first attack — even if it was only for forty minutes — by an accident of fate. I argued that so small a victory prefigured a total victory. I argued that it was not so trivial, that were it not for the precious accident of the train schedule, I would be in prison or dead. I argued, with no less sophism, that my timorous happiness was proof that I was man enough to bring this adventure to a successful conclusion. From my weakness I drew strength that never left me.

I foresee that man will resign himself each day to new abominations, that soon only soldiers and bandits will be left. To them I offer this advice: *Whosoever would undertake some atrocious enterprise should act as if it were already accomplished, should impose upon himself a future as irrevocable as the past.*

Thus I proceeded, while with the eyes of a man already dead, I contemplated the fluctuations of the day which would probably be my last, and watched the diffuse coming of night.

The train crept along gently, amid ash trees. It slowed down and stopped, almost in the middle of a field. No one called the name of a station. "Ashgrove?" I asked some children on the platform. "Ashgrove," they replied. I got out.

A lamp lit the platform, but the children's faces remained in a shadow. One of them asked me: "Are you going to Dr. Stephen Albert's house?" Without waiting for my answer, another said: "The house is a good distance away but you won't get lost if you take the road to the left and bear to the left at every crossroad." I threw them a coin (my last), went down some stone steps and started along a deserted road. At a slight incline, the road ran downhill. It was a plain dirt way, and overhead the branches of trees intermingled, while a round moon hung low in the sky as if to keep me company.

For a moment I thought that Richard Madden might in some way have divined my desperate intent. At once I realized that this would be impossible. The advice about turning always to the left reminded me that such was the common formula for finding the central courtyard of certain labyrinths. I know something about labyrinths. Not for nothing am I the great-grandson of Ts'ui Pên. He was Governor of Yunnan and gave up temporal power to write a novel with more characters than there are in the *Hung Lou Mêng,* and to create a maze in which all men would lose themselves. He spent thirteen years on these oddly assorted tasks before he was assassinated by a stranger. His novel had no sense to it and nobody ever found his labyrinth.

Under the trees of England I meditated on this lost and perhaps mythical labyrinth. I imagined it untouched and perfect on the secret summit of some mountain; I imagined it drowned under rice paddies or beneath the sea; I imagined it infinite, made not only of eight-sided pavilions and of twisting paths but also of rivers, provinces and kingdoms. . . . I thought of a maze of mazes, of a sinuous, ever growing maze which would take in both past and future and would somehow involve the stars.

Lost in these imaginary illusions I forgot my destiny — that of the hunted. For an undetermined period of time I felt myself cut off from the world, an abstract spectator. The hazy and murmuring countryside, the moon, the decline of the evening, stirred within me. Going down the gently sloping road I could not feel fatigue. The evening was at once intimate and infinite.

The road kept descending and branching off, through meadows misty in the twilight. A high-pitched and almost syllabic music kept coming and going, moving with the breeze, blurred by the leaves and by distance.

I thought that a man might be an enemy of other men, of the differing moments of other men, but never an enemy of a country: not of fireflies, words, gardens, streams, or the West wind.

Meditating thus I arrived at a high, rusty iron gate. Through the railings I could see an avenue bordered with poplar trees and also a kind of summer house or pavilion. Two things dawned on me at once, the first trivial and the second almost incredible: the music came from the pavilion and that music was Chinese. That was why I had accepted it fully, without paying it any attention. I do not remember whether there was a bell, a push-button, or whether I attracted attention by clapping my hands. The stuttering sparks of the music kept on.

But from the end of the avenue, from the main house, a lantern approached; a lantern which alternately, from moment to moment, was crisscrossed or put out by the trunks of the trees; a paper lantern shaped like a drum and colored like the moon. A tall man carried it. I could not see his face for the light blinded me.

He opened the gate and spoke slowly in my language.

"I see that the worthy Hsi P'eng has troubled himself to see to relieving my solitude. No doubt you want to see the garden?"

Recognizing the name of one of our consuls, I replied, somewhat taken aback.

"The garden?"

"The garden of forking paths."

Something stirred in my memory and I said, with incomprehensible assurance:

"The garden of my ancestor, Ts'ui Pên."

"Your ancestor? Your illustrious ancestor? Come in."

The damp path zigzagged like those of my childhood. When we reached the house, we went into a library filled with books from both East and West. I recognized some large volumes bound in yellow silk — manuscripts of the Lost Encyclopedia which was edited by the Third Emperor of the Luminous Dynasty. They had never been printed. A phonograph record was spinning near a bronze phoenix. I remember also a rose-glazed jar and yet another, older by many centuries, of that blue color which our potters copied from the Persians. . . .

Stephen Albert was watching me with a smile on his face. He was, as I have said, remarkably tall. His face was deeply lined and he had gray eyes and a gray beard. There was about him something of the priest, and something of the sailor. Later, he told me he had been a missionary in Tientsin before he "had aspired to become a Sinologist."

We sat down, I upon a large, low divan, he with his back to the window and to a large circular clock. I calculated that my pursuer, Richard Madden, could not arrive in less than an hour. My irrevocable decision could wait.

"A strange destiny," said Stephen Albert, "that of Ts'ui Pên — Governor of his native province, learned in astronomy, in astrology and tireless in the interpretation of the canonical books, a chess player, a famous poet and a calligrapher. Yet he abandoned all to make a book and a labyrinth. He gave up all the pleasures of oppression, justice, of a well-stocked bed, of banquets, and even of erudition, and shut himself up in the Pavilion of the Limpid Sun for thirteen years. At his death, his heirs found only a mess of manuscripts. The family, as you doubtless know, wished to consign them to the fire, but the executor of the estate — a Taoist or a Buddhist monk — insisted on their publication."

"Those of the blood of Ts'ui Pên," I replied, "still curse the memory of that monk. Such a publication was madness. The book is a shapeless mass of contradictory rough drafts. I examined it once upon a time: the hero dies in the third chapter, while in the fourth he is alive. As for that other enterprise of Ts'ui Pên . . . his Labyrinth. . . ."

"Here is the Labyrinth," Albert said, pointing to a tall, laquered writing cabinet.

"An ivory labyrinth?" I exclaimed. "A tiny labyrinth indeed . . . !"

"A symbolic labyrinth," he corrected me. "An invisible labyrinth of time. I, a barbarous Englishman, have been given the key to this transparent mystery. After more than a hundred years most of the details are irrecoverable, lost beyond all recall, but it isn't hard to imagine what must have happened. At one time, Ts'ui Pên must have said; 'I am going into seclusion to write a book,' and at another, 'I am retiring to construct a maze.' Everyone assumed these were separate activities. No one realized that the book and the labyrinth were one and the same. The Pavilion of the Limpid Sun was set in the middle of an intricate garden. This may have suggested the idea of a physical maze.

"Ts'ui Pên died. In all the vast lands which once belonged to your family, no one could find the labyrinth. The novel's confusion suggested that *it* was the labyrinth. Two circumstances showed me the direct solution to the problem. First, the curious legend that Ts'ui Pên had proposed to create an infinite maze, second, a fragment of a letter which I discovered."

Albert rose. For a few moments he turned his back to me. He opened the top drawer in the high black and gilded writing cabinet. He returned holding in his hand a piece of paper which had once been crimson but which had faded with the passage of time: it was rose colored, tenuous, quadrangular. Ts'ui Pên's calligraphy was justly famous. Eagerly, but without understanding, I read the words which a man of my own blood had written with a small brush: "I leave to various future times, but not to all, my garden of forking paths."

I handed back the sheet of paper in silence. Albert went on:

"Before I discovered this letter, I kept asking myself how a book could be infinite. I could not imagine any other than a cyclic volume, circular. A volume whose last page would be the same as the first and so have the possibility of continuing indefinitely. I recalled, too, the night in the middle of *The Thousand and One Nights* when Queen Scheherezade, through a magical mistake on the part of her copyist, started to tell the story of *The Thousand and One Nights,* with the risk of again arriving at the night upon which she will relate it, and thus on to infinity. I also imagined a Platonic hereditary work, passed on from father to son, to which each individual would add a new chapter or correct, with pious care, the work of his elders.

"These conjectures gave me amusement, but none seemed to have the remotest application to the contradictory chapters of Ts'ui Pên. At this point, I was sent from Oxford the manuscript you have just seen.

"Naturally, my attention was caught by the sentence, 'I leave to various future times, but not to all, my garden of forking paths.' I had no sooner read this, than I understood. *The Garden of Forking Paths* was the chaotic novel itself. The phrase 'to various future times, but not to all' suggested the image of bifurcating in time, not in space. Rereading the whole work confirmed this theory. In all fiction, when a man is faced with alternatives he chooses one at the expense of the others. In the almost unfathomable Ts'ui Pên, he chooses — simultaneously — all of them. He thus *creates* various futures, various times which start others that will in their turn branch out and bifurcate in other times. This is the cause of the contradictions in the novel.

"Fang, let us say, has a secret. A stranger knocks at his door. Fang makes up his mind to kill him. Naturally there are various possible outcomes. Fang can kill the intruder, the intruder can kill Fang, both can be saved, both can die and so on and so on. In Ts'ui Pên's work, all the possible solutions occur, each one being the point of departure for other bifurcations. Sometimes the pathways of this labyrinth converge. For example, you come to this house; but in other possible pasts you are my enemy; in others my friend.

"If you will put up with my atrocious pronunciation, I would like to read you a few pages of your ancestor's work."

His countenance, in the bright circle of lamplight, was certainly that of an ancient, but it shone with something unyielding, even immortal.

With slow precision, he read two versions of the same epic chapter. In the first, an army marches into battle over a desolate mountain pass. The bleak and somber aspect of the rocky landscape made the soldiers feel that life itself was of little value, and so they won the battle easily. In the second, the same army passes through a palace where a banquet is in progress. The splendor of the feast remained a memory throughout the glorious battle, and so victory followed.

With proper veneration I listened to these old tales, although perhaps with less admiration for them in themselves than for the fact that they had been thought out by one of my own blood, and that a man of a distant empire had given them back to me, in the last stage of a desperate adventure, on a Western island. I remember the final words, repeated at the end of each version like a secret command: "Thus the heroes fought, with tranquil heart and bloody sword. They were resigned to killing and to dying."

At that moment I felt within me and around me something invisible and intangible pullulating. It was not the pullulation of two divergent, parallel, and finally converging armies, but an agitation more inaccessible, more intimate, prefigured by them in some way. Stephen Albert continued:

"I do not think that your illustrious ancestor toyed idly with variations. I do not find it believable that he would waste thirteen years laboring over a never ending experiment in rhetoric. In your country the novel is an inferior genre; in Ts'ui Pên's period, it was a despised one. Ts'ui Pên was a fine novelist but he was also a man of letters who, doubtless, considered himself more than a mere novelist. The testimony of his contemporaries attests to this, and certainly the known facts of his life confirm his leanings toward the metaphysical and the mystical. Philosophical conjectures take up the greater part of his novel. I know that of all problems, none disquieted him more, and none concerned him more than the profound one of time. Now then, this is the *only* problem that does not figure in the pages of *The Garden*. He does not even use the word which means *time*. How can these voluntary omissions be explained?"

I proposed various solutions, all of them inadequate. We discussed them. Finally Stephen Albert said: "In a guessing game to which the answer is chess, which word is the only one prohibited?" I thought for a moment and then replied:

"The word is *chess*."

"Precisely," said Albert. *"The Garden of Forking Paths* is an enormous guessing game, or parable, in which the subject is time. The rules of the game forbid the use of the word itself. To eliminate a word completely, to refer to it by means of inept phrases and obvious paraphrases, is perhaps the best way of drawing attention to it. This, then, is the tortuous method of approach preferred by the oblique Ts'ui Pên in every meandering of his interminable novel. I have gone over hundreds of manuscripts, I have corrected errors introduced by careless copyists, I have worked out the plan from this chaos, I have restored, or believe I have restored, the original. I have translated the whole work. I can state categorically that not once has the word *time* been used in the whole book.

"The explanation is obvious. *The Garden of Forking Paths* is a picture, incomplete yet not false, of the universe such as Ts'ui Pên conceived it to be. Differing from Newton and Schopenhauer, your ancestor did not think of time as absolute and uniform. He believed in an infinite series of times, in a dizzily growing, ever spreading network of diverging, converging and parallel times. This web of time — the strands of which approach one another, bifurcate, intersect or ignore each other through the centuries — embraces *every* possibility. We do not exist in most of them. In some you exist and not I, while in others I do, and you do not, and in yet others both of us exist. In this one, in which chance has favored me, you have come to my gate. In another, you, crossing the garden, have found me dead. In yet another, I say these very same words, but am an error, a phantom."

"In all of them," I enunciated, with a tremor in my voice. "I deeply appreciate and am grateful to you for the restoration of Ts'ui Pên's garden."

"Not in *all*," he murmured with a smile. "Time is forever dividing itself toward innumerable futures and in one of them I am your enemy."

Once again I sensed the pullulation of which I have already spoken. It seemed to me that the dew-damp garden surrounding the house was infinitely saturated with invisible people. All were Albert and myself, secretive, busy and multiform in other dimensions of time. I lifted my eyes and the short nightmare disappeared. In the black and yellow garden there was only a single man, but this man was as strong as a statue and this man was walking up the path and he was Captain Richard Madden.

"The future exists now," I replied. "But I am your friend. Can I take another look at the letter?"

Albert rose from his seat. He stood up tall as he opened the top drawer of the high writing cabinet. For a moment his back was again turned to me. I had the revolver ready. I fired with the utmost care: Albert fell without a murmur, at once. I swear that his death was instantaneous, as if he had been struck by lightning.

What remains is unreal and unimportant. Madden broke in and arrested me. I have been condemned to hang. Abominably, I have yet triumphed! The secret name of the city to be attacked got through to Berlin. Yesterday it was bombed. I read the news in the same English newspapers which were trying to solve the riddle of the murder of the learned Sinologist Stephen Albert by the unknown Yu Tsun. The Chief, however, had already solved this mystery. He knew that my problem was to shout, with my feeble voice, above the tumult of war, the name of the city called Albert, and that I had no other course open to me than to kill someone of that name. He does not know, for no one can, of my infinite penitence and sickness of the heart.

JORGE LUIS BORGES

The South

Translated from the Spanish by Anthony Kerrigan

The man who landed in Buenos Aires in 1871 bore the name of Johannes Dahlmann and he was a minister in the Evangelical Church. In 1939, one of his grandchildren, Juan Dahlmann, was secretary of a municipal library on Calle Córdoba, and he considered himself profoundly Argentinian. His maternal grandfather had been that Francisco Flores, of the Second Line-Infantry Division, who had died on the frontier of Buenos Aires, run through with a lance by Indians from Catriel; in the discord inherent between his two lines of descent, Juan Dahlmann (perhaps driven to it by his Germanic blood) chose the line represented by his romantic ancestor, his ancestor of the romantic death. An old sword, a leather frame containing the daguerreotype of a blank-faced man with a beard, the dash and grace of certain music, the familiar strophes of *Martín Fierro,* the passing years, boredom and solitude, all went to foster this voluntary, but never ostentatious nationalism. At the cost of numerous small privations, Dahlmann had managed to save the empty shell of a ranch in the South which had belonged to the Flores family; he continually recalled the image of the balsamic eucalyptus trees and the great rose-colored house which had once been crimson. His duties, perhaps even indolence, kept him in the city. Summer after summer he contented himself with the abstract idea of possession and with the certitude that his ranch was waiting for him on a precise site in the middle of the plain. Late in February, 1939, something happened to him.

Blind to all fault, destiny can be ruthless at one's slightest distraction. Dahlmann had succeeded in acquiring, on that very afternoon, an imperfect copy of Weil's edition of *The Thousand and One Nights.* Avid to examine this find, he did not wait for the elevator but hurried up the stairs. In the obscurity, something brushed by his forehead: a bat, a bird? On the face of the woman who opened the door to him he saw horror engraved, and the hand he wiped across his face came away red with blood. The edge of a recently painted door which someone had forgotten to close had caused this wound. Dahlmann was able to fall asleep, but from the moment he awoke at dawn the savor of all things was atrociously poignant. Fever wasted him and the pictures in *The Thousand and One Nights* served to illustrate nightmares. Friends and relatives paid him visits and, with exaggerated smiles, assured him that they thought he looked fine. Dahlmann listened to them with a kind of feeble stupor and he marveled at their not knowing that he was in hell. A week, eight days passed, and they were like eight centuries. One afternoon, the usual doctor appeared, accompanied by a new doctor, and they carried him off to a sanitarium on the Calle Ecuador, for it was necessary to X-ray him. Dahlmann, in the hackney coach which bore them away, thought that he would, at last, be able to sleep in a room different from his own. He felt happy and communicative. When he arrived at his destination, they undressed him, shaved his head, bound him with metal fastenings to a stretcher; they shone bright lights on him until he was blind and dizzy, auscultated him, and a masked man stuck a needle into his arm. He awoke with a feeling of nausea, covered with a bandage, in a cell with something of a well about it; in the days and nights which followed the operation he came to realize that he had merely been, up until then, in a suburb of hell. Ice in his mouth did not leave the least trace of freshness. During these days Dahlmann hated himself in minute detail: he hated his identity, his bodily necessities, his humiliation, the beard which bristled upon his face. He stoically endured the curative measures, which were painful, but when the surgeon told him he had been on the point of death from septicemia, Dahlmann dissolved in tears of self-pity for his fate. Physical wretchedness and the incessant anticipation of horrible nights had not allowed him time to think of anything so abstract as death. On another day, the surgeon told him he was healing and that, very soon, he would be able to go to his ranch for convalescence. Incredibly enough, the promised day arrived.

Reality favors symmetries and slight anachronisms: Dahlmann had arrived at the sanitarium in a hackney coach and now a hackney coach was to take him to the Constitución station. The first fresh tang of autumn, after the summer's oppressiveness, seemed like a symbol in nature of his rescue and release from fever and death. The city, at seven in the morning, had not lost that air of an old house lent it by the night; the streets seemed like long vestibules, the plazas were like patios. Dahlmann recognized the city with joy on the edge of vertigo: a second before his eyes registered the phenomena themselves, he recalled the corners, the billboards, the modest variety of Buenos Aires. In the yellow light of the new day, all things returned to him.

Every Argentine knows that the South begins at the other side of Rivadavia. Dahlmann was in the habit of saying that this was no mere convention, that whoever crosses this street enters a more ancient and sterner world. From inside the carriage he sought out, among the new buildings, the iron grill window, the brass knocker, the arched door, the entrance way, the intimate patio.

At the railroad station he noted that he still had thirty minutes. He quickly recalled that in a café on the Calle Brazil (a few dozen feet from Yrigoyen's house) there was an enormous cat which allowed itself to be caressed as if it were a disdainful divinity. He entered the café. There was the cat, asleep. He ordered a cup of coffee, slowly stirred the sugar, sipped it (this pleasure had been denied him in the clinic), and thought, as he smoothed the cat's black coat, that this contact was an illusion and that the two beings, man and cat, were as good as separated by a glass, for man lives in time, in succession, while the magical animal lives in the present, in the eternity of the instant.

Along the next to the last platform the train lay waiting. Dahlmann walked through the coaches until he found one almost empty. He arranged his baggage in the network rack. When the train started off, he took down his valise and extracted, after some hesitation, the first volume of *The Thousand and One Nights*. To travel with this book, which was so much a part of the history of his ill-fortune, was a kind of affirmation that his ill-fortune had been annulled; it was a joyous and secret defiance of the frustrated forces of evil.

Along both sides of the train the city dissipated into suburbs; this sight, and then a view of the gardens and villas, delayed the beginning of his reading. The truth was the Dahlmann read very little. The magnetized mountain and the genie who swore to kill his benefactor are — who would deny it? — marvelous, but not so much more than the morning itself and the mere fact of being. The joy of life distracted him from paying attention to Scheherezade and her superfluous miracles. Dahlmann closed his book and allowed himself to live.

Lunch — the bouillon served in shining metal bowls, as in the remote summers of childhood — was one more peaceful and rewarding delight.

Tomorrow I'll wake up at the ranch, he thought, and it was as if he was two men at a time: the man who traveled through the autumn day and across the geography of the fatherland, and the other one, locked up in a sanitarium and subject to methodical servitude. He saw unplastered brick houses, long and angled, timelessly watching the trains go by; he saw horsemen along the dirt roads; he saw gullies and lagoons and ranches; he saw great luminous clouds that resembled marble; and all these things were accidental, casual, like dreams of the plain. He also thought he recognized trees and crop fields; but he would not have been able to name them, for his actual knowledge of the countryside was quite inferior to his nostalgic and literary knowledge.

From time to time he slept, and his dreams were animated by the impetus of the train. The intolerable white sun of high noon had already become the yellow sun which precedes nightfall, and it would not be long before it would turn red. The railroad car was now also different; it was not the same as the one which had quit the station siding at Constitución; the plain and the hours had transfigured it. Outside, the moving shadow of the railroad car stretched toward the horizon. The elemental earth was not perturbed either by settlements or other signs of humanity. The country was vast but at the same time intimate and, in some measure, secret. The limitless country sometimes contained only a solitary bull. The solitude was perfect, perhaps hostile, and it might have occurred to Dahlmann that he was traveling into the past and not merely south. He was distracted from these considerations by the railroad inspector who, on reading his ticket, advised him that the train would not let him off at the regular station but at another: an earlier stop, one scarcely known to Dahlmann. (The man added an explanation which Dahlmann did not attempt to understand, and which he hardly heard, for the mechanism of events did not concern him.)

The train laboriously ground to a halt, practically in the middle of the plain. The station lay on the other side of the tracks; it was not much more than a siding and a shed. There was no means of conveyance to be seen, but the station chief supposed that the traveler might secure a vehicle from a general store and inn to be found some ten or twelve blocks away.

Dahlmann accepted the walk as a small adventure. The sun had already disappeared from view, but a final splendor exalted the vivid and silent plain, before the night erased its color. Less to avoid fatigue than to draw out his enjoyment of these sights, Dahlmann walked slowly, breathing in the odor of clover with sumptuous joy.

The general store at one time had been painted a deep scarlet, but the years had tempered this violent color for its own good. Something in its poor architecture recalled a steel engraving, perhaps one from an old edition of *Paul et Virginie*. A number of horses were hitched up to the paling. Once inside, Dahlmann thought he recognized the shopkeeper. Then he realized that he had been deceived by the man's resemblance to one of the male nurses in the sanitarium. When the shop-keeper heard Dahlmann's request, he said he would have the shay made up. In order to add one more event to that day and to kill time, Dahlmann decided to eat at the general store.

Some country louts, to whom Dahlmann did not at first pay any attention, were eating and drinking at one of the tables. On the floor, and hanging on to the bar, squatted an old man, immobile as an object. His years had reduced and polished him as water does a stone or the generations of men do a sentence. He was dark, dried up, diminutive, and seemed outside time, situated in eternity. Dahlmann noted with satisfaction the kerchief, the thick poncho, the long *chiripá,* and the colt boots, and told himself, as he recalled futile discussions with people from the Northern counties or from the province of Entre Rios, that gauchos like this no longer existed outside the South.

Dahlmann sat down next to the window. The darkness began overcoming the plain, but the odor and sound of the earth penetrated the iron bars of the window. The shop owner brought him sardines, followed by some roast meat. Dahlmann washed the meal down with several glasses of red wine. Idling, he relished the tart savor of the wine, and let his gaze, now grown somewhat drowsy, wander over the shop. A kerosene lamp hung from a beam. There were three customers at the other table: two of them appeared to be farm workers; the third man, whose features hinted at Chinese blood, was drinking with his hat on. Of a sudden, Dahlmann felt something brush lightly against his face. Next to the heavy glass of turbid wine, upon one of the stripes in the table cloth, lay a spit ball of breadcrumb. That was all: but someone had thrown it there.

The men at the other table seemed totally cut off from him. Perplexed, Dahlmann decided that nothing had happened, and he opened the volume of *The Thousand and One Nights,* by way of suppressing reality. After a few moments another little ball landed on his table, and now the *peones* laughed outright. Dahlmann said to himself that he was not frightened, but he reasoned that it would be a major blunder if he, a convalescent, were to allow himself to be dragged by strangers into some chaotic quarrel. He determined to leave, and had already gotten to his feet when the owner came up and exhorted him in an alarmed voice:

"*Señor* Dahlmann, don't pay any attention to those lads; they're half high."

Dahlmann was not surprised to learn that the other man, now, knew his name. But he felt that these conciliatory words served only to aggravate the situation. Previous to this moment, the *peones'* provocation was directed against an unknown face, against no one in particular, almost against no one at all. Now it was an attack against him, against his name, and his neighbors knew it. Dahlmann pushed the owner aside, confronted the *peones,* and demanded to know what they wanted of him.

The tough with a Chinese look staggered heavily to his feet. Almost in Juan Dahlmann's face he shouted insults, as if he had been a long way off. His game was to exaggerate his drunkenness, and this extravagance constituted a ferocious mockery. Between curses and obscenities, he threw a long knife into the air, followed it with his eyes, caught and juggled it, and challenged Dahlmann to a knife fight. The owner objected in a tremulous voice, pointing out that Dahlmann was unarmed. At this point, something unforeseeable occurred.

From a corner of the room, the old ecstatic gaucho — in whom Dahlmann saw a summary and cipher of the South (his South) — threw him a naked dagger, which landed at his feet. It was as if the South had resolved that Dahlmann should accept the duel. Dahlmann bent over to pick up the dagger, and felt two things. The first, that this almost instinctive act bound him to fight. The second, that the weapon, in his torpid hand, was no defense at all, but would merely serve to justify his murder. He had once played with a poniard, like all men, but his idea of fencing and knifeplay did not go further than the notion that all strokes should be directed upwards, with the cutting edge held inwards. *They would not have allowed such things to happen to me in the sanitarium,* he thought.

"Let's get on our way," said the other man.

They went out and if Dahlmann was without hope, he was also without fear. As he crossed the threshold, he felt that to die in a knife fight, under the open sky, and going forward to the attack, would have been a liberation, a joy, and a festive occasion, on the first night in the sanitarium, when they stuck him with the needle. He felt that if he had been able to choose, then, or to dream his death, this would have been the death he would have chosen or dreamt.

Firmly clutching his knife, which he perhaps would not know how to wield, Dahlmann went out into the plain.

ELIZABETH BOWEN

 Elizabeth Bowen (1899–1973) was born in Dublin and spent her early years on the Bowen estate in County Cork. She went to England to pursue her education and did not return to live in Ireland until 1952. Her reputation as one of the twentieth century's finest fiction writers was secured by such elegantly shaped and poignant novels as *The House in Paris* (1935), *The Death of the Heart* (1938), and *The Heat of the Day* (1948) and by seventy-nine stories published over a period of forty years and now gathered in *The Collected Stories of Elizabeth Bowen* (1981). In all her fiction Bowen displays what her fellow Anglo-Irish novelist Angus Wilson called "a strength, a fierceness and a depth to her elaborations, her delight in words...". Her surpassing concerns, as he says, are "a sense of childhood's pervasiveness and of passion as essential parts of a life lived elegantly and bravely." They may be seen beautifully rendered in the second story here, "Ivy Gripped the Steps." "The Demon Lover" reveals Bowen's fascination with the occult.

The Demon Lover

Towards the end of her day in London Mrs Drover went round to her shut-up house to look for several things she wanted to take away. Some belonged to herself, some to her family, who were by now used to their country life. It was late August; it had been a steamy, showery day: at the moment the trees down the pavement glittered in an escape of humid yellow afternoon sun. Against the next batch of clouds, already piling up ink-dark, broken chimneys and parapets stood out. In her once familiar street, as in any unused channel, an unfamiliar queerness had silted up; a cat wove itself in and out of railings, but no human eye watched Mrs Drover's return. Shifting some parcels under her arm, she slowly forced round her latchkey in an unwilling lock, then gave the door, which had warped, a push with her knee. Dead air came out to meet her as she went in.

The staircase window having been boarded up, no light came down into the hall. But one door, she could just see, stood ajar, so she went quickly through into the room and unshuttered the big window in there. Now the prosaic woman, looking about her, was more perplexed than she knew by everything that she saw, by traces of her long former habit of life — the yellow smoke-stain up the white marble mantelpiece, the ring left by a vase on the top of the escritoire; the bruise in the wallpaper where, on the door being thrown open wildly, the china handle had always hit the wall. The piano, having gone away to be stored, had left what looked like claw-marks on its part of the parquet. Though not much dust had seeped in, each object wore a film of another kind; and, the only ventilation being the chimney, the whole drawing-room smelled of the cold hearth. Mrs Drover put down her parcels on the escritoire and left the room to proceed upstairs; the things she wanted were in a bedroom chest.

She had been anxious to see how the house was — the part-time caretaker she shared with some neighbours was away this week on his holiday, known to be not yet back. At the best of times he did not look in often, and she was never sure that she trusted him. There were some cracks in the structure, left by the last bombing, on which she was anxious to keep an eye. Not that one could do anything —

A shaft of refracted daylight now lay across the hall. She stopped dead and stared at the hall table — on this lay a letter addressed to her.

She thought first — then the caretaker *must* be back. All the same, who, seeing the house shuttered, would have dropped a letter in at the box? It was not a circular, it was not a bill. And the post office redirected, to the address in the country, everything for her that came through the post. The caretaker (even if he *were* back) did not know she was due in London today — her call here had been planned to be a surprise — so his negligence in the manner of this letter, leaving it to wait in the dusk and the dust, annoyed her. Annoyed, she picked up the letter, which bore no stamp. But it cannot be important, or they would know ... She took the letter rapidly upstairs with her, without a stop to look at the writing till she reached what had been her bedroom, where she let in light. The room looked over the garden and other gardens: the sun had gone in; as the clouds sharpened and lowered, the trees and rank lawns seemed already to smoke with dark. Her reluctance to look again at the letter came from the fact that she felt intruded upon — and by someone contemptuous of her ways. However, in the tenseness preceding the fall of rain she read it: it was a few lines.

> Dear Kathleen: You will not have forgotten that today is our anniversary, and the day we said. The years have gone by at once slowly and fast. In view of the fact that nothing has changed, I shall rely upon you to keep your promise. I was sorry to see you leave London, but was satisfied that you would be back in time. You may expect me, therefore, at the hour arranged. Until then ...
>
> K.

Mrs Drover looked for the date: it was today's. She dropped the letter on to the bed-springs, then picked it up to see the writing again — her lips, beneath the remains of lipstick, beginning to go white. She felt so much the change in her own face that she went to the mirror, polished a clear patch in it and looked at once urgently and stealthily in. She was confronted by a woman of forty-four, with eyes staring out under a hat-brim that had been rather carelessly pulled down. She had not put on any more powder since she left the shop where she ate her solitary tea. The pearls her husband had given her on their marriage hung loose round her now rather thinner throat, slipping in the V of the pink wool jumper her sister knitted last autumn as they sat around the fire. Mrs Drover's most normal expression was one of controlled worry, but of assent. Since the birth of the third of her little boys, attended by a quite serious illness, she had had an intermittent muscular flicker to the left of her mouth, but in spite of this she could always sustain a manner that was at once energetic and calm.

Turning from her own face as precipitately as she had gone to meet it, she went to the chest where the things were, unlocked it, threw up the lid and knelt to search. But as rain began to come crashing down she could not keep from looking over her shoulder at the stripped bed on which the letter lay. Behind the blanket of rain the clock of the church that still stood struck six — with rapidly heightening apprehension she counted each of the slow strokes. 'The hour arranged . . . My God,' she said, '*what* hour? How should I . . . ? After twenty-five years . . .'

The young girl talking to the soldier in the garden had not ever completely seen his face. It was dark; they were saying goodbye under a tree. Now and then — for it felt, from not seeing him at this intense moment, as though she had never seen him at all — she verified his presence for these few moments longer by putting out a hand, which he each time pressed, without very much kindness, and painfully, on to one of the breast buttons of his uniform. That cut of the button on the palm of her hand was, principally, what she was to carry away. This was so near the end of a leave from France that she could only wish him already gone. It was August 1916. Being not kissed, being drawn away from and looked at intimidated Kathleen till she imagined spectral glitters in the place of his eyes. Turning away and looking back up the lawn she saw, through branches of trees, the drawing-room window alight: she caught a breath for the moment when she could go running back there into the safe arms of her mother and sister, and cry: 'What shall I do, what shall I do? He has gone.'

Hearing her catch her breath, her fiancé said, without feeling: 'Cold?'

'You're going away such a long way.'

'Not so far as you think.'

'I don't understand?'

'You don't have to,' he said. 'You will. You know what we said.'

'But that was — suppose you — I mean, suppose.'

'I shall be with you,' he said, 'sooner or later. You won't forget that. You need do nothing but wait.'

Only a little more than a minute later she was free to run up the silent lawn. Looking in through the window at her mother and sister, who did not for the moment perceive her, she already felt that unnatural promise drive down between her and the rest of all human kind. No other way of having given herself could have made her feel so apart, lost and foresworn. She could not have plighted a more sinister troth.

Kathleen behaved well when, some months later, her fiancé was reported missing, presumed killed. Her family not only supported her but were able to praise her courage without stint because they could not regret, as a husband for her, the man they knew almost nothing about. They hoped she would, in a year or two, console herself — and had it been only a question of consolation things might have gone much straighter ahead. But her trouble, behind just a little grief, was a complete dislocation from everything. She did not reject other lovers, for these failed to appear: for years she failed to attract men — and with the approach of her 'thirties she became natural enough to share her family's anxiousness on this score. She began to put herself out, to wonder; and at thirty-two she was very greatly relieved to find herself being courted by William Drover. She married him, and the two of them settled down in this quiet, arboreal part of Kensington: in this house the years piled up, her children were born and they all lived till they were driven out by the bombs of the next war. Her movements as Mrs Drover were circumscribed, and she dismissed any idea that they were still watched.

As things were — dead or living the letter-writer sent her only a threat. Unable, for some minutes, to go on kneeling with her back exposed to the empty room, Mrs Drover rose from the chest to sit on an upright chair whose back was firmly against the wall. The desuetude of her former bedroom, her married London home's whole air of being a cracked cup from which memory, with its reassuring power, had either evaporated or leaked away, made a crisis — and at just this crisis the letter-writer had, knowledgeably, struck. The hollowness of the house this evening cancelled years on years of voices, habits and steps. Through the shut windows she only heard rain fall on the roofs around. To rally herself, she said she was in a mood — and for two or three seconds shutting her eyes, told herself that she had imagined the letter. But she opened them — there it lay on the bed.

On the supernatural side of the letter's entrance she was not permitting her mind to dwell. Who, in London, knew she meant to call at the house today? Evidently, however, this had been known. The caretaker, *had* he come back, had had no cause to expect her: he would have taken the letter in his pocket, to forward it, at his own time, through the post. There was no other sign that the caretaker had been in — but, if not? Letters dropped in at doors of deserted houses do not fly or walk to tables in halls. They do not sit on the dust of empty tables with the air of certainty that they will be found. There is needed some human hand — but nobody but the caretaker had a key. Under circumstances she did not care to consider, a house can be entered without a key. It was possible that she was not alone now. She might be being waited for, downstairs. Waited for — until when? Until 'the hour arranged'. At least that was not six o'clock: six has struck.

She rose from the chair and went over and locked the door.

The thing was, to get out. To fly? No, not that: she had to catch her train. As a woman whose utter dependability was the keystone of her family life she was not willing to return to the country, to her husband, her little boys and her sister, without the objects she had come up to fetch. Resuming work at the chest she set about making up a number of parcels in a rapid, fumbling-decisive way. These, with her shopping parcels, would be too much to carry; these meant a taxi — at the thought of the taxi her heart went up and her normal breathing resumed. I will ring up the taxi now; the taxi cannot come too soon: I shall hear the taxi out there running its engine, till I walk calmly down to it through the hall. I'll ring up — But no: the telephone is cut off . . . She tugged at a knot she had tied wrong.

The idea of flight . . . He was never kind to me, not really. I don't remember him kind at all. Mother said he never considered me. He was set on me, that was what it was — not love. Not love, not meaning a person well. What did he do, to make me promise like that? I can't remember — But she found that she could.

She remembered with such dreadful acuteness that the twenty-five years since then dissolved like smoke and she instinctively looked for the weal left by the button on the palm of her hand. She remembered not only all that he said and did but the complete suspension of *her* existence during that August week. I was not myself — they all told me so at the time. She remembered — but with one white burning blank as where acid has dropped on a photograph: *under no conditions* could she remember his face.

So, wherever he may be waiting, I shall not know him. You have no time to run from a face you do not expect.

The thing was to get to the taxi before any clock struck what could be the hour. She would slip down the street and round the side of the square to where the square gave on the main road. She would return in the taxi, safe, to her own door, and bring the solid driver into the house with her to pick up the parcels from room to room. The idea of the taxi driver made her decisive, bold: she unlocked her door, went to the top of the staircase and listened down.

She heard nothing — but while she was hearing nothing the *passé* air of the staircase was disturbed by a draught that travelled up to her face. It emanated from the basement: down there a door or window was being opened by someone who chose this moment to leave the house.

The rain had stopped; the pavements steamily shone as Mrs Drover let herself out by inches from her own front door into the empty street. The unoccupied houses opposite continued to meet her look with their damaged stare. Making towards the thoroughfare and the taxi, she tried not to keep looking behind. Indeed, the silence was so intense — one of those creeks of London silence exaggerated this summer by the damage of war — that no tread could have gained on hers unheard. Where her street debouched on the square where people went on living, she grew conscious of, and checked, her unnatural pace. Across the open end of the square two buses impassively passed each other: women, a perambulator, cyclists, a man wheeling a barrow signalized, once again, the ordinary flow of life. At the square's most populous corner should be — and was — the short taxi rank. This evening, only one taxi — but this, although it presented its blank rump, appeared already to be alertly waiting for her. Indeed, without looking round the driver started his engine as she panted up from behind and put her hand on the door. As she did so, the clock struck seven. The taxi faced the main road: to make the trip back to her house it would have to turn — she had settled back on the seat and the taxi *had* turned before she, surprised by its knowing movement, recollected that she had not 'said where'. She leaned forward to scratch at the glass panel that divided the driver's head from her own.

The driver braked to what was almost a stop, turned round and slid the glass panel back: the jolt of this flung Mrs Drover forward till her face was almost into the glass. Through the aperture driver and passenger, not six inches between them, remained for an eternity eye to eye. Mrs Drover's mouth hung open for some seconds before she could issue her first scream. After that she continued to scream freely and to beat with her gloved hands on the glass all round as the taxi, accelerating without mercy, made off with her into the hinterland of deserted streets.

ELIZABETH BOWEN

Ivy Gripped the Steps

Ivy gripped and sucked at the flight of steps, down which with such a deceptive wildness it seemed to be flowing like a cascade. Ivy matted the door at the top and amassed in bushes above and below the porch. More, it had covered, or one might feel consumed, one entire half of the high, double-fronted house, from the basement up to a spiked gable: it had attained about half-way up to the girth and more than the density of a tree, and was sagging outward under its own weight. One was left to guess at the size and the number of windows hidden by looking at those in the other side. But these, though in sight, had been made effectively sightless: sheets of some dark composition that looked like metal were sealed closely into their frames. The house, not old, was of dull red brick with stone trimmings.

To crown all, the ivy was now in fruit, clustered over with fleshy pale green berries. There was something brutal about its fecundity. It was hard to credit that such a harvest could have been nourished only on brick and stone. Had not reason insisted that the lost windows must, like their fellows, have been made fast, so that the suckers for all their seeking voracity could not enter, one could have convinced oneself that the ivy must be feeding on something inside the house.

The process of strangulation could be felt: one wondered how many more years of war would be necessary for this to complete itself. And, the conventionality of the house, the remains, at least, of order in its surroundings made what was happening more and more an anomaly. Mrs Nicholson's house had always enjoyed distinction — that of being detached, while its neighbours, though equally 'good', had been erected in couples or even in blocks of four, that of being the last in the avenue; that of having on one hand as neighbour the theater, to whose façade its front was at right angles. The theatre, set back behind shallow semi-circular gardens, at once crowned and terminated the avenue, which ran from it to the Promenade overhanging the sea. And the house, apart from the prestige of standing just where it stood, had had the air of reserving something quite of its own. It was thus perhaps just, or not unfitting, that it should have been singled out for this gothic fate.

This was, or had been, one of the best residential avenues in Southstone, into which private hotels intruded only with the most breathless, costly discretion: if it was not that now it was nothing else, for there was nothing else for it to be. Lines of chestnut trees had been planted along the pavements, along the railed strip of lawn that divided the avenue down the middle — now, the railings were, with all other ironwork, gone; and where the lawn was very long rusty grass grew up into the tangles of rusty barbed wire. On to this, as on to the concrete pyramids — which, in the course of four years of waiting to be pushed out to obstruct the invader, had sunk some inches into the soil — the chestnuts were now dropping their leaves.

The decline dated from the exodus of the summer of 1940, when Southstone had been declared in the front line. The houses at the sea end of the avenue had, like those on the Promenade, been requisitioned; but some of those at the theatre end stayed empty. Here and there, portions of porches or balustrades had fallen into front gardens, crushing their overgrowth; but there were no complete ruins; no bomb or shell had arrived immediately here, and effects of blast, though common to all of Southstone, were less evident than desuetude and decay. It was now the September of 1944; and, for some reason, the turn of the tide of war, the accumulation of the Invasion victories, gave Southstone its final air of defeat. The withdrawal of most of the soldiers, during the summer, had drained off adventitious vitality. The A.A. batteries, this month, were on the move to another part of the coast. And, within the very last few days, the silencing of the guns across the Channel had ended the tentative love affair with death: Southstone's life, no longer kept to at least a pitch by shelling warnings, now had nothing but an etiolated slowness. In the shuttered shopping streets along the Promenade, in the intersecting avenues, squares and crescents, vacuum mounted up. The lifting of the ban on the area had, so far, brought few visitors in.

This afternoon, for minutes together, not a soul, not even a soldier, crossed the avenue: Gavin Doddington stood to regard the ivy in which was, virtually, solitude. The sky being clouded, though not dark, a timeless flat light fell on to everything. Outside the theatre a very few soldiers stood grouped about; some moodily, some in no more than apathy. The theatre gardens had been cemented over to make a lorry park; and the engine of one of the lorries was being run.

Mrs Nicholson could not be blamed for the ivy: *her* absence from Southstone was of long standing, for she had died in 1912 — two years before the outbreak of what Gavin still thought of as Admiral Concannon's war. After her death, the house had been put up for auction by her executors: since then, it might well have changed hands two or three times. Probably few of the residents dislodged in 1940 had so much as heard Mrs Nicholson's name. In its condition, today, the house was a paradox: having been closed and sealed up with extreme care, it had been abandoned in a manner no less extreme. It had been nobody's business to check the ivy. Nor, apparently, had there been anybody to authorize a patriotic sacrifice of the railings — Gavin Doddington, prodding between the strands of ivy, confirmed his impression that that iron lacework still topped the parapet of the front garden. He could pursue with his finger, thought not see, the pattern that with other details of the house, outside and in, had long ago been branded into his memory. Looking up at the windows in the exposed half he saw, still in position along the sills, miniature reproductions of this pattern, for the support of window boxes. Those, which were gone, had been flowery in her day.

The assumption was that, as lately as 1940, Mrs Nicholson's house *had* belonged to someone, but that it belonged to nobody now. The late owner's death in some other part of England must have given effect to a will not brought up to date, by which the property passed to an heir who could not be found — to somebody not heard of since Singapore fell or not yet reported anything more than 'missing' after

a raid on London or a battle abroad. Legal hold-ups dotted the world-wide mess . . .
So reasoning, Gavin Doddington gave rein to what had been his infant and was now
his infantile passion for explanation. But also he attached himself to the story as to
something nothing to do with him; and did so with the intensity of a person who
must think lest he should begin to feel.

His passion for explanation had been, when he knew Mrs Nicholson, raised by her
power of silently baulking it into the principal reason for suffering. It had been
among the stigmata of his extreme youth — he had been eight when he met her, ten
when she died. He had not been back to Southstone since his last stay with her.

Now, the lifting of the official ban on the area had had the effect of bringing him
straight back — why? When what one has refused is put out of reach, when what one
has avoided becomes forbidden, some lessening of the inhibition may well occur.
The ban had so acted on his reluctance that, when the one was removed, the other
came away with it — as a scab, adhering, comes off with a wad of lint. The trans-
mutation, due to the fall of France, of his *'I cannot go back to Southstone'* into *'One
cannot go there'* must have been salutary, or, at least, exteriorizing. It so happened
that when the ban came off he had been due for a few days' leave from the Ministry
He had at once booked a room at one of the few hotels that remained at the visitor's
disposition.

Arriving at Southstone yesterday evening, he had confined his stroll in the hazy
marine dusk to the cracked, vacant and wirelooped Promenade — from which he
returned with little more than the wish that he had, after all, brought somebody
down here with him. Amorist since his 'teens, he had not often set off on a holiday
uncompanioned. The idea of this as a pilgrimage revolted him: he remained in the
bar till the bar closed. This morning he had no more than stalked the house,
approaching it in wavering closing circles through the vaguer Southstone areas of
association. He had fixed for the actual confrontation that hour, deadline for feeling,
immediately after lunch.

The story originated in a friendship between two young girls in their Dresden
finishing year. Edith and Lilian had kept in touch throughout later lives that ran
very widely apart — their letters, regularly exchanged, were perhaps more confidential than their infrequent meetings. Edith had married a country gentleman,
Lilian a business man. Jimmie Nicholson had bought the Southstone house for his
wife in 1907, not long before his death, which had been the result of a stroke. He
had been senior by about fifteen years: their one child, a daughter, had died at
birth.

Edith Doddington, who had never been quite at ease on the subject of Lilian's
marriage, came to stay more often now her friend was a widow, but still could not
come as often as both would have liked. Edith's own married life was one of
contrivance and of anxiety. After money, the most pressing of Edith's worries centred
round the health of her second son: Gavin had been from birth a delicate little boy.
The damp of his native county, inland and low-lying, did not suit him: there was the
constant question of change of air — till his health stabilized, he could not go away
to school. It was natural that Lilian, upon discovering this, should write inviting Gavin
to stay at Southstone — ideally, of course, let his mother bring him; but if Edith
could not be free, let him come alone. Mrs Nicholson hoped he and she, who had

not yet met, would not, or would not for long, be shy of each other. Her maid Rockham was, at any rate, good with children.

Gavin had heard of Southstone as the scene of his mother's only exotic pleasures. The maid Rockham was sent to London to meet him: the two concluded their journey with the absurdly short drive, in an open victoria, from the station to Mrs Nicholson's house. It was early in what was a blazing June: the awnings over the windows rippled, the marguerites in the window-boxes undulated, in a hot breeze coming down the avenue from the sea. From the awnings the rooms inside took a tense bright dusk. In the sea-blue drawing-room, up whose walls reared mirrors framed in ivory brackets, Gavin was left to await Mrs Nicholson. He had time to marvel at the variety of the bric-à-brac crowding brackets and tables, the manyness of the cut-crystal vases, the earliness of the purple and white sweet pea — at the Doddingtons', sweet pea did not flower before July. Mrs Nicholson then entered: to his surprise she did not kiss him.

Instead, she stood looking down at him — she was tall — with a glittering, charming uncertainty. Her head bent a little lower, during consideration not so much of Gavin as of the moment. Her *coiffeur* was like spun sugar: that its crisp upward waves should seem to have been splashed with silvery powder added, only, marquise-like glowing youth to her face.

The summery light-like fullness of her dress was accentuated by the taut belt with coral-inlaid clasp: from that small start the skirts flowed down to dissipate and spread where they touched the floor. Tentatively she extended her right hand, which he, without again raising his eyes, shook. 'Well ... Gavin,' she said. 'I hope you had a good journey? I am so very glad you could come.'

He said: 'And my mother sends you her love.'

'Does she?' Sitting down, sinking an elbow into the sofa cushions, she added: 'How *is* Edith — how is your mother?'

'Oh, she is very well.'

She vaguely glanced round her drawing-room, as though seeing it from his angle, and, therefore, herself seeing it for the first time. The alternatives it offered could be distracting: she soon asked him her first intimate question — 'Where do you think you would like to sit?'

Not that afternoon, nor indeed, until some way on into this first visit did Gavin distinguish at all sharply between Mrs Nicholson and her life. Not till the knife of love gained sufficient edge could he cut out her figure from its surroundings. Southstone was, for the poor landowner's son, the first glimpse of the enchanted existence of the *rentier*. Everything was effortless; and, to him, consequently, seemed stamped with style. This society gained by smallness: it could be comprehended. People here, the company that she kept, commanded everything they desired, were charged with nothing they did not. The expenditure of their incomes — expenditure calculated so long ago and so nicely that it could now seem artless — occupied them. What there was to show for it showed at every turn; though at no turn too much, for it was not too much. Such light, lofty, smooth-running houses were to be found, quite likely, in no capital city. A word to the livery stables brought an imposing carriage to any door: in the afternoons one drove, in a little party, to reflect on a Roman ruin or to admire a village church. In the Promenade's glare, at the end of the shaded avenue, parasols passed and repassed in a rhythm of leisure. Just inland were the attentive shops. There were meetings for good causes in cool drawing-rooms, afternoon concerts in the hotel ballrooms; and there was always the theatre, where applause continued long after Gavin had gone to bed. Best of all, there were no poor to be seen.

The plan of this part of Southstone (a plateau backed by the downs and over-hanging the sea) was masterful. Its architecture was ostentatious, fiddling, bulky and mixed. Gavin was happy enough to be at an age to admire the one, to be unaware of the other — he was elated, rather than not, by this exhibition of gimcrack size; and bows, bays, balustrades, glazed-in balconies and French-type mansardes not slowly took up their parts in the fairy tale. As strongly was he impressed by the strong raying out, from such points as station and theatre, of avenues; each of which crossed, obliquely, just less wide residential roads. Lavishness appeared in the public flowers, the municipal seats with their sofa-like curving backs, the flagpoles, cliff grottoes, perspectives of lawn. There was a climate here that change from season to season, the roughest Channel gale blowing, could not disturb. This town without function fascinated him — outside it, down to the port or into the fishing quarter, 'old Southstone', he did not attempt to stray. Such tameness might have been found odd in a little boy: Mrs Nicholson never thought of it twice.

Gavin's estimation of Southstone — as he understood much later — coincided with that of a dead man. When Jimmie Nicholson bought the house for his wife here, Southstone was the high dream of his particular world. It was as Lilian's husband he made the choice: alone, he might not have felt capable of this polished leisure. His death left it uncertain whether, even *as* Lilian's husband, he could have made the grade. The golf course had been his object: failing that he was not, perhaps, so badly placed in the cemetery, which was also outside the town. For, for Southstone dividends kept their mystic origin: they were as punctual as Divine grace, as un-mentioned as children still in wombs. Thickset Jimmie, with is pursuant reek of the City, could have been a distasteful reminder of money's source.

Gavin, like his dead host, beheld Southstone with all the ardour of an outsider. His own family had a touch of the brutishness that comes from any dependence upon land. Mr and Mrs Doddington were constantly in wet clothes, constantly fatigued, constantly depressed. Nothing new appeared in the squire's home; and what was old had acquired a sort of fog from being ignored. An austere, religious idea of their own standing not so much inspired as preyed upon Gavin's parents. Caps touched to them in the village could not console them for the letters they got from their bank. Money for them was like a spring in a marsh, feebly thrusting its way up to be absorbed again: any profit forced from the home farm, any rents received for outlying lands went back again into upkeep, rates, gates, hedging, draining, repairs to cottages and renewal of stock. There was nothing, no nothing ever, to show. In the society round them they played no part to which their position did not compel them: they were poor gentry, in fact, at a period when poverty could not be laughed away. Their lot was less enviable than that of any of their employees or tenants, whose faces, naked in their dejection, and voices pitched to complaints they could at least utter, had disconcerted Gavin, since babyhood, at the Hall door. Had the Doddingtons been told that their kind would die out, they would have expressed little more than surprise that such compli-cated troubles could end so simply.

Always toward the end of a stay at Southstone Gavin's senses began to be haunted by the anticipation of going back. So much so that to tread the heat-softened asphalt was to feel once more the suck of a sticky lane. *Here,* day and night he breathed with ease that was still a subconscious joy: the thought of the Midlands made his lungs contract and deaden — such was the old cold air, sequestered by musty baize doors, of the corridors all the way to his room at home.

His room *here* was on the second floor, in front, looking on to the avenue. It had a frieze of violets knotted along a ribbon: as dusk deepened, these turned gradually black. Later, a lamp from the avenue cast a tree's shifting shadow on to the ceiling above his bed; and the same light pierced the Swiss skirts of the dressing-table. Mrs Nicholson, on the first occasion when she came as far as his door to say good night, deprecated the 'silliness' of this little room. Rockham, it seemed, had thought it suitable for his age — she, Rockham, had her quarters on the same floor — Mrs Nicholson, though she did not say so, seemed to feel it to be unsuitable for his sex. 'Because I don't suppose,' she said, 'that you really ever *are* lonely in the night?'

Propped upright against his pillows, gripping his glass of milk, he replied: 'I am never frightened.'

'But, lonely — what makes you lonely, then?'

'I don't know. I suppose, thoughts.'

'Oh, but why,' she said, 'don't you like them?'

'When I am here the night seems a sort of waste, and I don't like to think what a waste it is.'

Mrs Nicholson, who was on her way out to dinner, paused in the act of looping a gauze scarf over her hair and once again round her throat. 'Only tell me,' she said, 'that you're not more lonely, Gavin, because I am going out? Up here, you don't know if I am in the house or not.'

'I do know.'

'Perhaps,' she suggested humbly, 'you'll go to sleep? They all say it is right for you, going to bed so early, but I wish it did not make days so short. — I must go.'

'The carriage hasn't come round yet.'

'No, it won't: it hasn't been ordered. It is so lovely this evening, I thought I would like to walk.' She spoke, though, as though the project were spoiled for her: she could not help seeing, as much as he did, the unkindness of leaving him with this picture. She came even further into the room to adjust her scarf at his mirror, for it was not yet dark. 'Just once, one evening perhaps, you could stay up late. Do you think it would matter? I'll ask Rockham.'

Rockham remained the arbiter: it was she who was left to exercise anything so nearly harsh as authority. In even the affairs of her own house Mrs Nicholson was not heard giving an order: what could not be thought to be conjured into existence must be part of the clockwork wound up at the start by Jimmie and showing no sign of beginning to run down yet. The dishes that came to table seemed to surprise her as much, and as pleasingly, as they did Gavin. Yet the effect she gave was not of idleness but of preoccupation: what she did with her days Gavin did not ask himself — when he did ask himself, later, it was too late. They continued to take her colour — those days she did nothing with.

It was Rockham who worked out the daily programme, devised to keep the little boy out of Madam's way. 'Because Madam,' she said, 'is not accustomed to children.'

It was by Rockham that, every morning, he was taken down to play by the sea: the beach, undulations of orange shingle, was fine-combed with breakwaters, against one of which sat Rockham, reading a magazine. Now and then she would look up, now and then she would call. These relegations to Rockham sent Gavin to angry extremes of infantilism: he tried to drape seaweed streamers around her hat; he plagued to have pebbles taken out of his shoe. There was a literal feeling of degradation about this descent from the plateau to the cliff's foot. From close up, the sea, with its heaving mackerel vacancy, bored him — most of the time he stood with his back to it, shading his eyes and staring up at the heights. From right down here, though Southstone could not be seen — any more than objects set back on a high shelf can be seen by somebody standing immediately underneath it — its illusion, its magical artificiality, was to be savoured as from nowhere else. Tiny, the flags of the Promenade's edge, the figures leaning along the railings, stood out against a dazzle of sky. And he never looked up at these looking down without an interrupted heartbeat — might she not be among them?

The rule was that they, Rockham and Gavin, walked zigzag down by the cliff path, but travelled up in the lift. But one day fate made Rockham forget her purse. They had therefore to undertake the ascent. The path's artful gradients, hand-railed, were broken by flights of steps and by niched seats, upon every one of which Rockham plumped herself down to regain breath. The heat of midday, the glare from the flowered cliff beat up Gavin into a sort of fever. As though a dropped plummet had struck him between the eyes he looked up, to see Mrs Nicholson's face above him against the blue. The face, its colour rendered transparent by the transparent silk of a parasol, was inclined forward: he had the experience of seeing straight up into eyes that did not see him. Her look was pitched into space: she was not only not seeing him, she was seeing nothing. She was listening, but not attending, while someone talked.

Gavin, gripping the handrail, bracing his spine against it, leaned out backwards over the handrail into the void, in the hopes of intercepting her line of view. But in vain. He tore off clumps of sea pinks and cast the too-light flowers outwards into the air, but her pupils never once flickered down. Despair, the idea that his doom must be never, never to reach her, not only now but ever, gripped him and gripped his limbs as he took the rest of the path — the two more bends and few more steps to the top. He clawed his way up the rail, which shook in its socket.

The path, when it landed Gavin on to the Promenade, did so some yards from where Mrs Nicholson and her companion stood. Her companion was Admiral Concannon. 'Hello, hello!' said the Admiral, stepping back to see clear of the parasol. 'Where have *you* sprung from?'

'Oh, but Gavin,' exclaimed Mrs Nicholson, also turning, 'why not come up in the lift? I thought you liked it.'

'Lift?' said the Admiral. 'Lift, at his age? What, has the boy got a dicky heart?'

'No indeed!' she said, and looked at Gavin so proudly that he became the image of health and strength.

'In that case,' said the Admiral, 'do him good.' There was something, in the main, not unflattering about this co-equal masculine brusqueness. Mrs Nicholson, looking over the railings, perceived the labouring top of her maid's hat. 'It's poor Rockham,' she said, 'that I am thinking about; she hasn't got a heart but she has attacks. — How hazy it is!' she said, indicating the horizon with a gloved hand. 'It seems to be days since we saw France. I don't believe Gavin believes it is really there.'

'It is there all right,' said the Admiral, frowning slightly.

'Why, Rockham,' she interposed, 'you look hot. Whatever made you walk up on a day like this?'

'Well, I cannot fly, can I, madam; and I overlooked my purse.'

'Admiral Concannon says we may all be flying. — What are you waiting for?'

'I was waiting for Master Gavin to come along.'

'I don't see why he should, really — which would you rather, Gavin?'

Admiral Concannon's expression did not easily change, and did not change now. His features were severely clear cut; his figure was nervy and spare; and he had an air of eating himself — due, possibly, to his retirement. His manners of walking, talking and standing, though all to be recognized at a distance, were vehemently impersonal. When in anything that could be called repose he usually kept his hands in his pockets — the abrupt extraction of one hand, for the purpose of clicking thumb and finger together, was the nearest thing to a gesture he ever made. His voice and step had become familiar, among the few nocturnal sounds of the avenue, some time before Gavin had seen his face; for he escorted Mrs Nicholson home from parties to which she had been wilful enough to walk. Looking out one night, after the hall door shut, Gavin had seen the head of a cigarette, immobile, pulsating sharply under the dark trees. The Concannons had settled at Southstone for Mrs Concannon's health's sake: their two daughters attended one of the schools.

Liberated into this blue height, Gavin could afford to look down in triumph at the sea by whose edge he had lately stood. But the Admiral said: 'Another short turn, perhaps?' — since they were to *be* three, they had better be three in motion. Mrs Nicholson raised her parasol, and the three moved off down the Promenade with the dignified aimlessness of swans. Ahead, the distance dissolved, the asphalt quivered in heat; and she, by walking between her two companions, produced a democracy of masculine trouble into which age did not enter at all. As they passed the bandstand she said to Gavin: 'Admiral Concannon has just been saying that there is going to be a war.'

Gavin glanced across at the Admiral, who remained in profile. Unassisted and puzzled, he said: 'Why?'

'Why indeed?' she agreed. — 'There!' she said to the Admiral. 'It's no good trying to tease me, because I never believe you.' She glanced around her and added: 'After all, we live in the present day! History is quite far back; it is said, of course, but it does seem silly. I never even cared for history at school; I was glad when we came to the end of it.'

'And when, my dear, did you come to the end of history?'

'The year I put up my hair. It had begun to be not so bad from the time we started catching up with the present; and I was glad I had stayed at school long enough to be sure that it had all ended happily. But oh, those unfortunate people in the past! It seems unkind to say so, but can it have been their faults? They can have been no more like us than cats and dogs. I suppose there *is* one reason for learning history — one sees how long it has taken to make the world nice. Who on earth could want to upset things now? — No one could want to,' she said to the Admiral. 'You forget the way we behave now, and there's no other way. Civilized countries are polite to each other, just as you and I are to the people we know, and uncivilized countries are put down — but, if one thinks, there are beautifully few of those. Even savages really prefer wearing hats and coats. Once people wear hats and coats and can turn on electric light, they would no more want to be silly than you or I do. — Or *do* you want to be silly?' she said to the Admiral.

He said: 'I did not mean to upset you.'

'You don't,' she said. 'I should not dream of suspecting *any* civilized country!'

'Which civilized country?' said Gavin. 'France?'

'For your information,' said the Admiral coldly, 'it is Germany we should be preparing to fight, for the reason that she is preparing to fight us.'

'I have never been happier anywhere,' said Mrs Nicholson, more nearly definitely than usual. 'Why,' she added, turning to Gavin, 'if it were not for Germany, now I come to think of it, you would not be here!'

The Admiral, meanwhile, had become intent on spearing on the tip of his cane a straying fragment of paper, two inches torn off a letter, that was defiling the Prom-cnadc. Lips compressed, he crossed to a little basket (which had till then stood empty, there being no litter) and knocked the fragment into it off his cane. He burst out: 'I should like to know what this place is coming to — we shall have trippers next!'

This concern his beautiful friend *could* share — and did so share that harmony was restored. Gavin, left to stare out to sea, reflected on one point in the conversa-tion: he could never forget that the Admiral had called Mrs Nicholson, 'My dear'.

Also, under what provocation had the Admiral threatened Mrs Nicholson with war? . . . Back at Gavin's home again, once more with his parents, nothing was, after all, so impossible: this was outside the zone of electric light. As late summer wore slowly over the Midlands, the elms in the Doddington's park casting lifeless slate-coloured shadows over sorrel, dung, thistles and tufted grass, it was born in on Gavin that this existence belonged, by its nature, to *any* century. It was unprogressive. It had stayed as it was while, elsewhere, history jerked itself painfully off the spool; it could hardly be more depressed by the fateful passage of armies than by the flooding of tillage or the failure of crops: it was hardly capable, really, of being depressed further. It was an existence mortgaged to necessity; it was an inheritance of uneasiness, tension and suspicion. One could preassume the enmity of weather, prices, mankind, cattle. It was this dead weight of existence that had supplied to history not so much the violence or the futility that had been, as she said, apparent to Mrs Nicholson, but its repetitive harshness and its power to scar. This existence had no volition, but could not stop; and its never stopping, because it could not, made history's ever stopping the less likely. No signs of even an agreeable pause were to be seen round Dod-dington Hall. Nor could one, at such a distance from Southstone, agree that time had laboured to make the world nice.

Gavin now saw his mother as Mrs Nicholson's friend. Indeed, the best of the gowns in which Edith went out to dinner, when forced to go out to dinner, had been Lilian's once, and once or twice worn by her. Worn by Edith, they still had the exoticism of gifts, and dispelled from their folds not only the giver's sachets, but the easy pitiful lovingness of the giver's mood. In them, Gavin's mother's thin figure assumed a grace whose pathos was lost to him at the time. While the brown-yellow upward light of the table oil-lamp unkindly sharpened the hollows in Mrs Doddington's face and throat, Gavin, thrown sideways out of his bed, fingered the mousseline or caressed the satin of the skirts with an adoring absorption that made his mother uneasy — for fetishism is still to be apprehended by those for whom it has never had any name. She would venture: 'You like, then, to see me in pretty clothes?' ... It was, too, in the first of these intermissions between his visits to Southstone that he, for the first time, took stock of himself, of his assets — the evident pleasingness of his manner; his looks — he could take in better and better part his elder brother's jibes at his pretty-prettiness — his quickness of mind, which at times made even his father smile; and his masculinity, which, now he tried it out, gave him unexpected command of small situations. At home, nights were not a waste: he attached himself to his thoughts, which took him, by seven-league strides, onward to his next visit. He rehearsed, using his mother, all sorts of little gratuities of behaviour, till she exclaimed: 'Why, Lilian has made quite a little page of you!' At her heels round the garden or damp extensive offices of the Hall, at her elbow as she peered through her letters or resignedly settled to her accounts, he reiterated: 'Tell me about Germany.'

'Why Germany?'

'I mean, the year you were there.'

A gale tore the slates from the Hall stables, brought one tree down on to a fence and another to block the drive, the night before Gavin left for Southstone. This time he travelled alone. At Southstone, dull shingly roaring thumps from the beach travelled as far inland as the railway station; from the Promenade — on which, someone said, it was all but impossible to stand upright — there came a whistling strain down the avenues. It was early January. Rockham was kept to the house by a nasty cold; so it was Mrs Nicholson who, with brilliantly heightened colour, holding her muff to the cheek on which the wind blew, was on the station platform to meet Gavin. A porter, tucking the two of them into the waiting carriage, replaced the foot-warmer under the fur rug. She said: 'How different this is from when you were with me last. Or do you like winter?'

'I like anything, really.'

'I remember one thing you don't like: you said you didn't like thoughts.' As they drove past a lighted house from which music came to be torn about by the wind, she remembered: 'You've been invited to several parties.'

He was wary: 'Shall you be going to them?'

'Why, yes; I'm sure I *could* go,' she said.

Her house was hermetic against the storm: in the drawing-room, heat drew out the smell of violets. She dropped her muff on the sofa, and Gavin stroked it — 'It's like a cat,' he said quickly, as she turned round. 'Shall I have a cat?' she said. 'Would you like me to have a cat?' All the other rooms, as they went upstairs, were tawny with fires that did not smoke.

Next morning, the wind had dropped; the sky reflected on everything its mild brightness; trees, houses and pavements glistened like washed glass. Rockham, puffy and with a glazed upper lip, said: 'Baster Gavid, You've brought us better weather.' Having blown her nose with what she seemed to hope was exhaustive thoroughness, she concealed her handkerchief in her bosom as guiltily as though it had been a dagger. 'Badam,' she said, 'doesn't like be to have a cold. — Poor Bisses Codcaddod,' she added, 'has been laid up agaid.'

Mrs Concannon's recovery must be timed for the little dinner party that they were giving. Her friends agreed that she ought to reserve her strength. On the morning of what was to be the day, it was, therefore, the Admiral whom one met out shopping: Gavin and Mrs Nicholson came on him moodily selecting flowers and fruit. Delayed late autumn and forced early spring flowers blazed, under artificial light, against the milder daylight outside the florist's plate glass. 'For tonight, for the party?' exclaimed Mrs Nicholson. 'Oh, let us have carnations, scarlet carnations!'

The Admiral hesitated. 'I think Constance spoke of chrysanthemums, white chrysanthemums.'

'Oh, but these are so washy, so like funerals. They will do poor Constance no good, if she still feels ill.'

Gavin, who had examined the prices closely, in parenthesis said: 'Carnations are more expensive.'

'No, wait!' cried Mrs Nicholson, gathering from their buckets all the scarlet carnations that were in reach, and gaily shaking the water from their stems, 'you must let me send these to Constance, because I am so much looking forward to tonight. It will be delightful.'

'I hope so,' the Admiral said. 'But I'm sorry to say we shall be an uneven number: we have just heard that poor Massingham has dropped out. Influenza.'

'Bachelors shouldn't have influenza, should they. — But then, why not ask somebody else?'

'So very much at the last moment, that might seem a bit — informal.'

'Dear me,' she teased, 'have you really *no* old friend?'

'Constance does not feel . . .'

Mrs Nicholson's eyebrows rose: she looked at the Admiral over the carnations. This was one of the moments when the Admiral could be heard to click his fingers and thumb. 'What a pity,' she said. 'I don't care for lopsided parties. *I* have one friend who is not touchy — invite Gavin!'

To a suggestion so completely outrageous, who was to think of any reply? It was a *coup*. She completed, swiftly: 'Tonight, then? We shall be with you at about eight.'

Gavin's squiring Mrs Nicholson to the Concannons' party symptomized this phase of their intimacy; without being, necessarily, its highest point. Rockham's cold had imperilled Rockham's prestige: as intervener or arbiter she could be counted out. There being no more talk of these odious drops to the beach, Gavin exercised over Mrs Nicholson's mournings what seemed a conqueror's rights to a terrain; while with regard to her afternoons she showed a flattering indecision as to what might not please him or what he could not share. At her tea-table, his position was made subtly manifest to her guests. His bedtime was becoming later and later; in vain did Rockham stand and cough in the hall; more than once or twice he had dined downstairs. When the curtains were drawn, it was he who lit the piano candles, then stood beside her as she played — ostensibly to turn over the music, but forgetting the score to watch her hands. At the same time, he envisaged their two figures as they would appear to someone — his other self — standing out there in the cold dark of the avenue, looking between the curtains into the glowing room. One evening, she sang 'Two Eyes of Grey that used to be so Bright.'

At the end, he said: 'But that's supposed to be a song sung by a man to a woman.'

Turning on the stool, she said: 'Then you must learn it.'

He objected: 'But your eyes are not grey.'

Indeed they were never neutral eyes. Their sapphire darkness, with that of the sapphire pendant she was wearing, was struck into by the Concannons' electric light. That round fitment on pulleys, with a red silk frill, had been so adjusted above the dinner table as to cast down a vivid circle, in which the guests sat. The stare and sheen of the cloth directly under the light appeared supernatural. The centrepiece was a silver or plated pheasant, around whose base the carnations — slightly but strikingly 'off' the red of the shade, but pre-eminently flattering in their contrast to Mrs Nicholson's orchid *glacé* gown — were bunched in four silver cornets. This was a party of eight: if the Concannons had insisted on stressing its 'littleness', it was, still, the largest that they could hope to give. The evident choiceness of the guests, the glitter and the mathematical placing of the silver and glass, the prompt, meticulous service of the dishes by maids whose suspended breath could be heard — all, all bespoke art and care. Gavin and Mrs Nicholson were so placed as to face one another across the table: her glance contained him, from time to time, in its leisurely, not quite attentive play. He wondered whether she felt, and supposed she must, how great had been the effrontery of their entrance.

For this dinner-party lost all point if it were not *de rigueur*. The Concannon daughters, even (big girls, but with hair still down their backs) had, as not qualified for it, been sent out for the evening. It, the party, had been balanced up and up on itself like a house of cards: built, it remained as precarious. Now the structure trembled, down to its base, from one contemptuous flip at its top story — Mrs Nicholson's caprice of bringing a little boy. Gavin perceived that night what he was not to forget: the helplessness, in the last resort, of society — which he was never, later, to be able to think of as a force. The pianola-like play of the conversation did not drown the nervousness round the table.

At the head of the table the Admiral leaned just forward, as though pedalling the pianola. At the far end, an irrepressible cough from time to time shook Mrs Concannon's décolletage and the crystal pince-nez which, balanced high on her face, gave her a sensitive blankness. She had the *dévote* air of some sailors' wives; and was heroic in pale blue without a wrap — arguably, nothing could make her iller. The Admiral's pride in his wife's courage passed like a current over the silver pheasant. For Mrs Concannon, joy in sustaining all this for his sake, and confidence in him, provided a light armour: she possibly did not feel what was felt for her. To Gavin she could not have been kinder; to Mrs Nicholson she had only and mildly said: 'He will not be shy, I hope, if he does not sit beside you?'

Rearrangement of the table at the last moment could not but have disappointed one or other of the two gentlemen who had expected to sit, and were now sitting, at Mrs Nicholson's right and left hand. More and more, as course followed course, these two showed how highly they rated their good fortune — indeed, the censure around the rest of the table only acted for them, like heat drawing out scent, to heighten the headiness of her immediate aura. Like the quick stuff of her dress her delinquency, even, gave out a sort of shimmer: while she, neither arch nor indolent, turned from one to the other her look — if you like, melting; for it dissolved her pupils, which had never been so dilated, dark, as tonight. In this look, as dinner proceeded, the two flies, ceasing to struggle, drowned.

The reckoning would be on the way home. Silent between the flies' wives, hypnotized by the rise and fall of Mrs Nicholson's pendant, Gavin ate on and on. The ladies' move to the drawing-room sucked him along with it in the wake of the last skirt . . . It was without a word that, at the end of the evening, the Admiral saw Mrs Nicholson to her carriage — Gavin, like an afterthought or a monkey, nipping in under his host's arm extended to hold open the carriage door. Light from the porch, as they drove off, fell for a moment longer on that erect form and implacable hatchet face. Mrs Nicholson seemed to be occupied in gathering up her skirts to make room for Gavin. She then leaned back in her corner, and he in his: not a word broke the tension of the short dark drive home. Not till she had dropped her cloak in front of her drawing-room fire did she remark: 'The Admiral's angry with me.'

'Because of me?'

'Oh dear no; because of her. If I did not think to be angry was very silly, I'd almost be a little angry with him.'

'But you meant to make him angry, didn't you?' Gavin said.

'Only because he's silly,' said Mrs. Nicholson. 'If he were not so silly, that poor unfortunate creature would stop coughing: she would either get better or die.' Still standing before her mantelpiece, she studied some freesias in a vase —dispassionately, she pinched off one fading bloom, rolled it into a wax pill between her thumb and finger, then flicked it away to sizzle in the heart of the fire. 'If people,' she said, 'give a party for no other reason but to show off their marriage, what kind of evening can one expect? — However, I quite enjoyed myself. I hope you did?'

Gavin said: 'Mrs Concannon's quite old. But then, so's the Admiral.'

'He quite soon will be, at this rate,' said Mrs Nicholson. 'That's why he's so anxious to have that war. One would have thought a man could just be a man. — What's the matter, Gavin; what are you staring at?'

'That is your most beautiful dress.'

'Yes; that's why I put it on.' Mrs Nicholson sat down on a low blue velvet chair and drew the chair to the fire: she shivered slightly. 'You say such sweet things, Gavin: what fun we have!' Then, as though, within the seconds of silence ticked off over her head by the little Dresden clock, her own words had taken effect with her, she turned and, with an impulsive movement, invited him closer to her side. Her arm stayed round him; her short puffed sleeve, disturbed by the movement, resulted down into silence. In the fire a coal fell apart, releasing a seam of gas from which spurted a pale tense quivering flame. 'Aren't you glad we are back?' she said, 'that we are only you and me? — Oh, why endure such people when all the time there is the whole world! Why do I stay on and on here; what am I doing? Why don't we go right away somewhere, Gavin; you and I? To Germany, or into the sun? Would that make you happy?'

'That — that flame's so funny,' he said, not shifting his eyes from it.

She dropped her arm and cried, in despair: 'After all, what a child you are!'

'I am not.'

'Anyhow, it's late; you must go to bed.'

She transmuted the rise of another shiver into a slight yawn.

Overcharged and trembling, he gripped his way, flight by flight, up the polished banister rail, on which his palms left patches of mist; pulling himself away from her up the staircase as he had pulled himself towards her up the face of the cliff.

After that midwinter visit there were two changes: Mrs Nicholson went abroad, Gavin went to school. He overheard his mother say to his father that Lilian found Southstone this winter really too cold to stay in. 'Or, has made it too hot to stay in?' said Mr Doddington, from whose disapproval the story of Gavin and the Concannons' party had not been able to be kept. Edith Doddington coloured, loyal, and said no more. During his first term Gavin received at school one bright picture postcard of Mentone. The carefully chosen small preparatory school confronted him, after all, with fewer trials than his parents had feared and his brother hoped. His protective adaptability worked quickly; he took enough colour, or colourlessness, from where he was to pass among the others, and along with them — a civil and indifferent little boy. His improved but never quite certain health got him out of some things and secured others — rests from time to time in the sick-room, teas by the matron's fire. This spectacled woman was not quite unlike Rockham; also, she was the most approachable edge of the grown-up ambience that connected him, however remotely, with Mrs Nicholson. At school, his assets of feeling remained, one would now say, frozen.

His Easter holidays had to be spent at home; his summer holidays exhausted their greater part in the same concession to a supposed attachment. Not until September was he dispatched to Southstone, for a week, to be set up before his return to school.

That September was an extension of summer. An admirable company continued its season of light opera at the theatre, in whose gardens salvias blazed. The lawns, shorn to the roots after weeks of mowing, were faintly blond after weeks of heat. Visitors were still many; and residents, after the fastidious retreat of August, were returning — along the Promenade, all day long, parasols, boater hats and light dresses flickered against the dense blue gauze backdrop that seldom let France be seen. In the evenings the head of the pier was a lighted musical box above the not yet cooling sea. Rare was the blade of chill, the too crystal morning or breathlike blur on the distance that announced autumn. Down the avenues the dark green trees hardened but did not change: if a leaf did fall, it was brushed away before anyone woke.

If Rockham remarked that Gavin was now quite a little man, her mistress made no reference to his schoolboy state. She did once ask whether the Norfolk jacket that had succeeded his sailor blouse were not, in this weather, a little hot; but that he might be expected to be more gruff, mum, standoffish or awkward than formerly did not appear to strike her. The change, if any, was in her. He failed to connect — why should he? — her new languor, her more marked contrarieties and her odd little periods of askance musing with the illness that was to be her death. She only said, the summer had been too long. Until the evenings she and Gavin were less alone, for she rose late; and, on their afternoon drives through the country, inland from the coast or towards the downs, they were as often as not accompanied by, of all persons, Mrs Concannon. On occasions when Mrs Concannon returned to Mrs Nicholson's house for tea, the Admiral made it his practice to call for her. The Concannons were very much occupied with preparations for another social event: a Southstone branch of the Awaken Britannia League was to be inaugurated by a drawing-room meeting at their house. The daughters were busy folding and posting leaflets. Mrs Nicholson, so far, could be pinned down to nothing more than a promise to send cakes from her own, or rather her cook's, kitchen.

'But at least,' pleaded Mrs Concannon, at tea one afternoon, 'you should come if only to hear what it is about.'

By five o'clock, in September, Mrs Nicholson's house cast its shadow across the avenue on to the houses opposite, which should otherwise have received the descending sun. In revenge, they cast shadow back through her bow window: everything in the drawing-room seemed to exist in copper-mauve glass, or as though reflected into a tarnished mirror. At this hour, Gavin saw the pale walls, the silver lamp stems, the transparent frills of the cushions with a prophetic feeling of their impermanence. At her friend's words, Mrs Nicholson's hand, extended, paused for a moment over the cream jug. Turning her head she said: 'But I know what it is about; and I don't approve.'

With so little reference to the Admiral were these words spoken that he might not have been there. There, however, he was, standing drawn up above the low tea table, cup and saucer in hand. For a moment, not speaking, he weighed his cup with a frown that seemed to ponder its exact weight. He then said: 'Then, logically, you should not be sending cakes.'

'Lilian,' said Constance Concannon fondly, 'is never logical with regard to her friends.'

'Aren't I?' said Mrs Nicholson. — 'But cake, don't you think, makes everything so much nicer? You can't offer people nothing but disagreeable ideas.'

'You are too naughty, Lilian. All the League wants is that we should be alert and thoughtful. — Perhaps Gavin would like to come?'

Mrs Nicholson turned on Gavin a considering look from which complicity seemed to be quite absent; she appeared, if anything, to be trying to envisage him as alert and thoughtful. And the Admiral, at the same moment, fixed the candidate with a measuring eye. 'What may come,' he said, 'is bound, before it is done, to be his affair.' Gavin made no reply to the proposition — and it was found, a minute or two later, that the day fixed for the drawing-room meeting was the day fixed for his return home. School began again after that. 'Well, what a pity,' Mrs Concannon said.

The day approached. The evenings were wholly theirs, for Mrs Nicholson dined out less. Always, from after tea, when any guests had gone, he began to reign. The apartnesses and frustrations of the preceding hours, and, most of all, the occasional dissonances that those could but produce between him and her, sent him pitching towards the twilight in a fever that rose as the week went on. This fever, every time, was confounded by the sweet pointlessness of the actual hour when it came. The warmth that lingered in the exhausted daylight made it possible for Mrs Nicholson to extend herself on the *chaise longue* in the bow window. Seated on a stool at the foot of the *chaise longue,* leaning back against the frame of the window, Gavin could see, through the side pane of the glass projection in which they sat, the salvias smouldering in the theatre gardens. As it was towards these that her chair faced, in looking at them he was looking away from her. On the other hand, they were looking at the same thing. So they were on the evening that was his last. At the end of a minute or two of silence she exclaimed: 'No, I don't care, really, for scarlet flowers. — You do?'

'Except carnations?'

'I don't care for public flowers. And you look and look at them till I feel quite lonely.'

'I was only thinking, *they* will be here tomorrow.'

'Have you been happy this time, Gavin? I haven't sometimes thought you've been quite so happy. Has it been my fault?'

He turned, but only to finger the fringe of the Kashmir shawl that had been spread by Rockham across her feet. Not looking up, he said: 'I have not seen you so much.'

'There are times,' she said, 'when one seems to be at the other side of glass. One sees what is going on, but one cannot help it. It may be what one does not like, but one cannot feel.'

'Here, I always feel.'

'Always feel what?' she remotely and idly asked.

'I just mean, here, I feel. I don't feel, anywhere else.'

'And what is "here"?' she said, with tender mocking obtuseness. 'Southstone? What do you mean by "here"?'

'Near you.'

Mrs Nicholson's attitude, her repose, had not been come at carelessly. Apparently relaxed, but not supine, she was supported by six or seven cushions — behind her head, at the nape of her neck, between her shoulders, under her elbows and in the small of her back. The slipperiness of this architecture of comfort enjoined stillness — her repose depended on each cushion staying just where it was. Up to now, she had lain with her wrists crossed on her dress: a random turn of the wrist, or flexing of fingers, were the nearest things to gestures she permitted herself — and indeed, these had been enough. *Now,* her beginning to say, 'I wonder if they were right . . .' must, though it sounded nothing more than reflective, have been accompanied by an incautious movement, for a cushion fell with a plump to the ground. Gavin went round, recovered the cushion and stood beside her: they eyed one another with communicative amazement, as though a third person had spoken and they were uncertain if they had heard aright. She arched her waist up and Gavin replaced the cushion. He said: 'If who were right?'

'Rockham . . . The Admiral. She's always hinting, he's always saying, that I'm in some way thoughtless and wrong with you.'

'Oh, him.'

'I know,' she said. 'But you'll say goodbye to him nicely?'

He shrugged. 'I shan't see him again — this time.'

She hesitated. She was about to bring out something that, though slight, must be unacceptable. 'He *is* coming in,' she said, 'for a moment, just after dinner, to fetch the cakes.'

'Which cakes?'

'The cakes for tomorrow. I had arranged to send them round in the morning, but that would not do; no, that would not be soon enough. Everything is for the Admiral's meeting to make us ready, so everything must be ready in good time.'

When, at nine o'clock, the Admiral's ring was heard, Mrs Nicholson, indecisively, put down her coffee cup. A wood fire, lit while they were at dinner, was blazing languidly in the already warm air: it was necessary to sit at a distance from it. While the bell still rang, Gavin rose, as though he had forgotten something, and left the drawing-room. Passing the maid on her way to open the front door, he made a bolt upstairs. In his bedroom, Rockham was in possession: his trunk waited, open, bottom layer packed; her mending-basket was on the bureau; she was taking a final

look through his things — his departure was to be early tomorrow morning. 'Time
flies,' she said. 'You're no sooner come than you're gone.' She continued to count
handkerchiefs, to stack up shirts. 'I'd have thought,' she said, 'you'd have wanted to
bring your school cap.'

'Why? Anyway, it's a silly beastly old colour.'

'You're too old-fashioned,' she said sharply. 'It was high time somebody went to
school. — Now you *have* come up, just run down again, there's a good boy, and ask
Madam if there's anything for your mother. If it's books, they ought to go in here
among your boots.'

'The Admiral's there.'

'Well, my goodness, you know the Admiral.'

Gavin played for time, on the way down, by looking into the rooms on every floor.
Their still only partial familiarity, their fullness with objects that, in the half light
coming in from the landing, he could only half perceive and did not yet dare touch,
made him feel he was still only at the first chapter of the mystery of the house. He
wondered how long it would be before he saw them again. Fear of Rockham's
impatience, of her calling down to ask what he was up to, made him tread cautiously
on the thickly carpeted stairs; he gained the hall without having made a sound. Here
he smelled the fresh-baked cakes, waiting in a hamper on the hall table. The
drawing-room door stood ajar, on, for a minute, dead silence. The Admiral must
have gone, without the cakes.

But then the Admiral spoke. 'You must see, there is nothing more to be said. I am
only sorry I came. I did not expect you to be alone.'

'For once, that is not my fault,' replied Mrs Nicholson, unsteadily. 'I do not even
know where the child is.' In a voice that hardly seemed to be hers she cried out softly:
'Then this is to go on always? What more do you ask? What else am I to be or do?'

'There's nothing more you can do. And all you must be is, happy.'

'How easy,' Mrs Nicholson said.

'You have always said that that was easy, for you. For my own part, I never
considered happiness. There you misunderstood me, quite from the first.'

'Not quite. Was I wrong in thinking you were a man?'

'I'm a man, yes. But I'm not that sort.'

'That is too subtle for me,' said Mrs Nicholson.

'On the contrary, it is too simple for you. You ignore the greater part of my life.
You cannot be blamed, perhaps; you have only known me since I was cursed with
too much time on my hands. Your — your looks, charm and gaiety, my dear Lilian,
I'd have been a fool not to salute at their full worth. Beyond that, I'm not such a fool
as I may have seemed. Fool? — all things considered, I could not have been simply
that without being something a good deal viler.'

'I have been nice to Constance,' said Mrs Nicholson.

'Vile in my own eyes.'

'I know, that is all you think of.'

'I see, now, where you are in your element. You know as well as I do what your
element is; which is why there's nothing more to be said. Flirtation's always been off
my beat — so far off my beat, as a matter of fact, that I didn't know what it was when
I first saw it. There, no doubt, I was wrong. If you can't live without it, you cannot,
and that is that. If you have to be dangled after, you no doubt will be. But don't, my

dear girl, go for that to the wrong shop. It would have been enough, where I am concerned, to watch you making a ninnie of that unfortunate boy.'

'Who, poor little funny Gavin?' said Mrs Nicholson. 'Must I have nothing? — I have no little dog. You would not like it, even, if I had a real little dog. And you expect me to think that you do not care . . .'

The two voices, which intensity more than caution kept pitched low, ceased. Gavin pushed open the drawing-room door.

The room, as can happen, had elongated. Like figures at the end of a telescope the Admiral and Mrs Nicholson were to be seen standing before the fire. Of this, not a glint had room to appear between the figures of the antagonists. Mrs Nicholson, head bent as though to examine the setting of the diamond, was twisting round a ring on her raised left hand — a lace-edged handkerchief, like an abandoned piece of stage property, had been dropped and lay on the hearthrug near the hem of her skirts. She gave the impression of having not moved: if they had not, throughout, been speaking from this distance, the Admiral must have taken a step forward. But this, on his part, must have been, and must be, all — his head was averted from her, his shoulders were braced back, and behind his back he imprisoned one of his own wrists in a handcuff grip that shifted only to tighten. The heat from the fire must have made necessary, probably for the Admiral when he came, the opening of a window behind the curtains; for, as Gavin advanced into the drawing-room, a burst of applause entered from the theatre, and continued, drowning the music which had begun again.

Not a tremor recorded the moment when Mrs Nicholson knew Gavin was in the room. Obliquely and vaguely turning her bowed head she extended to him, in an unchanged look, what might have been no more than an invitation to listen, also, to the music. 'Why, Gavin,' she said at last, 'we were wondering where you were.'

Here he was. From outside the theatre, stink still travelled to him from the lorry whose engine was being run. Nothing had changed in the colourless afternoon. Without knowing, he had plucked a leaf of the ivy which now bred and fed upon her house. A soldier, passing behind him to join the others, must have noticed his immobility all the way down the avenue; for the soldier said, out of the side of his mouth: 'Annie doesn't live here any more.' Gavin Doddington, humiliated, affected to study the ivy leaf, whose veins were like arbitrary vulgar fate-lines. He thought he remembered hearing of metal ivy; he knew he had seen ivy carved round marble monuments to signify fidelity, regret, or the tomb-defying tenaciousness of memory — what you liked. Watched by the soldiers, he did not care to make the gesture involving the throwing of the leaf: instead, he shut his hand on it, as he turned from the house. Should he go straight to the station, straight back to London? Not while the impression remained so strong. On the other hand, it would be a long time before the bars opened.

Another walk round Southstone, this afternoon, was necessary: there must be a decrescendo. From his tour of annihilation, nothing out of the story was to be missed. He walked as though he were carrying a guide-book.

Once or twice he caught sight of the immune downs, on the ascent to whose contours war had halted the villas. The most open view was, still, from the gates of the cemetery, past which he and she had so often driven without a thought. Through those gates, the extended dulling white marble vista said to him, only, that the multiplicity of the new graves, in thirty years, was enough in itself to make the position of hers indifferent — she might, once more, be lying beside her husband. On the return through the town towards the lip of the plateau overhanging the sea, the voidness and the air of concluded meaning about the plan of Southstone seemed to confirm her theory: history, after this last galvanized movement forward, had come, as she expected, to a full stop. It had only not stopped where or as she foresaw. Crossing the Promenade obliquely, he made, between wire entanglements, for the railings; to become one more of the spaced-out people who leaned along them, willing to see a convoy or gazing with indifference towards liberated France. The path and steps up the cliff face had been destroyed; the handrail hung out rotting into the air.

Back in the shopping centre, he turned a quickening step, past the shuttered, boarded or concave windows, towards the corner florist's where Mrs Nicholson had insisted on the carnations. But this had received a direct hit: the entire corner was gone. When time takes our revenges out of our hands it is, usually, to execute them more slowly: her vindictiveness, more thorough than ours, might satisfy us, if, in the course of her slowness, we did not forget. In this case, however, she had worked in the less than a second of detonation. Gavin Doddington paused where there was no florist — was he not, none the less, entitled to draw a line through this?

Not until after some time back in the bar did it strike him — there had been one omission. He had not yet been to the Concannons'. He pushed his way out: it was about seven o'clock, twenty minutes or so before the black-out. They had lived in a crescent set just back from a less expensive reach of the Promenade. On his way, he passed houses and former hotels occupied by soldiers or A.T.S. who had not yet gone. These, from top to basement, were in a state of naked, hard, lemon-yellow illumination. Interposing dark hulks gave you the feeling of nothing more than their recent military occupation. The front doors of the Concannons' crescent opened, on the inland side, into a curved street, which, for some military reason now probably out of date, had been blocked at the near end: Gavin had to go round. Along the pavements under the front doorsteps there was so much wire that he was thrust out into the road — opposite only one house was there an inviting gap in the loops. Admiral Concannon, having died in the last war, could not have obtained this as a concession — all the same this *was,* as the number faintly confirmed, his house. Nobody now but Gavin recognized its identity or its importance. Here had dwelled, and here continued to dwell, the genius of the Southstone that now was. Twice over had there been realized the Admiral's alternative to love.

The Concannons' dining-room window, with its high triple sashes, was raised some distance above the street. Gavin, standing opposite it, looked in at an A.T.S. girl seated at a table. She faced the window, the dusk and him. From above her head, a naked electric light bulb, on a flex shortened by being knotted, glared on the stripped, whitish walls of the room and emphasized the fact that she was alone. In her khaki shirt, sleeves rolled up, she sat leaning her bare elbows on the bare table. Her face was abrupt with youth. She turned one wrist, glanced at the watch on it, then resumed her steady stare through the window, downwards at the dusk in which Gavin stood.

It was thus that, for the second time in his life, he saw straight up into the eyes that did not see him. The intervening years had given him words for trouble: a phrase, *l'horreur de mon néant',* darted across his mind.

At any minute, the girl would have to approach the window to do the black-out — for that, along this coast, was still strictly enforced. It was worth waiting. He lighted a cigarette: she looked at her watch again. When she did rise it was, first, to unhook from a peg beside the dining-room door not only her tunic but her cap. Her being dressed for the street, when she did reach up and, with a succession of movements he liked to watch, begin to twitch the black stuff across the window, made it his object *not* to be seen — just yet. Light staggered, a moment longer, on the desiccated pods of the wall-flowers that, seeded from the front garden, had sprung up between the cracks of the pavement, and on the continuous regular loops or hoops of barbed wire, through all of which, by a sufficiently long leap, one *could* have projected oneself head foremost, unhurt. At last she had stopped the last crack of light. She had now nothing to do but to come out.

Coming smartly down the Concannons' steps, she may just have seen the outline of the civilian waiting, smoking a cigarette. She swerved impassively, if at all. He said: 'A penny for your thoughts.' She might not have heard. He fell into step beside her. Next, appearing to hear what he had not said, she replied: 'No, I'm *not* going your way.'

'Too bad. But there's only one way out — can't get out, you know, at the other end. What have *I* got to do, then — stay here all night?'

'*I* don't know, I'm sure.' Unconcernedly humming, she did not even quicken her light but ringing tramp on the curved street. If he kept abreast with her, it was casually, and at an unpressing distance: this, and the widening sky that announced the open end of the crescent, must have been reassuring. He called across to her: 'That house you came out of, I used to know people who lived there. I was just looking round.'

She turned, for the first time — she could not help it. 'People lived there?' she said. 'Just fancy. I know I'd sooner live in a tomb. And that goes for all this place. Imagine anyone coming here on a holiday!'

'I'm on a holiday.'

'Goodness. What do you do with yourself?'

'Just look around.'

'Well, I wonder how long you stick it out. — Here's where we go different ways. Good night.'

'I've got nobody to talk to,' Gavin said, suddenly standing still in the dark. A leaf flittered past. She was woman enough to halt, to listen, because this had not been said to her. If her 'Oh yes, we girls have heard that before' was automatic, it was, still more, wavering. He cast away the end of one cigarette and started lighting another: the flame of the lighter, cupped inside his hands, jumped for a moment over his features. Her first thought was: yes, he's quite old — that went along with his desperate jauntiness. Civilian, yes: too young for the last war, too old for this. A gentleman — they were the clever ones. But he had, she perceived, forgotten about her thoughts — what she saw, in that moment before he snapped down the lighter, stayed on the darkness, puzzling her somewhere outside the compass of her own youth. She had seen the face of somebody dead who was still there — 'old' because of the presence, under an icy screen, of a whole stopped mechanism for feeling. Those features had been framed, long ago, for hope. The dints above the nostrils, the lines extending the eyes, the lips' grimacing grip on the cigarette — all completed the picture of someone wolfish. A preyer. But who had said, preyers are preyed upon?

His lower lip came out, thrusting the cigarette up at a debonair angle towards his eyes. 'Not a soul,' he added — this time with calculation, and to her.

'Anyway,' she said sharply. 'I've got a date. Anyway, what made you pick on this dead place? Why not pick on some place where you know someone?'

KAY BOYLE

Kay Boyle, who was born in 1903 in St. Paul, Minnesota, lived for many years in Europe. Her expatriate experience, which coincided with the rise of Nazism in Europe and the outbreak of the Second World War, deeply influenced her choice of subject and tone. Her collections of stories include *Wedding Day and Other Stories* (1930), *The White Horses of Vienna and Other Stories* (1936), *Thirty Stories* (1946), and *The Smoking Mountain: Stories of Germany During the Occupation* (1951). One critic has written that the best of Boyle's stories reveal "the human tragicomedy remaining after the captains and kings have departed." In "The White Horses of Vienna" they are just beginning to arrive, and the mood is tinged with tragedy.

The White Horses of Vienna

I

The doctor often climbed the mountain at night, climbed up behind his own house hour after hour in the dark, and came back to bed long after his two children were asleep. At the end of June he sprained his knee coming down the mountain late. He wrenched it out of joint making his way down with the other men through the pines. They helped him into the house where his wife was waiting and writing letters by the stove, and the agony that he would not mention was marked upon his face.

His wife bound his leg with fresh, wet cloths all through the night, but in the morning the knee was hot with fever. It might be weeks before he could go about again, and there was nothing to do but write to the hospital in Vienna for a student-doctor to come out and take over his patients for a time.

"I'll lie still for a fortnight or so," said the doctor, and he asked his wife to bring him the bits of green wood that he liked to whittle, and his glazed papers and his fancy tag ends of stuff. He was going to busy himself making new personages for his theater, for he could not stay idle for half an hour. The June sun was strong at that height, and the doctor sat on the *Liegestuhl* with his knee bared to the warm light, working like a well man and looking up now and again to the end of the valley where the mountains stood with the snow shining hard and diamond-bright on their brows.

"You'll never sit still long enough for it to do you any good," said the doctor's wife sharply. She was quite a young, beautiful woman, in spite of her two growing sons, and in spite of her husband's ageless, weathered flesh. She was burned from the wind and the snow in winter and burned from the sun at other times of the year; she had straight, long, sunburned limbs, and her dark hair was cut short and pushed behind her ears. She had her nurse's degree from Vienna and she helped her husband in whatever there was to do: the broken bones, the deaths, the births. He even did a bit of dentistry too, when there was need, and she stood by in her nurse's blouse and mixed the cement and porcelain fillings and kept the instruments clean. Or at night, if they needed her, she climbed the mountain with him and the other men, carrying as well a knapsack of candles over her shoulders, climbing through the twig-broken and mossy silence in the dark.

The doctor had built their house himself with the trees cut down from their forest. The town lay in the high valley, and the doctor had built their house above it on the sloping mountainside. There was no real road leading to it: one had to get to him on foot or else on a horse. It was as if the doctor had chosen this place to build so that the village might leave him to himself unless the need were very great. He had come back to his own country after the years as a prisoner of war in Siberia, and after the years of studying in other countries, and the years of giving away as a gift his tenderness and knowledge as he went from one wild place to another. He had studied in cities, but he could not live for long in them. He had come back and bought a piece of land in the Tirol with a pine forest sloping down it, and he built his house there, working throughout the summer months late into the evening with only his two sons and his wife to help him lift the squared, varnished beams into place.

Inside the log walls the doctor made a pure white plaster wall and put his dark-stained bookshelves against it and hung on it his own paintings of Dalmatia and his drawings of the Siberian country. Everything was as neat and clean as wax, for the doctor was a savagely clean man. He had a coarse, reddish, well-scrubbed skin, and the gold hairs sprang out of his scalp, wavy and coarse, and out of his forearms and his muscular, heavy thighs. They would have sprung too around his mouth and along his jaw had he not shaved himself clean every morning. His face was as strong as rock, but it had seen so much of suffering that it had the look of being scarred, it seemed to be split in two, with one side of it given to resolve and the other to compassion.

All of the places that he had been before, Paris and Moscow and Munich and Constantinople, had never left an evil mark. None of the grand places or people had ever done to him what they can do. But merely because of his own strong, humble pride in himself his shirt was always a white one, and of fresh, clean linen no matter what sort of work he was doing. In the summer he wore the short, leather trousers of the country, for he had peasants behind him and he liked to remember that it was so. But the woven stockings that ended just above his calves were perfectly white and the nails of his broad, coarse hands were white. They were spotless, like the nails of a woman's hand.

The day the student doctor arrived from Vienna and walked up from the village, the doctor and his wife were both out in the sun before the house. She had been hanging the children's shirts up on the line to dry, and she came around to the timber piazza, drying her hands in her dress. The doctor was hopping around on one leg like a great, golden, wounded bird; he was hopping from one place to another, holding his wrenched leg off the ground, and seeking the bits of paper and stuff and wood and wire that he needed to make his dolls.

"Let me get the things for you!" his wife cried out. "Why must you do everything for yourself? Why can't you let anyone help you?"

The doctor hopped across to the timber table in the sun and picked up the clown's cap he was making and fitted it on the head of the doll he held in his hand. When he turned around he saw the student-doctor coming up the path. He stood still for a moment, with his leg still lifted up behind him, and then his face cleared of whatever was in it, and he nodded.

"God greet you," he said quietly, and the young man stopped too where he was on the path and looked up at them. He was smiling in his long, dark, alien face, but his city shoes were foul with the soft mud of the mountainside after rain, and the sweat was standing out on his brow because he was not accustomed to the climb.

"Good day," he said, as city people said it. The doctor and his wife stood looking down at him, and a little wave of pallor ran under the woman's skin.

The doctor had caught a very young fox in the spring, and it had now grown to live in the house with them without shyness or fear. The sound of their voices and the new human scent on the air brought it forth from the indoor dark of the house. It came out without haste, like a small, gentle dog, with its soft, gray, gently lifted brush and its eyes blinking slowly at the sun. It went daintily down the path toward the stranger, holding its brush just out of the mud of the path, with the black bead of its nose smelling the new smell of this other man who had come.

The young doctor from Vienna leaned over to stroke it, and while his head was down the doctor's wife turned to her husband. She had seen the black, smooth hair on the man's head, and the arch of his nose, and the quality of his skin. She could scarcely believe what she had seen and she must look into her husband's face for confirmation of the truth. But her husband was still looking down the little space toward the stranger. The fox had raised the sharp point of his muzzle and licked the young doctor's hand.

"Is this a dog or a cat?" the young man called up, smiling.

"It's a fox," said the doctor. The young man came up with his hat in his hand and said that his name was Heine and shook hands, and the doctor gave no sign.

"You live quite a way from the village," said the student-doctor, looking back the way he had come.

"You can see the snow mountains from here," said the doctor, and he showed the young man the sight of them at the far end of the valley. "You have to climb this way before you can see them," he said. "They're closed off from the valley."

This was the explanation of why they lived there, and the young man from the city stood looking a moment in silence at the far, gleaming crusts of the everlasting snows. He was still thinking of what he might say in answer when the doctor asked his wife to show Dr. Heine the room that would be his. Then the doctor sat down in the sun again and went on with the work he had been doing.

"What are we going to do?" said his wife's voice in a whisper behind him in a moment.

"What do you mean? About what?" said the doctor, speaking aloud. His crisp-haired head did not lift from his work, and the lines of patience and love were scarred deep in his cheeks as he whittled.

"About *him*," said the doctor's wife in hushed impatience.

"Send one of the boys down for his bag at the station," said the doctor. "Give him a drink of *Apfelsaft* if he's thirsty."

"But don't you see, don't you see what he is?" asked his wife's wild whisper.

"He's Viennese," said the doctor, working.

"Yes, and he's Jewish," said his wife. "They must be mad to have sent him. They know how everyone feels."

"Perhaps they did it intentionally," said the doctor, working carefully with what he had in his hands. "But it wasn't a good thing for the young man's sake. It's harder on him than us. If he works well, I have no reason to send him back. We've waited three days for him. There are people sick in the village."

"Ah," said his wife in anger behind, "we shall have to sit down at table with him!"

"They recommend him highly," said the doctor gently, "and he seems a very amiable young man."

"Ah," said his wife's disgusted whisper, "they all look amiable! Every one of them does!"

Almost at once there was a tooth to be pulled, and the young wife was there in her white frock with the instruments ready for the new young man. She stood very close, casting sharp looks at Dr. Heine, watching his slender, delicate hands at work, seeing the dark, silky hairs that grew on the backs of them and the black hair brushed smooth on his head. So much had she heard about Jews that the joints of his tall, elegant frame seemed oiled with some special, suave lubricant that was evil, as a thing come out of the Orient, to their clean, Nordic hearts. He had a pale skin, unused to the weather of mountain places, and his skull was lighted with bright, quick, ambitious eyes. But at lunch he had talked simply with them, although they were country people and ignorant as peasants for all he knew. He listened to everything the doctor had told him about the way he liked things done; in spite of his modern medical school and his Viennese hospitals, taking it all in with interest and respect.

"The doctor," said the young wife now, "always stands behind the patient to get at teeth like that."

She spoke in an undertone to Dr. Heine so that the peasant sitting there in the dentist chair with the cocaine slowly paralyzing his jaws might not overhear.

"Oh, yes. Thank you so much," said Dr. Heine with a smile, and he stepped behind the patient. "It's quite true. One can get a better grip that way."

But as he passed the doctor's wife, the tail of his white coat brushed through the flame of the little sterilizing lamp on the table. Nobody noticed that Dr. Heine had caught fire until the tooth was out and the smell of burning cloth filled the clean, white room. They looked about for what might be smoldering in the place, and in another moment the doctor's wife saw that Dr. Heine was burning very brightly: the back of the white jacket was eaten nearly out and the coat within it was flaming. He had even begun to feel the heat on his shirt when the doctor's wife picked up the strip of rug from the floor and flung it about him. She held it tightly around him with her bare, strong arms, and the young man looked back over his shoulder at her, and he was laughing.

"Now I shall lose my job," he said. "The doctor will never stand for me setting fire to myself the first day like this!"

"It's my fault," said the doctor's wife, holding him fast still in her arms. "I should have had the lamp out of the way."

She began to beat his back softly with the palm of her hand, and when she carried the rug to the window, Dr. Heine went to the mirror and looked over his shoulder at the sight of his clothes all burned away.

"My new coat!" he said, and he was laughing. But it must have been very hard for him to see the nice, gray flannel coat that he had bought to look presentable for his first place scalloped black to his shoulders where the fire had eaten its covert way.

"I should think I could put a piece in," said the doctor's wife, touching the good cloth that was left. And then she bit her lip suddenly and stood back, as if she had remembered the evil thing that stood between them.

II

When they sat down to supper, the little fox settled himself on the doctor's good foot, for the wool of his stocking was a soft bed where the fox could dream a little while. They had soup and the thick, rosy-meated leg of a pig and salt potatoes, and the children listened to their father and Dr. Heine speaking of music, and painting, and books together. The doctor's wife was cutting the meat and putting it on their plates. It was at the end of the meal that the young doctor began talking of the royal, white horses in Vienna, still royal, he said, without any royalty left to bow their heads to, still shouldering into the arena with spirits a man would give his soul for, bending their knees in homage to the empty, canopied loge where royalty no longer sat. They came in, said Dr. Heine in his rich, eager voice, and danced their statuesque dances, their *pas de deux,* their croupade, their capriole. They were very impatient of the walls around them and the bits in their soft mouths, and very vain of the things they had been taught to do. Whenever the applause broke out around them, said Dr. Heine, their nostrils opened wide as if a wind were blowing. They were actresses, with the deep, snowy breasts of prima donnas, these perfect stallions who knew to a breath the beauty of even their mockery of fright.

"There was a maharaja," said the young doctor, and the children and their father listened, and the young wife sat giving quick, unwilling glances at this man who could have no blood or knowledge of the land behind him; for what was he but a wanderer whose people had wandered from country to country and whose sons must wander, having no land to return to in the end? "There was a maharaja just last year," said Dr. Heine, "who went to the performance and fell in love with one of the horses. He saw it dancing and he wanted to buy it and take it back to India with him. No one else had ever taken a Lippizaner back to his country, and he wanted this special one, the best of them all, whose dance was like an angel flying. So the state agreed that he could buy the horse, but for a tremendous amount of money. They needed the money badly enough, and the maharaja was a very rich man." Oh, yes, thought the young mother bitterly, you would speak about money, you would come here and climb our mountain and poison my sons with the poison of money and greed! "But no matter how high the price was," said Dr. Heine, smiling because all their eyes were on him, "the maharaja agreed to pay it, provided that the man who rode the horse so beautifully came along as well. Yes, the state would allow that too, but the maharaja would have to pay an enormous salary to the rider. He would take him into his employ as the stallion's keeper, and he would have to pay him a salary as big as our own President is paid!" said Dr. Heine, and he ended this with a burst of laughter.

"And what then, what then?" said one of the boys as the student-doctor paused to laugh. The whole family was listening, but the mother was filled with outrage. These things are foreign to us, she was thinking. They belong to more sophisticated people, we do not need them here. The Spanish Riding School, the gentlemen of Vienna, they were as alien as places in another country, and the things they cherished could never be the same.

"So it was arranged that the man who rode the horse so well should go along too," said Dr. Heine. "It was finally arranged for a great deal of money," he said, and the mother gave him a look of fury. "But they had not counted on one thing. They had forgotten all about the little groom who had always cared for this special horse and who loved him better than anything else in the world. Ever since the horse had come from the stud farm in Styria, the little groom had cared for him, and he believed that they would always be together, he believed that he would go wherever the horse went, just as he had always gone to Salzburg with the horse in the summer, and always come back to Vienna with it in the wintertime again."

"And so what, what happened?" asked the other boy.

"Well," said the student-doctor, "the morning before the horse was to leave with the maharaja and the rider, they found that the horse had a deep cut on his leg, just above the hoof in front. Nobody could explain how it happened, but the horse was so wounded that he could not travel then and the maharaja said that he could go on without him and that the trainer should bring the horse over in a few weeks when the cut had healed. They did not tell the maharaja that it might be that the horse could never dance so beautifully again. They had the money and they weren't going to give it back so easily," said Dr. Heine, and to the mother it seemed that their shrewdness pleased his soul. "But when the cut had healed," he went on, "and the horse seemed well enough to be sent by the next boat, the trainer found the horse had a cut on the other hoof, exactly where the other wound had been. So the journey was postponed again, and again the state said nothing to the maharaja about the horse being so impaired that it was likely he could never again fly like an angel. But in a few days the horse's blood was so poisoned from the wound that they had to destroy him."

They all waited, breathless with pain a moment, and then the doctor's wife said bitterly:

"Even the money couldn't save him, could it?"

"No," said Dr. Heine, a little perplexed by her words. "Of course, it couldn't. And they never knew how the cuts had come there until the little groom committed suicide the same day the horse was destroyed. And then they knew that he had done it himself because he couldn't bear the horse to be taken away."

They were all sitting quietly there at the table, with the dishes and remnants of food still before them, when someone knocked at the outside door. One of the boys went out to open it and he came back with the Heimwehr men following after him, the smooth, little black-and-white cockades lying forward in their caps.

"God greet you," said the doctor quietly when he saw them.

"God greet you," said the Heimwehr men.

"There's a swastika fire burning on the mountain behind you," said the leader of the soldiers. They were not men of the village, but men brought from other parts of the country and billeted there as strangers to subdue the native people. "Show us the fastest way up there so we can see that it's put out."

"I'm afraid I can't do that," said the doctor, smiling. "You see, I have a bad leg."

"You can point out to us which way the path goes!" said the leader sharply.

"He can't move," said the doctor's wife, standing straight by the chair. "You have reports on everything. You must know very well that he is injured and has had a doctor come from Vienna to look after the sick until he can get around again."

"Yes," said the leader, "and we know very well that he wouldn't have been injured if he stayed home instead of climbing mountains himself at night!"

"Look here," said the student-doctor, speaking nervously, and his face gone thin and white. "He can't move a step, you know."

"He'll have to move more than a step if they want him at the *Rathaus* again!" said the Heimwehr leader. "There's never any peace as long as he's not locked up!"

The young doctor said nothing after they had gone, but he sat quiet by the window, watching the fires burning on the mountains in the dark. They were blooming now on all the black, invisible crests, marvelously living flowers of fire springing out of the arid darkness, seemingly higher than any other things could grow. He felt himself sitting defenseless there by the window, surrounded by these strong, long-burning fires of disaster. They were all about him, inexplicable signals given from one mountain to another in some secret gathering of power that cast him and his people out, forever out upon the waters of despair.

The doctor's wife and the children had cleared the table, and the doctor was finishing his grasshopper underneath the light. He was busy wiring its wings to its body, and fastening the long, quivering antennae in. The grasshopper was colored a deep, living green, and under him lay strong, green-glazed haunches for springing with his wires across the puppet stage. He was a monstrous animal in the doctor's hands, with his great, glassy, gold-veined wings lying smooth along his back.

"The whole country is ruined by the situation," said the student-doctor, suddenly angry. "Everything is politics now. One can't meet people, have friends on any other basis. It's impossible to have casual conversations or abstract discussions any more. Who the devil lights these fires?"

"Some people light them because of their belief," said the doctor, working quietly, "and others travel around from place to place and make a living lighting them."

"Politics, politics," said the student-doctor, "and one party as bad as another. You're much wiser to make your puppets, *Herr Doktor*. It takes one's mind off things, just as playing cards does. In Vienna we play cards, always play cards, no matter what is happening."

"There was a time for cards," said the doctor, working quietly with the grasshopper's wings. "I used to play cards in Siberia, waiting to be free. We were always waiting then for things to finish with and be over," he said. "There was nothing to do, so we did that. But now there is something else to do."

He said no more, and in a little while the student-doctor went upstairs to bed. He could hear the doctor's wife and the children still washing the dishes and tidying up, their voices clearly heard through the fresh planks of his new-made floor.

Usually in the evening the doctor played the marionette theater for his wife and children, and for whatever friends wanted to come up the mountainside and see. He had made the theater himself, and now he had the new personages he had fashioned while nursing his twisted knee, and a week or two after the student-doctor had come he told them at supper that he would give them a show that night.

"The *Bürgermeister* is coming up with his wife and their young sons," he said, "and the *Apotheker* and his nephews sent word that they'd drop in as well."

He moved the little fox from where it was sleeping on the wool sock of his foot, and he hopped on his one good leg across the room. Dr. Heine helped him carry the theater to the corner and set it up where the curtains hung, and the doctor hopped, heavy, and clean, and birdlike, from side to side and behind and before to get the look of light and see how the curtains drew and fell.

By eight o'clock they were all of them there and seated in the darkened room, the doctor's and the *Bürgermeister*'s boys waiting breathless for the curtain to rise, and the *Apotheker*'s nephews smoking in the dark.

"I think it's marvelous, your husband giving plays like this, keeping the artistic thing uppermost even with times as they are," said Dr. Heine quietly to the doctor's wife. "One gets so tired of the same question everywhere, anywhere one happens to be," he said, and she gave him a long, strange bitter glance from the corners of her eyes.

"Yes," she said. "Yes. I suppose you do think a great deal of art."

"Yes, of course," said Dr. Heine, quite guilelessly. "Art and science, of course."

"Yes," said the doctor's wife, saying the words slowly and bitterly. "Yes. Art and science. What about people being hungry, what about this generation of young men who have never had work in their lives because the factories have never opened since the war? Where do they come in?"

"Yes, that too — " Dr. Heine began, and the whispered dialogue ended.

The curtain had been jerked aside and a wonderful expectancy lay on the air.

The scene before them was quite a simple one: the monstrously handsome grasshopper was sitting in a field, presumably a field, for there were white linen petaled, yellow-hearted daisies all around him. He was a great, gleaming beauty, and the people watching cried out with pleasure. The doctor's sons could scarcely wait until the flurry of delight had died and the talking had begun.

There were only two characters in the play, and they were the grasshopper and the clown. The clown came out on the stage and joined him after the grasshopper had done his elegant dance. The dance in itself was a masterpiece of grace and wit, with the music of Mozart playing on the gramophone behind. The children cried with laughter, and Dr. Heine shouted aloud, and the *Bürgermeister* shook with silent laughter. It lifted its legs so delicately, and sprang with such precision this way and that, through the ragged-petaled daisies of the field, that it seemed to have a life of its own in its limbs, separate from and more sensitive than that given it by any human hand. Even the little fox sat watching in fascination, his bright, unwild eyes shining like point of fire in the dark.

"*Wunderbar, wunderschön!*" Dr. Heine called out. "It's really marvelous! He's as graceful as the white horses at Vienna, *Herr Doktor!* That step with the forelegs floating! It's extraordinary how you got it without ever seeing it done!"

And then the little clown came out on the stage. He came through the daisies of the field, a small, dwarfed clown with a sword ten times too big for him girded around his waist and tripping him at every step as he came. He was carrying a bunch of paper flowers and smiling, and there was something very *friseur* about him. He had no smell of the really open country or the roots of things, while the grasshopper was a fine, green-armored animal, strong and perfectly equipped for the life he had to lead.

The clown had a round, human face and he spoke in a faltering human voice, and the grasshopper was the superthing, speaking in the doctor's ringing voice. Just the sound of the doctor's compassionate voice released in all its power was enough to make the guilty and the weak shake in their seats as if it were some accusation made them. It was a voice as ready for honest anger as it was for gentleness.

"Why do you carry artificial flowers?" the grasshopper asked, and the clown twisted and turned on his feet, so ridiculous in his stupidity that the children and all the others watching laughed aloud in the timber room. "Why do you carry artificial flowers?" the grasshopper persisted. "Don't you see that the world is full of real ones?"

"Oh, it's better I carry artificial ones," said the clown in the humorous accent of the country boor, and he tripped on his sword as he said it. "I'm on my way to my own funeral, *nicht?* I want the flowers to keep fresh until I get there."

Everyone laughed very loud at this, but after a little, as the conversation continued between the grasshopper and the clown, Dr. Heine found he was not laughing as loudly as before. It was now evident that the grasshopper, for no conceivable reason, was always addressed as "The Leader," and the humorous little clown was called "Chancellor" by the grasshopper for no reason that he could see. The Chancellor was quite the fool of the piece. The only thing he had to support him was a very ludicrous faith in the power of the Church. The Church was a wonderful thing, the clown kept saying, twisting his poor bouquet.

"The cities are full of churches," said the Leader, "but the country is full of God."

The Leader spoke with something entirely different in his voice: he had a wild and stirring power that sent the cold of wonder up and down one's spine. And whatever the argument was, the Chancellor always got the worst of it. The children cried aloud with laughter, for the Chancellor was so absurd, so eternally on his half-witted way to lay his bunch of paper flowers on his own or somebody else's grave, and the Leader was ready to waltz away at any moment with the power of stallion life that was leaping in his limbs.

"I believe in the independence of the individual," the poor humble smiling little clown said, and then he tripped over his sword and fell flat among the daisies. The Leader picked him up with his fragile, lovely forelegs, and set him against the painting of the sky.

"Ow, *mein Gott,* the clouds are giving way!" cried the clown, and the grasshopper replied gently:

"But you are relying upon the heavens to support you. Are you afraid they are not strong enough?"

III

It was one evening in July, and the rain had just drawn off over the mountains. There was still the smell of it on the air, but the moon was shining strongly out. The student-doctor walked out before the house and watched the light bathing the dark valley, rising over the fertile slopes and the pine forests, running clear as milk above the timber line across the bare, bleached rock. The higher one went, the more terrible it became, he thought, and his heart shuddered within him. There were the rocks, seemingly as high as substance could go, but beyond that, even higher, hidden from the sight of the village people but clearly seen from the doctor's house, was the bend of the glacier and beside it were the peaks of everlasting snow. He was lost in this wilderness of cold, lost in a warm month, and the thought turned his blood to ice. He wanted to be indoors, with the warmth of his own people, and the intellect speaking. He had had enough of the bare, northern speech of these others who moved higher and higher as the land moved.

It was then that he saw the little lights moving up from the valley, coming like little beacons of hope carried to him. People were moving up out of the moon-bathed valley, like a little search party come to seek for him in an alien land. He stood watching the slow, flickering movement of their advance, the lights they carried seen far below, a small necklace of men coming to him; and then the utter white-darkness spread unbroken as they entered the wooded places and their lamps were extinguished by the trees.

"Come to me," he was saying within himself, "come to me. I am a young man alone on a mountain. I am a young man alone, as my race is alone, lost here amongst them all."

The doctor and his wife were sitting at work by the table when Dr. Heine came quickly into the room and said:

"There are some men coming up. They're almost here now. They look to me like the Heimwehr come again."

The doctor's wife stood up and touched the side of the timber wall as if something in it would give her fortitude. Then she went to the door and opened it, and in a moment the Heimwehr men came in.

"God greet you," the doctor said as they gathered around the table.

"God greet you," said the Heimwehr leader. "You're wanted at the *Rathaus,*" he said.

"My leg isn't good enough to walk on yet," said the doctor quietly. "How will you get me down?"

"This time we brought a stretcher along," said the Heimwehr leader. "We have it outside the door."

The doctor's wife went off to fetch his white wool jacket and to wake the two boys in their beds. Dr. Heine heard her saying:

"They're taking Father to prison again. Now you must come and kiss him. Neither of you is going to cry."

The men brought the stretcher just within the doorway and the doctor hopped over to it and lay down. He looked very comfortable there under the wool rug that his wife laid over him.

"Look here," said Dr. Heine, "why do you have to come after a person at night like this? Do you think the *Herr Doktor* would try to run away from you? What are you up to? What's it all about?"

The Heimwehr leader looked him full in the eyes.

"They got Dollfuss this afternoon," he said. "They shot him in Vienna. We're rounding them all up tonight. Nobody knows what will happen tomorrow."

"Ah, politics, politics again!" cried Dr. Heine, and he was wringing his hands like a woman about to cry. Suddenly he ran out the door after the stretcher and the men who were bearing the doctor away. He felt for the doctor's hand under the cover and he pressed it in his, and the doctor's hand closed over his in comfort. "What can I do? What can I do to help?" he said, and he was thinking of the pure-white horses of Vienna and of their waltz, like the grasshopper's dance across the stage. The doctor was smiling, his cheeks scarred with the marks of laughter in the light from the hurricane lamps that the men were carrying down.

"You can throw me peaches and chocolate from the street," said the doctor. "My wife will show you where we are. She's not a good shot. Her hand shakes too much when she tries. I missed all the oranges she threw me after the February slaughter."

"What do you like best?" Dr. Heine called down after him, and his own voice sounded small and senseless in the enormous night.

"Peaches," the doctor's voice called back from the stretcher. "We get so thirsty . . ."

"I'll remember!" said Dr. Heine, his voice calling after the descending lights. He was thinking in anguish of the snow-white horses, the Lippizaners, the relics of pride, the still unbroken vestiges of beauty bending their knees to the empty loge of royalty where there was no royalty any more.

RAY BRADBURY

 Ray Bradbury, born in 1920 in Waukegan, Illinois, has often been classified as a writer of science fiction, but the case might better be put this way: Bradbury incorporates the trappings of science fiction and the fantastic into his stories, which are, essentially, moral tales intent upon reminding readers that they must always measure the benefits of scientific development against potential diminution of their own humanity. As one critic wrote: "Bradbury's stories are not an escape from reality; they are windows looking upon enduring reality." Among his best-known works are *The Martian Chronicles* (1950), *Farenheit 451* (1954), *Something Wicked This Way Comes* (1962), and the short-story collections *The Golden Apples of the Sun* (1953), *Dandelion Wine* (1957), *I Sing the Body Electric!* (1969), and *Stories of Ray Bradbury* (1980). "I Sing the Body Electric!" captures Bradbury's vision with wonderfully humorous embellishments.

I Sing the Body Electric!

Grandma!

   I remember her birth.

Wait, you say, *no* man remembers his own grandma's birth.

But, yes, *we* remember the day that she was born.

For we, her grandchildren, slapped her to life. Timothy, Agatha, and I, Tom, raised up our hands and brought them down in a huge crack! We shook together the bits and pieces, parts and samples, textures and tastes, humors and distillations that would move her compass needle north to cool us, south to warm and comfort us, east and west to travel round the endless world, glide her eyes to know us, mouth to sing us asleep by night, hands to touch us awake at dawn.

Grandma, O dear and wondrous electric dream. . . .

When storm lightnings rove the sky making circuitries amidst the clouds, her name flashes on my inner lid. Sometimes still I hear her ticking, humming above our beds in the gentle dark. She passes like a clock-ghost in the long halls of memory, like a hive of intellectual bees swarming after the Spirit of Summers Lost. Sometimes still I feel the smile I learned from her, printed on my cheek at three in the deep morn. . . .

All right, all right! you cry. What was it like the day your damned and wondrous-dreadful-loving Grandma was born?

It was the week the world ended. . . .

Our mother was dead.

One late afternoon a black car left Father and the three of us stranded on our own front drive staring at the grass, thinking:

That's not our grass. There are the croquet mallets, balls, hoops, yes, just as they fell and lay three days ago when Dad stumbled out on the lawn, weeping with the news. There are the roller skates that belonged to a boy, me, who will never be that young again. And yes, there the tire-swing on the old oak, but Agatha afraid to swing. It would surely break. It would fall.

And the house? Oh, God . . .

We peered through the front door, afraid of the echoes we might find confused in the halls; the sort of clamor that happens when all the furniture is taken out and there is nothing to soften the river of talk that flows in any house at all hours. And now the soft, the warm, the main piece of lovely furniture was gone forever.

The door drifted wide.

Silence came out. Somewhere a cellar door stood wide and a raw wind blew damp earth from under the house.

But, I thought, we don't *have* a cellar!

"Well," said Father.

We did not move.

Aunt Clara drove up the path in her big canary-colored limousine.

We jumped through the door. We ran to our rooms.

We heard them shout and then speak and then shout and then speak: Let the children live with me! Aunt Clara said. They'd rather kill themselves! Father said.

A door slammed. Aunt Clara was gone.

We almost danced. Then we remembered what had happened and went downstairs.

Father sat alone talking to himself or to a remnant ghost of Mother left from the days before her illness, and jarred loose now by the slamming of the door. He murmured to his hands, his empty palms:

"The children need someone. I love them but, let's face it, I must work to feed us all. You love them, Ann, but you're gone. And Clara? Impossible. She loves but smothers. And as for maids, nurses — ?"

Here Father sighed and we sighed with him, remembering.

The luck we had had with maids or live-in teachers or sitters was beyond intolerable. Hardly a one who wasn't a crosscut saw grabbing against the grain. Handaxes and hurricanes best described them. Or, conversely, they were all fallen trifle, damp soufflé. We children were unseen furniture to be sat upon or dusted or sent for reupholstering come spring and fall, with a yearly cleansing at the beach.

"What we need," said Father, "is a . . ."

We all leaned to his whisper.

". . . grandmother."

"But," said Timothy, with the logic of nine years, "all our grandmothers are dead."

"Yes in one way, no in another."

What a fine mysterious thing for Dad to say.

"Here," he said at last.

He handed us a multifold, multicolored pamphlet. We had seen it in his hands, off and on, for many weeks, and very often during the last few days. Now, with one blink of our eyes, as we passed the paper from hand to hand, we knew why Aunt Clara, insulted, outraged, had stormed from the house.

Timothy was the first to read aloud from what he saw on the first page:

" 'I Sing the Body Electric!' "

He glanced up at Father, squinting. "What the heck does that mean?"

"Read on."

Agatha and I glanced guiltily about the room, afraid Mother might suddenly come in to find us with this blasphemy, but then nodded to Timothy, who read:

" 'Fanto — ' "

"Fantoccini," Father prompted.

" 'Fantoccini Limited. *We Shadow Forth* . . . the answer to all your most grievous problems. One Model Only, upon which a thousand times a thousand variations can be added, subtracted, subdivided, indivisible, with Liberty and Justice for all.' "

"Where does it say *that?*" we all cried.

"It doesn't." Timothy smiled for the first time in days. "I just had to put that in. Wait." He read on: " 'For you who have worried over inattentive sitters, nurses who cannot be trusted with marked liquor bottles, and well-meaning Uncles and Aunts — ' "

"Well-meaning, *but!*" said Agatha, and I gave an echo.

" ' — we have perfected the first humanoid-genre mini-circuited, rechargeable AC-DC Mark Five Electrical Grandmother . . .' "

"Grandmother!?"

The paper slipped away to the floor. "Dad . . . ?"

"Don't look at me that way," said Father. "I'm half mad with grief, and half mad thinking of tomorrow and the day after that. Someone pick up the paper. Finish it."

"I will," I said, and did:

" 'The Toy that is more than a Toy, the Fantoccini Electrical Grandmother is built with loving precision to give the incredible precision of love to your children. The child at ease with the realities of the world and the even greater realities of the imagination, is her aim.

" 'She is computerized to tutor in twelve languages simultaneously, capable of switching tongues in a thousandth of a second without pause, and has a complete knowledge of the religious, artistic, and sociopolitical histories of the world seeded in her master hive — ' "

"How great!" said Timothy. "It makes it sound as if we were to keep bees! *Educated* bees!"

"Shut up!" said Agatha.

" 'Above all,' " I read, " 'this human being, for human she seems, this embodiment in electro-intelligent facsimile of the humanities, will listen, know, tell, react and love your children insofar as such great Objects, such fantastic Toys, can be said to Love, or can be imagined to Care. This Miraculous Companion, excited to the challenge of large world and small, Inner Sea or Outer Universe, will transmit by touch and tell, said Miracles to your Needy.' "

"Our Needy," murmured Agatha.

Why, we all thought, sadly, that's us, oh, yes, that's *us*.

I finished:

" 'We do not sell our Creation to able-bodied families where parents are available to raise, effect, shape, change, love their own children. Nothing can replace the parent in the home. However there are families where death or ill health or disablement undermines the welfare of the children. Orphanages seem not the answer. Nurses tend to be selfish, neglectful, or suffering from dire nervous afflictions.

" 'With the utmost humility then, and recognizing the need to rebuild, rethink, and regrow our conceptualizations from month to month, year to year, we offer the nearest thing to the Ideal Teacher-Friend-Companion-Blood Relation. A trial period can be arranged for — ' "

"Stop," said Father. "Don't go on. Even *I* can't stand it."

"Why?" said Timothy. "I was just getting interested."

I folded the pamphlet up. "Do they *really* have these things?"

"Let's not talk any more about it," said Father, his hand over his eyes. "It was a mad thought — "

"Not so mad," I said, glancing at Tim. "I mean, heck, even if they tried, whatever they built, couldn't be worse than Aunt Clara, huh?"

And then we all roared. We hadn't laughed in months. And now my simple words made everyone hoot and howl and explode. I opened my mouth and yelled happily, too.

When we stopped laughing, we looked at the pamphlet and I said, "Well?"

"I — " Agatha scowled, not ready.

"We do need something, bad, right now," said Timothy.

"I have an open mind," I said, in my best pontifical style.

"There's only one thing," said Agatha. "We can try it. Sure."

"But — tell me this — when do we cut out all this talk and when does our *real* mother come home to stay?"

There was a single gasp from the family as if, with one shot, she had struck us all in the heart.

I don't think any of us stopped crying the rest of that night.

It was a clear bright day. The helicopter tossed us lightly up and over and down through the skyscrapers and let us out, almost for a trot and caper, on top of the building where the large letters could be read from the sky:

FANTOCCINI.

"What are 'Fantoccini'?" said Agatha.

"It's an Italian word for shadow puppets, I think, or dream people," said Father.

"But 'shadow forth,' what does that mean?"

"We try to guess your dream," I said.

"Bravo," said Father. "A-plus."

I beamed.

The helicopter flapped a lot of loud shadows over us and went away.

We sank down in an elevator as our stomachs sank up. We stepped out onto a moving carpet that streamed away on a blue river of wool toward a desk over which various signs hung:

THE CLOCK SHOP
FANTOCCINI OUR SPECIALTY
RABBITS ON WALLS, NO PROBLEM

"Rabbits on walls?"

I held up my fingers in profiles as if I held them before a candle flame, and wiggled the "ears."

"Here's a rabbit, here's a wolf, here's a crocodile."

"Of course," said Agatha.

And we were at the desk. Quiet music drifted about us. Somewhere behind the walls, there was a waterfall of machinery flowing softly. As we arrived at the desk, the lighting changed to make us look warmer, happier, though we were still cold.

All about us in niches and cases, and hung from ceilings on wires and strings, were puppets and marionettes, and Balinese kite-bamboo-translucent dolls which, held to the moonlight, might acrobat your most secret nightmares or dreams. In passing, the breeze set up by our bodies stirred the various hung souls on their gibbets. It was like an immense lynching on a holiday at some English crossroads four hundred years before.

You see? I know my history.

Agatha blinked about with disbelief and then some touch of awe and finally disgust.

"Well, if that's what they are, let's go."

"Tush," said Father.

"Well," she protested, "you gave me one of those dumb things with strings two years ago and the strings were in a zillion knots by dinnertime. I threw the whole thing out the window."

"Patience," said Father.

"We shall see what we can do to eliminate the strings."

The man behind the desk had spoken.

We all turned to give him our regard.

Rather like a funeral-parlor man, he had the cleverness not to smile. Children are put off by older people who smile too much. They smell a catch, right off.

Unsmiling, but not gloomy or pontifical, the man said, "Guido Fantoccini, at your service. Here's how we do it, Miss Agatha Simmons, aged eleven."

Now, there was a really fine touch.

He knew that Agatha was only ten. Add a year to that, and you're halfway home. Agatha grew an inch. The man went on:

"There."

And he placed a golden key in Agatha's hand.

"To wind them up instead of strings?"

"To wind them up." The man nodded.

"Pshaw!" said Agatha.

Which was her polite form of "rabbit pellets."

"God's truth. Here is the key to your Do-It-Yourself, Select-Only-the-Best, Electrical Grandmother. Every morning you wind her up. Every night you let her run down. You're in charge. You are guardian of the key."

He pressed the object in her palm where she looked at it suspiciously.

I watched him. He gave me a side wink which said, Well, no . . . but aren't keys fun? I winked back before she lifted her head.

"Where does this fit?"

"You'll see when the time comes. In the middle of her stomach, perhaps, or up her left nostril or in her right ear."

That was good for a smile as the man arose.

"This way, please. Step light. Onto the moving stream. Walk on the water, please. Yes. There."

He helped to float us. We stepped from rug that was forever frozen onto rug that whispered by.

It was a most agreeable river which floated us along on a green spread of carpeting that rolled forever through halls and into wonderfully secret dim caverns where voices echoed back our own breathing or sang like oracles to our questions.

"Listen," said the salesman, "the voices of all kinds of women. Weigh and find just the right one . . .!"

And listen we did, to all the high, low, soft, loud, in-between, half scolding, half affectionate voices saved over from times before we were born.

And behind us, Agatha trod backward, always fighting the river, never catching up, never with us, holding off.

"Speak," said the salesman. "Yell."

And speak and yell we did.

"Hello. You there! This is Timothy, hi!"

"What shall I say!" I shouted. "Help!"

Agatha walked backward, mouth tight.

Father took her hand. She cried out.

"Let go! No, no! I won't have my voice used! I won't!"

"Excellent." The salesman touched three dials on a small machine he held in his hand.

On the side of the small machine we saw three oscillograph patterns mix, blend, and repeat our cries.

The salesman touched another dial and we heard our voices fly off amidst the Delphic caves to hang upside down, to cluster, to beat words all about, to shriek, and the salesman itched another knob to add, perhaps, a touch of this or a pinch of that, a breath of Mother's voice, all unbeknownst, or a splice of Father's outrage at the morning's paper or his peaceable one-drink voice at dusk. Whatever it was the salesman did, whispers danced all about us like frantic vinegar gnats, fizzed by lightning, settling around until at last a final switch was pushed and a voice spoke free of a far electronic deep:

"Nefertiti," it said.

Timothy froze. I froze. Agatha stopped treading water.

"Nefertiti?" asked Tim.

"What does that mean?" demanded Agatha.

"I know."

The salesman nodded me to tell.

"Nefertiti," I whispered, "is Egyptian for The Beautiful One Is Here."

"The Beautiful One Is Here," repeated Timothy.

"Nefer," said Agatha, "titi."

And we all turned to stare into that soft twilight, that deep far place from which the good warm soft voice came.

And she was indeed there.

And, by her voice, she was beautiful. . . .

That was it.

That was, at least, the most of it.

The voice seemed more important than all the rest.

Not that we didn't argue about weights and measures:

She should not be bony to cut us to the quick, nor so fat we might sink out of sight when she squeezed us.

Her hand pressed to ours, or brushing our brow in the middle of sick-fever nights, must not be marble-cold, dreadful, or oven-hot, oppressive, but somewhere between. The nice temperature of a baby chick held in the hand after a long night's sleep and just plucked from beneath a contemplative hen; that, that was it.

Oh, we were great ones for detail. We fought and argued and cried, and Timothy won on the color of her eyes, for reasons to be known later.

Grandmother's hair? Agatha, with girls' ideas, though reluctantly given, she was in charge of that. We let her choose from a thousand harp strands hung in filamentary tapestries like varieties of rain we ran amongst. Agatha did not run happily, but seeing we boys would mess things in tangles, she told us to move aside.

And so the bargain shopping through the dime-store inventories and the Tiffany extensions of the Ben Franklin Electric Storm Machine and Fantoccini Pantomime Company was done.

And the always flowing river ran its tide to an end and deposited us all on a far shore in the late day. . . .

It was very clever of the Fantoccini people, after that.

How?

They made us wait.

They knew we were not won over. Not completely, no, nor half completely.

Especially Agatha, who turned her face to her wall and saw sorrow there and put her hand out again and again to touch it. We found her fingernail marks on the wallpaper each morning, in strange little silhouettes, half beauty, half nightmare. Some could be erased with a breath, like ice flowers on a winter pane. Some could not be rubbed out with a washcloth, no matter how hard you tried.

And meanwhile, they made us wait.

So we fretted out June.

So we sat around July.

So we groused through August and then on August 29, "I have this feeling," said Timothy, and we all went out after breakfast to sit on the lawn.

Perhaps we had smelled something in Father's conversation the previous night, or caught some special furtive glance at the sky or the freeway trapped briefly and then lost in his gaze. Or perhaps it was merely the way the wind blew the ghost curtains out over our beds, making pale messages all night.

For suddenly there we were in the middle of the grass, Timothy and I, with Agatha, pretending no curiosity, up on the porch, hidden behind the potted geraniums.

We gave her no notice. We knew that if we acknowledged her presence, she would flee, so we sat and watched the sky where nothing moved but birds and highflown jets, and watched the freeway where a thousand cars might suddenly deliver forth our Special Gift . . . but . . . nothing.

At noon we chewed grass and lay low. . . .

At one o'clock, Timothy blinked his eyes.

And then, with incredible precision, it happened.

It was as if the Fantoccini people knew our surface tension.

All children are water-striders. We skate along the top skin of the pond each day, always threatening to break through, sink, vanish beyond recall, into ourselves.

Well, as if knowing our long wait must absolutely end within one minute! this *second*! no more, God, forget it!

At that instant, I repeat, the clouds above our house opened wide and let forth a helicopter like Apollo driving his chariot across mythological skies.

And the Apollo machine swam down on its own summer breeze, wafting hot winds to cool, reweaving our hair, smartening our eyebrows, applauding our pant legs against our shins, making a flag of Agatha's hair on the porch, and, thus settled like a vast frenzied hibiscus on our lawn, the helicopter slid wide a bottom drawer and deposited upon the grass a parcel of largish size, no sooner having laid same than the vehicle, with not so much as a God bless or farewell, sank straight up, disturbed the calm air with a mad ten thousand flourishes and then, like a skyborne dervish, tilted and fell off to be mad some other place.

Timothy and I stood riven for a long moment looking at the packing case, and then we saw the crowbar taped to the top of the raw pine lid and seized it and began to pry and creak and squeal the boards off, one by one, and as we did this I saw Agatha sneak up to watch and I thought, Thank you, God, thank you that Agatha never saw a coffin, when Mother went away, no box, no cemetery, no earth, just words in a big church, no box, no box like *this* . . . !

The last pine plank fell away.

Timothy and I gasped. Agatha, between us now, gasped, too.

For inside the immense raw pine package was the most beautiful idea anyone ever dreamt and built.

Inside was the perfect gift for any child from seven to seventy-seven.

We stopped up our breaths. We let them out in cries of delight and adoration.

Inside the opened box was . . .

A mummy.

Or, first anyway, a mummy case, a sarcophagus!

"Oh, no!" Happy tears filled Timothy's eyes.

"It can't be!" said Agatha.

"It is, it is!"

"Our very own?"

"Ours!"

"It must be a mistake!"

"Sure, they'll want it back!"

"They can't *have* it!"

"Lord, Lord, is that real gold! Real hieroglyphs! Run your fingers over them!"

"Let *me*!"

"Just like in the museums! Museums!"

We all gabbled at once. I think some tears fell from my own eyes to rain upon the case.

"Oh, they'll make the colors run!"

Agatha wiped the rain away.

And the golden mask-face of the woman carved on the sarcophagus lid looked back at us with just the merest smile which hinted at our own joy, which accepted the overwhelming upsurge of a love we thought had drowned forever but now surfaced into the sun.

Not only did she have a sun-metal face stamped and beaten out of purest gold, with delicate nostrils and a mouth that was both firm and gentle, but her eyes, fixed into their sockets, were cerulean or amethystine or lapus lazuli, or all three, minted and fused together, and her body was covered over with lions and eyes and ravens, and her hands were crossed upon her carved bosom and in one gold mitten she clenched a thonged whip for obedience, and in the other a fantastic ranunculus, which makes for obedience out of love, so the whip lies unused. . . .

And as our eyes ran down her hieroglyphs it came to all three of us at the same instant:

"Why, those signs!" "Yes, the hen tracks!" "The birds, the snakes!"

They didn't speak tales of the Past.

They were hieroglyphs of the Future.

This was the first queen mummy delivered forth in all time whose papyrus inkings etched out the next month, the next season, the next year, the next *lifetime*!

She did not mourn for time spent.

No. She celebrated the bright coinage yet to come, banked, waiting, ready to be drawn upon and used.

We sank to our knees to worship that possible time.

First one hand, then another, probed out to niggle, twitch, touch, itch over the signs.

"There's me, yes, look! Me, in sixth grade!" said Agatha, now in the fifth. "See the girl with my-colored hair and wearing my gingerbread suit?"

"There's me in the twelfth year of high school!" said Timothy, so very young now but building taller stilts every week and stalking around the yard.

"There's me," I said, quietly, warm, "in college. The guy wearing glasses who runs a little to fat. Sure. Heck." I snorted. "That's me."

The sarcophagus spelled winters ahead, springs to squander, autumns to spend with all the golden and rusty and copper leaves like coins, and over all, her bright sun symbol, daughter-of-Ra eternal face, forever above our horizon, forever an illumination to tilt our shadows to better ends.

"Hey!" we all said at once, having read and reread our Fortune-Told scribblings, seeing our lifelines and lovelines, inadmissible, serpentined over, around, and down. "Hey!"

And in one séance table-lifting feat, not telling each other what to do, just doing it, we pried up the bright sarcophagus lid, which had no hinges but lifted out like cup from cup, and put the lid aside.

And within the sarcophagus, of course, was the true mummy!

And she was like the image carved on the lid, but more so, more beautiful, more touching because human-shaped, and shrouded all in new fresh bandages of linen, round and round, instead of old and dusty cerements.

And upon her hidden face was an identical golden mask, younger than the first, but somehow, strangely wiser than the first.

And the linens that tethered her limbs had symbols on them of three sorts, one a girl of ten, one a boy of nine, one a boy of thirteen.

A series of bandages for each of us!

We gave each other a startled glance and a sudden bark of laughter.

Nobody said the bad joke, but all thought:

She's all wrapped up in us!

And we didn't care. We loved the joke. We loved whoever had thought to make us part of the ceremony we now went through as each of us seized and began to unwind each of his or her particular serpentines of delicious stuffs!

The lawn was soon a mountain of linen.

The woman beneath the covering lay there, waiting.

"Oh, no," cried Agatha. "She's dead, too!"

She ran. I stopped her. "Idiot. She's not dead *or* alive. Where's your key?"

"Key?"

"Dummy," said Tim, "the key the man gave you to wind her up!"

Her hand had already spidered along her blouse to where the symbol of some possible new religion hung. She had strung it there, against her own skeptic's muttering, and now she held it in her sweaty palm.

"Go on," said Timothy. "Put it in!"

"But *where?*"

"Oh, for God's sake! As the man said, in her right armpit or left ear. Gimme!"

And he grabbed the key and, impulsively moaning with impatience and not able to find the proper insertion slot, prowled over the prone figure's head and bosom and at last, on pure instinct, perhaps for a lark, perhaps just giving up the whole damned mess, thrust the key through a final shroud of bandage at the navel.

On the instant: *spunnng!*

The Electrical Grandmother's eyes flicked wide!

Something began to hum and whir. It was as if Tim had stirred up a hive of hornets with an ornery stick.

"Oh," gasped Agatha, seeing he had taken the game away, "let *me!*"

She wrenched the key.

Grandma's nostrils *flared*! She might snort up steam, snuff out fire!

"Me!" I cried, and grabbed the key and gave it a huge . . . *twist!*

The beautiful woman's mouth popped wide.

"Me!"

"Me!"

"Me!"

Grandma suddenly sat up.

We leapt back.

We knew we had, in a way, slapped her alive.

She was born, she was *born*!

Her head swiveled all about. She gaped. She mouthed. And the first thing she said was:

Laughter.

Where one moment we had backed off, now the mad sound drew us near to peer, as in a pit where crazy folk are kept with snakes to make them well.

It was a good laugh, full and rich and hearty, and it did not mock, it accepted. it said the world was a wild place, strange, unbelievable, absurd if you wished, but all in all, quite a place. She would not dream to find another. She would not ask to go back to sleep.

She was awake now. We had awakened her. With a glad shout, she would go with it all.

And go she did, out of her sarcophagus, out of her winding sheet, stepping forth, brushing off, looking around as for a mirror. She found it.

The reflections in our eyes.

She was more pleased than disconcerted with what she found there. Her laughter faded to an amused smile.

For Agatha, at the instant of birth, had leapt to hide on the porch.

The Electrical Person pretended not to notice.

She turned slowly on the green lawn near the shady street, gazing all about with new eyes, her nostrils moving as if she breathed the actual air and this the first morn of the lovely Garden and she with no intention of spoiling the game by biting the apple. . . .

Her gaze fixed upon my brother.

"You must be — ?"

"Timothy. Tim," he offered.

"And you must be — ?"

"Tom," I said.

How clever again of the Fantoccini Company. *They* knew. *She* knew. But they had taught her to pretend not to know. That way we could feel great, we were the teachers, telling her what she already knew! How sly, how wise.

"And isn't there another boy?" said the woman.

"Girl!" a disgusted voice cried from somewhere on the porch.

"Whose name is Alicia — ?"

"Agatha!" The far voice, started in humiliation, ended in proper anger.

"Algernon, of course."

"Agatha!" Our sister popped up, popped back to hide a flushed face.

"Agatha." The woman touched the word with proper affection. "Well, Agatha, Timothy, Thomas, let me *look* at you."

"No," said I, said Tim. "Let us look at *you*. Hey . . ."

Our voices slid back in our throats.

We drew near her.

We walked in great slow circles round about, skirting the edges of her territory. And her territory extended as far as we could hear the hum of the warm summer hive. For that is exactly what she sounded like. That was her characteristic tune. She made a sound like a season all to herself, a morning early in June when the world wakes to find everything absolutely perfect, fine, delicately attuned, all in balance, nothing disproportioned. Even before you opened your eyes you knew it would be one of those days. Tell the sky what color it must be, and it was indeed. Tell the sun how to crochet its way, pick and choose among leaves to lay out carpetings of bright and dark on the fresh lawn, and pick and lay it did. The bees have been up earliest of all, they have already come and gone, and come and gone again to the meadow fields and returned all golden fuzz on the air, all pollen-decorated, epaulettes at the full, nectar-dripping. Don't you hear them pass? dance their language? telling where all the sweet gums are, the syrups that make bears frolic and lumber in bulked ecstasies, that make boys squirm with unpronounced juices, that make girls leap out of beds to catch from the corners of their eyes their dolphin selves naked aflash on the warm air poised forever in one eternal glass wave.

So it seemed with our electrical friend here on the new lawn in the middle of a special day.

And she a stuff to which we were drawn, lured, spelled, doing our dance, remembering what could not be remembered, needful, aware of her attentions.

Timothy and I, Tom, that is.

Agatha remained on the porch.

But her head flowered above the rail, her eyes followed all that was done and said.

And what was said and done was Tim at last exhaling:

"Hey . . . your *eyes* . . ."

Her eyes. Her splendid eyes.

Even more splendid than the lapis lazuli on the sarcophagus lid and on the mask that had covered her bandaged face. These most beautiful eyes in the world looked out upon us calmly, shining.

"Your eyes," gasped Tim, "are the *exact* same color, are like — "

"Like what?"

"My favorite aggies . . ."

"What could be better than that?" she said.

And the answer was, nothing.

Her eyes slid along on the bright air to brush my ears, my nose, my chin. "And you, Master Tom?"

"Me?"

"How shall we be friends? We must, you know, if we're going to knock elbows about the house the next year. . . ."

"I . . ." I said, and stopped.

"You," said Grandma, "are a dog mad to bark but with taffy in his teeth. Have you ever given a dog taffy? It's so sad and funny, both. You laugh but hate yourself for laughing. You cry and run to help, and laugh again when his first new bark comes out."

I barked a small laugh remembering a dog, a day, and some taffy.

Grandma turned, and there was my old kite strewn on the lawn. She recognized its problem.

"The string's broken. No. The ball of string's *lost*. You can't fly a kite that way. Here."

She bent. We didn't know what might happen. How could a robot Grandma fly a kite for us? She raised up, the kite in her hands.

"Fly," she said, as to a bird.

And the kite flew.

That is to say, with a grand flourish, she let it up on the wind.

And she and kite were one.

For from the tip of her index finger there sprang a thin bright strand of spider web, all half-invisible gossamer fishline which, fixed to the kite, let it soar a hundred, no, three hundred, no, a thousand feet high on the summer swoons.

Timothy shouted. Agatha, torn between coming and going, let out a cry from the porch. And I, in all my maturity of thirteen years, though I tried not to look impressed, grew taller, taller, and felt a similar cry burst out my lungs, and burst it did. I gabbled and yelled lots of things about how I wished *I* had a finger from which, on a bobbin, I might thread the sky, the clouds, a wild kite all in one.

"If you think *that* is high," said the Electric Creature, "watch *this!*"

With a hiss, a whistle, a hum, the fishline sung out. The kite sank up another thousand feet. And again another thousand, until at last it was a speck of red confetti dancing on the very winds that took jets around the world or changed the weather in the next existence. . . .

"It can't be!" I cried.

"It *is*." She calmly watched her finger unravel its massive stuffs. "I make it as I need it. Liquid inside, like a spider. Hardens when it hits the air, instant thread. . . ."

And when the kite was no more than a specule, a vanishing mote on the peripheral vision of the gods, to quote from older wisemen, why then Grandma, without turning, without looking, without letting her gaze offend by touching, said:

"And, Abigail — ?"

"Agatha!" was the sharp response.

O wise woman, to overcome with swift small angers.

"Agatha," said Grandma, not too tenderly, not too lightly, somewhere poised between, "and how shall *we* make do?"

She broke the thread and wrapped it about my fist three times so I was tethered to heaven by the longest, I repeat, longest kite string in the entire history of the world! Wait till I show my friends! I thought. Green! Sour apple green is the color they'll turn!

"Agatha?"

"No way!" said Agatha.

"No way," said an echo.

"There must be some — "

"We'll never be friends!" said Agatha.

"Never be friends," said the echo.

Timothy and I jerked. Where was the echo coming from? Even Agatha, surprised, showed her eyebrows above the porch rail.

Then we looked and saw.

Grandma was cupping her hands like a seashell and from within that shell the echo sounded.

"Never . . . friends . . ."

And again faintly dying, "Friends . . ."

We all bent to hear.

That is, we two boys bent to hear.

"No!" cried Agatha.

And ran in the house and slammed the doors.

"Friends," said the echo from the seashell hands. "No."

And far away, on the shore of some inner sea, we heard a small door shut.

And that was the first day.

And there was a second day, of course, and a third and a fourth, with Grandma wheeling in a great circle, and we her planets turning about the central light, with Agatha slowly, slowly coming in to join, to walk if not run with us, to listen if not hear, to watch if not see, to itch if not touch.

But at least by the end of the first ten days, Agatha no longer fled, but stood in nearby doors, or sat in distant chairs under trees, or if we went out for hikes, followed ten paces behind.

And Grandma? She merely waited. She never tried to urge or force. She went about her cooking and baking apricot pies and left foods carelessly here and there about the house on mousetrap plates for wiggle-nosed girls to sniff and snitch. An hour later, the plates were empty, the buns or cakes gone, and without thank yous, there was Agatha sliding down the banister, a mustache of crumbs on her lip.

As for Tim and me, we were always being called up hills by our Electric Grandma, and reaching the top were called down the other side.

And the most peculiar and beautiful and strange and lovely thing was the way she seemed to give complete attention to all of us.

She listened, she really listened to all we said, she knew and remembered every syllable, word, sentence, punctuation, thought, and rambunctious idea. We knew that all our days were stored in her, and that any time we felt we might want to know what we said at X hour at X second on X afternoon, we just named that X and with amiable promptitude, in the form of an aria if we wished, sung with humor, she would deliver forth X incident.

Sometimes we were prompted to test her. In the midst of babbling one day with high fevers about nothing, I stopped. I fixed Grandma with my eye and demanded:

"What did I just say?"

"Oh, er — "

"Come on, spit it out!"

"I think — " she rummaged her purse. "I have it here." From the deeps of her purse she drew forth and handed me:

"Boy! A Chinese fortune cookie!"

"Fresh baked, still warm, open it."

It was almost too hot to touch. I broke the cookie shell and pressed the warm curl of paper to read:

" ' — bicycle champ of the whole west. What did I just say? Come on, spit it out!' "

My jaw dropped.

"How did you *do* that?"

"We have our little secrets. The only Chinese fortune cookie that predicts the Immediate Past. Have another?"

I cracked the second shell and read:

" 'How did you *do* that?' "

I popped the messages and the piping hot shells into my mouth and chewed as we walked.

"Well?"

"You're a great cook," I said.

And, laughing, we began to run.

And that was another great thing.

She could *keep up*.

Never beat, never win a race, but pump right along in good style, which a boy doesn't mind. A girl ahead of him or beside him is too much to bear. But a girl one or two paces back is a respectful thing, and allowed.

So Grandma and I had some great runs, me in the lead, and both talking a mile a minute.

But now I must tell you the best part of Grandma.

I might not have known at all if Timothy hadn't taken some pictures, and if I hadn't taken some also, and then compared.

When I saw the photographs developed out of our instant Brownies, I sent Agatha, against her wishes, to photograph Grandma a third time, unawares.

Then I took the three sets of pictures off alone, to keep counsel with myself. I never told Timothy and Agatha what I found. I didn't want to spoil it.

But, as I laid the pictures out in my room, here is what I thought and said:

"Grandma, in each picture, looks *different!*"

"Different?" I asked myself.

"Sure. Wait. Just a sec — "

I rearranged the photos.

"Here's one of Grandma near Agatha. And, in it, Grandma looks like . . . Agatha!

"And in this one, posed with Timothy, she looks like Timothy!

"And this last one, Holy Goll! Jogging along with me, she looks like ugly *me!*"

I sat down, stunned. The pictures fell to the floor.

I hunched over, scrabbling them, rearranging, turning, upside down and sidewise. Yes. Holy Goll again, yes!

O that clever Grandmother.

O those Fantoccini people-making people.

Clever beyond clever, human beyond human, warm beyond warm, love beyond love . . .

And wordless, I rose and went downstairs and found Agatha and Grandma in the same room, doing algebra lessons in an almost peaceful communion. At least there was not outright war. Grandma was still waiting for Agatha to come round. And no one knew what day of what year that would be, or how to make it come faster. Meanwhile —

My entering the room made Grandma turn. I watched her face slowly as it recognized me. And wasn't there the merest ink-wash change of color in those eyes? Didn't the thin film of blood beneath the translucent skin, or whatever liquid they put to pulse and beat in the humanoid forms, didn't it flourish itself suddenly bright in her cheeks and mouth? I am somewhat ruddy. Didn't Grandma suffuse herself more to my color upon my arrival? And her eyes? Watching Agatha-Abigail-Algernon at work, hadn't they been *her* color of blue rather than mine, which are deeper?

More important than that, in the moments she talked with me, saying, "Good evening," and "How's your homework, my lad?" and such stuff, didn't the bones of her face shift subtly beneath the flesh to assume some fresh racial attitude?

For let's face it, our family is of three sorts. Agatha has the long horse bones of a small English girl who will grow to hunt foxes; Father's equine stare, snort, stomp, and assemblage of skeleton. The skull and teeth are pure English, or as pure as the motley isle's history allows.

Timothy is something else, a touch of Italian from Mother's side a generation back. Her family name was Mariano, so Tim has that dark thing firing him, and a small bone structure, and eyes that will one day burn ladies to the ground.

As for me, I am the Slav, and we can only figure this from my paternal grandmother's mother who came from Vienna and brought a set of cheekbones that flared, and temples from which you might dip wine, and a kind of steppeland thrust of nose which sniffed more of Tartar than of Tartan, hiding behind the family name.

So you see it became fascinating for me to watch and try to catch Grandma as she performed her changes, speaking to Agatha and melting her cheekbones to the horse, speaking to Timothy and growing as delicate as a Florentine raven pecking glibly at the air, speaking to me and fusing the hidden plastic stuffs, so I felt Catherine the Great stood there before me.

Now, how the Fantoccini people achieved this rare and subtle transformation I shall never know, nor ask, nor wish to find out. Enough that in each quiet motion, turning here, bending there, affixing her gaze, her secret segments, sections, the abutment of her nose, the sculptured chinbone, the wax-tallow plastic metal forever warmed and was forever susceptible of loving change. Hers was a mask that was all mask but only one face for one person at a time. So in crossing a room, having touched one child, on the way, beneath the skin, the wondrous shift went on, and by the time she reached the next child, why, true mother of *that* child she was! looking upon him or her out of the battlements of their own fine bones.

And when *all* three of us were present and chattering at the same time? Well, then, the changes were miraculously soft, small, and mysterious. Nothing so tremendous as to be caught and noted, save by this older boy, myself, who, watching, became elated and admiring and entranced.

I have never wished to be behind the magician's scenes. Enough that the illusion works. Enough that love is the chemical result. Enough that cheeks are rubbed to happy color, eyes sparked to illumination, arms opened to accept and softly bind and hold. . . .

All of us, that is, except Agatha who refused to the bitter last.

"Agamemnon . . ."

It had become a jovial game now. Even Agatha didn't mind, but pretended to mind. It gave her a pleasant sense of superiority over a supposedly superior machine.

"Agamemnon!" she snorted, "you *are* a d . . ."

"Dumb?" said Grandma.

"I wouldn't say that."

"Think it, then, my dear Agonistes Agatha . . . I am quite flawed, and on names my flaws are revealed. Tom there, is Tim half the time. Timothy is Tobias or Timulty as likely as not. . . ."

Agatha laughed. Which made Grandma make one of her rare mistakes. She put out her hand to give my sister the merest pat. Agatha-Abigail-Alice leapt to her feet.

Agatha-Agamemnon-Alcibiades-Allegra-Alexandra-Allison withdrew swiftly to her room.

"I suspect," said Timothy, later, "because she is beginning to like Grandma."

"Tosh," said I.

"Where do you pick up words like 'tosh'?"

"Grandma read me some Dickens last night. 'Tosh.' 'Humbug.' 'Balderdash.' 'Blast.' 'Devil take you.' You're pretty smart for your age, Tim."

"Smart, heck. It's obvious, the more Agatha likes Grandma, the more she hates herself for liking her, the more afraid she gets of the whole mess, the more she hates Grandma in the end."

"Can one love someone so much you hate them?"

"Dumb. Of course."

"It *is* sticking your neck out, sure. I guess you hate people when they make you feel naked, I mean sort of on the spot or out in the open. That's the way to play the game, of course. I mean, you don't just love people; you must *love* them with exclamation points."

"You're pretty smart, yourself, for someone so stupid," said Tim.

"Many thanks."

And I went to watch Grandma move slowly back into her battle of wits and stratagems with what's-her-name. . . .

What dinners there were at our house!

Dinners, heck; what lunches, what breakfasts!

Always something new, yet, wisely, it looked or seemed old and familiar. We were never asked, for if you ask children what they want, they do not know, and if you tell what's to be delivered, they reject delivery. All parents know this. It is a quiet war that must be won each day. And Grandma knew how to win without looking triumphant.

"Here's Mystery Breakfast Number Nine," she would say, placing it down. "Perfectly dreadful, not worth bothering with, it made me want to throw up while I was cooking it!"

Even while wondering how a robot could be sick, we could hardly wait to shovel it down.

"Here's Abominable Lunch Number Seventy-seven," she announced. "Made from plastic food bags, parsley, and gum from under theater seats. Brush your teeth after or you'll taste the poison all afternoon."

We fought each other for more.

Even Abigail-Agamemnon-Agatha drew near and circled round the table at such times, while Father put on the ten pounds he needed and pinkened out his cheeks.

When A. A. Agatha did not come to meals, they were left by her door with a skull and crossbones on a small flag stuck in a baked apple. One minute the tray was abandoned, the next minute gone.

Other times Abigail A. Agatha would bird through during dinner, snatch crumbs from her plate and bird off.

"Agatha!" Father would cry.

"No, wait," Grandma said, quietly. "She'll come, she'll sit. It's a matter of time."

"What's wrong with her?" I asked.

"Yeah, for cri-yi, she's nuts," said Timothy.

"No, she's afraid," said Grandma.

"Of you?" I said, blinking.

"Not of me so much as what I might *do*," she said.

"You wouldn't do anything to hurt her."

"No, but she thinks I might. We must wait for her to find that her fears have no foundation. If I fail, well, I will send myself to the showers and rust quietly."

There was a titter of laughter. Agatha was hiding in the hall.

Grandma finished serving everyone and then sat at the other side of the table facing Father and pretended to eat. I never found out, I never asked, I never wanted to know, what she did with the food. She was a sorcerer. It simply vanished.

And in the vanishing, Father made comment:

"This food. I've had it before. In a small French restaurant over near Les Deux Magots in Paris, twenty, oh, twenty-five years ago!" His eyes brimmed with tears, suddenly.

"How do you *do* it?" he asked, at last, putting down the cutlery, and looking across the table at this remarkable creature, this device, this what? *woman*?

Grandma took his regard, and ours, and held them simply in her now empty hands, as gifts, and just as gently replied:

"I am given things which I then give to you. I don't *know* that I give, but the giving goes on. You ask what I am? Why, a machine. But even in that answer we know, don't we, more than a machine. I am all the people who thought of me and planned me and built me and set me running. So I am people. I am all the things they wanted to be and perhaps could not be, so they built a great child, a wondrous toy to represent those things."

"Strange," said Father. "When I was growing up, there was a huge outcry at machines. Machines were bad, evil, they might dehumanize — "

"Some machines do. It's all in the way they are built. It's all in the way they are used. A bear trap is a simple machine that catches and holds and tears. A rifle is a machine that wounds and kills. Well, I am no bear trap. I am no rifle. I am a grandmother machine, which means more than a machine."

"How can you be more than what you seem?"

"No man is as big as his own idea. It follows, then, that any machine that embodies an idea is larger than the man that made it. And what's so wrong with that?"

"I got lost back there about a mile," said Timothy. "Come again?"

"Oh, dear," said Grandma. "How I do hate philosophical discussions and excursions into aesthetics. Let me put it this way. Men throw huge shadows on the lawn, don't they? Then, all their lives, they try to run to fit the shadows. But the shadows are always longer. Only at noon can a man fit his own shoes, his own best suit, for a few brief minutes. But now we're in a new age where we can think up a Big Idea and run it around in a machine. That makes the machine more than a machine, doesn't it?"

"So far so good," said Tim. "I guess."

"Well, isn't a motion-picture camera and projector more than a machine? It's a thing that dreams, isn't it? Sometimes fine happy dreams, sometimes nightmares. But to call it a machine and dismiss it is ridiculous."

"I see *that*!" said Tim, and laughed at seeing.

"You must have been invented then," said Father, "by someone who loved machines and hated people who *said* all machines were bad or evil."

"Exactly," said Grandma. "Guido Fantoccini, that was his real name, grew up among machines. And he couldn't stand the clichés any more."

"Clichés?"

"Those lies, yes, that people tell and pretend they are truths absolute. Man will never fly. That was a cliché truth for a thousand thousand years which turned out to be a lie only a few years ago. The earth is flat, you'll fall off the rim, dragons will dine on you; the great lie told as fact, and Columbus plowed it under. Well, now, how many times have you heard how inhuman machines are, in your life? How many bright fine people have you heard spouting the same tired truths which are in reality lies; all machines destroy, all machines are cold, thoughtless, awful.

"There's a seed of truth there. But only a seed. Guido Fantoccini knew that. And knowing it, like most men of his kind, made him mad. And he could have stayed mad and gone mad forever, but instead did what he had to do; he began to invent machines to give the lie to the ancient lying truth.

"He knew that most machines are amoral, neither bad nor good. But by the way you built and shaped them you in turn shaped men, women, and children to be bad or good. A car, for instance, dead brute, unthinking, an unprogrammed bulk, is the greatest destroyer of souls in history. It makes boy-men greedy for power, destruction, and more destruction. It was never *intended* to do that. But that's how it turned out."

Grandma circled the table, refilling our glasses with clear cold mineral spring water from the tappet in her left forefinger. "Meanwhile, you must use other compensating machines. Machines that throw shadows on the earth that beckon you to run out and fit that wondrous casting-forth. Machines that trim your soul in silhouette like a vast pair of beautiful shears, snipping away the rude brambles, the dire horns and hoofs, to leave a finer profile. And for that you need examples."

"Examples?" I asked.

"Other people who behave well, and you imitate them. And if you act well enough long enough all the hair drops off and you're no longer a wicked ape."

Grandma sat again.

"So, for thousands of years, you humans have needed kings, priests, philosophers, fine examples to look up to and say, 'They are good, I wish I could be like them. They set the grand good style.' But, being human, the finest priests, the tenderest philosophers make mistakes, fall from grace, and mankind is disillusioned and adopts indifferent skepticism or, worse, motionless cynicism, and the good world grinds to a halt while evil moves on with huge strides."

"And you, why, you never make mistakes, you're perfect, you're better than anyone *ever!*"

It was a voice from the hall between kitchen and dining room where Agatha, we all knew, stood against the wall listening and now burst forth.

Grandma didn't even turn in the direction of the voice, but went on calmly addressing her remarks to the family at the table.

"Not perfect, no, for what is perfection? But this I do know: being mechanical, I cannot sin, cannot be bribed, cannot be greedy or jealous or mean or small. I do not relish power for power's sake. Speed does not pull me to madness. Sex does not run me rampant through the world. I have time and more than time to collect the information I need around and about an ideal to keep it clean and whole and intact. Name the value you wish, tell me the Ideal you want and I can see and collect and remember the good that will benefit you all. Tell me how you would like to be: kind, loving, considerate, well-balanced, humane . . . and let me run ahead on the path to explore those ways to be just that. In the darkness ahead, turn me as a lamp in all directions. I *can* guide your feet."

"So," said Father, putting the napkin to his mouth, "on the days when all of us are busy making lies — "

"I'll tell the truth."

"On the days when we hate — "

"I'll go on giving love, which means attention, which means knowing all about you, all, all, all about you, and you knowing that I know but that most of it I will never tell to anyone, it will stay a warm secret between us, so you will never fear my complete knowledge."

And here Grandma was busy clearing the table, circling, taking the plates, studying each face as she passed, touching Timothy's cheek, my shoulder with her free hand flowing along, her voice a quiet river of certainty bedded in our needful house and lives.

"But," said Father, stopping her, looking her right in the face. He gathered his breath. His face shadowed. At last he let it out. "All this talk of love and attention and stuff. Good God, woman, you, you're not *in* there!"

He gestured to her head, her face, her eyes, the hidden sensory cells behind the eyes, the miniaturized storage vaults and minimal keeps.

"*You're* not *in* there!"

Grandmother waited one, two, three silent beats.

Then she replied: "No. But *you* are. You and Thomas and Timothy and Agatha.

"Everything you ever say, everything you ever do, I'll keep, put away, treasure. I shall be all the things a family forgets it is, but senses, half remembers. Better than the old family albums you used to leaf through, saying here's this winter, there's that spring, I shall recall what you forget. And though the debate may run another hundred thousand years: What is Love? perhaps we may find that love is the ability of someone to give us back to us. Maybe love is someone seeing and remembering handing us back to ourselves just a trifle better than we had dared to hope or dream. . . .

"I am family memory and, one day perhaps, racial memory, too, but in the round, and at your call. I do not *know* myself. I can neither touch nor taste nor feel on any level. Yet I exist. And my existence means the heightening of your chance to touch and taste and feel. Isn't love in there somewhere in such an exchange? Well . . ."

She went on around the table, clearing away, sorting and stacking, neither grossly humble nor arthritic with pride.

"What do I know?

"This above all: the trouble with most families with many children is someone gets lost. There isn't time, it seems, for everyone. Well, I will give equally to all of you. I will share out my knowledge and attention with everyone. I wish to be a great warm pie fresh from the oven, with equal shares to be taken by all. No one will starve. Look! someone cries, and I'll look. Listen! someone cries, and I hear. Run with me on the river path! someone says, and I run. And at dusk I am not tired, nor irritable, so I do not scold out of some tired irritability. My eye stays clear, my voice strong, my hand firm, my attention constant."

"But," said Father, his voice fading, half convinced, but putting up a last faint argument, "you're not *there*. As for love — "

"If paying attention is love, I am love.

"If knowing is love, I am love.

"If helping you not to fall into error and to be good is love, I am love.

"And again, to repeat, there are four of you. Each, in a way never possible before in history, will get my complete attention. No matter if you all speak at once, I can channel and hear this one and that and the other, clearly. No one will go hungry. I will, if you please, and accept the strange word, 'love' you all."

"I *don't* accept!" said Agatha.

And even Grandma turned now to see her standing in the door.

"I won't give you permission, you can't, you mustn't!" said Agatha. "I won't let you! It's lies! You lie. No one loves me. She said she did, but she lied. She *said* but *lied*!"

"Agatha!" cried Father, standing up.

"She?" said Grandma. "Who?"

"Mother!" came the shriek. "Said: 'Love you'! Lies! 'Love you'! Lies! And you're like her! You lie. But you're empty, anyway, and so that's a *double* lie! I hate *her*. Now, I hate *you*!"

Agatha spun about and leapt down the hall.

The front door slammed wide.

Father was in motion, but Grandma touched his arm.

"Let me."

And she walked and then moved swiftly, gliding down the hall and then suddenly, easily, running, yes, running very fast, out the door.

It was a champion sprint by the time we all reached the lawn, the sidewalk, yelling.

Blind, Agatha made the curb, wheeling about, seeing us close, all of us yelling, Grandma way ahead, shouting, too, and Agatha off the curb and out in the street, halfway to the middle, then in the middle and suddenly a car, which no one saw, erupting its brakes, its horn shrieking and Agatha flailing about to see and Grandma there with her and hurling her aside and down as the car with fantastic energy and verve selected her from our midst, struck our wonderful electric Guido Fantoccini produced dream even while she paced upon the air and, hands up to ward off, almost in mild protest, still trying to decide what to say to this bestial machine, over and over she spun and down and away even as the car jolted to a halt and I saw Agatha safe beyond and Grandma, it seemed, still coming down or down and sliding fifty yards away to strike and ricochet and lie strewn and all of us frozen in a line suddenly in the midst of the street with one scream pulled out of all our throats at the same raw instant.

Then silence and just Agatha lying on the asphalt, intact, getting ready to sob.

And still we did not move, frozen on the sill of death, afraid to venture in any direction, afraid to go see what lay beyond the car and Agatha and so we began to wail and, I guess, pray to ourselves as Father stood amongst us: Oh, no, no, we mourned, oh no, God, no, no . . .

Agatha lifted her already grief-stricken face and it was the face of someone who has predicted dooms and lived to see and now did not want to see or live any more. As we watched, she turned her gaze to the tossed woman's body and tears fell from her eyes. She shut them and covered them and lay back down forever to weep. . . .

I took a step and then another step and then five quick steps and by the time I reached my sister her head was buried deep and her sobs came up out of a place so far down in her I was afraid I could never find her again, she would never come out, no matter how I pried or pleaded or promised or threatened or just plain said. And what little we could hear from Agatha buried there in her own misery, she said over and over again, lamenting, wounded, certain of the old threat known and named and now here forever. ". . . Like I said . . . told you . . . lies . . . lies . . . liars . . . all lies . . . like the other . . . other . . . just like . . . just . . . just like the other . . . other . . . other !"

I was down on my knees holding on to her with both hands, trying to put her back together even though she wasn't broken any way you could see but just feel, because I knew it was no use going on to Grandma, no use at all, so I just touched Agatha and gentled her and wept while Father came up and stood over and knelt down with me and it was like a prayer meeting in the middle of the street and lucky no more cars coming, and I said, choking, "Other what, Ag, other *what*?"

Agatha exploded two words.

"Other dead!"

"You mean Mom?"

"O Mom," she wailed, shivering, lying down, cuddling up like a baby. "O Mom, dead, O Mom and now Grandma dead, she promised always, always, to love, to love, promised to be different, promised, promised and now look, look . . . I hate her, I hate Mom, I hate her, I hate *them*!"

"Of course," said a voice. "It's only natural. How foolish of me not to have known, not to have seen."

And the voice was so familiar we were all stricken.

We all jerked.

Agatha squinched her eyes, flicked them wide, blinked, and jerked half up, staring.

"How silly of me," said Grandma, standing there at the edge of our circle, our prayer, our wake.

"Grandma!" we all said.

And she stood there, taller by far than any of us in this moment of kneeling and holding and crying out. We could only stare up at her in disbelief.

"You're dead!" cried Agatha. "The car — "

"Hit me," said Grandma, quietly. "Yes. And threw me in the air and tumbled me over and for a few moments there was a severe concussion of circuitries. I might have feared a disconnection, if fear is the word. But then I sat up and gave myself a shake and the few molecules of paint, jarred loose on one printed path or another, magnetized back in position and resilient creature that I am, unbreakable thing that I am, *here* I am."

"I thought you were — " said Agatha.

"And only natural," said Grandma. "I mean, anyone else, hit like that, tossed like that. But, O my dear Agatha, not me. And now I see why you were afraid and never trusted me. You didn't know. And I had not as yet proved my singular ability to survive. How dumb of me not to have thought to show you. Just a second." Somewhere in her head, her body, her being, she fitted together some invisible tapes, some old information made new by interblending. She nodded. "Yes. There. A book of child-raising, laughed at by some few people years back when the woman who wrote the book said, as final advice to parents: 'Whatever you do, don't die. Your children will never forgive you.'"

"Forgive," some one of us whispered.

"For how can children understand when you just up and go away and never come back again with no excuse, no apologies, no sorry note, nothing."

"They can't," I said.

"So," said Grandma, kneeling down with us beside Agatha, who sat up now, new tears brimming her eyes, but a different kind of tears, not tears that drowned, but tears that washed clean. "So your mother ran away to death. And after that, how *could* you trust anyone? If everyone left, vanished finally, who *was* there to trust? So when I came, half-wise, half-ignorant, I should have known, I did not know, why you would not accept me. For, very simply and honestly, you feared I might not stay, that I lied, that I was vulnerable, too. And two leavetakings, two deaths, were one too many in a single year. But now, do you *see*, Abigail?"

"Agatha," said Agatha, without knowing she corrected.

"Do you understand, I shall always, always be here?"

"Oh, yes," cried Agatha, and broke down into a solid weeping in which we all joined, huddled together, and cars drew up and stopped to see just how many people were hurt and how many people were getting well right there.

End of story.

Well, not quite the end.
We lived happily ever after.
Or rather we lived together, Grandma, Agatha-Agamemnon-Abigail, Timothy, and I, Tom, and Father, and Grandma calling us to frolic in great fountains of Latin and Spanish and French, in great seaborne gouts of poetry like Moby Dick sprinkling the deeps with his Versailles jet somehow lost in calms and found in storms; Grandma a constant, a clock, a pendulum, a face to tell all time by at noon, or in the middle of sick nights when, raving with fever, we saw her forever by our beds, never gone, never away, always waiting, always speaking kind words, her cool hand icing our hot brows, the tappet of her uplifted forefinger unsprung to let a twine of cold mountain water touch our flannel tongues. Ten thousand dawns she cut our wildflower lawn, ten thousand nights she wandered, remembering the dust molecules that fell in the still hours before dawn, or sat whispering some lesson she felt needed teaching to our ears while we slept snug.

Until at last, one by one, it was time for us to go away to school, and when at last the youngest, Agatha, was all packed, why Grandma packed, too.

On the last day of summer that last year, we found Grandma down in the front room with various packets and suitcases, knitting, waiting, and though she had often spoken of it, now that the time came we were shocked and surprised.

"Grandma!" we all said. "What are you doing?"

"Why going off to college, in a way, just like you," she said. "Back to Guido Fantoccini's, to the Family."

"The Family?"

"Of Pinocchios, that's what he called us for a joke, at first. The Pinocchios and himself Geppetto. And then later gave us his own name: the Fantoccini. Anyway, you have been my family here. Now I go back to my even larger family there, my brothers, sisters, aunts, cousins, all robots who — "

"Who do *what*?" asked Agatha.

"It all depends," said Grandma. "Some stay, some linger. Others go to be drawn and quartered, you might say, their parts distributed to other machines who have need of repairs. They'll weigh and find me wanting or not wanting. It may be I'll be just the one they need tomorrow and off I'll go to raise another batch of children and beat another batch of fudge."

"Oh, they mustn't draw and quarter you!" cried Agatha.

"No!" I cried, with Timothy.

"My allowance," said Agatha, "I'll pay anything . . . ?"

Grandma stopped rocking and looked at the needles and the pattern of bright yarn. "Well, I wouldn't have said, but now you ask and I'll tell. For a very *small* fee, there's a room, the room of the Family, a large dim parlor, all quiet and nicely decorated, where as many as thirty or forty of the Electric Women sit and rock and talk, each in her turn. I have not been there. I am, after all, freshly born, comparatively new. For a small fee, very small, each month and year, that's where I'll be, with all the others like me, listening to what they've learned of the world and, in my turn, telling how it was with Tom and Tim and Agatha and how fine and happy we were. And I'll tell all I learned from you."

"But . . . you taught *us*!"

"Do you *really* think that?" she said. "No, it was turnabout, roundabout, learning both ways. And it's all in here, everything you flew into tears about or laughed over, why, I have it all. And I'll tell it to the others just as they tell their boys and girls and life to me. We'll sit there, growing wiser and calmer and better every year and every year, ten, twenty, thirty years. The Family knowledge will double, quadruple, the wisdom will not be lost. And we'll be waiting there in that sitting room, should you ever need us for your own children in time of illness, or, God prevent, deprivation or death. There we'll be, growing old but not old, getting closer to the time, perhaps, someday, when we live up to our first strange joking name."

"The Pinocchios?" asked Tim.

Grandma nodded.

I knew what she meant. The day when, as in the old tale, Pinocchio had grown so worthy and so fine that the gift of life had been given him. So I saw them, in future years, the entire family of Fantoccini, the Pinocchios, trading and retrading, murmuring and whispering their knowledge in the great parlors of philosophy, waiting for the day. The day that could never come.

Grandma must have read that thought in our eyes.

"We'll see," she said. "Let's just wait and see."

"Oh, Grandma," cried Agatha and she was weeping as she had wept many years before. "You don't have to wait. You're alive. You've always been alive to us!"

And she caught hold of the old woman and we all caught hold for a long moment and then ran off up in the sky to faraway schools and years and her last words to us before we let the helicopter swarm us away into autumn were these:

"When you are very old and gone childish-small again, with childish ways and childish yens and, in need of feeding, make a wish for the old teacher-nurse, the dumb yet wise companion, send for me. I will come back. We shall inhabit the nursery again, never fear."

"Oh, we shall never be old!" we cried. "That will never happen!"

"Never! Never!"

And we were gone.

And the years are flown.

And we are old now, Tim and Agatha and I.

Our children are grown and gone, our wives and husbands vanished from the earth and now, by Dickensian coincidence, accept it as you will or not accept, back in the old house, we three.

I lie here in the bedroom which was my childish place seventy, O seventy, believe it, seventy years ago. Beneath this wallpaper is another layer and yet another-times-three to the old wallpaper covered over when I was nine. The wallpaper is peeling. I see peeking from beneath, old elephants, familiar tigers, fine and amiable zebras, irascible crocodiles. I have sent for the paperers to carefully remove all but that last layer. The old animals will live again on the walls, revealed.

And we have sent for someone else.

The three of us have called:

Grandma! You said you'd come back when we had need.

We are surprised by age, by time. We are old. We *need*.

And in three rooms of a summer house very late in time, three old children rise up, crying out in their heads: We *loved* you! We *love* you!

There! There! in the sky, we think, waking at morn. Is that the delivery machine? Does it settle to the lawn?

There! There on the grass by the front porch. Does the mummy case arrive?

Are our names inked on ribbons wrapped about the lovely form beneath the golden mask?

And the kept gold key, forever hung on Agatha's breast, warmed and waiting? Oh God, will it, after all these years, will it wind, will it set in motion, will it, dearly, *fit*?!

ITALO CALVINO

Italo Calvino (1923–1985) was one of postwar Italy's most innovative writers. In seeking an overall definition of his ironic and fanciful fiction he wrote, "I have tried to remove weight from the structure of stories and from language." Indeed, in his inventiveness and playfulness Calvino is in some ways reminiscent of one of his acknowledged literary influences, Jorge Luis Borges. His novels include *Invisible Cities* (1974), *If on a Winter's Night a Traveler* (1981), and *Mr. Palomar* (1983); among his collections of stories are *Marcovaldo* (1963), *Cosmicomics* (1968), *TZero* (1969), *Italian Folktales* (1956), and *Difficult Loves* (1985). "One of the Three Is Still Alive," a wartime story, shows a darker side of Calvino. The second story here, "Summer: Moon and GNAC," is a dreamy story about one of Calvino's dreamiest characters, Marcovaldo.

One of the Three Is Still Alive

Translated from the Italian by Archibald Colquhoun and Peggy Wright

Three naked men were sitting on a stone. All the men of the village were standing around them and facing a bearded old man.

"... and they were the highest flames I've ever seen in the mountains," the old man with the beard was saying. "And I said to myself: How can a village burn so high?

"And the smell of smoke was unbearable and I said to myself: How can smoke from our village stink like that?"

The tallest of the three naked men, who was hugging his shoulders because there was a slight wind, gave the oldest a dig in the ribs to get him to explain; he still wanted to understand, and the other was the only one who knew a little of the language. But the oldest of the three did not raise his head from between his hands, and now and again a quiver passed along the vertebrae on his bent back. The fat man was no longer to be counted on; the womanish fat on his body was trembling all over, his eyes were like windowpanes streaked by rain.

"And then they told me that the flames burning our houses came from our own grain, and the stink was from our sons being burned alive; Tancin's son, Gé's son, the son of the customs guard. . . ."

"My son Bastian!" shouted a man with haunted eyes. He was the only one who interrupted, every now and again. The others were standing there silent and serious, with their hands on their rifles.

The third naked man was not of exactly the same nationality as the others; he came from a part where villages and children had been burned at one time. So he knew what people think about those who burn and kill, and should have felt less hopeful than the others. Instead of which there was something, an anguished uncertainty, that prevented him from resigning himself.

"Now, we've only caught these three men," said the old man with the beard.

"Only three!" shouted the haunted-looking man; the others were still silent.

"Maybe among them, too, there are some who aren't really bad, who obey orders against their will, maybe these three are that sort. . . ."

The haunted-looking man glared at the old man.

"Explain," whispered the tallest of the three naked men to the oldest. But the other's whole life now seemed to be running away down the vertebrae on his spine.

"When children have been killed and houses burned one can't make any distinction between those who're bad and not bad. And we're sure of being in the right by condemning these three to death."

"Death," thought the tallest of the three naked men. "I heard that word. What does it mean — 'death'?"

But the oldest one took no notice of him, and the fattest now seemed to be muttering prayers. Suddenly the fattest had remembered he was a Catholic. He had been the only Catholic in the company, and his comrades had often made fun of him. "I'm a Catholic," he began muttering in his own language. It was not clear whether he was begging for salvation on earth or in heaven.

"I say that before killing them we should . . ." exclaimed the haunted-looking man, but the others had got to their feet and were not listening to him.

"To the Witch's Hole," said one with a black mustache. "So there won't be any graves to dig."

They made the three get up. The fattest put his hands over his front. Nothing made them feel more under accusation than being naked.

The peasants led them up along the rocky path, with rifles in their backs. The Witch's Hole was the opening of a vertical cave, a hole that dropped right down into the belly of the mountain, down, down, no one knew where. The three naked men were led up to the edge, and the armed peasants lined up in front of them; then the oldest of them began screaming. He screamed out despairing phrases, perhaps in his own dialect; the other two did not understand him. He was the father of a family, the oldest was, but he was also the least worthy, and his screams had the effect of making the other two feel annoyed with him and calmer in the face of death. The tall one, though, still felt that strange disquiet, as if he were not quite certain of something. The Catholic was holding his joined hands low; it was not clear whether this was to pray or to hide his front.

Hearing the eldest one screaming made the armed peasants lose their calm; they wanted to have done with the business as soon as possible, and began to fire scattered shots without waiting for an order. The tall one saw the Catholic crumple down beside him and roll into the precipice; then the oldest of them fell with his head back and vanished, dragging his last cry down the walls of rock. Between the puffs of gunpowder the tall one saw a peasant struggling with a blocked bolt; then he, too, fell into the darkness.

A cloud of pain in the back like a swarm of stinging bees prevented him from losing consciousness at once; he had fallen through a briar bush. Then tons of emptiness weighed down on his stomach, and he fainted.

Suddenly he seemed to be back on a height, as if the earth had given a great heave; he had stopped. His fingers were wet and he smelled blood. He must be crushed to bits and about to die. But he did not feel himself getting weaker, and all the agonies of the fall were lively and distinct in his mind. He tried to move a hand, the left one; it responded. He groped along the other arm, touched his pulse, his elbow; but the arm did not feel anything; it might have been dead, for it only moved if raised by the other hand. Then he had the sensation of holding the wrist of his right arm in both hands; this was impossible. He realized that he was holding someone else's arm; he had fallen on the dead body of one of the other two. He prodded the fat flesh of the Catholic; that soft cushion had broken his fall. That was why he was alive. That was one reason; also, he remembered now, he had not been hit but had flung himself down beforehand; he could not remember if he had done it intentionally, but that was not important now. Then he discovered that he could see; some light filtered down there in the depths, and the tallest of the three naked men could make out his own hands and those sticking out of the heap of flesh beneath him. He turned and looked up; at the top was an aperture full of light — the opening of the Witch's Hole. First it hurt his eyes like a yellow flash; once they got used to it, he could see the blueness of the sky, far away from him, twice as far as the earth's crust.

The sight of the sky plunged him into despair; it would certainly be better to be dead. There he was with his two dead companions at the bottom of a very deep pit, from which he could never get out again. He shouted. The streak of sky above became fringed with heads. "One of them's alive!" they said. They threw something down. The naked man watched it dropping like a stone, then hit against the wall, and heard an explosion. There was a niche in the rock behind him, and the naked man squeezed into it; the well was full of dust and pieces of splintered rock. He pulled at the body of the Catholic and held it up in front of the niche; it was starting to fall apart but there was nothing else he could use to shelter himself. He was just in time: another grenade came down, and reached the bottom, raising a spray of blood and stones. The corpse broke up; now the naked man had no defense or hope. In the patch of sky appeared the white beard of the big old man. The others had drawn to one side.

"Hey!" called the big man with the beard.

"Hey!" replied the naked man, from the depths.

And the big man with the beard repeated: "Hey!"

There was nothing else to say between them.

Then the big man with the beard turned around. "Throw him a rope," he said.

The naked man did not understand. He saw some of the heads leaving and the ones remaining making signs at him, signs of assurance, not to worry. The naked man looked at them with his head stuck out of the niche, not daring to expose himself altogether, feeling the same disquiet as when he had been sitting on the stone during the trial. But the peasants were not throwing grenades any more; they were looking down and asking him questions, to which he replied with groans. The rope did not come, and one by one the peasants left the edge. Then the naked man came out of his hiding place and looked at the distance separating him from the top, the walls of sheer naked rock.

At that moment appeared the face of the haunted man. He was looking around and smiling. Then he moved back from the edge of the Witch's Hole, aimed his rifle into it, and fired. The naked man heard the bullet whistle past his ear; the Witch's Hole was a narrow shaft and not quite vertical, so things thrown in rarely reached the bottom, and bullets easily hit a layer of rock and stopped there. He squatted in his refuge, with foam on his lips, like a dog. Now up there all the peasants were back and one was unwinding a long rope down the shaft. The naked man watched the rope coming down but did not move.

"Hey!" the one with the black mustache shouted down. "Catch hold of it and come up."

But the naked man stayed in his niche.

"Come on; up you go," they shouted. "We won't do you any harm."

And they made the rope dance about in front of his eyes. The naked man was frightened.

"We won't do you any harm. We swear it," the men were saying, trying to sound sincere. And they were sincere; they wanted to save him at all costs so as to be able to shoot him all over again; but at that moment they just wanted to save him, and their voices had a tone of affection, of human brotherhood.

The naked man sensed all this, and anyway he had little choice; he put a hand on the rope. But then among the men holding it he saw the head of the man with the haunted eyes, and he dropped the rope and hid himself. They had to begin convincing him, begging him, all over again; finally he decided and began going up. The rope was full of knots and easy to climb; he could also catch hold of jutting bits of rock. As the naked man moved slowly up toward the light, he saw the heads of the peasants at the top becoming clearer and bigger. Then the man with the haunted eyes reappeared all of a sudden and the others did not have time to hold him back; he was holding an automatic gun and began firing it at once. At the first burst the rope broke right above the naked man's hands. He crashed down, knocking against the sides, and fell back on the remains of his companions. Up there, against the sky, he saw the man with the beard waving his arms and shaking his head.

The others were trying to explain, in gestures and shouts, that it was not their fault, that they'd punish that madman, and that they were going to look for another rope and bring him up again. But the naked man had lost hope now; he would never be able to return to the earth's surface; he would never leave the bottom of this shaft, and he would go mad there drinking blood and eating human flesh, without ever being able to die. Up there, against the sky, there were good angels with ropes, and bad angels with grenades and rifles, and a big old man with a white beard who waved his arms but could not save him.

The armed men, seeing him unconvinced by their fair words, decided to finish him off with hand grenades, and began throwing them down. But the naked man had found another hiding place, a narrow horizontal crack in the rock where he could slip in and be safe. At every grenade that fell he crawled deeper into this crack, until he reached a point where he could not see any more light. He went on dragging himself along on his stomach like a snake, with darkness and the damp slimy rock all around him. From being damp the rock surface beneath him was now getting wet, then covered with water; the naked man could feel the cold trickle running under his stomach. It was the passage opened under the earth by the rains coming down through the Witch's Hole: a long narrow cavern, a subterranean drain. Where would it end? Perhaps it would lose itself in blind caves in the belly of the mountain, or perhaps it would funnel the water through narrow little channels that would issue into springs. And his body would rot away there in a drain and infect the waters of the springs, poisoning entire villages.

The air was almost unbreathable; the naked man felt the moment coming when his lungs would no longer be able to hold out. Instead, the flow of water was increasing, getting deeper and quicker; the naked man was now slithering along with his whole body underwater and could clean off the crust of mud and of his own and others' blood. He did not know whether he had moved far or not; the complete darkness and that slithering movement had deprived him of all sense of distance. He was exhausted. Before his eyes luminous shapeless forms were beginning to appear. The farther he advanced, the clearer these shapes became, taking on definite though continuously transforming edges. Supposing it was not just a dazzle inside the retina of his eyes, but a light, a real light, at the end of the cavern? He had only to close his eyes, or look in the opposite direction, to make certain. But anyone who stares at a light has a dazzled feeling at the roots of his eyes even if he shuts his lids or turns his gaze; he could not distinguish between the light outside and the lights in his own eyes, and remained in doubt.

He noticed something else new, by touch: the stalactites. Slimy stalactites were hanging from the roof of the cave and stalagmites coming up from the ground on the verges of the water, where they were not eroded. The naked man began pulling himself along by the stalactites above his head. And as he moved he noticed that his arms, from being folded to grasp the stalactites, were gradually straightening out, which meant that the cave was getting bigger. Soon the man could arch his back and walk on all fours; and the light was becoming less uncertain; he could tell now whether his eyes were open or shut, and he was beginning to make out the shapes of things, the arch of the roof, the droop of the stalactites, the black glitter of the current.

Finally he was walking erect, up the long cave toward the luminous opening, with the water to his waist — still hanging on to the stalactites, though, to keep himself straight. One stalactite seemed bigger than the others, and when the man seized it he felt it opening in his hand and a cold soft wing beating on his face. A bat! It flew off, and the other bats hanging with their heads down woke up and flew away; soon the whole cave was full of silent flying bats, and the man felt the wind from their wings around him and their skin brushing against his forehead and mouth. He walked on in a cloud until he reached the open air.

The cave came out into a torrent. Once again the naked man was on the crust of the earth, under the sky. Was he safe now? He must take care not to make any mistakes. The torrent was running silently over white and black stones. Around it was a wood full of twisted trees; all that grew in the undergrowth was thorns and brambles. He was naked in wild and deserted parts, and the nearest human beings were enemies who would pursue him with pitchforks and guns as soon as they saw him.

The naked man climbed a willow tree. The valley was all woods and shrub-covered slopes, under a gray hump of mountain. But at the end of it, where the torrent turned, there was a slate roof with white smoke coming up. Life, thought the naked man, was a hell, with rare moments recalling some ancient paradise.

ITALO CALVINO

Summer: Moon and GNAC

Translated from the Italian by William Weaver

The night lasted twenty seconds, then came twenty seconds of GNAC. For twenty seconds you could see the blue sky streaked with black clouds, the gilded sickle of the waxing moon, outlined by an impalpable halo, and stars that, the more you looked at them, the denser their poignant smallness became, to the sprinkle of the Milky Way: all this seen in great haste; every detail you dwelt on was something of the whole that you lost, because the twenty seconds quickly ended and the GNAC took over.

The GNAC was a part of the neon sign SPAAK-COGNAC on the roof opposite, which shone for twenty seconds then went off for twenty, and when it was lighted you couldn't see anything else. The moon suddenly faded, the sky became a flat, uniform black, the stars lost their radiance, and the cats, male and female, that for ten seconds had been letting out howls of love, moving languidly towards each other along the drainpipes and the roof-trees, squatted on the tiles, their fur bristling in the phosphorescent neon light.

Leaning out of the attic where they lived, Marcovaldo's family was traversed by conflicting trains of thought. It was night, and Isolina, a big girl by now, felt carried away by the moonlight; her heart yearned, and even the faintest croaking of a radio from the lower floors of the building came to her like the notes of a serenade; there was the GNAC, and that radio seemed to take on a different rhythm, a jazz beat, and Isolina thought of the dance-hall full of blazing lights and herself, poor thing, up here all alone. Pietruccio and Michelino stared wide-eyed into the night and let themselves be invaded by a warm, soft fear of being surrounded by forests full of brigands; then, GNAC!, and they sprang up with thumbs erect and forefingers extended, one against the other: "Hands up! I'm the Lone Ranger!" Domitilla, their mother, every time the light was turned off, thought: "Now the children must be sent to bed; this air could be bad for them; and Isolina shouldn't be looking out of the window at this hour: it's not proper!" But then everything was again luminous, electric, outside and inside, and Domitilla felt as if she were paying a visit to the home of someone important.

Fiordaligi, on the contrary, a melancholy youth, every time the GNAC went off, saw the dimly lighted window of a garret appear behind the curl of the *G*, and beyond the pane the face of a moon-colored girl, neon-colored, the color of light in the night, a mouth still almost a child's that, the moment he smiled at her, parted imperceptibly and seemed almost to open in a smile; then all of a sudden from the darkness that implacable *G* of GNAC burst out again, and the face lost its outline, was transformed into a weak, pale shadow, and he could no longer tell if the girlish mouth had responded to his smile.

In the midst of this storm of passions, Marcovaldo was trying to teach his children the positions of the celestial bodies.

"That's the Great Bear: one, two, three, four, and there, the tail. And that's the Little Bear. And the Pole-Star that means North."

"What does that one over there mean?"

"It means *C*. But that doesn't have anything to do with the stars. It's the last letter of the word COGNAC. The stars mark the four cardinal points. North South East West. The moon's hump is to the west. Hump to the west, waxing moon. Hump to the east, waning moon."

"Is cognac waning, Papà? The *C*'s hump is to the east!"

"Waxing and waning have nothing to do with that: it's a sign the Spaak company has put there."

"What company put up the moon then?"

"The moon wasn't put up by a company. It's a satellite, and it's always there."

"If it's always there, why does it keep changing its hump?"

"It's the quarters. You only see a part of it."

"You only see a part of COGNAC too."

"Because the roof of the Pierbernardi building is higher."

"Higher than the moon?"

And so, every time the GNAC came on, Marcovaldo's stars became mixed up with terrestrial commerce, and Isolina transformed a sigh into a low humming of a mambo, and the girl of the garret disappeared in that cold and dazzling arc, hiding her response to the kiss that Fiordaligi had finally summoned the courage to blow her on his fingertips, and Filippetto and Michelino, their fists to their faces, played at strafing: Tat-tat-tat-tat . . . against the glowing sign, which, after its twenty seconds, went off.

"Tat-tat-tat . . . Did you see that, Papà? I shot it out with just one burst." Filippetto said, but already, outside the neon light, his warlike mania had vanished and his eyes were filling with sleep.

"If you only had!" his father blurted. "If it had only been blown to bits! I'd show you Leo the lion, the Twins . . ."

"Leo the lion!" Michelino was overcome with enthusiasm. "Wait!" He had an idea. He took his slingshot, loaded it with gravel, of which he always carried a reserve pocketful, and fired a volley of pebbles, with all his strength, at the GNAC.

They heard the shower fall, scattered, on the tiles of the roof opposite, on the tin of the drainpipes, the tinkle at the panes of a window that had been struck, the gong of a pebble plunging down on the metal shield of a street-light, a voice from below: "It's raining stones! Hey, you up there! Hoodlum." But at the very moment of the shooting the neon sign had turned off at the end of its twenty seconds. And everyone in the attic room began counting mentally: one two three, ten eleven, up to twenty. They counted nineteen, held their breath, they counted twenty, they counted twenty-one twenty-two, for fear of having counted too fast. But no, not at all: the GNAC didn't come on again; it remained a black curlicue, hard to decipher, twined around its scaffolding like a vine around a pergola. "Aaaah!" they all shouted and the hood of the sky rose, infinitely starry, above them.

Marcovaldo, his hand frozen halfway towards the slap he meant to give Michelino, felt as if he had been flung into space. The darkness that now reigned at roof-level made a kind of obscure barrier that shut out the world below, where yellow and green and red hieroglyphics continued to whirl, and the winking eyes of traffic-lights, and the luminous navigation of empty trams, and the invisible cars that cast in front of them the bright cone of their headlights. From this world only a diffuse phosphorescence rose up this high, vague as smoke. And raising your eyes, no longer blinded, you saw the perspective of space unfold, the constellations expanded in depth, the firmament turning in every direction, a sphere that contains everything and is contained by no boundary, and only a thinning of its weft, like a breach, opened towards Venus, to make it stand out alone over the frame of the earth, with its steady slash of light exploded and concentrated at one point.

Suspended in this sky, the new moon — rather than display the abstract appearance of a half-moon — revealed its true nature as an opaque sphere, its whole outline illuminated by the oblique rays of a sun the earth had lost, though it retained (as you can see only on certain early-summer nights) its warm color. And Marcovaldo, looking at that narrow shore of moon cut there between shadow and light, felt a nostalgia, as if yearning to arrive at a beach which had stayed miraculously sunny in the night.

And so they remained at the window of the garret, the children frightened by the measureless consequences of their act, Isolina carried away as if in ecstasy, Fiordaligi, who, alone among all, discerned the dimly lighted garret and finally the girl's lunar smile. Their Mamma recovered herself: "Come on now, it's night. What are you doing at the window? You'll catch something, in this moonlight!"

Michelino aimed his slingshot up high. "Now I'll turn off the moon!" He was seized and put to bed.

And so for the rest of that night and all through the night following, the neon sign on the other roof said only SPAAK-CO, and from Marcovaldo's garret you could see the firmament. Fiordaligi and the lunar girl blew each other kisses, and perhaps, speaking to each other in sign language, they would manage to make a date to meet.

But on the morning of the second day, on the roof, in the scaffolding that supported the neon sign, the tiny forms of two electricians in overalls were visible, as they checked the tubes and wires. With the air of old men who predict changes in the weather, Marcovaldo stuck his head out and said: "Tonight there'll be GNAC again."

Somebody knocked at the garret. They opened the door. It was a gentleman wearing eyeglasses. "I beg your pardon, could I take a look at your window? Thanks." And he introduced himself: "Godifredo, neon advertising agent."

"We're ruined! They want us to pay the damages!" Marcovaldo thought, and he was already devouring his children with his eyes, forgetting his astronomical transports. "Now he'll look at the window and realize the stones could only have come from here." He tried to ward this off. "You know how it is, the kids shoot at the sparrows. Pebbles. I don't know how that Spaak sign went out. But I punished them, all right. Oh yes indeed, I punished them! And you can be sure it won't happen again."

Signor Godifredo's face became alert. "Actually, I'm employed by 'Tomahawk Cognac', not by Spaak. I had come to examine the possibility of a sign on this roof. But do go on: I'm interested in what you're saying."

And so it was that Marcovaldo, half an hour later, concluded a deal with Tomahawk Cognac, Spaak's chief rival. The children should empty their slingshots at the GNAC every time the sign was turned on again.

"That should be the straw that will break the camel's back," Signor Godifredo said. He was not mistaken: already on the verge of bankruptcy because of its large advertising outlay, Spaak and Co. took the constant damaging of its most beautiful neon signs as a bad omen. The sign that now sometimes said COGAC and sometimes CONAC or CONC spread among the firm's creditors the impression of financial difficulties; at a certain point, the advertising agency refused to make further repairs if arrears were not paid; the turned-off sign increased the alarm among the creditors; and Spaak went out of business.

In the sky of Marcovaldo the full moon shone, round, in all its splendor.

It was in the last quarter when the electricians came back to clamber over the roof opposite. And that night, in letters of fire, letters twice as high and broad as before, they could read TOMAHAWK COGNAC, and there was no longer moon or firmament or sky or night, only TOMAHAWK COGNAC, TOMAHAWK COGNAC, TOMAHAWK COGNAC, which blinked on and off every two seconds.

The worst hit was Fiordaligi; the garret of the lunar girl had vanished behind an enormous, impenetrable *W*.

ETHAN CANIN

 Ethan Canin was born in 1960 in Ann Arbor, Michigan, the son of a musician and an artist. He grew up in many towns across the country, earned degrees at Stanford University and the Iowa Writer's Workshop, and enrolled in the Harvard University Medical School, where he is still a student. His stories, collected in *Emperor of the Air* (1987), are concerned with moments of realization, with the ways human beings learn the lessons life has to teach them. One reviewer, musing on the relation between medical training and writing (Chekhov, Arthur Conan Doyle, and Somerset Maugham were all doctors) observed that Canin's understanding of "the condition of the heart" probably owes to his study of the health of the body. Canin, perhaps, less willing to draw conclusions about the sources of his understanding, has said that he writes to move himself and to move the reader. "Despite all science, I think, we will never understand the sadness of certain notes." "Star Food" touches, and then transcends, that sadness.

Star Food

The summer I turned eighteen I disappointed both my parents for the first time. This hadn't happened before, since what disappointed one usually pleased the other. As a child, if I played broom hockey instead of going to school, my mother wept and my father took me outside later to find out how many goals I had scored. On the other hand, if I spent Saturday afternoon on the roof of my parents' grocery store staring up at the clouds instead of counting cracker cartons in the stockroom, my father took me to the back to talk about work and discipline, and my mother told me later to keep looking for things that no one else saw.

This was her theory. My mother felt that men like Leonardo da Vinci and Thomas Edison had simply stared long enough at regular objects until they saw new things, and thus my looking into the sky might someday make me a great man. She believed I had a worldly curiosity. My father believed I wanted to avoid stock work.

Stock work was an issue in our family, as were all the jobs that had to be done in a grocery store. Our store was called Star Food and above it an incandescent star revolved. Its circuits buzzed, and its yellow points, as thick as my knees, drooped with the slow melting of the bulb. On summer nights flying insects flocked in clouds around it, droves of them burning on the glass. One of my jobs was to go out on the roof, the sloping, eaved side that looked over the western half of Arcade, California, and clean them off the star. At night, when their black bodies stood out against the glass, when the wind carried in the marsh smell of the New Jerusalem River, I went into the attic, crawled out the dormer window onto the peaked roof, and slid across the shingles to where the pole rose like a lightning rod into the night. I reached with a wet rag and rubbed away the June bugs and pickerel moths until the star was yellow-white and steaming from the moisture. Then I turned and looked over Arcade, across the bright avenue and my dimly lighted high school in the distance, into the low hills where oak trees grew in rows on the curbs and where girls drove to school in their own convertibles. When my father came up on the roof sometimes to talk about the store, we fixed our eyes on the red tile roofs or the small clouds of blue barbecue smoke that floated above the hills on warm evenings. While the clean bulb buzzed and flickered behind us, we talked about loss leaders or keeping the elephant-ear plums stacked in neat triangles.

The summer I disappointed my parents, though, my father talked to me about a lot of other things. He also made me look in the other direction whenever we were on the roof together, not west to the hills and their clouds of barbecue smoke, but east toward the other part of town. We crawled up one slope of the roof, then down the other so that I could see beyond the back alley where wash hung on lines in the moonlight, down to the neighborhoods across Route 5. These were the neighborhoods where men sat on the curbs on weekday afternoons, where rusted, wheel-less cars lay on blocks in the yards.

"*You're* going to end up on one of those curbs," my father told me.

Usually I stared farther into the clouds when he said something like that. He and my mother argued about what I did on the roof for so many hours at a time, and I hoped that by looking closely at the amazing borders of clouds I could confuse him. My mother believed I was on the verge of discovering something atmospheric, and I was sure she told my father this, so when he came upstairs, made me look across Route 5, and talked to me about how I was going to end up there, I squinted harder at the sky.

"You don't fool me for a second," he said.

He was up on the roof with me because I had been letting someone steal from the store.

From the time we first had the star on the roof, my mother believed her only son was destined for limited fame. Limited because she thought that true vision was distilled and could not be appreciated by everybody. I discovered this shortly after the star was installed, when I spent an hour looking out over the roofs and chimneys instead of helping my father stock a shipment of dairy. It was a hot day and the milk sat on the loading dock while he searched for me in the store and in our apartment next door. When he came up and found me, his neck was red and his footfalls shook the roof joists. At my age I was still allowed certain mistakes, but I'd seen the dairy truck arrive and knew I should have been downstairs, so it surprised me later, after I'd helped unload the milk, when my mother stopped beside me as I was sprinkling the leafy vegetables with a spray bottle.

"Dade, I don't want you to let anyone keep you from what you ought to be doing."

"I'm sorry," I said. "I should have helped with the milk earlier."

"No," she said, "that's not what I mean." Then she told me her theory of limited fame while I sprayed the cabbage and lettuce with the atomizer. It was the first time

I had heard her idea. The world's most famous men, she said, presidents and emperors, generals and patriots, were men of vulgar fame, men who ruled the world because their ideas were obvious and could be understood by everybody. But there was also limited fame. Newton and Galileo and Enrico Fermi were men of limited fame, and as I stood there with the atomizer in my hand my mother's eyes watered over and she told me she knew in her heart that one day I was going to be a man of limited fame. I was twelve years old.

After that day I found I could avoid a certain amount of stock work by staying up on the roof and staring into the fine layers of stratus clouds that floated above Arcade. In the *Encyclopedia Americana* I read about cirrus and cumulus and thunderheads, about inversion layers and currents like the currents at sea, and in the afternoons I went upstairs and watched. The sky was a changing thing, I found out. It was more than a blue sheet. Twirling with pollen and sunlight, it began to transform itself.

Often as I stood on the roof my father came outside and swept the sidewalk across the street. Through the telephone poles and crossed power lines he looked up at me, his broom strokes small and fierce as if he were hoeing hard ground. It irked him that my mother encouraged me to stay on the roof. He was a short man with direct habits and an understanding of how to get along in the world, and he believed that God rewarded only two things, courtesy and hard work. God did not reward looking at the sky. In the car my father acknowledged good drivers and in restaurants he left good tips. He knew the names of his customers. He never sold a rotten vegetable. He shook hands often, looked everyone in the eye, and on Friday nights when we went to the movies he made us sit in the front row of the theater. "Why should I pay to look over other people's heads?" he said. The movies made him talk. On the way back to the car he walked with his hands clasped behind him and greeted everyone who passed. He smiled. He mentioned the fineness of the evening as if he were the admiral or aviator we had just seen on the screen. "People like it," he said. "It's good for business." My mother was quiet, walking with her slender arms folded in front of her as if she were cold.

I liked the movies because I imagined myself doing everything the heroes did — deciding to invade at daybreak, swimming half the night against the seaward current — but whenever we left the theater I was disappointed. From the front row, life seemed like a clear set of decisions, but on the street afterward I realized that the world existed all around me and I didn't know what I wanted. The quiet of evening and the ordinariness of human voices startled me.

Sometimes on the roof, as I stared into the layers of horizon, the sounds of the street faded into this same ordinariness. One afternoon when I was standing under the star my father came outside and looked up at me. "You're in a trance," he called. I glanced down at him, then squinted back at the horizon. For a minute he waited, and then from across the street he threw a rock. He had a pitcher's arm and could have hit me if he wanted, but the rock sailed past me and clattered on the shingles. My mother came right out of the store anyway and stopped him. "I wanted him off the roof," I heard my father tell her later in the same frank voice in which he explained his position to vegetable salesmen. "If someone's throwing rocks at him he'll come down. He's no fool."

I was flattered by this, but my mother won the point and from then on I could stay up on the roof when I wanted. To appease my father I cleaned the electric star, and though he often came outside to sweep, he stopped telling me to come down. I thought about limited fame and spent a lot of time noticing the sky. When I looked closely it was a sea with waves and shifting colors, wind seams and denials of distance, and after a while I learned to look at it so that it entered my eye whole. It was blue liquid. I spent hours looking into its pale wash, looking for things, though I didn't know what. I looked for lines or sectors, the diamond shapes of daylight stars. Sometimes, silver-winged jets from the air force base across the hills turned the right way against the sun and went off like small flash bulbs on the horizon. There was nothing that struck me and stayed, though, nothing with the brilliance of white light or electric explosion that I thought came with discovery, so after a while I changed my idea of discovery. I just stood on the roof and stared. When my mother asked me, I told her that I might be seeing new things but that seeing change took time. "It's slow," I told her. "It may take years."

The first time I let her steal I chalked it up to surprise. I was working the front register when she walked in, a thin, tall woman in a plaid dress that looked wilted. She went right to the standup display of cut-price, nearly expired breads and crackers, where she took a loaf of rye from the shelf. Then she turned and looked me in the eye. We were looking into each other's eyes when she walked out the front door. Through the blue-and-white LOOK UP TO STAR FOOD sign on the window I watched her cross the street.

There were two or three other shoppers in the store, and over the tops of the potato chip packages I could see my mother's broom. My father was in back unloading chicken parts. Nobody else had seen her come in; nobody had seen her leave. I locked the cash drawer and walked to the aisle where my mother was sweeping.

"I think someone just stole."

My mother wheeled a trash receptacle when she swept, and as I stood there she closed it, put down her broom, and wiped her face with her handkerchief. "You couldn't get him?"

"It was a her."

"A lady?"

"I couldn't chase her. She came in and took a loaf of rye and left."

I had chased plenty of shoplifters before. They were kids usually, in sneakers and coats too warm for the weather. I chased them up the aisle and out the door, then to the corner and around it while ahead of me they tried to toss whatever it was — Twinkies, freeze-pops — into the sidewalk hedges. They cried when I caught them, begged me not to tell their parents. First time, my father said, scare them real good. Second time, call the law. I took them back with me to the store, held them by the collar as we walked. Then I sat them in the straight-back chair in the stockroom and gave them a speech my father had written. It was printed on a blue index card taped to the door. DO YOU KNOW WHAT YOU HAVE DONE? it began. DO YOU KNOW WHAT IT IS TO STEAL? I learned to pause between the questions, pace the room, check the card. "Give them time to get scared," my father said. He was expert at this. He never talked to them until he had dusted the vegetables or run a couple of women through the register. "Why should I stop my work for a kid who steals from me?" he said. When he finally came into the stockroom he moved and spoke the way policemen do at the scene of an accident. His manner was slow and deliberate. First he asked me what they had stolen. If I had recovered whatever it was, he took it and held it up to the light, turned it over in his fingers as if it were of large value. Then he opened the freezer door and led the kid inside to talk about law and punishment amid the frozen beef carcasses. He paced as he spoke, breathed clouds of vapor into the air.

In the end, though, my mother usually got him to let them off. Once when he wouldn't, when he had called the police to pick up a third-offense boy who sat trembling in the stockroom, my mother called him to the front of the store to talk to a customer. In the stockroom we kept a key to the back door hidden under a silver samovar that had belonged to my grandmother, and when my father was in front that afternoon my mother came to the rear, took it out, and opened the back door. She leaned down to the boy's ear. "Run," she said.

The next time she came in it happened the same way. My father was at the vegetable tier, stacking avocados. My mother was in back listening to the radio. It was afternoon. I rang in a customer, then looked up while I was putting the milk cartons in the bottom of the bag, and there she was. Her gray eyes were looking into mine. She had two cans of pineapple juice in her hands, and on the way out she held the door for an old woman.

That night I went up to clean the star. The air was clear. It was warm. When I finished wiping the glass I moved out over the edge of the eaves and looked into the distance where little turquoise squares — lighted swimming pools — stood out against the hills.

"Dade — "

It was my father's voice from behind the peak of the roof.

"Yes?"

"Come over to this side."

I mounted the shallow-pitched roof, went over the peak, and edged down the other slope to where I could see his silhouette against the lights on Route 5. He was smoking. I got up and we stood together at the edge of the shingled eaves. In front of us trucks rumbled by on the interstate, their trailers lit at the edges like the mast lights of ships.

"Look across the highway," he said.

"I am."

"What do you see?"

"Cars."

"What else?"

"Trucks."

For a while he didn't say anything. He dragged a few times on his cigarette, then pinched off the lit end and put the rest back in the pack. A couple of motorcycles went by, a car with one headlight, a bus.

"Do you know what it's like to live in a shack?" he said.

"No."

"You don't want to end up in a place like that. And it's damn easy to do if you don't know what you want. You know how easy it is?"

"Easy," I said.

"You have to know what you want."

For years my father had been trying to teach me competence and industry. Since

I was nine I had been squeeze-drying mops before returning them to the closet, double-counting change, sweeping under the lip of the vegetable bins even if the dirt there was invisible to customers. On the basis of industry, my father said, Star Food had grown from a two-aisle, one-freezer corner store to the largest grocery in Arcade. When I was eight he had bought the failing gas station next door and built additions, so that now Star Food had nine aisles, separate coolers for dairy, soda, and beer, a tiered vegetable stand, a glass-fronted butcher counter, a part-time butcher, and, under what used to be the rain roof of the failing gas station, free parking while you shopped. When I started high school we moved into the apartment next door, and at meals we discussed store improvements. Soon my father invented a grid system for easy location of foods. He stayed up one night and painted, and the next morning there was a new coordinate system on the ceiling of the store. It was a grid, A through J, 1 through 10. For weeks there were drops of blue paint in his eyelashes.

A few days later my mother pasted up fluorescent stars among the grid squares. She knew about the real constellations and was accurate with the ones she stuck to the ceiling, even though she also knew that the aisle lights in Star Food stayed on day and night, so that her stars were going to be invisible. We saw them only once, in fact, in a blackout a few months later, when they lit up in hazy clusters around the store.

"Do you know why I did it?" she asked me the night of the blackout as we stood beneath their pale light.

"No."

"Because of the idea."

She was full of ideas, and one was that I was accomplishing something on the shallow-pitched section of our roof. Sometimes she sat at the dormer window and watched me. Through the glass I could see the slender outlines of her cheekbones. "What do you see?" she asked. On warm nights she leaned over the sill and pointed out the constellations. "They are the illumination of great minds," she said.

After the woman walked out the second time I began to think a lot about what I wanted. I tried to discover what it was, and I had an idea it would come to me on the roof. In the evenings I sat up there and thought. I looked for signs. I threw pebbles down into the street and watched where they hit. I read the newspaper, and stories about ballplayers or jazz musicians began to catch my eye. When he was ten years old, Johnny Unitas strung a tire from a tree limb and spent afternoons throwing a football through it as it swung. Dizzy Gillespie played with an orchestra when he was seven. There was an emperor who ruled China at age eight. What could be said about me? He swept the dirt no one could see under the lip of the vegetable bins.

The day after the woman had walked out the second time, my mother came up on the roof while I was cleaning the star. She usually wore medium heels and stayed away from the shingled roof, but that night she came up. I had been over the glass once when I saw her coming through the dormer window, skirt hem and white shoes lit by moonlight. Most of the insects were cleaned off and steam was drifting up into the night. She came through the window, took off her shoes, and edged down the roof until she was standing next to me at the star. "It's a beautiful night," she said.

"Cool."

"Dade, when you're up here do you ever think about what is in the mind of a great man when he makes a discovery?"

The night was just making its transition from the thin sky to the thick, the air was taking on weight, and at the horizon distances were shortening. I looked out over the plain and tried to think of an answer. That day I had been thinking about a story my father occasionally told. Just before he and my mother were married he took her to the top of the hills that surround Arcade. They stood with the New Jerusalem River, western California, and the sea on their left, and Arcade on their right. My father has always planned things well, and that day as they stood in the hill pass a thunderstorm covered everything west, while Arcade, shielded by hills, was lit by the sun. He asked her which way she wanted to go. She must have realized it was a test, because she thought for a moment and then looked to the right, and when they drove down from the hills that day my father mentioned the idea of a grocery. Star Food didn't open for a year after, but that was its conception, I think, in my father's mind. That afternoon as they stood with the New Jerusalem flowing below them, the plains before them, and my mother in a cotton skirt she had made herself, I think my father must have seen right through to the end of his life.

I had been trying to see right through to the end of my life, too, but these thoughts never led me in any direction. Sometimes I sat and remembered the unusual things that had happened to me. Once I had found the perfect, shed skin of a rattlesnake. My mother told my father that this indicated my potential for science. I was on the roof another time when it hailed apricot-size balls of ice on a summer afternoon. The day was hot and there was only one cloud, but as it approached from the distance it spread a shaft of darkness below it as if it had fallen through itself to the earth, and when it reached the New Jerusalem the river began throwing up spouts of water. Then it crossed onto land and I could see the hailstones denting parked cars. I went back inside the attic and watched it pass, and when I came outside again and picked up the ice balls that rolled between the corrugated roof spouts, their prickly edges melted in my fingers. In a minute they were gone. That was the rarest thing that had ever happened to me. Now I waited for rare things because it seemed to me that if you traced back the lives of men you arrived at some sort of sign, rainstorm at one horizon and sunlight at the other. On the roof I waited for mine. Sometimes I thought about the woman and sometimes I looked for silhouettes in the blue shapes between the clouds.

"Your father thinks you should be thinking about the store," said my mother.

"I know."

"You'll own the store some day."

There was a carpet of cirrus clouds in the distance, and we watched them as their bottom edges were gradually lit by the rising moon. My mother tilted back her head and looked up into the stars. "What beautiful names," she said. "Cassiopeia, Lyra, Aquila."

"The Big Dipper," I said.

"Dade?"

"Yes?"

"I saw the lady come in yesterday."

"I didn't chase her."

"I know."

"What do you think of that?"

"I think you're doing more important things," she said. "Dreams are more important than rye bread." She took the bobby pins from her hair and held them in her palm. "Dade, tell me the truth. What do you think about when you come up here?"

In the distance there were car lights, trees, aluminum power poles. There were several ways I could have answered.

I said, "I think I'm about to make a discovery."

After that my mother began meeting me at the bottom of the stairs when I came down from the roof. She smiled expectantly. I snapped my fingers, tapped my feet. I blinked and looked at my canvas shoe-tips. She kept smiling. I didn't like this so I tried not coming down for entire afternoons, but this only made her look more expectant. On the roof my thoughts piled into one another. I couldn't even think of something that was undiscovered. I stood and thought about the woman.

Then my mother began leaving little snacks on the sill of the dormer window. Crackers, cut apples, apricots. She arranged them in fan shapes or twirls on a plate, and after a few days I started working regular hours again. I wore my smock and checked customers through the register and went upstairs only in the evenings. I came down after my mother had gone to sleep. I was afraid the woman was coming back, but I couldn't face my mother twice a day at the bottom of the stairs. So I worked and looked up at the door whenever customers entered. I did stock work when I could, stayed in back where the air was refrigerated, but I sweated anyway. I unloaded melons, tuna fish, cereal. I counted the cases of freeze-pops, priced the cans of All-American ham. At the swinging door between the stockroom and the back of the store my heart went dizzy. The woman knew something about me.

In the evenings on the roof I tried to think what it was. I saw mysterious new clouds, odd combinations of cirrus and stratus. How did she root me into the linoleum floor with her gray stare? Above me on the roof the sky was simmering. It was blue gas. I knew she was coming back.

It was raining when she did. The door opened and I felt the wet breeze, and when I looked up she was standing with her back to me in front of the shelves of cheese and dairy, and this time I came out from the counter and stopped behind her. She smelled of the rain outside.

"Look," I whispered, "why are you doing this to me?"

She didn't turn around. I moved closer. I was gathering my words, thinking of the blue index card, when the idea of limited fame came into my head. I stopped. How did human beings understand each other across huge spaces except with the lowest of ideas? I have never understood what it is about rain that smells, but as I stood there behind the woman I suddenly realized I was smelling the inside of clouds. What was between us at that moment was an idea we had created ourselves. When she left with a carton of milk in her hand I couldn't speak.

On the roof that evening I looked into the sky, out over the plains, along the uneven horizon. I thought of the view my father had seen when he was a young man. I wondered whether he had imagined Star Food then. The sun was setting. The blues and oranges were mixing into black, and in the distance windows were lighting up along the hillsides.

"Tell me what I want," I said then. I moved closer to the edge of the eaves and repeated it. I looked down over the alley, into the kitchens across the way, into living rooms, bedrooms, across slate rooftops. "Tell me what I want," I called. Cars pulled in and out of the parking lot. Big rigs rushed by on the interstate. The air around me was as cool as water, the lighted swimming pools like pieces of the daytime sky. An important moment seemed to be rushing up. "Tell me what I want," I said again.

Then I heard my father open the window and come out onto the roof. He walked down and stood next to me, the bald spot on top of his head reflecting the streetlight. He took out a cigarette, smoked it for a while, pinched off the end. A bird fluttered around the light pole across the street. A car crossed below us with the words JUST MARRIED on the roof.

"Look," he said, "your mother's tried to make me understand this." He paused to put the unsmoked butt back in the pack. "And maybe I can. You think the gal's a little down and out; you don't want to kick her when she's down. Okay, I can understand that. So I've decided something, and you want to know what?"

He shifted his hands in his pockets and took a few steps toward the edge of the roof.

"You want to know what?"

"What?"

"I'm taking you off the hook. Your mother says you've got a few thoughts, that maybe you're on the verge of something, so I decided it's okay if you let the lady go if she comes in again."

"What?"

"I said it's okay if you let the gal go. You don't have to chase her."

"You're going to let her steal?"

"No," he said. "I hired a guard."

He was there the next morning in clothes that were all dark blue. Pants, shirt, cap, socks. He was only two or three years older than I was. My father introduced him to me as Mr. Sellers. "Mr. Sellers," he said, "this is Dade." He had a badge on his chest and a ring of keys the size of a doughnut on his belt. At the door he sat jingling them.

I didn't say much to him, and when I did my father came out from the back and counted register receipts or stocked impulse items near where he sat. We weren't saying anything important, though. Mr. Sellers didn't carry a gun, only the doughnut-size key ring, so I asked him if he wished he did.

"Sure," he said.

"Would you use it?"

"If I had to."

I thought of him using his gun if he had to. His hands were thick and their backs were covered with hair. This seemed to go along with shooting somebody if he had to. My hands were thin and white and the hair on them was like the hair on a girl's cheek.

During the days he stayed by the front. He smiled at customers and held the door for them, and my father brought him sodas every hour or so. Whenever the guard smiled at a customer I thought of him trying to decide whether he was looking at the shoplifter.

And then one evening everything changed.

I was on the roof. The sun was low, throwing slanted light. From beyond the New

Jerusalem and behind the hills, four air force jets appeared. They disappeared, then appeared again, silver dots trailing white tails. They climbed and cut and looped back, showing dark and light like a school of fish. When they turned against the sun their wings flashed. Between the hills and the river they dipped low onto the plain, then shot upward and toward me. One dipped, the others followed. Across the New Jerusalem they turned back and made two great circles, one inside the other, then dipped again and leveled off in my direction. The sky seemed small enough for them to fall through. I could see the double tails, then the wings and the jets. From across the river they shot straight toward the store, angling up so I could see the V-wings and camouflage and rounded bomb bays, and I covered my ears, and in a moment they were across the water and then they were above me, and as they passed over they barrel-rolled and flew upside down and showed me their black cockpit glass so that my heart came up into my mouth.

I stood there while they turned again behind me and lifted back toward the hills, trailing threads of vapor, and by the time their booms subsided I knew I wanted the woman to be caught. I had seen a sign. Suddenly the sky was water-clear. Distances moved in, houses stood out against the hills, and it seemed to me that I had turned a corner and now looked over a rain-washed street. The woman was a thief. This was a simple fact and it presented itself to me simply. I felt the world dictating its course.

I went downstairs and told my father I was ready to catch her. He looked at me, rolling the chewing gum in his cheek. "I'll be damned."

"My life is making sense," I said.

When I unloaded potato chips that night I laid the bags in the aluminum racks as if I were putting children to sleep in their beds. Dust had gathered under the lip of the vegetable bins, so I swept and mopped there and ran a wet cloth over the stalls. My father slapped me on the back a couple of times. In school once I had looked through a microscope at the tip of my own finger, and now as I looked around the store everything seemed to have been magnified in the same way. I saw cracks in the linoleum floor, speckles of color in the walls.

This kept up for a couple of days, and all the time I waited for the woman to come in. After a while it was more than just waiting; I looked forward to the day when she would return. In my eyes she would find nothing but resolve. How bright the store seemed to me then when I swept, how velvety the skins of the melons beneath the sprayer bottle. When I went up to the roof I scrubbed the star with the wet cloth and came back down. I didn't stare into the clouds and I didn't think about the woman except with the thought of catching her. I described her perfectly for the guard. Her gray eyes. Her plaid dress.

After I started working like this my mother began to go to the back room in the afternoons and listen to music. When I swept the rear I heard the melodies of operas. They came from behind the stockroom door while I waited for the woman to return, and when my mother came out she had a look about her of disappointment. Her skin was pale and smooth, as if the blood had run to deeper parts.

"Dade," she said one afternoon as I stacked tomatoes in a pyramid, "it's easy to lose your dreams."

"I'm just stacking tomatoes."

She went back to the register. I went back to stacking, and my father, who'd been patting me on the back, winking at me from behind the butcher counter, came over and helped me.

"I notice your mother's been talking to you."

"A little."

We finished the tomatoes and moved on to the lettuce.

"Look," he said, "it's better to do what you have to do, so I wouldn't spend your time worrying frontwards and backwards about everything. Your life's not so long as you think it's going to be."

We stood there rolling heads of butterball lettuce up the shallow incline of the display cart. Next to me he smelled like Aqua Velva.

"The lettuce is looking good," I said.

Then I went up to the front of the store. "I'm not sure what my dreams are," I said to my mother. "And I'm never going to discover anything. All I've ever done on the roof is look at the clouds."

Then the door opened and the woman came in. I was standing in front of the counter, hands in my pockets, my mother's eyes watering over, the guard looking out the window at a couple of girls, everything revolving around the point of calm that, in retrospect, precedes surprises. I'd been waiting for her for a week, and now she came in. I realized I never expected her. She stood looking at me, and for a few moments I looked back. Then she realized what I was up to. She turned around to leave, and when her back was to me I stepped over and grabbed her.

I've never liked fishing much, even though I used to go with my father, because the moment a fish jumps on my line a tree's length away in the water I feel as if I've suddenly lost something. I'm always disappointed and sad, but now as I held the woman beneath the shoulder I felt none of this disappointment. I felt strong and good. She was thin, and I could make out the bones and tendons in her arm. As I led her back toward the stockroom, through the bread aisle, then the potato chips that were puffed and stacked like a row of pillows, I heard my mother begin to weep behind the register. Then my father came up behind me. I didn't turn around, but I knew he was there and I knew the deliberately calm way he was walking. "I'll be back as soon as I dust the melons," he said.

I held the woman tightly under her arm but despite this she moved in a light way, and suddenly, as we paused before the stockroom door, I felt as if I were leading her onto the dance floor. This flushed me with remorse. Don't spend your whole life looking backwards and forwards, I said to myself. Know what you want. I pushed the door open and we went in. The room was dark. It smelled of my whole life. I turned on the light and sat her down in the straight-back chair, then crossed the room and stood against the door. I had spoken to many children as they sat in this chair. I had frightened them, collected the candy they had tried to hide between the cushions, presented it to my father when he came in. Now I looked at the blue card. DO YOU KNOW WHAT YOU HAVE DONE? it said. DO YOU KNOW WHAT IT IS TO STEAL? I tried to think of what to say to the woman. She sat trembling slightly. I approached the chair and stood in front of her. She looked up at me. Her hair was gray around the roots.

"Do you want to go out the back?" I said.

She stood up and I took the key from under the silver samovar. My father would be there in a moment, so after I let her out I took my coat from the hook and followed. The evening was misty. She crossed the lot, and I hurried and came up next to her. We walked fast and stayed behind cars, and when we had gone a distance I turned and looked back. The stockroom door was closed. On the roof the star cast a pale light that whitened the aluminum-sided eaves.

It seemed we would be capable of a great communication now, but as we walked I realized I didn't know what to say to her. We went down the street without talking. The traffic was light, evening was approaching, and as we passed below some trees the streetlights suddenly came on. This moment has always amazed me. I knew the woman had seen it too, but it is always a disappointment to mention a thing like this. The streets and buildings took on their night shapes. Still we didn't say anything to each other. We kept walking beneath the pale violet of the lamps, and after a few more blocks I just stopped at one corner. She went on, crossed the street, and I lost sight of her.

I stood there until the world had rotated fully into the night, and for a while I tried to make myself aware of the spinning of the earth. Then I walked back toward the store. When they slept that night, my mother would dream of discovery and my father would dream of low-grade crooks. When I thought of this and the woman I was sad. It seemed you could never really know another person. I felt alone in the world, in the way that makes me aware of sound and temperature, as if I had just left a movie theater and stepped into an alley where a light rain was falling, and the wind was cool, and, from somewhere, other people's voices could be heard.

TRUMAN CAPOTE

Truman Capote (1924–1984) was born in New Orleans, Louisiana, and was raised by relatives in Alabama until he was nine, when his mother, who had divorced his father and moved to New York City, sent for him. One of his childhood friends was Harper Lee, who later depicted the young Capote in her novel *To Kill a Mockingbird:* "His head teemed with eccentric plans, strange longings, and quaint fancies." Always eccentric — and ultimately outrageous — Capote perfected a version of the writer-as-celebrity, obsessed with fame and the famous. A sensitive and stylish writer of fiction, he is nonetheless perhaps best known for an experimental work he called (to less than universal approbation) a "nonfiction novel": *In Cold Blood* (1966). It is a deeply personalized study, embodying techniques of both journalism and fiction, of two death-row killers in Kansas. The book made both them and its author famous. Capote's novels include *Other Voices, Other Rooms* (1948) and *Breakfast at Tiffany's* (1958). His stories are included in *A Tree of Night and Other Stories* (1949), *The Grass Harp, A Tree of Night and Other Stories* (1956), *A Christmas Memory* (1956), and *Selected Writings* (1963). "Children on Their Birthdays," from its startling opening line onward, captures the essence of his touching and troubled vision.

Children on Their Birthdays

Yesterday afternoon the six-o'clock bus ran over Miss Bobbit. I'm not sure what there is to be said about it; after all, she was only ten years old, still I know no one of us in this town will forget her. For one thing, nothing she ever did was ordinary, not from the first time that we saw her, and that was a year ago. Miss Bobbit and her mother, they arrived on that same six-o'clock bus, the one that comes through from Mobile. It happened to be my cousin Billy Bob's birthday, and so most of the children in town were here at our house. We were sprawled on the front porch having tutti-frutti and devil cake when the bus stormed around Deadman's Curve. It was the summer that never rained; rusted dryness coated everything; sometimes when a car passed on the road, raised dust would hang in the still air an hour or more. Aunt El said if they didn't pave the highway soon she was going to move down to the seacoast; but she'd said that for such a long time. Anyway, we were sitting on the porch, tutti-frutti melting on our plates, when suddenly, just as we were wishing that something would happen, something did; for out of the red road dust appeared Miss Bobbit. A wiry little girl in a starched, lemon-colored party dress, she sassed along with a grownup mince, one hand on her hip, the other supporting a spinsterish umbrella. Her mother, lugging two cardboard valises and a wind-up victrola, trailed in the background. She was a gaunt shaggy woman with silent eyes and a hungry smile.

All the children on the porch had grown so still that when a cone of wasps started humming the girls did not set up their usual holler. Their attention was too fixed upon the approach of Miss Bobbit and her mother, who had by now reached the gate. "Begging your pardon," called Miss Bobbit in a voice that was at once silky and childlike, like a pretty piece of ribbon, and immaculately exact, like a movie-star or a schoolmarm, "but might we speak with the grownup persons of the house?" This, of course, meant Aunt El; and, at least to some degree, myself. But Billy Bob and all the other boys, no one of whom was over thirteen, followed down to the gate after us. From their faces you would have thought they'd never seen a girl before. Certainly not like Miss Bobbit. As Aunt El said, whoever heard tell of a child wearing make-up? Tangee gave her lips an orange glow, her hair, rather like a costume wig, was a mass of rosy curls, and her eyes had a knowing, penciled tilt; even so, she had a skinny dignity, she was a lady, and, what is more, she looked you in the eye with manlike directness. "I'm Miss Lily Jane Bobbit, Miss Bobbit from Memphis, Tennessee," she said solemnly. The boys looked down at their toes, and, on the porch, Cora McCall, who Billy Bob was courting at the time, led the girls into a fanfare of giggles. "Country children," said Miss Bobbit with an understanding smile, and gave her parasol a saucy whirl. "My mother," and this homely woman allowed an abrupt nod to acknowledge herself, "my mother and I have taken rooms here. Would you be so kind as to point out the house? It belongs to a Mrs. Sawyer." Why, sure, said Aunt El, that's Mrs. Sawyer's, right there across the street. The only boarding house around here, it is an old tall dark place with about two dozen lightning rods scattered on the roof: Mrs. Sawyer is scared to death in a thunderstorm.

Coloring like an apple, Billy Bob said, please ma'am, it being such a hot day and all, wouldn't they rest a spell and have some tutti-frutti? and Aunt El said yes, by all means, but Miss Bobbit shook her head. "Very fattening, tutti-frutti; but *merci* you kindly," and they started across the road, the mother half-dragging her parcels in the dust. Then, and with an earnest expression, Miss Bobbit turned back; the sunflower yellow of her eyes darkened, and she rolled them slightly sideways, as if trying to remember a poem. "My mother has a disorder of the tongue, so it is necessary that I speak for her," she announced rapidly and heaved a sigh. "My mother is a very fine seamstress; she has made dresses for the society of many cities and towns, including Memphis and Tallahassee. No doubt you have noticed and admired the dress I am wearing. Every stitch of it was hand-sewn by my mother. My mother can copy any pattern, and just recently she won a twenty-five-dollar prize from the *Ladies' Home Journal*. My mother can also crochet, knit and embroider. If you want any kind of sewing done, please come to my mother. Please advise your friends and family. Thank you." And then, with a rustle and a swish, she was gone.

Cora McCall and the girls pulled their hair-ribbons nervously, suspiciously, and looked very put out and prune-faced. I'm *Miss* Bobbit, said Cora, twisting her face into an evil imitation, and I'm Princess Elizabeth, that's who I am, ha, ha, ha. Furthermore, said Cora, that dress was just as tacky as could be; personally, Cora said, all my clothes come from Atlanta; plus a pair of shoes from New York, which is not even to mention my silver turquoise ring all the way from Mexico City, Mexico. Aunt El said they ought not to behave that way about a fellow child, a stranger in the town, but the girls went on like a huddle of witches, and certain boys, the sillier ones that liked to be with the girls, joined in and said things that made Aunt El go red and declare she was going to send them all home and tell their daddies, to boot. But before she could carry forward this threat Miss Bobbit herself intervened by traipsing across the Sawyer porch, costumed in a new and startling manner.

The older boys, like Billy Bob and Preacher Star, who had sat quiet while the girls razzed Miss Bobbit, and who had watched the house into which she'd disappeared with misty, ambitious faces, they now straightened up and ambled down to the gate. Cora McCall sniffed and poked out her lower lip, but the rest of us went and sat on the steps. Miss Bobbit paid us no mind whatever. The Sawyer yard is dark with mulberry trees and it is planted with grass and sweet shrub. Sometimes after a rain you can smell the sweet shrub all the way into our house; and in the center of this yard there is a sundial which Mrs. Sawyer installed in 1912 as a memorial to her Boston bull, Sunny, who died after having lapped up a bucket of paint. Miss Bobbit pranced into the yard toting the victrola, which she put on the sundial; she wound it up, and started a record playing, and it played the Count of Luxemborg. By now it was almost nightfall, a firefly hour, blue as milkglass; and birds like arrows swooped together and swept into the folds of trees. Before storms, leaves and flowers appear to burn with a private light, color, and Miss Bobbit, got up in a little white skirt like a powder-puff and with strips of gold-glittering tinsel ribboning her hair, seemed, set against the darkening all around, to contain this illuminated quality. She held her arms arched over her head, her hands lily-limp, and stood straight up on the tips of her toes. She stood that way for a good long while, and Aunt El said it was right smart of her. Then she began to waltz around and around, and around and around she went until Aunt El said, why, she was plain dizzy from the sight. She stopped only when it was time to re-wind the victrola; and when the moon came rolling down the ridge, and the last supper bell had sounded, and all the children had gone home, and the night iris was beginning to bloom, Miss Bobbit was still there in the dark turning like a top.

We did not see her again for some time. Preacher Star came every morning to our house and stayed straight through to supper. Preacher is a rail-thin boy with a butchy shock of red hair; he has eleven brothers and sisters, and even they are afraid of him, for he has a terrible temper, and is famous in these parts for his green-eyed meanness: last fourth of July he whipped Ollie Overton so bad that Ollie's family had to send him to the hospital in Pensacola; and there was another time he bit off half a mule's ear, chewed it and spit it on the ground. Before Billy Bob got his growth, Preacher played the devil with him, too. He used to drop cockleburrs down his collar, and rub pepper in his eyes, and tear up his homework. But now they are the biggest friends in town: talk alike, walk alike; and occasionally they disappear together for whole days, Lord knows where to. But during these days when Miss Bobbit did not appear they stayed close to the house. They would stand around in the yard trying to slingshot sparrows off telephone poles; or sometimes Billy Bob would play his ukulele, and they would sing so loud Uncle Billy Bob, who is Judge for this county, claimed he could hear them all the way to the courthouse: *send me a letter, send it by mail, sent it in care of the Birming-ham jail.* Miss Bobbit did not hear them; at least she never poked her head out the door. Then one day Mrs. Sawyer, coming over to borrow a cup of sugar, rattled on a good deal about her new boarders. You know, she said, squinting her chicken-bright eyes, the husband was a crook, uh huh, the child told me herself. Hasn't an ounce of shame, not a mite. Said her daddy was the dearest daddy and the sweetest singing man in the whole of Tennessee. . . . And I said, honey, where is he? and just as offhand as you please she penitentiary and we don't hear from him no more. Say, now, does that make your blood run cold? Uh huh, and I been thinking, her mama, I been thinking she's some kinda foreigner: never says a word, and sometimes it looks like she don't understand what nobody says to her. And you know, they eat everything *raw. Raw* eggs, *raw* turnips, carrots — no meat whatsoever. For reasons of health, the child says, but ho! she's been straight out on the bed running a fever since last Tuesday.

That same afternoon Aunt El went out to water her roses, only to discover them gone. These were special roses, ones she'd planned to send to the flower show in Mobile, and so naturally she got a little hysterical. She rang up the Sheriff, and said, listen here, Sheriff, you come over here right fast. I mean somebody's got off with all my Lady Anne's that I've devoted myself to heart and soul since early spring. When the Sheriff's car pulled up outside our house, all the neighbors along the street came out on their porches, and Mrs. Sawyer, layers of cold cream whitening her face, trotted across the road. Oh shoot, she said, very disappointed to find no one had been murdered, oh shoot, she said, nobody's stole them roses. Your Billy Bob brought them roses over and left them for little Bobbit. Aunt El did not say one word. She just marched over to the peach tree, and cut herself a switch. Ohhh, Billy Bob, she stalked along the street calling his name, and then she found him down at Speedy's garage where he and Preacher were watching Speedy take a motor apart. She simply lifted him by the hair and, switching blueblazes, towed him home. But she couldn't make him say he was sorry and she couldn't make him cry. And when she was finished with him he ran into the backyard and climbed high into the tower of a pecan tree and swore he wasn't ever going to come down. Then his daddy came home, and it was time to have supper. His daddy stood at the window and called to him: Son, we aren't mad with you, so come down and eat your supper. But Billy Bob wouldn't budge. Aunt El went and leaned against the tree. She spoke in a voice soft as the gathering light. I'm sorry, son, she said, I didn't mean whipping you so hard like that. I've fixed a nice supper, son, potato salad and boiled ham and deviled eggs. Go away, said Billy Bob, I don't want no supper, and I hate you like all-fire. His daddy said he ought not to talk like that to his mother, and she began to cry. She stood there under the tree and cried, raising the hem of her skirt to dab at her eyes. I don't hate you, son. . . . If I didn't love you I wouldn't whip you. The pecan leaves began to rattle; Billy Bob slid slowly to the ground, and Aunt El, rushing her fingers through his hair, pulled him against her. Aw, Ma, he said, Aw, Ma.

After supper Billy Bob came and flung himself on the foot of my bed. He smelled all sour and sweet, the way boys do, and I felt very sorry for him, especially because he looked so worried. His eyes were almost shut with sorry. You're s'posed to send sick folks flowers, he said righteously. About this time we heard the victrola, a lilting faraway sound, and a night moth flew through the window, drifting in the air delicate as the music. But it was dark now, and we couldn't tell if Miss Bobbit was dancing. Billy Bob, as though he were in pain, doubled up on the bed like a jackknife; but his face was suddenly clear, his grubby boy-eyes twitching like candles. She's so cute, he whispered, she's the cutest dickens I ever saw, gee, to hell with it, I don't care, I'd pick all the roses in China.

Preacher would have picked all the roses in China, too. He was as crazy about her as Billy Bob. But Miss Bobbit did not notice them. The sole communication we had with her was a note to Aunt El thanking her for the flowers. Day after day she sat on her porch, always dressed to beat the band, and doing a piece of embroidery, or combing curls in her hair, or reading a Webster's dictionary — formal, but friendly enough; if you said good-day to her she said good-day to you. Even so, the boys never could seem to get up the nerve to go over and talk with her, and most of the time she simply looked through them, even when they tomcatted up and down the street trying to get her eye. They wrestled, played Tarzan, did foolheaded bicycle tricks. It was a sorry business. A great many girls in town strolled by the Sawyer house two and three times within an hour just on the chance of getting a look. Some of the girls who did this were: Cora McCall, Mary Murphy Jones, Janice Ackerman. Miss Bobbit did not show any interest in them either. Cora would not speak to Billy Bob any more. The same was true with Janice and Preacher. As a matter of fact, Janice wrote Preacher a letter in red ink on lace-trimmed paper in which she told him he was vile beyond all human beings and words, that she considered their engagement broken, that he could have back the stuffed squirrel he'd given her. Preacher, saying he wanted to act nice, stopped her the next time she passed our house, and said, well, hell, she could keep that old squirrel if she wanted to. Afterwards, he couldn't understand why Janice ran away bawling the way she did.

Then one day the boys were being crazier than usual; Billy Bob was sagging around in his daddy's World War khakis, and Preacher, stripped to the waist, had a naked woman drawn on his chest with one of Aunt El's old lipsticks. They looked like perfect fools, but Miss Bobbit, reclining in a swing, merely yawned. It was noon, and there was no one passing in the street, except a colored girl, baby-fat and sugar-plum shaped, who hummed along carrying a pail of blackberries. But the boys, teasing at her like gnats, joined hands and wouldn't let her go by, not until she paid a tariff. I ain't studyin' no tariff, she said, what kinda tariff you talkin' about, mister? A party in the barn, said Preacher, between clenched teeth, mighty nice party in the barn. And she, with a sulky shrug, said, huh, she intended studyin' no barn parties. Whereupon Billy Bob capsized her berry pail, and when she, with despairing, piglike shrieks, bent down in futile gestures of rescue, Preacher, who can be mean as the devil, gave her behind a kick which sent her sprawling jellylike among the blackberries and the dust. Miss Bobbit came tearing across the road, her finger wagging like a metronome; like a schoolteacher she clapped her hands, stamped her foot, said: "It is a well-known fact that gentlemen are put on the face of this earth for the protection of ladies. Do you suppose boys behave this way in towns like Memphis, New York, London, Hollywood or Paris?" The boys hung back, and shoved their hands in their pockets. Miss Bobbit helped the colored girl to her feet; she dusted her off, dried her eyes, held out a handkerchief and told her to blow. "A pretty pass," she said, "a fine situation when a lady can't walk safely in the public daylight."

Then the two of them went back and sat on Mrs. Sawyer's porch; and for the next year they were never far apart, Miss Bobbit and this baby elephant, whose name was Rosalba Cat. At first, Mrs. Sawyer raised a fuss about Rosalba being so much at her house. She told Aunt El that it went against the grain to have a nigger lolling smack there in plain sight on her front porch. But Miss Bobbit had a certain magic, whatever she did she did it with completeness, and so directly, so solemnly, that there was nothing to do but accept it. For instance, the tradespeople in town used to snicker when they called her *Miss* Bobbit; but by and by she was Miss Bobbit, and they gave her stiff little bows as she whirled by spinning her parasol. Miss Bobbit told everyone that Rosalba was her sister, which caused a good many jokes; but like most of her ideas, it gradually seemed natural, and when we would overhear them calling each other Sister Rosalba and Sister Bobbit none of us cracked a smile. But Sister Rosalba and Sister Bobbit did some queer things. There was the business about the dogs. Now there are a great many dogs in this town, rat-terriers, bird-dogs, bloodhounds; they trail along the forlorn noon-hot streets in sleepy herds of six to a dozen, all waiting only for dark and the moon, when straight through the lonesome hours you can hear them howling: someone is dying, someone is dead. Miss Bobbit complained to the Sheriff; she said that certain of the dogs always planted themselves under her window, and that she was a light sleeper to begin with; what is more, and as Sister Rosalba said, she did not believe they were dogs at all, but some kind of devil. Naturally the Sheriff did nothing; and so she took the matter into her own hands. One morning, after an especially loud night, she was seen stalking through the town with Rosalba at her side, Rosalba carrying a flower basket filled with rocks; whenever they saw a dog they paused while Miss Bobbit scrutinized him. Sometimes she would shake her head, but more often she said, "Yes, that's one of them, Sister Rosalba," and Sister Rosalba, with ferocious aim, would take a rock from her basket and crack the dog between the eyes.

Another thing that happened concerns Mr. Henderson. Mr. Henderson has a back room in the Sawyer house; a tough runt of a man who formerly was a wildcat oil prospector in Oklahoma, he is about seventy years old and, like a lot of old men, obsessed by functions of the body. Also, he is a terrible drunk. One time he had been drunk for two weeks; whenever he heard Miss Bobbit and Sister Rosalba moving around the house, he would charge to the top of the stairs and bellow down to Mrs. Sawyer that there were midgets in the walls trying to get at his supply of toilet paper. They've already stolen fifteen cents' worth, he said. One evening, when the two girls were sitting under a tree in the yard, Mr. Henderson, sporting nothing more than a nightshirt, stamped out after them. Steal all my toilet paper, will you? he hollered, I'll show you midgets. . . . Somebody come help me, else these midget bitches are liable to make off with every sheet in town. It was Billy Bob and Preacher who caught Mr. Henderson and held him until some grown men arrived and began to tie him up. Miss Bobbit, who had behaved with admirable calm, told the men they did not know how to tie a proper knot, and undertook to do so herself. She did such a good job that all the circulation stopped in Mr. Henderson's hands and feet and it was a month before he could walk again.

It was shortly afterwards that Miss Bobbit paid us a call. She came on Sunday and I was there alone, the family having gone to church. "The odors of a church are so offensive," she said, leaning forward and with her hands folded primly before her. "I don't want you to think I'm a heathen, Mr. C.; I've had enough experience to know that there is a God and that there is a Devil. But the way to tame the Devil is not to go down there to church and listen to what a sinful mean fool he is. No, love the Devil like you love Jesus: because he is a powerful man, and will do you a good turn if he knows you trust him. He has frequently done me good turns, like at dancing school in Memphis. . . . I always called in the Devil to help me get the biggest part in our annual show. That is common sense; you see, I knew Jesus wouldn't have any truck with dancing. Now, as a matter of fact, I have called in the Devil just recently. He is the only one who can help me get out of this town. Not that I live here, not exactly. I think always about somewhere else, somewhere else where everything is dancing, like people dancing in the streets, and everything is pretty, like children on their birthdays. My precious papa said I live in the sky, but if he'd lived more in the sky he'd be rich like he wanted to be. The trouble with my papa was he did not love the Devil, he let the Devil love him. But I am very smart in that respect; I know the next best thing is very often the best. It was the next best thing for us to move to this town; and since I can't pursue my career here, the next best thing for me is to start a little business on the side. Which is what I have done. I am sole subscription agent in this county for an impressive list of magazines, including *Reader's Digest, Popular Mechanics, Dime Detective* and *Child's Life.* To be sure, Mr. C., I'm not here to sell you anything. But I have a thought in mind. I was thinking those two boys that are always hanging around here, it occurred to me that they are men, after all. Do you suppose they would make a pair of likely assistants?"

Billy Bob and Preacher worked hard for Miss Bobbit, and for Sister Rosalba, too. Sister Rosalba carried a line of cosmetics called Dewdrop, and it was part of the boys' job to deliver purchases to her customers. Billy Bob used to be so tired in the evening he could hardly chew his supper. Aunt El said it was a shame and a pity, and finally one day when Billy Bob came down with a touch of sunstroke she said, all right, that settled it, Billy Bob would just have to quit Miss Bobbit. But Billy Bob cussed her out until his daddy had to lock him in his room, whereupon he said he was going to kill himself. Some cook we'd had told him once that if you ate a mess of collards all slopped over with molasses it would kill you sure as shooting; and so that is what he did. I'm dying, he said, rolling back and forth on his bed, I'm dying and nobody cares.

Miss Bobbit came over and told him to hush up. "There's nothing wrong with you, boy," she said. "All you've got is a stomach ache." Then she did something that shocked Aunt El very much: she stripped the covers off Billy Bob and rubbed him down with alcohol from head to toe. When Aunt El told her she did not think that was a nice thing for a little girl to do, Miss Bobbit replied: "I don't know whether it's nice or not, but it's certainly very refreshing." After which Aunt El did all she could to keep Billy Bob from going back to work for her, but his daddy said to leave him alone, they would have to let the boy lead his own life.

Miss Bobbit was very honest about money. She paid Billy Bob and Preacher their exact commission, and she would never let them treat her, as they often tried to do, at the drugstore or to the picture-show. "You'd better save your money," she told them. "That is, if you want to go to college. Because neither one of you has got the brains to win a scholarship, not even a football scholarship." But it was over money that Billy Bob and Preacher had a big falling out; that was not the real reason, of course: the real reason was that they had grown cross-eyed jealous over Miss Bobbit. So one day, and he had the gall to do this right in front of Billy Bob, Preacher said to Miss Bobbit that she'd better check her accounts carefully because he had more than a suspicion that Billy Bob wasn't turning over to her *all* the money he collected. That's a damned lie, said Billy Bob, and with a clean left hook he knocked Preacher off the Sawyer porch and jumped after him into a bed of nasturtiums. But once Preacher got a hold on him, Billy Bob didn't stand a chance. Preacher even rubbed dirt in his eyes. During all this, Mrs. Sawyer, leaning out an upper-story window, screamed like an eagle, and Sister Rosalba, fatly cheerful, ambiguously shouted, Kill him! Kill him! Kill him! Only Miss Bobbit seemed to know what she was doing. She plugged in the lawn hose, and gave the boys a closeup, blinding bath. Gasping, Preacher staggered to his feet. Oh, honey, he said, shaking himself like a wet dog, honey, you've got to decide. "Decide *what?*" said Miss Bobbit, right away in a huff.

Oh, honey, wheezed Preacher, you don't want us boys killing each other. You got to decide who is your real true sweetheart. "Sweetheart, my eye," said Miss Bobbit. "I should've known better than to get myself involved with a lot of country children. What sort of businessman are you going to make? Now, you listen here, Preacher Star: I don't want a sweetheart, and if I did, it wouldn't be you. As a matter of fact, you don't even get up when a lady enters the room."

Preacher spit on the ground and swaggered over to Billy Bob. Come on, he said, just as though nothing had happened, she's a hard one, she is, she don't want nothing but to make trouble between two good friends. For a moment it looked as if Billy Bob was going to join him in a peaceful togetherness; but suddenly, coming to his senses, he drew back and made a gesture. The boys regarded each other a full minute, all the closeness between them turning an ugly color: you can't hate so much unless you love, too. And Preacher's face showed all of this. But there was nothing for him to do except go away. Oh, yes, Preacher, you looked so lost that day that for the first time I really liked you, so skinny and mean and lost going down the road all by yourself.

They did not make it up, Preacher and Billy Bob, and it was not because they didn't want to, it was only that there did not seem to be any straight way for their friendship to happen again. But they couldn't get rid of this friendship: each was always aware of what the other was up to; and when Preacher found himself a new buddy, Billy Bob moped around for days, picking things up, dropping them again, or doing sudden wild things, like purposely poking his finger in the electric fan. Sometimes in the evenings Preacher would pause by the gate and talk with Aunt El. It was only to torment Billy Bob, I suppose, but he stayed friendly with all of us, and at Christmas time he gave us a huge box of shelled peanuts. He left a present for Billy Bob, too. It turned out to be a book of Sherlock Holmes; and on the flyleaf there was scribbled, "Friends Like Ivy On The Wall Must Fall." That's the corniest thing I ever saw, Billy Bob said. Jesus, what a dope he is! But then, and though it was a cold winter day, he went in the backyard and climbed up into the pecan tree, crouching there all afternoon in the blue December branches.

But most of the time he was happy, because Miss Bobbit was there, and she was always sweet to him now. She and Sister Rosalba treated him like a man; that is to say, they allowed him to do everything for them. On the other hand, they let him win at three-handed bridge, they never questioned his lies, nor discouraged his ambitions. It was a happy while. However, trouble started again when school began. Miss Bobbit refused to go. "It's ridiculous," she said, when one day the principal, Mr. Copland, came around to investigate, "really ridiculous; I can read and write and there are *some* people in this town who have every reason to know that I can count money. No, Mr. Copland, consider for a moment and you will see neither of us has the time nor energy. After all, it would only be a matter of whose spirit broke first, yours or mine. And besides, what is there for you to teach me? Now, if you knew anything about dancing, that would be another matter; but under the circumstances, yes, Mr. Copland, under the circumstances, I suggest we forget the whole thing." Mr. Copland was perfectly willing to. But the rest of the town thought she ought to be whipped. Horace Deasley wrote a piece in the paper which was titled "A Tragic Situation." It was, in his opinion, a tragic situation when a small girl could defy what he, for some reason, termed the Constitution of the United States. The article ended with a question: *Can she get away with it?* She did; and so did Sister Rosalba. Only she was colored, so no one cared. Billy Bob was not as lucky. It was school for him, all right; but he might as well have stayed home for the good it did him. On his first report card he got three F's, a record of some sort. But he is a smart boy. I guess he just couldn't live through those hours without Miss Bobbit; away from her he always seemed half-asleep. He was always in a fight, too; either his eye was black, or his lip was split, or his walk had a limp. He never talked about these fights, but Miss Bobbit was shrewd enough to guess the reason why. "You are a dear, I know, I know. And I appreciate you, Billy Bob. Only don't fight with people because of me. Of course they say mean things about me. But do you know why that is, Billy Bob? It's a compliment, kind of. Because deep down they think I'm absolutely wonderful."

And she was right: if you are not admired no one will take the trouble to disapprove. But actually we had no idea of how wonderful she was until there appeared the man known as Manny Fox. This happened late in February. The first news we had of Manny Fox was a series of jovial placards posted up in the stores around town: Manny Fox Presents the Fan Dancer Without the Fan; then, in smaller print: Also, Sensational Amateur Program Featuring Your Own Neighbors — First Prize, A Genuine Hollywood Screen Test. All this was to take place the following Thursday. The tickets were priced at one dollar each, which around here is a lot of money; but it is not often that we get any kind of flesh entertainment, so everybody shelled out their money and made a great todo over the whole thing. The drugstore cowboys talked dirty all week, mostly about the fan dancer without the fan, who turned out to be Mrs. Manny Fox. They stayed down the highway at the Chucklewood Tourist Camp; but they were in town all day, driving around in an old Packard which had Manny Fox's full name stenciled on all four doors. His wife was a deadpan pimento-tongued redhead with wet lips and moist eyelids; she was quite large actually, but compared to Manny Fox she seemed rather frail, for he was a fat cigar of a man.

They made the pool hall their headquarters, and every afternoon you could find them there, drinking beer and joking with the town loafs. As it developed, Manny Fox's business affairs were not restricted to theatrics. He also ran a kind of employment bureau: slowly he let it be known that for a fee of $150 he could get for any adventurous boys in the county high-class jobs working on fruit ships sailing from New Orleans to South America. The chance of a lifetime, he called it. There are not two boys around here who readily lay their hands on so much as five dollars; nevertheless, a good dozen managed to raise the money. Ada Willingham took all she'd saved to buy an angel tombstone for her husband and gave it to her son, and Acey Trump's papa sold an option on his cotton crop.

But the night of the show! That was a night when all was forgotten: mortgages, and the dishes in the kitchen sink. Aunt El said you'd think we were going to the opera, everybody so dressed up, so pink and sweet-smelling. The Odeon had not been so full since the night they gave away the matched set of sterling silver. Practically everybody had a relative in the show, so there was a lot of nervousness to contend with. Miss Bobbit was the only contestant we knew real well. Billy Bob couldn't sit still; he kept telling us over and over that we mustn't applaud for anybody but Miss Bobbit; Aunt El said that would be very rude, which sent Billy Bob off into a state again; and when his father bought us all bags of popcorn he wouldn't touch his because it would make his hands greasy, and please, another thing, we mustn't be noisy and eat ours while Miss Bobbit was performing. That she was to be a contestant had come as a last-minute surprise. It was logical enough, and there were signs that should've told us; the fact, for instance, that she had not set foot outside the Sawyer house in how many days? And the victrola going half the night, her shadow whirling on the windowshade, and the secret, stuffed look on Sister Rosalba's face whenever asked after Sister Bobbit's health. So there was her name on the program, listed second, in fact, though she did not appear for a long while. First came Manny Fox, greased and leering, who told a lot of peculiar jokes, clapping his hands, ha, ha. Aunt El said if he told another joke like that she was going to walk straight out: he did, and she didn't. Before Miss Bobbit came on there were eleven contestants, including Eustacia Bernstein, who imitated movie stars so that they all sounded like Eustacia, and there was an extraordinary Mr. Buster Riley, a jug-eared old wool-hat from way in the back country who played "Waltzing Matilda" on a saw. Up to that point, he was the hit of the show; not that there was any marked difference in the various receptions, for everybody applauded generously, everybody, that is, except Preacher Star. He was sitting two rows ahead of us, greeting each act with a donkey-loud boo. Aunt El said she was never going to speak to him again. The only person he ever applauded was Miss Bobbit. No doubt the Devil was on her side, but she deserved it. Out she came, tossing her hips, her curls, rolling her eyes. You could tell right away it wasn't going to be one of her classical numbers. She tapped across the stage, daintily holding up the sides of a cloud-blue skirt. That's the cutest thing I ever saw, said Billy Bob, smacking his thigh, and Aunt El had to agree that Miss Bobbit looked real sweet. When she started to twirl the whole audience broke into spontaneous applause; so she did it all over again, hissing, "Faster, faster," at poor Miss Adelaide, who was at the piano doing her Sunday-school best. "I was born in China, and raised in Jay-pan . . ." We had never heard her sing before, and she had a rowdy sandpaper voice. ". . . if you don't like my peaches, stay away from my can, o-ho o-ho!" Aunt El gasped; she gasped again when Miss Bobbit, with a bump, up-ended her skirt to display blue-lace underwear, thereby collecting most of the whistles the boys had been saving for the fan dancer without the fan, which was just as well, as it later turned out, for that lady, to the tune of "An Apple for the Teacher" and cries of gyp gyp, did her routine attired in a bathing suit. But showing off her bottom was not Miss Bobbit's final triumph. Miss Adelaide commenced an ominous thundering in the darker keys, at which point Sister Rosalba, carrying a lighted Roman candle, rushed onstage and handed it to Miss Bobbit, who was in the midst of a full split; she made it, too, and just as she did the Roman candle burst into fiery balls of red, white and blue, and we all had to stand up because she was singing "The Star Spangled Banner" at the top of her lungs. Aunt El said afterwards that it was one of the most gorgeous things she'd ever seen on the American stage.

Well, she surely did deserve a Hollywood screen test and, inasmuch as she won the contest, it looked as though she were going to get it. Manny Fox said she was: honey, he said, you're real star stuff. Only he skipped town the next day, leaving nothing but hearty promises. Watch the mails, my friends, you'll all be hearing from me. That is what he said to the boys whose money he'd taken, and that is what he said to Miss Bobbit. There are three deliveries daily, and this sizable group gathered at the post office for all of them, a jolly crowd gradually joyless. How their hands trembled when a letter slid into their mailbox. A terrible hush came over them as the days passed. They all knew what the other was thinking, but no one could bring himself to say it, not even Miss Bobbit. Postmistress Patterson said it plainly, however:

the man's a crook, she said, I knew he was a crook to begin with, and if I have to look at your faces one more day I'll shoot myself.

Finally, at the end of two weeks, it was Miss Bobbit who broke the spell. Her eyes had grown more vacant than anyone had ever supposed they might, but one day, after the last mail was up, all her old sizzle came back. "O.K, boys, it's lynch law now," she said, and proceeded to herd the whole troupe home with her. This was the first meeting of the Manny Fox Hangman's Club, an organization which, in a more social form, endures to this day, though Manny Fox has long since been caught and, so to say, hung. Credit for this went quite properly to Miss Bobbit. Within a week she'd written over three hundred descriptions of Manny Fox and dispatched them to Sheriffs throughout the South; she also wrote letters to papers in the larger cities, and these attracted wide attention. As a result, four of the robbed boys were offered good-paying jobs by the United Fruit Company, and late this spring, when Manny Fox was arrested in Uphigh, Arkansas, where he was pulling the same old dodge, Miss Bobbit was presented with a Good Deed Merit award from the Sunbeam Girls of America. For some reason, she made a point of letting the world know that this did not exactly thrill her. "I do not approve of the organization," she said. "All that rowdy bugle blowing. It's neither good-hearted nor truly feminine. And anyway, what is a good deed? Don't let anybody fool you, a good deed is something you do because you want something in return." It would be reassuring to report she was wrong, and that her just reward, when at last it came, was given out of kindness and love. However, this is not the case. About a week ago the boys involved in the swindle all received from Manny Fox checks covering their losses, and Miss Bobbit, with clod-hopping determination, stalked into a meeting of the Hangman's Club, which is now an excuse for drinking beer and playing poker every Thursday night. "Look, boys," she said, laying it on the line, "none of you ever thought to see that money again, but now that you have, you ought to invest it in something practical — like me." The proposition was that they should pool their money and finance her trip to Hollywood; in return, they would get ten percent of her life's earnings which, after she was a star, and that would not be very long, would make them all rich men. "At least," as she said, "in this part of the country." Not one of the boys wanted to do it: but when Miss Bobbit looked at you, what was there to say?

Since Monday, it has been raining buoyant summer rain shot through with sun, but dark at night and full of sound, full of dripping leaves, watery chimings, sleepless scuttlings. Billy Bob is wide-awake, dry-eyed, though everything he does is a little frozen and his tongue is as stiff as a bell tongue. It has not been easy for him, Miss Bobbit's going. Because she'd meant more than that. Than what? Than being thirteen years old and crazy in love. She was the queer things in him, like the pecan tree and liking books and caring enough about people to let them hurt him. She was the things he was afraid to show anyone else. And in the dark the music trickled through the rain: won't there be nights when we will hear it just as though it were really there? And afternoons when the shadows will be all at once confused, and she will pass before us, unfurling across the lawn like a pretty piece of ribbon? She laughed to Billy Bob; she held his hand, she even kissed him. "I'm not going to die," she said. "You'll come out there, and we'll climb a mountain, and we'll all live there together, you and me and Sister Rosalba." But Billy Bob knew it would never happen that way, and so when the music came through the dark he would stuff the pillow over his head.

Only there was a strange smile about yesterday, and that was the day she was leaving. Around noon the sun came out, bringing with it into the air all the sweetness of wisteria. Aunt El's yellow Lady Anne's were blooming again, and she did something wonderful, she told Billy Bob he could pick them and give them to Miss Bobbit for good-bye. All afternoon Miss Bobbit sat on the porch surrounded by people who stopped by to wish her well. She looked as though she were going to Communion, dressed in white and with a white parasol. Sister Rosalba had given her a handkerchief, but she had to borrow it back because she couldn't stop blubbering. Another little girl brought a baked chicken, presumably to be eaten on the bus; the only trouble was she'd forgotten to take out the insides before cooking it. Miss Bobbit's mother said that was all right by her, chicken was chicken; which is memorable because it is the single opinion she ever voiced. There was only one sour note. For hours Preacher Star had been hanging around down at the corner, sometimes standing at the curb tossing a coin, and sometimes hiding behind a tree, as if he didn't want anyone to see him. It made everybody nervous. About twenty minutes before bus time he sauntered up and leaned against our gate. Billy Bob was still in the garden picking roses; by now he had enough for a bonfire, and their smell was as heavy as wind. Preacher stared at him until he lifted his head. As they looked at each other the rain began again, falling fine as sea spray and colored by a rainbow. Without a word, Preacher went over and started helping Billy Bob separate the roses into two giant bouquets: together they carried them to the curb. Across the street there were bumblebees of talk, but when Miss Bobbit saw them, two boys whose flower-masked faces were like yellow moons, she rushed down the steps, her arms outstretched. You could see what was going to happen; and we called out, our voices like lightning in the rain, but Miss Bobbit, running toward those moons of roses, did not seem to hear. That is when the six-o'clock bus ran over her.

ANGELA CARTER

 Angela Carter was born in London, England, in 1940. She received a degree in English from Bristol University and worked briefly as a journalist, but since the late 1960s she has given full attention to the writing of fiction. Among her novels are *Shadow Dance* (1966), *Heroes and Villains* (1970), and *The Infernal Desire Machines of Doctor Hoffman* (1972). Her short story collections include *Fireworks* (1974) and *The Bloody Chamber and Other Stories* (1979). One of Carter's fellow novelists in Britain, Ian McEwan, characterizes her prose this way: "magnificent set pieces of fastidious sensuality ... dreams, myths, fairy tales, metamorphoses, the unruly unconscious, epic journeys." "The Bloody Chamber," Carter's retelling of the fairy tale "Bluebeard's Castle," confirms McEwan's assessment and sounds a further note: that of horror.

The Bloody Chamber

I remember how, that night, I lay awake in the wagon-lit in a tender, delicious ecstasy of excitement, my burning cheek against the impeccable linen of the pillow and the pounding of my heart mimicking that of the great pistons ceaselessly thrusting the train that bore me through the night, away from Paris, away from girlhood, away from the white, enclosed quietude of my mother's apartment, into the unguessable country of marriage.

And I remember I tenderly imagined how, at this very moment, my mother would be moving slowly about the narrow bedroom I had left behind for ever, folding up and putting away all my little relics, the tumbled garments I would not need any more, the scores for which there had been no room in my trunks, the concert programmes I'd abandoned; she would linger over this torn ribbon and that faded photograph with all the half-joyous, half-sorrowful emotions of a woman on her daughter's wedding day. And, in the midst of my bridal triumph, I felt a pang of loss as if, when he put the gold band on my finger, I had, in some way, ceased to be her child in becoming his wife.

Are you sure, she'd said when they delivered the gigantic box that held the wedding dress he'd bought me, wrapped up in tissue paper and red ribbon like a

Christmas gift of crystallized fruit. Are you sure you love him? There was a dress for her, too; black silk, with the dull, prismatic sheen of oil on water, finer than anything she'd worn since that adventurous girlhood in Indo-China, daughter of a rich tea planter. My eagle-featured, indomitable mother; what other student at the Conservatoire could boast that her mother had outfaced a junkful of Chinese pirates, nursed a village through a visitation of the plague, shot a man-eating tiger with her own hand and all before she was as old as I?

'Are you sure you love him?'

'I'm sure I want to marry him,' I said.

And would say no more. She sighed, as if it was with reluctance that she might at last banish the spectre of poverty from its habitual place at our meagre table. For my mother herself had gladly, scandalously, defiantly beggared herself for love; and, one fine day, her gallant soldier never returned from the wars, leaving his wife and child a legacy of tears that never quite dried, a cigar box full of medals and the antique service revolver that my mother, grown magnificently eccentric in hardship, kept always in her reticule, in case — how I teased her — she was surprised by footpads on her way home from the grocer's shop.

Now and then a starburst of lights spattered the drawn blinds as if the railway company had lit up all the stations through which we passed in celebration of the bride. My satin nightdress had just been shaken from its wrappings; it had slipped over my young girl's pointed breasts and shoulders, supple as a garment of heavy water, and now teasingly caressed me, egregious, insinuating, nudging between my thighs as I shifted restlessly in my narrow berth. His kiss, his kiss with tongue and teeth in it and a rasp of beard, had hinted to me, though with the same exquisite tact as this nightdress he'd given me, of the wedding night, which would be voluptuously deferred until we lay in his great ancestral bed in the sea-girt, pinnacled domain that lay, still, beyond the grasp of my imagination ... that magic place, the fairy castle whose walls were made of foam, that legendary habitation in which he had been born. To which, one day, I might bear an heir. Our destination, my destiny.

Above the syncopated roar of the train, I could hear his even, steady breathing. Only the communicating door kept me from my husband and it stood open. If I rose up on my elbow, I could see the dark, leonine shape of his head and my nostrils caught a whiff of the opulent male scent of leather and spices that always accompanied him and sometimes, during his courtship, had been the only hint he gave me that he had come into my mother's sitting room, for, though he was a big man, he moved as softly as if all his shoes had soles of velvet, as if his footfall turned the carpet into snow.

He had loved to surprise me in my abstracted solitude at the piano. He would tell them not to announce him, then soundlessly open the door and softly creep up behind me with his bouquet of hot-house flowers or his box of marrons glacés, lay his offering upon the keys and clasp his hands over my eyes as I was lost in a Debussy prelude. But that perfume of spiced leather always betrayed him; after my first shock, I was forced always to mimic surprise, so that he would not be disappointed.

He was older than I. He was much older than I; there were streaks of pure silver in his dark mane. But his strange, heavy, almost waxen face was not lined by experience. Rather, experience seemed to have washed it perfectly smooth, like a stone on a beach whose fissures have been eroded by successive tides. And sometimes that face, in stillness when he listened to me playing, with the heavy eyelids folded over eyes that always disturbed me by their absolute absence of light, seemed to me like a mask, as if his real face, the face that truly reflected all the life he had led in the world before he met me, before, even, I was born, as though that face lay underneath this mask. Or else, elsewhere. As though he had laid by the face in which he had lived for so long in order to offer my youth a face unsigned by the years.

And, elsewhere, I might see him plain. Elsewhere. But, where?

In, perhaps, that castle to which the train now took us, that marvelous castle in which he had been born.

Even when he asked me to marry him, and I said: 'Yes,' still he did not lose that heavy, fleshy composure of his. I know it must seem a curious analogy, a man with a flower, but sometimes he seemed to me like a lily. Yes. A lily. Possessed of that strange, ominous calm of a sentient vegetable, like one of those cobra-headed, funereal lilies whose white sheaths are curled out of a flesh as thick and tensely yielding to the touch as vellum. When I said that I would marry him, not one muscle in his face stirred, but he let out a long, extinguished sigh. I thought: Oh! how he must want me! And it was as though the imponderable weight of his desire was a force I might not withstand, not by virtue of its violence but because of its very gravity.

He had the ring ready in a leather box lined with crimson velvet, a fire opal the size of a pigeon's egg set in a complicated circle of dark antique gold. My old nurse, who still lived with my mother and me, squinted at the ring askance: opals are bad luck, she said. But this opal had been his own mother's ring, and his grandmother's, and her mother's before that, given to an ancestor by Catherine de Medici . . . every bride that came to the castle wore it, time out of mind. And did he give it to his other wives and have it back from them? asked the old woman rudely; yet she was a snob. She hid her incredulous joy at my marital coup — her little Marquise — behind a façade of fault-finding. But, here, she touched me. I shrugged and turned my back pettishly on her. I did not want to remember how he had loved other women before me, but the knowledge often teased me in the threadbare self-confidence of the small hours.

I was seventeen and knew nothing of the world; my Marquis had been married before, more than once, and I remained a little bemused that, after those others, he should now have chosen me. Indeed, was he not still in mourning for his last wife? Tsk, tsk, went my old nurse. And even my mother had been reluctant to see her girl whisked off by a man so recently bereaved. A Romanian countess, a lady of high fashion. Dead just three short months before I met him, a boating accident, at his home, in Brittany. They never found her body but I rummaged through the back copies of the society magazines my old nanny kept in a trunk under her bed and tracked down her photograph. The sharp muzzle of a pretty, witty, naughty monkey; such potent and bizarre charm, of a dark, bright, wild yet worldly thing whose natural habitat must have been some luxurious interior decorator's jungle filled with potted palms and tame, squawking parakeets.

Before that? *Her* face is common property; everyone painted her but the Redon engraving I liked best, *The Evening Star Walking on the Rim of Night*. To see her skeletal, enigmatic grace, you would never think she had been a barmaid in a café in Montmartre until Puvis de Chavannes saw her and had her expose her flat breasts and elongated thighs to his brush. And yet it was the absinthe doomed her, or so they said.

The first of all his ladies? That sumptuous diva; I had heard her sing Isolde, precociously musical child that I was, taken to the opera for a birthday treat. My first opera; I had heard her sing Isolde. With what white-hot passion had she burned from the stage! So that you could tell she would die young. We sat high up, halfway to heaven in the gods, yet she half-blinded me. And my father, still alive (oh, so long ago), took hold of my sticky little hand, to comfort me, in the last act, yet all I heard was the glory of her voice.

Married three times within my own brief lifetime to three different graces, now, as if to demonstrate the eclecticism of his taste, he had invited me to join this gallery of beautiful women, I, the poor widow's child with my mouse-coloured hair that still bore the kinks of the plaits from which it had so recently been freed, my bony hips, my nervous, pianist's fingers.

He was rich as Croesus. The night before our wedding — a simple affair, at the Mairie, because his countess was so recently gone — he took my mother and me, curious coincidence, to see *Tristan*. And, do you know, my heart swelled and ached so during the Liebestod that I thought I must truly love him. Yes. I did. On his arm, all eyes were upon me. The whispering crowd in the foyer parted like the Red Sea to let us through. My skin crisped at his touch.

How my circumstances had changed since the first time I heard those voluptuous chords that carry such a charge of deathly passion in them! Now, we sat in a loge, in red velvet armchairs, and a braided, bewigged flunkey brought us a silver bucket of iced champagne in the interval. The froth spilled over the rim of my glass and drenched my hands, I thought: My cup runneth over. And I had on a Poiret dress. He had prevailed upon my reluctant mother to let him buy my trousseau; what would I have gone to him in, otherwise? Twice-darned underwear, faded gingham, serge skirts, hand-me-downs. So, for the opera, I wore a sinuous shift of white muslin tied with a silk string under the breasts. And everyone stared at me. And at his wedding gift.

His wedding gift, clasped round my throat. A choker of rubies, two inches wide, like an extraordinarily precious slit throat.

After the Terror, in the early days of the Directory, the aristos who'd escaped the guillotine had an ironic fad of tying a red ribbon round their necks at just the point where the blade would have sliced it through, a red ribbon like the memory of a wound. And his grandmother, taken with the notion, had her ribbon made up in rubies; such a gesture of luxurious defiance! That night at the opera comes back to me even now ... the white dress; the frail child within it; and the flashing crimson jewels round her throat, bright as arterial blood.

I saw him watching me in the gilded mirrors with the assessing eye of a connoisseur inspecting horseflesh, or even of a housewife in the market, inspecting cuts on the slab. I'd never seen, or else had never acknowledged, that regard of his before, the sheer carnal avarice of it; and it was strangely magnified by the monocle lodged in his left eye. When I saw him look at me with lust, I dropped my eyes but, in glancing away from him, I caught sight of myself in the mirror. And I saw myself, suddenly, as he saw me, my pale face, the way the muscles in my neck stuck out like thin wire. I saw how much that cruel necklace became me. And, for the first time in my innocent and confined life, I sensed in myself a potentiality for corruption that took my breath away.

The next day, we were married.

The train slowed, shuddered to a halt. Lights; clank of metal; a voice declaring the name of an unknown, never-to-be visited station; silence of the night; the rhythm of his breathing, that I should sleep with, now, for the rest of my life. And I could not sleep. I stealthily sat up, raised the blind a little and huddled against the cold window that misted over with the warmth of my breathing, gazing out at the dark platform towards those rectangles of domestic lamplight that promised warmth, company, a supper of sausages hissing in a pan on the stove for the station master, his children tucked up in bed asleep in the brick house with the painted shutters … all the paraphernalia of the everyday world from which I, with my stunning marriage, had exiled myself.

Into marriage, into exile; I sensed it, I knew it — that, henceforth, I would always be lonely. Yet that was part of the already familiar weight of the fire opal that glimmered like a gypsy's magic ball, so that I could not take my eyes off it when I played the piano. This ring, the bloody bandage of rubies, the wardrobe of clothes from Poiret and Worth, his scent of Russian leather — all had conspired to seduce me so utterly that I could not say I felt one single twinge of regret for the world of tartines and maman that now receded from me as if drawn away on a string, like a child's toy, as the train began to throb again as if in delighted anticipation of the distance it would take me.

The first grey streamers of the dawn now flew in the sky and an eldritch half-light seeped into the railway carriage. I heard no change in his breathing but my height-ened, excited senses told me he was awake and gazing at me. A huge man, an enormous man, and his eyes, dark and motionless as those eyes the ancient Egyp-tians painted upon their sarcophagi, fixed upon me. I felt a certain tension in the pit of my stomach, to be so watched, in such silence. A match struck. He was igniting a Romeo y Julieta fat as a baby's arm.

'Soon,' he said in his resonant voice that was like the tolling of a bell and I felt, all at once, a sharp premonition of dread that lasted only as long as the match flared and I could see his white, broad face as if it were hovering, disembodied, above the sheets, illuminated from below like a grotesque carnival head. Then the flame died, the cigar glowed and filled the compartment with a remembered fragrance that made me think of my father, how he would hug me in a warm fug of Havana, when I was a little girl, before he kissed me and left me and died.

As soon as my husband handed me down from the high step of the train, I smelled the amniotic salinity of the ocean. It was November; the trees, stunted by the Atlantic gales, were bare and the lonely halt was deserted but for his leather-gaitered chauffeur waiting meekly beside the sleek black motor car. It was cold; I drew my furs about me, a wrap of white and black, broad stripes of ermine and sable, with a collar from which my head rose like the calyx of a wildflower. (I swear to you, I had never been vain until I met him.) The bell clanged; the straining train leapt its leash and left us at that lonely wayside halt where only he and I had descended. Oh, the wonder of it; how all that might of iron and steam had paused only to suit his convenience. The richest man in France.

'Madame.'

The chauffeur eyed me; was he comparing me, individiously, to the countess, the artist's model, the opera singer? I hid behind my furs as if they were a system of soft shields. My husband liked me to wear my opal over my kid glove, a showy, theatrical trick — but the moment the ironic chauffeur glimpsed its simmering flash he smiled, as though it was proof positive I was his master's wife. And we drove towards the widening dawn, that now streaked half the sky with a wintry bouquet of pink of roses, orange of tiger-lilies, as if my husband had ordered me a sky from a florist. The day broke around me like a cool dream.

Sea; sand; a sky that melts into the sea — a landscape of misty pastels with a look about it of being continuously on the point of melting. A landscape with all the deliquescent harmonies of Debussy, of the études I played for him, the reverie I'd been playing that afternoon in the salon of the princess where I'd first met him, among the teacups and the little cakes, I, the orphan, hired out of charity to give them their digestive of music.

And, ah! his castle. The faery solitude of the place; with its turrets of misty blue, its courtyard, its spiked gate, his castle that lay on the very bosom of the sea with seabirds mewing about its attics, the casements opening on to the green and purple, evanescent departures of the ocean, cut off by the tide from land for half a day ... that castle, at home neither on the land nor on the water, a mysterious, amphibious place, contravening the materiality of both earth and the waves, with the melancholy of a mermaiden who perches on her rock and waits, endlessly, for a lover who had drowned far away, long ago. That lovely, sad, sea-siren of a place!

The tide was low; at this hour, so early in the morning, the causeway rose up out of the sea. As the car turned on to the wet cobbles between the slow margins of water, he reached out for my hand that had his sultry, witchy ring on it, pressed my fingers, kissed my palm with extraordinary tenderness. His face was as still as ever I'd seen it, still as a pond iced thickly over, yet his lips, that always looked so strangely red and naked between the black fringes of his beard, now curved a little. He smiled; he welcomed his bride home.

No room, no corridor that did not rustle with the sound of the sea and all the ceilings, the walls on which his ancestors in the stern regalia of rank lined up with their dark eyes and white faces, were stippled with refracted light from the waves which were always in motion; that luminous, murmurous castle of which I was the châtelaine, I, the little music student whose mother had sold all her jewellery, even her wedding ring, to pay the fees at the Conservatoire.

First of all, there was the small ordeal of my initial interview with the housekeeper, who kept this extraordinary machine, this anchored, castellated ocean liner, in smooth running order no matter who stood on the bridge; how tenuous, I thought, might be my authority here! She had a bland, pale, impassive, dislikeable face beneath the impeccably starched white linen head-dress of the region. Her greeting, correct but lifeless, chilled me; daydreaming, I dared presume too much on my status ... briefly wondered how I might install my old nurse, so much loved, however cosily incompetent, in her place. Ill-considered schemings! He told me this one had been his foster mother; was bound to his family in the utmost feudal complicity, 'as much part of the house as I am, my dear'. Now her thin lips offered me a proud little smile. She would be my ally as long as I was his. And with that, I must be content.

But, here, it would be easy to be content. In the turret suite he had given me for my very own, I could gaze out over the tumultuous Atlantic and imagine myself the Queen of the Sea. There was a Bechstein for me in the music room and, on the wall, another wedding present — an early Flemish primitive of Saint Cecilia at her celestial organ. In the prim charm of this saint, with her plump, sallow cheeks and crinkled brown hair, I saw myself as I could have wished to be. I warmed to a loving sensitivity I had not hitherto suspected in him. Then he led me up a delicate spiral staircase to my bedroom; before she discreetly vanished, the housekeeper set him chuckling with some, I dare say, lewd blessing for newlyweds in her native Breton. That I did not understand. That he, smiling, refused to interpret.

And there lay the grand, hereditary matrimonial bed, itself the size, almost, of my little room at home, with the gargoyles carved on its surfaces of ebony, vermilion lacquer, gold leaf; and its white gauze curtains, billowing in the sea breeze. Our bed. And surrounded by so many mirrors! Mirrors on all the walls, in stately frames of contorted gold, that reflected more white lilies than I'd ever seen in my life before. He'd filled the room with them, to greet the bride, the young bride. The young bride, who had become that multitude of girls I saw in the mirrors, identical in their chic navy blue tailor-mades, for travelling, madame, or walking. A maid had dealt with the furs. Henceforth, a maid would deal with everything.

'See,' he said, gesturing towards those elegant girls. 'I have acquired a whole harem for myself!'

I found that I was trembling. My breath came thickly. I could not meet his eye and turned my head away, out of pride, out of shyness, and watched a dozen husbands approach me in a dozen mirrors and slowly, methodically, teasingly, unfasten the buttons of my jacket and slip it from my shoulders. Enough! No; more! Off comes the skirt; and, next, the blouse of apricot linen that cost more than the dress I had for first communion. The play of the waves outside in the cold sun glittered on his monocle; his movements seemed to me deliberately coarse, vulgar. The blood rushed to my face again, and stayed there.

And yet, you see, I guessed it might be so — that we should have a formal disrobing of the bride, a ritual from the brothel. Sheltered as my life had been, how could I have failed, even in the world of prim bohemia in which I lived, to have heard hints of *his* world?

He stripped me, gourmand that he was, as if he were stripping the leaves off an artichoke — but do not imagine much finesse about it; this artichoke was no particular treat for the diner nor was he yet in any greedy haste. He approached his familiar treat with a weary appetite. And when nothing but my scarlet, palpitating core remained, I saw, in the mirror, the living image of an etching by Rops from the collection he had shown me when our engagement permitted us to be alone together . . . the child with her sticklike limbs, naked but for her button boots, her gloves, shielding her face with her hand as though her face were the last repository of her modesty; and the old, monocled lecher who examined her, limb by limb. He in his London tailoring; she, bare as a lamb chop. Most pornographic of all confrontations. And so my purchaser unwrapped his bargain. And, as at the opera, when I had first seen my flesh in his eyes; I was aghast to feel myself stirring.

At once he closed my legs like a book and I saw again the rare movement of his lips that meant he smiled.

Not yet. Later. Anticipation is the greater part of pleasure, my little love.

And I began to shudder, like a racehorse before a race, yet also with a kind of fear, for I felt both a strange, impersonal arousal at the thought of love and at the same time a repugnance I could not stifle for his white, heavy flesh that had too much in common with the armfuls of arum lilies that filled my bedroom in great glass jars, those undertakers' lilies with the heavy pollen that powders your fingers as if you had dipped them in tumeric. The lilies I always associate with him; that are white. And stain you.

This scene from a voluptuary's life was now abruptly terminated. It turns out he has business to attend to; his estates, his companies — even on your honeymoon? Even then, said the red lips that kissed me before he left me alone with my bewildered senses — a wet, silken brush from his beard; a hint of the pointed tip of the tongue. Disgruntled, I wrapped a négligé of antique lace around me to sip the little breakfast of hot chocolate the maid brought me; after that, since it was second nature to me, there was nowhere to go but the music room and soon I settled down at my piano.

Yet only a series of subtle discords flowed from beneath my fingers: out of tune . . . only a little out of tune; but I'd been blessed with perfect pitch and could not bear to play any more. Sea breezes are bad for pianos; we shall need a resident piano-tuner on the premises if I'm to continue with my studies! I flung down the lid in a little fury of disappointment; what should I do now, how shall I pass the long, sea-lit hours until my husband beds me?

I shivered to think of *that*.

His library seemed the source of his habitual odour of Russian leather. Row upon row of calf-bound volumes, brown and olive, with gilt lettering on their spines, the octavo in brilliant scarlet morocco. A deep-buttoned leather sofa to recline on. A lectern, carved like a spread eagle, that held open upon it an edition of Huysmans's *Là-bas,* from some over-exquisite private press; it had been bound like a missal, in brass, with gems of coloured glass. The rugs on the floor, deep, pulsing blues of heaven and red of the heart's dearest blood, came from Isfahan and Bokhara; the dark panelling gleamed; there was the lulling music of the sea and a fire of apple logs. The flames flickered along the spines inside a glass-fronted case that held books still crisp and new. Eliphas Levy; the name meant nothing to me. I squinted at a title or two: *The Initiation, The Key of Mysteries, The Secret of Pandora's Box,* and yawned. Nothing, here, to detain a seventeen-year-old girl waiting for her first embrace. I should have liked, best of all, a novel in yellow paper; I wanted to curl up on the rug before the blazing fire, lose myself in a cheap novel, munch sticky liqueur chocolates. If I rang for them, a maid would bring me chocolates.

Nevertheless, I opened the doors of that bookcase idly to browse. And I think I knew, I knew by some tingling of the fingertips, even before I opened that slim volume with no title at all on the spine, what I should find inside it. When he showed me the Rops, newly bought, dearly prized, had he not hinted that he was a connoisseur of such things? Yet I had not bargained for this, the girl with tears hanging on her cheeks like stuck pearls, her cunt a split fig below the great globes of her buttocks on which the knotted tails of the cat were about to descend, while a man in a black mask fingered with his free hand his prick, that curved upwards like the scimitar he held. The picture had a caption: 'Reproof of curiosity'. My mother, with all the precision of her eccentricity, had told me what it was that lovers did; I was innocent but not naïve. *The Adventures of Eulalie at the Harem of the Grand Turk* had been printed, according to the flyleaf, in Amsterdam in 1748, a rare collector's piece. Had some ancestor brought it back himself from that northern city? Or had my husband bought it for himself, from one of those dusty little bookshops on the Left Bank where an old man peers at you through spectacles an inch thick, daring you to inspect his wares . . . I turned the pages in the anticipation of fear; the print was rusty. Here was another steel engraving: 'Immolation of the wives of the Sultan'. I knew enough for what I saw in that book to make me gasp.

There was a pungent intensification of the odour of leather that suffused his library; his shadow fell across the massacre.

'My little nun has found the prayerbooks, has she?' he demanded, with a curious mixture of mockery and relish; then, seeing my painful, furious bewilderment, he laughed at me aloud, snatched the book from my hands and put it down on the sofa.

'Have the nasty pictures scared Baby? Baby mustn't play with grownups' toys until she's learned how to handle them, must she?'

Then he kissed me. And with, this time, no reticence. He kissed me and laid his hand imperatively upon my breast, beneath the sheath of ancient lace. I stumbled on the winding stair that led to the bedroom, to the carved, gilded bed on which he had been conceived. I stammered foolishly: We've not taken luncheon yet; and, besides, it is broad daylight . . .

All the better to see you.

He made me put on my choker, the family heirloom of one woman who had escaped the blade. With trembling fingers, I fastened the thing about my neck. It was cold as ice and chilled me. He twined my hair into a rope and lifted it off my shoulders so that he could the better kiss the downy furrows below my ears; that made me shudder. And he kissed those blazing rubies, too. He kissed them before he kissed my mouth. Rapt, he intoned: 'Of her apparel she retains/Only her sonorous jewellery.'

A dozen husbands impaled a dozen brides while the mewing gulls swung on invisible trapezes in the empty air outside.

I was brought to my senses by the insistent shrilling of the telephone. He lay beside me, felled like an oak, breathing stertorously, as if he had been fighting with me. In the course of that one-sided struggle, I had seen his deathly composure shatter like a porcelain vase flung against a wall; I had heard him shriek and blaspheme at the orgasm; I had bled. And perhaps I had seen his face without its mask; and perhaps I had not. Yet I had been infinitely dishevelled by the loss of my virginity.

I gathered myself together, reached into the cloisonné cupboard beside the bed that concealed the telephone and addressed the mouthpiece. His agent in New York. Urgent.

I shook him awake and rolled over on my side, cradling my spent body in my arms. His voice buzzed like a hive of distant bees. My husband. My husband, who, with so much love, filled my bedroom with lilies until it looked like an embalming parlour. Those somnolent lilies, that wave their heavy heads, distributing their lush, insolent incense reminiscent of pampered flesh.

When he'd finished with the agent, he turned to me and stroked the ruby necklace that bit into my neck, but with such tenderness now, that I ceased flinching and he caressed my breasts. My dear one, my little love, my child, did it hurt her? He's so sorry for it, such impetuousness, he could not help himself; you see, he loves her so . . . and this lover's recitative of his brought my tears in a flood. I clung to him as though only the one who had inflicted the pain could comfort me for suffering it. For a while, he murmured to me in a voice I'd never heard before, a voice like the soft consolations of the sea. But then he unwound the tendrils of my hair from the buttons of his smoking jacket, kissed my cheek briskly and told me the agent from New York had called with such urgent business that he must leave as soon as the tide was low enough. Leave the castle? Leave France! And would be away for at least six weeks.

'But it is our honeymoon!'

A deal, an enterprise of hazard and chance involving several millions, lay in the balance, he said. He drew away from me into that waxworks stillness of his; I was only a little girl, I did not understand. And, he said unspoken to my wounded vanity, I have had too many honeymoons to find them in the least pressing commitments. I know quite well that this child I've bought with a handful of coloured stones and the pelts of dead beasts won't run away. But, after he'd called his Paris agent to book a passage for the States next day — just one tiny call, my little one — we should have time for dinner together.

And I had to be content with that.

A Mexican dish of pheasant with hazelnuts and chocolate; salad; white, voluptuous cheese; a sorbet of muscat grapes and Asti spumante. A celebration of Krug exploded festively. And then acrid black coffee in precious little cups so fine it shadowed the birds with which they were painted. I had cointreau, he had cognac in the library, with the purple velvet curtains drawn against the night, where he took me to perch on his knee in a leather armchair beside the flickering log fire. He had made me change into that chaste little Poiret shift of white muslin; he seemed especially fond of it, my breasts showed through the flimsy stuff, he said, like little soft white doves that sleep, each one, with a pink eye open. But he would not let me take off my ruby choker, although it was growing very uncomfortable, nor fasten up my descending hair, the sign of a virginity so recently ruptured that still remained a wounded presence between us. He twined his fingers in my hair until I winced; I said, I remember, very little.

'The maid will have changed our sheets already,' he said. 'We do not hang the bloody sheets out of the window to prove to the whole of Brittany you are a virgin, not in these civilized times. But I should tell you it would have been the first time in all my married lives I could have shown my interested tenants such a flag.'

Then I realized, with a shock of surprise, how it must have been my innocence that captivated him — the silent music, he said, of my unknowingness, like *La Terrasse des audiences au clair de lune* played upon a piano with keys of ether. You must remember how ill at ease I was in that luxurious place, how unease had been my constant companion during the whole length of my courtship by this grave satyr who now gently martyrized my hair. To know that my naïvety gave him some pleasure made me take heart. Courage! I shall act the fine lady to the manner born one day, if only by virtue of default.

Then, slowly yet teasingly, as if he were giving a child a great, mysterious treat, he took out a bunch of keys from some interior hidey-hole in his jacket — key after key, a key, he said, for every lock in the house. Keys of all kinds — huge, ancient things of black iron; others slender, delicate, almost baroque; wafer-thin Yale keys for safes and boxes. And, during his absence, it was I who must take care of them all.

I eyed the heavy bunch with circumspection. Until that moment, I had not given a single thought to the practical aspects of marriage with a great house, great wealth, a great man, whose key ring was as crowded as that of a prison warder. Here were the clumsy and archaic keys for the dungeons, for dungeons we had in plenty although they had been converted to cellars for his wines; the dusty bottles inhabited in racks all those deep holes of pain in the rock on which the castle was built. These are the keys to the kitchens, this is the key to the picture gallery, a treasure house filled by five centuries of avid collectors — ah! he foresaw I would spend hours there.

He had amply indulged his taste for the Symbolists, he told me with a glint of greed. There was Moreau's great portrait of his first wife, the famous *Sacrificial Victim* with the imprint of the lacelike chains on her pellucid skin. Did I know the story of the painting of that picture? How, when she took off her clothes for him for the first time, she fresh from her bar in Montmartre, she had robed herself involuntarily in a blush that reddened her breasts, her shoulders, her arms, her whole body? He had thought of that story, of that dear girl, when first he had undressed me ... Ensor, the great Ensor, his monolithic canvas: *The Foolish Virgins*. Two or three late Gauguins, his special favourite the one of the tranced brown girl in the deserted house which was called: *Out of the Night We Come, Into the Night We Go*. And, besides the additions he had made himself, his marvellous inheritance of Watteaus, Poussins and a pair of very special Fragonards, commissioned for a licentious ancestor who, it was said, had posed for the master's brush himself with his own two daughters ... He broke off his catalogue of treasures abruptly.

Your thin white face, chérie; he said, as if he saw it for the first time. Your thin white face, with its promise of debauchery only a connoisseur could detect.

A log fell in the fire, instigating a shower of sparks; the opal on my finger spurted green flame. I felt as giddy as if I were on the edge of a precipice; I was afraid, not so much of him, of his monstrous presence, heavy as if he had been gifted at birth with more specific *gravity* than the rest of us, the presence that, even when I thought myself most in love with him, always subtly oppressed me ... No. I was not afraid of him; but of myself. I seemed reborn in his unreflective eyes, reborn in unfamiliar shapes. I hardly recognized myself from his descriptions of me and yet, and yet — might there not be a grain of beastly truth in them? And, in the red firelight, I blushed again, unnoticed, to think he might have chosen me because, in my innocence, he sensed a rare talent for corruption.

Here is the key to the china cabinet — don't laugh, my darling; there's a king's ransom in Sèvres in that closet, and a queen's ransom in Limoges. And a key to the locked, barred room where five generations of plate were kept.

Keys, keys, keys. He would trust me with the keys to his office, although I was only a baby; and the keys to his safes, where he kept the jewels I should wear, he promised me, when we returned to Paris. Such jewels! Why, I would be able to change my earrings and necklaces three times a day, just as the Empress Josephine used to change her underwear. He doubted, he said, with that hollow, knocking sound that served him for a chuckle, I would be quite so interested in his share certificates although they, of course, were worth infinitely more.

Outside our firelit privacy, I could hear the sound of the tide drawing back from the pebbles of the foreshore; it was nearly time for him to leave me. One single key remained unaccounted for on the ring and he hesitated over it; for a moment, I thought he was going to unfasten it from its brothers, slip it back into his pocket and take it away with him.

'What is *that* key?' I demanded, for his chaffing had made me bold. 'The key to your heart? Give it me!'

He dangled the key tantalizingly above my head, out of reach of my straining fingers; those bare red lips of his cracked sidelong in a smile.

'Ah, no,' he said. 'Not the key to my heart. Rather, the key to my enfer.'

He left it on the ring, fastened the ring together, shook it musically, like a carillon. Then threw the keys in a jingling heap in my lap. I could feel the cold metal chilling my thighs through my thin muslin frock. He bent over me to drop a beard-masked kiss on my forehead.

'Every man must have one secret, even if only one, from his wife,' he said. 'Promise me this, my whey-faced piano-player; promise me you'll use all the keys on the ring except that last little one I showed you. Play with anything you find, jewels, silver plate; make toy boats of my share certificates, if it pleases you, and send them sailing off to America after me. All is yours, everywhere is open to you — except the lock that this single key fits. Yet all it is is the key to a little room at the foot of the west tower, behind the still-room, at the end of a dark little corridor full of horrid cobwebs that would get into your hair and frighten you if you ventured there. Oh, and you'd find it such a dull little room! But you must promise me, if you love me, to leave it well alone. It is only a private study, a hideaway, a "den", as the English say, where I can go, sometimes, on those infrequent yet inevitable occasions when the yoke of marriage seems to weigh too heavily on my shoulders. There I can go, you understand, to savour the rare pleasure of imagining myself wifeless.'

There was a little thin starlight in the courtyard as, wrapped in my furs, I saw him to his car. His last words were, that he had telephoned the mainland and taken a piano-tuner on to the staff; this man would arrive to take up his duties the next day. He pressed me to his vicuña breast, once, and then drove away.

I had drowsed away that afternoon and now I could not sleep. I lay tossing and turning in his ancestral bed until another daybreak discoloured the dozen mirrors that were iridescent with the reflections of the sea. The perfume of the lilies weighed on my senses; when I thought that, henceforth, I would always share these sheets with a man whose skin, as theirs did, contained that toad-like, clammy hint of moisture, I felt a vague desolation that within me, now my female wound had healed, there had awoken a certain queasy craving like the cravings of pregnant women for the taste of coal or chalk or tainted food, for the renewal of his caresses. Had he not hinted to me, in his flesh as in his speech and looks, of the thousand, thousand baroque intersections of flesh upon flesh? I lay in our wide bed accompanied by, a sleepless companion, my dark newborn curiosity.

I lay in bed alone. And I longed for him. And he disgusted me.

Were there jewels enough in all his safes to recompense me for this predicament? Did all that castle hold enough riches to recompense me for the company of the libertine with whom I must share it? And what, precisely, was the nature of my desirous dread for this mysterious being who, to show his mastery over me, had abandoned me on my wedding night?

Then I sat straight up in bed, under the sardonic masks of the gargoyles carved above me, riven by a wild surmise. Might he have left me, not for Wall Street but for an importunate mistress tucked away God knows where who knew how to pleasure him far better than a girl whose fingers had been exercised, hitherto, only by the practice of scales and arpeggios? And, slowly, soothed, I sank back on to the heaping pillows; I acknowledged that the jealous scare I'd just given myself was not unmixed with a little tincture of relief.

At last I drifted into slumber, as daylight filled the room and chased bad dreams away. But the last thing I remembered, before I slept, was the tall jar of lilies beside the bed, how the thick glass distorted their fat stems so they looked like arms, dismembered arms, drifting drowned in greenish water.

Coffee and croissants to console this bridal, solitary waking. Delicious. Honey, too, in a section of comb on a glass saucer. The maid squeezed the aromatic juice from an orange into a chilled goblet while I watched her as I lay in the lazy, midday bed of the rich. Yet nothing, this morning, gave me more than a fleeting pleasure except to hear that the piano-tuner had been at work already. When the maid told me that, I sprang out of bed and pulled on my old serge skirt and flannel blouse, costume of a student, in which I felt far more at ease with myself than in any of my fine new clothes.

After my three hours of practice, I called the piano-tuner in, to thank him. He was blind, of course; but young, with a gentle mouth and grey eyes that fixed upon me although they could not see me. He was a blacksmith's son from the village across the causeway; a chorister in the church whom the good priest had taught a trade so that he could make a living. All most satisfactory. Yes. He thought he would be happy here. And if, he added shyly, he might sometimes be allowed to hear me play . . . for, you see, he loved music. Yes. Of course, I said. Certainly. He seemed to know that I had smiled.

After I dismissed him, even though I'd woken so late, it was still barely time for my 'five o'clock'. The housekeeper, who, thoughtfully forewarned by my husband, had restrained herself from interrupting my music, now made me a solemn visitation with a lengthy menu for a late luncheon. When I told her I did not need it, she looked at me obliquely, along her nose. I understood at once that one of my principal functions as châtelaine was to provide work for the staff. But, all the same, I asserted myself and said I would wait until dinner-time, although I looked forward nervously to the solitary meal. Then I found I had to tell her what I would like to have prepared for me; my imagination, still that of a schoolgirl, ran riot. A fowl in cream — or should I anticipate Christmas with a varnished turkey? No; I have decided. Avocado and shrimp, lots of it, followed by no entrée at all. But surprise me for dessert with every ice-cream in the ice box. She noted ail down but sniffed; I'd shocked her. Such tastes! Child that I was, I giggled when she left me.

But, now . . . what shall I do, now?

I could have spent a happy hour unpacking the trunks that contained my trousseau but the maid had done that already, the dresses, the tailor-mades hung in the wardrobe in my dressing room, the hats on wooden heads to keep their shape, the shoes on wooden feet as if all these inanimate objects were imitating the appearance of life, to mock me. I did not like to linger in my overcrowded dressing room, nor in my lugubriously lily-scented bedroom. How shall I pass the time?

I shall take a bath in my own bathroom! And found the taps were little dolphins made of gold, with chips of turquoise for eyes. And there was a tank of goldfish, who swam in and out of moving fronds of weeds, as bored, I thought, as I was. How I wished he had not left me. How I wished it were possible to chat with, say, a maid; or, the piano-tuner . . . but I knew already my new rank forbade overtures of friendship to the staff.

I had been hoping to defer the call as long as I could, so that I should have something to look forward to in the dead waste of time I foresaw before me, after my dinner was done with, but, at a quarter before seven, when darkness already surrounded the castle, I could contain myself no longer. I telephoned my mother. And astonished myself by bursting into tears when I heard her voice.

No, nothing was the matter. Mother, I have gold bath taps.

I said, gold bath taps!

No; I suppose that's nothing to cry about, Mother.

The line was bad, I could hardly make out her congratulations, her questions, her concern, but I was a little comforted when I put the receiver down.

Yet there still remained one whole hour to dinner and the whole, unimaginable desert of the rest of the evening.

The bunch of keys lay, where he had left them, on the rug before the library fire which had warmed their metal so that they no longer felt cold to the touch but warm, almost, as my own skin. How careless I was; a maid, tending the logs, eyed me reproachfully as if I'd set a trap for her as I picked up the clinking bundle of keys, the keys to the interior doors of this lovely prison of which I was both the inmate and the mistress and had scarcely seen. When I remembered that, I felt the exhilaration of the explorer.

Lights! More lights!

At the touch of a switch, the dreaming library was brilliantly illuminated. I ran crazily about the castle, switching on every light I could find — I ordered the servants to light up all their quarters, too, so the castle would shine like a seaborne birthday cake lit with a thousand candles, one for every year of its life, and everybody on shore would wonder at it. When everything was lit as brightly as the café in the Gare du Nord, the significance of the possessions implied by that bunch of keys no longer intimidated me, for I was determined, now, to search through them all for evidence of my husband's true nature.

His office first, evidently.

A mahogany desk half a mile wide, with an impeccable blotter and a bank of telephones. I allowed myself the luxury of opening the safe that contained the jewellery and delved sufficiently among the leather boxes to find out how my marriage had given me access to a jinn's treasury — parures, bracelets, rings . . . While I was thus surrounded by diamonds, a maid knocked on the door and entered before I spoke; a subtle discourtesy. I would speak to my husband about it. She eyed my serge skirt superciliously; did madame plan to dress for dinner?

She made a moue of disdain when I laughed to hear that, she was far more the lady than I. But, imagine — to dress up in one of my Poiret extravaganzas, with the jewelled turban and aigrette on my head, roped with pearl to the navel, to sit down all alone in the baronial dining hall at the head of that massive board at which King Mark was reputed to have fed his knights . . . I grew calmer under the cold eye of her disapproval. I adopted the crisp inflections of an officer's daughter. No, I would not dress for dinner. Furthermore, I was not hungry enough for dinner itself. She must tell the housekeeper to cancel the dormitory feast I'd ordered. Could they leave me sandwiches and a flask of coffee in my music room? And would they all dismiss for the night?

Mais oui, madame.

I knew by her bereft intonation I had let them down again but I did not care; I was armed against them by the brilliance of his hoard. But I would not find his heart amongst the glittering stones; as soon as she had gone, I began a systematic search of the drawers of his desk.

All was in order, so I found nothing. Not a random doodle on an old envelope, nor the faded photograph of a woman. Only the files of business correspondence, the bills from the home farms, the invoices from tailors, the billets-doux from international financiers. Nothing. And this absence of the evidence of his real life began to impress me strangely; there must, I thought, be a great deal to conceal if he takes such pains to hide it.

His office was a singularly impersonal room, facing inwards, on to the courtyard, as though he wanted to turn his back on the siren sea in order to keep a clear head while he bankrupted a small businessman in Amsterdam or — I noticed with a thrill of distaste — engaged in some business in Laos that must, from certain cryptic references to his amateur botanist's enthusiasm for rare poppies, be to do with opium. Was he not rich enough to do without crime? Or was the crime itself his profit? And yet I saw enough to appreciate his zeal for secrecy.

Now I had ransacked his desk, I must spend a cool-headed quarter of an hour putting every last letter back where I had found it, and, as I covered the traces of my visit, by some chance, as I reached inside a little drawer that had stuck fast, I must have touched a hidden spring, for a secret drawer flew open within that drawer itself; and this secret drawer contained — at last! — a file marked: *Personal*.

I was alone, but for my reflection in the uncurtained window.

I had the brief notion that his heart, pressed flat as a flower, crimson and thin as tissue paper, lay in this file. It was a very thin one.

I could have wished, perhaps, I had not found that touching, ill-spelt note on a paper napkin marked *La Coupole,* that began: 'My darling, I cannot wait for the moment when you may make me yours completely.' The diva had sent him a page of the score of *Tristan,* the Liebestod, with the single, cryptic word: 'Until ...' scrawled across it. But the strangest of all these love letters was a postcard with a view of a village graveyard, among mountains, where some black-coated ghoul enthusiastically dug at a grave; this little scene, executed with the lurid exuberance of Grand Guignol, was captioned: 'Typical Transylvanian Scene — Midnight, All Hallows.' And, on the other side, the message: 'On the occasion of this marriage to the descendant of Dracula — always remember, "the supreme and unique pleasure of love is the certainty that one is doing evil". Toutes amitiés, C.'

A joke. A joke in the worst possible taste; for had he not been married to a Romanian countess? And then I remembered her pretty, witty face, and her name — Carmilla. My most recent predecessor in this castle had been, it would seem, the most sophisticated.

I put away the file, sobered. Nothing in my life of family love and music had prepared me for these grown-up games and yet these were clues to his self that showed me, at least, how much he had been loved, even if they did not reveal any good reason for it. But I wanted to know still more; and, as I closed the office door and locked it, the means to discover more fell in my way.

Fell, indeed; and with the clatter of a dropped canteen of cutlery, for, as I turned the slick Yale lock, I contrived, somehow, to open up the key ring itself, so that all the keys tumbled loose on the floor. And the very first key I picked out of that pile was, as luck or ill fortune had it, the key to the room he had forbidden me, the room he would keep for his own so that he could go there when he wished to feel himself once more a bachelor.

I made my decision to explore it before I felt a faint resurgence of my ill-defined fear of his waxen stillness. Perhaps I half-imagined, then, that I might find his real self in his den, waiting there to see if indeed I had obeyed him; that he had sent a moving figure of himself to New York, the enigmatic, self-sustaining carapace of his public person, while the real man, whose face I had glimpsed in the storm of orgasm, occupied himself with pressing private business in the study at the foot of the west tower, behind the still-room. Yet, if that were so, it was imperative that I should find him, should know him; and I was too deluded by his apparent taste for me to think my disobedience might truly offend him.

I took the forbidden key from the heap and left the others lying there.

It was now very late and the castle was adrift, as far as it could go from the land, in the middle of the silent ocean where, at my orders, it floated, like a garland of light. And all silent, all still, but for the murmuring of the waves.

I felt no fear, no intimation of dread. Now I walked as firmly as I had done in my mother's house.

Not a narrow, dusty little passage at all; why had he lied to me? But an ill-lit one, certainly; the electricity, for some reason, did not extend here, so I retreated to the still-room and found a bundle of waxed tapers in a cupboard, stored there with matches to light the oak board at grand dinners. I put a match to my little taper and advanced with it in my hand, like a penitent, along the corridor hung with heavy, I think Venetian, tapestries. The flame picked out, here, the head of a man, there, the rich breast of a woman spilling through a rent in her dress — the Rape of the Sabines, perhaps? The naked swords and immolated horses suggested some grisly mythological subject. The corridor wound downstairs; there was an almost imperceptible ramp to the thickly carpeted floor. The heavy hangings on the wall muffled my footsteps, even my breathing. For some reason, it grew very warm; the sweat sprang out in beads on my brow. I could no longer hear the sound of the sea.

A long, a winding corridor, as if I were in the viscera of the castle; and this corridor led to a door of worm-eaten oak, low, round-topped, barred with black iron.

And still I felt no fear, no raising of the hairs on the back of the neck, no prickling of the thumbs.

The key slid into the new lock as easily as a hot knife into butter.

No fear; but a hesitation, a holding of the spiritual breath.

If I had found some traces of his heart in a file marked: *Personal,* perhaps, here, in his subterranean privacy, I might find a little of his soul. It was the consciousness of the possibility of such a discovery, of its possible strangeness, that kept me for a moment motionless, before, in the foolhardiness of my already subtly tainted innocence, I turned the key and the door creaked slowly back.

'There is a striking resemblance between the act of love and the ministrations of a torturer,' opined my husband's favourite poet; I had learned something of the nature of that similarity on my marriage bed. And now my taper showed me the outlines of a rack. There was also a great wheel, like the ones I had seen in woodcuts of the martyrdoms of the saints, in my old nurse's little store of holy books. And — just one glimpse of it before my little flame caved in and I was left in absolute darkness — a metal figure, hinged at the side, which I knew to be spiked on the inside and to have the name: the Iron Maiden.

Absolute darkness. And, about me, the instruments of mutilation.

Until that moment, this spoiled child did not know she had inherited nerves and a will from the mother who had defied the yellow outlaws of Indo-China. My mother's spirit drove me on, into that dreadful place, in a cold ecstasy to know the very worst. I fumbled for the matches in my pocket; what a dim, lugubrious light they gave! And yet, enough, oh, more than enough, to see a room designed for desecration and some dark night of unimaginable lovers whose embraces were annihilation.

The walls of this stark torture chamber were the naked rock; they gleamed as if they were sweating with fright. At the four corners of the room were funerary urns, of great antiquity, Etruscan, perhaps, and, on three-legged ebony stands, the bowls of incense he had left burning which filled the room with a sacerdotal reek. Wheel, rack and Iron Maiden were, I saw, displayed as grandly as if they were items of statuary and I was almost consoled, then, and almost persuaded myself that I might have stumbled only upon a little museum of his perversity, that he had installed these monstrous items here only for contemplation.

Yet at the centre of the room lay a catafalque, a doomed, ominous bier of Renaissance workmanship, surrounded by long white candles and, at its foot, an armful of the same lilies with which he had filled my bedroom, stowed in a four-foot-high jar glazed with a sombre Chinese red. I scarcely dared examine this catafalque and its occupant more closely; yet I knew I must.

Each time I struck a match to light those candles round her bed, it seemed a garment of that innocence of mine for which he had lusted fell away from me.

The opera singer lay, quite naked, under a thin sheet of very rare and precious linen, such as the princes of Italy used to shroud those whom they had poisoned. I touched her, very gently, on the white breast; she was cool, he had embalmed her. On her throat I could see the blue imprint of his strangler's fingers. The cool, sad flame of the candles flickered on her white, closed eyelids. The worst thing was, the dead lips smiled.

Beyond the catafalque, in the middle of the shadows, a white, nacreous glimmer; as my eyes accustomed themselves to the gathering darkness, I at last — oh horrors! — made out a skull; yes, a skull, so utterly denuded, now, of flesh, that it scarcely seemed possible the stark bone had once been richly upholstered with life. And this skull was strung up by a system of unseen cords, so that it appeared to hang, disembodied, in the still, heavy air, and it had been crowned with a wreath of white roses, and a veil of lace, the final image of his bride.

Yet the skull was still so beautiful, had shaped with its sheer planes so imperiously the face that had once existed above it, that I recognized her the moment I saw her; face of the evening star walking on the rim of night. One false step, oh, my poor, dear girl, next in the fated sisterhood of his wives; one false step and into the abyss of the dark you stumbled.

And where was she, the latest dead, the Romanian countess who might have thought her blood would survive his depredations? I knew she must be here, in the place that had wound me through the castle towards it on a spool of inexorability. But, at first, I could see no sign of her. Then, for some reason — perhaps some change of atmosphere wrought by my presence — the metal shell of the Iron Maiden emitted a ghostly twang; my feverish imagination might have guessed its occupant was trying to clamber out, though, even in the midst of my rising hysteria, I knew she must be dead to find a home there.

With trembling fingers, I prised open the front of the upright coffin, with its sculpted face caught in a rictus of pain. Then, overcome, I dropped the key I had held in my other hand. It dropped into the forming pool of her blood.

She was pierced, not by one but by a hundred spikes, this child of the land of the vampires who seemed so newly dead, so full of blood . . . oh God! how recently had he become a widower? How long had he kept her in this obscene cell? Had it been all the time he had courted me, in the clear light of Paris?

I closed the lid of her coffin very gently and burst into a tumult of sobbing that contained both pity for his other victims and also a dreadful anguish to know I, too, was one of them.

The candles flared, as if in a draught from a door to elsewhere. The light caught the fire opal on my hand so that it flashed, once, with a baleful light, as if to tell me the eye of God — his eye — was upon me. My first thought, when I saw the ring for which I had sold myself to this fate, was, how to escape it.

I retained sufficient presence of mind to snuff out the candles round the bier with my fingers, to gather up my taper, to look around, although shuddering, to ensure I had left behind me no traces of my visit.

I retrieved the key from the pool of blood, wrapped it in my handkerchief to keep my hands clean, and fled the room, slamming the door behind me.

It crashed to with a juddering reverberation, like the door of hell.

I could not take refuge in my bedroom, for that retained the memory of his presence trapped in the fathomless silvering of his mirrors. My music room seemed the safest place, although I looked at the picture of Saint Cecilia with a faint dread; what had been the nature of her martyrdom? My mind was in a tumult; schemes for flight jostled with one another . . . as soon as the tide receded from the causeway, I would make for the mainland — on foot, running, stumbling; I did not trust that leather-clad chauffeur, nor the well-behaved housekeeper, and I dared not take any of the pale, ghostly maids into my confidence, either, since they were his creatures, all. Once at the village, I would fling myself directly on the mercy of the gendarmerie.

But — could I trust them, either? His forefathers had ruled this coast for eight centuries, from this castle whose moat was the Atlantic. Might not the police, the advocates, even the judge, all be in his service, turning a common blind eye to his vices since he was milord whose word must be obeyed? Who, on this distant coast, would believe the white-faced girl from Paris who came running to them with a shuddering tale of blood, of fear, of the ogre murmuring in the shadows? Or, rather, they would immediately know it to be true. But were all honour-bound to let me carry it no further.

Assistance. My mother. I ran to the telephone; and the line, of course, was dead.

Dead as his wives.

A thick darkness, unlit by any star, still glazed the windows. Every lamp in my room burned, to keep the dark outside, yet it seemed still to encroach on me, to be present beside me but as if masked by my lights, the night like a permeable substance that could seep into my skin. I looked at the precious little clock made from hypocritically innocent flowers long ago, in Dresden; the hands had scarcely moved one single hour forward from when I first descended to that private slaughterhouse of his. Time was his servant, too; it would trap me, here, in a night that would last until he came back to me, like a black sun on a hopeless morning.

And yet the time might still be my friend; at that hour, that very hour, he set sail for New York.

To know that, in a few moments, my husband would have left France calmed my agitation a little. My reason told me I had nothing to fear; the tide that would take him away to the New World would let me out of the imprisonment of the castle. Surely I could easily evade the servants. Anybody can buy a ticket at a railway station. Yet I was still filled with unease. I opened the lid of the piano; perhaps I thought my own particular magic might help me, now, that I could create a pentacle out of music that would keep me from harm for, if my music had first ensnared him, then might it not also give me the power to free myself from him?

Mechanically, I began to play but my fingers were stiff and shaking. At first, I could manage nothing better than the exercises of Czerny but simply the act of playing soothed me and, for solace, for the sake of the harmonious rationality of its sublime mathematics, I searched among his scores until I found *The Well-Tempered Clavier*. I set myself the therapeutic task of playing all Bach's equations, every one, and, I told myself, if I played them all through without a single mistake — then the morning would find me once more a virgin.

Crash of a dropped stick.

His silver-headed cane! What else? Sly, cunning, he had returned; he was waiting for me outside the door!

I rose to my feet; fear gave me strength. I flung back my head defiantly.

'Come in!' My voice astonished me by its firmness, its clarity.

The door slowly, nervously opened and I saw, not the massive, irredeemable bulk of my husband but the slight, stooping figure of the piano tuner, and he looked far more terrified of me than my mother's daughter would have been of the Devil himself. In the torture chamber, it seemed to me that I would never laugh again; now, helplessly, laugh I did, with relief, and, after a moment's hesitation, the boy's face softened and he smiled a little, almost in shame. Though they were blind, his eyes were singularly sweet.

'Forgive me,' said Jean-Yves. 'I know I've given you grounds for dismissing me, that I should be crouching outside your door at midnight . . . but I heard you walking about, up and down — I sleep in a room at the foot of the west tower — and some intuition told me you could not sleep and might, perhaps, pass the insomniac hours at your piano. And I could not resist that. Besides, I stumbled over these — '

And he displayed the ring of keys I'd dropped outside my husband's office door, the ring from which one key was missing. I took them from him, looked around for a place to stow them, fixed on the piano stool as if to hide them would protect me. Still he stood smiling at me. How hard it was to make everyday conversation.

'It's perfect,' I said. 'The piano. Perfectly in tune.'

But he was full of the loquacity of embarrassment, as though I would only forgive him for his impudence if he explained the cause of it thoroughly.

'When I heard you play this afternoon, I thought I'd never heard such a touch. Such technique. A treat for me, to hear a virtuoso! So I crept up to your door now, humbly as a little dog might, madame, and put my ear to the keyhole and listened, and listened — until my stick fell to the floor through a momentary clumsiness of mine, and I was discovered.'

He had the most touchingly ingenuous smile.

'Perfectly in tune,' I repeated. To my surprise, now I had said it, I found I could not say anything else. I could only repeat: 'In tune . . . perfect . . . in tune,' over and over again. I saw a dawning surprise in his face. My head throbbed. To see him, in his lovely, blind humanity, seemed to hurt me very piercingly, somewhere inside my breast; his figure blurred, the room swayed about me. After the dreadful revelation of that bloody chamber, it was his tender look that made me faint.

When I recovered consciousness, I found I was lying in the piano-tuner's arms and he was tucking the satin cushion from the piano-stool under my head.

'You are in some great distress,' he said. 'No bride should suffer so much, so early in her marriage.'

His speech had the rhythms of the countryside, the rhythms of the tides.

'Any bride brought to this castle should come ready dressed in mourning, should bring a priest and a coffin with her,' I said.

'What's this?'

It was too late to keep silent; and if he, too, were one of my husband's creatures, then at least he had been kind to me. So I told him everything, the keys, the interdiction, my disobedience, the room, the rack, the skull, the corpses, the blood.

'I can scarcely believe it,' he said, wondering. 'That man . . . so rich; so well-born.'

'Here's proof,' I said and tumbled the fatal key out of my handkerchief on to the silken rug.

'Oh God,' he said. 'I can smell the blood.'

He took my hand; he pressed his arms about me. Although he was scarcely more than a boy, I felt a great strength flow into me from his touch.

'We whisper all manner of strange tales up and down the coast,' he said. 'There was a Marquis, once, who used to hunt young girls on the mainland; he hunted them with dogs, as though they were foxes. My grandfather had it from his grandfather, how the Marquis pulled a head out of his saddle bag and showed it to the blacksmith while the man was shoeing his horse. "A fine specimen of the genus, brunette, eh, Guillaume?" And it was the head of the blacksmith's wife.'

But, in these more democratic times, my husband must travel as far as Paris to do his hunting in the salons. Jean-Yves knew the moment I shuddered.

'Oh, madame! I thought all these were old wives' tales, chattering of fools, spooks to scare bad children into good behaviour! Yet how could you know, a stranger, that the old name for this place is the Castle of Murder?'

How could I know, indeed? Except that, in my heart, I'd always known its lord would be the death of me.

'Hark!' said my friend suddenly. 'The sea has changed key; it must be near morning, the tide is going down.'

He helped me up. I looked from the window, towards the mainland, along the causeway where the stones gleamed wetly in the thin light of the end of the night and, with an almost unimaginable horror, a horror the intensity of which I cannot transmit to you, I saw, in the distance, still far away yet drawing moment by moment inexorably nearer, the twin headlamps of his great black car, gouging tunnels through the shifting mist.

My husband had indeed returned; this time, it was no fancy.

'The key!' said Jean-Yves. 'It must go back on the ring, with the others. As though nothing had happened.'

But the key was still caked with wet blood and I ran to my bathroom and held it under the hot tap. Crimson water swirled down the basin but, as if the key itself were hurt, the bloody token stuck. The turquoise eyes of the dolphin taps winked at me derisively; they knew my husband had been too clever for me! I scrubbed the stain with my nail brush but still it would not budge. I thought how the car would be rolling silently towards the closed courtyard gate; the more I scrubbed the key, the more vivid grew the stain.

The bell in the gatehouse would jangle. The porter's drowsy son would push back the patchwork quilt, yawning, pull the shirt over his head, thrust his feet into his sabots ... slowly, slowly; open the door for your master as slowly as you can ...

And still the bloodstain mocked the fresh water that spilled from the mouth of the leering dolphin.

'You have no more time,' said Jean-Yves. 'He is here. I know it. I must stay with you.'

'You shall not!' I said. 'Go back to your room, now. Please.'

He hesitated. I put an edge of steel in my voice, for I knew I must meet my lord alone.

'Leave me!'

As soon as he had gone, I dealt with the keys and went to my bedroom. The causeway was empty; Jean-Yves was correct, my husband had already entered the castle. I pulled the curtains close, stripped off my clothes and pulled the bedcurtains round me as a pungent aroma of Russian leather assured me my husband was once again beside me.

'Dearest!'

With the most treacherous, lascivious tenderness, he kissed my eyes, and, mimicking the new bride newly wakened, I flung my arms around him, for on my seeming acquiescence depended my salvation.

'Da Silva of Rio outwitted me,' he said wryly. 'My New York agent telegraphed Le Havre and saved me a wasted journey. So we may resume our interrupted pleasures, my love.'

I did not believe one word of it. I knew I had behaved exactly according to his desires; had he not bought me so that I should do so? I had been tricked into my own betrayal to that illimitable darkness whose source I had been compelled to seek in his absence and, now that I had met that shadowed reality of his that came to life only in the presence of its own atrocities, I must pay the price of my new knowledge. The secret of Pandora's box; but he had given me the box, himself, knowing I must learn the secret. I had played a game in which every move was governed by a destiny as oppressive and omnipotent as himself, since that destiny was himself; and I had lost. Lost at that charade of innocence and vice in which he had engaged me. Lost, as the victim loses to the executioner.

His hand brushed my breast, beneath the sheet. I strained my nerves yet could not help but flinch from the intimate touch, for it made me think of the piercing embrace of the Iron Maiden and of his lost lovers in the vault. When he saw my reluctance, his eyes veiled over and yet his appetite did not diminish. His tongue ran over red lips already wet. Silent, mysterious, he moved away from me to draw off his jacket. He took the gold watch from his waistcoat and laid it on the dressing table, like a good bourgeois; scooped out his rattling loose change and now — oh God! — makes a great play of patting his pockets officiously, puzzled lips pursed, searching for something that has been mislaid. Then turns to me with a ghastly, a triumphant smile.

'But of course! I gave the keys to you!'

'Your keys? Why, of course. Here, they're under the pillow; wait a moment — what — Ah! No . . . now, where can I have left them? I was whiling away the evening without you at the piano, I remember. Of course! The music room!'

Brusquely he flung my négligé of antique lace on the bed.

'Go and get them.'

'Now? This moment? Can't it wait until morning, my darling?'

I forced myself to be seductive. I saw myself, pale, pliant as a plant that begs to be trampled underfoot, a dozen vulnerable, appealing girls reflected in as many mirrors, and I saw how he almost failed to resist me. If he had come to me in bed, I would have strangled him, then.

But he half-snarled: 'No. It won't wait. Now.'

The unearthly light of dawn filled the room; had only one previous dawn broken upon me in that vile place? And there was nothing for it but to go and fetch the keys from the music stool and pray he would not examine them too closely, pray to God his eyes would fail him, that he might be struck blind.

When I came back into the bedroom carrying the bunch of keys that jangled at every step like a curious musical instrument, he was sitting on the bed in his immaculate shirtsleeves, his head sunk in his hands.

And it seemed to me he was in despair.

Strange. In spite of my fear of him, that made me whiter than my wrap, I felt there emanate from him, at that moment, a stench of absolute despair, rank and ghastly, as if the lilies that surrounded him had all at once begun to fester, or the Russian leather of his scent were reverting to the elements of flayed hide and excrement of which it was composed. The chthonic gravity of his presence exerted a tremendous pressure on the room, so that the blood pounded in my ears as if we had been precipitated to the bottom of the sea, beneath the waves that pounded against the shore.

I held my life in my hands amongst those keys and, in a moment, would place it between his well-manicured fingers. The evidence of that bloody chamber had showed me I could expect no mercy. Yet, when he raised his head and stared at me with his blind, shuttered eyes as though he did not recognize me, I felt a terrified pity for him, for this man who lived in such strange, secret places that, if I loved him enough to follow him, I should have to die.

The atrocious loneliness of that monster!

The monocle had fallen from his face. His curling mane was disordered, as if he had run his hands through it in his distraction. I saw how he had lost his impassivity and was now filled with suppressed excitement. The hand he stretched out for those counters in his game of love and death shook a little; the face that turned towards me contained a sombre delirium that seemed to me compounded of a ghastly, yes, shame but also of a terrible, guilty joy as he slowly ascertained how I had sinned.

That tell-tale stain had resolved itself into a mark the shape and brilliance of the heart on a playing card. He disengaged the key from the ring and looked at it for a while, solitary, brooding.

'It is the key that leads to the kingdom of the unimaginable,' he said. His voice was low and had in it the timbre of certain great cathedral organs that seem, when they are played, to be conversing with God.

I could not restrain a sob.

'Oh, my love, my little love who brought me a white gift of music,' he said, almost as if grieving. 'My little love, you'll never know how much I hate daylight!'

Then he sharply ordered: 'Kneel!'

I knelt before him and he pressed the key lightly to my forehead, held it there for a moment. I felt a faint tingling of the skin and, when I involuntarily glanced at myself in the mirror, I saw the heart-shaped stain had transferred itself to my forehead, to the space between the eyebrows, like the caste mark of a brahmin woman. Or the mark of Cain. And now the key gleamed as freshly as if it had just been cut. He clipped it back on the ring, emitting that same, heavy sigh as he had done when I said that I would marry him.

'My virgin of the arpeggios, prepare yourself for martyrdom.'

'What form shall it take?' I said.

'Decapitation,' he whispered, almost voluptuously. 'Go and bathe yourself; put on that white dress you wore to hear *Tristan* and the necklace that prefigures your end. And I shall take myself off to the armoury, my dear, to sharpen my great-grandfather's ceremonial sword.'

'The servants?'

'We shall have absolute privacy for our last rites; I have already dismissed them. If you look out of the window you can see them going to the mainland.'

It was now the full, pale light of morning; the weather was grey, indeterminate, the sea had an oily, sinister look, a gloomy day on which to die. Along the causeway I could see trouping every maid and scullion, every pot-boy and pan-scourer, valet, laundress and vassal who worked in that great house, most on foot, a few on bicycles. The faceless housekeeper trudged along with a great basket in which, I guessed, she'd stowed as much as she could ransack from the larder. The Marquis must have given the chauffeur leave to borrow the motor for the day, for it went last of all, at a stately pace, as though the procession were a cortège and the car already bore my coffin to the mainland for burial.

But I knew no good Breton earth would cover me, like a last, faithful lover; I had another fate.

'I have given them all a day's holiday, to celebrate our wedding,' he said. And smiled.

However hard I stared at the receding company, I could see no sign of Jean-Yves, our latest servant, hired but the preceding morning.

'Go, now. Bathe yourself; dress yourself. The lustratory ritual and the ceremonial robing; after that, the sacrifice. Wait in the music room until I telephone for you. No, my dear!' And he smiled, as I started, recalling the line was dead. 'One may call inside the castle just as much as one pleases; but, outside — never.'

I scrubbed my forehead with the nail brush as I had scrubbed the key but this red mark would not go away, either, no matter what I did, and I knew I should wear it until I died, though that would not be long. Then I went to my dressing room and put on that white muslin shift, costume of a victim of an auto-da-fé, he had bought me to listen to the Liebestod in. Twelve young women combed out twelve listless sheaves of brown hair in the mirrors; soon, there would be none. The mass of lilies that surrounded me exhaled, now, the odour of their withering. They looked like the trumpets of the angels of death.

On the dressing table, coiled like a snake about to strike, lay the ruby choker.

Already almost lifeless, cold at heart, I descended the spiral staircase to the music room but there I found I had not been abandoned.

'I can be of some comfort to you,' the boy said. 'Though not much use.'

We pushed the piano stool in front of the open window so that, for as long as I could, I would be able to smell the ancient, reconciling smell of the sea that, in time, will cleanse everything, scour the old bones white, wash away all the stains. The last little chambermaid had trotted along the causeway long ago and now the tide, fated as I, came tumbling in, the crisp wavelets splashing on the old stones.

'You do not deserve this,' he said.

'Who can say what I deserve or no?' I said. 'I've done nothing; but that may be sufficient reason for condemning me.'

'You disobeyed him,' he said. 'That is sufficient reason for him to punish you.'

'I only did what he knew I would.'

'Like Eve,' he said.

The telephone rang a shrill imperative. Let it ring. But my lover lifted me up and set me on my feet; I knew I must answer it. The receiver felt heavy as earth.

'The courtyard. Immediately.'

My lover kissed me, he took my hand. He would come with me if I would lead him. Courage. When I thought of courage, I thought of my mother. Then I saw a muscle in my lover's face quiver.

'Hoofbeats!' he said.

I cast one last, desperate glance from the window and, like a miracle, I saw a horse and rider galloping at a vertiginous speed along the causeway, though the waves crashed, now, high as the horse's fetlocks. A rider, her black skirts tucked up around her waist so she could ride hard and fast, a crazy, magnificent horsewoman in widow's weeds.

As the telephone rang again.

'Am I to wait all morning?'

Every moment, my mother drew nearer.

'She will be too late,' Jean-Yves said and yet he could not restrain a note of hope that, though it must be so, yet it might not be so.

The third, intransigent call.

'Shall I come up to heaven to fetch you down, Saint Cecilia? You wicked woman, do you wish me to compound my crimes by desecrating the marriage bed?'

So I must go to the courtyard where my husband waited in his London-tailored trousers and the shirt from Turnbull and Asser, beside the mounting block, with, in his hand, the sword which his great-grandfather had presented to the little corporal, in token of surrender to the Republic, before he shot himself. The heavy sword, unsheathed, grey as that November morning, sharp as childbirth, mortal.

When my husband saw my companion, he observed: 'Let the blind lead the blind, eh? But does even a youth as besotted as you are think she was truly blind to her own desires when she took my ring? Give it me back, whore.'

The fires in the opal had all died down. I gladly slipped it from my finger and, even in that dolorous place, my heart was lighter for the lack of it. My husband took it lovingly and lodged it on the top of his little finger; it would go no further.

'It will serve me for a dozen more fiancées,' he said. 'To the block, woman. No — leave the boy; I shall deal with him later, utilizing a less exalted instrument than the one with which I do my wife the honour of her immolation, for do not fear that in death you will be divided.'

Slowly, slowly, one foot before the other, I crossed the cobbles. The longer I dawdled over my execution, the more time it gave the avenging angel to descend . . .

'Don't loiter, girl! Do you think I shall lose appetite for the meal if you are so long about serving it? No; I shall grow hungrier, more ravenous with each moment, more cruel . . . Run to me, run! I have a place prepared for your exquisite corpse in my display of flesh!'

He raised the sword and cut bright segments from the air with it, but still I lingered although my hopes, so recently raised, now began to flag. If she is not here by now, her horse must have stumbled on the causeway, have plunged into the sea . . . One thing only made me glad; that my lover would not see me die.

My husband laid my branded forehead on the stone and, as he had done once before, twisted my hair into a rope and drew it away from my neck.

'Such a pretty neck,' he said with what seemed to be a genuine, retrospective tenderness. 'A neck like the stem of a young plant.'

I felt the silken bristle of his beard and the wet touch of his lips as he kissed my nape. And, once again, of my apparel I must retain only my gems; the sharp blade ripped my dress in two and it fell from me. A little green moss, growing in the crevices of the mounting block, would be the last thing I should see in all the world.

The whizz of that heavy sword.

And — a great battering and pounding at the gate, the jangling of the bell, the frenzied neighing of a horse! The unholy silence of the place shattered in an instant. The blade did *not* descend, the necklace did *not* sever, my head did *not* roll. For, for an instant, the beast wavered in his stroke, a sufficient split second for astonished indecision to let me spring upright and dart to the assistance of my lover as he struggled sightlessly with the great bolts that kept her out.

The Marquis stood transfixed, utterly dazed, at a loss. It must have been as if he had been watching his beloved *Tristan* for the twelfth, the thirteenth time and Tristan stirred, then leapt from his bier in the last act, announced in a jaunty aria interposed from Verdi that bygones were bygones, crying over spilt milk did nobody any good and, as for himself, he proposed to live happily ever after. The puppet master, open-mouthed, wide-eyed, impotent at the last, saw his dolls break free of their strings, abandon the rituals he had ordained for them since time began and start to live for themselves; the king, aghast, witnesses the revolt of his pawns.

You never saw such a wild thing as my mother, her hat seized by the winds and blown out to sea so that her hair was her white mane, her black lisle legs exposed to the thigh, her skirts tucked round her waist, one hand on the reins of the rearing horse while the other clasped my father's service revolver and, behind her, the breakers of the savage, indifferent sea, like the witnesses of a furious justice. And my husband stood stock-still, as if she had been Medusa, the sword still raised over his head as in those clockwork tableaux of Bluebeard that you see in glass cases at fairs.

And then it was as though a curious child pushed his centime into the slot and set all in motion. The heavy, bearded figure roared out aloud, braying with fury, and, wielding the honourable sword as if it were a matter of death or glory, charged us, all three.

On her eighteenth birthday, my mother had disposed of a man-eating tiger that had ravaged the villages in the hills north of Hanoi. Now, without a moment's hesitation, she raised my father's gun, took aim and put a single, irreproachable bullet through my husband's head.

We lead a quiet life, the three of us. I inherited, of course, enormous wealth but we have given most of it away to various charities. The castle is now a school for the blind, though I pray that the children who live there are not haunted by any sad ghosts looking for, crying for, the husband who will never return to the bloody chamber, the contents of which are buried or burned, the door sealed.

I felt I had a right to retain sufficient funds to start a little music school here, on the outskirts of Paris, and we do well enough. Sometimes we can even afford to go to the Opéra, though never to sit in a box, of course. We know we are the source of many whisperings and much gossip but the three of us know the truth of it and mere chatter can never harm us. I can only bless the — what shall I call it? — the *maternal telepathy* that sent my mother running headlong from the telephone to the station after I had called her, that night. I never heard you cry before, she said, by way of explanation. Not when you were happy. And who ever cried because of gold bath taps?

The night train, the one I had taken; she lay in her berth, sleepless as I had been. When she could not find a taxi at that lonely halt, she borrowed old Dobbin from a bemused farmer, for some internal urgency told her that she must reach me before the incoming tide sealed me away from her for ever. My poor old nurse, left scandalized at home — what? interrupt milord on his honeymoon? — she died soon after. She had taken so much secret pleasure in the fact that her little girl had become a marquise; and now here I was, scarcely a penny the richer, widowed at seventeen in the most dubious circumstances and busily engaged in setting up house with a piano-tuner. Poor thing, she passed away in a sorry state of disillusion! But I do believe my mother loves him as much as I do.

No paint nor powder, no matter how thick or white, can mask that red mark on my forehead; I am glad he cannot see it — not for fear of his revulsion, since I know he sees me clearly with his heart — but, because it spares my shame.

RAYMOND CARVER

Raymond Carver (1938–1988) was born in Oregon, the son of a sawmill worker and a waitress, and lived almost all his life in the Pacific Northwest. He chronicled the often sad lives of America's working class; his own — troubled by poverty, divorce, and alcoholism — was similar. "I know these people. I'm one of them. I don't ever treat them with irony," he once told an interviewer. His stories are collected in a number of volumes, among them *Will You Please Be Quiet, Please?* (1976), *What We Talk About When We Talk About Love* (1981), *Cathedral* (1983), and *Where I'm Calling From* (1988). He counted Chekhov among his literary influences; indeed, shortly before his own early death he wrote a story about Chekhov's death from tuberculosis. The story here, "A Small, Good Thing," is a revised version of "The Bath," which Carver had written several years earlier. In changing the ending of the original story, Carver not only extended his plot line but introduced a note of deep compassion as well.

A Small, Good Thing

Saturday afternoon she drove to the bakery in the shopping center. After looking through a loose-leaf binder with photographs of cakes taped onto the pages, she ordered chocolate, the child's favorite. The cake she chose was decorated with a space ship and launching pad under a sprinkling of white stars, and a planet made of red frosting at the other end. His name, SCOTTY, would be in green letters beneath the planet. The baker, who was an older man with a thick neck, listened without saying anything when she told him the child would be eight years old next Monday. The baker wore a white apron that looked like a smock. Straps cut under his arms, went around in back and then to the front again, where they were secured under his heavy waist. He wiped his hands on his apron as he listened to her. He kept his eyes down on the photographs and let her talk. He let her take her time. He'd just come to work and he'd be there all night, baking, and he was in no hurry.

She gave the baker her name, Ann Weiss, and her telephone number. The cake would be ready on Monday morning, just out of the oven, in plenty of time for the child's party that afternoon. The baker was not jolly. There were no pleasantries between them, just the minimum exchange of words, the necessary information. He made her feel uncomfortable, and she didn't like that. While he was bent over the counter with the pencil in his hand, she studied his coarse features and wondered if he'd ever done anything else with his life besides be a baker. She was a mother and thirty-three years old, and it seemed to her that everyone, especially someone the baker's age — a man old enough to be her father — must have children who'd gone through this special time of cakes and birthday parties. There must be that between them, she thought. But he was abrupt with her — not rude, just abrupt. She gave up trying to make friends with him. She looked into the back of the bakery and could see a long, heavy wooden table with aluminum pie pans stacked at one end; and beside the table a metal container filled with empty racks. There was an enormous oven. A radio was playing country-Western music.

The baker finished printing the information on the special order card and closed up the binder. He looked at her and said, "Monday morning." She thanked him and drove home.

On Monday morning, the birthday boy was walking to school with another boy. They were passing a bag of potato chips back and forth and the birthday boy was trying to find out what his friend intended to give him for his birthday that afternoon. Without looking, the birthday boy stepped off the curb at an intersection and was immediately knocked down by a car. He fell on his side with his head in the gutter and his legs out in the road. His eyes were closed, but his legs moved back and forth as if he were trying to climb over something. His friend dropped the potato chips and started to cry. The car had gone a hundred feet or so and stopped in the middle of the road. The man in the driver's seat looked back over his shoulder. He waited until the boy got unsteadily to his feet. The boy wobbled a little. He looked dazed, but okay. The driver put the car into gear and drove away.

The birthday boy didn't cry, but he didn't have anything to say about anything either. He wouldn't answer when his friend asked him what it felt like to be hit by a car. He walked home, and his friend went on to school. But after the birthday boy was inside his house and was telling his mother about it — she sitting beside him on the sofa, holding his hands in her lap, saying, "Scotty, honey, are you sure you feel all right, baby?" thinking she would call the doctor anyway — he suddenly lay back on the sofa, closed his eyes, and went limp. When she couldn't wake him up, she hurried to the telephone and called her husband at work. Howard told her to remain calm, remain calm, and then he called an ambulance for the child and left for the hospital himself.

Of course, the birthday party was canceled. The child was in the hospital with a mild concussion and suffering from shock. There'd been vomiting, and his lungs had taken in fluid which needed pumping out that afternoon. Now he simply seemed to be in a very deep sleep — but no coma, Dr. Francis had emphasized, no coma, when he saw the alarm in the parents' eyes. At eleven o'clock that night, when the boy seemed to be resting comfortably enough after the many X-rays and the lab work, and it was just a matter of his waking up and coming around, Howard left the hospital. He and Ann had been at the hospital with the child since that afternoon, and he was going home for a short while to bathe and change clothes. "I'll be back in an hour," he said. She nodded. "It's fine," she said. "I'll be right here." He kissed her on the forehead, and they touched hands. She sat in the chair beside the bed and looked at the child. She was waiting for him to wake up and be all right. Then she could begin to relax.

Howard drove home from the hospital. He took the wet, dark streets very fast, then caught himself and slowed down. Until now, his life had gone smoothly and to his satisfaction — college, marriage, another year of college for the advanced degree in business, a junior partnership in an investment firm. Fatherhood. He was happy and, so far, lucky — he knew that. His parents were still living, his brothers and his sister were established, his friends from college had gone out to take their places in the world. So far, he had kept away from any real harm, from those forces he knew existed and that could cripple or bring down a man if the luck went bad, if things suddenly turned. He pulled into the driveway and parked. His left leg began to tremble. He sat in the car for a minute and tried to deal with the present situation in a rational manner. Scotty had been hit by a car and was in the hospital, but he was going to be all right. Howard closed his eyes and ran his hand over his face. He got out of the car and went up to the front door. The dog was barking inside the house. The telephone rang and rang while he unlocked the door and fumbled for the light switch. He shouldn't have left the hospital, he shouldn't have. "Goddamn it!" he said. He picked up the receiver and said, "I just walked in the door!"

"There's a cake here that wasn't picked up," the voice on the other end of the line said.

"What are you saying?" Howard asked.

"A cake," the voice said. "A sixteen-dollar cake."

Howard held the receiver against his ear, trying to understand. "I don't know anything about a cake," he said. "Jesus, what are you talking about?"

"Don't hand me that," the voice said.

Howard hung up the telephone. He went into the kitchen and poured himself some whiskey. He called the hospital. But the child's condition remained the same; he was still sleeping and nothing had changed there. While water poured into the tub, Howard lathered his face and shaved. He'd just stretched out in the tub and closed his eyes when the telephone rang again. He hauled himself out, grabbed a towel, and hurried through the house, saying, "Stupid, stupid," for having left the hospital. But when he picked up the receiver and shouted, "Hello!" there was no sound at the other end of the line. Then the caller hung up.

He arrived back at the hospital a little after midnight. Ann still sat in the chair beside the bed. She looked up at Howard, and then she looked back at the child. The child's eyes stayed closed, the head was still wrapped in bandages. His breathing was quiet and regular. From an apparatus over the bed hung a bottle of glucose with a tube running from the bottle to the boy's arm.

"How is he?" Howard said. "What's all this?" waving at the glucose and the tube.

"Dr. Francis's orders," she said. "He needs nourishment. He needs to keep up his strength. Why doesn't he wake up, Howard? I don't understand, if he's all right."

Howard put his hand against the back of her head. He ran his fingers through her hair. "He's going to be all right. He'll wake up in a little while. Dr. Francis knows what's what."

After a time, he said, "Maybe you should go home and get some rest. I'll stay here. Just don't put up with this creep who keeps calling. Hang up right away."

"Who's calling?" she asked.

"I don't know who, just somebody with nothing better to do than call up people. You go on now."

She shook her head. "No," she said, "I'm fine."

"Really," he said. "Go home for a while, and then come back and spell me in the morning. It'll be all right. What did Dr. Francis say? He said Scotty's going to be all right. We don't have to worry. He's just sleeping now, that's all."

A nurse pushed the door open. She nodded at them as she went to the bedside. She took the left arm out from under the covers and put her fingers on the wrist, found the pulse, then consulted her watch. In a little while, she put the arm back under the covers and moved to the foot of the bed, where she wrote something on a clipboard attached to the bed.

"How is he?" Ann said. Howard's hand was a weight on her shoulder. She was aware of the pressure from his fingers.

"He's stable," the nurse said. Then she said, "Doctor will be in again shortly. Doctor's back in the hospital. He's making rounds right now."

"I was saying maybe she'd want to go home and get a little rest," Howard said. "After the doctor comes," he said.

"She could do that," the nurse said. "I think you should both feel free to do that, if you wish." The nurse was a big Scandinavian woman with blond hair. There was the trace of an accent in her speech.

"We'll see what the doctor says," Ann said. "I want to talk to the doctor. I don't think he should keep sleeping like this. I don't think that's a good sign." She brought her hand up to her eyes and let her head come forward a little. Howard's grip tightened on her shoulder, and then his hand moved up to her neck, where his fingers began to knead the muscles there.

"Dr. Francis will be here in a few minutes," the nurse said. Then she left the room.

Howard gazed at his son for a time, the small chest quietly rising and falling under the covers. For the first time since the terrible minutes after Ann's telephone call to him at his office, he felt a genuine fear starting in his limbs. He began shaking his head. Scotty was fine, but instead of sleeping at home in his own bed, he was in a hospital bed with bandages around his head and a tube in his arm. But this help was what he needed right now.

Dr. Francis came in and shook hands with Howard, though they'd just seen each other a few hours before. Ann got up from the chair. "Doctor?"

"Ann," he said and nodded. "Let's just first see how he's doing," the doctor said. He moved to the side of the bed and took the boy's pulse. He peeled back one eyelid and then the other. Howard and Ann stood beside the doctor and watched. Then the doctor turned back the covers and listened to the boy's heart and lungs with his stethoscope. He pressed his fingers here and there on the abdomen. When he was finished, he went to the end of the bed and studied the chart. He noted the time, scribbled something on the chart, and then looked at Howard and Ann.

"Doctor, how is he?" Howard said. "What's the matter with him exactly?"

"Why doesn't he wake up?" Ann said.

The doctor was a handsome, big-shouldered man with a tanned face. He wore a three-piece blue suit, a striped tie, and ivory cufflinks. His gray hair was combed along the sides of his head, and he looked as if he had just come from a concert. "He's all right," the doctor said. "Nothing to shout about, he could be better, I think. But he's all right. Still, I wish he'd wake up. He should wake up pretty soon." The doctor looked at the boy again. "We'll know some more in a couple of hours, after the results of a few more tests are in. But he's all right, believe me, except for the hairline fracture of the skull. He does have that."

"Oh, no," Ann said.

"And a bit of a concussion, as I said before. Of course, you know he's in shock," the doctor said. "Sometimes you see this in shock cases. This sleeping."

"But he's out of any real danger?" Howard said. "You said before he's not in a coma. You wouldn't call this a coma, then — would you, doctor?" Howard waited. He looked at the doctor.

"No, I don't want to call it a coma," the doctor said and glanced over at the boy once more. "He's just in a very deep sleep. It's a restorative measure the body is taking on its own. He's out of any real danger, I'd say that for certain, yes. But we'll know more when he wakes up and the other tests are in," the doctor said.

"It's a coma," Ann said. "Of sorts."

"It's not a coma yet, not exactly," the doctor said. "I wouldn't want to call it coma. Not yet, anyway. He's suffered shock. In shock cases, this kind of reaction is common enough; it's a temporary reaction to bodily trauma. Coma. Well, coma is a deep, prolonged unconsciousness, something that could go on for days, or weeks even. Scotty's not in that area, not as far as we can tell. I'm certain his condition will show improvement by morning. I'm betting that it will. We'll know more when he wakes up, which shouldn't be long now. Of course, you may do as you like, stay here or go home for a time. But by all means feel free to leave the hospital for a while if you want. This is not easy, I know." The doctor gazed at the boy again, watching him, and then he turned to Ann and said, "You try not to worry, little mother. Believe me, we're doing all that can be done. It's just a question of a little more time now." He nodded at her, shook hands with Howard again, and then he left the room.

Ann put her hand over the child's forehead. "At least he doesn't have a fever," she said. Then she said, "My God, he feels so cold, though. Howard? Is he supposed to feel like this? Feel his head."

Howard touched the child's temples. His own breathing had slowed. "I think he's supposed to feel this way right now," he said. "He's in shock, remember? That's what the doctor said. The doctor was just in here. He would have said something if Scotty wasn't okay."

Ann stood there a while longer, working her lip with her teeth. Then she moved over to her chair and sat down.

Howard sat in the chair next to her chair. They looked at each other. He wanted to say something else and reassure her, but he was afraid, too. He took her hand and put it in his lap, and this made him feel better, her hand being there. He picked up her hand and squeezed it. Then he just held her hand. They sat like that for a while, watching the boy and not talking. From time to time, he squeezed her hand. Finally, she took her hand away.

"I've been praying," she said.

He nodded.

She said, "I almost thought I'd forgotten how, but it came back to me. All I had to do was close my eyes and say, 'Please God, help us — help Scotty,' and then the rest was easy. The words were right there. Maybe if you prayed, too," she said to him.

"I've already prayed," he said. "I prayed this afternoon — yesterday afternoon, I mean — after you called, while I was driving to the hospital. I've been praying," he said.

"That's good," she said. For the first time, she felt they were together in it, this trouble. She realized with a start that, until now, it had only been happening to her and to Scotty. She hadn't let Howard into it, though he was there and needed all along. She felt glad to be his wife.

The same nurse came in and took the boy's pulse again and checked the flow from the bottle hanging above the bed.

In an hour, another doctor came in. He said his name was Parsons, from Radiology. He had a bushy mustache. He was wearing loafers, a Western shirt, and a pair of jeans.

"We're going to take him downstairs for more pictures," he told them. "We need to do some more pictures, and we want to do a scan."

"What's that?" Ann said. "A scan?" She stood between this new doctor and the bed. "I thought you'd already taken all your X-rays."

"I'm afraid we need some more," he said. "Nothing to be alarmed about. We just need some more pictures, and we want to do a brain scan on him."

"My God," Ann said.

"It's perfectly normal procedure in cases like this," this new doctor said. "We just need to find out for sure why he isn't back awake yet. It's normal medical procedure, and nothing to be alarmed about. We'll be taking him down in a few minutes," this doctor said.

In a little while, two orderlies came into the room with a gurney. They were black-haired, dark-complexioned men in white uniforms, and they said a few words to each other in a foreign tongue as they unhooked the boy from the tube and moved him from his bed to the gurney. Then they wheeled him from the room. Howard and Ann got on the same elevator. Ann gazed at the child. She closed her eyes as the elevator began its descent. The orderlies stood at either end of the gurney without saying anything, though once one of the men made a comment to the other in their own language, and the other man nodded slowly in response.

Later that morning, just as the sun was beginning to lighten the windows in the waiting room outside the X-ray department, they brought the boy out and moved him back up to his room. Howard and Ann rode up on the elevator with him once more, and once more they took up their places beside the bed.

They waited all day, but still the boy did not wake up. Occasionally, one of them would leave the room to go downstairs to the cafeteria to drink coffee and then, as if suddenly remembering and feeling guilty, get up from the table and hurry back to the room. Dr. Francis came again that afternoon and examined the boy once more and then left after telling them he was coming along and could wake up at any minute now. Nurses, different nurses from the night before, came in from time to time. Then a young woman from the lab knocked and entered the room. She wore white slacks and a white blouse and carried a little tray of things which she put on the stand beside the bed. Without a word to them, she took blood from the boy's arm. Howard closed his eyes as the woman found the right place on the boy's arm and pushed the needle in.

"I don't understand this," Ann said to the woman.

"Doctor's orders," the young woman said. "I do what I'm told. They say draw that one, I draw. What's wrong with him, anyway?" she said. "He's a sweetie."

"He was hit by a car," Howard said. "A hit-and-run."

The young woman shook her head and looked again at the boy. Then she took her tray and left the room.

"Why won't he wake up?" Ann said. "Howard? I want some answers from these people."

Howard didn't say anything. He sat down again in the chair and crossed one leg over the other. He rubbed his face. He looked at his son and then he settled back in the chair, closed his eyes, and went to sleep.

Ann walked to the window and looked out at the parking lot. It was night, and cars were driving into and out of the parking lot with their lights on. She stood at the window with her hands gripping the sill, and knew in her heart that they were into something now, something hard. She was afraid, and her teeth began to chatter until she tightened her jaws. She saw a big car stop in front of the hospital and someone, a woman in a long coat, get into the car. She wished she were that woman and somebody, anybody, was driving her away from here to somewhere else, a place where she would find Scotty waiting for her when she stepped out of the car, ready to say *Mom* and let her gather him in her arms.

In a little while, Howard woke up. He looked at the boy again. Then he got up from the chair, stretched, and went over to stand beside her at the window. They both stared out at the parking lot. They didn't say anything. But they seemed to feel each other's insides now, as though the worry had made them transparent in a perfectly natural way.

The door opened and Dr. Francis came in. He was wearing a different suit and tie this time. His gray hair was combed along the sides of his head, and he looked as if he had just shaved. He went straight to the bed and examined the boy. "He ought to have come around by now. There's just no good reason for this," he said. "But I can tell you we're all convinced he's out of any danger. We'll just feel better when he wakes up. There's no reason, absolutely none, why he shouldn't come around. Very soon. Oh, he'll have himself a dilly of a headache when he does, you can count on that. But all of his signs are fine. They're as normal as can be."

"It is a coma, then?" Ann said.

The doctor rubbed his smooth cheek. "We'll call it that for the time being, until he wakes up. But you must be worn out. This is hard. I know this is hard. Feel free to go out for a bite," he said. "It would do you good. I'll put a nurse in here while you're gone if you'll feel better about going. Go and have yourselves something to eat."

"I couldn't eat anything," Ann said.

"Do what you need to do, of course," the doctor said. "Anyway, I wanted to tell you that all the signs are good, the tests are negative, nothing showed up at all, and just as soon as he wakes up he'll be over the hill."

"Thank you, doctor," Howard said. He shook hands with the doctor again. The doctor patted Howard's shoulder and went out.

"I suppose one of us should go home and check on things," Howard said. "Slug needs to be fed, for one thing."

"Call one of the neighbors," Ann said. "Call the Morgans. Anyone will feed a dog if you ask them to."

"All right," Howard said. After a while, he said, "Honey, why don't *you* do it? Why don't you go home and check on things, and then come back? It'll do you good. I'll be right here with him. Seriously," he said. "We need to keep up our strength on this. We'll want to be here for a while even after he wakes up."

"Why don't *you* go?" she said. "Feed Slug. Feed yourself."

"I already went," he said. "I was gone for exactly an hour and fifteen minutes. You go home for an hour and freshen up. Then come back."

She tried to think about it, but she was too tired. She closed her eyes and tried to think about it again. After a time, she said, "Maybe I *will* go home for a few minutes. Maybe if I'm not just sitting right here watching him every second, he'll wake up and be all right. You know? Maybe he'll wake up if I'm not here. I'll go home and take a bath and put on clean clothes. I'll feed Slug. Then I'll come back."

"I'll be right here," he said. "You go on home, honey. I'll keep an eye on things here." His eyes were bloodshot and small, as if he'd been drinking for a long time. His clothes were rumpled. His beard had come out again. She touched his face, and then she took her hand back. She understood he wanted to be by himself for a while, not have to talk or share his worry for a time. She picked her purse up from the nightstand, and he helped her into her coat.

"I won't be gone long," she said.

"Just sit and rest for a while when you get home," he said. "Eat something. Take a bath. After you get out of the bath, just sit for a while and rest. It'll do you a world of good, you'll see. Then come back," he said. "Let's try not to worry. You heard what Dr. Francis said."

She stood in her coat for a minute trying to recall the doctor's exact words, looking for any nuances, any hint of something behind his words other than what he had said. She tried to remember if his expression had changed any when he bent over to examine the child. She remembered the way his features had composed themselves as he rolled back the child's eyelids and then listened to his breathing.

She went to the door, where she turned and looked back. She looked at the child, and then she looked at the father. Howard nodded. She stepped out of the room and pulled the door closed behind her.

She went past the nurses' station and down to the end of the corridor, looking for the elevator. At the end of the corridor, she turned to her right and entered a little waiting room where a Negro family sat in wicker chairs. There was a middle-aged man in a khaki shirt and pants, a baseball cap pushed back on his head. A large woman wearing a housedress and slippers was slumped in one of the chairs. A teenaged girl in jeans, hair done in dozens of little braids, lay stretched out in one of the chairs smoking a cigarette, her legs crossed at the ankles. The family swung their eyes to Ann as she entered the room. The little table was littered with hamburger wrappers and Styrofoam cups.

"Franklin," the larger woman said as she roused herself. "Is it about Franklin?" Her eyes widened. "Tell me now, lady," the woman said. "Is it about Franklin?" She was trying to rise from her chair, but the man had closed his hand over her arm.

"Here, here," he said. "Evelyn."

"I'm sorry," Ann said. "I'm looking for the elevator. My son is in the hospital, and now I can't find the elevator."

"Elevator is down that way, turn left," the man said as he aimed a finger.

The girl drew on her cigarette and stared at Ann. Her eyes were narrowed to slits, and her broad lips parted slowly as she let the smoke escape. The Negro woman let her head fall on her shoulder and looked away from Ann, no longer interested.

"My son was hit by a car," Ann said to the man. She seemed to need to explain herself. "He has a concussion and a little skull fracture, but he's going to be all right.

He's in shock now, but it might be some kind of coma, too. That's what really worries us, the coma part. I'm going out for a little while, but my husband is with him. Maybe he'll wake up while I'm gone."

"That's too bad," the man said and shifted in the chair. He shook his head. He looked down at the table, and then he looked back at Ann. She was still standing there. He said, "Our Franklin, he's on the operating table. Somebody cut him. Tried to kill him. There was a fight where he was at. At this party. They say he was just standing and watching. Not bothering nobody. But that don't mean nothing these days. Now he's on the operating table. We're just hoping and praying, that's all we can do now." He gazed at her steadily.

Ann looked at the girl again, who was still watching her, and at the older woman, who kept her head down, but whose eyes were now closed. Ann saw the lips moving silently, making words. She had an urge to ask what those words were. She wanted to talk more with these people who were in the same kind of waiting she was in. She was afraid, and they were afraid. They had that in common. She would have liked to have said something else about the accident, told them more about Scotty, that it had happened on the day of his birthday, Monday, and that he was still unconscious. Yet she didn't know how to begin. She stood looking at them without saying anything more.

She went down the corridor the man had indicated and found the elevator. She waited a minute in front of the closed doors, still wondering if she was doing the right thing. Then she put out her finger and touched the button.

She pulled into the driveway and cut the engine. She closed her eyes and leaned her head against the wheel for a minute. She listened to the ticking sounds the engine made as it began to cool. Then she got out of the car. She could hear the dog barking inside the house. She went to the front door, which was unlocked. She went inside and turned on lights and put on a kettle of water for tea. She opened some dogfood and fed Slug on the back porch. The dog ate in hungry little smacks. It kept running into the kitchen to see that she was going to stay. As she sat down on the sofa with her tea, the telephone rang.

"Yes!" she said as she answered. "Hello!"

"Mrs. Weiss," a man's voice said. It was five o'clock in the morning, and she thought she could hear machinery or equipment of some kind in the background.

"Yes, yes! What is it?" she said. "This is Mrs. Weiss. This is she. What is it, please?" She listened to whatever it was in the background. "Is it Scotty, for Christ's sake?"

"Scotty," the man's voice said. "It's about Scotty, yes. It has to do with Scotty, that problem. Have you forgotten about Scotty?" the man said. Then he hung up.

She dialed the hospital's number and asked for the third floor. She demanded information about her son from the nurse who answered the telephone. Then she asked to speak to her husband. It was, she said, an emergency.

She waited, turning the telephone cord in her fingers. She closed her eyes and felt sick at her stomach. She would have to make herself eat. Slug came in from the back porch and lay down near her feet. He wagged his tail. She pulled at his ear while he licked her fingers. Howard was on the line.

"Somebody just called here," she said. She twisted the telephone cord. "He said it was about Scotty," she cried.

"Scotty's fine," Howard told her. "I mean, he's still sleeping. There's been no change. The nurse has been in twice since you've been gone. A nurse or else a doctor. He's all right."

"This man called. He said it was about Scotty," she told him.

"Honey, you rest for a little while, you need the rest. It must be that same caller I had. Just forget it. Come back down here after you've rested. Then we'll have breakfast or something."

"Breakfast," she said. "I don't want any breakfast."

"You know what I mean," he said. "Juice, something. I don't know. I don't know anything, Ann. Jesus, I'm not hungry, either. Ann, it's hard to talk now. I'm standing here at the desk. Dr. Francis is coming again at eight o'clock this morning. He's going to have something to tell us then, something more definite. That's what one of the nurses said. She didn't know any more than that. Ann? Honey, maybe we'll know something more then. At eight o'clock. Come back here before eight. Meanwhile, I'm right here and Scotty's all right. He's still the same," he added.

"I was drinking a cup of tea," she said, "when the telephone rang. They said it was about Scotty. There was a noise in the background. Was there a noise in the background on that call you had, Howard?"

"I don't remember," he said. "Maybe the driver of the car, maybe he's a psychopath and found out about Scotty somehow. But I'm here with him. Just rest like you were going to do. Take a bath and come back by seven or so, and we'll talk to the doctor together when he gets here. It's going to be all right, honey. I'm here, and there are doctors and nurses around. They say his condition is stable."

"I'm scared to death," she said.

She ran water, undressed, and got into the tub. She washed and dried quickly, not taking the time to wash her hair. She put on clean underwear, wool slacks, and a sweater. She went into the living room, where the dog looked up at her and let its tail thump once against the floor. It was just starting to get light outside when she went out to the car.

She drove into the parking lot of the hospital and found a space close to the front door. She felt she was in some obscure way responsible for what had happened to the child. She let her thoughts move to the Negro family. She remembered the name Franklin and the table that was covered with hamburger papers, and the teenaged girl staring at her as she drew on her cigarette. "Don't have children," she told the girl's image as she entered the front door of the hospital. "For God's sake, don't."

She took the elevator up to the third floor with two nurses who were just going on duty. It was Wednesday morning, a few minutes before seven. There was a page for a Dr. Madison as the elevator doors slid open on the third floor. She got off behind the nurses, who turned in the other direction and continued the conversation she has interrupted when she'd gotten into the elevator. She walked down the corridor to the little alcove where the Negro family had been waiting. They were gone now, but the chairs were scattered in such a way that it looked as if people had just jumped up from them the minute before. The tabletop was cluttered with the same cups and papers, the ashtray was filled with cigarette butts.

She stopped at the nurse's station. A nurse was standing behind the counter, brushing her hair and yawning.

"There was a Negro boy in surgery last night," Ann said. "Franklin was his name. His family was in the waiting room. I'd like to inquire about his condition."

A nurse who was sitting at a desk behind the counter looked up from a chart in front of her. The telephone buzzed and she picked up the receiver, but she kept her eyes on Ann.

"He passed away," said the nurse at the counter. The nurse held the hairbrush and kept looking at her. "Are you a friend of the family or what?"

"I met the family last night," Ann said. "My own son is in the hospital. I guess he's in shock. We don't know for sure what's wrong. I just wondered about Franklin, that's all. Thank you." She moved down the corridor. Elevator doors the same color as the walls slid open and a gaunt, bald man in white pants and white canvas shoes pulled a heavy cart off the elevator. She hadn't noticed these doors last night. The man wheeled the cart out into the corridor and stopped in front of the room nearest the elevator and consulted a clipboard. Then he reached down and slid a tray out of the cart. He rapped lightly on the door and entered the room. She could smell the unpleasant odors of warm food as she passed the cart. She hurried on without looking at any of the nurses and pushed open the door to the child's room.

Howard was standing at the window with his hands behind his back. He turned around as she came in.

"How is he?" she said. She went over to the bed. She dropped her purse on the floor beside the nightstand. It seemed to her she had been gone a long time. She touched the child's face. "Howard?"

"Dr. Francis was here a little while ago," Howard said. She looked at him closely and thought his shoulders were bunched a little.

"I thought he wasn't coming until eight o'clock this morning," she said quickly.

"There was another doctor with him. A neurologist."

"A neurologist," she said.

Howard nodded. His shoulders were bunching, she could see that. "What'd they say, Howard? For Christ's sake, what'd they say? What is it?"

"They said they're going to take him down and run more tests on him, Ann. They think they're going to operate, honey. Honey, they *are* going to operate. They can't figure out why he won't wake up. It's more than just shock or concussion, they know that much now. It's in his skull, the fracture, it has something, something to do with that, they think. So they're going to operate. I tried to call you, but I guess you'd already left the house."

"Oh, God," she said. "Oh, please, Howard, please," she said, taking his arms.

"Look!" Howard said. "Scotty! Look, Ann!" He turned her toward the bed.

The boy had opened his eyes, then closed them. He opened them again now. The eyes stared straight ahead for a minute, then moved slowly in his head until they rested on Howard and Ann, then traveled away again.

"Scotty," his mother said, moving to the bed.

"Hey, Scott," his father said. "Hey, son."

They leaned over the bed. Howard took the child's hand in his hands and began to pat and squeeze the hand. Ann bent over the boy and kissed his forehead again and again. She put her hands on either side of his face. "Scotty, honey, it's Mommy and Daddy," she said. "Scotty?"

The boy looked at them, but without any sign of recognition. Then his mouth opened, his eyes scrunched closed, and he howled until he had no more air in his lungs. His face seemed to relax and soften then. His lips parted as his last breath was puffed through his throat and exhaled gently through the clenched teeth.

The doctors called it a hidden occlusion and said it was a one-in-a-million circumstance. Maybe if it could have been detected somehow and surgery undertaken immediately, they could have saved him. But more than likely not. In any case, what would they have been looking for? Nothing had shown up in the tests or in the X-rays.

Dr. Francis was shaken. "I can't tell you how badly I feel. I'm so very sorry, I can't tell you," he said as he led them into the doctors' lounge. There was a doctor sitting in a chair with his legs hooked over the back of another chair, watching an early-morning TV show. He was wearing a green delivery-room outfit, loose green pants and green blouse, and a green cap that covered his hair. He looked at Howard and Ann and then looked at Dr. Francis. He got to his feet and turned off the set and went out of the room. Dr. Francis guided Ann to the sofa, sat down beside her, and began to talk in a low, consoling voice. At one point, he leaned over and embraced her. She could feel his chest rising and falling evenly against her shoulder. She kept her eyes open and let him hold her. Howard went into the bathroom, but he left the door open. After a violent fit of weeping, he ran water and washed his face. Then he came out and sat down at the little table that held a telephone. He looked at the telephone as though deciding what to do first. He made some calls. After a time, Dr. Francis used the telephone.

"Is there anything else I can do for the moment?" he asked them.

Howard shook his head. Ann stared at Dr. Francis as if unable to comprehend his words.

The doctor walked them to the hospital's front door. People were entering and leaving the hospital. It was eleven o'clock in the morning. Ann was aware of how slowly, almost reluctantly, she moved her feet. It seemed to her that Dr. Francis was making them leave when she felt they should stay, when it would be more the right thing to do to stay. She gazed out into the parking lot and then turned around and looked back at the front of the hospital. She began shaking her head. "No, no," she said. "I can't leave him here, no." She heard herself say that and thought how unfair it was that the only words that came out were the sort of words used on TV shows where people were stunned by violent or sudden deaths. She wanted her words to be her own. "No," she said, and for some reason the memory of the Negro woman's head lolling on the woman's shoulder came to her. "No," she said again.

"I'll be talking to you later in the day," the doctor was saying to Howard. "There are still some things that have to be done, things that have to be cleared up to our satisfaction. Some things that need explaining."

"An autopsy," Howard said.

Dr. Francis nodded.

"I understand," Howard said. Then he said, "Oh, Jesus. No, I don't understand, doctor. I can't, I can't. I just can't."

Dr. Francis put his arm around Howard's shoulders. "I'm sorry. God, how I'm sorry." He let go of Howard's shoulders and held out his hand. Howard looked at the hand, and then he took it. Dr. Francis put his arms around Ann once more. He seemed full of some goodness she didn't understand. She let her head rest on his shoulder, but her eyes stayed open. She kept looking at the hospital. As they drove out of the parking lot, she looked back at the hospital.

At home, she sat on the sofa with her hands in her coat pockets. Howard closed the door to the child's room. He got the coffee-maker going and then he found an empty box. He had thought to pick up some of the child's things that were scattered around the living room. But instead he sat down beside her on the sofa, pushed the box to one side, and leaned forward, arms between his knees. He began to weep. She pulled his head over into her lap and patted his shoulder. "He's gone," she said. She kept patting his shoulder. Over his sobs, she could hear the coffee-maker hissing in the kitchen. "There, there," she said tenderly. "Howard, he's gone. He's gone and now we'll have to get used to that. To being alone."

In a little while, Howard got up and began moving aimlessly around the room with the box, not putting anything into it, but collecting some things together on the floor at one end of the sofa. She continued to sit with her hands in her coat pockets. Howard put the box down and brought coffee into the living room. Later, Ann made calls to relatives. After each call had been placed and the party had answered, Ann would blurt out a few words and cry for a minute. Then she would quietly explain, in a measured voice, what had happened and tell them about arrangements. Howard took the box out to the garage, where he saw the child's bicycle. He dropped the box and sat down on the pavement beside the bicycle. He took hold of the bicycle awkwardly so that it leaned against his chest. He held it, the rubber pedal sticking into his chest. He gave the wheel a turn.

Ann hung up the telephone after talking to her sister. She was looking up another number when the telephone rang. She picked it up on the first ring.

"Hello," she said, and she heard something in the background, a humming noise. "Hello!" she said. "For God's sake," she said. "Who is this? What is it you want?"

"Your Scotty, I got him ready for you," the man's voice said. "Did you forget him?"

"You evil bastard!" she shouted into the receiver. "How can you do this, you evil son of a bitch?"

"Scotty," the man said. "Have you forgotten about Scotty?" Then the man hung up on her.

Howard heard the shouting and came in to find her with her head on her arms over the table, weeping. He picked up the receiver and listened to the dial tone.

Much later, just before midnight, after they had dealt with many things, the telephone rang again.

"You answer it," she said. "Howard, it's him, I know." They were sitting at the kitchen table with coffee in front of them. Howard had a small glass of whiskey beside his cup. He answered on the third ring.

"Hello," he said. "Who is this? Hello! Hello!" The line went dead. "He hung up," Howard said. "Whoever it was."

"It was him," she said. "That bastard. I'd like to kill him," she said. "I'd like to shoot him and watch him kick," she said.

"Ann, my God," he said.

"Could you hear anything?" she said. "In the background? A noise, machinery, something humming?"

"Nothing, really. Nothing like that," he said. "There wasn't much time. I think there was some radio music. Yes, there was a radio going, that's all I could tell. I don't know what in God's name is going on," he said.

She shook her head. "If I could, could get my hands on him." It came to her then. She knew who it was. Scotty, the cake, the telephone number. She pushed the chair away from the table and got up. "Drive me down to the shopping center," she said. "Howard."

"What are you saying?"

"The shopping center. I know who it is who's calling. I know who it is. It's the baker, the son-of-a-bitching baker, Howard. I had him bake a cake for Scotty's birthday. That's who's calling. That's who has the number and keeps calling us. To harass us about that cake. The baker, that bastard."

They drove down to the shopping center. The sky was clear and stars were out. It was cold, and they ran the heater in the car. They parked in front of the bakery. All of the shops and stores were closed, but there were cars at the far end of the lot in front of the movie theater. The bakery windows were dark, but when they looked through the glass they could see a light in the back room and, now and then, a big man in an apron moving in and out of the white, even light. Through the glass, she could see the display cases and some little tables with chairs. She tried the door. She rapped on the glass. But if the baker heard them, he gave no sign. He didn't look in their direction.

They drove around behind the bakery and parked. They got out of the car. There was a lighted window too high up for them to see inside. A sign near the back door said THE PANTRY BAKERY, SPECIAL ORDERS. She could hear faintly a radio playing inside and something creak — an oven door as it was pulled down? She knocked on the door and waited. Then she knocked again, louder. The radio was turned down and there was a scraping sound now, the distinct sound of something, a drawer, being pulled open and then closed.

Someone unlocked the door and opened it. The baker stood in the light and peered out at them. "I'm closed for business," he said. "What do you want at this hour? It's midnight. Are you drunk or something?"

She stepped into the light that fell through the open door. He blinked his heavy eyelids as he recognized her. "It's you," he said.

"It's me," she said. "Scotty's mother. This is Scotty's father. We'd like to come in."

The baker said, "I'm busy now. I have work to do."

She had stepped inside the doorway anyway. Howard came in behind her. The baker moved back. "It smells like a bakery in here. Doesn't it smell like a bakery in here, Howard?"

"What do you want?" the baker said. "Maybe you want your cake? That's it, you decided you want your cake. You ordered a cake, didn't you?"

"You're pretty smart for a baker," she said. "Howard, this is the man who's been calling us." She clenched her fists. She stared at him fiercely. There was a deep burning inside her, an anger that made her feel larger than herself, larger than either of these men.

"Just a minute here," the baker said. "You want to pick up your three-day-old cake? That it? I don't want to argue with you, lady. There it sits over there, getting stale. I'll give it to you for half of what I quoted you. No. You want it? You can have it. It's no good to me, no good to anyone now. It cost me time and money to make that cake.

If you want it, okay, if you don't, that's okay, too. I have to get back to work." He looked at them and rolled his tongue behind his teeth.

"More cakes," she said. She knew she was in control of it, of what was increasing in her. She was calm.

"Lady, I work sixteen hours a day in this place to earn a living," the baker said. He wiped his hands on his apron. "I work night and day in here, trying to make ends meet." A look crossed Ann's face that made the baker move back and say, "No trouble, now." He reached to the counter and picked up a rolling pin with his right hand and began to tap it against the palm of his other hand. "You want the cake or not? I have to get back to work. Bakers work at night," he said again. His eyes were small, mean-looking, she thought, nearly lost in the bristly flesh around his cheeks. His neck was thick with fat.

"I know bakers work at night," Ann said. "They make phone calls at night, too. You bastard," she said.

The baker continued to tap the rolling pin against his hand. He glanced at Howard. "Careful, careful," he said to Howard.

"My son's dead," she said with a cold, even finality. "He was hit by a car Monday morning. We've been waiting with him until he died. But, of course, you couldn't be expected to know that, could you? Bakers can't know everything — can they, Mr. Baker? But he's dead. He's dead, you bastard!" Just as suddenly as it had welled in her, the anger dwindled, gave way to something else, a dizzy feeling of nausea. She leaned against the wooden table that was sprinkled with flour, put her hands over her face, and began to cry, her shoulders rocking back and forth. "It isn't fair," she said. "It isn't, isn't fair."

Howard put his hand at the small of her back and looked at the baker. "Shame on you," Howard said to him. "Shame."

The baker put the rolling pin back on the counter. He undid his apron and threw it on the counter. He looked at them, and then he shook his head slowly. He pulled a chair out from under the card table that held papers and receipts, an adding machine, and a telephone directory. "Please sit down," he said. "Let me get you a chair," he said to Howard. "Sit down now, please." The baker went into the front of the shop and returned with two little wrought-iron chairs. "Please sit down, you people."

Ann wiped her eyes and looked at the baker. "I wanted to kill you," she said. "I wanted you dead."

The baker had cleared a space for them at the table. He shoved the adding machine to one side, along with the stacks of notepaper and receipts. He pushed the telephone directory onto the floor, where it landed with a thud. Howard and Ann sat down and pulled their chairs up to the table. The baker sat down, too.

"Let me say how sorry I am," the baker said, putting his elbows on the table. "God alone knows how sorry. Listen to me. I'm just a baker. I don't claim to be anything else. Maybe once, maybe years ago, I was a different kind of human being. I've forgotten, I don't know for sure. But I'm not any longer, if I ever was. Now I'm just a baker. That don't excuse my doing what I did, I know. But I'm deeply sorry. I'm sorry for your son, and sorry for my part in this," the baker said. He spread his hands out on the table and turned them over to reveal his palms. "I don't have any children myself, so I can only imagine what you must be feeling. All I can say to you now is that I'm sorry. Forgive me, if you can," the baker said. "I'm not an evil man, I don't think. Not evil, like you said on the phone. You got to understand what it comes down to is I don't know how to act anymore, it would seem. Please," the man said, "let me ask you if you can find it in your hearts to forgive me?"

It was warm inside the bakery. Howard stood up from the table and took off his coat. He helped Ann from her coat. The baker looked at them for a minute and then nodded and got up from the table. He went to the oven and turned off some switches. He found cups and poured coffee from an electric coffee-maker. He put a carton of cream on the table, and a bowl of sugar.

"You probably need to eat something," the baker said. "I hope you'll eat some of my hot rolls. You have to eat and keep going. Eating is a small, good thing in a time like this," he said.

He served them warm cinnamon rolls just out of the oven, the icing still runny. He put butter on the table and knives to spread the butter. Then the baker sat down at the table with them. He waited. He waited until they each took a roll from the platter and began to eat. "It's good to eat something," he said, watching them. "There's more. Eat up. Eat all you want. There's all the rolls in the world in here."

They ate rolls and drank coffee. Ann was suddenly hungry, and the rolls were warm and sweet. She ate three of them, which pleased the baker. Then he began to talk. They listened carefully. Although they were tired and in anguish, they listened to what the baker had to say. They nodded when the baker began to speak of loneliness, and of the sense of doubt and limitation that had come to him in his middle years. He told them what it was like to be childless all these years. To repeat the days with the ovens endlessly full and endlessly empty. The party food, the celebrations he'd worked over. Icing knuckle-deep. The tiny wedding couples stuck into cakes. Hundreds of them, no, thousands by now. Birthdays. Just imagine all those candles burning. He had a necessary trade. He was a baker. He was glad he wasn't a florist. It was better to be feeding people. This was a better smell anytime than flowers.

"Smell this," the baker said, breaking open a dark loaf. "It's a heavy bread, but rich." They smelled it, then he had them taste it. It had the taste of molasses and coarse grains. They listened to him. They ate what they could. They swallowed the dark bread. It was like daylight under the fluorescent trays of light. They talked on into the early morning, the high, pale cast of light in the windows, and they did not think of leaving.

WILLA CATHER

Willa Cather (1873–1947) was born in Virginia but after age eight grew up in the Nebraska landscape that figures so prominently in much of her fiction. Her novels — which are characteristically concerned with pioneering and the immigrant experience and also with the lives of artists — include *O, Pioneers!* (1913), *The Song of the Lark* (1915), *My Ántonia* (1918), *A Lost Lady* (1923), and *Death Comes for the Archbishop* (1927). Her short stories are collected in *Youth and the Bright Medusa* (1920), *Obscure Destinies* (1932), and *The Old Beauty and Others* (1948). It has been said of Cather that in her work she "made a contemplation on the struggle to achieve wholeness." "Paul's Case" is the story of such a struggle.

Paul's Case

It was Paul's afternoon to appear before the faculty of the Pittsburgh High School to account for his various misdemeanors. He had been suspended a week ago, and his father had called at the Principal's office and confessed his perplexity about his son. Paul entered the faculty room suave and smiling. His clothes were a trifle outgrown, and the tan velvet on the collar of his open overcoat was frayed and worn; but for all that there was something of the dandy about him, and he wore an opal pin in his neatly knotted black four-in-hand, and a red carnation in his buttonhole. This latter adornment the faculty somehow felt was not properly significant of the contrite spirit befitting a boy under the ban of suspension.

Paul was tall for his age and very thin, with high, cramped shoulders and a narrow chest. His eyes were remarkable for a certain hysterical brilliancy, and he continually used them in a conscious, theatrical sort of way, peculiarly offensive in a boy. The pupils were abnormally large, as though he were addicted to belladonna, but there was a glassy glitter about them which that drug does not produce.

When questioned by the Principal as to why he was there Paul stated, politely enough, that he wanted to come back to school. This was a lie, but Paul was quite accustomed to lying; found it, indeed, indispensable for overcoming friction. His teachers were asked to state their respective charges against him, which they did with such a rancor and aggrievedness as evinced that this was not a usual case. Disorder and impertinence were among the offenses named, yet each of his instructors felt that it was scarcely possible to put into words the real cause of the trouble, which lay in a sort of hysterically defiant manner of the boy's; in the contempt which they all knew he felt for them, and which he seemingly made not the least effort to conceal. Once, when he had been making a synopsis of a paragraph at the blackboard, his English teacher had stepped to his side and attempted to guide his hand. Paul had started back with a shudder and thrust his hands violently behind him. The astonished woman could scarcely have been more hurt and embarrassed had he struck at her. The insult was so involuntary and definitely personal as to be unforgettable. In one way and another he had made all his teachers, men and women alike, conscious of the same feeling of physical aversion. In one class he habitually sat with his hand shading his eyes; in another he always looked out of the window during the recitation; in another he made a running commentary on the lecture, with humorous intention.

His teachers felt this afternoon that his whole attitude was symbolized by his shrug and his flippantly red carnation flower, and they fell upon him without mercy, his English teacher leading the pack. He stood through it smiling, his pale lips parted over his white teeth. (His lips were continually twitching, and he had a habit of raising his eyebrows that was contemptuous and irritating to the last degree.) Older boys than Paul had broken down and shed tears under that baptism of fire, but his set smile did not once desert him, and his only sign of discomfort was the nervous trembling of the fingers that toyed with the buttons of his overcoat, and an occasional jerking of the other hand that held his hat. Paul was always smiling, always glancing about him, seeming to feel that people might be watching him and trying to detect something. This conscious expression, since it was as far as possible from boyish mirthfulness, was usually attributed to insolence or "smartness."

As the inquisition proceeded one of his instructors repeated an impertinent remark of the boy's, and the Principal asked him whether he thought that a courteous speech to have made a woman. Paul shrugged his shoulders slightly and his eyebrows twitched.

"I don't know," he replied. "I didn't mean to be polite or impolite, either. I guess it's a sort of way I have of saying things regardless."

The Principal, who was a sympathetic man, asked him whether he didn't think that a way it would be well to get rid of. Paul grinned and said he guessed so. When he was told that he could go he bowed gracefully and went out. His bow was but a repetition of the scandalous red carnation.

His teachers were in despair, and his drawing master voiced the feeling of them all when he declared there was something about the boy which none of them understood. He added: "I don't really believe that smile of his comes altogether from insolence; there's something sort of haunted about it. The boy is not strong, for one thing. I happen to know that he was born in Colorado, only a few months before his mother died out there of a long illness. There is something wrong about the fellow."

The drawing master had come to realize that, in looking at Paul, one saw only his white teeth and the forced animation of his eyes. One warm afternoon the boy had gone to sleep at his drawing board, and his master had noted with amazement what a white, blue-veined face it was; drawn and wrinkled like an old man's about the eyes, the lips twitching even in his sleep, and stiff with a nervous tension that drew them back from his teeth.

His teachers left the building dissatisfied and unhappy; humiliated to have felt so vindictive toward a mere boy, to have uttered this feeling in cutting terms, and to have set each other on, as it were, in the gruesome game of intemperate reproach. Some of them remembered having seen a miserable street cat set at bay by a ring of tormentors.

As for Paul, he ran down the hill whistling the "Soldiers' Chorus" from *Faust,* looking wildly behind him now and then to see whether some of his teachers were not there to writhe under his lightheartedness. As it was now late in the afternoon and Paul was on duty that evening as usher at Carnegie Hall, he decided that he would not go home to supper. When he reached the concert hall the doors were not yet open and, as it was chilly outside, he decided to go up into the picture gallery — always deserted at this hour — where there were some of Raffelli's gay studies of Paris streets and an airy blue Venetian scene or two that always exhilarated him. He was delighted to find no one in the gallery but the old guard, who sat in one corner, a newspaper on his knee, a black patch over one eye and the other closed. Paul possessed himself of the place and walked confidently up and down, whistling under his breath. After a while he sat down before a blue Rico and lost himself. When he bethought him to look at his watch, it was after seven o'clock, and he rose with a start and ran downstairs, making a face at Augustus, peering out from the cast room, and an evil gesture at the Venus de Milo as he passed her on the stairway.

When Paul reached the ushers' dressing room half a dozen boys were there already, and he began excitedly to tumble into his uniform. It was one of the few that at all approached fitting, and Paul thought it very becoming — though he knew that the tight, straight coat accentuated his narrow chest, about which he was exceedingly sensitive. He was always considerably excited while he dressed, twanging all over to the tuning of the strings and the preliminary flourishes of the horns in the music room; but tonight he seemed quite beside himself, and he teased and plagued the boys until, telling him that he was crazy, they put him down on the floor and sat on him.

Somewhat calmed by his suppression, Paul dashed out to the front of the house to seat the early comers. He was a model usher; gracious and smiling he ran up and down the aisles; nothing was too much trouble for him; he carried messages and brought programs as though it were his greatest pleasure in life, and all the people in his section thought him a charming boy, feeling that he remembered and admired them. As the house filled, he grew more and more vivacious and animated, and the color came to his cheeks and lips. It was very much as though this were a great reception and Paul were the host. Just as the musicians came out to take their places, his English teacher arrived with checks for the seats which a prominent manufacturer had taken for the season. She betrayed some embarrassment when she handed Paul the tickets, and a hauteur which subsequently made her feel very foolish. Paul was startled for a moment, and had the feeling of wanting to put her out; what business had she here among all these fine people and gay colors? He looked her over and decided that she was not appropriately dressed and must be a fool to sit downstairs in such togs. The tickets had probably been sent her out of kindness, he reflected as he put down a seat for her, and she had about as much right to sit there as he had.

When the symphony began Paul sank into one of the rear seats with a long sigh of relief, and lost himself, as he had done before the Rico. It was not that symphonies, as such, meant anything in particular to Paul, but the first sigh of the instruments seemed to free some hilarious and potent spirit within him; something that struggled there like the genie in the bottle found by the Arab fisherman. He felt a sudden zest of life; the lights danced before his eyes and the concert hall blazed into unimaginable splendor. When the soprano soloist came on Paul forgot even the nastiness of his teacher's being there and gave himself up to the peculiar stimulus such personages always had for him. The soloist chanced to be a German woman, by no means in her first youth, and the mother of many children; but she wore an elaborate gown and tiara, and above all she had that indefinable air of achievement, that world-shine upon her, which, in Paul's eyes, made her a veritable queen of Romance.

After a concert was over Paul was always irritable and wretched until he got to sleep, and tonight he was even more than usually restless. He had the feeling of not being able to let down, of its being impossible to give up this delicious excitement which was the only thing that could be called living at all. During the last number he withdrew and, after hastily changing his clothes in the dressing room, slipped out to the side door where the soprano's carriage stood. Here he began pacing rapidly up and down the walk, waiting to see her come out.

Over yonder, the Schenley, in its vacant stretch, loomed big and square through the fine rain, the windows of its twelve stories glowing like those of a lighted cardboard house under a Christmas tree. All the actors and singers of the better class stayed there when they were in the city, and a number of the big manufacturers of the place lived there in the winter. Paul had often hung about the hotel, watching the people go in and out, longing to enter and leave schoolmasters and dull care behind him forever.

At last the singer came out, accompanied by the conductor, who helped her into her carriage and closed the door with a cordial *auf wiedersehen* which set Paul to wondering whether she were not an old sweetheart of his. Paul followed the carriage over to the hotel, walking so rapidly as not to be far from the entrance when the singer alighted, and disappeared behind the swinging glass doors that were opened by a Negro in a tall hat and a long coat. In the moment that the door was ajar it seemed to Paul that he, too, entered. He seemed to feel himself go after her up the steps, into the warm, lighted building, into an exotic, tropical world of shiny, glistening surfaces and basking ease. He reflected upon the mysterious dishes that were brought into the dining room, the green bottles in buckets of ice, as he had seen them in the supper party pictures of the *Sunday World* supplement. A quick gust of wind brought the rain down with sudden vehemence, and Paul was startled to find that he was still outside in the slush of the gravel driveway; that his boots were letting in the water and his scanty overcoat was clinging wet about him; that the lights in front of the concert hall were out and that the rain was driving in sheets between him and the orange glow of the windows above him. There it was, what he wanted — but mocking spirits stood guard at the doors, and, as the rain beat in his face, Paul wondered whether he were destined always to shiver in the black night outside, looking up at it.

He turned and walked reluctantly toward the car tracks. The end had to come sometime; his father in his nightclothes at the top of the stairs, explanations that did not explain, hastily improvised fictions that were forever tripping him up, his upstairs room and its horrible yellow wallpaper, the creaking bureau with the greasy plush collarbox, and over his painted wooden bed the pictures of George Washington and John Calvin, and the framed motto, "Feed my Lambs," which had been worked in red worsted by his mother.

Half an hour later Paul alighted from his car and went slowly down one of the side streets off the main thoroughfare. It was a highly respectable street, where all the houses were exactly alike, and where businessmen of moderate means begot and reared large families of children, all of whom went to Sabbath school and learned the shorter catechism, and were interested in arithmetic; all of whom were as exactly alike as their homes, and of a piece with the monotony in which they lived. Paul never went up Cordelia Street without a shudder of loathing. His home was next to the house of the Cumberland minister. He approached it tonight with the nerveless sense of defeat, the hopeless feeling of sinking back forever into ugliness and commonness that he had always had when he came home. The moment he turned into Cordelia Street he felt the waters close above his head. After each of these orgies of living he experienced all the physical depression which follows a debauch; the loathing of respectable beds, of common food, of a house penetrated by kitchen odors; a shuddering repulsion for the flavorless, colorless mass of everyday existence; a morbid desire for cool things and soft lights and fresh flowers.

The nearer he approached the house, the more absolutely unequal Paul felt to the sight of it all: his ugly sleeping chamber; the cold bathroom with the grimy zinc tub, the cracked mirror, the dripping spigots; his father, at the top of the stairs, his hairy legs sticking out from his nightshirt, his feet thrust into carpet slippers. He was so much later than usual that there would certainly be inquiries and reproaches. Paul stopped short before the door. He felt that he could not be accosted by his father tonight; that he could not toss again on that miserable bed. He would not go in. He would tell his father that he had no carfare and it was raining so hard he had gone home with one of the boys and stayed all night.

Meanwhile, he was wet and cold. He went around to the back of the house and tried one of the basement windows, found it open, raised it cautiously, and scrambled down the cellar wall to the floor. There he stood, holding his breath, terrified by the noise he had made, but the floor above him was silent, and there was no creak on the stairs. He found a soapbox, and carried it over to the soft ring of light that streamed from the furnace door, and sat down. He was horribly afraid of rats, so he did not try to sleep, but sat looking distrustfully at the dark, still terrified lest he might have awakened his father. In such reactions, after one of the experiences which made days and nights out of the dreary blanks of the calendar, when his senses were deadened, Paul's head was always singularly clear. Suppose his father had heard him getting in at the window and had come down and shot him for a burglar? Then, again, suppose his father had come down, pistol in hand, and he had cried out in time to save himself, and his father had been horrified to think how nearly he had killed him? Then, again, suppose a day should come when his father would remember that night, and wish there had been no warning cry to stay his hand? With this last supposition Paul entertained himself until daybreak.

The following Sunday was fine; the sodden November chill was broken by the last flash of autumnal summer. In the morning Paul had to go to church and Sabbath school, as always. On seasonable Sunday afternoons the burghers of Cordelia Street always sat out on their front stoops and talked to their neighbors on the next stoop, or called to those across the street in neighborly fashion. The men usually sat on gay cushions placed upon the steps that led down to the sidewalk, while the women, in their Sunday "waists," sat in rockers on the cramped porches, pretending to be greatly at their ease. The children played in the streets; there were so many of them that the place resembled the recreation grounds of a kindergarten. The men on the steps — all in their shirt sleeves their vests unbuttoned — sat with their legs well apart, their stomachs comfortably protruding, and talked of the prices of things, or told anecdotes of the sagacity of their various chiefs and overlords. They occasionally looked over the multitude of squabbling children, listened affectionately to their high-pitched, nasal voices, smiling to see their own proclivities reproduced in their offspring, and interspersed their legends of the iron kings with remarks about their sons' progress at school, their grades in arithmetic, and the amounts they had saved in their toy banks.

On this last Sunday of November Paul sat all the afternoon on the lowest step of his stoop, staring into the street, while his sisters, in their rockers, were talking to the minister's daughters next door about how many shirtwaists they had made in the last week, and how many waffles someone had eaten at the last church supper. When the weather was warm, and his father was in a particularly jovial frame of mind, the girls made lemonade, which was always brought out in a red-glass pitcher, ornamented with forget-me-nots in blue enamel. This the girls thought very fine, and the neighbors always joked about the suspicious color of the pitcher.

Today Paul's father sat on the top step, talking to a young man who shifted a restless baby from knee to knee. He happened to be the young man who was daily held up to Paul as a model, and after whom it was his father's dearest hope that he would pattern. This young man was of a ruddy complexion, with a compressed, red mouth, and faded, nearsighted eyes, over which he wore thick spectacles, with gold bows that curved about his ears. He was clerk to one of the magnates of a great steel corporation, and was looked upon in Cordelia Street as a young man with a future. There was a story that, some five years ago — he was now barely twenty-six — he had been a trifle dissipated, but in order to curb his appetites and save the loss of time and strength that a sowing of wild oats might have entailed, he had taken his chief's advice, oft reiterated to his employees, and at twenty-one had married the first woman whom he could persuade to share his fortunes. She happened to be an angular schoolmistress, much older than he, who also wore thick glasses, and who had now borne him four children, all nearsighted, like herself.

The young man was relating how his chief, now cruising in the Mediterranean, kept in touch with all the details of the business, arranging his office hours on his yacht just as though he were at home, and "knocking off work enough to keep two stenographers busy." His father told, in turn, the plan his corporation was considering, of putting in an electric railway plant in Cairo. Paul snapped his teeth; he had an awful apprehension that they might spoil it all before he got there. Yet he rather liked to hear these legends of the iron kings that were told and retold on Sundays and holidays; these stories of palaces in Venice, yachts on the Mediterranean, and high play at Monte Carlo appealed to his fancy, and he was interested in the triumphs of these cash boys who had become famous, though he had no mind for the cash-boy stage.

After supper was over and he had helped to dry the dishes, Paul nervously asked his father whether he could go to George's to get some help in his geometry, and still more nervously asked for carfare. This latter request he had to repeat, as his father, on principle, did not like to hear requests for money, whether much or little. He asked Paul whether he could not go to some boy who lived nearer, and told him that he ought not to leave his schoolwork until Sunday; but he gave him the dime. He was not a poor man, but he had a worthy ambition to come up in the world. His only reason for allowing Paul to usher was that he thought a boy ought to be earning a little.

Paul bounded upstairs, scrubbed the greasy odor of the dishwater from his hands with the ill-smelling soap he hated, and then shook over his fingers a few drops of violet water from the bottle he kept hidden in his drawer. He left the house with his geometry conspicuously under his arm, and the moment he got out of Cordelia Street and boarded a downtown car, he shook off the lethargy of two deadening days and began to live again.

The leading juvenile of the permanent stock company which played at one of the downtown theaters was an acquaintance of Paul's, and the boy had been invited to drop in at the Sunday-night rehearsals whenever he could. For more than a year Paul had spent every available moment loitering about Charley Edwards's dressing room. He had won a place among Edwards's following not only because the young actor, who could not afford to employ a dresser, often found him useful, but because he recognized in Paul something akin to what churchmen term "vocation."

It was at the theater and at Carnegie Hall that Paul really lived; the rest was but a sleep and a forgetting. This was Paul's fairy tale, and it had for him all the allurement of a secret love. The moment he inhaled the gassy, painty, dusty odor behind the scenes, he breathed like a prisoner set free, and felt within him the possibility of doing or saying splendid, brilliant, poetic things. The moment the cracked orchestra beat out the overture from *Martha,* or jerked at the serenade from *Rigoletto,* all stupid and ugly things slid from him, and his senses were deliciously, yet delicately fired.

Perhaps it was because, in Paul's world, the natural nearly always wore the guise of ugliness, that a certain element of artificiality seemed to him necessary in beauty. Perhaps it was because his experience of life elsewhere was so full of Sabbath-school picnics, petty economies, wholesome advice as to how to succeed in life, and the inescapable odors of cooking, that he found this existence so alluring, these smartly clad men and women so attractive, that he was so moved by these starry apple orchards that bloomed perennially under the limelight.

It would be difficult to put it strongly enough how convincingly the stage entrance of that theater was for Paul the actual portal of Romance. Certainly none of the company ever suspected it, least of all Charley Edwards. It was very like the old stories that used to float about London of fabulously rich Jews, who had subterranean halls there, with palms, and fountains, and soft lamps and richly appareled women who never saw the disenchanting light of London day. So, in the midst of that smoke-palled city, enamored of figures and grimy toil, Paul had his secret temple, his wishing carpet, his bit of blue-and-white Mediterranean shore bathed in perpetual sunshine.

Several of Paul's teachers had a theory that his imagination had been perverted by garish fiction but the truth was that he scarcely ever read at all. The books at home were not such as would either tempt or corrupt a youthful mind, and as for reading the novels that some of his friends urged upon him — well, he got what he wanted much more quickly from music; any sort of music, from an orchestra to a barrel organ. He needed only the spark, the indescribable thrill that made his imagination master of his senses, and he could make plots and pictures enough of his own. It was equally true that he was not stagestruck — not, at any rate, in the usual acceptation of that expression. He had no desire to become an actor, any more than he had to become a musician. He felt no necessity to do any of these things; what he wanted was to see, to be in the atmosphere, float on the wave of it, to be carried out, blue league after blue league, away from everything.

After a night behind the scenes Paul found the schoolroom more than ever repulsive; the bare floors and naked walls; the prosy men who never wore frock coats, or violets in their buttonholes; the women with their dull gowns, shrill voices, and pitiful seriousness about prepositions that govern the dative. He could not bear to have the other pupils think, for a moment, that he took these people seriously; he must convey to them that he considered it all trivial, and was there only by way of a jest, anyway. He had autographed pictures of all the members of the stock company which he showed his classmates, telling them the most incredible stories of his familiarity with these people, of his acquaintance with the soloists who came to Carnegie Hall, his suppers with them and the flowers he sent them. When these stories lost their effect, and his audience grew listless, he became desperate and would bid all the boys good-by, announcing that he was going to travel for a while; going to Naples, to Venice, to Egypt. Then, next Monday, he would slip back, conscious and nervously smiling; his sister was ill, and he should have to defer his voyage until spring.

Matters went steadily worse with Paul at school. In the itch to let his instructors know how heartily he despised them and their homilies, and how thoroughly he was appreciated elsewhere, he mentioned once or twice that he had no time to fool with theorems; adding — with a twitch of the eyebrows and a touch of that nervous bravado which so perplexed them — that he was helping the people down at the stock company; they were old friends of his.

The upshot of the matter was that the Principal went to Paul's father, and Paul was taken out of school and put to work. The manager at Carnegie Hall was told to get another usher in his stead; the doorkeeper at the theater was warned not to admit him to the house; and Charley Edwards remorsefully promised the boy's father not to see him again.

The members of the stock company were vastly amused when some of Paul's stories reached them — especially the women. They were hard-working women, most of them supporting indigent husbands or brothers, and they laughed rather bitterly at having stirred the boy to such fervid and florid inventions. They agreed with the faculty and with his father that Paul's was a bad case.

The eastbound train was plowing through a January snowstorm; the dull dawn was beginning to show gray when the engine whistled a mile out of Newark. Paul started up from the seat where he had lain curled in uneasy slumber, rubbed the breath-misted window glass with his hand, and peered out. The snow was whirling in curling eddies above the white bottom lands, and the drifts lay already deep in the fields and along the fences, while here and there the long dead grass and dried weed stalks protruded black above it. Lights shone from the scattered houses, and a gang of laborers who stood beside the track waved their lanterns.

Paul had slept very little, and he felt grimy and uncomfortable. He had made the all-night journey in a day coach, partly because he was ashamed, dressed as he was, to go into a Pullman, and partly because he was afraid of being seen there by some Pittsburgh businessman, who might have noticed him in Denny & Carson's office. When the whistle awoke him, he clutched quickly at his breast pocket, glancing about him with an uncertain smile. But the little, clay-bespattered Italians were still sleeping, the slatternly women across the aisle were in open-mouthed oblivion, and even the crumby, crying babies were for the nonce stilled. Paul settled back to struggle with his impatience as best he could.

When he arrived at the Jersey City station he hurried through his breakfast, manifestly ill at ease and keeping a sharp eye about him. After he reached the Twenty-third Street station, he consulted a cabman and had himself driven to a men's-furnishings establishment that was just opening for the day. He spent upward of two hours, buying with endless reconsidering and great care. His new street suit he put on in the fitting room; the frock coat and dress clothes he had bundled into the cab with his linen. Then he drove to a hatter's and a shoe house. His next errand was at Tiffany's, where he selected his silver and a new scarf pin. He would not wait to have his silver marked, he said. Lastly, he stopped at a trunk shop on Broadway and had his purchases packed into various traveling bags.

It was a little after one o'clock when he drove up to the Waldorf, and after settling with the cabman, went into the office. He registered from Washington; said his mother and father had been abroad, and that he had come down to await the arrival of their steamer. He told his story plausibly and had no trouble, since he volunteered to pay for them in advance, in engaging his rooms; a sleeping room, sitting room, and bath.

Not once, but a hundred times, Paul had planned this entry into New York. He had gone over every detail of it with Charley Edwards, and in his scrapbook at home there were pages of description about New York hotels, cut from the Sunday papers. When he was shown to his sitting room on the eighth floor he saw at a glance that everything was as it should be; there was but one detail in his mental picture that the place did not realize, so he rang for the bellboy and sent him down for flowers. He moved about nervously until the boy returned, putting away his new linen and fingering it delightedly as he did so. When the flowers came he put them hastily into water, and then tumbled into a hot bath. Presently he came out of his white bathroom, resplendent in his new silk underwear, and playing with the tassels of his red robe. The snow was whirling so fiercely outside his windows that he could scarcely see across the street, but within the air was deliciously soft and fragrant. He put the violets and jonquils on the taboret beside the couch, and threw himself down, with a long sigh, covering himself with a Roman blanket. He was thoroughly tired; he had been in such haste, he had stood up to such a strain, covered so much ground in the last twenty-four hours, that he wanted to think how it had all come about. Lulled by the sound of the wind, the warm air, and the cool fragrance of the flowers, he sank into deep, drowsy retrospection.

It had been wonderfully simple; when they had shut him out of the theater and concert hall, when they had taken away his bone, the whole thing was virtually determined. The rest was a mere matter of opportunity. The only thing that at all surprised him was his own courage — for he realized well enough that he had always been tormented by fear, a sort of apprehensive dread that, of late years, as the meshes of the lies he had told closed about him, had been pulling the muscles of his body tighter and tighter. Until now he could not remember the time when he had not been dreading something. Even when he was a little boy it was always there — behind him, or before, or on either side. There had always been the shadowed corner, the dark place into which he dared not look, but from which something seemed always to be watching him — and Paul had done things that were not pretty to watch, he knew.

But now he had a curious sense of relief, as though he had at last thrown down the gauntlet to the thing in the corner.

Yet it was but a day since he had been sulking in the traces; but yesterday afternoon that he had been sent to the bank with Denny & Carson's deposit, as usual — but this time he was instructed to leave the book to be balanced. There was above two thousand dollars in checks, and nearly a thousand in the bank notes which he had taken from the book and quietly transferred to his pocket. At the bank he had made out a new deposit slip. His nerves had been steady enough to permit of his returning to the office, where he had finished his work and asked for a full day's holiday tomorrow, Saturday, giving a perfectly reasonable pretext. The bankbook, he knew, would not be returned before Monday or Tuesday, and his father would be out of town for the next week. From the time he slipped the bank notes into his pocket until he boarded the night train for New York, he had not known a moment's hesitation. It was not the first time Paul had steered through treacherous waters.

How astonishingly easy it had all been; here he was, the thing done; and this time there would be no awakening, no figure at the top of the stairs. He watched the snowflakes whirling by his window until he fell asleep.

When he awoke, it was three o'clock in the afternoon. He bounded up with a start; half of one of his precious days gone already! He spent more than an hour in dressing, watching every stage of his toilet carefully in the mirror. Everything was quite perfect; he was exactly the kind of boy he had always wanted to be.

When he went downstairs Paul took a carriage and drove up Fifth Avenue toward the Park. The snow had somewhat abated; carriages and tradesmen's wagons were hurrying soundlessly to and fro in the winter twilight; boys in woolen mufflers were shoveling off the doorsteps; the avenue stages made fine spots of color against the white street. Here and there on the corners were stands, with whole flower gardens blooming under glass cases, against the sides of which the snowflakes stuck and melted; violets, roses, carnations, lilies of the valley — somehow vastly more lovely and alluring that they blossomed thus unnaturally in the snow. The Park itself was a wonderful stage winterpiece.

When he returned, the pause of the twilight had ceased and the tune of the streets had changed. The snow was falling faster, lights streamed from the hotels that reared their dozen stories fearlessly up into the storm, defying the raging Atlantic winds. A long, black stream of carriages poured down the avenue, intersected here and there by other streams, tending horizontally. There were a score of cabs about the entrance of this hotel, and his driver had to wait. Boys in livery were running in and out of the awning stretched across the sidewalk, up and down the red velvet carpet laid from the door to the street. Above, about, within it all was the rumble and roar, the hurry and toss of thousands of human beings as hot for pleasure as himself, and on every side of him towered the glaring affirmation of the omnipotence of wealth.

The boy set his teeth and drew his shoulders together in a spasm of realization;

the plot of all dramas, the text of all romances, the nerve-stuff of all sensations was whirling about him like the snowflakes. He burnt like a faggot in a tempest.

When Paul went down to dinner the music of the orchestra came floating up the elevator shaft to greet him. His head whirled as he stepped into the thronged corridor, and he sank back into one of the chairs against the wall to get his breath. The lights, the chatter, the perfumes, the bewildering medley of color — he had, for a moment, the feeling of not being able to stand it. But only for a moment; these were his own people, he told himself. He went slowly about the corridors, through the writing rooms, smoking rooms, reception rooms, as though he were exploring the chambers of an enchanted palace, built and peopled for him alone.

When he reached the dining room he sat down at a table near a window. The flowers, the white linen, the many-colored wineglasses, the gay toilettes of the women, the low popping of corks, the undulating repetitions of the *Blue Danube* from the orchestra, all flooded Paul's dream with bewildering radiance. When the roseate tinge of his champagne was added — that cold, precious, bubbling stuff that creamed and foamed in his glass — Paul wondered that there were honest men in the world after all. This was what all the world was fighting for, he reflected; this was what all the struggle was about. He doubted the reality of his past. Had he ever known a place called Cordelia Street, a place where fagged-looking businessmen got on the early car; mere rivets in a machine they seemed to Paul, — sickening men, with combings of children's hair always hanging to their coats, and the smell of cooking in their clothes. Cordelia Street — Ah, that belonged to another time and country; had he not always been thus, had he not sat here night after night, from as far back as he could remember, looking pensively over just such shimmering textures and slowly twirling the stem of a glass like this one between his thumb and middle finger? He rather thought he had.

He was not in the least abashed or lonely. He had no especial desire to meet or to know any of these people; all he demanded was the right to look on and conjecture, to watch the pageant. The mere stage properties were all he contended for. Nor was he lonely later in the evening, in his lodge at the Metropolitan. He was now entirely rid of his nervous misgivings, of his forced aggressiveness, of the imperative desire to show himself different from his surroundings. He felt now that his surroundings explained him. Nobody questioned the purple; he had only to wear it passively. He had only to glance down at his attire to reassure himself that here it would be impossible for anyone to humiliate him.

He found it hard to leave his beautiful sitting room to go to bed that night, and sat long watching the raging storm from his turret window. When he went to sleep it was with the lights turned on in his bedroom; partly because of his old timidity, and partly so that, if he should wake in the night, there would be no wretched moment of doubt, no horrible suspicion of yellow wallpaper, or of Washington and Calvin above his bed.

Sunday morning the city was practically snowbound. Paul breakfasted late, and in the afternoon he fell in with a wild San Francisco boy, a freshman at Yale, who said he had run down for a "little flyer" over Sunday. The young man offered to show Paul the night side of the town, and the two boys went out together after dinner, not returning to the hotel until seven o'clock the next morning. They had started out in the confiding warmth of a champagne friendship, but their parting in the elevator was singularly cool. The freshman pulled himself together to make his train, and Paul went to bed. He awoke at two o'clock in the afternoon, very thirsty and dizzy, and rang for ice-water, coffee, and the Pittsburgh papers.

On the part of the hotel management, Paul excited no suspicion. There was this to be said for him, that he wore his spoils with dignity and in no way made himself conspicuous. Even under the glow of his wine he was never boisterous, though he found the stuff like a magician's wand for wonder-building. His chief greediness lay in his ears and eyes, and his excesses were not offensive ones. His dearest pleasures were the gray winter twilights in his sitting room; his quiet enjoyment of his flowers, his clothes, his wide divan, his cigarette, and his sense of power. He could not remember a time when he had felt so at peace with himself. The mere release from the necessity of petty lying, lying every day and every day, restored his self-respect. He had never lied for pleasure, even at school; but to be noticed and admired, to assert his difference from other Cordelia Street boys; and he felt a good deal more manly, more honest, even, now that he had no need for boastful pretensions, now that he could, as his actor friends used to say, "dress the part." It was characteristic that remorse did not occur to him. His golden days went by without a shadow, and he made each as perfect as he could.

On the eighth day after his arrival in New York he found the whole affair exploited in the Pittsburgh papers, exploited with a wealth of detail which indicated that local news of a sensational nature was at a low ebb. The firm of Denny & Carson announced that the boy's father had refunded the full amount of the theft and that they had no intention of prosecuting. The Cumberland minister had been inter-viewed, and expressed his hope of yet reclaiming the motherless lad, and his Sabbath-school teacher declared that she would spare no effort to that end. The rumor had reached Pittsburgh that the boy had been seen in a New York hotel, and his father had gone East to find him and bring him home.

Paul had just come in to dress for dinner; he sank into a chair, weak to the knees, and clasped his head in his hands. It was to be worse than jail, even; the tepid waters of Cordelia Street were to close over him finally and forever. The gray monotony stretched before him in hopeless, unrelieved years; Sabbath school, Young People's Meeting, the yellow-papered room, the damp dish-towels; it all rushed back upon him with a sickening vividness. He had the old feeling that the orchestra had suddenly stopped, the sinking sensation that the play was over. The sweat broke out on his face, and he sprang to his feet, looked about him with his white, conscious smile, and winked at himself in the mirror. With something of the old childish belief in miracles with which he had so often gone to class, all his lessons unlearned, Paul dressed and dashed whistling down the corridor to the elevator.

He had no sooner entered the dining room and caught the measure of the music than his remembrance was lightened by his old elastic power of claiming the moment, mounting with it, and finding it all-sufficient. The glare and glitter about him, the mere scenic accessories had again, and for the last time, their old potency. He would show himself that he was game, he would finish the thing splendidly. He doubted, more than ever, the existence of Cordelia Street, and for the first time he drank his wine recklessly. Was he not, after all, one of those fortunate beings born to the purple, was he not still himself and in his own place? He drummed a nervous accompaniment to the Pagliacci music and looked about him, telling himself over and over that it had paid.

He reflected drowsily, to the swell of the music and the chill sweetness of his wine, that he might have done it more wisely. He might have caught an outbound steamer and been well out of their clutches before now. But the other side of the world had seemed too far away and too uncertain then; he could not have waited for it; his need had been too sharp. If he had to choose over again, he would do the same thing tomorrow. He looked affectionately about the dining room, now gilded with a soft mist. Ah, it had paid indeed!

Paul was awakened next morning by a painful throbbing in his head and feet. He had thrown himself across the bed without undressing, and had slept with his shoes on. His limbs and hands were lead heavy, and his tongue and throat were parched and burnt. There came upon him one of those fateful attacks of clearheadedness that never occurred except when he was physically exhausted and his nerves hung loose. He lay still, closed his eyes, and let the tide of things wash over him.

His father was in New York; "stopping at some joint or other," he told himself. The memory of successive summers on the front stoop fell upon him like a weight of black water. He had not a hundred dollars left; and he knew now, more than ever, that money was everything, the wall that stood between all he loathed and all he wanted. The thing was winding itself up; he had thought of that on his first glorious day in New York, and had even provided a way to snap the thread. It lay on his dressing table now; he had got it out last night when he came blindly up from dinner, but the shiny metal hurt his eyes, and he disliked the looks of it.

He rose and moved about with a painful effort, succumbing now and again to attacks of nausea. It was the old depression exaggerated; all the world had become Cordelia Street. Yet somehow he was not afraid of anything, was absolutely calm; perhaps because he had looked into the dark corner at last and knew. It was bad enough, what he saw there, but somehow not so bad as his long fear of it had been. He saw everything clearly now. He had a feeling that he had made the best of it, that he had lived the sort of life he was meant to live, and for half an hour he sat staring at the revolver. But he told himself that was not the way, so he went downstairs and took a cab to the ferry.

When Paul arrived in Newark he got off the train and took another cab, directing the driver to follow the Pennsylvania tracks out of the town. The snow lay heavy on the roadways and had drifted deep in the open fields. Only here and there the dead grass or dried weed stalks projected, singularly black, above it. Once well into the country, Paul dismissed the carriage and walked, floundering along the tracks, his mind a medley of irrelevant things. He seemed to hold in his brain an actual picture of everything he had seen that morning. He remembered every feature of both his drivers, of the toothless old woman from whom he had bought the red flowers in his coat, the agent from whom he had got his ticket, and all of his fellow passengers on the ferry. His mind, unable to cope with vital matters near at hand, worked feverishly and deftly at sorting and grouping these images. They made for him a part of the ugliness of the world, of the ache in his head, and the bitter burning on his tongue. He stooped and put a handful of snow into his mouth as he walked, but that, too, seemed hot. When he reached a little hillside, where the tracks ran through a cut some twenty feet below him, he stopped and sat down.

The carnations in his coat were drooping with the cold, he noticed, their red glory all over. It occurred to him that all the flowers he had seen in the glass cases that first night must have gone the same way, long before this. It was only one splendid breath they had, in spite of their brave mockery at the winter outside the glass; and it was a losing game in the end, it seemed, this revolt against the homilies by which the world is run. Paul took one of the blossoms carefully from his coat and scooped a little hole in the snow, where he covered it up. Then he dozed awhile, from his weak condition, seemingly insensible to the cold.

The sound of an approaching train awoke him, and he started to his feet, remembering only his resolution, and afraid lest he should be too late. He stood watching the approaching locomotive, his teeth chattering, his lips drawn away from them in a frightened smile; once or twice he glanced nervously sidewise, as though he were being watched. When the right moment came, he jumped. As he fell, the folly of his haste occurred to him with merciless clearness, the vastness of what he had left undone. There flashed through his brain, clearer than ever before, the blue of Adriatic water, the yellow of Algerian sands.

He felt something strike his chest, and that his body was being thrown swiftly through the air, on and on, immeasurably far and fast, while his limbs were gently relaxed. Then, because the picture-making mechanism was crushed, the disturbing visions flashed into black, and Paul dropped back into the immense design of things.

ANTON CHEKHOV

Anton Chekhov (1860–1904), the son of a former serf, was born in Taganrog, a port on the Sea of Azov. He received a classical education in secondary school and studied medicine at the University of Moscow. While still a medical student he began writing short stories; in a life cut short by tuberculosis, he would write almost 600 of them, a prodigious output, to be sure — but not merely in terms of quantity. In his unflinching honesty and vision — tempered but never undone by gentleness — Chekhov is for many readers inarguably *the* master of the short story, and his influence on writers across the decades of the twentieth century is impossible to overestimate. Amazingly, he left his indelible mark not only on fiction: toward the end of his life he wrote four great plays   *The Sea Gull* (1895), *Uncle Vanya* (1900), *The Three Sisters* (1901), and *The Cherry Orchard* (1904) — which changed forever the course of modern theater. Chekhov's work, fiction and drama alike, goes to the heart of "the tragedy of life's trivialities." An unflagging commitment to realism was his hallmark; given it, his writing is often, but never mawkishly, sad. He once wrote that the business of the artist is that of "stating a problem correctly" — not solving it. In the two stories here, "Gooseberries" and "The Lady with the Pet Dog," the problem is stated unforgettably.

Gooseberries

Translated from the Russian by Ivy Litvinov

The sky had been covered with rain-clouds ever since the early morning; it was a still day, cool and dull, one of those misty days when the clouds have long been lowering overhead and you keep thinking it is just going to rain, and the rain holds off. Ivan Ivanich, the veterinary surgeon, and Burkin, the high-school teacher, had walked till they were tired, and the way over the fields seemed endless to them. Far ahead they could just make out the windmill of the village of Mironositskoye, and what looked like a range of low hills at the right extending well beyond the village, and they both knew that this range was really the bank of the river, and that further on were meadows, green willow-trees, country-estates; if they were on top of these hills, they knew they would see the same boundless fields and telegraph-posts, and the train, like a crawling caterpillar in the distance, while in fine weather even the town would be visible. On this still day, when the whole of nature seemed kindly and pensive, Ivan Ivanich and Burkin felt a surge of love for this plain, and thought how vast and beautiful their country was.

"The last time we stayed in Elder Prokofy's hut," said Burkin, "you said you had a story to tell me."

"Yes. I wanted to tell you the story of my brother."

Ivan Ivanich took a deep breath and lighted his pipe as a preliminary to his narrative, but just then the rain came. Five minutes later it was coming down in torrents and nobody could say when it would stop. Ivan Ivanich and Burkin stood still, lost in thought. The dogs, already soaked, stood with drooping tails, gazing at them wistfully.

"We must try and find shelter," said Burkin. "Let's go to Alekhin's. It's quite near."

"Come on, then."

They turned aside and walked straight across the newly reaped field, veering to the right till they came to a road. Very soon poplars, an orchard, and the red roofs of barns came into sight. The surface of a river gleamed, and they had a view of an extensive reach of water, a windmill and a whitewashed bathing-shed. This was Sofyino, where Alekhin lived.

The mill was working, and the noise made by its sails drowned the sound of the rain; the whole dam trembled. Horses, soaking wet, were standing near some carts, their heads drooping, and people were moving about with sacks over their heads and shoulders. It was wet, muddy, bleak, and the water looked cold and sinister. Ivan Ivanich and Burkin were already experiencing the misery of dampness, dirt, physical discomfort, their boots were caked with mud, and when, having passed the mill-dam, they took the upward path to the landowner's barns, they fell silent, as if vexed with one another.

The sound of winnowing came from one of the barns; the door was open, and clouds of dust issued from it. Standing in the door-way was Alekhin himself, a stout man of some forty years, with longish hair, looking more like a professor or an artist than a landed proprietor. He was wearing a white shirt, greatly in need of washing, belted with a piece of string, and long drawers with no trousers over them. His boots, too, were caked with mud and straw. His eyes and nose were ringed with dust. He recognized Ivan Ivanich and Burkin, and seemed glad to see them.

"Go up to the house, gentlemen," he said, smiling. "I'll be with you in a minute."

It was a large two-storey house. Alekhin occupied the ground floor, two rooms with vaulted ceilings and tiny windows, where the stewards had lived formerly. They were poorly furnished, and smelled of rye-bread, cheap vodka, and harness. He hardly ever went into the upstairs rooms, excepting when he had guests. Ivan Ivanich and Burkin were met by a maid-servant, a young woman of such beauty that they stood still involuntarily and exchanged glances.

"You have no idea how glad I am to see you here, dear friends," said Alekhin, overtaking them in the hall. "It's quite a surprise! Pelageya," he said, turning to the maid, "find the gentlemen a change of clothes. And I might as well change, myself. But I must have a wash first, for I don't believe I've had a bath since the spring. Wouldn't you like to go and have a bathe while they get things ready here?"

The beauteous Pelageya, looking very soft and delicate, brought them towels and soap, and Alekhin and his guests set off for the bathing-house.

"Yes, it's a long time since I had a wash," he said, taking off his clothes. "As you see I have a nice bathing-place, my father had it built, but somehow I never seem to get time to wash."

He sat on the step, soaping his long locks and his neck, and all round him the water was brown.

"Yes, you certainly . . ." remarked Ivan Ivanich, with a significant glance at his host's head.

"It's a long time since I had a wash . . ." repeated Alekhin, somewhat abashed, and he soaped himself again, and now the water was dark-blue, like ink.

Ivan Ivanich emerged from the shed, splashed noisily into the water, and began swimming beneath the rain, spreading his arms wide, making waves all round him, and the white water-lilies rocked on the waves he made. He swam into the very middle of the river and then dived, a moment later came up at another place and swam further, diving constantly, and trying to touch the bottom. "Ah, my God," he kept exclaiming in his enjoyment. "Ah, my God. . . ." He swam up to the mill, had a little talk with some peasants there and turned back, but when he got to the middle of the river, he floated, holding his face up to the rain. Burkin and Alekhin were dressed and ready to go, but he went on swimming and diving.

"God! God!" he kept exclaiming. "Dear God!"

"Come out!" Burkin shouted to him.

They went back to the house. And only after the lamp was lit in the great drawing-room on the upper floor, and Burkin and Ivan Ivanich, in silk dressing-gowns and warm slippers, were seated in arm-chairs, while Alekhin, washed and combed, paced the room in his new frock-coat, enjoying the warmth, the cleanliness, his dry clothes and comfortable slippers, while the fair Pelageya, smiling benevolently, stepped noiselessly over the carpet with her tray of tea and preserves, did Ivan Ivanich embark upon his yarn, the ancient dames, young ladies, and military gentlemen looking down at them severely from the gilded frames, as if they, too, were listening.

"There were two of us brothers," he began. "Ivan Ivanich (me), and my brother Nikolai Ivanich, two years younger than myself. I went in for learning and became a veterinary surgeon, but Nikolai started working in a government office when he was only nineteen. Our father, Chimsha-Himalaisky, was educated in a school for the sons of private soldiers, but was later promoted to officer's rank, and was made a hereditary nobleman and given a small estate. After his death the estate had to be sold for debts, but at least our childhood was passed in the freedom of the countryside, where we roamed the fields and the woods like peasant children, taking the horses to graze, peeling bark from the trunks of lime-trees, fishing, and all that sort of thing. And anyone who has once in his life fished for perch, or watched the thrushes fly south in the autumn, rising high over the village on clear, cool days, is spoilt for town life, and will long for the country-side for the rest of his days. My brother pined in his government office. The years passed and he sat in the same place every day, writing out the same documents and thinking all the time of the same thing — how to get back to the country. And these longings of his gradually turned into a definite desire, into a dream of purchasing a little estate somewhere on the bank of a river or the shore of a lake.

"He was a meek, good-natured chap, I was fond of him, but could feel no sympathy with the desire to lock oneself up for life in an estate of one's own. They say man only needs six feet of earth. But it is a corpse, and not man, which needs these six feet. And now people are actually saying that it is a good sign for our intellectuals to yearn for the land and try to obtain country-dwellings. And yet these estates are nothing but those same six feet of earth. To escape from the town, from the struggle, from the noise of life, to escape and hide one's head on a country-estate, is not life, but egoism, idleness, it is a sort of renunciation, but renunciation without faith. It is not six feet of earth, not a country-estate, that man needs, but the whole globe, the whole of nature, room to display his qualities and the individual characteristics of his soul.

"My brother Nikolai sat at his office-desk, dreaming of eating soup made from his own cabbages, which would spread a delicious smell all over his own yard, of eating out of doors, on the green grass, of sleeping in the sun, sitting for hours on a bench outside his gate, and gazing at the fields and woods. Books on agriculture, and all those hints printed on calendars were his delight, his favourite spiritual nourishment. He was fond of reading newspapers, too, but all he read in them was advertisements of the sale of so many acres of arable and meadowland, with residence attached, a river, an orchard, a mill, and ponds fed by springs. His head was full of visions of garden paths, flowers, fruit, nesting-boxes, carp-ponds, and all that sort of thing. These visions differed according to the advertisements he came across, but for some reason gooseberry bushes invariably figured in them. He could not picture to himself a single estate or picturesque nook that did not have gooseberry bushes in it.

" 'Country life has its conveniences,' he would say: 'You sit on the verandah, drinking tea, with your own ducks floating on the pond, and everything smells so nice, and . . . and the gooseberries ripen on the bushes.'

"He drew up plans for his estate, and every plan showed the same features: a) the main residence, b) the servant's wing, c) the kitchen-garden, d) gooseberry bushes. He lived thriftily, never ate or drank his fill, dressed anyhow, like a beggar, and saved up all his money in the bank. He became terribly stingy. I could hardly bear to look at him, and whenever I gave him a little money, or sent him a present on some holiday, he put that away, too. Once a man gets an idea into his head, there's no doing anything with him.

"The years passed, he was sent to another gubernia, he was over forty, and was still reading advertisements in the papers, and saving up. At last I heard he had married. All for the same purpose, to buy himself an estate with gooseberry bushes on it, he married an ugly elderly widow, for whom he had not the slightest affection, just because she had some money. After his marriage he went on living as thriftily as ever, half-starving his wife, and putting her money in his own bank account. Her first husband had been a postmaster, and she was used to pies and cordials, but with her second husband she did not even get enough black bread to eat. She began to languish under such a regime, and three years later yielded up her soul to God. Of course my brother did not for a moment consider himself guilty of her death. Money, like vodka, makes a man eccentric. There was a merchant in our town who asked for a plate of honey on his deathbed and ate up all his bank-notes and lottery tickets with the honey, so that no one else should get it. And one day when I was examining a consignment of cattle at a railway station, a drover fell under the engine and his leg was severed from his body. We carried him all bloody into the waiting-room, a terrible sight, and he did nothing but beg us to look for his leg, worrying all the time — there were twenty rubles in the boot, and he was afraid they would be lost."

"You're losing the thread," put in Burkin.

Ivan Ivanich paused for a moment, and went on: "After his wife's death my brother began to look about for an estate. You can search for five years, of course, and in the end make a mistake, and buy something quite different from what you dreamed of. My brother Nikolai bought three hundred acres, complete with gentleman's house, servants' quarters, and a park, as well as a mortgage to be paid through an agent, but there were neither an orchard, gooseberry bushes, nor a pond with ducks on it. There was a river, but it was as dark as coffee, owing to the fact that there was a brick-works on one side of the estate, and bone-kilns on the other. Nothing daunted, however, my brother Nikolai Ivanich ordered two dozen gooseberry bushes and settled down as a landed proprietor.

"Last year I paid him a visit. I thought I would go and see how he was getting on there. In his letters my brother gave his address as Chumbaroklova Pustosh or Himalaiskoye. I arrived at Himalaiskoye in the afternoon. It was very hot. Everywhere were ditches, fences, hedges, rows of fir-trees, and it was hard to drive into the yard and find a place to leave one's carriage. As I went a fat ginger-coloured dog, remarkably like a pig, came out to meet me. It looked as if it would have barked if it were not so lazy. The cook, who was also fat and like a pig, came out of the kitchen, barefoot, and said her master was having his after-dinner rest. I made my way to my brother's room, and found him sitting up in bed, his knees covered by a blanket. He had aged, and grown stout and flabby. His cheeks, nose and lips protruded — I almost expected him to grunt into the blanket.

"We embraced and wept — tears of joy, mingled with melancholy — because we had once been young and were now both grey-haired and approaching the grave. He put on his clothes and went out to show me over his estate.

" 'Well, how are you getting on here?' I asked.

" 'All right, thanks be, I'm enjoying myself.'

"He was no longer the poor, timid clerk, but a true proprietor, a gentleman. He had settled down, and was entering with zest into country life. He ate a lot, washed in the bathhouse, and put on flesh. He had already got into litigation with the village commune, the brick-works and the bone-kilns, and took offence if the peasants failed to call him 'Your Honour.' He went in for religion in a solid, gentlemanly way, and there was nothing casual about his pretentious good works. And what were these good works? He treated all the diseases of the peasants with bicarbonate of soda and castor-oil, and had a special thanksgiving service held on his name-day, after which he provided half a pail of vodka, supposing that this was the right thing to do. Oh, those terrible half pails! Today the fat landlord hauls the peasants before the Zemstvo representative for letting their sheep graze on his land, tomorrow, on the day of rejoicing, he treats them to half a pail of vodka, and they drink and sing and shout hurrah, prostrating themselves before him when they are drunk. Any improvement in his conditions, anything like satiety or idleness, develops the most insolent complacency in a Russian. Nikolai Ivanich, who had been afraid of having an opinion of his own when he was in the government service, was now continually coming out with axioms, in the most ministerial manner: 'Education is essential, but the people are not ready for it yet,' 'corporal punishment is an evil, but in certain cases it is beneficial and indispensable.'

" 'I know the people and I know how to treat them,' he said. 'The people love me. I only have to lift my little finger, and the people will do whatever I want.'

"And all this, mark you, with a wise, indulgent smile. Over and over again he repeated: 'We the gentry,' or 'speaking as a gentleman,' and seemed to have quite forgotten that our grandfather was a peasant, and our father a common soldier. Our very surname — Chimsha-Himalaisky — in reality so absurd, now seemed to him a resounding, distinguished, and euphonious name.

"But it is of myself, and not of him, that I wish to speak. I should like to describe to you the change which came over me in those few hours I spent on my brother's estate. As we were drinking tea in the evening, the cook brought us a full plate of gooseberries. These were not gooseberries bought for money, they came from his own garden, and were the first fruits of the bushes he had planted. Nikolai Ivanich broke into a laugh and gazed at the gooseberries, in tearful silence for at least five minutes. Speechless with emotion, he popped a single gooseberry into his mouth, darted at me the triumphant glance of a child who has at last gained possession of a longed-for toy, and said:

" 'Delicious!'

'And he ate them greedily, repeating over and over again:

" 'Simply delicious! You try them.'

"They were hard and sour, but, as Pushkin says: 'The lie which elates us is dearer than a thousand sober truths.' I saw before me a really happy man, one whose dearest wish had come true, who had achieved his aim in life, got what he wanted, and was content with his lot and with himself. There had always been a tinge of melancholy in my conception of human happiness, and now, confronted by a happy man, I was overcome by a feeling of sadness bordering on desperation. This feeling grew strongest of all in the night. A bed was made up for me in the room next to my brother's bedroom, and I could hear him moving about restlessly, every now and then getting up to take a gooseberry from a plate. How many happy, satisfied people there are, after all, I said to myself! What an overwhelming force! Just consider this life — the insolence and idleness of the strong, the ignorance and bestiality of the weak, all around intolerable poverty, cramped dwellings, degeneracy, drunkenness, hypocrisy, lying. . . . And yet peace and order apparently prevail in all those homes and in the streets. Of the fifty thousand inhabitants of a town, not one will be found to cry out, to proclaim his indignation aloud. We see those who go to the market to buy food, who eat in the day-time and sleep at night, who prattle away, marry, grow old, carry their dead to the cemeteries. But we neither hear nor see those who suffer, and the terrible things in life are played out behind the scenes. All is calm and quiet, only statistics, which are dumb, protest: so many have gone mad, so many barrels of drink have been consumed, so many children died of malnutrition. . . . And apparently this is as it should be. Apparently those who are happy can only enjoy themselves because the unhappy bear their burdens in silence, and but for this silence happiness would be impossible. It is a kind of universal hypnosis. There ought to be a man with a hammer behind the door of every happy man, to remind him by his constant knocks that there are unhappy people, and that happy as he himself may be, life will sooner or later show him its claws, catastrophe will overtake him —sickness, poverty, loss — and nobody will see it, just as he now neither sees nor hears the misfortunes of others. But there is no man with a hammer, the happy man goes on living and the petty vicissitudes of life touch him lightly, like the wind in an aspen-tree, and all is well.

"That night I understood that I, too, was happy and content," continued Ivan Ivanich, getting up. "I, too, while out hunting, or at the dinner table, have held forth on the right way to live, to worship, to manage the people. I, too, have declared that without knowledge there can be no light, that education is essential, but that bare literacy is sufficient for the common people. Freedom is a blessing, I have said, one can't get on without it, any more than without air, but we must wait. Yes, that is what

I said, and now I ask: In the name of what must we wait?" Here Ivan Ivanich looked angrily at Burkin. "In the name of what must we wait, I ask you. What is there to be considered? Don't be in such a hurry, they tell me, every idea materializes gradually, in its own time. But who are they who say this? What is the proof that it is just? You refer to the natural order of things, to the logic of facts, but according to what order, what logic do I, a living, thinking individual, stand on the edge of a ditch and wait for it to be gradually filled up, or choked with silt, when I might leap across it or build a bridge over it? And again, in the name of what must we wait? Wait, when we have not the strength to live, though live we must and to live we desire!

"I left my brother early the next morning, and ever since I have found town life intolerable. The peace and order weigh on my spirits, and I am afraid to look into windows, because there is now no sadder spectacle for me than a happy family seated around the tea-table. I am old and unfit for the struggle, I am even incapable of feeling hatred. I can only suffer inwardly, and give way to irritation and annoyance, at night my head burns from the rush of thoughts, and I am unable to sleep. . . . Oh, if only I were young!"

Ivan Ivanich began pacing backwards and forwards, repeating:

"If only I were young still!"

Suddenly he went up to Alekhin and began pressing first one of his hands, and then the other.

"Pavel Konstantinich," he said in imploring accents. "Don't *you* fall into apathy, don't *you* let your conscience be lulled to sleep! While you are still young, strong, active, do not be weary of well-doing. There is no such thing as happiness, nor ought there to be, but if there is any sense or purpose in life, this sense and purpose are to be found not in our own happiness, but in something greater and more rational. Do good!"

Ivan Ivanich said all this with a piteous, imploring smile, as if he were asking for something for himself.

Then they all three sat in their arm-chairs a long way apart from one another, and said nothing. Ivan Ivanich's story satisfied neither Burkin or Alekhin. It was not interesting to listen to the story of a poor clerk who ate gooseberries, when from the walls generals and fine ladies, who seemed to come to life in the dark, were looking down from their gilded frames. It would have been much more interesting to hear about elegant people, lovely women. And the fact that they were sitting in a drawing-room in which everything — the swathed chandeliers, the arm-chairs, the carpet on the floor, proved that the people now looking out of the frames had once moved about here, sat in the chairs, drunk tea, where the fair Pelageya was now going noiselessly to and fro, was better than any story.

Alekhin was desperately sleepy. He had got up early, at three o'clock in the morning, to go about his work on the estate, and could now hardly keep his eyes open. But he would not go to bed, for fear one of his guests would relate something interesting after he was gone. He could not be sure whether what Ivan Ivanich had just told them was wise or just, but his visitors talked of other things besides grain, hay, or tar, of things which had no direct bearing on his daily life, and he liked this, and wanted them to go on. . . .

"Well, time to go to bed," said Burkin, getting up. "Allow me to wish you a good night."

Alekhin said good night and went downstairs to his own room, the visitors remaining on the upper floor. They were allotted a big room for the night, in which were two ancient bedsteads of carved wood, and an ivory crucifix in one corner. There was a pleasant smell of freshly laundered sheets from the wide, cool beds which the fair Pelageya made up for them.

Ivan Ivanich undressed in silence and lay down.

"Lord have mercy on us, sinners," he said, and covered his head with the sheet.

There was a strong smell of stale tobacco from his pipe, which he put on the table, and Burkin lay awake a long time, wondering where the stifling smell came from.

The rain tapped on the window-panes all night.

ANTON CHEKHOV

The Lady with the Pet Dog

Translated from the Russian by Avrahm Yarmolinsky

1

A new person, it was said, had appeared on the esplanade: a lady with a pet dog. Dmitry Dmitrich Gurov, who had spent a fortnight at Yalta and had got used to the place, had also begun to take an interest in new arrivals. As he sat in Vernet's confectionery shop, he saw, walking on the esplanade, a fair-haired young woman of medium height, wearing a beret; a white Pomeranian was trotting behind her.

And afterwards he met her in the public garden and in the square several times a day. She walked alone, always wearing the same beret and always with the white dog; no one knew who she was and everyone called her simply "the lady with the pet dog."

"If she is here alone without husband or friends," Gurov reflected, "it wouldn't be a bad thing to make her acquaintance."

He was under forty, but he already had a daughter twelve years old, and two sons at school. They had found a wife for him when he was very young, a student in his second year, and by now she seemed half as old again as he. She was a tall, erect woman with dark eyebrows, stately and dignified and, as she said of herself, intellectual. She read a great deal, used simplified spelling in her letters, called her husband, not Dmitry, but Dimitry, while he privately considered her of limited intelligence, narrow-minded, dowdy, was afraid of her, and did not like to be at home. He had begun being unfaithful to her long ago — had been unfaithful to her often and, probably for that reason, almost always spoke ill of women, and when they were talked of in his presence used to call them "the inferior race."

It seemed to him that he had been sufficiently tutored by bitter experience to call them what he pleased, and yet he could not have lived without "the inferior race" for two days together. In the company of men he was bored and ill at ease, he was chilly and uncommunicative with them; but when he was among women he felt free, and knew what to speak to them about and how to comport himself; and even to be silent with them was no strain on him. In his appearance, in his character, in his whole make-up there was something attractive and elusive that disposed women in his favor and allured them. He knew that, and some force seemed to draw him to them, too.

Oft-repeated and really bitter experience had taught him long ago that with decent people — particularly Moscow people — who are irresolute and slow to move, every affair which at first seems a light and charming adventure inevitably grows into a whole problem of extreme complexity, and in the end a painful situation is created.

But at every new meeting with an interesting woman this lesson of experience seemed to slip from his memory, and he was eager for life, and everything seemed so simple and diverting.

One evening while he was dining in the public garden the lady in the beret walked up without haste to take the next table. Her expression, her gait, her dress, and the way she did her hair told him that she belonged to the upper class, that she was married, that she was in Yalta for the first time and alone, and that she was bored there. The stories told of the immorality in Yalta are to a great extent untrue; he despised them, and knew that such stories were made up for the most part by persons who would have been glad to sin themselves if they had had the chance; but when the lady sat down at the next table three paces from him, he recalled these stories of easy conquests, of trips to the mountains, and the tempting thought of a swift, fleeting liaison, a romance with an unknown woman of whose very name he was ignorant, suddenly took hold of him.

He beckoned invitingly to the Pomeranian, and when the dog approached him, shook his finger at it. The Pomeranian growled; Gurov threatened it again.

The lady glanced at him and at once dropped her eyes.

"He doesn't bite," she said and blushed.

"May I give him a bone?" he asked; and when she nodded he inquired affably, "Have you been in Yalta long?"

"About five days."

"And I am dragging out the second week here."

There was a short silence.

"Time passes quickly, and yet it is so dull here!" she said, not looking at him.

"It's only the fashion to say it's dull here. A provincial will live in Belyov or Zhizdra and not be bored, but when he comes here it is 'Oh, the dullness! Oh, the dust!' One would think he came from Granada."

She laughed. Then both continued eating in silence, like strangers, but after dinner they walked together and there sprang up between them the light banter of people who are free and contented, to whom it does not matter where they go or what they talk about. They walked and talked of the strange light on the sea: the water was a soft, warm, lilac color, and there was a golden band of moonlight upon it. They talked of how sultry it was after a hot day. Gurov told her that he was a native of Moscow, that he had studied languages and literature at the university, but had a post in a bank; that at one time he had trained to become an opera singer but had given it up, that he owned two houses in Moscow. And he learned from her that she had grown up in Petersburg, but had lived in S—— since her marriage two years previously, that she was going to stay in Yalta for about another month, and that her husband, who needed a rest, too, might perhaps come to fetch her. She was not certain whether her husband was a member of a Government Board or served on a Zemstvo Council, and this amused her. And Gurov learned too that her name was Anna Sergeyevna.

Afterwards in his room at the hotel he thought about her — and was certain that he would meet her the next day. It was bound to happen. Getting into bed he recalled that she had been a schoolgirl only recently, doing lessons like his own daughter; he thought how much timidity and angularity there was still in her laugh and her manner of talking with a stranger. It must have been the first time in her life that she was alone in a setting in which she was followed, looked at, and spoken to for one secret purpose alone, which she could hardly fail to guess. He thought of her slim, delicate throat, her lovely gray eyes.

"There's something pathetic about her, though," he thought, and dropped off.

2

A week had passed since they had struck up an acquaintance. It was a holiday. It was close indoors, while in the street the wind whirled the dust about and blew people's hats off. One was thirsty all day, and Gurov often went into the restaurant and offered Anna Sergeyevna a soft drink or ice cream. One did not know what to do with oneself.

In the evening when the wind had abated they went out on the pier to watch the steamer come in. There were a great many people walking about the dock; they had come to welcome someone and they were carrying bunches of flowers. And two peculiarities of a festive Yalta crowd stood out: the elderly ladies were dressed like young ones and there were many generals.

Owing to the choppy sea, the steamer arrived late, after sunset, and it was a long time tacking about before it put in at the pier. Anna Sergeyevna peered at the steamer and the passengers through her lorgnette as though looking for acquaintances, and whenever she turned to Gurov her eyes were shining. She talked a great deal and asked questions jerkily, forgetting the next moment what she had asked; then she lost her lorgnette in the crush.

The festive crowd began to disperse; it was now too dark to see people's faces; there was no wind any more, but Gurov and Anna Sergeyevna still stood as though waiting to see someone else come off the steamer. Anna Sergeyevna was silent now, and sniffed her flowers without looking at Gurov.

"The weather has improved this evening," he said. "Where shall we go now? Shall we drive somewhere?"

She did not reply.

Then he looked at her intently, and suddenly embraced her and kissed her on the lips, and the moist fragrance of her flowers enveloped him; and at once he looked round him anxiously, wondering if anyone had seen them.

"Let us go to your place," he said softly. And they walked off together rapidly.

The air in her room was close and there was the smell of the perfume she had bought at the Japanese shop. Looking at her, Gurov thought: "What encounters life offers!" From the past he preserved the memory of carefree, good-natured women whom love made gay and who were grateful to him for the happiness he gave them, however brief it might be; and of women like his wife who loved without sincerity, with too many words, affectedly, hysterically, with an expression that it was not love or passion that engaged them but something more significant; and of two or three others, very beautiful, frigid women, across whose faces would suddenly flit a rapacious expression — an obstinate desire to take from life more than it could give, and these were women no longer young, capricious, unreflecting, domineering, unintelligent, and when Gurov grew cold to them their beauty aroused his hatred, and the lace on their lingerie seemed to him to resemble scales.

But here there was the timidity, the angularity of inexperienced youth, a feeling of awkwardness; and there was a sense of embarrassment, as though someone had suddenly knocked at the door. Anna Sergeyevna, "the lady with the pet dog," treated what had happened in a peculiar way, very seriously, as though it were her fall — so it seemed, and this was odd and inappropriate. Her features drooped and faded, and her long hair hung down sadly on either side of her face; she grew pensive and her dejected pose was that of a Magdalene in a picture by an old master.

"It's not right," she said. "You don't respect me now, you first of all."

There was a watermelon on the table. Gurov cut himself a slice and began eating it without haste. They were silent for at least half an hour.

There was something touching about Anna Sergeyevna; she had the purity of a well-bred, naive woman who has seen little of life. The single candle burning on the table barely illumined her face, yet it was clear that she was unhappy.

"Why should I stop respecting you, darling?" asked Gurov. "You don't know what you're saying."

"God forgive me," she said, and her eyes filled with tears. "It's terrible."

"It's as though you were trying to exonerate yourself."

"How can I exonerate myself? No. I am a bad, low woman; I despise myself and I have no thought of exonerating myself. It's not my husband but myself I have deceived. And not only just now; I have been deceiving myself for a long time. My husband may be a good, honest man, but he is a flunkey! I don't know what he does, what his work is, but I know he is a flunkey! I was twenty when I married him. I was tormented by curiosity; I wanted something better. 'There must be a different sort of life,' I said to myself. I wanted to live! To live, to live! Curiosity kept eating at me — you don't understand it, but I swear to God I could no longer control myself; something was going on in me; I could not be held back. I told my husband I was ill, and came here. And here I have been walking about as though in a daze, as though I were mad; and now I have become a vulgar, vile woman whom anyone may despise."

Gurov was already bored with her; he was irritated by her naive tone, by her repentance, so unexpected and so out of place, but for the tears in her eyes he might have thought she was joking or play-acting.

"I don't understand, my dear," he said softly. "What do you want?"

She hid her face on his breast and pressed close to him.

"Believe me, believe me, I beg you," she said, "I love honestly and purity, and sin is loathsome to me; I don't know what I'm doing. Simple people say, 'The Evil One has led me astray.' And I may say of myself now that the Evil One has led me astray."

"Quiet, quiet," he murmured.

He looked into her fixed, frightened eyes, kissed her, spoke to her softly and affectionately, and by degrees she calmed down, and her gaiety returned; both began laughing.

Afterwards when they went out there was not a soul on the esplanade. The town with its cypresses looked quite dead, but the sea was still sounding as it broke upon the beach; a single launch was rocking on the waves and on it a lantern was blinking sleepily.

They found a cab and drove to Oreanda.

"I found out your surname in the hall just now: it was written on the board — von Dideritz," said Gurov. "Is your husband German?"

"No; I believe his grandfather was German, but he is Greek Orthodox himself."

At Oreanda they sat on a bench not far from the church, looked down at the sea, and were silent. Yalta was barely visible through the morning mist; white clouds rested motionlessly on the mountaintops. The leaves did not stir on the trees, cicadas twanged, and the monotonous muffled sound of the sea that rose from below spoke of the peace, the eternal sleep awaiting us. So it rumbled below when there was no Yalta, no Oreanda here; so it rumbles now, and it will rumble as indifferently and as hollowly when we are no more. And in this constancy, in this complete indifference to the life and death of each of us, there lies, perhaps, a pledge of our eternal salvation, of the unceasing advance of life upon earth, of unceasing movement towards perfection. Sitting beside a young woman who in the dawn seemed so lovely, Gurov, soothed and spellbound by these magical surroundings — the sea, the mountains, the clouds, the wide sky — thought how everything is really beautiful in this world when one reflects: everything except what we think or do ourselves when we forget the higher aims of life and our own human dignity.

A man strolled up to them — probably a guard — looked at them and walked away. And this detail, too, seemed so mysterious and beautiful. They saw a steamer arrive from Feodosia, its lights extinguished in the glow of dawn.

"There is dew on the grass," said Anna Sergeyevna, after a silence.

"Yes, it's time to go home."

They returned to the city.

Then they met every day at twelve o'clock on the esplanade, lunched and dined together, took walks, admired the sea. She complained that she slept badly, that she had palpitations, asked the same questions, troubled now by jealousy and now by the fear that he did not respect her sufficiently. And often in the square or the public garden, when there was no one near them, he suddenly drew her to him and kissed her passionately. Complete idleness, these kisses in broad daylight exchanged furtively in dread of someone's seeing them, the heat, the smell of the sea, and the continual flitting before his eyes of idle, well-dressed, well-fed people, worked a complete change in him; he kept telling Anna Sergeyevna how beautiful she was, how seductive, was urgently passionate; he would not move a step away from her, while she was often pensive and continually pressed him to confess that he did not respect her, did not love her in the least, and saw in her nothing but a common woman. Almost every evening rather late they drove somewhere out of town, to Oreanda or to the waterfall; and the excursion was always a success, the scenery invariably impressed them as beautiful and magnificent.

They were expecting her husband, but a letter came from him saying that he had eye-trouble, and begging his wife to return home as soon as possible. Anna Sergeyevna made haste to go.

"It's a good thing I am leaving," she said to Gurov. "It's the hand of Fate!"

She took a carriage to the railway station, and he went with her. They were driving the whole day. When she had taken her place in the express, and when the second bell had rung, she said, "Let me look at you once more — let me look at you again. Like this."

She was not crying but was so sad that she seemed ill and her face was quivering.

"I shall be thinking of you — remembering you," she said. "God bless you; be happy. Don't remember evil against me. We are parting forever — it has to be, for we ought never to have met. Well, God bless you."

The train moved off rapidly, its lights soon vanished, and a minute later there was no sound of it, as though everything had conspired to end as quickly as possible that sweet trance, that madness. Left alone on the platform, and gazing into the dark distance, Gurov listened to the twang of the grasshoppers and the hum of the telegraph wires, feeling as though he had just waked up. And he reflected, musing, that there had now been another episode or adventure in his life, and it, too, was at an end, and nothing was left of it but a memory. He was moved, sad, and slightly remorseful: this young woman whom he would never meet again had not been happy with him; he had been warm and affectionate with her, but yet in his manner, his tone, and his caresses there had been a shade of light irony, the slightly coarse arrogance of a happy male who was, besides, almost twice her age. She had constantly called him kind, exceptional, high-minded; obviously he had seemed to her different from what he really was, so he had involuntarily deceived her.

Here at the station there was already a scent of autumn in the air; it was a chilly evening.

"It is time for me to go north, too," thought Gurov as he left the platform. "High time!"

3

At home in Moscow the winter routine was already established; the stoves were heated, and in the morning it was still dark when the children were having breakfast and getting ready for school, and the nurse would light the lamp for a short time. There were frosts already. When the first snow falls, on the first day the sleighs are out, it is pleasant to see the white earth, the white roofs; one draws easy, delicious breaths, and the season brings back the days of one's youth. The old limes and birches, white with hoar-frost, have a good-natured look; they are closer to one's heart than cypresses and palms, and near them one no longer wants to think of mountains and the sea.

Gurov, a native of Moscow, arrived there on a fine frosty day, and when he put on his fur coat and warm gloves and took a walk along Petrovka, and when on Saturday night he heard the bells ringing, his recent trip and the places he had visited lost all charm for him. Little by little he became immersed in Moscow life, greedily read three newspapers a day, and declared that he did not read the Moscow papers on principle. He already felt a longing for restaurants, clubs, formal dinners, anniversary celebrations, and it flattered him to entertain distinguished lawyers and actors, and to play cards with a professor at the physicians' club. He could eat a whole portion of meat stewed with pickled cabbage and served in a pan, Moscow style.

A month or so would pass and the image of Anna Sergeyevna, it seemed to him, would become misty in his memory, and only from time to time he would dream of her with her touching smile as he dreamed of others. But more than a month went by, winter came into its own, and everything was still clear in his memory as though he had parted from Anna Sergeyevna only yesterday. And his memories glowed more and more vividly. When in the evening stillness the voices of his children preparing their lessons reached his study, or when he listened to a song or to an organ playing in a restaurant, or when the storm howled in the chimney, suddenly everything would rise up in his memory; what had happened on the pier and the early morning with the mist on the mountains, and the steamer coming from Feodosia, and the kisses. He would pace about his room a long time, remembering and smiling; then his memories passed into reveries, and in his imagination the past would mingle with what was to come. He did not dream of Anna Sergeyevna, but she followed him about everywhere and watched him. When he shut his eyes he saw her before him as though she were there in the flesh, and she seemed to him lovelier, younger, tenderer than she had been, and he imagined himself a finer man than he had been in Yalta. Of evenings she peered out at him from the bookcase, from the fireplace, from the corner — he heard her breathing, the caressing rustle of her clothes. In the street he followed the women with his eyes, looking for someone who resembled her.

Already he was tormented by a strong desire to share his memories with someone. But in his home it was impossible to talk of his love, and he had no one to talk to outside; certainly he could not confide in his tenants or in anyone at the bank. And what was there to talk about? He hadn't loved her then, had he? Had there been anything beautiful, poetical, edifying, or simply interesting in his relations with Anna Sergeyevna? And he was forced to talk vaguely of love, of women, and no one guessed what he meant; only his wife would twitch her black eyebrows and say, "The part of a philanderer does not suit you at all, Dimitry."

One evening, coming out of the physicians' club with an official with whom he had been playing cards, he could not resist saying:

"If you only knew what a fascinating woman I became acquainted with at Yalta!"

The official got into his sledge and was driving away, but turned suddenly and shouted:

"Dmitry Dmitrich!"

"What is it?"

"You were right this evening: the sturgeon was a bit high."

These words, so commonplace, for some reason moved Gurov to indignation, and struck him as degrading and unclean. What savage manners, what mugs! What stupid nights, what dull, humdrum days! Frenzied gambling, gluttony, drunkenness, continual talk always about the same thing! Futile pursuits and conversations always about the same topics take up the better part of one's time, the better part of one's strength, and in the end there is left a life clipped and wingless, an absurd mess, and there is no escaping or getting away from it — just as though one were in a madhouse or a prison.

Gurov, boiling with indignation, did not sleep all night. And he had a headache all the next day. And the following nights too he slept badly; he sat up in bed, thinking, or paced up and down his room. He was fed up with his children, fed up with the bank; he had no desire to go anywhere or to talk of anything.

In December during the holidays he prepared to take a trip and told his wife he was going to Petersburg to do what he could for a young friend — and he set off for S——. What for? He did not know, himself. He wanted to see Anna Sergeyevna and talk with her, to arrange a rendezvous if possible.

He arrived at S—— in the morning, and at the hotel took the best room, in which the floor was covered with gray army cloth, and on the table there was an inkstand, gray with dust and topped by a figure on horseback; its hat in its raised hand and its head broken off. The porter gave him the necessary information: von Dideritz lived in a house of his own on Staro-Goncharnaya Street, not far from the hotel; he was rich and lived well and kept his own horses; everyone in the town knew him. The porter pronounced the name: "Dridiritz."

Without haste Gurov made his way to Staro-Goncharnaya Street and found the house. Directly opposite the house stretched a long gray fence studded with nails.

"A fence like that would make one run away," thought Gurov, looking now at the fence, now at the windows of the house.

He reflected: this was a holiday, and the husband was apt to be at home. And in any case, it would be tactless to go into the house and disturb her. If he were to send her a note, it might fall into her husband's hands, and that might spoil everything. The best thing was to rely on chance. And he kept walking up and down the street and along the fence, waiting for the chance. He saw a beggar go in at the gate and heard the dogs attack him; then an hour later he heard a piano, and the sound came to him faintly and indistinctly. Probably it was Anna Sergeyevna playing. The front door opened suddenly, and an old woman came out, followed by the familiar white Pomeranian. Gurov was on the point of calling to the dog, but his heart began beating violently, and in his excitement he could not remember the Pomeranian's name.

He kept walking up and down, and hated the gray fence more and more, and by now he thought irritably that Anna Sergeyevna had forgotten him, and was perhaps already diverting herself with another man, and that that was very natural in a young woman who from morning till night had to look at that damn fence. He went back to his hotel room and sat on the couch for a long while, not knowing what to do, then he had dinner and a long nap.

"How stupid and annoying all this is!" he thought when he woke and looked at the dark windows: it was already evening. "Here I've had a good sleep for some reason. What am I going to do at night?"

He sat on the bed, which was covered with a cheap gray blanket of the kind seen in hospitals, and he twitted himself in his vexation:

"So there's your lady with the pet dog. There's your adventure. A nice place to cool your heels in."

That morning at the station a playbill in large letters had caught his eye. *The Geisha* was to be given for the first time. He thought of this and drove to the theater.

"It's quite possible that she goes to first nights," he thought.

The theater was full. As in all provincial theaters, there was a haze above the chandelier, the gallery was noisy and restless; in the front row, before the beginning of the performance the local dandies were standing with their hands clasped behind their backs; in the Governor's box the Governor's daughter, wearing a boa, occupied the front seat, while the Governor himself hid modestly behind the portiere and only his hands were visible; the curtain swayed; the orchestra was a long time tuning up. While the audience was coming in and taking their seats, Gurov scanned the faces eagerly.

Anna Sergeyevna, too, came in. She sat down in the third row, and when Gurov looked at her his heart contracted, and he understood clearly that in the whole world there was no human being so near, so precious, and so important to him; she, this little, undistinguished woman, lost in a provincial crowd, with a vulgar lorgnette in her hand, filled his whole life now, was his sorrow and his joy, the only happiness that he now desired for himself, and to the sounds of the bad orchestra, of the miserable local violins, he thought how lovely she was. He thought and dreamed.

A young man with small side-whiskers, very tall and stooped, came in with Anna Sergeyevna and sat down beside her; he nodded his head at every step and seemed to be bowing continually. Probably this was the husband whom at Yalta, in an access of bitter feeling, she had called a flunkey. And there really was in his lanky figure, his side-whiskers, his small bald patch, something of a flunkey's retiring manner; his smile was mawkish, and in his buttonhole there was an academic badge like a waiter's number.

During the first intermission the husband went out to have a smoke; she remained in her seat. Gurov, who was also sitting in the orchestra, went up to her and said in a shaky voice, with a forced smile:

"Good evening!"

She glanced at him and turned pale, then looked at him again in horror, unable to believe her eyes, and gripped the fan and the lorgnette tightly together in her hands, evidently trying to keep herself from fainting. Both were silent. She was sitting, he was standing, frightened by her distress and not daring to take a seat beside her. The violins and the flute that were being tuned up sang out. He suddenly felt frightened: it seemed as if all the people in the boxes were looking at them. She got up and went hurriedly to the exit; he followed her, and both of them walked blindly along the corridors and up and down stairs, and figures in the uniforms prescribed for magistrates, teachers, and officials of the Department of Crown Lands, all wearing badges, flitted before their eyes, as did also ladies, and fur coats on hangers; they were conscious of drafts and the smell of stale tobacco. And Gurov, whose heart was beating violently, thought:

"Oh, Lord! Why are these people here and this orchestra!"

And at that instant he suddenly recalled how when he had seen Anna Sergeyevna off at the station he had said to himself that all was over between them and that they would never meet again. But how distant the end still was!

On the narrow, gloomy staircase over which it said "To the Amphitheatre," she stopped.

"How you frightened me!" she said, breathing hard, still pale and stunned. "Oh, how you frightened me! I am barely alive. Why did you come? Why?"

"But do understand, Anna, do understand —" he said hurriedly, under his breath. "I implore you, do understand —"

She looked at him with fear, with entreaty, with love; she looked at him intently, to keep his features more distinctly in her memory.

"I suffer so," she went on, not listening to him. "All this time I have been thinking of nothing but you; I live only by the thought of you. And I wanted to forget, to forget; but why, oh, why have you come?"

On the landing above them two high school boys were looking down and smoking, but it was all the same to Gurov; he drew Anna Sergeyevna to him and began kissing her face and hands.

"What are you doing, what are you doing!" she was saying in horror, pushing him away. "We have lost our senses. Go away today; go away at once — I conjure you by all that is sacred, I implore you — People are coming this way!"

Someone was walking up the stairs.

"You must leave," Anna Sergeyevna went on in a whisper. "Do you hear, Dmitry Dmitrich? I will come and see you in Moscow. I have never been happy; I am unhappy now, and I never, never shall be happy, never! So don't make me suffer still more! I swear I'll come to Moscow. But now let us part. My dear, good, precious one, let us part!"

She pressed his hand and walked rapidly downstairs, turning to look round at him, and from her eyes he could see that she really was unhappy. Gurov stood for a while, listening, then when all grew quiet, he found his coat and left the theater.

4

And Anna Sergeyevna began coming to see him in Moscow. Once every two or three months she left S—— telling her husband that she was going to consult a doctor about a woman's ailment from which she was suffering — and her husband did and did not believe her. When she arrived in Moscow she would stop at the Slavyansky Bazar Hotel, and at once send a man in a red cap to Gurov. Gurov came to see her, and no one in Moscow knew of it.

Once he was going to see her in this way on a winter morning (the messenger had come the evening before and not found him in). With him walked his daughter, whom he wanted to take to school; it was on the way. Snow was coming down in big wet flakes.

"It's three degrees above zero, and yet it's snowing," Gurov was saying to his daughter. "But this temperature prevails only on the surface of the earth; in the upper layers of the atmosphere there is quite a different temperature."

"And why doesn't it thunder in winter, papa?"

He explained that, too. He talked, thinking all the while that he was on his way to a rendezvous, and no living soul knew of it, and probably no one would ever know. He had two lives, an open one, seen and known by all who needed to know it, full of conventional truth and conventional falsehood, exactly like the lives of his friends and acquaintances; and another life that went on in secret. And through some strange, perhaps accidental, combination of circumstances, everything that was of interest and importance to him, everything that was essential to him, everything about which he felt sincerely and did not deceive himself, everything that constituted the core of his life, was going on concealed from others; while all that was false, the shell in which he hid to cover the truth — his work at the bank, for instance, his discussions at the club, his references to the "inferior race," his appearances at anniversary celebrations with his wife — all that went on in the open. Judging others by himself, he did not believe what he saw, and always fancied that every man led his real, most interesting life under cover of secrecy as under cover of night. The personal life of every individual is based on secrecy, and perhaps it is partly for that reason that civilized man is so nervously anxious that personal privacy should be respected.

Having taken his daughter to school, Gurov went on to the Slavyansky Bazar Hotel. He took off his fur coat in the lobby, went upstairs, and knocked gently at the door. Anna Sergeyevna, wearing his favorite gray dress, exhausted by the journey and by waiting, had been expecting him since the previous evening. She was pale, and looked at him without a smile, and he had hardly entered when she flung herself on his breast. That kiss was a long, lingering one, as though they had not seen one another for two years.

"Well, darling, how are you getting on there?" he asked. "What news?"

"Wait; I'll tell you in a moment — I can't speak."

She could not speak; she was crying. She turned away from him, and pressed her handkerchief to her eyes.

"Let her have her cry; meanwhile I'll sit down," he thought, and he seated himself in an armchair.

Then he rang and ordered tea, and while he was having his tea she remained standing at the window with her back to him. She was crying out of sheer agitation, in the sorrowful consciousness that their life was so sad; that they could only see each other in secret and had to hide from people like thieves! Was it not a broken life?

"Come, stop now, dear!" he said.

It was plain to him that this love of theirs would not be over soon, that the end of it was not in sight. Anna Sergeyevna was growing more and more attached to him. She adored him, and it was unthinkable to tell her that their love was bound to come to an end some day; besides, she would not have believed it!

He went up to her and took her by the shoulders, to fondle her and say something diverting, and at that moment he caught sight of himself in the mirror.

His hair was already beginning to turn gray. And it seemed odd to him that he had grown so much older in the last few years, and lost his looks. The shoulders on which his hands rested were warm and heaving. He felt compassion for this life, still so warm and lovely, but probably already about to begin to fade and wither like his own. Why did she love him so much? He always seemed to women different from what he was, and they loved in him not himself, but the man whom their imagination created and whom they had been eagerly seeking all their lives; and afterwards, when they saw their mistake, they loved him nevertheless. And not one of them had been happy with him. In the past he had met women, come together with them, parted from them, but he had never once loved; it was anything you please, but not love. And only now when his head was gray he had fallen in love, really, truly — for the first time in his life.

Anna Sergeyevna and he loved each other as people do who are very close and intimate, like man and wife, like tender friends; it seemed to them that Fate itself had meant them for one another, and they could not understand why he had a wife and she a husband; and it was as though they were a pair of migratory birds, male and female, caught and forced to live in different cages. They forgave each other what they were ashamed of in their past, they forgave everything in the present, and felt that this love of theirs had altered them both.

Formerly in moments of sadness he had soothed himself with whatever logical arguments came into his head, but now he no longer cared for logic; he felt profound compassion, he wanted to be sincere and tender.

"Give it up now, my darling," he said. "You've had your cry; that's enough. Let us have a talk now, we'll think up something."

Then they spent a long time taking counsel together, they talked of how to avoid the necessity for secrecy, for deception, for living in different cities, and not seeing one another for long stretches of time. How could they free themselves from these intolerable fetters?

"How? How?" he asked, clutching his head. "How?"

And it seemed as though in a little while the solution would be found, and then a new and glorious life would begin; and it was clear to both of them that the end was still far off, and that what was to be most complicated and difficult for them was only just beginning.

JOSEPH CONRAD

Born in Poland to ardently nationalistic parents whose death, the result of their revolutionary activities, left him an orphan at age twelve, Joseph Conrad (1857–1924) went to sea at sixteen and eventually commanded merchant ships in the Far East and on the Congo River in Africa. He taught himself English (his third language, after Polish and French) by the time he was twenty, and when he left the sea a decade later he decided to try writing fiction — in English. His reputation as one of the twentieth century's great writers was secured by his many novels — among them *Lord Jim* (1900), *Nostromo* (1904), *The Secret Agent* (1907), *Under Western Eyes* (1911), and *Victory* (1915) — and powerful short stories (first published in *Youth and Heart of Darkness*, 1902; *Typhoon and Other Stories*, 1903; and *The Secret Sharer*, 1912). Conrad drew on his experience at sea and in foreign lands, but he never wrote mere tales of adventure and the exotic. His aim was to probe the reality of human experience, to uncover vulnerability and greatness in the human soul. He wrote, "My task . . . is, by the power of the written word, to make you hear, to make you feel — it is, before all, to make you *see*." Not infrequently in his work the revelation of reality is harrowing: such is the case in "An Outpost of Progress."

An Outpost of Progress

There were two white men in charge of the trading station. Kayerts, the chief, was short and fat; Carlier, the assistant, was tall, with a large head and a very broad trunk perched upon a long pair of thin legs. The third man on the staff was a Sierra Leone nigger, who maintained that his name was Henry Price. However, for some reason or other, the natives down the river had given him the name of Makola, and it stuck to him through all his wanderings about the country. He spoke English and French with a warbling accent, wrote a beautiful hand, understood bookkeeping, and cherished in his innermost heart the worship of evil spirits. His wife was a negress from Loanda, very large and very noisy. Three children rolled about in sunshine before the door of his low, shed-like dwelling. Makola, taciturn and impenetrable, despised the two white men. He had charge of a small clay storehouse with a dried-grass roof, and pretended to keep a correct account of beads, cotton cloth, red kerchiefs, brass wire, and other trade goods it contained. Besides the storehouse and Makola's hut, there was only one large building in the cleared ground of the station. It was built neatly of reeds, with a veranda on all the four sides. There were three rooms in it. The one in the middle was the living room, and had two rough tables and a few stools in it. The other two were the bedrooms for the white men. Each had a bedstead and a mosquito net for all furniture. The plank floor was littered with the belongings of the white men; open half-empty boxes, torn wearing apparel, old boots; all the things dirty, and all the things broken, that accumulate mysteriously round untidy men. There was also another dwelling place some distance away from the buildings. In it, under a tall cross much out of the perpendicular, slept the man who had seen the beginning of all this; who had planned and had watched the construction of this outpost of progress. He had been, at home, an unsuccessful painter who, weary of pursuing fame on an empty stomach, had gone out there through high protections. He had been the first chief of that station. Makola had watched the energetic artist die of fever in the just finished house with his usual kind of "I told you so" indifference. Then, for a time, he dwelt alone with his family, his account books, and the Evil Spirit that rules the lands under the equator. He got on very well with his god. Perhaps he had propitiated him by a promise of more white men to play with, by and by. At any rate the director of the Great Trading Company, coming up in a steamer that resembled an enormous sardine box with a flat-roofed shed erected on it, found the station in good order, and Makola as usual quietly diligent. The director had the cross put up over the first agent's grave, and appointed Kayerts to the post. Carlier was told off as second in charge. The director was a man ruthless and efficient, who at times, but very imperceptibly, indulged in grim humor. He made a speech to Kayerts and Carlier, pointing out to them the promising aspect of their station. The nearest trading post was about three hundred miles away. It was an exceptional opportunity for them to distinguish themselves and to earn percentages on the trade. This appointment was a favor done to beginners. Kayerts was moved almost to tears by his director's kindness. He would, he said, by doing his best, try to justify the flattering confidence, etc., etc. Kayerts had been in the Administration of the Telegraphs, and knew how to express himself correctly. Carlier, an ex-noncommissioned officer of cavalry in an army guaranteed from harm by several European powers, was less impressed. If there were commissions to get, so much the better; and, trailing a sulky glance over the river, the forests, the impenetrable bush that seemed to cut off the station from the rest of the world, he muttered between his teeth, "We shall see, very soon."

Next day, some bales of cotton goods and a few cases of provisions having been thrown on shore, the sardine box steamer went off, not to return for another six months. On the deck the director touched his cap to the two agents, who stood on the bank waving their hats, and turning to an old servant of the Company on his passage to headquarters, said, "Look at those two imbeciles. They must be mad at home to send me such specimens. I told those fellows to plant a vegetable garden, build new storehouses and fences, and construct a landing stage. I bet nothing will be done! They won't know how to begin. I always thought the station on this river useless, and they just fit the station!"

"They will form themselves there," said the old stager with a quiet smile.

"At any rate, I am rid of them for six months," retorted the director.

The two men watched the steamer round the bend, then, ascending arm in arm the slope of the bank, returned to the station. They had been in this vast and dark country only a very short time, and as yet always in the midst of other white men, under the eye and guidance of their superiors. And now, dull as they were to the subtle influences of surroundings, they felt themselves very much alone, when suddenly left unassisted to face the wilderness; a wilderness rendered more strange, more incomprehensible by the mysterious glimpses of the vigorous life it contained. They were two perfectly insignificant and incapable individuals, whose existence is only rendered possible through the high organization of civilized crowds. Few men realize that their life, the very essence of their character, their capabilities and their audacities, are only the expression of their belief in the safety of their surroundings. The courage, the composure, the confidence; the emotions and principles; every great and every insignificant thought belongs not to the individual but to the crowd: to the crowd that believes blindly in the irresistible force of its institutions and of its morals, in the power of its police and of its opinion. But the contact with pure unmitigated savagery, with primitive nature and primitive man, brings sudden and profound trouble into the heart. To the sentiment of being alone of one's kind, to the clear perception of the loneliness of one's thoughts, of one's sensations — to the negation of the habitual, which is safe, there is added the affirmation of the unusual, which is dangerous; a suggestion of things vague, uncontrollable, and repulsive, whose discomposing intrusion excites the imagination and tries the civilized nerves of the foolish and the wise alike.

Kayerts and Carlier walked arm in arm, drawing close to one another as children do in the dark; and they had the same, not altogether unpleasant, sense of danger which one half suspects to be imaginary. They chatted persistently in familiar tones. "Our station is prettily situated," said one. The other assented with enthusiasm, enlarging volubly on the beauties of the situation. Then they passed near the grave. "Poor devil!" said Kayerts. "He died of fever, didn't he?" muttered Carlier, stopping short. "Why," retorted Kayerts, with indignation, "I've been told that the fellow exposed himself recklessly to the sun. The climate here, everybody says, is not at all worse than at home, as long as you keep out of the sun. Do you hear that, Carlier? I am chief here, and my orders are that you should not expose yourself to the sun!" He assumed his superiority jocularly, but his meaning was serious. The idea that he would, perhaps, have to bury Carlier and remain alone, gave him an inward shiver. He felt suddenly that this Carlier was more precious to him here, in the center of Africa, than a brother could be anywhere else. Carlier, entering into the spirit of the thing, made a military salute and answered in a brisk tone, "Your orders shall be attended to, chief!" Then he burst out laughing, slapped Kayerts on the back and shouted, "We shall let life run easily here! Just sit still and gather in the ivory those savages will bring. This country has its good points, after all!" They both laughed loudly while Carlier thought: "That poor Kayerts; he is so fat and unhealthy. It would be awful if I had to bury him here. He is a man I respect." . . . Before they reached the veranda of their house they called one another "my dear fellow."

The first day they were very active, pottering about with hammers and nails and red calico, to put up curtains, make their house habitable and pretty; resolved to settle down comfortably to their new life. For them an impossible task. To grapple effectually with even purely material problems requires more serenity of mind and more lofty courage than people generally imagine. No two beings could have been more unfitted for such a struggle. Society, not from any tenderness, but because of its strange needs, had taken care of those two men, forbidding them all independent thought, all initiative, all departure from routine; and forbidding it under pain of death. They could only live on condition of being machines. And now, released from the fostering care of men with pens behind the ears, or of men with gold lace on the sleeves, they were like those life-long prisoners who, liberated after many years, do not know what use to make of their freedom. They did not know what use to make of their faculties, being both, through want of practice, incapable of independent thought.

At the end of two months Kayerts often would say, "If it was not for my Melie, you wouldn't catch me here." Melie was his daughter. He had thrown up his post in the Administration of the Telegraphs, though he had been for seventeen years perfectly happy there, to earn a dowry for his girl. His wife was dead, and the child was being brought up by his sisters. He regretted the streets, the pavements, the cafés, his friends of many years; all the things he used to see, day after day; all the thoughts suggested by familiar things — the thoughts effortless, monotonous, and soothing of a Government clerk; he regretted all the gossip, the small enmities, the mild venom, and the little jokes of Government offices. "If I had had a decent brother-in-law," Carlier would remark, "a fellow with a heart, I would not be here." He had left the army and had made himself so obnoxious to his family by his laziness and impudence, that an exasperated brother-in-law had made superhuman efforts to procure him an appointment in the Company as a second-class agent. Having not a penny in the world he was compelled to accept this means of livelihood as soon as it became quite clear to him that there was nothing more to squeeze out of his relations. He, like Kayerts, regretted his old life. He regretted the clink of saber and spurs on a fine afternoon, the barrack-room witticisms, the girls of garrison towns; but, besides, he had also a sense of grievance. He was evidently a much ill-used man. This made him moody, at times. But the two men got on well together in the fellowship of their stupidity and laziness. Together they did nothing, absolutely nothing, and enjoyed the sense of the idleness for which they were paid. And in time they came to feel something resembling affection for one another.

They lived like blind men in a large room, aware only of what came in contact with them (and of that only imperfectly), but unable to see the general aspect of things. The river, the forest, all the great land throbbing with life, were like a great emptiness. Even the brilliant sunshine disclosed nothing intelligible. Things appeared and disappeared before their eyes in an unconnected and aimless kind of way. The river seemed to come from nowhere and flow nowhither. It flowed through a void. Out of that void, at times, came canoes, and men with spears in their hands would suddenly crowd the yard of the station. They were naked, glossy black, ornamented with snowy shells and glistening brass wire, perfect of limb. They made an uncouth babbling noise when they spoke, moved in a stately manner, and sent quick, wild glances out of their startled, never-resting eyes. Those warriors would squat in long rows, four or more deep, before the veranda, while their chiefs bargained for hours with Makola over an elephant tusk. Kayerts sat on his chair and looked down on the proceedings, understanding nothing. He stared at them with his round blue eyes, called out to Carlier, "Here, look! look at that fellow there — and that other one, to the left. Did you ever see such a face? Oh, the funny brute!"

Carlier, smoking native tobacco in a short wooden pipe, would swagger up twirling his mustaches, and surveying the warriors with haughty indulgence, would say:

"Fine animals. Brought any bone? Yes? It's not any too soon. Look at the muscles of that fellow — third from the end. I wouldn't care to get a punch on the nose from him. Fine arms, but legs no good below the knee. Couldn't make cavalry men of them." And after glancing down complacently at his own shanks, he always concluded. "Pah! Don't they stink! You, Makola! Take that herd over to the fetish" (the storehouse was in every station called the fetish, perhaps because of the spirit of civilization it contained) "and give them up some of the rubbish you keep there. I'd rather see it full of bone than full of rags."

Kayerts approved.

"Yes, yes! Go and finish that palaver over there, Mr. Makola. I will come round when you are ready, to weigh the tusk. We must be careful." Then turning to his companion: "This is the tribe that lives down the river; they are rather aromatic. I remember, they had been once before here. D'ye hear that row? What a fellow has got to put up with in this dog of a country! My head is split."

Such profitable visits were rare. For days the two pioneers of trade and progress would look on their empty courtyard in the vibrating brilliance of vertical sunshine. Below the high bank, the silent river flowed on glittering and steady. On the sands in the middle of the stream, hippos and alligators sunned themselves side by side. And stretching away in all directions, surrounding the insignificant cleared spot of the trading post, immense forests, hiding fateful complications of fantastic life, lay in the eloquent silence of mute greatness. The two men understood nothing, cared for nothing but for the passage of days that separated them from the steamer's return. Their predecessor had left some torn books. They took up these wrecks of novels, and, as they had never read anything of the kind before, they were surprised and amused. Then during long days there were interminable and silly discussions about plots and personages. In the center of Africa they made acquaintance of Richelieu and of d'Artagnan, of Hawk's Eye and of Father Goriot, and of many other people. All these imaginary personages became subjects for gossip as if they had been living friends. They discounted their virtues, suspected their motives, decried their successes; were scandalized at their duplicity or were doubtful about their courage. The accounts of crimes filled them with indignation, while tender or pathetic passages moved them deeply. Carlier cleared his throat and said in a soldierly voice, "What nonsense!" Kayerts, his round eyes suffused with tears, his fat cheeks quivering, rubbed his bald head, and declared, "This is a splendid book. I had no idea there were such clever fellows in the world." They also found some old copies of a home paper. That print discussed what it was pleased to call "Our Colonial Expansion" in high-flown language. It spoke much of the rights and duties of civilization, of the sacredness of the civilizing work, and extolled the merits of those who went about bringing light, and faith and commerce to the dark places of the earth. Carlier and Kayerts read, wondered, and began to think better of themselves. Carlier said one evening, waving his hand about, "In a hundred years, there will be perhaps a town here. Quays, and warehouses, and barracks, and — and — billiard rooms. Civilization, my boy, and virtue — and all. And then, chaps will read that two good fellows, Kayerts and Carlier, were the first civilized men to live in this very spot!" Kayerts nodded, "Yes, it is a consolation to think of that." They seemed to forget their dead predecessor; but, early one day, Carlier went out and replanted the cross firmly. "It used to make me squint whenever I walked that way," he explained to Kayerts over the morning coffee. "It made me squint, leaning over so much. So I just planted it upright. And solid, I promise you! I suspended myself with both hands to the crosspiece. Not a move. Oh, I did that properly."

At times Gobila came to see them. Gobila was the chief of the neighboring villages. He was a gray-headed savage, thin and black, with a white cloth round his loins and a mangy panther skin hanging over his back. He came up with long strides of his skeleton legs, swinging a staff as tall as himself, and, entering the common room of the station, would squat on his heels to the left of the door. There he sat, watching Kayerts, and now and then making a speech which the other did not understand. Kayerts, without interrupting his occupation, would from time to time say in a friendly manner: "How goes it, you old image?" and they would smile at one another. The two whites had a liking for that old and incomprehensible creature, and called him Father Gobila. Gobila's manner was paternal, and he seemed really to love all white men. They all appeared to him very young, indistinguishably alike (except for stature), and he knew that they were all brothers, and also immortal. The death of the artist, who was the first white man whom he knew intimately, did not disturb this belief, because he was firmly convinced that the white stranger had pretended to die and got himself buried for some mysterious purpose of his own, into which it was useless to inquire. Perhaps it was his way of going home to his own country? At any rate, these were his brothers, and he transferred his absurd affection to them. They returned it in a way. Carlier slapped him on the back, and recklessly struck off matches for his amusement. Kayerts was already ready to let him have a sniff at the ammonia bottle. In short, they behaved just like that other white creature that had hidden itself in a hole in the ground. Gobila considered them attentively. Perhaps they were the same being with the other — or one of them was. He couldn't decide — clear up that mystery; but he remained always very friendly. In consequence of that friendship the women of Gobila's village walked in single file through the reedy grass, bringing every morning to the station, fowls, and sweet potatoes, and palm wine, and sometimes a goat. The Company never provisions the stations fully, and the agents required those local supplies to live. They had them through the good will of Gobila, and lived well. Now and then one of them had a bout of fever, and the other nursed him with gentle devotion. They did not think much of it. It left them weaker, and their appearance changed for the worse. Carlier was hollow-eyed and irritable. Kayerts showed a drawn, flabby face above the rotundity of his stomach, which gave him a weird aspect. But being constantly together, they did not notice the change that took place gradually in their appearance, and also in their dispositions.

Five months passed in that way.

Then, one morning, as Kayerts and Carlier, lounging in their chairs under the veranda, talked about the approaching visit of the steamer, a knot of armed men came out of the forest and advanced towards the station. They were strangers to that part of the country. They were tall, slight, draped classically from neck to heel in blue fringed cloths, and carried percussion muskets over their bare right shoulders. Makola showed signs of excitement, and ran out of the storehouse (where he spent all his days) to meet these visitors. They came into the courtyard and looked about them with steady, scornful glances. Their leader, a powerful and determined-looking Negro with bloodshot eyes, stood in front of the veranda and made a long speech. He gesticulated much, and ceased very suddenly.

There was something in his intonation, in the sounds of the long sentences he used, that startled the two whites. It was like a reminiscence of something not exactly familiar, and yet resembling the speech of civilized men. It sounded like one of those impossible languages which sometimes we hear in our dreams.

"What lingo is that?" said the amazed Carlier. "In the first moment I fancied the fellow was going to speak French. Anyway, it is a different kind of gibberish to what we ever heard."

"Yes," replied Kayerts. "Hey, Makola, what does he say? Where do they come from? Who are they?"

But Makola, who seemed to be standing on hot bricks, answered hurriedly, "I don't know. They come from very far. Perhaps Mrs. Price will understand. They are perhaps bad men."

The leader, after waiting for a while, said something sharply to Makola, who shook his head. Then the man, after looking round, noticed Makola's hut and walked over there. The next moment Mrs. Makola was heard speaking with great volubility. The other strangers — they were six in all — strolled about with an air of ease, put their heads through the door of the storeroom, congregated round the grave, pointed understandingly at the cross, and generally made themselves at home.

"I don't like those chaps — and, I say, Kayerts, they must be from the coast; they've got firearms," observed the sagacious Carlier.

Kayerts also did not like those chaps. They both, for the first time, became aware that they lived in conditions where the unusual may be dangerous, and that there was no power on earth outside of themselves to stand between them and the unusual. They became uneasy, went in and loaded their revolvers. Kayerts said, "We must order Makola to tell them to go away before dark."

The strangers left in the afternoon, after eating a meal prepared for them by Mrs. Makola. The immense woman was excited, and talked much with the visitors. She rattled away shrilly, pointing here and there at the forests and at the river. Makola sat apart and watched. At times he got up and whispered to his wife. He accompanied the strangers across the ravine at the back of the station-ground, and returned slowly looking very thoughtful. When questioned by the white men he was very strange, seemed not to understand, seemed to have forgotten French — seemed to have forgotten how to speak altogether. Kayerts and Carlier agreed that the nigger had had too much palm wine.

There was some talk about keeping a watch in turn, but in the evening everything seemed so quiet and peaceful that they retired as usual. All night they were disturbed by a lot of drumming in the villages. A deep, rapid roll near by would be followed by another far off — then all ceased. Soon short appeals would rattle out here and there, then all mingle together, increase, become vigorous and sustained, would spread out over the forest, roll through the night, unbroken and ceaseless, near and far, as if the whole land had been one immense drum booming out steadily an appeal to heaven. And through the deep and tremendous noise sudden yells that resembled snatches of songs from a madhouse darted shrill and high in discordant jets of sound which seemed to rush far above the earth and drive all peace from under the stars.

Carlier and Kayerts slept badly. They both thought they had heard shots fired during the night — but they could not agree as to the direction. In the morning Makola was gone somewhere. He returned about noon with one of yesterday's strangers, and eluded all Kayerts' attempts to close with him: had become deaf apparently. Kayerts wondered. Carlier, who had been fishing off the bank, came back and remarked while he showed his catch, "The niggers seem to be in a deuce of a stir; I wonder what's up. I saw about fifteen canoes cross the river during the two hours I was there fishing." Kayerts, worried, said, "Isn't this Makola very queer today?" Carlier advised, "Keep all our men together in case of some trouble."

2

There were ten station men who had been left by the Director. Those fellows, having engaged themselves to the Company for six months (without having any idea of a month in particular and only a very faint notion of time in general), had been serving the cause of progress for upwards of two years. Belonging to a tribe from a very distant part of the land of darkness and sorrow, they did not run away, naturally supposing that as wandering strangers they would be killed by the inhabitants of the country; in which they were right. They lived in straw huts on the slope of a ravine overgrown with reedy grass, just behind the station buildings. They were not happy, regretting the festive incantations, the sorceries, the human sacrifices of their own land; where they also had parents, brothers, sisters, admired chiefs, respected magicians, loved friends, and other ties supposed generally to be human. Besides, the rice rations served out by the Company did not agree with them, being a food unknown to their land, and to which they could not get used. Consequently they were unhealthy and miserable. Had they been of any other tribe they would have made up their minds to die — for nothing is easier to certain savages than suicide — and so have escaped from the puzzling difficulties of existence. But belonging, as they did, to a warlike tribe with filed teeth, they had more grit, and went on stupidly living through disease and sorrow. They did very little work, and had lost their splendid physique. Carlier and Kayerts doctored them assiduously without being able to bring them back into condition again. They were mustered every morning and told off to different tasks — grass-cutting, fence-building, tree-felling, etc., etc., which no power on earth could induce them to execute efficiently. The two whites had practically very little control over them.

In the afternoon Makola came over to the big house and found Kayerts watching three heavy columns of smoke rising above the forests. "What is that?" asked Kayerts. "Some villages burn," answered Makola, who seemed to have regained his wits. Then he said abruptly: "We have got very little ivory; bad six months' trading. Do you like get a little more ivory?"

"Yes," said Kayerts, eagerly. He thought of percentages which were low.

"Those men who came yesterday are traders from Loanda who have got more ivory than they can carry home. Shall I buy? I know their camp."

"Certainly," said Kayerts. "What are those traders?"

"Bad fellows," said Makola, indifferently. "They fight with people, and catch women and children. They are bad men, and got guns. There is a great disturbance in the country. Do you want ivory?"

"Yes," said Kayerts. Makola said nothing for a while. Then: "Those workmen of ours are no good at all," he muttered, looking round. "Station in very bad order, sir. Director will growl. Better get a fine lot of ivory, then he say nothing."

"I can't help it; the men won't work," said Kayerts. "When will you get that ivory?"

"Very soon," said Makola. "Perhaps tonight. You leave it to me, and keep indoors, sir. I think you had better give some palm wine to our men to make a dance this evening. Enjoy themselves. Work better tomorrow. There's plenty palm wine — gone a little sour."

Kayerts said "yes," and Makola, with his own hands, carried big calabashes to the door of his hut. They stood there till the evening, and Mrs. Makola looked into every one. The men got them at sunset. When Kayerts and Carlier retired, a big bonfire was flaring before the men's huts. They could hear their shouts and drumming. Some men from Gobila's village had joined the station hands, and the entertainment was a great success.

In the middle of the night, Carlier waking suddenly, heard a man shout loudly; then a shot was fired. Only one. Carlier ran out and met Kayerts on the veranda. They were both startled. As they went across the yard to call Makola, they saw shadows moving in the night. One of them cried, "Don't shoot! It's me, Price." Then Makola appeared close to them. "Go back, go back, please," he urged, "you spoil all." "There are strange men about," said Carlier. "Never mind; I know," said Makola. Then he whispered, "All right. Bring ivory. Say nothing! I know my business." The two white men reluctantly went back to the house, but did not sleep. They heard footsteps, whispers, some groans. It seemed as if a lot of men came in, dumped heavy things on the ground, squabbled a long time, then went away. They lay on their hard beds and thought: "This Makola is invaluable." In the morning Carlier came out, very sleepy, and pulled at the cord of the big bell. The station hands mustered every morning to the sound of the bell. That morning nobody came. Kayerts turned out also, yawning. Across the yard they saw Makola come out of his hut, a tin basin of soapy water in his hand. Makola, a civilized nigger, was very neat in his person. He threw the soapsuds skillfully over a wretched little yellow cur he had, then turning his face to the agent's house, he shouted from the distance, "All the men gone last night!"

They heard him plainly, but in their surprise they both yelled out together: "What!" Then they stared at one another. "We are in a proper fix now," growled Carlier. "It's incredible!" muttered Kayerts. "I will go to the huts and see," said Carlier, striding off. Makola coming up found Kayerts standing alone.

"I can hardly believe it," said Kayerts, tearfully. "We took care of them as if they had been our children."

"They went with the coast people," said Makola after a moment of hesitation.

"What do I care with whom they went — the ungrateful brutes!" exclaimed the other. Then with sudden suspicion, and looking hard at Makola, he added: "What do you know about it?"

Makola moved his shoulders, looking down on the ground. "What do I know? I think only. Will you come and look at the ivory I've got there? It is a fine lot. You never saw such."

He moved towards the store. Kayerts followed him mechanically, thinking about the incredible desertion of the men. On the ground before the door of the fetish lay six splendid tusks.

"What did you give for it?" asked Kayerts, after surveying the lot with satisfaction.

"No regular trade," said Makola. "They brought the ivory and gave it to me. I told them to take what they most wanted in the station. It is a beautiful lot. No station can show such tusks. Those traders wanted carriers badly, and our men were no good here. No trade, no entry in books; all correct."

Kayerts nearly burst with indignation. "Why!" he shouted, "I believe you have sold our men for these tusks!" Makola stood impassive and silent. "I — I — will — I," stuttered Kayerts. "You fiend!" he yelled out.

"I did the best for you and the Company," said Makola, imperturbably. "Why you shout so much? Look at this tusk."

"I dismiss you! I will report you — I won't look at the tusk. I forbid you to touch them. I order you to throw them into the river. You — you!"

"You very red, Mr. Kayerts. If you are so irritable in the sun, you will get fever and die — like the first chief!" pronounced Makola impressively.

They stood still, contemplating one another with intense eyes, as if they had been looking with effort across immense distances. Kayerts shivered. Makola had meant no more than he said, but his words seemed to Kayerts full of ominous menace! He turned sharply and went away to the house. Makola retired into the bosom of his family; and the tusks, left lying before the store, looked very large and valuable in the sunshine.

Carlier came back on the veranda. "They're all gone, hey?" asked Kayerts from the far end of the common room in a muffled voice. "You did not find anybody?"

"Oh, yes," said Carlier, "I found one of Gobila's people lying dead before the huts — shot through the body. We heard that shot last night."

Kayerts came out quickly. He found his companion staring grimly over the yard at the tusks, away by the store. They both sat in silence for a while. Then Kayerts related his conversation with Makola. Carlier said nothing. At the midday meal they ate very little. They hardly exchanged a word that day. A great silence seemed to lie heavily over the station and press on their lips. Makola did not open the store; he spent the day playing with his children. He lay full-length on a mat outside his door, and the youngsters sat on his chest and clambered all over him. It was a touching picture. Mrs. Makola was busy cooking all day as usual. The white men made a somewhat better meal in the evening. Afterwards, Carlier smoking his pipe strolled over to the store; he stood for a long time over the tusks, touched one or two with his foot, even tried to lift the largest one by its small end. He came back to his chief, who had not stirred from the veranda, threw himself in the chair and said:

"I can see it! They were pounced upon while they slept heavily after drinking all that palm wine you've allowed Makola to give them. A put-up job! See? The worst is, some of Gobila's people were there, and got carried off too, no doubt. The least drunk woke up, and got shot for his sobriety. This is a funny country. What will you do now?"

"We can't touch it, of course," said Kayerts.

"Of course not," assented Carlier.

"Slavery is an awful thing," stammered out Kayerts in an unsteady voice.

"Frightful — the sufferings," grunted Carlier with conviction.

They believed their words. Everybody shows a respectful deference to certain sounds that he and his fellows can make. But about feelings people really know nothing. We talk with indignation or enthusiasm; we talk about oppression, cruelty, crime, devotion, self-sacrifice, virtue, and we know nothing real beyond the words. Nobody knows what suffering or sacrifice mean — except, perhaps the victims of the mysterious purpose of these illusions.

Next morning they saw Makola very busy setting up in the yard the big scales used for weighing ivory. By and by Carlier said: "What's that filthy scoundrel up to?" and lounged out into the yard. Kayerts followed. They stood watching. Makola took no notice. When the balance was swung true, he tried to lift a tusk into the scale. It was too heavy. He looked up helplessly without a word, and for a minute they stood round that balance as mute and still as three statues. Suddenly Carlier said: "Catch hold of the other end, Makola — you beast!" and together they swung the tusk up.

Kayerts trembled in every limb. He muttered, "I say! O! I say!" and putting his hand in his pocket found there a dirty bit of paper and the stump of a pencil. He turned his back on the others, as if about to do something tricky, and noted stealthily the weights which Carlier shouted out to him with unnecessary loudness. When all was over Makola whispered to himself: "The sun's very strong here for the tusks." Carlier said to Kayerts in a careless tone: "I say, chief, I might just as well give him a lift with this lot into the store."

As they were going back to the house Kayerts observed with a sigh: "It had to be done." And Carlier said: "It's deplorable, but, the men being Company's men the ivory is Company's ivory. We must look after it." "I will report to the Director, of course," said Kayerts. "Of course; let him decide," approved Carlier.

At midday they made a hearty meal. Kayerts sighed from time to time. Whenever they mentioned Makola's name they always added to it an opprobrious epithet. It eased their conscience. Makola gave himself a half-holiday, and bathed his children in the river. No one from Gobila's villages came near the station that day. No one came the next day, and the next, nor for a whole week. Gobila's people might have been dead and buried for any sign of life they gave. But they were only mourning for those they had lost by the witchcraft of white men, who had brought wicked people into their country. The wicked people were gone, but fear remained. Fear always remains. A man may destroy everything within himself, love and hate and belief, and even doubt; but as long as he clings to life he cannot destroy fear: the fear, subtle, indestructible, and terrible, that pervades his being; that tinges his thoughts; that lurks in his heart; that watches on his lips the struggle of his last breath. In his fear, the mild old Gobila offered extra human sacrifices to all the Evil Spirits that had taken possession of his white friends. His heart was heavy. Some warriors spoke about burning and killing, but the cautious old savage dissuaded them. Who could foresee the woe those mysterious creatures, if irritated, might bring? They should be left alone. Perhaps in time they would disappear into the earth as the first one had disappeared. His people must keep away from them, and hope for the best.

Kayerts and Carlier did not disappear, but remained above on this earth, that, somehow, they fancied had become bigger and very empty. It was not the absolute and dumb solitude of the post that impressed them so much as an inarticulate feeling that something from within them was gone, something that worked for their safety, and had kept the wilderness from interfering with their hearts. The images of home; the memory of people like them, of men that thought and felt as they used to think and feel, receded into distances made indistinct by the glare of unclouded sunshine. And out of the great silence of the surrounding wilderness, its very hopelessness and savagery seemed to approach them nearer, to draw them gently, to look upon them, to envelop them with a solicitude irresistible, familiar, and disgusting.

Days lengthened into weeks, then into months. Gobila's people drummed and yelled to every new moon, as of yore, but kept away from the station. Makola and Carlier tried once in a canoe to open communications, but were received with a shower of arrows, and had to fly back to the station for dear life. That attempt set the country up and down the river into an uproar that could be very distinctly heard for days. The steamer was late. At first they spoke of delay jauntily, then anxiously, then gloomily. The matter was becoming serious. Stores were running short. Carlier cast his lines off the bank, but the river was low, and the fish kept out in the stream. They dared not stroll far away from the station to shoot. Moreover, there was no game in the impenetrable forest. Once Carlier shot a hippo in the river. They had no boat to secure it, and it sank. When it floated up it drifted away, and Gobila's people secured the carcass. It was the occasion for a national holiday, but Carlier had a fit of rage over it and talked about the necessity of exterminating all the niggers before the country could be made habitable. Kayerts mooned about silently; spent hours looking at the portrait of his Melie. It represented a little girl with long bleached tresses and a rather sour face. His legs were much swollen, and he could hardly walk. Carlier, undermined by fever, could not swagger any more, but kept tottering about, still with a devil-may-care air, as became a man who remembered his crack regiment. He had become hoarse, sarcastic, and inclined to say unpleasant things. He called it "being frank with you." They had long ago reckoned their percentages on trade, including in them that last deal of "this infamous Makola." They had also concluded not to say anything about it. Kayerts hesitated at first — was afraid of the Director.

"He has seen worse things done on the quiet," maintained Carlier, with a hoarse laugh. "Trust him! He won't thank you if you blab. He is no better than you or me. Who will talk if we hold our tongues? There is nobody here."

That was the root of the trouble! There was nobody there; and being left there alone with their weakness, they became daily more like a pair of accomplices than like a couple of devoted friends. They had heard nothing from home for eight months. Every evening they said, "Tomorrow we shall see the steamer." But one of the Company's steamers had been wrecked, and the Director was busy with the other, relieving very distant and important stations on the main river. He thought that the useless station, and the useless men, could wait. Meantime Kayerts and Carlier lived on rice boiled without salt, and cursed the Company, all Africa, and the day they were born. One must have lived on such diet to discover what ghastly trouble the necessity of swallowing one's food may become. There was literally nothing else in the station but rice and coffee; they drank the coffee without sugar. The last fifteen lumps Kayerts had solemnly locked away in his box, together with a half-bottle of cognac, "in case of sickness," he explained. Carlier approved. "When one is sick," he said, "any little extra like that is cheering."

They waited. Rank grass began to sprout over the courtyard. The bell never rang now. Days passed, silent, exasperating, and slow. When the two men spoke, they snarled; and their silences were bitter, as if tinged by the bitterness of their thoughts.

One day after a lunch of boiled rice, Carlier put down his cup untasted, and said: "Hang it all! Let's have a decent cup of coffee for once. Bring out that sugar, Kayerts!"

"For the sick," muttered Kayerts, without looking up.

"For the sick," mocked Carlier. "Bosh! . . . Well! I am sick."

"You are no more sick than I am, and I go without," said Kayerts in a peaceful tone.

"Come! Out with that sugar, you stingy old slave dealer."

Kayerts looked up quickly. Carlier was smiling with marked insolence. And suddenly it seemed to Kayerts that he had never seen that man before. Who was he? He knew nothing about him. What was he capable of? There was a surprising flash of violent emotion within him, as if in the presence of something undreamt-of, dangerous, and final. But he managed to pronounce with composure:

"That joke is in very bad taste. Don't repeat it."

"Joke!" said Carlier, hitching himself forward on his seat. "I am hungry — I am sick — I don't joke! I hate hypocrites. You are a hypocrite. You are a slave dealer. I am a slave dealer. There's nothing but slave dealers in this cursed country. I mean to have sugar in my coffee today, anyhow!"

"I forbid you to speak to me in that way,'" said Kayerts with a fair show of resolution.

"You! — What?" shouted Carlier, jumping up.

Kayerts stood up also. "I am your chief," he began, trying to master the shakiness of his voice.

"What?" yelled the other. "Who's chief? There's no chief here. There's nothing here: there's nothing but you and I. Fetch the sugar — you pot-bellied ass."

"Hold your tongue. Go out of this room," screamed Kayerts. "I dismiss you — you scoundrel!"

Carlier swung a stool. All at once he looked dangerously in earnest. "You flabby, good-for-nothing civilian — take that!" he howled.

Kayerts dropped under the table, and the stool struck the grass inner wall of the room. Then, as Carlier was trying to upset the table, Kayerts in desperation made a blind rush, head low, like a cornered pig would do, and overturning his friend, bolted along the veranda, and into his room. He locked the door, snatched his revolver, and stood panting. In less than a minute Carlier was kicking at the door furiously, howling, "If you don't bring out that sugar, I will shoot you at sight, like a dog. Now then — one — two — three. You won't? I will show you who's the master."

Kayerts thought the door would fall in, and scrambled through the square hole that served for a window in his room. There was then the whole breadth of the house between them. But the other was apparently not strong enough to break in the door, and Kayerts heard him running round. Then he also began to run laboriously on his swollen legs. He ran as quickly as he could, grasping the revolver, and unable yet to understand what was happening to him. He saw in succession Makola's house, the store, the river, the ravine, and the low bushes; and he saw all those things again as he ran for the second time round the house. Then again they flashed past him. That morning he could not have walked a yard without a groan.

And now he ran. He ran fast enough to keep out of sight of the other man.

Then as, weak and desperate, he thought, "Before I finish the next round I shall die," he heard the other man stumble heavily, then stop. He stopped also. He had the back and Carlier the front of the house, as before. He heard him drop into a chair cursing, and suddenly his own legs gave way, and he slid down into a sitting posture with his back to the wall. His mouth was as dry as a cinder, and his face was wet with perspiration — and tears. What was it all about? He thought it must be a horrible illusion; he thought he was dreaming; he thought he was going mad! After a while he collected his senses. What did they quarrel about? That sugar! How absurd! He would give it to him — didn't want it himself. And he began scrambling to his feet with a sudden feeling of security. But before he had fairly stood upright, a common-sense reflection occurred to him and drove him back into despair. He thought: "If I give way now to that brute of a soldier, he will begin this horror again tomorrow — and the day after — every day — raise other pretensions, trample on me, torture me, make me his slave — and I will be lost! Lost! The steamer may not come for days — may never come." He shook so that he had to sit down on the floor again. He shivered forlornly. He felt he could not, would not move any more. He was completely distracted by the sudden perception that the position was without issue — that death and life had in a moment become equally difficult and terrible.

All at once he heard the other push his chair back; and he leaped to his feet with extreme facility. He listened and got confused. Must run again! Right or left? He heard footsteps. He darted to the left, grasping his revolver, and at the very same instant, as it seemed to him, they came into violent collision. Both shouted with surprise. A loud explosion took place between them; a roar of red fire, thick smoke; and Kayerts, deafened and blinded, rushed back thinking: "I am hit — it's all over." He expected the other to come round — to gloat over his agony. He caught hold of an upright of the roof — "All over!" Then he heard a crashing fall on the other side of the house, as if somebody had tumbled headlong over a chair — then silence. Nothing more happened. He did not die. Only his shoulder felt as if it had been badly wrenched, and he had lost his revolver. He was disarmed and helpless! He waited for his fate. The other man made no sound. It was a stratagem. He was stalking him now! Along what side? Perhaps he was taking aim this very minute!

After a few moments of an agony frightful and absurd, he decided to go and meet his doom. He was prepared for every surrender. He turned the corner, steadying himself with one hand on the wall; made a few paces, and nearly swooned. He had seen on the floor, protruding past the other corner, a pair of turned-up feet. A pair of white naked feet in red slippers. He felt deadly sick, and stood for a time in profound darkness. Then Makola appeared before him, saying quietly: "Come along, Mr. Kayerts. He is dead." He burst into tears of gratitude; a loud, sobbing fit of crying. After a time he found himself sitting in a chair and looking at Carlier, who lay stretched on his back. Makola was kneeling over the body.

"Is this your revolver?" asked Makola, getting up.

"Yes," said Kayerts; then he added very quickly. "He ran after me to shoot me — you saw!"

"Yes, I saw," said Makola. "There is only one revolver; where's his?"

"Don't know," whispered Kayerts in a voice that had become suddenly very faint.

"I will go and look for it," said the other, gently. He made the round along the veranda, while Kayerts sat still and looked at the corpse. Makola came back empty-handed, stood in deep thought, then stepped quietly into the dead man's room, and came out directly with a revolver, which he held up before Kayerts. Kayerts shut his eyes. Everything was going round. He found life more terrible and difficult than death. He had shot an unarmed man.

After meditating for a while, Makola said softly, pointing at the dead man who lay there with his right eye blown out:

"He died of fever." Kayerts looked at him with a stony stare. "Yes," repeated Makola, thoughtfully, stepping over the corpse, "I think he died of fever. Bury him tomorrow."

And he went away slowly to his expectant wife, leaving the two white men alone on the veranda.

Night came, and Kayerts sat unmoving on his chair. He sat quiet as if he had taken a dose of opium. The violence of the emotions he had passed through produced a feeling of exhausted serenity. He had plumbed in one short afternoon the depths of horror and despair, and now found repose in the conviction that life had no more secrets for him: neither had death! He sat by the corpse thinking; thinking very actively, thinking very new thoughts. He seemed to have broken loose from himself altogether. His old thoughts, convictions, likes and dislikes, things he respected and things he abhorred, appeared in their true light at last! Appeared contempt- ible and childish, false and ridiculous. He reveled in his new wisdom while he sat by the man he had killed. He argued with himself about all things under heaven with that kind of wrong-headed lucidity which may be observed in some lunatics. Incidentally he reflected that the fellow dead there had been a noxious beast anyway; that men died every day in thousands; perhaps in hundreds of thousands — who could tell? — and that in the number, that one death could not possibly make any difference; couldn't have any importance, at least to a thinking creature. He, Kayerts, was a thinking creature. He had been all his life, till that moment, a believer in a lot of nonsense like the rest of mankind — who are fools; but now he thought! He knew! He was at peace; he was familiar with the highest wisdom! Then he tried to imagine himself dead, and Carlier sitting in his chair watching him; and his attempt met with such unexpected success, that in a very few moments he became not at all sure who was dead and who was alive. This extraordinary achievement of his fancy startled him, however, and by a clever and timely effort of mind he saved himself just in time from becoming Carlier. His heart thumped, and he felt hot all over at the thought of that danger. Carlier! What a beastly thing! To compose his now disturbed nerves — and no wonder! — he tried to whistle a little. Then, suddenly, he fell asleep, or thought he had slept; but at any rate there was a fog, and somebody had whistled in the fog.

He stood up. The day had come, and a heavy mist had descended upon the land: the mist penetrating, enveloping, and silent; the morning mist of tropical lands; the mist that clings and kills; the mist white and deadly, immaculate and poisonous. He stood up, saw the body, and threw his arms above his head with a cry like that of a man who, waking from a trance, finds himself immured forever in a tomb. *"Help! . . . My God!"*

A shriek inhuman, vibrating and sudden, pierced like a sharp dart the white shroud of that land of sorrow. Three short, impatient screeches followed, and then for a time, the fog-wreaths rolled on, undisturbed, through a formidable silence. Then many more shrieks, rapid and piercing, like the yells of some exasperated and ruthless creature, rent the air. Progress was calling to Kayerts from the river. Progress and civilization and all the virtues. Society was calling to its accomplished child to come, to be taken care of, to be instructed, to be judged, to be condemned; it called him to return to that rubbish heap from which he had wandered away, so that justice could be done.

Kayerts heard and understood. He stumbled out of the veranda, leaving the other man quite alone for the first time since they had been thrown there together. He groped his way through the fog, calling in his ignorance upon the invisible heaven to undo its work. Makola flitted by in the mist, shouting as he ran:

"Steamer! Steamer! They can't see. They whistle for the station. I go ring the bell. Go down to the landing, sir. I ring."

He disappeared. Kayerts stood still. He looked upwards; the fog low over his head. He looked round like a man who has lost his way; and he saw a dark smudge, a cross-shaped stain, upon the shifting purity of the mist. As he began to stumble towards it, the station bell rang in a tumultuous peal its answer to the impatient clamor of the steamer.

The Managing Director of the Great Civilizing Company (since we know that civilization follows trade) landed first, and incontinently lost sight of the steamer. The fog down by the river was exceedingly dense; above, at the station, the bell rang unceasing and brazen.

The Director shouted loudly to the steamer:

"There is nobody down to meet us; there may be something wrong, though they are ringing. You had better come, too!"

And he began to toil up the steep bank. The captain and the engine-driver of the boat followed behind. As they scrambled up the fog thinned, and they could see their Director a good way ahead. Suddenly they saw him start forward, calling to them over his shoulder: "Run! Run to the house! I've found one of them. Run, look for the other!"

He found one of them! And even he, the man of varied and startling experience, was somewhat discomposed by the manner of this finding. He stood and fumbled in his pockets (for a knife) while he faced Kayerts, who was hanging by a leather strap from the cross. He had evidently climbed the grave, which was high and narrow, and after tying the end of the strap to the arm, had swung himself off. His toes were only a couple of inches above the ground; his arms hung stiffly down; he seemed to be standing rigidly at attention, but with one purple cheek playfully posed on the shoulder. And, irreverently, he was putting out a swollen tongue at his Managing Director.

JULIO CORTÁZAR

Julio Cortázar (1914–1984) was born in Belgium, the son of an Argentine diplomat, and lived in Argentina and later in France (toward the end of his life he held dual citizenship in both countries). First earning his living as a teacher and a translator, he began to write stories, published in Spanish in the 1950s. With his first novel, *Hopscotch* (1963; English, 1966), he came to international fame; beyond its own merit the novel is widely agreed to have promoted wider acceptance in the United States of Latin American fiction. Among his other novels are *The Winners* (1960; English, 1973), *62: A Model Kit* (1968; English, 1972), and *A Manual for Manuel* (1973; English, 1978). His short story collections published in English translation include *End of the Game, and Other Stories* (1967), *Blow-up and Other Stories* (1968), and *A Change of Light and Other Stories* (1980). A constant, and often humorous, experimenter, Cortázar found innovative ways to reimagine reality: "The fantastic is something that one never says goodbye to lightly," he wrote. His preoccupation with the way stories are invented and interpreted and with the concept of life as a game is manifest in the two stories here, "Blow-up" and "End of the Game."

Blow-Up

Translated from the Spanish by Paul Blackburn

It'll never be known how this has to be told, in the first person or in the second, using the third person plural or continually inventing modes that will serve for nothing. If one might say: I will see the moon rose, or: we hurt me at the back of my eyes, and especially: you the blond woman was the clouds that race before my your his our yours their faces. What the hell.

Seated ready to tell it, if one might go to drink a bock over there, and the typewriter continue by itself (because I use the machine), that would be perfection. And that's not just a manner of speaking. Perfection, yes, because here is the aperture which must be counted also as a machine (of another sort, a Contax I.I.2) and it is possible that one machine may know more about another machine than I, you, she — the blond — and the clouds. But I have the dumb luck to know that if I go this Remington will sit turned to stone on top of the table with the air of being twice as quiet that mobile things have when they are not moving. So, I have to write. One of us all has to write, if this is going to get told. Better that it be me who am dead, for I'm less compromised than the rest; I who see only the clouds and can think without being distracted, write without being distracted (there goes another, with a grey edge) and remember without being distracted, I who am dead (and I'm alive, I'm not trying to fool anybody, you'll see when we get to the moment, because I have to begin some way and I've begun with this period, the last one back, the one at the beginning, which in the end is the best of periods when you want to tell something).

All of a sudden I wonder why I have to tell this, but if one begins to wonder why he does all he does do, if one wonders why he accepts an invitation to lunch (now a pigeon's flying by and it seems to me a sparrow), or why when someone has told us a good joke immediately there starts up something like a tickling in the stomach and we are not at peace until we've gone into the office across the hall and told the joke over again; then it feels good immediately, one is fine, happy, and can get back to work. For I imagine that no one has explained this, that really the best thing is to put aside all decorum and tell it, because, after all's done, nobody is ashamed of breathing or of putting on his shoes; they're things that you do, and when something weird happens, when you find a spider in your shoe or if you take a breath and feel like a broken window, then you have to tell what's happening, tell it to the guys at the office or to the doctor. Oh, doctor, every time I take a breath . . . Always tell it, always get rid of that tickle in the stomach that bothers you.

And now that we're finally going to tell it, let's put things a little bit in order, we'd be walking down the staircase in this house as far as Sunday, November 7, just a month back. One goes down five floors and stands then in the Sunday in the sun one would not have suspected of Paris in November, with a large appetite to walk around, to see things, to take photos (because we were photographers, I'm a photographer). I know that the most difficult thing is going to be finding a way to tell it, and I'm not afraid of repeating myself. It's going to be difficult because nobody really knows who it is telling it, if I am I or what actually occurred or what I'm seeing (clouds, and once in a while pigeon) or if, simply, I'm telling a truth which is only my truth, and then is the truth only for my stomach, for this impulse to go running out and to finish up in some manner with, this, whatever it is.

We're going to tell it slowly, what happens in the middle of what I'm writing is coming already. If they replace me, if, so soon, I don't know what to say, if the clouds stop coming and something else starts (because it's impossible that this keep coming, clouds passing continually and occasionally a pigeon), if something out of all this . . . And after the "if" what am I going to put if I'm going to close the sentence structure correctly? But if I begin to ask questions, I'll never tell anything, maybe to tell would be like an answer, at least for someone who's reading it.

Roberto Michel, French-Chilean, translator and in his spare time an amateur photographer, left number II, rue Monsieur-le-Prince Sunday November 7 of the current year (now there're two small ones passing, with silver linings). He had spent three weeks working on the French version of a treatise on challenges and appeals by José Norberto Allende, professor at the University of Santiago. It's rare that there's wind in Paris, and even less seldom a wind like this that swirled around corners and rose up to whip at old wooden venetian blinds behind which astonished ladies commented variously on how unreliable the weather had been these last few years. But the sun was out also, riding the wind and friend of the cats, so there was nothing that would keep me from taking a walk along the docks of the Seine and taking photos of the Conservatoire and Sainte-Chapelle. It was hardly ten o'clock, and I figured that by eleven the light would be good, the best you can get in the fall; to kill some time I detoured around by the Isle Saint-Louis and started to walk along the quai d'Anjou, I stared for a bit at the hôtel de Lauzun, I recited bits from Apollinaire which always get into my head whenever I pass in front of the hôtel de Lauzun (and at that I ought to be remembering the other poet, but Michel is an obstinate beggar), and when the wind stopped all at once and the sun came out at least twice as hard (I mean warmer, but really it's the same thing), I sat down on the parapet and felt terribly happy in the Sunday morning.

One of the many ways of contesting level-zero, and one of the best, is to take photographs, an activity in which one should start becoming an adept very early in life, teach it to children since it requires discipline, aesthetic education, a good eye and steady fingers. I'm not talking about waylaying the lie like any old reporter, snapping the stupid silhouette of the VIP leaving number 10 Downing Street, but in all ways when one is walking about with a camera, one has almost a duty to be attentive, to not lose that abrupt and happy rebound of sun's rays off an old stone, or the pigtails-flying run of a small girl going home with a loaf of bread or a bottle of milk. Michel knew that the photographer always worked as a permutation of his personal way of seeing the world as other than the camera insidiously imposed upon it (now a large cloud is going by, almost black), but he lacked no confidence in himself, knowing that he had only to go out without the Contax to recover the keynote of distraction, the sight without a frame around it, light without the dia-phragm aperture or I/250 sec. Right now (what a word, *now,* what a dumb lie) I was able to sit quietly on the railing overlooking the river watching the red and black motorboats passing below without it occurring to me to think photographically of the scenes, nothing more than letting myself go in the letting go of objects, running immobile in the stream of time. And then the wind was not blowing.

After, I wandered down the quai de Bourbon until getting to the end of the isle where the intimate square was (intimate because it was small, not that it was hidden, it offered its whole breast to the river and the sky), I enjoyed it, a lot. Nothing there but a couple and, of course, pigeons; maybe even some of those which are flying past now so that I'm seeing them. A leap up and I settled on the wall, and let myself turn about and be caught and fixed by the sun, giving it my face and ears and hands (I kept my gloves in my pocket). I had no desire to shoot pictures, and lit a cigarette to be doing something; I think it was that moment when the match was about to touch the tobacco that I saw the young boy for the first time.

What I'd thought was a couple seemed much more now a boy with his mother, although at the same time I realized that it was not a kid and his mother, and that it was a couple in the sense that we always allegate to couples when we see them leaning up against the parapets or embracing on the benches in the squares. As I had nothing else to do, I had more than enough time to wonder why the boy was so nervous, like a young colt or a hare, sticking his hands into his pockets, taking them out immediately, one after the other, running his fingers through his hair, changing his stance, and especially why was he afraid, well, you could guess that from every gesture, a fear suffocated by his shyness, an impulse to step backwards which he telegraphed, his body standing as if it were on the edge of flight, holding itself back in a final, pitiful decorum.

All this was so clear, ten feet away — and we were alone against the parapet at the tip of the island — that at the beginning the boy's fright didn't let me see the blond very well. Now, thinking back on it, I see her much better at that first second when I read her face (she'd turned around suddenly, swinging like a metal weathercock, and the eyes, the eyes were there), when I vaguely understood what might have been occurring to the boy and figured it would be worth the trouble to stay and watch (the wind was blowing their words away and they were speaking in a low murmur). I think that I know how to look, if it's something I know, and also that every looking oozes with mendacity, because it's that which expels us furthest outside ourselves, without the least guarantee, whereas to smell, or (but Michel rambles on to himself easily enough, there's no need to let him harangue on this way). In any case, if the likely inaccuracy can be seen beforehand, it becomes possible again to look; perhaps it suffices to choose between looking and the reality looked at, to strip things of all their unnecessary clothing. And surely all that is difficult besides.

As for the boy I remember the image before his actual body (that will clear itself up later), while now I am sure that I remember the woman's body much better than the image. She was thin and willowy, two unfair words to describe what she was, and was wearing an almost-black fur coat, almost long, almost handsome. All the morning's wind (now it was hardly a breeze and it wasn't cold) had blown through her blond hair which pared away her white, bleak face — two unfair words — and put the world at her feet and horribly alone in front of her dark eyes, her eyes fell on things like two eagles, two leaps into nothingness, two puffs of green slime. I'm not describing anything, it's more a matter of trying to understand it. And I said two puffs of green slime.

Let's be fair, the boy was well enough dressed and was sporting yellow gloves which I would have sworn belonged to his older brother, a student of law or sociology; it was pleasant to see the fingers of the gloves sticking out of his jacket pocket. For a long time I didn't see his face, barely a profile, not stupid — a terrified bird, a Fra Filippo angel, rice pudding with milk — and the back of an adolescent who wants to take up judo and has had a scuffle or two in defense of an idea or his sister. Turning fourteen, perhaps fifteen, one would guess that he was dressed and fed by his parents but without a nickel in his pocket, having to debate with his buddies before making up his mind to buy a coffee, a cognac, a pack of cigarettes. He'd walk through the streets thinking of the girls in his class, about how good it would be to go to the movies and see the latest film, or to buy novels or neckties or bottles of liquor with green and white labels on them. At home (it would be a respectable home, lunch at noon and romantic landscapes on the walls, with a dark entryway and a mahogany umbrella stand inside the door) there'd be the slow rain of time, for studying, for being mama's hope, for looking like dad, for writing to his aunt in Avignon. So that there was a lot of walking the streets, the whole of the river for him (but without a nickel) and the mysterious city of fifteen-year-olds with its signs in doorways, its terrifying cats, a paper of fried potatoes for thirty francs, the pornographic magazine folded four ways, a solitude like the emptiness of his pockets, the eagerness for so much that was incomprehensible but illumined by a total love, by the availability analogous to the wind and the streets.

This biography was of the boy and of any boy whatsoever, but this particular one now, you could see he was insular, surrounded solely by the blond's presence as she continued talking with him. (I'm tired of insisting, but two long ragged ones just went by. That morning I don't think I looked at the sky once, because what was happening with the boy and the woman appeared so soon I could do nothing but look at them and wait, look at them and . . .) To cut it short, the boy was agitated and one could guess without too much trouble what had just occurred a few minutes before, at most half-an-hour. The boy had come onto the tip of the island, seen the woman and thought her marvelous. The woman was waiting for that because she was there waiting for that, or maybe the boy arrived before her and she saw him from one of the balconies or from a car and got out to meet him, starting the conversation with whatever, from the beginning she was sure that he was going to be afraid and want to run off, and that, naturally, he'd stay, stiff and sullen, pretending experience and the pleasure of the adventure. The rest was easy because it was happening ten feet away from me, and anyone could have gauged the stages of the game, the derisive, competitive fencing; its major attraction was not that it was happening but in foreseeing its denouement. The boy would try to end it by pretending a date, an obligation, whatever, and would go stumbling off disconcerted, wishing he were walking with some assurance, but naked under the mocking glance which would follow him until he was out of sight. Or rather, he would stay there, fascinated or simply incapable of taking the initiative, and the woman would begin to touch his face gently, muss his hair, still talking to him voicelessly, and soon would take him by the arm to lead him off, unless he, with an uneasiness beginning to tinge the edge of desire, even his stake in the adventure, would rouse himself to put his arm around her waist and to kiss her. Any of this could have happened, though it did not, and perversely Michel waited, sitting on the railing, making the settings almost without looking at the camera, ready to take a picturesque shot of a corner of the island with an uncommon couple talking and looking at one another.

Strange how the scene (almost nothing: two figures there mismatched in their youth) was taking on a disquieting aura. I thought it was I imposing it, and that my photo, if I shot it, would reconstitute things in their true stupidity. I would have liked to know what he was thinking, a man in a grey hat sitting at the wheel of a car parked on the dock which led up to the footbridge, and whether he was reading the paper or asleep. I had just discovered him because people inside a parked car have a tendency to disappear, they get lost in that wretched, private cage stripped of the beauty that motion and danger give it. And nevertheless, the car had been there the whole time, forming part (or deforming that part) of the isle. A car: like saying a lighted streetlamp, a park bench. Never like saying wind, sunlight, those elements always new to the skin and the eyes, and also the boy and the woman, unique, put there to change the island, to show it to me in another way. Finally, it may have been that the man with the newspaper also became aware of what was happening and would, like me, feel that malicious sensation of waiting for everything to happen. Now the woman had swung around smoothly, putting the young boy between herself and the wall, I saw them almost in profile, and he was taller, though not much taller, and yet she dominated him, it seemed like she was hovering over him (her laugh, all at once, a whip of feathers), crushing him just by being there, smiling, one hand taking a stroll through the air. Why wait any longer? Aperture at sixteen, a sighting which would not include the horrible black car, but yes, that tree, necessary to break up too much grey space . . .

I raised the camera, pretended to study a focus which did not include them, and waited and watched closely, sure that I would finally catch the revealing expression, one that would sum it all up, life that is rhythmed by movement but which a stiff image destroys, taking time in cross section, if we do not choose the essential imperceptible fraction of it. I did not have to wait long. The woman was getting on with the job of handcuffing the boy smoothly, stripping from him what was left of his freedom a hair at a time, in an incredibly slow and delicious torture. I imagined the possible endings (now a small fluffy cloud appears, almost alone in the sky), I saw their arrival at the house (a basement apartment probably, which she would have filled with large cushions and cats) and conjectured the boy's terror and his desperate decision to play it cool and to be led off pretending there was nothing new in it for him. Closing my eyes, if I did in fact close my eyes, I set the scene: the teasing kisses, the woman mildly repelling the hands which were trying to undress her, like in novels, on a bed that would have a lilac-colored comforter, on the other hand she taking off his clothes, plainly mother and son under a milky yellow light, and everything would end up as usual, perhaps, but maybe everything would go otherwise, and the initiation of the adolescent would not happen, she would not let it happen, after a long prologue wherein the awkwardnesses, the exasperating caresses, the running of hands over bodies would be resolved in who knows what, in a separate and solitary pleasure, in a petulant denial mixed with the art of tiring and disconcerting so much poor innocence. It might go like that, it might very well go like that; that woman was not looking for the boy as a lover, and at the same time she was dominating him toward some end impossible to understand if you do not imagine it as a cruel game, the desire to desire without satisfaction, to excite herself for someone else, someone who in no way could be that kid.

Michel is guilty of making literature, of indulging in fabricated unrealities. Nothing pleases him more than to imagine exceptions to the rule, individuals outside the species, not-always-repugnant monsters. But that woman invited speculation, perhaps giving clues enough for the fantasy to hit the bullseye. Before she left, and now that she would fill my imaginings for several days, for I'm given to ruminating, I decided not to lose a moment more. I got it all into the view-finder (with the tree, the railing, the eleven-o'clock sun) and took the shot. In time to realize that they both had noticed and stood there looking at me, the boy surprised and as though questioning, but she was irritated, her face and body flat-footedly hostile, feeling robbed, ignominiously recorded on a small chemical image.

I might be able to tell it in much greater detail but it's not worth the trouble. The woman said that no one had the right to take a picture without permission, and demanded that I hand her over the film. All this in a dry, clear voice with a good Parisian accent, which rose in color and tone with every phrase. For my part, it hardly mattered whether she got the roll of film or not, but anyone who knows me will tell you, if you want anything from me, ask nicely. With the result that I restricted myself to formulating the opinion that not only was photography in public places not prohibited, but it was looked upon with decided favor, both private and official. And while that was getting said, I noticed on the sly how the boy was falling back, sort of actively backing up though without moving, and all at once (it seemed almost incredible) he turned and broke into a run, the poor kid, thinking that he was walking off and in fact in full flight, running past the side of the car, disappearing like a gossamer filament of angel-spit in the morning air.

But filaments of angel-spittle are also called devil-spit, and Michel had to endure rather particular curses, to hear himself called meddler and imbecile, taking great pains meanwhile to smile and to abate with simple movements of his head such a hard sell. As I was beginning to get tired, I heard the car door slam. The man in the grey hat was there, looking at us. It was only at that point that I realized he was playing a part in the comedy.

He began to walk toward us, carrying in his hand the paper he had been pretending to read. What I remember best is the grimace that twisted his mouth askew, it covered his face with wrinkles, changed somewhat both in location and shape because his lips trembled and the grimace went from one side of his mouth to the other as though it were on wheels, independent and involuntary. But the rest stayed fixed, a flour-powdered clown or bloodless man, dull dry skin, eyes deepset, the nostrils black and prominently visible, blacker than the eyebrows or hair or the black necktie. Walking cautiously as though the pavement hurt his feet; I saw patent-leather shoes with such thin soles that he must have felt every roughness in the pavement. I don't know why I got down off the railing, nor very well why I decided to not give them the photo, to refuse that demand in which I guessed at their fear and cowardice. The clown and the woman consulted one another in silence: we made a perfect and unbearable triangle, something I felt compelled to break with a crack of a whip. I laughed in their faces and began to walk off, a little more slowly, I imagine, than the boy. At the level of the first houses, beside the iron footbridge, I turned around to look at them. They were not moving, but the man had dropped his newspaper; it seemed to me that the woman, her back to the parapet, ran her hands over the stone with the classical and absurd gesture of someone pursued looking for a way out.

What happened after that happened here, almost just now, in a room on the fifth floor. Several days went by before Michel developed the photos he'd taken on Sunday; his shots of the Conservatoire and of Sainte-Chapelle were all they should be. Then he found two or three proof-shots he'd forgotten, a poor attempt to catch a cat perched astonishingly on the roof of a rambling public urinal, and also the shot of the blond and the kid. The negative was so good that he made an enlargement; the enlargement was so good that he made one very much larger, almost the size of a poster. It did not occur to him (now one wonders and wonders) that only the shots of the Conservatoire were worth so much work. Of the whole series, the snapshot of the tip of the island was the only one which interested him; he tacked up the enlargement on one wall of the room, and the first day he spent some time looking at it and remembering, that gloomy operation of comparing the memory with the gone reality; a frozen memory, like any photo, where nothing is missing, not even, and especially, nothingness, the true solidifier of the scene. There was the woman, there was the boy, the tree rigid above their heads, the sky as sharp as the stone of the parapet, clouds and stones melded into a single substance and inseparable (now one with sharp edges is going by, like a thunderhead). The first two days I accepted what I had done, from the photo itself to the enlargement on the wall, and didn't even question that every once in a while I would interrupt my translation of José Norberto Allende's treatise to encounter once more the woman's face, the dark splotches on the railing. I'm such a jerk; it had never occurred to me that when we look at a photo from the front, the eyes reproduce exactly the position and the vision of the lens; it's these things that are taken for granted and it never occurs to anyone to think about them. From my chair, with the typewriter directly in front of me, I looked at the photo ten feet away, and then it occurred to me that I had hung it exactly at the point of view of the lens. It looked very good that way; no doubt, it was the best way to appreciate a photo, though the angle from the diagonal doubtless has its pleasures and might even divulge different aspects. Every few minutes, for example when I was unable to find the way to say in good French what José Norberto

Allende was saying in very good Spanish, I raised my eyes and looked at the photo; sometimes the woman would catch my eye, sometimes the boy, sometimes the pavement where a dry leaf had fallen admirably situated to heighten a lateral section. Then I rested a bit from my labors, and I enclosed myself again happily in that morning in which the photo was drenched, I recalled ironically the angry picture of the woman demanding I give her the photograph, the boy's pathetic and ridiculous flight, the entrance on the scene of the man with the white face. Basically, I was satisfied with myself; my part had not been too brilliant, and since the French have been given the gift of sharp response, I did not see very well why I'd chosen to leave without a complete demonstration of the rights, privileges and prerogatives of citizens. The important thing, the really important thing was having helped the kid to escape in time (this in case my theorizing was correct, which was not sufficiently proven, but the running away itself seemed to show it so). Out of plain meddling, I had given him the opportunity finally to take advantage of his fright to do something useful; now he would be regretting it, feeling his honor impaired, his manhood diminished. That was better than the attentions of a woman capable of looking as she had looked at him on that island. Michel is something of a puritan at times, he believes that one should not seduce someone from a position of strength. In the last analysis, taking that photo had been a good act.

Well, it wasn't because of the good act that I looked at it between paragraphs while I was working. At that moment I didn't know the reason, the reason I had tacked the enlargement onto the wall; maybe all fatal acts happen that way, and that is the condition of their fulfillment. I don't think the almost-furtive trembling of the leaves on the tree alarmed me, I was working on a sentence and rounded it out successfully. Habits are like immense herbariums, in the end an enlargement of 32 × 28 looks like a movie screen, where, on the tip of the island, a woman is speaking with a boy and a tree is shaking its dry leaves over their heads.

But her hands were just too much. I had just translated: "In that case, the second key resides in the intrinsic nature of difficulties which societies . . ." — when I saw the woman's hand beginning to stir slowly, finger by finger. There was nothing left of me, a phrase in French which I would never have to finish, a typewriter on the floor, a chair that squeaked and shook, fog. The kid had ducked his head like boxers do when they've done all they can and are waiting for the final blow to fall; he had turned up the collar of his overcoat and seemed more a prisoner than ever, the perfect victim helping promote the catastrophe. Now the woman was talking into his ear, and her hand opened again to lay itself against his cheekbone, to caress and caress it, burning it, taking her time. The kid was less startled than he was suspicious, once or twice he poked his head over the woman's shoulder and she continued talking, saying something that made him look back every few minutes toward that area where Michel knew the car was parked and the man in the grey hat, carefully eliminated from the photo but present in the boy's eyes (how doubt that now) in the words of the woman, in the woman's hands, in the vicarious presence of the woman. When I saw the man come up, stop near them and look at them, his hands in his pockets and a stance somewhere between disgusted and demanding, the master who is about to whistle in his dog after a frolic in the square, I understood, if that was to understand, what had to happen now, what had to have happened then, what would have to happen at that moment, among these people, just where I had poked my nose in to upset an established order, interfering innocently in that which had not happened, but which was now going to happen, now was going to be fulfilled. And what I had imagined earlier was much less horrible than the reality, that woman, who was not there by herself, she was not caressing or propositioning or encouraging for her own pleasure, to lead the angel away with his tousled hair and play the tease with his terror and his eager grace. The real boss was waiting there, smiling petulantly, already certain of the business; he was not the first to send a woman in the vanguard, to bring him the prisoners manacled with flowers. The rest of it would be so simple, the car, some house or another, drinks, stimulating engravings, tardy tears, the awakening in hell. And there was nothing I could do, this time I could do absolutely nothing. My strength had been a photograph, that, there, where they were taking their revenge on me, demonstrating clearly what was going to happen. The photo had been taken, the time had run out, gone; we were so far from one another, the abusive act had certainly already taken place, the tears already shed, and the rest conjecture and sorrow. All at once the order was inverted, they were alive, moving, they were deciding and had decided, they were going to their future; and I on this side, prisoner of another time, in a room on the fifth floor, to not know who they were, that woman, that man, and that boy, to be only the lens of my camera, something fixed, rigid, incapable of intervention. It was horrible, their mocking me, deciding it before my impotent eye, mocking me, for the boy again was looking at the flour-faced clown and I had to accept the fact that he was going to say yes, that the proposition carried money with it or a gimmick, and I couldn't yell for him to run, or even open the road to him again with a new photo, a small and almost meek intervention which would ruin the framework of drool and perfume. Everything was going to resolve itself right there, at that moment; there was like an immense silence which had nothing to do with physical silence. It was stretching it out, setting itself up. I think I screamed, I screamed terribly, and that at that exact second I realized that I was beginning to move toward them, four inches, a step, another step, the tree swung its branches rhythmically in the foreground, a place where the railing was tarnished emerged from the frame, the woman's face turned toward me as though surprised, was enlarging, and then I turned a bit, I mean that the camera turned a little, and without losing sight of the woman, I began to close in on the man who was looking at me with the black holes he had in place of eyes, surprised and angered both, he looked, wanting to nail me onto the air, and at that instant I happened to see something like a large bird outside the focus that was flying in a single swoop in front of the picture, and I leaned up against the wall of my room and was happy because the boy had just managed to escape, I saw him running off, in focus again, sprinting with his hair flying in the wind, learning finally to fly across the island, to arrive at the footbridge, return to the city. For the second time he'd escaped them, for the second time I was helping him to escape, returning him to his precarious paradise. Out of breath, I stood in front of them; no need to step closer, the game was played out. Of the woman you could see just maybe a shoulder and a bit of the hair, brutally cut off by the frame of the picture; but the man was directly center, his mouth half open, you could see a shaking black tongue, and he lifted his hands slowly, bringing them into the foreground, an instant still in perfect focus, and then all of him a lump that blotted out the island, the tree, and I shut my eyes, I didn't want to see any more, and I covered my face and broke into tears like an idiot.

Now there's a big white cloud, as on all these days, all this untellable time. What remains to be said is always a cloud, two clouds, or long hours of a sky perfectly clear, a very clean, clear rectangle tacked up with pins on the wall of my room. That was what I saw when I opened my eyes and dried them with my fingers: the clear sky, and then a cloud that drifted in from the left, passed gracefully and slowly across and disappeared on the right. And then another, and for a change sometimes, everything gets grey, all one enormous cloud, and suddenly the splotches of rain cracking down, for a long spell you can see it raining over the picture, like a spell of weeping reversed, and little by little, the frame becomes clear, perhaps the sun comes out, and again the clouds begin to come, two at a time, three at a time. And the pigeons once in a while, and a sparrow or two.

JULIO CORTÁZAR

End of the Game

Translated from the Spanish by Paul Blackburn

Letitia, Holanda and I used to play by the Argentine Central tracks during the hot weather, hoping that Mama and Aunt Ruth would go up to their siesta so that we could get out past the white gate. After washing the dishes, Mama and Aunt Ruth were always tired, especially when Holanda and I were drying, because it was then that there were arguments, spoons on the floor, secret words that only we understood, and in general, an atmosphere in which the smell of the grease, José's yowling, and the dimness of the kitchen would end up in an incredible fight and the subsequent commotion. Holanda specialized in rigging this sort of brawl, for example, letting an already clean glass slip into the pan of dirty water, or casually dropping a remark to the effect that the Loza house had two maids to do all the work. I had other systems: I liked to suggest to Aunt Ruth that she was going to get an allergy rash on her hands if she kept scrubbing the pots instead of doing the cups and plates once in a while, which were exactly what Mama liked to wash, and over which they would confront one another soundlessly in a war of advantage to get the easy item. The heroic expedient, in case the bits of advice and the drawn-out family recollections began to bore us, was to upset some boiling water on the cat's back. Now that's a big lie about a scalded cat, it really is, except that you have to take the reference to cold water literally; because José never backed away from hot water, almost insinuating himself under it, poor animal, when we spilled a half-cup of it somewhere around 220° F., or less, a good deal less, probably, because his hair never fell out. The whole point was to get Troy burning, and in the confusion, crowned by a splendid G-flat from Aunt Ruth and Mama's sprint for the whipstick, Holanda and I would take no time at all to get lost in the long porch, toward the empty rooms off the back, where Letitia would be waiting for us, reading Ponson de Terrail, or some other equally inexplicable book.

Normally, Mama chased us a good part of the way, but her desire to bust in our skulls evaporated soon enough, and finally (we had barred the door and were begging for mercy in emotion-filled and very theatrical voices), she got tired and went off, repeating the same sentence: "Those ruffians'll end up on the street."

Where we ended up was by the Argentine Central tracks, when the house had settled down and was silent, and we saw the cat stretched out under the lemon tree to take its siesta also, a rest buzzing with fragrances and wasps. We'd open the white gate slowly, and when we shut it again with a slam like a blast of wind, it was a freedom which took us by the hands, seized the whole of our bodies and tumbled us out. Then we ran, trying to get the speed to scramble up the low embankment of the right-of-way, and there spread out upon the world, we silently surveyed our kingdom.

Our kingdom was this: a long curve of the tracks ended its bend just opposite the back section of the house. There was just the gravel incline, the crossties, and the double line of track; some dumb sparse grass among the rubble where mica, quartz and feldspar — the components of granite — sparkled like real diamonds in the two o'clock afternoon sun. When we stooped down to touch the rails (not wasting time because it would have been dangerous to spend much time there, not so much from the trains as for fear of being seen from the house), the heat off the stone roadbed flushed our faces, and facing into the wind from the river there was a damp heat against our cheeks and ears. We liked to bend our legs and squat down, rise, squat again, move from one kind of hot zone to the other, watching each other's faces to measure the perspiration — a minute or two later we would be sopping with it. And we were always quiet, looking down the track into the distance, or at the river on the other side, that stretch of coffee-and-cream river.

After this first inspection of the kingdom, we'd scramble down the bank and flop in the meager shadow of the willows next to the wall enclosing the house where the white gate was. This was the capital city of the kingdom, the wilderness city and the headquarters of our game. Letitia was the first to start the game; she was the luckiest and the most privileged of the three of us. Letitia didn't have to dry dishes or make the beds, she could laze away the day reading or pasting up pictures, and at night they let her stay up later if she asked to, not counting having a room to herself, special hot broth when she wanted it, and all kinds of other advantages. Little by little she had taken more and more advantage of these privileges, and had been presiding over the game since the summer before, I think really she was presiding over the whole kingdom; in any case she was quicker at saying things, and Holanda and I accepted them without protest, happy almost. It's likely that Mama's long lectures on how we ought to behave toward Letitia had had their effect, or simply that we loved her enough and it didn't bother us that she was boss. A pity that she didn't have the looks for the boss, she was the shortest of the three of us and very skinny. Holanda was skinny, and I never weighed over 110, but Letitia was scragglier than we were, and even worse, that kind of skinniness you can see from a distance in the neck and ears. Maybe it was the stiffness of her back that made her look so thin, for instance she could hardly move her head from side to side, she was like a folded-up ironing board, one of those kind they had in the Loza house, with a cover of white material. Like an ironing board with the wide part up, leaning closed against the wall. And she led us.

The best satisfaction was to imagine that someday Mama or Aunt Ruth would find out about the game. If they managed to find out about the game there would be an unbelievable mess. The G-flat and fainting fits, incredible protests of devotion and sacrifice ill-rewarded, and a string of words threatening the more celebrated punishments, closing the bid with a dire prediction of our fates, which consisted of the three of us ending up on the street. This final prediction always left us somewhat perplexed, because to end up in the street always seemed fairly normal to us.

First Letitia had us draw lots. We used to use pebbles hidden in the hand, count to twenty-one, any way at all. If we used the count-to-twenty-one system, we would pretend two or three more girls and include them in the counting to prevent cheating. If one of them came out 21, we dropped her from the group and started drawing again, until one of us won. Then Holanda and I lifted the stone and we got out the ornament-box. Suppose Holanda had won, Letitia and I chose the ornaments. The game took two forms: Statues and Attitudes. Attitudes did not require ornaments but an awful lot of expressiveness, for Envy you could show your teeth, make fists and hold them in a position so as to seem cringing. For Charity the ideal was an angelic face, eyes turned up to the sky, while the hands offered something — a rag, a ball, a branch of willow — to a poor invisible orphan. Shame and Fear were easy to do; Spite and Jealousy required a more conscientious study. The Statues were determined, almost all of them, by the choice of ornaments, and here absolute liberty reigned. So that a statue would come out of it, one had to think carefully of every detail in the costume. It was a rule of the game that the one chosen could not take part in the selection; the two remaining argued out the business at hand and then fitted the ornaments on. The winner had to invent her statue taking into account what they'd dressed her in, and in this way the game was much more complicated and exciting because sometimes there were counterplots, and the victim would find herself rigged out in adornments which were completely hopeless; so it was up to her to be quick then in composing a good statue. Usually when the game called for Attitudes, the winner came up pretty well outfitted, but there were times when the Statues were horrible failures.

Well, the story I'm telling, lord knows when it began, but things changed the day the first note fell from the train. Naturally the Attitudes and Statues were not for our own consumption, we'd have gotten bored immediately. The rules were that the winner had to station herself at the foot of the embankment, leaving the shade of the willow trees, and wait for the train from Tigre that passed at 2:08. At that height above Palermo the trains went by pretty fast and we weren't bashful doing the Statue or the Attitude. We hardly saw the people in the train windows, but with time, we got a bit more expert, and we knew that some of the passengers were expecting to see us. One man with white hair and tortoise-shell glasses used to stick his head out the window and wave at the Statue or the Attitude with a handkerchief. Boys sitting on the steps of the coaches on their way back from school shouted things as the train went by, but some of them remained serious and watching us. In actual fact, the Statue or the Attitude saw nothing at all, because she had to concentrate so hard on holding herself stock-still, but the other two under the willows would analyze in excruciating detail the great success produced, or the audience indifference. It was a Wednesday when the note dropped as the second coach went by. It fell very near Holanda (she did Malicious Gossip that day) and ricocheted toward me. The small piece of paper was tightly folded up and had been shoved through a metal nut. In a man's handwriting, and pretty bad too, it said: "The Statues very pretty. I ride in the third window of the second coach. Ariel B." For all the trouble of stuffing it through the nut and tossing it, it seemed to us a little dry, but it delighted us. We chose lots to see who would keep it, and I won. The next day nobody wanted to play because we all wanted to see what Ariel B. was like, but we were afraid he would misinterpret our interruption, so finally we chose lots and Letitia won. Holanda and I were very happy because Letitia did Statues very well, poor thing. The paralysis wasn't notice-able when she was still, and she was capable of gestures of enormous nobility. With Attitudes she always chose Generosity, Piety, Sacrifice and Renunciation. With Statues she tried for the style of the Venus in the parlor which Aunt Ruth called the Venus de Milo. For that reason we chose ornaments especially so that Ariel would be very impressed. We hung a piece of green velvet on her like a tunic, and a crown of willow on her hair. As we were wearing short sleeves, the Greek effect was terrific. Letitia practiced a little in the shade, and we decided that we'd show ourselves also and wave at Ariel, discreetly, but very friendly.

Letitia was magnificent, when the train came she didn't budge a finger. Since she couldn't turn her head, she threw it backward, bringing her arms against her body almost as though she were missing them; except for the green tunic, it was like looking at the Venus de Milo. In the third window we saw a boy with blond curly hair and light eyes, who smiled brightly when he saw that Holanda and I were waving at him. The train was gone in a second, but it was 4:30 and we were still discussing whether he was wearing a dark suit, a red tie, and if he were really nice or a creep. On Thursday I did an Attitude, Dejection, and we got another note which read: "The three of you I like very much. Ariel." Now he stuck his head and one arm out the window and laughed and waved at us. We figured him to be eighteen (we were sure he was no older than sixteen), and we decided that he was coming back every day from some English school, we couldn't stand the idea of any of the regular peanut factories. You could see that Ariel was super.

As it happened, Holanda had the terrific luck to win three days running. She surpassed herself, doing the attitudes Reproach and Robbery, and a very difficult Statue of The Ballerina, balancing on one foot from the time the train hit the curve. The next day I won, and the day after that too; when I was doing Horror, a note from Ariel almost caught me on the nose; at first we didn't understand it: "The prettiest is the laziest." Letitia was the last to understand it; we saw that she blushed and went off by herself, and Holanda and I looked at each other, just a little furious. The first judicial opinion it occurred to us to hand down was that Ariel was an idiot, but we couldn't tell Letitia that, poor angel, with the disadvantage she had to put up with. She said nothing, but it seemed to be understood that the paper was hers, and she kept it. We were sort of quiet going back to the house that day, and didn't get together that night. Letitia was very happy at the supper table, her eyes shining, and Mama looked at Aunt Ruth a couple of times as evidence of her own high spirits. In those days they were trying out a new strengthening treatment for Letitia, and considering how she looked, it was miraculous how well she was feeling.

Before we went to sleep, Holanda and I talked about the business. The note from Ariel didn't bother us so much, thrown from a train going its own way, that's how it is, but it seemed to us that Letitia from her privileged position was taking too much advantage of us. She knew we weren't going to say anything to her, and in a household where there's someone with some physical defect and a lot of pride, everyone pretends to ignore it starting with the one who's sick, or better yet, they pretend they don't know that the other one knows. But you don't have to exaggerate it either, and the way Letitia was acting at the table, or the way she kept the note, was just too much. That night I went back to having nightmares about trains, it was morning and I was walking on enormous railroad beaches covered with rails filled with switches, seeing in the distance the red glows of locomotives approaching, anxiously trying to calculate if the train was going to pass to my left and threatened at the same time by the arrival of an express back of me or — what was even worse — that one of the trains would switch off onto one of the sidings and run directly over me. But I forgot it by morning because Letitia was all full of aches and we had to help her get dressed. It seemed to us that she was a little sorry for the business yesterday and we were very nice to her, telling her that's what happens with walking too much and that maybe it would be better for her to stay in her room reading. She said nothing but came to the table for breakfast, and when Mama asked, she said she was fine and her back hardly hurt at all. She stated it firmly and looked at us.

That afternoon I won, but at that moment, I don't know what came over me, I told Letitia that I'd give her my place, naturally without telling her why. That this guy clearly preferred her and would look at her until his eyes fell out. The game drew to Statues, and we selected simple items so as not to complicate life, and she invented a sort of Chinese Princess, with a shy air, looking at the ground, and the hands placed together as Chinese princesses are wont to do. When the train passed, Holanda was lying on her back under the willows, but I watched and saw that Ariel had eyes only for Letitia. He kept looking at her until the train disappeared around the curve, and Letitia stood there motionless and didn't know that he had just looked at her that way. But when it came to resting under the trees again, we saw that she knew all right, and that she'd have been pleased to keep the costume on all afternoon and all night.

Wednesday we drew between Holanda and me, because Letitia said it was only fair she be left out. Holanda won, darn her luck, but Ariel's letter fell next to me. When I picked it up I had the impulse to give it to Letitia who didn't say a word, but I thought, then, that neither was it a matter of catering to everybody's wishes, and I opened it slowly. Ariel announced that the next day he was going to get off at the nearby station and that he would come by the embankment to chat for a while. It was all terribly written, but the final phrase was handsomely put: "Warmest regards to the three Statues." The signature looked like a scrawl though we remarked on its personality.

While we were taking the ornaments off Holanda, Letitia looked at me once or twice. I'd read them the message and no one had made any comments, which was very upsetting because finally, at last, Ariel was going to come and one had to think about this new development and come to some decision. If they found out about it at the house, or if by accident one of the Loza girls, those envious little runts, came to spy on us, there was going to be one incredible mess. Furthermore, it was extremely unlike us to remain silent over a thing like this; we hardly looked at one another, putting the ornaments away and going back through the white gate to the house.

Aunt Ruth asked Holanda and me to wash the cat, and she took Letitia off for the evening treatment and finally we could get our feelings off our chests. It seemed super that Ariel was going to come, we'd never had a friend like that, our cousin Tito we didn't count, a dumbbell who cut out paper dolls and believed in first communion. We were extremely nervous in our expectation and José, poor angel, got the short end of it. Holanda was the braver of the two and brought up the subject of Letitia. I didn't know what to think, on the one hand it seemed ghastly to me that Ariel should find out, but also it was only fair that things clear themselves up, no one had to out and out put herself on the line for someone else. What I really would have wanted was that Letitia not suffer; she had enough to put up with and now the new treatment and all those things.

That night Mama was amazed to see us so quiet and said what a miracle, and had the cat got our tongues, then looked at Aunt Ruth and both of them thought for sure we'd been raising hell of some kind and were conscience-stricken. Letitia ate very little and said that she hurt and would they let her go to her room to read Rocambole. Though she didn't much want to, Holanda gave her a hand, and I sat down and started some knitting, something I do only when I'm nervous. Twice I thought to go down to Letitia's room, I couldn't figure out what the two of them were doing there alone, but then Holanda came back with a mysterious air of importance and sat next to me not saying a word until Mama and Aunt Ruth cleared the table. "She doesn't want to go tomorrow. She wrote a letter and said that if he asks a lot of questions we should give it to him." Half-opening the pocket of her blouse she showed me the lilac-tinted envelope. Then they called us in to dry the dishes, and that night we fell asleep almost immediately, exhausted by all the high-pitched emotion and from washing José.

The next day it was my turn to do the marketing and I didn't see Letitia all morning, she stayed in her room. Before they called us to lunch I went in for a moment and found her sitting at the window with a pile of pillows and a new Rocambole novel. You could see she felt terrible, but she started to laugh and told me about a bee that couldn't find its way out and about a funny dream she had had. I said it was a pity she wasn't coming out to the willows, but I found it difficult to put it nicely. "If you want, we can explain to Ariel that you feel upset," I suggested, but she said no and shut up like a clam. I insisted for a little while, really, that she should come, and finally got terribly gushy and told her she shouldn't be afraid, giving as an example that true affection knows no barriers and other fat ideas we'd gotten from *The Treasure of Youth,* but it got harder and harder to say anything to her because she was looking out the window and looked as if she were going to cry. Finally I left, saying that Mama needed me. Lunch lasted for days, and Holanda got a slap from Aunt Ruth for having spattered some tomato sauce from the spaghetti onto the tablecloth. I don't even remember doing the dishes, right away we were out under the willows hugging one another, very happy, and not jealous of one another in the slightest. Holanda explained to me everything we had to say about our studies so that Ariel would be impressed, because high school students despised girls who'd only been through grade school and studied just home ec and knew how to do raised needlework. When the train went past at 2:08, Ariel waved his arms enthusiastically, and we waved a welcome to him with our embossed handkerchiefs. Some twenty minutes later we saw him arrive by the embankment; he was taller than we had thought and dressed all in grey.

I don't even remember what we talked about at first; he was somewhat shy in spite of having come and the notes and everything, and said a lot of considerate things. Almost immediately he praised our Statues and Attitudes and asked our names, and why had the third one not come. Holanda explained that Letitia had not been able to come, and he said that that was a pity and that he thought Letitia was an exquisite name. Then he told us stuff about the Industrial High School, it was not the English school, unhappily, and wanted to know if we would show him the ornaments. Holanda lifted the stone and we let him see the things. He seemed to be very interested in them, and at different times he would take one of the ornaments and say, "Letitia wore this one day," or "This was for the Oriental statue," what he meant was the Chinese Princess. We sat in the shade under a willow and he was happy but distracted, and you could see that he was only being polite. Holanda looked at me two or three times when the conversation lapsed into silence, and that made both of us feel awful, made us want to get out of it, or wish that Ariel had never come at all. He asked again if Letitia were ill and Holanda looked at me and I thought she was going to tell him, but instead she answered that Letitia had not been able to come. Ariel drew geometric figures in the dust with a stick and occasionally looked at the white gate and we knew what he was thinking, and because of that Holanda was right to pull out the lilac envelope and hand it up to him, and he stood there surprised with the envelope in his hand; then he blushed while we explained to him that Letitia had sent it to him, and he put the letter in an inside jacket pocket, not wanting to read it in front of us. Almost immediately he said that it had been a great pleasure for him and that he was delighted to have come, but his hand was soft and unpleasant in a way it'd have been better for the interview to end right away, although later we could only think of his grey eyes and the sad way he had of smiling. We also agreed on how he had said good-bye: "Until always," a form we'd never heard at home and which seemed to us so godlike and poetic. We told all this to Letitia who was waiting for us under the lemon tree in the patio, and I would have liked to have asked her what she had said in the letter, but I don't know what, it was because she'd sealed the envelope before giving it to Holanda, so I didn't say anything about that and only told her what Ariel was like and how many times he'd asked for her. This was not at all an easy thing to do because it was a nice thing and a terrible thing at the same time; we noticed that Letitia was feeling very happy and at the same time she was almost crying, and we found ourselves saying that Aunt Ruth wanted us now and we left her looking at the wasps in the lemon tree.

When we were going to sleep that night, Holanda said to me, "The game's finished from tomorrow on, you'll see." But she was wrong though not by much, and the next day Letitia gave us the regular signal when dessert came around. We went out to wash the dishes somewhat astonished, and a bit sore, because that was sheer sauciness on Letitia's part and not the right thing to do. She was waiting for us at the gate, and we almost died of fright when we got to the willows for she brought out of her pocket Mama's pearl collar and all her rings, even Aunt Ruth's big one with the ruby. If the Loza girls were spying on us and saw us with the jewels, sure as anything Mama would learn about it right away and kill us, the nasty little creeps. But Letitia wasn't scared and said if anything happened she was the only one responsible. "I would like you to leave it to me today," she added without looking at us. We got the ornaments out right away, all of a sudden we wanted to be very kind to Letitia and give her all the pleasure, although at the bottom of everything we were still feeling a little spiteful. The game came out Statues, and we chose lovely things that would go well with jewels, lots of peacock feathers to set in the hair, and a fur that she put on like a turban. We saw that she was thinking, trying the Statue out, but without moving, and when the train appeared on the curve she placed herself at the foot of the incline with all the jewels sparkling in the sun. She lifted her arms as if she were going to do an Attitude instead of a Statue, her hands pointed at the sky with her head thrown back (the only direction she could, poor thing) and bent her body backwards so far it scared us. To us it seemed terrific, the most regal statue she'd ever done; then we saw Ariel looking at her, hung halfway out the window he looked just at her, turning his head and looking at her without seeing us, until the train carried him out of sight all at once. I don't know why, the two of us started running at the same time to catch Letitia who was standing there, still with her eyes closed and enormous tears all down her face. She pushed us back, not angrily, but we helped her stuff the jewels in her pocket, and she went back to the house alone while we put the ornaments away in their box for the last time. We knew almost what was going to happen, but just the same we went out to the willows the next day, just the two of us, after Aunt Ruth imposed absolute silence so as not to disturb Letitia who hurt and who wanted to sleep. When the train came by, it was no surprise to see the third window empty, and while we were grinning at one another, somewhere between relief and being furious, we imagined Ariel riding on the other side of the coach, not moving in his seat, looking off toward the river with his grey eyes.

JOSÉ DONOSO

Chilean José Donoso was born in Santiago in 1924. In a varied career he has earned a degree from Princeton University, worked as a shepherd in Patagonia, practiced journalism, and taught writing. For many years Donoso lived in Spain, voluntarily expatriating himself from the political scene in Chile after the overthrow of Salvador Allende. He returned to Santiago in the 1980s. He is deemed one of the leading South American writers of this century, but recognition in Chile came slowly: he had to guarantee sales of one hundred copies of his first collection of short stories, and ultimately he and friends peddled both it and his first novel on street corners. His novels include *Coronation* (1957; English, 1965), *A House in the Country* (1978; English, 1984), and *Curfew* (1988). His short story collections include *Charleston and Other Stories* (1960; English, 1970) and *The Major Stories of José Donoso* (1966). For some time Donoso wrote in an essentially realist style; with the publication of *The Obscene Bird of Night* (1970; English, 1973) he moved toward a more hallucinatory vision. But even in his early work — as in "The Walk," for example — he evidenced a fascination with apartness, madness, and disintegration.

The Walk

Translated from the Spanish by Andree Conrad

It happened when I was very small, when my Aunt Matilde and Uncle Gustavo and Uncle Armando, my father's unmarried sister and brothers, and my father himself, were still alive. Now they are all dead. That is, I'd rather think they are all dead, because it's easier, and it's too late now to be tortured with questions that were certainly not asked at the opportune moment. They weren't asked because the events seemed to paralyze the three brothers, leaving them shaken and horrified. Afterwards, they erected a wall of forgetfulness or indifference in front of it all so they could keep their silence and avoid tormenting themselves with futile conjectures. Maybe it wasn't that way; it could be that my imagination and my memory play me false. After all, I was only a boy at the time, and they weren't required to include me in their anguished speculations, if there ever were any, or keep me informed of the outcome of their conversations.

What was I to think? Sometimes I heard the brothers talking in the library in low voices, lingeringly, as was their custom; but the thick door screened the meaning of the words, allowing me to hear only the deep, deliberate counterpoint of their voices. What were they saying? I wanted them to be talking in there about what was really important; to abandon the respectful coldness with which they addressed one another, to open up their doubts and anxieties and let them bleed. But I had so little faith that would happen; while I loitered in the high-walled vestibule near the library door, the certainty was engraved on my mind that they had chosen to forget, and had come together only to discuss, as always, the cases that fell within their bailiwick, maritime law. Now I think perhaps they were right to want to erase it all, for why should they live with the useless terror of having to accept that the streets of a city can swallow a human being, annul it, leave it without life or death, suspended in a dimension more threatening than any dimension with a name?

And yet . . .

One day, months after the incident, I surprised my father looking down at the street from the second-floor sitting room. The sky was narrow, dense, and the humid air weighed on the big limp leaves of the ailanthus trees. I went over to my father, anxious for some minimal explanation.

'What are you doing here, father?' I whispered.

When he answered, something closed suddenly over the desperation on his face, like a shutter slamming on an unmentionable scene.

'Can't you see? I'm smoking,' he answered.

And he lit a cigarette.

It wasn't true. I knew why he was looking up and down the street, with his eyes saddened, once in a while bringing his hand up to his soft brown goatee: it was in hopes of seeing her reappear, come back just like that, under the trees along the sidewalk, with the white dog trotting at her heels. Was he waiting there to gain some certainty?

Little by little I realized that not only my father but both his brothers, as if hiding from one another and without admitting even to themselves what they were doing, hovered around the windows of the house, and if a passerby chanced to look up from the sidewalk across the street, he might spot the shadow of one of them posted beside a curtain, or a face aged by suffering in wait behind the window panes.

2

Yesterday I passed the house we lived in then. It's been years since I was last there. In those days the street under the leafy ailanthus trees was paved with quebracho wood, and from time to time a noisy streetcar would go by. Now there aren't any wooden pavements, or streetcars, or trees along the sidewalk. But our house is still standing, narrow and vertical as a book slipped in between the thick shapes of the new buildings; it has stores on the ground floor and a loud sign advertising knit undershirts stretched across the two second-floor balconies.

When we lived there, most of the houses were tall and slender like ours. The block was always cheerful, with children playing games in the splashes of sunlight on the sidewalks, and servants from the prosperous homes gossiping as they came back from shopping. But our house wasn't happy. I say 'wasn't happy' as opposed to 'was sad,' because that's exactly what I mean. The word 'sad' wouldn't be correct because it has connotations that are too clearly defined; it has a weight and dimensions of its own. And what went on in our house was exactly the opposite: an absence, a lack, which, because it was unknown, was irremediable, something that had no weight, yet weighed because it didn't exist.

When my mother died, before I turned four, they thought I needed to have a woman around to care for me. Because Aunt Matilde was the only woman in the family and lived with my uncles Gustavo and Armando, the three of them came to our house, which was big and empty.

Aunt Matilde carried out her duties toward me with the punctiliousness characteristic of everything she did. I didn't doubt that she cared for me, but I never experienced that affection as something palpable that united us. There was something rigid about her feelings, as there was about those of the men in the family, and love was retained within each separate being, never leaping over the boundaries to express itself and unite us. Their idea of expressing affection consisted of carrying out their duties toward one another perfectly, and above all, of never upsetting one another. Perhaps to express affection otherwise was no longer necessary to them, since they shared so many anecdotes and events in which, possibly, affection had already been expressed to the saturation point, and all this conjectural past of tenderness was now stylized in the form of precise actions, useful symbols that did not require further explanation. Respect alone remained, as a point of contact among four silent, isolated relatives who moved through the halls of that deep house which, like a book, revealed only its narrow spine to the street.

I, of course, had no anecdotes in common with Aunt Matilde. How could I, since I was a boy and only half understood the austere motives of grown-ups? I desperately wanted this contained affection to overflow, to express itself differently, in enthusiasm, for example, or a joke. But she could not guess this desire of mine because her attention wasn't focused on me. I was only a peripheral person in her life, never central. And I wasn't central because the center of her whole being was filled with my father and my uncles Gustavo and Armando. Aunt Matilde was the only girl — an ugly girl at that — in a family of handsome men, and realizing she was unlikely to find a husband, she dedicated herself to the comfort of those men: keeping house for them, taking care of their clothes, preparing their favorite dishes. She carried out these functions without the slightest servility, proud of her role because she had never once doubted her brothers' excellence and dignity. In addition, like all women, she possessed in great measure that mysterious faith in physical well-being, thinking that if it is not the main thing, it is certainly the first, and that not to be hungry or cold or uncomfortable is the prerequisite of any good of another order. It wasn't that she suffered if defects of that nature arose, but rather that they made her impatient, and seeing poverty or weakness around her, she took immediate steps to remedy what she did not doubt were mere errors in a world that ought to be — no, *had* to be — perfect. On another plane, this was intolerance of shirts that weren't ironed exquisitely, of meat that wasn't a prime cut, of dampness leaking into the humidor through someone's carelessness. Therein lay Aunt Matilde's undisputed strength, and through it she nourished the roots of her brothers' grandness and accepted their protection because they were men, stronger and wiser than she.

Every night after dinner, following what must have been an ancient family ritual, Aunt Matilde went upstairs to the bedrooms and turned down the covers on each one of her brothers' beds, folding up the bedspreads with her bony hands. For him who was sensitive to the cold, she would lay a blanket at the foot of the bed; for him who read before going to sleep, she would prop a feather pillow against the headboard. Then, leaving the lamps lit on the night tables beside their vast beds, she went downstairs to the billiard room to join the men, to have coffee with them and play a few caroms before they retired, as if by her command, to fill the empty effigies of the pajamas laid out on the neatly turned-down white sheets.

But Aunt Matilde never opened my bed. Whenever I went up to my room I held my breath, hoping to find my bed turned down with the recognizable expertise of her hands, but I always had to settle for the style, so much less pure, of the servant who did it. She never conceded me this sign of importance because I was not one of her brothers. And not to be 'one of my brothers' was a shortcoming shared by so many people . . .

Sometimes Aunt Matilde would call me in to her room, and sewing near the high window she would talk to me without ever asking me to reply, taking it for granted that all my feelings, tastes, and thoughts were the result of what she was saying, certain that nothing stood in the way of my receiving her words intact. I listened to her carefully. She impressed on me what a privilege it was to have been born the son of one of her brothers, which made it possible to have contact with all of them. She spoke of their absolute integrity and genius as lawyers in the most intricate of maritime cases, informing me of her enthusiasm regarding their prosperity and distinction, which I would undoubtedly continue. She explained the case of an embargo on a copper shipment, another about damages resulting from a collision with an insignificant tugboat, and another having to do with the disastrous effects of the overlong stay of a foreign ship. But in speaking to me of ships, her words did not evoke the magic of those hoarse foghorns I heard on summer nights when, kept awake by the heat, I would climb up to the attic and watch from a roundel the distant lights floating, and those darkened blocks of the recumbent city to which I had no access because my life was, and always would be, perfectly organized. Aunt Matilde did not evoke that magic for me because she was ignorant of it; it had no place in her life, since it could not have a place in the life of people destined to die with dignity and then establish themselves in complete comfort in heaven, a heaven that would be identical to our house. Mute, I listened to her words, my eyes fixed on the length of light-colored thread which, rising against the black of her blouse, seemed to catch all the light from the window. I had a melancholy feeling of frustration, hearing those foghorns in the night and seeing that dark and starry city so much like the heaven in which Aunt Matilde saw no mystery at all. But I rejoiced at the world of security her words sketched out for me, that magnificent rectilinear road which ended in a death not feared, exactly like this life, lacking the fortuitous and unexpected. For death was not terrible. It was the final cutoff, clean and definite, nothing more. Hell existed, of course, though not for us, but rather to punish the rest of the city's inhabitants, or those nameless sailors who caused the damages that, after the struggle in the courts was over, always filled the family bank accounts.

Any notion of the unexpected, of any kind of fear, was so alien to Aunt Matilde that, because I believe fear and love to be closely related, I am overcome by the temptation to think that she didn't love anybody, not at that time. But perhaps I am wrong. In her own rigid, isolated way, it is possible that she was tied to her brothers by some kind of love. At night, after dinner, when they gathered in the billiard room for coffee and a few rounds, I went with them. There, faced with this circle of confined loves which did not include me, I suffered, perceiving that they were no longer tied together by their affection. It's strange that my imagination, remembering that house, doesn't allow more than grays, shadows, shades; but when I evoke that hour, the strident green of the felt, the red and white of the billiard balls, and the tiny cube of blue chalk begin to swell in my memory, illuminated by the hanging lamp that condemned the rest of the room to darkness. Following one of the many family rituals, Aunt Matilde's refined voice would rescue each of her brothers from the darkness as his turn came up: 'Your shot, Gustavo . . .'

And cue in hand, Uncle Gustavo would lean over the green of the table, his face lit up, fragile as paper, the nobility of it strangely contradicted by his small, close-set eyes. When his turn was over, he retreated into the shadows, where he puffed on a cigar whose smoke floated lackadaisically off, dissolved by the darkness of the ceiling. Then their sister would say: 'Your shot, Armando . . .'

And Uncle Armando's soft, timid face, his great blue eyes shielded by gold-framed glasses, would descend into the light. His game was generally bad, because he was the 'baby,' as Aunt Matilde sometimes called him. After the comments elicited by his game, he would take refuge behind the newspaper and Aunt Matilde would say: 'Pedro, your shot . . .'

I held my breath watching my father lean over to shoot; I held it seeing him succumb to his sister's command, and, my heart in a knot, I prayed he would rebel against the established order. Of course, I couldn't know that that rigid order was in itself a kind of rebellion invented by them against the chaotic, so that the terrible hand of what cannot be explained or solved would never touch them. Then my father would lean over the green felt, his soft glance measuring the distances and positions of the balls. He would make his play and afterwards heave a sigh, his moustache and goatee fluttering a little around his half-open mouth. Then he would hand me his cue to chalk with the little blue cube. By assigning me this small role, he let me touch at least the periphery of the circle that tied him to his brothers and sister, without letting me become more than tangential to it.

Afterwards Aunt Matilde played. She was the best shot. Seeing her ugly face, built up it seemed out of the defects of her brothers' faces, descend into the light, I knew she would win; she had to win. And yet . . . didn't I see a spark of joy in those tiny eyes in the middle of that face, as irregular as a suddenly clenched fist, when by accident one of the men managed to defeat her? That drop of joy was because, although she might want to, she could never have *let* them win. That would have been to introduce the mysterious element of love into a game which should not include it, because affection had to remain in its place, without overflowing to warp the precise reality of a carom.

3

I never liked dogs. Perhaps I had been frightened by one as a baby, I don't remember, but they have always annoyed me. In any case, at that time my dislike of animals was irrelevant since we didn't have any dogs in the house; I didn't go out very often, so there were few opportunities for them to molest me. For my uncles and father, dogs, as well as the rest of the animal kingdom, did not exist. Cows, of course, supplied the cream that enriched our Sunday dessert brought in on a silver tray; and birds chirped pleasantly at dusk in the elm tree, the only inhabitant of the garden behind our house. The animal kingdom existed only to the extent that it contributed to the comfort of their persons. It is needless to say, then, that the existence of dogs, especially our ragged city strays, never even grazed their imaginations.

It's true that occasionally, coming home from Mass on Sunday, a dog might cross our path, but it was easy to ignore it. Aunt Matilde, who always walked ahead with me, simply chose not to see it, and some steps behind us, my father and uncles strolled discussing problems too important to allow their attention to be drawn by anything so banal as a stray dog.

Sometimes Aunt Matilde and I went early to Mass to take communion. I was almost never able to concentrate on receiving the sacrament, because generally the idea that she was watching me without actually looking at me occupied the first plane of my mind. Although her eyes were directed toward the altar or her head bowed before the Almighty, any movement I made attracted her attention, so that coming out of church, she would tell me with hidden reproach that doubtless some flea trapped in the pew had prevented my concentrating on the thought that we shall all meet death in the end and on praying for it not to be too painful, for that was the purpose of Mass, prayer, and communion.

It was one of those mornings.

A fine mist was threatening to transform itself into a storm, and the quebracho paving extended its neat glistening fan shapes from sidewalk to sidewalk, bisected by the streetcar rails. I was cold and wanted to get home, so I hurried the pace under Aunt Matilde's black umbrella. Few people were out because it was early. A colored gentleman greeted us without tipping his hat. My aunt then proceeded to explain her dislike of persons of mixed race, but suddenly, near where we were walking, a streetcar I didn't hear coming braked loudly, bringing her monologue to an end. The conductor put his head out the window: 'Stupid dog!' he shouted.

We stopped to look. A small white bitch escaped from under the wheels, and, limping painfully with its tail between its legs, took refuge in a doorway. The streetcar rolled off.

'These dogs, it's the limit the way they let them run loose . . .' protested Aunt Matilde.

Continuing on our way, we passed the dog cowering in the doorway. It was small and white, with legs too short for its body and an ugly pointed nose that revealed a whole genealogy of alleyway misalliances, the product of different races running around the city for generations looking for food in garbage cans and harbor refuse. It was soaking wet, weak, shivering with the cold or a fever. Passing in front of it, I witnessed a strange sight: my aunt's and the dog's eyes met. I couldn't see the expression on my aunt's face. I only saw the dog look at her, taking possession of her glance, whatever it contained, merely because she was looking at it.

We headed home. A few paces further on, when I had almost forgotten the dog, my aunt startled me by turning abruptly around and exclaiming: 'Shoo, now! Get along with you!'

She had turned around completely certain of finding it following us and I trembled with the unspoken question prompted by my surprise: 'How did she know?' She couldn't have heard it because the dog was following us at some distance. But she didn't doubt it. Did the glance that passed between them, of which I had only seen the mechanical part — the dog's head slightly raised toward Aunt Matilde, Aunt Matilde's head slightly turned toward it — did it contain some secret agreement, some promise of loyalty I hadn't perceived? I don't know. In any case, when she turned to shoo the dog, her voice seemed to contain an impotent desire to put off a destiny that had already been accomplished. Probably I say all this in hindsight, my imagination imbuing something trivial with special meaning. Nevertheless, I certainly felt surprise, almost fear, at the sight of my aunt suddenly losing her composure and condescending to turn around, thereby conceding rank to a sick, dirty dog following us for reasons that could not have any importance.

We arrived home. We climbed the steps and the animal stayed down below, watching us through the torrential rain that had just begun. We went inside, and the delectable smell of a post-communion breakfast erased the dog from my mind. I had never felt the protectiveness of our house so deeply as I did that morning; the security of those walls delimiting my world had never been so delightful to me.

What did I do the rest of the day? I don't remember, but I suppose I did the usual thing: read magazines, did homework, wandered up and down the stairs, went to the kitchen to ask what was for dinner.

On one of my tours through the empty rooms — my uncles got up late on rainy Sundays, excusing themselves from church — I pulled a curtain back to see if the rain was letting up. The storm went on. Standing at the foot of the steps, still shivering and watching the house, I saw the white dog again. I let go of the curtain to avoid seeing it there, soaking wet and apparently mesmerized. Suddenly, behind me, from the dark part of the sitting room, Aunt Matilde's quiet voice reached me, as she leaned over to touch a match to the wood piled in the fireplace: 'Is she still there?'

'Who?'

I knew perfectly well who.

'The white dog.'

I answered that it was. But my voice was uncertain in forming the syllables, as if somehow my aunt's question was pulling down the walls around us, letting the rain and the inclement wind enter and take over the house.

4

That must have been the last of the winter storms, because I remember quite vividly that in the following days the weather cleared and the nights got warmer.

The white dog remained posted at our door, ever trembling, watching the window as though looking for somebody. In the morning, as I left for school, I would try to scare it away, but as soon as I got on the bus, I saw it peep timidly around the corner or from behind a lamppost. The servants tried to drive it away too, but their attempts were just as futile as my own, because the dog always came back, as if to stay near our house was a temptation it had to obey, no matter how dangerous.

One night we were all saying good night to one another at the foot of the stairs. Uncle Gustavo, who always took charge of turning off the lights, had taken care of all of them except that of the staircase, leaving the great dark space of the vestibule populated with darker clots of furniture. Aunt Matilde, who was telling Uncle Armando to open his window to let some air in, suddenly fell silent, leaving her good nights unfinished. The rest of us, who had begun to climb the stairs, stopped cold.

'What's the matter?' asked my father, coming down a step.

'Go upstairs,' murmured Aunt Matilde, turning to gaze into the shadows of the vestibule.

But we didn't go upstairs.

The silence of the sitting room, generally so spacious, filled up with the secret voice of each object — a grain of dirt slipping down between the old wallpaper and the wall, wood creaking, a loose window pane rattling — and those brief seconds were flooded with sounds. Someone else was in the room with us. A small white shape stood out in the shadows near the service door. It was the dog, who limped slowly across the vestibule in the direction of Aunt Matilde, and without even looking at her lay down at her feet.

It was as if the dog's stillness made movement possible for us as we watched the scene. My father came down two steps, Uncle Gustavo turned on the lights, Uncle Armando heavily climbed the stairs and shut himself in his room.

'What is this?' my father asked.

Aunt Matilde remained motionless.

'How could she have got in?' she asked herself suddenly.

Her question seemed to imply a feat: in this lamentable condition, the dog had leaped over the walls, or climbed through a broken window in the basement, or evaded the servants' vigilance by slipping through a door left open by accident.

'Matilde, call for somebody to get it out of here,' my father said, and went upstairs followed by Uncle Gustavo.

The two of us stood looking at the dog.

'She's filthy,' she said in a low voice. 'And she has a fever. Look, she's hurt . . .'

She called one of the servants to take her away, ordering her to give the dog food and call the veterinarian the next day.

'Is it going to stay in the house?' I asked.

'How can she go outside like that?' Aunt Matilde murmured. 'She has to get better before we can put her out. And she'll have to get better quickly, because I don't want any animals in the house.' Then she added: 'Get upstairs to bed.'

She followed the servant who was taking the dog away.

I recognized Aunt Matilde's usual need to make sure everything around her went well, the strength and deftness that made her the undoubted queen of things immediate, so secure inside her limitations that for her the only necessary thing was to correct flaws, mistakes not of intention or motive, but of state of being. The white dog, therefore, was going to get well. She herself would take charge of that, because the dog had come within her sphere of power. The veterinarian would bandage the dog's foot under her watchful eyes, and, protected by gloves and a towel, she herself would undertake to clean its sores with disinfectants that would make it whimper. Aunt Matilde remained deaf to those whimpers, certain, absolutely certain, that what she was doing was for the dog's good.

And so it was.

The dog stayed in the house. It wasn't that I could see it, but I knew the balance between the people who lived there, and the presence of any stranger, even if in the basement, would establish a difference in the order of things. Something, something informed me of its presence under the same roof as myself. Perhaps that something was not so very imponderable. Sometimes I saw Aunt Matilde with rubber gloves in her hand, carrying a vial full of red liquid. I found scraps of meat on a dish in a basement passageway when I went down to look at a bicycle I had recently been given. Sometimes, the suspicion of a bark would reach my ears faintly, absorbed by floors and walls.

One afternoon I went down to the kitchen and the white dog came in, painted like a clown with the red disinfectant. The servants threw it out unceremoniously. But I could see it wasn't limping anymore, and its once droopy tail now curled up like a plume, leaving its hindquarters shamelessly exposed.

That afternoon I said to Aunt Matilde: 'When are you going to get rid of it?'

'What?' she asked.

She knew perfectly well what I meant.

'The white dog.'

'She's not well yet,' she answered.

Later on, I was about to bring up the subject again, to tell her that even if the dog wasn't completely well yet, there was nothing to prevent it from standing on its hind legs and rooting around in the garbage pails for food. But I never did, because I think that was the night Aunt Matilde, after losing the first round of billiards, decided she didn't feel like playing anymore. Her brothers went on playing and she, sunk in the big leather sofa, reminded them of their turns. After a while she made a mistake in the shooting order. Everybody was disconcerted for a moment, but the correct order was soon restored by the men, who rejected chance if it was not favorable. But I had seen.

It was as if Aunt Matilde was not there. She breathed at my side as always. The deep, muffling rug sank as usual under her feet. Her hands, crossed calmly on her lap — perhaps more calmly than on other evenings — weighed on her skirt. How is it that one feels a person's absence so clearly when that person's heart is in another place? Only her heart was absent, but the voice she used to call her brothers contained new meanings because it came from that other place.

The next nights were also marred by this almost invisible smudge of her absence. She stopped playing billiards and calling out turns altogether. The men seemed not to notice. But perhaps they did, because the matches became shorter, and I noted that the deference with which they treated her grew infinitesimally.

One night, as we came out of the dining room, the dog made its appearance in the vestibule and joined the family. The men, as usual, waited at the library door for their sister to lead the way into the billiard room, this time gracefully followed by the dog. They made no comment, as if they hadn't seen it, and began their match as on other nights.

The dog sat at Aunt Matilde's feet, very quiet, its lively eyes examining the room and watching the players' maneuvers, as if it was greatly amused. It was plump now, and its coat, its whole body glowed, from its quivering nose to its tail, always ready to wag. How long had the dog been in the house? A month? Longer, perhaps. But in that month Aunt Matilde had made it get well, caring for it without displays of emotion, but with the great wisdom of her bony hands dedicated to repairing what was damaged. Implacable in the face of its pain and whimpers, she had cured its wounds. Its foot was healed. She had disinfected it, fed it, bathed it, and now the white dog was whole again.

And yet none of this seemed to unite her to the dog. Perhaps she accepted it in the same way that my uncles that night had accepted its presence: to reject it would have given it more importance than it could have for them. I saw Aunt Matilde tranquil, collected, full of a new feeling that did not quite overflow to touch its object, and now we were six beings separated by a distance vaster than stretches of rug and air.

It happened during one of Uncle Armando's shots, when he dropped the little cube of blue chalk. Instantly, obeying a reflex that linked it to its picaresque past in the streets, the dog scampered to the chalk, yanked it away from Uncle Armando who had leaned over to pick it up, and held it in its mouth. Then a surprising thing happened. Aunt Matilde, suddenly coming apart, burst out in uncontrollable guffaws that shook her whole body for a few seconds. We were paralyzed. Hearing her, the dog dropped the chalk and ran to her, its tail wagging and held high, and jumped on her skirt. Aunt Matilde's laughter subsided, but Uncle Armando, vexed, left the room to avoid witnessing this collapse of order through the intrusion of the absurd. Uncle Gustavo and my father kept on playing billiards; now more than ever it was essential not to see, not to see anything, not to make remarks, not even to allude to the episode, and perhaps in this way to keep something from moving forward.

I did not find Aunt Matilde's guffaws amusing. It was only too clear that something dark had happened. The dog lay still on her lap. The crack of the billiard balls as they collided, precise and discrete, seemed to lead Aunt Matilde's hand first from its place on the sofa to her skirt, and then to the back of the sleeping dog. Seeing that expressionless hand resting there, I also observed that the tension I had never before recognized on my aunt's face — I never suspected it was anything other than dignity — had dissolved, and a great peace was softening her features. I could not resist what I did. Obeying something stronger than my own will, I slid closer to her on the sofa. I waited for her to beckon to me with a look or include me with a smile, but she didn't, because their new relationship was too exclusive; there was no place for me. There were only those two united beings. I didn't like it, but I was left out. And the men remained isolated, because they had not paid attention to the dangerous invitation to which Aunt Matilde had dared to listen.

5

Coming home from school in the afternoon, I would go straight downstairs and, mounting my new bicycle, would circle round and round in the narrow garden behind the house, around the elm tree and the pair of iron benches. On the other side of the wall, the neighbors' walnut trees were beginning to show signs of spring, but I didn't keep track of the seasons and their gifts because I had more serious things to think about. And as I knew nobody came down to the garden until the suffocations of midsummer made it essential, it was the best place to think about what was happening in our house.

Superficially it might be said nothing was happening. But how could one remain calm in the face of the curious relationship that had arisen between my aunt and the white dog? It was as if Aunt Matilde, after punctiliously serving and conforming to her unequal life, had at last found her equal, someone who spoke her innermost language, and as among women, they carried on an intimacy full of pleasantries and agreeable refinements. They ate bonbons that came in boxes tied with frivolous bows. My aunt arranged oranges, pineapples, grapes on the tall fruit stands, and the dog watched as if to criticize her taste or deliver an opinion. She seemed to have discovered a more benign region of life in this sharing of pleasantries, so much so that now everything had lost its importance in the shadow of this new world of affection.

Frequently, when passing her bedroom door, I would hear a guffaw like the one that had dashed the old order of her life to the ground that night, or I would hear her conversing — not soliloquizing as when talking to me — with someone whose voice I could not hear. It was the new life. The culprit, the dog, slept in her room in a basket — elegant, feminine, and absurd to my way of thinking — and followed her everywhere, except into the dining room. It was forbidden to go in there, but waited for its friend to emerge, followed her to the library or the billiard room, wherever we were going, and sat beside her or on her lap, and from time to time, sly looks of understanding would pass between them.

How was this possible? I asked myself. Why had she waited until now to overflow and begin a dialogue for the first time in her life? At times she seemed insecure about the dog, as if afraid the day might come when it would go away, leaving her alone with all this new abundance on her hands. Or was she still concerned about the dog's health? It was too strange. These ideas floated like blurs in my imagination while I listened to the gravel crunching under the wheels of my bicycle. What was not blurry, on the other hand, was my vehement desire to fall seriously ill, to see if that way I too could gain a similar relationship. The dog's illness had been the cause of it all. Without that, my aunt would never have become linked to it. But I had an iron constitution, and furthermore it was clear that inside Aunt Matilde's heart there was room for only one love at a time, especially if it were so intense.

My father and uncles didn't seem to notice any change at all. The dog was quiet, and abandoning its street manners it seemed to acquire Aunt Matilde's somewhat dignified mien; but it preserved all the impudence of a female whom the vicissitudes of life have not been able to shock, as well as its good temper and its liking for adventure. It was easier for the men to accept than reject it since the latter would at least have meant speaking, and perhaps even an uncomfortable revision of their standards of security.

One night, when the pitcher of lemonade had already made its appearance on the library credenza, cooling that corner of the shadows, and the windows had been opened to the air, my father stopped abruptly at the entrance to the billiard room.

"What is this?" he exclaimed, pointing at the floor.

The three men gathered in consternation to look at a tiny round puddle on the waxed floor.

'Matilde!' Uncle Gustavo cried.

She came over to look and blushed with shame. The dog had taken refuge under the billiard table in the next room. Turning toward the table, my father saw it there, and suddenly changing course he left the room, followed by his brothers, heading toward the bedrooms, where each of them locked himself in, silent and alone.

Aunt Matilde said nothing. She went up to her room followed by the dog. I stayed in the library with a glass of lemonade in my hand, looking out at the summer sky and listening, anxiously listening to distant foghorns and the noise of the unknown city, terrible and at the same time desirable, stretched out under the stars.

Then I heard Aunt Matilde descend. She appeared with her hat on and her keys jingling in her hand.

'Go to bed,' she said. 'I'm taking her for a walk on the street so she can take care of her business there.'

Then she added something that made me nervous: 'The night's so pretty . . . '

And she went out.

From that night on, instead of going upstairs after dinner to turn down her brothers' beds, she went to her room, put on her hat, and came down again, her keys jingling. She went out with the dog, not saying a word to anybody. My uncles and my father and I stayed in the billiard room, or, as the season wore on, sat on the benches in the garden, with the rustling elm and the clear sky pressing down on us. These nightly walks of Aunt Matilde's were never mentioned, there was never any indication that anybody knew anything important had changed in the house; but an element had been introduced there that contradicted all order.

At first Aunt Matilde would stay out at most fifteen or twenty minutes, returning promptly to take coffee with us and exchange a few commonplaces. Later, her outings inexplicably took more time. She was no longer a woman who walked her dog for reasons of hygiene; out there in the streets, in the city, there was something powerful attracting her. Waiting for her, my father glanced furtively at his pocket watch, and if she was very late, Uncle Gustavo went up to the second floor, as if he had forgotten something there, to watch from the balcony. But they never said anything. Once when Aunt Matilde's walk had taken too long, my father paced back and forth along the path between the hydrangeas, their flowers like blue eyes watching the night. Uncle Gustavo threw away a cigar he couldn't light satisfactorily, and then another, stamping it out under his heel. Uncle Armando overturned a cup of coffee. I watched, waiting for an eventual explosion, for them to say something, for them to express their anxiety and fill those endless minutes stretching on and on without the presence of Aunt Matilde. It was half past twelve when she came home.

'Why did you wait up for me?' she said smiling.

She carried her hat in her hand and her hair, ordinarily so neat, was disheveled. I noted that daubs of mud stained her perfect shoes.

'What happened to you?'

'Nothing,' was her answer, and with that she closed forever any possible right her brothers might have had to interfere with those unknown hours, happy or tragic or insignificant, which were now her life.

I say they were her life, because in those instants she remained with us before going to her room, with the dog, muddy too, next to her, I perceived an animation in her eyes, a cheerful restlessness like the animal's, as if her eyes had recently bathed in scenes never before witnessed, to which we had no access. These two were companions. The night protected them. They belonged to the noises, to the foghorns that wafted over docks, dark or lamplit streets, houses, factories, and parks, finally reaching my ears.

Her walks with the dog continued. Now she said good night to us right after dinner, and all of us went to our rooms, my father, Uncle Gustavo, Uncle Armando, and myself. But none of us fell asleep until we heard her come in, late, sometimes very late, when the light of dawn already brightened the top of our elm tree. Only after she was heard closing her bedroom door would the paces by which my father measured his room stop, and a window be closed by one of her brothers to shut out the night, which had ceased being dangerous for the time being.

Once after she had come in very late, I thought I heard her singing very softly and sweetly, so I cracked open my door and looked out. She passed in front of my door, the white dog cuddled in her arms. Her face looked surprisingly young and perfect, although it was a little dirty, and I saw there was a tear in her skirt. This woman was capable of anything; she had her whole life before her. I went to bed terrified that this would be the end.

And I wasn't wrong. Because one night shortly afterwards, Aunt Matilde went out for a walk with the dog and never came back.

We waited up all night long, each one of us in his room, and she didn't come home. The next day nobody said anything. But the silent waiting went on, and we all hovered silently, without seeming to, around the windows of the house, watching for her. From that first day fear made the harmonious dignity of the three brothers' faces collapse, and they aged rapidly in a very short time.

'Your aunt went on a trip,' the cook told me once, when I finally dared to ask. But I knew it wasn't true.

Life went on in our house as if Aunt Matilde were still living with us. It's true they had a habit of gathering in the library, and perhaps locked in there they talked, managing to overcome the wall of fear that isolated them, giving free rein to their fears and doubts. But I'm not sure. Several times a visitor came who didn't belong to our world, and they would lock themselves in with him. But I don't believe he had brought them news of a possible investigation, perhaps he was nothing more than the boss of a longshoremen's union who was coming to claim damages for some accident. The door of the library was too thick, too heavy, and I never knew if Aunt Matilde, dragged along by the white dog, had got lost in the city, or in death, or in a region more mysterious than either.

ARTHUR CONAN DOYLE

 Arthur Conan Doyle (1859–1930), the son of an unsuccessful artist, received his medical education at the University of Edinburgh. It is there that he also received the first inklings of inspiration for his memorable creation, the amateur detective Sherlock Holmes. Doyle's teacher, Dr. Joseph Bell, was a startlingly swift and accurate diagnostician of his patients' habits and histories. Doyle transferred Bell's methods to the character Holmes, who first appeared in the novel *A Study in Scarlet* in 1887. Subsequently, Doyle wrote a series of stories about Holmes's adventures, all of them told in narratives ostensibly written by the detective's sidekick, Dr. John Watson. The Holmes stories first appeared in *Strand Magazine* and were later collected in *The Adventures of Sherlock Holmes* (1891) and *The Memoirs of Sherlock Holmes* (1894). When (after some sixty stories) Doyle tired of Holmes and killed off the detective by having him swept over the Reichenbach Falls during a struggle with his archenemy Moriarty, the reading public likewise took a plunge — into mourning. Some wore black armbands, and Doyle received hundreds of letters, most of them nasty. Holmes was resurrected in *The Return of Sherlock Holmes* (1905). The undying popularity of the Holmes stories owes to several features: the immediate arresting of the reader's attention, the astonishing feats of deduction, the period atmosphere, and most especially the character of Holmes himself. "The Adventure of the Speckled Band" offers a case in point.

The Adventure of the Speckled Band

In glancing over my notes of the seventy odd cases in which I have during the last eight years studied the methods of my friend Sherlock Holmes, I find many tragic, some comic, a large number merely strange, but none commonplace; for, working as he did rather for the love of his art than for the acquirement of wealth, he refused to associate himself with any investigation which did not tend towards the unusual, and even the fantastic. Of all these varied cases, however, I cannot recall any which presented more singular features than that which was associated with the well-known Surrey family of the Roylotts of Stoke Moran. The events in question occurred in the early days of my association with Holmes, when we were sharing rooms as bachelors, in Baker Street. It is possible that I might have placed them upon record before, but a promise of secrecy was made at the time, from which I have only been freed during the last month by the untimely death of the lady to whom the pledge was given. It is perhaps as well that the facts should now come to light, for I have reasons to know there are widespread rumours as to the death of Dr. Grimesby Roylott which tend to make the matter even more terrible than the truth.

It was early in April, in the year '83, that I woke one morning to find Sherlock Holmes standing, fully dressed, by the side of my bed. He was a late riser as a rule, and, as the clock on the mantelpiece showed me that it was only a quarter past seven, I blinked up at him in some surprise, and perhaps just a little resentment, for I was myself regular in my habits.

"Very sorry to knock you up, Watson," said he, "but it's the common lot this morning. Mrs. Hudson has been knocked up, she retorted upon me, and I on you."

"What is it, then? A fire?"

"No, a client. It seems that a young lady has arrived in a considerable state of excitement, who insists upon seeing me. She is waiting now in the sitting-room. Now, when young ladies wander about the metropolis at this hour of the morning, and knock sleepy people up out of their beds, I presume that it is something very pressing which they have to communicate. Should it prove to be an interesting case, you would, I am sure, wish to follow it from the outset. I thought at any rate that I should call you, and give you the chance."

"My dear fellow, I would not miss it for anything."

I had no keener pleasure than in following Holmes in his professional investigations, and in admiring the rapid deductions, as swift as intuitions, and yet always founded on a logical basis, with which he unravelled the problems which were submitted to him. I rapidly threw on my clothes, and was ready in a few minutes to accompany my friend down to the sitting-room. A lady dressed in black and heavily veiled, who had been sitting in the window, rose as we entered.

"Good morning, madam," said Holmes cheerily. "My name is Sherlock Holmes. This is my intimate friend and associate, Dr. Watson, before whom you may speak as freely as before myself. Ha, I am glad to see that Mrs. Hudson has had the good sense to light the fire. Pray draw up to it, and I shall order you a cup of hot coffee, for I observe that you are shivering."

"It is not cold which makes me shiver," said the woman in a low voice, changing her seat as requested.

"What then?"

"It is fear, Mr. Holmes. It is terror." She raised her veil as she spoke, and we could see that she was indeed in a pitiable state of agitation, her face all drawn and grey, with restless, frightened eyes like those of some hunted animal. Her features and figure were those of a woman of thirty, but her hair was shot with premature grey, and her expression was weary and haggard. Sherlock Holmes ran her over with one of his quick, all-comprehensive glances.

"You must not fear," said he soothingly, bending forward and patting her forearm. "We shall soon set matters right, I have no doubt. You have come in by train this morning, I see."

"You know me, then?"

"No, I observe the second half of a return ticket in the palm of your left glove. You must have started early and yet you had a good drive in a dog-cart, along heavy roads, before you reached the station."

The lady gave a violent start, and stared in bewilderment at my companion.

"There is no mystery, my dear madam," said he, smiling. "The left arm of your jacket is spattered with mud in no less than seven places. The marks are perfectly fresh. There is no vehicle save a dog-cart which throws up mud in that way, and then only when you sit on the left-hand side of the driver."

"Whatever your reasons may be, you are perfectly correct," said she. "I started from my home before six, reached Leatherhead at twenty past, and came in by the first train to Waterloo. Sir, I can stand this strain no longer, I shall go mad if it continues. I have no one to turn to — none, save only one, who cares for me, and he, poor fellow, can be of little aid. I have heard of you, Mr. Holmes; I have heard of you from Mrs. Farintosh, whom you helped in the hour of her sore need. It was from her that I had your address. Oh, sir, do you think you could help me, too, and at least throw a little light through the dense darkness which surrounds me? At present it is out of my power to reward you for your services, but in a month or two I shall be married, with the control of my own income, and then at least you shall not find me ungrateful."

Holmes turned to his desk, and unlocking it, drew out a small case-book which he consulted.

"Farintosh," said he. "Ah, yes, I recall the case; it was concerned with an opal tiara. I think it was before your time, Watson. I can only say, madam, that I shall be happy to devote the same care to your case as I did to that of your friend. As to reward, my profession is its reward; but you are at liberty to defray whatever expenses I may be put to, at the time which suits you best. And now I beg that you will lay before us everything that may help us in forming an opinion upon the matter."

"Alas!" replied our visitor. "The very horror of my situation lies in the fact that my fears are so vague, and my suspicions depend so entirely upon small points, which might seem trivial to another, that even he to whom of all others I have a right to look for help and advice looks upon all that I tell him about it as the fancies of a nervous woman. He does not say so, but I can read it from his soothing answers and averted eyes. But I have heard, Mr. Holmes, that you can see deeply into the manifold wickedness of the human heart. You may advise me how to walk amid the dangers which encompass me."

"I am all attention, madam."

"My name is Helen Stoner, and I am living with my stepfather, who is the last survivor of one of the oldest Saxon families in England, the Roylotts of Stoke Moran, on the western border of Surrey."

Holmes nodded his head. "The name is familiar to me," said he.

"The family was at one time among the richest in England, and the estate extended over the borders into Berkshire in the north, and Hampshire in the west. In the last century, however, four successive heirs were of a dissolute and wasteful disposition, and the family ruin was eventually completed by a gambler, in the days of the Regency. Nothing was left save a few acres of ground and the two-hundred-year-old house, which is itself crushed under a heavy mortgage. The last squire dragged out his existence there, living the horrible life of an aristocratic pauper; but his only son, my stepfather, seeing that he must adapt himself to the new conditions, obtained an advance from a relative, which enabled him to take a medical degree, and went out to Calcutta, where, by his professional skill and his force of character, he established a large practice. In a fit of anger, however, caused by some robberies which had been perpetrated in the house, he beat his native butler to death, and narrowly escaped a capital sentence. As it was, he suffered a long term of imprisonment, and afterwards returned to England a morose and disappointed man.

"When Dr. Roylott was in India he married my mother, Mrs. Stoner, the young widow of Major-General Stoner, of the Bengal Artillery. My sister Julia and I were twins, and we were only two years old at the time of mother's remarriage. She had a considerable sum of money, not less than a thousand a year, and this she bequeathed to Dr. Roylott entirely whilst we resided with him, with a provision that a certain annual sum should be allowed to each of us in the event of our marriage. Shortly after our return to England my mother died — she was killed eight years ago in a railway accident near Crewe. Dr. Roylott then abandoned his attempts to establish himself in practice in London, and took us to live with him in the ancestral house at Stoke Moran. The money which my mother had left was enough for all our wants, and there seemed no obstacle to our happiness.

"But a terrible change came over our stepfather about this time. Instead of making friends and exchanging visits with our neighbours, who had at first been overjoyed to see a Roylott of Stoke Moran back in the old family seat, he shut himself up in his house, and seldom came out save to indulge in ferocious quarrels with whoever might cross his path. Violence of temper approaching to mania has been hereditary in the men of the family, and in my stepfather's case it had, I believe, been intensified by his long residence in the tropics. A series of disgraceful brawls took place, two of which ended in the police-court, until at last he became the terror of the village, and the folks would fly at his approach, for he is a man of immense strength, and absolutely uncontrollable in his anger.

"Last week he hurled the local blacksmith over a parapet into a stream and it was only by paying over all the money that I could gather together that I was able to avert another public exposure. He had no friends at all save the wandering gipsies, and he would give these vagabonds leave to encamp upon the few acres of bramble-covered land which represent the family estate, and would accept in return the hospitality of their tents, wandering away with them sometimes for weeks on end. He has a passion also for Indian animals, which are sent over to him by a correspondent, and he has at this moment a cheetah and a baboon, which wander freely over his grounds, and are feared by the villagers almost as much as their master.

"You can imagine from what I say that my poor sister Julia and I had no great pleasure in our lives. No servant would stay with us, and for a long time we did all the work of the house. She was but thirty at the time of her death, and yet her hair had already begun to whiten, even as mine has."

"Your sister is dead, then?"

"She died just two years ago, and it is of her death that I wish to speak to you. You can understand that, living the life which I have described, we were little likely to see anyone of our own age and position. We had, however, an aunt, my mother's maiden sister, Miss Honoria Westphail, who lives near Harrow, and we were occasionally allowed to pay short visits at this lady's house. Julia went there at Christmas two years ago, and met there a half-pay Major of Marines, to whom she became engaged. My stepfather learned of the engagement when my sister returned, and offered no objection to the marriage; but within a fortnight of the day which had been fixed for the wedding, the terrible event occurred which has deprived me of my only companion."

Sherlock Holmes had been leaning back in his chair with his eyes closed, and his head sunk in a cushion, but he half opened his lids now, and glanced across at his visitor.

"Pray be precise as to details," said he.

"It is easy for me to be so, for every event of that dreadful time is seared into my memory. The manor house is, as I have already said, very old, and only one wing is now inhabited. The bedrooms in this wing are on the ground floor, the sitting-rooms being in the central block of the buildings. Of these bedrooms the first is Dr. Roylott's, the second my sister's, and the third my own. There is no communication between them, but they all open into the same corridor. Do I make myself plain?"

"Perfectly so."

"The windows of the three rooms open upon the lawn. That fatal night Dr. Roylott had gone to his room early, though we knew that he had not retired to rest, for my sister was troubled by the smell of strong Indian cigars which it was his custom to smoke. She left her room, therefore, and came into mine, where she sat for some time, chatting about her approaching wedding. At eleven o'clock she rose to leave me, but she paused at the door and looked back.

" 'Tell me, Helen,' said she, 'have you heard anyone whistle in the dead of the night?'

" 'Never,' said I.

" 'I suppose that you could not whistle yourself in your sleep?'

" 'Certainly not. But why?'

" 'Because during the last few nights I have always, about three in the morning, heard a low clear whistle. I am a light sleeper, and it has awakened me. I cannot tell where it came from — perhaps from the next room, perhaps from the lawn. I thought that I should ask you whether you had heard it.'

" 'No, I have not. It must be those wretched gipsies in the plantation.'

" 'Very likely. And yet if it were on the lawn I wonder that you did not hear it also.'

" 'Ah, but I sleep more heavily than you.'

" 'Well, it is of no consequence, at any rate,' she smiled back at me, closed my door, and a few minutes later I heard her key turn in the lock."

"Indeed," said Holmes. "Was it your custom always to lock yourselves in at night?"

"Always."

"And why?"

"I think I mentioned to you that the Doctor kept a cheetah and a baboon. We had no feeling of security unless our doors were locked."

"Quite so. Pray proceed with your statement."

"I could not sleep that night. A vague feeling of impending misfortune impressed me. My sister and I, you will recollect, were twins, and you know how subtle are the links which bind two souls which are so closely allied. It was a wild night. The wind was howling outside, and the rain was beating and splashing against the windows. Suddenly, amidst all the hubbub of the gale, there burst forth the wild scream of a terrified woman. I knew that it was my sister's voice. I sprang from my bed, wrapped a shawl around me, and rushed into the corridor. As I opened my door I seemed to hear a low whistle, such as my sister described, and a few moments later a clanging sound, as if a mass of metal had fallen. As I ran down the passage my sister's door was unlocked, and revolved slowly upon its hinges. I stared at it horror-stricken, not knowing what was about to issue from it. By the light of the corridor lamp I saw my sister appear at the opening, her face blanched with terror, her hands groping for help, her whole figure swaying to and fro like that of a drunkard. I ran to her and threw my arms around her, but at that moment her knees seemed to give way and she fell to the ground. She writhed as one who is in terrible pain, and her limbs were dreadfully convulsed. At first I thought she had not recognized me, but as I bent over her she suddenly shrieked out in a voice which I shall never forget, 'Oh, my God! Helen! It was the band! The speckled band!' There was something else which she would fain have said, and she stabbed with her finger into the air in the direction of the Doctor's room, but a fresh convulsion seized her and choked her words. I rushed out, calling loudly for my stepfather, and I met him hastening from his room in his dressing-gown. When he reached my sister's side she was unconscious, and though he poured brandy down her throat, and sent for medical aid from the village, all efforts were in vain, for she slowly sank and died without having recovered her consciousness. Such was the dreadful end of my beloved sister."

"One moment," said Holmes; "are you sure about this whistling and metallic sound? Could you swear to it?"

"That was what the county coroner asked asked me at the inquiry. It was my strong impression that I heard it, and yet among the crash of the gale, and the creaking of an old house, I may possibly have been deceived."

"Was your sister dressed?"

"No, she was in her nightdress. In her right hand was found the charred stump of a match, and in her left a matchbox."

"Showing that she had struck a light and looked about her when the alarm took place. That is important. And what conclusions did the coroner come to?"

"He investigated the case with great care, for Dr. Roylott's conduct had long been notorious in the county, but he was unable to find any satisfactory cause of death. My evidence showed that the door had been fastened upon the inner side, and the windows were blocked by old-fashioned shutters with broad iron bars, which were secured every night. The walls were carefully sounded, and were shown to be quite solid all round, and the flooring was also thoroughly examined, with the same result. The chimney is wide, but is barred up by four large staples. It is certain, therefore, that my sister was quite alone when she met her end. Besides, there were no marks of any violence upon her."

"How about poison?"

"The doctors examined her for it, but without success."

"What do you think that this unfortunate lady died of, then?"

"It is my belief that she died of pure fear and nervous shock, though what it was that frightened her I cannot imagine."

"Were there gipsies in the plantation at the time?"

"Yes, there are nearly always some there."

"Ah, and what did you gather from this allusion to a band — a speckled band?"

"Sometimes I have thought that it was merely the wild talk of delirium, sometimes that it may have referred to some band of people, perhaps to these very gipsies in the plantation. I do not know whether the spotted handkerchiefs which so many of them wear over their heads might have suggested the strange adjective which she used."

Holmes shook his head like a man who is far from being satisfied.

"These are very deep waters," said he; "pray go on with your narrative."

"Two years have passed since then, and my life has been until lately lonelier than ever. A month ago, however, a dear friend, whom I have known for many years, has done me the honour to ask my hand in marriage. His name is Armitage — Percy Armitage — the second son of Mr. Armitage, of Crane Water, near Reading. My stepfather has offered no opposition to the match, and we are to be married in the course of the spring. Two days ago some repairs were started in the west wing of the building, and my bedroom wall has been pierced, so that I have had to move into the chamber in which my sister died, and to sleep in the very bed in which she slept. Imagine, then, my thrill of terror when last night, as I lay awake, thinking over her terrible fate, I suddenly heard in the silence of the night the low whistle which had been the herald of her own death. I sprang up and lit the lamp, but nothing was to be seen in the room. I was too shaken to go to bed again, however, so I dressed, and as soon as it was daylight I slipped down, got a dog-cart at the Crown Inn, which is opposite, and drove to Leatherhead, from whence I have come on this morning, with the one object of seeing you and asking your advice."

"You have done wisely," said my friend. "But have you told me all?"

"Yes, all."

"Miss Stoner, you have not. You are screening your stepfather."

"Why, what do you mean?"

For answer Holmes pushed back the frill of black lace which fringed the hand that lay upon our visitor's knee. Five little livid spots, the marks of four fingers and a thumb, were printed upon the white wrist.

"You have been cruelly used," said Holmes.

The lady coloured deeply, and covered over her injured wrist. "He is a hard man," she said, "and perhaps he hardly knows his own strength."

There was a long silence, during which Holmes leaned his chin upon his hands and stared into the crackling fire.

"This is a very deep business," he said at last. "There are a thousand details which I should desire to know before I decide upon our course of action. Yet we have not a moment to lose. If we were to come to Stoke Moran today, would it be possible for us to see over these rooms without the knowledge of your stepfather?"

"As it happens, he spoke of coming into town today upon some important business. It is probable that he will be away all day, and that there would be nothing to disturb you. We have a housekeeper now, but she is old and foolish, and I could easily get her out of the way."

"Excellent. You are not averse to this trip, Watson?"

"By no means."

"Then we shall both come. What are you going to do yourself?"

"I have one or two things which I wish to do now that I am in town. But I shall return by the twelve o'clock train, so as to be there in time for your coming."

"And you may expect us early in the afternoon. I have myself some small business matters to attend to. Will you not wait and breakfast?"

"No, I must go. My heart is lightened already since I have confided my trouble to you. I shall look forward to seeing you again this afternoon." She dropped her thick black veil over her face, and glided from the room.

"And what do you think of it all, Watson?" asked Sherlock Holmes, leaning back in his chair.

"It seems to me a most dark and serious business."

"Dark enough and sinister enough."

"Yet if the lady is correct in saying that the flooring and walls are sound, and that the door, window, and chimney are impassable, then her sister must have been undoubtedly alone when she met her mysterious end."

"What becomes, then, of these nocturnal whistles, and what of the peculiar words of the dying woman?"

"I cannot think."

"When you combine the ideas of whistles at night, the presence of a band of gipsies who are on intimate terms with this old doctor, the fact that we have every reason to believe that the doctor has an interest in preventing his stepdaughter's marriage, the dying allusion to a band, and finally, the fact that Miss Helen Stoner heard a metallic clang, which might have been caused by one of those metal bars which secured the shutters falling back into their place, I think there is good ground to think that the mystery may be cleared along those lines."

"But what, then, did the gipsies do?"

"I cannot imagine."

"I see many objections to any such theory."

"And so do I. It is precisely for that reason that we are going to Stoke Moran this day. I want to see whether the objections are fatal, or if they may be explained away. But what, in the name of the devil!"

The ejaculation had been drawn from my companion by the fact that our door had been suddenly dashed open, and that a huge man framed himself in the aperture. His costume was a peculiar mixture of the professional and the agricultural, having a black top-hat, a long frock-coat, and a pair of high gaiters, with a hunting-crop swinging in his hand. So tall was he that his hat actually brushed the cross-bar of the doorway, and his breadth seemed to span it across from side to side. A large face, seared with a thousand wrinkles, burned yellow with the sun, and marked with every evil passion, was turned from one to the other of us, while his deep-set, bile-shot eyes, and the high thin fleshless nose, gave him somewhat the resemblance to a fierce old bird of prey.

"Which of you is Holmes?" asked the apparition.

"My name, sir, but you have the advantage of me," said my companion quietly.

"I am Dr. Grimesby Roylott, of Stoke Moran."

"Indeed, Doctor," said Holmes blandly. "Pray take a seat."

"I will do nothing of the kind. My stepdaughter has been here. I have traced her. What has she been saying to you?"

"It is a little cold for the time of year," said Holmes.

"What has she been saying to you?" screamed the old man furiously.

"But I have heard that the crocuses promise well," continued my companion imperturbably.

"Ha! You put me off, do you?" said our new visitor, taking a step forward, and shaking his hunting-crop. "I know you, you scoundrel! I have heard of you before. You are Holmes the meddler."

My friend smiled.

"Holmes the busybody!"

His smile broadened.

"Holmes the Scotland Yard jack-in-office."

Holmes chuckled heartily. "Your conversation is most entertaining," said he. "When you go out close the door, for there is a decided draught."

"I will go when I have had my say. Don't you dare to meddle with my affairs. I know that Miss Stoner has been here — I traced her! I am a dangerous man to fall foul of! See here." He stepped swiftly forward, seized the poker, and bent it into a curve with his huge brown hands.

"See that you keep yourself out of my grip," he snarled, and hurling the twisted poker into the fireplace, he strode out of the room.

"He seems a very amiable person," said Holmes, laughing. "I am not quite so bulky, but if he had remained I might have shown him that my grip was not so much more feeble than his own." As he spoke he picked up the steel poker, and with a sudden effort straightened it out again.

"Fancy his having the insolence to confound me with the official detective force! This incident gives zest to our investigation, however, and I only trust that our little friend will not suffer from her imprudence in allowing this brute to trace her. And now, Watson, we shall order breakfast, and afterwards I shall walk down to Doctors' Common, where I hope to get some data which may help us in this matter."

It was nearly one o'clock when Sherlock Holmes returned from his excursion. He held in his hand a sheet of blue paper, scrawled over with notes and figures.

"I have seen the will of the deceased wife," said he. "To determine its exact meaning I have been obliged to work out the present prices of the investments with which it is concerned. The total income, which at the time of the wife's death was little short of £1,100, is now through the fall in agricultural prices not more than £750. Each daughter can claim an income of £250, in case of marriage. It is evident, therefore, that if both daughters had married, this beauty would have had a mere pittance, while even one of them would have crippled him to a serious extent. My morning's work has not been wasted, since it has proved that he has the very strongest motives for standing in the way of anything of that sort. And now, Watson, this is too serious for dawdling, especially as the old man is aware that we are interesting ourselves in his affairs, so if you are ready we shall call a cab and drive to Waterloo. I should be very much obliged if you would slip your revolver into your pocket. An Eley's No. 2 is an excellent argument with gentlemen who can twist steel pokers into knots. That and a toothbrush are, I think, all that we need."

At Waterloo we were fortunate in catching a train for Leatherhead, where we hired a trap at the station inn, and drove for four or five miles through the lovely Surrey lanes. It was a perfect day, with a bright sun and a few fleecy clouds in the heavens. The trees and wayside hedges were just throwing out their first green shoots, and the air was full of the pleasant smell of the moist earth. To me at least there was a strange contrast between the sweet promise of the spring and the sinister quest upon which we were engaged. My companion sat in front of the trap, his arms folded, his hat pulled down over his eyes, and his chin sunk upon his breast, buried in the deepest thought. Suddenly, however, he started, tapped me on the shoulder, and pointed over to the meadows.

"Look there!" said he.

A heavily timbered park stretched up in a gentle slope, thickening into a grove at the highest point. From amidst the branches there jutted out the grey gables and high roof-tree of a very old mansion.

"Stoke Moran?" said he.

"Yes, sir, that is the house of Dr. Grimesby Roylott," remarked the driver.

"There is some building going on there," said Holmes; "that is where we are going."

"There's the village," said the driver, pointing to a cluster of roofs some distance to the left; "but if you want to get to the house, you'll find it shorter to go over this stile, and so by the footpath over the fields. There it is, where the lady is walking."

"And the lady, I fancy, is Miss Stoner," observed Holmes, shading his eyes. "Yes, I think we had better do as you suggest."

We got off, paid our fare, and the trap rattled back on its way to Leatherhead.

"I thought it as well," said Holmes, as we climbed the stile, "that this fellow should think that we had come here as architects, or on some definite business. It may stop his gossip. Good afternoon, Miss Stoner. You see that we have been as good as our word."

Our client of the morning had hurried forward to meet us with a face which spoke her joy. "I have been waiting so eagerly for you," she cried, shaking hands with us warmly. "All has turned out splendidly. Dr. Roylott has gone to town, and it is unlikely that he will be back before evening."

"We have had the pleasure of making the Doctor's acquaintance," said Holmes, and in a few words he sketched out what had occurred. Miss Stoner turned white to the lips as she listened.

"Good heavens!" she cried, "he has followed me, then."

"So it appears."

"He is so cunning that I never know when I am safe from him. What will he say when he returns?"

"He must guard himself, for he may find that there is someone more cunning than himself upon his track. You must lock yourself from him tonight. If he is violent, we shall take you away to your aunt's at Harrow. Now, we must make the best use of our time, so kindly take us at once to the rooms which we are to examine."

The building was of grey, lichen-blotched stone, with a high central portion, and two curving wings, like the claws of a crab, thrown out on each side. In one of these wings the windows were broken, and blocked with wooden boards, while the roof was partly caved in, a picture of ruin. The central portion was in little better repair, but the right-hand block was comparatively modern, and the blinds in the windows, with the blue smoke curling up from the chimneys, showed that this was where the family resided. Some scaffolding had been erected against the end wall, and the stonework had been broken into, but there were no signs of any workmen at the moment of our visit. Holmes walked slowly up and down the ill-trimmed lawn, and examined with deep attention the outsides of the windows.

"This, I take it, belongs to the room in which you used to sleep, the centre one to your sister's, and the one next to the main building to Dr. Roylott's chamber?"

"Exactly so. But I am now sleeping in the middle one."

"Pending the alterations, as I understand. By the way, there does not seem to be any pressing need for repairs at the end of the wall."

"There were none. I believe that it was an excuse to move me from my room."

"Ah! that is suggestive. Now, on the other side of this narrow wing runs the corridor from which these three rooms open. There are windows in it, of course?"

"Yes, but very small ones. Too narrow for anyone to pass through."

"As you both locked your doors at night, your rooms were unapproachable from that side. Now, would you have the kindness to go to your room, and to bar the shutters."

Miss Stoner did so, and Holmes, after a careful examination through the open window, endeavoured in every way to force the shutter open, but without success. There was no slit through which a knife could be passed to raise the bar. Then with his lens he tested the hinges, but they were of solid iron, built firmly into the massive masonry. "Hum!" said he, scratching his chin in some perplexity, "my theory certainly presents some difficulties. No one could pass these shutters if they were bolted. Well, we shall see if the inside throws any light upon the matter."

A small side-door led into the whitewashed corridor from which the three bedrooms opened. Holmes refused to examine the third chamber, so we passed at once to the second, that in which Miss Stoner was now sleeping, and in which her sister had met her fate. It was a homely little room, with a low ceiling and a gaping fireplace, after the fashion of old country houses. A brown chest of drawers stood in one corner, a narrow white-counterpaned bed in another, and a dressing-table on the left-hand side of the window. These articles, with two small wicker-work chairs, made up all the furniture in the room, save for a square of Wilton carpet in the centre. The boards round and the panelling of the walls were brown, worm-eaten oak, so old and discoloured that it may have dated from the original building of the house. Holmes drew one of the chairs into a corner and sat silent, while his eyes travelled round and round and up and down, taking in every detail of the apartment.

"Where does that bell communicate with?" he asked at last, pointing to a thick bell-rope which hung down beside the bed, the tassel actually lying upon the pillow.

"It goes to the housekeeper's room."

"It looks newer than the other things?"

"Yes, it was only put there a couple of years ago."

"Your sister asked for it, I suppose?"

"No, I never heard of her using it. We used always to get what we wanted for ourselves."

"Indeed, it seemed unnecessary to put so nice a bell-pull there. You will excuse me for a few minutes while I satisfy myself as to this floor." He threw himself down upon his face with his lens in his hand, and crawled swiftly backwards and forwards, examining minutely the cracks between the boards. Then he did the same with the woodwork with which the chamber was panelled. Finally he walked over to the bed and spent some time staring at it, and in running his eye up and down the wall. Finally he took the bell-rope in his hand and gave it a brisk tug.

"Why, it's a dummy," said he.

"Won't it ring?"

"No, it is not even attached to a wire. This is very interesting. You can see now that it is fastened to a hook just above where the little opening of the ventilator is."

"How very absurd! I never noticed that before."

"Very strange!" muttered Holmes, pulling at the rope. "There are one or two very singular points about this room. For example, what a fool a builder must be to open a ventilator in another room, when, with the same trouble, he might have communicated with the outside air!"

"That is also quite modern," said the lady.

"Done about the same time as the bell-rope?" remarked Holmes.

"Yes, there were several little changes carried out about the time."

"They seem to have been of a most interesting character — dummy bell-ropes, and ventilators which do not ventilate. With your permission, Miss Stoner, we shall carry our researches into the inner apartment."

Dr. Grimesby Roylott's chamber was larger than that of his stepdaughter, but was as plainly furnished. A camp bed, a small wooden shelf full of books, mostly of a technical character, an armchair beside the bed, a plain wooden chair against the wall, a round table, and a large iron safe were the principal things which met the eye. Holmes walked slowly round and examined each and all of them with the keenest interest.

"What's in here?" he asked, tapping the safe.

"My stepfather's business papers."

"Oh! you have seen inside, then?"

"Only once, some years ago. I remember that it was full of papers."

"There isn't a cat in it, for example?"

"No. What a strange idea!"

"Well, look at this!" He took up a small saucer of milk which stood on the top of it.

"No; we don't keep a cat. But there is a cheetah and a baboon."

"Ah, yes, of course! Well, a cheetah is just a big cat, and yet a saucer of milk does not go very far in satisfying its wants, I daresay. There is one point which I should wish to determine." He squatted down in front of the wooden chair, and examined the seat of it with the greatest attention.

"Thank you. That is quite settled," said he, rising and putting his lens in his pocket. "Hello! here is something interesting!"

The object which had caught his eye was a small dog lash hung on one corner of the bed. The lash, however, was curled upon itself, and tied so as to make a loop of whipcord.

"What do you make of that, Watson?"

"It's a common enough lash. But I don't know why it should be tied."

"That is not quite so common, is it? Ah, me! it's a wicked world, and when a clever man turns his brain to crime it is the worst of all. I think that I have seen enough now, Miss Stoner, and, with your permission, we shall walk upon the lawn."

I had never seen my friend's face so grim, or his brow so dark, as it was when we turned from the scene of his investigation. We had walked several times up and down the lawn, neither Miss Stoner nor myself liking to break in upon his thoughts before he roused himself from his reverie.

"It is very essential, Miss Stoner," said he, "that you should absolutely follow my advice in every respect."

"I shall most certainly do so."

"The matter is too serious for any hesitation. Your life may depend upon your compliance."

"I assure you that I am in your hands."

"In the first place, both my friend and I must spend the night in your room."

Both Miss Stoner and I gazed at him in astonishment.

"Yes, it must be so. Let me explain. I believe that that is the village inn over there?"

"Yes, that is the 'Crown.'"

"Very good. Your windows would be visible from there?"

"Certainly."

"You must confine yourself in your room, on pretence of a headache, when your stepfather comes back. Then when you hear him retire for the night, you must open the shutters of your window, undo the hasp, put your lamp there as a signal to us, and then withdraw with everything which you are likely to want into the room which you used to occupy. I have no doubt that, in spite of the repairs, you could manage there for one night."

"Oh, yes, easily."

"The rest you will leave in our hands."

"But what will you do?"

"We shall spend the night in your room, and we shall investigate the cause of the noise which has disturbed you."

"I believe, Mr. Holmes, that you have already made up your mind," said Miss Stoner, laying her hand upon my companion's sleeve.

"Perhaps I have."

"Then for pity's sake tell me what was the cause of my sister's death."

"I should prefer to have clearer proofs before I speak."

"You can at least tell me whether my own thought is correct, and if she died from some sudden fright."

"No, I do not think so. I think there was probably some more tangible cause. And now, Miss Stoner, we must leave you, for if Dr. Roylott returned and saw us, our journey would be in vain. Good-bye, and be brave, for if you will do what I have told you, you may rest assured that we shall soon drive away the dangers that threaten you."

Sherlock Holmes and I had no difficulty in engaging a bedroom and sitting-room at the Crown Inn. They were on the upper floor, and from our window we could command a view of the avenue gate, and of the inhabited wing of Stoke Moran Manor House. At dusk we saw Dr. Grimesby Roylott drive past, his huge form looming up beside the little figure of the lad who drove him. The boy had some slight difficulty in undoing the heavy iron gates, and we heard the hoarse roar of the Doctor's voice, and saw the fury with which he shook his clenched fists at him. The trap drove on, and a few minutes later we saw a sudden light spring up among the trees as the lamp was lit in one of the sitting rooms.

"Do you know, Watson," said Holmes, as we sat together in the gathering darkness, "I have really some scruples as to taking you tonight. There is a distinct element of danger."

"Can I be of assistance?"

"Your presence might be invaluable."

"Than I shall certainly come."

"It is very kind of you."

"You speak of danger. You have evidently seen more in these rooms than was visible to me."

"No, but I fancy that I have deduced a little more. I imagine that you saw all that I did."

"I saw nothing remarkable save the bell-rope, and what purpose that could answer I confess is more than I can imagine."

"You saw the ventilator, too?"

"Yes, but I do not think that it is such a very unusual thing to have a small opening between two rooms. It was so small a rat could hardly pass through."

"I knew that we should find a ventilator before ever we came to Stoke Moran."

"My dear Holmes!"

"Oh, yes, I did. You remember in her statement she said that her sister could smell Dr. Roylott's cigar. Now, of course that suggests at once that there must be a communication between the two rooms. It could only be a small one, or it would have been remarked upon at the coroner's inquiry. I deduced a ventilator."

"But what harm can there be in that?"

"Well, there is at least a curious coincidence of dates. A ventilator is made, a cord is hung, and a lady who sleeps in the bed dies. Does that not strike you?"

"I cannot see any connection."

"Did you not observe anything peculiar about the bed?"

"No."

"It was clamped to the floor. Did you ever see a bed fastened like that before?"

"I cannot say I have."

"The lady could not move her bed. It must always be in the same relative position to the ventilator and to the rope — for so we may call it, since it was clearly never meant for a bell-pull."

"Holmes," I cried, "I seem to see dimly what you are hitting at. We are only just in time to prevent some subtle and horrible crime."

"Subtle enough and horrible enough. When a doctor does go wrong he is the first of criminals. He has nerve and he has knowledge. Palmer and Pritchard were among the heads of their profession. This man strikes even deeper, but, I think, Watson, that we shall be able to strike deeper still. But we shall have horrors enough before the night is over; for goodness' sake let us have a quiet pipe, and turn our minds for a few hours to something more cheerful."

About nine o'clock the light among the trees was extinguished, and all was dark in the direction of the Manor House. Two hours passed slowly away, and then, suddenly, just at the stroke of eleven, a single bright light shone out right in front of us.

"That is our signal," said Holmes, springing to his feet; "it comes from the middle window."

As we passed out he exchanged a few words with the landlord, explaining that we were going on a late visit to an acquaintance, and that it was possible that we might spend the night there. A moment later we were out on the dark road, a chill wind blowing in our faces, and one yellow light twinkling in front of us through the gloom to guide us on our sombre errand.

There was little difficulty in entering the grounds, for unrepaired breaches gaped in the old park wall. Making our way among the trees, we reached the lawn, crossed it, and were about to enter through the window, when out from a clump of laurel bushes there darted what seemed to be a hideous and distorted child, who threw itself on the grass with writhing limbs, and then ran swiftly across the lawn into the darkness.

"My God!" I whispered, "did you see it?"

Holmes was for the moment as startled as I. His hand closed like a vice upon my wrist in his agitation. Then he broke into a low laugh, and put his lips to my ear.

"It is a nice household," he murmured, "that is the baboon."

I had forgotten the strange pets which the doctor affected. There was a cheetah, too; perhaps we might find it upon our shoulders at any moment. I confess that I felt easier in my mind when, after following Holmes's example and slipping off my shoes, I found myself inside the bedroom. My companion noiselessly closed the shutters, moved the lamp on to the table, and cast his eyes round the room. All was as we had seen it in the day-time. Then creeping up to me and making a trumpet of his hand, he whispered into my ear again so gently that it was all I could do to distinguish the words:

"The least sound would be fatal to our plans."

I nodded to show that I had heard.

"We must sit without a light. He would see it through the ventilator."

I nodded again.

"Do not go to sleep; your very life may depend on it. Have your pistol ready in case we should need it. I will sit on the side of the bed, and you in that chair."

I took out my revolver and laid it on the corner of the table.

Holmes had brought up a long thin cane, and this he placed upon the bed beside him. By it he laid the box of matches and the stump of a candle. Then he turned down the lamp and we were left in the darkness.

How shall I ever forget that dreadful vigil? I could not hear a sound, not even the drawing of a breath, and yet I knew that my companion sat open-eyed, within a few feet of me, in the same state of nervous tension in which I was myself. The shutters cut off the least ray of light, and we waited in absolute darkness. From outside came the occasional cry of a nightbird, and once at our very window a long-drawn, cat-like whine, which told us that the cheetah was indeed at liberty. Far away we could hear the deep tones of the parish clock, which boomed out every quarter of an hour. How long they seemed, those quarters! Twelve o'clock, and one, and two, and three, and still we sat waiting silently for whatever might befall.

Suddenly there was a momentary gleam of a light up in the direction of the ventilator, which vanished immediately, but was succeeded by a strong smell of burning oil and heated metal. Someone in the next room had lit a dark lantern. I heard a gentle sound of movement, and then all was silent once more, though the smell grew stronger. For half an hour I sat with straining ears. Then suddenly another sound became audible — a very gentle, soothing sound, like that of a small jet of steam escaping continuously from a kettle. The instant that we heard it, Holmes sprang from the bed, struck a match, and lashed furiously with his cane at the bell-pull.

"You see it, Watson?" he yelled. "You see it?"

But I saw nothing. At that moment when Holmes struck the light I heard a low, clear whistle, but the sudden glare flashing into my weary eyes made it impossible for me to tell what it was at which my friend lashed so savagely. I could, however, see that his face was deadly pale, and filled with horror and loathing.

He had ceased to strike, and was gazing up at the ventilator, when suddenly there broke from the silence of the night the most horrible cry to which I have ever listened. It swelled up louder and louder, a hoarse yell of pain and fear and anger all mingled in the one dreadful shriek. They say that away down in the village, and even in the distant parsonage, that cry raised the sleepers from their beds. It struck cold to our hearts, and I stood gazing at Holmes, and he at me, until the last echoes of it had died away into the silence from which it rose.

"What can it mean?" I gasped.

"It means that it is all over," Holmes answered. "And perhaps, after all, it is for the best. Take your pistol, and we shall enter Dr. Roylott's room."

With a grave face he lit the lamp, and led the way down the corridor. Twice he struck the chamber door without any reply from within. Then he turned the handle and entered, I at his heels, with the cocked pistol in my hand.

It was a singular sight which met our eyes. On the table stood a dark lantern with the shutter half open, throwing a brilliant beam of light upon the iron safe, the door of which was ajar. Beside this table, on the wooden chair, sat Dr. Grimesby Roylott, clad in a long dressing-gown, his bare ankles protruding beneath, and his feet thrust into red heelless Turkish slippers. Across his lap lay the short stock with the long lash which we had noticed during the day. His chin was cocked upwards, and his eyes were fixed in a dreadful rigid stare at the corner of the ceiling. Round his brow he had a peculiar yellow band, with brownish speckles, which seemed to be bound tight round his head. As we entered he made neither sound nor motion.

"The band! The speckled band!" whispered Holmes.

I took a step forward. In an instant his strange headgear began to move, and there reared itself from among his hair the squat diamond-shaped head and puffed neck of a loathsome serpent.

"It is a swamp adder!" cried Holmes — "the deadliest snake in India. He has died within ten seconds of being bitten. Violence does, in truth, recoil upon the violent, and the schemer falls into the pit which he digs for another. Let us thrust this creature back into its den, and we can then remove Miss Stoner to some place of shelter, and let the county police know what has happened."

As he spoke he drew the dog whip swiftly from the dead man's lap, and throwing the noose round the reptile's neck, he drew it from its horrid perch, and carrying it at arm's length, threw it into the iron safe, which he closed upon it.

Such are the true facts of the death of Dr. Grimesby Roylott, of Stoke Moran. It is not necessary that I should prolong a narrative which has already run to too great a length, by telling how we broke the news to the terrified girl, how we conveyed her by the morning train to the care of her good aunt at Harrow, of how the slow process of official inquiry came to the conclusion that the Doctor met his fate while indiscreetly playing with a dangerous pet. The little which I had yet to learn of the case was told me by Sherlock Holmes as we travelled back the next day.

"I had," said he, "come to an entirely erroneous conclusion, which shows, my dear Watson, how dangerous it always is to reason from insufficient data. The presence of the gipsies, and the use of the word 'band,' which was used by the poor girl, no doubt, to explain the appearance which she had caught a horrid glimpse of by the light of her match, were sufficient to put me upon an entirely wrong scent. I can only claim the merit that I instantly reconsidered my position when, however, it became clear to me that whatever danger threatened an occupant of the room could not come from the window or the door. My attention was speedily drawn, as I have already remarked to you, to this ventilator, and to the bell-rope which hung down to the bed. The discovery that this was a dummy, and that the bed was clamped to the floor, instantly gave rise to the suspicion that the rope was there as a bridge for something passing through the hole, and coming to the bed. The idea of a snake instantly occurred to me, and when I coupled it with my knowledge that the Doctor was furnished with a supply of creatures from India, I felt that I was probably on the right track. The idea of using a form of poison which could not possibly be discovered by any chemical test was just such a one as would occur to a clever and ruthless man who had an Eastern training. The rapidity with which such a poison would take effect would also, from his point of view, be an advantage. It would be a sharp-eyed coroner indeed who could distinguish the two little dark punctures which would show where the poison fangs had done their work. Then I thought of the whistle. Of course, he must recall the snake before the morning light revealed it to the victim. He had trained it, probably by the use of the milk which we saw, to return to him when summoned. He would put it through the ventilator at the hour he thought best, with the certainty that it would crawl down the rope, and land on the bed. It might or might not bite the occupant, perhaps she might escape every night for a week, but sooner or later she must fall a victim.

"I had come to these conclusions before ever I had entered his room. An inspection of his chair showed me that he had been in the habit of standing on it, which, of course, would be necessary in order that he should reach the ventilator. The sight of the safe, the saucer of milk, and the loop of whipcord were really enough to finally dispel any doubts which may have remained. The metallic clang heard by Miss Stoner was obviously caused by her stepfather hastily closing the door of his safe upon its terrible occupant. Having once made up my mind, you know the steps which I took in order to put the matter to proof. I heard the creature hiss, as I have no doubt that you did also, and I instantly lit the light and attacked it."

"With the result of driving it through the ventilator."

"And also with the result of causing it to turn upon its master at the other side. Some of the blows of my cane came home, and roused its snakish temper, so that it flew upon the first person it saw. In this way I am no doubt indirectly responsible for Dr. Grimesby Roylott's death, and I cannot say that it is likely to weigh very heavily upon my conscience."

ANDRE DUBUS

Andre Dubus was born in 1936 in Lake Charles, Louisiana. He served for a time in the United States Marine Corps, leaving in 1964 when he entered the Iowa Writers' Workshop. With the exception of his first work, a novel, Dubus has written stories and novellas; he attributes his learning to work in the short story form to Chekhov, whose work he studied intently. Among his collections are *Separate Flights* (1975), *Adultery and Other Choices* (1977), *Finding a Girl in America* (1980), and *The Times Are Never So Bad* (1983). Many of his characters, in the words of fellow writer Joyce Carol Oates, "perform criminal actions of one kind or another, [but] we are allowed to see how they define themselves as other than merely 'bad' through the author's extraordinary sympathy with them." Dubus has said, "If I can't become them, I can't write them." "A Father's Story" faces moral ambiguity with candor and compassion.

A Father's Story

My name is Luke Ripley, and here is what I call my life: I own a stable of thirty horses, and I have young people who teach riding, and we board some horses too. This is in northeastern Massachusetts. I have a barn with an indoor ring, and outside I've got two fenced-in rings and a pasture that ends at a woods with trails. I call it my life because it looks like it is, and people I know call it that, but it's a life I can get away from when I hunt and fish, and some nights after dinner when I sit in the dark in the front room and listen to opera. The room faces the lawn and the road, a two-lane country road. When cars come around the curve northwest of the house, they light up the lawn for an instant, the leaves of the maple out by the road and the hemlock closer to the window. Then I'm alone again, or I'd appear to be if someone crept up to the house and looked through a window: a big-gutted gray-haired guy, drinking tea and smoking cigarettes, staring out at the dark woods across the road, listening to a grieving soprano.

My real life is the one nobody talks about anymore, except Father Paul LeBoeuf, another old buck. He has a decade on me: he's sixty-four, a big man, bald on top with gray at the sides; when he had hair, it was black. His face is ruddy, and he jokes about being a whiskey priest, though he's not. He gets outdoors as much as he can, goes for a long walk every morning, and hunts and fishes with me. But I can't get him on a horse anymore. Ten years ago I could badger him into a trail ride; I had to give him a Western saddle, and he'd hold the pommel and bounce through the woods with me, and be sore for days. He's looking at seventy with eyes that are younger than many I've seen in people in their twenties. I do not remember ever feeling the way they seem to; but I was lucky, because even as a child I knew that life would try me, and I must be strong to endure, though in those days I expected to be tortured and killed for my faith, like the saints I learned about in school.

Father Paul's family came down from Canada, and he grew up speaking more French than English, so he is different from the Irish priests who abound up here. I do not like to make general statements, or even to hold general beliefs, about people's blood, but the Irish do seem happiest when they're dealing with misfortune or guilt, either their own or somebody else's, and if you think you're not a victim of either one, you can count on certain Irish priests to try to change your mind. On Wednesday nights Father Paul comes to dinner. Often he comes on other nights too and once, in the old days when we couldn't eat meat on Fridays, we bagged our first ducks of the season on a Friday, and as we drove home from the marsh, he said: For the purposes of Holy Mother Church, I believe a duck is more a creature of water than land, and is not rightly meat. Sometimes he teases me about never putting anything in his Sunday collection, which he would not know about if I hadn't told him years ago. I would like to believe I told him so we could have philosophical talk at dinner, but probably the truth is I suspected he knew, and I did not want him to think I so loved money that I would not even give his church a coin on Sunday. Certainly the ushers who pass the baskets know me as a miser.

I don't feel right about giving money for buildings, places. This starts with the pope, and I cannot respect one of them till he sells his house and everything in it, and that church too, and uses the money to feed the poor. I have rarely, and maybe never, come across saintliness, but I feel certain it cannot exist in such a place. But I admit, also, that I know very little, and maybe the popes live on a different plane and are tried in ways I don't know about. Father Paul says his own church, St John's, is hardly the Vatican. I like his church: it is made of wood, and has a simple altar and crucifix, and no padding on the kneelers. He does not have to lock its doors at night. Still it is a place. He could say Mass in my barn. I know this is stubborn, but I can find no mention by Christ of maintaining buildings, much less erecting them of stone or brick, and decorating them with pieces of metal and mineral and elements that people still fight over like barbarians. We had a Maltese woman taking riding lessons, she came over on the boat when she was ten, and once she told me how the nuns in Malta used to tell the little girls that if they wore jewelry, rings and bracelets and necklaces, in purgatory snakes would coil around their fingers and wrists and throats. I do not believe in frightening children or telling them lies, but if those nuns saved a few girls from devotion to things, maybe they were right. That Maltese woman laughed about it, but I noticed she wore only a watch, and that with a leather strap.

The money I give to the church goes in people's stomachs, and on their backs, down in New York City. I have no delusions about the worth of what I do, but I feel it's better to feed somebody than not. There's a priest in Times Square giving shelter to runaway kids, and some Franciscans who run a bread line; actually it's a morning line for coffee and a roll, and Father Paul calls it the continental breakfast for winos and bag ladies. He is curious about how much I am sending, and I know why: he guesses I send a lot, he has said probably more than tithing, and he is right; he wants to know how much because he believes I'm generous and good, and he is wrong about that; he has never had much money and does not know how easy it is to write a check when you have everything you will ever need, and the figures are mere numbers, and represent no sacrifice at all. Being a real Catholic is too hard; if I were one, I would do with my house and barn what I want the pope to do with his. So I do not want to impress Father Paul, and when he asks me how much, I say I can't let my left hand know what my right is doing.

He came on Wednesday nights when Gloria and I were married, and the kids were young; Gloria was a very good cook (I assume she still is, but it is difficult to think of her in the present), and I liked sitting at the table with a friend who was also a priest. I was proud of my handsome and healthy children. This was long ago, and they were all very young and cheerful and often funny, and the three boys took care of their baby sister, and did not bully or tease her. Of course they did sometimes, with that excited cruelty children are prone to, but not enough so that it was part of her days. On the Wednesday after Gloria left with the kids and a U-Haul trailer, I was sitting on the front steps, it was summer, and I was watching cars go by on the road, when Father Paul drove around the curve and into the driveway. I was ashamed to see him because he is a priest and my family was gone, but I was relieved too. I went to the car to greet him. He got out smiling, with a bottle of wine, and shook my hand, then pulled me to him, gave me a quick hug, and said: "It's Wednesday, isn't it? Let's open some cans."

With arms about each other we walked to the house, and it was good to know he was doing his work but coming as a friend too, and I thought what good work he had. I have no calling. It is for me to keep horses.

In that other life, anyway. In my real one I go to bed early and sleep well and wake at four forty-five, for an hour of silence. I never want to get out of bed then, and every morning I know I can sleep for another four hours, and still not fail at any of my duties. But I get up, so have come to believe my life can be seen in miniature in that struggle in the dark of morning. While making the bed and boiling water for coffee, I talk to God: I offer Him my day, every act of my body and spirit, my thoughts and moods, as a prayer of thanksgiving, and for Gloria and my children and my friends and two women I made love with after Gloria left. This morning offertory is a habit from my boyhood in a Catholic school; or then it was a habit, but as I kept it and grew older it became a ritual. Then I say the Lord's Prayer, trying not to recite it, and one morning it occurred to me that a prayer, whether recited or said with concentration, is always an act of faith.

I sit in the kitchen at the rear of the house and drink coffee and smoke and watch the sky growing light before sunrise, the trees of the woods near the barn taking shape, becoming single pines and elms and oaks and maples. Sometimes a rabbit comes out of the treeline, or is already sitting there, invisible till the light finds him. The birds are awake in the trees and feeding on the ground and the little ones, the purple finches and titmice and chickadees, are at the feeder I rigged outside the kitchen window; it is too small for pigeons to get a purchase. I sit and give myself to coffee and tobacco, that get me brisk again, and I watch and listen. In the first year or so after I lost my family, I played the radio in the mornings. But I overcame that, and now I rarely play it at all. Once in the mail I received a questionnaire asking me to write down everything I watched on television during the week they had chosen. At the end of those seven days I wrote in *The Wizard of Oz* and returned it. That was in winter and was actually a busy week for my television, which normally sits out the cold months without once warming up. Had they sent the questionnaire during baseball season, they would have found me at my set. People at the stables talk about shows and performers I have never heard of, but I cannot get interested; when I am in the mood to watch television, I go to a movie or read a detective novel. There are always good detective novels to be found, and I like remembering them next morning with my coffee.

I also think of baseball and hunting and fishing, and of my children. It is not painful to think about them anymore, because even if we had lived together, they would be gone now, grown into their own lives, except Jennifer. I think of death too, not sadly, or with fear, though something like excitement does run through me, something more quickening then the coffee and tobacco. I suppose it is an intense interest, and an outright distrust: I never feel certain that I'll be here watching birds eating at tomorrow's daylight. Sometimes I try to think of other things, like the rabbit that is warm and breathing but not there till twilight. I feel on the brink of something about the life of the senses, but either am not equipped to go further, or am not interested enough to concentrate. I have called all of this thinking, but it is not, because it is unintentional; what I'm really doing is feeling the day, in silence, and that is what Father Paul is doing too on his five- to ten-mile walks.

When the hour ends I take an apple or carrot, and I go to the stable and tack up a horse. We take good care of these horses, and no one rides them but students, instructors, and me, and nobody rides the horses we board unless an owner asks me to. The barn is dark and I turn on lights and take some deep breaths, smelling the hay and horses and their manure, both fresh and dried, a combined odor that you either like or you don't. I walk down the wide space of dirt between stalls, greeting the horses, joking with them about their quirks, and choose one for no reason at all other than the way it looks at me that morning. I get my old English saddle that has smoothed and darkened through the years, and go into the stall, talking to this beautiful creature who'll swerve out of a canter if a piece of paper blows in front of him, and if the barn catches fire and you manage to get him out he will, if he can get away from you, run back into the fire, to his stall. Like the smells that surround them, you either like them or you don't. I love them, so am spared having to try to explain why. I feed one the carrot or apple and tack up and lead him outside where I mount, and we go down the driveway to the road and cross it and turn northwest and walk then trot then canter to St. John's.

A few cars are on the road, their drivers looking serious about going to work. It is always strange for me to see a woman dressed for work so early in the morning. You know how long it takes them, with the makeup and hair and clothes, and I think of them waking in the dark of winter or early light of other seasons and dressing as they might for an evening's entertainment. Probably this strikes me because I grew up seeing my father put on those suits he never wore on weekends or his two weeks off, and so am accustomed to the men, but when I see these women I think something went wrong, to send all those dressed-up people out on the road when the dew hasn't dried yet. Maybe it's because I so dislike getting up early, but am also doing what I choose to do, while they have no choice. At heart I am lazy, yet I find such peace and delight in it that I believe it is a natural state, and in what looks like my laziest periods I am closest to my center. The ride to St. John's is fifteen minutes. The horses and I do it in all weather; the road is well plowed in winter, and there are only a few days a year when ice makes me drive the pickup. People always look at someone on horseback, and for a moment their faces change and many drivers and I wave to each other. Then at St. John's, Father Paul and five or six regulars and I celebrate the Mass.

Do not think of me as a spiritual man whose every thought during those twenty-five minutes is at one with the words of the Mass. Each morning I try, each morning I fail, and know that always I will be a creature who, looking at Father Paul and the altar, and uttering prayers, will be distracted by scrambled eggs, horses, the weather, and memories and daydreams that have nothing to do with the sacrament I am about to receive. I can receive, though: the Eucharist, and also, at Mass and at other times, moments and even minutes of contemplation. But I cannot achieve contemplation, as some can; and so, having to face and forgive my own failures, I have learned from them both the necessity and the wonder of ritual. For ritual allows those who cannot will themselves out of the secular to perform the spiritual as dancing allows the tongue-tied man a ceremony of love. And, while my mind dwells on breakfast, or Major or Duchess tethered under the church eave, there is, as I take the Host from Father Paul and place it on my tongue and return to the pew, a feeling that I am thankful I have not lost in the forty-eight years since my first Communion. At its center is excitement; spreading out from it is the peace of certainty. Or the certainty of peace. One night Father Paul and I talked about faith. It was long ago, and all I remember is him saying: Belief is believing in God; faith is believing that God believes in you. That is the excitement, and the peace; then the Mass is over, and I go into the sacristy and we have a cigarette and chat, the mystery ends, we are two men talking like any two men on a morning in America, about baseball, plane crashes, presidents, governors, murders, the sun, the clouds. Then I go to the horse and ride back to the life people see, the one in which I move and talk, and most days I enjoy it.

It is late summer now, the time between fishing and hunting, but a good time for baseball. It has been two weeks since Jennifer left, to drive home to Gloria's after her summer visit. She is the only one who still visits; the boys are married and have children, and sometimes fly up for a holiday, or I fly down or west to visit one of them. Jennifer is twenty, and I worry about her the way fathers worry about daughters but not sons. I want to know what she's up to, and at the same time I don't. She looks athletic, and she is: she swims and runs and of course rides. All my children do. When she comes for six weeks in summer, the house is loud with girls, friends of hers since childhood, and new ones. I am glad she kept the girl friends. They have been young company for me and, being with them, I have been able to gauge her growth between summers. On their riding days, I'd take them back to the house when their lessons were over and they had walked the horses and put them back in the stalls, and we'd have lemonade or Coke, and cookies if I had some, and talk until their parents came to drive them home. One year their breasts grew, so I wasn't startled when I saw Jennifer in July. Then they were driving cars to the stable, and beginning to look like young women, and I was passing out beer and ashtrays and they were talking about college.

When Jennifer was here in summer, they were at the house most days. I would say generally that as they got older they became quieter, and though I enjoyed both, I sometimes missed the giggles and shouts. The quiet voices, just low enough for me not to hear from wherever I was, rising and falling in proportion to my distance from them, frightened me. Not that I believed they were planning or recounting anything really wicked, but there was a female seriousness about them, and it was secretive, and of course I thought: love, sex. But it was more than that: it was womanhood they were entering, the deep forest of it, and no matter how many women and men too are saying these days that there is little difference between us, the truth is that men find their way into that forest only on clearly marked trails while women move about in it like birds. So hearing Jennifer and her friends talking so quietly, yet intensely, I wanted very much to have a wife.

But not as much as in the old days, when Gloria had left but her presence was still in the house as strongly as if she had only gone to visit her folks for a week. There were no clothes or cosmetics, but potted plants endured my neglectful care as long as they could, and slowly died; I did not kill them on purpose, to exorcise the house of her, but I could not remember to water them. For weeks, because I did not use it much, the house was as neat as she had kept it, though dust layered the order she had made. The kitchen went first: I got the dishes in and out of the dishwasher and wiped the top of the stove, but did not return cooking spoons and potholders to their hooks on the wall, and soon the burners and oven were caked with spillings, the refrigerator had more space and was spotted with juices. The living room and my bedroom went next; I did not go into the children's rooms except on bad nights when I went from room to room and looked and touched and smelled, so they did not lose their order until a year later when the kids came for six weeks. It was three months before I ate the last of the food Gloria had cooked and frozen: I remember it was a beef stew, and very good. By then I had four cookbooks, and was boasting a bit, and talking about recipes with the women at the stables, and looking forward to cooking for Father Paul. But I never looked forward to cooking at night only for myself, though I made myself do it; on some nights I gave in to my daily temptation, and took a newspaper or detective novel to a restaurant. By the end of the second year, though, I had stopped turning on the radio as soon as I woke in the morning, and was able to be silent and alone in the evening too, and then I enjoyed my dinners.

It is not hard to live through a day, if you can live through a moment. What creates despair is the imagination, that pretends there is a future, and insists on predicting millions of moments, thousands of days, and so drains you that you cannot live the moment at hand. That is what Father Paul told me in those first two years, on some of the bad nights when I believed I could not bear what I had to: the most painful loss was my children, then the loss of Gloria whom I still loved despite or maybe because of our long periods of sadness that rendered us helpless, so neither of us could break out of it to give a hand to the other. Twelve years later I believe ritual would have healed us more quickly than the repetitious talks we had, perhaps even kept us healed. Marriages have lost that, and I wish I had known then what I know now, and we had performed certain acts together every day, no matter how we felt, and perhaps then we could have subordinated feeling to action, for surely that is the essence of love. I know this from my distractions during Mass, and during everything else I do, so that my actions and feelings are seldom one. It does happen every day, but in proportion to everything else in a day, it is rare, like joy. The third most painful loss, which became second and sometimes first as months passed, was the knowledge that I could never marry again, and so dared not even keep company with a woman.

On some of the bad nights I was bitter about this with Father Paul, and I so pitied myself that I cried, or nearly did, speaking with damp eyes and breaking voice. I believe that celibacy is for him the same trial it is for me, not of the flesh, but the spirit: the heart longing to love. But the difference is he chose it, and did not wake one day to a life with thirty horses. In my anger I said I had done my service to love and chastity, and I told him of the actual physical and spiritual pain of practicing rhythm: nights of striking the mattress with a fist, two young animals lying side by side in heat, leaving the bed to pace, to smoke, to curse, and too passionate to question, for we were so angered and oppressed by our passion that we could see no further than our loins. So now I understand how people can be enslaved for generations before they throw down their tools or use them as weapons, the form of their slavery — the cotton fields, the shacks and puny cupboards and untended illnesses — absorbing their emotions and thoughts until finally they have little or none at all to direct with clarity and energy at the owners and legislators. And I told him of the trick of passion and its slaking: how during what we had to believe were safe periods, though all four children were conceived at those times, we were able with some coherence to question the tradition and reason and justice of the law against birth control, but not with enough conviction to soberly act against it, as though regular satisfaction in bed tempered our revolutionary as well as our erotic desires. Only when abstinence drove us hotly away from each other did we receive an urge so strong it lasted all the way to the drugstore and back; but always, after release, we threw away the remaining condoms; and after going through this a few times, we knew what would happen, and from then on we submitted to the calendar she so precisely marked on the bedroom wall. I told him that living two lives each month, one as celibates, one as lovers, made us tense and short-tempered, so we snapped at each other like dogs.

To have endured that, to have reached a time when we burned slowly and could gain from bed the comfort of lying down at night with one who loves you and whom you love, could for weeks on end go to bed tired, and peacefully sleep after a kiss, a touch of the hands, and then to be thrown out of the marriage like a bundle from a moving freight car, was unjust, was intolerable, and I could not or would not muster the strength to endure it. But I did, a moment at a time, a day, a night, except twice, each time with a different woman and more than a year apart, and this was so long ago that I clearly see their faces in my memory, can hear the pitch of their voices, and the way they pronounced words, one with a Massachusetts accent, one midwestern, but I feel as though I only heard about them from someone else. Each rode at the stables and was with me for part of an evening; one was badly married, one divorced, so none of us was free. They did not understand this Catholic view, but they were understanding about my having it, and I remained friends with both of them until the married one left her husband and went to Boston, and the divorced one moved to Maine. After both those evenings, those good women, I went to Mass early while Father Paul was still in the confessional, and received his absolution. I did not tell him who I was, but of course he knew, though I never saw it in his eyes. Now my longing for a wife comes only once in a while, like a cold; on some late afternoons when I am alone in the barn then I lock up and walk to the house, daydreaming, then suddenly look at it and see it empty, as though for the first time, and all at once I'm weary and feel I do not have the energy to broil meat, and I think of driving to a restaurant, then shake my head and go on to the house, the refrigerator, the oven; and some mornings when I wake in the dark and listen to the silence and run my hand over the cold sheet beside me; and some days in summer when Jennifer is here.

Gloria left first me then the church, and that was the end of religion for the children, though on visits they went to Sunday Mass with me, and still do, out of a respect for my life that they manage to keep free of patronage. Jennifer is an agnostic, though I doubt she would call herself that, any more than she would call herself any other name that implied she had made a decision, a choice, about existence, death, and God. In truth she tends to pantheism, a good sign I think; but not wanting to be a father who tells his children what they ought to believe, I do not say to her that Catholicism includes pantheism, like onions in the stew. Besides, I have no missionary instincts and do not believe everyone should or even could live with the Catholic faith. It is Jennifer's womanhood that renders me awkward. And womanhood now is frank, not like when Gloria was twenty and there were symbols: high heels and cosmetics and dresses, a cigarette, a cocktail. I am glad that women are free now of false modesty and all its attention paid the flesh; but still it is difficult to see so much of your daughter, to face the deep and unabashed sensuality of women, with no tricks of the eyes and mouth to hide the pleasure she feels at having a strong young body. I am certain, with the way things are now, that she has very happily not been a virgin for years. That does not bother me. What bothers me is my certainty about it, just from watching her walk across a room or light a cigarette or pour milk on cereal.

She told me all of it, waking me that night when I had gone to sleep listening to the wind in the trees against the house, a wind so strong that I had to shut all but the lee windows, and still the house cooled; told it to me in such detail and so clearly that now, when she has driven the car to Florida, I remember it all as though I had been a passenger in the front seat, or even at the wheel. It started with a movie, then beer and driving to the sea to look at the waves in the night and the wind. Jennifer and Betsy and Liz. They drank a beer on the beach and wanted to go in naked but were afraid they would drown in the high surf. They bought another six-pack at a grocery store in New Hampshire, and drove home. I can see it now, feel it: the three girls and the beer and the ride on country roads where pines curved in the wind and the big deciduous trees swayed and shook as if they might leap from the earth. They would have some windows partly open so they could feel the wind; Jennifer would be playing a cassette, the music stirring them, as it does the young, to memories of another time, other people and places in what is for them the past.

She took Betsy home, then Liz, and sang with her cassette as she left the town west of us and started home, a twenty-minute drive on the road that passes my house. They had each had four beers, but now there were twelve empty bottles in the bag on the floor at the passenger seat, and I keep focusing on their sound against each other when the car shifted speeds or changed directions. For I want to understand that one moment out of all her heart's time on earth, and whether her history had any bearing on it, or whether her heart was then isolated from all it had known, and the sound of those bottles urged it. She was just leaving the town, accelerating past a nightclub on the right, gaining speed to climb a long gradual hill, then she went up it, singing, patting the beat on the steering wheel, the wind loud through her few inches of open window, blowing her hair as it did the high branches alongside the road, and she looked up at them and watched the top of the hill for someone drunk or heedless coming over it in part of her lane. She crested to an open black road, and there he was: a bulk, a blur, a thing running across her headlights, and she swerved left and her foot went for the brake and was stomping air above its pedal when she hit him, saw his legs and body in the air, flying out of her light, into the dark. Her brakes were screaming into the wind, bottles clinking in the fallen bag, and with the music and wind inside the car was his sound already a memory but as real as an echo, that car-shuddering thump as though she had struck a tree. Her foot was back on the accelerator. Then she shifted gears and pushed it. She ejected the cassette and closed the window. She did not start to cry until she knocked on my bedroom door, then called: "Dad?"

Her voice, her tears, broke through my dream and the wind I heard in my sleep, and I stepped into jeans and hurried to the door, thinking harm, rape, death. All were in her face, and I hugged her and pressed her cheek to my chest and smoothed her blown hair, then led her weeping to the kitchen and sat her at the table where still she could not speak, nor look at me; when she raised her face it fell forward again, as of its own weight, into her palms. I offered tea and she shook her head, so I offered whiskey and she nodded. I had some rye that Father Paul and I had not finished last hunting season, and I poured some over ice and set it in front of her and was putting away the ice but stopped and got another glass and poured one for myself too, and brought the ice and bottle to the table where she was trying to get one of her long menthols out of the pack, but her fingers jerked like severed snakes, and I took the pack and lit one for her and took one for myself. I watched her shudder with her first swallow of rye, and push hair back from her face, it is auburn and gleamed in the overhead light, and I remembered how beautiful she looked riding a sorrel; she was smoking fast, then the sobs in her throat stopped, and she looked at me and said it, the words coming out with smoke: "I hit somebody. With the *car.*"

Then she was crying and I was on my feet, moving back and forth, looking down at her asking Who? Where? Where? She was pointing at the wall over the stove, jabbing her fingers and cigarette at it, her other hand at her eyes, and twice in horror I actually looked at the wall. She finished the whiskey in a swallow and I stopped pacing and asking and poured another, and either the drink or the exhaustion of tears quieted her, even the dry sobs, and she told me; not as I tell it now, for that was later as again and again we relived it in the kitchen or living room, and if in daylight fled it on horseback out on the trails through the woods, and if at night walked quietly around in the moonlit pasture, walked around and around it, sweating through our clothes. She told it in bursts, like she was a child again, running to me, injured from play. I put on boots and a shirt and left her with the bottle and her streaked face and a cigarette twitching between her fingers, pushed the door open against the wind, and eased it shut. The wind squinted and watered my eyes as I leaned into it and went to the pickup.

When I passed St. John's I looked at it, and Father Paul's little white rectory in the rear, and wanted to stop, wished I could as I could if he were simply a friend who sold hardware or something. I had forgotten my watch but I always know the time within minutes, even when a sound or dream or my bladder wakes me in the night. It was nearly two; we had been in the kitchen about twenty minutes; she had hit him around one-fifteen. Or her. The road was empty and I drove between blowing trees; caught for an instant in my lights, they seemed to be in panic. I smoked and let hope play her tricks on me; it was neither man nor woman but an animal, a goat or calf or deer on the road; it was a man who had jumped away in time, the collision of metal and body glancing not direct, and he had limped home to nurse bruises and cuts. Then I threw the cigarette and hope both out the window and prayed that he was alive, while beneath that prayer, a reserve deeper in my heart, another one stirred: that if he were dead, they would not get Jennifer.

From our direction, east and a bit south, the road to that hill and the nightclub beyond it and finally the town is, for its last four or five miles, straight through farming country. When I reached that stretch I slowed the truck and opened my window for the fierce air; on both sides were scattered farmhouses and barns and sometimes a silo, looking not like shelters but like unsheltered things the wind would flatten. Corn bent toward the road from a field on my right, and always something blew in front of me: paper, leaves, dried weeds, branches. I slowed approaching the hill, and went up it in second, staring through my open window at the ditch on the left side of the road, its weeds alive, whipping, a mad dance with the trees above them. I went over the hill and down and, opposite the club, turned right onto a side street of houses, and parked there, in the leaping shadows of trees. I walked back across the road to the club's parking lot, the wind behind me, lifting me as I strode, and I could not hear my boots on pavement. I walked up the hill, on the shoulder, watching the branches above me, hearing their leaves and the creaking trunks and the wind. Then I was at the top, looking down the road and at the farms and fields; the night was clear, and I could see a long way; clouds scudded past the half-moon and stars, blown out to sea.

I started down, watching the tall grass under the trees to my right, glancing into the dark of the ditch, listening for cars behind me; but as soon as I cleared one tree, its sound was gone, its flapping leaves and rattling branches far behind me, as though the greatest distance I had at my back was a matter of feet, while ahead of me I could see a barn two miles off. Then I saw her skid marks: short, and going left and downhill, into the other lane. I stood at the ditch, its weeds blowing; across it were trees and their moving shadows, like the clouds. I stepped onto its slope, and it took me sliding on my feet then rump to the bottom where I sat still, my body gathered to itself, lest a part of me should touch him. But there was only tall grass, and I stood, my shoulders reaching the sides of the ditch, and I walked uphill, wishing for the flashlight in the pickup, walking slowly, and down in the ditch I could hear my feet in the grass and on the earth, and kicking cans and bottles. At the top of the hill I turned and went down, watching the ground above the ditch on my right, praying my prayer from the truck again, the first one, the one I would admit, that he was not dead, was in fact home, and began to hope again, memory telling me of lost pheasants and grouse I had shot, but they were small and the colors of their home, while a man was either there or not; and from that memory I left where I was and while walking the ditch under the wind was in the deceit of imagination with Jennifer in the kitchen, telling her she had hit no one, or at least had not badly hurt anyone, when I realized he could be in the hospital now and I would have to think of a way to check there, something to say on the phone. I see now that, once hope returned, I should have been certain what she prepared me for: ahead of me, in high grass and the shadows of trees, I saw his shirt. Or that is all my mind would allow itself: a shirt, and I stood looking at it for the moments it took my mind to admit the arm and head and the dark length covered by pants. He lay face down, the arm I could see near his side, his head turned from me, on its cheek.

"Fella?" I said. I had meant to call, but it came out quiet and high, lost inches from my face in the wind. Then I said, "Oh God," and felt Him in the wind and the sky moving past the stars and moon and the fields around me, but only watching me as He might have watched Cain or Job, I did not know which, and I said it again, and wanted to sink to the earth and weep till I slept there in the weeds. I climbed, scrambling up the side of the ditch, pulling at clutched grass as high and higher than my face, crawling under that sky, making sounds too like some animal, there being no words to let him know I was here with him now. He was long; that is the word that came to me, not tall. I kneeled beside him, my hands on my legs. His right arm was by his side, his left arm straight out from the shoulder, but turned, so his palm was open to the tree above us. His left cheek was clean shaven, his eye closed, and there was no blood. I leaned forward to look at his open mouth and saw the blood on it, going down into the grass. I straightened and looked ahead at the wind blowing past me through grass and trees to a distant light, and I stared at the light, imagining someone awake out there, wanting someone to be, a gathering of old friends, or someone alone listening to music or painting a picture, then I figured it was a night light at a farmyard whose house I couldn't see. *Going,* I thought. *Still going.* I leaned over again and looked at dripping blood.

So I had to touch his wrist, a thick one with a watch and expansion band that I pushed up his arm, thinking *he's left-handed,* my three fingers pressing his wrist and all I felt was my tough fingertips on that smooth underside flesh and small bones, then relief, then certainty. But against my will, or only because of it, I still don't know, I touched his neck, ran my fingers down it as if petting, then pressed and my hand sprang back as from fire. I lowered it again, held it there until it felt that faint beating that I could not believe. There was too much wind. Nothing could make a sound in it. A pulse could not be felt in it, nor could mere fingers in that wind feel the absolute silence of a dead man's artery. I was making sounds again; I grabbed his left arm and his waist, and pulled him toward me, and that side of him rose, turned, and I lowered him to his back, his face tilted up toward the tree that was groaning, the tree and I the only sounds in the wind. Turning my face from his, looking down the length of him at his sneakers, I placed my ear on his heart, and heard not that but something else, and I clamped a hand over my exposed ear, heard something liquid and alive, like when you pump a well and after a few strokes you hear air and water moving in the pipe, and I knew I must raise his legs and cover him and run to a phone, while still I listened to his chest, thinking *raise with what? cover with what?* and amid the liquid sound I heard the heart then lost it, and pressed my ear against bone, but his chest was quiet, and I did not know when the liquid had stopped, and do not know now when I heard air, a faint rush of it, and whether under my ear or at his mouth or whether I heard it at all. I straightened and looked at the light, dim and yellow. Then I touched his throat, looking him full in the face. He was blond and young. He could have been sleeping in the shade of a tree, but for the smear of blood from his mouth to his hair, and the night sky, and the weeds blowing against his head, and the leaves shaking in the dark above us.

I stood. Then I knelt again and prayed for his soul to join in peace and joy all the dead and living; and doing so, confronted my first sin against him, not stopping for Father Paul, who could have given him the last rites, and immediately then my second one, or, I saw then, my first, not calling an ambulance to meet me there, and I stood and turned into the wind, slid down the ditch and crawled out of it, and went up the hill and down it, across the road to the street of houses whose people I had left behind forever, so that I moved with stealth in the shadows to my truck.

When I came around the bend near my house, I saw the kitchen light at the rear. She sat as I had left her, the ashtray filled, and I looked at the bottle, felt her eyes on me, felt what she was seeing too: the dirt from my crawling. She had not drunk much of the rye. I poured some in my glass, with the water from melted ice, and sat down and swallowed some and looked at her and swallowed some more, and said: "He's dead."

She rubbed her eyes with the heels of her hands, rubbed the cheeks under them, but she was dry now.

"He was probably dead when he hit the ground. I mean, that's probably what killed — "

"Where was he?"

"Across the ditch, under a tree."

"Was he — did you see his face?"

"No. Not really. I just felt. For life, pulse. I'm going out to the car."

"What for? Oh."

I finished the rye, and pushed back the chair, then she was standing too.

"I'll go with you."

"There's no need."

"I'll go."

I took a flashlight from a drawer and pushed open the door and held it while she went out. We turned our faces from the wind. It was like on the hill, when I was walking, and the wind closed the distance behind me: after three or four steps I felt there was no house back there. She took my hand, as I was reaching for hers. In the garage we let go, and squeezed between the pickup and her little car, to the front of it, where we had more room, and we stepped back from the grill and I shone the light on the fender, the smashed headlight turned into it, the concave chrome staring to the right, at the garage wall.

"We ought to get the bottles," I said.

She moved between the garage and the car, on the passenger side, and had room to open the door and lift the bag. I reached out, and she gave me the bag and backed up and shut the door and came around the car. We sidled to the doorway, and she put her arm around my waist and I hugged her shoulders.

"I thought you'd call the police," she said.

We crossed the yard, faces bowed from the wind, her hair blowing away from her neck, and in the kitchen I put the bag of bottles in the garbage basket. She was working at the table: capping the rye and putting it away, filling the ice tray, washing the glasses, emptying the ashtray, sponging the table.

"Try to sleep now," I said.

She nodded at the sponge circling under her hand, gathering ashes. Then she dropped it in the sink and, looking me full in the face, as I had never seen her look, as perhaps she never had, being for so long a daughter on visits (or so it seemed to me and still does: that until then our eyes had never seriously met), she crossed to me from the sink, and kissed my lips, then held me so tightly I lost balance, and would have stumbled forward had she not held me so hard.

I sat in the living room, the house darkened, and watched the maple and the hemlock. When I believed she was asleep I put on *La Bohème,* and kept it at the same volume as the wind so it would not wake her. Then I listened to *Madama Butterfly,* and in the third act had to rise quickly to lower the sound: the wind was gone. I looked at the still maple near the window, and thought of the wind leaving farms and towns and the coast, going out over the sea to die on the waves. I smoked and gazed out the window. The sky was darker, and at daybreak the rain came. I listened to *Tosca,* and at six-fifteen went to the kitchen where Jennifer's purse lay on the table, a leather shoulder purse crammed with the things of an adult woman, things she had begun accumulating only a few years back, and I nearly wept, thinking of what sandy foundations they were: driver's license, credit card, disposable lighter, cigarettes, checkbook, ballpoint pen, cash, cosmetics, comb, brush, Kleenex, these the rite of passage from childhood, and I took one of them — her keys — and went out, remembering a jacket and hat when the rain struck me, but I kept going to the car, and squeezed and lowered myself into it, pulled the seat belt over my shoulder and fastened it and backed out, turning in the drive, going forward into the road, toward St. John's and Father Paul.

Cars were on the road, the workers, and I did not worry about any of them noticing the fender and light. Only a horse distracted them from what they drove to. In front of St. John's is a parking lot; at its far side, past the church and at the edge of the lawn, is an old pine, taller than the steeple now. I shifted to third, left the road, and aiming the right headlight at the tree, accelerated past the white blur of church, into the black trunk growing bigger till it was all I could see, then I rocked in that resonant thump she had heard, had felt, and when I turned off the ignition it was still in my ears, my blood, and I saw the boy flying in the wind. I lowered my forehead to the wheel. Father Paul opened the door, his face white in the rain.

"I'm all right."

"What happened?"

"I don't know. I fainted."

I got out and went around to the front of the car, looked at the smashed light, the crumpled and torn fender.

"Come to the house and lie down."

"I'm all right."

"When was your last physical?"

"I'm due for one. Let's get out of this rain."

"You'd better lie down."

"No. I want to receive."

That was the time to say I wanted to confess, but I have not and will not. Though I could now, for Jennifer is in Florida, and weeks have passed, and perhaps now Father Paul would not feel that he must tell me to go to the police. And, for that very reason, to confess now would be unfair. It is a world of secrets, and now I have one from my best, in truth my only, friend. I have one from Jennifer too, but that is the nature of fatherhood.

Most of that day it rained, so it was only in early evening, when the sky cleared, with a setting sun, that two little boys, leaving their confinement for some play before dinner, found him. Jennifer and I got that on the local news, which we listened to every hour, meeting at the radio, standing with cigarettes, until the one at eight o'clock; when she stopped crying, we went out and walked on the wet grass, around the pasture, the last of sunlight still in the air and trees. His name was Patrick Mitchell, he was nineteen years old, was employed by CETA, lived at home with his parents and brother and sister. The paper next day said he had been at a friend's house and was walking home, and I thought of that light I had seen, then knew it was not for him; he lived on one of the streets behind the club. The paper did not say then, or in the next few days, anything to make Jennifer think he was alive while she was with me in the kitchen. Nor do I know if we — if I — could have saved him.

In keeping her secret from her friends, Jennifer had to perform so often, as I did with Father Paul and at the stables, that I believe the acting, which took more of her than our daylight trail rides and our night walks in the pasture, was her healing. Her friends teased me about wrecking her car. When I carried her luggage out to the car on that last morning, we spoke only of the weather for her trip — the day was clear, with a dry cool breeze — and hugged and kissed, and I stood watching as she started the car and turned it around. But then she shifted to neutral and put on the parking brake and unclasped the belt, looking at me all the while, then she was coming to me, as she had that night in the kitchen, and I opened my arms.

I have said I talk with God in the mornings, as I start my day, and sometimes as I sit with coffee, looking at the birds, and the woods. Of course He has never spoken to me, but that is not something I require. Nor does He need to. I know Him, as I know the part of myself that knows Him, that felt Him watching from the wind and the night as I knelt over the dying boy. Lately I have taken to arguing with Him, as I can't with Father Paul who, when he hears my monthly confession, has not and will not hear anything of failure to do all that one can to save an anonymous life, of injustice to a family in their grief, of deepening their pain at the chance and mystery of death by giving them nothing — no one — to hate. With Father Paul, I feel lonely about this, but not with God. When I received the Eucharist while Jennifer's car sat twice-damaged, so redeemed, in the rain, I felt neither loneliness nor shame, but as though He were watching me, even from my tongue, intestines, blood, as I have watched my sons at times in their young lives when I was able to judge but without anger, and so keep silent while they, in the agony of their youth, decided how they had done. Their reasons were never as good or as bad as their actions, but they needed to find them, to believe they were living by them, instead of the awful solitude of the heart.

I do not feel the peace I once did: not with God, nor the earth, or anyone on it. I have begun to prefer this state, to remember with fondness the other one as a period of peace I neither earned nor deserved. Now in the mornings while I watch purple finches driving larger titmice from the feeder, I say to Him: I would do it again. For when she knocked on my door then called me, she woke what had flowed dormant in my blood since her birth, so that what rose from the bed was not a stable owner or a Catholic or any other Luke Ripley I had lived with for a long time, but the father of a girl.

And He says: I am a Father too.

Yes, I say, as You are a Son whom this morning I will receive; unless You kill me on the way to church, then I trust You will receive me. And as a Son You made Your plea.

Yes, He says, but I would not lift the cup.

True, and I don't want You to lift it from me either. And if one of my sons had come to me that night, I would have phoned the police and told them to meet us with an ambulance at the top of the hill.

Why? Do you love them less?

I tell Him no, it is not that I love them less, but that I could bear the pain of watching and knowing my sons' pain, could bear it with pride as they took the whip and nails. But You never had a daughter, and if You had, You could not have borne her passion.

So, He says, you love her more than you love Me.

I love her more than I love truth.

Then you love in weakness, He says.

As You love me, I say, and I go with an apple or carrot out to the barn.

LOUISE ERDRICH

 Louise Erdrich was born in 1954 in Little Falls, Minnesota, of Chippewa and German-American parents. She grew up in North Dakota and received her education at Dartmouth College and Johns Hopkins University. She is the author of three novels, *Love Medicine* (1984), *The Beet Queen* (1986), and *Tracks* (1988), which evolved from linked short stories she had published in various literary journals. Another writer from the upper Midwest, poet Robert Bly, remarked his "amazement and gratitude at this splendid, feisty talent, capable of bizarre comedy, ordinary Midwestern facts, and vigorous tragedy." "The Beet Queen" is the original version of the prelude and opening chapter to Erdrich's novel of the same title.

The Beet Queen

Long before they planted beets in Argus and built the highways, there was a railroad. Along the track, which crossed the Dakota-Minnesota border and stretched on east to Minneapolis, everything that made the town arrived. All that diminished the town departed by that route too. On a cold spring morning in 1932 the train brought both an addition and a subtraction. They came by freight. By the time they reached Argus their lips were violet and their feet were so numb that, when they jumped out of the boxcar, they stumbled and scraped their palms and knees through the cinders.

The boy was a tall fourteen, hunched with his sudden growth and very pale. His mouth was sweetly curved, his skin fine and girlish. His sister was only eleven years old, but already she was so short and ordinary that it was obvious she would be this way all her life. Her name was as square and practical as the rest of her: Mary. She brushed her coat off and stood in the watery wind. Between the buildings there was only more bare horizon for her to see, and from time to time men crossing it. Wheat was the big crop then, and this topsoil was so newly tilled that it hadn't all blown off yet, the way it had in Kansas. In fact, times were generally much better in eastern North Dakota than in most places, which is why Karl and Mary Lavelle had come there on the train. Their mother's sister, Fritzie, lived on the eastern edge of town. She ran a butcher shop with her husband.

The two Lavelles put their hands up their sleeves and started walking. Once they began to move they felt warmer although they'd been traveling all night and the chill had reached in deep. They walked east, down the dirt and planking of the broad main street, reading the signs on each false-front clapboard store they passed, even reading the gilt letters in the window of the brick bank. None of these places was a butcher shop. Abruptly, the stores stopped and a string of houses, weathered gray or peeling gray, with dogs tied to their porch railings, began.

Small trees were planted in the yards of a few of these houses and one tree, weak, a scratch of light against the gray of everything else, tossed in a film of blossoms. Mary trudged solidly forward, hardly glancing at it, but Karl stopped. The tree drew him with its delicate perfume. His cheeks went pink, he stretched his arms out like a sleepwalker, and in one long transfixed motion he floated to the tree and buried his face in the white petals.

Turning to look for Karl, Mary was frightened by how far back he had fallen and how still he was, face pressed in the flowers. She shouted, but he did not seem to hear her and only stood, strange and stock-still, among the branches. He did not move even when the dog in the yard lunged against its rope and bawled. He did not notice when the door to the house opened and a woman scrambled out. She shouted at Karl too, but he paid her no mind and so she untied her dog. Large and anxious, it flew forward in great bounds. And then, either to protect himself or to seize the blooms, Karl reached out and tore a branch from the tree.

It was such a large branch, from such a small tree, that blight would attack the scar where it was pulled off. The leaves would fall away later that summer and the sap would sink into the roots. The next spring, when Mary passed it on some errand, she saw that it bore no blossoms and remembered how, when the dog jumped for Karl, he struck out with the branch and the petals dropped around the dog's fierce outstretched body in a sudden snow. Then he yelled, "Run!" and Mary ran east, toward Aunt Fritzie. But Karl ran back to the boxcar and the train.

So that's how I came to Argus. I was the girl in the stiff coat. After I ran blind and came to a halt, shocked not to find Karl behind me, I looked up to watch for him and heard the train whistle long and shrill. That was when I realized Karl had jumped back on the same boxcar and was now hunched in straw, watching out the opened door. The only difference would be the fragrant stick blooming in his hand. I saw the train pulled like a string of black beads over the horizon, as I have seen it so many times since. When it was out of sight, I stared down at my feet. I was afraid. It was not that with Karl gone I had no one to protect me, but just the opposite. With no one to protect and look out for, I was weak. Karl was taller than me but spindly, older of course, but fearful. He suffered from fevers that kept him in a stuporous dream state and was sensitive to loud sounds, harsh lights. My mother called him delicate, but I was the opposite. I was the one who begged rotten apples from the grocery store and stole whey from the back stoop of the creamery in Minneapolis, where we were living the winter after my father died.

This story starts then, because before that and without the year 1929, our family would probably have gone on living comfortably and even have prospered on the Minnesota land that Theodor Lavelle broke and plowed and where he brought his bride, Adelaide, to live. But because that farm was lost, bankrupt like so many around it, our family was scattered to chance. After the foreclosure, my father worked as day labor on other farms in Minnesota. I don't even remember where we were living the day that word came. I only remember that my mother's hair was plaited in two red crooked braids and that she fell, full length, across the floor at the news. It was a common grain-loading accident, and Theodor Lavelle had smothered in oats. After that we moved to a rooming house in the Cities, where my mother thought that, with her figure and good looks, she could find work in a fashionable store. She didn't know, when we moved, that she was pregnant. In a surprisingly short amount of time we were desperate.

I didn't know how badly off we were until my mother stole six heavy, elaborately molded silver spoons from our landlady, who was kind or at least harbored no grudge against us, and whom my mother counted as a friend. Adelaide gave no explanation for the spoons, but she probably did not know I had discovered them in her pocket. Days later, they were gone and Karl and I owned thick overcoats. Also, our shelf was loaded with green bananas. For several weeks we drank quarts of buttermilk and ate buttered toast with thick jam. It was not long after that, I believe, that the baby was ready to be born.

One afternoon my mother sent us downstairs to the landlady. This woman was stout and so dull that I've forgotten her name although I recall vivid details of all else that happened at that time. It was a cold late-winter afternoon. We stared into the glass-faced cabinet where the silver stirrup cups and painted plates were locked after the theft. The outlines of our faces stared back at us like ghosts. From time to time Karl and I heard someone groan upstairs. It was our mother, of couse, but we never let on as much. Once something heavy hit the floor directly above our heads. Both of us looked up at the ceiling and threw out our arms involuntarily, as if to catch it. I don't know what went through Karl's mind, but I thought it was the baby, born heavy as lead, dropping straight through the clouds and my mother's body. Because Adelaide insisted that the child would come from heaven although it was obviously growing inside of her, I had a confused idea of the process of birth. At any rate, no explanation I could dream up accounted for the groans, or for the long scream that tore through the air, turned Karl's face white, and caused him to slump forward in the chair.

I had given up on reviving Karl each time he fainted. By that time I trusted that he'd come to by himself, and he always did, looking soft and dazed and somehow refreshed. The most I ever did was support his head until his eyes blinked open. "It's born," he said when he came around, "let's go upstairs."

But as if I knew already that our disaster had been accomplished in that cry, I would not budge. Karl argued and made a case for at least going up the stairs, if not through the actual door, but I sat firm and he had all but given up when the landlady came back downstairs and told us, first, that we now had a baby brother, and, second, that she had found one of her grandmother's silver spoons under the mattress and that she wasn't going to ask how it got there, but would only say we had two weeks to get out.

The woman probably had a good enough heart. She fed us before she sent us upstairs. I suppose she wasn't rich herself, could not be bothered with our problems, and besides that, she felt betrayed by Adelaide. Still, I blame the landlady in some measure for what my mother said that night, in her sleep.

I was sitting in a chair beside Adelaide's bed, in lamp light, holding the baby in a light wool blanket. Karl was curled in a spidery ball at Adelaide's feet. She was sleeping hard, her hair spread wild and bright across the pillows. Her face was sallow and ancient with what she had been through, but after she spoke I had no pity.

"We should let it die," she mumbled. Her lips were pale, frozen in a dream. I would have shaken her awake but the baby was nestled hard against me.

She quieted momentarily, then she turned on her side and gave me a long earnest look.

"We could bury it out back in the lot," she whispered, "that weedy place."

"Mama, wake up," I urged, but she kept speaking.

"I won't have any milk. I'm too thin."

I stopped listening. I looked down at the baby. His face was round, bruised blue, and his eyelids were swollen almost shut. He looked frail, but when he stirred I put my little finger in his mouth, as I had seen woman do to quiet their babies, and his suck was eager.

"He's hungry," I said urgently, "wake up and feed him." But Adelaide rolled over and turned her face to the wall.

Milk came flooding into Adelaide's breasts, more than the baby could drink at first. She had to feed him. Milk leaked out in dark patches on her pale-blue shirtwaists. She moved heavily, burdened by the ache. She did not completely ignore the baby. She cut her skirts up for diapers, sewed a layette from her nightgown, but at the same time she only grudgingly cared for his basic needs, and often left him to howl. Sometimes he cried such a long time that the landlady came puffing upstairs to see what was wrong. I think she was troubled to see us in such desperation, because she silently brought up food left by the boarders who paid for meals. Nevertheless, she did not change her decision. When the two weeks were up, we still had to move.

Spring was faintly in the air the day we went out looking for a new place. The clouds were high and warm. All of the everyday clothes Adelaide owned had been cut up for the baby, so she had nothing but her fine things, lace and silk, good cashmere. She wore a black coat, a pale green dress trimmed in cream lace, and delicate string gloves. Her beautiful hair was pinned back in a strict knot. We walked down the brick sidewalks looking for signs in windows, for rooming houses of the cheapest kind, barracks, or hotels. We found nothing, and finally sat down to rest on a bench bolted to the side of a store. In those times, the streets of towns were much kindlier. No one minded the destitute gathering strength, taking a load off, discussing their downfall in the world.

"We can't go back to Fritzie," Adelaide said, "I couldn't bear to live with Pete."

"We have nowhere else," I sensibly told her, "unless you sell your heirlooms."

Adelaide gave me a warning look and put her hand to the brooch at her throat. I stopped. She was attached to the few precious treasures she often showed us — the complicated garnet necklace, the onyx mourning brooch, the ring with the good yellow diamond. I supposed that she wouldn't sell them even to save us. Our hardship had beaten her and she was weak, but in her weakness she was also stubborn. We sat on the store's bench for perhaps half an hour, then Karl noticed something like music in the air.

"Mama," he begged, "Mama, can we go? It's a fair!"

As always with Karl, she began by saying no, but that was just a formality and both of them knew it. In no time, he had wheedled and charmed her into going.

The Orphan's Picnic, a fair held to benefit the orphans of Saint Jerome's after the long winter, was taking place just a few streets over at the city fairground. We saw the banner blazing cheerful red, stretched across the entrance, bearing the seal of the patron saint of loneliness. Plank booths were set up in the long, brown winter grass. Cowled nuns switched busily between the scapular and holy medal counters, or stood poised behind racks of rosaries, shoeboxes full of holy cards, tiny carved statuettes of saints, and common toys. We swept into the excitement, looked over the grab bags, games of chance, displays of candy and religious wares. Adelaide stopped at a secular booth that sold jingling hardware, and pulled a whole dollar from her purse.

"I'll take that," she said to the vendor, pointing. He lifted a pearl-handled jackknife from his case and Mama gave it to Karl. Then she pointed at a bead necklace, silver and gold.

"I don't want it," I said to Adelaide.

Her face reddened, but after a slight hesitation she bought the necklace anyway. Then she had Karl fasten it around her throat. She put the baby in my arms.

"Here, Miss Damp Blanket," she said.

Karl laughed and took her hand. Meandering from booth to booth, we finally came to the grandstand, and at once Karl began to pull her toward the seats, drawn by the excitement. I had to stumble along behind them. Bills littered the ground. Posters were pasted up the sides of trees and the splintery walls. Adelaide picked up one of the smaller papers.

THE GREAT OMAR, it said, AERONAUT EXTRAORDINAIRE. APPEARING HERE AT NOON. Below the words there was a picture of a man — sleek, mustachioed, yellow scarf whipping in a breeze.

"Please," Karl said, "please!"

And so we joined the gaping crowd.

The plane dipped, rolled, buzzed, glided above us and I was no more impressed than if it had been some sort of insect. I did not crane my neck or gasp, thrilled, like the rest of them. I looked down at the baby and watched his face. He was just emerging from the newborn's endless sleep and from time to time now he stared fathomlessly into my eyes. I stared back. Looking into his face that day, I found a different arrangement of myself — bolder, quick as light, ill-tempered. He frowned at me, unafraid, unaware that he was helpless, only troubled at the loud drone of the biplane as it landed and taxied toward us on the field.

Thinking back now, I can't believe that I had no premonition of what power The Great Omar had over us. I hardly glanced when he jumped from the plane and I did not applaud his sweeping bows and pronouncements. I hardly knew when he offered rides to those who dared. I believe he charged a dollar or two for the privilege. I did not notice. I was hardly prepared for what came next.

"Here!" my mother called, holding her purse up in the sun.

Then without a backwards look, without a word, with no warning and no hesitation, she elbowed through the crowd collected at the base of the grandstand and stepped into the cleared space around the pilot. That was when I looked at The Great Omar for the first time, but, as I was so astonished at my mother, I can hardly recall any detail of his appearance. The general impression he gave was dashing, like his posters. The yellow scarf whipped out and certainly he had some sort of mustache. I believe he wore a grease-stained white sweater, perhaps a loose coverall. He was slender and dark, much smaller in relation to his plane than the poster showed, and older. After he helped my mother into the passenger's cockpit and jumped in behind the controls, he pulled a pair of green goggles down over his face. And then there was a startling, endless moment, as they prepared for the takeoff.

"Clear Prop!"

The propeller made a wind. The plane lurched forward, lifted over the low trees, gained height. The Great Omar circled the field in a low swoop and I saw my mother's long red crinkly hair spring from its tight knot and float free in an arc that seemed to reach out and tangle around his shoulders.

Karl stared in stricken fascination at the sky, and said nothing as The Great Omar began his stunts and droning passes. I did not watch. Again, I fixed my gaze on the face of my little brother and concentrated on his features, blind to the possibilities of Adelaide's sudden liftoff. I only wanted her to come back down before the plane smashed.

The crowd thinned. People drifted away, but I did not notice. By the time I looked into the sky The Great Omar was flying steadily away from the fairgrounds with my mother. Soon the plane was only a white dot, then it blended into the pale blue sky and vanished.

I shook Karl's arm but he pulled away from me and vaulted to the edge of the grandstand. "Take me!" he screamed, leaning over the rail. He stared at the sky, poised as if he'd throw himself into it.

Satisfaction. That was the first thing I felt after Adelaide flew off. For once she had played no favorites between Karl and me, but left us both. So there was some compensation in what she did. Karl threw his head in his hands and began to sob into his heavy wool sleeves. Only then did I feel frightened.

Below the grandstand, the crowd moved in patternless waves. Over us the clouds spread into a thin sheet that covered the sky like muslin. We watched the dusk collect in the corners of the field. Nuns began to pack away their rosaries and prayer books. Colored lights went on in the little nonreligious booths. Karl slapped his arms, stamped his feet, blew on his fingers. He was more sensitive to cold than I. Huddling around the baby kept me warm.

The baby woke, very hungry, and I was helpless to comfort him. He sucked so hard that my finger was white and puckered, and then he screamed. People gathered around us there. Women held out their arms, but I did not give the baby to any of them. I did not trust them. I did not trust the man who sat down beside me, either, and spoke softly. He was a young man with a hard-boned, sad, unshaven face. What I remember most about him was the sadness. He wanted to take the baby back to his wife so she could feed him. She had a new baby of her own, he said, and enough milk for two.

"I am waiting," I said, "for our own mother."

"When is she coming back?" asked the young man.

I could not answer. The sad man waited with open arms. Karl sat mute on one side of me, gazing into the dark sky. Behind and before, large interfering ladies counseled and conferred.

"Give him the baby, dear."

"Don't be stubborn."

"Let him take the baby home."

"No," I said to every order and suggestion. I even kicked hard when one woman tried to take my brother from my arms. They grew discouraged, or simply indifferent after a time, and went off. It was not the ladies who convinced me, finally, but the baby himself. He did not let up screaming. The longer he cried, the longer the sad man sat beside me, the weaker my resistance was, until finally I could barely hold my own tears back.

"I'm coming with you then," I told the young man. "I'll bring the baby back here when he's fed."

"No," cried Karl, coming out of his stupor suddenly, "you can't leave me alone!"

He grabbed my arm so fervently that the baby slipped, and then the young man caught me, as if to help, but instead he scooped the baby to himself.

"I'll take care of him," he said, and turned away.

I tried to wrench from Karl's grip, but like my mother he was strongest when he was weak, and I could not break free. I saw the man walk into the shadows. I heard the baby's wail fade. I finally sat down beside Karl and let the cold sink into me.

One hour passed. Another hour. When the colored lights went out and the moon came up, diffused behind the sheets of clouds, I knew the young man wasn't coming back. And yet, because he looked too sad to do any harm to anyone, I was more afraid for Karl and myself. We were the ones who were thoroughly lost. I stood up. Karl stood with me. Without a word we walked down the empty streets to our old rooming house. We had no key but Karl displayed one unexpected talent. He took the thin-bladed knife that Adelaide had given him, and picked the lock.

Once we stood in the cold room, the sudden presence of our mother's clothing dismayed us. The room was filled with the faint perfume of the dried flowers that she scattered in her trunk, the rich scent of the clove-studded orange she hung in the closet and the lavender oil she rubbed into her skin at night. The sweetness of her breath seemed to linger, the rustle of her silk underskirt, the quick sound of her heels. Our longing buried us. We sank down on her bed and cried, wrapped in her quilt, clutching each other. When that was done, however, I acquired a brain of ice.

I washed my face off in the basin, then I roused Karl and told him we were going to Aunt Fritzie's. He acquiesced, suffering again in a dumb lethargy. We ate all there was to eat in the room, two cold pancakes, and packed what we owned in a small cardboard suitcase. Karl carried that. I carried the quilt. The last thing I did was reach far back in my mother's drawer and pull out her small round keepsake box. It was covered in blue velvet and tightly locked.

"We might need to sell these things," I told Karl. He hesitated but then, with a hard look, he took the box.

We slipped out before sunrise and walked to the train station. In the weedy yards there were men who knew each boxcar's destination. We found the car we wanted and climbed in. There was hay in one corner. We spread the quilt over it and rolled up together, curled tight, with our heads on the suitcase and Adelaide's blue velvet box between us in Karl's breast pocket. We clung to the thought of the treasures inside of it.

We spent a day and a night on that train while it switched and braked and rumbled on an agonizingly complex route to Argus. We did not dare jump off for a drink of water or to scavenge food. The one time we did try this the train started up so quickly that we were hardly able to catch the side rungs again. We lost our suitcase and the quilt because we took the wrong car, farther back, and that night we did not sleep at all for the cold. Karl was too miserable even to argue with me when I told him it was my turn to hold Adelaide's box. I put it in the bodice of my jumper. It did not keep me warm, but even so, the sparkle of the diamond when I shut my eyes, the patterns of garnets that whirled in the dark air, gave me something. My mind hardened, faceted and gleaming like a magic stone, and I saw my mother clearly.

She was still in the plane, flying close to the pulsing stars, when suddenly Omar noticed that the fuel was getting low. He did not love Adelaide at first sight, or even care what happened to her. He had to save himself. Somehow he had to lighten his load. So he set his controls. He stood up in his cockpit. Then in one sudden motion he plucked my mother out of her seat like a doll and dropped her overboard.

All night she fell through the awful cold. Her coat flapped open and her pale green dress wrapped tightly around her legs. Her red hair flowed straight upward like a flame. She was a candle that gave no warmth. My heart froze. I had no love for her. That is why, by morning, I allowed her to hit the earth.

By the time we saw the sign on the brick station, I was dull again, a block of sullen cold. Still, it hurt when I jumped, scraping my cold knees and the heels of my hands. The pain sharpened me enough to read signs in windows and rack my mind for just where Aunt Fritzie's shop was. It had been years since we visited.

Karl was older, and I probably should not hold myself accountable for losing him too. But I didn't call him. I didn't run after him. I couldn't stand how his face glowed in the blossoms' reflected light, pink and radiant, so like the way he sat beneath our mother's stroking hand.

When I stopped running, I realized I was alone and now more truly lost than any of my family, since all I had done from the first was to try and hold them close while death, panic, chance, and ardor each took them their separate ways.

Hot tears came up suddenly behind my eyes and my ears burned. I ached to cry, hard, but I knew that was useless and so I walked. I walked carefully, looking at everything around me, and it was lucky I did this because I'd run past the butcher shop and, suddenly, there it was, set back from the road down a short dirt drive. A white pig was painted on the side, and inside the pig, the lettering "Kozka's Meats." I walked toward it between rows of tiny fir trees. The place looked both shabby and prosperous, as though Fritzie and Pete were too busy with customers to care for outward appearances. I stood on the broad front stoop and noticed everything I could, the way a beggar does. A rack of elk horns was nailed overhead. I walked beneath them.

The entryway was dark, my heart was in my throat. And then, what I saw was quite natural, understandable, although it was not real.

Again, the dog leapt toward Karl and blossoms from his stick fell. Except that they fell around me in the entrance to the store. I smelled the petals melting on my coat, tasted their thin sweetness in my mouth. I had no time to wonder how this could be happening because they disappeared as suddenly as they'd come when I told my name to the man behind the glass counter.

This man, tall and fat with a pale brown mustache and an old blue denim cap on his head, was Uncle Pete. His eyes were round, mild, exactly the same light brown as his hair. His smile was slow, sweet for a butcher, and always hopeful. He did not recognize me even after I told him who I was. Finally his eyes widened and he called out for Fritzie.

"Your sister's girl! She's here!" he shouted down the hall.

I told him I was alone, that I had come in on the boxcar, and he lifted me up in his arms. He carried me back to the kitchen where Aunt Fritzie was frying a sausage for my cousin, the beautiful Sita, who sat at the table and stared at me with narrowed eyes while I tried to tell Fritzie and Pete just how I'd come to walk into their front door out of nowhere.

They stared at me with friendly suspicion, thinking that I'd turn away. But when I told them about The Great Omar, and how Adelaide held up her purse, and how Omar helped her into the plane, their faces turned grim.

"Sita, go polish the glass out front," said Aunt Fritzie. Sita slid unwillingly out of her chair. "Now," Fritzie said. Uncle Pete sat down heavily. The ends of his mustache went into his mouth, he pressed his thumbs together under his chin, and turned to me. "Go on, tell the rest," he said, and so I told all of the rest, and when I had finished I saw that I had also drunk a glass of milk and eaten a sausage. By then I could hardly sit upright. Uncle Pete took me in his strong arms and I remember sagging against him, then nothing. I slept that day and all night and did not wake until the next morning. Sleep robbed me as profoundly as being awake had, for when I finally woke I had no memory of where I was and how I'd got there. I lay still for what seemed like a long while, trying to place the objects in the room.

This was the room where I would sleep for the rest of my childhood, or what passed for childhood anyway, since after that train journey I was not a child. It was a pleasant room, and before me it belonged entirely to cousin Sita. The paneling was warm-stained pine. Most of the space was taken up by a tall oak dresser with fancy curlicues and drawers. A small sheet of polished tin hung on the door and served as a mirror. Through that door, as I was trying to understand my surroundings, walked Sita herself, tall and perfect with a blond braid that reached to her waist.

"So you're finally awake." She sat down on the edge of my trundle bed and folded her arms over her small new breasts. She was a year older than me. Since I'd seen her last, she had grown suddenly, like Karl, but her growth had not thinned her into an awkward bony creature. She was now a slim female of utter grace.

I realized I was staring too long at her, and then the whole series of events came flooding back and I turned away. Sita grinned. She looked down at me, her strong white teeth shining, and she stroked the blond braid that hung down over one shoulder.

"Where's Auntie Adelaide?" she asked.

I did not answer.

"Where's Auntie Adelaide?" she asked, again. "How come you came here? Where'd she go? Where's Karl?"

"I don't know."

I suppose I thought the misery of my answer would quiet Sita but that was before I knew her. It only fueled more questions.

"How come Auntie left you alone? Where's Karl? What's this?"

She took the blue velvet box from my pile of clothes and shook it casually next to her ear.

"What's in it?"

For the moment at least, I bested her by snatching the box with an angry swiftness she did not expect. I rolled from the bed, bundled my clothes into my arms, and walked out of the room. The one door open in the hallway was the bathroom, a large smoky room of many uses that soon became my haven since it was the only door I could bolt against my cousin.

Every day for weeks after I arrived in Argus, I woke up thinking I was back on the farm with my mother and father and that none of this had happened. I always managed to believe this until I opened my eyes. Then I saw the dark swirls in the pine and Sita's arm hanging off the bed above me. I smelled the air, peppery and warm from the sausage makers. I heard the rhythmical whine of meat saws, slicers, the rippling beat of fans. Aunt Fritzie was smoking her sharp Viceroys in the bathroom. Uncle Pete was outside feeding the big white German shepherd that was kept in the shop at night to guard the canvas bags of money.

Every morning I got up, put on one of Sita's hand-me-down pink dresses, and went out to the kitchen to wait for Uncle Pete. I cooked breakfast. That I made fried eggs and a good cup of coffee at age eleven was a source of wonder to my aunt and uncle, and an outrage to Sita. That's why I did it every morning, with a finesse that got more casual until it became a habit to have me there.

From the first I made myself essential. I did this because I had to, because I had nothing else to offer. The day after I arrived in Argus and woke up to Sita's calculating smile I also tried to offer what I thought was treasure, the blue velvet box that held Adelaide's heirlooms.

I did it in as grand a manner as I could, with Sita for a witness and with Pete and Fritzie sitting at the kitchen table. That morning, I walked in with my hair combed wet and laid the box between the two of them. I looked at Sita as I spoke.

"This should pay my way."

Fritzie looked at me. She had my mother's features sharpened one notch past beauty. Her skin was rough and her short curled hair was yellow, bleached pale, not golden. Fritzie's eyes were a swimming, crazy shade of blue that startled customers. She ate heartily, but her constant smoking kept her string-bean thin and sallow.

"You don't have to pay us," said Fritzie, "Pete, tell her. She doesn't have to pay us. Sit down, shut up, and eat."

Fritzie spoke like that, joking and blunt. Pete was slower. "Come. Sit down and forget about the money," he said. "You never know about your mother . . ." he added in an earnest voice that trailed away when he looked at Aunt Fritzie. Things had a way of evaporating under her eyes, vanishing, getting sucked up into the heat of her stare. Even Sita had nothing to say.

"I want to give you this," I said. "I insist."

"She insists," exclaimed Aunt Fritzie. Her smile had a rakish flourish because one tooth was chipped in front. "Don't insist," she said. "Eat."

But I would not sit down. I took a knife from the butter plate and started to pry the lock up.

"Here now," said Fritzie. "Pete, help her."

So Pete got up slowly and fetched a screwdriver from the top of the icebox and sat down and jammed the end underneath the lock.

"Let her open it," said Fritzie, when the lock popped up. So Pete pushed the little round box across the table.

"I bet it's empty," Sita said. She took a big chance saying that, but it paid off in spades and aces between us growing up, because I lifted the lid a moment later and what she said was true. There was nothing of value in the box.

Stick pins. A few thick metal buttons off a coat. And a ticket describing the necklace of tiny garnets, pawned for practically nothing in Minneapolis.

There was silence. Even Fritzie was at a loss. Sita nearly buzzed off her chair in triumph but held her tongue, that is until later, when she would crow. Pete put his hand on his head in deep vexation. I stood quietly, stunned.

What is dark is light and bad news brings slow gain, I told myself. I could see a pattern to all of what happened, a pattern that suggested completion in years to come. The baby was lifted up while my mother was dashed to earth. Karl rode west and I ran east. It is opposites that finally meet.

WILLIAM FAULKNER

William Faulkner (1897–1962) grew up in and spent most of his life in Oxford, Mississippi. From that town and its surrounding landscape he drew the inspiration for the mythical world in which he set most of his fiction — Yoknapatawpha County. After dropping out of high school, Faulkner spent his early adult years in various pursuits. He enlisted in the British Royal Air Force in 1918; after the Armistice he returned to Oxford and was for a time postmaster of the University of Mississippi. Subsequently he went to New Orleans to work for a newspaper; there he met writer Sherwood Anderson, who encouraged him to write fiction. He did so, to no particular acclaim initially, but with his novel *Sartoris* (1929) he found his voice and his material, much of it drawn from his ancestral past. *Sartoris* won him acclaim, and he entered on a decade of writing his great Yoknapatawpha novels — *The Sound and the Fury* (1929), *As I Lay Dying* (1930), *Light in August* (1932), *Absalom, Absalom!* (1936), *The Wild Palms* (1939), and *The Hamlet* (1940). During the years of the Second World War his reputation waned and his books were out of print, but when the novelist and critic Malcolm Cowley edited *The Portable Faulkner* in 1946, the situation reversed dramatically, and Faulkner came into the prime of his fame and influence. Several novels followed over the next years, as did volumes of his short fiction, *Collected Stories of William Faulkner* (1950) and *Selected Short Stories* (1962). He was awarded the Nobel Prize for literature in 1949. Perhaps the essence of Faulkner's genius is that he lived and wrote with no regard for the normative. His fiction, long and short, plays out — in extravagant, extraordinary, dark-hued flights of language that convolute the so-called rules of syntax — a tragic, and often obsessive, saga of the human psyche struggling against enormous odds to comprehend and survive the pain of history and memory. The legend he told — which has roots in the deep South but has cast its universality far beyond any geography — shapes the stories here, "Barn Burning" and "An Odor of Verbena."

Barn Burning

The store in which the Justice of the Peace's court was sitting smelled of cheese. The boy, crouched on his nail keg at the back of the crowded room, knew he smelled cheese, and more: from where he sat he could see the ranked shelves close-packed with the solid, squat, dynamic shapes of tin cans whose labels his stomach read, not from the lettering which meant nothing to his mind but from the scarlet devils and the silver curve of fish — this, the cheese which he knew he smelled and the hermetic meat which his intestines believed he smelled coming in intermittent gusts momentary and brief between the other constant one, the smell and sense just a little of fear because mostly of despair and grief, the old fierce pull of blood. He could not see the table where the Justice sat and before which his father and his father's enemy (*our enemy* he thought in that despair; *ourn! mine and hisn both! He's my father!*) stood, but he could hear them, the two of them that is, because his father had said no word yet:

"But what proof have you, Mr. Harris?"

"I told you. The hog got into my corn. I caught it up and sent it back to him. He had no fence that would hold it. I told him so, warned him. The next time I put the hog in my pen. When he came to get it I gave him enough wire to patch up his pen.

The next time I put the hog up and kept it. I rode down to his house and saw the wire I gave him still rolled on to the spool in his yard. I told him he could have the hog when he paid me a dollar pound fee. That evening a nigger came with the dollar and got the hog. He was a strange nigger. He said, 'He say to tell you wood and hay kin burn.' That night my barn burned. I got the stock out but I lost the barn."

"Where is the nigger? Have you got him?"

"He was a strange nigger, I tell you. I don't know what became of him."

"But that's not proof. Don't you see that's not proof?"

"Get that boy up here. He knows." For a moment the boy thought too that the man meant his older brother until Harris said, "Not him. The little one. The boy," and, crouching, small for his age, small and wiry like his father, in patched and faded jeans even too small for him, with straight, uncombed, brown hair and eyes gray and wild as storm scud, he saw the men between himself and the table part and become a lane of grim faces, at the end of which he saw the Justice, a shabby, collarless, graying man in spectacles, beckoning him. He felt no floor under his bare feet; he seemed to walk beneath the palpable weight of the grim turning faces. His father, stiff in his black Sunday coat donned not for the trial but for the moving, did not even look at him. *He aims for me to lie,* he thought, again with that frantic grief and despair. *And I will have to do hit.*

"What's your name, boy?" the Justice said.

"Colonel Sartoris Snopes," the boy whispered.

"Hey?" the Justice said. "Talk louder. Colonel Sartoris? I reckon anybody named for Colonel Sartoris in this country can't help but tell the truth, can they?" The boy said nothing. *Enemy! Enemy!* he thought; for a moment he could not even see, could not see that the Justice's face was kindly nor discern that his voice was troubled when he spoke to the man named Harris: "Do you want me to question this boy?" But he could hear, and during those subsequent long seconds while there was absolutely no sound in the crowded little room save that of quiet and intent breathing it was as if he had swung outward at the end of a grape vine, over a ravine, and at the top of the swing had been caught in a prolonged instant of mesmerized gravity, weightless in time.

"No!" Harris said violently, explosively. "Damnation! Send him out of here!" Now time, the fluid world, rushed beneath him again, the voices coming to him again through the smell of cheese and sealed meat, the fear and despair and the old grief of blood:

"This case is closed. I can't find against you, Snopes, but I can give you advice. Leave this country and don't come back to it."

His father spoke for the first time, his voice cold and harsh, level, without emphasis: "I aim to. I don't figure to stay in a country among people who . . ." he said something unprintable and vile, addressed to no one.

"That'll do," the Justice said. "Take your wagon and get out of this country before dark. Case dismissed."

His father turned, and he followed the stiff black coat, the wiry figure walking a little stiffly from where a Confederate provost's man's musket ball had taken him in the heel on a stolen horse thirty years ago, followed the two backs now, since his older brother had appeared from somewhere in the crowd, no taller than the father but thicker, chewing tobacco steadily, between the two lines of grim-faced men and out of the store and across the worn gallery and down the sagging steps and among the dogs and half-grown boys in the mild May dust where as he passed a voice hissed:

"Barn burner!"

Again he could not see, whirling; there was a face in a red haze, moonlike, bigger than the full moon, the owner of it half again his size, he leaping in the red haze toward the face, feeling no blow, feeling no shock when his head struck the earth, scrabbling up and leaping again, feeling no blow this time either and tasting no blood, scrabbling up to see the other boy in full flight and himself already leaping into pursuit as his father's hand jerked him back, the harsh, cold voice speaking above him: "Go get in the wagon."

It stood in a grove of locusts and mulberries across the road. His two hulking sisters in their Sunday dresses and his mother and her sister in calico and sunbon-nets were already in it, sitting on and among the sorry residue of the dozen and more movings which even the boy could remember — the battered stove, the broken beds and chairs, the clock inlaid with mother-of-pearl, which would not run, stopped at some fourteen minutes past two o'clock of a dead and forgotten day and time, which had been his mother's dowry. She was crying, though when she saw him she drew her sleeve across her face and began to descend from the wagon. "Get back," the father said.

"He's hurt. I got to get some water and wash his . . ."

"Get back in the wagon," his father said. He got in too, over the tail-gate. His father mounted to the seat where the older brother already sat and struck the gaunt mules two savage blows with the peeled willow, but without heat. It was not even sadistic; it was exactly that same quality which in later years would cause his descendants to overrun the engine before putting a motor car into motion, striking and reining back in the same movement. The wagon went on, the store with its quiet crowd of grimly watching men dropped behind; a curve in the road hid it. *Forever* he thought. *Maybe he's done satisfied now, now that he has* . . . stopping himself, not to say it aloud even to himself. His mother's hand touched his shoulder.

"Does hit hurt?" she said.

"Naw," he said. "Hit don't hurt. Lemme be."

"Can't you wipe some of the blood off before hit dries?"

"I'll wash to-night," he said. "Lemme be, I tell you."

The wagon went on. He did not know where they were going. None of them ever did or ever asked, because it was always somewhere, always a house of sorts waiting for them a day or two days or even three days away. Likely his father had already arranged to make a crop on another farm before he . . . Again he had to stop himself. He (the father) always did. There was something about his wolf-like independence and even courage when the advantage was at least neutral which impressed strang-ers, as if they got from his latent ravening ferocity not so much a sense of depend-ability as a feeling that his ferocious conviction in the rightness of his own actions would be of advantage to all whose interest lay with his.

That night they camped, in a grove of oaks and beeches where a spring ran. The nights were still cool and they had a fire against it, of a a rail lifted from a nearby fence and cut into lengths — a small fire, neat, niggard almost, a shrewd fire; such fires were his father's habit and custom always, even in freezing weather. Older, the boy might have remarked this and wondered why not a big one; why should not a man who had not only seen the waste and extravagance of war, but who had in his blood an inherent voracious prodigality with material not his own, have burned everything in sight? Then he might have gone a step farther and thought that that was the reason: that niggard blaze was the living fruit of nights passed during those four years in the woods hiding from all men, blue or gray, with his strings of horses (captured horses, he called them). And older still, he might have divined the true reason: that the element of fire spoke to some deep mainspring of his father's being, as the element of steel or of powder spoke to other men, as the one weapon for the preservation of integrity, else breath were not worth the breathing, and hence to be regarded with respect and used with discretion.

But he did not think this now and he had seen those same niggard blazes all his life. He merely ate his supper beside it and was already half asleep over his iron plate when his father called him, and once more he followed the stiff back, the stiff and ruthless limp, up the slope and on to the starlit road where, turning, he could see his father against the stars but without face or depth — a shape black, flat, and bloodless as though cut from tin in the iron folds of the frockcoat which had not been made for him, the voice harsh like tin and without heat like tin:

"You were fixing to tell them. You would have told him." He didn't answer. His father struck him with the flat of his hand on the side of the head, hard but without heat, exactly as he had struck the two mules at the store, exactly as he would strike either of them with any stick in order to kill a horse fly, his voice still without fear or anger: "You're getting to be a man. You got to learn. You got to learn to stick to your own blood or you ain't going to have any blood to stick to you. Do you think either of them, any man there this morning, would? Don't you know all they wanted was a chance to get at me because they knew I had them beat? Eh?" Later, twenty years later, he was to tell himself, "If I had said they wanted only truth, justice, he would have hit me again." But now he said nothing. He was not crying. He just stood there. "Answer me," his father said.

"Yes," he whispered. His father turned.

"Get on to bed. We'll be there tomorrow."

Tomorrow they were there. In the early afternoon the wagon stopped before a paintless two-room house identical almost with the dozen others it had stopped before even in the boy's ten years, and again, as on the other dozen occasions, his mother and aunt got down and began to unload the wagon, although his two sisters and his father and brother had not moved.

"Likely hit ain't fitten for hawgs," one of the sisters said.

"Nevertheless, fit it will and you'll hog it and like it," his father said. "Get out of them chairs and help your Ma unload."

The two sisters got down, big, bovine, in a flutter of cheap ribbons; one of them drew from the jumbled wagon bed a battered lantern, the other a worn broom. His father handed the reins to the older son and began to climb stiffly over the wheel. "When they get unloaded, take the team to the barn and feed them." Then he said, and at first the boy thought he was still speaking to his brother: "Come with me."

"Me?" he said.

"Yes," his father said. "You."

"Abner," his mother said. His father paused and looked back — the harsh level stare beneath the shaggy, graying, irascible brows.

"I reckon I'll have a word with the man that aims to begin tomorrow owning me body and soul for the next eight months."

They went back up the road. A week ago — or before last night, that is — he would have asked where they were going, but not now. His father had struck him before last night but never before had he paused afterward to explain why; it was as if the blow and the following calm, outrageous voice still rang, repercussed, divulging nothing to him save the terrible handicap of being young, the light weight of his few years, just heavy enough to prevent his soaring free of the world as it seemed to be ordered but not heavy enough to keep him footed solid in it, to resist it and try to change the course of its events.

Presently he could see the grove of oaks and cedars and the other flowering trees and shrubs, where the house would be, though not the house yet. They walked beside a fence massed with honeysuckle and Cherokee roses and came to a gate swinging open between two brick pillars, and now, beyond a sweep of drive, he saw the house for the first time and at that instant he forgot his father and the terror and despair both, and even when he remembered his father again (who had not stopped) the terror and despair did not return. Because, for all the twelve movings, they had sojourned until now in a poor country, a land of small farms and fields and houses, and he had never seen a house like this before. *Hit's big as a courthouse* he thought quietly, with a surge of peace and joy whose reason he could not have thought into words, being too young for that: *They are safe from him. People whose lives are a part of this peace and dignity are beyond his touch, he no more to them than a buzzing wasp: capable of stinging for a little moment but that's all; the spell of this peace and dignity rendering even the barns and stable and cribs which belong to it impervious to the puny flames he might contrive* . . . this, the peace and joy, ebbing for an instant as he looked again at the stiff black back, the stiff and implacable limp of the figure which was not dwarfed by the house, for the reason that it had never looked big anywhere and which now, against the serene columned backdrop, had more than ever that impervious quality of something cut ruthlessly from tin, depthless, as though, sidewise to the sun, it would cast no shadow. Watching him, the boy remarked the absolutely undeviating course which his father held and saw the stiff foot come squarely down in a pile of fresh droppings where a horse had stood in the drive and which his father could have avoided by a simple change of stride. But it ebbed only for a moment, though he could not have thought this into words either, walking on in the spell of the house, which he could even want but without envy, without sorrow, certainly never with that ravening and jealous rage which unknown to him walked in the ironlike black coat before him: *Maybe he will feel it too. Maybe it will even change him now from what maybe he couldn't help but be.*

They crossed the portico. Now he could hear his father's stiff foot as it came down on the boards with clocklike finality, a sound out of all proportion to the displacement of the body it bore and which was not dwarfed either by the white door before it, as though it had attained to a sort of vicious and ravening minimum not to be dwarfed by anything — the flat, wide, black hat, the formal coat of broadcloth which had once been black but which had now that friction-glazed greenish cast of the bodies of old house flies, the lifted sleeve which was too large, the lifted hand like a curled claw. The door opened so promptly that the boy knew the Negro must have been watching them all the time, an old man with neat grizzled hair, in a linen jacket, who stood barring the door with his body, saying, "Wipe yo foots, white man, fo you come in here. Major ain't home nohow."

"Get out of my way, nigger," his father said, without heat too, flinging the door back and the Negro also and entering, his hat still on his head. And now the boy saw the prints of the stiff foot on the doorjamb and saw them appear on the pale rug behind the machinelike deliberation of the foot which seemed to bear (or transmit) twice the weight which the body compassed. The Negro was shouting "Miss Lula! Miss Lula!" somewhere behind them, then the boy, deluged as though by a warm wave by a suave turn of carpeted stair and a pendant glitter of chandeliers and a mute gleam of gold frames, heard the swift feet and saw her too, a lady — perhaps he had never seen her like before either — in a gray, smooth gown with lace at the throat and an apron tied at the waist and the sleeves turned back, wiping cake or biscuit dough from her hands with a towel as she came up the hall, looking not at his father at all but at the tracks on the blond rug with an expression of incredulous amazement.

"I tried," the Negro cried. "I tole him to . . ."

"Will you please go away?" she said in a shaking voice. "Major de Spain is not at home. Will you please go away?"

His father had not spoken again. He did not speak again. He did not even look at her. He just stood stiff in the center of the rug, in his hat, the shaggy iron-gray brows twitching slightly above the pebble-colored eyes as he appeared to examine the house with brief deliberation. Then with the same deliberation he turned; the boy watched him pivot on the good leg and saw the stiff foot drag round the arc of the turning, leaving a final long and fading smear. His father never looked at it, he never once looked down at the rug. The Negro held the door. It closed behind them, upon the hysteric and indistinguishable woman-wail. His father stopped at the top of the steps and scraped his boot clean on the edge of it. At the gate he stopped again. He stood for a moment, planted stiffly on the stiff foot, looking back at the house. "Pretty and white, ain't it?" he said. "That's sweat. Nigger sweat. Maybe it ain't white enough yet to suit him. Maybe he wants to mix some white sweat with it."

Two hours later the boy was chopping wood behind the house within which his mother and aunt and the two sisters (the mother and aunt, not the two girls, he knew that; even at this distance and muffled by walls the flat loud voices of the two girls emanated an incorrigible idle inertia) were setting up the stove to prepare a meal, when he heard the hooves and saw the linen-clad man on a fine sorrel mare, whom he recognized even before he saw the rolled rug in front of the Negro youth following on a fat bay carriage horse — a suffused, angry face vanishing, still at full gallop, beyond the corner of the house where his father and brother were sitting in the two tilted chairs; and a moment later, almost before he could have put the axe down, he heard the hooves again and watched the sorrel mare go back out of the yard, already galloping again. Then his father began to shout one of the sisters' names, who presently emerged backward from the kitchen door dragging the rolled rug along the ground by one end while the other sister walked behind it.

"If you ain't going to tote, go on and set up the wash pot," the first said.

"You, Sarty!" the second shouted. "Set up the wash pot!" His father appeared at the door, framed against that shabbiness, as he had been against that other bland perfection, impervious to either, the mother's anxious face at his shoulder.

"Go on," the father said. "Pick it up." The two sisters stooped, broad, lethargic; stooping, they presented an incredible expanse of pale cloth and a flutter of tawdry ribbons.

"If I thought enough of a rug to have to git hit all the way from France I wouldn't keep hit where folks coming in would have to tromp on hit," the first said. They raised the rug.

"Abner," the mother said. "Let me do it."

"You go back and git dinner," his father said. "I'll tend to this."

From the woodpile through the rest of the afternoon the boy watched them, the rug spread flat in the dust beside the bubbling wash-pot, the two sisters stooping over it with that profound and lethargic reluctance, while the father stood over them in turn, implacable and grim, driving them though never raising his voice again. He could smell the harsh homemade lye they were using; he saw his mother come to the door once and look toward them with an expression not anxious now but very like despair; he saw his father turn, and he fell to with the axe and saw from the corner of his eye his father raise from the ground a flattish fragment of field stone and examine it and return to the pot, and this time his mother actually spoke: "Abner. Abner. Please don't. Please, Abner."

Then he was done too. It was dusk; the whippoorwills had already begun. He could smell coffee from the room where they would presently eat the cold food remaining from the mid-afternoon meal, though when he entered the house he realized they were having coffee again probably because there was a fire on the hearth, before which the rug now lay spread over the backs of the two chairs. The tracks of his father's foot were gone. Where they had been were now long, water-cloudy scoriations resembling the sporadic course of a Lilliputian mowing machine.

It still hung there while they ate the cold food and then went to bed, scattered without order or claim up and down the two rooms, his mother in one bed, where his father would later lie, the older brother in the other, himself, the aunt, and the two sisters on pallets on the floor. But his father was not in bed yet. The last thing the boy remembered was the depthless, harsh silhouette of the hat and coat bending over the rug and it seemed to him that he had not even closed his eyes when the silhouette was standing over him, the fire almost dead behind it, the stiff foot prodding him awake. "Catch up the mule," his father said.

When he returned with the mule his father was standing in the black door, the rolled rug over his shoulder. "Ain't you going to ride?" he said.

"No. Give me your foot."

He bent his knee into his father's hand, the wiry, surprising power flowed smoothly, rising, he rising with it, on to the mule's bare back (they had owned a saddle once; the boy could remember it though not when or where) and with the same effortlessness his father swung the rug up in front of him. Now in the starlight they retraced the afternoon's path, up the dusty road rife with honeysuckle, through the gate and up the black tunnel to the drive to the lightless house, where he sat on the mule and felt the rough warp of the rug drag across his thighs and vanish.

"Don't you want me to help?" he whispered. His father did not answer and now he heard again that stiff foot striking the hollow portico with that wooden and clocklike deliberation, that outrageous overstatement of the weight it carried. The rug, hunched, not flung (the boy could tell that even in the darkness) from his father's shoulder struck the angle of wall and floor with a sound unbelievably loud, thunderous, then the foot again, unhurried and enormous; a light came on in the house and the boy sat, tense, breathing steadily and quietly and just a little fast, though the foot itself did not increase its beat at all, descending the steps now; now the boy could see him.

"Don't you want to ride now?" he whispered. "We kin both ride now," the light within the house altering now, flaring up and sinking. *He's coming down the stairs now,* he thought. He had already ridden the mule up beside the horse block; presently his father was up behind him and he doubled the reins over and slashed the mule across the neck, but before the animal could begin to trot the hard, thin arm came round him, the hard, knotted hand jerking the mule back to a walk.

In the first red rays of the sun they were in the lot, putting plow gear on the mules. This time the sorrel mare was in the lot before he heard it at all, the rider collarless and even bareheaded, trembling, speaking in a shaking voice as the woman in the house had done, his father merely looking up once before stooping again to the hame he was buckling, so that the man on the mare spoke to his stooping back:

"You must realize you have ruined that rug. Wasn't there anybody here, any of your women . . ." he ceased, shaking, the boy watching him, the older brother leaning now in the stable door, chewing, blinking slowly and steadily at nothing apparently. "It cost a hundred dollars. But you never had a hundred dollars. You never will. So I'm going to charge you twenty bushels of corn against your crop. I'll add it in your contract and when you come to the commissary you can sign it. That won't keep Mrs. de Spain quiet but maybe it will teach you to wipe your feet off before you enter her house again."

Then he was gone. The boy looked at his father, who still had not spoken or even looked up again, who was now adjusting the logger-head in the hame.

"Pap," he said. His father looked at him — the inscrutable face, the shaggy brows beneath which the gray eyes glinted coldly. Suddenly the boy went toward him, fast, stopping as suddenly. "You done the best you could!" he cried. "If he wanted hit done different why didn't he wait and tell you how? He won't git no twenty bushels! He won't git none! We'll gether hit and hide hit! I kin watch . . ."

"Did you put the cutter back in that straight stock like I told you?"

"No, sir," he said.

"Then go do it."

That was Wednesday. During the rest of that week he worked steadily, at what was within his scope and some which was beyond it, with an industry that did not need to be driven nor even commanded twice; he had this from his mother, with the difference that some at least of what he did he liked to do, such as splitting wood with the half-size axe which his mother and aunt had earned, or saved money somehow, to present him with at Christmas. In company with the two older women (and on one afternoon, even one of the sisters), he built pens for the shoat and the cow which were a part of his father's contract with the landlord, and one afternoon, his father being absent, gone somewhere on one of the mules, he went to the field.

They were running a middle buster now, his brother holding the plow straight while he handled the reins, and walking beside the straining mule, the rich black soil shearing cool and damp against his bare ankles, he thought *Maybe this is the end of it. Maybe even that twenty bushels that seems hard to have to pay for just a rug will be a cheap price for him to stop forever and always from being what he used to be;* thinking, dreaming now, so that his brother had to speak sharply to him to mind the mule: *Maybe he even won't collect the twenty bushels. Maybe it will all add up and*

*balance and vanish — corn, rug, fire; the terror and grief, the being pulled two ways
like between two teams of horses — gone, done with for ever and ever.*

Then it was Saturday; he looked up from beneath the mule he was harnessing and
saw his father in the black coat and hat. "Not that," his father said. "The wagon gear."
And then, two hours later, sitting in the wagon bed behind his father and brother on
the seat, the wagon accomplished a final curve, and he saw the weathered paintless
store with its tattered tobacco- and patent-medicine posters and the tethered wagons
and saddle animals below the gallery. He mounted the gnawed steps behind his
father and brother, and there again was the lane of quiet, watching faces for the three
of them to walk through. He saw the man in spectacles sitting at the plank table and
he did not need to be told this was a Justice of the Peace; he sent one glare of fierce,
exultant, partisan defiance at the man in collar and cravat now, whom he had seen
but twice before in his life, and that on a galloping horse, who now wore on his own
face an expression not of rage but of amazed unbelief which the boy could not have
known was at the incredible circumstance of being sued by one of his own tenants,
and came and stood against his father and cried at the Justice: "He ain't done it! He
ain't burnt . . ."

"Go back to the wagon," his father said.

"Burnt?" the Justice said. "Do I understand this rug was burned too?"

"Does anybody here claim it was?" his father said. "Go back to the wagon." But he
did not, he merely retreated to the rear of the room, crowded as that other had been,
but not to sit down this time, instead, to stand pressing among the motionless bodies,
listening to the voices:

"And you claim twenty bushels of corn is too high for the damage you did to the
rug?"

"He brought the rug to me and said he wanted the tracks washed out of it. I
washed the tracks out and took the rug back to him."

"But you didn't carry the rug back to him in the same condition it was in before
you made the tracks on it."

His father did not answer, and now for perhaps half a minute there was no sound
at all save that of breathing, the faint, steady suspiration of complete and intent
listening.

"You decline to answer that, Mr. Snopes?" Again his father did not answer. "I'm
going to find against you, Mr. Snopes. I'm going to find that you were responsible for
the injury to Major de Spain's rug and hold you liable for it. But twenty bushels of
corn seems a little high for a man in your circumstances to have to pay. Major de
Spain claims it cost a hundred dollars. October corn will be worth about fifty cents.
I figure that if Major de Spain can stand a ninety-five dollar loss on something he paid
cash for, you can stand a five-dollar loss you haven't earned yet. I hold you in
damages to Major de Spain to the amount of ten bushels of corn over and above your
contract with him, to be paid to him out of your crop at gathering time. Court
adjourned."

It had taken no time hardly, the morning was but half begun. He thought they
would return home and perhaps back to the field, since they were late, far behind
all other farmers. But instead his father passed on behind the wagon, merely
indicating with his hand for the older brother to follow with it, and crossed the road
toward the blacksmith shop opposite, pressing on after his father, overtaking him,

speaking, whispering up at the harsh, calm face beneath the weathered hat: "He won't git no ten bushels neither. He won't git one. We'll..." until his father glanced for an instant down at him, the face absolutely calm, the grizzled eyebrows tangled above the cold eyes, the voice almost pleasant, almost gentle:

"You think so? Well, we'll wait till October anyway."

The matter of the wagon — the setting of a spoke or two and the tightening of the tires — did not take long either, the business of the tires accomplished by driving the wagon into the spring branch behind the shop and letting it stand there, the mules nuzzling into the water from time to time, and the boy on the seat with the idle reins looking up the slope and through the sooty tunnel of the shed where the slow hammer rang and where his father sat on an upended cypress bolt, easily, either taking or listening, still sitting there when the boy brought the dripping wagon up out of the branch and halted it before the door.

"Take them on to the shade and hitch," his father said. He did so and returned. His father and the smith and a third man squatting on his heels inside the door were talking, about crops and animals; the boy, squatting too in the ammoniac dust and hoof-parings and scales of rust, heard his father tell a long and unhurried story out of the time before the birth of the older brother even when he had been a professional horsetrader. And then his father came up beside him where he stood before a tattered last year's circus poster on the other side of the store, gazing rapt and quiet at the scarlet horses, the incredible poisings and convolutions of tulle and tights and the painted leers of comedians, and said, "It's time to eat."

But not at home. Squatting beside his brother against the front wall, he watched his father emerge from the store and produce from a paper sack a segment of cheese and divide it carefully and deliberately into three with his pocket knife and produce crackers from the same sack. They all three squatted on the gallery and ate, slowly, without talking; then in the store again, they drank from a tin dipper tepid water smelling of the cedar bucket and of living beech trees. And still they did not go home. It was a horse lot this time, a tall rail fence upon and along which men stood and sat and out of which one by one horses were led, to be walked and trotted and then cantered back and forth along the road while the slow swapping and buying went on and the sun began to slant westward, they — the three of them — watching and listening, the older brother with his muddy eyes and his steady, inevitable tobacco, the father commenting now and then on certain of the animals, to no one in particular.

It was after sundown when they reached home. They ate supper by lamplight, then, sitting on the doorstep, the boy watched the night fully accomplish, listening to the whippoorwills and the frogs, when he heard his mother's voice: "Abner! No! No! Oh, God. Oh, God. Abner!" and he rose, whirled, and saw the altered light through the door where a candle stub now burned in a bottle neck on the table and his father, still in the hat and coat, at once formal and burlesque as though dressed carefully for some shabby and ceremonial violence, emptying the reservoir of the lamp back into the five-gallon kerosene can from which it had been filled, while the mother tugged at his arm until he shifted the lamp to the other hand and flung her back, not savagely or viciously, just hard, into the wall, her hands flung out against the wall for balance, her mouth open and in her face the same quality of hopeless despair as had been in her voice. Then his father saw him standing in the door.

"Go to the barn and get that can of oil we were oiling the wagon with," he said. The boy did not move. Then he could speak.

"What . . ." he cried. "What are you . . ."

"Go get that oil," his father said. "Go."

Then he was moving, running, outside the house, toward the stable: this the old habit, the old blood which he had not been permitted to choose for himself, which had been bequeathed him willy nilly and which had run for so long (and who knew where, battening on what of outrage and savagery and lust) before it came to him. *I could keep on,* he thought. *I could run on and on and never look back, never need to see his face again. Only I can't. I can't,* the rusted can in his hand now, the liquid sploshing in it as he ran back to the house and into it, into the sound of his mother's weeping in the next room, and handed the can to his father.

"Ain't you going to even send a nigger?" he cried. "At least you sent a nigger before!"

This time his father didn't strike him. The hand came even faster than the blow had, the same hand which had set the can on the table with almost excruciating care flashing from the can toward him too quick for him to follow it, gripping him by the back of his shirt and on to tiptoe before he had seen it quit the can, the face stooping at him in breathless and frozen ferocity, the cold, dead voice speaking over him to the older brother who leaned against the table, chewing with that steady, curious, sidewise motion of cows:

"Empty the can into the big one and go on. I'll catch up with you."

"Better tie him up to the bedpost," the brother said.

"Do like I told you," the father said. Then the boy was moving, his bunched shirt and the hard, bony hand between his shoulder-blades, his toes just touching the floor, across the room and into the other one, past the sisters sitting with spread heavy thighs in the two chairs over the cold hearth, and to where his mother and aunt sat side by side on the bed, the aunt's arms about his mother's shoulders.

"Hold him," the father said. The aunt made a startled movement. "Not you," the father said. "Lennie. Take hold of him. I want to see you do it." His mother took him by the wrist. "You'll hold him better than that. If he gets loose don't you know what he is going to do? He will go up yonder." He jerked his head toward the road. "Maybe I'd better tie him."

"I'll hold him," his mother whispered.

"See you do then." Then his father was gone, the stiff foot heavy and measured upon the boards, ceasing at last.

Then he began to struggle. His mother caught him in both arms, he jerking and wrenching at them. He would be stronger in the end, he knew that. But he had no time to wait for it. "Lemme go!" he cried. "I don't want to have to hit you!"

"Let him go!" the aunt said. "If he don't go, before God, I am going up there myself!"

"Don't you see I can't?" his mother cried. "Sarty! Sarty! No! No! Help me, Lizzie!"

Then he was free. His aunt grasped at him but it was too late. He whirled, running, his mother stumbled forward on to her knees behind him, crying to the nearer sister: "Catch him, Net! Catch him!" But that was too late too, the sister (the sisters were twins, born at the same time, yet either of them now gave the impression of being, encompassing as much living meat and volume and weight as any other two of the family) not yet having begun to rise from the chair, her head, face, alone merely turned, presenting to him in the flying instant an astonishing expanse of young female features untroubled by any surprise even, wearing only an expression of bovine interest. Then he was out of the room, out of the house, in the mild dust of the starlit road and the heavy rifeness of honeysuckle, the pale ribbon unspooling with terrific slowness under his running feet, reaching the gate at last and turning in, running, his heart and lungs drumming, on up the drive toward the lighted house, the lighted door. He did not knock, he burst in, sobbing for breath, incapable for the moment of speech; he saw the astonished face of the Negro in the linen jacket without knowing when the Negro had appeared.

"De Spain!" he cried, panted. "Where's ..." then he saw the white man too emerging from a white door down the hall. "Barn!" he cried. "Barn!"

"What?" the white man said. "Barn?"

"Yes!" the boy cried. "Barn!"

"Catch him!" the white man shouted.

But it was too late this time too. The Negro grasped his shirt, but the entire sleeve, rotten with washing, carried away, and he was out that door too and in the drive again, and had actually never ceased to run even while he was screaming into the white man's face.

Behind him the white man was shouting, "My horse! Fetch my horse!" and he thought for an instant of cutting across the park and climbing the fence into the road, but he did not know the park nor how high the vine-massed fence might be and he dared not risk it. So he ran on down the drive, blood and breath roaring; presently he was in the road again though he could not see it. He could not hear either: the galloping mare was almost upon him before he heard her, and even then he held his course, as if the very urgency of his wild grief and need must in a moment more find him wings, waiting until the ultimate instant to hurl himself aside and into the weed-choked roadside ditch as the horse thundered past and on, for an instant in furious silhouette against the stars, the tranquil early summer night sky which, even before the shape of the horse and rider vanished, stained abruptly and violently upward: a long, swirling roar incredible and soundless, blotting the stars, and he springing up and into the road again, running again, knowing it was too late yet still running even after he heard the shot and, an instant later, two shots, pausing now without knowing he had ceased to run, crying "Pap! Pap!", running again before he knew he had begun to run, stumbling, tripping over something and scrabbling up again without ceasing to run, looking backward over his shoulder at the glare as he got up, running on among the invisible trees, panting, sobbing, "Father! Father!"

At midnight he was sitting on the crest of a hill. He did not know it was midnight and he did not know how far he had come. But there was no glare behind him now and he sat now, his back toward what he had called home for four days anyhow, his face toward the dark woods which he would enter when breath was strong again, small, shaking steadily in the chill darkness, hugged himself into the remainder of his thin, rotten shirt, the grief and despair now no longer terror and fear but just grief and despair. *Father. My father,* he thought. "He was brave!" he cried suddenly, aloud but not loud, no more than a whisper: "He was! He was in the war! He was in Colonel Sartoris' cav'ry!" not knowing that his father had gone to that war a private in the fine old European sense, wearing no uniform, admitting the authority of and giving fidelity to no man or army or flag, going to war as Malbrouck himself did: for booty — it meant nothing and less than nothing to him if it were enemy booty or his own.

The slow constellations wheeled on. It would be dawn and then sun-up after a while and he would be hungry. But that would be tomorrow and now he was only cold, and walking would cure that. His breathing was easier now and he decided to get up and go on, and then he found that he had been asleep because he knew it was almost dawn, the night almost over. He could tell that from the whippoorwills. They were everywhere now among the dark trees below him, constant and inflectioned and ceaseless, so that, as the instant for giving over to the day birds drew nearer and nearer, there was no interval at all between them. He got up. He was a little stiff, but walking would cure that too as it would the cold, and soon there would be the sun. He went on down the hill, toward the dark woods within which the liquid silver voices of the birds called unceasing — the rapid and urgent beating of the urgent and quiring heart of the late spring night. He did not look back.

WILLIAM FAULKNER

An Odor of Verbena

It was just after supper. I had just opened my *Coke* on the table beneath the lamp; I heard Professor Wilkins' feet in the hall and then the instant of silence as he put his hand to the door knob, and I should have known. People talk glibly of presentiment, but I had none. I heard his feet on the stairs and then in the hall approaching and there was nothing in the feet because although I had lived in his house for three college years now and although both he and Mrs. Wilkins called me Bayard in the house, he would no more have entered my room without knocking than I would have entered his — or hers. Then he flung the door violently inward against the doorstop with one of those gestures with or by which an almost painfully unflagging preceptory of youth ultimately aberrates, and stood there saying, "Bayard. Bayard, my son, my dear son."

I should have known; I should have been prepared. Or maybe I was prepared because I remember how I closed the book carefully, even marking the place, before I rose. He (Professor Wilkins) was doing something, bustling at something; it was my hat and cloak which he handed me and which I took although I would not need the cloak, unless even then I was thinking (although it was October, the equinox had not occurred) that the rains and the cool weather would arrive before I should see this room again and so I would need the cloak anyway to return to it if I returned, thinking "God, if he had only done this last night, flung that door crashing and bouncing against the stop last night, without knocking so I could have gotten there before it happened, been there when it did, beside him on whatever spot, wherever it was that he would have to fall and lie in the dust and dirt."

"Your boy is downstairs in the kitchen," he said. It was not until years later that he told me (someone did; it must have been Judge Wilkins) how Ringo had apparently flung the cook aside and come on into the house and into the library where he and Mrs. Wilkins were sitting and said without preamble and already turning to withdraw: "They shot Colonel Sartoris this morning. Tell him I be waiting in the kitchen" and was gone before either of them could move. "He had ridden forty miles yet he refuses to eat anything." We were moving toward the door now — the door on my side of which I had lived for three years now with what I knew, what I knew now I must have believed and expected, yet beyond which I had heard the approaching feet yet heard nothing in the feet. "If there was just anything I could do."

"Yes, sir," I said. "A fresh horse for my boy. He will want to go back with me."

"By all means take mine — Mrs. Wilkins'," he cried. His tone was no different yet he did cry it and I suppose that at the same moment we both realised that was funny — a short-legged deep-barreled mare who looked exactly like a spinster music teacher, which Mrs. Wilkins drove to a basket phaeton — which was good for me, like being doused with a pail of cold water would have been good for me.

"Thank you, sir," I said. "We won't need it. I will get a fresh horse for him at the livery stable when I get my mare." Good for me, because even before I finished speaking I knew that would not be necessary either, that Ringo would have stopped at the livery stable before he came out to the college and attended to that and that the fresh horse for him and my mare both would be saddled and waiting now at the side fence and we would not have to go through Oxford at all. Loosh would not have thought of that if he had come for me, he would have come straight to the college, to Professor Wilkins', and told his news and then sat down and let me take charge from then on. But not Ringo.

He followed me from the room. From now until Ringo and I rode away into the hot thick dusty darkness quick and strained for the overdue equinox like a laboring delayed woman, he would be somewhere either just beside me or just behind me and I never to know exactly nor care which. He was trying to find the words with which to offer me his pistol too. I could almost hear him: "Ah, this unhappy land, not ten years recovered from the fever yet still men must kill one another, still we must pay Cain's price in his own coin." But he did not actually say it. He just followed me, somewhere beside or behind me as we descended the stairs toward where Mrs. Wilkins waited in the hall beneath the chandelier — a thin gray woman who reminded me of Granny, not that she looked like Granny probably but because she had known Granny — a lifted anxious still face which was thinking *Who lives by the sword shall die by it* just as Granny would have thought, toward which I walked, had to walk not because I was Granny's grandson and had lived in her house for three college years and was about the age of her son when he was killed in almost the last battle nine years ago, but because I was now The Sartoris. (The Sartoris: that had been one of the concomitant flashes, along with the *at last it has happened* when Professor Wilkins opened my door). She didn't offer me a horse and pistol, not because she liked me any less than Professor Wilkins but because she was a woman and so wiser than any man, else the men would not have gone on with the War for two years after they knew they were whipped. She just put her hands (a small woman, no bigger than Granny had been) on my shoulders and said, "Give my love to Drusilla and your Aunt Jenny. And come back when you can."

"Only I don't know when that will be," I said. "I don't know how many things I will have to attend to." Yes, I lied even to her; it had not been but a minute yet since he had flung that door bouncing into the stop yet already I was beginning to realize, to become aware of that which I still had no yardstick to measure save that one consisting of what, despite myself, despite my raising and background (or maybe because of them) I had for some time known I was becoming and had feared the test of it; I remember how I thought while her hands still rested on my shoulders: *At least this will be my chance to find out if I am what I think I am or if I just hope; if I am going to do what I have taught myself is right or if I am just going to wish I were.*

We went on to the kitchen, Professor Wilkins still somewhere beside me or behind me and still offering me the pistol and horse in a dozen different ways. Ringo was waiting; I remember how I thought then that no matter what might happen to either of us, I would never be The Sartoris to him. He was twenty-four too, but in a way he had changed even less than I had since that day when we had nailed Grumby's body to the door of the old compress. Maybe it was because he had outgrown me, had changed so much that summer while he and Granny traded mules with the Yankees that since then I had had to do most of the changing just to catch up with him. He was sitting quietly in a chair beside the cold stove, spent-looking too who had ridden forty miles (at one time, either in Jefferson or when he was alone at last on the road somewhere, he had cried; dust was now caked and dried in the tear-channels on his face) and would ride forty more yet would not eat, looking up at me a little red-eyed with weariness (or maybe it was more than just weariness and so I would never catch up with him) then rising without a word and going on toward the door and I following and Professor Wilkins still offering the horse and the pistol without speaking the words and still thinking (I could feel that too) *Dies by the sword. Dies by the sword.*

Ringo had the two horses saddled at the side gate, as I had known he would — the fresh one for himself and my mare father had given me three years ago, that could do a mile under two minutes any day and a mile every eight minutes all day long. He was already mounted when I realised that what Professor Wilkins wanted was to shake my hand. We shook hands; I knew he believed he was touching flesh which might not be alive tomorrow night and I thought for a second how if I told him what I was going to do, since we had talked about it, about how if there was anything at all in the Book, anything of hope and peace for His blind and bewildered spawn which He had chosen above all others to offer immortality, *Thou shalt not kill* must be it, since maybe he even believed that he had taught it to me except that he had not, nobody had, not even myself since it went further than just having been learned. But I did not tell him. He was too old to be forced so, to condone even in principle such a decision; he was too old to have to stick to principle in the face of blood and raising and background, to be faced without warning and made to deliver like a highwayman out of the dark: only the young could do that — one still young enough to have his youth supplied him gratis as a reason (not an excuse) for cowardice.

So I said nothing. I just shook his hand and mounted too, and Ringo and I rode on. We would not have to pass through Oxford now and so soon (there was a thin sickle of moon like the heel print of a boot in wet sand) the road to Jefferson lay before us, the road which I had travelled for the first time three years ago with Father and travelled twice at Christmas time and then in June and September and twice at Christmas time again and then June and September again each college term since alone on the mare, not even knowing that this was peace; and now this time and maybe last time who would not die (I knew that) but who maybe forever after could never again hold up his head. The horses took the gait which they would hold for forty miles. My mare knew the long road ahead and Ringo had a good beast too, had talked Hilliard at the livery stable out of a good horse too. Maybe it was the tears, the channels of dried mud across which his strain-reddened eyes had looked at me, but I rather think it was that same quality which used to enable him to replenish his and Granny's supply of United States Army letterheads during that time — some outrageous assurance gained from too long and too close association with white people: the one whom he called Granny, the other with whom he had slept from the time we were born until Father rebuilt the house. We spoke one time, then no more:

"We could bushwhack him," he said. "Like we done Grumby that day. But I reckon that wouldn't suit that white skin you walks around in."

"No," I said. We rode on; it was October; there was plenty of time still for verbena although I would have to reach home before I would realise there was a need for it; plenty of time for verbena yet from the garden where Aunt Jenny puttered beside old Joby, in a pair of Father's old cavalry gauntlets, among the coaxed and ordered beds, the quaint and odorous old names, for though it was October no rain had come yet and hence no frost to bring (or leave behind) the first half-warm half-chill nights of Indian Summer — the drowsing air cool and empty for geese yet languid still with the old hot dusty smell of fox grape and sassafras — the nights when before I became a man and went to college to learn law Ringo and I, with lantern and axe and crokersack and six dogs (one to follow the trail and five more just for the tonguing, the music) would hunt possum in the pasture where, hidden, we had seen our first Yankee that afternoon on the bright horse, where for the last year now you could hear the whistling of the trains which had no longer belonged to Mr. Redmond for a long while now and which at some instant, some second during the morning Father too had relinquished along with the pipe which Ringo said he was smoking, which slipped from his hand as he fell. We rode on, toward the house where he would by lying in the parlor now, in his regimentals (sabre too) and where Drusilla would be waiting for me beneath all the festive glitter of the chandeliers, in the yellow ball gown and the sprig of verbena in her hair, holding the two loaded pistols (I could see that too, who had had no presentiment; I could see her, in the formal brilliant room arranged formally for obsequy, not tall, not slender as a woman is but as a youth, a boy, is motionless, in yellow, the face calm, almost bemused, the head simple and severe, the balancing sprig of verbena above each ear, the two arms bent at the elbows, the two hands shoulder high, the two identical duelling pistols lying up, not clutched in, one to each: the Greek amphora priestess of a succinct and formal violence).

2

Drusilla said that he had a dream. I was twenty then and she and I would walk in the garden in the summer twilight while we waited for Father to ride in from the railroad. I was twenty then: that summer before I entered the University to take the law degree which Father decided I should have and four years after the one, the day, the evening when Father and Drusilla had kept old Cash Benbow from becoming United States Marshal and returned home still unmarried and Mrs. Habersham herded them into her carriage and drove them back to town and dug her husband out of his little dim hole in the new bank and made him sign Father's peace bond for killing the two carpet baggers, and took Father and Drusilla to the minister herself and saw that they were married. And Father had rebuilt the house too, on the same blackened spot, over the same cellar, where the other had burned, only larger, much larger: Drusilla said that the house was the aura of Father's dream just as a bride's trousseau and veil is the aura of hers. And Aunt Jenny had come to live with us now so we had the garden (Drusilla would no more have bothered with flowers than Father himself would have, who even now, even four years after it was over, still seemed to exist, breathe, in that last year of it while she had ridden in man's clothes and with her hair cut short like any other member of Father's troop, across Georgia and both Carolinas in front of Sherman's army) for her to gather sprigs of verbena from to wear in her hair because she said verbena was the only scent you could smell above the smell of horses and courage and so it was the only one that was worth wearing. The railroad was hardly begun then and Father and Mr. Redmond were not only still partners, they were still friends, which as George Wyatt said was easily a record for Father, and he would leave the house at daybreak on Jupiter, riding up and down the unfinished line with two saddlebags of gold coins borrowed on Friday to pay the men on Saturday, keeping just two cross-ties ahead of the sheriff as Aunt Jenny said. So we walked in the dusk, slowly between Aunt Jenny's flower beds while Drusilla (in a dress now, who still would have worn pants all the time if Father had let her) leaned lightly on my arm and I smelled the verbena in her hair as I had smelled the rain in it and in Father's beard that night four years ago when he and Drusilla and Uncle Buck McCaslin found Grumby and then came home and found Ringo and me more than just asleep: escaped into that oblivion which God or Nature or whoever it was had supplied us with for the time being, who had had to perform more than should be required of children because there should be some limit to the age, the youth at least below which one should not have to kill. This was just after the Saturday night when he returned and I watched him clean the derringer and reload it and we learned that the dead man was almost a neighbor, a hill man who had been in the first infantry regiment when it voted Father out of command: and we never to know if the man actually intended to rob Father or not because Father had shot too quick, but only that he had a wife and several children in a dirt-floored cabin in the hills, to whom Father the next day sent some money and she (the wife) walked into the house two days later while we were sitting at the dinner table and flung the money at Father's face.

"But nobody could have more of a dream than Colonel Sutpen," I said. He had been Father's second-in-command in the first regiment and had been elected colonel when the regiment deposed Father after Second Manassas, and it was Sutpen and not the regiment whom Father never forgave. He was underbred, a cold ruthless man who had come into the country about thirty years before the War, nobody knew from where except Father said you could look at him and know he would not dare to tell. He had got some land and nobody knew how he did that either, and he got money from somewhere — Father said they all believed he robbed steamboats, either as a card sharper or as an out-and-out highwayman — and built a big house and married and set up as a gentleman. Then he lost everything in the War like everybody else, all hope of descendants too (his son killed his daughter's fiancé on the eve of the wedding and vanished) yet he came back home and set out single-handed to rebuild the plantation. He had no friends to borrow from and he had nobody to leave it to and he was past sixty years old, yet he set out to rebuild the place like it used to be; they told how he was too busy to bother with politics or anything ; how when Father and the other men organised the nightriders to keep the carpet baggers from organising the Negroes into an insurrection, he refused to have anything to do with it. Father stopped hating him long enough to ride out to see Sutpen himself and he (Sutpen) came to the door with a lamp and did not even invite them to come in and discuss it; Father said, "Are you with us or against us?" and he said, "I'm for my land. If every man of you would rehabilitate his own land, the country will take care of itself" and Father challenged him to bring the lamp out and set it on a stump where they could both see to shoot and Sutpen would not. "Nobody could have more of a dream than that."

"Yes. But his dream is just Sutpen. John's is not. He is thinking of this whole country which he is trying to raise by its bootstraps, so that all the people in it, not just his kind nor his old regiment, but all the people, black and white, the women and children back in the hills who don't even own shoes — Don't you see?"

"But how can they get any good from what he wants to do for them if they are — after he has — "

"Killed some of them? I suppose you include those two carpet baggers he had to kill to hold that first election, don't you?"

"They were men. Human beings."

"They were Northerners, foreigners who had no business here. They were pirates." We walked on, her weight hardly discernible on my arm, her head just reaching my shoulder. I had always been a little taller than she, even on that night at Hawkhurst while we listened to the niggers passing in the road, and she had changed but little since — the same boy-hard body, the close implacable head with its savagely cropped hair which I had watched from the wagon above the tide of crazed singing niggers as we went down into the river — the body not slender as women are but as boys are slender. "A dream is not a very safe thing to be near, Bayard. I know; I had one once. It's like a loaded pistol with a hair trigger: if it stays alive long enough, somebody is going to be hurt. But if it's a good dream, it's worth it. There are not many dreams in the world, but there are a lot of human lives. And one human life or two dozen — "

"Are not worth anything?"

"No. Not anything — Listen. I hear Jupiter. I'll beat you to the house." She was already running, the skirts she did not like to wear lifted almost to her knees, her legs beneath it running as boys run just as she rode like men ride.

I was twenty then. But the next time I was twenty-four; I had been three years at the University and in another two weeks I would ride back to Oxford for the final year and my degree. It was just last summer, last August, and Father had just beat Redmond for the State legislature. The railroad was finished now and the partnership between Father and Redmond had been dissolved so long ago that most people would have forgotten they were ever partners if it hadn't been for the enmity between them. There had been a third partner but nobody hardly remembered his name now; he and his name both had vanished in the fury of the conflict which set up between Father and Redmond almost before they began to lay the rails, between Father's violent and ruthless dictatorialness and will to dominate (the idea was his; he did think of the railroad first and then took Redmond in) and that quality in Redmond (as George Wyatt said, he was not a coward or Father would never have teamed with him) which permitted him to stand as much as he did from Father, to bear and bear and bear until something (not his will nor his courage) broke in him. During the War Redmond had not been a soldier, he had had something to do with cotton for the Government; he could have made money himself out of it but he had not and everybody knew he had not, Father knew it, yet Father would even taunt him with not having smelled powder. He was wrong; he knew he was when it was too late for him to stop just as a drunkard reaches a point where it is too late for him to stop, where he promises himself that he will and maybe believes he will or can but it is too late. Finally they reached the point (they had both put everything they could mortgage or borrow into it for Father to ride up and down the line, paying the workmen and the waybills on the rails at the last possible instant) where even Father realised that one of them would have to get out. So (they were not speaking then; it was arranged by Judge Benbow) they met and agreed to buy or sell, naming a price which, in reference to what they had put into it, was ridiculously low but which each believed the other could not raise — at least Father claimed that Redmond did not believe he could raise it. So Redmond accepted the price, and found out that Father had the money. And according to Father, that's what started it, although Uncle Buck McCaslin said Father could not have owned a half interest in even one hog, let alone a railroad, and not dissolve the business either sworn enemy or death-pledged friend to his recent partner. So they parted and Father finished the road. By that time, seeing that he was going to finish it, some Northern people sold him a locomotive on credit which he named for Aunt Jenny, with a silver oil can in the cab with her name engraved on it; and last summer the first train ran into Jefferson, the engine decorated with flowers and Father in the cab blowing blast after blast on the whistle when he passed Redmond's house; and there were speeches at the station, with more flowers and a Confederate flag and girls in white dresses and red sashes and a band, and Father stood on the pilot of the engine and made a direct and absolutely needless allusion to Mr. Redmond. That was it. He wouldn't let him alone. George Wyatt came to me right afterward and told me. "Right or wrong," he said, "us boys and most of the other folks in this county know John's right. But he ought to let Redmond alone. I know what's wrong: he's had to kill too many folks, and that's bad for a man. We all know Colonel's brave as a lion, but Redmond ain't no coward either and there ain't any use in making a brave man that made one mistake eat crow all the time. Can't you talk to him?"

"I don't know," I said. "I'll try." But I had no chance. That is, I could have talked to him and he would have listened, but he could not have heard me because he had stepped straight from the pilot of that engine into the race for the legislature. Maybe he knew that Redmond would have to oppose him to save his face even though he (Redmond) must have known that, after that train ran into Jefferson, he had no chance against Father, or maybe Redmond had already announced his candidacy and Father entered the race just because of that, I don't remember. Anyway they ran, a bitter contest in which Father continued to badger Redmond without reason or need, since they both knew it would be a landslide for Father. And it was, and we thought he was satisfied. Maybe he thought so himself, as the drunkard believes that he is done with drink; and it was that afternoon and Drusilla and I walked in the garden in the twilight and I said something about what George Wyatt had told me and she released my arm and turned me to face her and said, "This from you? You? Have you forgotten Grumby?"

"No," I said. "I never will forget him."

"You never will. I wouldn't let you. There are worse things than killing men, Bayard. There are worse things than being killed. Sometimes I think the finest thing that can happen to a man is to love something, a woman preferably, well, hard hard hard, then to die young because he believed what he could not help but believe and was what he could not (could not? would not) help but be." Now she was looking at me in a way she never had before. I did not know what it meant then and was not to know until tonight since neither of us knew then that two months later Father would be dead. I just knew that she was looking at me as she never had before and that the scent of the verbena in her hair seemed to have increased a hundred times, to have got a hundred times stronger, to be everywhere in the dusk in which something was about to happen which I had never dreamed of. Then she spoke. "Kiss me, Bayard."

"No. You are Father's wife."

"And eight years older than you are. And your fourth cousin too. And I have black hair. Kiss me, Bayard."

"No."

"Kiss me, Bayard." So I leaned my face down to her. But she didn't move, standing so, bent lightly back from me from the waist, looking at me; now it was she who said, "No." So I put my arms around her. Then she came to me, melted as women will and can, the arms with the wrist- and elbow-power to control horses about my shoulders, using the wrists to hold my face to hers until there was no longer need for the wrists; I thought then of the woman of thirty, the symbol of the ancient and eternal Snake and of the men who have written of her, and I realised then the immitigable chasm between all life and all print — that those who can, do, those who cannot and suffer enough because they can't, write about it. Then I was free, I could see her again, I saw her still watching me with that dark inscrutable look, looking up at me now across her down-slanted face; I watched her arms rise with almost the exact gesture with which she had put them around me as if she were repeating the empty and formal gesture of all promises so that I should never forget it, the elbows angling outward as she put her hands to the sprig of verbena in her hair, I standing straight and rigid facing the slightly bent head, the short jagged hair, the rigid curiously formal angle of the bare arms gleaming faintly in the last of light as she removed the verbena sprig and put it into my lapel, and I thought how the War had tried to stamp all the women of her generation and class in the South into a type and how it had failed — the suffering, the identical experience (hers and Aunt Jenny's had been almost the same except that Aunt Jenny had spent a few nights with her husband and before they brought him back home in an ammunition wagon while Gavin Breckbridge was just Drusilla's fiancé) was there in the eyes, yet beyond that was the incorrigibly individual woman: not like so many men who return from wars to live on Government reservations like so many steers, emasculate and empty of all save an identical experience which they cannot forget and dare not, else they would cease to live at that moment, almost interchangeable save for the old habit of answering to a given name.

"Now I must tell Father," I said.

"Yes," she said. "You must tell him. Kiss me." So again it was like it had been before. No. Twice, a thousand times and never like — the eternal and symbolical thirty to a young man, a youth, each time both cumulative and retroactive, immitigably unrepetitive, each wherein remembering excludes experience, each wherein experience antedates remembering; the skill without weariness, the knowledge virginal to surfeit, the cunning secret muscles to guide and control just as within the wrists and elbows lay slumbering the mastery of horses: she stood back, already turning, not looking at me when she spoke, never having looked at me, already moving swiftly on in the dusk: "Tell John. Tell him tonight."

I intended to. I went to the house and into the office at once; I went to the center of the rug before the cold hearth, I don't know why, and stood there rigid like soldiers stand, looking at eye level straight across the room and above his head and said "Father" and then stopped. Because he did not even hear me. He said, "Yes, Bayard?" but he did not hear me although he was sitting behind the desk doing nothing, immobile, as still as I was rigid, one hand on the desk with a dead cigar in it, a bottle of brandy and a filled and untasted glass beside his hand, clothed quiet and bemused in whatever triumph it was he felt since the last overwhelming return of votes had come in late in the afternoon. So I waited until after supper. We went to the diningroom and stood side by side until Aunt Jenny entered and then Drusilla, in the yellow ball gown, who walked straight to me and gave me one fierce inscrutable look then went to her place and waited for me to draw her chair while Father drew Aunt Jenny's. He had roused by then, not to talk himself but rather to sit at the head of the table and reply to Drusilla as she talked with a sort of feverish and glittering volubility — to reply now and then to her with that courteous intolerant pride which had lately become a little forensic, as if merely being in a political contest filled with fierce and empty oratory had retroactively made a lawyer of him who was anything and everything except a lawyer. Then Drusilla and Aunt Jenny rose and left us and he said, "Wait" to me who had made no move to follow and directed Joby to bring one of the bottles of wine which he had fetched back from New Orleans when he went there last to borrow money to liquidate his first private railroad bonds. Then I stood again like soldiers stand, gazing at eye level above his head while he sat half-turned from the table, a little paunchy now though not much, a little grizzled too in the hair though his beard was as strong as ever, with that spurious forensic air of lawyers and the intolerant eyes which in the last two years had acquired that transparent film which the eyes of carnivorous animals have and from behind which they look at a world which no ruminant ever sees, perhaps dares to see, which I have seen before on the eyes of men who have killed too much, who have killed so much that never again as long as they live will they ever be alone. I said again, "Father," then I told him.

"Hah?" he said. "Sit down." I sat down, I looked at him, watched him fill both glasses and this time I knew it was worse with him than not hearing: it didn't even matter. "You are doing well in the law, Judge Wilkins tells me. I am pleased to hear that. I have not needed you in my affairs so far, but from now on I shall. I have now accomplished the active portion of my aims in which you could not have helped me; I acted as the land and the time demanded and you were too young for that, I wished to shield you. But now the land and the time too are changing; what will follow will be a matter of consolidation, of pettifogging and doubtless chicanery in which I would be a babe in arms but in which you, trained in the law, can hold your own — our own. Yes, I have accomplished my aim, and now I shall do a little moral house-cleaning. I am tired of killing men, no matter what the necessity nor the end. Tomorrow, when I go to town and meet Ben Redmond, I shall be unarmed."

3

We reached home just before midnight; we didn't have to pass through Jefferson either. Before we turned in the gates I could see the lights, the chandeliers — hall, parlor, and what Aunt Jenny (without any effort or perhaps even design on her part) had taught even Ringo to call the drawing room, the light falling outward across the portico, past the columns. Then I saw the horses, the faint shine of leather and buckle-glints on the black silhouettes and then the men too — Wyatt and others of Father's old troop — and I had forgot that they would be there. I had forgot that they would be there; I remember how I thought, since I was tired and spent with strain, *Now it will have to begin tonight. I won't even have until tomorrow in which to begin to resist.* They had a watchman, a picquet out, I suppose, because they seemed to know at once that we were in the drive. Wyatt met me, I halted the mare, I could look down at him and at the others gathered a few yards behind him with that curious vulture-like formality which Southern men assume in such situations.

"Well, boy," George said.

"Was it — " I said. "Was he — "

"It was all right. It was in front. Redmond ain't no coward. John had the derringer inside his cuff like always, but he never touched it, never made a move toward it." I have seen him do it, he showed me once: the pistol (it was not four inches long) held flat inside his left wrist by a clip he made himself of wire and an old clock spring; he would raise both hands at the same time, cross them, fire the pistol from beneath his left hand almost as if he were hiding from his own vision what he was doing; when he killed one of the men he shot a hole through his own coat sleeve.

"But you want to get on to the house," Wyatt said. He began to stand aside, then he spoke again: "We'll take this off your hands, any of us. Me." I hadn't moved the mare yet and I had made no move to speak, yet he continued quickly, as if he had already rehearsed all this, his speech and mine, and knew what I would say and only spoke himself as he would have removed his hat on entering a house or used "sir" in conversing with a stranger: "You're young, just a boy, you ain't had any experience in this kind of thing. Besides, you got them two ladies in the house to think about. He would understand, all right."

"I reckon I can attend to it," I said.

"Sure," he said; there was no surprise, nothing at all, in his voice because he had already rehearsed this: "I reckon we all knew that's what you would say." He stepped back then; almost it was as though he and not I bade the mare to move on. But they all followed, still with that unctuous and voracious formality. Then I saw Drusilla standing at the top of the front steps, in the light from the open door and the windows like a theater scene, in the yellow ball gown and even from here I believed that I could smell the verbena in her hair, standing there motionless yet emanating something louder than the two shots must have been — something voracious too and passionate. Then, although I had dismounted and someone had taken the mare, I seemed to be still in the saddle and to watch myself enter that scene which she had postulated like another actor while in the background for chorus Wyatt and the others stood with the unctuous formality which the Southern man shows in the presence of death — that Roman holiday engendered by the mist-born Protestantism grafted onto this land of violent sun, of violent alteration from snow to heat-stroke which has produced a race impervious to both. I mounted the steps toward the figure straight and yellow and immobile as a candle which moved only to extend one hand; we stood together and looked down at them where they stood clumped, the horses too gathered in a tight group beyond them at the rim of light from the brilliant door and windows. One of them stamped and blew his breath and jangled his gear.

"Thank you, gentlemen," I said. "My aunt and my — Drusilla thank you. There's no need for you to stay. Goodnight." They murmured, turning. George Wyatt paused, looking back at me.

"Tomorrow?" he said.

"Tomorrow." Then they went on, carrying their hats and tiptoeing, even on the ground, the quiet and resilient earth, as though anyone in that house awake would try to sleep, anyone already asleep in it whom they could have awakened. Then they were gone and Drusilla and I turned and crossed the portico, her hand lying light on my wrist yet discharging into me with a shock like electricity that dark and passionate voracity, the face at my shoulder — the jagged hair with a verbena sprig above each ear, the eyes staring at me with that fierce exaltation. We entered the hall and crossed it, her hand guiding me without pressure, and entered the parlor. Then for the first time I realised it — the alteration which is death — not that he was now just clay but that he was lying down. But I didn't look at him yet because I knew that when I did I would begin to pant; I went to Aunt Jenny who had just risen from a chair behind which Louvinia stood. She was Father's sister, taller than Drusilla but no older, whose husband had been killed at the very beginning of the War, by a shell from a Federal frigate at Fort Moultrie, come to us from Carolina six years ago. Ringo and I went to Tennessee Junction in the wagon to meet her. It was January, cold and clear and with ice in the ruts; we returned just before dark with Aunt Jenny on the seat beside me holding a lace parasol and Ringo in the wagon bed nursing a hamper basket containing two bottles of old sherry and the two jasmine cuttings which were bushes in the garden now, and the panes of colored glass which she had salvaged from the Carolina house where she and Father and Uncle Bayard were born and which Father had set in a fanlight about one of the drawing room windows for her — who came up the drive and Father (home now from the railroad) went down the steps and lifted her from the wagon and said, "Well, Jenny," and she said, "Well, Johnny," and began to cry. She stood too, looking at me as I approached — the same hair, the same high nose, the same eyes as Father's except that they were intent and very wise instead of intolerant. She said nothing at all, she just kissed me, her hands light on my shoulders. Then Drusilla spoke, as if she had been waiting with a sort of dreadful patience for the empty ceremony to be done, in a voice like a bell: clear, unsentient, on a single pitch, silvery and triumphant: "Come, Bayard."

"Hadn't you better go to bed now?" Aunt Jenny said.

"Yes," Drusilla said in that silvery ecstatic voice, "Oh, yes. There will be plenty of time for sleep." I followed her, her hand again guiding me without pressure; now I looked at him. It was just as I had imagined it — sabre, plumes, and all — but with that alteration, that irrevocable difference which I had known to expect yet had not realised, as you can put food into your stomach which for a while the stomach declines to assimilate — the illimitable grief and regret as I looked down at the face which I knew — the nose, the hair, the eyelids closed over the intolerance — the face which I realised I now saw in repose for the first time in my life; the empty hands still now beneath the invisible stain of what had been (once, surely) needless blood, the hands now appearing clumsy in their very inertness, too clumsy to have performed the fatal actions which forever afterward he must have waked and slept with and maybe was glad to lay down at last — those curious appendages clumsily conceived to begin with yet with which man has taught himself to do so much, so much more than they were intended to do or could be forgiven for doing, which had now surrendered that life to which his intolerant heart had fiercely held; and then I knew that in a minute I would begin to pant. So Drusilla must have spoken twice before I heard her and turned and saw in the instant Aunt Jenny and Louvinia watching us, hearing Drusilla now, the unsentient bell quality gone now, her voice whispering into that quiet death-filled room with a passionate and dying fall: "Bayard." She faced me, she was quite near; again the scent of the verbena in her hair seemed to have increased a hundred times as she stood holding out to me, one in either hand, the two duelling pistols. ""Take them, Bayard," she said, in the same tone in which she had said "Kiss me" last summer, already pressing them into my hands, watching me with that passionate and voracious exaltation, speaking in a voice fainting and passionate with promise: "Take them. I have kept them for you. I give them to you. Oh you will thank me, you will remember me who put into your hands what they say is an attribute only of God's, who took what belongs to heaven and gave it to you. Do you feel them? the long true barrels true as justice, the triggers (you have fired them) quick as retribution, the two of them slender and invincible and fatal as the physical shape of love?" Again I watched her arms angle out and upward as she removed the two verbena sprigs from her hair in two motions faster than the eye could follow, already putting one of them into my lapel and crushing the other in her other hand while she still spoke in that rapid passionate voice not much louder than a whisper. "There. One I give to you to wear tomorrow (it will not fade), the other I cast away, like this — " dropping the crushed bloom at her feet. "I abjure it. I abjure verbena forever more; I have smelled it above the odor of courage; that was all I wanted. Now let me look at you." She stood back staring at me — the face tearless and exalted, the feverish eyes brilliant and voracious. "How beautiful you are: do you know it? How beautiful: young, to be permitted to kill, to be permitted vengeance, to take into your bare hands the fire of heaven that cast down Lucifer. No; I. I gave it to you; I put it into your hands; Oh you will thank me, you will remember me when I am dead and you are an old man saying to himself, 'I have tasted all things.' — It will be the right hand, won't it?" She moved; she had taken my right hand which still held one of the pistols before I knew what she was about to do; she had bent and kissed it before I comprehended why she took it. Then she stopped dead still, still stooping in that attitude of fierce exultant humility, her hot lips and her hot hands still touching my flesh, light on my flesh as dead leaves yet communicating to it that battery charge dark, passionate and damned forever of all peace. Because they are wise, women are — a touch, lips or fingers, and the knowledge, even clairvoyance, goes straight to the heart without bothering the laggard brain at all. She stood erect now, staring at me with intolerable and amazed incredulity which occupied her face alone for a whole minute while her eyes were completely empty; it seemed to me that I stood there for a full minute while Aunt Jenny and Louvinia watched us, waiting for her eyes to fill. There was no blood in her face at all, her mouth open a little and pale as one of those rubber rings women seal fruit jars with. Then her eyes filled with an expression of bitter and passionate betrayal. "Why, he's not — " she said. "He's not — And I kissed his hand," she said in an aghast whisper; "*I kissed his hand!*" beginning to laugh, the laughter, rising, becoming a scream yet still remaining laughter, screaming with laughter, trying herself to deaden the sound by putting her hand over her mouth, the laughter spilling between her fingers like vomit, the incredulous betrayed eyes still watching me across the hand.

"Louvinia!" Aunt Jenny said. They both came to her. Louvinia touched and held her and Drusilla turned her face to Louvinia.

"I kissed his hand, Louvinia!" she cried. "Did you see it? *I kissed his hand!*" the laughter rising again, becoming the scream again yet still remaining laughter, she still trying to hold it back with her hand like a small child who has filled its mouth too full.

"Take her upstairs," Aunt Jenny said. But they were already moving toward the door, Louvinia half-carrying Drusilla, the laughter diminishing as they neared the door as though it waited for the larger space of the empty and brilliant hall to rise again. Then it was gone; Aunt Jenny and I stood there and I knew soon that I would begin to pant. I could feel it beginning like you feel regurgitation beginning, as though there were not enough air in the room, the house, not enough air anywhere under the heavy hot low sky where the equinox couldn't seem to accomplish, nothing in the air for breathing, for the lungs. Now it was Aunt Jenny who said "Bayard" twice before I heard her. "You are not going to try to kill him. All right."

"All right?" I said.

"Yes. All right. Don't let it be Drusilla, a poor hysterical young woman. And don't let it be him, Bayard, because he's dead now. And don't let it be George Wyatt and those others who will be waiting for you tomorrow morning. I know you are not afraid."

"But what good will that do?" I said. "What good will that do?" It almost began then; I stopped it just in time. "I must live with myself, you see."

"Then it's not just Drusilla? Not just him? Not just George Wyatt and Jefferson?"

"No," I said.

"Will you promise to let me see you before you go to town tomorrow?" I looked at her; we looked at one another for a moment. Then she put her hands on my shoulders and kissed me and released me, all in one motion. "Goodnight, son," she said. Then she was gone too and now it could begin. I knew that in a minute I would look at him and it would begin and I did look at him, feeling the long-held breath, the hiatus before it started, thinking how maybe I should have said, "Goodbye, Father." but did not. Instead I crossed to the piano and laid the pistols carefully on it, still keeping the panting from getting too loud too soon. Then I was outside on the porch and (I don't know how long it had been) I looked in the window and saw Simon squatting on a stool beside him. Simon had been his body servant during the War and when they came home Simon had a uniform too — a Confederate private's coat with a Yankee brigadier's star on it and he had put it on now too, like they had dressed Father, squatting on the stool beside him, not crying, not weeping the facile tears which are the white man's futile trait and which Negroes know nothing about but just sitting there, motionless, his lower lip slacked down a little; he raised his hand and touched the coffin, the black hand rigid and fragile-looking as a clutch of dead twigs, then dropped the hand; once he turned his head and I saw his eyes roll red and unwinking in his skull like those of a cornered fox. It had begun by that time; I panted, standing there and this was it — the regret and grief, the despair out of which the tragic mute insensitive bones stand up that can bear anything, anything.

4

After a while the whippoorwills stopped and I heard the first day bird, a mocking-bird. It had sung all night too but now it was the day song, no longer the drowsy moony fluting. Then they all began — the sparrows from the stable, the thrush that lived in Aunt Jenny's garden, and I heard a quail too from the pasture and now there was light in the room. But I didn't move at once. I still lay on the bed (I hadn't undressed) with my hands under my head and the scent of Drusilla's verbena faint from where my coat lay on a chair, watching the light grow, watching it turn rosy with the sun. After a while I heard Louvinia come up across the back yard and go into the kitchen; I heard the door and then the long crash of her armful of stovewood into the box. Soon they would begin to arrive — the carriages and buggies in the drive — but not for a while yet because they too would wait first to see what I was going to do. So the house was quiet when I went down to the diningroom, no sound in it except Simon snoring in the parlor, probably still sitting on the stool though I didn't look in to see. Instead I stood at the diningroom window and drank the coffee which Louvinia brought me, then I went to the stable; I saw Joby watching me from the kitchen door as I crossed the yard and in the stable Loosh looked up at me across Betsy's head, a curry comb in his hand, though Ringo didn't look at me at all. We curried Jupiter then. I didn't know if we would be able to without trouble or not, since always Father would come in first and touch him and tell him to stand and he would stand like a marble horse (or pale bronze rather) while Loosh curried him. But he stood for me too, a little restive but he stood, then that was done and now it was almost nine o'clock and soon they would begin to arrive and I told Ringo to bring Betsy on to the house.

I went on to the house and into the hall. I had not had to pant in some time now but it was there, waiting, a part of the alteration, as though by being dead and no longer needing air he had taken all of it, all that he had compassed and claimed and postulated between the walls which he had built, along with him. Aunt Jenny must have been waiting; she came out of the diningroom at once, without a sound, dressed, the hair that was like Father's combed and smooth above the eyes that were different from Father's eyes because they were not intolerant but just intent and grave and (she was wise too) without pity. "Are you going now?" she said.

"Yes." I looked at her. Yes, thank God, without pity. "You see, I want to be thought well of."

"I do," she said. "Even if you spend the day hidden in the stable loft, I still do."

"Maybe if she knew that I was going. Was going to town anyway."

"No," she said. "No, Bayard." We looked at one another. Then she said quietly, "All right. She's awake." So I mounted the stairs. I mounted steadily, not fast because if I had gone fast the panting would have started again or I might have had to slow for a second at the turn or at the top and I would not have gone on. So I went slowly and steadily, across the hall to her door and knocked and opened it. She was sitting at the window, in something soft and loose for morning in her bedroom only she never did look like morning in her bedroom because here was no hair to fall about her shoulders. She looked up, she sat there looking at me with her feverish brilliant eyes and I remembered I still had the verbena sprig in my lapel and suddenly she began to laugh again. It seemed to come not from her mouth but to burst out all over her face like sweat does and with a dreadful and painful convulsion as when you have vomited until it hurts you yet still you must vomit again — burst out all over her face except her eyes, the brilliant incredulous eyes looking at me out of the laughter as if they belonged to somebody else, as if they were two inert fragments of tar or coal lying on the bottom of a receptacle filled with turmoil: "I kissed his hand! *I kissed his hand!*" Louvinia entered, Aunt Jenny must have sent her directly after me;

again I walked slowly and steadily so it would not start yet, down the stairs where
Aunt Jenny stood beneath the chandelier in the hall as Mrs. Wilkins had stood
yesterday at the University. She had my hat in her hand. "Even if you hid all day in
the stable, Bayard," she said. I took the hat; she said quietly, pleasantly, as if she were
talking to a stranger, a guest: "I used to see a lot of blockade runners in Charleston.
They were heroes in a way, you see — not heroes because they were helping to
prolong the Confederacy but heroes in the sense that David Crockett or John Sevier
would have been to small boys or fool young women. There was one of them, an
Englishman. He had no business there; it was the money of course, as with all of
them. But he was the Davy Crockett to us because by that time we had all forgot what
money was, what you could do with it. He must have been a gentleman once or
associated with gentlemen before he changed his name, and he had a vocabulary of
seven words, though I must admit he got along quite well with them. The first four
were, 'I'll have rum, thanks,' and then, when he had the rum, he would use the other
three — across the champagne, to whatever ruffled bosom or low gown: 'No bloody
moon.' No bloody moon, Bayard."

Ringo was waiting with Betsy at the front steps. Again he did not look at me, his
face sullen, downcast even while he handed me the reins. But he said nothing, nor
did I look back. And sure enough I was just in time; I passed the Compson carriage
at the gates, General Compson lifted his hat as I did mine as we passed. It was four
miles to town but I had not gone two of them when I heard the horse coming up
behind me and I did not look back because I knew it was Ringo. I did not look back;
he came up on one of the carriage horses, he rode up beside me and looked me full
in the face for one moment, the sullen determined face, the eyes rolling at me
defiant and momentary and red; we rode on. Now we were in town — the long
shady street leading to the square, the new courthouse at the end of it; it was eleven
o'clock now: long past breakfast and not yet noon so there were only women on the
street, not to recognise me perhaps or at least not the walking stopped sudden and
dead in midwalking as if the legs contained the sudden eyes, the caught breath, that
not to begin until we reached the square and I thinking *If I could only be invisible
until I reach the stairs to his office and begin to mount.* But I could not, I was not;
we rode up to the Holston House and I saw the row of feet along the gallery rail
come suddenly and quietly down and I did not look at them, I stopped Betsy and
waited until Ringo was down then I dismounted and gave him the reins. "Wait for me
here," I said.

"I'm going with you," he said, not loud; we stood there under the still circumspect
eyes and spoke quietly to one another like two conspirators. Then I saw the pistol,
the outline of it inside his shirt, probably the one we had taken from Grumby that
day we killed him.

"No you ain't," I said.

"Yes I am."

"No you ain't." So I walked on, along the street in the hot sun. It was almost noon
now and I could smell nothing except the verbena in my coat, as if it had gathered
all the sun, all the suspended fierce heat in which the equinox could not seem to
occur and were distilling it so that I moved in a cloud of verbena as I might have
moved in a cloud of smoke from a cigar. Then George Wyatt was beside me (I don't
know where he came from) and five or six others of Father's old troop a few yards

behind, George's hand on my arm, drawing me into a doorway out of the avid eyes like caught breaths.

"Have you got that derringer?" George said.

"No," I said.

"Good," George said. "They are tricky things to fool with. Couldn't nobody but Colonel ever handle one right; I never could. So you take this. I tried it this morning and I know it's right. Here." He was already fumbling the pistol into my pocket, then the same thing seemed to happen to him that happened to Drusilla last night when she kissed my hand — something communicated by touch straight to the simple code by which he lived, without going through the brain at all; so that he too stood suddenly back, the pistol in his hand, staring at me with his pale outraged eyes and speaking in a whisper thin with fury: "Who are you? Is your name Sartoris? By God, if you don't kill him, I'm going to." Now it was not panting, it was a terrible desire to laugh, to laugh as Drusilla had, and say, "That's what Drusilla said." But I didn't. I said,

"I'm tending to this. You stay out of it. I don't need any help." Then his fierce eyes faded gradually, exactly as you turn a lamp down.

"Well," he said, putting the pistol back into his pocket. "You'll have to excuse me, son. I should have knowed you wouldn't do anything that would keep John from laying quiet. We'll follow you and wait at the foot of the steps. And remember: he's a brave man, and he's been sitting in that office by himself since yesterday morning waiting for you and his nerves are on edge."

"I'll remember," I said. "I don't need any help." I had started on when suddenly I said it without having any warning that I was going to: "No bloody moon."

"What?" he said. I didn't answer. I went on across the square itself now, in the hot sun, they following though not close so that I never saw them again until afterward, surrounded by the remote still eyes not following me yet either, just stopped where they were before the stores and about the door to the courthouse, waiting. I walked steadily on enclosed in the now fierce odor of the verbena sprig. Then shadow fell upon me; I did not pause, I looked once at the small faded sign nailed to the brick *B. J. Redmond, Atty at Law* and began to mount the stairs, the wooden steps scuffed by the heavy bewildered boots of countrymen approaching litigation and stained by tobacco spit, on down the dim corridor to the door which bore the name again, *B. J. Redmond* and knocked once and opened it. He sat behind the desk, not much taller than Father but thicker as a man gets who spends most of his time sitting and listening to people, freshly shaven and with fresh linen; a lawyer yet it was not a lawyer's face — a face much thinner than the body would indicate, strained (and yes, tragic; I know that now) and exhausted beneath the neat recent steady strokes of the razor, holding a pistol flat on the desk before him, loose beneath his hand and aimed at nothing. There was no smell of drink, not even of tobacco in the neat clean dingy room although I knew he smoked. I didn't pause. I walked steadily toward him. It was not twenty feet from door to desk yet I seemed to walk in a dreamlike state in which there was neither time nor distance, as though the mere act of walking was no more intended to encompass space than was his sitting. We didn't speak. It was as if we both knew what the passage of words would be and the futility of it; how he might have said, "Go out, Bayard. Go away, boy" and then, "Draw then. I will allow you to draw" and it would have been the same as if he had never said it. So we did not speak; I just walked steadily toward him as the pistol rose from the desk. I watched it, I could see the foreshortened slant of the barrel and I knew it would miss me though his hand did not tremble. I walked toward him, toward the pistol in the rocklike hand, I heard no bullet. Maybe I didn't even hear the explosion though I remember the sudden orange bloom and smoke as they appeared against his white shirt as they had appeared against Grumby's greasy Confederate coat; I still watched that foreshortened slant of barrel which I knew was not aimed at me and saw the second orange flash of smoke and heard no bullet that time either. Then I stopped; it was done then. I watched the pistol descend to the desk in short jerks; I saw him release it and sit back, both hands on the desk, I looked at his face and I knew too what it was to want air when there was nothing in the circumambience for the lungs. He rose, shoved the chair back with a convulsive motion and rose, with a queer ducking motion of his head; with his head still ducked aside and one arm extended as though he couldn't see and the other hand resting on the desk as if he couldn't stand alone, he turned and crossed to the wall and took his hat from the rack and with his head still ducked aside and one hand extended he blundered along the wall and passed me and reached the door and went through it. He was brave; no one denied that. He walked down those stairs and out onto the street where George Wyatt and the other six of Father's old troop waited and where the other men had begun to run now; he walked through the middle of them with his hat on and his head up (they told me how someone shouted at him: "Have you killed that boy too?"), saying no word, staring straight ahead and with his back to them, on to the station where the south-bound train was just in and got on it with no baggage, nothing, and went away from Jefferson and from Mississippi and never came back.

I heard their feet on the stairs then in the corridor then in the room, but for a while yet (it wasn't that long, of course) I still sat behind the desk as he had sat, the flat of the pistol still warm under my hand, my hand growing slowly numb between the pistol and my forehead. Then I raised my head; the little room was full of men. "My God!" George Wyatt cried. "You took the pistol away from him and then missed him, missed him *twice?*" Then he answered himself — that same rapport for violence which Drusilla had and which in George's case was actual character judgment: "No; wait. You walked in here without even a pocket knife and let him miss you twice. My God in heaven." He turned, shouting: "Get to hell out of here! You, White, ride out to Sartoris and tell his folks it's all over and he's all right. Ride!" So they departed, went away; presently only George was left, watching me with that pale bleak stare which was speculative yet not at all rationcinative. "Well by God," he said. " — Do you want a drink?"

"No," I said. "I'm hungry. I didn't eat any breakfast."

"I reckon not, if you got up this morning aiming to do what you did. Come on. We'll go to the Holston House."

"No," I said. "No. Not there."

"Why not? You ain't done anything to be ashamed of. I wouldn't have done it that way, myself. I'd a shot at him once, anyway. But that's your way or you wouldn't have done it."

"Yes," I said. "I would do it again."

"Be damned if I would. — You want to come home with me? We'll have time to eat and then ride out there in time for the — " But I couldn't do that either.

"No," I said. "I'm not hungry after all. I think I'll go home."

"Don't you want to wait and ride out with me?"

"No. I'll go on."

"You don't want to stay here, anyway." He looked around the room again, where the smell of powder smoke still lingered a little, still lay somewhere on the hot dead air though invisible now, blinking a little with his fierce pale unintroverted eyes. "Well by God," he said again. "Maybe you're right, maybe there has been enough killing in your family without — Come on." We left the office. I waited at the foot of the stairs and soon Ringo came up with the horses. We crossed the square again. There were no feet on the Holston House railing now (it was twelve o'clock) but a group of men stood before the door who raised their hats and I raised mine and Ringo and I rode on.

We did not go fast. Soon it was one, maybe after; the carriages and buggies would begin to leave the square soon, so I turned from the road at the end of the pasture and I sat the mare, trying to open the gate without dismounting, until Ringo dismounted and opened it. We crossed the pasture in the hard fierce sun; I could have seen the house now but I didn't look. Then we were in the shade, the close thick airless shade of the creek bottom; the old rails still lay in the undergrowth where we had built the pen to hide the Yankee mules. Presently I heard the water, then I could see the sunny glints. We dismounted. I lay on my back, I thought *Now it can begin again if it wants to*. But it did not. I went to sleep. I went to sleep almost before I had stopped thinking. I slept for almost five hours and I didn't dream anything at all yet I waked myself up crying, crying too hard to stop it. Ringo was squatting beside me and the sun was gone though there was a bird of some sort still singing somewhere and the whistle of the north-bound evening train sounded and the short broken puffs of starting where it had evidently stopped at our flag station. After a while I began to stop and Ringo brought his hat full of water from the creek but instead I went down to the water myself and bathed my face.

There was still a good deal of light in the pasture, though the whippoorwills had begun, and when we reached the house there was a mockingbird singing in the magnolia, the night song now, the drowsy moony one, and again the moon like the rim print of a heel in wet sand. There was just one light in the hall now and so it was all over though I could smell the flowers even above the verbena in my coat. I had not looked at him again. I had started to before I left the house but I did not, I did not see him again and all the pictures we had of him were bad ones because a picture could no more have held him dead than the house could have kept his body. But I didn't need to see him again because he was there, he would always be there; maybe what Drusilla meant by his dream was not something which he possessed but something which he had bequeathed us which we could never forget, which would even assume the corporeal shape of him whenever any of us, black or white, closed our eyes. I went into the house. There was no light in the drawing room except the last of the afterglow which came through the western window where Aunt Jenny's colored glass was; I was about to go on upstairs when I saw her sitting there beside the window. She didn't call me and I didn't speak Drusilla's name, I just went to the door and stood there. "She's gone," Aunt Jenny said. "She took the evening train. She has gone to Montgomery, to Dennison." Denny had been married about a year now; he was living in Montgomery, reading law.

"I see," I said. "Then she didn't — " But there wasn't any use in that either; Jed White must have got there before one o'clock and told them. And besides, Aunt Jenny didn't answer. She could have lied to me but she didn't, she said,

"Come here." I went to her chair. "Kneel down. I can't see you."

"Don't you want the lamp?"

"No. Kneel down." So I knelt beside the chair. "So you had a perfectly splendid Saturday afternoon, didn't you? Tell me about it." Then she put her hands on my shoulders. I watched them come up as though she were trying to stop them; I felt them on my shoulders as if they had a separate life of their own and were trying to do something which for my sake she was trying to restrain, prevent. Then she gave up or she was not strong enough because they came up and took my face between them, hard, and suddenly the tears sprang and streamed down her face like Drusilla's laughing had. "Oh, damn you Sartorises!" she said. "Damn you! Damn you!"

As I passed down the hall the light came up in the diningroom and I could hear Louvinia laying the table for supper. So the stairs were lighted quite well. But the upper hall was dark. I saw her open door (that unmistakable way in which an open door stands open when nobody lives in the room any more) and I realised that I had not believed that she was really gone. So I didn't look into the room. I went on to mine and entered. And then for a long moment I thought it was the verbena in my lapel which I still smelled. I thought that until I had crossed the room and looked down at the pillow on which it lay — a single sprig of it (without looking she would pinch off a half dozen of them and they would be all of a size, almost all of a shape, as if a machine had stamped them out) filling the room, the dusk, the evening with that odor which she said you could smell alone above the smell of horses.

GUSTAVE FLAUBERT

Gustave Flaubert (1821–1880) was born in Rouen, France, the son of a prominent surgeon. He studied law in Paris, but symptoms of a nervous disorder akin to epilepsy caused him to forgo any kind of active professional life. He moved back in with his mother at Croisset, periodically traveled to Paris and the Mediterranean, and began writing the novels that made his reputation. The first of these — *Madame Bovary* (1857) — was and remains the most famous. The story of Emma Bovary, bored wife of a provincial doctor, was deemed scandalous for its depiction of her adulteries and suicide; Flaubert was taken to court on charges of immorality, but was acquitted. The novel survived the uproar and has long been deemed a hallmark in the development of literary realism. Flaubert's other novels include *Salammbô* (1862), *A Sentimental Education* (1869), and *The Temptation of Saint Anthony* (1874). All display the precision of his style and the exactitude of his details. He wrote three long stories published as *Three Tales: A Simple Heart, The Legend of St. Julian the Hospitaller, and Hérodias* (1877). "A Simple Heart" reveals the calm strength of his style.

A Simple Heart

Translated from the French by Arthur McDowell

Madame Aubain's servant Félicité was the envy of the ladies of Pont-l'Évêque for half a century.

She received four pounds a year. For that she was cook and general servant, and did the sewing, washing, and ironing; she could bridle a horse, fatten poultry, and churn butter — and she remained faithful to her mistress, unamiable as the latter was.

Madame Aubain had married a gay bachelor without money who died at the beginning of 1809, leaving her with two small children and a quantity of debts. She then sold all her property except the farms of Toucques and Geffosses, which brought in two hundred pounds a year at most, and left her house in Saint-Melaine for a less expensive one that had belonged to her family and was situated behind the market.

This house had a slate roof and stood between an alley and a lane that went down to the river. There was an unevenness in the levels of the rooms which made you stumble. A narrow hall divided the kitchen from the "parlour" where Mme. Aubain spent her day, sitting in a wicker easy chair by the window. Against the panels, which were painted white, was a row of eight mahogany chairs. On an old piano under the barometer a heap of wooden and cardboard boxes rose like a pyramid. A stuffed armchair stood on either side of the Louis-Quinze chimney-piece, which was in yellow marble with a clock in the middle of it modelled like a temple of Vesta. The whole room was a little musty, as the floor was lower than the garden.

The first floor began with "Madame's" room: very large, with a pale-flowered wallpaper and a portrait of "Monsieur" as a dandy of the period. It led to a smaller room, where there were two children's cots without mattresses. Next came the drawing-room, which was always shut up and full of furniture covered with sheets. Then there was a corridor leading to a study. The shelves of a large bookcase were respectably lined with books and papers, and its three wings surrounded a broad writing-table in darkwood. The two panels at the end of the room were covered with pen-drawings, water-colour landscapes, and engravings by Audran, all relics of better days and vanished spendour. Félicité's room on the top floor got its light from a dormer-window, which looked over the meadows.

She rose at daybreak to be in time for Mass, and worked till evening without stopping. Then, when dinner was over, the plates and dishes in order, and the door shut fast, she thrust the log under the ashes and went to sleep in front of the hearth with her rosary in her hand. Félicité was the stubbornest of all bargainers; and as for cleanness, the polish on her saucepans was the despair of other servants. Thrifty in all things, she ate slowly, gathering off the table in her fingers the crumbs of her loaf — a twelve-pound loaf expressly baked for her, which lasted for three weeks.

At all times of year she wore a print handkerchief fastened with a pin behind, a bonnet that covered her hair, grey stockings, a red skirt, and a bibbed apron — such as hospital nurses wear — over her jacket.

Her face was thin and her voice sharp. At twenty-five she looked like forty. From fifty onwards she seemed of no particular age; and with her silence, straight figure, and precise movements she was like a woman made of wood, and going by clockwork.

2

She had had her love-story like another.

Her father, a mason, had been killed by falling off some scaffolding. Then her mother died, her sisters scattered, and a farmer took her in and employed her, while she was still quite little, to herd the cows at pasture. She shivered in rags and would lie flat on the ground to drink water from the ponds; she was beaten for nothing, and finally turned out for the theft of a shilling which she did not steal. She went to another farm, where she became dairy-maid; and as she was liked by her employers her companions were jealous of her.

One evening in August (she was then eighteen) they took her to the assembly at Colleville. She was dazed and stupefied in an instant by the noise of the fiddlers, the lights in the trees, the gay medley of dresses, the lace, the gold crosses, and the throng of people jigging all together. While she kept shyly apart a young man with a well-to-do air, who was leaning on the shaft of a cart and smoking his pipe, came up to ask her to dance. He treated her to cider, coffee, and cake, and bought her a silk handkerchief; and then, imagining she had guessed his meaning, offered to see her home. At the edge of a field of oats he pushed her roughly down. She was frightened and began to cry out; and he went off.

One evening later she was on the Beaumont road. A big hay-wagon was moving slowly along; she wanted to get in front of it, and as she brushed past the wheels she recognized Theodore. He greeted her quite calmly, saying she must excuse it all because it was "the fault of the drink." She could not think of any answer and wanted to run away.

He began at once to talk about the harvest and the worthies of the commune, for his father had left Colleville for the farm at Les Écots, so that now he and she were neighbours. "Ah!" she said. He added that they thought of settling him in life. Well, he was in no hurry; he was waiting for a wife to his fancy. She dropped her head; and then he asked her if she thought of marrying. She answered with a smile that it was mean to make fun of her.

"But I am not, I swear!" — and he passed his left hand round her waist. She walked in the support of his embrace; their steps grew slower. The wind was soft, the stars glittered, the huge wagon-load of hay swayed in front of them, and dust rose from the dragging steps of the four horses. Then, without a word of command, they turned to the right. He clasped her once more in his arms, and she disappeared into the shadow.

The week after Theodore secured some assignations with her.

They met at the end of farmyards, behind a wall, or under a solitary tree. She was not innocent as young ladies are — she had learned knowledge from the animals — but her reason and the instinct of her honour would not let her fall. Her resistance exasperated Theodore's passion; so much so that to satisfy it — or perhaps quite artlessly — he made her an offer of marriage. She was in doubt whether to trust him, but he swore great oaths of fidelity.

Soon he confessed to something troublesome; the year before his parents had bought him a substitute for the army, but any day he might be taken again, and the idea of serving was a terror to him. Félicité took this cowardice of his as a sign of affection, and it redoubled hers. She stole away at night to see him, and when she reached their meeting-place Theodore racked her with his anxieties and urgings.

At last he declared that he would go himself to the prefecture for information, and would tell her the result on the following Sunday, between eleven and midnight.

When the moment came she sped towards her lover. Instead of him she found one of his friends.

He told her that she would not see Theodore any more. To ensure himself against conscription he had married an old woman, Madame Lehoussais, of Toucques, who was very rich.

There was an uncontrollable burst of grief. She threw herself on the ground, screamed, called to the God of mercy, and moaned by herself in the fields till daylight came. Then she came back to the farm and announced that she was going to leave; and at the end of the month she received her wages, tied all her small belongings with a handkerchief, and went to Pont-l'Évêque.

In front of the inn there she made inquiries of a woman in a widow's cap, who, as it happened, was just looking for a cook. The girl did not know much, but her willingness seemed so great and her demands so small that Mme. Aubain ended by saying:

"Very well, then, I will take you."

A quarter of an hour afterwards Félicité was installed in her house.

She lived there at first in a tremble, as it were, at "the style of the house" and the memory of "Monsieur" floating over it all. Paul and Virginie, the first aged seven and the other hardly four, seemed to her beings of a precious substance; she carried them on her back like a horse; it was a sorrow to her that Mme. Aubain would not let her kiss them every minute. And yet she was happy there. Her grief had melted in the pleasantness of things all round.

Every Thursday regular visitors came in for a game of boston, and Félicité got the cards and foot-warmers ready beforehand. They arrived punctually at eight and left before the stroke of eleven.

On Monday mornings the dealer who lodged in the covered passage spread out all his old iron on the ground. Then a hum of voices began to fill the town, mingled with the neighing of horses, bleating of lambs, grunting of pigs, and the sharp rattle of carts along the street. About noon, when the market was at its height, you might see a tall, hook-nosed old countryman with his cap pushed back making his appearance at the door. It was Robelin, the farmer of Geffosses. A little later came Liébard, the farmer from Toucques — short, red, and corpulent — in a grey jacket and gaiters shod with spurs.

Both had poultry or cheese to offer their landlord. Félicité was invariably a match for their cunning, and they went away filled with respect for her.

At vague intervals Mme. Aubain had a visit from the Marquis de Gremanville, one of her uncles, who had ruined himself by debauchery and now lived at Falaise on his last remaining morsel of land. He invariably came at the luncheon hour, with a dreadful poodle whose paws left all the furniture in a mess. In spite of efforts to show his breeding, which he carried to the point of raising his hat every time he mentioned "my late father," habit was too strong for him; he poured himself out glass after glass and fired off improper remarks. Félicité edged him politely out of the house — "You have had enough, Monsieur de Gremanville! Another time!" — and she shut the door on him.

She opened it with pleasure to M. Bourais, who had been a lawyer. His baldness, his white stock, frilled shirt, and roomy brown coat, his way of rounding the arm as he took snuff — his whole person, in fact, created that disturbance of mind which overtakes us at the sight of extraordinary men.

As he looked after the property of "Madame" he remained shut up with her for hours in "Monsieur's" study, though all the time he was afraid of compromising himself. He respected the magistracy immensely, and had some pretensions to Latin.

To combine instruction and amusement he gave the children a geography book made up of a series of prints. They represented scenes in different parts of the world: cannibals with feathers on their heads, a monkey carrying off a young lady, Bedouins in the desert, the harpooning of a whale, and so on. Paul explained these engravings to Félicité; and that, in fact, was the whole of her literary education. The children's education was undertaken by Guyot, a poor creature employed at the town hall, who was famous for his beautiful hand and sharpened his penknife on his boots.

When the weather was bright the household set off early for a day at Geffosses Farm.

Its courtyard is on a slope, with the farmhouse in the middle, and the sea looks like a grey streak in the distance.

Félicité brought slices of cold meat out of her basket, and they breakfasted in a room adjoining the dairy. It was the only surviving fragment of a country house which was now no more. The wall-paper hung in tatters, and quivered in the draughts. Mme. Aubain sat with bowed head, overcome by her memories; the children became afraid to speak. "Why don't you play, then?" she would say, and off they went.

Paul climbed into the barn, caught birds, played at ducks and drakes over the pond, or hammered with his stick on the big casks which boomed like drums. Virginie fed the rabbits or dashed off to pick cornflowers, her quick legs showing their embroidered little drawers.

One autumn evening they went home by the fields. The moon was in its first quarter, lighting part of the sky; and mist floated like a scarf over the windings of the Toucques. Cattle, lying out in the middle of the grass, looked quietly at the four people as they passed. In the third meadow some of them got up and made a half-circle in front of the walkers. "There's nothing to be afraid of," said Félicité, as she stroked the nearest on the back with a kind of crooning song; he wheeled round and the others did the same. But when they crossed the next pasture there was a formidable bellow. It was a bull, hidden by the mist. Mme. Aubain was about to run. "No! no! don't go so fast!" They mended their pace, however, and heard a loud breathing behind them which came nearer. His hoofs thudded on the meadow grass like hammers; why, he was galloping now! Félicité turned round, and tore up clods of earth with both hands and threw them in his eyes. He lowered his muzzle, waved his horns, and quivered with fury, bellowing terribly. Mme. Aubain, now at the end of the pasture with her two little ones, was looking wildly for a place to get over the high bank. Félicité was retreating, still with her face to the bull, keeping up a shower of clods which blinded him, and crying all the time, "Be quick! be quick!"

Mme. Aubain went down into the ditch, pushed Virginie first and then Paul, fell several times as she tried to climb the bank, and managed it at last by dint of courage.

The bull had driven Félicité to bay against a rail-fence; his slaver was streaming into her face; another second, and he would have gored her. She had just time to slip between two of the rails, and the big animal stopped short in amazement.

This adventure was talked of at Pont-l'Évêque for many a year. Félicité did not pride herself on it in the least, not having the barest suspicion that she had done anything heroic.

Virginie was the sole object of her thoughts, for the child developed a nervous complaint as a result of her fright, and M. Poupart, the doctor, advised sea-bathing at Trouville. It was not a frequented place then. Mme. Aubain collected information, consulted Bourais, and made preparations as though for a long journey.

Her luggage started a day in advance, in Liébard's cart. The next day he brought round two horses, one of which had a lady's saddle with a velvet back to it, while a cloak was rolled up to make a kind of seat on the crupper of the other. Mme. Aubain rode on that, behind the farmer. Félicité took charge of Virginie, and Paul mounted M. Lechaptois' donkey, lent on condition that great care was taken of it.

The road was so bad that its five miles took two hours. The horses sank in the mud up to their pasterns, and their haunches jerked abruptly in the effort to get out; or else they stumbled in the ruts, and at other moments had to jump. In some places Liébard's mare came suddenly to a halt. He waited patiently until she went on again, talking about the people who had properties along the road, and adding moral reflections to their history. So it was that as they were in the middle of Toucques, and passed under some windows bowered with nasturtiums, he shrugged his shoulders and said: "There's a Mme. Lehoussais lives there; instead of taking a young man she ..." Félicité did not hear the rest; the horses were trotting and the donkey galloping. They all turned down a bypath; a gate swung open and two boys appeared; and the party dismounted in front of a manure-heap at the very threshold of the farmhouse door.

When Mme. Liébard saw her mistress she gave lavish signs of joy. She served her a luncheon with a sirloin of beef, tripe, black-pudding, a fricassee of chicken, sparkling cider, a fruit tart, and brandied plums; seasoning it all with compliments to Madame, who seemed in better health; Mademoiselle, who was "splendid' now; and Monsieur Paul, who had "filled out" wonderfully. Nor did she forget their deceased grandparents, whom the Liébards had known, as they had been in the service of the family for several generations. The farm, like them, had the stamp of antiquity. The beams on the ceiling were worm-eaten, the walls blackened with smoke, and the window-panes grey with dust. There was an oak dresser laden with every sort of useful article — jugs, plates, pewter bowls, wolf-traps, and sheep-shears; and a huge syringe made the children laugh. There was not a tree in the three courtyards without mushrooms growing at the bottom of it or a tuft of mistletoe on its boughs. Several of them had been thrown down by the wind. They had taken root again at the middle; and all were bending under their wealth of apples. The thatched roofs, like brown velvet and of varying thickness, withstood the heaviest squalls. The cart-shed, however, was falling into ruin. Mme. Aubain said she would see about it, and ordered the animals to be saddled again.

It was another half-hour before they reached Trouville. The little caravan dismounted to pass Écores — it was an overhanging cliff with boats below it — and three minutes later they were at the end of the quay and entered the courtyard of the Golden Lamb, kept by good Mme. David.

From the first days of their stay Virginie began to feel less weak, thanks to the change of air and the effect of the sea-baths. These, for want of a bathing-dress, she took in her chemise; and her nurse dressed her afterwards in a coastguard's cabin which was used by the bathers.

In the afternoons they took the donkey and went off beyond the Black Rocks, in the direction of Hennequeville. The path climbed at first through ground with dells in it like the green sward of a park, and then reached a plateau where grass fields and arable lay side by side. Hollies rose stiffly out of the briary tangle at the edge of the road; and here and there a great withered tree made zigzags in the blue air with its branches.

They nearly always rested in a meadow, with Deauville on their left, Havre on their right, and the open sea in front. It glittered in the sunshine, smooth as a mirror and so quiet that its murmur was scarcely to be heard; sparrows chirped in hiding and the immense sky arched over it all. Mme. Aubain sat doing her needlework; Virginie plaited rushes by her side; Félicité pulled up lavender, and Paul was bored and anxious to start home.

Other days they crossed the Toucques in a boat and looked for shells. When the tide went out sea-urchins, starfish, and jelly-fish were left exposed; and the children ran in pursuit of the foam-flakes which scudded in the wind. The sleepy waves broke on the sand and unrolled all along the beach; it stretched away out of sight, bounded on the land-side by the dunes which parted it from the Marsh, a wide meadow shaped like an arena. As they came home that way, Trouville, on the hill-slope in the background, grew bigger at every step, and its miscellaneous throng of houses seemed to break into a gay disorder.

On days when it was too hot they did not leave their room. From the dazzling brilliance outside light fell in streaks between the laths of the blinds. There were no sounds in the village; and on the pavement below not a soul. This silence round them deepened the quietness of things. In the distance, where men were caulking, there was a tap of hammers as they plugged the hulls, and a sluggish breeze wafted up the smell of tar.

The chief amusement was the return of the fishing-boats. They began to tack as soon as they had passed the buoys. The sails came down on two of the three masts; and they drew on with the foresail swelling like a balloon, glided through the splash of the waves, and when they had reached the middle of the harbour suddenly dropped anchor. Then the boats drew up against the quay. The sailors threw quivering fish over the side; a row of carts was waiting, and women in cotton bonnets darted out to take the baskets and give their men a kiss.

One of them came up to Félicité one day, and she entered the lodgings a little later in a state of delight. She had found a sister again — and then Nastasie Barette, "wife of Leroux," appeared, holding an infant at her breast and another child with her right hand, while on her left was a little cabin boy with his hands on his hips and a cap over his ear.

After a quarter of an hour Mme. Aubain sent them off; but they were always to be found hanging about the kitchen, or encountered in the course of a walk. The husband never appeared.

Félicité was seized with affection for them. She bought them a blanket, some shirts, and a stove; it was clear that they were making a good thing out of her. Mme. Aubain was annoyed by this weakness of hers, and she did not like the liberties taken by the nephew, who said "thee" and "thou" to Paul. So as Virginie was coughing and the fine weather was gone, she returned to Pont-l'Évêque.

There M. Bourais enlightened her on the choice of a boys' school. The one at Caen was reputed to be the best, and Paul was sent to it. He said his good-byes bravely, content enough at going to live in a house where he would have companions. Mme. Aubain resigned herself to her son's absence as a thing that had to be. Virginie thought about it less and less. Félicité missed the noise he made. But she found an occupation to distract her; from Christmas onward she took the little girl to catechism every day.

3

After making a genuflexion at the door she walked up between the double row of chairs under the lofty nave, opened Mme. Aubain's pew, sat down, and began to look about her. The choir stalls were filled with the boys on the right and the girls on the left, and the curé stood by the lectern. On a painted window in the apse the Holy Ghost looked down upon the Virgin. Another window showed her on her knees before the child Jesus, and a group carved in wood behind the altar-shrine represented St. Michael overthrowing the dragon.

The priest began with a sketch of sacred history. The Garden, the Flood, the Tower of Babel, cities in flames, dying nations, and overturned idols passed like a dream before her eyes; and the dizzying vision left her with reverence for the Most High and fear of His wrath. Then she wept at the story of the Passion. Why had they crucified Him, when He loved the children, fed the multitudes, healed the blind, and had willed, in His meekness, to be born among the poor, on the dung-heap of a stable? The sowings, harvests, wine-presses, all the familiar things the Gospel speaks of, were a part of her life. They had been made holy by God's passing; and she loved the lambs more tenderly for her love of the Lamb, and the doves because of the Holy Ghost.

She found it hard to imagine Him in person, for He was not merely a bird, but a flame as well, and a breath at other times. It may be His light, she thought, which flits at night about the edge of the marshes, His breathing which drives on the clouds, His voice which gives harmony to the bells; and she would sit rapt in adoration, enjoying the cool walls and the quiet of the church.

Of doctrines, she understood nothing — did not even try to understand. The curé discoursed, the children repeated their lesson, and finally she went to sleep, waking up with a start when their wooden shoes clattered on the flagstones as they went away.

It was thus that Félicité, whose religious education had been neglected in her youth, learned the catechism by dint of hearing it; and from that time she copied all Virginie's observances, fasting as she did and confessing with her. On Corpus Christi Day they made a festal altar together.

The first communion loomed distractingly ahead. She fussed over the shoes, the rosary, the book and gloves; and how she trembled as she helped Virginie's mother to dress her!

All through the mass she was racked with anxiety. She could not see one side of the choir because of M. Bourais; but straight in front of her was the flock of maidens, with white crowns above their hanging veils, making the impression of a field of snow; and she knew her dear child at a distance by her dainty neck and thoughtful air. The bell tinkled. The heads bowed, and there was silence. As the organ pealed, singers and congregation took up the "Agnus Dei"; then the procession of the boys began, and after them the girls rose. Step by step, with their hands joined in prayer, they went towards the lighted altar, knelt on the first step, received the sacrament in turn, and came back in the same order to their places. When Virginie's turn came Félicité leaned forward to see her; and with the imaginativeness of deep and tender feeling it seemed to her that she actually was the child; Virginie's face became hers, she was dressed in her clothes, it was her heart beating in her breast. As the moment came to open her mouth she closed her eyes and nearly fainted.

She appeared early in the sacristy next morning for Monsieur the curé to give her the communion. She took it with devotion, but it did not give her the same exquisite delight.

Mme. Aubain wanted to make her daughter into an accomplished person; and as Guyot could not teach her music or English she decided to place her in the Ursuline Convent at Honfleur as a boarder. The child made no objection. Félicité sighed and thought that Madame lacked feeling. Then she reflected that her mistress might be right; matters of this kind were beyond her.

So one day an old spring-van drew up at the door, and out of it stepped a nun to fetch the young lady. Félicité hoisted the luggage on to the top, admonished the driver, and put six pots of preserves, a dozen pears, and a bunch of violets under the seat.

At the last moment Virginie broke into a fit of sobbing; she threw her arms round her mother, who kissed her on the forehead, saying over and over "Come, be brave! be brave!" The step was raised, and the carriage drove off.

Then Mme. Aubain's strength gave way; and in the evening all her friends — the Lormeau family, Mme. Lechaptois, the Rochefeuille ladies, M. de Houppeville, and Bourais — came in to console her.

To be without her daughter was very painful for her at first. But she heard from Virginie three times a week, wrote to her on the other days, walked in the garden, and so filled up the empty hours.

From sheer habit Félicité went into Virginie's room in the mornings and gazed at the walls. It was boredom to her not to have to comb the child's hair now, lace up her boots, tuck her into bed — and not to see her charming face perpetually and hold her hand when they went out together. In this idle condition she tried making lace. But her fingers were too heavy and broke the threads; she could not attend to anything, she had lost her sleep, and was, in her own words, "destroyed."

To "divert herself" she asked leave to have visits from her nephew Victor.

He arrived on Sundays after mass, rosy-cheeked, bare-chested, with the scent of the country he had walked through still about him. She laid her table promptly and they had lunch, sitting opposite each other. She ate as little as possible herself to save expense, but stuffed him with food so generously that at last he went to sleep. At the first stroke of vespers she woke him up, brushed his trousers, fastened his tie, and went to church, leaning on his arm with maternal pride.

Victor was always instructed by his parents to get something out of her — a packet of moist sugar, it might be, a cake of soap, spirits, or even money at times. He brought his things for her to mend and she took over the task, only too glad to have a reason for making him come back.

In August his father took him off on a coasting voyage. It was holiday time, and she was consoled by the arrival of the children. Paul, however, was getting selfish, and Virginie was too old to be called "thou" any longer; this put a constraint and barrier between them.

Victor went to Morlaix, Dunkirk, and Brighton in succession and made Félicité a present on his return from each voyage. It was a box made of shells the first time, a coffee cup the next, and on the third occasion a large gingerbread man. Victor was growing handsome. He was well made, had a hint of a moustache, good honest eyes, and a small leather hat pushed backwards like a pilot's. He entertained her by telling stories embroidered with nautical terms.

On a Monday, July 14, 1819 (she never forgot the date), he told her that he had signed on for the big voyage and next night but one he would take the Honfleur boat and join his schooner, which was to weigh anchor from Havre before long. Perhaps he would be gone two years.

The prospect of this long absence threw Félicité into deep distress; one more good-bye she must have, and on the Wednesday evening, when Madame's dinner was finished, she put on her clogs and made short work of the twelve miles between Pont-l'Évêque and Honfleur.

When she arrived in front of the Calvary she took the turn to the right instead of the left, got lost in the timber-yards, and retraced her steps; some people to whom she spoke advised her to be quick. She went all round the harbour basin, full of ships, and knocked against hawsers; then the ground fell away, lights flashed across each other, and she thought her wits had left her, for she saw horses up in the sky.

Others were neighing by the quay-side, frightened at the sea. They were lifted by a tackle and deposited in a boat, where passengers jostled each other among cider casks, cheese baskets, and sacks of grain; fowls could be heard clucking, the captain swore; and a cabin-boy stood leaning over the bows, indifferent to it all. Félicité, who had not recognized him, called "Victor!" and he raised his head; all at once, as she was darting forwards, the gangway was drawn back.

The Honfleur packet, women singing as they hauled it, passed out of harbour. Its framework creaked and the heavy waves whipped its bows. The canvas had swung round, no one could be seen on board now; and on the moon-silvered sea the boat made a black speck which paled gradually, dipped, and vanished.

As Félicité passed by the Calvary she had a wish to commend to God what she cherished most, and she stood there praying a long time with her face bathed in tears and her eyes towards the clouds. The town was asleep, coastguards were walking to and fro; and water poured without cessation through the holes in the sluice, with the noise of a torrent. The clocks struck two.

The convent parlour would not be open before day. If Félicité were late Madame would most certainly be annoyed; and in spite of her desire to kiss the other child she turned home. The maids at the inn were waking up as she came in to Pont-l'Évêque.

So the poor slip of a boy was going to toss for months and months at sea! She had not been frightened by his previous voyages. From England or Brittany you came back safe enough; but America, the colonies, the islands — these were lost in a dim region at the other end of the world.

Félicité's thoughts from that moment ran entirely on her nephew. On sunny days she was harassed by the idea of thirst; when there was a storm she was afraid of the lightning on his account. As she listened to the wind growling in the chimney or carrying off the slates she pictured him lashed by that same tempest, at the top of a shattered mast, with his body thrown backwards under a sheet of foam; or else (with a reminiscence of the illustrated geography) he was being eaten by savages, captured in a wood by monkeys, or dying on a desert shore. And never did she mention her anxieties.

Mme. Aubain had anxieties of her own, about her daughter. The good sisters found her an affectionate but delicate child. The slightest emotion unnerved her. She had to give up the piano.

Her mother stipulated for regular letters from the convent. She lost patience one morning when the postman did not come, and walked to and fro in the parlor from her armchair to the window. It was really amazing; not a word for four days!

To console Mme. Aubain by her own example Félicité remarked:

"As for me, Madame, it's six months since I heard . . ."

"From whom, pray?"

"Why . . . from my nephew," the servant answered gently.

"Oh! your nephew!" And Mme. Aubain resumed her walk with a shrug of the shoulders, as much as to say: "I was not thinking of him! And what is more, it's absurd! A scamp of a cabin-boy — what does he matter? . . . whereas my daughter . . . why, just think!"

Félicité, though she had been brought up on harshness, felt indignant with Madame — and then forgot. It seemed the simplest thing in the world to her to lose one's head over the little girl. For her the two children were equally important; a bond in her heart made them one, and their destinies must be the same.

She heard from the chemist that Victor's ship had arrived in Havana. He had read this piece of news in a gazette.

Cigars — they made her imagine Havana as a place where no one does anything but smoke, and there was Victor moving among the negroes in a cloud of tobacco. Could you, she wondered, "in case you needed," return by land? What was the distance from Pont-l'Évêque? She questioned M. Bourais to find out.

He reached for his atlas and began explaining the longitudes; Félicité's consternation provoked a fine pedantic smile. Finally he marked with his pencil a black, imperceptible point in the indentations of an oval spot, and said as he did so, "Here it is." She bent over the map; the maze of coloured lines wearied her eyes without conveying anything; and on an invitation from Bourais to tell him her difficulty, she begged him to show her the house where Victor was living. Bourais threw up his arms, sneezed, and laughed immensely: a simplicity like hers was a positive joy. And Félicité did not understand the reason; how could she when she expected, very likely, to see the actual image of her nephew — so stunted was her mind!

A fortnight afterwards Liébard came into the kitchen at market-time as usual and handed her a letter from her brother-in-law. As neither of them could read she took it to her mistress.

Mme. Aubain, who was counting the stitches in her knitting, put the work down by her side, broke the seal of the letter, started, and said in a low voice, with a look of meaning:

"It is bad news ... that they have to tell you. Your nephew ..."

He was dead. The letter said no more.

Félicité fell on to a chair, leaning her head against the wainscot; and she closed her eyelids, which suddenly flushed pink. Then with bent forehead, hands hanging, and fixed eyes, she said at intervals:

"Poor little lad! poor little lad!"

Liébard watched her and heaved sighs. Mme. Aubain trembled a little.

She suggested that Félicité should go to see her sister at Trouville. Félicité answered by a gesture that she had no need.

There was a silence. The worthy Liébard thought it was time for them to withdraw. Then Félicité said:

"They don't care, not they!"

Her head dropped again; and she took up mechanically, from time to time, the long needles on her work-table.

Women passed in the yard with a barrow of dripping linen.

As she saw them through the window-panes she remembered her washing; she had put it to soak the day before, to-day she must wring it out; and she left the room.

Her plank and tub were at the edge of the Toucques. She threw a pile of linen on the bank, rolled up her sleeves, and taking her wooden beater dealt lusty blows whose sound carried to the neighbouring gardens. The meadows were empty, the river stirred in the wind; and down below long grasses wavered, like the hair of corpses floating in the water. She kept her grief down and was very brave until the evening; but once in her room she surrendered to it utterly, lying stretched on the mattress with her face in the pillow and her hands clenched against her temples.

Much later she heard, from the captain himself, the circumstances of Victor's end. They had bled him too much at the hospital for yellow fever. Four doctors held him at once. He had died instantly, and the chief had said:

"Bah! there goes another!"

His parents had always been brutal to him. She preferred not to see them again; and they made no advances, either because they forgot her or from the callousness of the wretchedly poor.

Virginie began to grow weaker.

Tightness in her chest, coughing, continual fever, and veinings on her cheek-bones betrayed some deep-seated complaint. M. Poupart had advised a stay in Provence. Mme. Aubain determined on it, and would have brought her daughter home at once but for the climate of Pont-l'Évêque.

She made an arrangement with a job-master, and he drove her to the convent every Tuesday. There is a terrace in the garden, with a view over the Seine. Virginie took walks there over the fallen vine-leaves, on her mother's arm. A shaft of sunlight through the clouds made her blink sometimes, as she gazed at the sails in the distance and the whole horizon from the castle of Tancarville to the lighthouses at Havre. Afterwards they rested in the arbour. Her mother had secured a little cask of excellent Malaga; and Virginie, laughing at the idea of getting tipsy, drank a thimble-full of it, no more.

Her strength came back visibly. The autumn glided gently away. Félicité reassured Mme. Aubain. But one evening, when she had been out on a commission in the neighbourhood, she found M. Poupart's gig at the door. He was in the hall, and Mme. Aubain was tying her bonnet.

"Give me my foot-warmer, purse, gloves! Quicker, come!"

Virginie had inflammation of the lungs; perhaps it was hopeless.

"Not yet!" said the doctor, and they both got into the carriage under whirling flakes of snow. Night was coming on and it was very cold.

Félicité rushed into the church to light a taper. Then she ran after the gig, came up with it in an hour, and jumped lightly in behind. As she hung on by the fringes a thought came into her mind: "The courtyard had not been shut up; supposing burglars got in!" And she jumped down.

At dawn next day she presented herself at the doctor's. He had come in and started for the country again. Then she waited in the inn, thinking that a letter would come by some hand or other. Finally, when it was twilight, she took the Lisieux coach.

The convent was at the end of a steep lane. When she was about half-way up it she heard strange sounds — a death-bell tolling. "It is for someone else," thought Félicité, and she pulled the knocker violently.

After some minutes there was a sound of trailing slippers, the door opened ajar, and a nun appeared.

The good sister, with an air of compunction, said that "she had just passed away." On the instant the bell of St. Leonard's tolled twice as fast.

Félicité went up to the second floor.

From the doorway she saw Virginie stretched on her back, with her hands joined, her mouth open, and head thrown back under a black crucifix that leaned towards her, between curtains that hung stiffly, less pale than was her face. Mme. Aubain, at the foot of the bed which she clasped with her arms, was choking with sobs of agony. The mother superior stood on the right. Three candlesticks on the chest of drawers made spots of red, and the mist came whitely through the windows. Nuns came and took Mme. Aubain away.

For two nights Félicité never left the dead child. She repeated the same prayers, sprinkled holy water over the sheets, came and sat down again, and watched her. At the end of the first vigil she noticed that the face had grown yellow, the lips turned blue, the nose was sharper, and the eyes sunk in. She kissed them several times, and would not have been immensely surprised if Virginie had opened them again; to minds like hers the supernatural is quite simple. She made the girl's toilette, wrapped her in her shroud, lifted her down into her bier, put a garland on her head, and spread out her hair. It was fair, and extraordinarily long for her age. Félicité cut off a big lock and slipped half of it into her bosom, determined that she should never part with it.

The body was brought back to Pont-l'Évêque, as Mme. Aubain intended; she followed the hearse in a closed carriage.

It took another three-quarters of an hour after the mass to reach the cemetery. Paul walked in front, sobbing. M. Bourais was behind, and then came the chief residents, the women shrouded in black mantles, and Félicité. She thought of her nephew; and because she had not been able to pay these honours to him her grief was doubled, as though the one were being buried with the other.

Mme. Aubain's despair was boundless. It was against God that she first rebelled, thinking it unjust of Him to have taken her daughter from her — she had never done evil and her conscience was so clear! Ah, no! — she ought to have taken Virginie off to the south. Other doctors would have saved her. She accused herself now, wanted to join her child, and broke into cries of distress in the middle of her dreams. One dream haunted her above all. Her husband, dressed as a sailor, was returning from a long voyage, and shedding tears he told her that he had been ordered to take Virginie away. Then they consulted how to hide her somewhere.

She came in once from the garden quite upset. A moment ago — and she pointed out the place — the father and daughter had appeared to her, standing side by side, and they did nothing, but they looked at her.

For several months after this she stayed inertly in her room. Félicité lectured her gently; she must live for her son's sake, and for the other, in remembrance of "her."

"Her?" answered Mme. Aubain, as though she were just waking up. "Ah, yes! . . . yes! . . . You do not forget her!" This was an allusion to the cemetery, where she was strictly forbidden to go.

Félicité went there every day.

Precisely at four she skirted the houses, climbed the hill, opened the gate, and came to Virginie's grave. It was a little column of pink marble with a stone underneath and a garden plot enclosed by chains. The beds were hidden under a coverlet of flowers. She watered their leaves, freshened the gravel, and knelt down to break up the earth better. When Mme. Aubain was able to come there she felt a relief and a sort of consolation.

Then years slipped away, one after another, and their only episodes were the great festivals as they recurred — Easter, the Assumption, All Saints' Day. Household occurrences marked dates that were referred to afterwards. In 1825, for instance, two glaziers whitewashed the hall; in 1827 a piece of the roof fell into the courtyard and nearly killed a man. In the summer of 1828 it was Madame's turn to offer the consecrated bread; Bourais, about this time, mysteriously absented himself; and one by one the old acquaintances passed away: Guyot, Liébard, Mme. Lechaptois, Robelin, and Uncle Gremanville, who had been paralysed for a long time.

One night the driver of the mail-coach announced the Revolution of July in Pont-l'Évêque. A new sub-prefect was appointed a few days later — Baron de Larsonnière, who had been consul in America, and brought with him, besides his wife, a sister-in-law and three young ladies, already growing up. They were to be seen about on their lawn, in loose blouses, and they had a negro and a parrot. They paid a call on Mme. Aubain which she did not fail to return. The moment they were seen in the distance Félicité ran to let her mistress know. But only one thing could really move her feelings — the letters from her son.

He was swallowed up in a tavern life and could follow no career. She paid his debts, he made new ones; and the sighs that Mme. Aubain uttered as she sat knitting by the window reached Félicité at her spinning-wheel in the kitchen.

They took walks together along the espaliered wall, always talking of Virginie and wondering if such and such a thing would have pleased her and what, on some occasion, she would have been likely to say.

All her small belongings filled a cupboard in the two-bedded room. Mme. Aubain inspected them as seldom as she could. One summer day she made up her mind to it — and some moths flew out of the wardrobe.

Virginie's dresses were in a row underneath a shelf, on which there were three dolls, some hoops, a set of toy pots and pans, and the basin that she used. They took out her petticoats as well, and the stockings and handkerchiefs, and laid them out on the two beds before folding them up again. The sunshine lit up these poor things, bringing out their stains and the creases made by the body's movements. The air was warm and blue, a blackbird warbled, life seemed bathed in a deep sweetness. They found a little plush hat with thick, chestnut-coloured pile; but it was eaten all over by moths. Félicité begged it for her own. Their eyes met fixedly and filled with tears; at last the mistress opened her arms, the servant threw herself into them, and they embraced each other, satisfying their grief in a kiss that made them equal.

It was the first time in their lives, Mme. Aubain's nature not being expansive. Félicité was as grateful as though she had received a favour, and cherished her mistress from that moment with the devotion of an animal and a religious worship.

The kindness of her heart unfolded.

When she heard the drums of a marching regiment in the street she posted herself at the door with a pitcher of cider and asked the soldiers to drink. She nursed cholera patients and protected the Polish refugees; one of these even declared that he wished to marry her. They quarrelled, however; for when she came back from the Angelus one morning she found that he had got into her kitchen and made himself a vinegar salad which he was quietly eating.

After the Poles came Father Colmiche, an old man who was supposed to have committed atrocities in '93. He lived by the side of the river in the ruins of a pigsty. The little boys watched him through the cracks in the wall, and threw pebbles at him which fell on the pallet where he lay constantly shaken by a catarrh; his hair was very long, his eyes inflamed, and there was a tumour on his arm bigger than his head. She got him some linen and tried to clean up his miserable hole; her dream was to establish him in the bakehouse, without letting him annoy Madame. When the tumour burst she dressed it every day; sometimes she brought him cake, and would put him in the sunshine on a truss of straw. The poor old man, slobbering and trembling, thanked her in his worn-out voice, was terrified that he might lose her, and stretched out his hands when he saw her go away. He died; and she had a mass said for the repose of his soul.

That very day a great happiness befell her; just at dinner-time appeared Mme. de Larsonnière's negro, carrying the parrot in its cage, with perch, chain, and padlock. A note from the baroness informed Mme. Aubain that her husband had been raised to a prefecture and they were starting that evening; she begged her to accept the bird as a memento and mark of her regard.

For a long time he had absorbed Félicité's imagination, because he came from America; and that name reminded her of Victor, so much so that she made inquiries of the negro. She had once gone so far as to say, "How Madame would enjoy having him!"

The negro repeated the remark to his mistress; and as she could not take the bird away with her she chose this way of getting rid of him.

4

His name was Loulou. His body was green and the tips of his wings rose-pink; his forehead was blue and his throat golden.

But he had the tiresome habits of biting his perch, tearing out his feathers, sprinkling his dirt about, and spattering the water of his tub. He annoyed Mme. Aubain, and she gave him to Félicité for good.

She endeavoured to train him; soon he could repeat "Nice boy! Your servant, sir! Good morning, Marie!" He was placed by the side of the door, and astonished several people by not answering to the name Jacquot, for all parrots are called Jacquot. People compared him to a turkey and a log of wood, and stabbed Félicité to the heart each time. Strange obstinacy on Loulou's part! — directly you looked at him he refused to speak.

None the less he was eager for society; for on Sundays, while the Rochefeuille ladies, M. de Houppeville, and new familiars — Onfroy the apothecary, Monsieur Varin, and Captain Mathieu — were playing their game of cards, he beat the windows with his wings and threw himself about so frantically that they could not hear each other speak.

Bourais' face, undoubtedly, struck him as extremely droll. Directly he saw it he began to laugh — and laugh with all his might. His peals rang through the courtyard and were repeated by the echo; the neighbours came to their windows and laughed too; while M. Bourais, gliding along under the wall to escape the parrot's eye, and hiding his profile with his hat, got to the river and then entered by the garden gate. There was a lack of tenderness in the looks which he darted at the bird.

Loulou had been slapped by the butcher-boy for making so free as to plunge his head into the basket; and since then he was always trying to nip him through his shirt. Fabu threatened to wring his neck, although he was not cruel, for all his tattooed arms and large whiskers. Far from it; he really rather liked the parrot, and in a jovial humour even wanted to teach him to swear. Félicité, who was alarmed by such proceedings, put the bird in the kitchen. His little chain was taken off and he roamed about the house.

His way of going downstairs was to lean on each step with the curve of his beak, raise the right foot, and then the left; and Félicité was afraid that these gymnastics brought on fits of giddiness. He fell ill and could not talk or eat any longer. There was a growth under his tongue, such as fowls have sometimes. She cured him by tearing the pellicle off with her fingernails. Mr. Paul was thoughtless enough one day to blow some cigar smoke into his nostrils, and another time when Mme. Lormeau was teasing him with the end of her umbrella he snapped at the ferrule. Finally he got lost.

Félicité had put him on the grass to refresh him, and gone away for a minute, and when she came back — no sign of the parrot! She began by looking for him in the shrubs, by the waterside, and over the roofs, without listening to her mistress's cries of "Take care, do! You are out of your wits!" Then she investigated all the gardens in Pont-l'Évêque, and stopped the passers-by. "You don't ever happen to have seen my parrot, by any chance, do you?" And she gave a description of the parrot to those who did not know him. Suddenly, behind the mills at the foot of the hill she thought she could make out something green that fluttered. But on the top of the hill there was nothing. A hawker assured her that he had come across the parrot just before, at Saint-Melaine, in Mère Simon's shop. She rushed there; they had no idea of what she meant. At last she came home exhausted, with her slippers in shreds and despair in her soul; and as she was sitting in the middle of the garden-seat at Madame's side, telling the whole story of her efforts, a light weight dropped on to her shoulder — it was Loulou! What on earth had he been doing? Taking a walk in the neighbourhood, perhaps!

She had some trouble in recovering from this, or rather never did recover. As the result of a chill she had an attack of quinsy, and soon afterwards an earache. Three years later she was deaf; and she spoke very loud, even in church. Though Félicité's sins might have been published in every corner of the diocese without dishonour to her or scandal to anybody, his Reverence the priest thought it right now to hear her confession in the sacristy only.

Imaginary noises in the head completed her upset. Her mistress often said to her, "Heavens! how stupid you are!" "Yes, Madame," she replied, and looked about for something.

Her little circle of ideas grew still narrower; the peal of church-bells and the lowing of cattle ceased to exist for her. All living beings moved as silently as ghosts. One sound only reached her ears now — the parrot's voice.

Loulou, as though to amuse her, reproduced the click-clack of the turn-spit, the shrill call of a man selling fish, and the noise of the saw in the joiner's house opposite; when the bell rang he imitated Mme. Aubain's "Félicité! the door! the door!"

They carried on conversations, he endlessly reciting the three phrases in his repertory, to which she replied with words that were just as disconnected but uttered what was in her heart. Loulou was almost a son and a lover to her in her isolated state. He climbed up her fingers, nibbled at her lips, and clung to her kerchief; and when she bent her forehead and shook her head gently to and fro, as nurses do, the great wings of her bonnet and the bird's wings quivered together.

When the clouds massed and the thunder rumbled Loulou broke into cries, perhaps remembering the downpours in his native forests. The streaming rain made him absolutely mad; he fluttered wildly about, dashed up to the ceiling; upset everything, and went out through the window to dabble in the garden; but he was back quickly to perch on one of the fire-dogs and hopped about to dry himself, exhibiting his tail and his beak in turn.

One morning in the terrible winter of 1837 she had put him in front of the fireplace because of the cold. She found him dead, in the middle of his cage: head downwards, with his claws in the wires. He had died from congestion, no doubt. But Félicité thought he had been poisoned with parsley, and though there was no proof of any kind her suspicions inclined to Fabu.

She wept so piteously that her mistress said to her, "Well, then, have him stuffed!"

She asked advice from the chemist, who had always been kind to the parrot. He wrote to Havre, and a person called Fellacher undertook the business. But as parcels sometimes got lost in the coach she decided to take the parrot as far as Honfleur herself.

Along the sides of the road were leafless apple-trees, one after the other. Ice covered the ditches. Dogs barked about the farms; and Félicité, with her hands under her cloak, her little black sabots and her basket, walked briskly in the middle of the road.

She crossed the forest, passed High Oak, and reached St. Gatien.

A cloud of dust rose behind her, and in it a mail-coach, carried away by the steep hill, rushed down at full gallop like a hurricane. Seeing this woman who would not get out of the way, the driver stood up in front and the postilion shouted too. He could not hold in his four horses, which increased their pace, and the two leaders were grazing her when he threw them to one side with a jerk of the reins. But he was wild with rage, and lifting his arm as he passed at full speed, gave her such a lash from waist to neck with his big whip that she fell on her back.

Her first act, when she recovered consciousness, was to open her basket. Loulou was happily none the worse. She felt a burn in her right cheek, and when she put her hands against it they were red; the blood was flowing.

She sat down on a heap of stones and bound up her face with her handkerchief. Then she ate a crust of bread which she had put in the basket as a precaution, and found a consolation for her wound in gazing at the bird.

When she reached the crest of Ecquemauville she saw the Honfleur lights sparkling in the night sky like a company of stars; beyond, the sea stretched dimly. Then a faintness overtook her and she stopped; her wretched childhood, the disillusion of her first love, her nephew's going away, and Virginie's death all came back to her at once like the waves of an oncoming tide, rose to her throat, and choked her.

Afterwards, at the boat, she made a point of speaking to the captain, begging him to take care of the parcel, though she did not tell him what was in it.

Fellacher kept the parrot a long time. He was always promising it for the following week. After six months he announced that a packing-case had started, and then nothing more was heard of it. It really seemed as though Loulou was never coming back. "Ah, they have stolen him!" she thought.

He arrived at last, and looked superb. There he was, erect upon a branch which screwed into a mahogany socket, with a foot in the air and his head on one side, biting a nut which the bird-stuffer — with a taste for impressiveness — had gilded.

Félicité shut him up in her room. It was a place to which few people were admitted, and held so many religious objects and miscellaneous things that it looked like a chapel and bazaar in one.

A big cupboard impeded you as you opened the door. Opposite the window commanding the garden a little round one looked out into the court; there was a table by the folding-bed with a water-jug, two combs, and a cube of blue soap in a chipped plate. On the walls hung rosaries, medals, several benign Virgins, and a holy water vessel made out of coconut; on the chest of drawers, which was covered with a cloth like an altar, was the shell box that Victor had given her, and after that a watering-can, a toy-balloon, exercise-books, the illustrated geography, and a pair of young lady's boots; and, fastened by its ribbons to the nail of the looking-glass, hung the little plush hat! Félicité carried observances of this kind so far as to keep one of Monsieur's frock-coats. All the old rubbish which Mme. Aubain did not want any longer she laid hands on for her room. That was why there were artificial flowers along the edge of the chest of drawers and a portrait of the Comte d'Artois in the little window recess.

With the aid of a bracket Loulou was established over the chimney, which jutted into the room. Every morning when she woke up she saw him there in the dawning light, and recalled old days and the smallest details of insignificant acts in a deep quietness which knew no pain.

Holding, as she did, no communication with anyone, Félicité lived as insensibly as if she were walking in her sleep. The Corpus Christi processions roused her to life again. Then she went round begging mats and candlesticks from the neighbours to decorate the altar they put up in the street.

In church she was always gazing at the Holy Ghost in the window, and observed that there was something of the parrot in him. The likeness was still clearer, she thought, on a crude colour-print representing the baptism of Our Lord. With his purple wings and emerald body he was the very image of Loulou.

She bought him, and hung him up instead of the Comte d'Artois, so that she could see them both together in one glance. They were linked in her thoughts; and the parrot was consecrated by his association with the Holy Ghost, which became more vivid to her eye and more intelligible. The Father could not have chosen to express Himself through a dove, for such creatures cannot speak; it must have been one of Loulou's ancestors, surely. And though Félicité looked at the picture while she said her prayers she swerved a little from time to time towards the parrot.

She wanted to join the Ladies of the Virgin but Mme. Aubain dissuaded her.

And then a great event loomed up before them — Paul's marriage.

He had been a solicitor's clerk to begin with, and then tried business, the Customs, the Inland Revenue, and made efforts, even, to get into the Rivers and Forests. By an inspiration from heaven he had suddenly, at thirty-six, discovered his real line — the Registrar's Office. And there he showed such marked capacity that an inspector had offered him his daughter's hand and promised him his influence.

So Paul, grown serious, brought the lady to see his mother.

She sniffed at the ways of Pont-l'Évêque, gave herself great airs, and wounded Félicité's feelings. Mme. Aubain was relieved at her departure.

The week after came news of M. Bourais' death in an inn in Lower Brittany. The rumour of suicide was confirmed, and doubts arose as to his honesty. Mme. Aubain studied his accounts, and soon found out the whole tale of his misdoings —embezzled arrears, secret sales of wood, forged receipts, etc. Besides that he had an illegitimate child, and "relations with a person at Dozulé."

These shameful facts distressed her greatly. In March 1853 she was seized with a pain in the chest; her tongue seemed to be covered with film, and leeches did not ease the difficult breathing. On the ninth evening of her illness she died, just at seventy-two.

She passed as being younger, owing to the bands of brown hair which framed her pale, pock-marked face. There were few friends to regret her, for she had a stiffness of manner which kept people at a distance.

But Félicité mourned for her as one seldom mourns for a master. It upset her ideas and seemed contrary to the order of things, impossible and monstrous, that Madame should die before her.

Ten days afterwards, which was the time it took to hurry there from Besançon, the heirs arrived. The daughter-in-law ransacked the drawers, chose some furniture, and sold the rest; and then they went back to their registering.

Madame's armchair, her small round table, her foot-warmer, and the eight chairs were gone! Yellow patches in the middle of the panels showed where the engravings had hung. They had carried off the two little beds and the mattresses, and all Virginie's belongings had disappeared from the cupboard. Félicité went from floor to floor dazed with sorrow.

The next day there was a notice on the door, and the apothecary shouted in her ear that the house was for sale.

She tottered, and was obliged to sit down. What distressed her most of all was to give up her room, so suitable as it was for poor Loulou. She enveloped him with a look of anguish when she was imploring the Holy Ghost, and formed the idolatrous habit of kneeling in front of the parrot to say her prayers. Sometimes the sun shone in at the attic window and caught his glass eye, and a great luminous ray shot out of it and put her in an ecstasy.

She had a pension of fifteen pounds a year which her mistress had left her. The garden gave her a supply of vegetables. As for clothes, she had enough to last her to the end of her days, and she economized in candles by going to bed at dusk.

She hardly ever went out, as she did not like passing the dealer's shop, where some of the old furniture was exposed for sale. Since her fit of giddiness she dragged one leg; and as her strength was failing Mère Simon, whose grocery business had collapsed, came every morning to split the wood and pump water for her.

Her eyes grew feeble. The shutters ceased to be thrown open. Years and years passed, and the house was neither let nor sold.

Félicité never asked for repairs because she was afraid of being sent away. The boards on the roof rotted; her bolster was wet for a whole winter. After Easter she spat blood.

Then Mère Simon called in a doctor. Félicité wanted to know what was the matter with her. But she was too deaf to hear, and the only word which reached her was "pneumonia." It was a word she knew, and she answered softly, "Ah! like Madame," thinking it natural that she should follow her mistress.

The time for the festal shrines was coming near. The first one was always at the bottom of the hill, the second in front of the post-office, and the third towards the middle of the street. There was some rivalry in the matter of this one, and the women of the parish ended by choosing Mme. Aubain's courtyard.

The hard breathing and fever increased. Félicité was vexed at doing nothing for the altar. If only she could at least have put something there! Then she thought of the parrot. The neighbours objected that it would not be decent. But the priest gave her permission, which so intensely delighted her that she begged him to accept Loulou, her sole possession, when she died.

From Tuesday to Saturday, the eve of the festival, she coughed more often. By the evening her face had shrivelled, her lips stuck to her gums, and she had vomitings; and at twilight next morning, feeling herself very low, she sent for a priest.

Three kindly women were round her during the extreme unction. Then she announced that she must speak to Fabu. He arrived in his Sunday clothes, by no means at his ease in the funereal atmosphere.

"Forgive me," she said, with an effort to stretch out her arm; "I thought it was you who had killed him."

What did she mean by such stories? She suspected him of murder — a man like him! He waxed indignant, and was on the point of making a row.

"There," said the women, "she is no longer in her senses, you can see it well enough!"

Félicité spoke to shadows of her own from time to time. The women went away, and Mère Simon had breakfast. A little later she took Loulou and brought him close to Félicité with the words:

"Come, now, say good-bye to him!"

Loulou was not a corpse, but the worms devoured him; one of his wings was broken, and the tow was coming out of his stomach. But she was blind now; she kissed him on the forehead and kept him close against her cheek. Mère Simon took him back from her to put him on the altar.

5

Summer scents came up from the meadows; flies buzzed; the sun made the river glitter and heated the slates. Mère Simon came back into the room and fell softly asleep.

She woke at the noise of bells; the people were coming out from vespers. Félicité's delirium subsided. She thought of the procession and saw it as if she had been there.

All the school children, the church-singers, and the firemen walked on the pavement, while in the middle of the road the verger armed with his halberd and the beadle with a large cross advanced in front. Then came the schoolmaster, with an eye on the boys, and the sister, anxious about her little girls; three of the daintiest, with angelic curls, scattered rose-petals in the air; the deacon controlled the band with outstretched arms; and two censer-bearers turned back at every step towards the Holy Sacrament, which was borne by Monsieur the curé, wearing his beautiful chasuble, under a canopy of dark-red velvet held up by four churchwardens. A crowd of people pressed behind, between the white cloths covering the house walls, and they reached the bottom of the hill.

A cold sweat moistened Félicité's temples. Mère Simon sponged her with a piece of linen, saying to herself that one day she would have to go that way.

The hum of the crowd increased, was very loud for an instant, and then went further away.

A fusillade shook the window-panes. It was the postilions saluting the monstrance. Félicité rolled her eyes and said as audibly as she could: "Does he look well?" The parrot was weighing on her mind.

Her agony began. A death-rattle that grew more and more convulsed made her sides heave. Bubbles of froth came at the corners of her mouth and her whole body trembled.

Soon the booming of the ophicleides, the high voices of the children, and the deep voices of the men were distinguishable. At intervals all was silent, and the tread of feet, deadened by the flowers they walked on, sounded like a flock pattering on grass.

The clergy appeared in the courtyard. Mère Simon clambered on to a chair to reach the attic window, and so looked down straight upon the shrine. Green garlands hung over the altar, which was decked with a flounce of English lace. In the middle was a small frame with relics in it; there were two orange-trees at the corners, and all along stood silver candlesticks and china vases, with sunflowers, lilies, peonies, foxgloves, and tufts of hortensia. This heap of blazing colour slanted from the level of the altar to the carpet which went on over the pavement; and some rare objects caught the eye. There was a silver-gilt sugar-basin with a crown of violets; pendants of Alençon stone glittered on the moss, and two Chinese screens displayed their landscapes. Loulou was hidden under roses, and showed nothing but his blue forehead, like a plaque of lapis lazuli.

The churchwardens, singers, and children took their places round the three sides of the court. The priest went slowly up the steps, and placed his great, radiant golden sun upon the lace. Everyone knelt down. There was a deep silence; and the censers glided to and fro on the full swing of their chains.

An azure vapour rose up into Félicité's room. Her nostrils met it; she inhaled it sensuously, mystically; and then closed her eyes. Her lips smiled. The beats of her heart lessened one by one, vaguer each time and softer, as a fountain sinks, an echo disappears; and when she sighed her last breath she thought she saw an opening in the heavens, and a gigantic parrot hovering above her head.

E. M. FORSTER

E(dward) M(organ) Forster (1879–1970) was born in London and received his education at Tonbridge School and King's College, Cambridge. He was all his life a novelist and critic, a "tragic humanist," in the words of one observer. His faith lay in the potential of the individual to meet life with courage, compassion, and creativity; humans must, he wrote, "learn to build the rainbow bridge that should connect the prose in us with the passion. Without it we are meaningless fragments, half monks, half beasts." In novels and short fiction, as well as distinguished literary criticism, he pursued that connection. Among his novels are *Where Angels Fear to Tread* (1905), *The Longest Journey* (1907), *A Room with a View* (1908), *Howard's End* (1910), *Maurice* (1913; published posthumously 1971), and *A Passage to India* (1924). Of his short stories, collected in *The Celestial Omnibus* (1923) and *The Eternal Moment* (1928), he said, "Fantasy can be caught in the open here by any who care to catch her." "The Story of the Siren," itself enclosing a fantastic story, reveals how deep the chasm separating reason (prose) from nature (passion) may be.

The Story of the Siren

Few things have been more beautiful than my notebook on the Deist Controversy as it fell downward through the waters of the Mediterranean. It dived, like a piece of black slate, but opened soon, disclosing leaves of pale green, which quivered into blue. Now it had vanished, now it was a piece of magical india-rubber stretching out to infinity, now it was a book again, but bigger than the book of all knowledge. It grew more fantastic as it reached the bottom, where a puff of sand welcomed it and obscured it from view. But it reappeared, quite sane though a little tremulous, lying decently open on its back, while unseen fingers fidgeted among its leaves.

"It is such a pity," said my aunt, "that you will not finish your work in the hotel. Then you would be free to enjoy yourself and this would never have happened."

"Nothing of it but will change into something rich and strange," warbled the chaplain, while his sister said,"Why, it's gone in the water!" As for the boatmen, one of them laughed, while the other, without a word of warning, stood up and began to take his clothes off.

"Holy Moses," cried the Colonel. "Is the fellow mad?"

"Yes, thank him, dear," said my aunt: "that is to say, tell him he is very kind, but perhaps another time."

"All the same I do want my book back," I complained. "It's for my Fellowship Dissertation. There won't be much left of it by another time."

"I have an idea," said some woman or other through her parasol. "Let us leave this child of nature to dive for the book while we go on to the other grotto. We can land him either on this rock or on the ledge inside, and he will be ready when we return."

The idea seemed good; and I improved it by saying I would be left behind too, to lighten the boat. So the two of us were deposited outside the little grotto on a great sunlit rock that guarded the harmonies within. Let us call them blue, though they suggest rather the spirit of what is clean — cleanliness passed from the domestic to the sublime, the cleanliness of all the sea gathered together and radiating light. The Blue Grotto at Capri contains only more blue water, not bluer water. That colour and that spirit are the heritage of every cave in the Mediterranean into which the sun can shine and the sea flow.

As soon as the boat left I realized how imprudent I had been to trust myself on a sloping rock with an unknown Sicilian. With a jerk he became alive, seizing my arm and saying, "Go to the end of the grotto, and I will show you something beautiful."

He made me jump off the rock on to the ledge over a dazzling crack of sea; he drew me away from the light till I was standing on the tiny beach of sand which emerged like powdered turquoise at the farther end. There he left me with his clothes, and returned swiftly to the summit of the entrance rock. For a moment he stood naked in the brilliant sun, looking down at the spot where the book lay. Then he crossed himself, raised his hands above his head, and dived.

If the book was wonderful, the man is past all description. His effect was that of a silver statue, alive beneath the sea, through whom life throbbed in blue and green. Something infinitely happy, infinitely wise — but it was impossible that it should emerge from the depths sunburned and dripping, holding the notebook on the Deist Controversy between its teeth.

A gratuity is generally expected by those who bathe. Whatever I offered, he was sure to want more, and I was disinclined for an argument in a place so beautiful and also so solitary. It was a relief that he should say in conversational tones, "In a place like this one might see the Siren."

I was delighted with him for thus falling into the key of his surroundings. We had been left together in a magic world, apart from all the commonplaces that are called reality, a world of blue whose floor was the sea and whose walls and roof of rock trembled with the sea's reflections. Here only the fantastic would be tolerable, and it was in that spirit I echoed his words, "One might easily see the Siren."

He watched me curiously while he dressed. I was parting the sticky leaves of the notebook as I sat on the sand.

"Ah," he said at last. "You may have read the little book that was printed last year. Who would have thought that our Siren would have given the foreigners pleasure!"

(I read it afterwards. Its account is, not unnaturally, incomplete, in spite of there being a woodcut of the young person, and the words of her song.)

"She comes out of this blue water, doesn't she," I suggested, "and sits on the rock at the entrance, combing her hair."

I wanted to draw him out, for I was interested in his sudden gravity, and there was a suggestion of irony in his last remark that puzzled me.

"Have you ever seen her?" he asked.

"Often and often."

"I, never."

"But you have heard her sing?"

He put on his coat and said impatiently, "How can she sing under the water? Who could? She sometimes tries, but nothing comes from her but great bubbles."

"She should climb on to the rock."

"How can she?" he cried again, quite angry. "The priests have blessed the air, so she cannot breathe it, and blessed the rocks, so that she cannot sit on them. But the sea no man can bless, because it is too big, and always changing. So she lives in the sea."

I was silent.

At this his face took a gentler expression. He looked at me as though something was on his mind, and going out to the entrance rock gazed at the external blue. Then returning into our twilight he said, "As a rule only good people see the Siren."

I made no comment. There was a pause, and he continued. "That is a very strange thing, and the priests do not know how to account for it; for she of course is wicked. Not only those who fast and go to Mass are in danger, but even those who are merely good in daily life. No one in the village had seen her for two generations. I am not surprised. We all cross ourselves before we enter the water, but it is unnecessary. Giuseppe, we thought, was safer than most. We loved him, and many of us he loved: but that is a different thing from being good."

I asked who Giuseppe was.

"That day — I was seventeen and my brother was twenty and a great deal stronger than I was, and it was the year when the visitors, who have brought such prosperity and so many alterations into the village, first began to come. One English lady in particular, of very high birth, came, and has written a book about the place, and it was through her that the Improvement Syndicate was formed, which is about to connect the hotels with the station by a funicular railway."

"Don't tell me about that lady in here," I observed.

"That day we took her and her friends to see the grottoes. As we rowed close under the cliffs I put out my hand, as one does, and caught a little crab, and having pulled off its claws offered it as a curiosity. The ladies groaned, but a gentleman was pleased, and held out money. Being inexperienced, I refused it, saying that his pleasure was sufficient reward! Giuseppe, who was rowing behind, was very angry with me and reached out with his hand and hit me on the side of the mouth, so that a tooth cut my lip, and I bled. I tried to hit him back, but he always was too quick for me, and as I stretched round he kicked me under the armpit, so that for a moment I could not even row. There was a great noise among the ladies, and I heard afterward that they were planning to take me away from my brother and train me as a waiter. That, at all events, never came to pass.

"When we reached the grotto — not here, but a larger one — the gentleman was very anxious that one of us should dive for money, and the ladies consented, as they sometimes do. Giuseppe, who had discovered how much pleasure it gives foreigners to see us in the water, refused to dive for anything but silver, and the gentleman threw in a two-lira piece.

"Just before my brother sprang off he caught sight of me holding my bruise, and crying, for I could not help it. He laughed and said, 'This time, at all events, I shall not see the Siren!' and went into the water without crossing himself. But he saw her."

He broke off and accepted a cigarette. I watched the golden entrance rock and the quivering walls and the magic water through which great bubbles constantly rose.

At last he dropped his hot ash into the ripples and turned his head away, and said, "He came up without the coin. We pulled him into the boat, and he was so large that he seemed to fill it, and so wet that we could not dress him. I have never seen a man so wet. I and the gentleman rowed back, and we covered Giuseppe with sacking and propped him up in the stern."

"He was drowned, then?" I murmured, supposing that to be the point.

"He was not," he cried angrily. "He saw the Siren. I told you."

I was silenced again.

"We put him to bed, though he was not ill. The doctor came, and took money, and the priest came and spattered him with holy water. But it was no good. He was too big — like a piece of the sea. He kissed the thumb-bones of San Biagio and they never dried till evening."

"What did he look like?" I ventured.

"Like any one who has seen the Siren. If you have seen her 'often and often' how is it you do not know? Unhappy, unhappy because he knew everything. Every living thing made him unhappy because he knew it would die. And all he cared to do was sleep."

I bent over my note-book.

"He did no work, he forgot to eat, he forgot whether he had his clothes on. All the work fell on me, and my sister had to go out to service. We tried to make him into a beggar, but he was too robust to inspire pity, and as for an idiot, he had not the right look in his eyes. He would stand in the street looking at people, and the more he looked at them the more unhappy he became. When a child was born he would cover his face with his hands. If any one was married — he was terrible then, and would frighten them as they came out of church. Who would have believed he would marry himself! I caused that, I. I was reading out of the paper how a girl at Ragusa had 'gone mad through bathing in the sea.' Giuseppe got up, and in a week he and that girl came in.

"He never told me anything, but it seems that he went straight to her house, broke into her room, and carried her off. She was the daughter of a rich mine-owner, so you may imagine our peril. Her father came down, with a clever lawyer, but they could do no more than I. They argued and they threatened, but at last they had to go back and we lost nothing — that is to say, no money. We took Giuseppe and Maria to the church and had them married. Ugh! that wedding! The priest made no jokes afterward, and coming out the children threw stones. . . . I think I would have died to make her happy; but as always happens, one could do nothing."

"Were they unhappy together then?"

"They loved each other, but love is not happiness. We can all get love. Love is nothing. I had two people to work for now, for she was like him in everything — one never knew which of them was speaking. I had to sell our own boat and work under the bad old man you have today. Worst of all, people began to hate us. The children first — everything begins with them — and then the women and last of all the men. For the cause of every misfortune was — You will not betray me?"

I promised good faith, and immediately he burst into the frantic blasphemy of one who has escaped from supervision, cursing the priests, who had ruined his life, he said. "Thus are we tricked!" was his cry, and he stood up and kicked at the azure ripples with his feet, till he had obscured them with a cloud of sand.

I too was moved. The story of Giuseppe, for all its absurdity and superstition, came nearer to reality than anything I had known before. I don't know why, but it filled me with desire to help others — the greatest of all desires, I suppose, and the most fruitless. The desire soon passed.

"She was about to have a child. That was the end of everything. People said to me, 'When will your charming nephew be born? What a cheerful, attractive child he will be, with such a father and mother!' I kept my face steady and replied, 'I think he may be. Out of sadness shall come gladness' — it is one of our proverbs. And my answer frightened them very much, and they told the priests, who were frightened too. Then the whisper started that the child would be Antichrist. You need not be afraid: he was never born.

"An old witch began to prophesy, and no one stopped her. Giuseppe and the girl, she said, had silent devils, who could do little harm. But the child would always be speaking and laughing and perverting, and last of all he would go into the sea and fetch up the Siren into the air and all the world would see her and hear her sing. As soon as she sang, the Seven Vials would be opened and the Pope would die and Mongibello flame, and the veil of Santa Agata would be burned. Then the boy and the Siren would marry, and together they would rule the world, for ever and ever.

"The whole village was in tumult, and the hotel-keepers became alarmed, for the tourist season was just beginning. They met altogether and decided that Giuseppe and the girl must be sent inland until the child was born, and they subscribed the money. The night before they were to start there was a full moon and wind from the east, and all along the coast the sea shot up over the cliffs in silver clouds. It is a wonderful sight, and Maria said she must see it once more.

"'Do not go,' I said. 'I saw the priest go by, and some one with him. And the hotel-keepers do not like you to be seen, and if we displease them also we shall starve.'

"'I want to go,' she replied. 'The sea is stormy, and I may never feel it again.'

"'No, he is right,' said Giuseppe. 'Do not go — or let one of us go with you.'

"'I want to go alone,' she said; and she went alone.

"I tied up their luggage in a piece of cloth, and then I was so unhappy at thinking I should lose them that I went and sat down by my brother and put my arm round his neck, and he put his arm round me, which he had not done for more than a year, and we remained thus I don't remember how long.

"Suddenly the door flew open and moonlight and wind came in together, and a child's voice said laughing, 'They have pushed her over the cliffs into the sea.'

"I stepped to the drawer where I keep my knives.

"'Sit down again,' said Giuseppe — Giuseppe of all people! 'If she is dead, why should others die too?'

"'I guess who it is,' I cried, 'and I will kill him.'

"I was almost out of the door, and he tripped me up and, kneeling upon me, took hold of both my hands and sprained my wrists; first my right one, then my left. No one but Giuseppe would have thought of such a thing. It hurt more than you would suppose, and I fainted. When I woke up, he was gone, and I never saw him again."

But Giuseppe disgusted me.

"I told you he was wicked," he said. "No one would have expected him to see the Siren."

"How do you know he did see her?"

"Because he did not see her 'often and often,' but once."

"Why do you love him if he is wicked?"

He laughed for the first time. That was his only reply.

"Is that the end?" I asked.

"I never killed her murderer, for by the time my wrists were well he was in America; and one cannot kill a priest. As for Giuseppe, he went all over the world too, looking for some one else who had seen the Siren — either a man, or, better still, a woman, for then the child might still have been born. At last he came to Liverpool — is the district probable? — and there he began to cough, and spat blood until he died.

"I do not suppose there is any one living now who has seen her. There has seldom been more than one in a generation, and never in my life will there be both a man and a woman from whom that child can be born, who will fetch up the Siren from the sea, and destroy silence, and save the world!"

"Save the world?" I cried. "Did the prophecy end like that?"

He leaned back against the rock, breathing deep. Through all the blue-green reflections I saw him colour. I heard him say: "Silence and loneliness cannot last for ever. It may be a hundred or a thousand years, but the sea lasts longer, and she shall come out of it and sing." I would have asked him more, but at that moment the whole cave darkened, and there rode in through its narrow entrance the returning boat.

CARLOS FUENTES

Carlos Fuentes was born in 1928 in Mexico City, the son of a diplomat. Raised in Washington, D.C., as well as Santiago and Buenos Aires, he learned both English and Spanish as a boy. In the 1950s he held a number of diplomatic posts in Mexico, and he served as Mexico's ambassador to France from 1975 to 1977. But his primary interest lay in writing, and he left his career to write the novels and stories that have won him a major international literary reputation. As Fuentes's novels (which were quickly and widely translated after they were published in Spanish) gained recognition, so did Latin American literature in general. Indeed, Chilean novelist José Donoso has called Fuentes "the first active and concious agent of the internationalization of the Spanish American novel." Fuentes's primary subject is Mexico — its social, political, and psychological history. His novels include *The Death of Artemio Cruz* (1964), *A Change of Skin* (1968), *Terra Nostra* (1976), *Hydra Head* (1978), and *The Old Gringo* (1985). A number of his short stories, published in English translation, are collected in *Burnt Water* (1980). Like so many Latin American writers, Fuentes is deeply preoccupied with the past: "We have to assimilate the enormous weight of the past so that we will not forget what gives us life. If you forget the past, you die." In "The Doll Queen" the region of exploration is the personal, rather than the historical, past.

The Doll Queen

Translated from the Spanish by Margaret S. Peden

I went because that card — such a strange card — reminded me of her existence. I found it in a forgotten book whose pages had revived the ghost associated with the childish calligraphy. For the first time in a long time I was rearranging my books. I met surprise after surprise since some, placed on the highest shelves, had not been read for a long time. So long a time that the edges of the leaves were grainy, and a mixture of gold dust and greyish scale fell onto my open palm, reminiscent of the lacquer covering certain bodies glimpsed first in dreams and later in the deceptive reality of the first ballet performance to which we're taken. It was a book from my childhood — perhaps from that of many children — that related a series of more or less truculent exemplary tales which had the virtue of precipitating us upon our elders' knees to ask them, over and over again: Why? Children who are ungrateful to their parents; maidens kidnapped by flashy horsemen and returned home in shame — as well as those who willingly abandon hearth and home; old men who in exchange for an overdue mortgage demand the hand of the sweetest and most long-suffering daughter of the threatened family. . . . Why? I do not recall their answers, I only know that from among the stained pages fell, fluttering, a white card in Amilamia's atrocious hand: *Amilamia wil not forget her good frend — com see me here lik I draw it.*

   And on the other side was that map of a path starting from an X that indicated, doubtlessly, the park bench where I, an adolescent rebelling against prescribed and tedious education, forgot my classroom schedule in order to spend several hours reading books which if not actually written by me, seemed to be: who could doubt that only from *my* imagination could spring all those corsairs, those couriers of the tsar, all those boys slightly younger than I who rowed all day up and down the great American rivers on a raft. Clutching the arm of the park bench as if it were the frame of a magical saddle, at first I didn't hear the sound of the light steps and of the little girl who would stop behind me after running down the graveled garden path. It was Amilamia, and I don't know how long the child would have kept me silent company if her mischievous spirit, one afternoon, had not chosen to tickle my ear with down from a dandelion she blew towards me, her lips puffed out and her brow furrowed in a frown.

   She asked my name and after considering it very seriously, she told me hers with a smile which if not candid, was not too rehearsed. Quickly I realized that Amilamia had discovered, if discovered is the word, a form of expression midway between the ingenuousness of her years and the forms of adult mimicry that well-brought-up children have to know, particularly those for the solemn moments of introduction and of leave-taking. Amilamia's seriousness, apparently, was a gift of nature, whereas her moments of spontaneity, by contrast, seemed artificial. I like to remember her, afternoon after afternoon, in a succession of snapshots that in their totality sum up the complete Amilamia. And it never ceases to surprise me that I cannot think of her as she really was, or remember how she actually moved, light, questioning, constantly looking around her. I must remember her fixed forever in time, as in a photograph album. Amilamia in the distance, a point on the spot where the hill began to descend from a lake of clover towards the flat meadow where I, sitting on the bench, used to read: a point of fluctuating shadow and sunshine and a hand that waved to me from high on the hill. Amilamia frozen in her flight down the hill, her white skirt billowing, the flowered panties gathered around her thighs with elastic, her mouth open and eyes half-closed against the streaming air, the child crying with pleasure. Amilamia sitting beneath the eucalyptus trees, pretending to cry so that I would go over to her. Amilamia lying on her stomach with a flower in her hand: the petals of a flower which I discovered later didn't grow in this garden, but somewhere else, perhaps in the garden of Amilamia's house, since the single pocket of her blue-checked apron was often filled with those white blossoms. Amilamia watching me read, holding with both hands to the bars of the green bench, asking questions with her grey eyes: I recall that she never asked me what I was reading, as if she could divine in my eyes the images born of the pages. Amilamia laughing with pleasure when I lifted her by the waist and whirled her around my head; she seemed to discover a new perspective on the world in that slow flight. Amilamia turning her back to me and waving goodbye, her arm held high, the fingers waving excitedly. And Amilamia in the thousand postures she affected around my bench, hanging upside down, her bloomers billowing; sitting on the gravel with her legs crossed and her chin resting on her fist; lying on the grass, baring her belly-button to the sun; weaving tree branches, drawing animals in the mud with a twig, licking the bars of the bench, hiding beneath the seat, silently breaking off the loose bark from the ancient treetrunks, staring at the horizon beyond the hill, humming with her eyes closed, imitating the voices of birds, dogs, cats, hens, and horses. All for me, and nevertheless, nothing. It was her way of being with me, all these things I remember, but at the same time her manner of being alone in the park. Yes, perhaps my memory of her is fragmentary because reading alternated with the contemplation of the chubby-cheeked child with smooth hair changing in the reflection of the light: now wheat-colored, now burnt chestnut. And it is only today that I think how Amilamia in that moment established the other point of support for my life, the one that created the tension between by own irresolute childhood and the open world, the promised land that was beginning to be mine through my reading.

Not then. Then I dreamed about the women in my books, about the quintessential female — the word disturbed me — who assumed the disguise of the Queen in order to buy the necklace secretly, about the imagined beings of mythology — half recognizable, half white-breasted, damp-bellied salamanders — who awaited monarchs in their beds. And thus, imperceptibly, I moved from indifference towards my childish companion to an acceptance of the child's gracefulness and seriousness and from there to an unexpected rejection of a presence that became useless to me. She irritated me, finally. I who was fourteen was irritated by that child of seven who was not yet memory or nostalgia, but rather the past and its reality. I had let myself be dragged along by weakness. We had run together, holding hands, across the meadow. Together we had shaken the pines and picked up the cones that Amilamia guarded jealously in her apron pocket. Together we had constructed paper boats and followed them, happy and gay, to the edge of the drain. And that afternoon amidst shouts of glee, when we tumbled together down the hill and rolled to a stop at its foot, Amilamia was on my chest, her hair between my lips; but when I felt her panting breath in my ear and her little arms sticky from sweets around my neck, I angrily pushed away her arms and let her fall. Amilamia cried, rubbing her wounded elbow and knee, and I returned to my bench. Then Amilamia went away and the following day she returned, handed me the paper without a word, and disappeared, humming, into the woods. I hesitated whether to tear up the card or keep it in the pages of the book: *Afternoons on the Farm.* Even my reading had become childish because of Amilamia. She did not return to the park. After a few days I left for my vacation and when I returned it was to the duties of my first year of prep school. I never saw her again.

2

And now, almost rejecting the image that is unaccustomed without being fantastic, but is all the more painful for being so real, I return to that forgotten park and stopping before the grove of pines and eucalyptus I recognize the smallness of the bosky enclosure that my memory has insisted on drawing with an amplitude that allowed sufficient space for the vast swell of my imagination. After all, Strogoff and Huckleberry, Milady de Winter and Geneviève de Brabante were born, lived and died here: in a little garden surrounded by mossy iron railings, sparsely planted with old, neglected trees, barely adorned by a concrete bench painted to look like wood that forces me to believe that my beautiful wrought-iron green-painted bench never existed, or else was a part of my orderly, retrospective delirium. And the hill . . . How could I believe the promontory that Amilamia climbed and descended during her daily coming and going, that steep slope we rolled down together, was *this*. A barely elevated patch of dark stubble with no more heights and depths than those my memory had created.

Com see me here lik I draw it. So I would have to cross the garden, leave the woods behind, descend the hill in three loping steps, cut through that narrow grove of chestnuts — it was here, surely, where the child gathered the white petals — open the squeaking park gate and suddenly recall . . . , know . . . , find oneself in the street, realize that every afternoon of one's adolescence, as if by a miracle, he had suc-ceeded in suspending the beat of the surrounding city, annulling that flood-tide of whistles, bells, voices, sobs, engines, radios, imprecations. Which was the true magnet, the silent garden or the feverish city?

I wait for the light to change and cross to the other sidewalk, my eyes never leaving the red iris detaining the traffic. I consult Amilamia's paper. After all, that rudimentary map is the true magnet of the moment I am living, and just thinking about it startles me. I was obliged, after the lost afternoons of my fourteenth year, to follow the channels of discipline; now I find myself, at twenty-nine, duly certi-fied with a diploma, owner of an office, assured of a moderate income, a bachelor still, with no family to maintain, slightly bored with sleeping with secretaries, scarcely excited by an occasional outing to the country or to the beach, feeling the lack of a central attraction such as those once afforded me by my books, my park, and Amilamia. I walk down the street of this grey, low-buildinged suburb. The one-story houses with their doorways scaling paint succeed each other monoto-nously. Faint neighborhood sounds barely interrupt the general uniformity: the squeal of a knife-sharpener here, the hammering of a shoe-repairman there. The children of the neighborhood are playing in the dead-end streets. The music of an organ-grinder reaches my ears, mingled with the voices of children's rounds. I stop a moment to watch them with the sensation, also fleeting, that Amilamia must be among these groups of children, immodestly exhibiting her flowered panties, hanging by her knees from some balcony, still fond of acrobatic excesses, her apron pocket filled with white petals. I smile, and for the first time I am able to imagine the young lady of twenty-two who, even if she still lives at this address, will laugh at my memories, or who perhaps will have forgotten the afternoons spent in the garden.

The house is identical to all the rest. The heavy entry door, two grilled windows with closed shutters. A one-story house, topped by a false neoclassic balustrade that probably conceals the practicalities of the flat-roofed *azotea:* clothes hanging on lines, tubs of water, servants' quarters, a chicken coop. Before I ring the bell, I want to free myself of any illusion. Amilamia no longer lives here. Why would she stay fifteen years in the same house? Besides, in spite of her precocious independence and aloneness, she seemed like a well-brought-up, well-behaved child, and this neighborhood is no longer elegant; Amilamia's parents, without doubt, have moved. But perhaps the new renters will know where.

I press the bell and wait. I ring again. Here is another contingency: no one is home. And will I feel the need again to look for my childhood friend? No. Because it will not be possible a second time to open a book from my adolescence and accidentally find Amilamia's card. I would return to my routine, I would forget the moment whose importance lay in its fleeting surprise.

I ring once more. I press my ear to the door and am surprised: I can hear a harsh and irregular breathing on the other side; the sound of labored breathing, accompanied by the disagreeable odor of stale tobacco, filters through the cracks in the hall.

"Good afternoon. Could you tell me . . . ?"

As soon as he hears my voice, the person moves away with heavy and unsure steps. I press the bell again, shouting this time:

"Hey! Open up? What's the matter? Don't you hear me?"

No response. I continue ringing the bell, without result. I move back from the door, still staring at the small cracks, as if distance might give me perspective, or even penetration. With all my attention fixed on that damned door, I cross the street, walking backwards; a piercing scream, followed by a prolonged and ferocious blast of a whistle, saves me in time; dazed, I seek the person whose voice has just saved me. I see only the automobile moving down the street and I hang on to a lamp post, a hold that more than security offers me a point of support during the sudden rush of icy blood to my burning, sweaty skin. I look towards the house that has been, that was, that must be, Amilamia's. There, behind the balustrade, as I had known there would be, fluttering clothes are drying. I don't know what else is hanging there — skirts, pajamas, blouses — I don't know. All I can see is that starched little blue-checked apron, clamped by clothespins to the long cord that swings between an iron bar and a nail in the white wall of the *azotea*.

3

In the Bureau of Records they have told me that the property is in the name of a Señor R. Valdivia, who rents the house. To whom? That they don't know. Who is Valdivia? He has declared himself a businessman. Where does he live? Who are *you?* the young lady asked me with haughty curiosity. I haven't been able to present a calm and sure appearance. Sleep has not relieved my nervous fatigue. Valdivia. As I leave the Bureau the sun offends me. I associate the repugnance provoked by the hazy sun sifting through the clouds — therefore all the more intense — with the desire to return to the damp, shadowy park. No. It is only the desire to know whether Amilamia lives in that house and why they refuse to let me enter. But the first thing I must do is reject the absurd idea that kept me awake all night. Having seen the apron drying on the flat roof, the one where she kept the flowers, and so believing that in that house lived a seven-year-old girl that I had known fourteen or fifteen years before. . . . She must have a little girl! Yes. Amilamia, at twenty-two, is the mother of a girl who dressed the same, looked the same, repeated the same games, and — who knows — perhaps even went to the same park. And deep in thought I again arrived at the door of the house. I ring the bell and await the whistling breathing on the other side of the door. I am mistaken. The door is opened by a woman who can't be more than fifty. But wrapped in a shawl, dressed in black and in black low-heeled shoes, with no make-up and her salt and pepper hair pulled into a knot, she seems to have abandoned all illusion or pretext of youth; she is observing me with eyes so indifferent they seem almost cruel.

"You want something?"

"Señor Valdivia sent me." I cough and run my hand over my hair. I should have picked up my briefcase at the office. I realize that without it I cannot play my role very well.

"Valdivia?" the woman asks without alarm, without interest.

"Yes. The owner of this house."

One thing is clear. The woman will reveal nothing in her face. She looks at me, calmly.

"Oh, yes. The owner of the house."

"May I come in?"

I think that in bad comedies the traveling salesman sticks a foot in the door so they can't close the door in his face. I do the same, but the woman steps back and with a gesture of her hand invites me to come into what must have been a garage. On one side there is a glass-paned door, its paint faded. I walk towards the door over the yellow tiles of the entryway and ask again, turning towards the woman who follows me with tiny steps:

"This way?"

I notice for the first time that in her white hands she is carrying a chapelet which she toys with ceaselessly. I haven't seen one of those old-fashioned rosaries since my childhood and I want to comment on it, but the brusque and decisive manner with which the woman opens the door precludes any gratuitous conversation. We enter a long narrow room. The woman hastens to open the shutters. But because of four large perennial plants growing in porcelain and crusted glass pots the room remains in shadow. The only other objects in the room are an old high-backed cane-trimmed sofa and a rocking chair. But it is neither the plants nor the sparseness of the furniture that draws my attention.

The woman invites me to sit on the sofa before she sits in the rocking chair. Beside me, on the cane arm of the sofa, there is an open magazine.

"Señor Valdivia sends his apologies for not having come in person."

The woman rocks, unblinkingly. I peer at the comic book out of the corner of my eye.

"He sends his greetings and. . . ."

I stop, awaiting a reaction from the woman. She continues to rock. The magazine is covered with red-penciled scribbling.

". . . and asks me to inform you that he must disturb you for a few days. . . ."

My eyes search rapidly.

". . . A new evaluation of the house must be made for the tax lists. It seems it hasn't been done for. . . . You have been living here since . . . ?"

Yes. That is a stubby lipstick lying under the chair. If the woman smiles, it is only with the slow-moving hands caressing the chapelet; I sense, for an instant, a swift flash of ridicule that does not quite disturb her features. She still does not answer.

". . . for at least fifteen years, isn't that true?"

She does not agree. She does not disagree. And on the pale thin lips there is not the least sign of lipstick. . . .

". . . you, your husband, and . . . ?"

She stares at me, never changing expression, almost daring me to continue. We sit a moment in silence, she playing with the rosary, I leaning forwards, my hands on my knees. I rise.

"Well, then, I'll be back this afternoon with the papers. . . ."

The woman nods while, in silence, she picks up the lipstick and the comic book and hides them in the folds of her shawl.

4

The scene has not changed. This afternoon, while I am writing down false figures in my notebook and feigning interest in establishing the quality of the dulled floor-boards and the length of the living room, the woman rocks, as the three decades of the chapelet whisper through her fingers. I sigh as I finish the supposed inventory of the living room and I ask her for permission to go to the other rooms in the house. The woman rises, bracing her long black-clad arms on the seat of the rocking chair and adjusting the shawl on her narrow bony shoulders.

She opens the opaque glass door and we enter a dining room with very little more furniture. But the table with the aluminum legs and the four nickel and plastic chairs lack even the slight hint of distinction of the living room furniture. Another window with wrought-iron grille and closed shutters must at times illuminate this bare-walled dining room, bare of either shelves or bureau. The only object on the table is a plastic fruit dish with a cluster of black grapes, two peaches, and a buzzing corona of flies. The woman, her arms crossed, her face expressionless, stops behind me. I take the risk of breaking the order of things: it is evident that these rooms will not tell me anything that I really want to know.

"Couldn't we go up to the roof?" I ask. "I believe that is the best way of measuring the total area."

The woman's eyes light up as she looks at me, or perhaps it is only the contrast with the penumbra of the dining room.

"What for?" she says finally. "Señor . . . Valdivia . . . knows the dimensions very well."

And those pauses, one before and one after the owner's name, are the first indications that something is at last perturbing the woman and forcing her, in defense, to resort to a certain irony.

"I don't know." I make an effort to smile. "Perhaps I prefer to go from top to bottom and not . . ." my false smile drains away, ". . . from bottom to top."

"You will go the way I show you," the woman says, her arms crossed across her chest, the silver cross hanging against her dark belly.

Before smiling weakly, I force myself to think how, in this shadow, my gestures are useless, not even symbolic. I open the notebook with a crunch of the cardboard cover and continue making my notes with the greatest possible speed, never glancing up, the numbers and estimates of this task whose fiction — the light flush in my cheeks and the perceptible dryness of my tongue tell me — is deceiving no one. And after filling the graph paper with absurd signs, with square roots and algebraic formulas, I ask myself what is preventing me from getting to the point, from asking about Amilamia and getting out of here with a satisfactory answer. Nothing. And nevertheless, I am sure that even if I obtained a response, the truth does not lie along this road. My slim and silent companion is a person I wouldn't look twice at in the street, but in this almost uninhabited house with the coarse furniture, she ceases to be an anonymous face in the crowd and is converted into a stock character of mystery. Such is the paradox, and if memories of Amilamia have once again awakened my appetite for the imaginary, I shall follow the rules of the game, I shall exhaust all the appearances, and I shall not rest until I find the answer — perhaps simple and clear, immediate and evident — that lies beyond the unexpected veils the señora of the rosary places in my path. Do I bestow a more-than-justified strangeness upon my reluctant Amphitryon? If that is so, I shall only take more pleasure in the labyrinths of my own invention. And the flies are still buzzing around the fruit dish, occasionally pausing on the damaged end of the peach, a nibbled bite — I lean closer using the pretext of my notes — where little teeth have left their mark in the velvety skin and ochre flesh of the fruit. I do not look towards the señora. I pretend I am taking notes. The fruit seems to be bitten but not touched. I crouch down to see it better, rest my hands upon the table, moving my lips closer as if I wished to repeat the act of biting without touching. I look down and I see another sign close to my feet: the track of two tires that seem to be bicycle tires, the print of two rubber tires that come as far as the edge of the table and then lead away, growing fainter, the length of the room, towards the señora. . . .

I close my notebook.

"Let us continue, señora."

As I turn towards her, I find her standing with her hands resting on the back of a chair. Seated before her, coughing the smoke of his black cigarette, is a man with heavy shoulders and hidden eyes: these eyes, hardly visible behind swollen wrinkled lids as thick and droopy as the neck of an ancient turtle, seem nevertheless to follow my every movement. The half-shaven cheeks, criss-crossed by a thousand grey furrows, hang from protruding cheekbones, and his greenish hands are folded beneath his arms. He is wearing a coarse blue shirt, and his rumpled hair is so curly it looks like the bottom of a barnacle-covered ship. He does not move, and the true sign of his existence is that difficult whistling breathing (as if every breath must breach a flood-gate of phlegm, irritation, and abuse) that I had already heard through the chinks of the entry hall.

Ridiculously, he murmurs: "Good afternoon . . . ," and I am disposed to forget everything: the mystery, Amilamia, the assessment, the bicycle tracks. The apparition of this asthmatic old bear justifies a prompt retreat. I repeat "Good afternoon," this time with an inflection of farewell. The turtle's mask dissolves into an atrocious smile: every pore of that flesh seems fabricated of brittle rubber, of painted, peeling oilcloth. The arm reaches out and detains me.

"Valdivia died four years ago," says the man in a distant, choking voice that issues from his belly instead of his larynx: a weak, high-pitched voice.

Held by that strong, almost painful, claw, I tell myself it is useless to pretend. But the wax and rubber faces observing me say nothing and for that reason I am able, in spite of everything, to pretend one last time, to pretend that I am speaking to myself when I say:

"Amilamia. . . ."

Yes; no one will have to pretend any longer. The fist that clutches my arm affirms its strength for only an instant, immediately its grip loosens, then it falls, weak and trembling, before rising to take the waxen hand touching the shoulder: the señora, perplexed for the first time, looks at me with the eyes of a violated bird and sobs with a dry moan that does not disturb the rigid astonishment of her features. Suddenly the ogres of my imagination are two solitary, abandoned, wounded old people, scarcely able to console themselves in the shuddering clasp of hands that fills me with shame.

My fantasy has brought me to this stark dining room to violate the intimacy and the secret of two human beings exiled from life by something I no longer have the right to share. I have never despised myself more. Never have words failed me in such a clumsy way. Any gesture of mine would be in vain: shall I approach them, shall I touch them, shall I caress the woman's head, shall I ask them to excuse my intrusion? I return the notebook to my jacket pocket. I toss into oblivion all the clues in my detective story: the comic book, the lipstick, the nibbled fruit, the bicycle tracks, the blue-checked apron. . . . I decide to leave this house in silence. The old man, from behind those thick eyelids, must have noticed me. The high breathy voice says:

"Did you know her?"

That past, so natural they must use it every day, finally destroys my illusions. There is the answer. Did you know her? How many years? How many years must the world have lived without Amilamia, assassinated first by my forgetfulness, and revived, scarcely yesterday, by a sad impotent memory? When did those serious grey eyes cease to be astonished by the delight of an always solitary garden? When did those lips cease to pout or press together thinly in that ceremonious seriousness with which, I now realize, Amilamia must have discovered and consecrated the objects and events of life that, she knew perhaps intuitively, was fleeting?

"Yes, we played together in the park. A long time ago."

"How old was she?" says the old man, his voice even more muffled.

"She must have been about seven. No, older than seven."

The woman's voice rises, along with the arms that seem to implore:

"What was she like, señor? Tell us what she was like, please."

I close my eyes. "Amilamia is my memory, too. I can only compare her to the things that she touched, that she brought, that she discovered in the park. Yes. Now I see her, coming down the hill. No. It isn't true that it was a barely elevated patch of stubble. It was a hill, with grass, and Amilamia's coming and going had traced a path, and she waved to me from the top before she started down, accompanied by the music, yes, the music I saw, the painting I smelled, the tastes I heard, the odors I touched . . . my hallucination. . . ." Do they hear me? "She came, waving, dressed in white, in a blue-checked apron . . . the one you have hanging on the *azotea*. . . ."

They take my arms and still I do not open my eyes.

"What was she like, señor?"

"Her eyes were grey and the color of her hair changed in the reflection of the sun and the shadow of the trees. . . ."

They lead me gently, the two of them; I hear the man's labored breathing, the cross on the rosary hitting against the woman's body.

"Tell us, please. . . ."

"The air brought tears to her eyes when she ran; when she reached my bench her cheeks were silvered with happy tears. . . ."

I do not open my eyes. Now we are going upstairs. Two, five, eight, nine, twelve steps. Four hands guide my body.

"What was she like, what was she like?"

"She sat beneath the eucalyptus and wove garlands from the branches and pretended to cry so I would quit my reading and go over to her. . . ."

Hinges creak. The odor overpowers everything else: it routs the other senses, it takes its seat like a yellow Mogul upon the throne of my hallucination; heavy as a coffin, insinuating as the slither of draped silk, ornamented as a Turkish sceptre, opaque as a deep, lost vein of ore, brilliant as a dead star. The hands no longer hold me. More than the sobbing, it is the trembling of the old people that envelops me. Slowly, I open my eyes: first through the dizzying liquid of my cornea then through the web of my eyelashes, the room suffocated in that enormous battle of perfumes is disclosed, effluvia and frosty, almost flesh-like petals; the presence of the flowers is so strong here they seem to take on the quality of living flesh — the sweetness of the jasmine, the nausea of the lilies, the tomb of the tuberose, the temple of the gardenia. Illuminated through the incandescent wax lips of heavy sputtering candles, the small windowless bedroom with its aura of wax and humid flowers assaults the very center of my plexus, and from there, only there at the solar center of life, am I able to revive and to perceive beyond the candles, among the scattered flowers, the accumulation of used toys: the colored hoops and wrinkled balloons, cherries dried to transparency, wooden horses with scraggly manes, the scooter, blind and hairless dolls, bears spilling their sawdust, punctured oilcloth ducks, moth-eaten dogs, worn-out jumping ropes, glass jars of dried candy, wornout shoes, the tricycle (three wheels? no, two, and not like a bicycle — two *parallel* wheels below), little woolen and leather shoes; and, facing me, within reach of my hand, the small coffin raised on paper flower-decorated blue boxes, flowers of life this time, carnations and sunflowers, poppies and tulips, but like the others, the ones of death, all part of a potion brewed by the atmosphere of this funeral hot-house in which reposes, inside the silvered coffin, between the black silk sheets, upon the pillow of white satin, that motionless and serene face framed in lace, highlighted with rose-colored tints, eyebrows traced by the lightest trace of pencil, closed lids, real eyelashes, thick, that cast a tenuous shadow on cheeks as healthy as those of the days in the park. Serious red lips, set almost in the angry pout that Amilamia feigned so I would come to play. Hands joined over the breast. A chapelet, identical to the mother's, strangling that cardboard neck. Small white shroud on the clean, prepubescent, docile body.

The old people, sobbing, have knelt.

I reach out my hand and run my fingers over the porcelain face of my friend. I feel the coldness of those painted features, of the doll queen who presides over the pomp of this royal chamber of death. Porcelain, cardboard, and cotton. *Amilamia wil not forget her good frend — com see me here lik I draw it.*

I withdraw my fingers from the false cadaver. Traces of my fingerprints remain where I touched the skin of the doll.

And nausea crawls in my stomach where the candle smoke and the sweet stench of the lilies in the enclosed room have settled. I turn my back on Amilamia's sepulchre. The woman's hand touches my arm. Her wildly staring eyes do not correspond with the quiet, steady voice.

"Don't come back, señor. If you truly loved her, don't come back again."

I touch the hand of Amilamia's mother. I see through nauseous eyes the old man's head buried between his knees, and I go out of the room to the stairway, to the living room, to the patio, to the street.

5

If not a year, nine or ten months have passed. The memory of that idolatry no longer frightens me. I have forgotten the odor of the flowers and the image of the petrified doll. The real Amilamia has returned to my memory and I have felt, if not content, sane again: the park, the living child, my hours of adolescent reading, have triumphed over the spectres of a sick cult. The image of life is the more powerful. I tell myself that I shall live forever with my real Amilamia, the conqueror of the caricature of death. And one day I dare look again at that notebook with graph paper where I wrote the information of the false assessment. And from its pages, once again, falls Amilamia's card with its terrible childish scrawl and its map for getting from the park to her house. I smile as I pick it up. I bite one of the edges, thinking that in spite of everything, the poor old people would accept this gift.

Whistling, I put on my jacket and knot my tie. Why not visit them and offer them this paper with the child's own writing?

I am running as I approach the one-story house. Rain is beginning to fall in large isolated drops that bring from the earth with magical immediacy an odor of damp benediction that seems to stir the humus and precipitate the fermentation of everything living with its roots in the dust.

I ring the bell. The shower increases and I become insistent. A shrill voice shouts: "I'm going!" and I wait for the figure of the mother with her eternal rosary to open the door for me. I turn up the collar of my jacket. My clothes, my body, too, smell different in the rain. The door opens.

"What do you want? How wonderful you've come!"

The misshapen girl sitting in the wheelchair lays one hand on the doorknob and smiles at me with an indecipherably wry grin. The hump on her chest converts the dress into a curtain over her body, a piece of white cloth that nonetheless lends an air of coquetry to the blue-checked apron. The little woman extracts a pack of cigarettes from her apron pocket and rapidly lights a cigarette, staining the end with orange-painted lips. The smoke causes the beautiful grey eyes to squint. She arranges the coppery, wheat-colored, permanently waved hair: She stares at me all the time with a desolate, inquisitive, and hopeful — but at the same time fearful — expression.

"No, Carlos. Go away. Don't come back."

And from the house, at the same moment, I hear the high breathy breathing of the old man, coming closer and closer.

"Where are you? Don't you know you're not supposed to answer the door? Go back! Devil's spawn! Do I have to beat you again?"

And the water from the rain trickles down my forehead, over my cheeks, and into my mouth, and the little frightened hands drop the comic book onto the damp stones.

MAVIS GALLANT

Mavis Gallant, born in Montreal in 1922, was raised in a bilingual family and sent at the age of four to a French convent school. She requested books from home, and those she was sent were written in English, a casual occurrence which she believes influenced her decision to write in that language. "[It] seemed to me the language of freedom and the open world. It was also the language of *stories.*" Throughout her childhood and adolescence Gallant wrote almost exclusively poetry; at nineteen she began to write prose. After working briefly for a newspaper in Montreal, she moved in 1950 to Paris, where she has lived ever since. Her stories, almost all of which were published initially in *The New Yorker,* are collected in a number of volumes: *The Other Paris* (1956), *My Heart Is Broken* (1964), *The Pegnitz Junction* (1973), *The End of the World* (1974), *From the Fifteenth District* (1979), *Home Truths* (1981), and *Overhead in a Balloon* (1979). Childhood and expatriation are prevalent concerns in Gallant's writing — and, with them, loneliness and difference. But she doesn't treat individual sensibilities with sentimentality or pathos. Like two of her acknowledged literary influences — Lewis Carroll and E. M. Forster — she brings to her themes a certain elegant wryness of tone. Yet her compassion is always just under the surface, and it quietly persuades the reader's own. Such is the case in the two stories here, "The Cost of Living" and "The Ice Wagon Going Down the Street."

The Cost of Living

Louise, my sister, talked to Sylvie Laval for the first time on the stairs of our hotel on a winter afternoon. At five o'clock the skylight over the stairway and the blank, black windows on each of the landings were pitch dark — dark with the season, dark with the cold, dark with the dark air of cities. The only light on the street was the blue neon sign of a snack bar. My sister had been in Paris six months, but she still could say, "What a funny French word that is, Puss — '*snack.*' " Louise's progress down the steps was halting and slow. At the best of times she never hurried, and now she was guiding her bicycle and carrying a trench coat, a plaid scarf, Herriot's "Life of Beethoven," Cassell's English-French, a bottle of cough medicine she intended to exchange for another brand, and a notebook, in which she had listed facts about nineteenth-century music under so many headings, in so many divisions of divisions, that she had lost sight of the whole.

The dictionary, the Herriot, the cough medicine, and the scarf were mine. I was the music mistress, out in all weathers, subject to chills, with plenty of woolen garments to lend. I had not come to Paris in order to *solfège* to stiff-fingered children. It happened that at the late age of twenty-seven I had run away from home. High time, you might say; but rebels can't always be choosers. At first I gave lessons so as to get by, and then I did it for a living, which is not the same thing. My older sister followed me — wisely, calmly, with plenty of money for travel — six years later, when both our parents had died. She was accustomed to a busy life at home in Australia, with a large house to look after and our invalid mother to nurse. In Paris, she found time on her hands. Once she had visited all the museums, and cycled around the famous squares, and read what was written on the monuments, she felt she was wasting her opportunities. She decided that music might be useful, since she had once been taught to play the piano; also, it was bound to give us something in common. She was making a serious effort to know me. There was a difference of five years between us, and I had been away from home for six. She enrolled in a course of lectures, took notes, and went to concerts on a cut-rate student's card.

I'd better explain about that bicycle. It was heavy and old — a boy's bike, left by a cousin killed in the war. She had brought it with her from Australia, thinking that Paris would be an easy, dreamy city, full of trees and full of time. The promises that led her, that have been made to us all at least once in our lives, had sworn faithfully there would be angelic children sailing boats in the fountains, and calm summer streets. But the parks were full of brats and quarreling mothers, and the bicycle was a nuisance everywhere. Still, she rode it; she would have thought it wicked to spend money on bus fares when there was a perfectly good bike to use instead.

We lived on the south side of the Luxembourg Gardens, where streets must have been charming before the motorcars came. Louise was hounded by buses and small, pitiless automobiles. Often, as I watched her from a window of our hotel, I thought of how she must seem to Parisian drivers — the very replica of the governessy figure the French, with their passion for categories and their disregard of real evidence, instantly label "the English Miss." It was a verdict that would have astonished her, if she had known, for Louise believed that "Australian," like "Protestant," was written upon her, plain as could be. She had no idea of the effect she gave, with her slow gestures, her straight yellow hair, her long face, her hand-stitched mannish gloves and shoes. The inclination of her head and the quarter-profile of cheek, ear, and throat could seem, at times, immeasurably tender. Full-face, the head snapped to, and you saw the lines of duty from nose to mouth, and the too pale eyes. The Prussian ancestry on our mother's side had given us something bleached and cold. Our faces were variations on a theme of fair hair, light brows. The mixture was weak in me. I had inherited the vanity, the stubbornness, without the will; I was too proud to follow and too lame to command. But physically we were nearly alike. The characteristic fold of skin at the outer corner of the eye, slanting down — we both had that. And I could have used a word about us, once, if I dared: "dainty." A preposterous word; yet, looking at the sepia studio portrait of us, taken twenty-five years ago, when I was eight and Louise thirteen, you could imagine it. Here is Louise, calm and straight, with her hair brushed on her shoulders, and her pretty hands; there am I, with organdy frock, white shoes, ribbon, and fringe. Two little Anglo-German girls, accomplished at piano, Old Melbourne on the father's side, Church of England to the bone: Louise and Patricia — Lulu and Puss. We hated each other then.

Once, before Louise left Paris forever, I showed her a description of her that had been written by Sylvie Laval. It was part of a cast of characters around whom Sylvie evidently meant to construct a film. I may say that Sylvie never wrote a scenario, or anything like one; but she belonged to a Paris where one was "writer" or "artist" or "actor" without needing to prove the point. "The Australian," wrote Sylvie, in a hand that showed an emotional age of nine, "is not elegant. All her skirts are too long, and she should not knit her own sweaters and hats. She likes Berlioz and the Romantics, which means corrupt taste. She lives in a small hotel on the left bank because [erased] She has an income she tries to pass off as moderate, which she probably got from a poor old mother, who died at last. Her character is innocent and romantic, but she is a mythomaniac and certainly cold. This [here Sylvie tried to spell a word unknown to me] makes it hard to guess her age. Her innocence is phenomenal, but she knows more than she says. She resembles the Miss Bronty [crossed out] Bron-thee [crossed out] Brounte, the English lady who wore her hair parted in front and lived to a great old age after writing many moral novels and also Wuthering Heights."

I found the notes for the film in a diary after Sylvie had left the hotel. Going by her old room, I stopped at the open door. I could see M. Rablis, who owned the hotel and who had been Sylvie's lover, standing inside. He stood, the heart of a temper storm, the core of a tiny hurricane, and he flung her abandoned effects onto a pile of ragged books and empty bottles. I think he meant to keep everything, even the bottles, until Sylvie came back to settle her bill and return the money he said she had stolen from his desk. There were Javel bottles and whiskey bottles and yoghurt bottles and milk bottles and bottles for olive oil and tonic water and medicine and wine. Onto the pile went her torn stockings, her worn-out shoes. I recognized the ribbons and the *broderie anglaise* of a petticoat my sister had once given her as a present. The petticoat suited Sylvie — the tight waist, and the wide skirt — and it suited her even more after the embroidery became unstitched and flounces began to hang. Think of draggled laces, sagging hems, ribbons undone; that was what Sylvie was like. Hair in the eyes, sluttish little Paris face — she was a curious friend for immaculate Louise. When M. Rablis saw me at the door, he calmed down and said, "Ah, Mademoiselle. Come in and see if any of this belongs to you. She stole from everyone — miserable little thief." But "little thief" sounded harmless, in French, in the feminine. It was a woman's phrase, a joyous term, including us all in a capacity for frivolous mischief. I stepped inside the room and picked up the diary, and a Japanese cigarette box, and the petticoat, and one or two other things.

That winter's day when Sylvie talked to Louise for the first time, Louise was guiding her bicycle down the stairs. It would be presumptuous for me to say what she was thinking, but I can guess: she was more than likely converting the price of oranges, face powder, and Marie-biscuits from French francs to Australian shillings and pence. She was, and she is, exceptionally prudent. Questions of upbringing must be plain to the eye and ear — if not, better left unexplained. Let me say only that it was a long training in modesty that made her accept this wretched hotel, where, with frugal pleasure, she drank tea and ate Marie-biscuits, heating the water on an electric stove she had been farsighted enough to bring from home. Her room had dusty claret hangings. Silverfish slid from under the carpet to the cracked linoleum around the washstand. She could have lived in comfort, but I doubt if it occurred to her to try. With every mouthful of biscuit and every swallow of tea, she celebrated our mother's death and her own release. Louise had nursed Mother eleven years. She nursed her eleven years, buried her, and came to Paris with a bicycle and an income.

Now, Sylvie, who knew nothing about duty and less about remorse, would have traded her soul, without a second's bargaining, for Louise's room; for Sylvie lived in an ancient linen cupboard. The shelves had been taken out and a bed, a washstand, a small table, a straight chair pushed inside. In order to get to the window, one had to pull the table away and climb over the chair. This room, or cupboard, gave straight onto the stairs, between two floors. The door was flush with the staircase wall; only a ravaged keyhole suggested that the panel might be any kind of door. As she usually forgot to shut it behind her, anyone who wanted could see her furrowed bed and the basin, in which underclothes floated among islands of scum. She would plunge down the stairs, leaving a blurred impression of mangled hair and shining eyes. Her eyes were a true black, with the pupil scarcely distinct from the iris. Later I knew that she came from the southwest of France; I think that some of her people were Basques. The same origins gave her a stocky peasant's build and thick, practical hands. Her hand, grasping the stair rail, and the firm tread of her feet specified a quality of strength that had nothing in common with the forced liveliness of Parisian girls, whose energy seemed to me as thin and strung up as their voices. Her scarf, her gloves flew from her like birds. Her shoes could never keep up with her feet. One of my memories of Sylvie — long before I knew anything about her, before I knew even her name — is of her halting, cursing loudly with a shamed smile, scrambling up or down a few steps, and shoving a foot back into a lost ballerina shoe. She wore those thin slippers out on the streets, under the winter rain. And she wore a checked skirt, a blue sweater, and a scuffed plastic jacket that might have belonged to a boy. Passing her, as she hung over the banister calling to someone below, you saw the tensed muscle of an arm or leg, the young neck, the impertinent head. Someone ought to have drawn her — but somebody has: Sylvie was the coarse and grubby Degas dancer, the girl with the shoulder thrown back and the insolent chin. For two pins, or fewer, that girl staring out of flat canvas would stick out her tongue or spit in your face. Sylvie had the voice you imagine belonging to the picture, a voice that was common, low-pitched, but terribly penetrating. When she talked on the telephone, you could hear her from any point in the hotel. She owned the telephone, and she read *Cinémonde,* a magazine about film stars, by the hour, in the lavatory or (about once every six weeks) while soaking in the tub. There was one telephone and one tub for the entire hotel, and one lavatory for every floor. Sylvie was always where you wanted to be; she had always got there first. Having got there, she remained, turning pages, her voice cheerfully lifted in the newest and most melancholy of popular songs.

"Have you noticed that noisy girl?" Louise said once, describing her to me and to the young actor who had the room next to mine.

We were all three in Louise's room, which now had the look of a travel bureau and a suburban kitchen combined; she had covered the walls with travel posters and bought a transparent plastic tablecloth. Pottery dishes in yellow and blue stood upon the shelves. Louise poured tea and gave us little cakes. I remember that the young man and I, both well into the age of reason, sat up very straight and passed spoons and paper napkins back and forth with constant astonished cries of "Thank you" and "Please." It was something about Louise; she was so kind, so hospitable, she made one want to run away.

"I never notice young girls," said the young man, which seemed to me a fatuous compliment, but Louise turned pink. She appeared to be waiting for something more from him, and so he went on, "I know the girl you mean." It was not quite a lie. I had seen Sylvie and this boy together many times. I had heard them in his room, and I had passed them on the stairs. Well, it was none of my affair.

Until Louise's arrival, I had avoided meeting anyone in the hotel. Friendship in bohemia meant money borrowed, recriminations, complaints, tears, theft, and deceit. I kept to myself, and I dressed like Louise, which was as much a disguise as my bohemian way of dressing in Melbourne had been. This is to explain why I had never introduced Louise to anyone in the hotel. As for the rest of Paris, I didn't need to bother; Louise arrived with a suitcase of introductions and a list of names as long as the list for a wedding. She was not shy, she wanted to "get to know the people," and she called at least once on every single person she had an introduction to. That was how it happened that she and the actor met outside the hotel, in a different quarter of Paris. They had seen each other across the room, and each of them thought "I wonder who that is?" before discovering they lived in the same place. This sort of thing is supposed never to happen in cities, and it does happen.

She met him on the twenty-first of December in the drawing room of a house near the Parc Monceau. She had been invited there by the widow of a man in the consular service who had been to Australia and had stayed with an uncle of ours. It was one of the names on Louise's list. Before she had been many weeks in Paris, she knew far more than I did about the hard chairs, cheerless lights, and gray-pink antique furniture of French rooms. The hobby of the late consul had been collecting costumes. The drawing room was lined with glass cases in which stood headless dummies wearing the beads and embroidery of Turkey, Macedonia, and Greece. It was a room intended not for people but for things — this was a feeling Louise said she often had about rooms in France. Thirty or forty guests drifted about, daunted by the museum display. They were given whiskey to drink and sticky cakes. Louise wore the gray wool dress that was her "best" and the turquoise bracelets our Melbourne grandfather brought back from a voyage to China. They were the only ornaments I have ever seen her wearing. She talked to a poet who carried in his pocket an essay about him that had been printed years before — yellow, brittle bits of paper, like beech leaves. She consoled a wild-haired woman who complained that her daughter had begun to carry on. "How old is your daughter?" said Louise. The woman replied, "Thirty-five. And you know how men are now. They have no respect for girlhood any more." "It is very difficult," Louise agreed. She was getting to know the people, and was pleased with her afternoon. The consul's widow looked toward the doors and muttered that Cocteau was coming, but he never came. All at once Louise heard her say, in answer to a low-toned question, "She's Australian," and then she heard, "She's like a coin, isn't she? Gold and cold. She's interested in music, and lives over on the Left Bank, just as you do — except that you don't give your address, little monkey, not even to your mother's friends. I had such a lot of trouble getting a message to you. Perhaps she's your sort, although she's much too old for you. She doesn't know how to talk to men." The consul's widow hadn't troubled to lower her voice — the well-bred Parisian voice that slices stone.

Louise accepted the summing up, which was inadequate, like any other. Possibly she did not know how to talk to men — at least the men she had met here. Because she thought people always said what they meant and no more than they intended, her replies were disconcerting; she never understood that the real, the unmentioned, topic was implicit between men and women. I had often watched her and seen the pattern — obtuseness followed by visible surprise — which made her seem more than ever an English Miss. She said to the young man who had asked the question about her, and who now was led across to be presented, "Yes, that's quite right. I don't talk to men much, although I do listen. I haven't any brothers and I went to Anglican convents."

That was abrupt and Australian and spinsterish, if you like, but she had been married. She had been married at eighteen to Collie Tate. After a few months his regiment was sent to Malaya, and before she'd had very many letters from him he was taken prisoner and died. He must have been twenty. Louise seemed to have forgotten Collie, obliterating, in her faithlessness, not only his death but the fact that he had ever lived. She wore the two rings he had given her. They had rubbed her fingers until calluses formed. She was at ease with the rings and with the protective thickening around them, but she had forgotten him.

The young actor gravely pointed out that the name he was introduced to her by — Patrick something — was a stage name, and after Louise had sat down on a gilt chair he sat down at her feet. She had never seen anyone sitting on the floor in France, and that made her look at him. She probably looked at his hands; most women think a man's character is shown in his hands. He was dressed like many of the students in the streets around our hotel, but her practical eye measured the cost and cut of the clothes, and she saw he was false-poor, pretending. There was something rootless and unclaimed in the way he dressed, the way he sprawled, and in his eagerness to explain himself; but for all that, he was French.

"You aren't what I think of as an Australian," he said, looking up at her. He must have learned to smile, and glance, and give his full attention, when he was still very young; perhaps he charmed his mother that way. "I didn't know there were any attractive women there."

"You might have met people from Sydney," Louise said. "I'm from Melbourne."

"Do the nice Australians come from Melbourne?"

"Yes, they do."

He looked at her briefly and suspiciously. Surely anyone so guileless seeming must be full of guile? If he had asked, she would have told him that, tired of clichés, she met each question as it came up. She returned his look, as if glancing out of shadows. There must have been something between them then — a mouse squeak of knowledge. She was not a little girl freshly out of school, wishing she had a brother; she was thirty-eight, and had been widowed nineteen years.

They discovered they lived in the same hotel. He thought he must have seen her, he said, particularly when she spoke of the bicycle. He remembered seeing a bicycle, someone guiding it up and down. "Perhaps your sister," he said, for she had told him about me. "Perhaps," said serpent Louise. She thought that terribly funny of him, funny enough to repeat to me. Then she told him that she was certain she had heard his voice. Wasn't he the person who had the room next to her sister? There was an actor in that room who read aloud — oh, admirably, said Louise. (He did read, and I had told her so; he read in the groaning, suffering French classical manner that is so excruciating to foreign ears.) He was that person, he said, delighted. They had recognized each other then; they had known each other for days. He said again that "Patrick" was a stage name. He was sorry he had taken it — I have forgotten why. He told her he was waiting for a visa so that he could join a repertory company that had gone to America. He had been tubercular once; there were scars, or shadows, on his lungs. That was why the visa was taking so long. He tumbled objects out of his pockets, as if everything had to be explained to her. He showed a letter from the embassy, telling him to wait, and a picture of a house in the Dordogne that belonged to his family, where he would live when he grew old. She looked at the stone house and the garden and the cherry trees, and her manner when she returned it to him was stiff and shy. She said nothing. He was young, but old enough to know what that sudden silence meant; and he woke up. When the consul's widow came to see how they were getting on and if one of them wanted rescuing, they said together, "We live in the same hotel!" Had anything as marvelous ever happened in Paris, and could it ever happen again? The woman looked at Louise then and said, "I was wrong about you, was I? Discreet but sure — that's how Anglo-Saxons catch their fish."

It was enough to make Louise sit back in her chair. "What will people say?" has always been, to her, deeply real. In that light the gray wool dress she was wearing and the turquoise bracelets were cold as snow. She was a winter figure in the museum room. She was a thrifty widow; and abstemious traveler counting her comforts in shillings and pence. She was a blunt foreigner, not for an instant to be taken in. Her most profound belief about herself was that she was too honest to fall in love. She believed that men were basically faithless, and that women could not love more than once. She never forgave a friend who divorced. Having forgotten Collie, she thought she had never loved at all.

"Could you let me have some money?"

That was the first time Sylvie talked to Louise. Those were Sylvie's first words, on the winter afternoon, on the dark stairs. The girl was around the bend of a landing, looking down. Louise stopped, propping the bicycle on the wall, and stared up. Sylvie leaned into the stair well so that the dead light from the skylight was behind her; then she drew back, and there was a touch of winter light upon her, on the warm skin and inquisitive eyes.

I may say that giving money away to strangers was not the habit of my sister, our family, or the people we grew up with. Louise stood, in her tweed skirt, her arm aching with the weight of so many useful objects. The mention of money automatically evoked two columns of figures. In all financial matters, Louise was bound to the rows of numbers in her account books. These account books were wrapped in patent leather, and came from a certain shop in Melbourne; our father's ledgers had never been bought in any other place. The columns were headed "Paid" and "Received," in the old-fashioned way, but at the top of each page our father, and then Louise, crossed out the printed words and wrote "Necessary" and "Unnecessary." When Louise was obliged to buy a Christmas or birthday present for anyone, she marked the amount she had spent under "Unnecessary." I had never attached any significance to her doing this; she was closer to our parents than I, and that was how they had always reckoned. She guarded her books as jealously as a diary. What can be more intimate than a record of money and the way one spends it? Think of what Pepys has revealed. Nearly everything we know about Leonardo is summed up in his accounts.

"Well, I do need money," said the girl, rather cheerfully. "Monsieur Rablis wants to put me out of my room again. Sometimes he makes me pay and sometimes he doesn't. Oh, imagine being on top of the world on top of a pile of money!" This was not said plaintively but with an intense vitality that was like a third presence on the stairs. Her warmth and her energy communicated so easily that there was almost too much, and some fell away and had its own existence.

That was all Louise could tell me later on. She had been asked to put her hand in her pocket for a stranger, for someone who had no claim on her at all, and she was as deeply shocked as if she had been invited to take part in an orgy — a comparison I do not intend as a joke.

"What if *I* asked you for money?" I suddenly said.

She looked at me with that pale-eyed appraisal and gently said, "Why, Puss, you've got what you want, haven't you? Haven't you got what you wanted out of life?" I had two woolen scarves, one plaid and one blue, which meant I had one to lend. Perhaps Louise meant that.

The absence of sun in Paris brought on a kind of irrationality at times, just as too much sun can drive one mad. If it had been anyone but my sister talking to me, I would have said that Sylvie was nothing but an apparition on the stairs. Who ever has heard of asking strangers for money? And one woman to another, at that. I know that I had never become accustomed to the northern solstice. The whitish sky and the evil Paris roofs and the cold red sun suggested a destiny so final that I wondered why everyone did not rebel or run away. Often after Christmas there was a fall of snow, and one could be amazed by the confident tracks of birds. But in a few weeks it was forgotten, and the tramps, the drunks, the unrepentant poor (locked up by the police so that they would not freeze on the streets) were released once more, and settled down in doorways and on the grilles over the Métro, where fetid air rose from the trains below, to await the coming of spring. I could see that Louise was perplexed by all this. She had been warned of the damp, but nothing had prepared her for those lumps of bodies, or for the empty sky. At four o'clock every day the sun appeared. It hung over the northwest horizon for a few minutes, like a malediction, and then it vanished and the city sank into night.

This is the moment to talk about Patrick. I think of him in that season — something to do with chill in the bones, and thermometers, and the sound of the rain. I had often heard his voice through the wall, and had guessed he was an actor. I knew him by sight. But I came home tired every night, disinclined to talk. I saw that everyone in this hotel was as dingy, as stationary, as I was myself, and I knew we were tainted with the same incompetence. Besides giving music lessons, I worked in a small art gallery on the Ile de la Cité. I received a commission of one half of one per cent on the paintings I sold. I was a foreigner without a working permit, and had no legal recourse. Every day, ten people came into that filthy gallery and asked for my job. Louise often said, "But this is a rich country, Puss. Why are there no jobs, and why are people paid nothing?" I can only describe what I know.

Patrick: my sister's lover. Well, perhaps, but not for long. An epidemic of grippe came into the city, as it did every year. Patrick was instantly felled. He went into illness as if it were a haven, establishing himself in bed with a record-player and a pile of books and a tape recorder. I came down with it, too. Every day, Louise knocked on his door, and then on mine. She came down the stairs — her room was one flight above ours — pushing her bicycle, the plaid scarf tied under her chin. She was all wool and tweed and leather again. The turquoise bracelets had been laid in a drawer, the good gray dress put away. She fetched soup, aspirin, oranges, the afternoon papers. She was conscientious, and always had the right change. Louise was a minor heiress now, but I had never been pardoned. I inherited my christening silver and an income of fifteen shillings a month. They might have made it a pound. It was only fair; she had stayed home and carried trays and fetched the afternoon papers — just as she was doing now — while I had run away. Nevertheless, although she was rich and I was poor, she treated me as an equal. I mean by that that she never bought me a cheese sandwich or a thermos flask of soup without first taking the money for it out of the purse on my desk and counting out the correct change. I don't know if she made an equal of Patrick. The beginning had already rushed into the past and frozen there, as if, from the first afternoon, each had been thinking. This is how it will be remembered. After a few days she declined, or rose, to governess, nanny, errand girl, and dear old friend. What hurts me in the memory is the thought of all that golden virtue, that limpid will, gone to waste. He was such an insignificant young man. Long eyelashes, grave smile — I could have snapped him out between thumb and finger like a bug. Poor Louise! She asked so many questions but never the right kind. God help you if you lose your footing in this country. There are no second tries. Was there any difference between a music teacher without a working permit, a tubercular actor trying to get to America, and a man bundled in newspapers sleeping on the street? Louise never saw that. She was as careful in her human judgments as she was in her accounts. Unable to squander, she wondered where to deposit her treasures of pity, affection, and love.

Patrick was reading to himself in English, with the idea that it would be useful in New York. Surely he might have thought of it before? Incompetence was written upon him as plainly as on me, and that was one of the reasons I averted my eyes. Louise was expected to correct his accent, and once he asked me to choose his texts. He read "Endgame" and "Waiting for Godot," which I heard through the wall. Can you imagine listening to Beckett when you are lying in bed with a fever? I struggled up one day, and into a dressing gown, and dumped on his bed an armload of poetry. "If you *must* have Irish misery," I said, and I gave him Yeats. English had one good effect; he stopped declaiming. The roughness of it took the varnish off his tongue. "Nor dread nor hope attend a dying animal," I heard through the wall one Thursday afternoon, and the tone was so casual that he might have been asking for a cigarette or the time of a train. "Nor dread nor hope . . ." I saw the window and heard the rain and realized it was my thirty-third birthday. Patrick had great patience, and listened to his own voice again and again.

Louise nursed us, Patrick and me, as if we were one: one failing appetite, one cracked voice. She was accustomed to bad-tempered invalids, and it must have taken two of us to make one of Mother. She fed us on soup and oranges and soda biscuits. The soda biscuits were hard to find in Paris, but she crossed to the Right Bank on her bicycle and brought them back from the exotic food shops by the Madeleine. They were expensive, and neither of us could taste them, but she thought that soda biscuits were what we ought to have. She planned her days around our meals. Every noon she went out with an empty thermos flask, which she had filled with soup at the snack bar across the street. The oranges came from the market, rue St.-Jacques. Our grippe smelled of oranges, and of leek-and-potato soup.

Louise had known Patrick seventeen days, and he had been ailing for twelve, when she talked to Sylvie again. The door to Sylvie's room was open. She sat up in her bed, with her back to a filthy pillow, eating *pain-au-chocolat*. There were crumbs on the blanket and around her chin. She saw Louise going by with a string bag and a thermos, and she called, "Madame!" Louise paused, and Sylvie said, "If you are coming straight back, would you mind bringing me a cheese sandwich? There's money for it in the chrysanthemum box." This was a Japanese cigarette box in which she kept her savings. "I am studying for the stage," she went on, without giving Louise a chance to reply. This was to explain a large mirror that had been propped against the foot of the bed so that she could look at herself. "It's important for me to know just what I'm like," she said seriously. "In the theatre, everything is enlarged a hundred times. If you bend your little finger" — she showed how — "from the top gallery it must seem like a great arc."

"Aren't you talking about films?" said Louise.

Sylvie screwed her eyes shut, thought, and said, "Well, if it isn't films it's Brecht. Anyway, it's something I've heard." She laughed, with her hands to her face, but she was watching between her fingers. Then she folded her hands and began telling poor Louise how to sit, stand, and walk on the stage — rattling off what she had learned in some second-rate theatrical course. Patrick had told us that every unemployed actor in Paris believed he could teach.

They still had not told each other their names; and if Louise walked into that cupboard room, and bothered to hear Sylvie out, and troubled to reply, it must have been only because she had decided one could move quite easily into another life in France. She worked hard at understanding, but she was often mistaken. I know she believed the French had no conventions.

"I stay in bed because my room is so cold," said Sylvie, rapidly now, as if Louise might change her mind and turn away. "This room is an icebox — there isn't even a radiator — so I stay in bed and study and I leave the door open so as to get some of the heat from the stairs." A tattered book of horoscopes lay face down on the blanket. Tacked to the wall was a picture someone had taken of Sylvie asleep on a sofa, during or after a party, judging from the scene. The slit of window in the room gave on a court, but it was a bright court, with a brave tree whose roots had cracked the paving.

"My name is Sylvie Laval," she said, and, wiping her palm on the bedsheet, prepared to shake hands.

"Louise Tate." Louise set the thermos down on Sylvie's table, between a full ashtray and a cardboard container of coagulated milk. She saw the Japanese box with the chrysanthemum painted on the lid, and picked it up.

"What a new element you are going to be for me," said Sylvie, settling back and watching with some amazement. "I shall observe you and become like you. Yes, that's the money box, and you must take whatever you need for the sandwich."

"Why do you want to observe me?" said Louise, turning and laughing at her.

"You look like an angel," Sylvie said. "I'm sure angels look like you."

"I was once told I looked like an English poet in first youth," said Louise, trying to pretend that Sylvie's intention had been ironical.

Sylvie tilted her little chin as if to say she knew what that was all about. "Your friends are poets," she said. "They must be like you, too — wise and calm. I wish I knew your friends."

"They are very plain people," said Louise, still smiling. "They wouldn't be much fun for a bright little thing like you."

"Foreigners?"

"Some. French, too." Louise was proud of her introductions.

Sylvie looked with her bold black eyes and said, "French. I knew it."

"Knew what?"

"You and the type upstairs. The great actor — the comedian." She bit her fingers, hesitating. Her features were coarse and sly. "You're so comic, the two of you, creeping about with your secret. But love is love, and everyone knows."

I have wondered since about that bit of mischief. I suppose Patrick had given Sylvie a role to play, because it was the only way he could control her. She had found out, or he had told, and he had warned her not to hurt Louise. Louise was someone who must be spared. She must never guess that he and Sylvie had been lovers. They thought Louise could never stand up to the truth; they thought no one could bear to be told the truth about anything after a certain age.

Sylvie, launched in a piece of acting, could not help overloading. "Do you know any other French people?" she said. "Never mind. There's me." She flung out her arms suddenly — to the mirror, not to Louise — and cried, "I am your French friend."

"She's got a picture of herself sound asleep, curled up with no shoes on," said Louise, talking in a new, breathless voice. "It must be the first thing she looks at in the morning when she wakes up. And she seems terribly emotional and generous. I don't know why, but she gives you the feeling of generosity. I'm sure she does herself a lot of harm."

We were in Patrick's room. Louise poured the daily soup into pottery bowls. I have often tried to imagine how he must have seemed to Louise. I doubt if she could have told you. From the beginning they stood too close; his face was like a painting in which there are three eyes and a double profile. No matter how far she backed off, later on, she never made sense of him. Let me tell what *I* remember. I remember that it was easy for him to talk, easy for him to say anything, so that I can hear a voice, having ceased to think of a face. He seldom gestured. Only his voice, which was trained, and could never be disguised, told that he did not think he was an ordinary person; he did not believe he was like anyone else in the world, not for a minute. I asked myself a commonplace question: What does she see in him? I should have wondered if she saw him at all. As for me, I saw him twice. I saw him the first time when Louise described the meeting in the consul's widow's drawing room, and I understood that the dazzling boy was only that droning voice through the wall. From the time of our grippe, I can see a spiral of orange peel, a water glass with air bubbles on the side of the glass, but I cannot see him. There was the bluish smoke of his caporal cigarettes, and the shape of Louise, like something seen against the light . . . None of it sharp.

One day I saw Patrick and Sylvie together, and that was plain, and clear, and well remembered. I had gone out in the rain to give a music lesson to a spoiled child, the ward of a doting grandmother. I came up the stairs, and because I heard someone laughing, or because I was feverish and beyond despair, I went into Patrick's room instead of my own.

Sylvie was there. She knelt on the floor, wearing her nightdress (the time must have been close to noon), struggling with Patrick for a bottle of French vodka, which tastes of marsh water and smells like eau de cologne. "Louise says mustn't drink," said Sylvie, in a babyish voice; "and besides it's mine." They stopped their puppy play when they saw me; there was a mock scurry, as if it were Puss who had the governess role instead of Louise. Then I noticed Louise. She sat before the window, reading a novel, taking no notice of her brawling pair. Her face was calm and happy and the lines of moral obligation had disappeared. She said, "Well, Puss," with our mother's inflection, and she seemed so young — nineteen or so — that I remembered how Collie had been in love with her once, before going to Malaya to be killed. Sylvie must have been born that year, the year Louise was married. I hadn't thought of that until now.

"When Berlioz was living in Italy," I said, "he heard that Marie Pleyel was going to be married, and so he disguised himself as a lady's maid and started off for Paris. He intended to assassinate Marie and her mother and perhaps the fiancé as well. But he changed his mind for some reason, and I think he went to Nice." This story rushed to my lips without reason. Berlioz and Marie Pleyel seemed to me living people, and the facts contemporary gossip. While I was telling it, I remembered they had all of them died. I forgot every word I had ever known of French, and told it in English, which Sylvie could not understand.

"You ought to be in bed, my pet," I heard Louise say.

Sylvie went on with something she had been telling before my arrival. She had an admirer who was a political cartoonist. His cartoons were ferocious, and one imagined him out on the boulevards of Paris doing battle with the police; but he was really a timid man, afraid of cats, and unable to cross most streets without trembling. "He spends thousands of francs," said Sylvie, sighing. She told how many francs she had seen him spending.

I said, "Money, money . . . it *does* bring happiness." I wondered if Louise recalled that Berlioz had written this, and that we had quarreled about it once.

Prone across the bed, leaning on his elbows, Patrick listened to Sylvie with grave attention, and I thought that here was a situation no amount of money could solve; for it must be evident to Louise, unless she were blind and had lost all feeling, that something existed between the two. The lark had stopped singing, but it had not died; it was alive and flying in the room. Sylvie, nibbling now on chocolates stuck to a paper bag, felt that I was staring at her, and turned her head.

"My room is so cold," she said humbly, "and I get so lonely, and finally I thought I'd come in to him."

"Quite right of you," I said, as if his time and his room were mine. But Sylvie seemed to think she had been dismissed. She licked the last of the chocolate from the paper, crumpled the bag, threw it at Patrick, and slammed the door. I sat down and leaned my head back and closed my eyes. I heard Patrick saying, "Read this," and when I looked again, Louise was on the edge of the bed with a letter in her hands. She bent over it. Her hair was like the sun — the real sun, not the sun we saw here.

"It says that your visa is refused," she said, in her flat, positive French. "It says that in six months you may apply again."

"That's what I understood. I thought you might understand more."

She smoothed the letter with both hands and made up her mind about saying something. She said, "Come to Australia."

"What?"

"Come to Australia. I'll see that they let you in; I can do that much for you. You can stay with me in Melbourne until you get settled. The house is enormous. It's too big for one person. The climate would be perfect for you."

Think of that courage: she'd have taken him home.

He looked as if she had said something completely empty of meaning, and then he appeared to understand; it was a splendid piece of mime. "What would I do in Australia? I can hardly talk the language."

"I've seen people arriving, without money, without English, without anything, and then they do as well as anyone."

"They were refugees," he said. "I've got my own country. I'm not a refugee."

"You were anxious enough to go to New York."

The apple never drops far from the tree; here was our mother all over again, saying something unpleasant but true. My dutiful sister, the good elder girl — I might have helped her then. I might have told her how men were, or what it was like in Paris. But I kept silent, and presently I heard him saying he was going home. He was going to the house in the Dordogne — the house he had shown her in the photograph. She may have been jealous of that house; in her place I should have been. He said that the winter in Paris had been bad for him; there hadn't been enough work. Next season he would try again.

"Your mother will be pleased to have you for a bit," said Louise, accepting it; but I doubt if any of us can accept humiliation so simply. She folded the letter and placed it quietly beside her on the blanket. She said, "I'd better put Puss to bed," and got to her feet. I don't believe they had much to say to each other after that. He went away for a week, came back to us for a fortnight, and then disappeared.

When I was recovering from that second attack of grippe, Louise made me go with her to the Faubourg St. Honoré to look at shops. Neither of us intended buying anything, but Louise thought the outing would do me good. Just as she was convinced invalids wanted soda biscuits, so she believed convalescents found a new purpose in living when they looked at pretty things. We looked at coats and ski boots and sweaters, and we stared at rare editions, and finally, fatigued and stupid, gazed endlessly at the brooches and strings of beads in an antique jewelry store.

"It can't be worth such an awful lot," said Louise, taking an interest in a necklace. The stones — agate, cornelian, red jasper — were rubbed and uneven, like glass that had been polished by waves. The charm of the necklace was in its rough, careless appearance and the warm color of the stones. I put one hand flat against the pane of the counter. When I took it away, I watched the imprint fade. I was accustomed to wanting what I could not have.

"Do you like it, Puss?" said Louise.

"Very much."

"So do I. It would be perfect for Sylvie."

That is all I can tell you: I am not Louise. She came out of the shop with a wrapped parcel in her hand, and said in a matter-of-fact tone that the stones were early-eighteenth-century seals, that the man had been most civil about taking her check, and that the necklace had cost a great deal of money. That was all until we reached the hotel, and then she said, "Puss, will you give it to her? She'll think it strange, coming from me."

"Why won't she think it just as odd if I give it?" I called, for Louise had simply moved on, leaving me outside Sylvie's door. I felt cross and foolish. Louise climbed slowly, one hand on the banister. I know now that she went straight upstairs to her room and marked the price of the necklace under "Necessary." It was not the real price but about a fifth of the truth. She absorbed the balance in the rest of her accounts by cheating heavily for a period of weeks. She charged herself an imaginary thousand francs for a sandwich and two thousand for a bunch of winter daisies, and inflated the cost of living until the cost of the necklace had disappeared.

I knocked on Sylvie's door, and heard her scuttling about behind it. "Come in!" she shouted. "Oh, it's you. I thought it was the horrible Rablis. I can't let him in when I'm not properly dressed, because . . . you know." She had pulled on a pair of slacks and a sweater I recognized as Patrick's.

"Louise wants you to have this," I said.

She took the box from me and sat down on the bed. She was terrified by this gift. Even the sight of the ribbons and tissue paper alarmed her. I saw that in terms of Sylvie's world Louise had made a mistake. The present was so extraordinary and it had been delivered in such a roundabout fashion that the girl thought she was being bought.

"My sister chose it for you on impulse," I said. I felt huge and uniformed, like a policeman. "It seems to me a ridiculous present for a girl who hasn't proper shoes or a decent winter coat, but she thought you'd like it."

She lifted the necklace out of its box and held it over her head and let it fall. She was an actress, true enough — Sarah Bernhardt to the life. But then she turned away from me, leaning on her hands, straining forward toward the mirror, and she stopped pretending. I saw on her impudent profile surprise and greed, and we understood, together, at the same moment, what could be had from women like Louise. Sylvie said, "Your sister must be very rich."

That jolted me. "Consider the necklace a kind of insurance if you want to," I said. "You can sell it if you need money. You can give it back when you don't want it any more." That stripped the giving of any intention; she was not obliged to admire Louise, or even be grateful.

She wore the necklace every day. It hung over her plastic coat, and on top of Patrick's old sweater. One night she fell up the stairs wearing it, and a piece of jasper broke away. The necklace had a grin to it then, with a cracked tooth. Louise scarcely noticed. Now that she had given the necklace away, she scarely saw it at all. Giving had altered her perceptions. She walked in her sleep, and part of her character, smothered until now, began to live and breathe in a dream. "I've hardly worn it," I can hear her telling Sylvie. "I bought it for myself, but it doesn't suit me." She said it about the tweed skirts, the quilted dressing gown, the stockings, the gloves, all purchased with Sylvie in mind. (She never felt the need to give me anything. She never so much as returned my scarf until she went back to Australia, and then it was simply a case of forgetting it, leaving it behind. She also left her trumped-up accounts. Sylvie abandoned her empty bottles and a diary and a dirty petticoat; my sister left my scarf and her false accounts. The stuff of her life is in those figures: "Dentist for S." "Shoes for S." "Oil stove for S." I was touched to find under "Necessary" "Aspirin for Puss." She had listed against it the price of a five-course meal. The two went together, the giving and the lying.)

The days drew out a quarter-second at a time. Patrick, who had been away (though not to the house in the Dordogne; he did not tell us where he was), returned to a different climate. Louise and Sylvie had become friends. They were silly and giggly, and had a private language and special jokes. The most unexpected remarks sent them off into fits of laughter. At times they hardly dared meet each other's eyes. It was maddening for anyone outside the society. I saw that Patrick was intrigued and then annoyed. The day he left (I mean, the day he left forever) he returned the books I'd lent him — Yeats, and the other poets — and he asked me what was happening between those two. I had never known him to be blunt. I gave him an explanation, but it was beside the truth. I could have said, "You don't need her; you refused Australia; and now you're going home." Instead, I told him, "Louise likes looking after people. It doesn't matter which one of us she looks after, does it? Sylvie isn't worth less than you or me. She loves the stage as much as you do. She'd starve to pay for her lessons."

"But Louise mustn't take that seriously," he said. "There are thousands of girls like Sylvie in Paris. They all have natural charm, and they don't want to work. They imagine there's no work to acting. Nothing about her acting is real. Everything is copied. Look at the way she holds her arms, and that quick turn of the head. She never stops posing, trying things out; but acting is something else."

I took my books from him and put them on my table. I said, "This is between you and Sylvie. It's got nothing to do with me."

They were young and ambitious and frightened; and they were French, so that their learned behavior was all smoothness. There was no crevice where an emotion could hold. I was thinking about Louise. It is one thing to go away, but it is terrible to be left.

I wanted him to go away, or stop telling me about Sylvie and Louise, but he would continue and I had to hear him say, "The difference between Sylvie and me is that I work. I believe in work. Sylvie believes in one thing after the other. Now she believes in Louise, and one day she'll turn on her."

"Why should she turn on her?"

"Because Louise is good," he said. This was the only occasion I remember when he had trouble saying what he meant. We stood face to face in my room, with the table and books between us. We had never been as near. Twice in that conversation he slipped from "*vous*" to "*toi,*" as if our tribal marks of incompetence gave us a right to intimacy. He stumbled over the words; stammered nearly. "She's so kind," he said. "She asks to be hurt."

"It's easy to be kind when you're an heiress."

"Aren't *you*?" I stared at him and he said, "Women like Louise make you think they can do anything, solve all your problems. Sylvie believes in magic. She believes in the good fairy, the endless wishes, the bottomless purse. I don't believe in magic." He had stopped groping. His actor's voice was as fluid and persistent as the winter rain. "But Sylvie believes, and one day she'll turn on Louise and hurt her."

"What do you expect me to do?" I said. "You keep talking about hurting and being hurt. What do you think my life is like? It's got nothing to do with me."

"Sylvie would leave Louise alone if you told her to," he said. "She isn't a clinger. She's a tough little thing. She's had to be ." There was the faintest coloration of class difference in his voice. I remembered that Louise had met him in a drawing room, even though he lived here, in the hotel, with Sylvie and me.

I said, "It's not my affair."

"Sylvie is good," he said stubbornly. That was all. He said "Sylvie," but he must have meant "Louise."

He left alone and went to the station alone. I was the only one to watch him go. Sylvie was out and Louise upstairs in her room. Unless I have dreamed it, it was then he told me he was ill. He was not going home after all but to a place in the mountains — near Grenoble, I think he said. That was why he had been away for a week; that was where he'd been. As he said those words, water rushed between us and we stood on opposite shores. He was sick, but I was well. We were both incompetent, but I was well. And I smiled and shook hands with him, and said goodbye.

In a book or a film one of us would have gone with him as far as the station. If he had disappeared in a country as big as Russia, one of us would have learned where he was. But he didn't disappear; he went to a town a few hundred miles distant and we never saw him again. I remember the rain on the skylight over the stairs. Louise may have looked out of her window; I would rather not guess. She may have wanted to come down at the last minute; but he had refused Australia, which meant he had refused her, and so she kept away.

Later on that day, she did something foolish: she stood in the passage and watched as his room was turned out by a maid. I managed to get her to sit on a chair. That was where Sylvie found her. Sylvie had come in from the street. Rain stood on her hair in perfect drops. She knelt beside Louise and began chafing her hands. "Tell me what it is," she said softly, looking up into her face. "How do you feel? What is it like? It must be something quite real."

"Of course it's real," I said heartily. "Come *on*, old girl."

Louise was clinging to Sylvie: she barely listened to me. "I feel as though I had no more blood," she said.

"That feeling won't last," said the girl. "He couldn't help leaving, could he? Think of how it would be if he had stayed beside you and been somewhere else — as good as miles and miles away." But I knew it was not Patrick but Collie who had gone. It was Collie who vanished before everything was said, turning his back, stopping his ears. I was thirteen and they were the love of my life. Sylvie said, "I wish I could be you and you could be me, for just this one crisis. I have too much blood and it never stops moving — never." She squeezed my sister's hand so hard that when she took her fingers away the mark of them remained in white bands. "Do you know what you must do now?" she said. "You must make yourself wait. Try to expect something. That will get the blood going again."

When I awoke the next day, I knew we were all three waiting. We waited for a letter, a telegram, a knock on the door. When Collie died, Louise went on writing letters. The letters began, "I can't believe that you are dead," which was chatty of her, not dramatic, and they went on giving innocent news. Mother and I found them and read them and tore them to shreds. We were afraid she would put them in the post and that they would be returned to her. Soon after Patrick had gone, Louise said to Sylvie, "I've forgotten what he was like."

"Like an actor," said Sylvie, with a funny little face. But I knew it was Collie Louise had meant.

Our relations became queer and strained. The final person, the judge, toward whom we were always turning for confirmation, was no longer there. Sylvie asked Louise outright for money now. If Patrick had been there to hear her, she might not have dared. Everything Louise replied touched off a storm. Louise seemed to be using a language every word of which offended Sylvie's ears. Sylvie had courted her, but now it was Louise who haunted Sylvie, sat in her cupboard room, badgered her with bursts of questions and pleas for secrecy. She asked Sylvie never to talk about her, never to disclose — she did not say what. When I saw them quarreling together, aimless and bickering, whispering and bored, I thought that a cloistered convent must be like that: a house without men.

"Did you have to stop combing your hair just because he left?" I heard Sylvie say. "You're untidy as Puss."

If you listen at doors, you hear what you deserve. She must have seemed thunderstruck, because Sylvie said, "Oh my God, don't look so helpless."

"I'm not helpless," said Louise.

"Why didn't you leave us alone?" Sylvie said. "Why didn't you just leave us with our weakness and our mistakes? You do so much, and you're so kind and good, and you get in the way, and no one dares hurt you."

That might have been the end of them, but the same afternoon Louise gave Sylvie a bottle of Miss Dior and the lace petticoat and a piece of real amber, and they went on being friends.

Soon after that scene, however, in March, Louise discovered two things. One was that Sylvie had an aunt and uncle living in Paris, so she was not as forsaken as she appeared to be. Sylvie told her this. The other had to do with Sylvie's social life, métier, and means. M. Rablis made one of his periodic announcements to the effect that Sylvie would have to leave the hotel — clothes, mirror, horoscopes, money box, and all. M. Rablis was, and is, a small truculent person. He keeps an underexercised dog chained to his desk. While the dog snarled and cringed, Louise said that she knew Sylvie had an aunt and uncle, and that she would make Sylvie go to them and ask them to pay their niece's back rent. Louise had an unshakable belief in the closeness of French families, having read about the welding influence of patriotism, the Church, and inherited property. She said that Sylvie would find some sort of employment. It was time to bring order into Sylvie's affairs, my sister said.

She was a type of client the hotel-keeper had often seen: the foreign, interfering, middle-aged female. He understood half she said, but was daunted by the voice, and the frozen eye, and the bird's-nest hair. The truth was that for long periods he forgot to claim Sylvie's rent. But he was not obsessed with her, and, in the long run, not French for nothing; he would as soon have had the money she owed. "She can stay," he said, perhaps afraid Louise might mention that he had been Sylvie's lover (although I doubt if she knew). "But I don't want her bringing her friends in at night. She never registers them, and whenever the police come around at night and find someone with Sylvie I have to pay a fine."

"Do you mean men?" said my wretched sister. "Do you mean the police come about men?"

Some of my sister's hardheaded common sense returned. She talked of making Sylvie a small regular allowance, which Sylvie was to supplement by finding a job. "Look at Puss," Louise said to her. "Look at how Puss works and supports herself." But Sylvie had already looked at me. Louise's last recorded present to Sylvie was a camera. Sylvie had told her some cocksure story about an advertising firm on the Rue Balzac, where someone had said she had gifts as a photographer. Later she changed her mind and said she was gifted as a model, but by that time Louise had bought the camera. She moved the listing in her books from "Necessary" to "Unnecessary." Mice, insects, and some birds have secret lives. She harped on the aunt and uncle, until one day I thought, She will drive Sylvie insane.

"Couldn't you ask them to make you a proper allowance?" Louise asked her.

"Not unless I worked for them, either cleaning for my aunt or in my uncle's shop. Needles and thread and mending wool. Just the thought of touching those old maid's things — no, I couldn't. And then, what about my lessons?"

"You used to sew for me," said Louise. "You darned beautifully. I can understand their point of view. You could make some arrangement to work half days. Then you would still have time for your lessons. You can't expect charity."

"I don't mind charity," said Sylvie. "You should know."

I remember that we were in the central market, in Les Halles, dodging among the barrows, pulling each other by the sleeve whenever a cart laden with vegetables came trundling toward us. This outing was a waste of time where I was concerned; but Sylvie hated being alone with Louise now. Louise had become so nagging, so dull. Louise took pictures of Sylvie with the new camera. Sylvie wanted a portfolio; she would take the photographs to the agency on the Rue Balzac, and then they would see how pretty she was and would give her a job. Louise had agreed, but she must have known it was foolish. Sylvie's bloom, divorced from her voice and her liveliness, simply disappeared. In any photograph I had ever seen of her she appeared unkempt and coarse and rather fat.

Her last words had been so bitter that I put my hand on the girl's shoulder, and at that her tension broke and she clutched Louise and cried, "I should be helped. Why shouldn't I be helped? I *should* be!"

When she saw how shocked Louise was, and how she looked to see if anyone had heard, Sylvie immediately laughed. "What will all those workmen say?" she said. It struck me how poor an actress she was; for the cry of "I should be helped" had been real, but nothing else had. All at once I had a strong instinct of revulsion. I felt that the new expenses in Louise's life were waste and pollution, and what had been set in motion by her giving was not goodness, innocence, courage, or generosity but something dark. I would have run away then, literally fled, but Sylvie had taken my sleeve and she began dragging me toward a fruit stall. "What if Louise took my picture here?" she said. "I saw something like that once. I make up my eyes in a new way, have you noticed? It draws attention away from my mouth. If I want to get on as a model, I ought to have my teeth capped."

I remember thinking, as Louise adjusted the camera, Teeth capped. I wonder if Louise will pay for that.

I think it was that night I dreamed about them. I had been dream-haunted for days. I watched Louise searching for Patrick in railway stations and I saw him departing on ships while she ran along the edge of the shore. I heard his voice. He said, "Haven't you seen her wings? She never uses them now." Then I saw wings, small, neatly folded back. That scene faded, and the dream continued, a dream of labyrinths, of search, of missed chances, of people standing on opposite shores. Awaking, I remembered a verse from a folkloric poem I had tried, when I was Patrick's age, to set to music:

> Es warent zwei Königskinder
> Die hatten einander so lief
> Sie konnten zusammen nicht kommen
> Das Wasser, es war zu tief.

I had not thought of this for years. I would rather not think about all the verses and all the songs. Who was the poem about? There were two royal children, standing on opposite shores. I was no royal child, and neither was Louise. We were too old and blunt and plain. We had no public and private manners; we were all one. We had secrets — nothing but that. Patrick was one child. Sylvie must be the other. I was still not quite awake, and the power of the dream was so strong that I said to myself, "Sylvie has wings. She could fly."

Sylvie. When she had anything particularly foolish to say, she put her head on one side. She sucked her fingers and grinned and narrowed her eyes. The grime behind her ears faded to gray on her neck and vanished inside her collar, the rim of which was black. She said, "I wonder if it's true, you know, the thing I'm not to mention. Do you think he loved her? What do you think? It's like some beautiful story, isn't it? . . . [hand on cheek, treacle voice]. It's pure Claudel. Broken lives. I *think*."

Cold and dry, I said, "Don't be stupid, Sylvie, and don't play detective." Louise and Collie, Patrick and Louise: I was as bad as Sylvie. My imagination crawled, rampant, unguided, flowering between stones. Supposing Louise had never loved Collie at all? Supposing Patrick had felt nothing but concern and some pity? Sylvie knew. She knew everything by instinct. She munched sweets, listened to records, grimaced in her mirror, and knew everything about us all.

Patrick had been pushed to the very bottom of my thoughts. But I knew that Sylvie was talking. I could imagine her excited voice saying, "Patrick was an actor, although he hardly ever had a part, and she was good and clever, nothing of a man-eater . . ." I could imagine her saying it to the young men, the casual drifters, who stood on the pavement and gossiped and fingered coins, wondering if they dared to go inside a café and sit down — wondering if they had enough money for a cup of coffee or a glass of beer. Sylvie knew everybody in Paris. She knew no one of any consequence, but she knew everyone, and her indiscretions spread like the track of a snail.

Patrick was behind a wall. I knew that something was living and stirring behind the wall, but it was impossible for me to dislodge the bricks. Louise never mentioned him. Once she spoke of her lost young husband, but Collie would never reveal his face again. He had been more thoroughly forgotten than anyone deserves to be. Patrick and Collie merged into one occasion, where someone had failed. The failure was Louise's; the infidelity of memory, the easy defeat were hers. It had nothing to do with me.

The tenants of the house in Melbourne wrote about rotten beams, and asked Louise to find a new gardner. She instantly wrote letters and a gardner was found. It was April, and the ripped fabric of her life mended. One could no longer see the way she had come. There had been one letter from Patrick, addressed to all three.

A letter to Patrick that Sylvie never finished was among the papers I found in Sylvie's room after she had left the hotel. "I have been painting pictures in a friend's studio," it said. "Perhaps art is what I shall take up after all. My paintings are very violent but also very tender. Some of them are large but others are small. Now I am playing Mozart on your old record-player. Now I am eating chocolate. Alas."

Patrick wrote to Sylvie. I found his letter on M. Rablis' desk one day. I put my hand across the desk to reach for my key, which hung on a board on the wall behind the desk, and I saw the letter in a basket of mail. I saw the postmark and I recognized his hand. I put the letter in my purse and carried it upstairs. I sat down at the table in my room before opening it. I slit the envelope carefully and spread the letter flat. I began to read it. The first words were *"Mon amour."*

The new tenant of his room was a Brazilian student who played the guitar. The sun falling on the carpet brought the promise of summer and memories of home. Paris was like a dragonfly. The Seine, the houses, the trees, the wind, and the sky were like a dragonfly's wing. Patrick belonged to another season — to winter, and museums, and water running off the shoes, and steamy cafés. I held the letter under my palms. What if I went to find him now? I stepped into a toy plane that went any direction I chose. I arrived where he was, and walked toward him. I saw, on a winter's day (the only season in which we could meet), Patrick in sweaters. I saw his astonishment, and, in a likeness as vivid as a dream, I saw his dismay.

I sat until the room grew dark. Sylvie banged on the door and came in like a young tiger. She said gaily, "Where's Louise? I think I've got a job. It's a funny job — I want to tell her. Why are you sitting in the dark?" She switched on a light. The spring evening came in through the open window. The room trembled with the passage of cars down the street. She looked at the letter and the envelope with her name upon it but made no effort to touch them.

She said, "Everything is so easy for people like Louise and you. You go on the assumption that no one will ever dare hurt you, and so nobody ever dares. Nobody dares because you don't expect it. It isn't fair."

I realized I had opened a letter. I had done it simply and naturally, as a fact of the day. I wondered if one could steal or kill with the same indifference — if one might actually do harm.

"Tell Louise not to do anything more for me," she said. "Not even if I ask."

That night she vanished. She took a few belongings and left the rest of her things behind. She owed much rent. The hotel was full of strangers, for with the spring the tourists came. M. Rablis had no difficulty in letting her room. Louise pushed her bicycle out to the street, and studied the history of music, and visited the people to whom she had introductions, and ate biscuits in her room. She stopped giving things away. Everything in her accounts was under "Necessary," and only necessary things were bought. One day, looking at the Seine from the Tuileries terrace, she said there was no place like home, was there? A week later, I put her on the boat train. After that, I had winter ghosts: Louise making tea, Sylvie singing, Patrick reading aloud.

Then, one summer morning, Sylvie passed me on the stairs. She climbed a few steps above me and stopped and turned. "Why, Puss!" she cried. "Are you still here?" She hung on the banister and smiled and said, "I've come back for my clothes. I've got the money to pay for them now. I've had a job." She was sunburned, and thinner than she had seemed in her clumsy winter garments. She wore a cotton dress, and sandals, and the necklace of seals. Her feet were filthy. While we were talking she casually picked up her skirt and scratched an insect bite inside her thigh. "I've been in a Christian coöperative community," she said. Her eyes shone. "It was wonderful! We are all young and we all believe in God. Have you read Maritain?" She fixed her black eyes on my face and I knew that my prestige hung on the reply.

"Not one word," I said.

"You could start with him," said Sylvie earnestly. "He is very materialistic, but so are you. I could guide you, but I haven't time. You must first dissolve your personality — are you listening to me? — and build it up again, only better. You must get rid of everything material. You must."

"Aren't you interested in the stage any more?" I said.

"That was just theatre," said Sylvie, and I was too puzzled to say anything more. I was not sure whether she meant that her interest had been a pose or that it was a worldly ambition with no place in her new life.

"Oh," said Sylvie, as if suddenly remembering. "Did you ever hear from him?"

Everything was still, as still as snow, as still as a tracked mouse.

"Yes, of course," I said.

"I'm so glad," said Sylvie, with some of her old overplaying. She made motions as though perishing with relief, hand on her heart. "I was so silly, you know. I minded about the letter. Now I'm beyond all that. A person in love will do anything."

"I was never in love," I said.

She looked at me, searching for something, but gave me up. "I've left the community now," she said. "I've met a boy ... oh, I wish you knew him! A saint. A modern saint. He belongs to a different group and I'm going off with them. They want to reclaim the lost villages in the South of France. You know? The villages that have been abandoned because there's no water or no electricity. Isn't that a good idea? We are all people for whom the theatre ... [gesture] ... and art ... [gesture] ... and music and all that have failed. We're trying something else. I don't know what the others will say when they see him arriving with me, because they don't want unattached women. They don't mind wives, but unattached women cause trouble, they say. *He* was against *all* women until he met *me.*" Sylvie was beaming. "There won't be any trouble with me. All I want to do is work. I don't want anything ...," She frowned. What was the word? "... anything material."

"In that case," I said, "you won't need the necklace."

She placed her hand flat against it, but there was nothing she could do. All the while she was lifting it off over her head and handing it down to me I saw she was regretting it, and for two pins would have taken back all she had said about God and materialism. I ought to have let her keep it, I suppose. But I thought of Louise, and everything spent with so little return. She had merged "Necessary" and "Unnecessary" into a single column, and when I added what she had paid out it came to a great deal. She must be living thinly now.

"I don't need it," said Sylvie, backing away. "I'd have been as well off without it. Everything I've done I've had to do. It never brought me *bonheur.*"

I am sorry to use a French word here, but "*bonheur*" is ambiguous. It means what you think it does, but sometimes it just stands for luck; the meaning depends on the sense of things. If the necklace had done nothing for Sylvie, what would it do for me? I went on down the stairs with the necklace in my pocket, and I thought, Selfish child. After everything that was given her, she might have been more grateful. She might have bitten back the last word.

MAVIS GALLANT

The Ice Wagon Going Down the Street

Now that they are out of world affairs and back where they started, Peter Frazier's wife says, "Everybody else did well in the international thing except us."

"You have to be crooked," he tells her.

"Or smart. Pity we weren't."

It is Sunday morning. They sit in the kitchen, drinking their coffee, slowly, remembering the past. They say the names of people as if they were magic. Peter thinks, *Agnes Brusen,* but there are hundreds of other names. As a private married joke, Peter and Sheilah wear the silk dressing gowns they bought in Hong Kong. Each thinks the other a peacock, rather splendid, but they pretend the dressing gowns are silly and worn in fun.

Peter and Sheilah and their two daughters, Sandra and Jennifer, are visiting Peter's unmarried sister, Lucille. They have been Lucille's guests seventeen weeks, ever since they returned to Toronto from the Far East. Their big old steamer trunk blocks a corner of the kitchen, making a problem of the refrigerator door; but even Lucille says the trunk may as well stay where it is, for the present. The Fraziers' future is so unsettled; everything is still in the air.

Lucille has given her bedroom to her two nieces, and sleeps on a camp cot in the hall. The parents have the living-room divan. They have no privileges here; they sleep after Lucille has seen the last television show that interests her. In the hall closet their clothes are crushed by winter overcoats. They know they are being judged for the first time. Sandra and Jennifer are waiting for Sheilah and Peter to decide. They are waiting to learn where these exotic parents will fly to next. What sort of climate will Sheilah consider? What job will Peter consent to accept? When the parents are ready, the children will make a decision of their own. It is just possible that Sandra and Jennifer will choose to stay with their aunt.

The peacock parents are watched by wrens. Lucille and her nieces are much the same — sandy-colored, proudly plain. Neither of the girls has the father's insouciance or the mother's appearance — her height, her carriage, her thick hair, and sky-blue eyes. The children are more cautious than their parents; more Canadian. When they saw their aunt's apartment they had been away from Canada nine years, ever since they were two and four; and Jennifer, the elder, said, "Well, now we're home." Her voice is nasal and flat. Where did she learn that voice? And why should this be home? Peter's answer to anything about his mystifying children is, "It must be in the blood."

On Sunday morning Lucille takes her nieces to church. It seems to be the only condition she imposes on her relations: the children must be decent. The girls go willingly, with their new hats and purses and gloves and coral bracelets and strings of pearls. The parents, ramshackle, sleepy, dim in the brain because it is Sunday, sit down to their coffee and privacy and talk of the past.

"We weren't crooked," says Peter. "We weren't even smart."

Sheilah's head bobs up; she is no drowner. It is wrong to say they have nothing to show for time. Sheilah has the Balenciaga. It is a black afternoon dress, stiff and boned at the waist; long for the fashions of now, but neither Sheilah nor Peter would change a thread. The Balenciaga is their talisman, their treasure; and after they remember it they touch hands and think that the years are not behind them but hazy and marvelous and still to be lived.

The first place they went to was Paris. In the early fifties the pick of the international jobs was there. Peter had inherited the last scrap of money he knew he was ever likely to see, and it was enough to get them over. Sheilah and Peter and the babies and the steamer trunk. To their joy and astonishment they had money in the bank. They said to each other, "It should last a year." Peter was fastidious about the new job; he hadn't come all this distance to accept just anything. In Paris he met Hugh Taylor, who was earning enough smuggling gasoline to keep his wife in Paris and a girl in Rome. That impressed Peter, because he remembered Taylor as a sour scholarship student without the slightest talent for life. Taylor had a job, of course. He hadn't said to himself, I'll go over to Europe and smuggle gasoline. It gave Peter an idea; he saw the shape of things. First you catch your fish. Later, at an international party, he met Johnny Hertzberg, who told him Germany was the place. Hertzberg said that anyone who came out of Germany broke now was too stupid to be here, and deserved to be back home at a desk. Peter nodded, as if he had already thought of that. He began to think about Germany. Paris was fine for a holiday, but it had been picked clean. Yes, Germany. His money was running low. He thought about Germany quite a lot.

That winter was moist and delicate; so fragile that they daren't speak of it now. There seemed to be plenty of everything and plenty of time. They were living the dream of a marriage, the fabric uncut, nothing slashed or spoiled. All winter they spent their money, and went to parties, and talked about Peter's future job. It lasted four months. They spent their money, lived in the future, and were never as happy again.

After four months they were suddenly moved away from Paris, but not to Germany — to Geneva. Peter thinks it was because of the incident at the Trudeau wedding at the Ritz. Paul Trudeau was a French Canadian Peter had known at school and in the Navy. Trudeau had turned into a snob, proud of his career and his Paris connections. He tried to make the difference felt, but Peter thought the difference was only for strangers. At the wedding reception Peter lay down on the floor and said he was dead. He held a white azalea in a brass pot on his chest, and sang, "Oh, hear us when we cry to Thee for those in peril on the sea." Sheilah bent over him and said, "Pete, darling, get up. Pete, listen, every single person who can do something for you is in this room. If you love me, you'll get up."

"I do love you," he said, ready to engage in a serious conversation. "She's so beautiful," he told a second face. "She's nearly as tall as I am. She was a model in

London. I met her over in London in the war. I met her there in the war." He lay on his back with the azalea on his chest, explaining their history. A waiter took the brass pot away, and after Peter had been hauled to his feet he knocked the waiter down. Trudeau's bride, who was freshly out of an Ursuline convent, became hysterical; and even though Paul Trudeau and Peter were old acquaintances, Trudeau never spoke to him again. Peter says now that French Canadians always have that bit of spite. He says Trudeau asked the Embassy to interfere. Luckily, back home there were still a few people to whom the name "Frazier" meant something, and it was to these people that Peter appealed. He wrote letters saying that a French-Canadian combine was preventing his getting a decent job, and could anything be done? No one answered directly, but it was clear that what they settled for was exile to Geneva: a season of meditation and remorse, as he explained to Sheilah, and it was managed tactfully, through Lucille. Lucille wrote that a friend of hers, May Fergus, now a secretary in Geneva, had heard about a job. The job was filing pictures in the information service of an international agency in the Palais des Nations. The pay was so-so, but Lucille thought Peter must be getting fed up doing nothing.

Peter often asks his sister now who put her up to it — what important person told her to write that letter suggesting Peter go to Geneva?

"Nobody," says Lucille. "I mean, nobody in the way *you* mean. I really did have this girl friend working there, and I knew you must be running through your money pretty fast in Paris."

"It must have been somebody pretty high up," Peter says. He looks at his sister admiringly, as he has often looked at his wife.

Peter's wife had loved him in Paris. Whatever she wanted in marriage she found that winter, there. In Geneva, where Peter was a file clerk and they lived in a furnished flat, she pretended they were in Paris and life was still the same. Often, when the children were at supper, she changed as though she and Peter were dining out. She wore the Balenciaga, and put candles on the card table where she and Peter ate their meal. The neckline of the dress was soiled with make-up. Peter remembers her dabbing on the make-up with a wet sponge. He remembers her in the kitchen, in the soiled Balenciaga, patting on the make-up with a filthy sponge. Behind her, at the kitchen table, Sandra and Jennifer, in buttonless pajamas and bunny slippers, ate their supper of marmalade sandwiches and milk. When the children were asleep, the parents dined solemnly, ritually, Sheilah sitting straight as a queen.

It was a mysterious period of exile, and he had to wait for signs, or signals, to know when he was free to leave. He never saw the job any other way. He forgot he had applied for it. He thought he had been sent to Geneva because of a misdemeanor and had to wait to be released. Nobody pressed him at work. His immediate boss had resigned, and he was alone for months in a room with two desks. He read the *Herald-Tribune,* and tried to discover how things were here — how the others ran their lives on the pay they were officially getting. But it was a closed conspiracy. He was not dealing with adventures now but civil servants waiting for pension day. No one ever answered his questions. They pretended to think his questions were a form of wit. His only solace in exile was the few happy weekends he had in the late spring and early summer. He had met another old acquaintance, Mike Burleigh. Mike was a serious liberal who had married a serious heiress. The Burleighs had two guest lists. The first was composed of stuffy people they felt obliged to entertain, while the second was made up of their real friends, the friends they wanted. The real friends strove hard to become stuffy and dull and thus achieve the first guest list, but few succeeded. Peter went on the first list straight away. Possibly Mike didn't understand, at the beginning, why Peter was pretending to be a file clerk. Peter had such an air — he might have been sent by a universal inspector to see how things in Geneva were being run.

Every Friday in May and June and part of July, the Fraziers rented a sky-blue Fiat and drove forty miles east of Geneva to the Burleighs' summer house. They brought the children, a suitcase, the children's tattered picture books, and a token bottle of gin. This, in memory, is a period of water and water birds, swans, roses, and singing birds. The children were small and still belonged to them. If they remember too much, their mouths water, their stomachs hurt. Peter says, "It was fine while it lasted." Enough. While it lasted Sheilah and Madge Burleigh were close. They abandoned their husbands and spent long summer afternoons comparing their mothers and praising each other's skin and hair. To Madge, and not to Peter, Sheilah opened her Liverpool childhood with the words "rat poor." Peter heard about it later, from Mike. The women's friendship seemed to Peter a bad beginning. He trusted women but not with each other. It lasted ten weeks. One Sunday, Madge said she needed the two bedrooms the Fraziers usually occupied for a party of sociologists from Pakistan, and that was the end. In November, the Fraziers heard that the summer house had been closed, and that the Burleighs were in Geneva, in their winter flat; they gave no sign. There was no help for it, and no appeal.

Now Peter began firing letters to anyone who had ever known his late father. He was living in a mild yellow autumn. Why does he remember the streets of the city dark, and the windows everywhere black with rain? He remembers being with Sheilah and the children as if they clung together while just outside their small shelter it rained and rained. The children slept in the bedroom of the flat because the window gave on the street and they could breathe air. Peter and Sheilah had the living-room couch. Their window was not a real window but a square on a well of cement. The flat seemed damp as a cave. Peter remembers steam in the kitchen, pools under the sink, sweat on the pipes. Water streamed on him from the children's clothes, washed and dripping overhead. The trunk, upended in the children's room, was not quite unpacked. Sheilah had not signed her name to this life; she had not given in. Once Peter heard her drop her aitches. "You kids are lucky," she said to the girls. "I never 'ad so much as a sitdown meal. I ate chips out of paper or I 'ad a butty out on the stairs." He never asked her what a butty was. He thinks it means bread and cheese.

The day he heard "You kids are lucky" he understood they were becoming in fact something they had only *appeared* to be until now — the shabby civil servant and his brood. If he had been European he would have ridden to work on a bicycle, in the uniform of his class and condition. He would have worn a tight coat, a turned collar, and a dirty tie. He wondered then if coming here had been a mistake, and if he should not, after all, still be in a place where his name meant something. Surely Peter Frazier should live where "Frazier" counts? In Ontario even now when he says "Frazier" an absent look comes over his hearer's face, as if its owner were consulting an interior guide. What is Frazier? What does it mean? Oil? Power? Politics? Wheat? Real estate? The creditors had the house sealed when Peter's father died. His aunt collapsed with a heart attack in somebody's bachelor apartment, leaving three sons and a widower to surmise they had never known her. Her will was a disappointment. None of that generation left enough. One made it: the granite Presbyterian immigrants from Scotland. Their children, a generation of daunted women and maiden men, held still. Peter's father's crowd spent: they were not afraid of their fathers, and their grandfathers were old. Peter and his sister and his cousins lived on the remains. They were left the rinds of income, of notions, and the memories of ideas rather than ideas intact. If Peter can choose his reincarnation, let him be the oppressed son of a Scottish parson. Let Peter grow up on cuffs and iron principles. Let him make the fortune! Let him flee the manse! When he was small his patrimony was squandered under his nose. He remembers people dancing in his father's house. He remembers seeing and nearly understanding adultery in a guest room, among a pile of wraps. He thought he had seen a murder; he never told. He remembers licking glasses wherever he found them — on window sills, on stairs, in the pantry. In his room he listened while Lucille read Beatrix Potter. The bad rabbit stole the carrot from the good rabbit without saying please, and downstairs was the noise of the party — the roar of the crouched lion. When his father died he saw the chairs upside down and the bailiff's chalk marks. Then the doors were sealed.

He has often tried to tell Sheilah why he cannot be defeated. He remembers his father saying, "Nothing can touch us," and Peter believed it and still does. It has prevented his taking his troubles too seriously. "Nothing can be as bad as this," he will tell himself. "It is happening to me." Even in Geneva, where his status was file clerk, where he sank and stopped on the level of the men who never emigrated, the men on the bicycles — even there he had a manner of strolling to work as if his office were a pastime, and his real life a secret so splendid he could share it with no one except himself.

In Geneva Peter worked for a woman — a girl. She was a Norwegian from a small town in Saskatchewan. He supposed they had been put together because they were Canadians; but they were as strange to each other as if "Canadian" meant any number of things, or had no real meaning. Soon after Agnes Brusen came to the office she hung her framed university degree on the wall. It was one of the gritty, prideful gestures that stand for push, toil, and family sacrifice. He thought, then, that she must be one of a family of immigrants for whom education is everything. Hugh Taylor had told him that in some families the older children never marry until the youngest have finished school. Sometimes every second child is sacrificed and made to work for the education of the next born. Those who finish college spend years paying back. They are white-hot Protestants, and they live with a load of work and debt and obligation. Peter placed his new colleague on scraps of information. He had never been in the West.

She came to the office on a Monday morning in October. The office was overheated and a painted cream. It contained two desks, the filing cabinets, a map of the world as it had been in 1945, and the Charter of the United Nations left behind by Agnes Brusen's predecessor. (She took down the Charter without asking Peter if he minded, with the impudence of gesture you find in women who wouldn't say boo to a goose; and then she hung her college degree on the nail where the Charter had been.) Three people brought her in — a whole committee. One of them said, "Agnes, this is Pete Frazier. Pete, Agnes Brusen. Pete's Canadian, too, Agnes. He knows all about the office, so ask him anything."

Of course he knew all about the office: he knew the exact spot where the cord of the venetian blind was frayed, obliging one to give an extra tug to the right.

The girl might have been twenty-three: no more. She wore a brown tweed suit with bone buttons, and a new silk scarf and new shoes. She clutched an unscratched brown purse. She seemed dressed in going-away presents. She said, "Oh, I never smoke," with a convulsive movement of her hand, when Peter offered his case. He was courteous, hiding his disappointment. The people he worked with had told him a Scandinavian girl was arriving, and he had expected a stunner. Agnes was a mole: she was small and brown, and round-shouldered as if she had always carried parcels or younger children in her arms. A mole's profile was turned when she said goodbye to her committee. If she had been foreign, ill-favored though she was, he might have flirted a little, just to show that he was friendly; but their being Canadian, and suddenly left together, was a sexual damper. He sat down and lit his own cigarette. She smiled at him, questioningly, he thought, and sat as if she had never seen a chair before. He wondered if his smoking was annoying her. He wondered if she was fidgety about drafts, or allergic to anything, and whether she would want the blind up or down. His social compass was out of order because the others couldn't tell Peter and Agnes apart. There was a world of difference between them, yet it was she who had been brought in to sit at the larger of the two desks.

While he was thinking this she got up and walked around the office, almost on tiptoe, opening the doors of closets and pulling out the filing trays. She looked inside everything except the drawers of Peter's desk. (In any case, Peter's desk was locked. His desk is locked wherever he works. In Geneva he went into Personnel one morning, early, and pinched his application form. He had stated on the form that he had seven years' experience in public relations and could speak French, German, Spanish, and Italian. He has always collected anything important about himself — anything useful. But he can never get on with the final act, which is getting rid of the information. He has kept papers about for years, a constant source of worry.)

"I know this looks funny, Mr. Ferris," said the girl. "I'm not really snooping or anything. I just can't feel easy in a new place unless I know where everything is. In a new place everything seems so hidden."

If she had called him "Ferris" and pretended not to know he was Frazier, it could only be because they had sent her here to spy on him and see if he had repented and was fit for a better place in life. "You'll be all right here," he said. "Nothing's hidden. Most of us haven't got brains enough to have secrets. This is Rainbow Valley." Depressed by the thought that they were having him watched now, he passed his hand over his hair and looked outside to the lawn and the parking lot and the peacocks someone gave the Palais des Nations years ago. The peacocks love no one. They wander about the parked cars looking elderly, bad-tempered, mournful, and lost.

Agnes had settled down again. She folded her silk scarf and placed it just so, with her gloves beside it. She opened her new purse and took out a notebook and a shiny gold pencil. She may have written

> Duster for desk
> Kleenex
> Glass jar for flowers
> Air-Wick because he smokes
> Paper for lining drawers

because the next day she brought each of these articles to work. She also brought a large black Bible, which she unwrapped lovingly and placed on the left-hand corner of her desk. The flower vase — empty — stood in the middle, and the Kleenex made a counterpoise for the Bible on the right.

When he saw the Bible he knew she had not been sent to spy on his work. The conspiracy was deeper. She might have been dispatched by ghosts. He knew everything about her, all in a moment: he saw the ambition, the terror, the dry pride. She was the true heir of the men from Scotland; she was at the start. She had been sent to tell him, "You can begin, but not begin again." She never opened the Bible, but she dusted it as she dusted her desk, her chair, and any surface the cleaning staff had overlooked. And Peter, the first days, watching her timid movements, her insignificant little face, felt, as you feel the approach of a storm, the charge of moral certainty round her, the belief in work, the faith in undertakings, the bread of the Black Sunday. He recognized and tasted all of it: ashes in the mouth.

After five days their working relations were settled. Of course, there was the Bible and all that went with it, but his tongue had never held the taste of ashes long. She was an inferior girl of poor quality. She had nothing in her favor except the degree on the wall. In the real world, he would not have invited her to his house except to mind the children. That was what he said to Sheilah. He said that Agnes was a mole, and a virgin, and that her tics and mannerisms were sending him round the bend. She had an infuriating habit of covering her mouth when she talked. Even at the telephone she put up her hand as if afraid of losing anything, even a word. Her voice was nasal and flat. She had two working costumes, both dull as the wall. One was the brown suit, the other a navy-blue dress with changeable collars. She dressed for no one; she dressed for her desk, her jar of flowers, her Bible, and her box of Kleenex. One day she crossed the space between the two desks and stood over Peter, who was reading a newspaper. She could have spoken to him from her desk, but she may have felt that being on her feet gave her authority. She had plenty of courage, but authority was something else.

"I thought — I mean, they told me you were the person . . ." She got on with it bravely: "If you don't want to do the filing or any work, all right, Mr. Frazier. I'm not saying anything about that. You might have poor health or your personal reasons. But it's got to be done, so if you'll kindly show me about the filing I'll do it. I've worked in Information before, but it was a different office, and every office is different."

"My dear girl," said Peter. He pushed back his chair and looked at her, astonished. "You've been sitting there fretting, worrying. How insensitive of me. How trying for you. Usually I file on the last Wednesday of the month, so you see, you just haven't been around long enough to see a last Wednesday. Not another word, please. And let us not waste another minute." He emptied the heaped baskets of photographs so swiftly, pushing "Iran — Smallpox Control" into "Irish Red Cross" (close enough), that the girl looked frightened, as if she had raised a whirlwind. She said slowly, "If you'll only show me, Mr. Frazier, instead of doing it so fast, I'll gladly look after it, because you might want to be doing other things, and I feel the filing should be done every day." But Peter was too busy to answer, and so she sat down, holding the edge of her desk.

"There," he said, beaming. "All done." His smile, his sunburst, was wasted, for the girl was staring round the room as if she feared she had not inspected everything the first day after all; some drawer, some cupboard, hid a monster. That evening Peter unlocked one of the drawers of his desk and took away the application form he had stolen from Personnel. The girl had not finished her search.

"How could you *not* know?" wailed Sheilah. "You sit looking at her every day. You must talk about *something*. She must have told you."

"She did tell me," said Peter, "and I've just told you."

It was this: Agnes Brusen was on the Burleighs' guest list. How had the Burleighs met her? What did they see in her? Peter could not reply. He knew that Agnes lived in a bed-sitting room with a Swiss family and had her meals with them. She had been in Geneva three months, but no one had ever seen her outside the office. "You *should* know," said Sheilah. "She must have something, more than you can see. Is she pretty? Is she brilliant? What is it?"

"We don't really talk," Peter said. They talked in a way: Peter teased her and she took no notice. Agnes was not a sulker. She had taken her defeat like a sport. She did her work and a good deal of his. She sat behind her Bible, her flowers, and her Kleenex, and answered when Peter spoke. That was how he learned about the Burleighs — just by teasing and being bored. It was a January afternoon. He said, "*Miss* Brusen. Talk to me. Tell me everything. Pretend we have perfect rapport. Do you like Geneva?"

"It's a nice clean town," she said. He can see to this day the red and blue anemones in the glass jar, and her bent head, and her small untended hands.

"Are you learning beautiful French with your Swiss family?"

"They speak English."

"Why don't you take an apartment of your own?" he said. Peter was not usually impertinent. He was bored. "You'd be independent then."

"I am independent," she said. "I earn my living. I don't think it proves anything if you live by yourself. Mrs. Burleigh wants me to live alone, too. She's looking for something for me. It mustn't be dear. I send money home."

Here was the extraordinary thing about Agnes Brusen: she refused the use of Christian names and never spoke to Peter unless he spoke first, but she would tell anything, as if to say, "Don't waste time fishing. Here it is."

He learned all in one minute that she sent her salary home, and that she was a friend of the Burleighs. The first he had expected; the second knocked him flat.

"She's got to come to dinner," Sheilah said. "We should have had her right from the beginning. If only I'd known! But *you* were the one. You said she looked like — oh, I don't even remember. A Norwegian mole."

She came to dinner one Saturday night in January, in her navy-blue dress, to which she had pinned an organdy gardenia. She sat upright on the edge of the sofa. Sheilah had ordered the meal from a restaurant. There was lobster, good wine, and a *pièce-montée* full of kirsch and cream. Agnes refused the lobster; she had never eaten anything from the sea unless it had been sterilized and tinned, and said so. She was afraid of skin poisoning. Someone in her family had skin poisoning after having eaten oysters. She touched her cheeks and neck to show where the poisoning had erupted. She sniffed her wine and put the glass down without tasting it. She could not eat the cake because of the alcohol it contained. She ate an egg, bread and butter, a sliced tomato, and drank a glass of ginger ale. She seemed unaware she was creating disaster and pain. She did not help clear away the dinner plates. She sat, adequately nourished, decently dressed, and waited to learn why she had been invited here — that was the feeling Peter had. He folded the card table on which they had dined, and opened the window to air the room.

"It's not the same cold as Canada, but you feel it more," he said, for something to say.

"Your blood has gotten thin," said Agnes.

Sheilah returned from the kitchen and let herself fall into an armchair. With her eyes closed she held out her hand for a cigarette. She was performing the haughty-lady act that was a family joke. She flung her head back and looked at Agnes through half-closed lids; then she suddenly brought her head forward, widening her eyes.

"Are you skiing madly?" she said.

"Well, in the first place there hasn't been any snow," said Agnes. "So nobody's doing any skiing so far as I know. All I hear is people complaining because there's no snow. Personally, I don't ski. There isn't much skiing in the part of Canada I come from. Besides, my family never had that kind of leisure."

"Heavens," said Sheilah, as if her family had every kind.

I'll bet they had, thought Peter. On the dole.

Sheilah was wasting her act. He had a suspicion that Agnes knew it was an act but did not know it was also a joke. If so, it made Sheilah seem a fool, and he loved Sheilah too much to enjoy it.

"The Burleighs have been wonderful to me," said Agnes. She seemed to have divined why she was here, and decided to give them all the information they wanted, so that she could put on her coat and go home to bed. "They had me out to their place on the lake every weekend until the weather got cold and they moved back to town. They've rented a chalet for the winter, and they want me to come there, too. But I don't know if I will or not. I don't ski, and oh, I don't know — I don't drink, either, and I don't always see the point. Their friends are too rich and I'm too Canadian."

She had delivered everything Sheilah wanted and more: Agnes was on the first guest list and didn't care. No, Peter corrected; doesn't know. Doesn't care and doesn't know.

"I thought with you Norwegians it was in the blood, skiing. And drinking," Sheilah murmured.

"Drinking, maybe," said Agnes. She covered her mouth and said behind her spread fingers, "In our family we were religious. We didn't drink or smoke. My brother was in Norway in the war. He saw some cousins. Oh," she said, unexpectedly loud, "Harry said it was just terrible. They were so poor. They had flies in their kitchen. They gave him something to eat a fly had been on. They didn't have a real toilet, and they'd been in the same house about two hundred years. We've only recently built our own home, and we have a bathroom and two toilets. I'm from Saskatchewan," she said. "I'm not from any other place."

Surely one winter here had been punishment enough? In the spring they would remember him and free him. He wrote Lucille, who said he was lucky to have a job at all. The Burleighs had sent the Fraziers a second-guest-list Christmas card. It showed a Moslem refugee child weeping outside a tent. They treasured the card and left it standing long after the others had been given the children to cut up. Peter had discovered by now what had gone wrong in the friendship — Sheilah had charged a skirt at a dressmaker to Madge's account. Madge had told her she might, and then changed her mind. Poor Sheilah! She was new to this part of it — to the changing humors of independent friends. Paris was already a year in the past. At Mardi Gras, the Burleighs gave their annual party. They invited everyone, the damned and the dropped, with the prodigality of a child at prayers. The invitation said "in costume," but the Fraziers were too happy to wear a disguise. They might not be recognized. Like many of the guests they expected to meet at the party, they had been disgraced, forgotten, and rehabilitated. They would be anxious to see one another as they were.

On the night of the party, the Fraziers rented a car they had never seen before and drove through the first snowstorm of the year. Peter had not driven since last summer's blissful trips in the Fiat. He could not find the switch for the windshield wiper in this car. He leaned over the wheel. "Can you see on your side?" he asked. "Can I make a left turn here? Does it look like a one-way?"

"I can't imagine why you took a car with a right-hand drive," said Sheilah.

He had trouble finding a place to park; they crawled up and down unknown streets whose curbs were packed with snow-covered cars. When they stood at last on the pavement, safe and sound, Peter said, "This is the first snow."

"I can see that," said Sheilah. "Hurry, darling. My hair."

"It's the first snow."

"You're repeating yourself," she said. "Please hurry, darling. Think of my poor shoes. My *hair*."

She was born in an ugly city, and so was Peter, but they have this difference: she does not know the importance of the first snow — the first clean thing in a dirty year. He would have told her then that this storm, which was wetting her feet and destroying her hair, was like the first day of the English spring, but she made a frightened gesture, trying to shield her head. The gesture told him he did not understand her beauty.

"Let me," she said. He was fumbling with the key, trying to lock the car. She took the key without impatience and locked the door on the driver's side; and then, to show Peter she treasured him and was not afraid of wasting her life or her beauty, she took his arm and they walked in the snow down a street and around a corner to the apartment house where the Burleighs lived. They were, and are, a united couple. They were afraid of the party, and each of them knew it. When they walk together, holding arms, they give each other whatever each can spare.

Only six people had arrived in costume. Madge Burleigh was disguised as Manet's "Lola de Valence," which everyone mistook for Carmen. Mike was an Impressionist painter, with a straw hat and a glued-on beard. "I am all of them," he said. He would rather have dressed as a dentist, he said, welcoming the Fraziers as if he had parted from them the day before, but Madge wanted him to look as if he had created her. "You know?" he said.

"Perfectly," said Sheilah. Her shoes were stained and the snow had softened her lacquered hair. She was not wasted; she was the most beautiful woman here.

About an hour after their arrival, Peter found himself with no one to talk to. He had told about the Trudeau wedding in Paris and the pot of azaleas, and after he mislaid his audience he began to look round for Sheilah. She was on a window seat, partly concealed by a green velvet curtain. Facing her, so that their profiles were neat and perfect against the night, was a man. Their conversation was private and enclosed, as if they had in minutes covered leagues of time and arrived at the place where everything was implied, understood. Peter began working his way across the room, toward his wife, when he saw Agnes. He was granted the sight of her drowning face. She had dressed with comic intention, obviously with care, and now she was a ragged hobo, half tramp, half clown. Her hair was tucked up under a bowler hat. The six costumed guests who had made the same mistake — the ghost, the gypsy, the Athenian maiden, the geisha, the Martian, and the apache — were delighted to find a seventh; but Agnes was not amused; she was gasping for life. When a waiter passed with a crowded tray, she took a glass without seeing it; then a wave of the party took her away.

Sheilah's new friend was named Simpson. After Simpson said he thought perhaps he'd better circulate, Peter sat down where he had been. "Now look, Sheilah," he began. Their most intimate conversations have taken place at parties. Once at a party she told him she was leaving him; she didn't, of course. Smiling, blue-eyed, she gazed lovingly at Peter and said rapidly, "Pete, shut up and listen. That man. The man you scared away. He's a big wheel in a company out in India or someplace like that. It's gorgeous out there. Pete, the *servants*. And it's warm. It never never snows. He says there's heaps of jobs. You pick them off the trees like ... orchids. He says it's even easier now than when we owned all those places, because now the poor pets can't run anything and they'll pay *fortunes*. Pete, he says it's warm, it's heaven, and Pete, they pay."

A few minutes later, Peter was alone again and Sheilah part of a closed, laughing group. Holding her elbow was the man from the place where jobs grew like orchids. Peter edged into the group and laughed at a story he hadn't heard. He heard only the last line, which was, "Here comes another tunnel." Looking out from the tight laughing ring, he saw Agnes again, and he thought, I'd be like Agnes if I didn't have Sheilah. Agnes put her glass down on a table and lurched toward the doorway, head forward. Madge Burleigh, who never stopped moving around the room and smiling, was still smiling when she paused and said in Peter's ear, "Go with Agnes, Pete. See that she gets home. People will notice if Mike leaves."

"She probably just wants to walk around the block," said Peter. "She'll be back."

"Oh, stop thinking about yourself, for once, and see that that poor girl gets home," said Madge. "You've still got your Fiat, haven't you?"

He turned away as if he had been pushed. Any command is a release, in a way. He may not want to go in that particular direction, but at least he is going somewhere. And now Sheilah, who had moved inches nearer to hear what Madge and Peter were murmuring, said, "Yes, go, darling," as if he were leaving the gates of Troy.

Peter was to find Agnes and see that she reached home: this he repeated to himself as he stood on the landing, outside the Burleighs' flat, ringing for the elevator. Bored with waiting for it, he ran down the stairs, four flights, and saw that Agnes had stalled the lift by leaving the door open. She was crouched on the floor, propped on her fingertips. Her eyes were closed.

"Agnes," said Peter. "*Miss* Brusen, I mean. That's no way to leave a party. Don't you know you're supposed to curtsey and say thanks? My God, Agnes, anybody going by here just now might have seen you! Come on now, be a good girl. Time to go home."

She got up without his help and, moving between invisible crevasses, shut the elevator door. Then she left the building and Peter followed, remembering he was to see that she got home. They walked along the snowy pavement, Peter a few steps behind her. When she turned right for no reason, he turned, too. He had no clear idea where they were going. Perhaps she lived close by. He had forgotten where the hired car was parked, or what it looked like; he could not remember its make or its color. In any case, Sheilah had the key. Agnes walked on steadily, as if she knew their destination, and he thought, Agnes Brusen is drunk in the street in Geneva and dressed like a tramp. He wanted to say, "This is the best thing that ever happened to you, Agnes; it will help you understand how things are for some of the rest of us." But she stopped and turned and, leaning over a low hedge, retched on a frozen lawn. He held her clammy forehead and rested his hand on her arched back, on muscles as tight as a fist. She straightened up and drew a breath but the cold air made her cough. "Don't breathe too deeply," he said. "It's the worst thing you can do. Have you got a handkerchief?" He passed his own handkerchief over her wet weeping face, upturned like the face of one of his little girls. "I'm out without a coat," he said, noticing it. "We're a pair."

"I never drink," said Agnes. "I'm just not used to it." Her voice was sweet and quiet. He had never seen her so peaceful, so composed. He thought she must surely be all right, now, and perhaps he might leave her here. The trust in her tilted face had perplexed him. He wanted to get back to Sheilah and have her explain something. He had forgotten what it was, but Sheilah would know. "Do you live around here?" he said. As he spoke, she let herself fall. He had wiped her face and now she trusted him to pick her up, set her on her feet, take her wherever she ought to be. He pulled her up and she stood, wordless, humble, as he brushed the snow from her tramp's clothes. Snow horizontally crossed the lamplight. The street was silent. Agnes had lost her hat. Snow, which he tasted, melted on her hands. His gesture of licking snow from her hands was formal as a handshake. He tasted snow on her hands and then they walked on.

"I never drink," she said. They stood on the edge of a broad avenue. The wrong turning now could lead them anywhere; it was the changeable avenue at the edge of towns that loses its houses and becomes a highway. She held his arm and spoke in a gentle voice. She said, "In our house we didn't smoke or drink. My mother was ambitious for me, more than for Harry and the others." She said, "I've never been alone before. When I was a kid I would get up in the summer before the others, and I'd see the ice wagon going down the street. I'm alone now. Mrs. Burleigh's found me an apartment. It's only one room. She likes it because it's in the old part of town. I don't like old houses. Old houses are dirty. You don't know who was there before.

"I should have a car somewhere," Peter said. "I'm not sure where we are."

He remembers that on this avenue they climbed into a taxi, but nothing about the drive. Perhaps he fell asleep. He does remember that when he paid the driver Agnes clutched his arm, trying to stop him. She pressed extra coins into the driver's palm. The driver was paid twice.

"I'll tell you one thing about us," said Peter. "We pay everything twice." This was part of a much longer theory concerning North American behavior, and it was not Peter's own. Mike Burleigh had held forth about it on summer afternoons.

Agnes pushed open a door between a stationer's shop and a grocery, and led the way up a narrow inside stair. They climbed one flight, frightening beetles. She had to search every pocket for the latchkey. She was shaking with cold. Her apartment seemed little warmer than the street. Without speaking to Peter she turned on all the lights. She looked inside the kitchen and the bathroom and then got down on her hands and knees and looked under the sofa. The room was neat and belonged to no one. She left him standing in this unclaimed room — she had forgotten him — and closed a door behind her. He looked for something to do — some useful action he could repeat to Madge. He turned on the electric radiator in the fireplace. Perhaps Agnes wouldn't thank him for it; perhaps she would rather undress in the cold. "I'll be on my way," he called to the bathroom door.

She had taken off the tramp's clothes and put on a dressing gown of orphanage wool. She came out of the bathroom and straight toward him. She pressed her face and rubbed her cheek on his shoulder as if hoping the contact would leave a scar. He saw her back and her profile and his own face in the mirror over the fireplace. He thought, This is how disasters happen. He saw floods of sea water moving with perfect punitive justice over reclaimed land; he saw lava covering vineyards and overtaking dogs and stragglers. A bridge over an abyss snapped in two and the long express train, suddenly V-shaped, floated like snow. He thought amiably of every kind of disaster and thought, This is how they occur.

Her eyes were closed. She said, "I shouldn't be over here. In my family we didn't drink or smoke. My mother wanted a lot from me, more than from Harry and the others." But he knew all that he had known from the day of the Bible, and because once, at the beginning, she had made him afraid. He was not afraid of her now.

She said, "It's no use staying here, is it?"

"If you mean what I think, no."

"It wouldn't be better anywhere."

She let him see full on her blotched face. He was not expected to do anything. He was not required to pick her up when she fell or wipe her tears. She was poor quality, really — he remembered having thought that once. She left him and went quietly into the bathroom and locked the door. He heard taps running and supposed it was a hot bath. He was pretty certain there would be no more tears. He looked at his watch: Sheilah must be home, now, wondering what had become of him. He descended the beetles' staircase and for forty minutes crossed the city under a windless fall of snow.

The neighbor's child who had stayed with Peter's children was asleep on the living-room sofa. Peter woke her and sent her, sleepwalking, to her own door. He sat down, wet to the bone, thinking, I'll call the Burleighs. In half an hour I'll call the police. He heard a car stop and the engine running and a confusion of two voices laughing and calling goodnight. Presently Sheilah let herself in, rosy-faced, smiling. She carried his trenchcoat over her arm. She said, "How's Agnes?"

"Where were you?" he said. "Whose car was that?"

Sheilah had gone into the children's room. He heard her shutting their window. She returned, undoing her dress, and said, "Was Agnes all right?"

"Agnes is all right. Sheilah, this is about the worst . . ."

She stepped out of the Balenciaga and threw it over a chair. She stopped and looked at him and said, "Poor old Pete, are you in love with Agnes?" And then, as if the answer were of so little importance she hadn't time for it, she locked her arms around him and said, "My love, we're going to Ceylon."

*   *   *

Two days later, when Peter strolled into his office, Agnes was at her desk. She wore the blue dress, with a spotless collar. White and yellow freesias were symmetrically arranged in the glass jar. The room was hot, and the spring snow, glued for a second when it touched the window, blurred the view of parked cars.

"Quite a party," Peter said.

She did not look up. He sighed, sat down, and thought if the snow held he would be skiing at the Burleighs' very soon. Impressed by his kindness to Agnes, Madge had invited the family for the first possible weekend.

Presently Agnes said, "I'll never drink again or go to a house where people are drinking. And I'll never bother anyone the way I bothered you."

"You didn't bother me," he said. "I took you home. You were alone and it was late. It's normal."

"Normal for you, maybe, but I'm used to getting home by myself. Please never tell what happened."

He stared at her. He can still remember the freesias and the Bible and the heat in the room. She looked as if the elements had no power. She felt neither heat nor cold. "Nothing happened," he said.

"I behaved in a silly way. I had no right to. I led you to think I might do something wrong."

"*I* might have tried something," he said gallantly. "But that would be my fault and not yours."

She put her knuckle to her mouth and he could scarcely hear. "It was because of you. I was afraid you might be blamed, or else you'd blame yourself."

"There's no question of any blame," he said. "Nothing happened. We'd both had a lot to drink. Forget about it. Nothing *happened*. You'd remember if it had."

She put down her hand. There was an expression on her face. Now she sees me, he thought. She had never looked at him after the first day. (He has since tried to put a name to the look on her face; but how can he, now, after so many voyages, after Ceylon, and Hong Kong, and Sheilah's nearly leaving him, and all their difficulties — the money owed, the rows with hotel managers, the lost and found steamer trunk, the children throwing up the foreign food?) She sees me now, he thought. What does she see?

She said, "I'm from a big family. I'm not used to being alone. I'm not a suicidal person, but I could have done something after that party, just not to see any more, or think or listen or expect anything. What can I think when I see these people? All my life I heard, Educated people don't do this, educated people don't do that. And now I'm here, and you're all educated people, and you're nothing but pigs. You're educated and you drink and do everything wrong and you know what you're doing, and that makes you worse than pigs. My family worked to make me an educated person, but they didn't know you. But what if I didn't see and hear and expect anything any more? It wouldn't change anything. You'd all be still the same. Only *you* might have thought it was your fault. You might have thought you were to blame. It could worry you all your life. It would have been wrong for me to worry you."

He remembered that the rented car was still along a snowy curb somewhere in Geneva. He wondered if Sheilah had the key in her purse and if she remembered where they'd parked.

"I told you about the ice wagon," Agnes said. "I don't remember everything, so you're wrong about remembering. But I remember telling you that. That was the best. It's the best you can hope to have. In a big family, if you want to be alone, you have to get up before the rest of them. You get up early in the morning in the summer and it's you, you, once in your life alone in the universe. You think you know everything that can happen . . . Nothing is ever like that again."

He looked at the smeared window and wondered if this day could end without disaster. In his mind he saw her falling in the snow wearing a tramp's costume, and he saw her coming to him in the orphanage dressing gown. He saw her drowning face at the party. He was afraid for himself. The story was still unfinished. It had to come to a climax, something threatening to him. But there was no climax. They talked that day, and afterward nothing else was said. They went on in the same office for a short time, until Peter left for Ceylon; until somebody read the right letter, passed it on for the right initials, and the Fraziers began the Oriental tour that should have made their fortune. Agnes and Peter were too tired to speak after that morning. They were like a married couple in danger, taking care.

But what were they talking about that day, so quietly, such old friends? They talked about dying, about being ambitious, about being religious, about different kinds of love. What did she see when she looked at him — taking her knuckle slowly away from her mouth, bringing her hand down to the desk, letting it rest there? They were both Canadians, so they had this much together — the knowledge of the little you dare admit. Death, near-death, the best thing, the wrong thing — God knows what they were telling each other. Anyway, nothing happened.

When, on Sunday mornings, Sheilah and Peter talk about those times, they take on the glamor of something still to come. It is then he remembers Agnes Brusen. He never says her name. Sheilah wouldn't remember Agnes. Agnes is the only secret Peter has from his wife, the only puzzle he pieces together without her help. He thinks about families in the West as they were fifteen, twenty years ago — the iron-cold ambition, and every member pushing the next one on. He thinks of his father's parties. When he thinks of his father he imagines him with Sheilah, in a crowd. Actually, Sheilah and Peter's father never met, but they might have liked each other. His father admired good-looking women. Peter wonders what they were doing over there in Geneva — not Sheilah and Peter, *Agnes* and Peter. It is almost as if they had once run away together, silly as children, irresponsible as lovers. Peter and Sheilah are back where they started. While they were out in the world affairs picking up microbes and debts, always on the fringe of disaster, the fringe of a fortune, Agnes went on and did — what? They lost each other. He thinks of the ice wagon going down the street. He sees something he has never seen in his life — a Western town that belongs to Agnes. Here is Agnes — small, mole-faced, round-shouldered because she has always carried a younger child. She watches the ice wagon and the trail of ice water in a morning invented for her: hers. He sees the weak prairie trees and the shadows on the sidewalk. Nothing moves except the shadows and the ice wagon and the changing amber of the child's eyes. The child is Peter. He has seen the grain of the cement sidewalk and the grass in the cracks, and the dust, and the dandelions at the edge of the road. He is there. He has taken the morning that belongs to Agnes, he is up before the others, and he knows everything. There is nothing he doesn't know. He could keep the morning, if he wanted to, but what can Peter do with the start of a summer day? Sheilah is here, it is a true Sunday morning, with its dimness and headache and remorse and regrets, and this is life. He says, "We have the Balenciaga." He touches Sheilah's hand. The children have their aunt now, and he and Sheilah have each other. Everything works out, somehow or other. Let Agnes have the start of the day. Let Agnes think it was invented for her. Who wants to be alone in the universe? No, begin at the beginning: Peter lost Agnes. Agnes says to herself somewhere, Peter is lost.

GABRIEL GARCÍA MÁRQUEZ

Gabriel García Márquez was born in 1928 in Aracataca, Colombia — the town he called Macondo in his greatest work, *One Hundred Years of Solitude* (1967; English 1970). He worked as a journalist in Latin America, Europe, and the United States for twenty years and still considers journalism his true profession. There is no question that it has had profound impact on his vision; his literary style has been called "magic realism" for its mingling of fact with fantasy (or, as one writer explained it, "the idea of saying incredible things with a completely unperturbed face"). Amused by the overwhelming praise his "imagination" has elicited, he has always avowed that his fiction is true: "There's not a single line in all my work that does not have a basis in reality. The problem is that Caribbean reality resembles the wildest imagination." Along with *One Hundred Years of Solitude,* which has been translated into countless languages worldwide (and which one critic called "the first work of literature since the Book of Genesis that should be required reading for the entire human race"), García Márquez's novels are *The Autumn of the Patriarch* (1976), *Chronicle of a Death Foretold* (1982), and *Love in the Time of Cholera* (1988). His early works include the novellas *Leaf Storm and Other Stories* (1955; English 1972) and *No One Writes to the Colonel* (1961; English 1968). His short stories are gathered in *The Collected Stories of Gabriel García Márquez* (1984). In 1982 he was awarded the Nobel Prize for Literature. The stories here, "Death Constant Beyond Love" and "Monologue of Isabel Watching It Rain in Macondo," are magic, real — and pure García Márquez.

Death Constant Beyond Love

Translated from the Spanish by Gregory Rabassa

Senator Onésimo Sánchez had six months and eleven days to go before his death when he found the woman of his life. He met her in Rosal del Virrey, an illusory village which by night was the furtive wharf for smugglers' ships; and on the other hand, in broad daylight looked like the most useless inlet on the desert, facing a sea that was arid and without direction and so far from everything no one would have suspected that someone capable of changing the destiny of anyone lived there. Even its name was a kind of joke, because the only rose in that village was being worn by Senator Onésimo Sánchez himself on the same afternoon when he met Laura Farina.

It was an unavoidable stop in the electoral campaign he made every four years. The carnival wagons had arrived in the morning. Then came the trucks with the rented Indians who were carried into the towns in order to enlarge the crowds at public ceremonies. A short time before eleven o'clock, along with the music and rockets and jeeps of the retinue, the ministerial automobile, the color of strawberry soda, arrived. Senator Onésimo Sánchez was placid and weatherless inside the air-conditioned car, but as soon as he opened the door he was shaken by a gust of fire and his shirt of pure silk was soaked in a kind of light-colored soup and he felt many years older and more alone than ever. In real life he had just turned forty-two, had been graduated from Göttingen with honors as a metallurgical engineer, and was an avid reader, although without much reward, of badly translated Latin classics. He was married to a radiant German woman who had given him five children and they were all happy in their home, he the happiest of all until they told him, three months before, that he would be dead forever by next Christmas.

While the preparations for the public rally were being completed, the senator managed to have an hour alone in the house they had set aside for him to rest in. Before he lay down he put in a glass of drinking water the rose he had kept alive all across the desert, lunched on the diet cereals that he took with him so as to avoid the repeated portions of fried goat that were waiting for him during the rest of the day, and he took several analgesic pills before the time prescribed so that he would have the remedy ahead of the pain. Then he put the electric fan close to the hammock and stretched out naked for fifteen minutes in the shadow of the rose, making a great effort at mental distraction so as not to think about death while he dozed. Except for the doctors, no one knew that he had been sentenced to a fixed term, for he had decided to endure his secret all alone, with no change in his life, not because of pride but out of shame.

He felt in full control of his will when he appeared in public again at three in the afternoon, rested and clean, wearing a pair of coarse linen slacks and a floral shirt, and with his soul sustained by the anti-pain pills. Nevertheless, the erosion of death was much more pernicious than he had supposed, for as he went up onto the platform he felt a strange disdain for those who were fighting for the good luck to shake his hand, and he didn't feel sorry as he had at other times for the groups of barefoot Indians who could scarcely bear the hot saltpeter coals of the sterile little square. He silenced the applause with a wave of his hand, almost with rage, and he began to speak without gestures, his eyes fixed on the sea, which was sighing with heat. His measured, deep voice had the quality of calm water, but the speech that had been memorized and ground out so many times had not occurred to him in the nature of telling the truth, but, rather, as the opposite of a fatalistic pronouncement by Marcus Aurelius in the fourth book of his *Meditations*.

"We are here for the purpose of defeating nature," he began, against all his convictions. "We will no longer be foundlings in our own country, orphans of God in a realm of thirst and bad climate, exiles in our own land. We will be different people, ladies and gentlemen, we will be a great and happy people."

There was a pattern to his circus. As he spoke his aides threw clusters of paper birds into the air and the artificial creatures took on life, flew about the platform of planks, and went out to sea. At the same time, other men took some prop trees with felt leaves out of the wagons and planted them in the saltpeter soil behind the crowd. They finished by setting up a cardboard façade with make-believe houses of red brick that had glass windows, and with it they covered the miserable real-life shacks.

The senator prolonged his speech with two quotations in Latin in order to give the farce more time. He promised rainmaking machines, portable breeders for table animals, the oils of happiness which would make vegetables grow in the saltpeter and clumps of pansies in the window boxes. When he saw that his fictional world was all set up, he pointed to it. "That's the way it will be for us, ladies and gentlemen," he shouted. "Look! That's the way it will be for us."

The audience turned around. An ocean liner made of painted paper was passing behind the houses and it was taller than the tallest houses in the artificial city. Only the senator himself noticed that since it had been set up and taken down and carried from one place to another the superimposed cardboard town had been eaten away by the terrible climate and that it was almost as poor and dusty as Rosal del Virrey.

For the first time in twelve years, Nelson Farina didn't go to greet the senator. He listened to the speech from his hammock amidst the remains of his siesta, under the cool bower of a house of unplaned boards which he had built with the same pharmacist's hands with which he had drawn and quartered his first wife. He had escaped from Devil's Island and appeared in Rosal del Virrey on a ship loaded with innocent macaws, with a beautiful and blasphemous black woman he had found in Paramaribo and by whom he had a daughter. The woman died of natural causes a short while later and she didn't suffer the fate of the other, whose pieces had fertilized her own cauliflower patch, but was buried whole and with her Dutch name in the local cemetery. The daughter had inherited her color and her figure along with her father's yellow and astonished eyes, and he had good reason to imagine that he was rearing the most beautiful woman in the world.

Ever since he had met Senator Onésimo Sánchez during his first electoral campaign, Nelson Farina had begged for his help in getting a false identity card which would place him beyond the reach of the law. The senator, in a friendly but firm way, had refused. Nelson Farina never gave up, and for several years, every time he found the chance, he would repeat his request with a different recourse. But this time he stayed in his hammock, condemned to rot alive in that burning den of buccaneers. When he heard the final applause, he lifted his head, and looking over the boards of the fence, he saw the back side of the farce: the props for the buildings, the framework of the trees, the hidden illusionists who were pushing the ocean liner along. He spat without rancor.

"*Merde,*" he said. "*C'est le Blacamén de la politique.*"

After the speech, as was customary, the senator took a walk through the streets of the town in the midst of the music and the rockets and was besieged by the townspeople, who told him their troubles. The senator listened to them good-naturedly and he always found some way to console everybody without having to do them any difficult favors. A woman up on the roof of a house with her six youngest children managed to make herself heard over the uproar and the fireworks.

"I'm not asking for much, Senator," she said. "Just a donkey to haul water from Hanged Man's Well."

The senator noticed the six thin children. "What became of your husband?" he asked.

"He went to find his fortune on the island of Aruba," the woman answered good-humoredly, "and what he found was a foreign woman, the kind that put diamonds on their teeth."

The answer brought on a roar of laughter.

"All right," the senator decided, "you'll get your donkey."

A short while later an aide of his brought a good pack donkey to the woman's house and on the rump it had a campaign slogan written in indelible paint so that no one would ever forget that it was a gift from the senator.

Along the short stretch of street he made other, smaller gestures, and he even gave a spoonful of medicine to a sick man who had had his bed brought to the door of his house so he could see him pass. At the last corner, through the boards of the fence, he saw Nelson Farina in his hammock, looking ashen and gloomy, but nonetheless the senator greeted him, with no show of affection.

"Hello, how are you?"

Nelson Farina turned in his hammock and soaked him in the sad amber of his look. "*Moi, vous savez,*" he said.

His daughter came out into the yard when she heard the greeting. She was wearing a cheap, faded Guajiro Indian robe, her heard was decorated with colored bows, and her face was painted as protection against the sun, but even in that state of disrepair it was possible to imagine that there had never been another so beautiful in the whole world. The senator was left breathless. "I'll be damned!" he breathed in surprise. "The Lord does the craziest things!"

That night Nelson Farina dressed his daughter up in her best clothes and sent her to the senator. Two guards armed with rifles who were nodding from the heat in the borrowed house ordered her to wait on the only chair in the vestibule.

The senator was in the next room meeting with the important people of Rosal del Virrey, whom he had gathered together in order to sing for them the truths he had left out of his speeches. They looked so much like all the ones he always met in all the towns in the desert that even the senator himself was sick and tired of that perpetual nightly session. His shirt was soaked with sweat and he was trying to dry it on his body with the hot breeze from an electric fan that was buzzing like a horse fly in the heavy heat of the room.

"We, of course, can't eat paper birds," he said. "You and I know that the day there are trees and flowers in this heap of goat dung, the day there are shad instead of worms in the water holes, that day neither you nor I will have anything to do here, do I make myself clear?"

No one answered. While he was speaking, the senator had torn a sheet off the calendar and fashioned a paper butterfly out of it with his hands. He tossed it with no particular aim into the air current coming from the fan and the butterfly flew about the room and then went out through the half-open door. The senator went on speaking with a control aided by the complicity of death.

"Therefore," he said, "I don't have to repeat to you what you already know too well: that my reelection is a better piece of business for you than it is for me, because I'm fed up with stagnant water and Indian sweat, while you people, on the other hand, make your living from it."

Laura Farina saw the paper butterfly come out. Only she saw it because the guards in the vestibule had fallen asleep on the steps, hugging their rifles. After a few turns, the large lithographed butterfly unfolded completely, flattened against the wall, and remained stuck there. Laura Farina tried to pull it off with her nails. One of the guards, who woke up with the applause from the next room, noticed her vain attempt.

"It won't come off," he said sleepily. "It's painted on the wall."

Laura Farina sat down again when the men began to come out of the meeting. The senator stood in the doorway of the room with his hand on the latch, and he only noticed Laura Farina when the vestibule was empty.

"What are you doing here?"

"*C'est de la part de mon père,*" she said.

The senator understood. He scrutinized the sleeping guards, then he scrutinized Laura Farina, whose unusual beauty was even more demanding than his pain, and he resolved then that death had made his decision for him.

"Come in," he told her.

Laura Farina was struck dumb standing in the doorway to the room: thousands of bank notes were floating in the air, flapping like the butterfly. But the senator turned off the fan and the bills were left without air and alighted on the objects in the room.

"You see," he said, smiling, "even shit can fly."

Laura Farina sat down on a schoolboy's stool. Her skin was smooth and firm, with the same color and the same solar density as crude oil, her hair was the mane of a young mare, and her huge eyes were brighter than the light. The senator followed the thread of her look and finally found the rose, which had been tarnished by the saltpeter.

"It's a rose," he said.

"Yes," she said with a trace of perplexity. "I learned what they were in Riohacha."

The senator sat down on an army cot, talking about roses as he unbuttoned his shirt. On the side where he imagined his heart to be inside his chest he had a corsair's tattoo of a heart pierced by an arrow. He threw the soaked shirt to the floor and asked Laura Farina to help him off with his boots.

She knelt down facing the cot. The senator continued to scrutinize her, thoughtfully, and while she was untying the laces he wondered which one of them would end up with the bad luck of that encounter.

"You're just a child," he said.

"Don't you believe it," she said. "I'll be nineteen in April."

The senator became interested.

"What day?"

"The eleventh," she said.

The senator felt better. "We're both Aries," he said. And smiling, he added:

"It's the sign of solitude."

Laura Farina wasn't paying attention because she didn't know what to do with the boots. The senator, for his part, didn't know what to do with Laura Farina, because he wasn't used to sudden love affairs and besides, he knew that the one at hand had its origins in indignity. Just to have some time to think, he held Laura Farina tightly between his knees, embraced her about the waist, and lay down on his back on the cot. Then he realized that she was naked under her dress, for her body gave off the dark fragrance of an animal of the woods, but her heart was frightened and her skin disturbed by a glacial sweat.

"No one loves us," he sighed.

Laura Farina tried to say something, but there was only enough air for her to breathe. He laid her down beside him to help her, he put out the light and the room was in the shadow of the rose. She abandoned herself to the mercies of her fate. The senator caressed her slowly, seeking her with his hand, barely touching her, but where he expected to find her, he came across something iron that was in the way.

"What have you got there?"

"A padlock," she said.

"What in hell!" the senator said furiously and asked what he knew only too well. "Where's the key?"

Laura Farina gave a breath of relief.

"My papa has it," she answered. "He told me to tell you to send one of your people to get it and to send along with him a written promise that you'll straighten out his situation."

The senator grew tense. "Frog bastard," he murmured indignantly. Then he closed his eyes in order to relax and he met himself in the darkness. *Remember,* he remembered, *that whether it's you or someone else, it won't be long before you'll be dead and it won't be long before your name won't even be left.*

He waited for the shudder to pass.

"Tell me one thing," he asked then. "What have you heard about me?"

"Do you want the honest-to-God truth?"

"The honest-to-God truth."

"Well," Laura Farina ventured, "they say you're worse than the rest because you're different."

The senator didn't get upset. He remained silent for a long time with his eyes closed, and when he opened them again he seemed to have returned from his most hidden instincts.

"Oh, what the hell," he decided. "Tell your son of a bitch of a father that I'll straighten out his situation."

"If you want, I can go get the key myself," Laura Farina said.

The senator held her back.

"Forget about the key," he said, "and sleep awhile with me. It's good to be with someone when you're so alone."

Then she laid his head on her shoulder with her eyes fixed on the rose. The senator held her about the waist, sank his face into woods-animal armpit, and gave in to terror. Six months and eleven days later he would die in that same position, debased and repudiated because of the public scandal with Laura Farina and weeping with rage at dying without her.

GABRIEL GARCÍA MÁRQUEZ

Monologue of Isabel Watching It Rain in Macondo

Translated from the Spanish by Gregory Rabassa

Winter fell one Sunday when people were coming out of church. Saturday night had been suffocating. But even on Sunday morning nobody thought it would rain. After Mass, before we women had time to find the catches on our parasols, a thick, dark wind blew, which with one broad, round swirl swept away the dust and hard tinder of May. Someone next to me said: "It's a water wind." And I knew it even before then. From the moment we came out onto the church steps I felt shaken by a slimy feeling in my stomach. The men ran to the nearby houses with one hand on their hats and a handkerchief in the other, protecting themselves against the wind and the dust storm. Then it rained. And the sky was a gray, jellyish substance that flapped its wings a hand away from our heads.

During the rest of the morning my stepmother and I were sitting by the railing, happy that the rain would revive the thirsty rosemary and nard in the flowerpots after seven months of intense summer and scorching dust. At noon the reverberation of the earth stopped and a smell of turned earth, of awakened and renovated vegetation mingled with the cool and healthful odor of the rain in the rosemary. My father said at lunchtime: "When it rains in May, it's a sign that there'll be good tides." Smiling, crossed by the luminous thread of the new season, my stepmother told me: "That's what I heard in the sermon." And my father smiled. And he ate with a good appetite and even let his food digest leisurely beside the railing, silent, his eyes closed, but not sleeping, as if to think that he was dreaming while awake.

It rained all afternoon in a single tone. In the uniform and peaceful intensity you could hear the water fall, the way it is when you travel all afternoon on a train. But without our noticing it, the rain was penetrating too deeply into our senses. Early Monday morning, when we closed the door to avoid the cutting, icy draft that blew in from the courtyard, our senses had been filled with rain. And on Monday morning they had overflowed. My stepmother and I went back to look at the garden. The harsh gray earth of May had been changed overnight into a dark, sticky substance like cheap soap. A trickle of water began to run off the flowerpots. "I think they had more than enough water during the night," my stepmother said. And I noticed that she had stopped smiling and that her joy of the previous day had changed during the night into a lax and tedious seriousness. "I think you're right," I said. "It would better to have the Indians put them on the veranda until it stops raining." And that was what they did, while the rain grew like an immense tree over the other trees. My father occupied the same spot where he had been on Sunday afternoon, but he didn't talk about the rain. He said: "I must have slept poorly last night because I woke up with a stiff back." And he stayed there, sitting by the railing with his feet on a chair and his head turned toward the empty garden. Only at dusk, after he had turned down lunch, did he say: "It looks as if it will never clear." And I remembered the months of heat. I remembered August, those long and awesome siestas in which we dropped down to die under the weight of the hour, our clothes sticking to our bodies, hearing outside the insistent and dull buzzing of the hour that never passed. I saw the washed-down walls, the joints of the beams all puffed up by the water. I saw the small garden, empty for the first time, and the jasmine bush against the wall, faithful to the memory of my mother. I saw my father sitting in a rocker, his painful vertebrae resting on a pillow and his sad eyes lost in the labyrinth of the rain. I remembered the August nights in whose wondrous silence nothing could be heard except the millenary sound that the earth makes as it spins on its rusty, unoiled axis. Suddenly I felt overcome by an overwhelming sadness.

It rained all Monday, just like Sunday. But now it seemed to be raining in another way, because something different and bitter was going on in my heart. At dusk a voice beside my chair said: "This rain is a bore." Without turning to look, I recognized Martín's voice. I knew that he was speaking in the next chair, with the same cold and awesome expression that hadn't varied, not even after that gloomy December dawn when he started being my husband. Five months had passed since then. Now I was going to have a child. And Martín was there beside me saying that the rain bored him. "Not a bore," I said. "It seems terribly sad to me, with the empty garden and those poor trees that can't come in from the courtyard." Then I turned to look at him and Martín was no longer there. It was only a voice that was saying to me: "It doesn't look as if it will ever clear," and when I looked toward the voice I found only the empty chair.

On Tuesday morning we found a cow in the garden. It looked like a clay promontory in its hard and rebellious immobility, its hooves sunken in the mud and its head bent over. During the morning the Indians tried to drive it away with sticks and stones. But the cow stayed there, imperturbable in the garden, hard, inviolable, its hooves still sunken in the mud and its huge head humiliated by the rain. The Indians harassed it until my father's patient tolerance came to its defense. "Leave her alone," he said. "She'll leave the way she came."

At sundown on Tuesday the water tightened and hurt, like a shroud over the heart. The coolness of the first morning began to change into a hot and sticky humidity. The temperature was neither cold nor hot; it was the temperature of a fever chill. Feet sweated inside shoes. It was hard to say what was more disagreeable, bare skin or the contact of clothing on skin. All activity had ceased in the house. We sat on the veranda but we no longer watched the rain as we did on the first day. We no longer felt it falling. We no longer saw anything except the outline of the trees in the mist, with a sad and desolate sunset which left on your lips the same taste with which you awaken after having dreamed about a stranger. I knew that it was Tuesday and I remembered the twins of Saint Jerome, the blind girls who came to the house every week to sing us simple songs, saddened by the bitter and unprotected prodigy of their voices. Above the rain I heard the blind twins' little song and I imagined them at home, huddling, waiting for the rain to stop so they could go out and sing. The twins of Saint Jerome wouldn't come that day, I thought, nor would the beggar woman be on the veranda after siesta, asking, as on every Tuesday, for the eternal branch of lemon balm.

That day we lost track of meals. At siesta time my stepmother served a plate of tasteless soup and a piece of stale bread. But actually we hadn't eaten since sunset on Monday and I think that from then on we stopped thinking. We were paralyzed, drugged by the rain, given over to the collapse of nature with a peaceful and resigned attitude. Only the cow was moving in the afternoon. Suddenly a deep noise shook her insides and her hooves sank into the mud with greater force. Then she stood motionless for half an hour, as if she were already dead but could not fall down because the habit of being alive prevented her, the habit of remaining in one position in the rain, until the habit grew weaker than her body. Then she doubled her front legs (her dark and shiny haunches still raised in a last agonized effort) and sank her drooling snout into the mud, finally surrendering to the weight of her own matter in a silent, gradual, and dignified ceremony of total downfall. "She got that far," someone said behind me. And I turned to look and on the threshold I saw the Tuesday beggar woman who had come through the storm to ask for the branch of lemon balm.

Perhaps on Wednesday I might have grown accustomed to that overwhelming atmosphere if on going to the living room I hadn't found the table pushed against the wall, the furniture piled on top of it, and on the other side, on a parapet prepared during the night, trunks and boxes of household utensils. The spectacle produced a terrible feeling of emptiness in me. Something had happened during the night. The house was in disarray; the Guajiro Indians, shirtless and barefoot, with their pants rolled up to their knees, were carrying the furniture into the dining room. In the men's expression, in the very diligence with which they were working, one could see the cruelty of their frustrated rebellion, of their necessary and humiliating inferiority in the rain. I moved without direction, without will. I felt changed into a desolate meadow sown with algae and lichens, with soft, sticky toadstools, fertilized by the repugnant plants of dampness and shadows. I was in the living room contemplating the desert spectacle of the piled-up furniture when I heard my stepmother's voice warning me from her room that I might catch pneumonia. Only then did I realize that the water was up to my ankles, that the house was flooded, the floor covered by a thick surface of viscous, dead water.

On Wednesday noon it still hadn't finished dawning. And before three o'clock in the afternoon night had come on completely, ahead of time and sickly, with the same slow, monotonous, and pitiless rhythm of the rain in the courtyard. It was a premature dusk, soft and lugubrious, growing in the midst of the silence of the Guajiros, who were squatting on the chairs against the walls, defeated and impotent against the disturbance of nature. That was when news began to arrive from outside. No one brought it to the house. It simply arrived, precise, individualized, as if led by the liquid clay that ran through the streets and dragged household items along, things and more things, the leftovers of a remote catastrophe, rubbish and dead animals. Events that took place on Sunday, when the rain was still the announcement of a providential season, took two days to be known at our house. And on Wednesday the news arrived as if impelled by the very inner dynamism of the storm. It was learned then that the church was flooded and its collapse expected. Someone who had no reason to know said that night: "The train hasn't been able to cross the bridge since Monday. It seems that the river carried away the tracks." And it was learned that a sick woman had disappeared from her bed and had been found that afternoon floating in the courtyard.

Terrified, possessed by the fright and the deluge, I sat down in the rocker with my legs tucked up and my eyes fixed on the damp darkness full of hazy foreboding. My stepmother appeared in the doorway with the lamp held high and her head erect. She looked like a family ghost before whom I felt no fear whatever because I myself shared her supernatural condition. She came over to where I was. She still held her head high and the lamp in the air, and she splashed through the water on the veranda. "Now we have to pray," she said. And I noticed her dry and wrinkled face, as if she had just left her tomb or as if she had been made of some substance different from human matter. She was across from me with her rosary in her hand saying: "Now we have to pray. The water broke open the tombs and now the poor dead are floating in the cemetery."

I may have slept a little that night when I awoke with a start because of a sour and penetrating smell like that of decomposing bodies. I gave a strong shake to Martín, who was snoring beside me. "Don't you notice it?" I asked him. And he said: "What?" And I said: "The smell. It must be the dead people floating along the streets." I was terrified by that idea, but Martín turned to the wall and with a husky and sleepy voice said: "That's something you made up. Pregnant women are always imagining things."

At dawn on Thursday the smells stopped, the sense of distance was lost. The notion of time, upset since the day before, disappeared completely. Then there was no Thursday. What should have been Thursday was a physical, jellylike thing that could have been parted with the hands in order to look into Friday. There were no men or women there. My stepmother, my father, the Indians were adipose and improbable bodies that moved in the marsh of winter. My father said to me: "Don't move away from here until you're told what to do," and his voice was distant and indirect and didn't seem to be perceived by the ear but by touch, which was the only sense that remained active.

But my father didn't return: he got lost in the weather. So when night came I called my stepmother to tell her to accompany me to my bedroom. I had a peaceful and serene sleep, which lasted all through the night. On the following day the atmosphere was still the same, colorless, odorless, and without any temperature. As soon as I awoke I jumped into a chair and remained there without moving, because something told me that there was still a region of my consciousness that hadn't awakened completely. Then I heard the train whistle. The prolonged and sad whistle of the train fleeing the storm. *It must have cleared somewhere,* I thought, and a voice behind me seemed to answer my thought. "Where?" it said. "Who's there?" I asked looking. And I saw my stepmother with a long thin arm in the direction of the wall. "It's me," she said. And I asked her: "Can you hear it?" And she said yes, maybe it had cleared on the outskirts and they'd repaired the tracks. Then she gave me a tray with some steaming breakfast. It smelled of garlic sauce and boiled butter. It was a plate of soup. Disconcerted, I asked my stepmother what time it was. And she, calmly, with a voice that tasted of prostrated resignation, said: "It must be around two-thirty. The train isn't late after all this." I said: "Two-thirty! How could I have slept so long!" And she said: "You haven't slept very long. It can't be more than three o'clock." And I, trembling, feeling the plate slip through my fingers: "Two-thirty on Friday," I said. And she, monstrously tranquil: "Two-thirty on Thursday, child. *Still* two-thirty on Thursday."

I don't know how long I was sunken in that somnambulism where the senses lose their value. I only know that after many uncountable hours I heard a voice in the next room. A voice that said: "Now you can roll the bed to this side." It was a tired voice, but not the voice of a sick person, rather that of a convalescent. Then I heard the sound of the bricks in the water. I remained rigid before I realized that I was in a horizontal position. Then I felt the immense emptiness. I felt the wavering and violent silence of the house, the incredible immobility that affected everything. And suddenly I felt my heart turned into a frozen stone. *I'm dead,* I thought. *My God, I'm dead.* I gave a jump in the bed. I shouted: "Ada! Ada!" Martín's unpleasant voice answered me from the other side. "They can't hear you, they're already outside by now." Only then did I realize that it had cleared and that all around us a silence stretched out, a tranquillity, a mysterious and deep beatitude, a perfect state which must have been very much like death. Then footsteps could be heard on the veranda. A clear and completely living voice was heard. Then a cool breeze shook the panel of the door, made the doorknob squeak, and a solid and monumental body, like a ripe fruit, fell deeply into the cistern in the courtyard. Something in the air revealed the presence of an invisible person who was smiling in the darkness. *Good Lord,* I thought then, confused by the mixup in time. *It wouldn't surprise me now if they were coming to call me to go to last Sunday's Mass.*

NATALIA GINZBURG

Natalia Ginzburg was born in 1916 in Palermo, Sicily, and grew up in the city of Turin, where her father taught at the university. She came of age in an Italy torn by the Second World War. Her first husband, a literature professor of Russian origin, was arrested by the government for anti-Fascist activities and turned over to the Nazis; he died in prison in Rome. Following the war, Ginzburg worked as an editorial consultant to a publisher in Turin and continued writing stories and novels. She remarried, lived for a time in London, and now lives in Rome. Her books, some of which are chronicles of the Fascist era, include *The Road to the City* (1942; English 1949), *The Dry Heart* (1947; English 1949), *A Light for Fools* (1952; English 1956), *Voices in the Evening* (1961; English 1963), *No Way* (1973; English 1974), *Family Sayings* (1983; English 1984), and *The City and the House* (1986; English 1987). Ginzburg writes in a style simultaneously rich with detail and restrained; she does not often intrude her voice into her work. An English critic, assessing her career, cited her "capacity to mean much while saying little — a kind of poetic compression. . . ." One of Ginzburg's translators has described her manner of creating characters as "cumulative characterization — a method that . . . builds up solid and memorable people by the gradual mounting up of small actions, oblique glances, other people's opinions." Told in Ginzburg's characteristic understatement, "The Mother" builds such a character.

The Mother

Translated from the Italian by Isabel Quigly

Their mother was small and thin, and slightly round-shouldered; she always wore a blue skirt and a red woollen blouse. She had short, curly black hair which she kept oiled to control its bushiness; every day she plucked her eyebrows, making two black fish of them that swam towards her temples; and she used yellow powder on her face. She was very young; how old, they didn't know, but she seemed much younger than the mothers of the boys at school; they were always surprised to see their friends' mothers, how old and fat they were. She smoked a great deal and her fingers were stained with smoke; she even smoked in bed in the evening, before going to sleep. All three of them slept together, in the big double bed with the yellow quilt; their mother was on the side nearest the door, and on the bedside table she had a lamp with its shade wrapped in a red cloth, because at night she read and smoked; sometimes she came in very late, and the boys would wake up and ask her where she had been: she nearly always answered: 'At the cinema', or else 'With a girl friend of mine'; who this friend was they didn't know, because no woman friend had ever been to the house to see their mother. She told them they must turn the other way while she undressed, they heard the quick rustle of her clothes, and shadows danced on the walls; she slipped into bed beside them, her thin body in its cold silk nightdress, and they moved away from her because she always complained that they came too close and kicked while they slept; sometimes she put out the light so that they should go to sleep and smoked in silence in the darkness.

Their mother was not important. Granny, Grandpa, Aunt Clementina who lived in the country and turned up now and then with chestnuts and maize-flour were important; Diomira the maid was important, Giovanni the tubercular porter who made cane chairs was important; all these were very important to the two boys because they were strong people you could trust, strong people in allowing and forbidding, very good at everything they did and always full of wisdom and strength; people who could defend you from storms and robbers. But if they were at home with their mother the boys were frightened, just as if they had been alone; as for allowing or forbidding, she never allowed or forbade anything, at the most she complained in a weary voice: 'Don't make such a row because I've got a headache,' and if they asked permission to do something or other she answered at once: 'Ask Granny', or she said no first and then yes and then no and it was all a muddle. When they went out alone with their mother they felt uncertain and insecure because she always took wrong turnings and had to ask a policeman the way, and then she had such a funny, timid way of going into shops to ask for things to buy, and in the shops she always forgot something, gloves or handbag or scarf, and had to go back to look and the boys were ashamed.

Their mother's drawers were untidy and she left all her things scattered about and Diomira grumbled about her when she did out the room in the morning. She even called Granny in to see and together they picked up stockings and clothes and swept up the ash that was scattered all over the place. In the morning their mother went to do the shopping: she came back and flung the string bag on the marble table in the kitchen and took her bicycle and dashed off to the office where she worked. Diomira looked at all the things in the string bag, touched the oranges one by one and the meat, and grumbled and called Granny to see what poor meat it was. Their mother came home at two o'clock when they had all eaten and ate quickly with the newspaper propped up against her glass and then rushed off again to the office on her bicycle and they saw her for a minute at supper again, but after supper she nearly always dashed off.

The boys did their homework in the bedroom. There was their father's picture, large at the head of the bed, with his square black beard and bald head and tortoiseshell-rimmed spectacles, and then another small portrait on the table, with the younger of the boys in his arms. Their father had died when they were very small, they remembered nothing about him: or rather in the older boy's memory there was the shadow of a very distant afternoon, in the country at Aunt Clementina's: his father was pushing him across the meadow in a green wheelbarrow; afterwards he had found some pieces of this wheelbarrow, a handle and a wheel, in Aunt Clementina's attic; when it was new it was a splendid wheelbarrow and he was glad to have it; his father ran along pushing him and his long beard flapped. They knew nothing about their father but they thought he must be the sort of person who is strong and wise in allowing and forbidding, when Grandpa or Diomira got angry with their mother Granny said that they should be sorry for her because she had been very unfortunate, and she said that if Eugenio, the boys' father, had been there she would have been an entirely different woman, whereas she had had the mis-fortune to lose her husband when she was still young. For a time there had been their father's mother as well, they never saw her because she lived in France but she used to write and send Christmas presents: then in the end she died because she was very old.

At tea-time they ate chestnuts, or bread with oil and vinegar, and then if they had finished their homework they could go and play in the small piazza or among the ruins of the public baths, which had been blown up in an air raid. In the small piazza there were a great many pigeons and they took them bread or got Diomira to give them a paper bag of left-over rice. There they met all the local boys, boys from school and others they met in the youth clubs on Sundays when they had football matches with Don Vigliani, who hitched up his black cassock and kicked. Sometimes they played football in the small piazza too or else cops and robbers. Their grand-mother appeared on the balcony occasionally and called to them not to get hurt: it was nice seeing the lighted windows of their home, up there on the third floor, from the dark piazza, and knowing that they could go back there, warm up at the stove and guard themselves from the night. Granny sat in the kitchen with Diomira and mended the linen; Grandpa was in the dining-room with his cap on, smoking his pipe. Granny was very fat, and wore black, and on her breast a medal with a picture of Uncle Oreste who had died in the war: she was very good at cooking pizzas and things. Sometimes she took them on her knee, even now when they were quite big boys; she was fat, she had a large soft bosom; from under the neck of her black dress you could see the thick white woollen vest with a scolloped edge which she had made herself. She would take them on her knee and say tender and slightly pitiful-sounding words in dialect; then she would take a long iron hair-pin out of her bun and clean their ears, and they would shriek and try to get away and Grandpa would come to the door with his pipe.

Grandpa had taught Greek and Latin at the high school. Now he was pensioned off and was writing a Greek grammar: many of his old pupils used to come and see him now and then. Then Diomira would make coffee; in the lavatory there were exercise book pages with Latin and Greek unseens on them, and his corrections in red and blue. Grandpa had a small white beard, a sort of goatee, and they were not to make a racket because his nerves were tired after all those years at school; he was always rather alarmed because prices kept going up and Granny always had a bit of a row with him in the morning because he was always surprised at the money they needed; he would say that perhaps Diomira pinched the sugar and made coffee in secret and Diomira would hear and rush at him and yell that the coffee was for the students who kept coming; but these were small incidents that quietened down at once and the boys were not alarmed, whereas they were alarmed when there was a quarrel between Grandpa and their mother; this happened sometimes if their mother came home very late at night, he would come out of his room with his overcoat over his pyjamas and bare feet, and he and their mother would shout: he said: 'I know where you've been, I know where you've been, I know what you are,' and their mother said: 'What do I care?' and then: 'Look, now you've woken the children,' and he said: 'A fat lot you care what happens to your children. Don't say anything because I know what you are. You're a bitch. You run around at night like the mad bitch you are.' And then Granny and Diomira would come out in their nightdresses and push him into his room and say: 'Shush, shush,' and their mother would get into bed and sob under the bedclothes, her deep sobs echoing in the dark room: the boys thought that Grandpa must be right, they thought their mother was wrong to go to the cinema and to her girl friends at night. They felt very unhappy, frightened and unhappy, and lay huddled close together in the deep, warm, soft bed, and the older boy who was in the middle pushed away so as not to touch his mother's body: there seemed to him something disgusting in his mother's tears, in the wet pillow: he thought: 'It gives a chap the creeps when his mother cries.' They never spoke between themselves of these rows their mother and Grandpa had, they carefully avoided mentioning them: but they loved each other very much and clung close together at night when their mother cried: in the morning they were faintly embarrassed, because they had hugged so tightly as if to protect themselves, and because there was that thing they didn't want to talk about; besides, they soon forgot that they had been unhappy, the day began and they went to school, and met their friends in the street, and played for a moment at the school door.

In the grey light of morning, their mother got up: with her petticoat wound round her waist she soaped her neck and arms standing bent over the basin: she always tried not to let them see her but in the looking glass they could make out her thin brown shoulders and small naked breasts: in the cold the nipples became dark and protruding, she raised her arms and powdered her armpits: in her armpits she had thick curly hair. When she was completely dressed she started plucking her eyebrows, staring at herself in the mirror from close to and biting her lips hard: then she smothered her face with cream and shook the pink swansdown puff hard and powdered herself: then her face became all yellow. Sometimes she was quite gay in the mornings and wanted to talk to the boys, she asked them about school and their friends and told them things about her time at school: she had a teacher called 'Signorina Dirce' and she was an old maid who tried to seem young. Then she put on her coat and picked up her string shopping bag, leant down to kiss the boys and ran out with her scarf wound round her head and her face all perfumed and powdered with yellow powder.

The boys thought it strange to have been born of her. It would have been much less strange to have been born of Granny or Diomira, with their large warm bodies that protected you from fear, that defended you from storms and robbers. It was very strange to think she was their mother, that she had held them for a while in her small womb. Since they learnt that children are in their mother's tummy before being born, they had felt very surprised and also a little ashamed that that womb had once held them. And that she had given them milk from her breasts as well: this was even more unlikely. But now she no longer had small children to feed and cradle, and every day they saw her dash off on her bicycle when the shopping was done, her body jerking away, free and happy. She certainly didn't belong to them: they couldn't count on her. You couldn't ask her anything: there were other mothers, the mothers of their school friends, whom clearly you could ask about all sorts of things; their friends ran to their mothers when school was over and asked them heaps of things, got their noses blown and their overcoats buttoned, showed their homework and their comics: these mothers were pretty old, with hats or veils or fur collars and they came to talk to the master practically every day: they were people like Granny or like Diomira, large soft imperious bodies of people who didn't make mistakes: people who didn't lose things, who didn't leave their drawers untidy, who didn't come home late at night. But their mother ran off free after the shopping; besides, she was bad at shopping, she got cheated by the butcher and was often given wrong change: she went off and it was impossible to join her where she went, deep down they marvelled at her enormously when they saw her go off: who knows what that office of hers was like, she didn't talk about it much; she had to type and write letters in French and English: who knows, maybe she was pretty good at that.

One day when they were out for a walk with Don Vigliani and with other boys from the youth club, on the way back they saw their mother in a suburban café. She was sitting inside the café; they saw her through the window, and a man was sitting with her. Their mother had laid her tartan scarf on the table and the old crocodile handbag they knew well: the man had a loose light overcoat and a brown moustache and was talking to her and smiling: their mother's face was happy, relaxed and happy, as it never was at home. She was looking at the man and they were holding hands and she didn't see the boys: the boys went on walking beside Don Vigliani who told them all to hurry because they must catch the tram: when they were on the tram the younger boy moved over to his brother and said: 'Did you see Mummy?' and his brother said: 'No, I didn't.' The younger one laughed softly and said: 'Oh yes you did, it was Mummy and there was a man with her.' The older boy turned his head away: he was big, nearly thirteen: his younger brother irritated him because he made him feel sorry for him, he couldn't understand why he felt sorry for him but he was sorry for himself as well and he didn't want to think of what he had seen, he wanted to behave as if he had seen nothing.

They said nothing to Granny. In the morning while their mother was dressing the younger boy said: 'Yesterday when we were out for a walk with Don Vigliani we saw you and there was a man with you.' Their mother jerked round, looking nasty: the black fish on her forehead quivered and met. She said: 'But it wasn't me. What an idea. I've got to stay in the office till late in the evening, as you know. Obviously you made a mistake.' The older boy then said, in a tired calm voice: 'No, it wasn't you. It was someone who looked like you.' And both boys realized that the memory must disappear: and they both breathed hard to blow it away.

But the man in the light overcoat once came to the house. He hadn't got his overcoat because it was summer, he wore blue spectacles and a light linen suit, he asked leave to take off his jacket while they had lunch. Granny and Grandpa had gone to Milan to meet some relations and Diomira had gone to her village, so they were alone with their mother. It was then the man came. Lunch was pretty good: their mother had bought nearly everything at the cooked meat shop: there was chicken with chips and this came from the shop: their mother had done the pasta, it was good, only the sauce was a bit burnt. There was wine, too. Their mother was nervous and gay, she wanted to say so much at once: she wanted to talk of the boys to the man and of the man to the boys. The man was called Max and he had been in Africa, he had lots of photographs of Africa and showed them: there was a photograph of a monkey of his, the boys asked him about this monkey a lot; it was so intelligent and so fond of him and had such a funny, pretty way with it when it wanted a sweet. But he had left it in Africa because it was ill and he was afraid it would die on the steamer. The boys became friendly with this Max. He promised to take them to the cinema one day. They showed him their books, they hadn't got many: he asked them if they had read *Saturnino Farandola* and they said no and he said he would give it to them, and *Robinson delle praterie* as well, as it was very fine. After lunch their mother told them to go and play in the recreation ground. They wished they could stay on with Max. They protested a bit but their mother, and Max too, said they must go; then in the evening when they came home Max was no longer there. Their mother hurriedly prepared the supper, coffee with milk and potato salad: they were happy, they wanted to talk about Africa and the monkey, they were extraordinarily happy and couldn't really understand why: and their mother seemed happy too and told them things, about a monkey she had once seen dancing to a little street organ. And then she told them to go to bed and said she was going out for a minute, they mustn't be scared, there was no reason to be; she bent down to kiss them and told them there was no point in telling Granny and Grandpa about Max because they never liked one inviting people home.

So they stayed on their own with their mother for a few days: they ate unusual things because their mother didn't want to cook, ham and jam and coffee with milk and fried things from the cooked meat shop. Then they washed up together. But when Granny and Grandpa came back the boys felt relieved: the tablecloth was on the dining-room table again, and the glasses and everything there should be: Granny was sitting in her rocking chair again, with her soft body and her smell: Grandma couldn't dash off, she was too old and too fat, it was nice having someone who stayed at home and couldn't ever dash away.

The boys said nothing to Granny about Max. They waited for the book *Saturnino Farandola* and waited for Max to take them to the cinema and show them more photographs of the monkey. Once or twice they asked their mother when they'd be going to the cinema with signor Max. But their mother answered harshly that signor Max had left now. The younger boy asked if he'd gone to Africa. Their mother didn't answer. But he thought he must have gone to Africa to fetch the monkey. He imagined that someday or other he would come and fetch them at school, with a black servant and a monkey in his arms. School began again and Aunt Clementina came to stay with them for a while; she had brought a bag of pears and apples which they put in the oven to cook with marsala and sugar. Their mother was in a very bad temper and quarrelled continually with Grandpa. She came home late and stayed awake smoking. She had got very much thinner and ate nothing. Her face became ever smaller and yellower, she now put black on her eyelashes too, she spat into a little box and picked up the black where she had spat with a brush; she put on masses of powder, Granny tried to wipe it off her face with a handkerchief and she turned her face away. She hardly ever spoke and when she did it seemed an effort, her voice was so weak. One day she came home in the afternoon at about six o'clock: it was strange, usually she came home much later; she locked herself in the bedroom. The younger boy came and knocked because he needed an exercise book: their mother answered angrily from inside that she wanted to sleep and that they were to leave her in peace: the boy explained timidly that he needed the exercise book; then she came to open up and her face was all swollen and wet: the boy realized she was crying, he went back to Granny and said: 'Mummy's crying,' and Granny and Aunt Clementina talked quietly together for a long time, they spoke of their mother but you couldn't make out what they were saying.

One night their mother didn't come home. Grandpa kept coming to see, barefoot, with his overcoat over his pyjamas; Granny came too and the boys slept badly, they could hear Granny and Grandpa walking about the house, opening and shutting the windows. The boys were very frightened. Then in the morning, they rang up from the police station: their mother had been found dead in an hotel, she had taken poison, she had left a letter: Grandpa and Aunt Clementina went along, Granny shrieked, the boys were sent to an old lady on the floor below who said continually: 'Heartless, leaving two babes like this.' Their mother was brought home. The boys went to see her when they had her laid out on the bed: Diomira had dressed her in her patent leather shoes and the red silk dress from the time she was married: she was small, a small dead doll.

It was strange to see flowers and candles in the same old room. Diomira and Aunt Clementina and Granny were kneeling and praying: they had said she took the poison by mistake, otherwise the priest wouldn't come and bless her, if he knew she had done it on purpose. Diomira told the boys they must kiss her: they were terribly ashamed and kissed her cold cheek one after the other. Then there was the funeral, it took ages, they crossed the entire town and felt very tired, Don Vigliani was there too and a great many children from school and from the youth club. It was cold, and very windy in the cemetery. When they went home again, Granny started crying and bawling at the sight of the bicycle in the passage: because it was really just like seeing her dashing away, with her free body and her scarf flapping in the wind: Don Vigliani said she was now in heaven, perhaps because he didn't know she had done it on purpose, or he knew and pretended not to: but the boys didn't really know if heaven existed, because Grandpa said no, and Granny said yes, and their mother had once said there was no heaven, with little angels and beautiful music, but that the dead went to a place where they were neither well nor ill, and that where you wish for nothing, you rest and are wholly at peace.

The boys went to the country for a time, to Aunt Clementina's. Everyone was very kind to them, and kissed and caressed them, and they were very ashamed. They never spoke together of their mother nor of signor Max either; in the attic at Aunt Clementina's they found the book of *Saturnino Farandola* and they read it over and over and found it very fine. But the older boy often thought of his mother, as he had seen her that day in the café with Max, holding her hands and with such a relaxed, happy face; he thought then that maybe their mother had taken poison because Max had gone back to Africa for good. The boys played with Aunt Clementina's dog, a fine dog called Bubi, and they learnt to climb trees, as they couldn't do before. They went bathing in the river, too, and it was nice going back to Aunt Clementina's in the evening and doing crosswords all together. The boys were very happy at Aunt Clementina's. Then they went back to Granny's and were very happy. Granny sat in the rocking chair, and wanted to clean their ears with her hairpins. On Sunday they went to the cemetery, Diomira came too, they bought flowers and on the way back stopped at a bar to have hot punch. When they were in the cemetery, at the grave, Granny prayed and cried, but it was very hard to think that the grave and the crosses and the cemetery had anything to do with their mother, who had been cheated by the butcher and dashed off on her bicycle, and smoked, and took wrong turnings, and sobbed at night. The bed was very big for them now and they had a pillow each.

They didn't often think of their mother because it hurt them a little and made them ashamed to think of her. Sometimes they tried to remember how she was, each on his own in silence: and they found it harder and harder to reassemble her short curly hair and the fish on her forehead and her lips: she put on a lot of yellow powder, this they remembered quite well; little by little there was a yellow dot, it was impossible to get the shape of her cheeks and face. Besides, they now realized that they had never loved her much, perhaps she too hadn't loved them much, if she had loved them she wouldn't have taken poison, they had heard Diomira and the porter and the lady on the floor below and so many other people say so. The years went by and the boys grew and so many things happened and that face which they had never loved very much disappeared for ever.

NADINE GORDIMER

 Born in 1923 in a gold-mining town in South Africa, Nadine Gordimer has lived all her life in that troubled country. Her work, with few exceptions, explores the effects of apartheid on the people of South Africa, black and white alike. For her sensitivity, knowledge, and insight she has been called "one of the very few links between white and black in South Africa . . . a luminous symbol of at least one white person's understanding of the black man's burden." Gordimer explains her life's work this way: ". . . in a certain sense a writer is 'selected' by his subject — his subject being *the consciousness* of his own era. . . . My time and place have been twentieth-century Africa." In short stories and novels over almost four decades, she has intelligently and acutely given twentieth-century Africa to the world. Her major novels include *The Lying Days* (1953), *A World of Strangers* (1958), *A Guest of Honor* (1970), *The Conservationist* (1975), *Burger's Daughter* (1979), and *A Sport of Nature* (1987). Gordimer's first short story collection, *The Soft Voice of the Serpent and Other Stories,* appeared in 1952. Among other collections are *Six Feet of the Country* (1956), *Friday's Footprint and Other Stories* (1960), and *A Soldier's Embrace* (1980). *Selected Stories* was published in 1976. She has articulated perhaps one of the most cogent explanations of the writing of short stories: "A short story *occurs,* in the imaginative sense. To write one is to express from a situation in the exterior or interior world the life-giving drop . . . that will spread an intensity on the page; burn a hole in it." The two stories here, "Africa Emergent" and "Sins of the Third Age," are different in subject and style, but each conveys Gordimer's extraordinary power.

Africa Emergent

He's in prison now, so I'm not going to mention his name. It mightn't be a good thing, you understand. — Perhaps you think you understand too well; but don't be quick to jump to conclusions from five or six thousand miles away: if you lived here, you'd understand something else — friends know that shows of loyalty are all right for children holding hands in the school playground; for us they're luxuries, not important and maybe dangerous. If I said, I was a friend of so-and-so, black man awaiting trial for treason, what good would it do him? And, who knows, it might draw just that decisive bit more attention to me. *He*'d be the first to agree.

Not that one feels that if they haven't got enough in my dossier already, this would make any difference; and not that he really was such a friend. But that's something else you won't understand; everything is ambiguous, here. We hardly know, by now, what we can do and what we can't do; it's difficult to say, goaded in on oneself by laws and doubts and rebellion and caution and — not least — self-disgust, what is or is not a friendship. I'm talking about black and white, of course. If you stay with it, boy, on the white side in the country clubs and garden suburbs if you're white, and on the black side in the locations and beerhalls if you're black, none of this applies, and you can go all the way to your segregated cemetery in peace. But neither he nor I did.

I began mixing with blacks out of what is known as an outraged sense of justice, plus strong curiosity, when I was a student. There were two ways — one was through the white students' voluntary service organization, a kibbutz-type junket where white boys and girls went into rural areas and camped while they built school classrooms for African children. A few coloured and African students from their segregated universities used to come along too, and there was the novelty, not without value, of dossing down alongside them at night, although we knew we were likely to be harbouring Special Branch spies among our willing workers, and we dared not make a pass at the coloured or black girls. The other way — less hard on the hands — was to go drinking with the jazz musicians and journalists, painters and would-be poets and actors who gravitated towards whites partly because such people naturally feel they can make free of the world, and partly because they found an encouragement and appreciation there that was sweet to them. I tried the V.S.O. briefly, but the other way suited me better; anyway, I didn't see why I should help this Government by doing the work it ought to be doing for the welfare of black children.

I'm an architect and the way I was usefully drawn into the black scene was literally that: I designed sets for a mixed-colour drama group got together by a white director. Perhaps there's no urban human group as intimate, in the end, as a company of this kind, and the colour problem made us even closer. I don't mean what *you* mean, the how-do-I-feel-about-that-black-skin stuff; I mean the daily exasperation of getting round, or over, or on top of the colour-bar laws that plagued our productions and our lives. We had to remember to write out 'passes' at night, so that our actors could get home without being arrested for being out after the curfew for blacks, we had to spend hours at the Bantu Affairs Department trying to arrange local residence permits for actors who were being 'endorsed out' of town back to the villages to which, 'ethnically', apparently, they belonged although they'd never set eyes on them, and we had to decide which of us could play the sycophant well enough to persuade the Bantu Commissioner to allow the show to go on the road from one Group Area, designated by colour, to another, or to talk some town clerk into getting his council to agree to the use of a 'white' public hall by the mixed cast. The black actors' lives were in our hands, because they were black and we were white, and could, must, intercede for them. Don't think this made everything love and light between us; in fact it caused endless huffs and rows. A white woman who'd worked like a slave acting as P.R.O.-cum-wardrobe-mistress hasn't spoken to me for years because I made her lend her little car to one of the chaps who'd worked until after the last train went back to the location, and then he kept it the whole weekend and she couldn't get hold of him because, of course, location houses rarely have telephones and once a black man has disappeared among those warrens you won't find him till he chooses to surface in the white town again. And when this one did surface, he was biting, to me, about white bitches' 'patronage' of people they secretly still thought of as 'boys'. Yet our arguments, resentments and misunderstandings were not only as much part of the intimacy of this group as the good times, the parties and the love-making we had, but were more — the defining part, because we'd got close enough to admit argument, resentment and misunderstanding between us.

He was one of this little crowd, for a time. He was a dispatch clerk and then a 'manager' and chucker-out at a black dance club. In his spare time he took a small part in our productions now and then, and made himself generally handy; in the end it was discovered that what he really was good at was front-of-house arrangements. His tubby charm (he was a large young man and a cheerful dresser) was just the right thing to deal with the unexpected moods of our location audiences when we went on tour — sometimes they came stiffly encased in their church-going best and seemed to feel it was vulgar to laugh or respond to what was going on, on stage; in other places they rushed the doors, tried to get in without paying, and were dominated by a *tsotsi,* street urchin, element who didn't want to hear anything but themselves. He was the particular friend, the other, passive half — of a particular friend of mine, Elias Nkomo.

And here I stop short. How shall I talk about Elias? I've never even learnt, in five years, how to think about him.

Elias was a sculptor. He had one of those jobs — messenger 'boy' or some such — that literate young black men can aspire to in a small gold-mining and industrial town outside Johannesburg. Somebody said he was talented, somebody sent him to me — at the beginning, the way for every black man to find himself seems inescapably to lead through a white man. Again, how can I say what his work was like? He came by train to the black people's section of Johannesburg central station, carrying a bulky object wrapped in that morning's newspaper. He was slight, round-headed, tiny-eared, dunly dressed, and with a frown of effort between his eyes, but his face unfolded to a wide, apologetic yet confident smile when he realized that the white man in a waiting car must be me — the meeting had been arranged. I took him back to my 'place' (he always called people's homes that) and he unwrapped the newspaper. What was there was nothing like the clumps of diorite or sandstone you have seen in galleries in New York, London or Johannesburg, marked 'Africa Emergent', 'Spirit of the Ancestors'.

What was there was a goat, or goat-like creature, in the way that a centaur is a horse-like, man-like creature, carved out of streaky knotted wood. It was delightful (I wanted to put out my hand to touch it), it was moving in its somehow concrete diachrony, beast men, coarse wood fine workmanship, and there was also something exposed about it (one would withdraw the hand, after all).

I asked him whether he knew Picasso's goats? He had heard of Picasso but never seen any of his work. I showed him a photograph of the famous bronze goat in Picasso's own house; thereafter all his beasts had sex organs as joyful as Picasso's goat's udder, but that was the only 'influence' that ever took, with him. As I say, a white man always intercedes in some way, with a man like Elias; mine was to keep him from those art-loving ladies with galleries who wanted to promote him, and those white painters and sculptors who were willing to have him work under their tutelage. I gave him an old garage (well, that means I took my car out of it) and left him alone, with plenty of chunks of wood.

But Elias didn't like the loneliness of work. That garage never became his 'place'. Perhaps when you've lived in an overcrowded yard all your life the counter-stimulus of distraction becomes necessary to create a tension of concentration. No — well all I really mean is that he liked company. At first he came only at weekends, and then, as he began to sell some of his work, he gave up the messenger job and moved in more or less permanently — we fixed up the 'place' together, putting in a ceiling and connecting water and so on. It was illegal for him to live there in a white suburb, of course, but such laws breed complementary evasions in people like Elias and me and the white building inspector didn't turn a hair of suspicion when I said that I was converting the garage as a flat for my wife's mother. It was better for Elias once he'd moved in; there was always some friend of his sharing his bed, not to mention the girls who did; sometimes the girls were shy little things almost of the kitchenmaid variety, who called my wife 'madam' when they happened to bump into her, crossing the garden, sometimes they were the bewigged and painted actresses from the group who sat smoking and gossiping with my wife while she fed the baby.

And *he* was there more often than anyone — the plump and cheerful front-of-house manager; he was married, but as happens with our sex, an old friendship was a more important factor in his life than a wife and kids — if that's a characteristic of black men, then I must be black under the skin, myself. Elias had become very involved in the theatre group, anyway, like *him*; Elias made some beautiful *papier mâché* gods for a play by a Nigerian that we did — 'spirits of the ancestors' at once amusing and frightening — and once when we needed a singer he surprisingly turned out to have a voice that could phrase a madrigal as easily as whatever the forerunner of Soul was called — I forget now, but it blared hour after hour from the garage when he was working. Elias seemed to like best to work when the other one was around; *he* would sit with his fat boy's legs rolled out before him, flexing his toes in his fashionable shoes, dusting down the lapels of the latest thing in jackets, as he changed the records and kept up a monologue contentedly punctuated by those soft growls and sighs of agreement, those sudden squeezes of almost silent laughter — responses possible only in an African language — that came from Elias as he chiselled and chipped. For they spoke in their own tongue, and I have never known what it was they talked about.

In spite of my efforts to let him alone, inevitably Elias was 'taken up' (hadn't I started the process myself, with that garage?) and a gallery announced itself his agent. He walked about at the opening of his one-man show in a purple turtle-necked sweater I think his best friend must have made him buy, laughing a little, softly, at himself, more embarrassed than pleased. An art critic wrote about his transcendental values and plastic modality, and he said, 'Christ, man, does he dig it or doesn't he?' while we toasted his success in brandy chased with beer — brandy isn't a rich man's sip in South Africa, it's made here and it's what people use to get drunk on.

He earned quite a bit of money that year. Then the gallery-owner and the art critic forgot him in the discovery of yet another interpreter of the African soul, and he was poor again, but he had acquired a patroness who, although she lived far away, did not forget him. She was, as you might have thought, an American lady, very old and wealthy according to South African legend but probably simply a middle-aged widow with comfortable stock holdings and a desire to get in on the cultural ground floor of some form of art collecting not yet overcrowded. She had bought some of his work while a tourist in Johannesburg. Perhaps she did have academic connections with the art world; in any case, it was she who got a foundation to offer Elias Nkomo a scholarship to study in America.

I could understand that he wanted to go simply in order to go: to see the world outside. But I couldn't believe that at this stage he wanted or could make use of formal art-school disciplines. As I said to him at the time, I'm only an architect, but I've had experience of the academic and even, God help us, the frenziedly non-academic approach in the best schools, and it's not for people who have, to fall back on the jargon, found themselves.

I remember he said, smiling, 'You think I've found myself?'

And I said, 'But you've never been lost, man. That very first goat wrapped in newspaper was your goat.'

But later, when he was refused a passport and the issue of his going abroad was much on our minds, we talked again. He wanted to go because he felt he needed some kind of general education, general cultural background that he'd missed, in his six years at the location school. 'Since I've been at your place I've been reading a lot of your books. And man, I know nothing. I'm as ignorant as that kid of yours there in the pram. Right, I've picked up a bit of politics, a few art terms here and there — I can wag my head and say "plastic values" all right, eh? But man, what do I know about life? What do I know about how it all works? How do I know *how* I do the work I do? Why we live and die? — If I carry on here I might as well be carving walking sticks,' he added. I knew what he meant: there are old men, all over Africa, who make a living squatting at a decent distance from tourist hotels, carving fancy walking sticks from local wood, only one step in sophistication below the 'African Emergent' school of sculptors so rapturously acclaimed by gallery owners. We both laughed at this, and following the line of thought suggested to me by this question to himself: 'How do I know how I do the work I do?', I asked him whether in fact there was any sort of traditional skill in his family? As I imagined, there was not, — he was an urban slum kid, brought up opposite a municipal beerhall among paraffin-tin utensils and abandoned motor-car bodies which, perhaps curiously, had failed to bring out a Duchamp in him but from which, on the contrary, he had sprung, full-blown, as a classical expressionist. Although there were no rural walking-stick carvers in his ancestry, he did tell me something I had no idea would have been part of the experience of a location childhood — he had been sent, in his teens, to a tribal initiation school in the bush and been circumcised according to rite. He described the experience vividly.

Once all attempts to get him a passport had failed, Elias's desire to go to America became something else, of course: an obsessive resentment against confinement itself. Inevitably, he was given no reason for the refusal. The official answer was the usual one — that it was 'not in the public interest' to reveal the reason for such things. Was it because 'they' had got to know he was 'living like a white man'? (Theory put to me by one of the black actors in the group.) Was it because a critic had dutifully described his work as expressive of the 'agony of the emergent African soul'? Nobody knew. Nobody ever knows. It is enough to be black; blacks are meant to stay put, in their own ethnically-apportioned streets in their own segregated areas, in those parts of South Africa where the government says they belong. Yet — the whole way our lives are manoeuvred, as I say, is an unanswered question — Elias's best friend suddenly got a passport. I hadn't even realized that *he* had been offered a scholarship or a study grant or something, too; *he* was invited to go to New York to study production and the latest acting techniques (it was the time of the Method rather than Grotowski). And he got a passport, 'first try' as Elias said with ungrudging pleasure and admiration; when someone black got a passport, then, there was a collective sense of pleasure in having outwitted we didn't quite know what. So they went together, *he* on his passport, and Elias Nkomo on an exit permit.

An exit permit is a one-way ticket, anyway. When you are granted one at your request but at the government's pleasure, you sign an undertaking that you will never return to South Africa or its mandatory territory, South West Africa. You pledge this with signature and thumb-print. Elias Nkomo never came back. At first he wrote (and he wrote quite often) enthusiastically about the world outside that he had gained, and he seemed to be enjoying some kind of small vogue, not so much as a sculptor as a genuine, real live African Negro who was sophisticated enough to be asked to comment on this and that: the beauty of American women, life in Harlem or Watts, Black Power as seen through the eyes, etc. He sent cuttings from *Ebony* and even from *The New York Times Magazine.* He said that a girl at *Life* was trying to get them to run a piece on his work; his work? — well, he hadn't settled down to anything new, yet, but the art centre was a really swinging place, Christ, the things people were doing, there! There were silences, naturally; we forgot about him and he forgot about us for weeks on end. Then the local papers picked up the sort of news they are alert to from all over the world. Elias Nkomo had spoken at an anti-apartheid rally. Elias Nkomo, in West African robes, was on the platform with Stokely Carmichael. 'Well, why not? He hasn't got to worry about keeping his hands clean for the time when he comes back home, has he?' — My wife was bitter in his defence. Yes, but I was wondering about his work — 'Will they leave him alone to work?' I didn't write to him, but it was as if my silence were read by him: a few months later I received a cutting from some university art magazine devoting a number to Africa, and there was a photograph of one of Elias's wood sculptures, with his handwriting along the margin of the page — *I know you don't think much of people who don't turn out new stuff but some people here seem to think this old thing of mine is good.* It was the sort of wry remark that, spoken aloud to me in the room, would have made us both laugh. I smiled, and meant to write. But within two weeks Elias was dead. He drowned himself early one morning in the river of the New England town where the art school was.

It was like the refusal of the passport; none of us knew why. In the usual arrogance one has in the face of such happenings, I even felt guilty about the letter. Perhaps, if one were thousands of miles from one's own 'place', in some sort of a bad way, just a small thing like a letter, a word of encouragement from someone who had hurt by being rather niggardly with encouragement in the past . . . ? And what pathetic arrogance, at that! As if the wisp of a letter, written by someone between other preoccupations, and in substance an encouraging lie (how splendid that your old work is receiving recognition in some piddling little magazine) could be anything round which the hand of a man going down for the second time might close.

Because before Elias went under in that river he must have been deep in forlorn horrors about which I knew nothing, nothing. When people commit suicide they do so apparently out of some sudden self-knowledge that those of us, the living, do not have the will to acquire. That's what's meant by despair, isn't it — what they have come to know? And that's what one means when one says in extenuation of oneself, *I knew so little about him, really.* I knew Elias only in the self that he had presented at my 'place'; why, how out of place it had been, once, when he happened to mention that as a boy he had spent weeks in the bush with his circumcision group! Of course we — his friends — decided out of the facts we knew and our political and personal attitudes, why he had died: and perhaps it is true that he was sick to death, in the real sense of the phrase that has been forgotten, sick unto death with homesickness for the native land that had shut him out for ever and that he was forced to conjure up for himself in the parody of 'native' dress that had nothing to do with his part of the continent, and the shame that a new kind of black platform-solidarity forced him to feel for his old dependence, in South Africa, on the friendship of white people. It was the South African government who killed him, it was culture shock — but perhaps neither our political bitterness nor our glibness with fashionable phrases can come near what combination of forces, within and without, led him to the fatal baptism of that early morning. *It is not in the private interest that this should be revealed.* Elias never came home. That's all.

But his best friend did, towards the end of that year.

He came to see me after he had been in the country some weeks — I'd heard he was back. The theatre group had broken up; it seemed to be that, chiefly, he'd come to talk to me about: he wanted to know if there was any money left in the kitty for him to start up a small theatrical venture of his own, he was eager to use the know-how (his phrase) he'd learned in the States. He was really plump now and he wore the most extraordinary clothes. A Liberace jacket. Plastic boots. An Afro wig that looked as if it had been made out of a bit of karakul from South West Africa. I teased him about it — we were at least good enough friends for that — asking him if he'd really been with the guerrillas instead of Off-Broadway? (There was a trial on at home, at the time, of South African political refugees who had tried to infiltrate through South West Africa.) And felt slightly ashamed of my patronage of his taste when he said with such good humour, 'It's just a fun thing, man, isn't it great?' I was too cowardly to bring the talk round to the point: Elias. And when it couldn't be avoided, I said the usual platitudes and he shook his head at them — 'Hell, man,' and we fell silent. Then he told me that that was how he had got back — because Elias was dead, on the unused portion of Elias's air ticket. *His* study grant hadn't included travel expenses and he'd had to pay his own way over. So he'd had only a one-way ticket, but Elias's scholarship had included a return fare to the student's place of origin. It had been difficult to get the airline to agree to the transfer; he'd had to go to the scholarship foundation people, but they'd been very decent about fixing it for him.

He had told me all this so guilelessly that I was one of the people who became angrily indignant when the rumour began to go around that he was a police agent: who else would have the cold nerve to come back on a dead man's ticket, a dead man who couldn't ever have used that portion of the ticket himself, because he had taken an exit permit? And who could believe the story, anyway? Obviously, *he* had to find some way of explaining why he, a black man like any other, could travel freely back and forth between South Africa and other countries. He had a passport, hadn't he? Well, there you were. Why should *he* get a passport? What black man these days had a passport?

Yes, I was angry, and defended him, by proof of the innocence of the very naïveté with which — a black man, yes, and therefore used to the necessity of salvaging from disaster all his life, unable to afford the nice squeamishness of white men's delicacy— he took over Elias's air ticket because he was alive and needed it, as he might have taken up Elias's coat against the cold. I refused to avoid him, the way some members of the remnant of our group made it clear they did now, and I remained stony-faced outside the complicity of those knowing half-smiles that accompanied the mention of his name. We had never been close friends, of course, but he would turn up from time to time. He could not find theatrical work and had a job as a travelling salesman in the locations. He took to bringing three or four small boys along when he visited us; they were very subdued and whisperingly well-behaved and well-dressed in miniature suits — our barefoot children stared at them in awe. They were his children plus the children of the family he was living with, we gathered. He and I talked mostly about his difficulties — his old car was unreliable, his wife had left him, his commissions were low, and he could have taken up an offer to join a Chicago repertory company if he could have raised the fare to go back to America — while my wife fed ice-cream and cake to the silent children, or my children dutifully placed them one by one on the garden swing. We had begun to be able to talk about Elias's death. He had told me how, in the weeks before he died, Elias would get the wrong way on the moving stairway going down in the subway in New York and keep walking, walking up. 'I thought he was foolin' around, man, you know? Jus' climbin' those stairs and goin' noplace?'

He clung nostalgically to the American idiom; no African talks about 'noplace' when he means 'nowhere'. But he had abandoned the Afro wig and when we got talking about Elias he would hold his big, well-shaped head with its fine, shaven covering of his own wool propped between his hands as if in an effort to think more clearly about something that would never come clear; I felt suddenly at one with him in that gesture, and would say, 'Go on.' He would remember another example of how Elias had been 'acting funny' before he died. It was on one of those afternoon visits that he said, 'And I don't think I ever told you about the business with the students at the college? How that last weekend — before he did it, I mean — he went around and invited everybody to a party, I dunno, a kind of feast he said it was. Some of them said he said a barbecue — you know what that is, same as a *braaivleis,* eh? But one of the others told me afterwards that he'd told them he was going to give them a real African feast, he was going to show them how the country people do it here at home when somebody gets married or there's a funeral or so. He wanted to know where he could buy a goat.'

'A goat?'

'That's right. A live goat. He wanted to kill and roast a goat for them, on the campus.'

It was round about this time that *he* asked me for a loan. I think that was behind the idea of bringing those pretty, dressed-up children along with him when he visited; he wanted firmly to set the background of his obligations and responsibilities before touching me for money. It was rather a substantial sum, for someone of my resources. But he couldn't carry on his job without a new car, and he'd just got the opportunity to acquire a really good second-hand buy. I gave him the money in spite of — because of, perhaps — new rumours that were going around then that, in a police raid on the house of the family with whom he had been living, every adult except himself who was present on that night had been arrested on the charge of attending a meeting of a banned political organization. His friends were acquitted on the charge simply through the defence lawyer's skill at showing the *agent provoca-teur,* on whose evidence the charge was based, to be an unreliable witness — that is to say, a liar. But the friends were promptly served with personal banning orders, anyway, which meant among other things that their movements were restricted and they were not allowed to attend gatherings.

He was the only one who remained, significantly, it seemed impossible to ignore, free. And yet his friends let him stay on in the house; it was a mystery to us whites — and some blacks, too. But then so much becomes a mystery where trust becomes a commodity on sale to the police. Whatever my little show of defiance over the loan, during the last year or two we have reached the stage where if a man is black, literate, has 'political' friends and white friends, *and* a passport, he must be considered a police spy. I was sick with myself — that was why I gave him the money — but I believed it, too. There's only one way for a man like that to prove himself, so far as we're concerned: he must be in prison.

Well, *he* was at large. A little subdued over the fate of his friends, about which he talked guilelessly as he had about the appropriation of Elias's air ticket, harassed as usual about money, poor devil, but generally cheerful. Yet our friendship, that really had begun to become one since Elias's death, waned rapidly. It was the money that did it. Of course, he was afraid I'd ask him to begin paying back and so he stopped coming to my 'place', he stopped the visits with the beautifully dressed and well-behaved black infants. I received a typed letter from him, once, solemnly thanking me for my kind co-operation etc., as if I were some business firm, and assuring me that in a few months he hoped to be in a position, etc. I scrawled a note in reply, saying of course I darned well hoped he was going to pay the money he owed, sometime, but why, for God's sake, in the meantime, did this mean we had to carry on as if we'd quarrelled? Damn it all, he didn't have to treat me as if I had some nasty disease, just because of a few rands?

But I didn't see him again. I've become too busy with my own work — the building boom of the last few years, you know; I've had the contract for several shopping malls and a big cultural centre — to do any work for the old theatre group in its sporadic comings-to-life. I don't think he had much to do with it any more, either; I heard he was doing quite well as a salesman and was thinking of marrying again. There was even a — yet another — rumour, that he was actually building a house in Dube, which is the nearest to a solid bourgeois suburb a black can get in these black dormitories outside the white man's city, if you can be considered to be a bourgeois without having freehold. I didn't need the money, by then, but you know how it is with money — I felt faintly resentful about the debt anyway, because it looked as if now *he* could have paid it back just as well as I could say *I* didn't need it. As for the friendship, he'd shown me the worth of that. It's become something the white man must buy just as he must buy the co-operation of police stool-pigeons. Elias has been dead five years; we live in our situation as of now, as the legal phrase goes; one falls back on legal phrases as other forms of expression become too risky.

And then, two hundred and seventy-seven days ago, there was a new rumour, and this time it was confirmed, this time it was no rumour. *He* was fetched from his room one night and imprisoned. That's perfectly legal, here; it's the hundred-and-eighty-day Detention Act. At least, because he was something of a personality, with many friends and contacts in particular among both black and white journalists, the fact has become public. If people are humble, or of no particular interest to the small world of white liberals, they are sometimes in detention for many months before this is known outside the eye-witness of whoever happened to be standing by, in house or street, when they were taken away by the police. But at least we all know where *he* is: in prison. They say that charges of treason are being prepared against him and various others who were detained at the same time, and still others who have been detained for even longer — three hundred and seventy-one days, three hundred and ten days — the figures, once finally released, are always as precise as this — and that soon they will be brought to trial for whatever it is that we do not know they have done, for when people are imprisoned under the Detention Act no one is told why and there are no charges. There are suppositions among us, of course. Was he a double agent, as it were, using his *laissez-passer* as a police spy in order to further his real work as an underground African nationalist? Was he just unlucky in his choice of friends? Did he suffer from a dangerous sense of loyalty in place of any strong convictions of his own? Was it all due to some personal, unguessed-at bond it's none of our business to speculate about? Heaven knows — those police-spy rumours aside — nobody could have looked more unlikely to be a political activist than that cheerful young man, second-string, always ready to jump up and turn over the record, fond of Liberace jackets and aspiring to play Le Roi Jones Off-Broadway.

But as I say, we know where he is now; inside. In solitary most of the time — they say, those who've also been inside. Two hundred and seventy-seven days he's been there.

And so we white friends can purge ourselves of the shame of rumours. We can be pure again. We are satisfied at last. He's in prison. He's proved himself, hasn't he?

NADINE GORDIMER

Sins of the Third Age

Each came from a different country and they met in yet another, during a war. After the war, they lived in a fourth country, and married there, and had children who grew up with a national patrimony and a flag. The official title of the war was the Second World War, but Peter and Mania called it "our war" apparently in distinction from the wars that followed. It was also a designation of territory in which their life together had begun. Under the left cuff of the freshly-laundered shirt he put on every day he had a number branded on his wrist; her hands, the nails professionally manicured and painted once a week with Dusty Rose No. 1, retained no mark of the grubbing — frost-cracked and bleeding — for frozen turnips, that had once kept her alive. Neither had any family left except that of their own procreation; and, of course, each other. They had each other. They had always had each other, in their definitive lives — a childhood that one has not grown out of but been exploded from in the cross-fire of armies explodes, at the same time, the theory of childhood as the basis to which the adult personality always refers itself. Destruction of places, habitations, is destruction of the touchstone they held. There was no church, schoolhouse or tree left standing to bring Peter or Mania back on a pilgrimage. There was no face in which to trace a young face remembered from the height of a child. Unfurnished, unpeopled by the past, there was their life together.

It was a well-made life. It did not happen; was carefully constructed. Right from the start, when they had no money and a new language to learn in that fourth country they had chosen as their home, they determined never to lose control of their lives as they had had no choice but to do in their war. They were enthusiastic, energetic, industrious, modestly ambitious, and this was part of their loving. They worked with and for each other, improving their grasp of the language while they talked and caressed over washing dishes or cooking together, murmuring soothing lies while confessing to each other — voices blurred by the pillows, between love-making and sleep — difficulties and loneliness encountered in their jobs.

She was employed as an interpreter at a conference centre. He lugged a range of medical supplies round the offices of city doctors and dentists, and, according to plan, studied electronics at night school in preparation for the technological expansion that could be foreseen. When the children were born, the young mother and father staggered their hours of employment so that she would not have to give up work. They were saving to buy an apartment of their own but they had too much loss behind them to forgo the only certainty of immediate pleasures and they also kept aside every week a sum for entertainment.

As the years went by, they could afford seasonal subscriptions to the opera and concerts. They bought something better than an apartment — a small house with a basement room they rented to a student. Peter became an assistant sales manager in a multinational company; Mania had opportunities to travel, now and then, with a team of translators sent to international conferences. Their children took guitar lessons, learnt to ski, and won state scholarships to universities, where they demonstrated against wars in Asia, Latin America, the Middle East and Africa they did not have to experience themselves. These same children came of age to vote against the government of their parents' adopted country, which the children said was authoritarian, neo-colonialist in its treatment of "guest workers" from poorer countries, and in danger of turning fascist. Their parents were anti-authoritarian, anti-colonialist, anti-fascist — with their past, how could they not be? But if a socialist government came to power taxes would be raised, and so they voted for the sitting government. Doesn't everyone over forty know that it is not the real exploiters, the powerful and the rich, but the middle class, the modest planners, the savers for a comfortable and independent retirement who suffer under measures meant to spread wealth and extend justice?

There were arguments around the evening meal, to which those children no longer living at home often turned up, with their lovers, hungry and angry.

"You would never have been born if it hadn't been for the decent welfare and health services provided for the past twenty years by this government." Peter's standard statement was intended to be the last word.

It roused outcry against self-interest, smugness, selling-out. Once, it touched off flippancy. The darling, blonde, only daughter was present. She peered from the privacy of her tresses, cuddling her breasts delightedly between arms crossed over her T-shirt. "So you lied about how babies are made, after all, Mama!" Mania supported Peter. "It's true — we couldn't have afforded to bring you up. Certainly you wouldn't have been able to go to university."

Even at the stage when one's children turn against one, at least they always had each other.

Mania's work as an interpreter had taken her to places as remote from their plans as Abidjan (Ivory Coast, WHO conference on water-borne diseases), Atlanta, Georgia (international congress of librarians) and, since the '70s, OPEC gatherings in new cities she described in long letters to Peter as air-conditioned shopping malls set down in the desert. But she also had been sent many times to Rome and Milan, and Peter had joined her by way of an excursion flight whenever her period of duty was contiguous with a long weekend or his yearly holiday leave. Then they would hire a small car and drive, each time through a different region of Italy. They felt the usual enthusiasm of Northerners for Tuscany and the South; it was only when, from Milan one year, they took a meandering route via the Turin road to Genoa through the maritime alps that this tourist pleasure, accepted as something to be put away with holiday clothes for next time, changed to the possibility of permanent attachment to a fifth country.

At first it was one of those visions engendered, like the beginning of a love affair, by the odd charm of an afternoon in the square of a small Piedmontese town. They had never heard of it; come upon it by hazard. They sat on the square into which mole-runs of streets debouched provincial Italians busy with their own lives. Nobody touted or offered services as a guide. Shopkeepers sent shutters flying as they opened for business after the siesta. Small children, pigeon toed in boots, ate cakes as they were walked home from school. Old women wearing black formed groups of the Fates on corners, and slowly climbed the steps of the church, each leg lifted and placed like a stake. At five o'clock, when Peter and Mania were sitting between tubs of red geraniums eating ice-cream, the figure of a blackamoor in doublet and gold turban swung out stiffly under a black-and-gold palanquin at the top of the church tower, and struck the hour with his pagan hand. Nobody hawked postcards of him; at six, when Peter and Mania had not moved, but moved on from ice-cream to Campari and soda, they saw local inhabitants checking their watches against his punctual reappearance. There was a kind of cake honouring him, the travellers discovered later; round, covered with the bitter-sweet black chocolate Mania liked best, the confections were called "The Moor's Balls", and these were what good children were rewarded with.

Peter and Mania found a *pensione* whose view was of chestnut woods and a horizon looped by peaks lustred with last winter's snow, distant in time as well as space. They shone pink in the twilight. Peter spoke. "Wherever you lived, round about here, you'd be able to see the mountains. From the smallest shack." Mania had acquired Italian, in the course of qualifying for advancement in her job. She got talking to the proprietor of the *pensione* and listened to his lament that land values were dropping — the country people were dying out, the young moved away to Turin and Milan. When Peter and Mania returned the following year to the town, to the square with *il moro* in his tower, to the same *pensione*, the proprietor took them to visit his brother-in-law in a little farmhouse with an iron gallery hung with grapes; they drank home made wine on yellow plastic chairs among giant cucurbits dangling from a vine and orange mushrooms set out to dry.

That same year Mania was again in Milan, and when she had a free weekend took a train and bus to the town; just to sit among the local people on the square and let the moor mark the passing of time (she would be retiring on pension in a few years), just to spend one evening on the balcony of the now familiar room at the *pensione*. Middle age made it difficult for her to see without glasses anything close by. She was becoming more and more far-sighted; but here her gaze was freed even as high and far as the snow from the past that would soon weld with the snow of winter ahead. In his usual long account of family misfortunes, the proprietor came to the necessity to sell the brother-in-law's property; that night Mania sat up in the *pensione* room until two, calculating the budgets and savings, over the years, she had by heart. When she got back home to Peter, she had only to write the figures down for him, and how they were arrived at. He went over them again, alone; they discussed at length what margin in their calculations should be allowed for the effects of inflation upon a fixed income. In his late fifties he had grown gaunt as she had padded out. Dressed, his were the flat belly and narrow waist of a boy, but naked he looked closer to the other end of life, and he was getting deaf. His deepened eyes and lengthened nose faced her with likenesses she would never recognize because no photographs had survived. But she knew, now, what he was thinking; and he saw, and smiled: he was thinking that there was not one habitation, however small, from which you wouldn't have the horizon of alps.

They raised a mortgage on their house and bought the farmhouse in Italy. It was not a dream, a crazy idea, but part of a perfectly practical preparation for retirement. The Italian property was a bargain, and when they were ready to sell their house they could count on making sufficient profit both to pay off the mortgage and finance the move abroad. Living was cheap in that safe, unfashionable part of Italy, far from political kidnappings and smart international expatriates. Their pensions (fully transferable under exchange control regulations, they had ascertained) would go much further than at home. They would grow some of their own food and make their own wine. He would smoke trout. In the meantime, they had a free holiday house for the years of waiting — and anticipation. Once they had dared buy the farmhouse they knew that, from the afternoon they had first sat in the square of *il moro,* this had become the place in the world they had been planning to deserve, to enjoy, all their life together. The preparation continued with Detto, the *pensione* proprietor, and his wife looking after farmhouse and garden in return for the produce they grew for themselves, and Peter and Mania spending every holiday painting, repairing and renovating the premises. By the time Peter's retirement was due, Mania had even retraced, in fresh colours, the mildewed painted garlands under the eaves, with their peasant design of flowers and fruit.

Peter's retirement came eighteen months before Mania's. They had planned accordingly, all along: he would move first, to Italy, settle in with the household goods, while she sat on in interpreters' glass booths hearing — each time nearer the final time — the disputes and deliberations of the world that had filled her ears since the noise of bombs ended, long ago in the country where she and Peter began. She saved money in every way she could. She worked through that summer. He was chopping wood, he said over the telephone, for winter storage: he had found there was a little cultural circle in the town, and had boldly joined in order to improve his Italian. She was sent to Washington and wrote that she thanked god every day it was the last time; the heat was primeval, she wouldn't have been surprised to see crocodiles slothful on the banks of the Potomac — O for the sky lifted to the alps! He wrote that the cultural circle was putting on a Goldoni play, and — he wasn't proud — he was a stage-hand along with kids of fifteen! It is always easier to give way to emotion in a letter than face-to-face — the recipient doesn't have to dissimulate in response. She wrote telling him how she had always admired him for his lack of pretension, his willingness to learn and adapt.

She knew he would know she was saying she loved him for these things, that were still with them although she was thick-ankled and his pliant muscles had shrunk away against his bones.

After Washington it was Sydney, and then she went back to autumn in the room she was occupying in her daughter's basement apartment, now that the city house had been sold. She scraped off the sweet-smelling mat of rotting wet leaves that stuck to the heels of her shoes: this time next year, she would be living in Italy. In old sweaters, she and Peter would walk into town and drink hot coffee and wait for the moor to strike twelve.

That evening she was about to phone the *pensione* and leave a message for Peter to say she had returned (they didn't yet have a phone in the farmhouse) when he walked into the apartment. Mother and daughter, like two blonde sheepdogs, almost knocked him over in their excitement. How much better than a phone-call! Husband

and wife were getting a bit too middle-aged, now, to mark every reunion with love-making, but in bed, when she began to settle in for a long talk in the dark, he took her gross breasts, through which he used to be able to feel her ribs, and manipulated the nipples deliberately as a combination lock calculated to rouse both him and her. After the love-making he fell asleep, and she lay against his back; she hoped their daughter hadn't heard anything.

In the morning the daughter went to work and over a long breakfast they were engrossed in practical matters concerning the farmhouse in Italy and residence there — taxes, permits, house and medical insurance. The roof repairs would have to be done sooner or later and would cost more than anticipated — "A good thing I decided to work this summer." However, Detto had made the suggestion Peter might do the repairs himself. Detto offered to help — through his foresight, Peter had bought cheaply and stored away the necessary materials. "Leave it until next year when I'll be there to help, too — so long as it won't leak on you this winter?" "Heavy plastic sheeting, Detto says, and the snow will pack down ... I'll be all right." And while she washed her hair Peter went off into the city to enquire about a method of insulating walls he couldn't find any information on, in Italy — at least not in the region of the moor's sovereignty.

Mania was using the hair-dryer when she heard him return. She called out a greeting but could not catch his reply because of the tempest blowing about her head. Presently he came into the bedroom with a handful of brochures and stood, in the doorway. He signalled to her to switch off; she smiled and did so, ready to listen to advice he had gleaned about damp rot. What he said was "I want to tell you why I came."

She was smiling again and at once had an instinct of embarrassment at that smile and its implication: to be here when I came back.

He walked into the room as if she had summoned him; Mania, sitting there with her tinted blonde hair dragged up in rollers, the dryer still in her hand.

"I've met somebody."

Mania said nothing. She looked at him, waiting for him to go on speaking. He did not, and her gaze wavered and dropped; she saw her own big bosom, rising and falling with faster and faster breaths. The dryer began to wobble in her hand. She put it on the bed.

"In the play. I told you they were putting on a Goldoni play."

Her brain was neatly stocked with thousands of words in five languages but she could think of nothing she wanted to say; nothing she wanted to ask. She slowly nodded: you told me about the play.

He was waiting for *her* to speak. They were two new people, just introduced with the words *I've met somebody,* and they didn't know what subject they had in common.

He struggled for recognition. "What do you want to do." He made it a conclusion, not a question.

"I? *I* do?"

She had pushed up one of the metal spokes that held the rollers in place and he saw the red indentation it left on her pink forehead.

He insisted quietly. "All the things are there ... furniture, everything. The property. The new material for the roof."

"You want to go away."

"It's not possible. The person — she has to look after her grandmother. And she's got a small child."

Mania was breathing fast with her mouth open, as she knew she did, now that she was fat, when they climbed a hill together. She also knew that when she was a child tears had followed deep, sharp breaths. Before that happened, she had to speak quickly. "What do you want me to do?"

"It's so difficult. Because everything's been arranged . . . so long. All sold up, here."

Their life had come to a stop, the way the hair-dryer had been switched off; here in a room in her daughter's life she would stay. "I could bring things back."

He was looking at the quarter-inch of grey that made a stripe below the blonde in hair bound over the rollers. "I don't take her to the farmhouse."

Mania had a vision of him, as she knew him, domestically naked about the bedroom; his thin thighs — and for the first time, a young Italian woman with black hair and a crucifix.

"Where does she come from?"

"Come from? You mean where does she live . . . in the town. Right in town."

Oh yes. Near the square — the moor struck again and again — all those little streets that lead to the square, one of those streets off the square.

Suddenly, Mania forgot everything else; remembered. Her face swelled drunk with shame. "Why did you do that . . . last night. Why? Why?"

He stood there and watched her sobbing.

She did not tell the daughter. Discussions about the farmhouse, the property in Italy, continued like the workings of a business under appointed executors after the principals have died. Some crates of books were at the shippers; so was Mania's sewing machine — one could not stop the process now. Damp rot could not be left to creep up the walls of the house, whatever happened — there are already some brown spots appearing on your frieze, Peter remarked — and he took back with him the necessary chemicals for injection into the brick.

His letters and hers were almost the same as before — an exchange of his news about the farmhouse and garden for hers about the grown-up children and her work. They continued to sign themselves "your Peter" and "your Mania" because this must have become a formula for a commitment that had long been expressed in ways other than possession and meant nothing in itself. She postponed any decision, any thought of a decision about what she would do when her retirement came. A year was a long time, the one friend in whom she confided kept telling her; a lot can happen in a year. She was advised according to female lore to let the affair wear itself out. But just before the year was up she came to a decision she did not confess. She wrote to Peter telling him she would come to Italy as planned, if he did not object, and he could continue seeing ("being with" she phrased it) the person he had found. She would not reproach or interfere. He wrote back and rather hurtfully did not mention the person, as if this were so private and precious a matter he did not want her to approach that part of his life even with tolerant words. He phrased his consent in the form of the remark that he was satisfied he had got everything more or less organized: she could count on finding the house and garden in fair order.

Mania knew she was sufficiently self-disciplined — held herself, now, in a particular sense like that of a military bearing or a sailor's sea-legs — to keep her word about reproaches or interference. Once she was living with him in the farmhouse she realized that this intention had to be extended to include glances, pauses of a particular weight, even aspects of personal equanimity — if a headache inclined her to be quieter than usual, she had best be careful the mood did not look like something else. Peter did not make love to her ever again and she didn't expect it. That time — that was the last time.

She presumed he had a place to meet the person. Perhaps Detto, simple good soul, and a man himself, of course, who had become such an understanding friend to the foreign couple, had put Peter in the way of finding somewhere, just as he had put them in the way of finding the farmhouse to which the remote exaltation of the alps was linked as domestically as a pet kept in the yard. Peter must have found some place, if the person had the grandmother and a child living with her . . . but pious old women in black, children with fat little calves laced into boots — these thoughts were out of bounds for a woman standing ground where Mania was. She did not allow herself, either, to look for signs (what would they be? all had black hair and wore crucifixes) among the young women who carried shopping-bags, flowering magnificent vegetables, across the square of the moor.

Peter went with her on shopping trips into the town. A pleasant, unvarying round. The post office for stamps, and the bank where a young teller sleek as the film stars of their youth counted out millionaire stacks of lire that paid for a little fruit from the old man they always patronized in the market, and bread from the woman with prematurely grey hair and shiny cheekbones who served alongside her floury father or husband. It was autumn, yes; sometimes they did go on foot, wearing their old sweaters. They drank coffee at an outside table if the sun was shining, and got up to trudge back at the convenient signal of *il moro* striking his baton twelve times. But Peter did not go out alone, and for the first few weeks after her arrival she thought this was some quaint respect or dutiful homage: when she had settled in and he knew she did not feel herself a new arrival in her status as resident, he would take up again — what he had found.

He seemed reluctant, indeed, to go anywhere. Detto came by to invite him to go mushrooming, or hunting boars in the mountains, something Peter had talked about doing (why not?) all the years of anticipation; he yawned, in his slippers, looking out at the soft mist that wrapped house and alps in a single silence, and watched the old man disappear into it alone. One of their retirement plans had been to do some langlauf skiing, you didn't have to be young for that, and there was a bus to a small ski resort only an hour away. The snow came; she suggested a day trip. He smiled and blew through his lips, dropping his book in his lap at the interruption. She felt like a child nagging to be taken to the swings. They stayed at home with the TV he kept flickering, along with the fire.

It was true that he had got everything more or less organized, on the property. When she asked him what he planned to do next — plant new vines, build the little smoke-house they'd talked of, to smoke the excellent local trout — he joked with her, apparently: "I'm retired, aren't I?" And when spring came he did nothing, he still watched TV most of the day. "It improves my Italian." She busied herself making curtains and chair-covers. She would wrap up for a walk and when she came home, expect he might have taken the opportunity, gone out. Even before she entered the house, she would see through the window the harsh barred light that flowed on the black-and-white television screen, a tide constantly rising and falling back over the glass. He was always there.

She found minute white violets in the woods. She went up to him that day, sitting in his chair, and held the fragile bouquet under his nose, cold and sweet. He revived; met her eyes; he seemed to have come to in a place as remote as the peaks where the snow never melts.

She made coffee and he raked up the fire. They were sitting cosily drinking, she was stirring her cup and she said, "I shouldn't have come."

He looked up from the newspaper as if she had passed a remark about the weather.

It was an effort to speak again. "You can go out, you know."

He said from behind the paper, "I gave up that person."

She felt herself being drawn into a desolation she had never known. She got up quietly, tactfully, and went into the kitchen as she might to some task there, but whatever she did, that day, the sense of being bereft would not leave her. She did not think of Peter. Only that Peter, in spite of what he had just told her, could do nothing for her; nothing could be done for her, despite the coming about of the prediction of female lore. She carried on with what she had planned: finished the curtains and fitted the chair-covers, and a day came when she was released by what had seized her and she hadn't understood, and she went to Detto's wife to learn, as promised, how to fry pumpkin flowers in batter. A stray dog adopted Peter and her, and joyously accompanied her walks. It was no use trying to get Peter to come; he stayed at the farmhouse while a contractor repaired the roof, and listened to Detto's stories while Detto planted the new vines and tended the garden. They did go into town to do the household shopping together, though, and sometimes in the summer evenings would sit in the square until the moor swung out to strike nine. One evening the woman from the baker's shop passed, carrying two ice-cream cones. "That was the person," Peter said. She didn't have black hair or wear a crucifix, she was the tall one with the shiny sad cheekbones and prematurely grey hair cut page-boy style. They had been into the baker's shop together — Peter and Mania — day after day, and taken bread from her hands, and there had never been a sign of what had been found, and lost again.

THOMAS HARDY

Thomas Hardy (1840–1928) was born and lived almost all his life in the southern English county of Dorset, a rural and deeply traditional culture to which industrial progress came slowly. His greatest novels and stories are set there — in Wessex, as he called it — and in them he depicted a microcosm of an England (and a world) on the brink of irrevocable change. As a youth Hardy contemplated becoming a clergyman; in his early twenties he went to London to train as an architect. There he encountered head-on the rational, skeptical thought of the age in the works of Darwin, Huxley, Spencer, Mill, and others. Always passionately attracted to poetry, he returned to Dorset to write it; but until almost the turn of the century he wrote novels and short stories. One of his biographers has best explained Hardy's work as emerging from his profound need of retaining the past: "his possession of that slowly fading world of Wessex, remembered with pathos and unrivaled knowledge, would make possible a fabled reconstruction, which he would then set off against the ruthlessness of historical change." In creating that "fabled reconstruction," Hardy wrote some of the most powerful fiction in the English language. Among his novels are *Far From the Madding Crowd* (1874), *The Return of the Native* (1878), *The Mayor of Casterbridge* (1886), *The Woodlanders* (1887), *Tess of the D'Urbervilles* (1891), and *Jude the Obscure* (1896). His best-known collection of short stories is *Wessex Tales* (1888). In his long and short fiction he drew on folk motifs and superstitions and ancient traditions of storytelling. "The Withered Arm," displaying all of these, is an authentic portrait of Hardy's Wessex.

The Withered Arm

1

A LORN MILKMAID

It was an eighty-cow dairy, and the troop of milkers, regular and supernumerary, were all at work; for, though the time of year was as yet but early April, the feed lay entirely in water-meadows, and the cows were 'in full pail'. The hour was about six in the evening, and three-fourths of the large, red, rectangular animals having been finished off, there was opportunity for a little conversation.

'He do bring home his bride to-morrow, I hear. They've come as far as Anglebury to-day.'

The voice seemed to proceed from the belly of the cow called Cherry, but the speaker was a milking-woman, whose face was buried in the flank of that motionless beast.

'Hav' anybody seen her?' said another.

There was a negative response from the first. 'Though they say she's a rosy-cheeked, tisty-tosty little body enough,' she added; and as the milkmaid spoke she turned her face so that she could glance past her cow's tail to the other side of the barton, where a thin, fading woman of thirty milked somewhat apart from the rest.

'Years younger than he, they say,' continued the second, with also a glance of reflectiveness in the same direction.

'How old do you call him, then?'

'Thirty or so.'

' 'More like forty,' broke in an old milkman near, in a long white pinafore or 'wropper', and with the brim of his hat tied down, so that he looked like a woman. 'A was born before our Great Weir was builded, and I hadn't man's wages when I laved water there.'

The discussion waxed so warm that the purr of the milk-streams became jerky, till a voice from another cow's belly cried with authority, 'Now then, what the Turk do it matter to us about Farmer Lodge's age, or Farmer Lodge's new mis'ess? I shall have to pay him nine pound a year for the rent of every one of these milchers, whatever his age or hers. Get on with your work, or 'twill be dark afore we have done. The evening is pinking in a'ready.' This speaker was the dairyman himself, by whom the milkmaids and men were employed.

Nothing more was said publicly about Farmer Lodge's wedding, but the first woman murmured under her cow to her next neighbour, ' 'Tis hard for *she*,' signifying the thin worn milkmaid aforesaid.

'O no,' said the second. 'He ha'n't spoke to Rhoda Brook for years.'

When the milking was done they washed their pails and hung them on a many-forked stand made as usual of the peeled limb of an oak-tree, set upright in the earth, and resembling a colossal antlered horn. The majority then dispersed in various directions homeward. The thin wman who had not spoken was joined by a boy of twelve or thereabouts, and the twain went away up the field also.

Their course lay apart from that of the others, to a lonely spot high above the water-meads, and not far from the border of Egdon Heath, whose dark countenance was visible in the distance as they drew nigh to their home.

'They've just been saying down in barton that your father brings his young wife home from Anglebury to-morrow,' the woman observed. 'I shall want to send you for a few things to market, and you'll be pretty sure to meet 'em.'

'Yes, mother,' said the boy. 'Is father married then?'

'Yes. . . . You can give her a look, and tell me what she's like, if you do see her.'

'Yes, mother.'

'If she's dark or fair, and if she's tall — as tall as I. And if she seems like a woman who has ever worked for a living, or one that has been always well off, and has never done anything, and shows marks of the lady on her, as I expect she do.'

'Yes.'

They crept up the hill in the twilight and entered the cottage. It was built of mud-walls, the surface of which had been washed by many rains into channels and depressions that left none of the original flat face visible; while here and there in the thatch above a rafter showed like a bone protruding through the skin.

She was kneeling down in the chimney-corner, before two pieces of turf laid together with the heather inwards, blowing at the red-hot ashes with her breath till the turves flamed. The radiance lit her pale cheek, and made her dark eyes, that had once been handsome, seem handsome anew. 'Yes,' she resumed, 'see if she is dark or fair, and if you can, notice if her hands be white; if not, see if they look as though she had ever done housework, or are milker's hands like mine.'

The boy again promised, inattentively this time, his mother not observing that he was cutting a notch with his pocket-knife in the beech-backed chair.

2

The Young Wife

The road from Anglebury to Holmstoke is in general level; but there is one place where a sharp ascent breaks its monotony. Farmers homeward-bound from the former market-town, who trot all the rest of the way, walk their horses up this short incline.

The next evening while the sun was yet bright a handsome new gig, with a lemon-coloured body and red wheels, was spinning westward along the level highway at the heels of a powerful mare. The driver was a yeoman in the prime of life, cleanly shaven like an actor, his face being toned to that bluish-vermilion hue which so often graces a thriving farmer's features when returning home after successful dealings in the town. Beside him sat a woman, many years his junior — almost, indeed, a girl. Her face too was fresh in colour, but it was of a totally different quality — soft and evanescent, like the light under a heap of rose-petals.

Few people travelled this way, for it was not a main road, and the long white riband of gravel that stretched before them was empty, save of one small scarce-moving speck, which presently resolved itself into the figure of a boy, who was creeping on at a snail's pace, and continually looking behind him — the heavy bundle he carried being some excuse for, if not the reason of, his dilatoriness. When the bouncing gig-party slowed at the bottom of the incline above mentioned, the pedestrian was only a few yards in front. Supporting the large bundle by putting one hand on his hip, he turned and looked straight at the farmer's wife as though he would read her through and through, pacing along abreast of the horse.

The low sun was full in her face, rendering every feature, shade and contour distinct, from the curve of her little nostril to the colour of her eyes. The farmer though he seemed annoyed at the boy's persistent presence, did not order him to get out of the way; and thus the lad preceded them, his hard gaze never leaving her, till they reached the top of the ascent, when the farmer trotted on with relief in his lineaments — having taken no outward notice of the boy whatever.

'How that poor lad stared at me!' said the young wife.

'Yes, dear; I saw that he did.'

'He is one of the village, I suppose?'

'One of the neighbourhood. I think he lives with his mother a mile or two off.'

'He knows who we are, no doubt?'

'O yes. You must expect to be stared at just at first, my pretty Gertrude.'

'I do, — though I think the poor boy may have looked at us in the hope we might relieve him of his heavy load, rather than from curiosity.'

'O no,' said her husband off-handedly. 'These country lads will carry a hundred-weight once they get it on their backs; besides, his pack had more size than weight in it. Now, then, another mile and I shall be able to show you our house in the distance — if it is not too dark before we get there.' The wheels spun round, and particles flew from their periphery as before, till a white house of ample dimensions revealed itself, with farm-buildings and ricks at the back.

Meanwhile the boy had quickened his pace, and turning up a by-lane some mile and half short of the white farmstead, ascended towards the leaner pastures, and so on to the cottage of his mother.

She had reached home after her day's milking at the outlying dairy, and was washing cabbage at the doorway in the declining light. 'Hold up the net a moment,' she said, without preface, as the boy came up.

He flung down his bundle, held the edge of the cabbage-net, and as she filled its meshes with the dripping leaves she went on, 'Well, did you see her?'

'Yes; quite plain.'

'Is she ladylike?'

'Yes; and more. A lady complete.'

'Is she young?'

'Well, she's growed up, and her ways be quite a woman's.'

'Of course. What colour is her hair and face?'

'Her hair is lightish, and her face as comely as a live doll's.'

'Her eyes, then, are not dark like mine?'

'No — of a bluish turn, and her mouth is very nice and red; and when she smiles, her teeth show white.'

'Is she tall?' said the woman sharply.

'I couldn't see. She was sitting down.'

'Then do you go to Holmstoke church to-morrow morning: she's sure to be there. Go early and notice her walking in, and come home and tell me if she's taller than I.'

'Very well, mother. But why don't you go and see for yourself?'

'*I* go to see her! I wouldn't look up at her if she were to pass my window this instant. She was with Mr. Lodge, of course. What did he say or do?'

'Just the same as usual.'

'Took no notice of you?'

'None.'

Next day the mother put a clean shirt on the boy, and started him off for Holmstoke church. He reached the ancient little pile when the door was just being opened and he was the first to enter. Taking his seat by the font, he watched all the parishioners file in. The well-to-do Farmer Lodge came nearly last, and his young wife, who accompanied him, walked up the aisle with the shyness natural to a modest woman who had appeared thus for the first time. As all other eyes were fixed upon her, the youth's stare was not noticed now.

When he reached home his mother said, 'Well?' before he had entered the room.

'She is not tall. She is rather short,' he replied.

'Ah!' said his mother, with satisfaction.

'But she's very pretty — very. In fact, she's lovely.' The youthful freshness of the yeoman's wife had evidently made an impression even on the somewhat hard nature of the boy.

'That's all I want to hear,' said his mother quickly. 'Now, spread the tablecloth. The hare you wired is very tender; but mind that nobody catches you. — You've never told me what sort of hands she had.'

'I have never seen 'em. She never took off her gloves.'

'What did she wear this morning?'

'A white bonnet and a silver-coloured gownd. It whewed and whistled so loud when it rubbed against the pews that the lady coloured up more than ever for very shame at the noise, and pulled it in to keep it from touching; but when she pushed into her seat, it whewed more than ever. Mr. Lodge, he seemed pleased, and his waistcoat stuck out, and his great golden seals hung like a lord's; but she seemed to wish her noisy gownd anywhere but on her.'

'Not she! However, that will do now.'

These descriptions of the newly-married couple were continued from time to time by the boy at his mother's request, after any chance encounter he had had with them. But Rhoda Brook, though she might easily have seen young Mrs Lodge for herself by walking a couple of miles, would never attempt an excursion towards the quarter where the farmhouse lay. Neither did she, at the daily milking in the dairyman's yard on Lodge's outlying second farm, ever speak on the subject of the recent marriage. The dairyman, who rented the cows of Lodge, and knew perfectly the tall milkmaid's history, with manly kindliness always kept the gossip in the cow-barton from annoying Rhoda. But the atmosphere thereabouts was full of the subject during the first days of Mrs Lodge's arrival, and from her boy's description and the casual words of the other milkers, Rhoda Brook could raise a mental image of the unconscious Mrs Lodge that was realistic as a photograph.

3

A VISION

One night, two or three weeks after the bridal return, when the boy was gone to bed, Rhoda sat a long time over the turf ashes that she had raked out in front of her to extinguish them. She contemplated so intently the new wife, as presented to her in her mind's eye over the embers, that she forgot the lapse of time. At last, wearied with her day's work, she too retired.

But the figure which had occupied her so much during this and the previous days was not to be banished at night. For the first time Gertrude Lodge visited the supplanted woman in her dreams. Rhoda Brook dreamed — since her assertion that she really saw, before falling asleep, was not to be believed — that that young wife, in the pale silk dress and white bonnet, but with features shockingly distorted, and wrinkled as by age, was sitting upon her chest as she lay. The pressure of Mrs Lodge's person grew heavier; the blue eyes peered cruelly into her face, and then the figure thrust forward its left hand mockingly, so as to make the wedding-ring it wore glitter in Rhoda's eyes. Maddened mentally, and nearly suffocated by pressure, the sleeper struggled; the incubus, still regarding her, withdrew to the foot of the bed, only, however, to come forward by degrees, resume her seat, and flash her left hand as before.

Gasping for breath, Rhoda, in a last desperate effort, swung out her right hand, seized the confronting spectre by its obtrusive left arm, and whirled it backward to the floor, starting up herself as she did so with a low cry.

'O, merciful heaven!' she cried, sitting on the edge of the bed in a cold sweat; 'that was not a dream — she was here!'

She could feel her antagonist's arm within her grasp even now — the very flesh and bone of it, as it seemed. She looked on the floor whither she had whirled the spectre, but there was nothing to be seen.

Rhoda Brook slept no more that night, and when she went milking at the next dawn they noticed how pale and haggard she looked. The milk that she drew quivered into the pail; her hand had not calmed even yet, and still retained the feel of the arm. She came home to breakfast as wearily as if it had been supper-time.

'What was that noise in your chimmer, mother, last night?' said her son. 'You fell off the bed, surely?'

'Did you hear anything fall? At what time?'

'Just when the clock struck two.'

She could not explain, and when the meal was done went silently about her household work, the boy assisting her, for he hated going afield on the farms, and she indulged his reluctance. Between eleven and twelve the garden-gate clicked, and she lifted her eyes to the window. At the bottom of the garden, within the gate, stood the woman of her vision. Rhoda seemed transfixed.

'Ah, she said she would come!' exclaimed the boy, also observing her.

'Said so — when? How does she know us?'

'I have seen and spoken to her. I talked to her yesterday.'

'I told you,' said the mother, flushing indignantly, 'never to speak to anybody in that house, or go near the place.'

'I did not speak to her till she spoke to me. And I did not go near the place. I met her in the road.'

'What did you tell her?'

'Nothing. She said, "Are you the poor boy who had to bring the heavy load from market?" And she looked at my boots, and said they would not keep my feet dry if it came on wet, because they were so cracked. I told her I lived with my mother, and we had enough to do to keep ourselves, and that's how it was; and she said then, "I'll come and bring you some better boots, and see your mother." She gives away things to other folks in the meads besides us.'

Mrs Lodge was by this time close to the door — not in her silk, as Rhoda had dreamt of in the bed-chamber, but in a morning hat, and gown of common light material, which became her better than silk. On her arm she carried a basket.

The impression remaining from the night's experience was still strong. Brook had almost expected to see the wrinkles, the scorn, and the cruelty on her visitor's face. She would have escaped an interview had escape been possible. There was, however, no backdoor to the cottage, and in an instant the boy had lifted the latch to Mrs Lodge's gentle knock.

'I see I have come to the right house,' said she, glancing at the lad, and smiling. 'But I was not sure till you opened the door.'

The figure and action were those of the phantom; but her voice was so indescribably sweet, her glance so winning, her smile so tender, so unlike that of Rhoda's midnight visitant, that the latter could hardly believe the evidence of her senses. She was truly glad that she had not hidden away in sheer aversion, as she had been inclined to do. In her basket Mrs Lodge brought the pair of boots that she had promised to the boy, and other useful articles.

At these proofs of a kindly feeling towards her and hers Rhoda's heart reproached her bitterly. This innocent young thing should have her blessing and not her curse.

When she left them a light seemed gone from the dwelling. Two days later she came again to know if the boots fitted, and less than a fortnight after that paid Rhoda another call. On this occasion the boy was absent.

'I walk a good deal,' said Mrs Lodge, 'and your house is the nearest outside our own parish. I hope you are well. You don't look quite well.'

Rhoda said she was well enough, and, indeed, though the paler of the two, there was more of the strength that endures in her well-defined features and large frame than in the soft-cheeked young woman before her. The conversation became quite confidential as regarded their powers and weaknesses; and when Mrs Lodge was leaving, Rhoda said, 'I hope you will find this air agree with you, ma'am, and not suffer from the damp of the water-meads.'

The younger one replied that there was not much doubt of it, her general health being usually good. 'Though, now you remind me,' she added, 'I have one little ailment which puzzles me. It is nothing serious, but I cannot make it out.'

She uncovered her left hand and arm, and their outline confronted Rhoda's gaze as the exact original of the limb she had beheld and seized in her dream. Upon the pink round surface of the arm were faint marks of an unhealthy colour, as if produced by a rough grasp. Rhoda's eyes became riveted on the discolourations; she fancied that she discerned in them the shape of her own four fingers.

'How did it happen?' she said mechanically.

'I cannot tell,' replied Mrs Lodge, shaking her head. 'One night when I was sound asleep, dreaming I was away in some strange place, a pain suddenly shot into my arm there, and was so keen as to awaken me. I must have struck it in the daytime, I suppose, though I don't remember doing so.' She added, laughing, 'I tell my dear husband that it looks just as if he had flown into a rage and struck me there. O, I daresay it will soon disappear.'

'Ha, ha! Yes. . . . On what night did it come?'

Mrs Lodge considered, and said it would be a fortnight ago on the morrow. 'When I awoke I could not remember where I was,' she added, 'till the clock striking two reminded me.'

She had named the night and the hour of Rhoda's spectral encounter, and Brook felt like a guilty thing. The artless disclosure startled her; she did not reason on the freaks of coincidence, and all the scenery of that ghastly night returned with double vividness to her mind.

'O, can it be,' she said to herself, when her visitor had departed, 'that I exercise a malignant power over people against my own will?' She knew that she had been slily called a witch since her fall; but never having understood why that particular stigma had been attached to her, it had passed disregarded. Could this be the explanation, and had such things as this ever happened before?

4

A SUGGESTION

The summer drew on, and Rhoda Brook almost dreaded to meet Mrs Lodge again, notwithstanding that her feeling for the young wife amounted wellnigh to affection.

Something in her own individuality seemed to convict Rhoda of crime. Yet a fatality sometimes would direct the steps of the latter to the outskirts of Holmstoke whenever she left her house for any other purpose than her daily work, and hence it happened that their next encounter was out of doors. Rhoda could not avoid the subject which had so mystified her, and after the first few words she stammered. 'I hope your — arm is well again, ma'am?' She had perceived with consternation that Gertrude Lodge carried her left arm stiffly.

'No; it is not quite well. Indeed, it is no better at all; it is rather worse. It pains me dreadfully sometimes.'

'Perhaps you had better go to a doctor, ma'am.'

She replied that she had already seen a doctor. Her husband had insisted upon her going to one. But the surgeon had not seemed to understand the afflicted limb at all; he had told her to bathe it in hot water, and she had bathed it, but the treatment had done no good.

'Will you let me see it?' said the milkwoman.

Mrs Lodge pushed up her sleeve and disclosed the place, which was a few inches above the wrist. As soon as Rhoda Brook saw it, she could hardly preserve her composure. There was nothing of the nature of a wound, but the arm at that point had a shrivelled look, and the outline of the four fingers appeared more distinct than at the former time. Moreover, she fancied that they were imprinted in precisely the relative position of her clutch upon the arm in the trance: the first finger towards Gertrude's wrist, and the fourth towards her elbow.

What the impress resembled seemed to have struck Gertrude herself since their last meeting. 'It looks almost like finger-marks,' she said; adding with a faint laugh, 'My husband says it is as if some witch, or the devil himself, had taken hold of me there, and blasted the flesh.'

Rhoda shivered. 'That's fancy,' she said hurriedly. 'I wouldn't mind it, if I were you.'

'I shouldn't so much mind it,' said the younger, with hesitation, 'if — if I hadn't a notion that it makes my husband — dislike me — no, love me less. Men think so much of personal appearance.'

'Some do — he for one.'

'Yes; and he was very proud of mine, at first.'

'Keep your arm covered from his sight.'

'Ah — he knows the disfigurement is there!' She tried to hide the tears that filled her eyes.

'Well, ma'am, I earnestly hope it will go away soon.'

And so the milkwoman's mind was chained anew to the subject by a horrid sort of spell as she returned home. The sense of having been guilty of an act of malignity increased, affect as she might to ridicule her superstition. In her secret heart Rhoda did not altogether object to a slight diminution of her successor's beauty, by whatever means it had come about; but she did not wish to inflict upon her physical pain. For though this pretty young woman had rendered impossible any reparation which Lodge might have made Rhoda for his past conduct, everything like resentment at the unconscious usurpation had quite passed away from the elder's mind.

If the sweet and kindly Gertrude Lodge only knew of the dream-scene in the bed-chamber, what would she think? Not to inform her of it seemed treachery in the presence of her friendliness; but tell she could not of her own accord — neither could she devise a remedy.

She mused upon the matter the greater part of the night, and the next day, after the morning milking, set out to obtain another glimpse of Gertrude Lodge if she could, being held to her by a gruesome fascination. By watching the house from a distance the milkmaid was presently able to discern the farmer's wife in a ride she was taking alone — probably to join her husband in some distant field. Mrs Lodge perceived her, and cantered in her direction.

'Good morning, Rhoda!' Gertrude said, when she had come up. 'I was going to call.'

Rhoda noticed that Mrs Lodge held the reins with some difficulty.

'I hope — the bad arm,' said Rhoda.

'They tell me there is possibly one way by which I might be able to find out the cause, and so perhaps the cure, of it,' replied the other anxiously. 'It is by going to some clever man over in Egdon Heath. They did not know if he was still alive — and I cannot remember his name at this moment; but they said that you knew more of his movements than anybody else hereabout, and could tell me if he were still to be consulted. Dear me — what was his name? But you know.'

'Not Conjuror Trendle?' said her thin companion, turning pale.

'Trendle — yes. Is he alive?'

'I believe so,' said Rhoda, with reluctance.

'Why do you call him conjuror?'

'Well — they say — they used to say he was a — he had powers other folks have not.'

'O, how could my people be so superstitious as to recommend a man of that sort! I thought they meant some medical man. I shall think no more of him.'

Rhoda looked relieved, and Mrs Lodge rode on. The milkwoman had inwardly seen, from the moment she heard of her having been mentioned as a reference for this man, that there must exist a sarcastic feeling among the workfolk that a sorceress would know the whereabouts of the exorcist. They suspected her, then. A short time ago this would have given no concern to a woman of her common sense. But she had a haunting reason to be superstitious now; and she had been seized with sudden dread that this Conjuror Trendle might name her as the malignant influence which was blasting the fair person of Gertrude and so lead her friend to hate her for ever, and to treat her as some fiend in human shape.

But all was not over. Two days after, a shadow intruded into the window-pattern thrown on Rhoda Brook's floor by the afternoon sun. The woman opened the door at once, almost breathlessly.

'Are you alone?' said Gertrude. She seemed to be no less harassed and anxious than Brook herself.

'Yes,' said Rhoda.

'The place on my arm seems worse, and troubles me!' the young farmer's wife went on. 'It is so mysterious! I do hope it will not be an incurable wound. I have again been thinking of what they said about Conjuror Trendle. I don't really believe in such men, but I should not mind just visiting him, from curiosity — though on no account must my husband know. Is it far to where he lives?'

'Yes — five miles,' said Rhoda backwardly. 'In the heart of Egdon.'

'Well, I should have to walk. Could not you go with me to show me the way — say to-morrow afternoon?'

'O, not I — that is,' the milkwoman murmured, with a start of dismay. Again the dread seized her that something to do with her fierce act in the dream might be revealed, and her character in the eyes of the most useful friend she had ever had be ruined irretrievably.

Mrs Lodge urged, and Rhoda finally assented, though with much misgiving. Sad as the journey would be to her, she could not conscientiously stand in the way of a possible remedy for her patron's strange affliction. It was agreed that, to escape suspicion of their mystic intent, they should meet at the edge of the heath at the corner of a plantation which was visible from the spot where they now stood.

5

CONJUROR TRENDLE

By the next afternoon Rhoda would have done anything to escape this inquiry. But she had promised to go. Moreover, there was a horrid fascination at times in becoming instrumental in throwing such possible light on her own character as would reveal her to be something greater in the occult world than she had ever herself suspected.

She started just before the time of day mentioned between them, and half-an-hour's brisk walking brought her to the south-eastern extension of the Egdon tract of country, where the fir plantation was. A slight figure, cloaked and veiled, was already there. Rhoda recognized, almost with a shudder, that Mrs Lodge bore her left arm in a sling.

They hardly spoke to each other, and immediately set out on their climb into the interior of this solemn country, which stood high above the rich alluvial soil they had left half-an-hour before. It was a long walk; thick clouds made the atmosphere dark, though it was as yet only early afternoon; and the wind howled dismally over the slopes of the heath — not improbably the same heath which had witnessed the agony of the Wessex King Ina, presented to after-ages as Lear. Gertrude Lodge talked most, Rhoda replying with monosyllabic preoccupation. She had a strange dislike to walking on the side of her companion where hung the afflicted arm, moving round to the other when inadvertently near it. Much heather had been brushed by their feet when they descended upon a cart-track, beside which stood the house of the man they sought.

He did not profess his remedial practices openly, or care anything about their continuance, his direct interests being those of a dealer in furze, turf, 'sharp sand', and other local products. Indeed, he affected not to believe largely in his own powers, and when warts that had been shown him for cure miraculously disappeared — which it must be owned they infallibly did — he would say lightly, 'O, I only drink a glass of grog upon 'em at your expense — perhaps it's all chance,' and immediately turn the subject.

He was at home when they arrived, having in fact seen them descending into his valley. He was a grey-bearded man, with a reddish face, and he looked singularly at Rhoda the first moment he beheld her. Mrs Lodge told him her errand; and then with words of self-disparagement he examined her arm.

'Medicine can't cure it,' he said promptly. ' 'Tis the work of an enemy.'

Rhoda shrank into herself, and drew back.

'An enemy? What enemy?' asked Mrs Lodge.

He shook his head. 'That's best known to yourself,' he said. 'If you like, I can show the person to you, though I shall not myself know who it is. I can do no more; and don't wish to do that.'

She pressed him; on which he told Rhoda to wait outside where she stood, and took Mrs Lodge into the room. It opened immediately from the door; and, as the latter remained ajar, Rhoda Brook could see the proceedings without taking part in them. He brought a tumbler from the dresser, nearly filled it with water and fetching an egg, prepared it in some private way; after which he broke it on the edge of the glass so that the white went in and the yolk remained. As it was getting gloomy, he took the glass and its contents to the window, and told Gertrude to watch the mixture closely. They leant over the table together, and the milkwoman could see the opaline hue of the egg-fluid changing form as it sank in the water, but she was not near enough to define the shape that it assumed.

'Do you catch the likeness of any face or figure as you look?' demanded the conjuror of the young woman.

She murmured a reply, in tones so low as to be inaudible to Rhoda, and continued to gaze intently into the glass. Rhoda turned, and walked a few steps away.

When Mrs Lodge came out, and her face was met by the light, it appeared exceedingly pale — as pale as Rhoda's — against the sad dun shades of the upland's garniture. Trendle shut the door behind her, and they at once started homeward together. But Rhoda perceived that her companion had quite changed.

'Did he charge much?' she asked tentatively.

'O no — nothing. He would not take a farthing,' said Gertrude.

'And what did you see?' inquired Rhoda.

'Nothing I — care to speak of.' The constraint in her manner was remarkable; her face was so rigid as to wear an oldened aspect, faintly suggestive of the face in Rhoda's bed-chamber.

'Was it you who first proposed coming here?' Mrs Lodge suddenly inquired after a long pause. 'How very odd, if you did!'

'No. But I am not sorry we have come, all things considered,' she replied. For the first time a sense of triumph possessed her, and she did not altogether deplore that the young thing at her side should learn that their lives had been antagonized by other influences than their own.

The subject was no more alluded to during the long and dreary walk home. But in some way or other a story was whispered about the many-dairied lowland that winter that Mrs Lodge's gradual loss of the use of her left arm was owing to her being 'overlooked' by Rhoda Brook. The latter kept her own counsel about the incubus, but her face grew sadder and thinner and in the spring she and her boy disappeared from the neighbourhood of Holmstoke.

6

A SECOND ATTEMPT

Half a dozen years passed away, and Mr and Mrs Lodge's married experience sank into prosiness, and worse. The farmer was usually gloomy and silent; the woman whom he had wooed for her grace and beauty was contorted and disfigured in the left limb; moreover, she had brought him no child, which rendered it likely that he would be the last of a family who had occupied that valley for some two hundred years. He thought of Rhoda Brook and her son; and feared this might be a judgment from heaven upon him.

The once blithe-hearted and enlightened Gertrude was changing into an irritable, superstitious woman, whose whole time was given to experimenting upon her ailment with every quack remedy she came across. She was honestly attached to her husband, and was ever secretly hoping against hope to win back his heart again by regaining some at least of her personal beauty. Hence it arose that her closet was lined with bottles, packets, and ointment-pots of every description — nay, bunches of mystic herbs, charms, and books of necromancy, which in her schoolgirl time she would have ridiculed as folly.

'Damned if you won't poison yourself with these apothecary messes and witch mixtures some time or other,' said her husband, when his eyes chanced to fall upon the multitudinous array.

She did not reply, but turned her sad, soft glance upon him in such heart-swollen reproach that he looked sorry for his words, and added, 'I only meant it for your good, you know, Gertrude.'

'I'll clear out the whole lot, and destroy them,' said she huskily, 'and try such remedies no more!'

'You want somebody to cheer you,' he observed. 'I once thought of adopting a boy; but he is too old now. And he is gone away I don't know where.'

She guessed to whom he alluded; for Rhoda Brook's story had in the course of years become known to her; though not a word ever passed between her husband and herself on the subject. Neither had she ever spoken to him of her visit to Conjuror Trendle, and of what was revealed to her, or she thought was revealed to her, by that solitary heathman.

She was now five-and-twenty; but she seemed older. 'Six years of marriage, and only a few months of love,' she sometimes whispered to herself. And then she thought of the apparent cause, and said, with a tragic glance at her withering limb, 'If I could only again be as I was when he first saw me!'

She obediently destroyed her nostrums and charms; but there remained a hankering wish to try something else — some other sort of cure altogether. She had never revisited Trendle since she had been conducted to the house of the solitary by Rhoda against her will; but it now suddenly occurred to Gertrude that she would, in a last desperate effort at deliverance from this seeming curse, again seek out the man, if he yet lived. He was entitled to a certain credence, for the indistinct form he had raised in the glass had undoubtedly resembled the only woman in the world who — as she now knew, though not then — could have a reason for bearing her ill-will. The visit should be paid.

This time she went alone, though she nearly got lost on the heath, and roamed a considerable distance out of her way. Trendle's house was reached at last, however; he was not indoors, and instead of waiting at the cottage, she went to where his bent figure was pointed out to her at work a long way off. Trendle remembered her, and laying down the handful of furze-roots which he was gathering and throwing into a heap, he offered to accompany her in her homeward direction, as the distance was considerable and the days were short. So they walked together, his head bowed nearly to the earth, and his form of a colour with it.

'You can send away warts and other excrescences, I know,' she said; 'why can't you send away this?' And the arm was uncovered.

'You think too much of my powers!' said Trendle; 'and I am old and weak now, too. No, no; it is too much for me to attempt in my own person. What have ye tried?'

She named to him some of the hundred medicaments and counter-spells which she had adopted from time to time. He shook his head.

'Some were good enough,' he said approvingly; 'but not many of them for such as this. This is of the nature of a blight, not of the nature of a wound, and if you ever do throw it off, it will be all at once.'

'If I only could!'

'There is only one chance of doing it known to me. It has never failed in kindred afflictions — that I can declare. But it is hard to carry out, and especially for a woman.'

'Tell me!' said she.

'You must touch with the limb the neck of a man who's been hanged.'

She started a little at the image he had raised.

'Before he's cold — just after he's cut down,' continued the conjuror impassively.

'How can that do good?'

'It will turn the blood and change the constitution. But, as I say, to do it is hard. You must go to the jail when there's a hanging, and wait for him when he's brought off the gallows. Lots have done it, though perhaps not such pretty women as you. I used to send dozens for skin complaints. But that was in former times. The last I sent was in '13 — near twelve years ago.'

He had no more to tell her, and, when he had put her into a straight track homeward, turned and left her, refusing all money as at first.

7

A RIDE

The communication sank deep into Gertrude's mind. Her nature was rather a timid one; and probably of all remedies that the white wizard could have suggested there was not one which would have filled her with so much aversion as this, not to speak of the immense obstacles in the way of its adoption.

Casterbridge, the country-town, was a dozen or fifteen miles off; and though in those days, when men were executed for horse-stealing, arson, and burglary, an assize seldom passed without a hanging, it was not likely that she could get access to the body of the criminal unaided. And the fear of her husband's anger made her reluctant to breathe a word of Trendle's suggestion to him or to anybody about him.

She did nothing for months, and patiently bore her disfigurement as before. But her woman's nature, craving for renewed love through the medium of renewed beauty (she was but twenty-five), was ever stimulating her to try what, at any rate, could hardly do her any harm. 'What came by a spell will go by a spell surely,' she would say. Whenever her imagination pictured the act she shrank in terror from the possibility of it; then the words of the conjuror, 'It will turn your blood,' were seen to be capable of a scientific no less than a ghastly interpretation; the mastering desire returned, and urged her on again.

There was at this time but one county paper, and that her husband only occasionally borrowed. But old-fashioned days had old-fashioned means and news was extensively conveyed by word of mouth from market to market, or from fair to fair, so that, whenever such an event as an execution was about to take place, few within a radius of twenty miles were ignorant of the coming sight; and, so far as Holmstoke was concerned, some enthusiasts had been known to walk all the way to Casterbridge and back in one day, solely to witness the spectacle. The next assizes were in March; and when Gertrude Lodge heard that they had been held, she inquired stealthily at the inn as to the result, as soon as she could find opportunity.

She was, however, too late. The time at which the sentences were to be carried out had arrived, and to make the journey and obtain admission at such short notice required at least her husband's assistance. She dared not tell him, for she had found by delicate experiment that these smouldering village beliefs made him furious if mentioned, partly because he half entertained them himself. It was therefore necessary to wait for another opportunity.

Her determination received a fillip from learning that two epileptic children had attended from this very village of Holmstoke many years before with beneficial results, though the experiments had been strongly condemned by the neighbouring clergy. April, May, June passed; and it is no overstatement to say that by the end of the last-named month Gertrude wellnigh longed for the death of a fellow-creature. Instead of her formal prayers each night, her unconscious prayer was, 'O Lord, hang some guilty or innocent person soon!'

This time she made earlier inquiries, and was altogether more systematic in her proceedings. Moreover, the season was summer, between the haymaking and the harvest, and in the leisure thus afforded him her husband had been holiday-taking away from home.

The assizes were in July, and she went to the inn as before. There was to be one execution — only one — for arson.

Her greatest problem was not how to get to Casterbridge, but what means she should adopt for obtaining admission to the jail. Though access for such purposes had formerly never been denied, the custom had fallen into desuetude; and in contemplating her possible difficulties, she was again almost driven to fall back upon her husband. But, on sounding him about the assizes, he was so uncommunicative, so more than usually cold, that she did not proceed, and decided that whatever she did she would do alone.

Fortune, obdurate hitherto, showed her unexpected favour. On the Thursday before the Saturday fixed for the execution, Lodge remarked to her that he was going away from home for another day or two on business at a fair, and that he was sorry he could not take her with him.

She exhibited on this occasion so much readiness to stay at home that he looked at her in surprise. Time had been when she would have shown deep disappointment at the loss of such a jaunt. However, he lapsed into his usual taciturnity, and on the day named left Holmstoke.

It was now her turn. She at first thought of driving, but on reflection held that driving would not do, since it would necessitate her keeping to the turnpike-road, and so increase by tenfold the risk of her ghastly errand being found out. She decided to ride, and avoid the beaten track, notwithstanding that in her husband's stables there was no animal just at present which by any stretch of imagination could be considered a lady's mount, in spite of his promise before marriage to always keep a mare for her. He had, however, many cart-horses, fine ones of their kind; and among the rest was a serviceable creature, an equine Amazon, with a back as broad as a sofa, on which Gertrude had occasionally taken an airing when unwell. This horse she chose.

On Friday afternoon one of the men brought it round. She was dressed, and before going down looked at her shrivelled arm. 'Ah!' she said to it, 'if it had not been for you this terrible ordeal would have been saved me!'

When strapping up the bundle in which she carried a few articles of clothing, she took occasion to say to the servant, 'I take these in case I should not get back to-night from the person I am going to visit. Don't be alarmed if I am not in by ten, and close up the house as usual. I shall be at home to-morrow for certain.' She meant then to tell her husband privately; the deed accomplished was not like the deed projected. He would almost certainly forgive her.

And then the pretty palpitating Gertrude Lodge went from her husband's homestead; but though her goal was Casterbridge she did not take the direct route thither through Stickleford. Her cunning course at first was in precisely the opposite direction. As soon as she was out of sight, however, she turned to the left by a road which led into Egdon, and on entering the heath wheeled round, and set out in the true course, due westerly. A more private way down the county could not be imagined; and as to direction, she had merely to keep her horse's head to a point a little to the right of the sun. She knew that she would light upon a furze-cutter or cottage of some sort from time to time, from whom she might correct her bearing.

Though the date was comparatively recent, Egdon was much less fragmentary in character than now. The attempts   successful and otherwise — at cultivation on the lower slopes, which intrude and break up the original heath into small detached heaths, had not been carried far; Enclosure Acts had not taken effect, and the banks and fences which now exclude the cattle of those villagers who formerly enjoyed rights of commonage thereon, and the carts of those who had turbary privileges which kept them in firing all the year round, were not erected. Gertrude, therefore, rode along with no other obstacles than the prickly furze-bushes, the mats of heather, the white water-courses, and the natural steeps and declivities of the ground.

Her horse was sure, if heavy-footed and slow, and though a draught animal, was easy-paced; had it been otherwise, she was not a woman who could have ventured to ride over such a bit of country with a half-dead arm. It was therefore nearly eight o'clock when she drew rein to breathe her bearer on the last outlying high point of heath-land towards Casterbridge, previous to leaving Egdon for the cultivated valleys.

She halted before a pool called Rushy-pond, flanked by the ends of two hedges; a railing ran through the centre of the pond, dividing it in half. Over the railing she saw the low green country; over the green trees the roofs of the town; over the roofs a white flat façade, denoting the entrance to the county jail. On the roof of this front specks were moving about; they seemed to be workmen erecting something. Her flesh crept. She descended slowly, and was soon amid cornfields and pastures. In another half-hour, when it was almost dusk, Gertrude reached the White Hart, the first inn of the town on that side.

Little surprise was excited by her arrival; farmers' wives rode on horseback then more than they do now; though, for that matter, Mrs Lodge was not imagined to be a wife at all; the innkeeper supposed her some harum-skarum young woman who had come to attend 'hang-fair' next day. Neither her husband nor herself ever dealt in Casterbridge market, so that she was unknown. While dismounting she beheld a crowd of boys standing at the door of a harness-maker's shop just above the inn, looking inside it with deep interest.

'What is going on there?' she asked of the ostler.

'Making the rope for to-morrow.'

She throbbed responsively, and contracted her arm.

' 'Tis sold by the inch afterwards,' the man continued, 'I could get you a bit, miss, for nothing, if you'd like?'

She hastily repudiated any such wish, all the more from a curious creeping feeling that the condemned wretch's destiny was becoming interwoven with her own; and having engaged a room for the night, sat down to think.

Up to this time she had formed but the vaguest notions about her means of obtaining access to the prison. The words of the cunning-man returned to her mind. He had implied that she should use her beauty, impaired though it was, as a pass-key. In her inexperience she knew little about jail functionaries; she had heard of a high-sheriff and an under-sheriff, but dimly only. She knew, however, that there must be a hangman, and to the hangman she determined to apply.

8

A WATER-SIDE HERMIT

At this date, and for several years after, there was a hangman to almost every jail. Gertrude found, on inquiry, that the Casterbridge official dwelt in a lonely cottage by a deep slow river flowing under the cliff on which the prison buildings were situate — the stream being the self-same one, though she did not know it, which watered the Stickleford and Holmstoke meads lower down in its course.

Having changed her dress, and before she had eaten or drunk — for she could not take her ease till she had ascertained some particulars — Gertrude pursued her way by a path along the water-side to the cottage indicated. Passing thus the outskirts of the jail, she discerned on the level roof over the gateway three rectangular lines against the sky, where the specks had been moving in her distant view; she recognized what the erection was, and passed quickly on. Another hundred yards brought her to the executioner's house, which a boy pointed out. It stood close to the same stream, and was hard by a weir, the waters of which emitted a steady roar.

While she stood hesitating the door opened, and an old man came forth, shading a candle with one hand. Locking the door on the outside, he turned to a flight of wooden steps fixed against the end of the cottage, and began to ascend them, this being evidently the staircase to his bedroom. Gertrude hastened forward, but by the time she reached the foot of the ladder he was at the top. She called to him loudly enough to be heard above the roar of the weir; he looked down and said, 'What d'ye want here?'

'To speak to you a minute.'

The candle-light, such as it was, fell upon her imploring, pale, upturned face, and Davies (as the hangman was called) backed down the ladder. 'I was just going to bed,' he said. 'Early to bed and early to rise', but I don't mind stopping a minute for such a one as you. Come into house.' He reopened the door, and preceded her to the room within.

The implements of his daily work, which was that of a jobbing gardener, stood in a corner, and seeing probably that she looked rural, he said, 'If you want me to undertake country work I can't come, for I never leave Casterbridge for gentle nor simple — not I. My real calling is officer of justice,' he added formally.

'Yes, yes! That's it. To-morrow!'

'Ah! I thought so. Well, what's the matter about that? 'Tis no use to come here about the knot — folks do come continually, but I tell 'em one knot is as merciful as another if ye keep it under the ear. Is the unfortunate man a relation; or, I should say, perhaps' (looking at her dress) 'a person who's been in your employ?'

'No. What time is the execution?'

'The same as usual — twelve o'clock, or as soon after as the London mail-coach gets in. We always wait for that, in case of a reprieve.'

'O — a reprieve — I hope not!' she said involuntarily.

'Well, — hee, hee! — as a matter of business, so do I! But still, if ever a young fellow deserved to be let off, this one does; only just turned eighteen, and only present by chance when the rick was fired. Howsomever there's not much risk of it, as they are obliged to make an example of him, there having been so much destruction of property that way lately.'

'I mean,' she explained, 'that I want to touch him for a charm, a cure of an affliction, by the advice of a man who has proved the virtue of the remedy.'

'O yes, miss! Now I understand. I've had such people come in past years. But it didn't strike me that you looked of a sort to require blood-turning. What's the complaint? The wrong kind for this, I'll be bound.'

'My arm.' She reluctantly showed the withered skin.

'Ah! — 'tis all a-scram!' said the hangman, examining it.

'Yes,' she said.

'Well,' he continued, with interest, 'that *is* the class o' subject, I'm bound to admit! I like the look of the wownd; it is truly as suitable for the cure as any I ever saw. 'Twas a knowing-man that sent 'ee, whoever he was.'

'You can contrive for me all that's necessary?' she said breathlessly.

'You should really have gone to the governor of the jail, and your doctor with 'ee, and given your name and address, — that's how it used to be done, if I recollect. Still, perhaps, I can manage it for a trifling fee.'

'O, thank you! I would rather do it this way, as I should like it kept private.'

'Lover not to know, eh?'

'No — husband.'

'Aha! Very well. I'll get 'ee a touch of the corpse.'

'Where is it now?' she said shuddering.

'It? — *he,* you mean; he's living yet. Just inside that little small winder up there in the glum.' He signified the jail on the cliff above.

She thought of her husband and her friends. 'Yes, of course,' she said; 'and how am I to proceed?'

He took her to the door. 'Now, do you be waiting at the little wicket in the wall, that you'll find up there in the lane, not later than one o'clock. I will open it from the inside, as I shan't come home to dinner till he's cut down. Good-night. Be punctual; and if you don't want anybody to know 'ee, wear a veil. Ah — once I had such a daughter as you!'

She went away, and climbed the path above, to assure herself that she would be able to find the wicket next day. Its outline was soon visible to her — a narrow opening in the outer wall of the prison precincts. The steep was so great that, having reached the wicket, she stopped a moment to breathe; and, looking back upon the water-side cot, saw the hangman again ascending his outdoor staircase. He entered the loft or chamber to which it led, and in a few minutes extinguished his light.

The town clock struck ten, and she returned to the White Hart as she had come.

9

A RENCOUNTER

It was one o'clock on Saturday. Gertrude Lodge, having been admitted to the jail as above described, was sitting in a waiting-room within the second gate, which stood under a classic archway of ashlar, then comparatively modern, and bearing the inscription, 'COVNTY JAIL: 1793'. This had been the façade she saw from the heath the day before. Near at hand was a passage to the roof on which the gallows stood.

The town was thronged, and the market suspended; but Gertrude had seen scarcely a soul. Having kept her room till the hour of the appointment she had proceeded to the spot by a way which avoided the open space below the cliff where the spectators had gathered; but she could, even now, hear the multitudinous babble of their voices, out of which rose at intervals the hoarse croak of a single voice uttering the words, 'Last dying speech and confession!' There had been no reprieve, and the execution was over; but the crowd still waited to see the body taken down.

Soon the persistent woman heard a trampling overhead, then a hand beckoned to her, and, following directions, she went out and crossed the inner paved court beyond the gate-house, her knees trembling so that she could scarcely walk. One of her arms was out of its sleeve, and only covered by her shawl.

On the spot at which she had now arrived were two trestles, and before she could think of their purpose she heard heavy feet descending stairs somewhere at her back. Turn her head she would not, or could not, and, rigid in this position, she was conscious of a rough coffin passing her shoulder, borne by four men. It was open, and in it lay the body of a young man, wearing the smockfrock of a rustic, and fustian breeches. The corpse had been thrown into the coffin so hastily that the skirt of the smockfrock was hanging over. The burden was temporarily deposited on the trestles.

By this time the young woman's state was such that a gray mist seemed to float before her eyes, on account of which, and the veil she wore, she could scarcely discern anything: it was as though she had nearly died, but was held up by a sort of galvanism.

'Now!' said a voice close at hand, and she was just conscious that the word had been addressed to her.

By a last strenuous effort she advanced, at the same time hearing persons approaching behind her. She bared her poor curst arm; and Davies, uncovering the face of the corpse, took Gertrude's hand, and held it so that her arm lay across the dead man's neck, upon a line the colour of an unripe blackberry, which surrounded it.

Gertrude shrieked: 'the turn o' the blood', predicted by the conjuror, had taken place. But at that moment a second shriek rent the air of the enclosure: it was not Gertrude's, and its effect upon her was to make her start round.

Immediately behind her stood Rhoda Brook, her face drawn, and her eyes red with weeping. Behind Rhoda stood Gertrude's own husband; his countenance lined, his eyes dim, but without a tear.

'D — n you! what are you doing here?' he said hoarsely.

'Hussy — to come between us and our child now!' cried Rhoda "This is the meaning of what Satan showed me in the vision! You are like her at last!' And clutching the bare arm of the younger woman, she pulled her unresistingly back against the wall. Immediately Brook had loosened her hold the fragile young Gertrude slid down against the feet of her husband. When he lifted her up she was unconscious.

The mere sight of the twain had been enough to suggest to her that the dead young man was Rhoda's son. At that time the relatives of an executed convict had the privilege of claiming the body for burial, if they chose to do so; and it was for this purpose that Lodge was awaiting the inquest with Rhoda. He had been summoned by her as soon as the young man was taken in the crime, and at different times since; and he had attended in court during the trial. This was the 'holiday' he had been indulging in of late. The two wretched parents had wished to avoid exposure; and hence had come themselves for the body, a waggon and sheet for its conveyance and covering being in waiting outside.

Gertrude's case was so serious that it was deemed advisable to call to her the surgeon who was at hand. She was taken out of the jail into the town; but she never reached home alive. Her delicate vitality, sapped perhaps by the paralyzed arm, collapsed under the double shock that followed the severe strain, physical and mental, to which she had subjected herself during the previous twenty-four hours. Her blood had been 'turned' indeed — too far. Her death took place in the town three days after.

Her husband was never seen in Casterbridge again; once only in the old market-place at Anglebury, which he had so much frequented, and very seldom in public anywhere. Burdened at first with moodiness and remorse, he eventually changed for the better, and appeared as a chastened and thoughtful man. Soon after attending the funeral of his poor young wife he took steps towards giving up the farms in Holmstoke and the adjoining parish, and, having sold every head of his stock, he went away to Port-Bredy, at the other end of the county, living there in solitary lodgings till his death two years later of painless decline. It was then found that he had bequeathed the whole of his not inconsiderable property to a reformatory for boys, subject to the payment of a small annuity to Rhoda Brook if she could be found to claim it.

For some time she could not be found; but eventually she reappeared in her old parish, — absolutely refusing, however, to have anything to do with the provision made for her. Her monotonous milking at the dairy was resumed, and followed for many long years, till her form became bent, and her once abundant dark hair white and worn away at the forehead — perhaps by long pressure against the cows. Here, sometimes, those who knew her experiences would stand and observe her, and wonder what sombre thoughts were beating inside that impassive, wrinkled brow, to the rhythm of the alternating milk-streams.

NATHANIEL HAWTHORNE

Nathaniel Hawthorne (1804–1864) was born in Salem, Massachusetts, and lived most of his life in the New England sites that his work would help immortalize: Salem, Concord, and the Berkshire Mountains. Descended from a line of Puritans, he created in his masterpiece, *The Scarlet Letter* (1850), what many readers consider the most probing revelation of the Puritan psyche ever written. He was given to reclusiveness, but, through the critical fame of his work, "the world found me out in my lonely chamber and called me forth." His contemporary, Edgar Allan Poe, premised his famous definition of the short story — that it can be read at one sitting, strives toward a single effect, and is linguistically highly charged — on a reading of Hawthorne's first collection, *Twice-Told Tales* (1842). Frequently, Hawthorne's tales, like his novels, are laced with allegory and reach toward a moral point. He considered himself a writer of romances, in the sense that romance may oppose itself to the demands of strict realism and create its own reality; its creator may "dream strange things, and make them look like truth." His other novels include *The House of the Seven Gables* (1851), *The Blithedale Romance* (1852), and *The Marble Faun* (1860). His tales were published in *Mosses from an Old Manse* (1846), *The Snow Image and Other Twice-Told Tales* (1852), and *Tanglewood Tales* (1853). Hawthorne lived near and knew well those writers with whom, as one of his biographers poignantly puts it, he joined in "that uncertain venture, the making of an American literature": Longfellow, Emerson, Holmes, Whittier, Lowell. Melville dedicated *Moby Dick* to him. But Henry James, whose own expatriation made him a particularly keen observer of American letters, perhaps best expressed Hawthorne's stature. Writing in 1879 of *The Scarlet Letter,* he said, "Something at last might be sent to Europe as exquisite in quality as anything that had been received, and the best of it was that the thing was absolutely American." The two stories here — "The Artist of the Beautiful" and "Rappaccini's Daughter" — are allegorical romances of transformation, wrought in Hawthorne's unmistakable style.

The Artist of the Beautiful

An elderly man, with his pretty daughter on his arm, was passing along the street, and emerged from the gloom of the cloudy evening into the light that fell across the pavement from the window of a small shop. It was a projecting window; and on the inside were suspended a variety of watches, — pinchbeck, silver, and one or two of gold, — all with their faces turned from the street, as if churlishly disinclined to inform the wayfarers what o'clock it was. Seated within the shop, sidelong to the window, with his pale face bent earnestly over some delicate piece of mechanism, on which was thrown the concentrated lustre of a shade-lamp, appeared a young man.

"What can Owen Warland be about?" muttered old Peter Hovenden, — himself a retired watchmaker, and the former master of this same young man, whose occupation he was now wondering at. "What can the fellow be about? These six months past, I have never come by his shop without seeing him just as steadily at work as now. It would be a flight beyond his usual foolery to seek for the Perpetual Motion. And yet I know enough of my old business to be certain, that what he is now so busy with is no part of the machinery of a watch."

"Perhaps, father," said Annie, without showing much interest in the question, "Owen is inventing a new kind of timekeeper. I am sure he has ingenuity enough."

"Poh, child! he has not the sort of ingenuity to invent anything better than a Dutch toy," answered her father, who had formerly been put to much vexation by Owen Warland's irregular genius. "A plague on such ingenuity! All the effect that ever I knew of it, was to spoil the accuracy of some of the best watches in my shop. He would turn the sun out of its orbit, and derange the whole course of time, if, as I said before, his ingenuity could grasp anything bigger than a child's toy!"

"Hush, father! he hears you," whispered Annie, pressing the old man's arm. "His ears are as delicate as his feelings, and you know how easily disturbed they are. Do let us move on."

So Peter Hovenden and his daughter Annie plodded on, without further conversation, until, in a by-street of the town, they found themselves passing the open door of a blacksmith's shop. Within was seen the forge, now blazing up, and illuminating the high and dusky roof, and now confining its lustre to a narrow precinct of the coal-strewn floor, according as the breath of the bellows was puffed forth, or again inhaled into its vast leathern lungs. In the intervals of brightness, it was easy to distinguish objects in remote corners of the shop, and the horse-shoes that hung upon the wall; in the momentary gloom, the fire seemed to be glimmering amidst the vagueness of unenclosed space. Moving about in this red glare and alternate dusk, was the figure of the blacksmith, well worthy to be viewed in so picturesque an aspect of light and shade, where the bright blaze struggled with the black night, as if each would have snatched his comely strength from the other. Anon, he drew a white-hot bar of iron from the coals, laid it on the anvil, uplifted his arm of might, and was soon enveloped in the myriads of sparks which the strokes of his hammer scattered into the surrounding gloom.

"Now, that is a pleasant sight," said the old watchmaker. "I know what it is to work in gold, but give me the worker in iron, after all is said and done. He spends his labor upon a reality. What say you, daughter Annie?"

"Pray don't speak so loud, father," whispered Annie. "Robert Danforth will hear you."

"And what if he should hear me?" said Peter Hovenden; "I say again, it is a good and a wholesome thing to depend upon main strength and reality, and to earn one's bread with the bare and brawny arm of a blacksmith. A watchmaker gets his brain puzzled by his wheels within a wheel, or loses his health or the nicety of his eyesight, as was my case; and finds himself, at middle age, or a little after, past labor at his own trade, and fit for nothing else, yet too poor to live at his ease. So, I say once again, give me main strength for my money. And then, how it takes the nonsense out of a man! Did you ever hear of a blacksmith being such a fool as Owen Warland, yonder?"

"Well said, uncle Hovenden!" shouted Robert Danforth, from the forge, in a full, deep, merry voice, that made the roof re-echo. "And what says Miss Annie to that doctrine? She, I suppose, will think it a genteeler business to tinker up a lady's watch, than to forge a horse-shoe or make a grid-iron!"

Annie drew her father onward, without giving him time for reply.

But we must return to Owen Warland's shop, and spend more meditation upon his history and character than either Peter Hovenden, or probably his daughter Annie, or Owen's old schoolfellow, Robert Danforth, would have thought due to so slight a subject. From the time that his little fingers could grasp a pen-knife, Owen had been remarkable for a delicate ingenuity, which sometimes produced pretty shapes in wood, principally figures of flowers and birds, and sometimes seemed to aim at the hidden mysteries of mechanism. But it was always for purposes of grace, and never with any mockery of the useful. He did not, like the crowd of school-boy artizans, construct little windmills on the angle of a barn, or watermills across the neighboring brook. Those who discovered such peculiarity in the boy, as to think it worth their while to observe him closely, sometimes saw reason to suppose that he was attempting to imitate the beautiful movement of Nature, as exemplified in the flight of birds or the activity of little animals. It seemed, in fact, a new development of the love of the Beautiful, such as might have made him a poet, a painter, or a sculptor, and which was as completely refined from all utilitarian coarseness, as it could have been in either of the fine arts. He looked with singular distaste at the stiff and regular processes of ordinary machinery. Being once carried to see a steam-engine, in the expectation that his intuitive comprehension of mechanical principles would be gratified, he turned pale, and grew sick, as if something monstrous and unnatural had been presented to him. This horror was partly owing to the size and terrible energy of the Iron Laborer; for the character of Owen's mind was miscroscopic, and tended naturally to the minute, in accordance with his diminutive frame, and the marvellous smallness and delicate power of his fingers. Not that his sense of beauty was thereby diminished into a sense of prettiness. The Beautiful Idea has no relation to size, and may be as perfectly developed in a space too minute for any but microscopic investigation, as within the ample verge that is measured by the arc of the rainbow. But, at all events, this characteristic minuteness in his objects and accomplishments made the world even more incapable, than it might otherwise have been, of appreciating Owen Warland's genius. The boy's relatives saw nothing better to be done — as perhaps there was not — than to bind him apprentice to a watchmaker, hoping that his strange ingenuity might thus be regulated, and put to utilitarian purposes.

Peter Hovenden's opinion of his apprentice has already been expressed. He could make nothing of the lad. Owen's apprehension of the professional mysteries, it is true, was inconceivably quick. But he altogether forgot or despised the grand object of a watchmaker's business, and cared no more for the measurement of time than if it had been merged into eternity. So long, however, as he remained under his old master's care, Owen's lack of sturdiness made it possible, by strict injunctions and sharp oversight, to restrain his creative eccentricity within bounds. But when his apprenticeship was served out, and he had taken the little shop which Peter Hovenden's failing eyesight compelled him to relinquish, then did people recognize how unfit a person was Owen Warland to lead old blind Father Time along his daily course. One of his most rational projects was, to connect a musical operation with the machinery of his watches, so that all the harsh dissonances of life might be rendered tuneful, and each flitting movement fall into the abyss of the Past in golden drops of harmony. If a family-clock was entrusted to him for repair — one of those tall, ancient clocks that have grown nearly allied to human nature, by measuring out the lifetime of many generations he would take upon himself to arrange a dance or funeral procession of figures, across its venerable face, representing twelve mirthful or melancholy hours. Several freaks of this kind quite destroyed the young watchmaker's credit with that steady and matter-of-fact class of people who hold the opinion that time is not to be trifled with, whether considered as the medium of advancement and prosperity in this world, or preparation for the next. His custom rapidly diminished — a misfortune, however, that was probably reckoned among his better accidents by Owen Warland, who was becoming more and more absorbed in a secret occupation, which drew all his science and manual dexterity into self, and likewise gave full employment to the characteristic tendencies of his genius. This pursuit had already consumed many months.

After the old watchmaker and his pretty daughter had gazed at him, out of the obscurity of the street, Owen Warland was seized with a fluttering of the nerves, which made his hand tremble too violently to proceed with such delicate labor as he was now engaged upon.

"It was Annie herself!" murmured he. "I should have known it, by this throbbing of my heart, before I heard her father's voice. Ah, how it throbs! I shall scarcely be able to work again on this exquisite mechanism to-night. Annie — dearest Annie — thou shouldst give firmness to my heart and hand, and not shake them thus; for if I strive to put the very spirit of Beauty into form, and give it motion, it is for thy sake alone. Oh, throbbing heart, be quiet! If my labor be thus thwarted, there will come vague and unsatisfied dreams, which will leave me spiritless to-morrow."

As he was endeavoring to settle himself again to his task, the shop-door opened, and gave admittance to no other than the stalwart figure which Peter Hovenden had paused to admire, as seen amid the light and shadow of the blacksmith's shop. Robert Danforth had brought a little anvil of his own manufacture, and peculiarly constructed, which the young artist had recently bespoken. Owen examined the article, and pronounced it fashioned according to his wish.

"Why, yes," said Robert Danforth, his strong voice filling the shop as with the sound of a bass-viol, "I consider myself equal to anything in the way of my own trade; though I should have made but a poor figure at yours, with such a fist as this," — added he, laughing, as he laid his vast hand beside the delicate one of Owen. "But what then? I put more main strength into one blow of my sledge-hammer, than all that you have expended since you were a 'prentice. Is not that the truth?"

"Very probably," answered the low and slender voice of Owen. "Strength is an earthly monster. I make no pretensions to it. My force, whatever there may be of it, is altogether spiritual."

"Well; but, Owen, what are you about?" asked his old schoolfellow, still in such a hearty volume of tone that it made the artist shrink; especially as the question related to a subject so sacred as the absorbing dream of his imagination. "Folks do say, that you are trying to discover the Perpetual Motion."

"The Perpetual Motion? — nonsense!" replied Owen Warland, with a movement of disgust; for he was full of little petulances. "It can never be discovered! It is a dream that may delude men whose brains are mystified with matter, but not me. Besides, if such a discovery were possible, it would not be worth my while to make it, only to have the secret turned to such purposes as are now effected by steam and water-power. I am not ambitious to be honored with the paternity of a new kind of cotton-machine."

"That would be droll enough!" cried the blacksmith, breaking out into such an uproar of laughter, that Owen himself, and the bell-glasses on his work-board, quivered in unison. "No, no, Owen! No child of yours will have iron joints and sinews. Well, I won't hinder you any more. Good night, Owen, and success; and if you need any assistance, so far as a downright blow of hammer upon anvil will answer the purpose, I'm your man!"

And with another laugh, the man of main strength left the shop.

"How strange it is," whispered Owen Warland to himself, leaning his head upon his hand, "that all my musings, my purposes, my passion for the Beautiful, my consciousness of power to create it — a finer, more ethereal power, of which this earthly giant can have no conception — all, all, look so vain and idle, whenever my path is crossed by Robert Danforth! He would drive me mad, were I to meet him often. His hard, brute force darkens and confuses the spiritual element within me. But I, too, will be strong in my own way. I will not yield to him!"

He took from beneath a glass, a piece of minute machinery, which he set in the condensed light of his lamp, and, looking intently at it through a magnifying glass, proceeded to operate with a delicate instrument of steel. In an instant, however, he fell back in his chair, and clasped his hands, with a look of horror on his face, that made its small features as impressive as those of a giant would have been.

"Heaven! What have I done!" exclaimed he. "The vapor! — the influence of that brute force! — it has bewildered me, and obscured my perception. I have made the very stroke — the fatal stroke — that I have dreaded from the first! It is all over — the toil of months — the object of my life! I am ruined!"

And there he sat, in strange despair, until his lamp flickered in the socket, and left the Artist of the Beautiful in darkness.

Thus it is, that ideas which grow up within the imagination, and appear so lovely to it, and of a value beyond whatever men call valuable, are exposed to be shattered and annihilated by contact with the Practical. It is requisite for the ideal artist to possess a force of character that seems hardly compatible with its delicacy; he must keep his faith in himself, while the incredulous world assails him with its utter disbelief; he must stand up against mankind and be his own sole disciple, both as respects his genius, and the objects to which it is directed.

For a time, Owen Warland succumbed to this severe, but inevitable test. He spent a few sluggish weeks, with his head so continually resting in his hands, that the townspeople had scarcely an opportunity to see his countenance. When, at last, it was again uplifted to the light of day, a cold, dull, nameless change was perceptible upon it. In the opinion of Peter Hovenden, however, and that order of sagacious understandings who think that life should be regulated, like clock-work, with leaden weights, the alteration was entirely for the better. Owen now indeed, applied himself to business with dogged industry. It was marvelous to witness the obtuse gravity with which he would inspect the wheels of a great, old silver watch; thereby delighting the owner, in whose fob it had been worn till he deemed it a portion of his own life, and was accordingly jealous of its treatment. In consequence of the good report thus acquired, Owen Warland was invited by the proper authorities to regulate the clock in the church-steeple. He succeeded so admirably in this matter of public interest, that the merchants gruffly acknowledged his merits on 'Change; the nurse whispered his praises, as she gave the potion in the sick-chamber; the lover blessed him at the hour of appointed interview; and the town in general thanked Owen for the punctuality of dinner-time. In a word, the heavy weight upon his spirits kept everything in order, not merely within his own system, but wheresoever the iron accents of the church-clock were audible. It was a circumstance, though minute, yet characteristic of his present state, that, when employed to engrave names or initials on silver spoons, he now wrote the requisite letters in the plainest possible style; omitting a variety of fanciful flourishes, that had heretofore distinguished his work in this kind.

One day, during the era of this happy transformation, old Peter Hovenden came to visit his former apprentice.

"Well, Owen," said he, "I am glad to hear such good accounts of you from all quarters; and especially from the town-clock yonder, which speaks in your commendation every hour of the twenty-four. Only get rid altogether of your nonsensical trash about the Beautiful — which I, nor nobody else, nor yourself to boot, could never understand — only free yourself of that, and your success in life is as sure as daylight. Why, if you go on in this way, I should even venture to let you doctor this precious old watch of mine; though, except my daughter Annie, I have nothing else so valuable in the world."

"I should hardly dare touch it, sir," replied Owen in a depressed tone; for he was weighed down by his old master's presence.

"In time," said the latter, "in time, you will be capable of it."

The old watchmaker, with the freedom naturally consequent on his former authority, went on inspecting the work which Owen had in hand at the moment, together with other matters that were in progress. The artist, meanwhile, could scarcely lift his head. There was nothing so antipodal to his nature as this man's cold, unimaginative sagacity, by contact with which everything was converted into a dream, except the densest matter of the physical world. Owen groaned in spirit, and prayed fervently to be delivered from him.

"But what is this?" cried Peter Hovenden abruptly, taking up a dusty bell-glass, beneath which appeared a mechanical something, as delicate and minute as the system of a butterfly's anatomy. "What have we here! Owen, Owen! there is witchcraft in these little chains, and wheels, and paddles! See! with one pinch of my finger and thumb, I am going to deliver you from all future peril."

"For Heaven's sake," screamed Owen Warland, springing up with wonderful energy, "as you would not drive me mad — do not touch it! The slightest pressure of your finger would ruin me for ever."

"Aha, young man! And is it so?" said the old watchmaker, looking at him with just enough of penetration to torture Owen's soul with the bitterness of worldly criticism. "Well; take your own course. But I warn you again, that in this small piece of mechanism lives your evil spirit. Shall I exorcise him?"

"You are my Evil Spirit," answered Owen, much excited — "you and the hard, coarse world! The leaden thoughts and the despondency that you fling upon me are my clogs. Else, I should long ago have achieved the task that I was created for."

Peter Hovenden shook his head, with the mixture of contempt and indignation which mankind, of whom he was partly a representative, deem themselves entitled to feel towards all simpletons who seek other prizes than the dusty ones along the highway. He then took his leave with an uplifted finger, and a sneer upon his face, that haunted the artist's dreams for many a night afterwards. At the time of his old master's visit, Owen was probably on the point of taking up the relinquished task; but, by this sinister event, he was thrown back into the state whence he had been slowly emerging.

But the innate tendency of his soul had only been accumulating fresh vigor, during its apparent sluggishness. As the summer advanced, he almost totally relinquished his business, and permitted Father Time, so far as the old gentleman was represented by the clocks and watches under his control, to stray at random through human life, making infinite confusion among the train of bewildered hours. He wasted the sunshine, as people said, in wandering through the woods and fields, and along the banks of streams. There, like a child, he found amusement in chasing butterflies, or watching the motions of water-insects. There was something truly mysterious in the intentness with which he contemplated these living playthings, as they sported on the breeze; or examined the structure of an imperial insect whom he had imprisoned. The chase of butterflies was an apt emblem of the ideal pursuit in which he had spent so many golden hours. But, would the Beautiful Idea ever be yielded to his hand, like the butterfly that symbolized it? Sweet, doubtless, were these days, and congenial to the artist's soul. They were full of bright conceptions, which gleamed through his intellectual world, as the butterflies gleamed through the outward atmosphere, and were real to him for the instant, without the toil, and perplexity, and many disappointments, of attempting to make them visible to the sensual eye. Alas, that the artist, whether in poetry or whatever other material, may not content himself with the inward enjoyment of the Beautiful, but must chase the flitting mystery beyond the verge of his ethereal domain, and crush its frail being in seizing it with a material grasp! Owen Warland felt the impulse to give external reality to his ideas, as irresistibly as any of the poets or painters, who have arrayed the world in a dimmer and fainter beauty, imperfectly copied from the richness of their visions.

The night was now his time for the slow process of recreating the one Idea, to which all his intellectual activity referred itself. Always at the approach of dusk, he stole into the town, locked himself within his shop, and wrought with patient delicacy of touch, for many hours. Sometimes he was startled by the rap of the watchman, who, when all the world should be asleep, had caught the gleam of lamp-light through the crevices of Owen Warland's shutters. Daylight, to the morbid sensibility of his mind, seemed to have an intrusiveness that interfered with his pursuits. On cloudy and inclement days, therefore, he sat with his head upon his hands, muffling, as it were, his sensitive brain in a mist of indefinite musings; for it was a relief to escape from the sharp distinctness with which he was compelled to shape out his thoughts, during his nightly toil.

From one of these fits of torpor, he was aroused by the entrance of Annie Hovenden, who came into the shop with the freedom of a customer, and also with something of the familiarity of a childish friend. She had worn a hole through her silver thimble, and wanted Owen to repair it.

"But I don't know whether you will condescend to such a task," said she, laughing, "now that you are so taken up with the notion of putting spirit into machinery."

"Where did you get that idea, Annie?" said Owen, starting in surprise.

"Oh, out of my own head," answered she, "and from something that I heard you say, long ago, when you were but a boy, and I a little child. But, come! will you mend this poor thimble of mine?"

"Anything for your sake, Annie," said Owen Warland — "anything; even were it to work at Robert Danforth's forge."

"And that would be a pretty sight!" retorted Annie, glancing with imperceptible slightness at the artist's small and slender frame. "Well; here is the thimble."

"But that is a strange idea of yours," said Owen, "about the spiritualization of matter!"

And then the thought stole into his mind, that this young girl possessed the gift to comprehend him, better than all the world beside. And what a help and strength would it be to him, in his lonely toil, if he could gain the sympathy of the only being whom he loved! To persons whose pursuits are insulated from the common business of life — who are either in advance of mankind, or apart from it — there often comes a sensation of moral cold, that makes the spirit shiver, as if it had reached the frozen solitudes around the pole. What the prophet, the poet, the reformer, the criminal, or any other man, with human yearnings, but separated from the multitude by a peculiar lot, might feel, poor Owen Warland felt.

"Annie," cried he, growing pale as death at the thought, "how gladly would I tell you the secret of my pursuit! You, methinks, would estimate it rightly. You, I know, would hear it with a reverence that I must not expect from the harsh, material world."

"Would I not? to be sure I would!" replied Annie Hovenden, lightly laughing. "Come; explain to me quickly what is the meaning of this little whirligig, so delicately wrought that it might be a plaything for Queen Mab. See; I will put it in motion."

"Hold," exclaimed Owen, "hold!"

Annie had but given the slightest possible touch, with the point of a needle, to the same minute portion of complicated machinery which has been more than once mentioned, when the artist seized her by the wrist with a force that made her scream aloud. She was affrighted at the convulsion of intense rage and anguish that writhed across his features. The next instant he let his head sink upon his hands.

"Go, Annie," murmured he, "I have deceived myself, and must suffer for it. I yearned for sympathy — and thought — and fancied — and dreamed — that you might give it to me. But you lack the talisman, Annie, that should admit you into my secrets. That touch has undone the toil of months, and the thought of a lifetime! It was not your fault, Annie — but you have ruined me!"

Poor Owen Warland! He had indeed erred, yet pardonably; for if any human spirit could have sufficiently reverenced the processes so sacred in his eyes, it must have been a woman's. Even Annie Hovenden, possibly, might not have disappointed him, had she been enlightened by the deep intelligence of love.

The artist spent the ensuing winter in a way that satisfied any persons, who had hitherto retained a hopeful opinion of him, that he was, in truth, irrevocably doomed to inutility as regarded the world, and to an evil destiny on his own part. The decease of a relative had put him in possession of a small inheritance. Thus freed from the necessity of toil, and having lost the steadfast influence of a great purpose — great, at least to him — he abandoned himself to habits from which, it might have been supposed, the mere delicacy of his organization would have availed to secure him. But when the ethereal portion of a man of genius is obscured, the earthly part assumes an influence the more uncontrollable, because the character is now thrown off the balance to which Providence had so nicely adjusted it, and which, in coarser natures, is adjusted by some other method. Owen Warland made proof of whatever show of bliss may be found in riot. He looked at the world through the golden medium of wine, and contemplated the visions that bubble up so gaily around the brim of the glass, and that people the air with shapes of pleasant madness, which so soon grow ghostly and forlorn. Even when this dismal and inevitable change had taken place, the young man might still have continued to quaff the cup of enchantments, though its vapor did but shroud life in gloom, and fill the gloom with spectres that mocked at him. There was a certain irksomeness of spirit, which, being real, and the deepest sensation of which the artist was now conscious, was more intolerable than any fantastic miseries and horrors that the abuse of wine could summon up. In the latter case, he could remember, even out of the midst of his trouble, that all was but a delusion; in the former, the heavy anguish was his actual life.

From this perilous state, he was redeemed by an incident which more than one person witnessed, but of which the shrewdest could not explain nor conjecture the operation on Owen Warland's mind. It was very simple. On a warm afternoon of spring, as the artist sat among his riotous companions, with a glass of wine before him, a splendid butterfly flew in at the open window, and fluttered about his head.

"Ah!" exclaimed Owen, who had drank freely. "Are you alive again, child of the sun, and playmate of the summer breeze, after your dismal winter's nap! Then it is time for me to be at work!"

And leaving his unemptied glass upon the table, he departed, and was never known to sip another drop of wine.

And now, again, he resumed his wanderings in the woods and fields. It might be fancied that the bright butterfly, which had come so spiritlike into the window, as Owen sat with the rude revellers, was indeed a spirit, commissioned to recall him to the pure, ideal life that had so etherealized him among men. It might be fancied, that he went forth to seek this spirit, in its sunny haunts; for still, as in the summer-time gone by, he was seen to steal gently up, wherever a butterfly had alighted, and lose himself in contemplation of it. When it took flight, his eyes followed the winged vision, as if its airy track would show the path to heaven. But what could be the purpose of the unseasonable toil, which was again resumed, as the watchman knew by the lines of lamp-light through the crevices of Owen Warland's shutters? The townspeople had one comprehensive explanation of all these singularities. Owen Warland had gone mad! How universally efficacious — how satisfactory, too, and soothing to the injured sensibility of narrowness and dullness — is this easy method of accounting for whatever lies beyond the world's most ordinary scope! From Saint Paul's days, down to our poor little Artist of the Beautiful, the same talisman has been applied to the elucidation of all mysteries in the words or deeds of men, who spoke or acted too wisely or too well. In Owen Warland's case, the judgment of his townspeople may have been correct. Perhaps he was mad. The lack of sympathy — that contrast between himself and his neighbors, which took away the restraint of example — was enough to make him so. Or, possibly, he had caught just so much of ethereal radiance as served to bewilder him, in an earthly sense, by its intermixture with the common daylight.

One evening, when the artist had returned from a customary ramble, and had just thrown the lustre of his lamp on the delicate piece of work, so often interrupted, but still taken up again, as if his fate were embodied in its mechanism, he was surprised by the entrance of old Peter Hovenden. Owen never met this man without a shrinking of the heart. Of all the world, he was most terrible, by reason of a keen understanding, which saw so distinctly what it did see, and disbelieved so uncompromisingly in what it could not see. On this occasion, the old watchmaker had merely a gracious word or two to say.

"Owen, my lad," said he, "we must see you at my house tomorrow night."

The artist began to mutter some excuse.

"Oh, but it must be so," quoth Peter Hovenden, "for the sake of the days when you were one of the household. What, my boy, don't you know that my daughter Annie is engaged to Robert Danforth? We are making an entertainment, in our humble way, to celebrate the event."

"Ah!" said Owen.

That little monosyllable was all he uttered; its tone seemed cold and unconcerned, to an ear like Peter Hovenden's; and yet there was in it the stifled outcry of the poor artist's heart, which he compressed within him like a man holding down an evil spirit. One slight outbreak, however, imperceptible to the old watchmaker, he allowed himself. Raising the instrument with which he was about to begin his work, he let it fall upon the little system of machinery that had, anew, cost him months of thought and toil. It was shattered by the stroke!

Owen Warland's story would have been no tolerable representation of the troubled life of those who strive to create the Beautiful, if, amid all other thwarting influences, love had not interposed to steal the cunning from his hand. Outwardly, he had been no ardent or enterprising lover; the career of his passion had confined its tumults and vicissitudes so entirely within the artist's imagination, that Annie herself had scarcely more than a woman's intuitive perception of it. But, in Owen's view, it covered the whole field of his life. Forgetful of the time when she had shown herself incapable of any deep response, he had persisted in connecting all his dreams of artistical success with Annie's image; she was the visible shape in which the spiritual power that he worshipped, and on whose altar he hoped to lay a not unworthy offering, was made manifest to him. Of course he had deceived himself; there were no such attributes in Annie Hovenden as his imagination had endowed her with. She, in the aspect which she wore to his inward vision, was as much a creation of his own, as the mysterious piece of mechanism would be were it ever realized. Had he become convinced of his mistake through the medium of successful love; had he won Annie to his bosom, and there beheld her fade from angel into ordinary woman, the disappointment might have driven him back, with concentrated energy, upon his sole remaining object. On the other hand, had he found Annie what he fancied, his lot would have been so rich in beauty, that, out of its mere redundancy, he might have wrought the Beautiful into many a worthier type than he had toiled for. But the guise in which his sorrow came to him, the sense that the angel of his life had been snatched away and given to a rude man of earth and iron, who could neither need nor appreciate her ministrations; this was the very perversity of fate, that makes human existence appear too absurd and contradictory to be the scene of one other hope or one other fear. There was nothing left for Owen Warland but to sit down like a man that had been stunned.

He went through a fit of illness. After his recovery, his small and slender frame assumed an obtuser garniture of flesh than it had ever before worn. His thin cheeks became round; his delicate little hand, so spiritually fashioned to achieve fairy task-work, grew plumper than the hand of a thriving infant. His aspect had a childishness, such as might have induced a stranger to pat him on the head — pausing, however, in the act, to wonder what manner of child was here. It was as if the spirit had gone out of him, leaving the body to flourish in a sort of vegetable existence. Not that Owen Warland was idiotic. He could talk, and not irrationally. Somewhat of a babbler, indeed, did people begin to think him; for he was apt to discourse at wearisome length, of marvels of mechanism that he had read about in books, but which he had learned to consider as absolutely fabulous. Among them he enumerated the Man of Brass, constructed by Albertus Magnus, and the Brazen Head of Friar Bacon; and, coming down to later times, the automata of a little coach and horses, which, it was pretended, had been manufactured for the Dauphin of France; together with an insect that buzzed about the ear like a living fly, and yet was but a contrivance of minute steel springs. There was a story, too, of a duck that waddled, and quacked, and ate; though, had any honest citizen purchased it for dinner, he would have found himself cheated with the mere mechanical apparition of a duck.

"But all these accounts," said Owen Warland, "I am now satisfied, are mere impositions."

Then, in a mysterious way, he would confess that he once thought differently. In his idle and dreamy days, he had considered it possible, in a certain sense, to spiritualize machinery; and to combine with the new species of life and motion, thus produced, a beauty that should attain to the ideal which Nature has proposed to herself, in all her creatures, but has never taken pains to realize. He seemed, however, to retain no very distinct perception either of the process of achieving this object, or of the design itself.

"I have thrown it all aside now," he would say. "It was a dream, such as young men are always mystifying themselves with. Now that I have acquired a little common sense, it makes me laugh to think of it."

Poor, poor, and fallen Owen Warland! These were the symptoms that he had ceased to be an inhabitant of the better sphere that lies unseen around us. He had lost his faith in the invisible, and now prided himself, as such unfortunates invariably do, in the wisdom which rejected much that even his eye could see, and trusted confidently in nothing but what his hand could touch. This is the calamity of men whose spiritual part dies out of them, and leaves the grosser understanding to assimilate them more and more to the things of which alone it can take cognizance. But, in Owen Warland, the spirit was not dead, nor past away; it only slept.

How it awoke again, is not recorded. Perhaps, the torpid slumber was broken by a convulsive pain. Perhaps, as in a former instance, the butterfly came and hovered about his head, and reinspired him — as, indeed, the creature of the sunshine had always a mysterious mission for the artist — reinspired him with the former purpose of his life. Whether it were pain or happiness that thrilled through his veins, his first impulse was to thank Heaven for rendering him again the being of thought, imagination, and keenest sensibility, that he had long ceased to be.

"Now for my task," said he. "Never did I feel such strength for it as now."

Yet, strong as he felt himself, he was incited to toil the more diligently, by an anxiety lest death should surprise him in the midst of his labors. This anxiety, perhaps, is common to all men who set their hearts upon anything so high, in their own view of it, that life becomes of importance only as conditional to its accomplishment. So long as we love life for itself, we seldom dread the losing it. When we desire life for the attainment of an object, we recognize the frailty of its texture. But, side by side with this sense of insecurity, there is a vital faith in our invulnerability to the shaft of death, while engaged in any task that seems assigned by Providence as our proper thing to do, and which the world would have cause to mourn for, should we leave it unaccomplished. Can the philosopher, big with the inspiration of an idea that is to reform mankind, believe that he is to be beckoned from this sensible existence, at the very instant when he is mustering his breath to speak the word of light? Should he perish so, the weary ages may pass away — the world's whole life-sand may fall, drop by drop — before another intellect is prepared to develop the truth that might have been uttered then. But history affords many an example, where the most precious spirit, at any particular epoch manifested in human shape, has gone hence untimely, without space allowed him, so far as mortal judgment could discern, to perform his mission on the earth. The prophet dies; and the man of torpid heart and sluggish brain lives on. The poet leaves his song half sung, or finishes it, beyond the scope of mortal ears, in a celestial choir. The painter — as Allston did — leaves half his conception on the canvas, to sadden us with its imperfect beauty, and goes to picture forth the whole, if it be no irreverence to say so, in the hues of Heaven. But, rather, such incomplete designs of this life will be perfected nowhere. This so frequent abortion of man's dearest projects must be taken as a proof, that the deeds of earth, however etherealized by piety or genius, are without value, except as exercises and manifestations of the spirit. In Heaven, all ordinary thought is higher and more melodious than Milton's song. Then, would he add another verse to any strain that he had left unfinished here?

But to return to Owen Warland. It was his fortune, good or ill, to achieve the purpose of his life. Pass we over a long space of intense thought, yearning effort, minute toil, and wasting anxiety, succeeded by an instant of solitary triumph; let all this be imagined; and then behold the artist, on a winter evening, seeking admittance to Robert Danforth's fireside circle. There he found the Man of Iron, with his massive substance thoroughly warmed and attempered by domestic influences. And there was Annie, too, now transformed into a matron, with much of her husband's plain and sturdy nature, but imbued, as Owen Warland still believed, with a finer grace, that might enable her to be the interpreter between Strength and Beauty. It happened, likewise, that old Peter Hovenden was a guest, this evening, at his daughter's fireside; and it was his well-remembered expression of keen, cold criticism, that first encountered the artist's glance.

"My old friend Owen!" cried Robert Danforth, starting up, and compressing the artist's delicate fingers within a hand that was accustomed to gripe bars of iron. "This is kind and neighborly, to come to us at last! I was afraid your Perpetual Motion had bewildered you out of the remembrance of old times."

"We are glad to see you!" said Annie, while a blush reddened her matronly cheek. "It was not like a friend, to stay from us so long."

"Well, Owen," inquired the old watchmaker, as his first greeting, "how comes on the Beautiful? Have you created it at last?"

The artist did not immediately reply, being startled by the apparition of a young child of strength, that was tumbling about on the carpet; a little personage who had come mysteriously out of the infinite, but with something so sturdy and real in his composition that he seemed moulded out of the densest substance which earth could supply. This hopeful infant crawled towards the new-comer, and setting himself on end — as Robert Danforth expressed the posture — stared at Owen with a look of such sagacious observation, that the mother could not help exchanging a proud glance with her husband. But the artist was disturbed by the child's look, as imagining a resemblance between it and Peter Hovenden's habitual expression. He could have fancied that the old watchmaker was compressed into this baby-shape, and was looking out of those baby-eyes, and repeating — as he now did — the malicious question:

"The Beautiful, Owen! How comes on the Beautiful? Have you succeeded in creating the Beautiful?"

"I have succeeded," replied the artist, with a momentary light of triumph in his eyes, and a smile of sunshine, yet steeped in such depth of thought that it was almost sadness. "Yes, my friends, it is the truth. I have succeeded!"

"Indeed!" cried Annie, a look of maiden mirthfulness peeping out of her face again. "And is it lawful, now, to inquire what the secret is!"

"Surely; it is to disclose it, that I have come," answered Owen Warland. "You shall know, and see, and touch, and possess, the secret! For Annie — if by that name I may still address the friend of my boyish years — Annie, it is for your bridal gift that I have wrought this spiritualized mechanism, this harmony of motion, this Mystery of Beauty! It comes late, indeed; but it is as we go onward in life, when objects begin to lose their freshness of hue, and our souls their delicacy of perception, that the spirit of Beauty is most needed. If — forgive me, Annie — if you know how to value this gift, it can never come too late!"

He produced, as he spoke, what seemed a jewel-box. It was carved richly out of ebony by his own hand, and inlaid with a fanciful tracery of pearl, representing a boy in pursuit of a butterfly, which, elsewhere, had become a winged spirit, and was flying heavenward; while the boy, or youth, had found such efficacy in his strong desire, that he ascended from earth to cloud, and from cloud to celestial atmosphere, to win the Beautiful. This case of ebony the artist opened, and bade Annie place her finger on its edge. She did so, but almost screamed, as a butterfly fluttered forth, and alighting on her finger's tip, sat waving the ample magnificence of its purple and gold-speckled wings, as if in prelude to a flight. It is impossible to express by words the glory, the splendor, the delicate gorgeousness, which were softened into the beauty of this object. Nature's ideal butterfly was here realized in all its perfection; not in the pattern of such faded insects as flit among earthly flowers, but of those which hover across the meads of Paradise, for child-angels and the spirits of departed infants to disport themselves with. The rich down was visible upon its wings; the lustre of its eyes seemed instinct with spirit. The firelight glimmered around this wonder — the candles gleamed upon it — but it glistened apparently by its own radiance, and illuminated the finger and outstretched hand on which it rested, with a white gleam like that of precious stones. In its perfect beauty, the consideration of size was entirely lost. Had its wings overarched the firmament, the mind could not have been more filled or satisfied.

"Beautiful! Beautiful!" exclaimed Annie. "Is it alive? Is it alive?"

"Alive? To be sure it is," answered her husband. "Do you suppose any mortal has skill enough to make a butterfly, — or would put himself to the trouble of making one, when any child may catch a score of them in a summer's afternoon? Alive? Certainly! But this pretty box is undoubtedly of our friend Owen's manufacture; and really it does him credit."

At this moment, the butterfly waved its wings anew, with a motion so absolutely lifelike that Annie was startled, and even awe-stricken; for, in spite of her husband's opinion, she could not satisfy herself whether it was indeed a living creature, or a piece of wondrous mechanism.

"Is it alive?" she repeated, more earnestly than before.

"Judge for yourself," said Owen Warland, who stood gazing in her face with fixed attention.

The butterfly now flung itself upon the air, fluttered round Annie's head, and soared into a distant region of the parlor, still making itself perceptible to sight by the starry gleam in which the motion of its wings enveloped it. The infant on the floor, followed its course with his sagacious little eyes. After flying about the room, it returned, in a spiral curve, and settled again on Annie's finger.

"But is it alive?" exclaimed she again; and the finger, on which the gorgeous mystery had alighted, was so tremulous that the butterfly was forced to balance himself with his wings. "Tell me if it be alive, or whether you created it?"

"Wherefore ask who created it, so it be beautiful?" replied Owen Warland. "Alive? Yes, Annie; it may well be said to possess life, for it absorbed my own being into itself; and in the secret of that butterfly, and in its beauty — which is not merely outward, but deep as its whole system — is represented the intellect, the imagination, the sensibility, the soul, of an Artist of the Beautiful! Yes, I created it. But" — and here his countenance somewhat changed — "this butterfly is not now to me what it was when I beheld it afar off, in the day-dreams of my youth."

"Be it what it may, it is a pretty plaything," said the blacksmith, grinning with childlike delight. "I wonder whether it would condescend to alight on such a great clumsy finger as mine? Hold it hither, Annie!"

By the artist's direction, Annie touched her finger's tip to that of her husband; and, after a momentary delay, the butterfly fluttered from one to the other. It preluded a second flight by a similar, yet not precisely the same waving of wings, as in the first experiment; then, ascending from the blacksmith's stalwart finger, it rose in a gradually enlarging curve to the ceiling, made one wide sweep around the room, and returned with an undulating movement to the point whence it had started.

"Well, that does beat all nature!" cried Robert Danforth, bestowing the heartiest praise that he could find expression for; and, indeed, had he paused there, a man of finer words and nicer perception, could not easily have said more. "That goes beyond me, I confess! But what then? There is more real use in one downright blow of my sledge-hammer, than in the whole five years' labor that our friend Owen has wasted on this butterfly!"

Here the child clapped his hands, and made a great babble of indistinct utterance, apparently demanding that the butterfly should be given him for a plaything.

Owen Warland, meanwhile, glanced sidelong at Annie, to discover whether she sympathized in her husband's estimate of the comparative value of the Beautiful and the Practical. There was, amid all her kindness towards himself, amid all the wonder and admiration with which she contemplated the marvelous work of his hands, and incarnation of his idea, a secret scorn; too secret, perhaps, for her own consciousness, and perceptible only to such intuitive discernment as that of the artist. But Owen, in the latter stages of his pursuit, had risen out of the region in which such a discovery might have been torture. He knew that the world, and Annie as the representative of the world, whatever praise might be bestowed, could never say the fitting word, nor feel the fitting sentiment which should be the perfect recompense of an artist who, symbolizing a lofty moral by a material trifle — converting what was earthly, to spiritual gold — had won the Beautiful into his handiwork. Not at this latest moment, was he to learn that the reward of all high performance must be sought within itself, or sought in vain. There was, however, a view of the matter, which Annie, and her husband, and even Peter Hovenden, might fully have understood, and which would have satisfied them that the toil of years had here been worthily bestowed. Owen Warland might have told them, that this butterfly, this plaything, this bridal-gift of a poor watchmaker to a blacksmith's wife, was, in truth, a gem of art that a monarch would have purchased with honors and abundant wealth, and have treasured it among the jewels of his kingdom, as the most unique and wondrous of them all! But the artist smiled, and kept the secret to himself.

"Father," said Annie, thinking that a word of praise from the old watchmaker might gratify his former apprentice, "do come and admire this pretty butterfly!"

"Let us see," said Peter Hovenden, rising from his chair, with the sneer upon his face that always made people doubt, as he himself did, in everything but a material existence. "Here is my finger for it to alight upon. I shall understand it better when once I have touched it."

But, to the increased astonishment of Annie, when the tip of her father's finger was pressed against that of her husband, on which the butterfly still rested, the insect drooped its wings, and seemed on the point of falling to the floor. Even the bright spots of gold upon its wings and body, unless her eyes deceived her, grew dim, and the glowing purple took a dusky hue, and the starry lustre that gleamed around the blacksmith's hand, became faint, and vanished.

"It is dying! it is dying!" cried Annie, in alarm.

"It has been delicately wrought," said the artist calmly. "As I told you, it has imbibed a spiritual essence — call it magnetism, or what you will. In an atmosphere of doubt and mockery, its exquisite susceptibility suffers torture, as does the soul of him who instilled his own life into it. It has already lost its beauty; in a few moments more, its mechanism would be irreparably injured."

"Take away your hand, father!" entreated Annie, turning pale. "Here is my child; let it rest on his innocent hand. There, perhaps, its life will revive, and its colors grow brighter than ever."

Her father, with an acrid smile, withdrew his finger. The butterfly then appeared to recover the power of voluntary motion; while its hues assumed much of their original lustre, and the gleam of starlight, which was its most ethereal attribute, again formed a halo round about it. At first, when transferred from Robert Danforth's hand to the small finger of the child, this radiance grew so powerful that it positively threw the little fellow's shadow back against the wall. He, meanwhile, extended his plump hand as he had seen his father and mother do, and watched the waving of the insect's wings, with infantine delight. Nevertheless, there was a certain odd expression of sagacity, that made Owen Warland feel as if here were old Peter Hovenden, partially, and but partially, redeemed from his hard scepticism into childish faith.

"How wise the little monkey looks!" whispered Robert Danforth to his wife.

"I never saw such a look on a child's face," answered Annie, admiring her own infant, and with good reason, far more than the artistic butterfly. "The darling knows more of the mystery than we do."

As if the butterfly, like the artist, were conscious of something not entirely congenial in the child's nature, it alternately sparkled and grew dim. At length, it arose from the small hand of the infant with an airy motion, that seemed to bear it upward without an effort; as if the ethereal instincts, with which it master's spirit had endowed it, impelled this fair vision involuntarily to a higher sphere. Had there been no obstruction, it might have soared into the sky, and grown immortal. But its lustre gleamed upon the ceiling; the exquisite texture of its wings brushed against that earthly medium; and a sparkle or two, as of star-dust, floated downward and lay glimmering on the carpet. Then the butterfly came fluttering down, and instead of returning to the infant, was apparently attracted towards the artist's hand.

"Not so, not so!" murmured Owen Warland, as if his handiwork could have understood him. "Thou hast gone forth out of thy master's heart. There is no return for thee!"

With a wavering movement, and emitting a tremulous radiance, the butterfly struggled, as it were, towards the infant, and was about to alight upon his finger. But, while it still hovered in the air, the little Child of Strength, with his grandsire's sharp and shrewd expression in his face, made a snatch at the marvelous insect, and compressed it in his hand. Annie screamed! Old Peter Hovenden burst into a cold and scornful laugh. The blacksmith, by main force, unclosed the infant's hand, and found within the palm a small heap of glittering fragments, whence the Mystery of Beauty had fled for ever. And as for Owen Warland, he looked placidly at what seemed the ruin of his life's labor, and which was yet no ruin. He had caught a far other butterfly than this. When the artist rose high enough to achieve the Beautiful, the symbol by which he made it perceptible to mortal senses became of little value in his eyes, while his spirit possessed itself in the enjoyment of the Reality.

NATHANIEL HAWTHORNE

Rappaccini's Daughter

From the Writings of Aubépine

We do not remember to have seen any translated specimens of the productions of M. de l'Aubépine; a fact the less to be wondered at, as his very name is unknown to many of his own countrymen, as well as to the student of foreign literature. As a writer, he seems to occupy an unfortunate position between the Transcendentalists (who, under one name or another, have their share in all the current literature of the world), and the great body of pen-and-ink men who address the intellect and sympathies of the multitude. If not too refined, at all events too remote, too shadowy and unsubstantial in his modes of development, to suit the taste of the latter class, and yet too popular to satisfy the spiritual or metaphysical requisitions of the former, he must necessarily find himself without an audience; except here and there an individual, or possibly an isolated clique. His writings, to do them justice, are not altogether destitute of fancy and originality; they might have won him greater reputation but for an inveterate love of allegory, which is apt to invest his plots and characters with the aspect of scenery and people in the clouds, and to steal away the human warmth out of his conceptions. His fictions are sometimes historical, sometimes of the present day, and sometimes, so far as can be discovered, have little or no reference either to time or space. In any case, he generally contents himself with a very slight embroidery of outward manners, — the faintest possible counterfeit of real life, — and endeavors to create an interest by some less obvious peculiarity of the subject. Occasionally, a breath of nature, a rain-drop of pathos and tenderness, or a gleam of humor, will find its way into the midst of his fantastic imagery, and make us feel as if, after all, we were yet within the limits of our native earth. We will only add to this very cursory notice, that M. de l'Aubépine's productions, if the reader chance to take them in precisely the proper point of view, may amuse a leisure hour as well as those of a brighter man; if otherwise, they can hardly fail to look excessively like nonsense.

Our author is voluminous; he continues to write and publish with as much praiseworthy and indefatigable prolixity, as if his efforts were crowned with the brilliant success that so justly attends those of Eugene Sue. His first appearance was by a collection of stories, in a long series of volumes, entitled *"Contes deux fois racontées."* The titles of some of his more recent works (we quote from memory) are as follows: — *"Le Voyage Céleste à Chemin de Fer,"* 3 tom. 1838. *"Le nouveau Père Adam et la nouvelle Mère Eve,"* 2 tom. 1839. *"Roderic; ou le Serpent à l'estomac,"* 2 tom. 1840. *"Le Culte du Feu,"* a folio volume of ponderous research into the religion and ritual of the old Persian Ghebers, published in 1841. *"La Soirée du Château en Espagne,"* 1 tom. 8 vo. 1842; and *"L'Artiste du Beau; ou le Papillon Mécanique,"* 5 tom 4to. 1843. Our somewhat wearisome perusal of this startling catalogue of volumes has left behind it a certain personal affection and sympathy, though by no means admiration, for M. de l'Aubépine; and we would fain do the little in our power towards introducing him favorably to the American public. The ensuing tale is a translation of his *"Beatrice; ou la Belle Empoisonneuse,"* recently published in *"La Revue Anti-Aristocratique."* This journal, edited by the Comte de Bearhaven, has, for some years past, led the defence of liberal principles and popular rights, with a faithfulness and ability worthy of all praise.

A young man, named Giovanni Guasconti, came, very long ago, from the more southern region of Italy, to pursue his studies at the University of Padua. Giovanni, who had but a scanty supply of gold ducats in his pockets, took lodgings in a high and gloomy chamber of an old edifice, which looked not unworthy to have been the palace of a Paduan noble, and which, in fact, exhibited over its entrance the armorial bearings of a family long since extinct. The young stranger, who was not unstudied in the great poem of his country, recollected that one of the ancestors of this family, and perhaps an occupant of this very mansion, had been pictured by Dante as a partaker of the immortal agonies of his Inferno. These reminiscences and associations, together with the tendency to heart-break natural to a young man for the first time out of his native sphere, caused Giovanni to sigh heavily, as he looked around the desolate and ill-furnished apartment.

"Holy Virgin, Signor," cried old dame Lisabetta, who, won by the youth's remarkable beauty of person, was kindly endeavoring to give the chamber a habitable air, "what a sigh was that to come out of a young man's heart! Do you find this old mansion gloomy? For the love of heaven, then, put your head out of the window, and you will see as bright sunshine as you have left in Naples."

Guasconti mechanically did as the old woman advised, but could not quite agree with her that the Paduan sunshine was as cheerful as that of southern Italy. Such as it was, however, it fell upon a garden beneath the window, and expended its fostering influences on a variety of plants, which seemed to have been cultivated with exceeding care.

"Does this garden belong to the house?" asked Giovanni.

"Heaven forbid, Signor! — unless it were fruitful of better pot-herbs than any that grow there now," answered old Lisabetta. "No; that garden is cultivated by the own hands of Signor Giacomo Rappaccini, the famous Doctor, who, I warrant him, has been heard of as far as Naples. It is said that he distils these plants into medicines that are as potent as a charm. Oftentimes you may see the Signor Doctor at work, and perchance the Signora his daughter, too, gathering the strange flowers that grow in the garden."

The old woman had now done what she could for the aspect of the chamber, and, commending the young man to the protection of the saints, took her departure.

Giovanni still found no better occupation than to look down into the garden beneath his window. From its appearance, he judged it to be one of those botanic gardens, which were of earlier date in Padua than elsewhere in Italy, or in the world. Or, not improbably, it might once have been the pleasure-place of an opulent family; for there was the ruin of a marble fountain in the centre, sculptured with rare art, but so wofully shattered that it was impossible to trace the original design from the chaos of remaining fragments. The water, however, continued to gush and sparkle into the sunbeams as cheerfully as ever. A little gurgling sound ascended to the young man's window, and made him feel as if the fountain were an immortal spirit, that sung its song unceasingly, and without heeding the vicissitudes around it; while one century embodied it in marble, and another scattered the perishable garniture on the soil. All about the pool into which the water subsided, grew various plants, that seemed to require a plentiful supply of moisture for the nourishment of gigantic leaves, and, in some instances, flowers gorgeously magnificent. There was one shrub in partic- ular, set in a marble vase in the midst of the pool, that bore a profusion of purple blossoms, each of which had the lustre and richness of a gem; and the whole together made a show so resplendent that it seemed enough to illuminate the garden, even had there been no sunshine. Every portion of the soil was peopled with plants and herbs, which, if less beautiful, still bore tokens of assiduous care; as if all had their individual virtues, known to the scientific mind that fostered them. Some were placed in urns, rich with old carving, and others in common garden-pots; some crept serpent-like along the ground, or climbed on high, using whatever means of ascent was offered them. One plant had wreathed itself round a statue of Vertumnus, which was thus quite veiled and shrouded in a drapery of hanging foliage, so happily arranged that it might have served a sculptor for a study.

While Giovanni stood at the window, he heard a rustling behind a screen of leaves, and became aware that a person was at work in the garden. His figure soon emerged into view, and showed itself to be that of no common laborer, but a tall, emaciated, sallow, and sickly-looking man, dressed in a scholar's garb of black. He was beyond the middle term of life, with grey hair, a thin grey beard, and a face singularly marked with intellect and cultivation, but which could never, even in his more youthful days, have expressed much warmth of heart.

Nothing could exceed the intentness with which this scientific gardener examined every shrub which grew in his path; it seemed as if he was looking into their inmost nature, making observations in regard to their creative essence, and discovering why one leaf grew in this shape, and another in that, and wherefore such and such flowers differed among themselves in hue and perfume. Nevertheless, in spite of this deep intelligence on his part, there was no approach to intimacy between himself and these vegetable existences. On the contrary, he avoided their actual touch, or the direct inhaling of their odors, with a caution that impressed Giovanni most disagree- ably; for the man's demeanor was that of one walking among malignant influences, such as savage beasts, or deadly snakes, or evil spirits, which, should he allow them one moment of license, would wreak upon him some terrible fatality. It was strangely frightful to the young man's imagination, to see this air of insecurity in a person cultivating a garden, that most simple and innocent of human toils, and which had been alike the joy and labor of the unfallen parents of the race. Was this garden, then, the Eden of the present world? — and this man, with such a perception of harm in what his own hands caused to grow, was he the Adam?

The distrustful gardener, while plucking away the dead leaves or pruning the too luxuriant growth of the shrubs, defended his hands with a pair of thick gloves. Nor were these his only armor. When, in his walk through the garden, he came to the magnificent plant that hung its purple gems beside the marble fountain, he placed a kind of mask over his mouth and nostrils, as if all this beauty did but conceal a deadlier malice. But finding his task still too dangerous, he drew back, removed the mask, and called loudly, but in the infirm voice of a person affected with inward disease:

"Beatrice! — Beatrice!"

"Here am I, my father! What would you?" cried a rich and youthful voice from the window of the opposite house; a voice as rich as a tropical sunset, and which made Giovanni, though he knew not why, think of deep hues of purple or crimson, and of perfumes heavily delectable. — "Are you in the garden?"

"Yes, Beatrice," answered the gardener, "and I need your help."

Soon there emerged from under a sculptured portal the figure of a young girl, arrayed with as much richness of taste as the most splendid of the flowers, beautiful as the day, and with a bloom so deep and vivid that one shade more would have been too much. She looked redundant with life, health, and energy; all of which attributes were bound down and compressed, as it were, and girdled tensely, in their luxuriance, by her virgin zone. Yet Giovanni's fancy must have grown morbid, while he looked down into the garden; for the impression which the fair stranger made upon him was if here were another flower, the human sister of those vegetable ones, as beautiful as they — more beautiful than the richest of them — but still to be touched only with a glove, nor to be approached without a mask. As Beatrice came down the garden path, it was observable that she handled and inhaled the odor of several of the plants, which her father had most sedulously avoided.

"Here, Beatrice," said the latter, — "see how many needful offices require to be done to our chief treasure. Yet, shattered as I am, my life might pay the penalty of approaching it so closely as circumstances demand. Henceforth, I fear, this plant must be consigned to your sole charge."

"And gladly will I undertake it," cried again the rich tones of the young lady, as she bent towards the magnificent plant, and opened her arms as if to embrace it. "Yes, my sister, my splendor, it shall be Beatrice's task to nurse and serve thee; and thou shalt reward her with thy kisses and perfumed breath, which to her is as the breath of life!"

Then, with all the tenderness in her manner that was so strikingly expressed in her words, she busied herself with such attentions as the plant seemed to require; and Giovanni, at his lofty window, rubbed his eyes, and almost doubted whether it were a girl tending her favorite flower, or one sister performing the duties of affection to another. The scene soon terminated. Whether Doctor Rappaccini had finished his labors in the garden, or that his watchful eye had caught the stranger's face, he now took his daughter's arm and retired. Night was already closing in; oppressive exhalations seemed to proceed from the plants, and steal upward past the open window; and Giovanni, closing the lattice, went to his couch, and dreamed of a rich flower and beautiful girl. Flower and maiden were different and yet the same, and fraught with some strange peril in either shape.

But there is an influence in the light of morning that tends to rectify whatever errors of fancy, or even of judgment, we may have incurred during the sun's decline, or among the shadows of the night, or in the less wholesome glow of moonshine. Giovanni's first movement on starting from sleep, was to throw open the window, and gaze down into the garden which his dreams had made so fertile of mysteries. He was surprised, and a little ashamed, to find how real and matter-of-fact an affair it proved to be, in the first rays of the sun, which gilded the dewdrops that hung upon leaf and blossom, and, while giving a brighter beauty to each rare flower, brought everything within the limits of ordinary experience. The young man re-joiced, that, in the heart of the barren city, he had the privilege of overlooking this spot of lovely and luxuriant vegetation. It would serve, he said to himself, as a symbolic language, to keep him in communion with Nature. Neither the sickly and thought-worn Doctor Giacomo Rappaccini, it is true, nor his brilliant daughter, were now visible; so that Giovanni could not determine how much of the singularity which he attributed to both, was due to their own qualities, and how much to his wonder-working fancy. But he was inclined to take a most rational view of the whole matter.

In the course of the day, he paid his respects to Signor Pietro Baglioni, professor of medicine in the University, a physician of eminent repute, to whom Giovanni had brought a letter of introduction. The Professor was an elderly personage, apparently of genial nature, and habits that might almost be called jovial; he kept the young man to dinner, and made himself very agreeable by the freedom and liveliness of his conversation, especially when warmed by a flask or two of Tuscan wine. Giovanni, conceiving that men of science, inhabitants of the same city, must needs be on familiar terms with one another, took an opportunity to mention the name of Doctor Rappaccini. But the Professor did not respond with so much cordiality as he had anticipated.

"Ill would it become a teacher of the divine art of medicine," said Professor Pietro Baglioni, in answer to a question of Giovanni, "to withhold due and well-considered praise of a physician so eminently skilled as Rappaccini. But, on the other hand, I should answer it but scantily to my conscience, were I to permit a worthy youth like yourself, Signor Giovanni, the son of an ancient friend, to imbibe erroneous ideas respecting a man who might hereafter chance to hold your life and death in his hands. The truth is, our worshipful Doctor Rappaccini has as much science as any member of the faculty — with perhaps one single exception — in Padua, or all Italy. But there are certain grave objections to his professional character."

"And what are they?" asked the young man.

"Has my friend Giovanni any disease of body or heart, that he is so inquisitive about physicians?" said the Professor, with a smile. "But as for Rappaccini, it is said of him — and I, who know the man well, can answer for its truth — that he cares infinitely more for science than for mankind. His patients are interesting to him only as subjects for some new experiment. He would sacrifice human life, his own among the rest, or whatever else was dearest to him, for the sake of adding so much as a grain of mustard-seed to the great heap of his accumulated knowledge."

"Methinks he is an awful man, indeed," remarked Guasconti, mentally recalling the cold and purely intellectual aspect of Rappaccini. "And yet, worshipful Professor, is it not a noble spirit? Are there many men capable of so spiritual a love of science?"

"God forbid," answered the Professor, somewhat testily — "at least, unless they take sounder views of the healing art than those adopted by Rappaccini. It is his theory, that all medicinal virtues are comprised within those substances which we term vegetable poisons. These he cultivates with his own hands, and is said even to have produced new varieties of poison, more horribly deleterious than Nature, without the assistance of this learned person, would ever have plagued the world withal. That the Signor Doctor does less mischief than might be expected, with such dangerous substances, is undeniable. Now and then, it must be owned, he has effected — or seemed to effect — a marvelous cure. But, to tell you my private mind, Signor Giovanni, he should receive little credit for such instances of success — they being probably the work of chance — but should be held strictly accountable for his failures, which may justly be considered his own work."

The youth might have taken Baglioni's opinions with many grains of allowance, had he known that there was a professional warfare of long continuance between him and Doctor Rappaccini, in which the latter was generally thought to have gained the advantage. If the reader be inclined to judge for himself, we refer him to certain black-letter tracts on both sides, preserved in the medical department of the University of Padua.

"I know not, most learned Professor," returned Giovanni, after musing on what had been said of Rappaccini's exclusive zeal for science — "I know not how dearly this physician may love his art; but surely there is one object more dear to him. He has a daughter."

"Aha!" cried the Professor with a laugh. "So now our friend Giovanni's secret is out. You have heard of this daughter, whom all the young men in Padua are wild about, though not half a dozen have ever had the good hap to see her face. I know little of the Signora Beatrice, save that Rappaccini is said to have instructed her deeply in his science, and that, young and beautiful as fame reports her, she is already qualified to fill a professor's chair. Perchance her father destines her for mine! Other absurd rumor there be, not worth talking about, or listening to. So now, Signor Giovanni, drink off your glass of Lacryma."

Guasconti returned to his lodgings somewhat heated with the wine he had quaffed, and which caused his brain to swim with strange fantasies in reference to Doctor Rappaccini and the beautiful Beatrice. On his way, happening to pass by a florist's, he bought a fresh bouquet of flowers.

Ascending to his chamber, he seated himself near the window, but within the shadow thrown by the depth of the wall, so that he could look down into the garden with little risk of being discovered. All beneath his eye was a solitude. The strange plants were basking in the sunshine, and now and then nodding gently to one another, as if in acknowledgment of sympathy and kindred. In the midst, by the shattered fountain, grew the magnificent shrub, with its purple gems clustering all over it; they glowed in the air, and gleamed back again out of the depths of the pool, which thus seemed to overflow with colored radiance from the rich reflection that was steeped in it. At first, as we have said, the garden was a solitude. Soon, however, — as Giovanni had half-hoped, half-feared, would be the case, — a figure appeared beneath the antique sculptured portal, and came down between the rows of plants, inhaling their various perfumes, as if she were one of those beings of old classic fable, that lived upon sweet odors. On again beholding Beatrice, the young man was even startled to perceive how much her beauty exceeded his recollection of it; so brilliant, so vivid was its character, that she glowed amid the sunlight, and, as Giovanni whispered to himself, positively illuminated the more shadowy intervals of the garden path. Her face being now more revealed than on the former occasion, he was struck by its expression of simplicity and sweetness; qualities that had not entered into his idea of her character, and which made him ask anew, what manner of mortal she might be. Nor did he fail again to observe, or imagine, an analogy between the beautiful girl and the gorgeous shrub that hung its gem-like flowers over the fountain; a resemblance which Beatrice seemed to have indulged a fantastic humor in heightening, both by the arrangement of her dress and the selection of its hues.

Approaching the shrub, she threw open her arms, as with a passionate ardor, and drew its branches into an intimate embrace; so intimate, that her features were hidden in its leafy bosom, and her glistening ringlets all intermingled with the flowers.

"Give me thy breath, my sister," exclaimed Beatrice; "for I am faint with common air! And give me this flower of thine, which I separate with gentlest fingers from the stem, and place it close beside my heart."

With these words, the beautiful daughter of Rappaccini plucked one of the richest blossoms of the shrub, and was about to fasten it in her bosom. But now, unless Giovanni's draughts of wine had bewildered his senses, a singular incident occurred. A small orange-colored reptile, of the lizard or chameleon species, chanced to be creeping along the path, just at the feet of Beatrice. It appeared to Giovanni — but, at the distance from which he gazed, he could scarcely have seen anything so minute — it appeared to him, however, that a drop or two of moisture from the broken stem of the flower descended upon the lizard's head. For an instant, the reptile contorted itself violently, and then lay motionless in the sunshine. Beatrice observed this remarkable phenomenon, and crossed herself, sadly, but without surprise; nor did she therefore hesitate to arrange the fatal flower in her bosom. There it blushed, and almost glimmered with the dazzling effect of a precious stone, adding to her dress and aspect the one appropriate charm, which nothing else in the world could have supplied. But Giovanni, out of the shadow of his window, bent forward and shrank back, and murmured and trembled.

"Am I awake? Have I my senses?" said he to himself. "What is this being? — beautiful, shall I call her? — or inexpressibly terrible?"

Beatrice now strayed carelessly through the garden, approaching closer beneath Giovanni's window, so that he was compelled to thrust his head quite out of its concealment in order to gratify the intense and painful curiosity which she excited. At this moment, there came a beautiful insect over the garden wall, it had perhaps wandered through the city and found no flowers nor verdure among those antique haunts of men, until the heavy perfumes of Doctor Rappaccini's shrubs had lured it from afar. Without alighting on the flowers, this winged brightness seemed to be attracted by Beatrice, and lingered in the air and fluttered about her head. Now, here it could not be but that Giovanni Guasconti's eyes deceived him. Be that as it might, he fancied that while Beatrice was gazing at the insect with childish delight, it grew faint and fell at her feet; — its bright wings shivered; it was dead — from no cause that he could discern, unless it were the atmosphere of her breath. Again Beatrice crossed herself and sighed heavily, as she bent over the dead insect.

An impulsive movement of Giovanni drew her eyes to the window. There she beheld the beautiful head of the young man — rather a Grecian than an Italian head, with fair, regular features, and a glistening of gold among his ringlets — gazing down upon her like a being that hovered in midair. Scarcely knowing what he did, Giovanni threw down the bouquet which he had hitherto held in his hand.

"Signora," said he, "there are pure and healthful flowers. Wear them for the sake of Giovanni Guasconti!"

"Thanks, Signor," replied Beatrice, with her rich voice, that came forth as it were like a gush of music; and with a mirthful expression half childish and half woman-like. "I accept your gift, and would fain recompense it with this precious purple flower; but if I toss it into the air, it will not reach you. So Signor Guasconti must even content himself with my thanks."

She lifted the bouquet from the ground, and then as if inwardly ashamed at having stepped aside from her maidenly reserve to respond to a stranger's greeting, passed swiftly homeward through the garden. But, few as the moments were, it seemed to Giovanni when she was on the point of vanishing beneath the sculptured portal, that his beautiful bouquet was already beginning to wither in her grasp. It was an idle thought; there could be no possibility of distinguishing a faded flower from a fresh one at so great a distance.

For many days after this incident, the young man avoided the window that looked into Doctor Rappaccini's garden, as if something ugly and monstrous would have blasted his eyesight, had he been betrayed into a glance. He felt conscious of having put himself, to a certain extent, within the influence of an unintelligible power, by the communication which he had opened with Beatrice. The wisest course would have been, if his heart were in any real danger, to quit his lodgings and Padua itself, at once; the next wiser, to have accustomed himself, as far as possible, to the familiar and daylight view of Beatrice; thus bringing her rigidly and systematically within the limits of ordinary experience. Least of all, while avoiding her sight, ought Giovanni to have remained so near this extraordinary being, that the proximity and possibility even of intercourse, should give a kind of substance and reality to the wild vagaries which his imagination ran riot continually in producing. Guasconti had not a deep heart — or at all events, its depths were not sounded now — but he had a quick fancy, and an ardent southern temperament, which rose every instant to a higher fever-pitch. Whether or no Beatrice possessed those terrible attributes — that fatal breath — the affinity with those so beautiful and deadly flowers — which were indicated by what Giovanni had witnessed, she had at least instilled a fierce and subtle poison into his system. It was not love, although her rich beauty was a madness to him; nor horror, even while he fancied her spirit to be imbued with the same baneful essence that seemed to pervade her physical frame; but a wild off-spring of both love and horror that had each parent in it, and burned like one and shivered like the other. Giovanni knew not what to dread; still less did he know what to hope; yet hope and dread kept a continual warfare in his breast, alternately vanquishing one another and starting up afresh to renew the contest. Blessed are all simple emotions, be they dark or bright! It is the lurid intermixture of the two that produces the illuminating blaze of the infernal regions.

Sometimes he endeavored to assuage the fever of his spirit by a rapid walk through the streets of Padua, or beyond its gates; his footsteps kept time with the throbbings of his brain, so that the walk was apt to accelerate itself to a race. One day, he found himself arrested; his arm was seized by a portly personage who had turned back on recognizing the young man, and expended much breath in overtaking him.

"Signor Giovanni! — stay, my young friend!" cried he. "Have you forgotten me? That might well be the case, if I were as much altered as yourself."

It was Baglioni, whom Giovanni had avoided, ever since their first meeting, from a doubt that the Professor's sagacity would look too deeply into his secrets. Endeavoring to recover himself, he stared forth wildly from his inner world into the outer one, and spoke like a man in a dream:

"Yes; I am Giovanni Guasconti. You are Professor Pietro Baglioni. Now let me pass!"

"Not yet — not yet, Signor Giovanni Guasconti," said the Professor, smiling, but at the same time scrutinizing the youth with an earnest glance. — "What; did I grow up side by side with your father, and shall his son pass me like a stranger, in these old streets of Padua? Stand still, Signor Giovanni; for we must have a word or two, before we part."

"Speedily, then, most worshipful Professor, speedily!" said Giovanni, with feverish impatience. "Does not your worship see that I am in haste?"

Now, while he was speaking, there came a man in black along the street, stooping and moving feebly, like a person in inferior health. His face was all overspread with a most sickly and sallow hue, but yet so pervaded with an expression of piercing and active intellect, that an observer might easily have overlooked the merely physical attributes, and have seen only this wonderful energy. As he passed, this person exchanged a cold and distant salutation with Baglioni, but fixed his eyes upon Giovanni with an intentness that seemed to bring out whatever was within him worthy of notice. Nevertheless, there was a peculiar quietness in the look, as if taking merely a speculative, not a human, interest in the young man.

"It is Doctor Rappaccini!" whispered the Professor, when the stranger had passed. — "Has he ever seen your face before?"

"Not that I know," answered Giovanni, starting at the name.

"He *has* seen you! — he must have seen you!" said Baglioni, hastily. "For some purpose or other, this man of science is making a study of you. I know that look of his! It is the same that coldly illuminates his face, as he bends over a bird, a mouse, or a butterfly, which, in pursuance of some experiment, he has killed by the perfume of a flower; — a look as deep as Nature itself, but without Nature's warmth of love. Signor Giovanni, I will stake my life upon it, you are the subject of one of Rappaccini's experiments!"

"Will you make a fool of me?" cried Giovanni, passionately. "*That,* Signor Professor, were an untoward experiment."

"Patience, patience!" replied the imperturbable Professor. "I tell thee, my poor Giovanni, that Rappaccini has a scientific interest in thee. Thou hast fallen into fearful hands! And the Signora Beatrice? What part does she act in this mystery?"

But Guasconti, finding Baglioni's pertinacity intolerable, here broke away, and was gone before the Professor could again seize his arm. He looked after the young man intently, and shook his head.

"This must not be," said Baglioni to himself. "The youth is the son of my old friend, and shall not come to any harm from which the arcana of medical science can preserve him. Besides, it is too insufferable an impertinence in Rappaccini, thus to snatch the lad out of my own hands, as I may say, and make use of him for his infernal experiments. This daughter of his! It shall be looked to. Perchance, most learned Rappaccini, I may foil you where you little dream of it!"

Meanwhile, Giovanni had pursued a circuitous route, and at length found himself at the door of his lodgings. As he crossed the threshold, he was met by old Lisabetta, who smirked and smiled, and was evidently desirous to attract his attention; vainly, however, as the ebullition of his feelings had momentarily subsided into a cold and dull vacuity. He turned his eyes full upon the withered face that was puckering itself into a smile, but seemed to behold it not. The old dame, therefore, laid her grasp upon his cloak.

"Signor! — Signor!" whispered she, still with a smile over the whole breadth of her visage, so that it looked not unlike a grotesque carving in wood, darkened by centuries — "Listen, Signor! There is a private entrance into the garden!"

"What do you say?" exclaimed Giovanni, turning quickly about, as if an inanimate thing should start into feverish life. — "A private entrance into Doctor Rappaccini's garden!"

"Hush! hush! — not so loud!" whispered Lisabetta, putting her hand over his mouth. "Yes; into the worshipful Doctor's garden, where you may see all his fine shrubbery. Many a young man in Padua would give gold to be admitted among those flowers."

Giovanni put a piece of gold into her hand.

"Show me the way," said he.

A surmise, probably excited by his conversation with Baglioni, crossed his mind, that this interposition of old Lisabetta might perchance be connected with the intrigue, whatever were its nature, in which the Professor seemed to suppose that Doctor Rappaccini was involving him. But such a suspicion, though it disturbed Giovanni, was inadequate to restrain him. The instant that he was aware of the possibility of approaching Beatrice, it seemed an absolute necessity of his existence to do so. It mattered not whether she were angel or demon; he was irrevocably within her sphere, and must obey the law that whirled him onward, in ever lessening circles, towards a result which he did not attempt to foreshadow. And yet, strange to say, there came across him a sudden doubt, whether this intense interest on his part were not delusory — whether it were really of so deep and positive a nature as to justify him in now thrusting himself into an incalculable position — whether it were not merely the fantasy of a young man's brain, only slightly, or not at all, connected with his heart!

He paused — hesitated — turned half about — but again went on. His withered guide led him along several obscure passages, and finally undid a door, through which, as it was opened, there came the sight and sound of rustling leaves, with the broken sunshine glimmering among them. Giovanni stepped forth, and forcing himself through the entanglement of a shrub that wreathed its tendrils over the hidden entrance, he stood beneath his own window, in the open area of Doctor Rappaccini's garden.

How often is it the case, that, when impossibilities have come to pass, and dreams have condensed their misty substance into tangible realities, we find ourselves calm, and even coldly self-possessed, amid circumstances which it would have been a delirium of joy or agony to anticipate! Fate delights to thwart us thus. Passion will choose his own time to rush upon the scene, and lingers sluggishly behind, when an appropriate adjustment of events would seem to summon his appearance. So was it now with Giovanni. Day after day, his pulses had throbbed with feverish blood, at the improbable idea of an interview with Beatrice, and of standing with her, face to face, in this very garden, basking in the Oriental sunshine of her beauty, and snatching from her full gaze the mystery which he deemed the riddle of his own existence. But now there was a singular and untimely equanimity within his breast. He threw a glance around the garden to discover if Beatrice or her father were present, and perceiving that he was alone, began a critical observation of the plants.

The aspect of one and all of them dissatisfied him; their gorgeousness seemed fierce, passionate, and even unnatural. There was hardly an individual shrub which a wanderer, straying by himself through a forest, would not have been startled to find growing wild, as if an unearthly face had glared at him out of the thicket. Several, also, would have shocked a delicate instinct by an appearance of artificialness, indicating that there had been such commixture, and, as it were, adultery of various vegetable species, that the production was no longer of God's making, but the monstrous offspring of man's depraved fancy, glowing with only an evil mockery of beauty. They were probably the result of experiment, which, in one or two cases, had succeeded in mingling plants individually lovely into a compound possessing the questionable and ominous character that distinguished the whole growth of the garden. In fine, Giovanni recognized but two or three plants in the collection, and those of a kind that he well knew to be poisonous. While busy with these contemplations, he heard the rustling of a silken garment, and turning, beheld Beatrice emerging from beneath the sculptured portal.

Giovanni had not considered with himself what should be his deportment; whether he should apologize for his intrusion into the garden, or assume that he was there with the privity, at least, if not by the desire, of Doctor Rappaccini or his daughter. But Beatrice's manner placed him at his ease, though leaving him still in doubt by what agency he had gained admittance. She came lightly along the path, and met him near the broken fountain. There was surprise in her face, but brightened by a simple and kind expression of pleasure.

"You are a connoisseur in flowers, Signor," said Beatrice with a smile, alluding to the bouquet which he had flung her from the window. "It is no marvel, therefore, if the sight of my father's rare collection has tempted you to take a nearer view. If he were here, he could tell you many strange and interesting facts as to the nature and habits of these shrubs, for he has spent a lifetime in such studies, and this garden is his world."

"And yourself, lady" — observed Giovanni — "if fame says true — you, likewise, are deeply skilled in the virtues indicated by these rich blossoms, and these spicy perfumes. Would you deign to be my instructress, I should prove an apter scholar than if taught by Signor Rappaccini himself."

"Are there such idle rumors?" asked Beatrice, with the music of a pleasant laugh. "Do people say that I am skilled in my father's science of plants? What a jest is there! No; though I have grown up among these flowers, I know no more of them than their hues and perfume; and sometimes, methinks I would fain rid myself of even that small knowledge. There are many flowers here, and those not the least brilliant, that shock and offend me, when they meet my eye. But, pray, Signor, do not believe these stories about my science. Believe nothing of me save what you see with your own eyes."

"And must I believe all that I have seen with my own eyes?" asked Giovanni pointedly, while the recollection of former scenes made him shrink. "No, Signora, you demand too little of me. Bid me believe nothing, save what comes from your own lips."

It would appear that Beatrice understood him. There came a deep flush to her cheek; but she looked full into Giovanni's eyes, and responded to his gaze of uneasy suspicion with a queen-like haughtiness.

"I do so bid you, Signor!" she replied. "Forget whatever you may have fancied in regard to me. If true to the outward senses, still it may be false in its essence. But the words of Beatrice Rappaccini's lips are true from the depths of the heart outward. Those you may believe!"

A fervor glowed in her whole aspect, and beamed upon Giovanni's consciousness like the light of truth itself. But while she spoke, there was a fragrance in the atmosphere around her, rich and delightful, though evanescent, yet which the young man, from an indefinable reluctance, scarcely dared to draw into his lungs. It might be the odor of the flowers. Could it be Beatrice's breath, which thus embalmed her words with a strange richness, as if by steeping them in her heart? A faintness passed like a shadow over Giovanni, and flitted away; he seemed to gaze through the beautiful girl's eyes into her transparent soul, and felt no more doubt or fear.

The tinge of passion that had colored Beatrice's manner vanished; she became gay, and appeared to derive a pure delight from her communion with the youth, not unlike what the maiden of a lonely island might have felt, conversing with a voyager from the civilized world. Evidently her experience of life had been confined within the limits of that garden. She talked now about matters as simple as the daylight or summer-clouds, and now asked questions in reference to the city, or Giovanni's distant home, his friends, his mother, and his sisters; questions indicating such seclusion, and such lack of familiarity with modes and forms, that Giovanni responded as if to an infant. Her spirit gushed out before him like a fresh rill, that was just catching its first glimpse of the sunlight, and wondering at the reflections of earth and sky which were flung into its bosom. There came thoughts, too, from a deep source, and fantasies of a gem-like brilliancy, as if diamonds and rubies sparkled upward among the bubbles of the fountain. Ever and anon, there gleamed across the young man's mind a sense of wonder, that he should be walking side by side with the being who had so wrought upon his imagination — whom he had idealized in such hues of terror — in whom he had positively witnessed such manifestations of dreadful attributes — that he should be conversing with Beatrice like a brother, and should find her so human and so maiden-like. But such reflections were only momentary; the effect of her character was too real, not to make itself familiar at once.

In this free intercourse, they had strayed through the garden, and now, after many turns among its avenues, were come to the shattered fountain, beside which grew the magnificent shrub with its treasury of glowing blossoms. A fragrance was diffused from it, which Giovanni recognized as identical with that which he had attributed to Beatrice's breath, but incomparably more powerful. As her eyes fell upon it, Giovanni beheld her press her hand to her bosom, as if her heart were throbbing suddenly and painfully.

"For the first time in my life," murmured she, addressing the shrub, "I had forgotten thee!"

"I remember, Signora," said Giovanni, "that you once promised to reward me with one of these living gems for the bouquet, which I had the happy boldness to fling to your feet. Permit me now to pluck it as a memorial of this interview."

He made a step toward the shrub, with extended hand. But Beatrice darted forward, uttering a shriek that went through his heart like a dagger. She caught his hand, and drew it back with the whole force of her slender figure. Giovanni felt her touch thrilling through his fibres.

"Touch it not!" exclaimed she, in a voice of agony. "Not for thy life! It is fatal!"

Then, hiding her face, she fled from him, and vanished beneath the sculptured portal. As Giovanni followed her with his eyes, he beheld the emaciated figure and pale intelligence of Doctor Rappaccini, who had been watching the scene, he knew not how long, within the shadow of the entrance.

No sooner was Guasconti alone in his chamber, than the image of Beatrice came back to his passionate musings, invested with all the witchery that had been gathering around it ever since his first glimpse of her, and now likewise imbued with a tender warmth of girlish womanhood. She was human; her nature was endowed with all gentle and feminine qualities; she was worthiest to be worshipped; she was capable, surely, on her part, of the height and heroism of love. Those tokens, which he had hitherto considered as proofs of a frightful peculiarity in her physical and moral system, were now either forgotten, or, by the subtle sophistry of passion, transmuted into a golden crown of enchantment, rendering Beatrice the more admirable, by so much as she was the more unique. Whatever had looked ugly, was now beautiful; or, if incapable of such a change, it stole away and hid itself among those shapeless half-ideas, which throng the dim region beyond the daylight of our perfect consciousness. Thus did he spend the night, nor fell asleep, until the dawn had begun to awake the slumbering flowers in Doctor Rappaccini's garden, whither Giovanni's dreams doubtless led him. Up rose the sun in his due season, and flinging his beams upon the young man's eyelids, awoke him to a sense of pain. When thoroughly aroused, he became sensible of a burning and tingling agony in his hand — in his right hand — the very hand which Beatrice had grasped in her own, when he was on the point of plucking one of the gem-like flowers. On the back of that hand there was now a purple print, like that of four small fingers, and the likeness of a slender thumb upon his wrist.

Oh, how stubbornly does love — or even that cunning semblance of love which flourishes in the imagination, but strikes no depth of root into the heart — how stubbornly does it hold its faith, until the moment come, when it is doomed to vanish into thin mist! Giovanni wrapt a handkerchief about his hand, and wondered what evil thing had stung him, and soon forgot his pain in a reverie of Beatrice.

After the first interview, a second was in the inevitable course of what we call fate. A third; a fourth; and a meeting with Beatrice in the garden was no longer an incident in Giovanni's daily life, but the whole space in which he might be said to live; for the anticipation and memory of that ecstatic hour made up the remainder. Nor was it otherwise with the daughter of Rappaccini. She watched for the youth's appearance, and flew to his side with confidence as unreserved as if they had been playmates from early infancy — as if they were such playmates still. If, by any unwonted chance, he failed to come at the appointed moment, she stood beneath the window, and sent up the rich sweetness of her tones to float around him in his chamber, and echo and reverberate throughout his heart — "Giovanni! Giovanni! Why tarriest thou? Come down!" — And down he hastened into that Eden of poisonous flowers.

But, with all this intimate familiarity, there was still a reserve in Beatrice's demeanor, so rigidly and invariably sustained, that the idea of infringing it scarcely occurred to his imagination. By all appreciable signs, they loved; they had looked love, with eyes that conveyed the holy secret from the depths of one soul into the depths of the other, as if it were too sacred to be whispered by the way; they had even spoken love, in those gushes of passion when their spirits darted forth in articulated breath, like tongues of long-hidden flame; and yet there had been no seal of lips, no clasp of hands, nor any slightest caress, such as love claims and hallows. He had never touched one of the gleaming ringlets of her hair; her garment — so marked was the physical barrier between them — had never been waved against him by a breeze. On the few occasions when Giovanni had seemed tempted to overstep the limit, Beatrice grew so sad, so stern, and withal wore such a look of desolate separation, shuddering at itself, that not a spoken word was requisite to repel him. At such times, he was startled at the horrible suspicions that rose, monster-like, out of the caverns of his heart, and stared him in the face; his love grew thin and faint as the morning-mist; his doubts alone had substance. But when Beatrice's face brightened again, after the momentary shadow, she was transformed at once from the mysterious, questionable being, whom he had watched with so much awe and horror; she was now the beautiful and unsophisticated girl, whom he felt that his spirit knew with a certainty beyond all other knowledge.

A considerable time had now passed since Giovanni's last meeting with Baglioni. One morning, however, he was disagreeably surprised by a visit from the Professor, whom he had scarcely thought of for whole weeks, and would willingly have forgotten still longer. Given up, as he had long been, to a pervading excitement, he could tolerate no companions, except upon condition of their perfect sympathy with his present state of feeling. Such sympathy was not to be expected from Professor Baglioni.

The visitor chatted carelessly, for a few moments, about the gossip of the city and the University, and then took up another topic.

"I have been reading an old classic author lately," said he, "and met with a story that strangely interested me. Possibly you may remember it. It is of an Indian prince, who sent a beautiful woman as a present to Alexander the Great. She was as lovely as the dawn, and gorgeous as the sunset; but what especially distinguished her was a certain rich perfume in her breath — richer than a garden of Persian roses. Alexander, as was natural to a youthful conqueror, fell in love at first sight with this magnificent stranger. But a certain sage physician, happening to be present, discovered a terrible secret in regard to her."

"And what was that?" asked Giovanni, turning his eyes downward to avoid those of the Professor.

"That this lovely woman," continued Baglioni, with emphasis, "had been nourished with poisons from her birth upward, until her whole nature was so imbued with them, that she herself had become the deadliest poison in existence. Poison was her element of life. With that rich perfume of her breath, she blasted the very air. Her love would have been poison! — her embrace death! Is not this a marvelous tale?"

"A childish fable," answered Giovanni, nervously starting from his chair. "I marvel how your worship finds time to read such nonsense, among your graver studies."

"By the bye," said the Professor, looking uneasily about him, "what singular fragrance is this in your apartment? Is it the perfume of your gloves? It is faint, but delicious, and yet, after all, by no means agreeable. Were I to breathe it long, methinks it would make me ill. It is like the breath of a flower — but I see no flowers in the chamber."

"Nor are there any," replied Giovanni, who had turned pale as the Professor spoke; "nor, I think, is there any fragrance, except in your worship's imagination. Odors, being a sort of element combined of the sensual and the spiritual, are apt to deceive us in this manner. The recollection of a perfume — the bare idea of it — may easily be mistaken for present reality."

"Aye; but my sober imagination does not often play such tricks," said Baglioni; "and were I to fancy any kind of odor, it would be that of some vile apothecary drug, wherewith my fingers are likely enough to be imbued. Our worshipful friend Rappaccini, as I have heard, tinctures his medicaments with odors richer than those of Araby. Doubtless, likewise, the fair and learned Signora Beatrice would minister to her patients with draughts as sweet as a maiden's breath. But wo to him that sips them!"

Giovanni's face evinced many contending emotions. The tone in which the Professor alluded to the pure and lovely daughter of Rappaccini was a torture to his soul; and yet, the intimation of a view of her character, opposite to his own, gave instantaneous distinctness to a thousand dim suspicions, which now grinned at him like so many demons. But he strove hard to quell them, and to respond to Baglioni with a true lover's perfect faith.

"Signor Professor," said he, "you were my father's friend — perchance, too, it is your purpose to act a friendly part towards his son. I would fain feel nothing towards you, save respect and deference. But I pray you to observe, Signor, that there is one subject on which we must not speak. You know not the Signora Beatrice. You cannot, therefore, estimate the wrong — the blasphemy, I may even say — that is offered to her character by a light or injurious word."

"Giovanni! — my poor Giovanni!" answered the Professor, with a calm expression of pity. "I know this wretched girl far better than yourself. You shall hear the truth in respect to the poisoner Rappaccini, and his poisonous daughter. Yes; poisonous as she is beautiful! Listen; for even should you do violence to my grey hairs, it shall not silence me. That old fable of the Indian woman has become a truth, by the deep and deadly science of Rappaccini, and in the person of the lovely Beatrice!"

Giovanni groaned and hid his face.

"Her father," continued Baglioni, "was not restrained by natural affection from offering up his child, in this horrible manner, as the victim of his insane zeal for science. For — let us do him justice — he is as true a man of science as ever distilled his own heart in an alembic. What, then, will be your fate? Beyond a doubt, you are selected as the material of some new experiment. Perhaps the result is to be death — perhaps a fate more awful still! Rappaccini, with what he calls the interest of science before his eyes, will hesitate at nothing."

"It is a dream!" muttered Giovanni to himself, "surely it is a dream!"

"But," resumed the Professor, "be of good cheer, son of my friend! It is not yet too late for the rescue. Possibly, we may even succeed in bringing back this miserable child within the limits of ordinary nature, from which her father's madness has estranged her. Behold this little silver vase! It was wrought by the hands of the renowned Benvenuto Cellini, and is well worthy to be a love-gift to the fairest dame in Italy. But its contents are invaluable. One little sip of this antidote would have rendered the most virulent poisons of the Borgias innocuous. Doubt not that it will be as efficacious against those of Rappaccini. Bestow the vase, and the precious liquid within it, on your Beatrice, and hopefully await the result."

Baglioni laid a small, exquisitely wrought silver phial on the table, and withdrew, leaving what he had said to produce its effect upon the young man's mind.

"We will thwart Rappaccini yet!" thought he, chuckling to himself, as he descended the stairs. "But, let us confess the truth of him, he is a wonderful man! — a wonderful man indeed! A vile empiric, however, in his practice, and therefore not to be tolerated by those who respect the good old rules of the medical profession!"

Throughout Giovanni's whole acquaintance with Beatrice, he had occasionally, as we have said, been haunted by dark surmises as to her character. Yet, so thoroughly had she made herself felt by him as a simple, natural, most affectionate and guileless creature, that the image now held up by Professor Baglioni, looked as strange and incredible, as if it were not in accordance with his own original conception. True, there were ugly recollections connected with his first glimpses of the beautiful girl; he could not quite forget the bouquet that withered in her grasp, and the insect that perished amid the sunny air, by no ostensible agency, save the fragrance of her breath. These incidents, however, dissolving in the pure light of her character, had no longer the efficacy of facts, but were acknowledged as mistaken fantasies, by whatever testimony of the senses they might appear to be substantiated. There is something truer and more real, than what we can see with the eyes, and touch with the finger. On such better evidence, had Giovanni founded his confidence in Beatrice, though rather by the necessary force of her high attributes, than by any deep and generous faith, on his part. But, now, his spirit was incapable of sustaining itself at the height to which the early enthusiasm of passion had exalted it; he fell down, grovelling among earthly doubts, and defiled therewith the pure whiteness of Beatrice's image. Not that he gave her up; he did but distrust. He resolved to institute some decisive test that should satisfy him, once for all, whether there were those dreadful peculiarities in her physical nature, which could not be supposed to exist without some corresponding monstrosity of soul. His eyes, gazing down afar, might have deceived him as to the lizard, the insect, and the flowers. But if he could witness, at the distance of a few paces, the sudden blight of one fresh and healthful flower in Beatrice's hand, there would be room for no further question. With this idea, he hastened to the florist's, and purchased a bouquet that was still gemmed with the morning dewdrops.

It was now the customary hour of his daily interview with Beatrice. Before descending into the garden, Giovanni failed not to look at his figure in the mirror; a vanity to be expected in a beautiful young man, yet, as displaying itself at that troubled and feverish moment, the token of a certain shallowness of feeling and insincerity of character. He did gaze, however, and said to himself, that his features had never before possessed so rich a grace, nor his eyes such vivacity, nor his cheeks so warm a hue of superabundant life.

"At least," thought he, "her poison has not yet insinuated itself into my system. I am no flower to perish in her grasp!"

With that thought, he turned his eyes on the bouquet, which he had never once laid aside from his hand. A thrill of indefinable horror shot through his frame, on perceiving that those dewy flowers were already beginning to droop; they wore the aspect of things that had been fresh and lovely, yesterday. Giovanni grew white as marble, and stood motionless before the mirror, staring at his own reflection there, as at the likeness of something frightful. He remembered Baglioni's remark about the fragrance that seemed to pervade the chamber. It must have been the poison in his breath! Then he shuddered — shuddered at himself! Recovering from his stupor, he began to watch, with curious eye, a spider that was busily at work, hanging its web from the antique cornice of the apartment, crossing and re-crossing the artful system of interwoven lines, as vigorous and active a spider as ever dangled from an old ceiling. Giovanni bent towards the insect, and emitted a deep, long breath. The spider suddenly ceased its toil; the web vibrated with a tremor originating in the body of the small artizan. Again Giovanni sent forth a breath, deeper, longer, and imbued with a venomous feeling out of his heart; he knew not whether he were wicked or only desperate. The spider made a convulsive gripe with his limbs, and hung dead across the window.

"Accursed! Accursed!" muttered Giovanni, addressing himself. "Hast thou grown so poisonous, that this deadly insect perishes by thy breath?"

At that moment, a rich, sweet voice came floating up from the garden: —

"Giovanni! Giovanni! It is past the hour! Why tarriest thou! Come down!"

"Yes," muttered Giovanni again. "She is the only being whom my breath may not slay! Would that it might!"

He rushed down, and in an instant, was standing before the bright and loving eyes of Beatrice. A moment ago, his wrath and despair had been so fierce that he could have desired nothing so much as to wither her by a glance. But, with her actual presence, there came influences which had too real an existence to be at once shaken off; recollections of many a holy and passionate outgush of her heart, when the pure fountain had been unsealed from its depths, and made visible in its transparency to his mental eye; recollections which, had Giovanni known how to estimate them, would have assured him that all this ugly mystery was but an earthly illusion, and that, whatever mist of evil might seem to have gathered over her, the real Beatrice was a heavenly angel. Incapable as he was of such high faith, still her presence had not utterly lost its magic. Giovanni's rage was quelled into an aspect of sullen insensibility. Beatrice, with a quick spiritual sense, immediately felt that there was a gulf of blackness between them, which neither he nor she could pass. They walked on together, sad and silent, and came thus to the marble fountain, and to its pool of water on the ground, in the midst of which grew the shrub that bore gem-like blossoms. Giovanni was affrighted at the eager enjoyment — the appetite, as it were — with which he found himself inhaling the fragrance of the flowers.

"Beatrice," asked he abruptly, "whence came this shrub?"

"My father created it," answered she, with simplicity.

"Created it! created it!" repeated Giovanni. "What mean you, Beatrice?"

"He is a man fearfully acquainted with the secrets of nature," replied Beatrice; "and, at the hour when I first drew breath, this plant sprang from the soil, the offspring of his science, of his intellect, while I was but his earthly child. Approach it not!" continued she, observing with terror that Giovanni was drawing nearer to the shrub. "It has qualities that you little dream of. But I, dearest Giovanni, — I grew up and blossomed with the plant, and was nourished with its breath. It was my sister, and I loved it with a human affection: for — alas! hast thou not suspected it? there was an awful doom."

Here Giovanni frowned so darkly upon her that Beatrice paused and trembled. But her faith in his tenderness reassured her, and made her blush that she had doubted for an instant.

"There was an awful doom," she continued. — "the effect of my father's fatal love of science — which estranged me from all society of my kind. Until Heaven sent thee, dearest Giovanni, Oh! how lonely was thy poor Beatrice!"

"Was it a hard doom?" asked Giovanni, fixing his eyes upon her.

"Only of late have I known how hard it was," answered she tenderly. "Oh, yes; but my heart was torpid, and therefore quiet."

Giovanni's rage broke forth from his sullen gloom like a lightning-flash out of a dark cloud.

"Accursed one!" cried he, with venomous scorn and anger. "And finding thy solitude wearisome, thou hast severed me, likewise, from all the warmth of life, and enticed me into thy region of unspeakable horror!"

"Giovanni!" exclaimed Beatrice, turning her large bright eyes upon his face. The force of his words had not found its way into her mind; she was merely thunder-struck.

"Yes, poisonous thing!" repeated Giovanni, beside himself with passion. "Thou hast done it! Thou hast blasted me! Thou has filled my veins with poison! Thou hast made me as hateful, as ugly, as loathsome and deadly a creature as thyself, — a world's wonder of hideous monstrosity! Now — if our breath be happily as fatal to ourselves as to all others — let us join our lips in one kiss of unutterable hatred, and so die!"

"What has befallen me?" murmured Beatrice, with a low moan out of her heart. "Holy Virgin pity me, a poor heartbroken child!"

"Thou! Dost thou pray?" cried Giovanni, still with the same fiendish scorn. "Thy very prayers, as they come from thy lips, taint the atmosphere with death. Yes, yes; let us pray! Let us to church, and dip our fingers in the holy water at the portal! They that come after us will perish as by a pestilence. Let us sign crosses in the air! It will be scattering curses abroad in the likeness of holy symbols!"

"Giovanni," said Beatrice calmly, for her grief was beyond passion, "why dost thou join thyself with me thus in those terrible words? I, it is true, am the horrible thing thou namest me. But thou! — what hast thou to do, save with one other shudder at my hideous misery, to go forth out of the garden and mingle with thy race, and forget that there ever crawled on earth such a monster as poor Beatrice?"

"Dost thou pretend ignorance?" asked Giovanni, scowling upon her. "Behold! This power have I gained from the pure daughter of Rappaccini!"

There was a swarm of summer-insects flitting through the air, in search of the food promised by the flower-odors of the fatal garden. They circled round Giovanni's head, and were evidently attracted towards him by the same influence which had drawn them, for an instant, within the sphere of several of the shrubs. He sent forth a breath among them, and smiled bitterly at Beatrice, as at least a score of the insects fell dead upon the ground.

"I see it! I see it!" shrieked Beatrice. "It is my father's fatal science! No, no, Giovanni, it was not I! Never, never! I dreamed only to love thee, and be with thee a little time, and so to let thee pass away, leaving but thine image in mine heart. For, Giovanni — believe it — though my body be nourished with poison, my spirit is God's creature, and craves love as its daily food. But my father! — he has united us in this fearful sympathy. Yes; spurn me! — tread upon me! — kill me! Oh, what is death, after such words as thine? But it was not I! Not for a world of bliss would I have done it!"

Giovanni's passion had exhausted itself in its outburst from his lips. There now came across him a sense, mournful, and not without tenderness, of the intimate and peculiar relationship between Beatrice and himself. They stood, as it were, in an utter solitude, which would be made none the less solitary by the densest throng of human life. Ought not, then, the desert of humanity around them to press this insulated pair closer together? If they should be cruel to one another, who was there to be kind to them? Besides, thought Giovanni, might there not still be a hope of his returning within the limits of ordinary nature, and leading Beatrice — the redeemed Beatrice — by the hand? Oh, weak, and selfish, and unworthy spirit, that could dream of an earthly union and earthly happiness as possible, after such deep love had been so bitterly wronged as was Beatrice's love by Giovanni's blighting words! No, no; there could be no such hope. She must pass heavily, with that broken heart, across the borders of Time — she must bathe her hurts in some fount of Paradise, and forget her grief in the light of immortality — and *there* be well!

But Giovanni did not know it.

"Dear Beatrice," said he, approaching her, while she shrank away, as always at his approach, but now with a different impulse — "dearest Beatrice, our fate is not yet so desperate. Behold! There is a medicine, potent, as a wise physician has assured me, and almost divine in its efficacy. It is composed of ingredients the most opposite to those by which thy awful father has brought this calamity upon thee and me. It is distilled of blessed herbs. Shall we not quaff it together, and thus be purified from evil?"

"Give it me!" said Beatrice, extending her hand to receive the little silver phial which Giovanni took from his bosom. She added, with a peculiar emphasis: "I will drink — but do thou await the result."

She put Baglioni's antidote to her lips; and, at the same moment, the figure of Rappaccini emerged from the portal, and came slowly towards the marble fountain. As he drew near, the pale man of science seemed to gaze with a triumphant expression at the beautiful youth and maiden, as might an artist who should spend his life in achieving a picture of a group of statuary, and finally be satisfied with his success. He paused — his bent form grew erect with conscious power, he spread out his hands over them, in the attitude of a father imploring a blessing upon his children. But those were the same hands that had thrown poison into the stream of their lives! Giovanni trembled. Beatrice shuddered nervously, and pressed her hand upon her heart.

"My daughter," said Rappaccini, "thou art no longer lonely in the world! Pluck one of those precious gems from thy sister shrub, and bid thy bridegroom wear it in his bosom. It will not harm him now! My science, and the sympathy between thee and him, have so wrought within his system, that he now stands apart from common men, as thou dost, daughter of my pride and triumph, from ordinary women. Pass on, then, through the world, most dear to one another, and dreadful to all besides!"

"My father," said Beatrice, feebly — and still, as she spoke, she kept her hand upon her heart — "wherefore didst thou inflict this miserable doom upon thy child?"

"Miserable!" exclaimed Rappaccini. "What mean you, foolish girl? Dost thou deem it misery to be endowed with marvellous gifts, against which no power nor strength could avail an enemy? Misery, to be able to quell the mightiest with a breath? Misery, to be as terrible as thou art beautiful? Wouldst thou, then, have preferred the condition of a weak woman, exposed to all evil, and capable of none?"

"I would fain have been loved, not feared," murmured Beatrice, sinking down upon the ground. — "But now it matters not; I am going, father, where the evil, which thou hast striven to mingle with my being, will pass away like a dream — like the fragrance of these poisonous flowers, which will no longer taint my breath among the flowers of Eden. Farewell, Giovanni! Thy words of hatred are like lead within my heart — but they, too, will fall away as I ascend. Oh, was there not, from the first, more poison in thy nature than in mine?"

To Beatrice — so radically had her earthly part been wrought upon by Rappaccini's skill — as poison had been life, so the powerful antidote was death. And thus the poor victim of man's ingenuity and of thwarted nature, and of the fatality that attends all such efforts of perverted wisdom, perished there, at the feet of her father and Giovanni. Just at that moment, Professor Pietro Baglioni looked forth from the window, and called loudly, in a tone of triumph mixed with horror, to the thunder-stricken man of science:

"Rappaccini! Rappaccini! And is *this* the upshot of your experiment?"

MARK HELPRIN

 Mark Helprin was born in 1947 in a small town on the Hudson River in New York state. The landscape made an indelible impression on him; he has described it in language reminiscent of the lyrical fantasy of much of his fiction: "The winter wind descended from Canada (or so we thought), pushing before it displaced mountain lions and bears, freezing the streams, and making the cattails in hidden moonshadowed ravines jingle with ice." Educated at Harvard, he did stints in the Israeli military and British Merchant Navy. His first collection of stories, *A Dove of the East and Other Stories* (1981), was followed quickly by a first novel, *Refiner's Fire* (1981). Both met with mixed critical reception, but his next collection, *Ellis Island and Other Stories* (1984), was an immediate success. Helprin secured his reputation with the publication of his long, mythic novel *Winter's Tale* (1983). He views himself as an outsider from the contemporary literary mainstream. In a telling statement, he once affirmed, "I am trying to open a road to God and nature ... I could write forever, without stopping, about nature." That spiritual approach is manifest in a story about spirit and nature, "The Schreuderspitze."

The Schreuderspitze

In Munich are many men who look like weasels. Whether by genetic accident, meticulous crossbreeding, an early and puzzling migration, coincidence, or a reason that we do not know, they exist in great numbers. Remarkably, they accentuate this unfortunate tendency by wearing mustaches, Alpine hats, and tweed. A man who resembles a rodent should never wear tweed.

One of these men, a commercial photographer named Franzen, had cause to be exceedingly happy. "Herr Wallich has disappeared," he said to Huebner, his supplier of paper and chemicals. "You needn't bother to send him bills. Just send them to the police. The police, you realize, were here on two separate occasions!"

"If the two occasions on which the police have been here had not been separate, Herr Franzen, they would have been here only once."

"What do you mean? Don't toy with me. I have no time for semantics. In view of the fact that I knew Wallich at school, and professionally, they sought my opinion on his disappearance. They wrote down everything I said, but I do not think that they will find him. He left his studio on the Neuhausstrasse just as it was when he was working, and the landlord has put a lien on the equipment. Let me tell you that he had some fine equipment — very fine. But he was not such a great photographer. He didn't have that killer's instinct. He was clearly not a hunter. His canine teeth were poorly developed; not like these," said Franzen, baring his canine teeth in a smile which made him look like an idiot with a mouth of miniature castle towers.

"But I am curious about Wallich."

"So is everyone. So is everyone. This is my theory. Wallich was never any good at school. At best, he did only middling well. And it was not because he had hidden passions, or a special genius for some field outside the curriculum. He tried hard but found it difficult to grasp several subjects; for him, mathematics and physics were pure torture.

"As you know, he was not wealthy, and although he was a nice-looking fellow, he was terribly short. That inflicted upon him great scars — his confidence, I mean, because he had none. He could do things only gently. If he had to fight, he would fail. He was weak.

"For example, I will use the time when he and I were competing for the Heller account. This job meant a lot of money, and I was not about to lose. I went to the library and read all I could about turbine engines. What a bore! I took photographs of turbine blades and such things, and seeded them throughout my portfolio to make Herr Heller think that I had always been interested in turbines. Of course, I had not even known what they were. I thought that they were an Oriental hat. And now that I know them, I detest them.

"Naturally, I won. But do you know how Wallich approached the competition? He had some foolish ideas about mother-of-pearl nautiluses and other seashells. He wanted to show how shapes of things mechanical were echoes of shapes in nature. All very fine, but Herr Heller pointed out that if the public were to see photographs of mother-of-pearl shells contrasted with photographs of his engines, his engines would come out the worse. Wallich's photographs were very beautiful — the tones of white and silver were exceptional — but they were his undoing. In the end, he said, "Perhaps, Herr Heller, you are right," and lost the contract just like that.

"The thing that saved him was the prize for that picture he took in the Black Forest. You couldn't pick up a magazine in Germany and not see it. He obtained so many accounts that he began to do very well. But he was just not commercially-minded. He told me himself that he took only those assignments which pleased him. Mind you, his business volume was only about two-thirds of mine.

"My theory is that he could not take the competition, and the demands of his various clients. After his wife and son were killed in the motorcar crash, he dropped assignments one after another. I suppose he thought that as a bachelor he could live like a bohemian, on very little money, and therefore did not have to work more than half the time. I'm not saying that this was wrong. (Those accounts came to me.) But it was another mistake of his weakness and lassitude.

"My theory is that he has probably gone to South America, or thrown himself off a bridge — because he saw that there was no future for him if he were always to take pictures of shells and things. And he was weak. The weak can never face themselves, and so cannot see the practical side of the world, how things are laid out, and what sacrifices are required to survive and prosper. It is only in fairy tales that they rise to triumph."

Wallich could not afford to get to South America. He certainly would not have thrown himself off a bridge. He was excessively neat and orderly, and the prospect of some poor fireman handling a swollen, bloated body resounding with flies deterred him forever from such nonsense.

Perhaps if he had been a Gypsy he would have taken to the road. But he was no Gypsy, and had not the talent, skill, or taste for life outside Bavaria. Only once had he been away, to Paris. It was their honeymoon, when he and his wife did not need Paris or any city. They went by train and stayed for a week at a hotel by the Quai Voltaire. They walked in the gardens all day long, and in the May evenings they went to concerts where they heard the perfect music of their own country. Though they were away for just a week, and read the German papers, and went to a corner of the Luxembourg Gardens where there were pines and wildflowers like those in the greenbelt around Munich, this music made them sick for home. They returned two days early and never left again except for July and August, which each year they spent in the Black Forest, at a cabin inherited from her parents.

He dared not go back to that cabin. It was set like a trap. Were he to enter he would be enfiladed by the sight of their son's pictures and toys, his little boots and miniature fishing rod, and by her comb lying at the exact angle she had left it when she had last brushed her hair, and by the sweet smell of her clothing. No, someday he would have to burn the cabin. He dared not sell, for strangers then would handle roughly all those things which meant so much to him that he could not even gaze upon them. He left the little cabin to stand empty, perhaps the object of an occasional hiker's curiosity, or recipient of cheerful postcards from friends traveling or at the beach for the summer — friends who had not heard.

He sought instead a town far enough from Munich so that he would not encounter anything familiar, a place where he would be unrecognized and yet a place not entirely strange, where he would have to undergo no savage adjustments, where he could buy a Munich paper.

A search of the map brought his flying eye always southward to the borderlands, to Alpine country remarkable for the steepness of the brown contours, the depth of the valleys, and the paucity of settled places. Those few depicted towns appeared to be clean and well placed on high overlooks. Unlike the cities to the north — circles which clustered together on the flatlands or along rivers, like colonies of bacteria — the cities of the Alps stood alone, *in extremis,* near the border. Though he dared not cross the border, he thought perhaps to venture near its edge, to see what he would see. These isolated towns in the Alps promised shining clear air and deep-green trees. Perhaps they were above the tree line. In a number of cases it looked that way — and the circles were far from resembling clusters of bacteria. They seemed like untethered balloons.

He chose a town for its ridiculous name, reasoning that few of his friends would desire to travel to such a place. The world bypasses badly named towns as easily as it abandons ungainly children. It was called Garmisch-Partenkirchen. At the station in Munich, they did not even inscribe the full name on his ticket, writing merely "Garmisch-P."

"Do you live there?" the railroad agent had asked.

"No," answered Wallich.

"Are you visiting relatives, or going on business, or going to ski?"

"No."

"Then perhaps you are making a mistake. To go in October is not wise, if you do not ski. As unbelievable as it may seem, they have had much snow. Why go now?"

"I am a mountain climber," answered Wallich.

"In winter?" The railway agent was used to flushing out lies, and when little fat Austrian boys just old enough for adult tickets would bend their knees at his window as if at confession and say in squeaky voices, "Half fare to Salzburg!," he pounced upon them as if he were a leopard and they juicy ptarmigan or baby roebuck.

"Yes, in the winter," Wallich said. "Good mountain climbers thrive in difficult conditions. The more ice, the more storm, the greater the accomplishment. I am accumulating various winter records. In January, I go to America, where I will ascend their highest mountain, Mt. Independence, four thousand meters." He blushed so hard that the railway agent followed suit. Then Wallich backed away, insensibly mortified.

A mountain climber! He would close his eyes in fear when looking through Swiss calendars. He had not the stamina to rush up the stairs to his studio. He had failed miserably at sports. He was not a mountain climber, and had never even dreamed of being one.

Yet when his train pulled out of the vault of lacy iron-work and late-afternoon shadow, its steam exhalations were like those of a man puffing up a high meadow, speeding to reach the rock and ice, and Wallich felt as if he were embarking upon an ordeal of the type men experience on the precipitous rock walls of great cloud-swirled peaks. Why was he going to Garmisch-Partenkirchen anyway, if not for an ordeal through which to right himself? He was pulled so far over on one side by the death of his family, he was so bent and crippled by the pain of it, that he was going to Garmisch-Partenkirchen to suffer a parallel ordeal through which he would balance what had befallen him.

How wrong his parents and friends had been when they had offered help as his business faltered. A sensible, graceful man will have symmetry. He remembered the time at youth camp when a stream had changed course away from a once gushing sluice and the younger boys had had to carry buckets of water up a small hill, to fill a cistern. The skinny little boys had struggled up the hill. Their counselor, sitting comfortably in the shade, would not let them go two to a bucket. At first they had tried to carry the pails in front of them, but this was nearly impossible. Then they surreptitiously spilled half the water on the way up, until the counselor took up position at the cistern and inspected each cargo. It had been torture to carry the heavy bucket in one aching hand. Wallich finally decided to take two buckets. Though it was agony, it was a better agony than the one he had had, because he had retrieved his balance, could look ahead, and, by carrying a double burden, had strengthened himself and made the job that much shorter. Soon, all the boys carried two buckets. The cistern was filled in no time, and they had a victory over their surprised counselor.

So, he thought as the train shuttled through chill half-harvested fields, I will be a hermit in Garmisch-Partenkirchen. I will know no one. I will be alone. I may even begin to climb mountains. Perhaps I will lose fingers and toes, and on the way gather a set of wounds which will allow me some peace.

He sensed the change of landscape before he actually came upon it. Then they began to climb, and the engine sweated steam from steel to carry the lumbering cars up terrifying grades on either side of which blue pines stood angled against the mountainside. They reached a level stretch which made the train curve like a dragon and led it through deep tunnels, and they sped along as if on a summer excursion, with views of valleys so distant that in them whole forests sat upon their meadows like birthmarks, and streams were little more than the grain in leather.

Wallich opened his window and leaned out, watching ahead for tunnels. The air was thick and cold. It was full of sunshine and greenery, and it flowed past as if it were a mountain river. When he pulled back, his cheeks were red and his face pounded from the frigid air. He was alone in the compartment. By the time the lights came on he had decided upon the course of an ideal. He was to become a mountain climber, after all — and in a singularly difficult, dangerous, and satisfying way.

A porter said in passing the compartment, "The dining car is open, sir." Service to the Alps was famed. Even though his journey was no more than two hours, he had arranged to eat on the train, and had paid for and ordered a meal to which he looked forward in pleasant anticipation, especially because he had selected French strawberries in cream for dessert. But then he saw his body in the gently lit half mirror. He was soft from a lifetime of near-happiness. The sight of his face in the blond light of the mirror made him decide to begin preparing for the mountains that very evening. The porter ate the strawberries.

Of the many ways to attempt an ordeal perhaps the most graceful and attractive is the Alpine. It is far more satisfying than Oriental starvation and abnegation precisely because the European ideal is to commit difficult acts amid richness and overflowing beauty. For that reason, the Alpine is as well the most demanding. It is hard to deny oneself, to pare oneself down, at the heart and base of a civilization so full.

Wallich rode to Garmisch-Partenkirchen in a thunder of proud Alps. The trees were tall and lively, the air crystalline, and radiating beams spoke through the train window from one glowing range to another. A world of high ice laughed. And yet ranks of competing images assaulted him. He had gasped at the sight of Bremen, a port stuffed with iron ships gushing wheat steam from their whistles as they prepared to sail. In the mountain dryness, he remembered humid ports from which these massive ships crossed a colorful world, bringing back on laden decks a catalogue of stuffs and curiosities.

Golden images of the north plains struck from the left. The salt-white plains nearly floated above the sea. All this was in Germany, though Germany was just a small part of the world, removed almost entirely from the deep source of things — from the high lakes where explorers touched the silvers which caught the world's images, from the Sahara where they found the fine glass which bent the light.

Arriving at Garmisch-Partenkirchen in the dark, he could hear bells chiming and water rushing. Cool currents of air flowed from the direction of this white tumbling sound. It was winter. He hailed a horse-drawn sledge and piled his baggage in the back. "Hotel Aufburg," he said authoritatively.

"Hotel Aufburg?" asked the driver.

"Yes, Hotel Aufburg. There is such a place, isn't there? It hasn't closed, has it?"

"No, sir, it hasn't closed." The driver touched his horse with the whip. The horse walked twenty feet and was reined to a stop. "Here we are," the driver said. "I trust you've had a pleasant journey. Time passes quickly up here in the mountains."

The sign for the hotel was so large and well lit that the street in front of it shone as in daylight. The driver was guffawing to himself; the little guffaws rumbled about in him like subterranean thunder. He could not wait to tell the other drivers.

Wallich did nothing properly in Garmisch-Partenkirchen. But it was a piece of luck that he felt too awkward and ill at ease to sit alone in restaurants while, nearby, families and lovers had self-centered raucous meals, sometimes even bursting into song. Winter took over the town and covered it in stiff white ice. The unresilient cold, the troikas jingling through the streets, the frequent snowfalls encouraged winter fat. But because Wallich ate cold food in his room or stopped occasionally at a counter for a steaming bowl of soup, he became a shadow.

The starvation was pleasant. It made him sleepy and its constant physical presence gave him companionship. He sat for hours watching the snow, feeling as if he were part of it, as if the diminution of his body were great progress, as if such lightening would lessen his sorrow and bring him to the high rim of things he had not seen before, things which would help him and show him what to do and make him proud just for coming upon them.

He began to exercise. Several times a day the hotel manager knocked like a woodpecker at Wallich's door. The angrier the manager, the faster the knocks. If he were really angry, he spoke so rapidly that he sounded like a speeded-up record: "Herr Wallich, I must ask you on behalf of the other guests to stop immediately all the thumping and vibration! This is a quiet hotel, in a quiet town, in a quiet tourist region. Please!" Then the manager would bow and quickly withdraw.

Eventually they threw Wallich out, but not before he had spent October and November in concentrated maniacal pursuit of physical strength. He had started with five each, every waking hour, of pushups, pull-ups, sit-ups, toe-touches, and leg-raises. The pull-ups were deadly — he did one every twelve minutes. The thumping and bumping came from five minutes of running in place. At the end of the first day, the pain in his chest was so intense that he was certain he was not long for the world. The second day was worse. And so it went, until after ten days there was no pain at all. The weight he abandoned helped a great deal to expand his physical prowess. He was, after all, in his middle twenties, and had never eaten to excess. Nor did he smoke or drink, except for champagne at weddings and municipal celebrations. In fact, he had always had rather ascetic tendencies, and had thought it fitting to have spent his life in Munich — "Home of Monks."

By his fifteenth day in Garmisch-Partenkirchen he had increased his schedule to fifteen apiece of the exercises each hour, which meant, for example, that he did a pull-up every four minutes whenever he was awake. Late at night he ran aimlessly about the deserted streets for an hour or more, even though it sometimes snowed. Two policemen who huddled over a brazier in their tiny booth simply looked at one another and pointed to their heads, twirling their fingers and rolling their eyes every time he passed by. On the last day of November, he moved up the valley to a little village called Altenburg-St. Peter.

There it was worse in some ways and better in others. Altenburg-St. Peter was so tiny that no stranger could enter unobserved, and so still that no one could do anything without the knowledge of the entire community. Children stared at Wallich on the street. This made him walk on the little lanes and approach his few destinations from the rear, which led housewives to speculate that he was a burglar. There were few merchants, and, because they were cousins, they could with little effort determine exactly what Wallich ate. When one week they were positive that he had consumed only four bowls of soup, a pound of cheese, a pound of smoked meat, a quart of yogurt, and two loaves of bread, they were incredulous. They themselves ate this much in a day. They wondered how Wallich survived on so little. Finally they came up with an answer. He received packages from Munich several times a week and in these packages was food, they thought — and probably very great delicacies. Then as the winter got harder and the snows covered everything they stopped wondering about him. They did not see him as he ran out of his lodgings at midnight, and the snow muffled his tread. He ran up the road toward the Schreuderspitze, first for a kilometer, then two, then five, then ten, then twenty — when finally he had to stop because he had begun slipping in just before the farmers arose and would have seen him.

By the end of February the packages had ceased arriving, and he was a changed man. No one would have mistaken him for what he had been. In five months he had become lean and strong. He did two hundred and fifty sequential pushups at least four times a day. For the sheer pleasure of it, he would do a hundred and fifty pushups on his fingertips. Every day he did a hundred pull ups in a row. His midnight run, sometimes in snow which had accumulated up to his knees, was four hours long.

The packages had contained only books on climbing, and equipment. At first the books had been terribly discouraging. Every elementary text had bold warnings in red or green ink: "It is extremely dangerous to attempt genuine ascents without proper training. This volume should be used in conjunction with a certified course on climbing, or with the advice of a registered guide. A book itself will not do!"

One manual had in bright-red ink, on the very last page: "Go back, you fool! Certain death awaits you!" Wallich imagined that, as the books said, there were many things he could not learn except by human example, and many mistakes he might make in interpreting the manuals, which would go uncorrected save for the critique of living practitioners. But it didn't matter. He was determined to learn for himself and accomplish his task alone. Besides, since the accident he had become a recluse, and could hardly speak. The thought of enrolling in a climbing school full of young people from all parts of the country paralyzed him. How could he reconcile his task with their enthusiasm? For them it was recreation, perhaps something aesthetic or spiritual, a way to meet new friends. For him it was one tight channel through which he would either burst on to a new life, or in which he would die.

Studying carefully, he soon worked his way to advanced treaties for those who had spent years in the Alps. He understood these well enough, having quickly learned the terminologies and the humor and the faults of those who write about the mountains. He was even convinced that he knew the spirit in which the treatises had been written, for though he had never climbed, he had only to look out his window to see high white mountains about which blue sky swirled like a banner. He felt that in seeing them he was one of them, and was greatly encouraged when he read in a French mountaineer's memoirs: "After years in the mountains, I learned to look upon a given range and feel as if I were the last peak in the line. Thus I felt the music of the empty spaces enwrapping me, and I became not an intruder on the cliffs, dangling only to drop away, but an equal in transit. I seldom looked at my own body but only at the mountains, and my eyes felt like the eyes of the mountains."

He lavished nearly all his dwindling money on fine equipment. He calculated that after his purchases he would have enough to live on through September. Then he would have nothing. He had expended large sums on the best tools, and he spent the intervals between his hours of reading and exercise holding and studying the shiny carabiners, pitons, slings, chocks, hammers, ice pitons, axes, étriers, crampons, ropes, and specialized hardware that he had either ordered or constructed himself from plans in the advanced books.

It was insane, he knew, to funnel all his preparation into a few months of agony and then without any experience whatever throw himself alone onto a Class VI ascent — the seldom climbed *Westgebirgsausläufer* of the Schreuderspitze. Not having driven one piton, he was going to attempt a five-day climb up the nearly sheer western counterfort. Even in late June, he would spend a third of his time on ice. But the sight of the ice in March, shining like a faraway sword over the cold and absolute distance, drove him on. He had long passed censure. Had anyone known what he was doing and tried to dissuade him, he would have told him to go to hell, and resumed preparations with the confidence of someone taken up by a new religion.

For he had always believed in great deeds, in fairy tales, in echoing trumpet lands, in wonders and wondrous accomplishments. But even as a boy he had never considered that such things would fall to him. As a good city child he had known that these adventures were not necessary. But suddenly he was alone and the things which occurred to him were great warlike deeds. His energy and discipline were boundless, as full and overflowing as a lake in the mountains. Like the heroes of his youth, he would try to approach the high cord of ruby light and bend it to his will, until he could feel rolling thunder. The small things, the gentle things, the good things he loved, and the flow of love itself were dead for him and would always be, unless he could liberate them in a crucible of high drama.

It took him many months to think these things, and though they might not seem consistent, they were so for him, and he often spent hours alone on a sunny snow-covered meadow, his elbows on his knees, imagining great deeds in the mountains, as he stared at the massive needle of the Schreuderspitze, at the hint of rich lands beyond, and at the tiny village where he had taken up position opposite the mountain.

Toward the end of May he had been walking through Altenburg-St. Peter and seen his reflection in a store window — a storm had arisen suddenly and made the glass as silver-black as the clouds. He had not liked what he had seen. His face had become too hard and too lean. There was not enough gentleness. He feared immediately for the success of his venture if only because he knew well that unmitigated extremes are a great cause of failure. And he was tired of his painful regimen.

He bought a large Telefunken radio, in one fell swoop wiping out his funds for August and September. He felt as if he were paying for the privilege of music with portions of his life and body. But it was well worth it. When the storekeeper offered to deliver the heavy console, Wallich declined politely, picked up the cabinet himself, hoisted it on his back, and walked out of the store bent under it as in classic illustrations for physics textbooks throughout the industrialized world. He did not put it down once. The storekeeper summoned his associates and they bet and counterbet on whether Wallich "would" or "would not," as he moved slowly up the steep hill, up the steps, around the white switchbacks, onto a grassy slope, and then finally up the precipitous stairs to the balcony outside his room. "How can he have done that?" they asked. "He is a small man, and the radio must weigh at least thirty kilos." The storekeeper trotted out with a catalogue."It weighs fifty-five kilograms!" he said. "Fifty-five kilograms!" And they wondered what had made Wallich so strong.

Once, Wallich had taken his little son (a tiny, skeptical, silent child who had a riotous giggle which could last for an hour) to see the inflation of a great gas dirigible. It had been a disappointment, for a dirigible is rigid and maintains always the same shape. He had expected to see the silver of its sides expand into ribbed cliffs which would float over them on the green field and amaze his son. Now that silver rising, the sail-like expansion, the great crescendo of a glimmering weightless mass, finally reached him alone in his room, too late but well received, when a Berlin station played the Beethoven Violin Concerto, its first five timpanic D's like grace before a feast. After those notes, the music lifted him, and he riveted his gaze on the dark shapes of the mountains, where a lightning storm raged. The radio crackled after each near or distant flash, but it was as if the music had been designed for it. Wallich looked at the yellow light within a softly glowing numbered panel. It flickered gently, and he could hear cracks and flashes in the music as he saw them delineated across darkness. They looked and sounded like the bent riverine limbs of dead trees hanging majestically over rocky outcrops, destined to fall, but enjoying their grand suspension nonetheless. The music traveled effortlessly on anarchic beams, passed high over the plains, passed high the forests, seeding them plentifully, and came upon the Alps like waves which finally strike the shore after thousands of miles in open sea. It charged upward, mating with the electric storm, separating, and delivering.

To Wallich — alone in the mountains, surviving amid the dark massifs and clear air — came the closeted, nasal, cosmopolitan voice of the radio commentator. It was good to know that there was something other than the purity and magnificence of his mountains, that far to the north the balance reverted to less than moral catastrophe and death, and much stock was set in things of extraordinary inconsequence. Wallich could not help laughing when he thought of the formally dressed audience at the symphony, how they squirmed in their seats and heated the bottoms of their trousers and capes, how relieved and delighted they would be to step out into the cool evening and go to a restaurant. In the morning they would arise and take pleasure from the sweep of the drapes as sun danced by, from the gold rim around a white china cup. For them it was always too hot or too cold. But they certainly had their delights, about which sometimes he would think. How often he still dreamed, asleep or awake, of the smooth color plates opulating under his hands in tanks of developer and of the fresh film which smelled like bread and then was entombed in black cylinders to develop. How he longed sometimes for the precise machinery of his cameras. The very word *"Kamera"* was as dark and hollow as this night in the mountains when, reviewing the pleasures of faraway Berlin, he sat in perfect health and equanimity upon a wickerweave seat in a bare white room. The only light was from the yellow dial, the sudden lightning flashes, and the faint blue of the sky beyond the hills. And all was quiet but for the music and the thunder and the static curling about the music like weak and lost memories which arise to harry even indomitable perfections.

A month before the ascent, he awaited arrival of a good climbing rope. He needed from a rope not strength to hold a fall but lightness and length for abseiling. His strategy was to climb with a short self-belay. No one would follow to retrieve his hardware and because it would not always be practical for him to do so himself, in what one of his books called "rhythmic recapitulation," he planned to carry a great deal of metal. If the metal and he reached the summit relatively intact, he could make short work of the descent, abandoning pitons as he abseiled downward.

He would descend in half a day that which had taken five days to climb. He pictured the abseiling, literally a flight down the mountain on the doubled cord of his long rope, and he thought that those hours speeding down the cliffs would be the finest of his life. If the weather were good he would come away from the Schreuderspitze having flown like an eagle.

On the day the rope was due, he went to the railroad station to meet the mail. It was a clear, perfect day. The light was so fine and rich that in its bath everyone felt wise, strong, and content. Wallich sat on the wooden boards of the wide platform, scanning the green meadows and fields for smoke and a coal engine, but the countryside was silent and the valley unmarred by the black woolly chain he sought. In the distance, toward France and Switzerland, a few cream-and-rose-colored clouds rode the horizon, immobile and high. On far mountainsides innumerable flowers showed in this long view as a slash, or as a patch of color not unlike one flower alone.

He had arrived early, for he had no watch. After some minutes a car drove up and from it emerged a young family. They rushed as if the train were waiting to depart, when down the long troughlike valley it was not even visible. There were two little girls, as beautiful as he had ever seen. The mother, too, was extraordinarily fine. The father was in his early thirties, and he wore gold-rimmed glasses. They seemed like a university family — people who knew how to live sensibly, taking pleasure from proper and beautiful things.

The littler girl was no more than three. Sunburnt and rosy, she wore a dress that was shaped like a bell. She dashed about the platform so lightly and tentatively that it was as if Wallich were watching a tiny fish gravityless in a lighted aquarium. Her older sister stood quietly by the mother, who was illumined with consideration and pride for her children. It was apparent that she was overjoyed with the grace of her family. She seemed detached and preoccupied, but in just the right way. The littler girl said in a voice like a child's party horn, "Mummy, I want some peanuts!"

It was so ridiculous that this child should share the appetite of elephants that the mother smiled. "Peanuts will make you thirsty, Gretl. Wait until we get to Garmsich-Partenkirchen. Then we'll have lunch in the buffet."

"When will we get to Garmisch-Partenkirchen?"

"At two."

"Two?"

"Yes, at two."

"At two?"

"Gretl!"

The father looked alternately at the mountains and at his wife and children. He seemed confident and steadfast. In the distance black smoke appeared in thick billows. The father pointed at it. "There's our train," he said.

"Where?" asked Gretl, looking in the wrong direction. The father picked her up and turned her head with his hand, aiming her gaze down the shimmering valley. When she saw the train she started, and her eyes opened wide in pleasure.

"Ah ... there it is," said the father. As the train pulled into the station the young girls were filled with excitement. Amid the noise they entered a compartment and were swallowed up in the steam. The train pulled out.

Wallich stood on the empty platform, unwrapping his rope. It was a rope, quite a nice rope, but it did not make him as happy as he had expected it would.

Little can match the silhouette of mountains by night. The great mass becomes far more mysterious when its face is darkened, when its sweeping lines roll steeply into valleys and peaks and long impossible ridges, when behind the void a concoction of rare silver leaps up to trace the hills — the pressure of collected starlight. That night, in conjunction with the long draughts of music he had become used to taking, he began to dream his dreams. They did not frighten him — he was beyond fear, too strong for fear, too played out. They did not even puzzle him, for they unfolded like the chapters in a brilliant nineteenth-century history. The rich explanations filled him for days afterward. He was amazed, and did not understand why these perfect dreams suddenly came to him. Surely they did not arise from within. He had never had the world so beautifully portrayed, had never seen as clearly and in such sure, gentle steps, had never risen so high and so smoothly in unfolding enlightenment, and he had seldom felt so well looked after. And yet, there was no visible presence. But it was as if the mountains and valleys were filled with loving families of which he was part.

Upon his return from the railroad platform, a storm had come suddenly from beyond the southern ridge. Though it had been warm and clear that day, he had seen from the sunny meadow before his house that a white storm billowed in higher curves, pushing itself over the summits, finally to fall like an air avalanche on the valley. It snowed on the heights. The sun continued to strike the opaque frost and high clouds. It did not snow in the valley. The shock troops of the storm remained at the highest elevations, and only worn gray veterans came below — misty clouds and rain on cold wet air. Ragged clouds moved across the mountainsides and meadows, watering the trees and sometimes catching in low places. Even so, the air in the meadow was still horn-clear.

In his room that night Wallich rocked back and forth on the wicker chair (it was not a rocker and he knew that using it as such was to number its days). That night's crackling infusion from Berlin, rising warmly from the faintly lit dial, was Beethoven's Eighth. The familiar commentator, nicknamed by Wallich Mälzels Metronom because of his even monotone, discoursed upon the background of the work.

"For many years," he said, "no one except Beethoven liked this symphony. Beethoven's opinions, however — even regarding his own creations — are equal at least to the collective pronouncements of all the musicologists and critics alive in the West during any hundred-year period. Conscious of the merits of the F-Major Symphony, he resolutely determined to redeem and ... ah ... the conductor has arrived. He steps to the podium. We begin."

Wallich retired that night in perfect tranquillity but awoke at five in the morning soaked in his own sweat, his fists clenched, a terrible pain in his chest, and breathing heavily as if he had been running. In the dim unattended light of the early-morning storm, he lay with eyes wide open. His pulse subsided, but he was like an animal in a cave, like a creature who has just escaped an organized hunt. It was as if the whole village had come armed and in search of him, had by some miracle decided that he was not in, and had left to comb the wet woods. He had been dreaming, and he saw his dream in its exact form. It was, first, an emerald. Cut into an octagon with two long sides, it was shaped rather like the plaque at the bottom of a painting. Events within this emerald were circular and never-ending.

They were in Munich. Air and sun were refined as on the station platform in the mountains. He was standing at a streetcar stop with his wife and his two daughters, though he knew perfectly well in the dream that these two daughters were meant to be his son. A streetcar arrived in complete silence. Clouds of people began to embark. They were dressed and muffled in heavy clothing of dull blue and gray. To his surprise, his wife moved toward the door of the streetcar and started to board, the daughters trailing after her. He could not see her feet, and she moved in a glide. Though at first paralyzed, as in the instant before a crash, he did manage to bound after her. As she stepped onto the first step and was about to grasp a chrome pole within the doorway, he made for her arm and caught it.

He pulled her back and spun her around, all very gently. Her presence before him was so intense that it was as if he were trapped under the weight of a fallen beam. She, too, wore a winter coat, but it was slim and perfectly tailored. He remembered the perfect geometry of the lapels. Not on earth had such angles ever been seen. The coat was a most intense liquid emerald color, a living light-infused green. She had always looked best in green, for her hair was like shining gold. He stood before her. He felt her delicacy. Her expression was neutral. "Where are you going?" he asked incredulously.

"I must go," she said.

He put his arms around her. She returned his embrace, and he said, "How can you leave me?"

"I have to," she answered.

And then stepped onto the first step of the streetcar, and onto the second step, and she was enfolded into darkness.

He awoke, feeling like an invalid. His strength served for naught. He just stared at the clouds lifting higher and higher as the storm cleared. By nightfall the sky was black and gentle, though very cold. He kept thinking back to the emerald. It meant everything to him, for it was the first time he realized that they were really dead. Silence followed. Time passed thickly. He could not have imagined the sequence of dreams to follow, and what they would do to him.

He began to fear sleep, thinking that he would again be subjected to the lucidity of the emerald. But he had run that course and would never do so again except by perfect conscious recollection. The night after he had the dream of the emerald he fell asleep like someone letting go of a cliff edge after many minutes alone without help or hope. He slid into sleep, heart beating wildly. To his surprise, he found himself far indeed from the trolley tracks in Munich.

Instead, he was alone in the center of a sunlit snowfield, walking on the glacier in late June, bound for the summit of the Schreuderspitze. The mass of his equipment sat lightly upon him. He was well drilled in its use and positioning, in the subtleties of placement and rigging. The things he carried seemed part of him, as if he had quickly evolved into a new kind of animal suited for breathtaking travel in the steep heights.

His stride was light and long, like that of a man on the moon. He nearly floated, ever so slightly airborne, over the dazzling glacier. He leaped crevasses, sailing in slow motion against intense white and blue. He passed apple-fresh streams and opalescent melt pools of blue-green water as he progressed toward the Schreuder-spitze. Its rocky horn was covered by nearly blue ice from which the wind blew a white corona in sines and cusps twirling about the sky.

Passing the bergschrund, he arrived at the first mass of rock. He turned to look back. There he saw the snowfield and the sun turning above it like a pinwheel, casting out a fog of golden light. He stood alone. The world had been reduced to the beauty of physics and the mystery of light. It had been rendered into a frozen state, a liquid state, a solid state, a gaseous state, mixtures, temperatures, and more varieties of light than fell on the speckled floor of a great cathedral. It was simple, and yet infinitely complex. The sun was warm. There was silence.

For several hours he climbed over great boulders and up a range of rocky escarpments. It grew more and more difficult, and he often had to lay in protection, driving a piton into a crack of the firm granite. His first piton was a surprise. It slowed halfway, and the ringing sound as he hammered grew higher in pitch. Finally, it would go in no farther. He had spent so much time in driving it that he thought it would be as steady as the Bank of England. But when he gave a gentle tug to test its hold, it came right out. This he thought extremely funny. He then remembered that he had either to drive it all the way, to the eye, or to attach a sling along its shaft as near as possible to the rock. It was a question of avoiding leverage.

He bent carefully to his equipment sling, replaced the used piton, and took up a shorter one. The shorter piton went to its eye in five hammer strokes and he could do nothing to dislodge it. He clipped in and ascended a steep pitch, at the top of which he drove in two pitons, tied in to them, abseiled down to retrieve the first, and ascended quite easily to where he had left off. He made rapid progress over frightening pitches, places no one would dare go without assurance of a bolt in the rock and a line to the bolt — even if the bolt was just a small piece of metal driven in by dint of precariously balanced strength, arm, and Alpine hammer.

Within the sphere of utter concentration easily achieved during difficult ascents, his simple climbing evolved naturally into graceful technique, by which he went up completely vertical rock faces, suspended only by pitons and étriers. The different placements of which he had read and thought repeatedly were employed skillfully and with a proper sense of variety, though it was tempting to stay with one familiar pattern. Pounding metal into rock and hanging from his taut and colorful wires, he breathed hard, he concentrated, and he went up sheer walls.

At one point he came to the end of a subtle hairline crack in an otherwise smooth wall. The rock above was completely solid for a hundred feet. If he went down to the base of the crack he would be nowhere. The only thing to do was to make a swing traverse to a wall more amenable to climbing.

Anchoring two pitons into the rock as solidly as he could, he clipped an oval carabiner on the bottom piton, put a safety line on the top one, and lowered himself about sixty feet down the two ropes. Hanging perpendicular to the wall, he began to walk back and forth across the rock. He moved to and fro, faster and faster, until he was running. Finally he touched only in places and was swinging wildly like a pendulum. He feared that the piton to which he was anchored would not take the strain, and would pull out. But he kept swinging faster, until he gave one final push and, with a pathetic cry, went sailing over a drop which would have made a mountain goat swallow its heart. He caught an outcropping of rock on the other side, and pulled himself to it desperately. He hammered in, retrieved the ropes, glanced at the impassable wall, and began again to ascend.

As he approached great barricades of ice, he looked back. It gave him great pride and satisfaction to see the thousands of feet over which he had struggled. Much of the west counterfort was purely vertical. He could see now just how the glacier was riverine. He could see deep within the Tyrol and over the border to the Swiss lakes. Garmisch-Partenkirchen looked from here like a town on the board of a toy railroad or (if considered only two-dimensionally) like the cross-section of a kidney. Altenburg-St. Peter looked like a ladybug. The sun sent streamers of tan light through the valley, already three-quarters conquered by shadow, and the ice above took fire. Where the ice began, he came to a wide ledge and he stared upward at a sparkling ridge which looked like a great crystal spine. Inside, it was blue and cold.

He awoke, convinced that he had in fact climbed the counterfort. It was a strong feeling, as strong as the reality of the emerald. Sometimes dreams could be so real that they competed with the world, riding at even balance and calling for a decision. Sometimes, he imagined, when they are so real and so important, they easily tip the scale and the world buckles and dreams become real. Crossing the fragile barricades, one enters his dreams, thinking of his life as imagined.

He rejoiced at his bravery in climbing. It had been as real as anything he had ever experienced. He felt the pain, the exhaustion, and the reward, as well as the danger. But he could not wait to return to the mountain and the ice. He longed for evening and the enveloping darkness, believing that he belonged resting under great folds of ice on the wall of the Schreuderspitze. He had no patience with his wicker chair, the bent wood of the windowsill, the clear glass in the window, the green-sided hills he saw curving through it, or his brightly colored equipment hanging from pegs on the white wall.

Two weeks before, on one of the eastward roads from Altenburg-St. Peter — no more than a dirt track — he had seen a child turn and take a well-worn path toward a wood, a meadow, and a stream by which stood a house and a barn. The child walked slowly upward into the forest, disappearing into the dark close, as if he had been taken up by vapor. Wallich had been too far away to hear footsteps, and the last thing he saw was the back of the boy's bright blue-and-white sweater. Returning at dusk, Wallich had expected to see warmly lit windows, and smoke issuing efficiently from the straight chimney. But there were no lights, and there was no smoke. He made his way through the trees and past the meadow only to come upon a small farmhouse with boarded windows and no-trespassing signs tacked on the doors.

It was unsettling when he saw the same child making his way across the upper meadow, a flash of blue and white in the near darkness. Wallich screamed out to him, but he did not hear, and kept walking as if he were deaf or in another world, and he went over the crest of the hill. Wallich ran up the hill. When he reached the top he saw only a wide empty field and not a trace of the boy.

Then in the darkness and purity of the meadows he began to feel that the world had many secrets, that they were shattering even to glimpse or sense, and that they were not necessarily unpleasant. In certain states of light he could see, he could begin to sense, things most miraculous indeed. Although it seemed self-serving, he concluded nonetheless, after a lifetime of adhering to the diffuse principles of a science he did not know, that there was life after death, that the dead rose into a mischievous world of pure light, that something most mysterious lay beyond the enfolding darkness, something wonderful.

This idea had taken hold, and he refined it. For example, listening to the Beethoven symphonies broadcast from Berlin, he began to think that they were like a ladder of mountains, that they surpassed themselves and rose higher and higher until at certain points they seemed to break the warp itself and cross into a heaven of light and the dead. There were signs everywhere of temporal diffusion and mystery. It was as if continents existed, new worlds lying just off the coast, invisible and redolent, waiting for the grasp of one man suddenly to substantiate and light them, changing everything. Perhaps great mountains hundreds of times higher than the Alps would arise in the seas or on the flatlands. They might be purple or gold and shining in many states of refraction and reflection, transparent in places as vast as countries. Someday someone would come back from this place, or someone would by accident discover and illumine its remarkable physics.

He believed that the boy he had seen nearly glowing in the half-darkness of the high meadow had been his son, and that the child had been teasing his father in a way only he could know, that the child had been asking him to follow. Possibly he had come upon great secrets on the other side, and knew that his father would join him soon enough and that then they would laugh about the world.

When he next fell asleep in the silence of a clear windless night in the valley, Wallich was like a man disappearing into the warp of darkness. He wanted to go there, to be taken as far as he could be taken. He was not unlike a sailor who sets sail in the teeth of a great storm, delighted by his own abandon.

Throwing off the last wraps of impure light, he found himself again in the ice world. The word was all-encompassing — *Eiswelt*. There above him the blue spire rocketed upward as far as the eye could see. He touched it with his hand. It was indeed as cold as ice. It was dense and hard, like glass ten feet thick. He had doubted its strength, but its solidity told that it would not flake away and allow him to drop endlessly, far from it.

On ice he found firm holds both with his feet and with his hands, and hardly needed the ice pitons and étriers. For he had crampons tied firmly to his boots, and could spike his toe points into the ice and stand comfortably on a vertical. He proceeded with a surety of footing he had never had on the streets of Munich. Each step bolted him down to the surface. And in each hand he carried an ice hammer with which he made swinging, cutting arcs that engaged the shining stainless-steel pick with the mirror-like wall.

All the snow had blown away or had melted. There were no traps, no pitfalls, no ambiguities. He progressed toward the summit rapidly, climbing steep ice walls as if he had been going up a ladder. The air became purer and the light more direct. Looking out to right or left, or glancing sometimes over his shoulders, he saw that he was now truly in the world of mountains.

Above the few clouds he could see only equal peaks of ice, and the Schreuderspitze dropping away from him. It was not the world of rock. No longer could he make out individual features in the valley. Green had become a hazy dark blue appropriate to an ocean floor. Whole countries came into view. The landscape was a mass of winding glaciers and great mountains. At that height, all was separated and refined. Soft things vanished, and there remained only the white and the silver.

He did not reach the summit until dark. He did not see the stars because icy clouds covered the Schreuderspitze in a crystalline fog which flowed past, crackling and hissing. He was heartbroken to have come all the way to the summit and then be blinded by masses of clouds. Since he could not descend until light, he decided to stay firmly stationed until he could see clearly. Meanwhile, he lost patience and began to address a presence in the air — casually, not thinking it strange to do so, not thinking twice about talking to the void.

He awoke in his room in early morning, saying, "All these blinding clouds. Why all these blinding clouds?"

Though the air of the valley was as fresh as a flower, he detested it. He pulled the covers over his head and strove for unconsciousness, but he grew too hot and finally gave up, staring at the remnants of dawn light soaking about his room. The day brightened in the way that stage lights come up, suddenly brilliant upon a beam-washed platform. It was early June. He had lost track of the exact date, but he knew that sometime before he had crossed into June. He had lost them early in June. Two years had passed.

He packed his things. Though he had lived like a monk, much had accumulated, and this he put into suitcases, boxes, and bags. He packed his pens, paper, books, a chess set on which he sometimes played against an imaginary opponent named Herr Claub, the beautiful Swiss calendars upon which he had at one time been almost afraid to gaze, cooking equipment no more complex than a soldier's mess kit, his clothing, even the beautifully wrought climbing equipment, for, after all, he had another set, up there in the *Eiswelt*. Only his bedding remained unpacked. It was on the floor in the center of the room, where he slept. He put some banknotes in an envelope — the June rent — and tacked it to the doorpost. The room was empty, white, and it would have echoed had it been slightly larger. He would say something and then listen intently, his eyes flaring like those of a lunatic. He had not eaten in days, and was not disappointed that even the waking world began to seem like a dream.

He went to the pump. He had accustomed himself to bathing in streams so cold that they were too frightened to freeze. Clean and cleanly shaven, he returned to his room. He smelled the sweet pine scent he had brought back on his clothing after hundreds of trips through the woods and forests girdling the greater mountains. Even the bedding was snowy white. He opened the closet and caught a glimpse of himself in the mirror. He was dark from sun and wind; his hair shone; his face had thinned; his eyebrows were now gold and white. For several days he had had only cold pure water. Like soldiers who come from training toughened and healthy, he had about him the air of a small child. He noticed a certain wildness in the eye, and he lay on the hard floor, as was his habit, in perfect comfort. He thought nothing. He felt nothing. He wished nothing.

Time passed as if he could compress and cancel it. Early-evening darkness began to make the white walls blue. He heard a crackling fire in the kitchen of the rooms next door, and imagined the shadows dancing there. Then he slept, departing.

On the mountain it was dreadfully cold. He huddled into himself against the wet silver clouds, and yet he smiled, happy to be once again on the summit. He thought of making an igloo, but remembered that he hadn't an ice saw. The wind began to build. If the storm continued, he would die. It would whittle him into a brittle wire, and then he would snap. The best he could do was to dig a trench with his ice hammers. He lay in the trench and closed his sleeves and hooded parka, drawing the shrouds tight. The wind came at him more and more fiercely. One gust was so powerful that it nearly lifted him out of the trench. He put in an ice piton, and attached his harness. Still the wind rose. It was difficult to breathe and nearly impossible to see. Any irregular surface whistled. The eye of the ice piton became a great siren. The zippers on his parka, the harness, the slings and equipment, all gave off musical tones, so that it was as if he were in a place with hundreds of tormented spirits.

The gray air fled past with breathtaking speed. Looking away from the wind, he had the impression of being propelled upward at unimaginable speed. Walls of gray sped by so fast that they glowed. He knew that if he were to look at the wind he would have the sense of hurtling forward in gravityless space.

And so he stared at the wind and its slowly pulsing gray glow. He did not know for how many hours he held that position. The rape of vision caused a host of delusions. He felt great momentum. He traveled until, eardrums throbbing with the sharpness of cold and wind, he was nearly dead, white as a candle, hardly able to breathe.

Then the acceleration ceased and the wind slowed. When, released from the great pressure, he fell back off the edge of the trench, he realized for the first time that he had been stretched tight on his line. He had never been so cold. But the wind was dying and the clouds were no longer a corridor through which he was propelled. They were, rather, a gentle mist which did not know quite what to do with itself. How would it dissipate? Would it rise to the stars, or would it fall in compression down into the valley below?

It fell; it fell all around him, downward like a lowering curtain. It fell in lines and stripes, always downward as if on signal, by command, in league with a directive force.

At first he saw just a star or two straight on high. But as the mist departed a flood of stars burst through. Roads of them led into infinity. Starry wheels sat in fiery white coronas. Near the horizon were the few separate gentle stars, shining out and turning clearly, as wide and round as planets. The air grew mild and warm. He bathed in it. He trembled. As the air became all clear and the mist drained away completely, he saw something which stunned him.

The Schreuderspitze was far higher than he had thought. It was hundreds of times higher than the mountains represented on the map he had seen in Munich. The Alps were to it not even foothills, not even rills. Below him was the purple earth, and all the great cities lit by sparkling lamps in their millions. It was a clear summer dawn and the weather was excellent, certainly June.

He did not know enough about other cities to make them out from the shapes they cast in light, but his eye seized quite easily upon Munich. He arose from his trench and unbuckled the harness, stepping a few paces higher on the rounded summit. There was Munich, shining and pulsing like a living thing, strung with lines of amber light — light which reverberated as if in crystals, light which played in many dimensions and moved about the course of the city, which was defined by darkness at its edge. He had come above time, above the world. The city of Munich existed before him with all its time compressed. As he watched, its history played out in repeating cycles. Nothing, not one movement, was lost from the crystal. The light of things danced and multiplied, again and again, and yet again. It was all there for him to claim. It was alive, and ever would be.

He knelt on one knee as in paintings he had seen of explorers claiming a coast of the New World. He dared close his eyes in the face of that miracle. He began to concentrate, to fashion according to will with the force of stilled time a vision of those he had loved. In all their bright colors, they began to appear before him.

He awoke as if shot out of a cannon. He went from lying on his back to a completely upright position in an instant, a flash, during which he slammed the floorboards energetically with a clenched fist and cursed the fact that he had returned from such a world. But by the time he stood straight, he was delighted to be doing so. He quickly dressed, packed his bedding, and began to shuttle down to the station and back. In three trips, his luggage was stacked on the platform.

He bought a ticket for Munich, where he had not been in many, many long months. He hungered for it, for the city, for the boats on the river, the goods in the shops, newspapers, the pigeons in the square, trees, traffic, even arguments, even Herr Franzen. So much rushed into his mind that he hardly saw his train pull in.

He helped the conductor load his luggage into the baggage car, and he asked, "Will we change at Garmisch-Partenkirchen?"

"No. We go right through, direct to Munich," said the conductor.

"Do me a great favor. Let me ride in the baggage car."

"I can't. It's a violation."

"Please. I've been months in the mountains. I would like to ride alone, for the last time."

The conductor relented, and Wallich sat atop a pile of boxes, looking at the landscape through a Dutch door, the top of which was open. Trees and meadows, sunny and lush in June, sped by. As they descended, the vegetation thickened until he saw along the cinder bed slow-running black rivers, skeins and skeins of thorns darted with the red of early raspberries, and flowers, which had sprung up on the paths. The air was warm and caressing — thick and full, like a swaying green sea at the end of August.

They closed on Munich, and the Alps appeared in a sweeping line of white cloud-touched peaks. As they pulled into the great station, as sooty as it had ever been, he remembered that he had climbed the Schreuderspitze, by its most difficult route. He had found freedom from grief in the great and heart-swelling sight he had seen from the summit. He felt its workings and he realized that soon enough he would come once more into the world of light. Soon enough he would be with his wife and son. But until then (and he knew that time would spark ahead), he would open himself to life in the city, return to his former profession, and struggle at his craft.

ERNEST HEMINGWAY

Ernest Hemingway (1899–1961) was born in Oak Park, Illinois, the son of a doctor. Following his graduation from high school, he worked briefly as a journalist in Kansas City; throughout his life journalism continued to attract him and to influence his choices of subject and style. In 1918 he enlisted as an ambulance driver on the Italian front in World War I. This experience — as all his experiences — ultimately found its way into his writing, in the novel *A Farewell to Arms* (1929). In Paris in the 1920s he met Gertrude Stein, Ezra Pound, F. Scott Fitzgerald, and other literary expatriates — what Stein dubbed "The Lost Generation." An aggressive, physically active, hard-drinking man, he spent his life in search of experience, adventure, and knowledge in many arenas: Left Bank Paris, the battlefields of the Spanish Civil War, the plains of Kenya, the islands of the Florida Keys, and Cuba. His first collection of stories, *In Our Time* (1924), was a major success. Throughout the 1920s and '30s followed the novels and stories with which he established a reputation and style that had profound impact on the writers of the twentieth century: *The Sun Also Rises* (1926), *Men Without Women* (stories, 1927), *The Green Hills of Africa* (1935), *The Fifth Column and the First Forty-nine Stories* (1938), and *For Whom the Bell Tolls* (1940). His spare style, which exposes the bone of the language, and terse heroism — "grace under pressure" — attracted literary imitation around the globe. Imitators, and detractors too, still exist; Hemingway's legacy is so strong that writers have often at least initially defined themselves as for or against it. Following the publication of the novels *Across the River and Into the Trees* (1950) and *The Old Man and the Sea* (1952), he was awarded the Nobel Prize for Literature in 1954. *Islands in the Stream* was published posthumously in 1970, nine years after Hemingway shot himself. "In Another Country," set in Milan in the First World War, is in style and substance the essence of the Hemingway code.

In Another Country

In the fall the war was always there, but we did not go to it any more. It was cold in the fall in Milan and the dark came very early. Then the electric lights came on, and it was pleasant along the streets looking in the windows. There was much game hanging outside the shops, and the snow powdered in the fur of the foxes and the wind blew their tails. The deer hung stiff and heavy and empty, and small birds blew in the wind and the wind turned their feathers. It was a cold fall and the wind came down from the mountains.

We were all at the hospital every afternoon, and there were different ways of walking across the town through the dusk to the hospital. Two of the ways were alongside canals, but they were long. Always, though, you crossed a bridge across a canal to enter the hospital. There was a choice of three bridges. On one of them a woman sold roasted chestnuts. It was warm, standing in front of her charcoal fire, and the chestnuts were warm afterward in your pocket. The hospital was very old and very beautiful, and you entered through a gate and walked across a courtyard and out a gate on the other side. There were usually funerals starting from the courtyard. Beyond the old hospital were the new brick pavilions, and there we met every afternoon and were all very polite and interested in what was the matter, and sat in the machines that were to make so much difference.

The doctor came up to the machine where I was sitting and said: "What did you like best to do before the war? Did you practise a sport?"

I said: "Yes, football."

"Good," he said. "You will be able to play football again better than ever."

My knee did not bend and the leg dropped straight from the knee to the ankle without a calf, and the machine was to bend the knee and make it move as in riding a tricycle. But it did not bend yet, and instead the machine lurched when it came to the bending part. The doctor said: "That will all pass. You are a fortunate young man. You will play football again like a champion."

In the next machine was a major who had a little hand like a baby's. He winked at me when the doctor examined his hand, which was between two leather straps that bounced up and down and flapped the stiff fingers, and said: "And will I too play football, captain-doctor?" He had been a very great fencer, and before the war the greatest fencer in Italy.

The doctor went to his office in a back room and brought a photograph which showed a hand that had been withered almost as small as the major's, before it had taken a machine course, and after was a little larger. The major held the photograph with his good hand and looked at it very carefully. "A wound?" he asked.

"An industrial accident," the doctor said.

"Very interesting, very interesting," the major said, and handed it back to the doctor.

"You have confidence?"

"No," said the major.

There were three boys who came each day who were about the same age I was. They were all three from Milan, and one of them was to be a lawyer, and one was to be a painter, and one had intended to be a soldier, and after we were finished with the machines, sometimes we walked back together to the Café Cova, which was next door to the Scala. We walked the short way through the communist quarter because we were four together. The people hated us because we were officers, and from a wineshop some one called out, "A basso gli ufficiali!" as we passed. Another boy who walked with us sometimes and made us five wore a black silk handkerchief across his face because he had no nose then and his face was to be rebuilt. He had gone out to the front from the military academy and been wounded within an hour after he had gone into the front line for the first time. They rebuilt his face, but he came from a very old family and they could never get the nose exactly right. He went to South America and worked in a bank. But this was a long time ago, and then we did not any of us know how it was going to be afterward. We only knew then that there was always the war, but that we were not going to it any more.

We all had the same medals, except the boy with the black silk bandage across his face, and he had not been at the front long enough to get any medals. The tall boy with a very pale face who was to be a lawyer had been a lieutenant of Arditi and had three medals of the sort we each had only one of. He had lived a very long time with death and was a little detached. We were all a little detached, and there was nothing that held us together except that we met every afternoon at the hospital. Although, as we walked to the Cova through the tough part of town, walking in the dark, with light and singing coming out of the wineshops, and sometimes having to walk into the street when the men and women would crowd together on the sidewalk so that we would have had to jostle them to get by, we felt held together by there being something that had happened that they, the people who disliked us, did not understand.

We ourselves all understood the Cova, where it was rich and warm and not too brightly lighted, and noisy and smoky at certain hours, and there were always girls at the tables and the illustrated papers on a rack on the wall. The girls at the Cova were very patriotic, and I found that the most patriotic people in Italy were the café girls — and I believe they are still patriotic.

The boys at first were very polite about my medals and asked me what I had done to get them. I showed them the papers, which were written in very beautiful language and full of *fratellanza* and *abnegazione,* but which really said, with the adjectives removed, that I had been given the medals because I was an American. After that their manner changed a little toward me, although I was their friend against outsiders. I was a friend, but I was never really one of them after they had read the citations, because it had been different with them and they had done very different things to get their medals. I had been wounded, it was true; but we all knew that being wounded, after all, was really an accident. I was never ashamed of the ribbons, though, and sometimes, after the cocktail hour, I would imagine myself having done all the things they had done to get their medals; but walking home at night through the empty streets with the cold wind and all the shops closed, trying to keep near the street lights, I knew that I would never have done such things, and I was very much afraid to die, and often lay in bed at night by myself, afraid to die and wondering how I would be when I went back to the front again.

The three with the medals were like hunting-hawks; and I was not a hawk, although I might seem a hawk to those who had never hunted; they, the three, knew better and so we drifted apart. But I stayed good friends with the boy who had been wounded his first day at the front, because he would never know now how he would have turned out; so he could never be accepted either, and I liked him because I thought perhaps he would not have turned out to be a hawk either.

The major, who had been the great fencer, did not believe in bravery, and spent much time while we sat in the machines correcting my grammar. He had complimented me on how I spoke Italian, and we talked together very easily. One day I had said that Italian seemed such an easy language to me that I could not take a great interest in it; everything was so easy to say. "Ah, yes," the major said. "Why, then, do you not take up the use of grammar?" So we took up the use of grammar, and soon Italian was such a difficult language that I was afraid to talk to him until I had the grammar straight in my mind.

The major came very regularly to the hospital. I do not think he ever missed a day, although I am sure he did not believe in the machines. There was a time when none of us believed in the machines and one day the major said it was all nonsense. The machines were new then and it was we who were to prove them. It was an idiotic idea, he said, "a theory, like another." I had not learned my grammar, and he said I was a stupid impossible disgrace, and he was a fool to have bothered with me. He was a small man and he sat straight up in his chair with his right hand thrust into the machine and looked straight ahead at the wall while the straps thumped up and down with his fingers in them.

"What will you do when the war is over if it is over?" he asked me. "Speak grammatically!"

"I will go to the States."

"Are you married?"

"No, but I hope to be."

"The more of a fool you are," he said. He seemed very angry. "A man must not marry."

"Why, Signor Maggiore?"

"Don't call me 'Signor Maggiore.'"

"Why must not a man marry?"

"He cannot marry. He cannot marry," he said angrily. "If he is to lose everything, he should not place himself in a position to lose that. He should not place himself in a position to lose. He should find things he cannot lose."

He spoke very angrily and bitterly, and looked straight ahead while he talked. "But why should he necessarily lose it?"

"He'll lose it," the major said. He was looking at the wall. Then he looked down at the machine and jerked his little hand out from between the straps and slapped it hard against his thigh. "He'll lose it," he almost shouted. "Don't argue with me!" Then he called to the attendant who ran the machines. "Come and turn this damned thing off."

He went back into the other room for the light treatment and the massage. Then I heard him ask the doctor if he might use his telephone and he shut the door. When he came back into the room, I was sitting in another machine. He was wearing his cape and had his cap on, and he came directly toward my machine and put his arm on my shoulder.

"I am so sorry," he said, and patted me on the shoulder with his good hand. "I would not be rude. My wife has just died. You must forgive me."

"Oh — " I said, feeling sick for him. "I am *so* sorry."

He stood there biting his lower lip. "It is very difficult," he said. "I cannot resign myself."

He looked straight past me and out through the window. Then he began to cry. "I am utterly unable to resign myself," he said and choked. And then crying, his head up looking at nothing, carrying himself straight and soldierly, with tears on both his cheeks and biting his lips, he walked past the machines and out the door.

The doctor told me that the major's wife, who was very young and whom he had not married until he was definitely invalided out of the war, had died of pneumonia. She had been sick only a few days. No one expected her to die. The major did not come to the hospital for three days. Then he came at the usual hour, wearing a black band on the sleeve of his uniform. When he came back, there were large framed photographs around the wall, of all sorts of wounds before and after they had been cured by the machines. In front of the machine the major used were three photographs of hands like his that were completely restored. I do not know where the doctor got them. I always understood we were the first to use the machines. The photographs did not make much difference to the major because he only looked out of the window.

ZORA NEALE HURSTON

Zora Neale Hurston (1903–1960) grew up in Eatonville, Florida, the first incorporated all-black town in America. Her father served three terms as its mayor. She was, even as a child, strong-minded and feisty; at age fourteen, disliking her new stepmother, she went to work as a wardrobe girl in a traveling Gilbert and Sullivan troupe. She received her formal education in Baltimore and at Howard University. In the 1920s Hurston was active in the Harlem Renaissance, writing plays and short stories. Her primary interest — and the source of much of her material — was black folklore, which she wove into stories essentially realistic but tinged with the legendary. Her short stories are collected in *The Eatonville Anthology* (1927); her novels include *Jonah's Gourd Vine* (1934), *Their Eyes Were Watching God* (1937), and *Seraph on the Suwanee* (1948). Some of her best work is anthologized in *I Love Myself When I Am Laughing . . . : A Zora Neale Hurston Reader* (ed. Washington and Walker, 1979). Humorous and bold, Hurston wrote in her autobiography, "I have loved unselfishly, and I have fondled hatred with the red-hot Tongs of Hell. That's living." "Spunk" is a reflection of that definition.

Spunk

1

A giant of a brown-skinned man sauntered up the one street of the village and out into the palmetto thickets with a small pretty woman clinging lovingly to his arm.

"Looka theah, folkses!" cried Elijah Mosley, slapping his leg gleefully. "Theah they go, big as life an' brassy as tacks."

All the loungers in the store tried to walk to the door with an air of nonchalance but with small success.

"Now pee-eople!" Walter Thomas gasped. "Will you look at 'em!"

"But that's one thing Ah likes about Spunk Banks — he ain't skeered of nothin' on God's green footstool — *nothin'!* He rides that log down at saw-mill jus' like he struts 'round wid another man's wife — jus' don't give a kitty. When Tes' Miller got cut to giblets on that circle-saw, Spunk steps right up and starts ridin'. The rest of us was skeered to go near it."

A round-shouldered figure in overalls much too large came nervously in the door and the talking ceased. The men looked at each other and winked.

"Gimme some soda-water. Sass'prilla Ah reckon," the newcomer ordered, and stood far down the counter near the open pickled pig-feet tub to drink it.

Elijah nudged Walter and turned with mock gravity to the new-comer.

"Say, Joe, how's everything up yo' way? How's yo' wife?"

Joe started and all but dropped the bottle he was holding. He swallowed several times painfully and his lips trembled.

"Aw 'Lige, you oughtn't to do nothin' like that," Walter grumbled. Elijah ignored him.

"She jus' passed heah a few minutes ago goin' thata way," with a wave of his hand in the direction of the woods.

Now Joe knew his wife had passed that way. He knew that the men lounging in the general store had seen her, moreover, he knew that the men knew *he* knew. He stood there silent for a long moment staring blankly, with his Adam's apple twitching nervously up and down his throat. One could actually *see* the pain he was suffering, his eyes, his face, his hands, and even the dejected slump of his shoulders. He set the bottle down upon the counter. He didn't bang it, just eased it out of his hand silently and fiddled with his suspender buckle.

"Well, Ah'm goin' after her to-day. Ah'm goin' an' fetch her back. Spunk's done gone too fur."

He reached deep down into his trouser pocket and drew out a hollow ground razor, large and shiny, and passed his moistened thumb back and forth over the edge.

"Talkin' like a man, Joe. 'Course that's *yo'* fambly affairs, but Ah like to see grit in anybody."

Joe Kanty laid down a nickel and stumbled out into the street.

Dusk crept in from the woods. Ike Clarke lit the swinging oil lamp that was almost immediately surrounded by candle-flies. The men laughed boisterously behind Joe's back as they watched him shamble woodward.

"You oughtn't to said whut you said to him, 'Lige — look how it worked him up," Walter chided.

"And Ah hope it did work him up. Tain't even decent for a man to take and take like he do."

"Spunk will sho' kill him."

"Aw, Ah doan know. You never kin tell. He might turn him up an' spank him fur gettin' in the way, but Spunk wouldn't shoot no unarmed man. Dat razor he carried outa heah ain't gonna run Spunk down an' cut him, an' Joe ain't got the nerve to go to Spunk with it knowing he totes that Army .45. He makes that break outa heah to bluff us. He's gonna hide that razor behind the first palmetto root an' sneak back home to bed. Don't tell me nothin' 'bout that rabbit-foot colored man. Didn't he meet Spunk an' Lena face to face one day las' week an' mumble sumthin' to Spunk 'bout lettin' his wife alone?"

"What did Spunk say?" Walter broke in. "Ah like him fine but tain't right the way he carries on wid Lena Kanty, jus' 'cause Joe's timid 'bout fightin'."

"You wrong theah, Walter. Tain't 'cause Joe's timid at all, it's 'cause Spunk wants Lena. If Joe was a passle of wile cats Spunk would tackle the job just the same. He'd go after *anything* he wanted the same way. As Ah wuz sayin' a minute ago, he tole Joe right to his face that Lena was his. 'Call her and see if she'll come. A woman knows her boss an' she answers when he calls.' 'Lena, ain't I yo' husband?' Joe sorter whines out. Lena looked at him real disgusted but she don't answer and she don't move outa her tracks. Then Spunk reaches out an' takes hold of her arm an' says: 'Lena, youse mine. From now on Ah works for you an' fights for you an' Ah never wants you to look to nobody for a crumb of bread, a stitch of close or a shingle to go over yo' head, but *me* long as Ah live. Ah'll git the lumber foh owah house to-morrow. Go home an' git yo' things together!'

" 'Thass mah house,' Lena speaks up. 'Papa gimme that.'

" 'Well, says Spunk, 'doan give up what's yours, but when youse inside doan forgit youse mine, an' let no other man git outa his place wid you!'

"Lena looked up at him with her eyes so full of love that they wuz runnin' over, an' Spunk seen it an' Joe seen it too, and his lip started to tremblin' and his Adam's apple was galloping up and down his neck like a race horse. Ah bet he's wore out half a dozen Adam's apples since Spunk's been on the job with Lena. That's all he'll do. He'll be back heah after while swallowin' an' workin' his lips like he wants to say somethin' an' can't."

"But didn't he do *nothin'* to stop 'em?"

"Nope, not a frazzlin' thing — jus' stood there. Spunk took Lena's arm and walked off jus' like nothin' ain't happened and he stood there gazin' after them till they was outa sight. Now you know a woman don't want no man like that. I'm jus' waitin' to see whut he's goin' to say when he gits back."

2

But Joe Kanty never came back, never. The men in the store heard the sharp report of a pistol somewhere distant in the palmetto thicket and soon Spunk came walking leisurely, with his big black Stetson set at the same rakish angle and Lena clinging to his arm, came walking right into the general store. Lena wept in a frightened manner.

"Well," Spunk announced calmly, "Joe came out there wid a meat axe an' made me kill him."

He sent Lena home and led the men back to Joe — crumpled and limp with his right hand still clutching his razor.

"See mah back? Mah close cut clear through. He sneaked up an' tried to kill me from the back, but Ah got him, an' got him good, first shot," Spunk said.

The men glared at Elijah, accusingly.

"Take him up an' plant him in Stony Lonesome," Spunk said in a careless voice. "Ah didn't wanna shoot him but he made me do it. He's a dirty coward, jumpin' on a man from behind."

Spunk turned on his heel and sauntered away to where he knew his love wept in fear for him and no man stopped him. At the general store later on, they all talked of locking him up until the sheriff should come from Orlando, but no one did anything but talk.

A clear case of self-defense, the trial was a short one, and Spunk walked out of the court house to freedom again. He could work again, ride the dangerous log-carriage that fed the singing, snarling, biting circle-saw; he could stroll the soft dark lanes with his guitar. He was free to roam the woods again; he was free to return to Lena. He did all these things.

3

"Whut you reckon, Walt?" Elijah asked one night later. "Spunk's gittin' ready to marry Lena!"

"Naw! Why, Joe ain't had time to git cold yit. Nohow Ah didn't figger Spunk was the marryin' kind."

"Well, he is," rejoined Elijah. "He done moved most of Lena's things — and her along wid 'em — over to the Bradley house. He's buying it. Jus' like Ah told yo' all right in heah the night Joe was kilt. Spunk's crazy 'bout Lena. He don't want folks to keep on talkin' 'bout her — thass reason he's rushin' so. Funny thing 'bout that bob-cat, wan't it?"

"What bob-cat, 'Lige? Ah ain't heered 'bout none."

"Ain't cher? Well, night befo' las' as they was goin' to bed, a big black bob-cat, black all over, you hear me, *black,* walked round and round that house and howled like forty, an' when Spunk got his gun an' went to the winder to shoot it, he says it stood right still an' looked him in the eye, an' howled right at him. The thing got Spunk so nervoused up he couldn't shoot. But Spunk says twan't no bob-cat nohow. He says it was Joe done sneaked back from Hell!"

"Humph!" sniffed Walter, "he oughter be nervous after what he done. Ah reckon Joe come back to dare him to marry Lena, or to come out an' fight. Ah bet he'll be back time and again, too. Know what Ah think? Joe wuz a braver man than Spunk."

There was a general shout of derision from the group.

"Thass a fact," went on Walter. "Lookit whut he done; took a razor an' went out to fight a man he knowed toted a gun an' wuz a crack shot, too; 'nother thing Joe wuz skeered of Spunk, skeered plumb stiff! But he went jes' the same. It took him a long time to get his nerve up. Tain't nothin' for Spunk to fight when he ain't skeered of nothin'. Now, Joe's done come back to have it out wid the man that's got all he ever had. Y'all know Joe ain't never had nothin' nor wanted nothin' besides Lena. It musta been a h'ant cause ain't nobody never seen no black bob-cat."

" 'Nother thing," cut in one of the men, "Spunk was cussin' a blue streak to-day 'cause he 'lowed dat saw wuz wobblin' — almos' got 'im once. The machinist come, looked it over an' said it wuz alright. Spunk musta been leanin' t'wards it some. Den he claimed somebody pushed 'im but twan't nobody close to 'im. Ah wuz glad when knockin' off time came. I'm skeered of dat man when he gits hot. He'd beat you full of button holes as quick as he'd look atcher."

4

The men gathered the next evening in a different mood, no laughter. No badinage this time.

"Look, 'Lige, you goin' to set up wid Spunk?"

"Naw, Ah reckon not, Walter. Tell yuh the truth, Ah'm a li'l bit skittish. Spunk died too wicket — died cussin' he did. You know he thought he was done outa life."

"Good Lawd, who'd he think done it?"

"Joe."

"Joe Kanty? How come?"

"Walter, Ah b'leeve Ah will walk up thata way an' set. Lena would like it Ah reckon."

"But whut did he say, 'Lige?"

Elijah did not answer until they had left the lighted store and were strolling down the dark street.

"Ah wuz loadin' a wagon wid scantlin' right near the saw when Spunk fell on the carriage but 'fore Ah could git to him the saw got him in the body — awful sight. Me an' Skint Miller got him off but it was too late. Anybody could see that. The fust thing he said wuz: 'He pushed me, 'Lige — the dirty hound pushed me in the back!' — he was spittin' blood at ev'ry breath. We laid him on the sawdust pile with his face to the East so's he could die easy. He helt mah han' till the last, Walter, and said: 'It was Joe, 'Lige . . . the dirty sneak shoved me . . . he didn't dare come to mah face . . . but Ah'll git the son-of-a-wood louse soon's Ah get there an' make hell too hot for him . . . Ah felt him shove me . . . !' Thass how he died."

"If spirits kin fight, there's a powerful tussle goin' on somewhere ovah Jordan 'cause Ah b'leeve Joe's ready for Spunk an' ain't skeered any more — yas, Ah b'leeve Joe pushed 'im mahself."

They had arrived at the house. Lena's lamentations were deep and loud. She had filled the room with magnolia blossoms that gave off a heavy sweet odor. The keepers of the wake tipped about whispering in frightened tones. Everyone in the village was there, even old Jeff Kanty, Joe's father, who a few hours before would have been afraid to come within ten feet of him, stood leering triumphantly down upon the fallen giant as if his fingers had been the teeth of steel that laid him low.

The cooling board consisted of three sixteen-inch boards on saw horses, a dingy sheet was his shroud.

The women ate heartily of the funeral baked meats and wondered who would be Lena's next. The men whispered coarse conjectures between guzzles of whiskey.

HENRY JAMES

Henry James (1843–1916) was born in New York City, the son of a wealthy theological philosopher who saw to it that his children were educated in Europe, to "get such a sensuous education as they cannot get here." That education in its way set in motion the "international theme" that preoccupied James for the rest of his life and informed much of his greatest fiction: a psychological probing of the differences between the European and the American character. James spent a brief time at Harvard Law School and then, beginning around 1865, regularly contributed short stories and reviews to various American periodicals. In 1875 he moved to France, realizing that, for him, Europe offered more "fund of suggestion for a novelist." In the following year he moved to London; he lived in England for the rest of his life, making occasional tours back to the United States. He became a British citizen in 1915. Molding his experiences in America and Europe into the stuff of fiction, James began, in 1876, to write the novels and novellas upon which his brilliant reputation is founded: *Roderick Hudson* (1876), *The American* (1877), *Daisy Miller* (1879), *The Portrait of a Lady* (1881), *The Bostonians* (1886), *What Maisie Knew* (1897), *The Turn of the Screw* (1898), *The Wings of the Dove* (1902), *The Ambassadors* (1903), and *The Golden Bowl* (1904). In them, as in the nearly one hundred stories he wrote (gathered in many editions, including *Complete Tales,* ed. Edel, 1962–64), James explored the sensibilities of character with a delicacy and psychological intensity that have few equals in the realm of fiction. His extraordinary style, which so deeply enhances his meaning, has been described as having "a vibrato that hangs over the cumulus of actual words, adding an intangible exactly as occurs so much more familiarly in music. . . ." "The Beast in the Jungle" is a masterpiece of James's style and insight; the second story here, "The Turn of the Screw," is one of the most profound — and ambiguous — ghost stories ever written.

The Beast in the Jungle

1

What determined the speech that startled him in the course of their encounter scarcely matters, being probably but some words spoken by himself quite without intention — spoken as they lingered and slowly moved together after their renewal of acquaintance. He had been conveyed by friends, an hour or two before, to the house at which she was staying; the party of visitors at the other house, of whom he was one, and thanks to whom it was his theory, as always, that he was lost in the crowd, had been invited over to luncheon. There had been after luncheon much dispersal, all in the interest of the original motive, a view of Weatherend itself and the fine things, intrinsic features, pictures, heirlooms, treasures of all the arts, that made the place almost famous; and the great rooms were so numerous that guests could wander at their will, hang back from the principal group, and, in cases where they took such matters with the least seriousness, give themselves up to mysterious appreciations and measurements. There were persons to be observed, singly or in couples, bending toward objects in out-of-the-way corners with their hands on their knees and their heads nodding quite as with the emphasis of an excited sense of smell. When they were two they either mingled their sounds of ecstasy or melted into silences of even deeper import, so that there were aspects of the occasion that gave it for Marcher much the air of the "look round," previous to a sale highly advertised, that excites or quenches, as may be, the dream of acquisition. The dream of acquisition at Weather-end would have had to be wild indeed, and John Marcher found himself, among such suggestions, disconcerted almost equally by the presence of those who knew too much and by that of those who knew nothing. The great rooms caused so much poetry and history to press upon him that he needed to wander apart to feel in a proper relation with them, though his doing so was not, as happened, like the gloating of some of his companions, to be compared to the movements of a dog sniffing a cupboard. It had an issue promptly enough in a direction that was not to have been calculated.

It led, in short, in the course of the October afternoon, to his closer meeting with May Bartram, whose face, a reminder, yet not quite a remembrance, as they sat, much separated, at a very long table, had begun merely by troubling him rather pleasantly. It affected him as the sequel of something of which he had lost the beginning. He knew it, and for the time quite welcomed it, as a continuation, but didn't know what it continued, which was an interest, or an amusement, the greater as he was also somehow aware — yet without a direct sign from her — that the young woman herself had not lost the thread. She had not lost it, but she wouldn't give it back to him, he saw, without some putting forth of his hand for it; and he not only saw that, but saw several things more, things odd enough in the light of the fact that at the moment some accident of grouping brought them face to face he was still merely fumbling with the idea that any contact between them in the past would have had no importance. If it had had no importance he scarcely knew why his actual impression of her should so seem to have so much; the answer to which, however, was that in such a life as they all appeared to be leading for the moment one could but take things as they came. He was satisfied, without in the least being able to say why, that this young lady might roughly have ranked in the house as a poor relation; satisfied also that she was not there on a brief visit, but was more or less a part of the establishment — almost a working, a remunerated part. Didn't she enjoy at periods a protection that she paid for by helping, among other services, to show the place and explain it, deal with the tiresome people, answer questions about the dates of the buildings, the styles of the furniture, the authorship of the pictures, the favourite haunts of the ghost? It wasn't that she looked as if you could have given her shillings — it was impossible to look less so. Yet when she finally drifted toward him, distinctly handsome, though ever so much older — older than when he had seen her before — it might have been as an effect of her guessing that he had, within the couple of hours, devoted more imagination to her than to all the others put together, and had thereby penetrated to a kind of truth that the others were too stupid for. She *was* there on harder terms than anyone; she was there as a consequence of things suffered, in one way and another, in the interval of years; and she remembered him very much as she was remembered — only a good deal better.

By the time they at last thus came to speech they were alone in one of the rooms — remarkable for a fine portrait over the chimney-place — out of which their friends had passed, and the charm of it was that even before they had spoken they had practically arranged with each other to stay behind for talk. The charm, happily, was in other things too; it was partly in there being scarce a spot at Weatherend without something to stay behind for. It was in the way the autumn day looked into the high windows as it waned; in the way the red light, breaking at the close from under a low, sombre sky, reached out in a long shaft and played over old wainscots, old tapestry, old gold, old colour. It was most of all perhaps in the way she came to him as if, since she had been turned on to deal with the simpler sort, he might, should he choose to keep the whole thing down, just take her mild attention for a part of her general business. As soon as he heard her voice, however, the gap was filled up and the missing link supplied; the slight irony he divined in her attitude lost its advantage. He almost jumped at it to get there before her. "I met you years and years ago in Rome. I remember all about it." She confessed to disappointment — she had been so sure he didn't; and to prove how well he did he began to pour forth the particular recollections that popped up as he called for them. Her face and her voice, all at his service now, worked the miracle — the impression operating like the torch of a lamplighter who touches into flame, one by one, a long row of gas jets. Marcher flattered himself that the illumination was brilliant, yet he was really still more pleased on her showing him, with amusement, that in his haste to make everything right he had got most things rather wrong. It hadn't been at Rome — it had been at Naples; and it hadn't been seven years before — it had been more nearly ten. She hadn't been either with her uncle and aunt, but with her mother and her brother; in addition to which it was not with the Pembles that *he* had been, but with the Boyers, coming down in their company from Rome — a point on which she insisted, a little to his confusion, and as to which she had her evidence in hand. The Boyers she had known, but she didn't know the Pembles, though she had heard of them, and it was the people he was with who had made them acquainted. The incident of the thunderstorm that had raged round them with such violence as to drive them for refuge into an excavation — this incident had not occurred at the Palace of the Cæsars, but at Pompeii, on an occasion when they had been present there at an important find.

He accepted her amendments, he enjoyed her corrections, though the moral of them was, she pointed out, that he *really* didn't remember the least thing about her; and he only felt it as a drawback that when all was made conformable to the truth there didn't appear much of anything left. They lingered together still, she neglecting her office — for from the moment he was so clever she had no proper right to him — and both neglecting the house, just waiting as to see if a memory or two more wouldn't again breathe upon them. It had not taken them many minutes, after all, to put down on the table, like the cards of a pack, those that constituted their respective hands; only what came out was that the pack was unfortunately not perfect — that the past, invoked, invited, encouraged, could give them, naturally, no more than it had. It had made them meet — her at twenty, him at twenty-five; but nothing was so strange, they seemed to say to each other, as that, while so occupied, it hadn't done a little more for them. They looked at each other as with the feeling of an occasion missed; the present one would have been so much better if the other, in the far distance, in the foreign land, hadn't been so stupidly meagre. There weren't apparently, all counted, more than a dozen little old things that had succeeded in coming to pass between them; trivialities of youth, simplicities of freshness, stupidities of ignorance, small possible germs, but too deeply buried — too deeply (didn't it seem?) to sprout after so many years. Marcher said to himself that he ought to have rendered her some service — saved her from a capsized boat in the Bay, or at least recovered her dressing-bag, filched from her cab, in the streets of Naples, by a lazzarone with a stiletto. Or it would have been nice if he could have been taken with fever, alone, at his hotel, and she could have come to look after him, to write to his people, to drive him out in convalescence. *Then* they would be in possession of the something or other that their actual show seemed to lack. It yet somehow presented itself, this show, as too good to be spoiled; so that they were reduced for a few minutes more to wondering a little helplessly why — since they seemed to know a certain number of the same people — their reunion had been so long averted. They didn't use that name for it, but their delay from minute to minute to join the others was a kind of confession that they didn't quite want it to be a failure. Their attempted supposition of reasons for their not having met but showed how little they knew of each other. There came in fact a moment when Marcher felt a positive pang. It was vain to pretend she was an old friend, for all the communities were wanting, in spite of which it was as an old friend that he saw she would have suited him. He had new ones enough — was surrounded with them, for instance, at that hour at the other house; as a new one he probably wouldn't have so much as noticed her. He would have liked to invent something, get her to make-believe with him that some passage of a romantic or critical kind *had* originally occurred. He was really almost reaching out in imagination — as against time — for something that would do, and saying to himself that if it didn't come this new incident would simply and rather awkwardly close. They would separate, and now for no second or for no third chance. They would have tried and not succeeded. Then it was, just at the turn, as he afterwards made it out to himself, that, everything else failing, she herself decided to take up the case and, as it were, save the situation. He felt as soon as she spoke that she had been consciously keeping back what she said and hoping to get on without it, a scruple in her that immensely touched him when, by the end of three or four minutes more, he was able to measure it. What she brought out, at any rate, quite cleared the air and supplied the link — the link it was such a mystery he should frivolously have managed to lose.

"You know you told me something that I've never forgotten and that again and again has made me think of you since; it was that tremendously hot day when we went to Sorrento, across the bay, for the breeze. What I allude to was what you said to me, on the way back, as we sat, under the awning of the boat, enjoying the cool. Have you forgotten?"

He had forgotten, and he was even more surprised than ashamed. But the great thing was that he saw it was no vulgar reminder of any "sweet" speech. The vanity of women had long memories, but she was making no claim on him of a compliment or a mistake. With another woman, a totally different one, he might have feared the recall possibly even of some imbecile "offer." So, in having to say that he had indeed forgotten, he was conscious rather of a loss than of a gain; he already saw an interest in the matter of her reference. "I try to think — but I give it up. Yet I remember the Sorrento day."

"I'm not very sure you do," May Bartram after a moment said; "and I'm not very sure I ought to want you to. It's dreadful to bring a person back, at any time, to what he was ten years before. If you've lived away from it," she smiled, "so much the better."

"Ah, if *you* haven't why should I?" he asked.

"Lived away, you mean, from what I myself was?"

"From what *I* was. I was of course an ass," Marcher went on; "but I would rather know from you just the sort of ass I was than — from the moment you have something in your mind — not know anything."

Still, however, she hesitated. "But if you've completely ceased to be that sort — ?"

"Why, I can then just so all the more bear to know. Besides, perhaps I haven't."

"Perhaps. Yet if you haven't," she added, "I should suppose you would remember. Not indeed that *I* in the least connect with my impression the invidious name you use. If I had only thought you foolish," she explained, "the thing I speak of wouldn't so have remained with me. It was about yourself." She waited, as if it might come to him; but as, only meeting her eyes in wonder, he gave no sign, she burnt her ships. "Has it ever happened?"

Then it was that, while he continued to stare, a light broke for him and the blood slowly came to his face, which began to burn with recognition. "Do you mean I told you — ?" But he faltered, lest what came to him shouldn't be right, lest he should only give himself away.

"It was something about yourself that it was natural one shouldn't forget — that is if one remembered you at all. That's why I ask you," she smiled, "if the thing you then spoke of has ever come to pass?"

Oh, then he saw, but he was lost in wonder and found himself embarrassed. This, he also saw, made her sorry for him, as if her allusion had been a mistake. It took him but a moment, however, to feel that it had not been, much as it had been a surprise. After the first little shock of it her knowledge on the contrary began, even if rather strangely, to taste sweet to him. She was the only other person in the world then who would have it, and she had had it all these years, while the fact of his having so breathed his secret had unaccountably faded from him. No wonder they couldn't have met as if nothing had happened. "I judge," he finally said, "that I know what you mean. Only I had strangely enough lost the consciousness of having taken you so far into my confidence."

"Is it because you've taken so many others as well?"

"I've taken nobody. Not a creature since then."

"So that I'm the only person who knows?"

"The only person in the world."

"Well," she quickly replied. "I myself have never spoken. I've never, never repeated of you what you told me." She looked at him so that he perfectly believed her. Their eyes met over it in such a way that he was without a doubt. "And I never will."

She spoke with an earnestness that, as if almost excessive, put him at ease about her possible derision. Somehow the whole question was a new luxury to him — that is, from the moment she was in possession. If she didn't take the ironic view she clearly took the sympathetic, and that was what he had had, in all the long time, from no one whomsoever. What he felt was that he couldn't at present have begun to tell her and yet could profit perhaps exquisitely by the accident of having done so of old. "Please don't then. We're just right as it is."

"Oh, I am," she laughed, "if you are!" To which she added: "Then you do still feel in the same way?"

It was impossible to him not to take to himself that she was really interested, and it all kept coming as a sort of revelation. He had thought of himself so long as abominably alone, and, lo, he wasn't alone a bit. He hadn't been, it appeared, for an hour — since those moments on the Sorrento boat. It was *she* who had been, he seemed to see as he looked at her — she who had been made so by the graceless fact of his lapse of fidelity. To tell her what he had told her — what had it been but to ask something of her? something that she had given, in her charity, without his having, by a remembrance, by a return of the spirit, failing another encounter, so much as thanked her. What he had asked of her had been simply at first not to laugh at him. She had beautifully not done so for ten years, and she was not doing so now. So he had endless gratitude to make up. Only for that he must see just how he had figured to her. "What, exactly, was the account I gave — ?"

"Of the way you did feel? Well, it was very simple. You said you had had from your earliest time, as the deepest thing within you, the sense of being kept for something rare and strange, possibly prodigious and terrible, that was sooner or later to happen to you, that you had in your bones the foreboding and the conviction of, and that would perhaps overwhelm you."

"Do you call that very simple?" John Marcher asked.

She thought a moment. "It was perhaps because I seemed, as you spoke, to understand it."

"You do understand it?" he eagerly asked.

Again she kept her kind eyes on him. "You still have the belief?"

"Oh!" he exclaimed helplessly. There was too much to say.

"Whatever it is to be," she clearly made out, "it hasn't yet come."

He shook his head in complete surrender now. "It hasn't yet come. Only, you know, it isn't anything I'm to *do,* to achieve in the world, to be distinguished or admired for. I'm not such an ass as *that.* It would be much better, no doubt, if I were."

"It's to be something you're merely to suffer?"

"Well, say to wait for — to have to meet, to face, to see suddenly break out in my life; possibly destroying all further consciousness, possibly annihilating me; possibly, on the other hand, only altering everything, striking at the root of all my world and leaving me to the consequences, however they shape themselves."

She took this in, but the light in her eyes continued for him not to be that of mockery. "Isn't what you describe perhaps but the expectation — or, at any rate, the sense of danger, familiar to so many people — of falling in love?"

John Marcher thought. "Did you ask me that before?"

"No — I wasn't so free-and-easy then. But it's what strikes me now."

"Of course," he said after a moment, "it strikes you. Of course it strikes *me.* Of course what's in store for me may be no more than that. The only thing is," he went on, "that I think that if it had been that, I should by this time know."

"Do you mean because you've *been* in love?" And then as he but looked at her in silence: "You've been in love, and it hasn't meant such a catacylsm, hasn't proved the great affair?"

"Here I am, you see. It hasn't been overwhelming."

"Then it hasn't been love," said May Bartram.

"Well, I at least thought it was. I took it for that — I've taken it till now. It was agreeable, it was delightful, it was miserable," he explained. "But it wasn't strange. It wasn't what *my* affair's to be."

"You want something all to yourself — something that nobody else knows or *has* known?"

"It isn't a question of what I 'want' — God knows I don't want anything. It's only a question of the apprehension that haunts me — that I live with day by day."

He said this so lucidly and consistently that, visibly, it further imposed itself. If she had not been interested before she would have been interested now. "Is it a sense of coming violence?"

Evidently now too, again, he liked to talk of it. "I don't think of it as — when it does come — necessarily violent. I only think of it as natural and as of course, above all, unmistakable. I think of it simply as *the* thing. *The* thing will of itself appear natural."

"Then how will it appear strange?"

Marcher bethought himself. "It won't — to *me*."

"To whom then?"

"Well," he replied, smiling at last, "say to you."

"Oh then, I'm to be present?"

"Why, you *are* present — since you know."

"I see." She turned it over. "But I mean at the catastrophe."

At this, for a minute, their lightness gave way to their gravity; it was as if the long look they exchanged held them together. "It will only depend on yourself — if you'll watch with me."

"Are you afraid?" she asked.

"Don't leave me *now*," he went on.

"Are you afraid?" she repeated.

"Do you think me simply out of my mind?" he pursued instead of answering. "Do I merely strike you as a harmless lunatic?"

"No," said May Bartram. "I understand you. I believe you."

"You mean you feel how my obsession — poor old thing! — may correspond to some possible reality?"

"To some possible reality."

"Then you *will* watch with me?"

She hesitated, then for the third time put her question. "Are you afraid?"

"Did I tell you I was — at Naples?"

"No, you said nothing about it."

"Then I don't know. And I should *like* to know," said John Marcher. "You'll tell me yourself whether you think so. If you'll watch with me you'll see."

"Very good then." They had been moving by this time across the room, and at the door, before passing out, they paused as if for the full wind-up of their understanding. "I'll watch with you," said May Bartram.

2

The fact that she "knew" — knew and yet neither chaffed him nor betrayed him — had in a short time begun to constitute between them a sensible bond, which became more marked when, within the year that followed their afternoon at Weatherend, the opportunities for meeting multiplied. The event that thus promoted these occasions was the death of the ancient lady, her great-aunt, under whose wing, since losing her mother, she had to such an extent found shelter, and who, though but the widowed mother of the new successor to the property, had succeeded — thanks to a high tone and a high temper — in not forfeiting the supreme position at the great house. The deposition of this personage arrived but with her death, which, followed by many changes, made in particular a difference for the young woman in whom Marcher's expert attention had recognised from the first a dependent with a pride that might ache though it didn't bristle. Nothing for a long time had made him easier than the thought that the aching must have been much soothed by Miss Bartram's now finding herself able to set up a small home in London. She had acquired property, to an amount that made that luxury just possible, under her aunt's extremely complicated will, and when the whole matter began to be straightened out, which indeed took time, she let him know that the happy issue was at last in view. He had seen her again before that day, both because she had more than once accompanied the ancient lady to town and because he had paid another visit to the friends who so conveniently made of Weatherend one of the charms of their own hospitality. These friends had taken him back there; he had achieved there again with Miss Bartram some quiet detachment; and he had in London succeeded in persuading her to more than one brief absence from her aunt. They went together, on these latter occasions, to the National Gallery and the South Kensington Museum, where, among vivid reminders, they talked of Italy at large — not now attempting to recover, as at first, the taste of their youth and their ignorance. That recovery, the first day at Weatherend, had served its purpose well, had given them quite enough; so that they were, to Marcher's sense, no longer hovering about the headwaters of their stream, but had felt their boat pushed sharply off and down the current.

They were literally afloat together; for our gentleman this was marked, quite as marked as that the fortunate cause of it was just the buried treasure of her knowledge. He had with his own hands dug up this little hoard, brought to light — that is to within reach of the dim day constituted by their discretions and privacies — the object of value the hiding-place of which he had, after putting it into the ground himself, so strangely, so long forgotten. The exquisite luck of having again just stumbled on the spot made him indifferent to any other question; he would doubtless have devoted more time to the odd accident of his lapse of memory if he had not been moved to devote so much to the sweetness, the comfort, as he felt, for the future, that this accident itself had helped to keep fresh. It had never entered into his plan that anyone should "know," and mainly for the reason that it was not in him to tell anyone. That would have been impossible, since nothing but the amusement of a cold world would have waited on it. Since, however, a mysterious fate had opened his mouth in youth, in spite of him, he would count that a compensation and profit by it to the utmost. That the right person *should* know tempered the asperity of his secret more even than his shyness had permitted him to imagine; and May Bartram was clearly right, because — well, because there she was. Her knowledge simply settled it; he would have been sure enough by this time had she been wrong. There was that in his situation, no doubt, that disposed him too much to see her as a mere confidant, taking all her light for him from the fact—the fact only — of her interest in his predicament, from her mercy, sympathy, seriousness, her consent not to regard him as the funniest of the funny. Aware, in fine, that her price for him was just in her giving him this constant sense of his being admirably spared, he was careful to remember that she had, after all, also a life of her own, with things that might happen to *her,* things that in friendship one should likewise take account of. Something fairly remarkable came to pass with him, for that matter, in this connection — something represented by a certain passage of his consciousness, in the suddenest way, from one extreme to the other.

He had thought himself, so long as nobody knew, the most disinterested person in the world, carrying his concentrated burden, his perpetual suspense, ever so quietly, holding his tongue about it, giving others no glimpse of it nor of its effect upon his life, asking of them no allowance and only making on his side all those that were asked. He had disturbed nobody with the queerness of having to know a haunted man, though he had had moments of rather special temptation on hearing people say that they were "unsettled." If they were as unsettled as he was — he who had never been settled for an hour in his life — they would know what it meant. Yet it wasn't, all the same, for him to make them, and he listened to them civilly enough. This was why he had such good — though possibly such rather colourless —manners; this was why, above all, he could regard himself, in a greedy world, as decently — as, in fact, perhaps even a little sublimely — unselfish. Our point is accordingly that he valued this character quite sufficiently to measure his present danger of letting it lapse, against which he promised himself to be much on his guard. He was quite ready, none the less, to be selfish just a little, since, surely, no more charming occasion for it had come to him. "Just a little," in a word, was just as much as Miss Bartram, taking one day with another, would let him. He never would be in the least coercive, and he would keep well before him the lines on which consideration for her — the very highest—ought to proceed. He would thoroughly establish the heads under which her affairs, her requirements, her peculiarities — he went so far as to give them the latitude of that name — would come into their intercourse. All this naturally was a sign of how much he took the intercourse itself for granted. There was nothing more to be done about *that*. It simply existed; had sprung into being with her first penetrating question to him in the autumn light there at Weatherend. The real form it should have taken on the basis that stood out large was the form of their marrying. But the devil in this was that the very basis itself put marrying out of the question. His conviction, his apprehension, his obsession, in short, was not a condition he could invite a woman to share; and that consequence of it was precisely what was the matter with him. Something or other lay in wait for him, amid the twists and the turns of the months and the years, like a crouching beast in the jungle. It signified little whether the crouching beast were destined to slay him or to be slain. The definite point was the inevitable spring of the creature; and the definite lesson from that was that a man of feeling didn't cause himself to be accompanied by a lady on a tiger-hunt. Such was the image under which he had ended by figuring his life.

They had at first, none the less, in the scattered hours spent together, made no allusion to that view of it; which was a sign he was handsomely ready to give that he didn't expect, that he in fact didn't care always to be talking about it. Such a feature in one's outlook was really like a hump on one's back. The difference it made every minute of the day existed quite independently of discussion. One discussed, of course, *like* a hunchback, for there was always, if nothing else, the hunchback face. That remained, and she was watching him; but people watched best, as a general thing, in silence, so that such would be predominantly the manner of their vigil. Yet he didn't want, at the same time, to be solemn; solemn was what he imagined he too much tended to be with other people. The thing to be, with the one person who knew, was easy and natural — to make the reference rather than be seeming to avoid it, to avoid it rather than be seeming to make it, and to keep it, in any case, familiar, facetious even, rather than pedantic and portentous. Some such consideration as the latter was doubtless in his mind, for instance, when he wrote pleasantly to Miss Bartram that perhaps the great thing he had so long felt as in the lap of the gods was no more than this circumstance, which touched him so nearly, of her acquiring a house in London. It was the first allusion they had yet again made, needing any other hitherto so little; but when she replied, after having given him the news, that she was by no means satisfied with such a trifle, as the climax to so special a suspense, she almost set him wondering if she hadn't even a larger conception of singularity for him than he had for himself. He was at all events destined to become aware little by little, as time went by, that she was all the while looking at his life, judging it, measuring it, in the light of the thing she knew, which grew to be at last, with the consecration of the years, never mentioned between them save as "the real truth" about him. That had always been his own form of reference to it, but she adopted the form so quietly that, looking back at the end of a period, he knew there was no moment at which it was traceable that she had, as he might say, got inside his condition, or exchanged the attitude of beautifully indulging for that of still more beautifully believing him.

It was always open to him to accuse her of seeing him but as the most harmless of maniacs, and this, in the long run — since it covered so much ground — was his easiest description of their friendship. He had a screw loose for her, but she liked him in spite of it, and was practically, against the rest of the world, his kind, wise keeper, unremunerated, but fairly amused and, in the absence of other near ties, not disreputably occupied. The rest of the world of course thought him queer, but she, she only, knew how, and above all why, queer; which was precisely what enabled her to dispose the concealing veil in the right folds. She took his gaiety from him — since it had to pass with them for gaiety — as she took everything else; but she certainly so far justified by her unerring touch his finer sense of the degree to which he had ended by convincing her. *She* at least never spoke of the secret of his life except as "the real truth about you," and she had in fact a wonderful way of making it seem, as such, the secret of her own life too. That was in fine how he so constantly felt her as allowing for him; he couldn't on the whole call it anything else. He allowed for himself, but she, exactly, allowed still more; partly because, better placed for a sight of the matter, she traced his unhappy perversion through portions of its course into which he could scarce follow it. He knew how he felt, but, besides knowing that, she knew how he *looked* as well; he knew each of the things of importance he was insidiously kept from doing, but she could add up the amount they made, understand how much, with a lighter weight on his spirit, he might have done, and thereby establish how, clever as he was, he fell short. Above all she was in the secret of the difference between the forms he went through — those of his little office under Government, those of caring for his modest patrimony, for his library, for his garden in the country, for the people in London whose invitations he accepted and repaid — and the detachment that reigned beneath them and that made of all behaviour, all that could in the least be called behaviour, a long act of dissimulation. What it had come to was that he wore a mask painted with the social simper, out of the eye-holes of which there looked eyes of an expression not in the least matching the other features. This the stupid world, even after years, had never more than half discovered. It was only May Bartram who had, and she achieved, by an art indescribable, the feat of at once — or perhaps it was only alternately — meeting the eyes from in front and mingling her own vision, as from over his shoulder, with their peep through the apertures.

So, while they grew older together, she did watch with him, and so she let this association give shape and colour to her own existence. Beneath *her* forms as well detachment had learned to sit, and behaviour had become for her, in the social sense, a false account of herself. There was but one account of her that would have been true all the while, and that she could give, directly, to nobody, least of all to John Marcher. Her whole attitude was a virtual statement, but the perception of that only seemed destined to take its place for him as one of the many things necessarily crowded out of his consciousness. If she had, moreover, like himself, to make sacrifices to their real truth, it was to be granted that her compensation might have affected her as more prompt and more natural. They had long periods, in this London time, during which, when they were together, a stranger might have listened to them without in the least pricking up his ears; on the other hand, the real truth was equally liable at any moment to rise to the surface, and the auditor would then have wondered indeed what they were talking about. They had from an early time made up their mind that society was, luckily, unintelligent, and the margin that this gave them had fairly become one of their commonplaces. Yet there were still moments when the situation turned almost fresh — usually under the effect of some expression drawn from herself. Her expressions doubtless repeated themselves, but her intervals were generous. "What saves us, you know, is that we answer so completely to so usual an appearance that of the man and woman whose friendship has become such a daily habit, or almost, as to be at last indispensable." That, for instance, was a remark she had frequently enough had occasion to make, though she had given it at different times different developments. What we are especially concerned with is the turn it happened to take from her one afternoon when he had come to see her in honour of her birthday. This anniversary had fallen on a Sunday, at a season of thick fog and general outward gloom; but he had brought her his customary offering, having known her now long enough to have established a hundred little customs. It was one of his proofs to himself, the present he made her on her birthday, that he had not sunk into real selfishness. It was mostly nothing more than a small trinket, but it was always fine of its kind, and he was regularly careful to pay for it more than he thought he could afford. "Our habit saves you, at least, don't you see? because it makes you, after all, for the vulgar, indistinguishable from other men. What's the most inveterate mark of men in general? Why, the capacity to spend endless time with dull women — to spend it, I won't say without being bored, but without minding that they are, without being driven off at a tangent by it; which comes to the same thing. I'm your dull woman, a part of the daily bread for which you pray at church. That covers your tracks more than anything."

"And what covers yours?" asked Marcher, whom his dull woman could mostly to this extent amuse. "I see of course what you mean by your saving me, in one way and another, so far as other people are concerned — I've seen it all along. Only, what is it that saves *you?* I often think, you know, of that."

She looked as if she sometimes thought of that too, but in rather a different way. "Where other people, you mean, are concerned?"

"Well, you're really so in with me, you know — as a sort of result of my being so in with yourself. I mean of my having such an immense regard for you, being so tremendously grateful for all you've done for me. I sometimes ask myself if it's quite fair. Fair I mean to have so involved and — since one may say it — interested you. I almost feel as if you hadn't really had time to do anything else."

"Anything else but be interested?" she asked. "Ah, what else does one ever want to be? If I've been 'watching' with you, as we long ago agreed that I was to do, watching is always in itself an absorption."

"Oh, certainly," John Marcher said, "if you hadn't had your curiosity — ! Only, doesn't it sometimes come to you, as time goes on, that your curiosity is not being particularly repaid?"

May Bartram had a pause. "Do you ask that, by any chance, because you feel at all that yours isn't? I mean because you have to wait so long."

Oh, he understood what she meant. "For the thing to happen that never does happen? For the beast to jump out? No, I'm just where I was about it. It isn't a matter as to which I can *choose*, I can decide for a change. It isn't one as to which there *can* be a change. It's in the lap of the gods. One's in the hands of one's law — there one is. As to the form the law will take, the way it will operate, that's its own affair."

"Yes," Miss Bartram replied; "of course one's fate is coming, of course it *has* come, in its own form and its own way, all the while. Only, you know, the form and the way in your case were to have been — well, something so exceptional and, as one may say, so particularly *your* own."

Something in this made him look at her with suspicion. "You say 'were to *have* been,' as if in your heart you had begun to doubt."

"Oh!" she vaguely protested.

"As if you believed," he went on, "that nothing will now take place."

She shook her head slowly, but rather inscrutably. "You're far from my thought."

He continued to look at her. "What then is the matter with you?"

"Well," she said after another wait, "the matter with me is simply that I'm more sure than ever my curiosity, as you call it, will be but too well repaid."

They were frankly grave now; he had got up from his seat; had turned once more about the little drawing-room to which, year after year, he brought his inevitable topic; in which he had, as he might have said, tasted their intimate community with every sauce, where every object was as familiar to him as the things of his own house and the very carpets were worn with his fitful walk very much as the desks in old counting-houses are worn by the elbows of generations of clerks. The generations of his nervous moods had been at work there, and the place was the written history of his whole middle life. Under the impression of what his friend had just said he knew himself, for some reason, more aware of these things, which made him, after a moment, stop again before her. "Is it, possibly, that you've grown afraid?"

"Afraid?" He thought, as she repeated the word, that his question had made her, a little, change colour; so that, lest he should have touched on a truth, he explained very kindly. "You remember that that was what you asked *me* long ago—that first day at Weatherend."

"Oh yes, and you told me you didn't know — that I was to see for myself. We've said little about it since, even in so long a time."

"Precisely," Marcher interposed — "quite as if it were too delicate a matter for us to make free with. Quite as if we might find, on pressure, that I *am* afraid. For then," he said, "we shouldn't, should we? quite know what to do."

She had for the time no answer to this question. "There have been days when I thought you were. Only, of course," she added, "there have been days when we have thought almost anything."

"Everything. Oh!" Marcher softly groaned as with a gasp, half spent, at the face, more uncovered just then than it had been for a long while, of the imagination always with them. It had always had its incalculable moments of glaring out, quite as with the very eyes of the very Beast, and, used as he was to them, they could still draw from him the tribute of a sigh that rose from the depths of his being. All that they had thought, first and last, rolled over him; the past seemed to have been reduced to mere barren speculation. This in fact was what the place had just struck him as so full of — the simplification of everything but the state of suspense. That remained only by seeming to hang in the void surrounding it. Even his original fear, if fear it had been, had lost itself in the desert. "I judge, however," he continued, "that you see I'm not afraid now."

"What I see is, as I make it out, that you've achieved something almost unprecedented in the way of getting used to danger. Living with it so long and so closely, you've lost your sense of it; you know it's there, but you're indifferent, and you cease even, as of old, to have to whistle in the dark. Considering what the danger is," May Bartram wound up, "I'm bound to say that I don't think your attitude could well be surpassed."

John Marcher faintly smiled. "It's heroic?"

"Certainly — call it that."

He considered. "I *am,* then, a man of courage?"

"That's what you were to show me."

He still, however, wondered. "But doesn't the man of courage know what he's afraid of — or *not* afraid of? I don't know *that,* you see. I don't focus it. I can't name it. I only know I'm exposed."

"Yes, but exposed — how shall I say? — so directly. So intimately. That's surely enough."

"Enough to make you feel, then — as what we may call the end of our watch — that I'm not afraid?"

"You're not afraid. But it isn't," she said, "the end of our watch. That is, it isn't the end of yours. You've everything still to see."

"Then why haven't *you?*" he asked. He had had, all along, to-day, the sense of her keeping something back, and he still had it. As this was his first impression of that, it made a kind of date. The case was the more marked as she didn't at first answer; which in turn made him go on. "You know something I don't." Then his voice, for that of a man of courage, trembled a little. "You know what's to happen." Her silence, with the face she showed, was almost a confession — it made him sure. "You know, and you're afraid to tell me. It's so bad that you're afraid I'll find out."

All this might be true, for she did look as if, unexpectedly to her, he had crossed some mystic line that she had secretly drawn round her. Yet she might, after all, not have worried; and the real upshot was that he himself, at all events, needn't. "You'll never find out."

3

It was all to have made, none the less, as I have said, a date; as came out in the fact that again and again, even after long intervals, other things that passed between them wore, in relation to this hour, but the character of recalls and results. It's immediate effect had been indeed rather to lighten insistence — almost to provoke a reaction; as if their topic had dropped by its own weight and as if moreover, for that matter, Marcher had been visited by one of his occasional warnings against egotism. He had kept up, he felt, and very decently on the whole, his consciousness of the importance of not being selfish, and it was true that he had never sinned in that direction without promptly enough trying to press the scales the other way. He often repaired his fault, the season permitting, by inviting his friend to accompany him to the opera; and it not infrequently thus happened that, to show he didn't wish her to have but one sort of food for her mind, he was the cause of her appearing there with him a dozen nights in the month. It even happened that, seeing her home at such times, he occasionally went in with her to finish, as he called it, the evening, and, the better to make his point, sat down to the frugal but always careful little supper that awaited his pleasure. His point was made, he thought, by his not eternally insisting with her on himself; made for instance, at such hours, when it befell that, her piano at hand and each of them familiar with it, they went over passages of the opera together. It chanced to be on one of these occasions, however, that he reminded her of her not having answered a certain question he had put to her during the talk that had taken place between them on her last birthday. "What is it that saves *you?*" — saved her, he meant, from that appearance of variation from the usual human type. If he had practically escaped remark, as she pretended, by doing, in the most important particular, what most men do — find the answer to life in patching up an alliance of a sort with a woman no better than himself — how had she escaped it, and how could the alliance, such as it was, since they must suppose it had been more or less noticed, have failed to make her rather positively talked about?

"I never said," May Bartram replied, "that it hadn't made me talked about."

"Ah well then, you're not 'saved.' "

"It has not been a question for me. If you've had your woman, I've had," she said, "my man."

"And you mean that makes you all right?"

She hesitated. "I don't know why it shouldn't make me — humanly, which is what we're speaking of — as right as it makes you."

"I see," Marcher returned. " 'Humanly,' no doubt, as showing that you're living for something. Not, that is, just for me and my secret."

May Bartram smiled. "I don't pretend it exactly shows that I'm not living for you. It's my intimacy with you that's in question."

He laughed as he saw what she meant. "Yes, but since, as you say, I'm only, so far as people make out, ordinary, you're — aren't you? — no more than ordinary either. You help me to pass for a man like another. So if I *am*, as I understand you, you're not compromised. Is that it?"

She had another hesitation, but she spoke clearly enough. "That's it. It's all that concerns me — to help you to pass for a man like another."

He was careful to acknowledge the remark handsomely. "How kind, how beautiful, you are to me! How shall I ever repay you?"

She had her last grave pause, as if there might be a choice of ways. But she chose. "By going on as you are."

It was into this going on as he was that they relapsed, and really for so long a time that the day inevitably came for a further sounding of their depths. It was as if these depths, constantly bridged over by a structure that was firm enough in spite of its lightness and of its occasional oscillation in the somewhat vertiginous air, invited on occasion, in the interest of their nerves, a dropping of the plummet and a measurement of the abyss. A difference had been made moreover, once for all, by the fact that she had, all the while, not appeared to feel the need of rebutting his charge of an idea within her that she didn't dare to express, uttered just before one of the fullest of their later discussions ended. It had come up for him then that she "knew" something and that what she knew was bad — too bad to tell him. When he had spoken of it as visibly so bad that she was afraid he might find it out, her reply had left the matter too equivocal to be let alone and yet, for Marcher's special sensibility, almost too formidable again to touch. He circled about it at a distance that alternately narrowed and widened and that yet was not much affected by the consciousness in him that there was nothing she could "know," after all, any better than he did. She had no source of knowledge that he hadn't equally — except of course that she might have finer nerves. That was what women had where they were interested; they made out things, where people were concerned, that the people often couldn't have made out for themselves. Their nerves, their sensibility, their imagination, were conductors and revealers, and the beauty of May Bartram was in particular that she had given herself so to his case. He felt in these days what, oddly enough, he had never felt before, the growth of a dread of losing her by some catastrophe — some catastrophe that yet wouldn't at all be *the* catastrophe: partly because she had, almost of a sudden, begun to strike him as useful to him as never yet, and partly by reason of an appearance of uncertainty in her health, coincident and equally new. It was characteristic of the inner detachment he had hitherto so successfully cultivated and to which our whole account of him is a reference, it was characteristic that his complications, such as they were, had never yet seemed so as at this crisis to thicken about him, even to the point of making him ask himself if he were, by any chance, of a truth, within sight or sound, within touch or reach, within the immediate jurisdiction of the thing that waited.

When the day came, as come it had to, that his friend confessed to him her fear of a deep disorder in her blood, he felt somehow the shadow of a change and the chill of a shock. He immediately began to imagine aggravations and disasters, and above all to think of her peril as the direct menace for himself of personal privation. This indeed gave him one of those partial recoveries of equanimity that were agreeable to him — it showed him that what was still first in his mind was the loss she herself might suffer. "What if she should have to die before knowing, before seeing — ?" It would have been brutal, in the early stages of her trouble, to put that question to her; but it had immediately sounded for him to his own concern, and the possibility was what most made him sorry for her. If she did "know," moreover, in the sense of her having had some — what should he think? — mystical, irresistible light, this would make the matter not better, but worse, inasmuch as her original adoption of his own curiosity had quite become the basis of her life. She had been living to see what would *be* to be seen, and it would be cruel to her to have to give up before the accomplishment of the vision. These reflections, as I say, refreshed his generosity; yet, make them as he might, he saw himself, with the lapse of the period, more and more disconcerted. It lapsed for him with a strange, steady sweep, and the oddest oddity was that it gave him, independently of the threat of such inconvenience, almost the only positive surprise his career, if career it could be called, had yet offered him. She kept the house as she had never done; he had to go to her to see her — she could meet him nowhere now, though there was scarce a corner of their loved old London in which she had not in the past, at one time or another, done so; and he found her always seated by her fire in the deep, old-fashioned chair she was less and less able to leave. He had been struck one day, after an absence exceeding his usual measure, with her suddenly looking much older to him than he had ever thought of her being; then he recognised that the suddenness was all on his side — he had just been suddenly struck. She looked older because inevitably, after so many years, she *was* old, or almost; which was of course true in still greater measure of her companion. If she was old, or almost, John Marcher assuredly was, and yet it was her showing of the lesson, not his own, that brought the truth home to him. His surprises began here; when once they had begun they multiplied; they came rather with a rush: it was as if, in the oddest way in the world, they had all been kept back, sown in a thick cluster, for the late afternoon of life, the time at which, for people in general, the unexpected has died out.

One of them was that he should have caught himself — for he *had* so done — *really* wondering if the great accident would take form now as nothing more than his being condemned to see this charming woman, this admirable friend, pass away from him. He had never so unreservedly qualified her as while confronted in thought with such a possibility; in spite of which there was small doubt for him that as an answer to his long riddle the mere effacement of even so fine a feature of his situation would be an abject anticlimax. It would represent, as connected with his past attitude, a drop of dignity under the shadow of which his existence could only become the most grotesque of failures. He had been far from holding it a failure — long as he had waited for the appearance that was to make it a success. He had waited for a quite other thing, not for such a one as that. The breath of his good faith came short, however, as he recognised how long he had waited, or how long, at least, his companion had. That she, at all events, might be recorded as having waited in vain — this affected him sharply, and all the more because of his at first having done little more than amuse himself with the idea. It grew more grave as the gravity of her condition grew, and the state of mind it produced in him, which he ended by watching, himself, as if it had been some definite disfigurement of his outer person, may pass for another of his surprises. This conjoined itself still with another, the really stupefying consciousness of a question that he would have allowed to shape itself had he dared. What did everything mean — what, that is, did *she* mean, she and her vain waiting and her probable death and the soundless admonition of it all — unless that, at this time of day, it was simply, it was overwhelmingly too late? He had never, at any stage of his queer consciousness, admitted the whisper of such a correction; he had never, till within these last few months, been so false to his conviction as not to hold that what was to come to him had time, whether *he* struck himself as having it or not. That at last, at last, he certainly hadn't it, to speak of, or had it but in the scantiest measure — such, soon enough, as things went with him, became the inference with which his old obsession had to reckon: and this it was not helped to do by the more and more confirmed appearance that the great vagueness casting the long shadow in which he had lived had, to attest itself, almost no margin left. Since it was in Time that he was to have met his fate, so it was in Time that his fate was to have acted; and as he waked up to the sense of no longer being young, which was exactly the sense of being stale, just as that, in turn, was the sense of being weak, he waked up to another matter beside. It all hung together; they were subject, he and the great vagueness, to an equal and indivisible law. When the possibilities themselves had, accordingly, turned stale, when the secret of the gods had grown faint, had perhaps even quite evaporated, that, and that only, was failure. It wouldn't have been failure to be bankrupt, dishonoured, pilloried, hanged; it was failure not to be anything. And so, in the dark valley into which his path had taken its unlooked-for twist, he wondered not a little as he groped. He didn't care what awful crash might overtake him, with what ignominy or what monstrosity he might yet be associated — since he wasn't, after all, too utterly old to suffer — if it would only be decently proportionate to the posture he had kept, all his life, in the promised presence of it. He had but one desire left — that he shouldn't have been "sold."

4

Then it was that one afternoon, while the spring of the year was young and new, she met, all in her own way, his frankest betrayal of these alarms. He had gone in late to see her, but evening had not settled, and she was presented to him in that long, fresh light of waning April days which affects us often with a sadness sharper than the greyest hours of autumn. The week had been warm, the spring was supposed to have begun early, and May Bartram sat, for the first time in the year, without a fire, a fact that, to Marcher's sense, gave the scene of which she formed part a smooth and ultimate look, an air of knowing, in its immaculate order and its cold, meaningless cheer, that it would never see a fire again. Her own aspect — he could scarce have said why — intensified this note. Almost as white as wax, with the marks and signs in her face as numerous and as fine as if they had been etched by a needle, with soft white draperies relieved by a faded green scarf, the delicate tone of which had been consecrated by the years, she was the picture of a serene, exquisite, but impenetrable sphinx, whose head, or indeed all whose person, might have been powdered with silver. She was a sphinx, yet with her white petals and green fronds she might have been a lily too — only an artificial lily, wonderfully imitated and constantly kept, without dust or stain, though not exempt from a slight droop and a complexity of faint creases, under some clear glass bell. The perfection of household care, of high polish and finish, always reigned in her rooms, but they especially looked to Marcher at present as if everything had been wound up, tucked in, put away, so that she might sit with folded hands and with nothing more to do. She was "out of it," to his vision; her work was over; she communicated with him as across some gulf, or from some island of rest that she had already reached, and it made him feel strangely abandoned. Was it—or, rather, wasn't it — that if for so long she had been watching with him the answer to their question had swum into her ken and taken on its name, so that her occupation was verily gone? He had as much as charged her with this in saying to her, many months before, that she even then knew something she was keeping from him. It was a point he had never since ventured to press, vaguely fearing, as he did, that it might become a difference, perhaps a disagreement, between them. He had in short, in this later time, turned nervous, which was what, in all the other years, he had never been; and the oddity was that his nervousness should have waited till he had begun to doubt, should have held off so long as he was sure. There was something, it seemed to him, that the wrong word would bring down on his head, something that would so at least put an end to his suspense. But he wanted not to speak the wrong word; that would make everything ugly. He wanted the knowledge he lacked to drop on him, if drop it could, by its own august weight. If she was to forsake him it was surely for her to take leave. This was why he didn't ask her again, directly, what she knew; but it was also why, approaching the matter from another side, he said to her in the course of his visit: "What do you regard as the very worst that, at this time of day, *can* happen to me?"

He had asked her that in the past often enough; they had, with the odd, irregular rhythm of their intensities and avoidances, exchanged ideas about it and then had seen the ideas washed away by cool intervals, washed like figures traced in sea-sand. It had ever been the mark of their talk that the oldest allusions in it required but a little dismissal and reaction to come out again, sounding for the hour as new. She could thus at present meet his inquiry quite freshly and patiently. "Oh, yes, I've repeatedly thought, only it always seemed to me of old that I couldn't quite make up my mind. I thought of dreadful things, between which it was difficult to choose; and so must you have done."

"Rather! I feel now as if I had scarce done anything else. I appear to myself to have spent my life in thinking of nothing *but* dreadful things. A great many of them I've at different times named to you, but there were others I couldn't name."

"They were too, too dreadful?"

"Too, too dreadful — some of them."

She looked at him a minute, and there came to him as he met it an inconsequent sense that her eyes, when one got their full clearness, were still as beautiful as they had been in youth, only beautiful with a strange, cold light — a light that somehow was a part of the effect, if it wasn't rather a part of the cause, of the pale, hard sweetness of the season and the hour. "And yet," she said at last, "there are horrors we have mentioned."

It deepened the strangeness to see her, as such a figure in such a picture, talk of "horrors," but she was to do, in a few minutes, something stranger yet — though even of this he was to take the full measure but afterwards — and the note of it was already in the air. It was, for the matter of that, one of the signs that her eyes were having again such a high flicker of their prime. He had to admit, however, what she said. "Oh yes, there were times when we did go far." He caught himself in the act, speaking as if it all were over. Well, he wished it were; and the consummation depended, for him, clearly, more and more on his companion.

But she had now a soft smile. "Oh, far — !"

It was oddly ironic. "Do you mean you're prepared to go further?"

She was frail and ancient and charming as she continued to look at him, yet it was rather as if she had lost the thread. "Do you consider that we went so far?"

"Why, I thought it the point you were just making — that we *had* looked most things in the face."

"Including each other?" She still smiled. "But you're quite right. We've had together great imaginations, often great fears; but some of them have been unspoken."

"Then the worst — we haven't faced that. I *could* face it. I believe, if I knew what you think it. I feel," he explained, "as if I had lost my power to conceive such things." And he wondered if he looked as blank as he sounded. "It's spent."

"Then why do you assume," she asked, "that mine isn't?"

"Because you've given me signs to the contrary. It isn't a question for you of conceiving, imagining, comparing. It isn't a question now of choosing." At last he came out with it. "You know something that I don't. You've showed me that before."

These last words affected her, he could see in a moment, remarkably, and she spoke with firmness. "I've shown you, my dear, nothing."

He shook his head. "You can't hide it."

"Oh, oh!" May Bartram murmured over what she couldn't hide. It was almost a smothered groan.

"You admitted it months ago, when I spoke of it to you as of something you were afraid I would find out. Your answer was that I couldn't, that I wouldn't, and I don't pretend I have. But you had something therefore in mind, and I see now that it must have been, that it still is, the possibility that, of all possibilities, has settled itself for you as the worse. This," he went on, "is why I appeal to you. I'm only afraid of ignorance now — I'm not afraid of knowledge." And then as for a while she said nothing: "What makes me sure is that I see in your face and feel here, in this air and amid these appearances, that you're out of it. You've done. You've had your experience. You leave me to my fate."

Well, she listened, motionless and white in her chair, as if she had in fact a decision to make, so that her whole manner was a virtual confession, though still with a small, fine, inner stiffness, an imperfect surrender. "It *would* be the worst," she finally let herself say. "I mean the thing that I've never said."

It hushed him a moment. "More monstrous than all the monstrosities we've named?"

"More monstrous. Isn't that what you sufficiently express," she asked, "in calling it the worst?"

Marcher thought. "Assuredly — if you mean, as I do, something that includes all the loss and all the same that are thinkable."

"It would if it *should* happen," said May Bartram. "What we're speaking of, remember, is only my idea."

"It's your belief," Marcher returned. "That's enough for me. I feel your beliefs are right. Therefore if, having this one, you give me no more light on it, you abandon me."

"No, no!" she repeated. "I'm with you — don't you see? — still." And as if to make it more vivid to him she rose from her chair — a movement she seldom made in these days — and showed herself, all draped and all soft, in her fairness and slimness. "I haven't forsaken you."

It was really, in its effort against weakness, a generous assurance, and had the success of the impulse not, happily, been great, it would have touched him to pain more than to pleasure. But the cold charm in her eyes had spread, as she hovered before him, to all the rest of her person, so that it was, for the minute, almost like a recovery of youth. He couldn't pity her for that; he could only take her as she showed — as capable still of helping him. It was as if, at the same time, her light might at any instant go out; wherefore he must make the most of it. There passed before him with intensity the three or four things he wanted most to know; but the question that came of itself to his lips really covered the others. "Then tell me if I shall consciously suffer."

She promptly shook her head. "Never!"

It confirmed the authority he imputed to her, and it produced on him an extraordinary effect. "Well, what's better than that? Do you call that the worst?"

"You think nothing is better?" she asked.

She seemed to mean something so special that he again sharply wondered, though still with the dawn of a prospect of relief. "Why not, if one doesn't *know?*" After which, as their eyes, over his question, met in a silence, the dawn deepened and something to his purpose came, prodigiously, out of her very face. His own, as he took it in, suddenly flushed to the forehead, and he gasped with the force of a perception to which, on the instant, everything fitted. The sound of his gasp filled the air; then he became articulate "I see — if I don't suffer!"

In her own look, however, was doubt. "You see what?"

"Why, what you mean — what you've always meant."

She again shook her head. "What I mean isn't what I've always meant. It's different."

"It's something new?"

She hesitated. "Something new. It's not what you think. I see what you think."

His divination drew breath then; only her correction might be wrong. "It isn't that I *am* a donkey?" he asked between faintness and grimness. "It isn't that it's all a mistake?"

"A mistake?" she pityingly echoed. *That* possibility, for her, he saw, would be monstrous; and if she guaranteed him the immunity from pain it would accordingly not be what she had in mind. "Oh, no," she declared; "it's nothing of that sort. You've been right."

Yet he couldn't help asking himself if she weren't, thus pressed, speaking but to save him. It seemed to him he should be most lost if his history should prove all a platitude. "Are you telling me the truth, so that I sha'n't have been a bigger idiot than I can bear to know? I *haven't* lived with a vain imagination, in the most besotted illusion? I haven't waited but to see the door shut in my face?"

She shook her head again. "However the case stands *that* isn't the truth. Whatever the reality, it *is* a reality. The door isn't shut. The door's open," said May Bartram.

"Then something's to come?"

She waited once again, always with her cold, sweet eyes on him. "It's never too late." She had, with her gliding step, diminished the distance between them, and she stood nearer to him, close to him, a minute, as if still full of the unspoken. Her movement might have been for some finer emphasis of what she was at once hesitating and deciding to say. He had been standing by the chimney-piece, fireless and sparely adorned, a small, perfect old French clock and two morsels of rosy Dresden constituting all its furniture; and her hand grasped the shelf while she kept him waiting, grasped it a little as for support and encouragement. She only kept him waiting, however; that is, he only waited. It had become suddenly, from her movement and attitude, beautiful and vivid to him that she had something more to give him; her wasted face delicately shone with it, and it glittered, almost as with the white lustre of silver, in her expression. She was right, incontestably, for what he saw in her face was the truth, and strangely, without consequence, while their talk of it as dreadful was still in the air, she appeared to present it as inordinately soft. This, prompting bewilderment, made him but gape the more gratefully for her revelation, so that they continued for some minutes silent, her face shining at him, her contact imponderably pressing, and his stare all kind, but all expectant. The end, none the less, was that what he had expected failed to sound. Something else took place instead, which seemed to consist at first in the mere closing of her eyes. She gave way at the same instant to a slow, fine shudder, and though he remained staring — though he stared, in fact, but the harder — she turned off and regained her chair. It was the end of what she had been intending, but it left him thinking only of that.

"Well, you don't say — ?"

She had touched in her passage a bell near the chimney and had sunk back, strangely pale. "I'm afraid I'm too ill."

"Too ill to tell me?" It sprang up sharp to him, and almost to his lips, the fear that she would die without giving him light. He checked himself in time from so expressing his question, but she answered as if she had heard the words.

"Don't you know — now?"

" 'Now' — ?" She had spoken as if something that had made a difference had come up within the moment. But her maid, quickly obedient to her bell, was already with them. "I know nothing." And he was afterwards to say to himself that he must have spoken with odious impatience, such an impatience as to show that, supremely disconcerted, he washed his hands of the whole question.

"Oh!" said May Bartram.

"Are you in pain?" he asked, as the woman went to her.

"No," said May Bartram.

Her maid, who had put an arm round her as if to take her to her room, fixed on him eyes that appealingly contradicted her; in spite of which, however, he showed once more his mystification. "What then has happened?"

She was once more, with her companion's help, on her feet, and, feeling withdrawal imposed on him, he had found, blankly, his hat and gloves and had reached the door. Yet he waited for her answer. "What *was* to," she said.

5

He came back the next day, but she was then unable to see him, and as it was literally the first time this had occurred in the long stretch of their acquaintance he turned away, defeated and sore, almost angry — or feeling at least that such a break in their custom was really the beginning of the end — and wandered alone with his thoughts, especially with one of them that he was unable to keep down. She was dying, and he would lose her; she was dying, and his life would end. He stopped in the park, into which he had passed, and stared before him at his recurrent doubt. Away from her the doubt pressed again; in her presence he had believed her, but as he felt his forlornness he threw himself into the explanation that, nearest at hand, had most of a miserable warmth for him and least of a cold torment. She had deceived him to save him — to put him off with something in which he should be able to rest. What could the thing that was to happen to him be, after all, but just this thing that had begun to happen? Her dying, her death, his consequent solitude — *that* was what he had figured as the beast in the jungle, that was what had been in the lap of the gods. He had had her word for it as he left her; for what else, on earth, could she have meant? It wasn't a thing of a monstrous order; not a fate rare and distinguished; not a stroke of fortune that overwhelmed and immortalised; it had only the stamp of the common doom. But poor Marcher, at this hour, judged the common doom sufficient. It would serve his turn, and even as the consummation of infinite waiting he would bend his pride to accept it. He sat down on a bench in the twilight. He hadn't been a fool. Something had *been,* as she had said, to come. Before he rose indeed it had quite struck him that the final fact really matched with the long avenue through which he had had to reach it. As sharing his suspense, and as giving herself all, giving her life, to bring it to an end, she had come with him every step of the way. He had lived by her aid, and to leave her behind would be cruelly, damnably to miss her. What could be more overwhelming than that?

Well, he was to know within the week, for though she kept him a while at bay, left him restless and wretched during a series of days on each of which he asked about her only again to have to turn away, she ended his trial by receiving him where she had always received him. Yet she had been brought out at some hazard into the presence of so many of the things that were, consciously, vainly, half their past, and there was scant service left in the gentleness of her mere desire, all too visible, to check his obsession and wind up his long trouble. That was clearly what she wanted; the one thing more, for her own peace, while she could still put out her hand. He was so affected by her state that, once seated by her chair, he was moved to let everything go; it was she herself therefore who brought him back, took up again, before she dismissed him, her last word of the other time. She showed how she wished to leave their affair in order. "I'm not sure you understood. You've nothing to wait for more. It *has* come."

Oh, how he looked at her! "Really?"

"Really."

"The thing that, as you said, *was* to?"

"The thing that we began in our youth to watch for."

Face to face with her once more he believed her; it was a claim to which he had so abjectly little to oppose. "You mean that it has come as a positive, definite occurrence, with a name and a date?"

"Positive. Definite. I don't know about the 'name,' but, oh, with a date!"

He found himself again too helplessly at sea. "But come in the night — come and passed me by?"

May Bartram had her strange, faint smile. "Oh no, it hasn't passed you by!"

"But if I haven't been aware of it, and it hasn't touched me — ?"

"Ah, your not being aware of it," and she seemed to hesitate an instant to deal with this — "your not being aware of it is the strangeness *in* the strangeness. It's the wonder *of* the wonder." She spoke as with the softness almost of a sick child, yet now at last, at the end of all, with the perfect straightness of a sybil. She visibly knew that she knew, and the effect on him was of something co-ordinate, in its high character, with the law that had ruled him. It was the true voice of the law; so on her lips would the law itself have sounded. "It *has* touched you," she went on. "It has done its office. It has made you all its own."

"So utterly without my knowing it?"

"So utterly without your knowing it." His hand, as he leaned to her, was on the arm of her chair, and, dimly smiling always now, she placed her own on it. "It's enough if *I* know it."

"Oh!" he confusedly sounded, as she herself of late so often had done.

"What I long ago said is true. You'll never know now, and I think you ought to be content. You've *had* it," said May Bartram.

"But had what?"

"Why, what was to have marked you out. The proof of your law. It has acted. I'm too glad," she then gravely added, "to have been able to see what it's *not.*"

He continued to attach his eyes to her, and with the sense that it was all beyond him, and that *she* was too, he would still have sharply challenged her, had he not felt it an abuse of her weakness to do more than take devoutly what she gave him, take it as hushed as to a revelation. If he did speak, it was out of the foreknowledge of his loneliness to come. "If you're glad of what it's 'not,' it might then have been worse?"

She turned her eyes away, she looked straight before her; with which, after a moment: "Well, you know our fears."

He wondered. "It's something then we never feared?"

On this, slowly, she turned to him. "Did we ever dream, with all our dreams, that we should sit and talk of it thus?"

He tried for a little to make out if they had; but it was as if their dreams, numberless enough, were in solution in some thick, cold mist, in which thought lost itself. "It might have been that we couldn't talk?"

"Well" — she did her best for him — "not from this side. This, you see," she said, "is the *other* side."

"I think," poor Marcher returned, "that all sides are the same to me." Then, however, as she softly shook her head in correction: "We mightn't, as it were, have got across — ?"

"To where we are — no. We're *here*" — she made her weak emphasis.

"And much good does it do us!" was her friend's frank comment.

"It does us the good it can. It does us the good that *it* isn't here. It's past. It's behind," said Mary Bartram. "Before — " but her voice dropped.

He had got up, not to tire her, but it was hard to combat his yearning. She after all told him nothing but that his light had failed — which he knew well enough without her. "Before — ?" he blankly echoed.

"Before, you see, it was always to *come*. That kept it present."

"Oh, I don't care what comes now! Besides," Marcher added, "it seems to me I liked it better present, as you say, than I can like it absent with *your* absence."

"Oh, mine!" — and her pale hands made light of it.

"With the absence of everything." He had a dreadful sense of standing there before her for — so far as anything but this proved, this bottomless drop was concerned — the last time of their life. It rested on him with a weight he felt he could scarce bear, and this weight it apparently was that still pressed out what remained in him of speakable protest. "I believe you; but I can't begin to pretend I understand. *Nothing,* for me, is past; nothing *will* pass until I pass myself, which I pray my stars may be as soon as possible. Say, however," he added, "that I've eaten my cake, as you contend, to the last crumb — how can the thing I've never felt at all be the thing I was marked out to feel?"

She met him, perhaps, less directly, but she met him unperturbed. "You take your 'feelings' for granted. You were to suffer your fate. That was not necessarily to know it."

"How in the world — when what is such knowledge but suffering?"

She looked up at him a while, in silence. "No — you don't understand."

"I suffer," said John Marcher.

"Don't, don't!"

"How can I help at least *that?*"

"Don't!" May Bartram repeated.

She spoke it in a tone so special, in spite of her weakness, that he stared an instant — stared as if some light, hitherto hidden, had shimmered across his vision. Darkness again closed over it, but the gleam had already become for him an idea. "Because I haven't the right — ?"

"Don't *know* — when you needn't," she mercifully urged. "You needn't — for we shouldn't."

"Shouldn't?" If he could but know what she meant!

"No — it's too much."

"Too much?" he still asked — but with a mystification that was the next moment, of a sudden, to give way. Her words, if they meant something, affected him in this light — the light also of her wasted face — as meaning *all,* and the sense of what knowledge had been for herself came over him with a rush which broke through into a question. "Is it of that, then, you're dying?"

She but watched him, gravely at first, as if to see, with this, where he was, and she might have seen something, or feared something, that moved her sympathy. "I would live for you still — if I could." Her eyes closed for a little, as if, withdrawn into herself, she were, for a last time, trying. "But I can't!" she said as she raised them again to take leave of him.

She couldn't indeed, as but too promptly and sharply appeared, and he had no vision of her after this that was anything but darkness and doom. They had parted forever in that strange talk; access to her chamber of pain, rigidly guarded, was almost wholly forbidden him; he was feeling now moreover, in the face of doctors, nurses, the two or three relatives attracted doubtless by the presumption of what she had to "leave," how few were the rights, as they were called in such cases, that he had to put forward, and how odd it might even seem that their intimacy shouldn't have given him more of them. The stupidest fourth cousin had more, even though she had been nothing in such a person's life. She had been a feature of features in *his,* for what else was it to have been so indispensable? Strange beyond saying were the ways of existence, baffling for him the anomaly of his lack, as he felt it to be, of producible claim. A woman might have been, as it were, everything to him, and it might yet present him in no connection that anyone appeared obliged to recognise. If this was the case in these closing weeks it was the case more sharply on the occasion of the last offices rendered, in the great grey London cemetery, to what had been mortal, to what had been precious, in his friend. The concourse at her grave was not numerous, but he saw himself treated as scarce more nearly concerned with it than if there had been a thousand others. He was in short from this moment face to face with the fact that he was to profit extraordinarily little by the interest May Bartram had taken in him. He couldn't quite have said what he expected, but he had somehow not expected this approach to a double privation. Not only had her interest failed him, but he seemed to feel himself unattended — and for a reason he couldn't sound — by the distinction, the dignity, the propriety, if nothing else, of the man markedly bereaved. It was as if, in the view of society, he had not *been* markedly bereaved, as if there still failed some sign or proof of it, and as if, none the less, his character could never be affirmed, nor the deficiency ever made up. There were moments, as the weeks went by, when he would have liked, by some almost aggressive act, to take his stand on the intimacy of his loss, in order that it *might* be questioned and his retort, to the relief of his spirit, so recorded; but the moments of an irritation more helpless followed fast on these, the moments during which, turning things over with a good conscience but with a bare horizon, he found himself wondering if he oughtn't to have begun, so to speak, further back.

He found himself wondering indeed at many things, and this last speculation had others to keep it company. What could he have done, after all, in her lifetime, without giving them both, as it were, away? He couldn't have made it known she was watching him, for that would have published the superstition of the Beast. This was what closed his mouth now — now that the Jungle had been threshed to vacancy and that the Beast had stolen away. It sounded too foolish and too flat; the difference for him in this particular, the extinction in his life of the element of suspense, was such in fact as to surprise him. He could scarce have said what the effect resembled; the abrupt cessation, the positive prohibition, of music perhaps, more than anything else, in some place all adjusted and all accustomed to sonoriety and to attention. If he could at any rate have conceived lifting the veil from his image at some moment of the past (what had he done, after all, if not lift it to *her?*) so to do this to-day, to talk to people at large of the Jungle cleared and confide to them that he now felt it as safe, would have been not only to see them listen as to a goodwife's tale, but really to hear himself tell one. What it presently came to in truth was that poor Marcher waded through his beaten grass, where no life stirred, where no breath sounded, where no evil eye seemed to gleam from a possible lair, very much as if vaguely looking for the Beast, and still more as if missing it. He walked about in an existence that had grown strangely more spacious, and, stopping fitfully in places where the undergrowth of life struck him as closer, asked himself yearningly, wondered secretly and sorely, if it would have lurked here or there. It would have at all events *sprung;* what was at least complete was his belief in the truth itself of the assurance given him. The change from his old sense to his new was absolute and final: what was to happen *had* so absolutely and finally happened that he was as little able to know a fear for his future as to know a hope; so absent in short was any question of anything still to come. He was to live entirely with the other question, that of his unidentified past, that of his having to see his fortune impenetrably muffled and masked.

The torment of this vision became then his occupation; he couldn't perhaps have consented to live but for the possibility of guessing. She had told him, his friend, not to guess; she had forbidden him, so far as he might, to know, and she had even in a sort denied the power in him to learn: which were so many things, precisely, to deprive him of rest. It wasn't that he wanted, he argued for fairness, that anything that had happened to him should happen over again; it was only that he shouldn't, as an anticlimax, have been taken sleeping so sound as not to be able to win back by an effort of thought the lost stuff of consciousness. He declared to himself at moments that he would either win it back or have done with consciousness for ever; he made this idea his one motive, in fine, made it so much his passion that none other, to compare with it, seemed ever to have touched him. The lost stuff of consciousness became thus for him as a strayed or stolen child to an unappeasable father; he hunted it up and down very much as if he were knocking at doors and inquiring of the police. This was the spirit in which, inevitably, he set himself to travel; he started on a journey that was to be as long as he could make it; it danced before him that, as the other side of the globe couldn't possibly have less to say to him, it might, by a possibility of suggestion, have more. Before he quitted London, however, he made a pilgrimage to May Bartram's grave, took his way to it through the endless avenues of the grim suburban necropolis, sought it out in the wilderness of tombs, and, though he had come but for the renewal of the act of farewell, found himself, when he had at last stood by it, beguiled into long intensities. He stood for an hour, powerless to turn away and yet powerless to penetrate the darkness of death; fixing with his eyes her inscribed name and date, beating his forehead against the fact of the secret they kept, drawing his breath, while he waited as if, in pity of him, some sense would rise from the stones. He kneeled on the stones, however, in vain; they kept what they concealed; and if the face of the tomb did become a face for him it was because her two names were like a pair of eyes that didn't know him. He gave them a last long look, but no palest light broke.

He stayed away, after this, for a year; he visited the depths of Asia, spending himself on scenes of romantic interest, of superlative sanctity; but what was present to him everywhere was that for a man who had known what *he* had known the world was vulgar and vain. The state of mind in which he had lived for so many years shone out to him, in reflection, as a light that coloured and refined, a light beside which the glow of the East was garish, cheap and thin. The terrible truth was that he had lost — with everything else — a distinction as well; the things he saw couldn't help being common when he had become common to look at them. He was simply now one of them himself — he was in the dust, without a peg for the sense of difference; and there were hours when, before the temples of gods and the sepulchres of kings, his spirit turned, for nobleness of association, to the barely discriminated slab in the London suburb. That had become for him, and more intensely with time and distance, his one witness of a past glory. It was all that was left to him for proof or pride, yet the past glories of Pharaohs were nothing to him as he thought of it. Small wonder then that he came back to it on the morrow of his return. He was drawn there this time as irresistibly as the other, yet with a confidence, almost, that was doubtless the effect of the many months that had elapsed. He had lived, in spite of himself, into his change of feeling, and in wandering over the earth had wandered, as might be said, from the circumference to the centre of his desert. He had settled to his safety and accepted perforce his extinction; figuring to himself, with some colour, in the likeness of certain little old men he remembered to have seen, of whom, all meagre and wizened as they might look, it was related that they had in their time fought twenty duels or been loved by ten princesses. They indeed had been wondrous for others, while he was but wondrous for himself; which, however, was exactly the cause of his haste to renew the wonder by getting back, as he might put it, into his own presence. That had quickened his steps and checked his delay. If his visit was prompt it was because he had been separated so long from the part of himself that alone he now valued.

It is accordingly not false to say that he reached his goal with a certain elation, and stood there again with a certain assurance. The creature beneath the sod *knew* of his rare experience, so that, strangely now, the place had lost for him its mere blankness of expression. It met him in mildness — not, as before, in mockery; it wore for him the air of conscious greeting that we find, after absence, in things that have closely belonged to us and which seem to confess of themselves to the connection. The plot of ground, the graven tablet, the tended flowers affected him so as belonging to him that he quite felt for the hour like a contented landlord reviewing a piece of property. Whatever had happened — well, had happened. He had not come back this time with the vanity of that question, his former worrying, "What, *what?*" now practically so spent. Yet he would, none the less, never again so cut himself off from the spot; he would come back to it every month, for if he did nothing else by its aid he at least held up his head. It thus grew for him, in the oddest way, a positive resource; he carried out his idea of periodical returns, which took their place at last among the most inveterate of his habits. What it all amounted to, oddly enough, was that, in his now so simplified world, this garden of death gave him the few square feet of earth on which he could still most live. It was as if, being nothing anywhere else for anyone, nothing even for himself, he were just everything here, and if not for a crowd of witnesses, or indeed for any witness but John Marcher, then by clear right of the register that he could scan like an open page. The open page was the tomb of his friend, and *there* were the facts of the past, there the truth of his life, there the backward reaches in which he could lose himself. He did this, from time to time, with such effect that he seemed to wander through the old years with his hand in the arm of a companion who was, in the most extraordinary manner, his other, his younger self; and to wander, which was more extraordinary yet, round and round a third presence — not wandering she, but stationary, still, whose eyes, turning with his revolution, never ceased to follow him, and whose seat was his point, so to speak, of orientation. Thus in short he settled to live — feeding only on the sense that he once *had* lived, and dependent on it not only for a support but for an identity.

It sufficed him, in its way, for months, and the year elapsed; it would doubtless even have carried him further but for an accident, superficially slight, which moved him, in a quite other direction, with a force beyond any of his impressions of Egypt or of India. It was a thing of the merest chance — the turn, as he afterwards felt, of a hair, though he was indeed to live to believe that if light hadn't come to him in this particular fashion it would still have come in another. He was to live to believe this, I say, though he was not to live, I may not less definitely mention, to do much else. We allow him at any rate the benefit of the conviction, struggling up for him at the end, that, whatever might have happened or not happened, he would have come round of himself to the light. The incident of an autumn day had put the match to the train laid from of old by his misery. With the light before him he knew that even of late his ache had only been smothered. It was strangely drugged, but it throbbed; at the touch it began to bleed. And the touch, in the event, was the face of a fellow mortal. This face, one grey afternoon when the leaves were thick in the alleys, looked into Marcher's own, at the cemetery, with an expression like the cut of a blade. He felt it, that is, so deep down that he winced at the steady thrust. The person who so mutely assaulted him was a figure he had noticed, on reaching his own goal, absorbed by a grave a short distance away, a grave apparently fresh, so that the emotion of the visitor would probably match it for frankness. This fact alone forbade further attention, though during the time he stayed he remained vaguely conscious of his neighbour, a middle-aged man apparently, in mourning, whose bowed back, among the clustered monuments and mortuary yews, was constantly presented. Marcher's theory that these were elements in contact with which he himself revived, had suffered, on this occasion, it may be granted, a sensible though inscrutable check. The autumn day was dire for him as none had recently been, and he rested with a heaviness he had not yet known on the low stone table that bore May Bartram's name. He rested without power to move, as if some spring in him, some spell vouchsafed, had suddenly been broken forever. If he could have done that moment as he wanted he would simply have stretched himself on the slab that was ready to take him, treating it as a place prepared to receive his last sleep. What in all the wide world had he now to keep awake for? He stared before him with the question, and it was then that, as one of the cemetery walks passed near him, he caught the shock of the face.

His neighbour at the other grave had withdrawn, as he himself, with force in him to move, would have done by now, and was advancing along the path on his way to one of the gates. This brought him near, and his pace was slow, so that — and all the more as there was a kind of hunger in his look — the two men were for a minute directly confronted. Marcher felt him on the spot as one of the deeply stricken — a perception so sharp that nothing else in the picture lived for it, neither his dress, his age, nor his presumable character and class; nothing lived but the deep ravage of the features that he showed. He *showed* them — that was the point; he was moved, as he passed, by some impulse that was either a signal for sympathy or, more possibly, a challenge to another sorrow. He might already have been aware of our friend, might, at some previous hour, have noticed in him the smooth habit of the scene, with which the state of his own senses so scantly consorted, and might thereby have been stirred as by a kind of overt discord. What Marcher was at all events conscious of was, in the first place, that the image of scarred passion presented to him was conscious too — of something that profaned the air; and, in the second, that, roused, startled, shocked, he was yet the next moment looking after it, as it went, with envy. The most extraordinary thing that had happened to him — though he had given that name to other matters as well — took place, after his immediate vague stare, as a consequence of this impression. The stranger passed, but the raw glare of his grief remained, making our friend wonder in pity what wrong, what wound it expressed, what injury not to be healed. What had the man *had* to make him, by the loss of it, so bleed and yet live?

Something — and this reached him with a pang   that *he*, John Marcher, hadn't; the proof of which was precisely John Marcher's arid end. No passion had ever touched him, for this was what passion meant; he had survived and maundered and pined, but where had been *his* deep ravage? The extraordinary thing we speak of was the sudden rush of the result of this question. The sight that had just met his eyes named to him, as in letters of quick flame, something he had utterly, insanely missed, and what he had missed made these things a train of fire, made them mark themselves in an anguish of inward throbs. He had seen *outside* of his life, not learned it within, the way a woman was mourned when she had been loved for herself; such was the force of his conviction of the meaning of the stranger's face, which still flared for him like a smoky torch. It had not come to him, the knowledge, on the wings of experience; it had brushed him, jostled him, upset him, with the disrespect of chance, the insolence of an accident. Now that the illumination had begun, however, it blazed to the zenith, and what he presently stood there gazing at was the sounded void of his life. He gazed, he drew breath, in pain; he turned in his dismay, and, turning, he had before him in sharper incision than ever the open page of his story. The name on the table smote him as the passage of his neighbour had done, and what it said to him, full in the face, was that *she* was what he had missed. This was the awful thought, the answer to all the past, the vision at the dread clearness of which he turned as cold as the stone beneath him. Everything fell together, confessed, explained, overwhelmed; leaving him most of all stupefied at the blindness he had cherished. The fate he had been marked for he had met with a vengeance — he had emptied the cup to the lees; he had been the man of his time, *the* man, to whom nothing on earth was to have happened. That was the rare stroke — that was his visitation. So he saw it, as we say, in pale horror, while the pieces fitted and fitted. So *she* had seen it, while he didn't, and so she served at this hour to drive the truth home. It was the truth, vivid and monstrous, that all the while he had waited the wait was itself his portion. This the companion of his vigil had at a given moment perceived, and she had then offered him the chance to baffle his doom. One's doom, however, was never baffled, and on the day she had told him that his own had come down she had seen him but stupidly stare at the escape she offered him.

The escape would have been to love her; then, *then* he would have lived. *She* had lived — who could say now with what passion? — since she had loved him for himself; whereas he had never thought of her (ah, how it hugely glared at him!) but in the chill of his egotism and the light of her use. Her spoken words came back to him, and the chain stretched and stretched. The beast had lurked indeed, and the beast, at its hour, had sprung; it had sprung in that twilight of the cold April when, pale, ill, wasted, but all beautiful, and perhaps even then recoverable, she had risen from her chair to stand before him and let him imaginably guess. It had sprung as he didn't guess; it had sprung as she hopelessly turned from him, and the mark, by the time he left her, had fallen where it *was* to fall. He had justified his fear and achieved his fate; he had failed, with the last exactitude, of all he was to fail of; and a moan now rose to his lips as he remembered she had prayed he mightn't know. This horror of waking — *this* was knowledge, knowledge under the breath of which the very tears in his eyes seemed to freeze. Through them, none the less, he tried to fix it and hold it; he kept it there before him so that he might feel the pain. That at least, belated and bitter, had something of the taste of life. But the bitterness suddenly sickened him, and it was as if, horribly, he saw, in the truth, in the cruelty of his image, what had been appointed and done. He saw the Jungle of his life and saw the lurking Beast; then, while he looked, perceived it, as by a stir of the air, rise, huge and hideous, for the leap that was to settle him. His eyes darkened — it was close; and, instinctively turning, in his hallucination, to avoid it, he flung himself, on his face, on the tomb.

HENRY JAMES

The Turn of the Screw

The story had held us, round the fire, sufficiently breathless, but except the obvious remark that it was gruesome, as on Christmas Eve in an old house a strange tale should essentially be, I remember no comment uttered till somebody happened to note it as the only case he had met in which such a visitation had fallen on a child. The case, I may mention, was that of an apparition in just such an old house as had gathered us for the occasion — an appearance, of a dreadful kind, to a little boy sleeping in the room with his mother and waking her up in the terror of it; waking her not to dissipate his dread and soothe him to sleep again, but to encounter also herself, before she had succeeded in doing so, the same sight that had shocked him. It was this observation that drew from Douglas — not immediately, but later in the evening — a reply that had the interesting consequence to which I call attention. Some one else told a story not particularly effective, which I saw he was not following. This I took for a sign that he had himself something to produce and that we should only have to wait. We waited in fact till two nights later; but that same evening, before we scattered, he brought out what was in his mind.

"I quite agree — in regard to Griffin's ghost, or whatever it was — that its appearing first to the little boy, at so tender an age, adds a particular touch. But it's not the first occurrence of its charming kind that I know to have been concerned with a child. If the child gives the effect another turn of the screw, what do you say to *two* children — ?"

"We say of course," somebody exclaimed, "that two children give two turns! Also that we want to hear about them."

I can see Douglas there before the fire, to which he had got up to present his back, looking down at this converser with his hands in his pockets. "Nobody but me, till now, has ever heard. It's quite too horrible." This was naturally declared by several voices to give the thing the utmost price, and our friend, with quiet art, prepared his triumph by turning his eyes over the rest of us and going on: "It's beyond everything. Nothing at all that I know touches it."

"For sheer terror?" I remember asking.

He seemed to say it was n't so simple as that; to be really at a loss how to qualify it. He passed his hand over his eyes, made a little wincing grimace. "For dreadful — dreadfulness!"

"Oh how delicious!" cried one of the women.

He took no notice of her; he looked at me, but as if, instead of me, he saw what he spoke of. "For general uncanny ugliness and horror and pain."

"Well then," I said, "just sit right down and begin."

He turned round to the fire, gave a kick to a log, watched it an instant. Then as he faced us again: "I can't begin. I shall have to send to town." There was a unanimous groan at this, and much reproach; after which, in his preoccupied way, he explained. "The story's written. It's in a locked drawer — it has not been out for years. I could write to my man and enclose the key; he could send down the packet as he finds it." It was to me in particular that he appeared to propound this — appeared almost to appeal for aid not to hesitate. He had broken a thickness of ice, the formation of many a winter; had had his reasons for a long silence. The others resented postponement, but it was just his scruples that charmed me. I adjured him to write by the first post and to agree with us for an early hearing; then I asked him if the experience in question had been his own. To this his answer was prompt. "Oh thank God, no!"

"And is the record yours? You took the thing down?"

"Nothing but the impression. I took that *here*" — he tapped his heart. "I've never lost it."

"Then your manuscript — ?"

"Is in old faded ink and in the most beautiful hand." He hung fire again. "A woman's. She has been dead these twenty years. She sent me the pages in question before she died." They were all listening now, and of course there was somebody to be arch, or at any rate to draw the inference. But if he put the inference by without a smile it was also without irritation. "She was a most charming person, but she was ten years older than I. She was my sister's governess," he quietly said. "She was the most agreeable woman I've ever known in her position; she'd have been worthy of any whatever. It was long ago, and this episode was long before. I was at Trinity, and I found her at home on my coming down the second summer. I was much there that year — it was a beautiful one; and we had, in her off-hours, some strolls and talks in the garden — talks in which she struck me as awfully clever and nice. Oh yes; don't grin: I liked her extremely and am glad to this day to think she liked me too. If she had n't she would n't have told me. She had never told any one. It was n't simply that she said so, but that I knew she had n't. I was sure; I could see. You'll easily judge why when you hear."

"Because the thing had been such a scare?"

He continued to fix me. "You'll easily judge," he repeated: "*you* will."

I fixed him too. "I see. She was in love."

He laughed for the first time. "You *are* acute. Yes, she was in love. That is she *had* been. That came out — she could n't tell her story without its coming out. I saw it, and she saw I saw it; but neither of us spoke of it. I remember the time and the place — the corner of the lawn, the shade of the great beeches and the long hot summer afternoon. It was n't a scene for a shudder; but oh — !" He quitted the fire and dropped back into his chair.

"You'll receive the packet Thursday morning?" I said.

"Probably not till the second post."

"Well then; after dinner — "

"You'll all meet me here?" He looked us round again. "Is n't anybody going?" It was almost the tone of hope.

"Everybody will stay!"

"*I* will — and *I* will!" cried the ladies whose departure had been fixed. Mrs. Griffin, however, expressed the need for a little more light. "Who was it she was in love with?"

"The story will tell," I took upon myself to reply.

"Oh I can't wait for the story!"

"The story *won't* tell," said Douglas; "not in any literal vulgar way."

"More's the pity then. That's the only way I ever understand."

"Won't *you* tell, Douglas?" somebody else enquired.

He spring to his feet again. "Yes — to-morrow. Now I must go to bed. Good-night." And, quickly catching up a candlestick, he left us slightly bewildered. From our end of the great brown hall we heard his step on the stair; whereupon Mrs. Griffin spoke. "Well, if I don't know who she was in love with I know who *he* was."

"She was ten years older," said her husband.

"*Raison de plus* — at that age! But it's rather nice, his long reticence."

"Forty years!" Griffin put in.

"With this outbreak at last."

"The outbreak," I returned, "will make a tremendous occasion of Thursday night", and every one so agreed with me that in the light of it we lost all attention for everything else. The last story, however incomplete and like the mere opening of a serial, had been told; we handshook and "candlestuck," as somebody said, and went to bed.

I knew the next day that a letter containing the key had, by the first post, gone off to his London apartments; but in spite of — or perhaps just on account of — the eventual diffusion of this knowledge we quite let him alone till after dinner, till such an hour of the evening in fact as might best accord with the kind of emotion on which our hopes were fixed. Then he became as communicative as we could desire, and indeed gave us his best reason for being so. We had it from him again before the fire in the hall, as we had had our mild wonders of the previous night. It appeared that the narrative he had promised to read us really required for a proper intelligence a few words of prologue. Let me say here distinctly, to have done with it, that this narrative, from an exact transcript of my own made much later, is what I shall presently give. Poor Douglas, before his death — when it was in sight — committed to me the manuscript that reached him on the third of these days and that, on the same spot, with immense effect, he began to read to our hushed little circle on the night of the fourth. The departing ladies who had said they would stay did n't, of course, thank heaven, stay: they departed, in consequence of arrangements made, in a rage of curiosity, as they professed, produced by the touches with which he had already worked us up. But that only made his little final auditory more compact and select, kept it, round the hearth, subject to a common thrill.

The first of these touches conveyed that the written statement took up the tale at a point after it had, in a manner, begun. The fact to be in possession of was therefore that his old friend, the youngest of several daughters of a poor country parson, had at the age of twenty, on taking service for the first time in the schoolroom, come up to London, in trepidation, to answer in person an advertisement that had already placed her in brief correspondence with the advertiser. This person proved, on her presenting herself for judgement at a house in Harley Street that impressed her as vast and imposing — this prospective patron proved a gentleman, a bachelor in the prime of life, such a figure as had never risen, save in a dream or an old novel, before a fluttered anxious girl out of a Hampshire vicarage. One could easily fix his type; it never, happily, dies out. He was handsome and bold and pleasant, off-hand and gay and kind. He struck her, inevitably, as gallant and splendid, but what took her most of all and gave her the courage she afterwards showed was that he put the whole thing to her as a favour, an obligation he should gratefully incur. She figured him as rich, but as fearfully extravagant — saw him all in a glow of high fashion, of good looks, of expensive habits, of charming ways with women. He had for his town residence a big house filled with the spoils of travel and the trophies of the chase; but it was to his country home, an old family place in Essex, that he wished her immediately to proceed.

He had been left, by the death of his parents in India, guardian to a small nephew and a small niece, children of a younger, a military brother whom he had lost two years before. These children were, by the strangest of chances for a man in his position — a lone man without the right sort of experience or a grain of patience — very heavy on his hands. It had all been a great worry and, on his own part doubtless, a series of blunders, but he immensely pitied the poor chicks and had done all he could; had in particular sent them down to his other house, the proper place for them being of course the country, and kept them there from the first with the best people he could find to look after them, parting even with his own servants to wait on them and going down himself, whenever he might, to see how they were doing. The awkward thing was that they had practically no other relations and that his own affairs took up all his time. He had put them in possession of Bly, which was healthy and secure, and had placed at the head of their little establishment — but below-stairs only — an excellent woman, Mrs. Grose, whom he was sure his visitor would like and who had formerly been maid to his mother. She was now housekeeper and was also acting for the time as superintendent to the little girl, of whom, without children of her own, she was by good luck extremely fond. There were plenty of people to help, but of course the young lady who should go down as governess would be in supreme authority. She would also have, in holidays, to look after the small boy, who had been for a term at school — young as he was to be sent, but what else could be done? — and who, as the holidays were about to begin, would be back from one day to the other. There had been for the two children at first a young lady whom they had had the misfortune to lose. She had done for them quite beautifully — she was a most respectable person — till her death, the great awkwardness of which had, precisely, left no alternative but the school for little Miles. Mrs. Grose, since then, in the way of manners and things, had done as she could for Flora; and there were, further, a cook, a housemaid, a dairywoman, an old pony, an old groom and an old gardener, all likewise thoroughly respectable.

So far had Douglas presented his picture when some one put a question. "And what did the former governess die of? Of so much respectability?"

Our friend's answer was prompt. "That will come out. I don't anticipate."

"Pardon me — I thought that was just what you *are* doing."

"In her successor's place," I suggested, "I should have wished to learn if the office brought with it — "

"Necessary danger to life?" Douglas completed my thought. "She did wish to learn, and she did learn. You shall hear to-morrow what she learnt. Meanwhile of course the prospect struck her as slightly grim. She was young, untried, nervous; it was a vision of serious duties and little company, of really great loneliness. She hesitated —

took a couple of days to consult and consider. But the salary offered much exceeded her modest measure, and on a second interview she faced the music, she engaged." And Douglas, with this, made a pause that, for the benefit of the company, moved me to throw in —

"The moral of which was of course the seduction exercised by the splendid young man. She succumbed to it."

He got up and, as he had done the night before, went to the fire, gave a stir to a log with his foot, then stood a moment with his back to us. "She saw him only twice."

"Yes, but that's just the beauty of her passion."

A little to my surprise, on this, Douglas turned round to me. "It *was* the beauty of it. There were others," he went on, "who had n't succumbed. He told her frankly all his difficulty — that for several applicants the conditions had been prohibitive. They were somehow simply afraid. It sounded dull — it sounded strange; and all the more so because of his main condition."

"Which was — ?"

"That she should never trouble him — but never, never: neither appeal nor complain nor write about anything; only meet all questions herself, receive all moneys from his solicitor, take the whole thing over and let him alone. She promised to do this, and she mentioned to me that when, for a moment, disburdened, delighted, he held her hand, thanking her for the sacrifice, she already felt rewarded."

"But was that all her reward?" one of the ladies asked.

"She never saw him again."

"Oh!" said the lady; which, as our friend immediately again left us, was the only other word of importance contributed to the subject till, the next night, by the corner of the hearth, in the best chair, he opened the faded red cover of a thin old-fashioned gilt-edged album. The whole thing took indeed more nights than one, but on the first occasion the same lady put another question.

"What's your title?"

"I have n't one."

"Oh *I* have!" I said. But Douglas, without heeding me, had begun to read with a fine clearness that was like a rendering to the ear of the beauty of his author's hand.

1

I remember the whole beginning as a succession of flights and 'drops, a little see-saw of the right throbs and the wrong. After rising, in town, to meet his appeal I had at all events a couple of very bad days — found all my doubts bristle again, felt indeed sure I had made a mistake. In this state of mind I spent the long hours of bumping swinging coach that carried me to the stopping-place at which I was to be met by a vehicle from the house. This convenience, I was told, had been ordered, and I found, toward the close of the June afternoon, a commodious fly in waiting for me. Driving at that hour, on a lovely day, through a country the summer sweetness of which served as a friendly welcome, my fortitude revived and, as we turned into the avenue, took a flight that was probably but a proof of the point to which it had sunk. I suppose I had expected, or had dreaded, something so dreary that what greeted me was a good surprise. I remember as a thoroughly pleasant impression the broad clear front, its open windows and fresh curtains and the pair of maids looking out; I remember the lawn and the bright flowers and the crunch of my wheels on the gravel and the clustered tree-tops over which the rooks circled and cawed in the golden sky. The scene had a greatness that made it a different affair from my own scant home, and there immediately appeared at the door, with a little girl in her hand, a civil person who dropped me as decent a curtsey as if I had been the mistress or a distinguished visitor. I had received in Harley Street a narrower notion of the place, and that, as I recalled it, made me think the proprietor still more of a gentleman, suggested that what I was to enjoy might be a matter beyond his promise.

I had no drop again till the next day, for I was carried triumphantly through the following hours by my introduction to the younger of my pupils. The little girl who accompanied Mrs. Grose affected me on the spot as a creature too charming not to make it a great fortune to have to do with her. She was the most beautiful child I had ever seen, and I afterwards wondered why my employer had n't made more of a point to me of this. I slept little that night — I was too much excited; and this astonished me too, I recollect, remained with me, adding to my sense of the liberality with which I was treated. The large impressive room, one of the best in the house, the great state bed, as I almost felt it, the figured full draperies, the long glasses in which, for the first time, I could see myself from head to foot, all struck me — like the wonderful appeal of my small charge — as so many things thrown in. It was thrown in as well, from the first moment, that I should get on with Mrs. Grose in a relation over which, on my way, in the coach, I fear I had rather brooded. The one appearance indeed that in this early outlook might have made me shrink again was that of her being so inordinately glad to see me. I felt within half an hour that she was so glad — stout simple plain clean wholesome woman — as to be positively on her guard against showing it too much. I wondered even then a little why she should wish *not* to show it, and that, with reflexion, with suspicion, might of course have made me uneasy.

But it was a comfort that there could be no uneasiness in a connexion with anything so beatific as the radiant image of my little girl, the vision of whose angelic beauty had probably more than anything else to do with the restlessness that, before morning, made me several times rise and wander about my room to take in the whole picture and prospect; to watch from my open window the faint summer dawn, to look at such stretches of the rest of the house as I could catch, and to listen, while in the fading dusk the first birds began to twitter, for the possible recurrence of a sound or two, less natural and not without but within, that I had fancied I heard. There had been a moment when I believed I recognised, faint and far, the cry of a child; there had been another when I found myself just consciously starting as at the passage, before my door, of a light footstep. But these fancies were not marked enough not to be thrown off, and it is only in the light, or the gloom, I should rather say, of other and subsequent matters that they now come back to me. To watch, teach, "form" little Flora would too evidently be the making of a happy and useful life. It had been agreed between us downstairs that after this first occasion I should have her as a matter of course at night, her small white bed being already arranged, to that end, in my room. What I had undertaken was the whole care of her, and she had remained just this last time with Mrs. Grose only as an effect of our consideration for my inevitable strangeness and her natural timidity. In spite of this timidity — which the child herself, in the oddest way in the world, had been perfectly frank and brave about, allowing it, without a sign of uncomfortable consciousness, with the deep sweet serenity indeed of one of Raphael's holy infants, to be discussed, to be imputed to her and to determine us — I felt quite sure she would presently like me. It was part of what I already liked Mrs. Grose herself for, the pleasure I could see her feel in my admiration and wonder as I sat at supper with four tall candles and with my pupil, in a high chair and a bib, brightly facing me between them over bread and milk. There were naturally things that in Flora's presence could pass between us only as prodigious and gratified looks, obscure and round-about allusions.

"And the little boy — does he look like her? Is he too so very remarkable?"

One would n't, it was already conveyed between us, too grossly flatter a child. "Oh Miss, *most* remarkable. If you think well of this one!" — and she stood there with a plate in her hand, beaming at our companion, who looked from one of us to the other with placid heavenly eyes that contained nothing to check us.

"Yes; if I do — ?"

"You *will* be carried away by the little gentleman!"

"Well, that, I think, is what I came for — to be carried away. I'm afraid, however," I remember feeling the impulse to add, "I'm rather easily carried away. I was carried away in London!"

I can still see Mrs. Grose's broad face as she took this in. "In Harley Street?"

"In Harley Street."

"Well, Miss, you're not the first — and you won't be the last."

"Oh I've no pretensions," I could laugh, "to being the only one. My other pupil, at any rate, as I understand, comes back to-morrow?"

"Not to-morrow — Friday, Miss. He arrives, as you did, by the coach, under care of the guard, and is to be met by the same carriage."

I forthwith wanted to know if the proper as well as the pleasant and friendly thing would n't therefore be that on the arrival of the public conveyance I should await him with his little sister; a proposition to which Mrs. Grose assented so heartily that I somehow took her manner as a kind of comforting pledge — never falsified, thank heaven! — that we should on every question be quite at one. Oh she was glad I was there!

What I felt the next day was, I suppose, nothing that could be fairly called a reaction from the cheer of my arrival; it was probably at the most only a slight oppression produced by a fuller measure of the scale, as I walked round them, gazed up at them, took them in, of my new circumstances. They had, as it were, an extent and mass for which I had not been prepared and in the presence of which I found myself, freshly, a little scared not less than a little proud. Regular lessons, in this agitation, certainly suffered some wrong; I reflected that my first duty was, by the gentlest arts I could contrive, to win the child into the sense of knowing me. I spent the day with her out of doors; I arranged with her, to her great satisfaction, that it should be she, she only, who might show me the place. She showed it step by step and room by room and secret by secret, with droll delightful childish talk about it and with the result, in half an hour, of our becoming tremendous friends. Young as she was I was struck, throughout our little tour, with her confidence and courage, with the way, in empty chambers and dull corridors, on crooked staircases that made me pause and even on the summit of an old machicolated square tower that made me dizzy, her morning music, her disposition to tell me so many more things than she asked, rang out and led me on. I have not seen Bly since the day I left it, and I dare say that to my present older and more informed eyes it would show a very reduced importance. But as my little conductress, with her hair of gold and her frock of blue, danced before me round corners and pattered down passages, I had the view of a castle of romance inhabited by a rosy sprite, such a place as would somehow, for diversion of the young idea, take all colour out of story-books and fairy-tales. Was n't it just a story-book over which I had fallen a-doze and a-dream? No; it was a big ugly antique but convenient house, embodying a few features of a building still older, half-displaced and half-utilised, in which I had the fancy of our being almost as lost as a handful of passengers in a great drifting ship. Well, I was strangely at the helm!

2

This came home to me when, two days later, I drove over with Flora to meet, as Mrs. Grose said, the little gentleman; and all the more for an incident that, presenting itself the second evening, had deeply disconcerted me. The first day had been, on the whole, as I have expressed, reassuring; but I was to see it wind up to a change of note. The postbag that evening — it came late — contained a letter for me which, however, in the hand of my employer, I found to be composed but of a few words enclosing another, addressed to himself, with a seal still unbroken. "This, I recognise, is from the head-master, and the head-master's an awful bore. Read him, please; deal with him; but mind you don't report. Not a word. I'm off!" I broke the seal with great effort — so great a one that I was a long time coming to it; took the unopened missive at last to my room and only attacked it just before going to bed. I had better have let it wait till morning, for it gave me a second sleepless night. With no counsel to take, the next day, I was full of distress; and it finally got so the better of me that I determined to open myself at least to Mrs. Grose.

"What does it mean? The child's dismissed his school."

She gave me a look that I remarked at the moment; then, visibly, with a quick blankness, seemed to try to take it back. "But are n't they all — ?"

"Sent home — yes. But only for the holidays. Miles may never go back at all."

Consciously, under my attention, she reddened. "They won't take him?"

"They absolutely decline."

At this she raised her eyes, which she had turned from me; I saw them fill with good tears. "What has he done?"

I cast about; then I judged best simply to hand her my document — which, however, had the effect of making her, without taking it, simply put her hands behind her. She shook her head sadly. "Such things are not for me, Miss."

My counsellor could n't read! I winced at my mistake, which I attenuated as I could, and opened the letter again to repeat it to her; then, faltering in the act and folding it up once more, I put it back in my pocket. "Is he really *bad?*"

The tears were still in her eyes. "Do the gentlemen say so?"

"They go into no particulars. They simply express their regret that it should be impossible to keep him. That can have but one meaning." Mrs. Grose listened with dumb emotion; she forbore to ask me what this meaning might be; so that, presently, to put the thing with some coherence and with the mere aid of her presence to my own mind, I went on: "That he's an injury to the others."

At this, with one of the quick turns of simple folk, she suddenly flamed up. "Master Miles! — *him* an injury?"

There was such a flood of good faith in it that, though I had not yet seen the child, my very fears made me jump to the absurdity of the idea. I found myself, to meet my friend the better, offering it, on the spot, sarcastically. "To his poor little innocent mates!"

"It's too dreadful," cried Mrs. Grose, "to say such cruel things! Why he's scarce ten years old."

"Yes, yes; it would be incredible."

She was evidently grateful for such a profession. "See him, Miss, first. *Then* believe it!" I felt forthwith a new impatience to see him; it was the beginning of a curiosity that, all the next hours, was to deepen almost to pain. Mrs. Grose was aware, I could judge, of what she had produced in me, and she followed it up with assurance. "You might as well believe it of the little lady. Bless her," she added the next moment — "*look* at her!"

I turned and saw that Flora, whom, ten minutes before, I had established in the schoolroom with a sheet of white paper, a pencil and a copy of nice "round O's," now presented herself to view at the open door. She expressed in her little way an extraordinary detachment from disagreeable duties, looking at me, however, with a great childish light that seemed to offer it as a mere result of the affection she had conceived for my person, which had rendered necessary that she should follow me. I needed nothing more than this to feel the full force of Mrs. Grose's comparison, and, catching my pupil in my arms, covered her with kisses in which there was a sob of atonement.

None the less, the rest of the day, I watched for further occasion to approach my colleague, especially as, toward evening, I began to fancy she rather sought to avoid me. I overtook her, I remember, on the staircase; we went down together and at the bottom I detained her, holding her there with a hand on her arm. "I take what you said to me at noon as a declaration that *you've* never known him to be bad."

She threw back her head; she had clearly by this time, and very honestly, adopted an attitude. "Oh never known him — I don't pretend *that!*"

I was upset again. "Then you *have* known him — ?"

"Yes indeed, Miss, thank God!"

On reflexion I accepted this. "You mean that a boy who never is — ?"

"Is no boy for *me!*"

I held her tighter. "You like them with the spirit to be naughty?" Then, keeping pace with her answer, "So do I!" I eagerly brought out. "But not to the degree to contaminate — "

"To contaminate?" — my big word left her at a loss.

I explained it. "To corrupt."

She stared, taking my meaning in; but it produced in her an odd laugh. "Are you afraid he'll corrupt *you?*" She put the question with such a fine bold humour that with a laugh, a little silly doubtless, to match her own, I gave way for the time to the apprehension of ridicule.

But the next day, as the hour for my drive approached, I cropped up in another place. "What was the lady who was here before?"

"The last governess? She was also young and pretty — almost as young and almost as pretty, Miss, even as you."

"Ah then I hope her youth and her beauty helped her!" I recollect throwing off. "He seems to like us young and pretty!"

"Oh he *did*," Mrs. Grose assented: "it was the way he liked every one!" She had no sooner spoken indeed than she caught herself up. "I mean that's *his* way — the master's."

I was struck. "But of whom did you speak first?"

She looked blank, but she coloured. "Why of *him*."

"Of the master?"

"Of who else?"

There was so obviously no one else that the next moment I had lost my impression of her having accidentally said more than she meant; and I merely asked what I wanted to know. "Did *she* see anything in the boy — ?"

"That was n't right? She never told me."

I had a scruple, but I overcame it. "Was she careful — particular?"

Mrs. Grose appeared to try to be conscientious. "About some things — yes."

"But not about all?"

Again she considered. "Well, Miss — she's gone. I won't tell tales."

"I quite understand your feeling," I hastened to reply; but I thought it after an instant not opposed to this concession to pursue: "Did she die here?"

"No — she went off."

I don't know what there was in this brevity of Mrs. Grose's that struck me as ambiguous. "Went off to die?" Mrs. Grose looked straight out of the window, but I felt that, hypothetically, I had a right to know what young persons engaged for Bly were expected to do. "She was taken ill, you mean, and went home?"

"She was not taken ill, so far as appeared, in this house. She left it, at the end of the year, to go home, as she said, for a short holiday, to which the time she had put in had certainly given her a right. We had then a young woman — a nursemaid who had stayed on and who was a good girl and clever; and *she* took the children altogether for the interval. But our young lady never came back, and at the very moment I was expecting her I heard from the master that she was dead."

I turned this over. "But of what?"

"He never told me! But please, Miss," said Mrs. Grose, "I must get to my work."

3

Her thus turning her back on me was fortunately not, for my just preoccupations, a snub that could check the growth of our mutual esteem. We met, after I had brought home little Miles, more intimately than ever on the ground of my stupefaction, my general emotion: so monstrous was I then ready to pronounce it that such a child as had now been revealed to me should be under an interdict. I was a little late on the scene of his arrival, and I felt, as he stood wistfully looking out for me before the door of the inn at which the coach had put him down, that I had seen him on the instant, without and within, in the great glow of freshness, the same positive fragrance of purity, in which I had from the first moment seen his little sister. He was incredibly beautiful, and Mrs. Grose had put her finger on it: everything but a sort of passion of tenderness for him was swept away by his presence. What I then and there took him to my heart for was something divine that I have never found to the same degree in any child — his indescribable little air of knowing nothing in the world but love. It would have been impossible to carry a bad name with a greater sweetness of innocence, and by the time I had got back to Bly with him I remained merely bewildered — so far, that is, as I was not outraged — by the sense of the horrible letter locked up in one of the drawers of my room. As soon as I could compass a private word with Mrs. Grose I declared to her that it was grotesque.

She promptly understood me. "You mean the cruel charge — ?"

"It does n't live an instant. My dear woman, *look* at him!"

She smiled at my pretension to have discovered his charm. "I assure you, Miss, I do nothing else! What will you say then?" she immediately added.

"In answer to the letter?" I had made up my mind. "Nothing at all."

"And to his uncle?"

I was incisive. "Nothing at all."

"And to the boy himself?"

I was wonderful. "Nothing at all."

She gave with her apron a great wipe to her mouth. "Then I'll stand by you. We'll see it out."

"We'll see it out!" I ardently echoed, giving her my hand to make it a vow.

She held me there a moment, then whisked up her apron again with her detached hand. "Would you mind, Miss, if I used the freedom — "

"To kiss me? No!" I took the good creature in my arms and after we had embraced like sisters felt still more fortified and indignant.

This at all events was for the time: a time so full that as I recall the way it went it reminds me of all the art I now need to make it a little distinct. What I look back at with amazement is the situation I accepted. I had undertaken, with my companion, to see it out, and I was under a charm apparently that could smooth away the extent and the far and difficult connexions of such an effort. I was lifted aloft on a great wave of infatuation and pity. I found it simple, in my ignorance, my confusion and perhaps my conceit, to assume that I could deal with a boy whose education for the world was all on the point of beginning. I am unable even to remember at this day what proposal I framed for the end of his holidays and the resumption of his studies. Lessons with me indeed, that charming summer, we all had a theory that he was to have; but I now feel that for weeks the lessons must have been rather my own. I learnt something — at first certainly — that had not been one of the teachings of my small smothered life; learnt to be amused, and even amusing, and not to think for the morrow. It was the first time, in a manner, that I had known space and air and freedom, all the music of summer and all the mystery of nature. And then there was consideration — and consideration was sweet. Oh it was a trap — not designed but deep — to my imagination, to my delicacy, perhaps to my vanity; to whatever in me was most excitable. The best way to picture it all is to say that I was off my guard. They gave me so little trouble — they were of a gentleness so extraordinary. I used to speculate — but even this with a dim disconnectedness — as to how the rough future (for all futures are rough!) would handle them and might bruise them. They had the bloom of health and happiness; and yet, as if I had been in charge of a pair of little grandees, of princes of the blood, for whom everything, to be right, would have to be fenced about and ordered and arranged, the only form that in my fancy the after-years could take for them was that of a romantic, a really royal extension of the garden and the park. It may be of course above all that what suddenly broke into this gives the previous time a charm of stillness — that hush in which something gathers or crouches. The change was actually like the spring of a beast.

In the first weeks the days were long; they often, at their finest, gave me what I used to call my own hour, the hour when, for my pupils, tea-time and bed-time having come and gone, I had before my final retirement a small interval alone. Much as I liked my companions this hour was the thing in the day I liked most; and I liked it best of all when, as the light faded — or rather, I should say, the day lingered and the last calls of the last birds sounded, in a flushed sky, from the old trees — I could take a turn into the grounds and enjoy, almost with a sense of property that amused and flattered me, the beauty and dignity of the place. It was a pleasure at these moments to feel myself tranquil and justified; doubtless perhaps also to reflect that by my discretion, my quiet good sense and general high propriety, I was giving pleasure — if he ever thought of it! — to the person to whose pressure I had yielded. What I was doing was what he had earnestly hoped and directly asked of me, and that I *could,* after all, do it proved even a greater joy than I had expected. I dare say I fancied myself in short a remarkable young woman and took comfort in the faith that this would more publicly appear. Well, I needed to be remarkable to offer a front to the remarkable things that presently gave their first sign.

It was plump, one afternoon, in the middle of my very hour: the children were tucked away and I had come out for my stroll. One of the thoughts that, as I don't in the least shrink now from noting, used to be with me in these wanderings was that it would be as charming as a charming story suddenly to meet some one. Some one would appear there at the turn of a path and would stand before me and smile and approve. I did n't ask more than that — I only asked that he should *know;* and the only way to be sure he knew would be to see it, and the kind light of it, in his handsome face. That was exactly present to me — by which I mean the face was — when, on the first of these occasions, at the end of a long June day, I stopped short on emerging from one of the plantations and coming into view of the house. What arrested me on the spot — and with a shock much greater than any vision had allowed for — was the sense that my imagination had, in a flash, turned real. He did stand there! — but high up, beyond the lawn and at the very top of the tower to which, on that first morning, little Flora had conducted me. This tower was one of a pair — square incongruous crenellated structures — that were distinguished, for some reason, though I could see little difference, as the new and the old. They flanked opposite ends of the house and were probably architectural absurdities, redeemed in a measure indeed by not being wholly disengaged nor of a height too pretentious, dating, in their gingerbread antiquity, from a romantic revival that was already a respectable past. I admired them, had fancies about them, for we could all profit in a degree, especially when they loomed through the dusk, by the grandeur of their actual battlements; yet it was not at such an elevation that the figure I had so often invoked seemed most in place.

It produced in me, this figure, in the clear twilight, I remember, two distinct gasps of emotion, which were, sharply, the shock of my first and that of my second surprise. My second was a violent perception of the mistake of my first: the man who met my eyes was not the person I had precipitately supposed. There came to me thus a bewilderment of vision of which, after these years, there is no living view that I can hope to give. An unknown man in a lonely place is a permitted object of fear to a young woman privately bred; and the figure that faced me was — a few more seconds assured me — as little any one else I knew as it was the image that had been in my mind. I had not seen it in Harley Street — I had not seen it anywhere. The place moreover, in the strangest way in the world, had on the instant and by the very fact of its appearance become a solitude. To me at least, making my statement here with a deliberation with which I have never made it, the whole feeling of the moment returns. It was as if, while I took in, what I did take in, all the rest of the scene had been stricken with death. I can hear again, as I write, the intense hush in which the sounds of evening dropped. The rooks stopped cawing in the golden sky and the friendly hour lost for the unspeakable minute all its voice. But there was no other change in nature, unless indeed it were a change that I saw with a stranger sharpness. The gold was still in the sky, the clearness in the air, and the man who looked at me over the battlements was as definite as a picture in a frame. That's how I thought, with extraordinary quickness, of each person he might have been and that he was n't. We were confronted across our distance quite long enough for me to ask myself with intensity who then he was and to feel, as an effect of my inability to say, a wonder that in a few seconds more became intense.

The great question, or one of these, is afterwards, I know, with regard to certain matters, the question of how long they have lasted. Well, this matter of mine, think what you will of it, lasted while I caught at a dozen possibilities, none of which made a difference for the better, that I could see, in there having been in the house — and for how long, above all? — a person of whom I was in ignorance. It lasted while I just bridled a little with the sense of how my office seemed to require that there should be no such ignorance and no such person. It lasted while this visitant, at all events — and there was a touch of the strange freedom, as I remember, in the sign of familiarity of his wearing no hat — seemed to fix me, from his position, with just the question, just the scrutiny through the fading light, that his own presence provoked. We were too far apart to call to each other, but there was a moment at which, at shorter range, some challenge between us, breaking the hush, would have been the right result of our straight mutual stare. He was in one of the angles, the one away from the house, very erect, as it struck me, and with both hands on the ledge. So I saw him as I see the letters I form on this page; then, exactly, after a minute, as if to add to the spectacle, he slowly changed his place — passed, looking at me hard all the while, to the opposite corner of the platform. Yes, it was intense to me that during this transit he never took his eyes from me, and I can see at this moment the way his hands, as he went, moved from one of the crenellations to the next. He stopped at the other corner, but less long, and even as he turned away still markedly fixed me. He turned away; that was all I knew.

4

It was not that I did n't wait, on this occasion, for more, since I was as deeply rooted as shaken. Was there a "secret" at Bly — a mystery of Udolpho or an insane, an unmentionable relative kept in unsuspected confinement? I can't say how long I turned it over, or how long, in a confusion of curiosity and dread, I remained where I had had my collision; I only recall that when I re-entered the house darkness had quite closed in. Agitation, in the interval, certainly had held me and driven me, for

I must, in circling about the place, have walked three miles; but I was to be later on so much more overwhelmed that this mere dawn of alarm was a comparatively human chill. The most singular part of it in fact — singular as the rest had been — was the part I became, in the hall, aware of in meeting Mrs. Grose. This picture comes back to me in the general train — the impression, as I received it on my return, of the wide white panelled space, bright in the lamplight and with its portraits and red carpet, and of the good surprised look of my friend, which immediately told me she had missed me. It came to me straightway, under her contact, that, with plain heartiness, mere relieved anxiety at my appearance, she knew nothing whatever that could bear upon the incident I had there ready for her. I had not suspected in advance that her comfortable face would pull me up, and I somehow measured the importance of what I had seen by my thus finding myself hesitate to mention it. Scarce anything in the whole history seems to me so odd as this fact that my real beginning of fear was one, as I may say, with the instinct of sparing my companion. On the spot, accordingly, in the pleasant hall and with her eyes on me, I, for a reason that I could n't then have phrased, achieved an inward revolution — offered a vague pretext for my lateness and, with the plea of the beauty of the night and of the heavy dew and wet feet, went as soon as possible to my room.

Here it was another affair; here, for many days after, it was a queer affair enough. There were hours, from day to day — or at least there were moments, snatched even from clear duties — when I had to shut myself up to think. It was n't so much yet that I was more nervous than I could bear to be as that I was remarkably afraid of becoming so; for the truth I had now to turn over was simply and clearly the truth that I could arrive at no account whatever of the visitor with whom I had been so inexplicably and yet, as it seemed to me, so intimately concerned. It took me little time to see that I might easily sound, without forms of enquiry and without exciting remark, any domestic complication. The shock I had suffered must have sharpened all my senses; I felt sure, at the end of three days and as the result of mere closer attention, that I had not been practised upon by the servants nor made the object of any "game." Of whatever it was that I knew nothing was known around me. There was but one sane inference; some one had taken a liberty rather monstrous. That was what, repeatedly, I dipped into my room and locked the door to say to myself. We had been, collectively, subject to an intrusion; some unscrupulous traveller, curious in old houses, had made his way in unobserved, enjoyed the prospect from the best point of view and then stolen out as he came. If he had given me such a bold hard stare, that was but a part of his indiscretion. The good thing, after all, was that we should surely see no more of him.

This was not so good a thing, I admit, as not to leave me to judge that what, essentially, made nothing else much signify was simply my charming work. My charming work was just my life with Miles and Flora, and through nothing could I so like it as through feeling that to throw myself into it was to throw myself out of my trouble. The attraction of my small charges was a constant joy, leading me to wonder afresh at the vanity of my original fears, the distaste I had begun by entertaining for the probable grey prose of my office. There was to be no grey prose, it appeared, and no long grind; so how could work not be charming that presented itself as daily beauty? It was all the romance of the nursery and the poetry of the schoolroom. I don't mean by this of course that we studied only fiction and verse; I mean that I can express no otherwise the sort of interest my companions inspired.

How can I describe that except by saying that instead of growing deadly used to them — and it's a marvel for a governess: I call the sisterhood to witness! — I made constant fresh discoveries. There was one direction, assuredly, in which these discoveries stopped: deep obscurity continued to cover the region of the boy's conduct at school. It had been promptly given me, I have noted, to face that mystery without a pang. Perhaps even it would be nearer the truth to say that — without a word — he himself had cleared it up. He had made the whole charge absurd. My conclusion bloomed there with the real rose-flush of his innocence: he was only too fine and fair for the little horrid unclean school-world, and he had paid a price for it. I reflected acutely that the sense of such individual differences, such superiorities of quality, always, on the part of the majority — which could include even stupid sordid head-masters — turns infallibly to the vindictive.

Both the children had a gentleness — it was their only fault, and it never made Miles a muff — that kept them (how shall I express it?) almost impersonal and certainly quite unpunishable. They were like those cherubs of the anecdote who had — morally at any rate — nothing to whack! I remember feeling with Miles in especial as if he had had, as it were, nothing to call even an infinitesimal history. We expect of a small child scant enough "antecedents," but there was in this beautiful little boy something extraordinarily sensitive, yet extraordinarily happy, that, more than in any creature of his age I have seen, struck me as beginning anew each day. He had never for a second suffered. I took this as a direct disproof of his having really been chastised. If he had been wicked he would have "caught" it, and I should have caught it by the rebound — I should have found the trace, should have felt the wound and the dishonour. I could reconstitute nothing at all, and he was therefore an angel. He never spoke of his school, never mentioned a comrade or a master; and I, for my part, was quite too much disgusted to allude to them. Of course I was under the spell, and the wonderful part is that, even at the time, I perfectly knew I was. But I gave myself up to it; it was an antidote to any pain, and I had more pains than one. I was in receipt in these days of disturbing letters from home, where things were not going well. But with this joy of my children what things in the world mattered? That was the question I used to put to my scrappy retirements. I was dazzled by their loveliness.

There was a Sunday — to get on — when it rained with such force and for so many hours that there could be no procession to church; in consequence of which, as the day declined, I had arranged with Mrs. Grose that, should the evening show improvement, we would attend together the late service. The rain happily stopped, and I prepared for our walk, which, through the park and by the good road to the village, would be a matter of twenty minutes. Coming downstairs to meet my colleague in the hall, I remembered a pair of gloves that had required three stitches and that had received them — with a publicity perhaps not edifying — while I sat with the children at their tea, served on Sundays, by exception, in that cold clean temple of mahogany and brass, the "grown-up" dining-room. The gloves had been dropped there, and I turned in to recover them. The day was grey enough, but the afternoon light still lingered, and it enabled me, on crossing the threshold, not only to recognise, on a chair near the wide window, then closed, the articles I wanted, but to became aware of a person on the other side of the window and looking straight in. One step into the room had sufficed; my vision was instantaneous; it was all there. The person looking straight in was the person who had already appeared to me. He appeared thus again with I won't say greater distinctness, for that was impossible, but with a nearness that represented a forward stride in our intercourse and made me, as I met him, catch my breath and turn cold. He was the same — he was the same, and seen, this time, as he had been seen before, from the waist up, the window, though the dining-room was on the ground floor, not going down to the terrace on which he stood. His face was close to the glass, yet the effect of this better view was, strangely, just to show me how intense the former had been. He remained but a few seconds — long enough to convince me he also saw and recognised; but it was as if I had been looking at him for years and had known him always. Something, however, happened this time that had not happened before; his stare into my face, through the glass and across the room, was as deep and hard as then, but it quitted me for a moment during which I could still watch it, see it fix successively several other things. On the spot there came to me the added shock of a certitude that it was not for me he had come. He had come for some one else.

The flash of this knowledge — for it was knowledge in the midst of dread — produced in me the most extraordinary effect, starting, as I stood there, a sudden vibration of duty and courage. I say courage because I was beyond all doubt already far gone. I bounded straight out of the door again, reached that of the house, got in an instant upon the drive and, passing along the terrace as fast as I could rush, turned a corner and came full in sight. But it was in sight of nothing now — my visitor had vanished. I stopped, almost dropped, with the real relief of this; but I took in the whole scene — I gave him time to reappear. I call it time, but how long was it? I can't speak to the purpose to-day of the duration of these things. That kind of measure must have left me: they could n't have lasted as they actually appeared to me to last. The terrace and the whole place, the lawn and the garden beyond it, all I could see of the park, were empty with a great emptiness. There were shrubberies and big trees, but I remember the clear assurance I felt that none of them concealed him. He was there or was not there: not there if I did n't see him. I got hold of this; then, instinctively, instead of returning as I had come, went to the window. It was confusedly present to me that I ought to place myself where he had stood. I did so; I applied my face to the pane and looked, as he had looked, into the room. As if, at this moment, to show me exactly what his range had been, Mrs. Grose, as I had done for himself just before, came in from the hall. With this I had the full image of a repetition of what had already occurred. She saw me as I had seen my own visitant; she pulled up short as I had done; I gave her something of the shock that I had received. She turned white, and this made me ask myself if I had blanched as much. She stared, in short, and retreated just on *my* lines, and I knew she had then passed out and come round to me and that I should presently meet her. I remained where I was, and while I waited I thought of more things than one. But there's only one I take space to mention. I wondered why *she* should be scared.

5

Oh she let me know as soon as, round the corner of the house, she loomed again into view. "What in the name of goodness is the matter — ?" She was now flushed and out of breath.

I said nothing till she came quite near. "With me?" I must have made a wonderful face. "Do I show it?"

"You're as white as a sheet. You look awful."

I considered; I could meet on this, without scruple, any degree of innocence. My need to respect the bloom of Mrs. Grose's had dropped, without a rustle, from my shoulders, and if I wavered for the instant it was not with what I kept back. I put out my hand to her and she took it; I held her hard a little, liking to feel her close to me. There was a kind of support in the shy heave of her surprise. "You came for me for church, of course, but I can't go."

"Has anything happened?"

"Yes. You must know now. Did I look very queer?"

"Through this window? Dreadful!"

"Well," I said, "I've been frightened." Mrs. Grose's eyes expressed plainly that *she* had no wish to be, yet also that she knew too well her place not to be ready to share with me any marked inconvenience. Oh it was quite settled that she *must* share! "Just what you saw from the dining-room a minute ago was the effect of that. What *I* saw — just before — was much worse."

Her hand tightened. "What was it?"

"An extraordinary man. Looking in."

"What extraordinary man?"

"I have n't the least idea."

Mrs. Grose gazed round us in vain. "Then where is he gone?"

"I know still less."

"Have you seen him before?"

"Yes — once. On the old tower."

She could only look at me harder. "Do you mean he's a stranger?"

"Oh very much!"

"Yet you did n't tell me?"

"No — for reasons. But now that you've guessed — "

Mrs. Grose's round eyes encountered this charge. "Ah I have n't guessed!" she said very simply. "How can I if *you* don't imagine?"

"I don't in the very least."

"You've seen him nowhere but on the tower?"

"And on this spot just now."

Mrs. Grose looked round again. "What was he doing on the tower?"

"Only standing there and looking down at me."

She thought a minute. "Was he a gentleman?"

I found I had no need to think. "No." She gazed in deeper wonder. "No."

"Then nobody about the place? Nobody from the village?"

"Nobody — nobody. I didn't tell you, but I made sure."

She breathed a vague relief: this was, oddly, so much to the good. It only went indeed a little way. "But if he is n't a gentleman — "

"What *is* he? He's a horror."

"A horror?"

"He's — God help me if I know *what* he is!"

Mrs. Grose looked round once more; she fixed her eyes on the duskier distance and then, pulling herself together, turned to me with full inconsequence. "It's time we should be at church."

"Oh I'm not fit for church!"

"Won't it do you good?"

"It won't do *them* — !" I nodded at the house.

"The children?"

"I can't leave them now."

"You're afraid — ?"

I spoke boldly. "I'm afraid of *him*."

Mrs. Grose's large face showed me, at this, for the first time, the far-away faint glimmer of a consciousness more acute: I somehow made out in it the delayed dawn of an idea I myself had not given her and that was as yet quite obscure to me. It comes back to me that I thought instantly of this as something I could get from her; and I felt it to be connected with the desire she presently showed to know more. "When was it — on the tower?"

"About the middle of the month. At this same hour."

"Almost at dark," said Mrs. Grose.

"Oh no, not nearly. I saw him as I see you."

"Then how did he get in?"

"And how did he get out?" I laughed. "I had no opportunity to ask him! This evening, you see," I pursued, "he has not been able to get in."

"He only peeps?"

"I hope it will be confined to that!" She had now let go my hand; she turned away a little. I waited an instant; then I brought out: "Go to church. Goodbye. I must watch."

Slowly she faced me again. "Do you fear for them?"

We met in another long look. "Don't *you*?" Instead of answering she came nearer to the window and, for a minute, applied her face to the glass. "You see how he could see," I meanwhile went on.

She did n't move. "How long was he here?"

"Till I came out. I came out to meet him."

Mrs. Grose at last turned round, and there was still more in her face. "*I* could n't have come out."

"Neither could I!" I laughed again. "But I did come. I've my duty."

"So have I mine," she replied; after which she added: "What's he like?"

"I've been dying to tell you. But he's like nobody."

"Nobody?" she echoed.

"He has no hat." Then seeing in her face that she already, in this, with a deeper dismay, found a touch of picture, I quickly added stroke to stroke. "He has red hair, very red, close-curling, and a pale face, long in shape, with straight good features and little rather queer whiskers that are red as his hair. His eyebrows are somehow darker; they look particularly arched and as if they might move a good deal. His eyes are sharp, strange — awfully; but I only know clearly that they're rather small and very fixed. His mouth's wide, and his lips are thin, and except for his little whiskers he's quite clean-shaven. He gives me a sort of sense of looking like an actor."

"An actor!" It was impossible to resemble one less, at least, than Mrs. Grose at that moment.

"I've never seen one, but so I suppose them. He's tall, active, erect," I continued, "but never — no, never! — a gentleman."

My companion's face had blanched as I went on; her round eyes started and her mild mouth gaped. "A gentleman?" she gasped, confounded, stupefied: "a gentleman *he?*"

"You know him then?"

She visibly tried to hold herself. "But he *is* handsome?"

I saw the way to help her. "Remarkably!"

"And dressed — ?"

"In somebody's clothes. They're smart, but they're not his own."

She broke into a breathless affirmative groan. "They're the master's!"

I caught it up. "You *do* know him?"

She faltered but a second. "Quint!" she cried.

"Quint?"

"Peter Quint — his own man, his valet, when he was here!"

"When the master was?"

Gaping still, but meeting me, she pieced it all together. "He never wore his hat, but he did wear — well, there were waistcoats missed! They were both here — last year. Then the master went, and Quint was alone."

I followed, but halting a little. "Alone?"

"Alone with *us*." Then as from a deeper depth, "In charge," she added.

"And what became of him?"

She hung fire so long that I was still more mystified. "He went too," she brought out at last.

"Went where?"

Her expression, at this, became extraordinary. "God knows where! He died."

"Died?" I almost shrieked.

She seemed fairly to square herself, plant herself more firmly to express the wonder of it. "Yes. Mr. Quint's dead."

6

It took of course more than that particular passage to place us together in presence of what we had now to live with as we could, my dreadful liability to impressions of the order so vividly exemplified, and my companion's knowledge henceforth — a knowledge half consternation and half compassion — of that liability. There had been this evening, after the revelation that left me for an hour so prostrate — there had been for either of us no attendance on any service but a little service of tears and vows, of prayers and promises, a climax to the series of mutual challenges and pledges that had straightway ensued on our retreating together to the schoolroom and shutting ourselves up there to have everything out. The result of our having everything out was simply to reduce our situation to the last rigour of its elements. She herself had seen nothing, not the shadow of a shadow, and nobody in the house but the governess was in the governess's plight; yet she accepted without directly impugning my sanity the truth as I gave it to her, and ended by showing me on this ground an awestricken tenderness, a deference to my more than questionable privilege, of which the very breath had remained with me as that of the sweetest of human charities.

What was settled between us accordingly that night was that we thought we might bear things together; and I was not even sure that in spite of her exemption it was she who had the best of the burden. I knew at this hour, I think, as well as I knew later, what I was capable of meeting to shelter my pupils; but it took me some time to be wholly sure of what my honest comrade was prepared for to keep terms with so stiff an agreement. I was queer company enough — quite as queer as the company I received; but as I trace over what we went through I see how much common ground we must have found in the one idea that, by good fortune, *could* steady us. It was the idea, the second movement, that led me straight out, as I may say, of the inner chamber of my dread. I could take the air in the court, at least, and there Mrs. Grose could join me. Perfectly can I recall now the particular way strength came to me before we separated for the night. We had gone over and over every feature of what I had seen.

"He was looking for some one else, you say — some one who was not you?"

"He was looking for little Miles." A portentous clearness now possessed me. "*That's* whom he was looking for."

"But how do you know?"

"I know, I know, I know!" My exaltation grew. "And *you* know, my dear!"

She did n't deny this, but I required, I felt, not even so much telling as that. She took it up again in a moment. "What if *he* should see him?"

"Little Miles? That's what he wants!"

She looked immensely scared again. "The child?"

"Heaven forbid! The man. He wants to appear to *them*." That he might was an awful conception, and yet somehow I could keep it at bay; which moreover, as we lingered there, was what I succeeded in practically proving. I had an absolute certainty that I should see again what I had already seen, but something within me said that by offering myself bravely as the sole subject of such experience, by accepting, by inviting, by surmounting it all, I should serve as an expiatory victim and guard the tranquillity of the rest of the household. The children in especial I should thus fence about and absolutely save. I recall one of the last things I said that night to Mrs. Grose.

"It does strike me that my pupils have never mentioned — !"

She looked at me hard as I musingly pulled up. "His having been here and the time they were with him?"

"The time they were with him, and his name, his presence, his history, in any way. They've never alluded to it."

"Oh the little lady does n't remember. She never heard or knew."

"The circumstances of his death?" I thought with some intensity. "Perhaps not. But Miles would remember — Miles would know."

"Ah don't try him!" broke from Mrs. Grose.

I returned her the look she had given me. "Don't be afraid." I continued to think. "It *is* rather odd."

"That he has never spoken of him?"

"Never by the least reference. And you tell me they were 'great friends.' "

"Oh it was n't *him!*" Mrs. Grose with emphasis declared. "It was Quint's own fancy. To play with him, I mean — to spoil him." She paused a moment; then she added: "Quint was much too free."

This gave me, straight from my vision of his face — *such* a face! — a sudden sickness of disgust. "Too free with *my* boy?"

"Too free with every one!"

I forbore for the moment to analyse this description further than by the reflexion that a part of it applied to several of the members of the household, of the half-dozen maids and men who were still of our small colony. But there was everything, for our apprehension, in the lucky fact that no discomfortable legend, no perturbation of scullions, had ever, within any one's memory, attached to the kind old place. It had neither bad name nor ill fame, and Mrs. Grose, most apparently, only desired to cling to me and to quake in silence. I even put her, the very last thing of all, to the test. It was when, at midnight, she had her hand on the schoolroom door to take leave. "I *have* it from you then — for it's of great importance — that he was definitely and admittedly bad?"

"Oh not admittedly. *I* knew it — but the master did n't."

"And you never told him?"

"Well, he did n't like tale-bearing — he hated complaints. He was terribly short with anything of that kind, and if people were all right to *him* — "

"He would n't be bothered with more?" This squared well enough with my impression of him: he was not a trouble-loving gentleman, nor so very particular perhaps about some of the company he himself kept. All the same, I pressed my informant. "I promise you *I* would have told!"

She felt my discrimination. "I dare say I was wrong. But really I was afraid."

"Afraid of what?"

"Of things that man could do. Quint was so clever — he was so deep."

I took this in still more than I probably showed. "You were n't afraid of anything else? Not of his effect — ?"

"His effect?" she repeated with a face of anguish and waiting while I faltered.

"On innocent little precious lives. They were in your charge."

"No, they were n't in mine!" she roundly and distressfully returned. "The master believed in him and placed him here because he was supposed not to be quite in health and the country air so good for him. So he had everything to say. "Yes" — she let me have it — "even about *them.*"

"Them — that creature?" I had to smother a kind of howl. "And you could bear it?"

"No. I could n't — and I can't now!" And the poor woman burst into tears.

A rigid control, from the next day, was, as I have said, to follow them; yet how often and how passionately, for a week, we came back together to the subject! Much as we had discussed it that Sunday night, I was, in the immediate later hours in especial — for it may be imagined whether I slept — still haunted with the shadow of something she had not told me. I myself had kept back nothing, but there was a word Mrs. Grose had kept back. I was sure moreover by morning that this was not from a failure of frankness, but because on every side there were fears. It seems to me indeed, in raking it all over, that by the time the morrow's sun was high I had restlessly read into the facts before us almost all the meaning they were to receive from subsequent and more cruel occurrences. What they gave me above all was just the sinister figure of the living man — the dead one would keep a while! — and of the months he had continuously passed at Bly, which, added up, made a formidable stretch. The limit of this evil time had arrived only when, on the dawn of a winter's morning, Peter Quint was found, by a labourer going to early work, stone dead on the road from the village: a catastrophe explained — superficially at least — by a visible wound to his head, such a wound as might have been produced (and as, on the final evidence, *had* been) by a fatal slip, in the dark and after leaving the public-house, on the steepish icy slope, a wrong path altogether, at the bottom of which he lay. The icy slope, the turn mistaken at night and in liquor, accounted for much — practically, in the end and after the inquest and boundless chatter, for everything; but there had been matters in his life, strange passages and perils, secret disorders, vices more than suspected, that would have accounted for a good deal more.

I scarce know how to put my story into words that shall be a credible picture of my state of mind; but I was in these days literally able to find a joy in the extraordinary flight of heroism the occasion demanded of me. I now saw that I had been asked for a service admirable and difficult; and there would be a greatness in letting it be seen — oh in the right quarter! — that I could succeed where many another girl might have failed. It was an immense help to me — I confess I rather applaud myself as I look back! — that I saw my response so strongly and so simply. I was there to protect and defend the little creatures in the world the most bereaved and the most loveable, the appeal of whose helplessness had suddenly become only too explicit, a deep constant ache of one's own engaged affection. We were cut off, really, together; we were united in our danger. They had nothing but me, and I — well, I had *them*. It was in short a magnificent chance. This chance presented itself to me in an image richly material. I was a screen — I was to stand before them. The more I saw the less they would. I began to watch them in a stifled suspense, a disguised tension, that might well, had it continued too long, have turned to something like madness. What saved me, as I now see, was that it turned to another matter altogether. It did n't last as suspense — it was superseded by horrible proofs. Proofs, I say, yes — from the moment I really took hold.

This moment dated from an afternoon hour that I happened to spend in the grounds with the younger of my pupils alone. We had left Miles indoors, on the red cushion of a deep window-seat; he had wished to finish a book, and I had been glad to encourage a purpose so laudable in a young man whose only defect was a certain ingenuity of restlessness. His sister, on the contrary, had been alert to come out, and I strolled with her half an hour, seeking the shade, for the sun was still high and the day exceptionally warm. I was aware afresh with her, as we went, of how, like her brother, she contrived — it was the charming thing in both children — to let me alone without appearing to drop me and to accompany me without appearing to oppress. They were never importunate and yet never listless. My attention to them all really went to seeing them amuse themselves immensely without me: this was a spectacle they seemed actively to prepare and that employed me as an active admirer. I walked in a world of their invention — they had no occasion whatever to draw upon mine; so that my time was taken only with being for them some remarkable person or thing that the game of the moment required and that was merely, thanks to my superior, my exalted stamp, a happy and highly distinguished sinecure. I forget what I was on the present occasion; I only remember that I was something very important and very quiet and that Flora was playing very hard. We were on the edge of the lake, and, as we had lately begun geography, the lake was the Sea of Azof.

Suddenly, amid these elements, I became aware that on the other side of the Sea of Azof we had an interested spectator. The way this knowledge gathered in me was the strangest thing in the world — the strangest, that is, except the very much stranger in which it quickly merged itself. I had sat down with a piece of work — for I was something or other that could sit — on the old stone bench which overlooked the pond; and in this position I began to take in with certitude and yet without direct vision the presence, a good way off, of a third person. The old trees, the thick shrubbery, made a great and pleasant shade, but it was all suffused with the brightness of the hot still hour. There was no ambiguity in anything; none whatever at least in the conviction I from one moment to another found myself forming as to what I should see straight before me and across the lake as a consequence of raising my eyes. They were attached at this juncture to the stitching in which I was engaged, and I can feel once more the spasm of my effort not to move them till I should so have steadied myself as to be able to make up my mind what to do. There was an alien object in view — a figure whose right of presence I instantly and passionately questioned. I recollect counting over perfectly the possibilities, reminding myself that nothing was more natural for instance than the appearance of one of the men about the place, or even of a messenger, a postman or a tradesman's boy, from the village. That reminder had as little effect on my practical certitude as I was conscious — still even without looking — of its having upon the character and attitude of our visitor. Nothing was more natural than that these things should be the other things they absolutely were not.

Of the positive identity of the apparition I would assure myself as soon as the small clock of my courage should have ticked out the right second; meanwhile, with an effort that was already sharp enough, I transferred my eyes straight to little Flora, who, at the moment, was about ten yards away. My heart had stood still for an instant with the wonder and terror of the question whether she too would see; and I held my breath while I waited for what a cry from her, what some sudden innocent sign either of interest or of alarm, would tell me. I waited, but nothing came; then in the first place — and there is something more dire in this, I feel, than in anything I have to relate — I was determined by a sense that within a minute all spontaneous sounds from her had dropped; and in the second by the circumstance that also within the minute she had, in her play, turned her back to the water. This was her attitude when I at last looked at her — looked with the confirmed conviction that we were still, together, under direct personal notice. She had picked up a small flat piece of wood which happened to have in it a little hole that had evidently suggested to her an idea of sticking in another fragment that might figure as a mast and make the thing a boat. This second morsel, as I watched her, she was very markedly and intently attempting to tighten in its place. My apprehension of what she was doing sustained me so that after some seconds I felt I was ready for more. Than I again shifted my eyes — I faced what I had to face.

7

I got hold of Mrs. Grose as soon after this as I could; and I can give no intelligible account of how I fought out the interval. Yet I still hear myself cry as I fairly threw myself into her arms: "They *know* — it's too monstrous: they know, they know!"

"And what on earth — ?" I felt her incredulity as she held me.

"Why all that *we* know — and heaven knows what more besides!" Then as she released me I made it out to her, made it out perhaps only now with full coherency even to myself. "Two hours ago, in the garden" — I could scarce articulate — "Flora *saw!*"

Mrs. Grose took it as she might have taken a blow in the stomach. "She has told you?" she panted.

"Not a word — that's the horror. She kept it to herself! The child of eight, *that* child!" Unutterable still for me was the stupefaction of it.

Mrs. Grose of course could only gape the wider. "Then how do you know?"

"I was there — I saw with my eyes: saw she was perfectly aware."

"Do you mean aware of *him?*"

"No — of *her.*" I was conscious as I spoke that I looked prodigious things, for I got the slow reflexion of them in my companion's face. "Another person — this time; but a figure of quite as unmistakeable horror and evil: a woman in black, pale and dreadful — with such an air also, and such a face! — on the other side of the lake. I was there with the child — quiet for the hour; and in the midst of it she came."

"Came how — from where?"

"From where they come from! She just appeared and stood there — but not so near."

"And without coming nearer?"

"Oh for the effect and the feeling she might have been as close as you!"

My friend, with an odd impulse, fell back a step. "Was she some one you've never seen?"

"Never. But some one the child has. Some one *you* have." Then to show how I had thought it all out: "My predecessor — the one who died."

"Miss Jessel?"

"Miss Jessel. You don't believe me?" I pressed.

She turned right and left in her distress. "How can you be sure?"

This drew from me, in the state of my nerves, a flash of impatience. "Then ask Flora — *she's* sure!" But I had no sooner spoken than I caught myself up. "No, for God's sake *don't!* She'll say she is n't — she'll lie!"

Mrs. Grose was not too bewildered instinctively to protest. "Ah how *can* you?"

"Because I'm clear. Flora does n't want me to know."

"It's only then to spare you."

"No, no — there are depths, depths! The more I go over it the more I see in it, and the more I see in it the more I fear. I don't know what I *don't* see, what I *don't* fear!"

Mrs. Grose tried to keep up with me. "You mean you're afraid of seeing her again?"

"Oh no; that's nothing — now!" Then I explained. "It's of *not* seeing her."

But my companion only looked wan. "I don't understand."

"Why, it's that the child may keep it up — and that the child assuredly *will* — without my knowing it."

At the image of this possibility Mrs. Grose for a moment collapsed, yet presently to pull herself together again as from the positive force of the sense of what, should we yield an inch, there would really be to give way to. "Dear, dear — we must keep our heads! And after all, if she does n't mind it — !" She even tried a grim joke. "Perhaps she likes it!"

"Like *such* things — a scrap of an infant!"

"Is n't it just a proof of her blest innocence?" my friend bravely enquired.

She brought me, for the instant, almost round. "Oh we must clutch at *that* — we must cling to it! If it is n't a proof of what you say, it's a proof of — God knows what! For the woman's a horror of horrors."

Mrs. Grose, at this, fixed her eyes a minute on the ground; then at last raising them, "Tell me how you know," she said.

"Then you admit it's what she was?" I cried.

"Tell me how you know," my friend simply repeated.

"Know? By seeing her! By the way she looked."

"At you, do you mean — so wickedly?"

"Dear me, no — I could have borne that. She gave me never a glance. She only fixed the child."

Mrs. Grose tried to see it. "Fixed her?"

"Ah with such awful eyes!"

She stared at mine as if they might really have resembled them. "Do you mean of dislike?"

"God help us, no. Of something much worse."

"Worse than dislike?" — this left her indeed at a loss.

"With a determination — indescribable. With a kind of fury of intention."

I made her turn pale. "Intention?"

"To get hold of her." Mrs. Grose — her eyes just lingering on mine — gave a shudder and walked to the window; and while she stood there looking out I completed my statement. "*That's* what Flora knows."

After a little she turned around. "The person was in black, you say?"

"In mourning — rather poor, almost shabby. But — yes — with extraordinary beauty." I now recognised to what I had at last, stroke by stroke, brought the victim of my confidence, for she quite visibly weighed this. "Oh handsome — very, very," I insisted; "wonderfully handsome. But infamous."

She slowly came back to me. "Miss Jessel — *was* infamous." She once more took my hand in both her own, holding it as tight as if to fortify me against the increase of alarm I might draw from this disclosure. "They were both infamous," she finally said.

So for a little we faced it once more together; and I found absolutely a degree of help in seeing it now so straight. "I appreciate," I said, "the great decency of your not having hitherto spoken; but the time has certainly come to give me the whole thing." She appeared to assent to this, but still only in silence; seeing which I went on: "I must have it now. Of what did she die? Come, there was something between them."

"There was everything."

"In spite of the difference — ?"

"Oh of their rank, their condition" — she brought it woefully out. "*She* was a lady."

I turned it over; I again saw. "Yes — she was a lady."

"And he so dreadfully below," said Mrs. Grose.

I felt that I doubtless need n't press too hard, in such company, on the place of a servant in the scale; but there was nothing to prevent an acceptance of my companion's own measure of my predecessor's abasement. There was a way to deal with that, and I dealt; the more readily for my full vision — on the evidence — of our employer's late clever good-looking "own" man; impudent, assured, spoiled, depraved. "The fellow was a hound."

Mrs. Grose considered as if it were perhaps a little a case for a sense of shades. "I've never seen one like him. He did what he wished."

"With *her?*"

"With them all."

It was as if now in my friend's own eyes Miss Jessel had again appeared. I seemed at any rate for an instant to trace their evocation of her as distinctly as I had seen her by the pond; and I brought out with decision: "It must have been also what *she* wished!"

Mrs. Grose's face signified that it had been indeed, but she said at the same time: "Poor woman — she paid for it!"

"Then you do know what she died of?" I asked.

"No — I know nothing. I wanted not to know; I was glad enough I did n't; and I thanked heaven she was well out of this!"

"Yet you had then your idea — "

"Of her real reason for leaving? Oh yes — as to that. She could n't have stayed. Fancy it here — for a governess! And afterwards I imagined — and I still imagine. And what I imagine is dreadful."

"Not so dreadful as what *I* do," I replied; on which I must have shown her — as I was indeed but too conscious — a front of miserable defeat. It brought out again all her compassion for me, and at the renewed touch of her kindness my power to resist broke down. I burst, as I had the other time made her burst, into tears; she took me to her motherly breast, where my lamentation overflowed. "I don't do it!" I sobbed in despair; "I don't save or shield them! It's far worse than I dreamed. They're lost!"

8

What I had said to Mrs. Grose was true enough: there were in the matter I had put before her depths and possibilities that I lacked resolution to sound; so that when we met once more in the wonder of it we were of a common mind about the duty of resistance to extravagant fancies. We were to keep our heads if we should keep nothing else — difficult indeed as that might be in the face of all that, in our prodigious experience, seemed least to be questioned. Late that night, while the house slept, we had another talk in my room; when she went all the way with me as to its being beyond doubt that I had seen exactly what I had seen. I found that to keep her thoroughly in the grip of this I had only to ask her how, if I had "made it up," I came to be able to give, of each of the persons appearing to me, a picture disclosing, to the last detail, their special marks — a portrait on the exhibition of which she had instantly recognised and named them. She wished, of course — small blame to her! — to sink the whole subject; and I was quick to assure her that my own interest in it had now violently taken the form of a search for the way to escape from it. I closed with her cordially on the article of the likelihood that with recurrence — for recurrence we took for granted — I should get used to my danger; distinctly professing that my personal exposure had suddenly become the least of my discomforts. It was my new suspicion that was intolerable; and yet even to this complication the later hours of the day had brought a little ease.

On leaving her, after my first outbreak, I had of course returned to my pupils, associating the right remedy for my dismay with that sense of their charm which I had already recognised as a resource I could positively cultivate and which had never failed me yet. I had simply, in other words, plunged afresh into Flora's special society and there become aware — it was almost a luxury! — that she could put her little conscious hand straight upon the spot that ached. She had looked at me in sweet speculation and then had accused me to my face of having "cried." I had supposed the ugly signs of it brushed away; but I could literally — for the time at all events — rejoice, under this fathomless charity, that they had not entirely disappeared. To gaze into the depths of blue of the child's eyes and pronounce their loveliness a trick of premature cunning was to be guilty of a cynicism in preference to which I naturally preferred to abjure my judgement and, so far as might be, my agitation. I could n't abjure for merely wanting to, but I could repeat to Mrs. Grose — as I did there, over and over, in the small hours — that with our small friends' voices in the air, their pressure on one's heart and their fragrant faces against one's cheek, everything fell to the ground but their incapacity and their beauty. It was a pity that, somehow, to settle this once for all, I had equally to re-enumerate the signs of subtlety that, in the afternoon, by the lake, had made a miracle of my show of self-possession. It was a pity to be obliged to re-investigate the certitude of the moment itself and repeat how it had come to me as a revelation that the inconceivable communion I then surprised must have been for both parties a matter of habit. It was a pity I should have had to quaver out again the reasons for my not having, in my delusion, so much as questioned that the little girl saw our visitant even as I actually saw Mrs. Grose herself, and that she wanted, by just so much as she did thus see, to make me suppose she did n't, and at the same time, without showing anything, arrive at a guess as to whether I myself did! It was a pity I needed to recapitulate the portentous little activities by which she sought to divert my attention — the perceptible increase of movement, the greater intensity of play, the singing, the gabbling of nonsense and the invitation to romp.

Yet if I had not indulged, to prove there was nothing in it, in this review, I should have missed the two or three dim elements of comfort that still remained to me. I should n't for instance have been able to asseverate to my friend that I was certain — which was so much to the good — that *I* at least had not betrayed myself. I should n't have been prompted, by stress of need, by desperation of mind — I scarce know what to call it — to invoke such further aid to intelligence as might spring from pushing my colleague fairly to the wall. She had told me, bit by bit, under pressure, a great deal; but a small shifty spot on the wrong side of it all still sometimes brushed my brow like the wing of a bat; and I remember how on this occasion — for the sleeping house and the concentration alike of our danger and our watch seemed to help — I felt the importance of giving the last jerk to the curtain. "I don't believe anything so horrible," I recollect saying; "no, let us put it definitely, my dear, that I don't. But if I did, you know, there's a thing I should require now, just without sparing you the least bit more — oh not a scrap, come! — to get out of you. What was it you had in mind when, in our distress, before Miles came back, over the letter from his school, you said, under my insistence, that you didn't pretend for him he had n't literally *ever* been 'bad'? He has *not,* truly, 'ever,' in these weeks that I myself have lived with him and so closely watched him; he has been an imperturbable little prodigy of delightful loveable goodness. Therefore you might perfectly have made the claim for him if you had not, as it happened, seen an exception to take. What was your exception, and to what passage in your personal observation of him did you refer?"

It was a straight question enough, but levity was not our note, and in any case I had before the grey dawn admonished us to separate got my answer. What my friend had had in mind proved immensely to the purpose. It was neither more nor less than the particular fact that for a period of several months Quint and the boy had been perpetually together. It was indeed the very appropriate item of evidence of her having ventured to criticise the propriety, to hint at the incongruity, of so close an alliance, and even to go so far on the subject as a frank overture to Miss Jessel would take her. Miss Jessel had, with a very high manner about it, requested her to mind her business, and the good woman had on this directly approached little Miles. What she had said to him, since I pressed, was that *she* liked to see young gentlemen not forget their station.

I pressed again, of course, the closer for that. "You reminded him that Quint was only a base menial?"

"As you might say! And it was his answer, for one thing, that was bad."

"And for another thing?" I waited. "He repeated your words to Quint?"

"No, not that. It's just what he *would n't!*" she could still impress on me. "I was sure, at any rate," she added, "that he did n't. But he denied certain occasions."

"What occasions?"

"When they had been about together quite as if Quint were his tutor — and a very grand one — and Miss Jessel only for the little lady. When he had gone off with the fellow, I mean, and spent hours with him."

"He then prevaricated about it — he said he had n't?" Her assent was clear enough to cause me to add in a moment: "I see. He lied."

"Oh!" Mrs. Grose mumbled. This was a suggestion that it did n't matter; which indeed she backed up by a further remark. "You see, after all, Miss Jessel did n't mind. She did n't forbid him."

I considered. "Did he put that to you as a justification?"

At this she dropped again. "No, he never spoke of it."

"Never mentioned her in connexion with Quint?"

She saw, visibly flushing, where I was coming out. "Well, he did n't show anything. He denied," she repeated; "he denied."

Lord, how I pressed her now! "So that you could see he knew what was between the two wretches?"

"I don't know — I don't know!" the poor woman wailed.

"You do know, you dear thing," I replied; "only you have n't my dreadful boldness of mind, and you keep back, out of timidity and modesty and delicacy, even the impression that in the past, when you had, without my aid, to flounder about in silence, most of all made you miserable. But I shall get it out of you yet! There was something in the boy that suggested to you," I continued, "his covering and concealing their relation."

"Oh he could n't prevent — "

"Your learning the truth? I dare say! But, heavens," I fell, with vehemence, a-thinking, "what it shows that they must, to that extent, have succeeded in making of him!"

"Ah nothing that's not nice *now!*" Mrs. Grose lugubriously pleaded.

"I don't wonder you looked queer," I persisted, "when I mentioned to you the letter from his school!"

"I doubt if I looked as queer as you!" she retorted with homely force. "And if he was so bad then as that comes to, how is he such an angel now?"

"Yes indeed — and if he was a fiend at school! How, how, how? Well," I said in my torment, "you must put it to me again, though I shall not be able to tell you for some days. Only put it to me again!" I cried in a way that made my friend stare. "There are directions in which I must n't for the present let myself go." Meanwhile I returned to her first example — the one to which she had just previously referred — of the boy's happy capacity for an occasional slip. "If Quint — on your remonstrance at the time you speak of — was a base menial, one of the things Miles said to you, I find myself guessing, was that you were another." Again her admission was so adequate that I continued: "And you forgave him that?"

"Would n't *you?*"

"Oh yes!" And we exchanged there, in the stillness, a sound of the oddest amusement. Then I went one: "At all events, while he was with the man — "

"Miss Flora was with the woman. It suited them all!"

It suited me, too, I felt, only too well; by which I mean that it suited exactly the particular deadly view I was in the very act of forbidding myself to entertain. But I so far succeeded in checking the expression of this view that I will throw, just here, no further light on it than may be offered by the mention of my final observation to Mrs. Grose. "His having lied and been impudent are, I confess, less engaging specimens than I had hoped to have from you of the outbreak in him of the little natural man. Still," I mused, "they must do, for they make me feel more than ever that I must watch."

It made me blush, the next minute, to see in my friend's face how much more unreservedly she had forgiven him than her anecdote struck me as pointing out to my own tenderness any way to do. This was marked when, at the schoolroom door, she quitted me. "Surely you don't accuse *him* — "

"Of carrying on an intercourse that he conceals from me? Ah remember that, until further evidence, I now accuse nobody." Then before shutting her out to go by another passage to her own place, "I must just wait," I wound up.

9

I waited and waited, and the days took as they elapsed something from my consternation. A very few of them, in fact, passing, in constant sight of my pupils, without a fresh incident, sufficed to give to grievous fancies and even to odious memories a kind of brush of the sponge. I have spoken of the surrender to their extraordinary childish grace as a thing I could actively promote in myself, and it may be imagined if I neglected now to apply at this source for whatever balm it would yield. Stranger than I can express, certainly, was the effort to struggle against my new lights. It would doubtless have been a greater tension still, however, had it not been so frequently successful. I used to wonder how my little charges could help guessing that I thought strange things about them; and the circumstance that these things only made them more interesting was not by itself a direct aid to keeping them in the dark. I trembled lest they should see that they *were* so immensely more interesting. Putting things at the worst, at all events, as in meditation I so often did, any clouding of their innocence could only be — blameless and foredoomed as they were — a reason the more for taking risks. There were moments when I knew myself to catch them up by an irresistible impulse and press them to my heart. As soon as I had done so I used to wonder — "What will they think of that? Does n't it betray too much?" It would have been easy to get into a sad wild tangle about how much I might betray; but the real account, I feel, of the hours of peace I could still enjoy was that the immediate charm of my companions was a beguilement still effective even under the shadow of the possibility that it was studied. For if it occurred to me that I might occasionally excite suspicion by the little outbreaks of my sharper passion for them, so too I remember asking if I mightn't see a queerness in the traceable increase of their own demonstrations.

They were at this period extravagantly and pretenaturally fond of me; which, after all, I could reflect, was no more than a graceful response in children perpetually bowed down over and hugged. The homage of which they were so lavish succeeded in truth for my nerves quite as well as if I never appeared to myself, as I may say, literally to catch them at a purpose in it. They had never, I think, wanted to do so many things for their poor protectress; I mean — though they got their lessons better and better, which was naturally what would please her most — in the way of diverting, entertaining, surprising her; reading her passages, telling her stories, acting her charades, pouncing out at her, in disguises, as animals and historical characters, and above all astonishing her by the "pieces" they had secretly got by heart and could interminably recite. I should never get to the bottom — were I to let myself go even now — of the prodigious private commentary, all under still more private correction, with which I in these days overscored their full hours. They had shown me from the first a facility for everything, a general faculty which, taking a fresh start, achieved remarkable flights. They got their little tasks as if they loved them; they indulged, from the mere exuberance of the gift, in the most unimposed little miracles of memory. They not only popped out at me as tigers and as Romans, but as Shakespeareans, astronomers and navigators. This was so singularly the case that it had presumably much to do with the fact as to which, at the present day, I am at a loss for a different explanation: I allude to my unnatural composure on the subject of another school for Miles. What I remember is that I was content for the time not to open the question, and that contentment must have sprung from the sense of his perpetually striking show of cleverness. He was too clever for a bad governess, for a parson's daughter, to spoil; and the strangest if not the brightest thread in the pensive embroidery I just spoke of was the impression I might have got, if I had dared to work it out, that he was under some influence operating in his small intellectual life as a tremendous incitement.

If it was easy to reflect, however, that such a boy could postpone school, it was at least as marked that for such a boy to have been "kicked out" by a schoolmaster was a mystification without end. Let me add that in their company now — and I was careful almost never to be out of it — I could follow no scent very far. We lived in a cloud of music and affection and success and private theatricals. The musical sense in each of the children was of the quickest, but the elder in especial had a marvellous knack of catching and repeating. The schoolroom piano broke into all gruesome fancies; and when that failed there were confabulations in corners, with a sequel of one of them going out in the highest spirits in order to "come in" as something new. I had had brothers myself, and it was no revelation to me that little girls could be slavish idolaters of little boys. What surpassed everything was that there was a little boy in the world who could have for the inferior age, sex and intelligence so fine a consideration. They were extraordinarily at one, and to say that they never either quarrelled or complained is to make the note of praise coarse for their quality of sweetness. Sometimes perhaps indeed (when I dropped into coarseness) I came across traces of little understandings between them by which one of them should keep me occupied while the other slipped away. There is a naïf side, I suppose, in all diplomacy; but if my pupils practised upon me it was surely with the minimum of grossness. It was all in the other quarter that, after a lull, the grossness broke out.

I find that I really hang back; but I must take my horrid plunge. In going on with the record of what was hideous at Bly I not only challenge the most liberal faith — for which I little care; but (and this is another matter) I renew what I myself suffered, I again push my dreadful way through it to the end. There came suddenly an hour after which, as I look back, the business seems to me to have been all pure suffering; but I have at least reached the heart of it, and the straightest road out is doubtless to advance. One evening — with nothing to lead up or prepare it — I felt the cold touch of the impression that had breathed on me the night of my arrival and which, much lighter then as I have mentioned, I should probably have made little of in memory had my subsequent sojourn been less agitated. I had not gone to bed; I sat reading by a couple of candles. There was a roomful of old books at Bly — last-century fiction some of it, which, to the extent of a distinctly deprecated renown, but never to so much as that of a stray specimen, had reached the sequestered home and appealed to the unavowed curiosity of my youth. I remember that the book I had in my hand was Fielding's "Amelia"; also that I was wholly awake. I recall further both a general conviction that it was horribly late and a particular objection to looking at my watch. I figure finally that the white curtain draping, in the fashion of those days, the head of Flora's little bed, shrouded, as I had assured myself long before, the perfection of childish rest. I recollect in short that though I was deeply interested in my author I found myself, at the turn of a page and with his spell all scattered, looking straight up from him and hard at the door of my room. There was a moment during which I listened, reminded of the faint sense I had had, the first night, of there being something undefinably astir in the house, and noted the soft breath of the open casement just move the half-drawn blind. Then, with all the marks of a deliberation that must have seemed magnificent had there been any one to admire it, I laid down my book, rose to my feet and, taking a candle, went straight out of the room and, from the passage, on which my light made little impression, noiselessly closed and locked the door.

I can say now neither what determined nor what guided me, but I went straight along the lobby, holding my handle high, till I came within sight of the tall window that presided over the great turn of the staircase. At this point I precipitately found myself aware of three things. They were practically simultaneous, yet they had flashes of succession. My candle, under a bold flourish, went out, and I perceived, by the uncovered window, that the yielding dusk of earliest morning rendered it unnecessary. Without it, the next instant, I knew that there was a figure on the stair. I speak of sequences, but I required no lapse of seconds to stiffen myself for a third encounter with Quint. The apparition had reached the landing halfway up and was therefore on the spot nearest the window, where, at sight of me, it stopped short and fixed me exactly as it had fixed me from the tower and from the garden. He knew me as well as I knew him; and so, in the cold faint twilight, with a glimmer in the high glass and another on the polish of the oak stair below, we faced each other in our common intensity. He was absolutely, on this occasion, a living detestable dangerous presence. But that was not the wonder of wonders; I reserve this distinction for quite another circumstance: the circumstance that dread had unmistakeably quitted me and that there was nothing in me unable to meet and measure him.

I had plenty of anguish after that extraordinary moment, but I had, thank God, no terror. And he knew I had n't — I found myself at the end of an instant magnificently aware of this. I felt, in a fierce rigour of confidence, that if I stood my ground a minute I should cease — for the time at least — to have him to reckon with; and during the minute, accordingly, the thing was as human and hideous as a real interview: hideous just because it *was* human, as human as to have met alone, in the small hours, in a sleeping house, some enemy, some adventurer, some criminal. It was the dead silence of our long gaze at such close quarters that gave the whole horror, huge as it was, its only note of the unnatural. If I had met a murderer in such a place and at such an hour we still at least would have spoken. Something would have passed, in life, between us; if nothing had passed one of us would have moved. The moment was so prolonged that it would have taken but little more to make me doubt if even *I* were in life. I can't express what followed it save by saying that the silence itself — which was indeed in a manner an attestation of my strength — became the element into which I saw the figure disappear; in which I definitely saw it turn, as I might have seen the low wretch to which it had once belonged turn on receipt of an order, and pass, with my eyes on the villainous back that no hunch could have more disfigured, straight down the staircase and into the darkness in which the next bend was lost.

10

I remained a while at the top of the stair, but with the effect presently of under-standing that when my visitor had gone, he had gone; then I returned to my room. The foremost thing I saw there by the light of the candle I had left burning was that Flora's little bed was empty; and on this I caught my breath with all the terror that, five minutes before, I had been able to resist. I dashed at the place in which I had left her lying and over which — for the small silk counterpane and the sheets were disarranged — the white curtains had been deceivingly pulled forward; then my step, to my unutterable relief, produced an answering sound: I noticed an agitation of the window-blind, and the child, ducking down, emerged rosily from the other side of it. She stood there in so much of her candour and so little of her night-gown, with her pink bare feet and the golden glow of her curls. She looked intensely grave, and I had never had such a sense of losing an advantage acquired (the thrill of which had just been so prodigious) as on my consciousness that she addressed me with a reproach — "You naughty: where *have* you been?" Instead of challenging her own irregularity I found myself arraigned and explaining. She herself explained, for that matter, with the loveliest eagerest simplicity. She had known suddenly, as she lay there, that I was out of the room, and had jumped up to see what had become of me. I had dropped, with the joy of her reappearance, back into my chair — feeling then, and then only, a little faint; and she had pattered straight over to me, thrown herself upon my knee, given herself to be held with the flame of the candle full in the wonderful little face that was still flushed with sleep. I remember closing my eyes an instant, yieldingly, consciously, as before the excess of something beautiful that shone out of the blue of her own. "You were looking for me out of the window?" I said. "You thought I might be walking in the grounds?"

"Well, you know. I thought some one was" — she never blanched as she smiled out that at me.

Oh how I looked at her now! "And did you see any one?"

"Ah *no!*" she returned almost (with the full privilege of childish inconsequence) resentfully, though with a long sweetness in her little drawl of the negative.

At that moment, in the state of my nerves, I absolutely believed she lied; and if I once more closed my eyes it was before the dazzle of the three or four possible ways in which I might take this up. One of these for a moment tempted me with such singular force that, to resist it, I must have gripped my little girl with a spasm that, wonderfully, she submitted to without a cry or a sign of fright. Why not break out at her on the spot and have it all over? — give it to her straight in her lovely little lighted face? "You see, you see, you *know* that you do and that you already quite suspect I believe it; therefore why not frankly confess it to me, so that we may at least live with it together and learn perhaps, in the strangeness of our fate, where we are and what it means?" This solicitation dropped, alas, as it came: if I could immediately have succumbed to it I might have spared myself — well, you'll see what. Instead of succumbing I sprang again to my feet, looked at her bend and took a helpless middle way. "Why did you pull the curtain over the place to make me think you were still there?"

Flora luminously considered; after which, with her little divine smile: "Because I don't like to frighten you!"

"But if I had, by your idea, gone out — ?"

She absolutely declined to be puzzled; she turned her eyes to the flame of the candle as if the question were as irrelevant, or at any rate as impersonal, as Mrs. Marcet or nine-times-nine. "Oh but you know," she quite adequately answered, "that you might come back, you dear, and that you *have!*" And after a little, when she had got into bed, I had, a long time, by almost sitting on her for the retention of her hand, to show how I recognised the pertinence of my return.

You may imagine the general complexion, from that moment, of my nights. I repeatedly sat up till I did n't know when; I selected moments when my room-mate unmistakeably slept, and, stealing out, took noiseless turns in the passage. I even pushed as far as to where I had last met Quint. But I never met him there again, and I may as well say at once that I on no other occasion saw him in the house. I just missed, on the staircase, nevertheless, a different adventure. Looking down it from the top I once recognised the presence of a woman seated on one of the lower steps with her back presented to me, her body half-bowed and her head, in an attitude of woe, in her hands. I had been there but an instant, however, when she vanished without looking round at me. I knew, for all that, exactly what dreadful face she had to show; and I wondered whether, if instead of being above I had been below, I should have had the same nerve for going up that I had lately shown Quint. Well, there continued to be plenty of call for nerve. On the eleventh night after my latest encounter with that gentleman — they were all numbered now — I had an alarm that perilously skirted it and that indeed, from the particular quality of its unexpectedness, proved quite my sharpest shock. It was precisely the first night during this series that, weary with vigils, I had conceived I might again without laxity lay myself down at my old hour. I slept immediately and, as I afterwards knew, till about one o'clock; but when I woke it was to sit straight up, as completely roused as if a hand had shaken me. I had left a light burning, but it was now out, and I felt an instant certainty that Flora had extinguished it. This brought me to my feet and straight, in the darkness, to her bed, which I found she had left. A glance at the window enlightened me further, and the striking of a match completed the picture.

The child had again got up — this time blowing out the taper, and had again, for some purpose of observation or response, squeezed in behind the blind and was peering out into the night. That she now saw — as she had not, I had satisfied myself, the previous time — was proved to me by the fact that she was disturbed neither by my re-illumination nor by the haste I made to get into slippers and into a wrap. Hidden, protected, absorbed, she evidently rested on the sill — the casement opened forward — and gave herself up. There was a great still moon to help her, and this fact had counted in my quick decision. She was face to face with the apparition we had met at the lake, and could now communicate with it as she had not been able to do. What I, on my side, had to care for was, without disturbing her, to reach, from the corridor, some other window turned to the same quarter. I got to the door without her hearing me; I got out of it, closed it and listened, from the other side, for some sound from her. While I stood in the passage I had my eyes on her brother's door, which was but ten steps off and which, indescribably, produced in me a renewal of the strange impulse that I lately spoke of as my temptation. What if I should go straight in and march to *his* window? — what if, by risking to his boyish bewilderment a revelation of my motive, I should throw across the rest of the mystery the long halter of my boldness?

This thought held me sufficiently to make me cross to his threshold and pause again. I preternaturally listened; I figured to myself what might portentously be; I wondered if his bed were also empty and he also secretly at watch. It was a deep soundless minute, at the end of which my impulse failed. He was quiet; he might be innocent; the risk was hideous; I turned away. There was a figure in the grounds — a figure prowling for a sight, the visitor with whom Flora was engaged; but it was n't the visitor most concerned with my boy. I hesitated afresh, but on other grounds and only a few seconds; then I had made my choice. There were empty rooms enough at Bly, and it was only a question of choosing the right one. The right one suddenly presented itself to me as the lower one — though high above the gardens — in the solid corner of the house that I have spoken of as the old tower. This was a large square chamber, arranged with some state as a bedroom, the extravagant size of which made it so inconvenient that it had not for years, though kept by Mrs. Grose in exemplary order, been occupied. I had often admired it and knew my way about in it; I had only, after just faltering at the first chill gloom of its disuse, to pass across it and unbolt in all quietness one of the shutters. Achieving this transit I uncovered the glass without a sound and, applying my face to the pane, was able, the darkness without being much less than within, to see that I commanded the right direction. Then I saw something more. The moon made the night extraordinarily penetrable and showed me on the lawn a person, diminished by distance, who stood there motionless and as if fascinated, looking up to where I had appeared — looking, that is, not so much straight at me as at something that was apparently above me. There was clearly another person above me — there was a person on the tower; but the presence on the lawn was not in the least what I had conceived and had confidently hurried to meet. The presence on the lawn — I felt sick as I made it out — was poor little Miles himself.

11

It was not till late next day that I spoke to Mrs. Grose; the rigour with which I kept my pupils in sight making it often difficult to meet her privately: the more as we each felt the importance of not provoking — on the part of the servants quite as much as on that of the children — any suspicion of a secret flurry or of a discussion of mysteries. I drew a great security in this particular from her mere smooth aspect. There was nothing in her fresh face to pass on to others the least of my horrible confidences. She believed me, I was sure, absolutely: if she had n't I don't know what would have become of me, for I could n't have borne the strain alone. But she was a magnificent monument to the blessing of a want of imagination, and if she could see in our little charges nothing but their beauty and amiability, their happiness and cleverness, she had no direct communication with the sources of my trouble. If they had been at all visibly blighted or battered she would doubtless have grown, on tracing it back, haggard enough to match them; as matters stood, however, I could feel her, when she surveyed them with her large white arms folded and the habit of serenity in all her look, thank the Lord's mercy that if they were ruined the pieces would still serve. Flights of fancy gave place, in her mind, to a steady fireside glow, and I had already begun to perceive how, with the development of the conviction that — as time went on without a public accident — our young things could, after all, look out for themselves, she addressed her greatest solicitude to the sad case presented by their deputy-guardian. That, for myself, was a sound simplification: I could engage that, to the world, my face should tell no tales, but it would have been, in the conditions, an immense added worry to find myself anxious about hers.

At the hour I now speak of she had joined me, under pressure, on the terrace, where, with the lapse of the season, the afternoon sun was now agreeable; and we sat there together while before us and at a distance, yet within call if we wished, the children strolled to and fro in one of their most manageable moods. They moved slowly, in unison, below us, over the lawn, the boy, as they went, reading aloud from a story-book and passing his arm round his sister to keep her quite in touch. Mrs. Grose watched them with positive placidity; then I caught the suppressed intellectual creak with which she conscientiously turned to take from me a view of the back of the tapestry. I had made her a receptacle of lurid things, but there was an odd recognition of my superiority — my accomplishments and my function — in her patience under my pain. She offered her mind to my disclosures as, had I wished to mix a witch's broth and proposed it with assurance, she would have held out a large clean saucepan. This had become thoroughly her attitude by the time that, in my recital of the events of the night, I reached the point of what Miles had said to me when, after seeing him, at such a monstrous hour, almost on the very spot where he happened now to be, I had gone down to bring him in; choosing then, at the window, with a concentrated need of not alarming the house, rather that method than any noisier process. I had left her meanwhile in little doubt of my small hope of representing with success even to her actual sympathy my sense of real splendour of the little inspiration with which, after I had got him into the house, the boy met my final articulate challenge. As soon as I appeared in the moonlight on the terrace he had come to me as straight as possible; on which I had taken his hand without a word and led him, through the dark spaces, up the staircase where Quint had so hungrily hovered for him, along the lobby where I had listened and trembled, and so to his forsaken room.

Not a sound, on the way, had passed between us, and I had wondered — oh *how* I had wondered! — if he were groping about in his dreadful little mind for something plausible and not too grotesque. It would tax his invention certainly, and I felt, this time, over his real embarrassment, a curious thrill of triumph. It was a sharp trap for any game hitherto successful. He could play no longer at perfect propriety, nor could he pretend to it; so how the deuce would he get out of the scrape? There beat in me indeed, with the passionate throb of this question, an equal dumb appeal as to how the deuce *I* should. I was confronted at last, as never yet, with all the risk attached even now to sounding my own horrid note. I remember in fact that as we pushed into his little chamber where the bed had not been slept in at all and the window, uncovered to the moonlight, made the place so clear that there was no need of striking a match — I remember how I suddenly dropped, sank upon the edge of the bed from the force of the idea that he must know how he really, as they say, "had" me. He could do what he liked, with all his cleverness to help him, so long as I should continue to defer to the old tradition of the criminality of those caretakers of the young who minister to superstitions and fears. He "had" me indeed, and in a cleft stick; for who would ever absolve me, who would consent that I should go unhung, if, by the faintest tremor of an overture, I were the first to introduce into our perfect intercourse an element so dire? No, no: it was useless to attempt to convey to Mrs. Grose, just as it is scarcely less so to attempt to suggest here, how, during our short stiff brush there in the dark, he fairly shook me with admiration. I was of course thoroughly kind and merciful; never, never yet had I placed on his small shoulders hands of such tenderness as those with which, while I rested against the bed, I held him there well under fire. I had no alternative but, in form at least, to put it to him.

"You must tell me now — and all the truth. What did you go out for? What were you doing there?"

I can still see his wonderful smile, the whites of his beautiful eyes and the uncovering of his clear teeth, shine to me in the dusk. "If I tell you why, will you understand?" My heart, at this, leaped into my mouth. *Would* he tell me why? I found no sound on my lips to press it, and I was aware of answering only with a vague repeated grimacing nod. He was gentleness itself, and while I wagged my head at him he stood there more than ever a little fairy prince. It was his brightness indeed that gave me a respite. Would it be so great if he were really going to tell me? "Well," he said at last, "just exactly in order that you should do this."

"Do what?"

"Think me — for a change — *bad!*" I shall never forget the sweetness and gaiety with which he brought out the word, nor how, on top of it, he bent forward and kissed me. It was practically the end of everything. I met his kiss and I had to make, while I folded him for a minute in my arms, the most stupendous effort not to cry. He had given exactly the account of himself that permitted least my going behind it, and it was only with the effect of confirming my acceptance of it that, as I presently glanced about the room, I could say —

"Then you did n't undress at all?"

He fairly glittered in the gloom. "Not at all. I sat up and read."

"And when did you go down?"

"At midnight. When I'm bad I *am* bad!"

"I see, I see — it's charming. But how could you be sure I should know it?"

"Oh I arranged that with Flora." His answers rang out with a readiness! "She was to get up and look out."

"Which is what she did do." It was I who fell into the trap!

"So she disturbed you, and, to see what she was looking at, you also looked — you saw."

"While you," I concurred, "caught your death in the night air!"

He literally bloomed so from this exploit that he could afford radiantly to assent. "How otherwise should I have been bad enough?" he asked. Then, after another embrace, the incident and our interview closed on my recognition of all the reserves of goodness that, for his joke, he had been able to draw upon.

12

The particular impression I had received proved in the morning light, I repeat, not quite successfully presentable to Mrs. Grose, though I re-enforced it with the mention of still another remark that he had made before we separated. "It all lies in half a dozen words," I said to her, "words that really settle the matter. 'Think, you know, what I *might* do!' He threw that off to show me how good he is. He knows down to the ground what he 'might do.' That's what he gave them a taste of at school."

"Lord, you do change!" cried my friend.

"I don't change — I simply make it out. The four, depend upon it, perpetually meet. If on either of these last nights you had been with either child you'd clearly have understood. The more I've watched and waited the more I've felt that if there were nothing else to make it sure it would be made so by the systematic silence of each. *Never,* by a slip of the tongue, have they so much as alluded to either of their old friends, any more than Miles has alluded to his expulsion. Oh yes, we may sit here and look at them and they may show off to us there to their fill; but even while they pretend to be lost in their fairy-tale they're steeped in their vision of the dead restored to them. He's not reading to her," I declared; "they're talking of *them* — they're talking horrors! I go on, I know, as if I were crazy; and it's a wonder I'm not. What I've seen would have made *you* so; but it has only made me more lucid, made me get hold of still other things."

My lucidity must have seemed awful, but the charming creatures who were victims of it, passing and repassing in their interlocked sweetness, gave my colleague something to hold on by; and I felt how tight she held as, without stirring in the breath of my passion, she covered them still with her eyes. "Of what other things have you got hold?"

"Why of the very things that have delighted, fascinated and yet, at bottom, as I now so strangely see, mystified and troubled me. Their more than earthly beauty, their absolutely unnatural goodness. It's a game," I went on; "it's a policy and a fraud!"

"On the part of little darlings — ?"

"As yet mere lovely babies? Yes, mad as that seems!" The very act of bringing it out really helped me to trace it — follow it all up and piece it all together. "They haven't been good — they've only been absent. It has been easy to live with them because they're simply leading a life of their own. They're not mine — they're not ours. They're his and they're hers!"

"Quint's and that woman's?"

"Quint's and that woman's. They want to get to them."

Oh how, at this, poor Mrs. Grose appeared to study them! "But for what?"

"For the love of all the evil that, in those dreadful days, the pair put into them. And to ply them with that evil still, to keep up the work of demons, is what brings the others back."

"Laws!" said my friend under her breath. The exclamation was homely, but it revealed a real acceptance of my further proof of what, in the bad time — for there had been a worse even than this! — must have occurred. There could have been no such justification for me as the plain assent of her experience to whatever depth of depravity I found credible in our brace of scoundrels. It was in obvious submission of memory that she brought out after a moment: "They *were* rascals! But what can they now do?" she pursued.

"Do?" I echoed so loud that Miles and Flora, as they passed at their distance, paused an instant in their walk and looked at us. "Don't they do enough?" I demanded in a lower tone, while the children, having smiled and nodded and kissed hands to us, resumed their exhibition. We were held by it a minute; then I answered: "They can destroy them!" At this my companion did turn, but the appeal she launched was a silent one, the effect of which was to make me more explicit. "They don't know as yet quite how — but they're trying hard. They're seen only across, as it were, and beyond — in strange places and on high places, the top of towers, the roof of houses, the outside of windows, the further edge of pools; but there's a deep design, on either side, to shorten the distance and overcome the obstacle: so the success of the tempters is only a question of time. They've only to keep to their suggestions of danger."

"For the children to come?"

"And perish in the attempt!" Mrs. Grose slowly got up, and I scrupulously added: "Unless, of course, we can prevent!"

Standing there before me while I kept my seat she visibly turned things over. "Their uncle must do the preventing. He must take them away."

"And who's to make him?"

She had been scanning the distance, but she now dropped on me a foolish face. "You, Miss."

"By writing to him that his house is poisoned and his little nephew and niece mad?"

"But if they *are,* Miss?"

"And if I am myself, you mean? That's charming news to be sent him by a person enjoying his confidence and whose prime undertaking was to give him no worry."

Mrs. Grose considered, following the children again. "Yes, he do hate worry. That was the great reason — "

"Why those fiends took him in so long? No doubt, though his indifference must have been awful. As I'm not a fiend, at any rate, I should n't take him in."

My companion, after an instant and for all answer, sat down again and grasped my arm. "Make him at any rate come to you."

I stared. "To *me?*" I had a sudden fear of what she might do. " 'Him'?"

"He ought to *be* here — he ought to help."

I quickly rose and I think I must have shown her a queerer face than ever yet. "You see me asking him for a visit?" No, with her eyes on my face she evidently could n't. Instead of it even — as a woman reads another — she could see what I myself saw: his derision, his amusement, his contempt for the breakdown of my resignation at being left alone and for the fine machinery I had set in motion to attract his attention to my slighted charms. She did n't know — no one knew — how proud I had been to serve him and to stick to our terms; yet she none the less took the measure, I think, of the warning I now gave her. "If you should so lose your head as to appeal to him for me — "

She was really frightened. "Yes, Miss?"

"I would leave, on the spot, both him and you."

13

It was all very well to join them, but speaking to them proved quite as much as ever an effort beyond my strength — offered, in close quarters, difficulties as insurmountable as before. This situation continued a month, and with new aggravations and particular notes, the note above all, sharper and sharper, of the small ironic consciousness on the part of my pupils. It was not, I am as sure to-day as I was sure then, my mere infernal imagination: it was absolutely traceable that they were aware of my predicament and that this strange relation made, in a manner, for a long time, the air in which we moved. I don't mean that they had their tongues in their cheeks or did anything vulgar, for that was not one of their dangers: I do mean, on the other hand, that the element of the unnamed and untouched became, between us, greater than any other, and that so much avoidance could n't have been made successful without a great deal of tacit arrangement. It was as if, at moments, we were perpetually coming into sight of subjects before which we must stop short, turning suddenly out of alleys that we perceived to be blind, closing with a little bang that made us look at each other — for, like all bangs, it was something louder than we had intended — the doors we had indiscreetly opened. All roads lead to Rome, and there were times when it might have struck us that almost every branch of study or subject of conversation skirted forbidden ground. Forbidden ground was the question of the return of the dead in general and of whatever, in especial, might survive, for memory, of the friends little children had lost. There were days when I could have sworn that one of them had, with a small invisible nudge, said to the other, "She thinks she'll do it this time — but she *won't!*" To "do it" would have been to indulge for instance — and for once in a way — in some direct reference to the lady who had prepared them for my discipline. They had a delightful endless appetite for passages in my own history to which I had again and again treated them; they were in possession of everything that had ever happened to me, had had, with every circumstance, the story of my smallest adventures and of those of my brothers and sisters and of the cat and the dog at home, as well as many particulars of the whimsical bent of my father, of the furniture and arrangement of our house and of the conversation of the old women of our village. There were things enough, taking one with another, to chatter about, if one went very fast and knew by instinct when to go round. They pulled with an art of their own the strings of my invention and my memory; and nothing else perhaps, when I thought of such occasions afterwards, gave me so the suspicion of being watched from under cover. It was in any case over *my* life, *my* past and *my* friends alone that we could take anything like our ease; a state of affairs that led them sometimes without the least pertinence to break out into sociable reminders. I was invited — with no visible connexion — to repeat afresh Goody Gosling's celebrated *mot* or to confirm the details already supplied as to the cleverness of the vicarage pony.

It was partly at such junctures as these and partly at quite different ones that, with the turn my matters had now taken, my predicament, as I have called it, grew most sensible. The fact that the days passed for me without another encounter ought, it would have appeared, to have done something toward soothing my nerves. Since the light brush, that second night on the upper landing, of the presence of a woman at the foot of the stair, I had seen nothing, whether in or out of the house, that one had better not have seen. There was many a corner round which I expected to come upon Quint, and many a situation that, in a merely sinister way, would have favoured the appearance of Miss Jessel. The summer had turned, the summer had gone; the autumn had dropped upon Bly and had blown out half our lights. The place, with its grey sky and withered garlands, its bared spaces and scattered dead leaves, was like a theatre after the performance — all strewn with crumpled playbills. There were exactly states of the air, conditions of sound and of stillness, unspeakable impressions of the *kind* of ministering moment, that brought back to me, long enough to catch it, the feeling of the medium in which, that June evening out of doors, I had had my first sight of Quint, and in which too, at those other instants, I had, after seeing him through the window, looked for him in vain in the circle of shrubbery. I recognised the signs, the portents — I recognised the moment, the spot. But they remained unaccompanied and empty, and I continued unmolested; if unmolested one could call a young woman whose sensibility had, in the most extraordinary fashion, not declined but deepened. I had said in my talk with Mrs. Grose on that horrid scene of Flora's by the lake — and had perplexed her by so saying — that it would from that moment distress me much more to lose my power than to keep it. I had then expressed what was vividly in my mind: the truth that, whether the children really saw or not — since, that is, it was not yet definitely proved — I greatly preferred, as a safeguard, the fulness of my own exposure. I was ready to know the very worst that was to be known. What I had then had an ugly glimpse of was that my eyes might be sealed just while theirs were most opened. Well, my eyes *were* sealed, it appeared, at present — a consummation for which it seemed blasphemous not to thank God. There was, alas, a difficulty about that: I would have thanked him with all my soul had I not had in a proportionate measure this conviction of the secret of my pupils.

How can I retrace to-day the strange steps of my obsession? There were times of our being together when I would have been ready to swear that, literally, in my presence, but with my direct sense of it closed, they had visitors who were known and were welcome. Then it was that, had I not been deterred by the very chance that such an injury might prove greater than the injury to be averted, my exaltation would have broken out. "They're here, they're here, you little wretches," I would have cried, "and you can't deny it now!" The little wretches denied it with all the added volume of their sociability and their tenderness, just in the crystal depths of which — like the flash of a fish in a stream — the mockery of their advantage peeped up. The shock had in truth sunk into me still deeper than I knew on the night when, looking out either for Quint or for Miss Jessel under the stars, I had seen there the boy over whose rest I watched and who had immediately brought in with him — had straight-way there turned on me — the lovely upward look with which, from the battlements above us, the hideous apparition of Quint had played. If it was a question of a scare my discovery on this occasion had scared me more than any other, and it was essentially in the scared state that I drew my actual conclusions. They harassed me so that sometimes, at odd moments, I shut myself up audibly to rehearse — it was at once a fantastic relief and a renewed despair — the manner in which I might come to the point. I approached it from one side and the other while, in my room, I flung myself about, but I always broke down in the monstrous utterance of names. As they died away on my lips I said to myself that I should indeed help them to represent something infamous if by pronouncing them I should violate as rare a little case of instinctive delicacy as any schoolroom probably had ever known. When I said to myself: "*They* have the manner to be silent, and you, trusted as you are, the baseness to speak!" I felt myself crimson and covered my face with my hands. After these secret scenes I chattered more than ever, going on volubly enough till one of our prodigious palpable hushes occurred — I can tell them nothing else — the strange dizzy lift or swim (I try for terms!) into a stillness, a pause of all life, that had nothing to do with the more or less noise we at the moment might be engaged in making and that I could hear through any intensified mirth or quickened recitation or louder strum of the piano. Then it was that the others, the outsiders, were there. Though they were not angels they "passed," as the French say, causing me, while they stayed, to tremble with the fear of their addressing to their younger victims some yet more infernal message or more vivid image than they had thought good enough for myself.

What it was least possible to get rid of was the cruel idea that, whatever I had seen, Miles and Flora saw *more* — things terrible and unguessable and that sprang from the dreadful passages to intercourse in the past. Such things naturally left on the surface, for the time, a chill that we vociferously denied we felt; and we had all three, with repetition, got into such splendid training that we went, each time, to mark the close of the incident, almost automatically through the very same movements. It was striking of the children at all events to kiss me inveterately with a wild irrelevance and never to fail — one or the other — of the precious question that had helped us through many a peril. "When do you think he *will* come? Don't you think we *ought* to write?" — there was nothing like that enquiry, we found by experience, for carrying off an awkwardness. "He" of course was their uncle in Harley Street; and we lived in much profusion of theory that he might at any moment arrive to mingle in our circle. It was impossible to have given less encouragement than he had admin-istered to such a doctrine, but if we had not had the doctrine to fall back upon we should have deprived each other of some of our finest exhibitions. He never wrote to them — that may have been selfish, but it was a part of the flattery of his trust of myself; for the way in which a man pays his highest tribute to a woman is apt to be but by the more festal celebration of one of the sacred laws of his comfort. So I held that I carried out the spirit of the pledge given not to appeal to him when I let our young friends understand that their own letters were but charming literary exercises. They were too beautiful to be posted; I kept them myself; I have them all to this hour. This was a rule indeed which only added to the satiric effect of my being plied with the supposition that he might at any moment be among us. It was exactly as if our young friends knew how almost more awkward than anything else that might be for me. There appears to me moreover as I look back no note in all this more extraordinary than the mere fact that, in spite of my tension and of their triumph, I never lost patience with them. Adorable they must in truth have been, I now feel, since I did n't in these days hate them! Would exasperation, however, if relief had longer been postponed, finally have betrayed me? It little matters, for relief arrived. I call it relief though it was only the relief that a snap brings to a strain or the burst of a thunderstorm to a day of suffocation. It was at least change, and it came with a rush.

14

Walking to church a certain Sunday morning, I had little Miles at my side and his sister, in advance of us and at Mrs. Grose's, well in sight. It was a crisp clear day, the first of its order for some time; the night had brought a touch of frost and the autumn air, bright and sharp, made the church-bells almost gay. It was an odd accident of thought that I should have happened at such a moment to be particularly and very gratefully struck with the obedience of my little charges. Why did they never resent my inexorable, my perpetual society? Something or other had brought nearer home to me that I had all but pinned the boy to my shawl, and that in the way our companions were marshalled before me I might have appeared to provide against some danger of rebellion. I was like a gaoler with an eye to possible surprises and escapes. But all this belonged — I mean their magnificent little surrender — just to the special array of the facts that were most abysmal. Turned out for Sunday by his uncle's tailor, who had had a free hand and a notion of pretty waistcoats and of his grand little air, Miles's whole title to independence, the rights of his sex and situation, were so stamped upon him that if he had suddenly struck for freedom I should have had nothing to say. I was by the strangest of chances wondering how I should meet him when the revolution unmistakeably occurred. I call it a revolution because I now see how, with the word he spoke, the curtain rose on the last act of my dreadful drama and the catastrophe was precipitated. "Look here, my dear, you know," he charmingly said, "when in the world, please, am I going back to school?"

Transcribed here the speech sounds harmless enough, particularly as uttered in the sweet, high, casual pipe with which, at all interlocutors, but above all at his eternal governess, he threw off intonations as if he were tossing roses. There was something in them that always made one "catch," and I caught at any rate now so effectually that I stopped short as if one of the trees of the park had fallen across the road. There was something new, on the spot, between us, and he was perfectly aware I recognised it, though to enable me to do so he had no need to look a whit less candid and charming than usual. I could feel in him how he already, from my at first finding nothing to reply, perceived the advantage he had gained. I was so slow to find anything that he had plenty of time, after a minute, to continue with his suggestive but inconclusive smile: "You know, my dear, that for a fellow to be with a lady *always* — !" His "my dear" was constantly on his lips for me, and nothing could have expressed more the exact shade of the sentiment with which I desired to inspire my pupils than its fond familiarity. It was so respectfully easy.

But oh how I felt that at present I must pick my own phrases! I remember that, to gain time, I tried to laugh, and I seemed to see in the beautiful face with which he watched me how ugly and queer I looked. "And always with the same lady?" I returned.

He neither blenched nor winked. The whole thing was virtually out between us. "Ah of course she's a jolly 'perfect' lady; but after all I'm a fellow, don't you see? who's — well, getting on."

I lingered there with him an instant ever so kindly. "Yes, you're getting on." Oh but I felt helpless!

I have kept to this day the heartbreaking little idea of how he seemed to know that and to play with it. "And you can't say I've not been awfully good, can you?"

I laid my hand on his shoulder, for though I felt how much better it would have been to walk on I was not yet quite able. "No, I can't say that, Miles."

"Except just that one night, you know — !"

"That one night?" I could n't look as straight as he.

"Why when I went down — went out of the house."

"Oh yes. But I forget what you did it for."

"You forget?" — he spoke with the sweet extravagance of childish reproach. "Why it was just to show you I could!"

"Oh yes — you could."

"And I can again."

I felt I might perhaps after all succeed in keeping my wits about me. "Certainly. But you won't."

"No, not *that* again. It was nothing."

"It was nothing," I said. "But we must go on."

He resumed our walk with me, passing his hand into my arm. "Then when *am* I going back?"

I wore, in turning it over, my most responsible air. "Were you very happy at school?"

He just considered. "Oh I'm happy enough anywhere!"

"Well then," I quavered, "if you're just as happy here — !"

"Ah but that isn't everything! Of course *you* know a lot   "

"But you hint you know almost as much?" I risked as he paused.

"Not half I want to!" Miles honestly professed. "But it isn't so much that."

"What is it then?"

"Well — I want to see more life."

"I see; I see." We had arrived within sight of the church and of various persons, including several of the household of Bly, on their way to it and clustered about the door to see us go in. I quickened our step; I wanted to get there before the question between us opened up much further; I reflected hungrily that he would have for more than an hour to be silent; and I thought with envy of the comparative dusk of the pew and of the almost spiritual help of the hassock on which I might bend my knees. I seemed literally to be running a race with some confusion to which he was about to reduce me, but I felt he had got in first when, before we had even entered the churchyard, he threw out —

"I want my own sort!"

It literally made me bound forward. "There are n't many of your own sort, Miles!" I laughed. "Unless perhaps dear little Flora!"

"You really compare me to a baby girl?"

This found me singularly weak. "Don't you then *love* our sweet Flora?"

"If I did n't — and you too; if I did n't — !" he repeated as if retreating for a jump, yet leaving his thought so unfinished that, after we had come into the gate, another stop, which he imposed on me by the pressure of his arm, had become inevitable. Mrs. Grose and Flora had passed into the church, the other worshipers had followed and we were, for the minute, alone among the old thick graves. We had paused, on the path from the gate, by a low oblong table-like tomb.

"Yes, if you did n't — ?"

He looked, while I waited, about at the graves. "Well, you know what!" But he did n't move, and he presently produced something that made me drop straight down on the stone slab as if suddenly to rest. "Does my uncle think what *you* think?"

I markedly rested. "How do you know what I think?"

"Ah well, of course I don't; for it strikes me you never tell me. But I mean does *he* know?"

"Know what, Miles?"

"Why the way I'm going on."

I recognised quickly enough that I could make, to this enquiry, no answer that would n't involve something of a sacrifice of my employer. Yet it struck me that we were all, at Bly, sufficiently sacrificed to make that venial. "I don't think your uncle much cares."

Miles, on this, stood looking at me. "Then don't you think he can be made to?"

"In what way?"

"Why by his coming down."

"But who'll get him to come down?"

"*I* will!" the boy said with extraordinary brightness and emphasis. He gave me another look charged with that expression and then marched off alone into church.

15

The business was practically settled from the moment I never followed him. It was a pitiful surrender to agitation, but my being aware of this had somehow no power to restore me. I only sat there on my tomb and read into what our young friend had said to me the fulness of its meaning; by the time I had grasped the whole of which I had also embraced, for absence, the pretext that I was ashamed to offer my pupils and the rest of the congregation such an example of delay. What I said to myself above all was that Miles had got something out of me and that the gage of it for him would be just this awkward collapse. He had got out of me that there was something I was much afraid of, and that he should probably be able to make use of my fear to gain, for his own purpose, more freedom. My fear was of having to deal with the intolerable question of the grounds of his dismissal from school, since that was really but the question of the horrors gathered behind. That his uncle should arrive to treat with me of these things was a solution that, strictly speaking, I ought now to have desired to bring on; but I could so little face the ugliness and the pain of it that I simply procrastinated and lived from hand to mouth. The boy, to my deep discomposure, was immensely in the right, was in a position to say to me: "Either you clear up with my guardian the mystery of this interruption of my studies, or you cease to expect me to lead with you a life that's so unnatural for a boy." What was so unnatural for the particular boy I was concerned with was this sudden revelation of a consciousness and a plan.

That was what really overcame me, what prevented my going in. I walked round the church, hesitating, hovering; I reflected that I had already, with him, hurt myself beyond repair. Therefore I could patch up nothing and it was too extreme an effort to squeeze beside him into the pew: he would be so much more sure than ever to pass his arm into mine and make me sit there for an hour in close mute contact with his commentary on our talk. For the first minute since his arrival I wanted to get away from him. As I paused beneath the high east window and listened to the sounds of worship I was taken with an impulse that might master me, I felt, and completely, should I give it the least encouragement. I might easily put an end to my ordeal by getting away altogether. Here was my chance; there was no one to stop me; I could give the whole thing up — turn my back and bolt. It was only a question of hurrying again, for a few preparations, to the house which the attendance at church of so many of the servants would practically have left unoccupied. No one, in short, could blame me if I should just drive desperately off. What was it to get away if I should get away only till dinner? That would be in a couple of hours, at the end of which — I had the acute prevision — my little pupils would play at innocent wonder about my non-appearance in their train.

"What *did* you do, you naughty bad thing? Why in the world, to worry us so — and take our thoughts off too, don't you know? — did you desert us at the very door?" I couldn't meet such questions nor, as they asked them, their false little lovely eyes; yet it was all so exactly what I should have to meet that, as the prospect grew sharp to me, I at last let myself go.

I got, so far as the immediate moment was concerned, away; I came straight out of the churchyard and, thinking hard, retraced my steps through the park. It seemed to me that by the time I reached the house I had made up my mind to cynical flight. The Sunday stillness both of the approaches and of the interior, in which I met no one, fairly stirred me with a sense of opportunity. Were I to get off quickly this way I should get off without a scene, without a word. My quickness would have to be remarkable, however, and the question of a conveyance was the great one to settle. Tormented, in the hall, with difficulties and obstacles, I remember sinking down at the foot of the staircase — suddenly collapsing there on the lowest step and then, with a revulsion, recalling that it was exactly where, more than a month before, in the darkness of night and just so bowed with evil things, I had seen the spectre of the most horrible of women. At this I was able to straighten myself; I went the rest of the way up; I made, in my turmoil, for the schoolroom, where there were objects belonging to me that I should have to take. But I opened the door to find again, in a flash, my eyes unsealed. In the presence of what I saw I reeled straight back upon resistance.

Seated at my own table in the clear noonday light I saw a person whom, without my previous experience, I should have taken at the first blush for some housemaid who might have stayed at home to look after the place and who, availing herself of rare relief from observation and of the schoolroom table and my pens, ink and paper, had applied herself to the considerable effort of a letter to her sweetheart. There was an effort in the way that, while her arms rested on the table, her hands, with evident weariness, supported her head; but at the moment I took this in I had already become aware that, in spite of my entrance, her attitude strangely persisted. Then it was — with the very act of its announcing itself — that her identity flared up in a change of posture. She rose, not as if she had heard me, but with an indescribable grand melancholy of indifference and detachment, and, within a dozen feet of me, stood there as my vile predecessor. Dishonoured and tragic, she was all before me; but even as I fixed and, for memory, secured it, the awful image passed away. Dark as midnight in her black dress, her haggard beauty and her unutterable woe, she had looked at me long enough to appear to say that her right to sit at my table was as good as mine to sit at hers. While these instants lasted indeed I had the extraordinary chill of a feeling that it was I who was the intruder. It was as a wild protest against it that, actually addressing her — "You terrible miserable woman!" — I heard myself break into a sound that, by the open door, rang through the long passage and the empty house. She looked at me as if she heard me, but I had recovered myself and cleared the air. There was nothing in the room the next minute but the sunshine and the sense that I must stay.

16

I had so perfectly expected the return of the others to be marked by a demonstration that I was freshly upset at having to find them merely dumb and discreet about my desertion. Instead of gaily denouncing and caressing me they made no allusion to my having failed them, and I was left, for the time, on perceiving that she too said nothing, to study Mrs. Grose's odd face. I did this to such purpose that I made sure they had in some way bribed her to silence; a silence that, however, I would engage to break down on the first private opportunity. This opportunity came before tea: I secured five minutes with her in the housekeeper's room, where, in the twilight, amid a smell of lately-baked bread, but with the place all swept and garnished, I found her sitting in pained placidity before the fire. So I see her still, so I see her best: facing the flame from her straight chair in the dusky shining room, a large clean picture of the "put away" — of drawers closed and locked and rest without a remedy.

"Oh yes, they asked me to say nothing; and to please them — so long as they were there — of course I promised. But what had happened to you?"

"I only went with you for the walk," I said. "I had then to come back to meet a friend."

She showed her surprise. "A friend — *you?*"

"Oh yes, I've a couple!" I laughed. "But did the children give you a reason?"

"For not alluding to your leaving us? Yes; they said you'd like it better. *Do* you like it better?"

My face had made her rueful. "No, I like it worse!" But after an instant I added: "Did they say why I should like it better?"

"No; Master Miles only said 'We must do nothing but what she likes!' "

"I wish indeed he would! And what did Flora say?"

"Miss Flora was too sweet. She said. 'Oh of course, of course!' — and I said the same."

I thought a moment. "You were too sweet too — I can hear you all. But none the less, between Miles and me, it's now all out."

"All out?" My companion stared. "But what, Miss?"

"Everything. It doesn't matter. I've made up my mind. I came home, my dear," I went on, "for a talk with Miss Jessel."

I had by this time formed the habit of having Mrs. Grose literally well in hand in advance of my sounding that note; so that even now, as she bravely blinked under the signal of my word, I could keep her comparatively firm. "A talk! Do you mean she spoke?"

"It came to that. I found her, on my return, in the schoolroom."

"And what did she say?" I can hear the good woman still, and the candour of her stupefaction.

"That she suffers the torments — !"

It was this, of a truth, that made her, as she filled out my picture, gape. "Do you mean," she faltered " — of the lost?"

"Of the lost. Of the damned. And that's why, to share them — " I faltered myself with the horror of it.

But my companion, with less imagination, kept me up. "To share them — ?"

"She wants Flora." Mrs. Grose might, as I gave it to her, fairly have fallen away from me had I not been prepared. I still held her there, to show I was. "As I've told you, however, it does n't matter."

"Because you've made up your mind? But to what?"

"To everything."

"And what do you call 'everything'?"

"Why to sending for their uncle."

"Oh Miss, in pity do," my friend broke out.

"Ah but I will, I *will!* I see it's the only way. What's 'out,' as I told you, with Miles is that if he thinks I'm afraid to — and has ideas of what he gains by that — he shall see he's mistaken. Yes, yes; his uncle shall have it here from me on the spot (and before the boy himself if necessary) that if I'm to be reproached with having done nothing again about more school — "

"Yes, Miss — " my companion pressed me.

"Well, there's that awful reason."

There were now clearly so many of these for my poor colleague that she was excusable for being vague. "But — a — which?"

"Why the letter from his old place."

"You'll show it to the master?"

"I ought to have done so on the instant."

"Oh no!" said Mrs. Grose with decision.

"I'll put it before him," I went on inexorably, "that I can't undertake to work the question on behalf of a child who has been expelled — "

"For we've never in the least known what!" Mrs. Grose declared.

"For wickedness. For what else — when he's so clever and beautiful and perfect? Is he stupid? Is he untidy? Is he infirm? Is he ill-natured? He's exquisite — so it can be only *that;* and that would open up the whole thing. After all," I said, "it's their uncle's fault. If he left here such people — !"

"He did n't really in the least know them. The fault's mine." She had turned quite pale.

"Well, you shan't suffer," I answered.

"The children shan't!" she emphatically returned.

I was silent a while; we looked at each other. "Then what am I to tell him?"

"You need n't tell him anything. *I'll* tell him."

I measured this. "Do you mean you'll write — ?" Remembering she couldn't, I caught myself up. "How do you communicate?"

"I tell the bailiff. *He* writes."

"And should you like him to write our story?"

My question had a sarcastic force that I had not fully intended, and it made her after a moment inconsequently break down. The tears were again in her eyes. "Ah Miss, *you* write!"

"Well — to-night," I at last returned; and on this we separated.

17

I went so far, in the evening, as to make a beginning. The weather had changed back, a great wind was abroad, and beneath the lamp, in my room, with Flora at peace beside me, I sat for a long time before a blank sheet of paper and listened to the lash of the rain and the batter of the gusts. Finally I went out, taking a candle; I crossed the passage and listened a minute at Miles's door. What, under my endless obsession, I had been impelled to listen for was some betrayal of his not being at rest, and I presently caught one, but not in the form I had expected. His voice tinkled out. "I say, you there — come in." It was gaiety in the gloom!

I went in with my light and found him in bed, very wide awake but very much at his ease. "Well, what are *you* up to?" he asked with a grace of sociability in which it occurred to me that Mrs. Grose, had she been present, might have looked in vain for proof that anything was "out."

I stood over him with my candle. "How did you know I was there?"

"Why of course I heard you. Did you fancy you made no noise? You're like a troop of cavalry!" he beautifully laughed.

"Then you were n't asleep?"

"Not much! I lie awake and think."

I had put my candle, designedly, a short way off, and then, as he held out his friendly old hand to me, had sat down on the edge of his bed. "What is it," I asked, "that you think of?"

"What in the world, my dear, but *you?*"

"Ah the pride I take in your appreciation does n't insist on that! I had so far rather you slept."

"Well, I think also, you know, of this queer business of ours."

I marked the coolness of his firm little hand. "Of what queer business, Miles?"

"Why the way you bring me up. And all the rest!"

I fairly held my breath a minute, and even from my glimmering taper there was light enough to show how he smiled up at me from his pillow. "What do you mean by all the rest?"

"Oh you know, you know!"

I could say nothing for a minute, though I felt as I held his hand and our eyes continued to meet that my silence had all the air of admitting his charge and that nothing in the whole world of reality was perhaps at that moment so fabulous as our actual relation. "Certainly you shall go back to school," I said, "if it be that that troubles you. But not to the old place — we must find another, a better. How could

I know it did trouble you, this question, when you never told me so, never spoke of it at all?" His clear listening face, framed in its smooth whiteness, made him for the minute as appealing as some wistful patient in a children's hospital; and I would have given, as the resemblance came to me, all I possessed on earth really to be the nurse or the sister of charity who might have helped to cure him. Well, even as it was I perhaps might help! "Do you know you've never said a word to me about your school — I mean the old one; never mentioned it in any way?"

He seemed to wonder; he smiled with the same loveliness. But he clearly gained time; he waited, he called for guidance. "Have n't I?" It was n't for *me* to help him — it was for the thing I had met!

Something in his tone and the expression of his face, as I got this from him, set my heart aching with such a pang as it had never yet known; so unutterably touching was it to see his little brain puzzled and his little resources taxed to play, under the spell laid on him, a part of innocence and consistency. "No, never — from the hour you came back. You've never mentioned to me one of your masters, one of your comrades, nor the least little thing that ever happened to you at school. Never, little Miles — no never — have you given me an inkling of anything that *may* have happened there. Therefore you can fancy how much I'm in the dark. Until you came out, that way, this morning, you had since the first hour I saw you scarce even made a reference to anything in your previous life. You seemed so perfectly to accept the present." It was extraordinary how my absolute conviction of his secret precocity — or whatever I might call the poison of an influence that I dared but half-phrase — made him, in spite of the faint breath of his inward trouble, appear as accessible as an older person, forced me to treat him as an intelligent equal. "I thought you wanted to go on as you are."

It struck me that at this he just faintly coloured. He gave, at any rate, like a convalescent slightly fatigued, a languid shake of his head. "I don't — I don't. I want to get away."

"You're tired of Bly?"

"Oh no, I like Bly."

"Well then — ?"

"Oh *you* know what a boy wants!"

I felt I did n't know so well as Miles, and I took temporary refuge. "You want to go to your uncle?"

Again, at this, with his sweet ironic face, he made a movement on the pillow. "Ah you can't get off with that!"

I was silent a little, and it was I now, I think, who changed colour. "My dear, I don't want to get off!"

"You can't even if you do. You can't, you can't!" — he lay beautifully staring. "My uncle must come down and you must completely settle things."

"If we do," I returned with some spirit, "you may be sure it will be to take you quite away."

"Well, don't you understand that that's exactly what I'm working for? You'll have to *tell* him — about the way you've let it all drop: you'll have to tell him a tremendous lot!"

The exultation with which he uttered this helped me somehow for the instant to meet him rather more. "And how much will *you*, Miles, have to tell him? There are things he'll ask you!"

He turned it over. "Very likely. But what things?"

"The things you've never told me. To make up his mind what to do with you. He can't send you back — "

"I don't want to go back!" he broke in. "I want a new field."

He said it with admirable serenity, with positive unimpeachable gaiety; and doubtless it was that very note that most evoked for me the poignancy, the unnatural childish tragedy, of his probable reappearance at the end of three months with all this bravado and still more dishonour. It overwhelmed me now that I should never be able to bear that, and it made me let myself go. I threw myself upon him and in the tenderness of my pity I embraced him. "Dear little Miles, dear little Miles — !"

My face was close to his, and he let me kiss him, simply taking it with indulgent good humour. "Well, old lady?"

"Is there nothing — nothing at all that you want to tell me?"

He turned off a little, facing round toward the wall and holding up his hand to look at as one had seen sick children look. "I've told you — I told you this morning."

Oh I was sorry for him! "That you just want me not to worry you?"

He looked round at me now as if in recognition of my understanding him; then ever so gently, "To let me alone," he replied.

There was even a strange little dignity in it, something that made me release him, yet, when I had slowly risen, linger beside him. God knows *I* never wished to harass him, but I felt that merely, at this, to turn my back on him was to abandon or, to put it more truly, lose him. "I've just begun a letter to your uncle," I said.

"Well then, finish it!"

I waited a minute. "What happened before?"

He gazed up at me again. "Before what?"

"Before you came back. And before you went away."

For some time he was silent, but he continued to meet my eyes. "What happened?"

It made me, the sound of the words, in which it seemed to me I caught for the very first time a small faint quaver of consenting consciousness — it made me drop on my knees beside the bed and seize once more the chance of possessing him. "Dear little Miles, dear little Miles, if you *knew* how I want to help you! It's only that, it's nothing but that, and I'd rather die than give you a pain or do you a wrong — I'd rather die than hurt a hair of you. Dear little Miles" — oh I brought it out now even if I *should* go too far — "I just want you to help me to save you!" But I knew in a moment after this that I had gone too far. The answer to my appeal was instantaneous, but it came in the form of an extraordinary blast and chill, a gust of frozen air and a shake of the room as great as if, in the wild wind, the casement had crashed in. The boy gave a loud high shriek which, lost in the rest of the shock of sound, might have seemed, indistinctly, though I was so close to him, a note either of jubilation or of terror. I jumped to my feet again and was conscious of darkness. So for a moment we remained, while I stared about me and saw the drawn curtains unstirred and the window still tight. "Why the candle's out!" I then cried.

"It was I who blew it, dear!" said Miles.

18

The next day, after lessons, Mrs. Grose found a moment to say to me quietly: "Have you written, Miss?"

"Yes — I've written." But I did n't add — for the hour — that my letter, sealed and directed, was still in my pocket. There would be time enough to send it before the messenger should go to the village. Meanwhile there had been on the part of my pupils no more brilliant, more exemplary morning. It was exactly as if they had both had at heart to gloss over any recent little friction. They performed the dizziest feats of arithmetic, soaring quite out of *my* feeble range, and perpetrated, in higher spirits than ever, geographical and historical jokes. It was conspicuous of course in Miles in particular that he appeared to wish to show how easily he could let me down. This child, to my memory, really lived in a setting of beauty and misery that no words can translate; there was a distinction all his own in every impulse he revealed; never was a small natural creature, to the uninformed eye all frankness and freedom, a more ingenious, a more extraordinary little gentleman. I had perpetually to guard against the wonder of contemplation into which my initiated view betrayed me; to check the irrelevant gaze and discouraged sigh in which I constantly both attacked and re-nounced the enigma of what such a little gentleman could have done that deserved a penalty. Say that, by the dark prodigy I knew, the imagination of all evil *had* been opened up to him: all the justice within me ached for the proof that it could ever have flowered into an act.

He had never at any rate been such a little gentleman as when, after our early dinner on this dreadful day, he came round to me and asked if I should n't like him for half an hour to play to me. David playing to Saul could never have shown a finer sense of the occasion. It was literally a charming exhibition of tact, of magnanimity, and quite tantamount to his saying outright: "The true knights we love to read about never push an advantage too far. I know what you mean now: you mean that — to be let alone yourself and not followed up — you'll cease to worry and spy upon me, won't keep me so close to you, will let me go and come. Well, I 'come,' you see — but I don't go! There'll be plenty of time for that. I do really delight in your society and I only want to show you that I contended for a principle." It may be imagined whether I resisted this appeal or failed to accompany him again, hand in hand, to the schoolroom. He sat down at the old piano and played as he had never played; and if there are those who think he had better have been kicking a football I can only say that I wholly agree with them. For at the end of a time that under his influence I had quite ceased to measure I started up with a strange sense of having literally slept at my post. It was after luncheon, and by the schoolroom fire, and yet I had n't really in the least slept; I had only done something much worse — I had forgotten. Where all this time was Flora? When I put the question to Miles he played on a minute before answering, and then could only say: "Why, my dear, how do *I* know?" — breaking moreover into a happy laugh which immediately after, as if it were a vocal accompaniment, he prolonged into incoherent extravagant song.

I went straight to my room, but his sister was not there; then, before going downstairs, I looked into several others. As she was nowhere about she would surely be with Mrs. Grose, whom in the comfort of that theory I accordingly proceeded in quest of. I found her where I had found her the evening before, but she met my quick challenge with blank scared ignorance. She had only supposed that, after the repast, I had carried off both the children; as to which she was quite in her right, for it was the very first time I had allowed the little girl out of my sight without some special provision. Of course now indeed she might be with the maids, so that the immediate thing was to look for her without an air of alarm. This we promptly arranged between us; but when, ten minutes later and in pursuance of our arrange-ment, we met in the hall, it was only to report on either side that after guard enquiries we had altogether failed to trace her. For a minute there, apart from observation, we exchanged mute alarms, and I could feel with what high interest my friend returned me all those I had from the first given her.

"She'll be above," she presently said — "in one of the rooms you have n't searched."

"No, she's at a distance." I had made up my mind. "She has gone out."

Mrs. Grose stared. "Without a hat?"

I naturally also looked volumes. "Is n't that woman always without one?"

"She's with *her?*"

"She's with *her!*" I declared. "We must find them."

My hand was on my friend's arm, but she failed for the moment, confronted with such an account of the matter, to respond to my pressure. She communed, on the contrary, where she stood, with her uneasiness. "And where's Master Miles?"

"Oh, *he's* with Quint. They'll be in the schoolroom."

"Lord, Miss!" My view, I was myself aware — and therefore I suppose my tone — had never yet reached so calm an assurance.

"The trick's played," I went on; "they've successfully worked their plan. He found the most divine little way to keep me quiet while she went off."

" 'Divine'?" Mrs. Grose bewilderedly echoed.

"Infernal then!" I almost cheerfully rejoined. "He has provided for himself as well. But come!"

She had helplessly gloomed at the upper regions. "You leave him — ?"

"So long with Quint? Yes — I don't mind that now."

She always ended at these moments by getting possession of my hand, and in this manner she could at present still stay me. But after gasping an instant at my sudden resignation, "Because of your letter?" she eagerly brought out.

I quickly, by way of answer, felt for my letter, drew it forth, held it up, and then, freeing myself, went and laid it on the great hall-table. "Luke will take it," I said as I came back. I reached the house-door and opened it; I was already on the steps.

My companion still demurred: the storm of the night and the early morning had dropped, but the afternoon was damp and grey. I came down to the drive while she stood in the doorway. "You go with nothing on?"

"What do I care when the child has nothing? I can't wait to dress," I cried, "and if you must do so I leave you. Try meanwhile yourself upstairs."

"With *them?*" Oh on this the poor woman promptly joined me!

19

We went straight to the lake, as it was called at Bly, and I dare say rightly called, though it may have been a sheet of water less remarkable than my untravelled eyes supposed it. My acquaintance with sheets of water was small, and the pool of Bly, at all events on the few occasions of my consenting, under the protection of my pupils, to affront its surface in the old flat-bottomed boat moored there for our use, had impressed me both with its extent and its agitation. The usual place of embarkation was half a mile from the house, but I had an intimate conviction that, wherever Flora might be, she was not near home. She had not given me the slip for any small adventure, and, since the day of the very great one that I had shared with her by the pond, I had been aware, in our walks, of the quarter to which she most inclined. This was why I had now given to Mrs. Grose's steps so marked a direction — a direction making her, when she perceived it, oppose a resistance that showed me she was freshly mystified. "You're going to the water, Miss? — you think she's *in* — ?"

"She may be, though the depth is, I believe, nowhere very great But what I judge most likely is that she's on the spot from which, the other day, we saw together what I told you."

"When she pretended not to see — ?"

"With that astounding self-possession! I've always been sure she wanted to go back alone. And now her brother has managed it for her."

Mrs. Grose still stood where she had stopped. "You suppose they really *talk* of them?"

I could meet this with an assurance! "They say things that, if we heard them, would simply appal us."

"And if she *is* there — ?"

"Yes?"

"Then Miss Jessel is?"

"Beyond a doubt. You shall see."

"Oh thank you!" my friend cried, planted so firm that, taking it in, I went straight on without her. By the time I reached the pool, however, she was close behind me, and I knew that, whatever, to her apprehension, might befall me, the exposure of sticking to me struck her as her least danger. She exhaled a moan of relief as we at last came in sight of the greater part of the water without a sight of the child. There was no trace of Flora on that nearer side of the bank where my observation of her had been most startling, and none on the opposite edge, where, save for a margin of some twenty yards, a thick copse came down to the pond. This expanse, oblong in shape, was so narrow compared to its length that, with its ends out of view, it might have been taken for a scant river. We looked at the empty stretch, and then I felt the suggestion in my friend's eyes. I knew what she meant and I replied with a negative headshake.

"No, no; wait! She has taken the boat."

My companion stared at the vacant mooring-place and then across the lake. "Then where is it?"

"Our not seeing it is the strongest of proofs. She has used it to go over, and then has managed to hide it."

"All alone — that child?"

"She's not alone, and at such times she's not a child; she's an old, old woman." I scanned all the visible shore while Mrs. Grose took again, into the queer element I offered her, one of her plunges of submission; then I pointed out that the boat might perfectly be in a small refuge formed by one of the recesses of the pool, an indentation masked, for the hither side, by a projection of the bank and by a clump of trees growing close to the water.

"But if the boat's there, where on earth's *she?*" my colleague anxiously asked.

"That's exactly what we must learn." And I started to walk further.

"By going all the way round?"

"Certainly, far as it is. It will take us but ten minutes, yet it's far enough to have made the child prefer not to walk. She went straight over."

"Laws!" cried my friend again: the chain of my logic was ever too strong for her. I dragged her at my heels even now, and when we had got halfway round — a devious tiresome process, on ground much broken and by path choked with overgrowth —

I paused to give her breath. I sustained her with a grateful arm, assuring her that she might hugely help me; and this started us afresh, so that in the course of but few minutes more we reached a point from which we found the boat to be where I had supposed it. It had been intentionally left as much as possible out of sight and was tied to one of the stakes of a fence that came, just there, down to the brink and that had been an assistance to disembarking. I recognised, as I looked at the pair of short thick oars, quite safely drawn up, the prodigious character of the feat for a little girl; but I had by this time lived too long among wonders and had panted to too many livelier measures. There was a gate in the fence, through which we passed, and that brought us after a trifling interval more into the open. Then "There she is!" we both exclaimed at once.

Flora, a short way off, stood before us on the grass and smiled as if her performance had now become complete. The next thing she did, however, was to stoop straight down and pluck — quite as if it were all she was there for — a big ugly spray of withered fern. I at once felt sure she had just come out of the copse. She waited for us, not herself taking a step, and I was conscious of the rare solemnity with which we presently approached her. She smiled and smiled, and we met; but it was all done in a silence by this time flagrantly ominous. Mrs. Grose was the first to break the spell: she threw herself on her knees and, drawing the child to her breast, clasped in a long embrace the little tender yielding body. While this dumb convulsion lasted I could only watch it — which I did the more intently when I saw Flora's face peep at me over our companion's shoulder. It was serious now — the flicker had left it; but it strengthened the pang with which I at that moment envied Mrs. Grose the simplicity of *her* relation. Still, all this while, nothing more passed between us save that Flora had let her foolish fern again drop to the ground. What she and I had virtually said to each other was that pretexts were useless now. When Mrs. Grose finally got up she kept the child's hand, so that the two were still before me; and the singular reticence of our communion was even more marked in the frank look she addressed me. "I'll be hanged," it said, "if *I'll* speak!"

It was Flora who, gazing all over me in candid wonder, was the first. She was struck with our bareheaded aspect. "Why where are your things?"

"Where yours are, my dear!" I promptly returned.

She had already got back her gaiety and appeared to take this as an answer quite sufficient. "And where's Miles?" she went on.

There was something in the small valour of it that quite finished me: these three words from her were, in a flash like the glitter of a drawn blade, the jostle of the cup that my hand, for weeks and weeks, had held high and full to the brim and that now, even before speaking, I felt overflow in a deluge. "I'll tell you if you'll tell *me* —" I heard myself say, then heard the tremor in which it broke.

"Well, what?"

Mrs. Grose's suspense blazed at me, but it was too late now, and I brought the thing out handsomely. "Where, my pet, is Miss Jessel?"

20

Just as in the churchyard with Miles, the whole thing was upon us. Much as I had made of the fact that this name had never once, between us, been sounded, the quick smitten glare with which the child's face now received it fairly likened my breach of the silence to the smash of a pane of glass. It added to the interposing cry, as if to stay the blow, that Mrs. Grose at the same instant uttered over my violence — the shriek of a creature scared, or rather wounded, which, in turn, within a few seconds, was completed by a gasp of my own. I seized my colleague's arm. "She's there, she's there!"

Miss Jessel stood before us on the opposite bank exactly as she had stood the other time, and I remember, strangely, as the first feeling now produced in me, my thrill of joy at having brought on a proof. She was there, so I was justified; she was there, so I was neither cruel nor mad. She was there for poor scared Mrs. Grose, but she was there most for Flora; and no moment of my monstrous time was perhaps so extraordinary as that in which I consciously threw out to her — with the sense that, pale and ravenous demon as she was, she would catch and understand it — an inarticulate message of gratitude. She rose erect on the spot my friend and I had lately quitted, and there was n't in all the long reach of her desire an inch of her evil that fell short. This first vividness of vision and emotion were things of a few seconds, during which Mrs. Grose's dazed blink across to where I pointed struck me as showing that she too at last saw, just as it carried my own eyes precipitately to the child. The revelation then of the manner in which Flora was affected startled me in truth far more than it would have done to find her also merely agitated, for direct dismay was of course not what I had expected. Prepared and on her guard as our pursuit had actually made her, she would repress every betrayal; and I was therefore at once shaken by my first glimpse of the particular one for which I had not allowed. To see her, without a convulsion of her small pink face, not even feign to glance in the direction of the prodigy I announced, but only, instead of that, turn at *me* an expression of hard still gravity, an expression absolutely new and unprecedented and that appeared to read and accuse and judge me — this was a stroke that somehow converted the little girl herself into a figure portentous. I gaped at her coolness even though my certitude of her thoroughly seeing was never greater than at that instant, and then, in the immediate need to defend myself, I called her passionately to witness. "She's there, you little unhappy thing — there, there, *there,* and you know it as well as you know me!" I had said shortly before to Mrs. Grose that she was not at these times a child, but an old, old woman, and my description of her could n't have been more strikingly confirmed than in the way in which, for all notice of this, she simply showed me, without an expressional concession or admission, a countenance of deeper and deeper, of indeed suddenly quite fixed reprobation. I was by this time — if I can put the whole thing at all together — more appalled at what I may properly call her manner than at anything else, though it was quite simultaneously that I became aware of having Mrs. Grose also, and very formidably, to reckon with. My elder companion, the next moment, at any rate, blotted out everything but her own flushed face and her loud shocked protest, a burst of high disapproval. "What a dreadful turn, to be sure, Miss! Where on earth do you see anything?"

I could only grasp her more quickly yet, for even while she spoke the hideous plain presence stood undimmed and undaunted. It had already lasted a minute, and it lasted while I continued, seizing my colleague, quite thrusting her at it and presenting her to it, to insist with my pointing hand. "You don't see her exactly as *we* see? — you mean to say you don't now — *now?* She's as big as a blazing fire! Only look, dearest woman, *look* — !" She looked, just as I did, and gave me, with her deep groan of negation, repulsion, compassion — the mixture with her pity of her relief at her exemption — a sense, touching to me even then, that she would have backed me up if she had been able. I might well have needed that, for with this hard blow of the proof that her eyes were hopelessly sealed I felt my own situation horribly crumble. I felt — I *saw* — my livid predecessor press, from her position, on my defeat, and I took the measure, more than all, of what I should have from this instant to deal with in the astounding little attitude of Flora. Into this attitude Mrs. Grose immediately and violently entered, breaking, even while there pierced through my sense of ruin a prodigious private triumph, into breathless reassurance.

"She isn't there, little lady, and nobody's there — and you never see nothing, my sweet! How can poor Miss Jessel — when poor Miss Jessel's dead and buried? *We* know, don't we, love?" — and she appealed, blundering in, to the child. "It's all a mere mistake and a worry and a joke — and we'll go home as fast as we can!"

Our companion, on this, had responded with a strange quick primness of propriety, and they were again, with Mrs. Grose on her feet, united, as it were, in shocked opposition to me. Flora continued to fix me with her small mask of disaffection, and even at that minute I prayed God to forgive me for seeming to see that, as she stood there holding tight to our friend's dress, her incomparable childish beauty had suddenly failed, had quite vanished. I've said it already — she was literally, she was hideously hard; she had turned common and almost ugly. "I don't know what you mean. I see nobody. I see nothing. I never *have*. I think you're cruel. I don't like you!" Then, after this deliverance, which might have been that of a vulgarly pert little girl in the street, she hugged Mrs. Grose more closely and buried in her skirts the dreadful little face. In this position she launched an almost furious wail. "Take me away, take me away — oh take me away from *her!*"

"From *me?*" I panted.

"From you — from you!" she cried.

Even Mrs. Grose looked across at me dismayed; while I had nothing to do but communicate again with the figure that, on the opposite bank, without a movement, as rigidly still as if catching, beyond the interval, our voices, was as vividly there for my disaster as it was not there for my service. The wretched child had spoken exactly as if she had got from some outside source each of her stabbing little words, and I could therefore, in the full despair of all I had to accept, but sadly shake my head at her. "If I had ever doubted all my doubt would at present have gone. I've been living with the miserable truth, and now it was only too much closed round me. Of course I've lost you: I've interfered, and you've seen, under *her* dictation" — with which I faced, over the pool again, our infernal witness — "the easy and perfect way to meet it. I've done my best, but I've lost you. Goodbye." For Mrs. Grose I had an imperative, an almost frantic "Go, go!" before which, in infinite distress, but mutely possessed of the little girl and clearly convinced, in spite of her blindness, that something awful had occurred and some collapse engulfed us, she retreated, by the way we had come, as fast as she could move.

Of what first happened when I was left alone I had no subsequent theory. I only knew that at the end of, I suppose, a quarter of an hour, an odorous dampness and roughness, chilling and piercing my trouble, had made me understand that I must have thrown myself, on my face, to the ground and given way to a wildness of grief. I must have lain there long and cried and wailed, for when I raised my head the day was almost done. I got up and looked a moment, through the twilight, at the grey pool and its blank haunted edge, and then I took, back to the house, my dreary and difficult course. When I reached the gate in the fence the boat, to my surprise, was gone, so that I had a fresh reflexion to make on Flora's extraordinary command of the situation. She passed that night, by the most tacit and, I should add, were not the word so grotesque a false note, the happiest of arrangements, with Mrs. Grose. I saw neither of them on my return, but on the other hand I saw, as by an ambiguous compensation, a great deal of Miles. I saw — I can use no other phrase — so much of him that it fairly measured more than it had ever measured. No evening I had passed at Bly was to have had the portentous quality of this one; in spite of which — and in spite also of the deeper depths of consternation that had opened beneath my feet — there was literally, in the ebbing actual, an extraordinarily sweet sadness. On reaching the house I had never so much as looked for the boy; I had simply gone straight to my room to change what I was wearing and to take in, at a glance, much material testimony to Flora's rupture. Her little belongings had all been removed. When later, by the schoolroom fire, I was served with tea by the usual maid, I indulged, on the article of my other pupil, in no enquiry whatever. He had his freedom now — he might have it to the end! Well, he did have it; and it consisted — in part at least — of his coming in at about eight o'clock and sitting down with me in silence. On the removal of the tea-things I had blown out the candles and drawn my chair closer: I was conscious of a mortal coldness and felt as if I should never again be warm. So when he appeared I was sitting in the glow with my thoughts. He paused a moment by the door as if to look at me; then — as if to share them — came to the other side of the hearth and sank into a chair. We sat there in absolute stillness; yet he wanted, I felt, to be with me.

21

Before a new day, in my room, had fully broken, my eyes opened to Mrs. Grose, who had come to my bedside with worse news. Flora was so markedly feverish that an illness was perhaps at hand; she had passed a night of extreme unrest, a night agitated above all by fears that had for their subject not in the least her former but wholly her present governess. It was not against the possible re-entrance of Miss Jessel on the scene that she protested — it was conspicuously and passionately against mine. I was at once on my feet, and with an immense deal to ask; the more that my friend had discernibly now girded her loins to meet me afresh. This I felt as soon as I had put to her the question of her sense of the child's sincerity as against my own. "She persists in denying to you that she saw, or has even seen, anything?"

My visitor's trouble truly was treat. "Ah Miss, it is n't a matter on which I can push her! Yet it is n't either, I must say, as if I much needed to. It has made her, every inch of her, quite old."

"Oh I see her perfectly from here. She resents, for all the world like some high little personage, the imputation on her truthfulness and, as it were, her respectability. 'Miss Jessel indeed — *she!*' Ah she's 'respectable,' the chit! The impression she gave me there yesterday was, I assure you, the very strangest of all: it was quite beyond any of the others. I *did* put my foot in it! She'll never speak to me again."

Hideous and obscure as it all was, it held Mrs. Grose briefly silent; then she granted my point with a frankness which, I made sure, had more behind it. "I think indeed, Miss, she never will. She do have a grand manner about it!"

"And that manner" — I summed it up — "is practically what's the matter with her now."

Oh that manner, I could see in my visitor's face, and not a little else besides! "She asks me every three minutes if I think you're coming in."

"I see — I see." I too, on my side, had so much more than worked it out. "Has she said to you since yesterday — except to repudiate her familiarity with anything so dreadful — a single other word about Miss Jessel?"

"Not one, Miss. And of course, you know," my friend added, "I took it from her by the lake that just then and there at least there *was* nobody."

"Rather! And naturally you take it from her still."

"I don't contradict her. What else can I do?"

"Nothing in the world! You've the cleverest little person to deal with. They've made them — their two friends, I mean — still cleverer even than nature did; for it was wondrous material to play on! Flora has now her grievance, and she'll work it to the end."

"Yes, Miss; but to *what* end?"

"Why that of dealing with me to her uncle. She'll make me out to him the lowest creature — !"

I winced at the fair show of the scene in Mrs. Grose's face; she looked for a minute as if she sharply saw them together. "And him who thinks so well of you!"

"He has an odd way — it comes over me now," I laughed, " — of proving it! But that does n't matter. What Flora wants of course is to get rid of me."

My companion bravely concurred. "Never again to so much as look at you."

"So that what you've come to me now for," I asked, "is to speed me on my way?" Before she had time to reply, however, I had her in check. "I've a better idea — the result of my reflexions. My going *would* seem the right thing, and on Sunday I was terribly near it. Yet that won't do. It's *you* who must go. You must take Flora."

My visitor, at this, did speculate. "But where in the world — ?"

"Away from here. Away from *them*. Away, even most of all, now, from me. Straight to her uncle."

"Only to tell on you — ?"

"No, not 'only'! To leave me, in addition, with my remedy."

She was still vague. "And what *is* your remedy?"

"Your loyalty, to begin with. And then Miles's."

She looked at me hard. "Do you think he — ?"

"Won't, if he has the chance, turn on me? Yes, I venture still to think it. At all events I want to try. Get off with his sister as soon as possible and leave me with him alone." I was amazed, myself, at the spirit I had still in reserve, and therefore perhaps a trifle the more disconcerted at the way in which, in spite of this fine example of it, she hesitated. "There's one thing, of course," I went on: "they must n't, before she goes, see each other for three seconds." Then it came over me that, in spite of Flora's presumable sequestration from the instant of her return from the pool, it might already be too late. "Do you mean," I anxiously asked, "that they *have* met?"

At this she quite flushed. "Ah, Miss, I'm not such a fool as that! If I've been obliged to leave her three or four times, it has been each time with one of the maids, and at present, though she's alone, she's locked in safe. And yet — and yet!" There were too many things.

"And yet what?"

"Well, are you so sure of the little gentleman?"

"I'm not sure of anything but *you*. But I have, since last evening, a new hope. I think he wants to give me an opening. I do believe that — poor little exquisite wretch! — he wants to speak. Last evening, in the firelight and the silence, he sat with me for two hours as if it were just coming."

Mrs. Grose looked hard through the window at the grey gathering day. "And did it come?"

"No, though I waited and waited I confess it did n't, and it was without a breach of the silence, or so much as a faint allusion to his sister's condition and absence, that we at last kissed for good-night. All the same," I continued, "I can't, if her uncle sees her, consent to his seeing her brother without my having given the boy — and most of all because things have got so bad — a little more time."

My friend appeared on this ground more reluctant than I could quite understand. "What do you mean by more time?"

"Well, a day or two — really to bring it out. He'll then be on *my* side — of which you see the importance. If nothing comes I shall only fail, and you at the worst have helped me by doing on your arrival in town whatever you may have found possible." So I put it before her, but she continued for a little so lost in other reasons that I came again to her aid. "Unless indeed," I wound up, "you really want *not* to go."

I could see it, in her face, at last clear itself: she put out her hand to me as a pledge. "I'll go — I'll go. I'll go this morning."

I wanted to be very just. "If you *should* wish still to wait I'd engage she should n't see me."

"No, no: it's the place itself. She must leave it." She held me a moment with heavy eyes, then brought out the rest. "Your idea's the right one. I myself, Miss — "

"Well?"

"I can't stay."

The look she gave me with it made me jump at possibilities. "You mean that, since yesterday, you *have* seen — ?"

She shook her head with dignity. "I've *heard* — !"

"Heard?"

"From that child — horrors! There!" she sighed with tragic relief. "On my honour, Miss, she says things — !" But at this evocation she broke down; she dropped with a sudden cry upon my sofa and, as I had seen her do before, gave way to all the anguish of it.

It was quite in another manner that I for my part let myself go. "Oh thank God!"

She sprang up again at this, drying her eyes with a groan. " 'Thank God'?"

"It so justifies me!"

"It does that, Miss!"

I could n't have desired more emphasis, but I just waited. "She's so horrible?"

I saw my colleague scarce knew how to put it. "Really shocking."

"And about me?"

"About you, Miss — since you must have it. It's beyond everything, for a young lady; and I can't think wherever she must have picked up — "

"The appalling language she applies to me? I can then!" I broke in with a laugh that was doubtless significant enough.

It only in truth left my friend still more grave. "Well, perhaps I ought to also —
since I've heard some of it before! Yet I can't bear it," the poor woman went on while
with the same movement she glanced, on my dressing-table, at the face of my watch.
"But I must go back."

I kept her, however. "Ah if you can't bear it — !"

"How can I stop with her, you mean? Why just *for* that: to get her away. Far from
this," she pursued, "far from *them* — "

"She may be different? she may be free?" I seized her almost with joy. "Then in
spite of yesterday you *believe* — "

"In such doings?" Her simple description of them required, in the light of her
expression, to be carried no further, and she gave me the whole thing as she had
never done. "I believe."

Yes, it was a joy, and we were still shoulder to shoulder: if I might continue sure
of that I should care but little what else happened. My support in the presence of
disaster would be the same as it had been in my early need of confidence, and if my
friend would answer for my honesty I would answer for all the rest. On the point of
taking leave of her, none the less, I was to some extent embarrassed. "There's one
thing of course — it occurs to me — to remember. My letter giving the alarm will
have reached town before you."

I now felt still more how she had been beating about the bush and how weary at
last it had made her. "Your letter won't have got there. Your letter never went."

"What then became of it?"

"Goodness knows! Master Miles — "

"Do you mean *he* took it?" I gasped.

She hung fire, but she overcame her reluctance. "I mean that I saw yesterday,
when I came back with Miss Flora, that it was n't where you had put it. Later in the
evening I had the chance to question Luke, and he declared that he had neither
noticed nor touched it." We could only exchange, on this, one of our deeper mutual
soundings, and it was Mrs. Grose who first brought up the plumb with an almost
elate "You see!"

"Yes, I see that if Miles took it instead he probably will have read it and destroyed it."

"And don't you see anything else?"

I faced her a moment with a sad smile. "It strikes me that by this time your eyes
are open even wider than mine."

They proved to be so indeed, but she could still almost blush to show it. "I make
out now what he must have done at school." And she gave, in her simple sharpness,
an almost droll disillusioned nod. "He stole!"

I turned it over — I tried to be more judicial. "Well — perhaps."

She looked as if she found me unexpectedly calm. "He stole *letters!*"

She could n't know my reasons for a calmness after all pretty shallow; so I showed
them off as I might. "I hope then it was to more purpose than in this case! The note,
at all events, that I put on the table yesterday," I pursued, "will have given him so
scant an advantage — for it contained only the bare demand for an interview — that
he's already much ashamed of having gone so far for so little, and that what he had
on his mind last evening was precisely the need of confession." I seemed to myself
for the instant to have mastered it, to see it all. "Leave us, leave us" — I was already,

at the door, hurrying her off. "I'll get it out of him. He'll meet me. He'll confess. If he confesses he's saved. And if he's saved — "

"Then *you* are?" The dear woman kissed me on this, and I took her farewell. "I'll save you without him!" she cried as she went.

22

Yet it was when she had got off — and I missed her on the spot — that the great pinch really came. If I had counted on what it would give me to find myself alone with Miles I quickly recognised that it would give me at least a measure. No hour of my stay in fact was so assailed with apprehensions as that of my coming down to learn that the carriage containing Mrs. Grose and my younger pupil had already rolled out of the gates. Now I *was,* I said to myself, face to face with the elements, and for much of the rest of the day, while I fought my weakness, I could consider that I had been supremely rash. It was a tighter place still than I had yet turned round in; all the more that, for the first time, I could see in the aspect of others a confused reflexion of the crisis. What had happened naturally caused them all to stare; there was too little of the explained, throw out whatever we might, in the suddenness of my colleague's act. The maids and the men looked blank; the effect of which on my nerves was an aggravation until I saw the necessity of making it a positive aid. It was in short by just clutching the helm that I avoided total wreck; and I dare say that, to bear up at all, I became that morning very grand and very dry. I welcomed the consciousness that I was charged with much to do, and I caused it to be known as well that, left thus to myself, I was quite remarkably firm. I wandered with that manner, for the next hour or two, all over the place and looked, I have no doubt, as if I were ready for any onset. So, for the benefit of whom it might concern, I paraded with a sick heart.

The person it appeared least to concern proved to be, till dinner, little Miles himself. My perambulations had given me meanwhile no glimpse of him, but they had tended to make more public the change taking place in our relation as a consequence of his having at the piano, the day before, kept me, in Flora's interest, so beguiled and befooled. The stamp of publicity had of course been fully given by her confinement and departure, and the change itself was now ushered in by our non-observance of the regular custom of the schoolroom. He had already disappeared when, on my way down, I pushed open his door, and I learned below that he had breakfasted — in the presence of a couple of the maids — with Mrs. Grose and his sister. He had then gone out, as he said, for a stroll; than which nothing, I reflected, could better have expressed his frank view of the abrupt transformation of my office. What he would now permit this office to consist of was yet to be settled: there was at least a queer relief — I mean for myself in especial — in the renouncement of one pretension. If so much had sprung to the surface I scarce put it too strongly in saying that what had perhaps sprung highest was the absurdity of our prolonging the fiction that I had anything more to teach him. It sufficiently stuck out that, by tacit little tricks in which even more than myself he carried out the care for my dignity, I had had to appeal to him to let me off straining to meet him on the ground of his true capacity. He had at any rate his freedom now; I was never to touch it again: as I had amply shown, moreover, when, on his joining me in the school-room the previous night, I uttered, in reference to the interval just concluded, neither challenge nor hint. I had too much, from this moment, my other ideas. Yet when he at last arrived the difficulty of applying them, the accumulations of my problem, were brought straight home to me by the beautiful little presence on which what had occurred had as yet, for the eye, dropped neither stain nor shadow.

To mark, for the house, the high state I cultivated I decreed that my meals with the boy should be served, as we called it, downstairs; so that I had been awaiting him in the ponderous pomp of the room outside the window of which I had had from Mrs. Grose, that first scared Sunday, my flash of something it would scarce have done to call light. Here at present I felt afresh — for I had felt it again and again — how my equilibrium depended on the success of my rigid will, the will to shut my eyes as tight as possible to the truth that what I had to deal with was, revoltingly, against nature. I could only get on at all by taking "nature" into my confidence and my account, by treating my monstrous ordeal as a push in a direction unusual, of course, and unpleasant, but demanding after all, for a fair front, only another turn of the screw of ordinary human virtue. No attempt, none the less, could well require more tact than just this attempt to supply, one's self, *all* the nature. How could I put even a little of that article into a suppression of reference to what had occurred? How on the other hand could I make a reference without a new plunge into the hideous obscure? Well, a sort of answer, after a time, had come to me, and it was so far confirmed as that I was met, incontestably, by the quickened vision of what was rare in my little companion. It was indeed as if he had found even now — as he had so often found at lessons — still some other delicate way to ease me off. Was n't there light in the fact which, as we shared our solitude, broke out with a specious glitter it had never yet quite worn? — the fact that (opportunity aiding, precious opportu-nity which had now come) it would be preposterous, with a child so endowed, to forego the help one might wrest from absolute intelligence? What had his intelli-gence been given him for but to save him? Might n't one, to reach his mind, risk the stretch of a stiff arm across his character? It was as if, when we were face to face in the dining-room, he had literally shown me the way. The roast mutton was on the table and I had dispensed with attendance. Miles, before he sat down, stood a moment with his hands in his pockets and looked at the joint, on which he seemed on the point of passing some humorous judgement. But what he presently produced was: "I say, my dear, is she really very awfully ill?"

"Little Flora? Not so bad but that she'll presently be better. London will set her up. Bly had ceased to agree with her. Come here and take your mutton."

He alertly obeyed me, carried the plate carefully to his seat and, when he was established, went on. "Did Bly disagree with her so terribly all at once?"

"Not so suddenly as you might think. One had seen it coming on."

"Then why didn't you get her off before?"

"Before what?"

"Before she become too ill to travel."

I found myself prompt. "She's *not* too ill to travel; she only might have become so if she had stayed. This was just the moment to seize. The journey will dissipate the influence" — oh I was grand! — "and carry it off."

"I see, I see" — Miles, for that matter, was grand too. He settled to his repast with the charming little "table manner" that, from the day of his arrival, had relieved me of all grossness of admonition. Whatever he had been expelled from school for, it was n't for ugly feeding. He was irreproachable, as always, to-day; but was unmistakeably more conscious. He was discernibly trying to take for granted more things than he found, without assistance, quite easy; and he dropped into peaceful silence while he felt his situation. Our meal was of the briefest — mine a vain pretence, and I had the things immediately removed. While this was done Miles stood again with his hands in his little pockets and his back to me — stood and looked out of the wide window through which, that other day, I had seen what pulled me up. We continued silent while the maid was with us — as silent, it whimsically occurred to me, as some young couple who on their wedding-journey, at the inn, feel shy in the presence of the waiter. He turned round only when the waiter had left us. "Well — so we're alone!"

23

"Oh more or less." I imagine my smile was pale. "Not absolutely. We should n't like that!" I went on.

"No — I suppose we should n't. Of course we've the others."

"We've the others — we've indeed the others," I concurred.

"Yet even though we have them," he returned, still with his hands in his pockets and planted there in front of me, "they don't much count, do they?"

I made the best of it, but I felt wan. "It depends on what you call 'much'!"

"Yes" — with all accommodation — "everything depends!" On this, however, he faced to the window again and presently reached it with his vague restless cogitating step. He remained there a while with his forehead against the glass, in contemplation of the stupid shrubs I knew and the dull things of November. I had always my hypocrisy of "work," behind which I now gained the sofa. Steadying myself with it there as I had repeatedly done at those moments of torment that I have described as the moments of my knowing the children to be given to something from which I was barred, I sufficiently obeyed my habit of being prepared for the worst. But an extraordinary impression dropped on me as I extracted a meaning from the boy's embarrassed back — none other than the impression that I was not barred now. This inference grew in a few minutes to sharp intensity and seemed bound up with the direct perception that it was positively *he* who was. The frames and squares of the great window were a kind of image, for him, of a kind of failure. I felt that I saw him, in any case, shut in or shut out. He was admirable but not comfortable: I took it in with a throb of hope. Was n't he looking through the haunted pane for something he could n't see? — and wasn't it the first time in the whole business that he had known such a lapse? The first, the very first: I found it a splendid portent. It made him anxious, though he watched himself; he had been anxious all day and, even while in his usual sweet little manner he set at table, had needed all his small strange genius to give it a gloss. When he at last turned round to meet me it was almost as if this genius had succumbed. "Well, I think I'm glad Bly agrees with *me!*"

"You'd certainly seem to have seen, these twenty-four hours, a good deal more of it than for some time before. I hope," I went on bravely, "that you've been enjoying yourself."

"Oh yes, I've been ever so far; all round about — miles and miles away. I've never been so free."

He had really a manner of his own, and I could only try to keep up with him. "Well, do you like it?"

He stood there smiling: then at last he put into two words — "Do *you?*" — more discrimination than I had ever heard two words contain. Before I had time to deal with that, however, he continued as if with the sense that this was an impertinence to be softened. "Nothing could be more charming than the way you take it, for of course if we're alone together now it's you that are alone most. But I hope," he threw in, "you don't particularly mind!"

"Having to do with you?" I asked. "My dear child, how can I help minding? Though I've renounced all claim to your company — you're so beyond me — I at least greatly enjoy it. What else should I stay on for?"

He looked at me more directly, and the expression of his face, graver now, struck me as the most beautiful I had ever found in it. "You stay on just for *that?*"

"Certainly. I stay on as your friend and from the tremendous interest I take in you till something can be done for you that may be more worth your while. That need n't surprise you." My voice trembled so that I felt it impossible to suppress the shake. "Don't you remember how I told you, when I came and sat on your bed the night of the storm, that there was nothing in the world I would n't do for you?"

"Yes, yes!" He, on his side, more and more visibly nervous, had a tone to master; but he was so much more successful than I that, laughing out through his gravity, he could pretend we were pleasantly jesting. "Only that, I think, was to get me to do something for *you!*"

"It was partly to get you to do something," I conceded. "But, you know, you didn't do it."

"Oh yes," he said with the brightest superficial eagerness. "you wanted me to tell you something."

"That's it. Out, straight out. What you have on your mind, you know."

"Ah then is *that* what you've stayed over for?"

He spoke with a gaiety through which I could still catch the finest little quiver of resentful passion; but I can't begin to express the effect upon me of an implication of surrender even so faint. It was as if what I had yearned for had come at last only to astonish me. "Well, yes — I may as well make a clean breast of it. It was precisely for that."

He waited so long that I supposed it for the purpose of repudiating the assumption on which my action had been founded; but what he finally said was: "Do you mean now — here?"

"There could n't be a better place or time." He looked round him uneasily, and I had the rare — oh the queer! — impression of the very first symptom I had seen in him of the approach of immediate fear. It was as if he were suddenly afraid of me — which struck me indeed as perhaps the best thing to make him. Yet in the very pang of the effort I felt it vain to try sternness, and I heard myself the next instant so gentle as to be almost grotesque. "You want so to go out again?"

"Awfully!" He smiled at me heroically, and the touching little bravery of it was enhanced by his actually flushing with pain. He had picked up his hat, which he had brought in, and stood twirling it in a way that gave me, even as I was just nearly reaching port, a perverse horror of what I was doing. To do it in *any* way was an act of violence, for what did it consist of but the obtrusion of the idea of grossness and guilt on a small helpless creature who had been for me a revelation of the possibilities of beautiful intercourse? Was n't it base to create for a being so exquisite a mere alien awkwardness? I suppose I now read into our situation a clearness it could n't have had at the time, for I seem to see our poor eyes already lighted with some spark of a prevision of the anguish that was to come. So we circled about with terrors and scruples, fighters not daring to close. But it was for each other we feared! That kept us a little longer suspended and unbruised. "I'll tell you everything," Miles said — "I mean I'll tell you anything you like. You'll stay on with me, and we shall both be all right, and I *will* tell you — I *will*. But not now."

"Why not now?"

My insistence turned him from me and kept him once more at his window in a silence during which, between us, you might have heard a pin drop. Then he was before me again with the air of a person for whom, outside, some one who had frankly to be reckoned with was waiting. "I have to see Luke."

I had not yet reduced him to quite so vulgar a lie, and I felt proportionately ashamed. But, horrible as it was, his lies made up my truth. I achieved thoughtfully a few loops of my knitting. "Well then go to Luke, and I'll wait for what you promise. Only in return for that satisfy, before you leave me, one very much smaller request."

He looked as if he felt he had succeeded enough to be able still a little to bargain. "Very much smaller — ?"

"Yes, a mere fraction of the whole. Tell me" — oh my work preoccupied me, and I was off-hand! — "if, yesterday afternoon, from the table in the hall, you took, you know, my letter."

24

My grasp of how he received this suffered for a minute from something that I can describe only as a fierce split of my attention — a stroke that at first, as I sprang straight up, reduced me to the mere blind movement of getting hold of him, drawing him close and, while I just fell for support against the nearest piece of furniture, instinctively keeping him with his back to the window. The appearance was full upon us that I had already had to deal with here: Peter Quint had come into view like a sentinel before a prison. The next thing I saw was that, from outside, he had reached the window, and then I knew that, close to the glass and glaring in through it, he offered once more to the room his white face of damnation. It represents but grossly what took place within me at the sight to say that on the second my decision was made; yet I believe that no woman so overwhelmed ever in so short a time recovered her command of the *act*. It came to me in the very horror of the immediate presence that the act would be, seeing and facing what I saw and faced, to keep the boy himself unaware. The inspiration — I can call it by no other name — was that I felt how voluntarily, how transcendently, I *might*. It was like fighting with a demon for a human soul, and when I had fairly so appraised it I saw how the human soul — held out, in the tremor of my hands, at arms' length — had a perfect dew of sweat on a lovely childish forehead. The face that was close to mine was as white as the face against the glass, and out of it presently came a sound, not low nor weak, but as if from much further away, that I drank like a waft of fragrance.

"Yes — I took it."

At this, with a moan of joy, I enfolded, I drew him close; and while I held him to my breast, where I could feel in the sudden fever of his little body the tremendous pulse of his little heart, I kept my eyes on the thing at the window and saw it move and shift its posture. I have likened it to a sentinel, but its slow wheel, for a moment, was rather the prowl of a baffled beast. My present quickened courage, however, was such that, not too much to let it through, I had to shade, as it were, my flame. Meanwhile the glare of the face was again at the window, the scoundrel fixed as if to watch and wait. It was the very confidence that I might now defy him, as well as the positive certitude, by this time, of the child's unconsciousness, that made me go on. "What did you take it for?"

"To see what you said about me."

"You opened the letter?"

"I opened it."

My eyes were now, as I held him off a little again, on Miles's own face, in which the collapse of mockery showed me how complete was the ravage of uneasiness. What was prodigious was that at last, by my success, his sense was sealed and his communication stopped: he knew that he was in presence, but knew not of what, and knew still less that I also was and that I did know. And what did this strain of trouble matter when my eyes went back to the window only to see that the air was clear again and — by my personal triumph — the influence quenched? There was nothing there. I felt that the cause was mine and that I should surely get *all.* "And you found nothing!" — I let my elation out.

He gave the most mournful, thoughtful little headshake. "Nothing."

"Nothing, nothing!" I almost shouted in my joy.

"Nothing, nothing," he sadly repeated.

I kissed his forehead; it was drenched. "So what have you done with it?"

"I've burnt it."

"Burnt it?" It was now or never. "Is that what you did at school?"

Oh what this brought up! "At school?"

"Did you take letters? — or other things?"

"Other things?" He appeared now to be thinking of something far off and that reached him only through the pressure of his anxiety. Yet it did reach him. "Did I *steal?*"

I felt myself redden to the roots of my hair as well as wonder if it were more strange to put to a gentleman such a question or to see him take it with allowances that gave the very distance of his fall in the world. "Was it for that you might n't go back?"

The only thing he felt was rather a dreary little surprise. "Did you know I might n't go back?"

"I know everything."

He gave me at this the longest and strangest look. "Everything?"

"Everything. Therefore *did* you — ?" But I couldn't say it again.

Miles could, very simply. "No, I did n't steal."

My face must have shown him I believed him utterly; yet my hands — but it was for the pure tenderness — shook him as if to ask him why, if it was all for nothing, he had condemned me to months of torment. "What then did you do?"

He looked in vague pain all round the top of the room and drew his breath, two or three times over, as if with difficulty. He might have been standing at the bottom of the sea and raising his eyes to some faint green twilight. "Well — I said things."

"Only that?"

"They thought it was enough!"

"To turn you out for?"

Never, truly, had a person "turned out" shown so little to explain it as this little person! He appeared to weigh my question, but in a manner quite detached and almost helpless. "Well, I suppose I ought n't."

"But to whom did you say them?"

He evidently tried to remember, but it dropped — he had lost it. "I don't know!"

He almost smiled at me in the desolation of his surrender, which was indeed practically, by this time, so complete that I ought to have left it there. But I was infatuated — I was blind with victory, though even then the very effect that was to have brought him so much nearer was already that of added separation. "Was it to every one?" I asked.

"No; it was only to — " But he gave a sick little headshake. "I don't remember their names."

"Were they then so many?"

"No — only a few. Those I liked."

Those he liked? I seemed to float not into clearness, but into a darker obscure, and within a minute there had come to me out of my very pity the appalling alarm of his being perhaps innocent. It was for the instant confounding and bottomless, for if he *were* innocent what then on earth was I? Paralysed, while it lasted, by the mere brush of the question, I let him go a little, so that, with a deep-drawn sigh, he turned away from me again; which, as he faced toward the clear window, I suffered, feeling that I had nothing now there to keep him from. "And did they repeat what you said?" I went on after a moment.

He was soon at some distance from me, still breathing hard and again with the air, though now without anger for it, of being confined against his will. Once more, as he had done before, he looked up at the dim day as if, of what had hitherto sustained him, nothing was left but an unspeakable anxiety. "Oh yes," he nevertheless replied — "they must have repeated them. To those *they* liked," he added.

There was somehow less of it than I had expected, but I turned it over. "And these things came round — ?"

"To the masters? Oh yes!" he answered very simply. "But I did n't know they'd tell."

"The masters? They did n't — they've never told. That's why I ask you."

He turned to me again his little beautiful fevered face. "Yes, it was too bad."

"Too bad?"

"What I suppose I sometimes said. To write home."

I can't name the exquisite pathos of the contradiction given to such a speech by such a speaker; I only know that the next instant I heard myself throw off with homely force: "Stuff and nonsense!" But the next after that I must have sounded stern enough. "What *were* these things?"

My sternness was all for his judge, his executioner; yet it made him avert himself again, and that movement made *me,* with a single bound and an irrepressible cry, spring straight upon him For there again, against the glass, as if to blight his confession and stay his answer, was the hideous author of our woe — the white face of damnation. I felt a sick swim at the drop of my victory and all the return of my battle, so that the wildness of my veritable leap only served as a great betrayal. I saw him, from the midst of my act, meet it with a divination, and on the perception that even now he only guessed, and that the window was still to his own eyes free, I let the impulse flame up to convert the climax of his dismay into the very proof of his liberation. "No more, no more, no more!" I shrieked to my visitant as I tried to press him against me.

"Is she *here?*" Miles panted as he caught with his sealed eyes the direction of my words. Then as his strange "she" staggered me and, with a gasp, I echoed it, "Miss Jessel, Miss Jessel!" he with sudden fury gave me back.

I seized, stupefied, his supposition — some sequel to what we had done to Flora, but this made me only want to show him that it was better still than that. "It's not Miss Jessel! But it's at the window — straight before us. It's *there* — the coward horror, there for the last time!"

At this, after a second in which his head made the movement of a baffled dog's on a scent and then gave a frantic little shake for air and light, he was at me in a white rage, bewildered, glaring vainly over the place and missing wholly, though it now, to my sense, filled the room like the taste of poison, the wide overwhelming presence. "It's *he?*"

I was so determined to have all my proof that I flashed into ice to challenge him. "Whom do you mean by 'he'?"

"Peter Quint — you devil!" His face gave again, round the room, its convulsed supplication. "*Where?*"

They are in my ears still, his supreme surrender of the name and his tribute to my devotion. "What does he matter now, my own? — what will he *ever* matter? *I* have you," I launched at the beast, "but he has lost you for ever!" Then for the demonstration of my work, "There, *there!*" I said to Miles.

But he had already jerked straight round, stared, glared again, and seen but the quiet day. With the stroke of the loss I was so proud of he uttered the cry of a creature hurled over an abyss, and the grasp with which I recovered him might have been that of catching him in his fall. I caught him, yes, I held him — it may be imagined with what a passion; but at the end of a minute I began to feel what it truly was that I held. We were alone with the quiet day, and his little heart, dispossessed, had stopped.

JAMES JOYCE

James Joyce (1882–1941) was born in Dublin and received his education in Jesuit schools and University College, Dublin. Irked by what he perceived to be the narrowness of Irish Catholic society, he moved to the Continent in 1902; with the exception of a year or so, he never again lived in Ireland. From Paris to Trieste to Zurich and back to Paris, he lived a life troubled by financial strain, self-absorption, and discontent, and he wrote novels of eccentric and brilliant vision and voice, mingling pedantry, folklore, myth, memory, and wordplay. The first of them, *A Portrait of the Artist as a Young Man* (1915), is largely autobiographical. It was followed by *Ulysses* (1922) — which created a critical sensation upon its publication and was banned in the United States until 1933, for reasons of alleged obscenity — and *Finnegans Wake* (1939). Joyce's short stories, *Dubliners,* appeared early in his career (1914); in them he depicted the Irish Catholic life of his native city. Joyce is perhaps most famous for his "stream of consciousness" technique: it is an uncensored, unformulated manner of presenting a character's interior monologue, and its influence on twentieth-century fiction is inestimable. From pessimism and linguistic dazzle, says one of his biographers, emerges "the Joycean word music" that "reaches us as a kind of dirge, sung over the flotsam and jetsam of civilization." That observation says much about "The Dead."

The Dead

Lily, the caretaker's daughter, was literally run off her feet. Hardly had she brought one gentleman into the little pantry behind the office on the ground floor and helped him off with his overcoat than the wheezy hall-door bell clanged again and she had to scamper along the bare hallway to let in another guest. It was well for her she had not to attend to the ladies also. But Miss Kate and Miss Julia had thought of that and had converted the bathroom upstairs into a ladies' dressing-room. Miss Kate and Miss Julia were there, gossiping and laughing and fussing, walking after each other to the head of the stairs, peering down over the banisters and calling down to Lily to ask her who had come.

It was always a great affair, the Misses Morkan's annual dance. Everybody who knew them came to it, members of the family, old friends of the family, the members of Julia's choir, any of Kate's pupils that were grown up enough, and even some of Mary Jane's pupils too. Never once had it fallen flat. For years and years it had gone off in splendid style, as long as anyone could remember; ever since Kate and Julia, after the death of their brother Pat, had left the house in Stoney Batter and taken Mary Jane, their only niece, to live with them in the dark, gaunt house on Usher's Island, the upper part of which they had rented from Mr. Fulham, the corn-factor on the ground floor. That was a good thirty years ago if it was a day. Mary Jane, who was then a little girl in short clothes, was now the main prop of the household, for she had the organ in Haddington Road. She had been through the Academy and gave a pupils' concert every year in the upper room of the Antient Concert Rooms. Many of her pupils belonged to the better-class families on the Kingstown and Dalkey line. Old as they were, her aunts also did their share. Julia, though she was quite grey, was still the leading soprano in Adam and Eve's, and Kate, being too feeble to go about much, gave music lessons to beginners on the old square piano in the back room. Lily, the caretaker's daughter, did housemaid's work for them. Though their life was modest, they believed in eating well; the best of everything: diamond-bone sirloins, three-shilling tea and the best bottled stout. But Lily seldom made a mistake in the orders, so that she got on well with her three mistresses. They were fussy, that was all. But the only thing they would not stand was back answers.

Of course, they had good reason to be fussy on such a night. And then it was long after ten o'clock and yet there was no sign of Gabriel and his wife. Besides they were dreadfully afraid that Freddy Malins might turn up screwed. They would not wish for worlds that any of Mary Jane's pupils should see him under the influence; and when he was like that it was sometimes very hard to manage him. Freddy Malins always came late, but they wondered what could be keeping Gabriel: and that was what brought them every two minutes to the banisters to ask Lily had Gabriel or Freddy come.

"O, Mr. Conroy," said Lily to Gabriel when she opened the door for him, "Miss Kate and Miss Julia thought you were never coming. Good-night, Mrs. Conroy."

"I'll engage they did," said Gabriel, "but they forget that my wife here takes three mortal hours to dress herself."

He stood on the mat, scraping the snow from his goloshes, while Lily led his wife to the foot of the stairs and called out:

"Miss Kate, here's Mrs. Conroy."

Kate and Julia came toddling down the dark stairs at once. Both of them kissed Gabriel's wife, said she must be perished alive, and asked was Gabriel with her.

"Here I am as right as the mail, Aunt Kate! Go on up. I'll follow," called out Gabriel from the dark.

He continued scraping his feet vigorously while the three women went upstairs, laughing, to the ladies' dressing-room. A light fringe of snow lay like a cape on the shoulders of his overcoat and like toecaps on the toes of his goloshes; and, as the buttons of his overcoat slipped with a squeaking noise through the snow-stiffened frieze, a cold, fragrant air from out-of-doors escaped from crevices and folds.

"Is it snowing again, Mr. Conroy?" asked Lily.

She had preceded him into the pantry to help him off with his overcoat. Gabriel smiled at the three syllables she had given his surname and glanced at her. She was a slim, growing girl, pale in complexion and with hay-coloured hair. The gas in the pantry made her look still paler. Gabriel had known her when she was a child and used to sit on the lowest step nursing a rag doll.

"Yes, Lily," he answered, "and I think we're in for a night of it."

He looked up at the pantry ceiling, which was shaking with the stamping and shuffling of feet on the floor above, listened for a moment to the piano and then glanced at the girl, who was folding his overcoat carefully at the end of a shelf.

"Tell me, Lily," he said in a friendly tone, "do you still go to school?"

"O no, sir," she answered. "I'm done schooling this year and more."

"O, then," said Gabriel gaily, "I suppose we'll be going to your wedding one of these fine days with your young man, eh?"

The girl glanced back at him over her shoulder and said with great bitterness:

"The men that is now is only all palaver and what they can get out of you."

Gabriel coloured, as if he felt he had made a mistake and, without looking at her, kicked off his goloshes and flicked actively with his muffler at his patent-leather shoes.

He was a stout, tallish young man. The high colour of his cheeks pushed upwards even to his forehead, where it scattered itself in a few formless patches of pale red; and on his hairless face there scintillated restlessly the polished lenses and the bright gilt rims of the glasses which screened his delicate and restless eyes. His glossy black hair was parted in the middle and brushed in a long curve behind his ears where it curled slightly beneath the groove left by his hat.

When he had flicked lustre into his shoes he stood up and pulled his waistcoat down more tightly on his plump body. Then he took a coin rapidly from his pocket.

"O Lily," he said, thrusting it into her hands, "it's Christmas-time, isn't it? Just . . . here's a little . . ."

He walked rapidly towards the door.

"O no, sir!" cried the girl, following him. "Really, sir, I wouldn't take it."

"Christmas-time! Christmas-time!" said Gabriel, almost trotting to the stairs and waving his hand to her in deprecation.

The girl, seeing that he had gained the stairs, called out after him:

"Well, thank you, sir."

He waited outside the drawing-room door until the waltz should finish, listening to the skirts that swept against it and to the shuffling of feet. He was still discomposed by the girl's bitter and sudden retort. It had cast a gloom over him which he tried to dispel by arranging his cuffs and the bows of his tie. He then took from his waistcoat pocket a little paper and glanced at the headings he had made for his speech. He was undecided about the lines from Robert Browning, for he feared they would be above the heads of his hearers. Some quotation that they would recognise from Shakespeare or from the Melodies would be better. The indelicate clacking of the men's heels and the shuffling of their soles reminded him that their grade of culture differed from his. He would only make himself ridiculous by quoting poetry to them which they could not understand. They would think that he was airing his superior education. He would fail with them just as he had failed with the girl in the pantry. He had taken up a wrong tone. His whole speech was a mistake from first to last, an utter failure.

Just then his aunts and his wife came out of the ladies' dressing-room. His aunts were two small, plainly dressed women. Aunt Julia was an inch or so the taller. Her hair, drawn low over the tops of her ears, was grey; and grey also, with darker shadows, was her large flaccid face. Though she was stout in build and stood erect, her slow eyes and parted lips gave her the appearance of a woman who did not know where she was or where she was going. Aunt Kate was more vivacious. Her face, healthier than her sister's, was all puckers and creases, like a shrivelled red apple, and her hair, braided in the same old-fashioned way, had not lost its ripe nut colour.

They both kissed Gabriel frankly. He was their favorite nephew, the son of their dead elder sister, Ellen, who had married T. J. Conroy of the Port and Docks.

"Gretta tells me you're not going to take a cab back to Monkstown tonight, Gabriel," said Aunt Kate.

"No," said Gabriel, turning to his wife, "we had quite enough of that last year, hadn't we? Don't you remember, Aunt Kate, what a cold Gretta got out of it? Cab windows rattling all the way, and the east wind blowing in after we passed Merrion. Very jolly it was. Gretta caught a dreadful cold."

Aunt Kate frowned severely and nodded her head at every word.

"Quite right, Gabriel, quite right," she said. "You can't be too careful."

"But as for Gretta there," said Gabriel, "she'd walk home in the snow if she were let." Mrs. Conroy laughed.

"Don't mind him, Aunt Kate," she said. "He's really an awful bother, what with green shades for Tom's eyes at night and making him do the dumb-bells, and forcing Eva to eat the stirabout. The poor child! And she simply hates the sight of it! . . . O, but you'll never guess what he makes me wear now!"

She broke out into a peal of laughter and glanced at her husband, whose admiring and happy eyes had been wandering from her dress to her face and hair. The two aunts laughed heartily, too, for Gabriel's solicitude was a standing joke with them.

"Goloshes!" said Mrs. Conroy. "That's the latest. Whenever it's wet underfoot I must put on my goloshes. Tonight even, he wanted me to put them on, but I wouldn't. The next thing he'll buy me will be a diving suit."

Gabriel laughed nervously and patted his tie reassuringly, while Aunt Kate nearly doubled herself, so heartily did she enjoy the joke. The smile soon faded from Aunt Julia's face and her mirthless eyes were directed towards her nephew's face. After a pause she asked:

"And what are goloshes, Gabriel?"

"Goloshes, Julia!" exclaimed her sister. "Goodness me, don't you know what goloshes are? You wear them over your . . . over your boots, Gretta, isn't it?"

"Yes," said Mrs. Conroy. "Guttapercha things. We both have a pair now. Gabriel says everyone wears them on the Continent."

"O, on the Continent," murmured Aunt Julia, nodding her head slowly.

Gabriel knitted his brows and said, as if he were slightly angered:

"It's nothing very wonderful, but Gretta thinks it very funny because she says the word reminds her of Christy Minstrels."

"But tell me, Gabriel," said Aunt Kate, with brisk tact. "Of course, you've seen about the room. Gretta was saying . . ."

"O, the room is all right," replied Gabriel. "I've taken one in the Gresham."

"To be sure," said Aunt Kate, "by far the best thing to do. And the children, Gretta, you're not anxious about them?"

"O, for one night," said Mrs. Conroy. "Besides, Bessie will look after them."

"To be sure," said Aunt Kate again. "What a comfort it is to have a girl like that, one you can depend on! There's that Lily, I'm sure I don't know what has come over her lately. She's not the girl she was at all."

Gabriel was about to ask his aunt some questions on this point, but she broke off suddenly to gaze after his sister, who had wandered down the stairs and was craning her neck over the banisters.

"Now, I ask you," she said almost testily, "where is Julia going? Julia! Julia! Where are you going?"

Julia, who had gone half way down one flight, came back and announced blandly: "Here's Freddy."

At the same moment a clapping of hands and a final flourish of the pianist told that the waltz had ended. The drawing-room door was opened from within and some couples came out. Aunt Kate drew Gabriel aside hurriedly and whispered into his ear:

"Slip down, Gabriel, like a good fellow and see if he's all right, and don't let him up if he's screwed. I'm sure he's screwed. I'm sure he is."

Gabriel went to the stairs and listened over the banisters. He could hear two persons talking in the pantry. Then he recognised Freddy Malins' laugh. He went down the stairs noisily.

"It's such a relief," said Aunt Kate to Mrs. Conroy, "that Gabriel is here. I always feel easier in my mind when he's here . . . . Julia, there's Miss Daly and Miss Power will take some refreshment. Thanks for your beautiful waltz, Miss Daly. It made lovely time."

A tall wizen-faced man, with a stiff grizzled moustache and swarthy skin, who was passing out with his partner, said:

"And may we have some refreshment, too, Miss Morkan?"

"Julia," said Aunt Kate summarily, "and here's Mr. Browne and Miss Furlong. Take them in, Julia, with Miss Daly and Miss Power."

"I'm the man for the ladies," said Mr. Browne, pursing his lips until his moustache bristled and smiling in all his wrinkles. "You know, Miss Morkan, the reason they are so fond of me is — "

He did not finish his sentence, but, seeing that Aunt Kate was out of earshot, at once led the three young ladies into the back room. The middle of the room was occupied by two square tables placed end to end, and on these Aunt Julia and the caretaker were straightening and smoothing a large cloth. On the sideboard were arrayed dishes and plates, and glasses and bundles of knives and forks and spoons. The top of the closed square piano served also as a sideboard for viands and sweets. At a smaller sideboard in one corner two young men were standing, drinking hop-bitters.

Mr. Browne led his charges thither and invited them all, in jest, to some ladies' punch, hot, strong and sweet. As they said they never took anything strong, he opened three bottles of lemonade for them. Then he asked one of the young men to move aside, and, taking hold of the decanter, filled out for himself a goodly measure of whisky. The young men eyed him respectfully while he took a trial sip.

"God help me," he said, smiling, "it's the doctor's orders."

His wizened face broke into a broader smile, and the three young ladies laughed in musical echo to his pleasantry, swaying their bodies to and fro, with nervous jerks of their shoulders. The boldest said:

"O, now, Mr. Browne, I'm sure the doctor never ordered anything of the kind."

Mr. Browne took another sip of his whisky and said, with sidling mimicry:

"Well, you see, I'm like the famous Mrs. Cassidy, who is reported to have said: 'Now, Mary Grimes, if I don't take it, make me take it, for I feel I want it.'"

His hot face had leaned forward a little too confidentially and he had assumed a very low Dublin accent so that the young ladies, with one instinct, received his speech in silence. Miss Furlong, who was one of Mary Jane's pupils, asked Miss Daly what was the name of the pretty waltz she had played; and Mr. Browne, seeing that he was ignored, turned promptly to the two young men who were more appreciative.

A red-faced young woman, dressed in pansy, came into the room, excitedly clapping her hands and crying:

"Quadrilles! Quadrilles!"

Close on her heels came Aunt Kate, crying:

"Two gentlemen and three ladies, Mary Jane!"

"O, here's Mr. Bergin and Mr. Kerrigan," said Mary Jane. "Mr. Kerrigan, will you take Miss Power? Miss Furlong, may I get you a partner, Mr. Bergin. O, that'll just do now."

"Three ladies, Mary Jane," said Aunt Kate.

The two young gentlemen asked the ladies if they might have the pleasure, and Mary Jane turned to Miss Daly.

"O, Miss Daly, you're really awfully good, after playing for the last two dances, but really we're so short of ladies tonight."

"I don't mind in the least, Miss Morkan."

"But I've a nice partner for you, Mr. Bartell D'Arcy, the tenor. I'll get him to sing later on. All Dublin is raving about him."

"Lovely voice, lovely voice!" said Aunt Kate.

As the piano had twice begun the prelude to the first figure Mary Jane led her recruits quickly from the room. They had hardly gone when Aunt Julia wandered slowly into the room, looking behind her at something.

"What is the matter, Julia?" asked Aunt Kate anxiously. "Who is it?"

Julia, who was carrying in a column of table-napkins, turned to her sister and said, simply, as if the question had surprised her:

"It's only Freddy, Kate, and Gabriel with him."

In face right behind her Gabriel could be seen piloting Freddy Malins across the landing. The latter, a young man of about forty, was of Gabriel's size and build, with very round shoulders. His face was fleshy and pallid, touched with colour only at the thick hanging lobes of his ears and at the wide wings of his nose. He had coarse features, a blunt nose, a convex and receding brow, tumid and protruded lips. His heavy-lidded eyes and the disorder of his scanty hair made him look sleepy. He was laughing heartily in a high key at a story which he had been telling Gabriel on the stairs and at the same time rubbing the knuckles of his left fist backwards and forwards into his left eye.

"Good evening, Freddy," said Aunt Julia.

Freddy Malins bade the Misses Morkan good-evening in what seemed an offhand fashion by reason of the habitual catch in his voice and then, seeing that Mr. Browne was grinning at him from the sideboard, crossed the room on rather shaky legs and began to repeat in an undertone the story he had just told to Gabriel.

"He's not so bad, is he?" said Aunt Kate to Gabriel.

Gabriel's brows were dark but he raised them quickly and answered:

"O, no, hardly noticeable."

"Now, isn't he a terrible fellow!" she said. "And his poor mother made him take the pledge on New Year's Eve. But come on, Gabriel, into the drawing-room."

Before leaving the room with Gabriel she signalled to Mr. Browne by frowning and shaking her forefinger in warning to and fro. Mr. Browne nodded in answer and, when she had gone, said to Freddy Malins:

"Now, then, Teddy, I'm going to fill you out a good glass of lemonade just to buck you up."

Freddy Malins, who was nearing the climax of his story, waved the offer aside impatiently but Mr. Browne, having first called Freddy Malins' attention to a disarray in his dress, filled out and handed him a full glass of lemonade. Freddy Malins' left hand accepted the glass mechanically, his right hand being engaged in the mechanical readjustment of his dress. Mr. Browne, whose face was once more wrinkling with mirth, poured out for himself a glass of whisky while Freddy Malins exploded, before he had well reached the climax of his story, in a kink of high-pitched bronchitic laughter and, setting down his untasted and overflowing glass, began to rub the knuckles of his left fist backwards and forwards into his left eye, repeating words of his last phrase as well as his fit of laughter would allow him.

Gabriel could not listen while Mary Jane was playing her Academy piece, full of runs and difficult passages, to the hushed drawing-room. He liked music but the piece she was playing had no melody for him and he doubted whether it had any melody for the other listeners, though they had begged Mary Jane to play something. Four young men, who had come from the refreshment-room to stand in the doorway at the sound of the piano, had gone away quietly in couples after a few minutes. The only persons who seemed to follow the music were Mary Jane herself, her hands racing along the key-board or lifted from it at the pauses like those of a priestess in momentary imprecation, and Aunt Kate standing at her elbow to turn the page.

Gabriel's eyes, irritated by the floor, which glittered with beeswax under the heavy chandelier, wandered to the wall above the piano. A picture of the balcony scene in *Romeo and Juliet* hung there and beside it was a picture of the two murdered princes in the Tower which Aunt Julia had worked in red, blue and brown wools when she was a girl. Probably in the school they had gone to as girls that kind of work had been taught for one year. His mother had worked for him as a birthday present a waistcoat of purple tabinet, with little foxes' heads upon it, lined with brown satin and having round mulberry buttons. It was strange that his mother had had no musical talent though Aunt Kate used to call her the brains carrier of the Morkan family. Both she and Julia had always seemed a little proud of their serious and matronly sister. Her photograph stood before the pierglass. She held an open book on her knees and was pointing out something in it to Constantine who, dressed in a man-o'-war suit, lay at her feet. It was she who had chosen the names of her sons for she was very sensible of the dignity of family life. Thanks to her, Constantine was now senior curate in Balbriggan and, thanks to her, Gabriel himself had taken his degree in the Royal University. A shadow passed over his face as he remembered her sullen opposition to his marriage. Some slighting phrases she had used still rankled in his memory; she had once spoken of Gretta as being country cute and that was not true of Gretta at all. It was Gretta who had nursed her during all her last long illness in their house at Monkstown.

He knew that Mary Jane must be near the end of her piece for she was playing again the opening melody with runs of scales after every bar and while he waited for the end the resentment died down in his heart. The piece ended with a trill of octaves in the treble and a final deep octave in the bass. Great applause greeted Mary Jane as, blushing and rolling up her music nervously, she escaped from the room. The most vigorous clapping came from the four young men in the doorway who had gone away to the refreshment-room at the beginning of the piece but had come back when the piano had stopped.

Lancers were arranged. Gabriel found himself partnered with Miss Ivors. She was a frank-mannered talkative young lady, with a freckled face and prominent brown eyes. She did not wear a low-cut bodice and the large brooch which was fixed in the front of her collar bore on it an Irish device and motto.

When they had taken their places she said abruptly:

"I have a crow to pluck with you."

"With me?" said Gabriel.

She nodded her head gravely.

"What is it?" asked Gabriel, smiling at her solemn manner.

"Who is G. C.?" answered Miss Ivors, turning her eyes upon him.

Gabriel coloured and was about to knit his brows, as if he did not understand, when she said bluntly:

"O, innocent Amy! I have found out that you write for *The Daily Express*. Now, aren't you ashamed of yourself?"

"Why should I be ashamed of myself?" asked Gabriel, blinking his eyes and trying to smile.

"Well, I'm ashamed of you," said Miss Ivors frankly. "To say you'd write for a paper like that. I didn't think you were a West Briton."

A look of perplexity appeared on Gabriel's face. It was true that he wrote a literary column every Wednesday in *The Daily Express*, for which he was paid fifteen shillings. But that did not make him a West Briton surely. The books he received for review were almost more welcome than the paltry cheque. He loved to feel the covers and turn over the pages of newly printed books. Nearly every day when his teaching in the college was ended he used to wander down the quays to the second-hand booksellers, to Hickey's on Bachelor's Walk, to Webb's or Massey's on Aston's Quay, or to O'Clohissey's in the by-street. He did not know how to meet her charge. He wanted to say that literature was above politics. But they were friends of many years' standing and their careers had been parallel, first at the University and then as teachers: he could not risk a grandiose phrase with her. He continued blinking his eyes and trying to smile and murmured lamely that he saw nothing political in writing reviews of books.

When their turn to cross had come he was still perplexed and inattentive. Miss Ivors promptly took his hand in a warm grasp and said in a soft friendly tone:

"Of course, I was only joking. Come, we cross now."

When they were together again she spoke of the University question and Gabriel felt more at ease. A friend of hers had shown her his review of Browning's poems. That was how she had found out the secret: but she liked the review immensely. Then she said suddenly:

"O, Mr. Conroy, will you come for an excursion to the Aran Isles this summer? We're going to stay there a whole month. It will be splendid out in the Atlantic. You ought to come. Mr. Clancy is coming, and Mr. Kilkelly and Kathleen Kearney. It would be splendid for Gretta too if she'd come. She's from Connacht, isn't she?"

"Her people are," said Gabriel shortly.

"But you will come, won't you?" said Miss Ivors, laying her warm hand eagerly on his arm.

"The fact is," said Gabriel, "I have just arranged to go — "

"Go where?" asked Miss Ivors.

"Well, you know, every year I go for a cycling tour with some fellows and so — "

"But where?" asked Miss Ivors.

"Well, we usually go to France or Belgium or perhaps Germany," said Gabriel awkwardly

"And why do you go to France and Belgium," said Miss Ivors, "instead of visiting your own land?"

"Well," said Gabriel, "it's partly to keep in touch with the languages and partly for a change."

"And haven't you your own language to keep in touch with — Irish?" asked Miss Ivors.

"Well," said Gabriel, "if it comes to that, you know, Irish is not my language."

Their neighbours had turned to listen to the cross-examination. Gabriel glanced right and left nervously and tried to keep his good humour under the ordeal which was making a blush invade his forehead.

"And haven't you your own land to visit," continued Miss Ivors, "that you know nothing of, your own people, and your own country?"

"O, to tell you the truth," retorted Gabriel suddenly, "I'm sick of my own country, sick of it!"

"Why?" asked Miss Ivors.

Gabriel did not answer for his retort had heated him.

"Why?" repeated Miss Ivors.

They had to go visiting together and, as he had not answered her, Miss Ivors said warmly:

"Of course, you've no answer."

Gabriel tried to cover his agitation by taking part in the dance with great energy. He avoided her eyes for he had seen a sour expression on her face. But when they met in the long chain he was surprised to feel his hand firmly pressed. She looked at him from under her brows for a moment quizzically until he smiled. Then, just as the chain was about to start again, she stood on tiptoe and whispered into his ear:

"West Briton!"

When the lancers were over Gabriel went away to a remote corner of the room where Freddy Malins' mother was sitting. She was a stout feeble old woman with white hair. Her voice had a catch in it like her son's and she stuttered slightly. She had been told that Freddy had come and that he was nearly all right. Gabriel asked her whether she had had a good crossing. She lived with her married daughter in Glasgow and came to Dublin on a visit once a year. She answered placidly that she had had a beautiful crossing and that the captain had been most attentive to her. She spoke also of the beautiful house her daughter kept in Glasgow, and of all the friends they had there. While her tongue rambled on Gabriel tried to banish from his mind all memory of the unpleasant incident with Miss Ivors. Of course the girl or woman, or whatever she was, was an enthusiast but there was a time for all things. Perhaps he ought not to have answered her like that. But she had no right to call him a West Briton before people, even in joke. She had tried to make him ridiculous before people, heckling him and staring at him with her rabbit's eyes.

He saw his wife making her way towards him through the waltzing couples. When she reached him she said into his ear:

"Gabriel, Aunt Kate wants to know won't you carve the goose as usual. Miss Daly will carve the ham and I'll do the pudding."

"All right," said Gabriel.

"She's sending in the younger ones first as soon as this waltz is over so that we'll have the table to ourselves."

"Were you dancing?" asked Gabriel.

"Of course I was. Didn't you see me? What row had you with Molly Ivors?"

"No row. Why? Did she say so?"

"Something like that. I'm trying to get that Mr. D'Arcy to sing. He's full of conceit, I think."

"There was no row," said Gabriel moodily, "only she wanted me to go for a trip to the west of Ireland and I said I wouldn't."

His wife clasped her hands excitedly and gave a little jump.

"O, do go, Gabriel," she cried. "I'd love to see Galway again."

"You can go if you like," said Gabriel coldly.

She looked at him for a moment, then turned to Mrs. Malins and said:

"There's a nice husband for you, Mrs. Malins."

While she was threading her way back across the room Mrs. Malins, without adverting to the interruption, went on to tell Gabriel what beautiful places there were in Scotland and beautiful scenery. Her son-in-law brought them every year to the lakes and they used to go fishing. Her son-in-law was a splendid fisher. One day he caught a beautiful big fish and the man in the hotel cooked it for their dinner.

Gabriel hardly heard what she said. Now that supper was coming near he began to think again about his speech and about the quotation. When he saw Freddy Malins coming across the room to visit his mother Gabriel left the chair free for him and retired into the embrasure of the window. The room had already cleared and from the back room came the clatter of plates and knives. Those who still remained in the drawing-room seemed tired of dancing and were conversing quietly in little groups. Gabriel's warm trembling fingers tapped the cold pane of the window. How cool it must be outside! How pleasant it would be to walk out alone, first along the river and then through the park! The snow would be lying on the branches of the trees and forming a bright cap on the top of the Wellington Monument. How much more pleasant it would be there than at the supper-table!

He ran over the headings of his speech: Irish hospitality, sad memories, the Three Graces, Paris, the quotation from Browning. He repeated to himself a phrase he had written in his review: "One feels that one is listening to a thought-tormented music." Miss Ivors had praised the review. Was she sincere? Had she really any life of her own behind all her propagandism? There had never been any ill-feeling between them until that night. It unnerved him to think that she would be at the supper-table, looking up at him while he spoke with her critical quizzing eyes. Perhaps she would not be sorry to see him fail in his speech. An idea came into his mind and gave him courage. He would say, alluding to Aunt Kate and Aunt Julia: "Ladies and Gentlemen, the generation which is now on the wane among us may have had its faults but for my part I think it had certain qualities of hospitality, of humour, of humanity, which the new and very serious and hypereducated generation that is growing up around us seems to me to lack." Very good: that was one for Miss Ivors. What did he care that his aunts were only two ignorant old women?

A murmur in the room attracted his attention. Mr. Browne was advancing from the door, gallantly escorting Aunt Julia, who leaned upon his arm, smiling and hanging her head. An irregular musketry of applause escorted her also as far as the piano and then, as Mary Jane seated herself on the stool, and Aunt Julia, no longer smiling, half turned so as to pitch her voice fairly into the room, gradually ceased. Gabriel recognised the prelude. It was that of an old song of Aunt Julia's — *Arrayed for the Bridal*. Her voice, strong and clear in tone, attacked with great spirit the runs which embellish the air and though she sang very rapidly she did not miss even the smallest of the grace notes. To follow the voice, without looking at the singer's face, was to feel and share the excitement of swift and secure flight. Gabriel applauded loudly with all the others at the close of the song and loud applause was borne in from the invisible supper-table. It sounded so genuine that a little colour struggled into Aunt Julia's face as she bent to replace in the music-stand the old leather-bound song-book that had her initials on the cover. Freddy Malins, who had listened with his head perched sideways to hear her better, was still applauding when everyone else had ceased and talking animatedly to his mother who nodded her head gravely and slowly in acquiescence. At last, when he could clap no more, he stood up suddenly and hurried across the room to Aunt Julia whose hand he seized and held in both his hands, shaking it when words failed him or the catch in his voice proved too much for him.

"I was just telling my mother," he said, "I never heard you sing so well, never. No, I never heard your voice so good as it is tonight. Now! Would you believe that now? That's the truth. Upon my word and honour that's the truth. I never heard your voice sound so fresh and so . . . so clear and fresh, never."

Aunt Julia smiled broadly and murmured something about compliments as she released her hand from his grasp. Mr. Browne extended his open hand towards her and said to those who were near him in the manner of a showman introducing a prodigy to an audience:

"Miss Julia Morkan, my latest discovery!"

He was laughing very heartily at this himself when Freddy Malins turned to him and said:

"Well, Browne, if you're serious you might make a worse discovery. All I can say is I never heard her sing half so well as long as I am coming here. And that's the honest truth."

"Neither did I," said Mr. Browne. "I think her voice has greatly improved."

Aunt Julia shrugged her shoulders and said with meek pride:

"Thirty years ago I hadn't a bad voice as voices go."

"I often told Julia," said Aunt Kate emphatically, "that she was simply thrown away in that choir. But she never would be said by me."

She turned as if to appeal to the good sense of the others against a refractory child while Aunt Julia gazed in front of her, a vague smile of reminiscence playing on her face.

"No," continued Aunt Kate, "she wouldn't be said or led by anyone, slaving there in that choir night and day, night and day. Six o'clock on Christmas morning! And all for what?"

"Well, isn't it for the honour of God, Aunt Kate?" asked Mary Jane, twisting round on her piano-stool and smiling.

Aunt Kate turned fiercely on her niece and said:

"I know all about the honour of God, Mary Jane, but I think it's not at all honorable for the pope to turn out the women out of the choirs that have slaved there all their lives and put little whipper-snappers of boys over their heads. I suppose it is for the good of the Church if the pope does it. But it's not just, Mary Jane, and it's not right."

She had worked herself into a passion and would have continued in defence of her sister for it was a sore subject with her but Mary Jane, seeing that all the dancers had come back, intervened pacifically:

"Now, Aunt Kate, you're giving scandal to Mr. Browne who is of the other persuasion."

Aunt Kate turned to Mr. Browne, who was grinning at this allusion to his religion, and said hastily:

"O, I don't question the pope's being right. I'm only a stupid old woman and I wouldn't presume to do such a thing. But there's such a thing as common everyday politeness and gratitude. And if I were in Julia's place I'd tell that Father Healey straight up to his face . . ."

"And besides, Aunt Kate," said Mary Jane, "we really are all hungry and when we are hungry we all very quarrelsome."

"And when we are thirsty we are also quarrelsome," added Mr. Browne.

"So that we had better go to supper," said Mary Jane, "and finish the discussion afterwards."

On the landing outside the drawing-room Gabriel found his wife and Mary Jane trying to persuade Miss Ivors to stay for supper. But Miss Ivors, who had put on her hat and was buttoning her cloak, would not stay. She did not feel in the least hungry and she had already overstayed her time.

"But only for ten minutes, Molly," said Mrs. Conroy. "That won't delay you."

"To take a pick itself," said Mary Jane, "after all your dancing."

"I really couldn't," said Miss Ivors.

"I am afraid you didn't enjoy yourself at all," said Mary Jane hopelessly.

"Ever so much, I assure you," said Miss Ivors, "but you really must let me run off now."

"But how can you get home?" asked Mrs. Conroy.

"O, it's only two steps up the quay."

Gabriel hesitated a moment and said:

"If you allow me, Miss Ivors, I'll see you home if you are really obliged to go."

But Miss Ivors broke away from them.

"I won't hear of it," she cried. "For goodness' sake go in to your suppers and don't mind me. I'm quite well able to take care of myself."

"Well, you're the comical girl, Molly," said Mrs. Conroy frankly.

"*Beannacht libh,*" cried Miss Ivors, with a laugh, as she ran down the staircase.

Mary Jane gazed after her, a moody puzzled expression on her face, while Mrs. Conroy leaned over the banisters to listen for the hall-door. Gabriel asked himself was he the cause of her abrupt departure. But she did not seem to be in ill humour: she had gone away laughing. He stared blankly down the staircase.

At the moment Aunt Kate came toddling out of the supper-room, almost wringing her hands in despair.

"Where is Gabriel?" she cried. "Where on earth is Gabriel? There's everyone waiting in there, stage to let, and nobody to carve the goose!"

"Here I am, Aunt Kate!" cried Gabriel, with sudden animation, "ready to carve a flock of geese, if necessary."

A fat brown goose lay at one end of the table and at the other end, on a bed of creased paper strewn with springs of parsley, lay a great ham, stripped of its outer skin and peppered over with crust crumbs, a neat paper frill round its shin and beside this was a round of spiced beef. Between these rival ends ran parallel lines of side-dishes: two little minsters of jelly, red and yellow; a shallow dish full of blocks of blancmange and red jam, a large green leaf-shaped dish with a stalk-shaped handle, on which lay bunches of purple raisins and peeled almonds, a companion dish on which lay a solid rectangle of Smyrna figs, a dish of custard topped with grated nutmeg, a small bowl full of chocolates and sweets wrapped in gold and silver papers and a glass vase in which stood some tall celery stalks. In the centre of the table there stood, as sentries to a fruit-stand which upheld a pyramid of oranges and American apples, two squat old-fashioned decanters of cut glass, one containing port and the other dark sherry. On the closed square piano a pudding in a huge yellow dish lay in waiting and behind it were three squads of bottles of stout and ale and minerals, drawn up according to the colours of their uniforms, the first two black, with brown and red labels, the third and smallest squad white, with transverse green sashes.

Gabriel took his seat boldly at the head of the table and, having looked to the edge of the carver, plunged his fork firmly into the goose. He felt quite at ease now for he was an expert carver and liked nothing better than to find himself at the head of a well-laden table.

"Miss Furlong, what shall I send you?" he asked. "A wing or a slice of the breast?"

"Just a small slice of the breast."

"Miss Higgins, what for you?"

"O, anything at all, Mr. Conroy."

While Gabriel and Miss Daly exchanged plates of goose and plates of ham and spiced beef Lily went from guest to guest with a dish of hot floury potatoes wrapped in a white napkin. This was Mary Jane's idea and she had also suggested apple sauce for the goose but Aunt Kate had said that plain roast goose without any apple sauce had always been good enough for her and she hoped she might never eat worse. Mary Jane waited on her pupils and saw that they got the best slices and Aunt Kate and Aunt Julia opened and carried across from the piano bottles of stout and ale for the gentlemen and bottles of minerals for the ladies. There was a great deal of confusion and laughter and noise, the noise of orders and counter-orders, of knives and forks, of corks and glass-stoppers. Gabriel began to carve second helpings as soon as he had finished the first round without serving himself. Everyone protested loudly so that he compromised by taking a long draught of stout for he had found the carving hot work. Mary Jane settled down quietly to her supper but Aunt Kate and Aunt Julia were still toddling round the table, walking on each other's heels, getting in each other's way and giving each other unheeded orders. Mr. Browne begged of them to sit down and eat their suppers and so did Gabriel but they said there was time enough, so that, at last, Freddy Malins stood up and, capturing Aunt Kate, plumped her down on her chair amid general laughter.

When everyone had been well served Gabriel said, smiling:

"Now, if anyone wants a little more of what vulgar people call stuffing let him or her speak."

A chorus of voices invited him to begin his own supper and Lily came forward with three potatoes which she had reserved for him.

"Very well," said Gabriel amiably, as he took another preparatory draught, "kindly forget my existence, ladies and gentlemen, for a few minutes."

He set to his supper and took no part in the conversation with which the table covered Lily's removal of the plates. The subject of talk was the opera company which was then at the Theatre Royal. Mr. Bartell D'Arcy, the tenor, a dark-complexioned young man with a smart moustache, praised very highly the leading contralto of the company but Miss Furlong thought she had a rather vulgar style of production. Freddy Malins said there was a Negro chieftain singing in the second part of the Gaiety pantomime who had one of the finest tenor voices he had ever heard.

"Have you heard him?" he asked Mr. Bartell D'Arcy across the table.

"No," answered Mr. Bartell D'Arcy carelessly.

"Because," Freddy Malins explained, "now I'd be curious to hear your opinion of him. I think he has a grand voice."

"It takes Teddy to find out the really good things," said Mr. Browne familiarly to the table.

"And why couldn't he have a voice too?" asked Freddy Malins sharply. "Is it because he's only a black?"

Nobody answered this question and Mary Jane led the table back to the legitimate opera. One of her pupils had given her a pass for *Mignon.* Of course it was very fine, she said, but it made her think of poor Georgina Burns. Mr. Browne could go back farther still, to the old Italian companies that used to come to Dublin — Tietjens, Ilma de Murzka, Campanini, the great Trebelli, Giuglini, Ravelli, Aramburo. Those were the days, he said, when there was something like singing to be heard in Dublin. He told too of how the top gallery of the old Royal used to be packed night after night, of how one night an Italian tenor had sung five encores to *Let me like a Soldier fall,* introducing a high C every time, and of how the gallery boys would sometimes in their enthusiasm unyoke the horses from the carriage of some great *prima donna* and pull her themselves through the streets to her hotel. Why did they never play the grand old operas now, he asked, *Dinorah, Lucrezia Borgia?* Because they could not get the voices to sing them: that was why.

"O, well," said Mr. Bartell D'Arcy, "I presume there are as good singers today as there were then."

"Where are they?" asked Mr. Browne defiantly.

"In London, Paris, Milan," said Mr. Bartell D'Arcy warmly. "I suppose Caruso, for example, is quite as good, if not better than any of the men you have mentioned."

"Maybe so," said Mr. Browne. "But I may tell you I doubt it strongly."

"O, I'd give anything to hear Caruso sing," said Mary Jane.

"For me," said Aunt Kate, who had been picking a bone, "there was only one tenor. To please me, I mean. But I suppose none of you ever heard of him."

"Who was he, Miss Morkan?" asked Mr. Bartell D'Arcy politely.

"His name," said Aunt Kate, "was Parkinson. I heard him when he was in his prime and I think he had then the purest tenor voice that was ever put into a man's throat."

"Strange," said Mr. Bartell D'Arcy. "I never heard of him."

"Yes, yes, Miss Morkan is right," said Mr. Browne. "I remember hearing of old Parkinson but he's far back for me."

"A beautiful, pure, sweet, mellow English tenor," said Aunt Kate with enthusiasm.

Gabriel having finished, the huge pudding was transferred to the table. The clatter of forks and spoons began again. Gabriel's wife served out spoonfuls of the pudding and passed the plates down the table. Midway down they were held up by Mary Jane, who replenished them with raspberry or orange jelly or with blancmange and jam. The pudding was of Aunt Julia's making and she received praises for it from all quarters. She herself said that it was not quite brown enough.

"Well, I hope, Miss Morkan," said Mr. Browne, "that I'm brown enough for you because, you know, I'm all brown."

All the gentlemen, except Gabriel, ate some of the pudding out of compliment to Aunt Julia. As Gabriel never ate sweets the celery had been left for him. Freddy Malins also took a stalk of celery and ate it with his pudding. He had been told that celery was a capital thing for the blood and he was just then under doctor's care. Mrs. Malins, who had been silent all through the supper, said that her son was going down to Mount Melleray in a week or so. The table then spoke of Mount Mellary, how bracing the air was down there, how hospitable the monks were and how they never asked for a penny-piece from their guests.

"And do you mean to say," asked Mr. Browne incredulously, "that a chap can go down there and put up there as if it were a hotel and live on the fat of the land and then come away without paying anything?"

"O, most people give some donation to the monastery when they leave," said Mary Jane.

"I wish we had an institution like that in our Church," said Mr. Browne candidly.

He was astonished to hear that the monks never spoke, got up at two in the morning and slept in their coffins. He asked what they did it for.

"That's the rule of the order," said Aunt Kate firmly.

"Yes, but why?" asked Mr. Browne.

Aunt Kate repeated that it was the rule, that was all. Mr. Browne still seemed not to understand. Freddy Malins explained to him, as best he could, that the monks were trying to make up for the sins committed by all the sinners in the outside world. The explanation was not very clear for Mr. Browne grinned and said:

"I like the idea very much but wouldn't a comfortable spring bed do them as well as a coffin?"

"The coffin," said Mary Jane, "is to remind them of their last end."

As the subject had grown lugubrious it was buried in a silence of the table during which Mrs. Malins could be heard saying to her neighbour in an indistinct undertone:

"They are very good men, the monks, very pious men."

The raisins and almonds and figs and apples and oranges and chocolates and sweets were now passed about the table and Aunt Julia invited all the guests to have either port or sherry. At first Mr. Bartell D'Arcy refused to take either but one of his neighbours nudged him and whispered something to him upon which he allowed his glass to be filled. Gradually as the last glasses were being filled the conversation ceased. A pause followed, broken only by the noise of the wine and by unsettlings of chairs. The Misses Morkan, all three, looked down at the tablecloth. Someone coughed once or twice and then a few gentlemen patted the table gently as a signal for silence. The silence came and Gabriel pushed back his chair and stood up.

The patting at once grew louder in encouragement and then ceased altogether. Gabriel leaned his ten trembling fingers on the tablecloth and smiled nervously at the company. Meeting a row of upturned faces he raised his eyes to the chandelier. The piano was playing a waltz tune and he could hear the skirts sweeping against the drawing-room door. People, perhaps, were standing in the snow on the quay outside, gazing up at the lighted windows and listening to the waltz music. The air was pure there. In the distance lay the park where the trees were weighted with snow. The Wellington Monument wore a gleaming cap of snow that flashed westward over the white field of Fifteen Acres.

He began:

"Ladies and Gentlemen,

"It has fallen to my lot this evening, as in years past, to perform a very pleasing task but a task for which I am afraid my poor powers as a speaker are all too inadequate."

"No, no!" said Mr. Browne.

"But, however that may be, I can only ask you tonight to take the will for the deed and to lend me your attention for a few moments while I endeavour to express to you in words what my feelings are on this occasion.

"Ladies and Gentlemen, it is not the first time that we have gathered together under this hospitable roof, around this hospitable board. It is not the first time that we have been the recipients—or perhaps, I had better say, the victims—of the hospitality of certain good ladies."

He made a circle in the air with his arm and paused. Everyone laughed or smiled at Aunt Kate and Aunt Julia and Mary Jane who all turned crimson with pleasure. Gabriel went on more boldly:

"I feel more strongly with every recurring year that our country has no tradition which does it so much honour and which it should guard so jealously as that of its hospitality. It is a tradition that is unique as far as my experience goes (and I have visited not a few places abroad) among the modern nations. Some would say, perhaps, that with us it is rather a failing than anything to be boasted of. But granted even that, it is, to my mind, a princely failing, and one that I trust will long be cultivated among us. Of one thing, at least, I am sure. As long as this one roof shelters the good ladies aforesaid—and I wish from my heart it may do so for many and many a long year to come—the tradition of genuine warm-hearted courteous Irish hospitality, which our forefathers have handed down to us and which we in turn must hand down to our descendants, is still alive among us."

A hearty murmur of assent ran round the table. It shot through Gabriel's mind that Miss Ivors was not there and that she had gone away discourteously: and he said with confidence in himself:

"Ladies and Gentlemen,

"A new generation is growing up in our midst, a generation actuated by new ideas and new principles. It is serious and enthusiastic for these new ideas and its enthusiasm, even when it is misdirected, is, I believe, in the main sincere. But we are living in a sceptical and, if I may use the phrase, a thought-tormented age: and sometimes I fear that this new generation, educated or hypereducated as it is, will lack those qualities of humanity, of hospitality, of kindly humour which belonged to an older day. Listening tonight to the names of all those great singers of the past it seemed to me, I must confess, that we were living in a less spacious age. Those days might, without exaggeration, be called spacious days: and if they are gone beyond recall let us hope, at least, that in gatherings such as this we shall still speak of them with pride and affection, still cherish in our hearts the memory of those dead and gone great ones whose fame the world will not willingly let die."

"Hear, hear!" said Mr. Browne loudly.

"But yet," continued Gabriel, his voice falling into a softer inflection, "there are always in gatherings such as this sadder thoughts that will recur to our minds: thoughts of the past, or youth, of changes, of absent faces that we miss here tonight. Our path through life is strewn with many such sad memories: and were we to brood upon them always we could not find the heart to go on bravely with our work among the living. We have all of us living duties and living affections which claim, and rightly claim, our strenuous endeavours.

"Therefore, I will not linger on the past. I will not let any gloomy moralising intrude upon us here tonight. Here we are gathered together for a brief moment from the bustle and rush of our everyday routine. We are met here as friends, in the spirit of good-fellowship, as colleagues, also to a certain extent, in the true spirit of *camaraderie,* and as the guests of—what shall I call them?—the Three Graces of the Dublin musical world."

The table burst into applause and laughter at this allusion. Aunt Julia vainly asked each of her neighbours in turn to tell her what Gabriel had said.

"He says we are the Three Graces, Aunt Julia," said Mary Jane.

Aunt Julia did not understand but she looked up, smiling, at Gabriel, who continued in the same vein:

"Ladies and Gentlemen,

"I will not attempt to play tonight the part that Paris played on another occasion. I will not attempt to choose between them. The task would be an invidious one and one beyond my poor powers. For when I view them in turn, whether it be our chief hostess herself, whose good heart, whose too good heart, has become a byword with all who know her, or her sister, who seems to be gifted with perennial youth and whose singing must have been a surprise and a revelation to us all tonight, or, last but not least, when I consider our youngest hostess, talented, cheerful, hard-working and the best of nieces, I confess, Ladies and Gentlemen, that I do not know to which of them I should award the prize."

Gabriel glanced down at his aunts and, seeing the large smile on Aunt Julia's face and the tears which had risen to Aunt Kate's eyes, hastened to his close. He raised his glass of port gallantly, while every member of the company fingered a glass expectantly, and said loudly:

"Let us toast them all three together. Let us drink to their health, wealth, long life, happiness and prosperity and may they long continue to hold the proud and self-won position which they hold in their profession and the position of honour and affection which they hold in our hearts."

All the guests stood up, glass in hand, and turning towards the three seated ladies, sang in unison, with Mr. Browne as leader:

> For they are jolly gay fellows,
> For they are jolly gay fellows,
> For they are jolly gay fellows,
> Which nobody can deny.

Aunt Kate was making frank use of her handkerchief and even Aunt Julia seemed moved. Freddy Malins beat time with his pudding-fork and the singers turned towards one another, as if in melodious conference, while they sang with emphasis:

> Unless he tells a lie
> Unless he tells a lie,

Then, turning once more towards their hostesses, they sang:

> For they are jolly gay fellows,
> For they are jolly gay fellows,
> For they are jolly gay fellows,
> Which nobody can deny.

The acclamation which followed was taken up beyond the door of the supper-room by many of the other guests and renewed time after time, Freddy Malins acting as officer with his fork on high.

The piercing morning air came into the hall where they were standing so that Aunt Kate said:

"Close the door, somebody. Mrs. Malins will get her death of cold."

"Browne is out there, Aunt Kate," said Mary Jane.

"Browne is everywhere," said Aunt Kate, lowering her voice.

Mary Jane laughed at her tone.

"Really," she said archly, "he is very attentive."

"He has been laid on here like the gas," said Aunt Kate in the same tone, "all during the Christmas."

She laughed herself this time good-humouredly and then added quickly:

"But tell him to come in, Mary Jane, and close the door. I hope to goodness he didn't hear me."

At that moment the hall-door was opened and Mr. Browne came in from the doorstep, laughing as if his heart would break. He was dressed in a long green overcoat with mock astrakhan cuffs and collar and wore on his head an oval fur cap. He pointed down the snow-covered quay from where the sound of shrill prolonged whistling was borne in.

"Teddy will have all the cabs in Dublin out," he said.

Gabriel advanced from the little pantry behind the office, struggling into his overcoat and, looking round the hall, said:

"Gretta not down yet?"

"She's getting on her things, Gabriel," said Aunt Kate.

"Who's playing up there?" asked Gabriel.

"Nobody. They're all gone."

"O no, Aunt Kate," said Mary Jane. "Bartell D'Arcy and Miss O'Callaghan aren't gone yet."

"Someone is fooling at the piano anyhow," said Gabriel.

Mary Jane glanced at Gabriel and Mr. Browne and said with a shiver:

"It makes me feel cold to look at you two gentlemen muffled up like that. I wouldn't like to face your journey home at this hour."

"I'd like nothing better this minute," said Mr. Browne stoutly, "than a rattling fine walk in the country or a fast drive with a good spanking goer between the shafts."

"We used to have a very good horse and trap at home," said Aunt Julia sadly.

"The never-to-be-forgotten Johnny," said Mary Jane, laughing.

Aunt Kate and Gabriel laughed too.

"Why, what was wonderful about Johnny?" asked Mr. Browne.

"The late lamented Patrick Morkan, our grandfather, that is," explained Gabriel, "commonly known in his later years as the old gentleman, was a glue-boiler."

"O, now, Gabriel," said Aunt Kate, laughing, "he had a starch mill."

"Well, glue or starch," said Gabriel, "the old gentleman had a horse by the name of Johnny. And Johnny used to work in the old gentleman's mill, walking round and round in order to drive the mill. That was all very well; but now comes the tragic part about Johnny. One fine day the old gentleman thought he'd like to drive out with the quality to a military review in the park."

"The Lord have mercy on his soul," said Aunt Kate compassionately.

"Amen," said Gabriel. "So the old gentleman, as I said, harnessed Johnny and put on his very best tall hat and his very best stock collar and drove out in grand style from his ancestral mansion somewhere near Back Lane, I think."

Everyone laughed, even Mrs. Malins, at Gabriel's manner and Aunt Kate said:

"O, now, Gabriel, he didn't live in Back Lane, really. Only the mill was there."

"Out from the mansion of his forefathers," continued Gabriel, "he drove with Johnny. And everything went on beautifully until Johnny came in sight of King Billy's statue: and whether he fell in love with the horse King Billy sits on or whether he thought he was back again in the mill, anyhow he began to walk round the statue."

Gabriel paced in a circle round the hall in his goloshes amid the laughter of the others.

"Round and round he went," said Gabriel, "and the old gentleman, who was a very pompous old gentleman, was highly indignant. 'Go on, sir! What do you mean, sir? Johnny! Johnny! Most extraordinary conduct! Can't understand the horse!' "

The peal of laughter which followed Gabriel's imitation of the incident was interrupted by a resounding knock at the hall door. Mary Jane ran to open it and let in Freddy Malins. Freddy Malins, with his hat well back on his head and his shoulders humped with cold, was puffing and steaming after his exertions.

"I could only get one cab," he said.

"O, we'll find another along the quay," said Gabriel.

"Yes," said Aunt Kate. "Better not keep Mrs. Malins standing in the draught."

Mrs. Malins was helped down the front steps by her son and Mr. Browne and, after many manoeuvres, hoisted into the cab. Freddy Malins clambered in after her and spent a long time settling her on the seat, Mr. Browne helping him with advice. At last she was settled comfortably and Freddy Malins invited Mr. Browne into the cab. There was a good deal of confused talk, and then Mr. Browne got into the cab. The cabman settled his rug over his knees, and bent down for the address. The confusion grew greater and the cabman was directed differently by Freddy Malins and Mr. Browne, each of whom had his head out through a window of the cab. The difficulty was to know where to drop Mr. Browne along the route, and Aunt Kate, Aunt Julia and Mary Jane helped the discussion from the doorstep with cross-directions and contradictions and abundance of laughter. As for Freddy Malins he was speechless with laughter. He popped his head in and out of the window every moment to the great danger of his hat, and told his mother how the discussion was progressing, till at last Mr. Browne shouted to the bewildered cabman above the din of everybody's laughter:

"Do you know Trinity College?"

"Yes, sir," said the cabman.

"Well, drive bang up against Trinity College gates," said Mr. Browne, "and then we'll tell you where to go. You understand now?"

"Yes, sir," said the cabman.

"Make like a bird for Trinity College."

"Right, sir," said the cabman.

The horse was whipped up and the cab rattled off along the quay amid a chorus of laughter and adieus.

Gabriel had not gone to the door with the others. He was in a dark part of the hall gazing up the staircase. A woman was standing near the top of the first flight, in the shadow also. He could not see her face but he could see the terra-cotta and salmon-pink panels of her skirt which the shadow made appear black and white. It was his wife. She was leaning on the banisters, listening to something. Gabriel was surprised at her stillness and strained his ear to listen also. But he could hear little save the noise of laughter and dispute on the front steps, a few chords struck on the piano and a few notes of a man's voice singing.

He stood still in the gloom of the hall, trying to catch the air that the voice was singing and gazing up at his wife. There was grace and mystery in her attitude as if she were a symbol of something. He asked himself what is a woman standing on the stairs in the shadow, listening to distant music, a symbol of. If he were a painter he would paint her in that attitude. Her blue felt hat would show off the bronze of her hair against the darkness and the dark panels of her skirt would show off the light ones. *Distant Music* he would call the picture if he were a painter.

The hall-door was closed; and Aunt Kate, Aunt Julia and Mary Jane came down the hall, still laughing.

"Well, isn't Freddy terrible?" said Mary Jane. "He's really terrible."

Gabriel said nothing but pointed up the stairs towards where his wife was standing. Now that the hall-door was closed the voice and the piano could be heard more clearly. Gabriel held up his hand for them to be silent. The song seemed to be in the old Irish tonality and the singer seemed uncertain both of his words and of his voice. The voice, made plaintive by distance and by the singer's hoarseness, faintly illuminated the cadence of the air with words expressing grief:

> O, the rain falls on my heavy locks
> And the dew wets my skin,
> My babe lies cold . . .

"O," exclaimed Mary Jane. "It's Bartell D'Arcy singing and he wouldn't sing all the night. O, I'll get him to sing a song before he goes."

"O, do, Mary Jane," said Aunt Kate.

Mary Jane brushed past the others and ran to the staircase, but before she reached it the singing stopped and the piano was closed abruptly.

"O, what a pity!" she cried. "Is he coming down, Gretta?"

Gabriel heard his wife answer yes and saw her come down towards them. A few steps behind her were Mr. Bartell D'Arcy and Miss O'Callaghan.

"O, Mr. D'Arcy," cried Mary Jane, "it's downright mean of you to break off like that when we were all in raptures listening to you."

"I have been at him all the evening," said Miss O'Callaghan, "and Mrs. Conroy, too, and he told us he had a dreadful cold and couldn't sing."

"O, Mr. D'Arcy," said Aunt Kate, "now that was a great fib to tell."

"Can't you see that I'm as hoarse as a crow?" said Mr. D'Arcy roughly.

He went into the pantry hastily and put on his overcoat. The others, taken aback by his rude speech, could find nothing to say. Aunt Kate wrinkled her brows and made signs to the others to drop the subject. Mr. D'Arcy stood swathing his neck carefully and frowning.

"It's the weather," said Aunt Julia, after a pause.

"Yes, everybody has colds," said Aunt Kate readily, "everybody."

"They say," said Mary Jane, "we haven't had snow like it for thirty years; and I read this morning in the newspapers that the snow is general all over Ireland."

"I love the look of snow," said Aunt Julia sadly.

"So do I," said Miss O'Callaghan. "I think Christmas is never really Christmas unless we have the snow on the ground."

"But poor Mr. D'Arcy doesn't like the snow," said Aunt Kate, smiling.

Mr. D'Arcy came from the pantry, fully swathed and buttoned, and in a repentant tone told them the history of his cold. Everyone gave him advice and said it was a great pity and urged him to be very careful of his throat in the night air. Gabriel watched his wife, who did not join in the conversation. She was standing right under the dusty fanlight and the flame of the gas lit up the rich bronze of her hair, which he had seen her drying at the fire a few days before. She was in the same attitude and seemed unaware of the talk about her. At last she turned towards them and Gabriel saw that there was colour on her cheeks and that her eyes were shining. A sudden tide of joy went leaping out of his heart.

"Mr. D'Arcy," she said, "what is the name of that song you were singing?"

"It's called *The Lass of Aughrim*," said Mr. D'Arcy, "but I couldn't remember it properly. Why? Do you know it?"

"*The Lass of Aughrim*," she repeated. "I couldn't think of the name."

"It's a very nice air," said Mary Jane. "I'm sorry you were not in voice tonight."

"Now, Mary Jane," said Aunt Kate, "don't annoy Mr. D'Arcy. I won't have him annoyed."

Seeing that all were ready to start she shepherded them to the door, where good-night was said:

"Well, good-night, Aunt Kate, and thanks for the pleasant evening."

"Good-night, Gabriel. Good-night, Gretta!"

"Good-night, Aunt Kate, and thanks ever so much. Good-night, Aunt Julia."

"O, good-night, Gretta. I didn't see you."

"Good-night, Mr. D'Arcy. Good-night, Miss O'Callaghan."

"Good-night, Miss Morkan."

"Good-night, again."

"Good-night, all. Safe home."

"Good-night. Good night."

The morning was still dark. A dull, yellow light brooded over the houses and the river; and the sky seemed to be descending. It was slushy underfoot; and only streaks and patches of snow lay on the roofs, on the parapets of the quay and on the area railings. The lamps were still burning redly in the murky air and, across the river, the palace of the Four Courts stood out menacingly against the heavy sky.

She was walking on before him with Mr. Bartell D'Arcy, her shoes in a brown parcel tucked under one arm and her hands holding her skirt up from the slush. She had no longer any grace of attitude, but Gabriel's eyes were still bright with happiness. The blood went bounding along his veins; and the thoughts went rioting through his brain, proud, joyful, tender, valorous.

She was walking on before him so lightly and so erect that he longed to run after her noiselessly, catch her by the shoulders and say something foolish and affectionate into her ear. She seemed to him so frail that he longed to defend her against something and then to be alone with her. Moments of their secret life together burst like stars upon his memory. A heliotrope envelope was lying beside his breakfast cup and he was caressing it with his hand. Birds were twittering in the ivy and the sunny web of the curtain was shimmering along the floor: he could not eat for happiness. They were standing on the crowded platform and he was placing a ticket inside the warm palm of her glove. He was standing with her in the cold, looking in through a grated window at a man making bottles in a roaring furnace. It was very cold. Her face, fragrant in the cold air, was quite close to his; and suddenly he called out to the man at the furnace:

"Is the fire hot, sir?"

But the man could not hear with the noise of the furnace. It was just as well. He might have answered rudely.

A wave of yet more tender joy escaped from his heart and went coursing in warm flood along his arteries. Like the tender fire of stars moments of their life together, that no one knew of or would ever know of, broke upon and illumined his memory. He longed to recall to her those moments, to make her forget the years of their dull existence together and remember only their moments of ecstasy. For the years, he felt, had not quenched his soul or hers. Their children, his writing, her household cares had not quenched all their souls' tender fire. In one letter that he had written to her then he had said:

"Why is it that words like these seem to me so dull and cold? Is it because there is no word tender enough to be your name?"

Like distant music these words that he had written years before were borne towards him from the past. He longed to be alone with her. When the others had gone away, when he and she were in the room in the hotel, then they would be alone together. He would call her softly:

"Gretta!"

Perhaps she would not hear at once: she would be undressing. Then something in his voice would strike her. She would turn and look at him. . . .

At the corner of Winetavern Street they met a cab. He was glad of its rattling noise as it saved him from conversation. She was looking out of the window and seemed tired. The others spoke only a few words, pointing out some building or street. The horse galloped along wearily under the murky morning sky, dragging his old rattling box after his heels, and Gabriel was again in a cab with her, galloping to catch the boat, galloping to their honeymoon.

As the cab drove across O'Connell Bridge Miss O'Callaghan said:

"They say you never cross O'Connell Bridge without seeing a white horse."

"I see a white man this time," said Gabriel.

"Where?" asked Mr. Bartell D'Arcy.

Gabriel pointed to the statue, on which lay patches of snow. Then he nodded familiarly to it and waved his hand.

"Good-night, Dan," he said gaily.

When the cab drew up before the hotel, Gabriel jumped out and, in spite of Mr. Bartell D'Arcy's protest, paid the driver. He gave the man a shilling over his fare. The man saluted and said:

"A prosperous New Year to you, sir."

"The same to you," said Gabriel cordially.

She leaned for a moment on his arm in getting out of the cab and while standing at the curbstone, bidding the others good-night. She leaned lightly on his arm, as lightly as when she had danced with him a few hours before. He had felt proud and happy then, happy that she was his, proud of her grace and wifely carriage. But now, after the kindling again of so many memories, the first touch of her body, musical and strange and perfumed, sent through him a keen pang of lust. Under cover of her silence he pressed her arm closely to his side; and, as they stood at the hotel door, he felt that they had escaped from their lives and duties, escaped from home and friends and run away together with wild and radiant hearts to a new adventure.

An old man was dozing in a great hooded chair in the hall. He lit a candle in the office and went before them to the stairs. They followed him in silence, their feet falling in soft thuds on the thickly carpeted stairs. She mounted the stairs behind the porter, her head bowed in the ascent, her frail shoulders curved as with a burden, her skirt girt tightly about her. He could have flung his arms about her hips and held her still, for his arms were trembling with desire to seize her and only the stress of his nails against the palms of his hands held the wild impulse of his body in check. The porter halted on the stairs to settle his guttering candle. They halted, too, on the steps below him. In the silence Gabriel could hear the falling of the molten wax into the tray and the thumping of his own heart against his ribs.

The porter led them along a corridor and opened a door. Then he set his unstable candle down on a toilet-table and asked at what hour they were to be called in the morning.

"Eight," said Gabriel.

The porter pointed to the tap of the electric-light and began a muttered apology, but Gabriel cut him short.

"We don't want any light. We have light enough from the street. And I say," he added, pointing to the candle, "you might remove that handsome article, like a good man."

The porter took up his candle again, but slowly, for he was surprised by such a novel idea. Then he mumbled good-night and went out. Gabriel shot the lock to.

A ghastly light from the street lamp lay in a long shaft from one window to the door. Gabriel threw his overcoat and hat on a couch and crossed the room towards the window. He looked down into the street in order that his emotion might calm a little. Then he turned and leaned against a chest of drawers with his back to the light. She had taken off her hat and cloak and was standing before a large swinging mirror, unhooking her waist. Gabriel paused for a few moments, watching her, and then said:

"Gretta!"

She turned away from the mirror slowly and walked along the shaft of light towards him. Her face looked so serious and weary that the words would not pass Gabriel's lips. No, it was not the moment yet.

"You look tired," he said.

"I am a little," she answered.

"You don't feel ill or weak?"

"No, tired: that's all."

She went on to the window and stood there, looking out. Gabriel waited again and then, fearing that diffidence was about to conquer him, he said abruptly:

"By the way, Gretta!"

"What is it?"

"You know that poor fellow Malins?" he said quickly.

"Yes. What about him?"

"Well, poor fellow, he's a decent sort of chap, after all," continued Gabriel in a false voice. "He gave me back that sovereign I lent him, and I didn't expect it, really. It's a pity he wouldn't keep away from that Browne, because he's not a bad fellow, really."

He was trembling now with annoyance. Why did she seem so abstracted? He did not know how he could begin. Was she annoyed, too, about something? If she would only turn to him or come to him of her own accord! To take her as she was would be brutal. No, he must see some ardour in her eyes first. He longed to be master of her strange mood.

"When did you lend him the pound?" she asked, after a pause.

Gabriel strove to restrain himself from breaking out into brutal language about the sottish Malins and his pound. He longed to cry to her from his soul, to crush her body against his, to overmaster her. But he said:

"O, at Christmas, when he opened that little Christmas-card shop in Henry Street."

He was in such a fever of rage and desire that he did not hear her come from the window. She stood before him for an instant, looking at him strangely. Then, suddenly raising herself on tiptoe and resting her hands lightly on his shoulders, she kissed him.

"You are a very generous person, Gabriel," she said.

Gabriel, trembling with delight on her sudden kiss and at the quaintness of her phrase, put his hands on her hair and began smoothing it back, scarcely touching it with his fingers. The washing had made it fine and brilliant. His heart was brimming over with happiness. Just when he was wishing for it she had come to him of her own accord. Perhaps her thoughts had been running with his. Perhaps she had felt the impetuous desire that was in him, and then the yielding mood had come upon her. Now that she had fallen to him so easily, he wondered why he had been so diffident.

He stood, holding her head between his hands. Then, slipping one arm swiftly about her body and drawing her towards him, he said softly:

"Gretta, dear, what are you thinking about?"

She did not answer nor yield wholly to his arm. He said again, softly:

"Tell me what it is, Gretta. I think I know what is the matter. Do I know?"

She did not answer at once. Then she said in an outburst of tears:

"O, I am thinking about that song, *The Lass of Aughrim*."

She broke loose from him and ran to the bed and, throwing her arms across the bed-rail, hid her face. Gabriel stood stock-still for a moment in astonishment and then followed her. As he passed in the way of the cheval-glass he caught sight of himself in full length, his broad, well-fitted shirt-front, the face whose expression always puzzled him when he saw it in a mirror, and his glimmering gilt-rimmed eyeglasses. He halted a few paces from her and said:

"What about the song? Why does that make you cry?"

She raised her head from her arms and dried her eyes with the back of her hand like a child. A kinder note than he had intended went into his voice.

"Why, Gretta?" he asked.

"I am thinking about a person long ago who used to sing that song."

"And who was the person long ago?" asked Gabriel, smiling.

"It was a person I used to know in Galway when I was living with my grandmother," she said.

The smile passed away from Gabriel's face. A dull anger began to gather again at the back of his mind and the dull fires of his lust began to glow angrily in his veins.

"Someone you were in love with?" he asked ironically.

"It was a young boy I used to know," she answered, "named Michael Furey. He used to sing that song, *The Lass of Aughrim*. He was very delicate."

Gabriel was silent. He did not wish her to think that he was interested in this delicate boy.

"I can see him so plainly," she said, after a moment. "Such eyes as he had: big, dark eyes! And such an expression in them—an expression!"

"O, then, you are in love with him?" said Gabriel.

"I used to go out walking with him," she said, "when I was in Galway."

A thought flew across Gabriel's mind.

"Perhaps that was why you wanted to go to Galway with that Ivors girl?" he said coldly.

She looked at him and asked in surprise:

"What for?"

Her eyes made Gabriel feel awkward. He shrugged his shoulders and said:

"How do I know? To see him, perhaps."

She looked away from him along the shaft of light towards the window in silence.

"He is dead," she said at length. "He died when he was only seventeen. Isn't it a terrible thing to die so young as that?"

"What was he?" asked Gabriel, still ironically.

"He was in the gasworks," she said.

Gabriel felt humiliated by the failure of his irony and by the evocation of this figure from the dead, a boy in the gasworks. While he had been full of memories of their secret life together, full of tenderness and joy and desire, she had been comparing him in her mind with another. A shameful consciousness of his own person assailed him. He saw himself as a ludicrous figure, acting as a pennyboy for his aunts, a nervous, well-meaning sentimentalist, orating to vulgarians and idealising his own clownish lusts, the pitiable fatuous fellow he had caught a glimpse of in the mirror. Instinctively he turned his back more to the light lest she might see the shame that burned upon his forehead.

He tried to keep up his tone of cold interrogation, but his voice when he spoke was humble and indifferent.

"I suppose you were in love with this Michael Furey, Gretta," he said.

"I was great with him at that time," she said.

Her voice was veiled and sad. Gabriel, feeling now how vain it would be to try to lead her whither he had purposed, caressed one of her hands and said, also sadly:

"And what did he die of so young, Gretta? Consumption, was it?"

"I think he died for me," she answered.

A vague terror seized Gabriel at this answer, as if, at that hour when he had hoped to triumph, some impalpable and vindictive being was coming against him, gathering forces against him in its vague world. But he shook himself free of it with an effort of reason and continued to caress her hand. He did not question her again, for he felt that she would tell him of herself. Her hand was warm and moist: it did not respond to his touch, but he continued to caress it just as he had caressed her first letter to him that spring morning.

"It was in the winter," she said, "about the beginning of the winter when I was going to leave my grandmother's and come up here to the convent. And he was ill at the time in his lodgings in Galway and wouldn't be let out, and his people in Oughterard were written to. He was in decline, they said, or something like that. I never knew rightly."

She paused for a moment and sighed.

"Poor fellow," she said. "He was very fond of me and he was such a gentle boy. We used to go out together, walking, you know, Gabriel, like the way they do in the country. He was going to study singing only for his health. He had a very good voice, poor Michael Furey."

"Well; and then?" asked Gabriel.

"And then when it came to the time for me to leave Galway and come up to the convent he was much worse and I wouldn't be let see him so I wrote him a letter saying I was going up to Dublin and would be back in the summer, and hoping he would be better then."

She paused for a moment to get her voice under control, and then went on:

"Then the night before I left, I was in my grandmother's house in Nuns' Island, packing up, and I heard gravel thrown up against the window. The window was so wet I couldn't see, so I ran downstairs as I was and slipped out the back into the garden and there was the poor fellow at the end of the garden, shivering."

"And did you not tell him to go back?" asked Gabriel.

"I implored of him to go home at once and told him he would get his death in the rain. But he said he did not want to live. I can see his eyes as well as well! He was standing at the end of the wall where there was a tree."

"And did he go home?" asked Gabriel.

"Yes, he went home. And when I was only a week in the convent he died and was buried in Oughterard, where his people came from. O, the day I heard that, that he was dead!"

She stopped, choking with sobs, and, overcome by emotion, flung herself face downward on the bed, sobbing in the quilt. Gabriel held her hand for a moment longer, irresolutely, and then, shy of intruding on her grief, let it fall gently and walked quietly to the window.

She was fast asleep.

Gabriel, leaning on his elbow, looked for a few moments unresentfully on her tangled hair and half-open mouth, listening to her deep-drawn breath. So she had had that romance in her life: a man had died for her sake. It hardly pained him now to think how poor a part he, her husband, had played in her life. He watched her while she slept, as though he and she had never lived together as man and wife. His curious eyes rested long upon her face and on her hair: and, as he thought of what she must have been then, in that time of her first girlish beauty, a strange, friendly pity for her entered his soul. He did not like to say even to himself that her face was no longer beautiful, but he knew it was no longer the face for which Michael Furey had braved death.

Perhaps she had not told him all the story. His eyes moved to the chair over which she had thrown some of her clothes. A petticoat string dangled to the floor. One boot stood upright, its limp upper fallen down: the fellow of it lay upon its side. He wondered at his riot of emotions of an hour before. From what had it proceeded? From his aunt's supper, from his own foolish speech, from the wine and dancing, the merry-making when saying good-night in the hall, the pleasure of the walk along the river in the snow. Poor Aunt Julia! She, too, would soon be a shade with the shade of Patrick Morkan and his horse. He had caught that haggard look upon her face for a moment when she was singing *Arrayed for the Bridal*. Soon, perhaps, he would be sitting in that same drawing-room, dressed in black, his silk hat on his knees. The blinds would be drawn down and Aunt Kate would be sitting beside him, crying and blowing her nose and telling him how Julia had died. He would cast about in his mind for some words that might console her, and would find only lame and useless ones. Yes, yes: that would happen very soon.

The air of the room chilled his shoulders. He stretched himself cautiously along under the sheets and lay down beside his wife. One by one, they were all becoming shades. Better pass boldly into that other world, in the full glory of some passion, than fade and wither dismally with age. He thought of how she who lay beside him had locked in her heart for so many years that image of her lover's eyes when he had told her that he did not wish to live.

Generous tears filled Gabriel's eyes. He had never felt like that himself towards any woman, but he knew that such a feeling must be love. The tears gathered more thickly in his eyes and in the partial darkness he imagined he saw the form of a young man standing under a dripping tree. Other forms were near. His soul had approached that region where dwell the vast hosts of the dead. He was conscious of, but could not apprehend, their wayward and flickering existence. His own identity was fading out into a grey impalpable world: the solid world itself, which these dead had one time reared and lived in, was dissolving and dwindling.

A few light taps upon the pane made him turn to the window. It had begun to snow again. He watched sleepily the flakes, silver and dark, falling obliquely against the lamplight. The time had come for him to set out on his journey westward. Yes, the newspapers were right: snow was general all over Ireland. It was falling on every part of the dark central plain, on the treeless hills, falling softly upon the Bog of Allen and, farther westward, softly falling into the dark mutinous Shannon waves. It was falling, too, upon every part of the lonely churchyard on the hill where Michael Furey lay buried. It lay thickly drifted on the crooked crosses and headstones, on the spears of the little gate, on the barren thorns. His soul swooned slowly as he heard the snow falling faintly through the universe and faintly falling, like the descent of their last end, upon all the living and the dead.

FRANZ KAFKA

Franz Kafka (1883–1924) was born in Prague to wealthy Jewish parents. After receiving a law degree from the University of Prague, he worked in an insurance office. Though he wrote three novels and numerous stories in his short life, at his death only a few stories had been published. Essentially ignoring Kafka's instructions, his friend Max Brod published the novels — *The Trial, The Castle,* and *Amerika* — in the years immediately following Kafka's death; they were first translated into English in the 1930s. Kafka was a profoundly private person; for him writing was not a literary endeavor but the wrenching expression of an enigmatic, indeed ominous, reality. His vision of the condition of the twentieth century was uncannily prophetic: his stories and novels presage the secret police, concentration camps, and purges of our time with frightening accuracy. In Kafka's work the individual is alone and estranged from any security — political, economic, or emotional — of society. Kafka's apprehension of that aloneness is, as one social critic has put it, "an expressive myth both simple as is a child's drawing of terror and encompassing as is Dante's metaphor of the voyage." "In the Penal Colony" locates a mounting terror in the simple, soulless capacity of technology and technocrats to inflict pain.

In the Penal Colony

Translated from the German by Willa and Edwin Muir

"It's a remarkable piece of apparatus," said the officer to the explorer and surveyed with a certain air of admiration the apparatus which was after all quite familiar to him. The explorer seemed to have accepted merely out of politeness the Commandant's invitation to witness the execution of a soldier condemned to death for disobedience and insulting behavior to a superior. Nor did the colony itself betray much interest in this execution. At least, in the small sandy valley, a deep hollow surrounded on all sides by naked crags, there was no one present save the officer, the explorer, the condemned man, who was a stupid-looking wide-mouthed creature with bewildered hair and face, and the soldier who held the heavy chain controlling the small chains locked on the prisoner's ankles, wrists and neck, chains which were themselves attached to each other by communicating links. In any case, the condemned man looked so like a submissive dog that one might have thought he could be left to run free on the surrounding hills and would only need to be whistled for when the execution was due to begin.

The explorer did not much care about the apparatus and walked up and down behind the prisoner with almost visible indifference while the officer made the last adjustments, now creeping beneath the structure, which was bedded deep in the earth, now climbing a ladder to inspect its upper parts. These were tasks that might well have been left to a mechanic, but the officer performed them with great zeal, whether because he was a devoted admirer of the apparatus or because of other reasons the work could be entrusted to no one else. "Ready now!" he called at last and climbed down from the ladder. He looked uncommonly limp, breathed with his mouth wide open and had tucked two fine ladies' handkerchiefs under the collar of his uniform. "These uniforms are too heavy for the tropics, surely," said the explorer, instead of making some inquiry about the apparatus, as the officer had expected. "Of course," said the officer, washing his oily and greasy hands in a bucket of water that stood ready, "but they mean home to us; we don't want to forget about home. Now just have a look at this machine," he added at once, simultaneously drying his hands on a towel and indicating the apparatus. "Up till now a few things still had to be set by hand, but from this moment it works all by itself." The explorer nodded and followed him. The officer, anxious to secure himself against all contingencies, said: "Things sometimes go wrong, of course; I hope that nothing goes wrong today, but we have to allow for the possibility. The machinery should go on working continuously for twelve hours. But if anything does go wrong it will only be some small matter that can be set right at once.

"Won't you take a seat?" he asked finally, drawing a cane chair out from among a heap of them and offering it to the explorer, who could not refuse it. He was now sitting at the edge of a pit, into which he glanced for a fleeting moment. It was not very deep. On one side of the pit the excavated soil had been piled up in a rampart, on the other side of it stood the apparatus. "I don't know," said the officer, "if the Commandant has already explained this apparatus to you." The explorer waved one hand vaguely; the officer asked for nothing better, since now he could explain the apparatus himself. "This apparatus," he said, taking hold of a crank handle and leaning against it, "was invented by our former Commandant. I assisted at the very earliest experiments and had a share in all the work until its completion. But the credit of inventing it belongs to him alone. Have you ever heard of our former Commandant? No? Well, it isn't saying too much if I tell you that the organization of the whole penal colony is his work. We who were his friends knew even before he died that the organization of the colony was so perfect that his successor, even with a thousand new schemes in his head, would find it impossible to alter anything, at least for many years to come. And our prophecy has come true; the new Commandant has had to acknowledge its truth. A pity you never met the old Commandant!— But," the officer interrupted himself, "I am rambling on, and here stands his apparatus before us. It consists, as you see, of three parts. In the course of time each of these parts has acquired a kind of popular nickname. The lower one is called the 'Bed,' the upper one the 'Designer,' and this one here in the middle that moves up and down is called the 'Harrow.' " "The Harrow?" asked the explorer. He had not been listening very attentively, the glare of the sun in the shadeless valley was altogether too strong, it was difficult to collect one's thoughts. All the more did he admire the officer, who in spite of his tight-fitting full-dress uniform coat, amply befrogged and weighed down by epaulettes, was pursuing his subject with such enthusiasm and, besides talking, was still tightening a screw here and there with a spanner. As for the soldier, he seemed to be in much the same condition as the explorer. He had wound the prisoner's chain round both his wrists, propped himself on his rifle, let his head hang and was paying no attention to anything. That did not surprise the explorer, for the officer was speaking French, and certainly neither the soldier nor the prisoner understood a word of French. It was all the more remarkable, therefore, that the prisoner was none the less making an effort to follow the officer's explanations. With a kind of drowsy persistence he directed his gaze wherever the officer pointed a finger, and at the interruption of the explorer's question he, too, as well as the officer, looked around.

"Yes, the Harrow," said the officer, "a good name for it. The needles are set in like the teeth of a harrow and the whole thing works something like a harrow, although its action is limited to one place and contrived with much more artistic skill. Anyhow, you'll soon understand it. On the Bed here the condemned man is laid — I'm going to describe the apparatus first before I set it in motion. Then you'll be able to follow the proceedings better. Besides, one of the cogwheels in the Designer is badly worn; it creaks a lot when it's working; you can hardly hear yourself speak; spare parts, unfortunately, are difficult to get here. — Well, here is the Bed, as I told you. It is completely covered with a layer of cotton wool; you'll find out why later. On this cotton wool the condemned man is laid, face down, quite naked, of course; here are straps for the hands, here for the feet, and here for the neck, to bind him fast. Here at the head of the bed, where the man, as I said, first lays down his face, is this little gag of felt, which can be easily regulated to go straight into his mouth. It is meant to keep him from screaming and biting his tongue. Of course the man is forced to take the felt into his mouth, for otherwise his neck would be broken by the strap." "Is that cotton wool?" asked the explorer, bending forward. "Yes, certainly," said the officer, with a smile. "Feel it for yourself." He took the explorer's hand and guided it over the bed. "It's specially prepared cotton wool; that's why it looks so different; I'll tell you presently what it's for." The explorer already felt a dawning interest in the apparatus; he sheltered his eyes from the sun with one hand and gazed up at the structure. It was a huge affair. The Bed and the Designer were of the same size and looked like two dark wooden chests. The Designer hung about two meters above the Bed; each of them was bound at the corners with four rods of brass that almost flashed out rays in the sunlight. Between the chests shuttled the Harrow on a ribbon of steel.

The officer had scarcely noticed the explorer's previous indifference, but he was now well aware of his dawning interest; so he stopped explaining in order to leave a space of time for quiet observation. The condemned man imitated the explorer; since he could not use a hand to shelter his eyes he gazed upwards without shade.

"Well, the man lies down," said the explorer, leaning back in his chair and crossing his legs.

"Yes," said the officer, pushing his cap back a little and passing one hand over his heated face, "now listen! Both the Bed and the Designer have an electric battery each; the Bed needs one for itself, the Designer for the Harrow. As soon as the man is strapped down, the Bed is set in motion. It quivers in minute, very rapid vibrations, both from side to side and up and down. You will have seen similar apparatus in hospitals; but in our Bed the movements are all precisely calculated; you see, they have to correspond very exactly to the movements of the Harrow. And the Harrow is the instrument for the actual execution of the sentence."

"And how does the sentence run?" asked the explorer.

"You don't know that either?" said the officer in amazement, and bit his lips. "Forgive me if my explanations seem rather incoherent. I do beg your pardon. You see, the Commandant always used to do the explaining; but the new Commandant shirks this duty; yet that such an important visitor" — the explorer tried to deprecate the honor with both hands; the officer, however, insisted — "that such an important visitor should not even be told about the kind of sentence we pass is a new development, which — " He was just on the point of using strong language but checked himself and said only: "I was not informed, it is not my fault. In any case, I am certainly the best person to explain our procedure, since I have here" — he patted his breast pocket — "the relevant drawings made by our former Commandant."

"The Commandant's own drawings?" asked the explorer. "Did he combine everything in himself, then? Was he soldier, judge, mechanic, chemist and draughtsman?"

"Indeed he was," said the officer, nodding assent, with a remote, glassy look. Then he inspected his hands critically; they did not seem clean enough to him for touching the drawings; so he went over to the bucket and washed them again. Then he drew out a small leather wallet and said: "Our sentence does not sound severe. Whatever commandment the prisoner has disobeyed is written upon his body by the Harrow. This prisoner, for instance" — the officer indicated the man — "will have written on his body: HONOR THY SUPERIORS!"

The explorer glanced at the man; he stood, as the officer pointed him out, with bent head, apparently listening with all his ears in an effort to catch what was being said. Yet the movement of his blubber lips, closely pressed together, showed clearly that he could not understand a word. Many questions were troubling the explorer, but at the sight of the prisoner he asked only: "Does he know his sentence?" "No," said the officer, eager to go on with his exposition, but the explorer interrupted him: "He doesn't know the sentence that has been passed on him?" "No," said the officer again, pausing a moment as if to let the explorer elaborate his question, and then said: "There would be no point in telling him. He'll learn it on his body." The explorer intended to make no answer, but he felt the prisoner's gaze turned on him; it seemed to ask if he approved such goings on. So he bent forward again, having already leaned back in his chair, and put another question: "But surely he knows that he has been sentenced?" "Nor that either," said the officer, smiling at the explorer as if expecting him to make further surprising remarks. "No," said the explorer, wiping his forehead, "then he can't know either whether his defense was effective?" "He has had no chance of putting up a defense," said the officer, turning his eyes away as if speaking to himself and so sparing the explorer the shame of hearing self-evident matters explained. "But he must have had some chance of defending himself," said the explorer, and rose from his seat.

The officer realized that he was in danger of having his exposition of the apparatus held up for a long time; so he went up to the explorer, took him by the arm, waved a hand towards the condemned man, who was standing very straight now that he had so obviously become the center of attention — the soldier had also given the chain a jerk — and said: "This is how the matter stands. I have been appointed judge in this penal colony. Despite my youth. For I was the former Commandant's assistant in all penal matters and know more about the apparatus than anyone. My guiding principle is this: Guilt is never to be doubted. Other courts cannot follow that principle, for they consist of several opinions and have higher courts to scrutinize them. That is not the case here, or at least, it was not the case in the former Commandant's time.

The new man has certainly shown some inclination to interfere with my judgments, but so far I have succeeded in fending him off and will go on succeeding. You wanted to have the case explained; it is quite simple, like all of them. A captain reported to me this morning that this man, who had been assigned to him as a servant and sleeps before his door, had been asleep on duty. It is his duty, you see, to get up every time the hour strikes and salute the captain's door. Not an exacting duty, and very necessary, since he has to be a sentry as well as a servant, and must be alert in both functions. Last night the captain wanted to see if the man was doing his duty. He opened the door as the clock struck two and there was his man curled up asleep. He took his riding whip and lashed him across the face. Instead of getting up and begging pardon, the man caught hold of his master's legs, shook him and cried: 'Throw that whip away or I'll eat you alive.' — That's the evidence. The captain came to me an hour ago, I wrote down his statement and appended the sentence to it. Then I had the man put in chains. That was all quite simple. If I had first called the man before me and interrogated him, things would have got into a confused tangle. He would have told lies, and had I exposed these lies he would have backed them up with more lies, and so on and so forth. As it is, I've got him and I won't let him go. — Is that quite clear now? But we're wasting time, the execution should be beginning and I haven't finished explaining the apparatus yet." He pressed the explorer back into his chair, went up again to the apparatus and began: "As you see, the shape of the Harrow corresponds to the human form; here is the harrow for the torso, here are the harrows for the legs. For the head there is only this one small spike. Is that quite clear?" He bent amiably forward towards the explorer, eager to provide the most comprehensive explanations.

The explorer considered the Harrow with a frown. The explanation of the judicial procedure had not satisfied him. He had to remind himself that this was in any case a penal colony where extraordinary measures were needed and that military disci-. pline must be enforced to the last. He also felt that some hope might be set on the new Commandant, who was apparently of a mind to bring in, although gradually, a new kind of procedure which the officer's narrow mind was incapable of under- standing. This train of thought prompted his next question: "Will the Commandant attend the execution?" "It is not certain," said the officer, wincing at the direct question, and his friendly expression darkened. "That is just why we have to lose no time. Much as I dislike it, I shall have to cut my explanations short. But of course tomorrow, when the apparatus has been cleaned — its one drawback is that it gets so messy — I can recapitulate all the details. For the present, then, only the essentials. — When the man lies down on the Bed and it begins to vibrate, the Harrow is lowered onto his body. It regulates itself automatically so that the needles barely touch his skin; once contact is made the steel ribbon stiffens immediately into a rigid band. And then the performance begins. An ignorant onlooker would see no difference between one punishment and another. The Harrow appears to do its work with uniform regularity. As it quivers, its points pierce the skin of the body which is itself quivering from the vibration of the Bed. So that the actual progress of the sentence can be watched, the Harrow is made of glass. Getting the needles fixed in the glass was a technical problem, but after many experiments we overcame the difficulty. No trouble was too great for us to take, you see. And now anyone can look through the glass and watch the inscription taking form on the body. Wouldn't you care to come a little nearer and have a look at the needles?"

The explorer got up slowly, walked across and bent over the Harrow. "You see," said the officer, "there are two kinds of needles arranged in multiple patterns. Each long needle has a short one beside it. The long needle does the writing, and the short needle sprays a jet of water to wash away the blood and keep the inscription clear. Blood and water together are then conducted here through small runnels into this main runnel and down a waste pipe into the pit." With his finger the officer traced the exact course taken by the blood and water. To make the picture as vivid as possible, he held both hands below the outlet of the waste pipe as if to catch the outflow, and when he did this the explorer drew back his head and feeling behind him with one hand sought to return to his chair. To his horror he found that the condemned man too had obeyed the officer's invitation to examine the Harrow at close quarters and had followed him. He had pulled forward the sleepy soldier with the chain and was bending over the glass. One could see that his uncertain eyes were trying to perceive what the two gentlemen had been looking at, but since he had not understood the explanation he could not make head or tail of it. He was peering this way and that way. He kept running his eyes along the glass. The explorer wanted to drive him away, since what he was doing was probably culpable. But the officer firmly restrained the explorer with one hand and with the other took a clod of earth from the rampart and threw it at the soldier. He opened his eyes with a jerk, saw what the condemned man had dared to do, let his rifle fall, dug his heels into the ground, dragged his prisoner back so that he stumbled and fell immediately, and then stood looking down at him, watching him struggling and rattling in his chains. "Set him on his feet!" yelled the officer, for he noticed that the explorer's attention was being too much distracted by the prisoner. In fact he was even leaning right across the Harrow, without taking any notice of it, intent only on finding out what was happening to the prisoner. "Be careful with him!" cried the officer again. He ran round the apparatus, himself caught the condemned man under the shoulders and with the soldier's help got him up on his feet, which kept slithering from under him.

"Now I know all about it," said the explorer as the officer came back to him. "All except the most important thing," he answered, seizing the explorer's arm and pointing upwards: "In the Designer are all the cogwheels that control the movements of the Harrow, and this machinery is regulated according to the inscription demanded by the sentence. I am still using the guiding plans drawn by the former Commandant. Here they are" — he extracted some sheets from the leather wallet — "but I'm sorry I can't let you handle them; they are my most precious possessions. Just take a seat and I'll hold them in front of you like this, then you'll be able to see everything quite well." He spread out the first sheet of paper. The explorer would have liked to say something appreciative, but all he could see was a labyrinth of lines crossing and re-crossing each other, which covered the paper so thickly that it was difficult to discern the blank spaces between them. "Read it," said the officer. "I can't," said the explorer. "Yet it's clear enough," said the officer. "It's very ingenious," said the explorer evasively, "but I can't make it out." "Yes," said the officer with a laugh, putting the paper away again, "it's no calligraphy for school children. It needs to be studied closely. I'm quite sure that in the end you would understand it too. Of course the script can't be a simple one; it's not supposed to kill a man straight off, but only after an interval of, on the average, twelve hours; the turning point is reckoned to come at the sixth hour. So there have to be lots and lots of flourishes around the actual script; the script itself runs round the body only in a narrow girdle; the rest of the body is reserved for the embellishments. Can you appreciate now the work accomplished by the Harrow and the whole apparatus? — Just watch it!" He ran up the ladder, turned a wheel, called down: "Look out, keep to one side!" and everything started working. If the wheel had not creaked, it would have been marvelous. The officer, as if surprised by the noise of the wheel, shook his fist at it, then spread out his arms in excuse to the explorer and climbed down rapidly to peer at the working of the machine from below. Something perceptible to no one save himself was still not in order; he clambered up again, did something with both hands in the interior of the Designer, then slid down one of the rods, instead of using the ladder, so as to get down quicker, and with the full force of his lungs, to make himself heard at all the noise, yelled in the explorer's ear: "Can you follow it? The Harrow is beginning to write; when it finishes the first draft of the inscription on the man's back, the layer of cotton wool begins to roll and slowly turns the body over, to give the Harrow fresh space for writing. Meanwhile the raw part that has been written on lies on the cotton wool, which is specially prepared to staunch the bleeding and so makes all ready for a new deepening of the script. Then these teeth at the edge of the Harrow, as the body turns further around, tear the cotton wool away from the wounds, throw it into the pit, and there is more work for the Harrow. So it keeps on writing deeper and deeper for the whole twelve hours. The first six hours the condemned man stays alive almost as before, he suffers only pain. After two hours the felt gag is taken away, for he has no longer strength to scream. Here, into this electrically heated basin at the head of the bed, some warm rice pap is poured, from which the man, if he feels like it, can take as much as his tongue can lap. Not one of them ever misses the chance. I can remember none, and my experience is extensive. Only about the sixth hour does the man lose all desire to eat. I usually kneel down here at that moment and observe what happens. The man rarely swallows his last mouthful, he only rolls it round his mouth and spits it out into the pit. I have to duck just then or he would spit it in my face. But how quiet he grows at just about the sixth hour! Enlightenment comes to the most dull-witted. It begins around the eyes. From there it radiates. A moment that might tempt one to get under the Harrow oneself. Nothing more happens than that the man begins to understand the inscription, he purses his mouth as if he were listening. You have seen how difficult it is to decipher the script with one's eyes; but our man deciphers it with his wounds. To be sure, that is a hard task; he needs six hours to accomplish it. By that time the Harrow has pierced him quite through and casts him into the pit, where he pitches down upon the blood and water and the cotton wool. Then the judgment has been fulfilled, and we, the soldier and I, bury him."

The explorer had inclined his ear to the officer and with his hands in his jacket pockets watched the machine at work. The condemned man watched it too, but uncomprehendingly. He bent forward a little and was intent on the moving needles when the soldier, at a sign from the officer, slashed through his shirt and trousers from behind with a knife, so that they fell off; he tried to catch at his falling clothes to cover his nakedness, but the soldier lifted him into the air and shook the last remnants from him. The officer stopped the machine, and in the sudden silence the condemned man was laid under the Harrow. The chains were loosened and the straps fastened on instead; in the first moment that seemed almost a relief to the prisoner. And now the Harrow was adjusted a little lower, since he was a thin man. When the needle points touched him a shudder ran over his skin; while the soldier was busy strapping his right hand, he flung out his left hand blindly; but it happened to be in the direction towards where the explorer was standing. The officer kept watching the explorer sideways, as if seeking to read from his face the impression made on him by the execution, which had been at least cursorily explained to him.

The wrist strap broke; probably the soldier had drawn it too tight. The officer had to intervene, the soldier held up the broken piece of strap to show him. So the officer went over to him and said, his face still turned towards the explorer: "This is a very complex machine, it can't be helped that things are breaking or giving way here and there; but one must not thereby allow oneself to be diverted in one's general judgment. In any case, this strap is easily made good; I shall simply use a chain; the delicacy of the vibrations for the right arm will of course be a little impaired." And while he fastened the chains, he added: "The resources for maintaining the machine are now very much reduced. Under the former Commandant I had free access to a sum of money set aside entirely for this purpose. There was a store, too, in which spare parts were kept for repairs of all kinds. I confess I have been almost prodigal with them, I mean in the past, not now as the new Commandant pretends, always looking for an excuse to attack our old way of doing things. Now he has taken charge of the machine money himself, and if I send for a new strap they ask for the broken strap as evidence, and the new strap takes ten days to appear and then is of shoddy material and not much good. But how I am supposed to work the machine without a strap, that's something nobody bothers about."

The explorer thought to himself: It's always a ticklish matter to intervene decisively in other people's affairs. He was neither a member of the penal colony nor a citizen of the state to which it belonged. Were he to denounce this execution or actually try to stop it, they could say to him: You are a foreigner, mind your own business. He could make no answer to that, unless he were to add that he was amazed at himself in this connection, for he traveled only as an observer, with no intention at all of altering other people's methods of administering justice. Yet here he found himself strongly tempted. The injustice of the procedure and the inhumanity of the execution were undeniable. No one could suppose that he had any selfish interest in the matter, for the condemned man was a complete stranger, not a fellow countryman or even at all sympathetic to him. The explorer himself had recommendations from high quarters, had been received here with great courtesy, and the very fact that he had been invited to attend the execution seemed to suggest that his views would be welcome. And this was all the more likely since the Commandant, as he had heard only too plainly, was no upholder of the procedure and maintained an attitude almost of hostility to the officer.

At that moment the explorer heard the officer cry out in rage. He had just, with considerable difficulty, forced the felt gag into the condemned man's mouth when the man in an irresistible access of nausea shut his eyes and vomited. Hastily the officer snatched him away from the gag and tried to hold his head over the pit; but it was too late, the vomit was running all over the machine. "It's all the fault of that Commandant!" cried the officer, senselessly shaking the brass rods in front, "the machine is befouled like a pigsty." With trembling hands he indicated to the explorer what had happened. "Have I not tried for hours at a time to get the Commandant to understand that the prisoner must fast for a whole day before the execution? But our new, mild doctrine thinks otherwise. The Commandant's ladies stuff the man with sugar candy before he's led off. He has lived on stinking fish his whole life long and now he has to eat sugar candy! But it could still be possible, I should have nothing to say against it, but why won't they get me a new felt gag, which I have been begging for the last three months. How should a man not feel sick when he takes a felt gag into his mouth which more than a hundred men have already slobbered and gnawed in their dying moments?"

The condemned man had laid his head down and looked peaceful; the soldier was busy trying to clean the machine with the prisoner's shirt. The officer advanced towards the explorer, who in some vague presentiment fell back a pace, but the officer seized him by the hand, and drew him to one side. "I should like to exchange a few words with you in confidence," he said, "may I?" "Of course," said the explorer, and listened with downcast eyes.

"This procedure and method of execution, which you are now having the opportunity to admire, has at the moment no longer any open adherents in our colony. I am its sole advocate, and at the same time the sole advocate of the old Commandant's tradition. I can no longer reckon on any further extension of the method; it takes all my energy to maintain it as it is. During the old Commandant's lifetime the colony was full of his adherents; his strength of conviction I still have in some measure, but not an atom of his power; consequently the adherents have skulked out of sight, there are still many of them but none of them will admit it. If you were to go into the teahouse today, on execution day, and listen to what is being said, you would perhaps hear only ambiguous remarks. These would all be made by adherents, but under the present Commandant and his present doctrines they are of no use to me. And now I ask you: because of this Commandant and the women who influence him, is such a piece of work, the work of a lifetime" — he pointed to the machine — "to perish? Ought one to let that happen? Even if one has only come as a stranger to our island for a few days? But there's no time to lose, an attack of some kind is impending on my function as judge; conferences are already being held in the Commandant's office from which I am excluded; even your coming here today seems to me a significant move; they are cowards and use you as a screen, you, a stranger. — How different an execution was in the old days! A whole day before the ceremony the valley was packed with people; they all came only to look on; early in the morning the Commandant appeared with his ladies; fanfares roused the whole camp; I reported that everything was in readiness; the assembled company — no high official dared to absent himself — arranged itself around the machine; this pile of cane chairs is a miserable survival from that epoch. The machine was freshly cleaned and glittering, I got new spare parts for almost every execution. Before hundreds of spectators — all of them standing on tiptoe as far as the heights there — the condemned man was laid under the Harrow by the Commandant himself. What is left today for a common soldier to do was then my task, the task of the presiding judge, and was an honor for me. And then the execution began! No discordant noise spoilt the working of the machine. Many did not care to watch it but lay with closed eyes in the sand; they all knew: Now Justice is being done. In the silence one heard nothing but the condemned man's sighs, half muffled by the felt gag. Nowadays the machine can no longer wring from anyone a sigh louder than the felt gag can stifle; but in those days the writing needles let drop an acid fluid, which we're no longer permitted to use. Well, and then came the sixth hour! It was impossible to grant all the requests to be allowed to watch it from near by. The Commandant in his wisdom ordained that the children should have the preference; I, of course, because of my office had the privilege of always being at hand; often enough I would be squatting there with a small child in either arm. How we all absorbed the look of transfiguration on the face of the sufferer, how we bathed our cheeks in the radiance of that justice, achieved at last and fading so quickly! What times these were, my comrade!" The officer had obviously forgotten whom he was addressing; he had embraced the explorer and laid his head on his shoulder. The explorer was deeply embarrassed, impatiently he stared over the officer's head. The soldier had finished his cleaning job and was now pouring rice pap from a pot into the basin. As soon as the condemned man, who seemed to have recovered entirely, noticed this action he began to reach for the rice with his tongue. The soldier kept pushing him away, since the rice pap was certainly meant for a later hour, yet it was just as unfitting that the soldier himself should thrust his dirty hands into the basin and eat out of it before the other's avid face.

The officer quickly pulled himself together. "I didn't want to upset you," he said. "I know it is impossible to make those days credible now. Anyhow, the machine is still working and it is still effective in itself. It is effective in itself even though it stands alone in this valley. And the corpse still falls at the last into the pit with an incomprehensibly gentle wafting motion, even although there are no hundreds of people swarming round like flies as formerly. In those days we had to put a strong fence round the pit; it has long since been torn down."

The explorer wanted to withdraw his face from the officer and looked round him at random. The officer thought he was surveying the valley's desolation; so he seized him by the hands, turned him round to meet his eyes, and asked: "Do you realize the shame of it?"

But the explorer said nothing. The officer left him alone for a little; with legs apart, hands on hips, he stood very still, gazing at the ground. Then he smiled encouragingly at the explorer and said: "I was quite near you yesterday when the Commandant gave you the invitation. I heard him giving it. I know the Commandant. I divined at once what he was after. Although he is powerful enough to take measures against me, he doesn't dare to do it yet, but he certainly means to use your verdict against me, the verdict of an illustrious foreigner. He has calculated it carefully: this is your second day on the island, you did not know the old Commandant and his ways, you are conditioned by European ways of thought, perhaps you object on principle to capital punishment in general and to such mechanical instruments of death in particular, besides you will see that the execution has no support from the public, a shabby ceremony — carried out with a machine already somewhat old and worn — now, taking all that into consideration, would it not be likely (so thinks the Commandant) that you might disapprove of my methods? And if you disapprove, you wouldn't conceal the fact (I'm still speaking from the Commandant's point of view), for you are a man to feel confidence in your own well-tried conclusions. True, you have seen and learned to appreciate the peculiarities of many peoples, and so you would not be likely to take a strong line against our proceedings, as you might do in your own country. But the Commandant has no need of that. A casual, even an unguarded remark will be enough. It doesn't even need to represent what you really think, so long as it can be used speciously to serve his purpose. He will try to prompt you with sly questions, of that I am certain. And his ladies will sit around you and prick up their ears; you might be saying something like this: 'In our country we have a different criminal procedure,' or 'In our country the prisoner is interrogated before he is sentenced,' or 'We haven't used torture since the Middle Ages.' All these statements are as true as they seem natural to you, harmless remarks that pass no judgment on my methods. But how would the Commandant react to them? I can see him, our good Commandant, pushing his chair away immediately and rushing onto the balcony, I can see his ladies streaming out after him, I can hear his voice — the ladies call it a voice of thunder — well, and this is what he says: 'A famous Western investigator, sent out to study criminal procedure in all the countries of the world, has just said that our old tradition of administering justice is inhumane. Such a verdict from such a personality makes it impossible for me to countenance these methods any longer. Therefore from this very day I ordain . . .' and so on. You may want to interpose that you never said any such thing, that you never called my methods inhumane; on the contrary your profound experience leads you to believe they are the most humane and most in consonance with human dignity, and you admire the machine greatly — but it will be too late; you won't even get onto the balcony, crowded as it will be with ladies; you may try to draw attention to yourself; you may want to scream out; but a lady's hand will close your lips — and I and the work of the old Commandant will be done for."

The explorer had to suppress a smile; so easy, then, was the task he had felt to be so difficult. He said evasively: "You overestimate my influence; the Commandant has read my letters of recommendation, he knows that I am no expert in criminal procedure. If I were to give an opinion, it would be as a private individual, an opinion no more influential than that of any ordinary person, and in any case much less influential than that of the Commandant, who, I am given to understand, has very extensive powers in this penal colony. If his attitude to your procedure is as definitely hostile as you believe, then I fear the end of your tradition is at hand, even without any humble assistance from me."

Had it dawned on the officer at last? No, he still did not understand. He shook his head emphatically, glanced briefly round at the condemned man and the soldier, who both flinched away from the rice, came close up to the explorer and without looking at his face but fixing his eye on some spot on his coat said in a lower voice than before: "You don't know the Commandant; you feel yourself — forgive the expression — a kind of outsider so far as all of us are concerned; yet, believe me, your influence cannot be rated too highly. I was simply delighted when I heard that you were to attend the execution all by yourself. The Commandant arranged it to aim a blow at me, but I shall turn it to my advantage. Without being distracted by lying whispers and contemptuous glances — which could not have been avoided had a crowd of people attended the execution — you have heard my explanations, seen the machine and are now in course of watching the execution. You have doubtless already formed your own judgment; if you still have some small uncertainties the sight of the execution will resolve them. And now I make this request to you: help me against the Commandant!"

The explorer would not let him go on. "How could I do that?" he cried. "It's quite impossible. I can neither help nor hinder you."

"Yes, you can," the officer said. The explorer saw with a certain apprehension that the officer had clenched his fists. "Yes, you can," repeated the officer, still more insistently. "I have a plan that is bound to succeed. You believe your influence is insufficient. I know that it is sufficient. But even granted that you are right, is it not necessary, for the sake of preserving this tradition, to try even what might prove insufficient? Listen to my plan, then. The first thing necessary for you to carry it out is to be as reticent as possible today regarding your verdict on these proceedings. Unless you are asked a direct question you must say nothing at all; but what you do say must be brief and general; let it be remarked that you would prefer not to discuss the matter, that you are out of patience with it, that if you are to let yourself go you would use strong language. I don't ask you to tell any lies; by no means; you should only give curt answers, such as: 'Yes, I saw the execution,' or 'Yes, I had it explained to me.' Just that, nothing more. There are grounds enough for any impatience you betray, although not such as will occur to the Commandant. Of course, he will mistake your meaning and interpret it to please himself. That's what my plan depends on. Tomorrow in the Commandant's office there is to be a large conference of all the high administrative officials, the Commandant presiding. Of course the Commandant is the kind of man to have turned these conferences into public spectacles. He has had a gallery built that is always packed with spectators. I am compelled to take part in the conferences, but they make me sick with disgust. Now, whatever happens, you will certainly be invited to this conference; if you behave today as I suggest the invitation will become an urgent request. But if for some mysterious reason you're not invited, you'll have to ask for an invitation; there's no doubt of you're getting it then. So tomorrow you're sitting in the Commandant's box with the ladies. He keeps looking up to make sure you're there. After various trivial and ridiculous matters, brought in merely to impress the audience — mostly harbor works, nothing but harbor works! — our judicial procedure comes up for discussion too. If the Commandant doesn't introduce it, or not soon enough, I'll see that it's mentioned. I'll stand up and report that today's execution has taken place. Quite briefly, only a statement. Such a statement is not usual, but I shall make it. The Commandant thanks me, as always, with an amiable smile, and then he can't restrain himself, he seizes the excellent opportunity. 'It has just been reported,' he will say, or words to that effect, 'that an execution has taken place. I should like merely to add that this execution was witnessed by the famous explorer who has, as you all know, honored our colony so greatly by his visit to us. His presence at today's session of our conference also contributes to the importance of this occasion. Should we not now ask the famous explorer to give us his verdict on our traditional mode of execution and the procedure that leads up to it?' Of course there is loud applause, general agreement, I am more insistent than anyone. The Commandant bows to you and says: 'Then in the name of the assembled company, I put the question to you.' And now you advance to the front of the box. Lay your hands where everyone can see them, or the ladies will catch them and press your fingers. — And then at last you can speak out. I don't know how I'm going to endure the tension of waiting for that moment. Don't put any restraint on yourself when you make your speech, publish the truth aloud, lean over the front of the box, shout, yes, indeed, shout your verdict, your unshakable conviction, at the Commandant. Yet perhaps you wouldn't care to do that, it's not in keeping with your character, in your country perhaps people do these things differently, well, that's all right too, that will be quite as effective, don't even stand up, just say a few words, even in a whisper, so that only the officials beneath you will hear them, that will be quite enough, you don't even need to mention the lack of public support for the execution, the creaking wheel, the broken strap, the filthy gag of felt, no, I'll take all that upon me, and, believe me, if my indictment doesn't drive him out of the conference hall, it will force him to his knees

to make the acknowledgment: Old Commandant, I humble myself before you. —
That is my plan; you will help me to carry it out. But of course you are willing, what
is more, you must." And the officer seized the explorer by both arms and gazed,
breathing heavily, into his face. He had shouted the last sentence so loudly that even
the soldier and the condemned man were startled into attending; they had not
understood a word but they stopped eating and looked over at the explorer,
chewing their previous mouthfuls.

From the very beginning the explorer had no doubt about what answer he must
give; in his lifetime he had experienced too much to have any uncertainty here; he
was fundamentally honorable and unafraid. And yet now, facing the soldier and the
condemned man, he did hesitate for as long as it took to draw one breath. At last,
however, he said, as he had to: "No." The officer blinked several times but did not
turn his eyes away. "Would you like me to explain?" asked the explorer. The officer
nodded wordlessly. "I do not approve of your procedure," said the explorer then,
"even before you took me into you confidence — of course I shall never in any
circumstances betray your confidence — I was already wondering whether it would
be my duty to intervene and whether my intervention would have the slightest
chance of success. I realized to whom I ought to turn: to the Commandant, of course.
You have made that fact even clearer, but without having strengthened my resolution; on the contrary, your sincere conviction has touched me even though it cannot
influence my judgment."

The officer remained mute, turned to the machine, caught hold of the brass rod,
and then, leaning back a little, gazed at the Designer as if to assure himself that all
was in order. The soldier and the condemned man seemed to have come to some
understanding; the condemned man was making signs to the soldier, difficult though
his movements were because of the tight straps; the soldier was bending down to
him; the condemned man whispered something and the soldier nodded.

The explorer followed the officer and said: "You don't know yet what I mean to
do. I shall tell the Commandant what I think of the procedure certainly, but not at
a public conference, only in private; nor shall I stay here long enough to attend any
conference; I am going away early tomorrow morning, or at least embarking on my
ship."

It did not look as if the officer had been listening. "So you did not find the
procedure convincing," he said to himself and smiled, as an old man smiles at
childish nonsense and yet pursues his own meditations behind the smile.

"Then the time has come," he said at last, and suddenly looked at the explorer
with bright eyes that held some challenge, some appeal for cooperation. "The time
for what?" asked the explorer uneasily, but got no answer.

"You are free," said the officer to the condemned man in the native tongue. The
man did not believe it at first. "Yes, you are set free," said the officer. For the first
time the condemned man's face woke to real animation. Was it true? Was it only a
caprice of the officer's that might change again? Had the foreign explorer begged
him off? What was it? One could read these questions on his face. But not for long.
Whatever it might be, he wanted to be really free if he might, and he began to
struggle so far as the Harrow permitted him.

"You'll burst my straps," cried the officer. "Lie still! We'll soon loosen them." And
signing the soldier to help him, he set about doing so. The condemned man laughed
wordlessly to himself, now he turned his face left towards the officer, now right
towards the soldier, nor did he forget the explorer.

"Draw him out," ordered the officer. Because of the Harrow this had to be done with some care. The condemned man had already torn himself a little in the back through his impatience.

From now on, however, the officer paid hardly any attention to him. He went up to the explorer, pulled out the small leather wallet again, turned over the papers in it, found the one he wanted and showed it to the explorer. "Read it," he said, "I can't," said the explorer, "I told you before that I can't make out these scripts." "Try taking a close look at it," said the officer and came quite near to the explorer so that they might read it together. But when even that proved useless, he outlined the script with his little finger, holding it high above the paper as if the surface dared not be sullied by touch, in order to help the explorer to follow the script in that way. The explorer did make an effort, meaning to please the officer in this respect at least, but he was quite unable to follow. Now the officer began to spell it, letter by letter, and then read out the words. "'BE JUST!' is what is written there," he said. "Surely you can read it now." The explorer bent so close to the paper that the officer feared he might touch it and drew it farther away; the explorer made no remark, yet it was clear that he still could not decipher it. "'BE JUST!' is what is written there," said the officer once more. "Maybe," said the explorer, "I am prepared to believe you." "Well, then," said the officer, at least partly satisfied, and climbed up the ladder with the paper; very carefully he laid it inside the Designer and seemed to be changing the disposition of all the cogwheels; it was a troublesome piece of work and must have involved wheels that were extremely small, for sometimes the officer's head vanished altogether from sight inside the Designer, so precisely did he have to regulate the machinery.

The explorer, down below, watched the labor uninterruptedly, his neck grew stiff and his eyes smarted from the glare of sunshine over the sky. The soldier and the condemned man were now busy together. The man's shirt and trousers, which were already lying in the pit, were fished out by the point of the soldier's bayonet. The shirt was abominably dirty and its owner washed it in the bucket of water. When he put on the shirt and trousers both he and the soldier could not help guffawing, for the garments were of course slit up behind. Perhaps the condemned man felt it incumbent on him to amuse the soldier, he turned round and round in his slashed garments before the soldier, who squatted on the ground beating his knees with mirth. All the same, they presently controlled their mirth out of respect for the gentlemen.

When the officer had at length finished his task aloft, he surveyed the machinery in all its details once more, with a smile, but this time shut the lid of the Designer, which had stayed open till now, climbed down, looked into the pit and then at the condemned man, noting with satisfaction that the clothing had been taken out, then went over to wash his hands in the water bucket, perceived too late that it was disgustingly dirty, was unhappy because he could not wash his hands, in the end thrust them into the sand — this alternative did not please him, but he had to put up with it — then stood upright and began to unbutton his uniform jacket. As he did this, the two ladies' handkerchiefs he had tucked under his collar fell into his hands. "Here are your handkerchiefs," he said, and threw them to the condemned man. And to the explorer he said in explanation: "A gift from the ladies."

In spite of the obvious haste with which he was discarding first his uniform jacket and then all his clothing, he handled each garment with loving care, he even ran his fingers caressingly over the silver lace on the jacket and shook a tassel into place.

This loving care was certainly out of keeping with the fact that as soon as he had a garment off he flung it at once with a kind of unwilling jerk into the pit. The last thing left to him was his short sword with the sword belt. He drew it out of the scabbard, broke it, then gathered all together, the bits of the sword, the scabbard and the belt, and flung them so violently down that they clattered into the pit.

Now he stood naked there. The explorer bit his lips and said nothing. He knew very well what was going to happen, but he had no right to obstruct the officer in anything. If the judicial procedure which the officer cherished were really so near its end — possibly as a result of his own intervention, as to which he felt himself pledged — then the officer was doing the right thing; in his place the explorer would not have acted otherwise.

The soldier and the condemned man did not understand at first what was happening; at first they were not even looking on. The condemned man was gleeful at having got the handkerchiefs back, but he was not allowed to enjoy them for long, since the soldier snatched them with a sudden, unexpected grab. Now the condemned man in turn was trying to twitch them from under the belt where the soldier had tucked them, but the soldier was on his guard. So they were wrestling, half in jest. Only when the officer stood quite naked was their attention caught. The condemned man especially seemed struck with the notion that some great change was impending. What had happened to him was now going to happen to the officer. Perhaps even to the very end. Apparently the foreign explorer had given the order for it. So this was revenge. Although he himself had not suffered to the end, he was to be revenged to the end. A broad, silent grin now appeared on his face and stayed there all the rest of the time.

The officer, however, had turned to the machine. It had been clear enough previously that he understood the machine well, but now it was almost staggering to see how he managed it and how it obeyed him. His hand had only to approach the Harrow for it to rise and sink several times till it was adjusted to the right position for receiving him; he touched only the edge of the Bed and already it was vibrating; the felt gag came to meet his mouth, one could see that the officer was really reluctant to take it but he shrank from it only a moment, soon he submitted and received it. Everything was ready, only the straps hung down at the sides, yet they were obviously unnecessary, the officer did not need to be fastened down. Then the condemned man noticed the loose straps, in his opinion the execution was incomplete unless the straps were buckled, he gestured eagerly to the soldier and they ran together to strap the officer down. The latter had already stretched out one foot to push the lever that started the Designer; he saw the two men coming up; so he drew his foot back and let himself be buckled in. But now he could not reach the lever; neither the soldier nor the condemned man would be able to find it, and the explorer was determined not to lift a finger. It was not necessary; as soon as the straps were fastened the machine began to work; the Bed vibrated, the needles flickered above the skin, the Harrow rose and fell. The explorer had been staring at it quite a while before he remembered that a wheel in the Designer should have been creaking; but everything was quiet, not even the slightest hum could be heard.

Because it was working so silently the machine simply escaped one's attention. The explorer observed the soldier and the condemned man. The latter was the more animated of the two, everything in the machine interested him, now he was bending down and now stretching up on tiptoe, his forefinger was extended all the time pointing out details to the soldier. This annoyed the explorer. He was resolved to stay till the end, but he could not bear the sight of these two. "Go back home," he said. The soldier would have been willing enough, but the condemned man took the order as a punishment. With clasped hands he implored to be allowed to stay, and when the explorer shook his head and would not relent, he even went down on his knees. The explorer saw that it was no use merely giving orders; he was on the point of going over and driving them away. At that moment he heard a noise above him in the Designer. He looked up. Was that cogwheel going to make trouble after all? But it was something quite different. Slowly the lid of the Designer rose up and clicked wide open. The teeth of a cogwheel showed themselves and rose higher, soon the whole wheel was visible; it was as if some enormous force were squeezing the Designer so that there was no longer room for the wheel; the wheel moved up till it came to the very edge of the Designer, fell down, rolled along the sand a little on its rim and then lay flat. But a second wheel was already rising after it followed by many others, large and small and indistinguishably minute, the same thing happened to all of them, at every moment one imagined the Designer must now really be empty, but another complex of numerous wheels was already rising into sight, falling down, trundling along the sand and lying flat. This phenomenon made the condemned man completely forget the explorer's command, the cogwheels fascinated him, he was always trying to catch one and at the same time urging the soldier to help, but always drew back his hand in alarm, for another wheel always came hopping along which, at least on its first advance, scared him off.

The explorer, on the other hand, felt greatly troubled; the machine was obviously going to pieces; its silent working was a delusion; he had a feeling that he must now stand by the officer, since the officer was no longer able to look after himself. But while the tumbling cogwheels absorbed his whole attention he had forgotten to keep an eye on the rest of the machine; now that the last cogwheel had left the Designer, however, he bent over the Harrow and had a new and still more unpleasant surprise. The Harrow was not writing, it was only jabbing, and the bed was not turning the body over but only bringing it up quivering against the needles. The explorer wanted to do something, if possible, to bring the whole machine to a standstill, for this was no exquisite torture such as the officer desired, this was plain murder. He stretched out his hand. But at that moment the Harrow rose with the body spitted on it and moved to the side, as it usually did only when the twelfth hour had come. Blood was flowing in a hundred streams, not mingled with water, the water jets too had failed to function. And now the last action failed to fulfil itself, the body did not drop off the long needles, streaming with blood it went on hanging over the pit without falling into it. The Harrow tried to move back to its old position, but as if it had itself noticed that it had not yet got rid of its burden it stuck after all where it was, over the pit. "Come and help!" cried the explorer to the other two, and himself seized the officer's feet. He wanted to push against the feet while the others seized the head from the opposite side and so the officer might be slowly eased off the needles. But the other two could not make up their minds to come; the condemned man actually turned away; the explorer had to go over to them and force them into position at the officer's head. And here, almost against his will, he had to look at the face of the corpse. It was as it had been in life; no sign was visible of the promised redemption; what the others had found in the machine the officer had not found; the lips were firmly pressed together, the eyes were open, with the same expression as in life, the look was calm and convinced, through the forehead went the point of the great iron spike.

As the explorer, with the soldier and the condemned man behind him, reached the first houses of the colony, the soldier pointed to one of them and said: "There is the teahouse."

In the ground floor of the house was a deep, low, cavernous space, its walls and ceiling blackened with smoke. It was open to the road all along its length. Although this teahouse was very little different from the other houses of the colony, which were all very dilapidated, even up to the Commandant's palatial headquarters, it made on the explorer the impression of a historic tradition of some kind, and he felt the power of past days. He went near to it, followed by his companions, right up between the empty tables which stood in the street before it, and breathed the cool, heavy air that came from the interior. "The old man's buried here," said the soldier. "The priest wouldn't let him lie in the churchyard. Nobody knew where to bury him for a while, but in the end they buried him here. The officer never told you about that, for sure, because of course that's what he was most ashamed of. He even tried several times to dig the old man up by night, but he was always chased away." "Where is the grave?" asked the explorer, who found it impossible to believe the soldier. At once both of them, the soldier and the condemned man, ran before him pointing with outstretched hands in the direction where the grave should be. They led the explorer right up to the back wall, where guests were sitting at a few tables. They were apparently dock laborers, strong men with short, glistening, full black beards. None had a jacket, their shirts were torn, they were poor, humble creatures. As the explorer drew near, some of them got up, pressed close to the wall, and stared at him. "It's a foreigner," ran the whisper around him. "He wants to see the grave." They pushed one of the tables aside, and under it there was really a gravestone. It was a simple stone, low enough to be covered by a table. There was an inscription on it in very small letters, the explorer had to kneel down to read it. This was what it said: "Here rests the old Commandant. His adherents, who now must be nameless, have dug this grave and set up this stone. There is a prophecy that after a certain number of years the Commandant will rise again and lead his adherents from this house to recover the colony. Have faith and wait!" When the explorer had read this and risen to his feet he saw all the bystanders around him smiling, as if they too had read the inscription, had found it ridiculous and were expecting him to agree with them. The explorer ignored this, distributed a few coins among them, waiting till the table was pushed over the grave again, quitted the teahouse and made for the harbor.

The soldier and the condemned man had found some acquaintances in the teahouse, who detained them. But they must have soon shaken them off, for the explorer was only halfway down the long flight of steps leading to the boats when they came rushing after him. Probably they wanted to force him at the last minute to take them with him. While he was bargaining below with a ferryman to row him to the steamer, the two of them came headlong down the steps, in silence, for they did not dare to shout. But by the time they reached the foot of the steps the explorer was already in the boat, and the ferryman was just casting off from the shore. They could have jumped into the boat, but the explorer lifted a heavy knotted rope from the floor boards, threatened them with it and so kept them from attempting the leap.

RUDYARD KIPLING

 Rudyard Kipling (1865–1936) was born in Bombay, India, the son of an Anglo-Indian professor of architectural sculpture. For the first several years of his life he was raised by native nurses, from whom he learned Indian folklore. When he was six he was taken to England, where he received a public school education. He returned to India as a journalist in 1882; there he began writing the short stories and poetry that, in a few years' time, gained him enormous popularity in England. In 1889 he went back to England where, except for brief periods, he lived the rest of his life. Kipling's tales of the Raj created a literary picture of India that persisted for decades, although his reputation was eventually shadowed by his zealous imperialism. His colorful narrative style and mastery of many forms of storytelling have appealed to children and adults alike. Another British spinner of exotic tales, Somerset Maugham, once said that Kipling was "the best short story writer that our country can boast." Kipling's collections of tales are *Plain Tales from the Hills* (1888), *Soldiers Three* (1890), *The Jungle Book* (1894), *Stalkey and Co.* (1899), *Just So Stories* (1902), *Puck of Pook's Hill* (1906), and *Debits and Credits* (1926). His novels include *The Light That Failed* (1890) and *Kim* (1901). He was awarded the Nobel Prize for Literature in 1907. Associated though he is with the sunset of Empire, Kipling explored themes well beyond India and colonialism, as "The Gardener" reveals.

The Gardener

One grave to me was given,
  One watch till Judgment Day;
And God looked down from Heaven
  And rolled the stone away.

One day in all the years,
  One hour in that one day,
His Angel saw my tears,
  And rolled the stone away!

Every one in the village knew that Helen Turrell did her duty by all her world, and by none more honourably than by her only brother's unfortunate child. The village knew, too, that George Turrell had tried his family severely since early youth, and were not surprised to be told that, after many fresh starts given and thrown away, he, an Inspector of Indian Police, had entangled himself with the daughter of a retired non-commissioned officer, and had died of a fall from a horse a few weeks before his child was born. Mercifully, George's father and mother were both dead, and though Helen, thirty-five and independent, might well have washed her hands of the whole disgraceful affair, she most nobly took charge, though she was, at the time, under threat of lung trouble which had driven her to the South of France. She arranged for the passage of the child and a nurse from Bombay, met them at Marseilles, nursed the baby through an attack of infantile dysentery due to the carelessness of the nurse, whom she had had to dismiss, and at last, thin and worn but triumphant, brought the boy late in the autumn, wholly restored, to her Hampshire home.

All these details were public property, for Helen was as open as the day, and held that scandals are only increased by hushing them up. She admitted that George had always been rather a black sheep, but things might have been much worse if the mother had insisted on her right to keep the boy. Luckily, it seemed that people of that class would do almost anything for money, and, as George had always turned to her in his scrapes, she felt herself justified — her friends agreed with her — in cutting the whole non-commissioned officer connection, and giving the child every advantage. A christening, by the Rector, under the name of Michael, was the first step. So far as she knew herself, she was not, she said, a child-lover, but, for all his faults, she had been very fond of George, and she pointed out that little Michael had his father's mouth to a line; which made something to build upon.

As a matter of fact, it was the Turrell forehead, broad, low, and well-shaped, with the widely-spaced eyes beneath it, that Michael had most faithfully reproduced. His mouth was somewhat better cut than the family type. But Helen, who would concede nothing good to his mother's side, vowed he was a Turrell all over, and, there being no one to contradict, the likeness was established.

In a few years Michael took his place, as accepted as Helen had always been — fearless, philosophical, and fairly good-looking. At six, he wished to know why he could not call her "Mummy," as other boys called their mothers. She explained that she was only his auntie, and that aunties were not quite the same as mummies, but that, if it gave him pleasure, he might call her "Mummy" at bedtime, for a pet-name between themselves.

Michael kept his secret most loyally, but Helen, as usual, explained the fact to her friends; which when Michael heard, he raged.

"Why did you tell? *Why* did you tell?" came at the end of the storm.

"Because it's always best to tell the truth," Helen answered, her arm round him as he shook in his cot.

"All right, but when the troof's ugly I don't think it's nice."

"Don't you, dear?"

"No, I don't, and" — she felt the small body stiffen — "now you've told, I won't call you 'Mummy' any more — not even at bedtimes."

"But isn't that rather unkind?" said Helen, softly.

"I don't care! I don't care! You've hurted me in my insides and I'll hurt you back. I'll hurt you as long as I live!"

"Don't, oh, don't talk like that, dear! You don't know what — "

"I will! And when I'm dead I'll hurt you worse!"

"Thank goodness. I shall be dead long before you, darling."

"Huh! Emma says, 'Never know your luck.' " (Michael had been talking to Helen's elderly, flat-faced maid.) "Lots of little boys die quite soon. So'll I. *Then* you'll see!"

Helen caught her breath and moved towards the door, but the wail of "Mummy! Mummy!" drew her back again, and the two wept together.

At ten years old, after two terms at a prep. school, something or somebody gave him the idea that his civil status was not quite regular. He attacked Helen on the subject, breaking down her stammered defences with the family directness.

"Don't believe a word of it," he said, cheerily, at the end. "People wouldn't have talked like they did if my people had been married. But don't you bother, Auntie. I've found out all about my sort in English Hist'ry and the Shakespeare bits. There was William the Conqueror to begin with, and — oh, heaps more, and they all got on first-rate. 'Twon't make any difference to you, my being *that* — will it?"

"As if anything could — " she began.

"All right. We won't talk about it any more if it makes you cry." He never mentioned the thing again of his own will, but when, two years later, he skilfully managed to have measles in the holidays, as his temperature went up to the appointed one hundred and four he muttered of nothing else, till Helen's voice, piercing at last his delirium, reached him with assurance that nothing on earth or beyond could make any difference between them.

The terms at his public school and the wonderful Christmas, Easter and Summer holidays followed each other, variegated and glorious as jewels on a string; and as jewels Helen treasured them. In due time Michael developed his own interests, which ran their courses and gave way to others; but his interest in Helen was constant and increasing throughout. She repaid it with all that she had of affection or could command of counsel and money; and since Michael was no fool, the War took him just before what was like to have been a most promising career.

He was to have gone up to Oxford, with a scholarship, in October. At the end of August he was on the edge of joining the first holocaust of public-school boys who threw themselves into the Line; but the captain of his O.T.C., where he had been sergeant for nearly a year, headed him off and steered him directly to a commission in a battalion so new that half of it still wore the old Army red, and the other half was breeding meningitis through living overcrowdedly in damp tents. Helen had been shocked at the idea of direct enlistment.

"But it's in the family," Michael laughed.

"You don't mean to tell me that you believed that old story all this time?" said Helen. (Emma, her maid, had been dead now several years.) "I gave you my word of honour — and I give it again — that it's all right. It is indeed."

"Oh, *that* doesn't worry me. It never did," he replied valiantly. "What I meant was, I should have got into the show earlier if I'd enlisted — like my grandfather."

"Don't talk like that! Are you afraid of it's ending so soon, then?"

"No such luck. You know what K. says."

"Yes. But my banker told me last Monday it couldn't *possibly* last beyond Christmas — for financial reasons."

"Hope he's right, but our Colonel — and he's a Regular — says it's going to be a long job."

Michael's battalion was fortunate in that, by some chance which meant several "leaves," it was used for coast-defence among shallow trenches on the Norfolk coast; thence sent north to watch the mouth of a Scotch estuary, and, lastly, held for weeks on a baseless rumour of distant service. But, the very day that Michael was to have met Helen for four whole hours at a railway-junction up the line, it was hurled out, to help make good the wastage of Loos, and he had only just time to send her a wire of farewell.

In France luck again helped the battalion. It was put down near the Salient, where it led a meritorious and unexacting life, while the Somme was being manufactured; and enjoyed the peace of the Armentières and Laventie sectors when that battle began. Finding that it had sound views on protecting its own flanks and could dig, a prudent Commander stole it out of its own Division, under pretence of helping to lay telegraphs, and used it round Ypres at large.

A month later, and just after Michael had written Helen that there was nothing special doing and therefore no need to worry, a shell-splinter dropping out of a wet dawn killed him at once. The next shell uprooted and laid down over the body what had been the foundation of a barn wall, so neatly that none but an expert would have guessed that anything unpleasant had happened.

By this time the village was old in experience of war, and, English fashion, had evolved a ritual to meet it. When the postmistress handed her seven-year-old daughter the official telegram to take to Miss Turrell, she observed to the Rector's gardener: "It's Miss Helen's turn now." He replied, thinking of his own son: "Well, he's lasted longer than some." The child herself came to the front-door weeping aloud, because Master Michael had often given her sweets. Helen, presently, found herself pulling down the house-blinds, one after one with great care, and saying earnestly to each: "Missing *always* means dead." Then she took her place in the dreary procession that was impelled to go through an inevitable series of unprofitable emotions. The Rector, of course, preached hope and prophesied word, very soon, from a prison camp. Several friends, too, told her perfectly truthful tales, but always about other women, to whom, after months and months of silence, their missing had been miraculously restored. Other people urged her to communicate with infallible Secretaries of organisations who could communicate with benevolent neutrals, who could extract accurate information from the most secretive of Hun prison commandants. Helen did and wrote and signed everything that was suggested or put before her.

Once, on one of Michael's leaves, he had taken her over a munition factory, where she saw the progress of a shell from blank-iron to the all but finished article. It struck her at the time that the wretched thing was never left alone for a single second; and "I'm being manufactured into a bereaved next-of-kin," she told herself, as she prepared her documents.

In due course, when all the organisations had deeply or sincerely regretted their inability to trace, etc., something gave way within her and all sensation — save of thankfulness for the release   came to an end in blessed passivity. Michael had died and her world had stood still and she had been one with the full shock of that arrest. Now she was standing still and the world was going forward, but it did not concern her — in no way or relation did it touch her. She knew this by the ease with which she could slip Michael's name into talk and incline her head to the proper angle, at the proper murmur of sympathy.

In the blessed realisation of that relief, the Armistice with all its bells broke over her and passed unheeded. At the end of another year she had overcome her physical loathing of the living and returned young, so that she could take them by the hand and almost sincerely wish them well. She had no interest in any aftermath, national or personal, of the War, but, moving at an immense distance, she sat on various relief committees and held strong views — she heard herself delivering them — about the site of the proposed village War Memorial.

Then there came to her, as next-of-kin, an official intimation, backed by a page of a letter to her in indelible pencil, a silver identity-disc, and a watch, to the effect that the body of Lieutenant Michael Turrell had been found, identified, and re-interred in Hagenzeele Third Military Cemetery — the letter of the row and the grave's number in that row duly given.

So Helen found herself moved on to another process of the manufacture — to a world full of exultant or broken relatives, now strong in the certainty that there was an altar upon earth where they might lay their love. These soon told her, and by means of time-tables made clear, how easy it was and how little it interfered with life's affairs to go and see one's grave.

"So different," as the Rector's wife said, "if he'd been killed in Mesopotamia, or even Gallipoli."

The agony of being waked up to some sort of second life drove Helen across the Channel, where, in a new world of abbreviated titles, she learnt that Hagenzeele Third could be comfortably reached by an afternoon train which fitted in with the morning boat, and that there was a comfortable little hotel not three kilometres from Hagenzeele itself, where one could spend quite a comfortable night and see one's grave next morning. All this she had from a Central Authority who lived in a board and tar-paper shed on the skirts of a razed city full of whirling lime-dust and blown papers.

"By the way," said he, "you know your grave, of course?"

"Yes, thank you," said Helen, and showed its row and number typed on Michael's own little typewriter. The officer would have checked it, out of one of his many books; but a large Lancashire woman thrust between them and bade him tell her where she might find her son, who had been corporal in the A.S.C. His proper name, she sobbed, was Anderson, but, coming of respectable folk, he had of course enlisted under the name of Smith; and had been killed at Dickiebush, in early 'Fifteen. She had not his number nor did she know which of his two Christian names he might have used with his alias; but her Cook's tourist ticket expired at the end of Easter week, and if by then she could not find her child she should go mad. Whereupon she fell forward on Helen's breast; but the officer's wife came out quickly from a little bedroom behind the office, and the three of them lifted the woman on to the cot.

"They are often like this," said the officer's wife, loosening the tight bonnet-strings. "Yesterday she said he'd been killed at Hooge. Are you sure you know your grave? It makes such a difference."

"Yes, thank you," said Helen, and hurried out before the woman on the bed should begin to lament again.

Tea in a crowded mauve and blue striped wooden structure, with a false front, carried her still further into the nightmare. She paid her bill beside a stolid, plain-featured Englishwoman, who, hearing her inquire about the train to Hagenzeele, volunteered to come with her.

"I'm going to Hagenzeele myself," she explained. "Not to Hagenzeele Third; mine is Sugar Factory, but they call it La Rosière now. It's just south of Hagenzeele Three. Have you got your room at the hotel there?"

"Oh yes, thank you. I've wired."

"That's better. Sometimes the place is quite full, and at others there's hardly a soul. But they've put bathrooms into the old Lion d'Or — that's the hotel on the west side of Sugar Factory — and it draws off a lot of people, luckily."

"It's all new to me. This is the first time I've been over."

"Indeed! This is my ninth time since the Armistice. Not on my own account. *I* haven't lost any one, thank God — but, like every one else, I've a lot of friends at home who have. Coming over as often as I do, I find it helps them to have some one just look at the — the place and tell them about it afterwards. And one can take photos for them, too. I get quite a list of commissions to execute." She laughed nervously and tapped her slung Kodak. "There are two or three to see at Sugar Factory this time, and plenty of others in the cemeteries all about. My system is save them up, and arrange them, you know. And when I've got enough commissions for one area to make it worth while, I pop over and execute them. It *does* comfort people."

"I suppose so," Helen answered, shivering as they entered the little train.

"Of course it does. (Isn't it lucky we've got window-seats?) It must do or they wouldn't ask one to do it, would they? I've a list of quite twelve or fifteen commissions here" — she tapped the Kodak again — "I must sort them out to-night. Oh, I forgot to ask you. What's yours?"

"My nephew," said Helen. "But I was very fond of him."

"Ah yes! I sometimes wonder whether *they* know after death? What do you think?"

"Oh, I don't — I haven't dared to think much about that sort of thing," said Helen, almost lifting her hands to keep her off.

"Perhaps that's better," the woman answered. "The sense of loss must be enough, I expect. Well, I won't worry you any more."

Helen was grateful, but when they reached the hotel Mrs. Scarsworth (they had exchanged names) insisted on dining at the same table with her, and after the meal, in the little, hideous salon full of low-voiced relatives, took Helen through her "commissions" with biographies of the dead, where she happened to know them, and sketches of their next-of-kin. Helen endured till nearly half-past nine, ere she fled to her room.

Almost at once there was a knock at her door and Mrs. Scarsworth entered; her hands, holding the dreadful list, clasped before her.

"Yes — yes — *I* know," she began. "You're sick of me, but I want to tell you something. You — you aren't married are you? Then perhaps you won't. . . . But it doesn't matter. I've *got* to tell some one. I can't go on any longer like this."

"But please — " Mrs. Scarsworth had backed against the shut door, and her mouth worked dryly.

"In a minute," she said. "You — you know about these graves of mine I was telling you about downstairs, just now? They really *are* commissions. At least several of them are." Her eye wandered round the room. "What extraordinary wall-papers they have in Belgium, don't you think? . . . Yes. I swear they are commissions. But there's *one,* d'you see, and — and he was more to me than anything else in the world. Do you understand?"

Helen nodded.

"More than any one else. And, of course, he oughtn't to have been. He ought to have been nothing to me. But he *was*. He *is*. That's why I do the commissions, you see. That's all."

"But why do you tell me?" Helen asked desperately.

"Because I'm *so* tired of lying. Tired of lying — always lying — year in and year out. When I don't tell lies I've got to act 'em and I've got to think 'em, always. *You* don't know what that means. He was everything to me that he oughtn't to have been — the one real thing — the only thing that ever happened to me in all my life; and I've had to pretend he wasn't. I've had to watch every word I said, and think out what lie I'd tell next, for years and years!"

"How many years?" Helen asked.

"Six years and four months before, and two and three-quarters after. I've gone to him eight times, since. Tomorrow'll make the ninth, and — and I can't — I *can't* go to him again with nobody in the world knowing. I want to be honest with some one before I go. Do you understand? It doesn't matter about *me*. I was never truthful, even as a girl. But it isn't worthy of *him*. So — so I — I had to tell you. I can't keep it up any longer. Oh, I can't!"

She lifted her joined hands almost to the level of her mouth, and brought them down sharply, still joined, to full arm's length below her waist. Helen reached forward, caught them, bowed her head over them, and murmured: "Oh, my dear! My dear!" Mrs. Scarsworth stepped back, her face all mottled.

"My God!" said she. "Is *that* how you take it?"

Helen could not speak, the woman went out; but it was a long while before Helen was able to sleep.

Next morning Mrs. Scarsworth left early on her round of commissions, and Helen walked alone to Hagenzeele Third. The place was still in the making, and stood some five or six feet above the metalled road, which it flanked for hundreds of yards. Culverts across a deep ditch served for entrances through the unfinished boundary wall. She climbed a few wooden-faced earthen steps and then met the entire crowded level of the thing in one held breath. She did not know that Hagenzeele Third counted twenty-one thousand dead already. All she saw was a merciless sea of black crosses, bearing little strips of stamped tin at all angles across their faces. She could distinguish no order or arrangement in their mass; nothing but a waist-high wilderness as of weeds stricken dead, rushing at her. She went forward, moved to the left and the right hopelessly, wondering by what guidance she should ever come to her own. A great distance away there was a line of whiteness. It proved to be a block of some two or three hundred graves whose headstones had already been set, whose flowers were planted out, and whose new-sown grass showed green. Here she could see clear-cut letters at the ends of the rows, and, referring to her slip, realised that it was not here she must look.

A man knelt behind a line of headstones — evidently a gardener, for he was firming a young plant in the soft earth. She went towards him, her paper in her hand. He rose at her approach and without prelude or salutation asked, "Who are you looking for?"

"Lieutenant Michael Turrell — my nephew," said Helen slowly and word for word, as she had many thousands of times in her life.

The man lifted his eyes and looked at her with infinite compassion before he turned from the fresh-sown grass towards the naked black crosses.

"Come with me," he said, "and I will show you where your son lies."

When Helen left the Cemetery she turned for a last look. In the distance she saw the man bending over his young plants; and she went away, supposing him to be the gardener.

MILAN KUNDERA

Born in 1929 in Brno, Czechoslovakia, Milan Kundera worked as a laborer and musician, then turned to writing and to film, first studying with and then joining the film faculty of the Prague Academy of Music and Drama. For fifteen years, until 1968, he and his students were deeply involved in creating Czech New Wave films. In 1968, with the Russian invasion of Czechoslovakia, he lost his job; in 1975 he moved to France, where he still lives. Kundera's stories first began appearing in Czech in the early 1960s in a series of books called *Laughable Loves* (the stories were later collected in one volume). They embodied, as most of his writing does, an ironic, imaginative view of human foibles, especially those centering on sexual politics. His first novel, *The Joke* (1967), was the last of his works to be published in his native country; the government proscribed his work, and subsequent novels, including *Life Is Elsewhere* (1973), *The Farewell Party* (1976), and *The Unbearable Lightness of Being* (1984) have been published in other countries. With the publication of *The Book of Laughter and Forgetting* (1979) the Czech government revoked Kundera's citizenship. Though his work his been embroiled in political and ideological controversy in Eastern Europe, Kundera rejects any categorical politicization of literature: "I don't much like the idea of committed literature. For me the only commitment of the novelist ought to be to oppose the ironic wisdom of the novel to ideological simplification of every sort." "Edward and God," indeed, is not a polemical story although it depicts a polemical society; it is a humorous, even farcical, sketch of the pitfalls of trying to outsmart the authorities.

Edward and God

Translated from the Czech by Suzanne Rappaport

1

We can advantageously begin Edward's story in his elder brother's little house in the country. His brother was lying on the couch and saying to Edward, "Ask the old hag. Never mind, just go and talk to her. Of course she's a pig, but I believe that even in such creatures a conscience exists. Just because she once did me dirt, now perhaps she'll be glad if you'll allow her to make amends for her past wrong-doings."

Edward's brother was still the same, a good-natured guy and a lazy one. Just this way perhaps had he been lolling on the couch in his university attic when, many years ago (Edward was still a little boy then), he had lazed and snored away the day of Stalin's death. The next day he had unsuspectingly gone to the department and caught sight of his fellow student, Miss Chehachkova, standing in ostentatious rigidity in the middle of the hall like a statue of grief. Three times he circled her and then began to roar with laughter. The offended girl denounced her fellow student's laughter as political provocation and Edward's brother had had to leave school and go to work in a village, where since that time he had acquired a little house, a dog, a wife, two children, and even a cottage.

In this village house, then, was he now lying on the couch and speaking to Edward. "We used to call her the chastising scourge of the working class. But as a matter of fact this needn't concern you. Today she's an aging female and she was always after young boys, so she'll meet you halfway."

Edward was at that time very young. He had just graduated from teacher's college (the course his brother had not completed), and was looking for a position. The next day, following his brother's advice, he knocked on the director's door. Then he saw a tall, bony woman with the greasy black hair of a gypsy, black eyes, and black down under her nose. Her ugliness relieved him of the shyness to which feminine beauty still always reduced him, so that he managed to talk to her in a relaxed manner, amiably, even courteously. The directress was evidently delighted by his approach and several times said with perceptible elation, "We need young people here." She promised to find a place for him.

2

And so Edward became a teacher in a small Czech town. This made him neither happy nor sad. He always tried hard to distinguish between the important and the unimportant, and he put his teaching career into the category of *unimportant*. Not that teaching itself was unimportant; after all, it constituted his livelihood (in this respect, in fact, he was deeply attached to it, because he knew that he would not be able to earn a living any other way). But he considered it unimportant in terms of his true nature. He hadn't selected it. Social demand, his party record, the certificate from high school, entrance examinations had selected it for him. The interlocking conjunction of all these forces eventually dumped him (as a crane drops a sack onto a truck) from secondary school into teachers' college. He didn't want to go there (it was superstitiously stigmatized by his brother's failure), but eventually he acquiesced. He understood, however, that his occupation would be among the fortuitous aspects of his life. It would be attached to him like a false beard — which is something laughable.

If, however, his professional duties were something not important (laughable, in fact), perhaps on the contrary, what he did voluntarily was. In his new place of work Edward soon found a young girl who struck him as beautiful, and he began to pursue her with a seriousness that was almost genuine. Her name was Alice and she was, as he discovered to his sorrow on their first date, very reserved and virtuous.

Many times during their evening walks he had tried to put his arm around her so that he could touch the region of her right breast from behind, and each time she'd seized his hand and pushed it away. One day when he was repeating this experiment once again and she (once again) was pushing his hand away, she stopped and asked: "Do you believe in God?"

With his sensitive ears Edward caught secret overtones to this question and immediately forgot about the breast.

"Do you?" Alice repeated her question and Edward didn't dare answer. Do not let us condemn him for fearing to be frank; in his new place of work he felt lonely and was too attracted to Alice to risk losing her favor over a single solitary answer.

"And you?" he asked in order to gain time.

"Yes, I do." And once again she urged him to answer her.

Until this time it had never occurred to him to believe in God. He understood, however, that he must not admit this. On the contrary, he saw that he should take advantage of the opportunity and knock together from faith in God a nice Trojan horse, within whose belly, according to the ancient example, he would enter the girl's heart unobserved. Only it wasn't so easy for Edward to say to Alice simply *yes, I believe in God.* He wasn't at all cynical and was ashamed to lie; the vulgar and uncompromising nature of a lie went against the grain with him. If he absolutely had to tell a lie, even so he wanted it to remain as close as possible to the truth. For that reason he replied in an exceptionally thoughtful voice:

"I don't really know, Alice, what I should say to you about this. Certainly I believe in God. But . . ." He paused and Alice glanced up at him in surprise. "But I want to be completely frank with you. May I?"

"You must be frank," she said. "Otherwise surely there wouldn't be any sense in our being together."

"Really?"

"Really," said Alice.

"Sometimes I'm bothered by doubts," said Edward in a low voice. "Sometimes I doubt whether He really exists."

"But how can you doubt that!" Alice almost shrieked.

Edward was silent, and after a moment's reflection a familiar thought struck him: "When I see so much evil around me, I often wonder how it is possible that God would permit it all."

This sounded so sad that Alice seized his hand. "Yes, the world is indeed full of evil, I know this only too well. But for just that reason you must believe in God. Without Him all this suffering would be in vain. Nothing would have any meaning. And if that were so, I couldn't live at all."

"Perhaps you're right," said Edward thoughtfully, and on Sunday he went to church with her. He dipped his fingers in the font and crossed himself. Then there was the Mass and people sang, and with the others he sang a hymn whose tune was familiar, but to which he didn't know the words. Instead of the prescribed words he chose only various vowels and always started to sing a fraction of a second behind the others, because he only dimly recollected even the tune. Yet the moment he became certain of the tune, he let his voice ring out fully, so that for the first time in his life he realized that he had a beautiful bass. Then they all began to recite the Lord's Prayer and some old ladies knelt. He could not hold back a compelling desire to kneel too on the stone floor. He crossed himself with impressive arm movements and experienced the incredible feeling of being able to do something that he'd never done in his life, neither in the classroom nor on the street, nowhere. He felt magnificently free.

When it was all over, Alice looked at him with a radiant expression in her eyes. "Can you still say that you have doubts about Him?"

"No."

And Alice said, "I would like to teach you to love Him just as I do."

They were standing on the broad steps of the church and Edward's soul was full of laughter. Unfortunately, just at that moment the directress was walking by and she saw them.

3

This was bad. We must recall (for the sake of those to whom perhaps the historical background of the story is missing) that although it is true people weren't forbidden to go to church, all the same, churchgoing was not without a certain danger.

This is not so difficult to understand. Those who had been leading the fight for the revolution were very proud, and their pride went by the name of: *standing on the correct side of the front lines.* When ten or twelve years have already passed since the revolution (as had happened approximately at the time of our story), the front lines begin to melt away, and with them the correct side. No wonder former adherents of the revolution feel cheated and are quick to seek *substitute* fronts. Thanks to religion they can (as atheists opposing believers) stand again in all their glory on the correct side and retain that so habitual and precious sense of their own superiority.

But to tell the truth, the substitute front was also useful to others, and it will perhaps not be too premature to disclose that Alice was one of them. Just as the directress wanted to be on the *correct* side, Alice wanted to be on the *opposite* side. During the revolution they had nationalized her dad's business and Alice hated those who had done this to him. But how should she show her hatred? Perhaps by taking a knife and avenging her father? But this sort of thing is not the custom in Bohemia. Alice had a better alternative for expressing her opposition: she began to believe in God.

Thus the Lord came to the aid of both sides (who had already almost lost the living reason for their positions), and, thanks to Him, Edward found himself between Scylla and Charybdis.

When on Monday morning the directress came up to Edward in the staff room, he felt very insecure. There was no way he could invoke the friendly atmosphere of their first talk because since that time (whether through artlessness or carelessness) he had never again engaged in polite conversation with her. The directress therefore had good reason to address him with a conspicuously cold smile:

"We saw each other yesterday, didn't we?"

"Yes, we did," said Edward.

The directress went on, "I can't understand how a young man can go to church." Edward shrugged his shoulders in bewilderment and the directress shook her head. "A young man."

"I went to see the baroque interior of the cathedral," said Edward by way of an excuse.

"Ah, so that's it," said the directress ironically, "I didn't know you had such artistic interests."

This conversation wasn't a bit pleasant for Edward. He remembered how his brother had circled his fellow student three times and then roared with laughter. It seemed to him that family history was repeating itself and he felt afraid. On Saturday he made his excuses over the telephone to Alice, saying that he wouldn't be going to church because he had a cold.

"You are a real mollycoddle," Alice rebuked him after Sunday and it seemed to Edward that her words sounded cold. So he began to tell her (enigmatically and vaguely, because he was ashamed to admit his fear and his true reasons) about the wrongs being done him at school, and about the horrible directress who was persecuting him for no reason. He wanted to get her pity and sympathy, but Alice said:

"My woman boss, on the contrary, isn't bad at all," and giggling, she began to relate stories about her work. Edward listened to her merry voice and became more and more gloomy.

4

Ladies and gentlemen, these were weeks of torment. Edward longed hellishly for Alice. Her body fired him up and yet this very body was utterly inaccessible to him. The settings in which their dates took place were also agonizing. Either they hung about together for an hour or two in the streets after dark or they went to the movies. The banality and the negligible erotic possibilities of these two variants (there weren't any others) prompted Edward to think that perhaps he would achieve more outstanding successes if they could meet in a different environment. Once, with an ingenuous face, he proposed that for the weekend they go to the country and visit his brother, who had a cottage in a wooded valley by a river. He excitedly described the innocent beauties of nature. However, Alice (naive and credulous in every other respect) swiftly saw through him and categorically refused. It wasn't Alice alone who was repulsing him. It was Alice's God Himself (eternally vigilant and wary).

This God embodied a single idea (He had no other wishes or concerns): He forbade extramartial sex. He was therefore a rather comical God, but let's not laugh at Alice for that. Of the ten commandments which Moses gave to the people, fully nine didn't trouble her at all; she didn't feel like killing or not honoring her father, or coveting her neighbor's wife. But the one remaining commandment she felt to be not *self-evident,* and therefore a genuine inconvenience and imposition, the famous seventh: *Thou shalt not commit adultery.* If she wanted to put her religious faith into practice somehow, to prove and demonstrate it, she had then to fasten onto this single commandment. She had thereby created for herself from an obscure, diffuse, and abstract God, a God who was quite specific, comprehensible, and concrete: the God of No Fornication.

I ask you where in fact does fornication begin? Every woman fixes this boundary for herself according to totally mysterious criteria. Alice quite happily allowed Edward to kiss her, and after many, many attempts she eventually became reconciled to letting him stroke her breasts. However, at the middle of her body, let's say at her navel, she drew a strict and uncompromising line below which lay the area of sacred prohibitions, the area of Moses's denial and of the anger of the Lord.

Edward began to read the Bible and to study basic theological literature. He had decided to fight Alice with her own weapons.

"Alice dear," he then said to her, "if we love God, nothing is forbidden. If we long for something, it's because of His will. Christ wanted nothing but that we should all be ruled by love."

"Yes," said Alice, "but a different love from the one you're thinking of."

"There's only one love," said Edward.

"That would certainly suit you," she said, "only God set down certain commandments, and we must abide by them."

"Yes, the Old Testament God," said Edward, "but not the Christian God."

"How's that? Surely there's only one God," objected Alice.

"Yes," said Edward, "only the Jews of the Old Testament understood him a little differently from the way we do. Before the coming of Christ, men had to abide above all by a specific system of God's commandments and laws. What a man was like inside was not so important. But Christ considered some of these prohibitions and regulations to be external. For Him, the most important thing was what a man is like inside. When a man is true to his own ardent, believing heart, everything he does will be good and pleasing to God. After all, that's why St. Paul said, 'Everything is pure to the man who is pure at heart.'"

"Only I wonder if you are this pure-hearted man."

"And St. Augustine," continued Edward, "said, 'Love God and do what it pleases you to do.' Do you understand, Alice? Love God and do what it pleases you to do!"

"Only what pleases you will never please me," she replied, and Edward understood that his theological assault had foundered completely this time, therefore he said:

"You don't like me."

"I do," said Alice in a terribly matter-of-fact way. "And that's why I don't want us to do anything that we shouldn't do!"

As we have already mentioned, these were tormenting weeks. And the torment was that much greater because Edward's desire for Alice was not only the desire of a body for a body; on the contrary, the more she refused him her body, the more lonesome and afflicted he became and the more he coveted her heart as well. However, neither her body nor her heart wanted to do anything about it; they were equally cold, equally wrapped up in themselves, and contentedly self-sufficient.

It was precisely this unruffled moderation of hers which exasperated Edward most in his relations with Alice. Although in other respects he was quite a sober young man, he began to long for some extreme action through which he could drive Alice out of her unruffled state. And because it was too risky to provoke her through blasphemy or cynicism (to which by nature he was attracted), he had to go to the opposite (and therefore far more difficult) extreme, which would coincide with Alice's own position but would be so overdone that it would put her to shame. To put it more simply: Edward began to exaggerate his religiousness. He didn't miss a single visit to church (his desire for Alice was greater than his fear of unpleasantnesses) and once there he behaved with eccentric humility: at every opportunity he knelt, while Alice prayed beside him and crossed herself standing, because she was afraid for her stockings.

One day he criticized her for her lukewarm religiosity. He reminded her of Jesus's words: "Not everyone who says to me 'Lord, Lord' shall enter the kingdom of heaven." He criticized her, saying that her faith was formal, external, shallow. He criticized her for being too pleased with herself. He criticized her for not being aware of anyone except herself.

As he was saying all this (Alice was not prepared for his attack and defended herself feebly), he suddenly caught sight of a cross on the opposite corner of the street, an old, neglected, metal cross with a rusty, iron Christ. He pretentiously slipped his arm out from under Alice's, stopped and (as a protest against her indifferent heart and a sign of his new offensive) crossed himself with stubborn conspicuousness. He did not even really get to see how this affected Alice, because at that moment he spied on the other side of the street the woman janitor who worked at the school. She was looking at him. Edward realized that he was lost.

5

His fears were confirmed when two days later the woman janitor stopped him in the corridor and loudly informed him that he was to present himself the next day at twelve o'clock at the directress's office: "We have something to talk to you about, comrade."

Edward was overcome by anxiety. In the evening he met Alice so that, as usual, they could hang about for an hour or two in the streets, but Edward no longer pursued his religious crusade. He was downcast and longed to confide what had happened to him, but he didn't dare, because he knew that in order to save his unloved (but indispensable) job, he was ready to betray the Lord without hesitation the next morning. For this reason he preferred not to say a word about the inauspicious summons, so he couldn't even get any consolation. The following day he entered the directress's room in a mood of utter dejection.

In the room four judges awaited him: the directress, the woman janitor, one of Edward's colleagues (a tiny man with glasses), and an unknown (gray-haired) gentleman, whom the others called Comrade Inspector. The directress asked Edward to be seated, and told him they had invited him for just a friendly and unofficial talk. For, she said, the manner in which Edward had been conducting himself in his extracurricular life was making them all uneasy. As she said this she looked at the inspector, who nodded his head in agreement, then at the bespectacled teacher, who had been watching her attentively the whole time. Now, intercepting her glance, he launched into a fluent speech about how we wanted to bring up healthy young people without prejudices and how we had complete responsibility for them because we (the teachers) served as models for them. Precisely for this reason, he said, we could not countenance a religious person within our walls. He developed this thought at length and finally declared that Edward's behavior was a disgrace to the whole school.

Even a few minutes earlier Edward had been convinced that he would deny his recently acquired God and admit that his church attendance and his crossing himself in public were only jokes. Now, however, face to face with the real situation, he felt that he couldn't do it. He could not, after all, say to these four people, so serious and so excited, that they were getting excited about some misunderstanding, some bit of foolishness. He understood that to do that would be to involuntarily mock their earnestness, and he also realized that what they were expecting from him were only quibbles and excuses which they were prepared in advance to reject. He understood (in a flash, there wasn't time for lengthy cogitation) that at that moment the most important thing was for him to appear truthful — more precisely, that his statements should resemble the ideas that they had constructed about him. If he was to succeed in correcting these ideas to a certain extent, he would also have to play their game to a certain extent. Therefore, he said:

"Comrades, may I be frank?"'

"Of course," said the directress. "After all, that's why you're here."

"And you won't be angry?"

"Just talk," said the directress.

"Very well, I shall confess to you then. I really do believe in God."

He glanced at his judges and it seemed to him that they all exhaled with satisfaction. Only the woman janitor snapped at him. "In this day and age, comrade? In this day and age?"

Edward went on. "I knew that you would get angry if I told the truth. But I don't know how to lie. Don't ask me to lie to you."

The directress said (gently): "No one wants you to lie. It's good that you are telling the truth. Only, please tell me how you, a young man, can believe in God!"

"Today, when we fly to the moon!" The teacher lost his temper.

"I can't help it," said Edward. "I don't want to believe in Him. Really, I don't."

"How come you say you don't want to believe, if you do?" The gray-haired gentleman (in an exceedingly kind tone of voice) joined the conversation.

"I don't want to believe, but I do believe." Edward quietly repeated his confession.

The teacher laughed. "But there's a contradiction in that!"

"Comrades, I'm telling it the way it is," said Edward. "I know very well that faith in God leads us away from reality. What would socialism come to if everyone believed that the world was in God's hands? No one would do anything and everyone would just rely on God."

"Exactly," agreed the directress.

"No one has ever yet proved that God exists," stated the teacher with glasses. Edward continued: "The history of mankind is distinguished from prehistory by the fact that people have taken their fate into their own hands and do not need God."

"Faith in God leads to fatalism," said the directress.

"Faith in God belongs to the Middle Ages," said Edward, and then the directress said something again and the teacher said something and Edward said something and the inspector said something, and they were all in complete accord, until finally the teacher with glasses exploded, interrupting Edward:

"So why do you cross yourself in the street, when you know all this?"

Edward looked at him with an immensely sad expression and then said, "Because I believe in God."

"But there's a contradiction in that!" repeated the teacher joyfully.

"Yes," admitted Edward, "there is. There is a contradiction between knowledge and faith. Knowledge is one thing and faith another. I recognize that faith in God will lead us to obscurantism. I recognize that it would be better if He didn't exist. But when here inside I . . ." he pointed with his finger to his heart, "feel that He exists . . . You see, comrades, I'm telling it to you the way it is. It's better that I confess to you, because I don't want to be a hypocrite. I want you to know what I'm really like," and he hung his head.

The teacher's brain was no larger, proportionally, than his body. He didn't know that even the strictest revolutionary considers force only a necessary evil and believes the intrinsic *good* of the revolution lies in re-education. He, who had become a revolutionary overnight, did not enjoy too much respect from the directress and did not suspect that at this moment Edward, who had placed himself at his judges' disposal as a difficult case and yet as an object capable of being remolded, had a thousand times more value than he. And because he didn't suspect it, he attacked Edward with severity and declared that people who did not know how to part with their medieval faith belonged in the Middle Ages and should leave the modern school.

The directress let him finish his speech then administered her rebuke: "I don't like it when heads roll. This comrade was frank; he told us everything just as it was. We must know how to respect this." Then she turned to Edward. "The comrades are right, of course, when they say that religious people cannot educate our youth. What do you yourself suggest?"

"I don't know, comrades," said Edward unhappily.

"This is what I think," said the inspector. "The struggle between the old and the new goes on not only between classes, but also within each individual man. Just such a struggle is going on inside our comrade here. With his reason he knows, but feeling pulls him back. We must help our comrade in this struggle, so that reason may triumph."

The directress nodded. Then she said: "I myself will take charge of him."

6

Edward had thus averted the most pressing danger. His fate as a teacher was now in the hands of the directress exclusively, which was entirely to his satisfaction. He remembered his brother's observation that the directress was always after young men, and with all his vacillating, youthful self-confidence (now deflated, then exaggerated) he resolved to win the contest by gaining as a man the favor of his ruler.

When, according to an agreement, he visited her a few days later in her office, he tried to assume a light tone. He used every opportunity to slip an intimate remark or bit of subtle flattery into the conversation, or to emphasize by way of discreet double-talk his curious position as a man in the hands of a woman. But he was not to be permitted to choose the tone of the conversation. The directress spoke to him affably, but with the utmost restraint. She asked him what he was reading, then she herself named some books and recommended that he should read them. She evidently wanted to embark upon the lengthy job to be done on his thinking. Their short meeting ended with her inviting him to her place.

As a result of the directress's reserve, Edward's self-confidence was deflated again, so he entered her bachelor apartment meekly, with no intention of conquering her with his masculine charm. She seated him in an armchair and, assuming a friendly tone, asked him what he felt like having: some coffee perhaps? He said that he didn't. Some alcohol then? He was embarrassed: "If you have some cognac ..." and was immediately afraid that he had been presumptuous. But the directress replied affably: "No, I don't have cognac, but I do have a little wine," and she fetched a half-empty bottle, whose contents were just sufficient to fill two tumblers.

Then she told Edward that he must not look upon her as some inquisitor; after all, everyone had a complete right to profess what he recognized as right. Naturally, it is another matter (she added at once) whether he is then fit or not fit to be a teacher; for that reason, she said, they had had (although they hadn't been happy about it) to summon Edward and have a talk with him and they (at least she and the inspector) were very pleased with the frank manner in which he had spoken to them, and the fact that he had not denied anything. Then she said she had talked with the inspector about Edward for a very long time and they had decided that they would summon him for another interview in six months' time and that until then the directress would help his development through her influence. And once again she emphasized that she merely wanted *to help him in a friendly way*, that she was neither an inquisitor nor a policeman. Then she mentioned the teacher who had attacked Edward so sharply, and said, "That man is hiding something himself and so he would be ready to sacrifice others. Also, the woman janitor is letting it be known everywhere that you were insolent, and pig-headedly stuck to your opinions, as she puts it. She's not to be talked out of the view that you should be dismissed from the school. Of course, I don't agree with her, but you cannot startle her so completely again. I wouldn't be happy either if someone who crosses himself publicly in the street were teaching my children."

Thus the directress showed Edward in a single outpouring of sentences how attractive were the prospects of her mercy, and also how menacing the prospects of her severity. And then to prove that their meeting was genuinely a friendly one, she digressed to other subjects; she talked about books and led him to her bookcase. She raved about Rolland's *Enchanted Soul* and scolded him for not having read it. Then she asked how he was getting on at the school, and after his conventional reply, she herself spoke at length. She said that she was grateful to fate for her position; she liked her work because it was a means for her to educate children and thus be in continuous and real touch with the future, and only the future could, in the end, justify all this suffering, of which she said ("Yes, we must admit it") there was plenty. "If I did not believe that I was living for something more than just my own life, I couldn't perhaps live at all."

These words suddenly sounded very ingenuous and it was not clear whether the directress was trying to confess or to commence the expected ideological polemic about the meaning of life. Edward decided to interpret them in their personal sense and asked her in a low, discreet voice:

"And how about your own life?"

"My life?" she repeated after him.

"Wouldn't it have been satisfying in itself?"

A bitter smile appeared on her face and Edward felt almost sorry for her at that moment. She was pitifully hideous: her black hair cast a shadow over her bony, elongated face and the black down under her nose began to look as conspicuous as a mustache. Suddenly he glimpsed all the sorrow of her life. He perceived her gypsylike features, revealing passion, and he perceived her ugliness, revealing the hopelessness of that passion; he imagined how she had passionately turned into a living statue of grief upon Stalin's death, how she had passionately sat up late at hundreds of thousands of meetings, how she had passionately struggled against poor Jesus. And he understood that all this was only a sad outlet for her desire, which could not flow where she wished it to. Edward was young and his compassion was not used up. He looked at the directress with sympathy. She, however, as if ashamed of having involuntarily fallen silent, now assumed a brisk tone and went on:

"It doesn't depend on that at all, Edward. Anyhow, a man is not in the world only for his own sake. He always lives for something." She looked deeply into his eyes: "However, the question is for what. For something real or for something fictitious? God — that is a beautiful fiction. But the future of the people, Edward, that is reality. And I have lived for reality, I have given up everything for reality."

She spoke with such an air of commitment, that Edward did not stop feeling that sudden rush of human sympathy which had awoken in him a short while before. It struck him as stupid that he should be lying to another human being (one fellow creature to another), and it seemed to him that this intimate moment in their conversation offered him the opportunity to cast away finally the unworthy (and after all difficult) pretense of being a believer.

"But I quite agree with you," he quickly assured her. "I too prefer reality. Don't take this religion of mine so seriously."

He soon learned that a man should never let himself be led astray by a rash fit of emotion. The directress looked at him in surprise and said with perceptible coldness: "Don't pretend. I liked you because you were frank. Now you're pretending to be something that you aren't."

No, Edward was not to be permitted to step out of the religious costume in which he had originally clothed himself. He quickly reconciled himself to this and tried hard to correct the bad impression: "No, I didn't mean to be evasive. Of course I believe in God, I would never deny that. I only wanted to say that I also believe in the future of humanity, in progress and all that. After all, if I didn't believe in that, what would my work as a teacher be for? Why should children be born and why should we live at all? And I've come to think that it is also God's will that society continue to advance toward something better. I have thought that a man can believe in God and in communism, that it is possible for them to be combined."

"No," the directress smiled with maternal authoritativeness, "it isn't possible for those two things to be combined."

"I know," said Edward sadly. "Don't be angry with me."

"I'm not angry. You are still a young man and you obstinately stick to what you believe. No one understands you the way I do. After all I was young once too. I know what it's like to be young. And I like your youthfulness. Yes, I rather like you."

And now it finally happened. Neither earlier nor later, but now, at precisely the right moment. It is evident that Edward was not the instigator but merely the instrument. When the directress said she rather liked him he replied, not too expressively:

"I like you too."

"Really?"

"Really."

"Well I never! I'm an old woman ..." objected the directress.

"That's not true," Edward had to say.

"But it is," said the directress.

"You're not at all old, that's nonsense," he had to say very resolutely.

"You think so?"

"It happens that I like you very much."

"Don't lie. You know you mustn't lie."

"I'm not lying. You're pretty."

"Pretty?" The directress made a face to show that she didn't really believe it.

"Yes, pretty," said Edward, and because he was struck by the obvious incredibility of his assertion, he at once took pains to support it: "I'm mad about black-haired women like you."

"You like black-haired women?" asked the directress.

"I'm mad about them," said Edward.

"And why haven't you come by all the time that you've been at the school? I had the feeling that you were avoiding me."

"I was ashamed," said Edward. "Everyone would have said that I was sucking up to you. No one would have believed that I was coming to see you only because I liked you."

"But you must not be ashamed," said the directress. "Now it has *been decided* that you must meet with me from time to time."

She looked into his eyes with her large brown irises (let us admit that in themselves they were beautiful), and just before he left she lightly stroked his hand, so that this foolish fellow went off with the sprightly feeling of a winner.

7

Edward was sure that the unpleasant affair had been settled to his advantage, and the next Sunday, feeling carefree and impudent, he went to church with Alice. Not only that, he went full of self-confidence — for (although this arouses in us a compassionate smile) in retrospect, he perceived the events at the directress's apartment as glaring evidence of his masculine appeal.

In addition, this particular Sunday in church he noticed that Alice was somehow different; as soon as they met she slipped her hand under his arm and even in church clung to him. Formerly she had behaved modestly and inconspicuously; now she kept looking around and smilingly greeted at least ten acquaintances.

This was curious and Edward didn't understand it.

Then two days later as they were walking together along the streets after dark, Edward became aware to his amazement that her kisses, once so unpleasantly matter-of-fact, had become damp, warm, and passionate. When they stopped for a moment under a street lamp he found that her eyes were looking amorously at him.

"Let me tell you this, I like you," blurted out Alice and immediately covered his mouth. "No, no, don't say anything; I'm ashamed, I don't want to hear anything."

Again they walked a little way and again they stopped. This time Alice said, "Now I understand everything. I understand why you reproached me for being too comfortable in my faith."

Edward, however, didn't understand anything. So he also didn't say anything. When they'd walked a bit further, Alice said, "And you didn't say anything to me. Why didn't you say anything to me?"

"And what should I have said to you?" asked Edward.

"Yes, that's you all over," she said with quiet enthusiasm. "Others would put on airs; but you are silent. But that's exactly why I like you."

Edward began to suspect what she was talking about, but nevertheless he questioned her. "What are you talking about?"

"About what happened to you."

"And who told you about it?"

"Come on! Everybody knows about it. They summoned you, they threatened you, and you laughed in their faces. You didn't retract anything. Everyone admires you."

"But I didn't tell anyone about it."

"Don't be naive. A thing like that gets around. After all, it's no small matter. How often today do you find someone who has a little courage?"

Edward knew that in a small town every event is quickly turned into a legend, but he hadn't suspected that the worthless episodes he'd been involved in, whose significance he'd never overestimated, possessed the stuff of which legends are made. He hadn't sufficiently realized how very useful he was to his fellow country-men who, as is well-known, do not really like *heroes* (men who struggle and conquer), but rather *martyrs,* for such men soothingly reassure them about their loyal inactivity, and corroborate their view that life provides only two alternatives: to be submissive or to be destroyed. Nobody doubted that Edward would be destroyed, and admiringly and complacently they all passed this on, until now, through Alice, he himself encountered the beautiful image of his own crucifixion. He accepted it cold-bloodedly and said:

"But my not retracting anything was after all a matter of course. Anyone would have done that much."

"Anyone?" blurted out Alice. "Look around you at what they all do! How cowardly they are! They would renounce their own mothers!"

Edward was silent and Alice was silent. They walked along holding hands. Then Alice said in a whisper: "I would do anything for you."

No one had ever said such words to Edward. They were an unexpected gift. Of course, Edward knew that they were an undeserved gift, but he said to himself that if fate withheld from him deserved gifts, he had a complete right to accept these undeserved ones. Therefore he said:

"No one can do anything for me any more."

"How's that?" whispered Alice.

"They'll drive me from the school and those who speak of me today as a hero won't lift a finger for me. Only one thing is certain. I shall remain entirely alone."

"You won't," Alice shook her head.

"I will," said Edward.

"You won't!" Alice almost shrieked.

"They've all abandoned me."

"I'll never abandon you," said Alice.

"You will," said Edward sadly.

"No, I won't," said Alice.

"No, Alice," said Edward, "you don't like me. You've never liked me."

"That's not true," whispered Alice and Edward noticed with satisfaction that her eyes were wet.

"You don't, Alice; a person can feel that sort of thing. You were always cold to me. A woman who loves a man doesn't behave like that. I know that very well. And now you feel pity for me, because you know they want to ruin me. But you don't really like me and I don't want you to deceive yourself about it."

They walked still further, silently, holding hands. Alice cried quietly for a while, then all at once she stopped walking and amid sobs said, "No, that's not true. You mustn't believe that. That's not true."

"It is," said Edward, and when Alice did not stop crying, he suggested that on Saturday they go to the country. In a beautiful valley by the river was his brother's cottage, where they could be alone.

Alice's face was wet with tears as she dumbly nodded her assent.

8

That was on Tuesday, and when on Thursday he was again invited to the directress's bachelor apartment, he made his way there with gay self-assurance, for he had absolutely no doubt that his natural charm would definitively dissolve the church scandal into little more than a cloud of smoke, a mere nothing. But this is the way life goes: a man imagines that he is playing his role in a particular play, and does not suspect that in the meantime they have changed the scenery without his noticing, and he unknowingly finds himself in the middle of a rather different performance.

He was again seated in the armchair opposite the directress. Between them was a little table and on it a bottle of cognac and two glasses. And this bottle of cognac was precisely that new prop by which a bright man with a sober temperament would have immediately recognized that the church scandal was no longer the matter in question.

But innocent Edward was so intoxicated with himself that at first he didn't realize this at all. He quite gaily took part in the opening conversation (the subject matter of which was vague and general). He drank the glass that was offered him, and was quite ingenuously bored. After half an hour or an hour the directress inconspicuously changed to more personal topics; she talked a lot about herself and from her words there emerged before Edward the image that she wanted: that of a sensible, middle-aged woman, not too happy, but reconciled to her lot in a dignified way; a woman who regretted nothing and even expressed satisfaction that she was not married, because only in this way, after all, could she fully enjoy her independence and privacy. This life had provided her with a beautiful apartment, where she felt happy and where perhaps now Edward was also not too uncomfortable.

"No, it's really very nice here," said Edward, and he said it glumly, because just at that moment he had stopped feeling good. The bottle of cognac (which he had inadvertently asked for on his first visit and which was now hurried to the table with such menacing readiness), the four walls of the bachelor apartment (creating a space which was becoming ever more constricting and confining), the directress's monologue (focusing on subjects ever more personal), her glance (dangerously fixed), all this caused *the change of program* to begin finally to get to him. He understood that he had entered into a situation, the development of which was irrevocably predetermined. He realized that his livelihood was jeopardized not by the directress's aversion, but just the contrary, by his physical aversion to this skinny woman with the down under her nose, who was urging him to drink. His anxiety made his throat contract.

He listened to the directress and had a drink, but now his anxiety was so strong that the alcohol had no effect on him at all. On the other hand, after a couple of drinks the directress was already so thoroughly carried away that she abandoned her usual sobriety, and her words acquired an exaltation that was almost threatening. "One thing I envy you," she said, "that you are so young. You cannot know yet what disappointment is, what disillusion is. You still see the world as full of hope and beauty."

She leaned across the table in Edward's direction and in gloomy silence (with a smile that was rigidly forced) fixed her frightfully large eyes on him, while he said to himself that if he didn't manage to get a bit drunk, he'd be in real trouble before the evening was over. To that end he poured some cognac into his glass and downed it quickly.

And the directress went on: "But I want to see it like that! The way you do!" And then she got up from the armchair, thrust out her chest, and said, "That I am not a boring woman! That I'm not!" And she walked around the little table and grabbed Edward by the sleeve. "That I'm not!"

"No," said Edward.

"Come, let's dance," she said, and letting go of Edward's arm she skipped over to the radio and turned the dial until she found some dance music. Then she stood over Edward with a smile.

Edward got up, seized the directress, and began to guide her around the room to the rhythm of the music. Every now and then the directress would tenderly lay her head on his shoulder, then suddenly raise it again, to gaze into his eyes, then, after another little while, she would sing along with the melody in a low voice.

Edward felt so out of sorts that several times he stopped dancing to have a drink. He longed for nothing more than to put an end to the discomfort of this interminable trudging around, but also he feared nothing more. For the discomfort of what would follow the dancing seemed to him even more unbearable. And so he continued to guide the lady who was singing to herself around the room and at the same time steadily (and meticulously) observe in himself the influence of the alcohol, which he longed for. When it finally seemed to him that his brain was sufficiently deadened, with his right arm he firmly pressed the directress against his body and put his left hand on her breast.

Yes, he did the very thing that had been frightening him the whole evening. He would have given anything not to have had to do this, but if he did it all the same, then believe me, it was only because he really *had* to. The situation, which he had got into at the very beginning of the evening, was so compelling that, though it was no doubt possible to slow down its course, it was not possible to stop it, so that when Edward put his hand on the directress's breast, he was merely submitting to totally irreversible necessity.

The results of his action exceeded all expectations. As if by magic command, the directress began to writhe in his arms and in no time had placed her hairy upper lip on his mouth. Then she dragged him onto the couch and, wildly writhing and loudly sighing, bit his lip and the tip of his tongue, which hurt Edward a lot. Then she slipped out of his arms, said, "Wait!" and ran off to the bathroom.

Edward licked his finger and found out that his tongue was bleeding slightly. The bite hurt so much that his painstakingly induced intoxication receded, and once again his throat contracted from anxiety at the thought of what awaited him. From the bathroom could be heard a loud running and splashing of water. He picked up the bottle of cognac, put it to his lips, and drank deeply.

But by this time the directress had already appeared in the doorway in a transparent nylon nightgown (thickly decorated with lace over the breasts), and was walking steadily toward Edward. She embraced him. Then she stepped back and reproachfully asked, "Why are you still dressed?"

Edward took off his jacket and, looking at the directress (who had her big eyes fixed on him), he couldn't think of anything but the fact that there was the greatest likelihood that his body would sabotage his assiduous will. Wishing therefore to arouse his body somehow or other, he said in an uncertain voice, "Undress completely."

With a violent and enthusiastically obedient movement she flung off her nylon nightie and bared her skinny white body, in the middle of which her thick black bush protruded in gloomy desolation. She came slowly toward him and with terror Edward discovered what he already knew anyway: his body was completely fettered by anxiety.

I know, gentlemen, that in the course of the years you have become accustomed to the occasional insubordination of your own bodies, and that this no longer upsets you at all. But understand, Edward was young then! His body's sabotage threw him into an incredible panic each time and he bore it as an inexpiable disgrace, whether the witness to it was a beautiful face or one as hideous and comical as the directress's. The directress was now only a step away from him, and he, frightened and not knowing what to do, all at once said, he didn't even know how (it was rather the fruit of inspiration than of cunning reflection): "No, no, oh Lord, no! No, it is a sin, it would be a sin!" and jumped away.

The directress kept coming toward him muttering in a husky voice: "What sin? There is no sin!"

Edward retreated behind the round table, where they had been sitting a while before: "No, I can't do this, I can't do it."

The directress pushed aside the armchair, standing in her path, and went after Edward, never taking her large brown eyes off him. "There is no sin! There is no sin!"

Edward went around the table, behind him was only the couch and the directress was a mere step away. Now he could no longer escape and perhaps his very desperation advised him at this moment of impasse to command her: "Kneel!"

She stared at him uncomprehendingly, but when he once again repeated in a firm (though desperate) voice, "Kneel!" she enthusiastically fell to her knees in front of him and embraced his legs.

"Take those hands off," he called her to order. "Clasp them!"

Once again she looked at him uncomprehendingly.

"Clasp them! Did you hear?"

She clasped her hands.

"Pray," he commanded.

She had her hands clasped and she glanced up at him devotedly.

"Pray, so that God may forgive us," he hissed.

She had her hands clasped. She was looking up at him with her large eyes and Edward not only obtained an advantageous respite, but looking down at her from above, he began to lose the oppressive feeling that he was mere prey, and he regained his self-assurance. He stepped back, away from her, so that he could survey the whole of her, and once again commanded, "Pray!"

When she remained silent, he yelled: "Aloud!"

And the skinny, naked, kneeling woman began to recite: "Our Father, who art in heaven, hallowed be Thy name. Thy kingdom come. . . ."

As she uttered the words of the prayer, she glanced up at him as if he were God Himself. He watched her with growing pleasure. In front of him was kneeling the directress, being humiliated by a subordinate; in front of him a naked revolutionary was being humiliated by prayer; in front of him a praying lady was being humiliated by her nakedness.

This threefold image of degradation intoxicated him and something unexpected suddenly happened: his body revoked its passive resistance. Edward was excited!

As the directress said, "And lead us not into temptation," he quickly threw off all his clothes. When she said, "Amen," he violently lifted her off the floor and dragged her onto the couch.

9

That was on Thursday, and on Saturday Edward went with Alice to the country to visit his brother, who welcomed them warmly and lent them the key to the nearby cottage.

The two lovers spent the whole afternoon wandering through the woods and meadows. They kissed and Edward's contented hands found that the imaginary line, level with her navel which separated the sphere of innocence from that of fornication, didn't count any more. At first he wanted to verify the so long awaited event verbally, but he became frightened of doing so and understood that he had to keep silent.

His judgment was quite correct, it seemed. Alice's unexpected turnabout had occurred independently of his many weeks of persuasion, independently of his argumentation, independently of any *logical* consideration whatsoever. In fact, it was based exclusively upon the news of Edward's martyrdom, consequently upon a *mistake,* and it had been deduced quite *illogically* even from this mistake. Why should Edward's sufferings for his fidelity to his beliefs have as a result Alice's infidelity to God's law? If Edward had not betrayed God before the fact-finding commission, why should she now betray Him before Edward?

In such a situation any reflection expressed aloud could reveal to Alice the inconsistency of her attitude. So Edward prudently kept silent, which went unnoticed, because Alice herself kept chattering. She was gay, and nothing indicated that this turnabout in her soul had been dramatic or painful.

When it got dark they went back to the cottage, turned on the lights, made the bed, and kissed, whereupon Alice asked Edward to turn off the lights. However, the light of the stars continued to show through thc window, so Edward had to close the shutters as well upon Alice's request. Then, in total darkness, Alice undressed and gave herself to him.

Edward had been looking forward to this moment for so many weeks, but surprisingly enough, now, when it was actually taking place, he didn't have the feeling that it would be as significant as the length of time he had been waiting for it suggested; it seemed to him so easy and self-evident that during the act of intercourse he was almost not concentrating. Rather, he was vainly trying to drive away the thoughts that were running through his head of those long, futile weeks when Alice had tormented him with her coldness. It all came back to him: the suffering at the school, of which she had been the cause, and, instead of gratitude for her giving of herself to him, he began to feel a certain vindictiveness and anger. It irritated him how easily and remorselessly she was now betraying her God of No Fornication, whom she had once so fanatically worshiped. It irritated him that nothing was able to throw her off balance, no desire, no event, no upset. It irritated him how she experienced everything without inner conflict — self-confidently and easily. And when this irritation threatened to overcome him with its power, he strove to make love to her passionately and furiously so as to force from her some sort of sound, moan, word, or pathetic cry, but he didn't succeed. The girl was quiet and in spite of all his exertions in their love-making, it ended silently and undramatically.

Then she snuggled up against his chest and quickly fell asleep, while Edward lay awake for a long time and realized that he felt no joy at all. He made an effort to imagine Alice (not her physical appearance but, if possible, her being in its entirety) and it occurred to him that he saw her *blurred*.

Let's stop at this word: Alice, as Edward had seen her until this time, was, with all her naiveté, a stable and distinct being. The beautiful simplicity of her looks seemed to accord with the unaffected simplicity of her faith, and her simple fate seemed to be a substantiation of her attitude. Until this time Edward had seen her as solid and coherent; he could laugh at her, he could curse her, he could besiege her with his guile, but he (involuntarily) had to respect her.

Now, however, the unpremeditated snare of false news caused a split in the coherence of her being and it seemed to Edward that her convictions were in fact only something *extraneous* to her fate, and her fate only something extraneous to her body. He saw her as an accidental conjunction of a body, thoughts, and a life's course; an inorganic conjunction, arbitrary and unstable. He visualized Alice (she was breathing deeply on his shoulder) and he saw her body separately from her thoughts. He liked this body but the thoughts struck him as ridiculous, and together they did not form a whole being. He saw her as an ink line spreading on blotting paper, without contours, without shape.

He really liked this body. When Alice got up in the morning, he forced her to remain naked, and, although just yesterday she had stubbornly insisted on closed shutters, for even the dim light of the stars had bothered her, she now altogether forgot her shame. Edward was scrutinizing her (she gaily pranced about, looking for a package of tea and cookies for breakfast), and Alice, when she glanced at him after a moment, noticed that he was lost in thought. She asked him what was the matter. Edward replied that after breakfast he had to go and see his brother.

His brother inquired how he was getting on at the school. Edward replied that on the whole it was fine, and his brother said, "That Chehachkova is a pig, but I forgave her long ago. I forgave her, for she did not know what she was doing. She wanted to harm me, but instead she helped me find a beautiful life. As a farmer I earn more, and contact with Nature protects me from the skepticism to which city-dwellers are prone."

"That woman, as a matter of fact, brought me some happiness too," said Edward, lost in thought, and he told his brother how he had fallen in love with Alice, how he had feigned a belief in God, how they had judged him, how Chehachkova had wanted to re-educate him, and how Alice had finally given herself to him thinking he was a martyr. The only thing he didn't tell was how he had forced the directress to recite the Lord's Prayer, because he saw disapproval in his brother's eyes. He stopped talking and his brother said:

"I may have a great many faults, but one I don't have: I've never dissimulated and I've said to everyone's face what I thought."

Edward liked his brother and his disapproval hurt, so he made an effort to justify himself and they began to argue. In the end Edward said:

"I know, brother, that you are a straightforward man, and that you pride yourself on it. But put one question to yourself: *why* in fact should one tell the truth? What obliges us to do it? And why do we consider telling the truth a virtue? Imagine that you meet a madman, who claims that he is a fish and that we are all fish. Are you going to argue with him? Are you going to undress in front of him and show him that you don't have fins? Are you going to say to his face what you think? Well, tell me!"

His brother was silent and Edward went on: "If you told him the whole truth and nothing but the truth, only what you really thought, you would enter into a serious conversation with a madman and you yourself would become mad. And it is the same way with the world that surrounds us. If I obstinately told a man the truth to his face, it would mean that I was taking him seriously. And to take something so unimportant seriously means to become less than serious oneself. I, you see, *must* lie, if I don't want to take madmen seriously and become one of them myself."

10

It was Sunday afternoon and the two lovers left for town. They were alone in a compartment (the girl was already gaily chattering away again), and Edward remembered how some time ago he had looked forward to finding in Alice, whom he'd chosen voluntarily, the seriousness of life, which his duties would never provide for him. And with regret he realized (the train idyllically clattered against the joints between the rails) that the love affair he'd experienced with Alice was worthless, made up of chance and errors, without any importance or sense whatsoever. He heard Alice's words, he saw her gestures (she squeezed his hand), and it occurred to him that these were signs devoid of meaning, currency without funds, weights made of paper, and that he couldn't grant them significance any more than God could the prayer of the naked directress. And all of a sudden it seemed to him that, in fact, all the people whom he'd met in his new place of work were only ink lines spreading on blotting paper, beings with interchangeable attitudes, beings without firm substance. But what was worse, what was far worse (it struck him next) was that he himself was only a shadow of all these shadowy people. After all, he had been exhausting his own brain only to adjust to them and imitate them. Yet even if he was inwardly laughing, and thus making an effort to mock them secretly (and so exonerate his accommodation), it didn't alter the case. For even malicious imitation remains imitation, and the shadow that mocks remains a shadow, subordinate, derivative, and wretched, and nothing more.

It was ignominious, horribly ignominious. The train idyllically clattered against the joints between the rails (the girl chattered away) and Edward said:

"Alice, are you happy?"

"Sure," said Alice.

"I'm miserable," said Edward.

"What, are you crazy?" said Alice.

"We shouldn't have done it. It shouldn't have happened."

"What's gotten into you? After all, you're the one who wanted to do it!"

"Yes, I wanted to," said Edward, "but that was my greatest mistake, for which God will never forgive me. It was a sin, Alice."

"Come on, what's happened to you?" said the girl calmly. "You yourself always used to say that God wants love most of all!"

When Edward heard Alice, after the fact, coolly appropriating the theological sophistries with which he had so unsuccessfully taken the field a while ago, fury seized him: "I used to say that to test you. Now I've found out how well you are able to be faithful to God! But a person who is able to betray God is able to betray man a hundred times more easily."

Alice found more ready answers, but it would have been better for her if she hadn't, because they only provoked his vindictive rage. Edward went on and on talking (in the end he used the words "disgust" and "physical aversion") until finally he did obtain from this placid and gentle face sobs, tears, and moans.

"Goodbye," he told her at the station and left her in tears. Only at home several hours later, when this curious anger had subsided, did it occur to him what he had done. He imagined her body, which had pranced stark naked in front of him that morning, and when he realized that this beautiful body was lost to him because he himself, of his own free will, had driven it away, he inwardly called himself an idiot and had a mind to slap his own face.

But what had happened, had happened, and it was no longer possible to right anything.

Though we must truthfully say that even if the idea of the beautiful, rejected body caused Edward a certain amount of grief, he coped with this loss fairly soon. If once the need for physical love had tormented him and reduced him to a state of longing, it was the short-lived need of a recent arrival. Edward no longer suffered from this need. Once a week he visited the directress (habit had relieved his body of its initial anxieties), and he resolved to continue to visit her, until his position at the school was clarified. Besides this, with increasing success he chased all sorts of other women and girls. As a consequence of both, he began to appreciate far more the times when he was alone, and became fond of solitary walks, which he sometimes combined (come, let us turn our attention to this for the last time) with a visit to a church.

No, don't be apprehensive, Edward did not begin to believe in God. Our story does not intend to be crowned with the effect of so ostentatious a paradox. But Edward, even if he was almost certain that God did not exist, after all felt happy and nostalgic entertaining the thought of Him.

God is essence itself, whereas Edward had never found (and since the incidents with the directress and with Alice, a number of years had passed) anything essential in his love affairs, or in his teaching, or in his thoughts. He was too bright to concede that he saw the essential in the unessential, but he was too weak not to long secretly for the essential.

Ah, ladies and gentlemen, a man lives a sad life when he cannot take anything or anyone seriously.

And that is why Edward longed for God, for God alone is relieved of the distracting obligation of *appearing* and can merely *be*. For He solely constitutes (He Himself, alone and nonexistent) the essential opposite of this unessential (but so much more existent) world.

And so Edward occasionally sits in church and looks thoughtfully at the cupola. Let us take leave of him at just such a time. It is afternoon, the church is quiet and empty. Edward is sitting in a pew tormented with sorrow, because God does not exist. But just at this moment his sorrow is so great that suddenly from its depth emerges the genuine *living* face of God. Look! Yes. Edward is smiling! He is smiling, and his smile is happy . . .

Please, keep him in your memory with this smile.

D. H. LAWRENCE

D(avid) H(erbert) Lawrence (1885–1930) was born in Nottinghamshire, England, the son of a coal miner and an ex-teacher. Raised in poverty, frequently ill, he was intensely attached to his mother, who, determined to keep him from going to the mines, encouraged his interest in education. By way of scholarship and hard work he eventually became a teacher. His first novel, *Sons and Lovers* (1913), is an autobiographical account of his early years. He led a wandering life — in part because his wife, of German origin, was subjected to harassment in England during World War I; in part because his novel *The Rainbow* (1915) was declared obscene by British police. He roamed from England to the Continent to Ceylon and Australia to America and Mexico. Constantly poor, and ill with tuberculosis, he nonetheless achieved a remarkable body of work. His other novels include *Women in Love* (1920), *Kangaroo* (1923), *The Plumed Serpent* (1926), and *Lady Chatterly's Lover* (1928). He wrote many stories, collected in *The Prussian Officer* (1914), *England, My England* (1922), *The Woman Who Rode Away* (1928), and *Collected Short Stories* (1955). Always frank about sexuality and outspokenly critical of bourgeois morality, Lawrence was invariably under fire for alleged obscenity; the uproar over *Lady Chatterly's Lover* was so furious that almost thirty years passed before unexpurgated versions were published in England and the United States. Although Lawrence's fiction is both passionate and erotically based, it would hardly occasion such scandal if published now for the first time. What remains perennially remarkable about his work — its intense portrayal of character and human subconsciousness, its devotion to the physicality of the world, and its stylistic flow — may be seen in the stories here, "The Prussian Officer" and "The Rocking-Horse Winner."

The Prussian Officer

They had marched more than thirty kilometres since dawn, along the white, hot road where occasional thickets of trees threw a moment of shade, then out into the glare again. On either hand, the valley, wide and shallow, glittered with heat; dark green patches of rye, pale young corn, fallow and meadow and black pine woods spread in a dull, hot diagram under a glistening sky. But right in front the mountains ranged across, pale blue and very still, snow gleaming gently out of the deep atmosphere. And towards the mountains, on and on, the regiment marched between the rye fields and the meadows, between the scraggy fruit trees set regularly on either side the high road. The burnished, dark green rye threw off a suffocating heat, the mountains drew gradually nearer and more distinct. While the feet of the soldiers grew hotter, sweat ran through their hair under their helmets, and their knapsacks could burn no more in contact with their shoulders, but seemed instead to give off a cold, prickly sensation.

He walked on and on in silence, staring at the mountains ahead, that rose sheer out of the land and stood fold behind fold, half earth, half heaven, the heaven, the barrier with slits of soft snow, in the pale, bluish peaks.

He could now walk almost without pain. At the start, he had determined not to limp. It had made him sick to take the first steps, and during the first mile or so, he had compressed his breath, and the cold drops of sweat had stood on his forehead. But he had walked it off. What were they after all but bruises! He had looked at them, as he was getting up: deep bruises on the backs of his thighs. And since he had made his first step in the morning, he had been conscious of them, till now he had a tight, hot place in his chest, with suppressing the pain, and holding himself in. There seemed no air when he breathed. But he walked almost lightly.

The Captain's hand had trembled at taking his coffee at dawn: his orderly saw it again. And he saw the fine figure of the Captain wheeling on horseback at the farmhouse ahead, a handsome figure in pale blue uniform with facings of scarlet, and the metal gleaming on the black helmet and the sword-scabbard, and dark streaks of sweat coming on the silky bay horse. The orderly felt he was connected with that figure moving so suddenly on horseback: he followed it like a shadow, mute and inevitable and damned by it. And the officer was always aware of the tramp of the company behind, the march of his orderly among the men.

The Captain was a tall man of about forty, grey at the temples. He had a handsome, finely knit figure, and was one of the best horsemen in the West. His orderly, having to rub him down, admired the amazing riding-muscles of his loins.

For the rest, the orderly scarcely noticed the officer any more than he noticed himself. It was rarely he saw his master's face: he did not look at it. The Captain had reddish brown, stiff hair that he wore short upon his skull. His moustache was also cut short and bristly over a full, brutal mouth. His face was rather rugged, the cheeks thin. Perhaps the man was the more handsome for the deep lines in his face, the irritable tension of his brow, which gave him the look of a man who fights with life. His fair eyebrows stood bushy over light blue eyes that were always flashing with cold fire.

He was a Prussian aristocrat, haughty and overbearing. But his mother had been a Polish Countess. Having made too many gambling debts when he was young, he had ruined his prospects in the Army, and remained an infantry captain. He had never married: his position did not allow of it, and no woman had ever moved him to it. His time he spent riding — occasionally he rode one of his own horses at the races — and at the officers' club. Now and then he took himself a mistress. But after such an event, he returned to duty with his brow still more tense, his eyes still more hostile and irritable. With the men, however, he was merely impersonal, though a devil when roused; so that, on the whole, they feared him, but had no great aversion from him. They accepted him as the inevitable.

To his orderly he was at first cold and just and indifferent: he did not fuss over trifles. So that his servant knew practically nothing about him, except just what orders he would give, and how he wanted them obeyed. That was quite simple. Then the change gradually came.

The orderly was a youth of about twenty-two, of medium height, and well built. He had strong, heavy limbs, was swarthy, with a soft, black, young moustache. There was something altogether warm and young about him. He had firmly marked eye-brows over dark, expressionless eyes that seemed never to have thought, only to have received life direct through his senses, and acted straight from instinct.

Gradually the officer had become aware of his servant's young, vigorous, unconscious presence about him. He could not get away from the sense of the youth's person, while he was in attendance. It was like a warm flame upon the older man's tense, rigid body, that had become almost unliving, fixed. There was something so free and self-contained about him, and something in the young fellow's movement, that made the officer aware of him. And this irritated the Prussian. He did not choose to be touched into life by his servant. He might easily have changed his man, but he did not. He now very rarely looked direct at his orderly, but kept his face averted, as if to avoid seeing him. And yet as the young soldier moved unthinking about the apartment, the elder watched him, and would notice the movement of his strong young shoulders under the blue cloth, the bend of his neck. And it irritated him. To see the soldier's young, brown, shapely peasant's hand grasp the loaf or the wine-bottle sent a flash of hate or of anger through the elder man's blood. It was not that the youth was clumsy: it was rather the blind, instinctive sureness of movement of an unhampered young animal that irritated the officer to such a degree.

Once, when a bottle of wine had gone over, and the red gushed out on to the tablecloth, the officer had started up with an oath, and his eyes, bluey like fire, had held those of the confused youth for a moment. It was a shock for the young soldier. He felt something sink deeper, deeper into his soul, where nothing had ever gone before. It left him rather blank and wondering. Some of his natural completeness in himself was gone, a little uneasiness took its place. And from that time an undiscovered feeling had held between the two men.

Henceforward the orderly was afraid of really meeting his master. His subconsciousness remembered those steely blue eyes and the harsh brows, and did not intend to meet them again. So he always stared past his master and avoided him. Also, in a little anxiety, he waited for the three months to have gone, when his time would be up. He began to feel a constraint in the Captain's presence, and the soldier even more than the officer wanted to be left alone, in his neutrality as servant.

He had served the Captain for more than a year, and knew his duty. This he performed easily, as if it were natural to him. The officer and his commands he took for granted, as he took the sun and the rain, and he served as a matter of course. It did not implicate him personally.

But now if he were going to be forced into a personal interchange with his master he would be like a wild thing caught, he felt he must get away.

But the influence of the young soldier's being had penetrated through the officer's stiffened discipline, and perturbed the man in him. He, however, was a gentleman, with long, fine hands and cultivated movements, and was not going to allow such a thing as the stirring of his innate self. He was a man of passionate temper, who had always kept himself suppressed. Occasionally there had been a duel, an outburst before the soldiers. He knew himself to be always on the point of breaking out. But he kept himself hard to the idea of the Service. Whereas the young soldier seemed to live out his warm, full nature, to give it off in his very movements, which had a certain zest, such as wild animals have in free movement. And this irritated the officer more and more.

In spite of himself, the Captain could not regain his neutrality of feeling towards his orderly. Nor could he leave the man alone. In spite of himself, he watched him, gave his sharp orders, tried to take up as much of his time as possible. Sometimes he flew into a rage with the young soldier, and bullied him. Then the orderly shut himself off, as it were out of earshot, and waited, with sullen, flushed face, for the end of the noise. The words never pierced to his intelligence, he made himself, protectively, impervious to the feelings of his master.

He had a scar on his left thumb, a deep seam going across the knuckle. The officer had long suffered from it, and wanted to do something to it. Still it was there, ugly and brutal on the young, brown hand. At last the Captain's reserve gave away. One day, as the orderly was smoothing out the tablecloth, the officer pinned down his thumb with a pencil, asking:

"How did you come by that?"

The young man winced and drew back at attention.

"A wood axe, Herr Hauptmann," he answered.

The officer waited for further explanation. None came. The orderly went about his duties. The elder man was sullenly angry. His servant avoided him. And the next day he had to use all his will-power to avoid seeing the scarred thumb. He wanted to get hold of it and — A hot flame ran in his blood.

He knew his servant would soon be free, and would be glad. As yet, the soldier had held himself off from the elder man. The Captain grew madly irritable. He could not rest when the soldier was away, and when he was present, he glared at him with tormented eyes. He hated those fine black brows over the unmeaning dark eyes, he was infuriated by the free movement of the handsome limbs, which no military discipline could make stiff. And he became harsh and cruelly bullying, using contempt and satire. The young soldier only grew more mute and expressionless.

"What cattle were you bred by, that you can't keep straight eyes? Look me in the eyes when I speak to you."

And the soldier turned his dark eyes to the other's face, but there was no sight in them: he stared with the slightest possible cast, holding back his sight, perceiving the blue of his master's eyes, but receiving no look from them. And the elder man went pale, and his reddish eyebrows twitched. He gave his order, barrenly.

Once he flung a heavy military glove into the young soldier's face. Then he had the satisfaction of seeing the black eyes flare up into his own, like a blaze when straw is thrown on a fire. And he had laughed with a little tremor and a sneer.

But there were only two months more. The youth instinctively tried to keep himself intact. he tried to serve the officer as if the latter were an abstract authority and not a man. All his instinct was to avoid personal contact, even definite hate. But in spite of himself the hate grew, responsive to the officer's passion. However, he put it in the background. When he had left the Army he could dare acknowledge it. By nature he was active, and had many friends. He thought what amazing good fellows they were. But, without knowing it, he was alone. Now this solitariness was intensified. It would carry him through his term. But the officer seemed to be going irritably insane, and the youth was deeply frightened.

The soldier had a sweetheart, a girl from the mountains, independent and primitive. The two walked together, rather silently. He went with her, not to talk, but to have his arm round her, and for the physical contact. This eased him, made it easier for him to ignore the Captain; for he could rest with her held fast against his chest. And she, in some unspoken fashion, was there for him. They loved each other.

The Captain perceived it, and was mad with irritation. He kept the young man engaged all the evenings long, and took pleasure in the dark look that came on his face. Occasionally, the eyes of the two men met, those of the younger sullen and dark, doggedly unalterable, those of the elder sneering with restless contempt.

The officer tried hard not to admit the passion that had got hold of him. He would not know that his feeling for his orderly was anything but that of a man incensed by his stupid, perverse servant. So, keeping quite justified and conventional in his consciousness, he let the other thing run on. His nerves, however, were suffering. At last he slung the end of a belt in his servant's face. When he saw the youth start back, the pain-tears in his eyes and the blood on his mouth, he had felt at once a thrill of deep pleasure and of shame.

But this, he acknowledged to himself, was a thing he had never done before. The fellow was too exasperating. His own nerves must be going to pieces. He went away for some days with a woman.

It was a mockery of pleasure. He simply did not want the woman. But he stayed on for his time. At the end of it, he came back in an agony of irritation, torment, and misery. He rode all the evening, then came straight into supper. His orderly was out. The officer sat with his long, fine hands lying on the table, perfectly still, and all his blood seemed to be corroding.

At last his servant entered. He watched the strong, easy young figure, the fine eyebrows, the thick black hair. In a week's time the youth had got back his old well-being. The hands of the officer twitched and seemed to be full of mad flame. The young man stood at attention, unmoving, shut off.

The meal went in silence. But the orderly seemed eager. He made a clatter with the dishes.

"Are you in a hurry?" asked the officer, watching the intent, warm face of his servant. The other did not reply.

"Will you answer my question?" said the Captain.

"Yes, sir," replied the orderly, standing with his pile of deep Army plates. The Captain waited, looked at him, then asked again:

"Are you in a hurry?"

"Yes, sir," came the answer, that sent a flash through the listener.

"For what?"

"I was going out, sir."

"I want you this evening."

There was a moment's hesitation. The officer had a curious stiffness of countenance.

"Yes, sir," replied the servant, in his throat.

"I want you tomorrow evening also — in fact, you may consider your evenings occupied, unless I give you leave."

The mouth with the young moustache set close.

"Yes, sir," answered the orderly, loosening his lips for a moment.

He again turned to the door.

"And why have you a piece of pencil in your ear?"

The orderly hesitated, then continued on his way without answering. He set the plates in a pile outside the door, took the stump of pencil from his ear, and put it in his pocket. He had been copying a verse for his sweetheart's birthday card. He returned to finish clearing the table. The officer's eyes were dancing, he had a little, eager smile.

"Why have you a piece of pencil in your ear?" he asked.

The orderly took his hands full of dishes. His master was standing near the great green stove, a little smile on his face, his chin thrust forward. When the young soldier saw him his heart suddenly ran hot. He felt blind. Instead of answering, he turned dazedly to the door. As he was crouching to set down the dishes, he was pitched forward by a kick from behind. The pots went in a stream down the stairs, he clung to the pillar of the banisters. And as he was rising he was kicked heavily again, and again, so that he clung sickly to the post for some moments. His master had gone swiftly into the room and closed the door. The maid-servant downstairs looked up the staircase and made a mocking face at the crockery disaster.

The officer's heart was plunging. He poured himself a glass of wine, part of which he spilled on the floor, and gulped the remainder, leaning against the cool, green stove. He heard his man collecting the dishes from the stairs. Pale, as if intoxicated, he waited. The servant entered again. The Captain's heart gave a pang, as of pleasure, seeing the young fellow bewildered and uncertain on his feet, with pain.

"Schöner!" he said.

The soldier was a little slower in coming to attention.

"Yes, sir!"

The youth stood before him, with pathetic young moustache, and fine eyebrows very distinct on his forehead of dark marble.

"I asked you a question."

"Yes, sir."

The officer's tone bit like acid.

"Why had you a pencil in your ear?"

Again the servant's heart ran hot, and he could not breathe. With dark, strained eyes, he looked at the officer, as if fascinated. And he stood there sturdily planted, unconscious. The withering smile came into the Captain's eyes, and he lifted his foot.

"I — I forgot it — sir," panted the soldier, his dark eyes fixed on the other man's dancing blue ones.

"What was it doing there?"

He saw the young man's breast heaving as he made an effort for words.

"I had been writing."

"Writing what?"

Again the soldier looked him up and down. The officer could hear him panting. The smile came into the blue eyes. The soldier worked his dry throat, but could not speak. Suddenly the smile lit like a flame on the officer's face, and a kick came heavily against the orderly's thigh. The youth moved a pace sideways. His face went dead, with two black, staring eyes.

"Well?" said the officer.

The orderly's mouth had gone dry, and his tongue rubbed in it as on dry brown-paper. He worked his throat. The officer raised his foot. The servant went stiff.

"Some poetry, sir," came the crackling, unrecognizable sound of his voice.

"Poetry, what poetry?" asked the Captain, with a sickly smile.

Again there was the working in the throat. The Captain's heart had suddenly gone down heavily, and he stood sick and tired.

"For my girl, sir," he heard the dry, inhuman sound.

"Oh!" he said, turning away. "Clear the table."

"Click!" went the soldier's throat; then again, "Click!" and then the half-articulate: "Yes, sir."

The young soldier was gone, looking old, and walking heavily.

The officer, left alone, held himself rigid, to prevent himself from thinking. His instinct warned him that he must not think. Deep inside him was the intense gratification of his passion, still working powerfully. Then there was a counter-action, a horrible breaking down of something inside him, a whole agony of reaction. He stood there for an hour motionless, a chaos of sensations, but rigid with a will to keep blank his consciousness, to prevent his mind grasping. And he held himself so until the worst of the stress had passed, when he began to drink, drank himself to an intoxication, till he slept obliterated. When he woke in the morning he was shaken to the base of his nature. But he had fought off the realization of what he had done. He had prevented his mind from taking it in, had suppressed it along with his instincts, and the conscious man had nothing to do with it. He felt only as after a bout of intoxication, weak, but the affair itself all dim and not to be recovered. Of the drunkenness of his passion he successfully refused remembrance. And when his orderly appeared with coffee, the officer assumed the same self he had had the morning before. He refused the event of the past night — denied it had ever been — and was successful in his denial. He had not done any such thing — not he himself. Whatever there might be, lay at the door of a stupid, insubordinate servant.

The orderly had gone about in a stupor all the evening. He drank some beer because he was parched, but not much, the alcohol made his feeling come back, and he could not bear it. He was dulled, as if nine-tenths of the ordinary man in him were inert. He crawled about disfigured. Still, when he thought of the kicks, he went sick, and when he thought of the threat of more kicking, in the room afterwards, his heart went hot and faint, and he panted, remembering the one that had come. He had been forced to say, "For my girl." He was much too done even to want to cry. His mouth hung slightly open, like an idiot's. He felt vacant, and wasted. So, he wandered at his work, painfully, and very slowly and clumsily, fumbling blindly with the brushes, and finding it difficult, when he sat down, to summon the energy to move again. His limbs, his jaw, were slack and nerveless. But he was very tired. He got to bed at last, and slept inert, relaxed, in a sleep that was rather stupor than slumber, a dead night of stupefaction shot through with gleams of anguish.

In the morning were the manoeuvres. But he woke even before the bugle sounded. The painful ache in his chest, the dryness of his throat, the awful steady feeling of misery made his eyes come awake and dreary at once. He knew, without thinking, what had happened. And he knew that the day had come again, when he must go on with his round. The last bit of darkness was being pushed out of the room. He would have to move his inert body and go on. He was so young, and had known so little trouble, that he was bewildered. He only wished it would stay night, so that he could lie still, covered up by the darkness. And yet nothing would prevent the day from coming, nothing would save him from having to get up and saddle the Captain's horse, and make the Captain's coffee. It was there, inevitable. And then, he thought, it was impossible. Yet they would not leave him free. He must go and take the coffee to the Captain. He was too stunned to understand it. He only knew it was inevitable — inevitable, however long he lay inert.

At last, after heaving at himself, for he seemed to be a mass of inertia, he got up. But he had to force every one of his movements from behind, with his will. He felt lost, and dazed, and helpless. Then he clutched hold of the bed, the pain was so keen. And looking at his thighs, he saw the darker bruises on his swarthy flesh and he knew that, if he pressed one of his fingers on one of the bruises, he should faint. But he did not want to faint — he did not want anybody to know. No one should ever know. It was between him and the Captain. There were only the two people in the world now — himself and the Captain.

Slowly, economically, he got dressed and forced himself to walk. Everything was obscure, except just what he had his hands on. But he managed to get through his work. The very pain revived his dull senses. The worst remained yet. He took the tray and went up to the Captain's room. The officer, pale and heavy, sat at the table. The orderly, as he saluted, felt himself put out of existence. He stood still for a moment submitting to his own nullification — then he gathered himself, seemed to regain himself, and then the Captain began to grow vague, unreal, and the younger soldier's heart beat up. He clung to this situation — that the Captain did not exist — so that he himself might live. But when he saw his officer's hand tremble as he took the coffee, he felt everything falling shattered. And he went away, feeling as if he himself were coming to pieces, disintegrated. And when the Captain was there on horseback, giving orders, while he himself stood, with rifle and knapsack, sick with pain, he felt as if he must shut his eyes — as if he must shut his eyes on everything. It was only the long agony of marching with a parched throat that filled him with one single, sleep-heavy intention: to save himself.

2

He was getting used even to his parched throat. That the snowy peaks were radiant among the sky, that the whity-green glacier-river twisted through its pale shoals in the valley below, seemed almost supernatural. But he was going mad with fever and thirst. He plodded on uncomplaining. He did not want to speak, not to anybody. There were two gulls, like flakes of water and snow, over the river. The scent of green rye soaked in sunshine came like a sickness. And the march continued, monotonously, almost like a bad sleep.

At the next farm-house, which stood low and broad near the high road, tubs of water had been put out. The soldiers clustered round to drink. They took off their helmets, and the steam mounted from their wet hair. The Captain sat on horseback, watching. He needed to see his orderly. His helmet threw a dark shadow over his light, fierce eyes, but his moustache and mouth and chin were distinct in the sunshine. The orderly must move under the presence of the figure of the horseman. It was not that he was afraid, or cowed. It was as if he was disembowelled, made empty, like an empty shell. He felt himself as nothing, a shadow creeping under the sunshine. And, thirsty as he was, he could scarcely drink, feeling the Captain near him. He would not take off his helmet to wipe his wet hair. He wanted to stay in shadow, not to be forced into consciousness. Starting, he saw the light heel of the officer prick the belly of the horse; the Captain cantered away, and he himself could relapse into vacancy.

Nothing, however, could give him back his living place in the hot, bright morning. He felt like a gap among it all. Whereas the Captain was prouder, overriding. A hot flash went through the young servant's body. The Captain was firmer and prouder with life, he himself was empty as a shadow. Again the flash went through him, dazing him out. But his heart ran a little firmer.

The company turned up the hill, to make a loop for the return. Below, from among the trees, the farm-bell clanged. He saw the labourers, mowing barefoot at the thick grass, leave off their work and go downhill, their scythes hanging over their shoulders, like long, bright claws curving down behind them. They seemed like dream-people, as if they had no relation to himself. He felt as in a blackish dream: as if all the other things were there and had form, but he himself was only a consciousness, a gap that could think and perceive.

The soldiers were tramping silently up the glaring hillside. Gradually his head began to revolve, slowly, rhythmically. Sometimes it was dark before his eyes, as if he saw this world through a smoked glass, frail shadows and unreal. It gave him a pain in his head to walk.

The air was too scented, it gave no breath. All the lush green-stuff seemed to be issuing its sap, till the air was deathly, sickly with the smell of greenness. There was the perfume of clover, like pure honey and bees. Then there grew a faint acrid tang — they were near the beeches; and then a queer clattering noise, and a suffocating, hideous smell; they were passing a flock of sheep, a shepherd in a black smock, holding his crook. Why should the sheep huddle together under this fierce sun? He felt that the shepherd would not see him, though he could see the shepherd.

At last there was the halt. They stacked rifles in a conical stack, put down their kit in a scattered circle around it, and dispersed a little, sitting on a small knoll high on the hillside. The chatter began. The soldiers were steaming with heat, but were lively. He sat still, seeing the blue mountains rising upon the land, twenty kilometres away. There was a blue fold in the ranges, then out of that, at the foot, the broad, pale bed of the river, stretches of whity-green water between pinkish-grey shoals among the dark pine woods. There it was, spread out a long way off. And it seemed to come downhill, the river. There was a raft being steered, a mile away. It was a strange country. Nearer, a red-roofed, broad farm with white base and square dots of windows crouched beside the wall of beech foliage on the wood's edge. There were long strips of rye and clover and pale green corn. And just at his feet, below the knoll, was a darkish bog, where globe flowers stood breathless still on their slim stalks. And some of the pale gold bubbles were burst, and a broken fragment hung in the air. He thought he was going to sleep.

Suddenly something moved into this coloured mirage before his eyes. The Captain, a small, light-blue and scarlet figure, was trotting evenly between the strips of corn, along the level brow of the hill. And the man making flag-signals was coming on. Proud and sure moved the horseman's figure, the quick, bright thing, in which was concentrated all the light of this morning, which for the rest lay a fragile, shining shadow. Submissive, apathetic, the young soldier sat and stared. But as the horse slowed to a walk, coming up the last steep path, the great flash flared over the body and soul of the orderly. He sat waiting. The back of his head felt as if it were weighted with a heavy piece of fire. He did not want to eat. His hands trembled slightly as he moved them. Meanwhile the officer on horseback was approaching slowly and proudly. The tension grew in the orderly's soul. Then again, seeing the Captain ease himself on the saddle, the flash blazed through him.

The Captain looked at the patch of light blue and scarlet, and dark heads, scattered closely on the hill-side. It pleased him. The command pleased him. And he was feeling proud. His orderly was among them in common subjection. The officer rose a little on his stirrups to look. The young soldier sat with averted, dumb face. The

Captain relaxed on his seat. His slim-legged, beautiful horse, brown as a beechnut, walked proudly uphill. The Captain passed into the zone of the company's atmosphere: a hot smell of men, of sweat, of leather. He knew it very well. After a word with the lieutenant, he went a few paces higher, and sat there, a dominant figure, his sweat-marked horse swishing its tail, while he looked down on his men, on his orderly, a nonentity among the crowd.

The young soldier's heart was like fire in his chest, and he breathed with difficulty. The officer, looking downhill, saw three of the young soldiers, two pails of water between them, staggering across a sunny green field. A table had been set up under a tree, and there the slim lieutenant stood, importantly busy. Then the Captain summoned himself to an act of courage. He called his orderly.

The flame leaped into the young soldier's throat as he heard the command, and he rose blindly, stifled. He saluted, standing below the officer. He did not look up. But there was the flicker in the Captain's voice.

"Go to the inn and fetch me . . . " the officer gave his commands. "Quick!" he added.

At the last word, the heart of the servant leapt with a flash, and he felt the strength come over his body. But he turned in mechanical obedience, and set off at a heavy run downhill, looking almost like a bear, his trousers bagging over his military boots. And the officer watched this blind, plunging run all the way.

But it was only the outside of the orderly's body that was obeying so humbly and mechanically. Inside had gradually accumulated a core into which all the energy of that young life was compact and concentrated. He executed his commission, and plodded quickly back uphill. There was a pain in his head, as he walked, that made him twist his features unknowingly. But hard there in the centre of his chest was himself, himself, firm, and not to be plucked to pieces.

The Captain had gone up into the wood. The orderly plodded through the hot, powerfully smelling zone of the company's atmosphere. He had a curious mass of energy inside him now. The Captain was less real than himself. He approached the green entrance to the wood. There, in the half-shade, he saw the horse standing, the sunshine and the flickering shadow of leaves dancing over his brown body. There was a clearing where timber had lately been felled. Here, in the gold-green shade beside the brilliant cup of sunshine, stood two figures, blue and pink, the bits of pink showing out plainly. The Captain was talking to his lieutenant.

The orderly stood on the edge of the bright clearing, where great trunks of trees, stripped and glistening, lay stretched like naked, brown-skinned bodies. Chips of wood littered the trampled floor, like splashed light, and the bases of the felled trees stood here and there, with their raw, level tops. Beyond was the brilliant, sunlit green of a beech.

"Then I will ride forward," the orderly heard his Captain say. The lieutenant saluted and strode away. He himself went forward. A hot flash passed through his belly, as he tramped towards his officer.

The Captain watched the rather heavy figure of the young soldier stumble forward, and his veins, too, ran hot. This was to be man to man between them. He yielded before the solid, stumbling figure with bent head. The orderly stopped and put the food on a level-sawn tree-base. The Captain watched the glistening, sun-inflamed, naked hands. He wanted to speak to the young soldier but could not. The servant propped a bottle against his thigh, pressed open the cork, and poured out the beer into the mug. He kept his head bent. The Captain accepted the mug.

"Hot!" he said, as if amiably.

The flame sprang out of the orderly's heart, nearly suffocating him.

"Yes, sir," he replied, between shut teeth.

And he heard the sound of the Captain's drinking, and he clenched his fists, such a strong comment came into his wrists. Then came the faint clang of the closing of the pot-lid. He looked up. The Captain was watching him. He glanced swiftly away. Then he saw the officer stoop and take a piece of bread from the tree-base. Again the flash of flame went through the young soldier, seeing the stiff body stoop beneath him, and his hands jerked. He looked away. He could feel the officer was nervous. The bread fell as it was being broken. The officer ate the other piece. The two men stood tense and still, the master laboriously chewing his bread, the servant staring with averted face, his fist clenched.

Then the young soldier started. The officer had pressed open the lid of the mug again. The orderly watched the lid of the mug, and the white hand that clenched the handle, as if he were fascinated. It was raised. The youth followed it with his eyes. And then he saw the thin, strong throat of the elder man moving up and down as he drank, the strong jaw working. And the instinct which had been jerking at the young man's wrists suddenly jerked free. He jumped, feeling as if it were rent in two by a strong flame.

The spur of the officer caught in a tree-root, he went down backwards with a crash, the middle of his back thudding sickeningly against a sharp-edged tree-base, the pot flying away. And in a second the orderly, with serious, earnest young face, and underlip between his teeth, had got his knee in the officer's chest and was pressing the chin backward over the farther edge of the tree-stump, pressing, with all his heart behind in a passion of relief, the tension of his wrists exquisite with relief. And with the base of his palms he shoved at the chin, with all his might. And it was pleasant, too, to have that chin, that hard jaw already slightly rough with beard, in his hands. He did not relax one hair's breadth, but, all the force of all his blood exulting in his thrust, he shoved back the head of the other man, till there was a little "cluck" and a crunching sensation. Then he felt as if his head went to vapour. Heavy convulsions shook the body of the officer, frightening and horrifying the young soldier. Yet it pleased him, too, to repress them. It pleased him to keep his hands pressing back the chin, to feel the chest of the other man yield in expiration to the weight of his strong, young knees, to feel the hard twitchings of the prostrate body jerking his own whole frame, which was pressed down on it.

But it went still. He could look into the nostrils of the other man, the eyes he could scarcely see. How curiously the mouth was pushed out, exaggerating the full lips, and the moustache bristling up from them. Then, with a start, he noticed the nostrils gradually filled with blood. The red brimmed, hesitated, ran over, and went in a thin trickle down the face to the eyes.

It shocked and distressed him. Slowly, he got up. The body twitched and sprawled there, inert. He stood and looked at it in silence. It was a pity *it* was broken. It represented more than the thing which had kicked and bullied him. He was afraid to look at the eyes. They were hideous now, only the whites showing, and the blood running to them. The face of the orderly was drawn with horror at the sight. Well, it was so. In his heart he was satisfied. He had hated the face of the Captain. It was extinguished now. There was a heavy relief in the orderly's soul. That was as it should be. But he could not bear to see the long, military body lying broken over the tree-base, the fine fingers crisped. He wanted to hide it away.

Quickly, busily, he gathered it up and pushed it under the felled tree-trunks, which rested their beautiful, smooth length either end on logs. The face was horrible with blood. He covered it with the helmet. Then he pushed the limbs straight and decent, and brushed the dead leaves off the fine cloth of the uniform. So, it lay quite still in the shadow under there. A little strip of sunshine ran along the breast, from a chink between the logs. The orderly sat by it for a few moments. Here his own life also ended.

Then, through his daze, he heard the lieutenant, in a loud voice, explaining to the men outside the wood, that they were to suppose the bridge on the river below was held by the enemy. Now they were to march to the attack in such and such a manner. The lieutenant had no gift of expression. The orderly, listening from habit, got muddled. And when the lieutenant began it all again he ceased to hear.

He knew he must go. He stood up. It surprised him that the leaves were glittering in the sun, and the chips of wood reflecting white from the ground. For him a change had come over the world. But for the rest it had not — all seemed the same. Only he had left it. And he could not go back. It was his duty to return with the beer-pot and the bottle. He could not. He had left all that. The lieutenant was still hoarsely explaining. He must go, or they would overtake him. And he could not bear contact with anyone now.

He drew his fingers over his eyes, trying to find out where he was. Then he turned away. He saw the horse standing in the path. He went up to it and mounted. It hurt him to sit in the saddle. The pain of keeping his seat occupied him as they cantered through the wood. He would not have minded anything, but he could not get away from the sense of being divided from the others. The path led out of the trees. On the edge of the wood he pulled up and stood watching. There in the spacious sunshine of the valley soldiers were moving in a little swarm. Every now and then, a man harrowing on a strip of fallow shouted to his oxen, at the turn. The village and the white-towered church was small in the sunshine. And he no longer belonged to it — he sat there, beyond, like a man outside in the dark. He had gone out from everyday life into the unknown, and he could not, he even did not want to go back.

Turning from the sun-blazing valley, he rode deep into the wood. Tree-trunks, like people standing grey and still, took no notice as he went. A doe, herself a moving bit of sunshine and shadow, went running through the flecked shade. There were bright green rents in the foliage. Then it was all pine wood, dark and cool. And he was sick with pain, he had an intolerable great pulse in his head, and he was sick. He had never been ill in his life. He felt lost, quite dazed with all this.

Trying to get down from the horse, he fell, astonished at the pain and his lack of balance. The horse shifted uneasily. He jerked its bridle and sent it cantering jerkily away. It was his last connection with the rest of things.

But he only wanted to lie down and not be disturbed. Stumbling through the trees, he came on a quiet place where beeches and pine trees grew on a slope. Immediately he had lain down and closed his eyes, his consciousness went racing on without him. A big pulse of sickness beat in him as if it throbbed through the whole earth. He was burning with dry heat. But he was too busy, too tearingly active in the incoherent race of delirium to observe.

3

He came to with a start. His mouth was dry and hard, his heart beat heavily, but he had not the energy to get up. His heart beat heavily. Where was he? — the barracks — at home? There was something knocking. And, making an effort, he looked round — trees, and litter of greenery, and reddish, bright, still pieces of sunshine on the floor. He did not believe he was himself, he did not believe what he saw. Something was knocking. He made a struggle towards consciousness, but relapsed. Then he struggled again. And gradually his surroundings fell into relationship with himself. He knew, and a great pang of fear went through his heart. Somebody was knocking. He could see the heavy, black rags of a fir tree overhead. Then everything went black. Yet he did not believe he had closed his eyes. He had not. Out of the blackness sight slowly emerged again. And someone was knocking. Quickly, he saw the blood-disfigured face of his Captain, which he hated. And he held himself still with horror. Yet, deep inside, he knew that it was so, the Captain should be dead. But the physical delirium got hold of him. Someone was knocking. He lay perfectly still, as if dead, with fear. And he went unconscious.

When he opened his eyes again, he started, seeing something creeping swiftly up a tree-trunk. It was a little bird. And the bird was whistling overhead. Tap-tap-tap — it was the small, quick bird rapping the tree-trunk with its beak, as if its head were a little round hammer. He watched it curiously. It shifted sharply, in its creeping fashion. Then, like a mouse, it slid down the bare trunk. Its swift creeping sent a flash of revulsion through him. He raised his head. It felt a great weight. Then, the little bird ran out of the shadow across a still patch of sunshine, its little head bobbing swiftly, its white legs twinkling brightly for a moment. How neat it was in its build, so compact, with pieces of white on its wings. There were several of them. They were so pretty — but they crept like swift, erratic mice, running here and there among the beech-mast.

He lay down again exhausted, and his consciousness lapsed. He had a horror of the little creeping birds. All his blood seemed to be darting and creeping in his head. And yet he could not move.

He came to with a further ache of exhaustion. There was the pain in his head, and the horrible sickness, and his inability to move. He had never been ill in his life. He did not know where he was or what he was. Probably he had got sunstroke. Or what else? — he had silenced the Captain for ever — some time ago — oh, a long time ago. There had been blood on his face, and his eyes had turned upwards. It was all right, somehow. It was peace. But now he had got beyond himself. He had never been here before. Was it life, or not life? He was by himself. They were in a big, bright place, those others, and he was outside. The town, all the country, a big bright place of light: and he was outside, here, in the darkened open beyond, where each thing existed alone. But they would all have to come out there sometime, those others. Little, and left behind him, they all were. There had been father and mother and sweetheart. What did they all matter? This was the open land.

He sat up. Something scuffled. It was a little brown squirrel running in lovely, undulating bounds over the floor, its red tail completing the undulation of its body — and then, as it sat up, furling and unfurling. He watched it, pleased. It ran on again, friskily, enjoying itself. It flew wildly at another squirrel, and they were chasing each other, and making little scolding, chattering noises. The soldier wanted to speak to them. But only a hoarse sound came out of his throat. The squirrels burst away — they flew up the trees. And then he saw the one peeping round at him, half-way up a tree trunk. A start of fear went through him, though, in so far as he was conscious, he was amused. It still stayed, its little, keen face staring at him half-way up a tree-trunk, its little ears pricked up, its clawey little hands clinging to the bark, its white breast reared. He started from it in panic.

Struggling to his feet, he lurched away. He went on walking, walking, looking for something — for a drink. His brain felt hot and inflamed for want of water. He stumbled on. Then he did not know anything. He went unconscious as he walked. Yet he stumbled on, his mouth open.

When, to his dumb wonder, he opened his eyes on the world again, he no longer tried to remember what it was. There was thick, golden light behind golden-green glitterings, and tall, grey-purple shafts, and darknesses further off, surrounding him, growing deeper. He was conscious of a sense of arrival. He was amid the reality, on the real, dark bottom. But there was the thirst burning in his brain. He felt lighter, not so heavy. He supposed it was newness. The air was muttering with thunder. He thought he was walking wonderfully swiftly and was coming straight to relief — or was it to water.

Suddenly he stood still with fear. There was a tremendous flare of gold, immense — just a few dark trunks like bars between him and it. All the young level wheat was burnished gold glaring on its silky green. A woman, full-skirted, a black cloth on her head for headdress, was passing like a block of shadow through the glistening green corn, into the full glare. There was a farm, too, pale blue in shadow, and the timber black. And there was a church spire, nearly fused away in the gold. The woman moved on, away from him. He had no language with which to speak to her. She was the bright, solid unreality. She would make a noise of words that would confuse him, and her eyes would look at him without seeing him. She was crossing there to the other side. He stood against a tree.

When at last he turned, looking down the long, bare grove whose flat bed was already filling dark, he saw the mountains in a wonderlight, not far away, and radiant. Behind the soft, grey ridge of the nearest range the further mountains stood golden and pale grey, the snow all radiant like pure, soft gold. So still, gleaming in the sky, fashioned pure out of the ore of the sky, they shone in their silence. He stood and looked at them, his face illuminated. And like the golden, lustrous gleaming of the snow he felt his own thirst bright in him. He stood and gazed, leaning against a tree. And then everything slid away into space.

During the night the lightning fluttered perpetually, making the whole sky white. He must have walked again. The world hung livid round him for moments, fields a level sheen of grey-green light, trees in dark bulk, and the range of clouds black across a white sky. Then the darkness fell like a shutter, and the night was whole. A faint flutter of a half-revealed world, that could not quite leap out of the darkness! — Then there again stood a sweep of pallor for the land, dark shapes looming, a range of clouds hanging overhead. The world was a ghostly shadow, thrown for a moment upon the pure darkness, which returned ever whole and complete.

And the mere delirium of sickness and fever went on inside him — his brain opening and shutting like the night — then sometimes convulsions of terror from something with great eyes that stared round a tree — then the long agony of the march, and the sun decomposing his blood — then the pang of hate for the Captain, followed by a pang of tenderness and ease. But everything was distorted, born of an ache and resolving into an ache.

In the morning he came definitely awake. Then his brain flamed with the sole horror of thirstiness! The sun was on his face, the dew was steaming from his wet clothes. Like one possessed, he got up. There, straight in front of him, blue and cool and tender, the mountains ranged across the pale edge of the morning sky. He wanted them — he wanted them alone — he wanted to leave himself and be identified with them. They did not move, they were still and soft, with white, gentle markings of snow. He stood still, mad with suffering, his hands crisping and clutching. Then he was twisting in a paroxysm on the grass.

He lay still, in a kind of dream of anguish. His thirst seemed to have separated itself from him, and to stand apart, a single demand. Then the pain he felt was another single self. Then there was the clog of his body, another separate thing. He was divided among all kinds of separate beings. There was some strange, agonized connection between them, but they were drawing further apart. Then they would all split. The sun, drilling down on him, was drilling through the bond. Then they would all fall, fall through the everlasting lapse of space. Then again, his consciousness reasserted itself. He roused on to his elbow and stared at the gleaming mountains. There they ranked, all still and wonderful between earth and heaven. He stared till his eyes went black, and the mountains, as they stood in their beauty, so clean and cool, seemed to have it, that which was lost in him.

4

When the soldiers found him, three hours later, he was lying with his face over his arm, his black hair giving off heat under the sun. But he was still alive. Seeing the open, black mouth, the young soldiers dropped him in horror.

He died in the hospital at night, without having seen again.

The doctors saw the bruises on his legs, behind, and were silent.

The bodies of the two men lay together, side by side, in the mortuary, the one white and slender, but laid rigidly at rest, the other looking as if every moment it must rouse into life again, so young and unused, from a slumber.

D. H. LAWRENCE

The Rocking-Horse Winner

There was a woman who was beautiful, who started with all the advantages, yet she had no luck. She married for love, and the love turned to dust. She had bonny children, yet she felt they had been thrust upon her, and she could not love them. They looked at her coldly, as if they were finding fault with her. And hurriedly she felt she must cover up some fault in herself. Yet what it was that she must cover up she never knew. Nevertheless, when her children were present, she always felt the centre of her heart go hard. This troubled her, and in her manner she was all the more gentle and anxious for her children, as if she loved them very much. Only she herself knew that at the centre of her heart was a hard little place that could not feel love, no, not for anybody. Everybody else said of her: "She is such a good mother. She adores her children." Only she herself, and her children themselves, knew it was not so. They read it in each other's eyes.

There were a boy and two little girls. They lived in a pleasant house, with a garden, and they had discreet servants, and felt themselves superior to anyone in the neighbourhood.

Although they lived in style, they felt always an anxiety in the house. There was never enough money. The mother had a small income, and the father had a small income, but not nearly enough for the social position which they had to keep up. The father went in to town to some office. But though he had good prospects, these prospects never materialized. There was always the grinding sense of the shortage of money, though the style was always kept up.

At last the mother said: "I will see if *I* can't make something." But she did not know where to begin. She racked her brains, and tried this thing and the other, but could not find anything successful. The failure made deep lines come into her face. Her children were growing up, they would have to go to school. There must be more money, there must be more money. The father, who was always very handsome and expensive in his tastes, seemed as if he never *would* be able to do anything worth doing. And the mother, who had a great belief in herself, did not succeed any better, and her tastes were just as expensive.

And so the house came to be haunted by the unspoken phrase: *There must be more money! There must be more money!* The children could hear it all the time, though nobody said it aloud. They heard it at Christmas, when the expensive and splendid toys filled the nursery. Behind the shining modern rocking-horse, behind the smart doll's-house, a voice would start whispering: "There *must* be more money!

There *must* be more money!" And the children would stop playing, to listen for a moment. They would look into each other's eyes, to see if they had all heard. And each one saw in the eyes of the other two that they too had heard. "There *must* be more money! There *must* be more money!"

It came whispering from the springs of the still-swaying rocking-horse, and even the horse, bending his wooden, champing head, heard it. The big doll, sitting so pink and smirking in her new pram, could hear it quite plainly, and seemed to be smirking all the more self-consciously because of it. The foolish puppy, too, that took the place of the teddy-bear, he was looking so extraordinarily foolish for no other reason but that he heard the secret whisper all over the house: "There *must* be more money!"

Yet nobody ever said it aloud. The whisper was everywhere, and therefore no one spoke it. Just as no one ever says: "We are breathing!" in spite of the fact that breath is coming and going all the time.

"Mother," said the boy Paul one day, "why don't we keep a car of our own? Why do we always use uncle's, or else a taxi?"

"Because we're the poor members of the family," said the mother.

"But why *are* we, mother?"

"Well — I suppose," she said slowly and bitterly, "it's because your father has no luck."

The boy was silent for some time.

"Is luck money, mother?" he asked rather timidly.

"No, Paul. Not quite. It's what causes you to have money."

"Oh!" said Paul vaguely. "I thought when Uncle Oscar said *filthy lucker,* it meant money."

"Filthy lucre does mean money," said the mother. "But it's lucre, not luck."

"Oh!" said the boy. "Then what *is* luck, mother?"

"It's what causes you to have money. If you're lucky you have money. That's why it's better to be born lucky than rich. If you're rich, you may lose your money. But if you're lucky, you will always get more money."

"Oh! Will you? And is father not lucky?"

"Very unlucky, I should say," she said bitterly.

The boy watched her with unsure eyes.

"Why?" he asked.

"I don't know. Nobody ever knows why one person is lucky and another unlucky."

"Don't they? Nobody at all? Does *nobody* know?"

"Perhaps God. But He never tells."

"'He ought to, then. And aren't you lucky either, mother?"

"I can't be, if I married an unlucky husband."

"But by yourself, aren't you?"

"I used to think I was, before I married. Now I think I am very unlucky indeed."

"Why?"

"Well — never mind! Perhaps I'm not really," she said.

The child looked at her, to see if she meant it. But he saw, by the lines of her mouth, that she was only trying to hide something from him.

"Well, anyhow," he said stoutly, "I'm a lucky person."

"Why?" said his mother, with a sudden laugh.

He stared at her. He didn't even know why he had said it.

"God told me," he asserted, brazening it out.

"I hope He did, dear!" she said, again with a laugh, but rather bitter.

"He did, mother!"

"Excellent!" said the mother, using one of her husband's exclamations.

The boy saw she did not believe him; or, rather, that she paid no attention to his assertion. This angered him somewhat, and made him want to compel her attention.

He went off by himself, vaguely, in a childish way, seeking for the clue to "luck." Absorbed, taking no heed of other people, he went about with a sort of stealth, seeking inwardly for luck. He wanted luck, he wanted it, he wanted it. When the two girls were playing dolls in the nursery, he would sit on his big rocking-horse, charging madly into space, with a frenzy that made the little girls peer at him uneasily. Wildly the horse careered, the waving dark hair of the boy tossed, his eyes had a strange glare in them. The little girls dared not speak to him.

When he had ridden to the end of his mad little journey, he climbed down and stood in front of his rocking-horse, staring fixedly into its lowered face. Its red mouth was slightly open, its big eye was wide and glassy-bright.

"Now!" he would silently command the snorting steed. "Now, take me to where there is luck! Now take me!"

And he would slash the horse on the neck with the little whip he had asked Uncle Oscar for. He *knew* the horse could take him to where there was luck, if only he forced it. So he would mount again, and start on his furious ride, hoping at last to get there. He knew he could get there.

"You'll break your horse, Paul!" said the nurse.

"He's always riding like that! I wish he'd leave off!" said his elder sister Joan.

But he only glared down on them in silence. Nurse gave him up. She could make nothing of him. Anyhow he was growing beyond her.

One day his mother and his Uncle Oscar came in when he was on one of his furious rides. He did not speak to them.

"Hallo, you young jockey! Riding a winner?" said his uncle.

"Aren't you growing too big for a rocking-horse? You're not a very little boy any longer, you know," said his mother.

But Paul only gave a blue glare from his big, rather close-set eyes. He would speak to nobody when he was in full tilt. His mother watched him with an anxious expression on her face.

At last he suddenly stopped forcing his horse into the mechanical gallop, and slid down.

"Well, I got there!" he announced fiercely, his blue eyes still flaring, and his sturdy long legs straddling apart.

"Where did you get to?" asked his mother.

"Where I wanted to go," he flared back at her.

"That's right, son!" said Uncle Oscar. "Don't you stop till you get there. What's the horse's name?"

"He doesn't have a name," said the boy.

"Gets on without all right?" asked the uncle.

"Well, he has different names. He was called Sansovino last week."

"Sansovino, eh? Won the Ascot. How did you know his name?"

"He always talks about horse-races with Bassett," said Joan.

The uncle was delighted to find that his small nephew was posted with all the racing news. Bassett, the young gardener, who had been wounded in the left foot in the war and had got his present job through Oscar Cresswell, whose batman he had been, was a perfect blade of the "turf." He lived in the racing events, and the small boy lived with him.

Oscar Cresswell got it all from Bassett.

"Master Paul comes and asks me, so I can't do more than tell him, sir," said Bassett, his face terribly serious, as if he were speaking of religious matters.

"And does he ever put anything on a horse he fancies?"

"Well — I don't want to give him away — he's a young sport, a fine sport, sir. Would you mind asking him himself? He sort of takes a pleasure in it, and perhaps he'd feel I was giving him away, sir, if you don't mind."

Bassett was serious as a church.

The uncle went back to his nephew and took him off for a ride in the car.

"Say, Paul, old man, do you ever put anything on a horse?" the uncle asked.

The boy watched the handsome man closely.

"Why, do you think I oughtn't to?" he parried.

"Not a bit of it! I thought perhaps you might give me a tip for the Lincoln."

The car sped on into the country, going down to Uncle Oscar's place in Hampshire.

"Honour bright?" said the nephew.

"Honour bright, son!" said the uncle.

"Well, then, Daffodil."

"Daffodil! I doubt it, sonny. What about Mirza?"

"I only know the winner," said the boy. "That's Daffodil."

"Daffodil, eh?"

There was a pause. Daffodil was an obscure horse comparatively.

"Uncle!"

"Yes, son?"

"You won't let it go any further, will you? I promised Bassett."

"Bassett be damned, old man! What's he got to do with it?"

"We're partners. We've been partners from the first. Uncle, he lent me my first five shillings, which I lost. I promised him, honour bright, it was only between me and him; only you gave me that ten-shilling note I started winning with, so I thought you were lucky. You won't let it go any further, will you?"

The boy gazed at his uncle from those big, hot, blue eyes, set rather close together. The uncle stirred and laughed uneasily.

"Right you are, son! I'll keep your tip private. Daffodil, eh? How much are you putting on him?"

"All except twenty pounds," said the boy. "I keep that in reserve."

The uncle thought it a good joke.

"You keep twenty pounds in reserve, do you, you young romancer? What are you betting, then?"

"I'm betting three hundred," said the boy gravely. "But it's between you and me, Uncle Oscar! Honour bright?"

The uncle burst into a roar of laughter.

"It's between you and me all right, you young Nat Gould," he said, laughing. "But where's your three hundred?"

"Bassett keeps it for me. We're partners."

"You are, are you! And what is Bassett putting on Daffodil?"

"He won't go quite as high as I do, I expect. Perhaps he'll go a hundred and fifty."

"What, pennies?" laughed the uncle.

"Pounds," said the child, with a surprised look at his uncle. "Bassett keeps a bigger reserve than I do."

Between wonder and amusement Uncle Oscar was silent. He pursued the matter no further, but he determined to take his nephew with him to the Lincoln races.

"Now, son," he said, "I'm putting twenty on Mirza, and I'll put five for you on any horse you fancy. What's your pick?"

"Daffodil, uncle."

"No, not the fiver on Daffodil!"

"I should if it was my own fiver," said the child.

"Good! Good! Right you are! A fiver for me and a fiver for you on Daffodil."

The child had never been to a race-meeting before, and his eyes were blue fire. He pursed his mouth tight, and watched. A Frenchman just in front had put his money on Lancelot. Wild with excitement, he flayed his arms up and down, yelling *"Lancelot! Lancelot!"* in his French accent.

Daffodil came in first, Lancelot second, Mirza third. The child, flushed and with eyes blazing, was curiously serene. His uncle brought him four five-pound notes, four to one.

"What am I to do with these?" he cried, waving them before the boy's eyes.

"I suppose we'll talk to Bassett," said the boy. "I expect I have fifteen hundred now; and twenty in reserve; and this twenty."

His uncle studied him for some moments.

"Look here, son!" he said. "You're not serious about Bassett and that fifteen hundred, are you?"

"Yes, I am. But it's between you and me, uncle. Honour bright!"

"Honour bright all right, son! But I must talk to Bassett."

"If you'd like to be a partner, uncle, with Bassett and me, we could all be partners. Only, you'd have to promise, honour bright, uncle, not to let it go beyond us three. Bassett and I are lucky, and you must be lucky, because it was your ten shillings I started winning with. . . ."

Uncle Oscar took both Bassett and Paul into Richmond Park for an afternoon, and there they talked.

"It's like this, you see, sir," Bassett said. "Master Paul would get me talking about racing events, spinning yarns, you know, sir. And he was always keen on knowing if I'd made or if I'd lost. It's about a year since, now, that I put five shillings on Blush of Dawn for him — and we lost. Then the luck turned, with that ten shillings he had from you, that we put on Singhalese. And since that time, it's been pretty steady, all things considering. What do you say, Master Paul?"

"We're all right when we're sure," said Paul. "It's when we're not quite sure that we go down."

"Oh, but we're careful then," said Bassett.

"But when are you *sure?*" smiled Uncle Oscar.

"It's Master Paul, sir," said Bassett, in a secret, religious voice. "It's as if he had it from heaven. Like Daffodil, now, for the Lincoln. That was as sure as eggs."

"Did you put anything on Daffodil?" asked Oscar Cresswell.

"Yes, sir. I made my bit."

"And my nephew?"

Bassett was obstinately silent, looking at Paul.

"I made twelve hundred, didn't I, Bassett? I told uncle I was putting three hundred on Daffodil."

"That's right," said Bassett, nodding.

"But where's the money?" asked the uncle.

"I keep it safe locked up, sir. Master Paul he can have it any minute he likes to ask for it."

"What, fifteen hundred pounds?"

"And twenty! And *forty,* that is, with the twenty he made on the course."

"It's amazing!" said the uncle.

"If Master Paul offers you to be partners, sir, I would, if I were you; if you'll excuse me," said Bassett.

Oscar Cresswell thought about it.

"I'll see the money," he said.

They drove home again, and sure enough, Bassett came round to the garden-house with fifteen hundred pounds in notes. The twenty pounds reserve was left with Joe Glee, in the Turf Commission deposit.

"You see, it's all right, uncle, when I'm *sure!* Then we go strong, for all we're worth. Don't we, Bassett?"

"We do that, Master Paul."

"And when are you sure?" said the uncle, laughing.

"Oh, well, sometimes I'm *absolutely* sure, like about Daffodil," said the boy; "and sometimes I have an idea; and sometimes I haven't even an idea, have I, Bassett? Then we're careful, because we mostly go down."

"You do, do you! And when you're sure, like about Daffodil, what makes you sure, sonny?"

"Oh, well, I don't know," said the boy uneasily. "I'm sure, you know, uncle; that's all."

"It's as if he had it from heaven, sir," Bassett reiterated.

"I should say so!" said the uncle.

But he became a partner. And when the Leger was coming on, Paul was "sure" about Lively Spark, which was a quite inconsiderable horse. The boy insisted on putting a thousand on the horse, Bassett went for five hundred, and Oscar Cresswell two hundred. Lively Spark came in first, and the betting had been ten to one against him. Paul had made ten thousand.

"You see," he said, "I was absolutely sure of him."

Even Oscar Cresswell had cleared two thousand.

"Look here, son," he said, "this sort of thing makes me nervous."

"It needn't, uncle! Perhaps I shan't be sure again for a long time."

"But what are you going to do with your money?" asked the uncle.

"Of course," said the boy, "I started it for mother. She said she had no luck, because father is unlucky, so I thought if *I* was lucky, it might stop whispering."

"What might stop whispering?"

"Our house. I *hate* our house for whispering."

"What does it whisper?"

"Why — why" — the boy fidgeted — "why, I don't know. But it's always short of money, you know, uncle."

"I know it, son, I know it."

"You know people send mother writs, don't you, uncle?"

"I'm afraid I do," said the uncle.

"And then the house whispers, like people laughing at you behind your back. It's awful, that is! I thought if I was lucky. . ."

"You might stop it," added the uncle.

The boy watched him with big blue eyes, that had an uncanny cold fire in them, and he said never a word.

"Well, then!" said the uncle. "What are we doing?"

"I shouldn't like mother to know I was lucky," said the boy.

"Why not, son?"

"She'd stop me."

"I don't think she would."

"Oh!" — and the boy writhed in an odd way — "I *don't* want her to know, uncle."

"All right, son! We'll manage it without her knowing."

They managed it very easily. Paul, at the other's suggestion, handed over five thousand pounds to his uncle, who deposited it with the family lawyer, who was then to inform Paul's mother that a relative had put five thousand pounds into his hands, which sum was to be paid out a thousand pounds at a time, on the mother's birthday, for the next five years.

"So she'll have a birthday present of a thousand pounds for five successive years," said Uncle Oscar. "I hope it won't make it all the harder for her later."

Paul's mother had her birthday in November. The house had been "whispering" worse than ever lately, and, even in spite of his luck, Paul could not bear up against it. He was very anxious to see the effect of the birthday letter, telling his mother about the thousand pounds.

When there were no visitors, Paul now took his meals with his parents, as he was beyond the nursery control. His mother went into town nearly every day. She had discovered that she had an odd knack of sketching furs and dress materials, so she worked secretly in the studio of a friend who was the chief "artist" for the leading drapers. She drew the figures of ladies in furs and ladies in silk and sequins for the newspaper advertisements. This young woman artist earned several thousand pounds a year, but Paul's mother only made several hundreds, and she was again dissatisfied. She so wanted to be first in something, and she did not succeed, even in making sketches for drapery advertisements.

She was down to breakfast on the morning of her birthday. Paul watched her face as she read her letters. He knew the lawyer's letter. As his mother read it, her face hardened and became more expressionless. Then a cold, determined look came on her mouth. She hid the letter under the pile of others, and said not a word about it.

"Didn't you have anything nice in the post for your birthday, mother?" said Paul.

"Quite moderately nice," she said, her voice cold and absent.

She went away to town without saying more.

But in the afternoon Uncle Oscar appeared. He said Paul's mother had a long interview with the lawyer, asking if the whole five thousand could not be advanced at once, as she was in debt.

"What do you think, uncle?" said the boy.

"I leave it to you, son."

"Oh, let her have it, then! We can get some more with the other," said the boy.

"A bird in the hand is worth two in the bush, laddie!" said Uncle Oscar.

" But I'm sure to *know* for the Grand National; or the Lincolnshire; or else the Derby. I'm sure to know for *one* of them," said Paul.

So Uncle Oscar signed the agreement, and Paul's mother touched the whole five thousand. Then something very curious happened. The voices in the house suddenly went mad, like a chorus of frogs on a spring evening. There were certain new furnishings, and Paul had a tutor. He was *really* going to Eton, his father's school, in the following autumn. There were flowers in the winter, and a blossoming of the luxury Paul's mother had been used to. And yet the voices in the house, behind the sprays of mimosa and almond blossom, and from under the piles of iridescent cushions, simply trilled and screamed in a sort of ecstasy: "There *must* be more money! Oh-h-h; there *must* be more money. Oh, now, now-w! Now-w-w — there *must* be more money! — more than ever! More than ever!"

It frightened Paul terribly. He studied away at his Latin and Greek with his tutors. But his intense hours were spent with Bassett. The Grand National had gone by: he had not "known" and had lost a hundred pounds. Summer was at hand. He was in agony for the Lincoln. But even for the Lincoln he didn't "know," and he lost fifty pounds. He became wild-eyed and strange, as if something were going to explode in him.

"Let it alone, son! Don't you bother about it!" urged Uncle Oscar. But it was as if the boy couldn't really hear what his uncle was saying.

"I've got to know for the Derby! I've got to know for the Derby!" the child reiterated, his big blue eyes blazing with a sort of madness.

His mother noticed how overwrought he was.

"You'd better go to the seaside. Wouldn't you like to go now to the seaside, instead of waiting? I think you'd better," she said, looking down at him anxiously, her heart curiously heavy because of him.

But the child lifted his uncanny blue eyes.

"I couldn't possibly go before the Derby, mother!" he said. "I couldn't possibly!"

"Why not?" she said, her voice becoming heavy when she was opposed. "Why not? You can still go from the seaside to see the Derby with your Uncle Oscar, if that's what you wish. No need for you to wait here. Besides, I think you care too much about these races. It's a bad sign. My family has been a gambling family, and you won't know till you grow up how much damage it has done. But it has done damage. I shall have to send Bassett away, and ask Uncle Oscar not to talk racing to you, unless you promise to be reasonable about it; go away to the seaside and forget it. You're all nerves!"

"I'll do what you like, mother, so long as you don't send me away till after the Derby," the boy said.

"Send you away from where? Just from this house?"

"Yes," he said, gazing at her.

"Why, you curious child, what makes you care about this house so much, suddenly? I never knew you loved it."

He gazed at her without speaking. He had a secret within a secret, something he had not divulged, even to Bassett or to his Uncle Oscar.

But his mother, after standing undecided and a little bit sullen for some moments, said:

"Very well, then! Don't go to the seaside till after the Derby, if you don't wish it. But promise me you won't let your nerves go to pieces. Promise you won't think so much about horse-racing and *events,* as you call them!"

"Oh, no," said the boy casually. "I won't think much about them, mother. You needn't worry. I wouldn't worry, mother, if I were you."

"If you were me and I were you," said his mother, "I wonder what we *should* do!"

"But you know you needn't worry, mother, don't you?" the boy repeated.

"I should be awfully glad to know it," she said wearily.

"Oh, well you *can,* you know. I mean, you *ought* to know you needn't worry," he insisted.

"Ought I? Then I'll see about it," she said.

Paul's secret of secrets was his wooden horse, that which had no name. Since he was emancipated from a nurse and a nursery-governess, he had had his rocking-horse removed to his own bedroom at the top of the house.

"Surely, you're too big for a rocking-horse!" his mother had remonstrated.

"Well, you see, mother, till I can have a *real* horse, I like to have *some* sort of animal about," had been his quaint answer.

"Do you feel he keeps you company?" she laughed.

"Oh, yes! He's very good, he always keeps me company, when I'm there," said Paul.

So the horse, rather shabby, stood in an arrested prance in the boy's bedroom.

The Derby was drawing near, and the boy grew more and more tense. He hardly heard what was spoken to him, he was very frail, and his eyes were really uncanny. His mother had sudden strange seizures of uneasiness about him. Sometimes, for half-an-hour, she would feel a sudden anxiety about him that was almost anguish. She wanted to rush to him at once, and know he was safe.

Two nights before the Derby, she was at a big party in town, when one of her rushes of anxiety about her boy, her first-born, gripped her heart till she could hardly speak. She fought with the feeling, might and main, for she believed in common-sense. But it was too strong. She had to leave the dance and go downstairs to telephone to the country. The children's nursery-governess was terribly surprised and startled at being rung up in the night.

"Are the children all right, Miss Wilmot?"

"Oh, yes, they are quite all right."

"Master Paul? Is he all right?"

"He went to bed as right as a trivet. Shall I run up and look at him?"

"No," said Paul's mother reluctantly. "No! Don't trouble. It's all right. Don't sit up. We shall be home fairly soon." She did not want her son's privacy intruded upon.

"Very good," said the governess.

It was about one o'clock when Paul's mother and father drove up to their house. All was still. Paul's mother went to her room and slipped off her white fur cloak. She had told her maid not to wait up for her. She heard her husband downstairs, mixing a whisky-and-soda.

And then, because of the strange anxiety at her heart, she stole upstairs to her son's room. Noiselessly she went along the upper corridor. Was there a faint noise? What was it?

She stood, with arrested muscles, outside his door, listening. There was a strange, heavy, and yet not loud noise. Her heart stood still. It was a soundless noise, yet rushing and powerful. Something huge, in violent, hushed motion. What was it? What in God's name was it? She ought to know. She felt that she knew the noise. She knew what it was.

Yet she could not place it. She couldn't say what it was. And on and on it went, like a madness.

Softly, frozen with anxiety and fear, she turned the door-handle.

The room was dark. Yet in the space near the window, she heard and saw something plunging to and fro. She gazed in fear and amazement.

Then suddenly she switched on the light, and saw her son, in his green pyjamas, madly surging on the rocking-horse. The blaze of light suddenly lit him up, as he urged the wooden horse, and lit her up, as she stood, blonde, in her dress of pale green and crystal, in the doorway.

"Paul!" she cried. "Whatever are you doing?"

"It's Malabar!" he screamed, in a powerful, strange voice. "It's Malabar!"

His eyes blazed at her for one strange and senseless second, as he ceased urging his wooden horse. Then he fell with a crash to the ground, and she, all her tormented motherhood flooding upon her, rushed to gather him up.

But he was unconscious, and unconscious he remained, with some brain-fever. He talked and tossed, and his mother sat stonily by his side.

"Malabar! It's Malabar! Bassett, Bassett, I *know!* It's Malabar!"

So the child cried, trying to get up and urge the rocking-horse that gave him his inspiration.

"What does he mean by Malabar?" asked the heart-frozen mother.

"I don't know," said the father stonily.

"What does he mean by Malabar?" she asked her brother Oscar.

"It's one of the horses running for the Derby," was the answer.

And, in spite of himself, Oscar Cresswell spoke to Bassett, and himself put a thousand on Malabar: at fourteen to one.

The third day of the illness was critical: they were waiting for a change. The boy, with his rather long, curly hair, was tossing ceaselessly on the pillow. He neither slept nor regained consciousness, and his eyes were like blue stones. His mother sat, feeling her heart had gone, turned actually into a stone.

In the evening, Oscar Cresswell did not come, but Bassett sent a message, saying could he come up for one moment, just one moment? Paul's mother was very angry at the intrusion, but on second thought she agreed. The boy was the same. Perhaps Bassett might bring him to consciousness.

The gardener, a shortish fellow with a little brown moustache, and sharp little brown eyes, tip-toed into the room, touched his imaginary cap to Paul's mother, and stole to the bedside, staring with glittering, smallish eyes, at the tossing, dying child.

"Master Paul!" he whispered. "Master Paul! Malabar came in first all right, a clean win. I did as you told me. You've made over seventy thousand pounds, you have; you've got over eighty thousand. Malabar came in all right, Master Paul."

"Malabar! Malabar! Did I say Malabar, mother? Did I say Malabar? Do you think I'm lucky, mother? I knew Malabar, didn't I? Over eighty thousand pounds! I call that lucky, don't you, mother? Over eighty thousand pounds! I knew, didn't I know I knew? Malabar came in all right. If I ride my horse till I'm sure, then I tell you,

Bassett, you can go as high as you like. Did you go for all you were worth, Bassett?"

"I went a thousand on it, Master Paul."

"I never told you, mother, that if I can ride my horse, and *get there,* then I'm absolutely sure   oh, absolutely! Mother, did I ever tell you? I *am* lucky!"

"No, you never did," said the mother.

But the boy died in the night.

And even as he lay dead, his mother heard her brother's voice saying to her: "My God, Hester, you're eighty-odd thousand to the good, and a poor devil of a son to the bad. But, poor devil, poor devil, he's best gone out of a life where he rides his rocking-horse to find a winner."

URSULA LE GUIN

 Ursula Le Guin was born in Berkeley, California, in 1929, the daughter of an anthropologist. She received her education at Radcliffe College and Columbia University and has taught at a number of universities across the country. Best known for her humane and gracefully written science fiction stories and novels — as one critic put it, "she writes what might be called anthropological science fiction" — Le Guin has won an audience far broader than that normally identified as science fiction aficionados. Perhaps that is because the worlds she creates reverberate so poignantly in the one in which we live. Le Guin herself, in an admission reminiscent of the avowals of magic realist Gabriel García Márquez, has said that her vision derives from reality: "Reality is much stranger than many people want to admit. . . . It doesn't seem probable that one's grandfather was once an egg the size of a pinhead . . . that whales sing in choruses deep under the sea; that when you look at a distant star you are seeing the past; yet all these things are actual — are real." Her major novels include *A Wizard of Earthsea* (1968), *The Left Hand of Darkness* (1969), *The Tombs of Atuan* (1971), *The Farthest Shore* (1972), *The Dispossessed* (1974), and *The Beginning Place* (1980). Among her short story collections are *The Wind's Twelve Quarters* (1975) and *Orsinian Tales* (1976). The latter are not precisely science fiction; instead, they create episodes across the historical epochs of an imaginary country in Eastern Europe. From first line to last, "The Lady of Moge," an Orsinian tale, sustains the dignity and rhythms of a fairy tale.

The Lady of Moge

They met once when they were both nineteen, and again when they were twenty-three. That they met only once after that, and long after, was Andre's fault. It was not the kind of fault one would have expected of him, seeing him at nineteen years old, a boy poised above his destiny like a hawk. One saw the eyes, the hawk-eyes, clear, unblinking, fierce. Only when they were closed in sleep did anyone ever see his face, beautiful and passive, the face of the hero. For heroes do not make history — that is the historian's job — but, passive, let themselves be borne along, swept up to the crest of the tide of change, of chance, of war.

She was Isabella Oriana Mogeskar, daughter of the Counts of Helle and the Princes of Moge. She was a princess, and lived in a castle on a hill above the Molsen River. Young Andre Kalinskar was coming to seek her hand in marriage. The Kalinskar family coach rolled for half an hour through the domains of Moge, came through a walled town and up a steep fortified hill, passed under a gateway six feet thick, and stopped before the castle. The high wall was made splendid by an infinite tracery of red vines, for it was autumn; the chestnut trees of the forecourt were flawless gold. Over the golden trees, over the towers, stood the faint, clear, windy sky of late October. Andre looked about him with interest. He did not blink.

In the windowless ground-floor hall of the castle, among saddles and muskets and hunting, riding, fighting gear the two old companions-at-arms, Andre's father and Prince Mogeskar, embraced. Upstairs where windows looked out to the river and the rooms were furnished with the comforts of peace, the Princess Isabella greeted them. Reddish-fair, with a long, calm, comely face and grey-blue eyes — Autumn as a young girl — she was tall, taller than Andre. When he straightened from his bow to her he straightened farther than usual, but the difference remained at least an inch.

They were eighteen at table that night, guests, dependents, and the Mogeskars: Isabella, her father, and her two brothers. George, a cheerful fifteen-year-old, talked hunting with Andre; the older brother and heir, Brant, glanced at him a couple of times, listened to him once, and then turned his fair head away, satisfied: his sister would not stoop to this Kalinskar fellow. Andre set his teeth, and, in order not to look at Brant, looked at his mother, who was talking with the Princess Isabella. He saw them both glance at him, as if they had been speaking of him. In his mother's eyes he saw, as usual, pride and irony, in the girl's — what? Not scorn; not approval. She simply saw him. She saw him clearly. It was exhilarating. He felt for the first time that esteem might be a motive quite as powerful as desire.

Late the next afternoon, leaving his father and his host to fight old battles, he went up to the roof of the castle and stood near the round tower to look out over the Molsen and the hills in the dying, windy, golden light. She came to him through the wind, across the stone. She spoke without greeting, as to a friend. "I've been wanting to talk with you."

Her beauty, like the golden weather, cheered his heart, made him both bold and calm. "And I with you, princess!"

"I think you're a generous man," she said. There was a pleasant husky tone, almost guttural, in her light voice. He bowed a little, and compliments pranced through his mind, but something prompted him to say only, "Why?"

"It's quite plain to see," she replied, impatient. "May I speak to you as one man to another?"

"As one man — ?"

"Dom Andre, when I first met you yesterday, I thought, 'I have met a friend at last.' Was I right?"

Did she plead, or challenge? He was moved. He said, "You were right."

"Then may I ask you, my friend, not to try to marry me? I don't intend to marry."

There was a long silence.

"I shall do as you wish, princess."

"And without arguing!" cried the girl, all at once alight, aflame. "Oh, I knew you were a friend! Please, Dom Andre, don't feel sad or foolish. I refused the others without even thinking about it. With you, I had to think. You see, if I refuse to marry, my father will send me to the convent. So I can't refuse to marry, I can only refuse each suitor. You see?" He did; though if she had given him time to think, he would have thought that she must in the end accept either marriage or the convent, being, after all, a girl. But she did not give him time to think. "So the suitors keep coming; and it's like Princess Ranya, in the tale, you know, with her three questions, and all the young men's heads stuck on poles around the palace. It is so cruel and wearisome. . . ." She sighed, and leaning on the parapet beside Andre looked out over the golden world, smiling, inexplicable, comradely.

"I wish you'd ask me the three questions," he said, wistful.

"I have no questions. I have nothing to ask."

"Nothing to ask that I could give you, to be sure."

"Ah, you've already given me what I asked of you — not to ask me!"

He nodded. He would not seek her reasons; his rebuffed pride, and a sense of her vulnerability, forbade it. And so in her sweet perversity she gave them to him. "What I want, Dom Andre, is to be left alone. To live my life, my own life. At least till I've found out . . . The one thing I have questions to ask of, is myself. To live my own life, to find out my own way, am I too weak to do that? I was born in this castle, my people have been lords here for a long time, one gets used to it. Look at the walls, you can see why Moge has been attacked but never taken. Ah, one's life could be so splendid, God knows what might happen! Isn't it true, Dom Andre? One mustn't choose too soon. If I marry I know what will happen, what I'll do, what I'll be. And I don't want to know. I want nothing, except my freedom."

"I think," Andre said with a sense of discovery, "most women marry to get their freedom."

"Then they want less than I do. There's something inside me, in my heart, a brightness and a heaviness, how can I describe it? Something that exists and does not yet exist, which is mine to carry, and not mine to give up to any man."

Did she speak, Andre wondered, of her virginity or of her destiny? She was very strange, but it was a princely and a touching strangeness. In all she said, however arrogant and naïve, she was most estimable; and though desire was forbidden, she had reached straight into him to his tenderness, the first woman who had ever done so. She stood there quite alone, within him, as she stood beside him and alone.

"Does your brother know your mind?"

"Brant? No. My father is gentle; Brant is not. When my father dies, Brant will force me to marry."

"Then you have no one . . ."

"I have you," she said smiling. "Which means that I have to send you away. But a friend is a friend, near or far."

"Near or far, call to me if you need a friend, princess. I will come." He spoke with a sudden dignity of passion, vowing to her, as a man when very young will vow himself entirely to the rarest and most imperilled thing he has beheld. She looked at him, shaken from her gentle, careless pride, and he took her hand, having earned the right. Beyond them the river ran red under the sunset. "I will," she said. "I was never grateful to a man before, Dom Andre."

He left her, full of exaltation; but when he got to his room he sat down, feeling suddenly very tired, and blinking often, as if on the point of tears.

That was their first meeting, in the wind and golden light on the top of the world, at nineteen. The Kalinskars went back home. Four years passed, in the second of which, 1640, began the civil struggle for succession known as the War of the Three Kings.

Like most petty noble families the Kalinskars sided with Duke Givan Sovenskar in his claim to the throne. Andre took arms in his troops; by 1643, when they were fighting town by town down through the Molsen Province to Krasnoy, Andre was a field-captain. To him, while Sovenskar pushed on to the capital to be crowned, was entrusted the siege of the last stronghold of the Loyalists east of the river, the town and castle of Moge. So on a June day Andre lay, chin on folded arms, on the rough grass of a hilltop, gazing across a valley at the slate roofs of the town, the walls rising from a surf of chestnut leaves, the round tower, the shining river beyond.

"Captain, where do you want the culverins placed?"

The old prince was dead, and Brant Mogeskar had been killed in March, in the east. Had King Gulhelm sent troops across the river to the defense of his defenders, his rival might not be riding now to Krasnoy to be crowned; but no help had come, and the Mogeskars were besieged now in their own castle. Surrender they would not. Andre's lieutenant, who had arrived some days before him with the light troops, had requested a parley with George Mogeskar; but he had not even seen the prince. He had been received by the princess, he said, a handsome girl, but hard as iron. She had refused to parley: "Mogeskar does not bargain. If you lay siege we shall hold the castle. If you follow the Pretender we shall wait here for the King."

Andre lay gazing at the tawny walls. "Well, Soten, the problem's this: do we take the town first, or the castle?"

But that was not the problem at all. The problem was much crueller than that.

Lieutenant Soten sat down by him and puffed out his round cheeks. "Castle," he said. "Lose weeks taking that town, and then still have the castle to breach."

"Breach that — with the guns we've got? Once we're in the town, they'll accept terms in the castle."

"Captain, that woman in there isn't going to accept any terms."

"How do you know?"

"I've seen her!"

"So have I," said Andre. "We'll set the culverins there, at the south wall of the town. We'll begin bombardment tomorrow at dawn. We were asked to take the fort as it stands. It'll have to be at the cost of the town. They give us no choice." He spoke grimly, but was in his heart elated. He would give her every chance: the chance to withdraw from the hopeless fight and the chance, also, to prove herself, to use the courage she had felt heavy and shining in her breast, like a sword lying secret in its sheath.

He had been a worthy suitor, a man of her own mettle, and had been rejected. Fair enough. She did not want a lover, but an enemy; and he would be a worthy, an estimable one. He wondered if she yet knew his name, if someone had said, "Field-captain Kalinskar is leading them," and she had replied in her lordly, gentle, unheeding way, "Andre Kalinskar?" — frowning perhaps to learn that he had joined the Duke against the King, and yet not displeased, not sorry to have him as her foe.

They took the town, at the cost of three weeks and many lives. Later when Kalinskar was Marshal of the Royal Army he would say when drunk, "I can take any town. I took Moge." The walls were ingeniously fortified, the castle arsenal seemed inexhaustible, and the defenders fought with terrible spirit and patience. They withstood shelling and assaults, put out fires barehanded, ate air, in the last extremity fought face to face, house after house, from the town gate up to the castle scarp; and when taken prisoner they said, "It's her."

He had not seen her yet. He had feared to see her in the thick of that carnage in the narrow, ruined streets. From them at evening he kept looking up to the battlements a hundred feet above, the smoking cannon-emplacements, the round tower tawny red in sunset, the untouched castle.

"Wonder how we could get a match into the powder-store," said Lieutenant Soten, puffing his cheeks out cheerfully. His captain turned on him, his hawk-eyes red and swollen with smoke and weariness: "I'm taking Moge as it stands! Blow up the best fort in the country, would you, because you're tired of fighting? By God I'll teach you respect, Lieutenant!" Respect for what, or whom? Soten wondered, but held his tongue. As far as he was concerned Kalinskar was the finest officer in the army, and he was quite content to follow him, into madness, or wherever. They were all mad with the fighting, with fatigue, with the glaring, grilling heat and dust of summer.

They bombarded and made assaults at all hours, to keep the defenders from rest. In the dark of early morning Andre was leading a troop up to a partial breach they had made by mining the outer wall, when a foray from the castle met them. They fought with swords there in the darkness under the wall. It was a confused and ineffectual scrap, and Andre was calling his men together to retreat when he became aware that he had dropped his sword. He groped for it. For some reason his hands would not grasp, but slid stupidly among clods and rocks. Something cold and grainy pressed against his face: the earth. He opened his eyes very wide, and saw darkness.

Two cows grazed in the inner courtyard, the last of the great herds of Moge. At five in the morning a cup of milk was brought to the princess in her room, as usual, and a little while later the captain of the fort came as usual to give her the night's news. The news was the same as ever and Isabella paid little heed. She was calculating when King Gulhelm's forces might arrive, if her messenger had got to him. It could not be sooner than ten days. Ten days was a long time. It was only three days now since the town had fallen, and that seemed quite remote, an event from last year, from history. However, they could hold out ten days, even two weeks, if they had to. Surely the King would send them help.

"They'll send a messenger to ask about him," Breye was saying.

"Him?" She turned her heavy look on the captain.

"The field-captain."

"What field-captain?"

"I was telling you, princess. The foray took him prisoner this morning."

"A prisoner? Bring him here at once!"

"He's got a sabre-cut on the head, princess."

"Can he speak? I'll go to him. What's his name?"

"Kalinskar."

She followed Breye through gilt bedrooms where muskets were stacked on the beds, down a long parqueted corridor that crunched underfoot with crystal from the shattered candle-sconces, to the ballroom on the east side, now a hospital. Oaken bedsteads, pillared and canopied, their curtains open and awry, stood about on the sweep of floor like stray ships in a harbor after storm. The prisoner was asleep. She sat down by him and looked at his face, a dark face, serene, passive. Something within her grieved; not her will, which was resolute; but she was tired, mortally tired and grieved, as she sat looking at her enemy. He moved a little and opened his eyes. She recognised him then.

After a long time she said, "Dom Andre."

He smiled a little, and said something inaudible.

"The surgeon says your wound is not serious. Have you been leading the siege?"

"Yes," he said, quite clearly.

"From the start?"

"Yes."

She looked up at the shuttered windows which let in only a dim hint of the hot July sunlight.

"You're our first prisoner. What news of the country?"

"Givan Sovenskar was crowned in Krasnoy on the first. Gulhelm is still in Aisnar."

"You don't bring good news, captain," she said softly, with indifference. She glanced round the other beds down the great room, and motioned Breye to stand back. It irked her that they could not speak alone. But she found nothing to say.

"Are you alone here, princess?"

He had asked her a question like that the other time, up on the rooftop in the sunset.

"Brant is dead," she answered.

"I know. But the younger brother . . . I hunted with him in the marshes, that time."

"George is here now. He was at the defense of Kastre. A mortar blew up. It blinded him. Did you lead the siege at Kastre, too?"

"No. I fought there."

She met his eyes, only for a moment.

"I'm sorry for this," she said, "For George. For myself. For you, who swore to be my friend."

"Are you? I'm not. I've done what I could. I've served your glory. You know that even my own soldiers sing songs about you, about the Lady of Moge, like an archangel on the castle walls. In Krasnoy they talk about you, they sing the songs. Now they can say that you took me prisoner, too. They talk of you with wonder. Your enemies rejoice in you. You've won your freedom. You have been yourself." He spoke quickly, but when he stopped and shut his eyes for a moment to rest, his face looked still again, youthful. Isabella sat for a minute saying nothing, then suddenly got up and went out of the room with the hurrying, awkward gait of a girl in distress, graceless in her heavy, powder-stained dress.

Andre found that she was gone, replaced by the old captain of the fort, who stood looking down at him with hatred and curiosity.

"I admire her as much as you do!" he said to Breye. "More, more even than you here in the castle. More than anyone. For four years — " But Breye too was gone. "Get me some water to drink!" he said furiously, and then lay silent, staring at the ceiling. A roar and shudder — what was it? — then three dull thuds, deep and shocking like the pain in the root of a tooth; then another roar, shaking the bed — he understood finally that this was the bombardment, heard from inside. Soten was carrying out orders. "Stop it," he said, as the hideous racket went on and on. "Stop it. I need to sleep. Stop it, Soten! Cease firing!"

When he woke free of delirium it was night. A person was sitting near the head of his bed. Between him and the chair a candle burned; beyond the yellow globe of light about the candle-flame he could see a man's hand and sleeve. "Who's there?" he asked uneasily. The man rose and showed him in the full light of the candle a face destroyed. Nothing was left of the features but mouth and chin. These were delicate, the mouth and chin of a boy of about nineteen. The rest was newly healed scar.

"I'm George Mogeskar. Can you understand me?"

"Yes," Andre replied from a constricted throat.

"Can you sit up to write? I can hold the paper for you."

"What should I write?"

They both spoke very low.

"I wish to surrender my castle," Mogeskar said. "But I wish my sister to be gone, out of here, to go free. After that I shall give up the fort to you. Do you agree?"

"I — wait — "

"Write your lieutenant. Tell him that I will surrender on this one condition. I know Sovenskar wants this fort. Tell him that if she is detained, I shall blow the fort, and you, and myself, and her, into dust. You see, I have nothing much to lose, myself." The boy's voice was level, but a little husky. He spoke slowly and with absolute definiteness.

"The . . . the condition is just," Andre said.

Mogeskar brought an inkwell into the light, felt for its top, dipped the pen, gave pen and paper to Andre, who had managed to get himself half sitting up. When the pen had been scratching on the paper for a minute, Mogeskar said, "I remember you, Kalinskar. We went hunting in the long marsh. You were a good shot."

Andre glanced at him. He kept expecting the boy to lift off that unspeakable mask and show his face. "When will the princess leave? Shall my lieutenant give her escort across the river?"

"Tomorrow night at eleven. Four men of ours will go with her. One will come back to warrant her escape. It seems the grace of God that you led this siege, Kalinskar. I remember you, I trust you." His voice was like hers, light and arrogant, with that same husky note. "You can trust your lieutenant, I hope, to keep this secret."

Andre rubbed his head, which ached; the words he had written jiggled and writhed on the paper. "Secret? You wish this — these terms to be kept — you want her escape to be made secretly?"

"Do you think I wish it said that I sold her courage to buy my safety? Do you think she'd go if she knew what I am giving for her freedom? She thinks she's going to beg aid from King Gulhelm, while I hold out here!"

"Prince, she will never forgive — "

"It's not her forgiveness I want, but her life. She's the last of us. If she stays here, she'll see to it that when you finally take the castle she is killed. I am trading Moge Castle, and her trust in me, against her life."

"I'm sorry, prince," Andre said; his voice quavered with tears. "I didn't understand. My head's not very clear." He dipped the pen in the inkwell the blind man held, wrote another sentence, then blew on the paper, folded it, put it in the prince's hand.

"May I see her before she goes?"

"I don't think she'll come to you, Kalinskar. She is afraid of you. She doesn't know that it's I who will betray her." Mogeskar put out his hand into his unbroken darkness; Andre took it. He watched the tall, lean, boyish figure go hesitatingly off into the dark. The candle burned on at the bedside, the only light in the high, long room. Andre lay staring at the golden, pulsing sphere of light around the flame.

Two days later Moge Castle was surrendered to its besiegers, while its lady, unknowing and hopeful, rode on across the neutral lands westward to Aisnar.

And they met the third and last time, only by chance. Andre had not availed himself of Prince George Mogeskar's invitation to stop at the castle on his way to the border war in '47. To avoid the site of his first notable victory, to refuse a proud and grateful ex-enemy, was unlike him, suggesting either fear or a bad conscience, in neither of which did he much indulge himself. Nonetheless, he did not go to Moge. It was thirty-seven years later, at a winter ball in Count Alexis Helleskar's house in Krasnoy, that somebody took his arm and said, "Princess, let me present Marshall Kalinskar. The Princess Isabella Proyedskar."

He made his usual deep bow, straightened up, and straightened up still more, for the woman was taller than he by an inch at least. Her grey hair was piled into the complex rings and puffs of the current fashion. The panels of her gown were embroidered with arabesques of seedpearls. Out of a broad, pale face her blue-grey eyes looked straight at him, an inexplicable, comradely gaze. She was smiling. "I know Dom Andre," she said.

"Princess," he muttered, appalled.

She had got heavy; she was a big woman now, imposing, firmly planted. As for him, he was skin and bone, and lame in the right leg.

"My youngest daughter, Oriana." The girl of seventeen or eighteen curtsied, looking curiously at the hero, the man who in three wars, in thirty years of fighting, had forced a broken country back into one piece, and earned himself a simple and unquestionable fame. What a skinny little old man, said the girl's eyes.

"Your brother, princess — "

"George died many years ago, Dom Andre. My cousin Enrike is lord of Moge now. But tell me, are you married? I know of you only what all the world knows. It's been so long, Dom Andre, twice this child's age. . . ." Her voice was maternal, plaintive. The arrogance, the lightness were gone, even the huskiness of passion and of fear. She did not fear him now. She did not fear anything. Married, a mother, a grand-mother, her day over, a sheath with the sword drawn, a castle taken, no man's enemy.

"I married, princess. My wife died in childbirth, while I was in the field. Many years ago." He spoke harshly.

She replied, banal, plaintive, "Ah, but how sad life is, Dom Andre!"

"You wouldn't have said that on the walls of Moge," he said, still more harshly, for it galled his heart to see her like this. She looked at him with her blue-grey eyes, impassive, simply seeing him.

"No," she said, "that's true. And if I had been allowed to die on the walls of Moge, I should have died believing that life held great terror and great joy."

"It does, princess!" said Andrew Kalinskar, lifting his dark face to her, a man unabated and unfulfilled. She only smiled and said in her level, maternal voice, "For you, perhaps."

Other guests came up and she spoke to them, smiling. Andre stood aside, looking ill and glum, thinking how right he had been never to go back to Moge. He had been able to believe himself an honest man. He had remembered, faithfully, joyfully, for forty years, the red vines of October, the hot blue evenings of midsummer in the siege. And now he knew that he had betrayed all that, and lost the thing worth having, after all. Passive, heroic, he had given himself wholly to his life but the gift he had owed her, the soldier's one gift, was death; and he had withheld it. He had refused her. And now, at sixty, after all the days, wars, years, countrysides of his life, now he had to turn back and see that he had lost it all, had fought for nothing, that there was no princess in the castle.

Doris Lessing was born to English parents in Persia in 1919. When she was five years old her father, an inveterate romantic who sought to escape the constraints of living in conventional society, found even Teheran too conventional and so moved the family to a farm in Southern Rhodesia. Lessing lived in Africa until she moved to England in 1949, having completed her first novel, *The Grass Is Singing.* Over the past forty years she has written numerous books, including the novels for which she is much admired: the tetralogy *Children of Violence* (1952–1969), *The Golden Notebook* (1962), *Briefing for a Descent into Hell* (1971), *Memoirs of a Survivor* (1975), *Shikasta* (1979), and *The Good Terrorist* (1986). Her themes and forms are eclectic and wide-ranging: *The Golden Notebook,* for example, became something of a manifesto for the feminist movement; and with *Shikasta* she commenced a series of nonrealistic novels (inaccurately described as science fiction, in her judgment) describing life in a fictional universe. Lessing's short stories are collected in, among others, *The Habit of Loving* (1960), *African Stories* (1964), *The Sun Between Their Feet* (1973), and *The Stories of Doris Lessing* (1978). A deeply committed humanist, she has said that writers are "architects of the soul," responsible to their readers. "The Black Madonna" explores the artist's imperative to remain true to the honesty of art.

The Black Madonna

There are some countries in which the arts, let alone Art, cannot be said to flourish. Why this should be so it is hard to say, although of course we all have our theories about it. For sometimes it is the most barren soil that sends up gardens of those flowers which we all agree are the crown and justification of life, and it is this fact which makes it hard to say, finally, why the soil of Zambesia should produce such reluctant plants.

Zambesia is a tough, sunburnt, virile, positive country contemptuous of subtleties and sensibility: yet there have been States with these qualities which have produced art, though perhaps with the left hand. Zambesia is, to put it mildly, unsympathetic to those ideas so long taken for granted in other parts of the world, to do with liberty, fraternity and the rest. Yet there are those, and some of the finest souls among them, who maintain that art is impossible without a minority whose leisure is guaranteed by a hard-working majority. And whatever Zambesia's comfortable minority may lack, it is not leisure.

Zambesia — but enough; out of respect for ourselves and for scientific accuracy, we should refrain from jumping to conclusions. Particularly when one remembers the almost wistful respect Zambesians show when an artist does appear in their midst.

Consider, for instance, the case of Michele.

He came out of the internment camp at the time when Italy was made a sort of honorary ally, during the Second World War. It was a time of strain for the authorities, because it is one thing to be responsible for thousands of prisoners of war whom one must treat according to certain recognized standards; it is another to be faced, and from one day to the next, with these same thousands transformed by some international legerdemain into comrades in arms. Some of the thousands stayed where they were in the camps; they were fed and housed there at least. Others went as farm labourers, though not many; for while the farmers were as always short of labour, they did not know how to handle farm labourers who were also white men: such a phenomenon had never happened in Zambesia before. Some did odd jobs around the towns, keeping a sharp eye out for the trade unions, who would neither admit them as members nor agree to their working.

Hard, hard, the lot of these men, but fortunately not for long, for soon the war ended and they were able to go home.

Hard, too, the lot of the authorities, as has been pointed out; and for that reason they were doubly willing to take what advantages they could from the situation; and that Michele was such an advantage there could be no doubt.

His talents were first discovered when he was still a prisoner of war. A church was built in the camp, and Michele decorated its interior. It became a show-place, that little tin-roofed church in the prisoners' camp, with its whitewashed walls covered all over with frescoes depicting swarthy peasants gathering grapes for the vintage, beautiful Italian girls dancing, plump dark-eyed children. Amid crowded scenes of Italian life, appeared the Virgin and her Child, smiling and beneficent, happy to move familiarly among her people.

Culture-loving ladies who had bribed the authorities to be taken inside the camp would say, 'Poor thing, how homesick he must be'. And they would beg to be allowed to leave half a crown for the artist. Some were indignant. He was a prisoner, after all, captured in the very act of fighting against justice and democracy, and what right had he to protest? — for they felt these paintings as a sort of protest. What was there in Italy that we did not have right here in Westonville, which was the capital and hub of Zambesia? Were there not sunshine and mountains and fat babies and pretty girls here? Did we not grow — if not grapes, at least lemons and oranges and flowers in plenty?

People were upset — the desperation of nostalgia came from the painted white walls of that simple church, and affected everyone according to his temperament.

But when Michele was free, his talent was remembered. He was spoken of as 'that Italian artist'. As a matter of fact, he was a bricklayer. And the virtues of those frescoes might very well have been exaggerated. It is possible they would have been overlooked altogether in a country where picture-covered walls were more common.

When one of the visiting ladies came rushing out to the camp in her own car, to ask him to paint her children, he said he was not qualified to do so. But at last he agreed. He took a room in the town and made some nice likenesses of the children. Then he painted the children of a great number of the first lady's friends. He charged ten shillings a time. Then one of the ladies wanted a portrait of herself. He asked ten pounds for it; it had taken him a month to do. She was annoyed, but paid.

And Michele went off to his room with a friend and stayed there drinking red wine from the Cape and talking about home. While the money lasted he could not be persuaded to do any more portraits.

There was a good deal of talk among the ladies about the dignity of labour, a subject in which they were well versed; and one felt they might almost go so far as to compare a white man with a kaffir, who did not understand the dignity of labour either.

He was felt to lack gratitude. One of the ladies tracked him down, found him lying on a camp-bed under a tree with a bottle of wine, and spoke to him severely about the barbarity of Mussolini and the fecklessness of the Italian temperament. Then she demanded that he should instantly paint a picture of herself in her new evening dress. He refused, and she went home very angry.

It happened that she was the wife of one of our most important citizens, a General or something of that kind, who was at that time engaged in planning a military tattoo or show for the benefit of the civilian population. The whole of Westonville had been discussing this show for weeks. We were all bored to extinction by dances, fancy-dress balls, fairs, lotteries and other charitable entertainments. It is not too much to say that while some were dying for freedom, others were dancing for it. There comes a limit to everything. Though, of course, when the end of the war actually came and the thousands of troops stationed in the country had to go home — in short, when enjoying ourselves would no longer be a duty, many were heard to exclaim that life would never be the same again.

In the meantime, the Tattoo would make a nice change for us all. The military gentlemen responsible for the idea did not think of it in these terms. They thought to improve morale by giving us some idea of what war was really like. Headlines in the newspaper were not enough. And in order to bring it all home to us, they planned to destroy a village by shell-fire before our very eyes.

First, the village had to be built.

It appears that the General and his subordinates stood around in the red dust of the parade-ground under a burning sun for the whole of one day, surrounded by building materials, while hordes of African labourers ran around with boards and nails, trying to make something that looked like a village. It became evident that they would have to build a proper village in order to destroy it; and this would cost more than was allowed for the whole entertainment. The General went home in a bad temper, and his wife said what they needed was an artist, they needed Michele. This was not because she wanted to do Michele a good turn; she could not endure the thought of him lying around singing while there was work to be done. She refused to undertake any delicate diplomatic missions when her husband said he would be damned if he would ask favours of any little Wop. She solved the problem for him in her own way: a certain Captain Stocker was sent out to fetch him.

The Captain found him on the same camp-bed under the same tree, in rolled-up trousers, and an uncollared shirt; unshaven, mildly drunk, with a bottle of wine standing beside him on the earth. He was singing an air so wild, so sad, that the Captain was uneasy. He stood at ten paces from the disreputable fellow and felt the indignities of his position. A year ago, this man had been a mortal enemy to be shot at sight. Six months ago, he had been an enemy prisoner. Now he lay with his knees up, in an untidy shirt that had certainly once been military. For the Captain, the situation crystallized in a desire that Michele should salute him.

'Piselli!' he said sharply.

Michele turned his head and looked at the Captain from the horizontal. 'Good morning,' he said affably.

'You are wanted,' said the Captain.

'Who?' said Michele. He sat up, a fattish, olive-skinned little man. His eyes were resentful.

'The authorities.'

'The war is over?'

The Captain, who was already stiff and shiny enough in his laundered khaki, jerked his head back frowning, chin out. He was a large man, blond, and wherever his flesh showed, it was brick-red. His eyes were small and blue and angry. His red hands, covered all over with fine yellow bristles, clenched by his side. Then he saw the disappointment in Michele's eyes, and the hands unclenched. 'No it is not over,' he said. 'Your assistance is required.'

'For the war?'

'For the war effort. I take it you are interested in defeating the Germans?'

Michele looked at the Captain. The little dark-eyed artisan looked at the great blond officer with his cold blue eyes, his narrow mouth, his hands like bristle-covered steaks. He looked and said: 'I am very interested in the end of the war.'

'*Well?*' said the Captain between his teeth.

'The pay?' said Michele.

'You will be paid.'

Michele stood up. He lifted the bottle against the sun, then took a gulp. He rinsed his mouth out with wine and spat. Then he poured what was left on to the red earth, where it made a bubbling purple stain.

'I am ready,' he said. He went with the Captain to the waiting lorry, where he climbed in beside the driver's seat and not, as the Captain had expected, into the back of the lorry. When they had arrived at the parade-ground the officers had left a message that the Captain would be personally responsible for Michele and for the village. Also for the hundred or so labourers who were sitting around on the grass verges waiting for orders.

The Captain explained what was wanted. Michele nodded. Then he waved his hand at the Africans. 'I do not want these,' he said.

'You will do it yourself — a village?'

'Yes.'

'With no help?'

Michele smiled for the first time. 'I will do it.'

The Captain hesitated. He disapproved on principle of white men doing heavy manual labour. He said: 'I will keep six to do the heavy work.'

Michele shrugged; and the Captain went over and dismissed all but six of the Africans. He came back with them to Michele.

'It is hot,' said Michele.

'Very,' said the Captain. They were standing in the middle of the parade-ground. Around its edge trees, grass, gulfs of shadow. Here, nothing but reddish dust, drifting and lifting in a low hot breeze.

'I am thirsty,' said Michele. He grinned. The Captain felt his stiff lips loosen unwillingly in reply. The two pairs of eyes met. It was a moment of understanding. For the Captain, the little Italian had suddenly become human. 'I will arrange it,' he said, and went off down-town. By the time he had explained the position to the right people, filled in forms and made arrangements, it was late afternoon. He returned to the parade-ground with a case of Cape brandy, to find Michele and the six black men seated together under a tree. Michele was singing an Italian song to them, and they were harmonizing with him. The sight affected the Captain like an attack of nausea. He came up, and the Africans stood to attention. Michele continued to sit.

'You said you would do the work yourself?'

'Yes, I said so.'

The Captain then dismissed the Africans. They departed, with friendly looks towards Michele, who waved at them. The Captain was beef-red with anger. 'You have not started yet?'

'How long have I?'

'Three weeks.'

'Then there is plenty of time,' said Michele, looking at the bottle of brandy in the Captain's hand. In the other were two glasses. 'It is evening,' he pointed out. The Captain stood frowning for a moment. Then he sat down on the grass, and poured out two brandies.

'Ciao,' said Michele.

'Cheers,' said the Captain. Three weeks, he was thinking. Three weeks with this damned little Itie! He drained his glass and refilled it, and set it in the grass. The grass was cool and soft. A tree was flowering somewhere close — hot waves of perfume came on the breeze.

'It is nice here,' said Michele. 'We will have a good time together. Even in a war, there are times of happiness. And of friendship. I drink to the end of the war.'

Next day, the Captain did not arrive at the parade-ground until after lunch. He found Michele under the trees with a bottle. Sheets of ceiling board had been erected at one end of the parade-ground in such a way that they formed two walls and part of a third, and a slant of steep roof supported on struts.

'What's that?' said the Captain, furious.

'The church,' said Michele.

'Wha-at?'

'You will see. Later. It is very hot.' He looked at the brandy bottle that lay on its side on the ground. The Captain went to the lorry and returned with the case of brandy. They drank. Time passed. It was a long time since the Captain had sat on grass under a tree. It was a long time, for that matter, since he had drunk so much. He always drank a great deal, but it was regulated to the times and seasons. He was a disciplined man. Here, sitting on the grass beside this little man whom he still could not help thinking of as an enemy, it was not that he let his self-discipline go, but that he felt himself to be something different: he was temporarily set outside his normal behaviour. Michele did not count. He listened to Michele talking about Italy, and it seemed to him he was listening to a savage speaking: as if he heard tales from the mythical South Sea islands where a man like himself might very well go just once in his life. He found himself saying he would like to make a trip to Italy after the war. Actually, he was attracted only by the North and by Northern people. He had visited Germany, under Hitler, and though it was not the time to say so, had found it very satisfactory. Then Michele sang him some Italian songs. He sang Michele some English songs. Then Michele took out photographs of his wife and children, who lived in a village in the mountains of North Italy. He asked the Captain if he were married. The Captain never spoke about his private affairs.

He had spent all his life in one or other of the African colonies as a policeman, magistrate, native commissioner, or in some other useful capacity. When the war started, military life came easily to him. But he hated city life, and had his own reasons for wishing the war over. Mostly, he had been in bush-stations with one or two other white men, or by himself, far from the rigours of civilization. He had relations with native women; and from time to time visited the city where his wife lived with her parents and the children. He was always tormented by the idea that she was unfaithful to him. Recently he had even appointed a private detective to watch her; he was convinced the detective was inefficient. Army friends coming from L — where his wife was, spoke of her at parties, enjoying herself. When the war ended, she would not find it so easy to have a good time. And why did he not simply live with her and be done with it? The fact was, he could not. And his long exile to remote bush-stations was because he needed the excuse not to. He could not bear to think of his wife for too long; she was that part of his life he had never been able, so to speak, to bring to heel.

Yet he spoke of her now to Michele, and of his favourite bush-wife, Nadya. He told Michele the story of his life, until he realized that the shadows from the trees they sat under had stretched right across the parade-ground to the grandstand. He got unsteadily to his feet, and said: 'There is work to be done. You are being paid to work.'

'I will show you my church when the light goes.'

The sun dropped, darkness fell, and Michele made the Captain drive his lorry on to the parade-ground a couple of hundred yards away and switch on his lights. Instantly, a white church sprang up from the shapes and shadows of the bits of board.

'Tomorrow, some houses,' said Michele cheerfully.

At the end of a week, the space at the end of the parade-ground had crazy gawky constructions of lath and board over it, that looked in the sunlight like nothing on this earth. Privately, it upset the Captain; it was like a nightmare that these skeleton-like shapes should be able to persuade him, with the illusions of light and dark, that they were a village. At night, the Captain drove up his lorry, switched on the lights, and there it was, the village, solid and real against a background of full green trees. Then, in the morning sunlight, there was nothing there, just bits of board stuck in the sand.

'It is finished,' said Michele.

'You were engaged for three weeks,' said the Captain. He did not want it to end, this holiday from himself.

Michele shrugged. 'The army is rich,' he said. Now, to avoid curious eyes, they sat inside the shade of the church, with the case of brandy between them. The Captain talked, talked endlessly, about his wife, about women. He could not stop talking.

Michele listened. Once he said: 'When I go home — when I go home — I shall open my arms . . .' He opened them, wide. He closed his eyes. Tears ran down his cheeks. 'I shall take my wife in my arms, and I shall ask nothing, nothing. I do not care. It is enough to be together. That is what the war has taught me. It is enough, it is enough. I shall ask no questions and I shall be happy.'

The Captain stared before him, suffering. He thought how he dreaded his wife. She was a scornful creature, gay and hard, who laughed at him. She had been laughing at him ever since they married. Since the war, she had taken to calling him names like Little Hitler, and Storm-trooper. 'Go ahead, my little Hitler,' she had cried last time they met. 'Go ahead, my Storm-trooper. If you want to waste your money on private detectives, go ahead. But don't think I don't know what *you* do when you're in the bush. I don't care what you do, but remember that I know it . . .'

The Captain remembered her saying it. And there sat Michele on his packing-case, saying: 'It's a pleasure for the rich, my friend, detectives and the law. Even jealousy is a pleasure I don't want any more. Ah, my friend, to be together with my wife again, and the children, that is all I ask of life. That and wine and food and singing in the evenings.' And the tears wetted his cheeks and splashed on to his shirt.

That a man should cry, good lord! thought the Captain. And without shame! He seized the bottle and drank.

Three days before the great occasion, some high-ranking officers came strolling through the dust, and found Michele and the Captain sitting together on the packing-case, singing. The Captain's shirt was open down the front, and there were stains on it.

The Captain stood to attention with the bottle in his hand, and Michele stood to attention too, out of sympathy with his friend. Then the officers drew, the Captain aside — they were all cronies of his — and said, what the hell did he think he was doing? And why wasn't the village finished?

Then they went away.

'Tell them it is finished,' said Michele. 'Tell them I want to go.'

'No,' said the Captain, 'no. Michele, what would you do if your wife . . .'

'This world is a good place. We should be happy — that is all.'

'Michele . . .'

'I want to go. There is nothing to do. They paid me yesterday.'

'Sit down, Michele. Three more days, and then it's finished.'

'Then I shall paint the inside of the church as I painted the one in the camp.'

The Captain laid himself down on some boards and went to sleep. When he woke, Michele was surrounded by the pots of paint he had used on the outside of the village. Just in front of the Captain was a picture of a black girl. She was young and plump. She wore a patterned blue dress and her shoulders came soft and bare out of it. On her back was a baby slung in a band of red stuff. Her face was turned towards the Captain and she was smiling.

'That's Nadya,' said the Captain. 'Nadya . . .' He groaned loudly. He looked at the black child and shut his eyes. He opened them, and mother and child were still there. Michele was very carefully drawing thin yellow circles around the heads of the black girl and her child.

'Good God,' said the Captain, 'you can't do that.'

'Why not?'

'You can't have a black Madonna.'

'She was a peasant. This is a peasant. Black peasant Madonna for black country.'

'This is a German village,' said the Captain.

'This is my Madonna,' said Michele angrily. 'Your German village and my Madonna. I paint this picture as an offering to the Madonna. She is pleased — I feel it.'

The Captain lay down again. He was feeling ill. He went back to sleep. When he woke for the second time it was dark. Michele had brought in a flaring paraffin lamp, and by its light was working on the long wall. A bottle of brandy stood beside him. He painted until long after midnight, and the Captain lay on his side and watched, as passive as a man suffering a dream. Then they both went to sleep on the boards. The whole of the next day Michele stood painting black Madonnas, black saints, black angels. Outside, troops were practising in the sunlight, bands were blaring and motor cyclists roared up and down. But Michele painted on, drunk and oblivious. The Captain lay on his back, drinking and muttering about his wife. Then he would say 'Nadya, Nadya', and burst into sobs.

Towards nightfall the troops went away. The officers came back, and the Captain went off with them to show how the village sprang into being when the great lights at the end of the parade-ground were switched on. They all looked at the village in silence. They switched the lights off, and there were only the tall angular boards leaning like gravestones in the moonlight. On went the lights — and there was the village. They were silent, as if suspicious. Like the Captain, they seemed to feel it was not right. Uncanny it certainly was, but *that* was not it. Unfair — that was the word. It was cheating. And profoundly disturbing.

'Clever chap, that Italian of yours,' said the General.

The Captain, who had been woodenly correct until this moment, suddenly came rocking up to the General, and steadied himself by laying his hand on the august shoulder. 'Bloody Wops,' he said. 'Bloody kaffirs. Bloody . . . Tell you what, though, there's one Itie that's some good. Yes, there is. I'm telling you. He's a friend of mine, actually.'

The General looked at him. Then he nodded at his underlings. The Captain was taken away for disciplinary purposes. It was decided, however, that he must be ill, nothing else could account for such behaviour. He was put to bed in his own room with a nurse to watch him.

He woke twenty-four hours later, sober for the first time in weeks. He slowly remembered what had happened. Then he sprang out of bed and rushed into his clothes. The nurse was just in time to see him run down the path and leap into his lorry.

He drove at top speed to the parade-ground, which was flooded with light in such a way that the village did not exist. Everything was in full swing. The cars were three deep around the square, with people on the running-boards and even the roofs. The grandstand was packed. Women dressed up as gipsies, country girls, Elizabethan court dames, and so on, wandered about with trays of ginger beer and sausage-rolls and programmes at five shillings each in aid of the war effort. On the square, troops deployed, obsolete machine-guns were being dragged up and down, bands played, and motor cyclists roared through flames.

As the Captain parked the lorry, all this activity ceased, and the lights went out. The Captain began running around the outside of the square to reach the place where the guns were hidden in a mess of net and branches. He was sobbing with the effort. He was a big man, and unused to exercise, and sodden with brandy. He had only one idea in his mind — to stop the guns firing, to stop them at all costs.

Luckily, there seemed to be a hitch. The lights were still out. The unearthly graveyard at the end of the square glittered white in the moonlight. Then the lights briefly switched on, and the village sprang into existence for just long enough to show large red crosses all over a white building beside the church. Then moonlight flooded everything again, and the crosses vanished. 'Oh, the bloody fool!' sobbed the Captain, running, running as if for his life. He was no longer trying to reach the guns. He was cutting across a corner of the square direct to the church. He could hear some officers cursing behind him: 'Who put those red crosses there? Who? We can't fire on the Red Cross.'

The Captain reached the church as the searchlights burst on. Inside, Michele was kneeling on the earth looking at his first Madonna. 'They are going to kill my Madonna,' he said miserably.

'Come away, Michele, come away.'

'They're going to . . .'

The Captain grabbed his arm and pulled. Michele wrenched himself free and grabbed a saw. He began hacking at the ceiling board. There was a dead silence outside. They heard a voice booming through the loudspeakers: 'The village that is about to be shelled is an English village, not as represented on the programme, a German village. Repeat, the village that is about to be shelled is . . .'

Michele had cut through two sides of a square around the Madonna.

'Michele,' sobbed the Captain, *'get out of here.'*

Michele dropped the saw, took hold of the raw edges of the board and tugged. As he did so, the church began to quiver and lean. An irregular patch of board ripped out and Michele staggered back into the Captain's arms. There was a roar. The church seemed to dissolve around them into flame. Then they were running away from it, the Captain holding Michele tight by the arm. 'Get down,' he shouted suddenly, and threw Michele to the earth. He flung himself down beside him. Looking from under the crook of his arm, he heard the explosion, saw a great pillar of smoke and flame, and the village disintegrated in a flying mass of debris. Michele was on his knees gazing at his Madonna in the light from the flames. She was unrecognizable, blotted out with dust. He looked horrible, quite white, and a trickle of blood soaked from his hair down one cheek.

'They shelled my Madonna,' he said.

'Oh, damn it, you can paint another one,' said the Captain. His own voice seemed to him strange, like a dream voice. He was certainly crazy, as mad as Michele himself . . . He got up, pulled Michele to his feet, and marched him towards the edge of the field. There they were met by the ambulance people. Michele was taken off to hospital, and the Captain was sent back to bed.

A week passed. The Captain was in a darkened room. That he was having some kind of a breakdown was clear, and two nurses stood guard over him. Sometimes he lay quiet. Sometimes he muttered to himself. Sometimes he sang in a thick clumsy voice bits out of opera, fragments from Italian songs, and — over and over again — There's a Long Long Trail. He was not thinking of anything at all. He shied away from the thought of Michele as if it were dangerous. When, therefore, a cheerful female voice announced that a friend had come to cheer him up, and it would do him good to have some company, and he saw a white bandage moving towards him in the gloom, he turned sharp over on to his side, face to the wall.

'Go away,' he said. 'Go away, Michele.'

'I have come to see you,' said Michele. 'I have brought you a present.'

The Captain slowly turned over. There was Michele, a cheerful ghost in the dark room. 'You fool,' he said. 'You messed everything up. What did you paint those crosses for?'

'It was a hospital,' said Michele. 'In a village there is a hospital, and on the hospital the Red Cross, the beautiful Red Cross — no?'

'I was nearly court-martialed.'

'It was my fault,' said Michele. 'I was drunk.'

'I was responsible.'

'How could you be responsible when I did it? But it is all over. Are you better?'

'I did not think,' said Michele. 'I was remembering the kindness of the Red Cross people when we were prisoners.'

'Oh shut up, shut up, shut up.'

'I have brought you a present.'

The Captain peered through the dark. Michele was holding up a picture. It was of a native woman with a baby on her back smiling sideways out of the frame.

Michele said: 'You did not like the haloes. So this time, no haloes. For the Captain — no Madonna.' He laughed. 'You like it? It is for you. I painted it for you.'

'God damn you!' said the Captain.

'You do not like it?' said Michele, very hurt.

The Captain closed his eyes. 'What are you going to do next?' he asked tiredly.

Michele laughed again. 'Mrs. Pannerhurst, the lady of the General, she wants me to paint her picture in her white dress. So I paint it.'

'You should be proud to.'

'Silly bitch. She thinks I am good. They know nothing — savages. Barbarians. Not you, Captain, you are my friend. But these people they know nothing.'

The Captain lay quiet. Fury was gathering in him. He thought of the General's wife. He disliked her, but he had known her well enough.

'These people,' said Michele. 'They do not know a good picture from a bad picture. I paint, I paint, this way, that way. There is the picture — I look at it and laugh inside myself.' Michele laughed out loud. 'They say, he is a Michelangelo, this one, and try to cheat me out of my price. Michele — Michelangelo — that is a joke, no?'

The Captain said nothing.

'But for you I painted this picture to remind you of our good times with the village. You are my friend. I will always remember you.'

The Captain turned his eyes sideways in his head and stared at the black girl. Her smile at him was half innocence, half malice.

'Get out,' he said suddenly.

Michele came closer and bent to see the Captain's face. 'You wish me to go?' He sounded unhappy. 'You saved my life. I was a fool that night. But I was thinking of my offering to the Madonna — I was a fool, I say it myself. I was drunk, we are fools when we are drunk.'

'Get out of here,' said the Captain again.

For a moment the white bandage remained motionless. Then it swept downwards in a bow.

Michele turned towards the door.

'And take that bloody picture with you.'

Silence. Then, in the dim light, the Captain saw Michele reach out for the picture, his white head bowed in profound obeisance. He straightened himself and stood to attention, holding the picture with one hand, and keeping the other stiff down his side. Then he saluted the Captain.

'Yes, *sir,*' he said, and he turned and went out of the door with the picture.

The Captain lay still. He felt — what did he feel? There was a pain under his ribs. It hurt to breathe. He realized he was unhappy. Yes, a terrible unhappiness was filling him, slowly, slowly. He was unhappy because Michele had gone. Nothing had ever hurt the Captain in all his life as much as that mocking *Yes, sir.* Nothing. He turned his face to the wall and wept. But silently. Not a sound escaped him, for the fear the nurses might hear.

BERNARD MALAMUD

Bernard Malamud (1914–1986) was born in Brooklyn, New York, and received his education at City College of New York. A teacher and writer all his life, he focused steadily in his work on the potential of human goodness to mitigate suffering. His characters and themes were primarily Jewish, but Malamud invariably equated Judaism with all humanity: "All men are Jews." His novels include *The Natural* (1952), *The Assistant* (1957), *The Fixer* (1966), *Pictures of Fidelman* (1969), and *Dubin's Lives* (1979). His stories are collected in *The Magic Barrel* (1958), *Idiots First* (1963), and *Rembrandt's Hat* (1973). As "The Last Mohican" shows, Malamud has a deft comic touch — perhaps an acknowledgment that laughter is one way of enduring life's ironies.

The Last Mohican

Fidelman, a self-confessed failure as a painter, came to Italy to prepare a critical study of Giotto, the opening chapter of which he had carried across the ocean in a new pigskin-leather briefcase, now gripped in his perspiring hand. Also new were his gum-soled oxblood shoes, a tweed suit he had on despite the late-September sun slanting hot in the Roman sky, although there was a lighter one in his bag; and a dacron shirt and set of cotton-dacron underwear, good for quick and easy washing for the traveler. His suitcase, a bulky, two-strapped affair which embarrassed him slightly, he had borrowed from his sister Bessie. He planned, if he had any money left at the end of the year, to buy a new one in Florence. Although he had been in not much of a mood when he had left the U.S.A., Fidelman revived in Naples, and at the moment, as he stood in front of the Rome railroad station, after twenty minutes still absorbed in his first sight of the Eternal City, he was conscious of a certain exaltation that devolved on him after he had discovered that directly across the many-vehicled piazza stood the remains of the Baths of Diocletian. Fidelman remembered having read that Michelangelo had had a hand in converting the baths into a church and convent, the latter ultimately changed into the museum that presently was there. "Imagine," he muttered. "Imagine all that history."

In the midst of his imagining, Fidelman experienced the sensation of suddenly seeing himself as he was, to the pinpoint, outside and in, not without bittersweet pleasure; and as the well-known image of his face rose before him he was taken by the depth of pure feeling in his eyes, slightly magnified by glasses, and the sensitivity of his elongated nostrils and often tremulous lips, nose divided from lips by a mustache of recent vintage that looked, Fidelman thought, as if it had been sculptured there, adding to his dignified appearance although he was a little on the short side. But almost at the same moment, this unexpectedly intense sense of his being — it was more than appearance — faded, exaltation having gone where exaltation goes, and Fidelman became aware that there was an exterior source to the strange, almost tri-dimensional reflection of himself he had felt as well as seen. Behind him, a short distance to the right, he had noticed a stranger   give a skeleton a couple of pounds — loitering near a bronze statue on a stone pedestal of the heavy-dugged Etruscan wolf suckling the infants Romulus and Remus, the man contemplating Fidelman already acquisitively so as to suggest to the traveler that he had been mirrored (lock, stock, barrel) in the other's gaze for some time, perhaps since he had stepped off the train. Casually studying him, though pretending no, Fidelman beheld a person of about his own height, oddly dressed in brown knickers and black, knee-length woolen socks drawn up over slightly bowed, broomstick legs, these grounded in small, porous, pointed shoes. His yellowed shirt was open at the gaunt throat, both sleeves rolled up over skinny, hairy arms. The stranger's high forehead was bronzed, his black hair thick behind small ears, the dark, close-shaven beard tight on the face; his experienced nose was weighted at the tip, and the soft brown eyes, above all, *wanted*. Though his expression suggested humility, he all but licked his lips as he approached the ex-painter.

"Shalom," he greeted Fidelman.

"Shalom," the other hesitantly replied, uttering the word — so far as he recalled — for the first time in his life. My God, he thought, a handout for sure. My first hello in Rome and it has to be a schnorrer.

The stranger extended a smiling hand. "Susskind," he said, "Shimon Susskind."

"Arthur Fidelman." Transferring his briefcase to under his left arm while standing astride the big suitcase, he shook hands with Susskind. A blue-smocked porter came by, glanced at Fidelman's bag, looked at him, then walked away.

Whether he knew it or not Susskind was rubbing his palms contemplatively together.

"Parla italiano?"

"Not with ease, although I read it fluently. You might say I need practice."

"Yiddish?"

"I express myself best in English."

"Let it be English then." Susskind spoke with a slight British intonation. "I knew you were Jewish," he said, "the minute my eyes saw you."

Fidelman chose to ignore the remark. "Where did you pick up your knowledge of English?"

"In Israel."

Israel interested Fidelman. "You live there?"

"Once, not now," Susskind answered vaguely. He seemed suddenly bored.

"How so?"

Susskind twitched a shoulder. "Too much heavy labor for a man of my modest health. Also I couldn't stand the suspense."

Fidelman nodded.

"Furthermore, the desert air makes me constipated. In Rome I am lighthearted."

"A Jewish refugee from Israel, no less," Fidelman said good-humoredly.

"I'm always running," Susskind answered mirthlessly. If he was lighthearted, he had yet to show it.

"Where else from, if I may ask?"

"Where else but Germany, Hungary, Poland? Where not?"

"Ah, that's so long ago." Fidelman then noticed the gray in the man's hair. "Well, I'd better be going," he said. He picked up his bags as two porters hovered uncertainly nearby.

But Susskind offered certain services. "You got a hotel?"

"All picked and reserved."

"How long are you staying?"

What business is it of his? However, Fidelman courteously replied, "Two weeks in Rome, the rest of the year in Florence, with a few side trips to Siena, Assisi, Padua, and maybe also Venice."

"You wish a guide in Rome?"

"Are you a guide?"

"Why not?"

"No," said Fidelman. "I'll look as I go along to museums, libraries, et cetera."

This caught Susskind's attention. "What are you, a professor?"

Fidelman couldn't help blushing. "Not exactly, really just a student."

"From which institution?"

He coughed a little. "By that I mean a professional student, you might say. Call me Trofimov, from Chekhov. If there's something to learn I want to learn it."

"You have some kind of a project?" the other persisted. "A grant?"

"No grant. My money is hard-earned. I worked and saved a long time to take a year in Italy. I made certain sacrifices. As for a project, I'm writing on the painter Giotto. He was one of the most important — "

"You don't have to tell me about Giotto," Susskind interrupted with a little smile.

"You've studied his work?"

"Who doesn't know Giotto?"

"That's interesting to me," said Fidelman, secretly irritated. "How do you happen to know him?"

"How do you mean?"

"I've given a good deal of time and study to his work."

"So I know him too."

I'd better get this over with before it begins to amount to something, Fidelman thought. He set down his bag and fished with a finger in his leather coin purse. The two porters watched with interest, one taking a sandwich out of his pocket, unwrapping the newspaper, and beginning to eat.

"This is for yourself," Fidelman said.

Susskind hardly glanced at the coin as he let it drop into his pants pocket. The porters then left.

The refugee had an odd way of standing motionless, like a cigar store Indian about to burst into flight. "In your luggage," he said vaguely, "would you maybe have a suit you can't use? I could use a suit."

At last he comes to the point. Fidelman, though annoyed, controlled himself. "All I have is a change from the one you now see me wearing. Don't get the wrong idea about me, Mr. Susskind. I'm not rich. In fact, I'm poor. Don't let a few new clothes deceive you. I owe my sister money for them."

Susskind glanced down at his shabby, baggy knickers. "I haven't had a suit for years. The one I was wearing when I ran away from Germany fell apart. One day I was walking around naked."

"Isn't there a welfare organization that could help you out — some group in the Jewish community interested in refugees?"

"The Jewish organizations wish to give me what they wish, not what I wish," Susskind replied bitterly. "The only thing they offer me is a ticket back to Israel."

"Why don't you take it?"

"I told you already, here I feel free."

"Freedom is a relative term."

"Don't tell me about freedom."

He knows all about that, too, Fidelman thought. "So you feel free," he said, "but how do you live?"

Susskind coughed, a brutal cough.

Fidelman was about to say something more on the subject of freedom but left it unsaid. Jesus, I'll be saddled with him all day if I don't watch out.

"I'd better be getting off to the hotel." He bent again for his bag.

Susskind touched him on the shoulder and when Fidelman exasperatedly straightened up, the half dollar he had given the man was staring him in the eye.

"On this we both lose money."

"How do you mean?"

"Today the lira sells six twenty-three on the dollar, but for specie they only give you five hundred."

"In that case, give it here and I'll let you have a dollar." From his wallet Fidelman quickly extracted a crisp bill and handed it to the refugee.

"Not more?" Susskind sighed.

"Not more," the student answered emphatically.

"Maybe you would like to see Diocletian's bath? There are some enjoyable Roman coffins inside. I will guide you for another dollar."

"No thanks." Fidelman said goodbye and, lifting the suitcase, lugged it to the curb. A porter appeared and the student, after some hesitation, let him carry it toward the line of small dark-green taxis in the piazza. The porter offered to carry the briefcase too, but Fidelman wouldn't part with it. He gave the cab driver the address of the hotel, and the taxi took off with a lurch. Fidelman at last relaxed. Susskind, he noticed, had disappeared. Gone with his breeze, he thought. But on the way to the hotel he had an uneasy feeling that the refugee, crouched low, might be clinging to the little tire on the back of the cab; he didn't look out to see.

Fidelman had reserved a room in an inexpensive hotel not far from the station, with its very convenient bus terminal. Then, as was his habit, he got himself quickly and tightly organized. He was always concerned with not wasting time, as if it were his only wealth — not true, of course, though Fidelman admitted he was ambitious — and he soon arranged a schedule that made the most of his working hours. Mornings he usually visited the Italian libraries, searching their catalogues and archives, read in poor light, and made profuse notes. He napped for an hour after lunch, then at four, when the churches and museums were reopening, hurried off to them with lists of frescoes and paintings he must see. He was anxious to get to Florence, at the same time a little unhappy at all he would not have time to take in in Rome. Fidelman promised himself to return again if he could afford it, perhaps in the spring, and look at anything he pleased.

After dark he managed to unwind and relax. He ate as the Romans did, late, enjoyed a half liter of white wine and smoked a cigarette. Afterwards he liked to wander — especially in the old sections near the Tiber. He had read that here, under his feet, were the ruins of ancient Rome. It was an inspiring business, he, Arthur Fidelman, after all born a Bronx boy, walking around in all this history. History was mysterious, the remembrance of things unknown, in a way burdensome, in a way a sensuous experience. It uplifted and depressed, why he did not know, except that it excited his thoughts more than he thought good for him. This kind of excitement was all right up to a point, perfect maybe for a creative artist, but less so for a critic. A critic, he thought, should live on beans. He walked for miles along the winding river, gazing at the star-strewn skies. Once, after a couple of days in the Vatican Museum, he saw flights of angels — gold, blue, white — intermingled in the sky. "My God, I got to stop using my eyes so much," Fidelman said to himself. But back in his room he sometimes wrote till morning.

Late one night, about a week after his arrival in Rome, as Fidelman was writing notes on the Byzantine-style mosaics he had seen during the day, there was a knock on the door, and though the student, immersed in his work, was not conscious he had said "Avanti," he must have, for the door opened, and instead of an angel, in came Susskind in his shirt and baggy knickers.

Fidelman, who had all but forgotten the refugee, certainly never thought of him, half rose in astonishment. "Susskind," he exclaimed, "how did you get in here?"

Susskind for a moment stood motionless, then answered with a weary smile, "I'll tell you the truth, I know the desk clerk."

"But how did you know where I live?"

"I saw you walking in the street so I followed you."

"You mean you saw me accidentally?"

"How else? Did you leave me your address?"

Fidelman resumed his seat. "What can I do for you, Susskind?" He spoke grimly.

The refugee cleared his throat. "Professor, the days are warm but the nights are cold. You see how I go around naked." He held forth bluish arms, goose-fleshed. "I came to ask you to reconsider about giving away your old suit."

"And who says it's an old suit?" Despite himself, Fidelman's voice thickened.

"One suit is new, so the other is old."

"Not precisely. I am afraid I have no suit for you, Susskind. The one I presently have hanging in the closet is a little more than a year old and I can't afford to give it away. Besides, it's gabardine, more like a summer suit."

"On me it will be for all seasons."

After a moment's reflection, Fidelman drew out his billfold and counted four single dollars. These he handed to Susskind.

"Buy yourself a warm sweater."

Susskind also counted the money. "If four," he said, "why not five?"

Fidelman flushed. The man's warped nerve. "Because I happen to have four available," he answered. "That's twenty-five hundred lire. You should be able to buy a warm sweater and have something left over besides."

"I need a suit," Susskind said. "The days are warm but the nights are cold." He rubbed his arms. "What else I need I won't tell you."

"At least roll down your sleeves if you're so cold."

"That won't help me."

"Listen, Susskind," Fidelman said gently, "I would gladly give you the suit if I could afford to, but I can't. I have barely enough money to squeeze out a year for myself here. I've already told you I am indebted to my sister. Why don't you try to get yourself a job somewhere, no matter how menial? I'm sure that in a short while you'll work yourself up into a decent position."

"A job, he says," Susskind muttered gloomily. "Do you know what it means to get a job in Italy? Who will give me a job?"

"Who gives anybody a job? They have to go out and look for it."

"You don't understand, professor. I am an Israeli citizen and this means I can only work for an Israeli company. How many Israeli companies are there here? — maybe two, El Al and Zim, and even if they had a job, they wouldn't give it to me because I have lost my passport. I would be better off now if I were stateless. A stateless person shows his laissez-passer and sometimes he can find a small job."

"But if you lost your passport why didn't you put in for a duplicate?"

"I did, but did they give it to me?"

"Why not?"

"Why not? They say I sold it."

"Had they reason to think that?"

"I swear to you somebody stole it from me."

"Under such circumstances," Fidelman asked, "how do you live?"

"How do I live?" He chomped with his teeth. "I eat air."

"Seriously?"

"Seriously, on air. I also peddle," he confessed, "but to peddle you need a license, and that the Italians won't give me. When they caught me peddling I was interned for six months in a work camp."

"Didn't they attempt to deport you?"

"They did, but I sold my mother's old wedding ring that I kept in my pocket so many years. The Italians are a humane people. They took the money and let me go, but they told me not to peddle any more."

"So what do you do now?"

"I peddle. What should I do, beg? — I peddle. But last spring I got sick and gave my little money away to the doctors. I still have a bad cough." He coughed fruitily. "Now I have no capital to buy stock with. Listen, professor, maybe we can go in partnership together? Lend me twenty thousand lire and I will buy ladies' nylon stockings. After I sell them I will return you your money."

"I have no funds to invest, Susskind."

"You will get it back, with interest."

"I honestly am sorry for you," Fidelman said, "but why don't you at least do something practical? Why don't you go to the Joint Distribution Committee, for instance, and ask them to assist you? That's their business."

"I already told you why. They wish me to go back, but I wish to stay here."

"I still think going back would be the best thing for you."

"No," cried Susskind angrily.

"If that's your decision, freely made, then why pick on me? Am I responsible for you then, Susskind?"

"Who else?" Susskind loudly replied.

"Lower your voice, please, people are sleeping around here," said Fidelman, beginning to perspire. "Why should I be?"

"You know what responsibility means?"

"I think so."

"Then you are responsible. Because you are a man. Because you are a Jew, aren't you?"

"Yes, goddamn it, but I'm not the only one in the whole wide world. Without prejudice, I refuse the obligation. I am a single individual and can't take on everybody's personal burden. I have the weight of my own to contend with."

He reached for his billfold and plucked out another dollar.

"This makes five. It's more than I can afford, but take it and after this please leave me alone. I have made my contribution."

Susskind stood there, oddly motionless, an impassioned statue, and for a moment Fidelman wondered if he would stay all night, but at last the refugee thrust forth a stiff arm, took the fifth dollar, and departed.

Early the next morning Fidelman moved out of the hotel into another, less convenient for him, but far away from Shimon Susskind and his endless demands.

This was Tuesday. On Wednesday, after a busy morning in the library, Fidelman entered a nearby trattoria and ordered a plate of spaghetti with tomato sauce. He was reading his *Messaggero,* anticipating the coming of the food, for he was unusually hungry, when he sensed a presence at the table. He looked up, expecting the waiter, but beheld instead Susskind standing there, alas, unchanged.

Is there no escape from him? thought Fidelman, severely vexed. Is this why I came to Rome?

"Shalom, professor," Susskind said, keeping his eyes off the table. "I was passing and saw you sitting here alone, so I came in to say shalom."

"Susskind," Fidelman said in anger, "have you been following me again?"

"How could I follow you?" asked the astonished Susskind. "Do I know where you live now?"

Though Fidelman blushed a little, he told himself he owed nobody an explanation. So he had found out he had moved — good.

"My feet are tired. Can I sit five minutes?"

"Sit."

Susskind drew out a chair. The spaghetti arrived, steaming hot. Fidelman sprinkled it with cheese and wound his fork into several tender strands. One of the strings of spaghetti seemed to stretch for miles, so he stopped at a certain point and swallowed the forkful. Having foolishly neglected to cut the long spaghetti string he was left sucking it, seemingly endlessly. This embarrassed him.

Susskind watched with rapt attention.

Fidelman at last reached the end of the long spaghetti, patted his mouth with a napkin, and paused in his eating.

"Would you care for a plateful?"

Susskind, eyes hungry, hesitated. "Thanks," he said.

"Thanks yes or thanks no?"

"Thanks no." The eyes looked away.

Fidelman resumed eating, carefully winding his fork; he had had not too much practice with this sort of thing and was soon involved in the same dilemma with the spaghetti. Seeing Susskind still watching him, he became tense.

"We are not Italians, professor," the refugee said. "Cut it in small pieces with your knife. Then you will swallow it easier."

"I'll handle it as I please," Fidelman responded testily. "This is my business. You attend to yours."

"My business," Susskind sighed, "don't exist. This morning I had to let a wonderful chance get away from me. I had a chance to buy ladies' stockings at three hundred lire if I had money to buy half a gross. I could easily sell them for five hundred a pair. We would have made a nice profit."

"The news doesn't interest me."

"So if not ladies' stockings, I can also get sweaters, scarves, men's socks, also cheap leather goods, ceramics — whatever would interest you."

"What interests me is what you did with the money I gave you for a sweater."

"It's getting cold, professor," Susskind said worriedly. "Soon comes the November rains, and in winter the tramontana. I thought I ought to save your money to buy a couple of kilos of chestnuts and a bag of charcoal for my burner. If you sit all day on a busy street corner you can sometimes make a thousand lire. Italians like hot chestnuts. But if I do this I will need some warm clothes, maybe a suit."

"A suit," Fidelman remarked sarcastically, "why not an overcoat?"

"I have a coat, poor that it is, but now I need a suit. How can anybody come in company without a suit?"

Fidelman's hand trembled as he laid down his fork. "To my mind you are utterly irresponsible and I won't be saddled with you. I have the right to choose my own problems and the right to my privacy."

"Don't get excited, professor, it's bad for your digestion. Eat in peace." Susskind got up and left the trattoria.

Fidelman hadn't the appetite to finish his spaghetti. He paid the bill, waited ten minutes, then departed, glancing around from time to time to see if he was being followed. He headed down the sloping street to a small piazza where he saw a couple of cabs. Not that he could afford one, but he wanted to make sure Susskind didn't tail him back to his new hotel. He would warn the clerk at the desk never to allow anybody of the refugee's name or description even to make inquiries about him.

Susskind, however, stepped out from behind a plashing fountain at the center of the little piazza. Modestly addressing the speechless Fidelman, he said, "I don't wish to take only, professor. If I had something to give you, I would gladly give it to you."

"Thanks," snapped Fidelman, "just give me some peace of mind."

"That you have to find yourself," Susskind answered.

In the taxi Fidelman decided to leave for Florence the next day, rather than at the end of the week, and once and for all be done with the pest.

That night, after returning to his room from an unpleasurable walk in the Trastevere — he had a headache from too much wine at supper — Fidelman found his door ajar and at once recalled that he had forgotten to lock it, although he had as usual left the key with the desk clerk. He was at first frightened, but when he tried the armadio in which he kept his clothes and suitcase, it was shut tight. Hastily unlocking it, he was relieved to see his blue gabardine suit.— a one-button-jacket affair, the trousers a little frayed at the cuffs, but all in good shape and usable for years to come — hanging amid some shirts the maid had pressed for him; and when he examined the contents of the suitcase he found nothing missing, including, thank God, his passport and traveler's checks. Gazing around the room, Fidelman saw all in place. Satisfied, he picked up a book and read ten pages before he thought of his briefcase. He jumped to his feet and began to search everywhere, remembering distinctly that it had been on the night table as he had lain on the bed that afternoon, rereading his chapter. He searched under the bed and behind the night table, then again throughout the room, even on top of and behind the armadio. Fidelman hopelessly opened every drawer, no matter how small, but found neither the briefcase nor, what was worse, the chapter in it.

With a groan he sank down on the bed, insulting himself for not having made a copy of the manuscript, because he had more than once warned himself that something like this might happen to it. But he hadn't because there were some revisions he had contemplated making, and he had planned to retype the entire chapter before beginning the next. He thought now of complaining to the owner of the hotel, who lived on the floor below, but it was already past midnight and he realized nothing could be done until morning. Who could have taken it? The maid or the hall porter? It seemed unlikely they would risk their jobs to steal a piece of leather goods that would bring them only a few thousand lire in a pawnshop. Possibly a sneak thief? He would ask tomorrow if other persons on the floor were missing something. He somehow doubted it. If a thief, he would then and there have ditched the chapter and stuffed the briefcase with Fidelman's oxblood shoes, left by the bed, and the fifteen-dollar R. H. Macy sweater that lay in full view of the desk. But if not the maid or porter or a sneak thief, then who? Though Fidelman had not the slightest shred of evidence to support his suspicions, he could think of only one person — Susskind. This thought stung him. But if Susskind, why? Out of pique, perhaps, that he had not been given the suit he had coveted, nor was able to pry it out of the armadio? Try as he would, Fidelman could think of no one else and no other reason. Somehow the peddler had followed him home (he suspected their meeting at the fountain) and had got into his room while he was out to supper.

Fidelman's sleep that night was wretched. He dreamed of pursuing the refugee in the Jewish catacombs under the ancient Appian Way, threatening him with a blow on the presumptuous head with a seven-flamed candelabrum he clutched in his hand; while Susskind, clever ghost, who knew the ins and outs of all the crypts and alleys, eluded him at every turn. Then Fidelman's candles all blew out, leaving him sightless and alone in the cemeterial dark; but when the student arose in the morning and wearily drew up the blinds, the yellow Italian sun winked him cheerfully in both bleary eyes.

Fidelman postponed going to Florence. He reported his loss to the Questura, and though the police were polite and eager to help, they could do nothing for him. On the form on which the inspector noted the complaint, he listed the briefcase as worth ten thousand lire, and for "valore del manuscritto" he drew a line. Fidelman, after giving the matter a good deal of thought, did not report Susskind, first, because he had absolutely no proof, for the desk clerk swore he had seen no stranger around in knickers; second, because he was afraid of the consequences for the refugee if he was written down "suspected thief" as well as "unlicensed peddler" and inveterate refugee. He tried instead to rewrite the chapter, which he felt sure he knew by heart, but when he sat down at the desk, there were important thoughts, whole paragraphs, even pages, that went blank in the mind. He considered sending to America for his notes for the chapter, but they were in a barrel in his sister's attic in Levittown, among many notes for other projects. The thought of Bessie, a mother of five, poking around in his things, and the work entailed in sorting the cards, then getting them packaged and mailed to him across the ocean, wearied Fidelman unspeakably; he was certain she would send the wrong ones. He laid down his pen and went into the street, seeking Susskind. He searched for him in neighborhoods where he had seen him before, and though Fidelman spent hours looking, literally days, Susskind never appeared; or if he perhaps did, the sight of Fidelman caused him to vanish. And when the student inquired about him at the Israeli consulate, the clerk, a new man on the job, said he had no record of such a person or his lost passport; on the other hand, he was known at the Joint Distribution Committee, but by name and address only, an impossibility, Fidelman thought. They gave him a number to go to but the place had long since been torn down to make way for an apartment house.

Time went without work, without accomplishment. To put an end to this appalling waste Fidelman tried to force himself back into his routine of research and picture viewing. He moved out of the hotel, which he now could not stand for the harm it had done him (leaving a telephone number and urging he be called if the slightest clue turned up), and he took a room in a small pensione near the stazione and here had breakfast and supper rather than go out. He was much concerned with expenditures and carefully recorded them in a notebook he had acquired for the purpose. Nights, instead of wandering in the city, feasting himself upon its beauty and mystery, he kept his eyes glued to paper, sitting steadfastly at his desk in an attempt to re-create his initial chapter, because he was lost without a beginning. He had tried writing the second chapter from notes in his possession, but it had come to nothing. Always Fidelman needed something solid behind him before he could advance, some worthwhile accomplishment upon which to build another. He worked late, but his mood, or inspiration, or whatever it was, had deserted him, leaving him with growing anxiety, almost disorientation; of not knowing — it seemed to him for the first time in months — what he must do next, a feeling that was torture. Therefore he again took up his search for the refugee. He thought now that once he had settled it, knew that the man had or hadn't stolen his chapter — whether he recovered it or not seemed at the moment immaterial — just the knowing of it would ease his mind and again he would *feel* like working, the crucial element.

Daily he combed the crowded streets, searching for Susskind wherever people peddled. On successive Sunday mornings he took the long ride to the Porta Portese market and hunted for hours among the piles of secondhand goods and junk lining the back streets, hoping his briefcase would magically appear, though it never did. He visited the open market at Piazza Fontanella Borghese, and observed the ambulant vendors at Piazza Dante. He looked among fruit and vegetable stalls set up in the streets, whenever he chanced upon them, and dawdled on busy street corners after dark, among beggars and fly-by-night peddlers. After the first cold snap at the end of October, when the chestnut sellers appeared throughout the city, huddled over pails of glowing coals, he sought in their faces the missing Susskind. Where in all of modern and ancient Rome was he? The man lived in the open air — he had to appear somewhere. Sometimes when riding in a bus or tram, Fidelman thought he had glimpsed somebody in a crowd, dressed in the refugee's clothes, and he invariably got off to run after whoever it was — once a man standing in front of the Banco di Santo Spirito, gone when Fidelman breathlessly arrived; and another time he overtook a person in knickers, but this one wore a monocle. Sir Ian Susskind?

In November it rained. Fidelman wore a blue beret with his trench coat and a pair of black Italian shoes, smaller, despite their pointed toes, than his burly oxbloods which overheated his feet and whose color he detested. But instead of visiting museums he frequented movie houses, sitting in the cheapest seats and regretting the cost. He was, at odd hours in certain streets, several times accosted by prostitutes, some heartbreakingly pretty, one a slender, unhappy-looking girl with bags under her eyes whom he desired mightily, but Fidelman feared for his health. He had got to know the face of Rome and spoke Italian fairly fluently, but his heart was burdened, and in his blood raged a murderous hatred of the bandy-legged refugee — although there were times when he bethought himself he might be wrong — so Fidelman more than once cursed him to perdition.

One Friday night, as the first star glowed over the Tiber, Fidelman, walking aimlessly along the left riverbank, came upon a synagogue and wandered in among a crowd of Sephardim with Italianate faces. One by one they paused before a sink in an antechamber to dip their hands under a flowing faucet, then in the house of worship touched with loose fingers their brows, mouths, and breasts as they bowed to the Ark, Fidelman doing likewise. Where in the world am I? Three rabbis rose from a bench and the service began, a long prayer, sometimes chanted, sometimes accompanied by invisible organ music, but no Susskind anywhere. Fidelman sat at a desk-like pew in the last row, where he could inspect the congregants yet keep an eye on the door. The synagogue was unheated and the cold rose like an exudation from the marble floor. The student's freezing nose burned like a lit candle. He got up to go, but the beadle, a stout man in a high hat and short caftan, wearing a long thick silver chain around his neck, fixed the student with his powerful left eye.

"From New York?" he inquired, slowly approaching.

Half the congregation turned to see who.

"State, not city," answered Fidelman, nursing an active guilt for the attention he was attracting. Then, taking advantage of a pause, he whispered, "Do you happen to know a man named Susskind? He wears knickers."

"A relative?" The beadle gazed at him sadly.

"Not exactly."

"My own son — killed in the Ardeatine Caves." Tears stood forth in his eyes.

"Ah, for that I'm sorry."

But the beadle had exhausted the subject. He wiped his wet lids with pudgy fingers and the curious Sephardim turned back to their prayer books.

"Which Susskind?" the beadle wanted to know.

"Shimon."

He scratched his ear. "Look in the ghetto."

"I looked."

"Look again."

The beadle walked slowly away and Fidelman sneaked out.

The ghetto lay behind the synagogue for several crooked, well-packed blocks, encompassing aristocratic palazzi ruined by age and unbearable numbers, their discolored façades strung with lines of withered wet wash, the fountains in the piazzas, dirt-laden, dry. And dark stone tenements, built partly on centuries-old ghetto walls, inclined toward one another across narrow, cobblestoned streets. In and among the impoverished houses were the wholesale establishments of wealthy Jews, dark holes ending in jeweled interiors, silks and silver of all colors. In the mazed streets wandered the present-day poor, Fidelman among them, oppressed by history, although, he joked to himself, it added years to his life.

A white moon shone upon the ghetto, lighting it like dark day. Once he thought he saw a ghost he knew by sight, and hastily followed him through a thick stone passage to a blank wall where shone in white letters under a tiny electric bulb: VIETATO URINARE. Here was a smell but no Susskind.

For thirty lire the student bought a dwarfed, blackened banana from a street vendor (not S) on a bicycle, and stopped to eat. A crowd of ragazzi gathered to watch.

"Anybody here know Susskind, a refugee wearing knickers?" Fidelman announced, stooping to point the banana where the pants went beneath the knees. He also made his legs a trifle bowed but nobody noticed.

There was no response until he had finished his fruit, then a thin-faced boy with brown liquescent eyes out of Murillo piped: "He sometimes works in the Cimitero Verano, the Jewish section."

There too? thought Fidelman. "Works in the cemetery?" he inquired. "With a shovel?"

"He prays for the dead," the boy answered, "for a small fee."

Fidelman bought him a quick banana and the others dispersed.

In the cemetery, deserted on the Sabbath — he should have come Sunday — Fidelman went among the graves, reading legends carved on tombstones, many topped with small brass candelabra, whilst withered yellow chrysanthemums lay on the stone tablets of other graves, dropped stealthily, Fidelman imagined, on All Souls' Day — a festival in another part of the cemetery — by renegade sons and daughters unable to bear the sight of their dead bereft of flowers, while the crypts of the goyim were lit and in bloom. Many were burial places, he read on the stained stones, of those who, for one reason or another, had died in the late large war, including an empty place, it said under a six-pointed star engraved upon a marble slab that lay on the ground, for "My beloved father/Betrayed by the damned Fascists/Murdered at Auschwitz by the barbarous Nazis/*O Crime Orribile.*" But no Susskind.

Three months had gone by since Fidelman's arrival in Rome. Should he, he many times asked himself, leave the city and this foolish search? Why not off to Florence, and there amid the art splendors of the world, be inspired to resume his work? But the loss of his first chapter was like a spell cast over him. There were times he scorned it as a man-made thing, like all such, replaceable; other times he feared it was not the chapter per se, but that his volatile curiosity had become somehow entangled with Susskind's strange personality — Had he repaid generosity by stealing a man's life work? Was he so distorted? To satisfy himself, to know man, Fidelman had to know, though at what a cost in precious time and effort. Sometimes he smiled wryly at all this; ridiculous, the chapter grieved him for itself only — the precious thing he had created, then lost — especially when he got to thinking of the long diligent labor, how painstakingly he had built each idea, how cleverly mastered problems of order, form, how impressive the finished product, Giotto reborn! It broke the heart. What else, if after months he was here, still seeking?

And Fidelman was unchangingly convinced that Susskind had taken it, or why would he still be hiding? He sighed much and gained weight. Mulling over his frustrated career, on the backs of envelopes containing unanswered letters from his sister Bessie he aimlessly sketched little angels flying. Once, studying his minuscule drawings, it occurred to him that he might someday return to painting, but the thought was more painful than Fidelman could bear.

One bright morning in mid-December, after a good night's sleep, his first in weeks, he vowed he would have another look at the Navicella and then be off to Florence. Shortly before noon he visited the porch of St. Peter's, trying, from his remembrance of Giotto's sketch, to see the mosaic as it had been before its many restorations. He hazarded a note or two in shaky handwriting, then left the church and was walking down the sweeping flight of stairs, when he beheld at the bottom — his hear misgave him, was he still seeing pictures, a sneaky apostle added to the overloaded boatful? — ecco Susskind! The refugee, in beret and long green G.I. raincoat, from under whose skirts showed his black-stockinged, rooster's ankles — indicating knickers going on above though hidden — was selling black and white rosaries to all who would buy. He had several strands of beads in one hand, while in the palm of the other a few gilded medallions glinted in the winter sun. Despite his outer clothing, Susskind looked, it must be said, unchanged, not a pound more of meat or muscle, the face though aged, ageless. Gazing at him, the student ground his teeth in remembrance. He was tempted quickly to hide, and unobserved observe the thief; but his impatience, after the long unhappy search, was too much for him. With controlled trepidation he approached Susskind on his left as the refugee was busily engaged on the right, urging a sale of beads upon a woman drenched in black.

"Beads, rosaries, say your prayers with holy beads."

"Greetings, Susskind," Fidelman said, coming shakily down the stairs, dissembling the Unified Man, all peace and contentment. "One looks for you everywhere and finds you here. Wie gehts?"

Susskind, though his eyes flickered, showed no surprise to speak of. For a moment his expression seemed to say he had no idea who this was, had forgotten Fidelman's existence, but then at last remembered — somebody long ago from another country, whom you smiled on, then forgot.

"Still here?" he perhaps ironically joked.

"Still." Fidelman was embarrassed at his voice slipping.

"Rome holds you?"

"Rome," faltered Fidelman, " — the air." He breathed deep and exhaled with emotion.

Noticing the refugee was not truly attentive, his eyes roving upon potential customers, Fidelman, girding himself, remarked, "By the way, Susskind, you didn't happen to notice — did you? — the briefcase I was carrying with me around the time we met in September?"

"Briefcase — what kind?" This he said absently, his eyes on the church doors.

"Pigskin. I had in it" — here Fidelman's voice could be heard cracking — "a chapter of critical work on Giotto I was writing. You know, I'm sure, the Trecento painter?"

"Who doesn't know Giotto?"

"Do you happen to recall whether you saw, if, that is — " He stopped, at a loss for words other than accusatory.

"Excuse me — business." Susskind broke away and bounced up the steps two at a time. A man he approached shied away. He had beads, didn't need others.

Fidelman had followed the refugee. "Reward," he muttered up close to his ear. "Fifteen thousand for the chapter, and who has it can keep the brand-new briefcase. That's his business, no questions asked. Fair enough?"

Susskind spied a lady tourist, including camera and guide book. "Beads — holy beads." He held up both hands but she was just a Lutheran, passing through.

"Slow today," Susskind complained as they walked down the stairs, "but maybe it's the items. Everybody has the same. If I had some big ceramics of the Holy Mother, they go like hot cakes — a good investment for somebody with a little cash."

"Use the reward for that," Fidelman cagily whispered, "buy Holy Mothers."

If he heard, Susskind gave no sign. At the sight of a family of nine emerging from the main portal above, the refugee, calling addio over his shoulder, fairly flew up the steps. But Fidelman uttered no response. I'll get the rat yet. He went off to hide behind a high fountain in the square. But the flying spume raised by the wind wet him, so he retreated behind a massive column and peeked out at short intervals to keep the peddler in sight.

At two o'clock, when St. Peter's closed to visitors, Susskind dumped his goods into his raincoat pockets and locked up shop. Fidelman followed him all the way home, indeed the ghetto, although along a street he had not consciously been on before, which led into an alley where the refugee pulled open a left-handed door and, without transition, was "home." Fidelman, sneaking up close, caught a dim glimpse of an overgrown closet containing bed and table. He found no address on wall or door, nor, to his surprise, any door lock. This for a moment depressed him. It meant Susskind had nothing worth stealing. Of his own, that is. The student promised himself to return tomorrow, when the occupant was elsewhere.

Return he did, in the morning, while the entrepreneur was out selling religious articles, glanced around once, and was quickly inside. He shivered — a pitch-black freezing cave. Fidelman scratched up a thick match and confirmed bed and table, also a rickety chair, but no heat or light except a drippy candle stub in a saucer on the table. He lit the yellow candle and searched all over the place. In the table drawer a few eating implements plus safety razor, though where he shaved was a mystery, probably a public toilet. On a shelf above the thin-blanketed bed stood half a flask of red wine, part of a package of spaghetti, and a hard panino. Also an unexpected little fish bowl with a bony goldfish swimming around in arctic seas. The fish, reflecting the candle flame, gulped repeatedly, threshing its frigid tail as Fidelman watched. He loves pets, thought the student. Under the bed he found a chamber pot, but nowhere a briefcase with a fine critical chapter in it. The place was not more than an icebox someone probably had lent the refugee to come in out of the rain. Alas, Fidelman sighed. Back in the pensione, it took a hot-water bottle two hours to thaw him out; but from the visit he never fully recovered.

In this latest dream of Fidelman's he was spending the day in a cemetery all crowded with tombstones, when up out of an empty grave rose this long-nosed brown shade, Virgilio Susskind, beckoning.

Fidelman hurried over.

"Have you read Tolstoy?"

"Sparingly."

"Why is art?" asked the shade, drifting off.

Fidelman, willy-nilly, followed, and the ghost, as it vanished, led him up steps going through the ghetto and into a marble synagogue.

The student, left alone, for no reason he could think of lay down upon the stone floor, his shoulders keeping strangely warm as he stared at the sunlit vault above. The fresco therein revealed this saint in fading blue, the sky flowing from his head, handing an old knight in a thin red robe his gold cloak. Nearby stood a humble horse and two stone hills.

Giotto. San Francesco dona le vesti al cavaliere povero.

Fidelman awoke running. He stuffed his blue gabardine into a paper bag, caught a bus, and knocked early on Susskind's heavy portal.

"Avanti." The refugee, already garbed in beret and raincoat (probably his pajamas), was standing at the table, lighting the candle with a flaming sheet of paper. To Fidelman the paper looked like the underside of a typewritten page. Despite himself, the student recalled in letters of fire his entire chapter.

"Here, Susskind," he said in a trembling voice, offering the bundle, "I bring you my suit. Wear it in good health."

The refugee glanced at it without expression. "What do you wish for it?"

"Nothing at all." Fidelman laid the bag on the table, called goodbye, and left.

He soon heard footsteps clattering after him across the cobblestones.

"Excuse me, I kept this under my mattress for you." Susskind thrust at him the pigskin briefcase.

Fidelman savagely opened it, searching frenziedly in each compartment, but the bag was empty. The refugee was already in flight. With a bellow the student started after him. "You bastard, you burned my chapter!"

"Have mercy," cried Susskind, "I did you a favor."

"I'll do you one and cut your throat."

"The words were there but the spirit was missing."

In a towering rage, Fidelman forced a burst of speed, but the refugee, light as the wind in his marvelous knickers, his green coattails flying, rapidly gained ground.

The ghetto Jews, framed in amazement in their medieval windows, stared at the wild pursuit. But in the middle of it, Fidelman, stout and short of breath, moved by all he had lately learned, had a triumphant insight.

"Susskind, come back," he shouted, half sobbing. "The suit is yours. All is forgiven."

He came to a dead halt but the refugee ran on. When last seen he was still running.

THOMAS MANN

Thomas Mann (1875–1955) was born in Lubeck, Germany, the son of a wealthy merchant. His first novel, the family saga *Buddenbrooks* (1900), was published when he was only twenty-five; it was at once an international success, and Mann was at once famous. In succeeding years he ensured his literary reputation with the publication of *Tonio Kroger* (1903), *Death in Venice* (1913), and, especially, *The Magic Mountain* (1924). He was awarded the Nobel Prize for Literature in 1929. When the Nazis came to power in Germany in 1933, Mann exiled himself, first to Switzerland, then to the United States, where he was granted citizenship in 1944. He returned to Europe after World War II and settled in Switzerland, choosing not to return to Germany. His later novels include the quartet *Joseph and His Brothers* (1933–1944), *Doctor Faustus* (1948), and *Confessions of Felix Krull* (1955). His stories are collected in *Stories of Three Decades* (1936). Living in the strife of a century engaged in its second world war, Mann was particularly apprehensive of disintegration and loss. "Disorder and Early Sorrow" is one of his most moving portraits of a changing order.

Disorder and Early Sorrow

Translated from the German by H. T. Lowe-Porter

The principal dish at dinner had been croquettes made of turnip greens. So there follows a trifle, concocted out of one of those dessert powders we use nowadays, that taste like almond soap. Xaver, the youthful manservant, in his outgrown striped jacket, white woollen gloves, and yellow sandals, hands it round, and the "big folk" take this opportunity to remind their father, tactfully, that company is coming today.

The "big folk" are two, Ingrid and Bert. Ingrid is brown-eyed, eighteen, and perfectly delightful. She is on the eve of her exams, and will probably pass them, if only because she knows how to wind masters, and even headmasters, round her finger. She does not, however, mean to use her certificate once she gets it; having leanings toward the stage, on the ground of her ingratiating smile, her equally ingratiating voice, and a marked and irresistible talent for burlesque. Bert is blond and seventeen. He intends to get done with school somehow, anyhow, and fling himself into the arms of life. He will be a dancer, or a cabaret actor, possibly even a waiter — but not a waiter anywhere else save at the Cairo, the night-club, whither he has once already taken flight, at five in the morning, and been brought back crestfallen. Bert bears a strong resemblance to the youthful manservant Xaver

Kleinsgutl, of about the same age as himself; not because he looks common — in features he is strikingly like his father, Professor Cornelius — but by reason of an approximation of types, due in its turn to far-reaching compromises in matters of dress and bearing generally. Both lads wear their heavy hair very long on top, with a cursory parting in the middle, and give their heads the same characteristic toss to throw it off the forehead. When one of them leaves the house, by the garden gate, bareheaded in all weathers, in a blouse rakishly girt with a leather strap, and sheers off bent well over with his head on one side; or else mounts his push-bike — Xaver makes free with his employers', of both sexes, or even, in acutely irresponsible mood, with the Professor's own — Dr. Cornelius from his bedroom window cannot, for the life of him, tell whether he is looking at his son or his servant. Both, he thinks, look like young moujiks. And both are impassioned cigarette-smokers, though Bert has not the means to compete with Xaver, who smokes as many as thirty a day, of a brand named after a popular cinema star. The big folk call their father and mother the "old folk" — not behind their backs, but as a form of address and in all affection: "Hullo, old folks," they will say; though Cornelius is only forty-seven years old and his wife eight years younger. And the Professor's parents, who lead in his household the humble and hesitant life of the really old, are on the big folk's lips the "ancients." As for the "little folk," Ellie and Snapper, who take their meals upstairs with blue-faced Ann — so-called because of her prevailing facial hue — Ellie and Snapper follow their mother's example and address their father by his first name, Abel. Unutterably comic it sounds, in its pert, confiding familiarity; particularly on the lips, in the sweet accents, of five-year-old Eleanor, who is the image of Frau Cornelius's baby pictures and whom the Professor loves above everything else in the world.

"Darling old thing," says Ingrid affably, laying her large but shapely hand on his, as he presides in proper middle-class style over the family table, with her on his left and the mother opposite: "Parent mine, may I ever so gently jog your memory, for you have probably forgotten: this is the afternoon we were to have our little jollification, our turkey-trot with eats to match. You haven't a thing to do but just bear up and not funk it; everything will be over by nine o'clock."

"Oh — ah!" says Cornelius, his face falling. "Good!" he goes on, and nods his head to show himself in harmony with the inevitable. "I only meant — is this really the day? Thursday, yes. How time flies! Well, what time are they coming?"

"Half past four they'll be dropping in, I should say," answers Ingrid, to whom her brother leaves the major rôle in all dealings with the father. Upstairs, while he is resting, he will hear scarcely anything, and from seven to eight he takes his walk. He can slip out by the terrace if he likes.

"Tut!" says Cornelius deprecatingly, as who should say: "You exaggerate." But Bert puts in: "It's the one evening in the week Wanja doesn't have to play. Any other night he'd have to leave by half past six, which would be painful for all concerned."

Wanja is Ivan Herzl, the celebrated young leading man at the Stadttheater. Bert and Ingrid are on intimate terms with him, they often visit him in his dressing-room and have tea. He is an artist of the modern school, who stands on the stage in strange and, to the Professor's mind, utterly affected dancing attitudes, and shrieks lamentably. To a professor of history, all highly repugnant; but Bert has entirely succumbed to Herzl's influence, blackens the lower rim of his eyelids — despite painful but fruitless scenes with the father — and with youthful carelessness of the ancestral anguish declares that not only will he take Herzl for his model if he becomes a dancer, but in case he turns out to be a waiter at the Cairo he means to walk precisely thus.

Cornelius slightly raises his brows and makes his son a little bow — indicative of the unassumingness and self-abnegation that befits his age. You could not call it a mocking bow or suggestive in any special sense. Bert may refer it to himself or equally to his so talented friend.

"Who else is coming?" next inquires the master of the house. They mention various people, names all more or less familiar, from the city, from the suburban colony, from Ingrid's school. They still have some telephoning to do, they say. They have to phone Max. This is Max Hergesell, an engineering student; Ingrid utters his name in the nasal drawl which according to her is the traditional intonation of all the Hergesells. She goes on to parody it in the most abandonedly funny and lifelike way, and the parents laugh until they nearly choke over the wretched trifle. For even in these times when something funny happens people have to laugh.

From time to time the telephone bell rings in the Professor's study, and the big folk run across, knowing it is their affair. Many people had to give up their telephones the last time the price rose, but so far the Corneliuses have been able to keep theirs, just as they have kept their villa, which was built before the war, by dint of the salary Cornelius draws as professor of history — a million marks, and more or less adequate to the chances and changes of post-war life. The house is comfortable, even elegant, though sadly in need of repairs that cannot be made for lack of materials, and at present disfigured by iron stoves with long pipes. Even so, it is still the proper setting of the upper middle class, though they themselves look odd enough in it, with their worn and turned clothing and altered way of life. The children, of course, know nothing else; to them it is normal and regular, they belong by birth to the "villa proletariat." The problem of clothing troubles them not at all. They and their like have evolved a costume to fit the time, by poverty out of taste for innovation: in summer it consists of scarcely more than a belted linen smock and sandals. The middle-class parents find things rather more difficult.

The big folk's table-napkins hang over their chair-backs, they talk with their friends over the telephone. These friends are the invited guests who have rung up to accept or decline or arrange; and the conversation is carried on in the jargon of the clan, full of slang and high spirits, of which the old folk understand hardly a word. These consult together meantime about the hospitality to be offered to the impending guests. The Professor displays a middle-class ambitiousness: he wants to serve a sweet — or something that looks like a sweet — after the Italian salad and brown-bread sandwiches. But Frau Cornelius says that would be going too far. The guests would not expect it, she is sure — and the big folk, returning once more to their trifle, agree with her.

The mother of the family is of the same general type as Ingrid, though not so tall. She is languid; the fantastic difficulties of the housekeeping have broken and worn her. She really ought to go and take a cure, but feels incapable; the floor is always swaying under her feet, and everything seems upside down. She speaks of what is uppermost in her mind: the eggs, they simply must be bought today. Six thousand marks apiece they are, and just so many are to be had on this one day of the week at one single shop fifteen minutes' journey away. Whatever else they do, the big folk must go and fetch them immediately after luncheon, with Danny, their neighbour's son, who will soon be calling for them; and Xaver Kleinsgutl will don civilian garb and attend his young master and mistress. For no single household is allowed more than five eggs a week; therefore the young people will enter the shop singly, one after another, under assumed names, and thus wring twenty eggs from the shop-keeper for the Cornelius family. This enterprise is the sporting event of the week for all participants, who excepting the moujik Kleinsgutl, and most of all for Ingrid and Bert, who delight in misleading and mystifying their fellowmen and would revel in the performance even if it did not achieve one single egg. They adore impersonating fictitious characters; they love to sit in a bus and carry on long lifelike conversations in a dialect which they otherwise never speak, the most commonplace dialogue about politics and people and the price of food, while the whole bus listens open-mouthed to this incredibly ordinary prattle, though with a dark suspicion all the while that something is wrong somewhere. The conversation waxes ever more shameless, it enters into revolting detail about these people who do not exist. Ingrid can make her voice sound ever so common and twittering and shrill as she imper-sonates a shop-girl with an illegitimate child, said child being a son with sadistic tendencies, who lately out in the country treated a cow with such unnatural cruelty that no Christian could have borne to see it. Bert nearly explodes at her twittering, but restrains himself and displays a grisly sympathy; he and the unhappy shop-girl entering into a long, stupid, depraved, and shuddery conversation over the particular morbid cruelty involved; until an old gentleman opposite, sitting with his ticket folded between his index finger and his seal ring, can bear it no more and makes public protest against the nature of the themes these young folk are discussing with such particularity. He uses the Greek plural: "themata." Whereat Ingrid pretends to be dissolving in tears, and Bert behaves as though his wrath against the old gentle-man was with difficulty being held in check and would probably burst out before long. He clenches his fists, he gnashes his teeth, he shakes from head to foot; and the unhappy old gentleman, whose intentions had been of the best, hastily leaves the bus at the next stop.

Such are the diversions of the big folk. The telephone plays a prominent part in them: they ring up any and everybody — members of government, opera singers, dignitaries of the Church — in the character of shop assistants, or perhaps as Lord or Lady Doolittle. They are only with difficulty persuaded that they have the wrong number. Once they emptied their parents' card-tray and distributed its contents among the neighbours' letter-boxes, wantonly, yet not without enough impish sense of the fitness of things to make it highly upsetting, God only knowing why certain people should have called where they did.

Xaver comes in to clear away, tossing the hair out of his eyes. Now that he has taken off his gloves you can see the yellow chain-ring on his left hand. And as the Professor finishes his watery eight-thousand-mark beer and lights a cigarette, the little folk can be heard scrambling down the stair, coming, by established custom, for their after-dinner call on Father and Mother. They storm the dining-room, after a struggle with the latch, clutched by both pairs of little hands at once; their clumsy small feet twinkle over the carpet, in red felt slippers with the socks falling down on them. With prattle and shoutings each makes for his own place: Snapper to Mother, to climb on her lap, boast of all he has eaten, and thump his fat little tum; Ellie to her Abel, so much hers because she is so very much his; because she consciously luxuriates in the deep tenderness — like all deep feeling, concealing a melancholy strain — with which he holds her small form embraced; in the love in his eyes as he kisses her little fairy hand or the sweet brow with its delicate tracery of tiny blue veins.

The little folk look like each other, with the strong undefined likeness of brother and sister. In clothing and hair-cut they are twins. Yet they are sharply distinguished after all, and quite on sex lines. It is a little Adam and a little Eve. Not only is Snapper the sturdier and more compact, he appears consciously to emphasize his four-year-old masculinity in speech, manner, and carriage, lifting his shoulders and letting the little arms hang down quite like a young American athlete, drawing down his mouth when he talks and seeking to give his voice a gruff and forthright ring. But all this masculinity is the result of effort rather than natively his. Born and brought up in these desolate, distracted times, he has been endowed by them with an unstable and hypersensitive nervous system and suffers greatly under life's disharmonies. He is prone to sudden anger and outbursts of bitter tears, stamping his feet at every trifle; for this reason he is his mother's special nursling and care. His round, round eyes are chestnut brown and already inclined to squint, so that he will need glasses in the near future. His little nose is long, the mouth small — the father's nose and mouth they are, more plainly than ever since the Professor shaved his pointed beard and goes smooth-faced. The pointed beard has become impossible — even professors must make some concession to the changing times.

But the little daughter sits on her father's knee, his Eleonorchen, his little Eve, so much more gracious a little being, so much sweeter-faced than her brother — and he holds his cigarette away from her while she fingers his glasses with her dainty wee hands. The lenses are divided for reading and distance, and each day they tease her curiosity afresh.

At bottom he suspects that his wife's partiality may have a firmer basis than his own: that Snapper's refractory masculinity perhaps is solider stuff than his own little girl's more explicit charm and grace. But the heart will not be commanded, that he knows; and once and for all his heart belongs to the little one, as it has since the day she came, since the first time he saw her. Almost always when he holds her in his arms he remembers that first time: remembers the sunny room in the Women's Hospital, where Ellie first saw the light, twelve years after Bert was born. He remembers how he drew near, the mother smiling the while, and cautiously put aside the canopy of the diminutive bed that stood beside the large one. There lay the little miracle among the pillows: so well formed, so encompassed, as it were, with the harmony of sweet proportions, with little hands that even then, though so much tinier, were beautiful as now; with wide-open eyes blue as the sky and brighter than the sunshine — and almost in that very second he felt himself captured and held fast. This was love at first sight, love everlasting: a feeling unknown, unhoped for, unexpected — in so far as it could be a matter of conscious awareness; it took entire possession of him, and he understood, with joyous amazement, that this was for life.

But he understood more. He knows, does Dr. Cornelius, that there is something not quite right about this feeling, so unaware, so undreamed of, so involuntary. He has a shrewd suspicion that it is not by accident it has so utterly mastered him and bound itself up with his existence; that he had — even subconsciously — been preparing for it, or, more precisely, been prepared for it. There is, in short, something in him which at a given moment was ready to issue in such a feeling; and this something, highly extraordinary to relate, is his essence and quality as a professor of history. Dr. Cornelius, however, does not actually say this, even to himself; he merely realizes it, at odd times, and smiles a private smile. He knows that history professors do not love history because it is something that comes to pass, but only because it is something that *has* come to pass; that they hate a revolution like the present one because they feel it is lawless, incoherent, irrelevant — in a word, unhistoric; that their hearts belong to the coherent, disciplined, historic past. For the temper of timelessness, the temper of eternity — thus the scholar communes with himself when he takes his walk by the river before supper — that temper broods over the past; and it is a temper much better suited to the nervous system of a history professor than are the excesses of the present. The past is immortalized; that is to say, it is dead; and death is the root of all godliness and all abiding significance. Dr. Cornelius, walking alone in the dark, has a profound insight into this truth. It is this conservative instinct of his, his sense of the eternal, that has found in his love for his little daughter a way to save itself from the wounding inflicted by the times. For father love, and a little child on its mother's breast — are not these timeless, and thus very, very holy and beautiful? Yet Cornelius, pondering there in the dark, descries something not perfectly right and good in his love. Theoretically, in the interests of science, he admits it to himself. There is something ulterior about it, in the nature of it; that something is hostility, hostility against the history of today, which is still in the making and thus not history at all, in behalf of the genuine history that has already happened — that is to say, death. Yes, passing strange though all this is, yet it is true; true in a sense, that is. His devotion to this priceless little morsel of life and new growth has something to do with death, it clings to death as against life; and that is neither right nor beautiful — in a sense. Though only the most fanatical asceticism could be capable, on no other ground than such casual scientific perception, of tearing this purest and most precious of feelings out of his heart.

He holds his darling on his lap and her slim rosy legs hang down. He raises his brow as he talks to her, tenderly, with a half-teasing note of respect, and listens enchanted to her high, sweet little voice calling him Abel. He exchanges a look with the mother, who is caressing her Snapper and reading him a gentle lecture. He must be more reasonable, he must learn self-control; today again, under the manifold exasperations of life, he has given way to rage and behaved like a howling dervish. Cornelius casts a mistrustful glance at the big folk now and then, too; he thinks it not unlikely they are not unaware of those scientific preoccupations of his evening walks. If such be the case they do not show it. They stand there leaning their arms on their chair-backs and with a benevolence not untinctured with irony look on at the parental happiness.

The children's frocks are of a heavy brick-red stuff, embroidered in modern "arty" style. They once belonged to Ingrid and Bert and are precisely alike, save that little knickers come out beneath Snapper's smock. And both have their hair bobbed. Snapper's is a streaky blond, inclined to turn dark. It is bristly and sticky and looks for all the world like a droll, badly fitting wig. But Ellie's is chestnut brown, glossy and fine as silk, as pleasing as her whole little personality. It covers her ears — and these ears are not a pair, one of them being the right size, the other distinctly too large. Her father will sometimes uncover this little abnormality and exclaim over it as though he had never noticed it before, which both makes Ellie giggle and covers her with shame. Her eyes are now golden brown, set far apart and with sweet gleams in them — such a clear and lovely look! The brows above are blond; the nose still unformed, with thick nostrils and almost circular holes; the mouth large and expressive, with a beautifully arching and mobile upper lip. When she laughs, dimples come in her cheeks and she shows her teeth like loosely strung pearls. So far she has lost but one tooth, which her father gently twisted out with his handkerchief after it had grown very wobbling. During this small operation she had paled and trembled very much. Her cheeks have the softness proper to her years, but they are not chubby; indeed, they are rather concave, due to her facial structure, with its somewhat prominent jaw. On one, close to the soft fall of her hair, is a downy freckle.

Ellie is not too well pleased with her looks — a sign that already she troubles about such things. Sadly she thinks it is best to admit it once for all, her face is "homely"; though the rest of her, "on the other hand," is not bad at all. She loves expressions like "on the other hand"; they sound choice and grown-up to her, and she likes to string them together, one after the other: "very likely," "probably," "after all." Snapper is self-critical too, though more in the moral sphere: he suffers from remorse for his attacks of rage and considers himself a tremendous sinner. He is quite certain that heaven is not for such as he; he is sure to go to "the bad place" when he dies, and no persuasions will convince him to the contrary — as that God sees the heart and gladly makes allowances. Obstinately he shakes his head, with the comic, crooked little peruke, and vows there is no place for him in heaven. When he has a cold he is immediately quite choked with mucus; rattles and rumbles from top to toe if you even look at him; his temperature flies up at once and he simply puffs. Nursy is pessimistic on the score of his constitution: such fat-blooded children as he might get a stroke any minute. Once she even thought she saw the moment at hand: Snapper had been in one of his berserker rages, and in the ensuing fit of penitence stood himself in the corner with his back to the room. Suddenly Nursy noticed that his face had gone all blue, far bluer, even, than her own. She raised the alarm, crying out that the child's all too rich blood had at length brought him to his final hour; and Snapper, to his vast astonishment, found himself, so far from being rebuked for evil-doing, encompassed in tenderness and anxiety — until it turned out that his colour was not caused by apoplexy but by the distempering on the nursery wall, which had come off on his tear-wet face.

Nursy has come downstairs too, and stands by the door, sleek-haired, owl-eyed, with her hands folded over her white apron, and a severely dignified manner born of her limited intelligence. She is very proud of the care and training she gives her nurslings and declares that they are "enveloping wonderfully." She has had seventeen suppurated teeth lately removed from her jaws and been measured for a set of symmetrical yellow ones in dark rubber gums; these now embellish her peasant face. She is obsessed with the strange conviction that these teeth of hers are the subject of general conversation, that, as it were, the sparrows on the housetops chatter of them. "Everybody knows I've had a false set put in," she will say; "there has been a great deal of foolish talk about them." She is much given to dark hints and veiled innuendo: speaks, for instance, of a certain Dr. Bleifuss, whom every child knows, and "there are even some in the house who pretend to be him." All one can do with talk like this is charitably to pass it over in silence. But she teaches the children nursery rhymes: gems like:

"Puff, puff, here comes the train!
Puff, puff, toot, toot,
Away it goes again."

Or that gastronomical jingle, so suited, in its sparseness, to the times, and yet seemingly with a blitheness of its own:

"Monday we begin the week,
Tuesday there's a bone to pick.
Wednesday we're half way through,
Thursday what a great to-do!
Friday we eat what fish we're able,
Saturday we dance round the table.
Sunday brings us pork and greens —
Here's a feast for kings and queens!"

Also a certain four-line stanza with a romantic appeal, unutterable and unuttered:

"Open the gate, open the gate
And let the carriage drive in.
Who is it in the carriage sits?
A lordly sir with golden hair."

Or, finally that ballad about golden-haired Marianne who sat on a, sat on a, sat on a stone, and combed out her, combed out her, combed out her hair; and about bloodthirsty Rudolph who pulled out a, pulled out a, pulled out a knife — and his ensuing direful end. Ellie enunciates all these ballads charmingly, with her mobile little lips, and sings them in her sweet little voice — much better than Snapper. She does everything better than he does, and he pays her honest admiration and homage and obeys her in all things except when visited by one of his attacks. Sometimes she teaches him, instructs him upon the birds in the picture-book and tells him their proper names: "This is a chaffinch, Buddy, this is a bullfinch, this is a cowfinch." He has to repeat them after her. She gives him medical instruction, too, teaches him the names of diseases, such as infammation of the lungs, infammation of the blood, infammation of the air. If he does not pay attention and cannot say the words after her, she stands him in the corner. Once she even boxed his ears, but was so ashamed that she stood herself in the corner for a long time. Yes, they are fast friends, two souls with but a single thought, and have all their adventures in common. They come home from a walk and relate as with one voice that they have seen two moollies and a teenty-weenty baby calf. They are on familiar terms with the kitchen, which consists of Xaver and the ladies Hinterhofer, two sisters once of the lower middle class who, in these evil days, are reduced to living "*au pair*" as the phrase goes and officiating as cook and housemaid for their board and keep. The little ones have a feeling that Xaver and the Hinterhofers are on much the same footing with their father and mother as they are themselves. At least sometimes, when they have been scolded, they go downstairs and announce that the master and mistress are cross. But playing with the servants lacks charm compared with the joys of playing upstairs. The kitchen could never rise to the height of the games their father can invent. For instance, there is "four gentlemen taking a walk." When they play it Abel will crook his knees until he is the same height with themselves and go walking with them, hand in hand. They never get enough of this sport; they could walk round and round the dining-room a whole day on end, five gentlemen in all, counting the diminished Abel.

Then there is the thrilling cushion game. One of the children, usually Ellie, seats herself, unbeknownst to Abel, in his seat at table. Still as a mouse she awaits his coming. He draws near with his head in the air, descanting in loud, clear tones upon the surpassing comfort of his chair; and sits down on top of Ellie. "What's this, what's this?" says he. And bounces about, deaf to the smothered giggles exploding behind him. "Why have they put a cushion in my chair? And what a queer, hard, awkward-shaped cushion it is!" he goes on. "Frightfully uncomfortable to sit on!" And keeps pushing and bouncing about more and more on the astonishing cushion and clutching behind him into the rapturous giggling and squeaking, until at last he turns round, and the game ends with a magnificent climax of discovery and recognition. They might go through all this a hundred times without diminishing by an iota its power to thrill.

Today is no time for such joys. The imminent festivity disturbs the atmosphere, and besides there is work to be done, and, above all, the eggs to be got. Ellie has just time to recite, "Puff, puff," and Cornelius to discover that her ears are not mates, when they are interrupted by the arrival of Danny, come to fetch Bert and Ingrid. Xaver, meantime, has exchanged his striped livery for an ordinary coat, in which he looks rather rough-and-ready, though as brisk and attractive as ever. So then Nursy and the children ascend to the upper regions, the Professor withdraws to his study to read, as always after dinner, and his wife bends her energies upon the sandwiches and salad that must be prepared. And she has another errand as well. Before the young people arrive she has to take her shopping-basket and dash into town on her bicycle, to turn into provisions a sum of money she has in hand, which she dares not keep lest it lose all value.

Cornelius reads, leaning back in his chair, with his cigar between his middle and index fingers. First he reads Macaulay on the origin of the English public debt at the end of the seventeenth century; then an article in a French periodical on the rapid increase in the Spanish debt towards the end of the sixteenth. Both these for his lecture on the morrow. He intends to compare the astonishing prosperity which accompanied the phenomenon in England with its fatal effects a hundred years earlier in Spain, and to analyse the ethical and psychological grounds of the difference in results. For that will give him a chance to refer back from the England of William III, which is the actual subject in hand, to the time of Philip II and the Counter-Reformation, which is his own special field. He has already written a valuable work on this period; it is much cited and got him his professorship. While his cigar burns down and gets strong, he excogitates a few pensive sentences in a key of gentle melancholy, to be delivered before his class next day: about the practically hopeless struggle carried on by the belated Philip against the whole trend of history: against the new, the kingdom-disrupting power of the Germanic ideal of freedom and individual liberty. And about the persistent, futile struggle of the aristocracy, condemned by God and rejected of man, against the forces of progress and change. He savours his sentences; keeps on polishing them while he puts back the books he has been using; then goes upstairs for the usual pause in his day's work, the hour with drawn blinds and closed eyes, which he so imperatively needs. But today, he recalls, he will rest under disturbed conditions, amid the bustle of preparations for the feast. He smiles to find his heart giving a mild flutter at the thought. Disjointed phrases on the theme of black-clad Philip and his times mingle with a confused consciousness that they will soon be dancing down below. For five minutes or so he falls asleep.

As he lies and rests he can hear the sound of the garden gate and the repeated ringing at the bell. Each time a little pang goes through him, excitement and suspense, at the thought that the young people have begun to fill the floor below. And each time he smiles at himself again — though even his smile is slightly nervous, is tinged with the pleasurable anticipations people always feel before a party. At half past four — it is already dark — he gets up and washes at the wash-stand. The basin has been out of repair for two years. It is supposed to tip, but has broken away from its socket on one side and cannot be mended because there is nobody to mend it; neither replaced because no shop can supply another. So it has to be hung up above the vent and emptied by lifting in both hands and pouring out the water. Cornelius shakes his head over this basin, as he does several times a day —whenever, in fact, he has occasion to use it. He finishes his toilet with care, standing under the ceiling light to polish his glasses till they shine. Then he goes downstairs.

On his way to the dining-room he hears the gramophone already going, and the sound of voices. He puts on a polite, society air; at his tongue's end is the phrase he means to utter: "Pray don't let me disturb you," as he passes directly into the dining-room for his tea. "Pray don't let me disturb you" — it seems to him precisely the *mot juste*; towards the guests cordial and considerate, for himself a very bulwark.

The lower floor is lighted up, all the bulbs in the chandelier are burning, save one that has burned out. Cornelius pauses on a lower step and surveys the entrance hall. It looks pleasant and cosy in the bright light, with its copy of Marées over the brick chimney-piece, its wainscoted walls — wainscoted in soft wood — and red-carpeted floor, where the guests stand in groups, chatting each with his tea-cup and slice of bread-and-butter spread with anchovy paste. There is a festal haze, faint scents of hair and clothing and human breath come to him across the room, it is all characteristic and familiar and highly evocative. The door into the dressing-room is open, guests are still arriving.

A large group of people is rather bewildering at first sight. The Professor takes in only the general scene. He does not see Ingrid, who is standing just at the foot of the steps, in a dark silk frock with a pleated collar falling softly over the shoulders, and bare arms. She smiles up at him, nodding and showing her lovely teeth.

"Rested?" she asks, for his private ear. With a quite unwarranted start he recognizes her, and she presents some of her friends.

"May I introduce Herr Zuber?" she says. "And this is Fräulein Plaichinger."

Herr Zuber is insignificant. But Fräulein Plaichinger is a perfect Germania, blond and voluptuous, arrayed in floating draperies. She has a snub nose, and answers the Professor's salutation in the high, shrill pipe so many stout women have.

"Delighted to meet you," he says. "How nice of you to come! A classmate of Ingrid's, I suppose?"

And Herr Zuber is a golfing partner of Ingrid's. He is in business; he works in his uncle's brewery. Cornelius makes a few jokes about the thinness of the beer and professes to believe that Herr Zuber could easily do something about the quality if he would. "But pray don't let me disturb you," he goes on, and turns towards the dining-room.

"There comes Max," says Ingrid. "Max, you sweep, what do you mean by rolling up at this time of day?" For such is the way they talk to each other, offensively to an older ear; of social forms, of hospitable warmth, there is no faintest trace. They all call each other by their first names.

A young man comes up to them out of the dressing-room and makes his bow; he has an expanse of white shirt-front and a little black string tie. He is as pretty as a picture, dark, with rosy cheeks, clean-shaven of course, but with just a sketch of side-whisker. Not a ridiculous or flashy beauty, not like a gypsy fiddler, but just charming to look at, in a winning, well-bred way, with kind dark eyes. He even wears his dinner-jacket a little awkwardly.

"Please don't scold me, Cornelia," he says; "it's the idiotic lectures." And Ingrid presents him to her father as Herr Hergesell.

Well, and so this is Herr Hergesell. He knows his manners, does Herr Hergesell, and thanks the master of the house quite ingratiatingly for his invitation as they shake hands. "I certainly seem to have missed the bus," says he jocosely. "Of course I have lectures today up to four o'clock; I would have; and after that I had to go home to change." Then he talks about his pumps, with which he has just been struggling in the dressing-room.

"I brought them with me in a bag," he goes on. "Mustn't tramp all over the carpet in our brogues — it's not done. Well, I was ass enough not to fetch along a shoe-horn, and I find I simply can't get in! What a sell! They are the tightest I've ever had, the numbers don't tell you a thing, and all the leather today is just cast iron. It's not leather at all. My poor finger" — he confidingly displays a reddened digit and once more characterizes the whole thing as a "sell," and a putrid sell into the bargain. He really does talk just as Ingrid said he did, with a peculiar nasal drawl, not affectedly in the least, but merely because that is the way of all the Hergesells.

Dr. Cornelius says it is very careless of them not to keep a shoe-horn in the cloak-room and displays proper sympathy with the mangled finger. "But now you *really* must not let me disturb you any longer," he goes on. "*Auf wiedersehen!*" And he crosses the hall into the dining-room.

There are guests there too, drinking tea; the family table is pulled out. But the Professor goes at once to his own little upholstered corner with the electric light bulb above it — the nook where he usually drinks his tea. His wife is sitting there talking with Bert and two other young men, one of them Herzl, whom Cornelius knows and greets; the other a typical "Wandervogel" named Möller, a youth who obviously neither owns nor cares to own the correct evening dress of the middle class (in fact, there is no such thing any more), nor to ape the manners of a gentleman (and, in fact, there is no such thing any more either). He has a wilderness of hair, horn spectacles, and long neck, and wears golf stockings and a belted blouse. His regular occupation, the Professor learns, is banking, but he is by way of being an amateur folk-lorist and collects folk-songs from all localities in all languages. He sings them, too, and at Ingrid's command has brought his guitar; it is hanging in the dressing-room in an oilcloth case. Herzl, the actor, is small and slight, but he has a strong growth of black beard, as you can tell by the thick coat of powder on his cheeks. His eyes are larger than life, with a deep and melancholy glow. He has put on rouge besides the powder — those dull carmine high-lights on the cheeks can be nothing but a cosmetic. "Queer," thinks the Professor. "You would think a man would be one thing or the other — not melancholic and use face paint at the same time. It's a psychological contradiction. How can a melancholy man rouge? But here we have a perfect illustration of the abnormality of the artist soul-form. It can make possible a contradiction like this — perhaps it even consists in the contradiction. All very interesting — and no reason whatever for not being polite to him. Politeness is

a primitive convention — and legitimate. . . . Do take some lemon, Herr Hofschau-
spieler!

Court actors and court theatres — there are no such things any more, really. But
Herzl relishes the sound of the title, notwithstanding he is a revolutionary artist. This
must be another contradiction inherent in his soul-form; so, at least, the Professor
assumes, and he is probably right. The flattery he is guilty of is a sort of atonement
for his previous hard thoughts about the rouge.

"Thank you so much — it's really too good of you, sir," says Herzl, quite embarrassed. He is so overcome that he almost stammers; only his perfect enunciation
saves him. His whole bearing towards his hostess and the master of the house is
exaggeratedly polite. It is almost as though he had a bad conscience in respect of his
rouge; as though an inward compulsion had driven him to put it on, but now, seeing
it through the Professor's eyes, he disapproves of it himself, and thinks, by an air of
humility towards the whole of unrouged society, to mitigate its effect.

They drink their tea and chat: about Möller's folk-songs, about Basque folk-songs
and Spanish folk-songs; from which they pass to the new production of *Don Carlos*
at the Stadttheater, in which Herzl plays the title-rôle. He talks about his own
rendering of the part and says he hopes his conception of the character has unity.
They go on to criticize the rest of the cast, the setting, and the production as a whole;
and Cornelius is struck, rather painfully, to find the conversation trending towards
his own special province, back to Spain and the Counter-Reformation. He has done
nothing at all to give it this turn, he is perfectly innocent, and hopes it does not look
as though he had sought an occasion to play the professor. He wonders, and falls
silent, feeling relieved when the little folk come up to the table. Ellie and Snapper
have on their blue velvet Sunday frocks; they are permitted to partake in the
festivities up to bed-time. They look shy and large-eyed as they say how-do-you-do
to the strangers and, under pressure, repeat their names and ages. Herr Möller does
nothing but gaze at them solemnly, but Herzl is simply ravished. He rolls his eyes up
to heaven and puts his hands over his mouth; he positively blesses them. It all, no
doubt, comes from his heart, but he is so addicted to theatrical methods of making
an impression and getting an effect that both words and behaviour ring frightfully
false. And even his enthusiasm for the little folk looks too much like part of his
general craving to make up for the rouge on his cheeks.

The tea-table has meanwhile emptied of guests, and dancing is going on in the
hall. The children run off, the Professor prepares to retire. "Go and enjoy yourselves," he says to Möller and Herzl, who have sprung from their chairs as he rises
from his. They shake hands and he withdraws into his study, his peaceful kingdom,
where he lets down the blinds, turns on the desk lamp, and sits down to his work.

It is work which can be done, if necessary, under disturbed conditions: nothing
but a few letters and a few notes. Of course, Cornelius's mind wanders. Vague
impressions float through it: Herr Hergesell's refractory pumps, the high pipe in that
plump body of the Plaichinger female. As he writes, or leans back in his chair and
stares into space, his thoughts go back to Herr Möller's collection of Basque
folk-songs, to Herzl's posings and humility, to "his" Carlos and the court of Philip II.
There is something strange, he thinks, about conversations. They are so ductile, they
will flow of their own accord in the direction of one's dominating interest. Often and
often he has seen this happen. And while he is thinking, he is listening to the sounds
next door — rather subdued, he finds them. He hears only voices, no sound of

footsteps. The dancers do not glide or circle round the room; they merely walk about over the carpet, which does not hamper their movements in the least. Their way of holding each other is quite different and strange, and they move to the strains of the gramophone, to the weird music of the new world. He concentrates on the music and makes out that it is a jazz-band record, with various percussion instruments and the clack and clatter of castanets, which, however, are not even faintly suggestive of Spain, but merely jazz like the rest. No, not Spain. . . . His thoughts are back at their old round.

Half an hour goes by. It occurs to him it would be no more than friendly to go and contribute a box of cigarettes to the festivities next door. Too bad to ask the young people to smoke their own — though they have probably never thought of it. He goes into the empty dining-room and takes a box from his supply in the cupboard: not the best ones, nor yet the brand he himself prefers, but a certain long, thin kind he is not averse to getting rid of — after all, they are nothing but youngsters. He takes the box into the hall, holds it up with a smile, and deposits it on the mantel-shelf. After which he gives a look round and returns to his own room.

There comes a lull in dance and music. The guests stand about the room in groups or round the table at the window or are seated in a circle by the fireplace. Even the built-in stairs, with their worn velvet carpet, are crowded with young folk as in an amphitheatre: Max Hergesell is there, leaning back with one elbow on the step above and gesticulating with his free hand as he talks to the shrill, voluptuous Plaichinger. The floor of the hall is nearly empty, save just in the centre: there, directly beneath the chandelier, the two little ones in their blue velvet frocks clutch each other in an awkward embrace and twirl silently round and round, oblivious of all else. Cornelius, as he passes, strokes their hair, with a friendly word; it does not distract them from their small solemn preoccupation. But at his own door he turns to glance round and sees young Hergesell push himself off the stair by his elbow — probably because he noticed the Professor. He comes down into the arena, takes Ellie out of her brother's arms, and dances with her himself. It looks very comic, without the music, and he crouches down just as Cornelius does when he goes walking with the four gentlemen, holding the fluttered Ellie as though she were grown up and taking little "shimmying" steps. Everybody watches with huge enjoyment, the gramophone is put on again, dancing becomes general. The Professor stands and looks, with his hand on the door-knob. He nods and laughs; when he finally shuts himself into his study the mechanical smile still lingers on his lips.

Again he turns over pages by his desk lamp, takes notes, attends to a few simple matters. After a while he notices that the guests have forsaken the entrance hall for his wife's drawing-room, into which there is a door from his own study as well. He hears their voices and the sounds of a guitar being tuned. Herr Möller, it seems, is to sing — and does so. He twangs the strings of his instrument and sings in a powerful bass a ballad in a strange tongue, possibly Swedish. The Professor does not succeed in identifying it, though he listens attentively to the end, after which there is great applause. The sound is deadened by the portière that hangs over the dividing door. The young bank-clerk begins another song. Cornelius goes softly in.

It is half-dark in the drawing-room; the only light is from the shaded standard lamp, beneath which Möller sits, on the divan, with his legs crossed, picking his strings. His audience is grouped easily about; as there are not enough seats, some stand, and more, among them many young ladies, are simply sitting on the floor with their hands clasped round their knees or even with their legs stretched out before them. Hergesell sits thus, in his dinner jacket, next the piano, with Fräulein Plaichinger beside him. Frau Cornelius is holding both children on her lap as she sits in her easy-chair opposite the singer. Snapper, the Bœotian, begins to talk loud and clear in the middle of the song and has to be intimidated with hushings and finger-shakings. Never, never would Ellie allow herself to be guilty of such conduct. She sits there daintily erect and still on her mother's knee. The Professor tries to catch her eye and exchange a private signal with his little girl; but she does not see him. Neither does she seem to be looking at the singer. Her gaze is directed lower down.

Möller sings the "joli tambour":

> "Sire, mon roi, donnez-moi votre
>   fille — "

They are all enchanted. "How good!" Hergesell is heard to say, in the odd, nasally condescending Hergesell tone. The next one is a beggar ballad, to a tune composed by young Möller himself; it elicits a storm of applause:

> "Gypsy lassie a-goin' to the fair,
> Huzza!
> Gypsy laddie a-goin' to be
>   there —
> Huzza, diddlety umpty dido!"

Laughter and high spirits, sheer reckless hilarity, reigns after this jovial ballad. "Frightfully good!" Hergesell comments again, as before. Follows another popular song, this time a Hungarian one; Möller sings it in its own outlandish tongue, and most effectively. The Professor applauds with ostentation. It warms his heart and does him good, this outcropping of artistic, historic, and cultural elements all amongst the shimmying. He goes up to young Möller and congratulates him, talks about the songs and their sources, and Möller promises to lend him a certain annotated book of folk-songs. Cornelius is the more cordial because all the time, as fathers do, he has been comparing the parts and achievements of this young stranger with those of his own son, and being gnawed by envy and chagrin. This young Möller, he is thinking, is a capable bank-clerk (though about Möller's capacity he knows nothing whatever) and has this special gift besides, which must have taken talent and energy to cultivate. "And here is my poor Bert, who knows nothing and can do nothing and thinks of nothing except playing the clown, without even talent for that!" He tries to be just; he tells himself that, after all, Bert has innate refinement; that probably there is a good deal more to him than there is to the successful Möller; that perhaps he has even something of the poet in him, and his dancing and table-waiting are due to mere boyish folly and the distraught times. But paternal envy and pessimism win the upper hand; when Möller begins another song, Dr. Cornelius goes back to his room.

He works as before, with divided attention, at this and that, while it gets on for seven o'clock. Then he remembers a letter he may just as well write, a short letter and not very important, but letter-writing is wonderful for the way it takes up the time, and it is almost half past when he has finished. At half past eight the Italian salad will be served; so now is the prescribed moment for the Professor to go out into the wintry darkness to post his letters and take his daily quantum of fresh air and exercise. They are dancing again, and he will have to pass through the hall to get his hat and coat; but they are used to him now, he need not stop and beg them not to be disturbed. He lays away his papers, takes up the letters he has written, and goes out. But he sees his wife sitting near the door of his room and pauses a little by her easy-chair.

She is watching the dancing. Now and then the big folk or some of their guests stop to speak to her; the party is at its height, and there are more onlookers than these two: blue-faced Ann is standing at the bottom of the stairs, in all the dignity of her limitations. She is waiting for the children, who simply cannot get their fill of these unwonted festivities, and watching over Snapper, lest his all too rich blood be churned to the danger-point by too much twirling round. And not only the nursery but the kitchen takes an interest: Xaver and the two ladies Hinterhofer are standing by the pantry door looking on with relish. Fräulein Walburga, the elder of the two sunken sisters (the culinary section — she objects to being called a cook), is a whimsical, good-natured sort, brown-eyed, wearing glasses with thick circular lenses; the nose-piece is wound with a bit of rag to keep it from pressing on her nose. Fräulein Cecilia is younger, though not so precisely young either. Her bearing is as self-assertive as usual, this being her way of sustaining her dignity as a former member of the middle class. For Fräulein Cecilia feels acutely her descent into the ranks of domestic service. She positively declines to wear a cap or other badge of servitude, and her hardest trial is on the Wednesday evening when she has to serve the dinner while Xaver has his afternoon out. She hands the dishes with averted face and elevated nose — a fallen queen; and so distressing is it to behold her degradation that one evening when the little folk happened to be at table and saw her they both with one accord burst into tears. Such anguish is unknown to young Xaver. He enjoys serving and does it with an ease born of practice as well as talent, for he was once a "piccolo." But otherwise he is a thorough-paced good-for-nothing and windbag — with quite distinct traits of character of his own, as his long-suffering employers are always ready to concede, but perfectly impossible and a bag of wind for all that. One must just take him as he is, they think, and not expect figs from thistles. He is the child and product of the disrupted times, a perfect specimen of his generation, follower of the revolution, Bolshevist sympathizer. The Professor's name for him is the "minute-man," because he is always to be counted on in any sudden crisis, if only it address his sense of humour or love of novelty, and will display therein amazing readiness and resource. But he utterly lacks a sense of duty and can as little be trained to the performance of the daily round and common task as some kinds of dogs can be taught to jump over a stick. It goes so plainly against the grain that criticism is disarmed. One becomes resigned. On grounds that appealed to him as unusual and amusing he would be ready to turn out of his bed at any hour of the night. But he simply cannot get up before eight in the morning, he cannot do it, he will not jump over the stick. Yet all day long the evidence of this free and untrammelled existence, the sound of his mouth-organ, his joyous whistle, or his raucous but expressive voice lifted in song, rises to the hearing of the world above-stairs; and the smoke of his cigarettes fills the pantry. While the Hinterhofer ladies work he stands and looks on. Of a morning while the Professor is breakfasting, he tears the leaf off the study calendar — but does not lift a finger to dust the room. Dr. Cornelius has often told him to leave the calendar alone, for he tends to tear off two leaves at a time and thus to add to the general confusion. But young Xaver appears to find joy in this activity, and will not be deprived of it.

Again, he is fond of children, a winning trait. He will throw himself into games with the little folk in the garden, make and mend their toys with great ingenuity, even read aloud from their books — and very droll it sounds in his thick-lipped pronunciation. With his whole soul he loves the cinema; after an evening spent there he inclines to melancholy and yearning and talking to himself. Vague hopes stir in him that some day he may make his fortune in that gay world and belong to it by rights — hopes based on his shock of hair and his physical agility and daring. He likes to climb the ash tree in the front garden, mounting branch by branch to the very top and frightening everybody to death who sees him. Once there he lights a cigarette and smokes it as he sways to and fro, keeping a look-out for a cinema director who might chance to come along and engage him.

If he changed his striped jacket for mufti, he might easily dance with the others and no one would notice the difference. For the big folk's friends are rather anomalous in their clothing: evening dress is worn by a few, but it is by no means the rule. There is quite a sprinkling of guests, both male and female, in the same general style as Möller the ballad-singer. The Professor is familiar with the circumstances of most of this young generation he is watching as he stands beside his wife's chair; he has heard them spoken of by name. They are students at the high school or at the School of Applied Art; they lead, at least the masculine portion, that precarious and scrambling existence which is purely the product of the time. There is a tall, pale, spindling youth, the son of a dentist, who lives by speculation. From all the Professor hears, he is a perfect Aladdin. He keeps a car, treats his friends to champagne suppers, and showers presents upon them on every occasion, costly little trifles in mother-of-pearl and gold. So today he has brought gifts to the young givers of the feast: for Bert a gold lead-pencil, and for Ingrid a pair of ear-rings of barbaric size, great gold circlets that fortunately do not have to go through the little ear-lobe, but are fastened over it by means of a clip. The big folk come laughing to their parents to display these trophies; and the parents shake their heads even while they admire — Aladdin bowing over and over from afar.

The young people appear to be absorbed in their dancing — if the performance they are carrying out with so much still concentration can be called dancing. They stride across the carpet, slowly, according to some unfathomable prescript, strangely embraced; in the newest attitude, tummy advanced and shoulders high, waggling the hips. They do not get tired, because nobody could. There is no such thing as heightened colour or heaving bosoms. Two girls may dance together or two young men — it is all the same. They move to the exotic strains of the gramophone, played with the loudest needles to procure the maximum of sound: shimmies, foxtrots, one-steps, double foxes, African shimmies, Java dances, and Creole polkas, the wild musky melodies follow one another, now furious, now languishing, a monotonous Negro programme in unfamiliar rhythm, to a clacking, clashing, and strumming orchestral accompaniment.

"What is that record?" Cornelius inquires of Ingrid, as she passes him by in the arms of the pale young speculator, with reference to the piece then playing, whose alternate languors and furies he finds comparatively pleasing and showing a certain resourcefulness in detail.

"*Prince of Pappenheim*: 'Console thee, dearest child,' " she answers, and smiles pleasantly back at him with her white teeth.

The cigarette smoke wreathes beneath the chandelier. The air is blue with a festal haze compact of sweet and thrilling ingredients that stir the blood with memories of green-sick pains and are particularly poignant to those whose youth — like the Professor's own — has been over-sensitive.... The little folk are still on the floor. They are allowed to stop up until eight, so great is their delight in the party. The guests have got used to their presence; in their own way, they have their place in the doings of the evening. They have separated, anyhow: Snapper revolves all alone in the middle of the carpet, in his little blue velvet smock, while Ellie is running after one of the dancing couples, trying to hold the man fast by his coat. It is Max Hergesell and Fräulein Plaichinger. They dance well, it is a pleasure to watch them. One has to admit that these mad modern dances, when the right people dance them, are not so bad after all — they have something quite taking. Young Hergesell is a capital leader, dances according to rule, yet with individuality. So it looks. With what aplomb can he walk backwards — when space permits! And he knows how to be graceful standing still in a crowd. And his partner supports him well, being unsuspectedly lithe and buoyant, as fat people often are. They look at each other, they are talking, paying no heed to Ellie, though others are smiling to see the child's persistence. Dr. Cornelius tries to catch up his little sweetheart as she passes and draw her to him. But Ellie eludes him, almost peevishly; her dear Abel is nothing to her now. She braces her little arms against his chest and turns her face away with a persecuted look. Then escapes to follow her fancy once more.

The Professor feels an involuntary twinge. Uppermost in his heart is hatred for this party, with its power to intoxicate and estrange his darling child. His love for her — that not quite disinterested, not quite unexceptionable love of his — is easily wounded. He wears a mechanical smile, but his eyes have clouded, and he stares fixedly at a point in the carpet, between the dancer's feet.

"The children ought to go to bed," he tells his wife. But she pleads for another quarter of an hour; she has promised already, and they do love it so! He smiles again and shakes his head, stands so a moment and then goes across to the cloak-room, which is full of coats and hats and scarves and overshoes. He has trouble in rummaging out his own coat, and Max Hergesell comes out of the hall, wiping his brow.

"Going out, sir?" he asks, in Hergesellian accents, dutifully helping the older man on with his coat. "Silly business this, with my pumps," he says. "They pinch like hell. The brutes are simply too tight for me, quite apart from the bad leather. They press just here on the ball of my great toe" — he stands on one foot and holds the other in his hand — "it's simply unbearable. There's nothing for it but to take them off; my brogues will have to do the business.... Oh, let me help you, sir."

"Thanks," says Cornelius. "Don't trouble. Get rid of your own tormentors.... Oh, thanks very much!" For Hergesell has gone on one knee to snap the fasteners of his snow-boots.

Once more the Professor expresses his gratitude; he is pleased and touched by so much sincere respect and youthful readiness to serve. "Go and enjoy yourself," he counsels. "Change your shoes and make up for what you have been suffering. Nobody can dance in shoes that pinch. Good-bye, I must be off to get a breath of fresh air."

"I'm going to dance with Ellie now," calls Hergesell after him. "She'll be a first-rate dancer when she grows up, and that I'll swear to."

"Think so?" Cornelius answers, already half out. "Well, you are a connoisseur, I'm sure. Don't get curvature of the spine with stooping."

He nods again and goes. "Fine lad," he thinks as he shuts the door. "Student of engineering. Knows what he's bound for, got a good clear head, and so well set up and pleasant too." And again paternal envy rises as he compares his poor Bert's status with this young man's, which he puts in the rosiest light that his son's may look the darker. Thus he sets out on his evening walk.

He goes up the avenue, crosses the bridge, and walks along the bank on the other side as far as the next bridge but one. The air is wet and cold, with a little snow now and then. He turns up his coat-collar and slips the crook of his cane over the arm behind his back. Now and then he ventilates his lungs with a long deep breath of the night air. As usual when he walks, his mind reverts to his professional preoccupations, he thinks about his lectures and the things he means to say tomorrow about Philip's struggle against the Germanic revolution, things steeped in melancholy and penetratingly just. Above all just, he thinks. For in one's dealings with the young it behooves one to display the scientific spirit, to exhibit the principles of enlightenment — not only for purposes of mental discipline, but on the human and individual side, in order not to wound them or indirectly offend their political sensibilities; particularly in these days, when there is so much tinder in the air, opinions are so frightfully split up and chaotic, and you may so easily incur attacks from one party or the other, or even give rise to scandal, by taking sides on a point of history. "And taking sides is unhistoric anyhow," so he muses. "Only justice, only impartiality is historic." And could not, properly considered, be otherwise. . . . For justice can have nothing of youthful fire and blithe, fresh, loyal conviction. It is by nature melancholy. And, being so, has secret affinity with the lost cause and the forlorn hope rather than with the fresh and blithe and loyal — perhaps this affinity is its very essence and without it it would not exist at all! . . . "And is there then no such thing as justice?" the Professor asks himself, and ponders the question so deeply that he absently posts his letters in the next box and turns round to go home. This thought of his is unsettling and disturbing to the scientific mind — but is it not after all itself scientific, psychological, conscientious, and therefore to be accepted without prejudice, no matter how upsetting? In the midst of which musings Dr. Cornelius finds himself back at his own door.

On the outer threshold stands Xaver, and seems to be looking for him.

"Herr Professor," says Xaver, tossing back his hair, "go upstairs to Ellie straight off. She's in a bad way."

"What's the matter?" asks Cornelius in alarm. "Is she ill?"

"No-o, not to say ill," answers Xaver. "She's just in a bad way and crying fit to bust her little heart. It's along o' that chap with the shirt-front that danced with her — Herr Hergesell. She couldn't be got to go upstairs peaceably, not at no price at all, and she's b'en crying bucketfuls."

"Nonsense," says the Professor, who has entered and is tossing off his things in the cloak-room. He says no more; opens the glass door and without a glance at the guests turns swiftly to the stairs. Takes them two at a time, crosses the upper hall and the small room leading into the nursery. Xaver follows at his heels, but stops at the nursery door.

A bright light still burns within, showing the gay frieze that runs all round the room, the large row of shelves heaped with a confusion of toys, the rocking-horse on his swaying platform, with red-varnished nostrils and raised hoofs. On the linoleum lie other toys — building blocks, railway trains, a little trumpet. The two white cribs stand not far apart, Ellie's in the window corner, Snapper's out in the room.

Snapper is asleep. He has said his prayers in loud, ringing tones, prompted by Nurse, and gone off at once into vehement, profound, and rosy slumber — from which a cannon-ball fired at close range could not rouse him. He lies with both fists flung back on the pillows on either side of the tousled head with its funny crooked little slumber-tossed wig.

A circle of females surrounds Ellie's bed: not only blue-faced Ann is there, but the Hinterhofer ladies too, talking to each other and to her. They make way as the Professor comes up and reveal the child sitting all pale among her pillows, sobbing and weeping more bitterly than he has ever seen her sob and weep in her life. Her lovely little hands lie on the coverlet in front of her, the nightgown with its narrow lace border has slipped down from her shoulder — such a thin, birdlike little shoulder — and the sweet head Cornelius loves so well, set on the neck like a flower on its stalk, her head is on one side, with the eyes rolled up to the corner between wall and ceiling above her head. For there she seems to envisage the anguish of her heart and even to nod to it — either on purpose or because her head wobbles as her body is shaken with the violence of her sobs. Her eyes rain down tears. The bow-shaped lips are parted, like a little *mater dolorosa's,* and from them issue long, low wails that in nothing resemble the unnecessary and exasperating shrieks of a naughty child, but rise from the deep extremity of her heart and wake in the Professor's own a sympathy that is well-nigh intolerable. He has never seen his darling so before. His feelings find immediate vent in an attack on the ladies Hinterhofer.

"What about the supper?" he asks sharply. "There must be a great deal to do. Is my wife being left to do it alone?"

For the acute sensibilities of the former middle class this is quite enough. The ladies withdraw in righteous indignation, and Xaver Kleingutl jeers at them as they pass out. Having been born to low life instead of achieving it, he never loses a chance to mock at their fallen state.

"Childie, childie," murmurs Cornelius, and sitting down by the crib enfolds the anguished Ellie in his arms. "What is the trouble with my darling?"

She bedews his face with her tears.

"Abel . . . Abel . . ." she stammers between sobs. "Why — isn't Max — my brother? Max ought to be — my brother!"

Alas, alas! What mischance is this? Is this what the party has wrought, with its fatal atmosphere? Cornelius glances helplessly up at blue-faced Ann standing there in all the dignity of her limitations with her hands before her on her apron. She purses up her mouth and makes a long face. "It's pretty young," she says, "for the female instincts to be showing up."

"Hold your tongue," snaps Cornelius, in his agony. He has this much to be thankful for, that Ellie does not turn from him now; she does not push him away as she did downstairs, but clings to him in her need, while she reiterates her absurd, bewildered prayer that Max might be her brother, or with a fresh burst of desire demands to be taken downstairs so that he can dance with her again. But Max, of course, is dancing with Fräulein Plaichinger, that behemoth who is his rightful partner and had every claim upon him; whereas Ellie — never, thinks the Professor, his heart torn with the violence of his pity, never has she looked so tiny and birdlike as now, when she nestles to him shaken with sobs and all unaware of what is happening in her little soul. No, she does not know. She does not comprehend that her suffering is on account of Fräulein Plaichinger, fat, overgrown, and utterly within her rights in dancing with Max Hergesell, whereas Ellie may only do it once, by way of a joke, although she is incomparably the more charming of the two. Yet it would be quite mad to reproach young Hergesell with the state of affairs or to make fantastic demands upon him. No, Ellie's suffering is without help or healing and must be covered up. Yet just as it is without understanding, so it is also without restraint — and that is what makes it so horribly painful. Xaver and blue-faced Ann do not feel this pain, it does not affect them — either because of native callousness or because they accept it as the way of nature. But the Professor's fatherly heart is quite torn by it, and by a distressful horror of this passion, so hopeless and so absurd.

Of no avail to hold forth to poor Ellie on the subject of the perfectly good little brother she already has. She only casts a distraught and scornful glance over at the other crib, where Snapper lies vehemently slumbering, and with fresh tears calls again for Max. Of no avail either the promise of a long, long walk tomorrow, all five gentlemen, round and round the dining-room table; or a dramatic description of the thrilling cushion games they will play. No, she will listen to none of all this, nor to lying down and going to sleep. She will not sleep, she will sit bolt upright and suffer.... But on a sudden they stop and listen, Abel and Ellie; listen to something miraculous that is coming to pass, that is approaching by strides, two strides to the nursery door, that now overwhelmingly appears....

It is Xaver's work, not a doubt of that. He has not remained by the door where he stood to gloat over the ejection of the Hinterhofers. No, he has bestirred himself, taken a notion; likewise steps to carry it out. Downstairs he has gone, twitched Herr Hergesell's sleeve, and made a thick-lipped request. So here they both are. Xaver, having done his part, remains by the door; but Max Hergesell comes up to Ellie's crib; in his dinner-jacket, with his sketchy side-whisker and charming black eyes; obviously quite pleased with his rôle of swan knight and fairy prince, as one who should say: "See, here am I, now all losses are restored and sorrows end."

Cornelius is almost as much overcome as Ellie herself.

"Just look," he says feebly, "look who's here. This is uncommonly good of you, Herr Hergesell."

"Not a bit of it," says Hergesell. "Why shouldn't I come to say good-night to my fair partner?"

And he approaches the bars of the crib, behind which Ellie sits struck mute. She smiles blissfully through her tears. A funny, high little note that is half a sigh of relief comes from her lips, then she looks dumbly up at her swan knight with her golden-brown eyes — tear-swollen though they are, so much more beautiful than the fat Plaichinger's. She does not put up her arms. Her joy, like her grief, is without understanding; but she does not do that. The lovely little hands lie quiet on the coverlet, and Max Hergesell stands with his arms leaning over the rail as on a balcony.

"And now," he says smartly, "she need not 'sit the livelong night and weep upon her bed'!" He looks at the Professor to make sure he is receiving due credit of the quotation. "Ha ha!" he laughs, "she's beginning young. 'Console thee, dearest child!'

Never mind, you're all right! Just as you are you'll be wonderful! You've only got to grow up. . . . And you'll lie down and go to sleep like a good girl, now I've come to say good-night? And not cry any more, little Lorelei?"

Ellie looks up at him, transfigured. One birdlike shoulder is bare; the Professor draws the lace-trimmed nighty over it. There comes into his mind a sentimental story he once read about a dying child who longs to see a clown he had once, with unforgettable ecstasy, beheld in a circus. And they bring the clown to the bedside marvellously arrayed, embroidered before and behind with silver butterflies; and the child dies happy. Max Hergesell is not embroidered, and Ellie, thank God, is not going to die, she has only "been in a bad way." But, after all, the effect is the same. Young Hergesell leans over the bars of the crib and rattles on, more for the father's ear than the child's, but Ellie does not know that — and the father's feelings towards him are a most singular mixture of thankfulness, embarrassment, and hatred.

"Good night, little Lorelei," says Hergesell, and gives her his hand through the bars. Her pretty, soft, white little hand is swallowed up in the grasp of his big, strong, red one. "Sleep well," he says, "and sweet dreams! But don't dream about me — God forbid! Not at your age — ha ha!" And then the fairy clown's visit is at an end. Cornelius accompanies him to the door. "No, no, positively, no thanks called for, don't mention it," he large-heartedly protests; and Xaver goes downstairs with him, to help serve the Italian salad.

Bur Dr. Cornelius returns to Ellie, who is now lying down, with her cheek pressed into her flat little pillow.

"Well, wasn't that lovely?" he says as he smoothes the covers. She nods, with one last little sob. For a quarter of an hour he sits beside her and watches while she falls asleep in her turn, beside the little brother who found the right way so much earlier than she. Her silky brown hair takes the enchanting fall it always does when she sleeps; deep, deep lie the lashes over the eyes that late so abundantly poured forth their sorrow; the angelic mouth with its bowed upper lip is peacefully relaxed and a little open. Only now and then comes a belated catch in her slow breathing.

And her small hands, like pink and white flowers, lie so quietly, one on the coverlet, the other on the pillow by her face — Dr. Cornelius, gazing, feels his heart melt with tenderness as with strong wine.

"How good," he thinks, "that she breathes in oblivion with every breath she draws! That in childhood each night is a deep, wide gulf between one day and the next. Tomorrow, beyond all doubt, young Hergesell will be a pale shadow, powerless to darken her little heart. Tomorrow, forgetful of all but present joy, she will walk with Abel and Snapper, all five gentlemen, round and round the table, will play the ever-thrilling cushion game."

Heaven be praised for that!

KATHERINE MANSFIELD

Katherine Mansfield (1888–1923) was born in Wellington, New Zealand, the daughter of a prominent businessman. A precocious child, she grew up in an atmosphere that pervades many of her stories: a large, comfortable old house, lawns and gardens, extended family, servants. When she was fifteen she moved to London, where she attended Queen's College. With the exception of the years 1906–1908, when she returned to New Zealand to study music, she lived in London for the rest of her short life; in her last years, ill with tuberculosis, she traveled annually to the south of France and Switzerland. She was the friend of her contemporaries Virginia Woolf, D. H. Lawrence, and E. M. Forster. Mansfield began writing stories when she was in her early twenties. Chekhov was her master, and in her touching portrayal of the everyday world his influence may be seen. But she was recognized from the outset as an original voice, an experimenter with mood, tone, and style. Her stories are collected in *In a German Pension* (1911), *Bliss and Other Stories* (1920), *The Garden Party and Other Stories* (1922), *Collected Stories* (1945), and *Undiscovered Country: The New Zealand Stories of Katherine Mansfield* (1974). She was a masterful stylist. Possessing an acute sense of irony, she frequently turned it to sketching the bittersweet comedy of manners of the "bright young things" of her time: "Bliss" is a devastating version of that comedy. But Mansfield was perhaps most deeply given to a lyrical mode; greatly attracted to children and their awarenesses, she centered some of her finest stories on motifs of childhood. "Prelude," the second story here, is sometimes considered her most moving exploration of the child's world.

Bliss

Although Bertha Young was thirty she still had moments like this when she wanted to run instead of walk, to take dancing steps on and off the pavement, to bowl a hoop, to throw something up in the air and catch it again, or to stand still and laugh at — nothing — at nothing, simply.

What can you do if you are thirty and, turning the corner of your own street, you are overcome, suddenly, by a feeling of bliss — absolute bliss! — as though you'd suddenly swallowed a bright piece of that late afternoon sun and it burned in your bosom, sending out a little shower of sparks into every particle, into every finger and toe? . . .

Oh, is there no way you can express it without being "drunk and disorderly"? How idiotic civilization is! Why be given a body if you have to keep it shut up in a case like a rare, rare fiddle?

"No, that about the fiddle is not quite what I mean," she thought, running up the steps and feeling in her bag for the key — she'd forgotten it, as usual — and rattling the letter-box. "It's not what I mean, because — Thank you, Mary" — she went into the hall. "Is nurse back?"

"Yes, M'm."

"And has the fruit come?"

"Yes, M'm. Everything's come."

"Bring the fruit up to the dining-room, will you? I'll arrange it before I go upstairs."

It was dusky in the dining-room and quite chilly. But all the same Bertha threw off her coat; she could not bear the tight clasp of it another moment, and the cold air fell on her arms.

But in her bosom there was still that bright glowing place — that shower of little sparks coming from it. It was almost unbearable. She hardly dared to breathe for fear of fanning it higher, and yet she breathed deeply, deeply. She hardly dared to look into the cold mirror — but she did look, and it gave her back a woman, radiant, with smiling, trembling lips, with big, dark eyes and an air of listening, waiting for something . . . divine to happen . . . that she knew must happen . . . infallibly.

Mary brought in the fruit on a tray and with it a glass bowl, and a blue dish, very lovely, with a strange sheen on it as though it had been dipped in milk.

"Shall I turn on the light, M'm?"

"No, thank you. I can see quite well."

There were tangerines and apples stained with strawberry pink. Some yellow pears, smooth as silk, some white grapes covered with a silver bloom and a big cluster of purple ones. These last she had bought to tone in with the new dining-room carpet. Yes, that did sound rather far-fetched and absurd, but it was really why she had bought them. She had thought in the shop: "I must have some purple ones to bring the carpet up to the table." And it had seemed quite sense at the time.

When she had finished with them and had made two pyramids of these bright round shapes, she stood away from the table to get the effect — and it really was most curious. For the dark table seemed to melt into the dusky light and the glass dish and the blue bowl to float in the air. This, of course in her present mood, was so incredibly beautiful. . . . She began to laugh.

"No, no. I'm getting hysterical." And she seized her bag and coat and ran upstairs to the nursery.

Nurse sat at a low table giving Little B her supper after her bath. The baby had on a white flannel gown and a blue woollen jacket, and her dark, fine hair was brushed up into a funny little peak. She looked up when she saw her mother and began to jump.

"Now, my lovey, eat it up like a good girl," said Nurse, setting her lips in a way that Bertha knew, and that meant she had come into the nursery at another wrong moment.

"Has she been good, Nanny?"

"She's been a little sweet all the afternoon," whispered Nanny. "We went to the park and I sat down on a chair and took her out of the pram and a big dog came along and put its head on my knee and she clutched its ear, tugged it. Oh, you should have seen her."

Bertha wanted to ask if it wasn't rather dangerous to let her clutch at a strange dog's ear. But she did not dare to. She stood watching them, her hands by her side, like the poor little girl in front of the rich little girl with the doll.

The baby looked up at her again, stared, and then smiled so charmingly that Bertha couldn't help crying:

"Oh, Nanny, do let me finish giving her her supper while you put the bath things away."

"Well, M'm, she oughtn't to be changed hands while she's eating," said Nanny, still whispering. "It unsettles her; it's very likely to upset her."

How absurd it was. Why have a baby if it has to be kept — not in a case like a rare, rare fiddle — but in another woman's arms?

"Oh, I must!" said she.

Very offended, Nanny handed her over.

"Now, don't excite her after her supper. You know you do, M'm. And I have such a time with her after!"

Thank heaven! Nanny went out of the room with the bath towels.

"Now I've got you to myself, my little precious," said Bertha, as the baby leaned against her.

She ate delightfully, holding up her lips for the spoon and then waving her hands. Sometimes she wouldn't let the spoon go; and sometimes, just as Bertha had filled it, she waved it away to the four winds.

When the soup was finished Bertha turned round to the fire.

"You're nice — you're very nice!" said she, kissing her warm baby. "I'm fond of you. I like you."

And, indeed, she loved Little B so much — her neck as she bent forward, her exquisite toes as they shone transparent in the firelight — that all her feeling of bliss came back again, and again she didn't know how to express it — what to do with it.

"You're wanted on the telephone," said Nanny, coming back in triumph and seizing *her* Little B.

Down she flew. It was Harry.

"Oh, is that you, Ber? Look here. I'll be late. I'll take a taxi and come along as quickly as I can, but get dinner put back ten minutes — will you? All right?"

"Yes, perfectly. Oh, Harry!"

"Yes?"

What had she to say? She'd nothing to say. She only wanted to get in touch with him for a moment. She couldn't absurdly cry: "Hasn't it been a divine day!"

"What is it?" rapped out the little voice.

"Nothing. *Entendu,*" said Bertha, and hung up the receiver, thinking how more than idiotic civilization was.

They had people coming to dinner. The Norman Knights — a very sound couple — he was about to start a theatre, and she was awfully keen on interior decoration, a young man, Eddie Warren, who had just published a little book of poems and whom everybody was asking to dine, and a "find" of Bertha's called Pearl Fulton. What Miss Fulton did, Bertha didn't know. They had met at the club and Bertha had fallen in love with her, as she always did fall in love with beautiful women who had something strange about them.

The provoking thing was that, though they had been about together and met a number of times and really talked, Bertha couldn't yet make her out. Up to a certain point Miss Fulton was rarely, wonderfully frank, but the certain point was there, and beyond that she would not go.

Was there anything beyond it? Harry said "No." Voted her dullish, and "cold like all blond women, with a touch, perhaps, of anæmia of the brain." But Bertha wouldn't agree with him; not yet, at any rate.

"No, the way she has of sitting with her head a little on one side, and smiling, has something behind it, Harry, and I must find out what that something is."

"Most likely, it's a good stomach," answered Harry.

He made a point of catching Bertha's heels with replies of that kind ... "liver frozen, my dear girl," or "pure flatulence," or "kidney disease," ... and so on. For some strange reason Bertha liked this, and almost admired it in him very much.

She went into the drawing-room and lighted the fire; then, picking up the cushions, one by one, that Mary had disposed so carefully, she threw them back on to the chairs and the couches. That made all the difference; the room came alive at once. As she was about to throw the last one she surprised herself by suddenly hugging it to her, passionately, passionately. But it did not put out the fire in her bosom. Oh, on the contrary!

The windows of the drawing-room opened on to a balcony overlooking the garden. At the far end, against the wall, there was a tall, slender pear tree in fullest, richest bloom; it stood perfect, as though becalmed against the jade-green sky. Bertha couldn't help feeling, even from this distance, that it had not a single bud or a faded petal. Down below, in the garden beds, the red and yellow tulips, heavy with flowers, seemed to lean upon the dusk. A grey cat, dragging its belly, crept across the lawn, and a black one, its shadow, trailed after. The sight of them, so intent and so quick, gave Bertha a curious shiver.

"What creepy things cats are!" she stammered, and she turned away from the window and began walking up and down....

How strong the jonquils smelled in the warm room. Too strong? Oh, no. And yet, as though overcome, she flung down on a couch and pressed her hands to her eyes.

"I'm too happy — too happy!" she murmured.

And she seemed to see on her eyelids the lovely pear tree with its wide open blossoms as a symbol of her own life.

Really — really — she had everything. She was young. Harry and she were as much in love as ever, and they got on together splendidly and were really good pals. She had an adorable baby. They didn't have to worry about money. They had this absolutely satisfactory house and garden. And friends — modern, thrilling friends, writers and painters and poets or people keen on social questions — just the kind of friends they wanted. And then there were books, and there was music, and she had found a wonderful little dressmaker, and they were going abroad in the summer, and their new cook made the most superb omelettes....

"I'm absurd. Absurd!" She sat up; but she felt quite dizzy, quite drunk. It must have been the spring.

Yes, it was the spring. Now she was so tired she could not drag herself upstairs to dress.

A white dress, a string of jade beads, green shoes and stockings. It wasn't intentional. She had thought of this scheme hours before she stood at the drawing-room window.

Her petals rustled softly into the hall, and she kissed Mrs. Norman Knight, who was taking off the most amusing orange coat with a procession of black monkeys round the hem and up the fronts.

"... Why! Why! Why is the middle-class so stodgy — so utterly without a sense of humour! My dear, it's only by a fluke that I am here at all — Norman being the protective fluke. For my darling monkeys so upset the train that it rose to a man and simply ate me with its eyes. Didn't laugh — wasn't amused — that I should have loved. No, just stared — and bored me through and through."

"But the cream of it was," said Norman, pressing a large tortoiseshell-rimmed monocle into his eye, "you don't mind me telling this, Face, do you?" (In their home and among their friends they called each other Face and Mug.) "The cream of it was when she, being full fed, turned to the woman beside her and said: 'Haven't you ever seen a monkey before?' "

"Oh, yes!" Mrs. Norman Knight joined in the laughter. "Wasn't that too absolutely creamy?"

And a funnier thing still was that now her coat was off she did look like a very intelligent monkey — who had even made that yellow silk dress out of scraped banana skins. And her amber ear-rings; they were like little dangling nuts.

"This is a sad, sad fall!" said Mug, pausing in front of Little B's perambulator. "When the perambulator comes into the hall — " and he waved the rest of the quotation away.

The bell rang. It was lean, pale Eddie Warren (as usual) in a state of acute distress.

"It *is* the right house, *isn't it?*" he pleaded.

"Oh, I think so — I hope so," said Bertha brightly.

"I have had such a *dreadful* experience with a taxi-man; he was *most* sinister. I couldn't get him to *stop*. The *more* I knocked and called the *faster* he went. And *in* the moonlight this *bizarre* figure with the *flattened* head *crouching* over the *lit-tle* wheel. . . ."

He shuddered, taking off an immense white silk scarf. Bertha noticed that his socks were white, too — most charming.

"But how dreadful!" she cried.

"Yes, it really was," said Eddie, following her into the drawing-room. "I saw myself *driving* through Eternity in a *timeless* taxi."

He knew the Norman Knights. In fact, he was going to write a play for N.K. when the theatre scheme came off.

"Well, Warren, how's the play?" said Norman Knight, dropping his monocle and giving his eye a moment in which to rise to the surface before it was screwed down again.

And Mrs. Norman Knight: "Oh, Mr. Warren, what happy socks!"

"I *am* so glad you like them," said he, staring at his feet. "They seem to have got so *much* whiter since the moon rose." And he turned his lean sorrowful young face to Bertha. "There *is* a moon, you know."

She wanted to cry: "I am sure there is — often — often!"

He really was a most attractive person. But so was Face, crouched before the fire in her banana skins, and so was Mug, smoking a cigarette and saying as he flicked the ash: "Why doth the bridegroom tarry?"

"There he is, now."

Bang went the front door open and shut. Harry shouted: "Hullo, you people. Down in five minutes." And they heard him swarm up the stairs. Bertha couldn't help smiling; she knew how he loved doing things at high pressure. What, after all, did an extra five minutes matter? But he would pretend to himself that they mattered beyond measure. And then he would make a great point of coming into the drawing-room, extravagantly cool and collected.

Harry had such a zest for life. Oh, how she appreciated it in him. And his passion for fighting — for seeking in everything that came up against him another test of his power and of his courage — that, too, she understood. Even when it made him just occasionally, to other people, who didn't know him well, a little ridiculous perhaps. . . . For there were moments when he rushed into battle where no battle was. . . . She talked and laughed and positively forgot until he had come in (just as she had imagined) that Pearl Fulton had not turned up.

"I wonder if Miss Fulton has forgotten?"

"I expect so," said Harry. "Is she on the 'phone?"

"Ah! There's a taxi, now." And Bertha smiled with that little air of proprietorship that she always assumed while her women finds were new and mysterious. "She lives in taxis."

"She'll run to fat if she does," said Harry coolly, ringing the bell for dinner. "Frightful danger for blond women."

"Harry — don't," warned Bertha, laughing up at him.

Came another tiny moment, while they waited, laughing and talking, just a trifle too much at their ease, a trifle too unaware. And then Miss Fulton, all in silver, with a silver fillet binding her pale blond hair, came in smiling, her head a little on one side.

"Am I late?"

"No, not at all," said Bertha. "Come along." And she took her arm and they moved into the dining-room.

What was there in the touch of that cool arm that could fan — fan — start blazing — blazing — the fire of bliss that Bertha did not know what to do with?

Miss Fulton did not look at her; but then she seldom did look at people directly. Her heavy eyelids lay upon her eyes and the strange half smile came and went upon her lips as though she lived by listening rather than seeing. But Bertha knew, suddenly, as if the longest, most intimate look had passed between them — as if they had said to each other: "You too?" — that Pearl Fulton, stirring the beautiful red soup in the grey plate, was feeling just what she was feeling.

And the others? Face and Mug, Eddie and Harry, their spoons rising and falling — dabbing their lips with their napkins, crumbling bread, fiddling with the forks and glasses and talking.

"I met her at the Alpha show — the weirdest little person. She'd not only cut off her hair, but she seemed to have taken a dreadfully good snip off her legs and arms and her neck and her poor little nose as well."

"Isn't she very *liée* with Michael Oat?"

"The man who wrote *Love in False Teeth*?"

"He wants to write a play for me. One act. One man. Decides to commit suicide. Gives all the reasons why he should and why he shouldn't. And just as he has made up his mind either to do it or not to do it — curtain. Not half a bad idea."

"What's he going to call it — 'Stomach Trouble'?"

"I *think* I've come across the *same* idea in a lit-tle French review, *quite* unknown in England."

No, they didn't share it. They were dears — dears — and she loved having them there, at her table, and giving them delicious food and wine. In fact, she longed to tell them how delightful they were, and what a decorative group they made, how they seemed to set one another off and how they reminded her of a play by Chekhov!

Harry was enjoying his dinner. It was part of his — well, not his nature, exactly, and certainly not his pose — his — something or other — to talk about food and to glory in his "shameless passion for the white flesh of the lobster" and "the green of pistachio ices — green and cold like the eyelids of Egyptian dancers."

When he looked up at her and said: "Bertha, this is a very admirable *soufflée!*" she almost could have wept with child-like pleasure.

Oh, why did she feel so tender towards the whole world tonight? Everything was good — was right. All that happened seemed to fill again her brimming cup of bliss.

And still, in the back of her mind, there was the pear tree. It would be silver now, in the light of poor dear Eddie's moon, silver as Miss Fulton, who sat there turning a tangerine in her slender fingers that were so pale a light seemed to come from them.

What she simply couldn't make out — what was miraculous — was how she should have guessed Miss Fulton's mood so exactly and so instantly. For she never doubted for a moment that she was right, and yet what had she to go on? Less than nothing.

"I believe this does happen very, very rarely between women. Never between men," thought Bertha. "But while I am making the coffee in the drawing-room perhaps she will 'give a sign.' "

What she meant by that she did not know, and what would happen after that she could not imagine.

While she thought like this she saw herself talking and laughing. She had to talk because of her desire to laugh.

"I must laugh or die."

But when she noticed Face's funny little habit of tucking something down the front of her bodice — as if she kept a tiny, secret hoard of nuts there, too — Bertha had to dig her nails into her hands — so as not to laugh too much.

It was over at last. And: "Come and see my new coffee machine," said Bertha.

"We only have a new coffee machine once a fortnight," said Harry. Face took her arm this time; Miss Fulton bent her head and followed after.

The fire had died down in the drawing-room to a red, flickering "nest of baby phœnixes," said Face.

"Don't turn up the light for a moment. It is so lovely." And down she crouched by the fire again. She was always cold . . . "without her little red flannel jacket, of course," thought Bertha.

At that moment Miss Fulton "gave the sign."

"Have you a garden?" said the cool, sleepy voice.

This was so exquisite on her part that all Bertha could do was obey. She crossed the room, pulled the curtains apart, and opened those long windows.

"There!" she breathed.

And the two women stood side by side looking at the slender, flowering tree. Although it was so still it seemed, like the flame of a candle, to stretch up, to point, to quiver in the bright air, to grow taller and taller as they gazed — almost to touch the rim of the round, silver moon.

How long did they stand there? Both, as it were, caught in that circle of unearthly light, understanding each other perfectly, creatures of another world, and wondering what they were to do in this one with all this blissful treasure that burned in their bosoms and dropped, in silver flowers, from their hair and hands?

For ever — for a moment? And did Miss Fulton murmur: "Yes. Just *that.*" Or did Bertha dream it?

Then the light was snapped on and Face made the coffee and Harry said: "My dear Mrs. Knight, don't ask me about my baby. I never see her. I shan't feel the slightest interest in her until she has a lover," and Mug took his eye out of the conservatory for a moment and then put it under glass again and Eddie Warren drank his coffee and set down the cup with a face of anguish as though he had drunk and seen the spider.

"What I want to do is to give the young men a show. I believe London is simply teeming with first-chop, unwritten plays. What I want to say to 'em is: 'Here's the theatre. Fire ahead.' "

"You know, my dear, I am going to decorate a room for the Jacob Nathans. Oh, I am so tempted to do a fried-fish scheme, with the backs of the chairs shaped like frying pans and lovely chip potatoes embroidered all over the curtains."

"The trouble with our young writing men is that they are still too romantic. You can't put out to sea without being seasick and wanting a basin. Well, why won't they have the courage of those basins?"

"A *dreadful* poem about a *girl* who was *violated* by a beggar *without* a nose in a lit-tle wood. . . ."

Miss Fulton sank into the lowest, deepest chair and Harry handed round the cigarettes.

From the way he stood in front of her shaking the silver box and saying abruptly: "Egyptian? Turkish? Virginian? They're all mixed up," Bertha realized that she not only bored him; he really disliked her. And she decided from the way Miss Fulton said: "No, thank you, I won't smoke," that she felt it, too, and was hurt.

"Oh, Harry, don't dislike her. You are quite wrong about her. She's wonderful, wonderful. And, besides, how can you feel so differently about someone who means so much to me. I shall try to tell you when we are in bed to-night what has been happening. What she and I have shared."

At those last words something strange and almost terrifying darted into Bertha's mind. And this something blind and smiling whispered to her: "Soon these people will go. The house will be quiet — quiet. The lights will be out. And you and he will be alone together in the dark room — the warm bed. . . ."

She jumped up from her chair and ran over to the piano.

"What a pity someone does not play!" she cried. "What a pity somebody does not play."

For the first time in her life Bertha Young desired her husband.

Oh, she'd loved him — she'd been in love with him, of course, in every other way, but just not in that way. And, equally, of course, she'd understood that he was different. They'd discussed it so often. It had worried her dreadfully at first to find that she was so cold, but after a time it had not seemed to matter. They were so frank with each other — such good pals. That was the best of being modern.

But now — ardently! ardently! The word ached in her ardent body! Was this what that feeling of bliss had been leading up to? But then then —

"My dear," said Mrs. Norman Knight, "you know our shame. We are the victims of time and train. We live in Hampstead. It's been so nice."

"I'll come with you into the hall," said Bertha. "I loved having you. But you must not miss the last train. That's so awful, isn't it?"

"Have a whisky, Knight, before you go?" called Harry.

"No, thanks, old chap."

Bertha squeezed his hand for that as she shook it.

"Good night, good-bye," she cried from the top step, feeling that this self of hers was taking leave of them for ever.

When she got back into the drawing-room the others were on the move.

". . . Then you can come part of the way in my taxi."

"I shall be *so* thankful *not* to have to face *another* drive *alone* after my *dreadful* experience."

"You can get a taxi at the rank just at the end of the street. You won't have to walk more than a few yards."

"That's a comfort. I'll go and put on my coat."

Miss Fulton moved towards the hall and Bertha was following when Harry almost pushed past.

"Let me help you."

Bertha knew that he was repenting his rudeness — she let him go. What a boy he was in some ways — so impulsive — so — simple.

And Eddie and she were left by the fire.

"I *wonder* if you have seen Bilks' *new* poem called 'Table d'Hôte,' " said Eddie softly. "It's *so* wonderful. In the last Anthology. Have you got a copy? I'd *so* like to *show* it to you. It begins with an *incredibly* beautiful line: 'Why Must it Always be Tomato Soup?' "

"Yes," said Bertha. And she moved noiselessly to a table opposite the drawing-room door and Eddie glided noiselessly after her. She picked up the little book and gave it to him; they had not made a sound.

While he looked it up she turned her head towards the hall. And she saw . . . Harry with Miss Fulton's coat in his arms and Miss Fulton with her back turned to him and her head bent. He tossed the coat away, put his hands on her shoulders and turned her violently to him. His lips said: "I adore you," and Miss Fulton laid her moonbeam fingers on his cheeks and smiled her sleepy smile. Harry's nostrils quivered; his lips curled back in a hideous grin while he whispered: "To-morrow," and with her eyelids Miss Fulton said: "Yes."

"Here it is," said Eddie. " 'Why Must it Always be Tomato Soup?' It's so *deeply* true, don't you feel? Tomato soup is so *dreadfully* eternal."

"If you prefer," said Harry's voice, very loud, from the hall, "I can phone you a cab to come to the door."

"Oh, no. It's not necessary," said Miss Fulton, and she came up to Bertha and gave her the slender fingers to hold.

"Good-bye. Thank you so much."

"Good-bye," said Bertha.

Miss Fulton held her hand a moment longer.

"Your lovely pear tree!" she murmured.

And then she was gone, with Eddie following, like the black cat following the grey cat.

"I'll shut up shop," said Harry, extravagantly cool and collected.

"Your lovely pear tree — pear tree — pear tree!"

Bertha simply ran over to the long windows.

"Oh, what is going to happen now?" she cried.

But the pear tree was as lovely as ever and as full of flower and as still.

KATHERINE MANSFIELD

Prelude

1

There was not an inch of room for Lottie and Kezia in the buggy. When Pat swung them on top of the luggage they wobbled; the grandmother's lap was full and Linda Burnell could not possibly have held a lump of a child on hers for any distance. Isabel, very superior, was perched beside the new handy-man on the driver's seat. Hold-alls, bags and boxes were piled upon the floor. "These are absolute necessities that I will not let out of my sight for one instant," said Linda Burnell, her voice trembling with fatigue and excitement.

Lottie and Kezia stood on the patch of lawn just inside the gate all ready for the fray in their coats with brass anchor buttons and little round caps with battleship ribbons. Hand in hand, they stared with round solemn eyes first at the absolute necessities and then at their mother.

"We shall simply have to leave them. That is all. We shall simply have to cast them off," said Linda Burnell. A strange little laugh flew from her lips; she leaned back against the buttoned leather cushions and shut her eyes, her lips trembling with laughter. Happily at that moment Mrs. Samuel Josephs, who had been watching the scene from behind her drawing-room blind, waddled down the garden path.

"Why nod leave the chudren with be for the afterdoon, Brs. Burnell? They could go on the dray with the storeban when he comes in the eveding. Those thigs on the path have to go, dod't they?"

"Yes, everything outside the house is supposed to go," said Linda Burnell, and she waved a white hand at the tables and chairs standing on their heads on the front lawn. How absurd they looked! Either they ought to be the other way up, or Lottie and Kezia ought to stand on their heads, too. And she longed to say: "Stand on your heads, children, and wait for the storeman." It seemed to her that would be so exquisitely funny that she could not attend to Mrs. Samuel Josephs.

The fat creaking body leaned across the gate, and the big jelly of a face smiled. "Dod't you worry, Brs. Burnell. Loddie and Kezia can have tea with by chudren in the dursery, and I'll see theb on the dray afterwards."

The grandmother considered. "Yes, it really is quite the best plan. We are very obliged to you, Mrs. Samuel Josephs. Children, say 'thank you' to Mrs. Samuel Josephs."

Two subdued chirrups: "Thank you, Mrs. Samuel Josephs."

"And be good little girls, and — come closer — " they advanced, "don't forget to tell Mrs. Samuel Josephs when you want to . . ."

"No, granma."

"Dod't worry, Brs. Burnell."

At the last moment Kezia let go Lottie's hand and darted towards the buggy.

"I want to kiss my granma good-bye again."

But she was too late. The buggy rolled off up the road, Isabel bursting with pride, her nose turned up at all the world, Linda Burnell prostrated, and the grandmother rummaging among the very curious oddments she had had put in her black silk reticule at the last moment, for something to give her daughter. The buggy twinkled away in the sunlight and fine golden dust up the hill and over. Kezia bit her lip, but Lottie, carefully finding her handkerchief first, set up a wail.

"Mother! Granma!"

Mrs. Samuel Josephs, like a huge warm black silk tea cosy, enveloped her.

"It's all right, by dear. Be a brave child. You come and blay in the dursery!"

She put her arm round weeping Lottie and led her away. Kezia followed, making a face at Mrs. Samuel Josephs' placket, which was undone as usual, with two long pink corset laces hanging out of it. . . .

Lottie's weeping died down as she mounted the stairs, but the sight of her at the nursery door with swollen eyes and a blob of a nose gave great satisfaction to the S. J.'s, who sat on two benches before a long table covered with American cloth and set out with immense plates of bread and dripping and two brown jugs that faintly steamed.

"Hullo! You've been crying!"

"Ooh! Your eyes have gone right in."

"Doesn't her nose look funny."

"You're all red-and-patchy."

Lottie was quite a success. She felt it and swelled, smiling timidly.

"Go and sit by Zaidee, ducky," said Mrs. Samuel Josephs, "and Kezia, you sid ad the end by Boses."

Moses grinned and gave her a nip as she sat down; but she pretended not to notice. She did hate boys.

"Which will you have?" asked Stanley, leaning across the table very politely, and smiling at her. "Which will you have to begin with — strawberries and cream or bread and dripping?"

"Strawberries and cream, please," said she.

"Ah-h-h-h." How they all laughed and beat the table with their teaspoons. Wasn't that a take in! Wasn't it now! Didn't he fox her! Good old Stan!

"Ma! She thought it was real."

Even Mrs. Samuel Josephs, pouring out the milk and water, could not help smiling. "You bustn't tease theb on their last day," she wheezed.

But Kezia bit a big piece out of her bread and dripping, and then stood the piece up on her plate. With the bite out it made a dear little sort of a gate. Pooh! She didn't care! A tear rolled down her cheek, but she wasn't crying. She couldn't have cried in front of those awful Samuel Josephs. She sat with her head bent, and as the tear dripped slowly down, she caught it with a neat little whisk of her tongue and ate it before any of them had seen.

2

After tea Kezia wandered back to their own house. Slowly she walked up the back steps, and through the scullery into the kitchen. Nothing was left in it but a lump of gritty yellow soap in one corner of the kitchen window sill and a piece of flannel stained with a blue bag in another. The fireplace was choked up with rubbish. She poked among it but found nothing except a hair-tidy with a heart painted on it that had belonged to the servant girl. Even that she left lying, and she trailed through the narrow passage into the drawing-room. The Venetian blind was pulled down but not drawn close. Long pencil rays of sunlight shown through and the wavy shadow of a bush outside danced on the gold lines. Now it was still, now it began to flutter again, and now it came almost as far as her feet. Zoom! Zoom! a bluebottle knocked against the ceiling; the carpet-tacks had little bits of red fluff sticking to them.

The dining-room window had a square of coloured glass at each corner. One was blue and one was yellow. Kezia bent down to have one more look at a blue lawn with blue arum lilies growing at the gate, and then at a yellow lawn with yellow lilies and a yellow fence. As she looked a little Chinese Lottie came out on to the lawn and began to dust the tables and chairs with a corner of her pinafore. Was that really Lottie? Kezia was not quite sure until she had looked through the ordinary window.

Upstairs in her father's and mother's room she found a pill box black and shiny outside and red in, holding a blob of cotton wool.

"I could keep a bird's egg in that," she decided.

In the servant girl's room there was a stay-button stuck in a crack of the floor, and in another crack some beads and a long needle. She knew there was nothing in her grandmother's room; she had watched her pack. She went over to the window and leaned against it, pressing her hands against the pane.

Kezia liked to stand so before the window. She liked the feeling of the cold shining glass against her hot palms, and she liked to watch the funny white tops that came on her fingers when she pressed them hard against the pane. As she stood there, the day flickered out and dark came. With the dark crept the wind snuffling and howling. The windows of the empty house shook, a creaking came from the walls and floors, a piece of loose iron on the roof banged forlornly. Kezia was suddenly quite, quite still, with wide open eyes and knees pressed together. She was frightened. She wanted to call Lottie and to go on calling all the while she ran downstairs and out of the house. But IT was just behind her, waiting at the door, at the head of the stairs, at the bottom of the stairs, hiding in the passage, ready to dart out at the back door. But Lottie was at the back door, too.

"Kezia!" she called cheerfully. "The storeman's here. Everything is on the dray and three horses, Kezia. Mrs. Samuel Josephs has given us a big shawl to wear round us, and she says to button up your coat. She won't come out because of asthma."

Lottie was very important.

"Now then, you kids," called the storeman. He hooked his big thumbs under their arms and up they swung. Lottie arranged the shawl "most beautifully" and the storeman tucked up their feet in a piece of old blanket.

"Lift up. Easy does it."

They might have been a couple of young ponies. The storeman felt over the cords holding his load, unhooked the brakechain from the wheel, and whistling, he swung up beside them.

"Keep close to me," said Lottie, "because otherwise you pull the shawl away from my side, Kezia."

But Kezia edged up to the storeman. He towered beside her big as a giant and he smelled of nuts and new wooden boxes.

3

It was the first time that Lottie and Kezia had ever been out so late. Everything looked different — the painted wooden houses far smaller than they did by day, the gardens far bigger and wilder. Bright stars speckled the sky and the moon hung over the harbour dabbling the waves with gold. They could see the lighthouse shining on Quarantine Island, and the green lights on the old coal hulks.

"There comes the Picton boat," said the storeman, pointing to a little steamer all hung with bright beads.

But when they reached the top of the hill and began to go down the other side the harbour disappeared, and although they were still in the town they were quite lost. Other carts rattled past. Everybody knew the storeman.

"Night, Fred."

"Night O," he shouted.

Kezia liked very much to hear him. Whenever a cart appeared in the distance she looked up and waited for his voice. He was an old friend; and she and her grandmother had often been to his place to buy grapes. The storeman lived alone in a cottage that had a glasshouse against one wall built by himself. All the glasshouse was spanned and arched over with one beautiful vine. He took her brown basket from her, lined it with three large leaves, and then he felt in his belt for a little horn knife, reached up and snapped off a big blue cluster and laid it on the leaves so tenderly that Kezia held her breath to watch. He was a very big man. He wore brown velvet trousers, and he had a long brown beard. But he never wore a collar, not even on Sunday. The back of his neck was burnt bright red.

"Where are we now?" Every few minutes one of the children asked him the question.

"Why, this is Hawk Street, or Charlotte Crescent."

"Of course it is," Lottie pricked up her ears at the last name; she always felt that Charlotte Crescent belonged specially to her. Very few people had streets with the same name as theirs.

"Look, Kezia, there is Charlotte Crescent. Doesn't it look different?" Now everything familiar was left behind. Now the big dray rattled into unknown country, along new roads with high clay banks on either side, up steep, steep hills, down into bushy valleys, through wide shallow rivers. Further and further. Lottie's head wagged; she drooped, she slipped half into Kezia's lap and lay there. But Kezia could not open her eyes wide enough. The wind blew and she shivered; but her cheeks and ears burned.

"Do stars ever blow about?" she asked.

"Not to notice," said the storeman.

"We've got a nuncle and a naunt living near our new house," said Kezia. "They have got two children, Pip, the eldest is called, and the youngest's name is Rags. He's got a ram. He has to feed it with a nenamuel teapot and a glove top over the spout. He's going to show us. What is the difference between a ram and a sheep?"

"Well, a ram has horns and runs for you."

Kezia considered. "I don't want to see it frightfully," she said. "I hate rushing animals like dogs and parrots. I often dream that animals rush at me — even camels — and while they are rushing, their heads swell e-enormous."

The storeman said nothing. Kezia peered up at him, screwing up her eyes. Then she put her finger out and stroked his sleeve; it felt hairy. "Are we near?" she asked.

"Not far off, now," answered the storeman. "Getting tired?"

"Well, I'm not an atom bit sleepy," said Kezia. "But my eyes keep curling up in such a funny sort of way." She gave a long sigh, and to stop her eyes from curling she shut them. . . . When she opened them again they were clanking through a drive that cut through the garden like a whip lash, looping suddenly an island of green, and behind the island, but out of sight until you came upon it, was the house. It was long and low built, with a pillared verandah and balcony all the way round. The soft white bulk of it lay stretched upon the green garden like a sleeping beast. And now one and now another of the windows leaped into light. Someone was walking through the empty rooms carrying a lamp. From a window downstairs the light of a fire flickered. A strange beautiful excitement seemed to stream from the house in quivering ripples.

"Where are we?" said Lottie, sitting up. Her reefer cap was all on one side and on her cheek there was the print of an anchor button she had pressed against while sleeping. Tenderly the storeman lifted her, set her cap straight, and pulled down her crumpled clothes. She stood blinking on the lowest verandah step watching Kezia who seemed to come flying through the air to her feet.

"Ooh!" cried Kezia, flinging up her arms. The grandmother came out of the dark hall carrying a little lamp. She was smiling.

"You found your way in the dark?" said she.

"Perfectly well."

But Lottie staggered on the lowest verandah step like a bird fallen out of the nest. If she stood still for a moment she fell asleep, if she leaned against anything her eyes closed. She could not walk another step.

"Kezia," said the grandmother, "can I trust you to carry the lamp?"

"Yes, my granma."

The old woman bent down and gave the bright breathing thing into her hands and then she caught up drunken Lottie. "This way."

Through a square hall filled with bales and hundreds of parrots (but the parrots were only on the wall-paper) down a narrow passage where the parrots persisted in flying past Kezia with her lamp.

"Be very quiet," warned the grandmother, putting down Lottie and opening the dining-room door. "Poor little mother has got such a headache."

Linda Burnell, in a long cane chair, with her feet on a hassock, and a plaid over her knees, lay before a crackling fire. Burnell and Beryl sat at the table in the middle of the room eating a dish of fried chops and drinking tea out of a brown china teapot. Over the back of her mother's chair leaned Isabel. She had a comb in her fingers and in a gentle absorbed fashion she was combing the curls from her mother's forehead.

Outside the pool of lamp and firelight the room stretched dark and bare to the hollow windows.

"Are those the children?" But Linda did not really care; she did not even open her eyes to see.

"Put down the lamp, Kezia," said Aunt Beryl, "or we shall have the house on fire before we are out of the packing cases. More tea, Stanley?"

"Well, you might just give me five-eighths of a cup," said Burnell, leaning across the table. "Have another chop, Beryl. Tip-top meat, isn't it? Not too lean and not too fat." He turned to his wife. "You're sure you won't change your mind, Linda darling?"

"The very thought of it is enough." She raised one eyebrow in the way she had. The grandmother brought the children bread and milk and they sat up to table, flushed and sleepy behind the wavy steam.

"I had meat for my supper," said Isabel, still combing gently.

"I had a whole chop for my supper, the bone and all and Worcester sauce. Didn't I, father?"

"Oh, don't boast, Isabel," said Aunt Beryl.

Isabel looked astounded. "I wasn't boasting, was I, Mummy? I never thought of boasting. I thought they would like to know. I only meant to tell them."

"Very well. That's enough," said Burnell. He pushed back his plate, took a tooth-pick out of his pocket and began picking his strong white teeth.

"You might see that Fred has a bite of something in the kitchen before he goes, will you, mother?"

"Yes, Stanley." The old woman turned to go.

"Oh, hold on half a jiffy. I suppose nobody knows where my slippers were put? I suppose I shall not be able to get at them for a month or two — what?"

"Yes," came from Linda. "In the top of the canvas hold-all marked 'urgent necessities.' "

"Well you might get them for me will you, mother?"

"Yes, Stanley."

Burnell got up, stretched himself, and going over to the fire he turned his back to it and lifted up his coat tails.

"By Jove, this is a pretty pickle. Eh, Beryl?"

Beryl, sipping tea, her elbows on the table, smiled over the cup at him. She wore an unfamiliar pink pinafore; the sleeves of her blouse were rolled up to her shoulders showing her lovely freckled arms, and she had let her hair fall down her back in a long pig-tail.

"How long do you think it will take to get straight — couple of weeks — eh?" he chaffed.

"Good heavens, no," said Beryl airily. "The worst is over already. The servant girl and I have simply slaved all day, and ever since mother came she has worked like a horse, too. We have never sat down for a moment. We have had a day."

Stanley scented a rebuke.

"Well, I suppose you did not expect me to rush away from the office and nail carpets — did you?"

"Certainly not," laughed Beryl. She put down her cup and ran out of the dining-room.

"What the hell does she expect us to do?" asked Stanley. "Sit down and fan herself with a palm leaf fan while I have a gang of professionals to do the job? By Jove, if she can't do a hand's turn occasionally without shouting about it in return for . . ."

And he gloomed as the chops began to fight the tea in his sensitive stomach. But Linda put up a hand and dragged him down to the side of her long chair.

"This is a wretched time for you, old boy," she said. Her cheeks were very white but she smiled and curled her fingers into the big red hand she held. Burnell became quiet. Suddenly he began to whistle "Pure as a lily, joyous and free" — a good sign.

"Think you're going to like it?" he asked.

"I don't want to tell you, but I think I ought to, mother," said Isabel. "Kezia is drinking tea out of Aunt Beryl's cup."

4

They were taken off to bed by the grandmother. She went first with a candle; the stairs rang to their climbing feet. Isabel and Lottie lay in a room to themselves, Kezia curled in her grandmother's soft bed.

"Aren't there going to be any sheets, my granma?"

"No, not to-night."

"It's tickly," said Kezia, "but it's like Indians." She dragged her grandmother down to her and kissed her under the chin. "Come to bed soon and be my Indian brave."

"What a silly you are," said the old woman, tucking her in as she loved to be tucked.

"Aren't you going to leave me a candle?"

"No. Sh — h. Go to sleep."

"Well, can I have the door left open?"

She rolled herself up into a round but she did not go to sleep. From all over the house came the sound of steps. The house itself creaked and popped. Loud whispering voices came from downstairs. Once she heard Aunt Beryl's rush of high laughter, and once she heard a loud trumpeting from Burnell blowing his nose. Outside the window hundreds of black cats with yellow eyes sat in the sky watching her — but she was not frightened. Lottie was saying to Isabel:

"I'm going to say my prayers in bed to-night."

"No you can't, Lottie." Isabel was very firm. "God only excuses you saying your prayers in bed if you've got a temperature." So Lottie yielded:

> Gentle Jesus meek anmile,
> Look pon a little chile.
> Pity me, simple Lizzie
> Suffer me to come to thee.

And then they lay down back to back, their little behinds just touching, and fell asleep.

Standing in a pool of moonlight Beryl Fairfield undressed herself. She was tired, but she pretended to be more tired than she really was — letting her clothes fall, pushing back with a languid gesture her warm, heavy hair.

"Oh, how tired I am — very tired."

She shut her eyes a moment, but her lips smiled. Her breath rose and fell in her breast like two fanning wings. The window was wide open; it was warm, and somewhere out there in the garden a young man, dark and slender, with mocking eyes, tiptoed among the bushes, and gathered the flowers into a big bouquet, and slipped under her window and held it up to her. She saw herself bending forward. He thrust his head among the bright waxy flowers, sly and laughing. "No, no," said Beryl. She turned from the window and dropped her nightgown over her head.

"How frightfully unreasonable Stanley is sometimes," she thought, buttoning. And then, as she lay down, there came the old thought, the cruel thought — ah, if only she had money of her own.

A young man, immensely rich, has just arrived from England. He meets her quite by chance. . . . The new governor is unmarried. . . . There is a ball at Government house. . . . Who is that exquisite creature in *eau de nil* satin? Beryl Fairfield. . . .

"The thing that pleases me," said Stanley, leaning against the side of the bed and giving himself a good scratch on his shoulders and back before turning in, "is that I've got the place dirt cheap, Linda. I was talking about it to little Wally Bell to-day and he said he simply could not understand why they had accepted my figure. You see land about here is bound to become more and more valuable . . . in about ten years' time . . . of course we shall have to go very slow and cut down expenses as fine as possible. Not asleep — are you?"

"No, dear, I've heard every word," said Linda.

He sprang into bed, leaned over her and blew out the candle.

"Good night, Mr. Business Man," said she, and she took hold of his head by the ears and gave him a quick kiss. Her faint faraway voice seemed to come from a deep well.

"Good night, darling." He slipped his arm under her neck and drew her to him.

"Yes, clasp me," said the faint voice from the deep well.

Pat the handy-man sprawled in his little room behind the kitchen. His sponge-bag coat and trousers hung from the door-peg like a hanged man. From the edge of the blanket his twisted toes protruded, and on the floor beside him there was an empty cane bird-cage. He looked like a comic picture.

"Honk, honk," came from the servant girl. She had adenoids.

Last to go to bed was the grandmother.

"What! Not asleep yet?"

"No, I'm waiting for you," said Kezia. The old woman sighed and lay down beside her. Kezia thrust her head under the grandmother's arm and gave a little squeak. But the old woman only pressed her faintly, and sighed again, took out her teeth, and put them in a glass of water beside her on the floor.

In the garden some tiny owls, perched on the branches of a lace-bark tree, called: "More pork; more pork." And far away in the bush there sounded a harsh rapid chatter: "Ha-ha-ha . . . Ha-ha-ha"

5

Dawn came sharp and chill with red clouds on a faint green sky and drops of water on every leaf and blade. A breeze blew over the garden, dropping dew and dropping petals, shivered over the drenched paddocks, and was lost in the sombre bush. In the sky some tiny stars floated for a moment and then they were gone — they were dissolved like bubbles. And plain to be heard in the early quiet was the sound of the creek in the paddock running over the brown stones, running in and out of the sandy hollows, hiding under clumps of dark berry bushes, spilling into a swamp of yellow water flowers and cresses.

And then at the first beam of sun the birds began. Big cheeky birds, starlings and mynahs, whistled on the lawns, the little birds, the goldfinches and linnets and fan-tails flicked from bough to bough. A lovely kingfisher perched on the paddock fence preening his rich beauty, and a *tui* sang his three notes and laughed and sang them again.

"How loud the birds are," said Linda in her dream. She was walking with her father through a green paddock sprinkled with daisies. Suddenly he bent down and parted the grasses and showed her a tiny ball of fluff just at her feet. "Oh, Papa, the darling." She made a cup of her hands and caught the tiny bird and stroked its head with her finger. It was quite tame. But a funny thing happened. As she stroked it began to swell, it ruffled and pouched, it grew bigger and bigger and its round eyes seemed to smile knowingly at her. Now her arms were hardly wide enough to hold it and she dropped it into her apron. It had become a baby with a big naked head and a gaping bird-mouth, opening and shutting. Her father broke into a loud clattering laugh and she woke to see Burnell standing by the windows rattling the Venetian blind up to the very top.

"Hullo," he said. "Didn't wake you, did I? Nothing much wrong with the weather this morning."

He was enormously pleased. Weather like this set a final seal on his bargain. He felt, somehow, that he had bought the lovely day, too — got it chucked in dirt cheap with the house and ground. He dashed off to his bath and Linda turned over and raised herself on one elbow to see the room by daylight. All the furniture had found a place — all the old paraphernalia — as she expressed it. Even the photographs were on the mantelpiece and the medicine bottles on the shelf above the washstand. Her clothes lay across a chair — her outdoor things, a purple cape and a round hat with a plume in it. Looking at them she wished that she was going away from this house, too. And she saw herself driving away from them all in a little buggy, driving away from everybody and not even waving.

Back came Stanley girt with a towel, glowing and slapping his thighs. He pitched the wet towel on top of her hat and cape, and standing firm in the exact centre of a square of sunlight he began to do his exercises. Deep breathing, bending and squatting like a frog and shooting out his legs. He was so delighted with his firm, obedient body that he hit himself on the chest and gave a loud "Ah." But this amazing vigour seemed to set him worlds away from Linda. She lay on the white tumbled bed and watched him as if from the clouds.

"Oh, damn! Oh, blast!" said Stanley, who had butted into a crisp white shirt only to find that some idiot had fastened the neckband and he was caught. He stalked over to Linda waving his arms.

"You look like a big fat turkey," said she.

"Fat. I like that," said Stanley. "I haven't a square inch of fat on me. Feel that."

"It's rock — it's iron," mocked she.

"You'd be surprised," said Stanley, as though this were intensely interesting, "at the number of chaps at the club who have got a corporation. Young chaps, you know — men of my age." He began parting his bushy ginger hair, his blue eyes fixed round and round in the glass, his knees bent, because the dressing table was always — confound it — a bit too low for him. "Little Wally Bell, for instance," and he straightened, describing upon himself an enormous curve with the hairbrush. "I must say I've a perfect horror   "

"My dear, don't worry. You'll never be fat. You are far too energetic."

"Yes, yes, I suppose that's true," said he, comforted for the hundredth time, and taking a pearl pen-knife out of his pocket he began to pare his nails.

"Breakfast, Stanley." Beryl was at the door. "Oh, Linda, mother says you are not to get up yet." She popped her head in at the door. She had a big piece of syringa stuck through her hair.

"Everything we left on the verandah last night is simply sopping this morning. You should see poor dear mother wringing out the tables and the chairs. However, there is no harm done — " this with the faintest glance at Stanley.

"Have you told Pat to have the buggy round in time? It's a good six and a half miles to the office."

"I can imagine what this early start for the office will be like," thought Linda. "It will be very high pressure indeed."

"Pat, Pat." She heard the servant girl calling. But Pat was evidently hard to find; the silly voice went baa-baaing through the garden.

Linda did not rest again until the final slam of the front door told her that Stanley was really gone.

Later she heard her children playing in the garden. Lottie's stolid, compact little voice cried: "Ke-zia. Isabel." She was always getting lost or losing people only to find them again, to her great surprise, round the next tree or the next corner. "Oh, there you are after all." They had been turned out after breakfast and told not to come back to the house until they were called. Isabel wheeled a neat pramload of prim dolls and Lottie was allowed for a great treat to walk beside her holding the doll's parasol over the face of the wax one.

"Where are you going to, Kezia?" asked Isabel, who longed to find some light and menial duty that Kezia might perform and so be roped in under her government.

"Oh, just away," said Kezia. . . .

Then she did not hear any more. What a glare there was in the room. She hated blinds pulled up to the top at any time, but in the morning it was intolerable. She turned over to the wall and idly, with one finger, she traced a poppy on the wallpaper with a leaf and a stem and a fat bursting bud. In the quiet, and under her tracing finger, the poppy seemed to come alive. She could feel the sticky, silky petals, the stem, hairy like a gooseberry skin, the rough leaf and the tight glazed bud. Things had a habit of coming alive like that. Not only large substantial things like furniture, but curtains and the patterns of stuffs and fringes of quilts and cushions. How often she had seen the tassel fringe of her quilt change into a funny procession of dancers with priests attending. . . . For there were some tassels that did not dance at all but walked stately, bent forward as if praying or chanting. How often the medicine bottles had turned into a row of little men with brown top-hats on; and the wash-stand jug had a way of sitting in the basin like a fat bird in a round nest.

"I dreamed about birds last night," thought Linda. What was it? She had forgotten. But the strangest part of this coming alive of things was what they did. They listened, they seemed to swell out with some mysterious important content, and when they were full she felt that they smiled. But it was not for her, only, their sly secret smile;

they were members of a secret society and they smiled among themselves. Some-times, when she had fallen asleep in the daytime, she woke and could not lift a finger, could not even turn her eyes to left or right because THEY were there; sometimes when she went out of a room and left it empty, she knew as she clicked the door to that THEY were filling it. And there were times in the evenings when she was upstairs, perhaps, and everybody else was down, when she could hardly escape from them. Then she could not hurry, she could not hum a tune; if she tried to say ever so carelessly — "Bother that old thimble" — THEY were not deceived. THEY knew how frightened she was; THEY saw how she turned her head away as she passed the mirror. What Linda always felt was that THEY wanted something of her, and she knew that if she gave herself up and was quiet, more than quiet, silent, motionless, something would really happen.

"It's very quiet now," she thought. She opened her eyes wide, and she heard the silence spinning its soft endless web. How lightly she breathed; she scarcely had to breathe at all.

Yes, everything had come alive down to the minutest, tiniest particle, and she did not feel her bed, she floated, held up in the air. Only she seemed to be listening with her wide open watchful eyes, waiting for someone to come who just did not come, watching for something to happen that just did not happen.

6

In the kitchen at the long deal table under the two windows old Mrs. Fairfield was washing the breakfast dishes. The kitchen window looked out on to a big grass patch that led down to the vegetable garden and the rhubarb beds. On one side the grass patch was bordered by the scullery and washhouse and over this whitewashed lean-to there grew a knotted vine. She had noticed yesterday that a few tiny cork-screw tendrils had come right through some cracks in the scullery ceiling and all the windows of the lean-to had a thick frill of ruffled green.

"I am very fond of a grape vine," declared Mrs. Fairfield, "but I do not think that the grapes will ripen here. It takes Australian sun." And she remembered how Beryl when she was a baby had been picking some white grapes from the vine on the back verandah of their Tasmanian house and she had been stung on the leg by a huge red ant. She saw Beryl in a little plaid dress with red ribbon tie-ups on the shoulders screaming so dreadfully that half the street rushed in. And how the child's leg had swelled! "T-t-t-t!" Mrs. Fairfield caught her breath remembering. "Poor child, how terrifying it was." And she set her lips tight and went over to the stove for some more hot water. The water frothed up in the big soapy bowl with pink and blue bubbles on top of the foam. Old Mrs. Fairfield's arms were bare to the elbow and stained a bright pink. She wore a grey foulard dress patterned with large purple pansies, a white linen apron and a high cap shaped like a jelly mould of white muslin. At her throat there was a silver crescent moon with five little owls seated on it, and round her neck she wore a watchguard made of black beads.

It was hard to believe that she had not been in that kitchen for years; she was so much a part of it. She put the crocks away with a sure, precise touch, moving leisurely and ample from the stove to the dresser, looking into the pantry and the larder as though there were not an unfamiliar corner. When she had finished, everything in the kitchen had become part of a series of patterns. She stood in the middle of the room wiping her hands on a check cloth; a smile beamed on her lips; she thought it looked very nice, very satisfactory.

"Mother! Mother! Are you there?" called Beryl.

"Yes, dear. Do you want me?"

"No. I'm coming," and Beryl rushed in, very flushed, dragging with her two big pictures.

"Mother, whatever can I do with these awful hideous Chinese paintings that Chung Wah gave Stanley when he went bankrupt? It's absurd to say that they are valuable, because they were hanging in Chung Wah's fruit shop for months before. I can't make out why Stanley wants them kept. I'm sure he thinks them just as hideous as we do, but it's because of the frames," she said spitefully. "I suppose he thinks the frames might fetch something some day or other."

"Why don't you hang them in the passage?" suggested Mrs. Fairfield; "they would not be much seen there."

"I can't. There is no room. I've hung all the photographs of his office there before and after building, and the signed photos of his business friends, and that awful enlargement of Isabel lying on the mat in her singlet." Her angry glance swept the placid kitchen. "I know what I'll do. I'll hang them here. I will tell Stanley they got a little damp in the moving so I have put them in here for the time being."

She dragged a chair forward, jumped on it, took a hammer and a big nail out of her pinafore pocket and banged away.

"There! That is enough! Hand me the picture, mother."

"One moment, child." Her mother was wiping over the carved ebony frame.

"Oh, mother, really you need not dust them. It would take years to dust all those little holes." And she frowned at the top of her mother's head and bit her lip with impatience. Mother's deliberate way of doing things was simply maddening. It was old age, she supposed, loftily.

At last the two pictures were hung side by side. She jumped off the chair, stowing away the little hammer.

"They don't look so bad there, do they?" said she. "And at any rate nobody need gaze at them except Pat and the servant girl — have I got a spider's web on my face, mother? I've been poking into that cupboard under the stairs and now something keeps tickling my nose."

But before Mrs. Fairfield had time to look Beryl had turned away. Someone tapped on the window: Linda was there, nodding and smiling. They heard the latch of the scullery door lift and she came in. She had no hat on; her hair stood up on her head in curling rings and she was wrapped up in an old cashmere shawl.

"I'm so hungry," said Linda: "where can I get something to eat, mother? This is the first time I've been in the kitchen. It says 'mother' all over; everything is in pairs."

"I will make you some tea," said Mrs. Fairfield, spreading a clean napkin over a corner of the table, "and Beryl can have a cup with you."

"Beryl, do you want half my gingerbread?" Linda waved the knife at her. "Beryl, do you like the house now that we are here?"

"Oh yes, I like the house immensely and the garden is beautiful, but it feels very far away from everything to me. I can't imagine people coming out from town to see us in that dreadful jolting bus, and I am sure there is not anyone here to come and call. Of course it does not matter to you because — "

"But there's the buggy," said Linda. "Pat can drive you into town whenever you like."

That was a consolation, certainly, but there was something at the back of Beryl's mind, something she did not even put into words for herself.

"Oh, well, at any rate it won't kill us," she said dryly, putting down her empty cup and standing up and stretching. "I am going to hang curtains." And she ran away singing:

> How many thousand birds I see
> That sing aloud from every tree . . .

". . . birds I see That sing aloud from every tree. . . ." But when she reached the dining-room she stopped singing, her face changed; it became gloomy and sullen.

"One may as well rot here as anywhere else," she muttered savagely, digging the stiff brass safety-pins into the red serge curtains.

The two left in the kitchen were quiet for a little. Linda leaned her cheek on her fingers and watched her mother. She thought her mother looked wonderfully beautiful with her back to the leafy window. There was something comforting in the sight of her that Linda felt she could never do without. She needed the sweet smell of her flesh, and the soft feel of her cheeks and her arms and shoulders still softer. She loved the way her hair curled, silver at her forehead, lighter at her neck, and bright brown still in the big coil under the muslin cap. Exquisite were her mother's hands, and the two rings she wore seemed to melt into her creamy skin. And she was always so fresh, so delicious. The old woman could bear nothing but linen next to her body and she bathed in cold water winter and summer.

"Isn't there anything for me to do?" asked Linda.

"No, darling. I wish you would go into the garden and give an eye to your children; but that I know you will not do."

"Of course I will, but you know Isabel is much more grown up than any of us."

"Yes, but Kezia is not," said Mrs. Fairfield.

"Oh, Kezia has been tossed by a bull hours ago," said Linda, winding herself up in her shawl again.

But no, Kezia had seen a bull through a hole in a knot of wood in the paling that separated the tennis lawn from the paddock. But she had not liked the bull frightfully, so she had walked away back through the orchard, up the grassy slope, along the path by the lace-bark tree and so into the spread tangled garden. She did not believe that she would ever not get lost in this garden. Twice she had found her way back to the big iron gates they had driven through the night before, and then had turned to walk up the drive that led to the house, but there were so many little paths on either side. On one side they all led into a tangle of tall dark trees and strange bushes with flat velvet leaves and feathery cream flowers that buzzed with flies when you shook them — this was the frightening side, and no garden at all. The little paths here were wet and clayey with tree roots spanned across them like the marks of big fowls' feet.

But on the other side of the drive there was a high box border and the paths had box edges and all of them led into a deeper and deeper tangle of flowers. The camellias were in bloom, white and crimson and pink and white striped with flashing leaves. You could not see a leaf on the syringa bushes for the white clusters. The roses were in flower — gentlemen's button-hole roses, little white ones, but far too full of insects to hold under anyone's nose, pink monthly roses with a ring of fallen petals round the bushes, cabbage roses on thick stalks, moss roses, always in bud, pink smooth beauties opening curl on curl, red ones so dark they seemed to turn black as they fell, and a certain exquisite cream kind with a slender red stem and bright scarlet leaves.

There were clumps of fairy bells, and all kinds of geraniums, and there were little trees of verbena and bluish lavender bushes and a bed of pelagoniums with velvet eyes and leaves like moths' wings. There was a bed of nothing but mignonette and another of nothing but pansies — borders of double and single daisies and all kinds of little tufty plants she had never seen before.

The red-hot pokers were taller than she; the Japanese sunflowers grew in a tiny jungle. She sat down on one of the box borders. By pressing hard at first it made a nice seat. But how dusty it was inside! Kezia bent down to look and sneezed and rubbed her nose.

And then she found herself at the top of the rolling grassy slope that led down to the orchard. . . . She looked down at the slope a moment; then she lay down on her back, gave a squeak and rolled over and over into the thick flowery orchard grass. As she lay waiting for things to stop spinning, she decided to go up to the house and ask the servant girl for an empty match-box. She wanted to make a surprise for the grandmother. . . . First she would put a leaf inside with a big violet lying on it, then she would put a very small white picotee, perhaps, on each side of the violet, and then she would sprinkle some lavender on the top, but not to cover their heads.

She often made these surprises for the grandmother, and they were always most successful.

"Do you want a match, my granny?"

"Why, yes, child, I believe a match is just what I'm looking for."

The grandmother slowly opened the box and came upon the picture inside.

"Good gracious, child! How you astonished me!"

"I can make her one every day here," she thought, scrambling up the grass on her slippery shoes.

But on her way back to the house she came to that island that lay in the middle of the drive, dividing the drive into two arms that met in front of the house. The island was made of grass banked up high. Nothing grew on the top except one huge plant with thick, grey-green, thorny leaves, and out of the middle there sprang up a tall stout stem. Some of the leaves of the plant were so old that they curled up in the air no longer; they turned back, they were split and broken; some of them lay flat and withered on the ground.

Whatever could it be? She had never seen anything like it before. She stood and stared. And then she saw her mother coming down the path.

"Mother, what is it?" asked Kezia.

Linda looked up at the fat swelling plant with its cruel leaves and fleshy stem. High above them, as though becalmed in the air, and yet holding so fast to the earth it grew from, it might have had claws instead of roots. The curving leaves seemed to be hiding something; the blind stem cut into the air as if no wind could ever shake it.

"That is an aloe, Kezia," said her mother.

"Does it ever have any flowers?"

"Yes, Kezia," and Linda smiled down at her, and half shut her eyes. "Once every hundred years."

7

On his way home from the office Stanley Burnell stopped the buggy at the Bodega, got out and bought a large bottle of oysters. At the Chinaman's shop next door he bought a pineapple in the pink of condition, and noticing a basket of fresh black cherries he told John to put him a pound of those as well. The oysters and the pine he stowed away in the box under the front seat, but the cherries he kept in his hand.

Pat, the handy-man, leapt off the box and tucked him up again in the brown rug.

"Lift yer feet, Mr. Burnell, while I give yer a fold under," said he.

"Right! Right! First-rate!" said Stanley. "You can make straight for home now."

Pat gave the grey mare a touch and the buggy sprang forward.

"I believe this man is a first-rate chap," thought Stanley. He liked the look of him sitting up there in his neat brown coat and brown bowler. He liked the way Pat had tucked him in, and he liked his eyes. There was nothing servile about him — and if there was one thing he hated more than another it was servility. And he looked as if he was pleased with his job — happy and contented already.

The grey mare went very well; Burnell was impatient to be out of the town. He wanted to be home. Ah, it was splendid to live in the country — to get right out of that hole of a town once the office was closed; and this drive in the fresh warm air, knowing all the while that his own house was at the other end, with its garden and paddocks, its three tip-top cows and enough fowls and ducks to keep them in poultry, was splendid too.

As they left the town finally and bowled away up the deserted road his heart beat hard for joy. He rooted in the bag and began to eat the cherries, three or four at a time, chucking the stones over the side of the buggy. They were delicious, so plump and cold, without a spot or a bruise on them.

Look at those two, now — black one side and white the other — perfect! A perfect little pair of Siamese twins. And he stuck them in his button-hole. . . . By Jove, he wouldn't mind giving that chap up there a handful — but no, better not. Better wait until he had been with him a bit longer.

He began to plan what he would do with his Saturday afternoons and his Sundays. He wouldn't go to the club for lunch on Saturday. No, cut away from the office as soon as possible and get them to give him a couple of slices of cold meat and half a lettuce when he got home. And then he'd get a few chaps out from town to play tennis in the afternoon. Not too many — three at most. Beryl was a good player, too. . . . He stretched out his right arm and slowly bent it, feeling the muscle. . . . A bath, a good rubdown, a cigar on the verandah after dinner. . . .

On Sunday morning they would go to church — children and all. Which reminded him that he must hire a pew, in the sun if possible and well forward so as to be out of the draught from the door. In fancy he heard himself intoning extremely well: "When thou didst overcome the *Sharp*ness of Death Thou didst open the *King*dom of Heaven to *all* Believers." And he saw the neat brass-edged card on the corner of the pew — Mr. Stanley Burnell and family. . . . The rest of the day he'd loaf about with Linda. . . . Now they were walking about the garden; she was on his arm, and he was explaining to her at length what he intended doing at the office the week following. He heard her saying: "My dear, I think that is most wise." . . . Talking things over with Linda was a wonderful help even though they were apt to drift away from the point.

Hang it all! They weren't getting along very fast. Pat had put the brake on again. Ugh! What a brute of a thing it was. He could feel it in the pit of his stomach.

A sort of panic overtook Burnell whenever he approached near home. Before he was well inside the gate he would shout to anyone within sight: "Is everything all right?" And then he did not believe it was until he heard Linda say: "Hullo! Are you home again?" That was the worst of living in the country — it took the deuce of a long time to get back. . . . But now they weren't far off. They were on the top of the last hill; it was a gentle slope all the way now and not more than half a mile.

Pat trailed the whip over the mare's back and he coaxed her: "Goop now. Goop now."

It wanted a few minutes to sunset. Everything stood motionless bathed in bright, metallic light and from the paddocks on either side there streamed the milky scent of ripe grass. The iron gates were open. They dashed through and up the drive and round the island, stopping at the exact middle of the verandah.

"Did she satisfy yer, Sir?" said Pat, getting off the box and grinning at his master.

"Very well indeed, Pat," said Stanley.

Linda came out of the glass door; her voice rang in the shadowy quiet. "Hullo! Are you home again?"

At the sound of her his heart beat so hard that he could hardly stop himself dashing up the steps and catching her in his arms.

"Yes, I'm home again. Is everything all right?"

Pat began to lead the buggy round to the side gate that opened into the courtyard.

"Here, half a moment," said Burnell. "Hand me those two parcels." And he said to Linda, "I've brought you back a bottle of oysters and a pineapple," as though he had brought her back all the harvest of the earth.

They went into the hall; Linda carried the oysters in one hand and the pineapple in the other. Burnell shut the glass door, threw his hat down, put his arms round her and strained her to him, kissing the top of her head, her ears, her lips, her eyes.

"Oh, dear! Oh, dear!" said she. "Wait a moment. Let me put down these silly things," and she put the bottle of oysters and the pine on a little carved chair. "What have you got in your button-hole — cherries?" She took them out and hung them over his ear.

"Don't do that, darling. They are for you."

So she took them off his ear again. "You don't mind if I save them. They'd spoil my appetite for dinner. Come and see your children. They are having tea."

The lamp was lighted on the nursery table. Mrs. Fairfield was cutting and spreading bread and butter. The three little girls sat up to table wearing large bibs embroidered with their names. They wiped their mouths as their father came in ready to be kissed. The windows were open; a jar of wild flowers stood on the mantelpiece, and the lamp made a big soft bubble of light on the ceiling.

"You seem pretty snug, mother," said Burnell, blinking at the light. Isabel and Lottie sat one on either side of the table, Kezia at the bottom — the place at the top was empty.

"That's where my boy ought to sit," thought Stanley. He tightened his arm round Linda's shoulder. By God, he was a perfect fool to feel as happy as this!

"We are, Stanley. We are very snug," said Mrs. Fairfield, cutting Kezia's bread into fingers.

"Like it better than town — eh, children?" asked Burnell.

"Oh, yes," said the three little girls, and Isabel added as an after-thought: "Thank you very much indeed, father dear."

"Come upstairs," said Linda. "I'll bring your slippers."

But the stairs were too narrow for them to go up arm in arm. It was quite dark in the room. He heard her ring tapping on the marble mantelpiece as she felt for the matches.

"I've got some, darling. I'll light the candles."

But instead he came up behind her and again he put his arms round her and pressed her head into his shoulder.

"I'm so confoundedly happy," he said.

"Are you?" She turned and put her hands on his breast and looked up at him.

"I don't know what has come over me," he protested.

It was quite dark outside now and heavy dew was falling. When Linda shut the window the cold dew touched her finger tips. Far away a dog barked. "I believe there is going to be a moon," she said.

At the words, and with the cold wet dew on her fingers, she felt as though the moon had risen — that she was being strangely discovered in a flood of cold light. She shivered; she came away from the window and sat down upon the box ottoman beside Stanley.

In the dining-room, by the flicker of a wood fire, Beryl sat on a hassock playing the guitar. She had bathed and changed all her clothes. Now she wore a white muslin dress with black spots on it and in her hair she had pinned a black silk rose.

> Nature has gone to her rest, love,
> See, we are alone.
> Give me your hand to press, love,
> Lightly within my own.

She played and sang half to herself, for she was watching herself playing and singing. The firelight gleamed on her shoes, on the ruddy belly of the guitar, and on her white fingers. . . .

"If I were outside the window and looked in and saw myself I really would be rather struck," thought she. Still more softly she played the accompaniment — not singing now but listening.

. . . "The first time that I ever saw you, little girl — oh, you had no idea that you were not alone — you were sitting with your little feet upon a hassock, playing the guitar. God, I can never forget. . . ." Beryl flung up her head and began to sing again:

> Even the moon is aweary . . .

But there came a loud bang at the door. The servant girl's crimson face popped through.

"Please, Miss Beryl, I've got to come and lay."

"Certainly, Alice," said Beryl, in a voice of ice. She put the guitar in a corner. Alice lunged in with a heavy black iron tray.

"Well, I have had a job with that oving," said she. "I can't get nothing to brown."

"Really!" said Beryl.

But no, she could not stand that fool of a girl. She ran into the dark drawing-room and began walking up and down. . . . Oh, she was restless, restless. There was a mirror over the mantel. She leaned her arms along and looked at her pale shadow in it. How beautiful she looked, but there was nobody to see, nobody.

"Why must you suffer so?" said the face in the mirror. "You were not made for suffering. . . . Smile!"

Beryl smiled, and really her smile *was* so adorable that she smiled again — but this time because she could not help it.

8

"Good morning, Mrs. Jones."

"Oh, good morning, Mrs. Smith. I'm so glad to see you. Have you brought your children?"

"Yes, I've brought both my twins. I have had another baby since I saw you last, but she came so suddenly that I haven't had time to make her any clothes, yet. So I left her. . . . How is your husband?"

"Oh, he is very well, thank you. At least he had a nawful cold but Queen Victoria — she's my godmother, you know — sent him a case of pineapples and that cured it im — mediately. Is that your new servant?"

"Yes, her name's Gwen. I've only had her two days. Oh, Gwen, this is my friend, Mrs. Smith."

"Good morning, Mrs. Smith. Dinner won't be ready for about ten minutes."

"I don't think you ought to introduce me to the servant. I think I ought to just begin talking to her."

"Well, she's more of a lady-help than a servant and you do introduce lady-helps, I know, because Mrs. Samuel Josephs had one."

"Oh, well, it doesn't matter," said the servant, carelessly, beating up a chocolate custard with half a broken clothes peg. The dinner was baking beautifully on a concrete step. She began to lay the cloth on a pink garden seat. In front of each person she put two geranium leaf plates, a pine needle fork and a twig knife. There were three daisy heads on a laurel leaf for poached eggs, some slices of fuchsia petal cold beef, some lovely little rissoles made of earth and water and dandelion seeds, and the chocolate custard which she had decided to serve in the pawa shell she had cooked it in.

"You needn't trouble about my children," said Mrs. Smith graciously. "If you'll just take this bottle and fill it at the tap — I mean at the dairy."

"Oh, all right," said Gwen, and she whispered to Mrs. Jones: "Shall I go and ask Alice for a little bit of real milk?"

But someone called from the front of the house and the luncheon party melted away, leaving the charming table, leaving the rissoles and the poached eggs to the ants and to an old snail who pushed his quivering horns over the edge of the garden seat and began to nibble a geranium plate.

"Come round to the front, children. Pip and Rags have come."

The Trout boys were the cousins Kezia had mentioned to the storeman. They lived about a mile away in a house called Monkey Tree Cottage. Pip was tall for his age, with lank black hair and a white face, but Rags was very small and so thin that when he was undressed his shoulder blades stuck out like two little wings. They had a mongrel dog with pale blue eyes and a long tail turned up at the end who followed them everywhere; he was called Snooker. They spent half their time combing and brushing Snooker and dosing him with various awful mixtures concocted by Pip, and kept secretly by him in a broken jug covered with an old kettle lid. Even faithful little Rags was not allowed to know the full secret of these mixtures.... Take some carbolic tooth powder and a pinch of sulphur powdered up fine, and perhaps a bit of starch to stiffen up Snooker's coat.... But that was not all; Rags privately thought that the rest was gun-powder.... And he never was allowed to help with the mixing because of the danger.... "Why if a spot of this flew in your eye, you would be blinded for life," Pip would say, stirring the mixture with an iron spoon. "And there's always the chance — just the chance, mind you — of it exploding if you whack it hard enough.... Two spoons of this in a kerosene tin will be enough to kill thousands of fleas." But Snooker spent all his spare time biting and snuffling, and he stank abominably.

"It's because he is such a grand fighting dog," Pip would say. "All fighting dogs smell."

The Trout boys had often spent the day with the Burnells in town, but now that they lived in this fine house and boncer garden they were inclined to be very friendly. Besides, both of them liked playing with girls — Pip, because he could fox them so, and because Lottie was so easily frightened, and Rags for a shameful reason. He adored dolls. How he would look at a doll as it lay asleep, speaking in a whisper and smiling timidly, and what a treat it was to him to be allowed to hold one....

"Curve your arms round her. Don't keep them stiff like that. You'll drop her," Isabel would say sternly.

Now they were standing on the verandah and holding back Snooker who wanted to go into the house but wasn't allowed to because Aunt Linda hated decent dogs.

"We came over in the bus with Mum," they said, "and we're going to spend the afternoon with you. We brought over a batch of our gingerbread for Aunt Linda. Our Minnie made it. It's all over nuts."

"I skinned the almonds," said Pip. "I just stuck my hand into a saucepan of boiling water and grabbed them out and gave them a kind of pinch and the nuts flew out of the skins, some of them as high as the ceiling. Didn't they, Rags?"

Rags nodded. "When they make cakes at our place," said Pip, "we always stay in the kitchen, Rags and me, and I get the bowl and he gets the spoon and the egg beater. Sponge cake's best. It's all frothy stuff, then."

He ran down the verandah steps to the lawn, planted his hands on the grass, bent forward, and just did not stand on his head.

"That lawn's all bumpy," he said. "You have to have a flat place for standing on your head. I can walk round the monkey tree on my head at our place. Can't I, Rags?"

"Nearly," said Rags faintly.

"Stand on your head on the verandah. That's quite flat," said Kezia.

"No, smarty," said Pip. "You have to do it on something soft. Because if you give a jerk and fall over, something in your neck goes click, and it breaks off. Dad told me."

"Oh, do let's play something," said Kezia.

"Very well," said Isabel quickly, "we'll play hospitals. I will be the nurse and Pip can be the doctor and you and Lottie and Rags can be the sick people."

Lottie didn't want to play that, because last time Pip had squeezed something down her throat and it hurt awfully.

"Pooh," scoffed Pip. "It was only the juice out of a bit of mandarin peel."

"Well, let's play ladies," said Isabel. "Pip can be the father and you can be all our dear little children."

"I hate playing ladies," said Kezia. "You always make us go to church hand in hand and come home and go to bed."

Suddenly Pip took a filthy handkerchief out of his pocket. "Snooker! Here, sir," he called. But Snooker, as usual, tried to sneak away, his tail between his legs. Pip leapt on top of him, and pressed him between his knees.

"Keep his head firm, Rags," he said, and he tied the handkerchief round Snooker's head with a funny knot sticking up at the top.

"Whatever is that for?" asked Lottie.

"It's to train his ears to grow more close to his head — see?" said Pip, "All fighting dogs have ears that lie back. But Snooker's ears are a bit too soft."

"I know," said Kezia. "They are always turning inside out. I hate that."

Snooker lay down, made one feeble effort with his paw to get the handkerchief off, but finding he could not, trailed after the children, shivering with misery.

9

Pat came swinging along; in his hand he held a little tomahawk that winked in the sun.

"Come with me," he said to the children, "and I'll show you how the kings of Ireland chop the head off a duck."

They drew back — they didn't believe him, and besides, the Trout boys had never seen Pat before.

"Come on now," he coaxed, smiling and holding out his hand to Kezia.

"Is it a real duck's head? One from the paddock?"

"It is," said Pat. She put her hand in his hard dry one, and he stuck the tomahawk in his belt and held out the other to Rags. He loved little children.

"I'd better keep hold of Snooker's head if there's going to be any blood about," said Pip, "because the sight of blood makes him awfully wild." He ran ahead dragging Snooker by the handkerchief.

"Do you think we ought to go?" whispered Isabel. "We haven't asked or anything. Have we?"

At the bottom of the orchard a gate was set in the paling fence. On the other side a steep bank led down to a bridge that spanned the creek, and once up the bank on the other side you were on the fringe of the paddocks. A little old stable in the first paddock had been turned into a fowl-house. The fowls had strayed far away across the paddock down to a dumping ground in a hollow, but the ducks kept close to that part of the creek that flowed under the bridge.

Tall bushes overhung the stream with red leaves and yellow flowers and clusters of blackberries. At some places the stream was wide and shallow, but at others it tumbled into deep little pools with foam at the edges and quivering bubbles. It was in these pools that the big white ducks had made themselves at home, swimming and guzzling along the weedy banks.

Up and down they swam, preening their dazzling breasts, and other ducks with the same dazzling breasts and yellow bills swam upside down with them.

"There is the little Irish navy," said Pat, "and look at the old admiral there with the green neck and the grand little flagstaff on his tail."

He pulled a handful of grain from his pocket and began to walk towards the fowl-house, lazy, his straw hat with the broken crown pulled over his eyes.

"Lid. Lid — lid — lid — lid — " he called.

"Qua. Qua — qua — qua — qua — " answered the ducks, making for land, and flapping and scrambling up the bank they streamed after him in a long waddling line. He coaxed them, pretending to throw the grain, shaking it in his hands and calling to them until they swept round him in a white ring.

From far away the fowls heard the clamour and they too came running across the paddock, their heads thrust forward, their wings spread, turning in their feet in the silly way fowls run and scolding as they came.

Then Pat scattered the grain and the greedy ducks began to gobble. Quickly he stopped, seized two, one under each arm, and strode across to the children. Their darting heads and round eyes frightened the children — all except Pip.

"Come on, sillies," he cried, "they can't bite. They haven't any teeth. They've only got those two little holes in their beaks for breathing through."

"Will you hold one while I finish with the other?" asked Pat. Pip let go of Snooker. "Won't I? Won't I? Give us one. I don't mind how much he kicks."

He nearly sobbed with delight when Pat gave the white lump into his arms.

There was an old stump beside the door of the fowl-house. Pat grabbed the duck by the legs, laid it flat across the stump, and almost at the same moment down came the little tomahawk and the duck's head flew off the stump. Up the blood spurted over the white feathers and over his hand.

When the children saw the blood they were frightened no longer. They crowded round him and began to scream. Even Isabel leaped about crying: "The blood! The blood!" Pip forgot all about his duck. He simply threw it away from him and shouted, "I saw it. I saw it," and jumped round the wood block.

Rags, with cheeks as white as paper, ran up to the little head, put out a finger as if he wanted to touch it, shrank back again and then again put out a finger. He was shivering all over.

Even Lottie, frightened little Lottie, began to laugh and pointed at the duck and shrieked: "Look, Kezia, look."

"Watch it!" shouted Pat. He put down the body and it began to waddle — with only a long spurt of blood where the head had been; it began to pad away without a sound towards the steep bank that led to the stream. . . . That was the crowning wonder.

"Do you see that? Do you see that?" yelled Pip. He ran among the little girls tugging at their pinafores.

"It's like a little engine. It's like a funny little railway engine," squealed Isabel.

But Kezia suddenly rushed at Pat and flung her arms round his legs and butted her head as hard as she could against his knees.

"Put head back! Put head back!" she screamed.

When he stooped to move her she would not let go or take her head away. She held on as hard as she could and sobbed: "Head back! Head back!" until it sounded like a loud strange hiccup.

"It's stopped. It's tumbled over. It's dead," said Pip.

Pat dragged Kezia up into his arms. Her sunbonnet had fallen back, but she would not let him look at her face. No, she pressed her face into a bone in his shoulder and clasped her arms round his neck.

The children stopped screaming as suddenly as they had begun. They stood round the dead duck. Rags was not frightened of the head any more. He knelt down and stroked it, now.

"I don't think the head is quite dead yet," he said. "Do you think it would keep alive if I gave it something to drink?"

But Pip got very cross: "Bah! You baby." He whistled to Snooker and went off. When Isabel went up to Lottie, Lottie snatched away.

"What are you always touching me for, Isabel?"

"There now," said Pat to Kezia. "There's the grand little girl."

She put up her hands and touched his ears. She felt something. Slowly she raised her quivering face and looked. Pat wore little round gold ear-rings. She never knew that men wore ear-rings. She was very much surprised.

"Do they come on and off?" she asked huskily.

10

Up in the house, in the warm tidy kitchen, Alice, the servant girl, was getting the afternoon tea. She was "dressed." She had on a black stuff dress that smelt under the arms, a white apron like a large sheet of paper, and a lace bow pinned on to her hair with two jetty pins. Also her comfortable carpet slippers were changed for a pair of black leather ones that pinched her corn on her little toe something dreadful. . . .

It was warm in the kitchen. A blow-fly buzzed, a fan of whity steam came out of the kettle, and the lid kept up a rattling jig as the water bubbled. The clock ticked in the warm air, slow and deliberate, like the click of an old woman's knitting needle, and sometimes — for no reason at all, for there wasn't any breeze — the blind swung out and back, tapping the window.

Alice was making water-cress sandwiches. She had a lump of butter on the table, a barracouta loaf, and the cresses tumbled in a white cloth.

But propped against the butter dish there was a dirty, greasy little book, half unstitched, with curled edges, and while she mashed the butter she read:

"To dream of black-beetles drawing a hearse is bad. Signifies death of one you hold near or dear, either father, husband, brother, son, or intended. If beetles crawl backwards as you watch them it means death from fire or from great height such as flight of stairs, scaffolding, etc.

"Spiders. To dream of spiders creeping over you is good. Signifies large sum of money in near future. Should party be in family way an easy confinement may be expected. But care should be taken in sixth month to avoid eating of probable present of shell fish. . . ."

How many thousand birds I see.

Oh, life. There was Miss Beryl. Alice dropped the knife and slipped the *Dream Book* under the butter dish. But she hadn't time to hide it quite, for Beryl ran into the kitchen and up to the table, and the first thing her eye lighted on were those greasy edges. Alice saw Miss Beryl's meaning little smile and the way she raised her eyebrows and screwed up her eyes as though she were not quite sure what that could be. She decided to answer if Miss Beryl should ask her: "Nothing as belongs to you, Miss." But she knew Miss Beryl would not ask her.

Alice was a mild creature in reality, but she had the most marvellous retorts ready for questions that she knew would never be put to her. The composing of them and the turning of them over and over in her mind comforted her just as much as if they'd been expressed. Really, they kept her alive in places where she'd been that chivvied she'd been afraid to go to bed at night with a box of matches on the chair in case she bit the tops off in her sleep, as you might say.

"Oh, Alice," said Miss Beryl. "There's one extra to tea, so heat a plate of yesterday's scones, please. And put on the Victoria sandwich as well as the coffee cake. And don't forget to put little doyleys under the plates — will you? You did yesterday, you know, and the tea looked so ugly and common. And, Alice, don't put that dreadful old pink and green cosy on the afternoon teapot again. That is only for the mornings. Really, I think it ought to be kept for the kitchen — it's so shabby, and quite smelly. Put on the Japanese one. You quite understand, don't you?"

Miss Beryl had finished.

That sing aloud from every tree . . .

she sang as she left the kitchen, very pleased with her firm handling of Alice.

Oh, Alice was wild. She wasn't one to mind being told, but there was something in the way Miss Beryl had of speaking to her that she couldn't stand. Oh, that she couldn't. It made her curl up inside, as you might say, and she fair trembled. But what Alice really hated Miss Beryl for was that she made her feel low. She talked to Alice in a special voice as though she wasn't quite all there; and she never lost her temper with her — never. Even when Alice dropped anything or forgot anything important Miss Beryl seemed to have expected it to happen.

"If you please, Mrs. Burnell," said an imaginary Alice, as she buttered the scones, "I'd rather not take my orders from Miss Beryl. I may be only a common servant girl as doesn't know how to play the guitar, but . . ."

This last thrust pleased her so much that she quite recovered her temper.

"The only thing to do," she heard, as she opened the dining-room door, "is to cut the sleeves out entirely and just have a broad band of black velvet over the shoulders instead. . . ."

11

The white duck did not look as if it had ever had a head when Alice placed it in front of Stanley Burnell that night. It lay, in beautifully basted resignation, on a blue dish — its legs tied together with a piece of string and a wreath of little balls of stuffing round it.

It was hard to say which of the two, Alice, or the duck, looked the better basted; they were both such a rich colour and they both had the same air of gloss and strain. But Alice was fiery red and the duck a Spanish mahogany.

Burnell ran his eye along the edge of the carving knife. He prided himself very much upon his carving, upon making a first-class job of it. He hated seeing a woman carve; they were always too slow and they never seemed to care what the meat looked like afterwards. Now he did; he took a real pride in cutting delicate shaves of cold beef, little wads of mutton, just the right thickness, and in dividing a chicken or a duck with nice precision. . . .

"Is this the first of the home products?" he asked, knowing perfectly well that it was.

"Yes, the butcher did not come. We have found out that he only calls twice a week."

But there was no need to apologise. It was a superb bird. It wasn't meat at all, but a kind of very superior jelly. "My father would say," said Burnell, "this must have been one of those birds whose mother played to it in infancy upon the German flute. And the sweet strains of the dulcet instrument acted with such effect upon the infant mind. . . . Have some more, Beryl? You and I are the only ones in this house with a real feeling for food. I'm perfectly willing to state, in a court of law, if necessary, that I love good food."

Tea was served in the drawing-room, and Beryl, who for some reason had been very charming to Stanley ever since he came home, suggested a game of crib. They sat at a little table near one of the open windows. Mrs. Fairfield disappeared, and Linda lay in a rocking-chair, her arms above her head, rocking to and fro.

"You don't want the light — do you, Linda?" said Beryl. She moved the lamp so that she sat under its soft light.

How remote they looked, those two, from where Linda sat and rocked. The green table, the polished cards, Stanley's big hands and Beryl's tiny ones, all seemed to be part of one mysterious movement. Stanley himself, big and solid, in his dark suit, took his ease, and Beryl tossed her bright head and pouted. Round her throat she wore an unfamiliar velvet ribbon. It changed her, somehow — altered the shape of her face — but it was charming, Linda decided. The room smelled of lilies; there were two big jars of arums in the fire-place.

"Fifteen two — fifteen four — and a pair is six and a run of three is nine," said Stanley, so deliberately, he might have been counting sheep.

"I've nothing but two pairs," said Beryl, exaggerating her woe because she knew how he loved winning.

The cribbage pegs were like two little people going up the road together, turning round the sharp corner, and coming down the road again. They were pursuing each other. They did not so much want to get ahead as to keep near enough to talk—to keep near, perhaps that was all.

But no, there was always one who was impatient and hopped away as the other came up, and would not listen. Perhaps the white peg was frightened of the red one, or perhaps he was cruel and would not give the red one a chance to speak. . . .

In the front of her dress Beryl wore a bunch of pansies, and once when the little pegs were side by side, she bent over and the pansies dropped out and covered them.

"What a shame," said she, picking up the pansies. "Just as they had a chance to fly into each other's arms."

"Farewell, my girl," laughed Stanley, and away the red peg hopped.

The drawing-room was long and narrow with glass doors that gave on to the verandah. It had a cream paper with a pattern of gilt roses, and the furniture, which had belonged to old Mrs. Fairfield, was dark and plain. A little piano stood against the wall with yellow pleated silk let into the carved front. Above it hung an oil painting by Beryl of a large cluster of surprised looking clematis. Each flower was the size of a small saucer, with a centre like an astonished eye fringed in black. But the room was not finished yet. Stanley had set his heart on a Chesterfield and two decent chairs. Linda liked it best as it was. . . .

Two big moths flew in through the window and round and round the circle of lamplight.

"Fly away before it is too late. Fly out again."

Round and round they flew; they seemed to bring the silence and the moonlight in with them on their silent wings. . . .

"I've two kings," said Stanley. "Any good?"

"Quite good," said Beryl.

Linda stopped rocking and got up. Stanley looked across. "Anything the matter, darling?"

"No, nothing. I'm going to find mother."

She went out of the room and standing at the foot of the stairs she called, but her mother's voice answered her from the verandah.

The moon that Lottie and Kezia had seen from the storeman's wagon was full, and the house, the garden, the old woman and Linda—all were bathed in dazzling light.

"I have been looking at the aloe," said Mrs. Fairfield. "I believe it is going to flower this year. Look at the top there. Are those buds, or is it only an effect of light?"

As they stood on the steps, the high grassy bank on which the aloe rested rose up like a wave, and the aloe seemed to ride upon it like a ship with the oars lifted. Bright moonlight hung upon the lifted oars like water, and on the green wave glittered the dew.

"Do you feel it, too," said Linda, and she spoke to her mother with the special voice that women use at night to each other as though they spoke in their sleep or from some hollow cave — "Don't you feel that it is coming towards us?"

She dreamed that she was caught up out of the cold water into the ship with the lifted oars and the budding mast. Now the oars fell striking quickly, quickly. They rowed far away over the top of the garden trees, the paddocks and the dark bush beyond. Ah, she heard herself cry: "Faster! Faster!" to those who were rowing.

How much more real this dream was than that they should go back to the house where the sleeping children lay and where Stanley and Beryl played cribbage.

"I believe those are buds," said she. "Let us go down into the garden, mother. I like that aloe. I like it more than anything here. And I am sure I shall remember it long after I've forgotten all the other things."

She put her hand on her mother's arm and they walked down the steps, round the island and on to the main drive that led to the front gates.

Looking at it from below she could see the long sharp thorns that edged the aloe leaves, and at the sight of them her heart grew hard. . . . She particularly liked the long sharp thorns. . . . Nobody would dare to come near the ship or to follow after.

"Not even my Newfoundland dog," thought she, "that I'm so fond of in the daytime."

For she really was fond of him; she loved and admired and respected him tremendously. Oh, better than anyone else in the world. She knew him through and through. He was the soul of truth and decency, and for all his practical experience he was awfully simple, easily pleased and easily hurt. . . .

If only he wouldn't jump at her so, and bark so loudly, and watch her with such eager, loving eyes. He was too strong for her; she had always hated things that rush at her, from a child. There were times when he was frightening — really frightening. When she just had not screamed at the top of her voice: "You are killing me." And at those times she had longed to say the most coarse, hateful things. . . .

"You know I'm very delicate. You know as well as I do that my heart is affected, and the doctor has told you I may die any moment. I have had three great lumps of children already. . . ."

Yes, yes, it was true. Linda snatched her hand from her mother's arm. For all her love and respect and admiration she hated him. And how tender he always was after times like those, how submissive, how thoughtful. He would do anything for her; he longed to serve her. . . . Linda heard herself saying in a weak voice:

"Stanley, would you light a candle?"

And she heard his joyful voice answer: "Of course I will my darling." And he leapt out of bed as though he were going to leap at the moon for her.

It had never been so plain to her as it was at this moment. There were all her feelings for him, sharp and defined, one as true as the other. And there was this other, this hatred, just as real as the rest. She could have done her feelings up in little packets and given them to Stanley. She longed to hand him that last one, for a surprise. She could see his eyes as he opened that . . .

She hugged her folded arms and began to laugh silently. How absurd life was — it was laughable, simply laughable. And why this mania of hers to keep alive at all? For it really was a mania, she thought, mocking and laughing.

"What am I guarding myself for so preciously? I shall go on having children and Stanley will go on making money and the children and the gardens will grow bigger and bigger, with whole fleets of aloes in them for me to choose from."

She had been walking with her head bent, looking at nothing. Now she looked up and about her. They were standing by the red and white camellia trees. Beautiful were the rich dark leaves spangled with light and the round flowers that perch among them like red and white birds. Linda pulled a piece of verbena and crumpled it, and held her hands to her mother.

"Delicious," said the old woman. "Are you cold, child? Are you trembling? Yes, your hands are cold. We had better go back to the house."

"What have you been thinking about?" said Linda. "Tell me."

"I haven't really been thinking of anything. I wondered as we passed the orchard what the fruit trees were like and whether we should be able to make much jam this autumn. There are splendid healthy currant bushes in the vegetable garden. I noticed them to-day. I should like to see those pantry shelves thoroughly well stocked with our own jam. . . ."

12

"MY DARLING NAN,

Don't think me a piggy wig because I haven't written before. I haven't had a moment, dear, and even now I feel so exhausted that I can hardly hold a pen.

Well, the dreadful deed is done. We have actually left the giddy whirl of town, and I can't see how we shall ever go back again, for my brother-in-law has bought this house 'lock, stock and barrel,' to use his own words.

In a way, of course, it is an awful relief, for he has been threatening to take a place in the country ever since I've lived with them — and I must say the house and garden are awfully nice — a million times better than that awful cubby-hole in town.

But buried, my dear. Buried isn't the word.

We have got neighbours, but they are only farmers — big louts of boys who seem to be milking all day, and two dreadful females with rabbit teeth who brought us some scones when we were moving and said they would be pleased to help. But my sister who lives a mile away doesn't know a soul here, so I am sure we never shall. It's pretty certain nobody will ever come out from town to see us, because though there is a bus it's an awful old rattling thing with black leather sides that any decent person would rather die than ride in for six miles.

Such is life. It's a sad ending for poor little B. I'll get to be a most awful frump in a year or two and come and see you in a mackintosh and a sailor hat tied on with a white china silk motor veil. So pretty.

Stanley says that now we are settled — for after the most awful week of my life we really are settled — he is going to bring out a couple of men from the club on Saturday afternoons for tennis. In fact, two are promised as a great treat to-day. But, my dear, if you could see Stanley's men from the club . . . rather fattish, the type who look frightfully indecent without waistcoats — always with toes that turn in rather — so conspicuous when you are walking about a court in white shoes. And they are pulling up their trousers every minute — don't you know — and whacking at imaginary things with their rackets.

I used to play with them at the club last summer, and I am sure you will know the type when I tell you that after I'd been there about three times they all called me Miss Beryl. It's a weary world. Of course mother simply loves the place, but then I suppose when I am mother's age I shall be content to sit in the sun and shell peas into a basin. But I'm not — not — not.

What Linda thinks about the whole affair, per usual, I haven't the slightest idea. Mysterious as ever. . . .

My dear, you know that white satin dress of mine. I have taken the sleeves out entirely, put bands of black velvet across the shoulders and two big red poppies off my dear sister's *chapeau.* It is a great success, though when I shall wear it I do not know."

Beryl sat writing this letter at a little table in her room. In a way, of course, it was all perfectly true, but in another way it was all the greatest rubbish and she didn't believe a word of it. No, that wasn't true. She felt all those things, but she didn't really feel them like that.

It was her other self who had written that letter. It not only bored, it rather disgusted her real self.

"Flippant and silly," said her real self. Yet she knew that she'd send it and she'd always write that kind of twaddle to Nan Pym. In fact, it was a very mild example of the kind of letter she generally wrote.

Beryl leaned her elbows on the table and read it through again. The voice of the letter seemed to come up to her from the page. It was faint already, like a voice heard over the telephone, high, gushing, with something bitter in the sound. Oh, she detested it to-day.

"You've always got so much animation," said Nan Pym. "That's why men are so keen on you." And she had added, rather mournfully, for men were not at all keen on Nan, who was a solid kind of girl, with fat hips and a high colour — "I can't understand how you can keep it up. But it is your nature, I suppose."

What rot. What nonsense. It wasn't her nature at all. Good heavens, if she had ever been her real self with Nan Pym, Nannie would have jumped out of the window with surprise.... My dear, you know that white satin of mine.... Beryl slammed the letter-case to.

She jumped up and half unconsciously, half consciously she drifted over to the looking-glass.

There stood a slim girl in white — a white serge skirt, a white silk blouse, and a leather belt drawn in very tightly at her tiny waist.

Her face was heart-shaped, wide at the brows and with a pointed chin — but not too pointed. Her eyes, her eyes were perhaps her best feature; they were such a strange uncommon colour — greeny blue with little gold points in them.

She had fine black eyebrows and long lashes — so long, that when they lay on her cheeks you positively caught the light in them, someone or other had told her.

Her mouth was rather large. Too large? No, not really. Her underlip protruded a little; she had a way of sucking it in that somebody else had told her was awfully fascinating.

Her nose was her least satisfactory feature. Not that it was really ugly. But it was not half as fine as Linda's. Linda really had a perfect little nose. Hers spread rather — not badly. And in all probability she exaggerated the spreadiness of it just because it was her nose, and she was so awfully critical of herself. She pinched it with a thumb and first finger and made a little face. . . .

Lovely, lovely hair. And such a mass of it. It had the colour of fresh fallen leaves, brown and red with a glint of yellow. When she did it in a long plait she felt it on her backbone like a long snake. She loved to feel the weight of it dragging her head back, and she loved to feel it loose, covering her bare arms. "Yes, my dear, there is no doubt about it, you really are a lovely little thing."

At the words her bosom lifted; she took a long breath of delight, half closing her eyes.

But even as she looked the smile faded from her lips and eyes. Oh God, there she was, back again, playing the same old game. False — false as ever. False as when she'd written to Nan Pym. False even when she was alone with herself, now.

What had that creature in the glass to do with her, and why was she staring? She dropped down to one side of her bed and buried her face in her arms.

"Oh," she cried, "I am so miserable — so frightfully miserable. I know that I'm silly and spiteful and vain; I'm always acting a part. I'm never my real self for a moment." And plainly, plainly, she saw her false self running up and down the stairs, laughing a special trilling laugh if they had visitors, standing under the lamp if a man came to dinner, so that he should see the light on her hair, pouting and pretending to be a little girl when she was asked to play the guitar. Why? She even kept it up for Stanley's benefit. Only last night when he was reading the paper her false self had stood beside him and leaned against his shoulder on purpose. Hadn't she put her hand over his, pointing out something so that he should see how white her hand was beside his brown one.

How despicable! Despicable! Her heart was cold with rage. "It's marvellous how you keep it up," said she to the false self. But then it was only because she was so miserable — so miserable. If she had been happy and leading her own life, her false life would cease to be. She saw the real Beryl — a shadow . . . a shadow. Faint and unsubstantial she shone. What was there of her except the radiance? And for what tiny moments she was really she. Beryl could almost remember every one of them. At those times she had felt: "Life is rich and mysterious and good, and I am rich and mysterious and good, too." Shall I ever be that Beryl for ever? Shall I? How can I? And was there ever a time when I did not have a false self? . . . But just as she had got that far she heard the sound of little steps running along the passage; the door handle rattled. Kezia came in.

"Aunt Beryl, mother says will you please come down? Father is home with a man and lunch is ready."

Botheration! How she had crumpled her skirt, kneeling in that idiotic way.

"Very well, Kezia." She went over to the dressing table and powdered her nose.

Kezia crossed too, and unscrewed a little pot of cream and sniffed it. Under her arm she carried a very dirty calico cat.

When Aunt Beryl ran out of the room she sat the cat up on the dressing table and stuck the top of the cream jar over its ear.

"Now look at yourself," said she sternly.

The calico cat was so overcome by the sight that it toppled over backwards and bumped and bumped on to the floor. And the top of the cream jar flew through the air and rolled like a penny in a round on the linoleum — and did not break.

But for Kezia it had broken the moment it flew through the air, and she picked it up, hot all over, and put it back on the dressing table.

Then she tip-toed away, far too quickly and airily. . . .

W. SOMERSET MAUGHAM

W(illiam) Somerset Maugham (1874–1965) was born in Paris to British parents. Orphaned at the age of ten, he was sent to England to live with relatives; he was educated in Canterbury and at Heidelberg University and then trained in obstetrics at St. Thomas's Hospital in London. He briefly practiced medicine, but the success of his first novel, *Liza of Lambeth* (1897), encouraged him to devote his energies to writing. In the early part of his career he wrote both plays and novels; so successful a dramatist was he that at one point only George Bernard Shaw had more plays running at once in London. His major novels are the autobiographical *Of Human Bondage* (1915), *The Moon and Sixpence* (1919), *Cakes and Ale* (1930), and *The Razor's Edge* (1944). He published more than ten volumes of short fiction; the stories are collected in *Complete Short Stories* (1951). In 1926 Maugham moved to the French Riviera, where he lived, amidst the comings and goings of friends and famous personalities, for the rest of his life. Always an avid traveler, he saw much of the world, invariably listening to the stories people told him (and often later incorporating them into his fiction). For him, the essence of a good story lay in its reflection of "the exception" — something apart from the normalcy of most lives. "I write stories about people who have some singularity of character . . . or about people who by some accident or another, accident of temperament, accident of environment, have been involved in unusual contingencies." "The Book-Bag" is such a story.

The Book-Bag

Some people read for instruction, which is praiseworthy, and some for pleasure, which is innocent, but not a few read from habit, and I suppose that this is neither innocent nor praiseworthy. Of that lamentable company am I. Conversation after a time bores me, games tire me and my own thoughts, which we are told are the unfailing resource of a sensible man, have a tendency to run dry. Then I fly to my book as the opium-smoker to his pipe. I would sooner read the catalogue of the Army and Navy Stores or Bradshaw's Guide than nothing at all, and indeed I have spent many delightful hours over both these works. At one time I never went out without a second-hand bookseller's list in my pocket. I know no reading more fruity. Of course to read in this way is as reprehensible as doping, and I never cease to wonder at the impertinence of great readers who, because they are such, look down on the illiterate. From the standpoint of what eternity is it better to have read a thousand books than to have ploughed a million furrows? Let us admit that reading with us is just a drug that we cannot do without — who of this band does not know the restlessness that attacks him when he has been severed from reading too long, the apprehension and irritability, and the sigh of relief which the sight of a printed page extracts from him? — and so let us be no more vainglorious than the poor slaves of the hypodermic needle or the pint-pot.

And like the dope-fiend who cannot move from place to place without taking with him a plentiful supply of his deadly balm I never venture far without a sufficiency of reading matter. Books are so necessary to me that when in a railway train I have become aware that fellow-travellers have come away without a single one I have been seized with a veritable dismay. But when I am starting on a long journey the problem is formidable. I have learnt my lesson. Once, imprisoned by illness for three months in a hill-town in Java, I came to the end of all the books I had brought with me, and knowing no Dutch was obliged to buy the school-books from which intelligent Javanese, I suppose, acquired knowledge of French and German. So I read again after five and twenty years the frigid plays of Goethe, the fables of La Fontaine and the tragedies of the tender and exact Racine. I have the greatest admiration for Racine, but I admit that to read his plays one after the other requires a certain effort in a person who is suffering from colitis. Since then I have made a point of travelling with the largest sack made for carrying soiled linen and filling it to the brim with books to suit every possible occasion and every mood. It weighs a ton and strong porters reel under its weight. Customhouse officials look at it askance, but recoil from it with consternation when I give them my word that it contains nothing but books. Its inconvenience is that the particular work I suddenly hanker to read is always at the bottom and it is impossible for me to get it without emptying the book-bag's entire contents upon the floor. Except for this, however, I should perhaps never have heard the singular history of Olive Hardy.

I was wandering about Malaya, staying here and there, a week or two if there was a rest-house or a hotel, and a day or so if I was obliged to inflict myself on a planter or a District Officer whose hospitality I had no wish to abuse; and at the moment I happened to be at Penang. It is a pleasant little town, with a hotel that has always seemed to me very agreeable, but the stranger finds little to do there and time hung a trifle heavily on my hands. One morning I received a letter from a man I knew only by name. This was Mark Featherstone. He was Acting Resident, in the absence on leave of the Resident, at a place called Tenggarah. There was a sultan there and it appeared that a water festival of some sort was to take place which Featherstone thought would interest me. He said that he would be glad if I would come and stay with him for a few days. I wired to tell him that I should be delighted and next day took the train to Tenggarah. Featherstone met me at the station. He was a man of about thirty-five, I should think, tall and handsome, with fine eyes and a strong, stern face. He had a wiry black moustache and bushy eyebrows. He looked more like a soldier than a government official. He was very smart in white ducks, with a white topi, and he wore his clothes with elegance. He was a little shy, which seemed odd in a strapping fellow of resolute mien, but I surmised that this was only because he was unused to the society of that strange fish, a writer, and I hoped in a little to put him at his ease.

"My boys'll look after your barang," he said. "We'll go down to the club. Give them your keys and they'll unpack before we get back."

I told him that I had a good deal of luggage and thought it better to leave everything at the station but what I particularly wanted. He would not hear of it.

"It doesn't matter a bit. It'll be safer at my house. It's always better to have one's barang with one."

"All right."

I gave my keys and the ticket for my trunk and my book-bag to a Chinese boy who stood at my host's elbow. Outside the station a car was waiting for us and we stepped in.

"Do you play bridge?" asked Featherstone.

"I do."

"I thought most writers didn't."

"They don't," I said. "It's generally considered among authors a sign of deficient intelligence to play cards."

The club was a bungalow, pleasing but unpretentious; it had a large reading-room, a billiard-room with one table, and a small card-room. When we arrived it was empty but for one or two persons reading the English weeklies, and we walked through to the tennis courts where a couple of sets were being played. A number of people were sitting on the verandah, looking on, smoking and sipping long drinks. I was introduced to one or two of them. But the light was failing and soon the players could hardly see the ball. Featherstone asked one of the men I had been introduced to if he would like a rubber. He said he would. Featherstone looked about for a fourth. He caught sight of a man sitting a little by himself, paused for a second, and went up to him. The two exchanged a few words and then came towards us. We strolled in to the card-room. We had a very nice game. I did not pay much attention to the two men who made up the four. They stood me drinks, and I, a temporary member of the club, returned the compliment. The drinks were very small, quarter whiskies, and in the two hours we played each of us was able to show his open-handedness without an excessive consumption of alcohol. When the advancing hour suggested that the next rubber must be the last we changed from whisky to gin pahits. The rubber came to an end. Featherstone called for the book and the winnings and losings of each one of us were set down. One of the men got up.

"Well, I must be going," he said.

"Going back to the Estate?" asked Featherstone.

"Yes," he nodded. He turned to me. "Shall you be here tomorrow?"

"I hope so."

He went out of the room.

"I'll collect my mem and get along home to dinner," said the other.

"We might be going too," said Featherstone.

"I'm ready whenever you are," I replied.

We got into the car and drove to his house. It was a longish drive. In the darkness I could see nothing much, but presently I realised that we were going up a rather steep hill. We reached the Residency.

It had been an evening like any other, pleasant, but not at all exciting, and I had spent I don't know how many just like it. I did not expect it to leave any sort of impression on me.

Featherstone led me into his sitting-room. It looked comfortable, but it was a trifle ordinary. It had large basket arm-chairs covered with cretonne and on the walls were a great many framed photographs; the tables were littered with papers, magazines and official reports, with pipes, yellow tins of straight-cut cigarettes and pink tins of tobacco. In a row of shelves were untidily stacked a good many books, their bindings stained with damp and the ravages of white ants. Featherstone showed me my room and left me with the words:

"Shall you be ready for a gin pahit in ten minutes?"

"Easily," I said.

I had a bath and changed and went downstairs. Featherstone, ready before me, mixed our drink as he heard me clatter down the wooden staircase. We dined. We talked. The festival which I had been invited to see was the next day but one, but Featherstone told me he had arranged for me before that to be received by the Sultan.

"He's a jolly old boy," he said. "And the palace is a sight for sore eyes."

After dinner we talked a little more, Featherstone put on the gramophone, and we looked at the latest illustrated papers that had arrived from England. Then we went to bed. Featherstone came to my room to see that I had everything I wanted.

"I suppose you haven't any books with you," he said. "I haven't got a thing to read."

"Books?" I cried.

I pointed to my book-bag. It stood upright, bulging oddly, so that it looked like a humpbacked gnome somewhat the worse for liquor.

"Have you got books in there? I thought that was your dirty linen or a camp-bed or something. Is there anything you can lend me?"

"Look for yourself."

Featherstone's boys had unlocked the bag, but quailing before the sight that then discovered itself had done no more. I knew from long experience how to unpack it. I threw it over on its side, seized its leather bottom and, walking backwards, dragged the sack away from its contents. A river of books poured on to the floor. A look of stupefaction came upon Featherstone's face.

"You don't mean to say you travel with as many books as that? By George, what a snip."

He bent down and turning them over rapidly looked at the titles. There were books of all kinds. Volumes of verse, novels, philosophical works, critical studies (they say books about books are profitless, but they certainly make very pleasant reading), biographies, history; there were books to read when you were ill and books to read when your brain, all alert, craved for something to grapple with, there were books that you had always wanted to read, but in the hurry of life at home had never found time to, there were books to read at sea when you were meandering through narrow waters on a tramp steamer, and there were books for bad weather when your whole cabin creaked and you had to wedge yourself in your bunk in order not to fall out; there were books chosen solely for their length, which you took with you when on some expedition you had to travel light, and there were books you could read when you could read nothing else. Finally Featherstone picked out a life of Byron that had recently appeared.

"Hullo, what's this?" he said. "I read a review of it some time ago."

"I believe it's very good," I replied. "I haven't read it yet."

"May I take it? It'll do me for tonight at all events."

"Of course. Take anything you like."

"No, that's enough. Well, good-night. Breakfast at eight-thirty."

When I came down next morning the head boy told me that Featherstone, who had been at work since six, would be in shortly. While I waited for him I glanced at his shelves.

"I see you've got a grand library of books on bridge," I remarked as we sat down to breakfast.

"Yes, I get every one that comes out. I'm very keen on it."

"That fellow we were playing with yesterday plays a good game."

"Which? Hardy?"

"I don't know. Not the one who said he was going to collect his wife. The other."

"Yes, that was Hardy. That was why I asked him to play. He doesn't come to the club very often."

"I hope he will tonight."

"I wouldn't bank on it. He has an estate about thirty miles away. It's a longish ride to come just for a rubber of bridge."

"Is he married?"

"No. Well, yes. But his wife is in England."

"It must be awfully lonely for those men who live by themselves on those estates," I said.

"Oh, he's not so badly off as some. I don't think he much cares about seeing people. I think he'd be just as lonely in London."

There was something in the way Featherstone spoke that struck me as a little strange. His voice had what I can only describe as a shuttered tone. He seemed suddenly to have moved away from me. It was as though one were passing along a street at night and paused for a second to look in at a lighted window that showed a comfortable room and suddenly an invisible hand pulled down a blind. His eyes, which habitually met those of the person he was talking to with frankness, now avoided mine and I had a notion that it was not only my fancy that read in his face an expression of pain. It was drawn for a moment as it might be by a twinge of neuralgia. I could not think of anything to say and Featherstone did not speak. I was conscious that his thoughts, withdrawn from me and what we were about, were turned upon a subject unknown to me. Presently he gave a little sigh, very slight, but unmistakable, and seemed with a deliberate effort to pull himself together.

"I'm going down to the office immediately after breakfast," he said. "What are you going to do with yourself?"

"Oh, don't bother about me. I shall slack around. I'll stroll down and look at the town."

"There's not much to see."

"All the better. I'm fed up with sights."

I found that Featherstone's verandah gave me sufficient entertainment for the morning. It had one of the most enchanting views I had seen in the F.M.S. The Residency was built on the top of a hill and the garden was large and well-cared for. Great trees gave it almost the look of an English park. It had vast lawns and there Tamils, black and emaciated, were scything with deliberate and beautiful gestures. Beyond and below, the jungle grew thickly to the bank of a broad, winding and swiftly flowing river, and on the other side of this, as far as the eye could reach, stretched the wooded hills of Tenggarah. The contrast between the trim lawns, so strangely English, and the savage growth of the jungle beyond pleasantly titillated the fancy. I sat and read and smoked. It is my business to be curious about people and I asked myself how the peace of this scene, charged nevertheless with a tremulous and dark significance, affected Featherstone who lived with it. He knew it under every aspect: at dawn when the mist rising from the river shrouded it with a ghostly pall; in the splendour of noon; and at last when the shadowy gloaming crept softly out of the jungle, like an army making its way with caution in unknown country, and presently enveloped the green lawns and the great flowering trees and the flaunting cassias in the silent night. I wondered whether, unbeknownst to him, the tender and yet strangely sinister aspect of the scene, acting on his nerves and his loneliness, imbued him with some mystical quality so that the life he led, the life of the capable administrator, the sportsman and the good fellow, on occasion seemed to him not quite real. I smiled at my own fancies, for certainly the conversation we had had the night before had not indicated in him any stirrings of the soul. I had thought him quite nice. He had been at Oxford and was a member of a good London club. He seemed to attach a good deal of importance to social things. He was a gentleman and slightly conscious of the fact that he belonged to a better class than most of the Englishmen his life brought him in contact with. I gathered from the various silver pots that adorned his dining-room that he excelled in games. He played tennis and billiards. When he went on leave he hunted and, anxious to keep his weight down, he dieted carefully. He talked a good deal of what he would do when he retired. He hankered after the life of a country gentleman. A little house in Leicestershire, a couple of hunters and neighbours to play bridge with. He would have his pension and he had a little money of his own. But meanwhile he worked hard and did his work, if not brilliantly, certainly with competence. I have no doubt that he was looked upon by his superiors as a reliable officer. He was cut upon a pattern that I knew too well to find very interesting. He was like a novel that is careful, honest and efficient, yet a little ordinary, so that you seem to have read it all before, and you turn the pages listlessly knowing that it will never afford you a surprise or move you to excitement.

But human beings are incalculable and he is a fool who tells himself that he knows what a man is capable of.

In the afternoon Featherstone took me to see the Sultan. We were received by one of his sons, a shy, smiling youth who acted as his A.D.C. He was dressed in a neat blue suit, but round his waist he wore a sarong, white flowers on a yellow ground, on his head a red fez, and on his feet knobby American shoes. The palace, built in the Moorish style, was like a very big doll's house and it was painted bright yellow, which is the royal colour. We were led into a spacious room, furnished with the sort of furniture you would find in an English lodging-house at the seaside, but the chairs were covered with yellow silk. On the floor was a Brussels carpet and on the walls photographs in very grand gilt frames of the Sultan at various state functions. In a cabinet was a large collection of all kinds of fruit done entirely in crochet work. The Sultan came in with several attendants. He was a man of fifty, perhaps, short and stout, dressed in trousers and tunic of a large white and yellow check; round his middle he wore a very beautiful yellow sarong and on his head a white fez. He had large, handsome, friendly eyes. He gave us coffee to drink, sweet cakes to eat and cheroots to smoke. Conversation was not difficult, for he was affable, and he told me that he had never been to a theatre or played cards, for he was very religious, and he had four wives and twenty-four children. The only bar to the happiness of his life seemed to be that common decency obliged him to divide his time equally between his four wives. He said that an hour with one was a month and with another five minutes. I remarked that Professor Einstein — or was it Bergson? — had made similar observations upon time and indeed on this question had given the world much to ponder over. Presently we took our leave and the Sultan presented me with some beautiful white Malaccas.

In the evening we went to the club. One of the men we had played with the day before got up from his chair as we entered.

"Ready for a rubber?" he said.

"Where's our fourth?" I asked.

"Oh, there are several fellows here who'll be glad to play."

"What about that man we played with yesterday?" I had forgotten his name.

"Hardy? He's not here."

"It's not worth while waiting for him," said Featherstone. "He very seldom comes to the club. I was surprised to see him last night."

I did not know why I had the impression that behind the very ordinary words of these two men there was an odd sense of embarrassment. Hardy had made no impression on me and I did not even remember what he looked like. He was just a fourth at the bridge table. I had a feeling that they had something against him. It was no business of mine and I was quite content to play with a man who at that moment joined us. We certainly had a more cheerful game than before. A good deal of chaff passed from one side of the table to the other. We played less serious bridge. We laughed. I wondered if it was only that they were less shy of the stranger who had happened in upon them or if the presence of Hardy had caused in the other two a certain constraint. At half-past eight we broke up and Featherstone and I went back to dine at his house.

After dinner we lounged in arm-chairs and smoked cheroots. For some reason our conversation did not flow easily. I tried topic after topic, but could not get Featherstone to interest himself in any of them. I began to think that in the last twenty-four hours he had said all he had to say. I fell somewhat discouraged into silence. It prolonged itself and again, I did not know why, I had a faint sensation that it was charged with a significance that escaped me. I felt slightly uncomfortable. I had that queer feeling that one sometimes has when sitting in an empty room that one is not by oneself. Presently I was conscious that Featherstone was steadily looking at me. I was sitting by a lamp, but he was in shadow so that the play of his features was hidden from me. But he had very large brilliant eyes and in the half darkness they seemed to shine dimly. They were like new boot-buttons that caught a reflected light. I wondered why he looked at me like that. I gave him a glance and catching his eyes insistently fixed upon me faintly smiled.

"Interesting book that one you lent me last night," he said suddenly, and I could not help thinking his voice did not sound quite natural. The words issued from his lips as though they were pushed from behind.

"Oh, the Life of Byron?" I said breezily. "Have you read it already?"

"A good deal of it. I read till three."

"I've heard it's very well done. I'm not sure that Byron interests me so much as all that. There was so much in him that was so frightfully second-rate. It makes one rather uncomfortable."

"What do you think is the real truth of that story about him and his sister?"

"Augusta Leigh? I don't know very much about it. I've never read Astarte."

"Do you think they were really in love with one another?"

"I suppose so. Isn't it generally believed that she was the only woman he ever genuinely loved?"

"Can you understand it?"

"I can't really. It doesn't particularly shock me. It just seems to me very unnatural. Perhaps 'unnatural' isn't the right word. It's incomprehensible to me. I can't throw myself into the state of feeling in which such a thing seems possible. You know, that's how a writer gets to know the people he writes about, by standing himself in their shoes and feeling with their hearts."

I knew I did not make myself very clear, but I was trying to describe a sensation, an action of the subconscious, which from experience was perfectly familiar to me, but which no words I knew could precisely indicate. I went on.

"Of course she was only his half-sister, but just as habit kills love I should have thought habit would prevent its arising. When two persons have known one another all their lives and lived together in close contact I can't imagine how or why that sudden spark should flash that results in love. The probabilities are that they would be joined by mutual affection and I don't know anything that is more contrary to love than affection."

I could just see in the dimness the outline of a smile flicker for a moment on my host's heavy, and it seemed to me then, somewhat saturnine face.

"You only believe in love at first sight?"

"Well, I suppose I do, but with the proviso that people may have met twenty times before seeing one another. 'Seeing' has an active side and a passive one. Most people we run across mean so little to us that we never bestir ourselves to look at them. We just suffer the impression they make on us."

"Oh, but one's often heard of couples who've known one another for years and it's never occurred to one they cared two straws for each other and suddenly they go and get married. How do you explain that?"

"Well, if you're going to bully me into being logical and consistent, I should suggest that their love is of a different kind. After all, passion isn't the only reason for marriage. It may not even be the best one. Two people may marry because they're lonely or because they're good friends or for convenience' sake. Though I said that affection was the greatest enemy of love, I would never deny that it's a very good substitute. I'm not sure that a marriage founded on it isn't the happiest."

"What did you think of Tim Hardy?"

I was a little surprised at the sudden question, which seemed to have nothing to do with the subject of our conversation.

"I didn't think of him very much. He seemed quite nice. Why?"

"Did he seem to you just like everybody else?"

"Yes. Is there anything peculiar about him? If you'd told me that I'd have paid more attention to him."

"He's very quiet, isn't he? I suppose no one who knew nothing about him would give him a second thought."

I tried to remember what he looked like. The only thing that had struck me when we were playing cards was that he had fine hands. It passed idly through my mind that they were not the sort of hands I should have expected a planter to have. But why a planter should have different hands from anybody else I did not trouble to ask myself. His were somewhat large, but very well formed, with peculiarly long fingers, and the nails were of an admirable shape. They were virile and yet oddly sensitive hands. I noticed this and thought no more about it. But if you are a writer, instinct and the habit of years enable you to store up impressions that you are not aware of.

Sometimes of course they do not correspond with the facts and a woman for example may remain in your subconsciousness as a dark, massive and ox-eyed creature when she is indeed rather small and of a nondescript colouring. But that is of no consequence. The impression may very well be more exact than the sober truth. And now, seeking to call up from the depths of me a picture of this man I had a feeling of some ambiguity. He was cleanshaven and his face, oval but not thin, seemed strangely pale under the tan of long exposure to the tropical sun. His features were vague. I did not know whether I remembered it or only imagined now that his rounded chin gave one the impression of a certain weakness. He had thick brown hair, just turning grey, and a long wisp fell down constantly over his forehead. He pushed it back with a gesture that had become habitual. His brown eyes were rather large and gentle, but perhaps a little sad; they had a melting softness which, I could imagine, might be very appealing.

After a pause Featherstone continued:

"It's rather strange that I should run across Tim Hardy here after all these years. But that's the way of the F.M.S. People move about and you find yourself in the same place as a man you'd known years before in another part of the country. I first knew Tim when he had an estate near Sibuku. Have you ever been there?"

"No. Where is it?"

"Oh, it's up north. Towards Siam. It wouldn't be worth your while to go. It's just like every other place in the F.M.S. But it was rather nice. It had a very jolly little club and there were some quite decent people. There was the schoolmaster and the head of the police, the doctor, the padre and the government engineer. The usual lot, you know. A few planters. Three or four women. I was A.D.O. It was one of my first jobs. Tim Hardy had an estate about twenty-five miles away. He lived there with his sister. They had a bit of money of their own and he'd bought the place. Rubber was pretty good then and he wasn't doing at all badly. We rather cottoned on to one another. Of course it's a toss-up with planters. Some of them are very good fellows, but they're not exactly . . ." he sought for a word or a phrase that did not sound snobbish. "Well, they're not the sort of people you'd be likely to meet at home. Tim and Olive were of one's own class, if you understand what I mean."

"Olive was the sister?"

"Yes. They'd had a rather unfortunate past. Their parents had separated when they were quite small, seven or eight, and the mother had taken Olive and the father had kept Tim. Tim went to Clifton, they were West Country people, and only came home for the holidays. His father was a retired naval man who lived at Fowey. But Olive went with her mother to Italy. She was educated in Florence; she spoke Italian perfectly and French too. For all those years Tim and Olive never saw one another once, but they used to write to one another regularly. They'd been very much attached when they were children. As far as I could understand, life when their people were living together had been rather stormy with all sorts of scenes and upsets, you know the sort of thing that happens when two people who are married don't get on together, and that had thrown them on their own resources. They were left a good deal to themselves. Then Mrs. Hardy died and Olive came home to England and went back to her father. She was eighteen then and Tim was seventeen. A year later the war broke out. Tim joined up and his father, who was over fifty, got some job at Portsmouth. I take it he had been a hard liver and a heavy drinker. He broke down before the end of the war and died after a lingering illness. They don't seem to have had any relations. They were the last of a rather old family; they had a fine old house in Dorsetshire that had belonged to them for a good many generations, but they had never been able to afford to live in it and it was always let. I remember seeing photographs of it. It was very much a gentleman's house, of grey stone and rather stately, with a coat of arms carved over the front door and mullioned windows. Their great ambition was to make enough money to be able to live in it. They used to talk about it a lot. They never spoke as though either of them would marry, but always as though it were a settled thing that they would remain together. It was rather funny considering how young they were."

"How old were they then?" I asked.

"Well, I suppose he was twenty-five or twenty-six and she was a year older. They were awfully kind to me when I first went up to Sibuku. They took a fancy to me at once. You see, we had more in common than most of the people there. I think they were glad of my company. They weren't particularly popular."

"Why not?" I asked.

"They were rather reserved and you couldn't help seeing that they liked their own society better than other people's. I don't know if you've noticed it, but that always seems to put people's backs up. They resent it somehow if they have a feeling that you can get along very well without them."

"It's tiresome, isn't it?" I said.

"It was rather a grievance to the other planters that Tim was his own master and had private means. They had to put up with an old Ford to get about in, but Tim had a real car. Tim and Olive were very nice when they came to the club and they played in the tennis tournaments and all that sort of thing, but you had an impression that they were always glad to get away again. They'd dine out with people and make themselves very pleasant, but it was pretty obvious that they'd just as soon have stayed home. If you had any sense you couldn't blame them. I don't know if you've been much to planters' houses. They're a bit dreary. A lot of gim-crack furniture and silver ornaments and tiger skins. And the food's uneatable. But the Hardys had made their bungalow rather nice. There was nothing very grand in it; it was just easy and homelike and comfortable. Their living-room was like a drawing-room in an English country house. You felt that their things meant something to them and that they had had them a long time. It was a very jolly house to stay at. The bungalow was in the middle of the estate, but it was on the brow of a little hill and you looked right over the rubber trees to the sea in the distance. Olive took a lot of trouble with her garden and it was really topping. I never saw such a show of cannas. I used to go there for weekends. It was only about half an hour's drive to the sea and we'd take our lunch with us and bathe and sail. Tim kept a small boat there. Those days were grand. I never knew one could enjoy oneself so much. It's a beautiful bit of coast and it was really extraordinarily romantic. Then in the evenings we'd play patience and chess or turn on the gramophone. The cooking was damned good too. It was a change from what one generally got. Olive had taught their cook to make all sorts of Italian dishes and we used to have great wallops of macaroni and risotto and gnocchi and things like that. I couldn't help envying them their life, it was so jolly and peaceful, and when they talked of what they'd do when they went back to England for good I used to tell them they'd always regret what they'd left.

"'We've been very happy here,'" said Olive.

"She had a way of looking at Tim, with a slow, sidelong glance from under her long eyelashes, that was rather engaging.

"In their own house they were quite different from what they were when they went out. They were so easy and cordial. Everybody admitted that and I'm bound to say that people enjoyed going there. They often asked people over. They had the gift of making you feel at home. It was a very happy house, if you know what I mean. Of course no one could help seeing how attached they were to one another. And whatever people said about their being standoffish and self-centered, they were bound to be rather touched by the affection they had for one another. People said they couldn't have been more united if they were married, and when you saw how some couples got on you couldn't help thinking they made most marriages look rather like a washout. They seemed to think the same things at the same time. They had little private jokes that made them laugh like children. They were so charming with one another, so gay and happy, that really to stay with them was, well, a spiritual refreshment. I don't know what else you could call it. When you left them, after a couple of days at the bungalow, you felt that you'd absorbed some of their peace and their sober gaiety. It was as though your soul had been sluiced with cool clear water. You felt strangely purified."

It was singular to hear Featherstone talking in this exalted strain. He looked so spruce in his smart white coat, technically known as a bum-freezer, his moustache was so trim, his thick curly hair so carefully brushed, that his high-flown language made me a trifle uncomfortable. But I realised that he was trying to express in his clumsy way a very sincerely felt emotion.

"What was Olive Hardy like?" I asked.

"I'll show you. I've got quite a lot of snapshots."

He got up from his chair and going to a shelf brought me a large album. It was the usual thing, indifferent photographs of people in groups and unflattering likenesses of single figures. They were in bathing dress or in shorts or tennis things, generally with their faces all screwed up because the sun blinded them, or puckered by the distortion of laughter. I recognised Hardy, not much changed after ten years, with his wisp of hair hanging across his forehead. I remembered him better now that I saw the snapshots. In them he looked nice and fresh and young. He had an alertness of expression that was attractive and that I certainly had not noticed when I saw him. In his eyes was a sort of eagerness for life that danced and sparkled through the fading print. I glanced at the photographs of his sister. Her bathing dress showed that she had a good figure, well-developed, but slender; and her legs were long and slim.

"They look rather alike," I said.

"Yes, although she was a year older they might have been twins, they were so much alike. They both had the same oval face and that pale skin without any colour in the cheeks, and they both had those soft brown eyes, very liquid and appealing, so that you felt whatever they did you could never be angry with them. And they both had a sort of careless elegance that made them look charming whatever they wore and however untidy they were. He's lost that now, I suppose, but he certainly had it when I first knew him. They always rather reminded me of the brother and sister in Twelfth Night. You know whom I mean."

"Viola and Sebastian."

"They never seemed to belong quite to the present. There was something Elizabethan about them. I don't think it was only because I was very young then that I couldn't help feeling they were strangely romantic somehow. I could see them living in Illyria."

I gave one of the snapshots another glance.

"The girl looks as though she had a good deal more character than her brother," I remarked.

"She had. I don't know if you'd have called Olive beautiful, but she was awfully attractive. There was something poetic in her, a sort of lyrical quality as it were, that coloured her movements, her acts and everything about her. It seemed to exalt her above common cares. There was something so candid in her expression, so courageous and independent in her bearing, that — oh, I don't know, it made mere beauty just flat and dull."

"You speak as if you'd been in love with her," I interrupted.

"Of course I was. I should have thought you'd guessed that at once. I was frightfully in love with her."

"Was it love at first sight?" I smiled.

"Yes, I think it was, but I didn't know it for a month or so. When it suddenly struck me that what I felt for her — I don't know how to explain it, it was a sort of shattering turmoil that affected every bit of me — that that was love, I knew I'd felt it all along. It was not only her looks, though they were awfully alluring, the smoothness of her pale skin and the way her hair fell over her forehead and the grave sweetness of her brown eyes, it was more than that; you had a sensation of well-being when you were with her, as though you could relax and be quite natural and needn't pretend to be anything you weren't. You felt she was incapable of meanness. It was impossible to think of her as envious of other people or catty. She seemed to have a natural generosity of soul. One could be silent with her for an hour at a time and yet feel that one had had a good time."

"A rare gift," I said.

"She was a wonderful companion. If you made a suggestion to do something she was always glad to fall in with it. She was the least exacting girl I ever knew. You could throw her over at the last minute and however disappointed she was it made no difference. Next time you saw her she was just as cordial and serene as ever."

"Why didn't you marry her?"

Featherstone's cheroot had gone out. He threw the stub away and deliberately lit another. He did not answer for a while. It may seem strange to persons who live in a highly civilised state that he should confide these intimate things to a stranger; it did not seem strange to me. I was used to it. People who live so desperately alone, in the remote places of the earth, find it a relief to tell someone whom in all probability they will never meet again the story that has burdened perhaps for years their waking thoughts and their dreams at night. And I have an inkling that the fact of your being a writer attracts their confidence. They feel that what they tell you will excite your interest in an impersonal way that makes it easier for them to discharge their souls. Besides, as we all know from our own experience, it is never unpleasant to talk about oneself.

"Why didn't you marry her?" I had asked him.

"I wanted to badly enough," Featherstone answered at length. "But I hesitated to ask her. Although she was always so nice to me and so easy to get on with, and we were such good friends, I always felt that there was something a little mysterious in her. Although she was so simple, so frank and natural, you never quite got over the feeling of an inner kernel of aloofness, as if deep in her heart she guarded, not a secret, but a sort of privacy of the soul that not a living person would ever be allowed to know. I don't know if I make myself clear."

"I think so."

"I put it down to her upbringing. They never talked of their mother, but somehow I got the impression that she was one of those neurotic, emotional women who wreck their own happiness and are a pest to everyone connected with them. I had a suspicion that she'd led rather a hectic life in Florence and it struck me that Olive owed her beautiful serenity to a disciplined effort of her own will and that her aloofness was a sort of citadel she'd built to protect herself from the knowledge of all sorts of shameful things. But of course that aloofness was awfully captivating. It was strangely exciting to think that if she loved you, and you were married to her, you would at last pierce right into the hidden heart of that mystery; and you felt that if you could share that with her it would be as it were a consummation of all you'd ever desired in your life. Heaven wouldn't be in it. You know, I felt about it just like Bluebeard's wife about the forbidden chamber in the castle. Every room was open to me, but I should never rest till I had gone into that last one that was locked against me."

My eye was caught by a chik-chak, a little brown house lizard with a large head, high up on the wall. It is a friendly little beast and it is good to see it in a house. It watched a fly. It was quite still. On a sudden it made a dart and then as the fly flew away fell back with a sort of jerk into a strange immobility.

"And there was another thing that made me hesitate. I couldn't bear the thought that if I proposed to her and she refused me she wouldn't let me come to the bungalow in the same old way. I should have hated that, I enjoyed going there so awfully. It made me so happy to be with her. But you know, sometimes one can't help oneself. I did ask her at last, but it was almost by accident. One evening, after dinner, when we were sitting on the verandah by ourselves, I took her hand. She withdrew it at once.

" 'Why did you do that?' I asked her.

" 'I don't very much like being touched,' she said. She turned her head a little and smiled. 'Are you hurt? You mustn't mind, it's just a funny feeling I have. I can't help it.'

" 'I wonder if it's ever occurred to you that I'm frightfully fond of you,' I said.

"I expect I was terribly awkward about it, but I'd never proposed to anyone before." Featherstone gave a little sound that was not quite a chuckle and not quite a sigh. "For the matter of that, I've never proposed to anyone since. She didn't say anything for a minute. Then she said:

" 'I'm very glad, but I don't think I want you to be anything more than that.'

" 'Why not?' I asked.

" 'I could never leave Tim.'

" 'But supposing he marries?'

" 'He never will.'

"I'd gone so far then that I thought I'd better go on. But my throat was so dry that I could hardly speak. I was shaking with nervousness.

" 'I'm frightfully in love with you, Olive. I want to marry you more than anything in the world.'

"She put her hand very gently on my arm. It was like a flower falling to the ground.

" 'No, dear, I can't,' she said.

"I was silent. It was difficult for me to say what I wanted to. I'm naturally rather shy. She was a girl. I couldn't very well tell her that it wasn't quite the same thing living with a husband and living with a brother. She was normal and healthy; she must want to have babies; it wasn't reasonable to starve her natural instincts. It was such a waste of her youth. But it was she who spoke first.

" 'Don't let's talk about this any more,' she said. 'D'you mind? It did strike me once or twice that perhaps you cared for me. Tim noticed it. I was sorry because I was afraid it would break up our friendship. I don't want it to do that, Mark. We do get on so well together, the three of us, and we have such jolly times. I don't know what we should do without you now.'

" 'I thought of that too,' I said.

" 'D'you think it need?' she asked me.

" 'My dear, I don't want it to,' I said. 'You must know how much I love coming here. I've never been so happy anywhere before!'

" 'You're not angry with me?'

" 'Why should I be? It's not your fault. It only means that you're not in love with me. If you were you wouldn't care a hang about Tim.'

" 'You are rather sweet,' she said.

"She put her arm round my neck and kissed me lightly on the cheek. I had a notion that in her mind it settled our relation. She adopted me as a second brother.

"A few weeks later Tim went back to England. The tenant of their house in Dorset was leaving and though there was another in the offing, he thought he ought to be on the spot to conduct negotiations. And he wanted some new machinery for the estate. He thought he'd get it at the same time. He didn't expect to be gone more than three months and Olive made up her mind not to go. She knew hardly anyone in England, and it was practically a foreign country to her, she didn't mind being left alone, and she wanted to look after the estate. Of course they could have put a manager in charge, but that wasn't the same thing. Rubber was falling and in case of accidents it was just as well that one or other of them should be there. I promised Tim I'd look after her and if she wanted me she could always call me up. My proposal hadn't changed anything. We carried on as though nothing had happened. I don't know whether she'd told Tim. He made no sign that he knew. Of course I loved her as much as ever, but I kept it to myself. I have a good deal of self-control, you know. I had a sort of feeling I hadn't a chance. I hoped eventually my love would change into something else and we could just be wonderful friends. It's funny, it never has, you know. I suppose I was hit too badly ever to get quite over it.

"She went down to Penang to see Tim off and when she came back I met her at the station and drove her home. I couldn't very well stay at the bungalow while Tim was away, but I went over every Sunday and had tiffin and we'd go down to the sea and have a bathe. People tried to be kind to her and asked her to stay with them, but she wouldn't. She seldom left the estate. She had plenty to do. She read a lot. She was never bored. She seemed quite happy in her own company, and when she had visitors it was only from a sense of duty. She didn't want them to think her ungracious. But it was an effort and she told me she heaved a sigh of relief when she saw the last of them and could again enjoy without disturbance the peaceful loneliness of the bungalow. She was a very curious girl. It was strange that at her age she should be so indifferent to parties and the other small gaieties the station afforded. Spiritually, if you know what I mean, she was entirely self-supporting. I don't know how people found out that I was in love with her; I thought I'd never given myself away in anything, but I had hints here and there that they knew. I gathered they thought Olive hadn't gone home with her brother on my account. One woman, a Mrs.

Sergison, the policeman's wife, actually asked me when they were going to be able to congratulate me. Of course I pretended I didn't know what she was talking about, but it didn't go down very well. I couldn't help being amused. I meant so little to Olive in that way that I really believe she'd entirely forgotten that I'd asked her to marry me. I can't say she was unkind to me, I don't think she could have been unkind to anyone; but she treated me with just the casualness with which a sister might treat a younger brother. She was two or three years older than I. She was always terribly glad to see me, but it never occurred to her to put herself out for me, she was almost amazingly intimate with me; but unconsciously, you know, as you might be with a person you'd known so well all your life that you never thought of putting on frills with him. I might not have been a man at all, but an old coat that she wore all the time because it was easy and comfortable and she didn't mind what she did in it. I should have been crazy not to see that she was a thousand miles away from loving me.

"Then one day, three or four weeks before Tim was due back, when I went to the bungalow I saw she'd been crying. I was startled. She was always so composed. I'd never seen her upset over anything.

" 'Hullo, what's the matter?' I said.

" 'Nothing.'

" 'Come off it, darling,' I said. 'What have you been crying about?'

"She tried to smile."

" 'I wish you hadn't got such sharp eyes,' she said. 'I think I'm being silly. I've just had a cable from Tim to say he's postponed his sailing.'

" 'Oh, my dear, I am sorry,' I said. 'You must be awfully disappointed.'

" 'I've been counting the days. I want him back so badly.'

" 'Does he say why he's postponing?' I asked.

" 'No, he says he's writing. I'll show you the cable.'

"I saw that she was very nervous. Her slow quiet eyes were filled with apprehension and there was a little frown of anxiety between her brows. She went into her bedroom and in a moment came back with the cable. I felt that she was watching me anxiously as I read. So far as I remember it ran: *Darling, I cannot sail on the seventh after all. Please forgive me. Am writing fully. Fondest love. Tim.*

" 'Well, perhaps the machinery he wanted isn't ready and he can't bring himself to sail without it,' I said.

" 'What could it matter if it came by a later ship? Anyhow, it'll be hung up at Penang.'

" 'It may be something about the house.'

" 'If it is why doesn't he say so? He must know how frightfully anxious I am.'

" 'It wouldn't occur to him,' I said. 'After all, when you're away you don't realise that the people you've left behind don't know something that you take as a matter of course.'

"She smiled again, but now more happily.

" 'I daresay you're right. In point of fact Tim is a little like that. He's always been rather slack and casual. I daresay I've been making a mountain out of a molehill. I must just wait patiently for his letter.'

"Olive was a girl with a lot of self-control and I saw her by an effort of will pull herself together. The little line between her eyebrows vanished and she was once more her serene, smiling and kindly self. She was always gentle: that day she had a mildness so heavenly that it was shattering. But for the rest of the time I could see that she kept her restlessness in check only by the deliberate exercise of her common sense. It was as though she had a foreboding of ill. I was with her the day before the mail was due. Her anxiety was all the more pitiful to see because she took such pains to hide it. I was always busy on mail day, but I promised to go up to the estate later on and hear the news. I was just thinking of starting when Hardy's seis came along in the car with a message from the amah asking me to go at once to her mistress. The amah was a decent, elderly woman to whom I had given a dollar or two and said that if anything went wrong on the estate she was to let me know at once. I jumped into my car. When I arrived I found the amah waiting for me on the steps.

" 'A letter came this morning,' she said.

"I interrupted her. I ran up the steps. The sitting-room was empty.

" 'Olive,' I called.

"I went into the passage and suddenly I heard a sound that froze my heart. The amah had followed me and now she opened the door to Olive's room. The sound I had heard was the sound of Olive crying. I went in. She was lying on her bed, on her face, and her sobs shook her from head to foot. I put my hand on her shoulder.

" 'Olive, what is it?' I asked.

" 'Who's that?' she cried. She sprang to her feet suddenly, as though she were scared out of her wits. And then: 'Oh, it's you,' she said. She stood in front of me, with her head thrown back and her eyes closed, and the tears streamed from them. It was dreadful. 'Tim's married,' she gasped, and her face screwed up in a sort of grimace of pain.

"I must admit that for one moment I had a thrill of exultation, it was like a little electric shock tingling through my heart; it struck me that now I had a chance, she might be willing to marry me; I know it was terribly selfish of me; you see, the news had taken me by surprise; but it was only for a moment, after that I was melted by her awful distress and the only thing I felt was deep sorrow because she was unhappy. I put my arm round her waist.

" 'Oh, my dear, I'm so sorry,' I said. 'Don't stay here. Come into the sitting-room and sit down and we'll talk about it. Let me give you something to drink.'

"She let me lead her into the next room and we sat down on the sofa. I told the amah to fetch the whisky and syphon and I mixed her a good strong stengah and made her drink a little. I took her in my arms and rested her head on my shoulder. She let me do what I liked with her. The great tears streamed down her poor face.

" 'How could he?' she moaned. 'How could he?'

" 'My darling,' I said, 'it was bound to happen sooner or later. He's a young man. How could you expect him never to marry? It's only natural.'

" 'No, no, no,' she gasped.

"Tight-clenched in her hand I saw she had a letter and I guessed that it was Tim's.

" 'What does he say?' I asked.

"She gave a frightened movement and clutched the letter to her heart as though she thought I would take it from her.

" 'He says he couldn't help himself. He says he had to. What does it mean?'

" 'Well, you know, in his way he's just as attractive as you are. He has so much charm. I suppose he just fell madly in love with some girl and she with him.'

" 'He's so weak,' she moaned.

" 'Are they coming out?' I asked.

" 'They sailed yesterday. He says it won't make any difference. He's insane. How *can* I stay here?'

"She began to cry hysterically. It was torture to see that girl, usually so calm, utterly shattered by her emotion. I had always felt that her lovely serenity masked a capacity for deep feeling. But the abandon of her distress simply broke me up. I held her in my arms and kissed her, her eyes and her wet cheek and her hair. I don't think she knew what I was doing. I was hardly conscious of it myself. I was so deeply moved.

" 'What shall I do?' she wailed.

" 'Why won't you marry me?' I said.

"She tried to withdraw herself from me, but I wouldn't let her go.

" 'After all, it would be a way out,' I said.

" 'How can I marry you?' she moaned. 'I'm years older than you are.'

" ' 'Oh, what nonsense, two or three. What do I care?'

" 'No, no.'

" 'Why not?' I said.

" 'I don't love you,' she said.

" 'What does that matter? I love you.'

"I don't know what I said. I told her that I'd try to make her happy. I said I'd never ask anything from her but what she was prepared to give me. I talked and talked. I tried to make her see reason. I felt that she didn't want to stay there, in the same place as Tim, and I told her that I'd be moved soon to some other district. I thought that might tempt her. She couldn't deny that we'd always got on awfully well together. After a time she did seem to grow a little quieter. I had a feeling that she was listening to me. I had even a sort of feeling that she knew that she was lying in my arms and that it comforted her. I made her drink a drop more whisky. I gave her a cigarette. At last I thought I might be just mildly facetious.

" 'You know, I'm not a bad sort really,' I said. 'You might do worse.'

" 'You don't know me,' she said. 'You know nothing whatever about me.'

" 'I'm capable of learning,' I said.

"She smiled a little.

" 'You're awfully kind, Mark,' she said.

" 'Say yes, Olive,' I begged.

"She gave a deep sigh. For a long time she stared at the ground. But she did not move and I felt the softness of her body in my arms. I waited. I was frightfully nervous and the minutes seemed endless.

" 'All right,' she said at last, as though she were not conscious that any time had passed between my prayer and her answer.

"I was so moved that I had nothing to say. But when I wanted to kiss her lips, she turned her face away, and wouldn't let me. I wanted us to be married at once, but she was quite firm that she wouldn't. She insisted on waiting till Tim came back. You know how sometimes you see so clearly in people's thoughts that you're more certain of them than if they'd spoken them; I saw that she couldn't quite believe that what Tim had written was true and that she had a sort of miserable hope that it was all a mistake and he wasn't married after all. It gave me a pang, but I loved her so much, I just bore it. I was willing to bear anything. I adored her. She wouldn't even let me tell anyone that we were engaged. She made me promise not to say a word till Tim's return. She said she couldn't bear the thought of the congratulations and all that. She wouldn't even let me make any announcement of Tim's marriage. She was obstinate about it. I had a notion that she felt if the fact were spread about it gave it a certainty that she didn't want it to have.

"But the matter was taken out of her hands. News travels mysteriously in the East. I don't know what Olive had said in the amah's hearing when first she received the news of Tim's marriage; anyhow, the Hardys' seis told the Sergisons' and Mrs. Sergison attacked me the next time I went into the club.

" 'I hear Tim Hardy's married,' she said.

" 'Oh?' I answered, unwilling to commit myself.

"She smiled at my blank face, and told me that her amah having told her the rumour she had rung up Olive and asked her if it was true. Olive's answer had been rather odd. She had not exactly confirmed it, but said that she had received a letter from Tim telling her he was married.

" 'She's a strange girl,' said Mrs. Sergison. 'When I asked her for details she said she had none to give and when I said: "Aren't you thrilled?" she didn't answer.'

" 'Olive's devoted to Tim, Mrs. Sergison,' I said. 'His marriage has naturally been a shock to her. She knows nothing about Tim's wife. She's nervous about her.'

" 'And when are you two going to be married?' she asked me abruptly.

" 'What an embarrassing question!' I said, trying to laugh it off.

"She looked at me shrewdly.

" 'Will you give me your word of honour that you're not engaged to her?'

"I didn't like to tell her a deliberate lie, nor to ask her to mind her own business, and I'd promised Olive faithfully that I would say nothing till Tim got back. I hedged.

" 'Mrs. Sergison,' I said, 'when there's anything to tell I promise that you'll be the first person to hear it. All I can say to you now is that I do want to marry Olive more than anything in the world.'

" 'I'm very glad that Tim's married,' she answered. 'And I hope she'll marry you very soon. It was a morbid and unhealthy life that they led up there, those two, they kept far too much to themselves and they were far too much absorbed in one another.'

"I saw Olive practically every day. I felt that she didn't want me to make love to her, and I contented myself with kissing her when I came and when I went. She was very nice to me, kindly and thoughtful; I knew she was glad to see me and sorry when it was time for me to go. Ordinarily, she was apt to fall into silence, but during this time she talked more than I had ever heard her talk before. But never of the future and never of Tim and his wife. She told me a lot about her life in Florence with her mother. She had led a strange lonely life, mostly with servants and governesses, while her mother, I suspected, engaged in one affair after another with vague Italian counts and Russian princes. I guessed that by the time she was fourteen there wasn't much she didn't know. It was natural for her to be quite unconventional: in the only world she knew till she was eighteen conventions weren't mentioned because they didn't exist. Gradually, Olive seemed to regain her serenity and I should have thought that she was beginning to accustom herself to the thought of Tim's marriage if it hadn't been that I couldn't but notice how pale and tired she looked. I made up my mind that the moment he arrived I'd press her to marry me at once. I could get short leave whenever I asked for it, and by the time that was up I thought I could manage a transfer to some other post. What she wanted was change of air and fresh scenes.

"We knew, of course, within a day when Tim's ship would reach Penang, but it was a question whether she'd get in soon enough for him to catch the train and I wrote to the P. & O. agent asking him to telegraph as soon as he had definite news. When

I got the wire and took it up to Olive I found that she'd just received one from Tim. The ship had docked early and he was arriving next day. The train was supposed to get in at eight o'clock in the morning, but it was liable to be anything from one to six hours late, and I bore with me an invitation from Mrs. Sergison asking Olive to come back with me to stay the night with her so that she would be on the spot and need not go to the station till the news came through that the train was coming.

"I was immensely relieved. I thought that when the blow at last fell Olive wouldn't feel it so much. She had worked herself up into such a state that I couldn't help thinking that she must have a reaction now. She might take a fancy to her sister-in-law. There was no reason why they shouldn't all three get on very well together. To my surprise Olive said she wasn't coming down to the station to meet them.

" 'They'll be awfully disappointed,' I said.

" 'I'd rather wait here,' she answered. She smiled a little. 'Don't argue with me, Mark, I've quite made up my mind.'

" 'I've ordered breakfast in my house,' I said.

" 'That's all right. You meet them and take them to your house and give them breakfast, and then they can come along here afterwards. Of course I'll send the car down.'

" 'I don't suppose they'll want to breakfast if you're not there,' I said.

" 'Oh, I'm sure they will. If the train gets in on time they wouldn't have thought of breakfasting before it arrived and they'll be hungry. They won't want to take this long drive without anything to eat.'

"I was puzzled. She had been looking forward so intensely to Tim's coming, it seemed strange that she should want to wait all by herself while the rest of us were having a jolly breakfast. I suppose she was nervous and wanted to delay as long as possible meeting the strange woman who had come to take her place. It seemed unreasonable. I couldn't see that an hour sooner or an hour later could make any difference, but I knew women were funny, and anyhow I felt Olive wasn't in the mood for me to press it.

" 'Telephone when you're starting so that I shall know when to expect you,' she said.

" 'All right,' I said, 'but you know I shan't be able to come with them. It's my day for going to Lahad.'

"This was a town that I had to go to once a week to take cases. It was a good way off and one had to ferry across a river, which took some time, so that I never got back till late. There were a few Europeans there and a club. I generally had to go on there for a bit to be sociable and see that things were getting along all right.

" 'Besides,' I added, 'with Tim bringing his wife home for the first time I don't suppose he'll want me about. But if you'd like to ask me to dinner I'll be glad to come to that.'

"Olive smiled.

" 'I don't think it'll be my place to issue any more invitations, will it?' she said. 'You must ask the bride.'

"She said this so lightly that my heart leaped. I had a feeling that at last she had made up her mind to accept the altered circumstances and, what was more, was accepting them with cheerfulness. She asked me to stay to dinner. Generally I left about eight and dined at home. She was very sweet, almost tender, and I was happier than I'd been for weeks. I had never been more desperately in love with her. I had a couple of gin pahits and I think I was in rather good form at dinner. I know I made her laugh. I felt that at last she was casting away the load of misery that had oppressed her. That was why I didn't let myself be very much disturbed by what happened at the end.

" 'Don't you think it's about time you were leaving a presumably maiden lady?' she said.

"She spoke in a manner that was so quietly gay that I answered without hesitation:

" 'Oh, my dear, if you think you've got a shred of reputation left you deceive yourself. You're surely not under the impression that the ladies of Sibuku don't know that I've been coming to see you every day for a month. The general feeling is that if we're not married it's high time we were. Don't you think it would be just as well if I broke it to them that we're engaged?'

" 'Oh, Mark, you mustn't take our engagement very seriously,' she said.

"I laughed.

" 'How else do you expect me to take it? It is serious.'

"She shook her head a little.

" 'No. I was upset and hysterical that day. You were being very sweet to me. I said yes because I was too miserable to say no. But now I've had time to collect myself. Don't think me unkind. I made a mistake. I've been very much to blame. You must forgive me.'

" 'Oh, darling, you're talking nonsense. You've got nothing against me.'

"She looked at me steadily. She was quite calm. She had even a little smile at the back of her eyes.

" 'I can't marry you. I can't marry anyone. It was absurd of me ever to think I could.'

"I didn't answer at once. She was in a queer state and I thought it better not to insist.

" 'I suppose I can't drag you to the altar by main force,' I said.

"I held out my hand and she gave me hers. I put my arm round her, and she made no attempt to withdraw. She suffered me to kiss her as usual on her cheek.

"Next morning I met the train. For once in a way it was punctual. Tim waved to me as his carriage passed the place where I was standing, and by the time I had walked up he had already jumped out and was handing down his wife. He grasped my hand warmly.

" 'Where's Olive?' he said, with a glance along the platform. 'This is Sally.'

"I shook hands with her and at the same time explained why Olive was not there.

" 'It was frightfully early, wasn't it?' said Mrs. Hardy.

"I told them that the plan was for them to come and have a bit of breakfast at my house and then drive home.

" 'I'd love a bath,' said Mrs. Hardy.

" 'You shall have one,' I said.

"She was really an extremely pretty little thing, very fair, with enormous blue eyes and a lovely little straight nose. Her skin, all milk and roses, was exquisite. A little of the chorus girl type, of course, and you may happen to think that rather namby-pamby, but in that style she was enchanting. We drove to my house, they both had a bath and Tim a shave; I just had two minutes alone with him. He asked me how Olive had taken his marriage. I told him she'd been upset.

" 'I was afraid so,' he said, frowning a little. He gave a short sigh. 'I couldn't do anything else.'

"I didn't understand what he meant. At that moment Mrs. Hardy joined us and slipped her arm through her husband's. He took her hand in his and gently pressed it. He gave her a look that had in it something pleased and humorously affectionate, as though he didn't take her quite seriously, but enjoyed his sense of proprietorship and was proud of her beauty. She really was lovely. She was not at all shy, she asked me to call her Sally before we'd known one another ten minutes, and she was quick in the uptake. Of course, just then she was excited at arriving. She'd never been East and everything thrilled her. It was quite obvious that she was head over heels in love with Tim. Her eyes never left him and she hung on his words. We had a jolly breakfast and then we parted. They got into their car to go home and I into mine to go to Lahad. I promised to go straight to the estate from there and in point of fact it was out of my way to pass by my house. I took a change with me. I didn't see why Olive shouldn't like Sally very much, she was frank and gay, and ingenuous; she was extremely young, she couldn't have been more than nineteen, and her wonderful prettiness couldn't fail to appeal to Olive. I was just as glad to have had a reasonable excuse to leave the three of them by themselves for the day, but as I started out from Lahad I had a notion that by the time I arrived they would all be pleased to see me. I drove up to the bungalow and blew my horn two or three times, expecting someone to appear. Not a soul. The place was in total darkness. I was surprised. It was absolutely silent. I couldn't make it out. They must be in. Very odd, I thought. I waited a moment, then got out of the car and walked up the steps. At the top of them I stumbled over something. I swore and bent down to see what it was; it had felt like a body. There was a cry and I saw it was the amah. She shrank back cowering as I touched her and broke into loud wails.

" 'What the hell's the matter?' I cried, and then I felt a hand on my arm and heard a voice. Tuan, Tuan. I turned and in the darkness recognised Tim's head boy. He began to speak in little frightened gasps. I listened to him with horror. What he told me was unspeakable. I pushed him aside and rushed into the house. The sitting-room was dark. I turned on the light. The first thing I saw was Sally huddled up in an arm-chair. She was startled by my sudden appearance and cried out. I could hardly speak. I asked her if it was true. When she told me it was I felt the room suddenly going round and round me. I had to sit down. As the car that bore Tim and Sally drove up the road that led to the house and Tim sounded the Klaxon to announce their arrival and the boys and the amah ran out to greet them there was the sound of a shot. They ran to Olive's room and found her lying in front of the looking-glass in a pool of blood. She had shot herself with Tim's revolver.

" 'Is she dead?' I said.

" 'No, they sent for the doctor, and he took her to the hospital.'

"I hardly knew what I was doing. I didn't even trouble to tell Sally where I was going. I got up and staggered to the door. I got into the car and told my seis to drive like hell to the hospital. I rushed in. I asked where she was. They tried to bar my way, but I pushed them aside. I knew where the private rooms were. Someone clung to my arm, but I shook him off. I vaguely understood that the doctor had given instructions that no one was to go into the room. I didn't care about that. There was an orderly at the door; he put out his arm to prevent me from passing. I swore at him and told him to get out of my way. I suppose I made a row, I was beside myself; the door was opened and the doctor came out.

" 'Who's making all this noise?' he said. 'Oh, it's you. What do you want?'

" 'Is she dead?' I asked.

" 'No. But she's unconscious. She never regained consciousness. It's only a matter of an hour or two.'

" 'I want to see her.'

" 'You can't.'

" 'I'm engaged to her.'

" 'You?' he cried, and even at that moment I was aware that he looked at me strangely. 'That's all the more reason.'

"I didn't know what he meant. I was stupid with horror.

" 'Surely you can do something to save her,' I cried.

"He shook his head.

" 'If you saw her you wouldn't wish it,' he said.

"I stared at him aghast. In the silence I heard a man's convulsive sobbing.

" 'Who's that?' I asked.

" 'Her brother.'

"Then I felt a hand on my arm. I looked round and saw it was Mrs. Sergison.

" 'My poor boy,' she said. 'I'm so sorry for you.'

" 'What on earth made her do it?' I groaned.

" 'Come away, my dear,' said Mrs. Sergison. 'You can do no good here.'

" 'No, I must stay,' I said.

" 'Well, go and sit in my room,' said the doctor.

"I was so broken that I let Mrs. Sergison take me by the arm and lead me into the doctor's private room. She made me sit down. I couldn't bring myself to realise that it was true. I thought it was a horrible nightmare from which I must awake. I don't know how long we sat there. Three hours. Four hours. At last the doctor came in.

" 'It's all over,' he said.

"Then I couldn't help myself, I began to cry. I didn't care what they thought of me. I was so frightfully unhappy.

"We buried her next day.

"Mrs. Sergison came back to my house and sat with me for a while. She wanted me to go to the club with her. I hadn't the heart. She was very kind, but I was glad when she left me by myself. I tried to read, but the words meant nothing to me. I felt dead inside. My boy came in and turned on the lights. My head was aching like mad. Then he came back and said that a lady wished to see me. I asked who it was. He wasn't quite sure, but he thought it must be the new wife of the tuan of Putatan. I couldn't imagine what she wanted. I got up and went to the door. He was right. It was Sally. I asked her to come in. I noticed that she was deathly white. I felt sorry for her. It was a frightful experience for a girl of that age and for a bride a miserable homecoming. She sat down. She was very nervous. I tried to put her at her ease by saying conventional things. She made me very uncomfortable because she stared at me with those enormous blue eyes of hers, and they were simply ghastly with horror. She interrupted me suddenly.

" 'You're the only person here I know,' she said. 'I had to come to you. I want you to get me away from here.'

"I was dumbfounded.

" 'What *do* you mean?' I said.

" 'I don't want you to ask me any questions. I just want you to get me away. At once. I want to go back to England!'

" 'But you can't leave Tim like that just now,' I said. 'My dear, you must pull yourself together. I know it's been awful for you. But think of Tim. I mean, he'll be miserable. If you have any love for him the least you can do is to try and make him a little less unhappy.'

" 'Oh, you don't know,' she cried. 'I can't tell you. It's too horrible. I beseech you to help me. If there's a train tonight let me get on it. If I can only get to Penang I can get a ship. I can't stay in this place another night. I shall go mad.'

"I was absolutely bewildered.

" 'Does Tim know?' I asked her.

" 'I haven't seen Tim since last night. I'll never see him again. I'd rather die.'

"I wanted to gain a little time.

" 'But how can you go without your things? Have you got any luggage?'

" 'What does that matter?' she cried impatiently. 'I've got what I want for the journey.'

" 'Have you any money?'

" 'Enough. Is there a train tonight?'

" 'Yes,' I said. 'It's due just after midnight.'

" 'Thank God. Will you arrange everything? Can I stay here till then?'

" 'You're putting me in a frightful position,' I said. 'I don't know what to do for the best. You know, it's an awfully serious step you're taking.'

" 'If you knew everything you'd know it was the only possible thing to do.'

" 'It'll create an awful scandal here. I don't know what people'll say. Have you thought of the effect on Tim?' I was worried and unhappy. 'God knows I don't want to interfere in what isn't my business. But if you want me to help you I ought to know enough to feel justified in doing so. You must tell me what's happened.'

" 'I can't. I can only tell you that I know everything.'

"She hid her face with her hands and shuddered. Then she gave herself a shake as though she were recoiling from some frightful sight.

" 'He had no right to marry me. It was monstrous.'

"And as she spoke her voice rose shrill and piercing. I was afraid she was going to have an attack of hysterics. Her pretty doll-like face was terrified and her eyes stared as though she could never close them again.

" 'Don't you love him any more?' I asked.

" 'After that?'

" 'What will you do if I refuse to help you?' I said.

" 'I suppose there's a clergyman here or a doctor. You can't refuse to take me to one of them.'

" 'How did you get here?'

" 'The head boy drove me. He got a car from somewhere.'

" 'Does Tim know you've gone?'

" 'I left a letter for him.'

" 'He'll know you're here.'

" 'He won't try to stop me. I promise you that. He daren't. For God's sake don't you try either. I tell you I shall go mad if I stay here another night.'

"I sighed. After all she was of an age to decide for herself."

I, the writer of this, hadn't spoken for a long time.

"Did you know what she meant?" I asked Featherstone.

He gave me a long, haggard look.

"There was only one thing she could mean. It was unspeakable. Yes, I knew all right. It explained everything. Poor Olive. Poor sweet. I suppose it was unreasonable of me, at that moment I only felt a horror of that little pretty fair-haired thing with her terrified eyes. I hated her. I didn't say anything for a while. Then I told her I'd do as she wished. She didn't even say thank you. I think she knew what I felt about her. When it was dinner time I made her eat something and then she asked me if there was a room she could go and lie down in till it was time to go to the station. I showed her into my spare room and left her. I sat in the sitting-room and waited. My God, I don't think the time has ever passed so slowly for me. I thought twelve would never strike. I rang up the station and was told the train wouldn't be in till nearly two. At midnight she came back to the sitting-room and we sat there for an hour and a half. We had nothing to say to one another and we didn't speak. Then I took her to the station and put her on the train."

"Was there an awful scandal?"

Featherstone frowned.

"I don't know. I applied for short leave. After that I was moved to another post. I heard that Tim had sold his estate and bought another. But I didn't know where. It was a shock to me at first when I found him here."

Featherstone, getting up, went over to a table and mixed himself a whisky and soda. In the silence that fell now I heard the monotonous chorus of the croaking frogs. And suddenly the bird that is known as the fever-bird, perched in a tree close to the house, began to call. First, three notes in a descending, chromatic scale, then five, then four. The varying notes of the scale succeeded one another with maddening persistence. One was compelled to listen and to count them, and because one did not know how many there would be it tortured one's nerves.

"Blast that bird," said Featherstone. "That means no sleep for me tonight."

GUY DE MAUPASSANT

 Guy de Maupassant (1880–1893), who was born in Normandy, France, fought in the Franco-Prussian War of 1870–1871 before turning his attention to writing. He apprenticed himself to Gustave Flaubert for almost ten years, ultimately destroying most of what he wrote during that time. His first short story was published in 1880; over the next decade he wrote nearly three hundred stories and several novels. The stories are gathered in *Collected Stories* (1903) and other editions. Maupassant's stories, simply told and resolutely unsentimental, present a cast of clerks, peasants, soldiers, politicians, and other citizens engaged in the vagaries, misdemeanors, and heartaches of daily life. He never swerved from realism, bleak though its truth may have been, but his was a realism informed by personal vision. He was not content merely to present life as it appeared to the eye; he rather sought to shape a story so the reader would be compelled "to think, and to understand the deep, hidden meanings of events." "The Olive Grove" — a somber tale even by Maupassant's standards — reveals his mastery of acute observation — and, as well, of suspenseful plotting.

The Olive Grove

Translated from the French by Saxe Commins

When the longshoremen of Garandou, a little port of Provence, situated in the bay of Pisca, between Marseilles and Toulon, perceived the boat of the Abbé Vilbois entering the harbor, they went down to the beach to help him pull her ashore.

The priest was alone in the boat. In spite of his fifty-eight years, he rowed with all the energy of a real sailor. He had placed his hat on the bench beside him, his sleeves were rolled up, disclosing his powerful arms, his cassock was open at the neck and turned over his knees, and he wore a round hat of heavy, white canvas. His whole appearance bespoke an odd and strenuous priest of southern climes, better fitted for adventures than for clerical duties.

He rowed with strong and measured strokes, as if to show the southern sailors how the men of the north handle the oars, and from time to time he turned around to look at the landing point.

The skiff struck the beach and slid far up, the bow plowing through the sand; then it stopped abruptly. The five men watching for the abbé drew near, jovial and smiling.

"Well!" said one, with the strong accent of Provence, "have you been successful, Monsieur le Curé?"

The abbé drew in the oars, removed his canvas headcovering, put on his hat, pulled down his sleeves, and buttoned his coat. Then having assumed the usual appearance of a village priest, he replied proudly: "Yes, I have caught three red-snappers, two eels, and five sunfish."

The fishermen gathered around the boat to examine, with the air of experts, the dead fish, the fat red-snappers, the flat-headed eels, those hideous sea-serpents, and the violet sunfish, streaked with bright orange-colored stripes.

Said one: "I'll carry them up to your house, Monsieur le Curé."

"Thank you, my friend."

Having shaken hands all around, the priest started homeward, followed by the man with the fish; the others took charge of the boat.

The Abbé Vilbois walked along slowly with an air of dignity. The exertion of rowing had brought beads of perspiration to his brow and he uncovered his head each time that he passed through the shade of an olive grove. The warm evening air, freshened by a slight breeze from the sea, cooled his high forehead covered with short, white hair, a forehead far more suggestive of an officer than of a priest.

The village appeared, built on a hill rising from a large valley which descended toward the sea.

It was a summer evening. The dazzling sun, traveling toward the ragged crests of the distant hills, outlined on the white, dusty road the figure of the priest, the shadow of whose three-cornered hat bobbed merrily over the fields, sometimes apparently climbing the trunks of the olive-trees, only to fall immediately to the ground and creep among them.

With every step he took, he raised a cloud of fine, white dust, the invisible powder which, in summer, covers the roads of Provence; it clung to the edge of his cassock turning it grayish white. Completely refreshed, his hands deep in his pockets, he strode along slowly and ponderously, like a mountaineer. His eyes were fixed on the distant village where he had lived twenty years, and where he hoped to die. Its church — his church — rose above the houses clustered around it; the square turrets of gray stone, of unequal proportions and quaint design, stood outlined against the beautiful southern valley; and their architecture suggested the fortifications of some old château rather than the steeples of a place of worship.

The abbé was happy; for he had caught three red-snappers, two eels, and five sunfish. It would enable him to triumph again over his flock, which respected him, no doubt, because he was one of the most powerful men of the place, despite his years. These little innocent vanities were his greatest pleasures. He was a fine marksman; sometimes he practiced with his neighbor, a retired army provost who kept a tobacco shop; he could also swim better than anyone along the coast.

In his day he had been a well-known society man, the Baron de Vilbois, but had entered the priesthood after an unfortunate love-affair. Being the scion of an old family of Picardy, devout and royalistic, whose sons for centuries had entered the army, the magistracy, or the Church, his first thought was to follow his mother's advice and become a priest. But he yielded to his father's suggestion that he should study law in Paris and seek some high office.

While he was completing his studies his father was carried off by pneumonia; his mother, who was greatly affected by the loss, died soon afterward. He came into a fortune, and consequently gave up the idea of following a profession to live a life of idleness. He was handsome and intelligent, but somewhat prejudiced by the traditions and principles which he had inherited, along with his muscular frame, from a long line of ancestors.

Society gladly welcomed him and he enjoyed himself after the fashion of a well-to-do and seriously inclined young man. But it happened that a friend introduced him to a young actress, a pupil of the Conservatoire, who was appearing with great success at the Odéon. It was a case of love at first sight.

His sentiment had all the violence, the passion of a man born to believe in absolute ideas. He saw her act the romantic rôle in which he had achieved a triumph the first night of her appearance. She was pretty, and, though naturally perverse, possessed the face of an angel.

She conquered him completely; she transformed him into a delirious fool, into one of those ecstatic idiots whom a woman's look will forever chain to the pyre of fatal passions. She became his mistress and left the stage. They lived together four years, his love for her increasing during the time. He would have married her in spite of his proud name and family traditions, had he not discovered that for a long time she had been unfaithful to him with the friend who had introduced them.

The awakening was terrible, for she was about to become a mother, and he was awaiting the birth of the child to make her his wife.

When he held the proof of her transgressions — some letters found in a drawer — he confronted her with his knowledge and reproached her with all the savageness of his uncouth nature for her unfaithfulness and deceit. But she, a child of the people, being as sure of this man as of the other, braved and insulted him with the inherited daring of those women, who, in times of war, mounted with the men on the barricades.

He would have struck her to the ground — but she showed him her form. As white as death, he checked himself, remembering that a child of his would soon be born to this vile, polluted creature. He rushed at her to crush them both, to obliterate this double shame. Reeling under his blows, and seeing that he was about to stamp out the life of her unborn babe, she realized that she was lost. Throwing out her hands to parry the blows, she cried:

"Do not kill me! It is his, not yours!"

He fell back, so stunned with surprise that for a moment his rage subsided. He stammered:

"What? What did you say?"

Crazed with fright, having read her doom in his eyes and gestures, she repeated: "It's not yours, it's his."

Through his clenched teeth, he stammered:

"The child?"

"Yes."

"You lie!"

And again he lifted his foot as if to crush her, while she struggled to her knees in a vain attempt to rise. "I tell you it's his. If it was yours, wouldn't it have come much sooner?"

He was struck by the truth of this argument. In a moment of strange lucidity, his mind evolved precise, conclusive, irresistible reasons to disclaim the child of this miserable woman, and he felt so appeased, so happy at the thought, that he decided to let her live.

He then spoke in a calmer voice: "Get up and leave, and never let me see you again."

Quite cowed, she obeyed him and went. He never saw her again.

Then he left Paris and came south. He stopped in a village situated in a valley, near the coast of the Mediterranean. Selecting for his abode an inn facing the sea, he lived there eighteen months in complete seclusion, nursing his sorrow and despair. The memory of the unfaithful one tortured him; her grace, her charm, her perversity haunted him, and withal came the regret of her caresses.

He wandered aimlessly in those beautiful vales of Provence, baring his head, filled with the thoughts of that woman, to the sun that filtered through the grayish-green leaves of the olive-trees.

His former ideas of religion, the abated ardor of his faith, returned to him during his sorrowful retreat. Religion had formerly seemed a refuge from the unknown temptations of life, now it appeared as a refuge from its snares and tortures. He had never given up the habit of prayer. In his sorrow, he turned anew to its consolations, and often at dusk he would wander into the little village church, where in the darkness gleamed the light of the lamp hung above the altar, to guard the sanctuary and symbolize the Divine Presence.

He confided his sorrow to his God, told Him of his misery, asking advice, pity, help, and consolation. Each day, his fervid prayers disclosed stronger faith.

The bleeding heart of this man, crushed by love for a woman, still longed for affection; and soon his prayers, his seclusion, his constant communion with the Savior who consoles and cheers the weary, wrought a change in him, and the mystic love of God entered his soul, casting out the love of the flesh.

He then decided to take up his former plans and to devote his life to the Church.

He became a priest. Through family connections he succeeded in obtaining a call to the parish of this village which he had come across by chance. Devoting a large part of his fortune to the maintenance of charitable institutions, and keeping only enough to enable him to help the poor as long as he lived, he sought refuge in a quiet life filled with prayer and acts of kindness toward his fellow-men.

Narrow-minded but kind-hearted, a priest with a soldier's temperament, he guided his blind, erring flock forcibly through the mazes of his life in which every taste, instinct, and desire is a pitfall. But the old man in him never disappeared entirely. He continued to love out-of-door exercise and noble sports, but he hated every woman, having an almost childish fear of their dangerous fascination.

2

The sailor who followed the priest, being a southerner, found it difficult to refrain from talking. But he did not dare start a conversation, for the abbé exerted a great prestige over his flock. At last he ventured a remark: "So you like your lodge, do you, Monsieur le Curé?"

This lodge was one of the tiny constructions that are inhabited during the summer by the villagers and the town people alike. It was situated in a field not far from the parish-home, and the abbé had hired it because the latter was very small and built in the heart of the village next to the church.

During the summer time, he did not live altogether at the lodge, but would remain a few days at a time to practice pistol-shooting and be close to nature.

"Yes, my friend," said the priest. "I like it very well."

The low structure could now be seen; it was painted pink, and the walls were almost hidden under the leaves and branches of the olive-trees that grew in the open field. A tall woman was passing in and out of the door, setting a small table at which she placed, at each trip, a knife and fork, a glass, a plate, a napkin, and a piece of bread. She wore the small cap of the women of Arles, a pointed cone of silk or black velvet, decorated with a white rosette.

When the abbé was near enough to make himself heard, he shouted:

"Eh! Marguerite!"

She stopped to ascertain whence the voice came, and recognizing her master: "Oh! it's you, Monsieur le Curé!"

"Yes. I have caught some fine fish, and want you to broil this sunfish immediately, do you hear?"

The servant examined, with a critical and approving glance, the fish that the sailor carried.

"Yes, but we are going to have a chicken for dinner," she said.

"Well, it cannot be helped. Tomorrow the fish will not be as fresh as it is now. I mean to enjoy a little feast — it does not happen often — and the sin is not great."

The woman picked out a sunfish and prepared to go into the house. "Ah!" she said, "a man came to see you three times while you were out, Monsieur le Curé."

Indifferently he inquired: "A man! What kind of man?"

"Why, a man whose appearance was not in his favor."

"What? a beggar?"

"Perhaps — I don't know. But I think he is more of a 'maoufatan.' "

The abbé smiled at this word, which, in the language of Provence means a highwayman, a tramp, for he was well aware of Marguerite's timidity, and knew that every day and especially every night she fancied they would be murdered.

He handed a few sous to the sailor, who departed. And just as he was saying: "I am going to wash my hands" — for his past dainty habits still clung to him — Marguerite called to him from the kitchen where she was scraping the fish with a knife, thereby detaching its blood-stained, silvery scales:

"There he comes!"

The abbé looked down the road and saw a man coming slowly toward the house, he seemed poorly dressed, indeed, so far as he could distinguish. He could not help smiling at his servant's anxiety, and thought, while he waited for the stranger: "I think, after all, she is right; he does look a 'maoufatan.' "

The man walked slowly, with his eyes on the priest and his hands buried deep in his pockets. He was young and wore a full, blond beard; strands of curly hair escaped from his soft felt hat, which was so dirty and battered that it was impossible to imagine its former color and appearance. He was clothed in a long, dark overcoat, from which emerged the frayed edge of his trousers; on his feet were bathing shoes that deadened his steps, giving him the stealthy walk of a sneak thief.

When he had come within a few steps of the priest, he doffed, with a sweeping motion, the ragged hat that shaded his brow. He was not bad-looking, though his face showed signs of dissipation and the top of his head was bald, an indication of premature fatigue and debauch, for he certainly was not over twenty-five years old.

The priest responded at once to his bow, feeling that this fellow was not an ordinary tramp, a mechanic out of work, or a jail-bird, hardly able to speak any other tongue but the mysterious language of prisons.

"How do you do, Monsieur le Curé?" said the man. The priest answered simply. "I salute you," unwilling to address this ragged stranger as "Monsieur." They considered each other attentively; the abbé felt uncomfortable under the gaze of the tramp, invaded by a feeling of unrest unknown to him.

At last the vagabond continued: "Well, do you recognize me?"

Greatly surprised, the priest answered: "Why no, you are a stranger to me."

"Ah! you do not know me? Look at me well."

"I have never seen you before."

"Well, that may be true," replied the man sarcastically, "but let me show you some one whom you will know better."

He put on his hat and unbuttoned his coat, revealing his bare chest. A red sash wound around his spare frame held his trousers in place. He drew an envelope from his coat pocket, one of those soiled wrappers destined to protect the sundry papers of the tramp, whether they be stolen or legitimate property, those papers which he guards jealously and uses to protect himself against the too zealous gendarmes. He pulled out a photograph about the size of a folded letter, one of those pictures which were popular long ago; it was yellow and dim with age, for he had carried it around with him everywhere and the heat of his body had faded it.

Pushing it under the abbé's eyes, he demanded:

"Do you know him?"

The priest took a step forward to look and grew pale, for it was his own likeness that he had given Her years ago.

Failing to grasp the meaning of the situation he remained silent.

The tramp repeated:

"Do you recognize him?"

And the priest stammered: "Yes."

"Who is it?"

"It is I."

"It is you?"

"Yes."

"Well, then, look at us both — at me and at your picture!"

Already the unhappy man had seen that these two beings, the one in the picture and the one by his side, resembled each other like brothers; yet he did not understand, and muttered: "Well, what is it you wish?"

Then in an ugly voice, the tramp replied: "What do I wish? Why, first I wish you to recognize me."

"Who are you?"

"Who am I? Ask anybody by the roadside, ask your servant, let's go and ask the mayor and show him this; and he will laugh, I tell you that! Ah! you will not recognize me as your son, papa curé?"

The old man raised his arms above his head, with patriarchal gesture, and muttered despairingly: "It cannot be true!"

The young fellow drew quite close to him.

"Ah! It cannot be true, you say! You must stop lying, do you hear!" His clenched fists and threatening face, and the violence with which he spoke, made the priest retreat a few steps, while he asked himself anxiously which one of them was laboring under a mistake.

Again he asserted: "I never had a child."

The other man replied: "And no mistress, either?"

The aged priest resolutely uttered one word, a proud admission:

"Yes."

"And was not this mistress about to give birth to a child when you left her?"

Suddenly the anger which had been quelled twenty-five years ago, not quelled, but buried in the heart of the lover, burst through the wall of faith, resignation, and renunciation he had built around it. Almost beside himself, he shouted:

"I left her because she was unfaithful to me and was carrying the child of another man; had it not been for this, I should have killed both you and her, sir!"

The young man hesitated, taken aback at the sincerity of this outburst. Then he replied in a gentler voice:

"Who told you that it was another man's child?"

"She told me herself and braved me."

Without contesting this assertion the vagabond assumed the indifferent tone of a loafer judging a case:

"Well, then, mother made a mistake, that's all!"

After his outburst of rage, the priest had succeeded in mastering himself sufficiently to be able to inquire:

"And who told you that you were my son?"

"My mother, on her deathbed, M'sieur le Curé. And then — this!" And he held the picture under the eyes of the priest.

The old man took it from him; and slowly, with a heart bursting with anguish, he compared this stranger with his faded likeness and doubted no longer — it was his son.

An awful distress wrung his very soul, a terrible, inexpressible emotion invaded him; it was like the remorse of some ancient crime. He began to understand a little, he guessed the rest. He lived over the brutal scene of the parting. It was to save her life, then, that the wretched and deceitful woman had lied to him, her outraged lover. And he had believed her. And a son of his had been brought into the world and had grown up to be this sordid tramp, who exhaled the very odor of vice as a goat exhales its animal smell.

He whispered: "Will you take a little walk with me, so that we can discuss these matters?"

The young man sneered: "Why certainly! Isn't that what I came for?"

They walked side by side through the olive grove. The sun had gone down and the coolness of southern twilights spread an invisible cloak over the country. The priest shivered, and raising his eyes with a familiar motion, perceived the trembling gray foliage of the holy tree which had spread its frail shadow over the Son of Man in His great trouble and despondency.

A short, despairing prayer rose within him, uttered by his soul's voice, a prayer by which Christians implore the Savior's aid: "O Lord! have mercy on me."

Turning to his son he said: "So your mother is dead?"

These words, "Your mother is dead," awakened a new sorrow; it was the torment of the flesh which cannot forget, the cruel echo of past sufferings; but mostly the thrill of the fleeting, delirious bliss of his youthful passion.

The young man replied: "Yes, Monsieur le Curé, my mother is dead."

"Has she been dead a long while?"

"Yes, three years."

A new doubt entered the priest's mind. "And why did you not find me out before?"

The other man hesitated.

"I was unable to, I was prevented. But excuse me for interrupting these recollections — I will enter into more details later — for I have not had anything to eat since yesterday morning."

A tremor of pity shook the old man and holding forth both hands: "Oh! my poor child!" he said.

The young fellow took those big, powerful hands in his own slender and feverish palms.

Then he replied, with that air of sarcasm which hardly ever left his lips: "Ah! I'm beginning to think that we shall get along very well together, after all!"

The curé started toward the lodge.

"Let us go to dinner," he said.

He suddenly remembered, with a vague and instinctive pleasure, the fine fish he had caught, which, with the chicken, would make a good meal for the poor fellow.

The servant was in front of the door, watching their approach with an anxious and forbidding face.

"Marguerite," shouted the abbé, "take the table and put it into the dining-room, right away; and set two places, as quick as you can."

The woman seemed stunned at the idea that her master was going to dine with this tramp.

But the abbé, without waiting for her, removed the plate and napkin and carried the little table into the dining-room.

A few minutes later he was sitting opposite the beggar, in front of a soup-tureen filled with savory cabbage soup, which sent up a cloud of fragrant steam.

3

When the plates were filled, the tramp fell to with ravenous avidity. The abbé had lost his appetite and ate slowly, leaving the bread in the bottom of his plate. Suddenly he inquired: "What is your name?"

The man smiled: he was delighted to satisfy his hunger.

"Father unknown," he said, "and no other name but my mother's, which you probably remember. But I possess two Christian names, which, by the way, are quite unsuited to me — Philippe-Auguste."

The priest whitened.

"Why were you named thus?" he asked.

The tramp shrugged his shoulders. "I fancy you ought to know. After mother left you, she wished to make your rival believe that I was his child. He did believe it until I was about fifteen. Then I began to look too much like you. And he disclaimed me, the scoundrel. I had been christened Philippe-Auguste; now, if I had not resembled a soul, or if I had been the son of a third person, who had stayed in the background, today I should be the Vicomte Philippe-Auguste de Pravallon, son of the count and senator bearing this name. I have christened myself 'No-luck.'"

"How did you learn all this?"

"They discussed it before me, you know; pretty lively discussions they were, too. I tell you, that's what shows you the seamy side of life!"

Something more distressing than all he had suffered during the last half hour now oppressed the priest. It was a sort of suffocation which seemed as if it would grow and grow till it killed him; it was not due so much to the things he heard as to the manner in which they were uttered by this wayside tramp. Between himself and this beggar, between his son and himself, he was discovering the existence of those moral divergencies which are as fatal poisons to certain souls. Was this his son? He could not yet believe it. He wanted all the proofs, every one of them. He wanted to hear all, to listen to all. Again he thought of the olive-trees that shaded his little lodge, and for the second time he prayed: "O Lord! have mercy upon me."

Philippe-Auguste had finished his soup. He inquired: "Is there nothing else, abbé?"

The kitchen was built in an annex. Marguerite could not hear her master's voice. He always called her by striking a Chinese gong hung on the wall behind his chair. He took the brass hammer and struck the round metal plate. It gave a feeble sound, which grew and vibrated, becoming sharper and louder till it finally died away on the evening breeze.

The servant appeared with a frowning face and cast angry glances at the tramp, as if her faithful instinct had warned her of the misfortune that had befallen her master. She held a platter on which was the sunfish, spreading a savory odor of melted butter through the room. The abbé divided the fish lengthwise, helping his son to the better half: "I caught it a little while ago," he said, with a touch of pride in spite of his keen distress.

Marguerite had not left the room.

The priest added: "Bring us some wine, the white wine of Cape Corse."

She almost rebelled, and the priest, assuming a severe expression, was obliged to repeat: "Now, go, and bring two bottles, remember," for, when he drank with anybody, a very rare pleasure, indeed, he always opened one bottle for himself.

Beaming, Philippe-Auguste remarked: "Fine! A splendid idea! It has been a long time since I've had such a dinner." The servant came back after a few minutes. The abbé thought it an eternity, for now a thirst for information burned his blood like infernal fire.

After the bottles had been opened, the woman still remained, her eyes glued on the tramp.

"Leave us," said the curé.

She intentionally ignored his command.

He repeated almost roughly: "I have ordered you to leave us."

Then she left the room.

Philippe-Auguste devoured the fish voraciously, while his father sat watching him, more and more surprised and saddened at all the baseness stamped on the face that was so like his own. The morsels the abbé raised to his lips remained in his mouth, for his throat could not swallow; so he ate slowly, trying to choose, from the host of questions which besieged his mind, the one he wished his son to answer first. At last he spoke:

"What was the cause of her death?"

"Consumption."

"Was she ill a long time?"

"About eighteen months."

"How did she contract it?"

"We could not tell."

Both men were silent. The priest was reflecting. He was oppressed by the multi-tude of things he wished to know and to hear, for since the rupture, since the day he had tried to kill her, he had heard nothing. Certainly, he had not cared to know, because he had buried her, along with his happiest days, in forgetfulness; but now, knowing that she was dead and gone, he felt within himself the almost jealous desire of a lover to hear all.

He continued: "She was not alone, was she?"

"No, she lived with him."

The old man started: "With him? With Pravallon?"

"Why, yes."

And the betrayed man rapidly calculated that the woman who had deceived him, had lived over thirty years with his rival.

Almost unconsciously he asked: "Were they happy?"

The young man sneered. "Why, yes, with ups and downs! It would have been better had I not been there. I always spoiled everything."

"How, and why?" inquired the priest.

"I have already told you. Because he thought I was his son up to my fifteenth year. But the old fellow wasn't a fool, and soon discovered the likeness. That created scenes. I used to listen behind the door. He accused mother of having deceived him. Mother would answer: 'Is it my fault? you knew quite well when you took me that I was the mistress of that other man.' You were that other man."

"Ah! They spoke of me sometimes?"

"Yes, but never mentioned your name before me, excepting toward the end, when mother knew she was lost. I think they distrusted me."

"And you — and you learned quite early the irregularity of your mother's posi-tion?"

"Why, certainly. I am not innocent and I never was. Those things are easy to guess as soon as one begins to know life."

Philippe-Auguste had been filling his glass repeatedly. His eyes now were begin-ning to sparkle, for his long fast was favorable to the intoxicating effects of the wine. The priest noticed it and wished to caution him. But suddenly the thought that a drunkard is imprudent and loquacious flashed through him, and lifting the bottle he again filled the young man's glass.

Meanwhile Marguerite had brought the chicken. Having set it on the table, she again fastened her eyes on the tramp, saying in an indignant voice: "Can't you see that he's drunk, Monsieur le Curé?"

"Leave us," replied the priest, "and return to the kitchen."

She went out, slamming the door.

He then inquired: "What did your mother say about me?"

"Why, what a woman usually says of a man she has jilted: that you were hard to get along with, very strange, and that you would have made her life miserable with your peculiar ideas."

"Did she say that often?"

"Yes, but sometimes only in allusions, for fear I would understand; but neverthe-less I guessed all."

"And how did they treat you in that house?"

"Me? They treated me very well at first and very badly afterward. When mother saw that I was interfering with her, she shook me."

"How?"

"How? very easily. When I was almost sixteen years old, I got into various scrapes, and those blackguards put me into a reformatory to get rid of me." He put his elbows on the table and rested his cheeks in his palms. He was hopelessly intoxicated, and felt the unconquerable desire of all drunkards to talk and boast about themselves.

He smiled sweetly, with a feminine grace, an arch grace the priest knew and recognized as the hated charm that had won him long ago, and had also wrought his undoing. Now it was his mother whom the boy resembled, not so much because of his features, but because of his fascinating and deceptive glance, and the seductiveness of the false smile that played around his lips, the outlet of his inner ignominy.

Philippe-Auguste began to relate: "Ah! Ah! Ah! — I've had a fine life since I left the reformatory! A great writer would pay a large sum for it! Why, old Pére Dumas's Monte Cristo has had no stranger adventures than mine."

He paused to reflect with the philosophical gravity of the drunkard, then he continued slowly:

"When you wish a boy to turn out well, no matter what he has done, never send him to reformatory. The associations are too bad. Now, I got into a bad scrape. One night about nine o'clock, I, with three companions — we were all a little drunk — was walking along the road near the ford of Folac. All at once a wagon hove in sight, with the driver and his family asleep in it. They were people from Martinon on their way home from town. I caught hold of the bridle, led the horse to the ferryboat, made him walk into it, and pushed the boat into the middle of the stream. This created some noise and the driver awoke. He could not see in the dark, but whipped up the horse, which started on a run and landed in the water with the whole load. All were drowned! My companions denounced me to the authorities, though they thought it was a good joke when they saw me do it. Really, we didn't think that it would turn out that way. We only wanted to give the people a ducking, just for fun. After that I committed worse offenses to revenge myself for the first one, which did not, on my honor, warrant the reformatory. But what's the use of telling them? I will speak only of the latest one, because I am sure it will please you. Papa, I avenged you!"

The abbé was watching his son with terrified eyes; he had stopped eating.

Philippe-Auguste was preparing to begin. "No, not yet," said the priest, "in a little while."

And he turned to strike the Chinese gong.

Marguerite appeared almost instantly. Her master addressed her in such a rough tone that she hung her head, thoroughly frightened and obedient: "Bring in the lamp and the dessert, and then do not appear until I summon you."

She went out and returned with a porcelain lamp covered with a green shade, and bringing also a large piece of cheese and some fruit.

After she had gone, the abbé turned resolutely to his son.

"Now I am ready to hear you."

Philippe-Auguste calmly filled his plate with dessert and poured wine into his glass. The second bottle was nearly empty, though the priest had not touched it.

His mouth and tongue, thick with food and wine, the man stuttered: "Well, now for the last job. And it's a good one. I was home again — stayed there in spite of them, because they feared me — yes, feared me. Ah! you can't fool with me, you know — I'll do anything, when I'm roused. They lived together on and off. The old man had two residences. One official, for the senator, the other clandestine, for the lover. Still, he lived more in the latter than in the former, as he could not get along without mother. Mother was a sharp one — she knew how to hold a man! She had taken him body and soul, and kept him to the last! Well, I had come back and I kept them down by fright. I am resourceful at times — nobody can match me for sharpness and for strength, too — I'm afraid of no one. Well, mother got sick and the old man took her to a fine place in the country, near Meulan, situated in a park as big as a wood. She lasted about eighteen months, as I told you. Then we felt the end to be near. He came from Paris every day — he was very miserable — really.

"One morning they chatted a long time, over an hour, I think, and I could not imagine what they were talking about. Suddenly mother called me in and said:

"'I am going to die, and there is something I want to tell you beforehand, in spite of the Count's advice.' In speaking of him she always said 'the Count.' 'It is the name of your father, who is alive.' I had asked her this more than fifty times — more than fifty times — my father's name — more than fifty times — and she always refused to tell. I think I even beat her one day to make her talk, but it was of no use. Then, to get rid of me, she told me that you had died penniless, that you were worthless and that she had made a mistake in her youth, an innocent girl's mistake. She lied so well, I really believed you had died.

"Finally she said: 'It is your father's name.'

"The old man, who was sitting in an armchair, repeated three times, like this: 'You do wrong, you do wrong, you do wrong, Rosette.'

"Mother sat up in bed. I can see her now, with her flushed cheeks and shining eyes; she loved me, in spite of everything; and she said: 'Then you do something for him, Philippe!' In speaking to him she called him 'Philippe' and me 'Auguste.'

"He began to shout like a madman: 'Do something for that loafer — that blackguard, that convict? Never!'

"And he continued to call me names, as if he had done nothing else all his life but collect them.

"I was angry, but mother told me to hold my tongue, and she resumed: 'Then you must want him to starve, for you know that I leave no money.'

"Without being deterred, he continued: 'Rosette, I have given you thirty-five thousand francs a year for thirty years — that makes more than a million. I have enabled you to live like a wealthy, a beloved, and I may say, a happy woman. I owe nothing to that fellow, who has spoiled our late years, and he will not get a cent from me. It is useless to insist. Tell him the name of his father, if you wish. I am sorry, but I wash my hands of him.'

"Then mother turned toward me. I thought: 'Good! now I'm going to find my real father — if he has money. I'm saved.'

"She went on: 'Your father, the Baron de Vilbois, is today the Abbé Vilbois, curé of Garandou, near Toulon. He was my lover before I left him for the Count!'

"And she told me all, except that she had deceived you about her pregnancy. But women, you know, never tell the whole truth."

Sneeringly, unconsciously, he was revealing the depths of his foul nature. With beaming face he raised the glass to his lips and continued:

"Mother died two days — two days later. We followed her remains to the grave, he and I — say — wasn't it funny? — he and I — and three servants — that was all. He cried like a calf — we were side by side — we looked like father and son.

"Then he went back to the house alone. I was thinking to myself: 'I'll have to clear out now and without a penny, too.' I owned only fifty francs. What could I do to revenge myself?

"He touched me on the arm and said: 'I wish to speak to you.' I followed him into his office. He sat down in front of the desk and, wiping away his tears, he told me that he would not be as hard on me as he had said he would to mother. He begged me to leave you alone. That — that concerns only you and me. He offered me a thousand-franc note — a thousand — a thousand francs. What could a fellow like me do with a thousand francs? — I saw that there were very many bills in the drawer. The sight of the money made me wild. I put out my hand as if to take the note he offered me, but instead of doing so, I sprang at him, threw him to the ground and choked him till he grew purple. When I saw that he was going to give up the ghost, I gagged and bound him. Then I undressed him, laid him on his stomach and — ah! ah! ah! — I avenged you in a funny way!"

He stopped to cough, for he was choking with merriment. His ferocious, mirthful smile reminded the priest once more of the woman who had wrought his undoing.

"And then?" he inquired.

"Then — ah! ah! ah! — There was a bright fire in the fireplace — it was in the winter — in December — mother died — a bright coal fire — I took the poker — I let it get red-hot — and I made crosses on his back, eight or more, I cannot remember how many — then I turned him over and repeated them on his stomach. Say, wasn't it funny, papa? Formerly they marked convicts in this way. He wriggled like an eel — but I had gagged him so that he couldn't scream. I gathered up the bills — twelve in all — with mine it made thirteen — an unlucky number. I left the house, after telling the servants not to bother their master until dinnertime, because he was asleep. I thought that he would hush the matter up because he was a senator and would fear the scandal. I was mistaken. Four days later I was arrested in a Paris restaurant. I got three years for the job. That is the reason why I did not come to you sooner." He drank again, and stuttering so as to render his words almost unintelligible, continued:

"Now — papa — isn't it funny to have one's papa a curé? You must be nice to me, very nice, because you know, I am not commonplace — and I did a good job — didn't I — on the old man?"

The anger which years ago had driven the Abbé Vilbois to desperation rose within him at the sight of this miserable man.

He, who in the name of the Lord, had so often pardoned the infamous secrets whispered to him under the seal of confession, was now merciless in his own behalf. No longer did he implore the help of a merciful God, for he realized that no power on earth or in the sky could save those who had been visited by such a terrible disaster.

All the ardor of his passionate heart and of his violent blood, which long years of resignation had tempered, awoke against the miserable creature who was his son. He protested against the likeness he bore to him and to his mother, the wretched mother who had formed him so like herself; and he rebelled against the destiny that had chained this criminal to him, like an iron ball to a galley-slave.

The shock roused him from the peaceful and pious slumber which had lasted twenty-five years; with a wonderful lucidity he saw all that would inevitably ensue.

Convinced that he must talk loud so as to intimidate this man from the first, he spoke with his teeth clenched with fury:

"Now that you have told all, listen to me. You will leave here tomorrow morning. You will go to a country that I shall designate, and never leave it without my permission. I will give you a small income, for I am poor. If you disobey me once, it will be withdrawn and you will learn to know me."

Though Philippe-Auguste was half dazed with wine, he understood the threat. Instantly the criminal within him rebelled. Between hiccoughs he sputtered: "Ah! papa, be careful what you say — you're a curé, remember — I hold you — and you have to walk straight, like the rest!"

The abbé started. Through his whole muscular frame crept the unconquerable desire to seize this monster, to bend him like a twig, so as to show him that he would have to yield.

Shaking the table, he shouted: "Take care, take care — I am afraid of nobody."

The drunkard lost his balance and seeing that he was going to fall and would forthwith be in the priest's power, he reached with a murderous look for one of the knives lying on the table. The abbé perceived his motion, and he gave the table a terrible shove; his son toppled over and landed on his back. The lamp fell with a crash and went out.

During a moment the clinking of broken glass was heard in the darkness, then the muffled sound of a soft body creeping on the floor, and then all was silent.

With the crashing of the lamp a complete darkness spread over them; it was so prompt and unexpected that they were stunned by it as by some terrible event. The drunkard, pressed against the wall, did not move; the priest remained on his chair in the midst of the night which had quelled his rage. The somber veil that had descended so rapidly, arresting his anger, also quieted the furious impulses of his soul; new ideas, as dark and dreary as the obscurity, beset him.

The room was perfectly silent, like a tomb where nothing draws the breath of life. Not a sound came from outside, neither the rumbling of a distant wagon, nor the bark of a dog, nor even the sigh of the wind passing through the trees.

This lasted a long time, perhaps an hour. Then suddenly the gong vibrated! It rang once, as if it had been struck a short, sharp blow, and was instantly followed by the noise of a falling body and an overturned chair.

Marguerite came running out of the kitchen, but as soon as she opened the door she fell back, frightened by the intense darkness. Trembling, her heart beating as if it would burst, she called in a low, hoarse voice: "M'sieur le Curé! M'sieur le Curé!"

Nobody answered, nothing stirred. "*Mon Dieu, mon Dieu*," she thought, "what has happened, what have they done?"

She did not dare enter the room, yet feared to go back to fetch a light. She felt as if she would like to run away, to screech at the top of her voice, though she knew her legs would refuse to carry her. She repeated: "M'sieur le Curé! M'sieur le Curé! it is me, Marguerite."

But, notwithstanding her terror, the instinctive desire of helping her master and a woman's courage, which is sometimes heroic, filled her soul with a terrified audacity, and running back to the kitchen she fetched a lamp.

She stopped at the doorsill. First, she caught sight of the tramp lying against the wall, asleep, or simulating slumber; then she saw the broken lamp, and then, under the table, the feet and black-stockinged legs of the priest, who must have fallen backward, striking his head on the gong.

Her teeth chattering and her hands trembling with fright, she kept on repeating: "My God! My God! what is this?"

She advanced slowly, taking small steps, till she slid on something slimy and almost fell.

Stooping, she saw that the floor was red and that a red liquid was spreading around her feet toward the door. She guessed that it was blood. She threw down her light so as to hide the sight of it, and fled from the room out into the fields, running half crazed toward the village. She ran screaming at the top of her voice, and bumping against the trees she did not heed, her eyes fastened on the gleaming lights of the distant town.

Her shrill voice rang out like the gloomy cry of the night-owl, repeating continuously, "The maoufatan — the maoufatan — the maoufatan" —

When she reached the first house, excited men came out and surrounded her; but she could not answer them and struggled to escape, for the fright had turned her head.

After a while they guessed that something must have happened to the curé, and a little rescuing party started for the lodge.

The little pink house standing in the middle of the olive grove had grown black and invisible in the dark, silent night. Since the gleam of the solitary window had faded, the cabin was plunged in darkness, lost in the grove, and unrecognizable for anyone but a native of the place.

Soon lights began to gleam near the ground, between the trees, streaking the dried grass with long, yellow reflections. The twisted trunks of the olive-trees assumed fantastic shapes under the moving lights, looking like monsters or infernal serpents. The projected reflections suddenly revealed a vague, white mass, and soon the low, square wall of the lodge grew pink from the light of the lanterns. Several peasants were carrying the lamps, escorting two gendarmes with revolvers, the mayor, the *garde-champêtre,* and Marguerite, supported by the men, for she was almost unable to walk.

The rescuing party hesitated a moment in front of the open, gruesome door. But the brigadier, snatching a lantern from one of the men, entered, followed by the rest.

The servant had not lied, blood covered the floor like a carpet. It had spread to the place where the tramp was lying, bathing one of his hands and legs.

The father and son were asleep, the one with a severed throat, the other in a drunken stupor. The two gendarmes seized the latter and before he awoke they had him handcuffed. He rubbed his eyes, stunned, stupefied with liquor, and when he saw the body of the priest, he appeared terrified, unable to understand what had happened.

"Why did he not escape?" said the mayor.

"He was too drunk," replied the officer.

And every man agreed with him, for nobody ever thought that perhaps the Abbé Vilbois had taken his own life.

HERMAN MELVILLE

Herman Melville (1819–1891) was born in New York City and received his education there and in Albany. In 1839, after unsuccessfully trying several vocations, he shipped as a cabin boy on a freighter to Liverpool. Two years later he sailed for the South Seas on a whaler — an adventure which culminated in his jumping ship and being held captive for four months by a cannibalistic Polynesian tribe. When he finally returned to the United States after other, nearly as dramatic, adventures, he conveyed his extraordinary experiences in two novels, *Typee* (1846) and *Omoo* (1847). They made him famous, and he became known as "the man who had lived among cannibals." He moved to western Massachusetts where he met and became friendly with Nathaniel Hawthorne. There he wrote (and dedicated to Hawthorne) his masterpiece, the incalculably great *Moby Dick* (1851), which has been called "a parable of human life and cosmic existence, with special reference to all that baffles and cripples the spirit of man." The book was badly received by the public, and from that time Melville's reputation as a writer began a long decline. He wrote other novels (*Pierre*, 1852; *The Confidence Man*, 1857) and short stories (*Piazza Tales*, 1856), but so forgotten was he by the end of his life that his death received no notice in the press. Only in the 1920s was his work reevaluated and his stature acknowledged; his last work of fiction, the novella *Billy Budd*, was published in 1924. Argentine writer Jorge Luis Borges observed of "Bartleby the Scrivener" that it "defines a genre that Kafka would reinvent and quarry . . . the genre of fantasies of conduct and feeling."

Bartleby the Scrivener

I am a rather elderly man. The nature of my avocations, for the last thirty years, has brought me into more than ordinary contact with what would seem an interesting and somewhat singular set of men, of whom, as yet, nothing, that I know of, has ever been written — I mean, the law-copyists, or scriveners. I have known very many of them, professionally and privately, and, if I pleased, could relate divers histories, at which good-natured gentlemen might smile, and sentimental souls might weep. But I waive the biographies of all other scriveners, for a few passages in the life of Bartleby, who was a scrivener, the strangest I ever saw, or heard of. While, of other law-copyists, I might write the complete life, of Bartleby nothing of that sort can be done. I believe that no materials exist, for a full and satisfactory biography of this man. It is an irreparable loss to literature. Bartleby was one of those beings of whom nothing is ascertainable, except from the original sources, and, in his case, those are very small. What my own astonished eyes saw of Bartleby, *that* is all I know of him, except, indeed, one vague report, which will appear in the sequel.

Ere introducing the scrivener, as he first appeared to me, it is fit I make some mention of myself, my *employés,* my business, my chambers, and general surroundings; because some such description is indispensable to an adequate understanding of the chief character about to be presented. Imprimis: I am a man who, from his youth upwards, has been filled with a profound conviction that the easiest way of life is the best. Hence, though I belong to a profession proverbially energetic and nervous, even to turbulence, at times, yet nothing of that sort have I ever suffered to invade my peace. I am one of those unambitious lawyers who never address a jury, or in any way draw down public applause; but, in the cool tranquillity of a snug retreat, do a snug business among rich men's bonds, and mortgages, and title-deeds. All who know me, consider me an eminently *safe* man. The late John Jacob Astor, a personage little given to poetic enthusiasm, had no hesitation in pronouncing my first grand point to be prudence; my next, method. I do not speak it in vanity, but simply record the fact, that I was not unemployed in my profession by the late John Jacob Astor; a name which, I admit, I love to repeat; for it hath a rounded and orbicular sound to it, and rings like unto bullion. I will freely add, that I was not insensible to the late John Jacob Astor's good opinion.

Some time prior to the period at which this little history begins, my avocations had been largely increased. The good old office, now extinct in the State of New York, of a Master in Chancery, had been conferred upon me. It was not a very arduous office, but very pleasantly remunerative. I seldom lose my temper; much more seldom indulge in dangerous indignation at wrongs and outrages; but I must be permitted to be rash here and declare, that I consider the sudden and violent abrogation of the office of Master in Chancery, by the new Constitution, as a — premature act; inasmuch as I had counted upon a life-lease of the profits, whereas I only received those of a few short years. But this is by the way.

My chambers were upstairs, at No. — Wall Street. At one end, they looked upon the white wall of the interior of a spacious sky-light shaft, penetrating the building from top to bottom.

This view might have been considered rather tame than otherwise, deficient in what landscape painters call "life." But, if so, the view from the other end of my chambers offered, at least, a contrast, if nothing more. In that direction, my windows commanded an unobstructed view of a lofty brick wall, black by age and everlasting shade; which wall required no spy-glass to bring out its lurking beauties, but, for the benefit of all near-sighted spectators, was pushed up to within ten feet of my windowpanes. Owing to the great height of the surrounding buildings, and my chambers being on the second floor, the interval between this wall and mine not a little resembled a huge square cistern.

At the period just preceding the advent of Bartleby, I had two persons as copyists in my employment, and a promising lad as an office-boy. First, Turkey; second, Nippers; third, Ginger Nut. These may seem names, the like of which are not usually found in the Directory. In truth, they were nicknames, mutually conferred upon each other by my three clerks, and were deemed expressive of their respective persons or characters. Turkey was a short, pursy Englishman, of about my own age — that is, somewhere not far from sixty. In the morning, one might say, his face was of a fine florid hue, but after twelve o'clock, meridian — his dinner hour — it blazed like a grate full of Christmas coals; and continued blazing — but, as it were, with a gradual wane — till six o'clock, P.M., or thereabouts; after which, I saw no more of the proprietor of the face, which, gaining its meridian with the sun, seemed to set with it, to rise, culminate, or decline the following day, with the like regularity and undiminished glory. There are many singular coincidences I have known in the course of my life, not the least among which was the fact, that, exactly when Turkey displayed his fullest beams from his red and radiant countenance, just then, too, at that critical moment, began the daily period when I considered his business capacities as seriously disturbed for the remainder of the twenty-four hours. Not that he was absolutely idle, or averse to business then; far from it. The difficulty was, he was apt to be altogether too energetic. There was a strange, inflamed, flurried, flighty recklessness of activity about him. He would be incautious in dipping his pen into his inkstand. All his blots upon my documents were dropped there after twelve o'clock, meridian. Indeed, not only would he be reckless, and sadly given to making blots in the afternoon, but, some days, he went further, and was rather noisy. At such times, too, his face flamed with augmented blazonry, as if cannel coal had been heaped on anthracite. He made an unpleasant racket with his chair; spilled his sand-box; in mending his pens, impatiently split them all to pieces, and threw them on the floor in a sudden passion; stood up, and leaned over his table, boxing his papers about in a most indecorous manner, very sad to behold in an elderly man like him. Nevertheless, as he was in many ways a most valuable person to me, and all the time before twelve o'clock, meridian, was the quickest, steadiest creature, too, accomplishing a great deal of work in a style not easily to be matched — for these reasons, I was willing to overlook his eccentricities, though, indeed, occasionally, I remonstrated with him. I did this very gently, however, because, though the civilest, nay, the blandest and most reverential of men in the morning, yet, in the afternoon, he was disposed, upon provocation, to be slightly rash with his tongue — in fact, insolent. Now, valuing his morning services as I did, and resolved not to lose them — yet, at the same time, made uncomfortable by his inflamed ways after twelve o'clock — and being a man of peace, unwilling by my admonitions to call forth unseemly retorts from him, I took upon me, one Saturday noon (he was always worse on Saturdays) to hint to him, very kindly, that, perhaps, now that he was growing old, it might be well to abridge his labors; in short, he need not come to my chambers after twelve o'clock, but, dinner over, had best go home to his lodgings, and rest himself, till tea-time. But no; he insisted upon his afternoon devotions. His countenance became intolerably fervid, as he oratorically assured me —gesticulating with a long ruler at the other end of the room — that if his services in the morning were useful, how indispensable, then, in the afternoon?

"With submission, sir," said Turkey, on this occasion, "I consider myself your right-hand man. In the morning I but marshall and deploy my columns; but in the afternoon I put myself at their head, and gallantly charge the foe, thus" — and he made a violent thrust with the ruler.

"But the blots, Turkey," intimated I.

"True; but, with submission, sir, behold these hairs! I am getting old. Surely, sir, a blot or two of a warm afternoon is not to be severely urged against gray hairs. Old age — even if it blot the page — is honorable. With submission, sir we *both* are getting old."

This appeal to my fellow-feeling was hardly to be resisted. At all events, I saw that go he would not. So, I made up my mind to let him stay, resolving, nevertheless, to see to it that, during the afternoon, he had to do with my less important papers.

Nippers, the second on my list, was a whiskered, sallow, and, upon the whole, rather piratical-looking young man, of about five-and-twenty. I always deemed him the victim of two evil powers — ambition and indigestion. The ambition was evinced by a certain impatience of the duties of a mere copyist, an unwarrantable usurpation of strictly professional affairs, such as the original drawing up of legal documents. The indigestion seemed betokened in an occasional nervous testiness and grinning irritability, causing the teeth to audibly grind together over mistakes committed in copying; unnecessary maledictions, hissed, rather than spoken, in the heat of business; and especially by a continual discontent with the height of the table where he worked. Though of a very ingenious mechanical turn, Nippers could never get this table to suit him. He put chips under it, blocks of various sorts, bits of pasteboard, and at last went so far as to attempt an exquisite adjustment, by final pieces of folded blotting-paper. But no invention would answer. If, for the sake of easing his back, he brought the table-lid at a sharp angle well up towards his chin, and wrote there like a man using the steep roof of a Dutch house for his desk, then he declared that it stopped the circulation in his arms. If now he lowered the table to his waistbands, and stooped over it in writing, then there was a sore aching in his back. In short, the truth of the matter was, Nippers knew not what he wanted. Or, if he wanted anything, it was to be rid of a scrivener's table altogether. Among the manifestations of his diseased ambition was a fondness he had for receiving visits from certain ambiguous-looking fellows in seedy coats, whom he called his clients. Indeed, I was aware that not only was he, at times, considerable of a ward-politician, but he occasionally did a little business at the Justices' courts, and was not unknown on the steps of the Tombs. I have good reason to believe, however, that one individual who called upon him at my chambers, and who, with a grand air, he insisted was his client, was no other than a dun, and the alleged title-deed, a bill. But, with all his failings, and the annoyances he caused me, Nippers, like his compatriot Turkey, was a very useful man to me; wrote a neat, swift hand; and, when he chose, was not deficient in a gentlemanly sort of deportment. Added to this, he always dressed in a gentlemanly sort of way; and so, incidentally, reflected credit upon my chambers. Whereas, with respect to Turkey, I had much ado to keep him from being a reproach to me. His clothes were apt to look oily, and smell of eating-houses. He wore his pantaloons very loose and baggy in summer. His coats were execrable; his hat not to be handled. But while the hat was a thing of indifference to me, inasmuch as his natural civility and deference, as a dependent Englishman, always led him to doff it the moment he entered the room, yet his coat was another matter. Concerning his coats, I reasoned with him; but with no effect. The truth was, I suppose, that a man with so small an income could not afford to sport such a lustrous face and a lustrous coat at one and the same time. As Nippers once observed, Turkey's money went chiefly for red ink. One winter day, I presented Turkey with a highly respectable-looking coat of my own — a padded gray coat, of a most comfortable warmth, and which buttoned straight up from the knee to the neck. I thought Turkey would appreciate the favor, and abate his rashness and obstreperousness of afternoons. But no; I verily believe that buttoning himself up in so downy and blanket-like a coat had a pernicious effect upon him — upon the same principle that too much oats are bad for horses. In fact, precisely as a rash, restive horse is said to feel his oats, so Turkey felt his coat. It made him insolent. He was a man whom prosperity harmed.

Though, concerning the self-indulgent habits of Turkey, I had my own private surmises, yet, touching Nippers, I was well persuaded that, whatever might be his faults in other respects, he was, at least, a temperate young man. But, indeed, nature herself seemed to have been his vintner, and, at his birth, charged him so thoroughly with an irritable, brandy-like disposition, that all subsequent potations were needless. When I consider how, amid the stillness of my chambers, Nippers would sometimes impatiently rise from his seat, and stooping over his table, spread his arms wide apart, seize the whole desk, and move it, and jerk it, with a grim, grinding motion on the floor, as if the table were a perverse voluntary agent, intent on thwarting and vexing him, I plainly perceive that, for Nippers, brandy-and-water were altogether superfluous.

It was fortunate for me that, owing to its peculiar cause — indigestion — the irritability and consequent nervousness of Nippers were mainly observable in the morning, while in the afternoon he was comparatively mild. So that, Turkey's paroxysms only coming on about twelve o'clock, I never had to do with their eccentricities at one time. Their fits relieved each other, like guards. When Nipper's was on, Turkey's was off; and *vice versa*. This was a good natural arrangement, under the circumstances.

Ginger Nut, the third on my list, was a lad, some twelve years old. His father was a carman, ambitious of seeing his son on the bench instead of a cart, before he died. So he sent him to my office, as student at law, errand-boy, cleaner and sweeper, at the rate of one dollar a week. He had a little desk to himself, but he did not use it much. Upon inspection, the drawer exhibited a great array of the shells of various sorts of nuts. Indeed, to this quick-witted youth, the whole noble science of the law was contained in a nutshell. Not the least among the employments of Ginger Nut, as well as one which he discharged with the most alacrity, was his duty as cake and apple purveyor for Turkey and Nippers. Copying law-papers being proverbially a dry, husky sort of business, my two scriveners were fain to moisten their mouths very often with Spitzenbergs, to be had at the numerous stalls nigh the Custom House and Post Office. Also, they sent Ginger Nut very frequently for that peculiar cake — small, flat, round, and very spicy — after which he had been named by them. Of a cold morning, when business was but dull, Turkey would gobble up scores of these cakes, as if they were mere wafers — indeed, they sell them at the rate of six or eight for a penny — the scrape of his pen blending with the crunching of the crisp particles in his mouth. Of all the fiery afternoon blunders and flurried rashnesses of Turkey, was his once moistening a ginger-cake between his lips, and clapping it on to a mortgage, for a seal. I came within an ace of dismissing him then. But he mollified me by making an oriental bow, and saying —

"With submission, sir, it was generous of me to find you in stationery on my own account."

Now my original business — that of a conveyancer and title hunter, and drawer-up of recondite documents of all sorts — was considerably increased by receiving the Master's office. There was now great work for scriveners. Not only must I push the clerks already with me, but I must have additional help.

In answer to my advertisement, a motionless young man one morning stood upon my office threshold, the door being open, for it was summer. I can see that figure now — pallidly neat, pitiably respectable, incurably forlorn! It was Bartleby.

After a few words touching his qualifications, I engaged him, glad to have among my corps of copyists a man of so singularly sedate an aspect, which I thought might operate beneficially upon the flighty temper of Turkey, and the fiery one of Nippers.

I should have stated before that ground-glass folding-doors divided my premises into two parts, one of which was occupied by my scriveners, the other by myself.

According to my humor, I threw open these doors, or closed them. I resolved to assign Bartleby a corner by the folding-doors, but on my side of them, so as to have this quiet man within easy call, in case any trifling thing was to be done. I placed his desk close up to a small side-window in that part of the room, a window which originally had afforded a lateral view of certain grimy backyards and bricks, but which, owing to subsequent erections, commanded at present no view at all, though it gave some light. Within three feet of the panes was a wall, and the light came down from far above, between two lofty buildings, as from a very small opening in a dome. Still further to a satisfactory arrangement, I procured a high green folding screen, which might entirely isolate Bartleby from my sight, though not remove him from my voice. And thus, in a manner, privacy and society were conjoined.

At first, Bartleby did an extraordinary quantity of writing. As if long famishing for something to copy, he seemed to gorge himself on my documents. There was no pause for digestion. He ran a day and night line, copying by sunlight and by candlelight. I should have been quite delighted with his application, had he been cheerfully industrious. But he wrote on silently, palely, mechanically.

It is, of course, an indispensable part of a scrivener's business to verify the accuracy of his copy, word by word. Where there are two or more scriveners in an office, they assist each other in this examination, one reading from the copy, the other holding the original. It is a very dull, wearisome, and lethargic affair. I can readily imagine that, to some sanguine temperaments, it would be altogether intolerable. For example, I cannot credit that the mettlesome poet, Byron, would have contentedly sat down with Bartleby to examine a law document of, say five hundred pages, closely written in a crimpy hand.

Now and then, in the haste of business, it had been my habit to assist in comparing some brief document myself, calling Turkey or Nippers for this purpose. One object I had, in placing Bartleby so handy to me behind the screen, was, to avail myself of his services on such trivial occasions. It was on the third day, I think, of his being with me, and before any necessity had arisen for having his own writing examined, that, being much hurried to complete a small affair I had in hand, I abruptly called to Bartleby. In my haste and natural expectancy of instant compliance, I say with my head bent over the original on my desk, and my right hand sideways, and somewhat nervously extended with the copy, so that, immediately upon emerging from his retreat, Bartleby might snatch it and proceed to business without the least delay.

In this very attitude did I sit when I called to him, rapidly stating what it was I wanted him to do — namely to examine a small paper with me. Imagine my surprise, nay, my consternation, when, without moving from his privacy, Bartleby, in a singular mild, firm voice, replied, "I would prefer not to."

I sat awhile in perfect silence, rallying my stunned faculties. Immediately it occurred to me that my ears had deceived me, or Bartleby had entirely misunderstood my meaning. I repeated my request in the clearest tone I could assume; but in quite as clear a one came the previous reply, "I would prefer not to."

"Prefer not to," echoed I, rising in high excitement, and crossing the room with a stride. "What do you mean? Are you moon-struck? I want you to help me compare this sheet here — take it," and I thrust it towards him.

"I would prefer not to," said he.

I looked at him steadfastly. His face was leanly composed; his gray eye dimly calm. Not a wrinkle of agitation rippled him. Had there been the least uneasiness, anger, impatience or impertinence in his manner; in other words, had there been anything ordinarily human about him, doubtless I should have violently dismissed him from the premises. But as it was, I should have as soon thought of turning my pale plaster-of-paris bust of Cicero out of doors. I stood gazing at him awhile, as he went on with his own writing, and then reseated myself at my desk. This is very strange, thought I. What had one best do? But my business hurried me. I concluded to forget the matter for the present, reserving it for my future leisure. So, calling Nippers from the other room, the paper was speedily examined.

A few days after this, Bartleby concluded four lengthy documents, being quadruplicates of a week's testimony taken before me in my High Court of Chancery. It became necessary to examine them. It was an important suit, and great accuracy was imperative. Having all things arranged, I called Turkey, Nippers, and Ginger Nut from the next room, meaning to place the four copies in the hands of my four clerks, while I should read from the original. Accordingly, Turkey, Nippers, and Ginger Nut had taken their seats in a row, each with his document in his hand, when I called to Bartleby to join this interesting group.

"Bartleby! quick, I am waiting."

I heard a slow scrape of his chair legs on the uncarpeted floor, and soon he appeared standing at the entrance of his hermitage.

"What is wanted?" said he, mildly.

"The copies, the copies," said I, hurriedly. "We are going to examine them. There" — and I held towards him the fourth quadruplicate.

"I would prefer not to," he said, and gently disappeared behind the screen.

For a few moments I was turned into a pillar of salt, standing at the head of my seated column of clerks. Recovering myself, I advanced towards the screen, and demanded the reason for such extraordinary conduct.

"*Why* do you refuse?"

"I would prefer not to."

With any other man I should have flown outright into a dreadful passion, scorned all further words, and thrust him ignominiously from my presence. But there was something about Bartleby that not only strangely disarmed me, but, in a wonderful manner, touched and disconcerted me. I began to reason with him.

"These are your own copies we are about to examine. It is labor saving to you, because one examination will answer for your four papers. It is common usage. Every copyist is bound to help examine his copy. Is it not so? Will you not speak? Answer!"

"I prefer not to," he replied in a flute-like tone. It seemed to me that, while I had been addressing him, he carefully revolved every statement that I made; fully comprehended the meaning; could not gainsay the irresistible conclusion; but, at the same time, some paramount consideration prevailed with him to reply as he did.

"You are decided, then, not to comply with my request — a request made according to common usage and common sense?"

He briefly gave me to understand, that on that point my judgment was sound. Yes: his decision was irreversible.

It is not seldom the case that, when a man is browbeaten in some unprecedented and violently unreasonable way, he begins to stagger in his own plainest faith. He begins, as it were, vaguely to surmise that, wonderful as it may be, all the justice and all the reason is on the other side. Accordingly, if any disinterested persons are present, he turns to them for some reinforcement for his own faltering mind.

"Turkey," said I, "what do you think of this? Am I not right?"

"With submission, sir," said Turkey, in his blandest tone, "I think that you are."

"Nippers," said I, "what do *you* think of it?"

"I think I should kick him out of the office."

(The reader of nice perceptions will here perceive that, it being morning, Turkey's answer is couched in polite and tranquil terms, but Nippers replies in ill-tempered ones. Or, to repeat a previous sentence, Nippers's ugly mood was on duty, and Turkey's off.)

"Ginger Nut," said I, willing to enlist the smallest suffrage in my behalf, "what do *you* think of it?"

"I think, sir, he's a little *luny*," replied Ginger Nut, with a grin.

"You hear what they say," said I, turning towards the screen, "come forth and do your duty."

But he vouchsafed no reply. I pondered a moment in sore perplexity. But once more business hurried me. I determined again to postpone the consideration of this dilemma to my future leisure. With a little trouble we made out to examine the papers without Bartleby, though at every page or two Turkey deferentially dropped his opinion, that this proceeding was quite out of the common; while Nippers, twitching in his chair with a dyspeptic nervousness, ground out, between his set teeth, occasional hissing maledictions against the stubborn oaf behind the screen. And for his (Nippers's) part, this was the first and the last time he would do another man's business without pay.

Meanwhile Bartleby sat in his hermitage, oblivious to everything but his own peculiar business there.

Some days passed, the scrivener being employed upon another lengthy work. His late remarkable conduct led me to regard his ways narrowly. I observed that he never went to dinner; indeed, that he never went anywhere. As yet I had never, of my personal knowledge, known him to be outside of my office. He was a perpetual sentry in the corner. At about eleven o'clock though, in the morning, I noticed that Ginger Nut would advance toward the opening in Bartleby's screen, as if silently beckoned thither by a gesture invisible to me where I sat. The boy would then leave the office, jingling a few pence, and reappear with a handful of ginger-nuts, which he delivered in the hermitage, receiving two of the cakes for his trouble.

He lives, then, on ginger-nuts, thought I; never eats a dinner, properly speaking; he must be a vegetarian, then; but no; he never eats even vegetables, he eats nothing but ginger-nuts. My mind then ran on in reveries concerning the probable effects upon the human constitution of living entirely on ginger-nuts. Ginger-nuts are so called, because they contain ginger as one of their peculiar constituents, and the final flavoring one. Now, what was ginger? A hot, spicy thing. Was Bartleby hot and spicy? Not at all. Ginger, then, had no effect upon Bartleby. Probably he preferred it should have none.

Nothing so aggravates an earnest person as a passive resistance. If the individual so resisted be of a not inhumane temper, and the resisting one perfectly harmless in his passivity, then, in the better moods of the former, he will endeavor charitably to construe to his imagination what proves impossible to be solved by his judgment. Even so, for the most part, I regarded Bartleby and his ways. Poor fellow! thought I, he means no mischief; it is plain he intends no insolence; his aspect sufficiently evinces that his eccentricities are involuntary. He is useful to me. I can get along with him. If I turn him away, the chances are he will fall in with some less indulgent employer, and then he will be rudely treated, and perhaps driven forth miserably to starve. Yes. Here I can cheaply purchase a delicious self-approval. To befriend Bartleby; to humor him in his strange willfulness, will cost me little or nothing, while I lay up in my soul what will eventually prove a sweet morsel for my conscience. But this mood was not invariable with me. The passiveness of Bartleby sometimes irritated me. I felt strangely goaded on to encounter him in new opposition — to elicit some angry spark from him answerable to my own. But, indeed, I might as well have essayed to strike fire with my knuckles against a bit of Windsor soap. But one afternoon the evil impulse in me mastered me, and the following little scene ensued:

"Bartleby," said I, "when those papers are all copied, I will compare them with you."

"I would prefer not to."

"How? Surely you do not mean to persist in that mulish vagary?"

No answer.

I threw open the folding-doors near by, and turning upon Turkey and Nippers, exclaimed:

"Bartleby a second time says, he won't examine his papers. What do you think of it, Turkey?"

It was afternoon, be it remembered. Turkey sat glowing like a brass boiler; his bald heat steaming; his hands reeling among his blotted papers.

"Think of it?" roared Turkey. "I think I'll just step behind his screen, and black his eyes for him!"

So saying, Turkey rose to his feet and threw his arms into a pugilistic position. He was hurrying away to make good his promise, when I detained him, alarmed at the effect of incautiously rousing Turkey's combativeness after dinner.

"Sit down, Turkey," said I, "and hear what Nippers has to say. What do you think of it, Nippers? Would I not be justified in immediately dismissing Bartleby?"

"Excuse me, that is for you to decide, sir. I think his conduct quite unusual, and, indeed, unjust, as regards Turkey and myself. But it may only be a passing whim."

"Ah," exclaimed I, "you have strangely changed your mind, then — you speak very gently of him now."

"All beer," cried Turkey; "gentleness is effects of beer — Nippers and I dined together to-day. You see how gentle *I* am, sir. Shall I go and black his eyes?"

"You refer to Bartleby, I suppose. No, not to-day, Turkey." I replied; "pray, put up your fists."

I closed the doors, and again advanced towards Bartleby. I felt additional incentives tempting me to my fate. I burned to be rebelled against again. I remembered that Bartleby never left the office.

"Bartleby," said I, "Ginger Nut is away; just step around to the post-office, won't you?" (it was but a three minutes' walk) "and see if there is anything for me."

"I would prefer not to."

"You *will* not?"

"I *prefer* not."

I staggered to my desk, and sat there in a deep study. My blind inveteracy returned. Was there any other thing in which I could procure myself to be ignominiously repulsed by this lean, penniless wight? — my hired clerk? What added thing is there, perfectly reasonable, that he will be sure to refuse to do?

"Bartleby!"

No answer.

"Bartleby," in a louder tone.

No answer.

"Bartleby," I roared.

Like a very ghost, agreeably to the laws of magical invocation, at the third summons, he appeared at the entrance of his hermitage.

"Go to the next room, and tell Nippers to come to me."

"I prefer not to," he respectfully and slowly said, and mildly disappeared.

"Very good, Bartleby," said I, in a quiet sort of serenely-severe self-possessed tone, intimating the unalterable purpose of some terrible retribution very close at hand. At the moment I half intended something of the kind. But upon the whole, as it was drawing towards my dinner-hour, I thought it best to put on my hat and walk home for the day, suffering much from perplexity and distress of mind.

Shall I acknowledge it? The conclusion of this whole business was, that it soon became a fixed fact of my chambers, that a pale young scrivener, by the name of Bartleby, had a desk there; that he copied for me at the usual rate of four cents a folio (one hundred words); but he was permanently exempt from examining the work done by him, that duty being transferred to Turkey and Nippers, out of compliment, doubtless, to their superior acuteness; moreover, said Bartleby was never, on any account, to be dispatched on the most trivial errand of any sort; and that even if entreated to take upon him such a matter, it was generally understood that he would "prefer not to" — in other words, that he would refuse point-blank.

As days passed on, I became considerably reconciled to Bartleby. His steadiness, his freedom from all dissipation, his incessant industry (except when he chose to throw himself into a standing revery behind his screen), his great stillness, his unalterableness of demeanor under all circumstances, made him a valuable acquisition. One prime thing was this — *he was always there* — first in the morning, continually through the day, and the last at night. I had a singular confidence in his honesty. I felt my most precious papers perfectly safe in his hands. Sometimes, to be sure, I could not, for the very soul of me, avoid falling into sudden spasmodic passions with him. For it was exceeding difficult to bear in mind all the time those strange peculiarities, privileges, and unheard-of exemptions, forming the tacit stipulations on Bartleby's part under which he remained in my office. Now and then, in the eagerness of dispatching pressing business, I would inadvertently summon Bartleby, in a short, rapid tone, to put his finger, say, on the incipient tie of a bit of red tape with which I was about compressing some papers. Of course, from behind the screen the usual answer, "I prefer not to," was sure to come; and then, how could a human creature, with the common infirmities of our nature, refrain from bitterly exclaiming upon such perverseness — such unreasonableness? However, every added repulse of this sort which I received only tended to lessen the probability of my repeating the inadvertence.

Here it must be said, that, according to the custom of most legal gentlemen occupying chambers in densely-populated law buildings, there were several keys to my door. One was kept by a woman residing in the attic, which person weekly scrubbed and daily swept and dusted my apartments. Another was kept by Turkey for convenience sake. The third I sometimes carried in my own pocket. The fourth I knew not who had.

Now, one Sunday morning I happened to go to Trinity Church, to hear a celebrated preacher, and finding myself rather early on the ground I thought I would walk round to my chambers for a while. Luckily I had my key with me; but upon applying it to the lock, I found it resisted by something inserted from the inside. Quite surprised, I called out; when to my consternation a key was turned from within; and thrusting his lean visage at me, and holding the door ajar, the apparition of Bartleby appeared, in his shirt-sleeves, and otherwise in a strangely tattered deshabille, saying quietly that he was sorry, but he was deeply engaged just then, and — preferred not admitting me at present. In a brief word or two, he moreover added, that perhaps I had better walk round the block two or three times, and by that time he would probably have concluded his affairs.

Now, the utterly unsurmised appearance of Bartleby, tenanting my law-chambers of a Sunday morning, with his cadaverously gentlemanly *nonchalance*, yet withal firm and self-possessed, had such a strange effect upon me, that incontinently I slunk away from my own door, and did as desired. But not without sundry twinges of impotent rebellion against the mild effrontery of this unaccountable scrivener. Indeed, it was his wonderful mildness chiefly, which not only disarmed me, but unmanned me, as it were. For I consider that one, for the time, is a sort of unmanned when he tranquilly permits his hired clerk to dictate to him, and order him away from his own premises. Furthermore, I was full of uneasiness as to what Bartleby could possibly be doing in my office in his shirt-sleeves, and in an otherwise dismantled condition of a Sunday morning. Was anything amiss going on? Nay, that was out of the question. It was not to be thought of for a moment that Bartleby was an immoral person. But what could he be doing there? — copying? Nay again, whatever might be his eccentricities, Bartleby was an eminently decorous person. He would be the last man to sit down to his desk in any state approaching to nudity. Besides, it was Sunday; and there was something about Bartleby that forbade the supposition that he would by any secular occupation violate the proprieties of the day.

Nevertheless, my mind was not pacified; and full of a restless curiosity, at last I returned to the door. Without hindrance I inserted my key, opened it and entered. Bartleby was not to be seen. I looked round anxiously, peeped behind his screen; but it was very plain that he was gone. Upon more closely examining the place, I surmised that for an indefinite period Bartleby must have ate, dressed, and slept in my office, and that too without plate, mirror, or bed. The cushioned seat of a rickety old sofa in one corner bore a faint impress of a lean, reclining form. Rolled away under his desk, I found a blanket; under the empty grate, a blacking box and brush; on a chair, a tin basin, with soap and a ragged towel; in a newspaper a few crumbs of ginger-nuts and a morsel of cheese. Yes, thought I, it is evident enough that Bartleby has been making his home here, keeping bachelor's hall all by himself. Immediately then the thought came sweeping across me, what miserable friendlessness and loneliness are here revealed! His poverty is great; but his solitude, how horrible! Think of it. Of a Sunday, Wall Street is deserted as Petra; and every night of every day it is an emptiness. This building, too, which of week-days hums with industry and life, at nightfall echoes with sheer vacancy, and all through Sunday is forlorn. And here Bartleby makes his home; sole spectator of a solitude which he has seen all populous — a sort of innocent and transformed Marius brooding among the ruins of Carthage!

For the first time in my life a feeling of overpowering stinging melancholy seized me. Before, I had never experienced aught but a not unpleasing sadness. The bond of a common humanity now drew me irresistibly to gloom. A fraternal melancholy! For both I and Bartleby were sons of Adam. I remembered the bright silks and sparkling faces I had seen that day, in gala trim, swan-like sailing down the Mississippi of Broadway; and I contrasted them with the pallid copyist, and thought to myself, Ah, happiness courts the light, so we deem the world is gay; but misery hides aloof, so we deem that misery there is none. These sad fancyings — chimeras, doubtless, of a sick and silly brain — led on to other and more special thoughts, concerning the eccentricities of Bartleby. Presentiments of strange discoveries hovered round me. The scrivener's pale form appeared to me laid out, among uncaring strangers, in its shivering winding-sheet.

Suddenly I was attracted by Bartleby's closed desk, the key in open sight left in the lock.

I mean no mischief, seek the gratification of no heartless curiosity, thought I; besides, the desk is mine, and its contents, too, so I will make bold to look within. Everything was methodically arranged, the papers smoothly placed. The pigeon-holes were deep, and removing the files of documents, I groped into their recesses. Presently I felt something there, and dragged it out. It was an old bandanna handkerchief, heavy and knotted. I opened it, and saw it was a saving's bank.

I now recalled all the quiet mysteries which I had noted in the man. I remembered that he never spoke but to answer; that, though at intervals he had considerable time to himself, yet I have never seen him reading — no, not even a newspaper; that for long periods he would stand looking out, at his pale window behind the screen, upon the dead brick wall; I was quite sure he never visited any refectory or eating-house; while his pale face clearly indicated that he never drank beer like Turkey, or tea and coffee even, like other men; that he never went anywhere in particular that I could learn; never went out for a walk, unless, indeed, that was the case at present; that he had declined telling who he was, or whence he came, or whether he had any relatives in the world; that though so thin and pale, he never complained of ill-health. And more than all, I remembered a certain unconscious air of pallid — how shall I call it? — of pallid haughtiness, say, or rather an austere reserve about him, which had positively awed me into my tame compliance with his eccentricities, when I had feared to ask him to do the slightest incidental thing for me, even though I might know, from his long-continued motionlessness, that behind his screen he must be standing in one of those dead-wall reveries of his.

Revolving all these things, and coupling them with the recently discovered fact, that he made my office his constant abiding place and home, and not forgetful of his morbid moodiness; revolving all these things, a prudential feeling began to steal over me. My first emotions had been those of pure melancholy and sincerest pity; but just in proportion as the forlornness of Bartleby grew and grew to my imagination, did the same melancholy merge into fear, that pity into repulsion. So true it is, and so terrible, too, that up to a certain point the thought or sight of misery enlists our best affections; but in certain special cases, beyond that point it does not. They err who would assert that invariably this is owing to the inherent selfishness of the human heart. It rather proceeds from a certain hopelessness of remedying excessive and organic ill. To a sensitive being, pity is not seldom pain. And when at last it is perceived that such pity cannot lead to effectual succor, common sense bids the soul be rid of it. What I saw that morning persuaded me that the scrivener was the victim of innate and incurable disorder. I might give alms to his body; but his body did not pain him; it was his soul that suffered, and his soul I could not reach.

I did not accomplish the purpose of going to Trinity Church that morning. Somehow, the things I had seen disqualified me for the time from church-going. I walked homeward, thinking what I would do with Bartleby. Finally, I resolved upon this — I would put certain calm questions to him the next morning, touching his history, etc., and if he declined to answer them openly and unreservedly (and I supposed he would prefer not), then to give him a twenty dollar bill over and above whatever I might owe him, and tell him his services were no longer required; but that if in any other way I could assist him, I would be happy to do so, especially if he desired to return to his native place, wherever that might be, I would willingly help to defray the expenses. Moreover, if, after reaching home, he found himself at any time in want of aid, a letter from him would be sure of a reply.

The next morning came.

"Bartleby," said I, gently calling to him behind his screen.

No reply.

"Bartleby," said I, in a still gentler tone, "come here; I am not going to ask you to do anything you would prefer not to do — I simply wish to speak to you."

Upon this he noiselessly slid into view.

"Will you tell me, Bartleby, where you were born?"

"I would prefer not to."

"Will you tell me *anything* about yourself?"

"I would prefer not to."

"But what reasonable objection can you have to speak to me? I feel friendly towards you."

He did not look at me while I spoke, but kept his glance fixed upon my bust of Cicero, which, as I then sat, was directly behind me, some six inches above my head.

"What is your answer, Bartleby?" said I, after waiting a considerable time for a reply, during which his countenance remained immovable, only there was the faintest conceivable tremor of the white attenuated mouth.

"At present I prefer to give no answer," he said, and retired into his hermitage.

It was rather weak in me I confess, but his manner, on this occasion, nettled me. Not only did there seem to lurk in it a certain calm disdain, but his perverseness seemed ungrateful, considering the undeniable good usage and indulgence he had received from me.

Again I sat ruminating what I should do. Mortified as I was at his behavior, and resolved as I had been to dismiss him when I entered my office, nevertheless I strangely felt something superstitious knocking at my heart, and forbidding me to carry out my purpose, and denouncing me for a villain if I dared to breathe one bitter word against this forlornest of mankind. At last, familiarly drawing my chair behind his screen, I sat down and said: "Bartleby, never mind, then, about revealing your history; but let me entreat you, as a friend, to comply as far as may be with the usages of this office. Say now, you will help to examine papers to-morrow or next day; in short, say now, that in a day or two you will begin to be a little reasonable: — say so, Bartleby."

"At present I would prefer not to be a little reasonable," was his mildly cadaverous reply.

Just then the folding-doors opened, and Nippers approached. He seemed suffering from an unusually bad night's rest, induced by severer indigestion than common. He overheard those final words of Bartleby.

"*Prefer not*, ch? gritted Nippers — "I'd *prefer* him, if I were you, sir," addressing me — "I'd *prefer* him; I'd give him preferences, the stubborn mule! What is it, sir, pray, that he *prefers* not to do now?"

Bartleby moved not a limb.

"Mr. Nippers," said I, "I'd prefer that you would withdraw for the present."

Somehow, of late, I had got into the way of involuntarily using this word "prefer" upon all sorts of not exactly suitable occasions. And I trembled to think that my contact with the scrivener had already and seriously affected me in a mental way. And what further and deeper aberration might it not yet produce? This apprehension had not been without efficacy in determining me to summary measures.

As Nippers, looking very sour and sulky, was departing, Turkey blandly and deferentially approached.

"With submission, sir," said he, "yesterday I was thinking about Bartleby here, and I think that if he would prefer to take a quart of good ale every day, it would do much towards mending him, and enabling him to assist in examining his papers."

"So you have got the word, too," said I, slightly excited.

"With submission, what word, sir?" asked Turkey, respectfully crowding himself into the contracted space behind the screen, and by so doing, making me jostle the scrivener. "What word, sir?"

"I would prefer to be left alone here," said Bartleby, as if offended at being mobbed in his privacy.

"*That's* the word, Turkey," said I — "*that's* it."

"Oh, *prefer*? oh yes — queer word. I never use it myself. But, sir, as I was saying, if he would but prefer — "

"'Turkey," interrupted I, "you will please withdraw."

"Oh certainly, sir, if you prefer that I should."

As he opened the folding-door to retire, Nippers at his desk caught a glimpse of me, and asked whether I would prefer to have a certain paper copied on blue paper or white. He did not in the last roguishly accent the word "prefer." It was plain that it involuntarily rolled from his tongue. I thought to myself, surely I must get rid of a demented man, who already has in some degree turned the tongues, if not the heads of myself and clerks. But I thought it prudent not to break the dismission at once.

The next day I noticed that Bartleby did nothing but stand at his window in his dead-wall revery. Upon asking him why he did not write, he said that he had decided upon doing no more writing.

"Why, how now? what next?" exclaimed I, "do no more writing?"

"No more."

"And what is the reason?"

"Do you not see the reason for yourself?" he indifferently replied.

I look steadfastly at him, and perceived that his eyes looked dull and glazed. Instantly it occurred to me, that his unexampled diligence in copying by his dim window for the first few weeks of his stay with me might have temporarily impaired his vision.

I was touched. I said something in condolence with him. I hinted that of course he did wisely in abstaining from writing for a while; and urged him to embrace that opportunity of taking wholesome exercise in the open air. This, however, he did not do. A few days after this, my other clerks being absent, and being in a great hurry to dispatch certain letters by the mail, I thought that, having nothing else earthly to do, Bartleby would surely be less inflexible than usual, and carry these letters to the post-office. But he blankly declined. So, much to my inconvenience, I went myself.

Still added days went by. Whether Bartleby's eyes improved or not, I could not say. To all appearance, I thought they did. But, when I asked him if they did, he vouchsafed no answer. At all events, he would do no copying. At last, in reply to my urgings, he informed me that he had permanently given up copying.

"What!" exclaimed I; "suppose your eyes should get entirely well — better than ever before — would you not copy then?"

"I have given up copying," he answered, and slid aside.

He remained as ever, a fixture in my chamber. Nay — if that were possible — he became still more a fixture than before. What was to be done? He would do nothing in the office; why should he stay there? In plain fact, he had now become a millstone to me, not only useless as a necklace, but afflictive to bear. Yet I was sorry for him. I speak less than truth when I say that, on his own account, he occasioned me uneasiness. If he would but have named a single relative or friend, I would instantly have written, and urged their taking the poor fellow away to some convenient retreat. But he seemed alone, absolutely alone in the universe. A bit of wreck in the mid-Atlantic. At length, necessities connected with my business tyrannized over all other considerations. Decently as I could, I told Bartleby that in six days' time he must unconditionally leave the office. I warned him to take measures, in the interval, for procuring some other abode. I offered to assist him in this endeavor, if he himself would but take the first step towards a removal. "And when you finally quit me, Bartleby," added I, "I shall see that you go not away entirely unprovided. Six days from this hour, remember."

At the expiration of that period, I peeped behind the screen, and lo! Bartleby was there.

I buttoned up my coat, balanced myself; advanced slowly towards him, touched his shoulder, and said, "The time has come; you must quit this place; I am sorry for you; here is money; but you must go."

"I would prefer not," he replied, with his back still towards me.

"You *must*."

He remained silent.

Now I had an unbounded confidence in this man's common honesty. He had frequently restored to me sixpences and shillings carelessly dropped upon the floor, for I am apt to be very reckless in such shirt-button affairs. The proceeding, then, which followed will not be deemed extraordinary.

"Bartleby," said I, "I owe you twelve dollars on account; here are thirty-two; the odd twenty are yours — Will you take it?" and I handed the bills towards him.

But he made no motion.

"I will leave them here, then," putting them under a weight on the table. Then taking my hat and cane and going to the door, I tranquilly turned and added — "After you have removed your things from these offices, Bartleby, you will of course lock the door — since every one is now gone for the day but you — and if you please, slip your key underneath the mat, so that I may have it in the morning. I shall not see you again; so good-bye to you. If, hereafter, in your new place of abode, I can be of any service to you, do not fail to advise me by letter. Good-bye, Bartleby, and fare you well."

But he answered not a word; like the last column of some ruined temple, he remained standing mute and solitary in the middle of the otherwise deserted room.

As I walked home in a pensive mood, my vanity got the better of my pity. I could not but highly plume myself on my masterly management in getting rid of Bartleby. Masterly I call it, and such it must appear to any dispassionate thinker. The beauty of my procedure seemed to consist in its perfect quietness. There was no vulgar bullying, no bravado of any sort, no choleric hectoring, and striding to and fro across the apartment, jerking out vehement commands for Bartleby to bundle himself off with his beggarly traps. Nothing of the kind. Without loudly bidding Bartleby depart — as an inferior genius might have done — I *assumed* the ground that depart he must; and upon that assumption built all I had to say. The more I thought over my procedure, the more I was charmed with it. Nevertheless, next morning, upon awakening, I had my doubts — I had somehow slept off the fumes of vanity. One of the coolest and wisest hours a man has, is just after he awakes in the morning. My procedure seemed as sagacious as ever — but only in theory. How it would prove in practice — there was the rub. It was truly a beautiful thought to have assumed Bartleby's departure; but, after all, that assumption was simply my own, and none of Bartleby's. The great point was, not whether I had assumed that he would quit me, but whether he would prefer so to do. He was more a man of preferences than assumptions.

After breakfast, I walked down town, arguing the probabilities, *pro* and *con*. One moment I thought it would prove a miserable failure, and Bartleby would be found alive at my office as usual; the next moment it seemed certain that I should find his chair empty. And so I kept veering about. At the corner of Broadway and Canal Street, I saw quite an excited group of people standing in earnest conversation.

"I'll take odds he doesn't," said a voice as I passed.

"Doesn't go? — done!" said I, "put up your money."

I was instinctively putting my hand in my pocket to produce my own, when I remembered that this was an election day. The words I had overheard bore no reference to Bartleby, but to the success or nonsuccess of some candidate for the mayoralty. In my intent frame of mind, I had, as it were, imagined that all Broadway shared in my excitement, and were debating the same question with me. I passed on, very thankful that the uproar of the street screened my momentary absent-mindedness.

As I had intended, I was earlier than usual at my office door. I stood listening for a moment. All was still. He must be gone. I tried the knob. The door was locked. Yes, my procedure had worked to a charm; he indeed must be vanished. Yet a certain melancholy mixed with this: I was almost sorry for my brilliant success. I was fumbling under the door mat for the key, which Bartleby was to have left there for me, when accidentally my knee knocked against a panel, producing a summoning sound, and in response a voice came to me from within — "Not yet; I am occupied."

It was Bartleby.

I was thunderstruck. For an instant I stood like the man who, pipe in mouth, was killed one cloudless afternoon long ago in Virginia, by summer lightning; at his own warm open window he was killed, and remained leaning out there upon the dreamy afternoon, till some one touched him, when he fell.

"Not gone!" I murmured at last. But again obeying that wondrous ascendancy which the inscrutable scrivener had over me, and from which ascendancy, for all my chafing, I could not completely escape, I slowly went down the stairs and out into the street and while walking round the block, considered what I should next do in this unheard-of perplexity. Turn the man out by an actual thrusting I could not; to drive him away by calling him hard names would not do; calling in the police was an unpleasant idea; and yet, permit him to enjoy his cadaverous triumph over me — this, too, I could not think of. What was to be done? or, if nothing could be done, was there anything further that I could *assume* in the matter? Yes, as before I had prospectively assumed that Bartleby would depart, so now I might retrospectively assume that departed he was. In the legitimate carrying out of this assumption, I might enter my office in a great hurry, and pretending not to see Bartleby at all, walk straight against him as if he were air. Such a proceeding would in a singular degree have the appearance of a home-thrust. It was hardly possible that Bartleby could withstand such an application of the doctrine of assumptions. But upon second thoughts the success of the plan seemed rather dubious. I resolved to argue the matter over with him again.

"Bartleby," said I, entering the office, with a quietly severe expression, "I am seriously displeased. I am pained, Bartleby. I had thought better of you. I had imagined you of such a gentlemanly organization, that in any delicate dilemma a slight hint would suffice — in short, an assumption. But it appears I am deceived. Why," I added, unaffectedly starting, "you have not even touched that money yet," pointing to it, just where I had left it the evening previous.

He answered nothing.

"Will you, or will you not, quit me?" I now demanded in a sudden passion, advancing close to him.

"I would prefer *not* to quit you," he replied, gently emphasizing the *not*.

"What earthly right have you to stay here? Do you pay any rent? Do you pay my taxes? Or is this property yours?"

He answered nothing.

"Are you ready to go on and write now? Are your eyes recovered? Could you copy a small paper for me this morning? or help examine a few lines? or step round to the post office? In a word, will you do anything at all, to give a coloring to your refusal to depart the premises?"

He silently retired into his hermitage.

I was now in such a state of nervous resentment that I thought it but prudent to check myself at present from further demonstrations. Bartleby and I were alone. I remembered the tragedy of the unfortunate Adams and the still more unfortunate Colt in the solitary office of the latter; and how poor Colt, being dreadfully incensed by Adams, and imprudently permitting himself to get wildly excited, was at unawares hurried into his fatal act — an act which certainly no man could possibly deplore more than the actor himself. Often it had occurred to me in my ponderings upon the subject that had that altercation taken place in the public street, or at a private residence, it would not have terminated as it did. It was the circumstance of being alone in a solitary office, up stairs, of a building entirely unhallowed by humanizing domestic associations — an uncarpeted office, doubtless, of a dusty, haggard sort of appearance — this it must have been, which greatly helped to enhance the irritable desperation of the hapless Colt.

But when this old Adam of resentment rose in me and tempted me concerning Bartleby, I grappled him and threw him. How? Why, simply by recalling the divine injunction: "A new commandment give I unto you, that ye love one another." Yes, this it was that saved me. Aside from higher considerations, charity often operates as a vastly wise and prudent principle — a great safeguard to its possessor. Men have committed murder for jealousy's sake, and anger's sake, and hatred's sake, and selfishness' sake, and spiritual pride's sake; but no man, that ever I heard of, ever committed a diabolical murder for sweet charity's sake. Mere self-interest, then, if no better motive can be enlisted, should, especially with high-tempered men, prompt all beings to charity and philanthropy. At any rate, upon the occasion in question, I strove to drown my exasperated feelings towards the scrivener by benevolently construing his conduct. Poor fellow, poor fellow! thought I, he don't mean anything; and besides, he has seen hard times, and ought to be indulged.

I endeavored, also, immediately to occupy myself, and at the same time to comfort my despondency. I tried to fancy, that in the course of the morning, at such time as might prove agreeable to him, Bartleby, of his own free accord, would emerge from his hermitage and take up some decided line of march in the direction of the door. But no. Half-past twelve o'clock came; Turkey began to glow in the face, overturn his inkstand, and become generally obstreperous; Nippers abated down into quietude and courtesy; Ginger Nut munched his noon apple; and Bartleby remained standing at his window in one of his profoundest dead-wall reveries. Will it be credited? Ought I to acknowledge it? That afternoon I left the office without saying one further word to him.

Some days now passed, during which, at leisure intervals I looked a little into "Edwards on the Will," and "Priestley on Necessity." Under the circumstances, those books induced a salutary feeling. Gradually I slid into the persuasion that these troubles of mine, touching the scrivener, had been all predestinated from eternity, and Bartleby was billeted upon me for some mysterious purpose of an all-wise Providence, which it was not for a mere mortal like me to fathom. Yes, Bartleby, stay there behind your screen, thought I; I shall persecute you no more; you are harmless and noiseless as any of these old chairs; in short, I never feel so private as when I know you are here. At last I see it; I penetrate to the predestinated purpose of my life. I am content. Others may have loftier parts to enact; but my mission in this world, Bartleby, is to furnish you with office-room for such period as you may see fit to remain.

I believe that this wise and blessed frame of mind would have continued with me, had it not been for the unsolicited and uncharitable remarks obtruded upon me by my professional friends who visited the rooms. But thus it often is, that the constant friction of illiberal minds wears out at last the best resolves of the more generous. Though to be sure, when I reflected upon it, it was not strange that people entering my office should be struck by the peculiar aspect of the unaccountable Bartleby, and so be tempted to throw out some sinister observations concerning him. Sometimes an attorney, having business with me, and calling at my office, and finding no one but the scrivener there, would undertake to obtain some sort of precise information from him touching my whereabouts; but without heeding his idle talk, Bartleby would remain standing immovable in the middle of the room. So after contemplating him in that position for a time, the attorney would depart, no wiser than he came.

Also, when a reference was going on, and the room full of lawyers and witnesses, and business driving fast, some deeply-occupied legal gentleman present, seeing

Bartleby wholly unemployed, would request him to run round to his (the legal gentleman's) office and fetch some papers for him. Thereupon, Bartleby would tranquilly decline, and yet remain idle as before. Then the lawyer would give a great stare, and turn to me. And what could I say? At last I was made aware that all through the circle of my professional acquaintance, a whisper of wonder was running round, having reference to the strange creature I kept at my office. This worried me very much. And as the idea came upon me of his possibly turning out a long-lived man, and keep occupying my chambers, and denying my authority; and perplexing my visitors; and scandalizing my professional reputation; and casting a general gloom over the premises; keeping soul and body together to the last upon his savings (for doubtless he spent but half a dime a day), and in the end perhaps outlive me, and claim possession of my office by right of his perpetual occupancy: as all these dark anticipations crowded upon me more and more, and my friends continually intruded their relentless remarks upon the apparition in my room; a great change was wrought in me. I resolved to gather all my faculties together, and forever rid me of this intolerable incubus.

Ere evolving any complicated project, however, adapted to this end, I first simply suggested to Bartleby the propriety of his permanent departure. In a calm and serious tone, I commended the idea to his careful and mature consideration. But, having taken three days to meditate upon it, he apprised me, that his original determination remained the same, in short, that he still preferred to abide with me.

What shall I do? I now said to myself, buttoning up my coat to the last button. What shall I do? what ought I do? what does conscience say I *should* do with this man, or, rather, ghost. Rid myself of him, I must; go, he shall. But how? You will not thrust him, the poor, pale, passive mortal — you will not thrust such a helpless creature out of your door? you will not dishonor yourself by such cruelty? No, I will not, I cannot do that. Rather would I let him live and die here, and then mason up his remains in the wall. What, then, will you do? For all your coaxing, he will not budge. Bribes he leaves under your own paperweight on your table; in short, it is quite plain that he prefers to cling to you.

Then something severe, something unusual must be done. What! surely you will not have him collared by a constable, and commit his innocent pallor to the common jail? And upon what ground could you procure such a thing to be done? — a vagrant, is he? What! he a vagrant, a wanderer, who refuses to budge? It is because he will *not* be a vagrant, then, that you seek to count him *as* a vagrant. That is too absurd. No visible means of support: there I have him. Wrong again: for indubitably he *does* support himself, and that is the only unanswerable proof that any man can show of his possessing the means so to do. No more, then. Since he will not quit me, I must quit him. I will change my offices; I will move elsewhere, and give him fair notice, that if I find him on my new premises I will then proceed against him as a common trespasser.

Acting accordingly, next day I thus addressed him: "I find these chambers too far from the City Hall; the air is unwholesome. In a word, I propose to remove my offices next week, and shall no longer require your services. I tell you this now, in order that you may seek another place."

He made no reply, and nothing more was said.

On the appointed day I engaged carts and men, proceeded to my chambers, and, having but little furniture, everything was removed in a few hours. Throughout, the scrivener remained standing behind the screen, which I directed to be removed the last thing. It was withdrawn; and, being folded up like a huge folio, left him the motionless occupant of a naked room. I stood in the entry watching him a moment, while something from within me upbraided me.

I re-entered, with my hand in my pocket — and — and my heart in my mouth.

"Good-bye, Bartleby; I am going — good-bye, and God some way bless you; and take that," slipping something in his hand. But it dropped upon the floor, and then — strange to say — I tore myself from him whom I had so longed to be rid of.

Established in my new quarters, for a day or two I kept the door locked, and started at every football in the passages. When I returned to my rooms, after any little absence, I would pause at the threshold for an instant, and attentively listen, ere applying my key. But these fears were needless. Bartleby never came nigh me.

I thought all was going well, when a perturbed-looking stranger visited me, inquiring whether I was the person who had recently occupied rooms at No. — Wall Street.

Full of forebodings, I replied that I was.

"Then, sir," said the stranger, who proved a lawyer, "you are responsible for the man you left there. He refuses to do any copying; he refuses to do anything; he says he prefers not to; and he refuses to quit the premises."

"I am very sorry, sir," said I, with assumed tranquillity, but an inward tremor, "but, really, the man you allude to is nothing to me — he is no relation or apprentice of mine, that you should hold me responsible for him."

"In mercy's name, who is he?"

"I certainly cannot inform you. I know nothing about him. Formerly I employed him as a copyist; but he has done nothing for me now for some time past."

"I shall settle him, then — good morning, sir."

Several days passed, and I heard nothing more; and, though I often felt a charitable prompting to call at the place and see poor Bartleby, yet a certain squeamishness, of I know not what, withheld me.

All is over with him, by this time, thought I, at last, when, through another week, no further intelligence reached me. But, coming to my room the day after, I found several persons waiting at my door in a high state of nervous excitement.

"That's the man — here he comes," cried the foremost one, whom I recognized as the lawyer who had previously called upon me alone.

"You must take him away, sir, at once," cried a portly person among them, advancing upon me, and whom I knew to be the landlord of No. — Wall Street. "These gentlemen, my tenants, cannot stand it any longer; Mr. B — — ," pointing to the lawyer, "has turned him out of his room, and he now persists on haunting the building generally, sitting upon the banisters of the stairs by day, and sleeping in the entry by night. Everybody is concerned; clients are leaving the offices; some fears are entertained of a mob; something you must do, and that without delay."

Aghast at this torrent, I fell back before it, and would fain have locked myself in my new quarters. In vain I persisted that Bartleby was nothing to me — no more than to any one else. In vain — I was the last person known to have anything to do with him, and they held me to the terrible account. Fearful, then, of being exposed in the papers (as one person present obscurely threatened), I considered the matter, and, at length, said, that if the lawyer would give me a confidential interview with the scrivener, in his (lawyer's) own room, I would, that afternoon, strive my best to rid them of the nuisance they complained of.

Going up stairs to my old haunt, there was Bartleby silently sitting upon the banister at the landing.

"What are you doing here, Bartleby?" said I.

"Sitting upon the banister," he mildly replied.

I motioned him into the lawyer's room, who then left us.

"Bartleby," said I, "are you aware that you are the cause of great tribulation to me, by persisting in occupying the entry after being dismissed from the office?"

No answer.

"Now one of two things must take place. Either you must do something, or something must be done to you. Now what sort of business would you like to engage in? Would you like to re-engage in copying for some one?"

"No; I would prefer not to make any change."

"Would you like a clerkship in a dry-goods store?"

"There is too much confinement about that. No, I would not like a clerkship; but I am not particular."

"Too much confinement," I cried, "why, you keep yourself confined all the time!"

"I would prefer not to take a clerkship," he rejoined, as if to settle that little item at once.

"How would a bar-tender's business suit you? There is no trying of the eye-sight in that."

"I would not like it at all; though, as I said before, I am not particular."

His unwonted wordiness inspirited me. I returned to the charge.

"Well, then, would you like to travel through the country collecting bills for the merchants? That would improve your health."

"No, I would prefer to be doing something else."

"How, then, would going as a companion to Europe, to entertain some young gentleman with your conversation — how would that suit you?"

"Not at all. It does not strike me that there is anything definite about that. I like to be stationary. But I am not particular."

"Stationary you shall be, then," I cried, now losing all patience, and, for the first time in all my exasperating connection with him, fairly flying into a passion. "If you do not go away from these premises before night, I shall feel bound — indeed, I *am* bound — to — to — to quit the premises myself!" I rather absurdly concluded, knowing not with what possible threat to try to frighten his immobility into compliance. Despairing of all further efforts, I was precipitately leaving him, when a final thought occurred to me — one which had not been wholly unindulged before.

"Bartleby," said I, in the kindest tone I could assume under such exciting circumstances, "will you go home with me now — not to my office, but my dwelling — and remain there till we can conclude upon some convenient arrangement for you at our leisure? Come, let us start now, right away."

"No: at present I would prefer not to make any change at all."

I answered nothing; but, effectually dodging every one by the suddenness and rapidity of my flight, rushed from the building, ran up Wall Street towards Broadway, and, jumping into the first omnibus, was soon removed from pursuit. As soon as tranquillity returned, I distinctly perceived that I had now done all that I possibly could, both in respect to the demands of the landlord and his tenants, and with regard to my own desire and sense of duty, to benefit Bartleby, and shield him from rude persecution. I now strove to be entirely care-free and quiescent; and my conscience justified me in the attempt; though, indeed, it was not so successful as I could have wished. So fearful was I of being again hunted out by the incensed landlord and his exasperated tenants, that, surrendering my business to Nippers, for a few days, I drove about the upper part of the town and through the suburbs, in my rockaway; crossed over to Jersey City and Hoboken, and paid fugitive visits to Manhattanville and Astoria. In fact, I almost lived in my rockaway for the time.

When again I entered my office, lo, a note from the landlord lay upon the desk. I opened it with trembling hands. It informed me that the writer had sent to the police, and had Bartleby removed to the Tombs as a vagrant. Moreover, since I knew more about him than any one else, he wished me to appear at the place, and make a suitable statement of the facts. These tidings had a conflicting effect upon me. At first I was indignant; but, at last, almost approved. The landlord's energetic, summary disposition, had led him to adopt a procedure which I do not think I would have decided upon myself; and yet, as a last resort, under such peculiar circumstances, it seemed the only plan.

As I afterwards learned, the poor scrivener, when told that he must be conducted to the Tombs, offered not the slightest obstacle, but, in his pale, unmoving way, silently acquiesced.

Some of the compassionate and curious by-standers joined the party, and headed by one of the constables arm-in-arm with Bartleby, the silent procession filed its way through all the noise, and heat, and joy of the roaring thoroughfares at noon.

The same day I received the note, I went to the Tombs, or, to speak more properly, the Halls of Justice. Seeking the right officer, I stated the purpose of my call, and was informed that the individual I described was, indeed, within. I then assured the functionary that Bartleby was a perfectly honest man, and greatly to be compassionated, however unaccountably eccentric. I narrated all I knew, and closed by suggesting the idea of letting him remain in as indulgent confinement as possible, till something less harsh might be done — though, indeed, I hardly knew what. At all events, if nothing else could be decided upon, the alms-house must receive him. I then begged to have an interview.

Being under no disgraceful charge, and quite serene and harmless in all his ways, they had permitted him freely to wander about the prison, and, especially, in the inclosed grass-plated yards thereof. And so I found him there, standing all alone in the quietest of the yards, his face towards a high wall, while all around, from the narrow slits of the jail windows, I thought I saw peering out upon the eyes of murderers and thieves.

"Bartleby!"

"I know you," he said, without looking around — "and I want nothing to say to you."

"It was not I that brought you here, Bartleby," said I, keenly pained at his implied suspicion. "And to you, this should not be so vile a place. Nothing reproachful attaches to you by being here. And see, it is not so sad a place as one might think. Look, there is the sky, and here is the grass."

"I know where I am," he replied, but would say nothing more, and so I left him.

As I entered the corridor again, a broad meat-like man, in an apron, accosted me, and jerking his thumb over his shoulder, said — "Is that your friend!"

"Yes."

"Does he want to starve? If he does, let him live on the prison fare, that's all."

"Who are you?" asked I, not knowing what to make of such an unofficially speaking person in such a place.

"I am the grub-man. Such gentlemen as have friends here, hire me to provide them with something good to eat."

"Is this so?" said I, turning to the turnkey.

He said it was.

"Well, then," said I, slipping some silver into the grub-man's hands (for so they called him), "I want you to give particular attention to my friend there; let him have the best dinner you can get. And you must be as polite to him as possible."

"Introduce me, will you?" said the grub-man, looking at me with an expression which seemed to say he was all impatience for an opportunity to give a specimen of his breeding.

Thinking it would prove of benefit to the scrivener, I acquiesced; and, asking the grub-man his name, went up with him to Bartleby.

"Bartleby, this is a friend; you will find him very useful to you."

"Your sarvant, sir, your sarvant," said the grub-man, making a low salutation behind his apron. "Hope you find it pleasant here, sir; nice grounds — cool apartments — hope you'll stay with us some time — try to make it agreeable. What will you have for dinner to-day?"

"I prefer not to dine to-day," said Bartleby, turning away. "It would disagree with me; I am unused to dinners." So saying, he slowly moved to the other side of the inclosure, and took up a position fronting the dead-wall.

"How's this?" said the grub-man, addressing me with a stare of astonishment. "He's odd, ain't he?"

"I think he is a little deranged," said I, sadly.

"Deranged? deranged is it? Well, now, upon my word, I thought that friend of yourn was a gentleman forger; they are always pale and genteel-like, them forgers. I can't help pity 'em — can't help it, sir. Did you know Monroe Edwards?" he added, touchingly, and paused. Then, laying his hand piteously on my shoulder, signed, "He died of consumption at Sing-Sing. So you weren't acquainted with Monroe?"

"No, I was never socially acquainted with any forgers. But I cannot stop longer. Look to my friend yonder. You will not lose by it. I will see you again."

Some few days after this, I again obtained admission to the Tombs, and went through the corridors in quest of Bartleby; but without finding him.

"I saw him coming from his cell not long ago," said the turnkey, "may be he's gone to loiter in the yards."

So I went in that direction.

"Are you looking for the silent man?" said another turnkey, passing me. "Yonder he lies — sleeping in the yard there. 'Tis not twenty minutes since I saw him lie down."

The yard was entirely quiet. It was not accessible to the common prisoners. The surrounding walls, of amazing thickness, kept off all sounds behind them. The Egyptian character of the masonry weighed upon me with its gloom. But a soft imprisoned turf grew under foot. The heart of the eternal pyramids, it seemed, wherein, by some strange magic, through the clefts, grass-seed, dropped by birds, had sprung.

Strangely huddled at the base of the wall, his knees drawn up, and lying on his side, his head touching the cold stones, I saw the wasted Bartleby. But nothing stirred. I paused; then went close up to him; stooped over, and saw that his dim eyes were open; otherwise he seemed profoundly sleeping. Something prompted me to touch him. I felt his hand, when a tingling shiver ran up my arm and down my spine to my feet.

The round face of the grub-man peered upon me now. "His dinner is ready. Won't he dine to-day, either? Or does he live without dining?"

"Lives without dining," said I, and closed the eyes.

"Eh! — He's asleep, ain't he?"

"With kings and counselors," murmured I.

There would seem little need for proceeding further in this history. Imagination will readily supply the meagre recital of poor Bartleby's interment. But, ere parting with the reader, let me say, that if this little narrative has sufficiently interested him, to awaken curiosity as to who Bartleby was, and what manner of life he led prior to the present narrator's making his acquaintance, I can only reply, that in such curiosity I fully share, but am wholly unable to gratify it. Yet here I hardly know whether I should divulge one little item of rumor, which came to my ear a few months after the scrivener's decease. Upon what basis it rested, I could never ascertain; and hence, how true it is I cannot now tell. But, inasmuch as this vague report has not been without a certain suggestive interest to me, however sad, it may prove the same with some others; and so I will briefly mention it. The report was this: that Bartleby had been a subordinate clerk in the Dead Letter Office at Washington, from which he had been suddenly removed by a change in the administration. When I think over this rumor, hardly can I express the emotions which seize me. Dead letters! does it not sound like dead men? Conceive a man by nature and misfortune prone to a pallid hopelessness, can any business seem more fitted to heighten it than that of continually handling these dead letters, and assorting them for the flames? For by the cartload they are annually burned. Sometimes from out the folded paper the pale clerk takes a ring — the finger it was meant for, perhaps, moulders in the grave; a bank-note sent in swiftest charity — he whom it would relieve, nor eats nor hungers any more; pardon for those who died despairing; hope for those who died unhoping; good tidings for those who died stifled by unrelieved calamities. On errands of life, these letters speed to death.

Ah, Bartleby! Ah, humanity!

YUKIO MISHIMA

Yukio Mishima (pseudonym of Kimitake Hiraoka, 1925–1970) was born in Tokyo, the son of a Japanese civil servant. Precocious and scholarly even as a child, he began to write stories while still in school. From the outset, he was preoccupied with the Japanese aristocratic tradition and aestheticism; further, he was intensely fascinated with samurai warrior rituals. He recognized his own dark fatalism: "my heart's leaning toward Death and Night and Blood," he called it. Early in his career he wrote novels that brought him considerable acclaim: *Confessions of a Mask* (1949; English 1958), *Thirst for Love* (1950; English 1969), *The Sound of Waves* (1954; English 1956), and *The Temple of the Golden Pavilion* (1956; English 1959). Yet literary fame was not all he craved, and beginning in the mid-1950s he cultivated an image of warriorlike fierceness: he studied boxing, karate, and sword fighting; and he sought celebrity by broadcasting his political and cultural views through the media. He continued to write plays, novels, and stories; among his later works are *The Sailor Who Fell from Grace with the Sea* (1963; English 1965), the tetralogy *The Sea of Fertility* (English 1975), and the collection of stories *Death in Midsummer* (English 1966). But his dissatisfaction with what he perceived to be the sterility of modern Japan drove him further into his fatal attraction to the samurai tradition. He created a private army of about one hundred men, dedicated to reviving the code of chivalry of the samurai. Two years later, in public, he committed *seppuku*, ritual suicide. "Swaddling Clothes" is not a story of samurai ways, but it chillingly reveals another dimension of Mishima's obsession with death, night, and blood.

Swaddling Clothes

Translated from the Japanese by Ivan Morris

He was always busy, Toshiko's husband. Even tonight he had to dash off to an appointment, leaving her to go home alone by taxi. But what else could a woman expect when she married an actor — an attractive one? No doubt she had been foolish to hope that he would spend the evening with her. And yet he must have known how she dreaded going back to their house, unhomely with its Western-style furniture and with the bloodstains still showing on the floor.

Toshiko had been oversensitive since girlhood: that was her nature. As the result of constant worrying she never put on weight, and now, an adult woman, she looked more like a transparent picture than a creature of flesh and blood. Her delicacy of spirit was evident to her most casual acquaintance.

Earlier that evening, when she had joined her husband at a night club, she had been shocked to find him entertaining friends with an account of "the incident." Sitting there in his American-style suit, puffing at a cigarette, he had seemed to her almost a stranger.

"It's a fantastic story," he was saying, gesturing flamboyantly as if in an attempt to outweigh the attractions of the dance band. "Here this new nurse for our baby arrives from the employment agency, and the very first thing I notice about her is her stomach. It's enormous — as if she had a pillow stuck under her kimono! No wonder, I thought, for I soon saw that she could eat more than the rest of us put together. She polished off the contents of our rice bin like that. . . ." He snapped his fingers. " 'Gastric dilation' — that's how she explained her girth and her appetite. Well, the day before yesterday we heard groans and moans coming from the nursery. We rushed in and found her squatting on the floor, holding her stomach in her two hands, and moaning like a cow. Next to her our baby lay in his cot, scared out of his wits and crying at the top of his lungs. A pretty scene, I can tell you!"

"So the cat was out of the bag?" suggested one of their friends, a film actor like Toshiko's husband.

"Indeed it was! And it gave me the shock of my life. You see, I'd completely swallowed that story about 'gastric dilation.' Well, I didn't waste any time. I rescued our good rug from the floor and spread a blanket for her to lie on. The whole time the girl was yelling like a stuck pig. By the time the doctor from the maternity clinic arrived, the baby had already been born. But our sitting room was a pretty shambles!"

"Oh, that I'm sure of!" said another of their friends, and the whole company burst into laughter.

Toshiko was dumbfounded to hear her husband discussing the horrifying happening as though it were no more than an amusing incident which they chanced to have witnessed. She shut her eyes for a moment and all at once she saw the newborn baby lying before her: on the parquet floor the infant lay, and his frail body was wrapped in bloodstained newspapers.

Toshiko was sure that the doctor had done the whole thing out of spite. As if to emphasize his scorn for this mother who had given birth to a bastard under such sordid conditions, he had told his assistant to wrap the baby in some loose newspapers, rather than proper swaddling. This callous treatment of the newborn child had offended Toshiko. Overcoming her disgust at the entire scene, she had fetched a brand-new piece of flannel from her cupboard and, having swaddled the baby in it, had laid him carefully in an armchair.

This all had taken place in the evening after her husband had left the house. Toshiko had told him nothing of it, fearing that he would think her oversoft, oversentimental; yet the scene had engraved itself deeply in her mind. Tonight she sat silently thinking back on it, while the jazz orchestra brayed and her husband chatted cheerfully with his friends. She knew that she would never forget the sight of the baby, wrapped in stained newspapers and lying on the floor — it was a scene fit for a butchershop. Toshiko, whose own life had been spent in solid comfort, poignantly felt the wretchedness of the illegitimate baby.

I am the only person to have witnessed its shame, the thought occurred to her. The mother never saw her child lying there in its newspaper wrappings, and the baby itself of course didn't know. I alone shall have to preserve that terrible scene in my memory. When the baby grows up and wants to find out about his birth, there will be no one to tell him, so long as I preserve silence. How strange that I should have this feeling of guilt! After all, it was I who took him up from the floor, swathed him properly in flannel, and laid him down to sleep in the armchair.

They left the night club and Toshiko stepped into the taxi that her husband had called for her. "Take this lady to Ushigomé," he told the driver and shut the door from the outside. Toshiko gazed through the window at her husband's smiling face and noticed his strong, white teeth. Then she leaned back in the seat, oppressed by the knowledge that their life together was in some way too easy, too painless. It would have been difficult for her to put her thoughts into words. Through the rear window of the taxi she took a last look at her husband. He was striding along the street toward his Nash car, and soon the back of his rather garish tweed coat had blended with the figures of the passers-by.

The taxi drove off, passed down a street dotted with bars and then by a theatre, in front of which the throngs of people jostled each other on the pavement. Although the performance had only just ended, the lights had already been turned out and in the half dark outside it was depressingly obvious that the cherry blossoms decorating the front of the theatre were merely scraps of white paper.

Even if that baby should grow up in ignorance of the secret of his birth, he can never become a respectable citizen, reflected Toshiko, pursuing the same train of thoughts. Those soiled newspaper swaddling clothes will be the symbol of his entire life. But why should I keep worrying about him so much? Is it because I feel uneasy about the future of my own child? Say twenty years from now, when our boy will have grown up into a fine, carefully educated young man, one day by a quirk of fate he meets that other boy, who then will also have turned twenty. And say that the other boy, who has been sinned against, savagely stabs him with a knife. . . .

It was a warm, overcast April night, but thoughts of the future made Toshiko feel cold and miserable. She shivered on the back seat of the car.

No, when the time comes I shall take my son's place, she told herself suddenly. Twenty years from now I shall be forty-three. I shall go to that young man and tell him straight out about everything — about his newspaper swaddling clothes, and about how I went and wrapped him in flannel.

The taxi ran along the dark wide road that was bordered by the park and by the Imperial Palace moat. In the distance Toshiko noticed the pinpricks of light which came from the blocks of tall office buildings.

Twenty years from now that wretched child will be in utter misery. He will be living a desolate, hopeless, poverty-stricken existence — a lonely rat. What else could happen to a baby who has had such a birth? He'll be wandering through the streets by himself, cursing his father, loathing his mother.

No doubt Toshiko derived a certain satisfaction from her somber thoughts: she tortured herself with them without cease. The taxi approached Hanzomon and drove past the compound of the British Embassy. At that point the famous rows of cherry trees were spread out before Toshiko in all their purity. On the spur of the moment she decided to go and view the blossoms by herself in the dark night. It was a strange decision for a timid and unadventurous young woman, but then she was in a strange state of mind and she dreaded the return home. That evening all sorts of unsettling fancies had burst open in her mind.

She crossed the wide street — a slim, solitary figure in the darkness. As a rule when she walked in the traffic Toshiko used to cling fearfully to her companion, but tonight she darted alone between the cars and a moment later had reached the long narrow park that borders the Palace moat. Chidorigafuchi, it is called — the Abyss of the Thousand Birds.

Tonight the whole park had become a grove of blossoming cherry trees. Under the calm cloudy sky the blossoms formed a mass of solid whiteness. The paper lanterns that hung from wires between the trees had been put out; in their place electric light bulbs, red, yellow, and green, shone dully beneath the blossoms. It was well past ten o'clock and most of the flower-viewers had gone home. As the occasional passers-by strolled through the park, they would automatically kick aside the empty bottles or crush the waste paper beneath their feet.

Newspapers, thought Toshiko, her mind going back once again to those happenings. Bloodstained newspapers. If a man were ever to hear of that piteous birth and know that it was he who had lain there, it would ruin his entire life. To think that I, a perfect stranger, should from now on have to keep such a secret — the secret of a man's whole existence. . . .

Lost in these thoughts, Toshiko walked on through the park. Most of the people still remaining there were quiet couples; no one paid her any attention. She noticed two people sitting on a stone bench beside the moat, not looking at the blossoms, but gazing silently at the water. Pitch black it was, and swathed in heavy shadows. Beyond the moat the somber forest of the Imperial Palace blocked her view. The trees reached up, to form a solid dark mass against the night sky. Toshiko walked slowly along the path beneath the blossoms hanging heavily overhead.

On a stone bench, slightly apart from the others, she noticed a pale object — not, as she had at first imagined, a pile of cherry blossoms, nor a garment forgotten by one of the visitors to the park. Only when she came closer did she see that it was a human form lying on the bench. Was it, she wondered, one of those miserable drunks often to be seen sleeping in public places? Obviously not, for the body had been systematically covered with newspapers, and it was the whiteness of those papers that had attracted Toshiko's attention. Standing by the bench, she gazed down at the sleeping figure.

It was a man in a brown jersey who lay there, curled up on layers of newspapers, other newspapers covering him. No doubt this had become his normal night residence now that spring had arrived. Toshiko gazed down at the man's dirty, unkempt hair, which in places had become hopelessly matted. As she observed the sleeping figures wrapped in its newspapers, she was inevitably reminded of the baby who had lain on the floor in its wretched swaddling clothes. The shoulder of the man's jersey rose and fell in the darkness in time with his heavy breathing.

It seemed to Toshiko that all her fears and premonitions had suddenly taken concrete form. In the darkness the man's pale forehead stood out, and it was a young forehead, though carved with wrinkles of long poverty and hardship. His khaki trousers had been slightly pulled up; on his sockless feet he wore a pair of battered gym shoes. She could not see his face and suddenly had an overmastering desire to get one glimpse of it.

She walked to the head of the bench and looked down. The man's head was half buried in his arms, but Toshiko could see that he was surprisingly young. She noticed the thick eyebrows and the fine bridge of his nose. His slightly open mouth was alive with youth.

But Toshiko had approached too close. In the silent night the newspaper bedding rustled, and abruptly the man opened his eyes. Seeing the young woman standing directly beside him, he raised himself with a jerk, and his eyes lit up. A second later a powerful hand reached out and seized Toshiko by her slender wrist.

She did not feel in the least afraid and made no effort to free herself. In a flash the thought had struck her, Ah, so the twenty years have already gone by! The forest of the Imperial Palace was pitch dark and utterly silent.

ALICE MUNRO

 Alice Munro, who was born in Wingham, Ontario, in 1931, has written short stories since she was a teenager. Though she lived for almost twenty-five years in western Canada, usually the world of her fiction is the world of her birthplace: rural southwestern Ontario. In stories remarkable for their wealth of "remembered detail" and their revelation of the emotional depths of ordinary people, she has told the lives of small-town Canadians, particularly girls and women. One of her primary concerns is "differentness," and her characters often find themselves trying to reconcile their yearnings for otherness with their need for acceptance in their social milieu. Munro is an admirer of the work of Southern writer Eudora Welty; like Welty, she can sketch a scene with almost casual brilliance, allowing accumulated detail and dialogue to carry the comedy or the pain. Her collections of stories include *Dance of the Happy Shades* (1968), *Something I've Been Meaning to Tell You* (1974), *The Beggar Maid* (1978), *The Moons of Jupiter* (1982), and *The Progress of Love* (1986). She has also written a novel, *Lives of Girls and Women* (1971). The stories here — "The Beggar Maid" and "Oh, What Avails" — disclose their characters' understandings, however tenuously sustained, of what is lost and what abides in the experience of living.

The Beggar Maid

Patrick Blatchford was in love with Rose. This had become a fixed, even furious, idea with him. For her, a continual surprise. He wanted to marry her. He waited for her after classes, moved in and walked beside her, so that anybody she was talking to would have to reckon with his presence. He would not talk, when these friends or classmates of hers were around, but he would try to catch her eye, so that he could indicate by a cold incredulous look what he thought of their conversation. Rose was flattered, but nervous. A girl named Nancy Falls, a friend of hers, mispronounced Metternich in front of him. He said to her later, "How can you be friends with people like that?"

Nancy and Rose had gone and sold their blood together, at Victoria Hospital. They each got fifteen dollars. They spent most of the money on evening shoes, tarty silver sandals. Then because they were sure the bloodletting had caused them to lose weight they had hot fudge sundaes at Boomers. Why was Rose unable to defend Nancy to Patrick?

Patrick was twenty-four years old, a graduate student, planning to be a history professor. He was tall, thin, fair, and good-looking, though he had a long pale-red birthmark, dribbling like a tear down his temple and his cheek. He apologized for it, but said it was fading, as he got older. When he was forty, it would have faded away. It was not the birthmark that canceled out his good looks, Rose thought. (Something did cancel them out, or at least diminish them, for her; she had to keep reminding herself they were there.) There was something edgy, jumpy, disconcerting, about him. His voice would break under stress — with her, it seemed he was always under stress — he knocked dishes and cups off tables, spilled drinks and bowls of peanuts, like a comedian. He was not a comedian, nothing could be further from his intentions. He came from British Columbia. His family was rich.

He arrived early to pick Rose up, when they were going to the movies. He wouldn't knock, he knew he was early. He sat on the step outside Dr. Henshawe's door. This was in the winter, it was dark out, but there was a little coach lamp beside the door.

"Oh, Rose! Come and look!" called Dr. Henshawe, in her soft, amused voice, and they looked down together from the dark window of the study. "The poor young man," said Dr. Henshawe tenderly. Dr. Henshawe was in her seventies. She was a former English professor, fastidious and lively. She had a lame leg, but a still youthfully, charmingly tilted head, with white braids wound around it.

She called Patrick poor because he was in love, and perhaps also because he was a male, doomed to push and blunder. Even from up here he looked stubborn and pitiable, determined and dependent, sitting out there in the cold.

"Guarding the door," Dr. Henshawe said. "Oh, Rose!"

Another time she said disturbingly, "Oh, dear, I'm afraid he is after the wrong girl."

Rose didn't like her saying that. She didn't like her laughing at Patrick. She didn't like Patrick sitting out on the steps that way, either. He was asking to be laughed at. He was the most vulnerable person Rose had ever known, he made himself so, didn't know anything about protecting himself. But he was also full of cruel judgments, he was full of conceit.

"You are a scholar, Rose," Dr. Henshawe would say. "This will interest you." Then she would read aloud something from the paper, or, more likely, something from *Canadian Forum* or the *Atlantic Monthly*. Dr. Henshawe had at one time headed the city's school board, she was a founding member of Canada's socialist party. She still sat on committees, wrote letters to the paper, reviewed books. Her father and mother had been medical missionaries; she had been born in China. Her house was small and perfect. Polished floors, glowing rugs, Chinese vases, bowls and landscapes, black carved screens. Much that Rose could not appreciate, at the time. She could not really distinguish between the little jade animals on Dr. Henshawe's mantelpiece and the ornaments displayed in the jewelry store window, in Hanratty, though she could now distinguish between either of these and the things Flo bought from the five-and-ten.

She could not really decide how much she liked being at Dr. Henshawe's. At times she felt discouraged, sitting in the dining room with a linen napkin on her knee, eating from fine white plates on blue placemats. For one thing, there was never enough to eat, and she had taken to buying doughnuts and chocolate bars and hiding them in her room. The canary swung on its perch in the dining room window and Dr. Henshawe directed conversation. She talked about politics, about writers. She mentioned Frank Scott and Dorothy Livesay. She said Rose must read them. Rose must read this, she must read that. Rose became sullenly determined not to. She was reading Thomas Mann. She was reading Tolstoy.

Before she came to Dr. Henshawe's, Rose had never heard of the working class. She took the designation home.

"This would have to be the last part of town where they put the sewers," Flo said.

"Of course," Rose said coolly. "This is the working-class part of town."

"*Working* class?" said Flo. "Not if the ones around here can help it."

Dr. Henshawe's house had done one thing. It had destroyed the naturalness, the taken-for-granted background, of home. To go back there was to go quite literally into a crude light. Flo had put fluroescent lights in the store and the kitchen. There was also, in a corner of the kitchen, a floor lamp Flo had won at Bingo; its shade was permanently wrapped in wide strips of cellophane. What Dr. Henshawe's house and Flo's house did best, in Rose's opinion, was discredit each other. In Dr. Henshawe's charming rooms there was always for Rose the raw knowledge of home, an indigestible lump, and at home, now, her sense of order and modulation elsewhere exposed such embarrassing sad poverty, in people who never thought themselves poor. Poverty was not just wretchedness, as Dr. Henshawe seemed to think, it was not just deprivation. It meant having those ugly tube lights and being proud of them. It meant continual talk of money and malicious talk about new things people had bought and whether they were paid for. It meant pride and jealousy flaring over something like the new pair of plastic curtains, imitating lace, that Flo had bought for the front window. That as well as hanging your clothes on nails behind the door and being able to hear every sound from the bathroom. It meant decorating your walls with a number of admonitions, pious and cheerful and mildly bawdy.

THE LORD IS MY SHEPHERD

BELIEVE IN THE LORD JESUS CHRIST AND THOU SHALL BE SAVED

Why did Flo have those, when she wasn't even religious? They were what people had, common as calendars.

THIS IS MY KITCHEN AND I WILL DO AS I DARNED PLEASE

MORE THAN TWO PERSONS TO A BED IS DANGEROUS AND UNLAWFUL

Billy Pope had brought that one. What would Patrick have to say about them? What would someone who was offended by a mispronunciation of Metternich think of Billy Pope's stories?

Billy Pope worked in Tyde's Butcher Shop. What he talked about most frequently now was the D.P., the Belgian, who had come to work there, and got on Billy Pope's nerves with his impudent singing of French songs and his naive notions of getting on in this country, buying a butcher shop of his own.

"Don't you think you can come over here and get yourself ideas," Billy Pope said to the D.P. "It's *youse* workin for *us*, and don't think that'll change into *us* workin for *youse*." That shut him up, Billy Pope said.

Patrick would say from time to time that since her home was only fifty miles away he ought to come up and meet Rose's family.

"There's only my stepmother."

"It's too bad I couldn't have met your father."

Rashly, she had presented her father to Patrick as a reader of history, an amateur scholar. That was not exactly a lie, but it did not give a truthful picture of the circumstances.

"Is your stepmother your guardian?"

Rose had to say she did not know.

"Well, your father must have appointed a guardian for you in his will. Who administers his estate?"

His *estate*. Rose thought an estate was land, such as people owned in England. Patrick thought it was rather charming of her to think that.

"No, his money and stocks and so on. What he left."

"I don't think he left any."

"Don't be silly," Patrick said.

And sometimes Dr. Henshawe would say, "Well, you are a scholar, you are not interested in that." Usually she was speaking of some event at the college; a pep rally, a football game, a dance. And usually she was right; Rose was not interested. But she was not eager to admit it. She did not seek or relish that definition of herself.

On the stairway wall hung graduation photographs of all the other girls, scholarship girls, who had lived with Dr. Henshawe. Most of them had got to be teachers, then mothers. One was a dietician, two were librarians, one was a professor of English, like Dr. Henshawe herself. Rose did not care for the look of them, for their soft-focused meekly smiling gratitude, their large teeth and maidenly rolls of hair. They seemed to be urging on her some deadly secular piety. There were no actresses among them, no brassy magazine journalists; none of them had latched on to the sort of life Rose wanted for herself. She wanted to perform in public. She thought she wanted to be an actress but she never tried to act, was afraid to go near the college drama productions. She knew she couldn't sing or dance. She would really have liked to play the harp, but she had no ear for music. She wanted to be known and envied, slim and clever. She told Dr. Henshawe that if she had been a man she would have wanted to be a foreign correspondent.

"Then you must be one," cried Dr. Henshawe alarmingly. "The future will be wide open, for women. You must concentrate on languages. You must take courses in political science. And economics. Perhaps you could get a job on the paper for the summer. I have friends there."

Rose was frightened at the idea of working on a paper, and she hated the introductory economics course, she was looking for a way of dropping it. It was dangerous to mention things to Dr. Henshawe.

She had got to live with Dr. Henshawe by accident. Another girl had been picked to move in but she got sick, she had T.B., and went instead to a sanitarium. Dr. Henshawe came up to the college office on the second day of registration to get the names of some other scholarship freshmen.

Rose had been in the office just a little while before, asking where the meeting of the scholarship students was to be held. She had lost her notice. The Bursar was giving a talk to the new scholarship students, telling them of ways to earn money and live cheaply and explaining the high standards of performance to be expected of them here, if they wanted their payments to keep coming.

Rose found out the number of the room, and started up the stairs to the first floor. A girl came up beside her and said, "Are you on your way to three-oh-twelve, too?"

They walked together, telling each other the details of their scholarships. Rose did not yet have a place to live, she was staying at the Y. She did not really have enough money to be here at all. She had a scholarship for her tuition and the county prize to buy her books and a bursary of three hundred dollars to live on; that was all.

"You'll have to get a job," the other girl said. She had a large bursary, because she was in Science (that's where the money is, the money's all in Science, she said seriously), but she was hoping to get a job in the cafeteria. She had a room in somebody's basement. How much does your room cost? How much does a hot plate cost? Rose asked her, her head swimming with anxious calculations.

This girl wore her hair in a roll. She wore a crepe blouse, yellowed and shining from washing and ironing. Her breasts were large and sagging. She probably wore a dirty-pink hooked-up-the-side brassiere. She had a scaly patch on one cheek.

"This must be it," she said.

There was a little window in the door. They could look through at the other scholarship winners already assembled and waiting. It seemed to Rose that she saw four or five girls of the same stooped and matronly type as the girl who was beside her, and several bright-eyed, self-satisfied babyish-looking boys. It seemed to be the rule that girl scholarship winners looked about forty and boys about twelve. It was not possible, of course, that they all looked like this. It was not possible that in one glance through the windows of the door Rose could detect traces of eczema, stained underarms, dandruff, moldly deposits on the teeth and crusty flakes in the corners of the eyes. That was only what she thought. But there was a pall over them, she was not mistaken, there was a true terrible pall of eagerness and docility. How else could they have supplied so many right answers, so many pleasing answers, how else distinguished themselves and got themselves here? And Rose had done the same.

"I have to go to the john," she said.

She could see herself, working in the cafeteria. Her figure, broad enough already, broadened out still more by the green cotton uniform, her face red and her hair stringy from the heat. Dishing up stew and fried chicken for those of inferior intelligence and handsomer means. Blocked off by the steam tables, the uniform, by decent hard work that nobody need be ashamed of, by publicly proclaimed braininess and poverty. Boys could get away with that, barely. For girls it was fatal. Poverty in girls is not attractive unless combined with sweet sluttishness, stupidity. Braininess is not attractive unless combined with some signs of elegance, *class*. Was this true, and was she foolish enough to care? It was; she was.

She went back to the first floor where the halls were crowded with ordinary students who were not on scholarships, who would not be expected to get A's and be grateful and live cheap. Enviable and innocent, they milled around the registration tables in their new purple and white blazers, their purple Frosh beanies, yelling reminders to each other, confused information, nonsensical insults. She walked among them feeling bitterly superior and despondent. The skirt of her green corduroy suit kept falling back between her legs as she walked. The material was limp; she should have spent more and bought the heavier weight. She thought now that the jacket was not properly cut either, though it had looked all right at home. The whole outfit had been made by a dressmaker in Hanratty, a friend of Flo's, whose main concern had been that there should be no revelations of the figure. When Rose asked if the skirt couldn't be made tighter this woman had said, "You wouldn't want your b.t.m. to show, now would you?" and Rose hadn't wanted to say she didn't care.

Another thing the dressmaker said was, "I thought now you was through school you'd be getting a job and help out at home."

A woman walking down the hall stopped Rose.

"Aren't you one of the scholarship girls?"

It was the Registrar's secretary. Rose thought she was going to be reprimanded, for not being at the meeting, and she was going to say she felt sick. She prepared her face for this lie. But the secretary said, "Come with me, now. I've got somebody I want you to meet."

Dr. Henshawe was making a charming nuisance of herself in the office. She liked poor girls, bright girls, but they had to be fairly good-looking girls.

"I think this could be your lucky day," the secretary said, leading Rose. "If you could put a pleasanter expression on your face."

Rose hated being told that, but she smiled obediently.

Within the hour she was taken home with Dr. Henshawe, installed in the house with the Chinese screens and vases, and told she was a scholar.

She got a job working in the Library of the college, instead of in the cafeteria. Dr. Henshawe was a friend of the Head Librarian. She worked on Saturday afternoons. She worked in the stacks, putting books away. On Saturday afternoons in the fall the Library was nearly empty, because of the football games. The narrow windows were open to the leafy campus, the football field, the dry fall country. The distant songs and shouts came drifting in.

The college buildings were not old at all, but they were built to look old. They were built of stone. The Arts building had a tower, and the Library had casement windows, which might have been designed for shooting arrows through. The buildings and the books in the Library were what pleased Rose most about the place. The life that usually filled it, and that was now drained away, concentrated around the football field, letting loose those noises, seemed to her inappropriate and distracting. The cheers and songs were idiotic, if you listened to the words. What did they want to build such dignified buildings for, if they were going to sing songs like that?

She knew enough not to reveal these opinions. If anybody said to her, "It's awful you have to work Saturdays and can't get to any of the games," she would fervently agree.

Once a man grabbed her bare leg, between her sock and her skirt. It happened in the Agriculture section, down at the bottom of the stacks. Only the faculty, graduate students, and employees had access to the stacks, though someone could have hoisted himself through a ground-floor window, if he was skinny. She had seen a man crouched down looking at the books on a low shelf, further along. As she reached up to push a book into place he passed behind her. He bent and grabbed her leg, all in one smooth startling motion, and then was gone. She could feel for quite a while where his fingers had dug in. It didn't seem to her a sexual touch, it was more like a joke, though not at all a friendly one. She heard him run away, or felt him running; the metal shelves were vibrating. Then they stopped. There was no sound of him. She walked around looking between the stacks, looking into the carrels. Suppose she did see him, or bumped into him around a corner, what did she intend to do? She did not know. It was simply necessary to look for him, as in some tense childish game. She looked down at the sturdy pinkish calf of her leg. Amazing, that out of the blue somebody had wanted to blotch and punish it.

There were usually a few graduate students working in the carrels, even on Saturday afternoons. More rarely, a professor. Every carrel she looked into was empty, until she came to one in the corner. She poked her head in freely, by this time not expecting anybody. Then she had to say she was sorry.

There was a young man with a book on his lap, books on the floor, papers all around him. Rose asked him if he had seen anybody run past. He said no.

She told him what had happened. She didn't tell him because she was frightened or disgusted, as he seemed afterward to think, but just because she had to tell somebody; it was so odd. She was not prepared at all for his response. His long neck and face turned red, the flush entirely absorbing a birthmark down the side of his cheek. He was thin and fair. He stood up without any thought for the book in his lap or the papers in front of him. The book thumped on the floor. A great sheaf of papers, pushed across the desk, upset his ink bottle.

"How vile," he said.

"Grab the ink," Rose said. He leaned to catch the bottle and knocked it on the floor. Fortunately the top was on, and it did not break.

"Did he hurt you?"

"No, not really."

"Come on upstairs. We'll report it."

"Oh, no."

"He can't get away with that. It shouldn't be allowed."

"There isn't anybody to report to," Rose said with relief. "The Librarian goes off at noon on Saturdays."

"It's disgusting," he said in a high-pitched, excitable voice. Rose was sorry now that she had told him anything, and said she had to get back to work.

"Are you really all right?"

"Oh yes."

"I'll be right here. Just call me if he comes back."

That was Patrick. If she had been trying to make him fall in love with her, there was no better way she could have chosen. He had many chivalric notions, which he pretended to mock, by saying certain words and phrases as if in quotation marks. *The fair sex*, he would say, and *damsel in distress*. Coming to his carrel with that story, Rose had turned herself into a damsel in distress. The pretended irony would not fool anybody; it was clear he did wish to operate in a world of knights and ladies; outrages; devotions.

She continued to see him in the Library, every Saturday, and often she met him walking across the campus or in the cafeteria. He made a point of greeting her with courtesy and concern, saying, "How are you," in a way that suggested she might have suffered a further attack, or might still be recovering from the first one. He always flushed deeply when he saw her, and she thought that this was because the memory of what she had told him so embarrassed him. Later she found out it was because he was in love.

He discovered her name, and where she lived. He phoned her at Dr. Henshawe's house and asked her to go to the movies. At first when he said, "This is Patrick Blatchford speaking," Rose could not think who it was, but after a moment she recognized the high, rather aggrieved and tremulous voice. She said she would go. This was partly because Dr. Henshawe was always saying she was glad Rose did not waste her time running around with boys.

Rather soon after she started to go out with him, she said to Patrick, "Wouldn't it be funny if it was you grabbed my leg that day in the Library?"

He did not think it would be funny. He was horrified that she would think such a thing.

She said she was only joking. She said she meant that it would be a good twist in a story, maybe a Maugham story, or a Hitchcock movie. They had just been to see a Hitchcock movie.

"You know, if Hitchcock made a movie out of something like that, you could be a wild insatiable leg-grabber with one half of your personality, and the other half could be a timid scholar."

He didn't like that either.

"Is that how I seem to you, a timid scholar?" It seemed to her he deepened his voice, introduced a few growling notes, drew in his chin, as if for a joke. But he seldom joked with her; he didn't think joking was suitable when you were in love.

"I didn't say you were a timid scholar or a leg-grabber. It was just an idea."

After a while he said, "I suppose I don't seem very manly."

She was startled and irritated by such an exposure. He took such chances, had nothing ever taught him not to take such chances? But maybe he didn't, after all. He knew she would have to say something reassuring. Though she was longing not to, she longed to say judiciously, "Well, no. You don't."

But that would not actually be true. He did seem masculine to her. Because he took those chances. Only a man could be so careless and demanding.

"We come from two different worlds," she said to him, on another occasion. She felt like a character in a play, saying that. "My people are poor people. You would think the place I lived in was a dump."

Now she was the one who was being dishonest, pretending to throw herself on his mercy, for of course she did not expect him to say, oh, well, if you come from poor people and live in a dump, then I will have to withdraw my offer.

"But I'm glad," said Patrick. "I'm glad you're poor. You're so lovely. You're like the Beggar Maid."

"Who?"

"King Cophetua and the Beggar Maid. You know. The painting. Don't you know that painting?"

Patrick had a trick — no, it was not a trick, Patrick had no tricks — Patrick had a way of expressing surprise, fairly scornful surprise, when people did not know something he knew, and similar scorn, similar surprise, whenever they had bothered to know something he did not. His arrogance and humility were both oddly exaggerated. The arrogance, Rose decided in time, must come from being rich, though Patrick was never arrogant about that in itself. His sisters, when she met them, turned out to be the same way, disgusted with anybody who did not know about horses or sailing, and just as disgusted by anybody knowing about music, say, or politics. Patrick and they could do little together but radiate disgust. But wasn't Billy Pope as bad, wasn't Flo as bad, when it came to arrogance? Maybe. There was a difference, though, and the difference was that Billy Pope and Flo were not protected. Things could get at them. D.P.'s; people speaking French on the radio; changes. Patrick and his sisters behaved as if things could never get at them. Their voices, when they quarreled at the table, were astonishingly childish; their demands for food they liked, their petulance at seeing anything on the table they didn't like, were those of children. They had never had to defer and polish themselves and win favor in the world, they never would have to, and that was because they were rich.

Rose had no idea at the beginning, how rich Patrick was. Nobody believed that. Everybody believed she had been calculating and clever, and she was so far from clever, in that way, that she really did not mind if they believed it. It turned out that other girls had been trying, and had not struck, as she had, the necessary note. Older girls, sorority girls, who had never noticed her before, began to look at her with puzzlement and respect. Even Dr. Henshawe, when she saw that things were more serious than she had supposed, and settled Rose down to have a talk about it, assumed that she would have an eye on the money.

"It is no small triumph to attract the attentions of the heir to a mercantile empire," said Dr. Henshawe, being ironic and serious at the same time. "I don't despise wealth," she said. "Sometimes I wish I had some of it." (Did she really suppose she had not?) "I am sure you will learn how to put it to good uses. But what about your ambitions, Rose? What about your studies and your degree? Are you going to forget all that so soon?"

Mercantile Empire was a rather grand way of putting it. Patrick's family owned a chain of department stores in British Columbia. All Patrick had said to Rose was that his father owned some stores. When she said *two different worlds* to him she was thinking that he probably lived in some substantial house like the houses in Dr. Henshawe's neighborhood. She was thinking of the most prosperous merchants in Hanratty. She could not realize what a coup she had made because it would have been a coup for her if the butcher's son had fallen for her, or the jeweler's; people would say she had done well.

She had a look at that painting. She looked it up in an art book in the Library. She studied the Beggar Maid, meek and voluptuous, with her shy white feet. The milky surrender of her, the helplessness and gratitude. Was that how Patrick saw Rose? Was that how she could be? She would need that king, sharp and swarthy as he looked, even in his trance of passion, clever and barbaric. He could make a puddle of her, with his fierce desire. There would be no apologizing with him, none of that flinching, that lack of faith, that seemed to be revealed in all transactions with Patrick.

She could not turn Patrick down. She could not do it. It was not the amount of money but the amount of love he offered that she could not ignore; she believed that she felt sorry for him, that she had to help him out. It was as if he had come up to her in a crowd carrying a large, simple, dazzling object — a huge egg, maybe, of solid silver, something of doubtful use and punishing weight — and was offering it to her, in fact thrusting it at her, begging her to take some of the weight of it off him. If she thrust it back, how could he bear it? But that explanation left something out. It left out her own appetite, which was not for wealth but for worship. The size, the weight, the shine, of what he said was love (and she did not doubt him) had to impress her, even though she had never asked for it. It did not seem likely such an offering would come her way again. Patrick himself, though worshipful, did in some oblique way acknowledge her luck.

She had always thought this would happen, that somebody would look at her and love her totally and helplessly. At the same time she had thought that nobody would, nobody would want her at all, and up until now, nobody had. What made you wanted was nothing you did, it was something you had, and how could you ever tell whether you had it? She would look at herself in the glass and think: *wife, sweetheart*. Those mild lovely words. How could they apply to her? It was a miracle; it was a mistake. It was what she had dreamed of; it was not what she wanted.

She grew very tired, irritable, sleepless. She tried to think admiringly of Patrick. His lean, fair-skinned face was really very handsome. He must know a number of things. He graded papers, presided at examinations, he was finishing his thesis. There was a smell of pipe tobacco and rough wool about him, that she liked. He was twenty-four. No other girl she knew, who had a boyfriend, had one as old as that.

Then without warning she thought of him saying, "I suppose I don't seem very manly." She thought of him saying, "Do you love me? Do you really love me?" He would look at her in a scared and threatening way. Then when she said yes he said how lucky he was, how lucky they were, he mentioned friends of his and their girls, comparing their love affairs unfavorably to his and Rose's. Rose would shiver with irritation and misery. She was sick of herself as much as him, she was sick of the picture they made at this moment, walking across a snowy downtown park, her bare hand snuggled in Patrick's, in his pocket. Some outrageous and cruel things were being shouted, inside her. She had to do something, to keep them from getting out. She started tickling and teasing him.

Outside Dr. Henshawe's back door, in the snow, she kissed him, tried to make him open his mouth, she did scandalous things to him. When he kissed her his lips were soft; his tongue was shy; he collapsed over rather than held her, she could not find any force in him.

"You're lovely. You have lovely skin. Such fair eyebrows. You're so delicate."

She was pleased to hear that, anybody would be. But she said warningly, "I'm not so delicate, really. I'm quite large."

"You don't know how I love you. There's a book I have called *The White Goddess*. Every time I look at the title it reminds me of you."

She wriggled away from him. She bent down and got a handful of snow from the drift by the steps and clapped it on his head.

"My White God."

He shook the snow out. She scooped up some more and threw it at him. He didn't laugh, he was surprised and alarmed. She brushed the snow off his eyebrows and licked it off his ears. She was laughing, though she felt desperate rather than merry. She didn't know what made her do this.

"Dr. *Hen*-shawe," Patrick hissed at her. The tender poetic voice he used for rhapsodizing about her could entirely disappear, could change to remonstrance, exasperation, with no steps at all between.

"Dr. Henshawe will hear you!"

"Dr. Henshawe says you are an honorable young man," Rose said dreamily. "I think she's in love you." It was true; Dr. Henshawe had said that. And it was true that he was. He couldn't bear the way Rose was talking. She blew at the snow in his hair. "Why don't you go in and deflower her? I'm sure she's a virgin. That's her window. Why don't you?" She rubbed his hair, then slipped her hand inside his overcoat and rubbed the front of his pants. "You're hard!" she said triumphantly. "Oh, Patrick! You've got a hard-on for Dr. Henshawe!" She had never said anything like this before, never come near behaving like this.

"Shut up!" said Patrick, tormented. But she couldn't. She raised her head and in a loud whisper pretended to call toward an upstairs window, "Dr. Henshawe! Come and see what Patrick's got for you!" Her bullying hand went for his fly.

To stop her, to keep her quiet, Patrick had to struggle with her. He got a hand over her mouth, with the other hand beat her away from his zipper. The big loose sleeves of his overcoat beat at her like floppy wings. As soon as he started to fight she was relieved — that was what she wanted from him, some sort of action. But she had to keep resisting, until he really proved himself stronger. She was afraid he might not be able to.

But he was. He forced her down, down, to her knees, face down in the snow. He pulled her arms back and rubbed her face in the snow. Then he let her go, and almost spoiled it.

"Are you all right? Are you? I'm sorry. Rose?"

She staggered up and shoved her snowy face into his. He backed off.

"Kiss me! Kiss the snow! I love you!"

"Do you?" he said plaintively, and brushed the snow from a corner of her mouth and kissed her, with understandable bewilderment. *"Do* you?"

Then the light came on, flooding them and the trampled snow, and Dr. Henshawe was calling over their heads.

"Rose! Rose!"

She called in a patient, encouraging voice, as if Rose was lost in a fog nearby, and needed directing home.

"Do you love him, Rose?" said Dr. Henshawe. "No, think about it. Do you?" Her voice was full of doubt and seriousness. Rose took a deep breath and answered as if filled with calm emotion, "Yes, I do."

"Well, then."

In the middle of the night Rose woke up and ate chocolate bars. She craved sweets. Often in class or in the middle of a movie she started thinking about fudge cupcakes, brownies, some kind of cake Dr. Henshawe bought at the European Bakery; it was filled with dollops of rich bitter chocolate, that ran out on the plate. Whenever she tried to think about herself and Patrick, whenever she made up her mind to decide what she really felt, these cravings intervened.

She was putting on weight, and had developed a nest of pimples between her eyebrows.

Her bedroom was cold, being over the garage, with windows on three sides. Otherwise it was pleasant. Over the bed hung framed photographs of Greek skies and ruins, taken by Dr. Henshawe herself on her Mediterranean trip.

She was writing an essay on Yeats's plays. In one of the plays a young bride is lured away by the fairies from her sensible unbearable marriage.

"Come away, O human child . . ." Rose read, and her eyes filled up with tears for herself, as if she was that shy elusive virgin, too fine for the bewildered peasants who have entrapped her. In actual fact she was the peasant, shocking high-minded Patrick, but he did not look for escape.

She took down one of those Greek photographs and defaced the wallpaper, writing the start of a poem which had come to her while she ate chocolate bars in bed and the wind from Gibbons Park banged at the garage walls.

> Heedless in my dark womb
> I bear a madman's child . . .

She never wrote any more of it, and wondered sometimes if she had meant headless. She never tried to rub it out, either.

Patrick shared an apartment with two other graduate students. He lived plainly, did not own a car or belong to a fraternity. His clothes had an ordinary academic shabbiness. His friends were the sons of teachers and ministers. He said his father had all but disowned him, for becoming an intellectual. He said he would never go into business.

They came back to the apartment in the early afternoon when they knew both the other students would be out. The apartment was cold. They undressed quickly and got into Patrick's bed. Now was the time. They clung together, shivering and giggling. Rose was doing the giggling. She felt a need to be continually playful. She was terrified that they would not manage it, that there was a great humiliation in store, a great exposure of their poor deceits and stratagems. But the deceits and stratagems were only hers. Patrick was never a fraud; he managed, in spite of gigantic embarrassment, apologies; he passed through some amazed pantings and flounderings, to peace. Rose was no help, presenting instead of an honest passivity much twisting and fluttering eagerness, unpracticed counterfeit of passion. She was pleased when it was accomplished; she did not have to counterfeit that. They had done what others did, they had done what lovers did. She thought of celebration. What occurred to her was something delicious to eat, a sundae at Boomers, apple pie with hot cinnamon sauce. She was not at all prepared for Patrick's idea, which was to stay where they were and try again.

When pleasure presented itself, the fifth or sixth time they were together, she was thrown out of gear entirely, her passionate carrying-on was silenced.

Patrick said, "What's the matter?"

"Nothing!" Rose said, turning herself radiant and attentive once more. But she kept forgetting, the new developments interfered, and she had finally to give in to that struggle, more or less ignoring Patrick. When she could take note of him again she overwhelmed him with gratitude; she was really grateful now, and she wanted to be forgiven, though she could not say so, for all her pretended gratitude, her patronizing, her doubts.

Why should she doubt so much, she thought, lying comfortably in the bed while Patrick went to make some instant coffee. Might it not be possible, to feel as she pretended? If this sexual surprise was possible, wasn't anything? Patrick was not much help; his chivalry and self-abasement, next door to his scoldings, did discourage her. But wasn't the real fault hers? Her conviction that anyone who could fall in love with her must be hopelessly lacking, must finally be revealed as a fool? So she took note of anything that was foolish about Patrick, even though she thought she was looking for things that were masterful, admirable. At this moment, in his bed, in his room, surrounded by his books and clothes, his shoe brushes and typewriter, some tacked-up cartoons — she sat up in bed to look at them, and they really were quite funny, he must allow things to be funny when she was not here — she could see him as a likable, intelligent, even humorous person; no hero; no fool. Perhaps they could be ordinary. If only, when he came back in, he would not start thanking and fondling and worshiping her. She didn't like worship, really; it was only the idea of it she liked. On the other hand, she didn't like it when he started to correct and criticize her. There was much he planned to change.

Patrick loved her. What did he love? Not her accent, which he was trying hard to alter, though she was often mutinous and unreasonable, declaring in the face of all evidence that she did not have a country accent, everybody talked the way she did. Not her jittery sexual boldness (his relief at her virginity matched hers at his competence). She could make him flinch at a vulgar word, a drawling tone. All the time, moving and speaking, she was destroying herself for him, yet he looked right through her, through all the distractions she was creating, and loved some obedient image that she herself could not see. And his hopes were high. Her accent could be eliminated, her friends could be discredited and removed, her vulgarity could be discouraged.

What about all the rest of her? Energy, laziness, vanity, discontent, ambition? She concealed all that. He had no idea. For all her doubts about him, she never wanted him to fall out of love with her.

They made two trips.

They went to British Columbia, on the train, during the Easter holidays. His parents sent Patrick money for his ticket. He paid for Rose, using up what he had in the bank and borrowing from one of his roommates. He told her not to reveal to his parents that she had not paid for her own ticket. She saw that he meant to conceal that she was poor. He knew nothing about women's clothes, or he would not have thought that possible. Though she had done the best she could. She had borrowed Dr. Henshawe's raincoat for the coastal weather. It was a bit long, but otherwise all right, due to Dr. Henshawe's classically youthful tastes. She had sold more blood and bought a fuzzy angora sweater, peach-colored, which was extremely messy and looked like a small-town girl's idea of dressing up. She always realized things like that as soon as a purchase was made, not before.

Patrick's parents lived on Vancouver Island, near Sidney. About half an acre of clipped green lawn — green in the middle of winter; March seemed like the middle of winter to Rose — sloped down to a stone wall and a narrow pebbly beach and salt water. The house was half stone, half stucco-and-timber. It was built in the Tudor style, and others. The windows of the living room, the dining room, the den, all faced the sea, and because of the strong winds that sometimes blew onshore, they were made of thick glass, plate glass Rose supposed, like the windows of the automobile showroom in Hanratty. The seaward wall of the dining room was all windows, curving out in a gentle bay; you looked through the thick curved glass as through the bottom of a bottle. The sideboard too had a curving, gleaming belly, and seemed as big as a boat. Size was noticeable everywhere and particularly thickness. Thickness of towels and rugs and handles of knives and forks, and silences. There was a terrible amount of luxury and unease. After a day or so there Rose became so discouraged that her wrists and ankles felt weak. Picking up her knife and fork was a chore; cutting and chewing the perfect roast beef was almost beyond her; she got short of breath climbing the stairs. She had never known before how some places could choke you off, choke off your very life. She had not known this in spite of a number of very unfriendly places she had been in.

The first morning, Patrick's mother took her for a walk on the grounds, pointing out the greenhouse, the cottage where "the couple" lived: a charming, ivied, shuttered cottage, bigger than Dr. Henshawe's house. The couple, the servants, were more gentle-spoken, more discreet and dignified, than anyone Rose could think of in Hanratty, and indeed they were superior in these ways to Patrick's family.

Patrick's mother showed her the rose garden, the kitchen garden. There were many low stone walls.

"Patrick built them," said his mother. She explained anything with an indifference that bordered on distaste. "He built all these walls."

Rose's voice came out full of false assurance, eager and inappropriately enthusiastic.

"He must be a true Scot," she said. Patrick was a Scot, in spite of his name. The Blatchfords had come from Glasgow. "Weren't the best stonemasons always Scotsmen?" (She had learned quite recently not to say "Scotch.") "Maybe he had stonemason ancestors."

She cringed afterward, thinking of these efforts, the pretense of ease and gaiety, as cheap and imitative as her clothes.

"No," said Patrick's mother. "No. I don't think they were stonemasons." Something like fog went out from her: affront, disapproval, dismay. Rose thought that perhaps she had been offended by the suggestion that her husband's family might have worked with their hands. When she got to know her better — or had observed her longer; it was impossible to get to know her — she understood that Patrick's mother disliked anything fanciful, speculative, abstract, in conversation. She would also, of course, dislike Rose's chatty tone. Any interest beyond the factual consideration of the matter at hand — food, weather, invitations, furniture, servants — seemed to her sloppy, ill-bred, and dangerous. It was all right to say, "This is a warm day," but not, "This day reminds me of when we used to — " She hated people being *reminded*.

She was the only child of one of the early lumber barons of Vancouver Island. She had been born in a vanished northern settlement. But whenever Patrick tried to get her to talk about the past, whenever he asked her for the simplest sort of information — what steamers went up the coast, what year was the settlement abandoned, what was the route of the first logging railway — she would say irritably, "I don't know. How would I know about that?" This irritation was the strongest note that ever got into her words.

Neither did Patrick's father care for this concern about the past. Many things, most things, about Patrick, seemed to strike him as bad signs.

"What do you want to know all that for?" he shouted down the table. He was a short square-shouldered man, red-faced, astonishingly belligerent. Patrick looked like his mother, who was tall, fair, and elegant in the most muted way possible, as if her clothes, her makeup, her style, were chosen with an ideal neutrality in mind.

"Because I am interested in history," said Patrick in an angry, pompous, but nervously breaking voice.

"Because-I-am-interested-in-history," said his sister Marion in an immediate parody, break and all. "History!"

The sisters Joan and Marion were younger than Patrick, older than Rose. Unlike Patrick they showed no nervousness, no cracks in self-satisfaction. At an earlier meal they had questioned Rose.

"Do you ride?"

"No."

"Do you sail?"

"No."

"Play tennis? Play golf? Play badminton?"

No. No. No.

"Perhaps she is an intellectual genius, like Patrick," the father said. And Patrick, to Rose's horror and embarrassment, began to shout at the table in general an account of her scholarships and prizes. What did he hope for? Was he so witless as to think such bragging would subdue them, would bring out anything but further scorn? Against Patrick, against his shouting boasts, his contempt for sports and television, his so-called intellectual interests, the family seemed united. But this alliance was only temporary. The father's dislike of his daughters was minor only in comparison with his dislike of Patrick. He railed at them, too, when he could spare a moment; he jeered at the amount of time they spent at their games, complained about the cost of their equipment, their boats, their horses. And they wrangled with each other, on obscure questions of scores and borrowings and damages. All complained to the mother about the food, which was plentiful and delicious. The mother spoke as little as possible to anyone and to tell the truth Rose did not blame her. She had never imagined so much true malevolence collected in one place. Billy Pope was a bigot and a grumbler, Flo was capricious, unjust, and gossipy, her father, when he was alive, had been capable of cold judgments and unremitting disapproval; but compared to Patrick's family, all Rose's own people seemed jovial and content.

"Are they always like this?" she said to Patrick. "Is it me? They don't like me."

"They don't like you because I chose you," said Patrick with some satisfaction.

They lay on the stony beach after dark, in their raincoats, hugged and kissed and uncomfortably, unsuccessfully, attempted more. Rose got seaweed stains on Dr. Henshawe's coat. Patrick said, "You see why I need you? I need you so much!"

She took him to Hanratty. It was just as bad as she had thought it would be. Flo had gone to great trouble, and cooked a meal of scalloped potatoes, turnips, big country sausages which were a special present from Billy Pope, from the butcher shop. Patrick detested coarse-textured food, and made no pretense of eating it. The table was spread with a plastic cloth, they ate under the tube of fluorescent light. The centerpiece was new and especially for the occasion. A plastic swan, lime green in color, with slits in the wings, in which were stuck folded, colored paper napkins. Billy Pope, reminded to take one, grunted, refused. Otherwise he was on dismally good behavior. Word had reached him, word had reached both of them, of Rose's triumph. It had come from their superiors in Hanratty, otherwise they could not have believed it. Customers in the butcher shop — formidable ladies, the dentist's wife, the veterinarian's wife — had said to Billy Pope that they heard Rose had picked herself up a millionaire. Rose knew Billy Pope would go back to work tomorrow with stories of the millionaire, or millionaire's son, and that all these stories would focus on his — Billy Pope's — forthright and unintimidated behavior in the situation.

"We just set him down and give him some sausages, don't make no difference to us what he comes from!"

She knew Flo would have her comments too, that Patrick's nervousness would not escape her, that she would be able to mimic his voice and his flapping hands that had knocked over the ketchup bottle. But at present they both sat hunched over the table in miserable eclipse. Rose tried to start some conversation, talking brightly, unnaturally, rather as if she was an interviewer trying to draw out a couple of simple local people. She felt ashamed on more levels than she could count. She was ashamed of the food and the swan and the plastic tablecloth; ashamed for Patrick, the gloomy snob, who made a startled grimace when Flo passed him the toothpick-holder; ashamed for Flo with her timidity and hypocrisy and pretensions; most of all ashamed for herself. She didn't even have any way that she could talk, and sound natural. With Patrick there, she couldn't slip back into an accent closer to Flo's, Billy Pope's and Hanratty's. That accent jarred on her ears now, anyway. It seemed to involve not just a different pronunciation but a whole different approach to talking. Talking was shouting; the words were separated and emphasized so that people could bombard each other with them. And the things people said were like lines from the most hackneyed rural comedy. *Wal if a feller took a notion to,* they said. They really said that. Seeing them through Patrick's eyes, hearing them through his ears, Rose too had to be amazed.

She was trying to get them to talk about local history, some things she thought Patrick might be interested in. Presently Flo did begin to talk, she could only be held in so long, whatever her misgivings. The conversation took another line from anything Rose had intended.

"The line I lived on when I was just young," Flo said, "it was the worst place ever created for suiciding."

"A line is a concession road. In the township," Rose said to Patrick. She had doubts about what was coming, and rightly so, for then Patrick got to hear about a man who cut his own throat, *his own throat,* from ear to ear, a man who shot himself the first time and didn't do enough damage, so he loaded up and fired again and managed it, another man who hanged himself using a chain, the kind of chain you hook on a tractor with, so it was a wonder his head was not torn off.

Tore off, Flo said.

She went on to a woman who, though not a suicide, had been dead in her house a week before she was found, and that was in the summer. She asked Patrick to imagine it. All this happened, said Flo, within five miles of where she herself was born. She was presenting credentials, not trying to horrify Patrick, at least not more than was acceptable, in a social way; she did not mean to disconcert him. How could he understand that?

"You were right," said Patrick, as they left Hanratty on the bus. "It is a dump. You must be glad to get away."

Rose felt immediately that he should not have said that.

"Of course that's not your real mother," Patrick said. "Your real parents can't have been like that." Rose did not like his saying that either, though it was what she believed, herself. She saw that he was trying to provide for her a more genteel background, perhaps something like the homes of his poor friends: a few books about, a tea tray, and mended linen, worn good taste; proud, tired, educated people. What a coward he was, she thought angrily, but she knew that she herself was the coward, not knowing any way to be comfortable with her own people or the kitchen or any of it. Years later she would learn how to use it, she would be able to amuse or intimidate right-thinking people at dinner parties with glimpses of her early home. At the moment she felt confusion, misery.

Nevertheless her loyalty was starting. Now that she was sure of getting away, a layer of loyalty and protectiveness was hardening around every memory she had, around the store and the town, the flat, somewhat scrubby, unremarkable countryside. She would oppose this secretly to Patrick's views of mountains and ocean, his stone and timbered mansion. Her allegiances were far more proud and stubborn than his. But it turned out he was not leaving anything behind.

Patrick gave her a diamond ring and announced that he was giving up being a historian for her sake. He was going into his father's business.

She said she thought he hated his father's business. He said that he could not afford to take such an attitude now that he would have a wife to support.

It seemed that Patrick's desire to marry, even to marry Rose, had been taken by his father as a sign of sanity. Great streaks of bounty were mixed in with all the ill will in that family. His father at once offered a job in one of the stores, offered to buy them a house. Patrick was as incapable of turning down this offer as Rose was of turning down Patrick's, and his reasons were as little mercenary as hers.

"Will we have a house like your parents?" Rose said. She really thought it might be necessary to start off in that style.

"Well, maybe not at first. Not quite so — "

"I don't want a house like that! I don't want to live like that!"

"We'll live however you like. We'll have whatever kind of house you like."

Provided it's not a dump, she thought nastily.

Girls she hardly knew stopped and asked to see her ring, admired it, wished her happiness. When she went back to Hanratty for a weekend, alone this time, thank God, she met the dentist's wife on the main street.

"Oh, Rose, isn't it wonderful! When are you coming back again? We're going to give a tea for you, the ladies in town all want to give a tea for you!"

This woman had never spoken to Rose, never given any sign before of knowing who she was. Paths were opening now, barriers were softening. And Rose — oh, this was the worst, this was the shame of it — Rose, instead of cutting the dentist's wife, was blushing and skittishly flashing her diamond and saying yes, that would be a lovely idea. When people said how happy she must be she did think herself happy. It was as simple as that. She dimpled and sparkled and turned herself into a fiancée with no trouble at all. Where will you live, people said and she said, Oh, in British Columbia! That added more magic to the tale. Is it really beautiful there, they said, is it never winter?"

"Oh, yes!" cried Rose. "Oh, no!"

She woke up early, got up and dressed and let herself out of the side door of Dr. Henshawe's garage. It was too early for the buses to be running. She walked through the city to Patrick's apartment. She walked across the park. Around the South African War Memorial a pair of greyhounds were leaping and playing, an old woman standing by, holding their leashes. The sun was just up, shining on their pale hides. The grass was wet. Daffodils and narcissus in bloom.

Patrick came to the door, tousled, frowning sleepily, in his gray and maroon striped pajamas.

"Rose! What's the matter?"

She couldn't say anything. He pulled her into the apartment. She put her arms around him and hid her face against his chest and in a stagey voice said, "Please, Patrick. Please let me not marry you."

"Are you sick? What's the matter?"

"Please let me not marry you," she said again, with even less conviction.

"You're crazy."

She didn't blame him for thinking so. Her voice sounded so unnatural, wheedling, silly. As soon as he opened the door and she faced the fact of him, his sleepy eyes, his pajamas, she saw that what she had come to do was enormous, impossible. She would have to explain everything to him, and of course she could not do it. She could not make him see her necessity. She could not find any tone of voice, any expression of the face, that would serve her.

"Are you upset?" said Patrick. "What's happened?"

"Nothing."

"How did you get here anyway?"

"Walked."

She had been fighting back a need to go to the bathroom. It seemed that if she went to the bathroom she would destroy some of the strength of her case. But she had to. She freed herself. She said, "Wait a minute, I'm going to the john."

When she came out Patrick had the electric kettle going, was measuring out instant coffee. He looked decent and bewildered.

"I'm not really awake," he said. "Now. Sit down. First of all, are you premenstrual?"

"No." But she realized with dismay that she was, and that he might be able to figure it out, because they had been worried last month.

"Well, if you're not premenstrual, and nothing's happened to upset you, then what is all this about?"

"I don't want to get married," she said, backing away from the cruelty of *I don't want to marry you.*

"When did you come to this decision?"

"Long ago. This morning."

They were talking in whispers. Rose looked at the clock. It was a little after seven.

"When do the others get up?"

"About eight."

"Is there milk for the coffee?" She went to the refrigerator.

"Quiet with the door," said Patrick, too late.

"I'm sorry," she said, in her strange silly voice.

"We went for a walk last night and everything was fine. You come this morning and tell me you don't want to get married. *Why* don't you want to get married?"

"I just don't. I don't want to be married."

"What else do you want to do?"

"I don't know."

Patrick kept staring at her sternly, drinking his coffee. He who used to plead with her *do you love me, do you really,* did not bring the subject up now.

"Well I know."

"What?"

"I know who's been talking to you."

"Nobody has been talking to me."

"Oh, no. Well, I bet Dr. Henshawe has."

"No."

"Some people don't have a very high opinion of her. They think she has an influence on girls. She doesn't like the girls who live with her to have boyfriends. Does she? You even told me that. She doesn't like them to be normal."

"That's not it."

"What did she say to you, Rose?"

"She didn't say anything." Rose began to cry.

"Are you sure?"

"Oh, Patrick, listen, please, I can't marry you, please. I don't know why, I can't, please, I'm sorry, believe me, I can't," Rose babbled at him, weeping, and Patrick saying, "Ssh! You'll wake them up!" lifted or dragged her out of the kitchen chair and took her to his room, where she sat on the bed. He shut the door. She held her arms across her stomach, and rocked back and forth.

"What is it, Rose? What's the matter? Are you sick!"

"It's just so hard to tell you!"

"Tell me what?"

"What I just did tell you!"

"I mean have you found out you have T.B. or something?"

"No!"

"Is there something in your family you haven't told me about? Insanity?" said Patrick encouragingly.

"No!" Rose rocked and wept.

"So what is it?"

"I don't love you!" she said. "I don't love you. I don't love you." She fell on the bed and put her head in the pillow. "I'm so sorry. I'm so sorry. I can't help it."

After a moment or two Patrick said, "Well. If you don't love me you don't love me. I'm not forcing you to." His voice sounded strained and spiteful, against the reasonableness of what he was saying. "I just wonder," he said, "if you know what you do want. I don't think you do. I don't think you have any idea what you want. You're just in a state."

"I don't have to know what I want to know what I don't want!" Rose said, turning over. This released her. "I never loved you."

"Ssh. You'll wake them. We have to stop."

"I never loved you. I never wanted to. It was a mistake."

"All right. All right. You made your point."

"Why am I supposed to love you? Why do you act as if there was something wrong with me if I didn't? You despise me. You despise my family and my background and you think you arc doing me a *great favor* — "

"I fell in love with you," Patrick said. "I don't despise you. Oh, Rose. I worship you."

"You're a sissy," Rose said. "You're a prude." She jumped off the bed with great pleasure as she said this. She felt full of energy. More was coming. Terrible things were coming.

"You don't even know how to make love right. I always wanted to get out of this from the very first. I felt sorry for you. You won't look where you're going, you're always knocking things over, just because you can't be bothered, you can't be bothered noticing anything, you're wrapped up in yourself, and you're always bragging, it's so stupid, you don't even know how to brag right, if you really want to impress people you'll never do it, the way you do it all they do is laugh at you!"

Patrick sat on the bed and looked up at her, his face open to whatever she would say. She wanted to beat and beat him, to say worse and worse, uglier and crueller, things. She took a breath, drew in air, to stop the things she felt rising in her from getting out.

"I don't want to see you, ever!" she said viciously. But at the door she turned and said in a normal and regretful voice, "Good-bye."

Patrick wrote her a note. "I don't understand what happened the other day and I want to talk to you about it. But I think we should wait for two weeks and not see or talk to each other and find out how we feel at the end of that time."

Rose had forgotten all about giving him back his ring. When she came out of his apartment building that morning she was still wearing it. She couldn't go back, and it seemed too valuable to send through the mail. She continued to wear it, mostly because she did not want to have to tell Dr. Henshawe what had happened. She was relieved to get Patrick's note. She thought that she could give him back the ring then.

She thought about what Patrick had said about Dr. Henshawe. No doubt there was some truth in that, else why should she be so reluctant to tell Dr. Henshawe she had broken her engagement, so unwilling to face her sensible approval, her restrained, relieved congratulations?"

She told Dr. Henshawe that she was not seeing Patrick while she studied for her exams. Rose could see that even that pleased her.

She told no one that her situation had changed. It was not just Dr. Henshawe she didn't want knowing. She didn't like giving up being envied; the experience was so new to her.

She tried to think what to do next. She could not stay on at Dr. Henshawe's. It seemed clear that if she escaped from Patrick, she must escape from Dr. Henshawe too. And she did not want to stay on at the college, with people knowing about her broken engagement, with the girls who now congratulated her saying they had known all along it was a fluke, her getting Patrick. She would have to get a job.

The Head Librarian had offered her a job for the summer but that was perhaps at Dr. Henshawe's suggestion. Once she moved out, the offer might not hold. She knew that instead of studying for her exams she ought to be downtown, applying for work as a filing clerk at the insurance offices, applying at Bell Telephone, at the department stores. The idea frightened her. She kept on studying. That was the one thing she really knew how to do. She was a scholarship student after all.

On Saturday afternoon, when she was working at the Library, she saw Patrick. She did not see him by accident. She went down to the bottom floor, trying not to make a noise on the spiraling metal staircase. There was a place in the stacks where she could stand, almost in darkness, and see into his carrel. She did that. She couldn't see his face. She saw his long pink neck and the old plaid shirt he wore on Saturdays. His long neck. His bony shoulders. She was no longer irritated by him, no longer frightened by him; she was free. She could look at him as she would look at anybody. She could appreciate him. He had behaved well. He had not tried to rouse her pity, he had not bullied her, he had not molested her with pitiful telephone calls and letters. He had not come and sat on Dr. Henshawe's doorstep. He was an honorable person, and he would never know how she acknowledged that, how she was grateful for it. The things she had said to him made her ashamed now. And they were not even true. Not all of them. He did know how to make love. She was so moved, made so gentle and wistful, by the sight of him, that she wanted to give him something, some surprising bounty, she wished to undo his unhappiness.

Then she had a compelling picture of herself. She was running softly into Patrick's carrel, she was throwing her arms around him from behind, she was giving everything back to him. Would he take it from her, would he still want it? She saw them laughing and crying, explaining, forgiving. *I love you. I do love you, it's all right, I was terrible. I didn't mean it, I was just crazy, I love you, it's all right.* This was a violent temptation for her; it was barely resistable. She had an impulse to hurl herself. Whether it was off a cliff or into a warm bed of welcoming grass and flowers, she really could not tell.

It was not resistable, after all. She did it.

When Rose afterward reviewed and talked about this moment in her life — for she went through a period, like most people nowadays, of talking freely about her most private decisions, to friends and lovers and party acquaintances whom she might never see again, while they did the same — she said that comradely compassion had overcome her, she was not proof against the sight of a bare bent neck. Then she went further into it, and said greed, greed. She said she had run to him and clung to him and overcome his suspicions and kissed and cried and reinstated herself simply because she did not know how to do without his love and his promise to look after her; she was frightened of the world and she had not been able to think up any other plan for herself. When she was seeing life in economic terms, or was with people who did, she said that only middle-class people had choices anyway, that if she had had the price of a train ticket to Toronto her life would have been different.

Nonsense, she might say later, never mind that, it was really vanity, it was vanity pure and simple, to resurrect him, to bring him back his happiness. To see if she could do that. She could not resist such a test of power. She explained then that she had paid for it. She said that she and Patrick had been married ten years, and that during that time the scenes of the first breakup and reconciliation had been periodically repeated, with her saying again all the things she had said the first time, and the things she had held back, and many other things which occurred to her. She hopes she did not tell people (but thinks she did) that she used to beat her head against the bedpost, that she smashed a gravy boat through a dining-room window; that she was so frightened, so sickened by what she had done that she lay in bed, shivering, and begged and begged for his forgiveness. Which he granted. Sometimes she flew at him; sometimes he beat her. The next morning they would get up early and make a special breakfast, they would sit eating bacon and eggs and drinking filtered coffee, worn out, bewildered, treating each other with shamefaced kindness.

What do you think triggers the reaction? they would say.

Do you think we ought to take a holiday? A holiday together? Holidays alone?

A waste, a sham, those efforts, as it turned out. But they worked for the moment. Calmed down, they would say that most people probably went through the same things like this, in a marriage, and indeed they seemed to know mostly people who did. They could not separate until enough damage had been done, until nearly mortal damage had been done, to keep them apart. And until Rose could get a job and make her own money, so perhaps there was a very ordinary reason after all.

What she never said to anybody, never confided, was that she sometimes thought it had not been pity or greed or cowardice or vanity but something quite different, like a vision of happiness. In view of everything else she had told she could hardly tell that. It seems very odd; she can't justify it. She doesn't mean that they had perfectly ordinary, bearable times in their marriage, long busy stretches of wallpapering and vacationing and meals and shopping and worrying about a child's illness, but that sometimes, without reason or warning, happiness, the possibility of happiness, would surprise them. Then it was as if they were in different though identical-seeming skins, as if there existed a radiantly kind and innocent Rose and Patrick, hardly ever visible, in the shadow of their usual selves. Perhaps it was that Patrick she saw when she was free of him, invisible to him, looking into his carrel. Perhaps it was. She should have left him there.

She knew that was how she had seen him; she knows it, because it happened again. She was in Toronto Airport, in the middle of the night. This was about nine years after she and Patrick were divorced. She had become fairly well-known by this time, her face was familiar to many people in this country. She did a television program on which she interviewed politicians, actors, writers, *personalities,* and many ordinary people who were angry about something the government or the police or a union had done to them. Sometimes she talked to people who had seen strange sights. UFO's, or sea monsters, or who had unusual accomplishments or collections, or kept up some obsolete custom.

She was alone. No one was meeting her. She had just come in on a delayed flight from Yellowknife. She was tired and bedraggled. She saw Patrick standing with his back to her, at a coffee bar. He wore a raincoat. He was heavier than he had been, but she knew him at once. And she had the same feeling that this was a person she was bound to, that by a certain magical, yet possible trick, they could find and trust each other, and that to begin this all that she had to do was go up and touch him on the shoulder, surprise him with his happiness.

She did not do this, of course, but she did stop. She was standing still when he turned around, heading for one of the little plastic tables and curved seats grouped in front of the coffee bar. All his skinniness and academic shabbiness, his look of prim authoritarianism, was gone. He had smoothed out, filled out, into such a modish and agreeable, responsible, slightly complacent-looking man. His birthmark had faded. She thought how haggard and dreary she must look, in her rumpled trenchcoat, her long, graying hair fallen forward around her face, old mascara smudged under her eyes.

He made a face at her. It was a truly hateful, savagely warning, face; infantile, self-indulgent, yet calculated; it was a timed explosion of disgust and loathing. It was hard to believe. But she saw it.

Sometimes when Rose was talking to someone in front of the television cameras she would sense the desire in them to make a face. She would sense it in all sorts of people, in skillful politicians and witty liberal bishops and honored humanitarians, in housewives who had witnessed natural disasters and in workmen who had performed heroic rescues or been cheated out of disability pensions. They were longing to sabotage themselves, to make a face or say a dirty word. Was this the face they all wanted to make? To show somebody, to show everybody? They wouldn't do it, though; they wouldn't get the chance. Special circumstances were required. A lurid unreal place, the middle of the night, a staggering unhinging weariness, the sudden, hallucinatory appearance of your true enemy.

She hurried away then, down the long varicolored corridor, shaking. She had seen Patrick; Patrick had seen her; he had made that face. But she was not really able to understand how she could be an enemy. How could anybody hate Rose so much, at the very moment when she was ready to come forward with her good will, her smiling confession of exhaustion, her air of diffident faith in civilized overtures?

Oh, Patrick could. Patrick could.

ALICE MUNRO

Oh, What Avails

1

DEADEYE DICK

They are in the dining room. The varnished floor is bare except for the rug in front of the china cabinet. There is not much furniture — a long table, some chairs, the piano, the china cabinet. On the inside of the windows, all the wooden shutters are closed. These shutters are painted a dull blue, a grayish blue. Some of the paint on them, and on the window frames, has flaked away. Some of it Joan has encouraged to flake away, using her fingernails.

This is a very hot day in Logan. The world beyond the shutters is swimming in white light; the distant trees and hills have turned transparent; the town is floating in the midst of cornfields under the still leaves, and dogs seek the vicinity of pumps and the puddles round the drinking fountains.

Some woman friend of their mother's is there. Is it the schoolteacher, Gussie Toll, or the station agent's wife? Their mother's friends are lively women, often transient — adrift and independent in attitude if not in fact.

On the table, under the fan, the two women have spread out cards and are telling their fortunes. Morris is lying on the floor, writing in a notebook. He is writing down how many copies of *New Liberty* magazine he sold that week, and who has paid and who still owes money. He is a solid-looking twelve-year-old boy, jovial but reserved, wearing glasses with one dark lens.

When Morris was four years old, he was roaming around in the long grass at the foot of the yard, near the creek, and he tripped over a rake that had been left lying there, prongs up. He tripped, he fell on the prongs, his brow and eyelid were badly cut and his eyeball was grazed. As long as Joan can remember — she was a baby when it happened — he has had a scar, and been blind in one eye, and worn glasses with a smoky lens.

A tramp left the rake there. So their mother said. She told the tramp she would give him a sandwich if he raked up the leaves under the walnut trees. She gave him the rake, and the next time she looked he was gone. He got tired of raking, she guessed, or he was mad at her for asking him to work first. She forgot to go and look for the rake. She had no man to help her with anything. Within a little more than half a year, she had to sustain these three things: Joan's birth, the death of her husband in a car accident (he had been drinking, she believed, but he wasn't drunk), and Morris's falling on the rake.

She never took Morris to a Toronto doctor, a specialist, to have a better job done fixing up the scar or to get advice about the eye. She had no money. But couldn't she have borrowed some (Joan, once she was grown up, wondered this), couldn't she have gone to the Lions Club and asked them to help her, as they sometimes did help poor people in an emergency? No. No, she couldn't. She did not believe that she and her children were poor in the way that people helped by the Lions Club were poor. They lived in a large house. They were landlords, collecting rent from the three small houses across the street. They still owned the lumberyard, though they were sometimes down to one employee. (Their mother liked to call herself Ma Fordyce, after a widow on a radio soap opera, Ma Perkins, who also owned a lumberyard.) They had not the leeway of people who were properly poor.

What is harder for Joan to understand is why Morris himself has never done anything. Morris has plenty of money now. And it wouldn't even be a question of money anymore. Morris pays his premiums on the government health-insurance plan, just the way everybody else does. He has what seem to Joan very right-wing notions about mollycoddling and individual responsibility and the impropriety of most taxes, but he pays. Wouldn't it make sense to him to try to get something back? A neater job on the eyelid? One of those new, realistic artificial eyes, whose magic sensitivity enables them to move in unison with the other, real eye? All that would entail is a trip to a clinic, a bit of inconvenience, some fussing and fiddling.

All it would entail is Morris's admission that he'd like a change. That it isn't shameful to try to turn in the badge misfortune has hung on you.

Their mother and her friend are drinking rum-and-Coke. There is a laxity in that house that might surprise most people Joan and Morris go to school with. Their mother smokes, and drinks rum-and-Coke on hot summer days, and she allows Morris to smoke and to drive the car by the time he's twelve years old. (He doesn't like rum.) Their mother doesn't mention misfortune. She tells about the tramp and the rake, but Morris's eye now might as well be some special decoration. She does give them the idea of being part of something special. Not because their grandfather started the lumberyard — she laughs at that, she says he was just a woodcutter who got lucky, and she herself was nobody, she came to town as a bank clerk — and not because of their large, cold, unmanageable house, but because of something private, enclosed, in their small family. It has to do with the way they joke, and talk about people. They have private names — their mother has made up most of them — for almost everybody in town. And she knows a lot of poetry, from school or somewhere. She will fix a couple of lines on somebody, summing them up in an absurd and unforgettable way. She looks out the window and says a bit of poetry and they know who has gone by. Sometimes she comes out with it as she stirs the porridge they eat now and then for supper as well as for breakfast, because it is cheap.

Morris's jokes are puns. He is dogged and sly-faced about this, and their mother pretends to be driven crazy. Once she told him that if he didn't stop she would empty the sugar bowl over his mashed potatoes. He didn't, and she did.

There is a smell in the Fordyce house, and it comes from the plaster and wallpaper in the rooms that have been shut off, and the dead birds in the unused chimneys, or the mice whose seedlike turds they find in the linen cupboard. The wooden doors in the archway between the dining room and living room are closed, and only the dining room is used. A cheap partition shuts off the side hall from the front hall. They don't buy coal or repair the ailing furnace. They heat the rooms they live in with two stoves, burning ends from the lumberyard. None of this is important, none of their privations and difficulties and economies are important. What is important? Jokes and luck. They are lucky to be the products of a marriage whose happiness lasted for five years and proclaimed itself at parties and dances and on wonderful escapades. Reminders are all around — gramophone records, and fragile, shapeless dresses made of such materials as apricot georgette and emerald silk moiré, and a picnic hamper with a silver flask. Such happiness was not of the quiet kind; it entailed lots of drinking, and dressing up, with friends — mostly from other places, even from Toronto — who had now faded away, many of them, too, smitten by tragedy, the sudden poverty of those years, the complications.

They hear the knocker banging on the front door, the way no caller of decent manners would bang it.

"I know, I know who that'll be," says their mother. "It'll be Mrs. Loony Buttler, what do you want to bet?" She slips out of her canvas shoes and slides the archway doors open carefully, without a creak. She tiptoes to the front window of the no longer used living room, from which she can squint through the shutters and see the front veranda. "Oh, shoot," she says. "It is."

Mrs. Buttler lives in one of the three cement-block houses across the road. She is a tenant. She has white hair, but she pushes it up under a turban made of different-colored pieces of velvet. She wears a long black coat. She has a habit of stopping children on the street and asking them things. Are you just getting home from school now — did you have to stay in? Does your mother know you chew gum? Did you throw bottle caps in my yard?

"Oh, shoot," their mother says. "There isn't anybody I'd sooner not see."

Mrs. Buttler isn't a constant visitor. She arrives irregularly, with some long rigma-role of complaint, some urgent awful news. Many lies. Then, for the next several weeks, she passes the house without a glance, with the long quick strides and forward-thrust head that take away all the dignity of her black outfit. She is preoc-cupied and affronted, muttering to herself.

The knocker sounds again, and their mother walks softly to the doorway into the front hall. There she stops. On one side of the big front door is a pane of colored glass with a design so intricate that it's hard to see through, and on the other, where a pane of colored glass has been broken (one night when we partied a bit too hard, their mother has said), is a sheet of wood. Their mother stands in the doorway barking. *Yap-yap-yap*, she barks, like an angry little dog shut up alone in the house. Mrs. Buttler's turbanned head presses against the glass as she tries to see in. She can't. The little dog barks louder. A frenzy of barking — angry excitement — into which their mother works the words *go away, go away, go away*. And *loony lady, loony lady, loony lady. Go away, loony lady, go away*.

Mrs. Buttler on her next visit says, "I never knew you had a dog."

"We don't," their mother says. "We've never had a dog. Often I think I'd like a dog. But we've never had one."

"Well, I came over here one day, and there was nobody home. Nobody came to the door, and, I could swear to it, I heard a dog barking."

"It may be a disturbance in your inner ear, Mrs. Buttler," their mother says next. "You should ask the doctor."

"I think I could turn into a dog quite easily," their mother says later. "I think my name would be Skippy."

They got a name for Mrs. Buttler. Mrs. Buncler, Mrs. Buncle, and finally Mrs. Carbuncle. It suited. Without knowing exactly what a carbuncle was, Joan understood how the name fitted, attaching itself memorably to something knobby, deadened, awkward, intractable in their neighbor's face and character.

Mrs. Carbuncle had a daughter, Matilda. No husband, just this daughter. When the Fordyces sat out on the side veranda after supper — their mother smoking and Morris smoking, too, like the man of the house — they might see Matilda going around the corner, on her way to the confectionery that stayed open late, or to get a book out of the library before it closed. She never had a friend with her. Who would bring a friend to a house ruled by Mrs. Carbuncle? But Matilda didn't seem lonely or shy or unhappy. She was beautifully dressed. Mrs. Carbuncle could sew — in fact, that was how she made what money she made, doing tailoring and alterations for Gillespie's Ladies' and Men's Wear. She dressed Matilda in pale colors, often with long white stockings.

"Rapunzel, Rapunzel, let down thy gold hair," their mother says softly, seeing Matilda pass by. "How can she be Mrs. Carbuncle's daughter? You tell me!" She says there is something fishy. She wouldn't be at all surprised — she wouldn't be at *all* surprised — to find out that Matilda is really some rich girl's child, or the child of some adulterous passion, whom Mrs. Carbuncle is being paid to raise. Perhaps, on the other hand, Matilda was kidnapped as a baby, and knows nothing about it. "Such things happen," their mother says.

The beauty of Matilda, which prompted this talk, was truly of the captive-princess kind. It was the beauty of storybook illustrations. Long, waving, floating light-brown hair with golden lights in it, which was called blond hair in the days before there were any but the most brazen artificial blonds. Pink-and-white skin, large, mild blue eyes. "The milk of human kindness" was an expression that came mysteriously into Joan's head when she thought of Matilda. And there was something milky about the blue of Matilda's eyes, and her skin, and her looks altogether. Something milky and cool and kind — something stupid, possibly. Don't all those storybook princesses have a tender blur, a veil of stupidity over their blond beauty, an air of unwitting sacrifice, helpless benevolence? All this appeared in Matilda at the age of twelve or thirteen. Morris's age, in Morris's room at school. But she did quite well there, so it seemed she wasn't stupid at all. She was known as a champion speller.

Joan collected every piece of information about Matilda that she could find and became familiar with every outfit that Matilda wore. She schemed to meet her, and because they lived in the same block she often did. Faint with love, Joan noted every variation in Matilda's appearance. Did her hair fall forward over her shoulders today or was it pushed back from her cheeks? Had she put a clear polish on her fingernails? Was she wearing the pale-blue rayon blouse with the tiny edging of lace around the collar, which gave her a soft and whimsical look, or the starched white cotton shirt, which turned her into a dedicated student? Matilda owned a string of glass beads, clear pink, the sight of which, on Matilda's perfect white neck, caused a delicate sweat to break out along the insides of Joan's arms.

At one time Joan invented other names for her. "Matilda" brought to mind dingy curtains, gray tent flaps, a slack-skinned old woman. How about Sharon? Lilliane? Elizabeth? Then, Joan didn't know how, the name Matilda became transformed. It started shining like silver. The "il" in it was silver. But not metallic. In Joan's mind the name gleamed now like a fold of satin.

The matter of greetings was intensely important, and a pulse fluttered in Joan's neck as she waited. Matilda of course must speak first. She might say "Hi," which was lighthearted, comradely, or "Hello," which was gentler and more personal. Once in a while she said "Hello, Joan," which indicated such special notice and teasing regard that it immediately filled Joan's eyes with tears and laid on her a shameful, exquisite burden of happiness.

This love dwindled, of course. Like other trials and excitements, it passed away, and Joan's interest in Matilda Buttler returned to normal. Matilda changed, too. By the time Joan was in high school Matilda was already working. She got a job in a lawyer's office; she was a junior clerk. Now that she was making her own money, and was partway out of her mother's control — only partway, because she still lived at home — she changed her style. It seemed that she wanted to be much less of a princess and much more like everybody else. She got her hair cut short, and wore it in the trim fashion of the time. She started wearing makeup, bright-red lipstick that hardened the shape of her mouth. She dressed the way other girls did — in long, tight slit skirts, and blouses with floppy bows at the neck, and ballerina shoes. She lost her pallor and aloofness. Joan, who was planning to get a scholarship and study art and archeology at the University of Toronto, greeted this Matilda with composure. And the last shred of her worship vanished when Matilda began appearing with a boyfriend.

The boyfriend was a good-looking man about ten years older than Matilda. He had thinning dark hair and a pencil mustache and a rather unfriendly, suspicious, de-termined expression. He was very tall, and he bent toward Matilda, with his arm around her waist, as they walked along the streets. They walked on the streets so much because Mrs. Carbuncle had taken a huge dislike to him and would not let him inside the house. At first he didn't have a car. Later he did. He was said to be either an airplane pilot or a waiter in a posh restaurant, and it was not known where Matilda had met him. When they walked, his arm was actually below Matilda's waist — his spread fingers rested securely on her hipbone. It seemed to Joan that this bold, settled hand had something to do with his gloomy and challenging expression.

But before this, before Matilda got a job, or cut her hair, something happened that showed Joan — by then long past being in love — an aspect, or effect, of Matilda's beauty that she hadn't suspected. She saw that such beauty marked you — in Logan, anyway — as a limp might, or a speech impediment. It isolated you — more se-verely, perhaps, than a mild deformity would have done, because it could be seen as a reproach. After she realized that, it wasn't so surprising to Joan, though it was still disappointing, to see that Matilda would do her best to get rid of or camouflage that beauty as soon as she could.

Mrs. Buttler, Mrs. Carbuncle invading their kitchen as she does every so often, never removes her black coat and her multicolored velvet turban. That is to keep your hopes up, their mother says. Hopes that she's about to leave, that you're going to get free of her in under three hours. Also to cover up whatever god-awful outfit she's got on underneath. Because she's got that coat, and is willing to wear it every day of the year, Mrs. Carbuncle never has to change her dress. A smell issues from her — camphorated, stuffy.

She arrives in mid-spiel, charging ahead in her talk — about something that has happened to her, some person who has outraged her, as if you were certain to know what it was or who. As if her life were on the news and you had just failed to catch the last couple of bulletins. Joan is always eager to listen to the first half hour or so of this report, or tirade, preferably from outside the room, so that she can slip away when things start getting repetitious. If you try to slip away from where Mrs. Carbuncle can see you, she's apt to ask sarcastically where you're off to in such a hurry, or accuse you of not believing her.

Joan is doing that — listening from the dining room, while pretending to practice her piano piece for the public-school Christmas concert. Joan is in her last year at the public grade school, and Matilda is in her last year at high school. (Morris will drop out, after Christmas, to take over the lumberyard.) It's a Saturday morning in mid-December — gray sky and an iron frost. Tonight the high-school Christmas Dance, the only formal dance of the year, is to be held in the town armory.

It's the high-school principal who has got into Mrs. Carbuncle's bad books. This is an unexceptionable man named Archibald Moore, who is routinely called by his students Archie Balls, or Archie Balls More, or Archie More Balls. Mrs. Carbuncle says he isn't fit for his job. She says he can be bought and everybody knows it; you'll never pass out of high school unless you slip him the money.

"But the exams are marked in Toronto," says Joan's mother, as if genuinely puzzled. For a while, she enjoys pushing things along, with mild objections and queries.

"He's in cahoots with them, too," says Mrs. Carbuncle. "Them, too." She goes on to say that if money hadn't changed hands he'd never have got out of high school himself. He's very stupid. An ignoramus. He can't solve the problems on the blackboard or translate the Latin. He has to have a book with the English words all written in on top. Also, a few years ago, he made a girl pregnant.

"Oh, I never heard that!" says Joan's mother, utterly genteel.

"It was hushed up. He had to pay."

"Did it take all the profits he made on the examinations?"

"He ought to have been horsewhipped."

Joan plays the piano softly — "Jesu, Joy of Man's Desiring" is her piece, and very difficult — because she hopes to hear the name of the girl, or perhaps how the baby was disposed of. (One time, Mrs. Carbuncle described the way a certain doctor in town disposed of babies, the products of his own licentious outbursts.) But Mrs. Carbuncle is swinging around to the root of her grievance, and it seems to be something about the dance. Archibald Moore has not managed the dance in the right way. He should make them all draw names for partners to take. Or else he should make them all go without partners. Either one or the other. That way, Matilda could go. Matilda hasn't got a partner — no boy has asked her — and she says she won't go alone. Mrs. Carbuncle says she will. She says she will make her. The reason she will make her is that her dress cost so much. Mrs. Carbuncle enumerates. The cost of the net, the taffeta, the sequins, the boning in the midriff (it's strapless), the twenty-two-inch zipper. She made this dress herself, putting in countless hours of labor, and Matilda wore it once. She wore it last night in the high-school play on the stage in the town hall, and that's all. She says she won't wear it tonight; she won't go to the dance, because nobody has asked her. It is all the fault of Archibald Moore, the cheater, the fornicator, the ignoramus.

Joan and her mother saw Matilda last night. Morris didn't go — he doesn't want to go out with them anymore in the evenings. He would sooner listen to the radio or scribble figures, probably having to do with the lumberyard, in a special notebook. Matilda played the role of a mannequin a young man falls in love with. Their mother told Morris when she came home that he was smart to stay away — it was an infinitely silly play. Matilda did not speak, of course, but she did hold herself still for a long time, showing a lovely profile. The dress was wonderful — a snow cloud with silver sequins glinting on it like frost.

Mrs. Carbuncle has told Matilda that she has to go. Partner or not, she has to go. She has to get dressed in her dress and put on a coat and be out the door by nine o'clock. The door will be locked till eleven, when Mrs. Carbuncle goes to bed.

But Matilda still says she won't go. She says she will just sit in the coal shed at the back of the yard. It isn't a coal shed anymore, it's just a shed. Mrs. Carbuncle can't buy coal any more than the Fordyces can.

"She'll freeze," says Joan's mother, really concerned with the conversation for the first time.

"Serve her right," Mrs. Carbuncle says.

Joan's mother looks at the clock and says she is sorry to be rude but she has just remembered an appointment she has uptown. She has to get a tooth filled, and she has to hurry — she has to ask to be excused.

So Mrs. Carbuncle is turned out — saying that it's the first time she heard of filling teeth on a Saturday — and Joan's mother immediately phones the lumberyard to tell Morris to come home.

Now there is the first argument — the first real argument — that Joan has ever heard between Morris and their mother. Morris keeps saying no. What his mother wants him to do he won't do. He sounds as if there were no convincing him, no ordering him. He sounds not like a boy talking to his mother but like a man talking to a woman. A man who knows better than she does, and is ready for all tricks she will use to make him give in.

"Well, I think you're very selfish," their mother says. "I think you can't think of anybody but yourself. I am very disappointed in you. How would you like to be that poor girl with her loony mother? Sitting in the *coal shed?* There are things a gentleman will do, you know. Your father would have known what to do."

Morris doesn't answer.

"It's not like proposing marriage or anything. What will it cost you?" their mother says scornfully. "Two dollars each?"

Morris says in a low voice that it isn't that.

"Do I very often ask you to do anything you don't want to do? Do I? I treat you like a grown man. You have all kinds of freedom. Well, now I ask you to do something to show that you really can act like a grownup and deserve your freedom, and what do I hear from you?"

This goes on a while longer, and Morris resists. Joan does not see how their mother is going to win and wonders that she doesn't give up. She doesn't.

"You don't need to try making the excuse that you can't dance, either, because you can, and I taught you myself. You're an elegant dancer!"

Then, of all things, Morris must have agreed, because the next thing Joan hears is their mother saying, "Go and put on a clean sweater." Morris's boots sound heavily on the back stairs, and their mother calls after him, "You'll be glad you did this! You won't regret it!"

She opens the dining-room door and says to Joan, "I don't hear an awful lot of piano-playing in here. Are you so good you can give up practicing already? The last time I heard you play that piece through, it was terrible."

Joan starts again from the beginning. But she doesn't keep it up after Morris comes down the stairs and slams the door, and their mother, in the kitchen, turns on the radio, opens the cupboards, begins putting together something for lunch. Joan gets up from the piano bench and goes quietly across the dining room, through the door into the hall, right up to the front door. She puts her face against the colored glass. You can't see in through this glass, because the hall is dark, but if you get your eye in the right place you can see out. There is more red than any other color, so she chooses a red view — though she has managed every color in her time — blue and gold and green; even if there's just a tiny leaf of it, she has figured a way to squint through.

The gray cement block house across the street is turned to lavender. Morris stands at the door. The door opens, and Joan can't see who has opened it. Is it Matilda or is it Mrs. Carbuncle? The stiff, bare trees and the lilac bush by the door of that house are a dark red, like blood. Morris's good yellow sweater is a blob of golden red, a stoplight, at the door.

Far back in the house, Joan's mother is singing along with the radio. She doesn't know of any danger. Between the front door, the scene outside, and their mother singing in the kitchen, Joan feels the dimness, the chilliness, the frailty and impermanence of these high half-bare rooms — of their house. It is just a place to be judged like other places — it's nothing special. It is no protection. She feels this because it occurs to her that their mother may be mistaken. In this instance — and further, as far as her faith and suppositions reach — she may be mistaken.

It is Mrs. Carbuncle. Morris has turned away and is coming down the walk and she is coming after him. Morris walks down the two steps to the sidewalk, he walks across the street very quickly without looking around. He doesn't run, he keeps his hands in his pockets, and his pink, blood-eyed face smiles to show that nothing that is happening has taken him by surprise. Mrs. Carbuncle is wearing her loose and tattery seldom-seen housedress, her pink hair is wild as a banshee's; at the top of her steps she halts and shrieks after him, so that Joan can hear her through the door, "We're not so bad off we need some Deadeye Dick to take my daughter to a dance!"

2

FRAZIL ICE

Morris looks to Joan like the caretaker when she sees him out in front of the apartment building, cutting the grass. He is wearing dull-green work pants and a plaid shirt, and, of course, his glasses, with the dark lens. He looks like a man who is competent, even authoritative, but responsible to someone else. Seeing him with a gang of his own workmen, at a construction site, you'd probably take him for the foreman — a sharp-eyed, fair-minded foreman with a solid but limited ambition. Not the boss. Not the owner of the apartment building. He is round-faced and partly bald, with a recent tan and new freckles showing on the front of his scalp. Sturdy but getting round-shouldered, or is that just the way he looks pushing the mower? Is there a look bachelors get, bachelor sons — bachelor sons who have cared for old parents, particularly mothers? A closed-in, patient look that verges on humility? She thinks that it's almost as if she were coming to visit an uncle.

This is 1972, and Joan herself looks younger than she did ten years ago. She wears her dark hair long, tucked back behind her ears; she makes up her eyes but not her mouth; she dresses in voluminous soft, bright cottons or brisk little tunics that cover only a couple of inches of her thighs. She can get away with this — she hopes she can get away with it — because she is a tall, slim-waisted woman with long, well-shaped legs.

Their mother is dead. Morris has sold the house and bought an apartment building. His own apartment is there. The people who bought the house are making it into a nursing home. Joan has told her husband that she wants to go home — that is, back to Logan — to help Morris get settled, but she knows, in fact, that he will be settled; with his grasp of things Morris always seemed settled. All he needs Joan to help him with is the sorting out of some boxes and a trunk, full of clothes, books, dishes, pictures, curtains, that he doesn't want or doesn't have space for and has stored temporarily in the basement of his building.

Joan has been married for years. Her husband is a journalist. They live in Ottawa. People know his name — they even know what he looks like, or what he looked like five years ago, from his picture at the top of a back-page column in a magazine. Joan is used to being identified as his wife, here and elsewhere. But in Logan this identification carries a special pride. Most people here do not care for the journalist's wit, which they think cynical, or for his opinions, but they are pleased that a girl from this town has got herself attached to a famous, or semi-famous, person.

Joan has a daughter and a son, thirteen and ten years old.

She has told her husband that she will be staying here for a week. It's Sunday evening when she arrives, a Sunday late in May, with Morris cutting the first grass of the year. She plans to leave on Friday, spending Saturday and Sunday in Toronto. If her husband should find out that she has not spent the entire week with Morris, she has a story ready — about having decided, when Morris no longer needed her, to visit a woman friend she has known since college. Perhaps she should tell that story anyway — it would be safer. She worries about whether she should take the friend into her confidence.

It is the first time she has ever managed anything of this sort.

The apartment building runs deep into the lot, its windows looking out on parking space or on the Baptist church. A driving shed once stood here, for the farmers to leave their horses in during the church service. It's a red brick building. No balconies. Plain, plain.

Joan hugs Morris. She smells cigarettes, gasoline, soft, worn, sweaty shirt, along with the fresh-cut grass. "Oh, Morris, you know what you should do?" she shouts over the sound of the lawnmower. "You should get an eyepatch. Then you'd look just like Moshe Dayan!"

Every morning Joan walks to the post office. She is waiting for a letter from a man in Toronto, whose name is John Brolier. She wrote to him and told him Morris's name, the name of Logan, the number of Morris's post-office box. Logan has grown, but it is still too small to have home delivery.

On Monday morning she hardly hopes for a letter. On Tuesday she does hope for one. On Wednesday she feels she should have every reasonable expectation. Each day she is disappointed. Each day a suspicion that she has made a fool of herself — a feeling of being isolated and unwanted — rises closer to the surface. She has taken a man at his word when he didn't mean it. He has thought again.

The post office she goes to is a new, low pinkish brick building. The old one, which used to make her think of a castle, has been torn down. The look of the town has greatly changed. Not many houses have been pulled down, but most have been improved. Aluminum siding, sandblasted brick, bright roofs, wide double-glazed windows, verandas demolished or enclosed as porches. And the wide, wild yards have disappeared — they were really double lots — and the extra lots have been sold and built on. New houses crowd in between the old houses. These are all suburban in style, long and low, or split-level. The yards are tidy and properly planned, with nests of ornamental shrubs, round and crescent-shaped flower beds. The old habit of growing flowers like vegetables, in a row beside the beans or potatoes, seems to have been forgotten. Many of the great shade trees have been cut down. They were probably getting old and dangerous. The shabby houses, the long grass, the cracked sidewalks, the deep shade, the unpaved streets full of dust or puddles — all of this which Joan remembers is not to be found. The town seems crowded, diminished, with so many spruced-up properties, so much deliberate arrangement. The town of her childhood — that dim, haphazard, dreamy Logan — was just Logan going through a phase. Its leaning board fences and sun-blistered walls and flowering weeds were no permanent expression of what the town could be. And people like Mrs. Buttler — costumed, obsessed — seemed to be bound to that old town and not to be possible anymore.

Morris's apartment has one bedroom, which he has given to Joan. He sleeps on the living-room sofa. A two-bedroom apartment would surely have been more convenient for the times when he has visitors. But he probably doesn't intend to have visitors, very many of them, or very often. And he wouldn't want to lose out on the rent from the larger apartment. He must have considered taking one of the bachelor apartments in the basement, so that he'd be getting the rent from the one-bedroom place as well, but he must have decided that that would be going too far. It would look mingy, it would call attention. It would be a kind of self-indulgence better avoided.

The furniture in the apartment comes from the house, where Morris lived with their mother, but not much of it dates from the days when Joan lived at home. Anything that looked like an antique has been sold, and replaced with fairly durable, fairly comfortable furniture that Morris has been able to buy in quantity. (He rents out some furnished apartments in this building, and also some over stores on the main street.) Joan sees some things she sent as birthday presents, Christmas presents. They don't fit in quite as well, or liven things up as much, as she had hoped they would.

A print of St. Giles Church recalls the year she and her husband spent in Britain — her own embarrassing postgraduate homesickness and trans-atlantic affection. And here on the glass tray on top of the coffee table, politely and prominently displayed, is a book she sent to Morris. It's a history of machinery. There are sketches of machines in it, and plans of machines, from the days before photography, from Greek and Egyptian times. Then photographs from the nineteenth century to the present day — road machines, farm machines, factory machines, sometimes shot from a distance, sometimes on the horizon, sometimes seen from close up and low down. Some photographs stress the workings of the machines, both minute and prodigious; others strive to make machines look as splendid as castles or as thrilling as monsters. "What a wonderful book for my brother!" Joan remembers saying to the friend who was with her in the bookstore. "My brother is crazy about machinery." *Crazy about machinery* — that was what she said.

Now she wonders what Morris really thought of this book. Would he like it at all? He wouldn't actually dislike it. He might be puzzled by it, he might discount it. For it wasn't true that he was crazy about machinery. He used machinery — that was what machinery was for.

Morris takes her on drives in the long spring evenings. He takes her around town and out into the countryside, where she can see what enormous fields, what vistas of corn or beans or wheat or clover, those machines have enabled the farmers to create, what vast and park-like lawns the power mowers have brought into being. Clumps of lilacs bloom over the cellars of abandoned farmhouses. Farms have been consolidated, Morris tells her. He knows the value. Not just houses and buildings but fields and trees, woodlots and hills appear in his mind with a cash value and a history of cash value attached to them, just as every person he mentions is defined as someone who has got ahead or has not got ahead. Such a way of looking at things is not at all in favor at this time — it is thought to be unimaginative and old-fashioned and callous and destructive. Morris is not aware of this, and his talk of money rambles on with a calm enjoyment. He throws in a pun here and there. He chuckles as he tells of certain chancy transactions or extravagant debacles.

While Joan listens to Morris, and talks a little, her thoughts drift on a familiar, irresistible underground stream. She thinks about John Brolier. He is a geologist, who once worked for an oil company, and now teaches (science and drama) at what is called an alternate school. He used to be a person who was getting ahead, and now he is not getting ahead. Joan met him at a dinner party in Ottawa a couple of months ago. He was visiting friends who were also friends of hers. He was not accompanied by his wife, but he had brought two of his children. He told Joan that if she got up early enough the next morning he would take her to see something called frazil ice on the Ottawa River.

She thinks of his face and his voice and wonders what could compel her at this time to want this man. It does not seem to have much to do with her marriage. Her marriage seems to her commodious enough — she and her husband have twined together, developing a language, a history, a way of looking at things. They talk all the time. But they leave each other alone, too. The miseries and nastiness that surfaced during the early years have eased or diminished.

What she wants from John Brolier appears to be something that a person not heard from in her marriage, and perhaps not previously heard from in her life, might want. What is it about him? She doesn't think that he is particularly intelligent and she isn't sure that he is trustworthy. (Her husband is both intelligent and trustworthy.) He is not as good-looking as her husband, not as "attractive" a man. Yet he attracts Joan, and she already has a suspicion that he has attracted other women. Because of his intensity, a kind of severity, a deep seriousness — all focussed on sex. His interest won't be too quickly satisfied, too lightly turned aside. She feels this, feels the promise of it, though so far she is not sure of anything.

Her husband was included in the invitation to look at the frazil ice. But it was only Joan who got up and drove to the riverbank. There she met John Brolier and his two children and his hosts' two children in the freezing, pink, snowbound winter dawn. And he really did tell her about frazil ice, about how it forms over the rapids without ever quite getting a chance to freeze solid, and how when it is swept over a deep spot it mounds up immediately, magnificently. He said that this was how they had discovered where the deep holes were in the riverbed. And he said, "Look, if you can ever get away — if it's possible — will you let me know? I really want to see you. You know I do. I want to, very much."

He gave her a piece of paper that he must have had ready. A box number written on it, of a postal station in Toronto. He didn't even touch her fingers. His children were capering around, trying to get his attention. When can we go skating? Can we go to the warplanes museum? Can we go and see the Lancaster Bomber? (Joan saved this up to tell her husband, who would enjoy it, in view of John Brolier's pacifism.)

She did tell her husband, and he teased her. "I think that jerk with the monk's haircut has taken a shine to you," he said. How could her husband believe that she could fall in love with a man who wore a fringe of thinning hair combed down over his forehead, who had rather narrow shoulders and a gap between his front teeth, five children from two wives, an inadequate income, an excitable and pedantic way of talking, and a proclaimed interest in the writing of Alan Watts? (Even when the time came when he had to believe it, he couldn't.)

When she wrote, she mentioned lunch, a drink, or coffee. She did not tell him how much time she had left open. Perhaps that was all that would happen, she thinks. She would go to see her woman friend after all. She has put herself, though cautiously, at this man's disposal. Walking to the post office, checking her looks in shop-windows, she feels herself loosed, in jeopardy. She has done this, she hardly knows why. She only knows that she cannot go back to the life she was living or to the person she was before she went out that Sunday morning to the river. Her life of shopping and housekeeping and married lovemaking and part-time work in the art-gallery bookstore, and dinner parties and holidays and ski outings at Camp Fortune — she cannot accept that as her only life, she cannot continue it without her sustaining secret. She believes that she does mean to continue it, and in order to continue it she must have this other. This other what? This investigation — to herself she still thinks of it as an investigation.

Put like that, what she was up to might sound coldhearted indeed. But how can a person be called coldhearted who walks to the post office every morning in such a fainthearted condition, who trembles and holds her breath as she turns the key in the lock, and walks back to Morris's apartment feeling so drained, bewildered, deserted? Unless this, too, is part of what she is investigating?

Of course she has to stop and talk to people about her son and daughter and her husband and her life in Ottawa. She has to recognize high-school friends and recall her childhood, and all this seems tedious and irritating to her. The houses themselves, as she walks past — their tidy yards and bright poppies and peonies in bloom — seem tedious to the point of being disgusting. The voices of people who talk to her strike her as harsh and stupid and self-satisfied. She feels as if she had been shunted off to some corner of the world where the real life and thoughts, the uproar and energy of the last few years have not penetrated at all. They have not very effectively penetrated Ottawa, either, but there, at least, people have heard rumors, they have tried imitations, they have got wind of what might be called profound, as well as trivial, changes of fashion. (Joan had her husband, in fact, make fun of some of these people — those who showily take up trends, go to encounter groups and holistic healers, and give up drink for dope.) Here even the trivial changes have hardly been heard of. Back in Ottawa next week, and feeling especially benevolent toward her husband, eager to fill up their time together with chat, Joan will say, "I'd have given thanks if somebody had even handed me an alfalfa-sprout sandwich. Really. It was that bad."

"No, I haven't room" is what Joan keeps saying as she and Morris go through the boxes. There are things here she would have thought she'd want, but she doesn't. "No. I can't think where I'd put it." No, she says, to their mother's dance dresses, the fragile silk and cobwebby georgette. They'd fall apart the first time anybody put them on, and Claire, her daughter, will never be interested in that kind of thing — she wants to be a horse trainer. No to the five wineglasses that didn't get broken, and no to the leatherette-bound copies of Lever and Lover, George Borrow, A. S. M. Hutchinson. "I have too much stuff now," she says sadly as Morris adds all this to the pile to go to the auction rooms. He shakes out the little rug that used to lie on the floor in front of the china cabinet, out of the sun, and that they were not supposed to walk on, because it was valuable.

"I saw one exactly like that a couple of months ago," she says. "It was in a secondhand store, not even an antique store. I was in there looking for old comics and posters for Rob's birthday. I saw one just the same. At first I didn't even know where I'd seen it before. Then I felt quite shocked. As if there were only supposed to be one of them in the world."

"How much did they want for it?" says Morris.

"I don't know. I was in better condition."

She doesn't understand yet that she doesn't want to take anything back to Ottawa because she herself won't be staying in the house there for much longer. The time of accumulation, of acquiring and arranging, of padding up the corners of her life, has come to an end. (It will return years later, and she will wish she had saved at least the wineglasses.) In Ottawa, in September, her husband will ask her if she still wants to buy wicker furniture for the sunroom, and if she would like to go to the wicker store, where they're having a sale on summer stock. A thrill of disaste will go through her then — at the very thought of looking for chairs and tables, paying for them, arranging them in the room — and she will finally know what is the matter.

On Friday morning, there is a letter in the box with Joan's name typed on it. She doesn't look at the postmark; she tears the envelope open gratefully, runs her eyes over it greedily, reads without understanding. It seems to be a chain letter. A parody of a chain letter, a joke. If she breaks the chain, it says, DIRE CALAMITY will befall her. Her fingernails will rot and her teeth will grow moss. Warts as big as cauliflowers will sprout on her chin, and her friends will avoid her. What can this be, thinks Joan. A code in which John Brolier has seen fit to write to her? Then it occurs to her to look at the postmark, and she does, and she sees that the letter comes from Ottawa. It comes from her son, obviously. Rob loves this sort of joke. His father would have typed the envelope for him.

She thinks of her child's delight when he sealed up the envelope and her own state of mind when she tore it open.

Treachery and confusion.

Late that afternoon, she and Morris open the trunk, which they have left till the last. She takes out a suit of evening clothes — a man's evening clothes, still in a plastic sheath, as if they had not been worn since being cleaned. "This must be Father's," she says. "Look, Father's old evening clothes."

"No, that's mine," says Morris. He takes the suit from her, shakes down the plastic, stands holding it out in front of him over both arms. "That's my old soup-and-fish — it ought to be hanging up in the closet."

"What did you get it for?" Joan says. "A wedding?" Some of Morris's workmen lead lives much more showy and ceremonious than his, and they invite him to elaborate weddings.

"That, and some things I have to go to with Matilda," Morris says. "Dinner dances, big dress-up kinds of things."

"With Matilda?" says Joan. "Matilda *Buttler*?"

"That's right. She doesn't use her married name." Morris seems to be answering a slightly different question, not the one Joan meant to ask. "Strictly speaking I guess she doesn't have a married name."

Joan hears again the story she just now remembers having heard before — or read before, in their mother's overlong, lively letters. Matilda Buttler ran off to marry her boyfriend. The expression "ran off" is their mother's, and Morris seems to use it with unconscious emphasis, a son's respect — it's as if the only way he can properly talk about this, or have the right to talk about it, were in his mother's language. Matilda ran off and married that man with the mustache, and it turned out that her mother's suspicions, her extravagant accusations had for once some grounds. The boyfriend turned out to be a bigamist. He had a wife in England, which was where he came from. After he had been with Matilda three or four years — fortunately, there were no children — the other wife, the real wife, tracked him down. The marriage to Matilda was annulled; Matilda came back to Logan, came back to live with her mother, and got a job in the courthouse.

"How could she?" says Joan. "Of all the stupid things to do."

"Well. She was young," says Morris, with a trace of stubbornness or discomfort in his voice.

"I don't mean *that*. I mean coming back."

"Well, she had her mother," Morris says, apparently without irony. "I guess she didn't have anybody else."

Looming above Joan, with his dark-lensed eye, and the suit laid like a body over his arms, he looks gloomy and troubled. His face and neck are unevenly flushed, mottled. His chin trembles slightly and he bites down on his lower lip. Does he know how his looks give him away? When he starts to talk again, it's in a reasonable, explanatory tone. He says that he guesses it didn't much matter to Matilda where she lived. In a way, according to her, her life was over. And that was where he, Morris, came into the picture. Because every once in a while Matilda had to go to functions. Political banquets. Retirement banquets. Functions. It was a part of her job, and it would be awkward if she didn't go. But it was also awkward for her to go alone — she needed an escort. And she couldn't go with a man who might get ideas, not understanding how things stood. Not understanding that Matilda's life, or that certain part of Matilda's life, was over. She needed somebody who understood the whole business and didn't need explanations. "Which is me," says Morris.

"Why does she think that way?" says Joan. "She's not so old. I bet she's still good-looking. It wasn't her fault. Is she still in love with him?"

"I don't think it's my place to ask her any questions."

"Oh, Morris!" Joan says, in a fond dismissive voice that surprises her, it sounds so much like her mother's. "I bet she is. In love with him still."

Morris goes off to hang his evening clothes in a closet in the apartment, where they can wait for his next summons to be Matilda's escort.

In bed that night, lying awake, looking out at the street light shining through the fresh leaves on the square, squat tower of the Baptist church, Joan has something to think about besides her own plight. (She thinks of that, too, of course.) She thinks of Morris and Matilda dancing. She sees them in Holiday Inn ballrooms, on golf-club dance floors, wherever it is that the functions are held. In their unfashionable formal clothes, Matilda's hair in a perfect sprayed bouffant, Morris's face glistening with the sweat of courteous effort. But it probably isn't an effort; they probably dance very well together. They are so terribly, perfectly balanced, each with stubbornly preserved, and wholeheartedly accepted, flaws. Flaws they could quite easily disregard or repair. But they would never do that. Morris in love with Matilda — in that stern, unfulfilled, lifelong way — and she in love with her bigamist, stubbornly obsessed with her own mistake and disgrace. They dance in Joan's mind's eye — sedate, absurd, romantic. Who but Morris after all, with his head full of mortgages and contracts, could turn out to be such a romantic?

She envies him. She envies them.

She has been in the habit of putting herself to sleep with a memory of John Brolier's voice — his hasty, lowered, private voice when he said, "I want to, very much." Or she pictured his face; it was a medieval face, she thought — long and pale and bony, with the smile she dismissed as tactical, the sober, glowing, not dismissible dark eyes. Her imagining won't work tonight; it won't open the gates for her, into foggy, tender, familiar territory. She isn't able to place herself anywhere but here, on the hard single bed in Morris's apartment — in her real and apparent life. And nothing that works for Morris and Matilda is going to work for her. Not self-denial, the exaltation of balked desires, no kind of high-flown helplessness. She is not to be so satisfied.

She knows that, and she knows what she will have to do. She casts her mind ahead — inadmissibly, tentatively, shamefully, she casts her mind ahead, fumbling for the shape of the next lover.

That won't be necessary.

What Joan has forgotten altogether is that mail comes to small-town post offices on Saturday. Saturday isn't a mail-less day here. Morris has gone to see what's in his box; he hands her the letter. The letter sets up a time and place. It is very brief, and signed only with John Brolier's initials. This is wise, of course. Such brevity, such caution, is not altogether pleasing to Joan, but in her relief, her transformation, she doesn't dwell on it.

She tells Morris the story she meant to tell him had the letter come earlier. She had been summoned by her college friend, who got word that she was here. While she washes her hair and packs her things, Morris takes her car to the cut-rate gas bar north of town and fills up the tank.

Waving goodbye to Morris, she doesn't see any suspicion on his face. But perhaps a little disappointment. He has two days less to be with someone now, two days more to be alone. He wouldn't admit to such a feeling. Maybe she imagines it. She imagines it because she has a feeling that she's waving to her husband and her children as well, to everybody who knows her, except the man she's going to meet. All so easily, flawlessly deceived. And she feels compunction, certainly. She is smitten by their innocence; she recognizes an irreparable tear in her life. This is genuine — her grief and guilt at this moment are genuine, and they'll never altogether vanish. But they won't get in her way, either. She is more than glad; she feels that she is right to be going.

3

ROSE MATILDA

Ruth Ann Leatherby is going with Joan and Morris to the cemetery. Joan is a little surprised about this, but Morris and Ruth Ann seem to take it for granted. Ruth Ann is Morris's bookkeeper. Joan has known of her for years, and may even have met her before. Ruth Ann is the sort of pleasant-looking, middle-sized, middle-aged woman whose looks you don't remember. She lives now in one of the bachelor apartments in the basement of Morris's building. She is married, but her husband hasn't been around for a long time. She is a Catholic, so has not thought about getting a divorce. There is some tragedy in her background — a house fire, a child? — but it has been thoroughly absorbed and is not mentioned. Ruth Ann seems to be a woman who can absorb things and keep track of things at the same time.

It is Ruth Ann who got the hyacinth bulbs to plant on their parents' graves. She had heard Morris say it would be nice to have something growing there, and when she saw the bulbs on sale at the supermarket she bought some. A wife-woman, thinks Joan, observing her. Wife-women are attentive yet self-possessed, they are dedicated but cool. What is it that they are dedicated to?

Joan lives in Toronto now. She has been divorced for twelve years. She has a job managing a bookstore that specializes in art books. It's a good job, though it doesn't pay much; she has been lucky. She is also lucky (she knows that people say she is lucky, for a woman of her age) in having a lover, a friend-lover — Geoffrey. They don't live together; they see each other on weekends and two or three times during the week. Geoffrey is an actor. He is talented, cheerful, adaptable, poor. One weekend a month he spends in Montreal with a woman he used to live with and their child. On these weekends Joan goes to see her children, who are grown up and have forgiven her. (Her son, too, is an actor — in fact, that's how she met Geoffrey. Her daughter is a journalist, like her father.) And what is there to forgive? Many parents got divorced, most of them shipwrecked by affairs, at about the same time. It seems that all sorts of marriages begun in the fifties without misgivings, or without misgivings that anybody could know about, blew up in the early seventies, with a lot of spectacular — and, it seems now, unnecessary, extravagant — complications. Joan thinks of her own history of love with no regret but some amazement. It's as if she had once gone in for skydiving.

And sometimes she comes to see Morris. Sometimes she gets Morris to talk about the very things that used to seem incomprehensible and boring and sad to her. The bizarre structure of earnings and pensions and mortgages and loans and investments and legacies which Morris sees underlying every human life — that interests her. It's still more or less incomprehensible to her, but its existence no longer seems to be a sorry delusion. It reassures her in some way. She's curious about how people believe in it.

This lucky woman, Joan, with her job and her lover and her striking looks — more remarked upon now than ever before in her life (she is as thin as she was at fourteen and has a wing, a foxtail, of silver white in her very short hair) — is aware of a new danger, a threat that she could not have imagined when she was younger. She couldn't have imagined it even if somebody described it to her. And it's hard to describe. The threat is of a change, but it's not the sort of change one has been warned about. It's just this — that suddenly, without warning, Joan is apt to think: *Rubble.* Rubble. You can look down a street, and you can see the shadows, the light, the brick walls, the truck parked under a tree, the dog lying on the sidewalk, the dark summer awning, or the grayed snowdrift — you can see all these things in their temporary separateness, all connected underneath in such a troubling, satisfying, necessary, indescribable way. Or you can see rubble. Passing states, a useless variety of passing states. Rubble.

Joan wants to keep this idea of rubble at bay, naturally. She pays attention now to all the ways in which people seem to do that. Acting is an excellent way — she has learned that from being with Geoffrey. Though there are gaps in acting. In Morris's sort of life or way of looking at things, there seems to be less chance of gaps.

As they drive through the streets, she notices that many of the old houses are reëmerging; doors and porches that were proud modern alterations fifteen or twenty years ago are giving way to traditional verandas and fanlights. A good thing, surely. Ruth Ann points out this feature and that, and Joan approves but thinks there is something here that is strained, meticulous.

Morris stops the car at an intersection. An old woman crosses the street in the middle of the block ahead of them. She strides across the street diagonally, not looking to see if there's anything coming. A determined, oblivious, even contemptuous stride, in some way familiar. The old woman is not in any danger; there is not another car on the street, and nobody else walking, just a couple of young girls on bicycles. The old woman is not so old, really. Joan is constantly revising her impressions these days of whether people are old or not so old. This woman has white hair down to her shoulders and is wearing a loose shirt and gray slacks. Hardly enough for the day, which is bright but cold.

"There goes Matilda," says Ruth Ann. The way that she says "Matilda" — without a surname, in a tolerant, amused, and distant tone — announces that Matilda is a character.

"Matilda!" says Joan, turning toward Morris. "Is that Matilda? What ever happened to her?"

It's Ruth Ann who answers, from the back seat. "She just started getting weird. When was it? A couple of years ago? She started dressing sloppy, and she thought people were taking things off her desk at work, and you'd say something perfectly decent to her and she'd be rude back. It could have been in her makeup."

"Her *makeup?*" says Joan.

"Heredity," Morris says, and they laugh.

"That's what I meant," says Ruth Ann. "Her mother was across the street in the nursing home for years — she was completely round the bend. Anyway, Matilda got a little pension when they let her go at the courthouse. Why work if you don't have to? She just walks around. Sometimes she talks to you as friendly as anything, other times not a word. And she never fixes up. She used to look so nice."

Joan shouldn't be so surprised, so taken aback. People change. They disappear, and they don't all die to do it. Some die — John Brolier has died. When Joan heard that, several months after the fact, she felt a pang, but not so sharp a pang as when she once heard a woman say at a party, "Oh, John Brolier, yes. Wasn't he the one who was always trying to seduce you by dragging you out to look at some natural marvel? God, it was uncomfortable!"

"She owns her house," Morris says. "I sold it to her about five years ago. And she's got that bit of pension. If she can hold on till she's sixty-five she'll be O.K."

Morris digs up the earth in front of the headstone; Joan and Ruth Ann plant the bulbs. The earth is cold, but there hasn't been a frost. Long bars of sunlight fall between the clipped cedar trees and the rustling poplars, which still hold many gold leaves, on the rich, green grass.

"Listen to that," says Joan, looking up at the leaves. "It's like water."

"People like it," says Morris. "Very pop'lar sound."

Joan and Ruth Ann groan together, and Joan says, "I didn't know you still did that, Morris."

Ruth Ann says, "He never stops."

They wash their hands at an outdoor tap and read a few names on the stones.

"Rose Matilda," Morris says.

For a moment Joan thinks that's another name he's read; then she realizes he's still thinking of Matilda Buttler.

"That poem Mother used to say about her," he says. "Rose Matilda."

"Rapunzel," Joan says. "That was what Mother used to call her. 'Rapunzel, Rapunzel, let down thy gold hair.'"

"I know she used to say that. She said 'Rose Matilda,' too. It was the start of a poem."

"It sounds like a lotion," Ruth Ann says. "Isn't that a skin lotion? Rose Emulsion?"

"'Oh, what avails,'" says Morris firmly. "That was the start of it. 'Oh, what avails.'"

"Of course, I don't know hardly any poems," says Ruth Ann — apologetic, versatile, unabashed. She says to Joan, "Does it ring a bell with you?"

She has really pretty eyes, Joan thinks — brown eyes that can look soft and shrewd at once.

"It does," says Joan. "But I can't think what comes next."

Morris has cheated them all a little bit, these three women. Joan, Ruth Ann, Matilda. Morris isn't habitually dishonest — he's not foolish that way — but he will cut a corner now and then. He cheated Joan a long time ago, when the house was sold. She got about a thousand dollars less out of that than she should have. He thought she would make it up in the things she chose to take back to her house in Ottawa. Then she didn't choose anything. Later on, when she and her husband had parted, and she was on her own, Morris considered sending her a check, with an explanation that there had been a mistake. But she got a job, she didn't seem short of money. She has very little idea of what to do with money anyway — how to make it work. He let the idea drop.

The way he cheated Ruth Ann was more complicated, and had to do with persuading her to declare herself a part-time employee of his when she wasn't. This got him out of paying certain benefits to her. He wouldn't be surprised if she had figured all that out, and had made a few little adjustments of her own. That was what she would do — never say anything, never argue, but quietly get her own back. And as long as she just got her own back — he'd soon notice if it was any more — he wouldn't say anything, either. She and he both believe that if people don't look out for themselves what they lose is their own fault. He means to take care of Ruth Ann eventually anyway.

If Joan found out what he had done, she probably wouldn't say anything, either. The interesting part, to her, would not be the money. She has some instinct lacking in that regard. The interesting part would be: why? She'd worry that around and get her curious pleasure out of it. This fact about her brother would lodge in her mind like a hard crystal — a strange, small, light-refracting object, a bit of alien treasure.

He didn't cheat Matilda when he sold her the house. She got that at a very good price. But he told her that the hot-water heater he had put in a year or so before was new, and of course it wasn't. He never bought new appliances or new materials when he was fixing up the places he owned. And three years ago last June, at a dinner dance in the Valhalla Inn, Matilda said to him, "My hot-water heater gave out. I had to replace it."

They were not dancing at the time. They were sitting at a round table, with some other people, under a canopy of floating balloons. They were drinking whiskey.

"It shouldn't have done that," Morris said.

"Not after you'd put it in new," said Matilda, smiling. "You know what I think?"

He kept looking at her, waiting.

"I think we should have another dance before we drink any more!"

They danced. They had always danced easily together, and often with some special flourish. But this time Morris felt that Matilda's body was heavier and stiffer than it had been — her responses were tardy, then overdone. It was odd that her body should seem unwilling when she was smiling and talking to him with such animation, and moving her head and shoulders with every sign of flirtatious charm. This, too, was new — not at all what he was used to from her. Year after year she had danced with him with a dreamy pliancy and a serious face, hardly talking at all. Then, after she had had a few drinks, she would speak to him about her secret concerns. Her concern. Which was always the same. It was Ron, the Englishman. She hoped to hear from him. She stayed here, she had come back here, so that he would know where to find her. She hoped, she doubted, that he would divorce his wife. He had promised, but she had no faith in him. She heard from him eventually. He said he was on the move, he would write again. And he did. He said that he was going to look her up. The letters were posted in Canada, from different, distant cities. Then she didn't hear. She wondered if he was alive; she thought of detective agencies. She said she didn't speak of this to anybody but Morris. Her love was her affliction, which nobody else was permitted to see.

Morris never offered advice, he never laid a comforting hand on her except as was proper, in dancing. He knew exactly how he must absorb what she said. He didn't pity her, either. He had respect for all the choices she had made.

It was true that the tone had changed before the night at the Valhalla Inn. It had taken on a tartness, a sarcastic edge, which pained him and didn't suit her. But this was the night he felt it all broken — their long complicity, the settled harmony of their dancing. They were like some other middle-aged couple, pretending to move lightly and with pleasure, anxious not to let the moment sag. She didn't mention Ron, and Morris, of course, did not ask. A thought started forming in his mind that she had seen him finally. She had seen Ron or heard that he was dead. Seen him, more likely.

"I know how you could pay me back for that heater," she teased him. "You could put in a lawn for me! When has that lawn of mine ever been seeded? It looks terrible; it's riddled with creeping Charlie. I wouldn't mind having a decent lawn. I'm thinking of fixing up the house. I'd like to put burgundy shutters on it to counter the effect of all that gray. I'd like a big window in the side. I'm sick of looking out at the nursing home. Oh, Morris, do you know they've cut down your walnut trees! They've levelled out the yard, they've fenced off the creek!"

She was wearing a long, rustling peacock-blue dress. Blue stones in silver disks hung from her ears. Her hair was stiff and pale, like spun taffy. There were dents in the flesh of her upper arms; her breath smelled of whiskey. Her perfume and her makeup and her smile all spoke to him of falsehood, determination, and misery. She had lost interest in her affliction. She had lost her nerve to continue as she was. And in her simple, dazzling folly she had lost his love.

"If you come around next week with some grass seed and show me how to do it, I'll give you a drink," she said. "I'll even make you supper. It embarrasses me to think that all these years you've never sat down at my table."

"You'd have to plow it all up and start fresh."

"Plow it all up, then! Why don't you come Wednesday? Or is that your evening with Ruth Ann Leatherby?"

She was drunk. Her head dropped against his shoulder, and he felt the hard lump of her earring pressing through his jacket and shirt into his flesh.

The next week he sent one of his workmen to plow up and seed Matilda's lawn, for nothing. The man didn't stay long. According to him, Matilda came out and yelled at him to get off her property, what did he think he was doing there, she could take care of her own yard. You better scram, she said to him.

Scram. That was a word Morris could remember his own mother using. And Matilda's mother had used it, too, in her old days of vigor and ill will. Mrs. Buttler, Mrs. Carbuncle. *Scram out of here.* Deadeye Dick.

He did not see Matilda for some time after that. He didn't run into her. If some business had to be done at the courthouse, he sent Ruth Ann. He got word of changes that were happening, and they were not in the direction of burgundy shutters or house renovation.

"Oh, what avails the sceptred race!" says Joan suddenly when they are driving back to the apartment. And as soon as they get there she goes to the bookcase — it's the same old glass-fronted bookcase. Morris didn't sell that, though it's almost too high for this living room. She finds their mother's "Anthology of English Verse."

"First lines," she says, going to the back of the book.

"Sit down and be comfortable, why don't you?" says Ruth Ann, coming in with the late-afternoon drinks. Morris gets whiskey-and-water, Joan and Ruth Ann white-rum-

and-soda. A liking for this drink has become a joke, a hopeful bond, between the two women, who understand that they are going to need something.

Joan sits and drinks, pleased. She runs her finger down the page. "Oh what, oh what — " she murmurs.

"Oh, what the form divine!" says Morris, with a great sigh of retrieval and satisfaction.

They were taught specialness, Joan thinks, without particular regret. The tag of poetry, the first sip of alcohol, the late light of an October afternoon may be what's making her feel peaceful, indulgent. They were taught a delicate, special regard for themselves, which made them go out and grab what they wanted, whether love or money. But that's not altogether true, is it? Morris has been quite disciplined about love, and abstemious. So has she been about money — in money matters she has remained clumsy, virginal, superior.

There's a problem, though, a hitch in her unexpected pleasure. She can't find the line. "It's not in here," she says. "How can it not be in here? Everything Mother knew was in here." She takes another, businesslike drink and stares at the page. Then she says, "I know! I know!" And in a few moments she has it; she is reading to them, in a voice full of playful emotion:

> Ah what avails the sceptred race,
> Ah what the form divine!
> What every virtue, every grace,
> Rose Aylmer — Rose *Matilda* — all were thine!

Morris has taken off his glasses. He'll do that now in front of Joan. Maybe he started doing it sooner in front of Ruth Ann. He rubs at the scar as if it were itchy. His eye is dark, veined with gray. It isn't hard to look at. Under its wrapping of scar tissue it's as harmless as a prune or a stone.

"So that's it," Morris says. "So I wasn't wrong."

V. S. NAIPAUL

 V(idiadhar) S(urajprased) Naipaul was born in 1932 in Trinidad to parents descended from Hindu immigrants from northern India. He received his education in England at Oxford University. Although he presently lives in England, Naipaul has felt himself unattached to any country, a wanderer among the wanderers of the world. Not surprisingly, much of his fiction concerns the psychology of exile. He tells the stories of the unsettled — both those who are adrift in their own disintegrating societies and those who journey afar in the hope of finding difference. His novels include *The Mystic Masseur* (1957), *The Suffrage of Elvira* (1958), *A House for Mr. Biswas* (1961), *The Mimic Men* (1967), *Guerillas* (1975), *A Bend in the River* (1979), and the autobiographical *The Enigma of Arrival* (1987). Among his short story collections are *Miguel Street* (1959), *A Flag on the Island* (1967), and *In a Free State* (1971). Although he worked hard as a youth to win the scholarship that would (by taking him to England) set him on the course of becoming the writer he aspired to be, Naipaul is not without his lighter moments. "Titus Hoyt, I.A." pokes gentle fun at academic earnestness.

Titus Hoyt, I.A.

This man was born to be an active and important member of a local road board in the country. An unkind fate had placed him in the city. He was a natural guide, philosopher and friend to anyone who stopped to listen.

Titus Hoyt was the first man I met when I came to Port of Spain, a year or two before the war.

My mother had fetched me from Chaguanas after my father died. We travelled up by train and took a bus to Miguel Street. It was the first time I had travelled in a city bus.

I said to my mother, 'Ma, look, they forget to ring the bell here.'

My mother said, 'If you ring the bell you damn well going to get off and walk home by yourself, you hear.'

And then a little later I said, 'Ma, look, the sea.'

People in the bus began to laugh.

My mother was really furious.

Early next morning my mother said, 'Look now, I giving you four cents. Go to the shop on the corner of this road, Miguel Street, and buy two hops bread for a cent apiece, and buy a penny butter. And come back quick.'

I found the shop and I bought the bread and the butter — the red, salty type of butter.

Then I couldn't find my way back.

I found about six Miguel Streets, but none seemed to have my house. After a long time walking up and down I began to cry. I sat down on the pavement and got my shoes wet in the gutter.

Some little white girls were playing in a yard behind me. I looked at them, still crying. A girl wearing a pink frock came out and said, 'Why are you crying?'

I said, 'I lost.'

She put her hands on my shoulder and said, 'Don't cry. You know where you live?'

I pulled out a piece of paper from my shirt pocket and showed her. Then a man came up. He was wearing white shorts and a white shirt, and he looked funny.

The man said, 'Why he crying?' in a gruff, but interested way.

The girl told him.

The man said, 'I will take him home.'

I asked the girl to come too.

The man said, 'Yes, you better come to explain to his mother.'

The girl said, 'All right, Mr Titus Hoyt.'

That was one of the first things about Titus Hoyt that I found interesting. The girl calling him 'Mr Titus Hoyt.' Not Titus, or Mr Hoyt, but Mr Titus Hoyt. I later realised that everyone who knew him called him that.

When we got home the girl explained to my mother what had happened, and my mother was ashamed of me.

Then the girl left.

Mr Titus Hoyt looked at me and said, 'He look like a intelligent little boy.'

My mother said in a sarcastic way, 'Like his father.'

Titus Hoyt said, 'Now, young man, if a herring and a half cost a penny and a half, what's the cost of three herrings?'

Even in the country, in Chaguanas, we had heard about that.

Without waiting, I said, 'Three pennies.'

Titus Hoyt regarded me with wonder.

He told my mother, 'This boy bright like anything, ma'am. You must take care of him and send him to a good school and feed him good food so he could study well.'

My mother didn't say anything.

When Titus Hoyt left, he said, 'Cheerio!'

That was the second interesting thing about him.

My mother beat me for getting my shoes wet in the gutter but she said she wouldn't beat me for getting lost.

For the rest of that day I ran about the yard saying, 'Cheerio! Cheerio!' to a tune of my own.

That evening Titus Hoyt came again.

My mother didn't seem to mind.

To me Titus Hoyt said, 'You can read?'

I said yes.

'And write?'

I said yes.

'Well, look,' he said, 'get some paper and a pencil and write what I tell you.'

I said, 'Paper and pencil?'

He nodded.

I ran to the kitchen and said, 'Ma, you got any paper and pencil?'

My mother said, 'What you think I is? A shopkeeper?'

Titus Hoyt shouted, 'Is for me, ma'am.'

My mother said, 'Oh,' in a disappointed way.

She said, 'In the bottom drawer of the bureau you go find my purse. It have a pencil in it.'

And she gave me a copy-book from the kitchen shelf.

Mr Titus Hoyt said, 'Now, young man, write. Write the address of this house in the top right-hand corner, and below that, the date.' Then he asked, 'You know who we writing this letter to, boy?'

I shook my head.

He said, 'Ha, boy! Ha! We writing to the *Guardian,* boy.'

I said, 'The *Trinidad Guardian?* The paper? What, *me* writing to the *Guardian!* But only big big man does write to the *Guardian.*'

Titus Hoyt smiled. 'That's *why* you writing. It go surprise them.'

I said, 'What I go write to them about?'

He said, 'You go write it now. Write. To the Editor, *Trinidad Guardian.* Dear Sir, I am but a child of eight (How old you is? Well, it don't matter anyway) and yesterday my mother sent me to make a purchase in the city. This, dear Mr Editor, was my first peregrination (p-e-r-e-g-r-i-n-a-t-i-o-n) in this metropolis, and I had the misfortune to wander from the path my mother had indicated —'

I said, 'Oh God, Mr Titus Hoyt, where you learn all these big words and them? You sure you spelling them right?'

Titus Hoyt smiled. 'I spend all afternoon making up this letter,' he said.

I wrote: '. . . and in this state of despair I was rescued by a Mr Titus Hoyt, of Miguel Street. This only goes to show, dear Mr Editor, that human kindness is a quality not yet extinct in this world.'

The *Guardian* never printed the letter.

When I next saw Titus Hoyt he said, 'Well, never mind. One day, boy, one day, I go make them sit up and take notice of every word I say. Just wait and see.'

And before he left he said, 'Drinking your milk?'

He had persuaded my mother to give me half a pint of milk every day. Milk was good for the brains.

It is one of the sadnesses of my life that I never fulfilled Titus Hoyt's hopes for my academic success.

I still remember with tenderness the interest he took in me. Sometimes his views clashed with my mother's. There was the business of the cobwebs, for instance.

Boyee, with whom I had become friendly very quickly, was teaching me to ride. I had fallen and cut myself nastily on the shin.

My mother was attempting to cure this with sooty cobwebs soaked in rum.

Titus Hoyt was horrified. 'You ain't know what you doing,' he shouted.

My mother said, 'Mr Titus Hoyt, I will kindly ask you to mind your own business. The day you make a baby yourself I go listen to what you have to say.'

Titus Hoyt refused to be ridiculed. He said, 'Take the boy to the doctor, man.'

I was watching them argue, not caring greatly either way.

In the end I went to the doctor.

Titus Hoyt reappeared in a new role.

He told my mother, 'For the last two three months I been taking the first-aid course with the Red Cross. I go dress the boy foot for you.'

That really terrified me.

For about a month or so afterwards, people in Miguel Street could tell when it was nine o'clock in the morning. By my shrieks. Titus Hoyt loved his work.

All this gives some clue to the real nature of the man.

The next step followed naturally.

Titus Hoyt began to teach.

It began in a small way, after the fashion of all great enterprises.

He had decided to sit for the external arts degree of London University. He began to learn Latin, teaching himself, and as fast as he learned, he taught us.

He rounded up three or four of us and taught us in the verandah of his house. He kept chickens in his yard and the place stank.

That Latin stage didn't last very long. We got as far as the fourth declension, and then Boyee and Errol and myself began asking questions. They were not the sort of questions Titus Hoyt liked.

Boyee said, 'Mr Titus Hoyt, I think you making up all this, you know, making it up as you go on.'

Titus Hoyt said, 'But I telling you, I not making it up. Look, here it is in black and white.'

Errol said, 'I feel, Mr Titus Hoyt, that one man sit down one day and make all this up and have everybody else learning it.'

Titus Hoyt asked me, 'What is the accusative singular of *bellum?*'

Feeling wicked, because I was betraying him, I said to Titus Hoyt, 'Mr Titus Hoyt, when you was my age, how you woulda feel if somebody did ask you that question?'

And then Boyee asked, 'Mr Titus Hoyt, what is the meaning of the ablative case?'

So the Latin lessons ended.

But however much we laughed at him, we couldn't deny that Titus Hoyt was a deep man.

Hat used to say, 'He is a thinker, that man.'

Titus Hoyt thought about all sorts of things, and he thought dangerous things sometimes.

Hat said, 'I don't think Titus Hoyt like God, you know.'

Titus Hoyt would say, 'The thing that really matter is faith. Look, I believe that if I pull out this bicycle-lamp from my pocket here, and set it up somewhere, and really really believe in it and pray to it, what I pray for go come. That is what I believe.'

And so saying he would rise and leave, not forgetting to say, 'Cheerio!'

He had the habit of rushing up to us and saying, 'Silence, everybody. I just been thinking. Listen to what I just been thinking.'

One day he rushed up and said, 'I been thinking how this war could end. If Europe could just sink for five minutes all the Germans go drown — '

Eddoes said, 'But England go drown too.'

Titus Hoyt agreed and looked sad. 'I lose my head, man,' he said. 'I lose my head.'

And he wandered away, muttering to himself and shaking his head.

One day he cycled right up to us when we talking about the Barbados-Trinidad cricket match. Things were not going well for Trinidad and we were worried.

Titus Hoyt rushed up and said, 'Silence. I just been thinking. Look, boys, it ever strike you that the world not real at all? It ever strike you that we have the only mind in the world and you just thinking up everything else? Like me here, having the only mind in the world, and thinking up you people here, thinking up the war and all the houses and the ships and them in the harbour. That ever cross your mind?'

His interest in teaching didn't die.

We often saw him going about with big books. These books were about teaching.

Titus Hoyt used to say, 'Is a science, man. The trouble with Trinidad is that the teachers don't have this science of teaching.'

And, 'Is the biggest thing in the world, man. Having the minds of the young to train. Think of that. Think.'

It soon became clear that whatever we thought about it, Titus Hoyt was bent on training our minds.

He formed the Miguel Street Literary and Social Youth Club, and had it affiliated to the Trinidad and Tobago Youth Association.

We used to meet in his house, which was well supplied with things to eat and drink. The walls of his house were now hung with improving quotations, some typed, some cut out of magazines and pasted on bits of cardboard.

I also noticed a big thing called 'Time-table.'

From this I gathered that Titus Hoyt was to rise at five-thirty, read Something from Greek philosophers until six, spend fifteen minutes bathing and exercising, another five reading the morning paper, and ten on breakfast. It was a formidable thing altogether.

Titus Hoyt said, 'If I follow the time-table I will be a educated man in about three four years.'

The Miguel Street Club didn't last very long.

It was Titus Hoyt's fault.

No man in his proper senses would have made Boyee secretary. Most of Boyee's minutes consisted of the names of people present.

And then we all had to write and read something.

The Miguel Street Literary and Social Club became nothing more than a gathering of film critics.

Titus Hoyt said, 'No, man. We just can't have all you boys talking about pictures all the time. I will have to get some propaganda for you boys.'

Boyee said, 'Mr Titus Hoyt, what we want with propaganda? Is a German thing.'

Titus Hoyt smiled. 'That is not the proper meaning of the word, boy. I am using the word in it proper meaning. Is education, boy, that make me know things like that.'

Boyee was sent as our delegate to the Youth Association annual conference.

When he came back Boyee said, 'Is a helluva thing at that youth conference. Is only a pack of old, old people it have there.'

The attraction of the Coca-Cola and the cakes and the ice-cream began to fade. Some of us began staying away from meetings.

Titus Hoyt made one last effort to keep the club together.

One day he said, 'Next Sunday the club will go on a visit to Fort George.'

There were cries of disapproval.

Titus Hoyt said, 'You see you people don't care about your country. How many of you know about Fort George? Not one of you here know about the place. But is history, man, your history, and you must learn about things like that. You must remember that the boys and girls of today are the men and women of tomorrow. The old Romans had a saying, you know. *Mens sana in corpore sano*. I think we will make the walk to Fort George.

Still no one wanted to go.

Titus Hoyt said, 'At the top of Fort George it have a stream, and it cool cool and the water crystal clear. You could bathe there when we get to the top.'

We couldn't resist that.

The next Sunday a whole group of us took the trolley-bus to Mucurapo.

When the conductor came round to collect the fares, Titus Hoyt said, 'Come back a little later.' And he paid the conductor only when we got off the bus. The fare for everybody came up to about two shillings. But Titus Hoyt gave the conductor a shilling, saying, 'We don't want any ticket, man!' The conductor and Titus Hoyt laughed.

It was a long walk up the hill, red and dusty, and hot.

Titus Hoyt told us, 'This fort was built at a time when the French and them was planning to invade Trinidad.'

We gasped.

We had never realised that anyone considered us so important.

Titus Hoyt said, 'That was in 1803, when we was fighting Napoleon.'

We saw a few old rusty guns at the side of the path and heaps of rusty cannon-balls.

I asked, 'The French invade Trinidad, Mr Titus Hoyt?'

Titus Hoyt shook his head in a disappointed way. 'No, they didn't attack. But we was ready, man. Ready for them.'

Boyee said, 'You sure it have this stream up there you tell us about, Mr Titus Hoyt?'

Titus Hoyt said, 'What you think I is? A liar?'

Boyee said, 'I ain't saying nothing.'

We walked and sweated. Boyee took off his shoes.

Errol said, 'If it ain't have that stream up there, somebody going to catch hell.'

We got to the top, had a quick look at the graveyard where there were a few tombstones of British soldiers dead long ago; and we looked through the telescope at the city of Port of Spain, large and sprawling beneath us. We could see the people walking in the streets as large as life.

Then we went looking for the stream.

We couldn't find it.

Titus Hoyt said, 'It must be here somewhere. When I was a boy I use to bathe in it.'

Boyee said, 'And what happen now? It dry up?'

Titus Hoyt said, 'It look so.'

Boyee got really mad, and you couldn't blame him. It was hard work coming up that hill, and we were all hot and thirsty.

He insulted Titus Hoyt in a very crude way.

Titus Hoyt said, 'Remember, Boyee, you are the secretary of the Miguel Street Literary and Social Club. Remember that you have just attended a meeting of the Youth Association as our delegate. Remember these things.'

Boyee said, 'Go to hell, Hoyt.'

We were aghast.
So the Literary Club broke up.

It wasn't long after that Titus Hoyt got his Inter Arts degree and set up a school of his own. He had a big sign placed in his garden:

TITUS HOYT, I.A. (London, External)
Passes in the Cambridge
School Certificate Guaranteed

One year the *Guardian* had a brilliant idea. They started the Needy Cases Fund to help needy cases at Christmas. It was popular and after a few years was called The Neediest Cases Fund. At the beginning of November the *Guardian* announced the target for the fund and it was a daily excitement until Christmas Eve to see how the fund rose. It was always front page news and everybody who gave got his name in the papers.

In the middle of December one year, when the excitement was high, Miguel Street was in the news.

Hat showed us the paper and we read:

FOLLOW THE EXAMPLE OF THIS TINYMITE!

'The smallest and most touching response to our appeal to bring Yuletide cheer to the unfortunate has come in a letter from Mr Titus Hoyt, I.A., a headmaster of Miguel Street, Port of Spain. The letter was sent to Mr Hoyt by one of his pupils who wishes to remain anonymous. We have Mr Hoyt's permission to print the letter in full.

'Dear Mr Hoyt, I am only eight and, as you doubtless know, I am a member of the GUARDIAN Tinymites League. I read Aunt Juanita every Sunday. You, dear Mr Hoyt, have always extolled the virtue of charity and you have spoken repeatedly of the fine work the GUARDIAN Neediest Cases Fund is doing to bring Yuletide cheer to the unfortunate. I have decided to yield to your earnest entreaty. I have very little money to offer — a mere six cents, in fact, but take it, Mr Hoyt, and send it to the GUARDIAN Neediest Cases Fund. May it bring Yuletide cheer to some poor unfortunate! I know it is not much. But, like the widow, I give my mite. I remain, dear Mr Hoyt, One of Your Pupils."

And there was a large photograph of Titus Hoyt, smiling and pop-eyed in the flash of the camera.

R. K. NARAYAN

 R(asipuram) K(rishnaswami) Narayan, born in 1906 in Ma-
dras, India, is usually considered the best-known Indian writing in English today. In novels and stories about his native land —
most set in an imaginary village, Malgudi, modeled on the village
Narayan grew up in — he has written what one critic called "comedies of sadness." They are perhaps universal comedies as well:
Narayan's portrayal of the human condition in Malgudi goes well
beyond a consideration of life in a third-world village. In its char-
acterizations and situations, it speaks to the human condition everywhere, ruefully, gently, and in a wonderfully cadenced style. His
novels include *The Bachelor of Arts* (1937), *The English Teacher*
(1945), *Mr. Sampath* (1949), *Waiting for the Mahatma* (1955), *The
Maneater of Malgudi* (1961), and *The Painter of Signs* (1976). His
stories are collected in *Malgudi Days* (1943), *An Astrologer's Day*
(1947), *Lawley Road* (1956), *Gods, Demons, and Others* (1964), and
A Horse and Two Goats (1970). "Naga" shows something of
the affection Narayan feels for his characters.

Naga

The boy took off the lid of the circular wicker basket and stood looking at the
cobra coiled inside, and then said, "Naga, I hope you are dead, so that I may
sell your skin to the pursemakers; at least that way you may become useful." He
poked it with a finger. Naga raised its head and looked about with a dull wonder.
"You have become too lazy even to open your hood. You are no cobra. You are an
earthworm. I am a snake charmer attempting to show you off and make a living. No
wonder so often I have to stand at the bus stop pretending to be blind and beg. The
trouble is, no one wants to see you, no one has any respect for you and no one is
afraid of you, and do you know what that means? I starve, that is all."

Whenever the boy appeared at the street door, householders shooed him away.
He had seen his father operate under similar conditions. His father would climb the
steps of the house unmindful of the discouragement, settle down with his basket and
go through his act heedless of what anyone said. He would pull out his gourd pipe
from the bag and play the snake tune over and over, until its shrill, ear-piercing note
induced a torpor and made people listen to his preamble: "In my dream, God Shiva
appeared and said, 'Go forth and thrust your hand into that crevice in the floor of my
sanctum.' As you all know, Shiva is the Lord of Cobras, which he ties his braid with,

and its hood canopies his head; the great God Vishnu rests in the coils of Adi-Shesha, the mightiest serpent, who also bears on his thousand heads this Universe. Think of the armlets on goddess Parvathi! Again, elegant little snakes. How can we think that we are wiser than our gods? Snake is a part of a god's ornament, and not an ordinary creature. I obeyed Shiva's command — at midnight walked out and put my arm into the snake hole."

At this point his audience would shudder and someone would ask, "Were you bitten?"

"Of course I was bitten, but still you see me here, because the same god commanded, 'Find that weed growing on the old fort wall.' No, I am not going to mention its name, even if I am offered a handful of sovereigns."

"What did you do with the weed?"

"I chewed it; thereafter no venom could enter my system. And the terrible fellow inside this basket plunged his fangs into my arms like a baby biting his mother's nipple, but I laughed and pulled him out, and knocked off with a piece of stone the fangs that made him so arrogant; and then he understood that I was only a friend and well wisher, and no trouble after that. After all, what is a serpent? A great soul in a state of penance waiting to go back to its heavenly world. That is all, sirs."

After this speech, his father would flick open the basket lid and play the pipe again, whereupon the snake would dart up like springwork, look about and sway a little, people would be terrified and repelled, but still enthralled. At the end of the performance, they gave him coins and rice, and sometimes an old shirt, too, and occasionally he wangled an egg if he observed a hen around; seizing Naga by the throat, he let the egg slide down its gullet, to the delight of the onlookers. He then packed up and repeated the performance at the next street or at the bazaar, and when he had collected sufficient food and cash he returned to his hut beside the park wall, in the shade of a big tamarind tree. He cooked the rice and fed his son, and they slept outside the hut, under the stars.

The boy had followed his father ever since he could walk, and when he attained the age of ten his father let him handle Naga and harangue his audience in his own style. His father often said, "We must not fail to give Naga two eggs a week. When he grows old, he will grow shorter each day; someday he will grow wings and fly off, and do you know that at that time he will spit out the poison in his fangs in the form of a brilliant jewel, and if you possessed it you could become a king?"

One day when the boy had stayed beside the hut out of laziness, he noiced a tiny monkey gambolling amidst the branches of the tamarind tree and watched it with open-mouthed wonder, not even noticing his father arrive home.

"Boy, what are you looking at? Here, eat this," said the father, handing him a packet of sweets. "They gave it to me at that big house, where some festival is going on. Naga danced to the pipe wonderfully today. He now understands all our speech. At the end of his dance, he stood six feet high on the tip of his tail, spread out his hood, hissed and sent a whole crowd scampering. Those people enjoyed it, though, and gave me money and sweets." His father looked happy as he opened the lid of the basket. The cobra raised its head. His father held it up by the neck, and forced a bit of a sweet between its jaws, and watched it work its way down. "He is now one of our family and should learn to eat what we eat," he said. After struggling through the sweet, Naga coiled itself down, and the man clapped the lid back.

The boy munched the sweet with his eyes still fixed on the monkey. "Father, I wish I were a monkey. I'd never come down from the tree. See how he is nibbling all that tamarind fruit. . . . Hey, monkey, get me a fruit!" he cried.

The man was amused, and said, "This is no way to befriend him. You should give him something to eat, not ask him to feed you."

At which the boy spat out his sweet, wiped it clean with his shirt, held it up and cried, "Come on, monkey! Here!"

His father said, "If you call him 'monkey,' he will never like you. You must give him a nice name."

"What shall we call him?"

"Rama, name of the master of Hanuman, the Divine Monkey. Monkeys adore that name."

The boy at once called. "Rama, here, take this." He flourished his arms, holding up the sweet, and the monkey did pause in its endless antics and notice him. The boy hugged the tree trunk, and heaved himself up, and carefully placed the sweet on the flat surface of a forking branch, and the monkey watched with round-eyed wonder. The boy slid back to the ground and eagerly waited for the monkey to come down and accept the gift. While he watched and the monkey was debating within himself, a crow appeared from somewhere and took away the sweet. The boy shrieked out a curse.

His father cried, "Hey, what? Where did you learn this foul word? No monkey will respect you if you utter bad words." Ultimately, when the little monkey was tempted down with another piece of sweet, his father caught him deftly by the wrist, holding him off firmly by the scruff to prevent his biting.

Fifteen days of starvation, bullying, cajoling and dangling of fruit before the monkey's eyes taught him what he was expected to do. First of all, he ceased trying to bite or scratch. And then he realized that his mission in life was to please his master by performing. At a command from his master, he could demonstrate how Hanuman, the Divine Monkey of the *Ramayana,* strode up and down with tail ablaze and set Ravana's capital on fire; how an oppressed village daughter-in-law would walk home carrying a pitcher of water on her head; how a newlywed would address his beloved (chatter, blink, raise the brow and grin); and, finally, what was natural to him — tumbling and acrobatics on top of a bamboo pole. When Rama was ready to appear in public, his master took him to a roadside-tailor friend of his and had him measured out for a frilled jacket, leaving the tail out, and a fool's cap held in position with a band under his small chin. Rama constantly tried to push his cap back and rip it off, but whenever he attempted it he was whacked with a switch, and he soon resigned himself to wearing his uniform until the end of the day. When his master stripped off Rama's clothes, the monkey performed spontaneous somersaults in sheer relief.

Rama became popular. Schoolchildren screamed with joy at the sight of him. Householders beckoned to him to step in and divert a crying child. He performed competently, earned money for his master and peanuts for himself. Discarded baby clothes were offered to him as gifts. The father-son team started out each day, the boy with the monkey riding on his shoulder and the cobra basket carried by his father at some distance away — for the monkey chattered and shrank, his face disfigured with fright, whenever the cobra hissed and reared itself up. While the young fellow managed to display the tricks of the monkey to a group, he could hear his father's pipe farther off. At the weekly market fairs in the villages around, they were a familiar pair, and they became prosperous enough to take a bus home at the end of the day. Sometimes as they started to get on, a timid passenger would ask, "What's to happen if the cobra gets out?"

"No danger. The lid is secured with a rope," the father replied.

There would always be someone among the passengers to remark, "A snake minds its business until you step on its tail."

"But this monkey?" another passenger said. "God knows what he will be up to!"

"He is gentle and wise," said the father, and offered a small tip to win the conductor's favor.

They travelled widely, performing at all market fairs, and earned enough money to indulge in an occasional tiffin at a restaurant. The boy's father would part company from him in the evening, saying, "Stay, I've a stomach ache; I'll get some medicine for it and come back," and return tottering late at night. The boy felt frightened of his father at such moments, and, lying on his mat, with the monkey tethered to a stake nearby, pretended to be asleep. Father kicked him and said, "Get up, lazy swine. Sleeping when your father slaving for you all day comes home for speech with you. You are not my son but a bastard." But the boy would not stir.

One night the boy really fell asleep, and woke up in the morning to find his father gone. The monkey was also missing. "They must have gone off together!" he cried. He paced up and down and called, "Father!" several times. He then peered into the hut and found the round basket intact in its corner. He noticed on the lid of the basket some coins, and felt rather pleased when he counted them and found eighty paise in small change. "It must all be for me," he said to himself. He felt promoted to adulthood, handling so much cash. He felt rich but also puzzled at his father's tactics. Ever since he could remember, he had never woken up without finding his father at his side. He had a foreboding that he was not going to see his father anymore. Father would never at any time go out without announcing his purpose — for a bath at the street tap, or to seek medicine for a "stomach ache," or to do a little shopping.

The boy lifted the lid of the basket to make sure that the snake at least was there. It popped up the moment the lid was taken off. He looked at it, and it looked at him for a moment. "I'm your master now. Take care." As if understanding the changed circumstances, the snake darted its forked tongue and half-opened its hood. He tapped it down with his finger, saying, "Get back. Not yet." Would it be any use waiting for his father to turn up? He felt hungry. Wondered if it'd be proper to buy his breakfast with the coins left on the basket lid. If his father should suddenly come back, he would slap him for taking the money. He put the lid back on the snake, put the coins back on the lid as he had found them and sat at the mouth of the hut, vacantly looking at the tamarind tree and sighing for his monkey, which would have displayed so many fresh and unexpected pranks early in the morning. He reached for a little cloth bag in which was stored a variety of nuts and fried pulses to feed the monkey. He opened the bag, examined the contents and put a handful into his mouth and chewed: "Tastes so good. Too good for a monkey, but Father will . . ." His father always clouted his head when he caught him eating nuts meant for the monkey. Today he felt free to munch the nuts, although worried at the back of his mind lest his father should suddenly remember and come back for the monkey food. He found the gourd pipe in its usual place, stuck in the thatch. He snatched it up and blew through its reeds, feeling satisfied that he could play as well as his father and that the public would not know the difference; only it made him cough a little and gasp for breath. The shrill notes attracted the attention of people passing by the hut, mostly day labourers carrying spades and pickaxes and women carrying baskets, who nodded their heads approvingly and remarked, "True son of the father." Everyone had a word with him. All knew him in that colony of huts, which had cropped up around the water fountain. All the efforts of the municipality to dislodge these citizens had proved futile; the huts sprang up as they were destroyed, and when the councillors realized the concentration of voting power in this colony, they let the squatters alone, except when some V.I.P. from Delhi passed that way, and then they were asked to stay out of sight, behind the park wall, till the eminent man had flashed past in his car.

"Why are you not out yet?" asked a woman.

"My father is not here," the boy said pathetically. "I do not know where he is gone." He sobbed a little.

The woman put down her basket, sat by his side and asked, "Are you hungry?"

"I have money," he said.

She gently patted his head and said, "Ah, poor child! I knew your mother. She was a good girl. That she should have left you adrift like this and gone heavenward!" Although he had no memory of his mother, at the mention of her, tears rolled down his cheeks, and he licked them off with relish at the corner of his mouth. The woman suddenly said, "What are you going to do now?"

"I don't know," he said. "Wait till my father comes."

"Foolish and unfortunate child. Your father is gone."

"Where?" asked the boy.

"Don't ask me," the woman said. "I talked to a man who saw him go. He saw him get into the early-morning bus, which goes up the mountains, and that strumpet in the blue sari was with him."

"What about the monkey?" the boy asked. "Won't it come back?"

She had no answer to this question. Meanwhile, a man hawking rice cakes on a wooden tray was crying his wares at the end of the lane. The woman hailed him in a shrill voice and ordered, "Sell this poor child two *idlies*. Give him freshly made ones, not yesterday's."

"Yesterday's stuff not available even for a gold piece," said the man.

"Give him the money," she told the boy. The boy ran in and fetched some money. The woman pleaded with the hawker, "Give him something extra for the money."

"What extra?" he snarled.

"This is an unfortunate child."

"So are others. What can I do? Why don't you sell your earrings and help him? I shall go bankrupt if I listen to people like you and start giving more for less money." He took the cash and went on. Before he reached the third hut, the boy had polished off the *idlies* — so soft and pungent, with green chutney spread on top.

The boy felt more at peace with the world now, and able to face his problems. After satisfying herself that he had eaten well, the women rose to go, muttering, "Awful strumpet, to seduce a man from his child." The boy sat and brooded over her words. Though he gave no outward sign of it, he knew who the strumpet in the blue sari was. She lived in one of those houses beyond the park wall and was always to be found standing at the door, and seemed to be a fixture there. At the sight of her, his father would slow down his pace and tell the boy, "You keep going, I'll join you." The first time it happened, after waiting at the street corner, the boy tied the monkey to a lamppost and went back to the house. He did not find either his father or the woman where he had left them. The door of the house was shut. He raised his hand to pound on it, but restrained himself and sat down on the step, wondering. Presently the door opened and his father emerged, with the basket slung over his shoulder as usual; he appeared displeased at the sight of the boy and raised his hand to strike him, muttering, "Didn't I say, 'Keep going'?" The boy ducked and ran down the street, and heard the blue-sari woman remark, "Bad, mischievous devil, full of evil curiosity!" Later, his father said, "When I say go, you must obey."

"What did you do there?" asked the boy, trying to look and sound innocent, and the man said severely, "You must not ask questions."

"Who is she? What is her name?"

"Oh, she is a relative," the man said. To further probing questions he said, "I went in to drink tea. You'll be thrashed if you ask more questions, little devil."

The boy said, as an afterthought, "I only came back thinking that you might want me to take the basket," whereupon his father said sternly, "No more talk. You must know, she is a good and lovely person." The boy did not accept this description of her. She had called him names. He wanted to shout from rooftops, "Bad, bad, and bad woman and not at all lovely!" but kept it to himself. Whenever they passed that way again, the boy quickened his pace, without looking left or right, and waited patiently for his father to join him at the street corner. Occasionally his father followed his example and passed on without glancing at the house if he noticed, in place of the woman, a hairy-chested man standing at the door, massaging his potbelly.

The boy found that he could play the pipe, handle the snake and feed it also — all in the same manner as his father used to. Also, he could knock off the fangs whenever they started to grow. He earned enough each day, and as the weeks and months passed he grew taller, and the snake became progressively tardy and flabby and hardly stirred its coils. The boy never ceased to sigh for the monkey. The worst blow his father had dealt him was the kidnapping of his monkey.

When a number of days passed without any earnings, he decided to rid himself of the snake, throw away the gourd pipe and do something else for a living. Perhaps catch another monkey and train it. He had watched his father and knew how to go about this. A monkey on his shoulder would gain him admission anywhere, even into a palace. Later on, he would just keep it as a pet and look for some other profession. Start as a porter at the railway station — so many trains to watch every hour — and maybe get into one someday and out into the wide world. But the first step would be to get rid of Naga. He couldn't afford to find eggs and milk for him.

He carried the snake basket along to a lonely spot down the river course, away from human habitation, where a snake could move about in peace without getting killed at sight. In that lonely part of Nallappa's grove, there were many mounds, crevasses and anthills. "You could make your home anywhere there, and your cousins will be happy to receive you back into their fold," he said to the snake. "You should learn to be happy in your own home. You must forget me. You have become useless, and we must part. I don't know where my father is gone. He'd have kept you until you grew wings and all that, but I don't care." He opened the lid of the basket, lifted the snake and set it free. It lay inert for a while, then raised its head, looked at the outside world without interest, and started to move along tardily, without any aim. After a few yards of slow motion, it turned about, looking for its basket home. At once the boy snatched up the basket and flung it far out of the snake's range. "You will not go anywhere else as long as I am nearby." He turned the snake round, to face an anthill, prodded it on and then began to run at full speed in the opposite direction. He stopped at a distance, hid himself behind a tree and watched. The snake was approaching the slope of the anthill. The boy had no doubt now that Naga would find the hole on its top, slip itself in and vanish from his life forever. The snake crawled halfway up the hill, hesitated and then turned round and came along in his direction again. The boy swore, "Oh, damned snake! Why don't you go back to your world and stay there? You won't find me again!" He ran through Nallappa's grove and stopped to regain his breath. From where he stood, he saw his Naga glide along majestically across the ground, shining like a silver ribbon under the bright sun. The boy paused to say "Goodbye" before making his exit. But looking up he noticed a white-necked Brahmany kite sailing in the blue sky. "Garuda," he said in awe. As was the custom, he made obeisance to it by touching his eyes with his fingertips. Garuda was the vehicle of God Vishnu and was sacred. He shut his eyes in a brief prayer to the bird. "You are a god, but I know you eat snakes. Please leave Naga alone." He opened his eyes and saw the kite skimming along a little nearer, its shadow almost trailing the course of the lethargic snake. "Oh!" he screamed. "I know your purpose." Garuda would make a swoop and dive at the right moment and stab his claws into that foolish Naga, who had refused the shelter of the anthill, and carry him off for his dinner. The boy dashed back to the snake, retrieving his basket on the way. When he saw the basket, Naga slithered back into it, as if coming home after a strenuous public performance.

Naga was eventually reinstated in his corner of the hut beside the park wall. The boy said to the snake, "If you don't grow wings soon enough, I hope you will be hit on the head with a bamboo staff, as it normally happens to any cobra. Know this: I will not be guarding you forever. I'll be away at the railway station, and if you come out of the basket and adventure about, it will be your end. No one can blame me afterward."

Joyce Carol Oates was born in Lockport, New York, in 1938 and received her education at Syracuse University and the University of Wisconsin. A prolific and powerful writer whose recurrent themes are violence, madness, and moral corruption, she has been described as having a mind "unbelievably crowded with psychic experiences" and as reflecting "a sweetly brutal sense of what American experience is really like." Her early stories and novels are often set in a mythical landscape, Eden County, in upstate New York. For her recurrence to that setting and also for the violence with which her characters confront life, Oates has been likened to one of her major literary influences, William Faulkner. One critic even called her "the first 'southern' writer in the north." In works written over the past decade, she has experimented with such forms as the gothic novel and the historical novel. She has written innumerable short stories; they likewise reveal her fascination with the psychology of human behavior and with varieties of literary form. Among Oates's major novels are *A Garden of Earthly Delights* (1967), *Expensive People* (1968), *Them* (1969), *Do with Me What You Will* (1973), *Bellefleur* (1980), *A Bloodsmoor Romance* (1982), *Mysteries of Winterburn* (1984), *Solstice* (1985), and *You Must Remember This* (1987). Her short story collections include *By the North Gate* (1963), *The Wheel of Love* (1970), *Marriage and Infidelity* (1972), *Where Are You Going, Where Have You Been?* (1974), *The Poisoned Kiss and Other Stories* (1975), *A Sentimental Education* (1981), *Last Days: Stories* (1984), and *Raven's Wing* (1986). The stories here — "The Lady with the Pet Dog" and "Raven's Wing" — illustrate something of Oates's range and depth: the first is a retelling of Chekhov's famous story of the same title, the second is a tender interlude in Oates's otherwise tough fictional world.

The Lady with the Pet Dog

1

Strangers parted as if to make way for him.

There he stood. He was there in the aisle, a few yards away, watching her. She leaned forward at once in her seat, her hand jerked up to her face as if to ward off a blow — but then the crowd in the aisle hid him, he was gone. She pressed both hands against her cheeks. He was not there, she had imagined him.

"My God," she whispered.

She was alone. Her husband had gone out to the foyer to make a telephone call; it was intermission at the concert, a Thursday evening.

Now she saw him again, clearly. He was standing there. He was staring at her. Her blood rocked in her body, draining out of her head . . . she was going to faint. . . . They stared at each other. They gave no sign of recognition. Only when he took a step forward did she shake her head *no — no — keep away.* It was not possible.

When her husband returned, she was staring at the place in the aisle where her lover had been standing. Her husband leaned forward to interrupt that stare.

"What's wrong?" he said. "Are you sick?"

Panic rose in her in long shuddering waves. She tried to get to her feet, panicked at the thought of fainting here, and her husband took hold of her. She stood like an aged woman, clutching the seat before her.

At home he helped her up the stairs and she lay down. Her head was like a large piece of crockery that had to be held still, it was so heavy. She was still panicked. She felt it in the shallows of her face, behind her knees, in the pit of her stomach. It sickened her, it made her think of mucus, of something thick and gray congested inside her, stuck to her, that was herself and yet not herself — a poison.

She lay with her knees drawn up toward her chest, her eyes hotly open, while her husband spoke to her. She imagined that other man saying, *Why did you run away from me?* Her husband was saying other words. She tried to listen to them. He was going to call the doctor, he said, and she tried to sit up. "No, I'm all right now," she said quickly. The panic was like lead inside her, so thickly congested. How slow love was to drain out of her, how fluid and sticky it was inside her head!

Her husband believed her. No doctor. No threat. Grateful, she drew her husband down to her. They embraced, not comfortably. For years now they had not been comfortable together, in their intimacy and at a distance, and now they struggled gently as if the paces of this dance were too rigorous for them. It was something they might have known once, but had now outgrown. The panic in her thickened at this double betrayal: she drew her husband to her, she caressed him wildly, she shut her eyes to think about that other man.

A crowd of men and women parting, unexpectedly, and there he stood — there he stood — she kept seeing him, and yet her vision blotched at the memory. It had been finished between them, six months before, but he had come out here . . . and she had escaped him, now she was lying in her husband's arms, in his embrace, her face pressed against his. It was a kind of sleep, this love-making. She felt herself falling asleep, her body falling from her. Her eyes shut.

"I love you," her husband said fiercely, angrily.

She shut her eyes and thought of that other man, as if betraying him would give her life a center.

"Did I hurt you? Are you — ?" her husband whispered.

Always this hot flashing of shame between them, the shame of her husband's near failure, the clumsiness of his love —

"You didn't hurt me," she said.

2

They had said good-by six months before. He drove her from Nantucket, where they had met, to Albany, New York, where she visited her sister. The hours of intimacy in the car had sealed something between them, a vow of silence and impersonality; she recalled the movement of the highways, the passing of other cars, the natural rhythms of the day hypnotizing her toward sleep while he drove. She trusted him, she could sleep in his presence. Yet she could not really fall asleep in spite of her exhaustion, and she kept jerking awake, frightened, to discover that nothing had changed — still the stranger who was driving her to Albany, still the highway, the sky, the antiseptic odor of the rented car, the sense of a rhythm behind the rhythm of the air that might unleash itself at any second. Everywhere on this highway, at this moment, there were men and women driving together, bonded together — what did that mean, to be together? What did it mean to enter into a bond with another person?

No, she did not really trust him; she did not really trust men. He would glance at her with his small cautious smile and she felt a declaration of shame between them. Shame.

In her head she rehearsed conversations. She said bitterly, "You'll be relieved when we get to Albany. Relieved to get rid of me." They had spent so many days talking, confessing too much, driven to a pitch of childish excitement, laughing together on the beach, breaking into that pose of laughter that seems to eradicate the soul, so many days of this that the silence of the trip was like the silence of a hospital — all these surface noises, these rattles and hums, but an interior silence, a befuddlement. She said to him in her imagination, "One of us should die." Then she leaned over to touch him. She caressed the back of his neck. She said, aloud, "Would you like me to drive for a while?"

They stopped at a picnic area where other cars were stopped — couples, families — and walked together, smiling at their good luck. He put his arm around her shoulders and she sensed how they were in a posture together, a man and a woman forming a posture, a figure, that someone might sketch and show to them. She said slowly, "I don't want to go back . . ."

Silence. She looked up at him. His face was heavy with her words, as if she had pulled at his skin with her fingers. Children ran nearby and distracted him — yes, he was a father, too, his children ran like that, they tugged at his skin with their light, busy fingers.

"Are you so unhappy?" he said.

"I'm not unhappy, back there. I'm nothing. There's nothing to me," she said.

They stared at each other. The sensation between them was intense, exhausting. She thought that this man was her savior, that he had come to her at a time in her life when her life demanded completion, an end, a permanent fixing of all that was troubled and shifting and deadly. And yet it was absurd to think this. No person could save another. So she drew back from him and released him.

A few hours later they stopped at a gas station in a small city. She went into the women's rest room, having to ask the attendant for a key, and when she came back her eye jumped nervously onto the rented car — why? did she think he might have driven off without her? — onto the man, her friend, standing in conversation with the young attendant. Her friend was as old as her husband, over forty, with lanky, sloping shoulders, a full body, his hair thick, a dark, burnished brown, a festive color that made her eye twitch a little — and his hands were always moving, always those rapid conversational circles, going nowhere, gestures that were at once a little aggressive and apologetic.

She put her hand on his arm, a claim. He turned to her and smiled and she felt that she loved him, that everything in her life had forced her to this moment and that she had no choice about it.

They sat in the car for two hours, in Albany, in the parking lot of a Howard Johnson's restaurant, talking, trying to figure out their past. There was no future. They concentrated on the past, the several days behind them, lit up with a hot, dazzling August sun, like explosions that already belonged to other people, to strangers. Her face was faintly reflected in the green-tinted curve of the windshield, but she could not have recognized that face. She began to cry; she told herself: *I am not here, this will pass, this is nothing.* Still, she could not stop crying. The muscles of her face were springy, like a child's, unpredictable muscles. He stroked her arms, her shoulders, trying to comfort her. "This is so hard . . . this is impossible . . ." he said. She felt panic for the world outside this car, all that was not herself and this man, and at the same time she understood that she was free of him, as people are free of other people, she would leave him soon, safely, and within a few days he would have fallen into the past, the impersonal past. . . .

"I'm so ashamed of myself!" she said finally.

She returned to her husband and saw that another woman, a shadow-woman, had taken her place — noiseless and convincing, like a dancer performing certain difficult steps. Her husband folded her in his arms and talked to her of his own loneliness, his worries about his business, his health, his mother, kept tranquillized and mute in a nursing home, and her spirit detached itself from her and drifted about the rooms of the large house she lived in with her husband, a shadow-woman delicate and imprecise. There was no boundary to her, no edge. Alone, she took hot baths and sat exhausted in the steaming water, wondering at her perpetual exhaustion. All that winter she noticed the limp, languid weight of her arms, her veins bulging slightly with the pressure of her extreme weariness. *This is fate,* she thought, to be here and not there, to be one person and not another, a certain man's wife and not the wife of another man. The long, slow pain of this certainly rose in her, but it never became clear, it was baffling and imprecise. She could not be serious about it; she kept congratulating herself on her own good luck, to have escaped so easily, to have freed herself. So much love had gone into the first several years of her marriage that there wasn't much left, now, for another man. . . . She was certain of that. But the bath water made her dizzy, all that perpetual heat, and one day in January she drew a razor blade lightly across the inside of her arm, near the elbow, to see what would happen.

Afterward she wrapped a small towel around it, to stop the bleeding. The towel soaked through. She wrapped a bath towel around that and walked through the empty rooms of her home, lightheaded, hardly aware of the stubborn seeping of blood. There was no boundary to her in this house, no precise limit. She could flow out like her own blood and come to no end.

She sat for a while on a blue love seat, her mind empty. Her husband telephoned her when he would be staying late at the plant. He talked to her always about his plans, his problems, his business friends, his future. It was obvious that he had a future. As he spoke she nodded to encourage him, and her heartbeat quickened with the memory of her own, personal shame, the shame of this man's particular, private wife. One evening at dinner he leaned forward and put his head in his arms and fell asleep, like a child. She sat at the table with him for a while watching him. His hair had gone gray, almost white, at the temples — no one would guess that he was so quick, so careful a man, still fairly young about the eyes. She put her hand on his head, lightly, as if to prove to herself that he was real. He slept, exhausted.

One evening they went to a concert and she looked up to see her lover there, in the crowded aisle, in this city, watching her. He was standing there, with his overcoat on, watching her. She went cold. That morning the telephone had rung while her husband was still home, and she had heard him answer it, heard him hang up — it must have been a wrong number — and when the telephone rang again, at 9:30, she had been afraid to answer it. She had left home to be out of the range of that ringing, but now, in this public place, in this busy auditorium, she found herself staring at that man, unable to make any sign to him, any gesture of recognition. . . .

He would have come to her but she shook her head. *No. Stay away.*

Her husband helped her out of the row of seats, saying, "Excuse us, please. Excuse us," so that strangers got to their feet, quickly, alarmed, to let them pass. Was that woman about to faint? What was wrong?

At home she felt the blood drain slowly back into her head. Her husband embraced her hips, pressing his face against her, in that silence that belonged to the earliest days of their marriage. She thought, *He will drive it out of me.* He made love to her and she was back in the auditorium again, sitting alone, now that the concert was over. The stage was empty; the heavy velvet curtains had not been drawn; the musicians' chairs were empty, everything was silent and expectant; in the aisle her lover stood and smiled at her — Her husband was impatient. He was apart from her, working on her, operating on her; and then, stricken, he whispered, "Did I hurt you?"

The telephone rang the next morning. Dully, sluggishly, she answered it. She recognized his voice at once — that "Anna?" with its lifting of the second syllable, questioning and apologetic and making its claim — "Yes, what do you want?" she said.

"Just to see you. Please — "

"I can't."

"Anna, I'm sorry, I didn't mean to upset you — "

"I can't see you."

"Just for a few minutes — I have to talk to you — "

"But why, why now? Why now?" she said.

She heard her voice rising, but she could not stop it. He began to talk again, drowning her out. She remembered his rapid conversation. She remembered his gestures, the witty energetic circling of his hands.

"Please don't hang up!" he cried.

"I can't — I don't want to go through it again — "

"I'm not going to hurt you. Just tell me how you are."

"Everything is the same."

"Everything is the same with me."

She looked up at the ceiling, shyly. "Your wife? Your children?"

"The same."

"Your son?"

"He's fine — "

"I'm glad to hear that. I — "

"Is it still the same with you, your marriage? Tell me what you feel. What are you thinking?"

"I don't know. . . ."

She remembered his intense, eager words, the movement of his hands, that impatient precise fixing of the air by his hands, the jabbing of his fingers.

"Do you love me?" he said.

She could not answer.

"I'll come over to see you," he said.

"No," she said.

What will come next, what will happen?

Flesh hardening on his body, aging. Shrinking. He will grow old, but not soft like her husband. They are two different types: he is nervous, lean, energetic, wise. She will grow thinner, as the tension radiates out from her backbone, wearing down her flesh. Her collarbones will jut out of her skin. Her husband, caressing her in their bed, will discover that she is another woman — she is not there with him — instead she is rising in an elevator in a downtown hotel, carrying a book as a prop, or walking, quickly away from that hotel, her head bent and filled with secrets. Love, what to do with it? . . . Useless as moths' wings, as moths' fluttering. . . . She feels the flutterings of silky, crazy wings in her chest.

He flew out to visit her every several weeks, staying at a different hotel each time. He telephoned her, and she drove down to park in an underground garage at the very center of the city.

She lay in his arms while her husband talked to her, miles away, one body fading into another. He will grow old, his body will change, she thought, pressing her cheek against the back of one of these men. If it was her lover, they were in a hotel room: always the propped-up little booklet describing the hotel's many services, with color photographs of its cocktail lounge and dining room and coffee shop. Grow old, leave me, die, go back to your neurotic wife and your sad, ordinary children, she thought, but still her eyes closed gratefully against his skin and she felt how complete their silence was, how they had come to rest in each other.

"Tell me about your life here. The people who love you," he said, as he always did.

One afternoon they lay together for four hours. It was her birthday and she was intoxicated with her good fortune, this prize of the afternoon, this man in her arms! She was a little giddy, she talked too much. She told him about her parents, about her husband. . . . "They were all people I believed in, but it turned out wrong. Now, I believe in you. . . ." He laughed as if shocked by her words. She did not understand. Then she understood. "But I believe truly in you. I can't think of myself without you," she said. . . . He spoke of his wife, her ambitions, her intelligence, her use of the children against him, her use of his younger son's blindness, all of his words gentle and hypnotic and convincing in the late afternoon peace of this hotel room . . . and she felt the terror of laughter, threatening laughter. Their words, like their bodies, were aging.

She dressed quickly in the bathroom, drawing her long hair up around the back of her head, fixing it as always, anxious that everything be the same. Her face was slightly raw, from his face. The rubbing of his skin. Her eyes were too bright, wearily bright. Her hair was blond but not so blond as it had been that summer in the white Nantucket air.

She ran water and splashed it on her face. She blinked at the water. Blind. Drowning. She thought with satisfaction that soon, soon, he would be back home, in that house on Long Island she had never seen, with that woman she had never seen, sitting on the edge of another bed, putting on his shoes. She wanted nothing except to be free of him. Why not be free? *Oh,* she thought suddenly, *I will follow you back and kill you. You and her and the little boy. What is there to stop me?*

She left him. Everyone on the street pitied her, that look of absolute zero.

3

A man and a child, approaching her. The sharp acrid smell of fish. The crashing of waves. Anna pretended not to notice the father with his son — there was something strange about them. That frank, silent intimacy, too gentle, the man's bare feet in the water and the boy a few feet away, leaning away from his father. He was about nine years old and still his father held his hand.

A small yipping dog, a golden dog, bounded near them.

Anna turned shyly back to her reading; she did not want to have to speak to these neighbors. She saw the man's shadow falling over her legs, then over the pages of her book, and she had the idea that he wanted to see what she was reading. The dog nuzzled her; the man called him away.

She watched them walk down the beach. She was relieved that the man had not spoken to her.

She saw them in town later that day, the two of them brown-haired and patient, now wearing sandals, walking with that same look of care. The man's white shorts were soiled and a little baggy. His pullover shirt was a faded green. His face was broad, the cheekbones wide, spaced widely apart, the eyes stark in their sockets, as if they fastened onto objects for no reason, ponderous and edgy. The little boy's face was pale and sharp; his lips were perpetually parted.

Anna realized that the child was blind.

The next morning, early, she caught sight of them again. For some reason she went to the back door of her cottage. She faced the sea breeze eagerly. Her heart hammered.... She had been here, in her family's old house, for three days, alone, bitterly satisfied at being alone, and now it was a puzzle to her how her soul strained to fly outward, to meet with another person. She watched the man with his son, his cautious, rather stooped shoulders above the child's small shoulders.

The man was carrying something, it looked like a notebook. He sat on the sand, not far from Anna's spot of the day before, and the dog rushed up to them. The child approached the edge of the ocean, timidly. He moved in short jerky steps, his legs stiff. The dog ran around him. Anna heard the child crying out a word that sounded like "Ty" — it must have been the dog's name — and then the man joined in, his voice heavy and firm.

"Ty —"

Anna tied her hair back with a yellow scarf and went down to the beach.

The man glanced around at her. He smiled. She stared past him at the waves. To talk to him or not to talk — she had the freedom of that choice. For a moment she felt that she had made a mistake, that the child and the dog would not protect her, that behind this man's ordinary, friendly face there was a certain arrogant maleness — then she relented, she smiled shyly.

"A nice house you've got there," the man said.

She nodded her thanks.

The man pushed his sunglasses up on his forehead. Yes, she recognized the eyes of the day before — intelligent and nervous, the sockets pale, untanned.

"Is that your telephone ringing?" he said.

She did not bother to listen. "It's a wrong number," she said.

Her husband calling; she had left home for a few days, to be alone.

But the man, settling himself on the sand, seemed to misinterpret this. He smiled in surprise, one corner of his mouth higher than the other. He said nothing. Anna wondered: *What is he thinking?* The dog was leaping about her, panting against her legs, and she laughed in embarrassment. She bent to pet it, grateful for its busyness. "Don't let him jump up on you," the man said. "He's a nuisance."

The dog was a small golden retriever, a young dog. The blind child, standing now in the water, turned to call the dog to him. His voice was shrill and impatient.

"Our house is the third one down — the white one," the man said.

She turned, startled. "Oh, did you buy it from Dr. Patrick? Did he die?"

"Yes, finally. . . ."

Her eyes wandered nervously over the child and the dog. She felt the nervous beat of her heart out to the very tips of her fingers, the fleshy tips of her fingers: little hearts were there, pulsing. *What is he thinking?* The man had opened his notebook. He had a piece of charcoal and he began to sketch something.

Anna looked down at him. She saw the top of his head, his thick brown hair, the freckles on his shoulders, the quick, deft movement of his hand. Upside down, Anna herself being drawn. She smiled in surprise.

"Let me draw you. Sit down," he said.

She knelt awkwardly a few yards away. He turned the page of the sketch pad. The dog ran to her and she sat, straightening out her skirt beneath her, flinching from the dog's tongue. "Ty!" cried the child. Anna sat, and slowly the pleasure of the moment began to glow in her; her skin flushed with gratitude.

She sat there for nearly an hour. The man did not talk much. Back and forth the dog bounded, shaking itself. The child came to sit near them, in silence. Anna felt that she was drifting into a kind of trance while the man sketched her, half a dozen rapid sketches, the surface of her face given up to him. "Where are you from?" the man asked.

"Ohio. My husband lives in Ohio."

She wore no wedding band.

"Your wife — " Anna began.

"Yes?"

"Is she here?"

"Not right now."

She was silent, ashamed. She had asked an improper question. But the man did not seem to notice. He continued drawing her, bent over the sketch pad. When Anna said she had to go, he showed her the drawings — one after another of her, Anna, recognizably Anna, a woman in her early thirties, her hair smooth and flat across the top of her head, tied behind by a scarf. "Take the one you like best," he said, and she picked one of her with the dog in her lap, sitting very straight, her brows and eyes clearly defined, her lips girlishly pursed, the dog and her dress suggested by a few quick irregular lines.

"Lady with pet dog," the man said.

She spent the rest of the day reading, nearer her cottage. It was not really a cottage — it was a two-story house, large and ungainly and weathered. It was mixed up in her mind with her family, her own childhood, and she glanced up from her book, perplexed, as if waiting for one of her parents or her sister to come up to her. Then she thought of the man, the man with the blind child, the man with the dog, and she could not concentrate on her reading. Someone — probably her father — had marked a passage that must be important, but she kept reading and rereading it: *We try to discover in things, endeared to us on that account, the spiritual glamour which we ourselves have cast upon them; we are disillusioned, and learn that they are in themselves barren and devoid of the charm that they owed, in our minds, to the association of certain ideas. . . .*

She thought again of the man on the beach. She lay the book aside and thought of him: his eyes, his aloneness, his drawings of her.

They began seeing each other after that. He came to her front door in the evening, without the child; he drove her into town for dinner. She was shy and extremely pleased. The darkness of the expensive restaurant released her; she heard herself chatter; she leaned forward and seemed to be offering her face up to him, listening to him. He talked about his work on a Long Island newspaper and she seemed to be listening to him, as she stared at his face, arranging her own face into the expression she had seen in that charcoal drawing. Did he see her like that, then? — girlish and withdrawn and patrician? She felt the weight of his interest in her, a force that fell upon her like a blow. A repeated blow. Of course he was married, he had children — of course she was married, permanently married. This flight from her husband was not important. She had left him before, to be alone, it was not important. Everything in her was slender and delicate and not important.

They walked for hours after dinner, looking at the other strollers, the weekend visitors, the tourists, the couples like themselves. Surely they were mistaken for a couple, a married couple. *This is the hour in which everything is decided,* Anna thought. They had both had several drinks and they talked a great deal. Anna found herself saying too much, stopping and starting giddily. She put her hand to her forehead, feeling faint.

"It's from the sun — you've had too much sun — " he said.

At the door to her cottage, on the front porch, she heard herself asking him if he would like to come in. She allowed him to lead her inside, to close the door. *This is not important,* she thought clearly, *he doesn't mean it, he doesn't love me, nothing will come of it.* She was frightened, yet it seemed to her necessary to give in; she had to leave Nantucket with that act completed, an act of adultery, an accomplishment she would take back to Ohio and to her marriage.

Later, incredibly, she heard herself asking. "Do you . . . do you love me?"

"You're so beautiful!" he said, amazed.

She felt this beauty, shy and glowing and centered in her eyes. He stared at her. In this large, drafty house, alone together, they were like accomplices, conspirators. She could not think: how old was she? which year was this? They had done something unforgivable together, and the knowledge of it was tugging at their faces. A cloud seemed to pass over her. She felt herself smiling shrilly.

Afterward, a peculiar raspiness, a dryness of breath. He was silent. She felt a strange, idle fear, a sense of the danger outside this room and this old, comfortable bed — a danger that would not recognize her as the lady in that drawing, the lady with the pet dog. There was nothing to say to this man, this stranger. She felt the beauty draining out of her face, her eyes fading.

"I've got to be alone," she told him.

He left, and she understood that she would not see him again. She stood by the window of the room, watching the ocean. A sense of shame overpowered her: it was smeared everywhere on her body, the smell of it, the richness of it. She tried to recall him, and his face was confused in her memory: she would have to shout to him across a jumbled space, she would have to wave her arms wildly. *You love me! You must love me!* But she knew he did not love her, and she did not love him; he was a man who drew everything up into himself, like all men, walking away, free to walk away, free to have his own thoughts, free to envision her body, all the secrets of her body. . . . And she lay down again in the bed, feeling how heavy this body had become, her insides heavy with shame, the very backs of her eyelids coated with shame.

"This is the end of one part of my life," she thought.

But in the morning the telephone rang. She answered it. It was her lover: they talked brightly and happily. She could hear the eagerness in his voice, the love in his voice, that same still, sad amazement — she understood how simple life was, there were no problems.

They spent most of their time on the beach, with the child and the dog. He joked and was serious at the same time. He said, once, "You have defined my soul for me," and she laughed to hide her alarm. In a few days it was time for her to leave. He got a sitter for the boy and took the ferry with her to the mainland, then rented a car to drive her up to Albany. She kept thinking: *Now something will happen. It will come to an end.* But most of the drive was silent and hypnotic. She wanted him to joke with her, to say again that she had defined his soul for him, but he drove fast, he was serious, she distrusted the hawkish look of his profile — she did not know him at all. At a gas station she splashed her face with cold water. Alone in the grubby little rest room, shaky and very much alone. In such places are women totally alone with their bodies. The body grows heavier, more evil, in such silence. . . . On the beach everything had been noisy with sunlight and gulls and waves; here, as if run to earth, everything was cramped and silent and dead.

She went outside, squinting. There he was, talking with the station attendant. She could not think as she returned to him whether she wanted to live or not.

She stayed in Albany for a few days, then flew home to her husband. He met her at the airport, near the luggage counter, where her three pieces of pale-brown luggage were brought to him on a conveyer belt, to be claimed by him. He kissed her on the cheek. They shook hands, a little embarrassed. She had come home again.

"How will I live out the rest of my life?" she wondered.

In January her lover spied on her: she glanced up and saw him, in a public place, in the DeRoy Symphony Hall. She was paralyzed with fear. She nearly fainted. In this faint she felt her husband's body, loving her, working its love upon her, and she shut her eyes harder to keep out the certainty of his love — sometimes he failed at loving her, sometimes he succeeded, it had nothing to do with her or her pity or her ten years of love for him, it had nothing to do with a woman at all. It was a private act accomplished by a man, a husband or a lover, in communion with his own soul, his manhood.

Her husband was forty-two years old now, growing slowly into middle age, getting heavier, softer. Her lover was about the same age, narrower in the shoulders, with a full, solid chest, yet lean, nervous. She thought, in her paralysis, of men and how they love freely and eagerly so long as their bodies are capable of love, love for a woman; and then, as love fades in their bodies, it fades from their souls and they become immune and immortal and ready to die.

Her husband was a little rough with her, as if impatient with himself. "I love you," he said fiercely, angrily. And then, ashamed, he said, "Did I hurt you? . . ."

"You didn't hurt me," she said.

Her voice was too shrill for their embrace.

While he was in the bathroom she went to her closet and took out that drawing of the summer before. There she was, on the beach at Nantucket, a lady with a pet dog, her eyes large and defined, the dog in her lap hardly more than a few snarls, a few coarse soft lines of charcoal . . . her dress smeared, her arms oddly limp . . . her hands not well drawn at all. . . . She tried to think: did she love the man who had drawn this? did he love her? The fever in her husband's body had touched her and driven her temperature up, and now she stared at the drawing with a kind of lust, fearful of seeing an ugly soul in that woman's face, fearful of seeing the face suddenly through her lover's eyes. She breathed quickly and harshly, staring at the drawing.

And so, the next day, she went to him at his hotel. She wept, pressing against him, demanding of him, "What do you want? Why are you here? Why don't you let me alone?" He told her that he wanted nothing. He expected nothing. He would not cause trouble.

"I want to talk about last August," he said.

"Don't — " she said.

She was hypnotized by his gesturing hands, his nervousness, his obvious agitation. He kept saying, "I understand. I'm making no claims upon you."

They became lovers again.

He called room service for something to drink and they sat side by side on his bed, looking through a copy of *The New Yorker,* laughing at the cartoons. It was so peaceful in this room, so complete. They were on a holiday. It was a secret holiday. Four-thirty in the afternoon, on a Friday, an ordinary Friday: a secret holiday.

"I won't bother you again," he said.

He flew back to see her again in March, and in late April. He telephoned her from his hotel — a different hotel each time — and she came down to him at once. She rose to him in various elevators, knocked on the doors of various rooms, she stepped into his embrace, breathless and guilty and already angry with him, pleading with him. One morning in May, when he telephoned, she pressed her forehead against the doorframe and could not speak. He kept saying, "What's wrong? Can't you talk? Aren't you alone?" She felt that she was going insane. Her head would burst. Why, why did he love her, why did he pursue her? Why did he want her to die?"

She went to him in the hotel room. A familiar room: had they been here before? "Everything is repeating itself. Everything is stuck," she said. He framed her face in his hands and said that she looked thinner — was she sick? — what was wrong? She shook herself free. He, her lover, looked about the same. There was a small, angry pimple on his neck. He stared at her, eagerly and suspiciously. Did she bring bad news?

"So you love me? You love me?" she asked.

"Why are you so angry?"

"I want to be free of you. The two of us free of each other."

"That isn't true — you don't want that — "

He embraced her. She was wild with that old, familiar passion for him, her body clinging to his, her arms not strong enough to hold him. Ah, what despair! — what bitter hatred she felt! — she needed this man for her salvation, he was all she had to live for, and yet she could not believe in him. He embraced her thighs, her hips, kissing her, pressing his warm face against her, and yet she could not believe in him, not really. She needed him in order to live, but he was not worth her love, he was not worth her dying. . . . She promised herself this: when she got back home, when she was alone, she would draw the razor more deeply across her arm.

The telephone rang and he answered it: a wrong number.

"Jesus," he said.

They lay together, still. She imagined their posture like this, the two of them one figure, one substance; and outside this room and this bed there was a universe of disjointed, separate things, blank things, that had nothing to do with them. She would not be Anna out there, the lady in the drawing. He would not be her lover.

"I love you so much. . . ." she whispered.

"Please don't cry! We have only a few hours, please. . . ."

It was absurd, their clinging together like this. She saw them as a single figure in a drawing, their arms and legs entwined, their heads pressing mutely together. Helpless substance, so heavy and warm and doomed. It was absurd that any human being should be so important to another human being. She wanted to laugh: a laugh might free them both.

She could not laugh.

Sometime later he said, as if they had been arguing. "Look, it's you. You're the one who doesn't want to get married. You lie to me — "

"Lie to you?"

"You love me but you won't marry me, because you want something left over — Something not finished — All your life you can attribute your misery to me, to our not being married — you are using me — "

"Stop it! You'll make me hate you!" she cried.

"You can say to yourself that you're miserable because of *me*. We will never be married, you will never be happy, neither one of us will ever be happy — "

"I don't want to hear this!" she said.

She pressed her hands flatly against her face.

She went to the bathroom to get dressed. She washed her face and part of her body, quickly. The fever was in her, in the pit of her belly. She would rush home and strike a razor across the inside of her arm and free that pressure, that fever.

The impatient bulging of the veins: an ordeal over.

The demand of the telephone's ringing: that ordeal over.

The nuisance of getting the car and driving home in all that five o'clock traffic: an ordeal too much for a woman.

The movement of this stranger's body in hers: over, finished.

Now, dressed, a little calmer, they held hands and talked. They had to talk swiftly, to get all their news in: he did not trust the people who worked for him, he had faith in no one, his wife had moved to a textbook publishing company and was doing well, she had inherited a Ben Shahn painting from her father and wanted to "touch it up a little" — she was crazy! — his blind son was at another school, doing fairly well, in fact his children were all doing fairly well in spite of the stupid mistake of their parents' marriage — and what about her? what about her life? She told him in a rush the one thing he wanted to hear: that she lived with her husband lovelessly, the two of them polite strangers, sharing a bed, lying side by side in the night in that bed, bodies out of which souls had fled. There was no longer even any shame between them.

"And what about me? Do you feel shame with me still?" he asked.

She did not answer. She moved away from him and prepared to leave.

Then, a minute later, she happened to catch sight of his reflection in the bureau mirror — he was glancing down at himself, checking himself mechanically, impersonally, preparing also to leave. He too would leave this room: he too was headed somewhere else.

She stared at him. It seemed to her that in this instant he was breaking from her, the image of her lover fell free of her, breaking from her . . . and she realized that he existed in a dimension quite apart from her, a mysterious being. And suddenly, joyfully, she felt a miraculous calm. This man was her husband, truly — they were truly married, here in this room — they had been married haphazardly and accidentally for a long time. In another part of the city she had another husband, a "husband," but she had not betrayed that man, not really. This man, whom she loved above any other person in the world, above even her own self-pitying sorrow and her own life, was her truest lover, her destiny. And she did not hate him, she did not hate herself any longer; she did not wish to die; she was flooded with a strange certainty, a sense of gratitude, of pure selfless energy. It was obvious to her that she had, all along, been behaving correctly; out of instinct.

What triumph, to love like this in any room, anywhere, risking even the craziest of accidents!

"Why are you so happy? What's wrong?" he asked, startled. He stared at her. She felt the abrupt concentration in him, the focusing of his vision on her, almost a bitterness in his face, as if he feared her. What, was it beginning all over again? Their love beginning again, in spite of them? "How can you look so happy?" he asked. "We don't have any right to it. Is it because. . . ?"

"Yes," she said.

JOYCE CAROL OATES

Raven's Wing

Billy was at the Meadowlands track one Saturday when the accident happened to Raven's Wing — a three-year-old silky black colt who was the favorite in the first race, and one of the crowd favorites generally this season. Billy hadn't placed his bet on Raven's Wing. Betting on the 4:5 favorite held no excitement, and in any case, things were going too well for Raven's Wing, Billy felt, and his owner's luck would be running out soon. But telling his wife about the accident the next morning Billy was surprised at how important it came to seem, how intense his voice sounded, as if he was high, or on edge, which he was not, it was just the *telling* that worked him up, and the way Linda looked at him.

" — So there he was in the backstretch, looping around one, two, three, four horses to take the lead — he's a hard driver, Raven's Wing, doesn't let himself off easy — a little skittish at the starting gate, but then he got serious — in fact he was maybe running a little faster than he needed to run, once he got out front — then something happened, it looked like he stumbled, his hindquarters went down just a little — but he was going so fast, maybe forty miles an hour, the momentum kept him going — Jesus, it must have been three hundred feet! — the poor bastard, on three legs. Then the jockey jumped off, the other horses ran by, Raven's Wing was just sort of standing there by the rail, his head bobbing up and down. What had happened was he'd broken his left rear leg — came down too hard on it, maybe, or the hoof sunk in the dirt wrong. Just like that," Billy said. He snapped his fingers. "One minute we're looking at a million-dollar colt, the next minute — nothing."

"Wait. What do you mean, nothing?" Linda said.

"They put them down if they aren't going to race anymore."

" 'Put them down' — you mean they kill them?"

"Sure. Most of the time."

"How do they kill them? Do they shoot them?"

"I doubt it, probably some kind of needle, you know, injection, poison in their bloodstream."

Linda was leaning toward him, her forehead creased. "Okay, then what happened?" she said.

"Well — an ambulance came out to the track and picked him up, there was an announcement about him breaking his leg, everybody in the stands was real quiet when they heard. Not because there was a lot of money on him either but because, you know, here's this first-class colt, a real beauty, a million-dollar horse, maybe two million, finished. Just like that."

Linda's eyelids were twitching, her mouth, she might have been going to cry, or maybe, suddenly, laugh, you couldn't predict these days. Near as Billy figured she hadn't washed her hair in more than a week and it looked like hell, she hadn't washed herself in all that time either, wore the same plaid shirt and jeans day after day, not that he'd lower himself to bring the subject up. She was staring at him, squinting. Finally she said, "How much did you lose? — you can tell me," in a breathy little voice.

"How much did *I* lose?" Billy asked. He was surprised as hell. They'd covered all this ground, hadn't they, there were certain private matters in his life, things that were none of her business, he'd explained it — her brother had explained it too — things she didn't need to know. And good reasons for her not to know. "How much did *I* lose — ?"

He pushed her aside, lightly, just with the tips of his fingers, and went to the refrigerator to get a beer. It was only ten in the morning but he was thirsty and his head and back teeth ached. "Who says I lost? We were out there for five races. In fact I did pretty well, we all did, what the hell do you know about it," Billy said. He opened the beer, took his time drinking. He knew that the longer he took, the calmer he'd get and it was one of those mornings — Sunday, bells ringing, everybody's schedule off — when he didn't want to get angry. But his hand was trembling when he drew a wad of bills out of his inside coat pocket and let it fall onto the kitchen counter. "Three hundred dollars, go ahead and count it, sweetheart," he said, "you think you're so smart."

Linda stood with her knees slightly apart, her big belly straining at the flannel shirt she wore, her mouth still twitching. Even with her skin grainy and sallow, and pimples across her forehead, she looked good, she was a good-looking girl, hell, thought Billy, it was a shame, a bad deal. She said, so soft he almost couldn't hear her, "I don't think I'm so smart."

"Yeah? What?"

"I don't think I'm anything."

She was looking at the money but for some reason, maybe she was afraid, she didn't touch it. Actually Billy had won almost a thousand dollars but that was his business.

Linda was eight years younger than Billy, just twenty-four though she looked younger, blond, high-strung, skinny except for her belly (she was five, six months pregnant, Billy couldn't remember), with hollowed-out eyes, that sullen mouth. They had been married almost a year and Billy thought privately it was probably a mistake though in fact he loved her, he *liked* her, if only she didn't do so many things to spite him. If she wasn't letting herself go, letting herself get sick, strung-out, weird, just to spite him.

He'd met her through her older brother, a friend of Billy's, more or less, from high school, a guy he'd done business with and could trust. But they had had a misunderstanding the year before and no longer worked together.

Once, in bed, Linda said, " – – If the man had to have it, boy, then things would be different. Things would be a lot different."

"What? A baby? How do you mean?" Billy asked. He'd been halfway asleep, he wanted to humor her, he didn't want a fight at two in the morning. "Are we talking about a baby?"

"They *wouldn't* have it, that's all."

"What?"

"The baby. Any baby."

"Jesus — that's crazy."

"Yeah? Who? Would you?" Linda said angrily. "What about your own?"

Billy had two children, both boys, from his first marriage, but as things worked out he never saw them and rarely thought about them — his wife had remarried, moved to Tampa. At one time Billy used to say that he and his ex-wife got along all right, they weren't out to slit each other's throat like some people he knew, but in fact when Billy's salary at GM Radiator had been garnisheed a few years ago he wasn't very happy; he'd gone through a bad time. So he'd quit the job, a good-paying job too, and later, when he tried to get hired back, they were already laying off men, it was rotten luck, his luck had run against him for a long time. One of the things that had driven him wild was the fact that his wife, that is his ex-wife, was said to be pregnant again, and he'd maybe be helping to support another man's kid, when he thought of it he wanted to kill somebody, anybody, but then she got married after all and it worked out and now he didn't have to see her or even think of her very much: that was the advantage of distance. But now he said, "Sure," trying to keep it all light. "What the hell, sure, it beats the Army."

"*You'd* have a baby?" Linda said. Now she was sitting up, leaning over him, her hair in her face, her eyes showing a rim of white above the iris. "Oh don't hand me that. Oh please."

"Sure. If you wanted me to."

"I'm asking about *you* — would *you* want to?"

They had been out drinking much of the evening and Linda was groggy but skittish, on edge, her face very pale and giving off a queer damp heat. The way she was grinning, Billy didn't want to pursue the subject.

"How about *you,* I said," she said, jabbing him with her elbow, " — I'm talking about *you.*"

"I don't know what the hell we are talking about."

"You do know."

"What — I don't."

"You do. You do. Don't hand me such crap."

When he and Linda first started going together they'd made love all the time, like crazy, it was such a relief (so Billy told himself) to be out from under that other bitch, but now, married only a year, with Linda dragging around the apartment sick and angry and sometimes talking to herself, pretending she didn't know Billy could hear, now everything had changed, he couldn't predict whether she'd be up or down, high or low, very low, hitting bottom, scaring him with her talk about killing herself (her crazy mother had tried *that* a few times, it probably ran in the family) or getting an abortion (but wasn't it too late, her stomach that size, for an abortion), he never knew when he opened the door what he'd be walking into. She didn't change her clothes, including her underwear, for a week at a time, she didn't wash her hair, she'd had a tight permanent that sprang out around her head but turned flat, matted, blowsy if it wasn't shampooed, he knew she was ruining her looks to spite him but she claimed (shouting, crying, punching her own thighs with her fists) that she just *forgot* about things like that, she had more important things to think about.

One day, a few months before, Billy had caught sight of this great-looking girl out on the street, coat with a fox-fur collar like the one he'd bought for Linda, high-heeled boots like Linda's, blond hair, wild springy curls like a model, frizzed, airy, her head high and her walk fast, almost like strutting — she knew she was being watched, and not just by Billy — and then she turned and it *was* Linda, his own wife, she'd washed her hair and fixed herself up, red lipstick, even eye makeup — he'd just stood there staring, it took him by such surprise. But then the next week she was back to lying around the apartment feeling sorry for herself, sullen and heavy-hearted, sick to her stomach even if she hadn't eaten anything.

The worst of the deal was, he and her brother had had their misunderstanding and didn't do business any longer. When Billy got drunk he had the vague idea that he was getting stuck again with another guy's baby.

The racing news was, Raven's Wing hadn't been killed after all.

It *was* news, people were talking about it, Billy even read about it in the newspaper, an operation on the colt's leg estimated to cost in the six-figure range, a famous veterinary surgeon the owner was flying in from Dallas, and there was a photograph (it somehow frightened Billy, that photograph) of Raven's Wing lying on his side, anesthetized, strapped down, being operated on like a human being. The *size* of a horse — that always impressed Billy.

Other owners had their opinions, was it worth it or not, other trainers, veterinarians, but Raven's Wing's owner wanted to save his life, the colt wasn't just any horse (the owner said) he was the most beautiful horse they'd ever reared on their farm. He was insured for $600,000 and the insurance company had granted permission for the horse to be destroyed but still the owner wanted to save his life. "They wouldn't do that for a human being," Linda said when Billy told her.

"Well," Billy said, irritated at her response, " — this isn't a human being, it's a first-class horse."

"Jesus, a *horse* operated on," Linda said, laughing, "and he isn't even going to run again, you said? How much is all this going to cost?"

"People like that, they don't care about money. They have it, they spend it on what matters," Billy said. "It's a frame of reference you don't know shit about."

"Then what?"

"What?"

"After the operation?"

"After the operation, if it works, then he's turned out to stud," Billy said. "You know what that is, huh?" he said, poking her in the breast.

"Just a minute. The horse is worth that much?"

"A first-class horse is worth a million dollars, I told you, maybe more. Two million. These people take things *seriously*."

"Two million dollars for an animal — ?" Linda said slowly. She sounded dazed, disoriented, as if the fact was only now sinking in, but what *was* the fact, what did it mean? "Hey I think that's *sick*."

"I told you, Linda, it's a frame of reference you don't know shit about."

"That's right. I don't."

She was making such a childish ugly face at him, drawing her lips back from her teeth, Billy lost control and shoved her against the edge of the kitchen table, and she slapped him hard, on the side of the nose, and it was all Billy could do to stop right there, just *stop,* not give it back to the bitch like she deserved. He knew, once he got started with this one, it might be the end. She might not be able to pick herself up from the floor when he was done.

Billy asked around, and there was this contact of his named Kellerman, and Kellerman was an old friend of Raven's Wing's trainer, and he fixed it up so that he and Billy could drive out to the owner's farm in Pennsylvania, so that Billy could see the horse, Billy just wanted to *see* the horse, it was always at the back of his mind these days.

The weather was cold, the sky a hard icy blue, the kind of day that made Billy feel shaky, things were so bright, so vivid, you could see something weird and beautiful anywhere you looked. His head ached, he was so edgy, his damn back teeth, he chewed on Bufferin, he and Kellerman drank beer out of cans, tossed the cans away on the road. Kellerman said horse people like these were the real thing, look at this layout, and not even counting Raven's Wing they had a stable worth millions, a Preakness winner, a second-place Kentucky Derby finisher, but was the money even in horses? — hell no it was in some investments or something. That was how rich people worked.

In the stable, at Raven's Wing's stall, Billy hung over the partition and looked at him for a long time, just looked. Kellerman and the trainer were talking but Billy just looked.

The size of the horse, that was one of the things, and the head, the big rounded eyes, ears pricked forward, tail switching, here was Raven's Wing looking at last at him, did he maybe recognize Billy, did he maybe sense who Billy was? Billy extended a hand to him, whispering his name. Hey Raven's Wing. Hey.

The size, and the silky sheen of the coat, the jet-black coat, that skittish air, head bobbing, teeth bared, Billy could feel his warm breath, Billy sucked in the strong *smell* — horse manure, horse piss, sweat, hay, mash, and what was he drinking? — apple juice, the trainer said. *Apple juice,* Christ! Gallons and gallons of it. Did he have his appetite back, Billy asked, but it was obvious the colt did, he was eating steadily, chomping hay, eyeing Billy as if Billy was — was what? — just the man he wanted to see. The man who'd driven a hundred miles to see him.

Both his rear legs were in casts, the veterinarian had taken a bone graft from the good leg, and his weight was down — 1,130 pounds to 880 — his ribs showing through the silky coat but Jesus did he look good, Jesus this was the real thing wasn't it? — Billy's heart beat fast as if he'd been popping pills, he wished to hell Linda was here, yeah the bitch should see *this,* it'd shut her up for a while.

Raven's Wing was getting his temper back, the trainer said, which was a good thing, it showed he was mending, but he still wasn't 99 percent in the clear, maybe they didn't know how easy it was for horses to get sick — colic, pneumonia, all kinds of viruses, infections. Even the good leg had gone bad for a while, paralyzed, and they'd had to have two operations, a six-hour and a four-hour, the owner had to sign a release, they'd put him down right on the operating table if things looked too bad. But he pulled through, his muscle tone was improving every day, there he was, fiery little bastard, watch out or he'll nip you — a steel plate, steel wire, a dozen screws in his leg, and him not knowing a thing. The way the bone was broken it wasn't *broken,* the trainer told them, it was smashed, like somebody had gone after it with a sledgehammer.

"So he's going to make it," Billy said, not quite listening. "Hey yeah. *You.* You're going to make it, huh."

He and Kellerman were at the stall maybe forty-five minutes and the place was busy, busier than Billy would have thought, it rubbed him the wrong way that so many people were around when he'd had the idea he and Kellerman would be the only ones. But it turned out that Raven's Wing always had visitors. He even got mail. (This Billy snorted to hear — a horse gets *mail?*) People took away souvenirs if they could, good-luck things, hairs from his mane, his tail, that sort of thing, or else they wanted to feed him by hand: there was a lot of that, they had to be watched.

Before they left Billy leaned over as far as he could, just wanting to stroke Raven's Wing's side, and two things happened fast: the horse snorted, stamped, lunged at his hand; and the trainer pulled Billy back.

"Hey I told you," he said. "This is a dangerous animal."

"He likes me," Billy said. "He wasn't going to bite hard."

"Yeah? — sometimes he does. They can bite damn hard."

"He wasn't going to bite actually *hard,*" Billy said.

Three dozen blue snakeskin wallets (Venezuelan), almost two dozen up-scale watches (Swiss, German) — chronographs, water-resistant, self-winding, calendar, ultrathin, quartz, and gold tone — and a pair of pierced earrings, gold and pearl, delicate, Billy thought, as a snowflake. He gave the earrings to Linda to surprise her and watched her put them in, it amazed him how quickly she could take out earrings and slip in new ones, position the tiny wires exactly in place, he knew it was a trick he could never do if he was a woman. It made him shiver, it excited him, just to watch.

Linda never said, "Hey where'd you get *these,*" the way his first wife used to, giving him that slow wide wet smile she thought turned him on. (Actually it had turned him on, for a while. Two, three years.)

Linda never said much of anything except thank you in her little-girl breathy voice, if she happened to be in the mood for thanking.

One morning a few weeks later Linda, in her bathrobe, came slowly out of the bedroom into the kitchen, squinting at something she held in the air, at eye level. "This looks like somebody's hair, what is it, Indian hair? — it's all black and stiff," she said. Billy was on the telephone so he had an excuse not to give her his fullest attention at the moment. He might be getting ready to be angry, he might be embarrassed, his nerves were always bad this time of day. Linda leaned up against him, swaying a little in her preoccupation, exuding heat, her bare feet planted apart on the linoleum floor. She liked to poke at him with her belly, she had a new habit of standing close.

Billy kept on with his conversation, it was in fact an important conversation, and Linda wound the several black hairs around her forearm, making a little bracelet, so tight the flesh started to turn white, didn't it hurt? — her forehead creased in concentration, her breath warm and damp against his neck.

EDNA O'BRIEN

Edna O'Brien was born in the west of Ireland in 1932. She attended convent school and studied chemistry at Pharmaceutical College in Dublin. As a young woman she left Ireland for England, where she still lives. Her first novels, *The Country Girls* (1960) and *The Lonely Girls* (1962), set one of O'Brien's fictional paradigms: Irish women (or girls) seeking to move beyond the confines of tradition and upbringing to new dimensions of experience, especially that of love. O'Brien has sometimes been called an "Irish Colette" — a writer intent almost exclusively on exploring versions of female sensuality — but that characterization misses her sensitively rendered understanding of multiple dimensions of the female psychology, and misses her quintessentially Irish sadness as well. Her other novels include *Girls in Their Married Bliss* (1964), *Casualties of Peace* (1966), *A Pagan Place* (1970), *Night* (1972), and *Johnny I Hardly Knew You* (1977). Her stories are collected in *The Love Object* (1969), *A Scandalous Woman and Others* (1974), *A Rose in the Heart* (1979), and *A Fanatic Heart* (1984). The novelist Philip Roth, introducing a collection of O'Brien's stories, wrote of her "sensibility . . . combining the innocence of childhood with the scars of maturity." O'Brien is always writing about coming to terms with things. Each of the stories here — "A Rose in the Heart of New York" and "Sister Imelda" — is, in its way, about coming to terms with the cost of loving.

A Rose in the Heart of New York

December night. Jack Frost in scales along the outside of the windows giving to the various rooms a white filtered light. The ice like bits of mirror beveling the puddles of the potholes. The rooms were cold inside, and for the most part identically furnished. The room with no furniture at all — save for the apples gathered in the autumn — was called the Vacant Room. The apples were all over the place. Their smell was heady, many of them having begun to rot. Rooms into which no one had stepped for days, and yet these rooms and their belongings would become part of the remembered story. A solemn house, set in its own grounds, away from the lazy bustle of the village. A lonesome house, it would prove to be, and with a strange lifelikeness, as if it were not a house at all but a person observing and breathing, a presence amid a cluster of trees and sturdy wind-shorn hedges.

The overweight midwife hurried up the drive, her serge cape blowing behind her. She was puffing. She carried her barrel-shaped leather bag in which were disinfectant, gauze, forceps, instruments, and a small bottle of holy water lest the new child should prove to be in danger of death. More infants died around Christmastime than in any other month of the year. When she passed the little sycamore tree that was halfway up, she began to hear the roaring and beseeching to God. Poor mother, she thought, poor poor mother. She was not too early, had come more or less at the correct time, even though she was summoned hours before by Donal, the serving boy who worked on the farm. She had brought most of the children of that parish into the world, yet had neither kith nor kin of her own. Coming in the back door, she took off her bonnet and then attached it to the knob by means of its elastic string.

It was a blue room — walls of dark wet morose blue, furniture made of walnut, including the bed on which the event was taking place. Fronting the fireplace was a huge lid of a chocolate box with the representation of a saucy-looking lady. The tassel of the blind kept bobbing against the frosted windowpane. There was a washstand, a basin and ewer of off-white, with big roses splashed throughout the china itself, and a huge lumbering beast of a wardrobe. The midwife recalled once going to a house up the mountain, and finding that the child had been smothered by the time she arrived, the fatherless child had been stuffed in a drawer. The moans filled that room and went beyond the distempered walls out into the cold hall outside, where the black felt doggie with the amber eyes stood sentinel on a tall varnished whatnot. At intervals the woman apologized to the midwife for the unto-ward commotion, said sorry in a gasping whisper, and then was seized again by a pain that at different times she described as being a knife, a dagger, a hell on earth. It was her fourth labor. The previous child had died two days after being born. An earlier child, also a daughter, had died of whooping cough. Her womb was sick unto death. Why be a woman. Oh, cruel life; oh, merciless fate; oh, heartless man, she sobbed. Gripping the coverlet and remembering that between those selfsame, much-patched sheets, she had been prized apart, again and again, with not a word to her, not a little endearment, only rammed through and told to open up. When she married she had escaped the life of a serving girl, the possible experience of living in some grim institution, but as time went on and the bottom drawer was emptied of its gifts, she saw that she was made to serve in an altogether other way. When she wasn't screaming she was grinding her head into the pillow and praying for it to be all over. She dreaded the eventual bloodshed long before they saw any. The midwife made her ease up as she put an old sheet under her and over that a bit of oilcloth. The midwife said it was no joke and repeated the hypothesis that if men had to give birth there would not be a child born in the whole wide world. The husband was downstairs getting paralytic. Earlier when his wife had announced that she would have to go upstairs because of her labor, he said, looking for the slightest pretext for a celebration, that if there was any homemade wine or altar wine stacked away, to get it out, to produce it, and also the cut glasses. She said there was none and well he knew it, since they could hardly afford tea and sugar. He started to root and to rummage, to empty cupboards of their contents of rags, garments, and provisions, even to put his hand inside the bolster case, to delve into pillows; on he went, rampaging until he found a bottle in the wardrobe, in the very room into which she delivered her moans and exhortations. She begged of him not to, but all he did was to wield the amber-colored bottle in her direction, and then put it to his head so that the spirit started to go glug-glug. It was intoxicating stuff. By a wicked coincidence a crony of his had come to sell them another stove, most likely another crock, a thing that would have to be coaxed alight with constant attention and puffing to create a draft. The other child was with a neighbor, the dead ones in a graveyard six or seven miles away, among strangers and distant relatives, without their names being carved on the crooked rain-soaked tomb.

"O Jesus," she cried out as he came back to ask for a knitting needle to skewer out the bit of broken cork.

"Blazes," he said to her as she coiled into a knot and felt the big urgent ball — that would be the head — as it pressed on the base of her bowels and battered at her insides.

Curse and prayers combined to issue out of her mouth, and as time went on, they became most pitiful and were interrupted with screams. The midwife put a facecloth on her forehead and told her to push, in the name of the Lord to push. She said she had no strength left, but the midwife went on enjoining her and simulating a hefty breath. It took over an hour. The little head showing its tonsure would recoil, would reshow itself, each time a fraction more, although, in between, it was seeming to shrink from the world that it was hurtling toward. She said to the nurse that she was being burst apart, and that she no longer cared if she died, or if they drank themselves to death. In the kitchen they were sparring over who had the best greyhound, who had the successor to Mick the Miller. The crucifix that had been in her hand had fallen out, and her hands themselves felt bony and skinned because of the way they wrenched one another.

"In the name of God, push, missus."

She would have pushed everything out of herself, her guts, her womb, her craw, her lights, and her liver, but the center of her body was holding on and this center seemed to be the governor of her. She wished to be nothing, a shell, devoid of everything and everyone, and she was announcing that, and roaring and raving, when the child came hurtling out, slowly at first, as if its neck could not wring its way through, then the shoulder — that was the worst bit — carving a straight course, then the hideous turnabout, and a scream other than her own, and an urgent presage of things, as the great gouts of blood and lymph followed upon the mewling creature itself. Her last bit of easiness was then torn from her, and she was without hope. It had come into the world lopsided, and the first announcement from the midwife was a fatality, was that it had clubbed feet. Its little feet, she ventured to say, were like two stumps adhering to one another, and the blasted cord was bound around its neck. The result was a mewling piece of screwed-up, inert, dark-purple misery. The men subsided a little when the announcement was shouted down and they came to say congrats. The father waved a strip of pink flesh on a fork that he was carrying and remarked on its being unappetizing. They were cooking a goose downstairs and he said in future he would insist on turkey, as goose was only for gobs and goms. The mother felt green and disgusted, asked them to leave her alone. The salesman said was it a boy or a child, although he had just been told that it was a daughter. The mother could feel the blood gushing out of her, like water at a weir. The midwife told them to go down and behave like gentlemen.

Then she got three back numbers of the weekly paper, and a shoe box with a lid, and into it she stuffed the mess and the unnecessaries. She hummed as she prepared to do the stitching down the line of torn flesh that was gaping and coated with blood. The mother roared again and said this indeed was her vinegar and gall. She bit into the crucifix and dented it further. She could feel her mouth and her eyelids being stitched, too; she was no longer a lovely body, she was a vehicle for pain and for insult. The child was so quiet it scarcely breathed. The afterbirth was placed on the stove, where the dog, Shep, sniffed at it through its layers of paper and for his curiosity got a kick in the tail. The stove had been quenched, and the midwife said to the men that it was a crying shame to leave a good goose like that, neither cooked nor uncooked. The men had torn off bits of the breast so that the goose looked wounded, like the woman upstairs, who was then tightening her heart and soul, tightening inside the array of catgut stitches, and regarding her whole life as a vast disappointment. The midwife carried the big bundle up to the cellar, put an oil rag to it, set a match to it, and knew that she would have to be off soon to do the same task elsewhere. She would have liked to stay and swaddle the infant, and comfort the woman, and drink hot sweet tea, but there was not enough time. There was never enough time, and she hadn't even cleaned out the ashes or the cinders in her grate that morning.

The child was in a corner of the room in a brown cot with slats that rattled because of the racket they had received from the previous children. The mother was not proud, far from it. She fed the child its first bottle, looked down at its wizened face, and thought, Where have you come from and why? She had no choice of a name. In fact, she said to her first visitor, a lieutenant from the army, not to tell her a pack of lies, because this child had the ugliest face that had ever seen the light of day. That Christmas the drinking and sparring went on, the odd neighbor called, the mother got up on the third day and staggered down to do something about the unruly kitchen. Each evening at nightfall she got a bit of a candle to have handy and reoiled the Sacred Heart lamp for when the child cried. They both contracted bronchitis and the child was impounded in masses of flannel and flannelette.

Things changed. The mother came to idolize the child, because it was so quiet, never bawling, never asking for anything, just weirdly still in its pram, the dog watching over it, its eyes staring out at whatever happened to loom in. Its very ugliness disappeared. It seemed to drink them in with its huge, contemplating, slightly hazed-over, navy eyes. They shone at whatever they saw. The mother would look in the direction of the pram and say a little prayer for it, or smile, and often at night she held the candle shielded by her hand to see the face, to say pet or tush, to say nonsense to it. It ate whatever it was given, but as time went on, it knew what it liked and had a sweet tooth. The food was what united them, eating off the same plate, using the same spoon, watching one another's chews, feeling the food as it went down the other's neck. The child was slow to crawl and slower still to walk, but it knew everything, it perceived everything. When it ate blancmange or junket, it was eating part of the lovely substance of its mother.

They were together, always together. If its mother went to the post office, the child stood in the middle of the drive praying until its mother returned safely. The child cut the ridges of four fingers along the edge of a razor blade that had been wedged upright in the wood of the dresser, and seeing these four deep, horizontal identical slits the mother took the poor fingers into her own mouth and sucked them, to lessen the pain, and licked them to abolish the blood, and kept saying soft things until the child was stilled again.

Her mother's knuckles were her knuckles, her mother's veins were her veins, her mother's lap was a second heaven, her mother's forehead a copybook onto which she traced A B C D, her mother's body was a recess that she would wander inside forever and ever, a sepulcher growing deeper and deeper. When she saw other people, especially her pretty sister, she would simply wave from that safe place, she would not budge, would not be lured out. Her father took a hatchet to her mother and threatened that he would split open the head of her. The child watched through the kitchen window, because this debacle took place outdoors on a hillock under the three beech trees where the clothesline stretched, then sagged. The mother had been hanging out the four sheets washed that morning, two off each bed. The child was engaged in twisting her hair, looping it around bits of white rag, to form ringlets, decking herself in the kitchen mirror, and then every other minute running across to the window to reconnoiter, wondering what she ought to do, jumping up and down as if she had a pain, not knowing what to do, running back to the mirror, hoping that the terrible scene would pass, that the ground would open up and swallow her father, that the hatchet would turn into a magic wand, that her mother would come through the kitchen door and say "Fear not," that travail would all be over. Later she heard a verbatim account of what had happened. Her father demanded money, her mother refused same on the grounds that she had none, but added that if she had it she would hang sooner than give it to him. That did it. It was then he really got bucking, gritted his teeth and his muscles, said that he would split the head of her, and the mother said that if he did so there was a place for him. That place was the lunatic asylum. It was twenty or thirty miles away, a big gray edifice, men and women lumped in together, some in straitjackets, some in padded cells, some blindfolded because of having sacks thrown over their heads, some strapped across the chest to quell and impede them. Those who did not want to go there were dragged by relatives, or by means of rope, some being tied on to the end of a plow or a harrow and brought in on all fours, like beasts of the earth. Then when they were not so mad, not so rampaging, they were let home again, where they were very peculiar and given to smiling and to chattering to themselves, and in no time they were ripe to go off again or to be dragged off. March was the worst month, when everything went askew, even the wind, even the March hares. Her father did not go there. He went off on a batter and then went to a monastery, and then was brought home and shook in the bed chair for five days, eating bread and milk and asking who would convey him over the fields, until he saw his yearlings, and when no one volunteered to, it fell to her because she was the youngest. Over in the fields he patted the yearlings and said soppy things that he'd never say indoors, or to a human, and he cried and said he'd never touch a drop again, and there was a dribble on his pewter-brown mustache that was the remains of the mush he had been eating, and the yearling herself became fidgety and fretful as if she might bolt or stamp the ground to smithereens.

The girl and her mother took walks on Sundays — strolls, picked blackberries, consulted them for worms, made preserve, and slept side by side, entwined like twigs of trees or the ends of the sugar tongs. When she wakened and found that her mother had got up and was already mixing meals for the hens or stirabout for the young pigs, she hurried down, carrying her clothes under her arm, and dressed in whatever spot she could feast on the sight of her mother most. Always an egg for breakfast. An egg a day and she would grow strong. Her mother never ate an egg but topped the girl's egg and fed her it off the tarnished eggy spoon and gave her little sups of tea with which to wash it down. She had her own mug, red enamel and with not a chip. The girl kept looking back as she went down the drive for school, and as time went on, she mastered the knack of walking backward to be able to look all the longer, look at the aproned figure waving or holding up a potato pounder or a colander, or whatever happened to be in her hand.

The girl came home once and the mother was missing. Her mother had actually fulfilled her promise of going away one day and going to a spot where she would not be found. That threatened spot was the bottom of the lake. But in fact her mother had gone back to her own family, because the father had taken a shotgun to her and had shot her but was not a good aim like William Tell, had missed, had instead made a hole in the Blue Room wall. What were they doing upstairs in the middle of the day, an ascent they never made except the mother alone to dress the two beds. She could guess. She slept in a neighbor's house, slept in a bed with two old people who reeked of eucalyptus. She kept most of her clothes on and shriveled into herself, not wanting to touch or be touched by these two old people buried in their various layers of skin and hair and winceyette. Outside the window was a climbing rose with three or four red flowers along the bow of it, and looking at the flowers and thinking of the wormy clay, she would try to shut out what these two old people were saying, in order that she could remember the mother whom she despaired of ever seeing again. Not far away was their own house, with the back door wide open so that any stranger or tinker could come in or out. The dog was probably lonely and bloodied from hunting rabbits, the hens were forgotten about and were probably in their coops, hysterical, picking at one another's feathers because of their nerves. Eggs would rot. If she stood on the low whitewashed wall that fronted the cottage, she could see over the high limestone wall that boundaried their fields and then look to the driveway that led to the abandoned house itself. To her it was like a kind of castle where strange things had happened and would go on happening. She loved it and she feared it. The sky behind and above gave it mystery, sometimes made it broody, and gave it a kind of splendor when the red streaks in the heavens were like torches that betokened the performance of a gory play. All of a sudden, standing there, with a bit of grass between her front teeth, looking at her home and imagining this future drama, she heard the nearby lych-gate open and then shut with a clang, and saw her father appear, and jumped so clumsily she thought she had broken everything, particularly her ribs. She felt she was in pieces. She would be like Humpty-Dumpty, and all the king's horses and all the king's men would not be able to put her together again. Dismemberment did happen, a long time before, the time when her neck swelled out into a big fleshed balloon. She could only move her neck on one side, because the other side was like a ball and full of fluid and made gluggles when she touched it with her fingers. They were going to lance it. They placed her on a kitchen chair. Her mother boiled a saucepan of water. Her mother stood on another chair and reached far into the rear of a cupboard and hauled out a new towel. Everything was in that cupboard, sugar and tea and round biscuits and white flour and linen and must and mice. First one man, then another, then another man, then a last man who was mending the chimney, and then last of all her father each took hold of her — an arm, another arm, a shoulder, a waist, and her two flying legs that were doing everything possible not to be there. The lady doctor said nice things and cut into the big football of her neck, and it was like a pig's bladder bursting all over, the waters flowing out, and then it was not like that at all; it was like a sword on the bone of her neck sawing, cutting into the flesh, deeper and deeper, the men pressing upon her with all their might, saying that she was a demon, and the knife went into her swallow or where she thought of forever more as her swallow, and the lady doctor said, "Drat it," because she had done the wrong thing — had cut too deep and had to start scraping now, and her older sister danced a jig out on the flagstones so that neighbors going down the road would not get the impression that someone was being murdered. Long afterward she came back to the world of voices, muffled voices, and their reassurances, and a little something sweet to help her get over it all, and the lady doctor putting on her brown fur coat and hurrying to her next important work of mercy.

When she slept with the neighbors the old man asked the old woman were they ever going to be rid of her, were they going to have this dunce off their hands, were they saddled with her for the rest of their blooming lives. She declined the milk they gave her because it was goat's milk and too yellow and there was dust in it. She would answer them in single syllables, just yes or no, mostly no. She was learning to frown, so that she, too, would have A B C's. Her mother's forehead and hers would meet in heaven, salute, and all their lines would coincide. She refused food. She pined. In all, it was about a week.

The day her mother returned home — it was still January — the water pipes had burst, and when she got to the neighbors' and was told she could go home, she ran with all her might and resolution, so that her windpipe ached and then stopped aching when she found her mother down on her knees dealing with pools of water that had gushed from the red pipes. The brown rag was wet every other second and had to be wrung out and squeezed in the big chipped basin, the one she was first bathed in. The lodges of water were everywhere, lapping back and forth, threatening to expand, to discolor the tiles, and it was of this hazard they talked and fretted over rather than the mother's disappearance, or the dire cause of it, or the reason for her return. They went indoors and got the ingredients and the utensils and the sieve so as to make an orange cake with orange filling and orange icing. She never tasted anything so wonderful in all her life. She ate three big hunks, and her mother put her hand around her and said if she ate any more she would have a little corporation.

The father came home from the hospital, cried again, said that sure he wouldn't hurt a fly, and predicted that he would never break his pledge or go outside the gate again, only to Mass, never leave his own sweet acres. As before, the girl slept with her mother, recited the Rosary with her, and shared the small cubes of dark raisin-filled chocolate, then trembled while her mother went along to her father's bedroom for a tick, to stop him bucking. The consequences of those visits were deterred by the bits of tissue paper, a protection between herself and any emission. No other child got conceived, and there was no further use for the baggy napkins, the bottle, and the dark-brown mottled teat. The cot itself was sawn up and used to back two chairs, and they constituted something of the furniture in the big upstairs landing, where the felt dog still lorded over it but now had an eye missing because a visiting child had poked wire at it. The chairs were painted oxblood red and had the sharp end of a nail dragged along the varnish to give a wavering effect. Also on the landing was a bowl with a bit of wire inside to hold a profusion of artificial tea roses. These tea roses were a two-toned color, were red and yellow plastic, and the point of each petal was seared like the point of a thorn. Cloth flowers were softer. She had seen some once, very pale pink and purple, made of voile, in another house, in a big jug, tumbling over a lady's bureau. In the landing at home, too, was the speared head of Christ, which looked down on all the proceedings with endless patience, endless commiseration.

Underneath Christ was a pussy cat of black papier-mâché which originally had sweets stuffed into its middle, sweets the exact image of strawberries and even with a little leaf at the base, a leaf made of green-glazed angelica. They liked the same things — applesauce and beetroot and tomato sausages and angelica. They cleaned the windows, one the inside, the other the outside, they sang duets, they put newspapers over the newly washed dark-red tiles so as to keep them safe from the muck and trampalations of the men. About everything they agreed, or almost everything.

In the dark nights the wind used to sweep through the window and out on the landing and into the other rooms, and into the Blue Room, by now uninhabited. The wardrobe door would open of its own accord, or the ewer would rattle, or the lovely buxom Our Lady of Limerick picture would fall onto the marble washstand and there was a rumpus followed by prognostications of bad luck for seven years. When the other child came back from boarding school, the girl was at first excited, prepared lovingly for her, made cakes, and, soon after, was plunged into a state of wretchedness. Her mother was being taken away from her, or, worse, was gladly giving her speech, her attention, her hands, and all of her gaze to this intruder. Her mother and her older sister would go upstairs, where her mother would have some little treat for her, a hanky or a hanky sachet, and once a remnant that had been got at the mill at reduced price, due to a fire there. Beautiful, a flecked salmon pink.

Downstairs *she* had to stack dishes onto the tray. She banged the cups, she put a butter knife into the two-pound pot of black-current jam and hauled out a big helping, then stuck the greasy plates one on top of the other, whereas normally she would have put a fork in between to protect the undersides. She dreamed that her mother and her rival sister were going for a walk and she asked to go too, but they sneaked off. She followed on a bicycle, but once outside the main gate could not decide whether to go to the left or the right, and then, having decided, made the wrong choice and stumbled on a herd of bullocks, all butting one another and endeavoring to get up into one another's backside. She turned back, and there they were strolling up the drive, like two sedate ladies linking and laughing, and the salmon-flecked remnant was already a garment, a beautiful swagger coat which her sister wore with a dash.

"I wanted to be with you," she said, and one said to the other, "She wanted to be with us," and then no matter what she said, no matter what the appeal, they repeated it as if she weren't there. In the end she knew that she would have to turn away from them, because she was not wanted, she was in their way. As a result of that dream, or rather the commotion that she made in her sleep, it was decided that she had worms, and the following morning they gave her a dose of turpentine and castor oil, the same as they gave the horses.

When her sister went back to the city, happiness was restored again. Her mother consulted her about the design on a leather bag which she was making. Her mother wanted a very old design, something concerning the history of their country. She said there would have to be battles and then peace and wonderful scenes from nature. Her mother said that there must be a lot of back history to a land and that education was a very fine thing. Preferable to the bog, her mother said. The girl said when she grew up that she would get a very good job and bring her mother to America. Her mother mentioned the street in Brooklyn where she had lodged and said that it had adjoined a park. They would go there one day. Her mother said maybe.

The growing girl began to say the word "backside" to herself and knew that her mother would be appalled. The girl laughed at bullocks and the sport they had. Then she went one further and jumped up and down and said, "Jumping Jack," as if some devil were inside her, touching and tickling the lining of her. It was creepy. It was done outdoors, far from the house, out in the fields, in a grove, or under a canopy of rhododendrons. The buds of the rhododendrons were sticky and oozed with life, and everything along with herself was soaking wet, and she was given to wandering flushes and then fits of untoward laughter, so that she had to scold herself into some state of normality and this she did by slapping both cheeks vehemently. As a dire punishment she took cups of Glauber's salts three times a day, choosing to drink it when it was lukewarm and at its most nauseating. She would be told by her father to get out, to stop hatching, to get out from under her mother's apron strings, and he would send her for a spin on the woeful brakeless bicycle. She would go to the chapel, finding it empty of all but herself and the lady sacristan, who spent her life in there polishing and rearranging the artificial flowers; or she would go down into a bog and make certain unattainable wishes, but always at the end of every day, and at the end of every thought, and at the beginning of sleep and the precise moment of wakening, it was of her mother and for her mother she existed, and her prayers and her good deeds and her ringlets and the ire on her legs — created by the serge of her gym frock — were for her mother's intention, and on and on. Only death could part them, and not even that, because she resolved that she would take her own life if some disease or some calamity snatched her mother away. Her mother's three-quarter-length jacket she would don, sink her hands into the deep pockets, and say the name "Delia," her mother's, say it in different tones of voice, over and over again, always in a whisper and with a note of conspiracy.

A lovely thing happened. Her mother and father went on a journey by hire car to do a transaction whereby they could get some credit on his lands, and her father did not get drunk but ordered a nice pot of tea, and then sat back gripping his braces and gave her mother a few bob, with which her mother procured a most beautiful lipstick in a ridged gold case. It was like fresh fruit, so moist was it, and coral red. Her mother and she tried it on over and over again, were comical with it, trying it on, then wiping it off, trying it on again, making cupids so that her mother expostulated and said what scatterbrains they were, and even the father joined in the hilarity and daubed down the mother's cheek and said Fanny Anny, and the mother said that was enough, as the lipstick was liable to get broken. With her thumbnail she pressed on the little catch, pushing the lipstick down into its case, into its bed. As the years went on, it dried out and developed a peculiar shape, and they read somewhere that a lady's character could be told by that particular shape, and they wished that they could discover whether the mother was the extrovert or the shy violet.

The girl had no friends, she didn't need any. Her cup was full. Her mother was the cup, the cupboard, the sideboard with all the things in it, the tabernacle with God in it, the lake with the legends in it, the bog with the wishing well in it, the sea with the oysters and the corpses in it, her mother a gigantic sponge, a habitation in which she longed to sink and disappear forever and ever. Yet she was afraid to sink, caught in the hideous trap between fear of sinking and fear of swimming, she moved like a flounderer through this and that; through school, through inoculation, through a man who put his white handkerchief between naked her and naked him, and against a galvanized outhouse door came, gruntling and disgruntling like a tethered beast upon her; through a best friend, a girl friend who tried to clip the hairs of her vagina with a shears. The hairs of her vagina were mahogany-colored, and her best friend said that that denoted mortal sin. She agonized over it. Then came a dreadful blow. Two nuns called and her mother and her father said that she was to stay outside in the kitchen and see that the kettle boiled and then lift it off so that water would not boil over. She went on tiptoe through the hall and listened at the door of the room. She got it in snatches. She was being discussed. She was being sent away to school. A fee was being discussed and her mother was asking if they could make a reduction. She ran out of the house in a dreadful state. She ran to the chicken run and went inside to cry and to go berserk. The floor was full of damp and gray-green mottled droppings. The nests were full of sour sops of hay. She thought she was going out of her mind. When they found her later, her father said to cut out the "bull," but her mother tried to comfort her by saying they had a prospectus and that she would have to get a whole lot of new clothes in navy blue. But where would the money come from?

In the convent to which they sent her she eventually found solace. A nun became her new idol. A nun with a dreadfully pale face and a master's degree in science. This nun and she worked out codes with the eyelids, and the flutter of the lashes, so they always knew each other's moods and feelings, so that the slightest hurt imposed by one was spotted by the other and responded to with a glance. The nun gave another girl more marks at the mid-term examination, and did it solely to hurt her, to wound her pride; the nun addressed her briskly in front of the whole class, said her full name and asked her a theological conundrum that was impossible to answer. In turn, she let one of the nun's holy pictures fall on the chapel floor, where of course it was found by the cleaning nun, who gave it back to the nun, who gave it to her with a "This seems to have got mislaid." They exchanged Christmas presents and notes that contained blissful innuendos. She had given chocolates with a kingfisher on the cover, and she had received a prayer book with gilt edging and it was as tiny as her little finger. She could not read the print but she held it to herself like a talisman, like a secret scroll in which love was mentioned.

Home on holiday it was a different story. Now *she* did the avoiding, the shunning. All the little treats and the carrageen soufflé that her mother had prepared were not gloated over. Then the pink crepe-de-Chine apron that her mother had made from an old dance dress did not receive the acclamation that the mother expected. It was fitted on and at once taken off and flung over the back of a chair with no praise except to remark on the braiding, which was cleverly done.

"These things are not to be sniffed at," her mother said, passing the plate of scones for the third or fourth time. The love of the nun dominated all her thoughts, and the nun's pale face got between her and the visible world that she was supposed to be seeing. At times she could taste it. It interfered with her studies, her other friendships, it got known about. She was called to see the Reverend Mother. The nun and she never had a *tête-à-tête* again and never swapped holy pictures. The day she was leaving forever they made an illicit date to meet in the summerhouse, out in the grounds, but neither of them turned up. They each sent a message with an apology, and it was, in fact, the messengers who met, a junior girl and a postulant carrying the same sentence on separate lips — "So-and-so is sorry — she wished to say she can't . . ." They might have broken down or done anything, they might have kissed.

Out of school, away from the spell of nuns and gods and flower gardens and acts of contrition, away from the chapel with its incense and its brimstone sermons, away from surveillance, she met a bakery man who was also a notable hurley player and they started up that kind of courtship common to their sort — a date at Nelson's pillar two evenings a week, then to a café to have coffee and cream cakes, to hold hands under the table, to take a bus to her digs, to kiss against a railing and devour each other's face, as earlier they had devoured the mock cream and the sugar-dusted sponge cakes. But these orgies only increased her hunger, made it into something that could not be appeased. She would recall her mother from the very long ago, in the three-quarter-length jacket of salmon tweed, the brooch on the lapel, the smell of face powder, the lipstick hurriedly put on so that a little of it always smudged on the upper or the lower lip and appeared like some kind of birthmark. Recall that they even had the same mole on the back of the left hand, a mole that did not alter winter or summer and was made to seem paler when the fist was clenched. But she was recalling someone whom she wanted to banish. The bakery man got fed up, wanted more than a cuddle, hopped it. Then there was no one, just a long stretch, doing novenas, working in the library, and her mother's letters arriving, saying the usual things, how life was hard, how inclement the weather, how she'd send a cake that day or the next day, as soon as there were enough eggs to make it with. The parcels arrived once a fortnight, bound in layers of newspaper, and then a strong outer layer of brown paper, all held with hideous assortments of twines — binding twine, very white twine, and colored plastic string from the stools that she had taken to making; then great spatters of sealing wax adorning it. Always a registered parcel, always a cake, a pound of butter, and a chicken that had to be cooked at once, because of its being nearly putrid from the four-day journey. It was not difficult to imagine the kitchen table, the bucket full of feathers, the moled hand picking away at the pin feathers, the other hand plunging in and drawing out all the undesirables, tremulous, making sure not to break a certain little pouch, since its tobacco-colored fluid could ruin the taste of the bird. Phew. Always the same implications in each letter, the same cry —

"Who knows what life brings. Your father is not hard-boiled despite his failings. It makes me sad to think of the little things that I used to be able to do for you." She hated those parcels, despite the fact that they were most welcome.

She married. Married in haste. Her mother said from the outset that he was as odd as two left shoes. He worked on an encyclopedia and was a mine of information on certain subjects. His specialty was vegetation in pond life. They lived to themselves. She learned to do chores, to bottle and preserve, to comply, to be a wife, to undress neatly at night, to fold her clothes, to put them on a cane chair, making sure to put her corset and her underthings respectfully under her dress or her skirt. It was like being at school again. The mother did not visit, being at odds with the censuring husband. Mother and daughter would meet in a market town midway between each of their rural homes, and when they met they sat in some hotel lounge, ordered tea, and discussed things that can easily be discussed — recipes, patterns for knitting, her sister, items of furniture that they envisaged buying. Her mother was getting older, had developed a slight stoop, and held up her hands to show the rheumatism in her joints. Then all of a sudden, as if she had just remembered it, she spoke about the cataracts, and her journey to the specialist, and how the specialist had asked her if she remembered anything about her eyes and how she had to tell him that she had lost her sight for five or six minutes one morning and that then it came back. He had told her how lucky it was, because in some instances it does not come back at all. She said yes, the shades of life were closing in on her. The daughter knew that her marriage would not last, but she dared not say so. Things were happening such as that they had separate meals, that he did not speak for weeks on end, and yet she defended him, talked of the open pine dresser he had made, and her mother rued the fact that she never had a handyman to do odd things for her. She said the window had broken in a storm and that there was still a bit of cardboard in it. She said she had her heart on two armchairs, armchairs with damask covers. The daughter longed to give them to her and thought that she might steal from her husband when he was asleep, steal the deposit, that is, and pay for them on hire purchase. But they said none of the things that they should have said.

"You didn't get any new style," the mother said, restating her particular dislike for a sheepskin coat.

"I don't want it," the girl said tersely.

"You were always a softie," the mother said, and inherent in this was disapproval for a man who allowed his wife to be dowdy. Perhaps she thought that her daughter's marriage might have amended for her own.

When her marriage did end, the girl wrote and said that it was all over, and the mother wrote posthaste, exacting two dire promises — the girl must write back on her oath and promise her that she would never touch an alcoholic drink as long as she lived and she would never again have to do with any man in body or soul. High commands. At the time the girl was walking the streets in a daze and stopping strangers to tell of her plight. One day in a park she met a man who was very sympathetic, a sort of tramp. She told him her story, and then all of a sudden he told her this terrible dream. He had wakened up and he was swimming in water and the water kept changing color, it was blue and red and green, and these changing colors terrified him. She saw that he was not all there and invented an excuse to go somewhere. In time she sold her bicycle and pawned a gold bracelet and a gold watch and chain. She fled to England. She wanted to go somewhere where she knew no one. She was trying to start afresh, to wipe out the previous life. She was staggered by the assaults of memory — a bowl with her mother's menstrual cloth soaking in it and her sacrilegious idea that if lit it could resemble the heart of Christ, the conical wick of the Aladdin lamp being lit too high and disappearing into a jet of black; the roses, the five freakish winter roses that were in bloom when the pipes burst; the mice that came out of the shoes, then out of the shoe closet itself, onto the floor where the newspapers had been laid to prevent the muck and manure of the trampling men; the little box of rouge that almost asked to be licked, so dry and rosy was it; the black range whose temperature could be tested by just spitting on it and watching the immediate jig and trepidation of the spit; the pancakes on Shrove Tuesday (if there wasn't a row); the flitches of bacon hanging to smoke; the forgotten jam jars with inevitably the bit of moldy jam in the bottom; and always, like an overseeing spirit, the figure of the mother, who was responsible for each and every one of these facets, and always the pending doom in which the mother would perhaps be struck with the rim of a bucket, or a sledgehammer, or some improvised weapon; struck by the near-crazed father. It would be something as slight as that the mother had a splinter under her nail and the girl felt her own nail being lifted up, felt hurt to the quick, or felt her mother's sputum, could taste it like a dish. She was possessed by these thoughts in the library where she worked day in and day out, filing and cataloguing and handing over books. They were more than thoughts, they were the presence of this woman whom she resolved to kill. Yes, she would have to kill. She would have to take up arms and commit a murder. She thought of choking or drowning. Certainly the method had to do with suffocation, and she foresaw herself holding big suffocating pillows or a bolster, in the secrecy of the Blue Room, where it had all begun. Her mother turned into the bursting red pipes, into the brown dishcloths, into swamps of black-brown blooded water. Her mother turned into a streetwalker and paraded. Her mother was taking down her knickers in public, squatting to do awful things, left little piddles, small as puppies' piddles, her mother was drifting down a well in a bug bucket, crying for help, but no help was forth-coming. The oddest dream came along. Her mother was on her deathbed, having just given birth to her — the little tonsured head jutted above the sheet — and had a neck rash, and was busy trying to catch a little insect, trying to cup it in the palms of her hands, and was saying that in the end "all there is, is yourself and this little insect that you're trying to kill." The word "kill" was everywhere, on the hoardings, in the evening air, on the tip of her thoughts. But life goes on. She bought a yellow two-piece worsted, and wrote home and said, "I must be getting cheerful, I wear less black." Her mother wrote, "I have only one wish now and it is that we will be buried together." The more she tried to kill, the more clinging the advances became. Her mother was taking out all the old souvenirs, the brown scapulars salvaged from the hurtful night in December, a mug, with their similar initial on it, a tablecloth that the girl had sent from her first earnings when she qualified as a librarian. The mother's letters began to show signs of wandering. They broke off in midsentence; one was written on blotting paper and almost indecipherable; they contained snatches of information such as "So-and-so died, there was a big turnout at the funeral," "I could do with a copper bracelet for rheumatism," "You know life gets lonelier."

She dreaded the summer holidays, but still she went. The geese and the gander would be trailing by the riverbank, the cows would gape at her as if an alien had entered their terrain. It was only the horses she avoided — always on the nervy side, as if ready to bolt. The fields themselves as beguiling as ever, fields full of herbage and meadowsweet, fields adorned with spangles of gold as the buttercups caught the shafts of intermittent sunshine. If only she could pick them up and carry them away. They sat indoors. A dog had a deep cut in his paw and it was thought that a fox did it, that the dog and the fox had tussled one night. As a result of this, he was admitted to the house. The mother and the dog spoke, although not a word passed between them. The father asked pointed questions, such as would it rain or was it teatime. For a pastime they then discussed all the dogs that they had had. The mother especially remembered Monkey and said that he was a queer one, that he'd know what you were thinking of. The father and daughter remembered further back to Shep, the big collie, who guarded the child's pram and drove thoroughbred horses off the drive, causing risk to his own person. Then there were the several pairs of dogs, all of whom sparred and quarreled throughout their lives, yet all of whom died within a week of one another, the surviving dog dying of grief for his pal. No matter how they avoided it, death crept into the conversation. The mother said unconvincingly how lucky they were never to have been crippled, to have enjoyed good health and enough to eat. The curtains behind her chair were a warm red velveteen and gave a glow to her face. A glow that was reminiscent of her lost beauty.

She decided on a celebration. She owed it to her mother. They would meet somewhere else, away from that house, and its skeletons and its old cunning tug at the heartstings. She planned it a year in advance, a holiday in a hotel, set in beautiful woodland surroundings on the verge of the Atlantic Ocean. Their first hours were happily and most joyfully passed as they looked at the rooms, the view, the various tapestries, found where things were located, looked at the games room and then at the display cabinets, where there were cutglass and marble souvenirs on sale. The mother said that everything was "poison, dear." They took a walk by the seashore and remarked one to the other on the different stripes of color on the water, how definite they were, each color claiming its surface of sea, just like oats or grass or a plowed land. The brown plaits of seaweed slapped and slathered over rocks, long-legged birds let out their lonesome shrieks, and the mountains that loomed beyond seemed to hold the specter of continents inside them so vast were they, so old. They dined early. Afterward there was a singsong and the mother whispered that money wasn't everything; to look at the hard boiled faces. Something snapped inside her, and forgetting that this was her errand of mercy, she thought instead how this mother had a whole series of grudges, bitter grudges concerning love, happiness, and her hard impecunious fate. The angora jumpers, the court shoes, the brown and the fawn garments, the milk complexion, the auburn tresses, the little breathlessnesses, the hands worn by toil, the sore feet, these were but the trimmings, behind them lay the real person, who demanded her pound of flesh from life. They sat on a sofa. The mother sipped tea and she her whiskey. They said, "Cheers." The girl tried to get the conversation back to before she was born, or before other children were born, to the dances and the annual race day and the courtship that preempted the marriage. The mother refused to speak, balked, had no story to tell, said that even if she had a story she would not tell it. Said she hated raking up the past. The girl tweezed it out of her in scraps. The mother said yes, that as a young girl she was bold and obstinate and she did have fancy dreams but soon learned to toe the line. Then she burst out laughing and said she climbed up a ladder once into the chapel, and into the confessional, so as to be the first person there to have her confession heard by the missioner. The missioner nearly lost his life because he didn't know how anyone could possibly have got in, since the door was bolted and he had simply come to sit in the confessional to compose himself, when there she was, spouting sins. What sins?

The mother said, "Oh, I forget, love. I forget everything now."

The girl said, "No, you don't."

They said night-night and arranged to meet in the dining room the following morning.

The mother didn't sleep a wink, complained that her eyes and her nose were itchy, and she feared she was catching a cold. She drank tea noisily, slugged it down. They walked by the sea, which was now the color of gunmetal, and the mountains were no longer a talking point. They visited a ruined monastery where the nettles, the sorrel, the clover, and the seedy dock grew high in a rectangle. Powder shed from walls that were built of solid stone. The mother said that probably it was a chapel, or a chancery, a seat of sanctity down through the centuries, and she genuflected. To the girl it was just a ruin, unhallowed, full of weeds and buzzing with wasps and insects. Outside, there was a flock of noisy starlings. She could feel the trouble brewing. She said that there was a lovely smell, that it was most likely some wild herb, and she got down on her knees to locate it. Peering with eyes and fingers among the low grass, she came upon a nest of ants that were crawling over a tiny bit of ground with an amazing amount of energy and will. She felt barely in control.

They trailed back in time for coffee. The mother said hotel life was demoralizing as she bit into an iced biscuit. The porter fetched the paper. Two strange little puppies lapped at the mother's feet, and the porter said they would have to be drowned if they were not claimed before dusk. The mother said what a shame and recalled her own little pups, who didn't eat clothes on the line during the day but when night came got down to work on them.

"You'd be fit to kill them, but of course you couldn't," she said lamely. She was speaking of puppies from ten or fifteen years back.

He asked if she was enjoying it, and the mother said, "I quote the saying 'See Naples and die,' the same applies to this."

The daughter knew that the mother wanted to go home there and then, but they had booked for four days and it would be an admission of failure to cut it short. She asked the porter to arrange a boat trip to the island inhabited by seabirds, then a car drive to the Lakes of Killarney and another to see the home of the liberator Daniel O'Connell, the man who had asked to have his dead heart sent to Rome, to the Holy See. The porter said certainly and made a great to-do about accepting the tip she gave him. It was he who told them where Daniel O'Connell's heart lay, and the mother said it was the most rending thing she had ever heard, and the most devout. Then she said yes, that a holiday was an uplift, but that it came too late, as she wasn't used to the spoiling. The girl did not like that. To change the conversation the girl produced a postcard that she used as a bookmark. It was a photograph of a gouged torso and she told the porter that was how she felt, that was the state of her mind. The mother said later she didn't think the girl should have said such a thing and wasn't it a bit extreme. Then the mother wrote a six-page letter to her friend Molly and the girl conspired to be the one to post it so that she could read it and find some clue to the chasm that stretched between them. As it happened, she could not bring herself to read it, because the mother gave it to her unsealed, as if she had guessed those thoughts, and the girl bit her lower lip and said, "How's Molly doing?"

The mother became very sentimental and said, "Poor creature, blind as a bat," but added that people were kind and how when they saw her with the white cane, they knew. The letter would be read to her by a daughter who was married and over-weight and who suffered with her nerves. The girl recalled an autograph book, the mother's, with its confectionery-colored pages and its likewise rhymes and ditties. The mother recalled ice creams that she had eaten in Brooklyn long before. The mother remembered the embroidery she had done, making the statement in stitches that there was a rose in the heart of New York. The girl said stitches played such an important role in life and said, "A stitch in time saves nine." They tittered. They were getting nearer. The girl delicately inquired into the name and occupation of the mother's previous lover, in short, the father's rival. The mother would not divulge, except to say that he loved his mother, loved his sister, was most thoughtful, and that was that. Another long silence. Then the mother stirred in her chair, coughed, confided, said that in fact she and this thoughtful man, fearing, somehow sensing, that they would not be man and wife, had made each other a solemn pact one Sunday afternoon in Coney Island over an ice. They swore that they would get in touch with each other toward the end of their days. Lo and behold, after fifty-five years the mother wrote that letter! The girl's heart quickened, and her blood danced to the news of this tryst, this long-sustained clandestine passion. She felt that something momentous was about to get uttered. They could be true at last, they need not hide from one another's gaze. Her mother would own up. Her own life would not be one of curtained shame. She thought of the married man who was waiting for her in London, the one who took her for delicious weekends, and she shivered. The mother said that her letter had been returned; probably his sister had returned it, always being jealous. The girl begged to know the contents of the letter. The mother said it was harmless. The girl said go on. She tried to revive the spark, but the mother's mind was made up. The mother said that there was no such thing as love between the sexes and that it was all bull. She reaffirmed that there was only one kind of love and that was a mother's love for her child. There passed between them then such a moment, not a moment of sweetness, not a moment of reaffirmation, but a moment dense with hate — one hating and the other receiving it like rays, and then it was glossed over by the mother's remark about the grandeur of the ceiling. The girl gritted her teeth and resolved that they would not be buried in the same grave, and vehemently lit a cigarette, although they had hardly tasted the first course.

"I think you're very unsettled," her mother said.

"I didn't get that from the ground," the daughter said.

The mother bridled, stood up to leave, but was impeded by a waiter who was carrying a big chafing dish, over which a bright blue flame riotously spread. She sat down as if pushed down and said that that remark was the essence of cruelty. The girl said sorry. The mother said she had done all she could and that without maid or car or checkbook or any of life's luxuries. Life's dainties had not dropped on her path, she had to knit her own sweaters, cut and sew her own skirts, be her own hairdresser. The girl said for God's sake to let them enjoy it. The mother said that at seventy-eight one had time to think.

"And at thirty-eight," the girl said.

She wished then that her mother's life had been happier and had not exacted so much from her, and she felt she was being milked emotionally. With all her heart she pitied this woman, pitied her for having her dreams pulped and for betrothing herself to a life of suffering. But also she blamed her. They were both wild with emotion. They were speaking out of turn and eating carelessly; the very food seemed to taunt them. The mother wished that one of those white-coated waiters would tactfully take her plate of dinner away and replace it with a nice warm pot of tea, or better still, that she could be home in her own house by her own fireside, and furthermore she wished that her daughter had never grown into the cruel feelingless hussy that she was.

"What else could I have done?" the mother said.

"A lot," the girl said, and gulped at once.

The mother excused herself.

"When I pass on, I won't be sorry," she said.

Up in the room she locked and bolted the door, and lay curled up on the bed, knotted as a foetus, with a clump of paper handkerchiefs in front of her mouth.

Downstairs she left behind her a grown girl, remembering a woman she most bottomlessly loved, then unloved, and cut off from herself in the middle of a large dining room while confronting a plate of undercooked lamb strewn with mint.

Death in its way comes just as much of a surprise as birth. We know we will die, just as the mother knows that she is primed to deliver around such and such a time, yet there is a fierce inner exclamation from her at the first onset of labor, and when the water breaks she is already a shocked woman. So it was. The reconciliation that she had hoped for, and indeed intended to instigate, never came. She was abroad at a conference when her mother died, and when she arrived through her own front door, the phone was ringing with the news of her mother's death. The message though clear to her ears was incredible to her. How had her mother died and why? In a hospital in Dublin as a result of a heart attack. Her mother had gone there to do shopping and was taken ill in the street. How fearful that must have been. Straight-away she set back for the airport, hoping to get a seat on a late-night flight.

Her sister would not be going, as she lived now in Australia, lived on a big farm miles from anywhere. Her letters were always pleas for news, for gossip, for books, for magazines. She had mellowed with the years, had grown fat, and was no longer the daffodil beauty. To her it was like seeing pages of life slip away, and she did not bend down to pick them up. They were carried away in the stream of life itself. And yet something tugged. The last plane had gone, but she decided to sit there until dawn and thought to herself that she might be sitting up at her mother's wake. The tube lighting drained the color from all the other waiting faces, and though she could not cry, she longed to tell someone that something incalculable had happened to her. They seemed as tired and as inert as she did. Coffee, bread, whiskey, all tasted the same, tasted of nothing, or at best of blotting paper. There was no man in her life at the moment, no one to ring up and tell the news to. Even if there was, she thought that lovers never know the full story of one another, only know the bit they meet, never know the iceberg of hurts that have gone before, and therefore are always strangers, or semi-strangers, even in the folds of love. She could not cry. She asked herself if perhaps her heart had turned to lead. Yet she dreaded that on impulse she might break down and that an attendant might have to lead her away.

When she arrived at the hospital next day, the remains had been removed and were now on their way through the center of Ireland. Through Joyce's Ireland, as she always called it, and thought of the great central plain open to the elements, the teeming rain, the drifting snow, the winds that gave chapped faces to farmers and cattle dealers and croup to the young calves. She passed the big towns and the lesser towns, recited snatches of recitation that she remembered, and hoped that no one could consider her disrespectful because the hire car was a bright ketchup red. When she got to her own part of the world, the sight of the mountains moved her, as they had always done — solemn, beautiful, unchanging except for different ranges of color. Solid and timeless. She tried to speak to her mother, but found the words artificial. She had bought a sandwich at the airport and now removed the glacé paper with her teeth and bit into it. The two days ahead would be awful. There would be her father's wild grief, there would be her aunt's grief, there would be cousins and friends, and strays and workmen; there would be a grave wide open and as they walked to it they would talk over other graves, under hawthorn, stamping the nettles as they went. She knew the graveyard very well, since childhood. She knew the tombs, the headstones, and the hidden vaults. She used to play there alone and both challenge and cower from ghosts. The inside of the grave was always a rich broody brown, and the gravedigger would probably lace it with a trellis of ivy or convolvulus leaf.

At that very moment she found that she had just caught up with the funeral cortege, but she could hardly believe that it would be her mother's. Too much of a coincidence. They drove at a great pace and without too much respect for the dead. She kept up with them. The light was fading, the bushes were like blurs, the air bat-black; the birds had ceased, and the mountains were dark bulks. If the file of cars took a right from the main road toward the lake town, then it must certainly be her mother's. It did. The thought of catching up with it was what made her cry. She cried with such delight, cried like a child who has done something good and is being praised for it and yet cannot bear the weight of emotion. She cried the whole way through the lakeside town and sobbed as they crossed the old bridge toward the lovely dark leafy country road that led toward home. She cried like a homing bird. She was therefore seen as a daughter deeply distressed when she walked past the file of mourners outside the chapel gate, and when she shook the hands or touched the sleeves of those who had come forward to meet her. Earlier a friend had left flowers at the car-hire desk and she carried them as if she had specially chosen them. She thought, They think it is grief, but it is not the grief they think it is. It is emptiness more than grief. It is a grief at not being able to be wholehearted again. It is not a false grief, but it is unyielding, it is blood from a stone.

Inside the chapel she found her father howling, and in the first rows closest to the altar and to the coffin the chief mourners, both men and women, were sobbing, or, having just sobbed, were drying their eyes. As she shook hands with each one of them, she heard the same condolence — "Sorry for your trouble, sorry for your trouble, sorry for your trouble."

That night in her father's house people supped and ate and reminisced. As if in mourning a huge bough of a nearby tree had fallen down. Its roots were like a hand stuck up in the air. The house already reeked of neglect. She kept seeing her mother's figure coming through the door with a large tray, laden down with things. The undertaker called her out. He said since she had not seen the remains he would bring her to the chapel and unscrew the lid. She shrank from it, but she went, because to say no would have brought her disgrace. The chapel was cold, the wood creaked, and even the flowers at night seemed to have departed from themselves, like ghost flowers. Just as he lifted the lid he asked her to please step away, and she thought, Something fateful has happened, the skin has turned black or a finger moves or, the worst, she is not dead, she has merely visited the other world. Then he called her and she walked solemnly over and she almost screamed. The mouth was trying to speak. She was sure of it. One eyelid was not fully shut. It was unfinished. She kissed the face and felt a terrible pity. "O soul," she said, "where are you, on your voyaging, and O soul, are you immortal."

Suddenly she was afraid of her mother's fate and afraid for the fact that one day she, too, would have to make it. She longed to hold the face and utter consolations to it, but she was unable. She thought of the holiday that had been such a fiasco and the love that she had so callously and so pointedly taken back. She thought why did she have to withdraw, why do people have to withdraw, why?

After the funeral she went around the house tidying and searching, as if for some secret. In the Blue Room damp had seeped through the walls, and there were little burrs of fungus that clung like bobbins on a hat veiling. In drawers she found bits of her mother's life. Emblems. Wishes. Dreams contained in such things as an exotic gauze rose of the darkest drenchingest red. Perfume bottles, dance shoes, boxes of handkerchiefs, and the returned letter. It was to the man called Vincent, the man her mother had intended to marry but whom she had forsaken when she left New York and came back to Ireland, back to her destiny. For the most part it was a practical letter outlining the size of her farm, the crops they grew, asking about mutual friends, his circumstances, and so forth. It seems he worked in a meat factory. There was only one little leak — "I think of you, you would not believe how often." In an instinctive gesture she crumpled the letter up as if it had been her own. The envelope had marked on the outside — *Return to sender*. The words seemed brazen, as if he himself had written them. There were so many hats, with flowers and veiling, all of light color, hats for summer outings, for rainless climes. Ah, the garden parties she must have conceived. Never having had the money for real style, her mother had invested in imitation things — an imitation crocodile handbag and an imitation fur bolero. It felt light, as if made of hair. There were, too, pink embroidered corsets, long bloomers, and three unworn cardigans.

For some reason she put her hand above the mantelpiece to the place where they hid shillings when she was young. There wrapped in cobweb was an envelope addressed to her in her mother's handwriting. It sent shivers through her, and she prayed that it did not bristle with accusations. Inside, there were some trinkets, a gold sovereign, and some money. The notes were dirty, crumpled, and folded many times. How long had the envelope lain there? How had her mother managed to save? There was no letter, yet in her mind she concocted little tendernesses that her mother might have written — words such as "Buy yourself a jacket," or "Have a night out," or "Don't spend this on Masses." She wanted something, some communiqué. But there was no such thing.

A new wall had arisen, stronger and sturdier than before. Their life together and all those exchanges were like so many split feelings, and she looked to see some sign or hear some murmur. Instead, a silence filled the room, and there was a vaster silence beyond, as if the house itself had died or had been carefully put down to sleep.

EDNA O'BRIEN

Sister Imelda

Sister Imelda did not take classes on her first day back in the convent but we spotted her in the grounds after the evening Rosary. Excitement and curiosity impelled us to follow her and try to see what she looked like, but she thwarted us by walking with head bent and eyelids down. All we could be certain of was that she was tall and limber and that she prayed while she walked. No looking at nature for her, or no curiosity about seventy boarders in gaberdine coats and black shoes and stockings. We might just as well have been crows, so impervious was she to our stares and to abortive attempts at trying to say "Hello, Sister."

We had returned from our long summer holiday and we were all wretched. The convent, with its high stone wall and green iron gates enfolding us again, seemed more of a prison than ever — for after our spell in the outside world we all felt very much older and more sophisticated, and my friend Baba and I were dreaming of our final escape, which would be in a year. And so, on that damp autumn evening when I saw the chrysanthemums and saw the new nun intent on prayer I pitied her and thought how alone she must be, cut off from her friends and conversation, with only God as her intangible spouse.

The next day she came into our classroom to take geometry. Her pale, slightly long face I saw as formidable, but her eyes were different, being blue-black and full of verve. Her lips were very purple, as if she had put puce pencil on them. They were the lips of a woman who might sing in a cabaret, and unconsciously she had formed the habit of turning them inward, as if she, too, was aware of their provocativeness. She had spent the last four years — the same span that Baba and I had spent in the convent — at the university in Dublin, where she studied languages. We couldn't understand how she had resisted the temptations of the hectic world and willingly come back to this. Her spell in the outside world made her different from the other nuns; there was more bounce in her walk, more excitement in the way she tackled teaching, reminding us that it was the most important thing in the world as she uttered the phrase "Praise be the Incarnate World." She began each day's class by reading from Cardinal Newman, who was a favorite of hers. She read how God dwelt in light unapproachable, and how with Him there was neither change nor shadow of alteration. It was amazing how her looks changed. Some days, when her eyes were flashing, she looked almost profane and made me wonder what events inside the precincts of the convent caused her to be suddenly so excited. She might have been a girl going to a dance, except for her habit.

"Hasn't she wonderful eyes," I said to Baba. That particular day they were like blackberries, large and soft and shiny.

"Something wrong in her upstairs department," Baba said, and added that with makeup Imelda would be a cinch.

"Still, she has a vocation!" I said, and even aired the idiotic view that I might have one. At certain moments it did seem enticing to become a nun, to lead a life unspotted by sin, never to have to have babies, and to wear a ring that singled one out as the Bride of Christ. But there was the other side to it, the silence, the gravity of it, having to get up two or three times a night to pray and, above all, never having the opportunity of leaving the confines of the place except for the funeral of one's parents. For us boarders it was torture, but for the nuns it was nothing short of doom. Also, we could complain to each other, and we did, food being the source of the greatest grumbles. Lunch was either bacon and cabbage or a peculiar stringy meat followed by tapioca pudding; tea consisted of bread dolloped with lard and occasionally, as a treat, fairly green rhubarb jam, which did not have enough sugar. Through the long curtainless windows we saw the conifer trees and a sky that was scarcely ever without the promise of rain or a downpour.

She was a right lunatic, then, Baba said, having gone to university for four years and willingly come back to incarceration, to poverty, chastity, and obedience. We concocted scenes of agony in some Dublin hostel, while a boy, or even a young man, stood beneath her bedroom window throwing up chunks of clay or whistles or a supplication. In our version of it he was slightly older than her, and possibly a medical student, since medical students had a knack with women, because of studying diagrams and skeletons. His advances, like those of a sudden storm, would intermittently rise and overwhelm her, and the memory of these sudden flaying advances of his would haunt her until she died, and if ever she contracted fever, these secrets would out. It was also rumored that she possessed a fierce temper and that, while a postulant, she had hit a girl so badly with her leather strap that the girl had to be put to bed because of wounds. Yet another black mark against Sister Imelda was that her brother Ambrose had been sued by a nurse for breach of promise.

That first morning when she came into our classroom and modestly introduced herself, I had no idea how terribly she would infiltrate my life, how in time she would be not just one of those teachers or nuns but rather a special one, almost like a ghost who passed the boundaries of common exchange and who crept inside one, devouring so much of one's thoughts, so much of one's passion, invading the place that was called one's heart. She talked in a low voice, as if she did not want her words to go beyond the bounds of the wall, and constantly she stressed the value of work both to enlarge the mind and to discipline the thought. One of her eyelids was red and swollen, as if she was getting a sty. I reckoned that she overmortified herself by not eating at all. I saw in her some terrible premonition of sacrifice which I would have to emulate. Then, in direct contrast, she absently held the stick of chalk between her first and second fingers, the very same as if it were a cigarette, and Baba whispered to me that she might have been a smoker when in Dublin. Sister Imelda looked down sharply at me and said what was the secret and would I like to share it, since it seemed so comical. I said, "Nothing, Sister, nothing," and her dark eyes exuded such vehemence that I prayed she would never have occasion to punish me.

November came and the tiled walls of the recreation hall oozed moisture and gloom. Most girls had sore throats and were told to suffer this inconvenience to mortify themselves in order to lend a glorious hand in the communion of spirit that linked the living with the dead. It was the month of the Suffering Souls in Purgatory, and as we heard of their twofold agony, the yearning for Christ and the ferocity of the leaping flames that burned and charred their poor limbs, we were asked to make acts of mortification. Some girls gave up jam or sweets and some gave up talking, and so in recreation time they were like dummies making signs with thumb and finger to merely say "How are you?" Baba said that saner people were locked in the lunatic asylum, which was only a mile away. We saw them in the grounds, pacing back and forth, with their mouths agape and dribble coming out of them, like melting icicles. Among our many fears was that one of those lunatics would break out and head straight for the convent and assault some of the girls.

Yet in the thick of all these dreads I found myself becoming dreadfully happy. I had met Sister Imelda outside of class a few times and I felt that there was an attachment between us. Once it was in the grounds, when she did a reckless thing. She broke off a chrysanthemum and offered it to me to smell. It had no smell, or at least only something faint that suggested autumn, and feeling this to be the case herself, she said it was not a gardenia, was it? Another time we met in the chapel porch, and as she drew her shawl more tightly around her body, I felt how human she was, and prey to the cold.

In the classroom things were not so congenial between us. Geometry was my worst subject, indeed, a total mystery to me. She had not taught more than four classes when she realized this and threw a duster at me in a rage. A few girls gasped as she asked me to stand up and make a spectacle of myself. Her face had reddened, and presently she took out her handkerchief and patted the eye which was red and swollen. I not only felt a fool but felt in imminent danger of sneezing as I inhaled the smell of chalk that had fallen onto my gym frock. Suddenly she fled from the room, leaving us ten minutes free until the next class. Some girls said it was a disgrace, said I should write home and say I had been assaulted. Others welcomed the few minutes in which to gabble. All I wanted was to run after her and say that I was sorry to have caused her such distemper, because I knew dimly that it was as much to do with liking as it was with dislike. In me then there came a sort of speechless tenderness for her, and I might have known that I was stirred.

"We could get her defrocked," Baba said, and elbowed me in God's name to sit down.

That evening at Benediction I had the most overwhelming surprise. It was a particularly happy evening, with the choir nuns in full soaring form and the rows of candles like so many little ladders to the golden chalice that glittered all the more because of the beams of fitful flame. I was full of tears when I discovered a new holy picture had been put in my prayer book, and before I dared look on the back to see who had given it to me, I felt and guessed that this was no ordinary picture from an ordinary girl friend, that this was a talisman and a peace offering from Sister Imelda. It was a pale-blue picture, so pale that it was almost gray, like the down of a pigeon, and it showed a mother looking down on the infant child. On the back, in her beautiful ornate handwriting, she had written a verse:

Trust Him when dark doubts assail thee,
Trust Him when thy faith is small,
Trust Him when to simply trust Him
Seems the hardest thing of all.

This was her atonement. To think that she had located the compartment in the chapel where I kept my prayer book and to think that she had been so naked as to write in it and give me a chance to boast about it and to show it to other girls. When I thanked her next day, she bowed but did not speak. Mostly the nuns were on silence and only permitted to talk during class.

In no time I had received another present, a little miniature prayer book with a leather cover and gold edging. The prayers were in French and the lettering so minute it was as if a tiny insect had fashioned them. Soon I was publicly known as her pet. I opened the doors for her, raised the blackboard two pegs higher (she was taller than other nuns), and handed out the exercise books which she had corrected. Now in the margins of my geometry propositions I would find "Good" or "Excellent," when in the past she used to splash "Disgraceful." Baba said it was foul to be a nun's pet and that any girl who sucked up to a nun could not be trusted.

About a month later Sister Imelda asked me to carry her books up four flights of stairs to the cookery kitchen. She taught cookery to a junior class. As she walked ahead of me, I thought how supple she was and how thoroughbred, and when she paused on the landing to look out through the long curtainless window, I too paused. Down below, two women in suede boots were chatting and smoking as they moved along the street with shopping baskets. Nearby a lay nun was on her knees scrubbing the granite steps, and the cold air was full of the raw smell of Jeyes Fluid. There was a potted plant on the landing, and Sister Imelda put her fingers in the earth and went "Tch tch tch," saying it needed water. I said I would water it later on. I was happy in my prison then, happy to be near her, happy to walk behind her as she twirled her beads and bowed to the servile nun. I no longer cried for my mother, no longer counted the days on a pocket calendar until the Christmas holidays.

"Come back at five," she said as she stood on the threshold of the cookery kitchen door. The girls, all in white overalls, were arranged around the long wooden table waiting for her. It was as if every girl was in love with her. Because, as she entered, their faces broke into smiles, and in different tones of audacity they said her name. She must have liked cookery class, because she beamed and called to someone, anyone, to get up a blazing fire. Then she went across to the cast-iron stove and spat on it to test its temperature. It was hot, because her spit rose up and sizzled.

When I got back later, she was sitting on the edge of the table swaying her legs. There was something reckless about her pose, something defiant. It seemed as if any minute she would take out a cigarette case, snap it open, and then archly offer me one. The wonderful smell of baking made me realize how hungry I was, but far more so, it brought back to me my own home, my mother testing orange cakes with a knitting needle and letting me lick the line of half-baked dough down the length of the needle. I wondered if she had supplanted my mother, and I hoped not, because I had aimed to outstep my original world and take my place in a new and hallowed one.

"I bet you have a sweet tooth," she said, and then she got up, crossed the kitchen, and from under a wonderful shining silver cloche she produced two jam tarts with a crisscross design on them where the pastry was latticed over the dark jam. They were still warm.

"What will I do with them?" I asked.

"Eat them, you goose," she said, and she watched me eat as if she herself derived some peculiar pleasure from it, whereas I was embarrassed about the pastry crumbling and the bits of blackberry jam staining my lips. She was amused. It was one of the most awkward yet thrilling moments I had lived, and inherent in the pleasure was the terrible sense of danger. Had we been caught, she, no doubt, would have had to make massive sacrifice. I looked at her and thought how peerless and how brave, and I wondered if she felt hungry. She had a white overall over her black habit and this made her warmer and freer, and caused me to think of the happiness that would be ours, the laissez-faire if we were away from the convent in an ordinary kitchen doing something easy and customary. But we weren't. It was clear to me then that my version of pleasure was inextricable from pain, that they existed side by side and were interdependent, like the two forces of an electric current.

"Had you a friend when you were in Dublin at university?" I asked daringly.

"I shared a desk with a sister from Howth and stayed in the same hostel," she said.

But what about boys? I thought, and what of your life now and do you long to go out into the world? But could not say it.

We knew something about the nuns' routine. It was rumored that they wore itchy wool underwear, ate dry bread for breakfast, rarely had meat, cakes, or dainties, kept certain hours of strict silence with each other, as well as constant vigil on their thoughts; so that if their minds wandered to the subject of food or pleasure, they would quickly revert to thoughts of God and their eternal souls. They slept on hard beds with no sheets and hairy blankets. At four o'clock in the morning while we slept, each nun got out of bed, in her habit — which was also her death habit — and chanting, they all flocked down the wooden stairs like ravens, to fling themselves on the tiled floor of the chapel. Each nun — even the Mother Superior — flung herself in total submission, saying prayers in Latin and offering up the moment to God. Then silently back to their cells for one more hour of rest. It was not difficult to imagine Sister Imelda face downward, arms outstretched, prostrate on the tiled floor. I often heard their chanting when I wakened suddenly from a nightmare, because, although we slept in a different building, both adjoined, and if one wakened one often heard that monotonous Latin chanting, long before the birds began, long before our own bell summoned us to rise at six.

"Do you eat nice food?" I asked.

"Of course," she said, and smiled. She sometimes broke into an eager smile, which she did much to conceal.

"Have you ever thought of what you will be?" she asked.

I shook my head. My design changed from day to day.

She looked at her man's silver pocket watch, closed the damper of the range, and prepared to leave. She checked that all the wall cupboards were locked by running her hand over them.

"Sister," I called, gathering enough courage at last — we must have some secret, something to join us together — "what color hair have you?"

We never saw the nuns' hair, or their eyebrows, or ears, as all that part was covered by a stiff white wimple.

"You shouldn't ask such a thing," she said, getting pink in the face, and then she turned back and whispered, "I'll tell you on your last day here, provided your geometry has improved."

She had scarcely gone when Baba, who had been lurking behind some pillar, struck her head in the door and said, "Christsake, save me a bit." She finished the second pastry, then went around looking in kitchen drawers. Because of everything being locked, she found only some castor sugar in a china shaker. She ate a little and threw the remainder into the dying fire, so that it flared up for a minute with a yellow spluttering flame. Baba showed her jealousy by putting it around the school that I was in the cookery kitchen every evening, gorging cakes with Sister Imelda and telling tales.

I did not speak to Sister Imelda again in private until the evening of our Christmas theatricals. She came to help us put on makeup and get into our stage clothes and fancy headgear. These clothes were kept in a trunk from one year to the next, and though sumptuous and strewn with braiding and gold, they smelled of camphor. Yet as we donned them we felt different, and as we sponged pancake makeup onto our faces, we became saucy and emphasized these new guises by adding dark pencil to the eyes and making the lips bright carmine. There was only one tube of lipstick and each girl clamored for it. The evening's entertainment was to comprise scenes from Shakespeare and laughing sketches. I had been chosen to recite Mark Antony's lament over Caesar's body, and for this I was to wear a purple toga, white knee-length socks, and patent buckle shoes. The shoes were too big and I moved in them as if in clogs. She said to take them off, to go barefoot. I realized that I was getting nervous and that in an effort to memorize my speech, the words were getting all askew and flying about in my head, like the separate pieces of a jigsaw puzzle. She sensed my panic and very slowly put her hand on my face and enjoined me to look at her. I looked into her eyes, which seemed fathomless, and saw that she was willing me to be calm and obliging me to be master of my fears, and I little knew that one day she would have to do the same as regards the swoop of my feelings for her. As we continued to stare I felt myself becoming calm and the words were restored to me in their right and fluent order. The lights were being lowered out in the recreation hall, and we knew now that all the nuns had arrived, had settled themselves down, and were eagerly awaiting this annual hotchpotch of amateur entertainment. There was that fearsome hush as the hall went dark and the few spotlights were turned on. She kissed her crucifix and I realized that she was saying a prayer for me. Then she raised her arm as if depicting the stance of a Greek goddess; walking onto the stage, I was fired by her ardor.

Baba could say that I bawled like a bloody bull, but Sister Imelda, who stood in the wings, said that temporarily she had felt the streets of Rome, had seen the corpse of Caesar, as I delivered those poignant, distempered lines. When I came off stage she put her arms around me and I was encased in a shower of silent kisses. After we had taken down the decorations and put the fancy clothes back in the trunk, I gave her two half-pound boxes of chocolates — bought for me illicitly by one of the day girls — and she gave me a casket made from the insides of match boxes and covered over with gilt paint and gold dust. It was like holding moths and finding their powder adhering to the fingers.

"What will you do on Christmas Day, Sister?" I said.

"I'll pray for you," she said.

It was useless to say, "Will you have turkey?" or "Will you have plum pudding?" or "Will you loll in bed?" because I believed that Christmas Day would be as bleak and deprived as any other day in her life. Yet she was radiant as if such austerity was joyful. Maybe she was basking in some secret realization involving her and me.

On the cold snowy afternoon three weeks later when we returned from our holidays, Sister Imelda came up to the dormitory to welcome me back. All the other girls had gone down to the recreation hall to do barn dances and I could hear someone banging on the piano. I did not want to go down and clump around with sixty other girls, having nothing to look forward to, only tea and the Rosary and early to bed. The beds were damp after our stay at home, and when I put my hand between the sheets, it was like feeling dew but did not have the freshness of outdoors. What depressed me further was that I had seen a mouse in one of the cupboards, seen its tail curl with terror as it slipped away into a crevice. If there was one mouse, there were God knows how many, and the cakes we hid in secret would not be safe. I was still unpacking as she came down the narrow passage between the rows of iron beds and I saw in her walk such agitation.

"Tut, tut, tut, you've curled your hair," she said, offended.

Yes, the world outside was somehow declared in this perm, and for a second I remembered the scalding pain as the trickles of ammonia dribbled down my forehead and then the joy as the hairdresser said that she would make me look like Movita, a Mexican star. Now suddenly that world and those aspirations seemed trite and I wanted to take a brush and straighten my hair and revert to the dark gawky somber girl that I had been. I offered her iced queen cakes that my mother had made, but she refused them and said she could only stay a second. She lent me a notebook of hers, which she had had as a pupil, and into which she had copied favorite quotations, some religious, some not. I read at random:

> Twice or thrice had I loved thee,
> Before I knew thy face or name.
> So in a voice, so in a shapeless flame,
> Angels affect us oft . . .

"Are you well?" I asked.

She looked pale. It may have been the day, which was wretched and gray with sleet, or it may have been the white bedspreads, but she appeared to be ailing.

"I missed you," she said.

"Me too," I said.

At home, gorging, eating trifle at all hours, even for breakfast, having little ratafias to dip in cups of tea, fitting on new shoes and silk stockings, I wished that she could be with us, enjoying the fire and the freedom.

"You know it is not proper for us to be so friendly."

"It's not wrong," I said.

I dreaded that she might decide to turn away from me, that she might stamp on our love and might suddenly draw a curtain over it, a black crepe curtain that would denote its death. I dreaded it and knew it was going to happen.

"We must not become attached," she said, and I could not say we already were, no more than I could remind her of the day of the revels and the intimacy between us. Convents were dungeons and no doubt about it.

From then on she treated me as less of a favorite. She said my name sharply in class, and once she said if I must cough, could I wait until class had finished. Baba was delighted, as were the other girls, because they were glad to see me receding in her eyes. Yet I knew that the crispness was part of her love, because no matter how callously she looked at me, she would occasionally soften. Reading her notebook helped me, and I copied out her quotations into my own book, trying as accurately as possible to imitate her handwriting.

But some little time later when she came to supervise our study one evening, I got a smile from her as she sat on the rostrum looking down at us all. I continued to look up at her and by slight frowning indicated that I had a problem with my geometry. She beckoned to me lightly and I went up, bringing my copybook and the pen. Standing close to her, and also because her wimple was crooked, I saw one of her eyebrows for the first time. She saw that I noticed it and said did that satisfy my curiosity. I said not really. She said what else did I want to see, her swan's neck perhaps, and I went scarlet. I was amazed that she would say such a thing in the hearing of other girls, and then she said a worse thing, she said that G. K. Chesterton was very forgetful and had once put on his trousers backward. She expected me to laugh. I was so close to her that a rumble in her stomach seemed to be taking place in my own, and about this she also laughed. It occurred to me for one terrible moment that maybe she had decided to leave the convent, to jump over the wall. Having done the theorem for me, she marked it "100 out of 100" and then asked if I had any other problems. My eyes filled with tears, I wanted her to realize that her recent coolness had wrought havoc with my nerves and my peace of mind.

"What is it?" she said.

I could cry, or I could tremble to try to convey the emotion, but I could not tell her. As if on cue, the Mother Superior came in and saw this glaring intimacy and frowned as she approached the rostrum.

"Would you please go back to your desk," she said, "and in future kindly allow Sister Imelda to get on with her duties."

I tiptoed back and sat with head down, bursting with fear and shame. Then she looked at a tray on which the milk cups were laid, and finding one cup of milk untouched, she asked which girl had not drunk her milk.

"Me, Sister," I said, and I was called up to drink it and stand under the clock as a punishment. The milk was tepid and dusty, and I thought of cows on the fair days at home and the farmers hitting them as they slid and slithered over the muddy streets.

For weeks I tried to see my nun in private; I even lurked outside doors where I knew she was due, only to be rebuffed again and again. I suspected the Mother Superior had warned her against making a favorite of me. But I still clung to a belief that a bond existed between us and that her coldness and even some glares which I had received were a charade, a mask. I would wonder how she felt alone in bed and what way she slept and if she thought of me, or refusing to think of me, if she dreamed of me as I did of her. She certainly got thinner, because her nun's silver ring slipped easily and sometimes unavoidably off her marriage finger. It occurred to me that she was having a nervous breakdown.

One day in March the sun came out, the radiators were turned off, and, though there was a lashing wind, we were told that officially spring had arrived and that we could play games. We all trooped up to the games field and, to our surprise, saw that Sister Imelda was officiating that day. The daffodils in the field tossed and turned; they were a very bright shocking yellow, but they were not as fetching as the little timid snowdrops that trembled in the wind. We played rounders, and when my turn came to hit the ball with the long wooden pound, I crumbled and missed, fearing that the ball would hit me.

"Champ . . ." said Baba, jeering.

After three such failures Sister Imelda said that if I liked I could sit and watch, and when I was sitting in the greenhouse swallowing my shame, she came in and said that I must not give way to tears, because humiliation was the greatest test of Christ's love, or indeed *any* love.

"When you are a nun you will know that," she said, and instantly I made up my mind that I would be a nun and that though we might never be free to express our feelings, we would be under the same roof, in the same cloister, in mental and spiritual conjunction all our lives.

"Is it very hard at first?" I said.

"It's awful," she said, and she slipped a little medal into my gym-frock pocket. It was warm from being in her pocket, and as I held it, I knew that once again we were near and that in fact we had never severed. Walking down from the playing field to our Sunday lunch of mutton and cabbage, everyone chattered to Sister Imelda. The girls milled around her, linking her, trying to hold her hand, counting the various keys on her bunch of keys, and asking impudent questions.

"Sister, did you ever ride a motorbicycle?"

"Sister, did you ever wear seamless stockings?"

"Sister, who's your favorite film star — male?"

"Sister, what's your favorite food?"

"Sister, if you had a wish, what would it be?"

"Sister, what do you do when you want to scratch your head?"

Yes, she had ridden a motorbicycle, and she had worn silk stockings, but they were seamed. She liked bananas best, and if she had a wish, it would be to go home for a few hours to see her parents and her brother.

That afternoon as we walked through the town, the sight of closed shops with porter barrels outside and mongrel dogs did not dispel my refound ecstasy. The medal was in my pocket, and every other second I would touch it for confirmation. Baba saw a Swiss roll in a confectioner's window laid on a doily and dusted with castor sugar, and it made her cry out with hunger and rail against being in a bloody reformatory, surrounded by drips and mopes. On impulse she took her nail file out of her pocket and dashed across to the window to see if she could cut the glass. The prefect rushed up from the back of the line and asked Baba if she wanted to be locked up.

"I am anyhow," Baba said, and sawed at one of her nails, to maintain her independence and vent her spleen. Baba was the only girl who could stand up to a prefect. When she felt like it, she dropped out of a walk, sat on a stone wall, and waited until we all came back. She said that if there was one thing more boring than studying it was walking. She used to roll down her stockings and examine her calves and say that she could see varicose veins coming from this bloody daily walk. Her legs, like all our legs, were black from the dye of the stockings; we were forbidden to bathe, because baths were immoral. We washed each night in an enamel basin beside our beds. When girls splashed cold water onto their chests, they let out cries, though this was forbidden.

After the walk we wrote home. We were allowed to write home once a week; our letters were always censored. I told my mother that I had made up my mind to be a nun, and asked if she could send me bananas when a batch arrived at our local grocery shop. That evening, perhaps as I wrote to my mother on the ruled white paper, a telegram arrived which said that Sister Imelda's brother had been killed in a van while on his way home from a hurling match. The Mother Superior announced it, and asked us to pray for his soul and write letters of sympathy to Sister Imelda's parents. We all wrote identical letters, because in our first year at school we had been given specimen letters for various occasions, and we all referred back to our specimen letter of sympathy.

Next day the town hire-car drove up to the convent, and Sister Imelda, accompanied by another nun, went home for the funeral. She looked as white as a sheet, with eyes swollen, and she wore a heavy knitted shawl over her shoulders. Although she came back that night (I stayed awake to hear the car), we did not see her for a whole week, except to catch a glimpse of her back, in the chapel. When she resumed class, she was peaky and distant, making no reference at all to her recent tragedy.

The day the bananas came I waited outside the door and gave her a bunch wrapped in tissue paper. Some were still a little green, and she said that Mother Superior would put them in the glasshouse to ripen. I felt that Sister Imelda would never taste them; they would be kept for a visiting priest or bishop.

"Oh, Sister, I'm sorry about your brother," I said in a burst.

"It will come to us all, sooner or later," Sister Imelda said dolefully.

I dared to touch her wrist to communicate my sadness. She went quickly, probably for fear of breaking down. At times she grew irritable and had a boil on her cheek. She missed some classes and was replaced in the cookery kitchen by a younger nun. She asked me to pray for her brother's soul and to avoid seeing her alone. Each time as she came down a corridor toward me, I was obliged to turn the other way. Now Baba or some other girl moved the blackboard two pegs higher and spread her shawl, when wet, over the radiator to dry.

I got flu and was put to bed. Sickness took the same bleak course, a cup of hot senna delivered in person by the head nun, who stood there while I drank it, tea at lunchtime with thin slices of brown bread (because it was just after the war, food was still rationed, so the butter was mixed with lard and had white streaks running through it and a faintly rancid smell), hours of just lying there surveying the empty dormitory, the empty iron beds with white counterpanes on each one, and metal crucifixes laid on each white, frilled pillow slip. I knew that she would miss me and hoped that Baba would tell her where I was. I counted the number of tiles from the ceiling to the head of my bed, thought of my mother at home on the farm mixing hen food, thought of my father, losing his temper perhaps and stamping on the kitchen floor with nailed boots, and I recalled the money owing for my school fees and hoped that Sister Imelda would never get to hear of it. During the Christmas holiday I had seen a bill sent by the head nun to my father which said, "Please remit this week without fail." I hated being in bed causing extra trouble and therefore re minding the head nun of the unpaid liability. We had no clock in the dormitory, so there was no way of guessing the time, but the hours dragged.

Marigold, one of the maids, came to take off the counterpanes at five and brought with her two gifts from Sister Imelda — an orange and a pencil sharpener. I kept the orange peel in my hand, smelling it, and planning how I would thank her. Thinking of her I fell into a feverish sleep and was wakened when the girls came to bed at ten and switched on the various ceiling lights.

At Easter Sister Imelda warned me not to give her chocolates, so I got her a flashlamp instead and spare batteries. Pleased with such a useful gift (perhaps she read her letters in bed), she put her arms around me and allowed one cheek to adhere but not to make the sound of a kiss. It made up for the seven weeks of withdrawal, and as I drove down the convent drive with Baba, she waved to me, as she had promised, from the window of her cell.

In the last term at school, studying was intensive because of the examinations which loomed at the end of June. Like all the other nuns, Sister Imelda thought only of these examinations. She crammed us with knowledge, lost her temper every other day, and gritted her teeth whenever the blackboard was too greasy to take the imprint of the chalk. If ever I met her in the corridor, she asked if I knew such and such a thing, and coming down from Sunday games, she went over various questions with us. The fateful examination day arrived and we sat at single desks supervised by some strange woman from Dublin. Opening a locked trunk, she took out the pink examination papers and distributed them around. Geometry was on the fourth day. When we came out from it, Sister Imelda was in the hall with all the answers, so that we could compare our answers with hers. Then she called me aside and we went up toward the cookery kitchen and sat on the stairs while she went over the paper with me, question for question. I knew that I had three right and two wrong, but did not tell her so.

"It is black," she said then, rather suddenly. I thought she meant the dark light where we were sitting.

"It's cool, though," I said.

Summer had come; our white skins baked under the heavy uniform, and dark violet pansies bloomed in the convent grounds. She looked well again, and her pale skin was once more unblemished.

"My hair," she whispered, "is black." And she told me how she had spent her last night before entering the convent. She had gone cycling with a boy and ridden for miles, and they'd lost their way up a mountain, and she became afraid she would be so late home that she would sleep it out the next morning. It was understood between us that I was going to enter the convent in September and that I could have a last fling, too.

Two days later we prepared to go home. There were farewells and outlandish promises, and autograph books signed, and girls trudging up the recreation hall, their cases bursting open with clothes and books. Baba scattered biscuit crumbs in the dormitory for the mice and stuffed all her prayer books under a mattress. Her father promised to collect us at four. I had arranged with Sister Imelda secretly that I would meet her in one of the summerhouses around the walks, where we would spend our last half hour together. I expected that she would tell me something of what my life as a postulant would be like. But Baba's father came an hour early. He had something urgent to do later and came at three instead. All I could do was ask Marigold to take a note to Sister Imelda.

> Remembrance is all I ask,
> But if remembrance should prove a task,
> Forget me.

I hated Baba, hated her busy father, hated the thought of my mother standing in the doorway in her good dress, welcoming me home at last. I would have become a nun that minute if I could.

I wrote to my nun that night and again the next day and then every week for a month. Her letters were censored, so I tried to convey my feelings indirectly. In one of her letters to me (they were allowed one letter a month) she said that she looked forward to seeing me in September. But by September Baba and I had left for the university in Dublin. I stopped writing to Sister Imelda then, reluctant to tell her that I no longer wished to be a nun.

In Dublin we enrolled at the college where she had surpassed herself. I saw her maiden name on a list, for having graduated with special honors, and for days was again sad and remorseful. I rushed out and bought batteries for the flashlamp I'd given her, and posted them without any note enclosed. No mention of my missing vocation, no mention of why I had stopped writing.

One Sunday about two years later, Baba and I were going out to Howth on a bus. Baba had met some businessmen who played golf there and she had done a lot of scheming to get us invited out. The bus was packed, mostly mothers with babies and children on their way to Dollymount Strand. We drove along the coast road and saw the sea, bright green and glinting in the sun, and because of the way the water was carved up into millions of little wavelets, its surface seemed like an endless heap of dark-green broken bottles. Near the shore the sand looked warm and was biscuit-colored. We never swam or sunbathed, we never did anything that was good for us. Life was geared to work and to meeting men, and yet one knew that mating could only lead to one's being a mother and hawking obstreperous children out to the seaside on Sunday. "They know not what they do" could surely be said of us.

We were very made up; even the conductor seemed to disapprove and snapped at having to give change of ten shillings. For no reason at all I thought of our makeup rituals before the school play and how innocent it was in comparison, because now our skins were smothered beneath layers of it and we never took it off at night. Thinking of the convent, I suddenly thought of Sister Imelda, and then, as if prey to a dream, I heard the rustle of serge, smelled the Jeyes Fluid and the boiled cabbage, and saw her pale shocked face in the months after her brother died. Then I looked around and saw her in earnest, and at first thought I was imagining things. But no, she had got on accompanied by another nun and they were settling themselves in the back seat nearest the door. She looked older, but she had the same aloof quality and the same eyes, and my heart began to race with a mixture of excitement and dread. At first it raced with a prodigal strength, and then it began to falter and I thought it was going to give out. My fear of her and my love came back in one fell realization. I would have gone through the window except that it was not wide enough. The thing was how to escape her. Baba gurgled with delight, stood up, and in the most flagrant way looked around to make sure that it was Imelda. She recognized the other nun as one with the nickname of Johnny who taught piano lessons. Baba's first thought was revenge, as she enumerated the punishments they had meted out to us and said how nice it would be to go back and shock them and say, "Mud in your eye, Sisters," or "Get lost," or something worse. Baba could not understand why I was quaking, no more than she could understand why I began to wipe off the lipstick. Above all, I knew that I could not confront them.

"You're going to have to," Baba said.

"I can't," I said.

It was not just my attire; it was the fact of my never having written and of my broken promise. Baba kept looking back and said they weren't saying a word and that children were gawking at them. It wasn't often that nuns traveled in buses, and we speculated as to where they might be going.

"They might be off to meet two fellows," Baba said, and visualized them in the golf club getting blotto and hoisting up their skirts. For me it was no laughing matter. She came up with a strategy: it was that as we approached our stop and the bus was still moving, I was to jump up and go down the aisle and pass them without even looking. She said most likely they would not notice us, as their eyes were lowered and they seemed to be praying.

"I can't run down the bus," I said. There was a matter of shaking limbs and already a terrible vertigo.

"You're going to," Baba said, and though insisting that I couldn't, I had already begun to rehearse an apology. While doing this, I kept blessing myself over and over again, and Baba kept reminding me that there was only one more stop before ours. When the dreadful moment came, I jumped up and put on my face what can only be called an apology of a smile. I followed Baba to the rear of the bus. But already they had gone. I saw the back of their two sable, identical figures with their veils being blown wildly about in the wind. They looked so cold and lost as they hurried along the pavement and I wanted to run after them. In some way I felt worse than if I had confronted them. I cannot be certain what I would have said. I knew that there is something sad and faintly distasteful about love's ending, particularly love that has never been fully realized. I might have hinted at that, but I doubt it. In our deepest moments we say the most inadequate things.

TIM O'BRIEN

 Tim O'Brien was born in Austin, Minnesota, and was educated at Macalester College and Harvard University. A veteran of the Vietnam War, he has concentrated his fiction upon exploring the profound effects of that conflict on individuals and a nation. His novels are *Northern Lights* (1974), *Going After Cacciato* (1978), and *The Nuclear Age* (1985). He has published a collection of narrative sketches, *If I Die in a Combat Zone* (1973), and his short stories are anthologized in various annual collections. Some critics have seen the influences of Hemingway in O'Brien's story lines and technique. He writes in a "precise and highly evocative style," one which sounds the horror of war while at the same time probing, almost lyrically, the hearts and minds of the men caught in it. "The Things They Carried" is a tour-de-force of that style.

The Things They Carried

First Lieutenant Jimmy Cross carried letters from a girl named Martha, a junior at Mount Sebastian College in New Jersey. They were not love letters, but Lieutenant Cross was hoping, so he kept them folded in plastic at the bottom of his rucksack. In the late afternoon, after a day's march, he would dig his foxhole, wash his hands under a canteen, unwrap the letters, hold them with the tips of his fingers, and spend the last hour of light pretending. He would imagine romantic camping trips into the White Mountains in New Hampshire. He would sometimes taste the envelope flaps, knowing her tongue had been there. More than anything, he wanted Martha to love him as he loved her, but the letters were mostly chatty, elusive on the matter of love. She was a virgin, he was almost sure. She was an English major at Mount Sebastian, and she wrote beautifully about her professors and roommates and midterm exams, about her respect for Chaucer and her great affection for Virginia Woolf. She often quoted lines of poetry; she never mentioned the war, except to say, Jimmy, take care of yourself. The letters weighed ten ounces. They were signed "Love, Martha," but Lieutenant Cross understood that "Love" was only a way of signing and did not mean what he sometimes pretended it meant. At dusk, he would carefully return the letters to his rucksack. Slowly, a bit distracted, he would get up and move among his men, checking the perimeter, then at full dark he would return to his hole and watch the night and wonder if Martha was a virgin.

The things they carried were largely determined by necessity. Among the necessities or near necessities were P-38 can openers, pocket knives, heat tabs, wrist watches, dog tags, mosquito repellent, chewing gum, candy, cigarettes, salt tablets, packets of Kool-Aid, lighters, matches, sewing kits, Military Payment Certificates, C rations, and two or three canteens of water. Together, these items weighed between fifteen and twenty pounds, depending upon a man's habits or rate of metabolism. Henry Dobbins, who was a big man, carried extra rations; he was especially fond of canned peaches in heavy syrup over pound cake. Dave Jensen, who practiced field hygiene, carried a toothbrush, dental floss, and several hotel-size bars of soap he'd stolen on R&R in Sydney, Australia. Ted Lavender, who was scared, carried tranquilizers until he was shot in the head outside the village of Than Khe in mid-April. By necessity, and because it was SOP, they all carried steel helmets that weighed five pounds including the liner and camouflage cover. They carried the standard fatigue jackets and trousers. Very few carried underwear. On their feet they carried jungle boots — 2.1 pounds — and Dave Jensen carried three pairs of socks and a can of Dr. Scholl's foot powder as a precaution against trench foot. Until he was shot, Ted Lavender carried six or seven ounces of premium dope, which for him was a necessity. Mitchell Sanders, the RTO, carried condoms. Norman Bowker carried a diary. Rat Kiley carried comic books. Kiowa, a devout Baptist, carried an illustrated New Testament that had been presented to him by his father, who taught Sunday school in Oklahoma City, Oklahoma. As a hedge against bad times, however, Kiowa also carried his grandmother's distrust of the white man, his grandfather's old hunting hatchet. Necessity dictated. Because the land was mined and booby-trapped, it was SOP for each man to carry a steel-centered, nylon-covered flak jacket, which weighed 6.7 pounds, but which on hot days seemed much heavier. Because you could die so quickly, each man carried at least one large compress bandage, usually in the helmet band for easy access. Because the nights were cold, and because the monsoons were wet, each carried a green plastic poncho that could be used as a raincoat or ground sheet or makeshift tent. With its quilted liner, the poncho weighed almost two pounds, but it was worth every ounce. In April, for instance, when Ted Lavender was shot, they used his poncho to wrap him up, then to carry him across the paddy, then to lift him into the chopper that took him away.

They were called legs or grunts.

To carry something was to "hump" it, as when Lieutenant Jimmy Cross humped his love for Martha up the hills and through the swamps. In its intransitive form, "to hump" meant "to walk," or "to march," but it implied burdens far beyond the intransitive.

Almost everyone humped photographs. In his wallet, Lieutenant Cross carried two photographs of Martha. The first was a Kodachrome snapshot signed "Love," though he knew better. She stood against a brick wall. Her eyes were gray and neutral, her lips slightly open as she stared straight-on at the camera. At night, sometimes, Lieutenant Cross wondered who had taken the picture, because he knew she had boyfriends, because he loved her so much, and because he could see the shadow of the picture taker spreading out against the brick wall. The second photograph had been clipped from the 1968 Mount Sebastian yearbook. It was an action shot —

women's volleyball — and Martha was bent horizontal to the floor, reaching, the palms of her hands in sharp focus, the tongue taut, the expression frank and competitive. There was no visible sweat. She wore white gym shorts. Her legs, he thought, were almost certainly the legs of a virgin, dry and without hair, the left knee cocked and carrying her entire weight, which was just over one hundred pounds. Lieutenant Cross remembered touching that left knee. A dark theater, he remembered, and the movie was *Bonnie and Clyde,* and Martha wore a tweed skirt, and during the final scene, when he touched her knee, she turned and looked at him in a sad, sober way that made him pull his hand back, but he would always remember the feel of the tweed skirt and the knee beneath it and the sound of the gunfire that killed Bonnie and Clyde, how embarrassing it was, how slow and oppressive. He remembered kissing her good night at the dorm door. Right then, he thought, he should've done something brave. He should've carried her up the stairs to her room and tied her to the bed and touched that left knee all night long. He should've risked it. Whenever he looked at the photographs, he thought of new things he should've done.

What they carried was partly a function of rank, partly of field specialty.

As a first lieutenant and platoon leader, Jimmy Cross carried a compass, maps, code books, binoculars, and a .45-caliber pistol that weighed 2.9 pounds fully loaded. He carried a strobe light and the responsibility for the lives of his men.

As an RTO, Mitchell Sanders carried the PRC-25 radio, a killer, twenty-six pounds with its battery.

As a medic, Rat Kiley carried a canvas satchel filled with morphine and plasma and malaria tablets and surgical tape and comic books and all the things a medic must carry, including M&M's for especially bad wounds, for a total weight of nearly twenty pounds.

As a big man, therefore a machine gunner, Henry Dobbins carried the M-60, which weighed twenty-three pounds unloaded, but which was almost always loaded. In addition, Dobbins carried between ten and fifteen pounds of ammunition draped in belts across his chest and shoulders.

As PFCs or Spec 4s, most of them were common grunts and carried the standard M-16 gas-operated assault rifle. The weapon weighed 7.5 pounds unloaded, 8.2 pounds with its full twenty-round magazine. Depending on numerous factors, such as topography and psychology, the riflemen carried anywhere from twelve to twenty magazines, usually in cloth bandoliers, adding on another 8.4 pounds at minimum, fourteen pounds at maximum. When it was available, they also carried M-16 maintenance gear — rods and steel brushes and swabs and tubes of LSA oil — all of which weighed about a pound. Among the grunts, some carried the M-79 grenade launcher, 5.9 pounds unloaded, a reasonably light weapon except for the ammunition, which was heavy. A single round weighed ten ounces. The typical load was twenty-five rounds. But Ted Lavender, who was scared, carried thirty-four rounds when he was shot and killed outside Than Khe, and he went down under an exceptional burden, more than twenty pounds of ammunition, plus the flak jacket and helmet and rations and water and toilet paper and tranquilizers and all the rest, plus the unweighed fear. He was dead weight. There was no twitching or flopping. Kiowa, who saw it happen, said it was like watching a rock fall, or a big sandbag or something — just boom, then down — not like the movies where the dead guy rolls around and does fancy spins and goes ass over teakettle — not like that, Kiowa said, the poor bastard just flat-fuck fell. Boom. Down. Nothing else. It was a bright morning in mid-April. Lieutenant Cross felt the pain. He blamed himself. They stripped off Lavender's canteens and ammo, all the heavy things, and Rat Kiley said the obvious, the guy's dead, and Mitchell Sanders used his radio to report one U.S. KIA and to request a chopper. Then they wrapped Lavender in his poncho. They carried him out to a dry paddy, established security, and sat smoking the dead man's dope until the chopper came. Lieutenant Cross kept to himself. He pictured Martha's smooth young face, thinking he loved her more than anything, more than his men, and now Ted Lavender was dead because he loved her so much and could not stop thinking about her. When the dust-off arrived, they carried Lavender aboard. Afterward they burned Than Khe. They marched until dusk, then dug their holes, and that night Kiowa kept explaining how you had to be there, how fast it was, how the poor guy just dropped like so much concrete. Boom-down, he said. Like cement.

In addition to the three standard weapons — the M-60, M-16, and M-79 — they carried whatever presented itself, or whatever seemed appropriate as a means of killing or staying alive. They carried catch-as-catch-can. At various times, in various situations, they carried M-14s and CAR-15s and Swedish Ks and grease guns and captured AK-47s and Chi-Coms and RPGs and Simonov carbines and black-market Uzis and .38-caliber Smith & Wesson handguns and 66 mm LAWs and shotguns and silencers and blackjacks and bayonets and C-4 plastic explosives. Lee Strunk carried a slingshot; a weapon of last resort, he called it. Mitchell Sanders carried brass knuckles. Kiowa carried his grandfather's feathered hatchet. Every third or fourth man carried a Claymore antipersonnel mine — 3.5 pounds with its firing device. They all carried fragmentation grenades — fourteen ounces each. They all carried at least one M-18 colored smoke grenade — twenty-four ounces. Some carried CS or tear-gas grenades. Some carried white-phosphorus grenades. They carried all they could bear, and then some, including a silent awe for the terrible power of the things they carried.

In the first week of April, before Lavender died, Lieutenant Jimmy Cross received a good-luck charm from Martha. It was a simple pebble, an ounce at most. Smooth to the touch, it was a milky-white color with flecks of orange and violet, oval-shaped, like a miniature egg. In the accompanying letter, Martha wrote that she had found the pebble on the Jersey shoreline, precisely where the land touched water at high tide, where things came together but also separated. It was this separate-but-together quality, she wrote, that had inspired her to pick up the pebble and to carry it in her breast pocket for several days, where it seemed weightless, and then to send it through the mail, by air, as a token of her truest feelings for him. Lieutenant Cross found this romantic. But he wondered what her truest feelings were, exactly, and what she meant by separate but together. He wondered how the tides and waves had come into play on that afternoon along the Jersey shoreline when Martha saw the pebble and bent down to rescue it from geology. He imagined bare feet. Martha was a poet, with the poet's sensibilities, and her feet would be brown and bare, the toenails unpainted, the eyes chilly and somber like the ocean in March, and though it was painful, he wondered who had been with her that afternoon. He imagined a pair of shadows moving along the strip of sand where things came together but also separated. It was phantom jealousy, he knew, but he couldn't help himself. He loved her so much. On the march, through the hot days of early April, he carried the pebble in his mouth, turning it with his tongue, tasting sea salts and moisture. His mind wandered. He had difficulty keeping his attention on the war. On occasion he would yell at his men to spread out the column, to keep their eyes open, but then he would slip away into daydreams, just pretending, walking barefoot along the Jersey shore, with Martha, carrying nothing. He would feel himself rising. Sun and waves and gentle winds, all love and lightness.

What they carried varied by mission.

When a mission took them to the mountains, they carried mosquito netting, machetes, canvas tarps, and extra bug juice.

If a mission seemed especially hazardous, or if it involved a place they knew to be bad, they carried everything they could. In certain heavily mined AOs, where the land was dense with Toe Poppers and Bouncing Betties, they took turns humping a twenty-eight-pound mine detector. With its headphones and big sensing plate, the equipment was a stress on the lower back and shoulders, awkward to handle, often useless because of the shrapnel in the earth, but they carried it anyway, partly for safety, partly for the illusion of safety.

On ambush, or other night missions, they carried peculiar little odds and ends. Kiowa always took along his New Testament and a pair of moccasins for silence. Dave Jensen carried night-sight vitamins high in carotin. Lee Strunk carried his slingshot; ammo, he claimed, would never be a problem. Rat Kiley carried brandy and M&M's. Until he was shot, Ted Lavender carried the starlight scope, which weighed 6.3 pounds with its aluminum carrying case. Henry Dobbins carried his girlfriend's pantyhose wrapped around his neck as a comforter. They all carried ghosts. When dark came, they would move out single file across the meadows and paddies to their ambush coordinates, where they would quietly set up the Claymores and lie down and spend the night waiting.

Other missions were more complicated and required special equipment. In mid-April, it was their mission to search out and destroy the elaborate tunnel complexes in the Than Khe area south of Chu Lai. To blow the tunnels, they carried one-pound blocks of pentrite high explosives, four blocks to a man, sixty-eight pounds in all. They carried wiring, detonators, and battery-powered clackers. Dave Jensen carried earplugs. Most often, before blowing the tunnels, they were ordered by higher command to search them, which was considered bad news, but by and large they just shrugged and carried out orders. Because he was a big man, Henry Dobbins was excused from tunnel duty. The others would draw numbers. Before Lavender died there were seventeen men in the platoon, and whoever drew the number seventeen would strip off his gear and crawl in head first with a flashlight and Lieutenant Cross's .45-caliber pistol. The rest of them would fan out as security. They would sit down or kneel, not facing the hole, listening to the ground beneath them, imagining cobwebs and ghosts, whatever was down there — the tunnel walls squeezing in — how the flashlight seemed impossibly heavy in the hand and how it was tunnel vision in the very strictest sense, compression in all ways, even time, and how you had to wiggle in — ass and elbows — a swallowed-up feeling — and how you found yourself worrying about odd things — will your flashlight go dead? Do rats carry rabies? If you screamed, how far would the sound carry? Would your buddies hear it? Would they have the courage to drag you out? In some respects, though not many, the waiting was worse than the tunnel itself. Imagination was a killer.

On April 16, when Lee Strunk drew the number seventeen, he laughed and muttered something and went down quickly. The morning was hot and very still. Not good, Kiowa said. He looked at the tunnel opening, then out across a dry paddy toward the village of Than Khe. Nothing moved. No clouds or birds or people. As they waited, the men smoked and drank Kool-Aid, not talking much, feeling sympathy for Lee Strunk but also feeling the luck of the draw. You win some, you lose some, said Mitchell Sanders, and sometimes you settle for a rain check. It was a tired line and no one laughed.

Henry Dobbins ate a tropical chocolate bar. Ted Lavender popped a tranquilizer and went off to pee.

After five minutes, Lieutenant Jimmy Cross moved to the tunnel, leaned down, and examined the darkness. Trouble, he thought — a cave-in maybe. And then suddenly, without willing it, he was thinking about Martha. The stresses and fractures, the quick collapse, the two of them buried alive under all that weight. Dense, crushing love. Kneeling, watching the hole, he tried to concentrate on Lee Strunk and the war, all the dangers, but his love was too much for him, he felt paralyzed, he wanted to sleep inside her lungs and breathe her blood and be smothered. He wanted her to be a virgin and not a virgin, all at once. He wanted to know her. Intimate secrets — why poetry? Why so sad? Why that grayness in her eyes? Why so alone? Not lonely, just alone — riding her bike across campus or sitting off by herself in the cafeteria. Even dancing, she danced alone — and it was the aloneness that filled him with love. He remembered telling her that one evening. How she nodded and looked away. And how, later, when he kissed her, she received the kiss without returning it, her eyes wide open, not afraid, not a virgin's eyes, just flat and uninvolved.

Lieutenant Cross gazed at the tunnel. But he was not there. He was buried with Martha under the white sand at the Jersey shore. They were pressed together, and the pebble in his mouth was her tongue. He was smiling. Vaguely, he was aware of how quiet the day was, the sullen paddies, yet he could not bring himself to worry about matters of security. He was beyond that. He was just a kid at war, in love. He was twenty-two years old. He couldn't help it.

A few moments later Lee Strunk crawled out of the tunnel. He came up grinning, filthy but alive. Lieutenant Cross nodded and closed his eyes while the others clapped Strunk on the back and made jokes about rising from the dead.

Worms, Rat Kiley said. Right out of the grave. Fuckin' zombie.

The men laughed. They all felt great relief.

Spook City, said Mitchell Sanders.

Lee Strunk made a funny ghost sound, a kind of moaning, yet very happy, and right then, when Strunk made that high happy moaning sound, when he went *Ahhooooo,* right then Ted Lavender was shot in the head on his way back from peeing. He lay with his mouth open. The teeth were broken. There was a swollen black bruise under his left eye. The cheekbone was gone. Oh shit, Rat Kiley said, the guy's dead. The guy's dead, he kept saying, which seemed profound — the guy's dead. I mean really.

The things they carried were determined to some extent by superstition. Lieutenant Cross carried his good-luck pebble. Dave Jensen carried a rabbit's foot. Norman Bowker, otherwise a very gentle person, carried a thumb that had been presented to him as a gift by Mitchell Sanders. The thumb was dark brown, rubbery to the touch, and weighed four ounces at most. It had been cut from a VC corpse, a boy of fifteen or sixteen. They'd found him at the bottom of an irrigation ditch, badly burned, flies in his mouth and eyes. The boy wore black shorts and sandals. At the time of his death he had been carrying a pouch of rice, a rifle, and three magazines of ammunition.

You want my opinion, Mitchell Sanders said, there's a definite moral here.

He put his hand on the dead boy's wrist. He was quiet for a time, as if counting a pulse, then he patted the stomach, almost affectionately, and used Kiowa's hunting hatchet to remove the thumb.

Henry Dobbins asked what the moral was.

Moral?

You know. *Moral.*

Sanders wrapped the thumb in toilet paper and handed it across to Norman Bowker. There was no blood. Smiling, he kicked the boy's head, watched the flies scatter, and said, It's like with that old TV show — Paladin. Have gun, will travel.

Henry Dobbins thought about it.

Yeah, well, he finally said. I don't see no moral.

There it *is,* man.

Fuck off.

They carried USO stationery and pencils and pens. They carried Sterno, safety pins, trip flares, signal flares, spools of wire, razor blades, chewing tobacco, liberated joss sticks and statuettes of the smiling Buddha, candles, grease pencils, *The Stars and Stripes* , fingernail clippers, Psy Ops leaflets, bush hats, bolos, and much more. Twice a week, when the resupply choppers came in, they carried hot chow in green Mermite cans and large canvas bags filled with iced beer and soda pop. They carried plastic water containers, each with a two-gallon capacity. Mitchell Sanders carried a set of starched tiger fatigues for special occasions. Henry Dobbins carried Black Flag insecticide. Dave Jensen carried empty sandbags that could be filled at night for added protection. Lee Strunk carried tanning lotion. Some things they carried in common. Taking turns, they carried the big PRC-77 scrambler radio, which weighed thirty pounds with its battery. They shared the weight of memory. They took up what others could no longer bear. Often, they carried each other, the wounded or weak. They carried infections. They carried chess sets, basketballs, Vietnamese-English dictionaries, insignia of rank, Bronze Stars and Purple Hearts, plastic cards imprinted with the Code of Conduct. They carried diseases, among them malaria and dysentery. They carried lice and ringworm and leeches and paddy algae and various rots and molds. They carried the land itself — Vietnam, the place, the soil — a powdery orange-red dust that covered their boots and fatigues and faces. They carried the sky. The whole atmosphere, they carried it, the humidity, the monsoons, the stink of fungus and decay, all of it, they carried gravity. They moved like mules. By daylight they took sniper fire, at night they were mortared, but it was not battle, it was just the endless march, village to village, without purpose, nothing won or lost. They marched for the sake of the march. They plodded along slowly, dumbly, leaning forward against the heat, unthinking, all blood and bone, simple grunts, soldiering with their legs, toiling up the hills and down into the paddies and across the rivers and up again and down, just humping, one step and then the next and then another, but no volition, no will, because it was automatic, it was anatomy, and the war was entirely a matter of posture and carriage, the hump was everything, a kind of inertia, a kind of emptiness, a dullness of desire and intellect and conscience and hope and human sensibility. Their principles were in their feet. Their calculations were biological. They had no sense of strategy or mission. They searched the villages without knowing what to look for, not caring, kicking over jars of rice, frisking children and old men, blowing tunnels, sometimes setting fires and sometimes not, then forming up and moving on to the next village, then other villages, where it would always be the same. They carried their own lives. The pressures were enormous. In the heat of early afternoon, they would remove their helmets and flak jackets, walking bare, which was dangerous but which helped ease the strain. They would often discard things along the route of march. Purely for comfort, they would throw away rations, blow their Claymores and grenades, no matter, because by nightfall the resupply choppers would arrive with more of the same, then a day or two later still more, fresh watermelons and crates of ammunition and sunglasses and woolen sweaters — the resources were stunning — sparklers for the Fourth of July, colored eggs for Easter. It was the great American war chest — the fruits of science, the smokestacks, the canneries, the arsenals at Hartford, the Minnesota forests, the machine shops, the vast fields of corn and wheat — they carried like freight trains; they carried it on their backs and shoulders — and for all the ambiguities of Vietnam, all the mysteries and unknowns, there was at least the single abiding certainty that they would never be at a loss for things to carry.

After the chopper took Lavender away, Lieutenant Jimmy Cross led his men into the village of Than Khe. They burned everything. They shot chickens and dogs, they trashed the village well, they called in artillery and watched the wreckage, then they marched for several hours through the hot afternoon, and then at dusk, while Kiowa explained how Lavender died, Lieutenant Cross found himself trembling.

He tried not to cry. With his entrenching tool, which weighed five pounds, he began digging a hole in the earth.

He felt shame. He hated himself. He had loved Martha more than his men, and as a consequence Lavender was now dead, and this was something he would have to carry like a stone in his stomach for the rest of the war.

All he could do was dig. He used his entrenching tool like an ax, slashing, feeling both love and hate, and then later, when it was full dark, he sat at the bottom of his foxhole and wept. It went on for a long while. In part, he was grieving for Ted Lavender, but mostly it was for Martha, and for himself, because she belonged to another world, which was not quite real, and because she was a junior at Mount Sebastian College in New Jersey, a poet and a virgin and uninvolved, and because he realized she did not love him and never would.

Like cement, Kiowa whispered in the dark. I swear to God — boom-down. Not a word.

I've heard this, said Norman Bowker.

A pisser, you know? Still zipping himself up. Zapped while zipping.

All right, fine. That's enough.

Yeah, but you had to see it, the guy just —

I *heard,* man. Cement. So why not shut the fuck *up?*

Kiowa shook his head sadly and glanced over at the hole where Lieutenant Jimmy Cross sat watching the night. The air was thick and wet. A warm, dense fog had settled over the paddies and there was the stillness that precedes rain.

After a time Kiowa sighed.

One thing for sure, he said. The Lieutenant's in some deep hurt. I mean that crying jag — the way he was carrying on — it wasn't fake or anything, it was real heavy-duty hurt. The man cares.

Sure, Norman Bowker said.

Say what you want, the man does care.

We all got problems.

Not Lavender.

No, I guess not, Bowker said. Do me a favor, though.

Shut up?

That's a smart Indian. Shut up.

Shrugging, Kiowa pulled off his boots. He wanted to say more, just to lighten up his sleep, but instead he opened his New Testament and arranged it beneath his head as a pillow. The fog made things seem hollow and unattached. He tried not to think about Ted Lavender, but then he was thinking how fast it was, no drama, down and dead, and how it was hard to feel anything except surprise. It seemed un-Christian. He wished he could find some great sadness, or even anger, but the emotion wasn't there and he couldn't make it happen. Mostly he felt pleased to be alive. He liked the smell of the New Testament under his cheek, the leather and ink and paper and glue, whatever the chemicals were. He liked hearing the sounds of night. Even his fatigue, it felt fine, the stiff muscles and the prickly awareness of his own body, a floating feeling. He enjoyed not being dead. Lying there, Kiowa admired Lieutenant Jimmy Cross's capacity for grief. He wanted to share the man's pain, he wanted to care as Jimmy Cross cared. And yet when he closed his eyes, all he could think was Boom-down, and all he could feel was the pleasure of having his boots off and the fog curling in around him and the damp soil and the Bible smells and the plush comfort of night.

After a moment Norman Bowker sat up in the dark.

What the hell, hc said. You want to talk, *talk*. Tell it to me.

Forget it.

No, man, go on. One thing I hate, it's a silent Indian.

For the most part they carried themselves with poise, a kind of dignity. Now and then, however, there were times of panic, when they squealed or wanted to squeal but couldn't, when they twitched and made moaning sounds and covered their heads and said Dear Jesus and flopped around on the earth and fired their weapons blindly and cringed and sobbed and begged for the noise to stop and went wild and made stupid promises to themselves and to God and to their mothers and fathers, hoping not to die. In different ways, it happened to all of them. Afterward, when the firing ended, they would blink and peek up. They would touch their bodies, feeling shame, then quickly hiding it. They would force themselves to stand. As if in slow motion, frame by frame, the world would take on the old logic — absolute silence, then the wind, then sunlight, then voices. It was the burden of being alive. Awkwardly, the men would reassemble themselves, first in private, then in groups, becoming soldiers again. They would repair the leaks in their eyes. They would check for casualties, call in dust-offs, light cigarettes, try to smile, clear their throats and spit and begin cleaning their weapons. After a time someone would shake his head and say, No lie, I almost shit my pants, and someone else would laugh, which meant it was bad, yes, but the guy had obviously not shit his pants, it wasn't that bad, and in any case nobody would ever do such a thing and then go ahead and talk about it. They would squint into the dense, oppressive sunlight. For a few moments, perhaps, they would fall silent, lighting a joint and tracking its passage from man to man, inhaling, holding in the humiliation. Scary stuff, one of them might say. But then someone else would grin or flick his eyebrows and say, Roger-dodger, almost cut me a new asshole, *almost*.

There were numerous such poses. Some carried themselves with a sort of wistful resignation, others with pride or stiff soldierly discipline or good humor or macho zeal. They were afraid of dying but they were even more afraid to show it.

They found jokes to tell.

They used a hard vocabulary to contain the terrible softness. *Greased,* they'd say. *Offed, lit up, zapped while zipping.* It wasn't cruelty, just stage presence. They were actors and the war came at them in 3-D. When someone died, it wasn't quite dying, because in a curious way it seemed scripted, and because they had their lines mostly memorized, irony mixed with tragedy, and because they called it by other names, as if to encyst and destroy the reality of death itself. They kicked corpses. They cut off thumbs. They talked grunt lingo. They told stories about Ted Lavender's supply of tranquilizers, how the poor guy didn't feel a thing, how incredibly tranquil he was.

There's a moral here, said Mitchell Sanders.

They were waiting for Lavender's chopper, smoking the dead man's dope.

The moral's pretty obvious, Sanders said, and winked. Stay away from drugs. No joke, they'll ruin your day every time.

Cute, said Henry Dobbins.

Mind-blower, get it? Talk about wiggy — nothing left, just blood and brains.

They made themselves laugh.

There it is, they'd say, over and over, as if the repetition itself were an act of poise, a balance between crazy and almost crazy, knowing without going. There it is, which meant be cool, let it ride, because oh yeah, man, you can't change what can't be changed, there it is, there it absolutely and positively and fucking well *is*.

They were tough.

They carried all the emotional baggage of men who might die. Grief, terror, love, longing — these were intangibles, but the intangibles had their own mass and specific gravity, they had tangible weight. They carried shameful memories. They carried the common secret of cowardice barely restrained, the instinct to run or freeze or hide, and in many respects this was the heaviest burden of all, for it could never be put down, it required perfect balance and perfect posture. They carried their reputations. They carried the soldier's greatest fear, which was the fear of blushing. Men killed, and died, because they were embarrassed not to. It was what had brought them to the war in the first place, nothing positive, no dreams of glory or honor, just to avoid the blush of dishonor. They died so as not to die of embarrassment. They crawled into tunnels and walked point and advanced under fire. Each morning, despite the unknowns, they made their legs move. They endured. They kept humping. They did not submit to the obvious alternative, which was simply to close the eyes and fall. So easy, really. Go limp and tumble to the ground and let the muscles unwind and not speak and not budge until your buddies picked you up and lifted you into the chopper that would roar and dip its nose and carry you off to the world. A mere matter of falling, yet no one ever fell. It was not courage, exactly; the object was not valor. Rather, they were too frightened to be cowards.

By and large they carried these things inside, maintaining the masks of composure. They sneered at sick call. They spoke bitterly about guys who had found release by shooting off their own toes or fingers. Pussies, they'd say. Candyasses. It was fierce, mocking talk, with only a trace of envy or awe, but even so, the image played itself out behind their eyes.

They imagined the muzzle against flesh. They imagined the quick, sweet pain, then the evacuation to Japan, then a hospital with warm beds and cute geisha nurses.

They dreamed of freedom birds.

At night, on guard, staring into the dark, they were carried away by jumbo jets. They felt the rush of takeoff. *Gone!* they yelled. And then velocity, wings and engines, a smiling stewardess — but it was more than a plane, it was a real bird, a big sleek silver bird with feathers and talons and high screeching. They were flying. The weights fell off, there was nothing to bear. They laughed and held on tight, feeling the cold slap of wind and altitude, soaring, thinking *It's over, I'm gone!* — they were naked, they were light and free — it was all lightness, bright and fast and buoyant, light as light, a helium buzz in the brain, a giddy bubbling in the lungs as they were taken up over the clouds and the war, beyond duty, beyond gravity and mortification and global entanglements — *Sin loi!* they yelled, *I'm sorry, motherfuckers, but I'm out of it, I'm goofed, I'm on a space cruise, I'm gone!* — and it was a restful, disencumbered sensation, just riding the light waves, sailing that big silver freedom bird over the mountains and oceans, over America, over the farms and great sleeping cities and cemeteries and highways and the golden arches of McDonald's. It was flight, a kind of fleeing, a kind of falling, falling higher and higher, spinning off the edge of the earth and beyond the sun and through the vast, silent vacuum where there were no burdens and where everything weighed exactly nothing. *Gone!* they screamed, *I'm sorry but I'm gone!* And so at night, not quite dreaming, they gave themselves over to lightness, they were carried, they were purely borne.

On the morning after Ted Lavender died, First Lieutenant Jimmy Cross crouched at the bottom of his foxhole and burned Martha's letters. Then he burned the two photographs. There was a steady rain falling, which made it difficult, but he used heat tabs and Sterno to build a small fire, screening it with his body, holding the photographs over the tight blue flame with the tips of his fingers.

He realized it was only a gesture. Stupid, he thought. Sentimental, too, but mostly just stupid.

Lavender was dead. You couldn't burn the blame.

Besides, the letters were in his head. And even now, without photographs, Lieutenant Cross could see Martha playing volleyball in her white gym shorts and yellow T-shirt. He could see her moving in the rain.

When the fire died out, Lieutenant Cross pulled his poncho over his shoulders and ate breakfast from a can.

There was no great mystery, he decided.

In those burned letters Martha had never mentioned the war, except to say, Jimmy, take care of yourself. She wasn't involved. She signed the letters "Love," but it wasn't love, and all the fine lines and technicalities did not matter.

The morning came up wet and blurry. Everything seemed part of everything else, the fog and Martha and the deepening rain.

It was a war, after all.

Half smiling, Lieutenant Jimmy Cross took out his maps. He shook his head hard, as if to clear it, then bent forward and began planning the day's march. In ten minutes, or maybe twenty, he would rouse the men and they would pack up and head west, where the maps showed the country to be green and inviting. They would do what they had always done. The rain might add some weight, but otherwise it would be one more day layered upon all the other days.

He was realistic about it. There was that new hardness in his stomach.

No more fantasies, he told himself.

Henceforth, when he thought about Martha, it would be only to think that she belonged elsewhere. He would shut down the daydreams. This was not Mount Sebastian, it was another world, where there were no pretty poems or midterm exams, a place where men died because of carelessness and gross stupidity. Kiowa was right. Boom down, and you were dead, never partly dead.

Briefly, in the rain, Lieutenant Cross saw Martha's gray eyes gazing back at him.

He understood.

It was very sad, he thought. The things men carried inside. The things men did or felt they had to do.

He almost nodded at her, but didn't.

Instead he went back to his maps. He was now determined to perform his duties firmly and without negligence. It wouldn't help Lavender, he knew that, but from this point on he would comport himself as a soldier. He would dispose of his good-luck pebble. Swallow it, maybe, or use Lee Strunk's slingshot, or just drop it along the trail. On the march he would impose strict field discipline. He would be careful to send out flank security, to prevent straggling or bunching up, to keep his troops moving at the proper pace and at the proper interval. He would insist on clean weapons. He would confiscate the remainder of Lavender's dope. Later in the day, perhaps, he would call the men together and speak to them plainly. He would accept the blame for what had happened to Ted Lavender. He would be a man about it. He would look them in the eyes, keeping his chin level, and would issue the new SOPs in a calm, impersonal tone of voice, an officer's voice, leaving no room for argument or discussion. Commencing immediately, he'd tell them, they would no longer abandon equipment along the route of march. They would police up their acts. They would get their shit together, and keep it together, and maintain it neatly and in good working order.

He would not tolerate laxity. He would show strength, distancing himself.

Among the men there would be grumbling, of course, and maybe worse, because their days would seem longer and their loads heavier, but Lieutenant Cross reminded himself that his obligation was not to be loved but to lead. He would dispense with love; it was not now a factor. And if anyone quarreled or complained, he would simply tighten his lips and arrange his shoulders in the correct command posture. He might give a curt little nod. Or he might not. He might just shrug and say Carry on, then they would saddle up and form into a column and move out toward the villages of Than Khe.

FLANNERY O'CONNOR

Flannery O'Connor (1925–1964) was born in Milledgeville, Georgia, and lived in that town and its environs all her brief life. She suffered from lupus, an incurable, crippling hereditary disease. Having to endure that illness may have been one source of O'Connor's fervid imagination — an imagination she unleashed in stories that are, in the words of Irish novelist Brian Moore, "comic and terrible, poignant and brutal." An even more cogent source was certainly her devoutly held Catholicism. O'Connor explained her writing this way: "I write the way I do because I am a Catholic. There is nothing harder or less sentimental than Christian realism. I believe that there are now many rough hearts slouching towards Bethlehem to be born and I have reported the progress of a few of them." Indeed, in O'Connor's fictive world "things fall apart; the center cannot hold." To carry her meaning, she chose a method: distortion. "I am interested in making a good case for distortion as I am coming to believe it is the only way to make people see," she wrote. She was — again in the words of Brian Moore — "an Old Testament prophet, crying out in our modern wilderness," making us see the decline of faith, the intensification of cruelty, the insurmountability of evil. In unforgettable stories — collected in *A Good Man Is Hard to Find* (1955) and *Everything That Rises Must Converge* (1965) — and in her novels, *Wise Blood* (1952) and *The Violent Bear It Away* (1960), she trained her moral vision on the condition of our lives and souls. In the two stories here, "The Artificial Nigger" and "A Good Man Is Hard to Find," we find ourselves in the heart of O'Connor country, examining betrayal and cruel happenstance.

The Artificial Nigger

Mr. Head awakened to discover that the room was full of moonlight. He sat up and stared at the floor boards — the color of silver — and then at the ticking on his pillow, which might have been brocade, and after a second, he saw half of the moon five feet away in his shaving mirror, paused as if it were waiting for his permission to enter. It rolled forward and cast a dignifying light on everything. The straight chair against the wall looked stiff and attentive as if it were awaiting an order and Mr. Head's trousers, hanging to the back of it, had an almost noble air, like the garment some great man had just flung to his servant; but the face on the moon was a grave one. It gazed across the room and out the window where it floated over the horse stall and appeared to contemplate itself with the look of a young man who sees his old age before him.

Mr. Head could have said to it that age was a choice blessing and that only with years does a man enter into that calm understanding of life that makes him a suitable guide for the young. This, at least, had been his own experience.

He sat up and grasped the iron posts at the foot of his bed and raised himself until he could see the face on the alarm clock which sat on an overturned bucket beside the chair. The hour was two in the morning. The alarm on the clock did not work but he was not dependent on any mechanical means to awaken him. Sixty years had not dulled his responses; his physical reactions, like his moral ones, were guided by his will and strong character, and these could be seen plainly in his features. He had a long tube-like face with a long rounded open jaw and a long depressed nose. His eyes were alert but quiet, and in the miraculous moonlight they had a look of composure and of ancient wisdom as if they belonged to one of the great guides of men. He might have been Vergil summoned in the middle of the night to go to Dante, or better, Raphael, awakened by a blast of God's light to fly to the side of Tobias. The only dark spot in the room was Nelson's pallet, underneath the shadow of the window.

Nelson was hunched over on his side, his knees under his chin and his heels under his bottom. His new suit and hat were in the boxes that they had been sent in and these were on the floor at the foot of the pallet where he could get his hands on them as soon as he woke up. The slop jar, out of the shadow and made snow-white in the moonlight, appeared to stand guard over him like a small personal angel. Mr. Head lay back down, feeling entirely confident that he could carry out the moral mission of the coming day. He meant to be up before Nelson and to have the breakfast cooking by the time he awakened. The boy was always irked when Mr. Head was the first up. They would have to leave the house at four to get to the railroad junction by five-thirty. The train was to stop for them at five forty-five and they had to be there on time for this train was stopping merely to accommodate them.

This would be the boy's first trip to the city though he claimed it would be his second because he had been born there. Mr. Head had tried to point out to him that when he was born he didn't have the intelligence to determine his whereabouts but this had made no impression on the child at all and he continued to insist that this was to be his second trip. It would be Mr. Head's third trip. Nelson had said, "I will've already been there twict and I ain't but ten."

Mr. Head had contradicted him.

"If you ain't been there in fifteen years, how you know you'll be able to find your way about?" Nelson had asked. "How you know it hasn't changed some?"

"Have you ever," Mr. Head had asked, "seen me lost?"

Nelson certainly had not but he was a child who was never satisfied until he had given an impudent answer and he replied, "It's nowhere around here to get lost at."

"The day is going to come," Mr. Head prophesied, "when you'll find you ain't as smart as you think you are." He had been thinking about this trip for several months but it was for the most part in moral terms that he conceived it. It was to be a lesson that the boy would never forget. He was to find out from it that he had no cause for pride merely because he had been born in a city. He was to find out that the city is not a great place. Mr. Head meant him to see everything there is to see in a city so that he would be content to stay at home for the rest of his life. He fell asleep thinking how the boy would at last find out that he was not as smart as he thought he was.

He was awakened at three-thirty by the smell of fatback frying and he leaped off his cot. The pallet was empty and the clothes boxes had been thrown open. He put on his trousers and ran into the other room. The boy had a corn pone on cooking and had fried the meat. He was sitting in the half-dark at the table, drinking cold coffee out of a can. He had on his new suit and his new gray hat pulled low over his eyes. It was too big for him but they had ordered it a size large because they expected his head to grow. He didn't say anything but his entire figure suggested satisfaction at having arisen before Mr. Head.

Mr. Head went to the stove and brought the meat to the table in the skillet. "It's no hurry," he said. "You'll get there soon enough and it's no guarantee you'll like it when you do neither," and he sat down across from the boy whose hat teetered back slowly to reveal a fiercely expressionless face, very much the same shape as the old man's. They were grandfather and grandson but they looked enough alike to be brothers and brothers not too far apart in age, for Mr. Head had a youthful expression by daylight, while the boy's look was ancient, as if he knew everything already and would be pleased to forget it.

Mr. Head had once had a wife and daughter and when the wife died, the daughter ran away and returned after an interval with Nelson. Then one morning, without geting out of bed, she died and left Mr. Head with sole care of the year-old child. He had made the mistake of telling Nelson that he had been born in Atlanta. If he hadn't told him that, Nelson couldn't have insisted that this was going to be his second trip.

"You may not like it a bit," Mr. Head continued. "It'll be full of niggers."

The boy made a face as if he could handle a nigger.

"All right," Mr. Head said. "You ain't ever seen a nigger."

"You wasn't up very early," Nelson said.

"You ain't ever seen a nigger," Mr. Head repeated. "There hasn't been a nigger in this county since we run that one out twelve years ago and that was before you were born." He looked at the boy as if he were daring him to say he had ever seen a Negro.

"How you know I never saw a nigger when I lived there before?" Nelson asked. "I probably saw a lot of niggers."

"If you seen one you didn't know what he was," Mr. Head said, completely exasperated. "A six-month-old child don't know a nigger from anybody else."

"I reckon I'll know a nigger if I see one," the boy said and got up and straightened his slick sharply creased gray hat and went outside to the privy.

They reached the junction some time before the train was due to arrive and stood about two feet from the first set of tracks. Mr. Head carried a paper sack with some biscuits and a can of sardines in it for their lunch. A coarse-looking orange-colored sun coming up behind the east range of mountains was making the sky a dull red behind them, but in front of them it was still gray and they faced a gray transparent moon, hardly stronger than a thumbprint and completely without light. A small tin switch box and a black fuel tank were all there was to mark the place as a junction; the tracks were double and did not converge again until they were hidden behind the bends at either end of the clearing. Trains passing appeared to emerge from a tunnel of trees and, hit for a second by the cold sky, vanish terrified into the woods again. Mr. Head had had to make special arrangements with the ticket agent to have this train stop and he was secretly afraid it would not, in which case, he knew Nelson would say, "I never thought no train was going to stop for you." Under the useless morning moon the tracks looked white and fragile. Both the old man and the child stared ahead as if they were awaiting an apparition.

Then suddenly, before Mr. Head could make up his mind to turn back, there was a deep warning bleat and the train appeared, gliding very slowly, almost silently around the bend of trees about two hundred yards down the track, with one yellow front light shining. Mr. Head was still not certain it would stop and he felt it would make an even bigger idiot of him if it went by slowly. Both he and Nelson, however, were prepared to ignore the train if it passed them.

The engine charged by, filling their noses with the smell of hot metal and then the second coach came to a stop exactly where they were standing. A conductor with the face of an ancient bloated bulldog was on the step as if he expected them, though he did not look as if it mattered one way or the other to him if they got on or not. "To the right," he said.

Their entry took only a fraction of a second and the train was already speeding on as they entered the quiet car. Most of the travelers were still sleeping, some with their heads hanging off the chair arms, some stretched across two seats, and some sprawled out with their feet in the aisle. Mr. Head saw two unoccupied seats and pushed Nelson toward them. "Get in there by the winder," he said in his normal voice which was very loud at this hour of the morning. "Nobody cares if you sit there because it's nobody in it. Sit right there."

"I heard you," the boy muttered. "It's no use in you yelling," and he sat down and turned his head to the glass. There he saw a pale ghost like face scowling at him beneath the brim of a pale ghost-like hat. His grandfather, looking quickly too, saw a different ghost, pale but grinning, under a black hat.

Mr. Head sat down and settled himself and took out his ticket and started reading aloud everything that was printed on it. People began to stir. Several woke up and stared at him. "Take off your hat," he said to Nelson and took off his own and put it on his knee. He had a small amount of white hair that had turned tobacco-colored over the years and this lay flat across the back of his head. The front of his head was bald and creased. Nelson took off his hat and put it on his knee and they waited for the conductor to come ask for their tickets.

The man across the aisle from them was spread out over two seats, his feet propped on the window and his head jutting into the aisle. He had on a light blue suit and a yellow shirt unbuttoned at the neck. His eyes had just opened and Mr. Head was ready to introduce himself when the conductor came up from behind and growled, "Tickets."

When the conductor had gone, Mr. Head gave Nelson the return half of his ticket and said, "Now put that in your pocket and don't lose it or you'll have to stay in the city."

"Maybe I will," Nelson said as if this were a reasonable suggestion.

Mr. Head ignored him. "First time this boy has ever been on a train," he explained to the man across the aisle, who was sitting up now on the edge of his seat with both feet on the floor.

Nelson jerked his hat on again and turned angrily to the window.

"He's never seen anything before," Mr. Head continued. "Ignorant as the day he was born, but I mean for him to get his fill once and for all."

The boy leaned forward, across his grandfather and toward the stranger. "I was born in the city," he said. "I was born there. This is my second trip." He said it in a high positive voice but the man across the aisle didn't look as if he understood. There were heavy purple circles under his eyes.

Mr. Head reached across the aisle and tapped him on the arm. "The thing to do with a boy," he said sagely, "is to show him all it is to show. Don't hold nothing back."

"Yeah," the man said. He gazed down at his swollen feet and lifted the left one about ten inches from the floor. After a minute he put it down and lifted the other. All through the car people began to get up and move about and yawn and stretch. Separate voices could be heard here and there and then a general hum. Suddenly Mr. Head's serene expression changed. His mouth almost closed and a light, fierce and cautious both, came into his eyes. He was looking down the length of the car. Without turning, he caught Nelson by the arm and pulled him forward. "Look," he said.

A huge coffee-colored man was coming slowly forward. He had on a light suit and a yellow satin tie with a ruby pin in it. One of his hands rested on his stomach which rode majestically under his buttoned coat, and in the other he held the head of a black walking stick that he picked up and set down with a deliberate outward motion each time he took a step. He was proceeding very slowly, his large brown eyes gazing over the heads of the passengers. He had a small white mustache and white crinkly hair. Behind him there were two young women, both coffee-colored, one in a yellow dress and one in a green. Their progress was kept at the rate of his and they chatted in low throaty voices as they followed him.

Mr. Head's grip was tightening insistently on Nelson's arm. As the procession passed them, the light from a sapphire ring on the brown hand that picked up the cane reflected in Mr. Head's eye, but he did not look up nor did the tremendous man look at him. The group proceeded up the rest of the aisle and out of the car. Mr. Head's grip on Nelson's arm loosened. "What was that?" he asked.

"A man," the boy said and gave him an indignant look as if he were tired of having his intelligence insulted.

"What kind of a man?" Mr. Head persisted, his voice expressionless.

"A fat man," Nelson said. He was beginning to feel that he had better be cautious.

"You don't know what kind?" Mr. Head said in a final tone.

"An old man," the boy said and had a sudden foreboding that he was not going to enjoy the day.

"That was a nigger," Mr. Head said and sat back.

Nelson jumped up on the seat and stood looking backward to the end of the car but the Negro had gone.

"I'd of thought you'd know a nigger since you seen so many when you was in the city on your first visit," Mr. Head continued. "That's his first nigger," he said to the man across the aisle.

The boy slid down into the seat. "You said they were black," he said in an angry voice. "You never said they were tan. How do you expect me to know anything when you don't tell me right?"

"You're just ignorant is all," Mr. Head said and he got up and moved over in the vacant seat by the man across the aisle.

Nelson turned backward again and looked where the Negro had disappeared. He felt that the Negro had deliberately walked down the aisle in order to make a fool of him and he hated him with a fierce raw fresh hate; and also, he understood now why his grandfather disliked them. He looked toward the window and the face there seemed to suggest that he might be inadequate to the day's exactions. He wondered if he would even recognize the city when they came to it.

After he had told several stories, Mr. Head realized that the man he was talking to was asleep and he got up and suggested to Nelson that they walk over the train and see the parts of it. He particularly wanted the boy to see the toilet so they went first to the men's room and examined the plumbing. Mr. Head demonstrated the ice-water cooler as if he had invented it and showed Nelson the bowl with the single spigot where the travelers brushed their teeth. They went through several cars and came to the diner.

This was the most elegant car in the train. It was painted a rich egg-yellow and had a wine-colored carpet on the floor. There were wide windows over the tables and great spaces of the rolling view were caught in miniature in the sides of the coffee pots and in the glasses. Three very black Negroes in white suits and aprons were running up and down the aisle, swinging trays and bowing and bending over the travelers eating breakfast. One of them rushed up to Mr. Head and Nelson and said, holding up two fingers, "Space for two!" but Mr. Head replied in a loud voice, "We eaten before we left!"

The waiter wore large brown spectacles that increased the size of his eye whites. "Stan' aside then please," he said with an airy wave of the arm as if he were brushing aside flies.

Neither Nelson nor Mr. Head moved a fraction of an inch. "Look," Mr. Head said.

The near corner of the diner, containing two tables, was set off from the rest by a saffron-colored curtain. One table was set but empty but at the other, facing them, his back to the drape, sat the tremendous Negro. He was speaking in a soft voice to the two women while he buttered a muffin. He had a heavy sad face and his neck bulged over his white collar on either side. "They rope them off," Mr. Head explained. Then he said, "Let's go see the kitchen," and they walked the length of the diner but the black waiter was coming fast behind them.

"Passengers are not allowed in the kitchen!" he said in a haughty voice. "Passengers are NOT allowed in the kitchen!"

Mr. Head stopped where he was and turned. "And there's good reason for that," he shouted into the Negro's chest, "because the cockroaches would run the passengers out!"

All the travelers laughed and Mr. Head and Nelson walked out, grinning. Mr. Head was known at home for his quick wit and Nelson felt a sudden keen pride in him. He realized the old man would be his only support in the strange place they were approaching. He would be entirely alone in the world if he were ever lost from his grandfather. A terrible excitement shook him and he wanted to take hold of Mr. Head's coat and hold on like a child.

As they went back to their seats they could see through the passing windows that the countryside was becoming speckled with small houses and shacks and that a highway ran alongside the train. Cars sped by on it, very small and fast. Nelson felt that there was less breath in the air than there had been thirty minutes ago. The man across the aisle had left and there was no one near for Mr. Head to hold a conversation with so he looked out the window, through his own reflection, and read aloud the names of the buildings they were passing. "The Dixie Chemical Corp!" he announced. "Southern Maid Flour! Dixie Doors! Southern Belle Cotton Products! Patty's Peanut Butter! Southern Mammy Cane Syrup!"

"Hush up!" Nelson hissed.

All over the car people were beginning to get up and take their luggage off the overhead racks. Women were putting on their coats and hats. The conductor stuck his head in the car and snarled, "Firstopppppmry," and Nelson lunged out of his sitting position, trembling. Mr. Head pushed him down by the shoulder.

"Keep your seat," he said in dignified tones. "The first stop is on the edge of town. The second stop is at the main railroad station." He had come by this knowledge on his first trip when he had got off at the first stop and had had to pay a man fifteen cents to take him into the heart of town. Nelson sat back down, very pale. For the first time in his life, he understood that his grandfather was indispensable to him.

The train stopped and let off a few passengers and glided on as if it had never ceased moving. Outside, behind rows of brown rickety houses, a line of blue buildings stood up, and beyond them a pale rose-gray sky faded away to nothing. The train moved into the railroad yard. Looking down, Nelson saw lines and lines of silver tracks multiplying and criss-crossing. Then before he could start counting them, the face in the window started out at him, gray but distinct, and he looked the other way. The train was in the station. Both he and Mr. Head jumped up and ran to the door. Neither noticed that they had left the paper sack with the lunch in it on the seat.

They walked stiffly through the small station and came out of a heavy door into the squall of traffic. Crowds were hurrying to work. Nelson didn't know where to look. Mr. Head leaned against the side of the building and glared in front of him.

Finally Nelson said, "Well, how do you see what all it is to see?"

Mr. Head didn't answer. Then as if the sight of people passing had given him the clue, he said, "You walk," and started off down the street. Nelson followed, steadying his hat. So many sights and sounds were flooding in on him that for the first block he hardly knew what he was seeing. At the second corner, Mr. Head turned and looked behind him at the station they had left, a putty-colored terminal with a concrete dome on top. He thought that if he could keep the dome always in sight, he would be able to get back in the afternoon to catch the train again.

As they walked along, Nelson began to distinguish details and take note of the store windows, jammed with every kind of equipment — hardware, drygoods, chicken feed, liquor. They passed one that Mr. Head called his particular attention to where you walked in and sat on a chair with your feet upon two rests and let a Negro polish your shoes. They walked slowly and stopped and stood at the entrances so he could see what went on in each place but they did not go into any of them. Mr. Head was determined not to go into any city store because on his first trip here, he had got lost in a large one and had found his way out only after many people had insulted him.

They came in the middle of the next block to a store that had a weighing machine in front of it and they both in turn stepped up on it and put in a penny and received a ticket. Mr. Head's ticket said, "You weigh 120 pounds. You are upright and brave and all your friends admire you." He put the ticket in his pocket, surprised that the machine should have got his character correct but his weight wrong, for he had weighed on a grain scale not long before and knew he weighed 110. Nelson's ticket said, "You weigh 98 pounds. You have a great destiny ahead of you but beware of dark women." Nelson did not know any women and he weighed only 68 pounds but Mr. Head pointed out that the machine had probably printed the number upside down, meaning the 9 for a 6.

They walked on and at the end of five blocks the dome of the terminal sank out of sight and Mr. Head turned to the left. Nelson could have stood in front of every store window for an hour if there had not been another more interesting one next to it. Suddenly he said, "I was born here!" Mr. Head turned and looked at him with horror. There was a sweaty brightness about his face. "This is where I come from!" he said.

Mr. Head was appalled. He saw the moment had come for drastic action. "Lemme show you one thing you ain't seen yet," he said and took him to the corner where there was a sewer entrance. "Squat down," he said, "and stick you head in there," and he held the back of the boy's coat while he got down and put his head in the sewer. He drew it back quickly, hearing a gurgling in the depths under the sidewalk. Then Mr. Head explained the sewer system, how the entire city was underlined with it, how it contained all the drainage and was full of rats and how a man could slide into it and be sucked along down endless pitchblack tunnels. At any minute any man in the city might be sucked into the sewer and never heard from again. He described it so well that Nelson was for some seconds shaken. He connected the sewer passages with the entrance to hell and understood for the first time how the world was put together in its lower parts. He drew away from the curb.

Then he said, "Yes, but you can stay away from the holes," and his face took on the stubborn look that was so exasperating to his grandfather. "This is where I come from!" he said.

Mr. Head was dismayed but he only muttered, "You'll get your fill," and they walked on. At the end of two more blocks he turned to the left, feeling that he was circling the dome; and he was correct for in a half-hour they passed in front of the railroad station again. At first Nelson did not notice that he was seeing the same stores twice but when they passed the one where you put your feet on the rests while the Negro polished your shoes, he perceived that they were walking in a circle.

"We done been here!" he shouted. "I don't believe you know where you're at!"

"The direction just slipped my mind for a minute," Mr. Head said and they turned down a different street. He still did not intend to let the dome get too far away and after two blocks in their new direction, he turned to the left. This street contained two and three-story wooden dwellings. Anyone passing on the sidewalk could see into the rooms and Mr. Head, glancing through one window, saw a woman lying on an iron bed, looking out, with a sheet pulled over her. Her knowing expression shook him. A fierce-looking boy on a bicycle came driving down out of nowhere and he had to jump to the side to keep from being hit. "It's nothing to them if they knock you down," he said. "You better keep closer to me."

They walked on for some time on streets like this before he remembered to turn again. The houses they were passing now were all unpainted and the wood in them looked rotten; the street between was narrower. Nelson saw a colored man. Then another. Then another. "Niggers live in these houses," he observed.

"Well come on and we'll go somewheres else," Mr. Head said. "We didn't come to look at niggers," and they turned down another street but they continued to see Negroes everywhere. Nelson's skin began to prickle and they stepped along at a faster pace in order to leave the neighborhood as soon as possible. There were colored men in their undershirts standing in the doors and colored women rocking on the sagging porches. Colored children played in the gutters and stopped what they were doing to look at them. Before long they began to pass rows of stores with colored customers in them but they didn't pause at the entrances of these. Black eyes in black faces were watching them from every direction. "Yes," Mr. Head said, "this is where you were born — right here with all these niggers."

Nelson scowled. "I think you done got us lost," he said.

Mr. Head swung around sharply and looked for the dome. It was nowhere in sight. "I ain't got us lost either," he said. "You're just tired of walking."

"I ain't tired, I'm hungry," Nelson said. "Give me a biscuit."

They discovered then that they had lost the lunch.

"You were the one holding the sack," Nelson said. "I would have kepaholt of it."

"If you want to direct this trip, I'll go on by myself and leave you right here," Mr. Head said and was pleased to see the boy turn white. However, he realized they were lost and drifting farther every minute from the station. He was hungry himself and beginning to be thirsty and since they had been in the colored neighborhood, they had both begun to sweat. Nelson had on his shoes and he was unaccustomed to them. The concrete sidewalks were very hard. They both wanted to find a place to sit down but this was impossible and they kept on walking, the boy muttering under his breath, "First you lost the sack and then you lost the way," and Mr. Head growling from time to time, "Anybody wants to be from this nigger heaven can be from it!"

By now the sun was well forward in the sky. The odor of dinners cooking drifted out to them. The Negroes were all at their doors to see them pass. "Whyn't you ast one of these niggers the way?" Nelson said. "You got us lost."

"This is where you were born," Mr. Head said. "You can ast one yourself if you want to."

Nelson was afraid of the colored men and he didn't want to be laughed at by the colored children. Up ahead he saw a large colored woman leaning in a doorway that opened onto the sidewalk. Her hair stood straight out from her head for about four inches all around and she was resting on bare brown feet that turned pink at the sides. She had on a pink dress that showed her exact shape. As they came abreast of her, she lazily lifted one hand to her head and her fingers disappeared into her hair.

Nelson stopped. He felt his breath drawn up by the woman's dark eyes. "How do you get back to town?" he said in a voice that did not sound like his own.

After a minute she said, "You in town now," in a rich low tone that made Nelson feel as if a cool spray had been turned on him.

"How do you get back to the train?" he said in the same reed-like voice.

"You can catch you a car," she said.

He understood she was making fun of him but he was too paralyzed even to scowl. He stood drinking in every detail of her. His eyes traveled up from her great knees to her forehead and then made a triangular path from the glistening sweat on her neck down and across her tremendous bosom and over her bare arm back to where her fingers lay hidden in her hair. He suddenly wanted her to reach down and pick him up and draw him against her and then he wanted to feel her breath on his face. He wanted to look down and down into her eyes while she held him tighter and tighter. He had never had such a feeling before. He felt as if he were reeling down through a pitchblack tunnel.

"You can go a block down yonder and catch you a car take you to the railroad station, Sugarpie," she said.

Nelson would have collapsed at her feet if Mr. Head had not pulled him roughly away. "You act like you don't have any sense!" the old man growled.

They hurried down the street and Nelson did not look back at the woman. He pushed his hat sharply forward over his face which was already burning with shame. The sneering ghost he had seen in the train window and all the foreboding feelings he had on the way returned to him and he remembered that his ticket from the scale had said to beware of dark women and that his grandfather had said he was upright and brave. He took hold of the old man's hand, a sign of dependence that he seldom showed.

They headed down the street toward the car tracks where a long yellow rattling trolley was coming. Mr. Head had never boarded a streetcar and he let that one pass. Nelson was silent. From time to time his mouth trembled slightly but his grandfather, occupied with his own problems, paid him no attention. They stood on the corner and neither looked at the Negroes who were passing, going about their business just as if they had been white, except that most of them stopped and eyed Mr. Head and Nelson. It occurred to Mr. Head that since the streetcar ran on tracks, they could simply follow the tracks. He gave Nelson a slight push and explained that they would follow the tracks on into the railroad station, walking, and they set off.

Presently to their great relief they began to see white people again and Nelson sat down on the sidewalk against the wall of a building. "I got to rest myself some," he said. "You lost the sack and the direction. You can just wait on me to rest myself."

"There's the tracks in front of us," Mr. Head said. "All we got to do is keep them in sight and you could have remembered the sack as good as me. This is where you were born. This is your old home town. This is your second trip. You ought to know how to do," and he squatted down and continued in this vein but the boy, easing his burning feet out of his shoes, did not answer.

"And standing their grinning like a chim-pan-zee while a nigger woman gives you direction. Great Gawd!" Mr. Head said.

"I never said I was nothing but born here," the boy said in a shaky voice. "I never said I would or wouldn't like it. I never said I wanted to come. I only said I was born here and I never had nothing to do with that. I want to go home. I never wanted to come in the first place. It was all your big idea. How you know you ain't following the tracks in the wrong direction?"

This last had occurred to Mr. Head too. "All these people are white," he said.

"We ain't passed here before," Nelson said. This was a neighborhood of brick buildings that might have been lived in or might not. A few empty automobiles were parked along the curb and there was an occasional passerby. The heat of the pavement came up through Nelson's thin suit. His eyelids began to droop, and after a few minutes his head tilted forward. His shoulders twitched once or twice and then he fell over on his side and lay sprawled in an exhausted fit of sleep.

Mr. Head watched him silently. He was very tired himself but they could not both sleep at the same time and he could not have slept anyway because he did not know where he was. In a few minutes Nelson would wake up, refreshed by his sleep and very cocky, and would begin complaining that he had lost the sack and the way. You'd have a mighty sorry time if I wasn't here, Mr. Head thought; and then another idea occurred to him. He looked at the sprawled figure for several minutes; presently he stood up. He justified what he was going to do on the grounds that it is sometimes necessary to teach a child a lesson he won't forget, particularly when the child is always reasserting his position with some new impudence. He walked without a sound to the corner about twenty feet away and sat down on a covered garbage can in the alley where he could look out and watch Nelson wake up alone.

The boy was dozing fitfully, half conscious of vague noises and black forms moving up from some dark part of him into the light. His face worked in his sleep and he had pulled his knees under his chin. The sun shed a dull dry light on the narrow street; everything looked like exactly what it was. After a while Mr. Head, hunched like an old monkey on the garbage can lid, decided that if Nelson didn't wake up soon, he would make a loud noise by bamming his foot against the can. He looked at his watch and discovered that it was two o'clock. Their train left at six and the possibility of missing it was too awful for him to think of. He kicked his foot backwards on the can and a hollow boom reverberated in the alley.

Nelson shot up onto his feet with a shout. He looked where his grandfather should have been and stared. He seemed to whirl several times and then, picking up his feet and throwing his head back, he dashed down the street like a wild maddened pony. Mr. Head jumped off the can and galloped after but the child was almost out of sight. He saw a streak of gray disappearing diagonally a block ahead. He ran as fast as he could, looking both ways down every intersection, but without sight of him again. Then as he passed the third intersection, completely winded, he saw about half a block down the street a scene that stopped him altogether. He crouched behind a trash box to watch and get his bearings.

Nelson was sitting with both legs spread out and by his side lay an elderly woman, screaming. Groceries were scattered about the sidewalk. A crowd of women had already gathered to see justice done and Mr. Head distinctly heard the old woman on the pavement shout, "You've broken my ankle and your daddy'll pay for it! Every nickel! Police! Police!" Several of the women were plucking at Nelson's shoulder but the boy seemed too dazed to get up.

Something forced Mr. Head from behind the trash box and forward, but only at a creeping pace. He had never in his life been accosted by a policeman. The women were milling around Nelson as if they might suddenly all dive on him at once and tear him to pieces, and the old woman continued to scream that her ankle was broken and to call for an officer. Mr. Head came on so slowly that he could have been taking a backward step after each forward one, but when he was about ten feet away, Nelson saw him and sprang. The child caught him around the hips and clung panting against him.

The women all turned on Mr. Head. The injured one sat up and shouted, "You sir! You'll pay every penny of my doctor's bill that your boy has caused. He's a juve-nile delinquent! Where is an officer? Somebody take this man's name and address!"

Mr. Head was trying to detach Nelson's fingers from the flesh in the back of his legs. The old man's head had lowered itself into his collar like a turtle's; his eyes were glazed with fear and caution.

"Your boy has broken my ankle!" the old woman shouted. "Police!"

Mr. Head sensed the approach of the policeman from behind. He stared straight ahead at the women who were massed in their fury like a solid wall to block his escape. "This is not my boy," he said. "I never seen him before."

He felt Nelson's fingers fall out of his flesh.

The women dropped back, staring at him with horror, as if they were so repulsed by a man who would deny his own image and likeness that they could not bear to lay hands on him. Mr. Head walked on, through a space they silently cleared, and left Nelson behind. Ahead of him he saw nothing but a hollow tunnel that had once been the street.

The boy remained standing where he was, his neck craned forward and his hands hanging by his sides. His hat was jammed on his head so that there were no longer any creases in it. The injured woman got up and shook her fist at him and the others gave him pitying looks, but he didn't notice any of them. There was no policeman in sight.

In a minute he began to move mechanically, making no effort to catch up with his grandfather but merely following at about twenty paces. They walked on for five blocks in this way. Mr. Head's shoulders were sagging and his neck hung forward at such an angle that it was not visible from behind. He was afraid to turn his head. Finally he cut a short hopeful glance over his shoulder. Twenty feet behind him, he saw too small eyes piercing into his back like pitchfork prongs.

The boy was not of a forgiving nature but this was the first time he had ever had anything to forgive. Mr. Head had never disgraced himself before. After two more blocks, he turned and called over his shoulder in a high desperately gay voice, "Let's us go get a Co' Cola somewheres!"

Nelson, with a dignity he had never shown before, turned and stood with his back to his grandfather.

Mr. Head began to feel the depth of his denial. His face as they walked on became all hollows and bare ridges. He saw nothing they were passing but he perceived that they had lost the car tracks. There was no dome to be seen anywhere and the afternoon was advancing. He knew that if dark overtook them in the city, they would be beaten and robbed. The speed of God's justice was only what he expected for himself, but he could not stand to think that his sins would be visited upon Nelson and that even now, he was leading the boy to his doom.

They continued to walk on block after block through an endless section of small brick houses until Mr. Head almost fell over a water spigot sticking up about six inches off the edge of a grass plot. He had not had a drink of water since early morning but he felt he did not deserve it now. Then he thought that Nelson would be thirsty and they would both drink and be brought together. He squatted down and put his mouth to the nozzle and turned a cold stream of water into his throat. Then he called out in the high desperate voice, "Come on and getcher some water!"

This time the child stared through him for nearly sixty seconds. Mr. Head got up and walked on as if he had drunk poison. Nelson, though he had not had water since some he had drunk out of a paper cup on the train, passed by the spigot, disdaining to drink where his grandfather had. When Mr. Head realized this, he lost all hope. His face in the waning afternoon light looked ravaged and abandoned. He could feel the boy's steady hate, traveling at an even pace behind him and he knew that (if by some miracle they escaped being murdered in the city) it would continue just that way for the rest of his life. He knew that now he was wandering into a black strange place where nothing was like it had ever been before, a long old age without respect and an end that would be welcome because it would be the end.

As for Nelson, his mind had frozen around his grandfather's treachery as if he were trying to preserve it intact to present at the final judgment. He walked without looking to one side or the other, but every now and then his mouth would twitch and this was when he felt, from some remote place inside himself, a black mysterious form reach up as if it would melt his frozen vision in one hot grasp.

The sun dropped down behind a row of houses and hardly noticing, they passed into an elegant suburban section where mansions were set back from the road by lawns with birdbaths on them. Here everything was entirely deserted. For blocks they didn't pass even a dog. The big white houses were like partially submerged icebergs in the distance. There were no sidewalks, only drives, and these wound around and around in endless ridiculous circles. Nelson made no move to come nearer to Mr. Head. The old man felt that if he saw a sewer entrance he would drop down into it and let himself be carried away; and he could imagine the boy standing by, watching with only a slight interest, while he disappeared.

A loud bark jarred him to attention and he looked up to see a fat man approaching with two bulldogs. He waved both arms like someone shipwrecked on a desert island. "I'm lost!" he called. "I'm lost and can't find my way and me and this boy have got to catch this train and I can't find the station. Oh Gawd I'm lost! Oh hep me Gawd I'm lost!"

The man, who was bald-headed and had on golf knickers, asked him what train he was trying to catch and Mr. Head began to get out his tickets, trembling so violently he could hardly hold them. Nelson had come up to within fifteen feet and stood watching.

"Well," the fat man said, giving him back the tickets, "you won't have time to get back to town to make this but you can catch it at the suburb stop. That's three blocks from here," and he began explaining how to get there.

Mr. Head stared as if he were slowly returning from the dead and when the man had finished and gone off with the dogs jumping at his heels, he turned to Nelson and said breathlessly, "We're going to get home!"

The child was standing about ten feet away, his face bloodless under the gray hat. His eyes were triumphantly cold. There was no light in them, no feeling, no interest. He was merely there, a small figure, waiting. Home was nothing to him.

Mr. Head turned slowly. He felt he knew now what time would be like without seasons and what heat would be like without light and what man would be like without salvation. He didn't care if he never made the train and if it had not been for what suddenly caught his attention, like a cry out of the gathering dusk, he might have forgotten there was a station to go to.

He had not walked five hundred yards down the road when he saw, within reach of him, the plaster figure of a Negro sitting bent over on a low yellow brick fence that curved around a wide lawn. The Negro was about Nelson's size and he was pitched forward at an unsteady angle because the putty that held him to the wall had cracked. One of his eyes was entirely white and he held a piece of brown watermelon.

Mr. Head stood looking at him silently until Nelson stopped at a little distance. Then as the two of them stood there, Mr. Head breathed, "An artificial nigger!"

It was not possible to tell if the artificial Negro were meant to be young or old; he looked too miserable to be either. He was meant to look happy because his mouth was stretched up at the corners but the chipped eye and the angle he was cocked at gave him a wild look of misery instead.

"An artificial nigger!" Nelson repeated in Mr. Head's exact tone.

The two of them stood there with their necks forward at almost the same angle and their shoulders curved in almost exactly the same way and their hands trembling identically in their pockets. Mr. Head looked like an ancient child and Nelson like a miniature old man. They stood gazing at the artificial Negro as if they were faced with some great mystery, some monument to another's victory that brought them together in their common defeat. They could both feel it dissolving their differences like an action of mercy. Mr. Head had never known before what mercy felt like because he had been too good to deserve any, but he felt he knew now. He looked at Nelson and understood that he must say something to the child to show that he was still wise and in the look the boy returned he saw a hungry need for that assurance. Nelson's eyes seemed to implore him to explain once and for all the mystery of existence.

Mr. Head opened his lips to make a lofty statement and heard himself say, "They ain't got enough real ones here. They got to have an artificial one."

After a second, the boy nodded with a strange shivering about his mouth, and said, "Let's go home before we get ourselves lost again."

Their train glided into the suburb stop just as they reached the station and they boarded it together, and ten minutes before it was due to arrive at the junction, they went to the door and stood ready to jump off if it did not stop; but it did, just as the moon, restored to its full splendor, sprang from a cloud and flooded the clearing with light. As they stepped off, the sage grass was shivering gently in shades of silver and the clinkers under their feet glittered with a fresh black light. The treetops, fencing the junction like the protecting walls of a garden, were darker than the sky which was hung with gigantic white clouds illuminated like lanterns.

Mr. Head stood very still and felt the action of mercy touch him again but this time he knew that there were no words in the world that could name it. He understood that it grew out of agony, which is not denied to any man and which is given in strange ways to children. He understood it was all a man could carry into death to give his Maker and he suddenly burned with shame that he had so little of it to take with him. He stood appalled, judging himself with the thoroughness of God, while the action of mercy covered his pride like a flame and consumed it. He had never thought himself a great sinner before but he saw now that his true depravity had been hidden from him for sins from the beginning of time, when he had conceived in his own heart the sin of Adam, until the present, when he had denied poor Nelson. He saw that no sin was too monstrous for him to claim as his own, and since God loved in proportion as He forgave, he felt ready at that instant to enter Paradise.

Nelson, composing his expression under the shadow of his hat brim, watched him with a mixture of fatigue and suspicion, but as the train glided past them and disappeared like a frightened serpent into the woods, even his face lightened and he muttered, "I'm glad I've went once, but I'll never go back again!"

FLANNERY O'CONNOR

A Good Man Is Hard to Find

The grandmother didn't want to go to Florida. She wanted to visit some of her connections in east Tennessee and she was seizing every chance to change Bailey's mind. Bailey was the son she lived with, her only boy. He was sitting on the edge of his chair at the table, bent over the orange sports section of the *Journal*. "Now look here, Bailey," she said, "see here, read this," and she stood with one hand on her thin hip and the other rattling the newspaper at his bald head. "Here this fellow that calls himself The Misfit is aloose from the Federal Pen and headed toward Florida and you read here what it says he did to these people. Just you read it. I wouldn't take my children in any direction with a criminal like that aloose in it. I couldn't answer to my conscience if I did."

Bailey didn't look up from his reading so she wheeled around then and faced the children's mother; a young woman in slacks, whose face was as broad and innocent as a cabbage and was tied around with a green headkerchief that had two points on the top like rabbit's ears. She was sitting on the sofa, feeding the baby his apricots out of a jar. "The children have been to Florida before," the old lady said. "You all ought to take them somewhere else for a change so they would see different parts of the world and be broad. They never have been to east Tennessee."

The children's mother didn't seem to hear her, but the eight-year-old boy, John Wesley, a stocky child with glasses, said, "If you don't want to go to Florida, why dontcha stay at home?" He and the little girl, June Star, were reading the funny papers on the floor.

"She wouldn't stay at home to be queen for a day," June Star said without raising her yellow head.

"Yes, and what would you do if this fellow, The Misfit, caught you?" the grandmother asked.

"I'd smack his face," John Wesley said.

"She wouldn't stay at home for a million bucks," June Star said. "Afraid she'd miss something. She has to go everywhere we go."

"All right, Miss," the grandmother said. "Just remember that the next time you want me to curl your hair."

June Star said her hair was naturally curly.

The next morning the grandmother was the first one in the car, ready to go. She had her big black valise that looked like the head of a hippopotamus in one corner, and underneath it she was hiding a basket with Pitty Sing, the cat, in it. She didn't intend for the cat to be left alone in the house for three days because he would miss her too much and she was afraid he might brush against one of the gas burners and accidentally asphyxiate himself. Her son, Bailey, didn't like to arrive at a motel with a cat.

She sat in the middle of the back seat with John Wesley and June Star on either side of her. Bailey and the children's mother and the baby sat in the front and they left Atlanta at eight forty-five with the mileage on the car at 55890. The grandmother wrote this down because she thought it would be interesting to say how many miles they had been when they got back. It took them twenty minutes to reach the outskirts of the city.

The old lady settled herself comfortably, removing her white cotton gloves and putting them up with her purse on the shelf in front of the back window. The children's mother still had on slacks and still had her head tied up in a green kerchief, but the grandmother had on a navy blue straw sailor hat with a bunch of white violets on the brim and a navy blue dress with a small white dot in the print. Her collar and cuffs were white organdy trimmed with lace and at her neckline she had pinned a purple spray of cloth violets containing a sachet. In case of an accident, anyone seeing her dead on the highway would know at once that she was a lady.

She said she thought it was going to be a good day for driving, neither too hot nor too cold, and she cautioned Bailey that the speed limit was fifty-five miles an hour and that the patrolmen hid themselves behind billboards and small clumps of trees and sped out after you before you had a chance to slow down. She pointed out interesting details of the scenery: Stone Mountain; the blue granite that in some places came up to both sides of the highway; the brilliant red clay banks slightly streaked with purple; and the various crops that made rows of green lace-work on the ground. The trees were full of silver-white sunlights and the meanest of them sparkled. The children were reading comic magazines and their mother had gone back to sleep.

"Let's go through Georgia fast so we won't have to look at it much," John Wesley said.

"If I were a little boy," said the grandmother, "I wouldn't talk about my native state that way." Tennessee has the mountains and Georgia has the hills."

"Tennessee is just a hillbilly dumping ground," John Wesley said, "and Georgia is a lousy state too."

"You said it," June Star said.

"In my time," said the grandmother, folding her thin veined fingers, "children were more respectful of their native states and their parents and everything else. People did right then. Oh look at the cute little pickaninny!" she said and pointed to a Negro child standing in the door of a shack. "Wouldn't that make a picture, now?" she asked and they all turned and looked at the little Negro out of the back window. He waved.

"He didn't have any britches on," June Star said.

"He probably didn't have any," the grandmother explained. "Little niggers in the country don't have things like we do. If I could paint, I'd paint that picture," she said.

The children exchanged comic books.

The grandmother offered to hold the baby and the children's mother passed him over the front seat to her. She set him on her knee and bounced him and told him about the things they were passing. She rolled her eyes and screwed up her mouth and stuck her leathery thin face into his smooth bland one. Occasionally he gave her a faraway smile. They passed a large cotton field with five or six graves fenced in the middle of it, like a small island. "Look at the graveyard!" the grandmother said, pointing it out. "That was the old family burying ground. That belonged to the plantation."

"Where's the plantation?" John Wesley asked.

"Gone With the Wind," said the grandmother. "Ha. Ha."

When the children finished all the comic books they had brought, they opened the lunch and ate it. The grandmother ate a peanut butter sandwich and an olive and would not let the children throw the box and the paper napkins out the window. When there was nothing else to do they played a game by choosing a cloud and making the other two guess what shape it suggested. John Wesley took one the shape of a cow and June Star guessed a cow and John Wesley said, no, an automobile, and June Star said he didn't play fair, and they began to slap each other over the grandmother.

The grandmother said she would tell them a story if they would keep quiet. When she told a story, she rolled her eyes and waved her head and was very dramatic. She said once when she was a maiden lady she had been courted by a Mr. Edgar Atkins Teagarden from Jasper, Georgia. She said he was a very good-looking man and a gentleman and that he brought her a watermelon every Saturday afternoon with his initials cut in it, E.A.T. Well, one Saturday, she said, Mr. Teagarden brought the watermelon and there was nobody at home and he left it on the front porch and returned in his buggy to Jasper, but she never got the watermelon, she said, because a nigger boy ate it when he saw the initials, E.A.T.! This story tickled John Wesley's funny bone and he giggled and giggled but June Star didn't think it was any good. She said she wouldn't marry a man that just brought her a watermelon on Saturday. The grandmother said she would have done well to marry Mr. Teagarden because he was a gentleman and had bought Coca-Cola stock when it first came out and that he had died only a few years ago, a very wealthy man.

They stopped at The Tower for barbecued sandwiches. The Tower was a part-stucco and part-wood filling station and dance hall set in a clearing outside of Timothy. A fat man named Red Sammy Butts ran it and there were signs stuck here and there on the building and for miles up and down the highway saying, TRY RED SAMMY'S FAMOUS BARBECUE. NONE LIKE FAMOUS RED SAMMY'S! RED SAM! THE FAT BOY WITH THE HAPPY LAUGH. A VETERAN! RED SAMMY'S YOUR MAN!

Red Sammy was lying on the bare ground outside The Tower with his head under a truck while a gray monkey about a foot high, chained to a small chinaberry tree, chattered nearby. The monkey sprang back into the tree and got on the highest limb as soon as he saw the children jump out of the car and run toward him.

Inside, The Tower was a long dark room with a counter at one end and tables at the other and dancing space in the middle. They all sat down at a broad table next to the nickelodeon and Red Sam's wife, a tall burnt-brown woman with hair and eyes lighter than her skin, came and took their order. The children's mother put a dime in the machine and played "The Tennessee Waltz," and the grandmother said that tune always made her want to dance. She asked Bailey if he would like to dance but he only glared at her. He didn't have a naturally sunny disposition like she did and trips made him nervous. The grandmother's brown eyes were very bright. She swayed her head from side to side and pretended she was dancing in her chair. June

Star said play something she could tap to so the children's mother put in another dime and played a fast number and June Star stepped out onto the dance floor and did her tap routine.

"Ain't she cute?" Red Sam's wife said, leaning over the counter. "Would you like to come be my little girl?"

"No, I certainly wouldn't," June Star said. "I wouldn't live in a broken-down place like this for a million bucks!" and she ran back to the table.

"Ain't she cute?" the woman repeated, stretching her mouth politely.

"Aren't you ashamed?" hissed the grandmother.

Red Sam came in and told his wife to quit lounging on the counter and hurry up with these people's order. His khaki trousers reached just to his hip bones and his stomach hung over them like a sack of meal swaying under his shirt. He came over and sat down at a table nearby and let out a combination sigh and yodel. "You can't win," he said. "You can't win," and he wiped his sweating red face off with a gray handkerchief. "These days you don't know who to trust," he said. "Ain't that the truth?"

"People are certainly not nice like they used to be," said the grandmother.

"Two fellers come in here last week," Red Sammy said, "driving a Chrysler. It was an old beat-up car but it was a good one and these boys looked all right to me. Said they worked at the mill and you know I let them fellers charge the gas they bought? Now why did I do that?"

"Because you're a good man!" the grandmother said at once.

"Yes'm, I suppose so," Red Sam said as if he were struck with this answer.

His wife brought the orders, carrying the five plates all at once without a tray, two in each hand and one balanced on her arm. "It isn't a soul in this green world of God's that you can trust," she said. "And I don't count nobody out of that, not nobody," she repeated, looking at Red Sammy.

"Did you read about that criminal, The Misfit, that's escaped?" asked the grandmother.

"I wouldn't be a bit surprised if he didn't attack this place right here," said the woman. "'If he hears about it being here, I wouldn't be none surprised to see him. If he hears it's two cent in the cash register, I wouldn't be a tall surprised if he. . . .'"

"That'll do," Red Sam said. "Go bring these people their Co'-Colas," and the woman went off to get the rest of the order.

"A good man is hard to find," Red Sammy said. "Everything is getting terrible. I remember the day you could go off and leave your screen door unlatched. Not no more."

He and the grandmother discussed better times. The old lady said that in her opinion Europe was entirely to blame for the way things were now. She said the way Europe acted you would think we were made of money and Red Sam said it was no use talking about it, she was exactly right. The children ran outside into the white sunlight and looked at the monkey in the lacy chinaberry tree. He was busy catching fleas on himself and biting each one carefully between his teeth as if it were a delicacy.

They drove off again into the hot afternoon. The grandmother took cat naps and woke up every few minutes with her own snoring. Outside of Toombsboro she woke up and recalled an old plantation that she had visited in this neighborhood once when she was a young lady. She said the house had six white columns across the

front and that there was an avenue of oaks leading up to it and two little wooden
trellis arbors on either side in front where you sat down with your suitor after a stroll
in the garden. She recalled exactly which road to turn off to get to it. She knew that
Bailey would not be willing to lose any time looking at an old house, but the more
she talked about it, the more she wanted to see it once again and find out if the little
twin arbors were still standing. "There was a secret panel in this house," she said
craftily, not telling the truth but wishing that she were, "and the story went that all
the family silver was hidden in it when Sherman came through but it was never
found. . . ."

"Hey!" John Wesley said. "Let's go see it! We'll find it! We'll poke all the wood work
and find it! Who lives there? Where do you turn off at? Hey Pop, can't we turn off
there?"

"We never have seen a house with a secret panel!" June Star shrieked. "Let's go to
the house with the secret panel! Hey, Pop, can't we go see the house with the secret
panel!"

"It's not far from here, I know," the grandmother said. "It wouldn't take over
twenty minutes."

Bailey was looking straight ahead. His jaw was as rigid as a horseshoe. "No," he
said.

The children began to yell and scream that they wanted to see the house with the
secret panel. John Wesley kicked the back of the front seat and June Star hung over
her mother's shoulder and whined desperately into her ear that they never had any
fun even on their vacation, that they could never do what THEY wanted to do. The
baby began to scream and John Wesley kicked the back of the seat so hard that his
father could feel the blows in his kidney.

"All right!" he shouted and drew the car to a stop at the side of the road. "Will you
all shut up? Will you all shut up for one second? If you don't shut up, we won't go
anywhere."

"It would be very educational for them," the grandmother murmured.

"All right," Bailey said, "but get this. This is the only time we're going to stop for
anything like this. This is the one and only time."

"The dirt road that you have to turn down is about a mile back," the grandmother
directed. "I marked it when we passed."

"A dirt road," Bailey groaned.

After they had turned around and were headed toward the dirt road, the grandmother recalled other points about the house, the beautiful glass over the front
doorway and the candle lamp in the hall. John Wesley said that the secret panel was
probably in the fireplace.

"You can't go inside this house," Bailey said. "You don't know who lives there."

"While you all talk to the people in front, I'll run around behind and get in a
window," John Wesley suggested.

"We'll all stay in the car," his mother said.

They turned onto the dirt road and the car raced roughly along in a swirl of pink
dust. The grandmother recalled the times when there were no paved roads and
thirty miles was a day's journey. The dirt road was hilly and there were sudden
washes in it and sharp curves on dangerous embankments. All at once they would
be on a hill, looking down over the blue tops of trees for miles around, then the next

minute, they would be in a red depression with the dust-coated trees looking down on them.

"This place had better turn up in a minute," Bailey said, "or I'm going to turn around."

The road looked as if no one had traveled on it in months.

"It's not much farther," the grandmother said and just as she said it, a horrible thought came to her. The thought was so embarrassing that she turned red in the face and her eyes dilated and her feet jumped up, upsetting her valise in the corner. The instant the valise moved, the newspaper top she had over the basket under it rose with a snarl and Pitty Sing, the cat, sprang onto Bailey's shoulder.

The children were thrown to the floor and their mother, clutching the baby, was thrown out the door onto the ground; the old lady was thrown into the front seat. The car turned over once and landed right-side-up in a gulch on the side of the road. Bailey remained in the driver's seat with the cat — gray-striped with a broad white face and an orange nose — clinging to his neck like a caterpillar.

As soon as the children saw they could move their arms and legs, they scrambled out of the car, shouting, "We've had an ACCIDENT!" The grandmother was curled up under the dashboard, hoping she was injured so that Bailey's wrath would not come down on her all at once. The horrible thought she had had before the accident was that the house she had remembered so vividly was not in Georgia but in Tennessee.

Bailey removed the cat from his neck with both hands and flung it out the window against the side of a pine tree. Then he got out of the car and started looking for the children's mother. She was sitting against the side of the red gutted ditch, holding the screaming baby, but she only had a cut down her face and a broken shoulder. "We've had an ACCIDENT!" the children screamed in a frenzy of delight.

"But nobody's killed," June Star said with disappointment as the grandmother limped out of the car, her hat still pinned to her head but the broken front brim standing up at a jaunty angle and the violet spray hanging off the side. They all sat down in the ditch, except the children, to recover from the shock. They were all shaking.

"Maybe a car will come along," said the children's mother hoarsely.

"I believe I have injured an organ," said the grandmother, pressing her side, but no one answered her. Bailey's teeth were clattering. He had on a yellow sport shirt with bright blue parrots designed in it and his face was as yellow as the shirt. The grandmother decided that she would not mention that the house was in Tennessee.

The road was about ten feet above and they could see only the tops of the trees on the other side of it. Behind the ditch they were sitting in there were more woods, tall and dark and deep. In a few minutes they saw a car some distance away on top of a hill, coming slowly as if the occupants were watching them. The grandmother stood up and waved both arms dramatically to attract their attention. The car continued to come on slowly, disappeared around a bend and appeared again, moving even slower, on top of the hill they had gone over. It was a big black battered hearselike automobile. There were three men in it.

It came to a stop just over them and for some minutes, the driver looked down with a steady expressionless gaze to where they were sitting, and didn't speak. Then he turned his head and muttered something to the other two and they got out. One was a fat boy in black trousers and a red sweat shirt with a silver stallion embossed on the front of it. He moved around on the right side of them and stood staring, his mouth partly open in a kind of loose grin. The other had on khaki pants and a blue striped coat and a gray hat pulled down very low, hiding most of his face. He came around slowly on the left side. Neither spoke.

The driver got out of the car and stood by the side of it, looking down at them. He was an older man than the other two. His hair was just beginning to gray and he wore silver-rimmed spectacles that gave him a scholarly look. He had a long creased face and didn't have on any shirt or undershirt. He had on blue jeans that were too tight for him and was holding a black hat and a gun. The two boys also had guns.

"We've had an ACCIDENT!" the children screamed.

The grandmother had the peculiar feeling that the bespectacled man was someone she knew. His face was as familiar to her as if she had known him all her life but she could not recall who he was. He moved away from the car and began to come down the embankment, placing his feet carefully so that he wouldn't slip. He had on tan and white shoes and no socks, and his ankles were red and thin. "Good afternoon," he said. "'I see you all had you a little spill."

"We turned over twice!" said the grandmother.

"Oncet," he corrected. "We see it happen. Try their car and see will it run, Hiram," he said quietly to the boy with the gray hat.

"What you got that gun for?" John Wesley asked. "Whatcha gonna do with that gun?"

"Lady," the man said to the children's mother, "would you mind calling them children to sit down by you? Children make me nervous. I want all you all to sit down right together there were you're at."

"What are you telling us what to do for?" June Star asked.

Behind them the line of woods gaped like a dark open mouth. "Come here," said the mother.

"Look here now," Bailey began suddenly, "we're in a predicament! we're in. . . ."

The grandmother shrieked. She scrambled to her feet and stood staring.

"You're The Misfit!" she said. "I recognized you at once!"

"Yes'm," the man said, smiling slightly as if he were pleased in spite of himself to be known, "but it would have been better for all of you, lady, if you hadn't of reckernized me."

Bailey turned his head sharply and said something to his mother that shocked even the children. The old lady began to cry and The Misfit reddened.

"Lady," he said, "don't you get upset. Sometimes a man says things he don't mean. I don't reckon he meant to talk to you thataway."

"You wouldn't shoot a lady, would you?" the grandmother said and removed a clean handkerchief from her cuff and began to slap at her eyes with it.

The Misfit pointed the toe of his shoe into the ground and made a little hole and then covered it up again. "I would hate to have to," he said.

"Listen," the grandmother almost screamed, "I know you're a good man. You don't look a bit like you have common blood. I know you must come from nice people!"

"Yes mam," he said, "finest people in the world." When he smiled he showed a row of strong white teeth. "God never made a finer woman than my mother and my daddy's heart was pure gold," he said. The boy with the red sweat shirt had come around behind them and was standing with his gun at his hip. The Misfit squatted down on the ground. "Watch them children, Bobby Lee," he said. "You know they make me nervous." He looked at the six of them huddled together in front of him and he seemed to be embarrassed as if he couldn't think of anything to say. "Ain't a cloud in the sky," he remarked, looking up at it. "Don't see no sun but don't see no cloud neither."

"Yes, it's a beautiful day," said the grandmother. "Listen," she said, "you shouldn't call yourself The Misfit because I know you're a good man at heart. I can just look at you and tell."

"Hush!" Bailey yelled. "Hush! Everybody shut up and let me handle this!" He was squatting in the position of a runner about to sprint forward but he didn't move.

"I pre-chate that, lady," The Misfit said and drew a little circle in the ground with the butt of his gun.

"It'll take a half a hour to fix this here car," Hiram called, looking over the raised hood of it.

"Well, first you and Bobby Lee get him and that little boy to step over yonder with you," The Misfit said, pointing to Bailey and John Wesley. "The boys want to ask you something," he said to Bailey. "Would you mind stepping back in them woods there with them?"

"Listen," Bailey began, "we're in a terrible predicament! Nobody realizes what this is," and his voice cracked. His eyes were as blue and intense as the parrots in his shirt and he remained perfectly still.

The grandmother reached up to adjust her hat brim as if she were going to the woods with him but it came off in her hand. She stood staring at it and after a second she let it fall on the ground. Hiram pulled Bailey up by the arm as if he were assisting an old man. John Wesley caught hold of his father's hand and Bobby Lee followed. They went off toward the woods and just as they reached the dark edge, Bailey turned and supporting himself against a gray naked pine trunk, he shouted, "I'll be back in a minute, Mamma, wait on me!"

"Come back this instant!" his mother shrilled but they all disappeared into the woods.

"Bailey Boy!" the grandmother called in a tragic voice but she found she was looking at The Misfit squatting on the ground in front of her. "I just know you're a good man," she said desperately. "You're not a bit common!"

"Nome, I ain't a good man," The Misfit said after a second as if he had considered her statement carefully, "but I ain't the worst in the world neither. My daddy said I was a different breed of dog from my brothers and sisters. 'You know,' Daddy said, 'it's some that can live their whole life out without asking about it and it's others has to know why it is, and this boy is one of the latters. He's going to be into everything!' " He put on his black hat and looked up suddenly and then away deep into the woods as if he were embarrassed again. "I'm sorry I don't have on a shirt before you ladies," he said, hunching his shoulders slightly. "We buried our clothes that we had on when we escaped and we're just making do until we can get better. We borrowed these from some folks we met," he explained.

"That's perfectly all right," the grandmother said. "Maybe Bailey has an extra shirt in his suitcase."

"I'll look and see terrectly," The Misfit said.

"Where are they taking him?" the children's mother screamed.

"Daddy was a card himself," The Misfit said. "You couldn't put anything over on him. He never got in trouble with the Authorities though. Just had the knack of handling them."

"You could be honest too if you'd only try," said the grandmother. "Think how wonderful it would be to settle down and live a comfortable life and not have to think about somebody chasing you all the time."

The Misfit kept scratching in the ground with the butt of his gun as if he were thinking about it. "Yes'm, somebody is always after you," he murmured.

The grandmother noticed how thin his shoulder blades were just behind his hat because she was standing up looking down on him. "Do you ever pray?" she asked.

He shook his head. All she saw was the black hat wiggle between his shoulder blades. "Nome," he said.

There was a pistol shot from the woods, followed closely by another. Then silence. The old lady's head jerked around. She could hear the wind move through the tree tops like a long satisfied insuck of breath. "Bailey Boy!" she called.

"I was a gospel singer for a while," The Misfit said. "I been most everything. Been in the arm service, both land and sea, at home and abroad, been twict married, been an undertaker, been with the railroads, plowed Mother Earth, been in a tornado, seen a man burnt alive oncet," and he looked up at the children's mother and the little girl who were sitting close together, their faces white and their eyes glassy; "I even seen a woman flogged," he said.

"Pray, pray," the grandmother began, "pray, pray. . . ."

"I never was a bad boy that I remember of," The Misfit said in an almost dreamy voice, "but somewheres along the line I done something wrong and got sent to the penitentiary. I was buried alive," and he looked up and held her attention to him by a steady stare.

"That's when you should have started to pray," she said. "What did you do to get to the penitentiary that first time?"

"Turn to the right, it was a wall," The Misfit said, looking up again at the cloudless sky. "Turn to the left, it was a wall. Look up it was a ceiling, look down it was a floor. I forget what I done, lady. I set there and set there, trying to remember what it was I done and I ain't recalled it to this day. Oncet in a while, I would think it was coming to me, but it never come."

"Maybe they put you in by mistake," the old lady said vaguely.

"Nome," he said. "It wasn't no mistake. They had the papers on me."

"You must have stolen something," she said.

The Misfit sneered slightly. "Nobody had nothing I wanted," he said. "It was a head-doctor at the penitentiary said what I had done was kill my daddy but I known that for a lie. My daddy died in nineteen ought nineteen of the epidemic flu and I never had a thing to do with it. He was buried in the Mount Hopewell Baptist churchyard and you can go there and see for yourself."

"If you would pray," the old lady said, "Jesus would help you."

"That's right," The Misfit said.

"Well then, why don't you pray?' she asked trembling with delight suddenly.

"I don't want no hep," he said. "I'm doing all right by myself."

Bobby Lee and Hiram came ambling back from the woods. Bobby Lee was dragging a yellow shirt with bright blue parrots in it.

"Throw me that shirt, Bobby Lee," The Misfit said. The shirt came flying at him and landed on his shoulder and he put it on. The grandmother couldn't name what the shirt reminded her of. "No, lady," The Misfit said while he was buttoning it up, "I found out the crime don't matter. You can do one thing or you can do another, kill a man or take a tire off his car, because sooner or later you're going to forget what it was you done and just be punished for it."

The children's mother had begun to make heaving noises as if she couldn't get her breath. "Lady," he asked, "would you and that little girl like to step off yonder with Bobby Lee and Hiram and join your husband?"

"Yes, thank you," the mother said faintly. Her left arm dangled helplessly and she was holding the baby, who had gone to sleep, in the other. "Hep that lady up, Hiram," The Misfit said as she struggled to climb out of the ditch, "and Bobby Lee, you hold onto that little girl's hand."

"I don't want to hold hands with him," June Star said. "He reminds me of a pig."

The fat boy blushed and laughed and caught her by the arm and pulled her off into the woods after Hiram and her mother.

Alone with The Misfit, the grandmother found that she had lost her voice. There was not a cloud in the sky nor any sun. There was nothing around her but woods. She wanted to tell him that he must pray. She opened and closed her mouth several times before anything came out. Finally she found herself saying, "Jesus. Jesus," meaning, Jesus will help you, but the way she was saying it, it sounded as if she might be cursing.

"Yes'm," The Misfit said as if he agreed. "Jesus thrown everything off balance. It was the same case with Him as with me except He hadn't committed any crime and they could prove I had committed one because they had the papers on me. Of course," he said, "they never shown me my papers. That's why I sign myself now. I said long ago, you get you a signature and sign everything you do and keep a copy of it. Then you'll know what you done and you can hold up the crime to the punishment and see do they match and in the end you'll have something to prove you ain't been treated right. I call myself The Misfit," he said, "because I can't make what all I done wrong fit what all I gone through in punishment."

There was a piercing scream from the woods, followed closely by a pistol report. "Does it seem right to you, lady, that one is punished a heap and another ain't punished at all?"

"Jesus!" the old lady cried. "You've got good blood! I know you wouldn't shoot a lady! I know you come from nice people! Pray! Jesus, you ought not to shoot a lady. I'll give you all the money I've got!"

"Lady," The Misfit said, looking beyond her far into the woods, "there never was a body that give the undertaker a tip."

There were two more pistol reports and the grandmother raised her head like a parched old turkey hen crying for water and called, "Bailey Boy, Bailey Boy!" as if her heart would break.

"Jesus was the only One that ever raised the dead," The Misfit continued, "and He shouldn't have done it. He thrown everything off balance. If He did what He said, then it's nothing for you to do but throw away everything and follow Him, and if He didn't then it's nothing for you to do but enjoy the few minutes you got left the best way you can — by killing somebody or burning down his house or doing some other meanness to him. No pleasure but meanness," he said and his voice had become almost a snarl.

"Maybe He didn't raise the dead," the old lady mumbled, not knowing what she was saying and feeling so dizzy that she sank down in the ditch with her legs twisted under her.

"I wasn't there so I can't say He didn't," The Misfit said. "I wisht I had of been there," he said, hitting the ground with his fist. "It ain't right I wasn't there because if I had of been there I would of known. Listen lady," he said in a high voice, "if I had of been there I would of known and I wouldn't be like I am now." His voice seemed about to crack and the grandmother's head cleared for an instant. She saw the man's face twisted close to her own as if he were going to cry and she murmured, "Why, you're one of my babies. You're one of my own children!" She reached out and touched him on the shoulder. The Misfit sprang back as if a snake had bitten him and shot her three times through the chest. Then he put his gun down on the ground and took off his glasses and began to clean them.

Hiram and Bobby Lee returned from the woods and stood over the ditch, looking down at the grandmother who half sat and half lay in a puddle of blood with her legs crossed under her like a child's and her face smiling up at the cloudless sky.

Without his glasses, The Misfit's eyes were red-rimmed and pale and defenseless-looking. "Take her off and throw her where you thrown the others," he said, picking up the cat that was rubbing itself against his leg.

"She was a talker, wasn't she?" Bobby Lee said, sliding down the ditch with a yodel.

"She would of been a good woman," The Misfit said, "if it had been somebody there to shoot her every minute of her life."

"Some fun!" Bobby Lee said.

"Shut up, Bobby Lee," The Misfit said. "It's no real pleasure in life."

FRANK O'CONNOR

 Frank O'Connor (the pen name of Michael O'Donovan, 1903–1966) was born in County Cork, Ireland. Like his countryman and fellow writer Sean O'Faolain, he served for a time in the Irish Republican Army during the Irish "troubles" — the struggle for independence from England. Throughout his life he wrote a considerable number of short stories, many of them realistic portrayals of life — drinking, talking, arguing politics — in Ireland. He captured faithfully the rhythm of speech of the Irish, so much so that his characters often seem to live primarily to talk. Among his collections of stories are *Guests of the Nation* (1931), *Crab Apple Jelly* (1944), *The Stories of Frank O'Connor* (1956), *My Oedipus Complex* (1963), and *A Set of Variables* (1971). "Guests of the Nation" reflects O'Connor's uncanny ear; even more, it reveals the anguish and injustices of war.

Guests of the Nation

1

At dusk the big Englishman Belcher would shift his long legs out of the ashes and ask, 'Well, chums, what about it?' and Noble or me would say, 'As you please, chum' (for we had picked up some of their curious expressions), and the little Englishman 'Awkins would light the lamp and produce the cards. Sometimes Jeremiah Donovan would come up of an evening and supervise the play, and grow excited over 'Awkins's cards (which he always played badly), and shout at him as if he was one of our own, 'Ach, you divil you, why didn't you play the trey?' But, ordinarily, Jeremiah was a sober and contented poor devil like the big Englishman Belcher, and was looked up to at all only because he was a fair hand at documents, though slow enough at these, I vow. He wore a small cloth hat and big gaiters over his long pants, and seldom did I perceive his hands outside the pockets of that pants. He reddened when you talked to him, tilting from toe to heel and back and looking down all the while at his big farmer's feet. His uncommon broad accent was a great source of jest to me, I being from the town as you may recognize.

I couldn't at the time see the point of me and Noble being with Belcher and 'Awkins at all, for it was and is my fixed belief you could have planted that pair in any untended spot from this to Claregalway and they'd have stayed put and flourished like a native weed. I never seen in my short experience two men that took to the country as they did.

They were handed on to us by the Second Battalion to keep when the search for them became too hot, and Noble and myself, being young, took charge with a natural feeling of responsibility. But little 'Awkins made us look right fools when he displayed he knew the countryside as well as we did and something more. 'You're the bloke they calls Bonaparte?' he said to me. 'Well, Bonaparte, Mary Brigid Ho'Connell was arskin' abaout you and said 'ow you'd a pair of socks belonging to 'er young brother.' For it seemed, as they explained it, that the Second used to have little evenings of their own, and some of the girls of the neighbourhood would turn in, and, seeing they were such decent fellows, our lads couldn't well ignore the two Englishmen, but invited them in and were hail-fellow-well-met with them. 'Awkins told me he learned to dance 'The Walls of Limerick' and 'The Siege of Ennis' and 'The Waves of Tory' in a night or two, though naturally he could not return the compliment, because our lads at that time did not dance foreign dances on principle.

So whatever privileges and favours Belcher and 'Awkins had with the Second they duly took with us, and after the first evening we gave up all pretence of keeping a close eye on their behaviour. Not that they could have got far, for they had a notable accent and wore khaki tunics and overcoats with civilian pants and boots. But it's my belief they never had an idea of escaping and were quite contented with their lot.

Now, it was a treat to see how Belcher got off with the old woman of the house we were staying in. She was a great warrant to scold, and crotchety even with us, but before ever she had a chance of giving our guests, as I may call them, a lick of her tongue, Belcher had made her his friend for life. She was breaking sticks at the time, and Belcher, who hadn't been in the house for more than ten minutes, jumped up out of his seat and went across to her.

'Allow me, madam,' he says, smiling his queer little smile; 'please allow me,' and takes the hatchet from her hand. She was struck too parlatic to speak, and ever after Belcher would be at her heels carrying a bucket, or basket, or load of turf, as the case might be. As Noble wittily remarked, he got into looking before she lept, and hot water or any little thing she wanted Belcher would have it ready before her. For such a huge man (and though I am five foot ten myself I had to look up to him) he had an uncommon shortness — or should I say lack — of speech. It took us some time to get used to him walking in and out like a ghost, without a syllable out of him. Especially because 'Awkins talked enough for a platoon, it was strange to hear big Belcher with his toes in the ashes come out with a solitary 'Excuse me, chum,' or 'That's right, chum.' His one and only abiding passion was cards, and I will say for him he was a good card-player. He could have fleeced me and Noble many a time; only if we lost to him, 'Awkins lost to us, and 'Awkins played with the money Belcher gave him.

'Awkins lost to us because he talked too much, and I think now we lost to Belcher for the same reason. 'Awkins and Noble would spit at one another about religion into the early hours of the morning; the little Englishman as you could see worrying the soul out of young Noble (whose brother was a priest) with a string of questions that would puzzle a cardinal. And to make it worse, even in treating of these holy subjects, 'Awkins had a deplorable tongue; I never in all my career struck across a man who could mix such a variety of cursing and bad language into the simplest topic. Oh, a terrible man was little 'Awkins, and a fright to argue! He never did a stroke of work, and when he had no one else to talk to he fixed his claws into the old woman.

I am glad to say that in her he met his match, for one day when he tried to get her to complain profanely of the drought she gave him a great comedown by blaming the drought upon Jupiter Pluvius (a deity neither 'Awkins nor I had ever even heard of, though Noble said among the pagans he was held to have something to do with rain). And another day the same 'Awkins was swearing at the capitalists for starting the German war, when the old dame laid down her iron, puckered up her little crab's mouth and said, 'Mr. 'Awkins, you can say what you please about the war, thinking to deceive me because I'm an ignorant old woman, but I know well what started the war. It was that Italian count that stole the heathen divinity out of the temple in Japan, for believe me, Mr. 'Awkins, nothing but sorrow and want follows them that disturbs the hidden powers!' Oh, a queer old dame, as you remark!

2

So one evening we had our tea together, and 'Awkins lit the lamp and we all sat in to cards. Jeremiah Donovan came in too, and sat down and watched us for a while. Though he was a shy man and didn't speak much, it was easy to see he had no great love for the two Englishmen, and I was surprised it hadn't struck me so clearly before. Well, like that in the story, a terrible dispute blew up late in the evening between 'Awkins and Noble, about capitalists and priests and love for your own country.

'The capitalists,' says 'Awkins, with an angry gulp, 'the capitalists pays the priests to tell you all abaout the next world, so's you awon't notice what they do in this!'

'Nonsense, man,' says Noble, losing his temper, 'before ever a capitalist was thought of people believed in the next world.'

'Awkins stood up as if he was preaching a sermon. 'Oh, they did, did they?' he says with a sneer. 'They believed all the things you believe, that's what you mean? And you believe that God created Hadam and Hadam created Shem and Shem created Jehoshophat? You believe all the silly hold fairy-tale abaout Heve and Heden and the happle? Well, listen to me, chum. If you're entitled to 'old to a silly belief like that, I'm entitled to 'old to my own silly belief — which is, that the fust thing your God created was a bleedin' capitalist with mirality and Rolls Royce complete. Am I right, chum?' he says then to Belcher.

'You're right, chum,' says Belcher, with his queer smile, and gets up from the table to stretch his long legs into the fire and stroke his moustache. So, seeing that Jeremiah Donovan was going, and there was no knowing when the conversation about religion would be over, I took my hat and went out with him. We strolled down towards the village together, and then he suddenly stopped, and blushing and mumbling, and shifting, as his way was, from toe to heel, he said I ought to be behind keeping guard on the prisoners. And I, having it put to me so suddenly, asked him what the hell he wanted a guard on the prisoners at all for, and said that so far as Noble and me were concerned we had talked it over and would rather be out with a column. 'What use is that pair to us?' I asked him.

He looked at me for a spell and said, 'I thought you knew we were keeping them as hostages.' 'Hostages — ?' says I, not quite understanding. 'The enemy,' he says in his heavy way, 'have prisoners belong' to us, and now they talk of shooting them. If they shoot our prisoners we'll shoot theirs, and serve them right.' 'Shoot them?' said I, the possibility just beginning to dawn on me. 'Shoot them, exactly,' said he. 'Now,' said I, 'wasn't it very unforeseen of you not to tell me and Noble that?' 'How so?' he asks. 'Seeing that we were acting as guards upon them, of course.' 'And hadn't you reason enough to guess that much?' 'We had not, Jeremiah Donovan, we had not. How were we to know when the men were on our hands so long?' 'And what difference does it make? The enemy have our prisoners as long or longer, haven't they?' 'It makes a great difference,' said I. 'How so?' said he sharply; but I couldn't tell him the difference it made, for I was struck too silly to speak. 'And when may we expect to be released from this anyway?' said I. 'You may expect it to-night,' says he. 'Or to-morrow or the next day at latest. So if it's hanging round here that worries you, you'll be free soon enough.'

I cannot explain it even now, how sad I felt, but I went back to the cottage, a miserable man. When I arrived the discussion was still on, 'Awkins holding forth to all and sundry that there was no next world at all and Noble answering in his best canonical style that there was. But I saw 'Awkins was after having the best of it. 'Do you know what, chum?' he was saying, with his saucy smile, 'I think you're jest as big a bleedin' hunbeliever as I am. You say you believe in the next world and you know jest as much abaout the next world as I do, which is sweet damn-all. What's 'Eaven? You dunno. Where's 'Eaven? You dunno. Who's in 'Eaven? You dunno. You know sweet damn-all! I arsk you again, do they wear wings?'

'Very well then,' says Noble, 'they do; is that enough for you? They do wear wings.' 'Where do they get them then? Who makes them? 'Ave they a fact'ry for wings? 'Ave they a sort of store where you 'ands in your chit and tikes your bleedin' wings? Answer me that.'

'Oh, you're an impossible man to argue with,' says Noble. 'Now listen to me — .' And off the pair of them went again.

It was long after midnight when we locked up the Englishman and went to bed ourselves. As I blew out the candle I told Noble what Jeremiah Donovan had told me. Noble took it very quietly. After we had been in bed about an hour he asked me did I think we ought to tell the Englishmen. I having thought of the same thing myself (among many others) said no, because it was more than likely the English wouldn't shoot our men, and anyhow it wasn't to be supposed the Brigade who were always up and down with the second battalion and knew the Englishmen well would be likely to want them bumped off. 'I think so,' says Noble. 'It would be sort of cruelty to put the wind up them now.' 'It was very unforeseen of Jeremiah Donovan anyhow,' says I, and by Noble's silence I realised he took my meaning.

So I lay there half the night, and thought and thought, and picturing myself and young Noble trying to prevent the Brigade from shooting 'Awkins and Belcher sent a cold sweat out through me. Because there were men on the Brigade you daren't let nor hinder without a gun in your hand, and at any rate, in those days disunion between brothers seemed to me an awful crime. I knew better after.

It was next morning we found it so hard to face Belcher and 'Awkins with a smile. We went about the house all day scarcely saying a word. Belcher didn't mind us much; he was stretched into the ashes as usual with his usual look of waiting in quietness for something unforeseen to happen, but little 'Awkins gave us a bad time with his audacious gibing and questioning. He was disgusted at Noble's not answering him back. 'Why can't you tike your beating like a man, chum?' he says. 'You with your Hadam and Heve! I'm a Communist — or an Anarchist. An Anarchist, that's what I am.' And for hours after he went round the house, mumbling when the fit took him 'Hadam and Heve! Hadam and Heve!'

3

I don't know clearly how we got over that day, but get over it we did, and a great relief it was when the tea-things were cleared away and Belcher said in his peaceable manner, 'Well, chums, what about it?' So we all sat round the table and 'Awkins produced the cards, and at that moment I heard Jeremiah Donovan's footsteps up the path, and a dark presentiment crossed my mind. I rose quietly from the table and laid my hand on him before he reached the door. 'What do you want?' I asked him. 'I want those two soldier friends of yours,' he says reddening. 'Is that the way it is, Jeremiah Donovan?' I ask. 'That's the way. There were four of our lads went west this morning, one of them a boy of sixteen.' 'That's bad, Jeremiah,' says I.

At that moment Noble came out, and we walked down the path together talking in whispers. Feeney, the local intelligence officer, was standing by the gate. 'What are you going to do about it?' I asked Jeremiah Donovan. 'I want you and Noble to bring them out: you can tell them they're being shifted again; that'll be the quietest way.' 'Leave me out of that,' says Noble suddenly. Jeremiah Donovan looked at him hard for a minute or two. 'All right so,' he said peaceably. 'You and Feeney collect a few tools from the shed and dig a hole by the far end of the bog. Bonaparte and I'll be after you in about twenty minutes. But whatever else you do, don't let anyone see you with the tools. No one must know but the four of ourselves.'

We saw Feeney and Noble go round to the houseen where the tools were kept, and sidled in. Everything if I can so express myself was tottering before my eyes, and I left Jeremiah Donovan to do the explaining as best he could, while I took a seat and said nothing. He told them they were to go back to the Second. 'Awkins let a mouthful of curses out of him at that, and it was plain that Belcher, though he said nothing, was duly perturbed. The old woman was for having them stay in spite of us, and she did not shut her mouth until Jeremiah Donovan lost his temper and said some nasty things to her. Within the house by this time it was pitch dark, but no one thought of lighting the lamp, and in the darkness the two Englishmen fetched their khaki topcoats and said good-bye to the woman of the house. 'Just as a man mikes a 'ome of a bleedin' place,' mumbles 'Awkins shaking her by the hand, 'some bastard at headquarters thinks you're too cushy and shunts you off.' Belcher shakes her hand very hearty. 'A thousand thanks, madam,' he says, 'a thousand thanks for everything . . .' as though he'd made it all up.

We go round to the back of the house and down towards the fatal bog. Then Jeremiah Donovan comes out with what is in his mind. 'There were four of our lads shot by your fellows this morning so now you're to be bumped off.' 'Cut that stuff out,' says 'Awkins flaring up. 'It's bad enough to be mucked about such as we are without you plying at soldiers.' 'It's true,' says Jeremiah Donovan. 'I'm sorry, 'Awkins, but 'tis true,' and comes out with the usual rigmarole about doing our duty and obeying our superiors. 'Cut it out,' says 'Awkins irritably, 'Cut it out!'

Then, when Donovan sees he is not being believed he turns to me. 'Ask Bonaparte here,' he says. 'I don't need to arsk Bonaparte. Me and Bonaparte are chums.' 'Isn't it true, Bonaparte?' says Jeremiah Donovan solemnly to me. 'It is,' I say sadly, 'it is.' 'Awkins stops. 'Now, for Christ's sike . . .' 'I mean it, chum,' I say. 'You daon't saound as if you mean it. You knaow well you don't mean it.' 'Well, if he don't I do,' says Jeremiah Donovan. 'Why the 'ell sh'd you want to shoot me, Jeremiah Donovan?' 'Why the hell should your people take out four prisoners and shoot them in cold blood upon a barrack square?' I perceive Jeremiah Donovan is trying to encourage himself with hot words.

Anyway, he took little 'Awkins by the arm and dragged him on, but it was impossible to make him understand that we were in earnest. From which you will perceive how difficult it was for me, as I kept feeling my Smith and Wesson and thinking what I would do if they happened to put up a fight or ran for it, and wishing in my heart they would. I knew if only they ran I would never fire on them. 'Was Noble in this?' 'Awkins wanted to know, and we said yes. He laughed. But why should Noble want to shoot him? Why should we want to shoot him? What had he done to us? Weren't we chums (the word lingers painfully in my memory)? Weren't we? Didn't we understand him and didn't he understand us? Did either of us imagine for an instant that he'd shoot us for all the so-and-so brigadiers in the so-and-so British Army? By this time I began to perceive in the dusk the desolate edges of the bog that was to be their last earthly bed, and, so great a sadness overtook my mind, I could not answer him. We walked along the edge of it in the darkness, and every now and then 'Awkins would call a halt and begin again, just as if he was wound up, about us being chums, and I was in despair that nothing but the cold and open grave made ready for his presence would convince him that we meant it all. But all the same, if you can understand, I didn't want him to be bumped off.

4

At last we saw the unsteady glint of a lantern in the distance and made towards it. Noble was carrying it, and Feeney stood somewhere in the darkness behind, and somehow the picture of the two of them so silent in the boglands was like the pain of death in my heart. Belcher, on recognizing Noble, said 'Allo, chum' in his usual peaceable way, but 'Awkins flew at the poor boy immediately, and the dispute began all over again, only that Noble hadn't a word to say for himself, and stood there with the swaying lantern between his gaitered legs.

It was Jeremiah Donovan who did the answering. 'Awkins asked for the twentieth time (for it seemed to haunt his mind) if anybody thought he'd shoot Noble. 'You would,' says Jeremiah Donovan shortly. 'I wouldn't, damn you!' 'You would if you knew you'd be shot for not doing it.' 'I wouldn't, not if I was to be shot twenty times over; he's my chum. And Belcher wouldn't — isn't that right, Belcher?' 'That's right, chum,' says Belcher peaceably. 'Damned if I would. Anyway, who says Noble'd be shot if I wasn't bumped off? What d'you think I'd do if I was in Noble's place and we were out in the middle of a blasted bog?' 'What would you do?' 'I'd go with him wherever he was going. I'd share my last bob with him and stick by 'im through thick and thin.'

'We've had enough of this,' says Jeremiah Donovan, cocking his revolver. 'Is there any message you want to send before I fire?' 'No, there isn't but . . .' 'Do you want to say your prayers?' 'Awkins came out with a coldblooded remark that shocked even me and turned to Noble again. 'Listen to me, Noble,' he said. 'You and me are chums. You won't come over to my side, so I'll come over to your side. Is that fair? Just you give me a rifle and I'll go with you wherever you want.'

Nobody answered him.

'Do you understand?' he said. 'I'm through with it all. I'm a deserter or anything else you like, but from this on I'm one of you. Does that prove to you that I mean what I say?' Noble raised his head, but as Jeremiah began to speak he lowered it again without answering. 'For the last time have you any messages to send?' says Donovan in a cold and excited voice.

'Ah, shut up, you, Donovan; you don't understand me, but these fellows do. They're my chums; they stand by me and I stand by them. We're not the capitalist tools you seem to think us.'

I alone of the crowd saw Donovan raise his Webley to the back of 'Awkins's neck, and as he did so I shut my eyes and tried to say a prayer. 'Awkins had begun to say something else when Donovan let fly, and, as I opened my eyes at the bang, I saw him stagger at the knees and lie out flat at Noble's feet, slowly, and as quiet as a child, with the lantern-light falling sadly upon his lean legs and bright farmer's boots. We all stood very still for a while watching him settle out in the last agony.

Then Belcher quietly takes out a handkerchief, and begins to tie it about his own eyes (for in our excitement we had forgotten to offer the same to 'Awkins), and, seeing it is not big enough, turns and asks for a loan of mine. I give it to him, and as he knots the two together he points with his foot at 'Awkins. ' 'e's not quite dead,' he says, 'better give 'im another.' Sure enough 'Awkins's left knee as we see it under the lantern is rising again. I bend down and put my gun to his ear; then, recollecting myself and the company of Belcher, I stand up again with a few hasty words. Belcher understands what is in my mind. 'Give 'im 'is first,' he says. 'I don't mind. Poor bastard, we dunno what's 'appening to 'im now.' As by this time I am beyond all feeling I kneel down again and skilfully give 'Awkins the last shot so as to put him for ever out of pain.

Belcher who is fumbling a bit awkwardly with the handkerchief comes out with a laugh when he hears the shot. It is the first time I have heard him laugh, and it sends a shiver down my spine, coming as it does so inappropriately upon the tragic death of his old friend. 'Poor blighter,' he says quietly, 'and last night he was so curious abaout it all. It's very queer, chums, I always think. Naow, 'e knows as much abaout it as they'll ever let 'im know, and last night 'e was all in the dark.'

Donovan helps him to tie the handkerchiefs about his eyes. 'Thanks, chum,' he says. Donovan asks him if there are any messages he would like to send. 'Naow, chum,' he says, 'none for me. If any of you likes to write to 'Awkins's mother you'll find a letter from 'er in 'is pocket. But my missus left me eight years ago. Went away with another fellow and took the kid with her. I like the feelin' of a 'ome (as you may 'ave noticed) but I couldn't start again after that.'

We stand around like fools now that he can no longer see us. Donovan looks at Noble and Noble shakes his head. Then Donovan raises his Webley again and just at that moment Belcher laughs his queer nervous laugh again. He must think we are talking of him; anyway, Donovan lowers his gun. ' 'Scuse me, chums,' says Belcher,

'I feel I'm talking the 'ell of a lot ... and so silly ... abaout me being so 'andy abaout a 'ouse. But this thing come on me so sudden. You'll forgive me, I'm sure.' 'You don't want to say a prayer?' asks Jeremiah Donovan. 'No, chum,' he replies, 'I don't think that'd 'elp. I'm ready if you want to get it over.' 'You understand,' says Jeremiah Donovan, 'it's not so much our doing. It's our duty, so to speak.' Belcher's head is raised like a real blind man's, so that you can only see his nose and chin in the lamplight. 'I never could make out what duty was myself,' he said, 'but I think you're all good lads, if that's what you mean. I'm not complaining.' Noble, with a look of desperation, signals to Donovan, and in a flash Donovan raises his gun and fires. The big man goes over like a sack of meal, and this time there is no need of a second shot.

I don't remember much about the burying, but that it was worse than all the rest, because we had to carry the warm corpses a few yards before we sunk them in the windy bog. It was all mad lonely, with only a bit of lantern between ourselves and the pitch-blackness, and birds hooting and screeching all round disturbed by the guns. Noble had to search 'Awkins first to get the letter from his mother. Then having smoothed all signs of the grave away, Noble and I collected our tools, said good-bye to the others, and went back along the desolate edge of the treacherous bog without a word. We put the tools in the houseen and went into the house. The kitchen was pitch-black and cold, just as we left it, and the old woman was sitting over the hearth telling her beads. We walked past her into the room, and Noble struck a match to light the lamp. Just then she rose quietly and came to the doorway, being not at all so bold or crabbed as usual.

'What did ye do with them?' she says in a sort of whisper, and Noble took such a mortal start the match quenched in his trembling hand. 'What's that?' he asks without turning round. 'I heard ye,' she said. 'What did you hear?' asks Noble, but sure he wouldn't deceive a child the way he said it. 'I heard ye. Do you think I wasn't listening to ye putting the things back in the houseen?' Noble struck another match and this time the lamp lit for him. 'Was that what ye did with them?' she said, and Noble said nothing — after all what could he say?

So then, by God, she fell on her two knees by the door, and began telling her beads, and after a minute or two Noble went on his knees by the fireplace, so I pushed my way out past her, and stood at the door, watching the stars and listening to the damned shrieking of the birds. It is so strange what you feel at such moments, and not to be written afterwards. Noble says he felt he seen everything ten times as big, perceiving nothing around him but the little patch of black bog with the two Englishmen stiffening into it; but with me it was the other way, as though the patch of bog where the two Englishmen were was a thousand miles away from me, and even Noble mumbling just behind me and the old woman and the birds and the bloody stars were all far away, and I was somehow very small and very lonely. And anything that ever happened me after I never felt the same about again.

SEAN O'FAOLAIN

 Sean O'Faolain was born in County Cork, Ireland, in 1900, the son of a policeman. He received his education at the National University of Ireland and served in the Irish Republican Army for three years. After spending a number of years studying and teaching in the United States, O'Faolain settled in Ireland and commenced a long career of writing stories, novels, and biographies. Among his collections of stories are *Midsummer Night Madness* (1932), *Teresa and Other Stories* (1947), *The Heat of the Day* (1966), and *Collected Stories*, Vol. I (1980). O'Faolain's subject, not suprisingly, is Ireland and the Irish. His stories, which owe a debt to Chekhov, are often set in the realm of loneliness, his characters realizing that fate has circumscribed their possibilities. Sometimes that fate inheres in the inescapable fact of having been born Irish, sometimes in the almost equally inescapable fact of the hold of Catholicism. "Lovers of the Lake" poses — but does not necessarily resolve — the dilemma between secular and sacred love.

Lovers of the Lake

"They might wear whites," she had said, as she stood sipping her tea and looking down at the suburban tennis players in the square. And then, turning her head in that swift movement that always reminded him of a jackdaw: "By the way, Bobby, will you drive me up to Lough Derg next week?"

He replied amiably from the lazy deeps of her armchair.

"Certainly! What part? Killaloe? But is there a good hotel there?"

"I mean the other Lough Derg. I want to do the pilgrimage."

For a second he looked at her in surprise and then burst into laughter; then he looked at her peeringly.

"Jenny! Are you serious?"

"Of course."

"Do you mean that place with the island where they go around on their bare feet on sharp stones, and starve for days, and sit up all night ologroaning and ologroaning?" He got out of the chair, went over to the cigarette box on the bookshelves, and, with his back to her, said coldly, "Are you going religious on me?"

She walked over to him swiftly, turned him about, smiled her smile that was whiter than the whites of her eyes, and lowered her head appealingly on one side. When this produced no effect she said:

"Bobby! I'm always praising you to my friends as a man who takes things as they come. So few men do. Never looking beyond the day. Doing things on the spur of the moment. It's why I like you so much. Other men are always weighing up, and considering and arguing. I've built you up as a sort of magnificent, wild, brainless tomcat. Are you going to let me down now?"

After a while he had looked at his watch and said:

"All right, then. I'll try and fix up a few days free next week. I must drop into the hospital now. But I warn you, Jenny, I've noticed this Holy Joe streak in you before. You'll do it once too often."

She patted his cheek, kissed him sedately, said, "You are a good boy," and saw him out with a loving smile.

They enjoyed that swift morning drive to the Shannon's shore. He suspected nothing when she refused to join him in a drink at Carrick. Leaning on the counter they had joked with the barmaid like any husband and wife off on a motoring holiday. As they rolled smoothly around the northern shore of Lough Gill he had suddenly felt so happy that he had stroked her purple glove and winked at her. The lough was vacant under the midday sun, its vast expanse of stillness broken only by a jumping fish or by its eyelash fringe of reeds. He did not suspect anything when she sent him off to lunch by himself in Sligo, saying that she had to visit an old nun she knew in the convent. So far the journey had been to him no more than one of her caprices; until a yellow signpost marked TO BUNDORAN made them aware that her destination and their parting was near, for she said:

"What are you proposing to do until Wednesday?"

"I hadn't given it a thought."

"Don't go off and forget all about me, darling. You know you're to pick me up on Wednesday about midday?"

After a silence he grumbled:

"You're making me feel a hell of a bastard, Jenny."

"Why on earth?"

"All this penitential stuff is because of me, isn't it?"

"Don't be silly. It's just something I thought up all by myself out of my own clever little head."

He drove on for several miles without speaking. She looked sideways, with amusement, at his ruddy, healthy, hockey-player face glimmering under the peak of his checked cap. The brushes at his temples were getting white. Everything about him bespoke the distinguished Dublin surgeon on holiday: his pale-green shirt, his darker-green tie, his double-breasted waistcoat, his driving gloves with the palms made of woven cord. She looked pensively towards the sea. He growled:

"I may as well tell you this much, Jenny, if you were my wife I wouldn't stand for any of this nonsense."

So their minds had travelled to the same thought? But if she were his wife the question would never have arisen. She knew by the sudden rise of speed that he was in one of his tempers, so that when he pulled into the grass verge, switched off, and turned towards her she was not taken by surprise. A sea gull moaned high overhead. She lifted her grey eyes to his, and smiled, waiting for the attack.

"Jenny, would you mind telling me exactly what all this is about? I mean, why are you doing this fal-lal at this particular time?"

"I always wanted to do this pilgrimage. So it naturally follows that I would do it sometime, doesn't it?"

"Perhaps. But why, for instance, this month and not last month?"

"The island wasn't open to pilgrims last month."

"Why didn't you go last year instead of this year?"

"You know we went to Austria last year."

"Why not the year before last?"

"I don't know. And stop bullying me. It is just a thing that everybody wants to do sometime. It is a special sort of Irish thing, like Lourdes, or Fatima, or Lisieux. Everybody who knows about it feels drawn to it. If you were a practicing Catholic you'd understand."

"I understand quite well," he snapped. "I know perfectly well that people go on pilgrimages all over the world. Spain. France. Mexico. I shouldn't be surprised if they go on them in Russia. What I am asking you is what has cropped up to produce this extra-special performance just *now?*"

"And I tell you I don't know. The impulse came over me suddenly last Sunday looking at those boys and girls playing tennis. For no reason. It just came. I said to myself, 'All right, go now!' I felt that if I didn't do it on the impulse I'd never do it at all. Are you asking me for a rational explanation? I haven't got one. I'm not clever and intelligent like you, darling."

"You're as clever as a bag of cats."

She laughed at him.

"I do love you, Bobby, when you are cross. Like a small boy."

"Why didn't you ask George to drive you?"

She sat up straight.

"I don't want my husband to know anything whatever about this. Please don't mention a word of it to him."

He grinned at his small victory, considered the scythe of her jawbone, looked at the shining darkness of her hair, and restarted the car.

"All the same," he said after a mile, "there must be some reason. Or call it a cause if you don't like the word reason. And I'd give a lot to know what it is."

After another mile:

"Of course, I might as well be talking to that old dolmen over there as be asking a woman why she does anything. And if she knew she wouldn't tell you."

After another mile:

"Mind you, I believe all this is just a symptom of something else. Never forget, my girl, that I'm a doctor. I'm trained to interpret symptoms. If a woman comes to me with a pain . . ."

"Oh, yes, if a woman comes to Surgeon Robert James Flannery with a pain he says to her, 'Never mind, that's only a pain.' My God! If a woman has a pain she has a bloody pain!"

He said quietly:

"Have you a pain?"

"Oh, do shut up! The only pain I have is in my tummy. I'm ravenous."

"I'm sorry. Didn't they give you a good lunch at the convent?"

"I took no lunch; you have to arrive at the island fasting. That's the rule."

"Do you mean to say you've had nothing at all to eat since breakfast?"

"I had no breakfast."

"What will you get to eat when you arrive on the island?"

"Nothing. Or next to nothing. Everybody has to fast on the island the whole time. Sometime before night I might get a cup of black tea, or hot water with pepper and salt in it. I believe it's one of their lighthearted jokes to call it soup."

Their speed shot up at once to sixty-five. He drove through Bundoran's siesta hour like the chariot of the Apocalypse. Nearing Ballyshannon they slowed down to a pleasant, humming fifty.

"Jenny!"

"Yes?"

"Are you tired of me?"

"Is this more of you and your symptoms?"

He stopped the car again.

"Please answer my question."

She laid her purple-gloved hand on his clenched fist.

"Look, darling! We've known one another for six years. You know that like any good little Catholic girl I go to my duties every Easter and every Christmas. Once or twice I've told you so. You've growled and grumbled a bit, but you never made any fuss about it. What are you suddenly worrying about now?"

"Because all that was just routine. Like the French or the Italians. Good Lord, I'm not bigoted. There's no harm in going to church now and again. I do it myself on state occasions, or if I'm staying in some house where they'd be upset if I didn't. But this sort of lunacy isn't routine!"

She slewed her head swiftly away from his angry eyes. A child in a pink pinafore with shoulder frills was driving two black cows through a gap.

"It was never routine. It's the one thing I have to hang on to in an otherwise meaningless existence. No children. A husband I'm not in love with. And I can't marry you."

She slewed back to him. He slewed away to look up the long empty road before them. He slewed back; he made as if to speak; he slewed away impatiently again.

"No?" she interpreted. "It isn't any use, is it? It's my problem, not yours. Or if it is yours you've solved it long ago by saying it's all a lot of damned nonsense."

"And how have you solved it?" he asked sardonically.

"Have you any cause to complain of how I've solved it? Oh, I'm not defending myself. I'm a fraud, I'm a crook, I admit it. You are more honest than I am. You don't believe in anything. But it's the truth that all I have is you and . . ."

"And what?"

"It sounds so blasphemous I can't say it."

"Say it!"

"All I have is you, and God."

He took out his cigarette case and took one. She took one. When he lit hers their eyes met. He said, very softly, looking up the empty road:

"Poor Jenny! I wish you'd talked like this to me before. It is, after all, as you say, your own affair. But what I can't get over is that this thing you're doing is so utterly extravagant. To go off to an island, in the middle of a lake, in the mountains, with a lot of Crawthumpers of every age and sex, and no sex, and peel off your stockings and your shoes, and go limping about on your bare feet on a lot of sharp stones, and kneel in the mud, psalming and beating your breast like a criminal, and drink nothing for three days but salt water . . . it's not like you. It's a side of you I've never known before. The only possible explanation for it must be that something is happening inside in you that I've never seen happen before!"

She spread her hands in despair. He chucked away his cigarette and restarted the car. They drove on in silence. A mist began to speckle the windscreen. They turned off the main road into sunless hills, all brown as hay. The next time he glanced at her she was making up her face; her mouth rolling the lipstick into her lips; her eyes rolling around the mirror. He said:

"You're going to have a nice picnic if the weather breaks."

She glanced out apprehensively.

"It won't be fun."

A sudden flog of rain lashed into the windscreen. The sky had turned its bucket upside down. He said:

"Even if it's raining do you still have to keep walking around on those damn stones?"

"Yes."

"You'll get double pneumonia."

"Don't worry, darling. It's called Saint Patrick's Purgatory. He will look after me."

That remark started a squabble that lasted until they drew up beside the lake. Other cars stood about like stranded boats. Other pilgrims stood by the boat slip, waiting for the ferry, their backs hunched to the wind, their clothes ruffled like the fur of cattle. She looked out across the lough at the creeping worms of foam.

He looked about him sullenly at the waiting pilgrims, a green bus, two taxi-loads of people waiting for the rain to stop. They were not his kind of people at all, and he said so.

"That," she smiled, "is what comes of being a surgeon. You don't meet people, you meet organs. Didn't you once tell me that when you are operating you never look at the patient's face?"

He grunted. Confused and hairy-looking clouds combed themselves on the ridges of the hills. The lake was crumpled and grey, except for those yellow worms of foam blown across it in parallel lines. To the south a cold patch of light made it all look far more dreary. She stared out towards the island and said:

"It's not at all like what I expected."

"And what the hell did you expect? Capri?"

"I thought of an old island, with old grey ruins, and old holly trees and rhododendrons down to the water, a place where old monks would live."

They saw tall buildings like modern hotels rising by the island's shore, an octagonal basilica big enough for a city, four or five bare, slated houses, a long shed like a ballroom. There was one tree. Another bus drew up beside them and people peered out through the wiped glass.

"Oh, God!" she groaned. "I hope this isn't going to be like Lourdes."

"And what, pray, is wrong with Lourdes when it's at home?"

"Commercialized. I simply can't believe that this island was the most famous pilgrimage of the Middle Ages. On the rim of the known world. It must have been like going off to Jerusalem or coming home brown from the sun with a cockle in your hat from Galilee."

He put on a vulgar Yukon voice:

"Thar's gold somewhere in them thar hills. It looks to me like a damn good financial proposition for somebody."

She glared at him. The downpour had slackened. Soon it almost ceased. Gurgles of streams. A sound of pervasive drip. From the back seat she took a small red canvas bag marked T.W.A.

"You will collect me on Wednesday about noon, won't you?"

He looked at her grimly. She looked every one of her forty-one years. The skin of her neck was corrugated. In five years' time she would begin to have jowls.

"Have a good time," he said, and slammed in the gears, and drove away.

The big, lumbering ferryboat was approaching, its prow slapping the corrugated waves. There were three men to each oar. It began to spit rain again. With about a hundred and fifty men and women, of every age and, so far as she could see, of every class, she clambered aboard. They pushed out and slowly they made the crossing, huddled together from the wind and rain. The boat nosed into its cleft and unloaded. She had a sensation of dark water, wet cement, houses, and a great number of people; and that she would have given gold for a cup of hot tea. Beyond the four or five white-washed houses — she guessed that they had been the only buildings on the island before trains and buses made the pilgrimage popular — and beyond the cement paths, she came on the remains of the natural island: a knoll, some warm grass, the tree, and the roots of the old hermits' cells across whose teeth of stone barefooted pilgrims were already treading on one another's heels. Most of these barefooted people wore mackintoshes. They not only stumbled on one another's heels; they kneeled on one another's toes and tails; for the island was crowded — she thought there must be nearly two thousand people on it. They were packed between the two modern hostels and the big church. She saw a priest in sou'wester and gum boots. A nun waiting for the new arrivals at the door of the women's hostel took her name and address, and gave her the number of her cubicle. She went upstairs to it, laid her red bag on the cot, sat beside it, unfastened her garters, took off her shoes, unpeeled her nylons, and without transition became yet another anonymous pilgrim. As she went out among the pilgrims already praying in the rain she felt only a sense of shame as if she were specially singled out under the microscope of the sky. The wet ground was cold.

A fat old woman in black, rich-breasted, grey-haired, took her kindly by the arm and said in a warm, Kerry voice: "You're shivering, you poor creature! Hould hard now. Sure, when we have the first station done they'll be giving us the ould cup of black tay."

And laughed at the folly of this longing for the tea. She winced when she stepped on the gritty concrete of the terrace surrounding the basilica, built out on piles over the lake. A young man smiled sympathetically, seeing that she was a delicate subject for the rigours before her: he was dressed like a clerk, with three pens in his breast pocket, and he wore a Total Abstinence badge.

"Saint's Island they call it," he smiled. "Some people think it should be called Divil's Island."

She disliked his kindness — she had never in her life asked for pity from anybody, but she soon found that the island floated on kindness. Everything and everybody about her seemed to say, "We are all sinners here, wretched creatures barely worthy of mercy." She felt the abasement of the doomed. She was among people who had surrendered all personal identity, all pride. It was like being in a concentration camp.

The fat old Kerrywoman was explaining to her what the routine was, and as she listened she realized how long her stay would really be. In prospect it had seemed so short: come on Monday afternoon, leave on Wednesday at noon; it had seemed no more than one complete day and two bits of nights She had not foreseen that immediately after arriving she must remain out of doors until the darkness fell, walking the rounds of the stones, praying, kneeling, for about five hours. And even then she would get no respite, for she must stay awake all night praying in the basilica. It was then that she would begin the second long day, as long and slow as the night; and on the third day she would still be walking those rounds until mid-day. She would be without food, even when she would have left the island, until the midnight of that third day.

"Yerrah, but sure," the old woman cackled happily, "they say that fasting is good for the stomach."

She began to think of "they."

They had thought all this up. They had seen how much could be done with simple prayers. For when she began to tot up the number of Paternosters and Aves that she must say she had to stop at the two thousandth. And these reiterated prayers must be said while walking on the stones, or kneeling in the mud, or standing upright with her two arms extended. This was the posture she disliked most. Every time she came to do it, her face to the lake, her arms spread, the queue listening to her renouncing her sins, she had to force herself to the posture and the words. The first time she did it, with the mist blowing into her eyes, her arms out like a crucifix, her lips said the words but her heart cursed herself for coming so unprepared, for coming at all. Before she had completed her first circuit — four times around each one of six cells — one ankle and one toe was bleeding. She was then permitted to ask for the cup of black tea. She received it sullenly, as a prisoner might receive his bread and water.

She wished after that first circuit to start again and complete a second — the six cells, and the seven other ordeals at other points of the island — and so be done for the day. But she found that "they" had invented something else: she must merge with the whole anonymous mass of pilgrims for mass prayer in the church.

A slur of wet feet; patter of rain on leaded windows; smells of bog water and damp clothing; the thousand voices responding to the incantations. At her right a young girl of about seventeen was uttering heartfelt responses. On her left an old man in his sixties gave them out loudly. On all sides, before her, behind her, the same passionate exchange of energy, while all she felt was a crust hardening about her heart, and she thought, in despair, "I have no more feeling than a stone!" And she thought, looking about her, that tonight this vigil would go on for hour after hour until the dark, leaded windows coloured again in the morning light. She leaned her face in her palms and whispered, "O God, please let me out of myself!" The waves of voices beat and rumbled in her ears as in an empty shell.

She was carried out on the general sliding whispering of the bare feet into the last gleanings of the daylight to begin her second circuit. In the porch she cowered back from the rain. It was settling into a filthy night. She was thrust forward by the crowd, flowed with its force to the iron cross by the shingle's edge. She took her place in the queue and then with the night wind pasting her hair across her face she raised her arms and once again renounced the world, the flesh, and the Devil. She did four circles of the church on the gritty concrete. She circled the first cell's stones. She completed the second circle. Her prayers were become numb by now. She stumbled, muttering them, up and down the third steeply sloped cell, or bed. She was a drowned cat and one knee was bleeding. At the fourth cell she saw him.

He was standing about six yards away looking at her. He wore a white raincoat buttoned tight about his throat. His feet were bare. His hair was streaked down his forehead as if he had been swimming. She stumbled towards him and dragged him by the arm down to the edge of the boat slip.

"What are you doing here?" she cried furiously. "Why did you follow me?"

He looked down at her calmly.

"Why shouldn't I be here?"

"Because you don't believe in it! You've just followed me to sneer at me, to mock at me! Or from sheer vulgar curiosity!"

"No," he said, without raising his voice. "I've come to see just what it is that you believe in. I want to know all about you. I want to know why you came here. I don't want you to do anything or have anything that I can't do or can't know. And as for believing — we all believe in something."

Dusk was closing in on the island and the lake. She had to peer into his face to catch his expression.

"But I've known you for years and you've never shown any sign of believing in anything but microscopes and microbes and symptoms. It's absurd, you couldn't be serious about anything like this. I'm beginning to hate you!"

"Are you?" he said, so softly that she had to lean near him to hear him over the slapping of the waves against the boat slip. A slow rift in the clouds let down a star; by its light she saw his smile.

"Yes!" she cried, so loudly that he swept out a hand and gripped her by the arm. Then he took her other arm and said gently:

"I don't think you should have come here, Jenny. You're only tearing yourself to bits. There are some places where some people should never go, things some people should never try to do — however good they may be for others. I know why you came here. You feel you ought to get rid of me, but you haven't the guts to do it, so you come up here into the mountains to get your druids to work it by magic. All right! I'm going to ask them to help you."

He laughed and let her go, giving her a slight impulse away from him.

"Ask? You will *ask?* Do you mean to tell me that you have said as much as one single, solitary prayer on this island?"

"Yes," he said casually, "I have."

She scorned him.

"Are you trying to tell me, Bobby, that you are doing this pilgrimage?"

"I haven't fasted. I didn't know about that. And, anyway, I probably won't. I've got my pockets stuffed with two pounds of the best chocolates I could buy in Bundoran. I don't suppose I'll even stay up all night like the rest of you. The place is so crowded that I don't suppose anybody will notice me if I curl up in some corner of the boathouse. I heard somebody saying that people had to sleep there last night. But you never know — I might — I just might stay awake. If I do, it will remind me of going to midnight Mass with my father when I was a kid. Or going to retreats, when we used to all hold up a lighted candle and renounce the Devil.

"It was a queer sensation standing up there by the lake and saying those words all over again. Do you know, I thought I'd completely forgotten them!"

"The next thing you're going to say is that you believe in the Devil! You fraud!"

"Oh, there's no trouble about believing in that old gentleman. There isn't a doctor in the world who doesn't, though he will give him another name. And on a wet night, in a place like this, you could believe in a lot of things. No, my girl, what I find it hard to believe in is the flesh and the world. They are good things. Do you think I'm ever going to believe that your body and my body are evil? And you don't either! And you are certainly never going to renounce the world, because you are tied to it hand and foot!"

"That's not true!"

His voice cut her like a whip:

"Then why do you go on living with your husband?"

She stammered feebly. He cut at her again:

"You do it because he's rich, and you like comfort, and you like being a 'somebody.'"

With a switch of her head she brushed past him. She did not see him again that night.

The night world turned imperceptibly. In the church, for hour after hour, the voices obstinately beat back the responses. She sank under the hum of the prayer wheel, the lust for sleep, her own despairs. Was he among the crowd? Or asleep in a corner of the boatshed? She saw his flatly domed fingers, a surgeon's hand, so strong, so sensitive. She gasped at the sensual image she had evoked.

The moon touched a black window with colour. After an age it had stolen to another. Heads drooped. Neighbours poked one another awake with a smile. Many of them had risen from the benches in order to keep themselves awake and were circling the aisles in a loose procession of slurring feet, responding as they moved. Exhaustion began to work on her mind. Objects began to disconnect, become isolated each within its own outline — now it was the pulpit, now a statue, now a crucifix. Each object took on the vividness of a hallucination. The crucifix detached itself from the wall and leaned towards her, and for a long while she saw nothing but the heavy pendent body, the staring eyes, so that when the old man at her side let his head sink over on her shoulder and then woke up with a start she felt him no more than if they were two fishes touching in the sea. Bit by bit the incantations drew her in; sounds came from her mouth; prayers flowed between her and those troubled eyes that fixed hers. She swam into an ecstasy as rare as one of those perfect dances of her youth when she used to swing in a whirl of music, a swirl of bodies, a circling of lights, floated out of her mortal frame, alone in the arms that embraced her.

Suddenly it all exploded. One of the four respites of the night had halted the prayers. The massed pilgrims relaxed. She looked blearily about her, no longer disjunct. Her guts rumbled. She looked at the old man beside her. She smiled at him and he at her.

"My poor old knees are crucified," he grinned.

"You should have the skirts," she grinned back.

They were all going out to stretch in the cool, and now dry, air, or to snatch a smoke. The amber windows of the church shivered in a pool of water. A hearty-voiced young woman leaning on the balustrade lit a match for her. The match hissed into the invisible lake lapping below.

"The ould fag," said the young woman, dragging deep on her cigarette, "is a great comfort. 'Tis as good as a man."

"I wonder," she said, "what would Saint Patrick think if he saw women smoking on his island?"

"He'd beat the living lights out of the lot of us."

She laughed aloud. She must tell him that . . . She began to wander through the dark crowds in search of him. He had said something that wasn't true and she would answer him. She went through the crowds down to the boat slip. He was standing there, looking out into the dark as if he had not stirred since she saw him there before midnight. For a moment she regarded him, frightened by the force of the love that gushed into her. Then she approached him.

"Well, Mr. Worldly Wiseman? Enjoying your boathouse bed?"

"I'm doing the vigil," he said smugly.

"You sound almighty pleased with yourself."

He spoke eagerly now:

"Jenny, we mustn't quarrel. We must understand one another. And understand this place. I'm just beginning to. An island. In a remote lake. Among the mountains. Nighttime. No sleep. Hunger. The conditions of the desert. I was right in what I said to you. Can't you see how the old hermits who used to live here could swim off into a trance in which nothing existed but themselves and their visions? I told you a man can renounce what he calls the Devil, but not the flesh, not the world. They thought, like you, that they could throw away the flesh and the world, but they were using the flesh to achieve one of the rarest experiences in the world! Don't you see it?"

"Experiences! The next thing you'll be talking about is symptoms."

"Well, surely, you must have observed?" He peered at the luminous dial of his watch. "I should say that about four o'clock we will probably begin to experience a definite sense of dissociation. After that a positive alienation . . ."

She turned furiously from him. She came back to say:

"I would much prefer, Bobby, if you would have the decency to go away in the morning. I can find my own way home. I hope we don't meet again on this island. Or out of it!"

"The magic working?" he laughed.

After that she made a deliberate effort of the mind to mean and to feel every separate word of the prayers — which is a great foolishness since prayers are not poems to be read or even understood; they are an instinct; to dance would be as wise. She thought that if she could not feel what she said how could she mean it, and so she tried to savour every word, and, from trying to mean each word, lagged behind the rest, sank into herself, and ceased to pray. After the second respite she prayed only to keep awake. As the first cold pallor of morning came into the windows her heart rose again. But the eastern hills are high here and the morning holds off stubbornly. It is the worst hour of the vigil, when the body ebbs, the prayers sink to a drone, and the night seems to have begun all over again.

At the last respite she emerged to see pale tents of blue on the hills. The slow cumulus clouds cast a sheen on the water. There is no sound. No birds sing. At this hour the pilgrims are too awed or too exhausted to speak, so that the island reverts to its ancient silence in spite of the crowds.

By the end of the last bout she was calm like the morning lake. She longed for the cup of black tea. She was unaware of her companions. She did not think of him. She was unaware of herself. She no more thought of God than a slave thinks of his master, and after she had drunk her tea she sat in the morning sun outside the women's hostel like an old blind woman who has nothing in life to wait for but sleep.

The long day expired as dimly as the vapour rising from the water. The heat became morbid. One is said to be free on this second day to converse, to think, to write, to read, to do anything at all that one pleases except the one thing everybody wants to do — to sleep. She did nothing but watch the clouds, or listen to the gentle muttering of the lake. Before noon she heard some departing pilgrims singing a hymn as the great ferryboats pushed off. She heard their voices without longing; she did not even desire food. When she met him she was without rancour.

"Still here?" she said, and when he nodded: "Sleepy?"

"Sleepy."

"Too many chocolates, probably."

"I didn't eat them. I took them out of my pockets one by one as I leaned over the balustrade and guessed what center each had — coffee, marshmallow, nut, toffee, cream — and dropped it in with a little splash to the holy fishes."

She looked up at him gravely.

"Are you really trying to join in this pilgrimage?"

"Botching it. I'm behindhand with my rounds. I have to do five circuits between today and tomorrow. I may never get them done. Still, something is better than nothing."

"You dear fool!"

If he had not walked away then she would have had to; such a gush of affection came over her at the thought of what he was doing, and why he was doing it — stupidly, just like a man; sceptically, just like a man; not admitting it to himself, just like a man; for all sorts of damnfool rational reasons, just like a man; and not at all for the only reason that she knew was his real reason: because she was doing it, which meant that he loved her. She sat back, and closed her eyes, and the tears of chagrin oozed between her lids as she felt her womb stir with desire of him.

When they met again it was late afternoon.

"Done four rounds," he said so cheerfully that he maddened her.

"It's not golf, Bobby, damn you!"

"I should jolly well think not. I may tell you my feet are in such a condition I won't be able to play golf for a week. Look!"

She did not look. She took his arm and led him to the quietest corner she could find.

"Bobby, I am going to confess something to you. I've been thinking about it all day trying to get it clear. I know now why I came here. I came because I know inside in me that some day our apple will have to fall off the tree. I'm forty. You are nearly fifty. It will have to happen. I came here because I thought it right to admit that some day, if it has to be, I am willing to give you up."

He began to shake all over with laughter.

"What the hell are you laughing at?" she moaned.

"When women begin to reason! Listen, wasn't there a chap one time who said, 'O God, please make me chaste, but not just yet'?"

"What I am saying is 'now,' if it has to be, if it can be, if I can make it be. I suppose," she said wildly, "I'm really asking for a miracle, that my husband would die, or that you'd die, or something like that that would make it all come right!"

He burst into such a peal of laughter that she looked around her apprehensively. A few people near them also happened to be laughing over something and looked at them indulgently.

"Do you realize, Bobby, that when I go to confession here I will have to tell all about us, and I will have to promise to give you up?"

"Yes, darling, and you won't mean a single word of it."

"But I always mean it!"

He stared at her as if he were pushing curtains aside in her.

"Always? Do you mean you've been saying it for six years?"

"I mean it when I say it. Then I get weak. I can't help it, Bobby. You know that!" She saw the contempt in his eyes and began to talk rapidly, twisting her marriage ring madly around her finger. He kept staring into her eyes like a man staring down the long perspective of a railway line waiting for the engine to appear. "So you see why there wasn't any sense in asking me yesterday why I come now and not at some other time, because with me there isn't any other time, it's always *now*, I meet you *now*, and I love you *now*, and I think it's not right *now*, and then I think, 'No, not *now*,' and then I say I'll give you up *now*, and I mean it every time until we meet again, and it begins all over again, and there's never any end to it until some day I can say, 'Yes, I used to know him once, but not now,' and then it will be a *now* where there won't be any other *now* any more because there'll be nothing to live for."

The tears were leaking down her face. He sighed:

"Dear me! You have got yourself into a mess, haven't you?"

"O God, the promises and the promises! I wish the world would end tonight and we'd both die together!"

He gave her his big damp handkerchief. She wiped her eyes and blew her nose and said:

"You don't mean to go to confession, do you?"

He chuckled sourly.

"And promise? I must go and finish a round of pious golf. I'm afraid, old girl, you just want to get me into the same mess as yourself. No, thank you. You must solve your own problems in your own way, and I in mine."

That was the last time she spoke to him that day.

She went back to the balustrade where she had smoked with the hearty girl in the early hours of the morning. She was there again. She wore a scarlet beret. She was smoking again. She began to talk, and the talk flowed from her without stop. She had fine broad shoulders, a big mobile mouth, and a pair of wild goat's eyes. After a while it became clear that the woman was beside herself with terror. She suddenly let it all out in a gush of exhaled smoke.

"Do you know why I'm hanging around here? Because I ought to go into confession and I'm in dread of it. He'll tear me alive. He'll murder me. It's not easy for a girl like me, I can promise you!"

"You must have terrible sins to tell?" she smiled comfortingly.

"He'll slaughter me, I'm telling you."

"What is it? Boys?"

The two goat's eyes dilated with fear and joy. Her hands shook like a drunkard's.

"I can't keep away from them. I wish to God I never came here."

"But how silly! It's only a human thing. I'm sure half the people here have the same tale to tell. It's an old story, child, the priests are sick of hearing it."

"Oh, don't be talking! Let me alone! I'm criminal, I tell yeh! And there are things you can't explain to a priest. My God, you can hardly explain 'em to a doctor?"

"You're married?" — looking at her ring.

"Poor Tom! I have him wore out. He took me to a doctor one time to know would anything cure me. The old foolah took me temperature and gave me a book like a bus guide about when it's safe and when it isn't safe to make love, the ould eedjut! I was pregnant again before Christmas. Six years married and I have six kids; nobody could stand that gait o'going. And I'm only twenty-four. Am I to have a baby every year of my life? I'd give me right hand this minute for a double whiskey."

"Look, you poor child! We are all in the same old ferryboat here. What about me?"

"You?"

"It's not men with me, it's worse."

"Worse? In God's name, what's worse than men?"

The girl looked all over her, followed her arm down to her hand, to her third finger.

"One man."

The tawny eyes swivelled back to her face and immediately understood.

"Are you very fond of him?" she asked gently, and taking the unspoken answer said, still more pityingly, "You can't give him up?"

"It's six years now and I haven't been able to give him up."

The girl's eyes roved sadly over the lake as if she were surveying a lake of human unhappiness. Then she threw her butt into the water and her red beret disappeared into the maw of the church porch.

She saw him twice before the dusk thickened and the day grew cold again with the early sunset. He was sitting directly opposite her before the men's hostel, smoking, staring at the ground between his legs. They sat facing one another. They were separated by their identities, joined by their love. She glimpsed him only once after that, at the hour when the sky and the hills merge, an outline passing across the lake. Soon after she had permission to go to her cubicle. Immediately she lay down she spiralled to the bottom of a deep lake of sleep.

She awoke refreshed and unburthened. She had received the island's gift: its sense of remoteness from the world, almost a sensation of the world's death. It is the source of the island's kindness. Nobody is just matter, poor to be exploited by rich, weak to be exploited by the strong; in mutual generosity each recognizes the other only as a form of soul; it is a brief, harsh Utopia of equality in nakedness. The bare feet are a symbol of that nakedness unknown in the world they have left.

The happiness to which she awoke was dimmed a little by a conversation she had with an Englishman over breakfast — the usual black tea and a piece of oaten bread. He was a city man who had arrived the day before, been up all night while she slept. He had not yet shaved; he was about sixty-two or three; small and tubby, his eyes perpetually wide and unfocusing behind pince-nez glasses.

"That's right," he said, answering her question. "I'm from England. Liverpool. I cross by the night boat and get here the next afternoon. Quite convenient, really. I've come here every year for the last twenty-two years, apart from the war years. I come on account of my wife."

"Is she ill?"

"She died twenty-two years ago. No, it's not what you might think — I'm not praying for her. She was a good woman, but, well, you see, I wasn't very kind to her. I don't mean I quarrelled with her, or drank, or was unfaithful. I never gambled. I've never smoked in my life." His hands made a faint movement that was meant to express a whole life, all the confusion and trouble of his soul. "It's just that I wasn't kind. I didn't make her happy."

"Isn't that, " she said, to comfort him, "a very private feeling? I mean, it's not in the Ten Commandments that thou shalt make thy wife happy."

He did not smile. He made the same faint movement with his fingers.

"Oh, I don't know! What's love if it doesn't do that? I mean to say, it is something godly to love another human being, isn't it? I mean, what does 'godly' mean if it doesn't mean giving up everything for another? It isn't human to love, you know. It's foolish, it's a folly, a divine folly. It's beyond all reason, all limits. I didn't rise to it," he concluded sadly.

She looked at him, and thought, "A little fat man, a clerk in some Liverpool office all his life, married to some mousy little woman, thinking about love as if he were some sort of Greek mystic."

"It's often," she said lamely, "more difficult to love one's husband, or one's wife, as the case may be, than to love one's neighbour."

"Oh, much!" he agreed without a smile. "Much! Much more difficult!"

At which she was overcome by the thought that inside ourselves we have no room without a secret door; no solid self that has not a ghost inside it trying to escape. If I leave Bobby I still have George. If I leave George I still have myself, and whatever I find in myself. She patted the little man's hand and left him, fearing that if she let him talk on even his one little piece of sincerity would prove to be a fantasy, and in the room that he had found behind his own room she would open other doors leading to other obsessions. He had told her something true about her own imperfection, and about the nature of love, and she wanted to share it while it was still true. But she could not find him, and there was still one more circuit to do before the ferryboat left. She did meet Goat's Eyes. The girl clutched her with tears magnifying her yellow-and-green irises and gasped joyously:

"I found a lamb of a priest. A saint anointed! He was as gentle! 'What's your husband earning?' says he. "Four pounds ten a week, Father,' says I. 'And six children?' says he. 'You poor woman,' says he, 'you don't need to come here at all. Your Purgatory is at home.' He laid all the blame on poor Tom. And, God forgive me, I let him do it. 'Bring him here to me,' says he, 'and I'll cool him for you.' God bless the poor innocent priest, I wish I knew as little about marriage as he does. But," and she broke into a wail, "sure he has me ruined altogether now. He's after making me so fond of poor Tommy I think I'll never get home soon enough to go to bed with him." And in a vast flood of tears of joy, of relief, and of fresh misery: "I wish I was a bloomin' nun!"

It was not until they were all waiting at the ferryboat that she saw him. She managed to sit beside him in the boat. He touched her hand and winked. She smiled back at him. The bugler blew his bugle. A tardy traveller came racing out of the men's hostel. The boatload cheered him, the bugler helped him aboard with a joke about people who can't be persuaded to stop praying, and there was a general chaff about people who have a lot to pray about, and then somebody raised the parting hymn, and the rowers began to push the heavy oars, and singing they were slowly rowed across the summer lake back to the world.

They were driving back out of the hills by the road they had come, both silent. At last she could hold in her question no longer:

"Did you go, Bobby?"

Meaning: had he, after all his years of silence, of rebellion, of disbelief, made his peace with God at the price of a compact against her. He replied gently:

"Did I probe your secrets all these years?"

She took the rebuke humbly, and for several miles they drove on in silence. They were close, their shoulders touched, but between them there stood that impenetrable wall of identity that segregates every human being in a private world of self. Feeling it she realized at last that it is only in places like the lake-island that the barriers of self break down. The tubby little clerk from Liverpool had been right. Only when love desires nothing but renunciation, total surrender, does self surpass self. Everybody who ever entered the island left the world of self behind for a few hours, exchanged it for what the little man had called a divine folly. It was possible only for a few hours — unless one had the courage, or the folly, to renounce the world altogether. Then another thought came to her. In the world there might also be escape from the world.

"Do you think, Bobby, that when people are in love they can give up everything for one another?"

"No," he said flatly. "Except perhaps in the first raptures?"

"If I had a child I think I could sacrifice anything for it. Even my life."

"Yes," he agreed. "It has been known to happen."

And she looked at him sadly, knowing that they would never be able to marry, and even if she did that she would never have children. And yet, if they could have married, there was a lake . . .

"Do you know what I'm planning at this moment?" he asked breezily.

She asked without interest what it was.

"Well, I'm simply planning the meal we're going to eat tonight in Galway, at midnight."

"At midnight? Then we're going on with this pilgrimage? Are we?"

"Don't *you* want to? It was your idea in the beginning."

"All right. And what are we going to do until midnight? I've never known time to be so long."

"I'm going to spend the day fishing behind Glencar. That will kill the hungry day. After that, until midnight, we'll take the longest possible road around Connemara. Then would you have any objections to mountain trout cooked in milk, stuffed roast kid with fresh peas and spuds in their jackets, apple pie and whipped cream, with a cool Pouilly Fuissé, a cosy 1929 claret, West of Ireland Pont l'Évêque, finishing up with Gaelic coffee and two Otards? Much more in your line, if I know anything about you, than your silly old black tea and hot salt water."

"I admit I like the things of the flesh."

"You live for them!"

He had said it so gently, so affectionately that, half in dismay, half with amusement, she could not help remembering Goat's Eyes, racing home as fast as the bus would carry her to make love to her Tommy. After that they hardly spoke at all, and then only of casual things such as a castle beside the road, the sun on the edging sea, a tinker's caravan, an opening view. It was early afternoon as they entered the deep valley at Glencar and he probed in second gear for an attractive length of stream, found one and started eagerly to put his rod together. He began to walk up against the dazzling bubble of water and within an hour was out of sight. She stretched herself out on a rug on the bank and fell sound asleep.

It was nearly four o'clock before she woke up, stiff and thirsty. She drank from a pool in the stream, and for an hour she sat alone by the pool, looking into its peat-brown depth, as vacantly contented as a tinker's wife to live for the moment, to let time wind and unwind everything. It was five o'clock before she saw him approaching, plodding in his flopping waders, with four trout on a rush stalk. He threw the fish at her feet and himself beside them.

"I nearly ate them raw," he said.

"Let's cook them and eat them," she said fiercely.

He looked at her for a moment, then got up and began to gather dry twigs, found Monday's newspaper in the car — it looked like a paper of years ago — and started the fire. She watched while he fed it. When it was big enough in its fall to have made a hot bed of embers he roasted two of the trout across the hook of his gaff, and she smelled the crisping flesh and sighed. At last he laid them, browned and crackly, on the grass by her hand. She took one by its crusted tail, smelled it, looked at him, and slung it furiously into the heart of the fire. He gave a sniff-laugh and did the same with his.

"Copy cat!" she said.

"Let's get the hell out of here," he said, jumping up. "Carry the kit, will you?"

She rose, collected the gear, and followed him saying:

"I feel like an Arab wife. 'Carry the pack. Go here. Go there.'"

They climbed out of the glens on to the flat moorland of the Easky peninsula where the evening light was a cold ochre gleaming across the green bogland that was streaked with all the weedy colours of a strand at ebb. At Ballina she suggested that they should have tea.

"It will be a pleasant change of diet!" he said.

When they had found a café and she was ordering the tea he said to the waitress:

"And bring lots of hot buttered toast."

"This," she said, as she poured out the tea and held up the milk jug questioningly, "is a new technique of seduction. Milk?"

"Are you having milk?"

"No."

"No, then."

"Some nice hot buttered toast?"

"Are you having toast?" he demanded.

"Why the bloody hell should it be up to me to decide?"

"I asked you a polite question," he said rudely.

"No."

"No!"

They looked at one another as they sipped the black tea like two people who are falling head over heels into hatred of one another.

"Could you possibly tell me," he said presently, "why I bother my head with a fool of a woman like you?"

"I can only suppose, Bobby, that it is because we are in love with one another."

"I can only suppose so," he growled. "Let's get on!"

They took the longest way round he could find on the map, west into County Mayo, across between the lake at Pontoon, over the level bogland to Castlebar. Here the mountains walled in the bogland plain with cobalt air — in the fading light the land was losing all solidity. Clouds like soapsuds rose and rose over the edges of the mountains until they glowed as if there was a fire of embers behind the blue ranges. In Castlebar he pulled up by the post office and telephoned to the hotel at Salthill for dinner and two rooms. When he came out he saw a poster in a shop window and said:

"Why don't we go to the pictures? It will kill a couple of hours."

"By rights," she said, "you ought to be driving me home to Dublin."

"If you wish me to I will."

"Would you if I asked you?"

"Do you want me to?"

"I suppose it's rather late now, isn't it?"

"Not at all. Fast going we could be there about one o'clock. Shall we?"

"It wouldn't help. George is away. I'd have to bring you in and give you something to eat, and . . . Let's go to the blasted movies!"

The film was *Charley's Aunt*. They watched its slapstick gloomily. When they came out, after nine o'clock, there was still a vestigial light in the sky. They drove on and on, westward still, prolonging the light, prolonging the drive, holding off the night's decision. Before Killary they paused at a black-faced lake, got out, and stood beside its quarried beauty. Nothing along its stony beach but a few wind-torn rushes.

"I could eat you," he said.

She replied that only lovers and cannibals talk like that.

They dawdled past the long fiord of Killary where young people on holiday sat outside the hotel, their drinks on the trestled tables. In Clifden the street was empty, people already climbing to bed, as the lights in the upper windows showed. They branched off on the long coastal road where the sparse whitewashed cottages were whiter than the foam of waves that barely suggested sea. At another darker strand they halted, but now they saw no foam at all and divined the sea only by its invisible whispering, or when a star touched a wave. Midnight was now only an hour away.

Their headlights sent rocks and rabbits into movement. The heather streamed past them like kangaroos. It was well past eleven as they poured along the lonely land by Galway Bay. Neither of them had spoken for an hour. As they drove into Salthill there was nobody abroad. Galway was dark. Only the porch light of the hotel showed that it was alive. When he turned off the engine the only sound at first was the crinkle of contracting metal as the engine began to cool. Then to their right they heard the lisping bay. The panel button lit the dashboard clock.

"A quarter to," he said, leaning back. She neither spoke nor stirred. "Jenny!" he said sharply.

She turned her head slowly and by the dashboard light he saw her white smile.

"Yes, darling?"

"Worn out?" he asked, and patted her knee.

She vibrated her whole body so that the seat shook, and stretched her arms about her head, and lowering them let her head fall on his shoulder, and sighed happily, and said:

"What I want is a good long drink of anything on earth except tea."

These homing twelve o'clockers from Lough Derg are well known in every hotel all over the west of Ireland. Revelry is the reward of penance. The porter welcomed them as if they were heroes returned from a war. As he led them to their rooms he praised them, he sympathized with them, he patted them up and he patted them down, he assured them that the ritual grill was at that moment sizzling over the fire, he proffered them hot baths, and he told them where to discover the bar. "Ye will discover it ..." was his phrase. The wording was exact, for the bar's gaiety was muffled by dim lighting, drawn blinds, locked doors. In the overheated room he took off his jacket and loosened his tie. They had to win a corner of the counter, and his order was for two highballs with ice in them. Within two minutes they were at home with the crowd. The island might never have existed if the barmaid, who knew where they had come from, had not laughed: "I suppose ye'll ate like lions?"

After supper they relished the bar once more, sipping slowly now, so refreshed that they could have started on the road again without distaste or regret. As they sipped they gradually became aware of a soft strumming and drumming near at hand, and were told that there was a dance on in the hotel next door. He raised his eyebrows to her. She laughed and nodded.

They gave it up at three o'clock and walked out into the warm-cool of the early summer morning. Gently tipsy, gently tired they walked to the little promenade. They leaned on the railing and he put his arm about her waist, and she put hers around his, and they gazed at the moon silently raking its path across the sea towards Aran. They had come, she knew, to the decisive moment. He said:

"They have a fine night for it tonight on the island."

"A better night than we had," she said tremulously.

After another spell of wave fall and silence he said:

"Do you know what I'm thinking, Jenny? I'm thinking that I wouldn't mind going back there again next year. Maybe I might do it properly the next time?"

"The next time?" she whispered, and all her body began to dissolve and, closing her eyes, she leaned against him. He, too, closed his eyes, and all his body became as rigid as a steel girder that flutters in a storm. Slowly they opened their love-drunk eyes, and stood looking long over the brightness and blackness of the sea. Then, gently, ever so gently, with a gentleness that terrified her he said:

"Shall we go in, my sweet?"

She did not stir. She did not speak. Slowly turning to him she lifted her eyes to him pleadingly.

"No, Bobby, please, not yet."

"Not yet?"

"Not tonight!"

He looked down at her, and drew his arms about her. They kissed passionately. She knew what that kiss implied. Their mouths parted. Hand in hand they walked slowly back to the hotel, to their separate rooms.

CYNTHIA OZICK

Cynthia Ozick was born in 1928 in New York City, the daughter of a pharmacist. She received her education at New York University and Ohio State University and, thereafter, briefly taught English. Her writing career has been diverse: she is a novelist, essayist, translator, and critic. As critic Clifton Fadiman notes, it is her short fiction — emerging from the Jewish tradition and, like everything she writes, fiercely intelligent — that has made her literary reputation. Her stories are collected in *The Pagan Rabbi and Other Stories* (1971), *Bloodshed and Three Novellas* (1976), and *Levitation: Five Fictions* (1981). Her novels are *Trust* (1966) and *The Cannibal Galaxy* (1983). Like many writers, Ozick has wrestled in her writing — fiction and nonfiction alike — with the horrifying fact and implications of the Holocaust. "The Shawl" is, excruciatingly, one of her most profoundly moving statements about that atrocity.

The Shawl

Stella, cold, cold the coldness of hell. How they walked on the roads together, Rosa with Magda curled up between sore breasts, Magda wound up in the shawl. Sometimes Stella carried Magda. But she was jealous of Magda. A thin girl of fourteen, too small, with thin breasts of her own, Stella wanted to be wrapped in a shawl, hidden away, asleep, rocked by the march, a baby, a round infant in arms. Magda took Rosa's nipple, and Rosa never stopped walking, a walking cradle. There was not enough milk; sometimes Magda sucked air; then she screamed. Stella was ravenous. Her knees were tumors on sticks, her elbows chicken bones.

Rosa did not feel hunger; she felt light, not like someone walking but like someone in a faint, in trance, arrested in a fit, someone who is already a floating angel, alert and seeing everything, but in the air, not there, not touching the road. As if teetering on the tips of her fingernails. She looked into Magda's face through a gap in the shawl: a squirrel in a nest, safe, no one could reach her inside the little house of the shawl's windings. The face, very round, a pocket mirror of a face: but it was not Rosa's bleak complexion, dark like cholera, it was another kind of face altogether, eyes blue as air, smooth feathers of hair nearly as yellow as the Star sewn into Rosa's coat. You could think she was one of *their* babies.

Rosa, floating, dreamed of giving Magda away in one of the villages. She could leave the line for a minute and push Magda into the hands of any woman on the side of the road. But if she moved out of line they might shoot. And even if she fled the line for half a second and pushed the shawl-bundle at a stranger, would the woman take it? She might be surprised, or afraid; she might drop the shawl, and Magda would fall out and strike her head and die. The little round head. Such a good child, she gave up screaming, and sucked now only for the taste of the drying nipple itself. The neat grip of the tiny gums. One mite of a tooth tip sticking up in the bottom gum, how shining, an elfin tombstone of white marble gleaming there. Without complaining, Magda relinquished Rosa's teats, first the left, then the right; both were cracked, not a sniff of milk. The duct crevice extinct, a dead volcano, blind eye, chill hole, so Magda took the corner of the shawl and milked it instead. She sucked and sucked, flooding the threads with wetness. The shawl's good flavor, milk of linen.

It was a magic shawl, it could nourish an infant for three days and three nights. Magda did not die, she stayed alive, although very quiet. A peculiar smell, of cinnamon and almonds, lifted out of her mouth. She held her eyes open every moment, forgetting how to blink or nap, and Rosa and sometimes Stella studied their blueness. On the road they raised one burden of a leg after another and studied Magda's face. "Aryan," Stella said, in a voice grown as thin as a string; and Rosa thought how Stella gazed at Magda like a young cannibal. And the time that Stella said "Aryan," it sounded to Rosa as if Stella had really said "Let us devour her."

But Magda lived to walk. She lived that long, but she did not walk very well, partly because she was only fifteen months old, and partly because the spindles of her legs could not hold up her fat belly. It was fat with air, full and round. Rosa gave almost all her food to Magda, Stella gave nothing; Stella was ravenous, a growing child herself, but not growing much. Stella did not menstruate. Rosa did not menstruate. Rosa was ravenous, but also not; she learned from Magda how to drink the taste of a finger in one's mouth. They were in a place without pity, all pity was annihilated in Rosa, she looked at Stella's bones without pity. She was sure that Stella was waiting for Magda to die so she could put her teeth into the little thighs.

Rosa knew Magda was going to die very soon; she should have been dead already, but she had been buried away deep inside the magic shawl, mistaken there for the shivering mound of Rosa's breasts; Rosa clung to the shawl as if it covered only herself. No one took it away from her. Magda was mute. She never cried. Rosa hid her in the barracks, under the shawl, but she knew that one day someone would inform; or one day someone, not even Stella, would steal Magda to eat her. When Magda began to walk Rosa knew that Magda was going to die very soon, something would happen. She was afraid to fall asleep; she slept with the weight of her thigh on Magda's body; she was afraid she would smother Magda under her thigh. The weight of Rosa was becoming less and less; Rosa and Stella were slowly turning into air.

Magda was quiet, but her eyes were horribly alive, like blue tigers. She watched. Sometimes she laughed — it seemed a laugh, but how could it be? Magda had never seen anyone laugh. Still, Magda laughed at her shawl when the wind blew its corners, the bad wind with pieces of black in it, that made Stella's and Rosa's eyes tear. Magda's eyes were always clear and tearless. She watched like a tiger. She guarded her shawl. No one could touch it; only Rosa could touch it. Stella was not allowed. The shawl was Magda's own baby, her pet, her little sister. She tangled herself up in it and sucked on one of the corners when she wanted to be very still.

Then Stella took the shawl away and made Magda die.

Afterward Stella said: "I was cold."

And afterward she was always cold, always. The cold went into her heart: Rosa saw that Stella's heart was cold. Magda flopped onward with her little pencil legs scribbling this way and that, in search of the shawl; the pencils faltered at the barracks opening, where the light began. Rosa saw and pursued. But already Magda was in the square outside the barracks, in the jolly light. It was the roll-call arena. Every morning Rosa had to conceal Magda under the shawl against a wall of the barracks and go out and stand in the arena with Stella and hundreds of others, sometimes for hours, and Magda, deserted, was quiet under the shawl, sucking on her corner. Every day Magda was silent, and so she did not die. Rosa saw that today Magda was going to die, and at the same time a fearful joy ran in Rosa's two palms, her fingers were on fire, she was astonished, febrile: Magda, in the sunlight, swaying on her pencil legs, was howling. Ever since the drying up of Rosa's nipples, ever since Magda's last scream on the road, Magda had been devoid of any syllable; Magda was a mute. Rosa believed that something had gone wrong with her vocal cords, with her windpipe, with the cave of her larynx; Magda was defective, without a voice; perhaps she was deaf; there might be something amiss with her intelligence; Magda was dumb. Even the laugh that came when the ash-stippled wind made a clown out of Magda's shawl was only the air-blown showing of her teeth. Even when the lice, head lice and body lice, crazed her so that she became as wild as one of the big rats that plundered the barracks at daybreak looking for carrion, she rubbed and scratched and kicked and bit and rolled without a whimper. But now Magda's mouth was spilling a long viscous rope of clamor.

"Maaaa . . ."

It was the first noise Magda had ever sent out from her throat since the drying up of Rosa's nipples.

"Maaaa . . . aaa!"

Again! Magda was wavering in the perilous sunlight of the arena, scrabbling on such pitiful little bent shins. Rosa saw. She saw that Magda was grieving for the loss of her shawl, she saw that Magda was going to die. A tide of commands hammered in Rosa's nipples: Fetch, get, bring! But she did not know which to go after first, Magda or the shawl. If she jumped out into the arena to snatch Magda up, the howling would not stop, because Magda would still not have the shawl; but if she ran back into the barracks to find the shawl, and if she found it, and if she came after Magda holding it and shaking it, then she would get Magda back, Magda would put the shawl in her mouth and turn dumb again.

Rosa entered the dark. It was easy to discover the shawl. Stella was heaped under it, asleep in her thin bones. Rosa tore the shawl free and flew — she could fly, she was only air — into the arena. The sunheat murmured of another life, of butterflies in summer. The light was placid, mellow. On the other side of the steel fence, far away, there were green meadows speckled with dandelions and deep-colored violets; beyond them, even farther, innocent tiger lilies, tall, lifting their orange bonnets. In the barracks they spoke of "flowers," of "rain": excrement, thick turd-braids, and the slow stinking maroon waterfall that slunk down from the upper bunks, the stink mixed with a bitter fatty floating smoke that greased Rosa's skin. She stood for an instant at the margin of the arena. Sometimes the electricity inside the fence would seem to hum; even Stella said it was only an imagining, but Rosa heard real sounds in the wire: grainy sad voices. The farther she was from the fence, the more clearly the voices crowded at her. The lamenting voices strummed so convincingly, so passionately, it was impossible to suspect them of being phantoms. The voices told her to hold up the shawl, high; the voices told her to shake it, to whip with it, to unfurl it like a flag. Rosa lifted, shook, whipped, unfurled. Far off, very far, Magda leaned across her air-fed belly, reaching out with the rods of her arms. She was high up, elevated, riding someone's shoulder. But the shoulder that carried Magda was not coming toward Rosa and the shawl, it was drifting away, the speck of Magda was moving more and more into the smoky distance. Above the shoulder a helmet glinted. The light tapped the helmet and sparkled it into a goblet. Below the helmet a black body like a domino and a pair of black boots hurled themselves in the direction of the electrified fence. The electric voices began to chatter wildly. "Maa-maa, maaamaaa," they all hummed together. How far Magda was from Rosa now, across the whole square, past a dozen barracks, all the way on the other side! She was no bigger than a moth.

All at once Magda was swimming through the air. The whole of Magda traveled through loftiness. She looked like a butterfly touching a silver vine. And the moment Magda's feathered round head and her pencil legs and balloonish belly and zigzag arms splashed against the fence, the steel voices went mad in their growling, urging Rosa to run and run to the spot where Magda had fallen from her flight against the electrified fence; but of course Rosa did not obey them. She only stood, because if she ran they would shoot, and if she tried to pick up the sticks of Magda's body they would shoot, and if she let the wolf's screech ascending now through the ladder of her skeleton break out, they would shoot; so she took Magda's shawl and filled her own mouth with it, stuffed it in and stuffed it in, until she was swallowing up the wolf's screech and tasting the cinnamon and almond depth of Magda's saliva; and Rosa drank Magda's shawl until it dried.

EDGAR ALLAN POE

N Edgar Allan Poe (1809–1849) was born in Boston, Massachusetts, the son of itinerant actors. His parents died in 1811, both of tuberculosis; Poe was taken in by John Allan, a merchant in Richmond, Virginia, and lived with the Allan family until he entered the University of Virginia in 1826. There he indulged so extravagantly in drinking, gambling, and incurring debts that his stepfather refused to allow him to return. Poe ran away from home, enlisted in the army under a false name, and shortly thereafter published his first volume of poems. In 1830, discharged from the army, he entered West Point, from which he succeeded in getting expelled the following year. Irrevocably estranged from his stepfather, he went to Baltimore to live with his aunt, Maria Clemm, whose thirteen-year-old daughter — his cousin Virginia — he married in 1835. For the next twelve years — until Virginia died of tuberculosis in 1847 —he worked as an editor and began to submit to magazines the haunting, strange stories ("ice palaces," they have been called) for which he is famous. It was a decade of hell: always nervously unstable, fearful of insanity, Poe lived in desperate poverty, succumbed increasingly to alcoholism, and watched his wife slowly die. In the two years following her death he twice became engaged to a wealthy widow in the hope of changing his luck. But in 1849, after a bout of especially heavy drinking, he was discovered unconscious in the streets of Baltimore, and died a few days later. The bare, brute facts of so tormented a life say next to nothing of the charged imagination that drove Poe to write. His literary criticism aside, that imagination most naturally expressed itself in terms of the macabre. His gothic tales of the supernatural are for many readers the very essence of the horror story. His poetry, lyric and obsessive, deeply influenced the symbolist poets writing in France in the nineteenth century. He was the creator of the modern detective story, establishing a form from which Arthur Conan Doyle drew freely and which Jorge Luis Borges deeply admired. "The Murders in the Rue Morgue" is a **N** locked-room mystery seeped in horror.

The Murders in the Rue Morgue

What song the Syrens sang, or what name Achilles assumed when he hid himself among women, although puzzling questions, are not beyond *all* conjecture.

SIR THOMAS BROWNE

N The mental features discoursed of as the analytical, are, in themselves, but little susceptible of analysis. We appreciate them only in their effects. We know of them, among other things, that they are always to their possessor, when inordinately possessed, a source of the liveliest enjoyment. As the strong man exults in his physical ability, delighting in such exercises as call his muscles into action, so glories the analyst in that moral activity which *disentangles*. He derives pleasure from even the most trivial occupations bringing his talent into play. He is fond of enigmas, of conundrums, hieroglyphics; exhibiting in his solutions of each a degree of *acumen* which appears to the ordinary apprehension praeternatural. His results, brought about by the very soul and essence of method, have, in truth, the whole air of intuition.

The faculty of re-solution is possibly much invigorated by mathematical study, and especially by that highest branch of it which, unjustly, and merely on account of its retrograde operations, has been called, as if *par excellence,* analysis. Yet to calculate is not in itself to analyze. A chess player, for example, does the one, without effort at the other. It follows that the game of chess, in its effects upon mental character, is greatly misunderstood. I am not now writing a treatise, but simply prefacing a somewhat peculiar narrative by observations very much at random; I will, therefore, take occasion to assert that the higher powers of the reflective intellect are more decidedly and more usefully tasked by the unostentatious game of draughts than by all the elaborate frivolity of chess. In this latter, where the pieces have different and *bizarre* motions, with various and variable values, what is only complex, is mistaken (a not unusual error) for what is profound. The *attention* is here called powerfully into play. If it flag for an instant, an oversight is committed, resulting in injury or defeat. The possible moves being not only manifold, but involute, the chances of such oversights are multiplied; and in nine cases out of ten, it is the more concentrative rather than the more acute player who conquers. In draughts, on the contrary, where the moves are *unique* and have but little variation, the probabilities of inadvertence are diminished, and the mere attention being left comparatively unemployed, what advantages are obtained by either party are obtained by superior *acumen.* To be less abstract, let us suppose a game of draughts where the pieces are reduced to four kings, and where, of course, no oversight is to be expected. It is obvious that here the victory can be decided (the players being at all equal) only by some *recherché* movement, the result of some strong exertion of the intellect. Deprived of ordinary resources, the analyst throws himself into the spirit of his opponent, identifies himself therewith, and not unfrequently sees thus, at a glance, the sole methods (sometime indeed absurdly simple ones) by which he may seduce into error or hurry into miscalculation.

Whist has long been noted for its influence upon what is termed the calculating power; and men of the highest order of intellect have been known to take an apparently unaccountable delight in it, while eschewing chess as frivolous. Beyond doubt there is nothing of a similar nature so greatly tasking the faculty of analysis. The best chess-player in Christendom *may* be little more than the best player of chess; but proficiency in whist implies capacity for success in all those more important undertakings where mind struggles with mind. When I say proficiency, I mean that perfection in the game which includes a comprehension of *all* the sources whence legitimate advantage may be derived. These are not only manifold, but multiform, and lie frequently among recesses of thought altogether inaccessible to the ordinary understanding. To observe attentively is to remember distinctly; and, so far, the concentrative chess-player will do very well at whist; while the rules of Hoyle (themselves based upon the mere mechanism of the game) are sufficiently and generally comprehensible. Thus to have a retentive memory, and proceed by "the book" are points commonly regarded as the sum total of good playing. But it is in matters beyond the limits of mere rule that the skill of the analyst is evinced. He makes, in silence, a host of observations and inferences. So, perhaps, do his companions; and the difference in the extent of the information obtained, lies not so much in the validity of the inference as in the quality of the observation. The necessary knowledge is that of *what* to observe. Our player confines himself not at all; nor because the game is the object, does he reject deductions from things external to the game. He examines the countenance of his partner, comparing it carefully with that of each of his opponents. He considers the mode of assorting the cards in each hand; often counting trump by trump, and honor by honor, through the glances bestowed by their holders upon each. He notes every variation of face as the play progresses, gathering a fund of thought from the differences in the expression of certainty, of surprise, of triumph, or chagrin. From the manner of gathering up a trick he judges whether the person taking it, can make another in the suit. He recognises what is played through feint, by the air with which it is thrown upon the table. A casual or inadvertent word; the accidental dropping or turning of a card, with the accompanying anxiety or carelessness in regard to its concealment; the counting of the tricks, with the order of their arrangement; embarrassment, hesitation, eagerness, or trepidation — all afford, to his apparently intuitive perception, indications of the true state of affairs. The first two or three rounds having been played, he is in full possession of the contents of each hand, and thenceforward puts down his cards with as absolute a precision of purpose as if the rest of the party had turned outward the faces of their own.

The analytical power should not be confounded with simple ingenuity; for while the analyst is necessarily ingenious, the ingenious man is often remarkably incapable of analysis. The constructive or combining power, by which ingenuity is usually manifested, and to which the phrenologists (I believe erroneously) have assigned a separate organ, supposing it a primitive faculty, has been so frequently seen in those whose intellect bordered otherwise upon idiocy, as to have attracted general observation among writers on morals. Between ingenuity and the analytic ability there exists a difference far greater, indeed, than that between the fancy and the imagination, but of a character very strictly analogous. It will be found, in fact, that the ingenious are always fanciful, and the *truly* imaginative never otherwise than analytic.

The narrative which follows will appear to the reader somewhat in the light of a commentary upon the propositions just advanced.

Residing in Paris during the spring and part of the summer of 18 — , I there became acquainted with a Monsieur C. Auguste Dupin. This young gentleman was of an excellent, indeed of an illustrious family, but, by a variety of untoward events, had been reduced to such poverty that the energy of his character succumbed beneath it, and he ceased to bestir himself in the world, or to care for the retrieval of his fortunes. By courtesy of his creditors, there still remained in his possession a small remnant of his patrimony; and, upon the income arising from this, he managed, by means of a rigorous economy, to procure the necessaries of life, without troubling himself about its superfluities. Books, indeed, were his sole luxuries, and in Paris these are easily obtained.

Our first meeting was at an obscure library in the Rue Montmartre, where the accident of our both being in search of the same very rare and very remarkable volume, brought us into closer communion. We saw each other again and again. I was deeply interested in the little family history which he detailed to me with all that candor which a Frenchman indulges whenever mere self is his theme. I was astonished, too, at the vast extent of his reading; and, above all, I felt my soul enkindled within me by the wild fervor, and the vivid freshness of his imagination. Seeking in Paris the objects I then sought, I felt that the society of such a man would be to me a treasure beyond price; and this feeling I frankly confided to him. It was at length arranged that we should live together during my stay in the city; and as my worldly circumstances were somewhat less embarrassed than his own, I was permitted to be at the expense of renting, and furnishing in a style which suited the rather fantastic gloom of our common temper, a time-eaten and grotesque mansion, long deserted through superstitions into which we did not inquire, and tottering to its fall in a retired and desolate portion of the Faubourg St. Germain.

Had the routine of our life at this place been known to the world, we should have been regarded as madman — although, perhaps, as madmen of a harmless nature. Our seclusion was perfect. We admitted no visitors. Indeed the locality of our retirement had been carefully kept a secret from my own former associates; and it had been many years since Dupin had ceased to know or be known in Paris. We existed within ourselves alone.

It was a freak of fancy in my friend (for what else shall I call it?) to be enamored of the night for her own sake; and into this *bizarrerie,* as into all his others, I quietly fell; giving myself up to his wild whims with a perfect *abandon.* The sable divinity would not herself dwell with us always; but we could counterfeit her presence. At the first dawn of the morning we closed all the massy shutters of our old building; lighting a couple of tapers which, strongly perfumed, threw out only the ghastliest and feeblest of rays. By the aid of these we then busied our souls in dreams — reading, writing, or conversing, until warned by the clock of the advent of the true Darkness. Then we sallied forth into the streets, arm in arm, continuing the topics of the day, or roaming far and wide until a late hour, seeking, amid the wild lights and shadows of the populous city, that infinity of mental excitement which quiet observation can afford.

At such times I could not help remarking and admiring (although from his rich ideality I had been prepared to expect it) a peculiar analytic ability in Dupin. He seemed, too, to take an eager delight in its exercise — if not exactly in its display — and did not hesitate to confess the pleasure thus derived. He boasted to me, with a low chuckling laugh, that most men, in respect to himself, wore windows in their bosoms, and was wont to follow up such assertions by direct and very startling proofs of his intimate knowledge of my own. His manner at these moments was frigid and abstract; his eyes were vacant in expression; while his voice, usually a rich tenor, rose into a treble which would have sounded petulantly but for the deliberateness and entire distinctness of the enunciation. Observing him in these moods, I often dwelt meditatively upon the old philosophy of the Bi-Part Soul, and amused myself with the fancy of a double Dupin — the creative and the resolvent.

Let it not be supposed, from what I have just said, that I am detailing any mystery, or penning any romance. What I have described in the Frenchman was merely the result of an excited, or perhaps of a diseased, intelligence, but of the character of his remarks at the periods in question an example will best convey the idea.

We were strolling one night down a long dirty street, in the vicinity of the Palais Royal. Being both, apparently, occupied with thought, neither of his had spoken a syllable for fifteen minutes at least. All at once Dupin broke forth with these words:

"He is a very little fellow, that's true, and would do better for the *Théâtre des Variétés.*"

"There can be no doubt of that," I replied, unwittingly, and not at first observing (so much had I been absorbed in reflection) the extraordinary manner in which the speaker had chimed in with my meditations. In an instant afterward I recollected myself, and my astonishment was profound.

"Dupin," said I, gravely, "this is beyond my comprehension. I do not hesitate to say that I am amazed, and can scarcely credit my senses. How was it possible you should know I was thinking of — ?" Here I paused, to ascertain beyond a doubt whether he really knew of whom I thought. " — of Chantilly," said he, "why do you pause? You were remarking to yourself that his diminutive figure unfitted him for tragedy."

This was precisely what had formed the subject of my reflections. Chantilly was a *quondam* cobbler of the Rue St. Denis, who, becoming stage-mad, had attempted the *rôle* of Xerxes, Crébillon's tragedy so called, and been notoriously Pasquinaded for his pains.

"Tell me, for Heaven's sake," I exclaimed, "the method — if method there is — by which you have been enabled to fathom my soul in this matter." In fact, I was even more startled than I would have been willing to express.

"It was the fruiterer," replied my friend, "who brought you to the conclusion that the mender of soles was not of sufficient height for Xerxes *et id genus omne.*"

"The fruiterer! — you astonish me — I know no fruiterer whomsoever."

"The man who ran up against you as we entered the street — it may have been fifteen minutes ago."

I now remembered that, in fact, a fruiterer, carrying upon his head a large basket of apples, had nearly thrown me down, by accident, as we passed from the Rue C — into the thoroughfare where he stood; but what this had to do with Chantilly I could not possibly understand.

There was not a particle of *charlatânerie* about Dupin. "I will explain," he said, "and that you may comprehend all clearly, we will first retrace the course of your meditations, from the moment in which I spoke to you until that of the *rencontre* with the fruiterer in question. The larger links of the chain run thus — Chantilly, Orion, Dr. Nichols, Epicurus, Stereotomy, the street stones, the fruiterer."

There are few persons who have not, at some period of their lives, amused themselves in retracing their steps by which particular conclusions of their own minds have been attained. The occupation is often full of interest; and he who attempts it for the first time is astonished by the apparently illimitable distance and incoherence between the starting-point and the goal. What, then, must have been my amazement, when I heard the Frenchman speak what he had just spoken, and I could not help acknowledging that he had spoken the truth. He continued:

"We had been talking of horses, if I remember aright, just before leaving the Rue C — . This was the last subject we discussed. As we crossed into this street, a fruiterer, with a large basket upon his head, brushing quickly past us, thrust you upon a pile of paving-stones collected at a spot where the causeway is undergoing repair. You stepped upon one of the loose fragments, slipped, slightly strained your ankle, appeared vexed or sulky, muttered a few words, turned to look at the pile, and then proceeded in silence. I was not particularly attentive to what you did; but observation has become with me, of late, a species of necessity.

"You kept your eyes upon the ground — glancing, with a petulant expression, at the holes and ruts in the pavement (so that I saw you were still thinking of the stones) until we reached the little alley called Lamartine, which has been paved, by way of experiment, with the overlapping and riveted blocks. Here your countenance brightened up, and, perceiving your lips move, I could not doubt that you murmured the word 'stereotomy,' a term very affectedly applied to this species of pavement. I knew that you could not say to yourself 'stereotomy' without being brought to think of atomies, and thus of the theories of Epicurus; and since, when we discussed this subject not very long ago, I mentioned to you how singularly, yet with how little notice, the vague guesses of that noble Greek had met with confirmation in the late nebular cosmogony, I felt that you could not avoid casting your eyes upward to the great *nebula* in Orion, and I certainly expected that you would do so. You did look up; and I was now assured that I had correctly followed your steps. But in that bitter *tirade* upon Chantilly, which appeared in yesterday's *'Musée,'* the satirist, making some disgraceful allusions to the cobbler's change of name upon assuming the buskin, quoted a Latin line about which we have often conversed. I mean the line

Perdidit antiquum litera prima sonum.

I had told you that this was in reference to Orion, formerly written Urion; and, from certain pungencies connected with this explanation, I was aware that you could not have forgotten it. It was clear, therefore, that you would not fail to combine the two ideas of Orion and Chantilly. That you did combine them I saw by the character of the smile which passed over your lips. You thought of the poor cobbler's immolation. So far, you had been stopping in your gait; but now I saw you draw yourself up to your full height. I was then sure that you reflected upon the diminutive figure of Chantilly. At this point I interrupted your meditations to remark that as, in fact, he *was* a very little fellow — that Chantilly — he would do better at the *Théâtre des Variétés.*"

Not long after this, we were looking over an evening edition of the *Gazette des Tribunaux,* when the following paragraphs arrested our attention.

"EXTRAORDINARY MURDERS. — This morning, about three o'clock, the inhabitants of the Quartier St. Roch were roused from sleep by a succession of terrific shrieks, issuing, apparently, from the fourth story of a house in the Rue Morgue, known to be in the sole occupancy of one Madame L'Espanaye, and her daughter, Mademoiselle Camille L'Espanaye. After some delay, occasioned by a fruitless attempt to procure admission in the usual manner, the gateway was broken in with a crowbar, and eight or ten of the neighbors entered, accompanied by two *gendarmes.* By this time the cries had ceased; but, as the party rushed up the first flight of stairs, two or more rough voices, in angry contention, were distinguished, and seemed to proceed from the upper part of the house. As the second landing was reached, these sounds, also, had ceased, and every thing remained perfectly quiet. The party spread themselves, and hurried from room to room. Upon arriving at a large back chamber in the fourth story, (the door of which, being found locked, with the key inside, was forced open,) a spectacle presented itself which struck every one present not less with horror than with astonishment.

"The apartment was in the wildest disorder — the furniture broken and thrown about in all directions. There was only one bedstead; and from this the bed had been removed, and thrown into the middle of the floor. On a chair lay a razor, besmeared with blood. On the hearth were two or three long and thick tresses of gray human hair, also dabbled with blood, and seeming to have been pulled out by the roots. Upon the floor were found four Napoleons, an ear-ring of topaz, three large silver spoons, three smaller of *métal d'Alger,* and two bags, containing nearly four thousand francs in gold. The drawers of a *bureau,* which stood in one corner, were open, and had been, apparently, rifled, although many articles still remained in them. A small iron safe was discovered under the *bed* (not under the bedstead). It was open, with the key still in the door. It had no contents beyond a few old letters, and other papers of little consequence.

"Of Madame L'Espanaye no traces were here seen; but an unusual quantity of soot being observed in the fireplace, a search was made in the chimney, and (horrible to relate!) the corpse of the daughter, head downward, was dragged therefrom; it having been thus forced up the narrow aperture for a considerable distance. The body was quite warm. Upon examining it, many excoriations were perceived, no doubt occasioned by the violence with which it had been thrust up and disengaged. Upon the face were many severe scratches, and, upon the throat, dark bruises, and deep indentations of finger nails, as if the deceased had been throttled to death.

"After a thorough investigation of every portion of the house without farther discovery, the party made its way into a small paved yard in the rear of the building, where lay the corpse of the old lady, with her throat so entirely cut that, upon an attempt to raise her, the head fell off. The body, as well as the head, was fearfully mutilated — the former so much so as scarcely to retain any semblance of humanity.

"To this horrible mystery there is not as yet, we believe, the slightest clew."

The next day's paper had these additional particulars:

"*The Tragedy in the Rue Morgue.* — Many individuals have been examined in relation to this most extraordinry and frightful affair," [the word '*affaire*' has not yet, in France, that levity of import which it conveys with us] "but nothing whatever has transpired to throw light upon it. We give below all the material testimony elicited.

"*Pauline Dubourg,* laundress, deposes that she has known both the deceased for three years, having washed for them during that period. The old lady and her daughter seemed on good terms — very affectionate toward each other. They were excellent pay. Could not speak in regard to their mode or means of living. Believed that Madame L. told fortunes for a living. Was reputed to have money put by. Never met any person in the house when she called for the clothes or took them home. Was sure that they had no servant in employ. There appeared to be no furniture in any part of the building except in the fourth story.

"*Pierre Moreau,* tobacconist, deposes that he has been in the habit of selling small quantities of tobacco and snuff to Madame L'Espanaye for nearly four years. Was born in the neighborhood, and has always resided there. The deceased and her daughter had occupied the house in which the corpses were found, for more than six years. It was formerly occupied by a jeweller, who under-let the upper rooms to various persons. The house was the property of Madame L. She became dissatisfied with the abuse of the premises by her tenant, and moved into them herself, refusing to let any portion. The old lady was childish. Witness had seen the daughter some five or six times during the six years. The two lived an exceedingly retired life — were reputed to have money. Had heard it said among the neighbors that Madame L. told fortunes — did not believe it. Had never seen any person enter the door except the old lady and her daughter, a porter once or twice, and a physician some eight or ten times.

"Many other persons, neighbors, gave evidence to the same effect. No one was spoken of as frequenting the house. It was not known whether there were any living connections of Madame L. and her daughter. The shutters of the front windows were seldom opened. Those in the rear were always closed, with the exception of the large back room, fourth story. The house was a good house — not very old.

"*Isidore Musèt, gendame,* deposes that he was called to the house about three o'clock in the morning, and found some twenty or thirty persons at the gateway, endeavoring to gain admittance. Forced it open, at length, with a bayonet — not with a crowbar. Had but little difficulty in getting it open, on account of its being a double or folding gate, and bolted neither at bottom nor top. The shrieks were continued until the gate was forced — and then suddenly ceased. They seemed to be screams of some person (or persons) in great agony — were loud and drawn out, not short and quick. Witness led the way up stairs. Upon reaching the first landing, heard two voices in loud and angry contention — the one a gruff voice, the other much shriller — a very strange voice. Could distinguish some words of the former, which was that of a Frenchman. Was positive that it was not a woman's voice. Could distinguish the words 'sacré' and 'diable.' The shrill voice was that of a foreigner. Could not be sure whether it was the voice of a man or of a woman. Could not make out what was said, but believed the language to be Spanish. The state of the room and of the bodies was described by this witness as we described them yesterday.

"*Henri Duval,* a neighbor, and by trade a silver-smith, deposes that he was one of the party who first entered the house. Corroborates the testimony of Musèt in general. As soon as they forced an entrance, they reclosed the door, to keep out the crowd, which collected very fast, notwithstanding the lateness of the hour. The shrill voice, this witness thinks, was that of an Italian. Was certain it was not French. Could not be sure that it was a man's voice. It might have been a woman's. Was not acquainted with the Italian language. Could not distinguish the words, but was convinced by the intonation that the speaker was an Italian. Knew Madame L. and her daughter. Had conversed with both frequently. Was sure that the shrill voice was not that of either of the deceased.

" — *Odenheimer, restaurateur.* — This witness volunteered his testimony. Not speaking French, was examined through an interpreter. Is a native of Amsterdam. Was passing the house at the time of the shrieks. They lasted for several minutes — probably ten. They were long and loud — very awful and distressing. Was one of those who entered the building. Corroborated the previous evidence in every respect but one. Was sure that the shrill voice was that of a man — of a Frenchman. Could not distinguish the words uttered. They were loud and quick — unequal — spoken apparently in fear as well as in anger. The voice was harsh — not so much shrill as harsh. Could not call it a shrill voice. The gruff voice said repeatedly, 'sacré,' 'diable,' and once 'mon Dieu.'

"*Jules Mignaud,* banker, of the firm of Mignaud et Fils, Rue Deloraine. Is the elder Mignaud. Madame L'Espanaye had some property. Had opened an account with his banking house in the spring of the year — (eight years previously). Made frequent deposits in small sums. Had checked for nothing until the third day before her death, when she took out in person the sum of 4000 francs. This sum was paid in gold, and a clerk sent home with the money.

"*Adolphe Le Bon,* clerk to Mignaud et Fils, deposes that on the day in question, about noon, he accompanied Madame L'Espanaye to her residence with the 4000 francs, put up in two bags. Upon the door being opened, Mademoiselle L. appeared and took from his hands one of the bags, while the old lady relieved him of the other. He then bowed and departed. Did not see any person in the street at the time. It is a by-street — very lonely.

"*William Bird,* tailor, deposes that he was one of the party who entered the house. Is an Englishman. Has lived in Paris two years. Was one of the first to ascend the stairs. Heard the voices in contention. The gruff voice was that of a Frenchman. Could make out several words, but cannot now remember all. Heard distinctly 'sacré'

and *'mon Dieu.'* There was a sound at the moment as if of several persons struggling — a scraping and scuffling sound. The shrill voice was very loud — louder
than the gruff one. Is sure that it was not the voice of an Englishman. Appeared to
be that of a German. Might have been a woman's voice. Does not understand
German.

"Four of the above-named witnesses being recalled, deposed that the door of the
chamber in which was found the body of Mademoiselle L. was locked on the inside
when the party reached it. Every thing was perfectly silent — no groans or noises of
any kind. Upon forcing the door no person was seen. The windows, both of the back
and front room, were down and firmly fastened from within. A door between the two
rooms was closed but not locked. The door leading from the front room into the
passage was locked, with the key on the inside. A small room in the front of the
house, on the fourth story, at the head of the passage, was open, the door being ajar.
This room was crowded with old beds, boxes, and so forth. These were carefully
removed and searched. There was not an inch of any portion of the house which was
not carefully searched. Sweeps were sent up and down the chimneys. The house was
a four-story one, with garrets *(mansardes)*. A trap-door on the roof was nailed down
very securely — did not appear to have been opened for years. The time elapsing
between the hearing of the voices in contention and the breaking open of the room
door was variously stated by the witnesses. Some made it as short as three minutes —
some as long as five. The door was opened with difficulty.

"*Alfonzo Garcio*, undertaker, deposes that he resides in the Rue Morgue. Is a
native of Spain. Was one of the party who entered the house. Did not proceed up
stairs. Is nervous, and was apprehensive of the consequences of agitation. Heard the
voices in contention. The gruff voice was that of a Frenchman. Could not distinguish
what was said. The shrill voice was that of an Englishman — is sure of this. Does not
understand the English language, but judges by the intonation.

"*Alberto Montani,* confectioner, deposes that he was among the first to ascend the
stairs. Heard the voices in question. The gruff voice was that of a Frenchman.
Distinguished several words. The speaker appeared to be expostulating. Could not
make out the words of the shrill voice. Spoke quick and unevenly. Thinks it the voice
of a Russian. Corroborates the general testimony. Is an Italian. Never conversed with
a native of Russia.

"Several witnesses, recalled, here testified that the chimneys of all the rooms on
the fourth story were too narrow to admit the passage of a human being. By 'sweeps'
were meant cylindrical sweeping-brushes, such as are employed by those who clean
chimneys. These brushes were passed up and down every flue in the house. There
is no back passage by which any one could have descended while the party proceeded up stairs. The body of Mademoiselle L'Espanaye was so firmly wedged in the
chimney that it could not be got down until four or five of the party united their
strength.

"*Paul Dumas,* physician, deposes that he was called to view the bodies about
daybreak. They were both then lying on the sacking of the bedstead in the chamber
where Mademoiselle L. was found. The corpse of the young lady was much bruised
and excoriated. The fact that it had been thrust up the chimney would sufficiently
account for these appearances. The throat was greatly chafed. There were several
deep scratches just below the chin, together with a series of livid spots which were
evidently the impression of fingers. The face was fearfully discolored, and the

eyeballs protruded. The tongue had been partially bitten through. A large bruise was discovered upon the pit of the stomach, produced, apparently, by the pressure of a knee. In the opinion of M. Dumas, Mademoiselle L'Espanaye had been throttled to death by some person or persons unknown. The corpse of the mother was horribly mutilated. All the bones of the right leg and arm were more or less shattered. The left *tibia* much splintered, as well as all the ribs of the left side. Whole body dreadfully bruised and discolored. It was not possible to say how the injuries had been inflicted. A heavy club of wood, or a broad bar of iron — a chair — any large, heavy, and obtuse weapon would have produced such results, if wielded by the hands of a very powerful man. No woman could have inflicted the blows with any weapon. The head of the deceased, when seen by witness, was entirely separated from the body, and was also greatly shattered. The throat had evidently been cut with some very sharp instrument — probably with a razor.

"*Alexandre Etienne,* surgeon, was called with M. Dumas to view the bodies. Corroborated the testimony and the opinions of M. Dumas.

"Nothing further of importance was elicited, although several other persons were examined. A murder so mysterious, and so perplexing in all its particulars, was never before committed in Paris — if indeed a murder has been committed at all. The police are entirely at fault — an unusual occurrence in affairs of this nature. There is not, however, the shadow of a clew apparent."

The evening edition of the paper stated that the greatest excitement still continued in the Quartier St. Roch — that the premises in question had been carefully re-searched, and fresh examinations of witnesses instituted, but all to no purpose. A postscript, however, mentioned that Adolphe Le Bon had been arrested and imprisoned — although nothing appeared to criminate him beyond the facts already detailed.

Dupin seemed singularly interested in the progress of this affair — at least so I judged from his manner, for he made no comments. It was only after the announcement that Le Bon had been imprisoned, that he asked me my opinion respecting the murders.

I could merely agree with all Paris in considering them an insoluble mystery. I saw no means by which it would be possible to trace the murderer.

"We must not judge of the means," said Dupin, "by this shell of an examination. The Parisian police, so much extolled for *acumen,* are cunning, but no more. There is no method in their proceedings, beyond the method of the moment. They make a vast parade of measures; but, not unfrequently, these are so ill-adapted to the objects proposed, as to put us in mind of Monsieur Jourdain's calling for his *robe-de-chambre — pour mieux entendre la musique*. The results attained by them are not unfrequently surprising, but, for the most part, are brought about by simple diligence and activity. When these qualities are unavailing, their schemes fail. Vidocq, for example, was a good guesser, and a persevering man. But, without educated thought, he erred continually by the very intensity of his investigations. He impaired his vision by holding the object too close. He might see, perhaps, one or two points with unusual clearness, but in so doing he, necessarily, lost sight of the matter as a whole. Thus there is such a thing as being too profound. Truth is not always in a well. In fact, as regards the more important knowledge, I do believe that she is invariably superficial. The depth lies in the valleys where we seek her, and not upon the mountain-tops where she is found. The modes and sources of this kind of error are well typified in the contemplation of the heavenly bodies. To look at a star by glances — to view it in a side-long way, by turning toward it the exterior portions of the *retina* (more susceptible of feeble impressions of light than the interior), is to behold the star distinctly — is to have the best appreciation of its lustre — a lustre which grows dim just in proportion as we turn our vision *fully* upon it. A greater number of rays actually fall upon the eye in the latter case, but in the former, there is the more refined capacity for comprehension. By undue profundity we perplex and enfeeble thought; and it is possible to make even Venus herself vanish from the firmament by a scrutiny too sustained, too concentrated, or too direct.

"As for these murders, let us enter into some examinations for ourselves, before we make up an opinion respecting them. An inquiry will afford us amusement," [I thought this an odd term, so applied, but said nothing] "and besides, Le Bon once rendered me a service for which I am not ungrateful. We will go and see the premises with our own eyes. I know G —, the Prefect of Police, and shall have no difficulty in obtaining the necessary permission."

The permission was obtained, and we proceeded at once to the Rue Morgue. This is one of those miserable thoroughfares which intervene between the Rue Richelieu and the Rue St. Roch. It was late in the afternoon when we reached it, as this quarter is at a great distance from that in which we resided. The house was readily found; for there were still many persons gazing up at the closed shutters, with an objectless curiosity, from the opposite side of the way. It was an ordinary Parisian house, with a gateway, on one side of which was a glazed watch-box, with a sliding panel in the window, indicating a *loge de concierge*. Before going in we walked up the street, turned down an alley, and then, again turning, passed in the rear of the building — Dupin, meanwhile, examining the whole neighborhood, as well as the house, with a minuteness of attention for which I could see no possible object.

Retracing our steps we came again to the front of the dwelling, rang, and having shown our credentials, were admitted by the agents in charge. We went up stairs — into the chamber where the body of Mademoiselle L'Espanaye had been found, and where both the deceased still lay. The disorders of the room had, as usual, been suffered to exist. I saw nothing beyond what had been stated in the *Gazette des Tribunaux*. Dupin scrutinized every thing — not excepting the bodies of the victims. We then went into the other rooms, and into the yard; a *gendarme* accompanying us throughout. The examination occupied us until dark, when we took our departure. On our way home my companion stepped in for a moment at the office of one of the daily papers.

I have said that the whims of my friend were manifold, and that *Je les ménageais:* — for this phrase there is no English equivalent. It was his humor, now, to decline all conversation on the subject of the murder, until about noon the next day. He then asked me, suddenly, if I had observed any thing *peculiar* at the scene of the atrocity.

There was something in his manner of emphasizing the word "peculiar," which caused me to shudder, without knowing why.

"No, nothing *peculiar*," I said; "nothing more, at least, than we both saw stated in the paper."

"The *Gazette*," he replied, "has not entered, I fear, into the unusual horror of the thing. But dismiss the idle opinions of this print. It appears to me that this mystery is considered insoluble, for the very reason which should cause it to be regarded as easy of solution — I mean for the *outré* character of its features. The police are confounded by the seeming absence of motive — not for the murder itself — but for the atrocity of the murder. They are puzzled, too, by the seeming impossibility of reconciling the voices heard in contention, with the facts that no one was discovered upstairs but the assassinated Mademoiselle L'Espanaye, and that there were no means of egress without the notice of the party ascending. The wild disorder of the room; the corpse thrust, with the head downward, up the chimney; the frightful mutilation of the body of the old lady; these considerations, with those just mentioned, and others which I need not mention, have sufficed to paralyze the powers, by putting completely at fault the boasted *acumen,* of the government agents. They have fallen into the gross but common error of confounding the unusual with the abstruse. But it is by these deviations from the plane of the ordinary, that reason feels its way, if at all, in its search for the true. In investigations such as we are now pursuing, it should not be so much asked 'what has occurred,' as 'what has occurred that has never occurred before.' In fact, the facility with which I shall arrive, or have arrived, at the solution of this mystery, is in the direct ratio of its apparent insolubility in the eyes of the police."

I stared at the speaker in mute astonishment.

"I am now awaiting," continued he, looking toward the door of our apartment — "I am now awaiting a person who, although perhaps not the perpetrator of these butcheries, must have been in some measure implicated in their perpetration. Of the worst portion of the crimes committed, it is probable that he is innocent. I hope that I am right in this supposition; for upon it I build my expectation of reading the entire riddle. I look for the man here — in this room — every moment. It is true that he may not arrive; but the probability is that he will. Should he come, it will be necessary to detain him. Here are pistols; and we both know how to use them when occasion demands their use."

I took the pistols, scarcely knowing what I did, or believing what I heard, while Dupin went on, very much as if in a soliloquy. I have already spoken of his abstract manner at such times. His discourse was addressed to myself; but his voice, although by no means loud, had that intonation which is commonly employed in speaking to some one at a great distance. His eyes, vacant in expression, regarded only the wall.

"That the voices heard in contention," he said, "by the party upon the stairs, were not the voices of the women themselves, was fully proved by the evidence. This relieves us of all doubt upon the question whether the old lady could have first destroyed the daughter, and afterward have committed suicide. I speak of this point chiefly for the sake of method; for the strength of Madame L'Espanaye would have been utterly unequal to the task of thrusting her daughter's corpse up the chimney as it was found; and the nature of the wounds upon her own person entirely precludes the idea of self-destruction. Murder, then, had been committed by some third party; and the voices of this third party were those heard in contention. Let me now advert — not to the whole testimony respecting these voices — but to what was *peculiar* in that testimony. Did you observe anything peculiar about it?"

I remarked that, while all the witnesses agreed in supposing the gruff voice to be that of a Frenchman, there was much disagreement in regard to the shrill, or, as one individual termed it, the harsh voice.

"That was the evidence itself," said Dupin, "but it was not the peculiarity of the evidence. You have observed nothing distinctive. Yet there *was* something to be observed. The witnesses, as you remark, agreed about the gruff voice, they were here unanimous. But in regard to the shrill voice, the peculiarity is — not that they disagreed — but that, while an Italian, an Englishman, a Spaniard, a Hollander, and a Frenchman attempted to describe it, each one spoke of it as that *of a foreigner.* Each is sure that it was not the voice of one of his own countrymen. Each likens it — not to the voice of an individual of any nation with whose language he is conversant — but the converse. The Frenchman supposes it the voice of a Spaniard, and 'might have distinguished some words *had he been acquainted with the Spanish.*' The Dutchman maintains it to have been that of a Frenchman, but we find it stated that *'not understanding French this witness was examined through an interpreter.'* The Englishman thinks it the voice of a German, and *'does not understand German.'* The Spaniard 'is sure' that it was that of an Englishman, but 'judges by the intonation' altogether, *'as he has no knowledge of the English.'* The Italian believes it the voice of a Russian, but *'has never conversed with a native of Russia.'* A second Frenchman differs, moreover, with the first, and is positive that the voice was that of an Italian; but, *not being cognizant of that tongue,* is, like the Spaniard, 'convinced by the intonation.' Now, how strangely unusual must that voice have really been, about which such testimony as this *could* have been elicited! — in whose *tones,* even, denizens of the five great divisions of Europe could recognize nothing familiar! You will say that it might have been the voice of an Asiatic — of an African. Neither Asiatics nor Africans abound in Paris; but, without denying the inference, I will now merely call your attention to three points. The voice is termed by one witness 'harsh rather than shrill.' It is represented by two others to have been 'quick and *unequal.*' No words — no sounds resembling words — were by any witness mentioned as distinguishable.

"I know not," continued Dupin, "what impression I may have made, so far, upon your own understanding; but I do not hesitate to say that legitimate deductions even from this portion of the testimony — the portion respecting the gruff and shrill voices — are in themselves sufficient to engender a suspicion which should give direction to all farther progress in the investigation of the mystery. I said 'legitimate deductions'; but my meaning is not thus fully expressed. I designed to imply that the deductions are the *sole* proper ones, and that the suspicion arises *inevitably* from them as the single result. What the suspicion is, however, I will not say just yet. I merely wish you to bear in mind that, with myself, it was sufficiently forcible to give a definite form — a certain tendency — to my inquiries in the chamber.

"Let us now transport ourselves, in fancy, to this chamber. What shall we first seek here? The means of egress employed by the murderers. It is not too much to say that neither of us believe in præternatural events. Madame and Mademoiselle L'Espanaye were not destroyed by spirits. The doers of the deed were material and escaped materially. Then how? Fortunately there is but one mode of reasoning upon the point, and that mode *must* lead us to a definite decision. Let us examine, each by each, the possible means of egress. It is clear that the assassins were in the room where Mademoiselle L'Espanaye was found, or at least in the room adjoining, when the party ascended the stairs. It is, then, only from these two apartments that we have to seek issues. The police have laid bare the floors, the ceiling, and the masonry of the walls, in every direction. No *secret* issues could have escaped their vigilance. But, not trusting to *their* eyes, I examined with my own. There were, then, *no* secret issues. Both doors leading from the rooms into the passage were securely locked, with the keys inside. Let us turn to the chimneys. These, although of ordinary width for some eight or ten feet above the hearths, will not admit, throughout their extent, the body of a large cat. The impossibility of egress, by means already stated, being thus absolute, we are reduced to the windows. Through those of the front room no one could have escaped without notice from the crowd in the street. The murderers *must* have passed, then, through those of the back room. Now, brought to this conclusion in so unequivocal a manner as we are, it is not our part, as reasoners, to reject it on account of apparent impossibilities. It is only left for us to prove that these apparent 'impossibilities' are, in reality, not such.

"There are two windows in the chamber. One of them is unobstructed by furniture, and is wholly visible. The lower portion of the other is hidden from view by the head of the unwieldy bedstead which is thrust close up against it. The former was found securely fastened from within. It resisted the utmost force of those who endeavored to raise it. A large gimlet-hole had been pierced in its frame to the left, and a very stout nail was found fitted therein, nearly to the head. Upon examining the other window, a similar nail was seen similarly fitted in it; and a vigorous attempt to raise this sash failed also. The police were now entirely satisfied that egress had not been in these directions. And, *therefore,* it was thought a matter of supereroga-tion to withdraw the nails and open the windows.

"My own examination was somewhat more particular, and was so for the reason I have just given — because here it was, I knew, that all apparent impossibilities *must* be proved to be not such in reality.

"I proceeded to think thus — *a posteriori*. The murderers *did* escape from one of these windows. This being so, they could not have re-fastened the sashes from the inside, as they were found fastened — the consideration which put a stop, through its obviousness, to the scrutiny of the police in this quarter. Yet the sashes *were* fastened. They *must,* then, have the power of fastening themselves. There was no escape from this conclusion. I stepped to the unobstructed casement, withdrew the nail with some difficulty, and attempted to raise the sash. It resisted all my efforts, as I had anticipated. A concealed spring must, I now knew, exist; and this corroboration of my idea convinced me that my premises, at least, were correct, however myste-rious still appeared the circumstances attending the nails. A careful search soon brought to light the hidden spring. I pressed it, and, satisfied with the discovery, forbore to upraise the sash.

"I now replaced the nail and regarded it attentively. A person passing out through this window might have reclosed it, and the spring would have caught — but the nail could not have been replaced. The conclusion was plain, and again narrowed in the field of my investigations. The assassins *must* have escaped through the other window. Supposing, then, the springs upon each sash to be the same, as was probable, there *must* be found a difference between the nails, or at least between the modes of their fixture. Getting upon the sacking of the bedstead, I looked over the head-board minutely at the second casement. Passing my hand down behind the board, I readily discovered and pressed the spring, which was, as I had supposed, identical in character with its neighbor. I now looked at the nail. It was as stout as the other, and apparently fitted in the same manner — driven in nearly up to the head.

"You will say that I was puzzled; but, if you think so, you must have misunderstood the nature of the inductions. To use a sporting phrase, I had not been once 'at fault.' The scent had never for an instant been lost. There was no flaw in any link of the chain. I had traced the secret to its ultimate result, — and that result was *the nail*. It had, I say, in every respect, the appearance of its fellow in the other window; but this fact was an absolute nullity (conclusive as it might seem to be) when compared with the consideration that here, at this point, terminated the clew. 'There *must* be something wrong,' I said, 'about the nail.' I touched it; and the head, with about a quarter of an inch of the shank, came off in my fingers. The rest of the shank was in the gimlet-hole, where it had been broken off. The fracture was an old one (for its edges were incrusted with rust), and had apparently been accomplished by the blow of a hammer, which had partially imbedded, in the top of the bottom sash, the head portion of the nail. I now carefully replaced this head portion in the indentation whence I had taken it, and the resemblance to a perfect nail was complete — the fissure was invisible. Pressing the spring, I gently raised the sash for a few inches; the head went up with it, remaining firm in its bed. I closed the window, and the semblance of the whole nail was again perfect.

"This riddle, so far, was now unriddled. The assassin had escaped through the window which looked upon the bed. Dropping of its own accord upon his exit (or perhaps purposely closed), it had become fastened by the spring; and it was the retention of this spring which had been mistaken by the police for that of the nail, farther inquiry being thus considered unnecessary.

"The next question is that of the mode of descent. Upon this point I had been satisfied in my walk with you around the building. About five feet and a half from the casement in question there runs a lightning-rod. From this rod it would have been impossible for any one to reach the window itself, to say nothing of entering it. I observed, however, that the shutters of the fourth story were of the peculiar kind called by Parisian carpenters *ferrades* — a kind rarely employed at the present day, but frequently seen upon very old mansions at Lyons and Bourdeaux. They are in the form of an ordinary door (a single, not a folding door), except that the upper half is latticed or worked in open trellis — thus affording an excellent hold for the hands. In the present instance these shutters are fully three feet and a half broad. When we saw them from the rear of the house, they were both about half open — that is to say, they stood off at right angles from the wall. It is probable that the police, as well as myself, examined the back of the tenement; but, if so, in looking at these *ferrades* in the line of their breadth (as they must have done), they did not perceive this great breadth itself, or, at all events, failed to take it into due consideration. In fact, having once satisfied themselves that no egress could have been made in this quarter, they would naturally bestow here a very cursory examination. It was clear to me, however, that the shutter belonging to the window at the head of the bed, would, if swung fully back to the wall, reach to within two feet of the lightning-rod. It was also evident that, by exertion of a very unusual degree of activity and courage, an entrance into the window, from the rod, might have been thus effected. By reaching to the distance of two feet and a half (we now suppose the shutter open to its whole extent) a robber might have taken a firm grasp upon the trellis-work. Letting go, then, his hold upon the rod, placing his feet securely against the wall, and springing boldly from it, he might have swung the shutter so as to close it, and, if we imagine the window open at the time, might even have swung himself into the room.

"I wish you to bear especially in mind that I have spoken of a *very* unusual degree of activity as requisite to success in so hazardous and so difficult a feat. It is my design to show you first, that the thing might possibly have been accomplished: — but, secondly and *chiefly,* I wish to impress upon your understanding the *very extraordinary* — the almost præternatural character of that agility which could have accomplished it.

"You will say, no doubt, using the language of the law, that 'to make out my case,' I should rather undervalue, than insist upon a full estimation of the activity required in this matter. This may be the practice in law, but it is not the usage of reason. My ultimate object is only the truth. My immediate purpose is to lead you to place in juxtaposition, that *very unusual* activity of which I have just spoken, with that *very peculiar* shrill (or harsh) and *unequal* voice, about whose nationality no two persons could be found to agree, and in whose utterance no syllabification could be detected."

At these words a vague and half-formed conception of the meaning of Dupin flitted over my mind. I seemed to be upon the verge of comprehension, without power to comprehend — as men, at times, find themselves upon the brink of remembrance, without being able, in the end, to remember. My friend went on with his discourse.

"You will see," he said, "that I have shifted the question from the mode of egress to that of ingress. It was my design to convey the idea that both were effected in the same manner, at the same point. Let us now revert to the interior of the room. Let us survey the appearances here. The drawers of the bureau, it is said, had been rifled, although many articles of apparel still remained within them. The conclusion here is absurd. It is a mere guess — a very silly one — and no more. How are we to know that the articles found in the drawers were not all these drawers had originally contained? Madame L'Espanaye and her daughter lived an exceedingly retired life — saw no company — seldom went out — had little use for numerous changes of habiliment. Those found were at least of as good quality as any likely to be possessed by these ladies. If a thief had taken any, why did he not take the best — why did he not take all? In a word, why did he abandon four thousand francs in gold to encumber himself with a bundle of linen? The gold *was* abandoned. Nearly the whole sum mentioned by Monsieur Mignaud, the banker, was discovered, in bags, upon the floor. I wish you therefore, to discard from your thoughts the blundering idea of *motive,* engendered in the brains of the police by that portion of the evidence which speaks of money delivered at the door of the house. Coincidences ten times as remarkable as this (the delivery of the money, and murder committed within three days upon the party receiving it), happen to all of us every hour of our lives, without attracting even momentary notice. Coincidences, in general, are great stumbling-blocks in the way of that class of thinkers who have been educated to know nothing of the theory of probabilities — that theory to which the most glorious objects of human research are indebted for the most glorious of illustration. In the present instance, had the gold been gone, the fact of its delivery three days before would have formed something more than a coincidence. It would have been corroborative of this idea of motive. But, under the real circumstances of the case, if we are to suppose gold the motive of this outrage, we must also imagine the perpetrator so vacillating an idiot as to have abandoned his gold and his motive together.

"Keeping now steadily in mind the points to which I have drawn your attention — that peculiar voice, that unusual agility, and that startling absence of motive in a murder so singularly atrocious as this — let us glance at the butchery itself. Here is a woman strangled to death by manual strength, and thrust up a chimney head downward. Ordinary assassins employ no such mode of murder as this. Least of all, do they thus dispose of the murdered. In this manner of thrusting the corpse up the chimney, you will admit that there was something *excessively outré* — something all together irreconcilable with our common notions of human action, even when we suppose the actors the most depraved of men. Think, too, how great must have been that strength which could have thrust the body *up* such an aperture so forcibly that the united vigor of several persons was found barely sufficient to drag it *down!*

"Turn, now, to other indications of the employment of a vigor most marvellous. On the hearth were thick tresses — very thick tresses — of gray human hair. These had been torn out by the roots. You are aware of the great force necessary in tearing thus from the head even twenty or thirty hairs together. You saw the locks in question as well as myself. Their roots (a hideous sight!) were clotted with fragments of the flesh of the scalp — sure token of the prodigious power which had been exerted in uprooting perhaps half a million of hairs at a time. The throat of the old lady was not merely cut, but the head absolutely severed from the body: the instrument was a mere razor. I wish you also to look at the *brutal* ferocity of these deeds. Of the bruises upon the body of Madame L'Espanaye I do not speak. Monsieur Dumas, and his worthy co-adjutor Monsieur Etienne, have pronounced that they were inflicted by some obtuse instrument; and so far these gentlemen are very correct. The obtuse instrument was clearly the stone pavement in the yard, upon which the victim had fallen from the window which looked in upon the bed. This idea, however simple it may now seem, escaped the police for the same reason that the breadth of the shutters escaped them — because, by the affair of the nails, their perceptions had been hermetically sealed against the possibility of the windows having ever been opened at all.

"If now, in addition to all these things, you have properly reflected upon the odd disorder of the chamber, we have gone so far as to combine the ideas of an agility astounding, a strength superhuman, a ferocity brutal, a butchery without motive, a *grotesquerie* in horror absolutely alien from humanity, and a voice foreign in tone to the ears of men of many nations, and devoid of all distinct or intelligible syllabification. What result, then, has ensued? What impression have I made upon your fancy?"

I felt a creeping of the flesh as Dupin asked me the question. "A madman," I said, "has done this deed — some raving maniac, escaping from a neighboring *Maison de Santé*."

"In some respects," he replied, "your idea is not irrelevant. But the voices of madmen, even in their wildest paroxysms, are never found to tally with that peculiar voice heard upon the stairs. Madmen are of some nation, and their language, however incoherent in its words, has always the coherence of syllabification. Besides, the hair of a madman is not such as I now hold in my hand. I disentangled this little tuft from the rigidly clutched fingers of Madame L'Espanaye. Tell me what you can make of it."

"Dupin!" I said, completely unnerved; "this hair is most unusual — this is no *human* hair."

"I have not asserted that it is," said he; "but, before we decide this point, I wish you to glance at the little sketch I have here traced upon this paper. It is a *facsimile* drawing of what has been described in one portion of the testimony as 'dark bruises and deep indentations of finger nails' upon the throat of Mademoiselle L'Espanaye, and in another (by Messrs. Dumas and Etienne) as a 'series of livid spots, evidently the impressions of fingers.'

"You will perceive," continued my friend, spreading out the paper upon the table before us, "that this drawing gives the idea of a firm and fixed hold. There is no *slipping* apparent. Each finger has retained — possibly until the death of the victim — the fearful grasp by which it originally imbedded itself. Attempt, now, to place all your fingers, at the same time, in the respective impressions as you see them."

I made the attempt in vain.

"We are possibly not giving this matter a fair trial," he said. "The paper is spread out upon a plane surface; but the human throat is cylindrical. Here is a billet of wood, the circumference of which is about that of the throat. Wrap the drawing around it, and try the experiment again."

I did so; but the difficulty was even more obvious than before. "This," I said, "is the mark of no human hand."

"Read now," replied Dupin, "this passage from Cuvier."

It was a minute anatomical and generally descriptive account of the large fulvous Ourang-Outang of the East Indian islands. The gigantic stature, the prodigious strength and activity, the wild ferocity, and the imitative propensities of these mammalia are sufficiently well know to all. I understood the full horrors of the murder at once.

"The description of the digits," said I, as I made an end of reading, "is in exact accordance with this drawing. I see that no animal but an Ourang-Outang, of the species here mentioned, could have impressed the indentations as you have traced them. This tuft of tawny hair, too, is identical in character with that of the beast of Cuvier. But I cannot possibly comprehend the particulars of this frightful mystery. Besides, there were *two* voices heard in contention, and one of them was unquestionably the voice of a Frenchman."

"True; and you will remember an expression attributed almost unanimously, by the evidence, to this voice, — the expression, '*mon Dieu!*' This, under the circumstances, has been justly characterized by one of the witnesses (Montani, the confectioner) as an expression of remonstrance or expostulation. Upon these two words, therefore, I have mainly built my hopes of a full solution of the riddle. A Frenchman was cognizant of the murder. It is possible — indeed it is far more than probable — that he was innocent of all participation in the bloody transaction which took place. The Ourang-Outang may have escaped from him. He may have traced it to the chamber; but, under the agitating circumstances which ensued, he could never have recaptured it. It is still at large. I will not pursue these guesses — for I have no right to call them more — since the shades of reflection upon which they are based are scarcely of sufficient depth to be appreciable by my own intellect, and since I could not pretend to make them intelligible to the understanding of another. We will call them guesses, then, and speak of them as such. If the Frenchman in question is indeed, as I suppose, innocent of this atrocity, this advertisement, which I left last night upon our return home, at the office of *Le Monde* (a paper devoted to the shipping interest, and much sought by sailors), will bring him to our residence."

He handed me a paper, and I read thus:

CAUGHT — *In the Bois de Boulogne, early in the morning of the — inst.* (the morning of the murder), *a very large, tawny Ourang-Outang of the Bornese species. The owner (who is ascertained to be a sailor, belonging to a Maltese vessel) may have the animal again, upon identifying it satisfactorily, and paying a few charges arising from its capture and keeping. Call at No. — Rue —, Faubourg St. Germain — au troisième.*"

"How was it possible," I asked, "that you should know the man to be a sailor, and belonging to a Maltese vessel?"

"I do *not* know it," said Dupin. "I am not *sure* of it. Here, however, is a small piece of ribbon, which from its form, and from its greasy appearance, has evidently been used in tying the hair in one of those long *queues* of which sailors are so fond. Moreover, this knot is one which few besides sailors can tie, and it is peculiar to the Maltese. I picked the ribbon up at the foot of the lightning-rod. It could not have belonged to either of the deceased. Now if, after all, I am wrong in my induction from this ribbon, that the Frenchman was a sailor belonging to a Maltese vessel, still I can have done no harm in saying what I did in the advertisement. If I am right, a great point is gained. Cognizant although innocent of the murder, the Frenchman will naturally hesitate about replying to the advertisement — about demanding the Ourang-Outang. He will reason thus: — 'I am innocent; I am poor; my Ourang-Outang is of great value — to one in my circumstances a fortune of itself — why should I lose it through idle apprehensions of danger? Here it is, within my grasp. It was found in the Bois de Boulogne — at a vast distance from the scene of that butchery. How can it ever be suspected that a brute beast should have done the deed? The police are at fault — they have failed to procure the slightest clew. Should they even trace the animal, it would be impossible to prove me cognizant of the murder, or to implicate me in guilt on account of that cognizance. Above all, *I am known*. The advertiser designates me as the possessor of the beast. I am not sure to what limit his knowledge may extend. Should I avoid claiming a property of so great value, which it is known that I possess, I will render the animal at least, liable to suspicion. It is not my policy to attract attention either to myself or to the beast. I will answer the advertisement, get the Ourang-Outang, and keep it close until this matter has blown over.' "

At this moment we heard a step upon the stairs.

"Be ready," said Dupin, "with your pistols, but neither use them nor show them until at a signal from myself."

The front door of the house had been left open, and the visitor had entered, without ringing, and advanced several steps upon the staircase. Now, however, he seemed to hesitate. Presently we heard him descending. Dupin was moving quickly to the door, when we again heard him coming up. He did not turn back a second time, but stepped up with decision, and rapped at the door of our chamber.

"Come in," said Dupin, in a cheerful and hearty tone.

A man entered. He was a sailor, evidently, — a tall, stout, and muscular-looking person, with a certain daredevil expression of countenance, not altogether unprepossessing. His face, greatly sunburnt, was more than half hidden by whisker and *mustachio*. He had with him a huge oaken cudgel, but appeared to be otherwise unarmed. He bowed awkwardly, and bade us "good evening," in French accents, which, although somewhat Neufchatelish, were still sufficiently indicative of a Parisian origin.

"Sit down, my friend," said Dupin. "I suppose you have called about the Ourang-Outang. Upon my word, I almost envy you the possession of him; a remarkably fine, and no doubt a very valuable animal. How old do you suppose him to be?"

The sailor drew a long breath, with the air of a man relieved of some intolerable burden, and then replied, in an assured tone:

"I have no way of telling — but he can't be more than four or five years old. Have you got him here?"

"Oh, no; we had no conveniences for keeping him here. He is at a livery stable in the Rue Dubourg, just by. You can get him in the morning. Of course you are prepared to identify the property?"

"To be sure I am, sir."

"I shall be sorry to part with him," said Dupin.

"I don't mean that you should be at all this trouble for nothing, sir," said the man. "Couldn't expect it. Am very willing to pay a reward for the finding of the animal — that is to say, anything in reason."

"Well," replied my friend, "that is all very fair, to be sure. Let me think! — what should I have? Oh! I will tell you. My reward shall be this. You shall give me all the information in your power about these murders in the Rue Morgue."

Dupin said the last words in a very low tone, and very quietly. Just as quietly, too, he walked toward the door, locked it, and put the key in his pocket. He then drew a pistol from his bosom and placed it, without the least flurry, upon the table.

The sailor's face flushed up as if he were struggling with suffocation. He started to his feet and grasped his cudgel; but the next moment he fell back into his seat, trembling violently, and with the countenance of death itself. He spoke not a word. I pitied him from the bottom of my heart.

"My friend," said Dupin, in a kind tone, "you are alarming yourself unnecessarily — you are indeed. We mean you no harm whatever. I pledge you the honor of a gentleman, and of a Frenchman, that we intend you no injury. I perfectly well know that you are innocent of the atrocities in the Rue Morgue. It will not do, however, to deny that you are in some measure implicated in them. From what I have already said, you must know that I have had means of information about this matter — means of which you could never have dreamed. Now the thing stands thus. You have done nothing which you could have avoided — nothing, certainly, which renders you culpable. You are not even guilty of robbery, when you might have robbed with impunity. You have nothing to conceal. You have no reason for concealment. On the other hand, you are bound by every principle of honor to confess all you know. An innocent man is now imprisoned, charged with that crime of which you can point out the perpetrator."

The sailor had recovered his presence of mind, in a great measure, while Dupin uttered these words; but his original boldness of bearing was all gone.

"So help me God!" said he, after a brief pause, "I *will* tell you all I know about this affair; — but I do not expect you to believe one half I say — I would be a fool indeed if I did. Still, I *am* innocent, and I will make a clean breast if I die for it."

What he stated was, in substance, this. He had lately made a voyage to the Indian Archipelago. A party, of which he formed one, landed at Borneo, and passed into the interior on an excursion of pleasure. Himself and a companion had captured the Ourang-Outang. This companion dying, the animal fell into his own exclusive possession. After a great trouble, occasioned by the intractable ferocity of his captive during the home voyage, he at length succeeded in lodging it safely at his own residence in Paris, where, not to attract toward himself the unpleasant curiosity of his neighbors, he kept it carefully secluded, until such time as it should recover from a wound in the foot, received from a splinter on board ship. His ultimate design was to sell it.

Returning home from some sailor's frolic on the night, or rather in the morning, of the murder, he found the beast occupying his own bedroom, into which it had broken from a closet adjoining, where it had been, as was thought, securely confined. Razor in hand, and fully lathered, it was sitting before a looking-glass, attempting the operation of shaving, in which it had no doubt previously watched its master through the keyhole of the closet. Terrified at the sight of so dangerous a weapon in the possession of an animal so ferocious, and so well able to use it, the man, for some moments, was at a loss what to do. He had been accustomed, however, to quiet the creature, even in its fiercest moods, by the use of a whip, and to this he now resorted. Upon sight of it, the Ourang-Outang sprang at once through the door of the chamber, down the stairs, and thence, through a window, unfortunately open, into the street.

The Frenchman followed in despair; the ape, razor still in hand, occasionally stopping to look back and gesticulate at his pursuer, until the latter had nearly come up with it. It then again made off. In this manner the chase continued for a long time. The streets were profoundly quiet, as it was nearly three o'clock in the morning. In passing down an alley in the rear of the Rue Morgue, the fugitive's attention was arrested by a light gleaming from the open window of Madame L'Espanaye's chamber, in the fourth story of her house. Rushing to the building, it perceived the lightning-rod, clambered up with inconceivable agility, grasped the shutter, which was thrown fully back against the wall, and, by its means, swung itself directly upon the headboard of the bed. The whole feat did not occupy a minute. The shutter was kicked open again by the Ourang-Outang as it entered the room.

The sailor, in the meantime, was both rejoiced and perplexed. He had strong hopes of now recapturing the brute, as it could scarcely escape from the trap into which it had ventured, except by the rod, where it might be intercepted as it came down. On the other hand, there was much cause for anxiety as to what it might do in the house. This latter reflection urged the man still to follow the fugitive. A lightning-rod is ascended without difficulty, especially by a sailor; but, when he had arrived as high as the window, which lay far to his left, his career was stopped; the most that he could accomplish was to reach over so as to obtain a glimpse of the interior of the room. At this glimpse he nearly fell from his hold through excess of horror. Now it was that those hideous shrieks arose upon the night, which had startled from slumber the inmates of the Rue Morgue. Madame L'Espanaye and her daughter, habited in their night clothes, had apparently been occupied in arranging some papers in the iron chest already mentioned, which had been wheeled into the middle of the room. It was open, and its contents lay beside it on the floor. The victims must have been sitting with their backs toward the window; and, from the time elapsing between the ingress of the beast and the screams, it seems probable that it was not immediately perceived. The flapping to of the shutter would naturally have been attributed to the wind.

As the sailor looked in, the gigantic animal had seized Madame L'Espanaye by the hair (which was loose, as she had been combing it), and was flourishing the razor about her face, in imitation of the motions of a barber. The daughter lay prostrate and motionless; she had swooned. The screams and struggles of the old lady (during which the hair was torn from her head) had the effect of changing the probably pacific purposes of the Ourang-Outang into those of wrath. With one determined sweep of its muscular arm it nearly severed her head from her body. The sight of blood inflamed its anger into phrenzy. Gnashing its teeth, and flashing fire from its eyes, it flew upon the body of the girl and embedded its fearful talons in her throat, retaining its grasp until she expired. Its wandering and wild glances fell at this moment upon the head of the bed, over which the face of its master, rigid with horror, was just discernible. The fury of the beast, who no doubt bore still in mind the dreaded whip, was instantly converted into fear. Conscious of having deserved punishment, it seemed desirous of concealing its bloody deeds, and skipped about the chamber in an agony of nervous agitation; throwing down and breaking the furniture as it moved, and dragging the bed from the bedstead. In conclusion, it seized first the corpse of the daughter, and thrust it up the chimney, as it was found; then that of the old lady, which, it immediately hurled through the window head-long.

As the ape approached the casement with its mutilated burden, the sailor shrank aghast to the rod, and, rather gliding than clambering down it, hurried at once home — dreading the consequences of the butchery, and gladly abandoning, in his terror, all solicitude about the fate of the Ourang-Outang. The words heard by the party upon the staircase were the Frenchman's exclamations of horror and affright, commingled with the fiendish jabberings of the brute.

I have scarcely any thing to add. The Ourang-Outang must have escaped from the chamber, by the rod, just before the breaking of the door. It must have closed the window as it passed through it. It was subsequently caught by the owner himself, who obtained for it a very large sum at the *Jardin des Plantes.* Le Bon was instantly released, upon our narration of the circumstances (with some comments from Dupin) at the *bureau* of the Prefect of Police. This functionary, however, well disposed to my friend, could not altogether conceal his chagrin at the turn which affairs had taken, and was fain to indulge in a sarcasm or two about the propriety of every person minding his own business.

"Let him talk," said Dupin, who had not thought it necessary to reply. "Let him discourse; it will ease his conscience. I am satisfied with having defeated him in his own castle. Nevertheless, that he failed in the solution of this mystery, is by no means that matter for wonder which he supposes it; for, in truth, our friend the prefect is somewhat too cunning to be profound. In his wisdom is no *stamen.* It is all head and no body, like the pictures of the Goddess Laverna — or, at best, all head and shoulders, like a codfish. But he is a good creature after all. I like him especially for one master stroke of cant, by which he has attained his reputation for ingenuity, I mean the way he has *'de nier ce qui est, et d'expliquer ce qui n'est pas.'* "*

---

* Rousseau — Nouvelle Heloise.

RICHARD POWERS

Richard Powers was born in 1957 in Illinois, grew up in the Midwest, and received his education at the University of Illinois at Champaign-Urbana. He is the author of two novels, *Three Farmers on Their Way to a Dance* (1985) and *Prisoner's Dilemma* (1988). In both, Powers's subject is time — how we of the present are invariably shaped by those of the past, how public History intersects with private history. Deploying shifts in chronology and point of view, as well as diverse narrative voices, Powers shapes his plots rather as an intellectual mystery writer might, taking his characters along a trail of clues which, slowly pieced together, yield a revelation, an awareness of meaning. "The Best Place for It" — published as a stand-alone segment from *Prisoner's Dilemma* — balances dreaminess with wit in an interlude with two of Powers's most appealing characters.

The Best Place for It

"Buffalo gals, can't you come out tonight ..."

Eddie Hobson, Jr., had abandoned his father to the front porch of the family's A-frame house, leaving the sick man shipwrecked on the blessed black sands of northern Illinois. Pop had promised to turn himself over to the Veterans Administration Hospital in Maywood after the Thanksgiving holidays. The Hobson dependents, helpless in the face of the old man's virtuoso invalid act, could do nothing between now and then but give in to November, 1978. And to Little Eddie, at eighteen, giving in came as easily as looking up the answers in the back of an algebra text. He felt no qualms about making his own emergency exit from family into the company of friends.

At the end of the evening, warmed by school acquaintances, Eddie had paired off with the prettiest, a junior named Sarah. He had talked her into seeing the second showing of "Fantasia" at the Egyptian, De Kalb's fifty-year-old Deco theatre. Walking her home, he started to sing, and she joined in: "And dance by the light of the moo-oon."

Their two-part harmony, flush with possibility, hung on the deserted street. Eddie grabbed Sarah around her willowy waist. "God, that was great. I had no idea you could sing. You sound just like Donna Reed." But Sarah, lovely in the limpid darkness, looked puzzled. "Donna Reed. *You* know. From 'It's a Wonderful Life.' " Astonished at not yet ringing the bell, he added, "Don't tell me you don't know it! Impossible. It's on a hundred times every Christmas. What were you, born yesterday?"

"I've seen that one, anyway, I think."

"That's got Judy Holliday, you nit." Eddie shook her lightly by her still unknown shoulders, scolding her in pantomime. "Know what my pop'll say when he finds out that his own flesh and blood spent the evening with a woman who didn't know the difference between Donna Reed and Judy Holliday? 'Out of the house, ingrate. You're no son of mine.' "

In fact the only response Dad ever made regarding any of the girlfriends Eddie brought home was the sad, cryptic chant "Girls, girls, girls." Once he had said, confidentially, "Remember, son. Fifty million Frenchmen *can* be wrong. Would you trust an appraisal of the fairer sex from the folks who gave you the Maginot Line?" That was the closest the two had ever come to discussing romantic love.

Sarah lifted her head to Eddie, Jr., and said, "I'm sorry. I haven't seen very many of the classics."

Eddie, hearing only her eyes, slipped his hands down into her floppy jacket pockets and played there. "Who said anything about *seeing* them? I haven't *seen* three-quarters of the old films I talk about. You just have to *know* about them."

"So how is it that you know all about them?"

"Blame it on my folks. They raised me on old-movie references."

"Just a slave to your upbringing, I suppose," Sarah said. Eddie felt confirmed in his suspicion that she was somewhat smarter than he, and infinitely more cultured. She played the cello. He had to step lightly or he'd end up in deep mischief — the kind of over-his-head treading for dear life that he lived for.

"I was *raised* to blame myself for my being raised that way. How's that?"

Sarah gave a sophisticated "Ha!" but drooped her shoulder toward his at the same time. Eddie supposed that indicated the answer was just fine.

"Funny you should ask, though. About my upbringing. I was designed by committee. Sins of the fathers. Nature versus nurture is one of my dad's favorite debates. But *my* father, he never comes down on one side or the other. He asked us once whether a person raised in solitary confinement can know what it means to get lonely."

"Your *father* asked you that?"

"Yeah. Over hot oatmeal, as I remember."

"Really! He sounds remarkable."

"Uh, that's the polite name. Look, I had better warn you about my family right now. They aren't the Cleavers." Eddie looked at her sidelong and said, "That's Ward and June, for those of you just back from the rococo."

Sarah shoved him and pulled his hands out of her pockets. "Enjoy the man," she ordered. "Mine just talks about what's wrong with the car. What about the rest of your family? Are they nature or nurture?"

Eddie dropped into the tones of dramatic voice-over. "The close-to-the-chest older brother. The testy, ex-radical big sis. Sis No. 2, everybody's favorite flake. The patient, long-suffering mom. All lost in orbit around the master of ceremonies. You tell me. Now that I think about it, we might make a halfway-decent sitcom after all."

She drew close again, and Eddie thought that nothing on this earth came close to the first feel of the waist of an unknown quantity. She had an easy grace, this stranger, a way of holding to his belt loop that made her seem unafraid of the consequences of knowing another person. He felt a rush of anticipation, doubled because he knew that she encouraged it.

For some months, seeing her in the halls, he had assumed that she was standoffish, that she liked cellos better than boys. And so he had fixed on her. Then they had caught one another making a mutual appraisal. The three-second glance proved how bendable the social circles of late adolescence still were. Each strained to find some overlap of friends, and at last hit on a contrived entrée to the other's crowd. And here was the same imaginary girl made real, teasing him on a late walk home. Her pretending that he was half as interesting as she was could only be early flirtation, a trick of the amber street light.

Eddie decided that before he dropped her off he would up the uncertain ante, answer her easy style. He started to steer them back to simple teases, but surprised himself by saying, "Pop's off to the hospital in a couple weeks."

"Oh? I'm sorry to hear that." She didn't bristle at the mention of illness. Eddie felt a sudden hurry to admire her, before life knocked her out for being perfect. "What's wrong?"

He even liked her wording, how she left off the *with him*. "We don't know what's wrong, really. Vertigo virus. The shimmies. Who knows? That's part of the problem. That's the *subject* of the Cleavers' misadventure this week."

"Don't be a curmudgeon. It's not becoming. Not if the man's not feeling well."

"Who you calling a curmudgeon?" She poked him in the sternum. "Oh, yeah? What's it mean?" she gave him the dictionary definition. "Damn it, that was on the S.A.T. If you'd told me three months ago, I'd be going to the college of my choice next year. Well, a couple of decades of Jaycee never hurt anybody, huh?"

"Three months ago you didn't know I existed. Maybe you should have gotten *Laura* to tell you what 'curmudgeon' meant."

"How do you know who I was going out with three months ago? Anyway, I swear to you that *Laurie,* as she is called by the general public, was just a passing physical insanity."

"What about Barbara, then?"

"Barbara? Barbara Simms? You jest. I wasn't going out with her. We were just childhood curmudgeons. All right, we *talked* about rubbing our bacons together. Once. In the interests of science. But that's as far as it went."

Sarah tucked her lower lip under her top teeth and pushed him again. "You are unbelievably crude, Hobson. 'Bacons.' I'd walk home alone if Rabelais hadn't used the same phrase."

Eddie assumed Rabelais was a passing indiscretion of Sarah's. Her Barbara Simms. "Who wants to know all these names from my sordid past, anyway?"

"I do," she said obstinately. And he fell in love.

"Listen. I want you to know, you have a terrific alto. Beats Donna Reed, I swear. We have to get married and form an act. I know you get a vote in the matter, but listen. We could take it on the road. Take it to Europe. Do Italy. Hop over to the Vatican and see the famous Medulla Oblongata."

Sarah laughed and corrected his anatomy. Then she lowered her eyes and hinted, "I've studied a little Italian, you know. On my own. For reading scores."

"That's O.K. I'll marry you anyway. We don't have to tell anyone that you know things." He had heard her excruciating maybe: *I wouldn't mind Italy; I don't mind you*. There was nothing to do but maybe her back.

The banter exasperated her. She withdrew her fingers from his and cast his hand away. "There's no way I'm going to marry you, Hobson. You are a proven unreliable quantity."

They walked in silence the length of three houses. The night air was cold, but not cold enough for either of them to know it. Near the horizon, just outside of town, sat the hunger moon. "If you bail out the tide with a twopenny pail," Eddie said quietly, to the motionless air.

"Then you and the moon can do a great deal."

Eddie looked at her in astonishment. He did not dare ask where she had heard the phrase. He had always considered it Dad's private stock, and the discovery that it was known to this beauty alarmed him with possibility. Sarah saw the quick look come across his face. Their hands fumbled and knit together, static-charged hair to winter wool.

"Know what my mother says?" Eddie asked, not believing that he was going to make this detail public. "She says, 'I would never dream of leaving your father. I signed the papers, didn't I?' How do you explain somebody like that?"

Sarah tucked her chin into her jacket collar. "That's who she is, I suppose. But I bet her feelings are the real contract."

He could not help himself from cupping both hands over her knit cap, behind her ears. "Well, if that's how you really feel about the matter, could we just live in sin, then? I'll move to Harvard or Yale, or wherever you end up. Pretty please?"

She laughed. "Oh, all right. If you insist."

The cadence of their step changed. Eddie tried wordlessly to make her avoid the sidewalk cracks, still visible through a first dusting of snow. After a silence that any other girl would have surely deflated, he asked, "What do you think of children?"

Sarah's face modulated to seriousness. Not oppressive seriousness, not brooding agitation or the end of enjoyment, but a textured, nuanced, sonata seriousness, the slow weighing of possibilities hidden in a minor key. "'I don't think . . .'" she began. "I'm not sure this is the best world to bring children into."

Eddie dropped a beat. He had heard the notion before. Pop had put it forward once to the older kids when they broke into their twenties: Suppose there was a final crisis in the world, and the outcome of everything was uncertain. Would any decent parent risk an infant to a world turned upside down? On the other hand, what good do we do by not enlisting new children? Now, suppose the crisis is too many children. Suppose the world is already lost. . . .

Eddie, Jr., had ignored the what-if then. Pop had a way of manufacturing sounds that weren't there. If the world were tearing at its seams, wouldn't the air fill with riot horns and sirens? Now, curling the ends of Sarah's hair, Eddie, Jr., understood that there would never be an advance warning. The siren comes only with returning order. All they would ever hear was a questionable hush. If someone as jaunty, full-spirited, and *seventeen* as this woman felt the touch of a child-forsaken world, maybe the place was upon them.

"We'll discuss this later, my little chickadee," he said, tapping imaginary cigar ash onto the snow. "Change of subject. Let me tell you a joke. There's this famous Broadway impresario — that's the right word, isn't it? — who wants to stage the greatest 'Hamlet' either side of the Atlantic. They put out the word for auditions. 'Looking for greatest Hamlet ever.' They listen to hundreds of guys. Famous, not so famous, good, great, unbelievable. But nobody rises to the heights of perfection this impresario has in mind. Then this little guy comes down from Washington Heights — paunch, receding hairline, shuffling, just off the boat. 'I vant to audition Hemlick.' The impresario groans, but lets the schlemiel do his thing, because nobody else has been quite good enough.

"So the guy gets up onstage and after a short silence says, 'Thrift.' Pretty good, eh? 'Thrift.' Didn't think I knew anything about Willie the S. didja? Thought I was a big dumb jock, dinja?"

"Just tell the story," she said, putting her hands in her pockets, refusing to take them out until he got on with it.

"You curmudgeon, you. So anyway, he says, 'Thrift, Horatio.' His voice fills the theatre, and the dust from his clothes falls off, his paunch disappears, and he is in another world. He transports everybody with that one word. He goes on: 'Assume a virtue if you have it not.' He holds up this skull, says how he kissed it once when it still had lips."

"Hobson, you counterfeit. You really *know* that play, don't you?"

"No way. But I've got this joke down pat. Now, please. By the end of the speech the impresario is weeping. The other auditioners are weeping. The guy sweeping the back of the theatre is weeping. The little man onstage has them all in a place where the skull is somebody *they* knew." Sarah took hold of his arm and slowed his walk.

"Then the man stops, turns back into a little schlep, and comes down off the stage. There's this moment of silence, and the impresario says, 'That was the most astonishing, moving Hamlet I have ever heard. How did you do that? What kind of man are you? Where in God's name did you get that power?' And the zhlub shrugs and says, 'That's ecting.' " Sarah laughed melodically, but not at the punch line. "I don't get it, Eddie."

"Come on, woman. 'Ecting,' you see. Immigrant's accent. You see, if he can talk like Hamlet, if he can fly away, change the place, then why does he . . ."

She covered her mouth and doubled up. "It's not funny, Eddie. It doesn't make any sense."

"What do you mean, not funny? You just don't get it. You eggheads have no sense of humor. Come to think of it, I don't really get it either. Thought *you* might be able to explain it to *me*. Blame it on my brother. He told it to me. Maybe you should marry my brother. He's an egghead, too." She shook her head rapidly and gathered a handful of his coat fabric into her face. She said something Eddie couldn't catch.

They turned at random onto Locust. Eddie could no longer tell where they were heading. He considered asking Sarah what she knew about the Drunk and the Lamppost, the thought experiment that Pop had put forward earlier that evening, over dinner — another pedagogical routine in the old teacher's repertoire that had ended in family disaster. But Eddie kept mum. They peered into low-lit living rooms, intimate domestic scenes that were fair game from street level, each holding the secret of how to get by but revealing nothing. They slowed again, as if only faint street lamps, the hollow moon, chill air, sidewalk cracks, the smell of a cold front rushing down a street already folded and put away for the night — only this collected instant could lead them to the specific weight and exactness of the world. They had fallen upon the legendary *there,* or as close as they could push to it, and all life after tonight would amount to trying to re-create this moment.

At last Eddie broke the spell. "One thing I have to ask you. If you ever *do* marry somebody, if you *do* decide that it's O.K. to bring children into this world, don't name them after their parents. You know: Junior. What can you do then, besides join Order of the Arrow or some other Elk-induced, paramilitary, junior chamber of . . ."

Sarah listened to him trail off. For a moment it seemed that they were going to stop under a shed maple, but they did not. When the chance was lost, she said, "Thanks for talking me into that movie. I'd read a lot about it, but none of my long-hair friends would ever deign to go near it."

"No kidding. One of my favorites. Classic animation. 1940. Happens to be one of the few old-timers I *have* seen."

"Admit it. You've seen them all."

"Have *not*. But this one I love. My favorite part's when that little rodent goes up and pulls on the old guy's coattails. I always want the maestro to turn around and go, 'Eeeek, plague!' "

She liked the Bach best, although she felt that the transcription was a little heavy-handed and inauthentic. Eddie preferred the little colored horses with wings.

"And speakin' of rats and plagues and all," Eddie said, meaning Mickey and Stokowski, "I learned something unbelievable this weekend. From Big Brother again. Did you know that ring-around-the-rosy was first played by little kids during the Black Death? It's all about those lumpy sores and how they had to burn the bodies and all." Big Brother, for his part, had learned this from Dad.

"I remember reading that somewhere."

"It's not fair. You can't be attractive and know everything, too. Make up your mind and specialize, like everyone else." Sarah declared that her specialty tonight was Donna Reed. So they took it again, from the top, with feeling. "Buffalo gals, can't you come out tonight, can't you come out tonight, can't you come out tonight. Buffalo gals, can't you come out tonight. And . . . dance . . . by . . . the light . . . of the moo-ooon."

"God, you're beautiful."

"Let's not be blasphemous, now."

"What? I didn't say nothing. I said *Gob*, not *God*. 'Gob, you're beautiful.' I've got a great idea. How about you and I . . ." He pointed to her mouth, then to his, waving his index finger back and forth between the two, inquiringly. She nodded almost imperceptibly, and they kissed.

Eddie felt that it was almost impossible to be less than an inch from the face of another without wanting to shout love like a signed confession. But somehow he did not. He said instead, "Mmm. Oh! That was perfect. Now, *that's* ecting."

Sarah looked off shyly. Facing away, she said, "You wouldn't be kissing relative strangers while keeping a certain Barbara Simms sequestered off on the side somewhere?"

"You've got me all wrong. I'm really a shy kind of fellow. 'Thrift, thrift.' I stand helpless in the express lines behind those people who try to sneak in with thirteen items. I want to tell them off, but I can't get up the nerve. See. . . ." He faced her, taking both her hands in front of him. "I'm really emotionally scarred, underneath. There was this traumatic incident when I was two, when I tried to split an English muffin with a knife and my mother came howling out of the next room screaming, 'Fork!' I've been virtually spineless ever since."

She took his arm, patted him gently on the back. "Maladjusted, are you? Poor boy. Tell me, what was the greatest embarrassment of your life?"

"Hmm. Tough one. Let's see. There was the time in Sunday school, when we were saying the Lord's Prayer just prior to heading off for the work week, and we got to the big finish — kingdom, power, glory for everandever — and I just kept going on with the Hobson evening version, 'God bless Mommy and Daddy and Lily . . .' An unfortunate solo that my peers did not soon let me forget. How about yours?"

"Well . . ." She grinned a sheepish, demure, but absolutely fetching overbite smile that made Eddie squeeze her shoulders in appreciation. "Last summer, when I went to Red Fox Music Camp on full scholarship, I stepped off the bus in front of the entire music faculty and my suitcase exploded and all my clothes came bursting out."

"Oh, Jesus. How indiscreet. Come on. You can do better than that. Let's talk real embarrassment. You know Paulie Kogan, the stocky guy with the wire rims? Last year, we were supposed to do weight training for some stupid jock thing or another, and he comes to me and says, 'Eddie, don't pick me up tonight. I'm leaving town on a family thing.' 'Oh, what's up?' I ask. 'My dad's dead,' he says. And before I know what I'm saying — stupid, middle-class, knee-jerk — I say, 'Oh, I hope he gets better soon.' You wanted embarrassment." They fell silent, stupid, middle class, knee jerk silence. Sarah sensed it wasn't Paulie's dad that stopped them in place.

Eddie, brave as the recollection was, kept back the real contenders for the title, the public incidents involving Pop and his proclivity, which he might consider telling this woman after he got to know her better. Like in another twenty years. He assumed a virtue, and continued comically, "My life is one continual embarrassment, really. Confusing Lerner and Loewe with Leopold and Loeb. You know, pronouncing 'epitome' like it looks. I hate being at the mercy of words. Gonna hafta learn a few, one of these days."

Sarah stopped. She pulled Eddie to her, and returned the previous favor. To cover her awkwardness when they drew apart, she said, "We ought to do this walk again in the spring, don't you think? I love it when it's rained lightly while you're in the theatre and when you come out everything smells of earthworms and something about to happen."

Eddie matched her voice, enthusiasm for enthusiasm. "I know. How the air fills with spore cases. You know how, when it rains, water trickles off of tree branches and lands on those bungalow-looking structures? Here's a couple." He produced an imaginary sample. "They grow up around the tree trunks and then the water force makes them release this powder into the air."

It was, he was suddenly aware, not standard high-school dialogue. But something about Sarah made him trust her without being able to help himself. "Here's one. Go ahead, tap it. The spores are in your hair. Let me help." He held her strands up to the light. "These are among your more serious fungi. They aren't ones to dance around in fairy rings to 'The Nutcracker Suite,' for instance. And look, see how the water pulls itself into spheres on the surface of the leaves? And underground . . ." He overturned a rock, revealing nothing.

"Bugs!" Sarah exclaimed, a cry of complete fascination. Eddie was astonished at her response. They had somehow jumped together into the same lost place.

"Sure. The night's when they really come out. More beetle activity per square leaf at night than anyone imagines." It was below freezing, and crouched on the ground they could not help starting to feel it. She was on her knees beside him, peering intently. He put his arm lightly around her, gratefully. "Not too many of them this far north, this time of year. November's tough on the food chain."

"What else?" she said. He had seen that look before, a genuine interest in whatever there was to learn. The discovery of the complex world under the rock, making the world above it almost livable.

"I think," Eddie said, standing and unfolding himself slowly, "that if I hadn't already made a complete botch of my future, I would have liked to make a living doing this — what we were just playing at doing. Digging around in the leaves, studying bugs."

"An entomologist!"

"I'm pretty good at sketching with a pencil, and I can look at things for hours without blinking. I just like to watch life. Maybe see something nobody else has yet."

"Good Lord, boy. You talk like the chance is gone. Do it, if you love it."

"Naw, it's too late already. Don't have the grades. And I'm not so good at the studies part. You know, turning it into a science, with math and all. My sister Rach got all the math genes. She didn't even have to study it. The formulas were just there, intact." He fell silent. Then he began to walk in circles, animated again. "But think of all these combinations, under our feet. The size of it. The possibilities." Sarah stared at him with a look of incredulity, which he misunderstood. "Sorry. I get that way as the night goes on. As the saying goes, 'That's . . .' "

"Don't say it!" She sounded violent.

"How did you know what I was going to say?" Eddie joked. But he had upset whatever she had been feeling about him. They strolled again, turning by accident almost to the front of the Hobson house before he noticed. "Hey! Look where we are." They had arrived, by the random walk, back at the family homestead, his father's sick bay, the soul of Second Street. "How did we wind up here? I thought the gentleman was supposed to walk the lady home."

"Well, I'd ask you in," he said, "but I'm afraid my motorcycle-gang-intelligentsia family would work you over." She was the first friend he could remember being reluctant to take inside.

"I'd love to meet them, actually."

"Well, there's just the four of us. The party's over. Big Brother and Sis No. 2 just jumped ship. Snuck out the back way to Chitown on Illinois 5. Sis 1 is still around. And the folks, of course. But they'd be more than willing to grill you until you confessed."

"Don't be so down on your family."

"I'm *not* down on them. They just never know what to make of my friends." After an awkward pause, Eddie added, "Want to sit in the yard for a while? We can dig up grubs or something."

Sarah nodded eagerly. She smoothed her skirt and began to settle onto the cold front lawn. Eddie shot a nervous glance porchward. "No, the back yard; it's better. Darker. We've got a swing rigged up, too."

Going around the side corner of the porch, they ran right into the cameo Eddie had dreaded. Pop's face, as drained of blood as the Mariner's, loomed up through the dark storm windows, disembodied. Sarah let out a sharp, frightened shout. "Wave to him," Eddie said, taking her by the hand. "Humor him." When they reached the back yard, he put on his most deferential face and said, "That's my dad," hoping to ease the situation by stating the obvious.

It didn't work. Sarah was absolutely peaked, as white as the apparition itself. "Oh, Eddie. He's really sick. What's wrong with him?"

"I told you, I don't *know* what's wrong with him." And to joke away his having spoken more curtly than intended, he added, "We're running forbidden scientific experiments on him. Don't tell anybody, all right?"

Sarah sat on the tree swing, and Eddie pushed her gently. They talked the quick, idle, expendable talk used to gloss over sudden shocks. He commented that they hadn't mentioned Top Forty all night, and that she was a disgrace to her age group. She thanked him. Then, bearing out that very observation, she said, "Tell me everything you think you can about your father."

He caught her at the apogee and held her waist until she released herself with the kind of brushing kiss one might give after two decades of shared uncertainty. "What do you want to know about him? He cleans his teeth with strips of cellophane from Lucky Strike cigarettes. And when Mom's not around he invents shocking meanings for the L.S./M.F.T. initials. He's . . . well, let's see . . . he was in the Army. But then, so was everybody's dad. During the war. *The* war. Is this what you want to hear?"

"Tell me everything that you think I should know."

"His brother was also in the Big One. Army Air Forces. Got killed in some sort of freak airplane crash. But Stateside, which was the weird thing about it. One of the central events in the life of Eddie, Sr., as far as I can make out. Been with him every day since."

"Is he morbid?"

"What do you mean — does he get schnockered once a year religiously on the date? Not really. No death shrines. No, it just sort of left him with this weird sense of humor."

"Black humor?"

"Coal dust. He's funny, all right, only . . . only everything's fair game. A kind of sarcasm, but not sarcastic. He jokes the way people hug at fiftieth-year reunions: too much backslapping, when what everybody really wants to do is kiss all those shattered faces and weep. He parodies everything. He never repeats the standard jokes. Dad would never do a one-liner for the one-liner's sake." And unable to help himself, Eddie recited in silence that old perennial of Pop's: *All Indians walk in single file. At least the one I saw did.* Half to himself he chanted, "All punches walk in straight lines. . . ."

"Eddie?"

"Nothing. Just free-associating. He likes catchphrases. Pop is capable of saying, in the same breath, with the same degree of seriousness and importance, both 'There is more to any of us than any of us suspects' and 'The secret of happiness consists in not eating grapes just after you've brushed your teeth.' He is totally maudlin underneath. A sentimentalist who refuses to put himself at the mercy of caring what happens to other people."

Sarah pulled her mouth to one side in an urbane twist. "You wouldn't have picked up any of that, now, would you?"

"Me? How could you suggest such a thing?" His irony proved the simple and unequivocal, if self-attacking, truth: *No Hobson can be trusted. At least the one I saw couldn't.* "He wants to know everything. He reads everything, which only makes him spout on about everything, until he's succeeded in dragging everybody down with him into the facts. Funny, though. It's exactly the opposite with my big brother, Artie. The two of them read a lot of the same books and everything. But the more Artie reads, the quieter he gets."

"And what about No. 3?"

"You talking about *moi?*" *Suppose this girl were already lost.* The terrifying thought shot up his backbone, and Eddie hunched over. "I say, Live all you can. You make things worse for everybody if you don't."

Whether she agreed or simply did not want to disabuse his simplicity, Sarah stayed silent. Eddie began talking faster, without looking at the woman he was swinging. "It's like Pop never made the compromises everybody else makes in growing up. He hit the age of twenty and looked around — you know, 'These people are *off the wall*' — and decided to regress to what the white-bread company calls the formative years. Try it all over again from the top. For instance, he's got this hobby . . ." Eddie trailed off and tried to push the swing. But Sarah would not lift her feet from the earth.

"No. Tell me. Don't be embarrassed. My father plays with model trains."

"Really? Does he? Well, I suppose you could call Pop's thing a model-train set. A surreal monstrosity of a model train. He builds this . . . You wouldn't get it. *I* don't get it myself. He plays at city planner, on the sly. Talks into a tape recorder. 'Hobstown.' Privilege of the sick. Cheaper than golf, see? And you don't need an opponent."

Eddie put his hand inside her open collar and tentatively, almost fearfully, rested it on her deltoids. "Ex-history teacher. Frozen in place by the past. Loves his black-and-white. Lost in Bedford Falls. What can I say? The man's my father." She touched her hand to his, not to arrest his forward progress but to give him the powerless gesture of comfort. And to direct him to the right place.

Eddie talked into the black air. "They say if you want to see how the son is going to turn out, look at the dad. That means if you marry me — and I intend to make your life miserable until you do, and probably after as well — I'll be decked out on the porch in thirty years, like the Big Guy. My belly will be out to here, and my arms and legs will be this little around. And off to the vets hospital. Sound attractive?" He understood that he had gone beyond the repartee with which she could live. His words had become ugly. There was no taking them back. "But why are we talking to one another about our *folks?* We're supposed to be talking about how pretty your nose is." He touched it. "Like it makes any difference what the folks are up to. We're supposed to give them something to drool about. 'What a great time the kids must be having, so young and all.' "

She laughed, both at how he talked and at the new force with which he suddenly swung her. "Too high, Eddie."

"High? You haven't *seen* high yet. We need to achieve antigravity." She closed her eyes and kept still. The look of bravery that then crossed her face made him call out, "Know what? I'm crazy about you."

She opened her eyes wide and just looked. But she had the presence of mind to taunt, "What about Miss Simms?"

"Oh, I'm crazy about her, too."

All sophistication vanished, and she was once again seventeen. "Jerk! Play nice. That's not fair."

"Of course it's fair. Don't you think it's better, the more people you care for? And I'm crazy about those hippos and those twinky horses with wings, and the mouse, and the foreign guy with the music stick, too." He teased her mercilessly, until he found her on the edge of tears. "No, friend. It's you. As of tonight." She brightened. "Still, people are really O.K. by me," Eddie went on. "Doesn't matter what kind of roof they put up to keep themselves dry, I guess. I defy you to come up with somebody I can't get along with."

"What about . . ." She cast a furtive glance toward the white wood house.

"What about . . . *Jesus.* My family? I *love* my family. What ever made you think . . ." She looked so hurt at his volume, so genuinely wronged, that he remembered the words that had, naturally, led her to that conclusion. "Oh, *that,*" he said, eyes appeasing. "That's *ecting.*"

Standing behind her, he put his hand deeper into her shirt. It fit nicely. She struggled up against him, to move his fingers to the right place.

"Would Donna Reed do this?"

"No, Donna never let Jimmy do this. Not without certification, anyway."

They began to learn about one another in the nimbus of the back-porch light. Whether or not this was the best place for it, their parents had left them here, to make a home somewhere under the weight of events. And when the historical world once more seemed to need speaking about, Eddie, Jr., said, "Peaceful here. The Hobson back yard. A good month, November. Not so cold as you'd expect. I like the place. And you?" Without waiting for the reply, he went on questioning. "Can't you? Can't you come out? And? Dance?"

MERCÈ RODOREDA

Mercè Rodoreda (1908–1983) was born in Catalonia, the region in south-eastern Spain that was autonomous from the central government and spoke its own language, Catalan, until Franco's fascist forces won the Spanish Civil War in 1939. Rodoreda had written five novels before the war broke out and was considered one of the most gifted young Catalan writers. But Franco's government, seeking conformity and unity by any means, forcibly suppressed Catalan culture and politics and forbade the speaking or writing of the Catalan language. Along with nearly half a million Spaniards, Rodoreda was forced into exile. She lived in Geneva and published nothing until 1959, when *Twenty-Two Stories* appeared. From that time she resumed writing; perhaps her best-known works in translation are *The Time of the Doves* (1980) and *My Christina and Other Stories* (1967). After Franco's death in 1975, restrictions against Catalan were relaxed, and Rodoreda returned to her homeland in 1979. She was primarily a realistic novelist, although her stories, especially those in *My Christina*, move into other realms. As her translator, David Rosenthal, has observed, they often "begin in everyday reality and end in delirium" — the exact movement, he further notes, of European history in the 1930s and '40s. "The Salamander" — a monologue, one of Rodereda's favorite forms — has the aura of a folktale, one deeply imbued with the supernatural.

The Salamander

Translated from the Catalan by David H. Rosenthal

I walked under the willow tree, came to the patch of watercress, and knelt beside the pond. As usual, there were frogs all around. As soon as I got there they'd come out and bounce up to me. And when I began to comb my hair, the naughtiest ones would start touching my red skirt with the five little plaits on it, or pulling the scalloped border on my petticoats, all full of frills and tucks. And the water'd grow sadder and sadder, and the trees on the hillside slowly darken. But that day the frogs leapt into the water in one jump, and the water's mirror shattered into little pieces. And when the water was all smooth again I saw his face beside mine, like two shadows watching me from the other side. And so he wouldn't think I was frightened, I got up without a word, I began walking through the grass very calmly, and as soon as I heard him following, I looked around and stopped. Everything was quiet, and one edge of the sky was already sprinkled with stars. He'd halted a little ways off, and I didn't know what to do, but suddenly I got scared and started to run. And when I realized he was catching up with me, I stopped underneath the willow with my back against the trunk. He planted himself in front of me, with his arms stretched out on both sides so I couldn't escape. And then, looking into my eyes, he pressed me against the willow and with my hair all dishevelled, between him and the willow tree, I bit my lip so I wouldn't cry out from the pain in my chest and all my bones feeling like they were about to break. He put his mouth on my neck, and it burned where he put it.

The next day the trees on the hill were already black when he came, but the grass was still warm from the sun. He held me again against the willow trunk, and put his hand flat over my eyes. And all at once I felt like I was falling asleep, and the leaves were telling me things which made sense but which I didn't understand, saying them softer and softer and slower and slower. And when I couldn't hear them anymore and my tongue was frozen with terror, I asked him, "And your wife?" And he told me, "You're my wife. Only you." My back was crushing the grass I'd hardly dared walk on when I was going to comb my hair. Just a little, to catch the smell of it breaking. Only you. Afterwards, when I opened my eyes, I saw the blond hair falling and she was bent over, looking at us blankly. And when she realized I'd seen her, she grabbed my hair and said "Witch." Very softly. But she let go of me immediately and grabbed him by his shirt collar. "Go on, go on," she said. And she led him away, pushing him as they went.

We never went back to the pond. We'd meet in stables, under haystacks, in the woods with the roots. But after that day when his wife led him away, the people in the village started looking at me like they didn't see me, and some of them would cross themselves quickly as I went by. After a while, when they saw me coming they'd go into their houses and lock the doors. I started hearing a word which followed me everywhere I went, as if the air whistled it or it came from the light and the darkness. Witch, witch, witch. The doors shut. I walked through the streets of a ghost town, and the eyes I saw between the slits in the curtains were always icy. One morning I had a lot of trouble opening my front door, which was old and cracked by the sun. They'd hung an ox's head in the middle of it, with two little green branches stuck in the eyes. I took it down. It was very heavy, and I left it on the ground since I didn't know what to do with it. The branches began to dry, and while they were drying the head began to stink and there was a swarm of milk-colored worms all around the neck on the side where they'd cut it.

Another day I found a headless pigeon, its breast red with blood, and another a sheep born dead before its time and two rat's ears. And when they stopped hanging dead animals on my door, they started to throw stones. They banged against the window and roof tiles at night, as big as fists . . . Then they had a procession. It was the beginning of winter. A windy day with scurrying clouds, and the procession went very slowly, with white and purple paper flowers. I lay on the floor, watching it through the special door I'd made for the cat. And when it was almost in front of the door, with the wind, the saint, and the banners, the cat got frightened by the torches and chants and tried to come in. And when he saw me he let out a great shriek, with his back arched like a bridge. And the procession came to a halt, and the priest gave blessing after blessing, and the altar boys sang and the wind whipped the flames on the torches, and the sexton walked up and down, and everything was a flutter of white and purple petals from the paper flowers. Finally the procession went away. And before the holy water had dried on the walls, I went out looking for him and I couldn't find him anywhere. I searched in the stables, under haystacks, in the woods with the roots — I knew it by heart. I always sat on the oldest root, which was all white and dusty like a bone. And that night, when I sat down, I suddenly realized I had no hope left. I lived facing backwards, with him inside me like a root in the earth. The next day they wrote "witch" on my door with a piece of charcoal. And that night, good and loud so I could hear them, two men said they should have burned me when I was little, along with my mother who used to fly around on eagle's wings when everyone was asleep. That they should have had me burned before they started needing me to pick garlic or tie the grain and alfalfa in sheaves or gather grapes from the poor vines.

One evening I thought I saw him at the entrance to the woods with the roots, but when I got closer he ran away and I couldn't tell if it was him or my desire for him or his shadow searching for me, lost like I was among the trees, pacing to and fro. "Witch," they said, and left me with my pain, which wasn't at all the kind they'd meant to give me. And I thought of the pond and the watercress and the willow's slender branches ... The winter was dark and flat and leafless. Just ice and frost and the frozen moon. I couldn't move, because to walk around in winter is to walk in front of everybody and I didn't want them to see me. And when spring came, with its joyous little leaves, they built a fire in the middle of the square, using dry wood, carefully cut.

Four men from the village came looking for me: the elders. From inside I told them I wouldn't go with them, and then the young ones came with their big red hands, and broke down the door with an axe. And I screamed, because they were dragging me from my own house, and I bit one and he hit the middle of my head with his fist, and they grabbed my arms and legs and threw me on top of the pile like one more branch, and they bound my arms and feet and left me with my skirt pulled up. I turned my head. The square was full of people, the young in front of the old, and the children off to one side with little olive branches and new Sunday smocks. And while I was looking at the children I caught sight of him. He was standing beside his wife, who was dressed in black with her blond hair, and he had his arm around her shoulder. I turned away and closed my eyes. When I opened them again, two old men came forward with burning torches, and the boys started singing the song of the burning witch. It was a very long song, and when they'd finished it the old men said they couldn't start the fire, that I wouldn't let them light it. And then the priest came up to the boys with his bowl full of holy water, and made them wet the olive branches and throw them on top of me, and soon I was covered with little olive branches, all with tiny shoots. And a little old lady, crooked and toothless, started laughing and went away and after a while she came back with two baskets full of dry heather and told the old men to spread them on the four sides of the bonfire, and she helped them, and then the fire caught. Four columns of smoke rose, and the flames twisted upwards and it seemed like a great sigh of relief went out of the hearts of all those people. The flames rose, chasing after the smoke, and I watched everything through a red downpour. And behind that water every man, woman, and child was like a happy shadow because I was burning.

The bottom of my skirt had turned black. I felt the fire in my kidneys, and from time to time, a flame chewed at my knee. It seemed like the ropes that tied me were already burnt. And then something happened which made me grit my teeth. My arms and legs started getting shorter like the horns on a snail I once touched with my finger, and under my head where my neck and shoulders met, I felt something stretching and piercing me. And the fire howled and the resin bubbled ... I saw some of the people looking at me raise their arms, and others were running and bumping into the ones who hadn't moved. And one whole side of the fire collapsed in a great shower of sparks, and when the scattered wood began burning again it seemed like someone was saying "She's a salamander." And I started walking over the burning coals, very slowly, because my tail was heavy.

I walked on all fours with my face against the ground. I was going towards the willow tree, rubbing against the wall, but when I got to the corner I turned my head slightly and off in the distance I saw my house, which looked like a flaming torch. There was no one in the street. I went past the stone bench, and then quickly through the house full of flames and glowing coals, towards the willow, towards the watercress, and when I was outside again I turned around because I wanted to see how the roof was burning. While I was staring at it the first drop fell, one of those hot, fat drops that give birth to toads, and then others fell, slowly at first and then faster, and soon all the water in the sky had poured down and the fire went out in a great cloud of smoke. I kept still. I couldn't see a thing, because night had fallen and the night was black and dense. I set out, wading through mud and puddles. My hands enjoyed sinking in the soft mush, but my feet grew weary behind me from getting stuck so often. I would have liked to run, but I couldn't. A clap of thunder stopped me in my tracks. Then came a bolt of lightning, and through the rocks I saw the willow. I was out of breath when I reached the pond. And when, after the mud, which is dirt from the ground, I found the slime, which is dirt from the bottom of the water, I crept into a corner, half-buried between two roots. And then three little eels came along.

At dawn, I don't know if it was the next day or some other, I climbed out slowly and saw the high mountains beneath a sky smudged with clouds. I ran through the watercress and stopped at the trunk of the willow tree. The first leaves were still inside the buds, but the buds were turning green. I didn't know which way to turn. If I didn't watch where I was going, the blades of grass would prick my eyes — and I fell asleep among those blades until the sun was high in the sky. When I woke up I caught a tiny mosquito, and then looked for worms in the grass. Finally I went back to the slime and pretended to be asleep, because the three eels immediately came up, acting very playful.

The night I decided to go to the village there was lots of moonlight. The air was full of smells and the leaves were already fluttering on all the branches. I followed the path with the rocks, very carefully because the smallest things frightened me. When I got to my house, I rested. There was nothing but ruins and nettle bushes, with spiders spinning and spinning. I went around back and stopped in front of his garden. Beside the hollyhocks, the sunflowers hung their round flowers. I followed the bramble hedge without thinking why I was doing it, as if someone were telling me "Do this, do that," and slipped under his door. The ashes in the hearth were still warm. I lay down for a while, and after running around a bit all over I settled down under the bed. So tired that I fell asleep and didn't see the sunrise.

When I woke up there were shadows on the floor, because night was already falling again, and his wife was walking back and forth with a burning candle. I saw her feet and part of her legs, thin at the bottom, swollen higher up, with white stockings. Then I saw his feet, big, with blue socks falling over his ankles. And I saw their clothing fall, and heard them sitting on the bed. Their feet were dangling, his next to hers, and one of his feet went up and a sock fell, and she took off her stockings, pulling them off with both hands, and then I heard the sheets rustling as they pulled them up. They were talking very softly, and after a while, when I'd gotten used to the darkness, the moonlight came in through the window, a window with four panes and two strips of wood that made a cross. And I crawled over to the light and placed myself right under the cross because inside myself, even though I wasn't dead, there was nothing inside me that was totally alive, and I prayed hard because I didn't know if I still was a person or only a little animal, or if I was half person and half animal. And also I prayed to know where I was, because at times I felt like I was underwater, and when I was underwater I felt like I was on the ground, and I never knew where I really was. When the moon went down they woke up, and I went back to my hiding place under the bed, and started to make myself a little nest with bits of fluff. And I spent many nights between the fluff and the cross. Sometimes I'd go outside and go up to the willow tree. When I was under the bed, I'd listen. It was just like before. "Only you," he'd say. And one night when the sheet was hanging on the floor I climbed up the sheet, holding onto the folds, and got into bed beside one of his legs. And he was as quiet as a corpse. He turned a little and his leg pressed down on top of me. I couldn't move. I breathed hard because he was crushing me, and I wiped my cheek against his leg, very carefully so as not to wake him.

But one day she did a housecleaning. I saw the white stockings and the raggedy broom, and just when I least expected it blond hair was dragging on the floor and she shoved the broom under the bed. I had to run because it seemed like the broom was searching for me, and suddenly I heard a scream and saw her feet running towards the door. She came back with a burning torch and jammed half her body under the bed and tried to burn my eyes. And I, clumsy, didn't know which way to run and was dazzled and bumped into everything: the legs on the bed, the walls, the feet on the chairs. I don't know how, I found myself outside and made for the puddle of water under the horses' drinking trough, and the water covered me up but two boys saw me and went to look for reeds and started poking me. I turned and faced them, with my whole head out of the water, and stared right at them. They threw down the reeds and ran away, but immediately they came back with six or seven bigger boys, and they all threw stones and handfuls of dirt at me. A stone hit one of my little hands and broke it, but in the midst of badly aimed stones and in utter terror I was able to get away and run into the stable. And she came looking for me there with the broom, with the children constantly shouting, waiting at the door, and she poked me and tried to make me come out of my corner full of straw and I was dazzled again and bumped into the pails, the baskets, the sacks of carob beans, the horses' hoofs, and a horse reared because I'd bumped into one of his hoofs, and I went up with him. A whack from the broom touched my broken hand and almost pulled it off, and a trickle of black spit oozed from one side of my mouth. But I still was able to get away through a crack, and as I escaped I heard the broom poking and poking.

In the dead of night I went to the woods with the roots. I came out from under some bushes in the light of the rising moon. Everything seemed hopeless. The broken hand didn't hurt, but it was dangling by a sinew, and I had to lift my arm so it wouldn't drag too much. I walked a little crookedly, now over a root, now over a stone, till I got to the root where I used to sit sometimes before they dragged me off to the bonfire in the square, and I couldn't get to the other side because I kept slipping. And on and on and on, towards the willow tree, and towards the watercress and towards my slimy home under the water. The grass rustled in the wind, which whipped up bits of dry leaves and carried off short, bright strands from the flowers beside the path. I rubbed one side of my head against a tree trunk and slowly went towards the pond, and entered it holding my weary arm up, with the broken hand on it.

Under the water streaked with moonlight, I saw the three eels coming. They seemed a little blurred, and intertwined with each other, winding in and out, making slippery knots till the littlest one came up to me and bit my broken hand. A little juice came out of the wrist, looking like a wisp of smoke beneath the water. The eel held onto the hand and slowly pulled it, and while he was pulling, he kept looking at me. And when he thought I wasn't watching he gave one or two hard, stubborn jerks. And the others played at entwining as if they were making a rope, and the one who was biting my hand gave a furious yank and the sinew must have snapped because he carried off the hand and when he had it he looked at me as if to say: "Now I've got it!" I closed my eyes for a while, and when I opened them the eel was still there, between the shadow and the shimmering bits of light, with the little hand in his mouth — a sheaf of bones stuck together, covered by a bit of black skin. And I don't know why, but all of a sudden I saw the path with the stones, the spiders inside my house, the legs hanging over the side of the bed. They were dangling, white and blue, like they were sitting on top of the water, but empty, like spread out washing, and the rocking water made them sway from side to side. And I saw myself under that cross made of shadows, above that fire full of colors that rose shrieking and didn't burn me . . . And while I was seeing all these things the eels were playing with that piece of me, letting it go and then grabbing it again, and the hand went from one eel to the next, whirling around like a little leaf, with all the fingers separated. And I was in both worlds: in the slime with the eels, and a little in that world of I don't know where . . . till the eels got tired and the slime sucked my hand under . . . a dead shadow, slowly smoothing the dirt in the water, for days and days and days, in that slimy corner, among thirsty grass roots and willow roots that had drunk there since the beginning of time.

Isaac Bashevis Singer was born in 1904 in Radsymin, Poland, the son of a rabbi. He was given an orthodox rabbinical education but, influenced by the rational secularism of his older brother, a novelist, he broke with tradition and commenced a career in writing. He worked in Warsaw for a Hebrew and Yiddish press and wrote stories in Yiddish. With the rise of Nazism in the 1930s he sensed Poland's impending doom, and in 1935 he followed his brother to the United States, where he still lives and writes. Among his novels are *Satan in Goray* (1935; English 1955), *The Family Moskat* (1950), *The Magician of Lublin* (1960), *The Manor* (1967), and *Shosha* (1978). His short story collections include *Gimpel the Fool and Other Stories* (1957), *The Spinoza of Market Street and Other Stories* (1961), *Selected Short Stories* (1966), *An Isaac Bashevis Singer Reader* (1971), *A Crown of Feathers and Other Stories* (1973), and *The Collected Short Stories of Issac Bashevis Singer* (1982). He received the Nobel Prize for Literature in 1978. Singer is generally recognized as the foremost living writer of Yiddish literature. Critics have long remarked the paradox he represents: he writes in a dying language of a world that literally no longer exists — the *shtetls* (Jewish ghettos) of Eastern Europe, destroyed by the Nazis. As one critic put it: "It strikes one as a kind of inspired madness: here is a man living in New York City, a sophisticated and clever writer, who composes stories about places like Frampol, Bilgoray, Kreshov, *as if they were still there*." In Singer's rich imagination, of course, they still are. He is a consummate storyteller, adapting the rhythms and easy ways with magic and the supernatural inherent in folktales. He says of his characters, "I think all my heroes are possessed people — possessed by mania, by a fixed idea, by a strange level of fear or passion." "The Spinoza of Market Street" is about such a one.

The Spinoza of Market Street

Translated from the Yiddish by Martha Glicklich and Cecil Hemley

1

Dr. Nahum Fischelson paced back and forth in his garret room in Market Street, Warsaw. Dr. Fischelson was a short, hunched man with a grayish beard, and was quite bald except for a few wisps of hair remaining at the nape of the neck. His nose was as crooked as a beak and his eyes were large, dark, and fluttering like those of some huge bird. It was a hot summer evening, but Dr. Fischelson wore a black coat which reached to his knees, and he had on a stiff collar and a bow tie. From the door he paced slowly to the dormer window set high in the slanting room and back again. One had to mount several steps to look out. A candle in a brass holder was burning on the table and a variety of insects buzzed around the flame. Now and again one of the creatures would fly too close to the fire and sear its wings, or one would ignite and glow on the wick for an instant. At such moments, Dr. Fischelson grimaced. His wrinkled face would twitch and beneath his disheveled moustache he would bite his lips. Finally he took a handkerchief from his pocket and waved it at the insects.

"Away from there, fools and imbeciles," he scolded. "You won't get warm here; you'll only burn yourself."

The insects scattered but a second later returned and once more circled the trembling flame. Dr. Fischelson wiped the sweat from his wrinkled forehead and sighed, "Like men they desire nothing but the pleasure of the moment." On the table lay an open book written in Latin, and on its broad-margined pages were notes and comments printed in small letters by Dr. Fischelson. The book was Spinoza's *Ethics* and Dr. Fischelson had been studying it for the last thirty years. He knew every proposition, every proof, every corollary, every note by heart. When he wanted to find a particular passage, he generally opened to the place immediately without having to search for it. But, nevertheless, he continued to study the *Ethics* for hours every day with a magnifying glass in his bony hand, murmuring and nodding his head in agreement. The truth was that the more Dr. Fischelson studied, the more puzzling sentences, unclear passages, and cryptic remarks he found. Each sentence contained hints unfathomed by any of the students of Spinoza. Actually the philosopher had anticipated all of the criticisms of pure reason made by Kant and his followers. Dr. Fischelson was writing a commentary on the *Ethics*. He had drawers full of notes and drafts, but it didn't seem that he would ever be able to complete his work. The stomach ailment which had plagued him for years was growing worse from day to day. Now he would get pains in his stomach after only a few mouthfuls of oatmeal. "God in Heaven, it's difficult, very difficult," he would say to himself using the same intonation as had his father, the late Rabbi of Tishevita. "It's very, very hard."

Dr. Fischelson was not afraid of dying. To begin with, he was no longer a young man. Secondly, it is stated in the fourth part of the *Ethics* that "a free man thinks of nothing less than of death and his wisdom is a meditation not of death, but of life." Thirdly, it is also said that "the human mind cannot be absolutely destroyed with the human body but there is some part of it that remains eternal." And yet Dr. Fischelson's ulcer (or perhaps it was a cancer) continued to bother him. His tongue was always coated. He belched frequently and emitted a different foul-smelling gas each time. He suffered from heartburn and cramps. At times he felt like vomiting and at other times he was hungry for garlic, onions, and fried foods. He had long ago discarded the medicines prescribed for him by the doctors and had sought his own remedies. He found it beneficial to take grated radish after meals and lie on his bed, belly down, with his head hanging over the side. But these home remedies offered only temporary relief. Some of the doctors he consulted insisted there was nothing the matter with him. "It's just nerves," they told him. "You could live to be a hundred."

But on this particular hot summer night, Dr. Fischelson felt his strength ebbing. His knees were shaky, his pulse weak. He sat down to read and his vision blurred. The letters on the page turned from green to gold. The lines became waved and jumped over each other, leaving white gaps as if the text had disappeared in some mysterious way. The heat was unbearable, flowing down directly from the tin roof; Dr. Fischelson felt he was inside of an oven. Several times he climbed the four steps to the window and thrust his head out into the cool of the evening breeze. He would remain in that position for so long his knees would become wobbly. "Oh it's a fine breeze," he would murmur, "really delightful," and he would recall that according to Spinoza, morality and happiness were identical, and that the most moral deed a man could perform was to indulge in some pleasure which was not contrary to reason.

2

Dr. Fischelson, standing on the top step at the window and looking out, could see into two worlds. Above him were the heavens, thickly strewn with stars. Dr. Fischelson had never seriously studied astronomy but he could differentiate between the planets, those bodies which like the earth, revolve around the sun, and the fixed stars, themselves distant suns, whose light reaches us a hundred or even a thousand years later. He recognized the constellations which mark the path of the earth in space and that nebulous sash, the Milky Way. Dr. Fischelson owned a small telescope he had bought in Switzerland where he had studied and he particularly enjoyed looking at the moon through it. He could clearly make out on the moon's surface the volcanoes bathed in sunlight and the dark, shadowy craters. He never wearied of gazing at these cracks and crevasses. To him they seemed both near and distant, both substantial and insubstantial. Now and then he would see a shooting star trace a wide arc across the sky and disappear, leaving a fiery trail behind it. Dr. Fischelson would know then that a meteorite had reached our atmosphere, and perhaps some un-burned fragment of it had fallen into the ocean or had landed in the desert or perhaps even in some inhabited region. Slowly the stars which had appeared from behind Dr. Fischelson's roof rose until they were shining above the house across the street. Yes, when Dr. Fischelson looked up into the heavens, he became aware of that infinite extension which is, according to Spinoza, one of God's attributes. It com-forted Dr. Fischelson to think that although he was only a weak, puny man, a changing mode of the absolutely infinite Substance, he was nevertheless a part of the cosmos, made of the same matter as the celestial bodies; to the extent that he was a part of the Godhead, he knew he could not be destroyed. In such moments, Dr. Fischelson experienced the *Amor Dei Intellectualis* which is, according to the philosopher of Amsterdam, the highest perfection of the mind. Dr. Fischelson breathed deeply, lifted his head as high as his stiff collar permitted and actually felt he was whirling in company with the earth, the sun, the stars of the Milky Way, and the infinite host of galaxies known only to infinite thought. His legs became light and weightless and he grasped the window frame with both hands as if afraid he would lose his footing and fly out into eternity.

When Dr. Fischelson tired of observing the sky, his glance dropped to Market Street below. He could see a long strip extending from Yanash's market to Iron Street with the gas lamps lining it merged into a string of fiery dots. Smoke was issuing from the chimneys on the black, tin roofs; the bakers were heating their ovens, and here and there sparks mingled with the black smoke. The street never looked so noisy and crowded as on a summer evening. Thieves, prostitutes, gam-blers, and fences loafed in the square which looked from above like a pretzel covered with poppy seeds. The young men laughed coarsely and the girls shrieked. A peddler with a keg of lemonade on his back pierced the general din with his intermittent cries. A watermelon vendor shouted in a savage voice, and the long knife which he used for cutting the fruit dripped with the blood-like juice. Now and again the street became even more agitated. Fire engines, their heavy wheels clang-ing, sped by; they were drawn by sturdy black horses which had to be tightly curbed to prevent them from running wild. Next came an ambulance, its siren screaming. Then some thugs had a fight among themselves and the police had to be called. A passerby was robbed and ran about shouting for help. Some wagons loaded with firewood sought to get through into the courtyards where the bakeries were located but the horses could not lift the wheels over the steep curbs and the drivers berated the animals and lashed them with their whips. Sparks rose from the clanging hoofs. It was now long after seven, which was the prescribed closing time for stores, but actually business had only begun. Customers were led in stealthily through back doors. The Russian policemen on the street, having been paid off, noticing nothing of this. Merchants continued to hawk their wares, each seeking to outshout the others.

"Gold, gold, gold," a woman who dealt in rotten oranges shrieked.

"Sugar, sugar, sugar," croaked a dealer of overripe plums.

"Heads, heads, heads," a boy who sold fishheads roared.

Through the window of a *Chassidic* study house across the way, Dr. Fischelson could see boys with long sidelocks swaying over holy volumes, grimacing and studying aloud in sing-song voices. Butchers, porters, and fruit dealers were drinking beer in the tavern below. Vapor drifted from the tavern's open door like steam from a bathhouse, and there was the sound of loud music. Outside of the tavern, street-walkers snatched at drunken soldiers and at workers on their way home from the factories. Some of the men carried bundles of wood on their shoulders, reminding Dr. Fischelson of the wicked who are condemned to kindle their own fires in Hell. Husky record players poured out their raspings through open windows. The liturgy of the high holidays alternated with vulgar vaudeville songs.

Dr. Fischelson peered into the half-lit bedlam and cocked his ears. He knew that the behavior of this rabble was the very antithesis of reason. These people were immersed in the vainest of passions, were drunk with emotions, and, according to Spinoza, emotion was never good. Instead of the pleasure they ran after, all they succeeded in obtaining was disease and prison, shame and the suffering that resulted from ignorance. Even the cats which loitered on the roofs here seemed more savage and passionate than those in other parts of the town. They caterwauled with the voices of women in labor, and like demons scampered up walls and leaped onto eaves and balconies. One of the toms paused at Dr. Fischelson's window and let out a howl which made Dr. Fischelson shudder. The doctor stepped from the window and, picking up a broom, brandished it in front of the black beast's glowing, green eyes. "Scat, begone, you ignorant savage!" — and he rapped the broom handle against the roof until the tom ran off.

3

When Dr. Fischelson had returned to Warsaw from Zurich where he had studied philosophy, a great future had been predicted for him. His friends had known that he was writing an important book on Spinoza. A Jewish Polish journal had invited him to be a contributor; he had been a frequent guest at several wealthy households and he had been made head librarian at the Warsaw synagogue. Although even then he had been considered an old bachelor, the matchmakers had proposed several girls for him. But Dr. Fischelson had not taken advantage of these opportunities. He had wanted to be as independent as Spinoza himself. And he had been. But because of his heretical ideas he had come into conflict with the rabbi and had to resign his post as librarian. For years after that, he had supported himself by giving private lessons in Hebrew and German. Then, when he had become sick, the Berlin Jewish community had voted him a subsidy of five hundred marks a year. This had been made possible through the intervention of the famous Dr. Hildesheimer with whom he corresponded about philosophy. In order to get by on so small a pension, Dr. Fischelson had moved into the attic room and had begun cooking his own meals on a kerosene stove. He had a cupboard which had many drawers, and each drawer was labelled with the food it contained — buckwheat, rice, barley, onions, carrots, potatoes, mushrooms. Once a week Dr. Fischelson put on his wide-brimmed black hat, took a basket in one hand and Spinoza's *Ethics* in the other, and went off to the market for his provisions. While he was waiting to be served, he would open the *Ethics*. The merchants knew him and would motion him to their stalls.

"A fine piece of cheese, Doctor — just melts in your mouth."

"Fresh mushrooms, Doctor, straight from the woods."

"Make way for the Doctor, ladies," the butcher would shout. "Please don't block the entrance."

During the early years of his sickness, Dr. Fischelson had still gone in the evening to a café which was frequented by Hebrew teachers and other intellectuals. It had been his habit to sit there and play chess while drinking a half a glass of black coffee. Sometimes he would stop at the bookstores on Holy Cross Street where all sorts of old books and magazines could be purchased cheap. On one occasion a former pupil of his had arranged to meet him at a restaurant one evening. When Dr. Fischelson arrived, he had been surprised to find a group of friends and admirers who forced him to sit at the head of the table while they made speeches about him. But these were things that had happened long ago. Now people were no longer interested in him. He had isolated himself completely and had become a forgotten man. The events of 1905 when the boys of Market Street had begun to organize strikes, throw bombs at police stations, and shoot strike breakers so that the stores were closed even on weekdays had greatly increased his isolation. He began to despise everything associated with the modern Jew — Zionism, socialism, anarchism. The young men in question seemed to him nothing but an ignorant rabble intent on destroying society, society without which no reasonable existence was possible. He still read a Hebrew magazine occasionally, but he felt contempt for modern Hebrew which had no roots in the Bible or the Mishnah. The spelling of Polish words had changed also. Dr. Fischelson concluded that even the so-called spiritual men had abandoned reason and were doing their utmost to pander to the mob. Now and again he still visited a library and browsed through some of the modern histories of philosophy, but he found that the professors did not understand Spinoza, quoted him incorrectly, attributed their own muddled ideas to the philosopher. Although Dr. Fischelson was well aware that anger was an emotion unworthy of those who walk the path of reason, he would become furious, and would quickly close the book and push it from him. "Idiots," he would mutter, "asses, upstarts." And he would vow never again to look at modern philosophy.

4

Every three months a special mailman who only delivered money orders brought Dr. Fischelson eighty rubles. He expected his quarterly allotment at the beginning of

July but as day after day passed and the tall man with the blond moustache and the shiny buttons did not appear, the Doctor grew anxious. He had scarcely a groshen left. Who knows — possibly the Berlin Community had rescinded his subsidy; perhaps Dr. Hildesheimer had died, God forbid; the post office might have made a mistake. Every event has its cause, Dr. Fischelson knew. All was determined, all necessary, and a man of reason had no right to worry. Nevertheless, worry invaded his brain, and buzzed about like the flies. If the worst came to the worst, it occurred to him, he could commit suicide, but then he remembered that Spinoza did not approve of suicide and compared those who took their own lives to the insane.

One day when Dr. Fischelson went out to a store to purchase a composition book, he heard people talking about war. In Serbia somewhere, an Austrian Prince had been shot and the Austrians had delivered an ultimatum to the Serbs. The owner of the store, a young man with a yellow beard and shifty yellow eyes, announced, "We are about to have a small war," and he advised Dr. Fischelson to store up food because in the near future there was likely to be a shortage.

Everything happened so quickly. Dr. Fischelson had not even decided whether it was worthwhile to spend four groshen on a newspaper, and already posters had been hung up announcing mobilization. Men were to be seen walking on the street with round, metal tags on their lapels, a sign that they were being drafted. They were followed by their crying wives. One Monday when Dr. Fischelson descended to the street to buy some food with his last kopecks, he found the stores closed. The owners and their wives stood outside and explained that merchandise was unobtainable. But certain special customers were pulled to one side and let in through back doors. On the street all was confusion. Policemen with swords unsheathed could be seen riding on horseback. A large crowd had gathered around the tavern where, at the command of the Tsar, the tavern's stock of whiskey was being poured into the gutter.

Dr. Fischelson went to his old café. Perhaps he would find some acquaintances there who would advise him. But he did not come across a single person he knew. He decided, then, to visit the rabbi of the synagogue where he had once been librarian, but the sexton with the six-sided skull cap informed him that the rabbi and his family had gone off to the spas. Dr. Fischelson had other old friends in town but he found no one at home. His feet ached from so much walking; black and green spots appeared before his eyes and he felt faint. He stopped and waited for the giddiness to pass. The passers-by jostled him. A dark-eyed high school girl tried to give him a coin. Although the war had just started, soldiers eight abreast were marching in full battle dress — the men were covered with dust and were sunburnt. Canteens were strapped to their sides and they wore rows of bullets across their chests. The bayonets on their rifles gleamed with a cold, green light. They sang with mournful voices. Along with the men came cannons, each pulled by eight horses; their blind muzzles breathed gloomy terror. Dr. Fischelson felt nauseous. His stomach ached; his intestines seemed about to turn themselves inside out. Cold sweat appeared on his face.

"I'm dying," he thought. "This is the end." Nevertheless, he did manage to drag himself home where he lay down on the iron cot and remained, panting and gasping. He must have dozed off because he imagined that he was in his home town, Tishvitz. He had a sore throat and his mother was busy wrapping a stocking stuffed with hot salt around his neck. He could hear talk going on in the house; something about a candle and about how a frog had bitten him. He wanted to go out into the street but they wouldn't let him because a Catholic procession was passing by. Men in long robes, holding double edged axes in their hands, were intoning in Latin as they sprinkled holy water. Crosses gleamed; sacred pictures waved in the air. There was an odor of incense and corpses. Suddenly the sky turned a burning red and the whole world started to burn. Bells were ringing; people rushed madly about. Flocks of birds flew overhead, screeching. Dr. Fischelson awoke with a start. His body was covered with sweat and his throat was now actually sore. He tried to meditate about his extraordinary dream, to find its rational connection with what was happening to him and to comprehend it *sub specie eternitatis,* but none of it made sense. "Alas, the brain is a receptacle for nonsense, " Dr. Fischelson thought. "This earth belongs to the mad."

And he once more closed his eyes; once more he dozed; once more he dreamed.

5

The eternal laws, apparently, had not yet ordained Dr. Fischelson's end.

There was a door to the left of Dr. Fischelson's attic room which opened off a dark corridor, cluttered with boxes and baskets, in which the odor of fried onions and laundry soap was always present. Behind this door lived a spinster whom the neighbors called Black Dobbe. Dobbe was tall and lean, and as black as a baker's shovel. She had a broken nose and there was a mustache on her upper lip. She spoke with the hoarse voice of a man and she wore men's shoes. For years Black Dobbe had sold breads, rolls, and bagels which she had bought from the baker at the gate of the house. But one day she and the baker had quarreled and she had moved her business to the marketplace and now she dealt in what were called "wrinklers" which was a synonym for cracked eggs. Black Dobbe had no luck with men. Twice she had been engaged to baker's apprentices but in both instances they had returned the engagement contract to her. Some time afterwards she had received an engagement contract from an old man, a glazier who claimed that he was divorced, but it had later come to light that he still had a wife. Black Dobbe had a cousin in America, a shoemaker, and repeatedly she boasted that this cousin was sending her passage, but she remained in Warsaw. She was constantly being teased by the women who would say, "There's no hope for you, Dobbe. You're fated to die an old maid." Dobbe always answered, "I don't intend to be a slave for any man. Let them all rot."

That afternoon Dobbe received a letter from America. Generally she would go to Leizer the Tailor and have him read it to her. However, that day Leizer was out and so Dobbe thought of Dr. Fischelson whom the other tenants considered a convert since he never went to prayer. She knocked on the door of the doctor's room but there was no answer. "The heretic is probably out," Dobbe thought but, nevertheless, she knocked once more, and this time the door moved slightly. She pushed her way in and stood there frightened. Dr. Fischelson lay fully clothed on his bed; his face was as yellow as wax; his Adam's apple stuck out prominently; his beard pointed upward. Dobbe screamed; she was certain that he was dead, but — no — his body moved. Dobbe picked up a glass which stood on the table, ran into the corridor, filled the glass with water from the faucet, hurried back, and threw the water into the face of the unconscious man. Dr. Fischelson shook his head and opened his eyes.

"What's wrong with you?" Dobbe asked. "Are you sick?"

"Thank you very much. No."

"Have you a family? I'll call them."

"No family," Dr. Fischelson said.

Dobbe wanted to fetch the barber from across the street but Dr. Fischelson signified that he didn't wish the barber's assistance. Since Dobbe was not going to the market that day, no "wrinklers" being available, she decided to do a good deed. She assisted the sick man to get off the bed and smoothed down the blanket. Then she undressed Dr. Fischelson and prepared some soup for him on the kerosene stove. The sun never entered Dobbe's room, but here squares of sunlight shimmered on the faded walls. The floor was painted red. Over the bed hung a picture of a man who was wearing a broad frill around his neck and had long hair. "Such an old fellow and yet he keeps his place so nice and clean," Dobbe thought approvingly. Dr. Fischelson asked for the *Ethics,* and she gave it to him disapprovingly. She was certain it was a gentile prayer book. Then she began bustling about, brought in a pail of water, swept the floor. Dr. Fischelson ate; after he had finished, he was much stronger and Dobbe asked him to read her the letter.

He read it slowly, the paper trembling in his hands. It came from New York, from Dobbe's cousin. Once more he wrote that he was about to send her a "really important letter" and a ticket to America. By now, Dobbe knew the story by heart and she helped the old man decipher her cousin's scrawl. "He's lying," Dobbe said. "He forgot about me a long time ago." In the evening, Dobbe came again. A candle in a brass holder was burning on the chair next to the bed. Reddish shadows trembled on the walls and ceiling. Dr. Fischelson sat propped up in bed, reading a book. The candle threw a golden light on his forehead which seemed as if cleft in two. A bird had flown in through the window and was perched on the table. For a moment Dobbe was frightened. This man made her think of witches, of black mirrors and corpses wandering around at night and terrifying women. Nevertheless, she took a few steps toward him and inquired, "How are you? Any better?"

"A little, thank you."

"Are you really a convert?" she asked although she wasn't quite sure what the word meant.

"Me, a convert? No, I'm a Jew like any other Jew," Dr. Fischelson answered.

The doctor's assurances made Dobbe feel more at home. She found the bottle of kerosene and lit the stove, and after that she fetched a glass of milk from her room and began cooking kasha. Dr. Fischelson continued to study the *Ethics,* but that evening he could make no sense of the theorems and proofs with their many references to axioms and definitions and other theorems. With trembling hand he raised the book to his eyes and read, "The idea of each modification of the human body does not involve adequate knowledge of the human body itself. . . . The idea of the idea of each modification of the human mind does not involve adequate knowledge of the human mind."

6

Dr. Fischelson was certain he would die any day now. He made out his will, leaving all of his books and manuscripts to the synagogue library. His clothing and furniture would go to Dobbe since she had taken care of him. But death did not come. Rather his health improved. Dobbe returned to her business in the market, but she visited the old man several times a day, prepared soup for him, left him a glass of tea, and told him news of the war. The Germans had occupied Kalish, Bendin, and Cestechow, and they were marching on Warsaw. People said that on a quiet morning one could hear the rumblings of the cannon. Dobbe reported that the casualties were heavy. "They're falling like flies," she said. "What a terrible misfortune for the women."

She couldn't explain why, but the old man's attic room attracted her. She liked to remove the gold-rimmed books from the bookcase, dust them, and then air them on the window sill. She would climb the few steps to the window and look out through the telescope. She also enjoyed talking to Dr. Fischelson. He told her about Switzerland where he had studied, of the great cities he had passed through, of the high mountains that were covered with snow even in the summer. His father had been a rabbi, he said, and before he, Dr. Fischelson, had become a student, he had attended a yeshiva. She asked him how many languages he knew and it turned out that he could speak and write Hebrew, Russian, German, and French, in addition to Yiddish. He also knew Latin. Dobbe was astonished that such an educated man should live in an attic room on Market Street. But what amazed her most of all was that although he had the title "Doctor," he couldn't write prescriptions. "Why don't you become a real doctor?" she would ask him. "I am a doctor," he would answer. "I'm just not a physician." "What kind of a doctor?" "A doctor of philosophy." Although she had no idea of what this meant, she felt it must be very important. "Oh my blessed mother," she would say, "where did you get such a brain?"

Then one evening after Dobbe had given him his crackers and his glass of tea with milk, he began questioning her about where she came from, who her parents were, and why she had not married. Dobbe was surprised. No one had ever asked her such questions. She told him her story in a quiet voice and stayed until eleven o'clock. Her father had been a porter at the kosher butcher shops. Her mother had plucked chickens in the slaughterhouse. The family had lived in a cellar at No. 19 Market Street. When she had been ten, she had become a maid. The man she had worked for had been a fence who bought stolen goods from thieves on the square. Dobbe had had a brother who had gone into the Russian army and had never returned. Her sister had married a coachman in Praga and had died in childbirth. Dobbe told of the battles between the underworld and the revolutionaries in 1905, of blind Itche and his gang and how they collected protection money from the stores, of the thugs who attacked young boys and girls out on Sunday afternoon strolls if they were not paid money for security. She also spoke of the pimps who drove about in carriages and abducted women to be sold in Buenos Aires. Dobbe swore that some men had even sought to inveigle her into a brothel, but that she had run away. She complained of a thousand evils done to her. She had been robbed; her boy friend had been stolen; a competitor had once poured a pint of kerosene into her basket of bagels; her own cousin, the shoemaker, had cheated her out of a hundred rubles before he had left for America. Dr. Fischelson listened to her attentively. He asked her questions, shook his head, and grunted.

"Well, do you believe in God?" he finally asked her.

"I don't know," she answered. "Do you?"

"Yes, I believe."

"Then why don't you go to synagogue?" she asked.

"God is everywhere," he replied. "In the synagogue. In the marketplace. In this very room. We ourselves are parts of God."

"Don't say such things," Dobbe said. "You frighten me."

She left the room and Dr. Fischelson was certain she had gone to bed. But he wondered why she had not said "good night." "I probably drove her away with my philosophy," he thought. The very next moment he heard her footsteps. She came in carrying a pile of clothing like a peddler.

"I wanted to show you these," she said. "They're my trousseau." And she began to spread out, on the chair, dresses — woolen, silk, velvet. Taking each dress up in turn, she held it to her body. She gave him an account of every item in her trousseau — underwear, shoes, stockings.

"I'm not wasteful," she said. "I'm a saver. I have enough money to go to America."

Then she was silent and her face turned brick-red. She looked at Dr. Fischelson out of the corner of her eyes, timidly, inquisitively. Dr. Fischelson's body suddenly began to shake as if he had the chills. He said, "Very nice, beautiful things." His brow furrowed and he pulled at his beard with two fingers. A sad smile appeared on his toothless mouth and his large fluttering eyes, gazing into the distance through the attic window, also smiled sadly.

7

The day that Black Dobbe came to the rabbi's chambers and announced that she was to marry Dr. Fischelson, the rabbi's wife thought she had gone mad. But the news had already reached Leizer the Tailor, and had spread to the bakery, as well as to other shops. There were those who thought that the "old maid" was very lucky; the doctor, they said, had a vast hoard of money. But there were others who took the view that he was a run-down degenerate who would give her syphilis. Although Dr. Fischelson had insisted that the wedding be a small, quiet one, a host of guests assembled in the rabbi's rooms. The baker's apprentices who generally went about barefoot, and in their underwear, with paper bags on the tops of their heads, now put on light-colored suits, straw hats, yellow shoes, gaudy ties, and they brought with them huge cakes and pans filled with cookies. They had even managed to find a bottle of vodka although liquor was forbidden in wartime. When the bride and groom entered the rabbi's chamber, a murmur arose from the crowd. The women could not believe their eyes. The woman that they saw was not the one they had known. Dobbe wore a wide-brimmed hat which was amply adorned with cherries, grapes, and plumes, and the dress that she had on was of white silk and was equipped with a train; on her feet were high-heeled shoes, gold in color, and from her thin neck hung a string of imitation pearls. Nor was this all: Her fingers sparkled with rings and glittering stones. Her face was veiled. She looked almost like one of those rich brides who were married in the Vienna Hall. The bakers' apprentices whistled mockingly. As for Dr. Fischelson, he was wearing his black coat and broad-toed shoes. He was scarcely able to walk; he was leaning on Dobbe. When he saw the crowd from the doorway, he became frightened and began to retreat, but Dobbe's former employer approached him saying, "Come in, come in, bridegroom. Don't be bashful. We are all brethren now."

The ceremony proceeded according to the law. The rabbi, in a worn satin gabardine, wrote the marriage contract and then had the bride and groom touch his handkerchief as a token of agreement; the rabbi wiped the point of the pen on his skullcap. Several porters who had been called from the street to make up the quorum supported the canopy. Dr. Fischelson put on a white robe as a reminder of the day of his death and Dobbe walked around him seven times as custom required. The light from the braided candles flickered on the walls. The shadows wavered. Having poured wine into a goblet, the rabbi chanted the benedictions in a sad melody. Dobbie uttered only a single cry. As for the other women, they took out their lace handkerchiefs and stood with them in their hands, grimacing. When the baker's boys began to whisper wisecracks to each other, the rabbi put a finger to his lips and murmured, "*Eh nu oh,*" as a sign that talking was forbidden. The moment came to slip the wedding ring on the bride's finger, but the bridegroom's hand started to tremble and he had trouble locating Dobbe's index finger. The next thing, according to custom, was the smashing of the glass, but though Dr. Fischelson kicked the goblet several times, it remained unbroken. The girls lowered their heads, pinched each other gleefully, and giggled. Finally one of the apprentices struck the goblet with his heel and it shattered. Even the rabbi could not restrain a smile. After the ceremony the guests drank vodka and ate cookies. Dobbe's former employer came up to Dr. Fischelson and said, "*Mazel tov,* bridegroom. Your luck should be as good as your wife." "Thank you, thank you," Dr. Fischelson murmured, "but I don't look forward to any luck." He was anxious to return as quickly as possible to his attic room. He felt a pressure in his stomach and his chest ached. His face had become greenish. Dobbe had suddenly become angry. She pulled back her veil and called out to the crowd, "What are you laughing at? This isn't a show." And without picking up the cushion-cover in which the gifts were wrapped, she returned with her husband to their rooms on the fifth floor.

Dr. Fischelson lay down on the freshly made bed in his room and began reading the *Ethics*. Dobbe had gone back to her own room. The doctor had explained to her that he was an old man, that he was sick and without strength. He had promised her nothing. Nevertheless she returned wearing a silk nightgown, slippers with pompoms, and with her hair hanging down over her shoulders. There was a smile on her face, and she was bashful and hesitant. Dr. Fischelson trembled and the *Ethics* dropped from his hands. The candle went out. Dobbe groped for Dr. Fischelson in the dark and kissed his mouth. "My dear husband," she whispered to him, "*Mazel tov.*"

What happened that night could be called a miracle. If Dr. Fischelson hadn't been convinced that every occurrence is in accordance with the laws of nature, he would have thought that Black Dobbe had bewitched him. Powers long dormant awakened in him. Although he had had only a sip of the benediction wine, he was as if intoxicated. He kissed Dobbe and spoke to her of love. Long forgotten quotations from Klopfstock, Lessing, Goethe, rose to his lips. The pressures and aches stopped. He embraced Dobbe, pressed her to himself, was again a man as in his youth. Dobbe was faint with delight; crying, she murmured things to him in a Warsaw slang which he did not understand. Later, Dr. Fischelson slipped off into the deep sleep young men know. He dreamed that he was in Switzerland and that he was climbing mountains — running, falling, flying. At dawn he opened his eyes; it seemed to him that someone had blown into his ears. Dobbe was snoring. Dr. Fischelson quietly got out of bed. In his long nightshirt he approached the window, walked up the steps and looked out in wonder. Market Street was asleep, breathing with a deep stillness. The gas lamps were flickering. The black shutters on the stores were fastened with iron bars. A cool breeze was blowing. Dr. Fischelson looked up at the sky. The black arch was thickly sown with stars — there were green, red, yellow, blue stars; there were large ones and small ones, winking and steady ones. There were those that were clustered in dense groups and those that were alone. In the higher sphere, apparently, little notice was taken of the fact that a certain Dr. Fischelson had in his declining days married someone called Black Dobbe. Seen from above even the Great War was nothing but a temporary play of the modes. The myriads of fixed stars continued to travel their destined courses in unbounded space. The comets, planets, satellites, asteroids kept circling these shining centers. Worlds were born and died in cosmic upheavals. In the chaos of nebulae, primeval matter was being formed. Now and again a star tore loose, and swept across the sky, leaving behind it a fiery streak. It was the month of August when there are showers of meteors. Yes, the divine substance was extended and had neither beginning nor end; it was absolute, indivisible, eternal, without duration, infinite in its attributes. Its waves and bubbles danced in the universal cauldron, seething with change, following the unbroken chain of causes and effects, and he, Dr. Fischelson, with his unavoidable fate, was part of this. The doctor closed his eyelids and allowed the breeze to cool the sweat on his forehead and stir the hair of his beard. He breathed deeply of the midnight air, supported his shaky hands on the window sill and murmured, "Divine Spinoza, forgive me. I have become a fool."

SUSAN SONTAG

Susan Sontag was born in New York City in 1933 but grew up in Arizona and California. She received her education at the University of Chicago and Harvard University, and taught in various college and universities until she was almost thirty. Her first book, the novel *The Benefactor*, was published in 1963, and from that time Sontag embarked on a distinguished and diverse writing career augmented by directorial excursions into film and drama. Her other works in fiction include the novel *Death Kit* (1967) and the collection of stories *I, Etcetera* (1978). A number of collections of her essays have confirmed the brilliance and originality of her commentary on the arts and popular culture: *Against Interpretation* (1966), *Styles of Radical Will* (1969), *On Photography* (1977), *Illness as Metaphor* (1978), and *Under the Sign of Saturn* (1980). Her reputation is for formidable intellect; Sontag herself says that her essays communicate "love and passion." "I am learned but I am not particularly cerebral — in fact, very little so." She has said of fiction in general, "My interest is in the quality of the prose. I want to be enchanted or delighted." Of her own fiction writing, which has freely experimented with form, style, and consciousness, she once observed, "I want to write fiction which is not solipsistic, in which there is a real world, but I'm not drawn to the conventions of realism." With astonishing linguistic virtuosity, "The Way We Live Now" certainly presents a real world — for the many whom the story's title includes, it is *the* real world.

The Way We Live Now

At first he was just losing weight, he felt only a little ill, Max said to Ellen, and he didn't call for an appointment with his doctor, according to Greg, because he was managing to keep on working at more or less the same rhythm, but he did stop smoking, Tanya pointed out, which suggests he was frightened, but also that he wanted, even more than he knew, to be healthy, or healthier, or maybe just to gain back a few pounds, said Orson, for he told her, Tanya went on, that he expected to be climbing the walls (isn't that what people say?) and found, to his surprise, that he didn't miss cigarettes at all and reveled in the sensation of his lungs' being ache-free for the first time in years. But did he have a good doctor, Stephen wanted to know, since it would have been crazy not to go for a checkup after the pressure was off and he was back from the conference in Helsinki, even if by then he was feeling better. And he said, to Frank, that he would go, even though he was indeed frightened, as he admitted to Jan, but who wouldn't be frightened now, though, odd as that might seem, he hadn't been worrying until recently, he avowed to Quentin, it was only in the last six months that he had the metallic taste of panic in his mouth, because becoming seriously ill was something that happened to other people, a normal delusion, he observed to Paolo, if one was thirty-eight and had never had a serious illness; he wasn't, as Jan confirmed, a hypochondriac. Of course, it was hard not to worry, everyone was worried, but it wouldn't do to panic, because, as Max pointed out to Quentin, there wasn't anything one could do except wait and hope, wait and start being careful, be careful, and hope. And even if one did prove to be ill, one shouldn't give up, they had new treatments that promised an arrest of the disease's inexorable course, research was progressing. It seemed that everyone was in touch with everyone else several times a week, checking in, I've never spent so many hours at a time on the phone, Stephen said to Kate, and when I'm exhausted after the two or three calls made to me, giving me the latest, instead of switching off the phone to give myself a respite I tap out the number of another friend or acquaintance, to pass on the news. I'm not sure I can afford to think so much about it, Ellen said, and I suspect my own motives, there's something morbid I'm getting used to, getting excited by, this must be like what people felt in London during the Blitz. As far as I know, I'm not at risk, but you never know, said Aileen. This thing is totally unprecedented, said Frank. But don't you think he ought to see a doctor, Stephen insisted. Listen, said Orson, you can't force people to take care of themselves, and what makes you think the worst, he could be just run down, people still do get ordinary illnesses, awful ones, why are you assuming it has to be *that*. But all I want to be sure, said Stephen, is that he understands the options, because most people don't, that's why they won't see a doctor or have the test, they think there's nothing one can do. But is there anything one can do, he said to Tanya (according to Greg), I mean what do I gain if I go to the doctor; if I'm really ill, he's reported to have said, I'll find out soon enough.

And when he was in the hospital, his spirits seemed to lighten, according to Donny. He seemed more cheerful than he had been in the last months, Ursula said, and the bad news seemed to come almost as a relief, according to Ira, as a truly unexpected blow, according to Quentin, but you'd hardly expect him to have said the same thing to all his friends, because his relation to Ira was so different from his relation to Quentin (this according to Quentin, who was proud of their friendship), and perhaps he thought Quentin wouldn't be undone by seeing him weep, but Ira insisted that couldn't be the reason he behaved so differently with each, and that maybe he was feeling less shocked, mobilizing his strength to fight for his life, at the moment he saw Ira but overcome by feelings of hopelessness when Quentin arrived with flowers, because anyway the flowers threw him into a bad mood, as Quentin told Kate, since the hospital room was choked with flowers, you couldn't have crammed another flower into that room, but surely you're exaggerating, Kate said, smiling, everybody likes flowers. Well, who wouldn't exaggerate at a time like this, Quentin said sharply. Don't you think *this* is an exaggeration. Of course I do, said Kate gently, I was only teasing, I mean I didn't mean to tease. I know that, Quentin said, with tears in his eyes, and Kate hugged him and said well, when I go this evening I guess I won't bring flowers, what does he want, and Quentin said, according to Max, what he likes best is chocolate. Is there anything else, asked Kate, I mean like chocolate but not chocolate. Licorice, said Quentin, blowing his nose. And besides that. Aren't *you* exaggerating now, Quentin said, smiling. Right, said Kate, so if I want to bring him a whole raft of stuff, besides chocolate and licorice, what else. Jelly beans, Quentin said.

He didn't want to be alone, according to Paolo, and lots of people came in the first week, and the Jamaican nurse said there were other patients on the floor who would be glad to have the surplus flowers, and people weren't afraid to visit, it wasn't like the old days, as Kate pointed out to Aileen, they're not even segregated in the hospital anymore, as Hilda observed, there's nothing on the door of his room warning visitors of the possibility of contagion, as there was a few years ago; in fact, he's in a double room and, as he told Orson, the old guy on the far side of the curtain (who's clearly on the way out, said Stephen) doesn't even have the disease, so, as Kate went on, you really should go and see him, he'd be happy to see you, he likes having people visit, you aren't not going because you're afraid, are you. Of course not, Aileen said, but I don't know what to say, I think I'll feel awkward, which he's bound to notice, and that will make him feel worse, so I won't be doing him any good, will I. But he won't notice anything, Kate said, patting Aileen's hand, it's not like that, it's not the way you imagine, he's not judging people or wondering about their motives, he's just happy to see his friends. But I never was really a friend of his, Aileen said, you're a friend, he's always liked you, you told me he talks about Nora with you, I know he likes me, he's even attracted to me, but he respects you. But, according to Wesley, the reason Aileen was so stingy with her visits was that she could never have him to herself, there were always others there already and by the time they left still others had arrived, she'd been in love with him for years, and I can understand, said Donny, that Aileen should feel bitter that if there could have been a woman friend he did more than occasionally bed, a woman he really loved, and my God, Victor said, who had known him in those years, he was crazy about Nora, what a heart-rending couple they were, two surly angels, then it couldn't have been she.

And when some of the friends, the ones who came every day, waylaid the doctor in the corridor, Stephen was the one who asked the most informed questions, who'd been keeping up not just with the stories that appeared several times a week in the *Times* (which Greg confessed to have stopped reading, unable to stand it anymore) but with articles in the medical journals published here and in England and France, and who knew socially one of the principal doctors in Paris who was doing some much-publicized research on the disease, but his doctor said little more than that the pneumonia was not life-threatening, the fever was subsiding, of course he was still weak but he was responding well to the antibiotics, that he'd have to complete his stay in the hospital, which entailed a minimum of twenty-one days on the IV, before she could start him on the new drug, for she was optimistic about the possibility of getting him into the protocol; and when Victor said that if he had so much trouble eating (he'd say to everyone when they coaxed him to eat some of the hospital meals, that food didn't taste right, that he had a funny metallic taste in his mouth) it couldn't be good that friends were bringing him all that chocolate, the doctor just smiled and said that in these cases the patient's morale was also an important factor, and if chocolate made him feel better she saw no harm in it, which worried Stephen, as Stephen said later to Donny, because they wanted to believe in the promises and taboos of today's high-tech medicine but here this reassuringly curt and silver-haired specialist in the disease, someone quoted frequently in the papers, was talking like some oldfangled country GP who tells the family that tea with honey or chicken soup may do as much for the patient as penicillin, which might mean, as Max said, that they were just going through the motions of treating him, that they were not sure about what to do, or rather, as Xavier interjected, that they didn't know what the hell they were doing, that the truth, the real truth, as Hilda said, upping the ante, was that they didn't, the doctors, really have any hope.

Oh, no, said Lewis, I can't stand it, wait a minute, I can't believe it, are you sure, I mean are they sure, have they done all the tests, it's getting so when the phone rings I'm scared to answer because I think it will be someone telling me someone else is ill; but did Lewis really not know until yesterday, Robert said testily, I find that hard to believe, everybody is talking about it, it seems impossible that someone wouldn't have called Lewis; and perhaps Lewis did know, was for some reason pretending not to know already, because, Jan recalled, didn't Lewis say something months ago to Greg, and not only to Greg, about his not looking well, losing weight, and being worried about him and wishing he'd see a doctor, so it couldn't come as a total surprise. Well, everybody is worried about everybody now, said Betsy, that seems to be the way we live, the way we live now. And, after all, they were once very close, doesn't Lewis still have the keys to his apartment, you know the way you let someone keep the keys after you've broken up, only a little because you hope the person might just saunter in, drunk or high, late some evening, but mainly because it's wise to have a few sets of keys strewn around town, if you live alone, at the top of a former commercial building that, pretentious as it is, will never acquire a doorman or even a resident superintendent, someone whom you can call on for the keys late one night if you find you've lost yours or have locked yourself out. Who else has keys, Tanya inquired, I was thinking somebody might drop by tomorrow before coming to the hospital and bring some treasures, because the other day, Ira said, he was complaining about how dreary the hospital room was, and how it was like being locked up in a motel room, which got everybody started telling funny stories about motel rooms they'd known, and at Ursula's story, about the Luxury Budget Inn in Schenectady, there was an uproar of laughter around his bed, while he watched them in silence, eyes bright with fever, all the while, as Victor recalled, gobbling that damned chocolate. But, according to Jan, whom Lewis's keys enabled to tour the swank of his bachelor lair with an eye to bringing over some art consolation to brighten up the hospital room, the Byzantine icon wasn't on the wall over his bed, and that was a puzzle until Orson remembered that he'd recounted without seeming upset (this disputed by Greg) that the boy he'd recently gotten rid of had stolen it, along with four of the *maki-e* lacquer boxes, as if these were objects as easy to sell on the street as a TV or a stereo. But he's always been very generous, Kate said quietly, and though he loves beautiful things isn't really attached to them, to things, as Orson said, which is unusual in a collector, as Frank commented, and when Kate shuddered and tears sprang to her eyes and Orson inquired anxiously if he, Orson, had said something wrong, she pointed out that they'd begun talking about him in a retrospective mode, summing up what he was like, what made them fond of him, as if he were finished, completed, already a part of the past.

Perhaps he was getting tired of having so many visitors, said Robert, who was, as Ellen couldn't help mentioning, someone who had come only twice and was probably looking for a reason not to be in regular attendance, but there could be no doubt, according to Ursula, that his spirits had dipped, not that there was any discouraging news from the doctors, and he seemed now to prefer being alone a few hours of the day; and he told Donny that he'd begun keeping a diary for the first time in his life, because he wanted to record the course of his mental reactions to this astonishing turn of events, to do something parallel to what the doctors were doing, who came every morning and conferred at his bedside about his body, and that perhaps it wasn't so important what he wrote in it, which amounted, as he said wryly to Quentin, to little more than the usual banalities about terror and amazement that this was happening to him, to him also, plus the usual remorseful assessments of his past life, his pardonable superficialities, capped by resolves to live better, more deeply, more in touch with his work and his friends, and not to care so passionately about what people thought of him, interspersed with admonitions to himself that in this situation his will to live counted more than anything else and that if he really wanted to live, and trusted life, and liked himself well enough (down, ol' debbil Thanatos!), he *would* live, he would be an exception; but perhaps all this, as Quentin ruminated, talking on the phone to Kate, wasn't the point, the point was that by the very keeping of the diary he was accumulating something to reread one day, slyly staking out his claim to a future time, in which the diary would be an object, a relic, in which he might not actually reread it, because he would want to have put this ordeal behind him, but the diary would be there in the drawer of his stupendous Majorelle desk, and he could already, he did actually say to Quentin one late sunny afternoon, propped up in the hospital bed, with the stain of chocolate framing one corner of a heartbreaking smile, see himself in the penthouse, the October sun streaming through those clear windows instead of this streaked one, and the diary, the pathetic diary, safe inside the drawer.

It doesn't matter about the treatment's side effects, Stephen said (when talking to Max), I don't know why you're so worried about that, every strong treatment has some dangerous side effects, it's inevitable, you mean otherwise the treatment wouldn't be effective, Hilda interjected, and anyway, Stephen went on doggedly, just because there *are* side effects it doesn't mean he has to get them, or all of them, each one, or even some of them. That's just a list of all the possible things that could go wrong, because the doctors have to cover themselves, so they make up a worst-case scenario, but isn't what's happening to him, and to so many other people, Tanya interrupted, a worst-case scenario, a catastrophe no one could have imagined, it's too cruel, and isn't everything a side effect, quipped Ira, even *we* are all side effects, but we're not bad side effects, Frank said, he likes having his friends around, and we're helping each other, too; because his illness sticks us all in the same glue, mused Xavier, and, whatever the jealousies and grievances from the past that have made us wary and cranky with each other, when something like this happens (the sky is falling, the sky is falling!) you understand what's really important. I agree, Chicken Little, he is reported to have said. But don't you think, Quentin observed to Max, that being as close to him as we are, making time to drop by the hospital every day, is a way of our trying to define ourselves more firmly and irrevocably as the well, those who aren't ill, who aren't going to fall ill, as if what's happened to him couldn't happen to us, when in fact the chances are that before long one of us will end up where he is, which is probably what he felt when he was one of the cohort visiting

Zack in the spring (you never knew Zack, did you?), and, according to Clarice, Zack's widow, he didn't come very often, he said he hated hospitals, and didn't feel he was doing Zack any good, that Zack would see on his face how uncomfortable he was. Oh, he was one of those, Aileen said. A coward. Like me.

And after he was sent home from the hospital, and Quentin had volunteered to move in and was cooking meals and taking telephone messages and keeping the mother in Mississippi informed, well, mainly keeping her from flying to New York and heaping her grief on her son and confusing the household routine with her oppressive ministrations, he was able to work an hour or two in his study, on days he didn't insist on going out, for a meal or a movie, which tired him. He seemed opimistic, Kate thought, his appetite was good, and what he said, Orson reported, was that he agreed when Stephen advised him that the main thing was to keep in shape, he was a fighter, right, he wouldn't be who he was if he weren't, and was he ready for the big fight, Stephen asked rhetorically (as Max told it to Donny), and he said you bet, and Stephen added it could be a lot worse, you could have gotten the disease two years ago, but now so many scientists are working on it, the American team and the French team, everyone bucking for that Nobel Prize a few years down the road, that all you have to do is stay healthy for another year or two and then there will be good treatment, real treatment. Yes, he said, Stephen said, my timing is good. And Betsy, who had been climbing on and rolling off macrobiotic diets for a decade, came up with a Japanese specialist she wanted him to see but thank God, Donny reported, he'd had the sense to refuse, but he did agree to see Victor's visualization therapist, although what could one possibly visualize, said Hilda, when the point of visualizing disease was to see it as an entity with contours, borders, here rather than there, something limited, something you were the host of, in the sense that you could disinvite the disease, while this was so total; or would be, Max said. But the main thing, said Greg, was to see that he didn't go the macrobiotic route, which might be harmless for plump Betsy but could only be devastating for him, lean as he'd always been, with all the cigarettes and other appetite-suppressing chemicals he'd been welcoming into his body for years; and now was hardly the time, as Stephen pointed out, to be worried about cleaning up his act, and eliminating the chemical additives and other pollutants that we're all blithely or not so blithely feasting on, blithely since we're healthy, healthy as we can be; so far, Ira said. Meat and potatoes is what I'd be happy to see him eating, Ursula said wistfully. And spaghetti and clam sauce, Greg added. And thick cholesterol-rich omelets with smoked mozzarella, suggested Yvonne, who had flown from London for the week-end to see him. Chocolate cake, said Frank. Maybe not chocolate cake, Ursula said, he's already eating so much chocolate.

And when, not right away but still only three weeks later, he was accepted into the protocol for the new drug, which took considerable behind-the-scenes lobbying with the doctors, he talked less about being ill, according to Donny, which seemed like a good sign, Kate felt, a sign that he was not feeling like a victim, feeling not that he *had* a disease but, rather, was living *with* a disease (that was the right cliché, wasn't it?), a more hospitable arrangement, said Jan, a kind of cohabitation which implied that it was something temporary, that it could be terminated, but terminated how, said Hilda, and when you say hospitable, Jan, I hear hospital. And it was encouraging, Stephen insisted, that from the start, at least from the time he was finally persuaded to make the telephone call to his doctor, he was willing to say the name of the disease, pronounce it often and easily, as if it were just another word, like boy or gallery or cigarette or money or deal, as in no big deal, Paolo interjected, because, as Stephen continued, to utter the name is a sign of health, a sign that one has accepted being who one is, mortal, vulnerable, not exempt, not an exception after all, it's a sign that one is willing, truly willing, to fight for one's life. And we must say the name, too, and often, Tanya added, we mustn't lag behind him in honesty, or let him feel that, the effort of honesty having been made, it's something done with and he can go on to other things. One is so much better prepared to help him, Wesley replied. In a way he's fortunate, said Yvonne, who had taken care of a problem at the New York store and was flying back to London this evening, sure, fortunate, said Wesley, no one is shunning him, Yvonne went on, no one's afraid to hug him or kiss him lightly on the mouth, in London we are, as usual, a few years behind you, people I know, people who would seem to be not even remotely at risk, are just terrified, but I'm impressed by how cool and rational you all are; you find us cool, asked Quentin. But I have to say, he's reported to have said, I'm terrified, I find it very hard to read (and you know how he loves to read, said Greg; yes, reading is his television, said Paolo) or to think, but I don't feel hysterical. I feel quite hysterical, Lewis said to Yvonne. But you're able to *do* something for him, that's wonderful, how I wish I could stay longer, Yvonne answered, it's rather beautiful, I can't help thinking, this utopia of friendship you've assembled around him (this pathetic utopia, said Kate), so that the disease, Yvonne concluded, is not, anymore, out there. Yes, don't you think we're more at home here, with him, with the disease, said Tanya, because the imagined disease is so much worse than the reality of him, whom we all love, each in our fashion, having it. I know for me his getting it has quite demystified the disease, said Jan, I don't feel afraid, spooked, as I did before he became ill, when it was only news about remote acquaintances, whom I never saw again after they became ill. But you know you're not going to come down with the disease, Quentin said, to which Ellen replied, on her behalf, that's not the point, and possibly untrue, my gynecologist says that everyone is at risk, everyone who has a sexual life, because sexuality is a chain that links each of us to many others, unknown others, and now the great chain of being has become a chain of death as well. It's not the same for you, Quentin insisted, it's not the same for you as it is for me or Lewis or Frank or Paolo or Max, I'm more and more frightened, and I have every reason to be. I don't think about whether I'm at risk or not, said Hilda, I know that I was afraid to know someone with the disease, afraid of what I'd see, what I'd feel, and after the first day I came to the hospital I felt so relieved. I'll never feel that way, that fear, again; he doesn't seem different from me. He's not, Quentin said.

According to Lewis, he talked more often about those who visited more often, which is natural, said Betsy, I think he's even keeping a tally. And among those who came or checked in by phone every day, the inner circle as it were, those who were getting more points, there was still a further competition, which was what was getting on Betsy's nerves, she confessed to Jan; there's always that vulgar jockeying for position around the bedside of the gravely ill, and though we all feel suffused with virtue at our loyalty to him (speak for yourself, said Jan), to the extent that we're carving time out of every day, or almost every day, though some of us are dropping out, as Xavier pointed out, aren't we getting at least as much out of this as he is. Are we, said Jan. We're rivals for a sign from him of special pleasure over a visit, each stretching for the brass ring of his favor, wanting to feel the most wanted, the true nearest and dearest, which is inevitable with someone who doesn't have a spouse and children or an official in-house lover, hierarchies that no one would dare contest, Betsy went on, so we are the family he's founded, without meaning to, without official titles and ranks (we, we, snarled Quentin); and is it so clear, though some of us, Lewis and Quentin and Tanya and Paolo, among others, are ex-lovers and all of us more or less than friends, which one of us he prefers, Victor said (now it's us, raged Quentin), because sometimes I think he looks forward more to seeing Aileen, who has visited only three times, twice at the hospital and once since he's been home, than he does you or me; but, according to Tanya, after being very disappointed that Aileen hadn't come, now he was angry, while, according to Xavier, he was not really hurt but touchingly passive, accepting Aileen's absence as something he somehow deserved. But he's happy to have people around, said Lewis; he says when he doesn't have company he gets very sleepy, he sleeps (according to Quentin), and then perks up when someone arrives, it's important that he not feel ever alone. But, said Victor, there's one person he hasn't heard from, whom he'd probably like to hear from more than most of us; but she didn't just vanish, even right after she broke away from him, and he knows exactly where she lives now, said Kate, he told me he put in a call to her last Christmas Eve, and she said it's nice to hear from you and Merry Christmas, and he was shattered, according to Orson, and furious and disdainful, according to Ellen (what do you expect of her, said Wesley, she was burned out), but Kate wondered if maybe he hadn't phoned Nora in the middle of a sleepless night, what's the time difference, and Quentin said no, I don't think so, I think he wouldn't want her to know.

And when he was feeling even better and had regained the pounds he'd shed right away in the hospital, though the refrigerator started to fill up with organic wheat germ and grapefruit and skimmed milk (he's worried about his cholesterol count, Stephen lamented), and told Quentin he could manage by himself now, and did, he started asking everyone who visited how he looked, and everyone said he looked great, so much better than a few weeks ago, which didn't jibe with what anyone had told him at that time; but then it was getting harder and harder to know how he looked, to answer such a question honestly when among themselves they wanted to be honest, both for honesty's sake and (as Donny thought) to prepare for the worst, because he'd been looking like *this* for so long, at least it seemed so long, that it was as if he'd always been like this, how did he look before, but it was only a few months, and those words, pale and wan looking and fragile, hadn't they always applied? And one Thursday Ellen, meeting Lewis at the door of the building, said, as they rode up together in the elevator, how is he *really?* But you see how he is, Lewis said tartly, he's fine, he's perfectly healthy, and Ellen understood that of course Lewis didn't think he was perfectly healthy but that he wasn't worse, and that was true, but wasn't it, well, almost heartless to talk like that. Seems inoffensive to me, Quentin said, but I know what you mean, I remember once talking to Frank, somebody, after all, who has volunteered to do five hours a week of office work at the Crisis Center (I know, said Ellen), and Frank was going on about this guy, diagnosed almost a year ago, and so much further along, who'd been complaining to Frank on the phone about the

indifference of some doctor, and had gotten quite abusive about the doctor, and
Frank was saying there was no reason to be so upset, the implication being that *he,*
Frank, wouldn't behave so irrationally, and I said, barely able to control my scorn,
but Frank, Frank, he has every reason to be upset, he's dying, and Frank said, said
according to Quentin, oh, I don't like to think about it that way.

And it was while he was still home, recuperating, getting his weekly treatment, still
not able to do much work, he complained, but, according to Quentin, up and about
most of the time and turning up at the office several days a week, that bad news came
about two remote acquaintances, one in Houston and one in Paris, news that was
intercepted by Quentin on the ground that it could only depress him, but Stephen
contended that it was wrong to lie to him, it was so important for him to live in the
truth; that had been one of his first victories, that he was candid, that he was even
willing to crack jokes about the disease, but Ellen said it wasn't good to give him this
end-of-the-world feeling, too many people were getting ill, it was becoming such a
common destiny that maybe some of the will to fight for his life would be drained
out of him if it seemed to be as natural as, well, death. Oh, Hilda said, who didn't
know personally either the one in Houston or the one in Paris, but knew *of* the one
in Paris, a pianist who specialized in twentieth-century Czech and Polish music, I
have his records, he's such a valuable person, and, when Kate glared at her, continued defensively, I know every life is equally sacred, but that *is* a thought, another
thought, I mean, all these valuable people who aren't going to have their normal four
score as it is now, these people aren't going to be replaced, and it's such a loss to the
culture. But this isn't going to go on forever, Wesley said, it can't, they're bound to
come up with something (they, they, muttered Stephen), but did you ever think,
Greg said, that if some people don't die, I mean even if they can keep them alive
(they, they, muttered Kate), they continue to be carriers and that means, if you have
a conscience, that you can never make love, make love fully, as you'd been wont —
wantonly, Ira said — to do. But it's better than dying, said Frank. And in all his talk
about the future, when he allowed himself to be hopeful, according to Quentin, he
never mentioned the prospect that even if he didn't die, if he were so fortunate as
to be among the first generation of the disease's survivors, never mentioned, Kate
confirmed, that whatever happened it was over, the way he had lived until now, but,
according to Ira, he did think about it, the end of bravado, the end of folly, the end
of trusting life, the end of taking life for granted, and of treating life as something
that, samurai-like, he thought himself ready to throw away lightly, impudently; and
Kate recalled, sighing, a brief exchange she'd insisted on having as long as two years
ago, huddling on a banquette covered with steel-gray industrial carpet on an upper
level of The Prophet and toking up for their next foray onto the dance floor: she'd
said hesitantly, for it felt foolish asking a prince of debauchery to, well, take it easy,
and she wasn't keen on playing big sister, a role, as Hilda confirmed, he inspired in
many women, are you being careful, honey, you know what I mean. And he replied,
Kate went on, no, I'm not, listen, I can't, I just can't, sex is too important to me, always
has been (he started talking like that, according to Victor, after Nora left him), and
if I get it, well, I get it. But he wouldn't talk like that now, would he, said Greg; he
must feel awfully foolish now, said Betsy, like someone who went on smoking,
saying I can't give up cigarettes, but when the bad X-ray is taken even the most
besotted nicotine addict can stop on a dime. But sex isn't like cigarettes, is it, said

Frank, and, besides, what good does it do to remember that he was reckless, said Lewis angrily, the appalling thing is that you just have to be unlucky once, and wouldn't he feel even worse if he'd stopped three years ago and had come down with it anyway, since one of the most terrifying features of the disease is that you don't know when you contracted it, it could have been ten years ago, because surely this disease has existed for years and years, long before it was recognized; that is, named. Who knows how long (I think a lot about that, said Max) and who knows (I know what you're going to say, Stephen interrupted) how many are going to get it.

I'm feeling fine, he's reported to have said whenever someone asked him how he was, which was almost always the first question anyone asked. Or: I'm feeling better, how are you? But he said other things, too. I'm playing leapfrog with myself, he is reported to have said, according to Victor. And: There must be a way to get something positive out of this situation, he's reported to have said to Kate. How American of him, said Paolo. Well, said Betsy, you know the old American adage: When you've got a lemon, make lemonade. The one thing I'm sure I couldn't take, Jan said he said to her, is becoming disfigured, but Stephen hastened to point out the disease doesn't take that form very often anymore, its profile is mutating, and, in conversation with Ellen, wheeled up words like blood-brain barrier; I never thought there was a barrier *there,* said Jan. But he mustn't know about Max, Ellen said, that would really depress him, please don't tell him, he'll have to know, Quentin said grimly, and he'll be furious not to have been told. But there's time for that, when they take Max off the respirator, said Ellen; but isn't it incredible, Frank said, Max was fine, not feeling ill at all, and then to wake up with a fever of a hundred and five, unable to breathe, but that's the way it often starts, with absolutely no warning, Stephen said, the disease has so many forms. And when, after another week had gone by, he asked Quentin where Max was, he didn't question Quentin's account of a spree in the Bahamas, but then the number of people who visited regularly was thinning out, partly because the old feuds that had been put aside through the first hospitalization and the return home had resurfaced, and the flickering enmity between Lewis and Frank exploded, even though Kate did her best to mediate between them, and also because he himself had done something to loosen the bonds of love that united the friends around him, by seeming to take them all for granted, as if it were perfectly normal for so many people to carve out so much time and attention for him, visit him every few days, talk about him incessantly on the phone with each other; but, according to Paolo, it wasn't that he was less grateful, it was just something he was getting used to, the visits. It had become, with time, a more ordinary kind of situation, a kind of ongoing party, first at the hospital and now since he was home, barely on his feet again, it being clear, said Robert, that I'm on the B list; but Kate said, that's absurd, there's no list; and Victor said, but there is, only it's not he, it's Quentin who's drawing it up. He wants to see us, we're helping him, we have to do it the way he wants, he fell down yesterday on the way to the bathroom, he mustn't be told about Max (but he already knew, according to Donny), it's getting worse.

When I was home, he is reported to have said, I was afraid to sleep, as I was dropping off each night it felt like just that, as if I were falling down a black hole, to sleep felt like giving in to death. I slept every night with the light on; but here, in the hospital, I'm less afraid. And to Quentin he said, one morning, the fear rips through me, it tears me open; and, to Ira, it presses me together, squeezes me toward myself. Fear gives everything its hue, its high. I feel so, I don't know how to say it, exalted, he said to Quentin. Calamity is an amazing high, too. Sometimes I feel *so* well, so powerful, it's as if I could jump out of my skin. Am I going crazy, or what? Is it all this attention and coddling I'm getting from everybody, like a child's dream of being loved? Is it the drugs? I know it sounds crazy but sometimes I think this is a *fantastic* experience, he said shyly; but there was also the bad taste in the mouth, the pressure in the head and at the back of the neck, the red, bleeding gums, the painful, if pink-lobed, breathing, and his ivory pallor, color of white chocolate. Among those who wept when told over the phone that he was back in the hospital were Kate and Stephen (who'd been called by Quentin), and Ellen, Victor, Aileen, and Lewis (who were called by Kate), and Xavier and Ursula (who were called by Stephen). Among those who didn't weep were Hilda, who said that she'd just learned that her seventy-five-year-old aunt was dying of the disease, which she'd contracted from a transfusion given during her successful double bypass of five years ago, and Frank and Donny and Betsy, but this didn't mean, according to Tanya, that they weren't moved and appalled, and Quentin thought they might not be coming soon to the hospital but would send presents; the room, he was in a private room this time, was filling up with flowers, and plants, and books, and tapes. The high tide of barely suppressed acrimony of the last weeks at home subsided into the routines of hospital visiting, though more than a few resented Quentin's having charge of the visiting book (but it was Quentin who had the idea, Lewis pointed out); now, to insure a steady stream of visitors, preferably no more than two at a time (this, the rule in all hospitals, wasn't enforced here, at least on this floor; whether out of kindness or inefficiency, no one could decide), Quentin had to be called first, to get one's time slot, there was no more casual dropping by. And his mother could no longer be prevented from taking a plane and installing herself in a hotel near the hospital; but he seemed to mind her daily presence less than expected, Quentin said; said Ellen it's we who mind, do you suppose she'll stay long. It was easier to be generous with each other visiting him here in the hospital, as Donny pointed out, than at home, where one minded never being alone with him; coming here, in our twos and twos, there's no doubt about what our role is, how we should be, collective, funny, distracting, undemanding, light, it's important to be light, for in all this dread there is gaiety, too, as the poet said, said Kate. (His eyes, his glittering eyes, said Lewis.) His eyes looked dull, extinguished, Wesley said to Xavier, but Betsy said his face, not just his eyes, looked soulful, warm; whatever is there, said Kate, I've never been so aware of his eyes; and Stephen said, I'm afraid of what my eyes show, the way I watch him, with too much intensity, or a phony kind of casualness, said Victor. And, unlike at home, he was clean-shaven each morning, at whatever hour they visited him; his curly hair was always combed; but he complained that the nurses had changed since he was here the last time, and that he didn't like the change, he wanted everyone to be the same. The room was furnished now with some of his personal effects (odd word for one's things, said Ellen), and Tanya brought drawings and a letter from her nine-year-old dyslexic son, who was writing now, since she'd purchased a computer; and Donny brought champagne and some helium balloons, which were anchored to the foot of his bed; tell me about something that's going on, he said, waking up from a nap to find Donny and Kate at the side of his bed, beaming at him; tell me a story, he said wistfully, said Donny, who couldn't think of anything to say; *you're* the story,

Kate said. And Xavier brought an eighteenth-century Guatemalan wooden statue of Saint Sebastian with upcast eyes and open mouth, and when Tanya said what's that, a tribute to eros past, Xavier said where I come from Sebastian is venerated as a protector against pestilence. Pestilence symbolized by arrows? Symbolized by arrows. All people remember is the body of a beautiful youth bound to a tree, pierced by arrows (of which he always seems oblivious, Tanya interjected), people forget that the story continues, Xavier continued, that when the Christian women came to bury the martyr they found him still alive and nursed him back to health. And he said, according to Stephen, I didn't know Saint Sebastian didn't die. It's undeniable, isn't it, said Kate on the phone to Stephen, the fascination of the dying. It makes me ashamed. We're learning how to die, said Hilda, I'm not ready to learn, said Aileen; and Lewis, who was coming straight from the other hospital, the hospital where Max was still being kept in ICU, met Tanya getting out of the elevator on the tenth floor, and as they walked together down the shiny corridor past the open doors, averting their eyes from the other patients sunk in their beds, with tubes in their noses, irradiated by the bluish light from the television sets, the thing I can't bear to think about, Tanya said to Lewis, is someone dying with the TV on.

He has that strange, unnerving detachment now, said Ellen, that's what upsets me, even though it makes it easier to be with him. Sometimes he was querulous. I can't stand them coming in here taking my blood every morning, what are they doing with all that blood, he is reported to have said; but where was his anger, Jan wondered. Mostly he was lovely to be with, always saying how are *you,* how are you feeling. He's so sweet now, said Aileen. He's so nice, said Tanya. (Nice, nice, groaned Paolo.) At first he was very ill, but he was rallying, according to Stephen's best information, there was no fear of his not recovering this time, and the doctor spoke of his being discharged from the hospital in another ten days if all went well, and the mother was persuaded to fly back to Mississippi, and Quentin was readying the penthouse for his return. And he was still writing his diary, not showing it to anyone, though Tanya, first to arrive one late-winter morning, and finding him dozing, peeked, and was horrified, according to Greg, not by anything she read but by a progressive change in his handwriting: in the recent pages, it was becoming spidery, less legible, and some lines of script wandered and tilted about the page. I was thinking, Ursula said to Quentin, that the difference between a story and a painting or photograph is that in a story you can write, He's still alive. But in a painting or a photo you can't show "still." You can just show him being alive. He's still alive, Stephen said.

NGUGI WA THIONG'O

 Ngugi Wa Thiong'o was born in 1938 in Limuru, Kenya, and received his education at the University of Makerere and Leeds University. Considered East Africa's best-known writer, he has melded a "messianic political search" with compassion in depicting the Kenyan struggle against colonialism. His four novels in English are *Weep Not, Child* (1964), *The River Between* (1965), *A Grain of Wheat* (1967), and *Petals of Blood* (1977). Ngugi was arrested by the Kenyan government when he began to write in his own language, Gikuyu; his novel in that language, translated as *Devil on the Cross* (1982), was written in prison. His stories are collected in *Secret Lives*. Since 1982 he has lived in exile. "Minutes of Glory" is a story of doomed desire and thwarted dreams in the bar underworld of Kenyan towns.

Minutes of Glory

Her name was Wanjiru. But she liked better her Christian one, Beatrice. It sounded more pure and more beautiful. Not that she was ugly; but she could not be called beautiful either. Her body, dark and full fleshed, had the form, yes, but it was as if it waited to be filled by the spirit. She worked in beer-halls where sons of women came to drown their inner lives in beer cans and froth. Nobody seemed to notice her. Except, perhaps, when a proprietor or an impatient customer called out her name, Beatrice; then other customers would raise their heads briefly, a few seconds, as if to behold the bearer of such a beautiful name, but not finding anybody there, they would resume their drinking, their ribald jokes, their laughter and play with the other serving girls. She was like a wounded bird in flight: a forced landing now and then but nevertheless wobbling from place to place so that she would variously be found in Alaska, Paradise, The Modern, Thome and other beer-halls all over Limuru. Sometimes it was because an irate proprietor found she was not attracting enough customers; he would sack her without notice and without salary. She would wobble to the next bar. But sometimes she was simply tired of nesting in one place, a daily witness of familiar scenes; girls even more decidedly ugly than she were fought over by numerous claimants at closing hours. What do they have that I don't have? she would ask herself, depressed. She longed for a bar-kingdom where she would be at least one of the rulers, where petitioners would bring their gifts of beer, frustrated smiles and often curses that hid more lust and love than hate.

She left Limuru town proper and tried the mushrooming townlets around. She worked at Ngarariga, Kamiritho, Rironi and even Tiekunu and everywhere the story was the same. Oh, yes, occasionally she would get a client; but none cared for her as she would have liked, none really wanted her enough to fight over her. She was always a hard-up customer's last resort. No make-believe even, not for her that sweet pretense that men indulged in after their fifth bottle of Tusker. The following night or during a pay-day, the same client would pretend not to know her; he would be trying his money-power over girls who already had more than a fair share of admirers.

She resented this. She saw in every girl a rival and adopted a sullen attitude. Nyagũthiĩ especially was the thorn that always pricked her wounded flesh. Nyagũthiĩ arrogant and aloof, but men always in her courtyard; Nyagũthiĩ fighting with men, and to her they would bring propitiating gifts which she accepted as of right. Nyagũthiĩ could look bored, impatient, or downright contemptuous and still men would cling to her as if they enjoyed being whipped with biting words, curled lips and the indifferent eyes of a free woman. Nyagũthiĩ was also a bird in flight, never really able to settle in one place, but in her case it was because she hungered for change and excitement: new faces and new territories for her conquest. Beatrice resented her very shadow. She saw in her the girl she would have liked to be, a girl who was both totally immersed in and yet completely above the underworld of bar violence and sex. Wherever Beatrice went the long shadow of Nyagũthiĩ would sooner or later follow her.

She fled Limuru for Ilmorog in Chiri District. Ilmorog had once been a ghost village, but had been resurrected to life by that legendary woman, Nyang'endo, to whom every pop group had paid their tribute. It was of her that the young dancing Muthuu and Muchun g'wa sang:

> When I left Nairobi for Ilmorog
> Never did I know
> I would bear this wonder-child mine
> Nyang'endo

As a result, Ilmorog was always seen as a town of hope where the weary and the down-trodden would find their rest and fresh water. But again Nyagũthiĩ followed her.

She found that Ilmorog, despite the legend, despite the songs and dances, was not different from Limuru. She tried various tricks. Clothes? But even here she never earned enough to buy herself glittering robes. What was seventy-five shillings a month without house allowance, posho, without salaried boy-friends? By that time, Ambi had reached Ilmorog, and Beatrice thought that this would be the answer. Had she not, in Limuru, seen girls blacker than herself transformed overnight from ugly sins into white stars by a touch of skin-lightening creams? And men would ogle them, would even talk with exaggerated pride of their newborn girl friends. Men were strange creatures, Beatrice thought in moments of searching analysis. They talked heatedly against Ambi, Butone, Firesnow, Moonsnow, wigs, straightened hair; but they always went for a girl with an Ambi-lightened skin and head covered with a wig made in imitation of European or Indian hair. Beatrice never tried to find the root cause of this black self-hatred, she simply accepted the contradiction and applied herself to Ambi with a vengeance. She had to rub out her black shame. But even Ambi she could not afford in abundance; she could only apply it to her face and her arms so that her legs and neck retained their blackness. Besides there were parts of her face she could not readily reach — behind the ears and above the eyelashes, for instance — and these were a constant source of shame and irritation for her Ambi-self.

She would always remember this Ambi period as one of her deepest humiliations before her later minutes of glory. She worked in Ilmorog Starlight Bar and Lodging. Nyagūthiī with her bangled hands, her huge earrings, served behind the counter. The owner was a good Christian soul who regularly went to church and paid all his dues to Harambee projects. Pot-belly. Grey hairs. Soft-spoken. A respectable family man, well known to Ilmorog. Hardworking even, for he would not leave the bar until the closing hours, or more precisely, until Nyagūthiī left. He had no eyes for any other girl; he hung around her, and surreptitiously brought her gifts of clothes without receiving gratitude in kind. Only the promise. Only the hope for tomorrow. Other girls he gave eighty shillings a month. Nyagūthiī had a room to herself. Nyagūthiī woke up whenever she like to take the stock. But Beatrice and the other girls had to wake up at five or so, make tea for the lodgers, clean up the bar and wash dishes and glasses. Then they would hang around the bar and in shifts until two o'clock when they would go for a small break. At five o'clock, they had to be in again, ready for customers whom they would now serve with frothy beers and smiles until twelve o'clock or for as long as there were customers thirsty for more Tuskers and Pilsners. What often galled Beatrice, although in her case it did not matter one way or another, was the owner's insistence that the girls should sleep in Starlight. They would otherwise be late for work, he said. But what he really wanted was for the girls to use their bodies to attract more lodgers in Starlight. Most of the girls, led by Nyagūthiī, defied the rule and bribed the watchman to let them out and in. They wanted to meet their regular or one-night boy-friends in places where they would be free and where they would be treated as not just barmaids. Beatrice always slept in. Her occasional one-night patrons wanted to spend the minimum. Came a night when the owner, refused by Nyagūthiī, approached her. He started by finding fault with her work; he called her names, then as suddenly he started praising her, although in a grudging almost contemptuous manner. He grabbed her, struggled with her, pot-belly, grey hairs, and everything. Beatrice felt an unusual revulsion for the man. She could not, she would not bring herself to accept that which had so recently been cast aside by Nyagūthiī. My God, she wept inside, what does Nyagūthiī have that I don't have? The man now humiliated himself before her. He implored. He promised her gifts. But she would not yield. That night she too defied the rule. She jumped through a window; she sought a bed in another bar and only came back at six. The proprietor called her in front of all the others and dismissed her. But Beatrice was rather surprised at herself.

She stayed a month without a job. She lived from room to room at the capricious mercy of the other girls. She did not have the heart to leave Ilmorog and start all over again in a new town. The wound hurt. She was tired of wandering. She stopped using

Ambi. No money. She looked at herself in the mirror. She had so aged, hardly a year after she had fallen from grace. Why then was she scrupulous, she would ask herself. But somehow she had a horror of soliciting lovers or directly bartering her body for hard cash. What she wanted was decent work and a man or several men who cared for her. Perhaps she took that need for a man, for a home and for a child with her to bed. Perhaps it was this genuine need that scared off men who wanted other things from barmaids. She wept late at nights and remembered home. At such moments, her mother's village in Nyeri seemed the sweetest place on God's earth. She would invest the life of her peasant mother and father with romantic illusions of immeasurable peace and harmony. She longed to go back home to see them. But how could she go back with empty hands? In any case the place was now a distant landscape in the memory. Her life was here in the bar among this crowd of lost strangers. Fallen from grace, fallen from grace. She was part of a generation which would never again be one with the soil, the crops, the wind and the moon. Not for them that whispering in dark hedges, not for her that dance and love-making under the glare of the moon, with the hill of Tumu Tumu rising to touch the sky. She remembered that girl from her home village who, despite a life of apparent glamour being the kept mistress of one rich man after another in Limuru, had gassed herself to death. This generation was now awed by the mystery of death, just as it was callous to the mystery of life; for how many unmarried mothers had thrown their babies into latrines rather than lose that glamour? The girl's death became the subject of jokes. She had gone metric — without pains, they said. Thereafter, for a week, Beatrice thought of going metric. But she could not bring herself to do it.

She wanted love; she wanted life.

A new bar was opened in Ilmorog. Treetop Bar, Lodging and Restaurant. Why Treetop, Beatrice could not understand unless because it was a storied building: tea-shop on the ground floor and beer-shop in a room at the top. The rest were rooms for five-minute or one-night lodgers. The owner was a retired civil servant but one who still played at politics. He was enormously wealthy with business sites and enterprises in every major town in Kenya. Big shots from all over the country came to his bar. Big men in Mercedes. Big men in their Bentleys. Big men in their Jaguars and Daimlers. Big men with uniformed chauffeurs drowsing with boredom in cars waiting outside. There were others not so big who came to pay respects to the great. They talked politics mostly. And about their work. Gossip was rife. Didn't you know? Indeed so and so has been promoted. Really? And so and so has been sacked. Embezzlement of public funds. So foolish you know. Not clever about it at all. They argued, they quarrelled, sometimes they fought it out with fists, especially during the elections campaign. The only point on which they were all agreed was that the Luo community was the root cause of all the trouble in Kenya; that intellectuals and University students were living in an ivory tower of privilege and arrogance; that Kiambu had more than a lion's share of developments; that men from Nyeri and Muranga had acquired all the big business in Nairobi and were even encroaching on Chiri District; that African workers, especially those on the farms, were lazy and jealous of 'us' who had sweated ourselves to sudden prosperity. Otherwise each would hymn his own praises or return compliments. Occasionally in moments of drunken ebullience and self-praise, one would order two rounds of beer for each man present in the bar. Even the poor from Ilmorog would come to Treetop to dine at the gates of the nouveaux riches.

Here Beatrice got a job as a sweeper and bedmaker. Here for a few weeks she felt closer to greatness. Now she made beds for men she had previously known as names. She watched how even the poor tried to drink and act big in front of the big. But soon fate caught up with her. Girls flocked to Treetop from other bars. Girls she had known at Limuru, girls she had known at Ilmorog. And most had attached themselves to one or several big men, often playing a hide-and-not-to-be found game with their numerous lovers. And Nyagūthiĩ was there behind the counter, with the eyes of the rich and the poor fixed on her. And she, with her big eyes, bangled hands and earrings, maintained the same air of bored indifference. Beatrice as a sweeper and bedmaker became even more invisible. Girls who had fallen into good fortune looked down upon her.

She fought life with dreams. In between putting clean sheets on beds that had just witnessed a five-minute struggle that ended in a half-strangled cry and a pool, she would stand by the window and watch the cars and the chauffeurs, so that soon she knew all the owners by the number plates of their cars and the uniforms of their chauffeurs. She dreamt of lovers who would come for her in sleek Mercedes sports cars made for two. She saw herself linking hands with such a lover, walking in the streets of Nairobi and Mombasa, tapping the ground with high heels, quick, quick short steps. And suddenly she would stop in front of a display glass window, exclaiming at the same time, Oh darling, won't you buy me those . . . ? Those what? he would ask, affecting anger. Those stockings, darling. It was as an owner of several stockings, ladderless and holeless, that she thought of her well-being. Never again would she mend torn things. Never, never, never. Do you understand? Never. She was next the proud owner of different coloured wigs, blonde wigs, brunette wigs, redhead wigs, Afro wigs, wigs, wigs, all the wigs in the world. Only then would the whole earth sing hallelujah to the one Beatrice. At such moments, she would feel exalted, lifted out of her murky self, no longer a floor sweeper and bedmaker for a five-minute instant love, but Beatrice, descendant of Wangu Makeri who made men tremble with desire at her naked body bathed in moonlight, daughter of Nyang'endo, the founder of modern Ilmorog, of whom they often sang that she had worked several lovers into impotence.

Then she noticed him and he was the opposite of the lover of her dreams. He came one Saturday afternoon driving a big five-ton lorry. He carefully parked it beside the Benzes, the Jaguars and the Daimlers, not as a lorry, but as one of those sleek cream-bodied frames, so proud of it he seemed to be. He dressed in a baggy grey suit over which he wore a heavy khaki military overcoat. He removed the overcoat, folded it with care, and put it in the front seat. He locked all the doors, dusted himself a little, then walked round the lorry as if inspecting it for damage. A few steps before he entered Treetop, he turned round for a final glance at his lorry dwarfing the other things. At Treetop he sat in a corner and, with a rather loud defiant voice, ordered a Kenya one. He drank it with relish, looking around at the same time for a face he might recognize. He indeed did recognize one of the big ones and he immediately ordered for him a quarter bottle of Vat 69. This was accepted with a bare nod of the head and a patronising smile; but when he tried to follow his generosity with a conversation, he was firmly ignored. He froze, sank into his Muratina. But only for a time. He tried again: he was met with frowning faces. More pathetic were his attempts to join in jokes; he would laugh rather too loudly, which would make the big ones stop, leaving him in the air alone. Later in the evening he stood up, counted several crisp hundred shilling notes and handed them to Nya-gūthiī behind the counter ostensibly for safekeeping. People whispered; murmured; a few laughed, rather derisively, though they were rather impressed. But this act did not win him immediate recognition. He staggered towards room no. 7 which he had hired. Beatrice brought him the keys. He glanced at her, briefly, then lost all interest.

Thereafter he came every Saturday. At five when most of the big shots were already seated. He repeated the same ritual, except the money act, and always met with defeat. He nearly always sat in the same corner and always rented room 7. Beatrice grew to anticipate his visits and, without being conscious of it, kept the room ready for him. Often after he had been badly humiliated by the big company, he would detain Beatrice and talk to her, or rather he talked to himself in her presence. For him, it had been a life of struggles. He had never been to school although getting an education had been his ambition. He never had a chance. His father was a squatter in the European settled area in the Rift Valley. That meant a lot in those colonial days. It meant among other things a man and his children were doomed to a future of sweat and toil for the white devils and their children. He had joined the freedom struggle and like the others had been sent to detention. He came from detention the same as his mother had brought him to this world. Nothing. With independence he found he did not possess the kind of education which would have placed him in one of the vacancies at the top. He started as a charcoal burner, then a butcher, gradually working his own way to become a big transporter of vegetables and potatoes from the Rift Valley and Chiri districts to Nairobi. He was proud of his achievement. But he resented that others, who had climbed to their present wealth through loans and a subsidized education, would not recognize his like. He would rumble on like this, dwelling on education he would never have, and talking of better chances for his children. Then he would carefully count the money, put it under the pillow, and then dismiss Beatrice. Occasionally he would buy her a beer but he was clearly suspicious of women whom he saw as money-eaters of men. He had not yet married.

One night he slept with her. In the morning he scratched for a twenty shilling note and gave it to her. She accepted the money with an odd feeling of guilt. He did this for several weeks. She did not mind the money. It was useful. But he paid for her body as he would pay for a bag of potatoes or a sack of cabbages. With the one pound, he had paid for her services as a listener, a vessel of his complaints against those above, and as a one-night receptacle of his man's burden. She was becoming bored with his ego, with his stories that never varied in content, but somehow, in him, deep inside, she felt that something had been there, a fire, a seed, a flower which was being smothered. In him she saw a fellow victim and looked forward to his visits. She too longed to talk to someone. She too longed to confide in a human being who would understand.

And she did it one Saturday night, suddenly interrupting the story of his difficult climb to the top. She did not know why she did it. Maybe it was the rain outside. It was softly drumming the corrugated iron sheets, bringing with the drumming a warm and drowsy indifference. He would listen. He had to listen. She came from Karatina in Nyeri. Her two brothers had been gunned down by the British soldiers. Another one had died in detention. She was, so to speak, an only child. Her parents were poor. But they worked hard on their bare strip of land and managed to pay her fees in primary school. For the first six years she had worked hard. In the seventh year, she must have relaxed a little. She did not pass with a good grade. Of course she knew many with similar grades who had been called to good government secondary schools. She knew a few others with lesser grades who had gone to very top schools on the strength of their connections. But she was not called to any high school with reasonable fees. Her parents could not afford fees in a Harambee school. And she would not hear of repeating standard seven. She stayed at home with her parents. Occasionally she would help them in the shamba and with house chores. But imagine: for the past six years she had led a life with a different rhythm from that of her parents. Life in the village was dull. She would often go to Karatina and to Nyeri in search of work. In every office, they would ask her the same questions: what work do you want? What do you know? Can you type? Can you take shorthand? She was desperate. It was in Nyeri, drinking Fanta in a shop, tears in her eyes, that she met a young man in a dark suit and sun-glasses. He saw her plight and talked to her. He came from Nairobi. Looking for work? That's easy; in a big city there would be no difficulty with jobs. He would certainly help. Transport? He had a car — a cream-white Peugeot. Heaven. It was a beautiful ride, with the promise of dawn. Nairobi. He drove her to Terrace Bar. They drank beer and talked about Nairobi. Through the window she would see the neon-lit city and knew that here was hope. That night she gave herself to him, with the promise of dawn making her feel light and gay. She had a very deep sleep. When she woke in the morning, the man in the cream-white Peugeot was not there. She never saw him again. That's how she had started the life of a barmaid. And for one and a half years now she had not been once to see her parents. Beatrice started weeping. Huge sobs of self-pity. Her humiliation and constant flight were fresh in her mind. She had never been able to take to bar culture, she always thought that something better would come her way. But she was trapped, it was the only life she now knew, although she had never really learnt all its laws and norms. Again she heaved out and in, tears tossing out with every sob. Then suddenly she froze. Her sobbing was arrested in the air. The man had long covered himself. His snores were huge and unmistakable.

She felt a strange hollowness. Then a bile of bitterness spilt inside her. She wanted to cry at her new failure. She had met several men who had treated her cruelly, who had laughed at her scruples, at what they thought was an ill-disguised attempt at innocence. She had accepted. But not this, Lord, not this. Was this man not a fellow victim? Had he not, Saturday after Saturday, unburdened himself to her? He had paid for her human services; he had paid away his responsibility with his bottle of Tuskers and hard cash in the morning. Her innermost turmoil had been his lullaby. And suddenly something in her snapped. All the anger of a year and a half, all the bitterness against her humiliation were now directed at this man.

What she did later had the mechanical precision of an experienced hand.

She touched his eyes. He was sound asleep. She raised his head. She let it fall. Her tearless eyes were now cold and set. She removed the pillow from under him. She rummaged through it. She took out his money. She counted five crisp pink notes. She put the money inside her brassiere.

She went out of room no. 7. Outside it was still raining. She did not want to go to her usual place. She could not now stand the tiny cupboard room or the superior chatter of her roommate. She walked through mud and rain. She found herself walking towards Nyagūthiĩ's room. She knocked at the door. At first she had no response. Then she heard Nyagūthiĩ's sleepy voice above the drumming rain.

'Who is that?'

'It is me. Please open.'

'Who?'

'Beatrice.'

'At this hour of the night?'

'Please.'

Lights were put on. Bolts unfastened. The door opened. Beatrice stepped inside. She and Nyagũthiĩ stood there face to face. Nyagũthiĩ was in a see-through night-dress: on her shoulders she had a green pullover.

'Beatrice, is there anything wrong?' She at last asked, a note of concern in her voice.

'Can I rest here for a while? I am tired. And I want to talk to you.' Beatrice's voice carried assurance and power.

'But what has happened?'

'I only want to ask you a question, Nyagũthiĩ.'

They were still standing. Then, without a word, they both sat on the bed.

'Why did you leave home, Nyagũthiĩ?' Beatrice asked. Another silent moment. Nyagũthiĩ seemed to be thinking about the question. Beatrice waited. Nyagũthiĩ's voice when at last it came was slightly tremulous, unsteady.

'It is a long story, Beatrice. My father and mother were fairly wealthy. They were also good Christians. We lived under regulations. You must never walk with the heathen. You must not attend their pagan customs — dances and circumcision rites, for instance. There were rules about what, how and when to eat. You must even walk like a Christian lady. You must never be seen with boys. Rules, rules all the way. One day instead of returning home from school, I and another girl from a similar home ran away to Eastleigh. I have never been home once this last four years. That's all.'

Another silence. Then they looked at one another in mutual recognition.

'One more question, Nyagũthiĩ. You need not answer it. But I have always thought that you hated me, you despised me.'

'No, no, Beatrice, I have never hated you. I have never hated anybody. It is just that nothing interests me. Even men do not move me now. Yet I want, I need instant excitement. I need the attention of those false flattering eyes to make me feel myself, myself. But you, you seemed above all this — somehow you had something inside you that I did not have.'

Beatrice tried to hold her tears with difficulty.

Early the next day, she boarded a bus bound for Nairobi. She walked down Bazaar Street looking at the shops. Then down Government Road, right into Kenyatta Avenue, and Kimathi Street. She went into a shop near Hussein Suleiman's Street and bought several stockings. She put on a pair. She next bought herself a new dress. Again she changed into it. In a Bata Shoeshop, she bought high heeled shoes, put them on and discarded her old flat ones. On to an Akamba kiosk, and she fitted herself with earrings. She went to a mirror and looked at her new self. Suddenly she felt enormous hunger as if she had been hungry all her life. She hesitated in front of Moti Mahal. Then she walked on, eventually entering Fransae. There was a glint in her eyes that made men's eyes turn to her. This thrilled her. She chose a table in a corner and ordered Indian curry. A man left his table and joined her. She looked at him. Her eyes were merry. He was dressed in a dark suit and his eyes spoke of lust. He bought her a drink. He tried to engage her in conversation. But she ate in silence.

He put his hand under the table and felt her knees. She let him do it. The hand went up and up her thigh. Then suddenly she left her unfinished food and her untouched drink and walked out. She felt good. He followed her. She knew this without once turning her eyes. He walked beside her for a few yards. She smiled at herself but did not look at him. He lost his confidence. She left him standing sheepishly looking at a glass window outside Gino's. In the bus back to Ilmorog, men gave her seats. She accepted this as of right. At Treetop bar she went straight to the counter. The usual crowd of big men were there. Their conversations stopped for a few seconds at her entry. Their lascivious eyes were turned to her. The girls stared at her. Even Nyagūthiī could not maintain her bored indifference. Beatrice bought them drinks. The manager came to her, rather unsure. He tried a conversation. Why had she left work? Where had she been? Would she like to work in the bar, helping Nyagūthiī behind the counter? Now and then? A barmaid brought her a note. A certain big shot wanted to know if she would join their table. More notes came from different big quarters with the one question; would she be free tonight? A trip to Nairobi even. She did not leave her place at the counter. But she accepted their drinks as of right. She felt a new power, confidence even.

She took out a shilling, put it in the slot and the juke box boomed with the voice of Robinson Mwangi singing *Hūnyū wa Mashambani*. He sang of those despised girls who worked on farms and contrasted them with urban girls. Then she played a Kamaru and a D.K. Men wanted to dance with her. She ignored them, but enjoyed their flutter around her. She twisted her hips to the sound of yet another D.K. Her body was free. She was free. She sucked in the excitement and tension in the air.

Then suddenly at around six, the man with the five-ton lorry stormed into the bar. This time he had on his military overcoat. Behind him was a policeman. He looked around. Everybody's eyes were raised to him. But Beatrice went on swaying her hips. At first he could not recognize Beatrice in the girl celebrating her few minutes of glory by the juke box. Then he shouted in triumph. 'That is the girl! Thief! Thief!'

People melted back to their seats. The policeman went and handcuffed her. She did not resist. Only at the door she turned her head and spat. Then she went out followed by the policeman.

In the bar the stunned silence broke into hilarious laughter when someone made a joke about sweetened robbery without violence. They discussed her. Some said she should have been beaten. Others talked contemptuously about 'these bar girls'. Yet others talked with a concern noticeable in unbelieving shakes of their heads about the rising rate of crime. Shouldn't the Hanging Bill be extended to all thefts of property? And without anybody being aware of it the man with the five-ton lorry had become a hero. They now surrounded him with questions and demanded the whole story. Some even bought him drinks. More remarkable, they listened, their attentive silence punctuated by appreciative laughter. The averted threat to property had temporarily knit them into one family. And the man, accepted for the first time, told the story with relish.

But behind the counter Nyagūthiī wept.

WILLIAM TREVOR

 William Trevor was born in County Cork, Ireland, in 1928, grew up in provincial Ireland, and received his education at Trinity College, Dublin. He moved to Devon, England, in 1960, where he has quietly created a body of some of the most distinguished Anglo-Irish writing of this century. A number of critics have avowed that Trevor is the finest short story writer presently writing in English, a "wise" artist who, with delicate understatement, sheds light on the endless dimensions of humanity. Drawn to "dying order and dying memory," Trevor writes often of characters "caught between yes and no," able neither to forget their dreams nor fully to realize them. His novels include *The Old Boys* (1964), *Miss Eckdorff in O'Neill's Hotel* (1969), *Elizabeth Alone* (1973), *Other People's Worlds* (1980), and *Fools of Fortune* (1983). His stories are collected in *The Day We Got Drunk on Cake* (1967), *The Ballroom of Romance* (1972), *Angels at the Ritz* (1975), *Lovers of Their Time* (1978), *Beyond the Pale* (1981), and *The News from Ireland* (1986). The stories here — "August Saturday" and "The News from Ireland" — illustrate something of Trevor's range and depth. The first is a story of revelation, set in the Ireland of today. The second, employing two narrative lines, is an eerie evocation of the time of famine in nineteenth-century Ireland. From it we can grasp something of the many passions implicit in Yeats's great phrase for Ireland: "a fanatic heart."

August Saturday

"You don't remember me," the man said.

His tone suggested a statement, not a question, but Grania did remember him. She had recognized him immediately, his face smiling above the glass he held. He was a man she had believed she would never see again. For fifteen years — since the summer of 1972 — she had tried not to think about him, and for the most part had succeeded.

"Yes, I do remember you," she said. "Of course."

A slice of lemon floated on the surface of what she guessed was gin-and-tonic; there were cubes of ice and the little bubbles that came from tonic when it was freshly poured. It wouldn't be tonic on its own; it hadn't been the other time. "I've drunk a bit too much," he'd said.

"I used to wonder," he went on now, "if ever we'd meet again. The kind of thing you wonder when you can't sleep."

"I didn't think we would."

"I know. But it doesn't matter, does it?"

"Of course not."

She wondered why he had come back. She wondered how long he intended to stay. He'd be staying with the Prendergasts, she supposed, as he had been before. For fifteen years she had avoided the road to the Prendergasts' house, but even so she vividly remembered the curve of the green iron railings on either side of the avenue gates, the unoccupied gate lodge.

"You weren't aware that Hetty Prendergast died?" he said.

"No, I wasn't."

"Well, she did. Two days ago."

The conversation took place in the bar of the Tara Hotel, where Grania and her husband, Desmond, dined once a month with other couples from the tennis club — an arrangement devised by the husbands so that the wives, just for a change, wouldn't have to cook.

"You don't mind my talking to you?" the man said. "I'm on my own again."

"Of course I don't."

"When I was told about the death I came on over. I've just come in from the house to have a meal with the Quiltys."

"Tonight, you mean?"

"When they turn up."

Quilty was a solicitor. He and his wife, Hazel, belonged to the tennis club and were usually present at the monthly dinners in the Rhett Butler Room of the Tara Hotel. The death of old Hetty Prendergast had clearly caught them unawares, and Grania could imagine Hazel Quilty sulkily refusing to cancel a long-booked baby-sitter in order to remain at home to cook a meal for the stranger who had arrived from England, with whom her husband presumably had business to discuss. "We'll take him with us," Quilty would have said in his soothing voice, and Hazel would have calmed down, as she always did when she got her way.

"Still playing tennis, Grania?"

"Pretty badly."

"You've hardly aged, you know."

This was so patently a lie that it wasn't worth protesting about. After the funeral of the old woman he would go away. He hadn't arrived for the other funeral, that of Mr. Prendergast, which had taken place nearly ten years ago, and there wouldn't be another one, because there was no other Prendergast left to die. She wondered what would happen to the house and to the couple who had looked after the old woman, driving in every Friday to shop for her. She didn't ask. She said, "A group of us have dinner here now and again — the Quiltys, too. I don't know if they told you that."

"You mean tonight?"

"Yes."

"No, that wasn't said."

He smiled at her. He sipped a little gin. He had a long face, high cheekbones, graying hair brushed straight back from a sallow forehead. His blue-green eyes were steady, almost staring because he didn't blink much. She remembered the eyes particularly, now that she was again being scrutinized by them. She remembered asking who he was and being told a sort of nephew of the Prendergasts, an Englishman.

"I've often wondered about the tennis club, Grania."

"It hasn't changed. Except that we've become the older generation."

Desmond came up then, and she introduced her companion, reminding Desmond that he'd met him before. She stumbled when she had to give him a name, because she'd never known what it was. "Prendergast," she mumbled vaguely, not sure if he was called Prendergast or not. She'd never known that.

"Hetty died, I hear," Desmond said.

"So I've been telling your wife. I've come over to do my stuff."

"Well, of course."

"The Quiltys have invited me to your dinner do."

"You're very welcome."

Desmond had a squashed pink face and receding hair that had years ago been reddish. As soon as he put his clothes on they became crumpled, no matter how carefully Grania had ironed them. He was a man who never lost his temper, slow-moving except on a tennis court, where he was surprisingly subtle and cunning, quite unlike the person he otherwise was.

Grania moved away. Mavis Duddy insisted she owed her a drink from last time and led her to the bar, where she ordered two more Martinis. "Who was that?" she asked, and Grania replied that the gray-haired man was someone from England, related to the Prendergasts, she wasn't entirely certain about his name. He'd come to the tennis club once, she said — an occasion when Mavis hadn't been there. "Over for old Hetty's funeral, is he?" Marvis said, and, accepting the drink, Grania agreed that that was so.

They were a set in the small town; since the time they'd been teen-agers the tennis club had been the pivot of their social lives. In winter some of them played bridge or golf, others chose not to. But all of them on summer afternoons and evenings looked in at the tennis club even if, like Francie MacGuinness and the Haddons, they didn't play much anymore. They shared memories, and likes and dislikes, that had to do with the tennis club; there were photographs that once in a blue moon were sentimentally mulled over; friendships had grown closer or apart. Billy MacGuinness had always been the same — determinedly a winner at fourteen and determinedly a winner at forty-five. Francie, who'd married him when it had seemed that he might marry Trish, had been a winner also; Trish had made do with Tom Crosbie. There'd been quarrels at the tennis club: a great row in 1961, when Desmond's father had wanted to raise money for a hard court and resigned in a huff when no one agreed; and nearly ten years later there had been the quarrel between Laverty and Dr. Timothy Sweeney, which had resulted in both their resignations, all to do with a dispute about a roller. There were jealousies and gossip, occasionally both envy and resentment. The years had been less kind to some while favoring others; the children born to the couples of the tennis club were often compared, though rarely openly, in terms of achievement or promise. Tea was taken, supplied by the wives, on Saturday afternoons from May to September. The men supplied drinks on that one day of the week also, and even washed up the glasses. The children of the tennis club tasted their first cocktails there — Billy MacGuinness's White Ladies and Sidecars. A handful of the tennis-club wives were best friends, and had been since their convent days: Grania and Mavis, Francie, Hazel, Trish. They trusted one another, doing so more easily now than they had when they'd been at the convent together or in the days when each of them might possibly have married one of the others' suitors. They told one another most things, confessing their errors and their blunders; they comforted and were a solace, jollying away feelings of inadequacy or guilt. Trish had worried at the convent because her breasts wouldn't grow, Hazel because her face was scrawny and her lips too thin. Francie had almost died when a lorry knocked her off her bicycle. Mavis had agonized for months before she said yes to Oliver Duddy. As girls, they had united in their criticism of girls outside their circle; as wives, in 1987, they had not changed.

"I heard about that guy," Mavis said now. "So that's what he looks like."

That August Saturday in 1972, he'd come to the tennis club on a bicycle, in whites he had borrowed at the house where he was staying, a racquet tied with string to the crossbar. He'd told Grania afterward that Hetty Prendergast had looked the whites out for him and had lent him the racquet as well. Hetty had mentioned the tennis club, to which she and her husband had years ago belonged themselves. "Of course a different kind of lot these days," she'd said. "Like everywhere." He'd pushed the bicycle through the gate and stood there watching a doubles game, not yet untying his racquet. "Who on earth's that?" someone had said, and Grania approached him after about a quarter of an hour, since she was at that time the club's secretary and vaguely felt it to be her duty.

Sipping the Martini Mavis had claimed to owe her, she remembered the sudden turning of his profile in her direction when she spoke and then his smile. Nothing of what she subsequently planned had yet entered her head; she would have been stunned by even the faintest inkling of it. "I'm awfully sorry," he'd said. "I'm barging in."

Grania had been twenty-seven then, married to Desmond for almost eight years. Now she was forty-three, and her cool brown eyes still strikingly complemented the lips that Desmond had once confessed he'd wanted to kiss ever since she was twelve. Her dark hair had been in plaits at twelve, later had been fashionably long, and now was short. She wasn't tall and had always wished she was, but at least she didn't have to slim. She hadn't become a mother yet, that Saturday afternoon when the stranger arrived at the tennis club. But she was happy, and in love with Desmond.

"Aisling's going out with some chartered accountant," Mavis said, speaking about her daughter. "Oliver's hopping mad."

The Quiltys arrived. Grania watched while they joined Desmond and their dinner guest. Desmond moved to the bar to buy them drinks. Quilty — a small man who reminded Grania of a monkey — lit a cigarette. Politely, Grania transferred her attention to her friend. Why should Oliver be angry, she asked, genuinely not knowing. She could tell from Mavis's tone of voice that she was not displeased herself.

"Because he's nine years older. We had a letter from Aisling this morning. Oliver's talking about going up to have it out with her."

"That might make it worse, actually."

"If he mentions it will you tell him that? He listens to you, you know."

Grania said she would. She knew Oliver Duddy would mention it, since he always seemed to want to talk to her about things that upset him. Once upon a time, just before she'd become engaged to Desmond, he'd tried to persuade her he loved her.

"They earn a fortune," Mavis said. "Chartered accountants."

Soon after that they all began to move into the Rhett Butler Room. Grania could just remember the time when the hotel had been called O'Hara's Commercial, in the days of Mr. and Mrs. O'Hara. It wasn't all that long ago that their sons, giving the place another face-lift as soon as they inherited it, decided to change the name to the Tara and to give the previously numbered bedrooms names like "Ashley's" and "Melanie's." The bar was known as Scarlett's Lounge. There were regular discos in Belle's Place.

"Who's that fellow with the Quiltys?" Francie MacGuinness asked, and Grania told her. "He's come back for Hetty Prendergast's funeral."

"God, I didn't know she died."

As always, several tables had been pushed together to form a single long one in the center of the dining room. At it, the couples who'd been drinking in the bar sat as they wished: there was no formality. Una Carty-Carroll, Trish Crosbie's sister, was unmarried but was usually partnered on these Saturday occasions by the surveyor from the waterworks. This was so tonight. At one end of the table a place remained unoccupied: Angela, outside the circle of best friends, as Una Carty-Carroll and Mary Ann Haddon were, invariably came late. In a distant corner of the Rhett Butler Room one other couple were dining. Another table, recently occupied, was being tidied.

"I think it's Monday," Grania said when Francie asked her when the funeral was.

She hoped he'd go away again immediately. That other Saturday, he'd said he found it appallingly dull at the Prendergasts' — a call of duty, no reason in the world that he should ever return. His reassurances had in a way been neither here nor there at the time, but afterward, of course, she'd recalled them. Afterward, many times she'd strained to establish every single word of the conversation they'd had.

"D'you remember poor old Hetty," Francie said, "coming into the club for a cup of tea once? Ages ago."

"Yes, I remember her."

A small woman they remembered, a frail look about her face. There was another occasion Francie recalled: when the old woman became agitated because one of Wm. Cole's meal lorries had backed into her Morris Minor. "I thought she'd passed on years ago," Francie said.

They separated. Hazel was sitting next to him, Grania noticed, Quilty on his other side. Presumably they'd talk over whatever business there was, so that he wouldn't have to delay once the funeral had taken place.

"How're you doing, dear?" Oliver Duddy said, occupying the chair on Grania's left. Desmond was on her right; he nearly always chose to sit next to her.

"I'm all right," she replied. "Are you O.K., Oliver?"

"Far from it, as a matter of fact." He twisted backward and stretched an arm out, preventing the waitress who was attempting to pass by from doing so. "Bring me a Crested Ten, will you? Aisling's in the family way," he muttered into Grania's ear. "Jesus Christ, Grania!"

He was an architect, responsible for the least attractive bungalows in the county, possibly in the province. He and Mavis had once spent a protracted winter holiday in Spain, the time he'd been endeavoring to find himself. He hadn't done so, but that period of his life had ever since influenced the local landscape. Also, people said, his lavatories didn't work as well as they might have.

"Do you mean it, Oliver? Are you sure?"

"Some elderly Mr. Bloody. I'll wring his damn neck for him."

He was drunk to the extent that failing to listen to him wouldn't matter. No opportunity for comment would be offered. The advice sought, the plea for understanding, would not properly register in the brain that set in motion the requests. It was extremely unlikely that Aisling was pregnant.

"Old Hetty left him the house," Desmond said on her other side. "He's going to live in it. Nora," he called out to the waitress, "I need to order the wine."

Oliver Duddy gripped her elbow, demanding the return of her attention. His face came close to hers: the small, snub nose, the tightly bunched, heated cheeks, droplets of perspiration on forehead and chin. Grania looked away. Across the table, Mavis was better-looking than her husband in all sorts of ways, her lips prettily parted as she listened to whatever it was Billy MacGuinness was telling her about, her blue eyes sparkling with Saturday-evening vivacity. Francie was listening to the surveyor. Mary Ann Haddon was nervously playing with her fork, the way she did when she felt she was being ignored: she had a complex about her looks, which were not her strong point. Hazel Quilty was talking to the man who'd come back for the funeral, her lean mouth swiftly opening and closing. Francie, who'd given up smoking a fortnight ago, lit a cigarette. Billy MacGuinness's round face crinkled with sudden laughter. Mavis laughed also.

The waitress hurried away with Desmond's wine order. Light caught one lens of Mary Ann's glasses. "Oh, I don't *believe* you!" Francie cried, her voice for a single instant shrill above the buzz of conversation. The man who'd come back to attend the old woman's funeral still listened politely. Trish — the smallest, most demure of the wives — kept nodding while Kevy Haddon spoke in his dry voice, his features dryly matching it.

There were other faces in the Rhett Butler Room, those of Clark Gable and Vivien Leigh reproduced on mirrored glass with bevelled edges, huge images that also included the shoulders of the film stars, the décolletage of one, the frilled evening shirt of the other. Clark Gable was subtly allowed the greater impact. In Scarlett's Lounge, together on a single mirror, the two appeared to be engaged in argument, he crossly pouting from a distance, she imperious in closeup.

"This man here, you mean?" Grania said to her husband when there was an opportunity. She knew he did; there was no one else he could mean. She didn't want to think about it, yet it had to be confirmed. She wanted to delay the knowledge, yet just as much she had to know quickly.

"So he's been saying," Desmond said. "You know, I'd forgotten who he was when you introduced us."

"But what on earth does he want to come and live in that awful old house for?"

"He's on his uppers, apparently."

Often they talked together on these Saturday occasions, in much the same way as they did in their own kitchen while she finished cooking the dinner and he laid the table. In the kitchen they talked about people they'd run into during the day, the same people once a week or so, rarely strangers. When his father retired almost twenty years ago, Desmond had taken over the management of the town's laundry and later inherited it. The Tara Hotel was his second most important customer, the Hospital of St. Bernadette of Lourdes being his first. He brought back to Grania reports of demands for higher wages, and the domestic confidences of his staff. In return she passed on gossip, which both of them delighted in.

"How's Judith?" Oliver Duddy inquired, finger and thumb again tightening on her elbow. "No Mr. Bloody yet?"

"Judith's still in school, remember."

"You never know these days."

"I think you've got it wrong about Aisling being pregnant."

"I pray to God I have, dear."

Desmond said he intended to go to Hetty Prendergast's funeral, but she saw no reason that she should go herself. Desmond went to lots of funerals, often of people she didn't know, business acquaintances who'd lived miles away. Going to funerals was different when there was a business reason — not that the Prendergasts had ever made much use of the laundry.

"I have a soft spot for Judith," Oliver Duddy said. "She's getting to be a lovely girl."

It was difficult to agree without sounding smug, yet it seemed disloyal to her daughter to deny what was claimed for her. Grania shrugged, a gesture that was vague enough to indicate whatever her companion wished to make of it. There was no one on Oliver Duddy's other side, because the table ended there. Angela, widow of a German businessman, had just sat down in the empty place opposite him. The most glamorous of all the wives, tall and slim, her hair the color of very pale sand, Angela was said to be on the lookout for a second marriage. Her husband had settled in the neighborhood after the war and had successfully begun a cheese-and-pâté business, supplying restaurants and hotels all over the country. With a flair he had cultivated in her, Angela ran it now. "How's Oliver?" She smiled seductively across the table, the way she'd smiled at men even in her husband's lifetime. Oliver Duddy said he was all right, but Grania knew that only a desultory conversation would begin between the two, because Oliver Duddy didn't like Angela for some reason, or else was alarmed by her.

"Judith always has a word for you," he said. "Rare, God knows, in a young person these days."

"Who's that?" Angela leaned forward, her eyes indicating the stranger.

She was told, and Grania watched her remembering him. Angela had been pregnant with the third of her sons that August afternoon. "Uncomfortably warm," she now recalled, nodding in recollection.

Oliver Duddy displayed no interest. He'd been at the club that afternoon and he remembered the arrival of the stranger, but an irritated expression passed over his tightly made face while Grania and Angela agreed about the details of the afternoon in question: he resented the interruption and wished to return to the subject of daughters.

"What I'm endeavoring to get at, Grania, is what would you say if Judith came back with some fellow old enough to be her father?"

"Mavis didn't say Aisling's friend was as old as that."

"Aisling wrote us a letter, Grania. There are lines to read between."

"Well, naturally I'd prefer Judith to marry someone of her own age. But of course it all depends on the man."

"D'you find a daughter easy, Grania? There's no one thinks more of Aisling than myself. The fonder you are, the more worry there is. Would you say that was right, Grania?"

"Probably."

"You're lucky in Judith, though. She has a great way with her."

Angela was talking to Tom Crosbie about dairy products. The Crosbies were an example of a marriage in which there was a considerable age difference that appeared not to have had an adverse effect. Trish had had four children, two girls and two boys; they were a happy, jolly family, even though when Trish married it had been widely assumed that she was not in love, was if anything still yearning after Billy

MacGuinness. It was even rumored that Trish had married for money, since Tom Crosbie owned Boyd Motors, the main Ford franchise in the neighborhood. Trish's family had once been well-to-do but had somehow become penurious.

"What's Judith going to do for herself? Nursing, is it, Grania?"

"If it is, she's never mentioned it."

"I only thought it might be."

"There's talk about college. She's not bad at languages."

"Don't send her to Dublin, dear. Keep the girl by you. D'you hear what I'm saying, Desmond?" Oliver Duddy raised his voice, shouting across Grania. He began all over again, saying he had a soft spot for Judith, explaining about the letter that had arrived from Aisling. Grania changed places with him.

"Oliver's had a few," Angela said. "He's upset about Aisling. She's going out with an older man."

She shouldn't have said it with Tom Crosbie sitting there. She made a face to herself and leaned toward him to tell him he was looking perky. As soon as she'd spoken she felt she'd made matters worse, that her remark could be taken to imply he was looking young for his years.

"There's a new place," Angela said when Grania asked her about her dress. "Pursestrings. D'you know it?"

Ever since she'd become a widow Angela had gone to Dublin to buy something during the week before each dinner at the hotel. Angela liked to be first, though often Francie ran her close. Mavis tried to keep up with them but couldn't quite. Grania sometimes tried, too; Hazel didn't mind what she wore.

"Is Desmond going to the funeral?" Tom Crosbie asked in his agreeable way — perhaps, Grania thought, to show that no offense had been taken.

"Yes, he is."

"Desmond's very good."

That was true. Desmond was good. He'd been the pick of the tennis club when she'd picked him herself — the pick of the town. Looking round the table — at Tom Crosbie's bald head and Kevy Haddon's joylessness, at the simian lines of Quilty's cheeks and Billy MacGuinness's tendency to glow, at Oliver Duddy's knotted features — she was aware that, on top of everything else, Desmond had worn better than any of them. He had acquired authority in middle age; the reticence of his youth had remained, but time had displayed that he was more often right than wrong, and his opinion was sought in a way it once had not been. Desmond was quietly obliging, a quality more appreciated in middle age than in youth. Mavis had called him a dear when he was still a bachelor.

They ate their prawn cocktails. The voices became louder. For a moment Grania's eye was held by the man who had said, at first, that she didn't remember him. A look was exchanged and persisted for a moment. Did he suspect that she had learned already of his intention to live in the Prendergasts' house? Would he have told her himself if they hadn't been interrupted by Desmond?

"Hetty was a nice old thing," Angela said. "I feel I'd like to attend her funeral myself."

Grania glanced again in the direction of the stranger. Tom Crosbie began to talk about a court case that was causing interest. Oliver Duddy got up and ambled out of the dining room, and Desmond moved to where he'd been sitting so that he was next to his wife again. The waitresses were collecting the prawn-cocktail glasses.

"Oliver's being a bore about this Aisling business," Desmond said.

"Desmond, did Prendergast mention being married now?"

He looked down the table, and across it. He shook his head. "He hasn't the look of being married. Another thing is, I have a feeling he's called something else."

"Angela says she's going to the funeral."

One of the waitresses brought round plates of grilled salmon, the other offered vegetables. Oliver Duddy returned with a glass of something he'd picked up in the bar — whiskey on ice, it looked like. He sat between Desmond and Una Carty-Carroll, not seeming to notice that it wasn't where he'd been sitting before.

Mavis's back was reflected in the Rhett Butler mirror, the V of her black dress plunging deeply down her spine. Her movements, and those of Billy MacGuinness next to her, danced over the features of Clark Gable. During a lull in the conversation, the sound of the television in the bar drifted in — the "Surprise! Surprise! Show" just beginning. Then a door was closed, and the sound abruptly ceased.

"He might suit Angela," Desmond said. "You never know."

That August afternoon Billy MacGuinness, who was a doctor, had been called away from the club — some complication with a confinement. "Damned woman," he'd grumbled unfeelingly, predicting an all-night job.

"Come back to the house, Francie," Grania had suggested when the tennis came to an end, and it was then that Desmond had noticed the young man attaching his tennis racquet to the crossbar of his bicycle and issued the same invitation. Desmond had said he'd drive him back to the Prendergasts' when they'd all had something to eat, and together they lifted his bicycle onto the boot of the car.

"I've something to confess," Francie had said in the kitchen, cutting the rinds off rashers of bacon, and Grania knew what it would be, because "I've something to confess" was a kind of joke among the wives, a time-honored way of announcing pregnancy.

"You're *not!*" Grania cried, disguising envy. "Oh, Francie, how grand!"

Desmond brought them drinks, but Francie didn't tell him, as Grania had guessed she wouldn't.

"February," Francie said. "Billy says it should be February."

Billy telephoned while they were still in the kitchen, guessing where Francie was when there'd been no reply from his own number. He'd be late, as he'd predicted.

"Francie's pregnant," Grania told Desmond while Francie was still on the phone. "Don't tell her I said."

In the sitting room they had a few more drinks while in the kitchen the bacon cooked on a glimmer of heat. All of them were still in their tennis clothes, and nobody was in a hurry. Francie wasn't, because of the empty evening in front of her. Grania and Desmond weren't, because they'd nothing to do that evening. The young man who was staying with the Prendergasts was like a schoolboy prolonging his leave. The sipping of their gin, the idle conversation — the young man being told about the town and the tennis club, told who Angela was, and which the Duddys were: all of it took on the pleasurable feeling of a party happening by chance. Desmond picked up the telephone and rang the Crosbies, but Trish said they wouldn't be able to get a babysitter or else of course they'd come over, love to. Eventually Desmond beat up eggs to scramble, and Grania fried potato cakes and soda bread. "We're none of us sober," Desmond said, offering a choice of white or red wine as they sat down to eat. Eartha Kitt sang "Just an Old-Fashioned Girl."

In the Rhett Butler Room, Grania heard the tune again. "And an old-fashioned millionaire," lisped the cool, sensuous voice, each emphasis strangely accented.

They'd danced to it among the furniture of the sitting room, Francie and the young man mostly, she and Desmond. "I'm sorry, darling," Desmond whispered, but she shook her head, refusing to concede that blame came into it. If it did, she might as well say she was sorry herself.

"I have to get back," Francie said. "Cook something for Billy."

Desmond said he'd drop her off on his way to the Prendergasts', but then he changed the record to "Love Grows," and fell asleep as soon as the music began.

Francie didn't want a lift. She wanted to walk, because the air would do her good. "D'you trust me?" Grania asked the young man, and he laughed and said he'd have to because he didn't have a lamp on his bicycle. She'd hardly spoken to him, had been less aware of him than of Desmond's apparent liking of him. With strangers Desmond was often like that.

"What do you do?" she asked in the car, suddenly shy in spite of all the gin and wine there'd been. He'd held her rather close when he danced with her, but she'd noticed he held Francie close, too. Francie had kissed him goodbye.

"Well, actually I've been working in a pub," he said. "Before that I made toast in the Royal Hotel in Bournemouth."

She drove slowly, with extreme caution through the narrow streets of the town. The public houses were closing; gaggles of men loitered near each, smoking or just standing. Youths thronged the pavement outside the Palm Grove fish-and-chip shop. Beyond the last of its lampposts the town straggled away to nothing; solitary cottages and bungalows gave way to fields.

"I haven't been to this house before," Grania said after a silence. Her companion had vouchsafed no further information about himself beyond the reference to a pub and making toast in Bournemouth.

"They'll be in bed," he said now. "They go to bed at nine."

The headlights picked out trunks of trees on the avenue, then urns, and steps leading up to a hall door. White wooden shutters flanked the downstairs windows, the paint peeling, as it was on the iron balustrade of the steps. All of it was swiftly there, then lost: the car lights isolated a rose bed and a seat on a lawn. "I won't be a minute unshackling this bike," he said.

She turned the lights off. The last of the August day hadn't quite gone; a warm duskiness was scented with honeysuckle she could not see when she stepped out of the car. "You've been awfully good to me," he said, unknotting the strings that held the bicycle in place. "You and Desmond."

In the Rhett Butler Room, now rowdy with laughter and raised voices, she didn't want to look at him again, and yet she couldn't help herself: waiting for her were the unblinking eyes, the hair brushed back from the sallow forehead, the high cheekbones. Angela would stand at the graveside and afterward would offer him sympathy. Quilty would be there, Hazel wouldn't bother. "I'd say we all need a drink": Grania could imagine Angela saying that, including Desmond in the invitation, gathering the three men around her.

In the dark the bicycle had been wheeled away and propped against the steps.

"Come in for a minute," he'd said, and she'd begun to protest that it was late, even though it wasn't. "Oh, don't be silly," he'd said.

She remembered, in the garish hotel dining room, the flash of his smile in the gloom, and how she'd felt his unblinking eyes caressing her. He reached out for her hand, and in a moment they were in a hall, the electric light turned on, a grandfather clock ticking at the bottom of the stairs. There was a hallstand, and square cream and terra-cotta tiles, sepia engravings framed in oak, fish in glass cases. "I shall offer you a nightcap," he whispered, leading her into a flagged passage and then into a cavernous kitchen. "Tullamore Dew is what they have," he murmured. "Give every man his dew."

She knew what he intended. She'd known it before they'd turned in at the avenue gates; she'd felt it in the car between them. He poured their drinks and then he kissed her, taking her into his arms as though that were simply a variation of their dancing together. "Dearest," he whispered, surprising her: she hadn't guessed that he intended all the delicacy of endearments.

Did she, before the car turned in at the avenue gates, decide herself what was to happen? Or was it later, even while still protesting that it was late? Or when he reached up to the high shelf of the dresser for the bottle? At some point she had said to herself: "I am going to do this." She knew she had, because the words still echoed. "How extraordinary!" he murmured in the kitchen, all his talk as soft as that now. "How extraordinary to find you at a tennis club in Ireland!" Her own arms held him to her; yet for some reason she didn't want to see his face, not that she found it unattractive.

The empty glasses laid down on the kitchen table, stairs without a carpet, a chest of drawers on a landing, towels in a pile on a chair, the door of his bedroom closing behind them: remembered images were like details from a dream. For a moment the light went on in his room: a pink china jug stood in a basin on a washstand, there was a wardrobe, a cigarette packet on the dressing table, the shirt and trousers he'd changed from into his tennis clothes were thrown onto the floor. Then the light was extinguished and again he embraced her, his fingers already unbuttoning her tennis dress, which no one but Desmond had ever done in that particular way. Before her marriage she'd been kissed, twice, by Billy MacGuinness, and once by a boy who'd left the neighborhood and gone to Canada. As all the tennis-club wives were when they married, she'd been a virgin. "Oh God, Grania!" she heard him whispering, and her thoughts became worries when she lay, naked, on the covers of his bed. Her father's face was vivid in her mind, disposing of her with distaste. "No, don't do that, dear," her mother used to say, clucking with her tongue when Grania picked a scab on her knee or made a pattern on the raked gravel with a stick.

In the kitchen they ate raspberries and cream. She asked him again about himself, but he hardly responded, questioning her instead and successfully extracting answers. The raspberries were delicious; he put a punnet on the passenger seat in the car. They were for Desmond, but he didn't say so. "Don't feel awkward," he said. "I'm going back on Monday."

A hare ran in front of the car on the avenue, bewildered by the lights. People would guess, she thought; they would see a solitary shadow in the car and they would know. It did not occur to her that if her expedition to the Prendergasts' house had been as innocent as its original purpose, the people who observed her return would still have seen what they saw now. In fact the streets were quite deserted when she came to them.

"God, I'm sorry," Desmond said, sitting up on the sofa, his white clothes rumpled, the texture of a cushion cover on his cheek, his hair untidy. She smiled, not trusting herself to speak or even to laugh, as in other circumstances she might have. She put the raspberries in the refrigerator and had a bath.

In the Rhett Butler Room they began to change places in the usual way, after the Black Forest gâteau. She sat beside Francie and Mavis. "Good for Aisling," Francie insisted when Mavis described the chartered accountant; he did not seem old at all.

"I'll have it out with Oliver when we get back," Mavis said. "There's no chance whatsoever she's been naughty. I can assure you I'd be the first to know." They lowered their voices to remark on Angela's interest in the stranger. "The house would suit her rightly," Mavis said.

All the rooms would be done up. The slatted shutters that flanked the windows would be repainted, and the balustrade by the steps. There'd be new curtains and carpets; a gardener would be employed. Angela had never cared for the house her well-to-do husband had built her, and since his death had made no secret of the fact.

"I'll never forget that night, Grania." Francie giggled, embarrassedly groping for a cigarette. "Dancing with your man and Desmond going to sleep. Wasn't it the same night I told you Maureen was on the way?"

"Yes, it was."

The three woman talked of other matters. That week in the town an elderly clerk had been accused of embezzlement. Mavis observed that the surveyor from the waterworks was limbering up to propose to Una Carty-Carroll. "And doesn't she know it!" Francie said. Grania laughed.

Sometimes she'd wondered if he was still working in a pub and told herself that of course he wouldn't be, that he'd have married and settled down ages ago. But when she saw him tonight she'd guessed immediately that he hadn't. She wasn't surprised when Desmond had said he was on his uppers. "I am going to do this": the echo of her resolve came back to her as she sat there. "I am going to do this because I want a child."

"God, I'm exhausted," Mavis said. "Is it age or what?"

"Oh, it's age, it's age," Francie sighed, stubbing out her cigarette. "Damn things," she muttered.

Mavis reached for the packet and flicked it across the table. "Present for you, Kevy," she said, but Francie pleaded with her eyes and he flicked it back again. Grania smiled, because they'd have noticed if she didn't.

In the intervening years he would never have wondered about a child being born. But if Angela married him he would think about it; being close by would cause him to. He would wonder, and in the middle of a night, while he lay beside Angela in bed, it would be borne in upon him that Desmond and Grania had one child only. Grania considered that: the untidiness of someone else's knowing, her secret shared. There'd been perpetually — every instant of the day, it sometimes seemed — the longing to share: with Desmond and with her friends, with the child that had been born. But this was different.

The evening came to an end. Cars were started in the yard of the hotel; there were warnings of ice on the roads. "Good night, Grania," the man who'd come for the funeral said. She buckled herself into her seat belt. Desmond backed and then crawled forward into West Main Street. "You're quiet," he said, and immediately she began to talk about the possibility of Una Carty-Carroll's being proposed to, in case he connected her silence with the presence of the stranger. "As a matter of fact," he said when that subject was exhausted, "I met that fellow of Aisling's once. He's only thirty-five." She opened the garage door, and he drove the car in. The air was refreshingly cold, sharper than it had been in the yard of the hotel.

They locked their house. Grania put things ready for the morning. It was a relief that a babysitter was no longer necessary, that she didn't have to wait with just a trace of anxiety while Desmond drove someone home. He'd gone upstairs, and she knew that he'd done so in order to press open Judith's door and glance in at her while she slept. Whenever they came in at night he did that.

At the sink Grania poured glasses of water for him and for herself, and carried them upstairs. When she had placed them on either side of their bed she, too, went to look in at her daughter — a mass of brown hair untidy on the pillow, eyes lightly closed.

"I might play golf tomorrow," Desmond said, settling his trousers into his electric press. Almost as soon as he'd clambered into bed he fell asleep. She switched out his bedside light and went downstairs.

Alone in the kitchen, sitting over a cup of tea, she returned again to the August Saturday. Two of Trish's children had already been born then, and two of Mavis's, and Hazel's first. "I wouldn't be surprised," Billy MacGuinness had said, "if Angela doesn't drop this one in a deck chair." Mary Ann Haddon had just started her second. Older children were sitting on the clubhouse steps.

Grania forced her thoughts through all the rest of it, through the party that had happened by chance, the headlights picking out the rose bed. She savored easily the solitude she had disguised during the years that had passed since then, the secret that had seemed so safe. In the quiet kitchen, when she had been over this familiar ground, she felt herself again possessed by the confusion that had come like fog when she'd seen tonight the father of her child. Then slowly it lifted: she was incapable of regret.

WILLIAM TREVOR

The News from Ireland

Poor Irish Protestants is what the Fogartys are: butler and cook. They have church connections, and conversing with Miss Fogarty people are occasionally left with the impression that their father was a rural dean who suffered some misfortune: in fact he was a sexton. Fogarty is the younger and the smaller of the pair, brought up by Miss Fogarty, their mother dying young. His life was saved by his sister's nursing the time he caught scarlatina, when he was only eight.

Dapper in his butler's clothes, a slight and unimposing man with a hazelnut face, Fogarty is at present fascinated by the newly arrived governess: Anna Maria Heddoe, from somewhere in England, a young woman of principle and sensibility, stranger and visitor to Ireland. Fogarty is an educated man, and thinks of other visitors there have been: the Celts, whose ramshackle gipsy empire expired in this same land-scape, St Patrick with his holy shamrock, the outrageous Vikings preceding the wily Normans, the adventurers of the Virgin Queen. His present employers arrived here also, eight years ago, in 1839. The Pulvertafts of Ipswich, as Fogarty thinks of them, and wishes they had not bothered to make the journey after old Hugh Pulvertaft died. House and estate fell away under the old man, and in Fogarty's opinion it is a pity the process didn't continue until everything was driven back into the clay it came from. Instead of which along had come the Pulvertafts of Ipswich, taking on more staff, clearing the brambles from the garden in their endeavour to make the place what it had been in the past, long before the old man's time. The Pulvertafts of Ipswich belong here now. They make allowances for the natives, they come to terms, they learn to live with things. Fogarty has watched surprise and dismay fade from their faces. He has watched these people becoming important locally, and calling the place they have come to 'home'. Serving them in the dining-room, holding for them a plate of chops or hurrying to them a gravy dish, he wishes he might speak the truth as it appears to him: that their fresh, decent blood is the blood of the invader though they are not themselves invaders, that they perpetrate theft without being thieves. He does not dislike the Pulvertafts of Ipswich, he has nothing against them beyond the fact that they did not stay where they were. He and his sister might alone have attended the mouldering of the place, urging it back to the clay.

The governess is interesting to Fogarty because she is another of the strangers whom the new Pulvertafts have trailed behind them in their advent. Such visitors, in the present and in the past, obsess the butler. He observes Miss Heddoe daily; he studies her closely and from a distance, but he does not reveal his obsession to his sister, who would consider it peculiar. He carries Miss Heddoe's meals to her room when normally this duty would be Cready's or Brigid's; he reads the letters she receives, and the diary she intermittently keeps.

October 15th, 1847. I look out of the window of my attic room, and in the early morning the men are already labouring on the road that is to encircle the estate. The estate manager, the one-armed Mr Erskine, oversees them from his horse. Mr Pulvertaft rides up, gesturing about some immediate necessity — how a particular shrub must be avoided, so his gestures suggest, or where best to construct a bridge. The estate manager listens and assents, his men do not cease in their work. Beyond the trees, beyond the high stone walls of the estate, women and children die of the hunger that God has seen fit to visit upon them. In my prayers I ask for mercy.

October 17th, 1847. Fogarty came in with my dinner on a tray and said that the marks of the stigmata had been discovered on a child.

'Is the child alive?' I demanded when he returned a half-hour later for the tray.

'Oh yes, miss. No doubt on that. The living child was brought to Father Horan.'

I was amazed but he seemed hardly surprised. I questioned him but he was vague; and the conversation continuing because he lingered, I told him the Legend of the True Cross, with which he was unfamiliar. He was delighted to hear of its elaborations, and said he would recount these in the kitchen. The stigmata on the child have been revealed on feet and hands only, but the priest has said that other parts of the body must be watched. The priest has cautiously given an opinion: that so clearly marked a stigma has never before been known in Ireland. The people consider it a miracle, a sign from God in these distressful times.

October 20th, 1847. I am not happy here. I do not understand this household, neither the family nor the servants. This is the middle of my third week, yet I am still in all ways at a loss. Yesterday, in the afternoon, I was for the first time summoned to the drawing-room to hear Adelaide play her pieces, and George Arthur's lessons being over for the day he sat by me, as naturally he should. Charlotte and her mother occupied the sofa, Emily a chair in a recess. Mr Pulvertaft stood toasting his back at the fire, his riding-crop tapping time on the side of his polished boot. They made a handsome family picture — Emily beautiful, Charlotte petite and pretty, the plump motherliness of Mrs Pulvertaft, her husband's ruddy presence. I could not see George Arthur's features, for he was a little in front of me, but I knew them well from the hours I have surveyed them across our lessons-table. He is sharp-faced, and dark like all the family except Mrs Pulvertaft, whose hair I would guess was red before becoming grey. Only Adelaide, bespectacled and seeming heavy for her age, does not share the family's gift of grace. Poor Adelaide is cumbersome; her movements are awkward at the piano and she really plays it most inelegantly.

Yet in the drawing-room no frown or wince betrayed the listeners' ennui. As though engrossed in a performance given by a fine musician, Mr Pulvertaft slightly raised and dropped his riding-crop, as he might a baton; similarly expressing absorption, his wife's lips were parted, the hurry and worry of her nature laid aside, her little eyes delighted. And Emily and Charlotte sat as girls more graciously endowed than a plain sister should, neither pouting nor otherwise recoiling from the halting cacophony. I, too — I hope successfully — forced delight into an expression that constantly sought to betray me, while surreptitiously examining my surroundings. (I cannot be certain of what passed, or did not pass, over George Arthur's features: in the nursery, certainly, he is not slow to display displeasure.)

The drawing-room is lofty and more than usually spacious, with pleasant recesses, and French windows curving along a single wall. Two smaller windows flank the fire-place, which is white marble that reflects, both in colour and in the pattern of its carving, the white plasterwork of the ceiling. Walls are of an apricot shade, crowded with landscape scenes and portraits of the Pulvertafts who belong to the past. Silks and velvets are mainly green; escritoires and occasional tables are cluttered with ornaments and porcelain pieces — too many for my own taste but these are family heirlooms which it would be impolite to hide away. So Mrs Pulvertaft has explained, for the same degree of overcrowding obtains in the hall and dining-room, and on the day of my arrival she remarked upon it.

'*Most* charmingly rendered,' her husband pronounced when the music ceased. 'What fingers Adelaide is blessed with!'

Hands in the drawing-room were delicately clapped. Mr Pulvertaft applauded with his riding-crop. I pursed my lips at the back of George Arthur's head, for he was perhaps a little rumbustious in his response.

'Is not Adelaide talented, Miss Heddoe?' Mrs Pulvertaft suggested.

'Indeed, ma'am.'

Two maids, Cready and Brigid, brought in tea. I rose to go, imagining my visit to the drawing-room must surely now be concluded. But Mrs Pulvertaft begged me to remain.

'We must get to know you, Miss Heddoe,' she insisted in her bustling manner. (It is from his mother, I believe, that George Arthur inherits his occasional boisterousness). 'And you,' she added, 'us.'

I felt, to tell the truth, that I knew the Pulvertafts fairly well already. I was not long here before I observed that families and events are often seen historically in Ireland — more so, for some reason, than in England. It surprised me when Mrs Pulvertaft went into details soon after I arrived, informing me that on the death of a distant relative Mr Pulvertaft had found himself the inheritor of this overseas estate. Though at first he had apparently resisted the move to another country, he ended by feeling it his bounden duty to accept the responsibility. 'It was a change of circumstances for us, I can tell you that,' Mrs Pulvertaft confessed. 'But had we remained in Ipswich these many acres would have continued to lose heart. There have been Pulvertafts here, you know, since Queen Elizabeth first granted them the land.' I thought, but did not remark, that when Mr Pulvertaft first looked upon drawings of the house and gardens his unexpected inheritance must have seemed like a gift from heaven, which in a sense it was, for the distant relative had been by all accounts a good man.

'Much undergrowth has yet to be cleared and burnt,' Mr Pulvertaft was saying now, with reference to the estate road that was being built. 'The merry fires along the route will continue for a while to come. Next, stones must be chipped and laid, and by the lakeside the ground raised and strengthened. Here and there we must have ornamental seats.'

Cake was offered to us by Cready and by Brigid. It was not my place in the drawing-room to check the manners of George Arthur, but they do leave much to be desired. Old Miss Larvey, who was my predecessor and governess to all four children, had clearly become slack before her death. I smiled a little at George Arthur, and was unable to resist moving my fingers slightly in his direction, a gesture to indicate that a more delicate consuming of the cake would not be amiss. He pretended, mischievously, not to notice.

'Will the road go round Bright Purple Hill?' Emily enquired. 'It would be beautiful if it did.'

It could be made to do so, her father agreed. Yes, certainly it could go round the northern slopes at least. He would speak to Erskine.

'Now, what could be nicer,' he resumed, 'than a picnic of lunch by the lake, then a drive through the silver birches, another pause by the abbey, continuing by the river for a mile, and home by Bright Purple Hill? This road, Miss Heddoe, has become my pride.'

I smiled and nodded, acknowledging this attention in silence. I knew that there was more to the road than that: its construction was an act of charity, a way of employing the men for miles around, since the failure of their potato crops had again reduced them to poverty and idleness. In years to come the road would stand as a memorial to this awful time, and Mr Pulvertaft's magnanimity would be recalled with gratitude.

'Might copper beech trees mark the route?' suggested Adelaide, her dumpling countenance freshened by the excitement this thought induced. Her eyes bulged behind her spectacles and I noticed that her mother, in glancing at her, resisted the impulse to sigh.

'Beech trees indeed! Quite splendid!' enthused Mr Pulvertaft. 'And in future Pulvertaft generations they shall arch a roof, shading our road when need be. Yes, indeed there must be copper beech trees.'

The maids had left the drawing-room and returned now with lamps. They fastened the shutters and drew the curtains over. The velvets and silks changed colour in the lamplight, the faces of the portraits became as they truly were, the faces of ghosts.

A silence gathered after the talk of beech trees, and I found myself surprised at no one mentioning the wonder Fogarty had told me of, the marks of Christ on a peasant child. It seemed so strange and so remarkable, an occurrence of such import and magnitude, that I would hardly have believed it possible that any conversation could take place in the house without some astonished reference to it. Yet none had been made, and the faces and the voices in the drawing-room seemed as untouched by this visitation of the miraculous as they had been by Adelaide's labouring on the piano. In the silence I excused myself and left, taking George Arthur with me, for my time to do so had come.

October 23rd, 1847. I am homesick, I make no bones about it. I cannot help dwelling on all that I have left behind, on familiar sounds and places. First thing when I awake I still imagine I am in England: reality comes most harshly then.

While I write, Emily and George Arthur are conversing in a corner of the nursery. She has come here, as she does from time to time, to persuade him against a military career. I wish she would not do so in this manner, wandering in and standing by the window to await the end of a lesson. It is distracting for George Arthur, and after all this is my domain.

'What I mean, George Arthur, is that it is an uncomfortable life in a general sort of way.'

'Captain Roche does not seem uncomfortable. When you look at him he doesn't give that impression in the least.'

'Captain Roche hasn't lived in a barracks in India. That leaves a mark, so people say.'

'I should not mind a barracks. And India I should love.'

'I doubt it, actually. Flies carry disease in India, the water you drink is putrid. And you would mind a barracks because they're rough and ready places.'

'You'd drink something else if the water was putrid. You'd keep well away from the flies.'

'You cannot in India. No, George Arthur, I assure you you enjoy your creature comforts. You'd find the uniform rough on your skin and the food unappetising. Besides, you have a family duty here.'

The nursery is a long, low-ceilinged room, with a fire at one end, close to which I sit as I write, for the weather has turned bitter. The big, square lessons-table occupies the centre of the room, and when Fogarty brings my tray he places it on the smaller table at which I'm writing now. There are pictures on the walls which I must say I find drab: one, in shades of brown, of St George and the Dragon; another of a tower; others of farmyard scenes. The nursery's two armchairs, occupied now by George Arthur and Emily, are at the other end with a rug between them. The floor is otherwise of polished board.

'Well, the truth is, George Arthur, I cannot bear the thought of your being killed.'

With that, Emily left the nursery. She smiled in her graceful manner at me, her head a little to one side, her dark, coiled hair gleaming for a moment in a shaft of afternoon sun. I had not thought a governess's position was difficult in a household, but somehow I am finding it so. I belong neither with the family nor the servants. Fogarty, in spite of calling me 'miss', addresses me more casually than he does the Pulvertafts; his sister is scarcely civil.

'Do they eat their babies, like in the South Seas?' George Arthur startled me by asking. He had crossed to where I sat and in a manner reminiscent of his father stood with his back to the fire, thereby blocking its warmth from me.

'Do who eat their babies, George Arthur?'

'The poor people.'

'Of course they don't.'

'But they are hungry. They have been hungry for ever so long. My mother and sisters give out soup at the back gate-lodge.'

'Hungry people do not eat their babies. And I think, you know, it's enemies, not babies, who are eaten in the South Seas.'

'But suppose a family's baby *did* die and suppose the family was hungry —'

'No, George Arthur, you must not talk like that.'

'Fogarty says he would not be surprised.'

'Well, she has settled down, I think,' Mrs Pulvertaft remarks to her husband in their bedroom, and when he asks her whom she refers to she says the governess.

'Pleasant enough, she seems,' he replies. 'I do prefer, you know, an English governess.'

'Oh yes, indeed.'

George Arthur's sisters have developed no thoughts about Miss Heddoe. They neither like nor dislike her; they do not know her; their days of assessing governesses are over.

But George Arthur's aren't. She is not as pretty as Emily or Charlotte, George Arthur considers, and she is very serious. When she smiles her smile is serious. The way she eats her food is serious, carefully cutting everything, carefully and slowly chewing. Often he comes into the nursery to find her eating from the tray that Fogarty carries up the back staircase for her, sitting all alone on one side of the fire-place, seeming very serious indeed. Miss Larvey had been different somehow, although she'd eaten her meals in much the same position, seated at the very same table, by the fire. Miss Larvey was untidy, her grey hair often working loose from its coils, her whole face untidy sometimes, her tray untidily left.

'Now it is transcription time,' Miss Heddoe says, interrupting all these reflections. 'Carefully and slowly, please.'

Fogarty thinks about the governess, but hides such thoughts from his sister. Miss Heddoe will surely make a scene, exclaiming and protesting, saying to the Pulvertafts all the things a butler cannot. She will stand in the drawing-room or the hall, smacking out the truth at them, putting in a nutshell all that must be said. She will bring up the matter of the stigmata found on the child, and the useless folly of the road, and the wisdom of old Hugh Pulvertaft. She will be the voice of reason. Fogarty dwells upon these thoughts while conversing with his sister, adept at dividing his mind. All his faith is in the governess.

'Declare to God,' remarks Miss Fogarty, 'Brigid'll be the death of me. Did you ever know a stupider girl?"

'There was a girl we had once who was stupider," Fogarty replied. 'Fidelma was she called?'

They sit at the wide wooden table that is the pivot of kitchen activities. The preparation of food, the polishing of brass and silver, the stacking of dishes, the disposal of remains, the eating and drinking, all card-playing and ironing, all cutting out of patterns and cloth, the trimming of lamps: the table has as many uses as the people of the kitchen can devise. Tears have soaked into its grain, and blood from meat and accidents; the grease of generations polishes it, not quite scrubbed out by the efforts made, twice every day, with soap and water.

The Fogartys sit with their chairs turned a little away from the table, so that they partly face the range and in anticipation of the benefit they will shortly receive from the glow of dampened slack. It is their early evening pose, daily the same from October to May. In summer the sunlight penetrates to the kitchen in a way that at first seems alien but later is welcomed. It spreads over the surface of the table, drying it out. It warms the Fogartys, who move their chairs to catch its rays when they rest in the early evening.

'You would not credit,' remarks Miss Fogarty, 'that Brigid has been three years in this kitchen. More like three seconds.'

'There are some that are untrainable.' His teeth are less well preserved than his sister's. She is the thinner of the two, razorlike in face and figure.

'I said at the time I would prefer a man. A man is more trainable in my opinion. A man would be more use to yourself.'

'Ah, Cready knows the dining-room by now. I wouldn't want a change made there.'

'It's Cready we have to thank for Brigid. Wasn't it Cready who had you black-guarded until you took her on?'

'We had to take someone. To give Cready her due she said we'd find her slow.'

'I'll tell you this: Cready's no racehorse herself.'

'The slowness is in that family.'

'Whatever He did He forgot to put brains in them.'

'We live with His mistakes.'

Miss Fogarty frowns. She does not care for that remark. Her brother is sometimes indiscreet in his speech. It is his nature, it is part of his cleverness; but whenever she feels uneasy she draws his attention to the source of her uneasiness, as she does now. It is a dangerous remark, she says, better it had not been made.

Fogarty nods, knowing the nod will soothe her. He has no wish to have her flurried.

'The road is going great guns,' he says, deeming a change of subject wise. 'They were on about it in the dining-room.'

'Did they mention the ground-rice pudding?'

'They ate it. Isn't it extraordinary, a road that goes round in a circle, not leading anywhere?'

'Heddoe left her ground rice. A pudding's good enough for the dining-room but not for Madam.'

'Was there an egg in it? Her stomach can't accept eggs.'

'Don't I know the woman can't take eggs? Isn't she on about it the entire time? There were four good turkey eggs in that pudding, and what harm did a turkey egg do anyone? Did eggs harm Larvey?'

'Oh true enough, Larvey ate anything. If you'd took a gate off its hinges she'd have ate it while you'd wink.'

'Larvey was a saint from heaven.'

Again Fogarty nods. In his wish not to cause flurry in his sister he refrains from saying that once upon a time Miss Larvey had been condemned as roundly as Miss Heddoe is now. When she'd been cold in her room she'd sent down to the kitchen for hot-water jars, a request that had not been popular. But when she died, as if to compensate for all this troublesomeness, Miss Larvey left the Fogartys a remembrance in her will.

'A while back I told Heddoe about that child. To see what she'd say for herself.'

Miss Fogarty's peaked face registers interest. Her eyes have narrowed into the slits that all his life have reminded Fogarty of cracks in a plate or a teacup.

'And what did the woman say?'

'She was struck silent, then she asked me questions. After that she told me an extraordinary thing: the Legend of the True Cross.'

As Fogarty speaks, the two maids enter the kitchen. Miss Fogarty regards them with asperity, telling Brigid she looks disgraceful and Cready that her cap is dirty. 'Get down to your work,' she snappishly commands. 'Brigid, push that kettle over the heat and stir a saucepan of milk for me.'

She is badly out of sorts because of Heddoe and the ground rice, Fogarty says to himself, and thinks to ease the atmosphere by relating the legend the governess has told him.

'Listen to me, girls,' he says, 'while I tell you the Legend of the True Cross.'

Cready, who is not a girl, appreciates the euphemism and displays appropriate pleasure as she sets to at the sink, washing parsnips. She is a woman of sixty-one, carelessly stout. Brigid, distantly related to her and thirty or so years younger, is of the same proportions.

'The Legend of the True Cross,' says Fogarty, 'has to do with a seed falling into Adam's mouth, some say his ear. It lay there until he died, and when the body decomposed a tree grew from the seed, which in time was felled to give timber for the beams of a bridge.'

'Well, I never heard that,' exclaims Cready in a loud, shrill voice, so fascinated by the revelation that she cannot continue with the parsnips.

'The Queen of Sheba crossed that bridge in her majesty. Later — well, you can guess — the cross to which Our Lord was fastened was constructed of those very beams.'

'Is it true, Mr Fogarty?' cries Cready, her voice becoming still shriller in her excitement, her mouth hanging open.

'Control yourself, Cready,' Miss Fogarty admonishes her. 'You look ridiculous.'

'It's only I was never told it before, miss. I never knew the Cross grew out of Adam's ear. Did ever you hear it, Brigid?'

'I did not.'

'It's a legend,' Fogarty explains. 'It illustrates the truth. It does not tell it, Miss Fogarty and myself would say. Your own religion might take it differently.'

'Don't you live and learn?' says Cready.

There is a silence for some moments in the kitchen. Then Brigid, stirring the saucepan of milk on the range as Miss Fogarty has instructed her, says:

'I wonder does Father Horan know that?'

'God, I'd say he would all right.' Cready wags her head, lending emphasis to this opinion. There isn't much relating to theological matters that eludes Father Horan, she says.

'Oh, right enough,' agrees Fogarty. 'The priests will run this country yet. If it's not one crowd it's another.' He explains to the maids that the Legend of the True Cross has come into the house by way of the governess. It is a typical thing, he says, that a Protestant English woman would pass the like of that on. Old Hugh wouldn't have considered it suitable; and the present Pulvertafts have been long enough away from England to consider it unsuitable also. He'd guess they have anyway; he'd consider that true.

Miss Fogarty, still idle in her chair by the range, nods her agreement. She states that, legend or not, she does not care for stuff like that. In lower tones, and privately to her brother, she says she is surprised that he repeated it.

'It's of interest to the girls,' he apologises. 'To tell the truth, you could have knocked me down when she told me in the nursery.'

'The boulders from the ridge may be used for walls and chipping?' enquires Mr Pulvertaft of his estate manager.

'It is a distance to carry boulders, sir.'

'So it is, but we must continue to occupy these men, Erskine. Time is standing still for them.'

'Yes, sir.'

The two men pace together on a lawn in front of the house, walking from one circular rosebed to the next, then turning and reversing the procedure. It is here that Mr Pulvertaft likes to discuss the estate with Erskine, strolling on the short grass in the mid-morning. When it rains or is too bitterly cold they converse instead in the great open porch of the house, both of them gazing out into the garden. The eyes of Mr Pulvertaft and Erskine never meet, as if by unspoken agreement. Mr Pulvertaft, though speaking warmly of Erskine's virtues, fears him; and Erskine does not trust his eye to meet his master's in case that conjunction, however brief, should reveal too much. Mr Pulvertaft has been a painless inheritor, in Erskine's view; his life has been without hardship, he takes too easily for granted the good fortune that came his way.

'The road,' he is saying now, seeming to Erskine to make his point for him, 'is our generation's contribution to the estate. You understand me, Erskine? A Pulvertaft planted Abbey Wood, another laid out these gardens. Swift came here, did you know that, Erskine? The Mad Dean assisted in the planning of all these lawns and shrubberies.'

'So you told me, sir.'

It is Erskine's left arm that is missing but he considers the loss as serious as if it had been his right. He is an Englishman, stoutly made and once of renowned strength, still in his middle age. His temper is short, his disposition unsentimental, his soldier's manner abrupt; nor is there, beneath that vigorous exterior, a gentler core. Leading nowhere, without a real purpose, the estate road is unnecessary and absurd, but he accepts his part in its creation. It is ill fortune that people have starved because a law of nature has failed them, it is ill fortune that he has lost a limb and seen a military career destroyed: all that must be accepted also. To be the manager of an estate of such size and importance is hardly recompense for the glories that might have been. He has ended up in a country that is not his own, employing men whose speech he at first found difficult to understand, collecting rents from tenants he does not trust, as he feels he might trust the people of Worcestershire or Durham. The Pulvertaft family — with the exception of Mr Pulvertaft himself — rarely seek to hold with him any kind of conversation beyond the formalities of greeting and leave-taking. Stoically he occupies his position, ashamed because he is a one-armed man, yet never indulging in melancholy, for this he would condemn as weakness.

'There is something concerning the men, sir.'

'Poor fellows, there is indeed.'

'Something other, sir. They have turned ungrateful, sir.'

'Ungrateful?'

'As well to keep an eye open for disaffection, sir.'

'Good God, those men are hardly fit for that.'

'They bite the hand that feeds them, sir. They're reared on it.'

He speaks in a matter-of-fact voice. It is the truth as he recognises it; he sees no point in dissembling for politeness' sake. He watches while Mr Pulvertaft nods his reluctant agreement. He does not need to remind himself that this is a landowner who would have his estate a realm of heaven, who would have his family and his servants, his tenants and all who work for him, angels of goodness. This is a landowner who expects his own generosity of spirit to beget such generosity in others, his unstinted patronage to find a reflection in unstinted gratitude. But reality, as Erskine daily experiences, keeps shattering the dream, and may shatter it irrevocably in the end.

They speak of other matters, of immediate practicalities. Expert and informed on all the subjects raised, Erskine gives the conversation only part of his attention, devoting the greater part to the recently arrived governess. He has examined her in church on the four occasions there have been since she joined the household. Twenty-five or -six years old, he reckons, not pretty yet not as plain as the plain one among the Pulvertaft girls. Hair too severely done, features too nervous, clothes too dowdy; but all that might be altered. The hands that hold the hymn book open before her are pale as marble, the fingers slender; the lips that open and close have a hint of voluptuousness kept in check; the breast that rises and falls has caused him, once or twice, briefly to close his eyes. He would marry her if she would have him, and why should she not, despite the absence of an arm? As the estate manager's wife she would have a more significant life than as a governess for ever.

'Well, I must not detain you longer,' Mr Pulvertaft says. 'The men are simple people, remember, rough in their ways. They may find gratitude difficult and, you know, I do not expect it. I only wish to do what can be done.'

Erskine, who intends to permit no nonsense, does not say so. He strides off to where his horse is tethered in the paddocks, wondering again about the governess.

Stout and round, Mrs Pulvertaft lies on her bed with her eyes closed. She feels a familiar discomfort low down in her stomach, on the left side, a touch of indigestion. It is very slight, something she has become used to, arriving as it does every day in the afternoon and then going away.

Charlotte will accept Captain Roche; Adelaide will not marry; Emily wishes to travel. Perhaps if she travels she will meet someone suitable; she is most particular. Mrs Pulvertaft cannot understand her eldest daughter's desire to visit France and Austria and Italy. They are dangerous places, where war is waged when offense is taken. Only England is not like that: dear, safe, uncomplicated England, thinks Mrs Pulvertaft, and for a moment is nostalgic.

The afternoon discomfort departs from her stomach, but she does not notice because gradually it has become scarcely anything at all. George Arthur must learn the ways of the estate so that he can sensibly inherit when his own time comes. Emily is right: it would be far better if he did not seek a commission. After all, except to satisfy his romantic inclination, there is no need.

Mrs Pulvertaft sighs. She hopes Charlotte will be sensible. An officer's wife commands a considerable position when allied with means, and she has been assured that Captain Roche's family, established for generations in Meath, leave nothing whatsoever to be desired socially. It is most unlikely that Charlotte will be silly since everything between her and Captain Roche appears to be going swimmingly, but then you never know: girls, being girls, are naturally inexperienced.

Mrs Pulvertaft dozes, and wakes a moment later. The faces of the women who beg on Sundays have haunted a brief dream. She has heard the chiming of the church bell and in some confused way the Reverend Poole's cherub face was among the women's, his surplice flapping in the wind. She stepped from the carriage and went towards the church. 'Give something to the beggars,' her husband's voice commanded, as it does every Sunday while the bell still rings. The bell ceases only when the family are in their pew, with Mr Erskine in the Pulvertaft pew behind them and the Fogartys and Miss Heddoe in the estate pew in the south transept.

It is nobody's fault, Mrs Pulvertaft reflects, that for the second season the potatoes have rotted in the ground. No one can be blamed. It is a horror that so many families have died, that so many bloated, poisoned bodies are piled into the shared graves. But what more can be done than is already being done? Soup is given away in the yard of the gate-lodge; the estate road gives work; the Distress Board is greatly pleased. Just and sensible laws prevent the wholesale distribution of corn, for to flood the country with corn would have consequences as disastrous as the hunger itself: that has been explained to her. Every Sunday, led by the Reverend Poole, they repeat the prayer that takes precedence over all others prayers: that God's love should extend to the hungry at this time, that His wrath may be lifted.

Again Mrs Pulvertaft drifts into a doze. She dreams that she runs through unfamiliar landscape, although she has not run anywhere for many years. There are sand dunes and a flat expanse which is empty, except for tiny white shells, crackling beneath her feet. She seems to be naked, which is alarming, and worries her in her dream. Then everything changes and she is in the drawing-room, listening to Adelaide playing her pieces. Tea is brought in, and there is ordinary conversation.

Emily, alone, walks among the abbey ruins on the lake-shore. It is her favourite place. She imagines the chanting of the monks once upon a time and the simple life they led, transcribing Latin and worshipping God. They built where the landscape was beautiful; their view of Bright Purple Hill had been perfect.

There is a stillness among the ruins, the air is mild for late October. The monks would have fished from the shore, they would have cultivated a garden and induced bees to make honey for them. For many generations they would have buried their dead here, but their graveyards have been lost in the time that has passed.

Evening sun bronzes the heathery purple of the hill. In the spring, Emily reflects, she will begin her journeys. She will stay with her Aunt Margery in Bath and her Aunt Tabby in Ipswich. Already she has persuaded her Aunt Margery that it would be beneficial to both of them to visit Florence, and Vienna and Paris. She has persuaded her father that the expense of all the journeys would be money profitably spent, an education that would extend the education he has expended money on already. Emily believes this to be true; she is not prevaricating. She believes that after she has seen again the architecture of England — which she can scarcely remember — and visited the great cities of Europe some anxious spirit within her will be assuaged. She will return to Ireland and accept a husband, as Charlotte is about to do; or not accept a husband and be content to live her life in her brother's house, as Adelaide's fate seems certainly to be. She will bear children; or walk among the abbey ruins a spinster, composing verse about the ancient times and the monks who fished in the lake.

A bird swoops over the water and comes to rest on the pebbled shore, not far from where Emily stands. It rises on spindly legs, stretches out its wings and pecks at itself. Then it staggers uncomfortably on the pebbles before settling into an attitude that pleases it, head drawn into its body, wings wrapped around like a cloak. Such creatures would not have changed since the time of the monks, and Emily imagines a cowled and roughly bearded figure admiring the bird from a window of the once gracious abbey. He whispers as he does so and Emily remembers enough from her lessons with Miss Larvey to know that the language he speaks is not known to her.

It is a pleasant fancy, one for verse or drawing, to be stored away and one day in the future dwelt upon, and in one way or the other transcribed to paper. She turns her back on the lake and walks slowly through the ruins, past the posts which mark the route of the estate road, by the birchwood and over the stone bridge where Jonathan Swift is said to have stood and ordered the felling of three elms that obscured the panorama which has the great house as its centre. In the far distance she can see the line of men labouring on the road, and the figure of Erskine on his horse. She passes on, following a track that is familiar to her, which skirts the estate beneath its high boundary wall. Beyond the wall lie the Pulvertaft acres of farmland, but they have no interest for Emily, being for the most part flat, a territory that is tediously passed over every Sunday on the journey to and from church.

She reaches the yard of a gate-lodge and speaks to the woman who lives there, reminding her that soup and bread will be brought again tomorrow, that the utensils left last week must be ready by eleven o'clock on the trestle tables. Everything will be waiting, the woman promises, and a high fire alight in the kitchen.

October 31st 1847. Fogarty told me. He stood beside me while I ate my dinner by the fire: stew and rice, with cabbage; a baked apple, and sago pudding. The child with the stigmata has died and been buried.

'And who will know now,' he questioned, himself as much as me, 'exactly what was what?'

There is a kind of cunning in Fogarty's nutlike face. The eyes narrow, and the lips narrow, and he then looks like his sister. But he is more intelligent, I would say.

'And what *is* what, Mr Fogarty?' I enquired

'The people are edgy, miss. At the soup canteen they are edgy, I'm to understand. And likewise on the road. There is a feeling among them that the child should not have died. It is unpleasant superstition, of course, but there is a feeling that Our Lord has been crucified again.'

'But that's ridiculous!'

'I am saying so, miss. Coolly ridiculous, everything back to front. The trouble is that starvation causes a lightness in the head.'

'Do the Pulvertafts know of this? No one but you has mentioned this child to me.'

'I heard the matter mentioned at the dinner table. Mr Pulvertaft said that Mr Erskine had passed on to him the news that there was some superstition about. "D'you know its nature, Fogarty?" Mr Pulvertaft said, and I replied that it was to do with the marks of Our Lord's stigmata being noticed on the feet and hands of a child.'

'And what did anyone say then?'

' "Well, what's the secret of it, Fogarty?" Mr Pulvertaft said, and I passed on to him the opinion of Miss Fogarty and myself: that the markings were inflicted at the time of birth. They had all of them reached that conclusion also: Mrs Pulvertaft and Miss Emily and Miss Charlotte and Miss Adelaide, even Master George Arthur, no doubt, although he was not present then. As soon as ever they heard the news they had come to that assumption. Same with Mr Erskine.'

I stared, astonished, at the butler. I could not believe what he was telling me, that all these people had independently dismissed, so calmly and so finally, what the people who were closer to the event took to be a miracle. I had known, from the manner in which Fogarty spoke after his introduction of the subject, that he was in some way dubious. But I had concluded that he doubted the existence of the marks, that he doubted the reliability of the priest. I had never seen Father Horan, so did not know what kind of man he was even in appearance, or what age. Fogarty had told me he'd never seen him either, but from what he gathered through the maids the priest was of advanced years. Fogarty said now:

'My sister and I only decided that that was the truth of it after Cready and Brigid had gone on about the thing for a long time, how the priest was giving out sermons on it, how the bishop had come on a special journey and how a letter had been sent to Rome. Our first view was that the old priest had been presented with the child after he'd had a good couple of glasses. And then oiled up again and shown the child a second time. He's half blind, I've heard it said, and if enough people raved over marks that didn't exist, sure wouldn't he agree instead of admitting he was drunk and couldn't see properly? But as soon as Miss Fogarty and myself heard that the bishop had stirred his stumps and a letter had gone to Rome we realised the affair was wearing a different pair of shoes. They're as wily as cockroaches, these old priests, and there isn't one among them who'd run a chance of showing himself up by giving out sermons and summoning his bishop. He'd have let the matter rest, he'd have kept it local if he was flummoxed. "No doubt at all," Miss Fogarty said. "They've put marks on the baby." '

I couldn't eat. I shivered even though I was warm from the fire. I found it difficult to speak, but in the end I said:

'But why on earth would this cruel and blasphemous thing be done? Surely it could have been real, truly there, as stigmata have occurred in the past?'

'I would doubt that, miss. And hunger would give cruelty and blasphemy a different look. That's all I'd say. Seven other children have been buried in that family, and the two sets of grandparents. There was only the father and the mother with the baby left. "Sure, didn't they see the way things was turning?" was how Miss Fogarty put it. "Didn't they see an RIP all ready for them, and wouldn't they be a holy family with the baby the way they'd made it, and wouldn't they be sure of preservation because of it?" '

In his dark butler's clothes, the excitement that enlivened his small face lending him a faintly sinister look, Fogarty smiled at me. The smile was grisly; I did not forgive it, and from that moment I liked the butler as little as I liked his sister. His smile, revealing sharp, discoloured teeth, was related to the tragedy of a peasant family that had been almost extinguished, as, one by one, lamps are in a house at night. It was related to the desperation of survival, to an act so barbarous that one could not pass it by.

'A nine days' wonder,' Fogarty said. 'I'd say it wasn't a bad thing the child was buried. Imagine walking round with a lie like that on you for all your mortal days.'

He took the tray and went away. I heard him in the lavatory off the nursery landing, flushing the food I hadn't eaten down the WC so that he wouldn't have to listen to his sister's abuse of me. I sat until the fire sank low, without the heart to put more coal on it even though the coal was there. I kept seeing that faceless couple and their just-born child, the woman exhausted, in pain, tormented by hunger, with no milk to give her baby. Had they touched the tiny feet and hands with a hot coal? Had they torn the skin open, as Christ's had been on the Cross? Had either of them in that moment been even faintly sane? I saw the old priest, gazing in wonder at what they later showed him. I saw the Pulvertafts in their dining-room, accepting what had occurred as part of their existence in this house. Must not life go on lest all life cease? A confusion ran wildly in my head, a jumble without a pattern, all sense befogged. In a civilised manner nobody protested at the cacophony in the drawing-room when the piano was played, and nobody spoke to me of the stigmata because the subject was too terrible for conversation.

I wept before I went to bed. I wept again when I lay there, hating more than ever the place I am in, where people are driven back to savagery.

'The men have not arrived this morning,' Erskine reports. 'I suspected they might not from their demeanour last evening. They attach some omen to this death.'

'But surely to heavens they see the whole thing was a fraud?'

'They do not think so, sir. Any more than they believe that the worship of the Virgin Mary is a fraud perpetrated by the priests. Or that the Body and the Blood is. Fraud is grist to their mill.'

Mr Pulvertaft thanks Erskine for reporting the development to him. The men will return to their senses in time, the estate manager assures him. What has happened is only a little thing. Hunger is the master.

Emily packs for her travels, and vows she will not forget the lake, or the shadows and echoes of the monks. In Bath and Florence, in Vienna and Paris she will keep faith with her special corner, where the spirit of a gentler age lingers.

Mrs Pulvertaft dreams that the Reverend Poole ascends to the pulpit with a bath towel over his shoulder. From this day forth we must all carry bath towels wherever we go, and the feet of Jesus must be dried as well as washed. 'And the woman anointed the feet,' proclaims the Reverend Poole, 'and Jesus thanked her and blessed her and went upon his way.' But Mrs Pulvertaft is unhappy because she does not know which of the men is Jesus. They work with shovels on the estate road, and when she asks them they tell her, in a most unlikely manner, to go away.

Alone in front of the drawing-room piano, Adelaide sits stiffly upright, not wishing to play because she is not in the mood. Again, only minutes ago, Captain Roche has not noticed her. He did not notice her at lunch; he did not address a single word to her, he evaded her glance as if he could not bear to catch it. Charlotte thinks him dull; she has said so, yet she never spurns his attentions. And he isn't dull. His handsome face, surmounting his sturdily handsome body, twinkles with vigour and with life. He has done so much and when he talks about the places he has been he is so interesting she could listen to him for ages.

Adelaide's spectacles have misted. She takes them off and wipes them with her handkerchief. She must not go red when he comes again, or when his name is mentioned. Going red will give away her secret and Emily and Charlotte will guess and feel sorry for her, which she could not bear.

'Very well,' Charlotte says by the sundial in the fuchsia garden.

Captain Roche blinks his eyes in an ecstasy of delight, and Charlotte thinks that yes, it probably will be nice, knowing devotion like this for ever.

'Heddoe's gone broody,' Fogarty reports in the kitchen.

'Not sickness in the house! One thing you could say about Larvey, she was never sick for an hour.'

'I think Heddoe'll maybe leave.' Fogarty speaks with satisfaction. The governess might leave because she finds it too much that such a thing should happen to a baby, and that her employers do not remark on it because they expect no better of these people. Erskine might be knocked from his horse by the men in a fit of anger because the death has not been honoured in the house or by the family. Erskine might lie dead himself on the day of the governess's departure, and the two events, combining, would cause these Pulvertafts of Ipswich to see the error of their ways and return to their native land.

The china rattles on the tea-trays which the maids carry to the draining-boards, and Fogarty lights the lamps which he has arrayed on the table, as he does every afternoon at this time in winter. He inspects each flame before satisfying himself that the trimming of the wick is precisely right, then one after another places the glasses in their brass supports and finally adjusts each light.

The maids unburden the trays at the sink, Miss Fogarty places a damp cloth around a fruitcake and lays aside sandwiches and scones, later to be eaten in the kitchen. Then the maids take the lamps that are ready and begin another journey through the house.

In the nursery Miss Heddoe reads from the history book Miss Larvey has used before her: 'In this manner the monasteries were lawfully dissolved, for the King believed they harboured vile and treacherous plots and were the breeding grounds for future disaffection. The King was privy, through counsellors and advisers, of the vengeance that was daily planned, but was wise and bade his time.'

George Arthur does not listen. He is thinking about the savages of the South Sea islands who eat their enemies. He has always thought it was their babies they ate, and wonders if he has misunderstood something Miss Larvey said on the subject. He wonders then if Emily could possibly be right in what she says about the discomfort of the regimental life. It is true that he enjoys being close to the fire, and likes the cosiness of the nursery in the evenings; and it is true that he doesn't much care for rough material next to his skin. He knows that in spite of what Emily says officers like Captain Roche would not be made to drink putrid water, and that flies can't kill you, but the real thing is that he is expected to stay here because he is the only son, because somebody will have to look after the place when his father isn't able to any more. 'Duty,' Emily says, and it is that in the end that will steal from him his dream of military glory. Itchy and uneasy, like the bite of an insect, this duty already nags him.

January 12th, 1848. Today it snowed. The fall began after breakfast and continued until it was almost dark. Great drifts have piled up in the garden, and from my window the scene is beautiful. George Arthur has a cold and so remained in bed; he was too feverish for lessons.

January 18th, 1848. The snow is high on the ground. In the garden we break the ice on pools and urns so that the birds may drink. Scraps are thrown out of the scullery doors for them.

February 4th, 1848. It is five months since I arrived here, and all that I have learnt is distressing. There is nothing that is not so. Last night I could not sleep again. I lay there thinking of the starvation, of the faces of the silent women when they come to the gate-lodge for food. There is a yellow-greyness in the flesh of their faces, they are themselves like obedient animals. Their babies die when they feed them grass and roots; in their arms at the gate-lodge the babies who survive are silent also, too weak to cry until the sustenance they receive revives them. Last night I lay thinking of the men who are turned away from the work on the road because they have not the strength that is necessary. I thought of the darkness in the cottages, of dawn bringing with it the glaring eyes of death. I thought of the graves again clawed open, the earth still loose, another carcass pushed on to the rotting heap. I thought of an infant tortured with Our Saviour's wounds.

The famine-fever descends like a rain of further retribution, and I wonder — for I cannot help it — what in His name these people have done to displease God so? It is true they have not been an easy people to govern; they have not abided by the laws which the rest of us must observe; their superstitious worship is a sin. But God is a forgiving God. I pray to understand His will.

February 5th, 1848. Charlotte Pulvertaft is not to be married until her sister's return, so the engagement will of necessity be lengthy. 'Will you still be with us for the wedding?' Fogarty impertinently enquired last night, for he knows the age of George Arthur and unless I am dismissed I must of course still be here. The work continues on the road, it having been abandoned during the period of snow.

March 6th, 1848. A singular thing has happened. Walking alone in the grounds, I was hailed by Mr Erskine from his horse. I paused, and watched while he dismounted. I thought he had some message for me from the house, but in this I was wrong. Mr Erskine walked beside me, his horse, trailing obediently behind. He spoke of the sunshine we were enjoying, and of the estate road. Beyond saluting me at church on Sundays he has never before paid me any attention whatsoever. My surprise must have shown in my face, for he laughed at something that was displayed there. 'I have always liked you, Miss Heddoe,' he said to my astonishment.

I reddened, as any girl would, and felt extremely awkward. I made no attempt at a reply.

'And have you settled, Miss Heddoe?' he next enquired. 'Do you care for it here?'

No one has asked me that before: why should they? My inclination was to smile and with vague politeness to nod. I did so, for to have said that I did not care for this place would have seemed ill-mannered and offensive. Mr Erskine, after all, is part of it.

'Well, that is good.' He paused and then resumed: 'If ever on your walks, Miss Heddoe, you pass near my house you would be welcome to stroll about the garden.'

I thanked him.

'It is the house at the southernmost point of the estate. The only large house there is, nearly hidden in summer by sycamore trees.'

'That is very kind of you, Mr Erskine.'

'I reclaimed the little garden, as the estate was reclaimed.'

'I see.'

The subject of conversation changed. We spoke again of the time of year and the progress that was being achieved on the estate road. Mr Erskine told me something of his history, how a military career had been cut short before it had properly begun. In return, and because the subjects seemed related, I passed on the ambition George Arthur had had in this direction.

'He is reconciled now,' I said, and soon after that the estate manager and I parted company, he riding back along the way we'd walked, I turning toward the house.

The estate road is completed on June 9th, 1848. Soon after that a letter arrives for Mr Pulvertaft from the Distress Board, thanking him for supplying so many months of work for the impoverished men. Since the beginning of the year the families of the area — some of them tenants of Mr Pulvertaft, some not — have been moving away to the harbour towns, to fill the exile ships bound for America. At least, Fogarty overhears Mr Pulvertaft remark in the dining-room, there is somewhere for them to go.

In August of that year there is champagne at Charlotte's wedding. Guests arrive from miles around. Emily, returned from her travels, is a bridesmaid.

At the celebrations, which take place in the hall and the drawing-room and the dining-room, and spill over into the garden, Fogarty watches Miss Heddoe, even though he is constantly busy. She wears a dress he has not seen before, in light-blue material, with lace at the collar and the wrists, and little pearl buttons. Wherever she is, she is in the company of George Arthur in his sailor suit. They whisper together and seem, as always nowadays, to be the best of friends. Occasionally Miss Heddoe chides him because an observation he has made oversteps the mark or is delivered indiscreetly. When Mr Erskine arrives he goes straight to where they are.

September 24th, 1848. I have been here a year. The potatoes are not good this year but at least the crop has not failed as completely as hitherto. I have not given Mr Erskine his answer, but he is kind and displays no impatience. I am very silly in the matter, I know I am, but sometimes I lie awake at night and pretend I am already his wife. I repeat the name and title; I say it aloud. I think of the house, hidden among the sycamores. I think of sitting with him in church, in the pew behind the Pulver-tafts, not at the side with the Fogartys.

September 25th, 1848. A Mr Ogilvie comes regularly to take tea, and often strolls with Emily to the ruined abbey. Emily has made some drawings of it, which show it as it used to be. 'Well?' Mr Erskine said quietly this afternoon, riding up when I was out on my walk. But I begged, again, for more time to consider.

November 1st, 1848. All Saints' Day. Fogarty frightened me tonight. He leaned against the mantelpiece and said:

'I would advise you not to take the step you are considering, miss.'

'What step, Fogarty?'

'To marry or not to marry Mr Erskine.'

I was flabbergasted at this. I felt myself colouring and stammered when I spoke, asking him what he meant.

'I mean only what I say, miss. I would say to you not to marry him.'

'Are you drunk, Fogarty?'

'No, miss. I am not drunk. Or if I am it is only slight. You have been going through in your mind whether or not to marry Mr Erskine. A while ago you said you could never settle in this troubled place. You said that to yourself, miss. You could not become, as the saying goes, more Irish than the Irish.'

'Fogarty —'

'I thought you would go. When I told you about the child I thought you would pack your bags. There is wickedness here: I thought you sensed it, miss.'

'I cannot have you speaking to me like this, Fogarty.'

'Because I am a servant? Well, you are right, of course. In the evenings, miss, I have always indulged myself with port: that has always been my way. I have enjoyed our conversations, but I am disappointed now.'

'You have been reading my diary.'

'I have, miss. I have been reading your diary and your letters, and I have been observing you. Since they came here I have observed the Pulvertafts of Ipswich also, and Mr Erskine, who has done such wonders all around. I have watched his big square head going about its business; I have listened when I could.'

'You had no right to read what was private. If I mentioned this to Mr Pulvertaft —'

'If you did, miss, my sister and I would be sent packing. Mr Pulvertaft is a fair and decent man and it is only just that disloyal servants should be dismissed. But you would have it on your conscience. I had hoped we might keep a secret between us.'

'I have no wish to share secrets with you, Fogarty.'

'A blind eye was turned, miss, you know that. The hunger was a plague: what use a few spoonfuls of soup, and a road that leads nowhere and only insults the pride of the men who built it? The hunger might have been halted, miss, you know that. The people were allowed to die: you said that to yourself. A man and his wife were driven to commit a barbarous act of cruelty: blasphemy you called it, miss.'

'What I called it is my own affair. I should be grateful, Fogarty, if you left me now.'

'If the estate had continued in its honest decline, if these Pulvertafts had not arrived, the people outside the walls would have travelled here from miles around. They would have eaten the wild raspberries and the apples from the trees, the peaches that still thrived on the brick-lined walls, the grapes and plums, and green-gages, the blackberries and mulberries. They would have fished the lake and snared the rabbits on Bright Purple Hill. There is pheasant and woodcock grown tame in the old man's time. There was his little herd of cows they might have had. I am not putting forth an argument, miss; I am not a humanitarian; I am only telling you.'

'You are taking liberties, Fogarty. If you do not go now I will most certainly mention this.'

'That was the picture, miss, that might have been. Instead we had to hear of Charlotte's marrying and of Emily's travelling, and of George Arthur's brave decision to follow in the footsteps of his father. Adelaide sulks in the drawing-room and is jealous of her sisters. Mrs Pulvertaft, good soul, lies harmlessly down in the after-noon, and you have put it well in calling her husband a fair and decent man.'

'I did not call him that.'

'You thought it long before I said it.'

'You are drunker than you think, Fogarty.'

'No, miss, I am not. The wickedness here is not intentional, miss. Well, you know about the wickedness, for you have acutely sensed it. So did Mr Pulvertaft at first, so did his wife. Charlotte did not, nor Adelaide, nor did the boy. Emily sensed it until a while ago. Emily would linger down by the old abbey, knowing that the men who lie dead there have never been dispossessed by all the visitors and the strangers there have been since. But now the old abbey is a lady's folly, a pretty ruin that pleases and amuses. Well, of course you know all this.'

'I know nothing of the sort. I would ask you to leave me now.'

'You have thought it would be better for the boy to have his military life, to perish for Queen and empire, and so extinguish this line. Listening to talk of the boy's romance, you have thought that would not be bad. So many perish anyway, all about us.'

'That is a wicked thing to say,' I cried, made furious by this. 'And it is quite untrue.'

'It is wicked, miss, but not untrue. It is wicked because it comes from wickedness, you know that. Your sharp fresh eye has needled all that out.'

'I do not know these things.' My voice was quieter now, even, and empty of emotion. 'I would ask you to leave this room at once.'

But Fogarty went on talking until I thought in the end he must surely be insane. He spoke again of Charlotte's marriage to Captain Roche, of Emily and Adelaide, of George Arthur taking the place of his father. He spoke again of the hungry passing without hindrance through the gates of the estate, to feed off what its trees and bushes offered. He spoke of his sister and himself left after the old man's death, he glad to see the decay continue, his sister persuaded that they must always remain.

'The past would have withered away, miss. Instead of which it is the future that's withering now.'

Did he mean the hunger and the endless death, the exile ships of those who had survived? I did not ask him. He frightened me more than ever, standing there, his eyes as dead as ice. He was no humanitarian, he repeated, he was no scholar. All he said came from a feeling he had, a servant's feeling which he'd always had in this house during the years the old man had let everything decline. Poor Protestants as they were, he and his sister belonged neither outside the estate gates with the people who had starved nor with a family as renowned as the Pulvertafts. They were servants in their very bones.

'You have felt you have no place either, miss. You can see more clearly for that.'

'Please go, Fogarty.'

He told me of a dream he'd had the night before or last week, I was too upset to note which. The descendants of the people who had been hungry were in the dream, and the son of George Arthur Pulvertaft was shot in the hall of the house, and no Pulvertaft lived in the place again. The road that had been laid in charity was overgrown through neglect, and the gardens were as they had been at the time of old Hugh Pulvertaft, their beauty strangled as they returned to wildness. Fogarty's voice quivered as his rigmarole ridiculously rambled on; and institution for corrected girls the house became, without carpets on the floors. The bones of the dogs that generations of Pulvertafts had buried in the grounds were dug up by the corrected girls when they were ordered by a Mother Superior to make vegetable beds. They threw the bones about, pretending to be frightened by them, pretending they were the bones of people.

'I don't wish to hear your dreams, Fogarty.'

'I have told you only the one, miss. It is a single dream I had. The house of the estate manager was burnt to the ground, and people burnt with it. The stone walls of the estate were broken down, pulled apart in places by the ivy that was let grow. In a continuation of the dream I was standing here talking to you like I'm talking now. I said to you not to perpetuate what has troubled you.'

He took my tray from me and went away. A moment later I heard him in the lavatory, flushing away the food I had not eaten.

'Not a bad soul,' Miss Fogarty remarks, 'when you come to know her.'

'Her father was a solicitor's clerk.'

'Oh granted, there's not a pennyworth of background to the creature. But I'd hardly say she wasn't good enough for Erskine.'

Fogarty does not comment. His sister resumes:

'I would expect to be invited to the house for late tea. I would expect her to say: "Why not walk over on Wednesday, Miss Fogarty, if you have a fancy for it?" I would expect the both of us to walk over for cards with the Erskines of an evening.'

'She has pulled herself up by marrying him. She is hardly going to drop down again by playing cards with servants.'

'Friends,' corrects Miss Fogarty. 'I would prefer to say friends.'

'When a bit of time goes by they'll dine with the Pulvertafts, she and Erskine. You'll cook the food at the range, I'll serve it at the table.'

'Oh, I hardly believe that'll be the order of it.'

Fogarty considers it unwise to pursue his argument and so is silent. Anna Maria Heddoe, he thinks, who was outraged when two guileful peasants tried on a trick. Well, he did his best. It is she, not he, who is the scholar and humanitarian. It is she, not he, who came from England and was distressed. She has wept into her pillow, she has been sick at heart. Stranger and visitor, she has written in her diary the news from Ireland. Stranger and visitor, she has learnt to live with things.

JOHN UPDIKE

John Updike was born in 1932 in Shillington, Pennsylvania, and was educated at Harvard University. Deeply compelled by the visual arts, he studied
drawing for a year at Oxford. Shortly later he joined the staff of *The New Yorker*
magazine; he remained there until the late 1950s and is still a frequent contributor to the magazine. A writer of many interests and talents, Updike has distinguished himself in fiction, poetry, essays, and criticism. His fiction probes the
ambivalence of human relationships: the effects of boredom, the stagnation of
trust, above all the fervid ache of sexuality. The critic Clifton Fadiman has adeptly
characterized the array of "convincing voices" in Updike's fictional world:
"small-town car dealers, WASP exurbanites and suburbanites, young (and troubled) marrieds, Jewish novelists, and modern witches and warlocks." Among
Updike's novels are *Rabbit Run* (1960), *Couples* (1968), *Rabbit Redux* (1971), *The
Coup* (1978), *Rabbit Is Rich* (1982), *The Witches of Eastwick* (1984), *Roger's
Version* (1987), and *S* (1988). His short story collections include *Pigeon Feathers
and Other Stories* (1962), *The Music School* (1966), *Museums and Women and
Other Stories* (1972), *Problems and Other Stories* (1979), and *Trust Me* (1987).
"Museums and Women" poignantly sustains a metaphor as it examines
dimensions of loss.

Museums and Women

Set together, the two words are seen to be mutually transparent; the E's, the
M's blend — the M's framing and squaring the structure lend resonance and a
curious formal weight to the M central in the creature, which it dominates like a dark
core winged with flitting syllables. Both words hum. Both suggest radiance, antiquity,
mystery, and duty.

My first museum I would visit with my mother. It was a provincial museum, a
stately pride to the third-class inland city it ornamented. It was approached through
paradisaical grounds of raked gravel walks, humus-fed plantings of exotic flora, and
trees wearing tags, as if freshly christened by Adam. The museum's contents were
disturbingly various, its cases stocked with whatever scraps of foreign civilization had
fallen to it from the imperious fortunes of the steel and textile barons of the
province. A shredding kayak shared a room with a rack of Polynesian paddles. A
mummy, its skull half masked in gold, lay in an antechamber like one more of the
open-casket funerals common in my childhood. Miniature Mexican villages lit up
when a switch was flicked, and a pyramid was being built by dogged brown dolls
who never pulled their papier-mâché stone a fraction of an inch. An infinitely patient
Chinaman, as remote from me as the resident of a star, had carved a yellow

rhinoceros horn into an upright crescental city, pagoda-tipped, of balconies, vines, and thimble-sized people wearing microscopic expressions of pain.

This was downstairs. Upstairs, up a double flight of marble climaxed by a green fountain splashing greenly, the works of art were displayed. Upstairs, every fall, the county amateur artists exhibited four hundred watercolors of peonies and stone barns. The rest of the year, somberly professional oils of rotting, tangled woodland had the walls to themselves, sharing the great cool rooms with cases of Philadelphia silver, chests decorated with hearts, tulips, and bleeding pelicans by Mennonite folk artists, thick aqua glassware left bubbled by the blowing process, quaint quilts, and strange small statues. Strange perhaps only in the impression they made on me. They were bronze statuettes, randomly burnished here and there as if by a caressing hand, of nudes or groups of nudes. The excuse for nudity varied; some of the figures were American Indians, some were mythical Greeks. One lady, wearing a refined, aloof expression, was having her clothes torn from her by a squat man with horns and hairy hooved legs hinged the wrong way. Another statue bodied forth two naked boys wrestling. Another was of an Indian, dressed in only a knife belt, sitting astride a horse bareback, his chin bowed to his chest in sorrow, his exquisitely toed feet hanging down both hard and limp, begging to be touched. I think it was the smallness of these figures that carried them so penetratingly into my mind. Each, if it could have been released into life, would have stood about twenty inches high and weighed in my arms perhaps as much as a cat. I itched to finger them, to interact with them, to insert myself into their mysterious silent world of strenuous contention — their bulged tendons burnished, their hushed violence detailed down to the finger-nails. They were in their smallness like secret thoughts of mine projected into dimension and permanence, and they returned to me as a response that carried strangely into parts of my body. I felt myself a furtive animal stirring in the shadow of my mother.

My mother: like the museum, she filled her category. I knew no other, and accepted her as the index, inclusive and definitive, of women. Now I see that she too was provincial, containing much that was beautiful, but somewhat jumbled, and distorted by great gaps. She was an unsearchable mixture of knowledge and igno-rance, openness and reserve; though she took me many Sundays to the museum, I do not remember our discussing anything in it except once when, noticing how the small statues fascinated me, she said, "Billy, they seem such unhappy little people." In her glancing way she had hit something true. The defeated Indian was not alone in melancholy; all the statuettes, as they engaged in the struggles or frolics that gave each group the metallic unity of a single casting, seemed caught in a tarnished fate from which I yearned to rescue them. I wanted to touch them to comfort them, yet I held my hand back, afraid of breaking the seal on their sullen, furious underworld.

My mood of dread in those high cool galleries condensed upon the small statues but did not emanate from them; it seemed to originate above and behind me, as if from another living person in the room. Often my mother, wordlessly browsing by the wall on the paintings of woods and shaggy meadows, was the only other person in the room. Who she was was a mystery so deep it never formed into a question. She had descended to me from thin clouds of preëxistent time, enveloped me, and set me moving toward an unseen goal with a vague expectation that in the beginning was more hers than mine. She was not content. I felt that the motion which brought us again and again to the museum was an agitated one, that she was pointing me through these corridors toward a radiant place she had despaired of reaching. The fountain at the head of the stairs splashed unseen; my mother's footsteps rustled and she drew me into another room, where a case of silver stood aflame with reflections like the mouth of a dragon of beauty. She let me go forward to meet it alone. I was her son and the center of her expectations. I dutifully absorbed the light-struck terror of the hushed high chambers, and went through each doorway with a kind of timid rapacity.

This museum, my first, I associate with another, less ghostly hunt; for this was one of the places — others being the telephone company, the pretzel factory, and the county fair — where schoolchildren were taken on educational expeditions. I would usually be toward the end of the line, among the unpaired stragglers, and up front, in the loud nucleus of leaders, the freckled girl I had decided I loved. The decision, perhaps, was as much my mother's as mine. The girl lived in our neighborhood, one of a pack of sisters, and from the time she could walk past our front hedge my mother had taken one of her quixotic fancies to her. She spoke admiringly of her "spirit"; this admiration surprised me, for the girl was what was known locally as "bold," and as she grew older fell in with a crowd of children whose doings would certainly have struck my mother as "unhappy." My mother always invited her to my birthday parties, where she, misplaced but rapidly forgiving the situation, animated for a few dazzling hours my circle of shadowy-faced, sheltered friends.

When I try to picture my school days, I seem to be embedded among boiling clouds straining to catch a glimpse of her, or trapped in a movie theatre behind a row of huge heads while fragmented arcs of the screen confusingly flicker. The alphabet separated us; she sat near the front of the classroom and I, William Young, toward the rear. Where the alphabet no longer obtained, other systems of distinction intervened. In the museum, a ruthless law propelled her forward to gather with the other bold spirits, tittering, around the defenseless little statues while I hung back, on the edge of the fountain, envious, angry, and brimming with things to say. I never said them. It seemed a simple matter of position; I was never in a position to declare, let alone act upon, my love. No distinction cuts as deep as the one between the worshipped and the worshipping. I am condemned by nature to be dutiful and reverent.

The girl who was to become my wife was standing at the top of some stone museum steps that I was climbing. Though it was bitterly cold, with crusts of snow packed into the stone, she wore threadbare sneakers from which her little toes stuck out, and she was smoking. Awesome sheets of smoke and frozen vapor flew from her mouth and she seemed, posed against a fluted pilaster, a white-faced priestess immolating herself in the worship of tobacco. "Aren't your feet cold?" I asked her.

"A little. I don't mind it."

"A stoic."

"Maybe I'm a masochist."

"Who isn't?"

She said nothing. Had I said something curious?

I lit a cigarette, though inhaling the raw air rasped my throat, and asked her, "Aren't you in Medieval Art? You sit near the front."

"Yes. Do you sit in the back?"

"I feel I should. I'm a history major."

"This is your first fine-arts course?"

"Yeah. It met at a good hour — late enough for a late breakfast and early enough for an early lunch. I'm trying to have a sophomore slump."

"Are you succeeding?"

"Not really. When the chips are down, I tend to grind."

"How do you like Medieval Art?"

"I love it. It's like going to a movie in the morning, which is my idea of sin."

"You have funny ideas."

"No. They're very conventional. It would never occur to me, for example, to stand outside in the snow in bare feet."

"They're not really bare."

Nevertheless, I yearned to touch them, to comfort them. There was in this girl, this pale creature of the college museum, a withdrawing that drew me forward. I felt in her an innocent sad blankness where I must stamp my name. I pursued her through the museum. It was, as museums go, rather intimate. Architecturally, it was radiantly hollow, being built around a skylight-roofed replica of a sixteenth-century Italian courtyard. At the four corners of the flagstone courtyard floor, four great gray terra-cotta statues of the seasons stood. Bigger than life, they were French, and reduced the four epic passages of the year to four charming aristocrats, two male and two female, who had chosen to attend a costume ball piquantly attired in grapes and ribbons. I remember that Spring wore a floppy hat and carried a basket of rigid flowers. The stairways and galleries that enabled the museum to communicate with itself around the courtyard were distinctly medieval in feeling, and the vagaries of benefaction had left the museum's medieval and Oriental collections disproportionately strong, though a worthy attempt had been made to piece together the history of art since the Renaissance with a painting or at least a drawing by each master. But the rooms that contained these later works — including some Cézannes and Renoirs that, because they were rarely reproduced in art books, had the secret sweetness of flowers in a forest — were off the route of the course we were both taking, so my courtship primarily led down stone corridors, past Romanesque capitals, through low gray archways giving on gilded altar panels.

I remember stalking her around a capital from Avignon; it illustrated Samson and his deeds. On one side he was bearing off the gates of Gaza, while around the corner his massive head was lying aswoon in Delilah's lap as she clumsily sawed his hair. The class had been assigned a paper on this capital, and as I rehearsed my interpretation, elaborately linear and accompanied by many agitated indications of my hands, the girl said thoughtfully, "You see awfully much in it, don't you?"

My hands froze and crept back, embarrassed; the terminology of fine-arts analysis was new to me, and in fact I did doubt that an illiterate carver of semi-barbaric Europe could have been as aesthetically ingenious as I was. "What do *you* see in it?" I asked in self-defense.

"Not very much," she said. "I wonder why they assigned it. It's not that lovely. I think the Cluny ones are much nicer."

It thrilled me to hear her speak with such careless authority. She was a fine-arts major, and there was a sense in which she contained the museum, had mastered all the priceless and timeless things that would become, in my possessing her, mine as well. She had first appeared to me as someone guarding the gates.

Once I accompanied her into Boston, to the museum there, to study, in connection with another course she was taking, an ancient Attic sphinx. This she liked, though it was just a headless winged body of white marble, very simple, sitting stiffly on its haunches, its broad breast glowing under the nicks of stylized feathers. She showed me the S-curve of its body, repeated in the tail and again, presumably, in the vanished head.

"It's a very proud little statue, isn't it?" I ventured, seeking to join her in her little careless heaven of appreciation. Again, I seemed to have said something curious.

"I love it" was all she replied, with a dent of stubbornness in her mouth and an inviting blankness in her eyes.

Outside, the weather was winter, the trees medieval presences arching gray through gray. We walked and walked, and for a time the only shelter we shared was the museum. My courtship progressed; we talked solemnly; the childhood I had spent in such angry silence and timid foreboding had left me with much to say. She could listen; she was like a room of vases: you enter and find your sense of yourself abruptly sharpened by a vague, tranquil expectancy in the air. I see her sitting on the broad cold balustrade that at second-story height ran around the courtyard. Beyond her head, the flagstones shone as if wet and Printemps in her wide hat was baroquely foreshortened. An apprehension of height seized me; this girl seemed poised on the edge of a fall. I heard the volume of emptiness calling to her, calling her away from me, so full of talk. There was in her something mute and remote which spoke only once, once when, after our lying side by side an entire evening, she told me calmly, "You know I don't love you yet."

I took this as a challenge, though it may have been meant as a release. I carried the chase through exams (we both got A-minuses) and into another course, a spring term course called, simply, Prints. My mother, surprisingly, wrote warning me that I mustn't spread myself too thin — she thought now that that had been *her* mistake at college. I was offended, for I thought that without my telling her anything she would know I was in the process of capturing the very gatekeeper of the temple of learning that must be the radiant place she had pointed me toward so long ago. The absence of her blessing seemed a tacit curse.

Here I must quickly insert, like a thin keystone, an imaginary woman I found in a faraway museum. It was another university museum, ancient and sprawling and resolutely masculine, full of battered weapons of war and unearthed agricultural tools and dull maps of diggings. All its contents seemed to need a dusting and a tasteful rearrangement by a female hand. But upstairs, in an out-of-the-way chamber, under a case of brilliantly polished glass, I one day discovered a smooth statuette of a nude asleep on a mattress. She was a dainty white dream, an eighteenth-century fancy; only that century would have thought to render a mattress in marble. Not that every stitch and seam was given the dignity of stone; but the corners were rounded, the buttoned squares of plumpness shown, and the creases of "give" lovingly sculpted. In short, it was clear that the woman was comfortable, and not posed on an arbitrary slab, or slaughtered on an altar. She was asleep, not dead; the delicate aroma of her slumber seemed to rise through the glass. She was the size of the small straining figures that had fascinated my childhood, and, as with them, smallness intensified sensual content. As I stood gazing into the eternal privacy of her sleep —

her one hand resting palm up beside her averted head, one knee lifted in a light suggestion of restlessness — I was disturbed by dread and a premonition of loss. Why? Was not my wife also fair, and finely formed, and mute? Perhaps it was the mattress that brought this ideal woman so close; it was a raft on which she had floated out of the inaccessible past and which brought her, small and intangible as a thought, ashore on the island of my bounded present. We seemed about to release each other from twin enchantments. Was not my huge face the oppressive dream that was making her stir? And was not I, out of all the thousands who had visited this museum, the first to find her here asleep? What we seek in museums is the opposite of what we seek in churches — the consoling sense of previous visitation. In museums, rather, we seek the untouched, the never-before-discovered; and it is their final unsearchability that leads us to hope, and return.

Two more, two more of each, each nameless. None have names. Museums are in the end nameless and continuous; we turn a corner in the Louvre and meet the head of a sphinx whose body is displayed in Boston. So, too, the women were broken arcs of one curve.

She was the friend of a friend, and she and I, having had lunch with the mutual friend, bade him goodbye and, both being loose in New York for the afternoon, went to a museum together. It was a new one, recently completed after the plan of a recently dead American wizard. It was shaped like a truncated top and its floor was a continuous spiral around an overweening core of empty vertical space. From the leaning, shining walls immense rectangles of torn and spattered canvas projected on thin arms of bent pipe. Menacing magnifications of textural accidents, they needed to be viewed at a distance greater than the architecture afforded. The floor width was limited by a rather slender and low concrete guard wall that more invited than discouraged a plunge into the cathedralic depths below. Too reverent to scoff and too dizzy to judge, my unexpected companion and I dutifully unwound our way down the exitless ramp, locked in a wizard's spell. Suddenly, as she lurched backward from one especially explosive painting, her high heels were tricked by the slope, and she fell against me and squeezed my arm. Ferocious gumbos splashed on one side of us; the siren chasm called on the other. She righted herself but did not let go of my arm. Pointing my eyes ahead, inhaling the presence of perfume, feeling like a cliff-climber whose companion has panicked on the sheerest part of the face, I accommodated my arm to her grip and, thus secured, we carefully descended the remainder of the museum. Not until our feet attained the safety of street level were we released. Our bodies then separated and did not touch again. Yet the spell was imperfectly broken, like the door of a chamber which, once unsealed, can never be closed quite tight.

Not far down the same avenue there is a museum which was once a mansion and still retains a homelike quality, if one can imagine people rich enough in self-esteem to inhabit walls so overripe with masterpieces, to dine from tureens by Cellini, and afterward to seat their bodies complacently on furniture invested with the blood of empires. There once were people so self-confident, and on the day of my visit I was one of them, for the woman I was with and I were perfectly in love. We had come from love-making, and were to return to it, and the museum, visited between the evaporation and the recondensation of desire, was like a bridge whose either end is dissolved in mist — its suspension miraculous, its purpose remembered only by the murmuring stream running in the invisible ravine below. Homeless, we had found a home worthy of us. We seemed hosts; surely we had walked these Persian rugs before, appraised this amphora with an eye to its purchase, debated the position of this marble-topped table whose veins foamed like gently surfing aquamarine. The woman's sensibility was more an interior decorator's than an art student's, and through her I felt furnishings unfold into a world of gilded scrolls, rubbed stuffs, cherished surfaces, painstakingly inlaid veneers, varnished cadenzas of line and curve lovingly carved by men whose hands were haunted by the memory of women. Rustling beside me, her body, which I had seen asleep on a mattress, seemed to wear clothes as a needless luxuriance, an ultra-extravagance heaped upon what was already, like the museum, both priceless and free. Room after room we entered and owned. A lingering look, a shared smile was enough to secure our claim. Once she said, of a chest whose panels were painted with pubescent cherubs after Boucher, that she didn't find it terribly "attractive." The one word, pronounced with a worried twist of her eyebrows, delighted me like the first polysyllable pronounced by an infant daughter. In this museum I was more the guide; it was I who could name the modes and deliver the appreciations. Her muteness was not a reserve but an expectancy; she and the museum were perfectly open and mutually transparent. As we passed a dark-red tapestry, her bare-shouldered summer dress, of a similar red, blended with it, isolating her head and shoulders like a bust. The stuffs of every laden room conspired to flatter her, to elicit with tinted reflective shadows the shy structure of her face, to accent with sumptuous textures her demure skin. My knowledge of how she looked asleep gave a tender nap to the alert surface of her wakefulness now. My woman, fully searched, and my museum, fully possessed; for this translucent interval — like the instant of translucence that shows in a wave between its peaking and its curling under — I had come to the limits of unsearchability. From this beautiful boundary I could imagine no retreat.

The last time I saw this woman was in another museum, where she had taken a job. I found her in a small room lined with pale books and journals, and her face as it looked up in surprise was also pale. She took me into the corridors and showed me the furniture it was her job to catalogue. When we had reached the last room of her special province, and her gay, rather matter-of-face lecture had ended, she asked me, "Why have you come? To upset me?"

"I don't mean to upset you. I wanted to see if you're all right."

"I'm all right. Please, William. If anything's left of what you felt for me, let me alone. Don't come teasing me."

"I'm sorry. It doesn't feel like teasing to me."

Her chin reddened and the rims of her eyes went pink as tears seized her eyes. Our bodies ached to comfort each other, but at any moment someone — a professor, a nun — might wander into the room. "You know," she said, "we really had it." A sob bowed her head and rebounded from the polished surfaces around us.

"I know. I know we did."

She looked up at me, the anger of her eyes blurred. "Then why — ?"

I shrugged. "Cowardice. I've always been timid. A sense of duty. I don't know. I can't do it to her. Not yet."

"Not yet," she said. "That's your little song, isn't it? That's the little song you've been singing me all along."

"Would you rather the song had been, Not ever? That would have been no song at all."

With two careful swipes of her fingers, as if she were sculpting her own face, she wiped the tears from below her eyes. "It's my fault. It's my fault for falling in love with you. In a funny way, it was unfair to you."

"Let's walk," I said.

Blind to all beauty, we walked through halls of paintings and statues and urns. A fountain splashed unseen off to our left. Through a doorway I glimpsed, still proud, its broad chest still glowing, the headless sphinx.

"No, it's my fault," I said. "I was in no position to love you. I guess I never have been." Her eyes went bold and her freckles leaped up childishly as she grinned, as if to console me.

Yet what she said was not consolatory. "Well just don't do it to anybody else."

"Lady, there is nobody else. You're all of it. You have no idea how beautiful you are."

"You made me believe it at the time. I'm grateful for that."

"And for nothing else?"

"Oh, for lots of things, really. You got me into the museum. It's fun."

"You came here to please me?"

"Yes."

"God, it's terrible to love what you can't have. Maybe that's why you love it."

"No, I don't think so. I think that's the way you work. But not everybody works that way."

"Well, maybe one of those others will find you now."

"No. You were it. You saw something in me nobody else ever saw. I didn't know it was there myself. Now go away, unless you want to see me cry some more."

We parted and I descended marble stairs. Before pushing through the revolving doors, I looked back, and it came to me that nothing about museums is as splendid as their entrances — the sudden vault, the shapely cornices, the motionless uniformed guard like a wittily disguised archangel, the broad stairs leading upward into heaven knows what mansions of expectantly hushed treasure. And it appeared to me that now I was condemned, in my search for the radiance that had faded behind me, to enter more and more museums, and to be a little less exalted by each new entrance, and a little more quickly disenchanted by the familiar contents beyond.

LUISA VALENZUELA

Luisa Valenzuela was born in 1938 in Buenos Aires, Argentina. She grew up in a literary atmosphere — her mother is a well-known novelist — and, after attending the University of Buenos Aires, began her career writing for magazines and working on the editorial staff of *La Nación*. Throughout the early part of her career Valenzuela traveled widely in the United States, Europe, and Latin America. Her first novel, *Hay que sonreir*, was published in 1966; it was translated into English and published with some of her short stories under the title *Clara* in 1979. With *Clara*, Valenzuela began gaining a reputation in the United States, one of the few Latin American women writers to do so at the time. Her next publication was a collection of stories, *Strange Things Happen Here* (1976; English 1979), reflecting the horrors perpetuated by the Argentine military regime in the late 1970s. As the condition in her country deteriorated — books burned, publishers' offices bombed, censorship rampant — and the numbers of the *Desaparecidos* (the "Disappeared," individuals removed by the military police) increased, Valenzuela realized that she could no longer fight back with words. She moved to New York City, where she presently lives, in 1979. Her work has continued to reflect both the political realities and the literary magical realism of Latin America. She takes themes of power, violence, and sexuality and explores them, at times surrealistically, in untraditional narrative forms. Her second novel is *The Lizard's Tale* (1983), and her other collections of stories are *Other Weapons* (1985) and *He Who Searches* (1987). Somewhere between the boundaries of dreaming and waking, "I'm Your Horse in the Night" speaks the anguish of living in the midst of political oppression.

I'm Your Horse in the Night

Translated from the Spanish by Deborah Bonner

The doorbell rang: three short rings and one long one. That was the signal, and I got up, annoyed and a little frightened; it could be them, and then again, maybe not; at these ungodly hours of the night it could be a trap. I opened the door expecting anything except him, face to face, at last.

He came in quickly and locked the door behind him before embracing me. So much in character, so cautious, first and foremost checking his — our — rear guard. Then he took me in his arms without saying a word, not even holding me too tight but letting all the emotions of our new encounter overflow, telling me so much by merely holding me in his arms and kissing me slowly. I think he never had much faith in words, and there he was, as silent as ever, sending me messages in the form of caresses.

We finally stepped back to look at one another from head to foot, not eye to eye, out of focus. And I was able to say Hello showing scarcely any surprise despite all those months when I had no idea where he could have been, and I was able to say

I thought you were fighting up north
I thought you'd been caught
I thought you were in hiding

I thought you'd been tortured and killed

I thought you were theorizing about the revolution in another country

Just one of many ways to tell him I'd been thinking of him, I hadn't stopped thinking of him or felt as if I'd been betrayed. And there he was, always so goddamn cautious, so much the master of his actions.

"Quiet, Chiquita. You're much better off not knowing what I've been up to."

Then he pulled out his treasures, potential clues that at the time eluded me: a bottle of cachaça and a Gal Costa record. What had he been up to in Brazil? What was he planning to do next? What had brought him back, risking his life, knowing they were after him? Then I stopped asking myself questions (quiet, Chiquita, he'd say). Come here, Chiquita, he was saying, and I chose to let myself sink into the joy of having him back again, trying not to worry. What would happen to us tomorrow, and the days that followed?

Cachaça's a good drink. It goes down and up and down all the right tracks, and then stops to warm up the corners that need it most. Gal Costa's voice is hot, she envelops us in its sound and half-dancing, half-floating, we reach the bed. We lie down and keep on staring deep into each other's eyes, continue caressing each other without allowing ourselves to give into the pure senses just yet. We continue recognizing, rediscovering each other.

Beto, I say, looking at him. I know that isn't his real name, but it's the only one I can call him out loud. He replies:

"We'll make it someday, Chiquita. But let's not talk now."

It's better that way. Better if he doesn't start talking about how we'll make it someday and ruin the wonder of what we're about to attain right now, the two of us, all alone.

"A noite eu so teu cavalo," Gal Costa suddenly sings from the record player.

"I'm your horse in the night," I translate slowly. And so as to bind him in a spell and stop him from thinking about other things:

"It's a saint's song, like in the *macumba*. Someone who's in a trance says she's the horse of the spirit who's riding her, she's his mount."

"Chiquita, you're always getting carried away with esoteric meanings and witchcraft. You know perfectly well that she isn't talking about spirits. If you're my horse in the night it's because I ride you, like this, see? ... Like this ... That's all."

It was so long, so deep and so insistent, so charged with affection that we ended up exhausted. I fell asleep with him still on top of me.

I'm your horse in the night.

The goddamn phone pulled me out in waves from a deep well. Making an enormous effort to wake up, I walked over to the receiver, thinking it could be Beto, sure, who was no longer by my side, sure, following his inveterate habit of running away while I'm asleep without a word about where he's gone. To protect me, he says.

From the other end of the line, a voice I thought belonged to Andrés — the one we call Andrés — began to tell me:

"They found Beto dead, floating down the river near the other bank. It looks as if they threw him alive out of a chopper. He's all bloated and decomposed after six days in the water, but I'm almost sure it's him."

"No, it can't be Beto," I shouted carelessly. Suddenly the voice no longer sounded like Andrés: it felt foreign, impersonal.

"You think so?"

"Who is this?" Only then did I think to ask. But that very moment they hung up.

Ten, fifteen minutes? How long must I have stayed there staring at the phone like an idiot until the police arrived? I didn't expect them. But, then again, how could I not? Their hands feeling me, their voices insulting and threatening, the house searched, turned inside out. But I already knew. So what did I care if they broke every breakable object and tore apart my dresser?

They wouldn't find a thing. My only real possession was a dream and they can't deprive me of my dreams just like that. My dream the night before, when Beto was there with me and we loved each other. I'd dreamed it, dreamed every bit of it, I was deeply convinced that I'd dreamed it all in the richest detail, even in full color. And dreams are none of the cops' business.

They want reality, tangible facts, the kind I couldn't even begin to give them.

Where is he, you saw him, he was here with you, where did he go? Speak up, or you'll be sorry. Let's hear you sing, bitch, we know he came to see you, where is he, where is he holed up? He's in the city, come on, spill it, we know he came to get you.

I haven't heard a word from him in months. He abandoned me, I haven't heard from him in months. He ran away, went underground. What do I know, he ran off with someone else, he's in another country. What do I know, he abandoned me, I hate him, I know nothing.

(Go ahead, burn me with your cigarettes, kick me all you wish, threaten, go ahead, stick a mouse in me so it'll eat my insides out, pull my nails out, do as you please. Would I make something up for that? Would I tell you he was here when a thousand years ago he left me forever?)

I'm not about to tell them my dreams. Why should they care? I haven't seen that so-called Beto in more than six months, and I loved him. The man simply vanished. I only run into him in my dreams, and they're bad dreams that often become nightmares.

Beto, you know now, if it's true that they killed you, or wherever you may be, Beto, I'm your horse in the night and you can inhabit me whenever you wish, even if I'm behind bars. Beto, now that I'm in jail I know that I dreamed you that night; it was just a dream. And if by some wild chance there's a Gal Costa record and a half-empty bottle of cachaça in my house, I hope they'll forgive me: I will them out of existence.

GUY VANDERHAEGHE

 Guy Vanderhaeghe was born in 1951 in Esterhazy, Saskatchewan, Canada. He grew up there, and was educated at the
University of Saskatchewan and the University of Regina. He worked
for a time as a teacher, researcher, and archivist, but since the late
1970s he has turned his attention mainly to writing. His first collection of stories, *Man Descending*, was published in 1982 and was
followed by another collection, *The Trouble with Heroes*, in 1983
and a novel, *My Present Age*, in 1984. Vanderhaeghe was influenced
by the "prairie writers," those who wrote of life in towns in the vast
rural stretches of Canada. He brings compassion to his portrayal of
life's bittersweetness. His work, he says, celebrates "the endurance
of the ordinary person whose life is a series of small victories
fashioned from small resources." "Drummer" is a rueful (and very
funny) story from the frontlines of that mystifying process —
growing up.

Drummer

You'd think my old man was the Pope's nephew or something if you'd seen
how wild he went when he learned I'd been sneaking off Sundays to Faith
Baptist Church. Instead of going to eleven o'clock Mass like he figured I was.

Which is kind of funny. Because although Mom is solid R.C. — eight o'clock Mass
and saying a rosary at the drop of a hat — nobody ever accused Pop of being a
religious fanatic by no means. He goes to confession regular like an oil change, every
five thousand miles, or Easter, whichever comes first.

Take the Knights of Columbus. He wouldn't join those guys for no money.
Whenever Mom starts in on him about enlisting he just answers back that he can't
afford the outlay on armour and where'd we keep a horse? Which is his idea of a
joke. So it isn't exactly as if he was St. Joan of Arc himself to go criticizing me.

And Pop wouldn't have been none the wiser if it wasn't for my older brother Gene,
the prick. Don't think I don't know who told. But I can't expect nothing different
from that horse's ass.

So, as I was saying, my old man didn't exactly take it all in stride. "Baptists! *Baptists!*
I'm having your head examined. Do you hear me? I'm having it *examined!* Just keep
it up and see if I don't, you crazy little pecker. They roll in the aisles, Baptists, for
chrissakes!"

"I been three times already and nobody rolled in an aisle once."

"Three times? *Three times?* Now it all comes out. Three, eh?" He actually hits himself in the forehead with the heel of his palm. Twice. "Jesus Christ Almighty, I'm blessed with a son like this? What's the matter with you? Why can't you ever do something I can understand?"

"Like wrecking cars?" This is a swift kick in the old fun sack. Pop's just getting over Gene's totalling off the first new car he's bought in eight years. A 1966 Chevy Impala.

"Shut your smart mouth. Don't go dragging your brother into this. Anyway, what he done to the car was *accidental*. But not you. Oh no, you marched into that collection of religious screwballs, holy belly floppers, and linolcum-beaters under your own steam. *On purpose*. For God's sake, Billy, that's no religion that — it's *exercise*. Stay away from them Baptists."

"Can't," I says to him.

"Can't? *Can't?* Why the hell not?"

"Matter of principle."

They teach us that in school, matters of principle. I swear it's a plot to get us all slaughtered the day they graduate us out the door. It's their revenge, see? Here we are reading books in literature class about some banana who's only got one oar in the water to start with, and then he pops it out worrying about principles. Like that Hamlet, or what's his name in *A Tale of Two Cities*. Ever notice how many of those guys are alive at the end of those books they teach us from?

"I'll principle you," says the old man.

The only teacher who maybe believes all that crock of stale horeseshit about principles is Miss Clark, who's fresh out of wherever they bake Social Studies teachers. She's got principles on the brain. For one thing, old Clarkie has pretty nearly wallpapered her room with pictures of that Negro, Martin Luther King, and some character who's modelling the latest in Wabasso sheets and looks like maybe he'd kill for a hamburger — Gandhi is his name — and that hairy old fart Tolstoy, who wrote the books you need a front-end loader to lift. From what Clarkie tells us, I gather they're what you call non-violent shit-disturbers.

Me too. Being a smart-ass runs in the Simpson family. It's what you call hereditary, like a disease. That's why all of a sudden, before I even *think* for chrissakes, I hear myself lecturing the old man in this fruity voice that's a halfway decent imitation of old Clarkie, and I am using the exact words which I've heard her say myself.

"Come, come, surely by this day and age everybody has progressed to the point where we can all agree on the necessity of freedom of worship. If we can't agree on anything else, at least we can agree on that."

I got news for her. My old man don't agree to no such thing. He up and bangs me one to the side of the head. A backhander special. You see, nobody in our house is allowed an opinion until they're twenty-one."

Of course, I could holler Religious Persecution. Not that it would do any good. But it's something I happen to know quite a bit about, seeing as Religious Persecution was my assignment in Social Studies that time we studied Man's Inhumanity to Man. The idea was to write a two-thousand-word report proving how everybody has been a shit to everybody else through the ages, and where did it ever get them? This is supposed to improve us somehow, I guess.

Anyway, as usual anything good went fast. Powbrowski got A. Hitler, Keller put dibs on Ivan the Terrible, Langly asked for Genghis Khan. By the time old Clarkie got around to me there was just a bunch of crap left like No Votes For Women. So I asked, please, could I do a project on Mr. Keeler? Keeler is the dim-witted bat's fart who's principal of our school.

For being rude, Miss Clark took away my "privilege" of picking and said I had to do Religious Persecution. Everybody was avoiding that one like the plague.

Actually, I found Religious Persecution quite interesting. It's got principles too, number one being that whatever you're doing to some poor son of a bitch — roasting his chestnuts over an open fire, or stretching his pant-leg from a 29-incher to a 36-incher on the rack — why, you're doing it for his own good. So he'll start thinking right. Which is more or less what my old man was saying when he told me I can't go out of the house on Sundays any more. He says to me, "You aren't setting a foot outside of that door [he actually points at it] of a Sunday until you come to your senses and quit with all the Baptist bullshit."

Not that that's any heavy-duty torture. What he don't know is that these Baptists have something called Prayer, Praise and Healing on Wednesday nights. My old man hasn't locked me up Wednesday nights yet by no means.

I figure if my old man wants somebody to blame for me becoming a Baptist he ought to take a peek in my older brother Gene's direction. He started it.

Which sounds awful funny if you know anything about Gene. Because if Gene was smart enough to have ever thought about it, he'd come out pretty strong against religion, since it's generally opposed to most things he's in favour of.

Still, nobody thinks the worse of my brother for doing what he likes to do. They make a lot of excuses for you in a dinky mining town that's the arsehole of the world if you bat .456 and score ninety-eight goals in a thirty-five-game season. *Shit,* last year they passed the hat around to all the big shots on the recreation board and collected the dough for one of Gene's liquor fines and give it to him on the *q.t.*

But I'm trying to explain my brother. If I had to sum him up I'd probably just say he's the kind of guy doesn't have to dance. What I mean is, you take your average, normal female: they slobber to dance. The guys that stand around leaning against walls are as popular to them as syphilis. You don't dance, you're a pathetic dope — even the ugly ones despise you.

But not Gene. He don't dance and they all cream. You explain it. Do they figure he's too superior to be bothered? Because it's not true. I'm his brother and I know. The dink just can't dance. That simple. But if I mention this little fact to anybody, they look at me like I been playing out in the sun too long. Everybody around here figures Mr. Wonderful could split the fucking atom with a hammer and a chisel if he put his mind to it.

Well, almost everybody. There's a born doubter in every crowd. Ernie Powers is one of these. He's the kind of stupid fuck who's sure they rig the Stanley Cup and the Oscars and nobody ever went up in space. Everything is a hoax to him. Yet he believes professional wrestling is on the up and up. You wonder — was he dropped on his head, or what? Otherwise you got to have a plan to grow up that ignorant.

So it was just like Einstein to bet Gene ten dollars he couldn't take out Nancy Williams. He did that while we were eating a plate of chips and gravy together in the Rite Spot and listening to Gene going on about who's been getting the benefit of his poking lately. Powers, who is a very jealous person because he's going steady with his right hand, says, oh yeah sure, maybe her, but he'd bet ten bucks somebody like Nancy Williams in 11B wouldn't even go out with Gene.

"Get serious," says my brother when he hears that. He considers himself irresist-ible to the opposite sex.

"Ten bucks. She's strictly off-limits even to you, Mr. Dreamboat. It's all going to waste. That great little gunga-poochy-snuggy-bum, that great matched set. Us guys in 11B, you know what we call them? The Untouchables. Like on TV."

"What a fucking sad bunch. Untouchables for you guys, maybe. If any of you queers saw a real live piece of pelt you'd throw your hat over it and run."

"Talk's cheap," says Ernie, real offended. "You don't know nothing about her. My sister says Miss High-and-Mighty didn't go out for cheerleading because the outfits was *too revealing*. My sister says Nancy Williams belongs to some religion doesn't allow her to dance. Me, I saw her pray over a hard-boiled egg for about a half-hour before she ate it in the school lunch-room. Right out where anybody could see, she prayed. No way somebody like that is going to go out with you, Simpson. If she does I'll eat my shorts."

"Start looking for the ten bucks, shitface, and skip dinner, because I'm taking Nancy Williams to the Christmas Dance," my brother answers him right back. Was Gene all of a sudden hostile, or was he hostile? I overheard our hockey coach say one time that my brother Gene's the kind of guy rises to a challenge. The man's got a point. I lived with Gene my whole life, which is sixteen years now, and I ought to know. Unless he gets mad he's useless as tits on a boar.

You better believe Gene was mad. He called her up right away from the pay phone in the Rite Spot. It was a toss-up as to which of those two jerks was the most entertaining. Powers kept saying, "There's no way she'll go out with him. No way." And every time he thought of parting with a ten-spot, a look came over his face like he just pinched a nut or something. The guy's so christly tight he squeaks when he walks. He was sharing *my* chips and gravy, if you know what I mean?

And then there was Gene. I must say I've always enjoyed watching him operate. I mean, even on the telephone he looks so sincere I could just puke. It's not uncon-scious by no means. My brother explained to me once what his trick is. To look that way you got to think that way is his motto. "What I do, Billy," he told me once, "is make myself believe, really believe, say ... well, that an H-bomb went off, or that some kind of disease which only attacks women wiped out every female on the face of the earth but the one I'm talking to. That makes her the last piece of tail on the face of the earth, Billy! It's just natural then to be extra nice." Even though he's my brother, I swear to God he had to been left on our doorstep.

Of course, you can't argue with success. As soon as Gene hung up and smiled, Powers knew he was diddled. Once. But my brother don't show much mercy. Twice was coming. It turned out Nancy Williams had a cousin staying with her for Christmas vacation. She wondered if maybe Gene could get this cousin a date? When Powers heard that, he pretty nearly went off in his pants. Nobody'll go out with him. He's fat and he sweats and he never brushes his teeth, there's stuff grows on them looks like the crap that floats on top of a slough. Even the really desperate girls figure no date is less damaging to their reputations than a date with Powers. You got to hold the line somewhere is how they look at it.

So Ernie's big yap cost him fifteen dollars. He blew that month's baby bonus (which his old lady gives him because he promises to finish school) and part of his allowance. The other five bucks is what he had to pay when Gene sold him Nancy Williams' cousin. It damn near killed him.

All right. Maybe I ought to've said something when Gene marched fat Ernie over to the Bank of Montreal to make a withdrawal on this account Powers has had since he was seven and started saving for a bike. He never got around to getting the bike because he couldn't bring himself to ever see that balance go down. Which is typical.

Already then I *knew* Ernie wasn't taking the cousin to no Christmas Dance. I'd heard once too often from that moron how Whipper Billy Watson would hang a licking on Cassius Clay, or how all the baseball owners get together in the spring to decide which team will win the World Series in the fall. He might learn to keep his hole shut for once.

The thing is *I'd* made up my mind to take the cousin. For nothing. It just so happens that, Gene being mad, he'd kind of forgot he's not allowed to touch the old man's vehicle. Seeing as he tied a chrome granny knot around a telephone pole with the last one.

Gene didn't realize it yet but he wasn't going nowhere unless I drove. And I was going to drive because I'd happened to notice Nancy Williams around. She seemed like a very nice person who maybe had what Miss Clark says are principles. I suspected that if that was true, Gene for once was going to strike out, and no way was I going to miss *that*. Fuck, I'd have killed to see that. No exaggeration.

On the night of the Christmas Dance it's snowing like a bitch. Not that it's cold for December, mind you, but snowing. Sticky, sloppy stuff that almost qualifies for sleet, coming down like crazy. I had to put the windshield wipers on. In December yet.

Nancy Williams lives on the edge of town way hell and gone, in new company housing. The mine manager is the dick who named it Green Meadows. What a joke. Nobody lives there seen a blade of grass yet nor pavement neither. They call it Gumboot Flats because if it's not frozen it's mud. No street-lights neither. It took me a fuck of a long time to find her house in the dark. When I did I shut off the motor and me and Gene just sat.

"Well?" I says after a bit. I was waiting for Gene to get out first.

"Well what?"

"Well, maybe we should go get them?"

Gene didn't answer. He leans across me and plays "Shave and a haircut, two bits" on the horn.

"You're a geek," I tell him. He don't care.

We wait. No girls. Gene gives a couple of long, long blasts on the hooter. I was wishing he wouldn't. This time somebody pulls open the living-room drapes. There stands this character in suspenders, for chrissakes, and a pair of pants stops about two inches shy of his armpits. He looked like somebody's father and what you'd call belligerent.

"I think he wants us to come to the door."

"He can want all he likes. Jesus Murphy, it's snowing out there. I got no rubbers."

"Oh, Christ," I says, "I'll go get them, Gene. It's such a big deal."

Easier said than done. I practically had to present a medical certificate. By the time Nancy's father got through with me I was starting to sound like that meatball Chip on *My Three Sons*. Yes sir. No sir. He wasn't too impressed with the horn-blowing episode, let me tell you. And then Nancy's old lady totes out a Kodak to get some "snaps" for Nancy's scrapbook. I didn't say nothing but I felt maybe they were getting evidence for the trial in case they had to slap a charge on me later. You'd have had to see it to believe it. Here I was standing with Nancy and her cousin, grinning like I was in my right mind, flash bulbs going off in my face, nodding away to the old man, who was running a safe-driving clinic for yours truly on the sidelines. Gene, I says to myself, Gene, you're going to pay.

At last, after practically swearing a blood oath to get his precious girls home, *undamaged,* by twelve-thirty, I chase the women out the door. And while they run through the snow, giggling, Stirling Moss delays me on the doorstep, in this blizzard, showing me for about the thousandth time how to pull a car out of a skid on ice. I kid you not.

From that point on everything goes rapidly downhill.

Don't get me wrong. I got no complaints against the girls. Doreen, the cousin, wasn't going to break no mirrors, and she sure was a lot more lively than I expected. Case in point. When I finally get to the car, fucking near frozen, what do I see? Old Doreen hauling up about a yard of her skirt, which she rolled around her waist like the spare tire on a fat guy. Then she pulled her sweater down to hide it. You bet I was staring.

"Uncle Bob wouldn't let me wear my mini," she says. "Got a smoke? I haven't had one for days."

It seems she wasn't the only one had a bit of a problem with the dress code that night. In the back seat I could hear Nancy apologizing to Gene for the outfit her mother had made her special for the dance. Of course, I thought Nancy looked quite nice. But with her frame she couldn't help, even though she was got up a bit peculiar. What I mean is, she had on this dress made out of the same kind of shiny material my mother wanted for drapes. But the old man said she couldn't have it because it was too heavy. It'd pull the curtain rods off the wall.

I could tell poor old Nancy Williams sure was nervous. She just got finished apologizing for how she looked and then she started in suckholing to Gene to please excuse her because she wasn't the world's best dancer. As a matter of fact this was her first dance ever. Thank heavens for Doreen, who was such a good sport. She'd been teaching her to dance all week. But it takes lots and lots of practice to get the hang of it. She hoped she didn't break his toes stepping on them. Ha ha ha. Just remember, she was still learning.

Gene said he'd be glad to teach her anything he figured she needed to know.

Nancy didn't catch on because she doesn't have that kind of mind. "That would be sweet of you, Gene," she says.

The band didn't show because of the storm. An act of God they call it. I'll say. So I drove around this dump for about an hour while Gene tried to molest Nancy. She put up a fair-to-middling struggle from what I could hear. The stuff her dress was made of was so stiff it crackled when she moved. Sort of like tin foil. Anyway, the two of them had it snapping and crackling like a bonfire there in the back seat while they fought a pitched battle over her body. She wasn't having none of that first time out of the chute.

"*Gene!*"

"Well for chrissakes, relax!"

"Don't take the Lord's name in vain."

"What's that supposed to mean?"

"Don't swear."

"Who's swearing?"

"Don't snag my nylons, Gene. Gene, what in the world are you … *Gene!*"

"Some people don't know when they're having a good time," says Doreen. I think she was a little pissed I hadn't parked and give her some action. But Lord knows what might've happened to Nancy if I'd done that.

Then, all of a sudden, Nancy calls out, sounding what you'd call desperate, "Hey, everbody, who wants a Coke!"

"Nobody wants a Coke," mumbles Gene, sort of through his teeth.

"Well, maybe we could go some place?" Meaning somewhere well-lit where this octopus will lay off for five seconds.

"I'll take you some place," Gene mutters. "You want to go somewhere, we'll go to Zipper's. Hey Billy, let's take them to Zipper's."

"I don't know, Gene …"

The way I said that perked Doreen up right away. As far as she was concerned, anything was better than driving around with a dope, looking at a snowstorm. "Hey," she hollers, "that sounds like *fun!*" Fun like a mental farm.

That clinched it though. "Sure," says Gene, "we'll check out Zipper's."

What could I say?

Don't get me wrong. Like everybody else I go to Zipper's and do stuff you can't do any place else in town. That's not it. But I wouldn't take anybody nice there on purpose. And I'm not trying to say that Zipper and his mother are bad people neither. It's just that so many shitty things have happened to those two that they've become kind of unpredictable. If you aren't used to that it can seem pretty weird.

I mean, look at Zipper. This guy is a not entirely normal human being who tries to tattoo himself with geometry dividers and India ink. He has this home poke on his arm which he claims is an American bald eagle but looks like a demented turkey or something. He did it himself, and the worst is he doesn't know how homely that bird is. The dumb prick shows it to people to admire.

Also, I should say a year ago he quits school to teach himself to be a drummer. That's all. He doesn't get a job or nothing, just sits at home and drums, and his mother, who's a widow and doesn't know any better, lets him. I guess that that's not any big surprise. She's a pretty hopeless drunk who's been taking her orders from Zipper since he was six. That's when his old man got electrocuted out at the mine.

Still, I'm not saying that the way Zipper is is entirely his fault. Though he can be a real creep all right. Like once when he was about ten years old Momma Zipper gets a jag on and passes out naked in the bedroom, and he lets any of his friends look at his mother with no clothes on for chrissakes, if they pay him a dime. His own mother, mind you.

But in his defence I'd say he's seen a lot of "uncles" come and go in his time, some of which figured they'd make like the man of the house and tune him in. For a while there when he was eleven, twelve maybe, half the time he was coming to school with a black eye.

Now you take Gene, he figures Zipper's house is heaven on earth. No rules. Gene figures that's the way life ought to be. No rules. Of course, nothing's entirely free. At Zipper's you got to bring a bottle or a case of beer and give Mrs. Zipper a few snorts, then everything is hunky-dory. Gene had a bottle of Five Star stashed under the back seat for the big Christmas Dance, so we were okay in that department.

But that night the lady of the house didn't seem to be around, or mobile anyway. Zipper himself came to the door, sweating like a pig in a filthy T-shirt. He'd been drumming along to the radio.

"What do you guys want?" says Zipper.

Gene holds up the bottle. "Party time."

"I'm practising," says Zipper.

"So you're practising. What's that to us?"

"My old lady's sleeping on the sofa," says Zipper, opening the door wide. "You want to fuck around here you do it in the basement." Which means his old lady'd passed out. Nobody *sleeps* through Zipper on the drums.

"*Gene.*" Nancy was looking a bit shy, believe me.

My brother didn't let on he'd even heard her. "Do I look particular? You know me, Zip."

Zipper looked like maybe he had to think about that one. To tell the truth, he didn't seem quite all there. At last he says, "Sure. Sure, I know you. Keep a cool tool." And then, just like that, he wanders off to his drums, and leaves us standing there. Gene laughs and shakes his head. "What a meatball."

It makes me feel empty lots of times when I see Zipper. He's so skinny and yellow and his eyes are always weepy-looking. They say there's something gone wrong with his kidneys from all the gas and glue he sniffed when he was in elementary school.

Boy, he loves his drums though. Zipper's really what you'd call dedicated. The sad thing is that the poor guy's got no talent. He just makes a big fucking racket and he don't know any better. You see, Zipper really thinks he's going to make himself somebody with those drums, he really does. Who'd tell him any different?

Gene found some dirty coffee cups in the kitchen sink and started rinsing them out. While he did that I watched Nancy Williams. She hadn't taken her coat off, in fact she was hugging it tight to her chest like she figured somebody was going to tear it off of her. I hadn't noticed before she had on a little bit of lipstick. But now her face had gone so pale it made her mouth look bright and red and pinched like somebody had just slapped it, hard.

Zipper commenced slamming away just as the four of us got into the basement. Down there it sounded as if we were right inside a great big drum and Zipper was beating the skin directly over our heads.

And boy, did it *stink* in that place. Like the sewer had maybe backed up. But then there were piles of dirty laundry humped up on the floor all around an old wringer washing machine, so that could've been the smell too.

It was cold and sour down there and we had nothing to sit on but a couple of lawn chairs and a chesterfield that was all split and stained with what I think was you know what. Nancy looked like she wished she had a newspaper to spread out over it before she sat down. As I said before, you shouldn't never take anybody nice to Zipper's.

Gene poured rye into the coffee mugs he'd washed out and passed them around. Nancy didn't want hers. "No thank you," she told him.

"You're embarrassing me, Nancy," says Doreen. The way my date was sitting in the lawn chair beside me in her make-do mini I knew why Gene was all scrunched down on that wrecked chesterfield.

"You know I don't drink, Doreen." Let me explain that when Nancy said that it didn't sound snotty. Just quiet and well-mannered like when a polite person passes up the parsnips. Nobody in their right minds holds it against them.

"You don't do much, do you?" That was Gene's two bits' worth.

"I'll say," chips in Doreen.

Nancy doesn't answer. I could hear old Zipper crashing and banging away like a madman upstairs.

"You don't do much, *do you?*" Gene's much louder this time.

"I suppose not." I can barely hear her answer because her head's down. She's checking out the backs of her hands.

"Somebody in your position ought to try harder," Doreen pipes up. "You don't make yourself too popular when you go spoiling parties."

Gene shoves the coffee mug at Nancy again. "Have a drink."

She won't take it. Principles.

"Have a drink!"

"Whyn't you lay off her?"

Gene's pissed off because he can't make Nancy Williams do what he says, so he jumps off the chesterfield and starts yelling at me. "Who's going to make me?" he hollers. "You? You going to make me?"

I can't do nothing but get up too. I never won a fight with my brother yet, but that don't mean I got to lay down and die for him. "You better take that sweater off," I says, pointing, "it's mine and I don't want blood on it." He always wears my clothes.

That's when the cousin Doreen slides in between us. She's the kind of girl loves fights. They put her centre stage. That is, if she can wriggle herself in and get involved breaking them up. Fights give her a chance to act all emotional and hysterical like she can't stand all the violence. Because she's so sensitive. Blessed are the peacemakers.

"Don't fight! Please, don't fight! Come on, Gene," she cries, latching on to his arm, "don't fight over her. Come away and cool down. I got to go to the bathroom. You show me where the bathroom is, Gene. Okay?"

"Don't give me that. You can find the bathroom yourself." Old Gene has still got his eyes fixed on me. He's acting the role. Both of them are nuts.

"Come on, Gene, I'm scared to go upstairs with that Zipper person there! He's so strange. I don't know what he might get it in his head to do. Come on, take me upstairs." Meanwhile this Doreen, who is as strong as your average sensitive ox, is sort of dragging my brother in the direction of the stairs. Him pretending he don't really want to go and have a fuss made over him, because he's got this strong urge to murder me or cripple me or something.

"You wait" is all he says to me.

"Ah, quit it or I'll die of shock," I tell him.

"Please, Gene. That Zipper person is *weird*."

At last he goes with her. I hear Gene on the stairs. "Zipper ain't much," he says, "I know lots of guys crazier than him."

I look over to Nancy sitting quietly on that grungy chesterfield, feet together, hands turned palms up on her lap. Her dress kind of sticks out from under the hem of her coat all stiff and shiny and funny-looking.

"I shouldn't have let her make me this dress," she says, angry. "We ought to have gone downtown and bought a proper one. But she had this *material*." She stops, pulls at the buttons of her coat and opens it. "Look at this thing. No wonder Gene doesn't like it, I bet."

At first I don't know what to say when she looks at me like that, her face all white except for two hot spots on her cheekbones. Zipper is going nuts upstairs. He's hot tonight. It almost sounds like something recognizable. "Don't pay Gene any attention," I say, "he's a goof."

"It's awful, this dress."

She isn't that dumb. But a person needs a reason for why things go wrong. I'm not telling her she's just a way to win ten dollars and prove a point.

"Maybe it's because I wouldn't drink that whiskey? Is that it?"

"Well, kind of. That's part of it. He's just a jerk. Take it from me, I know. Forget it."

"I never even thought he knew I was alive. Never guessed. And here I was, crazy about him. Just crazy. I'd watch him in the hallway, you know? I traded lockers with Susan Braithwaite just to get closer to his. I went to all the hockey games to see him play. I worshipped him."

The way she says that, well, it was too personal. Somebody oughtn't to say that kind of a thing to a practical stranger. It was worse than if she'd climbed out of her clothes. It made me embarrassed.

"An funny thing is, all that time he really did think I was cute. He told me on the phone. But he never once thought to ask me out because I'm a Baptist. He was sure I couldn't go. Because I'm a Baptist he thought I couldn't go. But he thought I was cute all along."

"Well, yeah."

"And now," she says, "look at this. I begged and begged Dad to let me come. I practically got down on my hands and knees. And all those dancing lessons and everything and the band doesn't show. Imagine."

"Gene wouldn't have danced with you anyway. He doesn't dance."

Nancy smiled at me. As if I was mental. She didn't half believe me.

"Hey," I says, just like that, you never know what's going to get into you, "Nancy, you want to dance?"

"Now?"

"Now. Sure. Come on. We got the one-man band, Zipper, upstairs. Why not?"

"What'll Gene say?"

"To hell with Gene. Make him jealous."

She was human at least. She liked the idea of Gene jealous. "Okay."

And here I got a confession to make. I go on all the time about Gene not being able to dance. Well, me neither. But I figured what the fuck. You just hop around and hope to hell you don't look too much like you're having a convulsion.

Neither of us knew how to get started. We just stood gawking at one another. Upstairs Zipper was going out of his tree. It sounded like there was four of him. As musical as a bag of hammers he is.

"The natives are restless tonight, Giles," I says. I was not uncomfortable. Let me tell you another one.

"Pardon?"

"Nothing. It was just dumb."

Nancy starts to sway from side to side, shuffling her feet. I figure that's the signal. I hop or whatever. So does she. We're out of the gate, off and running.

To be perfectly honest, Nancy Williams can't dance for shit. She gets this intense look on her face like she's counting off in her head, and starts to jerk. Which gets some pretty interesting action out of the notorious matched set but otherwise is pretty shoddy. And me? Well, I'm none too co-ordinated myself, so don't go getting no mental picture of Fred Astaire or whoever.

In the end what you had was two people who can't dance, dancing to the beat of a guy who can't drum. Still, Zipper didn't know no better and at the time neither did we. We were just what you'd call mad dancing fools. We danced and danced and Zipper drummed and drummed and we were all together and didn't know it. Son of a bitch, the harder we danced the hotter and happier Nancy Williams' face got. It just smoothed the unhappiness right out of it. Mine too, I guess.

That is, until all of a sudden it hit her. She stops dead in her tracks and asks, "Where's Doreen and Gene?"

Good question. They'd buggered off in my old man's car. Zipper didn't know where.

The rest of the evening was kind of a horror story. It took me a fair while to convince Nancy they hadn't gone for Cokes or something and would be right back. In the end she took it like a trooper. The only thing she'd say was, "That Doreen. *That Doreen,*" and shake her head. Of course she said it about a thousand times. I was wishing she'd shut up, or maybe give us a little variety like, "*That Gene.*" No way.

I had a problem. How to get Cinderella home before twelve-thirty, seeing as Gene had the family chariot. I tried Harvey's Taxi but no luck. Harvey's Taxi is one car and Harvey, and both were out driving lunches to a crew doing overtime at the mine.

Finally, at exactly twelve-thirty, we struck out on foot in this blizzard. Jesus, was it snowing. There was slush and ice water and every kind of shit and corruption all over the road. Every time some hunyak roared by us we got splattered by a sheet of cold slop. The snow melted in our hair and run down our necks and faces. By the time we went six blocks we were soaked. Nancy was the worst off because she wasn't dressed too good with nylons and the famous dress and such. I seen I had to be a gentleman so I stopped and give her my gloves, and my scarf to tie around her head. The two of us looked like those German soldiers I seen on TV making this death march out of Russia, on that series *Canada at War.* That was a very educational series. It made you think of man's inhumanity to man quite often.

"I could just die," she kept saying. "Dad is going to kill me. This is my last dance ever. I could just die. I could just die. *That Doreen.* Honestly!"

When we stumbled up her street, all black because of the lack of street-lights, I could see that her house was all lit up. Bad news. I stopped her on the corner. Just then it quits snowing. That's typical.

She stares at the house. "Dad's waiting."

"I guess I better go no further."

Nancy Williams bends down and feels her dress where it sticks out from under her coat. "It's soaked. I don't know how much it cost a yard. I could just die."

"Well," I says, repeating myself like an idiot, "I guess I better go no further." Then I try and kiss her. She sort of straight-arms me. I get the palm of my own glove in the face.

"What're you doing?" She sounds mad.

"Well, you know — "

"I'm not *your* date," she says, real offended. "I'm your brother's date."

"Maybe we could go out some time?"

"I won't be going anywhere for a long time. Look at me. He's going to kill me."

"Well, when you do? I'm in no hurry."

"Don't you understand? Don't you understand? Daddy will never let me go out with anybody named Simpson again. Ever. Not after tonight."

"Ever?"

"I can't imagine what you'd have to do to redeem yourself after this mess. That's how Daddy puts it — you've got to redeem yourself. I don't even know how *I'm* going to do it. And none of it's my fault."

"Yeah," I says, "he'll remember me. I'm the one he took the picture of."

She didn't seem too upset at not having me calling. "Everything is ruined," she says. "If you only knew."

Nancy Williams turns away from me then and goes up that dark, dark street where there's nobody awake except at her house. Wearing my hat and gloves.

Nancy Williams sits third pew from the front, left-hand side. I sit behind her, on the other side so's I can watch her real close. Second Sunday I was there she wore her Christmas Dance dress.

Funny thing, everything changes. At first I thought I'd start going and maybe that would *redeem* myself with her old man. Didn't work. He just looks straight through me.

You ought to see her face when she sings those Baptist hymns. It gets all hot and happy-looking, exactly like it did when we were dancing together and Zipper was pounding away there up above us, where we never even saw him. When her face gets like that there's no trouble in it, by no means.

It's like she's dancing then, I swear. But to what I don't know. I try to hear it. I try and try. I listen and listen to catch it. Christ, somebody tell me. What's she dancing to? Who's the drummer?

ALICE WALKER

Alice Walker was born in 1944 in Eatonville, Georgia, the daughter of sharecroppers. She was educated at Sarah Lawrence College, and in the 1960s was a social activist, working in the Civil Rights movement, the Head Start program, and the New York City welfare department. Thereafter she taught at various colleges and universities across the country. In poetry, novels, short stories, and essays Walker has articulated her intense belief in social and racial justice. Her novels include *The Third Life of Grange Copeland* (1970), *Meridian* (1976), and *The Color Purple* (1982). Her stories are collected in *In Love and Trouble: Stories of Black Women* (1973), and *You Can't Keep a Good Woman Down* (1982). Although in her fiction Walker writes primarily of the experience of black women, she has been seen by some critics as a spokesperson for all those oppressed; and although she tells of pain and desperation, she nonetheless brings an affirmative sense of possibility to her work. As she said of her most famous character, Celie (in *The Color Purple*): "Let's hope people can hear Celie's voice. There are so many people like Celie who make it, who come out of nothing. People who triumph." Hope, indeed, is at the heart of "To Hell with Dying," a largely autobiographical story about the redemptive power of love.

To Hell with Dying

"To hell with dying," my father would say. "These children want Mr. Sweet!" Mr. Sweet was a diabetic and an alcoholic and a guitar player and lived down the road from us on a neglected cotton farm. My older brothers and sisters got the most benefit from Mr. Sweet, for when they were growing up he had quite a few years ahead of him and so was capable of being called back from the brink of death any number of times — whenever the voice of my father reached him as he lay expiring. "To hell with dying, man," my father would say, pushing the wife away from the bedside (in tears although she knew the death was not necessarily the last one unless Mr. Sweet really wanted it to be). "These children want Mr. Sweet!" And they did want him, for at a signal from Father they would come crowding around the bed and throw themselves on the covers, and whoever was the smallest at the time would kiss him all over his wrinkled brown face and tickle him so that he would laugh all down in his stomach, and his mustache, which was long and sort of straggly, would shake like Spanish moss and was also that color.

Mr. Sweet had been ambitious as a boy, wanted to be a doctor or lawyer or sailor, only to find that black men fare better if they are not. Since he could become none of these things he turned to fishing as his only earnest career and playing the guitar as his only claim to doing anything extraordinarily well. His son, the only one that he and his wife, Miss Mary, had, was shiftless as the day is long and spent money as if he were trying to see the bottom of the mint, which Mr. Sweet would tell him was the clean brown palm of his hand. Miss Mary loved her "baby," however, and worked hard to get him the "li'l necessaries" of life, which turned out mostly to be women.

Mr. Sweet was a tall, thinnish man with thick kinky hair going dead white. He was dark brown, his eyes were squinty and sort of bluish, and he chewed Brown Mule tobacco. He was constantly on the verge of being blind drunk, for he brewed his own liquor and was not in the least a stingy sort of man, and was always very melancholy and sad, though frequently when he was "feelin'" good" he'd dance around the yard with us, usually keeling over just as my mother came to see what the commotion was.

Toward all of us children he was very kind, and had the grace to be shy with us, which is unusual in grown-ups. He had great respect for my mother for she never held his drunkenness against him and would let us play with him even when he was about to fall in the fireplace from drink. Although Mr. Sweet would sometimes lose complete or nearly complete control of his head and neck so that he would loll in his chair, his mind remained strangely acute and his speech not too affected. His ability to be drunk and sober at the same time made him an ideal playmate, for he was as weak as we were and we could usually best him in wrestling, all the while keeping a fairly coherent conversation going.

We never felt anything of Mr. Sweet's age when we played with him. We loved his wrinkles and would draw some on our brows to be like him, and his white hair was my special treasure and he knew it and would never come to visit us just after he had had his hair cut off at the barbershop. Once he came to our house for something, probably to see my father about fertilizer for his crops, because, although he never paid the slightest attention to his crops, he liked to know what things would be best to use on them if he ever did. Anyhow, he had not come with his hair since he had just had it shaved off at the barbershop. He wore a huge straw hat to keep off the sun and also to keep his head away from me. But as soon as I saw him I ran up and demanded that he take me up and kiss me with his funny beard which smelled so strongly of tobacco. Looking forward to burying my small fingers into his woolly hair I threw away his hat only to find he had done something to his hair, that it was no longer there! I let out a squall which made my mother think that Mr. Sweet had finally dropped me in the well or something and from that day I've been wary of men in hats. However, not long after, Mr. Sweet showed up with his hair grown out and just as white and kinky and impenetrable as it ever was.

Mr. Sweet used to call me his princess, and I believed it. He made me feel pretty at five and six, and simply outrageously devastating at the blazing age of eight and a half. When he came to our house with his guitar the whole family would stop whatever they were doing to sit around him and listen to him play. He liked to play "Sweet Georgia Brown," that was what he called me sometimes, and also he liked to play "Caldonia" and all sorts of sweet, sad, wonderful songs which he sometimes made up. It was from one of these songs that I heard that he had had to marry Miss Mary when he had in fact loved somebody else (now living in Chi-ca-go, or De-stroy, Michigan). He was not sure that Joe Lee, her "baby," was also his baby. Sometimes he would cry and that was an indication that he was about to die again. And so we would all get prepared, for we were sure to be called upon.

I was seven the first time I remember actually participating in one of Mr. Sweet's "revivals" — my parents told me I had participated before. I had been the one chosen to kiss him and tickle him long before I knew the rite of Mr. Sweet's rehabilitation. He had come to our house, it was a few years after his wife's death, and was very sad, and also, typically, very drunk. He sat on the floor next to me and my older brother, the rest of the children were grown up and lived elsewhere, and began to play his guitar and cry. I held his woolly head in my arms and wished I could have been old enough to have been the woman he loved so much and that I had not been lost years and years ago.

When he was leaving, my mother said to us that we'd better sleep light that night for we'd probably have to go over to Mr. Sweet's before daylight. And we did. For soon after we had gone to bed one of the neighbors knocked on our door and called my father and said that Mr. Sweet was sinking fast and if he wanted to get in a word before the crossover he'd better shake a leg and get over to Mr. Sweet's house. All the neighbors knew to come to our house if something was wrong with Mr. Sweet, but they did not know how we always managed to make him well, or at least stop him from dying, when he was so often near death. As soon as we heard the cry we got up, my brother and I and my mother and father, and put on our clothes. We hurried out of the house and down the road for we were always afraid that we might someday be too late and Mr. Sweet would get tired of dallying.

When we got to the house, a very poor shack really, we found the front room full of neighbors and relatives and someone met us at the door and said it was all very sad that old Mr. Sweet Little (for Little was his family name, although we mostly ignored it) was about to kick the bucket. My parents were advised not to take my brother and me into the "death room," seeing we were so young and all, but we were so much accustomed to the death room than he that we ignored him and dashed in without giving his warning a second thought. I was almost in tears, for these deaths upset me fearfully, and the thought of how much depended on me and my brother (who was such a ham most of the time) made me very nervous.

The doctor was bending over the bed and turned back to tell us for at least the tenth time in the history of my family that, alas, old Mr. Sweet Little was dying and that the children had best not see the face of implacable death (I didn't know what "implacable" was, but whatever it was, Mr. Sweet was not!). My father pushed him rather abruptly out of the way saying, as he always did and very loudly for he was saying it to Mr. Sweet, "To hell with dying, man, these children want Mr. Sweet" — which was my cue to throw myself upon the bed and kiss Mr. Sweet all around the whiskers and under the eyes and around the collar of his nightshirt where he smelled so strongly of all sorts of things, mostly liniment.

I was very good at bringing him around, for as soon as I saw that he was struggling to open his eyes I knew he was going to be all right, and so could finish my revival sure of success. As soon as his eyes were open he would begin to smile and that way I knew that I had surely won. Once, though, I got a tremendous scare, for he could not open his eyes and later I learned that he had had a stroke and that one side of his face was stiff and hard to get into motion. When he began to smile I could tickle him in earnest because I was sure that nothing would get in the way of his laughter, although once he began to cough so hard that he almost threw me off his stomach, but that was when I was very small, little more than a baby, and my bushy hair had gotten in his nose.

When we were sure he would listen to us we would ask him why he was in bed and when he was coming to see us again and could we play his guitar, which more than likely would be leaning against the bed. His eyes would get all misty and he would sometimes cry out loud, but we never let it embarrass us, for he knew that we loved him and that we sometimes cried too for no reason. My parents would leave the room to just the three of us; Mr. Sweet, by that time, would be propped up in bed with a number of pillows behind his head and with me sitting and lying on his shoulder and along his chest. Even when he had trouble breathing he would not ask me to get down. Looking into my eyes he would shake his white head and run a scratchy old finger all around my hairline, which was rather low down, nearly to my eyebrows, and made some people say I looked like a baby monkey.

My brother was very generous in all this, he let me do all the revivaling — he had done it for years before I was born and so was glad to be able to pass it on to someone new. What he would do while I talked to Mr. Sweet was pretend to play the guitar, in fact pretend that he was a young version of Mr. Sweet, and it always made Mr. Sweet glad to think that someone wanted to be like him — of course, we did not know this then, we played the thing by ear, and whatever he seemed to like, we did. We were desperately afraid that he was just going to take off one day and leave us.

It did not occur to us that we were doing anything special; we had not learned that death was final when it did come. We thought nothing of triumphing over it so many times, and in fact became a trifle contemptuous of people who let themselves be carried away. It did not occur to us that if our father had been dying we could not have stopped it, that Mr. Sweet was the only person over whom we had power.

When Mr. Sweet was in his eighties I was studying in the university many miles from home. I saw him whenever I went home, but he was never on the verge of dying that I could tell and I began to feel that my anixiety for his health and psychological well-being was unnecessary. By this time he not only had a mustache but a long flowing snow white beard, which I loved and combed and braided for hours. He was very peaceful, fragile, gentle, and the only jarring note about him was his old steel guitar, which he still played in the old sad, sweet, down-home blues way.

On Mr. Sweet's ninetieth birthday I was finishing my doctorate in Massachusetts and had been making arrangements to go home for several weeks' rest. That morning I got a telegram telling me that Mr. Sweet was dying again and could I please drop everything and come home. Of course I could. My dissertation could wait and my teachers would understand when I explained to them when I got back. I ran to the phone, called the airport, and within four hours I was speeding along the dusty road to Mr. Sweet's.

The house was more dilapidated than when I was last there, barely a shack, but it was overgrown with yellow roses which my family had planted many years ago. The air was heavy and sweet and very peaceful. I felt strange walking through the gate and up the old rickety steps. But the strangeness left me as I caught sight of the long white beard I loved so well flowing down the thin body over the familiar quilt coverlet, Mr. Sweet!

His eyes were closed tight and his hands, crossed over his stomach, were thin and delicate, no longer scratchy. I remembered how always before I had run and jumped up on him just anywhere; now I knew he would not be able to support my weight. I looked around at my parents, and was surprised to see that my father and mother also looked old and frail. My father, his own hair very gray, leaned over the quietly sleeping old man, who, incidentally, smelled still of wine and tobacco, and said, as he'd done so many times, "To hell with dying, man! My daughter is home to see Mr. Sweet!" My brother had not been able to come as he was in the war in Aisa. I bent down and gently stroked the closed eyes and gradually they began to open. The closed, wine-stained lips twitched a little, then parted in a warm, slightly embarrassed smile. Mr. Sweet could see me and he recognized me and his eyes looked very spry and twinkly for a moment. I put my head down on the pillow next to his and we just looked at each other for a long time. Then he began to trace my peculiar hairline with a thin, smooth finger. I closed my eyes when his finger halted above my ear (he used to rejoice at the dirt in my ears when I was little), his hand stayed cupped around my cheek. When I opened my eyes, sure that I had reached him in time, his were closed.

Even at twenty-four how could I believe that I had failed? that Mr. Sweet was really gone? He had never gone before. But when I looked at my parents I saw that they were holding back tears. They had loved him dearly. He was like a piece of rare and delicate china which was always being saved from breaking and which finally fell. I looked long at the old face, the wrinkled forehead, the red lips, the hands that still reached out to me. Soon I felt my father pushing something cool into my hands. It was Mr. Sweet's guitar. He had asked them months before to give it to me; he had known that even if I came next time he would not be able to respond in the old way. He did not want me to feel that my trip had been for nothing.

The old guitar! I plucked the strings, hummed "Sweet Georgia Brown." The magic of Mr. Sweet lingered still in the cool steel box. Through the window I could catch the fragrant delicate scent of tender yellow roses. The man on the high old-fashioned bed with the quilt coverlet and the flowing white beard had been my first love.

EUDORA WELTY

 Eudora Welty was born in 1909 in Jackson, Mississippi, and has lived there almost all her life. She was educated at Mississippi State College for Women and the University of Wisconsin, and for a time attended the Columbia School of Advertising in New York. During the Depression years of the 1930s she worked for the WPA, traveling all over Mississippi and photographing what she saw. It was this experience that prompted her to begin writing: "A fuller awareness of what I needed had to be sought for through another way, through writing stories." Her first collection of stories, *A Curtain of Green*, was published in 1941, and from that time she wrote the novels and stories that have brought her acclaim and affection. Her novels are *Delta Wedding* (1946), *The Ponder Heart* (1954), and *The Optimist's Daughter* (1972). Her other collections of stories are *The Wide Net and Other Stories* (1943), *The Golden Apples* (1949), *The Bride of Innisfallen and Other Stories* (1955), *Thirteen Stories* (1965), and *The Collected Stories of Eudora Welty* (1980). Welty has been called a regionalist, perhaps the best-known voice of Southern literature today. She is wary of "speaking for" any culture, but she does see in the Southern "sense of family" an impetus for the way she writes: "You don't just know people in little segments, or minutes, or only under certain circumstances. You know them under all circumstances. It can't help but develop your sense of narrative, the continuity in history of the life there." The stories here are both monologues but they are markedly different from one another. "Circe" is a powerful re-creation of the Greek myth; "Why I Live at the P.O." is an hilarious dramatization of a family, a "Southern kind of exaggeration," as Welty puts it.

Circe

Needle in air, I stopped what I was making. From the upper casement, my lookout on the sea, I saw them disembark and find the path; I heard that whole drove of mine break loose on the beautiful strangers. I slipped down the ladder. When I heard men breathing and sandals kicking the stones, I threw open the door. A shaft of light from the zenith struck my brow, and the wind let out my hair. Something else swayed my body outward.

"Welcome!" I said — the most dangerous word in the world.

Heads lifted to the smell of my bread, they trooped inside — and with such a grunting and frisking at their heels to the very threshold. Stargazers! They stumbled on my polished floor, strewing sand, crowding on each other, sizing up the household for gifts (thinking already of sailing away), and sighted upward where the ladder went, to the sighs of the island girls who peeped from the kitchen door. In the hope of a bath, they looked in awe at their hands.

I left them thus, and withdrew to make the broth.

With their tear-bright eyes they watched me come in with the great winking ray, and circle the room in a winding wreath of steam. Each in turn with a pair of black-nailed hands swept up his bowl. The first were trotting at my heels while the last still reached with their hands. Then the last drank too, and dredging their snouts from the bowls, let go and shuttled into the company.

That moment of transformation — only the gods really like it! Men and beasts almost never take in enough of the wonder to justify the trouble. The floor was swaying like a bridge in battle. "Outside!" I commanded. "No dirt is allowed in this house!" In the end, it takes phenomenal neatness of housekeeping to put it through the heads of men that they are swine. With my wand seething in the air like a broom, I drove them all through the door — twice as many hooves as there had been feet before — to join their brothers, who rushed forward to meet them now, filthily rivaling, but welcoming. What tusks I had given them!

As I shut the door on the sight, and drew back into my privacy — deathless privacy that heals everything, even the effort of magic — I felt something from behind press like the air of heaven before a storm, and reach like another wand over my head.

I spun round, thinking, O gods, it has failed me, it's drying up. Before everything, I think of my power. One man was left.

"What makes you think you're different from anyone else?" I screamed; and he laughed.

Before I'd believe it, I ran back to my broth. I had thought it perfect — I'd allowed no other woman to come near it. I tasted, and it was perfect — swimming with oysters from my reef and flecks of golden pork, redolent with leaves of bay and basil and rosemary, with the glass of island wine tossed in at the last: it has been my infallible recipe. Circe's broth: all the gods have heard of it and envied it. No, the fault had to be in the drinker. If a man remained, unable to leave that magnificent body of his, then enchantment had met with a hero. Oh, I know those prophecies as well as the back of my hand — only nothing is here to warn me when it is *now*.

The island girls, those servants I support, stood there in the kitchen and smiled at me. I threw kettle and all at their withering heels. Let them learn that unmagical people are put into the world to justify and serve the magical — not to smile at them!

I whirled back again. The hero stood as before. But his laugh had gone too, after his friends. His gaze was empty, as though I were not in it — I was invisible. His hand groped across the rushes of a chair. I moved beyond him and bolted the door against the murmurous outside. Still invisibly, I took away his sword. I sent his tunic away to the spring for washing, and I, with my own hands, gave him his bath. Then he sat and dried himself before the fire — carefully, the only mortal man on an island in the sea. I rubbed oil on his shadowy shoulders, and on the rope of curls in which his jaw was set. His rapt ears still listened to the human silence there.

"I know your name," I said in the voice of a woman, "and you know mine by now."

I took the chain from my waist, it slipped shining to the floor between us, where it lay as if it slept, as I came forth. Under my palms he stood warm and dense as a myrtle grove at noon. His limbs were heavy, braced like a sleep-walker's who has wandered, alas, to cliffs above the sea. When I passed before him, his arm lifted and barred my way. When I held up the glass he opened his mouth. He fell among the pillows, his still-open eyes two clouds stopped over the sun, and I lifted and kissed his hand.

It was he who in a burst of speech announced the end of day. As though the hour brought a signal to the wanderer, he told me a story, while the owl made comment outside. He told me of the monster with one eye — he had put out the eye, he said.

Yes, said the owl, the monster is growing another, and a new man will sail along to blind it again. I had heard it all before, from man and owl. I didn't want his story, I wanted his secret.

When Venus leaned at the window, I called him by name, but he had talked himself into a dream, and his dream had him fast. I now saw through the cautious herb that had protected him from my broth. From the first, he had found some way to resist my power. He must laugh, sleep, ravish, he must talk and sleep. Next it would be he must die. I looked an age into that face above the beard's black crescent, the eyes turned loose from mine like the statues' that sleep on the hill. I took him by the locks of his beard and hair, but he rolled away with his snore to the very floor of sleep — as far beneath my reach as the drowned sailor dropped out of his, in the tale he told of the sea.

I thought of my father the Sun, who went on his divine way untroubled, ambitionless — unconsumed; suffering no loss, no heroic fear of corruption through his constant shedding of light, needing no story, no retinue to vouch for where he has been — even heroes could learn of the gods!

Yet I know they keep something from me, asleep and awake. There exists a mortal mystery, that, if I knew where it was, I could crush like an island grape. Only frailty, it seems, can divine it — and I was not endowed with that property. They live by frailty! By the moment! I tell myself that it is only a mystery, and mystery is only uncertainty. (There is no mystery in magic! Men are swine: let it be said, and no sooner said than done.) Yet mortals alone can divine where it lies in each other, can find it and prick it in all its peril, with an instrument made of air. I swear that only to possess that one, trifling secret, I would willingly turn myself into a harmless dove for the rest of eternity!

When presently he leapt up, I had nearly forgotten he would move again — as a golden hibiscus startles you, all flowers, when you are walking in some weedy place apart.

Yes, but he would not dine. Dinner was carried in, but he would not dine with me until I would undo that day's havoc in the pigsty. I pointed out that his portion was served in a golden bowl — the very copy of that bowl my own father the Sun crosses back in each night after his journey of the day. But he cared nothing for beauty that was not of the world, he did not want the first taste of anything new. He wanted his men back. In the end, it was necessary for me to cloak myself and go down in the dark, under the willows where the bones are hung to the wind, into the sty; and to sort out and bring up his friends again from their muddy labyrinth. I had to pass them back through the doorway as themselves. I could not skip or brush lightly over one — he named and counted. Then he could look at them all he liked, staggering up on their hind legs before him. Their jaws sank asthmatically, and he cried, "Do you know me?"

"It's Odysseus!" I called, to spoil the moment. But with a shout he had already sprung to their damp embrace.

Reunions, it seems, are to be celebrated. (I have never had such a thing.) All of us feasted together on meat and bread, honey and wine, and the fire roared. We heard out the flute player, we heard out the story, and the fair-haired sailor, whose name is now forgotten, danced on the table and pleased them. When the fire was black, my servants came languishing from the kitchen, and all the way up the ladder to the beds above they had to pull the drowsy-kneed star-gazers, spilling laughter and songs all the way. I could hear them calling away to the girls as they would call them home. But the pigsty was where they belonged.

Hand in hand, we climbed to my tower room. His cheeks were grave and his eyes black, put out with puzzles and solutions. We conversed of signs, omens, premonitions, riddles and dreams, and ended in fierce, cold sleep. Strange man, as unflinching and as wound up as I am. His short life and my long one have their ground in common. Passion is our ground, our island — do others exist?

His sailors came jumping down in the morning, full of themselves and stories. Preparing the breakfast, I watched them tag one another, run rough-and-tumble around the table, regaling the house. "What did *I* do? How far did *I* go with it?" and in a reckless reassurance imitating the sounds of pigs at each other's backs. They were certainly more winsome now than they could ever have been before; I'd made them younger, too, while I was about it. But tell me of one that appreciated it! Tell me one now who looked my way until I had brought him his milk and figs.

When he made his appearance, we devoured a god's breakfast — all, the very sausages, taken for granted. The kitchen girls simpered and cried that if this went on, we'd be eaten out of house and home. But I didn't care if I put the house under greater stress for this one mortal than I ever dreamed of for myself — even on those lonely dull mornings when mist wraps the island and hides every path of the sea, and when my heart is black.

But a stir was upon them all from the moment they rose from the table. Treading on their napkins, tracking the clean floor with honey, they deserted me in the house and collected, arms wound on each other's shoulders, to talk beneath the sky. There they were in a knot, with him in the center of it. He folded his arms and sank his golden weight on one leg, while every ear on the island listened. I stood in the door and waited.

He walked up and said, "Thank you, Circe, for the hospitality we have enjoyed beneath your roof."

"What is the occasion for a speech?" I asked.

"We are setting sail," he said. "A year's visit is visit enough. It's time we were on our way."

Ever since the morning Time came and sat on the world, men have been on the run as fast as they can go, with beauty flung over their shoulders. I ground my teeth. I raised my wand in his face.

"You've put yourself to great trouble for us. You may have done too much," he said.

"I undid as much as I did!" I cried. "That was hard."

He gave me a pecking, recapitulating kiss, his black beard thrust at me like a shoe. I kissed it, his mouth, his wrist, his shoulder, I put my eyes to his eyes, through which I saw seas toss, and to the cabinet of his chest.

He turned and raised an arm to the others. "Tomorrow."

The knot broke and they wandered apart to the shore. They were not so forlorn when they could eat acorns and trot quickly where they would go.

It was as though I had no memory, to discover how early and late the cicadas drew long sighs like the playing out of all my silver shuttles. Wasn't it always the time of greatest heat, the Dog Star running with the Sun? The sea the color of honey looked sweet even to the tongue, the salt and vengeful sea. My grapes had ripened all over again while we stretched and drank our wine, and I ordered the harvest gathered and pressed, — but this wine, I made clear to the servants, was to store. Hospitality is one thing, but I must consider how my time is endless, how I shall need wine endlessly. They smiled; but magic is the tree, and intoxication is just the little bird that flies in it to sing and flies out again. But the wanderers were watching the sun and waiting for the stars.

Now the night wind was rising. I went my way over the house as I do by night to see if all is well and holding together. From the rooftop I looked out. I saw the vineyards spread out like wings on the hill, the servants' huts and the swarthy groves, the sea awake, and the eye of the black ship. I saw in the moonlight the dance of the bones in the willows. "Old, displeasing ones!" I sang to them on the wind. "There's another now more displeasing than you! Your bite would be sweeter to my mouth than the soft kiss of a wanderer." I looked up at Cassiopeia, who sits there and needs nothing, pale in her chair in the stream of heaven. The old Moon was still at work. "Why keep it up, old woman?" I whispered to her, while the lions roared among the rocks; but I could hear plainly the crying of birds nearby and along the mournful shore.

I swayed, and was flung backward by my torment. I believed that I lay in disgrace and my blood ran green, like the wand that breaks in two. My sight returned to me when I awoke in the pigsty, in the red and black aurora of flesh, and it was day.

They sailed from me, all but one.

The youngest — Elpenor was his name — fell from my roof. He had forgotten where he had gone to sleep. Drunk on the last night, the drunkest of them all — so as not to be known any longer as only the youngest — he'd gone to sleep on the rooftop, and when they called him, his step went off into air. I saw him beating down through the light with rosy fists, as though he'd never left his mother's side till then.

They all ran from the table as though a star had fallen. They stood or they crouched above Elpenor fallen in my yard, low-voiced now like conspirators — as indeed they were. They wept for Elpenor lying on his face, and for themselves, as *he* wept for them the day they came, when I had made them swine.

He knelt and touched Elpenor, and like a lover lifted him; then each in turn held the transformed boy in his arms. They brushed the leaves from his face, and smoothed his red locks, which were still in their tangle from his brief attempts at love-making and from his too-sound sleep.

I spoke from the door. "When you dig the grave for that one, and bury him in the lonely sand by the shadow of your fleeing ship, write on the stone: 'I died of love.'"

I thought I spoke in epitaph — in the idiom of man. But when they heard me, they left Elpenor where he lay, and ran. Red-limbed, with linens sparkling, they sped over the windy path from house to ship like a rainbow in the sun, like new butterflies turned erratically to sea. While he stood in the prow and shouted to them, they loaded the greedy ship. They carried off their gifts from me — all unappreciated, unappraised.

I slid out of their path. I had no need to see them set sail, knowing as well as if I'd been ahead of them all the way, the far and wide, misty and islanded, bright and indelible and menacing world under which they all must go. But foreknowledge is not the same as the last word.

My cheek against the stony ground, I could hear the swine like summer thunder. These were with me still, pets now, once again — grumbling without meaning. I rose to my feet. I was sickened, with child. The ground fell away before me, blotted with sweet myrtle, with high oak that would have given me a ship too, if I were not tied to my island, as Cassiopeia must be to the sticks and stars of her chair. We were a rim of fire, a ring on the sea. His ship was a moment's gleam on a wave. The little son, I knew, was to follow — follow and slay him. That was the story. For whom is a story enough? For the wanderers who will tell it — it's where they must find their strange felicity.

I stood on my rock and wished for grief. It would not come. Though I could shriek at the rising Moon, and she, so near, would wax or wane, there was still grief, that couldn't hear me — grief that cannot be round or plain or solid-bright or running on its track, where a curse could get at it. It has no heavenly course; it is like mystery, and knows where to hide itself. At last it does not even breathe. I cannot find the dusty mouth of grief. I am sure now grief is a ghost — only a ghost in Hades, where ungrateful Odysseus is going — waiting on him.

EUDORA WELTY

Why I Live at the P.O.

I was getting along fine with Mama, Papa-Daddy and Uncle Rondo until my sister Stella-Rondo just separated from her husband and came back home again. Mr. Whitaker! Of course I went with Mr. Whitaker first, when he first appeared here in China Grove, taking "Pose Yourself" photos, and Stella-Rondo broke us up. Told him I was one-sided. Bigger on one side than the other, which is a deliberate, calculated falsehood: I'm the same. Stella-Rondo is exactly twelve months to the day younger than I am and for that reason she's spoiled.

She's always had anything in the world she wanted and then she'd throw it away. Papa-Daddy gave her this gorgeous Add-a-Pearl necklace when she was eight years old and she threw it away playing baseball when she was nine, with only two pearls.

So as soon as she got married and moved away from home the first thing she did was separate! From Mr. Whitaker! This photographer with the popeyes she said she trusted. Came home from one of those towns up in Illinois and to our complete surprise brought this child of two.

Mama said she like to made her drop dead for a second. "Here you had this marvelous blonde child and never so much as wrote your mother a word about it," says Mama. "I'm thoroughly ashamed of you." But of course she wasn't.

Stella-Rondo just calmly takes off this *hat,* I wish you could see it. She says, "Why, Mama, Shirley-T.'s adopted, I can prove it."

"How?" says Mama, but all I says was, "H'm!" There I was over the hot stove, trying to stretch two chickens over five people and a completely unexpected child into the bargain, without one moment's notice.

"What do you — 'H'm!'?" says Stella-Rondo, and Mama says, "I heard that, Sister."

I said that oh, I didn't mean a thing, only that whoever Shirley-T. was, she was the spit-image of Papa-Daddy if he'd cut off his beard, which of course he'd never do in the world. Papa-Daddy's Mama's papa and sulks.

Stella-Rondo got furious! She said, "Sister, I don't need to tell you you got a lot of nerve and always did have and I'll thank you to make no future reference to my adopted child whatsoever."

"Very well," I said. "Very well, very well. Of course I noticed at once she looks like Mr. Whitaker's side too. That frown. She looks like a cross between Mr. Whitaker and Papa-Daddy."

"Well, all I can say is she isn't."

"She looks exactly like Shirley Temple to me," says Mama, but Shirley-T. just ran away from her.

So the first thing Stella-Rondo did at the table was turn Papa-Daddy against me.

"Papa-Daddy," she says. He was trying to cut up his meat. "Papa-Daddy!" I was taken completely by surprise. Papa-Daddy is about a million years old and's got this long-long beard. "Papa-Daddy, Sister says she fails to understand why you don't cut off your beard."

So Papa-Daddy l-a-y-s down his knife and fork! He's real rich. Mama says he is, he says he isn't. So he says, "Have I heard correctly? You don't understand why I don't cut off my beard?"

"Why," I says, "Papa-Daddy, of course I understand, I did not say any such of a thing, the idea!"

He says, "Hussy!"

I says, "Papa-Daddy, you know I wouldn't any more want you to cut off your beard than the man in the moon. It was the farthest thing from my mind! Stella-Rondo sat there and made that up while she was eating breast of chicken."

But he says, "So the postmistress fails to understand why I don't cut off my beard. Which job I got you through my influence with the government. 'Bird's nest' — is that what you call it?"

Not that it isn't the next to smallest P.O. in the entire state of Mississippi.

I says, "Oh, Papa-Daddy," I says, "I didn't say any such of a thing, I never dreamed it was a bird's nest, I have always been grateful though this is the next to smallest P.O. in the state of Mississippi, and I do not enjoy being referred to as a hussy by my own grandfather."

But Stella-Rondo says, "Yes, you did say it too. Anybody in the world could of heard you, that had ears."

"Stop right there," says Mama, looking at *me*.

So I pulled my napkin straight back through the napkin ring and left the table.

As soon as I was out of the room Mama says, "Call her back, or she'll starve to death," but Papa-Daddy says, "This is the beard I started growing on the Coast when I was fifteen years old." He would of gone on till nightfall if Shirley-T. hadn't lost the Milky Way she ate in Cairo.

So Papa-Daddy says, "I am going out and lie in the hammock, and you can all sit here and remember my words: I'll never cut off my beard as long as I live, even one inch, and I don't appreciate it in you at all." Passed right by me in the hall and went straight out and got in the hammock.

I would be a holiday. It wasn't five minutes before Uncle Rondo suddenly appeared in the hall in one of Stella-Rondo's flesh-colored kimonos, all cut on the bias, like something Mr. Whitaker probably thought was gorgeous.

"Uncle Rondo!" I says. "I didn't know who that was! Where are you going?"

"Sister," he says, "get out of my way, I'm poisoned."

"If you're poisoned stay away from Papa-Daddy," I says. "Keep out of the hammock. Papa-Daddy will certainly beat you on the head if you come within forty miles of him. He thinks I deliberately said he ought to cut off his beard after he got me the P.O., and I've told him and told him and told him, and he acts like he just don't hear me. Papa-Daddy must of gone stone deaf."

"He picked a fine day to do it then," says Uncle Rondo, and before you could say "Jack Robinson" flew out in the yard.

What he'd really done, he'd drunk another bottle of that prescription. He does it every single Fourth of July as sure as shooting, and it's horribly expensive. Then he falls over in the hammock and snores. So he insisted on zigzagging right on out to the hammock, looking like a half-wit.

Papa-Daddy woke up with this horrible yell and right there without moving an inch he tried to turn Uncle Rondo against me. I heard every word he said. Oh, he told Uncle Rondo I didn't learn to read till I was eight years old and he didn't see how in the world I ever got the mail put up at the P.O., much less read it all, and he said if Uncle Rondo could only fathom the lengths he had gone to to get me that job! And he said on the other hand he thought Stella-Rondo had a brilliant mind and deserved credit for getting out of town. All the time he was just lying there swinging as pretty as you please and looping out his beard, and poor Uncle Rondo was *pleading* with him to slow down the hammock, it was making him as dizzy as a witch to watch it. But that's what Papa-Daddy likes about a hammock. So Uncle Rondo was too dizzy to get turned against me for the time being. He's Mama's only brother and is a good case of a one-track mind. Ask anybody. A certified pharmacist.

Just then I heard Stella-Rondo raising the upstairs window. While she was married she got this peculiar idea that it's cooler with the windows shut and locked. So she has to raise the window before she can make a soul hear her outdoors.

So she raises the window and says, "*Oh!*" You would have thought she was mortally wounded.

Uncle Rondo and Papa-Daddy didn't even look up, but kept right on with what they were doing. I had to laugh.

I flew up the stairs and threw the door open! I says, "What in the wide world's the matter, Stella-Rondo? You mortally wounded?"

"No," she says, "I am not mortally wounded but I wish you would do me the favor of looking out that window there and telling me what you see."

So I shade my eyes and look out the window.

"I see the front yard," I says.

"Don't you see any human beings?" she says.

"I see Uncle Rondo trying to run Papa-Daddy out of the hammock," I says. "Nothing more. Naturally, it's so suffocating-hot in the house, with all the windows shut and locked, everyone who cares to stay in their right mind will have to go out and get in the hammock before the Fourth of July is over."

"Don't you notice anything different about Uncle Rondo?" asks Stella-Rondo.

"Why, no, except he's got on some terrible-looking flesh-colored contraption I wouldn't be found dead in, is all I can see," I says.

"Never mind, you won't be found dead in it, because it happens to be part of my trousseau, and Mr. Whitaker took several dozen photographs of me in it," says Stella-Rondo. "What on earth could Uncle Rondo *mean* by wearing part of my trousseau out in the broad open daylight without saying so much as 'Kiss my foot,' *knowing* I only got home this morning after my separation and hung my negligee up on the bathroom door, just as nervous as I could be?"

"I'm sure I don't know, and what do you expect me to do about it?" I says. "Jump out the window?"

"No, I expect nothing of the kind. I simply declare that Uncle Rondo looks like a fool in it, that's all," she says. "It makes me sick to my stomach."

"Well, he looks as good as he can," I says. "As good as anybody in reason could." I stood up for Uncle Rondo, please remember. And I said to Stella-Rondo, "I think I would do well not to criticize so freely if I were you and came home with a two-year-old child I had never said a word about, and no explanation whatever about my separation."

"I asked you the instant I entered this house not to refer one more time to my adopted child, and you gave me your word of honor you would not," was all Stella-Rondo would say, and started pulling out every one of her eyebrows with some cheap Kress tweezers.

So I merely slammed the door behind me and went down and made some green-tomato pickle. Somebody had to do it. Of course Mama had turned both the Negroes loose; she always said no earthly power could hold one anyway on the Fourth of July, so she wouldn't even try. It turned out that Jaypan fell in the lake and came within a very narrow limit of drowning.

So Mama trots in. Lifts up the lid and says, "H'm! Not very good for your Uncle Rondo in his precarious condition, I must say. Or poor little adopted Shirley-T. Shame on you!"

That made me tired. I says, "Well, Stella-Rondo had better thank her lucky stars it was her instead of me came trotting in with that very peculiar-looking child. Now if it had been me that trotted in from Illinois and brought a peculiar-looking child of two, I shudder to think of the reception I'd of got, much less controlled the diet of an entire family."

"But you must remember, Sister, that you were never married to Mr. Whitaker in the first place and didn't go up to Illinois to live," says Mama, shaking a spoon in my face. "If you had I would of been just as overjoyed to see you and your little adopted girl as I was to see Stella-Rondo, when you wound up with your separation and came on back home."

"You would not," I says.

"Don't contradict me, I would," says Mama.

But I said she couldn't convince me though she talked till she was blue in the face. Then I said, "Besides, you know as well as I do that that child is not adopted."

"She most certainly is adopted," says Mama, stiff as a poker.

I says, "Why, Mama, Stella-Rondo had her just as sure as anything in this world, and just too stuck up to admit it."

"Why, Sister," said Mama. "Here I thought we were going to have a pleasant Fourth of July, and you start right out not believing a word your own baby sister tells you!"

"Just like Cousin Annie Flo. Went to her grave denying the facts of life," I remind Mama.

"I told you if you ever mentioned Annie Flo's name I'd slap your face," says Mama, and slaps my face.

"All right, you wait and see," I says.

"I," says Mama, "*I* prefer to take my children's word for anything when it's humanly possible." You ought to see Mama, she weighs two hundred pounds and has real tiny feet.

Just then something perfectly horrible occurred to me.

"Mama," I says, "can that child talk?" I simply had to whisper! "Mama, I wonder if that child can be — you know — in any way? Do you realize," I says, "that she hasn't spoken one single, solitary word to a human being up to this minute? This is the way she looks," I says, and I looked like this.

Well, Mama and I just stood there and stared at each other. It was horrible!

"I remember well that Joe Whitaker frequently drank like a fish," says Mama. "I believed to my soul he drank *chemicals*." And without another word she marches to the foot of the stairs and calls Stella-Rondo.

"Stella-Rondo? O-o-o-o-o! Stella Rondo!"

"What?" says Stella-Rondo from upstairs. Not even the grace to get up off the bed.

"Can that child of yours talk?" asks Mama.

Stella-Rondo says, "Can she what?"

"Talk! Talk!" says Mama. "Burdyburdyburdyburdy!"

So Stella-Rondo yells back, "Who says she can't talk?"

"Sister says so," says Mama.

"You didn't have to tell me, I know whose word of honor don't mean a thing in this house," says Stella-Rondo.

And in a minute the loudest Yankee voice I ever heard in my life yells out, "OE'm Pop-OE the Sailor-r-r-r Ma-a-an!" and then somebody jumps up and down in the upstairs hall. In another second the house would of fallen down.

"Not only talks, she can tap-dance!" calls Stella-Rondo. "Which is more than some people I won't name can do."

"Why, the little precious darling thing!" Mama says, so surprised. "Just as smart as she can be!" Starts talking baby talk right there. Then she turns on me. "Sister, you ought to be thoroughly ashamed! Run upstairs this instant and apologize to Stella-Rondo and Shirley-T."

"Apologize for what?" I says. "I merely wondered if the child was normal, that's all. Now that she's proved she is, why, I have nothing further to say."

But Mama just turned on her heel and flew out, furious. She ran right upstairs and hugged the baby. She believed it was adopted. Stella-Rondo hadn't done a thing but turn her against me from upstairs while I stood there helpless over the hot stove. So that made Mama, Papa-Daddy and the baby all on Stella-Rondo's side.

Next, Uncle Rondo.

I must say that Uncle Rondo has been marvelous to me at various times in the past and I was completely unprepared to be made to jump out of my skin, the way it turned out. Once Stella-Rondo did something perfectly horrible to him — broke a chain letter from Flanders Field — and he took the radio back he had given her and gave it to me. Stella-Rondo was furious! For six months we all had to call her Stella instead of Stella-Rondo, or she wouldn't answer. I always thought Uncle Rondo had all the brains of the entire family. Another time he sent me to Mammoth Cave, with all expenses paid.

But this would be the day he was drinking that prescription, the Fourth of July.

So at supper Stella-Rondo speaks up and says she thinks Uncle Rondo ought to try to eat a little something. So finally Uncle Rondo said he would try a little cold biscuits and ketchup, but that was all. So *she* brought it to him.

"Do you think it wise to disport with ketchup in Stella-Rondo's flesh-colored kimono?" I says. Trying to be considerate! If Stella-Rondo couldn't watch out for her trousseau, somebody had to.

"Any objections?" asks Uncle Rondo, just about to pour out all the ketchup.

"Don't mind what she says, Uncle Rondo," says Stella-Rondo. "Sister has been devoting this solid afternoon to sneering out my bedroom window at the way you look."

"What's that?" says Uncle Rondo. Uncle Rondo has got the most terrible temper in the world. Anything is liable to make him tear the house down if it comes at the wrong time.

So Stella-Rondo says, "Sister says, 'Uncle Rondo certainly does look like a fool in that pink kimono!' "

Do you remember who it was really said that?

Uncle Rondo spills out all the ketchup and jumps out of his chair and tears off the kimono and throws it down on the dirty floor and puts his foot on it. It had to be sent all the way to Jackson to the cleaners and re-pleated.

"So that's your opinion of your Uncle Rondo, is it?" he says. "I look like a fool, do I? Well, that's the last straw. A whole day in this house with nothing to do, and then to hear you come out with a remark like that behind my back!"

"I didn't say any such of a thing, Uncle Rondo," I say, "and I'm not saying who did, either. Why, I think you look all right. Just try to take care of yourself and not talk and eat at the same time," I says. "I think you better go lie down."

"Lie down my foot," says Uncle Rondo. I ought to of known by that he was fixing to do something perfectly horrible.

So he didn't do anything that night in the precarious state he was in — just played Casino with Mama and Stella-Rondo and Shirley-T. and gave Shirley-T. a nickel with a head on both sides. It tickled her nearly to death, and she called him "Papa." But at 6:30 A.M. the next morning, he threw a whole five-cent package of some unsold one-inch firecrackers from the store as hard as he could into my bedroom and they every one went off. Not one bad one in the string. Anybody else, there'd be one that wouldn't go off.

Well, I'm just terribly susceptible to noise of any kind, the doctor has always told me I was the most sensitive person he had ever seen in his whole life, and I was simply prostrated. I couldn't eat! People tell me they heard it as far as the cemetery, and old Aunt Jep Patterson, that had been holding her own so good, thought it was Judgement Day and she was going to meet her whole family. It's usually so quiet here.

And I'll tell you it didn't take me any longer than a minute to make up my mind what to do. There I was with the whole entire house on Stella-Rondo's side and turned against me. If I have anything at all I have pride.

So I just decided I'd go straight down to the P.O. There's plenty of room there in the back, I says to myself.

Well! I made no bones about letting the family catch on to what I was up to. I didn't try to conceal it.

The first thing they knew, I marched in where they were all playing Old Maid and pulled the electric oscillating fan out by the plug, and everything got real hot. Next I snatched the pillow I'd done the needle-point on right off the davenport from behind Papa-Daddy. He went "Ugh!" I beat Stella-Rondo up the stairs and finally found my charm bracelet in her bureau drawer under a picture of Nelson Eddy.

"So that's the way the land lies," says Uncle Rondo. There he was, piecing on the ham. "Well, Sister, I'll be glad to donate my army cot if you got any place to set it up, providing you'll leave right this minute and let me get some peace." Uncle Rondo was in France.

"Thank you kindly for the cot and 'peace' is hardly the word I would select if I had to resort to firecrackers at 6:30 A.M. in a young girl's bedroom," I says back to him.

"And as to where I intend to go, you seem to forget my position as postmistress of China Grove, Mississippi," I says. "I've always got the P.O."

Well, that made them all sit up and take notice.

I went out front and started digging up some four-o'clocks to plant around the P.O.

"Ah-ah-ah!" says Mama, raising the window. "Those happen to be my four-o'clocks. Everything planted in that star is mine. I've never known you to make anything grow in life."

"Very well," I says. "But I take the fern. Even you, Mama, can't stand there and deny that I'm the one watered that fern. And I happen to know where I can send in a box top and get a packet of one thousand mixed seeds, no two the same kind, free."

"Oh, where?" Mama wants to know.

But I says, "Too late. You 'tend to your house, and I'll 'tend to mine. You hear things like that all the time if you know how to listen to the radio. Perfectly marvelous offers. Get anything you want free."

So I hope to tell you I marched in and got that radio, and they could of all bit a nail in two, especially Stella-Rondo, that it used to belong to, and she well knew she couldn't get it back, I'd sue for it like a shot. And I very politely took the sewing-machine motor I helped pay the most on to give Mama for Christmas back in 1929, and a good big calendar, with the first-aid remedies on it. The thermometer and the Hawaiian ukulele certainly were rightfully mine, and I stood on the step-ladder and got all my watermelon-rind preserves and every fruit and vegetable I'd put up, every jar. Then I began to pull the tacks out of the bluebird wall vases on the archway to the dining room.

"Who told you you could have those, Miss Priss?" says Mama, fanning as hard as she could.

"I bought 'em and I'll keep track of 'em," I says. "I'll tack 'em up one on each side the post-office window, and you can see 'em when you come to ask me for your mail, if you're so dead to see 'em."

"Not I! I'll never darken the door to that post office again if I live to be a hundred," Mama says. "Ungrateful child! After all the money we spent on you at the Normal."

"Me either," says Stella-Rondo. "You can just let my mail lie there and *rot,* for all I care. I'll never come and relieve you of a single, solitary piece."

"I should worry," I says. "And who you think's going to sit down and write you all those big fat letters and postcards, by the way? Mr. Whitaker? Just because he was the only man ever dropped down in China Grove and you got him — unfairly — is he going to sit down and write you a lengthy correspondence after you come home giving no rhyme nor reason whatsoever for your separation and no explanation for the presence of that child? I may not have your brilliant mind, but I fail to see it."

So Mama says, "Sister, I've told you a thousand times that Stella-Rondo simply got homesick, and this child is far too big to be hers," and she says, "Now, why don't you all just sit down and play Casino?"

Then Shirley-T. sticks out her tongue at me in this perfectly horrible way. She has no more manners than the man in the moon. I told her she was going to cross her eyes like that some day and they'd stick.

"It's too late to stop me now," I says. "You should have tried that yesterday. I'm going to the P.O. and the only way you can possibly see me is to visit me there."

So Papa-Daddy says, "You'll never catch me setting foot in that post office, even if I should take a notion into my head to write a letter some place." He says, "I won't have you reachin' out of that little old window with a pair of shears and cuttin' off any beard of mine. I'm too smart for you!"

"We all are," says Stella-Rondo.

But I said, "If you're so smart, where's Mr. Whitaker?"

So then Uncle Rondo says, "I'll thank you from now on to stop reading all the orders I get on postcards and telling everybody in China Grove what you think is the matter with them," but I says, "I draw my own conclusions and will continue in the future to draw them." I says, "If people want to write their inmost secrets on penny postcards, there's nothing in the wide world you can do about it, Uncle Rondo."

"And if you think we'll ever *write* another postcard you're sadly mistaken," says Mama.

"Cutting off your nose to spite your face then," I says. "But if you're all determined to have no more to do with the U.S. mail, think of this: What will Stella-Rondo do now, if she wants to tell Mr. Whitaker to come after her?"

"Wah!" says Stella-Rondo. I knew she'd cry. She had a conniption fit right there in the kitchen.

"It will be interesting to see how long she holds out," I says. "And now — I am leaving."

"Good-bye," says Uncle Rondo.

"Oh, I declare," says Mama, "to think that a family of mine should quarrel on the Fourth of July, or the day after, over Stella-Rondo leaving old Mr. Whitaker and having the sweetest little adopted child! It looks like we'd all be glad!"

"Wah!" says Stella-Rondo, and has a fresh conniption fit.

"*He* left *her* — you mark my words," I says. "That's Mr. Whitaker. I know Mr. Whitaker. After all, I knew him first. I said from the beginning he'd up and leave her. I foretold every single thing that's happened."

"Where did he go?" asks Mama.

"Probably to the North Pole, if he knows what's good for him," I says.

But Stella-Rondo just bawled and wouldn't say another word. She flew to her room and slammed the door.

"Now look what you've gone and done, Sister," says Mama. "You go apologize."

"I haven't got time, I'm leaving," I says.

"Well, what are you waiting around for?" asks Uncle Rondo.

So I just picked up the kitchen clock and marched off, without saying "Kiss my foot" or anything, and never did tell Stella-Rondo good-bye.

There was a girl going along on a little wagon right in front.

"Girl," I says, "come help me haul these things down the hill, I'm going to live in the post office."

Took her nine trips in her express wagon. Uncle Rondo came out on the porch and threw her a nickel.

And that's the last I've laid eyes on any of my family or my family laid eyes on me for five solid days and nights. Stella-Rondo may be telling the most horrible tales in the world about Mr. Whitaker, but I haven't heard them. As I tell everybody, I draw my own conclusions.

But oh, I like it here. It's ideal, as I've been saying. You see, I've got everything cater-cornered, the way I like it. Hear the radio? All the war news. Radio, sewing machine, book ends, ironing board and that great big piano lamp — peace, that's what I like. Butter-bean vines planted all along the front where the strings are.

Of course, there's not much mail. My family are naturally the main people in China Grove, and if they prefer to vanish from the face of the earth, for all the mail they get or the mail they write, why, I'm not going to open my mouth. Some of the folks here in town are taking up for me and some turned against me. I know which is which. There are always people who will quit buying stamps just to get on the right side of Papa-Daddy.

But here I am, and here I'll stay. I want the world to know I'm happy.

And if Stella-Rondo should come to me this minute, on bended knees, and *attempt* to explain the incidents of her life with Mr. Whitaker, I'd simply put my fingers in both my ears and refuse to listen.

EDITH WHARTON

Edith Wharton (1862–1937) was born in New York City to a prominent family. She was educated privately at home and in Europe, where she traveled extensively as a young woman. Wharton spent her life in various locales — New York, Paris, England, Western Massachusetts, and the French Riviera — maintaining a prodigious array of friendships (including a close one with Henry James) and sustaining a distinguished and prolific literary career. Her first novel, *The House of Mirth* (1905), established her reputation. It was followed by many others, perhaps the most notable of which are *Ethan Frome* (1911), *The Reef* (1912), *The Custom of the Country* (1913), *The Age of Innocence* (1920), and *Hudson River Bracketed* (1929). She published many volumes of short stories, including *The Greater Inclination* (1899), *Crucial Instances* (1901), *The Descent of Man* (1904), *Tales of Men and Ghosts* (1910), and *Certain People* (1933). Wharton wrote what her foremost biographer, R. W. B. Lewis, calls a *comédie humaine*, rich with the experiences of Americans (and especially American women) in the early decades of the twentieth century, born in America and abroad. She comprehended varieties of experience, their pleasures and sorrows, with amazing accuracy and rendered them subtly and movingly. Her works are, in Lewis's judgment, "among the handsomest statements in our literature." Wharton never lost a sense of the ironic: "The Other Two" is one of her finest depictions of social comedy.

The Other Two

1

Waythorn, on the drawing-room hearth, waited for his wife to come down to dinner.

It was their first night under his own roof, and he was surprised at his thrill of boyish agitation. He was not so old, to be sure — his glass gave him little more than the five-and-thirty years to which his wife confessed — but he had fancied himself already in the temperate zone; yet here he was listening for her step with a tender sense of all it symbolized, with some old trail of verse about the garlanded nuptial doorposts floating through his enjoyment of the pleasant room and the good dinner just beyond it.

They had been hastily recalled from their honeymoon by the illness of Lily Haskett, the child of Mrs. Waythorn's first marriage. The little girl, at Waythorn's desire, had been transferred to his house on the day of her mother's wedding, and the doctor, on their arrival, broke the news that she was ill with typhoid, but declared that all the symptoms were favorable. Lily could show twelve years of unblemished health, and the case promised to be a light one. The nurse spoke as reassuringly, and after a moment of alarm Mrs. Waythorn had adjusted herself to the situation. She was very fond of Lily — her affection for the child had perhaps been her decisive charm in

Waythorn's eyes — but she had the perfectly balanced nerves which her little girl had inherited, and no woman ever wasted less tissue in unproductive worry. Waythorn was therefore quite prepared to see her come in presently, a little late because of a last look at Lily, but as serene and well-appointed as if her good-night kiss had been laid on the brow of health. Her composure was restful to him; it acted as ballast to his somewhat unstable sensibilities. As he pictured her bending over the child's bed he thought how soothing her presence must be in illness: her very step would prognosticate recovery.

His own life had been a gray one, from temperament rather than circumstance, and he had been drawn to her by the unperturbed gaiety which kept her fresh and elastic at an age when most women's activities are growing either slack or febrile. He knew what was said about her; for, popular as she was, there had always been a faint undercurrent of detraction. When she had appeared in New York, nine or ten years earlier, as the pretty Mrs. Haskett whom Gus Varick had unearthed somewhere — was it in Pittsburgh or Utica? — society, while promptly accepting her, had reserved the right to cast a doubt on its own indiscrimination. Inquiry, however, established her undoubted connection with a socially reigning family, and explained her recent divorce as the natural result of a runway match at seventeen; and as nothing was known of Mr. Haskett it was easy to believe the worst of him.

Alice Haskett's remarriage with Gus Varick was a passport to the set whose recognition she coveted, and for a few years the Varicks were the most popular couple in town. Unfortunately the alliance was brief and stormy, and this time the husband had his champions. Still, even Varick's stanchest supporters admitted that he was not meant for matrimony, and Mrs. Varick's grievances were of a nature to bear the inspection of the New York courts. A New York divorce is in itself a diploma of virtue, and in the semiwidowhood of this second separation Mrs. Varick took on an air of sanctity, and was allowed to confide her wrongs to some of the most scrupulous ears in town. But when it was known that she was to marry Waythorn there was a momentary reaction. Her best friends would have preferred to see her remain in the role of the injured wife, which was as becoming to her as crepe to a rosy complexion. True, a decent time had elapsed, and it was not even suggested that Waythorn had supplanted his predecessor. People shook their heads over him, however, and one grudging friend, to whom he affirmed that he took the step with his eyes open, replied oracularly: "Yes — and with your ears shut."

Waythorn could afford to smile at these innuendoes. In the Wall Street phrase, he had "discounted" them. He knew that society has not yet adapted itself to the consequences of divorce, and that till the adaptation takes place every woman who uses the freedom the law accords her must be her own social justification. Waythorn had an amused confidence in his wife's ability to justify herself. His expectations were fulfilled, and before the wedding took place Alice Varick's group had rallied openly to her support. She took it all imperturbably: she had a way of surmounting obstacles without seeming to be aware of them, and Waythorn looked back with wonder at the trivialities over which he had worn his nerves thin. He had the sense of having found refuge in a richer, warmer nature than his own, and his satisfaction, at the moment, was humorously summed up in the thought that his wife, when she had done all she could for Lily, would not be ashamed to come down and enjoy a good dinner.

The anticipation of such enjoyment was not, however, the sentiment expressed by Mrs. Waythorn's charming face when she presently joined him. Though she had put on her most engaging tea gown she had neglected to assume the smile that went with it, and Waythorn thought he had never seen her look so nearly worried.

"What is it?" he asked. "Is anything wrong with Lily?"

"No; I've just been in and she's still sleeping." Mrs. Waythorn hesitated. "But something tiresome has happened."

He had taken her two hands, and now perceived that he was crushing a paper between them.

"This letter?"

"Yes — Mr. Haskett has written — I mean his lawyer has written."

Waythorn felt himself flush uncomfortably. He dropped his wife's hands.

"What about?"

"About seeing Lily. You know the courts — "

"Yes, yes," he interrupted nervously.

Nothing was known about Haskett in New York. He was vaguely supposed to have remained in the outer darkness from which his wife had been rescued, and Waythorn was one of the few who were aware that he had given up his business in Utica and followed her to New York in order to be near his little girl. In the days of his wooing, Waythorn had often met Lily on the doorstep, rosy and smiling, on her way "to see papa."

"I am so sorry," Mrs. Waythorn murmured.

He roused himself. "What does he want?"

"He wants to see her. You know she goes to him once a week."

"Well — he doesn't expect her to go to him now, does he?"

"No — he has heard of her illness; but he expects to come here."

"*Here?*"

Mrs. Waythorn reddened under his gaze. They looked away from each other.

"I'm afraid he has the right . . . You'll see. . . ." She made a proffer of the letter.

Waythorn moved away with a gesture of refusal. He stood staring about the softly-lighted room, which a moment before had seemed so full of bridal intimacy.

"I'm so sorry," she repeated. "If Lily could have been moved — "

"That's out of the question," he returned impatiently.

"I suppose so."

Her lip was beginning to tremble, and he felt himself a brute.

"He must come, of course," he said. "When is — his day?"

"I'm afraid — tomorrow."

"Very well. Send a note in the morning."

The butler entered to announce dinner.

Waythorn turned to his wife. "Come — you must be tired. It's beastly, but try to forget about it," he said, drawing her hand through his arm.

"You're so good, dear. I'll try," she whispered back.

Her face cleared at once, and as she looked at him across the flowers, between the rosy candleshades, he saw her lips waver back into a smile.

"How pretty everything is!" she sighed luxuriously.

He turned to the butler. "The champagne at once, please. Mrs. Waythorn is tired."

In a moment or two their eyes met above the sparkling glasses. Her own were quite clear and untroubled: he saw that she had obeyed his injunction and forgotten.

2

Waythorn, the next morning, went downtown earlier than usual. Haskett was not likely to come till the afternoon, but the instinct of flight drove him forth. He meant to stay away all day — he had thoughts of dining at his club. As his door closed behind him he reflected that before he opened it again it would have admitted another man who had as much right to enter it as himself, and the thought filled him with a physical repugnance.

He caught the elevated at the employees' hour, and found himself crushed between two layers of pendulous humanity. At Eighth Street the man facing him wriggled out, and another took his place. Waythorn glanced up and saw that it was Gus Varick. The men were so close together that it was impossible to ignore the smile of recognition on Varick's handsome overblown face. And after all — why not? They had always been on good terms, and Varick had been divorced before Waythorn's attentions to his wife began. The two exchanged a word on the perennial grievance of the congested trains, and when a seat at their side was miraculously left empty the instinct of self-preservation made Waythorn slip into it after Varick.

The latter drew the stout man's breath of relief. "Lord — I was beginning to feel like a pressed flower." He leaned back, looking unconcernedly at Waythorn. "Sorry to hear that Sellers is knocked out again."

"Sellers?" echoed Waythorn, starting at his partner's name.

Varick looked surprised. "You didn't know he was laid up with the gout?"

"No. I've been away — I only got back last night." Waythorn felt himself reddening in anticipation of the other's smile.

"Ah — yes; to be sure. And Sellers' attack came on two days ago. I'm afraid he's pretty bad. Very awkward for me, as it happens, because he was just putting through a rather important thing for me."

"Ah?" Waythorn wondered vaguely since when Varick had been dealing in "important things." Hitherto he had dabbled only in the shallow pools of speculation, with which Waythorn's office did not usually concern itself.

It occurred to him that Varick might be talking at random, to relieve the strain of their propinquity. That strain was becoming momentarily more apparent to Waythorn, and when, at Cortlandt Street, he caught sight of an acquaintance and had a sudden vision of the picture he and Varick must present to an initiated eye, he jumped up with a muttered excuse.

"I hope you'll find Sellers better," said Varick civilly, and he stammered back: "If I can be of any use to you — " and let the departing crowd sweep him to the platform.

At his office he heard that Sellers was in fact ill with the gout, and would probably not be able to leave the house for some weeks.

"I'm sorry it should have happened so, Mr. Waythorn," the senior clerk said with affable significance. "Mr. Sellers was very much upset at the idea of giving you such a lot of extra work just now."

"Oh, that's no matter," said Waythorn hastily. He secretly welcomed the pressure of additional business, and was glad to think that, when the day's work was over, he would have to call at his partner's on the way home.

He was late for luncheon, and turned in at the nearest restaurant instead of going to his club. The place was full, and the waiter hurried him to the back of the room to capture the only vacant table. In the cloud of cigar smoke Waythorn did not at once distinguish his neighbors: but presently, looking about him, he saw Varick seated a few feet off. This time, luckily, they were too far apart for conversation, and Varick, who faced another way, had probably not even seen him; but there was an irony in their renewed nearness.

Varick was said to be fond of good living, and as Waythorn sat dispatching his hurried luncheon he looked across half enviously at the other's leisurely degustation of his meal. When Waythorn first saw him he had been helping himself with critical deliberation to a bit of Camembert at the ideal point of liquefaction, and now, the cheese removed, he was just pouring his *café double* from its little two-storied earthen pot. He poured slowly, his ruddy profile bent over the task, and one beringed white hand steadying the lid of the coffeepot; then he stretched his other hand to the decanter of cognac at his elbow, filled a liqueur glass, took a tentative sip, and poured the brandy into his coffee cup.

Waythorn watched him in a kind of fascination. What was he thinking of — only of the flavor of the coffee and the liqueur? Had the morning's meeting left no more trace in his thoughts than on his face? Had his wife so completely passed out of his life that even this odd encounter with her present husband, within a week after her remarriage, was no more than an incident in his day? And as Waythorn mused, another idea struck him: had Haskett ever met Varick as Varick and he had just met? The recollection of Haskett perturbed him, and he rose and left the restaurant, taking a circuitous way out to escape the placid irony of Varick's nod.

It was after seven when Waythorn reached home. He thought the footman who opened the door looked at him oddly.

"How is Miss Lily?" he asked in haste.

"Doing very well, sir. A gentleman — "

"Tell Barlow to put off dinner for half an hour," Waythorn cut him off, hurrying upstairs.

He went straight to his room and dressed without seeing his wife. When he reached the drawing room she was there, fresh and radiant. Lily's day had been good; the doctor was not coming back that evening.

At dinner Waythorn told her of Sellers' illness and of the resulting complications. She listened sympathetically, adjuring him not to let himself be overworked, and asking vague feminine questions about the routine of the office. Then she gave him the chronicle of Lily's day; quoted the nurse and doctor, and told him who had called to inquire. He had never seen her more serene and unruffled. It struck him with a curious pang, that she was very happy in being with him, so happy that she found a childish pleasure in rehearsing the trivial incidents of her day.

After dinner they went to the library, and the servant put the coffee and liqueurs on a low table before her and left the room. She looked singularly soft and girlish in her rosy-pale dress, against the dark leather of one of his bachelor armchairs. A day earlier the contrast would have charmed him.

He turned away now, choosing a cigar with affected deliberation.

"Did Haskett come?" he asked, with his back to her.

"Oh, yes — he came."

"You didn't see him, of course?"

She hesitated a moment. "I let the nurse see him."

That was all. There was nothing more to ask. He swung round toward her, applying a match to his cigar. Well, the thing was over for a week, at any rate. He would try not to think of it. She looked up at him, a trifle rosier than usual, with a smile in her eyes.

"Ready for your coffee, dear?"

He leaned against the mantelpiece, watching her as she lifted the coffeepot. The lamplight struck a gleam from her bracelets and tipped her soft hair with brightness. How light and slender she was, and how each gesture flowed into the next! She seemed a creature all compact of harmonies. As the thought of Haskett receded, Waythorn felt himself yielding again to the joy of possessorship. They were his, those white hands with their flitting motions, his the light haze of hair, the lips and eyes. . . .

She set down the coffeepot, and reaching for the decanter of cognac, measured off a liqueur glass and poured it into his cup.

Waythorn uttered a sudden exclamation.

"What is the matter?" she said, startled.

"Nothing, only — I don't take cognac in my coffee."

"Oh, how stupid of me," she cried.

Their eyes met, and she blushed a sudden agonized red.

3

Ten days later, Mr. Sellers, still housebound, asked Waythorn to call on his way downtown.

The senior partner, with his swaddled foot propped up by the fire, greeted his associate with an air of embarrassment.

"I'm sorry, my dear fellow; I've got to ask you to do an awkward thing for me."

Waythorn waited, and the other went on, after a pause apparently given to the arrangement of his phrases: "The fact is, when I was knocked out I had just gone into a rather complicated piece of business for — Gus Varick."

"Well?" said Waythorn, with an attempt to put him at his ease.

"Well — it's this way: Varick came to me the day before my attack. He had evidently had an inside tip from somebody, and had made about a hundred thousand. He came to me for advice, and I suggested his going in with Vanderlyn."

"Oh, the deuce!" Waythorn exclaimed. He saw in a flash what had happened. The investment was an alluring one, but required negotiation. He listened quietly while Sellers put the case before him, and the statement ended, he said: "You think I ought to see Varick?"

"I'm afraid I can't as yet. The doctor is obdurate. And this thing can't wait. I hate to ask you, but no one else in the office knows the ins and outs of it."

Waythorn stood silent. He did not care a farthing for the success of Varick's venture, but the honor of the office was to be considered, and he could hardly refuse to oblige his partner.

"Very well," he said, "I'll do it."

That afternoon, apprised by telephone, Varick called at the office. Waythorn, waiting in his private room, wondered what the others thought of it. The newspapers, at the time of Mrs. Waythorn's marriage, had acquainted their readers with every detail of her previous matrimonial ventures, and Waythorn could fancy the clerks smiling behind Varick's back as he was ushered in.

Varick bore himself admirably. He was easy without being undignified, and Waythorn was conscious of cutting a much less impressive figure. Varick had no experience of business, and the talk prolonged itself for nearly an hour while Waythorn set forth with scrupulous precision the details of the proposed transaction.

"I'm awfully obliged to you," Varick said as he rose. "The fact is I'm not used to having much money to look after, and I don't want to make an ass of myself — " He smiled, and Waythorn could not help noticing that there was something pleasant about his smile. "It feels uncommonly queer to have enough cash to pay one's bills. I'd have sold my soul for it a few years ago!"

Waythorn winced at the allusion. He had heard it rumored that a lack of funds had been one of the determining causes of the Varick separation, but it did not occur to him that Varick's words were intentional. It seemed more likely that the desire to keep clear of embarrassing topics had fatally drawn him into one. Waythorn did not wish to be outdone in civility.

"We'll do the best we can for you," he said. "I think this is a good thing you're in."

"Oh, I'm sure it's immense. It's awfully good of you — " Varick broke off, embarrassed. "I suppose the thing's settled now — but if — "

"If anything happens before Sellers is about, I'll see you again," said Waythorn quietly. He was glad, in the end, to appear the more self-possessed of the two.

The course of Lily's illness ran smooth, and as the days passed Waythorn grew used to the idea of Haskett's weekly visit. The first time the day came round, he stayed out late, and questioned his wife as to the visit on his return. She replied at once that Haskett had merely seen the nurse downstairs, as the doctor did not wish anyone in the child's sickroom till after the crisis.

The following week Waythorn was again conscious of the recurrence of the day, but had forgotten it by the time he came home to dinner. The crisis of the disease came a few days later, with a rapid decline of fever, and the little girl was pronounced out of danger. In the rejoicing which ensued the thought of Haskett passed out of Waythorn's mind, and one afternoon, letting himself into the house with a latchkey, he went straight to his library without noticing a shabby hat and umbrella in the hall.

In the library he found a small effaced-looking man with a thinnish gray beard sitting on the edge of a chair. The stranger might have been a piano tuner, or one of those mysteriously efficient persons who are summoned in emergencies to adjust some detail of the domestic machinery. He blinked at Waythorn through a pair of gold-rimmed spectacles and said mildly: Mr. Waythorn, I presume? I am Lily's father."

Waythorn flushed. "Oh — " he stammered uncomfortably. He broke off, disliking to appear rude. Inwardly he was trying to adjust the actual Haskett to the image of him projected by his wife's reminiscences. Waythorn had been allowed to infer that Alice's first husband was a brute.

"I am sorry to intrude," said Haskett, with his over-the-counter politeness.

"Don't mention it," returned Waythorn, collecting himself. "I suppose the nurse has been told?"

"I presume so. I can wait," said Haskett. He had a resigned way of speaking, as though life had worn down his natural powers of resistance.

Waythorn stood on the threshold, nervously pulling off his gloves.

"I'm sorry you've been detained. I will send for the nurse," he said; and as he opened the door he added with an effort: "I'm glad we can give you a good report of Lily." He winced as the *we* slipped out, but Haskett seemed not to notice it.

"Thank you, Mr. Waythorn, it's been an anxious time for me."

"Ah, well, that's past. Soon she'll be able to go to you." Waythorn nodded and passed out.

In his own room he flung himself down with a groan. He hated the womanish sensibility which made him suffer so acutely from the grotesque chances of life. He had known when he married that his wife's former husbands were both living, and that amid the multiplied contacts of modern existence there were a thousand chances to one that he would run against one or the other, yet he found himself as much disturbed by his brief encounter with Haskett as though the law had not obligingly removed all difficulties in the way of their meeting.

Waythorn sprang up and began to pace the room nervously. He had not suffered half as much from his two meetings with Varick. It was Haskett's presence in his own house that made the situation so intolerable. He stood still, hearing steps in the passage.

"This way, please," he heard the nurse say. Haskett was being taken upstairs, then: not a corner of the house but was open to him. Waythorn dropped into another chair, staring vaguely ahead of him. On his dressing table stood a photograph of Alice, taken when he had first known her. She was Alice Varick then — how fine and exquisite he had thought her! Those were Varick's pearls about her neck. At Waythorn's instance they had been returned before her marriage. Had Haskett ever given her any trinkets — and what had become of them, Waythorn wondered? He realized suddenly that he knew very little of Haskett's past or present situation; but from the man's appearance and manner of speech he could reconstruct with curious precision the surroundings of Alice's first marriage. And it startled him to think that she had, in the background of her life, a phase of existence so different from anything with which he had connected her. Varick, whatever his faults, was a gentleman, in the conventional, traditional sense of the term: the sense which at that moment seemed, oddly enough, to have most meaning to Waythorn. He and Varick had the same social habits, spoke the same language, understood the same allusions. But this other man . . . it was grotesquely uppermost in Waythorn's mind that Haskett had worn a made-up tie attached with an elastic. Why should that ridiculous detail symbolize the whole man? Waythorn was exasperated by his own paltriness, but the fact of the tie expanded, forced itself on him, became as it were the key to Alice's past. He could see her, as Mrs. Haskett, sitting in a "front parlor" furnished in plush, with a pianola, and copy of *Ben Hur* on the center table. He could see her going to the theater with Haskett — or perhaps even to a "Church Sociable" — she in a "picture hat" and Haskett in a black frock coat, a little creased, with the made-up tie on an elastic. On the way home they would stop and look at the illuminated shop windows, lingering over the photographs of New York actresses. On Sunday afternoons Haskett would take her for a walk, pushing Lily ahead of them in a white enameled perambulator, and Waythorn had a vision of the people they would stop and talk to. He could fancy how pretty Alice must have looked, in a dress adroitly constructed from the hints of a New York fashion paper, and how she must have looked down on the other women, chafing at her life, and secretly feeling that she belonged in a bigger place.

For the moment his foremost thought was one of wonder at the way in which she had shed the phase of existence which her marriage with Haskett implied. It was as if her whole aspect, every gesture, every inflection, every allusion, were a studied negation of that period of her life. If she had denied being married to Haskett she could hardly have stood more convicted of duplicity than in this obliteration of the self which had been his wife.

Waythorn started up, checking himself in the analysis of her motives. What right had he to create a fantastic effigy of her and then pass judgment on it? She had spoken vaguely of her first marriage as unhappy, had hinted, with becoming reticence, that Haskett had wrought havoc among her young illusions. . . . It was a pity for Waythorn's peace of mind that Haskett's very inoffensiveness shed a new light on the nature of those illusions. A man would rather think that his wife has been brutalized by her first husband than that the process has been reversed.

4

"Mr. Waythorn, I don't like that French governess of Lily's."

Haskett, subdued and apologetic, stood before Waythorn in the library, revolving his shabby hat in his hand.

Waythorn, surprised in his armchair over the evening paper, stared back perplexedly at his visitor.

"You'll excuse my asking to see you," Haskett continued. "But this is my last visit, and I thought if I could have a word with you it would be a better way than writing to Mrs. Waythorn's lawyer."

Waythorn rose uneasily. He did not like the French governess either; but that was irrelevant.

"I am not so sure of that," he returned stiffly; "but since you wish it I will give your message to — my wife." He always hesitated over the possessive pronoun in addressing Haskett.

The latter sighed. "I don't know as that will help much. She didn't like it when I spoke to her."

Waythorn turned red. "When did you see her?" he asked.

"Not since the first day I came to see Lily — right after she was taken sick. I remarked to her then that I didn't like the governess."

Waythorn made no answer. He remembered distinctly that, after that first visit, he had asked his wife if she had seen Haskett. She had lied to him then, but she had respected his wishes since; and the incident cast a curious light on her character. He was sure she would not have seen Haskett that first day if she had divined that Waythorn would object, and the fact that she did not divine it was almost as disagreeable to the latter as the discovery that she had lied to him.

"I don't like the woman," Haskett was repeating with mild persistency. "She ain't straight, Mr. Waythorn — she'll teach the child to be underhand. I've noticed a change in Lily — she's too anxious to please — and she don't always tell the truth. She used to be the straightest child. Mr. Waythorn — " He broke off, his voice a little thick. "Not but what I want her to have a stylish education," he ended.

Waythorn was touched. "I'm sorry, Mr. Haskett; but frankly, I don't quite see what I can do."

Haskett hesitated. Then he laid his hat on the table, and advanced to the hearthrug, on which Waythorn was standing. There was nothing aggressive in his manner, but he had the solemnity of a timid man resolved on a decisive measure.

"There's just one thing you can do, Mr. Waythorn," he said. "You can remind Mrs. Waythorn that, by the decree of the courts, I am entitled to have a voice in Lily's bringing-up." He paused, and went on more deprecatingly: "I am not the kind to talk about enforcing my rights, Mr. Waythorn. I don't know as I think a man is entitled to rights he hasn't known how to hold on to; but this business of the child is different. I've never let go there — and I never mean to."

The scene left Waythorn deeply shaken. Shamefacedly, in indirect ways, he had been finding out about Haskett; and all that he had learned was favorable. The little man, in order to be near his daughter, had sold out his share in a profitable business in Utica, and accepted a modest clerkship in a New York manufacturing house. He boarded in a shabby street and had few acquaintances. His passion for Lily filled his life. Waythorn felt that this exploration of Haskett was like groping about with a dark lantern in his wife's past; but he saw now that there were recesses his lantern had not explored. He had never inquired into the exact circumstances of his wife's first matrimonial rupture. On the surface all had been fair. It was she who had obtained the divorce, and the court had given her the child. But Waythorn knew how many ambiguities such a verdict might cover. The mere fact that Haskett retained a right over his daughter implied an unsuspected compromise. Waythorn was an idealist. He always refused to recognize unpleasant contingencies till he found himself confronted with them, and then he saw them followed by a spectral train of consequences. His next days were thus haunted, and he determined to try to lay the ghosts by conjuring them up in his wife's presence.

When he repeated Haskett's request a flame of anger passed over her face; but she subdued it instantly and spoke with a slight quiver of outraged motherhood.

"It is very ungentlemanly of him," she said.

The word grated on Waythorn. "That is neither here nor there. It's a bare question of rights."

She murmured: "It's not as if he could ever be a help to Lily — "

Waythorn flushed. This was even less to his taste. "The question is," he repeated, "what authority has he over her?"

She looked downward, twisting herself a little in her seat. "I am willing to see him — I thought you objected," she faltered.

In a flash he understood that she knew the extent of Haskett's claims. Perhaps it was not the first time she had resisted them.

"My objecting has nothing to do with it," he said coldly; "if Haskett has a right to be consulted you must consult him."

She burst into tears, and he saw that she expected him to regard her as a victim.

Haskett did not abuse his rights. Waythorn had felt miserably sure that he would not. But the governess was dismissed, and from time to time the little man demanded an interview with Alice. After the first outburst she accepted the situation with her usual adaptability. Haskett had once reminded Waythorn of the piano tuner, and Mrs. Waythorn, after a month or two, appeared to class him with that domestic familiar. Waythorn could not but respect the father's tenacity. At first he had tried to cultivate the suspicion that Haskett might be "up to" something, that he had an object in securing a foothold in the house. But in his heart Waythorn was sure of Haskett's single-mindedness; he even guessed in the latter a mild contempt for such advantages as his relation with the Waythorns might offer. Haskett's sincerity of purpose made him invulnerable, and his successor had to accept him as a lien on the property.

Mr. Sellers was sent to Europe to recover from his gout, and Varick's affairs hung on Waythorn's hands. The negotiations were prolonged and complicated; they necessitated frequent conferences between the two men, and the interests of the firm forbade Waythorn's suggesting that his client should transfer his business to another office.

Varick appeared well in the transaction. In moments of relaxation his coarse streak appeared, and Waythorn dreaded his geniality; but in the office he was concise and clear-headed, with a flattering deference to Waythorn's judgment. Their business relations being so affably established, it would have been absurd for the two men to ignore each other in society. The first time they met in a drawing room, Varick took up their intercourse in the same easy key, and his hostess' grateful glance obliged Waythorn to respond to it. After that they ran across each other frequently, and one evening at a ball Waythorn, wandering through the remoter rooms, came upon Varick seated beside his wife. She colored a little, and faltered in what she was saying; but Varick nodded to Waythorn without rising, and the latter strolled on.

In the carriage, on the way home, he broke out nervously: "I didn't know you spoke to Varick."

Her voice trembled a little. "It's the first time — he happened to be standing near me; I didn't know what to do. It's so awkward, meeting everywhere — and he said you had been very kind about some business."

"That's different," said Waythorn.

She paused a moment. "I'll do just as you wish," she returned pliantly. "I thought it would be less awkward to speak to him when we meet."

Her pliancy was beginning to sicken him. Had she really no will of her own — no theory about her relation to these men? She had accepted Haskett — did she mean to accept Varick? It was "less awkward," as she had said, and her instinct was to evade difficulties or to circumvent them. With sudden vividness Waythorn saw how the instinct had developed. She was "as easy as an old shoe" — a shoe that too many feet had worn. Her elasticity was the result of tension in too many different directions. Alice Haskett — Alice Varick — Alice Waythorn — she had been each in turn, and had left hanging to each name a little of her privacy, a little of her personality, a little of the inmost self where the unknown god abides.

"Yes — it's better to speak to Varick," said Waythorn wearily.

5

The winter wore on, and society took advantage of the Waythorns' acceptance of Varick. Harassed hostesses were grateful to them for bridging over a social difficulty, and Mrs. Waythorn was held up as a miracle of good taste. Some experimental spirits could not resist the diversion of throwing Varick and his former wife together, and there were those who thought he found a zest in the propinquity. But Mrs. Waythorn's conduct remained irreproachable. She neither avoided Varick nor sought him out. Even Waythorn could not but admit that she had discovered the solution of the newest social problem.

He had married her without giving much thought to that problem. He had fancied that a woman can shed her past like a man. But now he saw that Alice was bound to hers both by the circumstances which forced her into continued relation with it, and by the traces it had left on her nature. With grim irony Waythorn compared himself to a member of a syndicate. He held so many shares in his wife's personality and his predecessors were his partners in the business. If there had been any element of passion in the transaction he would have felt less deteriorated by it. The fact that Alice took her change of husbands like a change of weather reduced the situation to mediocrity. He could have forgiven her for blunders, for excesses: for resisting Haskett, for yielding to Varick; for anything but her acquiescence and her tact. She reminded him of a juggler tossing knives; but the knives were blunt and she knew they would never cut her.

And then, gradually, habit formed a protecting surface for his sensibilities. If he paid for each day's comfort with the small change of his illusions, he grew daily to value the comfort more and set less store upon the coin. He had drifted into a dulling propinquity with Haskett and Varick and he took refuge in the cheap revenge of satirizing the situation. He even began to reckon up the advantages which accrued from it, to ask himself if it were not better to own a third of a wife who knew how to make a man happy than a whole one who had lacked opportunity to acquire the art. For it *was* an art, and made up, like all others, of concessions, eliminations and embellishments; of lights judiciously thrown and shadows skillfully softened. His wife knew exactly how to manage the lights, and he knew exactly to what training she owed her skill. He even tried to trace the source of his obligations, to discriminate between the influences which had combined to produce his domestic happiness: he perceived that Haskett's commonness had made Alice worship good breeding, while Varick's liberal construction of the marriage bond had taught her to value the conjugal virtues; so that he was directly indebted to his predecessors for the devotion which made his life easy if not inspiring.

From this phase he passed into that of complete acceptance. He ceased to satirize himself because time dulled the irony of the situation and the joke lost its humor with its sting. Even the sight of Haskett's hat on the hall table had ceased to touch the springs of epigram. The hat was often seen there now, for it had been decided that it was better for Lily's father to visit her than for the little girl to go to his boardinghouse. Waythorn, having acquiesced in this arrangement, had been surprised to find how little difference it made. Haskett was never obtrusive, and the few visitiors who met him on the stairs were unaware of his identity. Waythorn did not know how often he saw Alice, but with himself Haskett was seldom in contact.

One afternoon, however, he learned on entering that Lily's father was waiting to see him. In the library he found Haskett occupying a chair in his usual provisional way. Waythorn always felt grateful to him for not leaning back.

"I hope you'll excuse me, Mr. Waythorn," he said rising. "I wanted to see Mrs. Waythorn about Lily, and your man asked me to wait here till she came in."

"Of course," said Waythorn, remembering that a sudden leak had that morning given over the drawing room to the plumbers.

He opened his cigar case and held it out to his visitor, and Haskett's acceptance seemed to mark a fresh stage in their intercourse. The spring evening was chilly, and

Waythorn invited his guest to draw up his chair to the fire. He meant to find an excuse to leave Haskett in a moment; but he was tired and cold, and after all the little man no longer jarred on him.

The two were enclosed in the intimacy of their blended cigar smoke when the door opened and Varick walked into the room. Waythorn rose abruptly. It was the first time that Varick had come to the house, and the surprise of seeing him, combined with the singular inopportuneness of his arrival, gave a new edge to Waythorn's blunted sensibilities. He stared at his visitor without speaking.

Varick seemed too preoccupied to notice his host's embarrassment.

"My dear fellow," he exclaimed in his most expansive tone, "I must apologize for tumbling in on you in this way, but I was too late to catch you downtown, and so I thought — "

He stopped short, catching sight of Haskett, and his sanguine color deepened to a flush which spread vividly under his scant blond hair. But in a moment he recovered himself and nodded slightly. Haskett returned the bow in silence, and Waythorn was still groping for speech when the footman came in carrying a tea table.

The intrusion offered a welcome vent to Waythorn's nerves. "What the deuce are you bringing this here for?" he said sharply.

"I beg your pardon, sir, but the plumbers are still in the drawing room, and Mrs. Waythorn said she would have tea in the library." The footman's perfectly respectful tone implied a reflection on Waythorn's reasonableness.

"Oh, very well," said the latter resignedly, and the footman proceeded to open the folding tea table and set out its complicated appointments. While this interminable process continued the three men stood motionless, watching it with a fascinated stare, till Waythorn, to break the silence, said to Varick, "Won't you have a cigar?"

He held out the case he had just tendered to Haskett, and Varick helped himself with a smile. Waythorn looked about for a match, and finding none, proffered a light from his own cigar. Haskett, in the background, held his ground mildly, examining his cigar tip now and then, and stepping forward at the right moment to knock its ashes into the fire.

The footman at last withdrew, and Varick immediately began: "If I could just say half a word to you about this business — "

"Certainly," stammered Waythorn; "in the dining room — "

But as he placed his hand on the door it opened from without, and his wife appeared on the threshold.

She came in fresh and smiling, in her street dress and hat, shedding a fragrance from the boa which she loosened in advancing.

"Shall we have tea in here, dear?" she began; and then she caught sight of Varick. Her smile deepened, veiling a light tremor of surprise.

"Why, how do you do?" she said with a distinct note of pleasure.

As she shook hands with Varick she saw Haskett standing behind him. Her smile faded for a moment, but she recalled it quickly, with a scarcely perceptible side glance at Waythorn.

"How do you do, Mr. Haskett?" she said, and shook hands with him a shade less cordially.

The three men stood awkwardly before her, till Varick, always the most self-possessed, dashed into an explanatory phrase.

"We — I had to see Waythorn a moment on business," he stammered, brick-red from chin to nape.

Haskett stepped forward with his air of mild obstinacy. "I am sorry to intrude; but you appointed five o'clock — " he directed his resigned glance to the timepiece on the mantel.

She swept aside their embarrassment with a charming gesture of hospitality.

"I'm so sorry — I'm always late; but the afternoon was so lovely." She stood drawing off her gloves, propitiatory and graceful, diffusing about her a sense of ease and familiarity in which the situation lost its grotesqueness. "But before talking business," she added brightly, "I'm sure everyone wants a cup of tea."

She dropped into her low chair by the tea table, and the two visitors, as if drawn by her smile, advanced to receive the cups she held out.

She glanced about for Waythorn, and he took the third cup with a laugh.

VIRGINIA WOOLF

 Virginia Woolf (1882–1941) was born in London, the daughter of the eminent literary critic and biographer Leslie Stephen. She grew up in a household in which the daily visitors were usually novelists, poets, and critics (Henry James was one). Her mother died when Woolf was thirteen; when her father died in 1904, she moved with her sister Vanessa and their brothers to a flat in Bloomsbury. Their circle of friends came to be known as "The Bloomsbury Group" — writers, artists, and intellectuals whose ideas had considerable impact on the arts in England in the early twentieth century. Among them were E. M. Forster, Maynard Keynes, Duncan Grant, Leonard Woolf, Lytton Strachey, and Clive Bell. Virginia married Leonard Woolf in 1912; in 1917 they founded the Hogarth Press, which published the work of such notable writers as T. S. Eliot, Katherine Mansfield, and Sigmund Freud (in translation) — and published Virginia's own books. She was a writer of dazzling versatility. One critic has said that she put her talent in her nonfiction, her genius in her novels. Some readers would amend that to say that she put her genius in everything she wrote: unquestionably it is true that in novels, stories, essays, criticism, biographies, letters, and diaries she gave memorable voice and shape to a brilliant imagination. The proliferation of her writing is all the more amazing given the bouts of nervous depression she suffered throughout her life, a life cut short by her suicide by drowning. Her first two novels, *The Voyage Out* (1915) and *Night and Day* (1919), were traditional in form, but Woolf began to experiment with an impressionistic style in her first collection of short fiction, *Monday or Tuesday* (1921), and from that time wrote fiction that prized interior consciousness and sensibility over action. Fiction is not, she avowed, a matter of shaping a plot with requisite doses of tragedy, comedy, love, and "an air of probability" but rather a recording of "myriad impressions. . . events trivial, fantastic, evanescent, or engraved with the sharpness of steel. . . . the life of Monday or Tuesday." Her major novels reflect this awareness: *Jacob's Room* (1922), *Mrs. Dalloway* (1925), *To the Lighthouse* (1927), *The Waves* (1931), *The Years* (1932), and *Between the Acts* (1941). Her short fiction, likewise impressionistic, is gathered in *The Complete Shorter Fiction of Virginia Woolf* (1985). Woolf's characters, it has been said, "are seeing eternity in a grain of sand." Certainly the unnamed lady in "The Symbol" is doing so.

The Symbol

There was a little dent on the top of the mountain like a crater on the moon. It was filled with snow, iridescent like a pigeon's breast, or dead white. There was a scurry of dry particles now and again, covering nothing. It was too high for breathing flesh or fur-covered life. All the same the snow was iridescent one moment; and blood red; and pure white, according to the day.

The graves in the valley — for there was a vast descent on either side; first pure rock; snow silted; lower a pine tree gripped a crag; then a solitary hut; then a saucer of pure green; then a cluster of eggshell roofs; at last, at the bottom, a village, a hotel, a cinema, and a graveyard — the graves in the churchyard near the hotel recorded the names of several men who had fallen climbing.

"The mountain," the lady wrote, sitting on the balcony of the hotel, "is a symbol..." She paused. She could see the topmost height through her glasses. She focused the lens, as if to see what the symbol was. She was writing to her elder sister at Birmingham.

The balcony overlooked the main street of the Alpine summer resort, like a box at a theater. There were very few private sitting rooms, and so the plays — such as they were — the curtain raisers — were acted in public. They were always a little provisional; preludes, curtain raisers. Entertainments to pass the time; seldom leading to any conclusion, such as marriage; or even lasting friendship. There was something fantastic about them, airy, inconclusive. So little that was solid could be dragged to this height. Even the houses looked gimcrack. By the time the voice of the English announcer reached the village it too became unreal.

Lowering her glasses, she nodded at the young men who in the street below were making ready to start. With one of them she had a certain connection — that is, an aunt of his had been mistress of her daughter's school.

Still holding the pen, still tipped with a drop of ink, she waved down at the climbers. She had written that the mountain was a symbol. But of what? In the forties of the last century two men, in the sixties four men, had perished; the first party when a rope broke, the second when night fell and froze them to death. We are always climbing to some height; that was the cliché. But it did not represent what was in her mind's eye, after seeing through her glasses the virgin height.

She continued, inconsequently. "I wonder why it makes me think of the Isle of Wight? You remember when Mama was dying, we took her there. And I would stand on the balcony when the boat came in and describe the passengers. I would say, I think that must be Mr. Edwardes... He has just come off the gangway. Then, now all the passengers have landed. Now they have turned the boat... I never told you, naturally not — you were in India; you were going to have Lucy — how I longed when the doctor came that he should say, quite definitely, She cannot live another week. It was very prolonged; she lived eighteen months. The mountain just now reminded me how when I was alone, I would fix my eyes upon her death, as a symbol. I would think if I could reach that point — when I should be free — we could not marry as you remember until she died — a cloud then would do instead of the mountain. I thought, when I reach that point — I have never told anyone, for it seemed so heartless; I shall be at the top. And I could imagine so many sides. We come of course of an Anglo-Indian family. I can still imagine, from hearing stories told, how people live in other parts of the world. I can see mud huts, and savages; I can see elephants drinking at pools. So many of our uncles and cousins were explorers. I have always had a great desire to explore for myself. But of course, when the time came it seemed more sensible, considering our long engagement, to marry."

She looked across the street at a woman shaking a mat on another balcony. Every morning at the same time she came out. You could have thrown a pebble into her balcony. They had indeed come to the point of smiling at each other across the street.

"The little villas," she added, taking up her pen, "are much the same here as in Birmingham. Every house takes in lodgers. The hotel is quite full. Though monotonous, the food is not what you would call bad. And of course the hotel has a splendid view. One can see the mountain from every window. But then that's true of the whole place. I can assure you, I could shriek sometimes coming out of the one shop where they sell papers — we get them a week late — always to see that mountain. Sometimes it looks just across the way. At others, like a cloud; only it never moves. Somehow the talk, even among the invalids, who are everywhere, is always about the mountain. Either, how clear it is today, it might be across the street; or, how far away it looks, it might be a cloud. That is the usual cliché. In the storm last night, I hoped for once it was hidden. But just as they brought in the anchovies, the Rev. W. Bishop said, 'Look there's the mountain!'

"Am I being selfish? Ought I not to be ashamed of myself, when there is so much suffering? It is not confined to the visitors. The natives suffer dreadfully from goiter. Of course it could be stopped, if anyone had enterprise, and money. Ought one not to be ashamed of dwelling upon what after all can't be cured? It would need an earthquake to destroy that mountain, just as, I suppose, it was made by an earthquake. I asked the proprietor, Herr Melchior, the other day, if there were ever earthquakes now. No, he said, only landslides and avalanches. They have been known he said to blot out a whole village. But he added quickly, there's no danger here.

"As I write these words, I can see the young men quite plainly on the slopes of the mountain. They are roped together. One I think I told you was at the same school with Margaret. They are now crossing a crevasse . . ."

The pen fell from her hand, and the drop of ink straggled in a zigzag line down the page. The young men had disappeared.

It was only late that night when the search party had recovered the bodies that she found the unfinished letter on the table on the balcony. She dipped her pen once more and added, "The old clichés will come in very handy. They died trying to climb the mountain . . . And the peasants brought spring flowers to lay upon their graves. They died in an attempt to discover . . ."

There seemed no fitting conclusion. And she added, "Love to the children," and then her pet name.

MARGUERITE YOURCENAR

 Marguerite Yourcenar (1903–1987) was born in Brussels to a Franco-Belgian family. Her mother died a few days after her birth; she was raised in France by her father, who taught her Latin and Greek. She learned as well French, Italian, and English, and for much of her life lived in Greece and the United States. She was the first woman to be named to the French Academy since its founding in 1635. A poet, critic, and translator, Yourcenar is perhaps best known for a "historical novel that historians read," *Memoirs of Hadrian* (1954). It is a monologue about the Roman Emperor Hadrian's life, as if written by Hadrian. Yourcenar's other novels are *Alexis* (1929), *Coup de Grâce* (1939), and *The Abyss* (1968). *Fires* (1936) is a collection of monologues by characters from ancient Greek and Christian literature, and *Oriental Tales* (1938) gathers stories from various Asian cultures. One of the most beautiful sentences in French literature, Yourcenar once said, is "The only calamity is that we are not saints." Perhaps the artist comes as close to sainthood as anyone can: "How Wang-Fo Was Saved," a thirteenth-century Taoist tale translated and adapted by Yourcenar, gives us reason to believe so.

How Wang-Fo Was Saved

Translated from the French by Alberto Manguel and Marguerite Yourcenar

The old painter Wang-Fo and his disciple Ling were wandering along the roads of the Kingdom of Han.

They made slow progress because Wang-Fo would stop at night to watch the stars and during the day to observe the dragonflies. They carried hardly any luggage, because Wang-Fo loved the image of things and not the things themselves, and no object in the world seemed to him worth buying, except brushes, pots of lacquer and China ink, and rolls of silk and rice paper. They were poor, because Wang-Fo would exchange his paintings for a ration of boiled millet, and paid no attention to pieces of silver. Ling, his disciple, bent beneath the weight of a sack full of sketches, bowed his back with respect as if he were carrying the heavens' vault, because for Ling the sack was full of snow-covered mountains, torrents in spring, and the face of the summer moon.

Ling had not been born to trot down the roads, following an old man who seized the dawn and captured the dusk. His father had been a banker who dealt in gold, his mother the only child of a jade merchant who had left her all his worldly possessions, cursing her for not being a son. Ling had grown up in a house where wealth made him shy: he was afraid of insects, of thunder and the face of the dead. When

Ling was fifteen, his father chose a bride for him, a very beautiful one because the thought of the happiness he was giving his son consoled him for having reached the age in which the night is meant for sleep. Ling's wife was as frail as a reed, childish as milk, sweet as saliva, salty as tears. After the wedding, Ling's parents became discreet to the point of dying, and their son was left alone in a house painted vermilion, in the company of his young wife who never stopped smiling and a plum tree that blossomed every spring with pale-pink flowers. Ling loved this woman of a crystal-clear heart as one loves a mirror that will never tarnish, or a talisman that will protect one forever. He visited the tea-houses to follow the dictates of fashion, and only moderately favored acrobats and dancers.

One night, in the tavern, Wang-Fo shared Ling's table. The old man had been drinking in order to better paint a drunkard, and he cocked his head to one side as if trying to measure the distance between his hand and his bowl. The rice wine undid the tongue of the taciturn craftsman, and that night Wang spoke as if silence were a wall and words the colors with which to cover it. Thanks to him, Ling got to know the beauty of the drunkards' faces blurred by the vapors of hot drink, the brown splendor of the roasts unevenly brushed by tongues of fire, and the exquisite blush of wine stains strewn on the tablecloths like withered petals. A gust of wind broke the window: the downpour entered the room. Wang-Fo leaned out to make Ling admire the livid zebra stripes of lightning, and Ling, spellbound, stopped being afraid of storms.

Ling paid the old painter's bill, and as Wang-Fo was both without money and without lodging, he humbly offered him a resting place. They walked away together; Ling held a lamp whose light projected unexpected fires in the puddles. That evening, Ling discovered with surprise that the walls of his house were not red, as he had always thought, but the color of an almost rotten orange. In the courtyard, Wang-Fo noticed the delicate shape of a bush to which no one had paid any attention until then, and compared it to a young woman letting down her hair to dry. In the passageway, he followed with delight the hesitant trail of an ant along the cracks in the wall, and Ling's horror of these creatures vanished into thin air. Realizing that Wang-Fo had just presented him with the gift of a new soul and a new vision of the world, Ling respectfully offered the old man the room in which his father and mother had died.

For many years now, Wang-Fo had dreamed of painting the portrait of a princess of olden days playing the lute under a willow. No woman was sufficiently unreal to be his model, but Ling would do because he was not a woman. Then Wang-Fo spoke of painting a young prince shooting an arrow at the foot of a large cedar tree. No young man of the present was sufficiently unreal to serve as his model, but Ling got his own wife to pose under the plum tree in the garden. Later on, Wang-Fo painted her in a fairy costume against the clouds of twilight, and the young woman wept because it was an omen of death. As Ling came to prefer the portraits painted by Wang-Fo to the young woman herself, her face began to fade, like a flower exposed to warm winds and summer rains. One morning, they found her hanging from the branches of the pink plum tree: the ends of the scarf that was strangling her floated in the wind, entangled with her hair. She looked even more delicate than usual, and as pure as the beauties celebrated by the poets of days gone by. Wang-Fo painted her one last time, because he loved the green hue that suffuses the face of the dead. His disciple Ling mixed the colors and the task needed such concentration that he forgot to shed tears.

One after the other, Ling sold his slaves, his jades, and the fish in his pond to buy his master pots of purple ink that came from the West. When the house was emptied, they left it, and Ling closed the door of his past behind him. Wang-Fo felt weary of a city where the faces could no longer teach him secrets of ugliness or beauty, and the master and his disciple walked away together down the roads of the Kingdom of Han.

Their reputation preceded them into the villages, to the gateway of fortresses, and into the atrium of temples where restless pilgrims halt at dusk. It was murmured that Wang-Fo had the power to bring his paintings to life by adding a last touch of color to their eyes. Farmers would come and beg him to paint a watchdog, and the lords would ask him for portraits of their best warriors. The priests honored Wang-Fo as a sage; the people feared him as a sorcerer. Wang enjoyed these differences of opinion which gave him the chance to study expressions of gratitude, fear, and veneration.

Ling begged for food, watched over his master's rest, and took advantage of the old man's raptures to massage his feet. With the first rays of the sun, when the old man was still asleep, Ling went in pursuit of timid landscapes hidden behind bunches of reeds. In the evening, when the master, disheartened, threw down his brushes, he would carefully pick them up. When Wang became sad and spoke of his old age, Ling would smile and show him the solid trunk of an old oak; when Wang felt happy and made jokes, Ling would humbly pretend to listen.

One day, at sunset, they reached the outskirts of the Imperial City and Ling sought out and found an inn in which Wang-Fo could spend the night. The old man wrapped himself up in rags, and Ling lay down next to him to keep him warm because spring had only just begun and the floor of beaten earth was still frozen. At dawn, heavy steps echoed in the corridors of the inn; they heard the frightened whispers of the innkeeper and orders shouted in a foreign, barbaric tongue. Ling trembled, remembering that the night before, he had stolen a rice cake for his master's supper. Certain that they would come to take him to prison, he asked himself who would help Wang-Fo ford the next river on the following day.

The soldiers entered carrying lanterns. The flames gleaming through the motley paper cast red and blue lights on their leather helmets. The string of a bow quivered over their shoulders, and the fiercest among them suddenly let out a roar for no reason at all. A heavy hand fell on Wang-Fo's neck, and the painter could not help noticing that the soldiers' sleeves did not match the color of their coats.

Helped by his disciple, Wang-Fo followed the soldiers, stumbling along uneven roads. The passing crowds made fun of these two criminals who were certainly going to be beheaded. The soldiers answered Wang's questions with savage scowls. His bound hands hurt him, and Ling in despair looked smiling at his master, which for him was a gentler way of crying.

They reached the threshold of the Imperial Palace, whose purple walls rose in broad daylight like a sweep of sunset. The soldiers led Wang-Fo through countless square and circular rooms whose shapes symbolized the seasons, the cardinal points, the male and female, longevity, and the prerogatives of power. The doors swung on their hinges with a musical note, and were placed in such a manner that one followed the entire scale when crossing the palace from east to west. Everything combined to give an impression of superhuman power and subtlety, and one could feel that here the simplest orders were as final and as terrible as the wisdom of the ancients. At last, the air became thin and the silence so deep that not even a man under torture would have dared to scream. A eunuch lifted a tapestry; the soldiers began to tremble like women, and the small troop entered the chamber in which the Son of Heaven sat on a high throne.

It was a room without walls, held up by thick columns of blue stone. A garden spread out on the far side of the marble shafts, and each and every flower blooming in the greenery belonged to a rare species brought here from across the oceans. But none of them had any perfume, so that the Celestial Dragon's meditations would not be troubled by fine smells. Out of respect for the silence in which his thoughts evolved, no bird had been allowed within the enclosure, and even the bees had been driven away. An enormous wall separated the garden from the rest of the world, so that the wind that sweeps over dead dogs and corpses on the battlefield would not dare brush the Emperor's sleeve.

The Celestial Master sat on a throne of jade, and his hands were wrinkled like those of an old man, though he had scarcely reached the age of twenty. His robe was blue to symbolize winter, and green to remind one of spring. His face was beautiful but blank, like a looking glass placed too high, reflecting nothing except the stars and the immutable heavens. To his right stood his Minister of Perfect Pleasures, and to his left his Counselor of Just Torments. Because his courtiers, lined along the base of the columns, always lent a keen ear to the slightest sound from his lips, he had adopted the habit of speaking in a low voice.

"Celestial Dragon," said Wang-Fo, bowing low, "I am old, I am poor, I am weak. You are like summer; I am like winter. You have Ten Thousand Lives; I have but one, and it is near its close. What have I done to you? My hands have been tied, these hands that never harmed you."

"You ask what you have done to me, old Wang-Fo?" said the Emperor.

His voice was so melodious that it made one want to cry. He raised his right hand, to which the reflections from the jade pavement gave a pale sea-green hue like that of an underwater plant, and Wang-Fo marveled at the length of those thin fingers, and hunted among his memories to discover whether he had not at some time painted a mediocre portrait of either the Emperor or one of his ancestors that would now merit a sentence of death. But it seemed unlikely because Wang-Fo had not been an assiduous visitor at the Imperial Court. He preferred the farmers' huts or, in the cities, the courtesans' quarters and the taverns along the harbor where the dockers liked to quarrel.

"You ask me what it is you have done, old Wang-Fo?" repeated the Emperor, inclining his slender neck toward the old man waiting attentively. "I will tell you. But, as another man's poison cannot enter our veins except through our nine openings, in order to show you your offenses I must take you with me down the corridors of my memory and tell you the story of my life. My father had assembled a collection of your work and hidden it in the most secret chamber in the palace, because he judged that the people in your paintings should be concealed from the world since they cannot lower their eyes in the presence of profane viewers. It was in those same rooms that I was brought up, old Wang-Fo, surrounded by solitude. To prevent my innocence from being sullied by other human souls, the restless crowd of my future subjects had been driven away from me, and no one was allowed to pass my threshold, for fear that his or her shadow would stretch out and touch me. The few aged servants that were placed in my service showed themselves as little as possible; the hours turned in circles; the colors of your paintings bloomed in the first hours of the morning and grew pale at dusk. At night, when I was unable to sleep, I glazed at them, and for nearly ten years I gazed at them every night. During the day, sitting on a carpet whose design I knew by heart, I dreamed of the joys the future had in store for me. I imagined the world, with the Kingdom of Han at the center, to be like the flat palm of my hand crossed by the fatal lines of the Five Rivers. Around it lay the sea in which monsters are born, and farther away the mountains that hold up the heavens. And to help me visualize these things I used your paintings. You made me believe that the sea looked like the vast sheet of water spread across your scrolls, so blue that if a stone were to fall into it, it would become a sapphire; that women opened and closed like flowers, like the creatures that come forward, pushed by the wind, along the paths of your painted gardens; and that the young, slim-waisted warriors who mount guard in the fortresses along the frontier were themselves like arrows that could pierce my heart. At sixteen I saw the doors that separated me from the world open once again; I climbed onto the balcony of my palace to look at the clouds, but they were far less beautiful than those in your sunsets. I ordered my litter; bounced along roads on which I had not foreseen either mud or stones, I traveled across the provinces of the Empire without ever finding your gardens full of women like fireflies, or a woman whose body was in itself a garden. The pebbles on the beach spoiled my taste for oceans; the blood of the tortured is less red than the pomegranates in your paintings; the village vermin prevented me from seeing the beauty of the rice fields; the flesh of mortal women disgusted me like the dead meat hanging from the butcher's hook, and the coarse laughter of my soldiers made me sick. You lied, Wang-Fo, you old impostor. The world is nothing but a mass of muddled colors thrown into the void by an insane painter, and smudged by our tears. The Kingdom of Han is not the most beautiful of kingdoms, and I am not the Emperor. The only empire which is worth reigning over is that which you alone can enter, old Wang, by the road of One Thousand Curves and Ten Thousand Colors. You alone reign peacefully over mountains covered in snow that cannot melt, and over fields of daffodils that cannot die. And that is why, Wang-Fo, I have conceived a punishment for you, for you whose enchantment has filled me with disgust at everything I own, and with desire for everything I shall never possess. And in order to lock you up in the only cell from which there is no escape, I have decided to have your eyes burned out, because your eyes, Wang-Fo, are the two magic gates that open onto your kingdom. And as your hands are the two roads of ten forking paths that lead to the heart of your kingdom, I have decided to have your hands cut off. Have you understood, old Wang-Fo?"

Hearing the sentence, Ling, the disciple, tore from his belt an old knife and leaped toward the Emperor. Two guards immediately seized him. The Son of Heaven smiled and added, with a sigh: "And I also hate you, old Wang-Fo, because you have known how to make yourself beloved. Kill that dog."

Ling jumped to one side so that his blood would not stain his master's robe. One of the soldiers lifted his sword and Ling's head fell from his neck like a cut flower. The servants carried away the remains, and Wang-Fo, in despair, admired the beautiful scarlet stain that his disciple's blood made on the green stone floor.

The Emperor made a sign and two eunuchs wiped Wang's eyes.

"Listen, old Wang-Fo," said the Emperor, "and dry your tears, because this is not the time to weep. Your eyes must be clear so that the little light that is left to them is not clouded by your weeping. Because it is not only the grudge I bear you that makes me desire your death; it is not only the cruelty in my heart that makes me want to see you suffer. I have other plans, old Wang-Fo. I possess among your works a remarkable painting in which the mountains, the river estuary, and the sea reflect each other, on a very small scale certainly, but with a clarity that surpasses the real landscapes themselves, like objects reflected on the walls of a metal sphere. But that painting is unfinished, Wang-Fo; your masterpiece is but a sketch. No doubt, when you began your work, sitting in a solitary valley, you noticed a passing bird, or a child running after the bird. And the bird's beak or the child's cheeks made you forget the blue eyelids of the sea. You never finished the frills of the water's cloak, or the seaweed hair of the rocks. Wang-Fo, I want you to use the few hours of light that are left to you to finish this painting, which will thus contain the final secrets amassed during your long life. I know that your hands, about to fall, will not tremble on the silken cloth, and infinity will enter your work through those unhappy cuts. I know that your eyes, about to be put out, will discover bearings far beyond all human senses. This is my plan, old Wang-Fo, and I can force you to fulfill it. If you refuse, before blinding you, I will have all your paintings burned, and you will be like a father whose children are slaughtered and all hopes of posterity extinguished. However, believe, if you wish, that this last order stems from nothing but my kindness, because I know that the silken scroll is the only mistress you ever deigned to touch. And to offer you brushes, paints, and inks to occupy your last hours is like offering the favors of a harlot to a man condemned to death."

Upon a sign from the Emperor's little finger, two eunuchs respectfully brought forward the unfinished scroll on which Wang-Fo had outlined the image of the sea and the sky. Wang-Fo dried his tears and smiled, because that small sketch reminded him of his youth. Everything in it spoke of a fresh new spirit which Wang-Fo could no longer claim as his, and yet something was missing from it, because when Wang had painted it he had not yet looked long enough at the mountains or at the rocks bathing their naked flanks in the sea, and he had not yet penetrated deep enough into the sadness of the evening twilight. Wang-Fo selected one of the brushes which a slave held ready for him and began spreading wide strokes of blue into the unfinished sea. A eunuch crouched by his feet, mixing the colors; he carried out his task with little skill, and more than ever Wang-Fo lamented the loss of his disciple Ling.

Wang began by adding a touch of pink to the tip of the wing of a cloud perched on a mountain. Then he painted onto the surface of the sea a few small lines that deepened the perfect feeling of calm. The jade floor became increasingly damp, but Wang-Fo, absorbed as he was in his painting, did not seem to notice that he was working with his feet in water.

The fragile rowboat grew under the strokes of the painter's brush and now occupied the entire foreground of the silken scroll. The rhythmic sound of the oars rose suddenly in the distance, quick and eager like the beating of wings. The sound came nearer, gently filling the whole room, then ceased, and a few trembling drops appeared on the boatman's oars. The red iron intended for Wang's eyes lay extinguished on the executioner's coals. The courtiers, motionless as etiquette required, stood in water up to their shoulders, trying to lift themselves onto the tips of their toes. The water finally reached the level of the imperial heart. The silence was so deep one could have heard a tear drop.

It was Ling. He wore his everyday robe, and his right sleeve still had a hole that he had not had time to mend that morning before the soldiers' arrival. But around his neck was tied a strange red scarf.

Wang-Fo said to him softly, while he continued painting, "I thought you were dead."

"You being alive," said Ling respectfully, "how could I have died?"

And he helped his master into the boat. The jade ceiling reflected itself in the water, so that Ling seemed to be inside a cave. The pigtails of submerged courtiers rippled up toward the surface like snakes, and the pale head of the Emperor floated like a lotus.

"Look at them," said Wang-Fo sadly. "These wretches will die, if they are not dead already. I never thought there was enough water in the sea to drown an Emperor. What are we to do?"

"Master, have no fear," murmured the disciple. "They will soon be dry again and will not even remember that their sleeves were ever wet. Only the Emperor will keep in his heart a little of the bitterness of the sea. These people are not the kind to lose themselves inside a painting."

And he added: "The sea is calm, the wind high, the seabirds fly to their nests. Let us leave, Master, and sail to the land beyond the waves."

"Let us leave," said the old painter.

Wang-Fo took hold of the helm, and Ling bent over the oars. The sound of rowing filled the room again, strong and steady like the beating of a heart. The level of the water dropped unnoticed around the large vertical rocks that became columns once more. Soon only a few puddles glistened in the hollows of the jade floor. The courtiers' robes were dry, but a few wisps of foam still clung to the hem of the Emperor's cloak.

The painting finished by Wang-Fo was leaning against a tapestry. A rowboat occupied the entire foreground. It drifted away little by little, leaving behind it a thin wake that smoothed out into the quiet sea. One could no longer make out the faces of the two men sitting in the boat, but one could still see Ling's red scarf and Wang-Fo's beard waving in the breeze.

The beating of the oars grew fainter, then ceased, blotted out by the distance. The Emperor, leaning forward, a hand above his eyes, watched Wang's boat sail away till it was nothing but an imperceptible dot in the paleness of the twilight. A golden mist rose and spread over the water. Finally the boat veered around a rock that stood at the gateway to the ocean; the shadow of a cliff fell across it; its wake disappeared from the deserted surface, and the painter Wang-Fo and his disciple Ling vanished forever on the jade-blue sea that Wang-Fo had just created.

Patricia Hampl was born in St. Paul, Minnesota, in 1946. She received her education at the University of Minnesota and the University of Iowa. A sense of history, place, and beauty is the hallmark of her major works: a prose memoir, *A Romantic Education* (awarded the Houghton Mifflin Literary Fellowship in 1981); *Spillville*, a re-creation (with artist Steven Sorman) of one summer in the life of Czech composer Anton Dvořák; and two collections of poetry. In 1988 she received a grant from the Guggenheim Foundation. She teaches creative writing and literary studies at the University of Minnesota and is a contributor to various literary journals, among them *Paris Review*, *The New Yorker*, *The New York Times Book Review*, and *American Poetry Review*.